By the same author:

DISTURBING ELEMENT
LARGER THAN LIFE
SEVEN EMUS
CAPRICORNIA

POOR FELLOW MY COUNTRY

Xavier Herbert

ANGUS & ROBERTSON

A division of HarperCollins *Publishers*

AN ANGUS & ROBERTSON BOOK
An imprint of HarperCollinsPublishers

First published in Australia by William Collins Pty Ltd in 1975
Reprinted in 1988
Published by Collins/Angus & Robertson in 1990
Reprinted in 1991
CollinsAngus&Robertson Publishers Pty Limited (ACN 009 913 517)
A division of HarperCollinsPublishers (Australia) Pty Limited
4 Eden Park, 31 Waterloo Road, North Ryde, NSW 2113, Australia

HarperCollinsPublishers (New Zealand) Limited
31 View Road, Glenfield, Auckland 10, New Zealand

HarperCollinsPublishers Limited
77–85 Fulham Palace Road, London W6 8JB, United Kingdom

National Library of Australia
Cataloguing-in-Publication data:

Herbert, Xavier, 1901–1984.
Poor fellow my country.
ISBN 0 207 17040 1.

I. Title.

A823'.2

Printed in Hong Kong

8 7 6 5 4
95 94 93 92 91

PRINCIPAL CHARACTERS

Ah Loy, Willy *husband of Nellyerri*
Barbu, Ram ('Ali Barba') *Indian hawker*
Bickering, Mr Justice *Judge of the Supreme Court*
'Bloke' *official of Free Australia Movement*
Bobwirridirridi ('Cock-Eye Bob', the Pookarakka) *Aboriginal witch-doctor of the Rainbow-snake Cult*
Brew, Billy *donkey teamster*
Bullco *Superintendent of police*
Bundy *stipendiary magistrate*
Burrows, Oz *railway porter*
Cahoon, Dinny *police sergeant*
Candlemas, Aelfrieda ('Alfie') *authoress and reformer*
Candlemas, Frank *husband of Aelfrieda*
Chase, Chas *railway guard*
'Chief' *founder of Free Australia Movement*
Cobbity, Dr Cuthbert *Protector of Aborigines*
'Cock-Eye Bob' *see* Bobwirridirridi
Collings, Col *station master*
Cootes, Fabian *anthropologist*
Cullity, Con *publican, son-in-law of Shamus Finnucane*
Cullity, Bridie *daughter of Shamus Finnucane*
Curry, Mick *publican, son-in-law of Shamus Finnucane*
Curry, Colleen *daughter of Shamus Finnucane*
Delacy, Jeremy *father of Martin and Clancy, lessee of Lily Lagoons*
Delacy, Martin *elder son of Jeremy. Manager of Beatrice River Station, father of Prindy*
Delacy, Clancy *younger son of Jeremy. Manager of Catfish Station*
Delacy, Jumbo *halfcaste brother of Jeremy*
Dickey, Denzil *aide to Sir Mark Esk*
Doscas, Dicky *Clerk of Court*
Eaton, Rhoda *ex-wife of Jeremy Delacy, mother of Martin and Clancy*
Esk, General Sir Mark *British-appointed C-in-C of the Australian Army*
Ferris, Fergus *anthropologist and pilot*
Finnucane, Shamus ('Shame-on-us') *Irish proprietor of the Beatrice River Hotel*
Fox, Dr Felix *Flying Doctor*
Glascock, Father *missionary at the Leopold Islands*
Hannaford, Pat *engine driver and Communist agitator*
Hoff, Dr Kurt *Jewish refugee*
Jinbul *police tracker for Dinny Cahoon*
Jones, Porky *railway fireman*
'King George' (Njorjinga) *Aboriginal tribal uncle of Prindy*
Knowles, Nat *founder of Lily Lagoons*
Knowles, Ned *son of Nat Knowles*
Knowles, Nugget }
Knowles, Knobby } *sons of Ned Knowles*
Lilyponds, Phyllis *schoolteacher at Port Palmeston Aboriginal Compound*
Lyndbrooke-Esk, Lady Lydia *daughter of Sir Mark Esk, fiancée of Lord Vaisey*
Maltravers ('Malters') *aide to Sir Mark Esk*
Maryzic, Monsignor *missionary priest*
McCusky, Eddie *Administration officer of Aborigines*
McFee, Fay *a journalist*
McQuegg, Dr *Government medical officer*
Nanago *Jeremy Delacy's second wife, a halfcaste*
Nellyerri *halfcaste mother of Prindy*
Njorjinga *see* 'King George'
Okada, Capt. *Japanese pearler*
Pickles *Naval Chief Petty Officer, later Lieutenant*
Prindy *quarter-caste son of Nellyeri and Martin Delacy*
'Queeny Peg-leg' *'queen' of the Aboriginal Compound. Tribal sister of Nellyerri*
Rosen, Rifkah *refugee Jewess*
St Clair *Professor of Anthropology*
Sakamura *Japanese pearler*
Shane, Capt. Vic *pearling master*
'Silver Tongue' *a conservative Prime Minister*
Sims Sergeant, *Army Signal Corps*
'Storm the Barricades' *a socialist Prime Minister*
Stunke, Herbert *police constable*
Tasker, Rev. Mr *Protestant missionary*
Tinball, Jack *railway engine driver*
Toby, Capt. *naval officer*
Toohey, Tom *railway ganger, husband of Possum, father of Brumby and Micky*
Tripconny, Silas *politician, father of Alfie Candlemas*
Turkney, 'Tubby' *Superintendent of Aboriginal Compound, Port Palmeston*
Vaisey, Lord Alfred *British 'beef baron'*
Wyndeyer, Kitty *court reporter and telephonist*

Book One

TERRA AUSTRALIS

CHAPTER ONE

THE SMALL BOY was Aboriginal – distinctly so by cast of countenance, while yet so lightly coloured as to pass for any light-skinned breed, even tanned Caucasian. His skin was cream-caramel, with a hair-sheen of gold. There was also the glint of gold in his tow-tawny mop of curls. Then his eyes were grey – with a curious intensity of expression probably due to their being set in cavernous Australoid orbits where one would expect to see dark glinting as of shaded water. His nose, fleshed and curved in the mould of his savage ancestry, at the same time was given just enough of the beakiness of the other side to make it a thing of perfection. Likewise his lips. Surely a beautiful creature to any eye but the most prejudiced in the matter of race. Indeed, but for knowing the depth and breadth of prejudice against the very strain that gave him perfection, one might well be amazed to know that such a thing could stand up to the sight of him. Yet most people, at least of this remote northern part of the Australian Continent, would dismiss him as just a *boong*. He was aged about eight.

He was squatting beside a water-hole alone, fishing. He wore only khaki pants, the rent stern of which exposed a piece of his behind so closely matching the bleached cloth as to be scarcely noticeable. In one delicate truly Aboriginal hand he held a fishing line, in the other a fish-spear. As the Aboriginal fisherman or hunter must to ensure his catch, he was singing, softly:

Kowee, Tjala!
Long o' me come, Old Catfish
I sing you . . . Kowee, kowee, kowee!
Old Catfish, must you come . . .

It was not the mere monotone that mostly goes for Aboriginal singing, but oddly tuneful, and especially sweet as the only sound in all the small world thereabout, because everything else was sleeping out the midday heat, even the wind, so that the pool – emerald, silver, blue-enamel, gold – lay still as glass.

The pool was rockbound; by a sloping tumble on the side where the boy squatted amongst roots of a banyan that made the ruddy sandstone look as if crawling with grey snakes; on the other by a sheer wall grown with ferns and other clinging vegetation and topped with trees of which the branches mingled with those of the banyan.

I sing you . . . Kowee, kowee, kowee!
Old Tjala, you got 'o come . . . .

A golden flicker in the emerald depths. The slack line quickened. The grey eyes fairly blazed with intensity. The golden-brown hand drew the line. Up came the shadow. The fish-spear was poised. But the line fell slack and the shadow drifted down and vanished. The line came up without bait. The perfect lips moved to a soft throaty growl: 'Bloody bastard!'

He turned, to reach for a grubby cotton flour-sack hanging in the roots – to stiffen in that attitude. Only an eye of extraordinary sharpness could so quickly have discerned anything untoward, so much a part of the background was that which had intruded into it – or materialized out of it, as seemed as likely.

It was of human shape, greyish, or blackish made grey with dust and ashes and ancient body hair, so as to appear kindred to the crawling roots. It had stick legs, with shapeless lumpy feet and knobby knees, arms like a mantis, a tuft of grey hair sticking up like the crest of an angry bird out of a grubby ochred head-band, and whiskers plaited into a long goatee about slivers of cane or grass, an almost flat nose with slit septum dangling losely from enormous nostrils. It seemed to be sightless as a death's head – till suddenly there burnt within the black caverns that looked like live coals.

The seeming apparition wore no clothing, except the ceremonial loin-covering called the Hair Belt, a wide belly-band made of cord woven from human hair with a narrow pubic apron falling to the knees. The band was no mere covering, but also served for carrying numerous objects – *gungu*, or fire-lighting kit, quartz knife, *minga-minga* sticks for clicking accompaniment to singing, and a couple of boomerangs. Other articles were carried in dilly-bags of woven fibre slung round the scrub-turkey-like neck back and front, while the skeleton left arm was crooked about an assortment of spears, and the claw-like right hand held a womera. But what was of first importance in the rig-out, from an Aboriginal point of view, were the cicatrized markings in the slaty skin. Ridges were cut and brands burnt into upper arms, shoulders, breast, belly, thighs, some of very intricate design. From these a knowledgeable eye would read the wearer's status, which in this case must have been considerable.

Not a move from either. Both might have been spellbound.

The spell was broken by slight movement of the claw holding the womera – raising of the index finger. In common sign-language that meant 'Who are you?'

It was the proper way of greeting between strangers, for the elder to ask and the younger to respond, not with personal names, but the sign for his *Skin*, meaning his place in the relationship system, literally his Substance – although nothing could be more literal than the native interpretation, Skin. This was his eternal identity with the Dream Time and the factor determining his behaviour towards others, strangers or not. However, whatever the proprieties, there are strangers and strangers, and the *wisdom* of declaring one's identity to be considered. A stranger who seemed to have materialized out of nothing might well be a *Moomboo* or Devil-devil, wanting to know your Skin only to judge the propriety of eating you. The only response to the sign was a blink of grey eyes and slight quiver of lovely lip.

The grey whiskers parted in a wide grin, then jerked to cackling speech: '*Koyada kumeri.*'

Still no response. A moment of intense exchange of staring. Then the burning coals flicked to the pool. The grey glance followed. Again the golden shadow. The fair head turned, to see the mantis claws divesting themselves of dunnage. Rather like a grey spider, the unencumbered figure came slipping through the roots, to step into the shallow water a few feet from the boy, who stood as if ready to bolt. The mantis was intent now only on what was below. Swaying, and with claw to mouth, he began to chant, thin and nasal of tone, true blackfellow singing, C-sharp, E, C-sharp, each repeated four times, to accompaniment of slapping the water:

Mah-nah, mah-nah, mah-nah, mah-nah
Gu-dah, gu-dah, gu-dah, gu-dah
Mah-nah, gu-dah, mah-nah, gu-dah
Yuk!

A resounding slap went with the last note; then up an octave to repeat; down again. All the while the shadow circled and rose. Suddenly the claw left the mouth to make the gesture of spearing, while the red eyes shot a significant glance at the watchful grey eyes – without pause in chanting and slapping: '*Mah-nah, gu-dah, mah-nah, gu-dah – Yuk!*'

The boy caught on, raised the spear, stood poised to strike.

The long dorsal fin cut the surface.

Zip! The spear flew, struck, wobbled, spun violently, vanished into a bloody whirlpool. As grey eyes glanced again at the death's head, the latter split to cackle, 'Yakkarai . . . Properlee . . . . Numberr-one!'

Eyes back to the pool as the haft of the spear popped up to cut wild capers through the stained emerald, at last to collapse, to reveal its whiskery victim convulsing weakly on the barbs. The boy looked at the Master of Magic, received a nod, hesitated a moment, then slipped into the water, seized the spear, flung the fish ashore. It was a beauty, a good ten pounds in weight. Again the wide grin and the cackled comment: 'Properlee!'

The boy looked as wary as before on coming out. The death's head cackled at him, 'No-more fright!' The index finger rose again.

Again hesitation. Then a small hand gave the sign *Julama*.

Along with a still wider grin, the claw came up to give the same sign. This meant they were tribal brothers – or, because of the difference in age, paternal grandsire and grandson. Bond of blood wouldn't enter into it, not even had they been truly related, because theirs was a matrilinear social system, with male authority vested primarily in mother's brothers. Their bond would be one more of affection, no less strong for having its basis solely in tradition, their responsibility to each other simply exchange of the wisdom of age for the physical advantages of youth. This matter of responsibility was raised at once, when one of the claws reached to smooth a plump golden-brown shoulder in the Aboriginal way of expressing affection, while the cackle took on the whine customary in asking favours: 'Plenty beef you got him, eh? Goot tucker long o' dat place you sit down.' Curl of the perfect lips in a slight smile. 'Which way you sit down, Kumija?' At a questioning look in the grey eyes, the cackle added: 'Kumija . . . dat one Granny. Wha' nam' you call-yim?'

The answer was given in a whisper, but with breath inhaled in the native way: '*Mora*.'

'Ah! Where you sit down, *Mora*?'

To tell a stranger where one camped was to accept him. Likewise to use his language. A blink of the grey eyes first, then: 'Catfish Station . . . Kumija.'

A long red tongue flashed over whiskered lips: 'Ah . . . teeshon tucker!' The whine again: 'Too-much me hungry long o' dat one . . . bre'millik me like him. No-goot long o' *binji*.' A claw rubbed the brand-burnt stomach that seemed so hollow as to reveal the backbone.

Young Granny nodded understanding of what was required of him. Both looked at the fish gasping its last. Old Granny said, 'You tek him long o' teeshun, give him cook.' He pulled the quartz knife from his belt, slit a length of bark from a root, gave it to the boy. The boy slipped it through the fish's gills. Then he picked up his three small spears and the gunny-sack, and the fish, which he tossed over his shoulder. Old Granny nodded for him to go ahead. He climbed through the roots to the top of the tumble of rock. He stopped and looked back. No sign of Old Granny. He peered down. He looked around wide-eyed. Old Kumija had vanished the way he had appeared – as if by magic. The grey eyes rolled in wariness. Then with a swift movement he started away from the rocks and banyans, got out into the open. Still no sign. After a moment he set out southward, following the bank of a deep dry creek. He went with the swift easy lope of a blackfellow, but with the swift uneasy glances about of one travelling alone. In a land largely peopled by spirits one must be vigilant always. They had to materialize to do you harm. You had to be a jump ahead of them. It was probably concession to the boy's non-Aboriginal heritage that, Aboriginal enough as he seemed otherwise, he dared to be travelling alone.

The sandstone of the locality, projection of a distant Plateau to be just glimpsed through the ragged open forest to northward, and the dark red sandy soil and forest, soon gave way to grey plain with meaner growth and a profusion of small spiked grey termites' nests, or Ant Beds, as called in these parts, except along the creek-bank, where water-gums and coolibahs and the like grew stoutly, despite the dryness that would obtain for most of the year. The bed of the creek, now of white sand, blazed silver. So the boy travelled for about a mile and a half, when he came to a sharp bend in the creek, round which was revealed a very different vista. From a wide bar of rock that was the determining factor in the change of direction, shimmering blue water stretched away southward to vanishing point in the dense greenery of its banks. A ruddy smudge on the blue enamel of the sky in that direction told of dust blowing on the rising afternoon wind.

A halt to make a survey all round; then the boy climbed down to cross the bar. Galahs in the timber of the further bank spotted him, swept up like a mass of rosy blossoms torn from the trees by a freak wind, wheeled over him, screaming as if truly in frank fear of some devilish design on them – as native lore had it they always were through trouble with Tchamala, the Rainbow Serpent, back in the Dream Time, and as if the boy were thinking as he cocked his head to them and yelled in mockery, '*Yerrilgeenah, Yerrilgeenah . . . gully-gully Yerrilgeenah*!'

Legend had it that the *Yerrilgeenah*, spies of the Old Woman, the Earth Mother, Koonapippi, pursued by her enemy, Tchamala, the Snake in Arcady, had taken refuge in a hollow tree (as in fact their descendants do today) only to find themselves in the Old One's belly. Hence the tuneful little song with which the boy skipped across the rocks and up the other side:

Yerrilgeenah, Yerrilgeenah, gully-gully Yerrilgeenah
Shtinkit hide long hollit tree, find himself long Tchineke binj-ee.

The red beneath the mauve of the Galah's feathers was said to be blood shed by the Snake when the birds tore at his insides with fierce parrot bills and forced him to disgorge them. The boy looked up at the flash of crimson over him. There was a tale attached to everything in the land, just as a tail was too – except to Man, a freak mutation of the heroic creatures of the Dream Time.

He went bounding up a beaten track through the strip of aquatic jungle lining the great pool, to emerge to another marked change of scene. Here to eastward lay a vast expanse of treelessness, cut into three or four paddocks, the fences of which ran so far they ended climbing into silvery uplands of mirage where a few trees grew upside down and cattle were grazing in the sky. About a mile away southward, back about a quarter of a mile from the long pool, indistinct in heat-haze and a veil of dust, looking rather like a wobbly mushroom growth, dazzling white and shadow blue, stood the homestead of the cattle station known as Catfish Creek. This was one of the pioneer settlements of the district, although serving now only as an out-station in the international Vaisey Company's complex of grazing holdings centred for this region at Princess Beatrice River. It comprised half a dozen whitewashed iron buildings, embowered in planted greenery. The dust was rising from behind the homestead. Faintly at that distance and against the sou'deast wind came the sound of what was causing the dust; the bawling of yarded stock.

A fence ran parallel with the creek. The boy got onto a horse-pad beside it, broke into a trot. The galahs swept over him in a last sortie. A couple of egrets and a blue crane rose from the timber of the creek and came sailing to take a look at him, to swing away croaking contempt for such panic-merchants as took for the Old One or a henchman of his one small boy who wasn't even properly black.

The homestead rose out of the muddle of mirage to reveal itself in detail; the elevated water-tanks detaching from the mango trees, the high house of the Boss from the low kitchen, various sheds from each other, meat-house, fowl-house, goat-house, and those scarcely credible dog-houses to be found on the fringe of every homestead and township in the land – the humpies of the natives, built of anything, bark, bushes, flattened cans. A square of bright green garden surrounded the tanks from which water spilled in silver gouts to every turn of the windmill busily winding away on the edge of the creek timber. In the garden also, to be only glimpsed amongst the mangoes, was another bungalow building rather like the kitchen.

Coming to the garden, the boy slipped under the fence, making for the bungalow. He paused just short of it, at the tanks, to look up at a bunch of bananas beginning to ripen. He went on. The house was of corrugated iron, on a cemented sandstone foundation with bamboo-latticed verandahs all round, shutters admitting light. He went to the rear, skipped up the steps. The back verandah served as living-room, with furniture mostly of saplings built into the cement-like beaten stuff of ant-bed. At the end of the verandah was a bed of saplings and cowhide strips. He dropped all of his things on this, except the fish, then went rushing through a passage dividing two big central rooms, out onto the front verandah, down the steps, out of the garden.

First was what might be called the wood-yard, although it wasn't fenced; a stack of logs, a pile of billets, a waste of sawdust, a shed, a shady native plum tree, Mangan, against the axe-scarred trunk of which the wood-man squatted with idle axe, smoking a pipe. The man – or rather boy, as the conventions of the region would have dubbed him, despite the grey hair peeping through the broken top of his ancient stockman's hat – looked up as the young boy came through the garden gate, then at once averted his gaze. The boy did not look at all. Evidently the intimacy of exchanging glances was denied by the intricacies of relationship. But not so exchange of banter. The old fellow called out something in lingo to the distance. The boy responded similarly, while giving a skip that bounced the big fish on his back. The wood-boy laughed. The boy kept on towards the kitchen.

The kitchen also was on a stone foundation, with steps on this northern side and the western leading up to doorways in the lattice of the verandahs. As he reached the northern steps there appeared in the doorway a tall lean figure neatly clad in khaki trousers, white cotton singlet, apron. The face was dark as a well-used saddle, markedly both Australoid and Mongoloid of cast. The hair was a true Chinaman's bristly tarbrush. The combination slit of a mouth opened to reveal strong white teeth: 'Prindy, boy . . . where you been?'

Prindy was the name of the great Spotted Goanna.

The boy's teeth flashed in response as he bounded up the steps. He thrust the fish into the man's hands, only to have it thrust back, with the words: 'Eh . . . more better you givvit Mumma, I t'ink'.

The boy Prindy grimaced, muttered, 'Mumma don't like it blackfeller fashion.'

The exchange would refer to the Aboriginal custom whereby a son gave his mother the best of his hunting. The boy got rid of it again.

Now the man kept the fish, examined it, exclaiming, 'Which-way you been gitchim dat big bugger?'

First Prindy shot a searching glance into the kitchen, then turning away, answered on indrawn breath in lingo, concluding, '*Mahraghi-mahraghi* . . . *Yuk*! Got him!'

'*Gooruk bambulla*?'

The grey eyes met the popping black: 'Might be *Koornung*.'

The other's deep whisper was hoarse: 'Eh, look-out!'

There was fear in the black eyes, but not in the grey, whose owner said simply, 'Him all right long o' me. I call-yim Granny.'

They were interrupted by a screeching female voice inside: 'Who you talk to, Ah Loy?'

The Chinese eyes were hooded by their mongol folds. The mouth sucked in a whisper: 'Proper cranky today.'

A slap of bare feet. A young halfcaste woman clad in floral cotton dress and white apron suddenly was there, flinging the man aside, grabbing at the boy with chocolate hands, screeching, 'Where you been, boy? Wha's matter you mek me worrit sick? Next time, by-crise, I belt you!' But she hugged him close, burying dark handsome face in the fair hair, now moaning, 'Oh, wha's matter you go run-away like o' dat . . . t'ree day . . . oh, oh, oh!'

The man Ah Loy slipped inside with the fish.

Then as suddenly she pushed the boy away, demanding in high angry tones, 'Where you been go?'

'Mek him song.'

'You can mak him song stop home.'

'I like it quiet long o' bush.' Then the suppliant whine: 'Me hungry too-much, Mumma.'

'You like it live all-same blackfeller long o'bush . . . all right, you eat bush tucker.'

He slipped away from her, round the verandah, on the western side. A long trestle table was there with forms for seating, the bare scrubbed board set for a light meal with enamelware. He pounced on a pile of the sweet currant bread called Brownie, whooped, 'Smoke-o!' stuffed the slice in his mouth.

His mother came after him, pulled him away, snapped, 'Got steak-and-kidney pie for you.'

Just then a black stockman, grey with dust, came stamping up the steps in spurred elastic-sided riding-boots. Casting a mere glance at mother and son, he went on into the kitchen, bawling something in lingo that included the words Milk and Calf – or properly, Millik and Calfee. Prindy again dodged away from his mother to run in after the man and ply him with lingo. His mother came on his heels, snatched him away, screeching again: 'How many time I tell you not talk lingo?'

Looking at her, the stockman made the Aboriginal sound of contempt by blowing through thick lips: 'Brrrup!'

She turned the screech on him: 'Get out kitchen, black bastard!'

The man grunted, '*Goona*!' Ah Loy handed him two large buckets of milk evidently made from the dried powder, several cans of which stood on the kitchen table. The man went stamping out.

Now Ah Loy grunted: 'Wha's matter you hunt dat boy?'

'Dat black rubbitch no right kitchen.'

'He come tek him smoke-o o' stockyard. Who goin' o' tek him now?'

'Who been talk smoke-o long o' stockyard?'

'Boss been send word . . . want finish job.'

Ah Loy went to the back door, yelled at the khaki-clad figure under the mangan tree, 'Green-ant . . . gitchim hand-cart come.' Turning back inside, he spoke sharply to the woman: 'Nelyerri . . . get him two-feller smoke-o ready hand-cart. I mek tea.'

She scowled at him, perhaps because of the name he'd used to address her, a Skin Name, normally used only in formality, which could serve as rebuke spoken by an intimate. Use of names, of which one would have several to meet the complex demands of tribal life, was always a matter of delicacy. The boy's name, if his Totem or Dreaming Name, spoken by Ah Loy would declare the man husband to his mother, according to the rules of relationship if not in fact. Still, it could be a Nickname, used to avoid formality, as might be the case of the old wood-boy, Green-ant. Nicknaming was resorted to commonly in primitive conditions of Aboriginal society, but almost invariably in those of greater promiscuity resulting from dependence on the white man, when mostly they were to be had serving two purposes by twisting one of the proper names to semblance of those used by the masters. Thus Nelyerri probably was addressed usually as Nelly. A very intricate business of which whites mostly had no knowledge at all, or having some, little or no patience with.

Nelyerri took her scowl out to the side verandah.

Prindy, lingering, whispered to Ah Loy, 'Who dere long o' stockyard?'

Mention of two lots of smoke-o and the hand-cart would mean more whitemen than just the Boss.

Ah Loy answered in the same tone: 'Martin Delacy, Mullaka, new-feller Stock Inspector.'

The grey eyes grew wide with interest, while the whisper became excited: 'Mullaka! Close-up to Race Time. I go look-him.'

'More-better you wait, Joey. He come look-him you talk-about horse.'

'What-for dat-lot whitefeller come?'

'Sick cow. No-more millik. Too many calfee been die finish. Mullaka doctor him.'

'I go stockyard look-see.'

'Can't do it. Mumma cranky . . . mek too much trouble. You eat him pie.'

Ah Loy moved again to the back door, at which he stopped, to exclaim, 'Eh, who dat dere?' There was now a different person in khaki under the mangan tree, this one not with grey hair peeping out of hat, but in a top-knot out of what looked like a death's head.

Prindy came to look, said quickly, 'Dat old man I been tell-him 'bout . . . sing him fish.' As he looked out, a claw rose to signal greeting.

But Ah Loy's attention was diverted to the wood-shed, round which a black face under a battered hat was peeping. He murmured, 'Wha's matter Green-ant?' Then he bawled, 'Eh, old-man . . . gitchim hand-cart . . . quick-feller!'

The old fellow stared for a moment, disappeared behind the shed, to reappear coming at a run, heading not for the back steps but for the side. The man and boy looked at each other in surprise. Then there was Green-ant in the kitchen. Ah Loy went into him: 'Wha's matter, old-man?'

Green-ant answered on a deep inhalation: 'Dat-one Bobwirridirridi.'

Ah Loy responded similarly: 'Eh, look out!'

Prindy joined them, eyes averted from his theoretical wife's brother, or whatever old Green-ant was to him, asking 'Wha' name?'

Green-ant said to the roaring range, 'Bob-Big-Wind . . . Cock-Eye Bob . . . no-goot bugger dat-one. Me been see him long o' jail!'

Prindy asked Ah Loy, 'Wha' name no-goot?'

Green-ant answered, 'Belong o' Tchinek Bijnitch.'

The grey eyes widened.

Ah Loy turned to look out towards the wood-yard, where still the khaki figure squatted under the plum tree. He growled, 'Wha' for he come here?'

Prindy said quickly, 'I been promised him tucker.'

'Eh, look out!'

'Him all right. I call-yim Granny.'

'Green-ant breathed, 'Him *koornung*, dat one.'

'Da's right,' said Ah Loy. 'We got 'o hunt him.'

Prindy protested: 'No-more! I been promised . . . bre'millik . . . tchoup. He too-muchee hungry . . . no-goot long o' *binji*, he talk.'

Green-ant said to the range, 'Him got no *binji*, dat bugger. Him *koornung*. Him been burn-up in fire.'

Ah Loy's almond eyes quizzed the grey that were only shining with interest. Prindy said eagerly, 'You mek him bre'millik, tchoup . . . I go gitchim hand-cart.' He shot away towards the back door, out and down the steps, went racing to the mangan tree. The skeleton now in grubby khaki shirt and trousers remained seated. They were not old clothes, but by the look of them a recent jail issue. The red coals stared hard up into the staring grey eyes. An odd pair, this theoretical grandsire and grandson, making a new estimate of each other. Prindy spoke first: 'Close-up I bring him you bre'millik . . . Kumija.'

The appellative evidently pleased, the way the gaunt face split and the answer was given with a gusty exhalation: 'Ah . . . Mora!'

'I gitchim cart now.' The boy swung away to the hand-cart by the shed, seized its shafts, went racing with it to the side steps of the kitchen. As he left it to come leaping up the steps, his mother carrying a towel-covered box, demanded, 'What you doin'?'

'I tek smok-o long o' stockyard.'

'No you don't! You reckon hungry. You eat him dat steak-and-kidney pie.'

He bounded past her into the kitchen. Green-ant slipped past him, out onto the side verandah. Ah Loy stared at him. Prindy surveyed the table, where his pie awaited him heaped on an enamel plate. But it was not for that he looked. He asked, 'Where bre' millik?'

'You eat him pie.'

'I been promised him old-man . . . I call-yim Granny.'

Ah Loy's voice rose in protest: 'Dat-one Doctor Blackfeller!'

Stubbornly Prindy replied, 'I call-yim Granny.'

Ah Loy sighed: 'All Right . . . look out he no tuckered you. You eat him pie . . . I gitchim.'

Prindy wolfed the pie while watching Ah Loy mix bread and milk in a stockman's quart-pot. As he rose he said, 'Tchoup.' Without a word Ah Loy filled another pot with soup and bread.

The boy was picking up the pots when his mother came in, demanding, 'What you do now?'

'Tek him tucker long o' Granny.'

She snapped, 'Wha' nam' Granny?'

'Old-man I been find him long o' bush.'

Her voice rose to the screech: 'You no-more got him black feller granny. You white. All-day I got o' tell him you . . . you white, you white, you white . . . you no-more bloody blackfeller . . . come here!'

But Prindy was off with the pots, out by the back door. His mother ran after him, but to stop at the door and stand scowling at what amounted to a ritual giving, the way the donor knelt to make it with both hands, and the recipient took it likewise to bring each pot under his nose with something like a flourish to savour it then put it down and reach with claws to smooth the young shoulders.

However, he, called Bobwirridirridi, wasted no more time on niceties, but fell to the bread and soup, tossing it off in gulps that made his scrawny neck now look like that of an emu swallowing moya apples. Prindy knelt watching with interest.

'Ah . . . proper-lee!' The empty pot was set down. The red snake of tongue popped out to lick grey chops and express deep satisfaction.

Then the boy rose, saying, 'I go now, Granny.' Still he hesitated. A gift must always be met with a gift. A claw reached for the heap of dunnage, came back with the Minga-minga, the music sticks.

They were handed over with a cackle: '*Mundinjana* . . . Song Man. By'n'by me learn him you *maharaghi* song.'

The fair head nodded. The sticks were thrust into the waist of the khaki shorts. Prindy leapt away towards the garden gate. His mother screamed at him, 'Come here!' He ignored her, went through, ran to the house, through to his bed at the rear.

He stood a while clicking the sticks gently, while his lips moved in soundless snatches of song. Then he stopped, to cock his head to listen to sound outside. Nothing, seemingly, but the splash of water from the tanks. Still, the eyes sought the direction of the stockyard, from which keen hearing must have caught a sound. Hurriedly he slipped the sticks under his pillow, then dashed out by the back door, through the garden westward. He slipped through the fence onto a pad, went trotting towards that cloud of dust.

Soon the stockyard could be seen, standing away from the rest of the homestead, like a jail or madhouse outside a town. There were acres of it, high-railed, in a treeless clearing, built about the butchering-hoist that stood dimly in the swirling dust like a gallows-tree round which the goings on within brawled and bawled. Closer, the gallows could be seen to blossom with buzzard-kites and crows, awaiting dead eyes to pick, jockeying for position, adding raucous voices to the bellowing and shouting – *Hi, hi, hi*! – and crack of whips. Human figures loomed through the grey gloom, balanced on top rails, slashing with whips, poking with sticks. At one point, other human figures, diminutive these, for the most part naked, otherwise clothed in dust and looking rather like slim lizards foraging in cracks of a wall, darted in and out of the rails. At this point the din was at its height, by reason of being made by kids and calves.

Prindy arrived there, took a look, then slipped through the rails to join the fun. The black children were separating small calves from mothers and bundling them through a swing-gate where they were being fed milk by black women. Much of the fun was being caused by the objection of cows. Some of the picaninnies, emerging from hair-breadth escapes, clung to each other helpless with hilarity.

Had Prindy been in less hurry for fun, he must have noticed that it was not the usual cutting out of clean-skin calves that was in progress, but of such as bore a bright orange paint mark. These were the starveling calves. Evidently looking about for a worthy party to his soon-apparent prowess in stockyard bull-fighting, he chose a sturdy little red micky. It took up his challenge at once, snorted, dropped hornless head, charged. The young bull-fighter stood his ground to the last moment, then kicking dust into his adversary's eyes, stepped aside, to grab the high-held tail as it went sailing by, and swing the beast off balance. Down it came bawling in a swirl of dust. Next move was to get the head and twist it to the shoulder. Just as he was about to make it, something hurled him into a heap with his opponent. Both bawled. Prindy got to knees to meet a red and white face glowering down at him from under a pair of nasty horns on one of which hung half his trousers. The horns dropped for another rake at him. He lost the remainder of his pants in goanna-scuttling for the nearest rails, squeezed under the bottom rail as the horns crashed into it.

He looked up from where he lay naked in the dust. He was in a small yard beside the railed alley called the crush. There were no cattle here, only a group of humans, four of them white, and all staring at him hard.

It was on the faces of the white men, still to be seen as ruddy beneath sweat-streaked coatings of dust, that the grey eyes fixed. There were three pairs of light eyes, two blue, one grey and exactly like his own, the fourth greenish in a very red face as the sweat-streaks showed. It was on the grey eyes that the boy's finally dwelt, quickly, as if in flight from the others. The grey eyes twinkled, their owner, an oldish man, said, 'What 'smatter you runnin' round on your *binji* all-same you properly *prindy*?'

Red of lips and pearl of teeth broke the dust-grey Aboriginal mask: 'Old cow chase me, Mullaka.'

'Might-be think you calfee, eh?'

Chuckles from the black men and from the white man with the green eyes – while the faces of the blue-eyed ones remained shut tight. As if drawn to them, Prindy met the hard staring eyes; then as if repelled, turned back to the rails. He, called Mullaka, stopped him: 'Wait Sonny.'

There was a bloody weal on the boy's behind. Taking his arm, the man said, 'Better let me put something on it.' He propelled him to a trestle table beside the crush where there was medical and surgical gear, soused a bit of cotton from a bottle, dabbed the wound. Releasing the boy he said, 'Right. Look out you don't get another horn up the *loonga* . . . or you won't be able to ride races. I got a nice little horse for you. See you by'n'by.' Grinning, Prindy shinned to the top rail, disappeared.

The green-eyed young man said, 'Nice cut of kid . . . not a full-blood with that hair and those eyes, though, eh?' When no one answered, he looked around, surprised.

Mullaka broke the awkward little silence, saying in a dry tone, 'The genus *Homo sapiens*, despite its variety of breeds, doesn't excite much interest amongst cattlemen . . . at least around these parts, you'll find, Mr Bishoff. Let's get on with our bovines, to get 'em finished with before dark.'

The man Bishoff was the new Stock Inspector, obviously. The others were the Delacys, best known men of the district, father and sons, Jeremy, Martin, Clancy. Martin, the heavier built of the two sons and the elder, was the Big Boss of Vaiseys hereabout, the District Manager. Clancy was manager of Catfish Station. Jeremy, called Mullaka by the Aborigines, was an independent man, a stock expert.

It was not difficult to jump to the conclusion that the boy Prindy was a Delacy, too – not the son of Jeremy, judging by his dry remark, nor of the younger Clancy, the way his jaw set and eyes narrowed when, as it were in comment on what had been said, he looked at his brother. Not that Martin's face betrayed anything. But this would be in keeping with his position and the conventions of his breed regarding cross-bred bastards.

The boy himself must have some feeling of identity with his true father's tribe, if it were only something to be expressed by that wariness he had shown before the two young men. Then again, the indulgence of the grandfather was evident. Still, it did anything but follow that, semi-savage that he was, he understood the import of it. According to Aboriginal understanding of genetics, babies beget themselves. One's existence as tribesman or woman is eternal. One lives in the flesh for a spell, dies, goes back to an Elysian state of loitering in the Dreaming Place, until the urge to resume the fleshly role again takes hold, when one 'finds' oneself a father by whom to be presented to a woman destined by Skin to deliver one back into the bosom of the tribe. Ideally, the Finder is the physical protector of one's mother, that is her husband according to the laws of relationship, and also kin to oneself in the matter of one's dreaming. But in a pinch any man might serve who is not actually *wahji*, or taboo, according to the laws. Perhaps such concession had been made through dwindling numbers and intrusion of strangers with increased domination by the whiteman. At any rate, it had been extended even to include whitemen close enough to be chosen by the *Tjooloo*, the Baby Spirit. Copulation has no part in it. The *Tjooloo* simply attaches itself to the man, mostly without his being aware of it till later, and enters the mother with food he gives her, or even on his breath – but never, never by means of copulation.

Perhaps the last thing the Aborigine who has been bred in the old tradition surrenders to the rationalism of civilization is this Gooseberry Bush theory of the phenomenon of his existence. For with it goes the wonder of his existence, leaving him as what those who still cling to tradition so aptly call one of their kind who had abandoned it – a Bloody Nutching – which, in fact, is what the average white person is, if you look into him or her deeply enough. Take the wonder of Santa Claus from a civilized child, and you leave him or her with what? The very dubious kindness of real people?

II

Evening, with the work at the stockyard finished, the majority of the stock freed and gone to water, sick calves and cows still bawling for each other, the dusty day dying in whisps of heliotrope over the tall timber of the creek, a full moon rising vermilion out of the ragged scrub of the plain into a silver sky. At the Big House, the white men, bathed and changed, were in the latticed lower part that served as lounge and dining-room, sitting in cane chairs, drinking beer and talking sick cattle while awaiting the serving of the meal hereabout called Supper. It would seem that the sickness on hand was something hitherto unknown and under experimental treatment directed by Jeremy Delacy. Jeremy was telling of work he had been doing in his veterinary hospital on his own property, Lily Lagoons, while Bishoff, the Government Stock Inspector, kept bibbing in, evidently to air knowledge recenty acquired. Martin and Clancy Delacy were silent for the most part, staring at their father with expressions not easy to read.

Slap of bare feet caused all four men to glance casually as a female figure bearing a laden tray came into the light shed from an acetylene lamp hanging from the ceiling, heading for the dining table half-hidden behind bamboo screens. Two pairs of eyes remained casual in their interest. The others, those of the Delacy sons, widened with surprise. But while Martin continued to stare wide-eyed and slack-mouthed, his young brother's expression changed suddenly to unmistakable annoyance.

It was Nelyerri, rigged out in a bright floral dress of greens and reds, mane of wavy dark hair caught up with a red ribbon, highlights of excitement flashing from dark eyes. She cast the briefest glance in passing to become a shadow behind the screens. Clancy shot a glance at his brother, to find him gaping at the shadow. Martin, feeling the glance, started guiltily, raised his glass to drink. Clancy's face tightened still more. He glanced at his father, to find him eyeing both of them intently. Distinctly red of face now, he set his own glass down, mumbled, 'Excuse me,' rose, went swiftly towards the shadow.

Nelyerri, unloading the tray of soup-tureen, bread, plates, looked up wide-eyed at Clancy's appearance. Scowling now, he growled, 'What're you doing here?'

Drooping her head, she whispered on indrawn breath, 'Cocky not come from camp, Mister Clancy.'

'Why not? You know very well you're not supposed to serve.'

'Cocky too much fright' come.'

'Fright' of what?'

'One old man Doctor Blackfeller come station.'

'Well, you just go to the camp and tell Cocky to come and serve supper, or I'll come and get her myself . . . with the stock-whip. Now get!'

With head still drooped, she hastened away with the empty tray.

Clancy called to the others: 'Right. Soup's served. Bring the beer.' His eyes met his brother's in distinct challenge as Martin came to the table. Martin seemed to dismiss it with a blink.

After the soup they had to eat bread and butter and drink beer because of the delay in service continually called for by Clancy ringing the little bell. He began by apologizing, then explaining the cause of the holdup, burst out, 'I'll give 'em Doctor Blackfeller!'

When Bishoff asked what was meant, Clancy left it to his father to explain: 'Yes, a native doctor. But his job's as much causing illness as curing it. As malady is magic with them, the Doctor Blackfeller's first of all a magician. Although magic is the be-all end-all of Aboriginal existence, the accepted cause and effect of every contingency, acceptance is largely a matter of rote, so that confrontation with it, even with one of its practitioners, the *koornung*, is always cause for alarm. I wonder who this one is? We don't have many Doctor Blackfellers round these days. They were probably the first of the old things to go, because the blacks themselves didn't want 'em.'

At last there appeared a fat black woman, carrying a laden tray, panting with exertion and with face jerking in the way of the Aborigine under deep emotional stress. Evidently someone had accompanied her to the door. As she set down the big steak-and-kidney pie before Clancy, he demanded of her, 'Who you got out there?'

She breathed, 'My old man.'

'What's the matter with you all . . . buggerin' up my supper?'

Jeremy cut in: 'I'd like to ask her old man about this *koornung*.'

Clancy bawled, 'Green-ant . . . come here!'

The old fellow came sidling in, halted at a respectful distance. Jeremy asked, 'Wha' name Doctor Blackfeller, Jumbajinna?'

Green-ant answered in a deep whisper, 'Bobwirridirridi, Mullaka.'

'Ah . . . thank you, old-man. I give you somesing present Race Time.'

'Tahng you, Mullaka.' Green-ant slunk back outside.

'Old Cock-Eye Bob, eh,' said Jeremy to the others. 'No wonder they're scared . . . boss of the Snake Business.'

Martin growled, 'I thought the old bugger was in jail for life?'

'Must have got out on the Royal Amnesty. A couple of your own blacks were freed with this Edward the Eighth's Accession, weren't they . . . including Green-ant, if I'm not mistaken?'

Martin answered, 'I was first asked if I wanted 'em back. If they'd asked me about that bloody old pest, I'd've soon said No.'

'You don't employ him.'

'He wanders Vaisey country. I should've been asked.'

'Maybe they were glad of an opportunity to get him off their own hands. I understand he led 'em a dance in jail with his tricks."

They were eating now. Bishoff asked, 'What tricks?'

'*Koornungs* are very clever with natural faculties . . . hypnotism, ventriloquism, sleight-of-hand, and the like. Old Bob was supposed to break jail occasionally, by the simple process of detaching spirit from body, and going walk-about to cause trouble amongst the relatives of those who crossed him in jail. His trance-states were so near perfect that several times he was judged dead and nearly buried, and one time actually buried, only to turn up in the lively flesh in the Native Compound, and cause the entire population to go bush.'

Bishoff asked, 'How could he get out of a coffin and a grave?'

'They don't bury blacks in coffins in these parts, man . . . and even up in Town there's no proper cemetery for them. They're planted in a sandy waste that's part of the Sanitary Depot, called The Coconuts. They might have a bit of sacking for a shroud . . . but even sacking's too valuable a commodity to be wasted on someone whose bones are most likely dug up again in secret and taken away for proper native disposal. Planting 'em Long o' Coconuts, as it's called, is the authorities' idea. It can all be rather informal, seeing a blackfellow doesn't even have to have a Death Certificate . . . .'

'No Death Certificate?'

'No Birth Certificate, either . . . because no real citizenship . . . actually not subject to the Law of the Land . . . unless he breaks it!'

The lowering looks of the Delacy sons showed plainly that they didn't like the trend of talk. Apparently Bishoff was unobservant, since he declared, 'I never cease to be amazed by the way things are done in these parts.'

Not so Jeremy, who asked him, 'But how do you like the way this steak pie's done?'

'Must say it's just about perfect.'

'You did put sauce on it, though, I noticed.'

Bishoff looked up from his plate in surprise.

Jeremy chuckled: 'You could have offended the cook deeply, if he'd happened to be peeping . . . which isn't unlikely, because his old father used to do that when he worked as cook for my own old father. No matter how old Ah Loy would sweat to get dishes to Da's exact taste, the old fellow always added some condiment. It used to drive Ah Loy crazy. What he never found out was that Da didn't have any taste at all.'

'Would that be the ancient Chinaman I saw in at the Beatrice . . . running a couple thousand goats on public land?'

'That's him. This one here's half-Aboriginal . . . but no less a superb cook . . . eh?' He looked at his sons, now relaxed enough to nod. He added: 'You'll find those goats are really public property. Everyone makes use of 'em, but blames ownership onto everyone else. Who told you they were Ah Loy's?'

Bishoff laughed: 'As a matter of fact, Finnucane the Publican and McDodds the Storekeeper. No . . . they said they belonged to Ah Loy and Ali Barba, the Indian Hawker. It was Ali Barba told me they were Ah Loy's . . . only if you want one for Sunday dinner, you can get it either from Finnucane or McDodds.'

All laughed over it. The trend then turned to comical tales about the characters of the district. Thus till the meal was over. As they rose, Jeremy said to his sons, 'I'll relieve you of the presence of old Cock-Eye-Bob . . . take him away with me tomorrow. I'd like to hear more about Snake Business from him, if he'll talk. I'll go and see if I can find him now.' He added to Bishoff: 'Care to come?'

Passing out through the gate of the garden surrounding the Big House and out of earshot of those left behind, Jeremy murmured to his companion, 'I fancy the boys are in for a bit of a row . . . and are best left to it. Shows what a *koornung* can do. Everybody on edge. Listen.'

Bishoff's bristly fair hair glinted in the moonlight as he cocked his squarish head: 'Can't hear anything . . . only the stock.'

'That's just it. Normally, with full bellies, a full Moon, an exciting day behind them, the Murries should be corroboreeing full blast . . . dogs barking, kids yelling.'

'Would he be with them?'

'No fear. A *koornung*'s a solitary . . . and left to himself, unless wanted for use of his powers.'

'How'll you find him?'

'He'll have his eye and ear on us. If he gives a hint of his whereabouts, I'll let it be known I want to see him to have a talk about *Bijnitch* . . . which'll mean he'll be able to ask a present of me . . . .'

'*Bijnitch*?'

'Business. A handy term to embrace the complexities of Aboriginal culture . . . Blackfeller *Bijnitch* . . . Sunday, or Tjundi, Bijnitch, meaning Sacred . . . Wrong-side Bijnitch, on the wrong side of blackfellow's law. We'll probably run into him somewhere near Ah Loy's quarters, where there's plenty of cover for one reputed to be able to appear and disappear at will. I want to drop in on Ah Loy. Got something for him.'

They passed the big low batten-walled harness shed, heading for another shed that housed motor vehicles. Jeremy went into a utility truck, brought out of it a bundle of papers. He chuckled as he set off towards the kitchen: 'What they call Readin' Matter round these parts . . . catalogues from the big southern stores . . . favourite reading of all classes and breeds . . . even those who can't read. You must've noticed the stack in Clancy's place? It'll end up in the blacks' camp . . . to be studied just as avidly. They constitute the city shop windows . . . treasure caves . . . everything you want . . . dresses, suits, hats, boots, knives, saddles, spurs, tommy-axes. Even if you've got 'em, apparently it's sweet to dream over more . . . and if you can't get 'em . . . well, they're the stuff of dreams. You should see the wonder that shines in the face of a blackfellow for whom you've turned the dream of the catalogue picture into the reality of the mail-order you've got for him. Like a child at Christmas. Poor Clancy gets no such joy from his frequent mail-orders, because he's lost the faculty for wonder . . . like most whites in this country.' Jeremy sighed: 'That's what's wrong with us Australians. We left our sense of wonder behind with our ancestors.'

'How d'you mean?'

'I take it you're of German origin?'

'A fair way back.'

'Have you ever been to Germany?'

'Not yet. I hope to go.'

'Well, you must know something of its legends . . . of the nymphs of the Rhine and the giants of the Alps, and all the rest. Even as a stranger there . . . I spent a bit of time with the Army of Occupation . . . I couldn't help but feel the wonder of the place, because of its legends and history. It's the same everywhere . . . Britain, France, Egypt, Asia Minor . . . everywhere but here, where we live in a land the wonder of which, as damned and doomed Colonials, we've been unable to see. What wonder is in our lives is taken at second-hand, moth-eaten, only half comprehended, from our origins.'

'Well, we've got no real history yet.'

'I didn't say history alone . . . but legend, tradition . . . which this land's packed with.'

'Aboriginal legend . . . . '

'What's wrong with that? Are the legends of the Ancient Druids any the less satisfying to the English because based on culture long ante-dating the coming of the people who became the English . . . or the legends of Germany because dating from the Visigoths or someone?'

They were passing the dark kitchen, when after a pause, Jeremy said, 'See that tree ahead there, by the wood-heap. That's a mangan, a native plum. Apart from the fact that it has a good story concerning its origin in the Dream Time, it's supposed to have the power to attract and spellbind lovers, so that they may be crept up on and killed.'

'Why killed?'

'To Aborigines, love's always a matter of law-breaking. You only fall in love with someone *Wahji*, or Wrong-side to you, that is, not as permitted by laws of relationship. You fall in love only through magic . . . *Charada*, as love-magic is called. The Moon's involved in it . . . the Willy wagtail, too. Love is very real to Aborigines . . . not the fake thing it mostly is to us . . . a magic thing, and also a tragic thing.'

'Do they still kill people for it?'

'Wrong-side Business? Any whiteman who claims to know what the Murries do or don't do is a fool. They're a very secretive people, for all their seeming primitive simplicity. Well, here's your mangan. A common enough tree. When you come on it in your wanderings, knowing its power should add a bit more interest to surroundings otherwise meaningless to you . . . but, of course, be careful if there're any *Kweeais* about.'

'*Kweeais*?'

'Young lubras. It's the ladies who hold the secrets of *Charada*.'

'You sound as if you believe in these things.'

'In the power of *Charada*? I certainly do. It's a power of the mind . . . the greatest force in the Universe, surely. As to the magical power of the tree, I accept that.'

'How d'you mean?'

'As part of an environment I don't want to feel alien in . . . my own native land. According to the blackfellow there's magic in everything . . . every rock, tree, waterhole . . . even in the things he makes . . . his spears, dilly-bags. In fact, if you take the trouble, you yourself can find wonder in everything. We do in scientific things . . . what we see through a microscope, what takes place in chemical reaction. As geologists we'd find it in the rocks through rationalism. As zoologists in the pools, botanists in the trees. The blackfellow's reverence for things strikes me as much more intelligent than the blank disregard of the mass of our own people . . . who'd still be simple-minded enough to believe in the divinity of Christ and the sanctity of the Virgin Mary, the Holy Ghost, and all the rest of it.'

They were nearing the garden gate. Jeremy broke off to halt and look toward the Moon, against which, a short distance away, stood a biggish tree so thickly leafed as to look like a woolly black head. He said, 'There's another tree reputed to have special powers . . . *kumbitji*, the ironwood. It's believed that if you sleep under one at night you won't ever wake up again . . . unless you're a *koornung*.' After a pause he added: 'Two to one our old Pookarakka's camped there. Let's have a look.'

Sure enough, as they approached, there was a flicker as of movement in the deep shadow of the tree. However, there was neither sight nor sound of anyone's presence when they reached it. Jeremy said, 'He's done his famous disappearing trick.'

Bishoff asked, 'How does the tree kill lesser men?'

'With its poisonous breath. As a matter of fact, at a certain time of year the young leaves do contain a poisonous glucocide. In my early days of unbelief I did some experimenting to see what truth might be in it. Certainly it gives off CO_2 at night, like any other plant, and to a markedly greater degree because of the density of foliage . . . but in nothing like lethal quantity It's a general belief. Few if any whitemen . . . bushmen . . . will sleep under one.'

'Would you?'

'No.'

'Why . . . when you've disproved it scientifically?'

'Because I'd feel I was flouting the conventions of the country.'

'Eh? From what I've heard, you're the most unconventional man in it! I was told you even hung a stuffed french letter on the Anzac Memorial in Port Palmeston one Anzac Day . . . to the eternal outrage of the RSL'. The young man chuckled: 'Is that a fact?'

'To make a denial would be to deprive the community of one of its favorite furpheys . . . and the way I stand with my old comrades of the RSL, to confess, it would be like laying me down some night under the *kumbitji*. When I said conventions of the country I meant literally of the land . . . Terra Australis. For all that I was born of the land and would wish to be born nowhere else, I still feel that I'm the descendant of intruders, and am bound to watch my manners.' As they turned from the tree, Jeremy raised his voice: 'Where that Pookarakka? I want him learn him me something *bijnitch* . . . I give it present.' No response.

As they neared the garden gate again, Jeremy asked, 'Do you hear something?'

'Yes . . . singing, isn't it. That's not blacks singing, is it?'

It was a single voice, a sweet thin soprano, coming from the direction of Ah Loy's house, now to be seen as bars and triangles of bright light vying with dappled moonlight in the shadow of the mangoes.

'No . . . that's young Prindy . . . the quarter-caste boy you saw at the yard. Let's get closer and listen. He makes up songs of his own . . . a really remarkable thing in anyone like him!'

'How's that?'

'Well, Aborigines live by tradition, which naturally cancels out originality. Cross-breds, if they turn away from the Old People, as they call them . . . and mostly they do . . . go for the poorest of white man's music . . . Yankee hillbilly stuff.'

At the mangoes they stopped to listen. Now the words were plain:

. . . My Road, my Rown Road
I go look dat Road, my Rown, my Dream Road
Road belong 'o I, must-be find him by-'n'-by
My Road, my Rown Road . . .

Jeremy murmured, 'Your Road is the way you must go through life as the reincarnation of a Dream Time ancestor. Each child is taught its Road. This boy's would be that of the Goanna . . . because that's his Dreaming. But calling it My Rown Road . . . Own Road . . . suggests that he's seeking a Road of his own . . . ah!' The singing stopped abruptly. 'He's heard us. He's got the sharpest hearing I ever struck in a human being. We'll show ourselves.' As they neared, Jeremy called, 'Anybody home?'

Scurry of bare feet and a glint of gold that was surely the fair head, as they came round the back verandah. Prindy must have been sitting singing outside and ducked behind the wide trunk of a mango.

The two men halted at the glaring doorway. Inside an acetylene lamp flared on a kerosene case, on either side of which, in hide chairs, sat Ah Loy, who was making a saddle, stitching with double needles, and Nelyerri, who was examining a bright silk dress. Jeremy called, 'Evenin'.'

Ah Loy responded with a wide Chinese grin: 'Come on in, Mullaka. Have dring o' tea, eh.' He looked at Nelyerri: 'Light him Primus.' She rose, clutching her dress.

Jeremy said, 'No thanks . . . just finished supper. Only looked in having a stroll. Brought you some readin' matter. This is Mr Bishoff, new Stock Inspector, Willy.'

Bishoff shook hands heartily, while Willy Ah Loy all but kowtowed.

Nelyerri started for inside. Jeremy said to her, 'Getting ready for the Races, Nelly?'

She turned, met his eyes, then dropped her own dark gaze to her stumpy bare chocolate feet, answering, 'Yas, Mullaka.'

'I heard the boy singing . . . but he bolted before I could speak to him.'

She drew in her breath: 'He too-much myall dis time.'

'How's that?'

Willy answered, 'Aw . . . he runnin' too-much round bush . . . sometime two-t'ree day.'

'What . . . with the Murries?'

'No-more . . . himself-himself . . . all-same *koornung*.'

'Might-be he stop now . . . that old *koornung*, Cock-Eye Bob been come.'

'Nutching stop. He been find dat old bugger long o' bush, bring him here.'

'Go on, eh!' Then Jeremy chuckled: 'Might-be he grow up *koornung*.'

But father and mother looked anything but amused. Jeremy added: 'What about me taking him back Lily Lagoons . . . given him to Darcy, start school.'

Nelly raised her head with a jerk, stared evident hostility at Jeremy, then dropped her gaze again, scowling.

Looking at her, Willy said, 'Good idea, I reckon.'

Her breast heaved to a deep breath, which she exhaled forcefully, exclaiming, 'No-more!'

Willy said, 'All-day you reckon you don' wan' him grow up blackfeller . . . .'

Her eyes blazed at him as she hissed, 'He no-more blackfeller.'

'All right . . . you give him Mullaka grow him up whitefeller.'

The handsome dark face began to jerk.

Jeremy cut in quickly: 'All right . . . when you're ready.' He added: 'We'll be getting along now. If you see Bobwirridirridi, Willy, tell him I want to have a yarn with him, will you?'

Ah Loy grinned widely again: 'Spone I see dat old bugger, I bolt.'

Jeremy chuckled: 'Oh, well . . . goodnight. See you mornin'. I come kitchen early cup o' tea.'

Man and woman answered together, 'Gootnight, Mullaka . . . gootnight, Mist Bishp.'

The two men went on through the garden. Again a flicker of movement in the shadow of the clump of bananas beside the water-tanks. Bishoff was about to comment, but was stopped by a touch from Jeremy, who said loudly, 'Spone that Pookarakka come Lily Lagoons long o' me, I feed him plenty bread-and-milk.' He kept them going. At a little distance he murmured, 'That ought to fetch him . . . if that was the old chap and not his apprentice.'

'What's the lure about bread-and-milk?' asked Bishoff.

'He can't eat solid food. He's had his gut burnt out with arsenic.'

'How come?'

Jeremy left explaining till they were through the back fence of the garden and on that pad by which Prindy had come home: 'It happened a good while back . . . during the War . . . 'Sixteen or 'Seventeen. I was overseas at the time . . . mixed up in the filthy business, to my eternal shame.'

Bishoff glanced at the rugged face beside him, made more so by being against the moonlight, its shock of grey hair limned with silver, asked, 'Why shame? I'd've thought it'd be the adventure of a lifetime. I wish I'd've been old enough to have a go.'

'That was the trouble . . . the appeal to the immigrant adventure-seeking in us . . . at the cost of the greater, more positive, adventure, of establishing ourselves truly as a nation.'

'I've heard you're bitter about it because your brother was killed.'

'My brother's only a symbol of what we sacrificed in our stupidity. My bitterness is for the way our stupidity was exploited by the very people we sacrificed for . . . the British . . . and their agents here . . . the bastards!' The deep voice was vibrant with feeling. Bishoff glanced again.

They were still heading along the fence northward, with the silver and jet wall of the timber of the creek on their left. After a moment Jeremy went on: 'I'm telling you about Bobwirridirridi . . . so that you may get to understand the blackman better, and not make the mistakes most people do. You won't understand the country without understanding something of the original owners of it . . . or of the second dispossession of it . . . that is the robbing of *us*, the first robbers, but at least the ones who slaved and sweated and risked our lives . . . gave our lives in many cases . . . to make it ours. Actually that bloody war and the consequences of it that burn my own guts out with anger, are part of the story. His becoming a *koornung* coincides, you might say, with the selling out . . . or rather abject surrender . . . to the enemy, Britain . . . which is to say British Imperialism, economic as well as political . . . in the shape . . . shape of a bloody octopus . . . of Vaiseys Limited.'

Jeremy paused for a few paces, resumed: 'Just as it is now, most of the stock bred in this country was overlanded to the Southern States. Shortage of men for droving, through the War, soon put an end to that. Horsemen were the first to enlist . . . cavalry. Kitchener in his visit here had organized that. So most cattle runs, all of them small, still run by their founders, were out of business. That didn't mean they'd be sold up, or anything of the kind that may happen down South. Their lease-rentals were low. They could maintain things with their blacks for practically nothing, seeing they didn't have to pay them, and could feed them largely off the run. Anyway, there was no real excuse for the surrender to Vaiseys. Of course Vaiseys were already in control of grazing in the South American countries and Africa and supplying the world. What they were after here was a vast meat-canning industry. Cattle will breed in unlimited numbers here with little attention. They never fatten. But lean meat is what the canner wants. Bully beef was then in demand as never before. A huge meat works was built at Port Palmeston. It was hailed as an act of the first patriotism. The Big Boss, Alfred Vaisey, was made a lord for it.

'As I've said, it all happened while I was away helping to make the world safe for British Capitalism. I came home to find what I deserved in the circumstances, that Lord Vaisey had become *my* boss, too. The difference in my case was that I didn't consider it the great honour that the other graziers did, and promptly put in my resignation . . . with results you've probably heard of, namely that I have to maintain the scrap of leasehold I was able to hang onto by making a show of mining, as it's primarily a mining lease, and a living as a quack veterinary surgeon, am an utter stranger to the wife who bore my sons, and not much less a stranger to my sons. You haven't mentioned it . . but I guess you've met my first wife, now Mrs Eaton, wife of Vaiseys' General Manager for Australia, all set to become Lady Eaton with next Imperial Honours.'

Bishoff made a sympathetic sound.

Jeremy said, 'Don't get the impression that Vaiseys also dispossessed me of my wife. I was the cause of that bit of the change in my fortunes. I'm afraid I rather abandoned the lady to them. Not that she doesn't suit them and they her, as you must have noticed. And I'm well suited now as husband of a halfcaste wife.'

That seemed to embarrass Bishoff somewhat. As if to discomfort him more, Jeremy remained silent till the younger man spoke: 'You were telling me how the old *koornung* came to be poisoned with arsenic.'

'Yes . . . in effect how he became a *koornung*. Lord Vaisey, in his patriotic zeal, was taking over every property he, or his henchmen, rather, could lay hands on. They even went after holdings where the stock were still being speared by blacks. There were a couple of small runs just then opening up over in the Western Sandstone Country . . Queen Victoria and Alice River Districts. Wonderful place-names round these parts, aren't they . . . named after Queen Victoria and her brood. You'd think the explorers and early surveyors, tough fellows for a certainty, would have been above such sycophancy. Not only Royalty, of course, but some Bigwig. My own father, who was as good an Irishman as any, except when doing his duty as a policeman to the Queen of England, named two places he found during expeditions in that way . . . one after his immediate boss, the Police Superintendent, the other after the Administrator's wife, both of whom he actively disliked. As I found, the places had specially pleasant-sounding Aboriginal names. He didn't even ask these, as he admitted to me when I asked him years later. When I asked him why he'd named them as he did, he answered, 'Ye've got to be politic, me boy.' But I'm digressing. I guess I want to give you some idea of what this country's really like, before your fellow silver tails and the squattocracy bind you with their prejudices. You went so far as to consult me as a colleague in trouble with the stock . . . .'

'I consulted you as an expert.'

'That's nice of you . . . when your predecessor, old Stinker Daggenhart, spent the best part of his service trying to get me deregistered because I don't hold a degree.'

'That old dodderer . . . with his lion-hunter's hat!'

'He's a graduate of Leipzig University and a Fellow of the Royal Zoological Society.'

'And look at the muddle he's left the job in!'

'Well, it's nice to have you on my side to start with, anyway. But let's get on with the story. I like to finish a story I start. Besides, this one should give you a truer view of the Aboriginal Problem, so called, than the distorted one that's surely awaiting you. To me the Aboriginal Problem is a fundamental one, not only in this region, where it's still a very important issue in every aspect of life here, but for Australia generally . . . because only the other day, in terms of history, we stole this land we've been so quick to call our own, stole it with murder and mayhem and about the lowest forms of meanness a human being could stoop to . . . and we have to reconcile the matter someday, either by acknowledging the fact that we're bloody-handed thieves and being proud of it, or giving back what we stole, and not as an act of charity, but of downright humility.'

Bishoff, staring, exclaimed, 'But that's impossible!'

'I suppose it is. But it's the truth . . . and unless you face it, you can't live amongst these people, except as a downright rogue or hypocrite. Even those few people truly sympathetic towards them think of them as lowly creatures to be raised to our own exalted way of life. You'll find these good people mildly voicing the same objection to the blackfellow as drove the pioneers to destroy them in rage . . . that finally they're *useless*, because they won't give up their simple savage freedom, even if that amounts at last only to living like animals on the edge of the conquerors' towns . . . in short, won't join up with us as slaves to our own systems. What you'll see of the blackfellow mostly will make you feel he's pretty low. I'd like to put the idea into your mind that he's like that because he never gave in . . . for all the bullying, the sheer brutality and the pretended brotherly love, he has never, never given in. That's why I want to tell you the story of Bobwirridirridi. And speaking of the Pookarakka, the Wise One . . . I've a feeling we've got him with us.'

Bishoff looked around. Nothing but silvery grass and posts and wires of the fence: 'I don't see anything.'

Jeremy jerked his head towards the line of timber, went on to say, 'If you looked long enough you'd see a lot of things. That's what this country's like where it hasn't been defaced by our pale-faced brethren. I mean both real things and those that are unreal to the unknowing. This is a land of spirits. Don't forget that it was divined as such even before found by the unbelievers. The mariners who dreamt of its existence called it *Terra Australis del Espiritu Santo*, South Land of the Holy Spirit, from which at last the lovely name Australia, South Land, came. You'll have to make allowance for this magic quality to appreciate the story of the Pookarakka properly. I've inferred that magic is the be-all-end-all of Aboriginal existence. Even those who appear to be husks of men to you, the Bloody Nutchings who've lost their Dreaming, as the blackfellow who still has his would call them, see everything as magic, even the bottle of grog he gets for selling his wife, or the stick of *Niki-niki*, trade tobacco, he'll beg for without shame.'

Jeremy paused to clear his throat: 'Not used to so much talk-talk.'

'They told me that I'd be lucky if you talked to me at all . . . and just as unlucky if you did.'

'Oh? I haven't heard that one. They mean you'd regret it, because then I'd bash your ear?'

'Something like that. But please go on. I find everything you say quite fascinating. It gives a new slant to things I'd taken for granted.'

'Well . . . the early settlers over in that Princess Alice Country were left to settle their differences with the blacks their own way. The police kept out of it. It might have proved to be the best way in the end. Let everybody concerned get over their fear of each other . . . and then the traditional woman-lending starts. You're bound, as a blackfellow, to lend your women to a trusted stranger who has none. The boss's bed could have been the foundation of harmony . . . and a new society. The trouble was there were the white women to reckon with. Eventually they'd come looking for their men, find them Gin Jockeying, as they say, empty out their black rivals . . . and call in the police at any show of resentment. That's how the country was settled, man . . . settled and civilized. You've run into Piggy Trotters, I suppose? Well, he's Vaisey's manager at Alice River Downs. He pioneered that country. That halfcaste girl there, Ah Loy's wife, the little boy's mother, is a daughter of his. Not that Piggy would admit anything of the sort . . . or could if he would, with his squattocratic wife and daughters.' Jeremy chuckled.

He went on: 'Vaisey's took over the Princess Alice Country. The white ladies moved in. Soon the troopers arrived. As it was Vaisey cattle that were being speared now, and Lord Alfred had no idea of the old settlers' tolerance of it as a sort of tacit allowance for spoiling the hunting-grounds, Dispersal started. That was the official name for driving the tribes off their country. I understand they started off in a big way . . a punitive expedition . . . a dozen police officers, half of them white, the rest black. The black ones did the actual man-hunting. The black man would never have been so easily beaten, but for the treachery of his brethren. That treachery is hard to understand. The black policeman doesn't even get decently treated by his masters. He has no status, wears his master's cast-off uniforms, even gets only half the pay the regulations demand for other Aboriginal workers . . . that's to say, twenty shillings a month plus food and clothing. You have to understand that a blackfellow's loyalty, like everything else in his behaviour, is governed by the Relationship Laws, which have nothing to do with law as we know it, of course, but are based solely on mystic tradition.

'Well, it's rough country out there . . . and it took months to round up enough of the local tribesmen to ensure Detribalization, as it's called. In the end they were forced to abandon it, beaten by Wet Season. They were coming in starving, all of them, heading for the big new homestead, when just short of it they came on what had been the homestead in the old days. They looked in the hope of finding a bit of food . . . found a sack of flour. Nothing exactly is known of what happened. What is known is only what was told by Bobwirridirridi . . . or Tipperary, as for some odd reason he was called at that time. He became Cock-Eye Bob, or Bob the Big-Wind Man, only after his supernatural powers were recognized through this affair . . . that is by the blacks. Officially he was declared insane.

'Undoubtedly that flour was spiced with arsenic. It was an old trick of the grand old pioneers, the founders of our glorious young nation, to get rid of their pesky rivals for the land by leaving poisoned food about for them, as for the dingoes. Normally such a bag as was got on that occasion would have been bragged about. But, of course, half a dozen white policemen were included in it. It's generally believed that Piggy Trotters was responsible, and that's what's made of him the drunk he is. It wasn't till six months later that any trace of the party was found. First they found Bob wandering about as a living skeleton, claiming that he had wiped out the party himself. His story was that Tchamala, the Rainbow Snake, cut him out from the party, took him away up into the sky to where he lives, in that hole in the Milky Way we call the Coal Sack, and there gave him the powers of Boss Snake Man, and sent him back to earth as a python to swallow the party, police, prisoners and all. This he claimed to have done, and later to have vomited their bones and planted them in termites' nests. He took the search party and showed them these nests . . . and sure enough there were human bones in some. Termites do consume flesh and bone, and sometimes will build a new nest on top of the remains of some creature. In fact, an Aboriginal way to conceal a murder is to place the body in an ant-bed. The bones of the party would have been widely scattered by predatory and scavenging creatures. How much arsenic was found officially lord knows. Because it was Vaisey business, apparently it was glossed over by the Coroner, with a verdict of Misadventure. But no doubt about it, old Bob was a victim of arsenical poisoning. He was never able to eat solid food again. His diet in the bush was mainly *pijak*, or sugar-bag, the honey of native bees, for preference along with the lavae, and leaf-sugar, a kind of manna, and even crushed termites. He spent a couple of years up in town, in hospital or the Native Compound, feeding on bread and milk and soup. He used to go into those trances I was talking about, and claim afterwards that he'd been visiting his Country On Top, that is up with his Master, Tchamala, behind the Milky Way. I understand he used to howl for his celestial country much the same as an ordinary blackfellow does for his native haunts when away from them and feeling the deep nostalgia they often do . . . *Poor Fellow My Country*!'

They were cutting across to the creek timber beyond which was that rocky bar at the end of the long water-hole. Bishoff hissed, 'Thought I saw something over in the trees there.'

'That's the likely route he'd've taken.'

'But to cover that distance so quickly . . . across to the creek and then along!'

'He's supposed to be able to fly. Don't forget his proper country now is On Top.'

There was fluttering and faint scuffling as they neared the timber. Further back a Willy-wagtail could be heard faintly. Jeremy said, 'Everything's abroad tonight under the influence of old Igulgul, the Moon . . . except our black brethren, who even without a *koornung* round would be loath to take chances with the magic that's about . . . and my two sons, who prefer acetylene to moonlight anytime. You can't do justice to a store catalogue or a copy of *Man* magazine out in the moonlight.'

They passed through the timber in silence, listening to the squeaking, twittering, pattering, emerged to see the bar reared dark with the shadows of its unevenness against the blaze of the moonlit sand beyond. Bishoff hissed again, pointing, 'Look!'

Jeremy pulled his arm down, murmuring, 'Don't point with the finger. It's dangerous. You project a part of yourself at what you point. This's how you indicate things in these parts.' He protruded his lips towards an indistinct form that appeared in the middle of the bar and as quickly disappeared. They went on down to the bar, set out across. Bishoff, soon peering from side to side, said, 'We've just got to find him this time.'

'Why?'

'Just to see how smart he is.'

'You won't find him unless he wants you to.'

'You sound as if you credit him with special powers.'

'I told you that to live with these people without guilt or hatred you have to accept them as if one of them. If you question at all, it should be only to add to the richness of their complexity and to involve yourself more in it.'

Bishoff stopped his peeping into cracks and peeking after tracks in the sand below, sat down and stared at Jeremy: 'You are a strange man, you know . . . for one trained as a scientist.'

'I told you I was trained as a druggist, the nearest you could get to science in my day and environment . . . .'

'But you can buy and sell me scientifically, even though I've only been out of university three years . . . .'

'And I have a halfcaste Aboriginal wife.'

'What's that got to do with it? I found her an intelligent gracious lady.'

'Thank you. You're the first white person I've ever heard say it. She is all that. But what she's got to do with it is what I'm talking about. She'd rather have her finger cut off than point it, wouldn't eat possum if she were starving, because it's her totem and kin, wouldn't doubt for a moment that our friend here didn't come and go by magic. At the same time, because she was also mission-trained, she believes in God the Father, God the Son, and God the Holy Ghost . . . .'

'You don't believe in that stuff, though!'

'Definitely not. But I wouldn't interfere with anyone else's belief in it . . . unless they tried to shove it down my neck, as the missionaries do down the necks of the Aborigines, saying, Thou Shalt Have No Other Gods But Ours.'

'I'd've thought your rejection of Christianity would make you reject all religion.'

'You mean sects, I presume. Properly, Religion means having reverence for a divine conception. I can't think that a man can live fully without revering the marvel of the nature of things. Just take a look at what we see . . . that silver mirror that isn't a mirror at all, but a quantity of the stuff the likes of us call H_2O, a combination of two gases through heat . . . now teaming with fishes, weeds, a myriad things all living complexly . . . and the trees above and masses of other forms of life . . . and the sky above that . . . the Moon . . . the Milky Way with the Coal Sack . . . and who'll dare say Old Tchamala isn't peeping out of it to see where there's trouble he can make . . . which brings us back to our story about my old friend, the Pookarakka, that one I got plenty bread and milk for.'

No response. Jeremy said, 'It's embarrassing talking of present company, even if it can't be seen or heard. Let's get going back, eh, and have a drink. The boys ought've settled their difference by now.'

As they climbed back up to the timber, there was plainly movement of something like a human figure in its dappled shade. Bishoff muttered, 'Now, how the hell'd he do it?'

'Why not give him the credit of special powers . . . even if they're tricks like Houdini's? They do have special powers. I've known blacks tell when a man would die, almost to the minute, by Sun or Moon. I've checked with sticks, asking where the shadow would be. I've known 'em to tell of something happening a hundred miles away in a place and to people they haven't seen in months . . . and sure enough, the news turns up eventually. They customarily follow the fortunes of absent relatives through bodily sensations . . . itches, aches, numbness . . . each part of the body being representative. For instance, the right shoulder represents one's closest father, actually the man most likely to be your real father. An ache in that will cause you to say, 'Belong 'o me Daddy sick, I reckon. Better I go look-see.' You can just about bet it's right.'

As they went through the timber, Jeremy said, 'We'll follow the track close to the creek this time, to get a better view of things. But I wouldn't mind betting the next we'll see of him will be back at the water-tanks.' He went on: 'But I'd better finish the story about him . . . that is as far as it goes . . . because I have a feeling there's going to be an awful lot more, now he's back in circulation. Now, where was I? He was sick in town, yes. Then he vanished completely. The native supposition was that he had gone back On Top, to join Tchamala . . . and good riddance. Now, I'd best give you some idea of this Rainbow Snake Business. Not that I know a lot about it. Nobody I ever struck ever did . . . white that is. I've spoken to Anthropologists who've worked round here, who say there's no such cult at all, that it's only a racket worked by smart individuals to cause fear and hence get power. My own idea is that it's something very ancient that keeps waxing and waning in power. I suppose you know that Aboriginal beliefs are exasperatingly diverse. This is due, I think, to natural constant change in interpretation through the generations, and stiff rivalry between tribes . . . really language groups. There were supposed to be no less than five hundred of these groups in the Continent at the time of the coming of the *kuttabah*, the whiteman. Although they're great traders, in anything, from women to songs and legends, their trade contacts followed certain patterns that I'd say were dictated by economic history. What I mean is, because certain tribes could benefit from the economy of certain other ones, they'd make friends of these and enemies of others, and over a vast stretch of country would have cultural exchange, while quite close no contact at all, except say in battle. Thus you can find an elaborate system of, say, Young-man Making, initiation, cutting almost from Indian Ocean to Pacific, while from North to South, say, there'll be a band where the practice is entirely different. But I'm getting too complicated, perhaps. Let me say simply that much of what is ceremonial is unexplained. Even the words of the great chants are not understood. They are spoken just as the actions are made. Yet the purpose is quite clear to the actors.

'Only for the fact that you must always be on the lookout for the complexity in these allegedly simple people, speaking of these northern parts, where over say a million square miles there are a hundred languages, most still spoken, and half a dozen cultural systems that can be said to be distinct, you might say that the basic belief, even if much overlain with innovations, is that everything had its origin with the coming of the Earth Mother, called in these parts

Koonapippi, while over in the west, Bobwirridirridi's country, Kurrawaddi – and other names elsewhere, all sacred, not to be taken in vain. Apparently the name means, although not in current lingo, old woman, or rather, very old woman, which the blacks translate as Ol'Goomun-Ol'Goomun. Curiously, the Sun is supposed to be the old woman in the perpetual celestial existence to which the Dream Time heroes were translated, yet is not spoken of with any sort of reverence that I know of in that form. Perhaps the very obvious fact that the Sun is all-powerful in itself is enough. There is the Sun . . . there is the eternal one, as it were. It's only curious in that most else concerned with Koonapippi or Kurrawaddi is so damned sacred that the slightest sacrilege invites the direst punishment . . . even death.'

They were following a pad along the line of timber.

'Anyway, the Ol'Goomun-Ol'Goomun came out of the sea on the northern coast. She had with her a dilly-bag containing the *Shades*, or spirits, or souls . . . *Shades* is the blackfellow word . . . of all the creatures, animal and vegetable, that were eventually to stock the land, a magic wand with which she created the essentials of the landscape, and which spoke her bidding in its own voice . . . this is represented by the bullroarer used in sacred ceremonies . . . and a string made of stars for playing cat's cradle. You know the game children play . . . all children, or at least in my time . . . working string into designs for others to guess? The difference was that the old woman's cat's cradle was no mere guessing game, but the means by which the law of relationship is worked out. Aboriginal children are still taught their social responsibilities with cat's cradle. They become very skilled in it. In fact it serves as a means of communication . . . particularly in secret.

'Do you know the stars . . . the constellations . . . the main ones, anyway . . . Orion? Good. It's the wrong time of year, or rather of night, to see the old woman in her night attire with all her gear. But to the blacks she is the Pleiades . . . Seven Sisters, so-called by us. Tiny as that little cloud of stars is, it just fits the picture with the rest thrown in. She comes up dragging behind her the Dilly-bag, which is roughly the triangle we call Taurus. Then further back and southward trails the wonder of the Cat's Cradle . . . Orion, in all his blazing splendour. Beautiful, isn't it? Equal to anything the Greeks created . . . and so much more appropriate for the southern sky. And, yes . . . I forgot . . . Something the Greeks had in common with all this . . . Sirius, the Dog Star. That's *Wanjin* the Dingo, the only creature she brought with her in the flesh. Strange that they should have made this distinction . . . when the dingo is the one terrestial animal in all the myriad forms of life in Australia that's not strictly indigenous. The songs of the Dream Time, the *Kudijingah,* tell of how he came out of the sea at her heels, shook himself, cocked his leg and piddled. She brought *Wanjin* as companion and scout. He turned out to be mostly a nuisance . . . as indeed his descendants have remained to this day . . . too smart even for Alfred Vaisey, the new Lord of the Land.'

Bishoff chuckled. Jeremy continued: 'But that's only part of the creation of Terra Australis . . . as the bliss of Eden was of the world. There was Tchamala, the Serpent, who sneaked into the paradise Koonapippi had created, much as Satan sneaked into the Garden. That's if Satan did sneak in. He might have been there all the while, created by the Creator to balance things. Perhaps you need evil to give value to good, a sort of negative to positive to give potential, as in electrodynamics . . . otherwise you have inertia. Anyway, Tchamala was soon messing things up. He is the Lord of Storms. Koonapippi made the gentle breezes and the soft showers, to make living sweet for her children . . . only to have Tchamala turn them into hurricanes and deluges. She made the billabongs and streams for her water creatures to live in placidly. The old boy turned them into raging seas and torrents, flooded the sweet green land, and afterwards got underneath and drew the water off to leave arid plains and even deserts. He made the rivers in his rages. They are his tracks, tearing the gentle landscape apart. He made the ranges similarly. He still makes visitations, of course, has underground passages, into which he pops when he comes down from *on-top*, to pop out as the rainbow and rear over the land, threatening it, or to flatten and burn it with thunderstorms. More than interfering with Koonapippi's terrestial paradise, he fouled up the good she taught her people. For instance, he induced the Frog People to go *Wahji* in their selection of husbands and wives, with the result that they had a terrible fight and exterminated themselves as they were in the beginning, to become the silly little creatures they now are, able only to mate in storms and not male with female . . . males have to go make love to the female's eggs. Everything that was bad and wrong and uncomfortable and dangerous was due to Tchamala, the *tchineke-tchineke*, meaning big-big-snake. *Tchinek* is blackfellow English, believe it or not, the word snake being synonymous. To go *tchinekin* means to act with the subtlety of a snake. Anyway, that's a sort of outline to this Rainbow Serpent business. But don't take it as simple as I've made it sound. Our own forefathers' ideas about the evil one are by no means simple. He was called Satan, Lucifer, Mephistopheles, Beelzebub, Old Scratch, with a different conception attached to each name. The blackfellow's conception is similarly diverse and vague. The Cult of Koonapippi constitutes the Credo. All social behaviour is based on it. All males are initiated into it, and females, although rigidly denied communion, bound to observe its injunctions The cult of Tchamala is something quite different. It mightn't even be a cult in the proper sense of the term, which I take to mean a sort of congregation . . . and so the Anthropologists and police might be to a large degree right in saying it's only a sort of lurk worked by heads, as smart ones are called. That's why I want to find out more about it from the old man. How one becomes a snake man I've no idea. There's always one about somewhere. You don't have to be a *koornung* to be one. In fact Bobwirridirridi's the first I've known who was. A Snake Man, although leading an ordinary tribal life, more or less, is supposed to be in league with spirits that do Tchamala's bidding. In being so he can be dangerous. He can arrange for one's being bitten by a poisonous snake, taken by a crocodile, drowned in a flood, struck by lightning, or merely inconvenienced by being harrassed by mosquitoes, sand-flies, marsh-flies, leeches, ticks, all creatures of Tchamala's . . . or washed out of his humpy in the middle of a black night and have his fire put out and nothing to start another with. In a society where it is implicit that everything is controlled by magic, it's handy to have it known that you are in league with occult powers. At the same time, there is the disadvantage of being too greatly feared to lead a normal tribal life . . . '

Jeremy broke off as a large bird broke from the timber, and taking a half turn over them, croaking harshly, flapped away towards the ghostly white and jet hummock that was the homestead.

'What was that?' asked Bishoff.

'A night-heron. Also supposed to be in league with Snake Men, I think. Might've been old Bob cutting across ahead of us.'

'Eh?' The young man was staring again.

Jeremy chuckled: 'Well, I don't see how otherwise he's going to get across there without admitting to us that he's merely mortal.'

'But .. but .... '

'I'm not trying to do anything but impress you with the idea that it's as silly to measure these people by our own standards as to think we can convert this continent into another Europe. Leave it. Let's cut across now. Take it easy, so you don't miss any movement. Also I'm a long way off finishing the story.'

They had come back somewhat more than half the direct distance southward. The homestead lay across the strip of silver paddock, something like a third of a mile away. As they headed for the dark mass of the garden, Jeremy resumed his tale: 'As I've said, what happened to old Bob that I've told you of was while I was overseas. Well, as far as I know, during the next ten years, he might well have been *on-top* with Tchamala for all that was heard of him. Probably he was with the wild bush blacks of the nor'west. Anyway, civilization didn't hear of him again till the Beatrice River Riots in 1928 .... '

Bishoff exclaimed, 'Beatrice River Riots?'

'Sounds incredible, I know ... a town consisting of one pub, one store, a Chinese saddler, a Hindu hawker. But there were plenty of men there during the extension of the railway to Charlotte Springs. It was a transcontinental track they were supposed to be building, you know, the North-South Railway advocated at the beginning of the century to meet the Yellow Peril, but vetoed by Kitchener in favour of the East-West line, so's to get silly Aussies quicker to the war he was spoiling for with Von Hindenberg. What started the building of the North-South was not the Yellow Peril, but that bloody depression we got our share of through getting mixed up in that stinking war.' The vibrance of tone again caused Bishoff to glance at the rugged face. Jeremy grimaced: 'My hobby-horse ... the selling of our birthright, if you can call inherited stolen property that, to go strutting about the world in silly cocked hats, to go whoring as heroes in the same brothels that have served the soldiery of every warmonger since Alexander the Great to the Cockney-Welsh con-man into whose hands the destiny of the burgeoning Australian nation was so incredibly trusted. I suppose you know that building the East-West Railway was considered a great achievement in community endeavour, the sort of thing possible only in Soviet Russia ... and that was before the Russian Revolution, of course. The sort of thing on which the dream of Australia Felix was based ... the dream of the True Commonwealth. Before it was completed, we had sold our birthright ... or rather swapped it ... because we never got anything back but astronomical war-debts, Rolls of Honour, Anzac Day ... and, God save us! ... the RSL'. Jeremy himself laughed this time. He went on: 'This North-South Railway, although national property, was financed by international financiers, with the idea of giving work to men otherwise likely to become dangerous in idleness. But there couldn't have been enough profit in it, because they only got a hundred miles of the proposed thousand built, when along came a special representative of international finance, declared it too costly, and called it off.'

'You mean Sir Otto Niemeyer?'

'Yes . . . the British banker with the so un-British name.

'A bloody Jew!'

'You're wrong there, man. I was reading about him only the other day. He's completely English, of Dutch origin.'

'Still could be a Jew. Jews control the finances of the world. They were bleeding Germany white till Hitler took over.'

'According to what I've read, Hitler says it's the Treaty of Versailles that's bled Germany.'

'With the Jews operating it.' Now Bishoff's voice was vibrant.

Jeremy glanced at him: 'I wouldn't know that. I got to know a few Jews in the Army, who seemed to be ordinary men, doctors and lawyers and such, who didn't seem inordinately interested in money. Our own GOC, Monash, is a Jew . . . and renowned as an engineer. I saw a lot of Jews while serving in Palestine and other parts of Asia Minor, who weren't at all in powerful positions, although they struck me as the most intelligent, trustworthy, and generous people I had dealings with . . . in fact the only properly civilized people I did have dealings with, including many of my own comrades. Then there are the great Jews of science and philosophy . . . the Einsteins, Freuds, Spinozas . . . . '

'And the Rothschilds and money!'

'I never met them. But coming nearer home, while we're on the subject, seeing it's a touchy one with Hitler's now hounding the Jews out of Germany . . . what about Isaac Isaacs, the first man with the strength of character in our long history of colonial crawling, to save us the indignity of being ruled in the name of the King of England by some Pommy lordling . . . '

'Aw . . . he was pushed into the Governor-Generalship only as a political stooge for the Labor government!'

'Well that lets him off a charge of involvement in finance. Besides, he was Chief Justice of Australia, well known as a fair-minded and clever jurist. By the way, I had him as a guest when he was visiting these parts. He didn't strike me as anyone's stooge. Certainly he wasn't taken in by Lord Alfred Vaisey.'

They were entering the garden, and silent as they went up through the fruit trees. Then Jeremy whispered, 'Look on the tank-stand.'

His companion already had glimpsed the shadowy figure up amongst the top leaves of the bananas, and was gaping. It was gone again. Bishoff seemed to be about to go round the stand to take a closer look. Again Jeremy checked him, saying loudly as he guided him straight on, 'Old flying fox up there eating bananas, eh?'

The Ah Loy household was now dark and silent. They went on through the garden, were coming to the gate, when again Jeremy halted Bishoff, whispering, 'Someone there.' A figure could be seen to flit from the shadow of the mangan to the shed. Jeremy breathed, 'Bit of wrong side business, may be. Let's not disturb 'em. Come this way.' He drew the young man back a short distance, then turned him eastward along another path. They left the garden through the wires. Slowly they headed for the Big House, still lighted below. Jeremy resumed his story: 'I spoke of Wirridirridi's return to civilized ken as contemporary with those unemployed riots at Beatrice. That's not quite correct . . . although the riots had a bearing on his fortunes. It's also not right to blame the riots on Sir Otto Niemeyer. That other old *Tchamala*, Alf Vaisey, was primarily responsible. You see, as soon as the great military demand for bully-beef ceased, His Lordship closed down his Port Palmeston meat works . . . although industrial trouble was supposed to be the cause. Just as the Devil can quote scripture to his own ends, so I guess can the boss organize a strike, to save a sacking. Anyway, that's how the labour experts saw it. Remember that the social structure of this formerly purely rural community was greatly changed by the establishment of the meat works. Suddenly there was a large industrial population in Palmeston. Just as suddenly that population was unemployed. Vaisey removed a large part of it in his own ships, though at government expense. The men were actually *deported* . . . from a part of their own country. The alternative to leaving was jail. How it would stand tested in law I don't know. Anyway, there was no law but that of the policeman's baton. Those who objected were branded Bolsheviks. All went. However, it would be a lot of these men who came back to work on the railway construction some eight years later. The big joke was that, having had the joy of black velvet . . . Aboriginal women, you know . . . they had to come back.

'There was also an excuse for stopping the railway work without sacking. Early rain washed out some of the track, weakened a bridge that collapsed with a train-load of men. Unnecessary holdup of the work angered the men. Another strike. Another calling in of police . . . and deportation. That's how things were when Bobwirridirridi reappeared. But I must now take you back to what he was doing earlier. It seems that he first showed himself to his kind, the more civilized of it, at any rate, on Princess Alice Station, where he took part in an initiation ceremony, and also got together a small band to whom to teach the gospel of the Rainbow Snake . . . with the idea of getting rid of all whitemen, the way he had that party in the same locality. This was the Wet Season before. No work was being done on the property. The manager and other whites were away. The place was left in charge of a reliable halfcaste stockman, with the curious name of Blackman. His wife was the cook. She was only one quarter white, but possessed of all the potential volcanic violence that seethes in most crossbreeds with white blood . . . and more. She's still about . . . quite a figure in Palmeston now. You might have heard of her, Peg-leg Nelly, or Queen Nelly, or Queeny . . . Queen of the Compound, and boss of every black racket in Town . . . booze, opium, prostitution. You see her on Saturday nights outside the picture show, collecting from her black whores their earnings, and doling out to them what they need for entrance fee, ice-cream, *et cetera.* The rest goes towards credit for things bought at the store she runs at the compound with a character known as King George. I'm diverting again . . . but to give you the picture complete.'

They were coming up to the front of the house. Voices could be heard within. Jeremy asked, 'Well, have you had enough?'

'Lord, no . . . I'd like to hear it all. You're just coming to something, aren't you, I mean a specially interesting point?'

'Yes . . . but I'm afraid I can't talk freely before my sons. Could you do with some more walking?'

'Sure.'

'Well, let's go in and have a drink first. I'm dry from talking.'

They found the brothers pretending to read, Martin, *Man*, Clancy, a catalogue, looking hang-dog, even while they received the others eagerly enough and drank with them. The talk was only of the night, the weather, and again of stock. After Jeremy had drunk two brandies and Bishoff a bottle of beer, these two went out again, Jeremy saying, 'I'm telling him a few old yarns.' The Delacys seemed even glad to be rid of them, their jaws squaring belligerently for another private scrap. Outside the gate they had just entered, Jeremy sighed, 'I often think that what keeps those fellows for ever bickering is my neglect of them as a father . . . and wonder what would happen if I bumped their heads together now.'

This time they headed out onto the eastern plain, following a track well beaten by motor vehicles. Jeremy went on with his tale: 'Remember that we were at Princess Alice homestead, with an initiation in progress. The temporary manager, the half-caste blackman, was involved in this. As a good Kurrawaddi, man, he could not help but indulge the Pookarakka in the matter of special rations – that is bread and milk and soup. However, his wife, the cook, later called Peg-leg Nelly, was soon at loggerheads with the old boy, resenting his cult-boss's arrogance and he her cheek. Anyway, she hunted him with the rifle. From the evidence later produced in court it isn't clear whether he got his revenge by somehow luring her to the sacred initiation ground, the Ring Place, or she in her wilfulness deliberately intruded on it. I suppose you know that these places, equivalent to the old Bora grounds of the southern tribes, are forbidden women and children on pain of death? I must digress again to explain an oddity about this Kurrawaddi or Koonapippi business. Although it's a cult of masculinity to the very limit, legend shows plainly that it wasn't always so. This is as it should be, when the deity was female. The odd thing is despite this powerful advance towards a patriarchate, which seems to have been a normal process in the evolution of primitive societies, the *matrilineal* system of social control remains . . . although vested in mother's brothers. Legend has it that Ol'Goomun-Ol'Goomun entrusted the ritual necessary for maintaining the order of things to the women she created, but that the men, becoming jealous of their power, stole their magic paraphernalia, and so took command, to the utter exclusion of women . . . except, and here is another oddity, in the case of some very old woman who occasionally is taken into the cult to represent the *Ol'Goomun* in the flesh. The diabolical cruelty that goes with the execution of such women as intrude on the cult, suggests to me that the rebellion of the men was concerned with the diabolism of the Snake. I have no proof of this. The blacks are very close-mouthed about these things. I base my supposition on the fact that the ancient paintings, to be found in Snake Caves, often depict what might reasonably be taken to represent the traditional ceremonial rape that's part of the terrible business, and my hunch that some degree of diabolism is essential in human behaviour. I sometimes wonder if our propensity to murder, with which I include war, isn't due to this. We are the only mammalian species who do kill our kind deliberately . . . or rather, with respect to our brethren, the apes, I should say the only genus. I hope these philosophical digressions don't spoil my story.'

'Not at all. I think of you first as the scientist.'

'I'm not really . . . just a man, somewhat bewildered by my human intelligence. But it's nice to have someone to talk to about such things. Now, where was I? Yes . . . Nelly was caught in the sacred precincts, and subjected to the ancient and horrible ritual demanded . . . which consists of breaking arms and legs, literal rape by the participants, and a ceremonial business with the bull-roarer. Not only did Nelly catch it, but Blackman, who, apparently, objected. They killed him out of hand. Both were buried in termites' nests, which I think I told you is a way of concealing murder. It's interesting to note the tacit admission of guilt here. Why the need for concealment when the killing was supposed to be in accordance with law? It can't be laid to fear of the whiteman, because it's traditional. Besides, rarely would the whiteman ever hear of such secret things. Again, in this case, those involved immediately removed themselves from the scene. Perhaps they have to go, through fear of the vengeful *Shades* of their victims. Anyway, their bolting, when actually no one pursued, was their undoing.

'Remember I told you the Ol'Goomun-Ol'Goomun came ashore with Wanjin, the Dingo, as her companion and scout? Now, the dingo strain predominates in all blackfellows' dogs. Nelly had a dog, which she'd suckled at her own breast, having lost a baby. She's still got him, I think, as her protector, ancient as he must be now. I've seen him in town . . . a gross, yellow-eyed, snarling old wolf of a thing, pretty well pure-warrigal. She calls him Mate. Anyway, Mate was not involved in the sacrilegious business at the Ring Place . . . or else he'd have been killed, too. He must have been away somewhere, or deliberately made to stay at home. But subsequently he went looking for his mistress, sniffed her out, dug her out of the ant-bed . . . and, according to her, licked her back to life. The Cult men, of course, had gone. How she survived, I don't know. She lost one leg from the knee down, apparently through gangrene. She treated herself, with the aid of the other women of the place . . . using the inevitable pipe-clay. There's no doubt about the healing powers of pipe-clay . . . although the reason beats me. I've tried everything to find a scientific answer. It contains nothing but the common elements of clay . . . except some kind of spore-producing fungi. You'd think it'd make infection worse. In fact it does the opposite. If you sterilize the clay it becomes ineffective. Naturally, to the Murries it's plain magic. Anyhow, Nelly was able with her treatment to hang on long enough to be found by the boss, Piggy Trotters. He rushed her off to town and hospital. The police moved in for the good old manhunt.

'Of course you'll have met Sergeant Cahoon . . . and no doubt have heard of his henchman, Police Tracker Jinbul. Both have become quite famous since the southern press has taken an interest in the local scene and the local John Darms have been glamorized into a version of the Canadian Mounties. It was out of that case of Peg-leg Nelly's that Dinny Cahoon, then a plain trooper, or mounted constable to give the official designation, came to fame as the master mantracker. It was a tough assignment. Not being concerned with cattle-killing, Vaiseys weren't interested, and therefore not the top brass. Dinny had to battle on his own with a couple of trackers. He didn't have Jinbul to start with. Jinbul was on the other side . . . one of the hunted. He was the youngest of them, but well known as a nuisance round the Alice River. A great man with the girls . . . hence the name . . . gin bull . . . a nickname that became attached to him officially.

'It was this weakness of Jinbul for the ladies that led to Cahoon's ultimate great success in his calling. While doing a bit of *tchinekin* he was betrayed by jealous husbands, and captured. It took a good while for Cahoon to induce him to betray his comrades . . . but he did it, working on his conceit and the unusual detachment that would make him a Snake Man. Dinny plied him with drink and the promise of greater power as a policeman . . . a *dookyangana* . . . literally a camp destroyer in the native interpretation. At last Jinbul agreed to a plan to go through a semblance of escaping from custody and returning to his mates, eventually to lead them into a trap. The trap was to be baited with the weakness of the leader this time . . . Bobwirridirridi's weakness for bread and milk. The station chosen was Alexandra Downs, at the junction of the Beatrice and Alice Rivers. Jinbul, back with the fugitives, told the old man he could get him what he wanted through the offices of a black housemaid he was on with there. It worked. They took Cock-Eye Bob, along with the others. How he got away I don't know. I understand he was actually 'on the chain', as they say. Do you know that they chain Aboriginal prisoners by the neck? Of course, you can't hold such slim streamlined hands as theirs with any kind of device . . . and ankle-chains obstruct their walking. Not an easy thing to get out of, a neck-chain. He's supposed to have done it by magic, of course. He got clean away. Cahoon had to take his prisoners up to town and see them jailed without the ringleader. I guess Cahoon would have kept after him, but perhaps with no such zeal as circumstances gave him, and also no such luck. I now come to the Beatrice River Riots, which created those circumstances. How are your feet going? It's about half a mile to the top gate. Suit you if we go on to it and turn back there?'

'Sure. I'm a good walker.'

'You want to keep at it. The average whiteman round these parts couldn't walk a mile without knocking up. Well, as I think I told you, the rain came in early that year, caught 'em with their pants down . . . the railway construction people, I mean, and the job closed down. That left the best part of a thousand men, non-residents, idle. They were ordered to leave, not only the district, but the country. A cargo ship was called in to pick them up in Palmeston. But it didn't work as easily this time as last. I've said some of the men had been through the meat works deportation. There were Commos. There'd been a Communist cell in the land since the meat works days. They took charge. The few police on hand couldn't do much. Others were sent from Town, along with specials recruited from the Public Service. Dinny was one of the Johns. Now he had a chance to prove himself not only as a bush trooper herding blacks, but as a riot-breaker, which is more important to his masters. How things would have gone without him I don't know. The mob certainly had the other Johns bluffed till Dinny took charge. He's as brave and tough as an Irish terrier, and looks rather like one, with the sandy hair and green eyes. He got badly hurt . . . but not till the battle was won. I'm sure he suffered brain damage.

Anyway, it made him . . . what with that and his natural Irish capacity to fight and the driving force of the celibacy he lived in, chained to those repressed old biddies of sisters of his as he was.

'Although he saw the mob off on the special train, travelling like Murries in stock-waggons and on flat-tops . . . as I saw them myself in fact . . . his job wasn't done by any means. The two ring-leaders were still unaccounted for. Some men had got away southward by road, not an easy thing in those days. So the three or four police stations on the overland routes were able to screen them. There was no evidence that the leaders, Snowy Mack and Billy Bellairs, had left the country. In fact they had sworn not to go till it suited them. They weren't wanted merely for deportation, but for jailing on various charges.

'I don't suppose you've met Tom Toohey, boss of the Beatrice River railway fettling gang? No, you wouldn't. The only stock he has is creamy children. Besides, he's a self-effacing man. Like me he's also beyond the social pale for having a halfcaste wife . . . but lacks the status of having had a white wife who ranks close to First Lady of the Land.' Jeremy chuckled.

Then he sighed: 'Poor old Tom and his creamy kids! He'd had such hopes of raising them above the status of boong. He's always blamed the railway construction for their ruin. But I think he had a hand in it himself, hoping for too much from them. Anyway, the natural awful thing was that his girls became whores on reaching puberty. They'd already started before the railway construction did. One of them was carted off to town with gonorrhoea. The other, Tilly, became Snow Mack's mistress. It was she hid him and Bellairs at an old place down the river where there used to be a White Russian settlement . . . Vaiseys imported Russian aristocrats, *émigrés* from the Revolution . . . to spite the Bolsheviks, I guess. Mack and Bellairs had a plan to get to Town aboard a train driven by Pat Hannaford. Of course you've met Driver Hannaford? Well, Pat's a commo, of course. They would hide in Town, till they got legal representation to fight their case. Pat did eventually get them away, but not before there was a lot of trouble. Tracker Jinbull, now practically Cahoon's shadow, happened to see Tilly Toohey talking to Pat Hannaford in a way that suggested conspiracy to his natural policeman's mind. He reported to his master. Dinny grabbed Tilly for interrogation. The established method of getting your way with a boong is with a stockwhip . . . as you might have guessed from the incident at supper-time this evening. Cahoon chained Tilly up naked under the milk-wood used for that purpose at Beatrice River Police Station, and flogged her till she fainted. Failing to get results that way, he tried another method of making these secretive people talk. He stuck a stick down the dunny, and rubbed her face with the shit, forcing a bit into her mouth. I suppose that would be too much for any breed of person . . . unless a coprophile . . . but Aboriginal people are particularly sensitive concerning human excreta . . . magic, of course. You can kill a person with a bit of shit and the right words sung over it. Poor Tilly gave in. But meantime her brothers, Brumby and Micky, little more than kids, guessing the significance of the torture, ran and warned Snowey and his mate, got them away practically under Dinny's nose by rowing them up the river in heavy rain . . . and put them on the road to my place . . . .'

'Lily Lagoons?'

'That's right. As I told you when you came out, I'd always maintained it as much as a refuge for all creatures needing it as a retreat for myself. But I've never had occasion to shelter whitemen on the run before. Well, Cahoon was stumped by the trick. He may never have found out that the Toohey boys had been involved, had they not gone to him and confessed that they'd warned the Commos. They didn't tell the exact truth, however, and certainly not for the reason they gave for confessing, that is that they were sorry to have done *no good thing*. Determined to avenge their sister, they lured Dinny alone to a shed in the railway yards where they said the pair were hiding . . . and there gave him a belting that put him in hospital for a month. But for his own thirst for revenge, he should have stayed there longer. In fact he would have died from his injuries, if they hadn't sent down a special train with a doctor and nurses to attend to him. There was no Flying Doctor then.'

'What happened to the Toohey boys?'

'They came out to me, too. They were, of course, entitled to whatever protection I could give them. Brumby, the elder, had been out to me before, through trouble while working with the construction gang. After lying low for a while he went back and lost himself in the crowd. Mack and Bellairs were already there . . . on sufferance. They'd been frank with me, and I equally so. I said I wasn't going to jeopardize the condition of those dependent on me by involving myself so as to get into trouble with the police. I have to make only one slip-up . . . and the bureaucratic bastards who've been after my hide ever since I showed contempt for their phoney values would have it off me and pegged out. I told the two I have no time for their philosophy, which I regard as essentially inhuman, for all its preaching humanitarianism . . . .'

'Good on you . . . I hate bloody Commos, too.'

'I wouldn't say I hate 'em. They haven't done this country any particular harm that I can see . . . .'

'Give 'em half a chance and they'd take it over.'

'Off Lord Alfred Vaisey and his coronetted cobbers? I'd lend 'em a hand.'

Bishoff said quite savagely, 'Communists are low-down, scheming, ruthless, soulless bastards!'

'You certainly feel strongly about them. But I think you exaggerate in applying such epithets to the local talent. What I've seen of 'em, they're either big-mouthed Pommies with eyes on a political career, but not understanding the Australian way of going about it, that is with bullshit, and therefore getting nasty . . . like the local Party bosses, Scotty McClaggity and Geordie Jenks . . . or larrikin types with a streak of oddness that compels 'em to have some sort of respectable purpose for their larrikinism . . . like Pat Hannaford.'

'You surprise me telling me Hannaford's a Commo. I met him boozing in at the pub in Beatrice, while the train was camped the night. He struck me as a wag. There's no place for humour in Communism.'

'As I was saying . . . with the larrikin type it's more a game than anything else. For example . . . Pat had cooked up for this pair I had, a mad scheme to smuggle 'em up to Town under the coal in the tender of his engine . . . put 'em in a big tool-chest. That's what they told me. I said I'd give 'em the hospitality customary in the land . . . shelter for twenty-four hours and rations for the road . . . and if word came from Hannaford, I'd see they got it.'

'Thought you said you wouldn't get involved?'

'I didn't. I wasn't supposed to know they were fugitives from justice. When their twenty-four hours were up, I hunted 'em off to Corella Bore, on Vaisey property. They were supposed to work their way from there to the railway north of Beatrice, and wait somewhere for Pat to pick 'em up. I wasn't the slightest bit involved legally.'

'How'd it work out?'

'It didn't. They'd just set out for the Bore, when the Toohey boys turned up. They were scared . . . the boys . . . thinking they killed Cahoon. They wanted to hide up in the Painted Caves . . . back in the wall of the Plateau there. They knew the country well. Their idea was to hole up till the rains set in in earnest, then make their way across the Plateau to the northern coast, and there eventually to get picked up by Jap pearlers. Brumby had worked with the Japs. I guess they could have made it. However, when I told them about Mack and Bellairs, they went after them and generously offered to take them along. That pair would only have made a disaster of it. They all came back to get the extra gear to make a foursome of it. I argued against it. I must say the Comms showed themselves equally generous in involving themselves in what looked like murder. I advised them to get back to civilization and take the rap for their own simple bit of trouble, and leave the boys alone to battle out their destiny as blackfellows. But they wouldn't budge from their idea of helping the boys out of the country and away to the protection of the Party.'

'Did they make it?'

'They didn't have to. I'm sure they wouldn't have anyway, what with the country they had to traverse, two hundred miles of the roughest in the Continent, and the wildest . . . at such a season, with its fevers, its pests. As likely as not, the blacks, guessing they hadn't protection of the *dookyangana*, would have murdered them . . . or at least betrayed them at some mission station. But it happened that just as they were about to set out, who should turn up but Hannaford himself, with the thing all cut and dried.

'It was rather comical. As you know, with all the old crippled things we've got there, even although we've got no dogs, it's about impossible for any visitor to surprise us. We got the usual signals from the lookouts . . . butcher-birds, pee-wees, cockatoos . . . and rushed to get our guilty ones away . . . only to find that the potential enemy was none other than old Barbu, the hawker. He came driving his ancient van, drawn by the ancient horses . . . at a pace that for him was astonishing. Added to the general oddity of the situation was the fact that Barbu has long been barred from Lily Lagoons, because of his secondary trade as bird-trapper. The first thing he did was to beg my pardon for the intrusion and say he would never have made it but for fear of his life. Seems Pat Hannaford had commandeered him and his van at the point of a knife. Pat had first tried to drive the team, but not having a throttle or brake, made a complete mess of it. Pat had chosen the rather mad means of travel so as not to attract attention. It happened that he was the driver of that special medical train brought down for Dinny Cahoon. Means for a perfect get-away. The doctor was operating on the spot, but wouldn't be permitting Dinny's moving up to hospital till it could be done with absolute safety. Finding that his boys had vamoosed, Pat got it out of Tom Toohey where they had gone. Now he wanted a motor vehicle to take 'em back to sneak them onto the train, in a couple of big railway toolboxes this time, amongst a load of stuff from the construction being taken up to Town. I took him and the four fugitives myself, dumped them at the Racecourse. The odd thing about it is that for all the risk I took, the Commos still class me with the enemy. Only a week or so ago, Pat Hannaford called me a Fascist for refusing to subscribe to a collection he was making for the International Brigade fighting in Spain.'

'Stalin's boys, eh?'

'I suppose so. But on the other side they're just as bad, aren't they . . . Hitler's and Mussolini's boys? Poor Spaniards! Actually my objection wasn't on political grounds, but to preoccupation with evils on the other side of the world, when we have enough under our noses . . . the treatment of the Aborigines, for a start.'

They reached the gate. Turning, Jeremy said, 'Well, I'll have to finish the yarn on this leg, or I never will.'

'Did the Commos get away?'

'Oh, yes . . . and the Toohey boys. Hannaford picked them up at his first watering point north . . . Granite Springs. There's a cutting there blocks off view of the engine from the back of the train. Then up in Town, the Comrades smuggled them aboard the West Coast steamer.'

'Seamen's Union, eh?'

'I dare say. As Pat hadn't anything to do with that part of it, he couldn't brag beyond what he'd done himself . . . and the Comrades in town are typically tight-lipped. But get away the fugitives did . . . without leaving a clue for Dinny Cahoon when he woke up with his zeal for man-hunting doubled or trebled by what I'm sure was a brain lesion . . . Cock-Eye Bob's undoing.'

'How's that?'

'Well, as soon as he could set foot on the ground again, which was after some six weeks in hospital, Dinny had his nose to it again. . . the ground, I mean . . . along with his fellow-bloodhound, Jimbul. But catching up with the old boy was a sheer fluke. After he'd got away from Cahoon at Alexandra Downs, he'd come on alone up the Beatrice, following the track of his master, Tchamala, heading for the Snake Caves, back of my place. That's when I first met him. My people told me he was hanging about after bread and milk. I took it to him myself, with a drop of brandy. We soon became pally. I wanted to learn what I could about *Tchinek bijnitch* of course. But getting accurate information from Aborigines is a matter requiring infinite patience. For one thing, they're never in a hurry themselves . . . and who should be, dealing with the Infinite? Then they're always mistrustful of the *kuttabah*. Finally, they're shrewd enough traders to get all they can out of a deal. He let me know that he'd be in the locality for the duration of the Wet, touching up the snake paintings. I let him go with a swag of dried milk and flour for making his own bread and milk, and the arrangement to replenish the supply as needed and to have further yarns.

'It was just after New Year, '29, when Cahoon, looking a shadow even of his bony normal self, turned up at Lily Lagoons, with Jinbul and a couple of other trackers. Smart boy that he is, in looking for clues of the Toohey boys' whereabouts, he discovered that Barbu had a couple of fresh horses bearing my brand. I'd given these to the old fellow to spare those ancient prads of his the misery of dying while hauling him and his crossbred family on his annual beat round the stations. Cahoon knew I was crooked on Barbu, because I'd reported him for trapping and exporting rare protected birds. He sniffed something odd, and wormed it out of Barbu that he'd brought Pat out to me. He also knew that Pat and I weren't friends. Evidently Pat suggested Mack and Bellairs, and hence the Toohey boys. He tried trapping me into admission by pretending he knew all about it. I had my reason ready for why Pat had come to me. He and I had arranged it in case of inquiries. It was that Pat had become interested in racing and contemplated buying a horse from me . . . not a very good one, because Cahoon knew that Pat was crooked on the squatters and all the snobbery that goes with the Races here. Anyway, he headed out with his bloodhounds for the obvious hiding place, the Caves. I learnt from Jinbul bragging about his cleverness, how they took old Bob. First Jinbul, being a 'prentice Snake Man, observed the fresh painting, and, of course, had been associated with the Pookarakka in painting caves over in the Alice Country. Then he found a dried milk can. The old boy was famous for never leaving a track . . . but this was enough for the 'prentice *dookyángana*. He detached himself from the others, and went round making the secret call of Snake Men. It doesn't say much for old Bob's prescience as the earthly representative of Tchamala the all-knowing, that he didn't yet know that it was Jinbul who'd betrayed him before. So he presented himself to his young henchman . . . and thus to the chain, which they saw he didn't get out of this time. In fact, when I saw him, when Cahoon dropped in on me on the way back to demand the hospitality I was bound to give, they had three chains on him, each padlocked to a tracker. The old fellow seemed oblivious to me, wouldn't even take the bread and milk I offered him . . . oblivious to everything, perhaps shocked to find himself, the *protégé* of the all-powerful, powerless . . . crying to himself in lingo what was pretty obvious, but gloatingly translated by Cahoon through Jinbul, *Poor Fellow My Country*.'

'Poor old bastard!'

'Not so poor when you come to think of it. He was jailed for what is termed "His Majesty's Pleasure", meaning indefinitely. Odd how they cling to these moth-eaten things. Anyway, it worked nicely for the old boy, having a new King come along whose "Royal Pleasure" it was to set him free.'

'You're not interested in this Edward the Eighth, you say. But I think with the sort of freethinker he is, his reign should make a great difference . . . . '

'To whom . . . the English?'

'To the Commonwealth.'

'You mean the Commonwealth of Australia?'

'Well . . . really, the British Commonwealth.'

'Doesn't it offend you to have the title of your country ballsed up for ever by the high-handed act of Imperial Britain lumping it in with their own so-called Commonwealth of Nations . . . and the wretched supineness of our leaders to allow it?'

'Can't say I've thought much about it . . . although it's confusing sometimes to know what commonwealth's being referred to.'

'It makes my guts bleed!' The passion in Jeremy's voice made Bishoff turn and stare at him. 'The word commonwealth means the same thing as republic . . . *res publica* . . . the things of the people. How the hell can you have a king of a commonwealth, and commonwealth inside a commonwealth, as they say? British bullshit! Don't you feel it an insult to your intelligence even to have an hereditary monarch as the symbol of authority?'

The young man answered carefully, 'Yes . . . but I'm in the Public Service . . . and these days they're tough on the loyalty thing. You've got to mind what you say, if you want to keep your job. You're all right. You're a free man. I'm just starting my career . . . with a young wife.'

Jeremy put his hand on Bishoff's shoulder: 'Don't mind me, son. I'm not trying to involve you. I don't lead any movement. I'm a one-man band . . . the Scrub Bull, as they sometimes call me. Scrub bulls are solitary creatures.'

They were nearing the house, fell silent. Evidently the younger Delacys had retired. The light below was dying down. They went in. Murmuring goodnight, Bishoff went upstairs. Jeremy poured himself a brandy and sat awhile in the dimming light to drink it. Outside grew brighter and brighter. Now that Willy wagtail was singing close at hand, in the garden behind the kitchen: '*Kirri, kirri, kirrikijirrit* . . . . . *Sweet, sweet, Wrong-side Love*!'

Jeremy rose with a sigh, went aloft. The sleeping quarters were the verandahs that ran right round the place. Mosquito nets hooked to the ceiling reared in the filtered moonlight like shrouded ghosts. He went round to the western verandah, past a bed into which he glanced, to see his eldest son with big head dark against the pillow. No movement. He went on to the bed at the end of the verandah. He stripped to short underpants and singlet, got in, lay back with hands behind head. Still the *kirrikijirrit* sang in the kitchen garden . . . *Love, Sweet, sweet, Wrong-side Love*!

III

Martin Delacy, at sound of his father's snore, rose quickly from his pillow, sat listening, at length slipped out of bed, and as he was, clad only in undershorts, went tiptoeing through the luminous gloom of the stair-head. He stopped, to listen again. Someone was snoring round on the eastern verandah. He went downstairs like a shadow, made for the rear entrance, opened the lattice door and peered out. The whitewashed harness shed blazed in moonlight. He cocked his head to listen inside again. Then, taking a deep breath, he went out. At the gate of the bit of garden about the house he stopped to look about, most intently towards the kitchen. He stepped aside to piddle. Then he set out towards the kitchen, walking slowly at first, furtively, but with pace increasing and breathing deepening until his broad ginger-haired chest was heaving. He went past the kitchen, heading for the mangan plum. He reached the tree panting, pressed against the axe-scored trunk to obliterate himself as he looked about.

The Willy wagtail in the garden burst into song: '*Kirri, kirri, kirrikijirrit*!'

A sound – a slight cough. He looked quickly towards the woodshed, to see a shadow hanging in the less dark doorway. The shadow emerged, became the substance of Nelyerri Ah Loy, clad as before, a ribbon in her glossy mane, but with dark face gleaming now, eyes glowing as she came into the moonlight. She came slowly at first, then uttering a gasping subdued cry, with a rush that ended in his arms, mouth over his mouth, loins squirming into his. He was as ardent. As they broke away for want of breath he pushed her back a little, panting into her wild-bright face, 'Christ!'

She strained to him again, whimpering, 'I loff you!'

Still kissing her, he fumbled for the buttons of her dress, bared her small breasts, blobs of chocolate, and bent to them with greed, while she moaned and tore his hair.

Suddenly he seized her skirt, drew it about her waist, revealing her completely naked to the cup-like navel.

Hissing, he forced her down to the sawdust, bent over her hunched, while he tore off his own bit of clothing, then fell into the clutch of slender chocolate arms and legs she raised to him, almost puppy-yelping in the delight of coupling. He gasped, groaned. He fell limp upon her, creased ruddy forehead in the sawdust spread with ringlets of her hair. In the garden Willy wagtail sang: '*Sweet, sweet, Wrong-side Love*!'

After a while Martin groaned deeply, raised his head, stared at her, drew back when she tried to kiss him, freed himself of her clinging, lurched to knees, sank down again to sit with back to tree. She raised herself, to sit with bare legs drawn to chin, clutching at them, staring at him. Avoiding the glowing stare, he muttered, 'This's got to stop.'

She answered, 'I loff you.'

He sighed, groaned: 'I tell you it's got to stop, girl. I'm a married man now . . . with a baby.'

She dropped sideways onto hands and knees, came crawling the little distance to him, leaned against him, head on his shoulder, legs out-thrust with his. He made no response.

They sat a long while, almost as if sleeping. The wagtail sang and sang. Curlews were crying away towards the timber of the creek: '*Kweeluk, kweeluk!*'

She stirred, kissed his cheek, his lips, his eyes. She drew away from him, rose to knees pulled off the dress, to become completely naked. Even in the dappled light shed through the magic tree the difference in colour of the usually unexposed flesh was evident, a smoky sepia compared with the chocolate. Tossing the dress aside she drew to him again, kneeling, offering loins and breasts to his lips. He took them, slobbering, running hands over her writhing dusky slenderness. She sank down. Again they were straining, kissing. She rolled away, drawing him with lips, arms, legs, back to the sawdust. Now it was she who was yelping, to climax with a cry: 'Oh!'

Again they lay still. The Willy wagtail was still singing, but further away now. The curlews were in the garden, calling excitedly: '*Kweeluk, kweeluk, kweeeeeee-luk*!'

It was said that kweeluks called like that when, with the magic vision of those great eyes of theirs, they spied a Spirit baby wandering from its Dreaming Place, impatient to be reborn. Perhaps Martin knew of such things, even though he would hardly deign to believe them, despite the magic beaming all about him. Anyway, it seemed as if the persistent and still closer calling of the great birds roused him, he raised himself, and reaching for his pants, without looking at his partner, growled, 'No babies.'

With pants pulled on, he heaved himself to his feet, growling again, 'This can't go on.' Then looking at the ground he said, 'Don't forget to clean up my tracks . . . all the way up to the kitchen.'

'Yas,' she murmured. Then she leapt up, seized him, strained to him, whimpering, 'I loff you!' He suffered it for a moment, then disengaging her spidery arms, pushed her away.

He muttered, '*Mummuk*.' He turned away.

She breathed after him, '*Mummuk, yawarra*.'

He went swiftly, heading back, not troubling to look behind, breathing heavily, as if in exasperation, which feeling was also shown in his face. Then suddenly, as he neared the harness shed, the hangdog look was wiped off by alarm. From the gloomy interior a figure had appeared in the comparative brightness of the open entrance, or rather a whisp of greyness in human form, like a skeleton lately taken down from a burial platform for ritual distribution of its bones, a skeleton wearing a *bulkung* belt. Martin stopped dead, staring. A long moment. Then in a strangled voice he asked, 'Who're you?'

First a giggle, then the cackled answer: 'Me Cock-Eye Bob, Boss.'

The ginger bristles of the broad chest sparkled to a deep breath, which was released with a growl: 'What you doing here?'

'Me look-about, Boss.'

'Get to hell out of it!'

The cackle became the mendicant's whine: 'Give it lil bits grog, Boss . . . I go 'way.' It was the usual request of a blackfellow who felt himself able to take a liberty.

The ginger chest heaved again. The voice came grating: 'You sneakin' rotten blackmailin' old scare-crow. I'll give you more'n you bargained for, you don't get going.'

The whine rose: 'No-more growl, Boss. Lil bits lum.'

Again the chest heaved. The grating voice was kept low, but sounded no less menacing: 'I'll give you rum!' Martin darted past the skeleton figure, causing it to leap outside. Just ahead was a rack where stockwhips hung. He snatched one down, came rushing back, hissing now: 'Now get, you black bastard, get!' The whip whirled whistling, to wrap about the skeleton legs.

Bobwirridirridi hopped, emitting a cracked howl: 'No-more, Boss!'

Martin's face was twisted with rage, but still his voice subdued: 'Get goin' or I'll skin you alive.' He lashed again, at the skeleton torso.

The old man yelped: 'Ow!' He turned and ran, towards the gate of the Big House garden.

As the claw-like hands fumbled with the latch, Martin came leaping, with whip whirling: 'Out o'there, you black bastard!'

'Ow!' The whip cracked on the bony rump. The gate opened. Bob staggered inside. The whip caught him round the neck: 'Ow, ow!'

A rush of feet in the shadowy house.

As the old man was pulled off balance, to go staggering into a flower-bed, the whip caught him again, about the ribs.

A babble of voices as figures appeared in the moonlight: 'What's up . . . what's wrong?'

'Sneakin', thievin', no-good, black bastard!'

'Ow!'

Jeremy's voice rose: 'Go easy with that whip, boy!'

Martin was hissing again: 'I'm going to teach this bastard the lesson of his life.'

'No you're not. He's a frail old man.'

'He's a sneakin' black bastard.'

Now Jeremy was hissing: 'Give me that whip . . . or I'll take it off you and put it round you.' As the lash whirled again he grabbed it, snatched the whip out of Martin's hands.

Crouched and staring at him, Bobwirridirridi, whimpered, 'Me no-more been do it *wurruk* t'ing, Mullaka.'

Jeremy coiled the whip and flung it towards the house, saying, 'All right, Pookarakka. You go wait long o' motor-car.'

As the old man skipped past him, moving with remarkable agility, Martin roared at him, 'You ever come back this station again, I take the rifle to you.'

Jeremy said, 'I told you I was going to take him off your hands. What's the idea of putting the whip round him?'

'He was after grog.'

'He was probably after it off me. I've given it to him before.'

'No boong drinks grog on my run.'

'What . . . has His Lordship deeded his holdings to you?'

Dropping his head like an angry bull, Martin charged past him, into the house. As he vanished, Jeremy said to staring Clancy, 'You're in charge here. I want to give the old fellow a brandy and milk. Any objections?'

Clancy was looking hangdog now: 'So long's he doesn't make any more trouble.'

'What trouble's he made so far?'

But Clancy turned away, went back into the house. Jeremy followed, but only to go to the bubbling Icy Ball. Clancy had gone upstairs after his brother. Jeremy came out with a bottle of brandy and an enamel jug of goat's milk. Finding Bishoff still out in the garden, he said, 'Going to have a drink with the old man . . . care to be in it?'

'Yes, a brandy and milk would go well. Brandy's your favourite drink, I see.'

'Well, C_2H_5OH, really. But brandy's the cleanest and most intelligent way of taking it, in my opinion. It doesn't take so much of it to make you high, but a lot to make you rotten . . . and then you get really rotten.'

Bobwirridirridi was waiting outside the motor shed. He shook hands with Bishoff, cackled a bit over the conversation the young man tried to make about his release from jail, but as soon as he got the drink Jeremy dispensed for him in a stockman's quart-pot taken from the utility, backed off and did his disappearing trick. Jeremy called, 'You'n me two-feller go Lily Lagoons long o' motor-car tomorrow, eh, Pookarakka? See you daylight.'

Jeremy got out enamel pannikins for their own drinks. They had them stiff, finishing up the jug of milk, then headed back towards the house. Bishoff was interested in Bobwirridirridi's age and the average lifespan of Aborigines in general. Jeremy answered that despite the hard conditions under which they lived, both in the native state and as hangers-on to the *kuttabah's* society, they appeared to average about the same as the *kuttabah*. Regarding Bobwirridirridi's age he said, 'Don't forget he was supposed to have died back in about 1917. What's that . . . nineteen years. I didn't see him then, or till Cahoon took him out at my place in '29. That's seven years ago. He doesn't look a bit different from what he did then. He's about as near being what they call a living skeleton as you could get, I reckon. Amazing how he has the muscular power to get about, and so vigorously.'

As they were approaching the garden gate, voices that had been mumbling upstairs in the house rose so as to be heard distinctly.

'You're a lying bastard . . . you did go out to her.'

'You call me a lying bastard I'll knock your bloody block off.'

'Try it! I know you're a lying bastard because I found your bed empty.'

'Didn't I tell you I went to piss?'

'Pissin' for an hour and a half!'

'Same spying dirty little tell-tale shit you always were!'

'And you're the same dirty gin-rootin' bastard you always were . . . and always will be.' Sound of scraping of a chair and a couple of thumping steps. But no violence, because Clancy went on: 'If you're going to keep on rootin' that yeller bitch, do it some other place, not where I'm in charge.'

'Look out you stay in charge of any place under my jurisdiction.'

'You sack me and see what happens.'

'Aw, shut up and go to bed.'

'Are you going to take that yeller piece away from here?'

'I'll do anything . . . if only you'll shut up. I'm tired.'

'I'll bloody bet you are!'

Jeremy pulled Bishoff away from the gate: 'Let's have another little walk while they get over it. Feel up to it?'

'Wide awake.'

'You might as well get the low-down on the dispute from me. You're sure to hear a version someday. You've told me you're country-bred. There were still blacks in your district?'

'Only a handful of fullbloods. Fair number of crosses.'

'Well, I'm going to ask you a very personal question. You needn't answer, if it offends you. You know what Black Velvet is?'

'Of course . . . "Going the gins", as they say.'

'That's not the question. It is . . . Have you ever tried Black Velvet yourself?'

Bishoff chuckled: 'Can't say I have.'

'Nicely answered. If you'd reared up like most silvertails and said, "What do you take me for?" it wouldn't 've been worth going on. Now, I'm using the term Black Velvet not simply to apply to fullblood women, but any of obvious Aboriginal strain, "yeller girls," or "creamy pieces," as they're called, half and quarter.'

'Still not guilty.'

'You make it sound like a crime.'

Bishoff looked quickly, said, 'I'm sorry . . . I didn't mean . . . .'

'That's all right. It is actually against the law . . . to cohabit with an "Aboriginal Female," as the Ordinance puts it. They don't mention cohabitation with a male . . . presumably because a whitewoman's taking on a boong's unthinkable.'

'But, you can marry . . . . '

'Not without the consent of the Chief Protector of Aborigines . . and then not a fullblood. But don't let that worry you. Your "not guilty" bears me out in what I want to say. I'm not going to go so far as to ask if you felt like taking on one of these yeller or creamy girls . . . but could you say that there was a fair interest in them amongst the males of your town?'

'Why, sure. They were the town whores. Some dashed pretty girls among them, too. It was a pity to see 'em being preyed on by low types . . . I mean . . . . ',

'Take it easy. You don't have to apologize, son. Whatever else they call me it's not a Low Type. They'll call me a "Combo," along with any other whiteman who doesn't make a secret of having a coloured woman for wife or mistress. They just don't understand the fact that I don't make a secret of it. My son Martin is in the clear because he does just that. There's really nothing to going the gins in these parts. But never own up to it. That is definitely *not done.*'

Bishoff was obviously embarrassed, kicking up little spurts of dust as they went. Now they were headed along a direct track to the creek, with the Moon, now well down the sky, staring them in the face.

Jeremy went on: 'Have you ever thought what the Australian nation would have been like if the pioneers had succoured their hybrid offspring, had given even a little of the care they gave their stock . . . instead of letting them starve to death on the withered breasts of mothers starving because that very stock had destroyed the hunting grounds, or else were murdered in the camps when seen as pale-skinned monstrosities visited on them by devils?'

'No, it never occurred to me. It would've made us rather like the Latin American nations, I suppose.'

'Exactly. We'd have been a Creole Nation . . . of a different type again . . . unique. We might all have had the seat out of our pants . . but we'd've had that uniqueness to contribute to the world, in music, literature, politics . . . instead of being just lousy copies of the stock we came from. Do you know the literal meaning of Creole?'

'Half-breed?'

'No. It comes through Spanish and French from the Latin, meaning *created* . . . that is a created people, a new people. That's what we might have been. We'd have been largely a rural population . . . true peasants. There'd've been no need for planned immigration, because as hybrids we would have bred fast. How's it strike you?'

'Well . . . colourful. But you did say we'd've had the seat out of our pants like the South Americans.'

'But at least we'd have been free.'

'Don't the Yanks run South America? And what about the Vaiseys in Argentina and other places?'

'I guess the South Americans could get rid of them whenever they wanted to. They wouldn't be constitutionally stuck with them, as we are with the moth-eaten King of England, which makes us dominated by the British parliament, and ultimately by British capital.' Jeremy exhaled loudly, adding, 'But I'm back on my hobby-horse. What I want to tell you is enough about the reality of this business of my sons' you've just overheard, not to go away regarding it as just something dirty . . . . '

'Oh, I wouldn't do that.'

'I think you'd be bound to . . . unless you understood the implications. But let me get on . . . Remember I was telling you how the whitewomen came and broke up the liaisons their men had started with the blacks. Now, I guess the whitewomen of South America were just as jealous of their conjugal rights. But their men were different from ours. They weren't afraid of their women as Anglo-Celts are. Whereas it was the missus who put the stockwhip round the dusky interloper she found with her old man in this country, the Spanish-bred master would put it round his wife for intruding on his private business. I feel sure that but for the fear of their women, our forefathers would have been proud enough of their half-breed bastards at least to feed them . . . or rather honest enough in their pride, because the pride is there, still . . . in secret. I stress this thing about our women, because it's the crux of this thing, the whole Delacy thing. I do declare that all of us bushmen would have mated frankly with Aboriginal women, but for those prudish harridans, our Irish, Scotch, Welsh, and English mothers, sisters, aunts, cousins . . . all of them. They only have to see you treating an Aboriginal woman like a human being to raise the cry *Gin Jockey* . . . and we bolt like bandicoots at the howl of a dingo.

'The row you just heard not only exposed Martin as a Gin Jockey, but his brother as being jealous of him. It isn't that Clancy's going without. You'll soon enough hear he's got a Chinese girl-friend, one of the pure-blooded Ah Loy's. But I'll be bound he'd rather have someone out of the camp, because they were the first accessible females he'd seen . . . the more desirable because the more accessible. I suppose you know our sexual preferences are established quite early in life?'

'Yes . . . I've read Havelock Ellis . . . and all that.'

'The lonely bush-boy in puberty is naturally attracted to the pretty budding Creamies and Yelleries . . . and the girls themselves are quite mad to get a white boy. Beautiful as the girls though most of their menfolk are, the girls prefer the whiteman every time, even if he's rubbish. Whether it's physiological or psychological I've never worked out. But it's only too patent. Most of them will have a whiteman's baby as near to puberty as they can bear. That's no exaggeration. Most halfcaste families have one, two or more lighter than they ought to be kids in them. Husbands don't mind, as if it's normal . . . just as this Willy Ah Loy takes it.'

They reached the creek. Jeremy suggested they walk for a little. He resumed: 'My sons aren't really happy men. Why? They like the work they do . . . and I'm sure it's not their alienation from me, because they've grown up with it and are bound to it by allegiance to their mother, and also by temperament. No . . . I'm convinced that it's this Black Velvet business. They don't have sexual partners of their own natural choice. Martin's not long been married . . . to a squatter's daughter from the South . . . real blue-blood squattocracy that goes back to those horrible beginnings I've mentioned. That's what I mean. He married that girl to do the done thing. God forgive me, didn't I do the same myself?' You only have to watch the squatters with their wives to know that what I'm saying is the truth. Go to a bush party of any sort, and as soon as the concessions to snobbery are made, the men break away from the women . . . mostly to get out into the fresh air, because they're out-of-doors men, and booze and tell dirty yarns. Those poor women! You can see the humiliation in their eyes . . . and also the meanness in their tight mouths. They're as much victims as the men, of course . . . of the system. What's the use of a lady trained at the best ladies' school to a man who has to battle with this harsh country and needs a woman only to cook his tucker and root like an animal after watching animals root all day? The Squatter's Lady is the absolutely last choice of women for the bush. The first choice is the obvious one, the women with their roots in the soil itself . . . the Aboriginal woman . . . and I don't doubt that many, given the chance, would become something of ladies in their own right . . . and still be able to go out and bring in your dinner from the bush when things were bad, and save you having to go and raise the wind at the foreign-owned bank that eventually will foreclose on you and sell you out to the foreign-owned company that will do you the favour of letting you stay on as manager. I guarantee that if all the stations in these parts had had mistresses who'd had a slap of the tar-brush, it wouldn't be as it is today . . . hardly one remaining that belongs to the man who runs it . . . and I guess that'd go for practically the whole of Australia.'

The night heron again flew out of the timber croaking, heading for the homestead as before. 'Don't tell me!' exclaimed Bishoff.

'I should imagine he'd be sleeping off that heavy slug of brandy I gave him. Poor old Bob! He must have caught Martin with the girl and tried a little blackmail. That's an old Aboriginal custom. Use of his women by others means nothing to a blackfellow more than to do with friendship, relationship, or trade. The fact that the average whitefellow makes a secret of it that he's ready to pay to have kept is surely to be taken advantage of. You mustn't see old Bob as any less the Pookarakka for doing what to us would be unthinkable. Poor Martin, too! His state was surely indicated by his rage in dealing with the old fellow. Having the guts to sneak out under our noses and root the girl . . . but only to finish up acting like a boy who's been caught pulling his puddin'. Well, this ought to do us, eh? We'll get back. What's the time? Nearly three. Look . . . there's the stars I told you of rising . . . remember, concerning Koonapippi. Orion just popping up . . . the Cat's Cradle . . . and above, to the north, the Bull . . . the Dilly Bag of Shades . . . and there, the Pleiades . . . a bit hard to see in this bright moonlight . . . the Old Lady herself . . . Ol'Goomun-Ol'Goomun.'

As they set off to walk back, Jeremy asked, 'Have you guessed about the boy?'

'Eh?'

'Young Prindy, Nelly's quarter-caste son . . . Martin's son . . . my grandson.'

'Oh!'

'Don't let it worry you. He's not the only Delacy born on the wrong side of the slip-rails. My old Dad had one yeller-feller, Jumbo, so-called from his Skin name, Jumbajinna. He lives in Palmeston, a fair amount of the time in jail.

He gets away with a lot because he was a police inspector's son. Give the old man his due, he gave Jumbo as much recognition as he dared, with his job and his wife. My mother, of Welsh descent, was very prim and proper. Jumbo is my half-brother, of course. He married halfcaste and has a whole tribe of Delacys who are, of course, my nephews and nieces . . . cousins to my worthy sons. Then there are my brother Jack's son, Darcy, and his kids. I've told you my brother was killed on Gallipoli . . . by Winston Churchill and others!' The last bit came like the crack of a whip. Bishoff looked quickly. But Jeremy went on calmly enough: 'Darcy's mother is my wife, Nan, or Nanago. So Darcy is my stepson as well as my nephew. Nan was Jack's mistress when he went to war. I didn't inherit her in the hand-me-down system of the blacks. When I came home after the war, I found her starving and ill, actually deprived of what comfort and security Jack left her in by my lady wife, when there was no one to protect her. I think I've hinted that my first wife divorced me out of spite . . . using my taking Nan in as grounds . . . I took her in to physic and feed her . . . and I married Nan in the same spirit. But that doesn't mean that my Nan is a symbol of spite . . . at least as far as I am concerned. She's the sweetest woman I've ever known. And then, don't forget my ideas on miscegenation. I don't have to go *tchinekin* to get my heart's desire, like my son and the rest of the poor bastards.'

'You have no children . . . er . . . er . . . .'

'Creamies? No. Nan's illness prevented it. Perhaps for the best. I've had a lot of trouble with cross-breeds, trying to help them, as I thought. They're a different problem from the straight-out Aboriginal. Really a sociological one. I might have been too hard on my children, trying to make them perfect representatives of their race . . . Euraustralian . . . would have been, for a certainty. It's an easy way to get yourself roots in a country you want to belong to with all your being . . . too easy, I think. Properly a man should do it on his own.'

They were swinging back from the creek towards the homestead now sleeping whitely in the blaze of the Moon. Jeremy said, 'Well, that's about all . . . except a bit about Dinny Cahoon that you ought to know, in case what I tell you confuses you when you hear other tales. Remember I told you . . . or did I? . . . that this yeller girl, Nelly, is Piggy Trotter's daughter. Cahoon found her there in the camp after the Peg-Leg Nelly business, and took her out and sent her to his sisters as a housemaid. It's a common thing for police to do . . . as Protectors. Usually they take them at the age of eight or ten. The kids are glad enough of the better food, shelter, and protection, no matter what the treatment. Halfcastes are mostly neurotic and need and even appreciate discipline . . . other than that of the old people, which is, of course the cause of the neurosis. By fourteen or fifteen they have to be got rid of, sent to the Halfcastes' Home in Town, because if they haven't got involved with some male by then, usually white, the John himself will be looking at her in a way not to please his missus. At the time Dinny was stationed at Caroline River, not in charge, but under a sergeant. He had quarters with his sisters. They're all Irish born . . . emigrated on the death of their parents. Dinny was only a schoolboy. The old biddies are much older than he. They're very religious. I suppose Dinny is, too, in his way. He's hardly been out of their sight . . . except on bush-patrols. He rarely drinks . . . and then goes quite crazy . . . and his only dealings with a woman, I think, are those I'm going to relate.

'After the capture of Bobwirridirridi, Dinny was promoted to sergeant, and given the Beatrice Station . . . with the biddies in attendance, of course. He probably wanted it so as to keep an eye constantly on the Toohey household. They say that Jinbul visited Tom Toohey's place every day, looking for tracks . . . of Brumby and Micky. They brought their maid, Nelly, of course, a pretty thing, aged now about fourteen . . . and never been touched, thanks to the religious teaching and supervision of her mistresses. How Martin cut her out I don't know. He could've taken advantage of Race Time . . . it was about then . . . during the Races, or after, when Dinny would be away in Town seeing the people he'd pinched during the festivities through the court. It must've got out through blackfellow talk. Blame it on the Willy wagtail, who's supposed to watch these affairs with great interest and enjoyment, and then report them to the spoilsports. Dinny went quite mad, called Martin out, although Martin was only half his age, and gave him a sound thrashing. There were no witnesses to the fight . . . at least no white ones . . . but it was soon known far and wide. Also that Dinny went home and got Nelly, took her into the scrub and stripped her and flogged her . . . and then poked her himself. I suppose he'd been secretly desiring the kid for a long while. It seemed to settle him down. He even became friendly with Martin. The Irish are strange in matters of sex. Anyway, next thing she's up the duff. But to whom? Both boys have light complexions and light eyes. It took some time to tell . . . but I think it's pretty obvious now that the boy is Martin's . . . obvious, that is, to everyone but the pair themselves. Martin has shown no interest in the boy whatsoever. I've never seen him give the boy a second glance. But Cahoon even calls him Sonny Boy and buys him lollies . . . and's been known to brag that he's his son . . . when in drink. I guess the old biddies won't have such a sinful admission sober. Anyway, there it is. You'll soon hear about it. Apparently, although it's interesting to call the boy Martin Delacy's creamy bastard, there's piquancy in the idea that he might be Dinny's.'

They passed into the homestead paddock Jeremy said, 'I won't come back to the house. I've got all my gear out. I'd only embarrass 'em at breakfast. I'll camp in my ute till daylight, then get a bite at the kitchen, and piss off. There's nothing really to keep me around. Either those inoculations did the trick . . . or didn't. If you want any more help, let me know. Otherwise I'll see you at the Races, eh?'

'My word! I'd like my wife to meet you . . . your wife, too.'

As they came up to the motor shed, Jeremy said, 'There's an old chap works a donkey-team down inside, Billy Brew. He's got a lot of donks . . . a lot too many, according to squatters and stock inspectors. Your predecessor fairly hounded him. Not that it did old Stinker any good, because Billy's too good a bushman to corner. As he brags, he can hide his team in a hollow log if need be. I just wanted to say that he's a pretty good vet himself, and with a bit of co-operation from me, keeps his team in a lot better health than most of the complaining squatters keep their stock horses.

'When you meet up with him, start by giving him my regards. It'll save a lot of bother'. Jeremy chuckled: 'Well, I'll say *mummuk*.'

'*Mummuk?*'

'*Farewell* . . . in intertribal lingo hereabouts . . . and used by most whites, for that matter. Means simply: *I go.* Better add to it *yawarra*, seeing we'll soon be meeting again . . . means till return. *Mummuk, yawarra*, young fellow.'

'*Mummuk, yawarra* . . . Mullaka. That's what they call you, isn't it?'

Jeremy chuckled again: 'Means Old Man . . . but with respect and affection.'

'Well, that's what I feel for you.'

Jeremy grinned, waved a big hand, went into the shed.

IV

Jeremy turned out at first light, to find Bobwirridirridi awaiting him, clad in khaki again, a scarecrow figure against the luminescent milky East. The top-knot merely nodded to Jeremy's greeting. However, there was a flash of tongue and a cackle for the bottle of brandy he carried. The old man fell in behind as Jeremy headed for the kitchen. The place was ablaze with acetylene light and clamorous with activity.

Bread-baking was in progress, the bakers Willy Ah Loy and Prindy. Both greeted Jeremy's appearance with evident pleasure, then with very different expressions that of the scarecrow suddenly on the stairs outside. Jeremy said, 'I'm off home. How's the pot?' Then noting the changed faces, the one with Mongoloid eyes hooded and lips compressed to a crack, the other with Caucasian eyes that looked even odder in the Australoid setting, wide as with wonder, he added, 'I'm taking the Pookarakka with me. Can you give him a bite . . . bread and milk?'

Prindy gave the answer by leaping to cut a loaf. Jeremy got a couple of pannikins, set them on the table, sat down. Willy cast a glance after Prindy that might have signalled disapproval, but only said, 'I mek tea . . . fresh brea'n'butter, eh?'

As Prindy was about to dart out with the filled quart-pot, Jeremy grabbed at him: 'Here, sonny.' He added brandy. Prindy sniffed it, smiled with pleasure, then ran out.

Willy, coming to share the drink with Jeremy, looking out after the boy, who with his companion had vanished, muttered, 'Wha's matter he wan' him dat old bugger?' Meeting Jeremy's questioning glance, he added: 'He been get up dark-time go out look him.' He paused: 'Might-be dat old bastard sing him.'

Jeremy took it with a blink, said, 'Well, I'll be taking him away. I don't think he'll be coming back this way.'

Looking out into the milkiness, Ah Loy drew a deep breath, exhaled as he rose: 'I don' know.' Whether intentionally or not, his eyes sought the rifle slung on the wall, a heavy Winchester, used for killing the kitchen beef. He got tea and bread and goat's butter. They talked races till Jeremy left. Prindy did not return.

As they came out of the kitchen they saw the odd pair down in the woodyard.

'Look-him!' growled Willy.

Jeremy called, 'You right, Pookarakka . . . me two-feller go now.'

The pair rose from squatting, came up together, the old man laden with his weapons and other gear. Jeremy waited at the bottom of the steps, while Willy stood staring from above. The pair had eyes only for Jeremy, fixing him as they came up. He said, 'You two-feller mate, eh?'

'Belong me *mekullikulli*,' came the cackle.

'Wha' name . . . my boy, eh?'

Prindy answered, 'I call him Granny.'

'Ah, yes? Well . . . I'm taking your Granny to Lily Lagoons. You see him Race Time. All right, Pookarakka.' Jeremy turned to wave to Willy, set off back to the motor shed. Again Bobwirridirridi fell in behind, but this time with his *mekullikulli* at his side.

The old man was just as withdrawn in the matter of travelling, declining to get in the front with Jeremy. He was placed on sacks, with death's head sticking out from a loosened corner of the dust cover. Jeremy got in, glanced back through the peep-window in the canvas hood, to see the pair taking leave in the manner of Aborigines of close relationship, smoothing each other's arms. He started up. Driving away, he waved to Prindy, and got a short wave in return. The waving that continued evidently was intended for his passenger. He muttered to himself, 'An odd association . . . but a couple of odd ones, eh?'

The East was gilding as they passed through the home-paddock gate. Jeremy had to get out and open it. Evidently the Pookarakka was not that civilized as to know it was a boong's job. A short distance from the gate they turned southward, trailing a golden dust cloud. Thus till the Sun, the Earth Mother, came fairly popping from the plain, lighting the grass it seemed, the fire rushing to engulf them, but dying away just short. Soon afterwards they turned westward, came to the creek, dry but for a small waterhole dammed by the concreted causeway. A group of cattle were to be seen racing up the shadow-purpled sandy bed beyond. Far beyond was a heliotrope line, already wobbly in mirage. The wall of the Northern Plateau.

Ahead the bleached plain rolled like a sea as the sunlight swept it, white crests above long blue troughs. The trees were few enough to count, and really stunted, but magnified by isolation and the tricks of early light so as to stand as little giants. Here and there specks rose like fragments of bursting puffballs, to become kites and crows disturbed in feasting on swollen little humps of red or roan – the calves that had died when their mothers had dried up.

After a while there was to be seen what at first looked like another plateau wall ahead. Out of it rose a purple globe. Then the globe turned silver, and was seen to be a windmill. The wall proved to be cattle stringing along the horizon.

Although there was as yet no wind, the mill was turning. Then the force that was turning it became visible. A flock of birds, wheeling around it, settling on its sails, only to be started into flight again by gravitation. Some of the birds swept out in darting flight to meet the car with its high-flying tail of silver dust. They were corellas, pinkish white cockies with flashes of crimson under wings – cousins to the galahs, not so ruddy, because they hadn't been swallowed by Tchamala in the Dream Time, as legend had it, and not game to live anywhere but out on plains, lest Tchamala, who haunted the creeks and rivers he made, might deal with as with their gully-gully relatives.

Cattle raised heads from the water-troughs. Some tossed their heads and bolted. The so-called tank, the reservoir, was a hollow mound of earth scooped up about it, vivid green in contrast with the barrenness about, because fenced off. Within the fence stood the mill, with a shed fitted out to shelter stockmen in wet weather, open in the middle, with sapling table and lean-to fireplace, enclosed at each end as sleeping quarters separately for whites and blacks. Escorted by the screaming cockies, Jeremy did a turn in the car about the troughs, inspecting the cattle. No evidence of sickness here. He stopped to lean out and ask his passenger how he did. Bobwirridirridi's death's head, grey with dust, split in a grin.

Here they left the main track, which swung away southward, to continue on westward by a track much less used. Again there was a wall on the horizon, but of more substance than the last, as eventually revealed. Trees and rocks. Here was limestone country. Soon they were amongst huge outcrops of rock, like the grey tenements of city slums, only that they were thickly grown about with greenery. The road went tortuously here, with ruts and bumps to cause everything in the back to bounce. Jeremy drove slowly. At length, when they came to a creek where water flowed through limey ropes, he pulled up got out and said, 'Too rough ridin' in the back there, Pookarakka . . . more-better you come in front, eh?'

The scarecrow rose up from the canopy, then bent and hauled out spears and other gear. Jeremy said, 'Leave him.'

The red eyes fixed him, then turned to measure the distance to the ground. Like a grey spider Bobwirridirridi clambered down, reached up and got his equipment.

'What you goin' to do, old-man?' asked Jeremy.

'Me go look-about.'

'What about you come station . . . I give you tucker.'

'By'n'by.'

'I want a yarn with you.'

The top-knot nodded, while the eyes searched the irridescent water.

'You go look-about Snake Cave, eh?'

With eyes still on the water, Bobwirridirridi went a few paces along the low bank, to a clear spot, where, looking like a crouching spider, he bent and drank deeply.

Rising again, he belched, then looked at Jeremy with a grin, cackling, 'Proper-lee . . . numberr-one!'

'Rainbow water, eh? Good for Snake Man.'

Another belch.

'What you goin' to do about soft tucker.'

'Me find him.'

'Spone you come station, I give you swag tucker, bring you back.'

Bobwirridirridi came back, bent to pick up his belongings.

'All right, I'll get along then, Pookarakka.' Jeremy thrust out his hand. The red coals met the grey eyes. '*Mummuk, yawarra.*'

Bobwirridirridi took the hand lightly, grinned: '*Mummuk, yawarra,* Mullaka.' He began to load himself. Jeremy got back into the car, started up. When he looked out again – nothing. For a moment he stared, then with a shake of his head, slipped into gear, drove off.

He came to a place where the ground was paved with great slabs of limestone, all encrusted with dried greenish stuff that would be the roped growth in water. Twisted trees grew from interstices, showing that here a great volume of water flowed in wet season. No water now. The slabs gave out a hollow sound to the running of the utility. He crossed slowly by a fairly level line of slabs heaved up somewhat from the rest to form a sort of bar.

Then the limestone masses and thick scrub thinned out, giving glimpses of open country ahead. Here was quite different terrain, the soil yellowish volcanic stuff, sparkling with quartz and mica. From here the red wall of the Plateau could be seen plainly to the right. Intervening was a long low range, towards which the track was leading. Then ahead there was to be seen water, just silver glimpses among emerald seeming solid masses of reed at first. The track ran to skirt the water on the northern side, that is along the foot of the low red range. Miles of water there were soon seen to be, stretching away westward, water blue with the sky and electric heliotrope with masses of floating lilies. A few birds rose and wheeled. But that did not mean the birds were few. They were in masses on the water like the lilies, black birds, black and white, white, red, blue: geese and duck and ibis and jabiru and egret and crane.

The long low hill came slanting in, revealing itself as bare not so much by nature as by the hand of man, civilized man. The deep cuts in its slope, the heaps of rock on its summit, were much too rectilinear. Then was to be seen on the flat, stretching right from the foot of the hill into the water, an expanse of rubble, obviously the detritus of considerable mining. Further on, heaps of the rock of the hill that were bright orange in contrast with the dull brick-red showed that mining was still in progress. However, there was no such litter as must have been formerly, the washing of spoil evidently being done on top, to which a heavy pipe ran from the water. Here the slope was much more gradual, with a track running up a ridge. At the foot were several sheds, back some fifty yards from the water, and also, amongst a clump of small tea-trees and bottle-brushes, a group of native humpies. Jeremy swung in here.

Movement in the camp. Under a bark shelter, beside an ashy fire barely smoking, squatted a couple of skinny dusky figures, legs tucked under buttocks in blackfellow style. One was an old man, white-haired, white-whiskered, deeply cicatrized, completely naked. The other was an oldish woman, grey, with flaps of breasts, also naked, but with a black and white goose wing hiding her pudendum. Jeremy drew up, leaned out, called, 'Goooday, Jallyeri'

The man answered, 'Goottay, Mullaka.' The woman raised a slim dark chocolate hand to half hide her face.

Jeremy glanced at one of the bark gunyahs, with entrance just big enough to admit someone crawling. In the shadowy inside could be seen another dusky figure, prone. A glitter of watching eyes. Jeremy asked, '*Ol'Goomun* all right?'

'Him all right, Mullaka.'

'You don't want to come back yet?'

'No more yet.'

'Race Time, eh?'

'Yu.'

'Tobacco?'

The dark hand that held the goose wing let go to rise and extend in a graceful gesture, pink palm up. Jeremy turned to get several sticks of the trade tobacco called *niki-niki* from a box on the shelf above the seat. The man rose with a spidery movement and came to get it. Handing it over, Jeremy said, 'You savvy that old Pookarakka, Bobwirridirridi.'

The eyes in their deep sockets glinted like water in a well.

Jeremy jerked his head backwards: 'Him there long o' limestone.'

The eyes blinked. The comment was made in indrawn breath: 'Eh, look-out!'

'He no-more come this-a-way yet, I reckon. I think he go paint him Snake Cave.' A slight nod.

'Oh, well . . . you all right, eh? I'll get along. *Mummuk, yawarra.*' Jeremy slipped into gear, swung back to the main track, ran on beside the blazing blue water.

Hills and billabongs gave way to thickly timbered sandstone country, red sandy soil with a scatter of dark rocks. Deep ruts a short distance away showed where heavy traffic had gone through, many years ago, judging by the size of the trees that had reclaimed the right of way. Here the escarpment of the Plateau was no more than a mile away, to be glimpsed through the trees as splashes of crimson, orange, purple, where it angled to the sun. A well-beaten track branched off towards the wall. He did not take it, but kept on, with a southward turning. After a mile or so he came into yellow-soiled open forest, when he disturbed an emu with a yellow striped family at heel. A goanna raced him down the middle of the road at a good twenty-five, then gave up with a mighty spring to a stringy-bark.

The forest ended abruptly, to reveal a steel gate in a long barbed-wire fence. A broad paddock lay ahead. He stopped to open the gate, drove on. Bovine stock in no great number, but of a variety of breeds, European and Asiatic, were scattered about, looking up to watch his progress rolling a golden ball behind him. At distance beyond the paddock, a couple of miles perhaps, timber in a wobbly blue line marked the horizon. Another gate, this six feet high in a high netting fence. He let himself through.

In here the grass was green, irrigated, as to be seen from busy sprinklers. Here were no bovines, but beasts of many other species: horses, a few donkeys, kangaroos and wallabies, stalking birds, brolgas, bustards, an old emu that limped badly as it ran. The horses were mostly out in the middle, lined up at what was soon seen to be the railings of a race track. A couple of horses with riders were galloping within. When the horses outside became aware of the approaching vehicle, they turned to stare. Then a number came trotting to meet it at the gate.

As Jeremy drew up at the gate, the horses shoved in snuffling and whinnying. He put out a hand. Two of the beasts held back the others with snapping and lashing, gave noses to his touch, then turned teeth on each other, one a tubby bay mare, the other a rangy black stallion. He talked to them as to human beings: 'Never stop squabbling, do you. Time you grew up, you old buggers . . . eh, eh, don't bite me!'

Meantime the riders had come up. One, a shiny young black boy, opened the gate from his saddle, the other, a cross-bred young man with peculiar tan colouring, was having difficulty with his horse, a big roan. Jeremy drove through, while the black boy pushed back the other horses. He pulled up again. The big roan sniffed, extended his neck, came a few steps, then stopped. Jeremy held out his hand again. The horse snuffled, but would approach no nearer. Jeremy asked the rider, 'Giving you trouble, Darcy?'

'Playin' up a bit, Mullaka. You like to quiet him?' The young man had the grey Delacy eyes. One side of his face was badly scarred, evidently from burning.

Jeremy answered, 'Want a bit of breakfast first. Put him out with the others, and get another team and have a race. That'll punish the bugger, to be out of it.'

Darcy giggled. Jeremy started off again, across the course. Beyond the far railings the homestead bulked, green and white. As he approached the other gate, movement was to be seen behind the rails. Then small figures popped up on the rails to either side. The gate was opened for him. He increased speed, came tootling the horn, while massed black and brindle faces split to show gleaming teeth with bright eyes. As he went through, waving and laughing back, the children yelled, 'Mullaka . . . Mullaka!' He kept on.

To the left were small stockyards, to the right a big fenced garden plot, one half of it a lucern patch under sprinklers, the rest orchard and kitchen garden, stretching away to the bush timber. High concrete tanks and a windmill stood in the garden. He passed the yards. Now on the left were a group of neat cottages, shaded by big exotic trees of many types, to the right several sheds, ahead a grove of huge old mangoes. Black and brindle adults waved from the cottages. He tooted, ran on and through the grove.

He came into full view of the Big House, the rear of it. The front gate could be seen to the left, in a high netting fence, beyond bright patches of flower-garden. The house was truly big and well constructed, with two floors, the bottom glassed in, the top, under the big low-eaved bungalow roof, enclosed with wooden louvres. Down below was further sheltered with out-jutting trellis thickly grown with vines of several varieties, fruiting and flowering: granadillo, monsterio deliciosa, passion-fruit.

He did not keep going to the house, but swung to the right towards a very different building, this one low and long, in modern style, of asbestos and rippled glass. He ran the utility into a port attached to the place. Into the comparative silence falling with the cutting of the motor suddenly there were the sounds of the place itself: the bird-calls from grove and orchard, distant calling of children and what could almost be felt, like a heartbeat, the beat of the life force here.

Coming from the car, carrying his dunnage, which largely consisted of metal boxes of instruments and medicines, heading for a long back verandah, Jeremy cocked eye and ear towards the source of the beat, as if measuring its strength – *Home, Home, home, a-home, home, home, a-home, home, home*! The little power-house was plain to see beneath its array of heavy feeder cables, just off the verandah and just inside the garden, the fence of which ran parallel to this annexe.

The verandah ended at what, judging by its equipment, was an animal, hospital, empty just now. He went halfway along, to enter a door and a passage by which a few steps brought him to a door on the left leading into a spacious laboratory. He entered here and set down his boxes. Here also was a small hospital, for humans, just a screened-off corner with a couple of beds and bedside lockers. He left, to follow the passage through almost to the glazed front door, to turn again left into a large room that would serve as office, lounge, and library. He went to a telephone on the wall, cranked, listened, spoke: 'How's it for a feed? I'm starving. Good. As soon as I get the dust off I'll be over.'

A cross passage took him nearly the western length of the place, past store-rooms and a couple of bedrooms, to a well-equipped bathroom. He stripped, showered, shaved. Then to a bedroom to change into fresh light khaki. He returned to the middle passage, this time to go out through the front door. The space between annexe and house was simply gravelled with quartz and planted with clothes-lines. He crossed. The rear entrance, under a porch, was two fly screen doors in width, one of which opened to receive him, by the creamy chocolate hand of a plumpish woman of about forty, clad in a bright floral dress with a red ribbon in wavy brown hair and barefoot. Her lovely symmetrical soft features were bright with smiling. Jeremy gave his ruddy cheek for a peck.

Two young black girls were at the roaring range watching. Their teeth flashed at his nod. He sniffed the atmosphere of the kitchen: 'Smells good.'

The woman asked, 'You like tomato cocktail?'

He smacked his lips. They went through the kitchen to swing doors that brought them into a large dining-room with a view through eastern windows. A large table was set at one end for two. Through here and out by way of a hanging bamboo curtain, into a spacious loungeroom that occupied half of the downstairs space, except for a panelled corner on the western side, from which a fine stairway ran aloft. Through open windows and trellises and vines restricted view could be had on three sides. There was the big front gate, in the high mesh fence, the bush beyond.

They moved to a sort of cosy corner on the eastern side, where under the windows was concentrated most of the furniture of the place. While he seated himself in a deep partially upholstered rattan chair, she went to a mahogany ice-box. She fetched out a silver jug, set it up on a silver tray with silver mugs, brought it to a low table before him. When she gave him a cup, he sniffed, murmuring, 'The old familiar juice.'

Seating herself with her own drink, she asked, 'Too early?'

'Never too early for an old soak like me. To your bright eyes, Nan, darling!'

They were bright eyes, too, that looked over the silver cup, like brown agates shining through limpid water.

CHAPTER TWO

IT WAS A FACT that the Beatrice River Races constituted the social event of the year in those parts; the term Social meaning not simply the getting together of people, but that the occasion was something also favoured by those who thought themselves better than others, the Socialites, so-called, who hereabouts comprised the squattocracy and the gentry of the Government Service Senior Officers, lately augmented by the Military aristocracy being established along with the building of the Garrison in Port Palmeston. Doubtless the occasion was much improved by this quality of class distinction, even though the common herd might be limited merely to witnessing the strutting of their betters, since at least it brightened an otherwise mostly unlively existence; and deep down in Australians generally there must linger something of the ancestral Forelock Puller, else surely all forms of inequality in a nation calling itself a Commonwealth would have been done away with long ago, instead of being perpetuated as from the beginning of settlement.

Every big station in the land held its annual race meeting; but these were mere baronial concessions to serfs, handed down from the pioneering days, mere breaks in the otherwise ceaseless grind of the handling of stock during what was called The Season, the period between April and September. The difference in the case of the Beatrice River Meeting was that it signalled the end of the Season, that is apart from its social significance, and now considering this in its exacter sense of human congregation. It was through the Beatrice River Races that Bushies and Townies came to mingle in circumstances that enabled them to speak to themselves as Northerners, to join in ways comprehensible to all, the excitement of the race track, the *bonhomie* of the booze, the fraternal cavorting on the dance floor after the clod-hopping style of their forebears, the fun of sporting in the true old-fashioned sense of the term, by racing in sacks, chasing greased pigs, vying in tugs-of-war. Even the Blackfellow was permitted *almost* to rub shoulders with the Whitefellow.

Four special trains were provided for those able and willing to pack into any kind of railway vehicle, all kinds having to be used owing to the limited resources of the Railways Department. As the journeys both from Town and from the Head of the Road and back by rail were about the booziest part of the festival, few were fussy about how they made them. Many also came by road in motor vehicles, and a few even by aeroplane, because the Flying Doctor was always in attendance and brought someone along with him, and aircraft were becoming common enough in the land for there to be one or two others likely to drop in. But the horse was still the main means of transport for the bushies, even those of the squatter caste. It was only down South where they whisked racehorses about from meeting to meeting on wheels. Here even the champions walked the bush tracks, some over considerable distances. Drovers done droving for the season came in with their plants of horses, prads and packs. Ringers rode their fancy mounts. Even some of the blacks were mounted, if only on beasts given over to them for the occasion so that they might ride in the Blackboys' Races. The rest of the blacks walked. But then, they had been walking since the Dream Time.

After all, if only nominally, it was the carnival of the horse. For this occasion that animal ceased to be a mere accessory to man's perpetual harrassment of the unhappy bovine, to resume that relationship which is one of the few graces of this world given largely to depredation between species, namely the friendship of one species with another, most graceful of all being that between a noble horse and a man worthy of him.

The Carnival was timed for early September, when with cessation of the southeasters that had battered and chilled the land since June, it was warming up again, and when the working of stock was at an end, which is to say the mustering for branding and culling, the putting out to breeding or fattening, the *turn off*, or delivery to the drovers for taking to the distant markets. Beatrice River Races were the climax to it all, the pay-off, the reward. Pretty well everyone concerned with stock worked to see that the event took place to time. A date was fixed by the Committee and advertised far and wide.

Originally the date had depended on when the season ended. That was before Vaiseys took over. Since then it had been rather that the end of the season was fixed by that date; as if Lord Alfred Vaisey, in his financial wisdom, had seen it as means to more efficient working of his properties and further profit in reducing wages bills, since the common workers were employed only during those six months. If this were indeed the case, His Lordship might be asked to confirm it (if anyone were game to do so) because he would be blessing the event this year with his noble presence.

There was always a patron to give the baronial touch to it beloved by the squattocracy. To have the proceedings headed merely by the Chairman of Committees, who was always the Beatrice River Regional Manager for Vaiseys, was not enough. Several English lordlings, a couple even endowed with the Vice-regality of Governor General of the so-called Commonwealth of Australia, had served as patrons. In a pinch for patronage there was always His Honour the Administrator of the local Government set-up, First Gentleman of the Land, in fact, but when all was said and done, only a satrap compared with titled outsiders. But even these anointed ones faded into insignificance before the patronage of Lord Vaisey himself. He had done the job once before; only once, because that was just as many times as he had bothered to come this far to see how his dominions fared, so easy was it to dominate those who ran them for him; only once, a fact that might encourage some to think of him as an outsider also, but for the illogic of so dubbing one who held all the country worth a damn and had in his pocket every citizen of similar worth by what would be called Decent Standards. Perhaps the way the local conservative newspaper, *The Port Palmeston Times*, reported the announcement of his coming: 'This is wonderful news,' summed up the feelings of all those worth that damn. Even the comparatively radical paper, *The Palmeston Progressive*, mostly ready to belittle or berate anything that didn't conform with Labor politics, printed the news with no more adverse comment than: 'As no mention is made of a Lady Vaisey, presumably His Lordship is in that marital state which has been described as In Between Wives.' Lord Alfred was known as a much-married man.

Officially the shivoo lasted four days. That there was also an unofficial time was due to the fact that most of the country people had to arrive a couple of days earlier to set up camp and weren't in such a hurry to leave. Officially it began on a Wednesday, with a formal opening and some minor racing. The racing proper took place on Thursday and Friday, with the Cup Race on Friday. There would be a dance of sorts each night, then the Cup Ball on Friday night with presentation of the Cup. Saturday was Sports Day, part of the sport being the Blackboys' Races, which naturally could not be included with the official events. It all ended in a grand booze up on Saturday night. On Sunday, somehow the trains departed for their destinations with those with civilized responsibilities. Most of these travellers slept out their journeys. It said much for the stamina of the train crews that they always managed to get their passengers through without mishap, seeing that they, too, indulged along with the rest.

As accommodation in so small a township was of necessity very limited, camping, in the bush sense of sleeping and eating anywhere, was the order of the day. The bush people, used to attending several race meetings in a year, had more or less well organized camps, with claims pegged out, as it were, along the river bank, which is to say the Dry Season bank, down on the couch grass and soft sand under the big trees and right beside the lime-sweet flowing stream. The sapling timber and other material used for the structures that made up the average camp would be kept stored somewhere between meetings. Entire station staffs camped thus – the whites, of course. If they were Vaisey people and what is known as Socially Acceptable, the Boss and his lady would stay at the Big House of Beatrice River Station, biggest of the Big Houses of the land, as guests of the virtual mistress, Mrs Rhoda Eaton, the former Mrs Jeremy Delacy. The big wigs from Town would also be her guests.

Less important gentry were accommodated at the Princess Beatrice Hotel, owned by one Shamus Finnucane, better known (but behind his back since he was a man of considerable power) as old Shame-on-us. The hotel was specially constructed to meet the annual demand, upon which its business largely depended. Still lesser ones camped either in the vehicles that had brought them by rail or road, or, becoming indifferent to comfort or propriety or both, just dropped down anywhere. It really didn't matter where you slept, except from the point of view of propriety. At that time of year the weather was perfect.

It has been said that black and white were brought by the festivities almost to the point of rubbing shoulders. However, this was confined to the Racecourse, where everybody, other than the elite who occupied the little grandstand, needs must mingle. (Of course more than shoulder-rubbing took place between the races, since it was only by means of prostitution that most of the blacks could get the wherewithal to take part in the festival; but this was, of necessity, furtive, and to respectable people non-existent.) As regards camping there was a definite line of demarcation, which was the space between the two means of crossing the river: the concrete causeway down in the Dry Season bed, called the Crossing, and the high steel girder railway bridge a couple of hundred yards upstream. Whites camped above the crossing, blacks below; for the obvious reason that both had to use the water, and it was unthinkable that anyone with a white skin could use it *after* a blackfellow. Anyway, it was the accepted mode of water usage of the country. Blacks' camps were always downsteam from the homesteads. When black and white stockmen travelling together stopped to drink at running water, the former always retired discreetly a little way on the downside; or if the drinking were done at waterhole or tank or out of a waterbag or pack-canteen, the blackfellow must use his own pannikin or pint-pot, which usually he kept strapped to his saddle.

In the circumstances, it was proper that the Lily Lagoons people, being non-white save for that single one they called Mullaka, should camp downstream. What would not be considered proper was the fact that the head of the household should camp along with his mob of savages and in a manner surely calculated to offend those with any sense of true values. In fact the Lily Lagoons camp was above all the rest of those downstream, which would classify it as being uncontaminated by anything but its own self. The trouble was that it was by far the best appointed camp on the river, a showpiece even, with its striped awnings, electric lighting and refrigeration, the best of picnic-type furnishings. It was right beside the Crossing, where everybody passing to and fro, as everybody of any dignity must, because the Racecourse was over the other side, must take a look at it, unless deliberately ignore it, and taking the compulsive look meant seeing boongs lounging about in style that – that was surely little short of sacrilegious!

The spirit prevailing during the Races, from the moment the mob poured itself out of the trains (such being the way the alcoholic detrainments were described) on the Wednesday afternoon to that when, by those responsible for getting them home again, they were poured back on, was surely as near to Carnival, in its true sense of behaviour with riotous excess, as was possible in a community predominantly Anglo-Celtic; yet its functioning was directed by formalism that in the circumstances was scarcely credible. One might think that it began with the invasion of the township by the boozy mob off the first train, roaring up from the railway station to the hotel like a bacchanalian rout somewhat after three in the afternoon. But that was by no means so. It did not even do any such common or garden thing as begin: it was Inaugurated. First item on the printed program, under the heading *Princess Beatrice River Racing Club* was Inaugural Luncheon of Committees. This took place at the Big House, in the great dining-room, with Martin Delacy, grave in his responsibilities as Chairman of Committees at the head of the table, and his lady mother, as President of the Social Subcommittee, at the foot. It was all very nicely done. A first-class meal from a kitchen run by the best cook in the country, Lim Yu, served by Chinese waiters brought from Palmeston for the occasion. (Normally the servants, except for Li Yu, were halfcaste women, all carefully culled and trained by Madam herself.) There was a short address in which Mr Chairman welcomed those who retained committee membership from the last occasion and greeted anyone newly invited to join for this, then declared proceedings inaugurated. After lunch the male company adjourned to one of the wide verandahs set up for the seeming essentials of Reading the Minutes of Last Meeting, Presenting Balance Sheet, Electing Office Bearers – those in favour say Aye, those against say No – carried unanimously! The Social Committee withdrew to Rhoda's Drawing Room to do their stuff also in the interests of good behaviour in the midst of riot, or out of *noblesse oblige*, or just plain stuffiness, or whatever it was back of this compulsive formality.

There were always new faces in Committee, even though it remained the same old stuff that was in debate, because there was always more for the Committee to do than it had numbers and time for catering for low tastes while trying to get a swig or two from the flowing cup themselves. Strangers were always welcome, provided, of course, they were of the right kind. This time there were a couple of horse-faced and sheep-visaged young women, scions of southern squattocracy, visiting amongst their local kind, and a young jackaroo who was the son of a titled judge. Another female newcomer was Mrs Betty Bishoff, wife of the stock inspector, a pretty bright little woman, not *quaite* the thing, since only of *Junior* Government Officer standing and giving herself away as *common* with her nervousness; still, it wouldn't have been easy to ignore her and expect the best from her husband in his onerous office of Steward of the Course (his predecessor had happily been a bachelor) and there was always the Horseshoe Selling to fob off on the like of her, not a job for a lady who was particular whom she talked to.

Golden Horseshoes were badges of a sort, made of gilded cardboard, really tokens of subscription to the cost of the shivoo, which otherwise was free. Only the very meanest failed to buy them, pricey though they were at five pounds a pop. But the incentive to subscribe was not merely a sense of the propriety of sharing, or boozy weakness in the face of the lady-seller's blandishments. In fact the Horseshoes could prove to be the equivalent of pure gold for some buyers, because they also happened to be tokens in a lottery. Each was numbered; and there was at the Cup Ball on the Friday night a draw. There were several prizes, such as people of the bush would value: a radio set, a kerosene refrigerator, saddlery, stockwhips, all contributions from the big stations, which in effect meant Lord Vaisey – but best of all, a young horse, colt or filly, of such breeding as very likely to turn out to be a racing champion. If you'd rather have the cash, there were always plenty ready to buy. The very favourite for this year's Cup, Rajah of Timor, had been won a couple of years back by a linesman working on the Overland Telegraph, and sold for a goodly sum to the man whose hopes were now pinned on him before all others who fancied him, Mr Percival Trotters, better known as Piggy, Vaisey manager of Alice River Downs.

It was all the same old committee stuff: the consideration of the nominations, the decisions in handicap, the allotment of the genteel duties for the ladies, yet with an exciting difference that every now and again expressed itself with the mention of a magic name, Lord Vaisey! An oft-repeated question concerning an item of procedure was: *Will it suit Lord Vaisey*? No one as yet was game to speak of him as His Lordship, except one, the only one who'd had more than the briefest dealings with him, she who was called Her Ladyship behind her stiff back. In fact, only one other had had any dealings with him at all, who had been of small account socially when Lord Alfred was there before, back in the

Twenties. The rest, comparatively, were Johnnies-come-lately. But Rhoda had been hostess to him while he made Beatrice River his headquarters during his one previous tour of his Antipodean domains, and more than that, had been his guest at his baronial domicile, Castle Kenny, in Ireland, while abroad with her present husband, Lord Alfred's general manager for Australia, Clement Eaton. Just now Mr Eaton was with His Lordship, somewhere in the air between here and Port Palmeston. Lord Alfred now travelled in his own private aircraft. All ears were cocked for the sound of it now. Indeed, proceedings were brought to an abrupt halt somewhere about three o'clock by a drone unmistakeable as that of an aircraft; and everybody rushed out to see, with the exception of Her Ladyship, who never rushed. It turned out to be only the Flying Doctor. As usual, he did a few steep turns over the Big House and one over the blacks' camp behind the stockyards. Usually his bit of aerobatics here was greeted as elsewhere, with demonstrations of the pleasure of people who had little excitement in their lives; but today he got only a few half-hearted waves. Likewise, whereas one of the more important members of the household, at times even Rhoda herself, would have gone to the airstrip lying between the homestead and the township and in the big car to pick him up, today it was left to the Assistant Bookkeeper. But, of course, everybody else was so busy with committee work; and the big car was standing nicely dusted waiting to pick up His Lordship.

Dr Fox (the Flyin' Fox as they called him) also did his usual stuff for those at the township, and with a good deal more zest, since having no prize bulls or stallions or milch cows to upset with the racket or Madam to show disapproval of such juvenile conduct in one of so serious a calling. The only animals to scare here were the legion of goats, with whom no one had any sympathy, not even the owners who mostly disowned them, and Ali Barba's horses, long past being upset by anything. He did a couple of barrel rolls and stall turns, scattered the Aboriginal crowd waiting at the railway station by appearing to dive on them, then mustering the goats with a wide low sweep of the area, put them on the run, so that for hours afterwards they were seen only as a cloud of red dust away over the bush to eastward, to the calculated effect that the township would be rid of their pestiferous presence throughout the Races.

The aeronautical antics and uproar diverted the crowd from the very purpose for its assembly, namely to welcome the trains. Normally the best ears would have heard the rumbling over the trestle causeways spanning the Racecourse Billabongs some three miles beyond the bridge. As it was the first train had reached the Racecourse, only just across the river, and was already tootling salute to those attending the horses there before it was heard. Young Prindy Ah Loy heard it, while still the doctor's aircraft was in the air. He yelled, 'Treen come!'

The cry went up: *Treen! Treen! Treen!*

Then in no time she was on the bridge, to be seen only as a shadow flitting through the high red lattice of the girders, because the bridge lay at an acute angle viewed from the railway yards, and as a trailing feather of steam from her unceasing whistling – no smoke, because she was now what the knowing would call 'rollin' in.'

'Ah!' The concerted exhalation announced the bursting of the engine into view.

Cock-a-doodle, she was screaming . . . . *Cock-a-doodle-doo!*

She was pulling a truly mixed train, of open waggons, box-cars, flat-tops, with three passenger coaches and a brake-van at the rear. That all were packed to capacity became evident when she swung round the curve to show all those heads and shoulders hanging out and a list to port far in excess of what the camber of the track would have given her . . . *Cock-a-doodle-doo*!

Even as she turned into the straight nearly half a mile away, to come running into the yards, sharp eyes had identified the driver. Another yell: 'T'annaford . . . 'T'annaford . . . Pa'tannaford!'

The carroty head sticking out of the cab glinted like bright copper in the sun. Soon to be seen was the lean freckled face beneath it, with wide crack of a mouth yelling back at the crowd what was lost in the din of their greeting and the grinding of his brakes and the last long scream of his whistle.

There was puke on the sides of some of the waggons and all of the coaches; and the first act of some of those who alighted was to stagger to some point amongst the handy stacks of railway material to do the trick with some degree of privacy. Nothing daunted, save for a few who remained aboard oblivious of the fact that the journey was ended, and a couple who found it impossible to cross the railway tracks lying between the station and the single line of some half a dozen buildings comprising the business section of the town. Scarcely was the train halted when the time-honoured Bacchantes' rush for the Princess Beatrice Hotel began.

Shamus Finnucane was standing on his front verandah, to be sure a fine figure of a man, as they said of him, with his height and his bulk, his shock of iron-grey hair above the ruddy Irish countenance, the black eyes with great bushy brows above that could so effectively emphasize the expression of his always excessive sentiments, the white silk shirt with discreet little black bow tie and well pressed black lustre trousers, that made him look every inch the prosperous innkeeper he was and liked to be, out to greet with the joy of a man who loved money, that annual tide of it sweeping in a roaring wave to engulf him: 'Goo' ol' Shame-on-us . . . Goo' ol' Shame-on-us . . . 'ere we are 'ere we are, 'ere we are again!'

Grasping at the flailing hands, he raised his great voice above the uproar: 'Ah, me bonny boys . . . and it's good to be seein' ye all agin and not lookin' a day older anny o' ye . . . Charlie, Andy, Vince, Mike, Bogga . . . and a hearty welcome to ye all . . . and as usual 'tis drinks on the house to begin wit'.'

Behind the bar, similarly attired, stood his two barmen, ruddy as himself from sun that would ever be alien to them, one dark as he, the other ginger. They were also his sons-in-law, in from other down-country pubs of his, to manage which he'd imported them from his motherland, with the bright promise of sharing it all with him after they'd married his daughters. How they felt about him was surely expressed by the ginger fellow's saying to his mate, as they proceeded to fill the lined-up glasses from foaming jugs, 'Sure, the ginerosity of it fair brings tears to me ears!'

Escaping the mob, as it surged to pack the three rectangular counters of this, the big public bar, Finnucane slipped into his office behind, and out of it again into the still bigger dining-room, and through there to the huge kitchen. Here some six or seven people were madly busy with the preparation of piles of food. One was Willy Ah Loy from Catfish Station, another a full Chinese of middle age wearing a chef's cap. The rest were women, three youngish and mostly comely, another thin and small and grey with age, with the bony bitter face of the Irish shrew. Addressing her as Mother, Shamus asked where the food for the bar was. She flung him a black look and pointed through a side door. He went out into a passage, where there was a table laden with trays of sandwiches and such things, presumably prepared to absorb the alcoholic excess already in his clients' guts and make room for more. The passage gave view of the rear of the premises, which consisted of a sizeable three-sided pavilion of groups of small rooms, fronted with common verandahs to each group and built about a concrete courtyard with a rotunda in the middle, all bright with new paint and potted greenery, and hung with bunting and coloured lights. He took a sharp look at it, then hoisted a couple of the trays and proceeded with them back to the bar, where he was hailed again: 'G'wole Shame-on-us . . . G'wole Bung!'

The rush to the pub didn't mean that the entire trainload had gone with it. Some were heading that way with more or less seemliness, carrying suitcases and the canvas-covered hold-alls of the bushies called swags. Others were still hanging about the station, talking with friends they'd met. A couple of these were Police Sergeant Cahoon and his henchman Tracker Jinbull, not actually together, but close enough to be of the one company without breaking the rules. Cahoon was a lanky gingerish man of forty or so, with long narrow green eyes of which the glances seemed to be darting all over the place, while yet he talked easily with his companions. These were Constable Stunke, the local officer, stocky, squarish, dark, and his not dissimilarly looking wife, and Col Collings, the Station Master. Both policemen were in uniform, khaki shirt and trousers, silver buttons that glinted in the sun, short riding boots of the strap-over type, wide-awake hats with white puggaree and badges. While the Sergeant wore his hat on the back of his head so that a lock of ginger hair hung over his narrow forehead, the Constable had his pulled down so that he seemed to look out from under it furtively. Jinbull also a lanky fellow, similarly dressed but in obvious cast-offs, with a long black moustache at which he tugged, was talking with the two local black trackers. Like his master, and indeed all of the policemen, his eyes darted everywhere.

Those green eyes of Cahoon's kept coming back to the Lily Lagoons group, who were crowded about Jumbo Delacy, halfcaste brother to Jeremy, a lean saddle-coloured man of about forty, and his thin worried-looking wife, Possy, and their numerous brood, all just off the train from town. Prindy and his mother were in the group. It was perhaps at Prindy that Cahoon was taking those swift looks, because the boy seemed to be aware of them and to get behind someone out of range, as if having had experience of the like before. Jeremy also was there, although not exactly of the coloured group. He was standing a little apart, talking with Tom Toohey, ganger of the local railway fettlers. Toohey was still in working clothes, the conventional outfit of the fettler: rough grey shirt and dungarees, flat-topped wide-awake and sweat-rag round the neck. He would be in his middle fifties, like Jeremy, but was of very different type, slight and dark, with drooping grey moustache and seamed troubled face.

Another one slow to leave the station was Mr Eddy McCusky, Assistant Protector of Aborigines, a man of considerable importance in the land, and showing it with his strutting about amongst the black and tan groups, looking them over, calling this and that one by name, shaking hands with some, looking rather like a politician on a visit to his constituents, talking all the while, seeming to be inquiring about grievances he could rectify, offering assistance where needed, but not stopping long enough with anyone to be involved. He was a slight man, fairish, thirty-five or so, nattily attired in Chinese-tailored grey poplin, with a panama worn at a rakish angle. It was perhaps the tilt of the hat that gave the impression that he strutted rather than walked.

McCusky came up to Jeremy and Toohey, thrusting out his hand. Both shook with him, obviously without heartiness, but evidently also without damping the man's air of *bonhomie*, the cause of at least some of which was detectable on his breath. He asked Toohey, 'Any news of the boys?' Tom Toohey merely shrugged. Would one speak of sons who were fugitives from justice to a Government Official, even if that one were classified as a Protector? But evidently the question was just another bit of Eddy's politician-like rhetoric. Without waiting for an answer he turned to Jeremy: 'And how's the set-up out your way, Jerry?'

Jeremy answered with a dry-sounding question: 'What would you be meaning by set-up?'

'Regards my own department, of course . . . Aborigines. I must get out there and take another look at that school of yours.'

In the same tone Jeremy asked, 'You're not thinking of emulating our methods by any chance?'

McCusky emitted a beery belch and guffawed, 'That'll be the day when our departmental Estimates allow for play schools!'

Jeremy snapped, 'It'll be the bloody day when your departmental Estimates allow for anything much more than the salaries you blokes cop.'

'Now, now, Jerry . . . you know very well that getting the money's been our big trouble always. But things're changing. You'll be surprised at what's coming up, man.'

'Give me an idea . . . so's I won't die of shock when I see it . . . because I'll be a lot older and feebler when I do . . . if your department sticks true to form.'

'Next year's Estimates'll definitely include the cost of building a new Compound on a new site . . . Native Settlement, rather . . . the old term compound's been officially dropped.'

'A shit-house by any other name . . . '

'Come into my office next time you're in Town, I'll show you the draft . . . . '

'Draft my arse!'

'With a letter of recommendation signed by the Minister attached . . . new site named and all. It can't go wrong. It'll be quoted in the Budget Estimates in Parliament.'

'Then they must be wanting the old site for something pretty important. That's where the Shell Oil Company's going to build the new tanks, eh?'

'No . . . the old site's going to be used for the new hospital. Building that's to start definitely next financial year.'

'Ah . . . new hospital! It always comes back to medical matters. Your boss is the medical man, first, last, and always.'

'Public health man.'

'That's what I mean. He was appointed as just that . . . Director of Public Health. Protector of Aborigines comes a long way second. The Aboriginal Problem's a Health Problem to him. The Aborigines are a disease, like malaria and leprosy. He was appointed to the job without the slightest knowledge of Aborigines. You were, too. You're just a Public Service officer, an Estimates man . . . .'

'We've done our best to learn. You can't deny its complexities. You can't deny we haven't improved things mightily . . . .'

'Who did you consult . . . the likes of Cahoon there?'

'Certainly not. You know very well the Doc's on the outer with the coppers for boong-bashing, with the squatters for exploitation. Do you see him here? Does he ever come to the Races?'

A strangely resonant bass voice intruded into the lively conversation: 'Did I hear me name taken in vain be anny chance?' There was a slight brogue to it.

They turned to find Cahoon with them.

McCusky cried, 'Ah, Dinny!'

The bass voice demanded, 'What's the big argument?'

McCusky answered, 'The usual one . . . the Aborigines.'

'Boongs,' said Cahoon flatly, as if by way of correction.

Jeremy asked dryly, 'Do you know what the word boong means, Sergeant?'

Cahoon's slit of a mouth twisted in a grin: 'I know what a boong is . . . that's good enough for me.'

'You might be surprised to know it's a Malay word for brother . . . first used by Malays working with blacks on the pearling luggers.'

The grin widened: 'It don't mean brother to me, man.'

Grey eyes and green eyes were locked in antagonism.

McCusky said hastily, 'I was telling Jerry about the New Settlement.'

The deep bass rasped: 'What we need's a new jail for the black bastards. Blue Bay's bustin' apart with 'em.'

Jeremy said in the same dry tone, 'I guess that was the idea of letting them out under the Royal Amnesty . . . more to ease pressure than to express His Majesty's Pleasure, as it said in the Proclamation'.

'That's about it . . . and they all be back inside of a year.'

Jeremy, turning away, said with a hard grin, 'Thanks to you, eh, Sergeant?'

The voice rasped: 'Thanks to any officer of the law 't's doin' his duty.'

'But doesn't that rather make a case of an officer of the Crown running counter to the wishes of the Crown in his sense of duty?'

The slit twisted again: 'Maybe it does. But whether the King let 'em out or not, I'm runnin' 'em back in if I find 'em breakin' the law ag'in . . . . And speakin' o' them as got out under the Amnesty, I hear tell that old murderin' madman Cock-Eye Bob's out your way. Is that correct?'

'I'm not a police informer, Sergeant . . . goodday to you.' Jeremy turned away, saying to Toohey, 'Coming down the camp for a drink, Tom?' But he had gone only a step or two, when he swung back, and eyeing McCusky, asked,

'You were saying you want to come out to Lily Lagoons to take a look at the school. May I ask why?'

McCusky pushed his hat a fraction further over his left eye: 'The new order's providing for the education of all part-Aboriginal children.'

'Why . . . is there any objection to my educating full-bloods as well?'

'Not at all. But we'll be wanting the others. We'll be bringing them all in.'

'In where?'

'The Estimates provide for a school for girls and small boys on Lady Beaumont Island . . . for bigger boys at an institution being built down in the Centre.'

'What're you going to teach 'em?'

'To take their place in our system of society.'

'On several occasions I've heard you running down our system of society. Is there some new Public Service rule that's forced you to change your politics? I've heard they're getting tough.'

Another tilt of the hat: 'That'll be the day when anyone forces me to change my politics, man!'

'You sound like a Conservative now, instead of a Labor man. Anyway, the youngsters out our way are being just as well schooled as you'll ever do it . . . and better . . . because no one's going to shove 'em out afterwards into a society that you'll admit yourself can't treat its own kind properly, let alone coloured waifs out of Government orphanages.'

'Sorry, Jerry . . . but you don't have qualified teachers . . . and we have.'

'Qualified in what . . . understanding of the Aboriginal mind? Because that's the first qualification required . . . and who's going to have that who hasn't lived his life with Aborigines and identified himself with them?'

Cahoon came in with the slit grin and the basso: 'Is there such a thing as an Aboriginal mind?'

The grey eyes met the green again: 'You wouldn't know, Sergeant. You don't find it with a stockwhip and a stickful of shit.' Jeremy swung away, with the green eyes blazing after him.

McCusky said quickly to Cahoon, 'Been a dry argument. Come and have a drink, Dinny . . . or we'll miss out on old Shame-on-us's free beer.'

It was a moment before Cahoon could answer, and then with a heavy exhalation: 'Okay.'

Then he glanced again at the Lily Lagoons crowd, seeming to cause them to shrink together. Now Prindy and his mother were not of it. He remarked on it: 'Where's that kid from Catfish got to?' He advanced on the crowd, demanding, 'Where young Prindy?'

Shrinking more, they hung their heads. Cahoon snapped at Darcy, 'You?'

Darcy, face aquiver, giggled nervously: 'I don't know, Boss.'

'Where he camped . . . with you?'

'No-more wit' me-feller, Boss.'

The green eyes shrivelled the crowd for a moment longer. Then Cahoon turned away to the waiting McCusky. As they went he asked, 'You're goin' to pick up that boy too?'

'Sure . . . they've all got to come in sooner or later. Not quite ready for 'em yet. After next Wet.'

The Sergeant raspingly cleared his throat: 'My sisters wouldn't mind takin' the kid. They'd teach him some good . . . like they did his mother. What d'you say?'

McCusky, quizzing from under the panama, answered, 'I don't know Dinny. The boss would have to say. I'll put it to him if you like.'

Cahoon said hastily, 'No, for christ' sake, keep Cobbity out of it. Surely you can fix it, can't you?'

'No . . . the Doc's the man with the say.'

'You ask me, he's got too much bloody say. No man should have as much power as he's got.'

'Gwahn! What about you blokes?'

'P'lice? Jesus man, we're handcuffed with bloody regulations at every turn!'

'What about your mate McKinn? In the Marraningo business he gets up in court and says: *I shot everything that put its head up*. Just like that . . . and not a word said officially.'

'That was a punitive expedition, man, to punish a tribe of bloody savages that murdered a whiteman . . . . '

'A whole friggin' tribe for one dirty old combo . . . . '

Cahoon stopped in his tracks, with eyes narrowed and mouth tight: 'Now, Eddy, if you're goin' to talk like a bloody missionary, or that trouble-makin' rat-bag Delacy . . . . '

McCusky patted the narrow khaki back affectionately: 'Gwahn, Dinny . . . only kiddin' you. Come on and get that drink.'

Prindy and Nelyerri were down in the Lily Lagoons camp. As Jeremy and Tom Toohey arrived, Nanago was giving them lemon squash from the refrigerator. Jeremy and Tom, settling into deck chairs under the wide striped awning that served as lounge and dining-room, while Nanago waited on them, were talking of the very thing that their enemy Cahoon had just now complained of to Eddy McCusky, namely the all-abiding authority Dr Cobbity, Protector of Aborigines, held over anyone of Aboriginal blood. They were discussing the Ordinance under the Aboriginal Act, whereby anyone deemed to be Aboriginal in the opinion of the Protector was so in law, unless able to prove otherwise, onus of proof being on the person so-deemed. Nanago joined them in discussion of a recent local instance of the operation of the Ordinance, in which he who was generally known as Ali Barba, the Indian hawker, properly called Rabindratha Barbu, had his wife and two adolescent daughters taken from him on the report of Constable Stunke that they were conducting a house of ill fame. They were not charged with any offence, but simply arrested on an order issued by the Protector on receipt of the police report, to the effect that, being Aboriginal, they were to be brought to Port Palmeston and there confined to the Adult Female Halfcaste section of the Aboriginal Compound. Barbu tried to institute court proceedings to effect their release, declaring that they were not of Aboriginal blood at all, but pure Indian. He claimed that he had found his wife in a mining camp of the interior peopled by so-called Afghans, remnants of the cameleers imported from India during the gold rushes in the west at the end of the last Century. Certainly the people as a whole were Aboriginal mixtures; but Barbu swore that his wife was purely Asiatic, daughter of a true

Afghan and a woman of South India. Unfortunately she, the wife, looked a South Indian type, a Dravidian, which resembles the Australoid closer than any other race, according to ethnologists. But there were no ethnologists in Port Palmeston. Nor did Barbu have the money to hire one or even to hire a lawyer with enough interest to try to trace the Indian mother. There was no court case. Barbu made a personal appeal to Dr Cobbity, who called him a 'dirty old bludger' for living on the immoral earnings of his wife and daughters, and warned him that his other daughter, a child too young to be suspected even by Constable Stunke of sullying the fair name of the town of Princess Beatrice River by having it known that there was a brothel for what properly took place down on the river bank, or in flood times or Race times under old Jimmy Ah Loy's mangoes, or amongst his pumpkins and sweet potatoes, or in his goat-house.

'I wonder why Cobbity's got to act like that?' mused Jeremy. 'He seems a more than ordinarily intelligent man. He's a doctor of some distinction in his field of public health. Why want to tyrannize over simple people . . . the simplest people on the earth, at that?'

Tom Toohey grunted: 'He strikes me more as a copper than a doctor.'

'Maybe all doctors are to some degree like policemen . . . like priests. Power, eh? They have special power. And as they say: All power corrupts . . . .'

He was interrupted by a cry from Prindy: 'Aer'plin come!'

It was evident that no one else heard, but so certain the reliance on those sharp ears that all looked whither the grey gaze was directed, across the river sou'westward. A good twenty seconds passed before the concerted breathing of 'Ah!' told that it had been heard generally. Still it was a murmur no louder than *pijak* bees deep in an ironwood. Then it was a kind of music, an aerial drone-pipe, a didjeridoo in the sky. At last there she was, a silver bird skimming the trees far off, rising higher, higher. The white cockatoos, just settled back into the river timber from having been disturbed by Flyin' Fox, rose again shrieking their hatred of these perpetual disturbers of the peace, the human race.

But here was something very different from Dr Fox's little old biplane. She was a shiny metal thing, with but two wings, low set so that she looked like a great predatory bird. She had twin engines, howling now in close proximity and in the added power she was using in the steep turn round the town. Faces could be seen looking down from her many windows. Jeremy remarked: 'His bloody Lordship for a certainty.' Prindy and the rest of the piccaninnies, brown and black, set off at a gallop along the river pad that would at a point take them up through Jimmy Ah Loy's garden in a short cut to the air-strip. When the aircraft landed, out of it spilled quite a crowd, all looking at a loss to find themselves groundings again and at the mercy of what Mother Earth had to offer its children: the heat, the dust, the swarming flies. All soon had out their handkerchiefs, wiping, swiping. To perfect her hostess-ship, Rhoda should have had some sort of fanning and fly-spraying device to greet such distinguished ones with. Besides Lord Alfred, a big paunchy man, sweating profusely and hence a natural target for the flies, were His Honour the Administrator, Colonel Close, Judge Bickering, Colonel Cadogan of the Garrison, Police Superintendent Bullco, Mr Clem Eaton, Australian Manager for Vaiseys, and others to make up a dozen or more, including a fragile-looking youth whom His

Lordship introduced as My Son and a skinny fair-haired young woman he named simply as Lydia, who didn't seem to want to be introduced at all. But for all the discomfort of it, Lord Alfred, looking the perfect squatter in tusser silk and wide-awake and elastic sides, greeted his hostess most graciously, taking both her hands and calling her Dear Lady. She put him in the back of the big car with his son. Whom she would have chosen to sit with them she wasn't given the chance to show, because fairly under her arm holding the door wide went Lydia. Rhoda gave her a look, but without effect, even without being seen herself it seemed; for no doubt about it, for all her pushing manner, Lydia was an aristocrat. It was left for Rhoda to jam their two Honours, Administrator and Judge, into the front seat with herself, the driver. Clancy and Martin with other cars and the Bookkeeper with the utility, dealt with the rest.

Over the very genteel afternoon tea with which the guests were settled in, Lord Alfred, guzzling the dainties that were the result of the co-operative art of Rhoda and Tommy Lim Yu, remarked on the famous Australian Bush Hospitality – which he might have done well to put to test by turning up somewhere incognito. The proof of hospitality is not in the lavish giving of your pudding, but in the matter of whom you give it to and why.

The Sun went down on all these activities of Wednesday, leaving for a while a saffron sky in which the young Moon hung above the tall trees of the river and into which the smoke of the supper fires of the campers rose like whisps of violet silk, and the flying foxes, looking much like charred bits of rag similarly rising, fluttered undecided whether to work on the paper-bark blossoms above the Crossing, where it was safe but discommoding for their pur-blind kind by reason of the glare of acetylene and kerosene lighting, or below where only the tiny fires of blacks were the distraction but there lay the risk of being brought down with a boomerang and finishing up sizzling as supper on one of those fires. The white cockatoos, usually the loud-voiced bosses of the river timber, had departed after the second aeronautical assault on their territory, and now could be heard far down the river disputing roosts with others of their kind. The curlews also were down river tonight, calling along the western bank, doubtless driven off by the whiteman's glaring lights, but also having no business with people whose baby spirits, stored in hospitals or some such safe places, weren't subject to the hazards of those of the Old People.

After moonset, to creatures of the surrounding wilderness looking from afar, it would look, according to the direction of looking, as if either the Moon had got stuck just down below the horizon or another was rising, so bright must have been the glare of the Beatrice River settlement in the deep purple of the night. At the station homestead the big power-plant was thumping out full amperage to light pretty well every lamp on the place. The verandahs of the Big House blazed, and the windows of the several staff quarters and of the big block of offices and stores, and the swimming pool and tennis court with their floodlamps. In fact the only section not ablaze was the dining-room, where the lighting was of the shadowless type built into cornices, bright enough to give full effect to furniture, plate, crystal, napery, and the elegance of the dishes, but so soft as to give grace where it was lacking: as in Lord Vaisey's beefy baggy features, Police Superintendent Bullco's bullet head and bruiser's jaw, the aristocratic Miss Lydia's colourlessness, Rhoda's once lovely neck and shoulders so recklessly revealed by her evening gown, and in many a face seared by fierce Australian suns and winds in pursuit of an ungentle calling while wanting to look like English gentlemen and ladies, and in some whom the very pursuit of gentility itself had worn to rags.

Since it was a warm night, the company withdrew to the verandah adjoining the dining room, where the lights were promptly dimmed. Then, somewhat tardily, the lights were extinguished, in response to a remark by Miss Lydia that she would like to see the stars and could not do so to advantage with lights on – any lights. Off went all lights outside. The tardiness was due initially to Rhoda's evident waiting for His Lordship's sanction to the request. He seemed to realize it, at length saying quickly, 'Yes, yes . . . Lydia's a great star-gazer, don't y'know.'

The view was sou'western, with a diamond blaze of stars ranging from Antares in the very cream of the Milky Way at the verandah's edge to two great glittering bloodshot orbs, bloodied by the dust no doubt, lying in the black velvet of the horizon. When Lydia stepped to the edge of the tessellation His Lordship did likewise, although slowly through having difficulty owing to his bulk and age. The rest then rose with alacrity.

Lydia stepped onto the lawn, remarking, 'You people are reahlly lucky, don't y'know, with your quaite mah-vellous southern skay!'

No response. In fact there was dead silence for the best part of a minute while she made a wide sweeping survey of the celestial scene. She was half-turned back to the verandah when she spoke again: 'I expect you know your Constellations?'

Response now, but only in uneasy stirring and some throaty sounds. Then she swung fully on the dim gathering, demanding, 'My God . . . don't tell me you're ignorant of the identity of these . . . these mah-vellous gifts Nature lavishes on you every night?'

Lord Vaisey cleared his throat noisily.

Rhoda spoke, rather stiffly: 'We live out-of-doors a lot, you know. What seems wonderful to strangers becomes commonplace to us.'

'What?' Lydia almost screamed, 'Scorpio, Libra, the Centaur . . . commonplace?'

Again His Lordship hawked.

Rhoda said with increased stiffness, 'Here we have different names for the stars.'

Lydia swung away, and her skinny arm was seen pointing at the twin rubies now on the point of vanishing: 'Well, what're your names for those?'

Rhoda's voice was vibrant now; 'My sons will know.' She turned to Martin beside her.

Martin had to hawk, too. Pointing to the southernmost he said: 'We call that the Drover's Star.'

Lydia asked, 'Why?'

'Well . . . it goes down about the time the drover's night watch starts.'

'I see.' Lydia seemed to be considering it. Then suddenly she asked, 'But I understand the droving season's over.'

Martin answered; 'Yes . . . that's right.'

'When does it start?'

'Oh . . . about June.'

The skinny arm shot towards the zenith and her aristocratic voice rose with it: 'In June that star would be theah!'

You could hear Martin swallow. After a terrible moment be said huskily, 'It must be another one we call the Drover's Star.'

The response came icily: 'It certainly must be!'

Lord Alfred spoke: 'Lydia, m'dear . . . '

But she went on: 'What would you call the other one . . . the one that's just gone down?'

Martin muttered, 'I don't know that one.'

Up rose the aristocratic bray again: 'Well, you might be interested to know that it's *Arcturus*, chief star in the Constellation *Bootes*, the *Herdsman*.' A moment, then it came, like a whip-lash: 'Being a herdsman yourself, I'd've thought you'd know that!'

By the sound of caught breaths the lash whipped just about everyone.

Lord Alfred stepped onto the lawn, took a thin arm, saying, 'Lydia, m'dear . . . . '

She answered with a sigh: 'Yes . . . I am a bit tired, Alfred. It's been a dashed long day.' Then she addressed the dim gathering: 'Sorry, chaps, and all that . . . but Alfred did warn you . . . about me and the stars, I mean. Think I'll toddle, if you'll excuse.'

Rhoda said quickly and easily, 'I'll see you to your room dear.'

But Lord Alfred intervened: 'Leave it to me, dear lady.'

Now arm in arm they moved off. Lydia swung back on the gathering: 'I do take those old stars seriously, don't y'know. You have to take 'em seriously . . . cos they've been there such a long while . . . like Alfred heah . . . night-night!'

Lord Alfred guffawed. There was a responding titter and a chorus of good night.

Out of the long moment of intense silence that followed the disappearance of the couple, Rhoda spoke quietly: 'We reahlly must learn something about them . . . the stars, I mean. There're charts, I believe.'

Out of earshot Lydia was being nothing like so well-bred: 'The stupid, ignorant oafs! The more I see of Australians the more I detest 'em.'

His Lordship murmured: 'But Lyd dear . . . you said you loved it all!'

'Australia, which is a lovely land . . . *but not Australians* . . . . who're just colonial louts and toadies!'

'Rilly, m'dear!'

'It's true. Look at the way they're treating me . . . because they think I'm your mistress . . . while they grovel to you . . . yes, positively grovel . . . Yes, Your Lordship, No, Your Lordship . . . and you say there's no class distinction heah!'

'I mean the way it is at Home. Class means nothing to these people rilly. It's only because I'm the boss that they treat me the way they do.'

'That makes it worse. That makes them sycophants as well as snobs.' Lydia's voice had risen.

'Shh, m'dear . . . for God's sake!'

'As if they'd do anything about it if they heard me . . . the . . . the crawlin' spawn of convicts!'

'Oh, my God!'

Lydia chuckled: 'It's all right, Alfie . . . I'll play it soft.'

He sighed: 'If only you'd let me tell 'em who you are . . . and that we're engaged.'

'And have 'em fawnin' on me too? Not bally likely! And we're not reahlly engaged, old deah, till it's in *The Times*. Goodnight, dear old thing.'

They kissed lightly.

'Goodnight, old gal . . . sleep tight.'

Back with the company, which he found all standing by their chairs as if sprung to attention at his step, His Lordship seated himself with the aid of half a dozen eager hands. He said, 'It's Lydia's upbringin', don't y'know . . . grand-daughter of a crazy duke and all that . . . apple of the old man's eye. He's a positive crank on the stars . . . own observatory. I expect she learnt her stars with her ABC. By the way . . . we're engaged, don' y' know . . . but she wants it kept secret till we get back home . . . *The Times*, and all that rot . . . not *The Port Palmeston Times* . . . ha, ha, ha! . . . fusty old London *Times*. She's secretive about her title, too . . . doesn't like the Lady business . . . all right for 'em's had it a thousand years or so, I suppose, not like us parvenus . . . ha, ha, ha! If you'll only keep the little secret for me . . . eh, what?'

A chorus answered: 'Oo, yis . . . Your Lordship!'

'Good, good . . . or as you put it yourselves . . . ha, ha, ha! . . . Good-o! I expect those lights there are Finnucane's pub, what? I must look him up. My last visit here he promised to have for my next a supply of my favorite tipple, Tullamore Dew . . . wonderful stuff, distilled by the Little People themselves, the Irish say. I wonder if he reahlly got any . . . or didn't drink it all himself?'

Martin assured Lord Alfred that indeed there was a stock of Tullamore Dew at the Princess Beatrice Hotel, broached on the very rarest of occasions.

'Good-o . . . I'll drop in on him tomorrow after the races.'

Rhoda protested: 'But an awful crowd gets into the hotel then, Your Lordship!'

'I'd like that, deah lady. I like your crowds. I like your Jack's-as-good-as his-master attitude.'

Now, where Lord Vaisey got the idea that class distinction meant nothing in Australia would be impossible to say. Perhaps it's a foreign fiction like our hospitality. But there it was in full sway over at the Princess Alice Hotel also – second-class-distinction to be sure, but no less strict, even for being merrier through being less stiff. There had been a grand dinner at which those of social eminence insufficient to get them a place at the Big House table had been guests of old Shame-on-us – people like Eddy McCusky, the two Police Inspectors, Mr and Mrs Bishoff, Col Collings the Station Master, other lesser silvertails and business men from Town, some squatters lacking the gentility to be classed squattocracy in a social sense, among these latter even a couple of Vaisey managers, one being Piggy Trotters. It was a gathering of a score and more. Finnucane himself had presided and made one of those speeches of his that were considered highlights of the festival; and Eddy McCusky, who despite his silvertail assertiveness, was a natural-born showman, had replied in like comic vein for the guests. The food had been excellent, probably to beat that at the Big House since less fancy. Hock had been the drink. Champagne would be reserved for the Cup Dinner that would be put on for the Cup winner (human) on Friday night. The festive board, made up of table sections of special design, had occupied all one side of the large dining-room, and the feast partaken of in the presence of the other diners; that is the lesser ones with the lesser fare that they had to pay for, so that everybody could have some share in it, meaning everybody qualified for admittance to the dining-room at this season, which was certainly not anybody.

But when the dinner was over, it was everybody from the dining-room who trouped outside to the colourfully lit courtyard to take part in the fun and games there. Outsiders of the proper kind were also admitted here, people from the camps mostly, the train crews, who were accommodated in their own barracks (but not including Pat Hannaford) the lesser policemen, camped at the Police Station, among them Dinny Cahoon, (if one could speak of him as being a lesser member of his kind) and some soldiers from the garrison who had bivouacked in military style on the other side of the river, making a sort of military manoeuvre of it perhaps so as to do it at the public's expense, much as the Navy converges on Melbourne at the time of the Melbourne Cup. Police, but not soldiers, were in mufti. The latter were an asset in that they augmented the usually indifferent orchestra with a couple of accomplished bandsmen, a trumpeter and a drummer. With them were playing two of the old regulars, Bridie Cullity, one of the Finnucane girls, at the piano, and Eileen, another, on the fiddle. Master of Ceremonies and doing it very well was Eddy McCusky. There was dancing, singing and reciting. Best voice of all was that of old Shame-on-us himself-himself, a fine Irish tenor, Irish because that's all he sang, and with effect to bring tears to many an eye in a gathering largely Irish at least at second-hand. Apart from his solos, he sang a couple of duets with his third daughter, Colleen. The crowd roared the choruses. Another good voice, a baritone, was that of Dinny Cahoon, who oddly enough chose Australian songs, so-called, which are mostly concerned with lawlessness, of course: *The Wild Colonial Boy, Since Dad Got Put in Jail, The Jolly Swagman.* Perhaps his holy sisters had made a policeman out of him to prevent his becoming a criminal. Eddy McCusky recited comic verse. Occasionally someone from the packed bars up front, carried away by the music, would wander in, usually with shirt-tail out if he were a ringer or fly half-gaping if he were railway fettler, fencer, well-sinker, but always to be gentled out again by Shamus and his blarney, his promise of a free drink tomorrow, and his talk of the better fun to be had along at the Dance Hall. Here was no real trouble at all with intruders, as if in this famous egalitarian society everybody knew their place quite well. The occasional intrusion might even make the intruded-upon feel snugger and smugger in their exclusiveness. Surely sight of the faces, black, brown, and·yellow, peeping from just beyond the lamplight through spaces between the groups of rooms, must have had that effect on those within. The yellow faces were those of the veritable little horde of Ah Loys of the district. For a short while there were also a couple of white faces, although not wearing the expressions of respectful interest of the others, but rather of disdain over the boozy frolicking of people who should know better. These were the McDodds, the storekeepers, skinny old Angus and fat old Fan, who confined their junketing to a single day and night of the year, Hogmannay, and were always at daggers drawn with the Finnucanes. In fact few of the peepers stayed for long, there being that other show to divert them, the romp of the really common herd at the Dance Hall.

The Dance Hall was across the railway from the rest of the town, just beyond the eastern termination of the shunting yards, but easy enough to locate just then by reason of the acetylene glare from open doors and wide-canted louvers, and the glitter of what was claimed to be the biggest heap of broken bottles in the land. It was just a big corrugated iron barn, sapling-framed on a concrete floor, with the entire lower part of the walls louvred to permit maximum ventilation and observation from the outside to suit a community where most of its members were debarred from inside. Benches flanked the walls, while a small platform stood in a rear corner to accommodate now the orchestra of four young coloured men, two guitarists, a piano-accordionist, a drummer. There was a goodly crowd dancing, mostly crossbred girls dancing with whitemen of the ringer type with shirt-tails out. The louver spaces were crowded with blacks and brindles, while round about were giggling and guffawing groups of blacks, a lot of them tipsy. Jinbul and his black brethren of the law were there, in uniform, and more or less drunk by the look of them. There wasn't a truly black person within the walls, except one of the musicians, who appeared to be some sort of Torres Strait Islander. The whites would barely number two dozen, four of them being slatternly women with snotty kids, perhaps belonging to men of the newly arrived road-workers' gangs and not yet aware of their distinction, but even so sitting apart from the dusky ones. Nelyerri was there, dancing in high-heel shoes on which she wobbled when walking back to her seat. Young Prindy was perched in a louver space with a bunch of the Lily Lagoon kids.

Pat Hannaford had danced with Nelyerri. He was MC, naming the dances, calling the movements of the old-style set-dances. He himself was married to a halfcaste, but not now in possession of his wife or creamy child, who had left him to go off with a half-caste drover. It wasn't that Pat hadn't treated his wife well, but the contrary, according to him. 'You've got 'o belt 'em,' he would say. 'Cantankerousness's part o' their make-up. I couldn't belt a woman.' But others said she left him because he talked nothing but politics.

But it wasn't long before Hannaford was yawning, and most of the company with him, and a number slumped sound asleep on the benches. Prindy had fallen asleep in his window and been picked up and passed out to Willy Ah Loy, on whose shoulders he now slept. That it was likewise in more select quarters was soon revealed to these lowly ones by the indrawn hiss through the crowd of *dookyangana*. Those who didn't do the disappearing trick on the instant began to yawn the louder and prepare to depart. Sharp eyes had spotted the lanky silhouettes against the stars and known them for what they were despite the lack of buttons and badges. They were Constable Stunke, officer in charge here, Constable Gobally of Caroline River, and his nibs, Sergeant Cahoon, in a moment standing blinking in the bright doorway. Assuming the twisted slit of a grin, Cahoon asked, 'How you all doin'?'

Pat Hannaford answered, 'Fine . . . till you come along.' Then he turned to the orchestra: 'Okay, boys . . . pack it up.' He looked round the hall, in every direction but that where the policemen stood, adding: 'Goodnight all . . . see's tomorro'.' With that he stalked out by the back door. Suddenly the lights went out. There was scuffling in the darkness, and the sound of Cahoon's vocal vibrance as he and his colleagues walked away.

The Ah Loys – that is to say the Catfish Creek Station branch of this multitudinous and multifarious family, Willy, Prindy, Nelyerri – had been amongst the first to leave, going along with the left-branch Delacys, down to the Lily Lagoons camp. Evidently it was a customary thing, since Jeremy and Nanago, sitting in their lounge tent, showed no surprise at their arrival, and Nan went to the refrigerator for refreshments while the others settled themselves down. Prindy, still sleeping, was lain on a cane lounge. Nelly was now barefoot and rubbing sore feet. Nan brought brandy and rum and milk and certain essences, with which Jeremy proceeded to concoct nightcaps. The rum drink was for Willy. They talked of the dance and then of Jumbo Delacy, Jeremy's halfcaste brother, who was down from Town not simply to attend the Races, but to ride for Piggy Trotters.

Jumbo, Jerry's junior by a score and more years, was considered the best racing rider in the land. He had been riding in the Beatrice River Races since their inauguration by his father when only a small boy. It was through Jumbo's riding that the custom of permitting employment of halfcaste jockeys along with whites had persisted. From the conversation now it seemed as if Jumbo, mostly drunk, was strictly on the water-waggon at times like this, and keeping so by staying at the Toohey homestead, where drink was never allowed for fear of trouble for Tom himself from the law for ever keeping tab on him, he being the only one of the household legally permitted the privilege. The way the company were talking, it seemed as if Jumbo was very likely to carry off this year's Cup too. The only serious rival to his mount, Rajah of Timor, was the Lagoons horse Red Rory, as yet not to be relied on. Darcy Delacy, Nan's son by Jeremy's dead brother Jack hence Jumbo's nephew in whiteman style, would be riding Red Rory. He was considered almost Jumbo's rival as a rider. Jumbo didn't get along with the Lagoons people, hence the fact of his camping with the Tooheys. In fact Jumbo didn't get along with anyone.

The talk was interrupted by faint strange-sounding cries from Prindy, still asleep but half-risen from the lounge. When Jeremy inquired what was wrong with the boy, Willy Ah Loy whispered, 'He goin' 'o sing . . . might-be walk-about too.'

'Sing?'

'Yeah . . . like o' dat now time he get too-muchee what-you-call-yum 'cited.'

'He walks in his sleep, too?'

Mother and stepfather shook their heads to express concern about the boy. Aborigines believed that a sleepwalker was under the influence of a *moomboo*. Nelyerri muttered: 'Dat old *koornung* been do it, I reckon.'

'Old Cock-Eye Bob?'

'Where dat old-man now?'

'He's up in the Painted Caves.'

'He been do it sumpin long o' my lil boy. All-day he walk-about look-about him.'

Ah Loy whispered, 'He reckon dat old-man goin' learn him sumpin. No-goot bijnitch dat.'

But Prindy was not going to walk. He sank back, gasping. Evidently the singing, if the few sweet strangled sounds he uttered could be so called, caused him great effort. Jeremy rose and bent over the boy, whispering; 'Sleep, little man . . . sleep . . . you can sing me your song tomorrow.' The boy murmured, then fell silent, sleeping peacefully. Jeremy turned back to the others, saying, 'That old-man can't hurt him. He been promised me he no-more hurt nobody round here. Better take him home now, eh?'

Ah Loy picked the boy up with the greatest care, since to wake anyone suddenly was to risk parting *Shade* from body permanently. As the *Shade* might wander far during sleep, time must be given for it to get back home. For one to wake without one's *Shade*, meant to live out the rest of one's mortal existence as an idiot, a husk, while the *Shade* went wandering as a *poot-poot*, a tick, for ever looking for a body.

Still sound asleep, the boy locked his legs round the man's shoulders and arms about his neck, dropping his pale cheek to the black Chinese fuzz of hair. They followed the water's edge, walking in the single file of blackfellows, the man ahead, past the bark and bough humpies of the blacks, mostly invisible in the gloom, only a glimpse here and there where a fire burnt brightly round which the campers still sat, giggling and guffawing softly while passing the bottle round, their restraint due as much to the convention concerning others sleeping as to wariness of the *dookyangana*. Likewise the dogs beside the fires that were but glowing embers gave warning to their people only in soft growling.

It was a very different matter with dogs when they swung up the bank and, coming to a fence of netting and barbed wire, entered a gate, and what seemed to be man-eating mastiffs roared and raged at various points of the wide garden. Evidently the dogs were chained, since they made only a noise about their misanthropy. Through the groves of pawpaws, bananas, and other plants, could be glimpsed a few dim lights. They were almost up to them, when a flashlight caught them, causing them to drop their heads. A squeaky old Chinese voice spoke in its own lingo. Willy replied to it similarly. The light was dowsed. They went on past iron houses, odd-shaped structures of the Chinese style that adds bits and pieces as required, at length entering one, a mere shed, as revealed when Willy struck a match and put it to a hurricane lamp. There were a couple of hide-strip beds and a sapling table, built into ant-bed. Willy set Prindy down on one of the beds, straightening the rumpled blanket and the canvas roll that served as pillow. In a moment Nelyerri had her flowered dress off, to hang it on a peg. Her shoes she placed beneath the bed. She had nothing on now but cotton drawers. Thus attired, she got into the bed with the boy, slipped a slender arm about him, whereupon he cuddled up to her, setting lips to one of her small dark breasts and sucked. Willy, stripping to the buff, did no more than glance, as one used to the sight – as well he might be, when it was the convention of those he lived amongst for mothers to give their breasts to children of all ages to puberty. Ah Loy blew out the light, settled down in the other bed with a gusty sigh.

II

The racing began at eleven on Thursday, after the customary Address by the Patron, delivered from the steps of the little corrugated iron grandstand. The difference on this occasion was that it was listened to generally as not for many a year. This was proper, seeing who the Patron was, not merely His Lordship, as those about him called him, but the Big Boss, as called by lesser ones, and by the least ones, who knew so many bosses, little and big, Boss Number One, the last surely the most apt appellative, seeing that he, almost utter stranger though he was, virtually was monarch of all he surveyed as he stood there. Not that he even hinted of his great power, but rather belittled himself, saying in concluding his address: 'You don't know what it means to be amongst you as one of you in this good Australian style, paying homage to what, after all, is the true king of Australia, the horse.' And he asked for three cheers for the equine species – although not in those terms, else, scarcely anyone would have understood what he meant, literate nation though Australia is supposed to be, at least as far as its white citizens are concerned.

Only one person in all the gathering of hundreds ignored the address. That was Jeremy Delacy, who remained with the Lily Lagoons horses in their stalls. The rest of his household were there, even Nanago, very nicely and even expensively dressed, to match any lady in the grandstand, but without the floral or frilly headpiece that seemed to mean so much, hers being a squatter's wide-awake, black, with a band of fine silver. Also, very sensibly for that dusty place, she wore no shoes. Most of the young halfcaste women were wobbling round in high heels, and even a couple of the blacks.

Even that high priest of class-consciousness, Pat Hannaford, listened, in the very front of the crowd, primarily to provoke by the leer he presented, but only to be disconcerted himself by getting a friendly smile from Lady Lydia when she caught his leery eye. Turning very red, he gave a wobbly grin in reply. When later he heard that she was a duchess, as everybody was soon saying, despite that injunction of His Lordship's, he muttered, 'Christ . . . and I smiled back at her!'

There was nothing elaborate about the Racecourse, as there never is about such places in the bush, for all the swank that goes with them. Besides the grandstand, which was self-contained to protect the elite from the mob, with its own privies and lunch-room beneath, there were some half a dozen tin lean-tos, serving as totalizator, scales room, jockeys' room, privies for the mob (tacitly for whites only), and largest of all, the bar, with annexes of bough-covered saplings for those who chose to drink sitting down instead of holding up the counter. Of course blacks of all shades were barred from here by law. Here old Shame-on-us and his slave sons-in-law laboured, while most of the females of the Finnucane family swilled the myriad glasses. It was generally referred to as Finnucane's Gold Mine. Other bush-shelters lined the rails of the course proper on the flats to either side of the grandstand for the convenience of the mob (white). A couple of others served as annexes to the refreshment booths run by Barbu and his little daugher, and the Ah Loy family. Barbu specialized in curry, with fly-whisks made by himself from cows' tails, and cheap dark glasses imported from India as sidelines, and the Ah Loys in Chinese delicacies as well as common-herd tack like meat pies and saveloys. Barbu would also give you a winner for a fee by consulting some sort of occult apparatus. Ah Loy's sideline was grog for the blacks in the guise of what was called lolly water. The horse stalls were also of bush materials, a shelter and a yard with a water-trough for each string of beasts of which there would be a good hundred.

The Patron's call for cheers for the horse was the signal for the parade of all the beasts that would be racing – a circling of the area between grandstand and post by excited animals led by nervous owners and trainers, round and round, prancing, rearing, bay and chestnut, black and white and roan and grey – while the mob packed along the rails of the flat named them – Bonny Beau, Silver Lad, Franjipani, Red Rory, Night Queen, Rajah of Timor, Last Toss, Last Hope and all the rest – and pronounced grave judgments on their chances with statistics of their breeding. Included in the parade was the youngster who would be First Prize in the Golden Horseshoe lottery, a handsome little black colt named Sir Brunette, donated by the *North Australian Pastoral Company*, another great foreign land-holder, subsidiary of British banking interests.

At the head of the parade, mounted on a white horse and tricked out in the get-up of an English huntsman, was the steward, otherwise known as Charlie Bishoff, the stock inspector.

First race the Maiden Stakes, with untried colts and fillies, fearful of the crowd and suspicious of each other, quivering, sweating, champing, stamping, bucking, striving with might and main against the intentions of their exasperated jockeys and Charlie Bishoff's directions, bunching at the barrier, tangling, swinging from it, essaying to run the race the other way, coming back to tangle and bunch again, a hopeless mess of variegated horseflesh, of tossing names and swishing tails, of multicoloured silks and flaying whips – until, as if by the intervention of some unseen power, chaos for an instant became order, the field was strung out behind the barrier, and the steward signalled, the barrier shot up – '*They're off*!'

The shuffle of hoofs became a sudden steady drumming, waxing to rolling thunder, as heaving rumps and flying tails and flickering hoofs and the flapping silks of crouching backs vanished in a cloud of dust, and the thunder waned with distance, only to be seen as a flying ruddy cloud at which the crowd stared in silence. Then round the first curving quarter of the great oval of the course, the two-furlong mark, the creatures of the storm appeared again as what they were, hard striving units of flesh and blood. Binoculars were raised, and voices: '*Blue Bob's leading*' – '*Last Hope Lassie next*' – '*Come on Blue Bob*!'

The course was one mile, the distance for every race, except the Cup, which was a gruelling two. No fancy little gallops and sprints for these beasts, emphasis being placed on stamina as much as speed and more so, since the underlying purpose was to breed horses for stockwork. Rarely was a gelding run. The champions of these events became the stations' studs. Nevertheless it was racing, chief interest of the so-called Nation of Australia.

There was a grand view across the weedy waste, the field strung out now, still with Blue Bob out in front but the placings different. Short people were jumping up and down for glimpses over the shoulders of the tall, while the gabble became excited: '*Coolibah second*' – '*Grand Slam*' – '*Bill Bailley*' – '*Last Hope Lassie*!'

But no – past the fourth furlong Last Hope Lassie was third and gaining ground. '*Come on, Blue Bob – Grand Slam – Lassie, you little beauty*!'

Round the southern curve and coming up to six furlongs, and significance lost by change of view so that they appeared to bunch again, just a madly heaving mass against the rails backed by the red dust cloud.

But here they come, with the straight ahead – into the straight, with the leaders bunched but the others strung out, the leaders Grand Slam, Blue Bob, Last Hope Lassie – anyone's race – stamina for the last burst would decide it: '*Come on Slam – Bob – Lassie – Lassie, you little beauty – look at the mare: Billy Button, look at your mare, she's out in front – no, no, Blue Bob's got her*' – they're girth and girth – they're neck and neck – the post ahead and neck and neck they come before the screaming crowd, their thunder and the storm of their breathing drowning out the little human sound – '*the mare a head ahead – the mare, the mare*' – the post – and it's Last Hope Lassie's by a head – and Billy Button is crying into his wide-awake.

Poor old Billy Button, railway ganger at the Caroline, married to a yeller piece, father of a mob o' creamies, got a bit of a stock-run, tryin' to win a race for twenty years – and now he's done it! 'Good on you Billy, come'n'ave a drink. I did me dough on Blue Bob – but come'n'ave one on me, jes' the same!'

Then it happened all over again, this time in somewhat more orderly fashion to begin with because the horses were better experienced. It was listed as the Trial Handicap, with rather good mounts that aspired, or more truly their owners did so through them, to run in next year's Cup race. But still it was much the same thing, the jostling, the cavorting, the patient marshalling of Charlie Bishoff in the guise of John Peel, the miracle of the lining up, and – '*They're off*!' But no less excitement for the repetition – even more so – the wild staring after the heaving rumps and flying silks, the dumbness with lost vision at the second, the goggling and the gabbling at the fourth, the shouting and the screaming as they swing into the straight and come a-roarin' and a-thunderin' in to leave half the mob whooping for joy and the other half groaning. The same old thing each time – yet always different.

Flying Welter. President's Trophy. Ladies' Committee's Bracelet. It mattered not the name.

Then the break for lunch. Those in the grandstand came down in stately fashion to their cold meat and salads and chablis, hock and lager, served by the Chinese waiters from the Big House; while the mob (white) pressed and buzzed like blue-bottles on a carcass about Finnucane's bar and vied like meat ants for the savories of Ali Barba and the Ah Loys. As to the boongs, none in this classless society knew their place better. What they drank they did so in the bushes behind the stinking privies, while what they ate was what was left when the *kuttabah* had had his fill, and at twice the price for the privilege.

At two-thirty the racing was resumed. The same old thing, but with the difference now of seeing the field between the third and fifth furlong racing in mirage in the sky and then coming into the straight as a great rolling blob of quicksilver. Still there were people who tipped the placings in these conditions and rushed to the tote to bet on them. And always there was that subtle something that made it different and no less but even more exciting every time.

It ended at five-thirty with the copper Sun glinting on the dust-encrusted tree tops beyond the course, and soon to be obliterated by the cloud of dust raised by the rush back to the township. It was Finnucane's they were mostly headed for, the man himself and his minions having hastily departed earlier for just this. Even Lord Vaisey was in the rush, with the Delacy Boys and some of the less of other Big House guests, including Lady Lydia. They had no need to expose themselves to such crudity, when there was a private road running up the river on that side and another causeway by which to cross to the Big House. But His Lordship said he wanted to go with the mob, for the fun of it, and also because he wanted to take a dram of that Tullamore Dew.

Jeremy Delacy, having seen two of his horses win minor races, had left the Racecourse well before the mob. He was in his camp when it rolled by in its cloud of dust and gasolene fumes, out of sight of it himself and with all tents closed to keep out the contamination. He emerged from the sleeping tent on hearing his name called. A big truck stood near, driven by Tom Toohey, and packed with crossbreeds of various shades. Billy Button alighted. He was to go up with Jeremy to join the small drinking party that Finnucane customarily put on for owners of winning horses. Perhaps Jeremy, who so far during the festival had not had any dealings with Finnucane, was going as a kindness to the nervous carroty little man. Jeremy took him into the lounge tent to have a drink, while Toohey and his mob, which included Billy's creamy family and Jumbo's halfcaste, drove on. Jeremy and Billy Button waited till the mob were past and the dust a little settled.

They walked up to the pub, a distance of about a third of a mile from the river, went round the verandah to the private bar reserved for such occasions, to find the lucky owners there, with filled glasses before them on the counter, but no host. Jeremy asked, 'Where's the bung?'

The others looked towards the open door leading to Finnucane's own sanctum, which served as both office and place of very special entertainment; and one said in a voice hushed with the momentous news, 'Lord Vaisey's in there.'

Another hissed, 'With that young duchess.'

Then Finnucane appeared, again in his hostellier's neat rigout, ruddy face glowing with evident pleasure. His black eyes lit on Jeremy, and the bushy brows shot up: 'Ah, Jerry, my boy . . . 'tis good to see ye! I know 'tis but little winnin's for the loike o' ye ye've had today. 'Twas good o' ye to come along and join us.' He swung to address his guests generally, lowering his head like an old bull and lowering his voice, rumbled: 'His Lordship says he'd loike to do the honours be ye too . . . so if ye'll shtep t'is way, gintlemin.' He reached with a great hairy black hand for the flap in the counter and raised it. When no one moved, he urged softly: 'Now, don't be shoy . . . he'll not ate ye . . . he's the most amiable of gintlemen as a matter of fact.'

They began to file through. 'Go right insoide,' said Finnucane.

Jeremy, the last outside the bar, reached for the flap and lowered it between himself and Finnucane. The black brows came down on narrowed black eyes. Finnucane rumbled, 'Ye'll not be joinin' us then?'

Jeremy answered shortly, 'You ought've known I wouldn't.'

Finnucane cast a glance at the last of the crowd pushing through the office door, then leant over the counter hissing, 'I didn't anticipate ye'r comin'.'

'I wouldn't have, only to bring Billy Button.'

The hiss became more intense: 'Always the same stiff-necked bloody fool, now aren't ye!'

Jeremy answered quite loudly, 'And you're always the same sneaking, crawling hypocrite.'

The brows shot up and the hiss was like a jet of steam: 'Don't ye hypocrite me, ye . . . ye misanthropical sod, ye!'

In the same loud voice Jeremy replied, 'You don't mind the sneak and the crawler . . . it's the hypocrite that hurts, eh? Talking nothing but the total independence of Ireland . . . . '

The steam was rumbling under pressure: 'Will ye koindly lave me house, Delacy?'

'Until along comes one of the greatest curses of your benighted country, and the all-abiding curse of mine, the English Landlord . . . . '

The rumble became a subdued roar: 'I'm askin' ye to lave me house!'

'And not only do you let him piss in your pocket, but import the stuff for him to piss with.'

Finnucane choked down a bellow, let off the mighty head of steam by bringing a hairy hand down on the counter with a clap that made the glasses dance, then said hoarsely, 'Shame on us for kaipin' in our midst the loike o' ye . . . son of a good Irishman, son of a man who through knowin' how to be politic saved this counthry from becomin' the blacks' camp the loike o' ye'd'a'-had it be now . . . but for the quality o' that man in there!' The hairy hand was flung towards the inner door, and the fierce black gaze with it – to see standing watching it all and listening with head cocked, His Lordship himself, with Lady Lydia peering with evident interest over his shoulder.

Jeremy looked too, held the blue-eyed stares for a moment, then swung away from the counter towards the outer door. As he strode out of it, Finnucane roared after him, 'An' good riddance to bad rubbish!'

Jeremy chuckled as he stepped from the hotel verandah onto the gravel, looking away to the crescent Moon all bloodied from the dust of the day. He went on chuckling down to his camp, repeating some of the things he had said. Nanago greeted him with a wide inquiring look. He answered, 'Had a bit of a barney with old Shame-on-us . . . right in front of His Holiness the Big Boss, too . . . ha, ha, ha! Give us a brandy, dear . . . a stiff un.'

He drank with relish, still watching the Moon, still chuckling.

The Moon went down – and the fun and games started as last night, but with a good deal more purpose for enjoyment, as was evident from the different quality of the noise, even of that refined murmur that went for noise at the Big House, where they played a game new to these parts, called Bingo, organized by Lady Lydia, whom everybody was treating with great cordiality now. The singers at the hotel were in such fine voice that they could be heard word for word down on the river. The Dance Hall throbbed and thumped till midnight. When the Ah Loys came down to get their nightcap, Nanago gave it to them in whispers, saying that Mullaka had taken a pill to get in a good sleep for Cup Day; then she sent them on their way.

III

Cup Day dawned cloudless as all days at this season of the year. But the silver quickly darkened to blood owing to the dust of yesterday. Jeremy walked the mile to the Racecourse by way of a bridle pad, arriving to find those attendant on the Lily Lagoons horses, Darcy and a couple of blackboys, dead to the world in snuggeries of straw, and likewise the chief object of their attention, Red Rory. The big beast was lying on his side, stretched out as if dead. Jeremy, staring at the scene, frowned, but not in annoyance with the somnolent attendants, as was evident when, after waking them by quietly moving about, he spoke: 'Looks bad . . . the bugger's down to it again.' It didn't mean that the horse was sick, because he rose lively enough when roused, to create a storm of chaff and dust with a mighty shaking of his brindle hide. From the conversation that went on between Jeremy and Darcy it would seem that the horse's taking it easy when others of his trained-to-the-limit ilk were restless was an ill omen for success. Jeremy expressed his puzzlement over it saying, 'Do we train him so that he gets muscle-bound and has to flake out like this to relax? Or does he just decide to give up when he knows we want the best out of him? He's the strangest cuss I've ever had to deal with.' He sighed. 'Well, get the bugger moving. See if you can get him alongside the Rajah this time with young Prindy's help. The Rajah was definitely interested in that little mare of Prindy's yesterday. If we can get the three of 'em close together and make the two stallions jealous, we'll get this one interested in winning . . . perhaps.'

While the boys curry-combed Red Rory, Jeremy went along to fondle his old black stallion Electron, there only to share the excitement of the season.

Soon there was Prindy, breathless from his long run from Ah Loy's, giving a salivary grin in reply to his grandfather's greeting, going to the saddle-rail for the wherewithall for the pony mare Sugarbag, whom he would be riding in the Blackboys' Races tomorrow and had come to exercise.

The Sun rose bloody as bandit's gold, to pick the gold out of Red Rory's glistening roan hide as, prancing along with the little mare, he headed for the Course for exercise. There was nothing sleepy about him now. He played up, trying to throw Darcy, till Jeremy came and lectured him on his fate if he failed them: 'It's definitely the crows, Rory boy, if you don't behave.' The horse stopped his tricks, evidently out of regard for the man, but without the whinnying affection of Electron, his sire.

The scheme they had worked out to bring Red Rory and Rajah of Timor together for a preliminary encounter that might fire them for a great battle of rivalry in the afternoon's race did not work, for the reason, evidently, that Jumbo Delacy saw through it and kept his mount away from them. There was nothing Jumbo need be told about horseracing tricks.

The brassiness of early morning changed to the blue enamel. A breeze sprang up. The flies sprang out. The crowd began to roll back to the Racecourse.

Ten-thirty – and it was on again – the prads parading, showing either their conceit with arching necks and mincing steps, or their nervousness with sweating, champing, rolling of eyes – the proud owners, the nervous trainers, the tight-lipped jockeys going with them round and round – the shining horse-flesh and the gleaming silk – the jostling – then, '*They're off*!'

The drumming, the thunder, the dust, the screaming, yelling, agony of the home run to triumph or defeat. Again – and yet again – the same thing, and yet subtly so different.

Then lunch, with the same dignified descent of patricians, and, even though there was much more time for it today, the same starveling scramble of the plebs. The Cup Race, last event of the day and hence of the season, excepting the Blackboys' events of the morrow, which really did not count, was timed for three.

Everybody belonging to Lily Lagoons was round their champion during the interval, munching on refreshments dished out by Nanago and her girls. Prindy and his mother were with the Catfish crew.

Red Rory was restive enough now, in a foul mood, lashing and snapping even at those who were keeping the flies off him. Jeremy's talk of handing him over to the crows had no effect. He seemed to know they were all depending on him, and was making them pay for it.

Then it was three and the bell tolling for the weighing-in. They had to keep a halter on Rory to get him moving. Then he defied them to remove it when they set about bridling him, as if perversely wanting to add to his already top weight of ten stone two. Darcy on the scales was shivering, so that the Clerk of Scales, Clancy Delacy, his unofficial cousin, asked him if he felt all right.

Then out to the Grand Parade. It took Jeremy all his strength to hold the great roan head. When he talked of the crows, Rory tried to bite him.

Charlie Bishoff in his coat so gay manoeuvred them somehow to the barrier.

'*They're off*.'

Red Rory shot away in the lead, then seemed to regret it and fell back into the ruck even before the dust enveloped them. Soon the crowd were yelling the placings at the second furlong: '*Sovereign out in front*,' then Rhymer followed by Winsome, Arafura, Rajah of Timor, Red Rory, the lesser half-dozen strung out, all taking it fairly easy; yet as they crossed the direct line of vision of the half-mile and were running in the sky, they were streaking like lesser horses at their best. Round and into the straight, in much the same order, with a thunder of hoof-beats and storm of straining lungs, and past the stand like a flash of tattered rainbow.

Now was the test, the second mile – that awful gruelling second mile. The crowd now on their toes. Furlong ten. They were bunching now, really trying, boring in for that position on the rail. Furlong twelve across the way saw them bunched in the sky like a dark cloud driven by a hurricane; yet there were those who with binoculars dared declare the placings: the twin favourites in the lead – yes, but who of the leaders leading? '*It's the Rajah – It's Red Rory – No, the Rajah – I'll give you ten to one the Rajah*!' But who could tell when both horses soaked with sweat were the same colour now – and what price jockeys' colours in mirage?

But there it was plain enough at the twelfth. Rajah of Timor in front, Red Rory on his heels. The crowd were yelling – hoarse. But not Jeremy, who groaned to Nanago, squatter-hatted and barefoot at his side, 'Same old thing . . . follow-my-leader . . . unless he's chasing a bloody mare!'

Into the straight – the home straight this time and the end in sight and the crowd gone mad because of the half-and-half fancy of most of them.

'*Come on Red Rory, you can beat him. Stick to it Rajah, he can't catch you – Rory, Rajah, Rajah, Rory*' – while the thunder waxed and the storm came raging. The post – and it was over – with Rajah of Timor winning by that length it seemed Red Rory could have snatched off him even in the last ten yards. Half the crowd crowing, the other half groaning.

Piggy Trotters being helped down from the grandstand to waddle out to meet his champion as he came in heaving, steaming, with smirking Jumbo on his back. When Piggy tried to kiss the flaring muzzle the horse swung away from the grog-blossom presented to it and that boozy breath. A great cheer went up for gross man and graceful beast as they came through the gate. Jeremy was first to take Trotters' trembling hand. They weren't friends; but it was a great occasion. 'Thanks, Delacy,' Piggy wheezed.

Jeremy took the reins of Red Rory and led him heaving through the crowd, many of whom snarled, 'Shoot the bastard, Delacy . . . he could'a' won!'

From the scale room the Lily Lagoons people walked with their shame back to the stalls. So often had they seen The Chairman come down from his dais on the grandstand to take the hands of their Mullaka and their clever boy Darcy in congratulation on winning the Cup that they had no interest when the victor was someone else. But Prindy stayed with his mother, surely not knowing that the hunk of red meat in the squatter's tusser silk and wide-awake was equally his Granny with the one he called Mullaka.

As a matter of fact, it wasn't the Chairman who offered congratulations this time; or at least not he alone. It was only fitting that the job be left to the Patron of patrons. Lord Vaisey came down with Martin Delacy. Grasping the sweaty shaky trotter of Piggy, he said, 'A victory for Vaiseys too, by Jove! Congratulations to us all, eh, what?'

When Jumbo's surname was given in introducing him, His Lordship, reaching up to take the lean mahogany hand, stared into the smirking mottled brown face, murmuring, 'Delacy?'

His sudden blinking surely showed he'd realized the *faux pas* almost as he made it; but by what gentlemanly means he would have extricated himself he was not given the chance of showing, because Jumbo answered promptly and loudly, 'Da's right, Boss . . . I old-man Paddy's boy. I huncle long Martin 'ere.'

Lord Alfred couldn't have missed the deepening of Martin's natural ruddiness. He responded: 'H'm . . . I knew your father . . . grand old gentleman, and a great horseman . . . and you're a credit to him, Jumbo . . . as a horseman . . . a credit.' He shook hands heartily.

There was no hope of beating the mob in their wild townward rush this evening. Jeremy was still at the stalls, waiting with his people for the dust to settle before going down to the camp, and watching the rubbing down of Red Rory, when a stir amongst those about him caused him to turn, to find just behind him Lord Vaisey and Lady Lydia. His Lordship said, 'Mr Jeremy Delacy, I presume?'

Colouring and swallowing, Jeremy replied stiffly, 'That's me.'

Smiling, Lord Alfred extended a plump red hand: 'I'm Vaisey.'

Without responding to the gesture, Jeremy answered, somewhat breathlessly, 'I'm sorry . . . but I don't take hand shaking lightly.'

Vaisey's colour deepened too; and he dropped his hand, but said easily enough, 'I understand . . . I should have known better.'

A little silence, which Jeremy broke, saying stiffly, 'You want to see me about something?'

'Oh, simply to pay my respects.'

'Respects?'

'Well . . . I've heard a lot about you. I knew your father, of course.'

'Of course.'

'He was a grand old man.'

'If you've really heard a lot about me, you'll know I have a very different opinion of my father.'

Vaisey cleared his throat: 'Well, yes . . . I understand that . . . er . . . oh, I'm sorry . . . but may I present Miss Lydia Lindbrooke-Esk?'

Jeremy met the cool blue eyes of Lydia, who smiled, and extended a thin white hand. His face flamed. For a moment he hesitated. Then he met the challenge, met the hand, saying huskily, 'How d'you do?'

She shook like a man, but spoke like the lady she was. 'I'm honoured, Mr Delacy.' Then she swung towards Red Rory, saying, 'He's a handsome beast.'

Evidently somewhat at a loss, Jeremy said, 'He's not popular with us at the moment.'

'Poor old boy!' she said, and put out the white hand to touch the horse.

'Careful! said Jeremy. 'He's a biter.'

Nothing daunted, she touched the sweat-soaked ruffled neck. Red Rory swung towards her, but only to rub his head against her arm.

Vaisey said, 'Lydia's got a way with horses.'

Lydia looked at Jeremy and smiled slowly, as if she had a way with men as well, despite her aristocratic plainness. Her eyes were intense blue, her lips full, and rosy with more than make-up. She brushed away the flies. She said, 'I'd like to ride him!

Jeremy said, 'He'd be too rough for you.'

'I ride fairly well.'

Vaisey put in: 'She's a dashed good rider.'

'You'd have to be a rough-rider for this one.'

She asked, 'Do you ride him?'

'Only when he plays up.'

'Plays up . . . meaning misbehaves, I take it? I like that. I'll have to use it at home.'

Lord Vaisey came into it again: 'You wouldn't care to sell him, would yon, old man?'

Jeremy answered shortly, 'No.'

'Pitay . . . I'd like him.'

'He'd be useless for the lady. When I say he's rough he really is. It takes half a dozen of us sometimes to sweat the misanthropy out of him.'

Lady Lydia chuckled again: 'Misanthropy . . . I like that, too.'

His Lordship said, 'I was thinkin' of him for racin' reahlly. I race, don't y'know.'

'He'd be useless for your kind of racing, too. We breed for stamina here, more than speed.'

'That's what we need. We're losin' stamina over there. Your horse could've won that race if he'd wanted to He wasn't nearly as blown as the winner.'

Jeremy asked, 'Where's Over There?'

'Ireland. I'm an Irishman, don't y'know.'

'Transplanted, eh?'

'No . . . born. Very proud of it's matter of fact. You're of Irish descent yourself, of course.'

'My mother was Welsh.'

'Ah . . . a true Celt! A mighty combination Welsh and Irish.'

'More a *complication* than anything else, I'm afraid.'

'How so?'

'We're aliens in this country . . . those of us not of Aboriginal blood. The more complex our origins, the more alien we are.'

'You surprise me. I understood it was us you regarded as the aliens.'

'Vaiseys, you mean?'

'Exactly.'

Jeremy's face darkened again as he said, 'More than aliens.' When they both looked at him quickly, he added: 'Enemies.'

Both blinked. A moment. Then His Lordship said, 'Come now, old man . . .'

Jeremy was breathless again. 'You must have heard what I said to Finnucane last night about the all-abiding curse of his country and mine . . . the English landlord?'

The blue eyes were regarding him intently. Another moment. Then Jeremy moved to turn away, saying, 'Well . . . if you'll excuse me . . . I have my horse to see to . . . and I want to get my people back to camp.'

He turned right away, to speak to Darcy: 'Give him a *bogie,* son. He looks as if he needs it.'

Lydia's voice asked, 'What's a *bogie*, Mr Delacy?'

Jeremy swung round to find the pair still there. He blinked. She added: 'A medicine?'

Throatily he answered, 'No . . . a swim . . . a bath. He . . . he likes the water.'

She asked, 'May I watch you swim him? I love to see horses swim.'

Plainly at a loss, Jeremy looked away, glanced over the deserted flat even a little desperately, saying, 'It's rather late. Won't your people be waiting to take you home?'

Lydia said, 'They've gone without us.'

He looked at her quickly.

Vaisey cleared his throat: 'As a matter of fact, old man, we . . . er . . . that is to say . . . well, we rather hoped to go along with you.'

Jeremy stared at him: 'With me . . . where?'

'Well . . . to that very cosy-looking camp of yours . . . like to see it at close quarters.'

Jeremy took a moment to reply, and showed his uneasiness in his hesitancy: 'I hardly bargained for anything . . . like this. I don't like being inhospitable . . . but you must realize the depth of my enmity to you.'

Vaisey said, 'Can't say I do, old man. Anyway, isn't it something we ought to iron out, so to speak, what?'

Jeremy was red again: 'You'll never iron that out.'

'At least let me hear your views.'

'It'd be a waste of time . . . so long as you hold a stake in this country.'

Lady Lydia, watching him intently, shook her head slightly and said with almost a sigh, 'We were warned.' She turned to Vaisey, who looked back at her blankly.

Jeremy swallowed hard. 'Well . . . seeing you've got no transport, you'll have to go in one of my vehicles. I don't use cars, though.'

The others said together, 'Thank you.'

Jeremy turned to Darcy and said, 'I'll take the horse now. Drive these people down to the camp, will you.' He looked at Nanago: 'You can look after them, eh, dear.' He turned back to the pair, saying shortly, 'My wife. She'll be your hostess. There's a tradition of hospitality in the land . . . but it doesn't force one to be host where one doesn't want to be . . . at least not me. Hope you don't mind. Dissemblance is something I can't bear.'

Lydia nodded, murmuring, 'So I should imagine.'

As the utility came up, Jeremy said, 'There's seating for only two in front, besides the driver. My wife doesn't drive. So that means one of you . . . not my wife, of course . . . will have to ride in the back.' He looked at Vaisey, saying, 'It'd better be you, I suppose. Your fiancée looks as if she'll stand the bumps better. Well, I'll leave you to it.' He turned away towards the horse-stall.

Lydia called after him, 'Wheah'd you get this fiancée business?

Jeremy looked back: 'Sorry if I've offended you. I'd been given to understand you were to be married.'

Lydia looked at Vaisey, who reddened, then back at Jeremy, who was turning away again: 'Who gave you to understand it, Mr Delacy?'

Jeremy shrugged: 'I just heard it . . . and if I heard it . . . well, the dogs must be barking it.' He went on his way.

Lydia swung on His Lordship, snapping, 'You bastard, Alfred . . . you bastard!'

She wheeled on high heels and swung away towards the flat. Jeremy, hearing the sharp retort, looked back, stopped. Vaisey, standing at the door of the utility, looked helpless. He called after her rather weakly: 'Lydia, old gal!'

Without turning, she called back, 'I'm not coming with you.'

'But . . . for God's sake m'dear . . . how are you going to get back?'

She swung right round, stood, looked at Jeremy: 'Will you take me . . . with the horse?'

Jeremy stared at her for a moment, then looked at His Lordship, then at Nanago watching wide-eyed. Then he turned back to Lydia and said shortly, 'All right.' He swung away again towards the horse.

Lydia came strolling back. To His Lordship she said coolly, 'Be seeing you, Alfred.' Whereupon he let himself be assisted into the car by Darcy. She stood by while the car started up, arms folded, thin legs apart, in mannish stance. As the car moved off she waved, to those with which the rear was packed as well as to those in the front, then went after Jeremy.

As Jeremy set off leading Red Rory by the halter she fell into step with him, saying, 'Refreshing to see someone standing up to Alfred.'

Jeremy took a moment to answer: 'He isn't an easy man to stand up to. I mean his manner's so pleasant it . . . it cramps your style.'

She chuckled: 'Cramps your style . . . I like that. Yes, he is persuasive. Still, you didn't appear to find it so hard.'

'Well . . . I'm not in his power . . . and feeling about him as I do, I'd take an awful lot of persuading.'

'How do you feel about him, reahlly?'

'It's not the man personally . . . it's the concern . . . Vaiseys. I'm afraid that's just about my *bête noire*.'

They were heading straight for the river, now down a steep track well-trodden by much coming and going of horses. She was forced away from him by the roughness onto another pad. She was going awkwardly in her high heels. He appeared not to notice. She seemed in no way daunted. She asked, 'Why do you say afraid?'

Jeremy shrugged: 'Sort of apology, I suppose . . . for excess of feeling.'

'You don't seem the apologetic kind.'

'I'm trying to be polite.'

'Are you finding it hard?'

'No madam . . . I find nothing hard I have to do.'

She chuckled again: 'I asked for that.'

The difficulty of the track forced her behind somewhat. He didn't slacken pace. But at the bottom of the slope, which was hedged with thick prickly growth, he stopped and called back: 'Careful how you go through this rubbish . . . it might scratch . . . and it stinks.' The growth was flowering. He passed through with the horse onto the grassy verge. He slipped the long lead from the horse's neck and let the beast, straining with impatience now, go down the slight bank to the big waterhole below.

She came up sniffing at a piece of stuff she'd picked, saying, 'It does stink, too . . . what is it?

'A damn weed with half a dozen names. Everything you see around here's weeds . . . except the big trees . . . and they wouldn't be here only they want the shade for the Race camps.'

'I've heard about your passion for conservation of the pristine landscape.'

Holding hard to the rope as Red Rory swam snorting for the joy of it in circles, he looked at her, saying, 'I'm pretty sure you never heard it put like that.'

'Like what?'

'Conservation and pristine landscape . . . they're not the sort of words they use round here.'

She laughed: 'Well, no . . . as a matter of fact they said you want to put the country back the way it was and give it back to the blacks.

He muttered, 'The fools . . . they've no idea that the destruction they do is cumulative and must catch up with them sooner or later.'

'It's an offly big country to destroy, though, isn't it?'

'What've you seen of it?'

'Well . . . mostly from the air, of course . . . but a lot of stations.'

'You probably never saw a bit of natural growth about the station homesteads. The rule is to cut down every native tree . . . well, they want it for firewood and fencing. But it could be replaced. It'll replace itself if given a chance. But they must plant alien trees . . . and the weeds . . . the rubbish of the earth they've brought in here.' He waved his hand towards the township, adding: 'Behind the buildings there you'll find nothing but rubbish . . . weeds, weeds, weeds . . . old iron scattered everywhere, heaps of broken glass . . . a million goats, rats, cats, every abomination known to man . . . and none of it here till the whiteman came . . . and all of it eradicable even now.' He hauled on the rope, calling to the horse, 'That'll do you boy. Come on out.' He spoke to the girl without looking at her: 'Better stand clear . . . or you'll get a shower when he shakes himself.'

Rory came up and gave a mighty shake. Jeremy looked round and saw that Lydia hadn't moved and had been well and truly spattered from flowered wide hat to dusty shoes. 'Your lovely clothes!' he exclaimed.

She shrugged: 'Silly things to wear in a place like this. I wanted to put on jodhpurs and riding-boots. Alfred wouldn't hear of it.'

'That'd be mean. This is the one chance of the year for a lot of these women to dress up . . . even some of the black women.'

He replaced the rope on Red Rory's neck and began to lead him up river towards the crossing. She asked, 'Why do you say even the black women?'

'You seem to question my every utterance.'

'I think what you say is mostly significant.'

'Well . . . I hope it's not just empty words to you.'

'I assure you it isn't.'

'Well . . . black women mostly aren't interested in dress like white women.'

'I saw quite a lot dressed up quite fantastically.'

'They'd be halfcastes. It's the black man who likes dressing up, if he's got the chance. You must have noticed the red and yellow shirts and coloured sombreros. It's like that in their native state. The women even have to give their hair to make string for male decorations.'

'Is it true you want to give the country back to the blacks?'

'They don't want it back.'

'But is it true what they say?'

'Is this some kind of interrogation? Because I wouldn't iron things out with Vaisey, as he put it, have you been sent along to do the job?'

'That's lousy!'

'I'm sorry . . . but Vaisey's my sworn enemy so long as he holds this land.'

'Would it be any different if anyone else held it?'

'The fact that it's held by an absentee landlord's the galling thing.'

'Alfred didn't grab it, you know. What was occupied he bought . . . and what he's added to those leases was granted to him readily enough by your Government.' When he looked at her, she added: 'I know all about it. There was something in a left wing paper in Sydney when he arrived about his taking over the country.'

Jeremy sighed: 'That's the pity of it . . . Australians are to blame.'

'Doesn't that make the Black Beast Vaisey rather an image of your own creation?'

When he looked at her again she smiled: 'No . . . it's not an interrogation. Didn't I start by complimenting you on standing up to him? I meant it. I think you're a brave man. Because Alfred could break you, you know.'

He looked at her swiftly. She added: 'He has enormous power.'

As he turned away he said, 'I have nothing to be broken but a resolve.'

'To free the land of Vaisey?'

'No . . . simply to learn to love it enough to feel something of what those it was stolen from feel for it . . . so as not to die feeling like an alien and a thief.'

He looked at her again, to find her blue eyes serious: 'Any more questions?'

She shook her head: 'No . . . not after that.'

They were approaching the crossing. She asked suddenly: 'May I take your arm?'

He looked surprised. She didn't wait for his answer, but slipped her thin silk-clad arm into his. Thus they crossed the river in full view of the people in the Lily Lagoons camp: Lord Vaisey seated at a table in the lounge tent with bottle and glass, with him Nanago, Darcy, and Water-Lily, Darcy's wife.

Near the tent Jeremy disengaged his arm, and went on with Rory, turning to her to say shortly, 'Goodbye, Miss . . . er . . .'

'Lindbrooke-Esk,' she said, then added: 'We'll be seeing you to-night, I expect?'

He halted: 'Where's this?'

'Isn't it the Cup Ball tonight?'

'I never go.'

'Oh. . . . Well, tomorrow at the races . . . .'

'Only Blackboys' races tomorrow.'

'I should think that rather fun.'

He said stiffly, 'They take it rather seriously.'

She answered at once, 'So shall I.'

He nodded, went on to put Rory to grass, turning towards the tent and calling to Darcy: 'Take this lady and gentlemen in the ute, will you please son . . . wherever they want to go.'

As Darcy moved to obey, Lydia said to him, 'No thank you . . . we'll walk . . . only going up to the pub. Ready, Alfred?'

His Lordship, already risen, turned beaming to his hostess, took her plump brown hand and bent over it, saying, 'Thank you, deah lady . . . thank you.' And he shook hands with Darcy and Mrs Darcy, as he called her. Then he went to the waiting Lydia, who took his arm, giving a wave and a smile to the watching halfcastes. A small crowd of whites was gathering up the road to watch the royal progress.

The Cup Ball actually began with the Cup Banquet, held at Finnucane's. This was no treat of old Shame-on-us's, whose part was only to dance attendance at the head of his slaves on the chosen ones, who were of the Committees and such owners of winning horses as, being not of the elite, were also not too shy to attend. It was held out in the courtyard of the hotel, at a table arranged to represent a horse-shoe, decorated with green and gold, not in concession to Finnucane's nationality, but to the Beatrice River Racing Club, whose colours they were, initiated by its founder, the late Patrick Delacy, to whom a toast in champagne was always drunk on this occasion. Not a very elaborate or lengthy affair, for all its high-sounding title of banquet and the drinking of champagne. It had to be over in an hour to permit reasonably early start of the ball proper, with its plenitude of initial formality.

As already observed, the Cup Ball was for everybody, and pretty well everybody attended; but few except the boldest did more than stand about outside and watch the somebodies whose show it really was. Those formalities with which it began were surely enough to put off anyone who went there for sheer enjoyment. In fact, presentation of the Cup was the very purpose of it; and that had to be led up to with the Chairman of Committees' speech to say how wonderful it all had been and how they looked forward to next year's meeting, and the speech of the President of the Social Committee to thank all the ladies, and then the presentation, and finally that which alone interested the mob, the drawing of the Golden Horseshoe prizes. The couple of hours of very proper gliding about the floor in waltz or foxtrot, with an occasional stately romp in a lancer or Sir Roger de Coverly and the genteel supper were really only a concession to social convention.

For the primary purpose the little stage otherwise used by the dance band and now decorated with the Club's Colours was occupied by such leaders of the Committees as it would hold, the rest being seated on a long church-like pew before it. For the rest the place was tricked out in red, white and blue, presumably the colours of the Nation, with streamers and balloons, and looked very different from the bare barn it had been.

The speeches dragged through. There was, however, variation in the actual presentation, because again the Chairman deferred to his master, Lord Vaisey, which obviously meant much to those looking on, to judge by their goggling at the great man as if truly believing in the literal meaning of the word aristocrat, *one privileged to rule because of the best*, and accepting this paunchy, jowly, jolly old fellow as *best* while they were least. And then there was the tragi-comedy of the Cup's actual reception by poor old Piggy Trotters, who was so drunk they had to heave him up out of his seat and steady his progress to the dais, then catch him when he bowed in gratitude to his Master, since otherwise he would have made an old-time Chinese job of it by bumping his bald head on the floor. It raised a titter within from the less refined, and a guffaw without from everyone, and very obviously also raised the blood pressure of Mrs Trotters, sitting so stiff in silks and stays and swank, awaiting this crowning glory to her long long climb upward to true gentility. Surely next year they'd have her in the Big House? Perhaps there was more to Piggy's chronic drunkenness than that reputed guilt of his for the manslaughter of three or four white policemen when he had meant merely to murder a tribe of blacks.

The prize drawing was also done by His Lordship. Mrs Betty Bishoff, looking very pretty and important, handed to him the butts of the receipts she'd given with each Golden Horseshoe sold, he put them in the little lottery barrel and twirled it a bit, then drew out first prize. The prize was, of course, little Sir Brunette, who was tethered under a tree not far away, with a couple of other horses to keep him company, awaiting his lucky owner.

The winner was named as Knobby Knowles. He was outside with the common herd, to which he certainly belonged, by the look of him, when at length he was pushed inside. He was aged about twenty-five, a ringer by his outfit, mean-faced, low-browed, lanky, awkward of step in his laughin'-sides, all of a dither with excitement and embarrassment, and of course with a bit of shirt-tail showing. He handled his wide-awake just as his English yokel ancestors must have in the presence of their betters, twirling it, crumpling it, in lean grubby hands. A typical Australian bushman, one might say. At least it looked as if the eyes of his betters about him now were saying it. Lord Alfred would have talked to him a little, it seemed; but he fled, back to the mob, to whom he could be heard shouting that he'd never won anything in his life before – and now look at him – he was a racehorse owner, than which there is no higher order of citizen in the Commonwealth of Australia.

There was a rush with Knobby Knowles to see him take possession of his prize. He was rather drunk, like most, and blubbered a bit in embracing the little beast. The instant affection was not mutual. Sir Brunette broke free of the hug, snorted, reared, then tried to bring his hind hoofs round to settle the matter. Knobby was for showing him who was boss; but the crowd dragged him clear.

Someone offered Knobby twenty pounds for the horse. Another made it fifty. Knobby only guffawed: 'I wouldn' take nothin' f'im . . . 'e's go'n' 'o make me a big man, that lil 'orse . . . a big man!'

One lean tall fellow was shoving in: 'I'll give yo' 'undred, mate.'

'Wouldn't take two 'un'red.'

'Make it two-fifty,' the thin nasal voice persisted.

'Balls!'

Here another voice rose above the general babble, urgent, that of a man quite unlike Knobby in most respects, being shorter and thick-set, although in fact his older brother, Nugget Knowles. He was urging Knobby to take the cash. Knobby's answer to him was the same: 'Balls!' and he flung off the hand lain on his arm.

The thin voice said: 'Toss yo' for it.'

Knobby yelped, 'Toss me for what . . . me 'orse? Don' be bloody jitty!'

'Toss you two-hundred-and-fifty . . . you win, you get the dough and the 'orse . . . I win, you still get the dough . . . I on'y get the 'orse.'

'Say't again? demanded Knobby.

It was repeated slowly.

Knobby growled, 'Wha's yo' game? Gi' donkey-walloped!'

But the tall fellow was persistent: 'Yo' got 'o 'ave money to train 'im, ain't yo'? 'Ere's yo' chance, mate. It's yo' lucky day.'

' 'S me lucky day all right,' Knobby chuckled 'First lucky break I ever 'ad.'

Nugget Knowles was urging his brother again to take the money: 'We need it, Knob.'

The thin voice was also urging, and now the crowd: 'G'im a go, Knobby . . . 's yo' lucky day.'

Knobby asked, 'Wha' yo' say . . . I win you gi' me two-fifty an' I keep the 'orse . . . I lose I still get two-fifty?'

'That's it, cobber . . . you won' get better odds'n'at.'

'Gi'm a go, Knobby!' howled the crowd.

'I will, too,' declared Knobby. ' 'S me lucky day.'

There was movement towards the bright light of the doorway. Some of those inside, hearing of it, began to move out. Someone started explaining to Lord Vaisey that Australians were inveterate gamblers. He said, 'I know . . . good losers, too.' Perhaps he was referring to the ease with which they'd let him relieve them of their heritage.

It was to be an odds or evens toss, by an umpire. Pat Hannaford was umpire. He asked the contestants to call. The tall man who'd started it said to Knobby, 'You first call.'

'Right,' said Knobby, and thought a while. He nodded to Pat, who tossed the two pennies. 'Evens'. called Knobby.

The coins jingled on the concrete. Umpire and contestants bent over them.

'Evens she is!' called Pat.

Knobby shrieked for joy: 'I win . . . I win . . . didn' I tell yo's me lucky day? Wha' 'bout me two-fifty, mate?'

'She'll be right,' the thin voice answered. 'Finnucane'll cash me cheque. But wha' 'bout double or quits?'

'Wha' yo' mean double or quits?'

'Make it another two-fifty. You win you get five 'undred and keep the 'orse.'

'Wha'f I lose?'

'You lose on'y the 'orse . . . seein' you ain't put up no dough.'

'Aw . . . I don' know . . . '

Nugget was hissing again, 'Don't do it, Knob. Hang onto what you got and sell 'm the 'orse.'

Again Knobby shrugged him off. The thin voice was urging again, the crowd yelling: 'Gi'm a go, Knobby . . . 's yo' lucky day!'

Knobby muttered, 'Yeah . . . it is me lucky day, too . . . never won nothin' me life before. Okay, mate . . . I'll 'ave yo'. Your call.'

Up went the coins again. The thin voice called: 'Odds!'

They bent over the spilled coins lying in the acetylene glare. Hannaford said, 'She's odds all right.'

'My 'orse,' said the tall man promptly, and went off to get it.

Someone gave Knobby a bottle, from which he took a long long pull. Then he went reeling away. His brother went after him, but to be told to 'Go to buggery.' He went reeling up to the pub, where tossing off drink after drink, he told the lone barman there, the ginger fellow, Con Cullity, his sad story. Con's only comment was: 'Och, man . . . if I could only lay me hands on two hundred and fifty fiddleys that aisey, I know't I'd be doin' roight now.'

'Wha'd yo' be doin' mate, if yo's 'n unlucky rint like me?'

'I'd blow me brains out first . . . but not in the bar here, if ye plaise . . . there's enough to clain up as 'tis. But I was tellin' you what I'd do meself wit that much money . . . I'd be down there before iverybody, payin' that ould dog Finnucane what he claims I owe him for the whiskey I've drunk in me misery as slave to him in the loneness of t' wilderness . . . and let it be known that he charged me not wholesale price, mind ye, and not aven price by the bhottle . . . but by the nip, bedad . . . by the bloody nip!'

Down in the hall the prizes were all distributed with a handshake from His Lordship that by the look of them the recipients prized even more. Then it was time to dance. The black orchestra took over the rostrum, and Eddy McCusky as MC. Pat Hannaford, being a bold fellow, led in the few who dared step it with their betters, with none other than Tess Toohey, renowned as a harlot and cheeky baggage. Both leered at those they whirled about, perhaps as much out of pride in the fact that they were the best dancers on the floor as provocation, but to get only blank looks from all except Lord Vaisey and his Lady Lydia, who smiled back pleasantly. Later, after what seemed a long spell of making up his mind, staring at her from the doorway, Pat approached Her Ladyship and asked her, as he put it: 'How 'bout a dance?' She readily agreed, but with the warning that she was a poor dancer. He must have seen that, but might have blamed her partners. The fact was she danced so badly that he was probably too much preoccupied with handling her to do more in the way of conversation than utter a few almost polite remarks, when it might have been expected he would give her a round dissertation on the Class Struggle. He didn't ask her again.

It went on till midnight, when McCusky called for *God Save the King*. Most went home worn out. However, a grand party went on all night down on the river below Toohey's, chief drunk of which was Jumbo Delacy, off the water-waggon for another year. Jumbo's first expression of triumph and liberty from moral restraint was to issue a challenge calculated soon to have him under restraint again in normal circumstances. An old enemy of his was Sergeant Cahoon, who during Jumbo's recent period of sobriety had taunted him by telling him he'd soon have him 'yarded' again. The burden of Jumbo's drunken yelling was: 'Come on, Cahoon, yo' khaki bastard . . . come an' try yardin' me now!' But it happened that poor Dinny was 'yarded' himself, having gone on a bender, as it was his weakness to do occasionally, and been locked in a cell by his comrades, who wouldn't want to add to his raving with another of his like.

IV

Saturday and Sport's Day. Its events, as those of the other days of the festival, were timed to start at ten-thirty. However, the excesses of Cup Day and Night and the fact that the sports were generally regarded as a joke, meant as usual a straggling start near noon. Today the officials were different, although Martin Delacy was there still as Chairman and Lord Vaisey still extended his patronage. Much of the running, jumping, stock-whip cracking, sack-racing, was really only clowning. There was no official break for lunch. You just boozed and ate and boozed again as you felt inclined. The Blackboys' Races were timed for two-thirty.

There were four of these races, run not according to properly constituted Racing Association rules, but on a rough and ready classification system worked out in the saddling paddock. Mounts were judged by age and known and apparent prowess. There was no handicapping. Weights of jockeys, all spidery creatures, men and boys, or of gear, which was that used in common stock work, did not count. The one race with anything like conditions to it was the Pony Race, in which mounts must not be more than three years old or of height exceeding thirteen hands, and jockeys no older than to be reasonably classed as picaninnies. Also, this must be ridden bareback.

The totalizator was not used. However, betting between individuals was always lively, for the reason that the stock-riding fraternity knew the horses, owned them, in fact, and were very interested in results. There were no black owners. Not that there was any bar. It was just that blackfellows didn't own anything; not even their wives or the pants they stood up in, such being the peculiar system of their economy.

Lord Vaisey showed special interest in all the proceedings, no doubt as an act of *noblesse oblige* to those who, after all, were the mainstay of his monarchy hereabout. What would his managers have done without their black stockriders, their black household staffs? It was traditional to say that they weren't worth their tucker, which was pricing them pretty low, seeing the kind of tucker they got, inferior stuff specially imported for them. Besides this poor fare, they were given occasional issue of rough clothing. Certain ones were paid something like one pound per month, deposited in Government Trust, and left to the honesty of some police officer to pay out when wanted for such occasions as this annual bean-feast. If a station could claim that it was keeping a worker's dependants, they need not pay him at all, even while they worked the dependants also. 'But what's the use of givin' 'em money, when they only spend it on booze?' So said the station people, and most others. They said it to Lord Vaisey when he expressed a wish to add a small gift of money to the prizes given the winners of these races, things like sombreros, fancy belts, spurs, laughin'-side boots. The incongruity of the fact that those who said it to him themselves reeked with booze didn't seem to occur to anyone.

While the ponies were being looked over, His Lordship, coming to Sugarbag and noting the pale-faced, grey-eyed, fair-haired boy on her back, exclaimed, 'But you're not a blackboy!'

Jeremy, who was at the little mare's head, on the other side, perhaps deliberately keeping out of sight, looked over, saying shortly, 'According to the law of the land he's just as much a blackfellow as any of 'em.'

Vaisey looked at him: 'Ah . . . it's you, Mr Delacy! What's that you're saying?'

'I was just remarking, in case you're thinking of debarring the boy on account of the lightness of his colour, that he enjoys exactly the same lack of rights and privileges as if he were coal-black . . . something you ought to be conversant with, seeing you're by far the biggest employer of Aboriginal labour in the land.'

'Am I, begad!'

His Lordship was looking somewhat ruddier, but in no less control of himself: 'I'll confess I've left it to my managers, Mr Delacy . . . but I'll look into it.' He turned back to Prindy, patted the bare brown knee, saying, 'Go in and win, laddie, and I'll give you a special prize . . . I'll give you a fiver. No, let's make it properly sporting . . . guineas, eh what?'

Prindy was silent. Jeremy said dryly, 'He hardly understands a word you're saying.'

Vaisey looked at Jeremy again: 'You mean he doesn't speak English?'

'I mean he's never been taught anything but the crudest kind of it. School's not for the like of him . . . unless it's on a Mission or a Government Settlement . . . which wouldn't make him much better off.'

'Rilly!' Lord Alfred blinked a little before Jeremy's hard stare. Then he looked back at the boy, stared a moment, then again at Jeremy. Cause of his sudden change of expression was obvious.

In the same dry tone Jeremy said, 'In your circles you'd call it *bar sinister*, I guess.'

His Lordship blinked rapidly, cleared his throat, gave horse and rider another pat, then moved on. Martin at his heels looked very red. Lady Lydia beside Martin was all blue-eyed interest.

The Pony Race was the last event. Prindy and Sugerbag won it easily. The listed prize was half a dozen bottles of Lolly Water and a can of boiled sweets. As Martin presented it, seeming not to see his son even while shaking hands with him, Vaisey said, 'My five guineas, don't forget.' He pulled out his wallet.

Jeremy was lurking. He said, 'Notes are meaningless to these people. It'll have to be in silver . . . that's all they get in wages . . . if any at all.'

Even without blinking His Lordship said, 'Silver, eh? Silver it shall be. I'll get it from Finnucane as soon as we get back. A hundred and five bob . . . why, we'll have to get you a bag to carry it away!' He rumpled the fair hair, adding: 'Handsome young feller-me-lad you are, too.' He turned away.

Jeremy, alone now, found Lady Lydia beside him. He had stiffly greeted her earlier on. Now he was silent. She asked, 'Is that lovely boy your son?'

He answered shortly, 'No.'

'You did mention the *bar sinister*.'

'He could be anybody's bastard . . . it's not done to acknowledge relations with mothers like his.'

'With that hair and those eyes . . . !'

'People don't talk about those things here.'

'People have been talking to me.'

'Then why ask?'

'I'd like to know the truth.'

'About the paternity of one poor little creamy boy?'

'No . . . about you. It's you I've been hearing about.'

'Then it's a wonder you talk to me at all . . . seeing who your informants must be.'

'Don't be so difficult! You sound like the only person in the country worth talking to.'

'Thanks . . . but it might mean I'm only the best of a very bad job.'

'I'd like to talk to you.'

'Go right ahead . . . but I'll have to go and see to my people and my horses.'

'I mean alone.'

He looked at her. She added: 'I'd like to see your station . . . I hear it's a wonderful place.'

He scratched his jaw: 'Sorry . . . no Vaiseys admitted . . . no alien creatures of any kind. It has what's called in these parts a Pest Fence round it.'

'So I've heard. But I don't happen to be a Vaisey.'

'All those connected with . . . .'

'Your *bête noire* . . . I know. But I'm not at the moment. The engagement's broken off.'

He stared: 'Since when?'

'Since you let the cat out of the bag yesterday.'

'What cat? I don't have any dealings with cats. They're destructive animals in these parts. I'm a mad conservationist, you know.'

'Will you please answer my question . . . will you let me see your place . . . the lagoons, the Painted Caves, the things you've bred?'

'Well . . . if you come out alone?'

'I want you to take me.'

'You can come along with the crowd. We'll be going home on Monday.'

'I won't be heah on Monday.'

'Too bad . . . another time then.'

'I'd like you to run me out tomorrow . . . it's only forty miles, isn't it?'

He grinned: 'Your Ladyship is so used to giving orders . . . . '

Her thin face looked strained. 'I'm not giving orders.' I'm asking a great favour. I'm desperate!'

He stared: 'For what?'

'For a spell of relief from these people here . . . from Alfred . . . particularly from Alfred at the moment.' As he continued to stare, she asked, with something like desperation in her voice now, 'Won't you take me . . . please?'

He drew a deep breath, exhaled it: 'All right.'

She pressed his arm quickly: 'Thank you.' Her face was glowing now.

Still he eyed her searchingly. He said, 'You'll need a chaperon.'

Her eyes blazed: 'Rubbish!'

'Not rubbish at all. I'm a married man. I'd insist on my wife's accompanying us, only I know she wouldn't want to . . . wants to run her camp and see to breaking it up and getting it back home. It's a ritual with her. She's very proud of her household and efficient in the control of it. I'm not just having her humiliated to suit the whim of a spoilt child of a system of society I have only contempt for.'

Lydia had become very red and the blaze in the blue eyes increased. But if she had been made angry she swallowed it, and even smiled slightly in saying, 'All right . . . a chaperon.'

He swallowed, too, evidently momentarily at a loss through her aplomb. He said, 'None of your ladies-in-waiting.'

'I told you I wanted to get away from them. What about the little boy . . . your bastard son.'

'He's not my son.'

'Well grandson.'

'All right. But we'll probably have to take his mother too. It's only forty miles to the homestead . . . but past there the going's rough and slow. We'll have to leave at daybreak. Can you get to my camp by then?'

'Can't you pick me up?'

'No . . . I never go near the Beatrice homestead. I've never been near it. I never will go near it while it's Vaisey's.'

Staring at him, she said, 'You're a bugger of a man . . . but I'll be there.'

'Right . . . I'll be seeing you.' Jeremy swung away.

Saturday night, and the party at the Dance Hall with which the festival would be wound up. It began respectably enough, although without any sort of formality. Both McCusky and Hannaford acted as MCs. As the jollity increased with the consumption of booze the more respectable withdrew. The squattocracy was well represented – and more, the British aristocracy. The Delacy boys were there, with Lady Lydia. Clancy made bold to dance with his doxy, pretty Selina Ah Loy, who was pure Chinese. Martin wasn't anything so brave, although his eyes often followed Nelyerri as she danced with others – and hers scarcely left him. They did not speak. Clancy disappeared with Selina; and Martin soon took Her Ladyship home.

Tonight was the great occasion for adding to the famous heap of bottles. It was said that the heap had its beginnings away back when the Overland Telegraph was being built and a party of teamsters, after a mighty struggle with Christmas stores across the flooded river, had decided they deserved some of the cheer they carried for the linesmen down inland, and one sip had led to another until they had broached the lot. Then the diggers of the Knowles Creek Tin Rush at the turn of the Century had, in accordance with the pioneering tradition of the land, raised it as a monument. Most bottles emptied locally in a spirit of conviviality had gone to augment it ever since; however, the contribution made on the last night of the Races was not so much a mere disposal as a ritual, like Edinburgh Scots' smashing their emptied whisky bottles on the steps of the Tron Kirk to mark the end of the bawdy founess of Hogmanay and the beginning of a dour New Year.

Bottles were now being emptied for the sheer creative joy of the augmentation – *Crash! Crash! Crash!* – nor emptied on the ground to be sure. Those who hadn't gullets wide enough to do the job quickly enough to suit the yelling mob were relieved of their contributions. Black and brown hands did as much snatching as white. Nelyerri Ah Loy and Pat Hannaford consumed a quart of Square gin in mutual snatching. When Pat gave up in the interests of his duties of the morrow, the Knowles brothers took Nellie over from him. Knobby, very drunk, tried to do more than drink with her. Lots of whitemen were doing similarly with coloured female partners, but with more discretion. Knobby looked like having her on the heap of broken glass. His brother hauled him off. Willy An Loy, with good Chinese sense, whisked his spouse away, even while she dealt with him as violently as she had been dealing with Knobby. Meanwhile the Knowles brothers fought it out, till they fell into each other's arms weeping their love.

Down at the Lily Lagoons camp, when Willy arrived with the now weeping Nelyerri, Jeremy suggested that he take her home and leave sleeping Prindy with him and so save him having to come for him in the morning, adding that it would be good for the boy to go with him alone.

V

It was still so dark when Lady Lydia arrived at the Lily Lagoons camp on Sunday morning that the car that brought her had its headlights on. Jeremy was waiting, sitting with Prindy drinking coffee. It was Clancy who was Her Ladyship's driver, as seen when he alighted and came running through the headlight beams to open the door for her. She herself, in the light of the camp, was seen to be wearing black jodhpurs with a yellow silk blouse and a black wide-awake and elastic sides. 'Well, here I am!' she cried. 'Top o' the mornin'!'

Jeremy murmured a response. Neither he nor Clancy exchanged greetings. In fact Jeremy did not appear to see the boy, who stood by the car staring.

Jeremy asked Lydia, 'Like some coffee? Bit early for breakfast. We'll have that out on the road.'

'Rah-ther! Do I smell *café royal*?'

'Yes . . . I've royalled mine up a bit. Like yours the same?

'Love it.'

Nanago was there in a moment with more cups. The two women exchanged smiles. Nan looked at Clancy, then at Jeremy pouring only one extra cup. Jeremy said he preferred his sweetened with honey and asked Lydia if she'd like hers that way, she said yes, but absently, glancing at Clancy, evidently having become aware of the situation. At her glance Clancy gave her a slight wave and turned to get back into the car. She half-rose, calling to him, 'Thank you, deah boy!' She watched the car swing away, then looked at Jeremy, who was concentrating on his coffee cup. He looked up and met her gaze steadily. She sipped her coffee.

Jeremy asked, 'To your liking?'

'Divine!' she cried, 'Simply divine . . . first time I've tried it with honey.'

Nanago came from the kitchen tent lugging a fair-sized metal box with handles. Jeremy took it from her, at the same time kissing her dusky cheek, and loaded it into the back of the utility. He said to Prindy, already there, 'Going to be dusty . . . better get in the front.' But the boy ignored him. Settling into the front with Lydia, Jeremy remarked, 'Probably never ridden anywhere but in the back before. It's hard to get 'em in front.'

They set off without lights. As they crossed the causeway the river lay like mother-o'-pearl to either side. Lydia said, 'How lovely!'

A little further on was another sight, a man and a woman sprawled in the dusty grass beside the road, the man with pale behind bare because his pants were down around his knees, the woman scarcely visible because of her blackness. As Jeremy revved up to start the climb up the bank he said, 'Not so lovely!'

Lydia responded easily: 'Must have been quite a night in the old town. We saw several like that. Poor Clancy was quite embarrassed.' She chuckled.

'You find it amusing?'

'Well . . . it's pretty crude, I know . . . but, frankly, I didn't think Australians had that much go in 'em. They're awfully tame the ones I've met.'

'I think you'll find most of 'em the same. The credit for this you'd have to give to the blacks. They're the true bacchanalians.'

They climbed to the top, swung along the Racecourse road, past the place, on to a narrow winding track that took them northwestward. At some distance the numerous white buildings of Beatrice Homestead could be seen ghostly in the silvery light. She broke a lengthy silence: 'I was surprised that you didn't ask your son to join us at coffee.'

'Yes . . . so I noticed.'

'May I ask why?'

'Well . . . for a start he didn't ask.'

'Would he have to? You're not that much out of friends with your family, are you? He spoke quite well of you to me . . . telling me about the wonderful things you do with breeding things . . . your research laboratory . . . '

'He hasn't seen it since he was a little boy . . . Do you know, that's the first time he's ever been near that Race-time camp of mine in all the years it's been there?'

'Is that so?'

'And his only reason for coming was to bring you . . . a stranger, a guest of his mother's, a titled lady. Why didn't they send one of their staff to drive you?'

'I asked Clancy especially.'

'You see!'

'You sound the bitter man I've heard you are.'

'Where'd you hear that?'

She shrugged. Then she exclaimed, 'Oh, look . . . a thing . . . a snake, isn't it?

A snake-like head was peering at them over tall dry grass beside the road. They were now back near the river, to be seen in silver glimpses through the trees, far below.

'It's a bustard . . . generally called Plain Turkey round here. See, there're several. Australians have a faculty for giving everything half a dozen names . . . ignoring the native ones . . . *Beenook* in this case.' The birds rose on great wings.

'What huge things!'

'Yes . . . they can weigh up to twenty pounds dressed.'

'They're good to eat?'

'Too good.'

'Why do you say that?'

'They're being wiped out. What with their tastiness and their fatal curiosity. The done thing would have been to slow down when we saw them looking from the grass, wait till they came up . . . and pot 'em.'

'You don't pot 'em.'

'No.'

'I see you have a gun, though.' A rifle was slung above the windscreen.

'Probably more for defence than offence.'

'But no one's likely to attack you, is there . . . blacks or anything?'

'Least of all the poor beaten blacks. No . . . it's a habit. We like to go armed. Most cars you'll find carry a rifle in the bush. Every camp and homestead has a rifle handy . . . too handy, often. Shooting matches are quite common. There isn't a station in all the wide North that hasn't had its shooting match or two. Something goes wrong . . . *'Grab the gun,'* as they say. The courts regard it less as murder than a sort of justifiable homicide. It's supposed to be due to the loneliness.'

'Why do you say Supposed to be?'

'Well . . . how can you be lonely if you've got someone to shoot at? No . . . in my belief it's something deeper . . . something to do with not truly belonging to the land. It's a wide silent land . . . a brooding land . . . and full of spirit things, even if you don't believe in them. Unless you can come to love it, you come to hate it . . . like either loving or hating a woman. Most Australians . . . bush Australians . . . the others aren't really Australians at all, just transplanted Pommies or something equally alien . . . hate it. They live in it only because they have to. They get to town as often as possible. The shooting is hate . . . hate of your mate, hate of the boss, hate of the blacks . . . on the surface . . . but deep down, hate of the land, because it's for ever strange to you, and you need it, as every creature needs earth of its own, and you're left frustrated. Again it's like a woman to you . . . like loving an unresponsive woman . . . .'

'Have you done that?'

He looked at her quickly, turned back to the road, was silent.

After a while she said, 'When I told you yesterday they say you want to give the country back to the blacks, you didn't answer me. Do you?'

'If they wanted what I have I'd give it to them. But they don't. So I try to share it with them.'

'I must say I haven't been much impressed with what I've seen of the Aborigines . . . on the contrary, some I saw in a camp at the station made me feel quite ill.'

'Those you saw were old and sick. The others were at the Races.'

'Can't say I was impressed with what I saw there, either.'

'Were you impressed by what you saw of the majority of the whites?'

'Well . . . hardly.'

'There are some very handsome Aborigines, male and female. Truly beautiful people of any race are rarities. The mother of that boy behind is a handsome creature . . . . '

'But she'd be halfcaste, wouldn't she?'

'If you mean it's her white blood that made her so . . . then I must tell you the awful truth that Piggy Trotters is her father.'

'Oh, lord!'

'So you see. As a matter of fact most crossbreeds are good-looking. It seems to me that the perfect symmetry of the Aboriginal face makes up for the lack of it in the average white face. In my opinion a beautiful breed of people could have been created if only our forefathers'd had the courage to breed with the Aborigines like men, instead of like dirty little boys . . . and one that would have loved the land because they truly belonged to it . . . . ' Jeremy launched into his subject of what Australia might have been as a Creole nation.

She listened with close attention, even while interrupting him occasionally to ask about some of the things she saw as they went winding their way up the river: the parrots of so many varieties, cockatoos, great water birds sweeping up from the stream to watch from lofty perches in the tall timber growing in the lower dampness, a huge spotted *prindy* that galloped along ahead of them, head over shoulder, forked tongue flickering, then sprang to a tree beside the track, to peep from behind the trunk and set her laughing with the quaintness of it. Perhaps owing to the many interruptions, he finished rather lamely: 'Well, how's it strike you?'

She thought a moment: 'After all, it's only a dream . . . and, if I may say so, a rather bad one.'

He swallowed: 'How's that?'

'Well . . . for a start I think it's only born of your bitterness . . . the bitterness you feel because your fellow countrymen are such a poor lot generally.'

He asked sharply, 'Are yours any better . . . generally?'

'I expect not. But they're not a bastard people . . . and that's what you advocate as the best kind for this country . . . .'

'Because they'd belong . . . .'

'Let me finish. You spoke of the South Americans. You've been there?'

'No.'

'I had a feeling you hadn't. You'd be shocked if you did so and saw the poverty and ignorance and superstition . . . the grinding rackets of those of your so-called Creoles smart enough to get a shirt on their backs . . . and behind it all the Spanish or Portuguese aristocratic pretenders.'

'Why pretenders in their case?'

'Because the Spanish and Portuguese have been bastard breeds ever since the Moors overran them. If they were true patricians the frightful conditions would never have resulted . . . . '

'But poverty, tyranny, are the direct results of aristocracy . . . the Russian Romanovs . . . the French aristocracy . . . .'

'According to socialist literature . . . besides, they were in a degenerate state. Only a true aristocrat can rule. The people want their rule.'

He glanced at her, met the cool blue eyes. Turning back to the road he asked, 'Do you consider yourself a true aristocrat?'

'Naturally . . . my family came over with The Conqueror.'

'And that gives you a special right to rule?'

'If we can . . . and we do, don't y'know . . . we rule most of the world.'

He nodded to the road.

She went on: 'Only aristocracy can break the rule of aristocracy.'

'What about the Russians?'

'It's temporary.'

'What about the North Americans?'

'They love us, reahlly . . . we're gradually infusing their rulers with our blood.'

After a little silence she added: 'The only people out heah who ever looked like breaking our rule were aristocrats.'

'Yes? And who were they?'

'The Macarthur-Onslows. Do you know them?'

'Only as the Kings of the Squatters. I've never been one to think others better than myself . . . I mean socially.'

'That's because you're an aristocrat yourself.'

He went red, glanced at her, turned away, laughing: 'God save us . . . I the son of an Irish policeman!'

'The fair Irish are of Norman stock.'

'I told you I'm Welsh on my mother's side.'

'The Normans went quickly into Wales. Wales is still in fact a fiefdom of English aristocrats. I'd say you're definitely of Norman stock. It shows no better than in that little boy, for all his Aboriginal blood.'

'Which makes us aristocrats and natural rulers of this land held in fief by Lord Vaisey?'

'If you chose to be.'

He glanced again, and away. She was looking very serious. She added: 'If you'd drop your silly pretence of socialism . . . . '

'Who says I'm a socialist?'

'Everything I've heard about you, and everything you've said about yourself, points to it. You've founded a community based on liberty, equality, fraternity . . . with your dream of the Creole Nation at the back of it.'

'All right . . . where's the pretence, then?'

'Because it's obvious to me that what you've reahlly done is set yourself up as a sort of Robber Baron in the middle of your fief-lord's domain.'

He reddened again, took a deep breath, and exhaling said, 'Lady, you talk like the Domesday Book.'

'My ancestors' names are in the Domesday Book . . . as the rulers of England.'

'For a seemingly very intelligent lady, you're dragging back a bit in the past aren't you?'

'We still rule England.'

'Despite the boasted British system of Government by Parliament?'

'We still rule England . . . and we'll prove it soon by doing away with Parliamentary humbug.'

He looked at her quickly, searchingly. Now her normal pallor was gone, her eyes shining. He looked back to the road. After a moment she said, 'I'm a British Fascist.'

He seemed to ponder it for a moment, then said, 'I thought Fascists were Italian.'

'Properly, yes . . . but the name's caught on for any right-wing movement. We're reahlly called British Unionists.'

'Sounds like a labour movement.'

'It's anything but . . . I assure you!'

'That's the Oswald Mosley thing, is it?'

'It's hardly a thing, my deah man . . . in fact it's the greatest thing that's happened to Britain since Cromwell.'

'Yes? I thought it was just a cheap imitation of the Hitler and Mussolini stuff . . . black shirts and Roman salutes and all that.'

'There's nothing cheap about it, I do assure you. Most of the aristocracy of England now belong to it.'

He said dryly, 'Although I might be an aristocrat myself, according to the family-tree you've wished on me, I can't say that impresses me much.'

'I've told you the aristocracy rules England.'

'So what?'

'So when the time's ripe for taking over the Government of England . . . of the Empire . . . *Greater Britain*, as we shall call it . . . it'll be done like that!' She snapped thin white fingers.

'And this time . . . this ripe time . . . when'll that be?'

'When Adolf Hitler has crushed the Russian Bolsheviks and the world is liberated from the myth of the dictatorship of the proletariat.'

He was silent. After a while she remarked coldly, 'You don't seem much impressed.'

He glanced: 'Sorry . . . but I can't say I'm interested in anything that happens in Europe. Europocentricity is one of Australia's sicknesses. I don't suffer from it myself. I left mad Europe behind me when I climbed out of the trenches of Normandy in 1918 . . . your ancestral land of Normandy, where, by the way, I saw more moron types than anywhere else I've been . . . .'

'The fight of Fascism against Bolshevism will be worldwide.'

He grinned through the wind-screen: 'Well . . . if it comes here, I'll be doing what the bushies say they'll do when there's talk of trouble . . . I'll be lookin' fo' a 'oller log.'

'You . . . a soldier and an aristocrat?'

'I was so little of a soldier, lady, that they removed my name from the Reserve of Officers soon after I was demobbed . . . and it's only you've given me the accolade of aristocracy.' He glanced at her again, smiling, and looking back to the road, added: 'Don't want to offend you . . . but I'm not interested in politics . . . and I'm rather surprised to find you are. I brought you out to show you the country. Just up here's a lovely place called the Rainbow Pool. I thought we'd go in there and have breakfast . . . suit you?'

She smiled rather stiffly, but replied easily, 'Jolly good show . . . and no politics with meals, eh what?'

He chuckled, reached and touched the white hand resting on a black knee. At once she brought her other hand over and clasped his so tightly that he looked at her in surprise. Her face had another expression now, a brightness that made her look even beautiful. He snatched his hand away to prevent the car from running off the road. 'Sorry,' he murmured.

They came to a turnoff to the right, where a track that was just a pair of wheel ruts in the grass, ran towards the river, hereabout some distance off and located now in rocky country. Swinging onto the track, Jeremy stopped and alighted and spoke to Prindy standing with hands on the cabin, yellow with dust: 'Might-be more better you stop here, young feller.'

The grey eyes stared inquiringly.

Jeremy went on: 'I want to show Missus one place in there.' He jerked his jaw towards the river. '*Wurruk* that place. I give you some tucker, you sit down here wait, eh?'

Without moving, Prindy asked, 'Wha' nam' *wurruk*, Mullaka?'

'Belong 'o *tchinek* business.' Jeremy was watching the grey eyes closely.

Just one blink, and Prindy answered, 'I no-more fright *tchinek* Bijnitch Mullaka.'

'What for like-o'-dat?'

'Dat old-man . . . Wirridirridi . . . he *tchinek* man . . . he mate long o' me.'

'Might be your mumma growl spone I take you in there.'

Prindy made the sound of contempt with his lips: 'All day mumma growl sumpin. Dat old-man been promised learn him me good t'ing. He been come dis country, ain't it?'

'Yes . . . he's over this way.'

'I wan' 'o talk long o' him.'

'All right . . . but be it on your own head.'

Jeremy got back into the car. When Lady Lydia asked him he explained the situation at length. Her comment was: 'Good for him . . . brave little boy!'

'I don't think you've grasped the significance of witchcraft to these people.'

She said shortly, 'The boy isn't a black savage. I told you what he is . . . an aristocrat.'

Jeremy sighed: 'I hope you're around to convince his mother if and when she finds out.'

A couple of hundred yards of bumpy going through thick brush brought them suddenly onto a grassy verge and into a view of water, rock, and vegetation so pleasant that Lydia cried out about its loveliness. As the roar of the engine ceased in rushed the quiet roar of water.

Prindy leapt down at once, with grey gaze intent on the scene, seeming to search every inch of the further shore of the wide pool before them. The pool would be on average some fifteen yards across. The other shore was rocky, but only three or four feet above the water that lay along there emerald with reflexion of ferny and mossy growth. Beyond was thick brush. It was perhaps fifty feet in length, beginning at a higher and less overgrown wall down which water ran in several silver streams, and ending at rapids to which it suddenly converged to race away. It was the rapids that made the watery roar. The near shore was sandy, although with grass growing almost into the water. A curious thing was the seeming glassy stillness of the pool, while being fed by a lively little waterfall and spilled out in rapids. Only near fall and rapids was there apparent movement.

Prindy quickly moved to the water's edge, touched it with a toe, bent and tasted, drank with sucking lips. When he looked up at the others now behind him, Jeremy said, 'All-same water long o' Catfish.' When Prindy nodded, Jeremy added, 'Taste different over there.' He projected his lips towards the further shore.

Rising, Prindy began to peel off his dusty clothes, khaki shirt and shorts, saying, 'I *bogie*.'

Jeremy said, 'I told you this *wurruk* place.'

Prindy shrugged, dumped his clothes, and dived, or rather simply vanished, so smooth was his entry and long his submergence. Staring at the still water, Lydia murmured, 'What's *wurruk*?'

'Bad . . . sinister.'

She exhaled a pent breath as the yellow head popped up and yellow-brown hands dashed water from grey eyes and white teeth and red gums flashed in a broad gasping grin. She asked, 'What's it like in?'

He answered gaspingly, 'Properly!' then promptly showed his caramel-cream behind in another dive.

Lydia bent to the water, touched it, rose saying, 'It's warm.'

'The water's always warm in these parts . . . except in flood time.'

'D'y'know, I think I'll take a dip too.'

'It's a dangerous place.'

'*Wurruk*!' she said contemptuously, and dropped down to the grass and began to take off her boots.

'No . . . I mean it's physically dangerous, too. A number of whites have been drowned here . . . during the tin mining. It probably got its bad reputation with the blacks, from drowning some of them too, away back.'

She was pulling her jodhpurs down over her bottom as she sat. She said, 'Well, it isn't drowning that small boy.' Prindy had appeared again over under the other wall and was heading swiftly towards the waterfall.

Jeremy called to him, 'Careful, sonny . . . no good place up there . . . might pull you down.'

Sitting in scanty drawers, struggling with the tight pants, Lydia said: 'These things were made for skinny Indians . . . or fat ones with wallahs to pull 'em off.'

With gaze averted, Jeremy said; 'There's a strange inflow down below there. This is the actual head of the Beatrice, which's quite a big river just down a bit. All that water couldn't come over those little falls. For certain there's an underground stream that drains all the country back to the limestone. The Beatrice's limey, you'll have noticed. But here on this side of the pool it's a sandstone taste. That's from the falls there. That's the end of the creek that flows through my place . . . sandstone country. This is mixed-up country round here . . . a couple of great rock faults that give you sandstone, limestone, shale, all within a few yards . . . careful sonny!' Prindy, near the falls and apparently having felt the pull of something, waved acknowledgement and came swimming back.

'What a beautiful swimmer he is.' said Lydia, struggling now to get the pants over her feet, showing long thin white legs. Then looking up at Jeremy, she asked, 'Be my wallah, will you, old boy?'

Red-faced he bent and pulled the jodhpurs clear.

She rose, pulled off the blouse, to reveal nothing but a brassière encasing tiny breasts. Observing his embarrassment she chuckled. He gave her a twisted smile, saying, 'I'm not used to the ways of aristocracy.'

'You must learn, deah boy . . . seeing you're one of us.' So saying, she unhooked the brassière and let it fall, then slid hands down slim hips to remove the drawers, bending thin legs as she slipped out of them. Looking up at the astonished Jeremy she laughed merrily. Prindy, now down near the rapids and standing in water only calf-deep, was also staring. She turned to him, saying to Jeremy, 'What a lovely boy he is . . . like a little golden Adonis.' At that she stepped into the water.

'Wait a minute!' exclaimed Jeremy.

She flopped into the pool, thrashed about a bit, then evidently with her stern on the bottom, since she raised a white knee as she looked back at him, she asked, 'You were saying?'

'It's too late now . . . but there's a superstition that anyone who swims in the Rainbow Pool must come back to this country to die.'

'Superstition!' she jeered. '*Wurruk*! You've lived too long with the blacks, my deah.' Thereupon she stood up, to reveal herself in all her schoolgirlish gangling entirety, from bony shoulders to knees, undeveloped tits in a ribby chest, flat belly, a wisp of pubic hair yellow as her head. She added: 'I don't care where I die . . . so long as I have fun living in the meantime.' She turned her back, to show a rather pretty bum, then slipped down again into the water, and breaststroke, began to swim to Prindy. Soon they were swimming together, splashing and laughing.

Jeremy turned away to the utility, got out the insulated tucker-box, began to prepare a picnic spot on the grass on the side remote from where the clothes lay. After a while he called to them that breakfast was ready and tossed tea-towels onto their clothes with which to dry themselves, then went back and sat down. Giggling together like a couple of kids they dressed, came to join him sparkling. Lydia asked, 'You're not shocked by my bathing in the nuddy, are you, old thing?'

'No.'

'Was it really superstition about the place that stopped you from coming in with us?'

'I've swum in it many a time.'

'Then why not just now'?

'An old fellow like me swim naked with a couple of lovely youngsters?'

She smiled: 'That's sweet of you. I'm just a bony old bag.'

'You can't be a day over twenty-two . . . and you've got . . . er . . . your good points.'

'Spoken like the gentleman you are! I'm twenty-five, actually. And you're not a day over fifty . . . and you're as fine a figure of a man as I've ever seen. Where'd your grandson get his beauty from, if not from you?'

'I'm fifty-three . . . and where'd you get this grandson business?'

'I asked him if you were his father . . . and he said you're his white granny.'

'The term hasn't the same meaning to him as it has to us. He's got blacks he calls granny, too . . . haven't you sonny?'

'Wha' nam', Mullaka?'

'You got him blackfeller granny, too . . . ain't it?'

'Yu-ai.'

'Why do you talk to him in that outlandish way?'

'Because it's what he understands best.'

'Why don't you teach him to speak properly?'

'What d'you mean properly?'

'Decent English, of course.'

'I won't ask you what you mean by decent . . . but he gets by for the time on the English he has. They actually prefer speaking that patois of theirs. My wife, who had some education in a mission to start with and has become quite well educated by her own efforts . . . runs a school now . . . prefers it. It expresses their own idiom best, I think. Anyway, the boy speaks a native language . . . which is more useful to him at present than English.'

'But surely you're going to have him educated?'

'He's being educated now in the best way I think possible for him . . . in the knowledge of his country and his people . . . '

'But he isn't black!'

'I told you the other day the depth of his colour doesn't make much difference to his status in the eyes of the law. Besides, those of them brought up with the Old People, as they call them, don't get into the state of conflict others do by being ashamed of them. If he needs my protection he'll seek it. I'm forcing nothing on him.'

Lydia looked at Prindy, who all the while was wolfing sandwiches of which there were a large quantity and swigging tea poured from one of a couple of big vacuum flasks, and staring at the other side of the pool as if expecting to see something. She asked, 'Can't he understand us?'

'I don't think he's even concerned with us. He's got something else on his mind much more important to him.'

'Such as?'

'I wouldn't know . . . nor would he tell me, probably. They're secretive people . . . except with those they're bound to be frank with.'

Lydia had been eating heartily too. Suddenly she said, 'By jove . . . these sandwiches are reahlly mahvellous, don't y'know . . . what are they?'

'The meat's roast bustard.'

'Thought you didn't kill native things!'

'I don't . . . nor do I permit the killing of them anywhere near my homestead. But it's native game . . . and I have natives . . . or rather they have me. They like their own food . . . feel deep need for it at times. I like it too. I encourage them to hunt . . . in the old way . . . no firearms. Game's abundant where there's some degree of conservation. It can even become overabundant and upset the balance of things. The blacks have lived with that balance for longer than anyone will probably ever know. If there's superabundance, I buy it from them. What they get for me they kill to suit my special taste . . . it must be bled and salted. Now, what say we get on the move again?'

Still Prindy refused to get in front. Jeremy made him wrap in a strip of canvas and wear his own hat so as to keep the dust off. As they drove away, Jeremy remarked to Lydia at the boy's disinclination to sit with them as proof of the true attitude of Aborigines to whites: 'They distrust us all, even me they call *mullaka*, which means more than boss . . . rather patron. You can force 'em into association with you that they'll accept so cheerfully you'll think you've bridged the gulf. But the plain truth is they don't want us for anything but what they can get out of us. It's been like that from the beginning. I think it always will be . . . and with the relationship worsening as they become more aware of our limitations and we of their complexity. It's to the children you have to look for the truth. The adults, knowing their need of us, become cunning. I don't think it's conscious cunning always. They just know they're in the grip of something beyond coping with and have to put on an act to adjust themselves. You see that plainly on the missions. The children are unaware of the situation, and hence, like all children, act naturally. To Aboriginal children we are bogeymen. The first reaction of a black baby to sight of a whiteman or woman is to shrink into its mother's arms.'

'Why did that one come with us, then, if he distrusts us?'

'I've wondered about that. For a start, we got him alone with us only because his mother was drunk last night and couldn't come. I've often wanted to get him out here alone . . . but she wouldn't let me. As a matter of fact, this's the first time he's ever been with me without someone of his own kind. But I heard the other night that he was mixed up with an old witch-doctor who's out this way now . . . and that he'd been behaving strangely. He's a strange little boy in many ways, makes up songs and goes walking in the bush alone, which isn't the Aboriginal way of doing things. Actually that's why we went to the Rainbow Pool. I wanted to see what he'd do.'

'How d'you mean . . . you said we were going there for breakfast?'

'I've never taken an Aboriginal person near it before. I know how they feel about it. You only have to tell 'em a place strange to them is *wahji* or *wurruk*, and they'll stay behind and wait for you. Remember what he said when I told him it was like that? He asked, *what name?* . . . meaning what kind of taboo business was it . . . and when he heard it was Snake Business, said that kind was all right long o' him. I knew then he was looking for the *koornung*. It seems they've got some sort of secret arrangement. His parents . . . well, his mother and the halfcaste who stands in relationship to him as father, don't like it . . . any more than any ordinary Aboriginal person would. We'll have to keep the fact that he was at the pool with us a secret . . . for his sake. They'll be avoiding him as a *koornung* if they find out, or at any rate as one bedevilled.'

'But will he keep it secret?'

'I'm pretty sure he will.'

'And here have I been wondering how to stop him from telling everybody that I went bathing naked!'

They laughed. She asked, 'Tell me about this old man . . . this . . . *koor-nung* chappie.'

'I'll have to tell you about the Rainbow Snake Business first . . . about Old Tchamala, the Rainbow Serpent, the Great Upheavalist. Do you know the local map at all?'

'Oh, yes . . . I flew in front with our pilot most of the way. I've done a bit of flying training, don't y'know. He showed me his charts.'

'Well, you'll have some idea of the great Queen Victoria River system, which this's part of. Tchamala made it all in his raging, starting at the Rainbow Pool. Although he lives now mostly up behind the Milky Way, down under the pool there is one of his favourite haunts on earth. If there's a rainbow on it, as there often is in Wet Season when there's a lot of water running over the falls, you can bet he's in residence. The rainbow is one of his numerous Shades, or spiritual selves.' Jeremy went on to tell about Tchamala and Bobwirridirridi.

She remarked at length: 'You really believe in this business, don't you!'

'I explained to you that unless you accept the beliefs as part of the land, you can't live happily in it. Can't you see that? You have your King Arthur and Merlin the Druid and such things . . . the Germans their Siegfried . . . everybody's got something mythical, semi-historical even, like your William the Conqueror, that makes them one with their environment . . . except us poor damned colonials, who're supposed to get through on what's handed down to us from our forebears, when our environment is utterly different.'

'Yes, I see that. What I mean's you actually believe in the magical properties of that pool, say. I could tell by the way you spoke when you told me I'd be certain to die in this country because I swam in it.'

'I guess I do, to some degree. You see, I've never known anyone who ever bathed there to die elsewhere . . . and there was one particular case of someone who didn't bathe there who did die elsewhere . . .'

'How would you know all the people who've bathed there or haven't?'

'Haven't I lived most of my life hereabouts? I'd know pretty well everybody who'd bathed there in say the past thirty-five years . . . allowing for the time I was away at the war. They're not many. Bush people are superstitious. The bush makes them so. And the place had a bad name from those drownings during the tin mining . . . the Knowles Creek Tin Rush, as it was called.'

She was watching him closely. He went on: 'The particular case I mentioned was that of my brother Jack . . . Flash Jack, as they called him, because of his horsemanship. He rode a horse not simply to get around, but to show the bond there could be between two intelligent and handsome creatures of different species. As you know, it takes first of all courage to handle a horse . . . a real horse. In fact he was a man of great courage. Yet nothing would induce him to swim in that pool. He died on Gallipoli.'

'Thousands of men did.'

'Spoken like a true Daughter of the Regiment! I'll bet you belong to a military family.'

Well . . . as a matter of fact my father was Sandhurst . . . . '

'That'll do me . . . we won't pursue the subject any further.'

'I didn't mean to sound callous about the thousands of men. I know it was an awful mess. I only meant that your brother's dying there didn't prove anything about the pool.'

Jeremy was silent.

She said after a while, 'I heard you were bitter about the war.'

'Why shouldn't I be? It decimated our manhood and bankrupted us.'

'It did the same to us.'

'You were not a developing community . . . besides, it was your bloody war, not ours!'

'Then why did you yourself come into it? You had no conscription, I understand. And you held the rank of Major, no less.'

'I don't want to talk about it.'

'I don't blame you. It came to be a stinking thing. The stink's still around . . . and will be until we've cleaned things up.'

He looked at her: 'We? . . Oh, your British Fascists.'

'And other Fascists . . . Australian, too, I guess.'

'Yes, I suppose someone'll start something like that here . . . Australians have to copy . . . and, of course, follow Old England.'

'As a matter of fact, your Australian Fascist Party's already in formation . . . and as for following Old England, it just does not do that. It's called the Free Australia Movement . . . and what seems to be its chief aim is to get rid of what they call the British Garrison in Australia.'

He looked at her. She went on to say that she'd come to Australia with greetings to the Movement from Sir Oswald Mosley, with whom there'd been correspondence, and had been received at their headquarters, in Sydney. She hadn't been much impressed. Those she'd met seemed to be crackpots. Anglophobia seemed to be the chief incentive. They had baited her for a Pommy, a term she'd later learnt was applied only to English of lower class.

Jeremy sighed: 'So much even for home-spun Fascism in Australia. The only *-ism* that could even flourish here is toadyism. You're right about the Pommy business. For all our vaunted Jack's-as-good-as-his-master, we are sneaks to the boss.'

'Yes, I'm afraid I've found the toadyism rather nauseating. That's why I asked Alfred to keep my title and our engagement secret. It was bad enough watching them fawn on him.'

'You should be glad of it . . . it's what established him here.'

'Why should I be glad of it?'

'You're going to marry him and share the billions.'

'I told you I'd broken the engagement . . . anyway, it wasn't official.'

'I'm going to be popular with him . . . refusing to shake hands with him, losing him his girl . . . taking his girl away swimming in the nude!'

'Oh, he won't greatly care. I think he was a bit chary of it. He's getting pretty old, don't y'know . . . and I'm afraid I'm a bit harem-scarem.'

'He's been married half a dozen times, hasn't he?'

'Four times, actually. But this time was different. He was really after blood this time.'

He looked: 'Blood?'

'My blood.'

'Oh . . . I see . . . the blue blood.'

'Of course. It was my blood for the Vaisey billions..

'Sorry I've done your dough for you.'

'What's that?'

'Local idiom . . . lost you your money.'

'You're laughing at me!'

'Of course . . . it's all too ridiculous.' He chuckled deeply.

She shrugged: 'That's how it's done, old dear.'

He looked, to meet her blue eyes. Turning back to the road he asked, 'But how's that sort of thing fit in with your Fascism? I understand Fascism to be a kind of socialism . . . National Socialism . . . isn't that what the Germans call theirs?'

'Oh, that's just a sop to get the *petite bourgeoisie* in.'

'Then Fascism's really only a patrician swindle?'

'All's fair in love and war. I told you . . . we Patricians are at war with the Proletariat. We have to win now . . . or go down for good.'

He shrugged: 'I've told you I don't like war.'

'Love?' she asked.

He shrugged again. He was slowing down. He said, 'We're coming close to the homestead. You'll see it through the trees. I have to slow down to give the cripples a chance to get to the gate. The signal's gone up by now that someone's coming. You have to be pretty smart to take Lily Lagoons by surprise. But this time of year it's different. Pretty well the whole household's away for a full week . . . and I fancy those left behind get the notion they've been abandoned. Hence the rush to greet the first who come home. They're a jealous lot. You have to be careful you don't run someone down in the mêlée.'

Rather sharply she asked, 'What cripples?'

'You'll see . . . and there's the homestead now.'

Unlike the northern approach, with its open paddocks, this from southward gave a view of the place somewhat obscured by trees, mainly big trees, stringybark, ironbark, bloodwood, thinned-out forest. A number of birds flew in from various quarters to northward, to wheel about the car, some to land in trees peeking, others to go flapping or skimming along ahead: butcher birds and parrots in number, a hawk, a couple of pee-wees. 'The scouts,' remarked Jeremy.

'The Robber Baron's fastness,' she said.

'More of a keep, a refuge. It's my own refuge from a society that mostly sickens me . . . and I feel bound to share it with others wanting to escape from the predatory world.'

She eyed him searchingly.

Soon they were at the big white double iron gate in the high netting fence. An odd assortment of beasts and birds were crowding about the entrance, most of them kept back from the gate by an iron grid. There were three emus, one so tall that he could look over the fence with stretching neck, even with but one leg to stand on. There were several brolgas, a jabiru, numerous magpie geese, pee-wees, plovers, doves; it was impossible to pick them all out by breed or number, such was the jostling, the awkward flapping and lurching of maimed things, and the din of it, the screaming, honking, croaking. The beasts were several kangaroos and wallabies and bandicoots, a huge goanna without a tail, a frilled lizard with only half his frill and one front claw to wave as he stood on tail as if signalling greeting.

Lady Lydia exclaimed, 'Good heavens!'

Prindy was staring over the cabin open-mouthed.

Jeremy alighted to unlatch the gate, did merely that, then returned to the truck and moved it slowly to push the gate open, stopping again when the vehicle was just clear, and alighted to close it, while some of the animals crowded up to nuzzle him. For all the eagerness of the greeting, most were wary. 'My cripples,' said Jeremy as he got back to the wheel and set the car slowly moving. 'Now they can go back to their holes and corners and relax for another year.' He looked at Lydia, whose face was pinched with an expression of displeasure. He asked, 'What's the matter . . . don't you like it?'

She shrugged: 'Can't say I do. What makes a man like you collect maimed animals like an old maid?'

He laughed a little: 'I hardly collect them. They have a way of turning up here themselves. The place's got a reputation in the animal world as a refuge, I suppose, as it has with the blacks . . . . ' When she looked at him doubtfully, he added: 'Animals have a lot more savvy than most people give them credit for. I suppose you know I'm a Veterinary Surgeon . . . of sorts?

'Yes.'

'Well . . . when we started off as graziers, the veterinary part of the job was mine. I needed practice. I'd attend to any sick or injured animal. There are always plenty about . . . what with dingoes, crocodiles, pythons, predatory birds . . . and our own murderous species. My mother and sister . . . particularly my sister, who was an old maid . . . were gentle souls. They did the collecting. Then the creatures just took to coming of their own accord. There're ways for them to get in. Dingoes . . . the worst of the maimers . . . are too wary to follow . . . but, of course, I've got to have a dingo-proof fence to keep 'em from sneaking in at night . . . and also to keep the other things from going out before they're ready. Those that can't get in are usually located in time by those scouts of ours, and brought in. Actually I regard it as a bit of a nuisance . . . but then, as I've said, how dare I have a refuge unless I share it . . . and it's satisfying to be trusted and good for you to honour the trust.'

They were halted before the porch-like entrance through the trellis at the front of the Big House. As they alighted he looked at her, saw her frowning at the creatures still lurching and hopping about, and said, 'It's upset you?'

She grimaced: 'I don't like crippled things.'

'Why's that . . . excess of compassion, or lack of it?'

She shrugged: 'I don't know . . . bit of both, I expect.' She turned her back on the cripples: 'It's all right for you . . . you' re like a doctor with sick people . . . it's your job. I'd have to have them done away with.'

'Life's a peculiarly precious thing . . . surely to everything that possesses it.' He paused. then added: 'Do you know . . . the first quarrel I had with my first wife was over the same thing. She couldn't stand the sight of the poor brutes. I had to keep them in a special compound. You know who my first wife is, of course?'

'Yes . . . I don't like her and she doesn't like me . . . but she's the nearest thing to a lady I've met in a long while.'

Jeremy sighed: 'That's why I married her . . . God forgive me.'

She looked at him quickly: 'Tell me about it.'

'Later. Let's go in and have a quick drink . . . and you can look over the place while I'm attending to some things. I've got some old and sick blacks down the back . . . and a couple of old horses . . . hear'em neighing? . . . and other small chores. It might interest you to know that I built this house for Rhoda . . . to bring her into as my bride.'

She exclaimed, 'Ah . . . I've got it . . . the cause of the bitterness . . . a woman!'

'Wrong . . . a man.'

'A man . . . what man?'

'Vaisey . . . always Vaisey . . . but I'll explain later. You ought to know about it, seeing you've done the Vaisey dough.'

'Who says I have?'

'You said you're not marrying him now.'

'What's wrong with marrying his son?' When he stared at her she added, 'They still get the blood . . . with more chance of mixing theirs with it.'

Jeremy, still staring, shook his head. Then he turned to Prindy, standing by the car, and asked, 'Want to come inside?' Prindy was silent. Jeremy went on: 'All right . . . have a look around. We won't be long. By'n'by we go look lagoon . . . and after that to Painted Caves. Might-be we see that old-man there.'

The grey eyes widened.

Before leaving the Big House, Jeremy got stuff from the kitchen store and refrigerator and loaded it into the utility. Then with Prindy in the back again they set out northward. Some of the old blacks were out to wave to them. Lady Lydia remarked on the neatness of the cottages compared with those at Beatrice homestead, adding that Clancy, in showing her round there, had said it was impossible to get blacks to live in any other way than squalor. 'How do you manage it?' she asked.

'Simply by having a rule for sanitary living on the place, and seeing it's enforced . . . but not by the people themselves. Cleanliness as we know it means nothing to them. In their natural state they're as clean as animals . . . which is really being cleaner than humans, when you know animals. Humans accumulate dirt through living in one place. These people in their natural state are always on the move. The squalor comes only when they're forced to live in one place . . . like animals in a zoo. I keep a crew to clean up for them. I don't expect them to do it themselves . . . although some do. And when they get sick of living so unnaturally, as literally they do, I see to it that they go bush for a while. If they're old and sick or crippled, I see they're transported wherever they want to go, and brought back when they're ready. It's the only way it'll work, I'm sure. The information might be useful to you when you come back to run things as Lady Vaisey.'

'Who says I'm coming back?'

'Didn't you swim in the Rainbow Pool?'

'Oh, that! Well, if I do, I won't be coddling them like that . . . nor the way they do at Beatrice. I'd pay them properly, and expect them to work and live like civilized beings.'

'What if they didn't want to?'

'Then they could get back to the bush and live like animals . . . as you said yourself.'

'With their hunting grounds spoilt by Vaisey's stock, their water fouled?'

She shrugged.

They came to the racecourse. Prindy dropped down to remove the rails.

As they went on, Jeremy began what he called, 'The sad story of my first marriage.' He told how his Irish father had been a trooper of mounted police in South Australia, how the old man's ambition had always been to make his family Landed Gentry. 'It was with that in mind,' he said, 'that when we settled in a biggish country town after a lot of wandering in the bush there, he had us . . . myself and my brother Jack, apprenticed to trades that would be useful . . . essential in our case . . . when eventually we went on the land. The old-time trooper was the watchdog of the squatter . . . '*Up came the squatter, mounted on his thoroughbred, up came the troopers, one, two, three*!' . . . and Da was shrewd enough to know that the only country we could get would be that which the rich man didn't want because of the difficulty of raising stock on it owing to climate, disease, poisonous plants, *et cetera*. Expert knowledge would be required to overcome the difficulties. He apprenticed Jack to a farrier . . . in case you don't know what a farrier properly is . . . .'

'Of course I do . . . a blacksmith . . . .'

'You're wrong . . . he's a shoe-smith . . . and in the old days he was also a veterinary surgeon. The druggist was his medical aide. There was no such thing as degrees in Veterinary Science and Pharmacy in those days. I was apprenticed to a druggist . . . or Chemist and Druggist, as they were then called. We both took to our jobs with pleasure. Botany, a very important thing in old-time medicine, had always interested me. Chemistry opened up a new world of understanding of nature. My master was a learned old fellow. The old-time chemist and druggist was a man of wide knowledge and in demand for it. He had to be horse-doctor, plant expert, mineral assayer. At eighteen I was doing everything from pulling teeth . . . human or animal . . . to classifying poisonous plants and identifying minerals. Jack had always loved horses. Da was a great horseman, but a cruel one, which rather spoils it. Jack was the kindest man I've ever known with horses. That's what made him, as I've told you, the leading horseman in this land of crack riders . . . Flash Jack!'

He paused while the big white gate was being opened, and directed Lydia's attention to the glimpses of the red wall of the Plateau away beyond the trees where eventually they would be going.

He went on: 'We were common Laceys before we became squatters. Da claimed that the *De* was real enough, that he had dropped it when becoming a common policeman, so as not to antagonize his superiors . . . mostly Irishmen . . . by appearing to be superior. One of his favourite sayings. . . when you argued with him about some dodge he was up to . . . was: "Ye've got to be politic, me boy!" I never was that.' He sighed.

'Well, this was the land of opportunity to Da. He used to hear about it from fellow officers who'd done duty here. He was always after a tour of such duty himself. He organized it to coincide with our coming out of our time as apprentices, Jack and I. He sent Mother and my sister Kathleen round by boat . . . the usual way. He took us boys with him overland . . . most of it camel-riding. Da already was as good with a camel as a horse. He soon had us riding like Bedouins. They used to think it was all camel country up here in those days. Horses and cattle wouldn't live here, they reckoned. In fact Jack and I brought the first bovine stock in to this district.'

'Da . . . by being politic . . . quickly climbed the police ladder. In no time he was Inspector, and as such wielding a lot of power. He had come here as such with the Knowles Creek Tin Rush. In those days the railway came only as far South as the Princess Caroline. Everything had to be packed in across country. No one thought of bringing cattle. The miners were living like blacks on lily-roots and native game. Da sent Jack and me racing round the stations newly founded down on the rich Eastern Downs country, which were too far away to know of the advantage offering, and had us buy up any stock they would sell. We came back with a big mob of store cattle we'd got for a song. Da got a fine herd of breeders by confiscating a mob he found being overlanded from the South and suspected of having been stolen. But meantime, Jack and I, with Shamus Finnucane, who had a grog shanty on the tin fields, were running a thriving butchering business. We didn't deal in money. It was a pound of tin for a pound of meat . . . and the meat meant by the quarter, bones and hide and hoofs and all. Da sold the tin to Chinese in Port Palmeston. He had a lot of them in his pocket too.

'When the tin petered out, as it soon did, because there was really only a pocket of it . . . and a lot of the stuff they'd mined as tin turned out to be Tantalite, quite valueless at the time . . . we were ready to set up as graziers. I'd already taken up the nice bit of country back there on Knowles Creek on a mining homestead lease. We put our breeders on it. It may not convey anything much to you . . . but it's typical of the country, that when I asked that the name of the place be put on the map as Lulalla-goon, the native name, the Lands Office made it Lily Lagoons, arguing, when I protested, that native names have no significance! Their alternative was Knowles Creek, which would have perpetuated the name of Nat Knowles, who'd hunted the local blacks off the lagoons because they wouldn't work for him, destroying them. Poor devils had to come back and work for the miners when the rush started simply to live . . . or rather put their women to work . . . the blackmen didn't know how to work . . . and the women were handy for other purposes. It was then I began to feel guilty about the Old People. Before that I'd blithely accepted the general idea that they were only animals in the form of humans, much less valuable than a horse . . . that's how we were brought up . . . that's how most Australians still think of them. The local horde was practically wiped out . . .

not actually murdered, although there were a number shot, women mostly, for giving the whitemen who used them Gonorrhoea they'd contracted from other whitemen! There was no venereal disease before the whites came. The blacks of the coast have a disease of their own of the kind, Granuloma . . . but whites rarely contract it. Fortunately this disease has made them immune to Syphilis, which has done so much to wipe out the blacks of the Centre and the South. But how Gonorrhoea didn't wipe out those of the North, too, by rendering them sterile, beats me. There's still an awful lot of it about . . . and no real treatment for it, because of the ill-treatment in the beginning. As I've said, one of the methods was to quietly murder any woman known to be infected. The official one was to put the suspects on the chain and march them up to the Railhead and dump them in the Aboriginal Compound at Port Palmeston . . . but what am I using the past tense for? That's still the official method. According to my inquiries, treatment is practically non-existent . . . there seems to be a token of it, and that's about all. It's something no official will talk about or let you look into. Anyway, I started treatment of a kind even back in those days. There's a very useful species of *santalis* grows up on the Plateau there. I still distil the oil from it. In those days treatment of VD by a druggist was quite legal. It isn't now . . . but I defy the Health Department to try to stop me, till I see them giving treatment as good as my own. I sometimes wonder if it isn't official policy to exterminate the unfortunates with disease . . . but I see the subject's distasteful to you . . . sorry, Your Ladyship!' He said it with a wry smile; but his voice became vibrant with anger when he added, 'My lady wife didn't like to hear about it, either!'

She reddened. They drove for a while in silence, till he said, 'We're coming to the lagoons now . . . or billabongs, as properly they should be called.'

She asked, 'What's the difference?'

'Properly a lagoon is a salt-water arm . . . but inland can be any sort of depression filled with water during Wet Season and holding it for some time. A billabong's a backwater of a regular stream that becomes one with it during floods. A great river runs through here during heavy spells of rain . . . we can get up to ten inches in a single night. The so-called lagoons are what's left of it during the Dry. See that ridge ahead? Well that's where they are . . . Knowles' Ridge as it's called on the map . . . called by the blacks Numburra, which means a *gunyah*, or humpy, that is a native hut, as called generally in Australia . . . because the Old Woman, the Earth Mother, was supposed to have camped there when she made the billabongs. The ridge was what caused all the trouble subsequently, because that's where the mineral is, a lode outcropping in the middle of a plain . . . there you see it . . . one bit of a hump in the middle of acres of water. He drew up: 'Take a good look at it as a whole. See how there seems to be an electric blue glow over it all . . . that's the lilies. The wave-like motion's made by the birds swimming . . . thousands of birds . . . water-birds . . . of every kind. You see there're few trees anywhere near the water, except round the ridge. The clumps of stuff you see round the edges and out on the flats there are pandanus palms. That's how it would be in its pristine state . . . I assume from seeing other places like it, still unspoiled. I say I assume, because . . . well, when first I saw it the mining was in full swing and it . . . well, it was just torn to pieces. They'd even pumped the billabongs dry, running the water out over the dry plains, to get at the rich lode they reckoned ran underneath. I put it back as it is . . . or helped to. Nature only wanted a hand . . . but she demanded an awful lot of time, and money, too. I had to keep a tribe of blacks. I like to think she's paid me back . . . not merely with the great satisfaction I feel in the accomplishment, but in actual cash. That valueless stuff, the Tantalite they mined so much of and had to dump, has since become worth ten times the price of tin. You see I've got a bit of a mine on the ridge there. When I feel like working it I do. I have to, occasionally, to keep the mining lease I hold on it . . . but it's mainly from the Tantalite dump I make the money. By the way, my best customers are friends of yours.'

'Of mine?'

'Yes . . . Krupps of Germany. It's used in making special kinds of steel. I presume they're making things to exterminate those Bolsheviks of yours.'

'I hope so!'

'For my part I'm indifferent. What I'm concerned with is stopping the extermination of the people this land was robbed from . . . and Krupp's money's as good as anyone else's to maintain that robber baron's castle, as you call it, to do it in. They could use it against the English for all I cared. In fact, I think I'd regard it as poetic justice . . . because Nat Knowles was English, and most of his dirty poxy murderous mob!' Again the vibrance of anger.

He drew a deep breath, saying, 'You'll have to excuse the outbursts. To me it's holy ground we tread. Now, let's take a quick run round to show you the birds . . . then we'll cut across to the Caves, where we'll have lunch.'

There was no doubt about Lydia's delight in the scene, particularly the myriad birds as part of it.

As they were coming back from a round tour of it, Jeremy drew in to the blacks' camp at the foot of the ridge, saying as he alighted, 'Some of my old folk. Have to pay my respects. Don't suppose you want to come?'

Looking frankly askance at the scene, Lydia replied, 'Why not?' and got out to join him. Prindy stayed where he was, probably through fear of offending against etiquette, and handed down a packet to Jeremy, containing tea and tobacco.

There were four old couples now, all staring warily, squatting in ashes about an almost dead fire, before the two humpies. All were stark naked, so skinny as to seem scarcely fleshed, the women, with withered dugs, sitting, after the manner of their kind in similar circumstances, each with a heel in her crotch to prevent the intrusion of spirit things in the shape of insects, the men cross-legged, with an elbow covering pubes probably out of deference to the white woman. One old woman sucked an empty pipe. All four were crawling with flies they seemed not to be aware of. Three were caked to the neck with reddish-grey mud glistening with mica, evidently through having been grubbing for lily roots, a small heap of which lay by the smokeless fire. A dead goose, swarming with meat ants, hung by a yellow leg from a branch of a small sheltering tea-tree, its twisted neck showing that probably it had been pulled under water while the lily-rooting was in progress. The large wing of a goose lay in the ashes, to fan up the fire when need be, near it a black-caked billy-can the contents of which looked like black syrup. Ants of various kind, black, red, green, swarmed everywhere. A few spears and digging sticks leaned against the tree, and woven dilly bags hung from broken twigs. Jeremy asked, 'Everybody all right?'

They answered together, 'Yu-ai, Mullaka.'

'Present for you.' Long-fingered claws, black on the outside, smoky pink on the inside, snatched at tea and tobacco. The woman with the pipe began to shred the tobacco with a long thumbnail. Jeremy said, 'You gettin' too-muchee bone-bugger. More-better you come back station I tucker you.'

'By'n'by, Mullaka,' answered one of the men. The others cackled with amusement, showing apparent interest in the staring Lydia.

'All right, said Jeremy. 'Time you ready . . . I go now . . . *mummuk*.'

'*Mummuk, yawarra*, Mullaka.'

As Jeremy helped Lydia back into the car he asked: 'Shocked?'

She murmured, 'Can't say I was delighted.'

As he got in behind the wheel and started up he said, 'That's the natural state . . . but, of course, in a typical camp you'd find babies crawling about, kids laughing and playing, young girls giggling, strapping men painted up for corroboree or hunting . . . .'

'All stark naked and crawling with ants and flies?'

'That's the true Aborigine!'

She stared at him: 'And you like them!'

He waved a hand out of the window: 'With all the rest of it.'

'But . . . but . . . . '

'But what?'

'Do you want me to say it?'

'Don't say anything to please me.'

'Well . . . well, then, to me they seemed just animals.'

'Of the species *homo sapiens*.'

'How can you accept them as fellow creatures?'

He looked at her. Her eyes were wide, face flushed and troubled. Turning away he asked, 'Who speaks thus . . . the patrician or the Fascist?'

She snapped: 'I think you regard them much as you do those crippled animals of yours.'

'And how's that?'

She said fiercely. 'As some sort of escape from the realities of life.'

'What are they?'

'Civilized things . . . world politics . . . . '

'They seem to me quite *un*real!'

'Then love . . you've dodged love!'

'What do *you* know about love?' He met her staring eyes. Turning away, he added, 'Except as a form of blood-transfusion?'

They were silent until he turned into a track running towards the Plateau, when she said, 'Go on with the story about Rhoda.'

He said, 'I was thinking about my mother just then . . . and how she loved my father . . . if she really did love him and not just fear him. I never had a chance to ask her. She died while I was at the war.'

Jeremy was silent for a moment, then went on: 'Mother was just a little mouse of a thing. She was the daughter of Welsh parents. Her father was a miner . . . worked in the copper mines of Moonta. South Australia was founded largely on Welsh and Cornish mining stock . . . so much for the aristocrat in me! She was a music teacher when Da met her. God knows what the attraction was. There was even the barrier of religion. She was Bible-thumping Baptist, and he Catholic . . . and being Catholic in those days was something black . . . Black Irish. This land of liberty has a beautiful history of bigotry, believe me. The religious bigotry's largely gone . . . but I'm sure the bigot is still in us. Anyway, she became a Catholic to marry Da. Her parents wiped her for it. I never met them . . . I'm glad to say. I suppose it was all Da's doing . . . the big walk-you-down talk-you-down Irish policeman. What he wanted must have been a wife who simply wouldn't interfere with what he wanted to do . . . . '

'Not a Rhoda type?'

'Exactly . . . yet he and Rhoda got on famously . . . and it was really through him that I came to marry her.'

'Your father chose your wife for you?' She was staring again.

He grimaced: 'More or less. There was something of your blood-transfusion business about it. You see, we grew up with the idea of marrying well, as Da used to put it . . . and Ma echoed him. Of course with the idea of becoming Landed Gentry. Rhoda was squattocracy, but without acres. She was the daughter of the local Administrator of the day, Colonel Johns, a Boer War veteran and scion of southern squattocracy with more scions than square miles to share. Her mother was connected with your Macarthur-Onslows, no less. Da as Police Inspector gave us some social status to begin with. People tend to forget that inspectors were originally only common coppers. I suppose it stems from the old days when those who ran the police were military men. The Administrator here is also Commissioner of Police and a retired military man. You've met old Bullco, of course. He started as a mounted trooper, just like Da. He's always one of the elite at Race Time. Well, there was Rhoda, brought up to look for a young man to marry who had the means to make her a true member of the class she was born into and who also had the need of that connexion of hers to accept it as her dowry. She was a handsome girl . . . .'

'She's still very handsome.'

'She was nineteen when I met her . . . I twenty-three. We had a fine town house, originally belonging to a Chinese tycoon of the Caroline Gold Rush days, acquired by Da through his power as a policeman over the Chinese community. We were guests at Government House. We were already *De*lacys and the makings of squatters. Jack and I had taken our holdings in that name. Da didn't come into it officially till he'd retired from the police. Then we were Delacy and Sons. An important thing to remember of what I'm telling you is that I personally held the Lu-lalla-goon, or Knowles Creek, bit of country on a mining lease. Da wasn't concerned about it, because he foresaw the building of the railway on down to the Beatrice, and planned eventual setting up of our homestead and headquarters there. What we first had on Knowles Creek was only a sapling and ant-bed and corrugated iron affair.' He concentrated for a while on negotiating a washed-out creek crossing, saying that this track was very little used. The country was becoming rough.

He resumed his story: 'Rhoda and I became engaged . . . and my preoccupation to build the finest homestead in the land. Don't forget I was taking my bride out of the grandest household, Government House. Da raised little objection to my insistence on remaining at Lu-lalla-goon. After all, I was the means to our end as squattocracy. Rhoda wasn't concerned about the location. She'd heard my enthusiastic descriptions of my choice, and my plans for building . . . installation of the first electricity and cold storage outside of Port Palmeston. Besides, like all squatters' ladies she would be spending at least half her time in Town. Da had his Chinese minions build it for me. Although there's no worse jerry-builder than a Chinaman, there's also no tradesman like him, either, when he wants to be. That house is dowelled from top to bottom, and not a stick of it but what's proof against rot and termites. They milled their timber on the spot, all of it the best of local stuff, and pit-sawn by hand. They even built into it a Chinese blessing. As soon as it was finished I married my bride. But I didn't take her straight there. That would've been too much like the selector, the cocky farmer as he's called down South, taking his wife bush after the wedding to the bark humpy he's built for her on his newly cleared selection. We were squatters. We had to have our honeymoon abroad . . . and going abroad in these parts meant what was called 'going East.' It would be laughable but for the danger of our future as a nation . . . but, believe it or not, what we called The East, and still do, actually lies northwest of us mainly . . . such being our orientation, our bearings taken eternally from our spiritual centre, the British Isles! It was the done thing to go East. It still is. It gives you the *Tuan* touch. You learn to clap your hands to summon your coloured servants, instead of yelling . . . to drink stengahs, instead of plain whisky, to speak of lunch as *tiffin* . . . God help us!' He chuckled deeply.

Then he sighed: 'But the honeymoon could not have been more pleasant. I considered myself very much in love . . . I was! I believed myself the luckiest man in the world. In fact, the only unpleasantness I can recall in all our years of being actually together was the occasion I mentioned . . . when she objected to my weakness, as she called it, for succouring maimed and sick creatures. Even that didn't make a lot of difference. I called her hard. I think she even liked to be told so. She was hard on the blacks, our servants . . . not cruel . . . just strict to the point of never permitting a smile to pass between them and herself, or a laugh or giggle between themselves in her presence. She declared it was the proper way to treat them to get the best service . . . and, on results, she was right. I insisted on indulging that so-called weakness of mine, but had to keep my creatures, including sick blacks, out of her sight. I set up a kind of hospital-cum-menagerie well away from the Big House. The fact that I was a Veterinary Surgeon . . . through Da's pull I'd been registered as such . . . was something even to my *discredit* with her. Having scientific knowledge of animal husbandry was perhaps permissible in a squatter . . . but the Vet was the fellow you called in to attend some beast you considered too valuable to shoot.'

They were now in a great bight of the escarpment through the tumbled wilderness of trees and rock of which the bright cliffs could be glimpsed from three sides. She remarked on the colourfulness: 'Those reds! Is that why it's called the Painted Caves?'

'No . . . the caves are literally galleries of Aboriginal paintings . . . not really caves at all, but overhangs of the cliff faces . . . there wouldn't be much sense in painting in caves, where there was no sunlight . . . although it is done in cases of deep secrecy . . . or was, rather. No one paints here any more, except that old fellow I was telling you about, and that's only in special galleries. His galleries are over that way.' He jerked his chin northward. 'Ours are in there.' This time the indication was westward. There was a glimpse of the galvanized iron shed ahead. 'Our dinner-camp,' he said. In a moment they emerged onto the little flat where the shed and small stockyard stood beside the waterhole.

Alighting and taking hold of the tucker-box behind, Jeremy said to Prindy, 'Get some firewood . . . pipey stuff, because I want to grill some meat . . . and look-about track . . . that old-man, mate belong o' you, might be round here.'

Carrying the tucker box to the shelter, he said to Lydia, already out and looking about, 'We're trespassing really. This shed belongs to His Lordship. But I guess he'd rather you ate here than with the ants.'

She smiled: 'As I feel about him at the moment I'd as soon eat with the ants.'

'Ah . . . but what about the ants? *They* might object. It's only the transplanted things of this land that'd love you for your blue blood. Others might find it even objectionable.'

'What are you getting at?'

'The boy there . . . did you notice he wrinkled his nose as he passed you just now?'

Her eyes widened. He added, 'No offence meant . . . maybe it was your perfume he didn't like.'

She snapped: 'I don't use perfume . . . except on occasions.'

'Then it must have been your body odour.'

She opened her mouth, shut it. He went on: 'I told you no offence meant. He's not used to the smell of white women, that's all.'

She snapped: 'I hope I don't smell like one of those old black women!'

'You couldn't . . . no matter how dirty you were . . . nor they like you, no matter how clean. Body odour's a matter of race. The awful truth is we stink a bit to them as they to us. Just thought you'd like to know . . . along with other things that seem like the realities of life to me.' He turned to Prindy, bringing wood: 'You see any track?'

'Dat old-man can't leave him track.'

'Hum . . . you're right . . . I forgot. We'll make a smoke for him, anyway. He's sure to see it. . . or smell it.' Jeremy turned back to Lydia: 'I'm going to grill some steak. Hope you like grills?'

'Love 'em.'

'This one'll be in real bush fashion . . . bush meat, eaten the bushman's way.'

'What . . . is it native food?'

'No . . . not native in the least. The only difference from the ordinary steak you get round here is it doesn't belong either to Boss Vaisey or *Bos Taurus* . . . if you follow me.'

'I don't. Is the latter another of your black beasts?'

He chuckled: 'No . . . but the late owner of this steak was rather that . . . *Bos Bubalus.*'

'You're talking in riddles.'

'Rather . . . but I hope you'll enjoy it as no other meat you've ever tasted.' He proceeded to start the fire.

'Go on with the story of your wife.'

'My first wife. I'd quite forgotten her.'

'She hasn't forgotten you.'

'How would you know?'

'Women know these things.'

Now cutting green twigs with a clasp knife, sharpening some of them, Jeremy resumed his story: 'Well . . . I'd got the Delacy dynasty established for Da. He remained the virtual head of it as long as it lasted . . . was spared the grief it certainly would've cost him to see it brought down. He and Jack . . . and Rhoda, who showed increasing interest in the management . . . ran the place. My part became more and more in the laboratory. We have some bad poisonous plants round here. They had to be identified, located, eradicated if possible or else made inaccessible to stock. Bad seasons'll drive 'em to eat all kinds of things. Then there were diseases . . . swamp-cancer, fly-fevers . . . the pleuro, black-leg, red-water . . . everything bad from outside the country was brought in to add to what was bad inside it, of course. What had looked easy at first . . . wide fertile land got for the asking, good stock acquired for a song . . . proved to be something very different. They were inclined to think I made too much of the scientific side, having their own troubles. We'd started in a period of boom. We had to learn about markets . . . or they did, anyway. We were all preoccupied in our way. Rhoda had the additional preoccupation of the two children and her precious social position. We didn't know it . . . but we were drifting apart from the start. It happens to most couples, of course. Statistics, which can be very useful things, despite the dishonesty that can be worked with 'em, show that the average marriage becomes a sort of compromise, from the disillusionments following the honeymoon period to a point between the fifth and eighth year, when either something like true mateship's established, or the thing goes to pieces. Meantime the thing hangs together through the habit of sexual congress . . . .'

'Habit?'

'It's largely habit in marriage.'

'Was she frigid?'

'No . . . quite the contrary.'

'I shouldn't have thought so . . . with a man like you.'

He turned from her quickly to attend the fire.

'She's frigid now,' she added.

He answered as if absently, 'That's her business, I guess.' He went on: 'The fire's about right. Now . . . you've got to do your own grilling. Just watch us. Take these.' He handed her an enamel plate on which was a thick slice of bread and an opened clasp knife. The steak, already salted, stood ready in a dish. 'Right, boy . . . you show Missus.'

Prindy cleared away ashes from the coals with a brush of leaves, then dropped green twigs on them. Then, taking up a piece of steak on one of the sharpened sticks, he dropped it onto the others smoking on the coals.

'Smells good,' said Lydia.

Prindy turned the meat. It was quickly done. He lifted it onto his slice of bread, wrapped the bread round it, was lifting the combination to his mouth, when Jeremy said sharply, 'No-more . . . white feller ringer fashion . . . use the knife.'

Prindy reached for the clasp knife, when, holding the folded bread and beef in his left hand, with thumb sticking up, and gripped the knife similarly in the right, bringing the whole level with his mouth, he proceeded to slice off a chunk, collecting it with fingers freeing themselves somewhat from the knife handle, and with the knife brought almost to his nose, stuffed the morsel in his mouth. Juice oozed from his lips to his vigorous chewing.

Jeremy did the same, while Lydia watched. He looked at her after despatching his portion, saying, 'The knife work'll be too much for you. Likely to cut yourself. Just wanted to show you how it's done. Bush etiquette. Just chuck yours onto the bread and gorge it.'

She said, 'I'll try the knife . . . since it's etiquette.'

But her attempt was useless and dangerous. He took the knife, saying, 'Go on . . . eat it like what a good bushman would call a pig.'

She bit into the folded piece, chewed, with juice exuding. She swallowed it, wiped the juice from her chin with a white hand, said, 'Delicious!'

'Nice to see you enjoying it . . . although a bit disgusting to one used to good manners round a camp fire.'

She choked over the next bite, then laughing said, 'You're really bent on cutting me down to size, aren't you!'

'Not really . . . only trying to show you there're other ways of living than by the code you think's holy because it's yours.'

'I don't think anything of the sort. But aren't you eating any more yourself?'

'I've trained myself in the habit of only two meals a day. You carry on. I'll just sip beer and go on with the story. Where was I?'

'You were talking of the critical period in marriage . . . the fifth to the eighth year . . . and the habit of sexual congress, as you called it. I understood it was children kept married people together after love had flown out the window . . . .'

'No . . . habit. Habit's one of the strongest forces in nature. You can't make habits of children. They largely bewilder you by their constant changing . . . But let me get on with it. In our eighth and most critical year we were parted by the War . . . .'

'That War parted a lot of people . . . including my own parents. You put the blame on Vaiseys.'

'Madam, you're speaking with your mouth full, which while perfectly good bush etiquette, isn't good for the digestion. You've a long walk and a stiff climb. Besides, if you don't stop eating you won't be able to walk at all . . . By the way, the steak was buffalo . . . *Bos Bubalus* to a Vet.'

A look of alarm seized her. He said quickly, 'Don't tell me that after finding it so delicious learning what it is is going to turn you up?'

She swallowed: 'No . . . but they're such horrible-looking things.'

'Where'd you see buffalo?'

'From the plane. We flew low over some in a swamp. They came out . . . hundreds of them . . . hideous, slimy things.' She shuddered.

'I don't like the look of 'em myself . . . and I shoot 'em on sight as imported pests . . . but surely they're no worse than a pig . . . and you eat pork?' She nodded, wiping her greasy mouth with her hand. 'There you are again . . . prejudice against the unknown . . . habit. Now go and wash up.'

Lydia came back from the waterhole smiling: 'I wasn't sick. I was just surprised. I really did enjoy it.'

'Good girl!' Jeremy turned to Prindy: 'Sonny, we go now. You stop here. Might be old man come. You tell him wait for me, eh?'

Jeremy led the way along a rough track, instructing her to take it easy and to call on him to stop whenever she felt the pace too hard; and as they went he resumed his story: 'My brother Jack was off to the War like a shot. He'd badly wanted to drop his apprenticeship and go to the Boer War . . . but Da had prevented it, calling it a British War of Oppression ... behind closed doors, of course, because he was a loyal officer of the Queen outside. But I think Da was mainly concerned for those plans of his. This time was different. In fact it was the squatter thing to do, to get into khaki and a hat with emu's feathers . . . and, of course, pips on your shoulders. Our democratic system's against the officer and gentleman business of the British Army. You don't automatically become an officer because you're well placed. You've got to enlist as a private soldier like everybody else. You can't expect a commission till you've had your uniforms tailored. Have a blow, eh?'

They sat down in shade. Here the tumble made it impossible to see the wall ahead of them; but there was the sense of the mass of it in the background.

'There was no recruiting and training depot in these outlandish parts, of course . . . you had to go South. Jack was off on the first boat. Within a week or two of getting there he was a Lieutenant of Light Horse. He'd wanted me to go along with him; as I could easily have done, for all Rhoda or Da cared. The cattle business was in the doldrums. They were well enough staffed, with Aboriginal labour, and a couple of reliable old white stockmen as overseers. They had nothing to worry about. There's no better boss's man than the famous Australian Ringer. There'd be no squattocracy but for him. So Da and Rhoda were able to spend most of their time in Town. That was the only place you could get any immediate news of War in those days, of course. Not that they were worried about it a bit the last I saw of them . . . or anybody else, for that matter . The general opinion was that it'd be over in a matter of months. In fact the spirit of those interested was one of "Hurry along or you'll miss the show." Well, let's get on again, eh?'

He continued as they walked: 'Why I didn't go with Jack, when I followed so closely behind him, I don't know. I can't recollect my feelings then . . . except that I was troubled about losing him. Rhoda'd said I could go if I liked. All of her brothers were in khaki. I guess she wanted me in it, too. She never really liked Jack, for all his nice ways. She could've been a bit jealous of her status as Squatter's Lady in not having her man doing the done thing . . . especially one such as "Following the Flag" . . . the Union Jack, of course.'

Jeremy halted while she clambered over a rocky pinch, resuming: 'It was quickly made clear that Australia's part'd be to deal with the Turks, who'd naturally be out to seize the Suez Canal. We were the boys to stop 'em . . . the world's best cavalrymen. But for Jack's going, I don't think I'd've gone myself. Surely I'd've thought about it and seen through it as an Imperial racket . . . even though I didn't have much interest in or knowledge of politics in those days . . . . '

'Do you now?'

'I hear enough on the radio and read enough in the papers just to maintain my long-established belief that it all stinks of power-grabbing. Ready to go on? Good. Well . . . the very fact that when I left to go South with the expressed intention of only going to see Jack off on his troopship is surely indication of reluctance. At that stage of the War you could see your warriors off right beside the ship. There he was, aboard the biggest ship I'd ever seen, one of a vast khaki mob . . . a faceless mass, of uniforms, boots, hats, arms . . . which is what an army is. Not that he was with the common mob, packing the hatches, the rails, the ratlines, but up on the passenger deck with his brother officers. I can see it plainly as a picture yet . . . Flash Jack, my handsome winsome brother, so smart in his well-fitting uniform, the plumed hat at just the right rakish angle, the gleaming leather of Sam Brown and leggings. I looked right into his smiling eyes. That's how I saw him go . . . out of my life . . . taking my heart with him. I hadn't realized the depth of my hero worship of my elder brother . . . I was still the young brother at thirty-two. I knew then I'd have to go after him . . . to save him from what I suddenly realized was War, which for all the talk of glory, really meant destruction and death. I wrote home that night to say I thought of enlisting. It would take a fortnight for them to get the letter. Two days later I wired it, asking were there any objections. Within a few hours I got word back to say: *None whatever, best of luck and love, Rhoda, Da, the Boys*. Next day I got another from Mother and Kathleen, saying: *God go with you both* . . . Here, let me get you a stick. It'll make walking over these rocks easier . . . three legs are better than two.'

After getting her the walking stick he continued: 'I was commissioned within a couple of weeks . . . Light Horse, naturally. They called us the Flower of the Nation. The cheers we'd get riding through the streets of Adelaide . . . so many of us for the last time! It's always the Flower that's destroyed . . . why not the runts?'

'Runts don't go to war.'

'Oh, yes they do . . . with a bayonet at their backside . . . and make no less soldiers than the others. I've seen too many brave conscripts.'

'But Australians were not conscripted.'

'No . . . they refused to be . . . but only because the Irish were in rebellion against England at the time . . . and as the rest of our mixed Anglo-Celtic population had gone off to 'Follow the Flag,' that left a majority of Irish at home to fight the Conscription Issue, which meant really to fight for old Ireland . . . in the way that expatriate Irishmen prefer it . . . *with their tongues*!' He paused to help her.

'Well, I became one of the faceless khaki mass too . . . to be loaded into the troopship *Medic*, an old White Star liner . . . we and our horses, the best horses in the land and the best men . . . but just beasts to the big boys running it. I had an awful sense of being trapped as I walked up the *Medic's* gangway . . . especially on seeing the faces of those on board waiting to receive us . . . British faces, naval and military officers. It was like betrayal of one's own country. They looked so foreign.' Jeremy fell silent, as if reliving the experience.

'Well . . . we went straight to where they wanted us . . . El Kantara, in the Palestinian desert, on the Suez Canal. It was May, burning by day and bitterly cold of nights. I had something much more bitter to put up with than the weather, though. News came to me there that Jack had been killed on Gallipoli while I was at sea. What made it worse was what I'd learnt of militarism in the meantime. Some of those British officers we had on board were of quite high rank . . . had been in Australia organizing things. We were, of course, under British command. Their contempt for us was so frank as to be a joke with us. I don't know if you've heard the one about the British General who, when asked what he thought of Australian officers under his command, said: "Great soldiers . . . but impossible as gentlemen!" It was worse even than that with us, because as yet we hadn't proved ourselves as soldiers. We were just damned colonials. If we'd had two penn'oth of guts we'd have mutinied. Instead, we took it as a joke . . . even accepted it, I suppose.'

'You too?'

'Not quite. I hit back a bit . . . to my military detriment . . . and perhaps the eventual saving of my life at the hands of the callous bastards. Military men are like elephants. They never forget . . . that is anything that's a slight to their rank, which is their power over other men. But it wasn't simply their personal arrogance I objected to. It was the essential evil of what they stood for. Britain was supposed to be fighting to avenge brave little Belgium, to make the world safe for democracy . . . when in fact the British General Staff was embarked on a grand-scale military adventure. Our presence in Asia Minor was supposed to be, as I've said, to outflank any movement of Boche and Turk threatening the British Empire in that direction. The frank declaration of these brass-bound yahoos was to the effect that we were there to bring down the Ottoman Empire and add it to our own. What fascinated them was to be following in the footsteps of Alexander the Great. Evidently every military adventurer dreams of that. They knew everything about Alexander's campaigns . . . taught 'em at Sandhurst as the Great Example, maybe. One monster I was involved with aimed to get from Baghdad to Bokhara simply because Alexander had failed to do it. He . . . the monster . . . made three attempts at it, lost men and animals by the thousands, through starvation, thirst, cold, heat, disease, enemy action . . . gave it up disgruntled only after someone somewhere told him there weren't any more men and horses left to give him. I can imagine him saying . . . in some Brass Hat's mess in Cairo: "Rotten luck, don't y'know . . . another ten thousand or so men and horses and I'd've done the bally thing and gone down in history." I saw a lot of that sort of thing, because I had a sort of roving commission. Being branded a bad type because of those remarks of mine on the troopship, I was eased out of my unit. Militarism's such a mad thing that if it judges you incompetent it's as likely to promote you as cashier you. They hadn't grounds to do the latter with me . . . so up I went. They made me a sort of super horse-coper, an officer farrier . . . the limit in rank of which was only that of sergeant. Not that anything much was done for the beautiful beasts we'd brought, except shoe 'em . . . or shoot 'em. The only treatment a sick or injured horse got usually was a bullet. Eventually all were shot. Those wonderful beasts who really won the campaigns with their stamina and courage over the enemy's cavalry . . . even those that carried the conquering generals into Jerusalem, Beirut, Damascus . . . all shot out of hand. Not a single horse was brought home out of scores of thousands . . . not even one as a gesture to the nobility of the species!' Jeremy's voice became rough with emotion. 'We're a people without compassion,' he said. 'What sort of nation could do what we do, to animals and simple savages? Only one that could accept as its war-time leader and hero an artful dodger from the slums of London, the Cockney runt they hailed as the Little Digger!'

He stopped, breathless with anger. After a moment he said, 'Forgive the outburst. You probably don't know whom I'm referring to.'

'Oh yes I do . . . but I've never heard him described in those terms, I must say.'

They were at the foot of the escarpment now, right up against the towering red wall. In a little overhang were yellow limned stencils of human hands. When she asked about them he said he didn't understand the significance truly. The few local blacks remaining, either knew little about the galleries or pretended ignorance; and he himself had been too whiteman-stupid to find out what he might have while there was still the chance. The stencils were made by blowing yellow ochreous paint from the mouth. 'One thing you can be sure of, they weren't done just for the fun of it. No blackfellow ever did anything like that except with deep purpose. Perhaps these indicate, by number or position, the type of cave in the vicinity. There are several types. Some are very sacred. That's why I didn't bring the boy. Let's sit down here till I finish the story. It's nice and cool, with a bit of a view.'

Through tree tops could be seen the limitless wilderness below, violet in the noonday heat.

He said, 'I got my field rank eventually so as to save anybody with seniority the trouble and embarrassment of having to give such a type the warrants necessary for movement. I was then able to detach myself from everybody and go pretty well anywhere I wished. I tell you this so's you won't have any illusions about my being a soldier. I was in several actions . . . but only as a witness. I went armed . . . but only for my own safety. I've never killed a fellow man nor been party to such killing.'

After a pause he went on: 'Now for the Vaisey business. I was still in Asia Minor when I received word from home that Vaisey was going to build a great meatworks in Port Palmeston to can meat for the fighting forces . . . hence our fortunes were reassured. It didn't trouble me at first. In fact I was pleased. At least it stopped the perpetual complaint from both Da and Rhoda about the hard times at home . . . that is to say they weren't making the money they'd expected. Being parted from Rhoda and freed from the bad old habit that had maintained enough of the primary need and admiration responsible for joining us to perpetuate it, I'd soon begun to see her as a stranger. I was particularly affected by her evident indifference to my sorrow over loss of my brother. She replied by reminding me that thousands of men were dying similarly . . . . ' he paused significantly, but did not look at Lydia, who coloured slightly . . . 'and after all it was for King and Country. Da wasn't much more sympathetic. I believe it was his callousness helped to kill my mother, whose favourite Jack was. Within a year of his death she was dead, too. My sister, who stayed with her always, hinted at something of the sort.'

'Your sister didn't marry, you said.'

'No . . . she had that streak of the nun common in the Celtic women. It was as well, seeing how her own death would have affected her family, if she'd had one.'

'She's dead, then?'

'She died about ten years ago . . . at the Peel Island Leper Station.'

Lydia looked aghast, murmuring, 'Leprosy?'

'Don't be scared. It isn't really as infectious as people think. Where and how she contracted it, God knows. It's always much of a mystery. But had it she did. It was properly diagnosed. I saw to that. If she hadn't been white she'd have been run across on the Leper launch to Mud Island, off Palmeston and left to rot. As it was, she was quietly smuggled out aboard a steamer going South . . . But I'm telling you about Vaiseys . . . .'

'It seems to me that Vaiseys are only a means of your expressing the bitterness you feel over all the other things you've told me of.'

He said sharply, 'Vaiseys and their kind, the absentee landlords are the abomination of this land. Hear me out, please!' After a moment he went on quietly: 'Next came the news of the terms of the new prosperity. All stations selling stock to the Vaisey meatworks would be taken over by the Company. Cash would be paid for all buildings, plant, stock, along with shares to certain value in the concern . . . and all owners retained as managers on generous salaries. Gone for good would be the old insecurity, the hazards of weather, markets, all the rest. We would be part of an international organization that needn't care two hoots in hell if there were drought here, pleuro there, union trouble somewhere else, revolution, flood, fire, war . . . some places of ours would be functioning easily and bringing in the dough. I wrote back in haste to say that we would also be losing our independence, our very nationality. Da wrote to me in very clever Irish policeman's terms about the need to be politic.

'It wasn't long after that I was sent to Europe. The Alexandrine adventure was over. We'd beaten the Turk but not *Arabia Deserta*, for all that our generals had the advantage over Alexander in being Sandhurst. Also, our brother the Boche was proving himself more than our match in the grand old game of war, again without the benefit of Sandhurst. Because of my name, perhaps, and the aim to embarrass me, they first sent me to Ireland to take charge of a gang of British military thugs there to express the bit of Hun that seems to me to be in every Englishman . . .'

'Oh, I say . . . reahlly!'

'I thought you admired the Germans?'

'Not as Huns, dear boy!'

'These goose-stepping Jew-murdering *Schutz Staffel* elite of your hero Hitler strike *me* as being Huns . . . But we declared a truce on politics, didn't we?

'You broke it!'

'I apologize. Let me get on with the story. I mentioned Ireland only to let you know that I know something of Irish reality. Most of the trouble was that politic of Da's. Through it half the Irish were at the other half's throats. Anyway, I wasn't there long . . . only long enough to learn that it was as foreign to me as any other country I'd been in. I refused duty there . . . and was sent to France, evidently for elimination in the general wholesale slaughter then taking place.'

Jeremy took a look at the wall above, saying, 'We've got to wait for a certain amount of light to get into the gallery for best effect. It's a bit early yet.'

He went on with his story: 'I'd given Rhoda Power of Attorney over my share in the property. It was what a soldier had to do to protect his interests. Jack put his in Da's hands . . . of course, with his will. Rhoda could do anything at all in my name. But you'll recall that I told you I'd actually founded the place on a homestead *mining* lease, which is something very different from a *grazing* lease. I also held the Lagoons area by Miner's Right, because something had made me feel that Tantalite was really valuable stuff . . . the chemist, the metallurgist, you see. All soldiers were granted indefinite exemption from the laws governing tenure and such things. Fortunately, Da and Rhoda hadn't thought of that, nor I to mention it in my objections to their sell-out. What they'd signed away was grazing rights and property. If they'd known, they might have found a way round it with your smart boy Alfred at hand. But he'd soon cleared out, leaving his minions to carry on. Da was soon gone, too. On the eve of the end of the War he was killed by a horse . . . as all men who ill-use horses should be. Da was a fine horseman, but a cruel one. I think it was his cruelty that made both Jack and me as gentle as we were with horses . . . and with much better results. In fact there was a double Nemesis in Da's death. You know Jumbo Delacy, the halfcaste jockey who rode the Cup winner . . . and that he's my half-brother?'

'Of course.'

'Well, Da begot him soon after arrival in the North. All the old police had their halfcaste bastards . . . repudiated, of course. But Da only half-repudiated Jumbo . . . Jumbajinna, to give him his proper name. He took him out of the blacks camp where he was born and let him grow up on the station. Jumbo worshipped him . . . used to follow him about wherever he went . . . which was mostly on horseback, Jumbo riding any sort of beast, bareback. He became so expert with horses that when he was scarcely in his 'teens he took over the horse-breaking for the station when Jack went off to war. There was another of the *bar sinister* side of the family had to be included in the household with Jack's going . . . his favourite yeller girl, Nanago, and her baby, Darcy. In case you haven't guessed, the same Nanago is now my wife. When I say household, I mean they lived on the homestead, somewhat better than the blacks. I saw Nanago and her baby arrive. Jack had formerly kept them out of sight, down on the Beatrice. As a dyed-in-the-wool Squatter's Lady, Rhoda hated the blacks. There're two reasons for this hatred of the squatters' . . . for one reason they've been unable to enslave the blackfellow as they'd have liked . . . and then there's the miscegenation thing. Well, with us away at the War and Da more and more under her influence, Rhoda pretty soon got rid of the three Delacys disgracing the name by not being the right colour . . . or rather two, since poor Nanago was only a victim of the clan. She and her baby were not only driven off the station, but hunted out of the district. Rhoda had the Beatrice River policeman see to that. Jumbo was able to hang around, although not about the homestead, because Da wanted him for occasional horsebreaking and the racing. If temporarily at the homestead, he had to camp with the blacks. He took it badly. According to him, he killed Da. Not that you can believe much that poor Jumbo boasts about. Da had a bad habit of quieting a horse that was playing up by giving it a clout behind the ear with the butt of his stockwhip. He used a special steel-butted whip for the purpose. It can give a horse a bad headache. Jumbo claims that he trained a colt to go berserk when it was done to him, especially to get Da. Sure enough, a colt went mad when Da did just that to him, threw him, then trampled him to death. As I say, I don't know how true it is . . . but, anyway, it's become a legend now.' Jeremy sighed, took another look at the wall.

'I came home from the War to find Rhoda in full command . . . and by some stroke of good luck also to find Clem Eaton at the homestead. There was nothing between them, I'm sure . . . so don't go jumping to conclusions. He's an English gentleman, titled connexions, related to the Vaiseys. She liked him, of course, as she would even if only for that. But he's also a very pleasant fellow. He was there when I found them together, purely as Vaiseys General Manager . . . and just as pleased to see me as she was . . . and surprised, because I'd come home unannounced. It was just that the fact of his presence gave me something to make my stand on, make my declaration of war. He'd been in the British Army, a Major of Cavalry, too . . . had fought the *Uhlans*, no less, and been wounded and invalided out. I was full to the crop of the stink of the War and made no bones about it . . . nor about officers and gentlemen and the English and Vaiseys . . . and, well just about everything offensive I could throw at him. He stalked out in a very English fashion . . . with Rhoda and the two boys at his heels . . . because she'd been just as offended as he, as I'd intended. I remember eternally how they chugged away in a huge old Daimler car he used to get about in, thinking to myself as they went through the gate: "I wonder what I've done?" 'Jeremy sighed again.

'It was only then they found out about the mining lease the homestead stood on. When I'd arrived in Palmeston, the first thing I'd done was to go on to the Mines Office and look up the Mining Warden, always a friend of mine, regarding me more as the chemist than the squatter. He disliked squatters as a true mining man always does. We soon established the legality of my tenure. It wasn't long before Eaton was back again, swallowing the English pride for the sake of his master, Lord Alfred, trying to persuade me to give it up . . . for my family's sake, as he put it. Rhoda also tried a bit of persuasion in the same line . . . but she did it by letter. She never came back to Lily Lagoons . . . nor did the boys. How it would have worked out but for my discovery of what she'd done to Nanago I don't know. I did feel responsible for the boys. Of course I'd have had her and them back only on my own terms . . . which, perhaps, would have been impossible for her. But I did find out about Nanago. More than that, I found the girl herself, living in a blacks' camp down the Beatrice, sick to the point of death, with a blind baby, begotten by God knows whom, dying in her arms, and young Darcy all set for septicaemia through terrible burns to his face, sustained by falling into the fire in a fit. They'd all been in the Native Compound in Palmeston, supposed to be under medical care . . . but had absconded for the very lack of it, to save their lives. Christ!' Jeremy was heaving with feeling. It took him a moment to get control of himself.

He went on quietly enough: 'It's my philosophy that a man should excuse a woman for just about anything. She's the female of the species and should be indulged in everything that may be considered female . . . but . . . .' His voice suddenly became harsh again '. . . unkindness, cruelty, isn't one of these. Apart from driving out the inoffensive creature Nanago, and her baby, to live like what she'd call animals, when Rhoda heard that she, Nanago, was back at the homestead . . . and not merely at the homestead but living in the Big House, the house that was built for her . . . as she probably heard from Clem Eaton, who was here and saw Nanago working as my housekeeper . . . she wrote to me saying that I was deliberately humiliating her and that if I didn't give her immediate assurance that I'd turned the creature out, she would lay a charge against me for cohabiting with an Aboriginal female, which in this land of liberty is a legal offence. I ignored the letter. Next thing I have the Beatrice policeman out investigating . . . rather apologetically, because he had a couple of halfcaste bastards himself. Nothing happened as regards the charge. Oh, what a scene there would have been in the Port Palmeston Court if I'd been arraigned! There was nothing for it but to sue me for divorce, naming Nanago as co-respondent. I ignored that, too. I got my revenge by marrying Nanago as soon as the decree was issued . . . with the kind permission of the Protector, of course, her legal and so-kindly guardian. Soon afterwards Rhoda married Eaton. I doubt if she regrets it, whatever you imply about her sexual life. I certainly don't regret what I did in the matter. Nanago to me is the perfect wife. I guess I should have married a yellow girl to begin with . . . .'

'Why didn't you?'

'I thought I'd made that clear?'

'The explanation might stand for other men . . . but not for you.'

'There's no time for that now. The Sun's just right. Come on up the wall.'

He led the way up a steep path formed by the oblique cracking of the sheer rock face and the forward slipping of the mass. Thus up some twenty feet to a wide horizontal shelf formed by detritus fallen from above supported by great slabs below that had once been the part of the cliff face. They were now heading for a perpendicular point beyond which seemed nothing but the violet sky. When she remarked on the intensity of the colouring of the sky he replied, 'It's but the true blue of heaven . . . untainted by the dust and smoke of man . . . particularly by that man Vaisey.'

She asked, 'Does he own this?'

'No . . . this wall's his northern boundary. But if it and what lies North of here was worth two bob to him, I guess he'd have it too.'

They reached the point, rounded it, to see the wall blazing in the slightly westerned Sun and that it reared above concavities made by vertical slipping of the face. He said, 'The galleries are in those overhangs.' He asked her if she knew anything of graphic art. She said she thought she did, that she had studied if for a while with the illusion that she had talent, and had seen all the great art galleries of the world and lots of exhibitions. He said that he also had seen some of the great art works, without much understanding of them through ignorance, but that since becoming interested in what he called, this sort of stuff, had as much study of the subject of art generally as was possible through books. He added, 'It's not easily understood. I've had lots of discerning people here to see them and give me an opinion on Aboriginal art that'll satisfy me . . . because I've never been able to form one . . . and all I've got is something either different from everybody else's or the conventional stuff of the Anthropologists . . . symbolic equivalence, ethnographic parallels, and the like, which I think's all academic humbug. I'll be very interested in the effect it has on you.'

There was no decoration in any of the overhangs they passed under to begin with, except Nature's, in the form of streaks of all possible shades of red from palest pink to puce over the general terracotta, due to the chemical action of seepage. Then suddenly they were in a deep concavity that stretched back some fifteen feet from bottom lip to base of wall, the roof curving up from base to the top lip, which would be twenty feet above the bottom at its outer brush-grown and broken-toothed extremity, the whole about fifty feet in length, with a flat sandy floor marked recently only by the tracks of tiny animals and reptiles. That the curvature was a mass of decoration was evident on sight; but Jeremy halted the girl before she could give more than a glance to them, making her sit down and accustom her eyes to the shade after the glare from the wall. He got her to look out on the view that stretched to infinity southwestward, olive green, with here and there, like islets in a sea, bits of blue that were the few prominences thereabout. He said with a sigh, 'Well, there it is . . . *Terra Australis*. You couldn't get a more typical view of it. How does it greet your alien eye?'

Lydia stared for a while before answering, 'Monotony . . . awful monotony.'

'Yet you saw the teeming variety as we came along . . . or I hope you did. No place on earth has natural variety in any way comparable with Australia . . . in vegetation, animal, reptilian, insect life. You have to think of it like that to truly see it. That's the way the blackfellow sees it, I think . . . with a kind of intellectual telescope and X-ray apparatus functioning along with his normal vision . . . knowing what's in there, and there, and there . . . he sees it, even though so many miles away. What colour is it to you?'

'Grey . . . no, green-grey . . . a drab green-grey. Does that offend you?'

'Not a bit. It's the way most people see it . . . people born for generations in it . . . not truly native, of course. To me it's filled with colour.' For once he indicated with his hand, sweeping it over the whole scene. 'To start with, it has a blue iridescence over it. It's always like that in bright sunshine from about eleven to two. Then there are the bits of deeper blue and the quality of their depth. See!' He pointed with his finger 'There . . . there . . . there! And the browns . . . see . . . and shades of green . . . and all meaning something. You can mark the watercourses if you concentrate, see where the sandstone ends and the limestone begins, by the change in colour. There it's schist. That litmus blue streak is the ridge where we saw the old blacks. The green that seems to be in the sky marks the lagoons . . . the billabongs. That yellowish patch . . . that's the Rainbow Pool.'

But she was paying more attention to his animation. She said, 'You truly love it, don't you!'

He looked into the searching blue eyes: 'How terrible it'd be if I didn't.'

'Why terrible?'

'Because my heart would be empty.'

'If you had a woman to love?'

'A man's love of woman should be a passing thing. Only stupid men remain enthralled by women. But this . . . . ' His sweeping hand seemed to caress the scene. Then he turned suddenly to her: 'But come . . . let's see what must prove surely the strangest of all the art shows you've ever seen.'

Not a square inch of the roof, from where it started in the sand to where at its outer extremity the roughness of weathering made it impossible, but was painted, by how many artists in how many designs for how many ages would surely never be known even with the use of the most expert devices of detection. Picture had been painted over picture. What had been coarse rock as elsewhere was here silky smooth with uncountable layers of pigment, the colours of this earth, the innumerable reds, the yellows, pipe-clay white, fixed with saliva, plant-juice, blood drawn from the painters' own arms. Figures of all shapes, from spidery fine to gross. Animals recognizable as local creatures, kangaroos, emus, goannas, echidna, fish . . . and humans . . . but all so different from reality. Some of the animals were depicted with entrails shown, and always their genitals. Curiously the entrails of the human figures were not shown, but again always the genitals, and in proportions ranging from mere indications of sex to monstrosities that had character of their own and might be said to have human-like figures appended rather than to be appendages. There were mere faces, round or elliptical, but never square, with ears that hung down or stuck out or up, animals' ears, or had no ears at all – with eyes and noses but no mouths – with rays like the Sun rising from craniums or growths like trees sprouting from brains – with necks as long as bodies, or no necks at all – arms and legs as thick as bodies or the whole figure thin as sticks – hands with five fingers or six – feet with as many toes – all with genitals – and all, all with latent force beyond description.

Lady Lydia's interest was even intense. She swung from here to there in the soft red sand. Jeremy followed her, watching. She looked at every bit of it, touched some with a long white finger. Not a word said, till at last she swung to him, met his questing eyes, held them for a moment, then asked, 'What do you want me to say?'

He looked at a loss.

'I can't say anything without prompting.'

'Wouldn't that be dishonest?'

'I don't know. If you asked me if I liked them, I'd say no. If you asked me how they affected me, I'd say they only bewildered me. If you asked me if it's art, I'd say, perhaps the art of children . . . but not done by children, nor for children's purposes . . . . ' She stopped, swung away from him.

'Anything else?'

'No . . . only take me out of here. I feel as if I don't belong in here . . . nor am wanted in here . . . by anything . . . the spirit of the place, or . . . or . . . ' her voice rose hysterically ' . . . or even by you!' She rushed back to the point of entry, stopped there, staring out upon the wilderness.

He watched her for a while, then went out to her. She met him with a face hard and haughty. He said they'd better be getting down. They spoke little as they went, and nothing about the paintings. She complained of thirst. He got her a pebble to suck. He told her of native methods of getting water in dry places, of how animals in such places subsisted on dew. Thus back to the waterhole, the shed, the utility.

While she went to the hole to drink, he cupped his hands and called to Prindy.

No sight or sound of the boy. Jeremy got out a vacuum flask and poured tea. He was sitting with Lydia, sipping tea, when suddenly he rose and went to the utility and looked in the back. The rations for Bobwirridirridi were gone. He looked about for tracks. None but his own. Seeing him frown, Lydia called, 'What's the matter?'

'That old Snake Man's been here . . . and it looks as if the boy's gone off with him.' He cupped his hands again, and this time called mightily: 'Kuuuuu . . . Prindy!'

The red cliffs flung the echo back . . . *oo* . . . *oo* . . . *indy* . . . *indy*!

He waited. He called again. Nothing but the echoes. He swore: 'Godammit!'

He turned northward, to where the bight ended, beyond which, as he had told Lydia earlier, the Snake Caves lay. He called: 'Kuuuuu . . . old-man . . . Wirri . . . dirrid . . . dee!'

Only the echoes in reply.

He tried again: 'Old-man . . . you . . . been . . . promised . . . me . . . no . . . trouble!'

As the echoes died, a voice called from the cliff about where they had just come from, faint but clear: 'Ko . . . Mullaka!'

Jeremy called back: 'Kuuuuu . . . old-man!'

'No-more . . . trouble . . . Mullaka!'

'Bring . . . that . . . boy . . . back . . . here!'

'By'n'by . . . Mullaka!'

'I . . . want . . . him . . . now!'

'Me . . . two . . . feller . . . go . . . walkabout . . . *mummuk* . . . Mullaka!'

'You . . . make trouble . . . long . . . o' . . . me . . . bring back boy now!'

'No more trouble . . . Mullaka . . . *mummuk* . . . *yawarra*!'

This last came from a point at least ninety degrees North of the last. Involuntarily Jeremy swung to it. 'Listen . . . old-man!'

The answer came from yet another direction: '*Mummuk* . . . *yawarra*!' And yet another: '*Mummuk* . . . *yawarra*!' Too many times and too clear to be merely echoes.

When Lydia looked at Jeremy with surprise in her eyes he said in a ragged voice, 'Ventriloquism . . . one of a *koornung's* tricks.'

He called again: 'Old-man!' Again. Only the echoes now. He stood a moment, staring helplessly round the ring of cliff-face, at length said 'What's the use? God knows where they are.'

'Will he do the boy harm?'

'I shouldn't think so. They're friends. Old blackfellows do get attached to boys like that . . . often adopt 'em. Nothing sinister about it. They're not paederasts. The boy probably wanted to go with him.'

'What's there to worry about, then?'

Worry was plain in Jeremy's face: 'It's going to upset everybody.'

'The blacks?'

'Yes. His mother for a start. She hates him having anything to do with blacks. And they're going to regard him as *tulli-tulli* . . . and shun him.'

'But you said old blackfellows adopt young boys . . . .'

'The fact that this one's a *koornung*'ll make all the difference. I'll get the blame. I brought the old fellow here. What little trust they had in me I'll lose now. A man's a fool for monkeying in their business . . . . '

'I'm glad you see that at last . . . wasting your great substance on Stone Age savages, when the real world's in turmoil!'

He looked at her: 'I didn't mean it like that. I value their trust more than anything. I meant I'm a fool for blundering into something to alienate me, like any other fool whiteman.'

She shrugged: 'I suppose you blame me?'

'What for?'

'For making you bring me out here.'

'You didn't make me do anything I didn't want to do. Come on, let's pack up. We've got a long run home . . . and trouble ahead.'

They didn't speak again until they were in the car and on the move, now taking the better and more direct route towards home. It was she who broke the silence: 'You said I didn't make you bring me. Does that mean you really wanted to?'

He answered shortly, 'I was pleased enough to take you once it was fixed.'

'Why . . . to give Alfred one in the eye . . . or because you don't really hate me as you pretend to?'

He glanced at her: 'Sorry if I've given you the impression of hating you. It's only that you're connected with the Vaiseys.'

'Can't you forget that?'

'I've forgotten it most of the day. I was glad to show you the country. You're intelligent, sensitive, and a stranger . . . I wanted to see the effect it had on you.'

'Are you pleased with the effect?'

'You're asking too many questions. I'm worried about the boy. If you want to talk, tell me about yourself . . . about your old duke . . . anything . . . ask me about the birds and the trees and things, if you like . . . but don't force me into arguments about things you think are real and I think are as silly as you think the things I believe in are.'

'All right,' she said, and put a hand on his on the wheel, and held it there. After a while she asked, 'Mind if I lean on you? I feel a bit sleepy.' She dropped her fair head to his shoulder. The going like that was too rough to begin with. She gave up the attempt with a smile. But when they were out of the rough and speeding along a good stretch of road, she dropped her head to him again, and this time slept out most of the rest of the journey.

It was close to sunset when they came in sight again of Beatrice homestead. He wanted to put her down so that she might cross over by the private causeway; but she insisted on coming with him to witness what happened when he reported the disappearance of Prindy. The Sun was setting as they crossed the main causeway and drew into the Lily Lagoons camp. Waiting with the household were the Ah Loys, Nelyerri and Willy.

Nelyerri was already standing on tiptoe looking for her son. As soon as the car stopped she came hurrying to look in the back, then confronted Jeremy as he alighted, demanding, 'Where my boy?'

He answered casually enough, 'He stop Lily Lagoons.' He kissed Nanago's cheek, saying, 'Let's have something to drink, dear.'

With voice rising, Nell followed him: 'Why you leave him behind?'

Seating Lydia, Jeremy answered, 'He no want to come back with me.'

'Who dere long o' Lily Lagoon?'

'Some old people.'

'Where dat *koornung*?'

Seating himself, Jeremy said, 'I don't know.' He began to pour the beer that Nanago had brought, adding, 'Have a drink, Nell . . . come on Willy.'

Nell ignored him: 'I been hear dat *koornung* dere long o' Lagoon.' She was panting now.

'I never see him.'

'You been bring him from Catfish.'

'I tell you, girl, I never see him this time.'

The girl bent over him, her voice rising to a shriek: 'What for you steal him my boy?'

'Don't be silly. Sit down and have a drink.'

'You been steal him 'way be-fore deelight!'

'That's because you were too drunk to come. I asked you and Willy the night before to come out with us. That right, Willy, eh?'

'Da's right, Mullaka.'

Nelyerri raised clenched hands, screeched through them into Jeremy's face: 'You take me out Lily Lagoon.'

'You can go out there with everybody tomorrow.'

'You take me now . . . now . . . now!' She grabbed his shoulders.

Jeremy called to Ah Loy: 'Come and get hold of her, Willy.'

Willy leapt up, seized the girl from behind. She swung on him, shrieking: 'Le' me 'lone, you Chinee bastard!'

But Willy kept his grip, pinioned her arms behind, avoiding her kicking feet, while she yelled, 'Dat bloody white bastard been steal him my boy . . . He wan' 'o put him long o' school . . . .'

Jeremy cried, 'If you don't let me have the boy for my school, McCusky'll take him away from you, put him Compound school.'

'You bloody white bastard . . . you been steal him my boy. You been leave him long o' dat no-goot bloody puggin old black bastard *koornung*!' Her tone changed to a wail.

Jeremy said to Nanago, 'Look after her, dear,' and beckoning her close, whispered, 'Give her a tablet.' Nan nodded, went to Nell and put her arms around her, and kept putting her arms back as they were flung off, and at length got the girl, now sobbing, into her own sleeping tent.

Lydia was watching with wide blue eyes. Jeremy seemed to have forgotten her. He beckoned to Ah Loy, who when he came, addressing him with the formal name of Jumara, he told what had happened. Willy, with eyes popping, commented with indrawn breath: 'Eh, look out!'

'Sorry I give you trouble, mate. I pay you. Go out with her tomorrow with the mob. Don't tell her properly yet.'

'She goin' 'o go look-about him, Mullaka.'

'She'll never find him. Nobody can find that old man. When I come back I'll go with more bre'-milk and brandy. That'll fetch him.'

'Where you go now, Mullaka?'

'I go for a run down Inland. Go and tell Nanago I want her.'

Mingled howls and sobs were coming from the tent. But soon Nanago came; and Jeremy repeated what he had told Ah Loy, while she listened with great dark eyes. He concluded: 'It'll be all right. Sorry to leave it to you. But if I were round it'd only make things worse. I'll be back in a week or so and fix it. Roll my swag for me, will you dear . . . and send Darcy up to the pub with the ute. I've got to take this lady up there so's someone from the station can come and fetch her. I'll wait there.'

He rose, and as she rose with him, put his arms about her and kissed her lips. She clung to him for a moment, then released him, murmuring, '*Mummuk, yawarra.*' He repeated the farewell.

Nanago turned to Lydia, smiled: 'Goodbye, Missus.'

Lydia returned the smile, saying, '*Mummuk, yawarra.*'

It was almost dark now. The Moon, nearing first quarter, hung westward in the unstained violet of the gathering night. As they walked up the road toward the township Lydia took Jeremy's arm, saying, 'Well, you handled it nicely.'

'I'm afraid I only handled it. The poor thing's a bundle of tension all the time. There's a case of a halfcaste taken too early from the blacks.'

'But I'm surprised at your running away.'

'I'm not really running away. I mostly take a trip off somewhere after the Races. Simple return home's too much of an anti-climax after the spell of intense purpose, win or lose. I usually go and get on the booze. Haven't they told you that?'

'Yes . . . but I didn't believe it.'

'Why not. This is the land of what they call the booze artist.'

'You seemed too balanced.'

'That's a compliment, from one who so lately declared I was wasting my substance on a dream!'

'I know you better now.' She squeezed his arm. When he squeezed back, she reached for his cheek and kissed it.

'Careful!' he muttered, and disengaged himself, adding: 'Old Shame-on-us is out on his verandah, if I'm not mistaken.'

There was light in the hotel, but not as before on the verandah, nor, in fact light anywhere now but for a spot here and there, where during the festivities there had been brilliance. Even the reek of goats was back in the air.

Jeremy said, 'You'd think old Shame-on-us would still be in his counting-house, counting the money he's made.' Then he quoted: '*I wonder what the vintner buys* . . . .'

She finished for him: '*One half so precious as the goods he sells.* I'm fascinated by this idea of your going on the booze, as they say.'

'Drunkenness breaks tension as nothing else in all Man's inventory of remedies for the same.'

'I couldn't imagine you drunk.'

'I wouldn't let you see me. When you reach the proper state of what's aptly called rottenness, you must hide yourself.'

'How can you, when you're . . . rotten, as you call it. I know when I'm rotten, I make a silly ass of myself, don't know what I'm doing.'

'A lady should never get drunk without a reliable male escort . . . and a man never without dignity. A man's dignity, which is very different from a woman's, is the last thing to go under. It's that that stops the room spinning long enough for you to get out of it after having said to your fellow topers: "'Scuse me genlm'n, I have to shee a dog 'bout a man." You enter the stage of rottenness in strict privacy, crawl out of it similarly, regain your dignity, then back to your crazy purpose of living catharticized, a new man.'

'D'y'know, I'd love to go on the booze with you.'

'It wouldn't work.'

'Why?'

'As I've said . . . a woman must not drink without a reliable escort . . . and a drunken man is not reliable . . . .'

'Not a man of dignity?'

'The man of dignity never gets really drunk while he has a responsibility.'

'I'd still like to get molo with you.'

'When you come back as Lady Vaisey, eh? Shush now! We can't have Himself hearing such lewd talk . . . or we'll be the talk of the country an hour after the phones start operating tomorrow morning.'

Seeing who was coming caused Finnucane to retreat into his lighted doorway. Handing Lydia up the step onto the verandah, Jeremy said easily, 'Goodnight, Shamus.'

Finnucane responded quite heartily: 'Ah . . . gootnoight to ye, Jeremy . . . and gootnoight to Your Ladyship!'

'Good evening, Mr Finnucane.'

'Ah!' breathed Finnucane, standing back to permit their entry and half bowing them in: ''Tis aiv'nin we call anny toime after noon, and noight is noight in these benoighted parts . . . isn't that so now, Jeremy?'

'Very well put in the Irish idiom that's responsible for it,' answered Jeremy.

A black brow cocked with suspicion: 'And what's that ye sayin' about Irish idiom?'

Jeremy looked at Lydia: 'The usage evening for afternoon is Irish, really . . . and so many of us round these parts are of Irish origin.' He turned back to old Shame-on-us: 'I've been showing Miss Lindbrooke-Esk round the district and instructing her in local usages.'

'Ah!' commented Finnucane, but still with suspicion in the black eye.

Jeremy went on: 'She'll be wanting someone to come from the Big House and pick her up. I thought we might have a drink while she's waiting.'

'Sure . . . sure!' cried Finnucane. 'Ye'll be wantin' to use the telephone then, Me Lady. Ye'll foind it switched t'rough to the Big House. Then we'll adjourn to me office for a quoiet wan.'

'I'd like to have it in the bar,' said Lydia. 'I haven't had a chance to stand up in a bar and drink.'

Old Shame-on-us hesitated just a moment, probably because of the impropriety, indeed the local illegality, of serving women in an open bar, but then said, 'If it plaise Your Ladyship . . . but I insist on ye doin' me the honour of takin' a dram of the Dew agin, and not just some common tipple off these shelves.'

'Thank you,' she said.

'Well, I lave you to your telephonin', bewhilst I get a bhottle.'

Finnucane went. Lydia turned to Jeremy standing by and said pointedly, 'Excuse me.'

Jeremy looked slightly surprised, but bowed slightly: 'Of course.' He went into the lighted public bar.

Finnucane and Lydia came into the bar together, old Shame-on-us to duck under the counter flap and proceed to set up special glasses and the bottle of Tullamore Dew. As he poured the third glass he looked under brows at Jeremy, saying, 'Ye have no objections, I presume, Jeremy?'

'On the contrary, I'm honoured,' said Jeremy, but gave Lydia a slight wink as Finnucane gave his attention back to the glass.

'Well,' said Finnucane, 'here's to our meetin' again in the same happy circumstances.'

They drank. 'Very nice,' commented Jeremy.

' 'Tis better than noice, me boy . . . 'tis superb!' Finnucane slapped his long moustachioed top lip: 'But then, ye've never had a proper Irishman's taste for whisky. Now, your old Da . . . .'

But the utility was drawing up at the step. Jeremy said, 'Excuse me . . . I must have a word with Darcy.' He went out.

Darcy got out, giggled, 'Full up oil, benzine, everything, Mullaka.'

'Thanks, son. See you in a week or so. Keep your eye on things. If I'm wanted urgently, wire me. They'll know along the Telegraph Line where I am.'

'Yas, Mullaka.'

'*Mummuk*, son.'

'*Mummuk, yawarra*, Mullaka.'

Jeremy returned to the bar to find another glass poured out. As they drank, Finnucane asked, 'Ye'd be takin' the usual little thrip away, then, Jeremy?'

'Yes.'

'Would ye be anny chanst goin' Cornelius Cullity's way?'

'Yes . . . I was thinking of heading for the Centre . . . and I'll certainly drop in on Con and Bridie. Any message?'

The broad red face hardened and the rumbling voice lost its smoodging quality: 'As a matther of actual fact I have a letter for the man. He left in a bit of a hurry. I'd be obloiged to ye for takin' it and savin' the week's delay the mail'll take. I'll get it.'

Finnucane was back in a moment, casting a professional eye on the bottle on the counter and saying, 'Ah . . . and whyn't ye help yeselves to another dhrop?'

As they were drinking again another car was heard and soon the braked wheels on the gravel outside. Finnucane said, 'Dhrink up . . . and we'll have another wid whoever's come for ye, Me Lady.'

Lydia said with haste, 'No thanks . . . I've had enough.'

She turned to the outer door. Footsteps on the verandah. It was Mr Gilling, Head Bookkeeper of Beatrice Station. He was holding a small suitcase.

Jeremy and Finnucane were coming out. As they emerged, Lydia took the case from Gilling's hand, and gave him her own, saying, 'Goodbye, Mr Gilling . . . give my regards to everybody.'

Gilling bent over her hand murmuring, cast a look at the two staring men beyond Lydia, then nodding to them, stepped off the verandah and back to the big car. As the car started up, Jeremy asked, 'What's this?'

Lydia heaved a sigh: 'I just couldn't go back there after all the excitement.

I've arranged with Lord Alfred to pick me up in the plane at Boulder Creek. As you're going Inland, Mr Delacy, would you be so kind as to give me a lift?'

From staring at her, Jeremy looked at Finnucane. The black eyebrows had never been higher than now. He swallowed, looked at Lydia again, took a deep breath and said dryly, 'One can't refuse a lift to anyone in this country . . . especially a lady.' He turned to Finnucane: 'Isn't that right, Shamus?'

Old Shame-on-us had scarcely the breath to answer: ' 'Tis truth and all.'

Lydia smiled: 'Thanks offly, Mr Delacy.' She handed him the suitcase, then turned to Finnucane, offering her white hand, which the hairy paw took with evident embarrassment: 'Goodbye, Mr Finnucane . . . and thanks for everything . . . especially for the Tullamore Dew.'

Finnucane's rumble could scarcely be heard: 'Gootbye, Your Ladyship.'

She stepped off the verandah, went to the door of the cabin of the car, opened it, looking back. Jeremy hadn't yet moved. Then with a nod to Finnucane he followed, going to the rear to lift the dust sheet now covering it and put her suitcase in. He went round to the driving side, got in, started up at once. The distant mob of goats was revealed by the headlights as a mass of twinkling golden gems. The car was moving, Lydia waving to the staring Finnucane. Jeremy dowsed the lights, switched on again to reveal that the goats were gone, but leaving powerful evidence of their presence as they ran through the spot where the mob had been. Lydia held her nose, smirking at Jeremy. He took no notice of her.

They ran on in silence through the township, came onto the red road lined with scrubby trees. Staring at his grim profile, lit by the dashboard lights and the reflection of the glare ahead, she asked, 'Well?'

He snapped at the road: 'Well what?'

'Just well.'

He was silent. She sighed, settled back in her corner.

VI

They ran on for half an hour in silence. Lydia, by her attitude, was asleep; but when in the red barrel of the road ahead two sets of fiery sparks appeared and Jeremy slowed down and momentarily dowsed the lights again, she sat up asking, 'What was that?'

Jeremy answered shortly, 'Dingoes.'

'Anybody else would have run them down, I expect?'

'For sure.' Jeremy got up speed again.

'Tell me about dingoes.'

He glanced at her and turning back to the road asked, 'For your true edification or just to make you feel more at ease?'

'Do you wish me to be ill at ease?'

'I haven't got over wishing you weren't here yet.'

'Will you?'

'Depends on your behaviour.'

'How must I behave to please you?'

'Are you so irresponsible that you have to be told how to behave?'

She was silent for a while, then asked, 'Have I done something so terrible?'

'Evidently you are irresponsible. But why? Is it bad upbringing, or because the class you belong to doesn't feel it has responsibility to others . . . sort of *Dieu et mon Droit*?'

'Don't rub my class in, please.' She sounded humble.

He fell silent, staring grimly ahead and driving at what was high speed on that ill-made road. The road ran dead straight, towards the Southern Cross, hanging above reach of the headlights in what looked like black void. The Moon was now peering at them through the flying trees.

At last he said, 'May I ask what you said when you phoned Beatrice homestead?'

'Of course. I spoke to Alfred, and told him that I'd had such a marvellous time with you I just couldn't face people who hated you . . . and as you were about to take a trip Inland, would he mind much if I went with you, and he came and picked me up somewhere later.'

'Just like that?'

'Almost word for word.'

'And he said?'

'What he always does . . . "Just as you wish, old gal!" '

'You make a practice of this sort of thing?'

'What sort of thing?'

'Attaching yourself to strange men?'

She was silent, for so long that several times he glanced at her huddled in her corner. At last he asked, 'Are you crying?'

The answer came in a sob. Then suddenly she flung herself against him. He cried, 'Steady! I'm doing fifty . . . which is a lot for this road.'

She withdrew somewhat, but kept her head against his shoulder, sniffling now into her handkerchief. After another long silence he said, 'I presume you never had the slightest realization of the implications of your act?' When she didn't answer he added. 'That it'd start the biggest scandal in the country since . . . since . . . '

She raised her face suddenly: 'Since your wife Rhoda divorced you for adultery with a halfcaste?'

He swallowed, keeping eyes on the road.

'Are you afraid your halfcaste wife will now divorce you for adultery with a white woman?'

He remained silent. She demanded, 'Well . . . are you?'

'No . . . my halfcaste wife's got too much sense.'

'That's what I thought, too. So what are you afraid of?'

He swallowed on that one, too, but answered at length, 'You.'

She sat up straight, staring at him. He added hastily, 'Don't get me wrong. It isn't you the woman I'm afraid of . . . but you the irresponsible spoilt child of charlatans whose racket is to hold place and power by kidding half-wits that a thousand years of inbreeding makes them somehow holy.' He ended with voice vibrant with feeling.

She drew a deep breath: 'Christ . . . you do love us, don't you!'

After another lengthy silence she asked; 'Well, explain how it is that this

. . . this despicable, wretched, inbred creature you describe makes you afraid. I don't get it.'

He sighed: 'Because she's made me responsible for her. Because I have to drag her half a thousand miles and more introducing her as Lady Something-or-other, fiancée to my enemy Lord Vaisey, and suffer the lunatic toadying of the nitwits I present her to and her arrogance in the face of it all.'

'I'm not being presented to anybody dear boy. I'm taking a trip through the wilds of Australia with the greatest Australian of them all to show me the wilds.'

'No . . . by God you're not! Every homestead, every pub, every telegraph station, all the way to Boulder Creek . . . I take you in and present you for what you are!'

She was breathing heavily. After a moment she said, 'You bastard . . . Jeremy Delacy!'

'You were probably warned that I'm just that, My Lady.'

She was silent. After a longish while and in a different voice she asked, 'How else could I have done it? You wouldn't have taken me if I'd asked you beforehand, would you?'

'No.'

'Why not?'

'Because of the goddam implications I spoke of, for a start. The moment the telephone system and the Flying Doctor radio network starts to operate tomorrow morning, it'll be blabbed all over the country. Didn't you see stupid Finnucane staring? I'll bet at this moment he and his two biddies back there are just talking themselves hoarse about it . . . '

Her voice had changed again: 'You make it sound as if you haven't been involved with other women in exactly the same way before.' When he was silent she added: 'I told you I'd heard a lot about you. What about those other women you've taken overland after the Races?'

'At least they did ask me first . . . and the circumstances were different. They were heading somewhere South, or East, or West.'

'That's what I'm doing.'

'They had a real purpose for going . . . if it was only that they were tramps and had been ordered out of the country.'

'So have I a purpose.'

'State it.'

She swallowed first, then in a strangled voice said, 'I . . . I've fallen in love with you!'

He stiffened, swallowed, stared at the rushing road. A moment of staring at his dim-lit profile, the craggy manly beauty of it; then she leaned against his arm and wept again.

She fell asleep weeping, stayed like that, undisturbed by frequent gearing down and revving up, in the negotiation of sudden curves, sand-drifts, the avoidance of kangaroos, curlews, an owl that hit the windscreen. Twice they passed through railway settlements where figures stood out to stare at them from lighted doorways.

She slept out the best part of an hour, no doubt exhausted by the efforts of the long day and dopey from the Tullamore Dew, looking very much the child in the little light. He must have been cramped with the weight of her, but made no move to disburden himself. The Moon went down. She was wakened at last by a mighty cacophony, to start up and stare out on a veritable heaving grey sea of hairy backs and flopping ears. She gasped, 'What on earth?'

'Donkeys,' he said.

A seemingly limitless mass of the beasts blocked the road. He kept shoving into it, adding the braying of the horn to the unearthly din.

'What huge things,' she commented. 'I've never seen donkeys like that.'

'A special breed . . . team-donkeys . . . bred by Billy Brew. He must have at least five hundred of 'em. The squatters hate the sight of them and him, but daren't do anything. For one thing, old Billy's cartage rates are about half those of the truck carriers . . . for another, he can get stuff to 'em where the trucks can't . . . and for a third, he's sworn that when the stations stop employing him, he's going to distribute his donks in small mobs over the best parts of the country. Donkeys breed fast. They could become an awful nuisance. So long as Billy's got control of 'em, the squatters're safe. He's one of the few free spirits in this land of alleged liberty.'

'Good for Billy Brew! I'd like to meet him.'

'You pretty soon will.'

'How's that?'

'We're getting close to Charlotte Springs. He's sure to be in the pub there. The mob back from the Races'll still be boozing.'

'Are we going to the pub?'

'Where else will you sleep?'

'I thought we'd be camping out.'

'You didn't bring a swag.'

'Swag?'

'Bedding.'

'Oh!'

'You see what doing things rashly in this country means. You need more than a toothbrush and pyjamas when you travel here.'

After a little silence she asked, 'Are you still angry with me?'

Without looking, he replied, 'How could I be angry, when you've paid me the greatest compliment a woman can pay a man . . . even if she really doesn't mean it.'

'Oh, but I do mean it!' She snuggled up to him, murmuring, 'Dear Jeremy.'

He shrugged her off. 'You make it hard driving on this rough road. And please remember what I said about being afraid of your irresponsibility. There'll be people at the Charlotte. I hope you'll behave nicely.'

'For you I'll do anything.'

'Well, here we are.'

An iron shed appeared . . . goats . . . a fleeing cat . . . lights. In a minute or two they were running into the tiny township: just a couple of iron buildings across the way from the whitewashed sheds and water tanks of the railway. From one of the buildings the glare of acetylene gas spilled onto a low verandah where figures could be seen seated on forms and packing cases. Jeremy caught the group, all glass in hand, in his headlights as he swung from the road to run up a lane and reveal at the rear something like the accommodation set-up of the Beatrice River Hotel, although much meaner and all in corrugated iron. 'The hotel suites,' said Jeremy, letting her take a good look before switching off the lights. He added: 'But first we've got to see if they'll have us.' Dogs began to bark as they alighted.

She asked, 'Why shouldn't they have us?'

'It's a Finnucane pub . . . run by his daughter Colleen and one of his imported slave sons-in-law, Mick Curry. You wouldn't know, perhaps, that of all the sins in the catalogue, the one that Finnucane can't tolerate is that listed in the Catholic Church as, against chastity, or as Finnucane himself calls it, indeed roars it when confronted with it, *farnication*. People can do what they like, says he, provided they're not objectionable to others . . . in his pubs, he means . . . "But farnication I'll not abide under anny circumstances!" Many's the couple Finnucane's thrown out when he's discovered they've been occupying his daicent beds without a marriage certificate . . . and the travelling lady come to the Races on the make. Didn't you see the eyebrows raised at us? Only for knowing the reception he'd've got had he tried to rouse the men at the Telegraph Station, sleeping it off with their yeller girls, I'll bet he'd have made a special request to be put through on the phone to warn 'em here of what to expect. Please act the Lady Lydia . . . No, don't take my arm . . . it isn't done in these parts.'

Faces peering round the corner of the front verandah vanished as they came into sight. They reached the verandah to find everybody seated again and looking indifferent. Jeremy said easily, 'Goodnight, all.' A mumble of replies.

He guided Lydia into a narrow passage, lit only by the glare from a door opening onto the bar and serving window further in. He stopped her at the window. Behind the bar were thin Mick Curry and his plump dark Colleen, all eyes and alertness. Jeremy called to them, 'Hello, Colleen . . . Hello, Mick. You know Lady Lydia Lindbrooke-Esk, Lord Vaisey's fiancée, don't you?'

Those outside were crowding into the outer door of the bar, those inside gaping.

Colleen came to the window and dropped a sort of curtsy. Lydia smiled and extended the white hand, saying, 'We haven't been introduced . . . but I saw you, of course . . . at the Races.'

Colleen wiped her hand on her dress first, murmuring, 'Your Ladyship.'

Jeremy said, 'I'm giving Lady Lydia a lift through to Boulder Creek, where Lord Vaisey'll pick her up in his aeroplane. She wants to see the Inland. Can you put her up for the night?'

Flushed and breathless, Colleen answered, 'Oh . . . but . . . but . . .'

Jeremy said, 'Don't worry about what sort of room. I've warned her what the Inland's like.'

Smiling still, Lydia said, 'I want to see the real Australia.'

Colleen recovered, gasped, 'Oh, yes, Your Ladyship . . . certainly, Your Ladyship. But I must get a room ready for you . . . .'

Jeremy cut in: 'Let's have a drink first, eh?'

'Oh, yes!' Colleen sprang to obey.

'In the bar, if you don't mind. She wants to meet everybody.'

Colleen gaped: 'In the *bar*?'

Jeremy nudged Lydia back to the communicating door and into the bar.

He addressed the gaping dozen or so: 'How's everybody?' Then he introduced the girl as he had to Colleen, adding, 'You must've seen her with the Big Boss at the races. I won't introduce you by name. You can get to know her yourselves . . . except you, Billy Brew. She wants to meet you personally.'

A little old man, leathern brown and wrinkled as bark, with blue eyes and fuzz of white beard, gaped more than all the rest, murmuring, 'Me?'

'Yes . . . I told her one of these days you and Lord Vaisey are going to have to shoot it out over those donks of yours . . . and seeing she's going to marry the bloke, she's naturally interested.'

The old fellow gasped, 'You told 'er that, Delacy?'

Lydia laughed: 'No, he didn't Mr Brew. But he did tell me a lot of nice things about you, when we met your donkeys along the road. I'm so glad to meet you.' She went to him with hand outstretched. The famous squatter-baiter took it as in a dream.

Then she swung on the others, with hand out: 'I'm glad to meet you all . . . please shake hands.' She had to insist to move them. Each took the hand as if it were porcelain.

'My shout,' said Jeremy, turning to the bar counter. 'Come on, everybody!'

Everybody had warmish beer, including Lydia, but excluding Jeremy, who had the usual brandy. He called another round. Billy Brew, recovered now, and even looking perky, declared that the next was his. Lydia said, 'Then mine.'

'Can't 'ave a lady buyin' drinks,' said Billy, 'Specially a titled one.'

Jeremy said, 'What about all the dough her old man's done you for?'

'Wasn't 'er ol' man . . . was them lousy managers of 'is.'

At her insistence eventually they let her shout, wherewith, she went onto brandy with Jeremy. 'Bung-ho!' she cried as she tossed it off. Everybody laughed.

They drank again. Jeremy loaded Lydia's glass, watched sharply by Colleen. Billy Brew called for rum as well as beer, using the beer to chase it. Billy waxed bold, declaring his feuding with Vaisey managers. Jeremy said, 'Tell us the yarn about Delhunty and the donkey in the bed, Billy.'

The old fellow protested: 'Eh look out! That ain't for the ears of a lady.'

'She isn't a lady, Billy . . . she's more than that. She's really a duchess.'

Old Billy's beard gaped wide: ''S a fact, Missus, you're a dutch-ess?'

Lydia, catching a slight wink from Jeremy, answered, 'Something like that, Billy.' Her voice was slurring.

'An' I shook 'an's 't a dutch-ess!'

'Tell her the yarn,' Jeremy insisted.

Colleen tried to interfere, muttering about no dirty yarns. But Jeremy kept insisting: 'It isn't dirty . . . only funny. Tell it, Billy.'

'Yesh . . . tell't Billy,' cried Lydia.

'Well . . .' mumbled Billy, tearing at his beard in embarrassment ' . . . . if Yo' Dutch-ess-ship insists . . . well, there was this ba . . . er, Vaisey's manager Delhunty, o' Lake Leichhardt Downs . . . .'

It seemed that in the course of clashing with Billy over the intrusion of the donkeys into the sacred precincts of his homestead, Mr Delhunty had declared, 'One o' these nights I'll be goin' to me bed to find one o' your bloody hairy canaries asleep in it.' That had set Billy thinking. So next time a donkey died on him, he removed the hide from its head and stuffed it. But how to get it into the Big House at Leichhardt? Impossible. Ah, but something better offered. Mr Delhunty had a fancy piece amongst the yeller girls working there and housed her so that he could conveniently sneak out to her of nights when his wife happened to be away visiting. Billy camped on Leichhardt Creek against the day, having bribed the girl to co-operate, with finery for the next races such as Delhunty would never give her. So it was that one dark night Mr Delhunty came *tchinekin*, as they say, and with his flashlight found exactly what he'd predicted – and what's more, a donkey *snoring* in the bed he considered his, Billy himself being under the bed – and more again, one that let out a terrific hee-hawing as the gentleman went galloping for home.'

Lydia laughed till she wept. Jeremy had a brandy ready for her that nearly choked her with its potency; but she downed it like the donkey teamster his rum.

Jeremy said to Billy, 'What about Piggy Trotters' mare?'

Billy, getting drunk himself, roared with laughter: 'Ha, ha, ha! Piggy Trotters' mare . . . ho, ho, ho!'

'That'll do for yarns,' said Colleen, but without strength. She turned to her husband, who merely shrugged.

Jeremy said, 'If you call a yarn about horses dirty, you shouldn't be living in the bush. The lady's a horsewoman, too . . . .'

''Orsewoman, are yo', Dutch-ess, m'dear?' cried Billy. 'Good on yo'!'

There was a chorus of good-on-yous. They had a drink on the strength of it. Now Lydia was holding the bar up somewhat, standing with her back to it, jodhpured legs and elastic sides well apart for better support.

Billy wiped his beard clear of the dark stain of rum and froth of beer, proceeded to tell how he'd got even with Piggy Trotters for a certain meanness done him, by taking a hand in a bit of horse-breeding Piggy was essaying in his striving after the Beatrice Cup: 'He's got this mare, Belmont Belle. She's good. She cost him a whole heap o' dough. She's got speed . . . but no stamina. He reckons she'll get that speed combined with stamina through puttin' her to a Lily Lagoons 'orse. There was a good 'orse, Magnet, son of that wonder 'orse of Jeremy's 'ere, Elektron. Magnet was a Vaisey sire. Piggy borrees him when his lady mare comes in her time.' Billy paused, then said to Lydia, 'Bein' a laidy, Dutch-ess, you wouldn't know nothin' 'bout Bromide, would yo'?'

Jeremy explained to her, 'It's used as an anaphrodisiac for males.'

Lydia nodded, repeating the medical term with care and a giggle.

'Wha' you call it?' Billy demanded.

'Get on with the yarn.'

'Not under the stockwhip, I don't mate!'

'All right . . . it's the polite way to say it puts a male off his oats.'

Billy guffawed: 'That's a good 'un. Write it down fo' me. That's what I want . . . a lot o' polite ways o' tellin' me yarns, so's to beat Colleen 'ere.' Colleen scowled at him.

Billy resumed: 'Well, Dutch-ess, I got 'o use this Bromide stuff a lot, yo' see, wit' all them Jack donks o' mine, which can be a fo . . . a flamin' nuisance when they're ruttin'. Now, me luck's dead in to get even with Piggy. I'm camped on the Alice when they bring Magnet in and put him in a paddock near by to rest him 'cause he's come a long way. He's got a trough there to drink out o'. I sneaks in and Bromide's his trough. Next day they puts the mare in with him. She's all for it. But poor ol' Magnet . . . he don't even try. They think he's still tired. But they leave the mare in with him, 'cause she's that mad she's workin' on him. As soon's it's dark I opens the fence and lets in me ol' Jack donkey, Walloper. He fixes her right away. That's the nice thing about animals. They ain't fussy like humans when it comes to doin' what comes natural.' Billy cocked an eye at Colleen and got another scowl. Lydia could scarcely contain her giggling.

Billy went on: 'Course I had me ol' Jack out o' there toot sweet, and drained the trought, and run clean water in. Next day Magnet's feeling better. He's got over the what-y'-call-it, Alfie-daisy-oc, and does a bit o' stuff . . . and everybody's satisfied, includin' Piggy, and specially yours truly. Naturateivly, in due course, Piggy finds himself the proud owner of a promisin' little colt with a donkey tail and the Cross o' Calvary on his back . . . ho, ho, ha, ha, ha, wow!'

The place rocked with laughter. Even the grim faces behind the bar unstiffened a bit. Lydia, in tears, would have buried her face in Jeremy's breast, but evidently anticipating it, he sidestepped so that she landed on Billy, who embraced her, till he woke up to what he was doing. As Billy pushed her away, Jeremy said to him, 'Wait till Vaisey hears you've been playing around with his girl, too!'

Lydia reeled. Taking advantage of the general hilarity, Jeremy guided her to the door, at the same time signalling to Colleen with his brows. Colleen was out in the passage to meet them. Between them they supported her, all but helpless with laughter as well as the grog, to the room quite elaborately prepared for her next to the Currys' own quarters. Jeremy went to get her suitcase. When he returned he left it at the door, saying to Colleen, who was helping her undress, that they would be departing at daybreak and would require nothing but a cup of coffee, since he had food with him.

Back in the bar he found the crowd silent and subdued.

'Where is she?' demanded Billy Brew.

'She's gone to bed. She's pretty tired from a long day . . . and you leave her alone, you old Jack Donkey.'

There were a couple more rounds of drinks. But the fun had gone out of things. Within an hour Mick closed the bar. Jeremy went to the car and got his swag and found a room in the tin complex, a bare little box with a fly-wire door, a hinged shutter for a window, a bare iron bed, a chair, an old-fashioned washstand with enamel jug, basin, and po, standard hotel equipment of the land. He unrolled his swag, took out the clothes neatly wrapped in the middle, stripped to under-drawers, lay down, and was soon asleep.

Jeremy was up at first light, rousing the dogs as he went to shower under the tank that took its chalky tepid water from the big square railways tank, which in turn was supplied from a bore. There was light in the detached kitchen as he came back. He went there to find Colleen with the Primus burning and the kettle on. She replied to his greeting stiffly, and when he asked if she had called the lady, took a key from her apron pocket and handed it to him. He asked, 'What'd you lock her in for?'

'Well . . . those drunks . . . and her behaviour.'

Handing the key back, he said shortly, 'Won't she still be needing protection from us? It isn't daylight yet. Besides, you'll have to take her to the shower.'

Colleen scowled as she passed him. When he glanced at the bulge beneath her pinny as she passed him she scowled again. But when she came back with Lydia she was as pleasant as could be, with every second sentence: Your Ladyship. Evidently she had washed and ironed Her Ladyship's yellow silk blouse in the night and pressed the black jodhpurs, so fresh did the lady look. They had *café royal* with toast. Then farewelled by Colleen and several of her brood, they were off and away, into the copper-red morning.

The copper became brass. The blue lane they followed became a scarlet ribbon through eternal silver-grey, with the slender silver poles of the Overland Telegraph line to count the miles in leaping chains. Lydia babbled like a happy little girl about the fun of the night before. How glad she was to be away from the toadies, she declared. He looked at her a couple of times as if he might tell her that no ordinary woman traveller would have been so indulged, but did not want to spoil her fun.

The country they sped through was of hard red soil scattered with pebbles of purple ironstone and flat as concrete, grown with as many spiky antbeds as stunted trees so that it was a wonder either trees or termites managed to survive. No water, save at intervals a bore, a windmill either turning slowly or hanging inert in dead air, an earthen tank, a line of troughing, with sometimes a flock of bright birds drinking. Never an animal, nor a blade of grass within sight. Jeremy said that, being a stock route, it had long since been eaten to the roots by travelling stock and the roots eaten out by termites, but that a single shower of rain would miraculously bring it back to life again.

After an hour or so of running they stopped for breakfast at a bore. The heat smote them. The flies appeared from nowhere. He got her out a fly-veil under which to eat her sandwiches and drink her tea. 'What a country,' she remarked. 'The silence presses down on you.'

'Listen, and you'll hear things,' he said. 'Insects, birds . . . hear the telegraph line humming. It's probably alive with talk about us.'

Breakfast done, he went off into the scrub. She looked up to find him gone, stood rigid, staring. When he came back she said breathlessly, 'Please don't leave me like that again.'

'They don't put up public lavatories in these places. Don't you want to go yourself?'

'I couldn't go away there.'

'Go behind the tank.'

'Oh, no!'

'Well, I will.'

'No . . . don't go . . . don't go out of sight.'

He walked a little way along the trough.

She pulled her pants down, squatted, gave the parched earth a drink such as it never had before. She called Jeremy back while she was still buttoning up, standing boldly over the damp erosion, and smirked at his evident embarrassment. As they got back into the car she kissed his cheek, to his further embarrassment, and this time laughed at him.

They went on, to come at length to what he called Black Soil country, but which was really grey, and differed in carrying tufted bleached white grass and less antbeds. A gate. Stock now staring at them. He said they were on Ilfracombe, one of the Vaisey properties. She laughed at the name, asking had he seen the English beauty spot beside the sea it was named after. He said he hadn't, but added, 'The whole country's full of names like that, stations and towns . . . Stratfords, Avons, Northamptons, Southamptons, Ilfords, Guilfords, all so different from the originals you'd think those who named them were making a deliberate joke of the contrariness of it. But apparently it was nostalgia, prompted by fear of losing identity if they'd called it what the blacks did.' He said they wouldn't be stopping here, because the manager and his wife were still back at Beatrice, and the humbler white members of the staff had been in the Charlotte pub last night: 'There'll be only the Chinese cook there and the blacks.'

As they sped by the village of whitewashed buildings comprising the homestead a few blacks stood out to stare at them and wave back when they waved.

At the end of the Black Soil was York Waters Telegraph Station. The two telegraphists were out waiting, proving Jeremy's prediction that the land would be electrically buzzing with the news. They were two middle-aged men, much embarrassed by the call. Jeremy produced a bottle of O.P. rum, but only made things worse by increasing Lydia's attempting to be matey and hence the simpletons' fear of her. They were solemnly conducted over the station, shown the relay system. As they drove off again Jeremy directed the girl's attention to the blacks' camp of hovels of scraps of iron and flattened cans and the several yellow children amongst the naked youngsters: 'They neglected to introduce us to their families.'

They climbed what Jeremy called the Jump Up, a steep incline he described as being the beginning of the vast Inland Plateau. They stopped on top to alight and look back at the smoky blue infinity that stretched away hundreds of miles to the northern sea, and for Lydia to pee again while squatting smirking at the broad back in grey poplin turned to her.

They stopped for lunch beside a tree-lined waterhole white as milk. Lydia wanted to bathe in it, and would have, but for Jeremy's showing her that she would bog to the knees in mud and declaring quite definitely that he would do nothing to help her get the mud off. After lunch they rested a while under a shady coolibah. Somehow she got into his arms, to lie with her back against his breast, and eventually to pull his hands onto her own breasts and try to get him to kiss her. He kissed her hair, then heaved her off, saying they must be going, and went to the utility. She followed. She sat sulking as they went their way, then probably through boredom and too much brandy with lunch, curled up to him and fell asleep.

She woke when he stopped to open a gate. They were at Mount Prince Albert, he told her, an independent station where they would spend the night. She declared that she wanted to spend the night in the open like a real Overlander, even if she had to roll up in a bit of canvas. He said, 'No fear . . . not with your name on every lip along the route!'

She cried, 'What sort of bloody country is it where a woman's watched even out in the middle of the wilderness?'

'Did you know you were locked in your room last night, so none of us could get at you?'

'What? Oh, the narrow-minded Colonial bastards!' Then she added, 'All of you!'

He only shrugged, and drove her up to the little whitewashed bungalow standing amidst a tumble of red rock grown with spiky spinifex and reeking of goats. A wire ran up to it from the OTL. Awaiting them on the stone steps leading up to the front verandah were a couple who might have been taken for halfcastes, so age-withered and weatherbeaten were they, but for the glint of faded blue peeping out of squinting eyelids and false teeth gleaming in fixed sycophantic grins and their rig-outs of squatter's finery and the fact that no Aborigines of any breed had as yet stood out before any sort of homestead as obvious lords of it.

Jeremy drew up so that the steps were on his side. He merely nodded to the dolled-up ancients, and leaving the engine running, alighted quickly and went round to help Lydia out. As he brought her round, the pair, now at the bottom step, ducked and chuckled like a couple of English yokels. He addressed them shortly: ''Day, Ned . . .'Day, Missus . . . Well, here she is, Lady Lindbrooke-Esk, Lord Vaisey's intended. Your Ladyship, Mr and Mrs Knowles.'

Rather red and with her smile rather thin, Lydia gave the white hand, saying, 'How'd'y'do?' The Knowleses bobbed and babbled.

Jeremy made no attempt to join in the hand-shaking, but turned and got Lydia's case from the back and placed it on the steps, saying, 'Well, she'll be all right with you for the night. I'll go and camp on the waterhole. See you in the morning, M'Lady.'

Lydia turned on him with face aflame and eyes blazing. But he was already in the car and not looking, and in a moment was moving off.

Jeremy had told her that Ned Knowles was a son of Nat Knowles, destroyer of Lu-lalla-goon and father to the lout who'd won the Golden Horseshoe Prize at the Races. However, he hadn't confided what was more important, namely that he was himself the declared enemy of all Knowleses, considered by them to have robbed them of that Tantalite their ancestor had so conveniently dug and thrown away, on account of which they'd had him to court and, failing to get a verdict against him legally, had sworn to settle matters someday with the gun. Nor had he told her that old Ned had been trying to sell his wretched property to Vaiseys ever since the great takeover of 1917, and certainly would try to involve her in the matter, as well as try to interest her in the million or so pounds' worth of gold he reckoned were in them there red rocks of which his holding largely consisted, but which had been so niggard in yield to himself, even with his sons' help, that he'd been unable to keep the louts at home.

All this she learnt for herself, as with acerbity she made known to Jeremy when, after being bowed down the steps next morning, she was driving away with him and he asked her how she had got along. She said to him, 'You must really hate me to play a trick on me like that.'

'It wasn't a trick, my dear. I told you how it was going to be.'

'Do you hate me?'

'Of course not.'

'Do you like me?'

'Quite a lot.'

'Then kiss me!'

His face darkened in a flush: 'What . . . and wreck the car amongst these goats and rocks!'

'Then stop the car.'

'And remember our first kiss whenever I run into the reek of goats?'

She laughed, snuggled up to him, saying, 'I do love you, don't y'know! I'd've come looking for you last night if I'd known where to find you.'

'I counted on that. Did you hear the dingoes howling?'

'Is that what the awful noise was?'

They ran on out of the barren ranges, down to a plain where the dust lay on the road in heaps like yellowed flour. They stopped at a bore for her to piddle within sight of him. When he came back with eyes averted, she laughed again, grabbed him and kissed him on the mouth, clinging till he was kissing her back. When they broke away panting, she was glowing, he burning, 'That's better,' she said, 'Let's do it again.'

But he broke away, looked round, muttering, 'What a hell of a place to make love in!' Some skinny cattle were staring from beyond the windmill.

Evidently annoyed, she cried, 'Where else is there in this God-forsaken country?'

'I told you before. This road only follows the OT Line, straight as a die wherever possible. When God . . . or Koonapippi . . . laid things out, it wasn't to suit the convenience of the like of us. Of course there're lovely places . . . even away in the deserts.'

'Take me to one.'

'All in good time. We have another call to make.'

'I don't want to make any more calls . . . I want to make love to you.'

He flamed and swallowed, said huskily, 'You heard old Finnucane ask me to take a letter to his son-in-law, Con Cullity.'

'Another pub?'

'Yes. We should get there about midday.'

'And then?'

'We'll have a few drinks. You might strike some more characters. They serve a gold-mining community back in the ranges.'

'And get locked in my room again?'

'Bridie Cullity wouldn't do a thing like that.'

They went on. It was near enough to noon when the narrow lane of road and telegraph line suddenly expanded into a patch of waste, in which stood a small whitewashed bungalow, with detached kitchen behind and the line of tin cabins and isolated privies that declared it for what it must be in those parts, a hotel. To Lydia's surprised inquiry as they approached – 'How came a hotel to stand so isolated?' – Jeremy replied that old Shame-on-us, the owner, had declared that whereas the thirst of the miners of the goldfield some twenty miles to westward would drive them to the place in any case and the distance keep them longer at the bar than had it been closer, passers by, of whom there could be many during the droving season, were far more likely to quench theirs at the bore beside which the place stood than travel forty miles out of their way. The only signs of life, if indeed these could be called such when they showed no hint of movement, were a huddle of blacks under a bough shelter by the bore tank, a line of kites perched on the trough, a small flock of staring goats.

'My God . . . what a place!' muttered Lydia.

'You said you wanted to see the Inland.'

There was no one on the verandah of the hotel, bare except for a couple of cane chairs and a bench beneath a window inscribed BAR. The chairs stood on either side of a gaping doorway that gave a glimpse through a hallway of the kitchen out in the backyard. Next to the bar window was another gaping door. Above the verandah was a sign: PROSPECTOR'S ALMS, the L having been roughly substituted for the still visible original R. Nor was there sound of life. As Jeremy drew up before the place and cut the motor, into the silence swept the hum of the telegraph line.

They alighted, crossed to the verandah, stepped onto it, headed with resounding steps for the bar door. Behind the bar, like dummy figures, staring, were the Cullitys, plump pretty Bridie, rangy ruddy ginger Con. Jeremy hailed them. They answered flatly, 'Goodday, Jeremy.'

Grinning, he said, 'Well, I guess we haven't taken you by surprise . . . unless your phone's out of order . . .'

Bridie cut in, so sharp of tone that Jeremy's eyes widened in surprise: 'No, our phone's all right . . . but we certainly were surprised . . . *at you*!' Her plump cheeks were flaming now, her dark eyes wide with anger.

Jeremy looked at Con, also redder, but stony-faced as before, and rocking on his heels and staring outside. He opened his mouth to speak; but Bridie got in first, asking, in a barmaid's voice, 'What'll you have?'

At a loss, Jeremy said, 'Well . . . of all people, I thought you knew my poison.'

She looked past him at the wide-eyed staring Lydia: 'Your Ladyship?'

Jeremy answered, shortly now, 'Don't bung it on, Bridie! Her name's Lydia . . . and she drinks the same as me . . . and you. So three double brandies . . . and Con a whisky, eh?' He took money from his pocket.

Con said to the outside world, ' 'Tis on the house.' Then he swung away to get glasses and bottles from the towel-covered shelves behind.

Bridie, bending over the Icy Ball, said, 'If you'll go along to the parlour it'll be brought to you.'

Jeremy snapped, 'We'll have it here, thanks.' With a touch to Lydia's elbow he urged her towards the bar counter. Then as Bridie set soda bottles down on the counter rather heavily, he asked her, 'What's the cool reception in aid of?'

Whipping the tops off the sodas Bridie asked, 'What'd you expect . . . the red carpet?'

Again at a loss, Jeremy fished in his shirt pocket: 'Brought you a letter, Con.'

Con glanced at it as Jeremy set it down on the counter, grunting, 'Ahhgh!'

Bridie said, 'Help yourselves to soda,' and attended to her own glass, then said, again in the barmaid's voice, 'Here's luck!'

She swigged hers off, as did Con, while the others sipped. Then Bridie said, 'Well, if you'll excuse me . . . I'm getting our dinner.' She turned to the flap that would let her out into the hall, sweeping the couple a dark glance as she did so.

Jeremy said quickly, 'We were hoping to dine with you.'

Bridie swung round as she lifted the flap. 'What . . . on goat?'

'Goat's just what we wanted.'

The black eyes shot from one to the other. The red mouth buttoned tight. Down came the flap – *Bang*! Bridie vanished.

Jeremy drained his glass, put it back on the counter, asked, 'What's the matter with her, Con, boy?'

Con, proceeding to fill the glasses again, eyes down, said, 'Ahhh . . . all this rarin' and tearin' to get back home.'

'When'd you get back?'

'Yesterday noonin'.'

'That's travelling, man, on that road.'

'You got to travel wit' the divil behoint ye.'

'Meaning old Shame-on-us?'

'Mainin' none but the same, Jeremy . . . and here's luck to you, and bad cess to the wan as mintioned!'

They drank again.

Jeremy said, 'I must go and put things right with her other ladyship. I'll leave you to look after this one.' He turned to Lydia, who shot him a questioning glance: 'Excuse me, m'dear.' Then he whipped out to the verandah, into the hall.

'Arrah!' cried Con. 'Two ladyships in the house . . . ha! ha!'

Jeremy strode through the hall and out by the gangway leading to the detached kitchen. Bridie was at the range as he opened the fly-door. She cast him a look out of the corner of an eye and bent to the oven, opened it. He said, 'Smells good.' Ignoring him, she turned to get a cloth. He grabbed it before her, saying, 'Let me,' and bent and took the sizzling dish out and set it on top of the range. There were two haunches of kid, surrounded by browned sweet potatoes and pumpkin. 'Hmmm!' he said. 'Must have some of that.'

Still ignoring him, she went to a cupboard for dishes. He asked, 'What's wrong, sweetheart?'

She blazed at him. 'Don't call me sweetheart!'

'But I always have.'

'Well don't do it any more.' She clattered the dishes down on the big table, snatched open a drawer.

'If it has to do with the lady inside . . . .'

'You know very well it has.'

'She isn't the grand duchess I've been kidding everybody she is. She wants people to forget she's titled.'

Busy with implements and utensils, Bridie said flatly, 'Well, I'm not going to forget it, see!'

'Why?'

She swung on him blazing: 'Because she's making a bloody fool of *you*!'

Going very red, he stared at her. She held his stare, after a moment demanding, 'Well isn't she?'

'In the telephone conversations didn't anyone tell you how she forced herself on to me?'

Bridie laughed, the high harsh laugh of an angry woman: 'Twisted your arm for you, didn't she?' As he went beetroot red, she went on: 'You walked her home from the races Cup Day. You were with her on the course the next day. Next day you took her out to Lily Lagoons ... *and she's been with you ever since!*'

He sighed: 'You can ask your old man exactly what happened. What could I do but give her a lift?'

'You could've been the man you've always been before with Vaiseys.'

'What's Vaiseys got to do with it?'

'Everything, surely!'

'She's broken off her engagement to Vaisey.'

'She tell you that?'

'Yes.'

'And you believed her!'

'Why not? It seemed genuine enough.'

'For godsake!' panted Bridie, rushing to get the smoking meat. As she came back and slammed the dish on the table, she said, 'I could see it in your face as you came in from the car ... that goofy look of a man who's done his balls on a woman completely.'

He swallowed: 'Well ... I've never heard you talk like that before.'

'I never thought .... .' her voice quavered 'I never ever thought I'd have to speak like that of Jeremy Delacy.' She broke off, choking.

He stood at a loss, watching her quivering face. At length he murmured, 'Do you really want us to go?'

She looked at him through tears, blinked them back, bit trembling lip to stiffness, then muttered, 'D'you think I could sit up and eat and drink with someone I knew was ruining the life of my best friend?'

'Ruining my life?'

'What else? Haven't you given your life to fighting Vaiseys?'

'Well ... hardly that. But I still feel the same about 'em as I ever did ... and always will.'

'After Lord Vaisey's girlfriend has seduced you ... with his blessing?'

'Seduced my foot!'

'It isn't your foot she's concerned with. Look at me and tell me you're not in love with her!'

He was very red, but smiling, as he looked at her: 'Not guilty!'

She stared at him hard, said after a moment, 'She's been playing around with you, though.'

'She's a girl who's used to playing around with men, I suppose ... but so long as I don't play around with her.'

Still staring, she went on: 'I don't trust you with her. Where were you going from here?'

'Boulder Creek. I've been putting her up somewhere every night. I'll continue to do so.'

'Why couldn't you put her up here?'

'That's a good one, after saying you wouldn't eat or drink with her .... '

'Do you think I'm going to sneak to a skinny Pommy bitch with a title?'

'I've told you she doesn't like people sneaking to her. Why don't you see for yourself by asking us for dinner ... and see how much I've been seduced by Vaiseys, into the bargain?'

She eyed him long and earnestly. He held the gaze of the big black eyes.

Her expression was changing. What had been hard lines of anger and suspicion softened to something else: excitement, eagerness. Her colour rose. Her eyes glowed. At length she swallowed, and said breathlessly, 'Yes . . . all right . . . but not just for dinner . . . for the night.'

He grimaced: 'I'll have to ask her, of course.'

Anger flared in the black eyes again: 'Ask her?'

'Well, you haven't been very nice about it, have you?'

'If you're not going to stop the night . . . . '

'I am . . . but it'll have to be done discreetly. We start by staying to dinner. You ask her . . . . '

'Me ask her?'

'Well, you're the hostess . . . Look, I'll go back to the bar and say something about a lovely roast . . . how lovely roast kid is . . . especially this one. Then you come back . . . and be nice. We'll have another drink. Then you ask us . . . eh?'

Bridie blinked on it for a moment, then said, 'All right.'

'Okay . . . I'll be getting back to the bar.'

As he went out, Bridie drew a deep breath, and exhaling it, still staring after his dim figure to be seen going up the passage through the fly-wire, said, 'Yes!'

Lydia, smiling from something Con had been telling her, eyed Jeremy intently as he entered the bar. Con also shot him a sharp look. He said, 'Everything's in order now. How about another gargle, Con?' As Con hastened to comply, Jeremy turned to Lydia: 'A bit bothered about the lady-business, that's all. One of my pupils in anti-toadyism . . . and anti-Vaiseyism.'

'One of your pupils?' Lydia asked dryly.

'One of my first. I've known her all her life.'

Lydia was staring hard, but Jeremy meeting the stare frankly. 'Have a drink,' he said, handing her a brandy and soda. 'Cheers!' he said. Having drunk, he said to Con, 'That's a lovely bit of venison she's cooked.'

Con cried, 'She's a queen of cooks, is me darlint Bridie. The wonder is I ain't loike Piggy Trotters himself.'

'Venison?' asked Lydia.

'Local name for goat-meat.' explained Jeremy. 'I suppose you've eaten it . . . goat . . . you must've, travelling around the way you have.'

'Oh, I love it . . . roast kid . . . the way the Arabs do it. When I was with my father in Palestine . . . . '

But there was Bridie, in a bright new dress and wearing a brighter smile, coming through the flap, and saying, 'How many drinks am I behind?'

Con leapt to pour her a brandy and soda. 'Here's luck!' she said. She smiled over her bubbling glass at the watchful Lydia, who smiled back.

After a moment Jeremy said to Bridie, 'Lydia was just saying she likes kid goat.'

Black eyes and blue eyes flew to meet each other, clashed gently, as women's eyes do in combat, searched deeply, then called truce in another smile. 'Do you, really?' asked Bridie, and getting a pleasant nod, added, 'Would you like to have dinner with us?'

'Love to,' said Lydia.

Bridie turned quickly to Con: 'We've got to have something to drink with it. What've we cold, hock?'

Con whipped open the Icy Ball, pronounced: 'Sparklin' hock four bhottles.'

Bridie looked again at Lydia: 'Like hock?'

Lydia cried, 'Huhmmm . . . hock and venison . . . that's reahlly something!'

'The hock's my shout,' said Jeremy quickly.

'You're our guests,' protested Bridie.

'But if you charge it to yourselves you'll have to pay for it be the nip instead o' be the bhottle,' said Jeremy lapsing into the Irish.

Con cried, 'Ye heard about that did ye now?'

'Yes . . . Tom Toohey told me. But you tell us.'

'I'll be tellin' the woide wurruld, man. This here's the bill, I will be bound, because I made me departure wit'out it. The mean ould dog!' Con grabbed at the letter Jeremy had brought.

Bridie said, 'I'll have to go and lay the table.' She looked at Lydia.

Lydia smiled and asked, 'Mind if I come and help?'

'Thank you . . . but you'll be wanting to freshen up. I'll show you a room.

Bridie went out through the flap, to be joined in a moment by Lydia in the passage. 'It's terribly primitive, you'll find,' said Bridie. 'But that's the way you like it, Jerry says. That right?'

'Hhhhu.'

'Have another wan,' said Con to Jeremy, and pouring for him, spread the letter on the counter and read it. 'Oh, gawd!' he cried. 'Look at this!'

It was a single page, written in a large sprawling hand beginning by stating that Con was in arrears with his bar accounting to the tune of £63.14.0 and that no wages would be paid him until his books were balanced, and concluding: '*If you'd pay more attention to your marital duties like a true man, and less to sucking the whisky bottle like your Mam's titty, you'd be having the family it's your constant coronach that you haven't, and thereby conduct yourself with some of the dignity a man is entitled to expect in the husbands of his daughters.*'

'That ould Wexford Wolf!' howled Con. 'I cust the day I set oyes on him!'

Con was still babbling about Finnucane, and by the look of the whisky bottle he'd not so long ago freshly uncorked doing just what old Shame-on-us had accused him of, when Bridie came to call them to dinner. She shot a glance at the bottle. Then she picked up the letter, and flamed crimson, crumpling it in her hand. Con would have started off again; but she said shortly, 'Shut up, Con. Get the hock. And don't go talking about it to her. Everything's going nicely . . . and I want to keep it like that.'

Things did go nicely. Although they dined in the kitchen, the table was nicely laid, and the food as good as it smelt and looked. Con was a bit morose to start with, ignoring attempts by Lydia to get him to tell her more funny stories about the local prospectors he'd evidently been entertaining her with in the bar before. However, when Bridie took to telling the yarns, the story-teller in him got the better of the slighted man, rousing him to say, 'Arrah . . . let me tell the story prhoperly, now!' Thereupon things became even merry. They drank the other two bottles of hock, on the house, at Con's insistence and with his initial toast: 'To me bankruptcy at ten bob a nip!' He then told the story of how Finnucane had charged him for his own drinking, 'Be the nip, bedad . . . be the flamin' nip!' He would have quoted from the letter, too, only for a furious look that Bridie flung him.

But Con had sworn to tell the wurruld; and on making a trip later to the bar to get brandy and whisky to suppliment the vanished hock, and meeting Lydia, who'd gone out to pee beside the utility, he confided the libel levelled at him by Finnucane to her: ''Tis herself, poor darlint, can't have babies. Ahhh . . . if there was only a prhoper doctor in this benoighted land, and not just a gang o' Government quacks!' While this was going on, Bridie was confiding to Jeremy that what was in the letter was true, and that it looked as if Con would be doing what she called getting on it again.

The party went on till 3.30 p.m. when suddenly everybody was drunk, except Bridie, who had been taking it easy, and who suggested a lay-off, so that they might have another session in the night. She saw them all off to beds in the little iron boxes behind.

It was dark, or rather bright moonlight, when Bridie roused Lydia, calling gently into the ear peeping out of a tangle of pale hair on the pillow, 'Lydia . . . Lydia, dear . . . wakee, wakee, Lydee dear!'

A groan for first answer, then a heaving up of the yellow silk blouse and the pale face just a blur in the blaze coming in through the fly-door: 'Who's it . . . wazzer time?'

'Half-past six, dear. Like to get up and fresh-up a bit?'

Lydia dropped her bare white feet to the floor, and head to hands, groaning again.

Bridie said, 'You'll be right as pie with a hair of the dog. Just have a sluice and a pee . . . you'll find everything there on the wash-stand . . . then come along to the kitchen.'

Lydia stretched and yawned, asked, 'Wheah's Jeremy?'

'Listen!' From the next box came the sound of heavy snoring. Bridie said, 'The boys had another bash at it.'

'Why'n't you call me?'

'Thought you'd rather be in good form for a party tonight.'

'Party?'

'Well . . . another bit of a binge. I'll leave you to it.'

Freshed-up at length and wearing elastic sides again, Lydia came out of the room, to stand a while on the moonlit verandah, first staring at the bit of daylight still lingering in the west, then at the door from which the snoring issued. She went to the door, opened it, went in. Jeremy lay sprawled on the bed, his face dark against the pillow, his mouth slightly open. She spoke: 'Jeremy!' A snort. 'Jeremy . . . wake up!' A deeper snore. She laid a white hand on his shoulder, shook it. He groaned, snored again, louder than ever.

She stood for a moment, then shuddered, turned away, went out and to the kitchen, where a pressure lamp was burning brightly. 'Ah, there you are!' said Bridie. 'Sit down and drink this.'

'What is it?'

'No questions. I'm a barmaid . . . skilled in the art of resuscitation.'

Lydia sipped, warily at first, then with evident relief. It was a long lemony drink. 'Thanks,' she muttered.

'You'll be sparking in a minute.'

Bridie went out, to be heard soon inside the hotel shutting doors, When at length she returned she was carrying a handbag. 'Feeling better?' she asked.

'Fine.'

'Like something to eat?'

'No thanks.'

'Sorry I won't be able to leave you in here. I'll have to lock up everything . . . because of the blacks.'

'The blacks?'

'Yes . . . there's a mob of desert blacks camped back in the bush there . . . waiting for the miners to come in . . . to get booze off 'em. Knowing I wasn't here and the boys out to it, they'd help themselves . . . and then, God help us!'

Lydia stared with blue eyes wide: 'You're going away somewhere?'

'Yes . . . I have to go to Boulder Creek to get some things we need. Can't let Con go like he is. And most likely tomorrow we'll have some miners in. Sorry to leave you. You'd best stay in your room. Our own blacks can't be trusted. Well, I must be off. Won't be long. Only about three hours. The boys should be right again by then. Coming out to the car with me?' Bridie's face was flushed, her eyes shining, her actions quick and nervous. Lydia kept staring at her.

Bridie dowsed the light, shut the wooden door of the kitchen and locked it. They went round the hotel in shadow, with all the world elsewhere ablaze. Away to the West a mournful sound. Lydia looked towards it. 'Dingoes,' said Bridie. 'There're mobs round here . . . although it might be blacks. They use animal sounds as signals.'

They went to Jeremy's utility. Opening the door on the driving side, Bridie said, 'I'll fill her up in town for you.' She flopped into the seat. From staring at her, Lydia looked back at the still and silent hotel, all silver-white and jet. Bridie asked, rather breathlessly: 'You wouldn't like to come for the run, would you?'

Lydia hesitated, then muttered, 'All right,' and went round to the other side. Bridie reached to open the door for her. Her lips moved as she started up. Lydia asked, 'What'd you say?'

Bridie turned with a smile: 'I was just praying.'

'Praying . . . why?'

'Oh . . . safe, successful journey. Brought up religious.'

'Oh!'

The car was moving, gathering speed. In top gear and settled down, Bridie said, 'I suppose you went to some swell ladies' college. My school was only the little old convent in Palmeston.'

'No. I had governesses . . . and my grandfather taught me a lot.'

'Your grandfather's a Duke, isn't he?'

Lydia sighed: 'Yes.'

'Tell me about it?'

'About what?'

'Being a Duchess, and all that.'

'I'm not a Duchess . . . and I'd rather you told me about yourself.'

'What's to tell about poor me. Just a barmaid married to a barman . . . running a blood-house in the desert.'

'What's a blood-house?'

'Don't know exactly. Name for a bush pub. Where they suck men's blood, I suppose it means . . . rob 'em while they're drunk.'

Lydia looked at her: 'You wouldn't do anything like that?'

Bridie shrugged: 'You don't know me.'

'Jeremy likes you.'

Now Bridie glanced at the dim white face: 'What's that mean?'

'Well . . . he wouldn't like anyone unless there was something speical about them'.

Their eyes clung for an instant, causing the car to skid in bull-dust. Bridie concentrated on her driving. Lydia leaned back. They were silent for a long while, as the car sped on.

At length Lydia asked, 'How far is it to . . . this place you're going?'

'Boulder Creek? About fifty miles. It's a bit slow here, 'cause of the bull-dust . . . but the other side of the range is gravel, and you can make it up on there. Like to stop and pee or something?'

'Not yet.'

'I always stop for a pee on top of the range. So does everybody. Piss Ridge they call it. I suppose Jeremy told you about it.'

'No. Why should he?'

'Well . . . he's supposed to be showing you the country, isn't he?'

'He *is* showing me the country.'

'He naturally would. It's his first love . . . *Terra Australis*. I suppose he's talked about it all the time to you?'

'Not all the time.'

Another long silence, broken this time by Bridie: 'Jeremy once told me this . . . we were talking about love . . . he said: "A man's only happy when he's pursuing a mad idea or a bad woman!" '

Lydia was slow in asking: 'What's that supposed to mean?'

'What it says, I guess.'

'I mean . . . what's your telling me supposed to mean?'

'Oh, nothing. I just thought of it . . . 'cause we were talking about Jeremy and love.'

'We were talking about Jeremy and Australia, weren't we?'

'Well, that's the same thing to Jeremy. That's his mad idea, like.'

Another silence, till Bridie said, 'If it's right a man's happy only when he's pursuing a mad idea or a bad woman. . . a bad woman would be happy only pursuing a man with a mad idea, eh?'

Lydia replied, 'I'm afraid I'm not up to riddles at the moment.'

'Poor dear . . . all that brandy, and hock. We'll have a snort when we get up the hill. Jeremy's always got a bottle of brandy aboard.'

'You know a lot about him, don't you.'

'Known him all my life.'

After a moment Lydia asked, 'Do you love him?'

Bridie started visibly, but didn't turn, and when she answered it was with a shrug: 'What's the good of loving a man with a mad idea?'

'Perhaps it's men with mad ideas that women really do love.'

Bridie glanced then: 'You could be right at that.' After a while she added, 'But, of course, there's love and love, isn't there.'

'How'd'you mean?'

'Well . . . if a woman loved a man with a mad idea so's to help him with it, her love would be different from that of a woman who only wanted to take it off of him . . . Look, there's the ridge. See, it's like a wall. It's quite steep.'

Soon they were running in coarse gravelly stuff that caused Bridie to slow down. A couple of dark wallabies dashed into the light, which she dowsed to let them get away, remarking, 'Rock wallabies. What they live on here, God knows . . . no grass, no water.'

Then they were climbing the ridge. It took them up some three hundred feet, with engine roaring and fenders clangorous with the pounding of upflung stones. Neither spoke. At last they were on top, on a little stretch of flat, along which Bridie ran for a hundred yards or so before stopping. Moonlight revealed heaps of rock on either side. 'Pee,' she said, and alighted. Lydia did likewise. Bridie began to move away to the right. Lydia came hurrying round the car in pursuit of her. Bridie said, 'Better stay here. Pretty rough over these rocks. I'm only going to try my luck . . . What's the matter, you scared?' She stood, regarding Lydia for a moment, then said, 'Oh, this'll do. I can try my luck any time.' She hitched up her dress, pulled down her drawers, squatted, piddled voluminously as a mare. Lydia, longer on the job by reason of her outfit, was still at it when Bridie rose, and putting herself to rights, said, 'You showed no curiosity about why they call it Piss Ridge . . . but I'd better tell you, seeing no one else's likely to, and you're supposed to be getting to know the country.'

Lydia, up now, was staring at her. Bridie continued: 'This's a fairly new road. The old one was the camel pad following the OTL through bad sand over that way.' She nodded eastward. 'Well, when the motor vehicles started coming this way, there was a man named Noble, who got out here to have a pee . . . and what'd he see in the rock he pee'd on but gold. It started a bit of a rush. That's what led 'em to the gold over West there. They still find prospects here. So everybody pees here . . . hence the name . . . which they changed on the map to Pisgah.' She chuckled, adding, 'Aren't you interested to see if you've had any luck yourself?' When Lydia merely glanced at the dark patch she'd left, Bridie said, 'But a bit of gold wouldn't interest you, eh . . . with the Vaisey millions?'

Lydia looked up sharply. Bridie headed back to the car, but stopped short of it, to turn back to Lydia at her heels and say in a different voice, vibrant and somewhat breathless, 'Want to talk to Your Ladyship, before we go on . . . if we're going on.'

Lydia looked scared, but asked in a haughty tone, 'What is it you want with me?'

'To make a kind of bargain.'

Lydia swallowed: 'Is this some kind of trick?'

'No trick. You came of your own free will.'

'Well?'

'Well, you see . . . while you were snoring off with the boys . . . by the way, they didn't really have another session . . . I drugged 'em . . . . '

'You . . . . '

'Wait. While you were asleep I phoned through to the Boulder and arranged accommodation for you . . . best hotel, of course . . . not anything like so grand as you're used to . . . but they'll give you the red carpet treatment. Then I got onto the Post Office there and sent a wire for you to Lord Vaisey . . . .'

'How dare you!'

'Yes . . . it's a cheek, isn't it. But they're used to me sending wires for drunks. I said in the wire that you'd be waiting for him in his plane at Boulder Creek. That was the arrangement, I understand, that he was to pick you up somewhere when you'd finished with Jeremy, wasn't it? At least that's what they've been saying on the phone from Palmeston to the Centre since yesterday morning. And seeing that you've now finished with Jeremy . . . .'

'Who says I'm finished with him?'

'I do . . . now wait, listen. I've worked this all out carefully. Unless you agree to go quietly into that hotel and take the room I've booked for you, and stop there till your sugar-daddy comes to pick you up, you won't only be finished with Jeremy, but with everybody and everything . . . 'cause, lady, I'm going to leave you right here. Now, you haven't met anyone along the road, I mean travelling, in five hundred miles, have you? Shows you what this road's like this time of the year. Droving's finished. People from the Boulder don't go to the Beatrice Races. So your luck'd be dead in if anyone came along here within a week . . . and you'd be well and truly dead long before that. It's only twenty-five mile to the Boulder, or back to our place . . . but twenty-five mile's a long long walk for anyone not used to it, with no hat, no water, laughin'-side boots, and the murderous Sun . . . to say nothing of adders, dingoes, and wild blacks. You wouldn't do five mile before you lay down and perished, like so many who've tried to do it a lot better equipped than you. I'd have it on my soul. But it wouldn't be as bad as having on it the crime of letting you ruin that lovely man . . . .'

'What d'you mean ruin him?'

'Don't tell me you don't think everybody in the country, except the poor silly man himself, doesn't know what your game is?'

'My game . . . what game?'

'To get him in your clutches so's he won't be able to fight Vaiseys.'

Lydia's voice was strangled as she said, 'If you think that, you're mad . . . I love him!'

'Ahhh . . . don't give me that!' Bridie's breathlessness was quite gone.

Lydia was heaving for breath now: 'I do . . . I do! I never felt for any other man what I do for him.'

'That's no proof you love him. Anyway . . . do you agree to what I say?'

Lydia shrugged: 'Oh, I agree. But has it occurred to you that I can hire somebody to drive me straight back here?'

'You can try . . . but I doubt if you'll get anybody after what I told 'em.'

'What did you tell them?'

'It'll keep . . . but the chief thing is Lord Vaisey coming to pick you up.'

'I don't give a damn about Lord Vaisey. It's Jeremy Delacy I want.'

'And if you had him, what'd you do with him?'

'That's my business.' Lydia was haughty again.

'I'll bet it is. It wouldn't be his.'

'What d'you mean by that?'

'That bad woman with the good man with the mad idea.'

'He's as he is only because he's been disappointed in love.'

'You reckon?'

'I know. He told me his life story.'

'I've watched his life story being told since I was a baby. It didn't make me want to steal his ideals from him.'

'I don't want to steal anything from him. I want to *give* to him.'

'Like what?'

'A child, for a start. He's a natural aristocrat . . . . '

'Don't make me laugh!' Bridie actually giggled.

'You haven't any cause to laugh.'

'Haven't I? Shows you how much you understand Jeremy Delacy . . . him with a son an English duke or something . . . ha, ha, ha!' The mirth was genuine.

Lydia snapped, 'You couldn't have children by him at all!'

Bridie stiffened: 'Where'd you get that?'

'Your own husband told me.'

'My own husband?'

'Yes . . . I'm sorry to be cruel . . . but you've asked for it.'

Bridie stared at her for a moment, then said shortly, 'Go on . . . get in.'

As Lydia took her seat she said to Bridie starting up, 'You can't win, you know.'

'We'll see about that.' Bridie's lips were moving again.

Lydia sneered: 'Praying again? Praying to God to strike me or something?'

'Praying to the Virgin Mary for something you wouldn't understand.'

'Why wouldn't I understand . . . because I didn't go to school in a convent?'

'Just because you're what you are.'

Lydia shrugged. They were running on. From the southern edge of the ridge could be seen a faint glow on the horizon just under the low-hung Cross, which Bridie remarked on as being from the lights of the township of Boulder Creek. Lydia made no reply. Nor was there any exchange between them for the best part of half an hour, during which they sped, as Bridie had predicted, at a great bat, along a dead straight road of hard red gravel. The silence was broken as they were coming so close to the township that its glow had become individual pricks of light. Bridie, said, 'If you're thinking of rushing back to Jeremy and get the chance, which I very much doubt, you'll be wasting your time, because he'll be out to it for quite a while. If you're also thinking of ringing him up tomorrow, you can forget that, too, 'cause the phone'll be off the hook.'

Lydia answered now, calmly, 'Don't you realize the risk you've taken drugging us? What if I were to inform the police?'

'I didn't drug you, duckey . . . you just keeled over on your own. As for informing on me . . . it's old-established practice in these parts to drug drunks. It isn't called drugging, by the way, but knockin' 'em . . . giving them the knock-out-drops. We often have to do it to stop men from drinking themselves crazy . . . for their own sakes as much as our own.'

'And to rob them more easily too, eh what? You did mention robbing them, you know.'

'You mustn't forget, Your Ladyship, that we're the descendants of criminal types.'

'I was beginning to remember it, as a matter of fact.'

'I guess it was your mob made 'em criminals.'

'My mob?'

'Your bloomin' ancestors!' After a moment Bridie added, 'But don't be scared of 'em drugging and robbing you in the Boulder. The pub you're going to's run by a Greek. Now, they *do* know how to treat a lady, these Greeks. Ever since that royal princess of theirs married that English prince of yours . . . I forget their names . . . they've acted like they'd all married into the British Royal Family. No dinky-die Aussie boy would dream of marrying a Greek girl, of course. Must be different with the English. But then, a dinky-die Aussie'd think twice about marrying a Pommy, too . . . . '

'Didn't you?'

'He's Irish. It's only the English are Poms.'

Lydia said nothing. Now tin shacks in ragged gardens appeared beside the road. There were electric lights slung on wires across a main street wide enough to drove a fair-sized cattle station's whole year's turnoff through. A few shops, with windows barred to save them from reeling drunks. A few of the latter, and the little low-roofed iron blood-houses they'd come out of, places with names like *Imperial Hotel, Royal Arms, The Grand.* Then the most dignified structure of all, two-storied, with railed balcony above, and below not just a couple of scratched frosted windows painted with the word BAR, but a blaze of lighted fluted glass with blinds and curtains, bars labelled *Public, Private, Saloon,* and a wide doorway giving entrance to a hall carpeted in red and ornamented with ebony stands carved to represent black boys holding aloft brass bowls filled with artificial flowers – the *Princess Marina.*

As Bridie halted the car before the hallway, Lydia asked coldly, 'What was it you told them here about my coming?'

'I was just going to tell you for your own sake. I said the boys got on the booze, and you thought it no place for a lady to spend the night. They know what it's like when the miners get in there . . . and they're not to know there aren't any there now. They also know that Con gets on it pretty bad. You've got your name up large enough in these parts already, lady, for hooking onto Jeremy like you did. You'll do it altogether by asking to be driven back there . . . But here's your host.'

A plump and swarthy little man, surely dressed up for the occasion, in the black and starched-white of the true *maître d'hôtel*, was coming bouncing from the hall. Bridie got out, and saying, 'Hello, Nicko,' went to get Lydia's suitcase from the rear.

Nicko had Lydia's door open in a flash, and bent double as she stepped out. There was a sudden explosion of faces out of doors and windows behind him. Bridie handed the case to Nicko, who took it without looking at her. Then she said, 'The Duchess of Lyndhaven.'

Nicko bowed even lower, mumbling, 'Your Gryce!'

Bridie leapt back behind the wheel, slipped into gear, grinned at the blank-faced Lydia, calling, 'Cheeri-ho, old bean . . . pip, pip!' and shot away, laughing . . . but only to be crying within fifty yards. She pulled up before a store, sat dabbing her eyes, till a man roused her.

'Hello, Bride . . . where's your royal passenger? What, you been cryin'? Wha' wen' wrong?'

'Nothing wrong, Sam. Only sad to lose her. She was such a dear. Got the groceries ready? I'll go and get 'em while you fill the tank . . . and the drum in the back there, too.'

She got out of talking to inquisitive people in the shop first by going to the lavatory, and then by saying she was in a hurry to get back home. With the car loaded, she swung it round, heading for home, with just a glance at the Princess Marina Hotel as she passed on the other side. Then in no time she was out on the long red road again, and speeding so that the flying gravel roared in the fenders like ore in a ball-mill, and praying most of the time, by the moving of her lips, voicing the prayer at last as she came to the ridge again and began to climb it: 'Hail Bridie, full of Grace, the Lord is with thee. Blessed art thou among women at last, and blessed will be the fruit of thy womb. Holy Mary, Mother of God, pray for me now, and in my hour of conception . . . and forgive me my sin, if it is one . . . but I've got to do it, or my heart will die . . . Amen.'

At the top she halted where they had before, and got out, saying, 'Yes . . . I'll pee on top of where she did, for luck.'

Then on down the hill, with the Moon now well down the sky on her left and with tree-shadows making the dusty road still more hazardous to travel, but by no means reducing her speed. Twice she almost slewed the car right round, gasping, 'Mother of God!'

As she drew up to the Prospector's Alms her headlights revealed a figure seated in a cane chair on the verandah. It rose – a grey-haired man in pearl grey shirt and trousers. He came out to meet her as she stopped at the step. He opened the door for her. She didn't move, but staring at him, asked, 'Well?'

He countered quietly: 'Well what?'

'Aren't you going to ask me what I did?'

He regarded her for a moment, then said, 'I presume you didn't do anything cruel or mean.'

'I don't think so.'

'Right . . . forget it. But what about opening the joint and getting me a drink. I'm doing a perish.'

She came sliding out, and getting her feet on the ground, flung herself upon him, kissing him quickly on the mouth, then, still clinging, dropped her dark head on his breast. He held her lightly, murmuring, 'What's this in aid of?'

She didn't answer, but clung a little longer, then let go, reached for the handbag on the seat and asked him would he get the box of groceries from the back, and started towards the verandah. She opened up, the bar as well, and by the slanting moonlight in the hall got a bottle of brandy and a couple of soda waters, saying to Jeremy as he came into the hall, 'Let's go to the kitchen.'

Settled in the kitchen, over their first drink, she asked, 'When'd you wake?'

'When I heard you start the ute. But I was a bit too dopey to get up for a while. What'd you give me . . . Hexobarbitone?'

'Yes. I left you strong coffee in a Thermos to help you get over it quickly. Did you find it?'

'Yes . . . but I could've done with a hair of the dog as well.'

'You told me never to let Con have a drink too soon after it, or it'd knock him again.'

'That was for the long-acting stuff, Barbitone. But what's the idea of giving a man who wasn't really drunk knock-drops, and at the same time coffee to get over it quickly?'

She ignored the question, asked another, 'Are you hungry?'

'Starving.'

'I brought some fresh bread. We'll have venison sandwiches, with mustard, eh? And brandy . . . lashings of brandy.'

'What . . . are we going to have another party?'

She looked at him frankly: 'I hope so.' She had risen, was going to get the food. She paused beside him, pressed her belly against his arm, and stroked his wavy grey hair. Flushing, he looked up, saying, 'I did ask you what the show of affection was in aid of.'

'Well, you've lost your girlfriend . . . so I thought you'd like to . . . to replace what you've lost.'

He murmured, 'Lost, stolen, or strayed.'

She asked quickly, 'Are you sorry to lose her?'

'Not really. She was a bit of an embarrassment.'

'Oh, go on! You were just goofy about her when you arrived.'

'You imagined it.'

'I was watching.'

'For just that. Just because you'd heard who I was with. I've been through here with other females . . . and you didn't have to go and lose 'em.'

'I could have shot 'em, though!'

He chuckled. She bent and kissed his hair. Then she went to get the food. He sliced the meat, while she cut bread and buttered it. While they were eating and drinking she said, 'It's an awful long while since we were alone together . . . for more than a few minutes, I mean.'

He nodded. She said, 'I still feel the same about you.'

'You should have grown up in that time. What's it . . . sixteen years?'

'Yes. But you can't say now you're twice my age.'

'Pretty near it.'

'A long way off it. You'd have to be ten years older than you are. Besides, you were twice her age . . . and more!'

'What's that got to do with it?'

'You'd have gone to bed with *her*, wouldn't you?'

'You're speaking about a lady I know.'

'A high-class trollop, you mean!'

He shook his head as if sadly, but with a smile about his lips and in his grey eyes. They finished eating in silence. When she had cleared away, she came and poured more drinks and knelt beside him to drink hers, looking up at him with face burning, eyes aglow: 'You said that time I came into your room and tried to get into bed with you that you'd love to have me . . . only I was too young, and under my father's roof . . . Remember?'

'Could I ever forget?'

'I'm not too young now, Jeremy . . . and I'm not under my father's roof.'

'Try telling your old man this isn't his roof!'

'Be serious . . .' cause I'm being serious . . . more serious than ever in my life.'

He met the glowing black eyes. She went on: 'You saw the letter and you know it's true. Con only wants me when he's drunk . . . '

'Oh, go on! He adores you.'

'I mean he only wants to . . . to have it, when he's drunk. It's 'cause he's frightened . . . afraid he can't do it. So he gets himself rotten . . . and tries and tries . . . and's so drunk he thinks he does. It's my fault. I've always kidded him he does, to pacify him.'

He stared at her: 'You mean he's *never* done it?'

'No . . . he's managed it a couple of times . . . but always at the *wrong* time.'

'What d'you mean the wrong time?'

'Out of my fertile period.'

'What do you know about fertile periods?'

'Aren't I a good Catholic, with a little prayer-wheel thing to stop me going to hell for using contraceptives?'

'You're not sterile, then?'

'No. I've had myself examined. They said there's nothing to prevent me having babies.'

'Why did you ask me that time to give you something?'

She lowered her eyes: 'I . . I was really asking you to give me a baby, Jeremy.'

'Oh!' He blinked, swallowed.

She stroked his thigh, went on, murmuring, eyes still downcast, 'I'm at my fertile period now. I always get desperate when I am. Poor Con can feel it. He'll get drunk and try again, and . . . oh, it'll be just the same old thing. When I heard you were with *her* . . . up there at Beatrice, and then coming down here, I . . . I got so mad jealous . . . . '

He put his arm about her drooped shoulders. She straightened up quickly, seizing his fingers, squeezing them. She went on: 'I've often thought of doing it with another man . . . some fair man, so's Con wouldn't know. But it felt too sinful . . . even if it'd be good for Con, as I'm sure it would be . . . and might even cure him of his fear.' She paused, and looked at him earnestly: 'But it wouldn't be sinful with you, I'm sure . . . not with you, Jeremy.' She dropped her dark curly head again and shoved it against his belly, murmuring, ' 'Cause I love you . . . have always loved you.'

He bent and kissed her burning cheek. She raised her face quickly, seized his lips with her own, while he, with face as burning as hers, put both arms about her and drew at her drawing mouth.

They broke away panting. She drew back a little and looked at him, the strain gone from her face, laughter lighting it. She said softly, quickly, 'Let's go to the bedroom.'

He nodded, rose with her. She reached for the brandy bottle, saying, 'You'll want that.'

He took it from her, put it back on the table, said huskily, 'All I want is you, sweetheart.'

She flung herself into his arms.

The Moon went down. The kweeluks found a baby spirit wandering, danced around it in the starlight, calling, calling:' *Kweeluk . . . kweeluk . . . kweeluk-kweeluk . . . kweeeeeluk*!'

CHAPTER THREE

THE LILY LAGOONS household was in turmoil owing to the intrusion of Nelyerri Ah Loy in search of her son. Having forced Willy to divulge what he knew of the matter of Prindy's escapade, she had him and Darcy take her to the Plateau, where she spent a whole day calling the boy and forcing her reluctant companions to add their voices to hers, punctuating appeals with threats to his alleged abductor, till the voices of all gave out. The search extended from the point of Prindy's disappearance, up the escarpment, and round from Painted Caves to Snake Caves, although without looking into either of these *wahji* localities. Not a sound or a sign of those sought. Because Nell would not give up even after their voices had failed, it looked as if the hunt might go on into the night, the Moon being as it was and the sky clear. The Sun went down ruddy into Lord Vaisey's dust. The dust was flaming like a bushfire, when the first sound of the long hard day was heard – '*Mooboo*!' A single call to begin with, faint and far away in the waste of rock. They stopped to listen. Again – '*Mooboo*!' But now it came from the rim of the escarpment. It could be a pair of *goguls*, or mopokes, beginning their night rounds.

If it were *goguls* calling, there could be nothing sinister round about here, neither *moomboos*, nor such as they were familiar with, *koornungs*. Willy was explaining the significance of this, when there came another call from so close at hand as to make them start – '*Mooboo*!' Darcy whispered that mopokes are never to be found within calling distance in more than pairs. Then another call from another point. Another. Suddenly the purpling rocks all round were ringing – '*Mooboo, mooboo, mooboo, mooboo*!' Igulgul, that other old harrier of scary mortals, peering through the ragged bush, seemed to be laughing – '*Hoo, hoo, hoo, hoo, hoo*!'

The party fled to the glowing edge of the escarpment, soon found a place to descend, went crashing down in such haste as to rouse the roosting birds for half a mile around and scatter the rock-wallabies at their evening play. Down below, recovering her breath and a thread of her torn voice, Nell looked back up the wall and screeched, 'All right, you bloody ol' *koornung* bastard . . . I gitchim Targen Coon-Coon!'

Back at the homestead, Nell refused to take the dose of Barbitone with which Nanago had been keeping the peace of nights since Sunday, accusing her now of being party to the abduction and of giving her poison. Worn out with the howling and the threatening, Nanago took the dose herself – and so failed in the vigil she had kept the past two nights, with Nell sleeping with her in the Big House. She woke unusually late on Wednesday to find her charge gone. Sharp eyes soon discovered that Nelyerri had set out at picaninny daylight, which would be as early as she would have dared to venture forth alone, and that she was headed not back to the Plateau, but for Beatrice – to carry out her threat to get Sergeant Cahoon! Nanago ordered out the big truck, and along with Willy and Darcy, followed.

It was one thing to catch up with Nell, but quite another to catch her. She had got almost to the turnoff to the Rainbow Pool, when, evidently hearing them coming, she went bush. There was no sense in trying to follow her through the scrub. They dawdled down the road a bit, yelling to her to have sense, and back, and down again, but only to the annoyance of the cockatoos and butcher birds. They even offered to take her into the township, without getting a reply. They kept it up till noon, then decided to go on in and report the matter to the police as they themselves understood it.

The Police Station, like all other institutions of its kind in the land, was a dun-coloured wooden bungalow raised on stilts, the space beneath, partitioned, being for official use, that above, with verandahs latticed all round, the residence. It was fenced, with a tidy garden in front. Behind was the cell-block, looking like a row of privies. There were some sheds, and a tumbledown shack that was the tracker's residence.

Constable Stunke was in his office, doing what he would call 'paperwork,' the bane of all policemen's lives and perhaps the cause of his surly reception of his callers from Lily Lagoons, expressed by his keeping them a full hour before even acknowledging their presence and the scant attention he gave them subsequently. However, there was the fact that he still had Dinny Cahoon sick and sorry on his hands, and the prospect of having to suffer Dinny's sisters, Kit and Tess, due in on this afternoon's train and not due out before the train's return to Town on Friday. He grunted: 'If it's true that the old bugger promised your boss he'd bring the kid back, what're you wasting my time for?' He scarcely listened to what they said about Nelyerri's mad coming. He only grunted again: 'Nobody's seeing Sergeant Cahoon. Now get . . . I got work to do before the train comes in.'

As they left, Tracker Jinbul assailed them and tried to pump them, but without success. They went on to see the train come in.

The Cahoon sisters were an odd pair: Kit tall and gaunt like Dinny, and probably ginger in her day, Tess comparatively short and plump, with a bloated veiny face and popping eyes. But that they were alike in disposition was evident even before they alighted and were seen to be crazily gathering their luggage while squawking like a couple of wet hens. Part of their baggage was a case containing special foods and drugs for their darlint, who it would seem from their babbling they believed was down wit' the fever.

Straight after seeing the train in, Nanago and Darcy set out for home, taking Willy along in the hope of meeting Nell within reasonable distance. They came on Nell's tracks about eight miles out. Again they called, but without getting an answer. Willy dropped off, letting the others go on. After walking back about a mile he found her on the road again, ran to join her. Her greeting was: 'Don' you talk me, Chinee bastard!' She was soaked with sweat and smothered in flies and limping. Still she kept on at full belt. He fell in behind her, silent.

At last, there through the river trees were the white roofs of Beatrice homestead, lolly-pink in the sunset. She turned towards it, dropping down diagonally to the private causeway. It was no shorter to go that way than to keep straight on; but she may have wanted, in her misery, to get near that tardy lover of hers. Perhaps it was down on the grassy bank here where she stopped to drink and bathe her bruised feet and stand for a while looking wistfully about, that the tardy one first took her and in joy of it was conceived the cause of all this madness. They didn't go any nearer the Big House than would be proper for their kind, and were seen by no one at the station but the blacks in the camp, who came out to stare, perhaps wondering at the odd sight of an Aboriginal woman's walking in front of her man, not behind.

It was only a little more than a mile from Beatrice homestead to the township; yet by the time they had completed their journey, it was dark enough for lights to be shining in windows. The upstairs part of the Police Station was lit as for a party and as noisy with the claque of women's tongues. Nelyerri flung open the garden gate and marched boldly in. Willy stopped outside.

Nell's precipitousness took her only to the foot of the steep steps leading up to the front door of the residence. She stopped with a hand on a rail, staring up. She turned swiftly when a shadowy figure appeared from out the office section. A male Aboriginal voice, labial-nasal in tone, asked, 'Wha' nam' you want him?'

It was Jinbul. She stared at him for a moment, before answering, 'I talk Targen Coon-Coon.'

'Can't talk Targen. Him sick. Wha' you want?'

She turned away from him, began to ascend the stairs. He grabbed her arm. She flung off his hand, went bounding up, to yell through the open doorway, 'Targen Coon-Coon!'

The vocal din within fell silent. Jinbul was leaping up the stairs. As he grabbed her again, Nell screeched, 'Targen Coon-Coon!'

Thump of booted feet. There was Stunke, roaring, 'What the hell you think you're doing?'

Her breast was heaving, face jerking. She gasped, 'Wan' talk Targen . . . .'

'Sergeant Cahoon's sick.'

'Dat old blackfeller steal him my boy . . . . '

'I heard all about it's afternoon. Now get out!'

Her voice rose, ragged, 'Targen Coon-Coon!'

Stunke snapped at Jinbul, 'Chuck her out' and shut the door.

Jinbul locked her arm behind her, put a hand over her mouth when she screamed, knee'd her in the behind when she bit him, propelled her to the bottom. Still keeping his hold on her arm, but releasing her mouth, he demanded, 'Whaffor you want him Coon-Coon?'

She panted, 'Dat Cock-Eye Bob been steal him my lil boy . . . I want Targen gitchim.'

'Targen can't do nutching. I gitchim for you.'

'Le' me go!'

'Coon-Coon go long o' Town Friday. I stop behind run-him-up dat oldman.'

She swung her head to stare at him.

He leered: 'How much wages you pay me?'

'How much you want wages?'

'I want for puggim you.'

She caught her breath, but after a moment answered, 'All right. First-time you get him back my boy.'

'I want for puggim you now.'

'No-more . . . after . . . .'

Tightening his grip, he forced her towards the passage running under the house, hissing, 'Come on . . . in cell.'

She fought against him, panting protest, then as they emerged she yelled, 'Targen Coon-Coon!'

He clapped the hand over her mouth again: 'Shut up . . . I break bloody arm!'

She bit herself free, screamed, 'Targen . . . Targen!'

A white figure appeared on the rear stairway. A husky voice demanded, 'What's goin' on?'

Jinbul called up, 'I chuck him out, Boss . . . mek trouble.'

Nell wrenched away from him, swung to the foot of the stairs: 'He been wan' 'o puggim me, Targen!'

The husk rose to a hoarse roar as Cahoon, clad in pyjamas, came leaping down the stairs. Jinbul bolted. Nell flung herself on Cahoon's bony breast, sobbed her story, while he held her, ignoring the shrill protestations from his sisters at the head of the stairs – 'Bad gurrl . . . wicked gurrl . . . after all we done for her!'

Willy came. Cahoon passed Nell to him, saying, 'I'll go out and get him tomorrow. Take her home now, Willy. It's all right, little girl . . . it's all right . . . have him back in a couple o' days.'

Kit and Tess descended on their darlint, to drag him back to bed, protesting against his doing anything for that hussy. But he insisted: 'I got 'o go and find that boy . . . I got 'o . . . it's me duty!'

Thus it was that at Lily Lagoons, in mid-morning of Thursday, those watch-keepers, the crippled butcher birds, the parrots, the droop-winged falcon, came flapping their awkward way over the homestead sounding the warning of impending intrusion, and the timid groundlings peeped, and the indrawn whisper *dookyangana* swept through the place, rising to a little storm when it was seen who it was – *Coon-Coon*!

The yellow police utility rolled through the front gate. Sergeant Cahoon was driving, looking gaunter than ever, with green eyes shot with red. Nelyerri was beside him. In the back, identical in their disguise of dust till they alighted and shook themselves, were Willy and Jinbul. Cahoon drove straight past the Big House and through the grove of mangoes, leapt out, and with Jinbul on his heels, made a rush for the Aboriginal quarters. Finding no one there he wanted, he headed with stalking gait back towards the Big House. He paused at the annexe, to peer boldly through windows, went on his way.

He went to the back door of the Big House, rattled the fly-screen, called in that grating voice of his 'Annybody home?'

Nan was waiting. She opened the door, met the quizzing green eyes calmly. He said, 'Goodday.'

She responded shortly: 'Mullaka not home.'

The slit mouth twisted in a grin: 'I know. He's gone bush with Lady Whatsit. Likes a bit o' white stuff now'n'agin . . . eh?' He looked past her at the two blacks maids, called to them, 'You-two-feller . . . 'ere!'

They came to him with hanging heads. He demanded their names, which they gave in in-drawn whispers: Cocky, Nolly. He demanded of Nan: 'They properly signed up?' He was referring to the official system under which Aborigines were employed, which although far more breached than honoured, was useful when officialdom wished to cause embarrassment.

Nan answered calmly, although her plump brown cheeks betrayed a quiver, 'Everybody work here properly sign up, Sergeant.'

'Papers?'

'Lock up in Mullaka's office.'

He tried to batter down the brown eyes with his stare, but only made them blink. He said, 'I'm lookin' for a quarter-caste boy, Prindy Ah Loy, alleged to've been abducted. What d'you know about it?'

'Nutching.'

A moment more of staring, then he snapped, 'All right. I go look-about. This my base camp. Annything I want . . . tucker, men, horses, accommodation . . . I'm entitled to on requisition. You understand that?'

'Yas.'

'Bread and cooked beef for three men for two days . . . tea and sugar.' He turned away, headed back whence he had come.

He would not have Nelyerri in the expedition, silencing her protests by threatening to put her on the chain. Within an hour, he and Jinbul and Willy set out for the Plateau in the utility. After dinner at the Turtle Hole stockyard, they headed for the Snake Caves.

Perhaps Dinny was still suffering recovery from that alleged fever of his, since what with the negative report of the previous search-party and his own and Jinbul's knowledge of the wiliness of the quarry they were after, he could have expected small result. Certainly Bobwirridirridi had been here, judging by the fresh painting in the caves and tracks of someone with six-toed feet, the latter being a Snake Man's cipher. Not another trace of human going, but explainable as due to the use of a brush of a brushtail wallaby for erasure. The region abounded with these creatures. According to native lore, the brush of the *marmaroo*, called *bornji* in local lingo, had magic properties. Evidently Jinbul accepted this as fact, while not respecting it, believing the boasted magical powers of his master to be superior. Another matter according to lore that showed the futility of the endeavour was the nightly calling of mopokes that the locality was free of *wurruk* bijnitch. Nevertheless, Cahoon kept at it for four full days, half of it on grilled parrakeets and the baked seeds of *larrama*, the so-called native kapok, till he was looking as gaunt almost as that bloody old black bastard he constantly raged about. The brushtails only mocked them by leaping about their miserable camps of nights. You had to be a practising Snake Man to bag one of those. All the while poor Willy, worn out with unaccustomed exertion and fear of intrusion into places *wahji* to ordinary mortals, kept hinting that all they had to do, really, was to wait till Cock-Eye Bob brought the boy back, as he had promised Mullaka to do. But even in giving up on the fifth day, Cahoon paid no concession to Willy's Chinaman's good sense, only declaring that he was going back to Lily Lagoons to organize a full-scale expedition to trace that bloody old black bastard if need be to the sea.

II

Meanwhile the hunted ones had come almost in sight of the sea. Almost was enough to suit their purpose, namely, that the novice should see how their master, Tchamala, had begun the wondrous things they had sung of while following his ancient track back across this broken land which was one of the first of his negative creations:

Kunderak, kunderak
Tjeritjeru, widjijeru
Alga agula, Numeriji
Tjeritjeru, widjijeru
Alga agula
Tchamala, Tchamala, Tchamala.

The sea, *burrulka*, was revealed by magic, when Igulgul, mate of Tchamala, came climbing up the eastern sky, blown to the full. The Pookarakka sang of the mateship between these old ones dedicated to *wurruk bijnitch.* Igulgul had come into being as one of Koonapippi's creations, but had made himself a humbug by flouting of her laws regarding marriage, and been banished by her to the sky. In his vindictiveness he had cursed all the Ol'Goomun-Ol'Goomun's creatures with age and death, reserving for himself the power of resurrection at will:

Igulgul n'gir n'gir n'bulgin wahji
N'bulgin wahji, n'buljin wahji
N'gir, n'gir, n'gir.

The odd pair, Wise-one and Neophyte, painted from head to foot for ceremony, squatted in their high place at the top of the northern escarpment of the Plateau, looking out across the maritime swamplands. The sea was that glow caught by the bases of the far-off cloud-mountains. Serpentine reaches of it were to be seen, seeming, in the magic sheen from above, to wriggle towards the watchers like those pythons of Tchamala's, of which the Pookarakka sang, to the beat of his prentice's *minga-minga:*

Ba na burranji
Ba na burranji
Wallakawoo, wallakawoo
Ba na burranji
Tchamalaaaaaah!

The song told the story of Tchamala's first intrusion into Koonapippi's Eden. The Ol'Goomun-Ol'Goomun came out of the sea, carried on a white cloud, the spirits of which she made into *booroolooloogun*, the nutmeg pigeons. She created the *mukkinboro,* the banyan trees, with their figs for the pigeons to feed on and their leafy branches for roost. She went on inland, followed by her dog, Wanjin, who pissed on everything she made, till she hit him with her yam-stick. Thus were the rank swamps made. It was then that Tchamala came out of the sea. He came as the rainbow, and landing, peeled strips off himself to make his pythons. These he hung from the branches of the banyans to look like the aerial roots of the great trees, telling them to wait till night, then crawl up and gobble the roosting pigeons. What birds survived fled to the islands just off the coast (made by Koonapippi for the *kudjalinga*, the salt water turtles) and camped there in the jungles and made their nests, coming over to feed in the banyans only in daylight. But Tchamala had to look out for his snakes: so one night he got them to uproot the banyans and push them back through the swamps to the foot of the Plateau, which he himself had made in a rage against Koonapippi's paradise. The great trees were to be seen below there now, clinging like snakes to the rock. The winding reaches away there were the tracks the pythons left:

Ba na burranji
Ba na burranji
Kintijibil-kintibil
Tchamalaaaaah!

The pigeons could fly inland to feed by day, but not back and forth continuously to bring food to their nestlings, which began to die of hunger. Then old Googoowinji the Cormorant, created as boss of the swamps by the Ol'-Goomun, came to the rescue. He showed the pigeons how to stuff food in their gizzards as he did for feeding his young. Thus were the pythons outdone. Still, Tchamala made things hard for the *boorooloologun*. He created the South-East wind to blow them out of the country, which it did every time it came up at the end of the wet season, when the squabs were mature. But there was always Koonapippi's nor'wester to blow them back again with the rains. The trouble was that those that returned were the squabs of last season, which must be taught Googoowinji's trick all over again. This was done now by the people of the Cormorant Dreaming, who held a great coroborree here every year when the pigeons returned, and instructed them in song and dance. This happened immediately after the first storm of the season.

The Pookarakka told how the pigeons came from the sea in a great cloud that lined the horizon from end to end, black like a storm-cloud to begin with, paling, till white like the sea itself in a storm, it washed up here in the bayans. He sang:

Wallakawoo, wallakawoo
Alga agula
Boorooolooloogun
Wallakawoo, wallakawoooooo!

He said they must someday come back here in the Season and scare off the Pigeon People, who were deadly afraid of Snake Men. Meantime they would repaint the Snake Caves hereabout, and leave *tchineke* signs where the coroborree was held just to make the Boorooolooloogun nervous during their next ceremonial.

Prindy made up a song of his own about it, to the delight of his master:

Pigeon come, like o' cloud he come
Wallakawoo, wallakawoo

For tucker fig, dat banyan fig
Wallakawoo, wallakawoo
Tchineke man fright him, hoo-hoo-hoo
Wallakawoo, wallakawoo!

Old Bob cried out, '*Marana nunga dunaitji* . . . properly Song Man, *mekullikulli*!'

III

Jeremy arrived back at Lily Lagoons to find Sergeant Cahoon and Jinbul camped in his harness shed, and Nelyerri and Willy Ah Loy with relations in the Aboriginal quarters. Nanago reported that Cahoon, after returning from his futile expedition, had gone straight in to Beatrice, and had come back only yesterday, ignoring her. Jeremy reckoned that Dinny must have heard from the telephone gossips of his own impending return. He went to the shed. Dinny was sitting at a table improvised from fittings of the place, appearing to be busy with paperwork, from under which peeped catalogues. Jinbul stood beside him as if in ready attendance for pressing duty. Bunks had been made up on strip-hide shelves used for stowing harness. Jeremy entered, saying dryly, 'Made yourselves at home, I see.'

The green eyes met the grey in a hard stare. The grating voice replied, 'As much at home as the famous hospitality of Lily Lagoons offers annyone but fugitives from justice, thank you kindly.'

'I'm sure that if hospitality were offered you, Sergeant, much better accommodation would have been found you than this.'

'That's just what I mean. Offered no assistance in the execution of me duty, I've had to establish meself be requisition.'

'What exactly is this duty you're executing?'

'My duty as a police officer.'

'Be specific. What law has been broken that entitled you to intrude on my privacy?'

'A child has been abducted.'

'Balls!'

The green eyes blazed: 'I warn you against using insulting language to a police officer.'

'Balls again . . . and charge me for it.'

'If you're not careful, Delacy, I'll charge you with aidin' and abettin' the said abduction.'

'Why wasn't I charged by the District Police Officer, then? I was talking to him only a couple of hours back. He made no mention of abduction. He told me you were out here in a private capacity.'

'He's not concerned in the matter at all. I'm his superior officer.'

'It'd be interesting to hear what *your* superiors would have to say to that. We'll soon know, too . . . if you don't remove yourself from my property . . . because I'll get on the radio to your Superintendent and lay a charge against you for trespass.'

Cahoon rose, grating: 'I can lay a charge of actual abduction against you. You had no right to bring that boy out here in the first place.'

'He came of his own free will, to take part in a picnic, at the request of a distinguished visitor. His mother was supposed to come, too, but got lost by the wayside.'

'You're well aware that no Aboriginal person is allowed to go anywhere without the permission of a Protector. By transporting the boy without that permission, you've committed an offence under the Aboriginal Act.'

'Okay . . . charge me, and arrest me. You'll have to take the case to Town, because I'll fight it . . . and be glad to, to expose the Aboriginal Act in all its brutal stupidity. And won't your Bolshie mates of *The Palmeston Progressive* be glad to have a crack at you again . . . and especially Fay McFee!'

Obviously the lady's name hit Dinny hard, the way he blinked and buttoned his thin mouth. Fay McFee, leftish journalist and vituperative castigator of the social anomalies peculiar to these parts, had embarrassing connexions with powerful Southern newspapers eager for outlandish sensationalism.

Jeremy went on: 'Apart from exposing the rotten system you're part of, you'll make a fool of yourself by showing how you've wasted the time the taxpayer pays for by interfering in what amounts only to a blackfellow's walkabout . . . . '

The mouth unbuttoned to grate: 'Now listen to me, Delacy . . . . '

'You're listening to me, Dinny . . . or I go straight in and get on the radio to Bullco. I understand your tracker's been paying daily visits to the Plateau. You know old Bob made a bargain with me to bring the boy back, and that he won't show up while the police are hanging round. So will you just remove yourself and your Man Friday, and let things take their natural course?'

'I'll take no orders from you.'

'Suit yourself. I'll pass the word on to your boss, then. It's a pity. I understand your sisters are just living for the day they'll see their Dinny an inspector. That so?' The green eyes blinked. Jeremy turned to go, saying, 'I'm going to have a meal now. It'll take about an hour. The Flying Doctor schedule will be coming up just about then. Goodday.'

Jeremy had gone only a few yards when his attention was caught by a rush of bare feet behind and to the left. He looked to see Nelyerri rushing towards him. She came up panting, whimpering, 'You get him back my boy, Mullaka . . . my lil boy!'

Jeremy patted her arm, saying loudly, 'I get him back for you quick-feller, Nell, spone that-lot policeman go away.' As she turned to look at the glaring officers, he gave her a slight shove towards them, went on his way.

Jeremy was still at table with Nanago, when the police utility was seen through the dining-room windows, whizzing towards the front gate. He said, 'Poor old Dinny! Always does the wrong thing at the right time. I'll just have to see that I don't do the same. Better get going right out to see if they've turned up. I reckon the old fellow'd come back after the full Moon. But pack us about three days' tucker in case we have to wait. Better give me something extra for old Bob, too. He mightn't want to come in . . . and I must have a present for him.'

He set out for the Plateau in the utility, accompanied by Darcy, Nellyeri, and Willy. They stopped at the Turtle Hole to make camp, had just got the truck unloaded, when from the tumble of rock filling that deep bay in the red wall there, a call: *Ku*! It sounded as from about halfway in, say quarter of a mile. Jeremy answered. The voice again: 'Mullaka . . . you come yo'self-yo'self.' The wall echoed it all round: *Yo'self, yo'self*!

Jeremy took up the sugar-sack of stuff for Bobwirridirridi, set out northward. It was rough and tough going, over and under and round the great hot rocks, shoving through the tangled scrub. He kept on. After about fifteen minutes he must have reckoned he had covered the distance, the way he slowed down and looked about. But another call: *Ku*! It was away to westward, about the same distance off as the first, its source the very foot of the escarpment now. He sighed, mopped his steaming face, changed course. Another ten minutes: *Ku*! It was close, but to the left now, southward. He stopped, stared that way, groaned: 'Lord, what game is the old bugger playing?' He answered the call, but spelled for a couple of minutes before heading as directed. Five minutes now: *Ku*! Again to the left, and as far-off-sounding as the first and second calls. 'For godsake!' he muttered. The new heading would take him back whence he had come. He stood a minute, mopping, muttering, 'Trying to show me how clever he is, I suppose.' He answered, went on. But after only twenty yards or so, hearing a rattle of falling stones behind, he swung round, to see standing on a rock above him a skeleton figure, accoutred in *bulkung* belt and ochre. The death's head with its top-knot split in a grin at Jeremy's evident surprise. A cackled greeting: 'Goottay, Mullaka!'

Jeremy looked further. No one else in sight. He looked back to find the skeleton vanished. Then here it was beside him, grinning impishly, a claw extended. Jeremy took the claw, asked, 'Where boy?'

The top-knotted head was canted to the sky. The cackle: 'Too hot. Close-up rain.'

Jeremy swallowed. The red coals fixed him: 'You been walkabout lo-ong way long o' motor-car, eh Mullaka?'

Jeremy breathed, '*Yu-ai*.'

The coals fixed on the sack. Jeremy said, 'Present for you.'

'Ah!'

Jeremy handed it over. A claw groped in it, came out with a bottle of brandy. 'Ah!' The sack was set down. The cork was pulled from the bottle. The wide nostrils of the pierced and whitened nose dilated in sniffing. The turkey-throat convulsed. The bottle was upturned. 'Ah . . . properly!' The bottle was handed to Jeremy, who took a swig, gave it back. Up with the bottle again. Then: 'Properly goot-feller dat one plendy . . . ah!' It was stowed away in the sack again, the sack slung over a skinny shoulder. The claw was extended again. Jeremy took it in surprise. 'Me go now, Mullaka.'

'Eh?' Jeremy gaped. 'What about the boy?'

'Him all right.'

'Ain't you comin' to my place?'

'By'n'by.'

'But you promised . . . . '

'By'n'by break him in dat young-feller.'

'Eh . . . but he's too young!'

'*Kirrikijirrit* . . . you savvy.'

Jeremy nodded. A *kirrikijirrit* initiation was a limited form for boys not yet of the age of puberty but considered to have too much knowledge of secret business to be permitted the utterly undisciplined life of children. It was named from the Willy wagtail, who was supposed to advise the *Kudijingera*, or Tribal Elders, in such matters.

Obviously at a loss as he stared into the surely mocking face, Jeremy muttered, 'Too much trouble I been catch him from you take away boy.'

The eyes looked past him, in the direction of the Turtle Hole. A claw came up to the mouth. The call was ear-piercing: '*Hoo-hoo-hoo*!'

A moment. It came back, from about the distance the hole was away: '*Hoo-hoo-hoo*! Jeremy turned to it. He looked back. He was alone. He stared. Not a sign. Not a sound. He sighed heavily, shook his head, turned about again, went heading towards that last call, but not without looking back several times.

Prindy was at the Turtle Hole, dressed in the khakis in which Jeremy last had seen him, the clothes badly rumpled from having been stowed somewhere and with traces of ochre still on fair hair and face. He was eating bread and beef, being cut by his mother who was still sniffling and wet-cheeked from what evidently had been, for her at any rate, an emotional reunion. Willy and Darcy squatted a little distance away, aloof from the pair, it seemed, even embarrassed, the way they rose in haste to meet Jeremy. Jeremy was the only one to speak, addressing Prindy: 'Well, young feller . . . have a good walkabout?' The grey eyes looking over a huge sandwich did not even blink. For a moment grey eyes held grey eyes. Then, murmuring, 'Hmm!' Jeremy turned to the men and said, 'Better load up again, eh?'

Nelyerri would have shoved Prindy up in the back of the utility, only Jeremy pushed them both in front. They obeyed in silence. As they drove off, Jeremy said to the boy beside him, 'By'n'by you got to learn to drive motor car.' The grey eyes met his. 'You like that?' No answer . Jeremy asked, 'What name . . . you *koynainjil*?' The term meant under ban of silence, not infrequently imposed for various reasons by native custom.

Prindy answered promptly, 'No-more.'

'Hmm!' was Jeremy's comment again, turning to the road with mouth pursed and brows rumpled, as if contemplating the propriety of the situation: Someone returns from having supped with the Devil – how do you receive him? It must be embarrassing if you truly believe in *dibble* bijnitch. Here was the mother, so happy to have her son back, now scowling, the men in the back blank-faced. Jeremy said, 'I reckon we'll go straight back to Catfish, eh?' No answer. He added, 'We'll stop at the lagoons and get some geese. How are you on goose hunt, sonny?' Prindy smiled.

They turned eastward at the crossroads. As they sped on their way, Jeremy asked, 'You know that yarn about Old Crocodile been pull him down that goose, Nuttagul, Dream Time?' The boy nodded. 'All right . . . you tell-him-'bout.'

Prindy shook his head: 'Can't do it.'

'Wha' name?'

'That-one yarn no-more belong o' me.'

'I see. All right . . . tell-him 'bout one yarn belong o' you.'

But Prindy was silent. Thus they ran on to the mine and the lagoons.

The native camp there was deserted. They drew up at the site. Prindy and Darcy stripped for the hunt, gathered rushes, strung them into mats a couple of feet long, shaped them into barrels, which they slipped over head and shoulders. Thus accoutred, bearing no weapons but their hands, they entered the water, made their way imperceptibly out to the busy noisy flotilla of birds. The method of slaughter was to float amongst the birds as part of the mass of vegetation everywhere, pull them down and strangle them without a squawk. Thus had Yinganga, the Fresh Water Crocodile, done it in the beginning – and it had worked ever since. Jeremy left the silent watching Nelyerri and Willy, to go up to take a look at the mine. It was an open cut, driven into the red schist hill from the western side.

The hunters were back within an hour with half a dozen Nuttagul geese and a couple of brace of Pigmies.

The journey was resumed. When they reached the limestone, Prindy showed such great interest in that natural causeway of great mossy slabs over which a veritable river must run in Wet Season, that Jeremy stopped and alighted and had the boy out. He asked him what he knew about the place, but without getting an answer. Prindy looked intently away back into the tumble of great marble rocks and the verdant jungle growing around them, from which the flood would come, and away whence it would go, over slabs scattered as far as eye could see, out of the interstices of which grew bent and twisted trees crippled by the seasonal violence. No doubt its history would be concerned with Tchamala, and the boy knew something of it, the way he blinked when his grandfather told him that away, away there lay the Rainbow Pool. But no word in response. They got back into the ute, went on their way.

As they came into the grey plain beyond which lay Catfish Creek, Jeremy said to his small companion, 'What about you tell me one yarn belong to you?' The boy looked at him meaningfully. Storytelling was a matter for trade, like everything else – dancing, ceremonial, handicraft, marriage. One had only a certain repertoire, performance of which must be paid for. It was a curious thing that the *kuttabah*, who did little for nothing himself, was mostly blind to this very important aspect of Aboriginal culture (as shown only too blatantly in seizure of tribal lands) believing that the simpletons had no economic sense at all, hence considering the asking for reward only beggary and resenting it. But not Jeremy Delacy. Smiling into the grey eyes, he said, 'I give you anything present.' His glance went on to the mother, who looked as if about to protest, presumably against what she would call Blackfeller Bijnitch, and added, 'I give your mumma present, too . . . hair-oil, eh?' Nelyerri relaxed. Brilliantine was prized by women.

Prindy smiled, nodded. For a while he stared through the windscreen towards sepia mirage where the homestead would be, then chuckled, 'Dat old Marmaroo . . . time he gitchim brushtail.'

Bright-eyed, he talked over it to himself silently for a minute or two. Then he began. Translated from the Murringlitch, in which surely it would have sounded better, since the idiom would not be lost (as for instance when Marmaroo, the Brush-tailed Rock Wallaby and Wanjin, the Dingo, were travelling fast, the former in flight, the latter in slavering pursuit, sound echoed the sense of their speeding with *tull-tull-tull-tull-tulli-tull-tull!*) it went:

In the Dreamtime, Marmaroo, who was then just an ordinary rock-wallaby with a long thin tail, while travelling through poor country that offered no provender, fell in with Wanjin. Although Wanjin was friendly, Marmaroo was scared of him, knowing of his cunning and greed. He didn't like the way the Dog's jaws dripped when he looked at him, and hence kept well out of reach of him as they went together, and when they camped, always got up on a rock too steep for Wanjin to climb. He was becoming weak with hunger and the taxing pace with Wanjin fairly snapping at his tail, when camped one night he met Yang, the Lizard. Hearing of his fears, Yang suggested that he adopt his own method of shaking off predators, which is to drop a piece of tail, which with its contortions diverts them and also serves to stay their ravening and gives good time for a get-away. Yang taught him the magic for accomplishing the trick, and also for returning the tail to normal. Thus knowledgeable, when Marmaroo set out next day and found Wanjin slavering worse than ever on his tail, he worked the *mahraghi*, shed the tip of his tail, and sped on his way, leaving the greedy Wanjin well behind, and soon was clean away. But he'd given heed only to the magic of the shedding, so that when he came to try to Sing the tip back on, what did he get but the tuft he carries to this day. Still, there was advantage in it. The magic that had gone wrong was concentrated in the brush, so that by means of it he became able to wipe out his tracks completely, not only as to sign but as to scent, which latter makes his kind safe from the dingo as no other creature is, since the dog tracks with his nose. In fact no one but a python or a *Tchenek* Man can gitchim *marmaroo*. Even the brush of brushtail taken by a *Tchenek* Man can be used to the same effect.

The last was said somewhat breathlessly and wide-eyed, so as to sound like a little boy's boast. Holding the wide eyes, Jeremy asked, 'You got him brush-tail now?' The eyes blinked, swung back to the horizon. Jeremy touched the khaki shoulder beside him, giving it a slight conventional stroke, saying 'Properly good yarn. What about you make him up song about that, eh?'

The answer was given on indrawn breath: 'Been mek him.'

'Well, what about you sing for me . . . 'nother-one present.'

The eyes blinked at the distance, held it, the crazy shape of the top gate wobbling in a flood of silver. Shyness or secrecy? Jeremy's eyes looked quizzical as he looked at the perfect profile. Then he asked, 'What name present you want?'

The eyes swung back, held. The answer was given in another breath: 'Horse.'

'Horse, eh? Spoken like a true Delacy. What about young Sugar Bag? She'll never be a big horse . . . pony type. Saddle and bridle, too?'

Again the breath: '*Yu-ai.*'

'You'll have to come over and get her.'

Eyes of both son and mother looked wary.

His own eyes on the road, Jeremy asked, 'When you come?'

No answer. A moment, then Jeremy said, 'What about Christmas . . . I send horse in with Christmas mob, eh?'

A sigh of relief. Then: 'How long Critchmitch?'

'Aw . . . couple of months yet . . . no more long time.'

They were at a gate. Soon they were at the homestead. Clancy was out at the garden gate, waiting. Jeremy swung round to draw up at a little distance and with his passengers on the off-side, no doubt with deliberate intent to let them slip out and away without too close scrutiny from the Boss. Mother and son and foster father set out at once towards the kitchen. Darcy also dropped down on the far side, to dust himself down out of sight. Jeremy didn't move.

Clancy came stolling out: 'Gooday, father.'

'Gooday, son.'

'Unexpected visit.'

'Brought you some geese. They forgot to take 'em, I think. Darcy, son . . . give Clancy the geese.'

Darcy giggled as he handed the sack to his cousin, to have it received stiffly and without comment.

Clancy asked his father, 'Coming in?'

'Darcy's with me.'

Grey eyes and blue met in what must be an old challenge, which could only mean: No acceptance of your coloured cousin socially, no sociability.

The blue eyes blinked: 'Where'd the kid get to?'

'He didn't say.'

'Where's the old bloke?'

'Went bush again.'

Another blinking. Then: 'Cahoon's looking for him.'

'Cahoon's always looking for someone, isn't he?' A pause. Then Jeremy said, 'If you're going in to meet next train you should run into him. If you like, tell him the boy's back home . . . safe and well.'

Clancy nodded. Jeremy signalled to Darcy to get in with him, started up, gave a slight wave to his son, drove off. For a long while Clancy stood staring after the ball of grey dust rolling back westward, with face puckered like a wilful but unhappy boy.

IV

The return of the Sorcerer's Apprentice to the bosom of his clan appeared to have little or no effect on his status therein. Perhaps it was the very peculiarity of his original status that was responsible for the seemingly odd lack of curiosity about his adventure. Still, those who truly believe in the Devil surely would want to hear as little about him as possible, other than what might serve as protection against his wiles. A truly Aboriginal child who had come so close to supping with the Devil as this one could not be expected to return to his people. But there was a way to ignore the contamination in this case; he was what could be classed as Another Kind, one accepted and yet not – as in fact crossbreds really were ever since the days when, regarded as devil-foisted monstrosities, they were dispatched at birth. At any rate, things went much as usual for Prindy after his return. Green-ant still cracked jokes with him without looking him in the eye. His tribal grannies and mothers-in-law in the camp still took the food he brought them from the kitchen, honouring his tribal duties, and no less encouraged to do so by his Finder-Father, Willy. He still swam with the black kids in the creek, played games with them of warring with spear-grass spears. The only difference was in himself, and that shown simply by his singing songs of his own that he kept to himself. Often he went to the catfish hole upstream, obviously in some expectation of meeting someone there, and spending the time singing in lingo but in his own tuneful way songs that he must have learnt from his *koornung* master. Probably the words of the songs were unknown to him, or to anyone, the verbal meaning having been lost in antiquity, as that of most in Aboriginal ceremonial, the *whole* having meaning rather than *parts*. However, he did have some renderings of his own:

I follow him, I follow him, my Rown Road
Follow, follow, follow, follow Rown Road
Boss Tchamala by'n'by
Learn me kill him Whiteman die
Dat my Road, my proper road
My Rown Road.

All the while the weather changed with those cloud mountains slowly drifting from the northern sea – till there they were over Catfish Station, cooling the blazing land with vast blue shadows. In imagination one could go into the mountains, to scale the silver peaks, or go scary walkabout into the dark valleys and caverns, in search of Waianga, the Spirits who built the clouds and sailed them hither and yon in accordance with Koonoopippi's plan for replenishing the waters of the earth. That replenishment by rights should always be gentle, as, indeed, mostly it was. But usually things were very ungentle at the start of Wet Season, when the Shade of Tchamala would sneak into the mountains and panic the sleepy Waianga into dropping their store of water so as to cause havoc. Thunder and lightning were his voice and his destructive hand, the storm winds his breath. After the battle was over, if you were one of those privileged through familiarity with the Old One not to fear to look, you might see his Shade cavorting in the sky in colourfulness that put the rest of Creation to shame, chasing his tail into one of his countless tcheneke-holes and out by another. While he thus displayed, ordinary mortals kept their heads down and avoided creeks and waterholes and hid their children. His familiars would join in the hallelujah chorus of the frogs just released from dryseason-bondage deep in clay-holes:

Kunderak, kunderak
Tjeritjeru, tjeritjeru
Old One, Old One, Old One!

Already there had been a couple of heavy thunderstorms. However, the advantages therefrom well outweighed the bit of panic and havoc that had been wrought. Most important: the grass, for the most part vanished from the dusty earth these couple of months, was sprung again, to fat all creatures, particularly those on which the people of the land generally now had become most dependent, the Boss's bullocks, Bone-bugger this long while, but now putting on poundage that also put the Boss himself in better mood – so *yakkarai*!

Sweet pickin', the station people called the green green miracle.

A couple of heavy thunderstorms to start with usually presaged a full-time steady Wet Season, with all the natural benefits this would ensue – but something more to these people less dependent on Nature's bounty now, indeed much more, since it replaced some of the spiritual satisfaction lost with that dependence, namely, a dry Christmas.

As a nominally Christian community, the supposed birthday of Jesus Christ was its chief festival. Beatrice River Races has also been described as a festival, but with the qualification that it was the community's chief Social Event. There was no rubbing shoulders with everybody at Christmas. As everywhere else in Christendom, people frankly celebrated the occasion in groups of their own classification. All that is expected of one at Christmas is that one act in accord with the Spirit of Christmas, which is to be generous to others within one's means, part of which are one's prejudices.

The Christmas Spirit was appropriately expressed locally in the attitude of whites to blacks and vice versa. Officially it was the time when those Aborigines classified as Indigent, meaning those in contact with civilization who could not be made to contribute to it by doing some job of work, were given the annual handout of clothing, blankets, tobacco pipes, and other things considered necessary for civilized living for the like of them. This was apart from what was called Subsistence, the monthly doling out of rations, usually done by the police. At Christmas the District Police Officer became Santa Claus to the blacks, handing out not merely the official largesse, but contributions from institutions moved to special charitableness, like religious sects, Country Woman's Association (to which, of course, no black or yellow woman could belong) and the RSL (which boasted that it gave a Christmas present to every accessible child in the land, irrespective of colour or creed). Thus for the townships. The cattle stations had their own way of doing it, with a grand slaughter of bullocks, paying of wages in kind to willing workers, distributing gifts like red calico for loincloths, clasp knives, scented soap, brilliantine, lollies, to all who lined up with pink palm extended and the proper acknowledgement: *Tahng you Boss – Mary Critchmitch.*

Peace on Earth, Goodwill towards All Mankind.

The blacks didn't expect to join the festivities of their masters. They made their own, gorging, boozing if possible, corroboreeing, sweethearting, gambling away the gifts, invariably winding up with a battle-royal that left them bruised, battered, bloody, but content to meet another year. As shelter was always minimal in their way of life and taxed far beyond that when they congregated, a wet Christmas could be a poor affair indeed. In fact, if Wet Season set in early (the Season proper started with onset of the Intertropic Frontal System, or Monsoon as erroneously called in these parts, of which the initial thunderstorms had no true part) there would be no Critchmitch at all.

The Christmas Spirit already was dominating the household at Catfish Creek, since it had been ascertained from the Boss that the beginning of festivities was within calculable distance: which is to say the count down could be done on fingers and toes. In fact the counting now was down to fingers. The weather still looked promising. Tchamala's interference with the Waiaṅga amounted to no more than a flashing and crashing away up in the cloud mountains of nights, with only a scattering of large warm raindrops as the result. Igulgul was close to full, as usual round about Critchmitch. Everybody was happy and expressing it by saying Mary Critchmitch on all possible occasions.

Then suddenly a change set in – not of weather; although that also eventuated to spoil things utterly – but of spirit. The merriment died away. In fact the merriest, like Green-ant and Splinter, always a couple of wags, had disappeared, along with other males. Deserting the place meant nothing to the Boss now, when there were only odd jobs to do and the less to feed. No one asked questions. Awareness of a state of *jungara*, of taboo business, was practically instinctive with such people. Prindy, seeing his father Willy chopping his own kindling early in the morning of the ninth day before Christmas went to help him without a word. Even Nelyerri, despite eloquent looks and gestures to show contempt for whatever mad Blackfeller bijnitch was throwing the household out of gear and the fact that Willy himself was the most silent of all and looked even worried, said nothing about it.

Willy looked particularly worried when, during the after-breakfast clean-up of the kitchen on the third day of *jungara*, getting Prindy out of earshot of his busy mother, he whispered, 'Somebody dere wan' him you . . . long o' rocky-bar.' Avoiding the wide grey stare, he returned to his job. For a moment Prindy stood, then slipped out. In Murringlitch, Somebody meant a person or persons unnameable by propriety. Prindy paused but a moment, then slipped away, through woodyard, garden. He paused another moment outside his home, then ran in and got from under his bed two small spears and a womera and a dilly bag. Out again and through the back of the garden and away southward at a trot along the horse-pad.

He reached the bit of aquatic jungle at the end of the big pool, entered it, was halfway through, when – *whitt*! The sound was from behind. He swung around. No one there. But what at first looked like moving clumps of undergrowth suddenly converged on the track behind his back. Again he swung, but to be seized by skinny ochred arms that in a trice disarmed him, locked him, clamped his mouth, hooded him with a cone of woven grass. He struggled. A voice: '*Koyada koomeri*.' He relaxed. It was the voice of Splinter, skin-named Jelyerri, maternal uncle to him tribal-wise and chief authority concerning his behaviour.

There were four men, all elaborately decorated, with ochres of different colours and stuck-on birds' down, and wearing ***bulkung*** belts in which they carried boomerangs. One was Green-ant, Skin-name Jumbajinna, related as wife's father and having certain rights of authority. He it was guided the hooded captive as the party set forth. Through the jungle and down to and across the bar, and up along the creek, to skirt the catfish hole guarded by its snake-rooted banyan, and just past there to come into rocky country and call halt. One of the men trailed well behind, erasing the tracks. The other three sat waiting for him, while leaving the captive stand. As the man came up, Jumbajinna raised a hand to his mouth, wobbling it as he called out, to give the ululation known as *Tjangaluma* – *yoodle-oodle-oodle-oodle-ooooo*!

Silence, except for the *whirr-whirr-whirr* of insects – silence of listening here. Then a droning, augmenting the insect-sounds at first, but waxing to drown them out – *bidooz, bidooz, bidooz, bidooz* – like giant insects in flight, coming from somewhere amidst the rocks – *bidooz, bidooz, bidooz, bidooz*!

Green-ant struck a pose, began to stamp and chant: 'Koonapippi, Koonapippi, Koonapipp-eeeee!' The other men joined in.

Then Green-ant broke off to give the *Tjangaluma* again. With that the procession proceeded, heading for the Voice, which swelled till there was no other sound on earth – *bidooz, bidooz, bidooz, bidooz*! – the voice of Koonapippi, the Creator.

Suddenly the Voice ceased, but leaving tiny voices singing all round, it seemed.

In silence the party proceeded, soon to come to a halt again. Yet again Green-ant gave the *Tjangaluma*. Close at hand a voice called in lingo. Green-ant answered with a word. Each of the other men in turn did likewise. The hidden voice called: '*Goydai!*' They went on, in a moment to come upon a circular clearing – a Ring Place, Boree, or as called hereabouts, *Kunjan* –amphitheatre of primitive man. In the middle was a small gunyah of fresh-cut boughs, and round the edge six or seven like it. On the far side, in semi-circle, stood half a dozen decorated men. One other squatted – cross-legged on the ground to the right of the group, he more elaborately decorated than the rest, and with plaited beard and topknot and skeleton skinniness, recognizable as Bobwirridirridi. He was tapping *minga-minga* sticks inaudibly. At the appearance of the party the standing men gave the *Tjangaluma*, which the party echoed. The *minga-minga* sounded as it died away – *click-a-click, click-a-click, click, click, click*!

The captive was marched to the central gunyah, turned with back to it, made to squat on haunches, while his uncle and father-in-law ranged themselves standing on either side of him, and the others went to join the semi-circle – *click-a-click, click-a-click, click*! The group began to shuffle and sway. Bobwirridirridi raised his voice in a thin nasal chant:

Maringah, maringah
Mar widji, widji ma
Koonapippi, Koonapippi!

The others joined in, raising the dust as they stamped:

Marungah, marungah
Ma widji, widji ma-ah-ah-ah-ah!
Nahgunidah!

The group fell back into their semi-circle. Splinter and Green-ant raised Prindy, marched him off the ground into the tumble of rocks behind. As they disappeared, Bobwirridirridi took from under a sheet of bark beside him an object wrapped in a coil of hair-string. He rose, unwrapped the object, disclosing it for a flat oval of engraved and painted wood – the *bidu-bidu*, Bullroarer, symbol of the oldest of Old Ones, Koonapippi. He loosened the string, with a flourish, tossed the oval away and swung it, swung it, faster, faster, causing it to hiss, to whistle, to whine, to drone, to find full voice that filled the world – *bidooz, bidooz, bidooz, bidooz, bidooz, bidooz, bidooz!*

Back at the homestead, Nelyerri began to fret about her boy's absence after failure to come for his dinner. When she went back to their quarters for the afternoon spell she looked under his bed, and finding some of his things gone, cried, 'He gone walk-about again.'

Taking no notice, Willy went into the bedroom. She followed him, demanding, 'You been give him tucker for walkabout?'

'Nutching.' He cast himself down on his bed.

She stood in the doorway, hesitant, speaking as if to herself: 'Bloody Sunday bijnitch goin' on.' Willy turned his back. She came to him: 'Wha' dey doin' Sunday bijnitch?'

He grunted, 'I don' know.'

'Course you know. Where dat bijnitch? Might-be he get mix-up dat lot.'

He didn't answer. She turned away, went back to the passage-way, to stand there irresolute, alternatively staring in at him and out through the doorway of the back verandah.

Properly, she should have been warned by Willy. In accordance with ancient custom, he should have come to her with his spears, one of which he should have broken, and when asked by her why he did it, to droop his head and say, 'Your son is dead.' At that she would shriek, seize something with which to cut her head. All close female relatives would come and join her in her grief. Actually all would know the truth of the matter, even although it had not been spoken of except in secret by the male elders, the *Kudijingera*. Despite the secrecy surrounding initiation rites, it was something to be expected as boys approached puberty. Even a case of *Kirrikijirrit* might be presumed from precocious behaviour. Those dealing with Prindy would expect Willy to deal with the mother, his wife. How she took it was his lookout.

Her voice rose now: 'Spone he get mix-up dat-lot?'

Willy sighed: 'Dey can't hurt him!'

She swung back to him: 'Where dat-lot now?'

He groaned: 'Lo-ong way. Shut up. I wan' tchillip.'

She glared at him for a moment, then flung out again, this time to the back verandah, to stare into the garden. After a while she withdrew, flung herself, scowling, into a sack-and-sapling lounge chair.

When Prindy was still missing at supper time, Nell abused Willy so roundly about Sunday-business that, surely embarrassed by the presence of blackmen, he gave her a clout to shut her up, only to make things worse. The brawl was stopped by those on the verandah, not by their physical intrusion, but cries of warning: '*Danook*! Boss him singin' out.'

The rising of a great cloud in the northwest brought on early night. But there was Igulgul in the East. The cloud-mountain peaks blazed to make the eyes ache. Riot could be seen and heard within it. Back in their quarters, Nell whimpered to Willy, 'Big rain come . . . my boy out dere!'

Igulgul dived into the cloud to join the fun. Darkness. Then the world was split apart with light and sound. Nell's howling for her boy was drowned in the roar of rain. It was soon over, as usual, leaving Igulgul laughing, but tonight looking out of a rainbow like a tight-coiled snake, which was not usual and not a good omen for a dry Christmas, as borne out by the basso-profundo comments of the big tree-toads in the mangoes: 'Wet come, Wet come, I reckon, don't you?'

Nelyerri snivelled herself to sleep.

First thing in the morning, in the kitchen, Nell suddenly declared her intention of going to look for Prindy after breakfast. Willy ignored her, and kept on doing so till she said fiercely, 'I tek him rifle. Spone dat-lot got my boy, I shoot him bloody black bastard!'

He turned on her: 'You mek him more trouble, I go tell him Boss hunt him you . . . hunt him for goot!'

That shut her up. Breakfast was dealt with, all chores concerning it done quietly. But that didn't mean that work was finished. Nevertheless, Nell took off her apron, started for the back door. As if he had been waiting the move, Willy leapt to head her off, demanding, 'Where you go?'

'Lie down.'

'Wha' 'bout bread-sponge?'

'Puggim bread!'

He shut the door: 'You stop here.'

'I tired . . . wan' 'o tchillip.'

'I reckon you go look-about.'

She tried to get at the door. He turned the key in the lock, pocketed it.

She hissed at him: 'Dat bloody bastard got my boy, ain't it?'

He turned away. She leapt after him, grabbed his lean brown arm, shrieked into his face, 'Dey mek him young-man!'

He blinked. She went on: 'He only lil boy . . . dey kill him!'

He jerked out of her grip, growling, 'Him all right.'

She started for the side door, crying, 'I go tell him Boss!'

He leapt again, caught her arm. She shrieked in his face, 'Boss call him p'lice long o' radio.'

He twisted her arm, forced her to the table, hissing now: 'You listen . . . dat only Kirrikijirrit business . . . .'

'Le' me go . . . I yell for Boss!'

'You don' mek trouble. Dis goot way dey do. Got 'o do it. He been mix-up *koornung*, ain't it?'

She stiffened, stared, then screamed, 'Dat bloody *koornung* come back!'

She broke free, collided with the butcher's block. As he came at her she snatched up a knife: 'You stop me go Boss, I kill him you die, Chinee bastard!'

With a sideways swipe of a long lean hand he struck her wrist. The knife went flying. She reached for the chopper. He used the same hand in the same way on her neck. She grunted, fell senseless.

He knelt and raised her to a sitting posture, back to the block, smoothed the dark curls of her lolling head. Then he rose, went padding on big bare feet to the side door, went out. No one was on the verandah. He shut the door, locked it. He peered back inside, through the fly-wire backed by stout mesh that constituted the upper half of the door. Still Nell sat lolling. He turned, went down the steps, headed for the Big House. Blackmen working in the harness shed stared out at him.

Clancy was in the lounge-room under the house, sitting digesting breakfast ogling glossy naked white girls in *Man* magazine. He started at Willy's cough, stared at him in the doorway, grunted, 'What you want?'

'My missus, Boss . . . .'

'You've my permission to give her a bloody good beltin'. That's what she needs.'

Willy drooped, fiddling with his apron: 'Wan' 'o talk you, Boss.'

'All right. Come on in.'

Still drooping and fiddling, Willy told of Prindy's *Kirrikijirrit* initiation.

Clancy cut in: 'But he's only a picaninny. They can't cut him yet.'

'No-more cut him cock, Boss. Only lil bits long o' skin.' He indicated the cicatrices on his own upper arms.

'What the hell's it for?'

Willy shrugged: 'Old-man been reckon more-better.'

'What old man?'

'Dat-lot *Kudijingera*.'

'Them old bastards still throwin' their weight around? I thought we'd put a stop to all that mad blackfeller business.'

'Can't stop him old way yet, Boss.'

Staring hard, Clancy remarked, 'You're still a blackfeller, Willy, eh?'

Willy's face puckered as with misery.

'Well, what you want me to do?'

'Nutching, Boss.' Willy went on to explain that he only wanted Clancy to ignore Nell's panic and let the thing go through, concluding 'Only two-t'ree day, Boss. I reckon dey bring him back tomorro'.'

'You sure of that? I don't want that mad woman of yours disturbin' the peace for Christmas.'

'Dat lot wan' 'o come in for Critchmitch.'

'Well, if they don't, I'll call the police, and they'll spend Christmas in jail . . . and that woman of yours, if she makes trouble. Tell her I don't want to see her . . . if she comes I'll put the stockwhip round her.'

'Tahng you, Boss.'

Back at the kitchen, Willy found his spouse so well recovered as to be in the act of hacking her way out with chopper. When she saw him, she dropped the chopper, to snatch up something else. The barrel of the killing rifle was poked out through the hole. She screeched, 'Spone you don' le' me out I shoot you daid, you bastard!' He blinked, fished out the key, opened the door. As she burst out, he snatched the rifle from her. She turned and struck at him: 'Bloody puggim Chinee black bastard!'

He panted: 'You mad bugger.'

She stood a moment glaring, then swung away, leapt down the steps, headed as he had. He yelled after her, 'Boss belt him you, you go dere!' She was gone.

He sighed, turned with the rifle to replace it on the wall. It was a big old-fashioned repeating rifle, with magazine under the barrel. He jerked the magazine to clear it, letting the shiny cartridges spill onto the floor, hung the weapon again, then picked up the ammunition and slipped it into a pocket of his pants. With another sigh he turned to his culinary duties.

Some ten minutes later, as Willy, perched on his stool, was chopping onions, he looked up quickly on hearing quick shod steps outside. Then Clancy, red and blue-pop-eyed with anger, burst in, shouting, 'I've had a bloody 'nough of this bitch of yours . . . and her bloody kid, too. You go right out and get him. I'm taking 'em in to Beatrice after dinner . . . and dumping 'em there for good.'

Willy blinked watery almond eyes, gasped, 'Aw . . . tomorro', Boss . . . . '

'I said bloody now!'

Willy was panting: 'Can't do it, Boss. Spone I go dere, old-man mek me *tjungara* one munce . . . I can't come back.'

'I don't care if they *tjungara* you for one bloody year. You go and get that boy or I'll call the police to get him.'

Willy's face was quivering in that Aboriginal way under deep stress: 'Only one day, Boss . . . I promised.'

'Are you going now . . . or do I call the police?'

Willy swallowed hard, spoke on indrawn breath: 'All right, Boss . . . I go.'

'Right. Take a horse . . . take a rifle if you're fright', and tell them black bastards *I'll* be out with the rifle, if that boy isn't back here by dinner time.'

Willy went to the sink and washed his hands, removed apron and hung it beneath the rifle. Watched by Clancy he went out. Nell was on the verandah, crouched, snivelling. As he passed her he breathed, '*Goona*!'

Clancy, following him, heard and said, 'Shit's right.' Then he barked at the girl, 'Go and roll your swag . . . because, be jees, you're getting out of here today.' The way she stood made plain the fact that she was pregnant. He blazed at her, 'You bloody whore!' She slunk inside.

Clancy went to the harness shed and watched the men at work there, till Willy, mounted on a big bay, went cantering past along the track following the fence northward, then went back to the house and *Man* magazine.

Nelyerri was also watching from the kitchen. Seeing both men disappear, she flung about, slipped to where the rifle hung, got it down, opened the lock slightly, to reveal a cartridge in the breach. Then covering the weapon with Willy's apron, she went back to the verandah, peeped, then went round to the rear, down by the steps there, through the woodyard, the garden, out onto the pad, to follow Willy's tracks.

Willy didn't bother to follow tracks, but kept on up the creek on the western side, till some distance beyond the bar the pad dropped down into the creek to cross it. He rode on at an amble, soon came to the rocky region beyond the banyan pool. He dismounted, took hobbles from where they hung about the horse's neck, hobbled it, slipped the bit and tied the reins to the neck-strap. Then he went on through the rocks, with face set in a true Chinaman's mask, not hastily, or slowly, but with a sort of stooped deliberateness. At the right spot he stopped, put hand to mouth, gave the *Tjangaluma*. He had to do it again before the answer came – *yoodle-oodle-oodle-oo-oo-oo*!'

He went on, giving the call again, again. Then a voice, quite close, called: '*Nunyardil*!'

Demanding his identity. He gave it slowly and at length. Only fellow initiates would know his full name.

The voice called: '*Goydai*!'

In a moment he was at the Ring Place. The group, in full decoration, evidently interrupted in their business, were all standing staring at him, The subject of the ceremonial was not to be seen, no doubt shut in the gunyah in the middle, the entrance to which was closed.

Splinter began to speak to Willy in lingo and he to reply, when Bobwirridirridi cut in sharply: 'No-more lingo'!

A moment of hesitation. But evidently he had the authority. Willy went on to explain the situation in Murringlitch. The others tried to discuss it in lingo. But again the *Pookarakka* intervened: 'Wha' name you talk?'

Green-ant answered, 'More-better finish him bijnitch.'

The red eyes glared. The cackling voice rose sharply: '*Kaiu kahlu*!'

Green-ant's seamed old face puckered under its paint: 'Too muchee trouble.'

The crack of a mouth blew contemptuously: 'Trouble! All-day *ngeinya kumeri* long o' *kuttabah*. By'n'by kill-him-die dat lot . . . poff!'

The group stared at him out of painted rings, except Willy, who blinking Chinese eyes, said weakly, 'Boss gitchim p'liceman, spone no-more finish now.'

'Brrrup! *dookyangana* can't beat him me.' The coals flipped over Willy's whiteman's outfit. The cackle was peremptory: 'Take him out clodje . . . paint him all-same. You *tjungara*.'

The coals swung on Splinter, '*Beraga ningari*!'

The terms were too powerful in meaning, the authority of the speaker too great, to be gainsaid. Splinter went to the central gunyah, opened it, to reveal the small crouched figure, painted white from head to foot: '*Goydai*!' The boy rose stiffly, came out, to stand with head bowed. Raw cuts on his arms near the shoulder.

The group formed into the semi-circle to face the boy, while Bowirridirridi sank down with his music-sticks, and Willy Ah Loy stood drooped and staring. '*Click-a-click-click-a-click* . . . . Shuffle and stamp and chant:

Marungah, marungah
Ma widji, widji ma
Koonapippi, Koonapipeeee!

Thus – till the *Pookarakka* suddenly stopped it, not simply by ceasing to beat his sticks, but by tossing one to land at Green-ant's feet. All stared at him, except the drooping little subject. Plaited beard was raised high in lip-pointing to the rocks to southward, while the wide nostrils were flared as if sniffing hard. Then the old man swung without rising and with spider-like movement scuttled to a gunyah behind. He rose up spear in hand, turned back whence he had been sniffing – *BANG*! He yelped, fell thrashing the dust. The rocks rang. Blue smoke floating into the Ring. The painted group leapt for cover in the rocks behind. Only the Initiate and Willy stood, both staring through the smoke, to see Nelyerri rise out of the rocks there.

Wirridirridi, clutching his left leg from which bright blood oozed, also looked, then snatched up the fallen spear.

The loading mechanism of the rifle fairly clashed to fierce operation. The spent shell flew sparkling in the Sun. The lever crashed home again. Rifle and spear were raised together.

Whist! The spear flew, missed by a fraction, clattered in the rocks.

From the rifle – *Click*!

Like a wounded spider now, dragging his left leg, Bobwirridirridi went scrabbling after another spear, cackling shrilly, '*Tchil makoon* . . . *tchil makoon*!'

He got a spear with long blade attached – a shovel-spear, so called. As he aimed, the rifle clicked again. He yelled, '*Liwatchungun nanyog ningun* ... kill him die dat woman!'

The spear was snatched from the black hand by a yellow one. The red coals looked up into the slant eyes of a crazy Chinaman. Then there was Splinter, flying across the Ring, leaping at Nelyerri as she raised the rifle again, grabbing the weapon, twisting it in her grasp – *Snap*! She shrieked as her arm broke, stumbled, fell. Then Willy leaping at Splinter, to snatch the rifle away from him, but to turn on Nelyerri as she rose screaming like a wounded cockatoo, and strike her on the neck with the heel of his hand. She fell inert. Heaving for breath, Willy looked back at the Ring, to see the *Pookarakka* dragging himself towards the discarded shovel-spear. His hand shot to his pocket, took out a cartridge, shoved it in the breach of the rifle.

Bobwirridirridi got the spear, crouched to level it, squawking, '*Barrugun Kurrawaddi.*'

Willy held his fire. But not the *Pookarakka*. With a hiss he drove the spear. It struck Willy in the midriff, entered to the haft.

BANG! The bullet howled away over the rocks. Again the rocks rang. Blue smoke drifted.

Willy sagged to knees, with the long haft of the spear striking the rocks and bending to his weight. He struggled with the rifle, ejected the spent cartridge, slipped in another. Blood was spurting from his stomach, bubbling from his mouth.

Prindy stood staring.

Willy coughed – a great gout of blood that splashed on his thighs.

Wirridirridi was spider-crawling back for another spear. Willy croaked at him, 'No-more, old-man ... you go ... you go'way ... huh!' It ended in another bloody cough.

The *Pookarakka* got his spear, and a womera, turned and stared at Willy. The rifle lay across Willy's knees. The old man lowered his spear, called over his shoulder, 'Carry-him-me-up!' Movement amongst the rocks. He looked at Prindy, called '*Mekullikulli* ... *goydai*!'

The boy looked. Willy gasped, '*Joey*!'

When Prindy looked that way, the old man cackled, '*Jungara-Jungara, mekullikulli.*'

The grey eyes sought the distance, blinking.

The men came out of the rocks, looking dazed. The old man spoke sharply, in mixed lingo and Murringlitch, directing them to carry him and collect his belongings. He called in Splinter to bring the boy. One man took him on his back. As they moved off, Bobwirridirridi addressed the still squatting staring Willy: 'You die finish, Chinaman. Properly I been kill-him-you-die for bugger-him-up bijnitch ... *mummuk*!'

Willy nodded, as if accepting the verdict, coughed, spattering the rifle with blood.

The party disappeared westward. Willy let the rifle fall, lay hands on the spear, tried to rise, sank back gasping and groaning.

Nelyerri stirred, groaned, cried out, sat up clutching her broken arm. She became aware of Willy, who gasped at her, 'Gi' me hand.'

She got to knees, looked about wildly, lurched to feet, squealing, 'Where my boy?'

'Gi' me hand.' Willy coughed blood again.

'Where my boy?'

'Him all right . . . gi' me . . . huh, huh!'

'Chinee bastard – where my boy?'

He took up the rifle: 'Spone you . . . mek trouble . . . shoot him you . . . huh, huh!'

She stared at him. He gasped, 'Come here.' When she came, clinging to her arm, he added, 'Gitchim rock . . . break him . . . spear.' He had to make threatening motions with the rifle to move her. She got a sharp-edged rock He dropped the rifle again, jerked the haft onto a ridge of rock, hammered through the tough wood. When she bent to get the rifle he swung at her with the rock.

Free of the haft, he took up the rifle to raise himself. Standing swaying, bubbling blood, he said, 'We go . . . station . . . g'won.'

She moved slowly whimpering now, with little yelps of pain. He followed, using the rifle for support. Thus for some fifty yards. Then she broke into a run. He tried to call, but only coughed.

She reached the hobbled horse, to find that it had a chestnut companion, likewise saddled and bridled. Then she saw Clancy, looking about for tracks, a rifle in his hands, which he swung up with a scared look when he heard her. She rushed to him, babbling of what had happened. All he could say was, 'Christ . . . Jesus Bloody Christ! Come on . . . we got to get Willy.'

They found Willy given up, bloodily gasping that he was finished. Clancy forced him to come on, all but carrying him, got him to the horses, and up onto the bay. Nelyerri, whimpering still despite the Boss's curses, climbed up behind. Clancy mounted his chestnut, took the other in lead.

Back at the homestead, Clancy hurried to the radio, a small pedal-driven set as used on the so-called Flying Doctor network, and immediately got in on a schedule, and thus through to Radio Palmeston. Meanwhile, Willy had been placed on a mattress of sacking in the back of a utility truck, where he lay palely yellow as a true Chinaman. Clancy gave him a slug of whisky, told him that in no time he would be in hospital and for certain sitting up to eat Christmas dinner. He ordered Nell up in the back, too, along with a couple of blacks, got in the front alone. Thus away before dinner, as he had decreed, although hardly as he had intended.

V

Dr Fox was already at Beatrice Homestead when the party from Catfish arrived, together with Sergeant Cahoon and Tracker Jinbul, who had come down with him, and Constable Stunke and his man Treacle.

Dinny lost no time in getting to work on Willy, all the more importunate for being told by the doctor that Willy was close to death. Fox said that the only thing to save him was immediate blood-transfusion and surgery, while all he could do himself was to maintain the flicker of life left in him with Dextrose,

Saline, and Adrenalin. Leaving Willy on his blood-soaked death-bed, they parked the utility so as to give him the intravenous fluid from a bottle hitched to a post of the office verancah. As he revived, Cahoon urged him: 'Come on, Willy, I want you tell me who done it.'

Willy whispered, 'Rown fault, Boss.'

'Don't give me that. Who been spear you?'

'*Kudijinera* bijnitch.'

'I want to know which one . . . so I can put the bastard long o' jail for kill him my old mate, Willy.'

'I been do it wrong t'ing.'

'You never do wrong thing. You all-day good boy. Tell me name that muddrin bastard.'

Willy appeared to faint. Cahoon shook his shoulder. The doctor intervened: 'Go easy, Dinny . . . he's dying.'

Cahoon snapped, 'I want his testimony before he does.'

'Even if you have to hasten his death?'

'Give him something more . . . Keep him alive . . . Eh, what you sayin', Willy?'

Willy was whispering, on outflowing breath now: '*Koonapippi* . . *Koo-na-pipp-eeeee* . . .'

'Willy!'

'You've missed out, Dinny. He's had it.'

'Bugger it!'

Cahoon swung on snivelling Nelly: 'What happened, Nell . . . what d'you know?'

'Nutching.'

'You were there. Come on now, tell me.' He put an arm about her, causing her to yelp.

Dr Fox intervened again: 'Let her alone, Dinny, I want to fix her arm. Bad fracture.' She yelped again as Fox touched the swollen hanging arm. He said, 'I'll give you something.' He took hypodermic gear from his case.

Still Cahoon insisted: 'What happened, Nell?'

'For godsake!' snapped the doctor. 'I want to set her arm and splint it. If you can't keep out of it, give me a hand. Just shut up and hold her shoulder. Have to get her down on the floor.'

Kneeling beside her and taking a grip on the slender chocolate shoulder, with cheek in her dark hair, Cahoon said as soothingly as that grating voice would allow, 'You're goin' to tell me all about it, ain't you, little girl.'

She blubbered, 'You get him back my lil boy.'

'Course I will. We'll have him in for Christmas. Now, who speared Willy?

'I don't know . . . I never see . . . Ow, ow, eeeeee!'

'She's fainted,' said the doctor. 'Let her head down. This ought've been splinted hours ago.'

Cahoon looked up at those standing round, fixed on Clancy, demanded gratingly, 'Why didn't you put a splint on for the poor kid?'

Clancy growled, 'Didn't I have enough to do with Willy?' He walked away.

Nell recovered from the faint, only to lapse into drugged sleep. Cahoon carried her to the police utility, placed her in the front seat, went back to the office to get a statement from Clancy.

The doctor declared that there was no need for autopsy on Willy, since it was evident how he had died, and thus gave permission for his burial. No need for a death certificate for one without citizenship. He would have taken Nelly with him for delivery to hospital in Palmeston, only Dinny insisted that she would fret wildly till her boy was restored to her. Thus she was left in Dinny's care. He took her away, still sleeping, in Stunke's car, leaving Stunke to deliver Willy into the bosom of his Chinese family. The doctor himself declined the usual invitation to stay overnight at the homestead, saying that he wanted to go on to the Catholic Mission in the Prince Leopold Islands, directly to the North. After afternoon tea at the Big House he returned to his aircraft, driven by Martin.

Martin returned to the big white bungalow to find his brother still at the tea-table on the west-side verandah, alone. He came up to him, scowling: 'Proper bloody mess you made of things, eh?'

Clancy scowled back: 'What d'you mean by that?'

'Why didn't you do what the poor bastard said?'

'What're you talking about?'

'Willy. You told Cahoon he wanted them to break the kid in.'

Clancy's voice rose: 'But that bloody bitch of yours wouldn't have it!'

Martin reddened deeply, growled, 'I reckon you made the trouble yourself . . . deliberately . . . to give you the excuse to bring 'em in.'?

'And what you wanted was to have your bastard initiated as a blackfellow, so's you'd have less responsibility for him still.'

Martin's blue eyes popped: 'You bloody rat!' He turned away.

Clancy took a deep breath, called after him, 'And what about the other one?'

Martin swung back.

Clancy sneered: 'Have to have another initiation someday, eh?'

'What're you yappin' about?'

'Don't tell me you don't know she's up the duff again.'

Martin's heavy face jerked. He swallowed: 'I warned you that I'd run you off the place . . . .'

Clancy's voice rose higher: 'So's you can gin root to your heart's content!'

Martin leapt towards him, hissing. 'You little prick.'

But he stopped dead, at sight of his mother in the dining-room doorway. Clancy followed his startled glance.

Rhoda stepped onto the verandah, grey of handsome face, haggard of fine blue eye. Although her breast heaved, her voice was subdued: 'Nice conduct in my gentlemen sons, I must say.' She looked from one to the other.

Clancy was the first to speak: 'He accused me of causing the trouble at Catfish.'

She said stiffly, 'From what I heard you tell the police, it looks as if you could have stopped it with a little tact.'

'With that yeller bitch screaming in my ear to get her kid back for her?' Clancy swung on his brother: 'I asked him to get rid of her long ago. I knew there'd be trouble.'

'Even if you had to cause it yourself,' growled Martin, and turned away.

His mother said sharply, 'Wait!' He turned back, scowling. She sighed heavily: 'All I want to say is that I'm disgusted with you both. You're nothing but a pair of louts. It's in your blood. It's in the land . . . this rotten country!'

Martin snapped, 'Why do you live here, then?'

'What would it be like if people like myself didn't?'

Martin dropped his eyes before the icy stare, grunted, turned and walked away.

The cold eyes smote Clancy: 'This *is* all your doing.'

Clancy cried, 'Mine? For godsake . . . that bitch and that brat of his . . . .'

'There's no proof about that child. You're ridiculously, stupidly jealous of your elder brother. If you have to go to court about this thing . . . if you say anything to lower him, us . . . I'm finished with you . . . finished!' Rhoda turned back to the dining-room, vanished into it.

VI

Willy Ah Loy's last words surely entitled him to burial according to the rites of his Aboriginal side. This would mean his being wrapped in bark and placed on a platform in a tree, there to lie till his Shade departed to its Dreaming Place, which could be reckoned by his having ceased to stink; whereupon, with due ceremony, his bones would be cleaned and appropriately apportioned to his relatives, to be carried about for a certain season, then with final ceremony stowed away in some rocky reliquary and thenceforth forgotten. Instead, his Chinese side built him a square coffin from packing-case timber, sat him upright in it, with bits of the funereal baked meats to sustain his Shade on its way to Paradise and funeral money to ensure his admission therein, waked him with a grand feast (to which everybody in the community was invited, except blacks, who nevertheless sneaked the Demons' share of it left at the grave) then planted him in the Asiatic section of the cemetery.

Tiny as the township of Beatrice was, having long been a centre of pioneering activity, it had a necropolis of no mean order. It stood on the river bank at the western end of the one street, just beyond the Police Station and across the way from the Racecourse. It was plain to see from far off by reason of its two sizable monuments. One of these stood in the middle, a Celtic cross cut from the limestone of the country, inscribed: *Sacred to the Memory of Patrick Delacy, Pioneer of This District, RIP*. The other, at the entrance, was the Anzac Memorial, exact replica of the thousands that stand throughout Australia: a concrete soldier in the silly cocked hat, standing drooping over a reversed rifle – an Italian job, it seemed, fashioned by a sculptor whose idea of an Australian soldier had been got from a photograph sent along by whomever it was got the contract for *en masse* production. The cocked hat looked even sillier than in reality. A number of names of local lads were inscribed on the plinth, among them those of the Delacy Brothers, Jeremy and Jack, with a cross against the latter's to show that his glory was supreme. A ceremony of sorts was still held at the Memorial on Anzac Days, but nothing like that of most centres, as say Port Palmeston, where the anniversary was the Day of Days.

The Ah Loys were lucky to be able to bury Willy, instead of sink him, as surely they would have had to do had the funeral been delayed but a few hours. For a storm that had been threatening from about the moment of his death came roaring down from the North, as if it had something to do with it, and as indeed simpler people were supposing. The Weather Office in Palmeston reported a cyclone on the Northern Coast. However, Bobwirridirridi was not so named for nothing; and certainly just now he had reason to use those powers he was credited with, seeing that Coon-Coon and Jinbul were out hunting him. At any rate, whatever the cause of the weather, Christmas was going to be a poor affair for those who would have to spend it out of doors.

VII

The Pookarakka, with his apprentice, was holed up in a cave in the limestone eastward of Lily Lagoons. The boy was sorcerer's prentice again rather than cult novitiate, because the rest of the *Kudijingera* had deserted without finishing the job, and the job now was to assist the stricken Wise One with the magic necessary to beat the surely threatening circumstances that prevailed. As the others were not Snakemen, it was too much to expect them to remain in the hideously uncomfortable and scary conditions supposedly due to the machinations of Tchamala. There could be no doubt but that Bobwirridirridi had invoked the storm and deliberately sought this refuge as Snakeman Number One. Stricken as he was, with a thigh-bone shattered, he was soon in a state to frighten away anyone not sure of immunity from such *moah*. Burning, sweating, panting, sucking up for its magic the white water that soon was seeping through the place, he told of how when last here the Old One had appeared to him and told him how he could destroy the *dookyangana*, every *kuttabah* in fact, by leading them to a certain spot near here. This while the lightning ripped the rocks apart and sent them crashing so that the single pair of ears that wanted to hear the wonderous chant had to lean close, although it was fairly screamed:

Alga agula
Numeriji ga
Kill-him-die dat kuttabah
Dat kuttabah
Gwalla gwallu Tchamala
Whiteman kill-him-die.

The others simply vanished.

Prindy got the pipe-clay and the sugar-bag honey to mix with it to plaster the injured limb, which from skeleton skinniness had swelled like a cheeky-yam with onset of the rain, and bound it with paper-bark and hibiscus fibre, and plied his master with the magic water.

Then suddenly, out of the chaos, into the refuge leapt what looked and indeed proved virtually to be a squad of shiny black devils. Perhaps Prindy could have dodged past them in their moment of pause to take in the sight, but paused himself to look at his crippled master, and in that moment was lost.

A strong lean hand, not exactly white but unmistakably that of a *kuttabah*, stretching out of an oilskin sleeve, clamped on his naked arm, on the still oozing cicatrices, and a lean pale face looking out from under a dripping sou'wester split in a grin, and a well-known voice came grating: 'Don't be fright, Sonny Boy. It's only Coon-Coon, your Daddy-o.'

The grin was turned on the death's head out of which even in the gloom of the cave the coals were seen to glow: 'Got y' agin, you tricky old bastard . . . and for good this time. Reckon your magic more-better'n mine, eh? Ha, ha, ho! Put him on the chain . . . neck and leg.'

It was soon revealed how easily it had been done. There were the deserters, chained by the neck, naked as when last seen, but shivering and drooping in the sheeting rain, the paint and pride of *Kudijingera* scoured out of them. Coon-Coon caused them to droop lower still, by loading onto their shoulders him they had betrayed, trussed to a pole and with chains connecting him to those professional betrayers of their kind, Trackers Jinbul and Treacle. The police were mounted, Constable Stunke leading. Coon-Coon himself rode at the rear, with his Sonny Boy up on his saddle-pummel and fastened to it with a monkey-strap about a wrist, but sheltered under the oilskin and with his Daddy-o's warm arm about him and grating voice telling him of cosy things: 'Christmas Day tomorro'. What-'o-you-t'ink-o'-dat, eh? We camp there long o' Police Station, me-two-feller. I give you prejent. Daddy Critchmitch, eh? Ha, ha, ho!'

Evidently the place of execution of the *kuttabah* shown to the Pookarakka by the Old One was that giant's causeway of great slabs of rock, where now the white water ran knee-deep to man and beast, with a pull that would have washed the men away, but for the greater strength of the beasts they were chained to. For out in the middle Bobwirridirridi began to swing on the pole and sing:

Alga agula
Numeriji ga
Gwalla gwallu Tchamala . . . .

Cahoon shouted, 'Watch the old bastard!'

Too late. The bearers staggered, fell, were swept into the deep – but held by the swift movement of Jinbul, causing his horse to rear. Treacle's horse stumbled and would have gone over, too, but for Cahoon's spurring forward to lend his mount's shoulder to holding him up. Prindy watched with wide grey eyes. His Daddy-o left him to get down and sort things out with roaring and kicking and good use of the slack of the chains. They got the bearing party back on their feet, half-drowned. Swung up again, the Pookarakka howled: '*Ngoo ninji . . . ninji ngoo!*'

Back in the saddle, Coon-Coon cuddled his shivering charge close again, asking, 'You savvy wha' name old-man been sing out?'

The wet mop of fair curls shook.

'I'll tell you, then. That's his lingo for Poor Feller My Country. I've heard him before. It means he knows he's beat.' Coon-Coon chuckled deeply: 'Can't beat old Coon-Coon, yo' know . . . aaaaaaah!'

On arrival at Beatrice Police Station, Prindy was snatched from his Daddy-o by his mother, who first hugged him to her with her one good arm, then rushed him through the rain to quarters made up for her in the fuel-shed, where she examined him anxiously for injury. The cicatrices caused her to howl, 'Bloody black bastard . . . I kill-him-die properly next time!' Then she dressed him in cast-offs of the Stunke boy.

The Stunke children, a boy and a girl, down from the Convent in Town for the holidays, were out in the rain in oilskins and rubber boots, watching the locking up of the prisoners. Prindy watched from the shed. Later he lay down on the bed made up with sacks on cases of gasolene. His mother lay down with him, offered her breast in the time-honoured way, but to have him turn his back on it.

At dusk Tracker Treacle's lubra, who skivvied for the white folks, brought them supper of beef and bread, plus a slice each of iced Christmas cake. Later, sounds of revelry were heard from the house, faintly above the roar of the rain on the iron roof and the distant bellowing of Numeriji, the great white snake that the river had become. Coon-Coon's tenor could be heard distinctly:

Silent night, holy night
All is calm, all is bright . . . .

Prindy woke his mother in the middle of the night, murmuring the tune in his sleep.

Early on Christmas morning there was Coon-Coon himself with breakfast of porridge and ham and eggs, grating cheerfully, 'Merry Christmas . . . Merry Christmas.' He said he'd cooked the food for them himself. He had a parcel, which he opened to reveal brand-new clothing: boy's khaki shirt and pants and a bright print dress: 'Prejent,' he said. 'By'n'by more prejent from Christmas tree. I come get you. You wash-up nicely and put on clean clothes. Be seein' you.'

He came for them just before noon, all the jollier for a bit of booze by the smell of him – till he observed the bulge in Nell's belly, made more noticeable because the new dress was too small for her. The look he then gave her caused her to droop her head. He fairly flung at her the oilskin coat he'd brought. But he smiled again on his Sonny Boy, even though the outfit this time was rather on the big side. He took him up under his own coat. As they went out into the rain he said, 'Let's take a look at our caged canaries,' and swung towards the cell-block. They did not enter, but looked through the wire mesh enclosing the verandah. The Pookarakka was in an end cell, alone, lying on the concrete floor, chained to something. Jinbul and Treacle were on guard inside the mesh. Coon-Coon called, 'Eh . . . old man!' The death's head was raised. The coals glowed on meeting the grey staring out at him. Coon-Coon called again, 'How 'bout stop him rain . . . I give you drink o' rum . . . ahahah!' As they swung away he said to his Sonny Boy, 'Silly bugger blackfeller reckon old Cock-Eye Bob make this big rain . . . flood us out. Well, he'll be the one to get drownded, any way, eh? Ha, ha!'

The Christmas tree was on the side verandah remote from the weather, a very elaborate affair, presumably in the German tradition, because hung with bright captions in German as well as presents. Also, the children sang several songs in German before the ceremony of present-giving began. Prindy's eyes showed how intently he was listening as he stood on one side with his mother. Constable Stunke played Santa Klaus only to his family. Daddy-o Coon-Coon gave the gifts to the others: to her he had lately called his Little Girl a small suitcase, in which was a mirror, towel, scented soap, comb, brilliantine, and another dress: to his Sonny Boy a still smaller case, with a flashlight and belt with toy pistol in holster. Buckling the belt on him, he pointed out that it was fitted with a proper police buckle that he had fitted himself. It was, in fact, slightly out of date, bearing the insignia G V R whereas the one he wore himself was E VIII R. He said to the gathering, 'There you are . . . little p'lice-man. He's goin' to be a big p'liceman when he grows up . . . ain't you, Sonny Boy?'

Sonny Boy was silent. The Stunke boy piped up, 'I ain't goin' to be p'liceman, but.'

'What,' demanded Cahoon, 'Not goin' to be a p'liceman like your big daddy?'

'I'm goin' to be a engine driver, like big Pat Hannaford.'

The obvious embarrassment was relieved by the girl's saying, 'I'm going to marry a p'liceman.'

'Good on you sweetheart,' said Cahoon. 'I'll wait for you to grow up . . . aweeah!'

The Ah Loys, mother and son, had their dinner down in the gasolene-stinking quarters: roast pork, ham, plum pudding, nuts, lollies. Coon-Coon came down to them later with crackers for them to pull with him. Despite the gesture, he wasn't in a good mood, probably from having been sleeping off the festivities and wakened with a sore head. He betrayed his mood as he was about to go, frowning again at Nell's belly and growling at her. 'Thought you were goin' to have a bit o' sense. Who was it . . . Martin, or Clancy?' When she only drooped, he grated, 'Bloody rubbish . . . that's all you are!'

They watched him go – not back into the house, but away out to the street, with oilskins flapping to his angry stride.

It was to Finnucane's Dinny went. The place was full – an abnormal state of things for this time of year, when everybody from hereabouts and down the line who could get away would have been up in Town truly making merry for Christmas. The reason was the weather. The mail-train had not been able to get through owing to washaways; and the road was impassable. A grand thing for old Shame-on-us, it might be thought. But to be sure he was not enjoying the music of his cash-register as normally. Again it was the weather. While his customers kept reminding him that it was a time for nought but good cheer, he insisted on recalling the Old Man Flood of 1914 that had all but swept the town away and actually had swept away a consignment of goods he had foolishly left in the railway goods-shed and not got a penny compensation because it was judged an Act of God, bedad! He kept looking out through the rain for signs of the White Snake, which by the sound of it was knocking the bridge down. Snakes and bandicoots and a couple of Vaisey bullocks had appeared on the street coughing water. The drunks made things worse by harping on the yarn that was going round that it was due to the fact that Cock-Eye Bob was amongst them. It was being said that old Shame-on-us had been seen down on his knees in his office, although not decided whether he was praying or looking for a lost zac.

If it was praying Finnucane had been, then his magic proved more powerful than old Bob's, because on the day after Boxing Day the rain ceased abruptly and the Weather Bureau announced the passing of the cyclone. The day after that the railway appeared, undamaged hereabout, according to Ganger Toohey. Then Col Collings reported that a train with ballast waggons and workmen was on its way down to repair the washaways, and reckoned that it would get through to Beatrice to be able to take to Town those who wanted to see the New Year in there.

CHAPTER FOUR

STATION MASTER COLLINGS's reckoning to get the train away from Beatrice River for Town on New Year's Eve was so accurate that the time of departure might have been the usual one for the mail-train, (7 a.m.), despite the fact that almost a week of celebrating the Festive Season made it necessary to deal with many of the passengers as at the end of the Racing Festival, which is to say Pour 'Em Aboard. What went wrong was Mr Collings's too great reliance on his own authority, or on someone else's, combined with underestimation of the person he was asserting it on, namely Driver Hannaford.

Collings and Hannaford were old enemies. Enmity between engine crews and those called Traffic Men, the officials who control the enginemen's movements and hence restrict the liberty they enjoy more than other railway workers, is common enough, as known to anyone who knows railways. However, that between these two was something much deeper: a temperamental matter to begin with, the one being a big larrikin type with an ideology behind his nonconformism, the other a small man, self-important, a Boss's Man, as the other would say. The feeling between the two was shown in a clash at Finnucane's only the night before, when Hannaford had been soliciting the drunks for contributions to a fund to help the Leftist faction in the Spanish Civil War, and Collings, half molo, had questioned even the stated purpose of the fund. There was no fight. Hannaford was no sort of bully in his bellowing. It amounted to no more than an exchange of insults – Bolshevik Bastard and Fascist Shithead – with audience participation according to political bias or sense of humour.

Another enmity involved in the upset was that between Hannaford and Sergeant Cahoon. Naturally Cahoon as an enemy of Pat's and a pal of Collings'. For a certainty there was collusion between station master and police officer in the matter that caused the trouble; but whether with deliberate intent to provoke their enemy or through inability to refrain from expressing natural inclination when opportunity presented itself, even at risk of causing themselves embarrassment, would be difficult to say. As Pat Hannaford later said to his fireman, Porky Jones, 'Now why should the bastards want to do a thing like that? They must 'a' known it couldn't do 'em any good. That's what bein' a Fascist is, I reckon . . . a runt who's got 'o make himself big by having someone to stamp on as a kind of natural right. Course these boongs're useless bastards. But they're human bein's. Plenty whites're useless bastards, too.'

Sergeant Cahoon hadn't been at Finnucane's that night. The collusion between him and his pal would have nothing to do with the incident there. In fact it could have been entered into about the same time as Col Collings made his prediction concerning getting the ballast train away in lieu of a mail-train.

Anyway, as usual in order to make what would be scheduled in the Train Notice as Dep. Beatrice R. 7.00 a.m., Pat and Porky climbed aboard their engine at six to prepare her for the journey. She was in the little engine shed, into which she was run always of nights, not so much for shelter as for the facilities there for ash-dropping and tube-blowing and the rest of the things to be done at the end of a long day of operations. Porky had banked his fire and needed only to rake and shake it into life to get up steam. The train was marshalled ready from the evening before. It comprised ten ballast hoppers and two small flats packed with the gear the fettlers had been using in their repair work, two passenger coaches in which the men had travelled and camped, and the brake-van. The coaches were of the single type used locally, old-fashioned things like everything else on this railroad, each consisting of two compartments, with wooden seats running lengthwise so that one sat with one's back to the windows and looked out through those opposite, the compartments divided by tiny lavatories, one on either side, with a swinging door between, and with platforms at either end.

The rain had ceased. The Sun gilded the first high-flung puffs from the engine as she cleared the shed hissing and squealing. As she came rolling up to pass the parked train, Chas Chase, the guard, a stocky figure in the khaki uniform and wide-awake of the traffic man, dropped down out of his van to stand beside the track in an attitude of waiting. Pat Hannaford pulled up when he reached him. Chase climbed aboard, and shouted above the din of steam and open fire-box, 'Col wants us to pick up a stock waggon.'

Pat nodded, and whirled the wheel that would reverse her, gave her steam and set her rolling back, looking towards the stockyard where a rake of stock cars stood as usual. No more was said. Engine-men never waste words on traffic men. Chas dropped down to the bottom step, jumped off a couple of times to change points, coupled the stock car, and signalling to go ahead, rode the way back and up past the train, standing on the waggon's brake lever. Then back to couple with the train. The couplings were of a simple early type, a single spring buffer in the middle, split to hold the heavy hooks of the two vehicles, one hook being pivoted on, and the other falling to grip a stout pin running through the middle of the buffer. There was no automatic train brake. The engine had an air brake for its own exclusive use. Each vehicle had its own hand braking device. For train braking the driver needed to call on the guard by whistling to have him apply his heavy handbrake in the van. Not infrequently the driver had to call on the guard to release the brake, source of never-ending contentions between each end. There were also a brace of chains on either side of the couplings of each vehicle, these to hold the train together in the case of breaking of the couplings proper for long enough to bring the train to a halt and, if possible, rectify the damage. Spare hooks and pins were carried in the van. However, there was no roadside way of repairing broken safety chains.

With the train coupled up for starting and only the Pourin' Aboard process to be completed, Pat, leaning from the cab and looking backward and seeing the porter, Oz Burrows, trundling a baggage barrow up towards the head of the train loaded with tarpaulins, remarked to Porky, 'Who'd be truckin' blood-stock this time o' year?'

Tarpaulins were thrown over stock waggons only when the stock was very valuable and there was the fear of their being blinded by flying cinders, the waggons being for the most part open to the rush of smoke-laden air. Tarpaulins had also been used to cover such waggons when used, as they had been until a year or so ago, for transporting Aborigines by the police. It was Pat Hannaford, by causing a row that had roused national interest and involved wide industrial trouble and eventually won reluctant veto from top authorities, who had put an end to the practice.

Then scarcely had Pat made the remark, when the answer came to him in the form of unusual movements in the vicinity of the station. There was little Col Collings coming strutting up the train in his khakis, with his lanky khaki mate Cahoon beside him, while converging on the stock waggon was the yellow police utility so heavily laden that she swayed to scrape wheels on rear mudguards, laden with human freight wearing the prison garb of grey and khaki with chains that glinted in the sunlight. Hannaford exploded: 'Jesus bloody Christ!' and went leaping down to meet it.

The police car swung so as to back towards the waggon, Trackers Jinbul and Treacle leaping down to come running to open the doors, which were at the end remote from the engine, two upper outward-swinging, a single wide one at the bottom that fell downward. Pat yelled at Collings and Cahoon, 'What the bloody hell you think you're goin' 'o do?'

Cahoon assumed the twisted grin. Collings, reddening, looked at the utility, about to back across their path, signalling the driver of it, Constable Stunke, to keep backing.

Pat yelled across the back of the ute, 'I'm not haulin' human bein's in stock waggons . . . and don't you bloody think so.'

Cahoon now gave his attention to directing things. The trackers, up in the car, hauled out the men in chains who were standing up, then came and got him who was chained to an ambulance stretcher. Oz Burrows and Collings were unfolding the dumped tarpaulins.

Pat yelled, 'Okay, you Nazi bastards!' and turned about and went back towards the engine, but not to go past the end of the tender, in between which and the waggon he disappeared.

Col Collings and his mate, with one eye on him since he'd turned, dropped what they were doing, and went sprinting round the truck to see what he was doing. He had already done it when they got up there – uncoupled the engine from the train.

Collings demanded, 'What d'you think you're doing?'

Pat snapped, 'That's just what I asked you. I'll answer you when you've answered me.'

Collings snapped back, 'I'm loading the train, Driver. I'll ask you not to interfere in what doesn't concern you.' He moved to go in and re-couple.

Pat blocked his way: 'It's my concern not to break railway regulations, mate. That's why I uncoupled my injin. Don't you interfere, that's all.'

'What regulations?' demanded Collings.

'Regulations say no Aborigine's to be conveyed in any other vehicle but what's designed specif'cally for human use . . . . '

'That's not a regulation . . . it's a ruling . . . '

'Well, the rulin'll do me. Take them poor black bastards out o' that waggon . . . or I don't take the train.'

'You don't know your regulations *or* your rulings. The ruling states . . . *except in cases of emergency*. If you want to see it . . . here it is.' Collings fished an official-looking booklet from his pocket.

Pat sneered: 'I'll take your word for it. I know you're a regulations expert. All runts like you are. Just tell me what the emergency is in this case.'

'Ordinary passenger accommodation taxed to the limit . . . . '

'Havin' a full train don't constitute an emergency. You only have to leave this lot behind for the mail-train.'

'The emergency's a police matter. The police want these prisoners off their hands as soon as possible.'

Pat looked at Cahoon, stared into the other green eyes for a moment, then with a sudden glint in his own: 'That's unusual, isn't it! I always thought . . . . ' Then an answering glint in those eyes stopped him. It was generally said that the police kept their prisoners down country as long as possible, because they were paid personally so much per head per day for maintaining them, which could be means to a tidy bit made on the side if you knew your onions.

Cahoon urged, even amiable of tone: 'You were saying, Driver?'

Pat swallowed it, asked, 'Mind telling me exactly what this emergency is, Sergeant?'

Cahoon grinned: 'I don't have to tell you anything, Driver.'

'Right!' said Pat. 'If somebody don't tell me something, and mighty quick, I'm runnin' this injin back into the shed and phonin' my immediate superior, the Loco foreman, that I can't proceed because of a breach of regulations Traffic's tryin' to put over me.'

'Then you'll be wasting your time,' said Collings. 'I don't have to tell you anything, either, Driver, except to take this train away . . . . '

'I take orders only from my Guard, Station Master.'

'Your Guard takes 'em from me, as deputy in this district to the Railways Manager. But I'll tell you what you want to know, to save the railway's time. This matter's been gone into thoroughly with the Railways Manager, the Superintendent of Police, the Chief Protector of Aborigines, and the Government Medical Officer . . . and it's been deemed by those authorities that these prisoners can't be kept here any longer in these weather conditions, as a matter of police expediency, and humanity . . . they're all dangerous criminals charged with murder . . . there isn't enough food to feed them . . . and one of 'em's in urgent need of qualified medical treatment. Now . . . will you kindly take this train away?'

Pat swallowed, took a deep breath. Obviously he was struggling with an urge to knock the pompous little man down. In a strangled voice at last he said, 'I'll have it from the Guard, if you don't mind.'

'Please yourself.' Collings turned to his porter, who was directing the spreading aloft of the tarpaulin by those old-time experts the trackers: 'Oz . . . get Chas.'

The gangling Oz broke into a knock-kneed run.

Pat turned towards his engine, but as he moved, snapped back at Collings: 'Touch them couplin's and I pull the injin away and blow her off . . . and you can do what you bloody like . . . but you won't be usin' her to pull no Nazi prison train.' He went up to the cab, climbed aboard, said to the gaping Porky, 'The bastards 'a' got it all sewed up. I got 'o think fast, boy.'

'What you goin' 'o do?'

'I don' know . . . 'cept I ain't pullin' them poor black bastards like that, anyway. Bloody Nazi Germany! Let 'em get away with it . . . and they'll have *us* in stock waggons yet . . . takin' us to concentration camps. I said I'd take orders only from Chas. They're chuckin' the regulations at me. I'm chuckin' 'em back.'

'But ain't it agin regulations what they tryin' 'o do . . . after what you done that time to beat 'em?'

'Agin a rulin' only . . . with bloody loopholes in it, course . . . the bastards!'

Chas Chase came climbing up to the cab, looking worried. Collings and Cahoon were now standing just below; and a little behind them what looked like all those off the train who could stand. Chas asked, 'What's the trouble, Pat?'

Pat snarled, 'Like you don't know, you bastard!'

Chase said miserably, 'I didn't have nothing to do with it . . . dinkum. They jes sprung it on me . . . regulations and all . . . .'

'Why'n't you tell me?'

'Man gets a great chance tellin' you anything, don't he!'

'Well, spill it. . . ask me am I goin' 'o take the train?'

'Are you?'

'You know I won't.'

'You can't win, Pat. They got it all worked out. If you won't they'll suspend you, and call on Porky here. If Porky refuses, they got Bill Bolger . . . and he'll do it to nark you.'

'Yes . . . the Catholic Action bastard!'

Bill Bolger, officially classified as Pumper Bolger, was the man who operated the water-pumping system locally, formerly a locomotive driver who'd been compelled to give up the job because of ill health, and a bitter enemy of Communism and hence of Pat Hannaford.

Chase asked, 'You still won't take her?'

'That's it, comrade,'

'Oh, well . . . .' Chase began to step down

Collings raised his voice: 'Driver Hannaford!'

Pat's ginger head popped out: '*Ja, Mein Führer*!'

A titter from the crowd.

Collings scowled: 'I hereby suspend you from duty.'

Hannaford gave the Nazi salute, calling, 'Danke, danke, Mein Leader-schnozzel! If vos load o' poor bloody Jews or vorkers vot wouldn't lick your puggin' arse 'ole, I vould do like shot. But dey only poor bloody mob o' boongs, not fit for *unsen* o' der Master Race, eh, vot?'

A whoop from the crowd. Collings flung them a fierce look, then turned it on Pat, to yell back, 'If it was a stock train full o' poor bastards being taken to Siberia, though, it'd be different, eh?'

Pat flamed as darkly as Collings, and spat back, 'It ain't the poor bastards get sent to Siberia no more, brother . . . but the likes o' you and your long khaki mate there, who've got to make 'emselves big by makin' others little!'

The crowd was laughing – some of it, anyway. Some were stony-faced.

Collings looked past Pat, calling, 'Fireman Jones!'

Porky, goggle eyed, was hanging back. Pat grabbed him, pushed him into the place where he had stood himself. Collings said, 'I order you to take this train to Port Palmeston.'

Porky goggled down at him: 'What . . . me?'

Pat hissed above the steam, 'Take it!'

Porky tried to turn to argue; but Pat, out of sight by those below, shoved him back, still hissing, 'Take it . . . so long's I don't have to.'

Collings demanded, 'Well?'

Porky, with sweat streaming from his dimpled cheeks, had to get a prod in the back to answer, 'Okay.'

Collings, plainly taken aback, glanced at Cahoon. Then he turned back to Porky: 'I'll get you a fireman.'

Pat hissed behind, 'I'll fire for you.'

Porky called down, 'Pat'll fire for me.'

'He can't . . . he's suspended. I'll give you Pumper Bolger.'

Pat still hissing: 'Bolger's a sick man.'

Porky said, 'Don' wan' Bolger . . . he's a sick man. Pat'll do me.'

'But he's suspended.'

The ginger head popped out of the cab: 'You suspended me as driver. That's what you addressed me as . . . Driver Hannaford. That's how suspensions're made on the footplate. Guard comes up and says to Driver: "You're suspended. Hand over to the Fireman." Fireman takes over regulator. Driver picks up the banjo. You ought to know that, Mr Collings. You were on the footplate yourself firin', down New South Wales, till you wouldn't go on strike with your mates . . . and you had to get out and come all the way up here to get a job, 'cause this shows run by a Big Scab . . . eh?'

He who was named as a Big Scab was the local Manager, Mr Broadbeam, who'd also been involved, on the Boss's side, in some railway union trouble in the South.

Collings said, 'I don' know what you're up to Hannaford . . . .'

'But I know what you're up to, mate . . . you're up to shit!'

'You're not the driver of this engine. If you do anything to interfere with the driving of it, I'll see you're prosecuted according to the law. You remember that, too, Jones. You're responsible now.'

Pat Hannaford leered at Collings, extended the leer of Cahoon, who was eyeing him suspiciously, then looked over the crowd, calling, 'So long as no one can say that *I* stooped to haulin' poor black bastards like animals . . . or like the mates of these couple o' khaki Hitlers here in Germany are doin' with women and children and old men . . . arhhh!' He dismissed Collings and Cahoon together with a savagely upjerked thumb, then turned to Jones, saying, 'She's all yours, Porky, boy. Handle her nicely.' Then he retired to the fireman's side.

Down below was the call of *All Aboard* – and then the clank of the couplings as the engine was reunited to the train. Porky turned his pop eyes on Pat: 'You ain't goin' 'o give into 'em like that, are you?'

'I haven't, have I? I ain't haulin' the train, boy . . . you are.'

'You made me.'

'So what?'

'I never ever thought . . . .'

'Stop thinkin', boy, and leave it to me. That's what I want. Time to think.' Pat grabbed up the shovel, knocked open the firebox door, turned to get a shovelful of coal from the bunker, turned again to shoot it into the fire, his face tight with thinking. Porky looked at him helplessly.

Pat said, 'Get your 'ead out and watch for the right-o'-way.'

Porky looked out. After a while he looked in again, shot Pat a glance, then reached for the whistle – *Boo-hoot*!

He looked out again, now with a hand on the regulator, gave her steam slowly – *Hissss*!

She was moving – slowly – *Puff! – Puff! – Puff!*

They were rolling. Two whistle blasts to acknowledge Chas Chase's signal that he was aboard. Now *Puff-puff-puff-puff-puff-puff-puff* – they were striding towards the bridge.

Onto the bridge, with the White Snake only a foot below the track and the force of it such as to be felt right through the steel and into the structure of the train . . . at least into that rear part where Prindy and his mother rode, he kneeling on a seat and staring out at the swirling whiteness, with a blink as each red girder reared as if aiming a blow at him in passing. This was the back compartment of the rear coach, usually occupied by the like of these two only, they the only two of their like today, the rest whitemen, to judge by what little could be seen of most of them, so filthy were all from having been working for days in mud, and some even filthier from having rolled in it drunk after spending their earnings with Finnucane.

Over the river and past the yellow lake that had been the Racecourse, where flocks of black ibis and white ibis were rooting with long bills in the mud and keeping as aloof from each other as if being black and white ibis meant as much as being black and white men, the difference being that each kind were doing their own rooting and seemed equally proud of their breed. The grandstand and tin buildings looked strange mirrored in the lake. Slow over the Racecourse causeway, which spanned what was really a billabong of the river filled only by Old-man Floods and from which now such a mighty hallelujah chorus of frogs arose as to drown out the roll and squealing of the wheels on rusty steel. Turtles too. Look . . . tuttle, tuttle, tuttle! An old man Jabiru, looking like the old Pookarakka he was in the story in which he settled the dispute between the Frogmen started by old Tchamala. A cloud of black duck on the wing. White duck. Rainbow-tinted pigmy geese. And behind it all the trees running round and round like a big mob blackfellow in corroboree.

Across the swamps that were usually plains where Tchamala's Dust Devils played. Where all that-lot white ant go in old-man flood? Where all that-lot red ant go? Reckon he can swim like all-about. Out of the swamps and into hills all bright emerald with sweet pickin' and where silver rocks spouted fountains that joined to become molten red copper gushing under every culvert, drowning the grass. Kangaroos leaping up the hills, going for their lives because of the engine's *Boo-hoot, Boo-hoo-hoot*! Then clanging through winding granite cuttings, with the sweet wet smoke blotting out the dripping walls and filling the compartment till you coughed to the engine's laboured coughing: *Huff-huff-huff-huff-huff*!

Music in it all to sing to: *Click-clack-click-clack, boo-hoo-hoot, Old-Man Kangaroo, doin' a scoot! . . . Roholing wheel, Sihilent night, All is fair, All is bright, Roholing whee-el, boo-hoot, a-click-clack . . . la-la-la-la-la-la-la, laha, la-la-la!*

Granite Springs was the first watering point on the run to Town. Nothing there but the big red tank into which the water spilled of itself the whole year round, a mere trickle in the Dry, but more than enough to meet the needs of the little traffic of this road, so that normally it overflowed into a grating that took it away somewhere amongst the rocks; but now a white waterfall leaping down the ferny wall and roaring away into some booming cavern; that and a small whitewashed shed and a rusty bit of loop-line. The engine drew up at the tank. The curve of the cutting made it impossible to see from the rear what was going on up front, at least on the right side travelling up, that on which the track hugged the almost sheer wall.

True to the decree of Station Master Collings, it was Hannaford up on the coal, filling the engine's tank, and Porky Jones going over rods and links with the oil-can, when Sergeant Cahoon came loping along between the main line and the loop to take a look at his prisoners. Porky went round the other side, as if the sight offended him. But Pat, leaning against the gushing hydrant, stared rudely. Cahoon didn't come right up to the door to look in at his prisoners, the door on that side being just behind the engine, but looked in through one of the wide spaces between the timbers. Surely he wouldn't be intimidated by that rude staring. He stayed talking to the trackers riding with the prisoners, till the hydrant was swung back from the tender. Then he went loping back towards the coaches, perhaps thinking that those Commo types up front were not above starting without warning and leaving him flat-footed on the ground.

But the boys up front were in no such hurry. There were two ways to get down from the tender, the simpler one to walk over the coal and drop into the cab. The other was by steps onto the rear couplings and round and up. Pat Hannaford chose the longer, and soon showed why he did so, by producing a ball-peen hammer, and at the very moment that Porky chose to blow off steam with a mighty bellow, gave the pin in the coupling a couple of good seemingly soundless welts. The pin had a hinged end to facilitate its placing and prevent its pulling out. Pat drove the hinged part, which would be quite weak, in so that when the engine began to pull it would be taking the full weight of the train. He could not be seen from the stock waggon there, because the ends were not open like the sides. In a moment he was out and round on the blind side and climbing up into the cab. He winked at Porky, who immediately closed the blow-off cock and reached for the whistle. Pat stowed the hammer and took up his fireman's position, from which he looked back for the guard's signal. He got it, turned to Porky, who whistled again – *Boo-hoot*!

Pat was watching Porky closely as he eased off the brake, eased on the steam. Ever so gently she got away, to roll almost imperceptibly over the points of the loop. Then she was running smoothly in the narrowing walls of the cutting.

Thus for half a mile. Then out onto a green hillside, with the track sloping gently to a small trestle bridge from which as gently it climbed the other side. Red kangaroos went leaping off the track, but without interesting the engine crew – the one, Pat, keeping eyes fixed on the road ahead, the other with eyes on Pat. Halfway down the slope Pat signalled: *Steam off*. A slight jerk as the engine took the momentum of the train. Onto the bridge: *Give it to her*.

Puffa-puff, puffa-puff, puffa-puff!

Crack! It was more felt than heard.

Pat signalling: *Easy*.

Again the train shoving as they began to climb, but only for a moment. This time Pat shouted it, 'Give her the gun!'

Porky pulled open the regulator . . . *puffa-puff, puffa-puff, puffa-puff*!

Bang! The engine leapt forward without load, went pounding up the hill. Pat signalled: *Easy*.

The train like a headless snake came blundering a short way up the slope, faltered, halted, then began to roll back slowly. Heads craning out of coaches and van, but not out of caboose, because the guard would be busy with his brake. His wide-awake appeared as she settled to a stop, straddling the bridge. Then Chas came leaping down, to trot along the cess. Another khaki figure jumped down to join him, to come loping, buttons glinting. Then passengers on their heels.

The engine looked remote, standing up there black against the green of the hill, smoke curling up slowly into the blue.

The two khaki figures running along the train stooped now and again, evidently looking for the pieces of the break along the track, which for a certainty would be lying in the brawling creek beneath the bridge.

'Look at the silly bastards!' chuckled Hannaford.

There was no crossing the bridge with the train on it. Chas Chase climbed into a hopper to cross from one to another. Cahoon disappeared down into the bed of the creek. Only half a dozen passengers followed by one way or the other. Then there were Chase and Cahoon together again, the sergeant with legs wet to the knees and a coupling hook in his hand. They both stood to examine the snapped safety chains.

'Right,' said Hannaford. 'Reckon you can handle it, mate?'

Sweat was streaming down Jones's fat face and his voice somewhat husky, but his answer brave enough: 'She's right!'

'Just remember you've got to get stuck right into 'em. Don't give 'em a chance to get a word in. Blame Chas for havin' his brake on. Demand to have everything put in writin' on Form B-Seventeen. Ignore the copper. I can deal with him. They can't beat us. We got the regulations on our side. Either the train goes back to Granite Springs and that waggon's shunted off . . . or we refuse duty under protest, and everybody's stranded. Right?'

Porky said grimly, 'I said she's right, mate.'

'Right . . . let her go.'

The engine came rolling back down to the two khaki figures standing now with arms folded, authority waiting for delinquency that must come to them for punishment. But obviously they hadn't counted on the astuteness of the delinquents. Stopping within a dozen feet of them, Porky leapt down, came back roaring about the brake in the van: 'Silly bastard!' Chas Chase was at a loss, driven to protest when he should have been accusing.

Cahoon tried to be the accuser, only to be silenced immediately by Hannaford, yelling at him to mind his own bloody business: 'This's a railway matter, copper. Keep your long nose out of it.' No matter Cahoon's trying to tell Chase that he was being taken for a ride by two Communist smart alecs who'd done this deliberately to beat himself. Chas said feebly that it was against regulations to do more than take the waggon to the nearest siding and shunt it off. As to the charge of doing it deliberately, Hannaford demanded that the sergeant put it in writing and sign it and it be attached to Form B-Seventeen. The sergeant refused, whereupon Pat yelled at him, 'Then, shut your bloody trap!'

So Chas Chase had to go back to his van and take the brake off while the others trailed behind him, one breathing vengeance, most of the others grinning privily, and the engine crew, back on their foot-plate, embraced each other shaking with suppressed laughter. Then at a signal from Chas the engine gave the loudest and longest *Boo-hoo-hoot*! so far and began to push the train back up the hill and along through the cutting to Granite Springs again. They didn't wait for the guard to come along to uncouple the stock waggon. Pat did it, and hooked one of the stout engine chains to the intact buffer pin of the waggon to pull it clear of the train, and stood on the brake of the waggon as Porky shunted it on wheels squealing like stuck pigs round the rusty loop and up to the van.

The engine need not have stayed there while the prisoners were being transferred to the baggage compartment of the brake van, out of which a bunch of drunken navvies and their swags had been cleared; but it did, while its crew, in full voice sang *The Red Flag*. The navvies took up the song. Soon half the train was bawling it:

The workers' Flag is deepest red, its dye the blood of martyred dead.
Mistrust all other flags, my friends, they're Boss's tools for Boss's ends.
So lift the Scarlet Banner high, beneath its folds we'll live and die.
Though cowards cringe and traitors sneer, we'll keep the Red Flag flying here.

The best part of it all was Dinny Cahoon's expression. Those who saw it and were out of sight of those sharp green eyes, howled over it with mirth.

Boo-hoot! The engine was back on the train again. The train was moving again. The engine was cock-a-doodling. *Boot-a-hoot-a-hoooooot*!

Though cowards cringe, and traitors sneer, we'll keep the Red Flag flying here.

Prindy sang it softly to himself, not the words, but the lilt of it! *La-la-l'-la, la-la-l'-la, la-la-la-la-la-la-l'-la*, as he knelt staring out on the miles of sweet pickin' where the kangaroos, blue now, and some emus, and Lord Vaisey's bulls and cows and calves, and a small herd of buffalo, went racing from this hooting puffing smoking disturbing element of man the dangerous-most of all creation – *Boo-hoo-hoot*! – and the swamps shadowed by bird-clouds, – blue hills in far distance, sudden silver curtains of rain – *La-la-l'-la, la-la-l'-la*!

Cahoon coming through to take a look at his prisoners, as he did every now and then, for all that they were chained to every ring and staple in the van and Cock-Eye Bob also to his stretcher, happened to stop behind the fair head and before reaching to tousle it as usual, heard the singing, listened, then said, 'Hey . . . stop that! That no-good song, belong to no-good man. I belt him you I hear you singin' that again.' Then the tousle and the grin that meant Old Coon-Coon couldn't belt his Sonny Boy. As soon as he disappeared, Sonny Boy started in to sing again – and a couple of the pack of drunks in the compartment who'd heard the injunction joined in:

The Copper Class may kiss me arse
We'll keep the Red Flag flyin' . . . .

Next stop was Alice River, to take water again, and to set down those of the local fettlers who had been in the repair gang, the drunkest of the lot because this would be the end of their drinking for a while. Here was nothing but the water tank, the half dozen fettlers' cottages, the pump-house beside the shallow roaring river, a big iron shed that was the storage depot for Alice Downs Station, some fifty miles away westward where the Alice joined her royal sister Beatrice. The drunken hilarity of the muddy homecomers to their peeping black mistresses was suddenly silenced by a procession coming from the Alice Station Depot: four men in stockmen's outfits, one white, three black, bearing between them an ambulance stretcher on which beneath a blanket a bulk that surely needed four men to take the weight of it: 'Piggy Trotters . . . he's dyin' . . . he's dead . . . boozed himself to death durin' the rain . . . .' so ran the news through the crowd, through the train.

Piggy wasn't dead – not quite. Chas Chase, who had an ambulance certificate, gave the prognosis that replaced *The Red Flag* as the theme of the wheels when again they got rolling: '*Poor old Piggy . . . he won't see the New Year in . . . won't see the New Year in . . . won't see the New Year in.*'

It seemed that Piggy should have gone to Town aboard the Christmas Eve train to join his lady wife there. But they'd got it on the Flying Doctor Network, so Piggy's head stockman said, that there'd be no such train. So Piggy, who'd been holding himself in on a promise to his missus, hit the bottle, O.P. rum. He hadn't been taken with the ding-bats, but with a stroke or something. 'Coma,' said Chas Chase. 'Alcoholic Poisoning.'

Piggy's face, mostly purple before, with grog and the exertion needed to move his bulk about, lay grey-faced, with slatey eyes half-open, scarcely breathing, in the back section of the rear car on the stretcher on the floor between the seats. He had only two fellow passengers, because with the easing of accommodation pressure all the others moved in elsewhere, it being no place to wish each other happy New Year, pledging with tilted bottles, over one who was not going to see the old year out. Cahoon doing his rounds asked the pair left behind if they knew who he was there lying at their feet. They nodded. Didn't everybody know Piggy Trotters? But did they know who he was in respect to themselves? Evidently Nell knew that Piggy was her father, whatever they might mean to her semi-savage understanding. Obviously it meant nothing to her emotionally. Prindy, on being told that it was his grandfather, gave his Daddy-o one of those blank grey glances that to one more intelligent would surely have been interpreted as: *I don't know what you're talking about, nor want to know, but have to pretend to listen to you.* Cahoon just rumpled the fair hair. Prindy turned back to watch the flying world, the corroboree of trees and rocks dancing to the *minga-minga* music of the wheels, and the now-brown waters still rushing westward.

Then suddenly the water was flowing eastward and the train labouring through walls of quartz, to emerge at last into a torn land, a land torn by the *kuttabah* and the Chinee-man, no soil left on which sweet pickin' might ever grow again, scarcely a tree worth the name, only scattered sheets of rusting iron, old boilers, funnels, trommels, busted pipes, heaps of cans, of broken bottles with here and there leaning baulks of timber, rotting in the weather because even the termites were gone. The old Caroline Goldfield, Cahoon explained in passing. He wouldn't be able to explain what it had looked like in its pristine state. Perhaps no one was left who could do that, not even some old blackfellow singing his last days out under a sheet of tin on the outskirts of the tumbledown tin township soon looming up amidst the waste because it would mostly have been blasted from his memory with the dynamite they'd used, leached and bleached out of his soul with the grog and the opium he had got for the sale of his womenfolk.

The engine, *Boo-hooting*, pulled into Caroline River siding, while the dozen or so whites of the populace and the *dookyangana* and the thousand goats came rushing down to greet her, to grasp the hands of those who fell off to meet them, and pound backs and cry: Happy New Year . . . Happy New Year!

The whites came trooping through to take a look at the three passengers in the last compartment and take up the theme: 'Poor old Piggy . . . he won't see the New Year in.' Then they and all the others went rushing up to the sagging white building with its sign *Hotel Croesus*.

The blacks stood off in a close-packed ragged mob staring into the van through its big wide-open sliding door, well off, because it was known that one of those in there on the chain was Cock-Eye Bob the *koornung*, and only too well known that one of the hard-staring trackers was that most dingo-doggedest of all his kind, Jinbul.

Then the engine was yelling to those rocking the *Hotel Croesus* with their alcoholic goodwill. The mob came running, lurching, some to fall and have to be gone back for and dragged the rest of the way and heaved into that back coach where even a man's dying could not disturb their slumbering. *Boo-hoot*! And away again.

The murdered country fell behind. The drunks snored. Grandfather Trotters stared and stared at his first glimpse of eternity. All water now ran eastward. Prindy shifted to that side to watch it vanish like swift-moving snakes into the greenery. Now he was singing to the song of the wheels: *He won't see the New Year in.*

There were other bits of murdered landscape with shanty towns sitting in the midst of them, each with its sagging-verandahed pub to which these passengers still with use of legs went lurching. At one, Golden Grove, Daddy-o Cahoon brought beef sandwiches and lolly-water to his Sonny Boy and she he used to call My Girl but now only looked at with a tightening of eyes and lips that made her droop. More people came to look at Piggy and pronounce the inevitable that made the song of the unconcerned unknowing grandson.

It came on to rain, so that they drove through a silver tunnel with everything obliterated but the gouting silver underneath vanishing eastward. Prindy lay down on the seat beside his dying grandsire and slept. He woke to the clatter of points and *Boo-hooting*. They were at Helena River. Again Cahoon came with sandwiches and lemonade, and this time noting that Piggy's complexion had changed from grey to yellow and his eyes widened to full revelation of the unknown, he bent and pulled the blanket over the baldy head, saying, 'He's dead, Sonny Boy . . . your Gran'pa's dead!'

The grey eyes, squinting down past the neck of the upturned bottle, looked interested at last. A dead Granny was something to stare at. Likewise a dead pal, all blanketed up so that you couldn't see him, was evidently more interesting than one staring at you without knowing you but still with the capacity for knowing, to judge by the way the file of all those who came to look, just about everybody but those who were chained up next door, lingered as they hadn't before, saying, 'Poor old Piggy . . . just missed seein' New Year in.'

It was getting dark. The guard came along with lighted hurricane lamps to hang one in each compartment. A swarm of flying ants followed him, settled on the lamp hanging above the bulbous remains of Piggy Trotters, and shed their gossamer wings so that they fell like tears.

Boo-hoot! And they were on the way again – a funeral-train now as well as a prison-train. *Boo-hoo-hoot*! Over the Helena River, as she went brawling underneath, not to meet a royal sister, for all her being made regal by the sycophants who had stolen her from the simpletons who'd owned her – Princess Helena, another of Queen Victoria's brood – but to the king of all waters, the sea, just a short way down there through the showery darkness, and the jungles and the swamps. *Boo-hoot*! – with the headlight slicing the forest down on the curves. Twice they stopped, where there were little lights in tiny houses and pale faces and dark faces looking up at the windows and calling Happy New Year. And again *Click-a-click-click* to the music of the wheels and the soft singing from the eastern window – till the fair head drooped to the breast ever ready for it, not to suck any more, because only little boys suck, not young men, but just in sleep.

Again a clattering of points – more points than ever this time – and lights, many lights, electric lights strung on poles, sheds and railway waggons, and white faces by the track. It was the loco siding just outside of Town. While Pat Hannaford and Porky and Chas Chase were getting rid of the ballast hoppers, people crowded aboard to take a look at poor old Piggy under his blanket and scattering of frozen tears – and said it. But it was not only on account of dead Piggy that they came. They were travelling to Town to the several parties that were being held tonight. In the midst of death we are in life.

Boo-hoot! – and on the move again, with the engine so close now that the laughter of the crowd aboard it came sweeping back into the coaches with the steamy smoke. Sergeant Cahoon, sitting with his Sonny Boy to show him the sights as they came to them, frowned. Could they be laughing about him? At least they weren't singing the *Red Flag*.

Lights now everywhere, and bright-eyed cars racing them. It was fine here. You could see the stars, soon see them glinting on water. The Harbour, Daddy-o explained. Those other watery lights, the long golden splashes, were from the pearling luggers – the Japs. That bright-lit shed built over the water was the Japanee House, where they were celebrating New Year: 'Like we do . . . not like them bloody Chinee mob, got silly New Year their own.' And that big house blazing up there on the hill was Captain Vic Shane's, the Pearling Master – Big Man. And here we are, coming into Port Palmeston Station. The lights. The cars. The people. 'Right, Sonny Boy . . . I got 'o go, I'll see they look out for you all right. And you . . . you bloody rubbish Nelly . . . you behave yourself . . . or I'll let 'em put you long o' jail.' One last rumple of the fair hair – and Daddy-o went loping through to the van.

Clatter of points and squeal of brakes. They were slowing down. They were stopped amidst a sea of white faces, in a reek of grog and *kuttabah* and the babble of *kuttabah* speech – Happy New Year, Bill – same to you, Harry – Happy New Year . . . Happy New Year all!

The yellow ambulance was there, as ordered from early morning to pick up Piggy Trotters for conveyance to the Hospital. He would still be going there, but to the morgue, instead of to that pleasant louvered corner overlooking the Harbour, reserved for the sick elite. Mrs Piggy was also there, throwing herself upon the unresponsive lump as they loaded it, weeping wildly, but whether for the loss of her pig just when he had become a prize one, or for the inconvenience he was causing her by choosing such a time to die, probably not even she would ever know. Her two classy daughters were with her, looking even sulky about it, although that may have been their particular way of showing grief. The fact remained that it was the party night of the year; and they were great party gals, all three. There was Captain Shane's party, the grandest of all, although a bit on the vulgar side. There was Rhoda Eaton's, so refined. There was the RSL binge, for everybody who was white and loyal, the loyalty being to the Traditions of Anzac and Old England. A real party-goer would drop in at the lot, that is if acceptable at all, finishing up at the RSL, since part of the famous Traditions was to get as rotten as possible after winding things up officially by singing *God Save the King*. Piggy would have done the rounds with wife and daughters, and ended up at the RSL and stayed on to become the rottenest of all. Wife and daughters could hardly be in any of it now. But there was no reason why a damper should be put on anyone else's jollity; for as they were saying, although out of earshot of Piggy's bereaved: 'That's the way old Piggy would have liked it.' Time enough to mourn at his funeral. When's his funeral? Christ, not tomorrow, New Year's Day, with everybody hungover! They'd have to pack him in ice till the day after.

Dr McQuegg, Government Medical Officer, took a look at Piggy to make sure. There was no doubt about it. He was beginning to stink already. Then he took a hasty look at the other two patients he'd been advised of, hasty because he was a Committee Member of the RSL and a keen party-goer. But he was kind to these humble ones, gave Nell something out of his bag to take when she went to bed, because she said she suffered pain at night, and said he'd do an X-ray on her later. He said she'd be all right at the Compound. Perhaps he was being considerate of the one or two nurses only who would be on duty at the Hospital that night because of the partying. He greeted Bobwirridirridi like an old mate: 'You old bugger, you're back again, eh? Couldn't keep away from the bre'-milk and lum. Made a good job of your leg, eh? You're a better doctor than I am, Ghunga Din. Let's write a medical paper together on the use of clay in surgical dressings, eh? Ha, ha, ha!' Old Bob cackled as if in mirth.

The doctor added to the police crowding round: 'Yes, you can put him in a cell, seeing you're so scared he'll do a bolt on you . . . on only one leg. But I want to X-ray him before you put him in jail.'

The police loaded Bob into their utility with the other prisoners. Prindy and he had time to exchange a sign before Nell snatched the boy away. A tall lean halfcaste came to take possession of them, introducing himself as Barney Bynoe. 'You know me,' he said. 'See you long o' Races.' To Prindy he added: 'Long o' your lingo you call 'm me *Baranga*, ain't it? Dis one, my Mumma . . . he-he-eeeeee!' He nodded at his tribal mother, Nelyerri, who frowned at the liberty.

Barney Bynoe was pannikin-boss at the Compound. He had another halfcaste with him, a little fellow with a limp, whom he referred to as Hoppy. Barney said, 'Dis first time you come Town, eh? Tarjen Coon-Coon tell me give you run roun' look-see. You goot friend' long o' old Coon-Coon, eh? He-he-eeeee!'

He was in charge of a big yellow truck, up into the front seat of which he helped mother and son, while Hoppy jumped up into the back. There were no other Aborigines about. As Barney explained as they drove slowly up the hill from the station behind the weaving line of tail-lights of other vehicles heading into the centre of the town, such as they were not allowed out of the Aboriginal Compound, or places where they were permitted to reside as servants of a household, on any nights but Saturdays between sunset and sunrise, except in possession of a pass issued in the name of the Protector. A special proclamation was made in the Government Gazette by that gentleman every week to the effect that his charges were permitted 'To enter the Town Area for the purpose of attending the Pictures.' Barney put it in no such words and quite without bitterness, in fact even with something like glee, since he was able to add that when what he called citizen rights were proclaimed, as expected soon, types like themselves, that is crossbreeds, would be able to move at will – and booze. 'We can go in to pub like whiteman!' As if that were the acme of the longed-for grace of acceptance. He didn't add that there were a lot of whitemen saying that any pub that served a bloody boong was going to be blackballed.

They swung from the traffic to the left, into what Barney described as Chinatown – although there were Greek names on many of the shops interspersed with those with garish Chinese signs; where swarthy whitemen, with moustachios and bellies like Grand Turks, were sitting out in cane chairs close to where skinny Chinamen in pantaloons and high-necked jackets sat on hunkers squabbling over games of chance, or fat rich yellow-faced tycoons lay on cane lounges with pretty silk-clad wives around them and yellow children rolled in play in littered gutters. 'You can buy anyt'ing you want in Chinatown,' said Barney. 'Spone you got him money. But pretty harcarse girl can mek plenty money.' He turned to Prindy, as if remembering something: 'You Chinaman, ain't it . . . Ah Loy . . . *yu na mukka hai lo*! . . . he-heeeee!' The incongruity evidently tickled him deeply.

They came through Chinatown to the edge of a cliff, over which they had a full view of the wide harbour; or rather of what could be seen of it in the darkness, only a black line over the other side with the stars dropping down behind it; but almost immediately below them the bright-lit shipping section, the L-shaped jetty with its L of lights and a blazing steamer at the end. Another blaze of light was the floodlit Flying Boat base, with a big boat, looking with spread wings and fat body like a giant pelican just landed. Barney explained that both ship and flying boat plied between what even he called The East (which was north-west) and the South.

They turned from there to pass other shops, then come to the Government Offices. 'Protector dere . . . Dr Cobbity,' said Barney. 'Boss number-one longo we-lot. Nex' door dere . . . das Cop Shop . . . see dem khaki bastard inside dere! You don' wan' o' get in dere, eh, young feller? He-he-eeeee! But you got him mate, dere, ain't it . . . old Coon-Coon . . . Eeeeee!'

Round again. There was Government House, so called, the residence of the Administrator. 'Boss over everybody.' explained Barney.

The Anzac Memorial, with the concrete soldier wearing an Italian's comic version of the comic hat. 'Anzac Day,' said Barney. 'All-lot kid from Compound come down 'ere. Blowin' the bugle, an' singin'. Den everybody go long Oval and sports . . . lollies and lolly-water, cakes, good fun.'

Round to show all the pubs, all packed and uproarious and reeking of the goods they sold, crawling past, so that Barney could look inside in obvious proud anticipation of that day next year when he would be able to breast the bar like a whiteman. 'Nex' year!' he whooped. 'Da's tomorro', next year . . . you savvy date? Da's what for Happy New Year bijnitch, and all them white peoples goin' mad.'

They pulled up across the road from the RSL where the crowd were beginning to gather. It was a big bungalow-type place, on high piers, the bottom part serving as refreshment room, as evident from the laden tables and the mob, the men in starched whites, the women in all colours, standing with glasses about that biggest of the tables packed with bottles. 'Look-it all dat bloody grog!' said Barney, and smacked his lips.

'Pretty dress,' remarked Nell.

No hope of their kind ever getting in there.

Down a long long street of houses obviously too big and well built for anyone like them, and mostly in darkness because of the crowding into town. Then down a hill and through a grove of trees, to be suddenly confronted with a blaze of light. Well-dressed white people could be seen on the wide front verandah and the flood-lit lawn before it. 'Mitchis Eaton . . . you know, Mitchis Delacy before,' said Barney, and cast a look at his passengers as if to show he knew of their relationship to the luxuriance. Both stared with interest. 'Dey got good place over 'nother side . . . Rainbow Head,' Barney went on, jerking his lips forward, where through the windscreen above a line of trees could be seen the dark luminosity of the sea against the black line and starlight of the western horizon. 'Big picnic dere tomorro' New Year Day . . . white peoples. You see him tomorro' from Compound. We lot got picnic tomorro' too. New Year Day big holiday.'

Down the hill and swing to the right, with the silhouette of coconuts against the stars and below a glimmer of light. 'Das Jumbo Delacy place. Old Jumbo him in jail . . . for goin' mad Chritchmitch. Him mad bugger, dat Jumbo. Him mitchis dere, and mob kid. Poor bugger.'

They swung round the cemeteries. Only two here, European and Asiatic, the latter being very large. Aborigines were buried in what was shown on the map of the town as the Sanitary Reserve, also used for the dumping of rubbish. Along through a coconut grove, with no sight of the sea but strong smell of it for nostrils not used to it and now flaring to sniff at it. Then up another hill and back onto the long promontory on which the town of Palmeston was built, to have revealed in the headlights that part of this community of human beings reserved for those to whom the land it was built on had belonged and whose compensation for having it taken from them in the name of civilization was to live on subsistence rations behind that barbed wire fence on which was a notice declaring what it was: *Aboriginal Reserve. Any person entering upon this Reserve without authority may be prosecuted according to the Law. Protector of Aborigines* – A ghostly looking city of whitewashed hovels. 'Compound,' said Barney Bynoe shortly. The passengers, who must have heard so much of it, since it constituted the *ne plus ultra* of their kind, the place that eventually would swallow them and obliterate them, stared out at it. There were a few dim lights, a few small fires with ghostly figures standing or crouched beside them. But for the sound of the motor they might have heard the old familiar click of the *minga-minga*, the drone of dijeridoo, a stanza or two of the ancient chanting, sadly, from those who still remembered, or the whoops and squeals of those who had learnt to forget – with the grog.

Across the corner of the place was to be seen a big bright house. It was outside the city of hovels, as revealed when they turned the corner and headed for it. Barney said, 'Boss live dere . . . Sup'tendent Turkney . . . good bloke . . . spone you don' mek him wild. Havin' big party tonight . . . so all-lot inside . . . ' he jerked his head to the ghost-city ' . . . havin' party too . . . He-he-eeeee!'

He pulled up with a squeal of brakes as well as mirth before the Superintendent's residence. He shut off the engine. Sound of hilarity within and blare of gramophone music. The sounds from the hovels across the way also swept in. As Barney got down to go into the house he nodded to a similarly built place next door to it that was in complete darkness. 'Da's you call-yim Harcase Home . . . for kid.' Then he disappeared through the wire gate leading into a well-kept garden of shrubs. The garden could be pretty plainly seen from light shed from the latticed verandahs above. As usual, the house stood on high piers. But below this one was in darkness.

After some minutes a tubby figure in white came out of the gate, swinging a bunch of keys in one hand, in the other a flashlight, which, coming up to the truck, he shone into the cabin, calling in a thick boozy voice, 'Hello . . . hello . . . who we got here, eh . . . the Ah Loys? Eh . . . where you get that name Ah Loy, young feller, with that hair and those Irish eyes? . . . *When Irish eyes are smilin'*. Ah . . . I see it all now . . . why old Coon-Coon rings me up and says: 'Want you take special care that boy. Ha, ha, ha, ho, ho! I heard somethin' like that . . . but didn't b'lieve it . . . ho, ho, ho! . . . wait'll I tell 'em inside. Ah Loy, eh? That's good! Come on . . . get down . . . I'll show you where you sleep tonight.'

He swung the torch on the white gate that was the entrance to the Compound. Not a sound out of there now. Silence had fallen as if by magic at Mr Turkney's emergence. He took them to the gate, unlocked it. As they went in he flashed his light on a big building on the right: 'That's my office . . . where I keep the cane to belt him cheeky boys.' Then, chuckling, he rumpled Prindy's hair, he added: 'I no-more belt him boy . . . I only gammon.' He turned the beam to another sizeable building on that side: 'That's the laundry. My girls work there. Keeps 'em out of no-good business . . . ha, ha, ho!'

Still jollying, he led them to the left, where there were other bigger buildings, these of whitewashed iron and soon seen to be behind a fence of their own. There was a glimmer of light here and there, but no sound. As he unlocked another gate he said, 'I wonder what the buggers're up to? They're only quiet when they're up to no good.'

There were half a dozen of these buildings, not much better than sheds it could be seen at closer quarters, with shut doors and windows consisting of tin shutters, open but backed with stout wire mesh. A prison, it might be thought. But as it was a place of protection, not correction, such a thing could not be said.

Turkney, after some fumbling with keys, opened one of the blank-faced doors. His light revealed nothing inside but some institutional furniture, bare table, forms. There were a couple of other rooms behind, light in one of them. He called in, 'Wha's matter . . . all-about been die-finish, eh?'

Silence. He added: '*Yu-ai*, he been die all right. I can smell him . . . pooh!'

A titter from within.

He said, 'Must be dibble I can hear him. I ain't goin' in there. Go on, you two. Goodnight.' Then he raised his voice: 'Happy New Year, girls!'

An answering chorus of rough, half-Aboriginal female voices: 'Hap' New Year, Mist Turk'ey!' He shut the door, locked it. His footsteps receded on the gravel.

A torch flashed from the rear, dazzling them. Then someone came with a hurricane lantern and placed it on the table, saying, shyly, 'Ullo.' She was about sixteen, a quarter-caste, wearing a one-piece pale blue cotton dress with darker blue fine stripes and thick blue hems to short sleeves and skirt.

Then there was a rush of figures similarly clad, and a babble of voices and dark hand grasping.

'Nelyerri!'

'Prindy!'

'Nelly . . . my cujin . . . Nelly!'

'Julama!'

It was the Barbu women, mother and dirty daughters, whom Constable Stunke had had removed from Beatrice for the good of the morality of that community. They were panting questions about those they'd left behind there, old Ali Barba, Savitra their sister and daughter. There was a strong smell of grog on them. Maggie the mother whispered on intaken breath, 'We got bottle lum for New Year. You like lil bits, Nelly . . . cujin Nell?'

They produced the bottle and pannikins and cake.

Over at the residence they were whooping it up: *Roll out the barrel, We'll have a barrel of fun* . . . .

The *minga-mingas* were clicking all around, the chanting voices raised: *Kah-kai, kah-kai, imberrunni kah-kai . . . Brau, brau, brau*!

The black drunks were yelling, screaming: *Bloody puggin bastard*!

The white drunks bellowing, shrilling: *Show me the way to go home* . . . .

Then the tooting of cars and banging of cans and a bang or two of explosives from near and far, the giant's dijeridoo of the steamer at the distant jetty –

Boomb-boomba-booooooo! and the crowd with Mr Turkney bellowing and shrilling to beat it all: *Should auld acquaintance be forgot and never brought to mind . . . should auld acquaintance be forgot in days of auld lang syne . . . Happy New Year, everybody . . . Happy New Year*!

It dwindled away to silence – to silence over which Igulgul rose, misshapen almost unto death. As if his peeping through the prisoner-protecting wire had to do with it, Prindy sleeping on sacks in a corner of that room with the big table, began to murmur, to try to sing in that sweet strangled voice:

Oh lif a scarla banna high, aneet a fol ee lin ee die
For day a ol land syne.

The others woke, muttered. His mother whispered. There was a little giggling.

Then it began again, stronger, while the listeners sat up, straining to hear, eyes now goggling and glistening in the little light:

I follow him, I follow him, my Rown Road
Follow, follow, follow, follow Rown Road
Boss Tchamala by'n'by
Learn me kill him whiteman die
Dat my Road, my Road, my proper Road
My Rown Road.

A concert of startled indrawn whispering. 'Eh, look out!'

Then as the sweet small voice fell silent with a sigh, Nell began to whimper softly, 'Dat old *koornung* been do it . . . been mek him *tulli-tulli* . . . oh, my lil boy!'

A clicking of tongues in sympathy, then whispered demands for more information. Someone lit a hurricane lamp. The gloom was too scary. Then someone else got out canned food and biscuits. Prindy slept on.

CHAPTER FIVE

AS ONLY TO BE EXPECTED, no one who was part of that institution called the Compound was out and about early that New Year's Day, even those whose share in the jollification attendant upon the heralding of it had been limited to being kept awake thereby. Nevertheless, there was to its tardy starting the business of the day a quality that was a revelation of what sort of place it really was, what sort of thing the system was that it was part of, despite that word *Protection*, perhaps even what sort of Nation it was in which such a system, such a place, such a circumstance, could function in the name of authority. The immediate authority was Superintendent Turkney, who held the keys to the locks that restrained those of the inmates whose liberty was restricted as a considered part of their protection. The first Sun of the year was halfway to the zenith before Mr Turkney made a move. The girls in the Adult Halfcaste Women's Home, so-called, had been ramping for a couple of hours: 'Wha's matter, Tur'key, you bloody puggin rotten drunk bastard . . . come on . . . get out o' bed, Tur'key . . . come 'n' le's out o' here . . . Tur'key . . . Tur'key!' but not loud enough to carry across the way. There were rules. Bad behaviour could be punished by more restriction of liberty. What finally roused him could not have been that carefully subdued ramping, else surely he would have had something to say about it, surly as he was, nor could it have been much concern for them personally, since not only did he not apologize, but answered their Good Morning, Mr Tur'key, with a grunt. Probably what got him out was the pressure in his bladder. But what was more significant than the petty despotism revealed was the docile acceptance of it. Plainly the resentment was no stronger than that of well-trained dogs kept overlong on the chain by a master whose authority was completely accepted, even if there were no love for him. Indeed, it was with something like the frolicsomeness of released puppies that they came leaping out of their opened cages as he turned his fat back on them. The same sort of thing had happened across the road at the place next to the Superintendent's residence where the youngsters of their breed were housed. Some thirty children of all sizes from about six to twelve, mostly girls, and clad in pale blue, were racing round the bare yard there, to be called to order by the loud clapping of hands and a loud authoritative female voice calling, 'Quiet, children . . . quiet!' A white woman, clad in white and with mop of yellow hair, was to be seen emerging into the bare yard from the greenery that surrounded the residence.

Not that there was anything into which to direct that joy of release, here in the Adults' Home any more than over the way there where the fun to be got out of childish romping and squealing had been so quickly stifled Here the yard was likewise bare, except for a few outbuildings of exactly similar design, a dining-room that was just a peak-roofed shed on a concrete floor with built-in table and seats running down the middle, a tin wash-house, a couple of tin privies. Those who had the best of the cursed-for liberty were the ones whose turn it was to do the chores, like emptying the commode pots, or going to fetch breakfast from the common kitchen where a triangle was dinning as the result of Mr Turkney's having kicked the cooks into activity.

Those with the chores went about them swinging, laughing. The others did a turn or two about the yard, staring through the high netting fence as if bored to death with what they saw, then retired from the blasting sunlight to the dining-room, to flop down on the benches fixed to the table, to lean on elbows, a couple even to drop faces to downflung arms. Not all them. The Barbus, with a couple of others, were showing the Ah Loys the sights. Then when the bored ones saw there were newcomers amongst them they sat up, leapt up, came crowding. An excited chorus of: 'Hullo! ' Staring and smiling. A couple made Skin signs, but as if from sheer habit and not caring how they would be received. In fact, that was all the introducing there was. For the moment the interest lay entirely in showing things. They all gabbled the information. That was home for halfcaste kid. School there, too. They kept you there till they saw you going to have baby. Then you come here. That playground belong to kid. They got hole for tchinekin out under fence and going down in gully gitchim cocky-apple and plum and mango. Sometime gitchim goat and milk 'im. Big girl sometime meet halfcaste boy down there, play-about in long grass. You got to look out down there, but. Bandicoot tick. You get tick-bite Matron Turk'ey know where you been. The kid all careful looking for tick on somebody been down in grass. Over there across the gully was the Kerosine – the Soldier Place – the iron roofs just peeping above the trees. Dat-lot soldier mad for halfcaste girl. But Boss soldier make trouble because pox. Now soldier get put Kerosine Jail for play-about colour girl. Two bloody white moll down town doing it for soldier. But we lot go tchinekin. Picture Night – dat's best time. Down there through tree, that's Compound Beach. All-lot go picnic today-afternoon. Dat Missionary mob come, Bible-basher. But good tucker and plenty fun. Might be can go tchinekin long o' grass for play-about wit' halfcaste boy. But look out that lot black bastard! They gitchim you, they puggim you – all-lot, bloody black bastard! Across the way, beside Mr Turk'ey's office, was Laundry. Some girl work there, washin' for Government people, and Kerosene. Next to that Sewing Room, where girl make uniforms for Compound and Jail. You can earn money Washin' and Sewin' – but nothin' so good's play-about wit' soldier. Money you get workin' here they keep in trust, give only when they like, won't let you buy what they call foolish thing. Money you get from soldier that's all yours. You can buy nice thing from Catalogue.

Then the girls arrived with breakfast, lugging between them battered army dixies, containing porridge, sliced bread, tea, skim-milk made from powder, as well as a couple of cans of treacle. As they all sat down to it, someone said, 'Bloody rubbitch!' It was taken up as a chorus. Nor was the complaint so far from truth. The porridge, cooked the day before, already was sour and roped from the mould in it, and when dowsed with the thin milk, gave up the corpses of weevils by the score. The bread was even worse, stringy grey wrapped about congealed glue, the whole cased in charcoal. The tea had most of the leaves floating on top. One of the girls, called Dolly, a big handsome creature, in the family way, as at least half of them seemed to be, declared, 'Dem bloody bastard Islander!' Then everybody proceeded to tell the newcomers that the kitchen was run by what sounded like a gang of crooks, blackmen from the adjacent Coburg Islands, who didn't have their own women with them, because these were forbidden by the mission controlling them to come to the Mainland, and who thinking themselves better than mainlanders, from whom they did in fact differ in many respects, presumed to think they had a right to dealings with yeller girls rather than black, and because the former rebuffed them, took revenge by serving them always the worst of their bad cooking. Apparently they had great rows about it at times, in which Mr Turk'ey had to intervene. But the girls didn't care today. They still had some biscuits and tinned stuff got from the Kerosene. Besides, there was the picnic this afternoon. A few had a nibble of bread and treacle to stay their hunger, and all drank the tea, spitting out the leaves. Prindy and his mother merely sniffed at the poor stuff and rejected it. Dolly said they would throw it in their rubbish-hole, since if they sent it back to the kitchen, the black bastards from the Coburgs would only sell it to the other blacks.

Then they began to talk about the lovely new place Mr McCusky said was soon going to be built for them, and kept at it, despite Dolly's sneers that she'd been hearing about that lovely place since she came in here as a kid. She added: 'Dey mek dat place for blackfeller. On'y halfcaste go dere's dat-lot dey want work laundry and sewin'. All rest got 'o go long o' Mission. Da's too puggin right. I been hear him dat missionary Mist' Tasker, talk. He been growl-growl 'cause we lot no-more go silly Sunday School long o' kid dere. "All right," he say, "we gitchim all-lot you sinner next year when Old Compound finish and you got to come live long o' Mission." Da's I tell him you straight. I ain't goin' no mission. I run away long o' Japanee lugger.'

There was diversion round about noon, when cars began to arrive at the Superintendent's residence, delivering men in white and women in bright colours, all of whom were greeted with great enthusiasm by Mist' Turk'ey. The knowledgeable girls named those they knew, claiming to have worked for this and that one as housemaid, and told what they knew about them, none to their former employers' credit. These people were all of the Junior Officer type, not eligible for the Eaton-Delacy party over at Rainbow Beach. Among them were Mr McCusky and his wife – the Mick Cuskys, as they were called. Dolly commented: 'Dat bloody skinny bitch Mitchis Mick Cusky! I got 'o work her one whole year. Jes 'bout break every china she got so's I can get away. But, bloody bastard, she know what for I do it and keep me nark me . . . get him new china from Govmin' cause reckon train me housework. White bastard!' Still, for all the vigour of the denunciation, there seemed to be no real resentment behind it. It sounded more like description of even pleasurable feuding.

There arrived also Dr Cobbity, a biggish man, but with a little round head and very red face that looked like a tomato on a long stalk. So striking were his blue eyes in the red face that when he looked straight across at the girls, they cringed visibly. He did not wave, as Mick Cusky had, just gave them that long hard stare, and went inside. He was alone. It was interesting that the hilarity that had been working up in the place since the visitors had begun arriving fell noticeably with his entry, then rose again when, after about half an hour, he left. Of course he was Turkney's and McCusky's boss, and a Senior Officer amongst juniors. Still, there must have been more to it than that, something about the man himself. Even the children romping in their playground visibly were pulled up as his pale blue sports car went flying past them heading back to town. Again no wave. Dolly said, 'Bloody bastard, Dr Cobbity!' But still no resentment.

Soon after Dr Cobbity's departure, the kitchen triangle rang for dinner, a good hour behind time. But there was no response from either of the halfcastes' homes. It would only be Rubbitch as usual, the knowing ones told the newcomers, beef stew, with not a lot of beef in it, and that bread, – always beef stew, sometimes with a bit of rice with weevils – and in no time the Missionaries would be along with the cakes and the lollies and the lolly-water. 'Sun like o' dat!' said Big Dolly, projecting her lips to a point in the blue and blazing silver above where the Sun should be at about two.

It was likewise with the children across the way. Dutifully they had come to their dining-room from the playground at the ringing of the gong; but no bevvy of them came skipping and hopping and giggling to get the food as in response to that announcing breakfast. Matron Turkney appeared, apparently expecting the indifference to the Rubbitch today, since she stood for only a moment or two talking to them, then turned and went back to her now raucous guests. The children went the other way, with a rush, through the underneath part that served as their schoolroom, to go crowding up the inner stairway to their sleeping quarters, housing for some thirty of them, in exactly the same space as occupied by Mr and Mrs Turkney. The reason for the rush was soon apparent. There was no rush down again. In their best clothes, the girls in flowered prints, the half dozen little boys in grey instead of khaki, they came decorously, some to sit at the school desks, others to go to line the fence that made caged birds of them. No running, no yelling. All their energy concentrated in the rumbling anticipation of stomachs starved for change of diet and in eyes longing for sights different from those eternal ones within range of the cage.

The Sun was exactly where Dolly had said it would be when the first of the cars appeared round the bend of the road from town, a big old-fashioned thing, bright red, high on its wheels and with a wide high canvas hood. The know-alls exclaimed: 'Mist' Tasker.'

The Reverend Mr Tasker was the head of the local Protestant Mission Society. He had with him a couple of other clergymen of similar persuasion, as seen when, with much donkey-like braying on his old-fashioned Klaxon horn, he drew up outside the residence, but on the Compound side of the road from it, and alighted with two other males wearing clerical collars and a whole bevy of females who had the look of having their minds on higher things than most women. Directly outside the residence were the cars of those noisy guests of the Turkneys'. Not that there was any noise from them now. The hilarity had not simply subsided as with the entry of Dr Cobbity, but fallen into dead silence at sound of the Klaxon. Mr Tasker, a stout squarish figure in tussore and brown topee, and his friends, made no move even to approach the residence, but gave their immediate attention to those craning in their cages in wait for them, waving and smiling. Nor was there need of their approaching it, because in a moment there were Messrs McCusky and Turkney coming out to greet them, while Mrs Turkney appeared in the yard of the children's home, waving her greetings, heading for the gate to let the children out onto the road.

In view of the well-known enmity between missioners and the Department of Aboriginal Protection, arising from their eternal rivalry over the objects of their interest, it was surprising to see the warmth of greetings, the hearty handshaking, the crying of Happy New Year! But then, Messrs McCusky and Turkney must have been somewhat drunk, and the others would be acting out of Christian Charity. As the greetings were being exchanged more Mission vehicles arrived to draw up near Mr Tasker's, except one, a big truck, which pulled in so as to be ready to go through the gate of the Compound when it was opened. The smaller vehicles contained mostly white people of prim and proper appearance, with a few coloured folk of mixed blood. The truck was driven by a coloured man of unusual type, yellow-skinned, slant-eyed, thick-set and handsome, most likely a cross between Japanese and Aboriginal, and manned by other coloureds who by their woolly heads were Melanesian and Polynesian, the usual type of pannikin boss connected with missions. The truck also carried a stack of folded canvas chairs, an harmonium, and a huge barrel almost entirely covered with wet sacks.

Mrs Turkney, coming with the ordered line of children, did her part in the handshaking, then headed back for home, leaving her charges in the care of certain ladies who greeted them with *Happy New Year, children*, and got a sing-song response. Mr Turkney opened the gate, and together with Mr McCusky and the three clergymen, entered the Compound. The others followed, those with the children at the rear. Turkney signalled to the big girls to come. Their gate was not locked. They came. McCusky called to them, 'Happy New Year, girls!' The cry was taken up by the rest of the white party. The girls responded as they came to join the procession, some getting caught up by the white ladies and the few respectable coloureds, the rest falling in with the children, except Nell and Prindy, who being caught sight of by McCusky as they trailed behind those out of the adult home, were called by him: 'Nelly Ah Loy . . . come here . . . and the boy!' The procession halted while the pair approached slowly. McCusky turned to those about him, saying, 'They're the ones the trouble was about . . . murder . . . down Catfish Creek.'

A soft chorus of Oh! and the turning of eyes.

As mother and son, hand in hand, came up, watching with eyes looking from lowered brows, McCusky cried, 'Hello, you two! Everything all right?'

Nell whispered, 'Yas, Boss.'

McCusky rumpled Prindy's hair: 'You all right, sonny boy?'

Prindy's grey eyes flicked up for a second at the name, met the bleary blue ones. McCusky grinned at him. Prindy's nose wrinkled, probably at the reek of beer puffed into his face. McCusky said, 'Going to have a picnic this afternoon with these nice people, eh? Don't go eating too much cake and things and makin' yourself *barcoo*, now . . . aaaah!' Prindy stood with head hanging.

McCusky gave the head another tousle, then said, 'Okay . . . you can go along with the others. I'll be up to see you tomorrow.'

As the pair turned to go, Mrs Tasker, a dumpy little woman with a crop of downy whiskers sprouting from her plump red cheeks, said, 'Come with us, dears.' She reached for Prindy. But, staring at her, he shrunk away. 'Don't you want to?' asked Mrs Tasker. For answer Nell cast her a scarey glance and drew away. Then she and Prindy went hurrying rearward.

Mrs Tasker said, 'Poor thing!'

The procession was on the move again. McCusky said, 'As a matter of fact she's a bit of a dam-er-darn nuisance. Led her poor old man a dance. From what I hear she was really the cause of all the trouble.'

Mrs Tasker said with emphasis, 'Poor thing!'

Mr Tasker cleared his throat: 'Ahem!'

McCusky said, 'Yeah.' He gave Turkney beside him a swift wink. Then he said, 'Get your lolly bags out . . . here they come!'

Blacks were coming running from the collection of whitewashed iron hovels, to line the route the procession would be taking. Some of the ladies, from baskets they carried, began to take little bags of sweets and hand them to others. In a moment black hands were snatching for them.

'I'll back them for the world's champion cadgers,' remarked McCusky.

Mrs Tasker said with still more emphasis, 'Poor things!'

Another wink between the two officials.

Prindy and Nell fell in with the Barbus at the end of the line, with the big truck growling in low gear on their heels and the yellow-faced driver tootling lightly on his horn and giving Prindy a toothy grin every time he looked back at him. But for all this silly business behind, apparently Prindy was missing nothing: the crowding, gobbling, staring blacks, most of them in rags if adult, naked if children and snotty-nosed, and staring at him – the hovels and skinny dogs and cats the earth treeless and grassless to this point, red gravel with all fertility trodden out of it long ago. But suddenly there was sand and patches of grass, and ahead a thicket of stunted wind-bent trees, through which silvery flashes of the sea. Prindy was staring at the sea, when his attention was caught by an odd-looking hovel amongst twisted tea-trees, made out of a couple of big corrugated iron water tanks, rusty and badly dinted and distorted, wreckage of some storm, seemingly half buried in the sand and joined together and with a door cut in an end and a tin chimney and a bit of a porch, to make a substantial dwelling, and round about stacks of metal drums and crates and piled bottles. But odder than the house was its occupant, standing out on her porch watching the procession. She was a big woman, strikingly dressed in yellow with touches of red, nothing cast-off for sure and nicely laundered, and strikingly handsome of face, which metallic brown and shining, in profile looked like the intaglio of some savage queen on a copper coin, regal quality given to it by the way her grey hair was dressed, no mere mop of curls as affected by practically all Aboriginal women of all breeds, but pulled back and tied in a knot on her nape and half covered with a spotted red bandana. Not that the oddity lay in this difference from other inmates of this poorest of all poor-houses in the land. She had but one leg, the other being a so-called peg, and stood supported by a crutch. She was smiling and waving at everybody, and getting the same in return. but her smile vanished as she caught sight of Prindy and his mother. She stared sharply. Then she raised a hand to give the Skin sign *Nelyerri*. Nell's free hand half rose to reply, then dropped back. Then the woman tried it on Prindy. He gave back *Julama*. She smiled widely, showing bright teeth, and came lurching towards them: 'Eh, ullo!' she cried in a high musical voice, then broke into lingo, addressing Nell. For answer Nell drooped her head. 'Wha's matter . . . you lose him lingo?' Nell nodded.

The truck blared behind them. The woman caught Nell by her free arm and pulled her clear. As he passed, the driver leaned out, and with slant eyes on Nell and Prindy, called: 'Don' you have nothin' do dat one Peg-leg . . . she no-goot woman!'

Peg-leg screeched back at him, 'You go an' git pug, you bloody missionary.' Then she said to Nell: 'You forget me, eh? I chister belong you.' She broke into more lingo.

Nell looked at her with something like recognition, but with fear also. Peg-leg stroked her arm, saying, 'No-more fright, *burruwa*. I look out my lil chister. I been hear about trouble. Dat same bloody bastard, Bobwirridirridi, been mek'm dat trouble for me.' With a movement she indicated the truncated leg and the other one, which was twisted, and showed a misshapen arm, and scowling now, she hissed: 'I kill-him-die by'n'by, kill him finish! 'Then she looked at Prindy, smiling again: 'I look out my *ngaggun* too . . . you pretty boy!' She smoothed the golden hair, the caramel cheek. She swung on Nell: 'Me . . . I boss long o' Compound, Queen.' She projected her lips back towards her strange dwelling: 'I got him store dere . . . anysing!'

'Hullo, hullo, hullo!' They all swung towards the loud voice.

Messrs McCusky and Turkney were coming back up the steep sandy bank through the trees. It was McCusky's voice. He added: 'Getting' in early procurin' new blood for your whoreshop, eh, Queeny?'

'What you talkin' about?'

McCusky leered at her: 'You know very well what I'm talkin' about. Leave the girl alone.'

'She my chister.' There was nothing like the usual sycophancy in the quick reply.

'I know all about your sisters.'

'Dis one properly my chister from Alice River.'

'Yeah? That doesn't mean you won't sell her to some soldier or bloke down town and take half the money she gets.'

'What you talkin' about?'

'Course you don't know . . . you don't know nothing but what suits you.' McCusky turned to Nell and Prindy: 'Go on . . . you go along with the picnic mob. They're tapping the ginger beer.' The two went off at once.

Looking back at Queeny, McCusky asked, 'How much money'd you make sellin' grog to the blacks over Christmas?'

She snapped, 'I don't sell grog nobody.'

McCusky turned to Turkney: 'What about we'll take a look see if she's got any grog in her joint?'

'Sure, sure!'

They started towards the tanks. Queeny swung on her crutch, and with a couple of loping strides got ahead of them, and turned, saying, 'What about you mek bet you find'm grog?' They both chuckled. 'Come on,' she said. 'I bet you five pound.'

They both burst out laughing, Turkney saying, 'No doubt about you, Queeny!'

Turkney said, 'You won't find anything, Eddy. I raided her Boxing Day.'

'You fright' mek bet, eh?' Queeny jeered.

'I'm not bettin' with you!' chuckled McCusky. Then to Turkney he said, 'We'll take her word for it, eh, Tub . . . the word of an honest woman . . . ha, ha, ha!' He swung away from the place, heading back towards the track, calling over his shoulder, 'Happy New Year, Queeny!'

She answered readily, 'Happy New Year, Boss. Happy New Year, Mist' Turk'ey.'

Turkney called back, 'Same to you, Queeny, love. Keep your legs together.'

She answered with a peal of laughter, turning from them to watch her tribal sister and nephew disappearing through the belt of marine scrub, then after shooting a glance back at the whitemen and seeing them preoccupied in laughing conversation, swung on her crutch to go down after the others.

Nell and Prindy came out onto a grassy stretch, a sort of ledge between the scrub and the steep beach, to see the picnic crowd milling round the rear of the truck as the ginger beer barrel was being slid down to a stand, but to give it scant attention, in view of the wonder expanding vastly before them, the sea. From where they stood, not only could they see much of the harbour at its widest part, up to six miles across, but also a slice of the infinity of the ocean beyond. It was an expanse of blazing silver, lying motionless with the tide at neap and unruffled by wind, mirroring the westerning Sun and a colossus of white cloud rising as if to meet it. Due westward the shore was most distant, low, a mere green line of mangroves. Southwestward, much nearer, because it was actually an island, connected only at low water with a neck of land splitting off a part of the harbour, was Rainbow Head, blazing of itself and mirroring itself, because it was composed of micaceous quartz, not entirely bare of vegetation, but with so slight a capping of it as not to matter. Beyond it, still southwestward, was Rainbow Beach, again a dazzling thing, since composed of the same stuff as the headland, as indeed were all the beaches hereabout, with a glimpse of the red roofs of the buildings there, and of the several launches and luggers riding the silver offshore. Then the view was cut off in that direction by the red wall of Point Lookout surmounted by its lately erected paraphenalia belonging to what was known in this quarter as the Kerosene: a signal mast, gun-turrets, and the like.

Nor was it distant strangeness that seized their obvious wonder. A short distance away along the Compound Beach, towards Point Lookout, fish-netting was in progress, being conducted by a couple of blackmen wearing nothing but red *nagas*, or breach-clouts, and a host of naked black children. There was the wide arc of corks, round which two dug-out canoes patrolled, each packed precariously with children using hands for propulsion, while also splashing and yelling to discourage fish that could be seen here and there leaping the invisible fence. Other children were hauling with the men at the water's edge. As they stood gaping, Queeny Peg-leg reached them, saying, 'First time you been look-him sea, eh?' They gave their affirmation in swift glances. Then back to the wonder of it.

But they were not here for sight-seeing. At least not as far as their picnic mates thought. Maggy Barbu called to them: 'Eh . . . come gitchim ginger beer!' That attracted the attention of others, among them Mrs Tasker, who stood out and called, and being white must be obeyed. Dragging their eyes from the sea, they headed for the truck. Queeny stayed behind. They were pounced on out of the crowd by more old friends: the Jumbo Delacys, mother and children. Jumbo was there too, but standing off, sour-faced, either not wanted by the respectable ones or not wanting them.

Mr Tootle, manufacturer of softdrinks for the locality and the leading advocate of temperance, had just tapped the keg and drawn the first glass for sampling by Mr Tasker. The Reverend Gentleman sipped, smacked, swigged, looked at Mr Tootle and said, 'You've surpassed yourself, my dear Enoch. Superb!'

Mr Tootle replied in a broad North-County English accent, 'Aye . . . I thought 'twould please you, Reverend.'

'My dear . . . your glass!' Mr Tasker cried to his wife, then drained his own, and as Mr Tootle filled his spouse's, shoved his own forward for refilling. Then he turned to the crowd and said, 'Now, hurry up and fill your glasses and pannikins . . . because we're going to drink a toast to the New Year.'

With professional celerity Mr Tootle charged the multitude of vessels thrust at him, just a mouthful for the toast, as he kept saying – plenty for everyone afterwards. There was a lot of sly sipping during the waiting, by whites as well as darkies. But soon they all had something. Mr Tasker raised his full glass: 'And now, dear friends, I ask you to drink to a Happy, Prosperous, and Godly New Year to all of us!' The response came trailing out. Then up went the vessels, down the drink. Then a rush for replenishment.

Maggy Barbu asked Prindy, 'How you like him, Prindy?'

Prindy smacked his lips over it: 'Goot-feller!'

'Well, come on we gitchim some more.'

Prindy joined the throng pressing towards the barrel, but with eyes turned back to the fishing. Now the net was halfway in and a great upheaval going on within it, and not without a bit of fun owing to the capsize of one of the canoes.

Mr Tasker halted the general hogging of Mr Tootle's brew by reminding the gathering of the games they were to play and the prizes to win. Included amongst the boxes and baskets being unloaded with folding tables and chairs from the truck was a pack of pretty picture books. Still Prindy was more interested in what was going on down there along the beach, judging by his frequent glances, even in the midst of a ring game he was shoved into.

Prindy was standing out of a game for girls only, giving all his attention to that *coup de main* of net-fishing, the final slow haul when the convulsing belly of the net, if the catch is good as this one was, becomes a veritable cornucopia, symbol of the abundance of earth and the waters thereunder and man's easy lordship of it all. He turned on hearing a step, to find his great-uncle Jumbo beside him. Jumbo grinned: 'Ullo . . . you never see fishin' like dat before, eh?

Come on down, we look him close-up.' He put an arm round the boy's shoulders, looked down at him as readily Prindy went along with him, adding, 'How you doin' eh? I been hear him you get mix up trouble . . . da's right, eh?' Prindy looked away from the quizzing dark eyes. Jumbo went on: 'Must be you witch-nitch long o' Court. I come look him you.'

Prindy may not have been listening, so intent were the grey eyes on the fabulous sight ahead. The black kids formed an almost solid wall behind the overflowing net, beating back the leaping silver. As if carried away with it, Prindy broke into a run, went leaping into the water to fill a sudden breach in the wall caused by diversion elsewhere and taken instant advantage of by the fish, and grabbed at a huge spiny-finned salmon in the act of flapping itself to freedom, got a poke from a spine and a dash of salt water in the face that evidently made him as surprised with the taste of it as all the rest, the way he kept licking himself. Black kids who had seen his tussle with the fish shrilled with laughter. That fish got away. But there was half a ton of others, of many varieties and sizes, now safely (for the fishermen) up out of the water, gasping and flopping on the silky silver sand. Even the sand was a wonder, the way the grey eyes stared at it, and brown hand reached down to take up a handful of it. As different from the coarse-grained stuff of inland streams as this harsh pungent water was from the sweet stuff of the creeks and rivers. He bent breathless over the catch, while everybody looked at him, if not attracted simply by his obvious naïveté, then surely by his odd appearance. Queeny standing propped on her crutch, declared the former in that high soparano with a fruity laugh: 'Him myall . . . he never see sea before!'

Eyes and teeth sparkled in black faces to silent laughter.

One of the two blackmen, a stocky fellow, grey-haired, fat with good living as few of his kind ever got to be, caught the grey eyes, and raised his right index finger. Prindy hesitated, then gave his Skin sign. The black face split in a smile as the hand gave back the sign *Jelyerri*, which meant they were maternal uncle and nephew. The old man approached him, to touch him and to ask, 'Where you come from, my-boy?'

But as Prindy opened his mouth to answer the attention of everybody was diverted to something behind and beyond him; and he turned with the others to see his mother coming running towards him. She let out a screech, 'Boy . . . what you doin' dere . . . come here!'

Prindy stood his ground. She grabbed him as she came up to him, but with eyes popping at the fish. Queeny swung up beside her, saying 'You like him one goot fish, *Burrawa*, I cook him for you, eh?' When Nell looked at her she added: 'Half dat-lot fish belong 'o me.' She shot what looked like a challenging glance at grey-head, who looked away and spat.

Another diversion, from the same direction. Maggie Barbu was calling. Beside her was Mrs Tasker. Nell said, 'We got 'o go back.'

'I cook him you fish for you supper, chister,' said Queeny.

The grey head spoke to Prindy: '*Mummuk, Kokanjinni* . . . by'n'by you come hellip him me long o' fish-trap, eh?' He jerked his lips towards a pattern of stakes running out from the beach further down. Prindy nodded. There was more yelling, and now waving, from those wanting them back at the picnic. Nell drew Prindy away.

Jumbo fell in beside them. He said, 'Dat old-man . . . he call himself huncle belong you. Dat-one King George,' He chuckled. 'Smart old bugger. He King o' Compound . . . on'y dat Peg-leg Queeny too goot for him.' Then catching Prindy by the shoulder, he swung him so that he looked towards Rainbow Head, saying, 'Dat mob Delacy dere . . . our mob. Your properly father dere . . . Martin . . . properly father, whiteman way.' He looked at Nell, who had swung to stare with them. 'Dat right, ain't it?' he asked. She didn't answer.

More yelling from Maggie Barbu, to be heard now, 'We goin' 'o have tea . . . hurry up!'

As they turned to obey, Jumbo said to Prindy, 'Don' you let dat Delacy mob beat you. You Delacy. Don' you forget it, sonny boy.'

As they came up to the picnic crowd, Mrs Tasker popped out from somewhere to say to Jumbo, 'Now, we don't want you, Jumbo. This's for children and mothers . . . . '

Jumbo sneered: 'What about all them white bloke . . . and your old man . . . dey children and mother, eh?'

'Now, go away, there's a good man, and don't make trouble. Let your wife and little ones have a bit of a treat for once.'

'Gi's a drink o' ginger beer, then.'

Mrs Tasker spoke sharply: 'I'll give you nothing. You're only here to make trouble. Go . . . or I'll send for Mr Turkney.'

Jumbo leered: 'T'ink I drink dat rubbitch? I on'y gammon.'

'Pity you didn't drink that instead of beer . . . and wine . . . and any of the real rubbish you drink and make your family unhappy with.'

'Arrh! grunted Jumbo. 'You on'y drink ginger beer 'cause you got 'o drink sumpin . . . but you fright' real stuff . . . . '

Mrs Tasker went very red: 'I warned you, Jumbo Delacy . . . another word out of you . . . . '

'Arrrh!' Jumbo swung away, back to the fish.

The children of the picnic party and such coloured female adults as had come along with them were seated in a rough semi-circle on the grass facing the sea, with the food tables behind them and before them, as if that should be the focus of their attention rather than the view, the harmonium with a thin smallish lady with fair frizzy hair seated at it, and beside her the Reverend Mr Tasker with a pale hand half raised to imply that he was waiting for everyone to settle down so that they all might sing. Those seated had paper plates and their pannikins before them. The Mission people, ready with the goodies on large enamel dishes and the ginger beer in big enamel jugs each crowned with golden foam, were lined up behind. The Sun was not dazzling now because mostly hidden by the silvery edges of that southward drifting berg of cloud. Prindy and Nell were pushed into a place already held for them by the Barbu children and Big Dolly, while everybody stared at them, particularly at Prindy in his wet khaki clothes.

At last everybody was settled. Mr Tasker nodded to the organist, who played, with a merry little trill, the opening bars of the hymn *Old Hundredth*. Then he raised the poised hand and beat: One, Two, Three – and the voices rose with the music: *Be present at our table, Lord* . . . .

Prindy, in line to see something of what the organist was doing with feet and hands, stared at her so intently as to catch her eye, causing her to smile at him and nod to the music, perhaps to encourage him to join in. Since his lips did not move as seen when previously he had heard new music of a kind that obviously had affected him emotionally, evidently his interest was not so much in the music itself as in the device that produced it. His experience of musical instruments so far would have been confined to those he'd heard played at dances during Race Meetings, good enough for its purpose, but lacking something an ear like his might need especially, melody closer to natural sound, no doubt, since he was adept at bird mimicry. Not that there was anything so natural-sounding, at least to an ordinarily perceptive ear, about what that wheezy old organ was pumping out.

'Amen!' called Mr Tasker at the end of it. Then he dashed off to help his fellows in good-doing to serve the humbler ones, but not before he had taken a good big swig of ginger beer like any common toss-pot and smacked his lips over it the same. But the organist stayed where she was, and kept on playing, all hymns, probably favourites of the children, because many of them beefed out bits between bites, in accompaniment with the Mission people, all of whom sang as they went about serving – the sandwiches with *What Can We Do For Jesus' Sake* – the little cakes with *Jesus Loves Me* – the tarts with *What a Friend We have In Jesus* – the big chunks of iced plum cake with *Gentle Jesus* – and toper's swigs of ginger beer with the lot of it.

Prindy ate and drank everything given him, but more or less mechanically, keeping his eyes on the organist, with such persistent interest that before long, smiling and nodding still, she was playing for him of all of them. When the eating was over, and Mr Tasker had offered up a prayer of thanks for it and said, 'Now, we'll all sit down and have a good old sing-song till it's time to go home,' the organist beckoned Prindy to her. He went at once.

'Hello, little boy,' she said, with that nice smile. 'What's your name?'

A difficult question when you have several names for various uses, until you have been given one by people who don't matter in your scheme of things. He hung his head. She took one of the golden brown hands: 'Don't be shy. My name's Kitty Windeyer.' She giggled slightly, adding, 'Silly name for an organist, isn't it?' When the grey eyes rose questioningly she said, 'But you wouldn't understand the joke, would you. You do understand when I ask your name, though, don't you?'

He nodded. She waited. But he was staring at the keyboard. She asked, 'You like music?'

He looked at her questioningly again. She asked, 'Do you know what music is?'

He shook his head.

'I can see you have lots to learn. You've just come from the bush, haven't you? Now, you know what a song is, I suppose?'

He nodded, his eyes looking eager.

'Well, music means singing songs, and the playing of songs on an instrument . . . like this . . . . ' She gave a couple of pumps with her feet, opened a stop, and played a few melodious notes.

The grey eyes shone with interest. She asked, 'Like to try. Come on. Give me your hand again. Middle C.' She pressed the little index finger down. The note peeled forth. She laughed with delight into the delighted face. 'I can see we're going to make a musician out of you. Now let's run up the scale from C. I'll show you.' She sang the notes as she played them with her own bony white forefinger.' C, D, E, F, G, A, B, C!' Again she smiled at his delight. 'Now you.' He did it almost perfectly.

'What's this?' asked a deep voice.

They looked up to see the square red face under its shock of bristly grey hair and above its dog-collar of Mr Tasker. He added, 'A music lesson?'

Miss Windeyer beamed, 'I do believe we've found a budding musical genius, Mr Tasker.'

'Well, well!' rumbled the Reverend Gentleman, and rumpled the golden hair. 'Isn't that something! Er . . . but Miss Windeyer, let's leave the music lesson for another time, shall we?'

She blushed, murmuring, 'Of course, Mr Tasker . . . I was only . . . '

'Yes, yes . . . if only we *can* make an organist out of him. But now . . . what about some of our new favourites, *God is Love*, and such . . . of our Plagiarisms, I believe you called them, eh? . . . Ha, ha, ha!'

Miss Windeyer went very red, muttering, 'Oh, I didn't call them that, Reverend!

Mr Tasker chuckled. 'A little bird told me, Miss Windeyer . . . a very reliable little bird at that.'

She panted in her embarrassment. 'The word I used, Mr Tasker, was Purloined.'

He laughed heartily. 'Yes, I believe it was, now. I dare say there's a difference. But when it comes to purloining something beautiful for the greater glory of God, it's hardly a sin, is it?'

'Oh, I didn't mean it as a sin. It's only that I've known them as Classics not connected with religion . . . '

'And now all the better that they are, eh? I'm sure that's how you feel about it. You play them with such . . . shall I say gusto? Let's have *God is Love*, then, shall we?'

'Of course, Reverend, of course!' Her thin prettyish face was quivering as she turned it, smiling again on Prindy, to whom she said, 'I'm going to play real music now. See how you like it.'

She swung back to her keyboard and pedal-boards, ran a little flourish, then played the opening bars of Shubert's *Serenade*, then at Mr Tasker's third beat began the lovely melody, to which the gathering sang.

Do you hear the whisper on the breeze,
God is Love, God is Love, . . .
Do you hear the murmur in the trees,
God is Lo-ove, God is Love . . . .

She glanced a few times at Prindy, to see his lips moving. When it was over she swung to him. It was unnecessary to ask him if he liked it. The expression on his face was beatific. For a moment she stared into the wide staring grey eyes, then swiftly bent to him, kissed him on the mouth. He seemed to start awake. He smiled. Redder than ever, she swung back to the little gasper of an instrument out of which she had forced such sweetness.

Next it was Mendelssohn's *Spring Song*. Next Verdi's *Back to Our Mountains*. Then, of all things, *La Donna e Mobile*, giving rollicking praise to the Lord . . . '*Praise, praise, prai-ise ye the Lord* . . . . '

It went on while the great cloud crimsoned to the setting Sun and the sea became a lake of blood now flowing slowly, because the neap was past, and Rainbow Head went through colour changes to purple, and golden lights like stars on the horizon began to twinkle where the rich Delacys and their high-class friends were still celebrating the New Year. Prindy held hands with Miss Windeyer while the Mission darkies loaded the precious music maker onto the truck with all the other gear. She seemed as if she would have kept hold of him, only that his mother came and took him away, and Mrs Tasker took possession of her for the procession back up through the Compound. One last glance back at the pewter sea, the purpling skyline, the ghost-white beach, then plunge into the scrub.

There was Queeny Peg-leg waiting with a newspaper parcel of fish she said she'd just now cooked, to press into Nell's hands, calling her Chister and saying she'd see her tomorro' by'n'by. A little further up, on the opposite side King George was waiting with a similar parcel for him he addressed as *Kokanjinni* and a like injunction for the future.

In the ghostly hovels there were hurricane lamps or fires that revealed ghostly figures. Mr Turkney was waiting outside his office. While everybody else said goodnight and God bless you to the adult girls and their one small male companion, he escorted them to their prison, jollying them for a lot of no-goods who'd been playing the goody-goody for what they could get out of it, predicted that they'd be most of them spending the night on the commodes with belly-ache, then locked them up and departed in haste to do the goody-goody act himself with the departing guest-hosts.

The adult girls, worn out with it all, settled down yawning, talked a little. Prindy was soon asleep. So were the rest. But then suddenly the rest were startled awake by the sound of singing, a sweet strangled version of *The Spring Song*.

There was that breathed-in comment of the night before: *Eh, look out*! since it was a wondrous thing that disturbed them, but with nothing like the sharpness of fear to it as last night, when those terrible words had been uttered: *Kill-him dat whiteman die*!

II

When Mr Eddy McCusky told Prindy and his mother that he would be seeing them tomorrow, as he did when greeting them on New Year's Day, he was not being merely boozily patronising to people who, because he was officially responsible for them, might, by such as he, be thought to feel in need of his patronage, as soon revealed. Most likely what he had told them had made no impression on them whatsoever. The need to see them was all his. Evidently he had arranged with Mr Turkney to have them on hand for his dealings with them first thing that promised day.

As things turned out, Mr Turkney had them, as he put it himself when driven at last to complain about his superior's inordinate failure to comply with what he had committed himself to, not merely in hand but *on his hands* for three full days of waiting, on each of which McCusky had declared by telephone that he would be along as soon as he got things sorted out. Probably it wouldn't have mattered so much to Turkney, surely used to having people on his hands, since the population of the Compound ran into hundreds, had it not been raining hard during those three days, and the man, being told to have the pair on hand and not being completely heartless and having no other handy shelter for them, had been compelled to have them close enough to be irritated by their presence – by their windging, as he called it, because they naturally grew irritable hanging about. He did not have them actually in his office, but in a passage that led through to storerooms and the medical clinic, still with them in constant view. His first complaints were to his wife over the house telephone. Being ironic about McCusky over the house-phone seemed to be a sport of theirs, or perhaps rather a form of release from pressures he put upon them as their boss.

They had a long and droll conversation of the kind after McCusky's admission at last on the fourth day that the sorting-out process had him temporarily beaten, and to Turkney's asking what he should do with the pair, replied, 'Do what you bloody well like.' Then he corrected that: 'No . . . let him run around in the truck a bit with Barney Bynoe. He knows Barney. Have a word with Barney, and tell him to get him to talk about the Catfish affair. I'll have a word with Barney, too . . . and with Jumbo Delacy. The trouble is the kid's said nothing . . . absolutely bloody nothing. Dinny Cahoon tried to kid me he got it all out of him. But I've proved that's a lie. I've seen the Police Statement. The point is: Is the kid a witness for the Defence or the Prosecution? I want him for the Defence, naturally. His testimony's vital. He's actually the only reliable witness to what happened. It isn't that I want to get Old Bob off scot-free. He'll have to go to jail. He's a damn nuisance to 'em out there . . . but he'd be a bigger one out free, even out with you. But we've got to make a showing of defence, now the people down South are watching these cases. Already there's a complication. Bill Billings'll be briefed as Defence Council, as usual, of course . . . but he tells me Jeremy Delacy's been in touch with him, offering himself as Prisoner's Friend . . . ever heard of it? I hadn't. But it seems it's right in law for these parts. As Prisoner's Friend he's offering to testify in the prisoner's favour, to say he was to some extent responsible for letting the boy pass into Old Bob's care, and also to get a qualified Anthropologist up from South to give expert evidence. We don't want it, of course. And now, bugger me, Dinny Cahoon's come up with the idea of adopting the kid to outwit Delacy. He did ask me before. Course it's impossible. Silly cow likes to think he's the boy's father . . . when he's full. His sisters're against it, naturally. . . and the Superintendent and the Administrator . . . and Cobbity. We want to send the boy away, of course. Dinny's got some old-fashioned idea of draggin' him round on police expeditions and makin' a copper out of him. Cobbity's doing nothing as usual, except poke borac. So you see what I'm up against. Like I said . . . give the boy to Barney to run around. We might get him yet.'

Mrs Turkney had been trying to get through to the office while the long explanation went on. When she demanded to know who it was, Turkney said with a groan, 'Our learned friend McCusky. He's become the big bush-lawyer. Christ . . . I've got a cauliflower ear from the bashin' he gave it. All about the Ah Loy kid.'

'Well, I want fish. It's Friday, remember . . . and I've promised half a dozen people. Has the truck gone down yet?'

'No. Tide a bit late, I think. But I'll send Barney now.'

Turkney went out yelling for Barney Bynoe and the truck, and as it came up, went to Prindy and Nell and said, 'Look, Mr McCusky can't come. Nell . . . you go into the laundry and give 'em a hand there. You sonny . . . you can go for a ride with Barney.'

Nell tried to argue that she wanted Prindy to be with her. Turkney raised his voice: 'Do as I tell you, get off to the laundry. The boy'll be all right. What're you frightened of? Ain't I here to look out for him? Go on . . . off you go. You got one good arm. You can help 'em sort the dirty linen.'

The rain had ceased. It was in bright sunshine that Prindy saw that other wondrous sight to eyes not used to the sea – low water, an exaggerated business hereabout, because mean rise and fall of spring tides was something like thirty feet and the seabed such, at least off the beaches, as to be exposed for up to a mile from the normal shore-line when the tide was right out. As the spring tides were then only beginning to make, the conditions were not so extreme as they could be, but enough to cause Barney Bynoe, not a very perceptive person one would gather from his general conduct, to see the wonder in the wide grey eyes and halt the truck in running it out to the fish-trap so as to give full scope to the viewing. Before that Barney had been saying what good mates they were, how they would be going about everywhere together in the truck, and how his little mate would be telling him all about the Muddrin' bijnitch, eh, now, wouldn't he? Almost as soon as Barney had installed Prindy in the cabin of the truck, putting his usual mate Hoppy up behind probably as part of the subtlety he had in mind, he began the questioning. Prindy's response was to give him that wide calm grey glance which anybody knowing him and having any awareness would immediately take as meaning: *No-more savvy nutching*.

There was much more to the scene than a wide stretch of terra firma where an infinitude of silver water had been before. The sand was silver, too, but chased with a myriad ripple lines that gave it a pattern that seemed of itself to flow, the effect perhaps enhanced by the teeming tiny crustacean life upon it and the fact that at its extremity there was a suggestion of violence, due to the play of mirage with the receding water, which gave to it all a quality of calm in storm, a lovely safety granted as a gift as if in temporary concession by an element in otherwise permanent enmity with solid earth. Prindy's lips were moving as he stared, as if being deeply moved by it to song.

King George and his helpers were to be seen simply as black figures inside the apex of the angle of high wire netting that constituted the trap, the contraption being set up to fence what probably would be the final streaming of the outgoing tide, a slightly depressed region lying off a little bay into which debouched the gully between the heights on which the Compound stood and those of Point Lookout. The rippled micaceous wet sand was so hard as scarcely to show the track of the big truck. Barney drove on towards the fishermen, while Prindy now gaped out at the tiny crabs, some with houses on their backs of all shapes and sizes trying to make a brave show but finally having to go indoors, roll over, and dig smartly out of sight, others to run backwards maintaining defiance to the last, still others forming into serried ranks to turn and flee like defeated armies on the run, then suddenly to vanish as literally the earth opened up and swallowed them. A stream of water was soon seen to be flowing from the gully, through banks that kept collapsing in miniature earthquakes. Barney pulled up short of this, at a point about fifty yards from where the blackmen were robbing the trap of its still living silver trove and dumping it into baskets. He said they'd wait there for the fishermen to bring the baskets to them, and went to explain that the trap was King George's own and that he sold his catches through the Compound for his own profit. 'Don't belong to properly King George, all-same nother-one Guvmin t'ing,' Barney said with a laugh. Then, since it was evident that Prindy hadn't seen the joke, he asked, 'You savvy dat King George business?'

Prindy protruded his lips towards the fishermen. 'I savvy dat dat one King George.'

'No-more him,' said Barney; and he went on to give a somewhat confused account of what had been happening of late with regard to the Throne of England, saying that there'd been a King George before and then a King Edward who'd got the sack, and now another King George, who wasn't properly king yet, till he got his crown on, which would be in a couple of month's time, when there'd be a big holiday and sports and a picnic in town. Evidently he wasn't the only one confused over the issue. Chuckling, he said, 'Silly bugger blackfeller been t'ink old George here dat King. Time dat nother-one George been die las' year, Guvmin been let him go prisoner from jail, mek him good-binji, like, long o' new-feller King. Dat-lot been tink it old George been do it . . . ha, ha, ha! . . . dat silly old bugger been tink he do it, too . . . he get pretty big in head dat time, I can tell you.' He added, chuckling, 'Look out you don' go gettin' dem two mix-up time you go Court and you 'ear 'em say . . . King George agin Cock-Eye Bob!'

Looking interested, but also at a loss, Prindy asked, with another projection of the lips forward, 'Dat old-man King George go long o' Court?'

Barney sighed and grimaced, as one used to trying in vain to talk of civilized things to uncivilized people, saying, 'No . . . no . . . you got it all wrong. Dis one no-more properly King George. Dat on'y nickname dey give him. Properly his name Njorjinga . . . dey used to call him Jingo George . . . den King George . . . like o' dat, see? He been mix up in dat Snake bijnitch trouble long o' old Cock-Eye Bob . . . lo-ong time, now. He been go jail. He been come 'ere for what dey call Holdin'. Den by'n'by he King George, King de Compound. I bet you dat day dey put crown long o' that big feller King, old George here goin' 'o reckon it belong 'o him . . . aaaah!' Seeing that Prindy still couldn't see the joke, he stopped laughing, saying, 'I tell you all about King bijnitch by'n'by. I show you picture, too. I tek'm you long o' my house. Plenty book dere. My kid go 'o State School. Den you tell me all about dat Muddrin bijnitch, eh?'

But Prindy was staring at him called Njorjinga and King George, as he came towards them with the other blackmen, lugging their piled buckets of fish. The grey eyes were wide, perhaps from more than interest in the fish, since mention had been made of what probably was the most interesting of all things to him now, the Snake.

Old George smiled at Prindy as he came up, and again addressed him as *Kokanjinni*, a western lingo for Nephew. He also looked at him, as Prindy craned out to watch the loading of the fish, with an expression that seemed to suggest he read more in the grey-eyed glance than the mere display of nepotal deference he might expect by convention. But no other word or sign was exchanged between them. George climbed into the truck with the others. Barney swung the truck back for the shore-line, sending the crabs scuttling again, headed up the beach and through the Compound, to halt outside Mr Turkney's office and there have the catch weighed on the big scales and duly entered in a ledger. It was obvious that George understood neither operation, although he watched with interest verging on suspicion.

As a matter of fact, his industry was very much curtailed. By law he was prevented from what was called Managing his Estate, which virtually meant from conducting any kind of business without the patronage of his Protectors. What money accrued from his fishing was held in trust for him by the Aborigines Protection Department, which doled it out to him as it thought fit. But the shrewd old fellow had a way of beating that. He could buy what he liked from the Compound Canteen Store on credit against his Trust Account. He did so liberally, and realized handsomely on the stuff in cash through some system of brokerage dealings with other inmates of the institution that had never been elucidated by the authorities, to whom he was known as a Head.

It was curious that when their declared policy was to assimilate their charges into the civilized community, and complained of their general lack of what was called economic sense, they disapproved of the display of the very essence of it, Private Enterprise. King George and his female counterpart in the matter, Queeny Peg-leg, were joked about mainly in Official circles. Still the disapproval was there always in evidence. They were accused of exploiting their simpler brethren. As if just about every civilized person in the land did not do exactly that in some form or other, if it were only in foisting Jesus onto them or taking salaries for protecting them.

Old George now went into the store to collect his dues, while Prindy went off in the truck with Barney and Hoppy to deliver the goods, at much greater profit to the Department than to George.

The delivery first took them into the region reserved for the residences of Junior Government Officers, their first call being at the McCusky home, evidently to give Mrs McCusky the pick of the catch, the way she, a thin tight-lipped fairish lady, went through it. Looking at Prindy, she asked, 'That the boy?' As they left her, Barney remarked on the interest that was being taken in him and hinted at the much greater that would follow his appearance in Court, and got onto the subject of the bijnitch again under the guise of being able to help him see the embarrassing business through more easily if he knew all about it. Still Prindy was silent.

Next they called at the Garrison, where they dallied for some little time beside the cook-house owing to Prindy's interest in company drill that was going on. So struck was he by the patent absurdity of a body of men's heading in one direction with such positive purpose only to turn and do the like in the opposite that he asked, 'Wha's matter dat-lot . . . he like old bull walkin' up-an'-down fence?' He also remarked on the Drill Sergeant's yelling, which must have struck him like the bawling out of defaulting black stockmen by his uncle Clancy and others. 'Wha's matter dat-one all-time growl-growl-growl?'

From the Garrison to the Hospital, where there was the strange sight to see of people lying in bed in whole groups with the Sun halfway up the sky, and the chilling sound of a woman's screaming as if being beaten fair to death. Of the latter, Barney remarked, 'White lady havin' a baby.' Black ladies, at least living in their natural state more or less, never inflicted their pangs of parturition on male ears, always being removed into isolation at time of delivery.

Then to the Jail. It wasn't the prisoners who got the fish, but the jailers, the pick of it here being taken by the wife of the Chief Jailer, Major O'Dowdy. So thorough was her picking that it allowed quite a time for looking about at what could be seen, which included a glimpse inside through the big wooden doors, where a group of blackmen, all clad alike in grey shirts and khaki pants, decorated with that emblem of the King of England, the broad arrow, were squatting in groups cutting logs of wood with cross-cut saws, while chanting in corroboree style. There were other men similarly coloured and clad working in the bright gardens that lay between the high white washed iron walls and the line of Officers' residences. All were interested in Prindy, perhaps already having been appraised of his identity and appearance by the grapevine that was known to function most efficiently between jail and town. Mrs O'Dowdy knew of him, anyway. Having mauled all of the fish several times, looking in their gills and sniffing them, a fat fair woman with silly wobbly blue eyes, she asked Barney, 'That him?' Then, as if Prindy were some dumb animal, proceeded to inquire about his parentage: 'Is it a fact that his father's Martin Delacy . . . or Dinny Cahoon like they say?' Barney was obviously careful with his answers, as if knowing her as one not to be trusted. While it was going on, Major O'Dowdy himself appeared from inside the prison, a heavily built white-haired red-faced man, dressed rather like a policeman. He spoke to Barney about bringing more wood for his sawyers. The logs used were cut by gangs of more or less forced labourers who were inmates of the Compound with nothing better, from an official point of view, to do. The resultant wood was issued as fuel to Government Officers.

As they left the Jail, Barney had another go at getting Prindy to talk, even suggesting now that his stubborn silence might land him behind that high wall to saw wood all day – but quite without effect.

The baskets were empty of fish now. However, there remained a box, covered with a sack and serving so far as a seat for Hoppy and not included in the weighing-in at the Compound, which proved to hold the best of all the catch, a dozen or so large Trevally, or White Fish as they were called locally, at least by Chinese, who prized them highly. These were destined for the Chinese. On the way back from the Jail towards Town, Barney took a sudden turn up a narrow road that brought them into what was obviously the domain of Chinese gardeners. As in all such places, there were large chained dogs to announce their presence. A skinny old pantalooned Chinese woman came to them with a basket, took a look and a sniff at the fish, and when it had been handed over to her, gave Barney a small paper packet. No word was said. Evidently it was a commonplace deal, with what was called opium ash, a low-grade form of the drug pedlared to the blacks by Chinamen.

The itinerary now led by way of that road down which Barney had taken Prindy and his mother the night of their arrival. They went through a timbered region, with a glimpse of the old Delacy residence, down to the coconuts, but off to the left now before reaching the cemeteries and over the wastes of maritime marsh to the home of Jumbo Delacy. It was quite a substantial place, even if in bad repair, an iron bungalow with verandahs screened in the old style with split bamboo strung on wire, well shaded with mangoes and other leafy trees and a couple of coconuts. Jumbo and Possum, his wife, and their numerous brood came rushing out at sound of the horn. It was then revealed that still more fish were being transported unofficially, when Barney handed over a sugar sack he'd had on the ledge behind him in the cabin. As it was just about time for dinner, and the visitors accepted Jumbo's invitation to stop and have it with them, Possum set to work at once, with the help of a couple of the bigger children, to clean and cook the fish. Evidently Jumbo had been appraised of the need to get Prindy talking about the Catfish affair, as Mr McCusky had said he would be, because he and Barney at once fell to discussing the matter over a bottle of beer also produced from the cabin of the truck by Barney, while Prindy went off with younger children, at Jumbo's urging, to look for coconuts. During the meal the pair continued to discuss it, at first as if Prindy weren't there, advancing their own theories – I reckon – no-more, I reckon – then suddenly swung on Prindy and asked what he reckoned. The stratagem didn't work. The grey eyes were as blank as ever. Exasperated, Jumbo demanded, 'Wha's matter . . . you been chillip dat time?'

Prindy said simply, 'I don' know.'

Jumbo went on: 'Crise . . . wha'-for you fright? Dat-lot old-man can't hurt you spone you talk. He dere long o' jeel, ain't he? You fright' long o' dat lot Delacy, eh?'

Prindy shook his head.

'Yes . . . I reckon you fright' long o' dat-lot. You fright' dat-one Clancy put him stock-whip roun' you, spone you talk, ain't it?'

The grey eyes widened. Jumbo seemed to take the expression for admission of fear: 'Yeah . . . da's it.' Evidently he'd heard, like most people in the land by this time, surely, seeing what a place it was for passing the word around, that the affair had been in some degree due to Clancy's interference. He went on: 'Mr McCusky . . . and me-two-feller Barney . . . we wan' 'o help you. No matter 'bout who been start dat row. Dat one Clancy been start it all right. We know. All you got 'o do you tell him me-feller what happen dere long o' Ring Place. Den we can mek trouble for Clancy. More better we mek trouble long o' Delacy mob, eh? You no-more like him dat-one Clancy, eh?' Prindy shook his head. 'You no-more like'm Martin, eh?' Again the fair head shook. 'Well, there y'are, see. We after dat-lot white Delacy. Now you tell-him-'bout.'

The head shook again: 'I don' know.'

Barney checked Jumbo's impatience, got him aside and said he'd leave the boy with him. He then departed. Prindy appeared to be quite ready to stay. Soon after Barney left, he joined the other children in a trip to the beach just across the way through the maritime scrub, and had his first taste of the joy of swimming in salt water.

Arrived back at the Compound, Barney Bynoe went straight to Mr Turkney in his office to report on what he'd done. Turkney's reply was to the effect that he had done well, but that he himself had better check with the Boss, and promptly rang Mr McCusky. McCusky not only approved of the idea of leaving Jumbo to work on Prindy, but added that he thought it a good idea to have the boy stay with Jumbo's family for the time being, seeing they had no proper place for him at the Compound. Turkney asked what he would do about the mother. McCusky said, 'Hang on to her. It might be her who's stopping him from talking. Besides, she's supposed to be under medical attention, isn't she?' Turkney explained that so far Dr McQuegg hadn't been to see her. McCusky laughed: 'He hasn't got over Hogmanay yet . . . or Piggy Trotters' wake. Issue some special rations to Jumbo for the boy, otherwise I'll have him on my back for money. By the way, I've just heard that poor old Piggy was that yeller piece's old man . . . you ever hear it? Dinny told me . . . and he ought to know. So really the kid's name's Trotters. I was thinking of using it. We can't put him up in Court as Ah Loy, or into our new institution . . . it's too ridiculous. But it'd be too hard on old Elsie and the girls. Still, we got to get him a proper name. That's our policy now. No blackfeller names. No crazy nicknames. That Prindy business'll have to go. Means a bloody goanna. You got anything in mind, Tub?'

Tubby Turkney, feet now up on the table and phone cradled on shoulder, wearing that look of resignation which was part of his dealings with his superior, answered with deliberation that might well have been taken as irony by a more perceptive questioner, 'Not a thing, Eddy, not a thing.'

'Right, then. Leave it to me So long.'

Mr Turkney lowered feet and phone together with relief so evident that Barney smirked in turning towards the door. But that relief lasted only as long as it took Barney to get outside, when it was shattered by a shrieking revelation of something of what McCusky actually had left to him. Evidently Nell had been on the lookout for the return of her boy, and not seeing him, rushed at Barney, wanting to know where he was, and being told, demanded to be taken to him, shrieking down his assurances and objections, and proceeding to do violence on him, when Turkney came lumbering out, roaring. 'Here . . . cut that out . . . what's going on?'

Nell turned on him. 'Bloody harcarse bastard been steal my boy!'

'He never steal him . . . he leave him Jumbo Delacy place . . . and I told him to.'

'I wan' 'o go dere long o' my boy.'

'Well, you can't. He's all right there.'

She swung from him back to Barney, who was retreating to the truck, rushed after him and grabbed him by the blue shirt, pulling it out of his trousers, screeching, 'You tek me long o' my boy, you bloody bastard.'

Struggling to get free of her, Barney lost half his shirt. He leapt out of reach. As she went after him again, Turkney went after her, grabbed her sound arm. She swung on him to menace him with the splinted arm, with the cockatoo screeching rising higher, 'Le' me 'lone, you bloody bastard!'

Turkney was bellowing now: 'Don't you swear at me, you bloody bitch!'

A crowd was coming running, blacks and the girls from the Adults Home. Nell's voice cracked as she got it out: 'Bloody puggim white bastard!' She broke free, turned to run towards the gate. Turkney yelled to Barney to stop her. She kicked Barney in the shin, but stumbled in doing so saved herself from hitting the ground with the hand of her good arm. Yelling for someone to go and get his missus, Turkney pounced on her, tangled with her in her fierce resistance, grabbed the hand of the broken arm, twisted it, causing her to give a final piercing shriek and fall in a faint. The inadvertency of his act was surely shown in his sudden paling and gasping, 'Christ!' as he bent over her. He looked up at his wife's arrival, saying miserably, 'I must've hurt her arm . . . but she was going crazy. I'd better get the doctor.'

He trotted back to his office and called Dr McQuegg, who started off with a testy implication that the girl had been neglected. As testily Turkney replied, 'You can hardly blame me for that. I arranged about an X-ray and everything with the hospital.'

McQuegg grunted, 'Bloody holidays. Send her over the Hospital and I'll be right out to take a look at her.'

Nell had recovered consciousness by the time Turkney returned. She was struggling again, but with no such violence, and sobbing for her lost Lil Boy instead of shrieking, soothed somewhat now by her friends from the home and Mrs Turkney, who was saying, 'Now everything's going to be all right.'

Turkney briskly told Barney to take her to the Hospital in the truck, and then told Big Dolly to accompany her. Nell's too ready compliance with his directing her to get into the truck should have given a hint of the fact, as quickly disclosed, that she thought she was being taken to Prindy. She realized that something other than her own intention was being carried out when the truck, having passed through the gateway, swung right instead of left, which was the direction they'd come in from, that night of arrival. She was sitting between Barney and Dolly. Wildly she began to look about, then demanded, 'Where we go?' Barney told her to the Hospital. She started shrieking again, 'I don' wan' 'o go Hospital . . . you tek me my boy!' Then as they tried to soothe her she swore at them, struggled to get out. Dolly got a grip on her as she tried to squeeze across her bulging belly. Still Barney kept going, passed the Children's Home and their playground, beyond which the road narrowed, running through scrub, its surface rather rough, being the natural rock of the locality, a slag-like laterite. They had just got onto this narrow stretch, with Nell well and truly in Dolly's grasp but still struggling, when she kicked Barney in the ribs, knocking the wind out of him and causing him to lose control. The truck veered off the road, bounced over some lumps of laterite, hit a tree – *Bang*!

The impact threw Dolly and Nell out, Nell to fall underneath. Another shriek. Then silence. Dolly dragged herself off her cushion to find it inert. She called to Barney, 'She faint again. Look her arm!'

Barney and Hoppy came down to take a look. One of the splints was splintered and half the bandages snapped. A glance at the truck showed it was undamaged. Barney leapt back into it, started up, backed onto the road. Then he got down again to help Dolly and Hoppy lift the still unconscious Nell into the back. As they did so, Hoppy, who had her by the legs as the others hauled her up, exclaimed: 'Crise!' When they looked at him he showed a pink palm red with blood.

In a few minutes they were at the Hospital, to find Dr McQuegg already waiting and with some excuse for his testiness now after hearing what had happened meanwhile. 'Bloody halfwits! She ought've been sent in the ambulance. Bone fragmented . . . miscarriage, too, I'll bet. What a bloody mess!'

As Nell began to rally and struggle again they gave her Morphine. Examination proved the doctor's prognostication correct. It was dark when they wheeled her out of the Operating Theatre, with her arm in plaster, her belly deflated, and put her in a bed in that corner of one of the verandahs reserved for the like of her. The Matron, a stocky red-faced woman with popping blue eyes silenced the worried doctor's final attempt to blame everybody but himself by saying, 'Blame the booze, doctor. Anyway, does it matter all that much? She's only a halfcaste.'

Just about then, over at Jumbo's, Prindy was being taken up that scrubby hill in the pale light of a half Moon mostly clouded over, by Jumbo and two of Jumbo's bigger boys, with the intention of showing him how his rich relations lived. The big old Delacy home (the modified palace of a Chinese tycoon somehow outwitted by the late Inspector Delacy, now become the leading squatter's town-house of the land) was ablaze with light. The visit was, of necessity, secret, but easily enough made; for one reason that evidently Jumbo had made it so often as to have perfected it as a piece of stratagem; for another that watch-dogs were not kept, as probably by the former owners. In fact the modification of the place was such that whereas the mainstay of the domestic service down at Beatrice River was Chinese, here it was Japanese, the very opposite. The major-domo was an ancient Japanese named Hanno, another shrewd acquisition of old-man Delacy's, according to what Jumbo told Prindy about this family of theirs, at once to express his own all-abiding bitterness in his own rejection by them, and evidently to arouse the same in the boy with a view to getting his confidence. It seemed that Hanno, an old-time pearler, had been involved in murdering business with his compatriots that could have cost him his life either at the hands of these or of the hangman, was delivered from both through the power of Police Inspector Delacy, as the result of which, out of a Nipponese sense of obligation or need of perpetual protection, had enlisted himself in perpetuity as bondsman to the family. Although Jumbo spoke of Hanno as a friend of his, it was obvious that he envied him his position in the household. As he said, when pointing Hanno out as they crept up to watch the family, with several friends, at dinner in the big dining-room, 'Wha' dat bloody Jap doin' dere, and we-lot got 'o stay outside, eh?'

They were able to go right into the verandah conservatory adjoining the dining-room and see and hear everything. Clem Eaton was at the head of the grand table, Rhoda at the foot, with Martin and Clancy interspersed among the half-dozen or so superior looking guests. Hanno, a stocky figure with a bristly frizz of white hair and clad immaculately in white with tunic buttoned to his chin, stood by a large dinner-waggon, to and from which he moved in attending the diners with such celerity that most of his time was spent standing. A couple of times he glanced into the conservatory as if he knew someone was there behind the ferns and orchids, as indeed was made apparent when at last he made a move in that direction which caused Jumbo to hiss to the others and to withdraw.

'Dere y'are,' said Jumbo as they went home, 'Da's dem bloody white Delacy bastard. Wha' dey care 'bout you, eh? And close-up you white, too. Spone you tell me 'bout dat Muddrin bijnitch, we mek proper fool dat Clancy long o' Court . . . eh?'

Apparently Prindy was quite unaffected in the manner Jumbo had hoped for. Back home, finding Barney and Hoppy there with a couple of bottles of beer, Jumbo gave him up in disgust. But a couple of hours later, while the visitors were still there, and Prindy sleeping on a bed of sacks out on a side verandah with the other smaller kids and he began to sing *My Rown Road* and the startled kids came running to report the phenomenon, Jumbo hissed, 'Now we goin' 'o hear sumpin!' and went rushing on tip-toe to hear.

Prindy struggled through the song as usual, but to end as he had that first disturbed night of sleeping in these so different from usual circumstances.

I find him by'n'by
Kill dat whiteman, kill-him-die
My Road, My Road, My Road, My Ro-own Road.

It was received with the same startled in-breathed exclamation. All who heard it stared at one another, the fearful question in their dark eyes: *Kill the whiteman*?

Talking about it afterwards, in voices subdued compared with what they had been, the three men came to the conclusion that what they'd heard was the result of Cock-Eye Bob's interference with the boy, and the fact that he would not talk was due to the old man's having *Sung* him.

Over at the Hospital, as if the emotional upsurging of the son had communicated itself to the mother, Nell woke from her long sleep, and finding herself not only in strange surroundings but immobilized by the hospital device called the Restraining Sheet, began to whimper, then to yell.

It happened that the Matron was handy and came hurrying with the Night Charge. Finding no medical evidence for the trouble, Matron snapped: 'Shut up! There's nothing wrong with you now. There's lots sicker people in the place than you. So don't disturb them . . . Shut up, I tell you!'

Nell quit yelling, but continued to whimper for her Lil Boy. Matron said, 'Give her another quarter grain, Sister.'

The Sister was soon there with the syringe – and soon the whimpering died away – 'My Lil Boy . . . my Lil Boy . . . Lil . . . Lil . . . Boy . . . '

Curlews were crying on the Hospital beach, perhaps through having found the *tjooloo* belonging to that bloody something they'd thrown into the white enamel waste bucket in the hospital theatre earlier on, and were concerned with getting it back to a place of safety. Or were they playing a joke on the whitefeller by deciding to present it to that white lady moaning in delayed parturition over in Maternity? For it happened just then that the lady began to yell again. The Night Charge went racing to see, then leapt to the telephone to call Dr McQuegg.

Next morning at the Hospital, Nell still under restraint and still whimpering, but softly, suddenly found the cause of all her troubles at her side, with Mr

McCusky also there, panama over one eye and a hand on Prindy's shoulder and a twinkle in his eye. She had eyes for only the one, and as best she could in the contraption restraining her, seized him, hugged him to her, gasping and gurgling of her Lil Boy, completely ignoring the fatherly advice that McCusky at once proceeded to give her concerning her behaviour. When he essayed to take the boy away with him, he had to say it all over again. He told her he intended to have Prindy stay with Jumbo's family until after what he described as Court business, that he would keep an eye on him himself, and see to it that she saw him every day – so long as she behaved herself. If she would promise him now not to leave the hospital or do any other *tulli-tulli* thing, he would see Dr McQuegg about getting her out of that thing. Whimpering again, she promised.

Man and boy went off hand in hand, the man in his jaunty way hailing everybody he passed, the boy taking in everything with wide grey-eyed interest. Getting into McCusky's car, Prindy settled with ease. McCusky headed for town, talking all the while, mostly of the wonderful things he was going to do for all halfcaste kids in the near future, and especially for him he called his mate. He put his hand on the bare golden-brown knee as they pulled in at the Government Offices, saying, 'You and me proper mates . . . ain't we?' Prindy nodded, but without responding to the wide grin. 'Right,' added McCusky. 'Let's get inside and fix things up for you. You like that new name I've got for you, eh? Well, I'll show you what it looks like in writing . . . and in no time you'll be writing it yourself.'

As they entered McCusky's office, the man said to the two people who looked up from desks at their entry, 'Well, here he is . . . Prendegast Alroy.' They smiled. McCusky went to his own desk and took up an official folder. The name was printed in a corner. He pointed it out to Prindy, saying, 'There it is. I'll spell it to you.' He did so, then said, 'Say it.'

'Prendegast Alroy.' So perfect was the delivery that it must have been well rehearsed. The clerk laughed and the typist giggled. Prindy joined in the mirth. But not McCusky, who asked somewhat shortly, 'What's funny about it? That's the best name I've thought up yet.' Red-faced, his subordinates concentrated on their work. But he had their attention again in a moment, saying 'You know, that's the first time I've heard him laugh. Maybe it's a talisman. Yes, by jings! Maybe he'll talk now . . . .'

He broke off when Prindy looked quickly towards the doorway of an inner room, and turned, to see Dr Cobbity standing staring – literally staring – with those intense blue eyes out of the brick-red face. Prindy's grey eyes, meeting the stare, widened visibly, as in alarm. The doctor transferred the stare to McCusky, whom he addressed in what sounded like a mocking tone and with a grin: 'Well, let's see the talisman work . . . Bring him in.' He turned back into his sanctum.

McCusky, whose usual bossy manner had changed on the instant, bent to Prindy, saying softly, 'Come on . . . don't be fright.' He put an arm about the small shoulders. Prindy went readily enough.

By the time they got in, Dr Cobbity was seated behind his big barish glass-topped table, leaning back in a swivel chair, elbows on the arm rests, hands clasped to support his chin. Again he fixed Prindy with the glassy stare, but was evidently addressing McCusky when he spoke: 'Well, what's the latest?'

McCusky said, 'I reckon he's been hypnotized, Doc.'

The grin started, but was quickly sucked in by the ruddy cheeks. The eyes swung on McCusky, who had read the signs of mockery, and reddening, began to expostulate: 'Dinkum, Doc . . . Jumbo and Barney heard him singing in his sleep last night . . . .'

'How's that prove hypnosis?'

'They reckon he's been *Sung*.'

This time the doctor erased the grin by altering his pose to reach onto the table for his pipe. McCusky said with haste, 'These old *koornungs*'ve got strange powers.'

Addressing his pipe as he stuffed it from the pouch, Dr Cobbity said, 'There's nothing strange about hypnosis.'

'That's what I mean, Doc. The old feller had him hypnotized. He won't talk, because he was told not to.'

Cobbity lit the pipe and hid behind the smoke. He said, 'And your ground for this theory is that Jumbo and Barney heard him singing in his sleep. Any kid could sing in his sleep. If he were hypnotized he'd only sing what he was instructed to.'

McCusky said quickly, 'Ah . . . that's just what he did do, Doc!'

The half-mockery fled in a flash: 'What'd he sing?'

McCusky was himself again. He answered slowly and with full dramatic effect, ' "Kill that whiteman die." '

Cobbity looked at Prindy, stared at him, was stared out by the grey eyes, gave his attention again to McCusky, who was awaiting it posed in all his cocksureness, and promptly said, 'Don't forget Cock-Eye Bob's dedicated to wiping out the whiteman.'

The doctor puffed his pipe, said out of the smoke, 'Cock-Eye Bob's insane.'

'According to our standards.'

The mockery was in the voice again: 'What others do you propose we should conform to?'

McCusky was deflated again: 'But . . . but if it proves the old man's interfered with the boy's mind.'

'Where's it going to get you?'

'Well, now the Prosecution's conceded him as our witness, and we can't make him talk, we've got an excuse for his silence.'

'What excuse?'

'Tribal matter. He was under the influence of an elder putting him through an initiation, in which the halfcaste mother and so-called father interfered to the point of threatening the life of the elder, who did the killing in self-defence.'

Dr Cobbity blew out a great cloud of smoke: 'I told you the self-defence plea'll only make things worse by working the Prosecution up and prolonging the case.'

'But you said you don't want the Protection of Native Races mob and their Anthropologists poking their noses into it.'

'They're already into it. I'm informed that Dr Fabian Cootes'll be honouring us with his presence again.'

'That boofhead!'

'Boofhead or not, he's out to get us. I'm Public Enemy Number One to him.'

'That means we've got to fight like hell for the Defence so they've got nothing on us.'

'Whatever we did they'd break it down so as to stop me going on with my ideas for integration. They want menageries for their Stone Age Men, with mission stations next door so that as the savages come out of the Stone Age they walk into the arms of Jesus. I've given too much bloody work to what I want to do with the boongs, to be kicked out now. I pulled the bloody thing out of Nineteenth Century slavery. I've got everybody against me, black and white. I'm not going to be beaten now. The bigger the case, the more the publicity. That's what the Anthrops and the bible-bashers want. We've got to defend ourselves first . . . and the only way to do that is to have no case at all.'

McCusky gaped: 'No case?'

The grin widened. The smoke puffed. The mocking voice said, 'We'll plead insanity. Not even Cootes would call the old man sane. He's always been considered mad. He had a special corner in the Jail. If we'd had a mad-house, he'd've been in that instead of jail. He shouldn't have been released under the Amnesty. They only did it because they wanted to get rid of him and his bread-and-milk diet, and that mad judge making a mate of him. What's he do when he's released? Goes and lures away a little half-wit boy, gets a crazy notion to initiate him, scares the local mob into compliance. Just naturally kills the half-wit's father for interfering. No anthropology. No sociology. No criminology. Just plain unadulterated lunacy, for which myself and McQuegg will issue a certificate for presentation to the judge.'

McCusky swallowed: 'You think the boy's a half-wit?'

Cobbity fixed his blue stare on the grey, held it for a while, then raised a smoke screen, as if to ease the strain on himself, and said, 'I think it's obvious. Nobody can get a squeak out of him, except that laugh just now . . . and he only laughed because someone else did. Sign of insanity. Say something, anything . . . and laugh . . . and you'll see . . . go on!'

Eddy McCusky swallowed again, said weakly, 'I can't.'

The grin, the puffing pipe. Then fixing the grey eyes again, the doctor asked, 'What's your name, boy?'

The grey eyes blinked once. Cobbity waited, keeping up the smokescreen, asked, 'Where you come from?'

Another blink. Cobbity blew out a great puff that caused the grey eyes to blink rapidly, and turned from them to McCusky. 'Obviously *non compos mentis*. From what I've been hearing from the Hospital, the mother's a border-line case of insanity, too. Maybe after the business is over, we'll certify 'em both and get rid of 'em . . . . ' Evidently noting the scary look in McCusky's eyes, Cobbity added: 'You don't want to start off your new Settlement by including a loony bin in it, do you? Anyway, the Estimates are too tight as they are . . . and speaking of bloody Estimates . . . . ' He reached for a pile of papers on the desk.

McCusky took the hint, put a hand on Prindy's shoulder, turned him towards the door. As he was opening it, Cobbity said, with the grin, 'Sorry to cramp your style in forensic histrionics, Eddy . . . but maybe you can put on something of a show with the insanity plea.'

McCusky went red, but answered with a weak grin, went out.

In the other office, clerk and typist looked up with what appeared to be routine expectancy. McCusky addressed them without looking at them, out of the side of the mouth: 'No doubt about him . . . our Cuthbert's a brainy bastard.' He added: 'Off to the Compound. See you later.'

When they were back in the car, McCusky turned and stared at Prindy, who stared back in the usual way. After a moment McCusky asked, 'Are you really as dumb as you make out to be . . . or are you havin' us on? Funny if you were, wouldn't it . . . heeee . . . haaaa? . . . Oh no!' For Prindy was echoing the laugh. McCusky turned away, started up, drove off in silence. He dropped Prindy off at Jumbo's. Jumbo himself was absent. While Prindy went off looking for the children, McCusky told Possum that he and Dr Cobbity had come to the conclusion that Prindy wasn't what he called all-there, tapping his head. Possum clicked her tongue, as if in sympathy. But ready response of the kind was typically Aboriginal and more expression of courtesy than emotion. She might as well have been showing sympathy for Messrs Cobbity and McCusky for having a half-wit to deal with when they needed someone really smart. The Aboriginal attitude to such a person was much less sympathetic than indulgent.

McCusky went on to the Compound and reported the matter to Turkney, who promptly said he'd guessed it all along: 'That stare of his . . . and that mad bloody mother. Do I have to have her back here?'

'Yes. I wouldn't trust her with the boy alone. She'd do a bolt, I reckon . . . and we want her for the trial.'

'When'll that be?'

'Christ knows . . . when Judge Bickering makes up his mind that he's had enough of the Law Vacation. The Inquest'll be next week. I'll keep the mother in hospital till then. Now, don't forget. Barney's to pick the kid up every day and take him to his mother when he calls at the Hospital, and see he gets home to Jumbo's every night.'

That's the way it went, except that Prindy soon learnt to find his own way home. He spent his time by no means mostly at his mother's bedside. In fact the nursing staff discouraged him from hanging about her; and it was obvious that he didn't need much discouragement. He was sent to eat with the halfcaste domestic staff, male and female, on the back verandah of the kitchen. All treated him with special kindness, perhaps from having heard that he was what locally was called *jitti*. Being used to helping in a kitchen, he soon made friends with the Greek cook, who took him down to a nearby beach and introduced him to the Greek boat-builders. Apart from the boat-building, which appeared to interest him greatly, there was the fascination of the seashore. A small creek ran into the sea there with a bit of mud and mangroves and the odd things that live in such places: the red-armed fiddler crabs and mudskippers. Then there was the Pharmacist, who besides having bottles of medicines on his shelves, had a fine collection of zoological specimens of medical interest; snakes, scorpions, centripedes, and the like, and venomous sea creatures. Finding Prindy peeping one day, he offered him a closer look. Prindy was wary to begin with, but soon showed marked interest. The Pharmacist also got him to take a peep into his microscope, to the boy's evident wonder, especially when he saw what one of the golden hairs of his own head looked like, and a drop of his blood produced with a pin-prick. He was there one day when Dr Cobbity came in. Prindy promptly ran out. On Cobbity's inquiring what he was doing there, the Pharmacist told him of the boy's interest in things, adding: 'He doesn't seem anything like a half-wit to me.'

Dr Cobbity said, 'Being interested in snakes and things in bottles is no criterion of intelligence. Young apes show a lively interest in everything. The point is, has he *talked* to you?'

'Well, no . . . I can't say I've heard him say a word.'

Then there at Jumbo's one morning, instead of Barney with the Compound truck, was Mr McCusky with his car, and a neat little outfit in galatea for him to put on in place of those too-big khakis Daddy Christmas Cahoon had given him. They were going to Court, said McCusky. From Jumbo's they went on to the Hospital to pick up Nell, who was already dressed up, in the pretty Cahoon dress, which fitted her much better now. Evidently she had been instructed to be ready, but thought she was merely leaving hospital, because she looked scared when Court was mentioned. Doubtless McCusky had experience of losing Aboriginal witnesses through too early talk of Court. As it was he delivered them into the Courtroom a matter of minutes before the proceedings of the Inquest began.

So many eyes leaping to challenge the grey eyes – blue eyes, green, grey, brown, black – and the grey widening to meet them but never flinching. So intense was the staring at him in that moment of his appearance that he might have been seen for what he really was if only he chose to be, the star witness. He looked first to the left, since when entering from the verandah fronting the street that was the side where the assemblage was most dense, packed as it seemed to be by reason of the limited capacity of the place. There were, in fact, only three rows of seating forms, long church-like things with backs to them, six in all, since there was an aisle between them leading from a door at the rear. The aisle served also as division between those concerned with Prosecution and Defence, who were seated in the front row, with desk-like tables before them, the former being the further in, seeing that Daddy-o Cahoon was there, with his long legs stuck out under a desk and arms folded, and others of his khaki-clad kind with him, and seeing that the newcomers were halted at the first bench and pushed into places there with several strangers. Daddy-o waved and smiled at them. They only stared their recognition. There was another familiar face in the bench behind them, ruddy and grey-eyed and grey-haired, near enough to lean forward and say, 'Hello, sonny.' Prindy looked into those eyes so like his own, the Mullaka's, but could do no more.

And then in being seated, they were confronted with the other so different aspect, the reared bench, above it the Royal Arms, below the desk of the Clerk of Court, Mr Doscas, so vast of girth as to take up the room of three ordinary persons and breathing like a stranded dugong, at the inner end of the desk another presence, a familiar one, Miss Kitty Windeyer, the Court Reporter, seated at her typewriter, nodding and smiling to her little friend. These were directly in front. To the left was the Dock, ranged along the pale green wall, also elevated, and fully occupied, with forms in uniform prison grey, above which soon to be made out were familiar black faces; Uncle Splinter, Father-in-law Green-ant and others of the station staff – but that gaunt face at the far end, clean-shaved, topped with a fuzz of clipped grey hair, beneath it the clothes, surely unrecognizable to one who knew it looking so different, yet the eyes, those burning coals of eyes, unforgettable, and seizing now the grey eyes and with their intensity surely reading the mind behind. A slight twist of the crack of a mouth perhaps to show that what was read was good. Then the red eyes flicked away, to concentrate on the Royal Arms of England. The grey eyes were drawn with them. A great garish thing, it was as flamboyant as the Kings of England must have been in their truly kingly beginnings – white and red and blue and gold, the Lion and the Unicorn, a-fighting for the Crown – *Honi Soit Qui Mal y Pense* on a princely buckler, *Dieu et Mon Droit* on a ribbon of royal blue – the alien totem, the symbol of the *kuttabah*, the white stranger in all his ruthless might.

The burning eyes came back to meet the grey, as if to read again. Again the twist of smile. Then they looked straight ahead, over the bald dome of Fatty Doscas, over the tables of Miss Kitty and the two newspaper reporters, a fair fat woman and a lean dark man, over the empty jury pews, out through the wide open windows giving perfect view of the harbour, right across and to include almost all of the western shore. Again the grey eyes turned as if by order. Their view was through the wide doorway. The tide was out, so that some of the near shore with its careened vessels of many sorts could clearly be seen over the edge of the cliff across the road from the Court House. There was the jetty, there another steamboat, another flying-boat; but what was most striking of all by far and surely was what was ordered to be looked at was Rainbow Head standing high out of water and fairly blazing in the morning sunlight, with behind it, straggling away southward out of view, a line of jagged rocks past which the incoming tide was seething with such force that, aided by mirage, the whole thing looked like a mighty monster swimming. That was the treacherous Rainbow Reef, one of the few geographical features in the land named by the whiteman after the geography of the blackmen, who believed it to be one of the Shades, and perhaps the most dangerous, of the Rainbow Snake. But there was no time for another exchange of glances to show whether the significance was understood. Scarcely had Prindy set eyes on the amazing thing when there was a shout: '*Silence in Court . . . be upstanding*!' And the grey eyes, startled, turned to be arrested by the sight of an old whiteman, white-haired and white-moustached and wearing a black silk gown, come through a small door directly under the English King's totem, and to be hauled to his feet by Mr McCusky. The old man, bowed slightly to the assembly, some of whom returned the gesture, including Mr Doscas, who in the process exposed the outlines of a prodigious arse and what must have been veritable pack-bags of testicles dangling between his legs. The old man seated himself on his throne. The assembly sank down again, with the exception of Mr Doscas, doubtless through knowing that he would soon have to rise again and what the effort would cost.

The enthroned old gentleman was Mr Bundy, Stipendiary Magistrate, and Coroner. He began proceedings by lowering his head to take a look at his audience over his spectacles, a long and searching look, as if wanting to know whom he had to deal with. Certainly it was not a mere gesture of authority, that is to say an act put on to give weight to his personal insignificance, like the bright insignia hanging above his bleached old head, because it was clear that he looked at Jeremy Delacy with recognition, and with curiosity at the men beside him, one a plump dark little fellow, Dr Fabian Cootes, noted Anthropologist, and a fair young man with the suggestion of a harelip, Dr Cootes's assistant, a Mr Fergus Ferris. It was also evident that Prindy caught his eye. Having thus appraised things for himself, he then gave a tap with his gavel and said in a thin old man's voice but with a ring to it from long use of it in such circumstances, 'This Coronial Inquiry is sitting . . . proceed.'

Mr Doscas then stated, reading from a paper of official blue, what they were there for, in the name of His Most Gracious Majesty, his Peace and Dignity, concluding by naming as first witness Constable Stunke. Stunke rose from the form across the way and came stomping past in his policeman's riding boots, climbed into the Witness Box, to which the Court Usher, another policeman, he who had shouted for silence, went to present him with the Bible. 'Take the Bible in your right hand . . .' Stunke went through it all like drill, going on to affirm that he was Herbert Stunke, Constable of Police, stationed at Beatrice River, and how on such and such a day he received certain information, all in measured sentences so that Miss Windeyer could get it down on her clacking typewriter, to the wonderment of Prindy watching her long white fingers flying over the little keys as when they had been extracting sweet droning sounds from the bigger keys of the harmonium – and to the apparent boredom of the Pookarakka up there at the head of the line of prisoners who shut his eyes and dropped his hairless bony chin into the grey collar of his shirt, surely showing himself to be a wise one by sleeping through what he had experienced several times and still had not the slightest understanding of or respect for. At last Herbert Stunke stood down and stomped away.

Next witness was Dr Fox, revealed as being first-named Felix. He said this, and that, and identified something extracted from a large envelope and handed to him as the object he had withdrawn from the stomach of the corpse of one Willy Ah Loy, who in his opinion had died from haemorrhage caused by the said exhibit. Next was Clancy Francis Delacy, who told *something* of the truth about his part in the affair, despite his having started off by declaring: 'I swear before Almighty God to speak the truth, the *whole* truth, and nothing but the truth.' Then it was Dennis Aloisius Cahoon, Sergeant of Police, telling how he had done this, that, and the other, leading to the arrest of certain persons he could see there in the Dock, one of them, to wit Cock-Eye Bob, also known as Bobwirridirridi, on a charge of wilful murder, the others that of being accessories before and after the fact. He submitted statements made by the six accessories. Cock-Eye Bob had declined to make a statement. He also submitted a statement made by Nelly Ah Loy, wife of the deceased, who was at the scene of the crime. As Dennis Aloisius stepped down, the Coroner asked for Nelly Ah Loy. Dinny paused momentarily in passing her to give her a grin of encouragement and to extend the grin to Sonny Boy and reach to give a rumple to the golden hair, perhaps not an act in strict accordance with court procedure; but whoever might have objected would be stuffy indeed.

The Usher had to come for Nell and guide her reluctant feet, wobbly in high heels, to the Witness Box. There began a discussion between Coroner and Clerk whether this witness need be sworn. Mr McCusky rose to submit respectfully that the swearing be foregone, only to have Sergeant Cahoon shoot up with his own respectful submission that the witness had to his personal knowledge received religious instruction. Thereupon Mr Bundy asked the witness: 'Do you understand the nature of an oath?' Nell drooped her head.

The Coroner snapped, 'Forego the swearing.'

Then Mr Doscas spoke to her in kindly tone: 'You understand Nelly, you got to talk true-feller, no-more tell lie, only properly what you been see with rown eye, and what you been hear with rown ear?'

She muttered, 'Yas.'

Prindy staring at her, as she had the story dragged out of her almost word by word by the Coroner, with the assistance of Mr Doscas, Mr McCusky, and Sergeant Cahoon, became aware of another pair of pale blue eyes under frizzy fair hair regarding him almost as intently as had Miss Windeyer until duty called her to her type-writer. Had he but known it, he was drawing the attention of one whom most people preferred to be ignored by, the redoubtable Fay McFee, special writer for *The Palmeston Progressive* and local representative of several radical southern newspapers. Across the table from her, the gaunt dark male was the reporter from the rival conservative *Northern Times*. Miss McFee nodded to Prindy and smiled, perhaps to show that she understood and sympathized with him in the terrible business he had endured according to his mother. Poor pretty little boy, at the mercy of a horde of sadistic savage blackmen!

Prindy kept trying to look past her at the shade of Old Tchamala gradually vanishing beneath the glittering flow of jade and silver. Then he found that he was being nudged to attend to the business of the Court. He had to stand, to stare at the old whiteman under the blazing animal thing.

Coroner Bundy had a note that had been handed to him by Mr McCusky. He said, 'Whatever Dr Cobbity says about the boy's mentality, I'd still like to examine him. Call him, please.'

The Usher called, 'Prendegast Alroy, otherwise known as Prindy Ah Loy.'

Sergeant Cahoon's grin was so wide as the boy was ushered to the box that Mr Bundy asked, 'Is there some joke, Sergeant?'

Dinny's grin vanished: 'Ahem . . . no, Your Worship, no.'

But His Worship was not satisfied: 'I take it the Aborigines Department has renamed him . . . for obvious reasons. But why Alroy? Is he connected with the Alroy family?'

McCusky rose: 'No, Your Worship. I just used the name of their station, Alroy Downs.'

'Did you consult them?'

'Well . . . no, Your Worship.'

'I would if I were you, Mr McCusky . . . lest you find yourself in legal difficulties.'

Very red, McCusky muttered, 'Yes, Sir,' and sat down, but with eyes on Fay McFee writing rapidly. The Coroner also gave her a sharp glance, thus permitting the indulgence of another wide grin on the part of Dinny Cahoon, out of his line of vision.

Mr Bundy concentrated on Prindy, who stood high because the Usher had put a small stool in for him. 'What's your name, young man?'

Prindy stared at the bits of blue behind the twinkling glasses.

'They call you Prindy, don't they?'

No answer. 'Haven't you got a tongue, boy?'

Apparently not. 'Put out your tongue to show me.'

Just that wide grey stare.

Mr Bundy looked at a loss. But he tried again. 'Where you come from?' A moment longer of suffering the stare. Then Mr Bundy sighed, looked away, at Mr McCusky again, saying, 'Perhaps the doctor's right. He may stand down.'

In that moment of release Prindy looked at the Pookarakka, who looked very much awake and whose crack of a mouth moved ever so slightly in a grin. The Usher lifted Prindy down. Both Miss Windeyer and Miss McFee looked sadly at him as he resumed his seat.

Then began the examination of the witnesses in custody, beginning with Green-ant. There was immediate diversion resulting from the Coroner's asking the witness what was his blackfellow name. Green-ant promptly replied, 'Da's him, Boss . . . Green-ant . . . make him whitefeller name from blackfeller name.'

The Green Ant would probably be his Dreaming.

'Ah,' said Mr Bundy. 'A literal translation.'

That caused a general titter, but Green-ant to answer promptly, 'Da's right, Boss.'

Bundy stared at him. 'Do you understand the word translate?'

Green-ant furrowed his brow for a moment, then replied, 'Yas, Boss.'

Everybody was staring now.

'Well . . . what's it mean?'

'Long o' railway . . . spone injin bugger-up . . . tra'ns late . . . . '

The laughter started like the rustle of the little wind in trees that suddenly becomes the whirling force which rips the leaves off. Everybody laughed, even Bobwirridirridi. The Coroner had had to remove his glasses. Then he rapped; and the Usher got control of himself and cried, '*Silence in Court*!'

But there was one man in the body of the Courtroom standing, as the Coroner saw when he replaced his glasses and then looked over them, Jeremy Delacy. The Coroner asked, 'You wish to say something, Mr Delacy?'

Jeremy cleared his throat. 'Yes, Sir . . . I'd like to point out that it's a sad reflexion on our attitude to the Aborigines that such ignorance after a hundred and forty-nine years of our civilizing influence can be treated as a joke.'

Clackety-clack went Miss Windeyer's flying fingers. Mr Bundy, flushing perceptibly, glanced down at her, then up again at Jeremy, swallowed, spoke somewhat throatily: 'Are you by any chance rebuking me, Mr Delacy?'

Clackety-clack-clack-clack!

'No, Sir. I confess I laughed myself, until I realized the anomaly. If my remark suggests rebuke, then it's for the Australian Nation.'

Clack-clack-clackety!

Mr Bundy withdrew his spectacles from the grey eyes and swept them over the gaping gathering, then came back to Jeremy to say dryly, 'This is a Coroner's Inquest, Mr Delacy, not a public meeting where anyone can chip in. I'll ask you to refrain from making any more remarks, unless they're pertinent to the inquest.'

Mr Bundy was bending over to speak to Miss Windeyer, whose eye he had caught, when Jeremy said, 'With all due respect, Sir, I regard my remark as very pertinent.'

The spectacles came up flashing. 'Do you indeed!'

Clackety-clackety-clack!

'Yes, Sir. The joke was due to the witness's poor grasp of English, the language of the Court. His testimony without an interpreter makes a travesty of it.'

Clackety-clack-clackety!

The white head with the now burning red face bent to Miss Windeyer again: 'Miss Windeyer!'

'Yes, Your Worship?'

'Kindly refrain from including this interruption of proceedings in the record.'

'Yes, Sir.'

The head came up again with glasses glinting, but not to look at the interrupter, instead at Miss McFee scribbling in her notebook for her very life, so intent upon her task that a tip of her tongue protruded from one corner of a fair moustachioed lip. Then the glasses hit the grey eyes again. 'Are you capable of acting as interpreter in this case, Mr Delacy?'

Jeremy swallowed: 'No, Sir . . . I regret to say.'

Mr Bundy's voice became a little shrill: 'Then leave the Court!'

Jeremy stood for a moment as if in defiance of the authority beneath the Alien Totem, then bowed slightly, reached for his hat. But as his head came up again he glanced at the dock, down the line of black faces above the grey shirts, from standing Green-ant to sitting Bobwirridirridi at the end, and met the red coals, held them as if trying to convey a message, a silent *Mummuk Yawarra*. Then he turned and blundered out over legs that surely expressed the disapproval of most of their owners by their reluctant giving way.

The proceedings resumed, without further interruption, without further laughter, indeed without even another titter, although there was scope for mirth aplenty in the black simpletons' quaint expression of themselves in self-committal: as for instance, when Splinter, describing the shooting of Bobwirridirridi, said, 'Poom . . . yeel . . . dat old-man him go arse-over-head now . . . .' – and Green-ant, on being asked why, when requested by Ah Loy on the authority of Mr Clancy Delacy to return the boy at once, having first agreed to do so, he still complied with Cock-Eye Bob's insistence on completing the initiation: 'Too many bloody boss give rorder, mek belong me 'ead go roun'-roun' . . . . ' because it still seemed as if that spoilsport with the grey eyes and the grey head stood there ready to declare what sane men thought funny to be injustice.

There was a stir of expectancy when at last the principal witness was called upon to testify. He may not have heard, so stonily did he sit with red eyes fixed on the last of the five-miles-long backbone of the Shade of the only master he recognized. Mr Bundy called on him thrice, then asked Mr McCusky had he anything to say for his protégé. McCusky rose, saying, 'Nothing, Your Worship,' and sat down.

Mr Bundy had timed it so nicely that it was all over and done with before lunch. He declared he found that Willy Ah Loy had met his death as the result of violence feloniously done upon him by Cock-Eye Bob, otherwise known as Bobwirridirridi, with some degree of compliance from the other six held with him in custody. He then stacked his papers into a neat pile, but instead of rising and so causing the rest to rise because he was the representative there of The Most Gracious One whose medallion hung upon the wall, leaned over to say in a low voice to Mr Doscas, 'Might as well get the committal over now, Dickey, eh? We haven't got anything else this week. Be able to catch up on some back work.' Dickey nodded, but heaved himself up and rolled back to confer for a moment with Mr McCusky and the police. He turned to the Bench to nod that all were in agreement.

Mr Bundy then assumed his regular role of Police Magistrate, and without ado committed Cock-Eye Bob for trial, on a charge of wilful murder and his accomplices on that of being accessories before and after the fact, at the next Quarter Sessions. Then he rose, bowed, was bowed to, and was gone, out through the door under the Royal Insignia, as if through the navel of a colossus into its guts.

Prindy, known as Prendegast, although being shoved by him who had so altered his identity, lingered looking over his left shoulder at the filing out of the prisoners, down from the dock to the door on that side, shepherded by their khaki keepers, last of them, loping along on crutches, with a coal-red glance and a slit of a grin for him in disappearing. Mr McCusky, talking over his own right shoulder to the Anthropologists, Dr Cootes and Mr Ferris, about meeting for lunch at the pub, did not notice. Indeed, so wrapt in conversation with the two scholars was Mr McCusky that he let go Prindy as they got free of the seats, so that the boy went out to the verandah alone, where promptly he was pounced on by no less than three females, all gabbling to him at once – his mother, Miss Kitty Windeyer, and Miss Fay McFee. His mother wrested physical possession of him from the others, taking advantage of the evident mutual animosity of the other two which caused them to be diverted from the object of their primary attention to glare at one another. Both had been trying to make dates with him, Fay to talk to him, she said, Kitty to play him some more musics. Mr McCusky pounced upon the lot of them, demanding, 'Hey, what's all this . . . what're you up to, Fay?'

For answer Miss McFee bared her teeth at him and stalked away. But Miss Kitty gushed to him about the boy's interest in music that day at the beach, and couldn't she have him at least to Sunday School at the Compound school? McCusky said, 'Wait till the school opens. He'll be going there till we send him away.'

'Send him away . . . where to?'

'A new school for boys we're opening down the Centre.'

'Oh, that's a long way off, isn't it!' Miss Kitty sounded relieved.

McCusky snapped, 'What d'you mean's a long way off, the new school or the Centre? We start the new school with the Financial Year.'

'Then he'll be quite a time yet at the Compound school.' Miss Kitty ruffled the fair hair, smiling happily. 'School starts week after next . . . after Australia Day . . . why, and of course we'll be having another picnic on Australia Day . . . at the Oval, with sports and things . . . if it's fine, of course. Will you be coming to that P-er-Prendegast?'

McCusky answered, somewhat gruffly, 'Yes . . . he'll be there. Now come on, you two, I want to take you home. I have to get back to town to lunch.'

As he ushered mother and son out to his car, Miss Windeyer stood watching, and smiled and waved as they drove away, and sighed and looked sad and lonely as she went back into the deserted Courtroom, to her typewriter and the pile of depositions.

III

It turned out that bad weather caused cancellation of the Australia Day Sports that would have meant a picnic at the Oval for the Compound kids and made impossible all other sorts of outdoor fun and games. It was what you had to expect in these parts, considering the time of year. The Sports were listed as an annual event simply to be in line with the rest of the Nation, most of which, considering it as populace and not as earth, being in what is called the Temperate Zone, could expect fine weather. A Nation of Sports, Australia, predominantly and pre-eminently, without much nationality. Hence Australia Day should be primarily a sports day. What to do with the day if sports were impossible? Well, this was not the Temperate Zone, and Temperance was here considered a virtue only by a few. There were always the pubs, for the men, at any rate. For women with children there was the chance to make extra-last-minute preparations for getting the kids off to school next day, first day of the school year. For the kids it could be an extra day of grubby liberty. White kids, that is. Certainly the spoiling of the day for outdoors activities wouldn't mean something more in the way of a contribution to Australian Nationalism on this Australia's National Day. Indeed, it would mean less contribution than there would have been, because had there been the Sports, the Town Band would have been there and included in its repertoire such stirring renderings of Australian patriotism as *Advance Australia Fair, Australia Will Be There*, and *The Road To Gundagai*, of course along with *God Save The King*. Anyway, what did it really mean, this National Day? Until recently it had been called *Foundation Day*, because primarily it celebrated the founding of the Penal Settlement of New South Wales, perpetuated that day on which the First Fleet sailed into Port Jackson, and gentry with muskets and cat-o'-nine-tails, after having stood guard over their several hundred fellow countrymen who'd spent the voyage of half a year coming halfway round the world chained in the ships' holds, stepped ashore to receive what remained of the chained ones and to add balls to their chains in case they might be thinking that here was a Land of Liberty. Cause for patriotic fervor, this reminder of what the Nation had sprung from? Perhaps there was some unconscious subtle irony about the choice of the anniversary as National Day for such a Nation.

But however the white folks and the black folks and the yellow folks of Port Palmeston spent that Australia Day of roaring rain, what of the particoloured Compound kids to whom any sort of day out of their cage was one of delirious flight?

Only Miss Kitty Windeyer asked the question. She asked it of several people who should have been primarily interested, beginning with the Reverend

Mr Tasker, who said, 'Yes, I suppose the poor kids will be disappointed. But what can you do to entertain them on a day like this? We can't even feed them. All arrangements for refreshments were cancelled.'

'There's the ginger beer,' she said.

Mr Tasker looked as if he didn't like that bit. Mr Tootle, the soft-drink maker, had already prepared and presented the keg of that precious stuff. Perhaps Mr Tasker thought it better that he drink it himself than let it go to waste. Miss Kitty added that she could have a whip-round amongst friends and get a few cakes and things. 'But what'll you do with the children? It's such a wretched place to do anything when it's raining and blowing like this . . . even pray.'

'I'll take the harmonium . . . and we'll have a sing-song and tell stories.'

'All day!'

'I just can't disappoint them, Reverend.'

'All right, then. But you can't expect anyone else to go with you.'

'Oh, I don't . . . only David, to bring the harmonium.'

'And you'd better let him come back . . . and call for you later. And you'll have to ring the Turkneys and see if it's all right with them.'

It was not all right with the Turkneys. Mr Turkney said that they'd had to feed the children in the school-room that morning. When Miss Kitty said that that's where they'd have their picnic, he said he'd have to put Mrs T on. Mrs T was quite a while in coming, and only to say flatly No. The school-room was all ready for school tomorrow, and she couldn't have it upset. It was bad enough having to feed the children their meals in there – but a picnic! Impossible. Miss Kitty said she'd see that the place was left exactly as she found it. Impossible, repeated Mrs Turkney, adding, 'You don't know what a mess these children make. Also, you don't know what a fuss-pot that teacher, Miss Lilyponds is. Slightest thing wrong and she's reporting to her head-teacher, and he to Dr Cobbity. Sorry, but definitely, No.'

'But they'll be so disappointed.'

'Not as much as you think. Anyway, it isn't your fault . . . it's nobody's fault . . . only the weather.'

Then it occurred to Miss Windeyer to have the children down to their own Mission Hall – all the room in the world and the harmonium and the picnic things already there! Mr Tasker frowned over it slightly, beginning by saying, 'Really, Miss Windeyer!' But he agreed, adding: 'Ring up Turkneys again, though, first. They'll tell you they'll have to have McCusky's permission, and that may well not be forthcoming. You know how their Department is about us, always thinking we're trying to steal a march on them.' To that Mr Tasker added something more, and bitter-sounding. 'But I wonder would our Mr McCusky be as suspicious of the designs of his own Church on his charges . . . what he'd say if Father Gorgon or Mother Mary Joseph asked instead?'

Mr Tasker was right about it all. 'Very definitely No,' said Mr McCusky. 'You know our policy with our own charges. We don't interfere with yours.'

Sounding rather desperate, Miss Kitty asked McCusky, 'Well, might I have just the little boy, Prendegast . . . . '

'He's not at the Compound yet. He's at Jumbo Delacy's.'

'I know. I would have picked him up. It was really on account of him that

I didn't want to disappoint them. He's musical, you know . . . and I promised to play for him.'

'No . . . sorry, Miss Windeyer . . . but it would be creating a precedent by giving you permission to take certain children from the Compound.'

'But he doesn't belong to the Compound . . . you said yourself . . . . '

'He'll start belonging to the Compound when he starts school there tomorrow. Sorry, Miss Windeyer. Goodbye!'

Mr Tasker shrugged over Miss Kitty's obvious dejection. 'I warned you my dear. Now, off you go and forget about it. I've a lot of writing to do . . . and I'm sure you'll be able to fill the day with good works of some sort.'

But what seems good works to some may be judged sheer evil by others. The corollary perhaps is that there is neither good nor evil. The trouble is that corollaries are the deductions of minds, which is to say, in most if not all cases, prejudice.

Certainly Miss Kitty Windeyer would not have filled the day with the wickedness that her works thereof were subsequently called had it not been for the extraordinary temptation to which she was exposed. But perhaps the greater the temptation the greater the sin of yielding, since little ones might sneak up on you and naughty you before you know it. Without doubt, clad in her rain clothes, she was going to get her bike from where it stood in the bicycle rack on the Mission Hall verandah, when she found waiting there with the truck David, the Mission Centre's factotum, the halfcaste Japanese, if that was what he was. David had been standing by when Kitty asked Mr Tasker about having the picnic at the Compound, and on hearing him agree, evidently as eager for the excursion as she, had gone off to get the truck. He told her now that everything was ready. Harmonium and ginger beer keg were in the back of the truck covered with tarpaulin. She hesitated just one moment – was lost, and let him help her into the cabin of the truck. No one else was aboard.

She was flushed, silent, obviously very guilty. But David appeared to be preoccupied with business of his own, kept his slant eyes on the streaming road, made only a few remarks about the weather. It wasn't until they were coming to the turn-off of the Compound that she spoke, saying they weren't going there, but to Jumbo Delacy's place. David was surprised, and concerned, so much that he stopped the truck. Avoiding the slant eyes she told him a little of what had taken place, making it sound as if Mr Tasker had agreed to their at least having a picnic with Jumbo's family. He shook his head: 'That Jumbo Delacy no goot man, Missus. I bet he drinkin' dere. All-lot halfcaste gone mad drinkin' now dey got permit. Jumbo don't get permit. But dat other lot go dere makin' party.' She said no matter, they were going there. He was sulky now as he drove her.

That David was more conversant with the wicked ways of the town than to be expected in a Missionary Man was soon revealed, beginning with their arrival at Jumbo's to find things just as he had predicted. Half a dozen halfcaste men were there, making enough noise for half a hundred, celebrating Australia Day for the first time as true Australians, at least all except Jumbo, who by law was considered not competent to bend his elbow with enough propriety, as indeed he showed when he saw who the visitors were, and from roaring: 'Home, home on de range, where de deer an' de buffalo roam . . ' suddenly changed his tune to: 'Wha' you puggim Bible-bashers wan' comin' my place, eh? I don' wan' no bloody puggim Jesus bijnitch 'ere. Get'ell out o' it!'

Rumple-faced Possum apologized to Miss Kitty out in the rain, while the mob inside howled with laughter over the idea of Sunday School at Jumbo Delacy's, a couple of them hooting things that would suggest to anyone listening closely that David wasn't the Missionary Man he ought to be. David was listening all right, the way he cringed and looked to see if Miss Kitty heard. But she had her ears blocked with goody-goodiness against dirty words and suggestions, and besides by the look of her was preoccupied with disappointment in being led into sin only thus far and no further. Or so it seemed – until Possum suggested that she take Prindy back to the Mission Hall and play to him there. 'Yes . . . yes, that's a good idea!' exclaimed Miss Kitty. And Prindy was got from the shed where, perhaps he had taken refuge from the cacophony that had been going for music in the resonant iron house. When told what was afoot, he fairly flew to the truck.

David looked particularly sour about going back to the Hall, but needn't have, because as he soon learnt, they weren't going there at all. How could they? For one thing it would be regarded with disapproval by all those who had the power to hand out that unpleasant thing, and must come to naught. For another, this was sin; and sin's something to be done properly or not at all. They were going to Miss Kitty's home. She looked at David, as if expecting disapproval first from him. Instead he even looked pleased. He looked even more pleased when she said Yes to his suggestion that he should take the ginger beer and deliver it at the Compound after setting her and Prindy down. She asked him to come back to pick them up somewhere about three in the afternoon. It was then around eleven. Right smartly David carried the harmonium into Kitty's sitting-room, then vanished into the rain.

You couldn't hear the rain here nearly so much as in most places, because it was old-fashioned with a high peaked roof that the rain rather skidded off than crashed onto, and thickly ceiled and lined, a gentleman's house of the old days, no doubt, and built by Chinamen. Now it was paintworn and in many ways dilapidated, surrounded by the little tin and cypress boxes of the working class. It was actually two houses, as Miss Kitty explained to Prendegast as she made tea and sandwiches for them because he'd said he was hungry when she asked him. See, those doors were nailed up. On the other side of them lived Miss Fay McFee. She sighed a little, saying, 'We shared it together once. But we fell out. It's a pity. Because we did get on so well, She's awfully demanding . . . but I couldn't do what she last demanded of me . . . even for the piano. The piano's hers. I miss it. That's why I joined the Mission people to be able to play the organ. But my love is the piano. I'm saving up to buy one. But they're awfully dear here . . . twice the price they are down South, because of freight . . . special freight, you see. And poor Fay can't play so well, really. That's why I left the Telephone Exchange to work as Court Reporter. The money's so much better . . . although the work's so terribly exacting, and I make mistakes, which are very worrying, because what you write may be vital to someone's case. I like the Exchange. I like people's voices. They sound better through a telephone, too. Have you ever talked on a telephone? Don't you even know what a telephone is? My! I don't suppose you even know half of what I'm saying to you. So I can tell you, what I've wanted to tell someone, but dare not. Fay's a journalist, of course . . . quite dedicated, oh yes. But to betray my responsibility as a telephonist, even if the people were bad and wanted exposing, was too . . . too . . . well, I don't know what to call it . . . but I couldn't do it. And so we fell out. People say it's because we were living like lesbians. You don't know what that means, I'm sure. People have hinted at it. It isn't a bit true. Fay isn't like that. She just dislikes men. But I mustn't go on chatting, when we have the Musics, as you call it, to play . . . the lovely musics. You've had enough to eat? All right, then, let's to our Wurlitzer . . .heeeee! Poor little old thing, isn't it . . . so tinny sounding. I wish I could play you the piano . . . Bach, Chopin . . . .'

'Do you know, dear,' she added, as she sat down at the harmonium, 'I had a dream of you as a great composer . . . while yet a child, like the great geniuses of music. You were on the stage in a great crowded theatre, a little boy in a velvet suit, sitting at a grand piano. I was there in front . . . and so proud of you!' Her pale blue eyes swam with tears as she looked at him. She sniffed them back, turning hastily, saying, 'Silly old thing, aren't I!' and pumped vigorously for a moment, then did a little *scherzando*. 'What'll we have first . . . the *Melody in F*, if I remember, was your favourite? Away we go then.'

She played all of those sweet things that Mr Tasker had chided her with having said had been purloined in the name of the Lord – without intrusion of the Lord into any of them now. She la-la-la-dee-dahed any she was moved to express herself vocally over, but mostly was content to rock her fair thin frizzy head in keeping time and to smile the joy it gave her, watching the boundless appreciation of her small audience, standing with eyes fixed on her cavorting fingers and lips moving as if they savoured and drank in the sweetness. Then she gave him some Grieg, *Butterflies*, a Delibes, *Dance from Coppelia*, Chopin's *Fantaisie Impromtue*. She said, 'I could go on for hours . . . and still the well would not be dry.' She sighed: 'That's what I'd love to do all day . . . just play and play . . . on a good piano, of course. I dreamt of being a concert pianist when I was young. But I haven't the strength . . . physical or moral. First, my mother and father hated me playing scales. Poor Mother used to yell at me: "For God's sake, girl, if you've got to play, play something tuneful . . . and something we know." You have to practise and practise to be good, of course. That takes a lot of stamina. I showed how little I have by giving in to them . . . poor dears! But we've got to practise and practise don't we? Now come on. The Major scales to begin with. Remember? C-D-E-F-G-A-B- and C again. La-la-la-la- la-la-la-La! Heeeee! That's it . . . that's it. Now do it backwards . . . Oh, I'm so excited I'm forgetting to pump!'

And so it went. For variety she had him pick out the *Melody in F* with one finger.

There came, at length, a thumping and bumping next door that caused Kitty to say, 'That's Fay. She'll be making tea, after being out in the rain somewhere looking for news, or sending it off, or something. I'd love to call her in to join us. But she can be so rude. And she'd only want to ask you questions . . . who your father is, and all that. What's it matter who your father is? Perhaps it's better even not to know.' She sighed again, and to his urging began to play again, Mozart, *Divertissement in E-Flat*. She said when she'd finished it, 'They call it the most perfect thing in an imperfect world. But there're so many perfect things, really . . . I mean not only in music. But what about some of your own music? I've been hearing that you sing at night . . . your own songs. Is that true? Then sing me one.'

Prindy sang *My Rown Road*, while she stared amazed. There was no *whiteman kill-him-die* in this version. 'Let's try and play it, shall we?' she asked. It was she who did it – and soon got it. But he didn't look pleased. She asked him why he didn't like it. He only shook his head. She said, 'I think it's the instrument. That's a very simple melody. It's like a bird-song. That's how you sing it. The reed-sound is too harsh. It needs sweetness . . . the simple sweetness of wood-wind. If only we had a flute . . . but I can't play one. Even a tin-whistle would do. Yes . . . I'll see if I can buy one . . . for next time. But let's try it again . . . in a higher key . . . Oh, but there's David back!' Sound of steps out on the verandah. She looked at her wrist watch. Only two-thirty. Hammering on the outside door. As she rose to go to the door she said, 'Maybe he'll stay and have a cup of tea with us . . . and that'll make it a little longer, eh?'

It was not David, but the Reverend Mr Tasker, and wearing such an expression as to cause Miss Kitty's face, glowing with happiness all these hours, to blanch. She had every reason to expect the Reverend Gentleman to be annoyed with her, even angry, but never to see him eyeing her with such blazing rage. For greeting he fairly shouted in her face, 'How dare you . . . how dare you place me in this invidious position!'

The blood swept back to her face, so that her hair looked pale as dead grass in red earth. Clinging to the door-handle she began to gasp an explanation: 'As the truck was loaded . . . and David . . . . '

'David!' he roared. 'That reprobate . . . and with your connivance, Madam, your cunning connivance!'

'I . . . I didn't mean to connive, Reverend . . . I . . . . '

'You don't think it connivance and deceit to make a bargain with that . . . that serpent I have nurtured . . . so that you both could have the use of the truck for your improper and illicit business?'

Miss Kitty breathed incredulously, 'Illicit?'

'Yes . . . illicit, nefariously illegal, and . . . . '

Out of the tail of her goggling eye she saw a movement of the other door like this along the verandah as a gust of the wet wind tried to pull it from the hand holding it open a crack, and after a swift glance, she gasped, 'Won't you come in Reverend?'

He had seen the glance and guessed its meaning, and shut his wide-jerking mouth so that his face was a red hard square again. As she stepped back, he followed her in. He stared at Prindy, standing in the doorway of the sitting-room staring at him. As Miss Kitty got him into the sitting-room she turned and said, 'I'm really very sorry, Reverend . . . but I didn't think it would matter so much . . . . '

'Not matter so much to risk betraying our sacred institutions into the hands of our secular enemies, at such a critical time as this in affairs . . . and for the mere whim of occupying your idleness on a wet day?'

Staring at him, she muttered, 'Betraying?'

Mr Tasker had stopped shouting; but his voice was harsh with pent feelings. 'There's no other word for it that I can say. You don't belong to our faith, I know . . . and I've sometimes doubted your respect for it. But I felt sorry for you in your rejection by your own church people, your Anglicans, who refused you access to their organ because of your supposed reputation.'

Miss Kitty flushed and demanded with some spirit, 'My reputation?'

'I'm sorry to refer to it . . . but I've heard insinuations about you and . . . .' His eyes made the slightest movement towards Fay McFee's quarters. 'I repeat I felt sorry for you in your need for expression of your musical talent and took you as our organist. And this is how you repay me. If that's not betrayal, tell me what is!'

Kitty drooped before the glaring eyes.

The little silence that followed was broken by more steps on the verandah. A tap at the door. She said hastily, heading for the door, 'That'll be David now. He'll explain.'

Mr Tasker snapped, 'David is in the Lock Up!'

She stopped, to goggle at him, to clutch at her slack mouth. Tasker added: 'That will be Mr McCusky come to take the boy away.'

She went to the door. It was Eddy McCusky, hat over one eye, which he didn't bother to touch in salutation to a lady. In fact his only greeting was: 'Where's the boy?'

She struggled for the words. 'I'll . . . I'll get him.' She returned to the sitting-room, beckoned to Prindy, put an arm about him as she led him to the door, leant a little against him, whispering, 'I'll see you soon.'

McCusky heard it: 'You *won't* be seeing the boy again, Miss Windeyer. I haven't made up my mind yet whether to prosecute you or not over this affair. But I certainly shall if I find you interfering with him further.'

He took Prindy from her, pushed him out onto the verandah. Miss Kitty gasped, 'Prosecute me?'

McCusky half turned away, pulling the hat down a little further. 'You were specifically informed that you were not to take the boy out of the custody I'd placed him in. You've deliberately committed an offence under the Protection of Aborigines Act. Your superior informs me that it wasn't with his connivance . . . . '

Mr Tasker, just behind Kitty, shouted, 'How dare you use the word connivance in connexion with me, Sir?'

McCusky swung on him, eyed him insolently: 'It sounded mighty like connivance to me. You started off by wanting to hold some sort of shivoo at the Compound . . . .'

'I started off nothing, Sir!'

McCusky went on unperturbed: 'Next you want the children down at the Mission . . . . '

'Leave me out of it, I tell you!'

'I certainly won't leave you out of my report on the matter . . . .'

Kitty cut in: 'Mr Tasker hadn't anything to do with it, Mr McCusky. It was all my doing. I . . . well, I just couldn't help myself.'

McCusky eyed her for a moment, then asked, 'Are you pleading that it was a mental aberration that caused you to plan the whole thing?'

She murmured, 'Mental aberration?'

'Well . . . you're a . . . a maiden lady . . . frustrated motherhood and all that. There's a half-witted boy . . . . '

She cried out, 'Oh, don't say that. He's a genius!'

McCusky said, 'I won't prosecute you, Miss Windeyer. But kindly keep away from the boy. Goodday to you . . . and to you, Your Reverence!' He touched his hat this time, turning to push Prindy out off the verandah.

Mr Tasker shouted, 'I'm not Your Reverence . . . I'm not a papist priest!'

McCusky leered: 'Have it your own way, Mister,' and grabbed Prindy and did a rush with him through the rain to his car.

Mr Tasker said to Kitty, 'You will also kindly keep away from the Mission Centre, Miss Windeyer. I'll send someone to pick up the harmonium. God be with you!'

Miss Kitty was more interested for the moment in waving to Prindy, a glimpse of whom could be seen looking out through a celluloid window in Mr McCusky's side-screens. She waved. Then as Tasker reached the edge of the verandah she asked quickly, 'Why did they have to lock David up?'

He turned for a moment: 'If you don't think they had every reason for doing so, then I can only pity you.' With that he went.

Miss Kitty stared till his big old car disappeared into the rain. Then suddenly, with a choking cry she turned and rushed into the house, flung herself sobbing into an arm chair. A moment later a strong stout arm was flung about her shoulders, and through her tears she saw Fay McFee, and dropped a head onto the ample bosom that went with the arm. 'There now, there!' crooned Fay. 'What've the bastards done to you . . . the Bible-bashing and Fascist-strutting bloody bastards? Here . . . I'll get you a whisky . . . that'll make you feel better.'

There was to be whisky-drinking also up at the Compound when Mr McCusky arrived and handed the innocent cause of all the trouble over to Mr Turkney. It happened that as McCusky's car pulled up before the Superintendent's residence, Nell, watching from the Adult Quarters, no doubt expecting them, since news of things of Compound concern travelled swiftly there, went rushing over through the rain, to arrive looking so dishevelled and distraught that, when Turkney would have hunted her, perhaps less indulgent out of deference to his superior, the latter in his official bigness said, 'Aw, let her stay a while. She won't be seeing so much of him later. Christ, Tub, I could do a drink!'

From the conversation over the whisky between Mr McCusky and Mr and Mrs Turkney, while mother and son sat huddled together in the conservatory below, peeped at by bright-dark eyes from slits in the flapping canvas blinds of the similar place across the way that served as school room, something of the circumstances that must have so bewildered Miss Kitty Windeyer in the last half-hour were revealed. It would seem that Missionary Man David had been conducting a liaison with one of the big girls of the Children's Home, a quarter-caste, Wilhelmina Whitehead (surely one of Mr McCusky's namings!) and that they had been taking advantage of the picnics to indulge their passion and had intended to do likewise during the affair planned for today had it come off. This much Wilhelmina had confessed. Well, when David had arrived this morning with the keg of ginger beer, being trusted as a Missionary Man, he had been allowed to take it right into the home unescorted to set it up for the children, and while there had made an assignation with his lady-love and given her a screwdriver as a means to keeping it, the same to be used to remove the front of one of the boxes covering the sanitary pans in the privy, (or dunny as those discussing the business called it, in accordance with local usage.) 'Fancy crawling through a dunny to get it,' Mrs Turkney declared. 'They'll come at anything!'

The dunnies of both halfcaste homes were built against the fence with the doors of the boxes outside, through which the nightmen could remove the pans without entering the premises, a very necessary arrangement in the opinion of those responsible for the girls, since the nightmen were themselves halfcastes.

Thus Wilhelmina had got out, taking advantage of the rain, and made her way to David waiting off the Hospital road in the truck. They then drove away to Shelly Beach, the beach below Jumbo Delacy's place, where the coconut grove was, a favourite place for lovers. He'd said they had hours and had nothing to fear because Miss Windeyer had made a bargain with him to use the truck to take Wilhelmina out for taking that little boy and the organ to her home. It wasn't the sort of day you'd expect to find other lovers at Shelly Beach. But there was another couple, no other than Miss Lilyponds, the Compound schoolteacher, and her boy friend. Although David had declared that he was positive Miss Lilyponds had not seen them as they passed the parked car, he was soon proved wrong.

Evidently Miss Lilyponds, ever a spoilsport, had lost no time in reporting the matter to the police, who had come and caught them clipping in the cabin and done all that might be expected of guardians of public decency, which included charging David with an offence under the Aboriginal Ordinance.

Mrs Turkney said she didn't relish the idea of having that idiot boy put in with her kids. He was too big a boy to begin with. You never knew what he might get up to with the girls – 'Or the girls with him!' said Mr McCusky with a guffaw. 'D'you know, when I was running this show, those kids used to ride each other . . . the girls. We caught 'em at it a couple o' times . . . I think I told you, didn' I . . . .'

Mrs Turkney, looking displeased, said stiffly, 'Yes . . . you did.' And she shot a significant glance from her husband to the bottle, because it was evident that Mr McCusky was getting under the weather.

Turkney said, 'Well, one for the road, eh? We've got to see to feedin' the brutes. No chance of whippin' the kid back to Jumbo's, eh?'

McCusky, rising, said thickly, 'Not a 'ope in 'ell.'

Turkney slipped an arm about his shoulders. 'But he's been doing all right there . . . .'

His wife chipped in. 'Besides, his mad mother might give us more trouble if he's here all the time . . . and we've got trouble enough as it is.'

McCusky, who perhaps had seen that glance of hers, turned on them as he was about to go out and, banging his hat on and pulling it over an eye, snapped slurrily, ' 's wha' you get paid for. If you can't take it . . . it's plenty more'd like the job . . . see you!' He went out onto the rain-swept stairs, descended uncertainly, then went running to his car.

Turkney showed his teeth at his receding back, snarling, 'You bastard!'

Mrs Turkney wasted no time in sending Nell back to her quarters, telling her that she could see the boy once a day, for half an hour after he finished school – provided they both behaved themselves. She kept Prindy waiting under the house until the girls, looking like some brown monster heaved up out of the sea and taken quivering and lurching and full of strange sound to the land, came over from the kitchen under a sheet of tarpaulin. Then gathering him under her big umbrella, she took him across to the home.

Supper consisted of two thick slices of that stuff they called bread, one to be spread with beef dripping, the other with apricot jam – with, as a treat because of the auspicious day it was and the unexpected evil thereof, ginger beer. Where was Wilhelmina? Up in the dormitory crying, Matron. Matron went to look. Last time she asked for her, at midday dinner, they'd said was in the dunny with the gripes from drinking too much ginger beer – and she, poor fool, had believed them. Never believe 'em – that's what everybody said.

Every crumb had to be swept up because of Miss Lilyponds in the morning. Whatever the weather was like tomorrow they'd have to eat in the dining-room, because of Miss Lilyponds. One crumb and she'd complain. 'And I've got trouble enough,' said Mrs Turkney.

It was customary for them to go up to the dormitory at sundown. They did it earlier tonight, because you didn't know when it was sundown, anyway. Prindy was allotted a cot in a corner of the verandah closest to the house. 'So that I'll hear you if you play up,' said Mrs Turkney. Then she left them, locking them in.

Most played quiet games in the dark. The exceptions were Prindy, whom they ignored, and Wilhelmina, who lay and cried and cried. Later Prindy added to the entertainment by singing in his sleep, all manner of songs. Even Wilhelmina stopped crying to listen. They whispered amongst themselves, 'He *jitty* . . . he pretty boy . . . but he *jitty*.'

Then it was another day. Breakfast of that porridge and that bread and treacle, had out in the dining-room without much inconvenience, because the rain had eased considerably and the wind dropped. No one complained here about the food, and not simply because Mrs Turkney was sitting at the head of the table, as was evident from the way they put every scrap of it away, weevils and all, even Prindy and Wilhelmina.

When Miss Lilyponds arrived at nine she had a little chat with Mrs Turkney about the affair of yesterday. She was young, was Miss Lilyponds, only about twenty, and prettyish, although it could have been the heavy make-up and the very nicely marcelled blond hair. All the girls admired that hair, even though they detested Miss Lilyponds. She said to Mrs Turkney, quite loudly, so that everybody in the schoolroom could hear, 'Never believe 'em. I told you that when you first came here. Never believe 'em . . . and never trust 'em out of your sight. They're dingo niggers, remember . . . dingo niggers.'

When Miss Lilyponds had got everybody settled down to the school work she reckoned they were capable of doing, she took a look at Prindy, stared into his grey eyes with her own grey-green, asked him a question or two, and getting no answer but the stare, said, 'We'll put you in a corner down the back. Here's a slate for you, and a slate pencil. Just amuse yourself.'

When the next issue of *The Palmeston Progressive* came out it carried a carefully written bit in Fay McFee's column reserved for such things, about the goings on of certain Missionary Men, reverend and otherwise, and certain officers of a certain Government Department noted for its leanings towards the methods of Adolf Hitler in dealing with its fellow men. It was too carefully worded for legal repercussions, Fay having sheer genius for libel without action. But there were others. First there was the renailing up of the doors between the quarters of the Misses McFee and Windeyer. Then there was the request by the Crown Law Office for Miss Windeyer's resignation as Court Reporter on the ground of incompetency. Certainly she had been making a lot of mistakes of late; and, as Mr Doscas told her with much trembling of his chins, 'You can't afford to make mistakes in depositions, you know, Kitty . . . why, if we had Capital Punishment, it might even cost someone his life, mightn't it? I'm terribly sorry. But they're pushing me from on top. You'll be able to get your old job back in the Post Office, I'm sure.'

Indeed, within a week of leaving the Crown Law Office, Kitty was again on the Post Office switchboard. And within a week of that again, she overheard a conversation between Father Gorgon and one of his Faithful, in which His Reverence complained that he didn't know what he was going to do about an organist for the Church, seeing that Mr Dealney was leaving on the next boat, and Easter would be coming up, and no one in the town who could play anything better than a tin-whistle. That night she presented herself at the Presbytery.

It was not Father Gorgon she saw, because he was out, but old Monsignor Maryzic, long since pushed out of active clerical work by reason of his age and tactlessness, and just hanging about, as he sometimes himself said to those who still were friends of his, 'Makingk a nuisance of meinself.' He was an Eastern European of some sort, had been a great force in the establishment of Catholic Missions in the Australasian tropics. Miss Kitty told the Monsignor that she was not a Catholic, but would gladly convert to Catholicism to become the Catholic Church organist. 'You have a beautiful organ,' she said. He chuckled deeply at that, causing her first to stare in surprise and then to blush deeply, faltering, 'I've often gone into your church to listen.'

He said, 'Mein dear, you do not haf to be of our faith to play or sing for us. Der Catholic Church haf alvays been liberal mit der arts. Ve vant der best. Ve get der best. Ve pay for it. Let me hear you play. Vot can you play? Not der hymn. Can you play Mozart . . . yes? Goot!'

The result was that Miss Kitty got the job, at a small salary, and on her own condition that she be permitted to convert to Catholicism anyway. Monsignor Maryzic undertook to instruct her for conversion in return for an organ recital of his favourite music after each lesson.

Somewhat later there appeared in *The Progressive* an exceedingly bitter attack on religion in general, and the Catholic Church in particular, as the Opium of the People and the Father of Fascism, by Fay McFee. It was also rumoured round the town that she had put nails in her *side* of the doors now.

IV

It was not long before Prindy was copying off Miss Lilypond's blackboard onto his slate, not mere *ABC* and words like *Cat* and *Fat* and *Mat,* but sentences like *I did put one pig in a bag,* and arithmetical calculations involving numbers up to 10, and was able to sing the Multiplication Table right up to 100 with the seniors. The other children observed his cleverness long before their teacher did, and whispered that it was due to his having been stolen away one time by a *koornung,* as they had heard. Some of the bigger girls tried to get him to talk about that experience, but without getting a word out of him. Then it was whispered that he'd had a *Kirrikijirrit* initiation and was circumcised. The oldest of the girls, Elizabeth Lake, challenged him to show his *darra.* When he ignored them they climbed up the wall of the boys' shower to peep at him. It was like that for a couple of weeks, with his mother, sitting with him for half an hour each afternoon in Mrs Turkney's conservatory, the only person he talked to – except for a couple of chats through the fence with King George as he was passing.

Nell was working in the Compound laundry, still at her one-armed dirty-linen sorting, by means of which she earned a few shillings a week that she spent with Peg-leg Queeny on lollies and biscuits she brought to Prindy.

He seemed content enough, spending his leisure mostly in Mrs Turkney's garden weeding for her, while singing to himself. The job of weeding was given him on his first Sunday as alternative to attending Sunday School, where he had given offence by covering ears with hands during the singing of hymns. The Mission people, talking to Mrs Turkney about it, suggested that it must have something to do with the influence *that* Miss Windeyer had had on him. Yet he had looked even delighted when he saw the harmonium carried in to the school room and the organist sit down to it, even if it were another lady. The hymns he had objected to before being removed for naughtiness were *Jesus Loves Me, Tell me the Old, Old Story, Safe in the Arms of Jesus.*

When Miss Lilyponds heard about the hands-on-ears business she told Mrs Turkney that he always did it when the children were singing with her those songs that were the delight of their schooling, it would seem: *There was a Crooked Man who walked a Crooked Mile, Jack and Jill, Barney Google* – the last her own particular favourite, because that was what she called her boy friend, whose name was Barney. Perhaps there was something wrong with the child's ears, said Mrs Turkney. She would get Dr McQuegg to take a look at him next time he was along. The doctor was along quite soon, took the look, and over whisky with the Turkneys, reported that he could find nothing the matter, except an evident hypersensitivity to sound. He said, 'Maybe he just doesn't like the Bible-bashers' voices . . . or Filly Lilyponds', either. I know I don't . . . but what would only be dissonance to people with normal hearing, could be sheer cacophony to someone like him.'

Turkney said: 'Cacophony . . . that's a good one. Sounds like something out of the dunny . . . ha, ha, ho!'

'That's actually the literal meaning of it,' said the doctor. 'The caco part, anyway . . . something that stinks.' They all laughed over it, even Mrs Turkney, who threw one of those double-barrel glances of hers at the whisky bottle and her husband.

Unfortunately, or so it seemed at the time, Mrs Turkney's dislike for Miss Lilyponds was such that she could not help but use that word when relating the doctor's report to her. Now, of several unpleasant things about Phyllis Lilyponds was that strident voice of hers; and it was not unlikely that she knew it. She must have gone away and looked up a dictionary to get the meaning. Next day when Prindy closed his ears with his hands as she began to lead the singing lesson with *Barney Google*, she leapt at him and struck his hands down, shrieking, 'You don't like my voice, don't you, you little white nigger? Well . . . you're going to hear it, whether you like it or not.' So he had to hear it out: *Barney Google, with his great big Googley Eyes* . . . .

Prindy was wise enough even to restrain his blinking with pain thereafter during the singing, even though it got actually worse, the children flatter and Filly sharper, for knowing that they were being listened to with much the same feeling as one had when the lid of one of the dunny seats was left up. He made up for it by singing to himself what he remembered of the sweetness he had heard from the gentle white hands of Miss Windeyer and his own songs, in corners of Mrs Turkney's garden and in his own little corner of the dormitory when asleep and when the other kids crowded round and listened and marvelled, whispered of his being *tulli-tulli*, and hence at last endeared.

So Wet Season passed, leaving the land languishing in that Edenesque tranquility and fruitfulness its creator, the Ol'Goomun-Ol'Goomun, had intended for it always.

The Compound kids, that is the captive yeller ones, were able again to make full use of their playground since it had ceased to be only a wallow fit for pigs – Prindy with the rest of them, so that his mother, with the three or four others permitted contact with their children, had to spend her half-hour of an afternoon largely yearning after him at a distance through the fence. The ingenious escape system under the fence still operated for those venturesome enough to go get the cocky-apples and bush-plums and leaf-sugar now to be gathered down in the gully below the Kerosene and smuggled in for sharing and those old enough and bold enough for what was called *tchinekin*. This was the bad time for ticks – shell-backs. Everybody who went out had to be as carefully looked over as monkeys by their mates, although with much more discretion. Shell-backs were hard to kill, at least by persons whose every action was viewed with suspicion. Pounding one with a rock, if not seen from the Boss's house would be heard, even in the midst of a beery party. The established method of disposal was to put them in a *Goona* Tin, in which the big girls going to the kitchen for meals would take them for throwing in the fire. A *Goona* Tin was a tiny ointment tin issued to everyone weekly to put a bit of their *goona* in for a Hookworm Check. There had been no hookworm cases lately, because Prindy was supplying all the *goona*, as was the custom for new kids to do until they contracted. Having hookworm was not nearly so bad as having to take the Carbon Tetrachloride that made one's food taste like *goona* for a day or so afterwards. Besides, the hookies in *their* hunger made you all the more hungry for that rubbitch tucker.

On the black grapevine it came through to Wilhelmina that her Tweet'art

David would be down in the gully any afternoon, calling like a coucal. David had done a month's jail for his crime in connexion with her, and of course had lost his job with the Protestant Mission Centre. However the Catholics had taken him over, not out of Christian Charity, but because he was good with motors and they needed a new engineer for their mission schooner. How the Bible-bashers must have sneered at this double-barrel evidence of Papists' cynical disregard of Christian Ethics to meet expedience! David sent word to say that he would be leaving for the Leopold Islands Mission soon, so don't fail him.

Wilhelmina didn't fail him. But the ticks she gathered in her trysting! They just about filled the *goona* tin that someone gave Prindy to hide in the chink of the concrete pier at the back of the class-room where he always sat.

It was surely significant of the strange docility of the Aboriginal Race with regard to white people, that none of the many so ill-treated children who had passed through this House of Humiliation called the Halfcastes' Home and had held in their hands so often so potent a weapon of revenge as contained, like a piece of explosive Mercuric Fulminate, in those *goona* tins, had not thought to use it – until now – and perhaps significant of the non-Aboriginal heritage and instruction in the ways of Tchamala the disrupter of him who saw the opportunity and was moved to use it – he whose name was written on the roll as Prendegast Alroy.

It happened that Miss Lilyponds was in a particularly bad mood, perhaps through having difficulty with her Barney Google, whom even the kids had heard she was pursuing ruthlessly, a somewhat simple cadet Government Officer recently from the South. She had been giving the kids hell. She had even stood beside Prindy with head bent listening while he sang those favourite songs of hers with the rest, including *Barney Google*. It also happened that she kept her bike just behind where Prindy sat, and always hung her wide straw hat by its chin-ribbon on one of the handlebars. Just before dismissing the school for the day she turned her back on it and saw to her synthetic looks in her compact mirror, because she always rode down town to pick up Barney as he came from work. Prindy must have had it in mind for some time. Without rising he hooked the *goona* tin out of its hiding place, pulled off the lid under cover of his desk, and in a swift movement emptied the contents into the upturned hat. Anyone who knows shellback bandicoot ticks knows how grimly they cling to anything that smells of a likely suck. Turning, Miss Lilyponds, buttoned up the face that had been smiling at itself, and told the class it could get to hell. Then she went to her bike, donned her hat, and rode away. Only Prindy was interested in her departure. The other kids were racing for the playground.

They were able to play all next day, because Miss Lilyponds didn't turn up – and the next, and the next. It took that long for them to learn that the lady was in hospital in a bad way. They got it not over the grapevine, but from Mrs Turkney, whose relish in the news could not be disguised in the slightest by her referring to Filly as a Poor Thing. Not only was the Poor Thing in great pain with the several tick-bites she had sustained on the head, but treatment had required the shaving of her scalp, and worse, when her young man Barney had come to visit her he had been obviously shocked by her appearance, and not only failed to visit her again, but had suddenly resigned from his job and caught the train down bush – or, as Mrs Turkney had put it, almost with a chuckle, Had Blown Through.

Perhaps the tongue-clicking with which most of the children heard the news expressed genuine sympathy, being what they were, even though they had all learned long before this how it had come about. Even their asking if they might be taken by Barney Bynoe to visit her could have sprung from sympathy as much as curiosity about her looks without that one redeeming feature, the marcelled hair, and surely a small wish to gloat over one who had treated them so meanly. But Mrs Turkney said that the Poor Thing was refusing to see anyone, was lying in a darkened room, weeping her heart out . . . eeeee . . . ahem. They would be getting a special new teacher in a day or two, Mrs Alfie Candlemas, wife of the new Health Inspector, that nice tall dark man they had seen come round looking at the dunnies with Dr Cobbity.

The children cried out, 'Alfie . . . dat name for boy!'

'I know,' said Mrs Turkney. 'But that's what she calls herself, I'm told . . . and she's a very nice young lady, they say.'

'How you spell name . . . Kennelmitch?'

'It isn't my job to teach you spelling . . . but it isn't anything to do with Kennels, but Candles . . . and Christmas, like. Now, say it properly . . . Can-del-mass . . . Mrs Alfie Candlemas.'

The kids all sang it in their sing-song way, and went on singing it after Mrs Turkney had left them, gradually getting it back to the way they liked it – *Kennelmitch.*

They had another song to sing that night, softly in the dormitory, the first of many made for them by Prindy the Songmaker, strangely, or perhaps not really so in the circumstances, to that tune which evidently had previously so offended his ears, *Barney Google.*

Barney Google, wit' his great big googley eyes,
Go long Hospital, gitchim great big surprise,
Mitchis Lilypon' got no hair . . .
Now she cryin': 'Where, Oh, where,
Where gone my Barney, wit' his great big googley eyes?'

When Mrs Alfie Candlemas arrived at the Compound it was in regal style, not because there was anything queenly about the slight young thing; but she was riding in a Rolls Royce – and a Rolls, whatever its age or condition, is like royalty, for ever royal. It was quite an old bus, and battered from a long hard journey overland. But even the kids crowding the fence, saw the difference in it from other cars the way they stared; and the Turkneys said frankly, 'Well, what d'you know . . . a Rolls Royce!' And the Candlemases, because both of them were there, smiled apologetically, as common people do who come by such uncommon things. Mrs Candlemas showed that she was a nice lady from the moment of arrival by waving to the children and wanting to go to them first, instead of up to have a drink with the Turkneys. She also kissed Mrs Turkney on the hard hairy cheek in greeting.

Naturally the first thing that had to be done over the drinks up on Turkney's potted-palm and fern-hung verandah was to explain that Alfie business. The lady explained that properly her name was Aelfrieda, an old Saxon name, the feminine of Alfred, and meaning the same thing, *enchanted*. She said this with a pretty girlish laugh, adding, 'Ratbag!' But what a dainty bag for rats! That's what Mr Turkney's pop-eyes plainly said, a fact that did not miss his old pudding-bag of a missus, the way her own eyes narrowed slightly. Alfie didn't say it, but it was probable that she'd been given the name because of her funny little pixie-like pointed ears and that her father, of whom she spoke with the affection of a little girl, My Daddy, was surely a romantic type. She was talkative. In no time she had told of her origins, her vicissitudes, her aspirations. She was not beautiful. Her little turned-up nose and over-wide mouth left her looks far short of perfection. But it was truly a pretty face. Her cheeks were darkly rosy, her eyes quite black, her brows too, while there was a hint of black hair on her wide and mobile upper lip and on those pixie ears. Her hair, however, a curly mop, was brown. She said she was from Cornish stock on her father's, My Daddy's, side.

Daddy was Silas Tripconny, originally a schoolteacher by profession (as she herself was by training) turned politician, as which he had been something of a celebrity in Federal Labor politics, but now in the political wilderness and writing and lecturing for a living. She said, 'Poor Daddy . . . the pangs of plebiscites are too much for him now.' But it seemed that he had passed on his yearning for a better world with his genes, because, as she said, 'Frank and I are determined to leave the world a better place than when we came into it . . . aren't we, darling?'

Frank's smile was answer enough. It said: *Anything you say, my enchanted one.* But it wasn't the vapid smile of a man simply lost in love. As he turned it on the others it curled slightly as if in challenge, as if to add: *She is truly a fairy, and being her consort makes me a fairy king.*

She told how they had married with the intention of going to some land of poverty, ignorance, and disease: 'Where we could use our qualifications,' she said. 'There are plenty of doctors and nurses and Bible-thumpers going into places like India, Malaya. What they want is teachers and sanitary engineers . . . their need is first education and sanitation. What's the good of food and physic in the midst of ignorance and filth? We came to Frank's job here as a sort of stepping-stone to Asia, just across the way. I was only going to write for the time being, while we got together enough money to go on. I hadn't any idea of all this.' She waved a hand in a way to indicate the squalor of the Compound as a whole. 'Down South we didn't realize an Aboriginal Problem existed. We thought they'd just about died out, except for a few pockets living happily in reserves in remote places untouched by whites. My Daddy often used to speak of the great wrong we'd done them. I hadn't any idea we were still doing it . . . and how! We were appalled as we came overland, getting further and further North, at what we saw . . . and the hostility of whites if you said anything! Why go to Asia, we asked ourselves? Our job's here . . . right here. I saw Dr Cobbity, and asked if he could find me something to do. He's awfully nice, isn't he. He said, not just yet . . . but big things are coming up. I realize from what he told me that it's a terrific task. Everybody against you . . . even the unfortunates themselves. But I've so wanted to be in it. Frank's all right. He's got surveys coming up, looking for leprosy, malaria, VD and things.

But poor little me! There were only the Bible-bashers . . . and . . . I hope you're not religious . . . but my Daddy's a died-in-the-wool atheist. And suddenly there's this lovely job offered me. Poor Miss Lilyponds . . . I do feel sorry for her . . . but I'm awfully glad, too. I feel even as if it was something fatal . . . fateful, I mean . . . as if it were done by someone deliberately for me.'

Mrs Turkney said, a little stiffly, 'As a matter of fact, *we* were thinking it might have been done deliberately by someone, too. I wouldn't put it past those kids . . . . '

Alfie looked aghast: 'What . . . the . . . the Aboriginal children?'

Mrs Turkney smiled, a little sadly, and shook her head: 'I don't want to dampen your enthusiasm, dear . . . but you've got a job ahead of you there. It's best you know . . . .'

Alfie turned her wide black eyes on what evidently she could handle better than the female of her species, the tubby male Turkney, who cleared his throat, saying, 'We've all been through it . . . the enthusiasm, the disappointment . . . all of us, from Cobbity and Co. down.'

'Cobbity and Co?' murmured Alfie.

'Dr Cobbity and Mr McCusky,' said Mrs Turkney. 'You'll find that's another element in the battle . . . . '

When Alfie's dark eyes flashed as if in readiness to defend friends, her man Frank said hastily, with that easy smile of his, 'Alfie's a regular warhorse for a battle.'

Mrs Turkney said, 'Well, she'll have to be prepared to lose this one . . . or get hurt.'

'I don't understand!' cried Alfie.

'No, my dear . . . but you will,' said Mrs Turkney. 'All I'm trying to do is save you from being hurt. And those across the way there,' she nodded towards the Childrens' Home, 'will be the first to hurt you, if you're not ready for 'em. Never trust 'em. Never trust any Aboriginal person. Start with that in your mind . . . and you can't go wrong . . . isn't that so, Oscar?' She turned to Tub.

Tub sighed: 'I'm afraid it is, my dear. The chief thing in the Aboriginal Problem's the Aborigines. The plain fact is that they don't appreciate anything we do for them. All they want is what they can get out of us. They don't want schooling. School's alien to their minds. You've got to see them as they really are. They're nomadic savages. Children are allowed to do what they like till puberty . . . just what they bloomin' well like. At puberty they're initiated into the tribal laws. That's all right when there's a tribe. But when there isn't . . . what? Just puberty. And you'll soon find out what that means with your charges across the way . . . Oh, I'm so sorry . . . I'm truly only trying to help you!' Alfie's black eyes had suddenly begun to swim, her wide lip to tremble.

Frank laid a lean brown hand on the little-girl hand quivering on the table. She looked at him with a wobbly smile, blinked back the tears, turned to the others, sniffed and said, 'I'm sorry. I'm silly. Yes . . . Dr Cobbity told me how hard it is, too. It's . . . it's just that it means so much to me. I do want to do a good job . . . . '

'I'm sure you will, too, dear,' said Mrs Turkney. 'And I'll tell you frankly I'm glad to see you in place of that screaming bully Lilyponds, especially as you're one of us, not Education Department stuck-ups. If the kids did put the ticks on her . . . well, she deserved it. But just watch out they don't do it to you.'

'To me?' murmured Alfie. 'Would they put ticks on me?'

Turkney, who had been mopping it up as usual, chuckled, 'Half the luck of the ticks!'

Mrs Turkney gave him and the bottle one of those looks again, then shot a swift glance at Frank, who only smiled, as if used to such remarks as the owner of a Fairy Fay.

'One for the road,' said Turkney.

'No . . . not for me,' said Alfie. Then she smiled widely and shrewdly, adding, 'Looks as if I'll have to have my wits about me.'

Tub poured generously for himself and Frank, saying, 'You only have to call on us, dear lady . . . I'll be at your shervish any time.'

Mrs Turkney rose and everybody did likewise. Then she led Alfie away to go down by the inner stairs and into the conservatory. At the stairs Alfie called to her husband, standing watching her and looking so slim and tall and handsome beside boozy little goggling Tub, saying, 'You'll call for me this afternoon, darling.'

Frank grinned at her: 'Let's know if you'll be wanting the Rolls or the ambulance.' They all laughed, 'You're a shport,' said Turkney as the ladies disappeared, 'I like shports. Have 'nother drink.'

'Well, just a little one. I've got to go and look at the drainage in Chinatown.'

'Ho, ho . . . you'll need all your wits about you there!'

Down below, entering the yard of the Children's Home, Mrs Turkney was saying, 'I *do* like your husband, Mrs Candlemas.'

'Please call me Alfie . . . yes, he is a dear.' Alfie's eyes were on the children crowding into their seats in the schoolroom, but all turned to her, all staring with wide-eyed expectancy. She looked daunted, so that that rosiness left her cheeks and her drooping mouth drew lines in them. Perhaps it was in seeing the Problem in the flesh *en masse* for the first time, a mass of faces differing from those she was accustomed to by the evolution of a million years: primitive faces, as they would be called, simply because of different structure, the jaws, the brows, the lips, the eyes no darker than her own, but so cavernous. Oh, but one pair of eyes to save the situation, for all their deep setting – one pair of eyes of grey! She sighed, as if in relief. She smiled at the grey eyes. A moment. Then they smiled back at her. She giggled like a little girl to Mrs Turkney, saying, 'Well . . . here I go!'

They entered the schoolroom, stood before the rows of seats. Mrs Turkney told the children who it was and ordered them to say: *How do you do, Mrs Candlemas.*

They sang it – in their own way. It made Alfie blink and twist her face slightly. She swallowed and turned to Mrs Turkney and said, 'Thank you, Mrs Turkney . . . I think I can manage now.'

'Sit down, children,' she said, as Mrs Turkney walked away. She sat down herself, looking them over with a wobbly smile while they stared at her or dropped their heads or hid their faces in their hands, according to disposition. The grey eyes regarded her steadily from the back. As Mrs Turkney disappeared into her fernery, Alfie said, 'Well, the first thing we've got to do is get to know each other. We'll just sit and talk, eh? You can tell me about yourselves. Now, we mustn't be shy with each other. I'd like to kiss you all.' All the faces popped up, the eyes popped out. 'Who's going to let me kiss them first? What about you, young man?' She was looking into the grey eyes. They merely blinked. She looked at Wilhelmina, beckoned. Wilhelmina wriggled like a forked goanna, but came. Alfie kissed the dusky blotchy cheek, then had Whilhemina kiss hers. Not only Wilhemina giggled. After that it was easy.

They spent the rest of the morning playing games. Alfie had dinner with them, gobbling the stew and stuff called bread as if it weren't choking her, while Mrs Turkney sat and watched. Miss Lilyponds had always gone home for dinner, leaving the children to sit around till she chose to return. Alfie went over to the playground with them for an hour, and let them show her games of their own invention. The afternoon was spent in singing mostly. She had no sort of voice. But when Prindy covered his ears at revelation of it, she only laughed.

When Frank Candlemas called in the Rolls at four, the Turkneys wanted them up for a drink before they left. But Alfie asked to be excused, saying she felt exhausted. That she was not lying was evident enough when just out of sight of the Compound, after the great waving with which the children saw her off, she asked Frank to stop the car because she wanted to lean on him and cry. She did just that. He said nothing, just held her.

Up in the Turkney residence Tub asked his spouse how she thought the girl had gone. Mrs Turkney said tersely, 'Well, if she goes on like that for long, there won't be any holding 'em.'

'Yes? She's a nice kid, though.'

'Kid? She's twenty-five if she's a day.'

'Well . . . '

'You mean she's a kid to you, you old fool. I saw the way your were ogling her.'

'Arrrh!' Turkney swigged off a large whisky and went back to his office.

V

Mrs Turkney's frankly expressed gladness over the replacement of Miss Lilyponds by someone of more amiable disposition, not a Screaming Bully, and especially by One Of Us, that is to say of the Aborigines Department rather than of Education, was quite short lived. It had little to do with her husband's undisguised admiration for this Alfie person. She herself too frankly despised old Tub. She had shown how she felt about him during that first week or so while she and Alfie were still speaking, one day when all four of them had been having the after-school drink that Tub had tried to make a ritual of, and Alfie had said she believed success in marriage was based on having something in common outside the couple's own personal interests, and Mrs Turkney, or Vi as her old man called her, turned to him and asked, 'What've we got in common?' and when he only blinked blearily, she gave the answer herself: 'Just being common, eh?' Besides, Tub's love of the lassie was so undangerous that he was obviously just as pleased to have all the other fellows who had fallen for her, or as Vi put it crudely to Tub, Done Their Dangles on her, hanging about her with him, and even more so, judging by his guffaws to be heard at the residence from the office when she was in there with him along with either McCusky, Cobbity, McQuegg, or all three, whereas alone with her his breathless gabbling showed he was as much in conflict as an adolescent boy with a pretty girl. Nor could it be blamed onto ordinary female jealousy, because even while Vi in speaking of the matter to her couple of close friends referred to the general male interest in Alfie as being like dogs running after a bitch, she always conceded the girl's attractiveness, and use of the word bitch was literal and not spiteful, as evident in Vi's always adding that it was Alfie's sheer childishly innocent enthusiasm that was responsible for the muck-up being made of things.

It would seem then that the trouble was simply that Alfie was doing something with ease that poor old Vi, for all her manner of a poor-house keeper, had wanted, as a childless woman and a nurse by dedication, to do, truly take care of these waifs given into her care, but had been frustrated by so many things that she herself, through training, dispostion, experience of the wicked world, was incapable of beating: the antagonism of the Master Race, the interference of bureaucracy, the stinginess of Government spending, the resistance to care of the very people to be cared for because their instinct was that they were the children of Nature, the Ol'Goomun-Ol'Goomun, whose bounty might vary but could never fail.

The trouble began on the third or fourth day, when Mrs Turkney, remarking on Alfie's persistent unnecessary attendance at the midday dinner table, said that she might as well leave full superintendence of the meal to Alfie and free herself for other duties. Quite failing to grasp the irony patent in the remark, Alfie replied eagerly, 'Yes . . . leave it all to me.' Vi did just that, immediately, and by so doing put into her enemy's hands the very weapon she needed to start waging the battle for which the husband had given warning that she was a Regular Warhorse. Turkney was short with Vi when she complained to him, saying she ought to be only too glad to be relieved of the job. That stung her to saying that if she was going to be relieved of it for the one meal she might as well hand the feeding of the children over completely. Tub told her not to be silly. For that, perhaps, she put the proposition with a smile to Alfie over the whisky. Alfie looked the silly one by jumping at it. Without the smile, Vi reminded her of the implications, having to be on the job at 7 a.m. instead of 9, and until 5 or 6 p.m. instead of 4. Alfie, like a cheerful idiot, said she didn't mind what the hours were. Tub looked at her as if he thought she was just that. When Vi, with a smirk of one about to deliver the K.O. to such an easy opponent asked What about Weekends, and Alfie took it on the chin as if she were punchy, Frank, her husband, looked at her as Tub had. Vi went red. But it wasn't the flush of victory, as betrayed when later she insisted in private to her husband, as Superintendent, to make the arrangement official so that there would be no backing out When She Gets Sick Of It. Tub tried to get out of that. But Vi forced him to put it to McCusky and Dr Cobbity, who'd already begun to hang about the place instead of coming to it with grumpy reluctance only when repeatedly requested; and they, getting Alfie's quick bright nod, because it was a sort of official gathering, said, Why not?

One of the last remarks that Mrs Violet Turkney made to Mrs Alfie Candlemas, except in the way of official necessity, was: 'You'll be sorry!'

But it wasn't Alfie who became the sorry one. Nor was it only Vi.

The weapon that Vi had handed Alfie was the matter of the children's food; not merely that of feeding them, but of the food they were given to eat, which was bad by anybody's standards, even those of the black Coburg Islanders who ran the kitchen and dished it out as the worst of the Rubbitch they turned out generally, for the reason that it was Rubbitch they were given with which to cook.

Alfie the warhorse began her battle in the kitchen. Instead of leaving it to the kids to get their food, she went along too, and seeing the difference in what was about to be dished out to them from that in other pots, demanded of Big Butcher, the Boss Cook, that they be given the other. It was still bad. Big Butcher whined that he didn't put the maggots in the meat or the weevils in the flour, the oatmeal, and the rice. That's how he got it from the town butcher every morning and from Mist' Turk'ey's store. She took the battle to Mist' Turk'ey, who gave in at once about the meat, the moment he'd smelt it. He blamed the town butcher who had the Compound contract, said he was putting it over. Alfie stood over him while he dealt with the butcher on the phone. The butcher tried to be funny about it; but Turkney said, 'You'd better be careful, mate. Mrs Candlemas's husband's the new Health Inspector. No more meat like that . . . *if* you don't mind!'

Tub blamed the Wet Season for the condition of the cereals. She demanded to see his stocks. There was enough to take them through the *next* Wet Season. She demanded to see samples of it all. He complied without resistance, only babbling, 'Everything goes mouldy here during the Wet. You've got to expect it.'

'But you don't expect the children to go on eating that?' she asked.

He shrugged: 'What can we do?'

'Chuck it out!'

'You can't do that . . . it's Government Stores!'

'Why . . . are Government Stores holy, or something?' For that's the way his horrified exclamation had made it sound.

'Well . . . they're Government property, and can't be disposed of except in the proper manner.'

'What's that . . . with Bell, Book, and Candle?'

He guffawed: 'No doubt about you . . . you're a . . . you're a wag!' By the look of him he was going to say something nicer than that.

She certainly looked nice enough to kiss out of hand, so was she glowing and sparkling in her indignation. She demanded, 'How would you go about getting rid of the rubbish?'

'Well . . . I'd have to notify McCusky . . . and he Cobbity . . . who'd have to get in touch with the Auditor. Then there'd be an inspection. It has to be officially condemned as not fit for human consumption.'

'Does it happen often?'

'Well . . . no . . . only a couple of times to my knowledge . . . when we had some pretty bad stuff.'

'Worse than this?'

'Oh . . . lots worse . . . just a couple of bags of stuff.'

'Do you consider this fit for human consumption?'

He guffawed nervously: 'Well, I'm no judge.'

'Would you eat it yourself?'

'If I was very hungry, I suppose.'

'Like those children of mine?'

He was silent. She went on. 'Oscar . . . I'm sure you're a good-hearted man . . . and that you wouldn't give children stuff to eat that you wouldn't eat yourself. What about doing something about it, eh?'

He giggled nervously. 'What *can* I do?'

'Start the process rolling to get this officially condemned.'

He hesitated a moment, then said, 'Okay.'

'At once . . . to please me?'

He swallowed. 'Okay.' He got on the phone to McCusky.

McCusky was out in ten minutes. He put on a great performance . . . at poor Tub's expense. 'Certainly the stuff will be condemned,' he declared. 'It should never have been kept so long. Its condition should've been reported long ago.' In vain did Tub say that it had arrived like that.

Dr Cobbity came out in the afternoon, inclined to make a joke of it, to say, 'Now, weevils aren't classed as noxious. You might even say that the lavae adds protein to the diet.' Then he argued: 'What's the good of good flour if you have bad cooks? We've never been able to get anyone to make good bread here.'

'Have you ever employed a proper baker?'

'Where would we get the money?'

'Will you have a proper baker at the new place you talk about?'

'I sincerely hope so.'

'Is it only on hope you base your plans, Doctor?'

Cobbity made a comical face. 'Estimates, my dear, Estimates . . . it's always Estimates first . . . . '

'And humanity last!'

'Now . . . I say!'

'I don't mean to be offensive. I know what you're all up against. But I think you've been up against it so long that it's exhausting you . . . '

'Hear, hear, hear!' cried everybody crowded round, Tubby Turkney, Eddy McCusky, Cuthbert Cobbity.

She went on, spinning daintily on high heels as she spoke, so that she spoke to each of them, giving them all that same dark rosy black-eyed amorous look which held them spellbound. 'I happen to have a proper baker I can put straight into the kitchen . . . . '

'Who's going to pay him?' asked Cobbity.

'It's a she . . . already employed in this place . . . handling dirty linen in the laundry. Nelly Ah Loy. She was baker on the station she came from.'

Cobbity and McCusky turned on Tub, who cringed. 'No one told me she was a baker . . . . '

Cobbity said to Alfie, 'There you are . . . we've got our baker for the next place!'

'What about now?'

'That's up to you . . . and Tub, here.'

'She can't make good bread with that flour, though, can she.'

'I don't know . . . I'm not a cooking expert.'

'Well, I do know. We'll need new flour.'

There was a gasp all round. But new flour they got, from a Chinese wholesaler down town, enough to last till the next steamer came in with more as Government Stores, about which a memo had been sent in ordering that it be inspected before shipment. There was also new rice, new oatmeal, stuff for making cakes and custards, dried fruit, canned full-cream milk, butter. The Coburg Islanders were kicked out of the kitchen, and their places taken by women from the Adult Halfcaste Home. No one got paid. But everybody began to be better fed; and that was enough, at least for the time. The only scoffer was Vi Turkney, who said it wouldn't last. But one evening, with a bit too much whisky in her and much too much about Alfie Candlemas from Tub, she broke down and cried, 'After all my years of trying . . . and along comes a chit of a thing with a pretty face and . . . oh, oh, oh, ah!'

In the *Government Gazette* published that day, as supplement to the *Port Palmeston Times*, there appeared under the heading of *Appointments*: Aelfrieda Tripconny Candlemas, as Protector of Aborigines. The ladies of the community were scoffing, saying: What a name to go to bed with! But the gentlemen were saying: Yes . . . but what a gal . . . phwee-phew!

So far the Candlemases were taking little or no part in the social life of the town. For one thing they were unable to do the proper thing in the matter of routine entertaining, having not yet been allotted Government quarters, the house they lived in being a little old cottage in that run-down locality shared by those two semi-sharers Kitty Windeyer and Fay McFee; for another, Alfie, busy as a little bee from dawn to dark for seven days a week, was worn out of nights, so much so that often she fell asleep soon after the meal they always had sent round to them from a Chinese restaurant; for a third they would not be much interested in the frivolous sociality of the community they were part of; and then, despite the male appreciation of Alfie as a female, resentment was already being expressed by both sexes concerning what they called Spoiling the Black Bastards: 'If you want to live on the fat of the land for nothing, black your face and go up and live at the Compound. You won't be able to do anything with the BB's soon.' It was a fact that halfcaste maids were becoming more difficult to get, now that good food was available for only a token of work and no bullying; and there were always the boys of the Kerosene to provide a bit of money, which didn't have to go into Government Trust for niggardly doling out by Mick Cusky. First of the white ladies to suffer in this regard were those who should have been the last, Mesdames Cobbity and McCusky, who could do no better now out of Tub Turkney, than to have him say he'd see what he could do, and Vi, who told them even shortly, that it was now out of her hands and that they'd best ask their husbands, with the inference that it was these who had brought the situation about. Each of the ladies, in asking their husbands said something like: 'That woman's making a fool of you.' They had to be content, like the common herd, with the service of what they called Gins, meaning full-blood black women. They weren't above calling any woman of Aboriginal blood a Gin. But it was mostly reserved for use in insult: 'You clumsy dirty Gin!' Halfcaste women could be deeply hurt by it, but not the blacks, who were used to it simply as a name for a woman of their kind. Of course the word really meant simply *woman* in classic Greek, *gyn*, of very ancient usage, without malicious intent, like *nigger*, simply being from the Latin, *niger, black*. It was perhaps as well that the whites were as poorly educated as they were, despite their airs, since it must have cramped their style badly to know that they were using classical words as insults.

However, the Candlemases might have made friends quickly enough and even of a sort that might have suited them, had it not been for Frank's shrewd judgment that it would not be politic in the circumstances to accept them. There were the people of the *Palmeston Progressive*: Rollo Ramstones, the Editor, who claimed to have known Si Tripconny in his political fighting days and to have seen Alfie alongside him on several platforms as a little girl, and now wanted to do a special article on Old Si with mention of what his fighting daughter was doing for the underdog – and Fay McFee, wanting to do a Pen Portrait of Alfie. Frank knew enough about the feud between the local Government set-up and their critics to realize that, whatever his Enchanted One's enchantment of Cobbity and Co., involvement with what were called the Bolshies would bring the fairy castle she was building tumbling down. One had only to watch him watching her in her enthusiasm to realize that it wasn't a bit what his darling was doing that interested him as her joy in doing it. An article did appear in *The Progressive* about Silas Tripconny, but with a slighting reference to his daughter as having joined the ranks of the Government nobs. Fay was put off her Pen Portrait with a promise of something lively to come. Instead Alfie was taken up by *The Times*, which referred to her efforts as *Preliminary to the Institution of the Plans the Government had in Hand in the Matter of Aboriginal Affairs for Later in the Year*.

Frank was even careful in their dealings with Jeremy Delacy and his Anthropologists, Cootes and Ferris. These three were back in town from a trip down country in search of anthropological data and interpreters with which to strengthen the interference they planned in the case of The King against Cock-Eye Bob when it came up, as listed, after Easter, only a couple of weeks away. They had done the trip by air, as in fact the Anthropologists had done that from the South, Mr Ferris being also an airman and having some arrangement with the German Junkers Company to demonstrate their aircraft in Australia. Frank's caution cost Alfie a private flight with Ferris, and himself probably with pain of so deeply disappointing her as obviously he had. But he insisted on the unwisdom of the association at the moment. Apart from the team's being regarded as natural enemies by Cobbity and Co., there was the fact that Fergus Ferris, as waggish a young fellow as his mate, Cootes, was ponderous, had already antagonized McCusky by making a fool of him in a pub in town. There could well have been an element of protection of his darling from a bit of a lad in Frank's holding young Fergus off her, because that was what the fellow was for a certainty. It was he who had brought the others to the Candlesmases, having heard what the boys were saying about Alfie in town, and being one for the ladies. He had made the first approach to her at the Compound, calling on the evident pretence of being interested in her school. He'd tried to get to see her kitchen, too, and would have, but for being barred by Turkney. There was that strict rule that no one was allowed on the Reserve without the express permission of the Protector, otherwise Prosecution

According to the Law. Even an attempt at wheedling Cobbity on the phone by Alfie herself didn't work. When she said it was because Ferris was an Anthropologist that she wanted to get him in, he snapped, 'They're just the buggers we want to keep out.'

'But why?' she asked.

'Because they want to undo everything I've spent all these years doing. They want to get a look at that place to use in evidence against me. It isn't mine. I inherited it. I'm just about to disburden myself of it. Least of all people I'd like to help cruel things for me is you . . . sweetheart!' He said the last word almost with a sigh, as if it had been squeezed out in spite of him and not as one of the common appelations of the day. It silenced her.

Fergus Ferris's response to the rebuff was a split-lip grin: 'I'll get in there, sweetheart, you'll see . . . and I won't be Prosecuted According to the Law.' It was a very different sounding sweetheart; still there was no doubt about his interest in her.

He was a pretty boy, except for that suggestion of harelip concealed as near as possible under a largish fair moustache of the kind aeronautical types were just then making a kind of cult of. He was slight, with a dancer's grace, with a fine pair of greenish-grey eyes that he used to as much effect in his dealings with Alfie as to make those roses keep blooming in her cheeks. When he offered to Take her for a Flip in his aircraft, to land on a marvellous salt-pan he knew Across That-a-way, jerking his lips Aboriginal-fashion across the harbour, the roses glowed. Perhaps the fact that she said what one would not expect of her, that she'd have to ask her husband, was as much in self-defence as Frank's subsequent dissuasion of her doing so was not really a matter of being politic.

She got to know Jeremy through seeking a meeting with him. Fergus had told her about the school at Lily Lagoons and Jeremy's theory that the education of Aborigines, full-blood or part, should follow the pattern of their ancient ways, that is that children should be permitted to pick up as they liked till puberty, then suddenly whipped into discipline by respect for their elders. She was excited by it, for the reason that so far her work in the school had been, as she thought, a complete failure. Half the school-time period she had spent with the children down on the Compound beach, trying to get into their heads what was in the Curriculum inherited from Miss Lilyponds, while they sported in the sea like young dugongs or went running miles after fleeing armies of crabs or listened to what King George told them about crocodile hunting down on the Queen Victoria River, or Peg-leg Queeny about preparing and cooking different kinds of bush tucker. Mrs Turkney had reported the matter privily to the Head Teacher at the State School, who had in turn complained to Dr Cobbity, who'd made a joke about it: 'Have your fun with them while you can. When you get to the New Settlement there'll be no sea to play around in . . . no more playing at school then. These kids have got to be equipped to take their place in our society . . . they've got to learn the value of money, the nature of contract . . . but have your fun now. Blow the State School. They didn't want anything to do with it when we never had anyone. They can go jump in the harbour now we have.'

Jeremy came on Good Friday night, along with the Anthropologists and a load of liquor. In phoning him at his hotel, Alfie had said that although she wanted to talk seriously to him, she was also in something of a party mood and had heard he was something of a party man on occasions. Her own occasion, she said, was the fact that this was her first day off the job since she'd got it, her charges having been taken over for the day by the Mission people, for the purpose, as she put it: 'Of celebrating the execution of one, Jesus of Nazareth, a colonial trouble-maker in Imperial Roman times.' Jeremy was stiffish on the phone to begin with; but that made him chuckle, and moved him to say that as she wanted it both ways, intelligent discussion with the party spirit, the spirit was brandy, and might he bring some?

Jeremy was jolly enough in the early stages of the party , too – as who could not help be with the constant intelligent clowning of young Fergus Ferris and so good-humoured a host as Frank Candlemas? Although Fergus couldn't get more than snickers out of his mate, Fabian Cootes, whose academic dignity probably he had outraged too often already, Frank had Cootes, quickly under the influence despite his quite small whisky nipping, giggling most of the while. The way Frank made it sound, there was no more entertaining job than that of a Health Inspector with a sense of humour. Already he had a score of funny stories about his experiences with the Chinese and Greeks of Port Palmeston with their utter lack of comprehension of Anglo-Saxon ideas on sanitation except as a means of harassing people who had lived so long with filth that they had no fear of it, until they anted-up the *cumshaw*. He told of one old Chinese woman who produced a ham and a live rooster even in Court to prevent her prosecution. But things changed somewhat as Alfie, not heeding Jeremy's warning that, while brandy did not make one ordinarily drunk it still did the job, and drank too much too quickly, got into the bellicose state of drunkenness and took to fighting with him. Most likely the trouble between them began with his resistance to her trying to take possession of him and his obvious manoeuvring to fob her off on Fergus. Fergus was quite ready to flirt with her and in fact did at every opportunity to get her alone, as when she left the company in pursuit of her duties as hostess. Evidently Alfie was not used to failing to take possession of males of her species if she chose it. The thing flared up when she learnt, through his inquiry about Prindy, that the boy was his grandson, or as he put it to her annoyance, allegedly so. She charged him with repudiating the child. In vain did he try to point out that it was up to the child to claim him rather than vice versa, that the boy would do better growing up to understand the reality of his place in Australian society than having it hidden from him, that anyway, it was a matter for her colleagues Cobbity & Co. to decide According to the Law. She declared that his attitude to the Aboriginal Problem was negative, and all but called him a coward. Afterwards she became contrite, even got him away and wept a little on his breast. He spoilt it all for her by refusing to put his arms round her and in telling her that she had now reached the third stage of alcoholic indulgence, lachrimosity, and wouldn't be long in reaching the third and last. He wouldn't tell her what that was; so she asked Frank, and when he replied, 'the comatose,' she flounced out, and didn't come back. Frank took it with good humour. Jeremy apologized for having caused it with that grand old trouble-maker for those not used to handling it, brandy.

On Easter Monday there was another Mission picnic for the Compound kids, Alfie took part in this after getting Dr Cobbity's permission to hold it on Shelly Beach as a change from the Compound beach, which meant nothing to the kids as it had in the past. It was the same old thing, with Mr Tasker and the ginger beer and the harmonium, only no renegades like Miss Kitty Windeyer and David to liven things up. Bored after a while, Alfie went walking through the coconuts, and ran into Jumbo Delacy, lurking as usual on the outskirts of a picnic his family was included in. She spoke to him. He knew who she was, and responded in nothing like his usual surly manner with his betters, telling her that he'd heard what a good job she was doing with the kids. She was instantly interested in him when she heard his name, and soon knew much of his history of misfortune, according to Jumbo's interpretation of it, including the last bit of it, which was his imminent dispossession of his last shred of dignity as a man and a Delacy, namely loss of his own home, about to be pulled down to make room for oil tanks the Shell Oil Company would soon be building on the site. Mention of the Shell Oil Company had even more electrifying effect on Alfie than the name of Delacy. Forgetting about the picnic, she went up with Jumbo to have a look at his doomed home and a peep at that eternally safe and sound one of his rich relations, one of whom, as Jumbo had made it sound, was that somehow specially irritating but rather attractive old man, Jeremy. Jumbo had told her that once he had lived with his half-brother Jeremy, but had fallen out with him because Jeremy only wanted to use him to turn Lily Lagoons into a private park to live in like a squatter without doing any squatter work. He said, 'He start what he call Euraustralia League . . . get all halfcaste come live dere . . . learn what he call Dignity o' Race. We go all right. Da's what we want. But how we goin' 'o get rich like whiteman, eh? We wan' 'o run stock. He won't let us. We got to work, work, work . . . all-day bloody work, fixin' up de lagoon so he can have plen'y duck and goose and ev't 'ing shoot when he want. We soon wake up, we lot. He don' care 'bout Aborigines. All he want's dat big place . . . and people workin' for him for nutching.'

'The old time Lord of the Manor and his serfs, eh?' suggested Alfie.

'Da's it, Missus . . . da's just it. So bugger him, I say.'

'That's what I say, too,' declared Alfie, rosy with indignation. 'The Delacys . . . what a mob! Living like lords . . . and leave one poor little boy in the Compound like in a waifs' home . . . and you and your poor wife and children to be swept aside by the greatest greediest monster the world has ever known . . . the Shell Oil Company . . . my god!'

She went home to Frank full of it. Frank said he knew something about it, but understood that although Jumbo's father, the Inspector, had provided the house for him, there was some doubt about his right to the land, that anyway, as he had heard things, Jumbo and his family would be better in quarters provided for them in the new Aboriginal Settlement when it was built.

'But he doesn't want to go to the Settlement!' cried Alfie. 'He says he wants to be free.'

Frank shrugged. 'I suppose that's up to your mates, Cobbity & Co.'

'Don't use that expression! I'm getting sick of it. It's only people opposed to the reforms who use it. They make it sound like . . . like . . . well, something like Shell Oil!'

Next day Alfie phoned Dr Cobbity and told him what she'd learnt and asked him what was he going to do about it. He asked, 'What do you want me to do?'

'Fight,' she said, 'fight!'

'Fight who?'

'That Shell Oil Company, for a start.'

'Now, come off it, Alfie, dear!' he said it so nicely.

'But you've fought everybody else . . . the squatters, the boong-bashers . . . "He is thrice armed whose cause is just".'

'But the Shell Oil Company! That's a job for an army . . . two or three armies . . . why, they own the blooming armies!'

'All the more reason to fight them!'

He sighed, then said suddenly, 'Speaking of the Delacys . . . I hear you had the king of 'em at a boozy party the other night.'

'So what?'

'Well . . . he's not exactly on our side, you know.'

'It's all right . . . I don't like him. He's pompous. And after hearing this Jumbo thing, I like him less.'

'Ah . . . that's my girl!'

She asked a little stiffly, 'What's that mean?'

He chuckled: 'Leave it for the moment. And how about leaving this Jumbo business for the time being, too? I've got this Court case on my mind. It's on today. All your mates'll be in on it . . . the Ape Men, Jeremy Delacy, Fay McFee, Tasker . . . .'

'They're no friends of mine!'

He chuckled again, and said again, 'That's my girl, Alfie!'

She wasn't stiff this time. 'Okay,' she said. 'Good luck with the case. Be seeing you!'

Later that same morning an aged halfcaste woman who looked to have some Chinese blood came to Alfie while she was down on the Compound beach with the children. The woman said she lived with black relatives in one of the Compound hovels. She came almost cringing, saying, 'Pleeje, Mitchis, pleeje, Mitchis!' till Alfie, in evident embarrassment, asked her not to talk like that. The woman didn't appear to understand. Still cringing, she said she'd come to her because she'd heard she was a Good Kind Mitchis, and hoped she might help her to join her husband, who was in the Leper Lazaret. What she babbled out in the patois, that Alfie had some difficulty in gathering for a while, was to the effect that she loved her husband, Albert Snowball, also a halfcaste, dearly, and would like to spend her last days with him. Their children were gone. Their black relations didn't want her. If there was a chance of his coming out of the lazaret she would wait patiently. But if not, she would like to go there to be with him to the end. She had already approached Dr Cobbity but he had refused to let her go to the Island, saying that it was only for lepers. She had tried sneaking over in a canoe with blacks, but only to be turned away when found by the Superintendent there. Could Mitchis speak to Dr Cobbity for her? Alfie said she certainly would, that she had heard that leprosy was now curable, and there shouldn't be any difficulty. But she asked Lucy, as the woman said she was called, to be patient for just a little longer, because at the moment Dr Cobbity was very busy with a court case. 'Trust me,' she said. And to seal it, she kissed Lucy's dirty smelly cheek, to the astonishment of Lucy and of all who were watching, whose comment on it was that which always followed on the amazing or fearsome, the in-breathed: 'Eh, look out!'

VI

The Court of Oyer and Terminer and General Jail Delivery (the setting for the *Case of The King Against Cock-Eye Bob*) was called. It was so announced in that same little old courtroom by the same massive Clerk of Courts, the wheezy Mr Doscas. Old World stuff, with all the Old World trappings, of wigs and gowns and tipstaff, as well as the Lion and Unicorn, looking insanely outlandish when taken with that wide view through door and window of Terra Australis, the Southern Land of the Holy Spirit, venue for Australia Felix, the dreamed-of Nation where the insanity and inanity of the old world might be forgot and men true brothers be.

Judge Bickering sat on his throne beneath the symbol of the Power and the Glory, the Peace and Dignity, invested in him by Him of Westminster, London, announced by Mr Doscas, puffing like a stranded dugong, as *Our Sovereign Lord the King*. The Judge was a bulky ruddy man, in full-bottom wig descending to the scarlet hood of his Doctor's gown, and a compulsive wink of a watery left eye which his associates knew meant he was in a merry mood for commencing his Sessions: so woe to anyone who didn't laugh readily at his witticisms, including those in the Dock.

Gowned and wigged were those two secondary players in the Sixteenth Century Charade, Counsel for Prosecution and Defence. Gowned also was Dr Fabian Cootes, there to assist Defending Counsel in his capacity as Anthropologist, and kidded into wearing his regalia by that joker, his own assistant, Fergus Ferris, who'd told him he'd heard that Old Bickers wouldn't listen to him unless he wore it. Now that he'd learnt from Defence Counsel that he'd had his leg pulled, he could do nothing but sit in the front bench with face as crimson as his Doctor's hood. It was off that poor fellow, The Coot, as cheeky Fergus called him, that Judge Bickering scored his first laugh. Spotting the flash of crimson, the watery winking eye concentrated on it, and His Honour asked dryly, 'Do you also wear it to the bathroom, Dr Cootes?'

Loud laughter – till the winking froze into a glare, when the Usher took the cue and cried, 'Silence in Court!'

His Honour began to wink again and asked that the first case be called.

Mr Doscas called it: '*The King against Cock-Eye Bob.*'

The judicial eye winked rapidly again and the dry voice proclaimed: 'With all due humility to Our Sovereign Lord, and respect to yourself, Mr Clerk, you *do* make it sound rather like Canute against the Tide.'

It must have been one of his best yet, because he let the laughter go on for quite a while before he gave the cue to the Usher.

Prosecution muttered to his learned friend, Defence, 'The old boy's fairly dripping with it today. If you can make your Defendant laugh you might even get an acquittal.'

That most valuable of all the laughter was indeed forthcoming, but not through connivance of the Defence. When Bobwirridirridi was duly escorted into the dock and Judge Bickering looked at him amiably, he grinned broadly, saying, 'Gootay, Boss!'

Judge Bickering was well known at the Jail, not simply as Chiefest of Turnkeys, Master of Screws, but as an amiable visitor, who often went out to see how those who had lost the game with him were getting along, to consider releases, even to take small gifts. He called it Tempering Justice with Mercy, and often declared in his Court that while he enjoyed his power as a judge he preferred the exercise of it rather in ordering release of a prisoner than in committing one. Now he winked rapidly at old Bob, but addressed him in a tone of true judicial gravity: 'Prisoner at the Bar, know you that you are in flagrant contempt in so addressing me? Nevertheless, Gootay to you, too!'

Bobwirridirridi flung his grey head back and opened the crack of a mouth wide in joining the wholesale laughter.

'Silence in Court!'

'Arraign the Prisoner.'

Fatty Doscas went through the rigmarole of the Indictment, while Wirridirridi, having glanced over the Court for familiar faces and not seeing the one he was probably looking for, because the Witnesses would be admitted only as required, looked over the now-packed Jury Box, out of the window, at what could be seen in a neap tide of the local Shade of his own particular sovereign lord, until his name was spoken again: 'Cock-Eye Bob . . . how plead you, Guilty or Not Guilty?'

The question in the case of an Aboriginal prisoner was only a formality. Mr McCusky, in his best white suit and wearing a bright yellow tie, leapt to his feet to give the answer, strode to the foot of the dock and turned dramatically, to answer in a loud clear voice: 'Guilty!'

A gasp from the Court. His Honour, whose eye had started winking as if making ready to say something about the theatricality, looked as astonished almost as the rest. McCusky held it for the perfect moment, then added: 'Guilty but Insane!'

Sighs of pent breaths. Sensing something untoward, Bobwirridirridi's red eyes burned over the crowded room. Counsel were staring at each other. The unofficial Defence Group were gaping. The Jury had sagged, done out of several days' entertainment with pay. There were smirks only on the faces of Police Superintendent Bullco and Sergeant Cahoon.

Mr McCusky then strode towards the Bench, and handing up a document in a wax-sealed envelope, said, 'If it please Your Honour, the Certification.'

His Honour took it, broke the seal, glanced at the document. Then the eye began to wink again. The dry voice spoke into the utter silence: 'Well, well . . . a shrewd plea, and not to be gainsaid.' The eye fell on Dr Cootes. The voice went on: 'But I must admit a slight disappointment on my own behalf. With the array of talent that we have here today, not merely judicial, but sociological . . . and may I even say zoological?' The eye fell on Jeremy who reddened ' . . . I had expected some fireworks.'

The laugh came from everywhere, but rather weakly.

'Hmm . . . do I detect the anticlimactic effect of a damp squib generally?'

The laugh was much louder. When the Usher had called silence, His Honour asked the Crown Prosecutor if he were satisfied. That gentleman replied yes. The Judge didn't ask Defending Counsel Billings, nor address him, although he winked at him as if he would have liked to say something like: *Pity about your fee, mate*! Certainly that's the way he looked at Mr Billings. Evidently his clients, the Aborigines Department, had not taken him into their confidence.

His Honour went on to say that, had the indictment been contested, whatever the verdict, he himself would have ruled that the Defendant be subject to psychiatric examination with Anthropologists in attendance with medical men: 'I say this, not only from what I have read in the Indictment, in its lines and between them, but from what I know of the Defendant . . . or Prisoner as we must call him now . . . whom I have known and been interested in for a long while. I say this not by reason of the offence for which he was committed, but that of his obsession with the Cult of the Rainbow Snake, for which I can find no grounds in my own anthropological reading. It may be remembered . . . it will be by the police, I'm sure . . . . ' The eye that had winked before glared for a moment at Police Officers Bullco and Cahoon until they dropped their own ' . . . that it was I who recommended his release under the Amnesty granted at the Accession of His Ex-Majesty, Edward the Eighth. Just before his release I asked him if he intended to pursue the Cult and he ignored me, which I took to mean that he did. I presumed it a harmless personal lunacy, since he seems to be alone in it. Jesus Christ was considered harmless until he got a following. I daresay that if the Pope of Rome were to stand as an unknown before a Rabbinical or Mohammedan Court and state his beliefs they would think him crazy, too. I am not passing judgment on the beliefs of Bobwirridirridi, as I prefer to call him, but only on their likely danger to the community. For it has been demonstrated that, even though greatly feared and avoided, he had been able to command a following and hence to feel power and to want to exercise it. That is why I like the plea. I want to see him put away. However, I am making a ruling. I shall in a moment formally sentence him to detention during His Majesty's Pleasure, but in doing so I shall rule that he be not removed from this Jurisdiction, not for judicial reasons, but because sending him to a Southern mad-house would kill him. I've heard him crying before, *Poor Fellow My Country*, have had him ask me to let him have a Walk-about so that he might not, as he said, lose his Dreaming. I gave it him when the opportunity offered . . . at the cost of a man's life . . . although I am of the opinion from what I have read of the evidence, that the fatality might easily have been avoided.' The eye fixed on Clancy, who flamed, swallowed, and looked down. 'It can't happen again, except in some incredible contingency. The fault is to some degree mine, owing to the weakness I have, if you wish to call it so, often expressed in this court, that I would much rather use my judicial powers to liberate a man than to imprison him For that reason I wish to make amends to the Prisoner with that ruling, and with another, which I want inserted in the document of committal as seriously as the first, namely that with the bread-and-milk that the medical authorities prescribed as his daily diet, he be given a tot of rum, as on occasions when he was in a low state and put in hospital . . . a tot by my ruling being one fluid ounce, apothecaries' measure, since this is a medicinal matter . . . Yes, Mr Delacy?'

For Jeremy had risen from his seat. His Honour winked. 'Do you wish to give me the pleasure of committing you for Contempt of Court?'

Jeremy, very red, answered, 'No, Your Honour. I thought I might be able to be of assistance in the matter of the Prisoner's tot. I also feel that I need to make amends to him . . . . '

The Judge interrupted: 'When I used the word Pleasure in the matter of committing you, Mr Delacy, I did not mean that it would actually please me to do so. On the contrary . . . I respect you for some of your views and your courageous outspokenness in support of them. What I meant . . . .' The eye was winking hard ' . . . was that the case has been so much without incident that a little wouldn't hurt and that you were going to do me the favour of providing it. Yes, Sir . . . what is it you would like to say about the tot?'

'As you know, I am a registered Pharmacist. In that capacity, while I was associated with the Prisoner before the affair that caused him to be removed from my district, I gave him brandy with the bread-and-milk, and found that he greatly appreciated it. It would do him far more good medicinally than rum, also. I am willing to meet the cost of the brandy.'

'Very good of you, Mr Delacy . . . and I must say, very shrewd of you legally to use your pharmaceutical qualifications to get round a charge of supplying liquor to an Aboriginal. But let us ask the Prisoner.' The Pookarakka was drinking it in. The red coals met the wet winking blue eye: 'Prisoner at the Bar . . . which one you like more better, that-one rum, or that-one brandy?'

The coals glowed, the lips smacked, the voice cackled: 'Plendy, Boss . . . proper goot one dat plendy!'

Judge Bickering looked at the new Court Reporter, a stony faced young woman with red hair: 'Alter the transcript to brandy, will you please, Miss Williams.' He then looked at Jeremy: 'The cost will be met by the Government, Mr Delacy.'

'Thank you, Sir.' Jeremy sat down.

The eye fixed on Dr Cootes: 'Have you anything to say, Doctor?'

The Coot rose looking sheepish in his gown, gasped, 'No, Your Honour.'

'Not on the subject of the cult of the Rainbow Snake?'

'No, Your Honour. I consider it quite unauthentic anthropologically.'

'Would you expound that?'

Conscious of all the eyes on him the way his own popping black eyes rolled, Cootes stammered, 'Well . . . there's nothing in anthropological literature to . . . to . . . well, it seems to me to be . . . a sort of racket worked on occasions by types who want to gain their ends by intimidation.'

'A *racket*, Doctor? Does that word fit into an anthropological dissertation?'

Cootes was at a loss. Old Bickers' eye was winking hard again: 'You don't have anything more to say on the subject, Doctor?'

The Coot quavered, 'N-no, Sir.'

'A pity . . . attired like that you look the perfect part for a learned discussion.'

As Cootes sat down there was a titter. A guffaw. A howl of laughter, in which Bobwirridirridi joined. Then 'Silence in Court!'

His Honour then duly sentenced Bobwirridirridi, who waved to him as he was led away, and to Jeremy also.

The eye began winking as His Honour set it on both Prosecutor and Defence: 'In view of the verdict, you learned gentlemen have quite a problem to face in the matter of the trial of the Prisoner's accomplices. I understand they are charged with being Accessories Before and After the Fact of the Wilful Murder. In view of the finding of Insanity, what are you going to do? Is one who is accessory to the act of a madman also a madman? I leave it to you for the time being. Meantime, we adjourn. Thank you, gentlemen!'

'The Court will rise!'

Judge Bickering rose, bowed, was swallowed by the King's Beasts.

VII

It was Frank Candlemas who first approached Dr Cobbity with the request of Lucy Snowball concerning her husband confined in the Leper Lazaret. Cobbity's reply, reported back to Alfie by Frank, was a definite No. Frank said he had tried arguing on the grounds of what he had read about the modern attitude to leprosy, but without a chance, because not only did Cobbity stand on his dignity as a medical man, but could claim to have specialized in the study of the disease while doing his D.P.H. abroad. The doctor had said that until he had it on what he called Proper Authority that leprosy was curable, those people he sent to the lazaret were to be regarded as there for life, while as for permitting exposure to infection by the disease such as this woman – this crazy woman, he had called her – wanted, not only would it be creating an exceedingly dangerous precedent, but was against all Medical Ethics, and Frank ought to know better than to ask.

'Sounds a bit arrogant, doesn't he,' commented Alfie.

'He can be, too,' Frank conceded. 'But who are we to buck the verdict of a medical man . . . and a specialist?'

Alfie said, 'I'll have a go at him.'

Alfie had that go at Cobbity one day when he came to the Compound Children's Home with another medical specialist, this one in diseases of the Ear, Nose, and Throat, who happened to be passing through on the steamer for the co-called East, to examine Prindy. Cobbity had already taken another look at Prindy on the report of Dr McQuegg and the insistence of Alfie that his alleged mental defectiveness was due to abnormality of hearing. Cobbity had spent an hour, with face rather close to watching Alfie's, twanging a tuning-fork in the boy's ear, so much to Prindy's delight that his reaction was recorded as further evidence of his being *non compos mentis*. The instant Prindy heard the sound his eyes glowed and he whispered, inward: 'Cee!' The significance of the remark was evidently lost on the two non-musical observers. Having got prompt normal physical reaction, the doctor remarked that there certainly wasn't anything much the matter with his hearing, and would have put the fork away, only that Prindy asked for more of it, and assumed a wrapt expression, with lips moving silently, surely indicating that his mind was running up and down the scale. But it looked so silly, that the kids, crowded at a little distance, began to giggle. Then when Cobbity tried to put the fork away again, Prindy took hold of it, took possession of it, even forcibly, and tried, by manipulation, to do what should have been obvious, that is make the ringing metal play a tune. Alfie did suggest that that was what he might be attempting; but Dr Cobbity said, no, it was the classic monkey-trick of a Cretin, get your paws on a pretty thing, and refuse to let it go. He snatched the fork back and shoved it in his pocket, receiving such a look from the grey eyes that he remarked, 'Look . . . you just have to look at him!'

The ENT Specialist, a thin little sniffly man, did the best he could with the very limited equipment Dr Cobbity had to lend him for peeking into Prindy's ears. He said he couldn't make a full diagnosis with such gear. Seeing that he was having a sort of busman's holiday, else he wouldn't have dropped in on Cobbity and gotten himself involved, it was a wonder he hadn't brought his apparatus with him. But then, busmen on holidays don't take their ticket-clippers with them. All the ENT man could say was that one of the boy's ears looked Rather Dingy. Then he looked into the other kids' ears and found a lot of dinginess, and a couple who were deaf. When he suggested hearing aids for the deafies, Cobbity laughed and said, 'We're flat out getting money to feed 'em.'

Perhaps Alfie was a bit piqued at being more or less ignored during this visit of the otherwise always eagerly regardful Cobbity in her presence, not knowing that while a medical man can also be a man when left to himself, with another or more of his kind he becomes part of a Medical Faculty, which, of course, is a kind of Theocracy, beyond common human ken. Anyway, to that remark of Cobbity's she added a tart one of her own: 'I pay the cook out of my salary.'

The ENT Man looked at her over his rimless glasses, sniffling, 'Do you indeed!' Then he looked at his colleague for conformation.

Cobb was looking red and angry. He snapped, 'She doesn't have to do it. She's been told not to.'

Now it was Alfie who was red: 'If I didn't pay her, we'd have no cook. Then where would we be?'

Cobbity got control of himself and grinned at her, saying, 'On much better terms with the Government Auditor than we've been since you came along and appointed your own catering staff.' He laughed. The ENT man laughed. Alfie made a little face to show she took it in good part.

But to disprove that showing, as the two doctors were leaving, after taking a quick look at the black part of the menagerie, and happened to meet her near Turkney's office and paused to say goodbye to her, she, having just a few minutes ago had to deal with Lucy Snowball, who was still sitting in a weeping huddle against the office wall, asked the ENT man, 'Doctor . . . do you happen to have heard that leprosy is now curable and considered not as contagious as it was?'

The medical gentleman should properly have consulted his colleague first, especially as he must have known that Cobbity would know more about the disease than he, even if Cobbity hadn't told him of his qualifications, as was likely, because while often arrogant, he was never pompous. But perhaps for the first time he had noticed how pretty this young lady was, prettier for being angry too, and so far forgot his Theocratic Oath as to reply, 'Why, yes . . . I believe that it's got such a new look they've given it a new name . . . Hansen's Disease . . . Isn't that so, Doctor. Ahem!' It was plain enough to see by the look of Cobbity that a frightful mistake in Medical Ethics had been made.

Alfie must have realized, too, that she had made a mistake, because when later she phoned Cobbity it was with due humility of tone. He was stiff to begin with, very official, wanting to know what official business it was she wanted him for. She told him it was only to say that she was sorry, that she wouldn't have done it only he was so mean about the cook business. She said, 'You made it sound as if I'm just a damn nuisance.'

He answered, but with the stiffness gone, 'You are, too.'

'Well, why don't you fire me?'

He sighed: 'And take out of my life the only joy that's left in it?' She was silent. He asked, 'Are you there?'

'Of course.'

'Then say something?'

'What is there to say?'

'Lots, actually . . . but . . . but . . . .'

'But what?'

He was the silent one now, till he broke it, saying, 'Look, what about coming to Vic Shane's party on Anzac Night?'

'I can't stand that vain old man.'

'Oh, old Vic's not so bad. But if you don't like the party, we could go for a drive somewhere while they're boozing . . . and have a talk. We never get to talk about anything but bloody boongs.'

'I thought bloody boongs were your chief interest in life.'

'They were. Not now.'

She was silent. Then she said softly, 'Cuthbert . . . .'

She must have heard him catch his breath. He answered slowly, 'Yes?'

'I know it's not the time to ask . . . but I'm worried about that poor woman, Lucy Snowball . . . .'

He cut in sharply: 'Now listen, if you're going to . . . .'

She cut in on him: 'All right, all right . . . I won't. I just wanted to ask for her, because she asked me to.'

'I told your husband.'

'I know. I'm sorry. But I had to ask.'

After a moment he said, 'Fair enough . . . and now, what about that party?'

'Okay,' she said. 'Anzac night. When's that . . . about a week? I'll have to go with Frank, of course.'

'Of course.'

'Okay.'

'Okay . . . sweetheart.'

It was a fact that Alfie was paying the Compound Cook, Nelly Ah Loy. To be sure it was only a few shillings a week, mostly spent on buying things for the allegedly half-wit son, a bit for the pictures of Saturday nights. Dr Cobbity told Alfie to tell Nell to wait until they were out at the New Settlement, the Estimates of which allowed for wages for a cook. But the New Settlement would not even be begun building until July – a long while to wait to go to the pictures and buy a new dress and a couple of pairs of drawers, let alone the pretty things the girls who traded with the men of the Kerosene got, even rouge and lipstick and silk stockings and handbags. Queeny Peg-leg, who managed the trade, often told Nell what a fool she was not to be in it: 'Pretty girl like o' you

. . . crise . . . you can get tcharjent tcholdier!' Anzac Day was a particularly good day for business, she said, because the Kerosene men all got drunk and had a great party in the night and it was a simple matter to get in there with them. In fact she always organized it: 'Wha' you say, eh?'

And there at length it was that Day of All Days to the Australian Nation, Anzac Day. The Christ may have been born on December 25th and died on the First Friday after the Full Moon that falls on or next after March 21; Captain Cook may have first set eyes on the continent called Terra Australis on April 29 and renamed it New Wales and the property of King George III of England; Captain Phillip may have landed with his lags to found the Nation on January 26; the Diggers of Eureka may have hoisted the Five-starred Flag for the first time on December 3 (and been shot down and jailed for it); God may have finished building the Earth on Saturday evening and proclaimed every Sunday a holiday thereafter; but nothing that ever happened on any day, anywhere, at any time in history, compares in importance to Australians with the Day of Anzac.

Why is it? No one ever really found out. From its Inauguration schoolchildren (white) have been asked to write essays about it for prizes, perhaps in the hope that out of the mouth of some inspired babe someday the truth will come. The nearest anyone has ever got to it, of all that has been spouted annually, like the periodic puking of geysers, out of the mouths of Priests, Parsons, Poets, Politicians, Boy Scouts, and Bemedalled Soldiery, is that *On That Day the Australian Nation was Blooded*. An English term that, *Blooded*, in the huntin', fishin', shootin' tradition, referring to the actual bespattering with a victim creature's blood of a novice huntsman to mark his first bit of slaughter. But how can it be appropriate to the so-called Tradition of Anzac when it was the victims who were bespattered and the blood their own?

But to say those Heroes of Anzac were victims, is to deny them their undying heroism and risk bringing down upon one's head not simply the wrath of the God of War but what is ten times more thunderous, at least in Australia, that of the R.S.S.A.I.L.A. or as it is more generally called, perhaps because it's much more easy when you're drunk, on Anzac Day, the RSL – and who would dare? Therefore let the story of how it came about be told, while the bugle of Lefty Larkins sings of its glory in *Reveille* at the initiatory ceremony at four in the morning before the concrete statue of a soldier in a comical slouch hat, the Cenotaph so called, outside Government House, Port Palmeston.

There was a podgy little Englishman, lived in England, who thought he was a military genius because he was descended from the Duke of Marlborough, had seen service in the British War of Suppression of the Boers as a newspaper correspondent, and as Home Secretary had taken part in the so-called Sydney Street Siege, London, in which poor madmen dubbed Anarchists were shot for refusing to believe in the glory of institutions like, say, Marlborough House (a famous photograph shows the fat little fellow directing the shooting in a top hat). Well, this little man was a Big Man in the British War Office, and conceived the bright idea that on April 25, 1915, the Turks could be knocked out of the war by someone's sneaking up behind them over the Heights of Gallipoli and bayoneting the Sultan into the Bosphorus, and even if it didn't do the immediate enemy, the Hun, much harm, it could mean adding the Ottoman

Empire to that of Imperial Britain. The right boys to do it were almost right on the job, the Aussies, a mob who called themselves the Imperial Force, yet were wasting their time and substance in the brothels of Sister Street, Alexandria, Egypt. A tough lot – as you might expect of the descendants of the sweepings of the British Prisons of a hundred odd years before. So the brothels were emptied, and the thing happened at four on that Morning of Glory according to plan. The little fat man would have been in bed at the time; or if awaiting word of how it went, indulging a disgusting gustatory habit he was famous for, eating sandwiches made with a mixture of Marmite and sardines. Would he have been put off his food by the terrible news when it came? Some men would have hanged themselves in the privy with their braces. But such men would not be the descendants of dukes.

That fat-arsed old Sultan of Turkey, called Mohammed Reshad Effendi, was not as silly as he looked from the British War Office. His nation had been repelling invaders while the War Office chappies were still painting themselves with woad. Do the Turks celebrate Anzac Day; and if so, is it as one of the silliest things the Unbeliever ever tried on them, with laughter and dancing in the streets, or with silence and a sense of guilt at having taken simpletons like those poor Aussie boys who'd come boasting halfway round the world at such disadvantage? But even if they'd laughed while they watched the impending blooding of the Heroes in their own blood through the sights of their artillery hidden in those supposedly empty hills, could they be blamed, men being what they are?,

So Lefty Larkin's bugle rang, rather flatly, as ever, in remembrance of that Hour of Glory, that bright black morning in Port Palmeston twenty-two years later, while the waters of the harbour reflecting the stars of the Milky Way poured to the sea, and the Southern Cross swung round her invisible axis. They might have had a first-rate bugler from the Garrison, if they'd liked. But as was said when the offer was made with the establishment of the Garrison a couple of years back, old Lefty would have been hurt; and besides, he was one of the only two of the gathering who'd seen action on Gallipoli. Not that the last mattered so much. So long as you were a member of the RSL you were an Anzac, and you could be that so long as you had been a member of the Australian Imperial Force and had left Australian shores, even if all the action you'd seen had been behind the counter of a Quartermaster's Store or Pay Office, so long as you had been prepared to die outside your own country. 'Up the Old Diggers!'

As well as the bugler there was a parson, since they were conjuring the spirits of the dead: the Reverend Mr Tasker, wearing his campaign medals like the rest, won for dishing out Holy Communion to those about to kill their fellow men. It didn't last long. Just a bit of mumbling and head-hanging and the flat bugling and sobs in the background from one lone invisible woman; then led by His Honour, the Administrator, Colonel Close, they marched into Government House, where the traditional rum and curry were awaiting them along with the ladies of the RSL Anzac Day Committee, who would dish it out, or at any rate the curry. Apparently that was what the men of Anzac had gone to their death with in their bellies, because there was something holy about the partaking of it. Even a ginger beer drinker like Mr Tasker, while not partaking of the OP rum, showed none of his usual antagonism to alcoholic liquor. As tradition has it, they stayed on there till the Sun came up, by which time most were silly drunk. But this was only the beginning. Anzac Day is the Day of the Great Drink Up. Drunks are a nuisance other days; but on the Day of Anzac the Booze Artist comes into his own. The drunker you get the more you are honoured, because it means that you saw more action than the others, saw more of your mates' guts hanging out, did the bravest deeds – at least that's how the drunkest made it seem. Those who were well under the weather already were driven home by others and made to lie down to sleep it off in readiness for the Anzac Day Parade that would culminate with the laying of wreaths on the Cenotaph so-called, the full-dress eulogy by Mr Tasker, who would conclude with: *They shall grow not old as we that are left grow old . . .* and *At the going down of the sun and in the morning we will remember them* – the singing of the *Old Hundred* as *Oh, God our Help in Ages Past, our Hope in Years to Come,* without thought to the dirty versions the troops had used to divert themselves – the playing of the *Last Post,* this time by the Garrison bugler because the troops would be there with their band, that Holiest of the Holy Acts of this Holy Boozy Day, the Two Minutes Silence, during which probably no one thought of anything but how long two minutes silence seems in the noisy world of Man – then the raising of the Flag, the blue banner composed of the Five Stars the men of Eureka fought for, superimposed by the Union Jack of those who shot them for it, from half-mast to peak – then a lively Reveille by the Garrison's cornetist – and as that died away, the Garrison Band would break into some such good old Australian military marching tune as *It's a Long Way to Tipperary,* or *Soldiers of the King.* After that it was the booze *ad lib.*

So it was this Anzac day of 1937, with nothing untoward, except that a dog nipped in and piddled on a wreath, probably not out of the disrespect it was taken for, judging by the indignation hurled at him with stones, but out of pride of ownership, because his master had put it there. The same dog, at a safe distance now, howled during the sounding of the *Last Post,* again most likely moved by feeling deeper than the stony-faced humans were capable of.

As usual everybody was there, except a few of the type called Bolsheviks (they would have been called Anarchists earlier on) blacks as well as whites, and the kids from the Halfcaste Home, who were always given free lollies. There was only one Aboriginal member of the local RSL, a halfcaste, and he was missing this day. Before this year of grace, only on Anzac Day would he be permitted to take alcoholic liquor, which went to show rather that the RSL was beyond the Law – like the Ku Klux Klan, according to its enemies, the Bolshies. His absence wasn't due to the fact that, having at last got the right to drink simply as a man, he didn't give a damn any more about being a Digger. Indeed, he had been perhaps the proudest Digger of them all, seeing that The Day conferred upon him not only the status of a hero but also of a full citizen of the land he had fought for. That was his wife, the invisible woman weeping at the Dawn Service, Mrs Lucy Snowball.

Alfie Candlemas, taking her children back to the Compound in the truck, also took Lucy, and heard all about Digger Albert Snowball, from her driver, Barney Bynoe. Lucy, still weeping, would have told her all about it, too, and how her old man must be feeling sitting out there in his hut in the lazaret today; but Alfie, looking as if about to weep herself, fled from her. She also abandoned her children much earlier than usual, giving them a kind of picnic tea, so that she may be in good time to prepare for that party she had promised to go to at Captain Vic Shane's. She told the children of the party; and they were interested and asked her to tell them all about it tomorrow; and also, a couple of the big ones, hinted that there was also to be a party at the Kerosene that night, which some of the adult girls would be attending. As a Protector she should have done something about that information. But what? Dr Cobbity, who was Captain Cobbity today, and celebrating the part he had taken in the blooding of the Nation in the Officers' Mess at the Garrison; and Tubby Turkney, today a Corporal and jangling medals, although on duty, was pretty drunk and singing with some old comrades in his residence: '*Ol' solyers neffer doy, dey sim'ly fyde awye* . . . . '

Besides, how dare one stop others going to a party when one was bound for a party oneself?

The adult girls had a way of getting out of their cages when it suited them and it was safe. There were six of them, including that Big Dolly, who'd long since had her baby and was leaving it for an older one to mind, and Nell, whom Queeny Peg-leg, her tribal sister, had at last persuaded. Queeny saw them safely out through their bolt hole in the dusk like a string of bandicoots emerging from a hollow log and down to the beach and along and over the little tide creek. The escort was essential in a place where no undefended woman was safe at night, and particularly on the night of such a day when many of the male inmates of the Compound had been emulating the behaviours of their civilized masters in celebrating the Blooding of the Nation that denied them citizenship. Queeny, with her bulk and her crutch and her hatred of blackmen, was as good as a guard with fixed bayonets. She didn't have to go beyond the creek, because an Old Woman lived in the tumble of rocks at the foot of Point Look-out, had always lived there, it seemed, on shell-fish and crabs and things, and also men, it was believed, if she could lay hands on them. This Old Woman was said to have red hair, like the Ol'Goomun-Ol'Goomun, and to be able to change herself to look young and alluring. No one of the present generation had set eyes on her, except King George, so he claimed; although her tracks occasionally were seen in the sand, after the tide had been over it. Some believed she was the Ol'Goomun-Ol'Goomun, who hated men for stealing her secrets. Others were of the opinion that she was just a debil-debil. Anyway, women had nothing to fear from her. Nevertheless, the girls left the beach as quickly as possible, to head for the heights on which the Kerosine stood within its high barbed wire enclosure, following a pad that led up through the scrub. It wasn't really dark. The young Moon hung silvering the purple tide racing out to sea.

Suddenly there was the wire fence, although no sign of life within, but plenty of distant sounds of it: *Ol' solyers neffer doy* . . . . They followed the fence until they came to a piece of newspaper hanging on it with ostensible innocence. There they stopped, while Dolly unhooked several strands of the cruel wire from a steel post. They entered, crossed through scrub to the gravel road that ran between the barracks, back towards town, and the big guns installed above the Ol'Goomun's hide-out. Now they followed the road, soon to glimpse lights, soon indeed to be confronted with a veritable little city of blazing buildings.

There was a view across the wide parade ground to the entrance with its guard-house and flaring spotlights. The girls went nowhere near the lights, but coming amongst stacks of building material and unlighted sheds, veered leftward. A girl named Nancy was leading. She took them to an unlighted building that had evidently been some sort of mess-hut or recreational hall in the early stages of establishment. There they sat on a porch, and watched by Igulgul, the wrong-side love-match maker, giggling over stories Doll and Nancy were telling about former parties here.

Half an hour or so, with Igulgul winking through the trees, when heavy hasty lurching steps. The girls rose. The dark bulk of men. Flashlights blazing in the girls' dark faces, revealing also the khaki linen of the men. Guffaws and greetings: ' 'Lo girls . . . 'lo . . . who's here . . . Where's Dolly?'

'Me here.'

'Aw . . . my girl, Nancy . . . Come on Nancy . . . 'ad a 'orn all day thinkin' 'bout you . . . Come on.' One big fellow grabbed Nancy, rushed her into the hut.

Loud guffaws: 'Dinsey don' waste no time!'

'Dinsey's the bloke they reckon when he goes on leave the second thing he does's take his pack off.'

'Ho, ho, ho!' The girls were giggling, except Nell, who was shrinking back behind the others, looking scared.

'Dinsey don' even wait t' unbutton 'is fly . . . the buttons fly off 'emselves.'

'Ha, ha, ho!'

'Come on, Doll. Got some whisky for yous. Where's the grog, blokes?'

'Here she is. Come on in. Christ look at Dinsey . . . ha, ha, ha, ho, ho!'

'Where you got to, Nancy? I want my girl Nancy.'

'They're all the same in the dark, mate.'

'Not my Nancy . . . ah, there y' are, love!'

They all went barging into the hall leaving Nell outside. Squeals and guffaws within and thumping and bumping. Nell, leaning against the wall, had her head turned towards the doorway, almost indescernible in her flowered frock in the fading light. Then more steps coming. She stiffened. The man nearly passed her on the porch, glimpsed her out of the tail of his eye, stopped, stared, flashed his torch on her, said, ' 'Lo, love.'

She drooped and blinked in the light.

He came up to her. 'Ain't seed you before.'

She shrank away from him. He reeked of drink.

'Wha's matter . . . you shy, eh?' He tried to put his arm about her. She slipped free.

He went after her. 'Come on . . . don' be frighten' . . . gi's a kiss.'

He tried to grab her again. She jumped off the porch. He went after. She ran. He ran after her, calling, 'Don' run away, love . . . I got bottle o' whisky . . . I give you a quid . . . I give you two . . . 'ere . . . eh . . . don' be diff'cult!'

She got out of sight behind another building. Evidently she'd lost him, because his footsteps could be heard blundering at a distance. There was a scuffling and thumping and then a stream of dirty words. He must have fallen over. The laughter and squealing in the hall was faint from here. The noise from the barracks was louder. She waited a while, then began to move, towards the glow of the Moon, away from which she had been forced to go before. She came round the building, went round a stack of timber, ran bang into him. He yelped, 'Gotcher!'

She slipped out of his grip, turned, ran the other way, now towards the light. There was no one to be seen, only that open gate, beckoning as a way of escape. He called to her 'Hey . . . hey . . . don't go that way, you silly bastard!"

She went all the harder – and he too, catching up with her, panting, 'Fo' christ sake come back . . . you'll get us all in the bloody brig!'

As she ran onto the parade ground he stopped with a slither of gravel, nearly fell. Natty khaki figures were emerging from the Officer's Mess. Nell, in full view, slackened pace, looked back at the halted pursuer, then turned towards the gate again, flying.

A babble of voices from the officers, one barking, 'What goes on here?'

Then a shout, 'Guard!'

Nell was almost at the gate, already in the glare.

'Guard . . . guard . . . Goddammit!'

A khaki figure with a rifle, the bayonet flickering in the light like silver moths' wings, came blundering in big red boots, saw the charging enemy, struck the appropriate pose, cried, 'Halt!'

She tried to get around him; but the glinting steel designed for murder burnt before her frightened eyes, forcing her to the guard-house wall. There was another one coming with a bayonet – and the officers running, to stop as they came up, all goggling drunkenly, some chuckling comicalities, one whooping, 'Bring on the dancing girls!'

The press gave way to a stiff striding figure, ruddy, grey-haired, Colonel Chivvy, OC Troops: 'What's this woman doing here . . . black woman?'

A chorus: 'Don' know, Sir . . . trying to get out, Sir.'

'What the hell's she doing in?'

Another officer was coming up with the late pursuer.

Colonel Chivvy turned. 'What's this?'

The officer said, 'Corporal Blanco here, Sir . . . says he caught the woman snooping round.'

The Colonel looked at the goggling dishevelled soldier, demanding, 'Snooping round? How'd she get in here?'

The Corporal had snapped to swaying attention: 'Don' know, Sir. Seen 'er . . . challenged 'er . . . she done a bunk.'

Colonel Chivvy concentrated on the gasping, crouching prisoner. 'Where'd you come from? . . . . Come on . . . answer up.'

Nell panted, 'Compound.'

'How'd you get in here?'

'T'rough fence.'

'On your own?'

'Other girl dere.'

'Where?'

She looked back whence she'd come. 'I don' know properly . . . behin'.'

'What'd you come here for?'

'Party long o' tcholdier . . . dey reckon.'

The Colonel roared, 'Party long o' soldier . . . for Christ's sake, what's going on in my barracks? Orderly Officer . . . Sar'-Major!'

'Sah!'

'Sah!'

'What party's going on here with black women in it?'

'Don't know, Sir.'

'No party, Sah!'

'Well, there's a black woman from the Compound says she was in a party.' He snapped at her, 'You . . . what are you, a prostitute?'

No answer – only a lower dropping of the dark curly head.

'You've been with soldiers in here tonight?'

She muttered, 'I been runned away.'

'From what?'

'Tcholdier.'

'After coming to a party here?'

'I come for money.'

'You *are* a whore? Sar'-Major!'

The tall thin Sergeant-Major became a ramrod. 'Sah!'

'Have my barracks been turned into a whore-house?'

'Not to my knowledge, Sah.'

'Your knowledge is supposed to embrace every phase of the life and duty of every other-rank in this Garrison, is it not?'

'Yessah!'

'Yet you don't know what a black whore is doing here who says she came for a party and money from soldiers?'

'I'll very promptly have the facts and submit them to you, Sah!' The Sergeant-Major was struggling with his words alcoholically.

'I'll bloody well see you do!'

'Yessah!'

'Sar'-Major.'

'Sah!'

'We have two men down with the clap, have we not?'

'That ish c'rect, Sah!'

'You declared that you couldn't for the life of you see how they had got it, when the three known whores in town were cleared by the MO and you were convinced . . . *convinced*, Sar'-Major . . . that no man was breaking the rule against consorting with coloured women.' The Colonel's tone was that of a man who had drunk much and been asleep and wakened with a sore head.

'Yessah!'

'Are you convinced now?'

'Nosah.'

'You're not convinced of what, Sar'-Major?'

'Er . . . er, of whatever it wash I wasn't convinshed of before, Sah.'

'You're drunk, Sar'-Major!'

'It's Anzac Day, Sah.'

'An excuse in your case, but not in the case of the great majority of my men, who not only have seen no action, but aren't even soldiers, but bloody tradesmen dressed up in the King's uniform. You will investigate this matter at once, and parade every man suspected of being concerned before the Orderly Officer, and arrange for a short-arm inspection of all OR's tomorrow morning . . . get going!'

'Yessah!'

'Orderly Officer!'

'Sah!'

'Have his woman confined to the guard-house and held till the the civil police call for her . . . also any others that are picked up.'

'Police, Sir?'

'I said it. I'll inform them on my way to Captain Shane's and lay the charges . . . Where's my staff-car . . . Dammit, where's my car?'

Captain Vic Shane's mansion was rather like what was still called the Delacy Town House, Chinese built, and although on the other side of the promontory on which the town stood, similarly situated, which is to say on a hillside above a tidal inlet, and most likely with the same smart intention, namely acquisition of a huge tract of land that, because occasionally, at most once a year and then depending on unusual circumstances, it was inundated by the so-called King Tide, was subject to no deed of entitlement since said to be below High Water. That was Jumbo Delacy's trouble now in that matter of dispossession by the Shell Oil Co. Captain Shane had been a good deal cleverer than Jumbo. He'd reclaimed the land somewhat, applied to the Lands Department for entitlement, and had got it for a song. Old Vic was ever ready to tell new acquaintances how clever he was, or rather how lucky, since that's how he described the successfulness of his shrewdness, Shane's Luck, probably much less to appear modest than anointed. He lost no time in telling Alfie Candlemas about Shane's Luck, as, taking possession of her upon arrival at his party, he showed her over the place.

Down below, dim in the last light of the Moon, but pricked at many points by their own bright illumination, were his boat-sheds and pearl-shell packing-sheds, quarters of his men, all still standing on stilts since it was not so long since he'd effected that reclamation. He'd employed as many as a thousand men at a time he said, sailed upwards of fifty ships. He didn't go into details about those men of his, to tell her that they were, according to the covenants of this land, semi-slaves, imported under what was called the Indenture System from Asiatic countries: Japan, the Dutch East Indies, Malaya. This Indenture System was a way by which the prohibition of Asiatic immigration under the White Australia Policy could be overcome so as not to interfere with the profits and powers of such people as Captain Shane, who had enjoyed them since before the Policy was initiated. It was claimed that exploitation of the great pearl-shell banks off the North Australians coast, all well beyond legal territorial limits, would be lost to the Nation unless Japanese divers, incomparable in their aptitude for the work and willing to do it for little better than coolie wages, with other cheap labour to assist, were employed. The Pearling Masters, so called, were allowed to recruit such persons and sign them on at their own terms for limited periods, usually three years at a time. There was no such Bolshevistic humbug as award rates and workers' compensation.

If a man died in the course of his job, as many hundreds of Lucky Shane's had over the years (one had only to pay a visit to the Asiatic Section of the Cemetery to see) it was just that he wasn't as lucky as his Master. All the Master had to do was send his recruiting man into the poverty-stricken seafaring communities of what, in their unchangeable Europo-centricity they called The

East, and take the ablest young men into bondage for a down payment of half their wages for the period of indenture, the other half forfeit if a man hadn't the luck to make the full time. Not that it was quite like that nowadays. The Japanese had got smarter. They still might work only under Indenture, but had it so arranged that secretly the smartest of them were virtually masters in their own right, simply hiring the ships and gear they used from the Big Man and giving him a royalty on their catch. Some had even gone beyond that, had bought their own vessels and now operated out of near Asiatic ports on exactly the same banks, coming into Port Palmeston only to look up old friends and booze and gamble. Old Vic didn't mind that. As he so often said, and told Alfie now, he had made his pile. He also told her now that she was a witch, and tried to kiss her. She got away from him through the fortuitous intrusion of his latest mistress, a red-haired Russian from Shanghai, who in terrible English reminded him of his duty to his other guests, and something in Cantonese or some such language that made him scowl at her. Alfie fled back to Frank – and Dr Cobbity.

It was round about midnight, when the party was getting quite silly, that Dr Cobbity said to Alfie, 'What about that spin in the car?'

As they sped away in his smart sports car with the hood down he said, 'Pity it's not moonlight?'

'Why?'

'Moonlight becomes you, Madam.'

'How do you know?'

'I was watching for you when you arrived and the Moon was up.'

'Moonlight becomes any woman.'

'You're a creature of the moonlight.'

'Like a cat?'

He laughed, threw an arm along the back of the seat behind her shoulders. They were speeding out along the long gravel road leading to the Compound, but swung away by that other leading down to the flat and the coconut grove behind which Jumbo's place still stood, to be seen only as a pinpoint of light. She remarked, 'Poor Jumbo!'

He grunted, 'Poor Jumbo, be blowed! He's just a semi-savage, drinking himself into insanity, starving his wife and family.'

'It's the way he's been treated that's made him like that.'

'How do you know?'

'He told me his history.'

Cobbity laughed. 'Jumbo Delacy's the biggest liar in the community. He even claims to have killed his father. Did he tell you that?' He withdrew his arm, which she was obviously keeping clear of.

'Something . . . but it was a bit complicated . . . about training a horse to do it.'

'That's the yarn. He really believes it by now.'

'Maybe he did. He hates white people.'

'He doesn't. He only wants to be thought he's white himself.'

She was silent for a while, as they sped up from the flat to another part of the heights that gave them a view of the dark starry sea, along a cliff above which they were now travelling, northward. She said, 'You know, you're a hard man in many ways.'

'You have to be, in a position like mine.'

'I don't see it. It seems to me that the main thing that's wrong with these people is that no one's ever been kind to them.'

He put his arm back again as they sped by the ghostly bulk of the white-washed Jail. He said, 'Wait'll you've had a bit more to do with 'em!'

'You talk as bitterly about them as other people . . . the people who hate *you* for what you've done for them . . . and are doing.'

'You get a bit bitter with the disappointments they give you.'

'Just because you can't change them in a day.'

'I've been at it for ten years and more . . . and the Anthropologists and the Missionaries, as well as the rest of 'em, would have me booted out tomorrow if they had a chance.'

'Isn't that rather your own fault?'

'How come?'

'Well . . . that hardness I mentioned . . . even a bit of arrogance, at times.'

'Sounds like you don't care much for me.'

'But I do.'

'Yes?' He slipped his arm about her shoulder, drew her to him . . . but had to let go quickly, because they were running through a bit of maritime jungle, and there were wallabies on the road. They came out on an expanse of cliff-top that gave them a seemingly limitless view of the dark sea. 'Want to get out?' he asked.

'No . . . I'd just as soon sit.'

He pulled the windscreen up to give a better view, then put his arm about her properly, drew her to him. She rested her curly head against his shoulder. She sighed. He asked, 'What's that for?'

'I was just thinking that here we are, almost on the rim of Asia, with its teeming millions and its poverty . . . and here there are so few of us . . . and we are so rich . . . at least us white people.'

'Old Jumbo's crept back into it again, eh?'

'Well . . . I can't forget him . . . and the rest of the poor things.'

'How about forgetting about everybody but me for a while, eh?'

He bent and kissed her on the mouth. She was submissive. He kissed more ardently, turning round to her. Still she was compliant, if not eager. He ran a long thin hand down over her creamy bare shoulder to the small protuberance of her breast. She struggled away. 'No, Doctor!'

He uttered a bit of a grunt; 'Doctor . . . eh?'

'I'm sorry . . . but . . . .'

'You're not interested, eh?'

'Not . . . not just now.'

'Maybe later?'

'I . . . don't know.'

He drew a deep breath, turning away to look out to sea. 'Depends on Jumbo Delacy, eh?'

She was silent for a moment, then said, 'It could.'

He looked at her. 'You mean . . .'

'I mean if you show yourself less hard . . less . . . well, bureaucratic.'

He almost sniggered, 'Bureaucratic is it now? I'll see if I can mend my ways.' He reached for the ignition key, switched on, started up, without a word swung the car round, heading back for home. They were silent back as far as the Jail, after which he began to talk easily about plans formulating for the new Aboriginal Settlement, due to have its foundations laid on the First of July. Then he spoke of Captain Shane, who he said would be having one of his picnic cruises in his schooner soon, but this a very special one, something not to miss: 'During Coronation Weekend,' he said.

She asked: 'When's Coronation Day?'

'May 12. Big day for us. Don't know what the Boss'll be handing out.'

'What boss?'

'The King, of course.'

'He's not my boss.'

'Hey . . . disloyalty! You're a servant of the Crown now. You'll have the Loyalty Swearers down on you, if you're not careful.'

'Blow 'em!' she snapped.

He chuckled, and turned quickly and kissed her on the cheek.

They were coming close to Captain Shane's, the hilarity from which could be heard above the engine of the car. As they pulled up, Cobbity asked, 'Enjoy the spin?'

'Immensely.'

'Any chance of doing it again?'

'Every chance.' He chuckled, reached for her hand and squeezed it, then got out. She got out and joined him. As they went up the stairs together they were hailed by the Captain himself, coming striding from a group on the verandah scuffling in some hilarious game.

'What's this?' cried the Captain. 'Romance, scandal, or what? What's this sawbones got that I haven't, m'dear, that you desert my party for him?'

'Purely business, you superannuated old gubbernaut,' said the doctor chuckling.

'Ho, ho, ho!' was Shane's comment. 'Well . . . come'n have a drink.'

The Captain showed plainly that he wanted possession of his pretty guest again; and with a wink, Cobbity left her to him. The old fellow was not drunk, because he drank so much as to be able to act with reasonable rationality always. He was only more-so Lucky Shane than before. He put an arm about her, with fingers rather close to her tit, and took her down to walk in the lighted garden and tell her more about his luck – how as a penniless cabin-boy he had laid the foundations of that pile of his, with a handful of Brazilian gold coins given him by a shopkeeper of Rio to leave his young daughter alone. Alfie was beginning to sigh and weary of those sneaking bony old fingers and kept looking up at the rowdy house for relief, when her interest was caught by what he was yawping, about the latest favour conferred upon him by his sweetheart, Lady Luck. It concerned his property here, which it seemed he'd all but lost through having no legal title to the tide-flat, when someone *very high* had decided to allot it to the Shell Oil Company as a site for what were called Strategic Oil Tanks.

It was no mere local authority he had to deal with, not even a National one, but no less than the Imperial High Command: 'Part of Imperial Defence, Singapore Base, and all that.'

He seemed a bit surprised at Alfie's sudden interest and inclined to close up, till she leaned against him and let the claw have its way. 'You *are* a witch, you know . . . you got witch's ears . . . but they're lovely!' He kissed one.

Smothering the shudder, she asked, 'How'd you find out what was happening, when it was all so terribly hush-hush, as you say?'

'The old Shane Luck. The Imperial Brass was here from Singapore. They were here to see the opening of the Garrison. I ignored 'em myself. Never could get along with Brass . . . naval or military. Don't mind this Chivvy chap . . . but I never go to *his* joint . . . he's got to come here. So I missed what was going on. It'd been all decided. Nothing left to do but put it on paper with thc Imperial Coat of Arms and God Save the King and all that damn rot, giving me the order of the boot, with nothing but a lousy compensation for my rather ancient buildings there. But Lady Luck was hanging about looking after the interests of her white-haired boy. It happened that the Imperial Brass, used to taking disease into consideration, wanted to know if there was Malaria to be contended with in the project, which caused their medical experts to confer with a certain someone, who although he's on the Garrison staff, for want of a proper military MO, doesn't like the Poms. It also happens that the certain someone is a good mate of mine . . . and so I got the hot tip, and promptly acted on it.'

'You mean that's when you started reclaiming the tide flat?'

'Clever girl . . . what lovely little titties you got!'

'Stop, stop . . . they might see us from the verandah!'

'They'll only see what they expect from Old Vic.'

'But my husband! Now behave like a good boy . . . and tell me about how you beat the Pommies . . . because I hate 'em too.'

'Do you, now? I thought by that lovely complexion of yours, the roses under the brown, that you were one. Well, where was I? Yes . . . the reclamation. Well, I got together all my men and have 'em bag up hundreds of tons of dirt . . . sort of thing they were bred to . . . coolie types, you know. Did it during the low slack tides of the middle of the year. So I beat old King Canute, and dammed the tide. I then got a bulldozer . . . first ever used in this country . . . sold it at a profit to Works Department afterwards . . . and filled the whole thing in . . . and having friends in high places here . . . well, it was a simple thing to apply for title and get it. Naturally the local lads didn't know anything about what the Imperial Brass had in mind.'

'And so Shell Oil has to use the Coconuts Inlet instead.'

'That's right . . . and were they mad! They wanted this place, they said, because it was strategically better placed. But that's nonsense. Anyone bombing or shelling Port Palmeston could just as easily hit this place as the Coconuts. They didn't like being outwitted, of course.' He chuckled, adding, 'Or maybe they'd reckoned that if it was Japs attacking the place they'd keep clear of my property . . . and they'd get the benefit of it. Japs're like that. No matter how high they rise, you're always the Master to 'em. Pretty sure some of my men had Jap naval connexions and'd be in the vanguard of an attack . . . '

She interrupted, a little sharply, drawing away, 'They never found out who told you?'

'Eh . . . who tipped me off, you mean? No. Probably never dreamt I was tipped off. Thought it'd just happened . . . Shane's Luck, like . . . ha, ha, ha!'

She drew a deep breath; 'I know who it was, though.'

'You? Bet you don't!'

'Like to bet?'

'I'll lay you a kiss to a case of champagne you don't.'

'Right . . . our friend Dr Cobbity.'

He gaped at her, then muttered, 'How did you know that?'

'You said I'm a witch.'

'You are, too. Well . . . bang goes my case of bubbly. But look here . . . you won't say anything, will you? I don't suppose it can hurt the Doc, really. He doesn't like being MO for the Garrison much. But if there's a war, he'll be automatically in it . . . and you never know, they might take it out of him somehow . . . the Imperial Brass, I mean. I'll give you the bubbly on Coronation Day. Something to celebrate with, what?'

'You can have your kiss now, though.'

'Eh?' The seamed old face lit up.

She gave him her lips. He was devouring her, when she broke away, laughed breathlessly, fled, as he gasped after her, 'Witch . . . wonderful witch!'

Just round a corner of the verandah she found Frank. She grabbed him, dragged him out of the crowd, whispered, 'I want to go home . . . come on.'

'What's up? What's happened?'

'Plenty. But let's get out of here . . . without being seen. I feel a little sick.'

'What . . . too much booze?'

'No . . . the people . . . the awful people!'

VIII

Next morning, that is of the day after Anzac Day, Alfie Candlemas was riding the bike she now used, heading into the Compound to see about the children's breakfast, when Mr Turkney popped out of his office, hailing her. She swung to meet him. He said, 'Afraid you got no cook, this morning, Alfie.'

'How come?'

He told her of Nell's arrest and confinement in the lock-up in town, the only one captured. He scowled across at the Adult Home, but didn't express his feelings about the others, instead, complaining, 'It never rains but it bloody pours. Now they tell me Lucy Snowball's been eaten by a shark.'

Alfie, quite pale, gasped. He went on: 'The silly buggers think she was taken by the Rainbow Snake, or something. Mob coming over from the other side by canoe saw her body hung up on the beacon on the reef there, with the legs eaten off.'

'Good God!'

'King George reckons she took his dinghy last night . . . it's gone and her tracks're there. Must've been trying to get to the lazaret again. Big tide last night. Must've got stuck on the reef, and lost the boat . . . terrible rip there . . . and tied herself onto the beacon . . . and the sharks got at her when the tide came back . . . Oh, I say . . . sorry!' Alfie put her face in a hand and began to cry. Tub took the bike from her, put an arm about her, talked soothingly while she wept, now into both hands, quite unrestrainedly. 'Clumsy of me . . . just didn't think. There, now, dear. Poor thing's better off . . . she wasn't happy as she was . . . Here, boy, take this bike.' He led Alfie into his office.

She soon recovered, sat blinking and sniffling. He said, 'What I really wanted was to ask you if you'd do the Court trick for me this morning.'

She mumbled, 'Court trick?'

'You know . . . how when anyone out of the Compound's pinched, I have to go into the Police Court to defend 'em. It's only a formality, really . . . as long as there's a Protector there not a member of the Police Force. There's this Nelly Ah Loy business. I'll have to go out in the launch and get Lucy. The blacks won't. And I'd as soon keep out of this Nelly Ah Loy business, because there'll be enough row about it as it is . . . and I don't want old Bundy rooting me for a start. He can be an old bastard of a Monday morning, or after a holiday. But he wouldn't pick on you. Wouldn't have any reason. Will you do it for me?'

Sniffling a bit still, she asked, 'But what do I do?'

'Nothing. Like I said . . . your appearance is only a formality. The prisoner's charged with such and such. The Prosecuting Sergeant does his spiel. All you've got to say is *Guilty* . . . they're not able to plead for 'emselves, unless freed from the Act . . . .'

'What if they're not guilty?'

'They wouldn't be there if they weren't. They've got it all worked out. Most Aboriginal offenders've got a record. The old boy goes on that mostly. A month for this, three months for that . . . considering the record, how much of a nuisance they are, and how things are out at the Jail . . . wood-cutting and things.'

'Has this Nelly got a record?'

'I wouldn't know. She's new here. But he'll go easy on her . . . unless she gives him cheek, like that silly bitch Dolly. She'll get a week or a fortnight . . . depends on whether old Dotty needs anyone . . . . '

'Dotty?'

'Mrs Dorothy O'Dowdy, wife of the Jailer. Has At Homes, and likes to show off the halfcaste maids she gets for nothing. You'd be doing me a great favour . . . .'

'I'd like to do it, Oscar. I'd like to see how it's done. It all sounds rather callous though . . . . ' She was searching for her handkerchief.

'Now, don't go getting yourself too involved. You're doing a grand job as it is. Put in a good word for her and say she's a good cook and mostly well behaved, if you like. You'll soon have her back.' He sighed: 'It wouldn't've happened only that brass-bound bugger, Colonel Chivvy, caught her himself. Anyone else would've rung *me* up, not called the cops. Right . . . now, you have to be there by ten. Don't be late, for godsake. There'll probably be other cases of blacks picked up drunk in town. You'll have do 'em all. They'll be no-hopers. Just say *Guilty*, and leave it at that. You'll be back by lunch-time . . . might be back with Nelly. Right? Thanks a lot. Now I'll have to go and . . . sorry! Mind if I wipe your face myself? I . . . I'd like to have such nice tears on my hanky . . . eeeee!'

Alfie arrived at Court in plenty of time, to surprise Fatty Doscas and Miss Williams, the new Court Reporter, and also Fay McFee, who smiled at her, but stiffly, and then stopped smiling altogether when she heard Doscas ask Alfie how things had gone at Old Vic's party. Then when Alfie explained why she was there, Fay bounced up to stare out at the Rainbow Reef from the verandah, and for a while looked as if she couldn't make up her mind where she ought to be keeping tabs on the drama of life. There was hardly anybody in the public seats. The Police – Usher and Prosecuting Sergeant Nullity – didn't come in until just before Stipendiary Magistrate Bundy slipped in from what seemed like the belly of His Gracious Majesty, Our Sovereign Lord, like a slight black gnome. For a certainty his face was buttoned up with misanthropy, due, some said, to the fact that he was a reformed drunk, the reformer being his large wife, not himself. The Clerk quickly explained Alfie's presence to the surprised and somewhat arch-looking Sergeant, and then again to His Worship, who merely grunted.

After some shuffling of papers and muttering between Mr Bundy and Mr Doscas, the first case was called, that of three ragged blackfellows with crazy whitemen's names, charged with having consumed intoxicating liquor in contravention of the Ordinance, this that and the other – in fact for being drunk and fighting behind the RSL Hall, it all came out when the arresting Constable was called. But first Mr Doscas asked Alfie how she pleaded. She rose and said very weakly, 'Guilty.'

After the Constable, the Sergeant read the Records of the accused, adding that they were pests. In no time His Worship grunted, 'Three months with hard labour.'

Next it was Billy Noseda, a halfcaste, charged with having supplied the former prisoners with the drink, himself being an Exempted Person within the Ordinance. How did he plead? Alfie voiced the plea with more confidence this time. There was also a difference in procedure in that the Prosecuting Sergeant helped out the Defence by telling His Worship that the Defendant was the foreman of the night-cart crew and that there might be some inconvenience if he was jailed. Mr Bundy was impressed. He said to the Defendant, 'Listen, Billy . . . if you do it again, I'll give you six months, understand?'

'Yes, Boss.'

'Fined Five Pounds . . . to be paid at the rate of one pound per week out of his pay. Next case.'

'Nelly Ah Loy!'

Nell was marched in from the dungeons region by a young policeman and shoved into the dock. The scene should be familiar enough to her, but the aspect so different that she gave a frightened look at those below. Alfie smiled at her. But she only blinked, drooped.

Fatty Doscas wheezed, 'Nelly Ah Loy, you are hereby charged that on the night of the 25th April in the year of our Lord 1937, you did make unlawful and unwarranted intrusion and trespass upon an area declared prohibited under the Defence of the Commonwealth Act, Section 34, sub-section iii, to wit the military establishment known as Point Lookout Barracks. How do you plead, Guilty or Not Guilty?'

Looking troubled, Alfie rose slowly, hesitated so long as to attract every eye. At length she faltered to the Bench, 'Isn't it a rather serious charge?'

Mr Bundy snapped, 'Of course it is!'

'Then . . . then . . . should I plead guilty for her?'

'It's not for me to tell you how to plead, Madam. Haven't you been appraised of the case?'

'Well . . . no. I . . . I was told just to . . . that it was a mere formality.'

'To do what?'

Sergeant Nullity bent to her, whispering, 'There isn't much to it . . . not like Intent to Spy or anything like that. Just a formality.'

She whispered back, 'Should I plead Guilty?'

'Save a lot of bother.'

She looked up at the Bench, which snapped, 'Well?'

She said, weak again, 'Guilty.'

Sergeant Nullity rose and began to spout from a paper: 'At 8.15 p.m. on the night of April 25, information was received from the OC Troops that Defendant had been apprehended at the Barracks, with a request that she be taken into custody . . . .' Sergeant Nullity paused to reach for a document in an envelope, with which he walked towards the bench, saying, 'I have here a communication from Colonel Chivvy, Your Worship.' He handed it up, then returned to his place to conclude giving details of the arrest, while Mr Bundy opened the envelope and perused its contents. Nell was staring out at freedom beckoning from the familiar wilderness.

His Worship looked up and demanded of the Sergeant, 'It says here that she was at the Barracks for an immoral purpose. If that's so, why wasn't she charged under Section 28, instead of under this Defence Act thing?'

'There was no actual evidence of immorality, Your Worship.'

'You can't have it both ways. You charge her under the Defence Act . . . and Colonel Chivvy asks me to make an example of her in order to stamp out what he calls an immoral traffic. How expect me to make an example of her for an offence she's not charged with?'

The Sergeant bowed his head slightly, sighed, said, 'Mentioned lack of evidence, Your Worship.'

Old Bundy turned his meaty eyes on Alfie: 'You, Madam . . . are you aware of any immoral traffic between the Compound and the Garrison?'

Alfie, risen, hesitated, perhaps remembering a hint she'd heard yesterday of just such a thing, and wondering about the propriety of lying in a Court of Law as Counsel for Defence. She swallowed: 'No, Your Worship.'

'Are you aware of what Colonel Chivvy's written here?'

'No, Your Worship.'

'Then you ought to be. Read it!'

She took the letter from him, read slowly, to his evident impatience, then looked up, at a loss.

Bundy demanded of her. 'Why were you sent here, having no experience of this sort of thing?'

'Mr Turkney was busy . . . . '

'In other words he fobbed something off on you that he might be held responsible for . . . . '

'No, Sir . . . he was . . . was otherwise very seriously engaged . . . one of the inmates . . . . '

The meaty eyes swung away from her to Nell, whom he addressed sharply:

'Tell me how you got into the Garrison.' When she drooped her head and twined her fingers, he raised his voice, 'Answer up . . . do you hear me?' He repeated the question.

Nell gasped, 'T'rough fence.'

'Tell me about it . . . I want to know all about it . . . come on, now!'

He dragged the sorry story out of Nell – while she writhed in terror, with dark eyes leaping again and again to the wilderness . . . while the Court Reporter's typewriter clacked and clattered, spelling it into the Criminal Records, and Fay McFee and her male opposite-number turned it into twiggles and dots – while Sergeant Nullity leaned back with arms folded, stifling yawns – while tears swam in Alfie's eyes and she bit her lip to hold them.

When he had done, His Worship turned to Counsel, grunting, 'Clearly she was there for an immoral purpose. Whether carried out or not is of no concern in law. Any convictions?'

The Sergeant answered, 'None, Your Worship.'

The meaty eyes fell on Alfie again; 'Have you anything to say for Defendant?'

Alfie positively leapt up, sniffed, said eagerly, 'I'm sure she's a good girl. She has a little boy I teach. She's the Compound cook . . . . '

He cut in dryly: 'But not above sneaking out at night to prey on decent young men whose association with her might easily lead to their ruin.' He swung back to Nell: 'Prisoner . . . I've been asked to make an example of you . . . and I'm inclined to do so. We can't have the kind of thing you've been doing . . . not now this town's become a garrison town. I find you guilty of soliciting for an immoral purpose . . . . '

Alfie leapt up again, rosy now, eyes all shiny bright from those tears and from something else: 'But . . . Your Worship . . . . '

He swung on her. 'Yes?'

She was panting: 'The charge is Unwarranted Trespass, or something . . . not Immorality . . . . '

The ruddy face went purple. It took a moment for him to get it out: 'But for your unwarranted interruption, Madam, I would have added to the verdict: "*While trespassing on a military reserve.*" Are you satisfied?' The last was said with heavy sarcasm.

Still Alfie stood. She swallowed, panted, 'No . . . I'm not!'

The purpling paled with the rage behind it now and the sharp voice came throatily: 'Indeed! And in what way, may I ask, are you not satisfied with the verdict of the Court?'

'Because . . . because . . . you said yourself, at first . . . that they couldn't have it both ways.'

The purple came back with a rush. The meaty eyes blazed. But she stuck to it. 'You said you . . . you couldn't make an example of her for an offence she's not charged with . . . . '

He shouted, 'Sit down.'

She flamed, and shouted back, 'I won't . . . I'm here to defend that poor girl . . . . '

Half risen in his throne, old Bundy yelled, 'If you don't sit down, I'll have you committed for contempt!'

She gasped, 'It's a travesty of justice . . . . '

'How dare you, Madam . . . Usher . . . remove that woman from the Court . . . and send for someone from the Aborigines Department.'

'Yessir!'

The tears had burst. The Usher took Alfie gently by the elbow. She tried to look round and say something, but instead broke into sobs.

'In all my experience on the Bench!' bellowed Bundy. 'If there was a place for white women in the jail I'd . . . I'd send her along with this one. In all my experience . . . . '

Eddy McCusky came running in, took a wild look round, noted the faces, the weeping woman out at the verandah rail. 'Yes, Your Worship?'

'Mr McCusky . . . kindly assume the Protector's office while I commit the Prisoner. I had to dismiss your colleague for unseemly behaviour. Please see to it that that hysterical young woman makes no more appearances in my Court.'

'As Your Worship pleases.'

'Nelly Ah Loy, I find you guilty as charged, and sentence you to imprisonment in Blue Bay Jail for three months.'

Even Sergeant Nullity whistled under his breath at the severity of the sentence: 'Phew!'

Having heard it, Alfie staggered down the steps of the Court verandah, groped for her bike, made her wobbly way back to the Compound.

The children were in the playground. They came rushing to the fence as she came up, calling, 'Prindy mumma go long o' jeel, eh?'

She asked tonelessly; 'How do you know?'

Someone said, 'Spone she no go jeel, p'lice car bring her back.'

Alfie looked at Prindy, who appeared to be merely interested, like the others. She said, 'Well . . . I suppose we'd better do a bit of school before lunch, eh?'

As she unpadlocked the gate to let them out, they babbled of Lucy Snowball, half-gobbled by sharks or by the Rainbow Snake – but without direct mention of her name, since to do so could mean to call her wandering Shade to worry them till it went its way to Jesus – 'Dat mitjish belong to Albert long o' leper 'teetion.'

It was pretty evident from Tubby Turkney's behaviour when Alfie passed his office on the way to see about the midday meal that he had heard about the affair in court and was embarrassed thereby. She hailed him as usual; but instead of coming out as usual, he only waved and grinned. Further evidence that the news had spread widely without much credit to herself was forthcoming when she went to see about the tea, and Dolly, now in charge of the kitchen, who earlier on had ramped about the heavy sentence Old Bundy Bastard had handed out to her mate, this time remarked frankly, 'She get dat t'ree month for *you* givin' dat Old Bundy Bastard cheek, eh?' Useless to try to explain to Dolly and the others helping her. Their faces remained blank.

When Alfie reached home she found Frank waiting at the gate for her. He was smiling. When she asked had he heard, he answered, 'The town's talking of nothing else. I'd've liked to come out to you, but thought it best to make it look as if it didn't matter much . . . to us.'

She kissed him. 'Thank you, darling. That was wise. But I would have liked to see you . . . to cry on. I cried in the court, did you hear?'

'That's not what I heard . . . but what I *knew*.'

'What'd you *hear*?'

'That you took hysterics.'

She drooped, with his arm about her. 'What a fool I am for crying always!'

He kissed her cheek. 'Proves you're a girl, and not the boy you sometimes say you're afraid you are mostly. Let's have a drink and tell me all about it.'

When she'd told him, she asked what Dr Cobbity had said about it. He shrugged, saying, 'He laughed . . . called you that little fire-eater of yours.'

'But he didn't like it?'

He shrugged again.

She said, 'I guessed he wouldn't . . . or he'd've come out. Nobody came. Nobody official said a word about it. Turkney practically ignored me.'

'The official mind, darling. You bucked authority. It isn't done in Public Service.'

'I bucked an absolute travesty of justice!'

'To them you bucked absolute power. Those who have it in their own little department, don't like to see it kicked around. Those who haven't got it, hope to get it later.'

'But what a state of things? How are we going to get progress, proper human dignity, when an old dog like that magistrate, who isn't qualified to deal with . . . with cats, even . . . can do what he did, just because he got a letter from some pompous popinjay of a military colonel?'

He sighed: 'By being patient . . . and doing our own jobs properly, I suppose.'

'But I *was* doing my job . . . I was sent into the court to defend that poor thing!'

'You had something fobbed off on you. Turkney has it fobbed off on him too. Either Cobbity or McCusky should be doing it . . . or, the correct thing would be to employ a lawyer. You're a teacher, my little love . . . .'

'I haven't any proper facilities to do even that. I've had to start by *feeding* the children.'

'Well, there you are. You've done a wonderful thing . . . . '

'For which people say, "If you want to live on the fat of the land and lie on the flat of your back all day, go to the Compound!" '

'No matter what they say . . . you've achieved that. The children are being properly fed at last. They've got a proper teacher at last. Soon you'll have proper housing for them, a proper school . . . . '

'I wonder!'

' "It's all there in the Estimates." ' He had mimicked the tone of McCusky. She laughed and took his hand and pressed it to her breast. He caressed it, came close and kissed her, then with cheek against hers, and still playing with her breast, said, 'Just play it safe for a while. Don't give 'em an excuse to leave you out of things later.'

She withdrew to look at him: 'Would they want an excuse . . . when they've said I've done a good job already?'

'If they thought you were dangerous to 'em.'

'You're talking about Cobbity?'

'In a way . . . but Cobbity's got a boss, too, don't forget.'

'You said he made a joke of it.'

'I said he laughed over it, and called you a little fire-eater. I think he was dropping me a hint to keep you under control . . . . '

'Why, the arrogant . . . . '

'He's the boss, my love. He likes you . . . even a bit too much, maybe . . . but he likes himself best. I laughed over it too . . . as if I took it as a bit of fun . . . as if you'd fallen foul of that old bugger just by accident . . . because you didn't know your way about, like. That's why I didn't come out, as I said . . . as if it wasn't important . . . although, Jesus, my little one, I could have gone and kicked that old cow in the balls . . . if he's got any . . . because I knew how you'd be feeling if you cried. Will you pretend to treat it as a joke, too . . . for the time being?'

She dropped her head to his shoulder, nodding it, but sighing: 'A joke . . . while that poor girl's in jail . . . and all through my stupid handling of it, they say . . . even the halfcastes . . . oh, Frank, oh, oh, oh!' She sobbed while he held her close.

At about that time, Nelyerri was being conducted to the sleeping quarters she would be occupying for the next ninety days, according to the law, her escort a burly white guard in khaki uniform and a little old black woman in the striped cotton uniform of female prisoners, not much different from that used at the Compound, except in the matter of braiding and a couple of Broad Arrows. The black woman was one known as Jenny Lifer, well known as much outside of Blue Bay Jail as in it, because while she wore the prison garb and ate the poor food the place provided and slept within its tar and phenyle-reeking confines and behind its many locks, she did so from choice rather than necessity. She might be said to be there in an honourary capacity. She had entered the place to serve a ten-year sentence for the murder of her husband over a tribal matter, so long ago that only the prison records could say when. Her sentence served, she had stayed on inside out of fear of what awaited her outside in the matter of tribal law. As she had explained to Nell, while she had cropped her hair and seen her bathed and rigged out for her stay, 'I been lòse him my Dreamin' lo-long time now. Wha' for I wan' 'o go back long o' bush?' Occasionally she went to town with the Jailer, Major O'Dowdy, in the prison utility. Often she went fishing and crabbing on the beach. But she was always there to receive new female inmates and gentle them into the strangeness of it all.

They came along several corridors of stone, tarred halfway up, whitewashed for the rest. There were four sections to the jail, one for whitemen, another for blackmen, a third for Asiatic males, the fourth, a small corner, for, as they put it, Gins. White or Asiatic women who offended sufficiently to be regarded as a menace to the community were deported.

After passing several grilled doors leading elsewhere, they came to a small group of barred-doored cells. The guard opened one of them, saw them in, shut and locked it after them, departed. It was a small place, tarred and whitewashed and reeking of phenyle. At the rear were two high-placed small barred windows through which the ruddy evening sky could be seen. Most light came through the grill of the door from a lamp in the roof of the corridor. The furniture consisted of two tiered bunks on either side, a commode, a can of water.

On a top bunk, propped on an elbow, watching the newcomers with narrow

Mongoloid eyes in Aboriginal sockets, was a thin aged woman, dark as old leather. Jenny Lifer said, 'Dat-one Lucy Leong . . . dis one Nelly Ah Loy . . . two Chinee . . . eeeeee!'

'No-more Chinee!' shrilled the other one. Then she asked Jenny 'Bring him tucker?'

'Venus bring him by'n'by. I come hearly, bring him dis one.'

The one on top whispered inwardly, 'Wha' nam' dat-one belong o' Albert leper-'teeshun?' So the grape-vine had got the news through to the Jail. Jenny explained, while instructing Nell to strip to blue cotton drawers and take the other top bunk.

While the grim story was being told, there was sound of steps in the passage, and voices, the guard's guffawing, a female's squealing: 'Gertch . . . you bloody bastard . . . tek you 'and 'way!'

The door opened again, to admit a biggish handsome young woman, quarter-caste by her blotchy pallid duskiness, who at once took out of the bosom of her dress a newspaper package and handed it up to old Ruby. It was meat and bread and apple-pie. The old woman began to munch greedily.

Jenny introduced the young woman as Venus. 'Seen you come in,' said Venus. 'Bloody bastard give you three months, eh? Too much. Dat white woman mek trouble for you, eh? But dat not long time. I get seven year.'

Nell looked as if she didn't understand the significance of the time. Perhaps Jenny thought she should help educate her. She said, with a cackle of ancient laughter, 'Venus been kill him one whiteman . . . shoot him daid.'

Nell's eye opened wide. Venus said, 'Bloody old bastard.' Later on, after she'd questioned Nell about herself, showing in the process that she knew quite a lot already, Venus told the story of her crime. She came from somewhere down the Centre. Her mother, evidently a drunken knockabout, had sold her to an elderly whiteman with a small cattle-run away on the Eastern Downs. She was then about thirteen. She had lived with the squatter as his wife for six years, had one baby that had died. There were no other whites on the place but the Boss. 'But I like white woman den,' she said. 'Goot clo'hes . . . any'ting I want . . . only, go to town, we got 'o camp on creek. Da's all right. Den dis young feller come along. Da's Harry . . . whiteman. He borin' contractor. He's big feller . . . blue eye, yeller hair . . . pretty man. We start makin' love, *tchinekin*. Da's all right. But Harry got 'o go away when finish contract. He want me come too. We clear out together. But dat old feller o' mine . . . he foller him up. Dey have big row. He shoot Harry. I want dat Harry too much now. So I shoot him Boss. I get seven year.' She ended with a little laugh, probably through seeing tears in Nell's eyes, because she added: 'More better you laugh dis place, tchister . . . no goot cry. Dat right, ain't it, Jenny?

Jenny cackled, 'Plen'y fun long o' kitchen. You work dere. You t'ree-feller Millie. Dat-one old Dotty, all-day growl-growl-growl. Don' you tek notice. Him jitty, dat one. Spone he get too rough, her old man shut him up quick . . . dat Major O'Dowdy, Boss. Him all right . . . ain't it, Venus . . . eeeeee!'

All three had a good giggle over something private. They told Nell funny stories about Old Dotty, as they called their mistress, and her airs, till, apparently exhausted, she fell asleep.

The guard had them out at dawn. Nell, Venus, and Millie, a slight little smiling thing, sharp-faced and almost toothless, were escorted from the big front gate by Jenny, through the trim line of gardens separating the officers' quarters from the jail wall, to the biggest of the high-built houses. Jenny stopped below to play with a cat, while the others went up the back stairs and into the kitchen. There was the fire to light and tea and toast to be made for themselves. Conversation was carried on in whispers. It was revealed that Millie had committed double murder, a whiteman and a black woman, and got five years for it: 'Wha' you mek o' dat?' asked Venus. 'I kill one, I get seven year . . . Millie kill two, she get five.' They giggled over it as if it were a long-standing joke.

At sound of movement in the house, more tea and toast was made and a tray set up. Millie went inside with the tray. Soon Major Dowdy came out, white-haired, red-faced, moustachioed, who bawled, 'Good morning girls!' and pinched Venus's bottom as he passed her to go out by the back door.

Somewhat later there was a thudding and thumping within that made the wooden house shake. 'Here she come!' hissed Venus.

Into the kitchen doorway came the bulky figure of her called Dotty, consisting of two or three bundles, it seemed, so was she trussed up in bathgown and with a towel about her large head.

There was no greeting this time, just a blue-eyed glare from one to another. It lit on Nell, who was making porridge. 'You!' wheezed Dotty. 'Let me look at you.'

Nell came drooping. Dotty looked her over as one would an animal, but without touching her. 'Are you clean? Can you make beds and sweep floors, and scrub and polish . . . . ' Dotty ran out of breath. Nell nodded to each question. Dotty got her breath back: 'Well, come in and do my room . . . while I bath.' She led the way in to her cluttered scent-reeking bedroom.

When Dotty returned, now scent-reeking herself, she looked over everything with an eye ready to pounce on anything not done properly, and found a dozen things wrong and nagged about them, then said, 'Do my hair,' and sat before her dressing-table mirror, a heaving, blubbery mass of flesh, staring unhappily at the same thing looking back at her. She wheezed, 'Tell me about yourself . . . and don't tell lies . . . because I know all about you.'

Part of that early conversation in the cell last night had been about Dotty's passion for hearing of the sexual experiences of her coloured domestic staff, with the advice to tell her, tell her anything, but tell her, because she could have you put back into the jail to clean *goona* buckets and mend the male prisoners' dirty clothes, or out in the garden, where you were likely to be raped by the black bastards who worked there too. Still Nell had to have it dragged out of her: 'Who been puggim you first-time . . . blackman, whiteman? . . . Come on, you tell me!'

So hungry was Dotty for the details that the heavy steps of the Major were clomping through from the back before the young ringer, whose name Nell said she didn't know, had properly got started, and Dotty had to interrupt, saying, 'It's breakfast.' By the look of her, food meant even more than sex. She added, 'You can be my housemaid, and tell me while you work.'

Thus Nelyerri, probably for the first time in all the years of her obsession with it, told of her love for Martin Delacy, had to be in jail to tell it, to one virtually her jailer. The dragging out process didn't last long. Soon it was outpouring, with tears that fell on the things she swept, scrubbed, polished, dusted, folded, set out in neat rows – not bitter tears, the way the lips curled in smiling reminiscence that brought forth the flow most copiously and the tongue took them from the lips and swallowed them as part of the sweetness of it all – and the way Dotty's painted and powdered old wreck of a phiz would rumple up in sympathy and she would have a sniff and blink and use her own lacy hanky to mop up those falling attar drops. Yes, admitted Nell, without much pressing, it was Martin, and without having Dotty say, as most white women would: *These bloody whitemen . . . and him with a white wife and young baby, too*! Instead, Dotty said, 'It doesn't matter who or what the man is you love . . . so long as you love.' She would say, after the interruptions forced on them, 'Tell me more.' Sometimes she was saying it with *dear* . . . 'Tell me more about it, dear . . . how you killed the babies, because *he* wanted you to . . . with a pointed piece of rush, you say. I wish I had a baby . . . oh, I have wished and wished! . . . But I would kill my baby for my lover. Tell me more, dear . . . I'll never tell a soul, I swear. You are blessed among women because you *love*. It's given to so few of us. It comes from above. It's like your Old People say . . . "the magic of Igulgul, the Moon" . . . . '

The other girls thought it a rare joke at first, and taunted Nell with what they called 'Play lick-lick' with Dotty in the bedroom. But the change in Dotty was so great that they began to wonder, began to whisper, 'Wha' nam' . . . you been sing him dat one?' For Dotty went off her food, comparatively, and off her customary bullying of them, but wonder of wonders, was being nice to her old man, instead of grow-growl-growl at him every time he came into the house. Nell had nothing to say about it, having fallen back into her dream of love, so that the girls whispered behind her back that she looked as if she were *gulli-gulli*, love-bewitched. Their own love affairs had been so different. Venus had killed her old master for denying her right of possession of another whiteman, a young one. Millie's story was that she had been the slave of a whiteman, a trepang fisher, from puberty to the early aging that had come upon her through his infecting her with what she called the Pox, which had caused her several babies to be born dead. Then he had taken a young black girl into his bunk, leaving the mere slavery to Millie. She said she didn't mind the work, but objected to their constantly deriding her with the worst of insults, puggim before her eyes. So one day while they were at it and she at the cooking stove on deck, she took the tommyhawk and finished them . . . eeeeeeee!

Not only did Dotty train Nell to serve tea in the correct manner for her At Homes, but told her that the first one would be for guests who were coming to see *her*, Nell, rather than herself. Dot would say no more, except that they would be there tomorrow, and for the occasion she might wear her own dress, nicely laundered.

'Why didn't you kill that first baby?' she asked.

'Martin not tell me.'

'S'pose he told you . . . would you have?'

'I don' know dat-one. Dat-one differen'. Martin find dat-one . . . gi'me for present. Spone I lose him Martin . . . I got dat-one, belong 'o him.'

'But the others were his babies too . . . or don't you know about where the babies really come from . . . like the blacks?'

'I been hear dat whiteman way.'

'Don't you believe it?'

'I don' know!'

'It's a beautiful belief, really . . . the blackfellow one . . . like we all believed as children. Tell me . . . did that Chinaman ever give you a baby?'

'Nutching.'

'You used to let him puggim you, though?'

'No-more. He on'y look out for me. He got black lubra in camp for properly wife.'

'He was a good man . . . a kind man . . . I heard.'

'Yas.'

'You've never had another man . . . only Martin?'

'Two t'ree . . . whiteman and halfcaste been gitchim me sometime I can't get away . . . Race Time . . . I drink too much, might-be. Dat time Tarjen Cahoon, I been tell him 'bout.'

'Yes . . . poor old Dinny. I think he loves you. He rang up Major on telephone, to ask him to look out for you good. Are you sure that boy doesn't belong to him? Lots of people say he does . . . and that Dinny says so, too, when he's drunk.'

'Belong to Martin . . . I know.'

Dotty had undertaken to inquire daily after Prindy for Nell.

Friday was Dotty's At Home day that caused all the mirth in her kitchen and in the cells where her housemaids slept, with their mimicry of her airs and graces. Venus was chief mimic. She would pretend to ring the little bell: 'Ting-ting-ting . . . where dat maid . . . where dat gal? Rilly, Mitchis Cobbity, dese gals dey a try! But have 'nother coop o' tay. Tray one dese cake. My cook, Millie, she mek 'em wid Arsenic . . . dey rilly good . . . Ah, dere you are, gal . . . 'bout time, too! Bring some more Arsenic cake. Mitchis Bundy like 'em too much . . . ting-ting-ting!' The ladylike way of holding a teacup was a source of great amusement, too. But not to Nell, lost in *gulli-gulli*.

It was Friday afternoon. There was the old Rolls Royce drawing up at Dotty's front gate, with the sea blazing jade and silver behind it. Dotty opened the latticed door and stood smiling in her silly way, while up the stairs, hand in hand, came Alfie Candlemas and he now known officially (unless Mr McCusky had been intimidated to change it by Mr Bundy) as Prendegast Alroy.

Dotty gave Alfie the high how'd'y'do handshake proper for At Homes, then put a fat red hand on Prindy's golden head and smiled into the calm-staring grey eyes, saying, 'We've met before, young man, haven't we . . . remember the day you came round with the fish.' Then aside to Alfie: 'I must take him to his mother. Won't you sit down. I always take tea out heah . . . the view is, I always say, the grandest in the world . . . with imagination you can see the Island of Bali, and those lovely girls dancing naked to the waist . . . eeeee!'

Dotty duly delivered Prindy into his mother's snatching arms, leaving him staring just as calmly at the smirking Venus and Millie, to return to her ladylike duties. She said to Alfie, 'He's a beautiful child, isn't he . . . despite the Abo features.'

Alfie said boldly, black eyes fixed on the watery blue, 'Perhaps it's *because* of them. I've seen some *very* handsome Aborigines.'

Dotty blinked. It wouldn't be the kind of talk she was used to. But her responses had changed mightily during these past three or four days. She replied mildly, 'Well, yes . . . I suppose there are. It's only that we're used to our own type of face . . . yes, the mother's really quite pretty.'

'Beautiful, I think.'

'Yes . . . beautiful . . . with a beautiful heart, too. But tell me about yourself I've heard so much about you. That brush with old Bundy you had the other day. He is an old pig at times. But, oh dear, it was taking an awful risk, wasn't it?'

Evidently in these few days Alfie had learnt much in dealing with Government people. She laughed, saying, 'It was all a mistake, really.'

Dotty looked relieved. And so the little bell went *ting-ting-ting* in reality, and Nell came with the tray, with the tay and Millie's Arsenic Cakes, and smiled dutifully when Alfie smiled at her; and the two ladies sat and sipped their tay with fingers stuck out and stared at imaginary Bali rising like ivory out of the jade. Dotty had said she wanted to hear about Alfie, but apparently wasn't so interested now she found her as just another little Junior Officer's wife, when she herself was a Senior Officer's.

She did most of the talking herself, about what was the all-absorbing social topic of the period, Coronation Day, and all that would be happening. There would be the Levee at Government House on the Night of the Day, beginning at eight, so as to coincide with the actual crowning of the King at eleven in the morning of the same day on the other side of the world. Even Dotty said it sounded mad: 'But . . . how could the Honours be conferred unless His Majesty was actually crowned? That'd make a complete farce of it. I'll let you in on a secret . . . but not a word to anyone, mind . . . I can trust you? Robert . . . that's the Major, my husband . . . will be getting the M.B.E. It's all supposed to be secret, you know . . . only those who're to get Honours know. But of course everybody knows that that old braggart, Vic Shane's getting something. He hasn't really said anything . . . but quite enough. That's what the schooner party's for, of course. He'll have to have us this time . . . because he's said it's for all those who get Honours . . . and others, too, of course. The old thing! What would he be entitled to Royal Honours for . . . sleeping with Japanese and Chinese women he brings back from his trips, the dirty old man! It's his money, of course. We've never been friends with him. He was rude to me at one of his boozy parties years ago . . . and Robert never forgave him. But, of course, it would be like *lèse-majesté* not to go on the cruise. We'll have one Knight and one Lady . . . the Eatons. Everybody's known that, since Edward the Eighth. Clem Eaton entertained Edward when he was here as Prince of Wales. It'll make a difference to the tone of the country having a Knight and a Lady, don't you think?'

Alfie murmured, 'I suppose so.'

So it went on for an hour or so, till Alfie said she must be getting back to feed her children. Dotty said, 'I believe you're having real fun with them . . .

that you're like a real mother to them. Tell me, my dear . . . can't you have children yourself?'

Alfie reddened. 'As far as I know . . . yes. But Frank and I decided against it till . . . well, till we'd done something to make the world a place more fit to bring children into.'

'So you use contraceptives?'

Redder, and sounding somewhat aggressive, perhaps in anticipation of a rebuke, Alfie answered, 'Yes.'

But Dotty only sighed, and said, 'I wish I could have had a child. I would have been so happy. It seems that those who want them can't have them, and those who can won't, or have too many. That poor girl told me that she did away with several . . . Oh, I'm sorry, I didn't mean to say it! I promised not to. Please don't repeat it.'

Dotty looked quite earnest in her request.

Alfie relaxed, smiled in a kindly way, saying, 'Of course I won't. I feel too bad about her myself.'

'Bad?'

'For getting her that long sentence with my foolishness.'

'Oh, don't worry about that. She'll soon be out.'

'Yes?'

'Yes . . . there'll be another Royal Amnesty. I've already made up my mind that Robert shall recommend her release. Judge Bickering, who makes the decisions, is sure to agree to it, just to annoy Bundy. Rest assured of that.'

'Oh, thank you, thank you, dear Mrs O'Dowdy . . . I've not had a proper night's sleep since it happened.'

Ting-ting-ting!

Nell came. Dotty told her to bring Prindy. Dotty kissed Prindy on the brow in taking leave of him. Then Alfie kissed Dotty, whose pale eyes swam with tears. She and Nell stood in the door waving the Rolls out of sight.

Alfie reached home to find her Frank at the gate again, wearing that quizzical smile. She asked, 'How have I sinned against the Holy Writ of Government Service now?' He shrugged. She went on: 'They wouldn't let me visit her unless on business connected with the Aborigines Department, when you can visit white prisoners for no other reason than friendship, compassion. They wouldn't give me permission. So I paid a social call on the Jailer's wife . . . Old Dotty, as they call her . . . who's got more kindliness in her little finger . . . '

'It wasn't your going out to the Jail,' he said, putting an arm about her.

Her face was rosy, eyes flashing. He kissed her. She pulled away. 'Then what?'

'The silly papers,' he said, and went to the ice-box for drinks.

Palmeston Times and *Palmeston Progressive*, just off the press, were spread out on the cane table. Both announced the thing identically in their biggest type: *SCENE IN POLICE COURT*.

The *Times*'s sub-heading was: *Magistrate Ejects Abo. Dept. Officer*. The *Progressive* had it: *Abo. Protector Calls Magistrate's Finding Travesty of Justice*.

How differently can the same tale be told with differing design! The *Times* gave twice the space to it to justify justice as done in this best of all possible systems. *Progressive* reported chiefly the bits that made the system stink. Alfie looked up from quick reading to say, 'Everybody knew all that days ago. We laughed it off, didn't we?'

He handed her a glass of sherry, then opened the *Progressive*. The second page was almost entirely filled with a special article by Fay McFee, what amounted to the Pen Portrait that Fay had been asked to leave for a more appropriate time. Alfie took a swig of wine, and read all about the fighting daughter of that grand old fighter for social justice, Silas Tripconny. It told how she, a woman of youth, beauty, charm, everything to put her in the forefront of the legion of female parasites of the Community who called themselves Socialites, had gone into the Compound, that impregnable fortress hitherto of those who would perpetuate slavery, and within hours had had the rubbish bought as food by a heartless and heedless administration for the virtually imprisoned inmates, condemned and destroyed and replaced with something fit for human beings – how out of a Concentration Camp for unwanted waifs, by working ten hours a day for seven days a week for a pittance, she had made a happy home of laughing healthy children – how finally, she had stood in a Court of Law and done properly the job that every other officer of the Aborigines Department hitherto had squibbed, had exposed a glaring piece of injustice, and out of the goodness of her heart, when ordered from the precincts for having dared to do her duty, had wept in pity for the victim of it, and been officially dubbed Hysterical! At last, at long last, in the lovely and gracious form of Aelfrieda Tripconny Candlemas, there was hope for those most ill-used people on the face of the earth, the Australian Aborigines!

Alfie, flushed again, drank off the wine, looked at Frank watching her intently. She smiled: 'Quite a wrap-up, isn't it . . . only much more what I'd like to be like than what I am.'

He smiled back, that slow, easy smile: 'I got put on the mat for it.'

'What?'

He refilled her glass: 'I'm supposed to put you on it, too.'

'What on earth are you talking about?'

He sat her down and set about explaining. It seemed that when the weekly papers first came off the press the Administrator, or Old Man, as Frank called him, had the right, by reason of the fact that Government Pronouncements were printed by both, to exercise a covert censorship before they were put into circulation. Of course he had nothing to fear from the *Times*. It was the *Progressive* he was always after, and they had to make the concession as the price for their share of Government printing. When he saw something that enraged him particularly, he had the Crown Law Officer read it. There had been numerous suppressions of editions and court actions over the years, so many of the latter that had gone in favour of the *Progressive*, which with much experience had become very smart in out-witting him, that His Honour had been ordered by the distant Bigger Fleas who rode him to go easy. He'd had the Crown Law man study this Pen Portrait thing. Then he had had Dr Cobbity in on the mat to take out on him what, on advice, he couldn't on Fay and her editor. His order to Cobbity was to the effect that if Mrs Candlemas got any more favourable publicity from the *Palmeston Progressive* her services were to be dispensed with. So Cobbity had had Frank in on *his* mat, and said, according to Frank, 'Tell the little lady to go easy.'

'Go easy on what?' demanded Alfie. 'What have I done? I didn't write the damn thing!'

Frank shrugged: 'As I said at the time of the Bundy business . . . Public Service. Petty power.'

'But we can't go creeping round in fear of offending their sense of their own importance. We're dedicated to better things. If we're going to let these Little Hitlers . . . .'

He came to her and put his arm about her. 'Sweetheart . . . I told you before. You're in. While you're in there's the chance to do the better things when the time comes . . . the New Settlement. Just take it easy till then. Come on, now . . . let's have dinner.'

For a moment she stared at him as if doubting him. But he met her gaze steadily, gave that easy smile again, and bent and kissed her. She sighed: 'All right,' and let him help her up, take her in his arms and kiss her again.

The couple had not long finished dinner and were listening to the radio, to the BBC and an argument between a group of Intellectuals over the Spanish Civil War. It seemed that Italy was sending troops into Spain to fight against the Republicans with the insurgent General Franco, while the British Government, under Prime Minister Baldwin, was preventing even the passage of volunteers to go to help the legitimate Spanish Government against what was being called hotly 'Fascist Aggression' as opposed to the other side of the argument's cold 'Bolshevik Interference'. A loud knocking at the door. Frank and Alfie exchanged glances. Then Frank rose and went to the door. It was Fay McFee. Her penetrating contralto rose above the radio. 'Those bloody Fascists . . . may I come in?' Frank looked troubled. But Fay was already leaning in and shouting to Alfie, 'Hullo, there! Thought I'd drop in with a peace-offering.' She held up a bottle of whisky. 'I suppose you're mad at me? Heard that the Brass has been kicking up a row.' She was in, and in a moment with her big behind jammed in a cane chair, talking Spanish Civil War, while Frank turned down the talked-down BBC and got glasses and ginger ale.

Suddenly Fay asked, 'Well, how'd you like the Pen Portrait?'

The popping grey eyes stared down their embarrassment with evident growing indignation as the silence lengthened. Alfie broke it, panting slightly, rosy of cheeks. 'You promised to wait a while . . . . '

'Promised nothing!' Fay snapped. 'I never make promises in my work . . . . '

Frank cut in: 'I distinctly heard you say you'd agree to wait a while.'

'And haven't I . . . about three months?'

Alfie snapped now, 'I expected you to consult me first.'

Frank was hesitating with the bottle. Fay assumed a sort of leer, saying, 'I like mine straight, thanks,' then added, 'That sounds like Dr Cobbity.' When Alfie didn't answer, Fay went on, 'If I'd've consulted you, you'd then have had to consult him, eh . . . is that it?'

Frank handed her the drink, and proceeded to pour the others with ginger ale, saying, 'We're trying to be careful till the right time comes.'

Fay leered again: 'Till the sweet by'n'by, like . . . cheers!'

The others drank, but in silence.

The grey eyes challenged them again. Frank said, 'If Alfie's to do any good for the Aborigines the best way will be from inside the Department . . . .'

'Taking orders from Cobbity and Co.!' Fay finished her drink, shoved her glass out for another. As he poured it, she added, 'Looks like she's got to take orders from her old man, too.' She bared her teeth in a grin at him.

Going red, he said, 'Indeed, she doesn't.'

Fay took a swig, then demanded, 'Then why the hell're you doing all the talking?' The challenging glare turned on Alfie. 'I thought you had a mind of your own. You seemed to in court the other day. D'you have to get away from *him* to use it?' She jerked her fairish frizz contemptuously towards Frank.

Quite red now, and with black eyes ablaze, Alfie panted, 'Really!'

Fay said to her, 'Looks like Rollo Ramstones, my editor, was right about you . . . you're just a pretty kid playing a game.'

Frank said stiffly, 'If you don't mind, Madam . . . '

She turned on him with teeth really bared now: 'You keep out of this! I wrote that thing out of admiration of your wife . . . for her guts in standing up to tyranny. Leave her alone. Let her do what she was born to do . . . which is to work to make a better world, not crawl to a bloody boss.' She swung back to Alfie: 'Because that's what you're doing . . . at the instigation of this . . . this silvertail!' She stressed the term with the utmost contempt and a glance at Frank to show she meant it. 'If you're going to give in to these petty bosses, you'll never be anything but one of them. I asked you a question when I came in . . . How did you like my Pen Portrait of you? . . . I want your answer.'

Alfie's little bosom was heaving as she met glare with glare. She drew a deep breath, let it out with a rush: 'I like it very much . . . *but I don't like you!*' Tears sprang to drown the glare. She turned and rushed out to the kitchen.

From watching her go, Frank swung on Fay and said coldly, 'And now, Madam . . . if you'll excuse us . . . . '

Bouncing up out of the chair, Fay snapped, 'I'll excuse you nothing. Give me my whisky. You can get plenty as cumshaw off the Chows.'

He flamed, but answered evenly, 'Be careful what you say.'

She showed all her teeth at him: 'I always am careful what I say . . . and that's how I get away with it. But I *do* say it, Mr Silvertail . . . so just *you* be careful what you *do*. Goodbye . . . and bugger you!'

Fay marched out. Frank stood gaping after her till he heard her car start up, then turned and went hurrying to the kitchen, to stop and gape again, on finding Alfie leaning against the sink, helpless with silent laughter. For a moment he stared, then grinned. Then they fell into each other's arms laughing.

'Oh, that last bit!' cried Alfie. 'Oh, oh, ha, ha, ha!'

'There's no doubt about her . . . ha, ha, ha, ho, ho!'

But when they'd got over it, Alfie, sniffling back the tears it had brought, said, 'She's right, though. If we keep on giving in to them, we'll get to be like them. We have to fight them.'

'Not yet, my dear . . . not yet.'

When she looked at him with big eyes, he asked, 'Don't you trust me? There's only one thing I want . . . my darling's happiness. You know that.'

She dropped her head to his breast, sighing: 'Yes, darling . . . I know. Yes, I trust you.'

'Then play it safe till the time's right.'

She raised her head suddenly: 'But there's one thing I'm not going to do, and that's go on that cruise with all those damn snobs and prigs, with their O.B.E.'s and Knighthoods. I couldn't stand it. I'll take the kids for a picnic instead.'

'Aren't they supposed to be at the public shivoo at the Oval . . . to get flags and medals and lollies and things?'

'Let the white kids and the black kids get 'em. What reason have my yeller kids got for celebrating the crowning of a halfwit on the other side of the world? I'd rather they never heard about it.'

'Thank God you didn't say that in front of old Fay!'

'At least it'd've shown her I don't have to ask your permission to say things.'

They laughed and embraced again. Then he said, 'But you'll have to go to the Levee, you know.'

'Who says?'

'It's a command . . . a Royal Command. Didn't you read the invitations?'

They went back into the lounge-room, where he took from the sideboard the cards sent from the Residency, headed, *You Are Commanded To Attend* . . . .

'Well, blow me down!' she exploded. 'The cheek of it . . . .'

'The Old Man's assumed the Royal Prerogative . . . whether rightly or not I don't know. But if we don't go, we're looking for trouble, I guess.'

'That settles it . . . It's mediaeval tyranny! I'm not going. You can.'

He sighed: 'My little fire-eater, as our immediate master said! It might be fun, you know, to see the snobs. What chance'll you ever get again to go to a Vice-regal Levee?'

'None that I'd take, any more than I'll take this one. I'll do my job. I'll shut my mouth. But I won't go on the *command* of a puffed-up little tin-god like the Old Man, as you call him. No, I won't!'

He sighed again, taking her in his arms: 'Okay. That settles it. I won't go, either. They'll probably not notice us, anyway. I'll be glad to keep out of the other thing . . . Shane's schooner party. Can I come to your picnic?'

'Of course. I tell you what we'll do . . . we'll have a cruise, too. King George . . . for God's sake . . . I mean that old blackfellow, the fisherman, at the Compound . . . he was telling me the turtles are laying their eggs now over on the beaches, just outside the harbour. What say we hire a launch . . . and go and gather turtle eggs?'

'Great idea!' he cried. 'Willie Pak Poy's got a big launch. I might get him to take us for nothing by forgetting about his dirty dunny!'

Alfie's revolt went according to plan – except that afterwards Alfie admitted regretting not having attended the Levee, on hearing that Jumbo Delacy had done so *without* the Royal Command and caused a diversion of which she had to say, 'I'd have loved to have seen it!' It seemed that Jumbo had leapt from the watching crowd of commoners outside Government House, just as his white-side nephew, Martin, on the spotlit dais on the front lawn, was having the ribbon and medallion of the Order of the British Empire hung about his neck by that stand-in for Him just then having the Crown placed upon his holy head some ten thousand miles away, Colonel Close, and shouted something like: 'The bastard got quarter-caste kid in Compound!' Nobody who spoke of it later either could, or would, describe it clearly. They said it had happened so swiftly. Almost as soon as Jumbo had shown himself amongst his betters and got that bit out, the King's Men in khaki, who should have been more alert than to have let it happen at all, pounced, and stifling anything else Jumbo had to say, dragged him away. The wonder was that His Honour had not then withheld the M.B.E. he had for Police Superintendent Bullco and the Police Medal for Sergeant Cahoon, granted, as the Royal Citation had it, *For Devotion to Duty*. When Alfie made that remark of hers, Frank's reply to it was to the effect that thank God she hadn't been there, else *she* might have piped up with something about the Shell Oil Company. She said, 'I might have, too, seeing who the gongs were being handed out to!' She would mean Captain Shane, who got an O.B.E., *For Service to the Pearling Industry*, and Dr Cobbity, who got the same Order, *For Services to Tropical Medicine*.

As anticipated, other recipients were Major O'Dowdy, M.B.E., *For Devotion to Duty*, and Clement John Eaton, K.C.M.G., which might have been cited as for the same purpose, seeing that it was with something like devotion that he did his duty by his master, Lord Vaisey, but instead repeated the citation that went with his step-son's O.B.E. So at last Rhoda was truly Her Ladyship. Alfie couldn't mock at that, not yet having had the honour of meeting the lady or enough knowledge of her to be interested. She also didn't mock at the O'Dowdy thing, but instead, early next morning rang Dotty and congratulated her, then came out with her real purpose, which was to ask if Nelly Ah Loy would be free to join in her picnic. Dotty said she hadn't anything official, for one reason that Robert was not yet awake, but rest assured that Nelly would be waiting for them on the beach below the Jail.

There was plenty of room in Willie Pak Poy's launch *Maskee* for several other mothers also. Alfie took them without the permission she should have had, because Mr. Turkney, also, could not be roused from the slumber he was wrapt in through having taken part in a party Dr Cobbity had thrown after the Levee, and Mrs Turkney ignored Alfie's attempt to get *her* advice in the matter. So Alfie said, '*Maskee*!' having just learnt that the name of the boat was Malay for *What's it Matter*! In that mood she also included Queeny Peg-leg when that one, seeing and hearing what was going on, asked if she might be in it. The tide was at neap, which made embarkation easy from the Compound beach and the picking up some twenty minutes later of Nell. Alfie kissed her as she came aboard, much to Nell's surprise, but only for a moment, since she had real interest obviously only in her but slightly interested son. Prindy had fishing line out, ready for spinning, under the direction of King George, and in no time after they got under way again had a kingfish so big that George had to help him in with it. Other kids wanted to use the spinner; but Prindy, his grey eyes shining with excitement, would not hand it over.

Thus out through the harbour's mouth and into the ocean, turquoise today, and along the western shore to Turtle Bay – a lovely spot, with a creek in the middle for anchoring the launch, and pandanus, casuarina, and tea-tree growing to the very edge of the ledge that marked spring-tide high-water. George had already shown them the tracks of turtles on the long white heach. They lost no time in getting ashore and sharpening sticks as George directed; and then, the bigger ones swinging the kerosene-can buckets they were to bring it home in, went racing to the buried treasure – Alfie well out in front and very conspicuous in a one-piece crimson bathing suit. Only grey-haired Willie Pak Poy with Peg-leg stayed behind, Willie to look after the boat, he said, and she because she was no salt-water woman and found it hard going in sand. George, taking it easy with Frank, gave it as his opinion that the pair were going to have a bit of Play-about. He added: 'Dat bloody woman no goot!' He and Queeny had kept as far apart as possible during the voyage, and not simply because they were tribal brother and sister. They were well known as enemies from a long way back.

While being quite careless about leaving tracks, turtles show great cunning in concealing their nests. Even those of the kids who'd come from salt-water tribes hadn't located any eggs before George came up and did it for them. It was only a matter of shoving the pointed stick deep in the soft dry sand and if it came up with sand sticking to it, there was a nest. But where, oh where, in a waste of turtle-flipper-scored sand! George got one first pop. Then everybody dug, like terriers. Two and a half feet down; and there they were, like a mass of billiard balls, till you touched them, and their flexible shells rumpled. Fifty-seven in that first nest. They robbed another of exactly fifty, a third of nearly seventy. Alfie became concerned about wiping out the species. But George said there would be nests for miles, all round the coast, and out of each nest only a few picaninny turtles survived, what with birds and sharks and things waiting on their birthday; even so, the seas hereabout teemed with full-grown turtles: 'Some-feller proper old-man,' he added. 'Me only picaninny long o' him . . . eeeeeeee!'

But Alfie called a halt at three nests. Anyway, it was all they had cans enough to carry. Then they headed back to the launch, and near it, beside the creek, made a dinner camp under leafy trees, and using a huge frying pan from the Compound kitchen, after separating non-coagulable whites from yokes, made mighty omelets, eaten with tomato sauce and bread and butter, and washed down with lemonade from Mr Tootle's. While they were eating, they saw the schooner *San Toy* go gliding by, a lovely sight with all sails set and leaning to the gentle breeze, a fitting vessel for all those grand ones aboard her. But as Alfie said, 'I'd rather be here eating tuttle, wouldn't you?' The answering cry was a general hearty *Yu-ai*!

As they were coming home in the evening *San Toy* passed them again just as they were entering the harbour, close enough to distinguish the faces of those aboard. There they all were, the accoladed ones, and their hangers-on. Dr Cobbity and Captain Shane and the O'Dowdys responded cheerily enough in response to the *Maskee* crew's waving; but the rest were stiffish, if they deigned at all. She went on, the lovely thing, to pass the Rainbow Reef beacon and head in towards the Delacy place, where there was to be a grand finale to this wondrous day for colonial snobs and toadies.

Quite tired-out, the Compound commoners landed, to trudge up to their respective quarters. Alfie kissed everybody in saying Goodnight, even George, who cried, 'Eh, look-out!' The children fell into bed.

No one came out of the residence to greet Alfie and Frank. It had been another day of junketing, of course. So they got into the old Rolls and headed for home. Alfie leaned her head against Frank's shoulder, murmuring sleepy-sounding as the kids, 'I think it's been about the happiest day of my life.'

He kissed her cheek, 'Let's hope they don't do anything to spoil it for you.'

'What can they do?'

'You never know. We stood 'em up on the Levee. Notice the Old Man didn't wave?'

'That pompous old bastard . . . let him do what he likes . . . he can't take this lovely lovely thing away from me . . . oooh!' She curled up to him, fell asleep.

IX

It was just a week after the Crowning, Anointing, and otherwise rendering of that inoffensive, stuttering, in-bred, German-Danish-anything-but-English, young Englishman, erstwhile called Albert, something entirely different from the common run of men born of common women, George VI, by the Grace of God, King of the Pommies, Defender of the Anglican Faith, Emperor of India, Sovereign Lord of His Dominions Beyond the Seas (which would be about the time it took for his subjects in that remote part of his Imperium called Port Palmeston to recover sufficiently from the booziness and general lunacy attendant upon the event to get back to their mean work-a-day) that Alfie Candlemas had an official visitor call on her at the Compound School, but in no way concerning the school. It was a policeman, as the kids announced with indrawn breaths the moment the yellow utility truck came into view. It was, in fact, more than a common policeman – no less an officer of the law than Sergeant Dennis Cahoon, Police Medal.

Dinny came strolling in, with the grin and the greenish eyes shooting all over the place, and particularly at the scared young dusky faces, till they lit on one paler than most and with staring grey eyes, when the grin altered somewhat and a hand was raised in greeting. But the Sergeant was there on official business. He continued on his way towards the teacher, standing by her blackboard. He saluted, saying, 'Mornin' Mrs Candlemas . . . see you a moment privately?'

She looked surprised: 'Yes . . . of course, Sergeant.' Then she told the children to run along and play.

'How's young Prindy doing?' Dinny asked, watching them go.

'Quite well,' said Alfie. 'But he really needs special schooling . . . .'

'They say it's his ears.'

'No . . . I meant, he's too big a boy for this place, and advanced. Evidently his mother gave him his ABC and things . . . .'

'My sisters taught her.'

'So I understand. What I mean is he's a particularly bright boy . . . in my opinion. He's withdrawn . . . but what intelligent child with his background wouldn't be?'

'I'd like my sisters to take him, like they did her mother, but . . . but they're gettin' a bit old now. I'd adopt him myself, only for that.' When she met the green eyes with surprise they blinked, and turned away. The truth as Alfie wouldn't know through being too busy to know much of what was other people's business, was that Dinny's sisters had unequivocally denied him the indulgence of *de facto* recognition of his alleged bastard. He changed the subject quickly, saying, 'I've a small official matter for you to attend to.' From his breast pocket he took papers and a small black book that had made it bulge hugely. He set the things down on the table. Alfie showed obvious surprise on seeing that the little book was entitled in gold: *Holy Bible*. Dinny handed her one of the papers, which was in an envelope bearing the printed letters O.H.M.S. She opened it. Most certainly was the matter *On His Majesty's Service*. She read:

> It has been noted that you have not yet taken the Oath of Allegiance prerequisite in appointment to Public Service. You are hereby requested to undergo the formality without delay.
>
> *Signed: E.P.N. Twigg*
> *Government Secretary.*

She looked up at Dinny in surprise: 'What's this in aid of?'

He grinned: 'Just a formality. Here's the Oath.' He unfolded a paper and gave it to her.

Her eyes rolled as they went over the heavy print that with a lot of jargon in legalistic style would bind her in Loyalty and Obedience to Our Sovereign Lord the King and his Ministers of Government appointed by him, so help her God. She looked up to meet the green eyes again, face rosy now and black eyes flashing, saying, 'But this is ridiculous!'

He grinned: 'It's the rule.'

She put the paper back on the table, demanding, 'Is this something being done to . . . harass me?'

'Lord, no! Everybody's got ‹o swear it who's a servant of the Crown. I did.'

'But you're a policeman. I'm only a teacher.'

'What's the difference . . . we're both servants of the Crown.'

'No . . . I don't like this. This's something being done to me. I remember that that man the Federal Attorney-General, brought it in . . . to get at Communists.'

'You're not a Commo, though?'

'No . . I'm not. But I object to being treated with suspicion.'

'But I've told you . . . it's only a formality.'

'I don't mean to be rude . . . to you, Sergeant . . . but I don't believe in it . . . and I won't do it.'

He stared at her, with her head high and cheeks rosy and dark eyes wide and angry, looking very lovely. Then he shook his head. 'It might cause trouble for you if you don't.'

'I don't care!'

'I'll have to report back, of course, that you refused.'

'Of course.'

He was silent a moment. Then: 'Leave it till you've spoken to your husband, eh?'

She snapped, 'As far as I'm concerned, the matter's closed.' She took up papers and Bible and handed them to him.

As he took them he shook his head again. 'I'll still wait till you've spoken to your husband, lady. Goodday to you.' He saluted withdrew.

The children came rushing back, divining that something was amiss, but too polite to ask. She couldn't go on with school. She said they'd go and get a picnic lunch from Nell in the kitchen and go down the beach and have it and play. As she passed the Superintendent's office she slipped in and asked Tubby did he have to swear an Oath of Allegiance on appointment. He said, 'Lord no!' Nor had he ever sworn or signed anything. 'Something new, eh?' he suggested, and looked cagey.

Venus, Nell's cell-mate in jail, freed with her under the Royal Amnesty. was now also working in the kitchen. She came down to the beach with them. Others also released were Green-ant and Splinter, and the rest concerned in the Catfish Creek Affair. Prindy left Alfie and the others to go talk to them in King George's hut, asking them about Bobwirridirridi. George looked troubled. It seemed that he was being credited again in some quarters with being the one who had brought the releases about. Certainly the Catfish men believed he'd been responsible, and had given him their brand-new discharged-prisoner outfits, of khaki shirts and trousers, in payment for the favour, according to inviolate Aboriginal custom, and in place of them bought from him on promise of payment later, well-worn stuff he traded in. What was worrying George was not his conscience, because it was evident he more than half believed that he had done the trick again, but that Bobwirridirridi was getting impatient about his own expected release, sending almost daily messages through Barney Bynoe. It was from Barney, who was getting a lot of fun out of it, that Prindy heard of the business between the two old fellows. Barney told it to Prindy as a joke, but without getting him to see it. Prindy only asked when the old man would be free, perhaps in the hope of returning with him to Catfish, whither the others were going by next train. Mr Turkney was also in the joke, so that when George went and asked him could he hurry up old Bob's release, he said he'd see what he could do, then phoned the Aborigines' Department Office and put them into fits with it.

Another piece of information the very knowledgeable Barney Bynoe had to relate, and this not in jest, was that Jumbo Delacy, in jail since Coronation Day, being held on a charge of being Drunk and Disorderly, was to be certified insane by Drs Cobbity and McQuegg and sent to an asylum in the South. He told Alfie about it. When Alfie cried out in protest he said, 'More better, I reckon. Poor old Jumbo, too much he mek trouble for everybody.'

Alfie, on reaching home, was immediately asked by Frank, 'What's happened?' When he heard he nodded as if he'd expected it.

She asked, 'Did you have to swear the Oath?'

'Yes.'

'When?'

'When I was appointed.'

'Why didn't you tell me?'

'I didn't think it worth it. Seems to be routine now . . . like the medical examination, when they ask you have you had VD and you just say no, and that's that.'

'But you regard the King of England the same as I do . . . as something alien to people like Australians . . . all right for the English, if they want to cling to old trappings of authority. But we're citizens of a properly constituted Commonwealth. How can you have that with a King and his nobles and all the old-fashioned rest of it? It's just historical to us. Having to swear an oath of allegiance to it seems to me like swearing against all our principles . . . *against Australia* even.'

'Probably most Australians feel that way about it . . . but don't think it matters. It's only been in a couple of years . . . anti-Communist business.'

'Yes, I thought of that . . . red-baiting.'

'Silly . . . because the Comms swear it just the same . . . end justifies the means, you know.'

'Do we have to be dishonest because the Communists are?'

'We do have an *end* in view, you know.'

'Which we'll never get so long as we give in to them. I feel sure this is something vindictive. We didn't go to the Levee, nor on the cruise. I remember those hard faces looking at us from the *San Toy*. It seems like they're looking at me now. They haven't forgotten what I said in Court that day. You said I'd bucked authority. Authority's out to get me. If I bow down to Our Sovereign Lord the bloody King of England, I bow down to His Bloody Honour the Administrator . . . then to Cobbity, then to McCusky, then to Turkney . . . . '

He slipped an arm about her. 'Then to me?'

She pulled away: 'I won't do it, Frank . . . I won't, I won't!'

He smiled that smile of his: 'Okay, darling. Let's have a drink. Maybe they'll forget about it.'

But the men of power never forget when the principles of their power are threatened. There was Sergeant Cahoon at the Compound School again first thing next morning. Alfie saved him from coming in by going to meet him saying, 'No, Sergeant . . definitely no!'

He looked at her seriously. 'I'll have to report it, of course.'

'Do so . . . with my best disrespects to everyone concerned!' She swung round and went back to her class, head high, eyes flashing, face aglow. She said to the staring kids, 'I'll tell you about the Eureka Stockade . . . the only time the people who call themselves Australians ever showed any courage . . . and they mightn't have been Australian-born, either. My great-grandfather fought in it, as a rebel . . . and he was English.'

Two hours later there was the police car again. Alfie cried out, 'Oh, no!' But it wasn't Cahoon; instead, young Constable Gobally, looking rather red and awkward, as he handed her another O.H.M.S. envelope. He simply saluted and departed.

It was another communication from the Government Secretary, just a couple of lines, reading: *You are hereby requested to present yourself at the Office of His Honour the Administrator immediately.*

Alfie said to the kids, 'Let's go down the beach again.'

They got to the beach in time to see King George, with a couple of black helpers, running out his net to take a haul from the tide just beginning to ebb. The children rushed to be in it. Alfie squatted in the sand to watch, soon to be joined by Queeny, who proceeded to pump her concerning official matters, evidently leading to that of the New Settlement, about her own place in it which she, with all her vested interests here, must be especially concerned about. Alfie's declaiming knowledge, and even saying that she did not think she herself would be having anything to do with the new place, didn't put Queeny off, used as she was, no doubt, to being put off by officialdom.

The fish were almost landed, making a last boiling fight for liberty and life, with half a hundred kids, black and yellow and creamy, making it hard for them on the side where it lay, with their splashing and yelling, and Peg-leg still doing her stuff, with Alfie sitting drooping, staring blankly, playing with the sand – when a sudden change came over things. The children fell silent Some black ones dropped down into the water to render themselves less conspicuous. George and his adult helpers turned – and Queeny, too, to breathe 'Eh, look out!' and heave herself up on peg and crutch and go loping for the scrub. Alfie was the last to turn. A tall figure clad in gleaming whites and wearing a topee had just come onto the grassy stretch from the track from above – Dr Cobbity. Alfie didn't move, just sat staring.

Cobbity came up to her, took off the topee, grinned a greeting, 'What a life you and your pupils have!'

Still sitting, she met his smiling blue eyes, said stiffly, 'Better than keeping them cooped up in that place up there . . . .'

'Prison, Fay McFee called it, didn't she . . . virtual prison, wasn't it? May I sit down?'

She was rosy, wide-eyed, heaving a bit for breath. She answered, 'Why ask? It's your property.'

'Now, now!' he said, stretching out long legs as he settled down. 'That isn't very nice.' He got out his pipe.

'It's what it says on the notice board in front.'

'Hardly that. But what's got into you, Alfie? I thought we were friends.'

She resumed her playing with the sand, watching those of the children, her own, who, unlike the blacks, had not taken advantage of their Protector's momentary preoccupation with sitting down, to vanish. The others were watching under lowered brows, except the one with the fair hair and grey eyes, who was busy basketing the fish with King George.

When she didn't answer, Cobbity went on: 'I've told you I want you in the new place. I believed in your enthusiasm . . . when others were inclined to say you were only a little girl having a game. Have you got sick of the game?'

She glanced at him: 'It's not a game to me. It means everything to me. She lifted her fingers from the sand to wave towards the children.

He caught the slim brown hand as she drew it in, pressed it down on the sand beside him with his own, ruddy and ginger-haired. She let him hold it. He puffed on his pipe then asked, 'Then why not be reasonable?'

'What have I done now that's considered unreasonable?'

'For godsake . . . you stood the Old Man up!'

'So what?'

'Don't you understand he's the Big Boss . . . that the whole of the Public Service here's under his control?'

'Of course.'

'Then why did you disobey the order sent you to present yourself to him?'

'To save his time and my own.'

'What d'you mean by that?'

She pulled her hand from under his, but left it lying by her thigh. She said, 'He only wanted to bully me into swearing that silly oath.'

He got the hand again, smoothed it now: 'There's no need for you to go to him now.'

She looked at him quickly. Through smoke he went on: 'I fixed it with him. I explained that you're young, inexperienced in Public Service . . . and that I want you for the new place.'

'The Oath doesn't matter now?'

'I told him I'd fix that.'

'What's that mean?'

'You needn't swear anything, if you don't want to . . . just sign that paper . . . .'

She withdrew her hand again: 'Which says I have sworn the Oath.'

He went red: 'For godsake, girl . . . why do you go on about that bloody Oath?'

'Because swearing it's against my conscience.'

'You can't have any conscience in a matter like this without declaring yourself a rebel . . . I mean a real rebel. You're a subject of the King, and therefore automatically owe allegiance to him. To refuse to acknowledge it constitutes a crime . . . do you realize that?' He puffed vigorously.

She stared at him for a moment, then asked, 'Is that part of the price you have to pay for an O.B.E. . . . to preach the gospel of the out-of-date Imperialism that gave it to you?'

His face went redder, his voice sharp: 'I told you I'm trying to keep you with me. You told me you want to stay. The Old Man's ramping. No one but myself could have made such a bargain with him . . . .'

'What bargain?'

'That I'd handle the matter of the Oath if he'd let bullying you drop.'

Their eyes clung for a moment. His mouth slipped into a grin again; and again he took her hand: 'Alfie, dear . . . .'

She interrupted: 'I'll make a bargain with you, then.'

The grin vanished: 'Well?'

'First . . . is it true that you're going to certify Jumbo Delacy insane?'

He went redder than ever, swallowed, let her hand go, asked stiffly, 'Where'd you get that?'

'I find this's a great place for things getting about. Well?'

He hid in smoke, muttered, 'Such matters are strictly confidential.'

The smoke cleared to show her eyes still on him. But now no change to a grin on his part. She broke the little silence: 'That's as good as yes to me. The bargain is . . . you call off that dreadful thing, and I'll swear your silly Oath.

'What dreadful thing?'

'Declaring an unfortunate man insane to get rid of him because he's an embarrassment to the people who made him what he is.'

'What are you talking about?'

'How long have you considered Jumbo insane?'

Puffing, he took a moment to answer, 'Pretty well as long as I've known him.'

'Then why after all the years decide now to have him put away?'

'I told you this is a confidential matter . . . a medical matter.'

'And my opinion is that because of what Jumbo did on the night the Delacys got their knighthoods and O.B.E.'s and things, *plus* the Shell Oil Company thing, you've been asked by someone in a high place to get rid of him . . . '

He blazed: 'Madam!'

She was panting now: 'Is that the bargain you made with your boss, your master, your Old Man . . . bosom friend of the Delacys, servant of the Vaiseys . . . and Captain Shane and Shell Oil?'

He heaved himself to his feet, to blaze down at her: 'How dare you!'

She stayed where she was, to pant up, 'How dare I question the motives of another tin god?'

He barked at her, 'Oh . . . you're . . . you're impossible!' He swung away.

She cried after him, 'I thought you were going to say I was insane.'

He turned back to bark, 'The way you behave, you might be!'

She leapt up: 'Why don't you certify me? Why don't you, and that fat little drunken colleague of yours, use your God-given powers to do the same to me as . . . as . . . oh . . . oh!' He was striding away . . . and she was struggling with those all-too-ready tears of hers. The tears beat her. She dropped face to hands, sank to the sand again. Cobbity, turning into the track again, glanced back to her, for a moment hesitated, then went on, disappeared. As he vanished, the children from the home, all but the one busy with the fish, came running to comfort her.

They had dinner on the beach: fish grilled on the coals, a gift from King George and Prindy, with bread and butter. Then a blackfellow's sleep-it-off in the shade of the casuarinas. Prindy spent the sleepy time in King George's hut, till hauled out of there by his mother, come down after finishing her work in the kitchen. Nell called George a Black Bastard. He appeared to take no notice, evidently well used to being so-called by Queeny. Prindy's other black mates, the Catfish men, were gone, heading for home on today's mail train There could be no holding them in the Compound for what was known as the adaptation period, which usually followed a spell in jail and was useful in keeping a pool of five-bob-a-week house-boy labour for the town, because these were Vaisey slaves, and the Season was about to begin. George was one of those held for adaptation, and had been so since release from jail some ten years back for involvement in the affair that had got Bobwirridirridi life imprisonment and Queeny her peg-leg and crutch. He had been telling Prindy how the Pookarakka had wanted him to come back to the bush with him when he, George, had got him out of jail last year, and how he had intended to go *tchinekin* off after him eventually. 'Spone I get him out dis time,' he told Prindy. 'Me-two-feller go long o' him, eh?' Prindy had agreed readily.

Returning with the children in the afternoon, Alfie was pounced on by Tubby Turkney, wanting to know what had happened on the beach: 'The bloke looked as if someone had kicked him in the guts,' he added, when Alfie answered only with a wry smile.

After eyeing him for a moment, she said, 'Maybe it was rather like that to him. I offered to make a bargain with him.'

'A bargain?'

'Yes . . . that I'd swear that silly Oath of his, if he'd promise not to certify Jumbo Delacy.'

With eyes popping, Tubby breathed, 'Christ!'

Alfie said, 'I guess I'm on my way out of the Department now.'

When Frank heard about it on her arrival home, he said he reckoned that he would also be on his way out. Not that he minded, he added with that smile of his: 'The Service stinks worse than Chinatown, really . . . and we mustn't get contaminated . . . not that anyone could contaminate my lovely little fire-eater!'

'Do I look like a dragon?' she asked.

'Dragons aren't fire-eaters, but fire-breathers.'

'That's what he meant I was, of course.'

'Well, if he didn't poor old Saint Cuthbert, O.B.E., lost a battle he'd very much liked to have won with what must be the loveliest dragon there ever was.'

Alfie was right in her guessing. Next morning, Thursday, she had yet another call from young Constable Gobally, with yet another missive stated to be O.H.M.S.:

Dear Madam,

I am instructed to inform you that your services will no longer be required from the end of the current pay period. As your appointment is of a temporary nature, you will be paid one month's salary in lieu of the usual notice.

Yours faithfully,
E.P.N. Twigg,
Government Secretary.

Alfie took the children to Shelly Beach this time, in the Compound truck, and with the permission of Mr Turkney, who said when it was asked of him, 'Why not? The kids're going to miss you . . . who isn't!' Alfie sent Barney Bynoe to get Possum Delacy and the couple of kids she had home from State School to join them. Possum was very doleful. Asked if *she* thought Jumbo mad, she replied, 'He on'y halfcaste mad, and bit more, too, 'cause he Delacy.' Over Alfie's swearing to move heaven and earth to see that he wasn't sent away, Possum only shook her head, saying, 'Dat lot Govmin too strong. Nobody can beat him.'

Also while at Shelly Beach, looking out across the harbour, Alfie had another idea for using up the last few hours of her time with the children – tomorrow being the end of the current pay period – a picnic by launch again, but inside the harbour this time, not out to sea. What about it? The children yelled for joy. What about it, she asked Tubby when she got back. He said that, of course he'd have to get permission from the Office, then seeing her face fall, added, 'But why not do it off your own hook? You did it before. You've got nothing to lose. Just bring the launch round, pick up the kids, and off. But just forget you told me, eh?'

Willy Pak Poy took them again, on the in-running tide, past Rainbow Head with its quartz-and-mica substance sparkling with a myriad little rainbows in the early sunlight, along the reef, where the growth on the outcroppings trailed like long green hair in the rush of the limpid waters, so that Prindy, up in the bow with King George beside him telling him about Old Tchamala's doings round about here, stared as if fascinated, quite missing the beacon on which Lucy Snowball had died and which was the focal point of fascination for the rest. The beacon stood on a flat expanse of rock to mark the low-water channel in to Rainbow Beach, just a stout wooden post supporting a barred triangle, its base elephantine with growth of weed and shellfish, out of which, higher up, protruded spikes for climbing to the top. Poor Lucy had never reached the spikes. Crabs of many kinds and molluscs scampered and crept and rolled about the mossy flat, evidently in preparation for the flood that would soon come rushing over them; or perhaps in anticipation of more torn flesh to gnaw at, seeing human beings round again.

They came to the channel, swung towards the snowy shore with its backing of low green upland, some three-quarters of a mile away, too far to see the Delacy place as more than a patch of lower and darker green with a hint of red-roofed buildings amidst it. King George up in front and Willie Pak Poy in the stern, announced what it was. George said softly to Prindy, 'Belong 'o you mob.' Prindy appeared to be interested only in the scene.

There were sandbanks intervening, which the racing tide cut down and levelled as it reached them, the water dancing over the crumbling remains as if in delight in its might. Willy slowed down, to approach the shore crabwise, nosing into the flood as he made his way. Dark spots appeared on the steep beach, a pair of them, that were seen to be human figures at length, women, a couple of old halfcastes who looked after the place, Willy explained to Alfie, adding, 'Can't go 'shore there. Delacy no like.' But they got near enough to take a good look.

The buildings, a big bungalow and a couple of sheds on one side, mean humpies on the other, stood in a grove of shady trees, mostly of indigenous type, probably original growth of the little gully for which the place had been chosen for settlement, for space and for water, stretching back from the beach to the indented wall of micaceous rock that was the promontory behind. A windmill could be seen turning slowly back inside. The beach northward ended in a tumble of rock that at low water connected it with Rainbow Head, which was really the end of the promontory. But now the Head stood as an island, as the head of the fast disappearing reef, as the head of this very special Shade of the Old One, Tchamala. Willie waved to the watching halfcaste women, who waved back. Then everybody began to wave. Willy swung his launch southward to run along the beach.

Another heap of rocks guarded the sacred property of the Delacys on that side. Beyond it was another stretch of beach, a very long one. Near a creek they saw a number of canoes above high-water mark, and after a while several black figures, who evidently had been in hiding until able to make out who the newcomers were. More waving. Willy at his end, and George at his, explained that they were Koonyarrikin people, from back in the Paper-bark country. George told Prindy they were 'half-countrymen' of his. A lot of no-good loafers, according to Willy, who went on to explain to Alfie that this was the jumping-off place for blacks who liked to come and go between bush and town as it suited them, keeping clear of the Compound, having hide-outs of their own in the town area. 'Damn nuisance,' he said. Nevertheless, it was the Chinese community mostly who supported these illegal migrants and profited by their cheap labour and the favours of their women.

Coming to another creek, Willie swung into it, one very different from that out on the ocean beach, as revealed soon after entry, the sandy banks and varied maritime scrub giving way to walls of bluish mud backed by jungles of mangroves. They were here to hunt the giant mud crab, a sport known to most of them, since the creatures were to be found near the Compound, but of necessity, being so toothsome, rarely. Here they were in superabundance, according to those knowledgeable ones, Willie and George. They had sugar-sacks to dump them in as caught, kerosene-can buckets to cook them in, lengths of fencing wire for hooking them out of their holes.

Again Peg-leg and Willie stayed aboard, while the rest, stripped to drawers, except Alfie in her red bathing-togs, scrambled up the slippery southern bank; with the exception of King George and Prindy, who, to the disconcertment of Nell when she saw they had outwitted her, went off down the creek again in the dinghy, taking the cans and the food that was to go with the crabs, to make a dinner camp on the beach. They would come back to meet the others, who would work towards them in a direction arranged by George.

Catching the crabs was a simple if exciting business. All you had to do was to find one of the great cave-like holes in which they lived at low water, shove in the long hooked wire, waggle it about, and if anyone were at home, he or she invariably came out clinging to the wire, whereupon you dumped it in the sack, where usually it would release its grip on the wire, and tackled the stuff of the sack. The excitement lay in getting the creatures into the sack before they woke up to what was going on and tackled you. A nip from one of those terrible claws could mean loss of a toe or finger.

But the going was tough, in mud that would bog you till the tide came in and drowned you and left you for the crabs and crocodiles to finish off, unless you kept close to the mangroves, whose aim was to punish you for intrusion by tripping you up with masses of semi-aerial roots that seemed to reach out like skinny clutching hands. Not that anybody minded, not even the newchum Alfie, soon so mud-bespattered as to be indistinguishable from the rest.

Meanwhile, Prindy and George had fixed things for the dinner camp in a shady spot where the tiny black and red seeds of the jerquity bean, much used in decoration by coastal tribes, lay about in profusion. Prindy pounced on them to gather them, but was told by George to leave them for a while, because he wanted to take him somewhere to see something special. They made up a fire of driftwood, filled the buckets with sea water and set them to boil. Then they got back into the dinghy and went on southward along the shore for somewhat less than half a mile, where there was another creek like that they had left. They entered it, travelling swiftly on the flowing tide, through mangroves, to come soon to a rocky region, where the country rose steeply from the creek as ragged bush. George tied the boat to a tree well up the bank. Then rapidly he led the way up through the bush. It would be a climb of about three hundred feet, quite a height in that low region, in fact the highest prominence around the harbour, called the King's Table by the *kuttabah*, as George explained, adding with a giggle, 'Belong 'o me, eh?'

From the top they had a view of everything from the ocean back to the town. But it was in the opposite direction that George wanted Prindy to look, southwest, where above the horizon of a grey-green sea of trees could be seen a spot of violet. 'Dat-one Mooragetaghee . . . proper big hill,' said George, and repeated the name slowly: 'Moo-ra-get-a-ghee . . . mean porkypine, lingo dat country. Belong 'o Porkypine Dreamin'.'

'Country belong 'o you?'

'Half-country. My mumma from dat way. Dat country you gitchim wife from 'nother-one mob. My properly country lo-long way more far.' George lifted his projecting chin, still in the same direction, and sighed, in nostalgia so obvious that Prindy looked at him.

Prindy asked, 'When you go back country?'

George shook his head: 'I don' know, *Kokanjinni*.'

Evidently Prindy had heard, probably from the talkative Barney Bynoe, that George was forbidden to return home. He asked, 'Wha's matter you nomore go *tchinekin*?'

George looked at him: 'Might-be . . . by'n'by . . . you'n-me-two-feller, eh?' He laughed and rumpled the fair hair. Prindy nodded gravely. Then George said they must be getting back, because they must eat before the turn of the tide so that Willie could take them home on the ebb.

In no time they were down the hill, and rowing down the creek on the now slackening flood. Round and up the beach again, to find the water bubbling merrily in the cans, and to hear laughter in the bush behind. Then the muddy ladies burst out upon the beach with their bulging squirming sugar sacks. The smallest ones rushed to gather the bright seeds but were soon stopped by the others, saying they all must bathe first. George took the bags and shook out the contents of three of them into the seething cans, giving rise at each shaking to death-shrieks scarcely audible, except to one, whose brow knitted above his grey eyes, and who murmured, 'Poor bugger!'

The girls went racing to the sea, now close and swirling up the beach in silver loops. 'Look out shark!' they yelled, but plunged in as if unheeding. What a feed the sharks would have had if they'd known about it, with all those round brown bottoms and one white one bobbing about while their owners rung out their muddy bits of garments. But all were decently clad, at least to the navel, except the one in red who had hers covered, as they came up to feast. There, too, was Willy coming sailing up the beach, to drop anchor off shore, while George went out to him with the dinghy. Queeny came ashore this time, and showed that her alleged difficulty in getting about in sand was all what one would say with a blowing out of lips: *Burrup*!

Even the claw of a great mud crab makes a meal. But everybody ate at least one whole crab, and some more. The next thing was sleep. But there was no time for sleeping ashore, with the little quartz pebbles rolling backwards now and the hermit crabs popping out of the sand where they had hidden to avoid the buffeting. The kids grabbed up the abrus seeds by the handful to make into a double necklace as a prejent for her they now called, with unconscious appropriateness, Mitchis Elvy. Then out in the dinghy to the launch in several down-to-the gunnel batches. Old Tchamala's Shade, invisible this long while, was beginning to show again in sea-serpent-like humps.

This time they steered straight across the harbour, close enough to the leper island to wave to those who crowded the shore, and over some of whom, known to those aboard, some of the picnickers wept a little. Then most fell asleep as they swept down the harbour to the Compound.

Then ashore, and for the last time up through the scrub, saying goodbye to King George and Queeny Peg-leg, while they clicked their tongues for the pity of it, and Alfie blinked back her tears. Saying *mummuk*. No *yawarra*. Saying *mummuk* to everyone she passed, embracing and kissing the girls in the kitchen and giving them each a present of money she'd brought for the purpose, including the equivalent of that one month's salary in lieu of, for Nell. Saying goodbye to Tubby Turkney, who when he heard that Frank would be calling for her, said, 'Well, why can't we all go into the house and have a drink?' But there was no Mrs Turkney out to corroborate.

An hour or so in the schoolroom with the children tangling about her, fondling her, saying that they would soon have her necklace done and give it to Mrs Turkney to give to her, and when they grew up they'd ask if they might go out and work for her. She wept most of the while.

Then there was the old Rolls Royce honking up the road as if it were all a bit of fun. Turkney came running out, made a last plea for a last drink – but still no Mrs Turkney, at least not outside. Surely she saw her Tubby kissed Goodbye – *and the way he kissed the creature back*! Then they were gone, in a storm of weeping and honking: *mummuk* . . . *mummuk* . . . but no *yawarra*!

When Tubby Turkney went inside he grunted to his Vi, 'You might've asked her in.'

'What for?'

'To have a drink and a proper civilized goodbye.'

'If that was a civilized goodbye you gave her out in front of everybody, what'd it've been like when you'd filled yourself with booze?'

'Arrh!' He went into his bedroom, came out after a few minutes in whites, said shortly, 'I'm going down town.'

'To say goodbye again?'

'Arrrh!' He rushed down to his car.

End of pay period night meant a foregathering at the Queen Victoria, the *best* hotel, of all Junior Public Servants, except the very stuffiest, for a drink or two – or three or more. Seniors went to the Residency for cocktails. It was to the Queen Vic that Tubby Turkney went, there to join his immediate boss, Eddy McCusky, already somewhat molo, but under the watchful eye of his skinny wife. The subject of conversation was, naturally enough, mainly Alfie. And there, suddenly, Alfie was, on the arm of her husband, as on former occasions of the kind, both smiling easily and nodding to this one and that, but choosing a table to themselves on the back verandah. It rather cramped the general style. Tubby came over and had a round with them, then excused himself, since supposed to be on duty. No one else came. Junior Officers must be careful.

Then suddenly there was Eddy McCusky, breaking away from his wife as they were on their way out to go home, coming wobbling up to them, burbling 'Goo' on yo' . . . goo' on yo' both. You stoo' up to 'im, an' tol' 'im where t'ge'off. He needed it. He 'ad it comin' to 'im. It took you, Alfie . . . it took you. Now *all* their lousy mouths'll be shut up. I wan' 'o shake y'and. . . . '

While Eddy was shaking and reeling, Frank asked, 'What's this about shutting *all* their mouths?'

'Wha' they been sayin' 'bout the bloke keepin' Alfie on so's 'e can get 'o bed with 'er.'

'They said that?'

'They said that, brother. Bu' I . . . I nev' b'lieved it. I respec' you both too much. I'm Labor man meself. I'll sing yo' *Red Flag* . . . *So lif the shcarlet banner 'igh, 'neath 'sfol's live' die* . . . *though cowards cringe and traitors shneer, we'll keep the Red Flag flyin' 'ere* . . . .' The last was really beefed out, to be interrupted by a sharp female voice.

'Eddy!'

Eddy swung to meet his wife's thin face and blazing blue eyes: 'On'y sayin' goo'bye to me lil frien' Alfie . . . . '

'You're making a fool of yourself. Come here!'

Eddy swung back to the Candlemases with a beery sigh, blinked at Frank, asking, 'How'd yo' be, ol' feller, with a wife like that?'

Alfie, meeting the blue eyes blazing down the verandah, whispered, 'Better go. Come and see us.'

'Shertnly will . . . bu' gi' me a kiss before I go. You don' min' if I kiss your lovely lovely wife, Frank, ol' man?'

Frank smiled: 'It's entirely up to her.'

'What a lovely 'usban' you got, too, Alfie. Tha's what the lousy bastards been sayin' . . . *Franks's easy*. Yeah . . . he might be, I said . . . but Alfie ain't. Kiss me, Alfie.'

She leaned towards him, with lips protruded. He drank of them greedily, gripping the table for support. When she withdrew, he sighed in her face: 'That I'll never forget!' Then he wheeled about, went marching unsteadily to his spouse, who looked as if she never would forget it, either. She grabbed his arm.

As they vanished into the hall, Alfie murmured, 'Lousy bastards is right, isn't it!'

Frank smiled the easy smile: 'People are like that everywhere. They mostly don't really mean what they say.'

'Well let's get out of here, anyway. Let's go down to the Terminus, and talk to some lying old drovers or miners or fettlers or someone we can trust.'

CHAPTER SIX

ON THE SUNDAY NIGHT following Alfie Candlemas's dismissal from His Majesty's Service, she and her husband were sitting listening to a radio play about the famous Beau Brummel and his association with King George IV, which rather showed how unmajestic one called Sovereign Lord could be – when there was loud knocking at the door. Frank toned the set down and went to see. It was Fay McFee again, declaring in her brassy contralto that she supposed she ought to throw her hat in first, but didn't have one. 'Hats don't suit me,' she said, 'Except the tweedy sort . . . and I just hate to be taken for the tweedy sort, although I suppose I am. May I come in? I've brought a peace-offering that I'm sure you'll appreciate.'

What would have stopped her, short of a gang of strong-arm men?

She marched in, showing a carton, from which she drew a bottle of very high-class whisky. 'Smuggled,' she said, 'And all the better for being so.' When they only stared at her, she demanded, 'Well, do something . . . kick me out, or ask me to sit down.'

Frank looked at Alfie, then said, 'Sit down, by all means.'

Fay handed him the whisky, sank into a chair with a gusty sigh: 'Just dropped by to congratulate you . . . and ask what're your plans now?'

Frank said, 'I'm still with the enemy.' He got glasses.

'I know that. Scared I'll get you in bad with 'em?'

'Not a bit . . . now I know that *you too* get your whisky through the Chows.'

Fay guffawed, and raised the glass he'd poured for her: 'Well . . . congratulations. It was a famous victory.'

'Thanks,' said Alfie, taking a sip. 'But it did me out of a job I loved . . . and half the town's not speaking to me.'

'You should worry about that lousy half. How about sinking the rotten ship of state completely by giving me the story in full?'

Again they stared at her. She went on: 'I know all about it, of course. Turkney spilt the beans first that night. Then Fergus Ferris and I paid that promised visit to the Compound this morning. We had the great good misfortune to have a forced landing on the beach there, with what you might call engine trouble. Nice beach to land on, that, at low tide. Fergus had taken me on a flight round the harbour, supposed to be taking photographs for the Garrison people. We even had a couple of officers aboard, friends of Fergus's. It was they we sent up to tell Tubby Turkney and call a mechanic from the aerodrome . . . while *we* did a bit more photography on the ground, as well as a bit of what you might call scientific survey work with my dictaphone. Poor old Tubby was too hung-over and generally confused with militarism and aeronautical bullshit from Fergus to suspect anything. The only thing he didn't like was the sight of me talking to Queeny Peg-leg . . . and he told me either to get off the Reserve, under his escort, or back to the aeroplane, or he'd call the police. I said first that I'd go under escort, to give Fergus time to get the cameras and dicto back into his plane. Then up at the gate I used what they call a woman privilege and changed my mind, which gave Fergus still more time while Tubby argued with me. Anyway, we have the photos we want of the dirty old dump they thought they were going to destroy without evidence of its existence, plus *viva voce* interviews with people who thought Alfie the most wonderful person who'd ever worked for them, and who also saw Dr Cobbity come down to the beach and bully her till she cried . . . two days before he sacked her. But before that we did an aerial survey of the town, to show the comparison with the hovels of the Compound . . . especially Cobbity's big house, and the Delacy places, and Vic Shane's. We were lucky to find Shane out in his schooner with the mob . . . including Cobbity. We buzzed 'em. They thought it fun. We got beaut pictures. All I want now, to sink this stinking ship, as I said, with all hands, is Alfie's story. How about it?'

The Candlemases exchanged quick glances. Alfie looked back to ask, 'What story?'

'The whole of your experience with them.'

'With whom?'

'Cobbity and Co., of course . . . and all the rest of 'em.'

'Actually they treated me very well . . . especially Dr Cobbity.'

Fay bared her teeth: 'Come off it! What about the court case? What about the Oath business? What about how he treated you over, first, Lucy Snowball, and then Jumbo Delacy? It's because you dared ask him to act with compassion to poor helpless people that he set you . . . and sacked you. He's an arrogant dog.''

Alfie, with cheeks flushing, said, 'He introduced the only reforms there've ever been made. He's got himself hated by everybody.'

Fay sneered: 'Don't tell me you had a crush on him, too, like he had on you . . . .'

Frank cut in: 'If you want to stay, Miss McFee . . . you'll have to behave.'

She swung on him: 'Don't tell me you don't know what the mob's been saying about why Cobbity took her on.'

Alfie answered sharply, 'We know . . . and it isn't true. He was nice to me . . . just like everybody else. He made no advances to me . . . '

Fay bared her teeth: 'He only kicked you out because you dared to do your job properly, eh?'

'Well . . . that's Government Service, isn't it? I had no right to try to make bargains with someone who was my superior officer.'

Fay downed a full glass of whisky, then yelled, 'Good Christ . . . what's got into you? I repeat that you uncovered several instances of callous bureaucratic treatment of poor simple people and made an approach to the man on their behalf . . . and what happened?'

Flushed and shiny-eyed though Alfie was, she looked more scary-angry than genuinely irate. She said somewhat breathlessly, 'When I asked for the improvement in the matter of the food he did it readily enough . . . . '

'Because he couldn't have done otherwise. The food would have been officially condemned . . . and him with it. There was no one to gainsay him in the matter of Lucy Snowball or Jumbo Delacy . . . so what did he do?'

Alfie blinked. Fay answered for her: 'He started off by telling you to mind your own bloody business . . . and when you wouldn't, he sacked you. That's the plain truth of it. Listen . . . . ' Fay leaned forward with finger outstretched: 'You gave me to understand that you were going to *fight* these people. You gave Lucy Snowball the promise that you'd fight to get her to her husband . . . yes, I know that Fate intervened there . . . but you also promised Possum Delacy to fight to the last ditch to get Jumbo released . . . don't deny it, because she told me. And what are you doing?'

Frank spoke up again: 'Now, Miss McFee.'

Without looking at him, she waved him away, saying, 'Fay's the name to you, brother . . . and this girl can look after herself.' She raised her big finger again to Alfie: 'You're in this, sister. You started it. I'm running the story with you as the centre of it. You're in it at least up to the middle . . . so you might as well be in it up to the neck.'

Alfie panted, 'There's such a thing as libel.'

'As if I didn't know . . . and learnt to beat it every time.'

Frank cut in: 'The greater the truth, the greater the libel, don't they say?'

Still without looking at him, Fay answered, 'The first consideration in law is truth uttered for the public good. If this isn't telling the truth for the public good . . . tell me what is?' She swung on Frank now.

He shrugged. She demanded, 'Are you afraid of losing *your* job by being mixed up with me?'

'No.'

'You have no need to be. We'll get you another job.'

'Who's we?'

'Trades and Labour . . . the *Progressive* . . . unless, of course,' she bared her teeth, 'You wouldn't like working with the likes of us!'

He only smiled that easy smile.

She swung back to Alfie: 'I've got a job for you whenever you want it?'

'What?' asked Alfie.

'We're losing a proof-reader off the paper. Soon teach you the job if you don't know it. Want it?'

Alfie smiled weakly: 'This a kind of bargain?'

'We don't make bargains in our turn-out.'

Alfie flamed: 'Is that a crack at me for trying to bargain with Dr Cobbity?'

'Not a bit of it. You did the only thing you could do . . . for a humane purpose. It was wonderful of you. That's why I want your story as told by yourself. You won't even have to write it. You can talk it onto the dicto. Start off saying: "One day Dr Cobbity came to me . . . or sent for me . . . and asked me would I take over the teaching at the Compound School. I went there and found that what the children needed before the ABC was food. What they were eating was hogwash . . . et cetera" . . . right through to where you offered to forego your principles to save an unfortunate man who you believed was being put into a lunatic asylum to save the faces of snobs . . . . '

'That'd land *her* for libel for a certainty,' said Frank.

'I told you I have the recorded evidence of a witness . . . Queeny Peg-leg.

She heard it all . . . and is a pretty smart piece. Besides, this would all go through the expert hands of *Truth*'s legal advisers first . . . .'

'*Truth*?' cried Alfie.

'Making a national issue of it . . . and *Truth*'s the national paper. *Truth*'s fought and won that many libels that only those who have an exhibitionist complex dare take 'em to court any more.'

'It hasn't got a very savoury reputation," Frank remarked.

'But it has a vast circulation,' said Fay, 'and with all the sex and the rest of it, has effected more reform in this country than any other institution that's ever been in it. Speaking of savoury reputations, I don't have one either . . . in the opinion of your Government Service mates. But I don't stink in their nostrils one half as much as they do in mine . . . and as they will in the noses of the whole nation, when this gets out.' Fay swung on Alfie: 'Well, girl . . . are you for us or agin us?'

Alfie swallowed. Fay added, 'Because you're *in* with us . . . whether you like it or not.'

Alfie looked at Frank, who caressed her with his eyes and smiled. Then she said to Fay, 'I'd rather do it myself.'

'What d'you mean by that?'

'As a matter of fact *I hadn't* given up . . . about Jumbo, I mean. I was going to have another go at Dr Cobbity . . . .'

'If he wouldn't listen to you the first time and went and sacked you after it, what chance'd you have again?'

'I've got another shot in my locker.'

'What's that supposed to mean?'

'I happen to know something else that might make him change his mind.'

'Like what?'

'I'm not going to tell you that.'

'Why . . . did you have a love affair with him after all, then?'

Alfie flamed: 'No . . . I didn't!'

Undaunted, Fay said, 'I'm glad of that, because *that* would be libel. Why can't you tell me?'

'Because I'm thinking of Jumbo first. That's my job . . . what I promised . . . to get Jumbo released.'

'And you reckon you've got something up your sleeve that'll make him?'

'Yes,' said Alfie. Now Frank was looking at Alfie wide-eyed.

'Then why haven't you done it?' demanded Fay.

'I've been thinking about it.'

'You'll have to think quick, sister. I'm getting this off for next Sunday's *Truth*. Jumbo'll be a national martyr this time next week.'

Alfie went very red, took a big swig of her whisky and ginger ale, with which she had been going very easy. She said, 'I'll tell Dr Cobbity what you're doing.'

Fay stared at her. Then she bared her teeth in a sneer: 'Won't make the slightest bit of difference . . . only make him shit himself for a week waiting for it.'

Still red, and breathless again, Alfie said, 'If he agrees to what I ask, I'll repudiate all you say about me.'

Now Fay flamed. But she had control of herself, and soon bared the teeth again: 'You can't. What I'll be saying will be known facts about you.'

'I'll stick up for him. I'll tell the other papers that I think he's tried hard to do a good job, but has been prevented.'

'Like he tried hard to let Lucy Snowball go to her husband . . . and she went to the sharks instead!'

Alfie was silent, flushed, blinking, a tremor on her lovely lips.

Fay regarded her for a moment, then said, 'You must have something pretty good to chuck at him. Still, it won't do you any good . . . even if you score a bull's-eye . . . because I've got enough on him to sink him.'

'Why do you want to sink him? He's tried.'

'He's an arrogant bureaucrat. He's definitely *not* the man to be in charge of the new deal that had to be handed out to the Aborigines. He's a doctor. He's thinking in terms of medicine. He wants the old Compound site first for a new hospital for whites. Next he wants a place where he can practise medical eugenics on the blacks. He's a scientist, if you like. But what is wanted for this job before all else is a humanitarian, someone who'll weep over these people in their dreadful state, someone who won't be able to sleep at night till he's seen this wicked destruction of a race of people stopped. That man of yours isn't even human. Blacks and halfcastes bolt when they see him. I have it in the simple words of Queeny and that old King George what happened when he came down to you on the beach that day. And that's the man you'd have to be the Big Boss of what the likes of myself have fought to get for him, while he's hated us . . . what he couldn't get for himself because he wanted mostly to be boss.'

Alfie drooped her head.

Fay waited a while, then demanded, 'Well?'

Alfie looked up: 'I want to do it my own way. I don't want to be charged with being treacherous, or vindictive. I promised first for Jumbo. I'll ring him up . . . and tell him what I have to say . . . and what you're going to do. I'll try to make another bargain with him.'

'When are you going to ring him?'

'I'll ring him first thing tomorrow morning.'

'Will you ring me to tell me the result?'

Alfie hesitated, looked at Frank, who only looked back intently. Then she answered, 'Yes.'

'Okay,' said Fay, proceeding to heave herself up. 'I guess I'm hardly wanted now. So, till tomorrow. No, Frank . . . keep the whisky. Give her a good slug of it to drown that bloomin' conscience she's got about someone who never had any. Goodnight!'

Fay got into her tinny little car and drove into the centre of town and round the back of the Hotel Queen Victoria, which was closed. She went in through the yard, headed for a lighted parlour, where men were laughing loudly. She stopped in the doorway for a moment before being seen. Fergus Ferris was telling some yarn that had half a dozen men sitting with drinks about him very tickled. Then someone saw her and shut up. They all looked and were silent, some scowling. She bared her teeth at them, saying, 'Sorry to intrude, *gentlemen*!' There was no doubting the contempt in the stressed appellative. She looked at Fergus: 'Urgent business.' When he rumpled his brows with annoyance, she snapped, 'Are you working with me . . . or aren't you?'

He bit the fair harelip, then answered briskly, 'Yessir.' He rose, and excused himself to the others, adding, 'Duty and beauty calls!' The response was a general snigger.

She got her revenge as he joined her, saying to him loudly, 'Clowning for drinks, eh? Sparrin', they call it, don't they . . . what broken-down boxers do. But you'll find this mob of louts are as broke as you when it comes to paying the bill.'

The lip cocked in a grin: 'You win, Boss.'

Fergus was now on his own, his master, Fabian Cootes, having returned to the South and the cloisters where he pontificated about primitive man amongst ten thousand artifacts and scores of grinning skulls stolen from their sacred places. Jeremy was back at Lily Lagoons. Fergus was battling for a living with his borrowed German aeroplane, and evidently doing a bit of espionage on the side for Fay. Without showing any more respect for him than for a dog at heel, she led him to her car, got into it, started up, and driving off, said to him, 'I couldn't get her to come in. She wants to talk to Cobbity first . . . try him again on the Jumbo business . . . another bargain.'

'Throwing herself in this time, too, eh?'

'Don't be funny. She isn't like that.'

'How do you know? You said you reckoned she had a bit of a crush on him.'

'I know women better than you . . . and don't try and be funny about that, or you can get to hell.'

'Yessir. What d'you want me to do . . . work on her?'

'I don't know. From what she said, she's got something on him . . . and it's not sexual. She knows something. We've got to find out what it is. I tried bluffing her by saying we could run the story without her co-operation. She appeared to believe it. We could, of course . . . but it wouldn't be worth two bob. Besides . . . I doubt if *Truth* would be in it without her. They'd reckon *she* could bring action. Her appointment, discoveries and reforms, and then dismissal, is what makes it. She has to be the centre of it. She sort of agreed to come in if he refused her next bit of bargaining. But I doubt it. Besides, he's sure to bluff her, whatever it is.'

They reached her home. Next door was in darkness. Miss Windeyer would be at religious instruction with her Monsignor Maryzic, following her organ-playing for Vespers. They went in. Fay produced a bottle of whisky, with the injunction to go easy with it, because she wanted him to use his wits. 'Now, if only I had tits instead of wits,' he said, 'I might work on Cuthbert himself . . . .'

She snapped, 'Shut up!'

After a while she said, 'She's going to phone him first thing tomorrow, she said. If we can get in on that phone call, and it's something really nifty she's got on him . . . then we're set.'

'Well, tap the phone.'

'How?'

'Hell . . . every newspaper's got a phone-tapping system . . . don't tell me the mighty *Palmeston Progressive* only listens at keyholes!'

'This's very different from down in the cities, where people can get in and out of places without being noticed. We've planted our dictaphone more than once, I can tell you. But the trouble with phones is getting into places. I can get the mechanic, all right. But is Cobbity going to let him into his office on some pretext of fixing the phone? Are the Candlemases going to let him look 'em up just tomorrow morning? Do you know any way? You say you were in the racing game . . . that's *all* phone-tapping, isn't it?

'It's done through exchanges. Anyway, I was an apprentice jockey, not a telephone mechanic. What about your own exchange . . . the Post Office? Didn't you say the dame next door works there?'

'You won't get anything out of her. For a start we don't speak. And that's how the trouble between us started. I tried to get her to let us record a talk between two big shots over a snide deal they worked to sell the land now used as the Aerodrome to the Department of Civil Aviation. I'd've had 'em on toast if she had. But her bloody conscience wouldn't let her.'

'What about other telephonists?'

'There're only four altogether, one working at a time. The others are Government Officers' daughters. They all hate me.'

'It's that endearing way you have . . . . '

'Shut up! We've got to get this done somehow.'

'Want me to work on the female next door?'

'This's got to be done before nine tomorrow morning.'

'I'm a fast worker . . . '

'You're a conceited ass! I brought you here because I thought, with your smart-alecry and your racing experience you'd see a way. Don't forget, the money you get depends on what's got from the story. At the moment it looks like nil.'

Fergus stroked his fair moustache, after a moment asked, 'No harm in trying the lady next door. Could promise her a flight. Where's she now?' Fay explained, with frank contempt.

Fergus said, 'I want to meet old Maryzic myself. Want to try to get some charter work from their missions.'

Fay had a swig of whisky, grunted, 'Bugger your charters! I want this story.'

Suddenly he looked excited, tossed off his drink, said, 'Listen . . . Maryzic hates Cobbity and Co., doesn't he?'

'The boot's on the other foot, more likely. He's been a great critic of 'em. He's been more or less retired by the Church for picking at 'em.'

'Well, he's going to be glad about what we did today, eh? About the thing for *Truth*, eh?'

'I suppose so. But what's that got to do with the bloody phone-tapping?'

'Everything . . . if my hunch's correct. I haven't met him. The Coot kept me away from him . . . at least he didn't take me with him when he went to see him, because the old boy had been poking borak at him about anthropology, and he thought, I suppose, that I'd make it worse. I want to meet him for business. You take me round to introduce me . . . .'

'He won't have a bar of me!'

'Why?'

'Because I attack the Church. I wrote an attack on it as the agency of Fascism only a few weeks back . . . just after Easter.'

'What'd he do?'

'Nothing.'

'Well, what the hell? Maybe he believes you're right. There's plenty of Catholic clergy against it. They're persecuting 'em in Germany. Doesn't he speak to you?'

'Only sarcastically.'

'Can't you take it?'

'Why should I?'

'For the cause, gal, the cause.'

'What cause? You don't share any of my causes. You're a bloody Fascist yourself!'

Fergus shot his hand up in the Fascist salute, crying, 'Heil . . . *Viva da Musso*!' When she showed her teeth at him, he went on eagerly: 'I'm talking about *our* cause, sweetheart . . . this *Truth* thing. You take me round to the old boy in all humility . . . .'

'Me humble myself to that old tyrant?'

'Like I was saying . . . in all proper humility of one tyrant to another . . . you've got nice teeth, you know, but you don't show 'em to advantage with the way you smile . . . like this's the way. Now, you go round there smiling nicely. You introduce us. We tell him about what we did at the Compound today and why we did it. If he's what I've heard he is, he'll be delighted . . . . '

'And he'll get someone to tap the telephone for us tomorrow!' Fay said it with heavy sarcasm. Then her eyes popped, and she cried, 'Hey . . . I've got it!'

'Exactly! We've got to catch 'em together, your coy telephonist and him. We've got to talk the ethics of telephone-tapping to down tyrants, to overthrow bureaucracy, to smash an evil system . . . *Viva il Papa*!'

Her hairy face was flushed, her grey eyes popping, with excitement; but she had to bare those teeth and say, 'You'll come at anything, won't you!'

'That makes two of us, sweetheart. Now, we've got to move, so's to get your girlfriend with him . . . and you've got to be nice to her . . . introduce her to me, and I'll promise her a flight, promise to go to bed with her, if you like. Yes . . . I have it. You bring up that matter of why you fell out. Yes . . . yes . . . that's it! You discuss the ethics of *that* . . . not of this job. If he supports betrayal of the confessional by the Hello-girls when they hear evil things, then we've got this Windy Kitty of yours . . . eh?'

They perfected their planning rapidly while they drove round to the Catholic Church, stopping en route, as part of the plan, at the Queen Vic, to pick up a bottle of first-class whisky. The Church itself was dark, save for the red eye of God winking from the altar. Next door was the lighted Presbytery, from which came the sound of male laughter and the clink of glass. They went to a building on the other side, down a gravel pathway, a rambling old place as seen by the bit of moonlight shining through the big fig and mango trees, originally the Convent, but since the new one had been built on the main road beside the Church, serving now as a town centre for the Church's mission people and a portion of it as quarters for Monsignor Maryzic. There was only one light to be seen, spilling onto a side verandah. Fay led the way thither.

A glimpse through the wide-open double glass doors of a huge high chamber built in the old style. On a cane lounge, protuberant of belly, cassock-clad, a red-edged biretta propped up on one of the top corner pieces of the lounge, feet in Japanese sandals, lay a massive figure, face brown and seamed and broad in the Slavic way, with a whisp of white hair, head clasped in hands as he lay back on a cushion. At a barish desk near by sat Kitty Windeyer, taking notes out of a book. Both looked out at sounds of steps on the verandah. Monsignor Maryzic called, 'Who isht zere?'

Fay, looking rather red, showed herself in the doorway. The old priest stared at her in surprise. Kitty looked alarmed. Breathlessly, Fay said, 'Hope I'm not intruding . . . just brought a young man round to meet you, Monsignor . . . Mr Fergus Ferris . . . he's an aviator . . . and . . . and . . . .'

'Anthropologist,' the old man finished. Fergus had shoved into the doorway, with split lip twisted in a grin. 'How do you do, young man.' The Monsignor heaved his huge body up from the lounge. 'I haf heard about you. Vot vood you be vontingk mit me?' Hard slatey blue eyes were fixed on Fergus, who reddened under them.

Fergus said, 'Well . . . it's about getting some flying to do for your missions, Your Excellency.'

'I am not Excellency, my son . . . Fader vill do. Come in.'

Kitty, gathering up her things, said hastily, 'I'll go, Father.'

Fay said as quickly, 'Oh, no, Kitty . . . don't let us intrude.'

Kitty stared at her.

Maryzic now looked at Fay for the first time: 'You knew she vos here . . . vy are you concerned not to intrude?'

Fay went crimson: 'I thought she may have left by now, Monsignor.'

'But vy should you come at all?'

'I told you . . . to bring Mr Ferris.'

'Has a man who can fly across der Continent mitout seeink der ground, I presume, got to be led across zis little town to find der most prominent place in it, der Church?'

Fergus cut in: 'To tell you the truth, Father, I was scared to come on my own.'

'Scared?'

'Well . . . you did appear to be something of a *bête noire* to my colleague, Dr Cootes.'

The broad face split in a grin; and the fat belly began to shake. The old man laughed heartily: 'Ha, ha, ha! Der learned doctor . . . Ho, ho, ho!'

Fergus echoed him: 'Ha, ha, ha!'

Maryzic stopped laughing suddenly to glare and demand, 'Vell, vot has brought you?'

Fergus produced the bottle of whisky: 'A little gift, Father.'

The old man waved to a side table: 'Put it zere.' And as Fergus came back from doing so, he added, 'Bevare der Greek who comes mit gift.'

Fergus smiled that split-lip smile, attractive in its being at once insolent and pathetic: 'I am not a Greek, Your Reverence.'

'But you are a sly fellow, I can see. Sit down . . . both of you. I am very glad to haf you. I vont to say a vord or two to your female accomplice mit regard to false statements made by her in jealous rage over der loss to der Church of somevun she vonted to dominate herself. Attack on der Church herself can be forgifen. Der Church isht human. Zat is ze greatness of der Catholic Church. She isht composed of peoples who know zere frailty and confess it . . . from Pope to peasant . . . but keep on beingk frail because zey are human. Zere isht no institution in der vorld so human zan der Catholic Church. Zere are no people in der vorld of simple frail human beingks so happy as Catholics. Ven you, Fay McFee, still told your beads and vore your Veil of Mary, you vere a lot happier zan since you haf taken to followingk der Red Banner of vot isht claimed as Rationalism . . . as if any human beingk can be rational zis side of der grave! I say zat attack on der Church herself for her own sake isht forgivable easily . . . but not not ven it is borne of personal spite, as vos yours last Easter.'

Fay's face was purplish, her bosom heaving.

The booming voice went on, getting louder: 'Your friend found joy in our organ. You've denied her der joy of your piano. Because she isht generous, she vonted to pay by converting. She need not haf. But she had glimpsed der beauty of zis human zing you yourself vos born into as your heritage and turned your back on because it deprived you of personal power, demanded humility of you. So she haf found another joy . . . vile all you find is some-zingk to make yourself a nuisance about so as to attract attention to yourself.' The voice suddenly dropped: 'All right . . . I haf vot I vont. Now tell me vot *you* vont?'

Fay looked capable only of rushing at him and throttling him or of bursting into tears and fleeing. Fergus, with his eye on her, took over: 'Father . . . did you hear that we had a forced landing on the Compound beach this morning?'

'I hear of most zings zat happen in zis little town, my boy. Vot has it to do mit me?'

Fergus started from the point of effecting the ruse to photograph the squalor of the Compound before it could be hidden for ever by those who had created and perpetuated it. The old man smiled with satisfaction. Fergus went on to tell the whole thing. Only once did the priest interrupt his early part of the story, when he said, 'Are you doink this for der Aborigines, my son?'

'No, father. I know it stinks, the whole thing. But the truth is I'm in it for what I'm being paid.'

'Goot . . . proceed! No . . . first open der bottle. Zere are glasses in der cupboard . . . and vater outside if you vont it. No, you get it, my dear,' Maryzic added to Kitty.

When it came to the need for phone-tapping the old man laughed again: 'Ha, ha, ha, ha, ho!'

He kept them waiting while he took a long drink. Then he said, 'You led up to zis mit reference to der confidence of der confessional. Zere is no rule or law concerningk such confidence. It is a matter for der conscience of der priest. If evil haf been done zat must be undone or paid for, it isht der duty of der priest to see to it, even if he haf to betray his trust. He isht not zere to protect der conscience of der evil-doer, but to encourage der confession of evil and der condemnation of it. I vill say zat Miss Vindeyer here, ven she refused to divulge to Miss McFee vot she chanced to hear of zat zing about der aerodrome did right . . . but *not* in keepingk it to herself just because of a rule made by der Post Office to discourage tattlingk about ozer people's business. Der proper protection of der public who use der telephone is der law. If people are silly enough to tattle zomezingk zat vill be tattled about, it isht zere own fault. Zere isht no sin called tattlingk. Zere isht no sin in eavesdroppink. Zere is sin only in bearingk valse vitness against zy neighbour. I am interested in zis story of Mrs Candlemas. I haf heard a lot about der lady. I vood like to see zis vicious bureaucracy broken. I vill concede that Fay McFee is der person to do der job, newspaper publicity beink vot it lamentably isht in zese days. I am villingk to say zat a goot zing vill be done if some ozer bureaucratical evil of Dr Cobbity's is uncovered by tappingk his telephone. Zere is no law against eavesdroppingk of any kind, only against trespassing for ozer purposes. But der matter must be left to the conscience of Miss Kitty. She must be left der night to deal vis der matter. Zen, if she decide to comply mit your request to haf der svitchingk of her board arranged so zat a recordingk can be made of der conversation, I vood advise her *not* to permit der switchingk to der office of der *Progressive*, but to me here. I haf a telephone in anozer room. I vill be der eavesdropper, truly in ze name of ze betterment of ze Aborigines. If I consider zat purpose served, I vill advise Miss Kitty to zat effect. Does zat satisfy everybody? Goot! Zen let us drink to its success.'

It was at five-thirty next morning that Kitty Windeyer knocked on the nailed-up door, and rousing Fay McFee, told her she'd decided to do as she asked. Fay asked her in to have a cup of tea. Then in the ruddy dawn, Fay drove round to the home of Mossie Makins, PMG mechanic, and after having some difficulty in waking him from boozy slumber explained her need. He agreed readily enough, evidently more for mercenary reasons than political ones, since he haggled over the fee.

Kitty went into the Exchange to relieve the night-shift girl at seven, looking so distraught that the other remarked on it, and when Kitty said she'd only had a bad night, offered to get one of the other girls for her. Kitty was made more distraught by the girl's hanging about talking. Then the girl was gone; and Mossie came in and got behind the switchboard, soon to emerge to say cheerfully, 'She's sweet,' while Kitty in her earphones hung her burning face.

There were a couple of calls to the aerodrome concerning the flight of the mail-plane later in the day, and one from the Hospital for Dr McQuegg – then suddenly, just after eight, there was the Candlemas' indicator blinking. Kitty plugged in, panting, 'Number please?' It was Alfie, asking for the number of Dr Cobbity's residence. Kitty reached automatically for the plug, almost pulled it, then looked at the clock above the board, then wildly at the board itself. A moment. Then she gasped, 'Hold the line, please.' Her right hand flew to another plug, her left to the magneto handle. She cranked madly. Fay's voice answered. When she heard the gasped news she told Kitty to check with the Monsignor, but that she thought everything would be in order, because she'd told Mossie the call could be made privately. Kitty gave another breathless *hold the line* to Alfie, checked, heard His Very Reverence say, 'She sveet.' Then with a sigh she plugged in the Cobbity residence, cranked her little handle, – heard a female voice, said to Alfie, 'You are through.'

It was Mrs Cobbity, who began by being nasty, saying that Alfie had no business ringing the doctor at his private house and indeed no business to be ringing him at all, since she had been dismissed from the Service. She was interrupted in the middle of a sentence. A male voice, somewhat hoarse, came in: 'Yes . . . what is it?'

'It's me,' said Alfie.

Cobbity was silent for a moment, then asked, 'What would you be wanting?'

'Just a word with you.'

'I can't get you your job back, if that's what it is.'

'It isn't . . . it's another bargain.'

'I don't make bargains. You ought to know that.'

She was silent so long that he asked, 'Well . . . does that settle the matter?'

Alfie came out with it breathlessly: 'No . . . it doesn't.'

'Well, don't make it too long . . I have to shave.'

'Right. I'm being asked by newspaper people to give my story of everything I saw while at the Compound . . . everything that was done to me . . . .'

'Fay McFee.'

'I understand it'll be a much bigger thing than just something in the *Progressive*.'

'And you're going to tell how you took over an institution already condemned by the Administration and about to be replaced in a matter of weeks, and proceeded to reform it by sitting on the beach all day, and got dismissed for refusing to comply with simple Public Service regulations . . . eh?'

'I didn't want to tell anything. I wanted to save you from having everything you've said you've worked for for years taken from you.'

'That was kind of you. But the kindness's is misplaced. I've got along pretty well all these years without you, and guess I'll continue to do so. In fact, things've only got messed up since I was silly enough to get mixed up with you.'

She was silent again, till he said, 'Well?'

She cleared her throat: 'What you say you've done pretty well all these years is now on photographic record for publishing to the Nation. They did an aerial and ground survey yesterday. They landed at the Compound.'

Now it was he who was silent. Then he said, 'Anyone who was on the Compound reserve without my permission will be prosecuted. I'll see to that as soon as I get into the office.'

'I guess they'd rather like that as further evidence of the whole crux of the matter.'

'Which is?'

'I've told you before . . . your own official arrogance.'

He drew a deep breath exhaled it in a word: 'Madam!'

She went on, somewhat breathless again: 'It's that that'll bring you down. It's that I wanted to make sure of. And your callousness . . . .'

'Would you mind letting me get to the bathroom?'

'It's the callousness they want me to speak of . . . about Lucy Snowball and Jumbo Delacy . . . . '

'I don't want to be rude and ring off in your ear, Madam . . . '

'I happen to know that it was through you that Captain Shane was able to hold his tide-flats and turn them into valuable property, while poor Jumbo Delacy, whom you've declared insane, is having his, the only thing he thought he owned in the world, and under your protection by the law, taken over by the Shell Oil Company.'

He was silent again.

She went on: 'Captain Shane told me all about it . . . how you overheard what the Imperial Brass Hats were going to do, while you were supposed to be an Officer of the Garrison, and you tipped him off. He told me that night of the Anzac Day party. He was bragging about his cleverness. That was the first shock I got about you. I trusted you up till then. I believed you when you said you were trying to do something for the Aborigines but had been prevented. When I heard that you were going to declare Jumbo insane because he made that scene at the Coronation Levee that embarrassed the rich relations who treated him like a blackfellow . . . . '

He cut in: 'Would you come up to my office and make these allegations in front of witnesses?'

'Gladly . . . provided I've got someone to see that you and Dr McQuegg don't declare me insane!'

'We might find ground for that, too . . . the way you're behaving.'

'It must be very convenient to be able to declare someone insane who's a nuisance to you and have them put away.'

'Madam . . . I'm going to ring off. I'll be seeing you in court.'

'That'll be fun . . . because *Truth's* lawyers are noted for their cross-examinations of people who try suing them for libel. I'd like to hear them beating the arrogance and callousness and conceit out of you . . . Goodbye, Doctor . . . I've learnt a lot about Australian Bureaucracy since meeting you. I wouldn't have believed it . . . Goodbye!'

Alfie sank down into a chair beneath the wall telephone and stared at staring Frank. Her lips were quivering. She tried to smile, muttering, 'Same old arrogance . . . oh, ah!' She dropped head to an arm. Frank leapt to soothe her.

Down at Cobbity's the doctor was standing by his telephone, staring out across the harbour at Old Tchamala's Shade rising from the jade sea, but very evidently seeing nothing of it. So for several minutes. Then he swung to the telephone, cranked, snapped at Kitty's breathless acknowledgement, 'Get me Captain Shane . . . his residence.'

Shane was a long while coming, and none too pleasant even when he learnt who it was: 'For christ sake, man . . . I've got the world's worst bloody hangover, and you got to drag me out of bed this hour! Send me over something to put me right. What is it, anyway, what is it?'

'I want to see you about something right away.'

'Nobody's seein' me about nothin' all this day . . . or I'll shoot 'em!'

'Listen, Vic . . . this's serious . . . . '

'I'm dead serious, too. I think the ol' liver's goin' on me. I never felt so sick before . . . . '

'Listen, you bloody fool!'

'Who you callin' a fool?'

'You . . . with your big mouth. You've started something, with your bragging and magging . . . . '

'Here . . . mind what you're saying, Cobbity . . . . '

'I want you over here, I said . . . right now. It's urgent.'

'Then tell me what it is.'

'Not over the phone.'

'S'like that, eh? Wife left you? Ha, ha, ha! Come over here'n tell me . . . an' we'll shelebrate some more.'

'Listen, you bloody old fool . . . *Truth*'s onto the Oil Tank site business. Now . . . get your pants on and get right over here . . . to my residence.'

'Truth . . . Truth . . . you mean newspaper *Truth*?'

'I'm not saying any more . . . *except get over here at once*!' The last of it was shouted.

Skinny, unhappy-looking Mrs Cobbity spoke to her husband as he left the phone: 'Something wrong, dear?'

He snapped, 'Nothing!'

'It's that woman. I knew she'd cause trouble.'

'Aw, shut up!'

'Why don't you give up this horrible job . . . and be a proper doctor again. You've been in nothing but trouble ever since you took it. You're not an administrator . . . you're a doctor . . . .'

'Didn't I tell you to shut up?' Cobbity marched through from the hall to the dining-room, took a whisky bottle from the sideboard, poured a stiff drink.

Alfie had just seen Frank off to work at eight-thirty, he with the laughing remark that he should be home again within the hour and for good, she saying that she would ring Fay after nine – when there was Fay hammering at her door again, and not alone, but, to Alfie's evident surprise, with a fat old clergyman wearing grubby tussore silk and a grubbier panama hat. Fay said hastily, 'Monsignor Maryzic, Alfie . . . Mrs Candlemas, Your Reverence. Can we come in, Alfie . . . it's urgent . . . about the *Truth* business . . . you're alone?'

Alfie let them in, eyeing the odd-looking cedar box that Fay was carrying. Quickly Fay explained what was going on, asked a question or two about the Oil Tanks business, remarking that it was wonderful to have Cobbity tied in with Shane and this on top of all the rest, said, 'Monsignor here's known old Shane for more years than he cares to remember, and's convinced that he'll come here from Cobbity and try either to bluff you into saying something silly or bribe you to shut up. He's seen him in action. He's had trouble with him over his pearling crews' stealing black women from his missions . . . bluff or buy . . . that's old Vic Shane. Now, we've got here a dictaphone, with microphone attached. We'll plant the mike in here, and the dicto somewhere it can't be heard working. Also, if you'll let His Reverence hide somewhere. Doesn't matter if he hears anything, because the dicto'll do all that. But he thinks it'd be a good idea for him to show himself at the end of it. That'd sink Shane if he's made anything like an admission. What I mean is if there were any court action. Monsignor Maryzic is a man of great standing . . . and Shane as crooked as they come. See what I mean? We don't want court action. The less chance there is of it, the more of the truth we can tell. Now, I leave it to you two. I'll duck out the back, in case he may be coming. I left my car round the corner. Right?' Fay didn't wait for answer.

Monsignor Maryzic chuckled, 'How zat voman keeps zat condition and yet rushes about as she does isht to me a mystery.'

Alfie eyed him shyly, while he was smilingly bold in his appraisal of her. He said, 'I can joost zee zat silly old man givink avay his secrets to impress a pretty young voman like you. But ve moost make der preparations. Vere der microphone? Vere vill he sit or stand, or votever? Can you manouvre him into position? Are you anyzing of an actress, mein dear?'

'I'm afraid not, Your Reverence,' she said. 'I'm scared.'

'All der better. It vill look more natural . . . and he'll be less on guard. Let us put der mike behind zis cane lounge, yes? Fortunately he isht a loud-mout'ed man. Now you vill show me a place to hide der mechanical eaves-dropper, and meinself, der common-or-garden human type?'

They chose the bedroom, with the wardrobe for the dictaphone and the adjacent corner, screened by the furled mosquito net of the bed, for himself. If and when the Captain came, he would start the machine, close the door on it, and get out of sight. They were still in the bedroom, the old man asking Alfie about herself, she answering absently, when she heard a car stop. He motioned her back to the lounge-room.

Sure enough, it was the gallant captain, in gleaming fresh whites and topee, wielding an ebony stick and carrying a lidded picnic basket out of which poked a couple of gold-foiled corks, but looking anything but fresh-faced, despite the toothy smile he gave in greeting: 'Ah, my lovely little friend, Alfie! Just dropped by to have a word with you. D'you know I still owe you a case of champagne? Why haven't you collected it? Why haven't you been out in *San Toy*? In fact, why, why, why everything? May I come in?'

As she stood back to admit him, looking very flushed and scared and lovely, he turned towards his great car outside, with an Asiatic of some sort at the wheel, adding, 'Take you for a spin afterwards, if you like. You're alone, I take it? Don't mind having a gentleman caller this time of day . . . ha, ha!'

Setting the basket down on the table, he said, 'Some bubbly in there. Shall we have a drop?'

She murmured, 'Oh . . . it's a bit early.'

'To tell you the truth, I'm perishing. Quite a day and a night, yesterday.'

'I'll get you a glass . . . . '

'No, two . . . I make it a rule never, never, never to drink alone. I'll need a napkin or something to open the bottle. Mind if I come into the kitchen with you?' He simply followed her with a bottle, opened it wrapped in a tea-cloth, let the first of it bubble into the tumbler she offered saying she was sorry they had no champagne glasses. 'Must make you a present of some,' he said. Got to have 'em for that case, eh . . . ha, ha, ha!'

She led him back to the lounge. He dropped into a cane chair, raised his glass to her: 'Here's to your bright eyes!' He took it in one swig, sighed: 'Ah . . . that's better!'

She took only a sip of hers. 'Come on,' he said, 'drink up!'

'No,' she said. 'Too early for me.'

'Well you won't mind me, will you.' He poured another tumber, half emptied it, sighed again, then smiling at her, said, 'I've just been talking to Cuth Cobbitty. I thought you two were great pals. How come you to fall out like that?'

She took a deep breath to answer, 'I just don't like the things he does.'

'Lots of us don't like the things he does. But he's really a great chap. He says you've even threatened to make trouble for him in that dirty rag *Truth.* That can't be true, can it?'

Alfie took another deep breath: 'Are you suggesting that your friend lied to you about me?'

Shane guffawed, but was watching her closely with meaty, baggy eyes: 'Lord no! But women do strange things when they like a man.'

'What do you mean by that?'

'Well, you and Cuthbert were thick as thieves . . . then you fall out for some reason or other best known to yourselves, and you threaten him.'

'I didn't threaten him. I asked him to stop persecuting Jumbo Delacy . . . and if he did, I wouldn't take part in the newspaper campaign already started attacking him for his callous and bureaucratic handling of the Aboriginal Problem.'

'That constitutes a threat, my dear. And take an old hand's advice . . . getting mixed up with Fay McFee and her gang will get you into serious trouble.'

'For telling the truth?'

'The greater the truth, the greater the libel, they say, you know . . . or don't you?'

'I know.'

'Here . . . let me fill your glass up.' Alfie had drunk half of what he'd given her. She didn't hand him the glass. He reached over with the bottle and filled it, then filled his own. He swigged, then asked, 'Why in the name of thunder did you want to drag me into your row with him?'

She didn't touch the glass. She answered breathlessly, 'Because you were involved with him in the matter of the persecution of Jumbo Delacy.'

'Now you sound as crazy as Jumbo, m'dear. What'd I have to do with persecuting that lunatic . . . for godsake?'

'You told me that night of your Anzac Day party that you'd beaten the Imperial General Staff and Shell Oil for that tidal land of yours because someone in their confidence had tipped you off . . . and so poor Jumbo had to suffer . . . .'

The Captain guffawed again: 'You *are* crazy, lady . . . like Cuthbert said. As if I'd tell a total stranger a thing like that . . . even if I'd done it!'

'You admitted just now that you told me.'

'What's this . . . am I hearing right?'

'You admitted that you owe me a case of champagne for a bet we made. You even said you'd get me glasses to drink it.'

'What if I did?'

'The bet was that I didn't know who it was tipped you off about resumption of that land . . . you made it yourself . . . a kiss to a case of bubbly, you said. I told you it was Dr Cobbity gave you the tip . . . and you conceded defeat. I gave you the kiss . . . and just now you admitted you hadn't paid your part of the debt.'

He finished the glass, filled it again, swigged again, then said, shaking his head, with a wry grin, 'There's no doubt about women!'

'You admit it?'

'I admit nothing. I'm just astonished that you should take a little bit of fun like that, between a man and a pretty girl at a boozy party, and use it to such an end.'

'The end was to stop Dr Cobbity from persecuting that unfortunate man. I used every weapon I had . . . for the common good, which cancels out libel, in case you don't know.'

'You're not going to give *Truth* this yarn about reclamation of the land, are you?'

'I certainly am.'

'But it was only a comical yarn . . . told to amuse you. I'm notorious for my yarns, don't y'know?'

'You admit telling me about being tipped off by someone you later conceded was Dr Cobbity, and so outwitted the Imperial Brass, as you called it?'

'I told you I admit nothing. Anyway, what good'll it do to this cause of yours? Cobbity didn't take your threat, did he now.'

'No.'

'Well then . . . you'll only lose my friendship, and everybody else's round here, because they're all my friends. Your husband'll lose his job . . . .'

'Why should he? He's done nothing to offend anyone.'

'He hasn't given you the damn good hiding I think you need. Look, little lady . . . be your age. I'm the most powerful man in this community. If I say a man's to lose his job he loses it . . . Government Service or no. If the Administrator himself was to go against me I'd have him out. Do you realize that? Answer me?'

She swallowed, nodded: 'Yes . . . I think I do.'

'Well, there you are, then. Cross me and you're ruined. Come on my side . . . and, why, I'll even make Cobbity release your crazy yeller-feller, Jumbo Delacy.'

She stared at him: 'You could do that?'

'I could . . . and what's more I would.'

'You'd put it in writing?'

'I put nothing in writing but what's legal. But you have my word as a gentleman. Cobbity knows how close he is to being pushed out . . . . '

'He didn't give in to me.'

'He will to me . . . if you come in on my side.'

'What's that?'

'Simply forget that silly business about the bet. You haven't told anyone but Cobbity?'

She hesitated, then said, 'No.'

He suddenly glared at her, half rising, snarling at her, 'You *have*, you bitch!'

She gasped, 'Only my husband.'

He was on his feet, advancing on her with long thin finger outstretched, bellowing now, 'You've told those newspaper bastards already . . . I can see it in your eyes . . . by Jesus, you bitch, if . . . '

A huge figure lumbered in from the bedroom. Shane turned to it, gaping. Monsignor Maryzic's square face split in a wide grin: 'By Jesus vot, Capitan?'

Shane turned goggling to Alfie, who looked almost as astonished herself, but shouted, 'You bastards . . . this is a trick!'

'It vos yourself who turned der trick, Capitan. I zink der little lady in her compassion for poor Jumbo might haf made a bargain mit you . . . . '

Shane swung quickly on Alfie again. But the old priest went on before he could say anything, now addressing Alfie: 'Vich vood haf been tantamount to makingk a bargain mit der Devil, my dear. I beg your pardon for startlingk you by intrudingk not accordingk to der plan.' He looked again at the panting captain: 'You may go now Capitan Shane. Ve haf finished mit you . . . . '

Old Vic was purple, struggling for breath: 'By God, but I haven't finished with you . . . either of you!'

Maryzic smiled: 'Better to svear by your old frient der Devil, Vic. God isht not goingk to take mooch notice of you. Shane's Luck, you know. Zat is der Devil's Luck. Vun day he vill be along to claim der price of it . . . Take your basket and your ozzer bottle. I don't like champagne myself . . . ha, ha, ha!'

The laugh was for old Vic's snatching up his things and rushing to the door and out. For a moment there was the boom of his gubbernautical voice addressing his chauffeur. Then the slam of a metal door, muffled thunder of a starting engine. The old priest turned his grin on Alfie, to see her face crumple, her eyes swim. She came towards him. He put out his arms. She fell against his protuberance weeping wildly. 'Zere, zere!' he crooned, raising a hand to stroke her dark curls: 'Zere, zere, my pretty vun. It isht all over bar der shoutingk!'

Monday was the day the weekly air-mail went South – Sunday the day it came in. Today's mail had already left before all that was required for the great story Fay promised *Truth* for next Sunday's issue was in hand. Nevertheless she was able to wire Sydney headquarters that she would be delivering the goods on time. She worked on it right through the rest of Monday, into the early hours of Tuesday. Then at dawn that day Fergus Ferris took off with copy, pictures, and phono-records, to fly East and hand the stuff over to another air-mail by which it would go down the East Coast. On Thursday Fay received a telegram from *Truth* describing the stuff as magnificent, a terrific indictment, assuring publication in next issue, and offering congratulations to all concerned. Fay was thus able, in Friday's *Progressive*, to announce a treat in store for Port Palmeston and district next Sunday, being quite frank about it, even to passing on those congratulations literally to *all* concerned, the sheep with the goats, naming them. There was great activity that afternoon between that department of Government House called The Lion's Den, meaning the Old Man's sanctum, and the Crown Law Office. Still the *Palmeston Progressive* appeared on time and as printed. But the activity of the official libel hunters that day was nothing in comparison with what it was on Sunday afternoon, never had been, and probably never would be again. Bolshies and other low types even congregated about the Anzac Memorial to watch the running to and fro. A couple of policemen were stationed at the gates, as if a riot were expected. Perhaps the Old Man had even ordered his launch to be got ready to get him out by the back way in case of trouble, as had been done by another Administrator at the time of the Bolshie demonstrations over the sudden closure of Lord Vaisey's meatworks. But there was nothing angry about this mob. In fact they were mostly laughing. Still, laughing at high authority perhaps could constitute riotous behaviour and call for a police charge with batons.

A number of people of the town made a practice of making the run out to the aerodrome by car of Sunday afternoons to see the mail plane come in and to collect the southern papers it always brought. But this Sunday it seemed as if *everybody* was out there, with the notable exception of those who might be termed the goats in the expected *divertissement*, or rather the chief goats, since what the thing really was was epitomized in the great banner headlines: TERRIFIC INDICTMENT OF OFFICIAL CALLOUSNESS – which could apply to at least half of those snatching their copies of *Truth* from old Frobisher, the newsagent, as fast as he could unpack them and take the money. That was how *Truth* had got away with it. The indictment was not of persons but of persons-in-positions. Names might be named, but the blame put on the job, not on the man who did it. Anyway, there was no legal action. In fact the only apparent repercussion was the reappearance in the community of him over whom it all seemed to have started and whom few were likely to welcome back, that self-confessed public nuisance, Jumbo Delacy. All Jumbo had to say was that Major O'Dowdy had taken him in his utility on Monday morning, merely telling him he was free, and dumping him off at the Coconuts. Jumbo knew nothing about the national stir he had caused, nor cared about it or about anything for the moment but getting some booze to relieve what he called the Dry Horrors, developed during his period of enforced sobriety.

The slightness of the effect of it all caused Alfie, now working at proof-reading on the *Progressive* staff, to complain to Fay about the futility of doing anything to break bureaucracy. She said, 'They're even keeping Frank on, although I'm working here, as if out of contempt for anything we can do.'

Fay said, 'You've got to be patient, and keep at 'em and at 'em. How d'you think I feel after fighting 'em for years, exposing one piece of tyrrany after another, and still seeing the same old gang in the high places? But I know it's working slowly. Every time you hit the bastards you put a crack in 'em and their rotten system . . . and eventually they and it are going to fall to pieces.'

Alfie also complained that for all the vast publicity given the matter of Jumbo's dispossession, the Shell Oil Co. were still laying the foundations for their tanks on the Coconuts Flats and getting nearer and nearer to his house, while their supervising engineer and other officers were attending parties given by Captain Shane. To that Fay replied, 'Well, why don't you have a go at causing trouble on the job. Organize something industrial as a protest.'

'You mean get the men to strike?'

'You won't do that. They're mostly Greeks, newly imported. The union had a tough enough job getting them to take out tickets. But you might try boycotting delivery of stuff to the site through the militants. Go and see the Commo heads, Scotty McClaggity and Geordie Jenks. If you can get them interested, they might get the Waterside Workers' Branch to declare anything black being unloaded from ships for Shell, and seamen, too . . . they're all tied up with the Party.'

'Would they listen to me?'

'Well, they wouldn't listen to *me*. They hate me as much as the other side do. But Pat Hannaford, the engine driver, isn't so bad. Go and see him. He had a halfcaste wife who left him . . . and he's pretty crooked on halfcastes because of it . . . but he's not a bad bloke. He'd introduce you to the Kremlin boys.

Anyway, if they don't do anything, you can have a crack at 'em in the paper . . . good practice in your new career.'

Alfie did see Pat, who evidently succumbed to her female charm and started something that ended in a grand row in the offices called the Kremlin. Comrades McClaggity, President of the local Communist Party, and Jenks, Secretary, refused to do anything for Jumbo, because he had worked in a strike-breaking gang during a dispute on the wharf a couple of years back, and berated Pat for taking up the cause of a scab in order to make his alley good with a designing female who was on one side today and any other tomorrow. When Alfie heard of it, she wrote a scathing piece for the *Progressive* that caused Rollo Ramstones, the Editor, to take her onto the literary staff proper and to say, along with Fay, that undoubtedly her future lay in writing. Alfie confessed that she had long dreamt of being a writer.

The effect of Alfie's article was to rouse the crew of the night cart to action that was hardly what might be called direct, or even efficacious, but made itself at least stink strongly. McClaggity and Jenks had declared to Alfie that all halfcastes were born scabs and not worth bothering about. Alfie had quoted them exactly. The night cart crew, all halfcastes, and all men of pride since having been given the legal right to drink, privily declared the sanitary pans of the Kremlin and the homes of Comrades McClaggity and Jenks black. The Sanitary Contractor had to do the job himself. It made him ill, so that he had to go to hospital. The Comrades complained to their old enemies the Administration, who took so long about it that they, Scotty and Geordie, had to do it *themselves*. That was too much for them. Apparently blacklegging someone for something by professionals in that way is a very different thing from being blacklegged oneself. They decided on direct action, laid an ambush composed of Comrades on the night the Kremlin's pan should have been emptied and it was anticipated that the cart would drive past as usual, 'forgettin' ' as the crew always said when charged with the omission, and sprang out with a prepared barricade and pick-handles to enforce their rights as respectable citizens. The crew could do nothing but stop and pick up the well-filled pan. The barricade was not removed till the pan was tossed up to the men on top who would stow it, and Scotty McClaggity, in his broad accent, with his comrades beside him, standing beside the stinking vehicle, had delivered himself of an oration which amongst much else declared that this same apparatus would be applied every due night until the scabby scabs came round to doing their duty. Then, as the barricade was moved away and the truck started up, the three men on top, emptied the contents of not only the proletarians own pan onto those below but of two others that could have come from the dunnies of their worst enemies.

Fay wrote that piece up, with such gusto that the Party met and discussed an action for libel. They had already discussed taking legal action against the night-cart crew, but had been overruled by those who had been out of range that night. Fay mentioned that, adding that the occasion of the discussion was the only one on which laughter had been heard at the Kremlin, but that no one had been inclined to investigate the cause, because of the stink that hung over the place. '*Will it ever quite fade away*?' asked Fay in her piece. The motion to sue the *Progressive* was also defeated. As Pat Hannaford, one of those lucky ones that night, said, the less said about it now the better. He reported that Alfie had told him that her husband had spoken to the nightmen and been given an assurance that now they felt their honour vindicated, things would proceed normally.

The official reply to the *Truth* story was made through the big southern daily newspapers, which traditionally supported conservative Government policy, in the form of a statement by the Minister on the program of works about to be started for the betterment of the lot of Aborigines of the North. While making no specific reference to the *Truth* publication, the Minister spoke of 'Sensation-mongers and Subversive Elements, who preferred to capitalize on the mistakes of the past and to ignore the abundant evidence of the better deal the Aborigines were now getting.' Dr Cobbity was described as a dedicated scientist and humane reformer, who had recently been honoured by the King. To prove that the old system was gone for good, facts and figures were given regarding the work in hand by the Public Works to replace the old Palmeston Compound with a model settlement at Sweet Creek, outside of the town, where there would be every facility for effecting the reforms for which Dr Cobbity had been working for years: good living-quarters, canteens, schools, sanitation. More than that, a world-famous Anthropologist was being appointed to make a survey of the Aboriginal Affairs of Australia generally, with the view to establishing a Commonwealth Department of Aboriginal Welfare, under an expert Director.

His Honour the Administrator received the statement ahead of publication in a telegram sent from his superiors down South, who evidently wanted to cheer him up. It was then his duty to cheer up the smaller flea beneath himself, Dr Cobbity, whom he called to the Lion's Den. With that grin of his, after reading the telegram, Cobbity commented: 'The Anthrops are going to push me out all right. Is this to warn me?'

'Certainly not. The thing has nothing but praise for you.'

'But there's going to be an expert Director . . . and that's not going to be me, is it? I wonder what he'll be expert in, the bastard . . . the head-shrinkers of the Amazon, or the zombi-dancers of Zamboanga, or some bloody rubbish equally unrealistic as regards this thankless job? After all I've given to it, I'll go out discredited.'

'Discredited nothing, man! Look what you're getting with the new Financial Year . . . this settlement, a new lazaret, a new hospital . . . . '

'And an Irishman's rise, I'll bet you.'

'I'll stand by you, man.'

Cobbity grinned again, and rose to go. The Old Man halted him with a meaningful cough. Cobbity looked at him. Fiddling with things on his desk, His Honour said, 'You've heard, I suppose, that that Mrs Candlemas is working on the *Progressive*?'

'Of course.'

His Honour cleared his throat again, looked up: 'What about her husband, then?'

Cobbity demanded, 'What about him?'

The Colonel reddened. He was not used to being spoken to without one or other of his titles, or Sir, at least. He snapped, 'Rather anomalous, isn't it . . . one of our officers, with a wife like that?'

Cobbity was silent, staring with the glassy eyes, perhaps thinking about having *a wife like that.* His Honour went on: 'Have you said anything to him about it?'

'No.'

'Don't you think you ought to?'

'Why should I? He's a level-headed fellow. He does a good job.'

'Well, I can't say *I* much like it. If you won't tackle him, I will . . . .'

Now it was Cobbity who went red, and the eyes blazed. From easy insolent leaning with hands on the table he stood erect. He snapped, 'With all due respect, Sir, if you interfere with an officer of mine, you'll have my resignation.'

Flaming, the Old Man glared back. Cobbity went on: 'That man's first class at his job. I want him for the drainage lay-out of these places. I want him for a down-country disease survey . . . the things I've always wanted done and been deprived of by you or whoever else was sitting behind this desk cheese-paring for the blokes down South who only appointed you because you're a Yes man . . . '

The Colonel shouted, 'How dare you, Sir!'

'Do you want my resignation?'

His Honour struggled with his dignity and the truth of his position, came out with a compromise: 'I make allowance for what you've been through lately, Doctor.'

'I don't want any allowances, Your Honour. All I want is for you to keep off my back till I get these things done I've tried so long for. You won't have to kick me out when they're done. Neither will those bastards with their ape men. I'll be off under my own steam. I asked you did you want my resignation. Will you kindly answer yes or no?'

His Honour choked over it: 'No . . . no, Cobbity . . . no.'

Cobbity sighed heavily, said, 'Well, if you'll excuse me, Sir . . . I've a lot to do.'

'Certainly, Doctor, certainly . . . Goodday.'

As Dr Cobbity was marching towards the Government Offices, past the Cenotaph, so-called, an old Rolls Royce swung round the corner, slowed to allow him to get across. His long legs hastened their gait. He was across. Then he looked back, met the black eyes staring at him, so intently that the car was swinging to the wrong side. A moment. Then he grinned, waved. Alfie smiled, waved back. He went on his way, loped up the steps of the Offices, disappeared.

CHAPTER SEVEN

THERE WAS no doubting the sincerity of the official statement that the Aborigines were in for a new deal, because even two weeks before the declared date of implementing it, July 1, there was Mr McCusky out at that dirty old dump which had served the purpose of what was called Aboriginal Protection for so long, the Palmeston Compound, making arrangements, in his vigorous fashion for doing anything, for its complete elimination by due date. Poor old Tubby Turkney bore the brunt of it. It was one thing for McCusky to go strutting through the place telling the inmates that the Millennium had come for them and allotting them their several parts thereinafter, but quite another to get the co-operation of people who, along with their forefathers for a hundred years or so, had learnt to expect nothing from the *kuttabah*, except having to do something you didn't want to do, without the application, actual or equivalent of one of those several time-honoured incentives: the stock-whip, the hobble-chain, or the *dookyangana's* boot.

Tubby was supposed to organize the able-bodied into gangs who would assist with the building of the new place at Sweet Creek, beginning with clearing the site and erecting temporary dwellings and other structures with the material of clearing. The less robust were to be got rid of, temporarily or permanently, by sending them back to where they'd come from, with rail-warrants if they came from down the line, with rations for a month if they could be expected to walk back to their countries, or placed in the care of the missionaries if from distant points along the coast. Their hovels here were to be knocked down and burnt as evacuated. What happened in most cases was that allotments were swapped, the young ones taking the older ones' rations, and if not going bush for a holiday, joined the smart boys and girls who lived independently if illegally in and around town, while the older ones, no longer fit for the hardships of bush-living, turned up at Sweet Creek, to camp hungry in the surrounding bush watching the halfcastes and the whitemen work. When all was said and done, these latter were being paid. Some of the very old had to be removed forcibly; and a few sneaked back and tried to set up home again down in the Kerosene gully, using the wreckage for building. There were no more of those happy boozy sessions of evenings at the Superintendent's residence. Poor old Tubby was on the go morning noon and night, with McCusky, dashing from one to another of the fronts under his generalship, popping in at all hours to keep him hustling. Dr Cobbity, concerned only with the grand plan, rarely came out of his office.

Amongst those given rail-warrants and told to go home and never come back, on pain of imprisonment if they did, were King George and Queeny Peg-leg. Shrewdies, that they were, anticipating dispossession of their accumulated wealth along with destruction of their dwellings, they joined forces after years of enmity and had their stuff as it were spirited away by night aboard Willy Pak Poy's launch, taken out of the harbour and round the eastern shore and inland on high tide, well up the tidal reach of Sweet Creek to the Sanitary Depot, not so far from the site of the new Settlement. When they were found to be missing when the roll was called for those booked to board the train, Eddy McCusky only laughed, saying, 'They'll show up sometime. Just as we're building our canteen they'll open theirs. Let 'em go. I can see 'em somewhere out in the scrub tryin' to sell their rubbish to one another . . . eeeeeahhh!'

The fact was that George had already sold his stuff to Queeny, because he *wanted* to go home, but was waiting to pick up Prindy to take him along, too, such being what he was told to do in the last orders received from Bobwirridirridi. The Pookarakka had at last accepted George's miserable admission that he could not effect his release this time because something contrary was at work, most likely Tarjen Coon-Coon, and that he would have to rely on his own resources. From what George had told Prindy, speaking to him through the Halfcaste Children's Home fence, beyond which they never went now, when next Wet Season came round and conditions were right for it, the Pookarakka would sing a great storm to wreck the jail and would come down on the wind to join them, in the distant Princess Alice country. Prindy was quite agreeable. The fact that he had been told by Mr McCusky that shortly he was to be sent down to the Centre, with Jumbo's bigger boys and a couple of other yeller kids, to enter the Home for Halfcaste Boys already functioning there, evidently had made no impression on him at all. George also knew what McCusky's intentions were concerning the boy, but apparently saw no urgency about removing him.

McCusky's plans, or rather Dr Cobbity's, although Eddy made them sound very much like his own, first concerned settling the full-blood Aborigines in conditions that, even without considering the people themselves, would not make oneself look more like the keeper of a tumble-down piggery than a social and medical scientist supposed to be dealing with the Nation's most pressing problems in these departments of science.

For the time, the Compound halfcastes, that is the females and boys under eight, were to be given into the care of Mr Tasker and his people, who would hold them at one of their island missions until the Government institution planned and budgeted for establishment on Echo Island were ready. The Compound kitchen still functioned to feed them, with Nelly Ah Loy in charge. The makeshift kitchen operating at the new place pending the proper building was being run by Possum Delacy, already appointed as permanent cook for the place.

McCusky himself, determined to rehabilitate Jumbo, perhaps to give the lie to the nationally disseminated impression that those who were supposed to be protecting him were actually persecuting him, had had Jumbo's house removed, by courtesy of the Shell Oil Co. who pulled it down, to Sweet Creek, where it was actually the first building to be erected, and repaired and painted to look like new. As it was intended to run a small herd of cattle to make the Settlement independent for its beef supply as well as for training young full-bloods in the handling of stock, Jumbo had been appointed Head Stockman.

Both he and his wife would be paid. Jumbo seemed to like the idea, perhaps because at last he had become some sort of boss. McCusky had offered Nell the job as baker for the settlement after the Halfcaste Homes were disbanded; but she had said she wanted to return to Beatrice River. He had told her of his intention to send Prindy to the Centre, only to have her forthrightly tell him of her own plans regarding the boy, which was that she would take him to Lily Lagoons and let his uncle Darcy teach him. Perhaps because he realized that it was no use arguing with her, or was too much preoccupied with other things, McCusky said no more to her about it.

It was Alfie Candlemas who brought Nell and McCusky to sharp awareness of the difference of their intentions. She did it quite inadvertently in the course of her duties as a reporter for the *Progressive* coupled with interest in old friends and places. The Aborigines Department showed no such coyness about its functioning now as in the past. When Alfie went to the Compound to take a peep at what was going on there, and found McCusky hustling Turkney, she was taken on a tour of inspection to see the piles of smoking remnants of what had been its former glory as a National Institution, awaiting transportation to the rubbish dump where much of it had come from. Dropping in for a word with the girls in the kitchen, she learnt from Nell that she would be returning to the Beatrice with Prindy as soon as the place was closed down altogether, and parted with her saying that she would be seeing her there when she and her husband attended the Races in September, as they surely would be doing, because Frank would then be down country doing that health survey and she along with him. Afterwards Alfie had been permitted by Mrs Turkney, half-friendly, to spend a little time with the kids, who were still making her necklace, the boring of a couple of hundred hard jirquities with a single needle and the making of the fine string from hybiscus bark being slow work. She was to pick up the prejent from them when she would be seeing them off to the missions in a week or two. A few days later, on a Monday, Alfie was out taking a look at how things were going at Sweet Creek and taking tea with Possum in the bright transplanted Delacy quarters there and listening to Possum's sniffling complaint about the impending loss of most of her children, when she met up with the ubiquitous McCusky again. He joined them at tea. She said to him, 'Seeing this sending the kids away is only a temporary measure, why not let Possum's go along to that school of old Jeremy Delacy's with the other Delacy boy?'

'What other Delacy boy?' asked McCusky.

'Well, whatever he is, Nelly Ah Loy's boy.'

'Who says he's going to Lily Lagoons?'

'She does.'

'Does she, then! As a matter of fact he'll be off with the couple of others I'm sending to the Centre on Wednesday's train. I'll have to put that right . . . or we'll have a bloody riot on our hands on Wednesday morning.' When Alfie offered to take mother and son along in her car for parting at the train, he said definitely No, that would really be starting a riot: 'You don't know that Nelly when she gets worked up. The boys're going down with a couple of coppers as escort. She'll think they're being taken to jail or something. I'll go and explain to her on the way back to town.' McCusky then discussed the Lily Lagoons school with Alfie, saying that it was worse than useless in the scheme of things he and Cobbity were putting into practice, which was, essentially, that '... Every Aboriginal person shall understand the value of money and the nature of work and of contracting to work, so as eventually to be able to take part in the general economy of the Nation.' Cobbity, whom McCusky honoured greatly for what he called his concise thinking, must have had that written down somewhere.

McCusky had something of a riot on his hands as it was. Knowing Nell, he would have done best simply to have stolen Prindy away. Instead, as he had said he would, he dropped in at the old Compound on the way home. Nell was preparing tea for the yeller folk at the Homes. He ate a piece of her excellent brownie while explaining the facts, adding that she really was a first-class baker and he would pay her well if she'd come work for him out at Sweet Creek. He was obviously startled when she leapt at him, screeching, 'You bloody bastard ... you can't tek my boy 'way ... I get Tarjen Coon-Coon fix you.'

Turkney came running to his master's aid, seeing him leap from the uproarious kitchen. At a safe distance, McCusky cocked his hat over an eye and said, 'Now listen, Nelly ... that boy's going away on Wednesday's train ... and if you give any trouble, you'll be going back to jail. You'll get your boy back soon. Soon he'll be a man, with a good job, looking out for you when you get old. Now shut up!' He turned away with Turkney.

'You bloody puggin bastard!' Nell yelled after him, then fell into the arms of her helpers, weeping wildly: 'Dey tek my lil boy 'way ... my lil boy ... oh, ah ... my lil boy ... oh, oh, ah!'

Then suddenly she ceased to weep, and declared, 'I beat dat bloody bastard. I steal him my boy. I tek him Lily Lagoon meself.'

There was a general exclamation: *Eh, look out*!

'Yas,' she went on. 'I can do it. I go tell him 'bout now .... '

'You can't do it like o' dat!' cried Venus. 'Old Turk'ey stop you.'

The children were still in the playground. Staring away in that direction, Nell said, 'I go tell him get out, go down gully, before lock up. I meet him dere.' She swung on the others, Dolly, Maggie Barbu: 'Get me tucker ready ... brea'n'beef .... '

Dolly squealed, 'You jitty! Can't do it like o' dat. Policeman gitchim you right-away .... '

'P'liceman can't gitchim my boy. He too goot long o' bush. He been beat him all-lot before ... dat-lot Coon-Coon, Jinbul ... I go!'

She flung off her apron, went hurrying towards the gate. Turkney came puffing from his office: 'Where you think you're going?'

'I wan' 'o see my boy.'

'You been see him this afternoon.'

'Boss been say he goin' 'o tek him 'way.'

'He's not going till day after tomorrow.'

From staring defiantly, Nell suddenly drooped her head, began to whimper, 'I on'y wan' talk him lil bits more, Boss ... please you let me.'

He sighed heavily: 'All right, then ... but no causing trouble ... no upsetting that boy. If I hear you kickin' up a row I'll call p'liceman.'

'No more trouble, Boss.'

'Okay, then. Hurry up. It'll soon be tea-time.'

Prindy, in the middle of a last-minute game, was disinclined to come to the fence. She had to get Wilhelmina Whitehead to bring him by explaining that he was to get out of the place at once. Then all of the kids crowded round to hear, and were greatly excited. Nell seemed as if inclined to wait till she saw Prindy out. But Turkney was standing out before his office watching. She turned away, heading back to the Compound, while the children began the lively game they always played when someone was going out or coming in by way of their bandicoot hole. Turkney went back into his office.

The girls in the kitchen had a calico flour-sack of food ready. Nell simply snatched it, and without even answering the whispered *mummuk yawarra*, shot out of the back door, and with the kitchen covering any sight of her from beyond it, went running down to the scrub, avoiding the track, and through it down to the beach. The tide was coming in, a spring tide, with Igulgul very young again, just turning silver in the gilding sky. She ran towards Point Lookout, with the tidal wavelets, licking the sand like curling frothy tongues, conveniently wiping out her tracks almost as she made them. She found Prindy waiting knee-deep in the little creek that ran in and out of the gully, trying to corner a largish fish in a tiny bay. He came splashing to meet her, then dashed ahead, wading the way to the rocks.

He was onto the rocks and climbing towards a sort of platform, with the alacrity of a rock wallaby, while she toiled behind with the food sack, although less encumbered by the physical burden than by fear, and more fear of what might lie ahead than be in pursuit, it was evident from her wild-eyed watchfulness in that direction. The tumult of the swiftly rising waters was unnerving enough in itself, without the reputation of the place, the gurgling, the suck and slap, the moan of trapped air seeking escape from deep cavities. He had to lean down and take the sack from her to help her make the almost sheer last of it. Above the platform was an overhang, the crack between them at the back a depthless black haunt for any monstrosity. Seeing her fearfulness, Prindy said, 'No-more fright. Dat-one Ol'Goomun dibble can't hurt you'n'me . . . on'y *Kudijingera* man.'

She breathed, 'You been mix up dat bijnitch.'

'No matter. My huncle, dat-one King George, been tell him 'bout. Dis place he been tell him me wait. He come long o' canoe. I swim out.' He helped himself to the beef sandwiches. 'Where King George now?' he mumbled. She said she didn't know. It soon became evident that he had mistaken her intention in getting him out of bondage as helping him to make his rendezvous with George. When at length he grasped that they were having nothing at all to do with George, but heading for Beatrice River down the railway line, most likely with the police after them, he just sat and stared.

The West was red now, young Igulgul laughing at his long reflexion in the swift running blood of the sea.

Then together they spotted the dim figures on the beach, away back where the picnics used to be held – one in white. Prindy said they were calling, but couldn't make out the voices with all that watery noise. The figures – there appeared to be three – went the other way, towards the rocks of Blackfellow Point, the other extremity of the Compound beach. Only the one in white was soon to be seen. The sea was purpling, the West darkening to rust, Igulgul down amongst the western trees.

It might have been a trick of Igulgul's before he vanished, cutting a shape out of the shadows of the rocks - but there they saw a figure flitting from rock to rock just below them, crouched and skinny like an old old woman, but with glinting golden hair - and were those her fiery eyes? Was that babbling her voice? They clung to each other, still staring after, as in a flash, whatever it was was gone. Igulgul went with it.

Then Prindy swung to look along the beach again, saying 'Dey come dis-a-way now. Dey singin' out.'

It was quite dark now back from the luminosity of the water, which was just about at top level. Those who were singin' out, as Prindy said, would be walking the strip of maritime couch between the top lip of the beach and the scrub. Soon he said, 'Dey singin' out us. Mist' Mick Cuskey, Mist' Turk'ey . . . 'nother-one I tink Barney Bynoe.'

'Wha'-nam singin' out?'

'Come on you two . . . come on out o' dat. You can't get away. Spone you don' come back tonight, we get him tracker . . . Like o' dat.'

Then Nell herself could hear, Barney Bynoe calling: "Ku!" and McCusky, in a torn voice, telling her not to be a Mad Bugger, warning her that he would put her back in jail.

Prindy said, 'Dey stop nother side creek. Dey can't get crost now . . . too deep.' Then the voices grew fainter. 'Dey go up gully,' Prindy said.

His mother asked, 'Wha' you reckon . . . he come back dis side?'

'I don' know. Might-be he go gitchim p'liceman.'

She said quickly, 'Better we go.'

'Where we goin' 'o go?'

'Like I been talk . . . we go long o' railway. You can find him all right?'

'Yu. We go back long o' beach . . . long o' water. We go over Blackfeller Point . . . long o' Coconut.'

'Jumbo no more dere. Dey pull down dat house . . . tek long o' Sweet Creek.'

'I know. Railway 'nother side dat hill behin' Coconut.'

'All right . . . we go.'

They were in for another shock as they dropped from the rocks to the shallow water and saw it blaze with fire about their feet. 'Eh, look out!' they both gasped, and leapt back to safety, to stare at what had been out of sight higher up; a veritable watery hell, as creatures, large and small, darted about, most likely in pursuit and flight, through labyrinths of phosphorescence. Too much for ones steeped in the magic of existence to take risks with it. Even while keeping ears cocked for pursuit from this side of the gully, they waited for the tide to fall. How swiftly does tide flow except when waited on! Lights in the big houses over on the other point diminished one by one.

At last they got down onto the oozing rippled sand, to find still a hint of the fearful fire in the myriad tiny movements about their own sparkling feet. Thus across the bay of the Compound. Now up the other rocks. No monsters here to be scared of, except those whose names are Protection and Justice and the civilized like, living up the road there in those dark bulks against the stars.

Over the road warily, and into the scrub, and down again to the flats of the Coconuts. No crossing the flats directly as formerly. Silhouetted against the northern stars were not only the heads of the few coconuts left standing, but a crane-jib and scaffolding. There was a whitish huddle of new asbestos buildings, workers' quarters, a couple of which were lit, their occupants Greek by the tinkling gramophone music. They skirted the place, reached the road they wanted by also skirting the cluster of whitemen's and yellowmen's cemeteries with their crowds of marble ghosts – nothing to be afraid of there, since you aren't one of these breeds and like haunts only like. So up the hill again, past Gran'ma Lady Eaton's, referred to in a whisper as they went as *Delacy Place* – no one at home, apparently, except Hanno the factotum, judging by a single lighted window in a cottage at the rear. What price refuge in there, even if Granny were at home? The refugees would not know, just as in their ignorance they did not know that she was away on the other side of the world they knew nothing of, having gone by flying-boat to visit Lord Vaisey and be truly a Ladyship in his castle.

They turned into that narrow road running through the scrub into the district of Chinese, setting all the chained dogs roaring of their going and rousing one or two suspicious Chinamen to relight their lamps. They hurried, came out on a main road, to be caught by the headlights of a motor vehicle swinging in from another side track. They were back in the scrub in a flash. But they had been seen. The vehicle, the night-cart obviously by the stink of it, halted before turning into the track they'd just come out from, while a couple of flashlights probed for them, and voices gabbled in the patois: 'Yeah . . . I been see all right . . . two-feller . . . blackfeller, I reckon.' Then the truck moved on its way in to rouse the dogs again. The pair came out of hiding, got onto the hard gravel, in a moment were on the railway crossing. There were no houses near, only the two dully-gleaming rails and the ghostly arms of the warning signs. Still Nell whispered, asking which way they were to go. Prindy pulled her to the left, to follow the railway track.

It was safe enough going here, through a low long cutting topped with scrub. What houses there were along the way were well back beyond the paralleling road. So for about a mile, when against the southern stars there began to loom the somewhat massive structures, at least for these parts, of the Loco Depot: the tall tanks, the engine sheds, a signal; and the simple steel-bound track they followed became intricate with diverging alleyways and obstructions to be watched for closely in the gloom so as to save more of the toe-stubbing with which the new conditions began. Not a light anywhere, nor any sound, except the drip of water, which Prindy heard. 'Wadder . . . me t'ursty.' He led the way to it: a leaky tank outside the shed where engines were to be seen, three of them on as many tracks, against the starry open further end, like sleeping monsters, one of them softly hissing in its sleep. Having drunk from a tap, Prindy took a peep. Then he complained that he was hungry. Having eaten he complained that he was sleepy. His mother herself sighed wearily, and sank to the night-black ashy ground, with back to the dingy whitewashed wall of the shed, and drew him onto her lap. He was quickly asleep. Soon she was nodding over him.

Prindy woke suddenly, said, 'Motor car!'

They sat listening. The sound came from beyond the little station, which was out of their line of sight because a rake of waggons intervened. Across the road from the station was the line of railwaymen's quarters. The motor stopped. Then there was heard the familiar sounds of the nightmen at their operations, in which invariably they showed as little regard for the populace they served as probably it felt for them.

The pair beside the engine house sat listening. The racket came to the station dunnies, ended there. Now there was only talk and laughter. But suddenly, to Prindy's acute ears, sound of bare footsteps: 'Somebody come!'

They leapt up. A flashlight beamed through the couplings of waggons right before them. The flashlight leapt up with its owner's climbing over the couplings. Snatching at Prindy, Nell dragged him towards the entrance to the shed, just a step or two. But the beam caught them even as they turned the corner. Someone shouted, 'Lookit!' The entire crew were coming through couplings, evidently heading for the water tank.

Nell dragged Prindy into the gloom, heading for the black bulk of an engine, stepped into an ash-pit, fell sprawling in cold ashes, with the boy on top of her. They disentangled in a flash, but to lie still, as bare feet came thudding in, beams of light darting overhead. Then a beam found them – more beams – behind them a panted chorus: 'Eh, look out!'

A gabble of voices identified the crouching blinking captives. Then one asked, 'Wha's matter . . . you run-away, eh?'

Only blinking for answer. Then the face of Billy Noseda, the foreman, showed itself in the light. He said, 'No-more fright'. We on'y nightman. Come on out o' dere.' He extended a hand that stank of his occupation even as he shoved it down to help.

Although the pair, dragged up and surrounded with torches and quizzing faces and voices, would not speak at first, their silence was as unnecessary as their fear, as they were being told over and over: 'You steal him kid from Mick Cusky tek him way. We savvy all right. We ain't goin' tell nobody. We ain't p'liceman. We nightman . . . eeeeeahhhh! But you can't do it like o' dat. P'lice gitchim you. Where you reckon you go . . . where you reckon you go . . . where you reckon you go he can't gitchim you?'

At last Nell told them she was going to Lily Lagoons: 'Dat Mullaka he look-out for we.'

The men admitted it. 'Yeah . . . but how you goin' 'o get dere? Dat hundred-hundred mile?'

'Foller him up railway line.'

'What 'bout fettler . . . he goin' o' see you?'

'We plant him long o' bush spone somebody come.'

'Too many whiteman down dere now. Dey's buildin' new road. Big mob gang dere now . . . camp all dem sidin' . . . Helena River, Caroline, Alice.'

'What you goin' 'o do tucker?'

Someone giggled: 'Tchileep long o' gang, eh?'

There was a general guffaw.

Someone else said, 'P'liceman goin' 'o tell dat lot keep eye out for you two-feller.'

Prindy piped up, 'We go long o' Mooragetaghee.'

Another chorus of: 'Eh look-out!'

One asked, 'You no-more savvy Mooragetaghee?'

'I savvy all right . . . him dat-a-way.' Prindy jerked his chin sou'westward.

'Das right!' someone exclaimed. 'How you savvy? Dat not you country.'

'My huncle been show him me. He tell him he tek me dere. I reckon he sit down dere now. We gitchim up, he look-out we.'

'Wha' nam' huncle, young feller?' asked Noseda.

'Dat-one King George.'

A chorus of exclamations. Noseda said, 'Dat King George, he no-more long o' bush . . . he dere now, long o' Sanitary Depot . . . him-two-feller Peg-leg.'

Now the pair exclaimed, although surely from different reasons of interest. 'Where dat place?' they both asked.

The others said they themselves were heading there now, had finished their round, and were only going to wash up at the tap. 'You wait . . . we tek him you.'

As the half dozen of them went towards the water tank, Noseda turned back, said to Nell, 'Spone I tek him you, you gi' me, eh?'

She drew a deep breath, nodded, breathed out, 'Yu.'

The men were ready in about ten minutes. As they came back one of them took Prindy by the hand, saying he was his uncle, and helped him through the couplings and across to the smellful truck, and bumped him up into the cabin after his mother. The awful atmosphere was left behind with the truck's moving off. They ran on past the shunting yard, crossed the railway where it became a single track again, turned into a waste of torn trees and earth through which a strip of new yellow gravel ran straight as a die, the beginnings of what was intended to be the Transcontinental Highway, being constructed, like those oil tanks of Shell's, for strategic purposes, so it was said. A dismal prospect for people used to travelling by tracks that were part of the bush itself, as much pathways for wild things as for men, winding from water to water, dodging the bigger trees and rocks.

They went thus for a couple of miles, with here and there a dry gully with all resemblance to what it had been gone, slabs of concrete serving as the beds of the creeks that had bottomed them, creeks that perhaps had been so dealt with as never to run again, except as drains. Then a white notice loomed in the headlights on the left: SWEET CREEK ABORIGINAL SETTLEMENT, with an arrow pointing. Noseda slowed down and turned into another straight road of recent making, but not nearly so broad, since not designed for the transport of men and their guns in battalions. They followed this down through sparse timber for half a mile, then swung left again onto a bush-track, where there were curlews to be seen blinking for a moment in the headlights, then winging upward, and a couple of wallabies. Suddenly they were in dense scrub, bumping over timbered corduroy, slow enough to have the essence of their load envelope them again, along with the miasma of maritime mud. A short distance; and there ahead was a clearing, with several white buildings, big and small, and what looked like a shiny black wall, but was seen at closer range as a long line of stacked sanitary cans freshly tarred.

The truck ran on through the clearing, to stop at last where there was the glint of water ahead. 'Here we are,' said Noseda, and cut his engine and his lights, then got out and came round to let the others out, because they were having trouble with the door. The three were alone, the rest of the crew, by the sound of talk and laughter back where the houses were, evidently having dropped off as they came through. Lamps were being lit there. Noseda led his charges towards them, along with a whining swarm of mosquitoes. He told them that the crew would be having crib after they'd showered, and that he would light a bin of mangrove leaves to drive the mosquitoes away. He took them to a shed used for eating in, and left them slapping at the mosquitoes, only to have them coughing and weeping soon in a cloud of acrid smoke pouring from a drum he had set match to.

The crew came at last, wearing clean clothes, and made tea and cut up bread and beef, and told how George and Peg-leg were camped *dat-a-way*, with jerks of lips and chins, to be reached only when the tide was low and the bar across Sweet Creek exposed. Prindy fell asleep with fair head on the table, to be picked up and carried off by his new-found uncle, to a hut where there were stretcher beds, on one of which he was lain.

Noseda, carrying a hurricane lantern, took Nell to another hut where there were similar beds. He blew out the light, and without further ado, flung her down on a bed, and dealt with her. When he got up and went outside, and she was sitting up to put on her drawers again, someone else burst into the hut and pushed her down and did likewise. He went also. She was at the door when the third came. No more after that. Perhaps relationship forbade it. She came out warily. Some of the men were still sitting in the dining-shed, talking and laughing. Watching them, she went like a wraith across the clearing in the direction Prindy had been taken. There were several small buildings. She stared at them for a while, then went and sat down beside the one furthest from the men and out of sight of them. A mopoke was calling that the district was clear of evil things, while she swatted at the mosquitoes. At last she lay down, and still swatting, and scratching where she had failed to swat, slept fitfully.

Nell woke wide at last to find a small form standing over her, distinct against the pearl of dawn. She heaved herself up, looked about through the smellful gloom. After a moment she whispered, 'Where dat-lot?'

'All lot tchileep.'

'We go find Queeny Peg-leg.'

'Dat-way, he reckon.' Prindy turned eastward. He looked back at his mother, then turned again and led the way.

Fifty yards or so brought them to a wall of mangroves, but with a gap in it, and the damp mud well trodden. They entered it, soon to hear the click-clack of the life of mangrove swamps now familiar to them, and to have a myriad mosquitoes join them. Then the glint of water. They emerged to find a wide silvery expanse of estuary, chased with the agitated movements of fish trying to get back to the deep through ambuscades of large predators who occasionally betrayed themselves with skimming fins or spines. The bar was just beginning to show, like the broken top of a sunken wall some three to four feet wide. A slippery track led down to it through gravelly mud. They went down, leaving most of their mosquito escort, only to enter a veritable haze of sandflies. Almost as fast as they went out on the slimy wall it rose above the water. Several times they had to stop at gaps through which the water boiled, not only with its own force, but with leaping fish. Prindy remarked on how easy it would be to fill a sugar-sack if you had a spear; but his mother was more concerned with what might be behind them in human form, and kept looking that way – while the sky ahead turned from pearl to rose. It was gilding as they climbed up through a similar gap in a mangrove jungle on the other side.

A well-defined track went on through open forest, with several branches off, but no chance of going wrong, because there were the tracks of Peg-leg's having gone that way a couple of times. There were also recent tracks of a small dog. After something like half a mile they came to a bit of fresh-water swamp, thickly grown with rushes and pandanus, but with scarcely a bucketful of water to be dipped out of the muddy hole to which it had contracted. At the hole was ample evidence of Peg-leg's presence in the locality. The track away from it led to rising stony ground. As they were climbing Prindy said he heard a cough. They halted. His mother cocked her ear. No sound but a duet of butcher-birds a long way off. Prindy said he heard it again, indicating a point diagonally up the hill. Then he put a hand to mouth and called, '*Ku*!' No answer for ordinary ears; but he said: 'Dog dere. Been squeak. Sombody been hit him.' He called again, '*Ku-uuuuu . . . Ngaggun*!' Again, drawing out the relationship name, '*Nah-gag-gun*!'

The reply came, at a fair distance: '*Ko*!'

'*Ku*!'

'*Ko . . . Kokanjinni*!'

Smiling, Prindy led the way at a trot. The track led almost to the top of the low hill, to a point where the eroded conglomerate that capped it had been weathered into bits of caverns. Two of the caverns had been made into dwellings with screens of boughs, the latter surely put up less for privacy, even though the owners, as tribal brother and sister as well as old enemies, might be expected to have as little to do with one another as possible, than a shelter from the sou'-easter that could come up blustering and cool of afternoons and evenings at this time of year. They were each standing outside their respective domiciles, with a little dog between them, a little yellow and white mongrel with one ear cocked in the way of his dingo ancestry, the other flopping to other responses of his variety of canine genes, both flickering in agitated hearkening to a master and mistress who would not let him do what half his nature craved, which was to bark at intruders like a white-fellow dog – as bark, indeed, he did, shrilly and without restraint, when the parties rushed to greet each other, sister to sister, uncle to nephew, crying their delight in reunion, embracing, fondling, the women even weeping over each other – till Queeny, herself again, took a swing at him with her crutch, yelling, 'Bloody *mungus* dog . . . *kai-atulli*!' He squeaked and fled.

While Nell told briefly how came they there, to the accompaniment of cries of *Hallelujah*! from Queeny and a fit of coughing by King George, Prindy made friendly signs to the little dog, which came to him writhing on its belly. Queeny's comment on Nell's tale was simply, 'Jesus been sent you . . . I been prayed.' A hint of the extremes that had brought her to praying, as well as of the reason for the excessive affection of the welcome just now, was forthcoming with her making another swipe at the dog, yelling, 'Dat bloody dog belong 'o shit man . . . him on'y shit dog . . . Gwon 'way, *mungus* dog . . . shit!' She then explained how the pit-diggers of the Depot across the way had fobbed the animal off on her as part payment for a huge debt they owed her for goods more or less forcibly extracted from her store, tobacco, grog, clothes: 'Bloody yeller puggin shit-diggin' robber bastard!' she yelled, turning towards the Depot as if she might be heard there. Then she proceeded to tell the sorry tale of her own experiences since leaving the Compound, while George went off to get food for breakfast from a hiding place. She declared that but for hiding what remained of her possessions, by now she would have nothing, thanks to those – and again she turned and raised her powerful voice to express her opinion of the neighbours.

George stirred up the fire and put on the billy for tea and produced crackers and canned beef to eat, behaving as if Queeny with her excited angry gabbling were not there; as she also did with regard to him. The *mungus* dog squatted quivering at a distance, waiting for the bits that now and again Prindy tossed him. Perhaps the halfcastes of the Sanitary Depot had given the poor little mongrel to her in deliberate jest. She said she had told them to get her a big savage animal as a watchdog. Some of them could have been amongst the many simpletons she herself had robbed in her long and ruthless career in business.

She had been ruthlessly dealt with from the very start of the adventure, according to her version of it. Willy Pak Poy, whom she had regarded as more than a friend and supposed would have done what she asked of him for not much more than a token fee, had charged her no less than fifty pounds, half her capital, for the trip from the Compound, demanding payment before he landed them at their destination, on the threat of taking them right back again and putting them ashore not on the Compound beach, but right in town: 'The bloody slant-eye Chinee puggin bastard . . . *yhuna mukka hai lo*!' she cried, and added more Chinese obscenities, concluding: 'I gitchim dat bastard some time . . . I tell him 'bout dat opium he pick up what Chinee steamer man chuck long o' sea . . . I know all 'bout it. I put him long o' jail. I wan' 'o belt dat bugger long o' crutch . . . but spone I do it like o' dat, who goin' 'o work dat launch?'

It seemed that, having got his fee, Pak Poy simply dumped the pair ashore with their goods and King George's boat, which he'd had in tow, on the first bit of open shore he came to, which happened to be the clearing in the mangroves of the estuary where the pits, in which what was politely and officially called Night Soil, was dumped, drained through the salt marshes on the sea. They'd had to call on the diggers and dumpers for further help, which included finding a suitable place to camp. These had begun by helping themselves to the goods, particularly to the rum and tobacco, first on demand as payment for their services, then on no less peremptory demand with the promise to pay later; part of the payment being the poor little Mungus. They had shifted them across the water and to this spot; and ever since, whenever they wanted anything, they came and took it, until they'd hidden it. What use the signatures of those who could write their names and the crosses of those who couldn't, so glibly made against what was debited to them in her account book? Again Queeny turned westward and at the top of her rich contralto delivered her opinion of the rogues.

Now their water, which they had been told was fed by a spring and to be relied on throughout the year, was definitely about to fail; and there was no other fresh water nearer than the New Settlement, except that in the tanks across the way, which it looked as if they'd soon have to be buying at the price of rum: 'Bloody stinkin' shit-diggin' bastard!' Queen yelled.

They would have got out before this, and gone back into the harbour and set up camp on the creek South of Rainbow Beach, only they couldn't get the boat back into the water. The spring tide they'd come in on was higher than this last one, and the Shit-diggin' Bastards had taken them up a creek as high as they could to make carrying to this point easier. Their efforts to launch the boat had failed through George's lack of strength and Queeny's inability to move about in the deep mud. George had cut corduroy to slide the boat down on, but was unable unaided to both lift the boat and get the timber under her. To ask the help of the *goona* shovellin' bloody buggers would surely mean complete dispossession. Queeny wanted the last of her goods to set up a trading station on that creek for dealing with the *Koonyarrakung* people who passed to and from their own still wild country, buying crocodile and buffalo hides and tin from them, as she used to on occasions at the Compound, but now to do it in a big way. She needed goods to start with. It was to the end of getting the boat afloat while the tides were still high that she had been praying Jesus to lend a hand, she said. That's all they needed: a couple of strong hands attached to feet that wouldn't leave you stuck in the mud for the crabs and the crocodiles – and 'Hallelujah, praise de Lord Sweet Jesus, das what we got now, ain't it?'

It took some talking over with those Jesus had sent along; that is to say Nell, since Prindy showed little interest in anything but the dog Mungus, except when George told him that if they went to Rainbow Creek they would be able to make that trip to Mt Mooragetaghee. Nell had but one idea in mind, and that to get back to the Beatrice as quickly as possible. She took a lot of convincing that it was even easier to get there by travelling by water what was obviously westward from here when her homing instinct told her it was sou'sou'east by terra firma, following a railway line. She would know the reputation this pair had as smarties who played the poor darkies for the simpletons they mostly were. But what else could she do, especially when Queeny predicted that the shit-diggers would be over in force tonight to deal with her, for sure, because they'd had a go at her too, only that she was, as she put it: 'All bugger up inside from what dat-lot bloody black bastard . . . this bloody one here, too . . . . ' she jerked her lips at indifferent George ' . . . been do it to me . . . Bloody puggin black bastard!' she yelled, and took a swipe at George, which he very skilfully dodged, as if he'd had lots of practise at it.

At last, on George's promise to take her and Prindy to the railway at the first opportunity after reaching Rainbow Creek, Nell agreed. Thereupon the move began. The cache of remaining goods, clothes, blankets, tobacco, pipes, matches, canned foods, was opened up, and carried down to the boat in the creek; and up and down again, for several hours, the procession went, so as to be ready to catch the tide tonight. It was a simple matter to get the boat ready for launching, with George and Nell heaving on a lever while Prindy poked the sticks beneath the keel. The only trouble was with sandflies and mosquitoes. They daren't light a fire for fear of rousing the suspicion of their neighbours and having them come to interfere.

Then everything was ready, and nothing to do but watch Igulgul come smirking looking a bit fatter out of the deepening blue, while oily brown water came up and up, with the mud-skippers leaping ahead of it and the crabs darting about and the big creatures of the deep harrying the little ones in the endless struggle for survival. Mungus was there. Queeny was for leaving him behind, tied up for the mob to find him tonight. But Prindy wanted him: 'For learn him properly bush-dog way,' as he said. He was so excited that someone had to keep an eye on him all the while to stop him from barking, instead of which he squeaked.

The lapping water was crimson as they shoved the boat into it. Then there was the rush to load those stores left out so as not to make the job too heavy. Then Mungus, with a hand over his muzzle to silence what could not now possibly have been restrained with mere threats of the violence that no one of Aboriginal upbringing could ever do to child or dog. They were on their way, keeping to the creek till it was good and dark and the water pulling back towards the sea. George had stepped his mast with the leg-of-mutton sail ready for use, but for the time was poling her along with an oar. Soon they were racing in the tide stream, soon out of the estuary and tossing in the swell of the open sea. With a light wind off the land and the current running parallel to it, George unfurled the sail, went into the stern to steer with an oar and work the sheet, heading northwestward, following the dark line of the shore, all the darker for the blaze of the setting Moon. Nor'nor'west of them blinked what George said was the Point Albert Lighthouse.

George told Prindy that the breeze would drop when Igulgul went down into his hole, because he sucked it, just as Old Tchamala sucked the sea and made the tide. Queeny's comment on that, made with a lilting laugh of derision, was: 'Dat blackfeller rubbitch, boy. Don't you tek notice. Bible say God mek him wind and sea and ev't'ing.'

Ignoring her, George said that moonset would bring them to a beach where there were coconuts, remnants of an old plantation, and where they would spend the night. Sure enough, there was Igulgul soon winking through tall palms and as he vanished the wind dropped. George took the depth with his oar, said they were almost on the bottom, and jumped out, with a blaze of phosphorescence that made Prindy cry out. George explained that it was nothing but the light Igulgul left behind him so that fishes and things could see where they were going in the dark: 'All-same you tek fire-stick from fire for look-about,' he explained, 'You come on in, gi' me hand.' Somewhat gingerly Prindy went overboard, but in a moment to be delighting in the wonder, which he described as being like someone lighting matches under water. George giggled, saying, 'Might be dat-one Jesus, eh?' A snort from Queeny.

When the boat grounded, George brought out his home-made kellick to moor her for the night. The bottom was hard sand. George said that she would be floating well inshore when they wanted her in the morning. Then, with dunnage for camping for the night, all four made their way up to the warm dry sand at the edge of the scrub, with Mungus leaping madly about squeaking on the edge of barking, while Queeny's flashlight struck at him like an extension of her crutch. When a fire was lit, Prindy wanted to take the flashlight and go look for coconuts with Mungus, but to the loud objection of the others, saying you didn't know what might be in there. By the sounds, after they had settled down, a lively little world was in there: the squeaks, the cracklings, rustlings, while flying foxes flapped and gabbled up in the coconuts. Not that Prindy paid much attention to it. Scarcely had he eaten when he fell asleep against George. His mother, on his other side, was not long in going off herself. Mungus dug a hole for himself at a safe distance from Queeny. The others sat for a goodly while, in stony silence, staring at the Point Albert light, Queeny smoking cigarette after cigarette, George a couple of pipes of opium.

Queeny was the last to drop down to the silky sand, pulling a blanket over her, but to wake after only an hour or so crying out so as to arouse the others. Panting, she told Nell that she had dreamt that a big black flying fox had her in his claws and was carrying her away. It was small wonder that she should dream of flying foxes, with the racket going on up top there; still, she declared that it was ominous, that in her country, away over East, to dream of the flying fox meant that someone close to you was soon to die, might be you'self. Prindy went off again at once; but the others took so long about it as to need to brew a billy of tea. Then George had to take himself off a little way because he was seized with coughing, and Queeny objected. When he was out of earshot Queeny muttered to Nell, 'He de one goin' 'o die, I reckon.' Then she added savagely: 'Might-be I kill de bloody black bastard!' Nell's comment was the indrawn whisper: Eh, look out!

Prindy and Mungus, well rested, had the others out at picaninny daylight with a noisy assault on the crab armies marching ahead of the incoming tide. The boat was well afloat. Prindy and the dog swam out to it, while Nell shrieked of sharks and Queeny called on Jesus. Prindy, already something of a boatman, had anchor up and boat ashore in no time. He would have loaded her with coconuts, only that there was scarcely room to move about in her as it was. He consumed one with his breakfast and took along another four. George said they must make the eastern horn of the harbour before the tide turned and Igulgul got up to come tchinekin, as he did by day, and blowing the sou'easter before him; otherwise they would be swept out to sea. He predicted a windy day, talking only to Prindy, but for the benefit of all. What they would do, he said, was to cross the harbour at the mouth, and lay up for the day in a little cove just inside West Point. Then with the aid of his Patrons, Igulgul and Tchamala, they would make their way in secret and with ease to their destination. He made no bones about reliance on those Patrons of his, perhaps largely in refutation of Queeny's too-ready mockery of blackfeller rubbitch.

But however the Old Ones had dealt with George in the past, they weren't a bit helpful today. Tchamala was already sucking the tide out at full rip again they reached the harbour, the invisible Igulgul breathing at some twenty knots at least – conditions that could have been disastrous for a less skilled boatman with a boat not so well equipped to meet them. There was no beating up against that wind and tide in what was a mere row-boat with a sail that was useless in any but a following wind. He kept her only as much into the wind as would give him steerway westwards, where there was land, if ever so far away, and not an horizon blank of anything but ivory bits of cloud out of which to make imaginary Isles of Spice. He was lucky in not having Queeny's mockery to make things worse. She started off well enough when it was evident that they were not heading as planned, but desisted as the sea got up and laid her low. All got seasick except George; even Mungus, but Queeny worst of all. She was beyond even caring for the spoiling of much of her precious merchandise by the swamping seas. Prindy recovered as soon as he'd got rid of his breakfast of coconut. He then took a hand, bailing. It was the turning of the tide again that saved them from a voyage to the so-called East away up there to north-westward, or return to their Dreaming Places in the spirit. Evidently George was counting on the turn to counter northerly drift when he pressed more to windward.

Thus in the middle of the afternoon he got them ashore on Prince Albert Peninsula, so close to Point Albert Lighthouse that the stripes about it were plain to see, but so far from Port Palmeston that the place was only a few purplish humps floating in heaving mirage from which Queeny, crying her thanks to Jesus for delivering her, turned looking as if white-ochred again. However, it wasn't long before Queeny, taking stock of things, delivered herself in her customary manner. George ignored her, going off with Prindy and Mungus to dig turtle eggs, this being a nice bit of beach and turtle tracks fresh on it.

They had the good luck to catch a turtle that, having been mauled by a shark or some such creature, was too stricken to return to the sea from its last-night's laying. They had that baked in its upturned shell, for supper, along with eggs cooked in hot ashes, and a damper of sorts made with soggy flour. Igulgul appeared to be laughing at them as he slipped down behind the scrub. They slept in the soft sand as the night before, but with no such interruptions. The lighthouse winked and winked, but without troubling them, because they knew, on George's information, that no one was there except the mysterious contraption that gave forth the light. There was nothing to fear from the *kuttabah's* magic, only from the *kuttabah* himself.

As the idea of chance can have no place in Aboriginal philosophy, it would be wrong to say that George was taking no chances with tomorrow's wind and tide when he took the precautions he did to avail himself of the very best conditions for navigation to suit his purpose. He anchored the boat in a bit of a creek with a channel that would fill with the first incoming water, unloaded her so as to have her floating at the first possible moment, and roused the camp at the first lap of the turning tide, declared breakfast off, had everybody racing to load up again when it was possible, and was under way while yet the light left by Igulgul from the night before blazed to the long strokes of his oars. Conditions were perfect. The sea was like a billabong at midday for smoothness, the tide set to sweep them towards Port Palmeston even if they'd lain down and slept once they got out into the run of it, the only wind that made by their progress. So easy was the going that George declined Prindy's assistance on the oars, telling him to throw the spinner out and hook a few of the multitude of fishes to be heard and seen about them, so that they might breakfast well on arrival at their destination. Prindy showed the true Aboriginal philosophy by asking him to Sing the *White Fish*, and joined in with him with a much more musical version of the chant, despite the snickering of Queeny.

Soon there were the lights of the Jail to be seen. They should pass it in daylight too faint for anyone watching even with a spyglass to take them for other than Greek fishermen, so said the knowledgeable George. But he was forgetting that one in the Jail who he believed needed no such things as white-man's magic to know what was going on and who was particularly concerned with his own, that is to say George's, business just then. He soon had cause to remember the Pookarakka. Normally, at this time of year, the wind, the Trade Wind of the southern tropics, would rise with the Sun, as a breeze that developed in strength with the heat of the day. Later it could be expected to get earlier as the continental Inland got colder with advance of winter and the northern seas by contrast warmer, until for several weeks it would be blowing all the while. There might have been a cold snap down Inland last night – might, that is, if blackfellow logic were to be ignored. The breeze caught them while they were off Turtle Beach. Then would have been the time to act upon that logic, had wisdom prevailed. But how act upon it readily in these days when it was held in such contempt that a master of it like the Pookarakka was kept in a cage, when things had come to such a pass that a man was reduced to travelling with tribal sisters, even to have them pissing in one's presence, as that peg-legged rubbitch did without shame in the bailer tin? So George kept on, even when the breeze was so stiff as to need Prindy's help on the oars. He said that as things were they'd never make their destination today. Instead they would make for West Point and wait in a salt-arm till dark. But they never got within cooee of the harbour's mouth. Such was the wind by sunrise as to defeat all advantage to be had from the tide, which meant at last to have the tide against them, too. It was then that George admitted openly what privily was probably nagging his mind for a long while, the way he kept casting worried glances at the pile of shimmering whiteness on the harbour's eastern shore that was the Jail: 'Old Pookarakka been sing him wind, I reckon. Him *koola* long o' me.' It was to Prindy, as always, he spoke, and softly, since it was masculine business. But the women heard; and Queeny sniggered to Nell about silly-bugger blackfeller. George said nothing to that, but swung the boat round, shipped his oars, gave one to Prindy to steer with while he unfurled the bit of sail.

Queeny demanded, 'Wha' you doin' . . . where you go?'

Ignoring her, George took the steering, heading for Turtle Bay.

But they were in the middle of the tide stream, running nor'west. There was no getting clear of it to make the shore. The Pookarakka was doing things properly. George knew better than to waste energy trying to beat him. He eased the sheet, let the boat have her way with the following wind and sea. How she spanked along!

Queeny demanded, 'Wha' you doin' . . . goin' 'o bloody China?'

Soon they were abeam the camping place of last night, and quickly overhauling the lighthouse. Queeny sitting amidships, amidst her dunnage, and Nell, up near the bow, kept looking ashore and astern and ahead and at each other with evident increasing concern. As they swept on past the beach, Queeny raised her voice again: 'Wha's matter . . . you go jitty, old-man . . . where you goin' to?'

George gave his answer through Prindy: 'Behin' point dere, no-more big wind, no-more sitrong tide.'

That's how it turned out – although the Pookarakka made things so lively as they turned Point Albert that it looked as if his intentions were not mere harrassment but sheer deadly. The sea was boiling in a rip that at times seemed to lift the small vessel clean out of the water and dump her down again so that she wallowed in green wells. Queeny screamed to Jesus. Even old George was crying out in lingo what sounded like appeals to the Wise One. Nell and Mungus crouched together, whimpering and vomiting. Prindy, large-eyed, simply hung on.

Then there they were, in comparatively quiet water, running westerly past a high rocky shore, above the sheer cliffs of which the heaving of the trees showed how the wind was piping. No chance of a landing there, even though the water inshore was glassy smooth. Then round another point and running now sou'westward.

'Look-see!' said George to Prindy.

Far ahead of them the shore turned due westward, so far away as to be seen only as a dun line. But reared behind it was a violet pyramid – Mt Mooragetaghee. Prindy recognized it with a smile. 'We go dere now,' said George.

'Where you goin'?' demanded Queeny.

Nell added her voice: 'We wan' 'o go long o' railway line.'

George said to Prindy, 'Railway line dere behin' river dere. Whiteman call-yim Finish River . . . from time dat-lot come overland . . . dey finish dere. Mooragetaghee dey call-yim Mt. Finish. We go up dat river . . . go, go . . . we come Mooragetaghee By'n'by we go long o' railway line '

Queeny yelled, 'I wan' 'o go long o' Rainbow Beach '

George said to his mate, 'I reckon Pookarakka want him me tek you long o' Mooragetaghee. Dat *Tchinek* place. Might be we wait long o' him dere. We meet him blackfeller dere. I send him word long old-man. Dat my half-country, I been tell him you '

Queeny yelled louder, 'I wan' 'o go Rainbow Beach '

George answered but without looking at her, 'All right . . . jump overboard, tchwim!'

She shut up, at length fell asleep amongst her sodden and mostly ruined goods. She woke to find the boat tossing again. 'Silly black bastard . . . what you doin' now?' she cried.

They had just cleared the high shores of the northern part of the peninsula which constituted that region, and were come into a long bay backed with mangrove swamps that curved all the way round to where, at its western extremity, it dissolved in mirage. The wind, blowing over low country, was as fierce here as round the other side, and seemed all the worse after the spell of quietude. But whereas on the eastern side the sea had run wild, here there was not enough of it to raise a wave worthy of the name, because the tide was now low and the bay for the most part stinking mud. Queeny woke to find George struggling with an oar to keep them off a mud-bank. There was no leaving it to the sail here. They had to row, following winding channels that sometimes proved to be *culs-de-sac* and had to be rowed all over again, or that were connected with others so shallow that those who could get out without getting stuck for good had to do so to pull her across. Queeny, the one who hadn't to do anything, cursed George for messing up her goods with the foul mud. He forgot himself again several times to curse her back, telling her that if she didn't *kai-atulli* he'd heave her stuff overboard and make their going easier.

The tide was coming in again; and they were sailing again, helped again in heading across wind by the set of the tide as it rushed in to fill the swamps. They were making great way, with higher country looming up to southward to give promise of a landing for the night. Already they could see the silvery gap in the grey-green of the southern shore that George told Prindy was the mouth of the Finish River – and all the while Mooragetaghee, rising higher and higher from the wilderness. They were hugging the shore as close as possible now to take advantage of its shelter, because further out the white horses were tossing their manes out of the coffee-coloured water. They would be about half a mile offshore. Now there were no mud banks. They had scraped over the last of them away back. The shore was still lined with mangroves, but behind could be glimpsed the eucalypts of higher ground than the tides could touch. Everything looking lovely – when the Pookarakka struck again – *CRASH*! They all fell in a yelling heap as the boat stopped dead. The water was too dirty to see what it was; but George quickly found it with an oar. A reef – shoved up right in front of them, and so hard that there was a gaping hole in the bow with the milky coffee gushing in. George grabbed a sack of Queen's flour to plug it, and had Nell sit on it, while he and Prindy heaved everything else into the stern, including the shrieking Queeny and the yelping Mungus. Then he tried shoving the boat off. She wouldn't budge, except to swing her stern from the tide and tear still more out of her torn bow. The water poured in. Queeny yelled to Jesus to save her. George called on the Pookarakka: 'Wha's matter, old-man . . . you too rough . . . I do it ever't'ing you ask him me . . . go easy, Pookarakka!' Nell grabbed Prindy, only to be pushed away, as he turned to help George heave the cargo overboard. There was no need for that. Soon what could float was floating out, as the stern rose with the rushing tide and the jammed bow went under.

'We got 'o tchwim shore,' yelled George. 'Grab hold someping.' The flour sacks were floating, but sweeping out of reach. Prindy went shooting after them, got hold of two. His mother came up and got one. George had the oars. Queeny was floating on her crutch and peg. Mungus came paddling in the rear. Still Queeny talked to Jesus, about sharks and crocodiles now: 'I never been do it wrong t'ing, Jesus . . . you look-out me now I go mission-church ev' Sunday . . . sweet Jesus, you look-out me now!'

They needed to swim only to keep together. The tide was sweeping them ashore along with all the rubbish of the mangroves it had previously swept out. It looked at first as if the succour awaiting them ashore (if they were not prevented from reaching it by one of the invisible things making the mullet leap like bubbles of silver out of the slimy brown) was to be no better than that of the egrets they could see here and there perched in the mangroves watching them. Then George saw a creek, and called on them to head for it. They were soon in it, just a filthy channel running through the mangroves. Here the tide was racing. They turned several bends, then came suddenly into a region of rising banks of mud. George said they'd keep on and come to hard ground. But scarcely had he said it, when Prindy cried, 'Look-it!'

Not fifty yards ahead of them there was a momentary swirl of water that revealed a scaly back and tail and head, fifteen feet and more in length – just a glimpse – then there were only four small protuberances in quadrigeminal pattern – nostrils and eyes.

George yelled, 'Crocodile!' let go his oar and with arms and legs boiling the water into coffee froth, headed for the bank. The others did likewise, Queeny at the tail, yelling to Jesus, Mungus going round in rings at a loss to understand it all – till he saw the pattern come cutting the water towards the group, saw the westerning Sun reflected by the yellow eyes – then he swung towards the thing, barking at the top of his shrill voice, one ear up and one ear down: '*Kai, kai, kai, kai, kai* . . . !'

The rush stopped. The golden eyes blinked. Still Mungus kept on: *Kai, kai, kai, kai*!'

Nostrils and eyes vanished.

Mungus looked round to see his people struggling up the slimy bank. Yelping in fear of being left behind, he set out splashing after them. Prindy pulled the dog out of the water while his mother tried to pull him back. But his mother took the muddy little mongrel to her bosom and like all the others and particularly Queeny, wept over him: 'My lil dog . . . my lil doggie . . . wha' Jesus been gi' me to save my life . . . oh, my darlin' lil Mungus-dog!'

It was no great distance through the belt of mangroves. As soon as the top of the bank was reached the glaring brightness of the saltpan backing it could be seen. Yet it took almost till sundown to get through to it, owing to the disability of Queeny, who had to do it on hands and knees and with peg removed because it entangled with the tricky roots. Her Christian joy in deliverance was soon discarded for fierce complaint about her lot in being involved with black bastards, not entirely due to the discomfort of the moment; for George had countered her calling Mungus an agent of Jesus by telling Prindy that they had been in no real danger from the crocodile, since the creatures never attached Snake Men – this despite the tremendous haste of his own retreat. The fact that a crocodile is an inveterate coward and will only pursue what won't stand up to him, something at least George and Queeny would know, was out of the question in the circumstances.

At last they gained dry ground, a strip of glistening saltpan untouched by tides since the greater ones early in the year. Beyond lay a fringe of maritime jungle, backed by rising forest country. Prindy broke off a couple of stout mangrove sticks to enable Queeny, with her peg strapped back on, to hobble across. In the process of putting on the peg, Queeny drew from the elastic-gripping leg of her drawers a sodden package, at which she took a swift and somewhat secret look: bank-notes.

The Sun was already down in the trees. Peg-leg was now complaining of thirst. George informed Prindy that there was no hope of getting fresh water in such a place, and evidently being either in no such need of it as the complaining one or pleased to suffer to make her suffer more, did nothing about seeking a place more likely. He said they would camp there. They settled down in the red evening, with Igulgul laughing at them through the trees and the mosquitoes and sandflies from the mangroves to add to the joke, and Queeny moaning about the gross of tins of wax vestas that had gone down with the ship, since a certain black bastard hadn't the blackfeller savvy to make a fire otherwise, Maybe she wanted the fire as much to dry her bank-notes, which she lay out again with a show of secrecy, on the baked warm salty ground.

They were fortunate in being largely protected from the insects through being coated with mud. Prindy promised them fire as soon as he could lay hands on a bit of dry ironwood. He did so repeatedly throughout a night that for people less naturally endowed to suffer such a state of things might well have been described as hideous. Queeny must make it worse by dreaming again of the big black flying fox. 'Somebody goin' 'o die,' she moaned. 'Somebody goin' 'o die all right . . . might be me . . . oh, poor-feller me!'

George had them on the move at first light, sticking to the maritime strip westward – easy going for Queeny – compensating for its much winding in following the contour of the mangrove swamp. She was soon able to swing along in something like her usual lope when a sapling was found that she could use as a crutch. Prindy also found his ironwood in the form of a piece that had been washed up by the tide, and soon with a piece of quartz found in a dry creek bed, began to fashion the drill-part of an *ingornu* outfit as they went. They crossed several of these dry creeks, up a couple of which they looked for water, but only to find that they were mere Wet Season washouts. Queeny, settled down to what after all was something that came natural to her, ceased to complain, easing her thirst by sucking a pebble, and otherwise occupying herself by questioning Nell about the Beatrice River country, her interest such as to suggest that she was thinking of going along to look the place over as one to suit her for the future.

There was plenty of game about: wallabies, goannas, ground birds like quail and squatter pigeons; but water was their concern of the moment. Anyway, hunting wouldn't have been so easy, with Mungus racing yapping after everything. He was driven to the rear with dire threats a hundred times.

Thus till nearly noon, when they found themselves confronted with a salt arm that turned them suddenly southward and soon had them in rising rocky country following what evidently was the mouth of a fair-sized creek. No easy track here. The banks of both sides ended abruptly in the top branches of a fringe of mangroves clinging to sheer walls of mud. The tide was out, the stream not much more than a sluggish brown gutter beside which the armies of small crabs manoeuvred. A half-sized crocodile, basking in the mud, slid into the water at sound of their noisy progress over the rocks, George's puffing and Queeny's clattering. Mungus would have gone after him and found to his cost that while a crocodile may be a coward he isn't a fool and knows just the right moment to snap or grab, according to the size of the unwary one; but Prindy, beginning to get control of him, halted him with a snap of the fingers, even if he couldn't stop him from making the rocks ring with his *kai-kai-kai-ing*.

Then just when Queeny was starting again to talk about black bastards and her ruin by them, they came to a bar of rock rearing high above the mud as a whiteman's dam, the smooth red top of it surely due to the cascading of fresh water during the rains, and water trickling over it now in places, although it was muddy. For certain there would be fresh water behind it. Almost as they saw it, Prindy clicked his tongue in signal to George ahead of him, and when he stopped told him he could hear *tilbyuk* – duck. George signalled for silence.

Ahead of them was a low ridge, of which the bar was part. They topped it to see ahead of them on their side, the left, a grassy expanse, lying between the creek, which here was lined with tallish paperbarks and other fresh-water trees, and a true billabong, overflow from what must be a considerable stream in wet weather. Everybody could hear the ducks now, and see them, in glimpses, as they swam amongst the lilies. Prindy had almost to throttle Mungus to impress on him the need for silence. Poor Mungus accepted the situation, but at such cost of emotion as to stand shaking as if about to take a fit.

Prindy and George, as true blackfellows, were already armed after a fashion, with likely bits of wood for effective throwing. George conferred quickly with Prindy, then sent him ahead, and signalled the women to stop where they were with Mungus. Prindy went up the ridge a little under cover of the rocks, then came down in tall grass. George went directly, from cover to cover of small bushes growing on the flat. The billabong itself was conveniently screened, with small bushes and pandanus. Its inner-shore was the rock of the hillside.

There were two groups of birds swimming and feeding, a dozen or so whistler ducks in pairs, one pair of green pigmy geese. The geese were up at the near-end, the ducks all over the place. Prindy came in close to the little geese, signalled to George that he had something at hand. George went on, now on his belly, came in by the water halfway along its length. The hunters had each other in view most of the while. Soon the strategy was disclosed. George signalled. Prindy rose quickly, hurled his stick at the geese, skimming it so, that it struck both. The ducks nearby quacked the alarm, turned into the wind, took off with whistling wings, bunching together, half a dozen or more. George downwind from them, rose and sent his stick whirling into their midst. Four came down. He pounced on them. Prindy was already in the water finishing off the disabled geese – and Mungus was coming *kai-kai-kai-kai-ing* to join Prindy, who gave him a thump with the dead birds as he came out of the water, sending him off to hide in the grass, squeaking with humiliation.

The women, neither of them likely to be concerned about the proprieties of the life they were now leading, came hurrying down to drink without awaiting the signal permitting them to do so. George took his revenge by walking off with Prindy, when the pair, having drunk flung themselves down to enjoy the luxury of a bellyfull of water after a long parch, lying in shade on couch grass with bruised feet in cool sweet water. He led Prindy across the flat and up the creek a little, crossed the creek, stopping to taste and feel the faintly muddy water. He looked up the creek, saying, 'White feller up dere, I reckon, minin.' When Prindy asked how far, he answered, 'Little-bit long way. Might-be half-day foot-walk.'

They chose a bit of flat under a big flood-bent paperbark, to make camp. George dropped down to rest, puffing, against the shaggy silky trunk of the tree, to watch Prindy set to work with his *ingornu*, already about right to operate. It comprised the hardwood drill, a piece of softwood with a hole scooped with a bit of quartz to take the former, and a slip of teased stringybark. In the approved cross-legged squatting posture, Prindy twirled the drill between his palms. George smiled at the facility of it. In no time the smoke was rising in a tiny whisp. The drill twirled back and forth so fast as to appear only as a blur in the increasing little haze of smoke. Then Prindy stopped, blew into the smoking sawdust, quickly touched it with the teased bark. A burst of smoke – a tongue of flame. George cried: '*Yakkarai*!' Prindy grinned at him, reached for a handful of leaves, looked up to see the two women watching from the water. Queeny smiled broadly at him. But not his mother. Nor did she show any gratification when George said to Prindy, 'Gi'm pi'my gootch you Mumma, boy.'

Soon the ducks and geese were sizzling and popping on a heap of coals. Nothing had been done to pluck or gut them. Anyway, the feathers were burnt off, and the guts blew out – and by the way they were eaten, to the scraps that were tossed to Mungus, nothing of their natural sweetness had been lost by so crude a mode of cookery. George pointed out some little fan palms the hearts of which made good eating, he said, adding that they would later look about for a sharp rock to chop them with. When Prindy asked what about making spears, George answered that they'd better wait till they went to the whiteman's mine and could borrow a tommy'awk to do the job easily. Mention of the mine caused Nell alarm. Even when she heard George tell Prindy that only he himself would go, she declared, 'We wan' o' go long o' railway line.'

'Yeah,' cried Queeny. 'We go find him railway line. We wan' 'o go Beatrice.'

George said to Prindy, 'Come on, *Kokanjinni* . . . we go look him dat sharp rock. Bring him dog. We learn him.'

That was the way a man must deal with a sister and a nephew. Prindy went without a word to the women. Queeny's comment was: 'Arrrh . . . bloody blackfeller!'

George cracked a piece of the red granite of the locality to make a sharp axe-head, then showed Prindy how to chop out the tender heart stuff of a palm, the base of the sprouting frond. *Pam*, as it was called in Murringlitch, consisted of a cylindrical rod of what looked like ivory, three to four inches long by about an inch in diameter, the tip of it the embryonic frond. The taste was sweetly nutty. They ate two themselves, then chopped a couple of palms down and took them back to the camp for the women to open up themselves. As George said, 'Dat-one job belong 'o woman.' George also showed him how the sheaths at the base of the mature leaves could be used for smoking by stuffing them with tobacco, which caused him to bemoan the fact that he had nothing to smoke. 'Long o' my properly country,' he said, 'got him dat-one Pituri . . . you can smoke him . . . goot-feller, all-same hopium.' He sighed. 'Dis country nutching.'

They left the women, to go back to the billabong, to get tortoises or turtles, for supper, so George said, but really to have that luxurious camp denied the women. While they camped, George told Prindy bits of legends about the locality, including that of how, in the Dream Time, old Goorawundanji, the Saltwater Crocodile, came to take the form and habits such creatures have today. 'Dat Goorawundanji, he got three-feller wife and big mob picaninny. He look-out dat-lot properly. He good huntin' man. Proper fat dat-lot belong 'o him from goot tucker. But by'n'by one big-feller python he been try gitchim, dat-one bite him. He get sick now. Can't go huntin'. All-day sit down long o' camp, wait for dat-lot mob belong him tucker him. Dey get plenty lil-feller tucker . . . yam, lily, bandicoot, possum, sugar-bag. But dey eat him long o' bush, come back camp say nutching tucker. He stop fat dat-lot. But dat old-man get pretty poor. By'n'by he proper bone-bugger, too weak. Dat mob belong him leave him now. He goin' 'o die finish. He crawl down long o' mangrove. Can't walk no more. Tide come, take him 'way . . . lo-ong way he go, right down dere long Old Tchamala. Dat Old-one now, he say: "Wha's matter you?" Goorawundanji tell him 'bout. Old Tchamala say: "Well, da's wha' for you been huntin' my mate Python. You le'm 'lone. Spone you le'm 'lone altogether *Tchenek, Tchenek Man*, I tucker you plenty fish." All right, he been do it like o' dat. Goorawundanji been change shape, like dat crocodile now, and he stop long o' salt water, eat him fish. But he got 'o get square long o' dat wife and picaninny, dat no-goot woman and kid belong'o him. He come up from saltwater, wait long o' creek crossin', long o' drinkin' place. One day he gitchim all-lot drinkin'. He been grab him tuckered him. He been lie down sleep. But dat lot kick round in him guts. He *barcoo* him. He rock now, dat mob. Him dere now, long o' Finish River Crossing. I show him you time I tek you long o' Mooragetaghee.'

Turtle hunting was really woman's business, George said; nevertheless, he and Prindy and Mungus caught five between them. They also dug some lily-roots. But, George declared, those women would have to do their stuff in food gathering when they themselves had the weapons they needed for big game, otherwise they, the women, could go without. They returned to the camp across the creek as the Sun got down in the trees.

While the tortoises were sizzling savourily in their shells on the coals and the lily roots baking with steamy fragrance in hot ashes, pied butcher birds, come to spend the night nearby so as to be the first to pick up the scraps next day, gave throat in melodious chorus to farewell the passing day. Prindy mimicked the birds: *Gool-gool gee gool-gool* . . . . George took advantage of the situation to tell Prindy the yarn about how Gurrawirrilyuma, the Butcher Bird, came to adopt the practice of hiding the results of his hunting, the frogs and lizards and nestling birds and things, spiked in thorny bushes. Like Old Gorrawundanji, the Crocodile, Old Gurrawirrilyuma had numerous wives and lots of kids, and was a great provider; but his trouble wasn't that he got sick and was neglected to the point of death; instead his women were too lazy to go out with the children to get the small foodstuffs to supplement the big meats, and hung about camp all day sleeping and talking, telling him the same lie as had Goorawundanji's mob. When he woke up to the truth he turned the tables on them by tuckering himself out in the bush and hiding what was left over, returning to say that there was no game about. Queeny caught the inference and replied to it with a grunt, 'Urrh . . . we-feller ain't you bloody wife and kid.'

But if George failed to score a point with the women then, he did later, when not long after the Moon had set and the night seemed very dark and menacing and a crocodile was heard bellowing down in the salt-arm, he told Prindy that it was probably the same old bull they had encountered the day before, come round looking for the women, told where they were by the dotterels, who were mates of crocodiles and who had watched their own progress round the swamps. He suggested to Prindy that they two shift camp, because Old Tchamala might be annoyed with them if they stopped where they were and spoilt the hunting of one of his friends, and it wasn't likely that the crocodile would come while they were there. Queeny cried, 'Dat on'y bloody puggin blackfeller gammon

. . . but spone you go 'way, I don' give you no money for buy tobacco and tommy'awk from dat tin miner.'

George had been throwing out hints about money for those things. He now told Prindy that he would tell the crocodile that the women were no longer here, and raised his voice to call something in lingo. It seemed to work. The bellowing was not heard again. All slept soundly, worn out by the long hard day and comforted by mopokes telling them that the district was clear of forces likely to do them harm.

The butcher birds had them out with the first flush of dawn, singing for those scraps, as Prindy put it in a little song he sang back to them:

Gool-gool, gee gool-gool,
Butcher Bird in tree,
Singin' for breakfas',
Gool-gool gool gee gee!

'*Yakkarai*! cried George. 'Properly *Mundinjana* my-boy . . . properly Song Man!'

The bold birds came swooping down, sounding their usual sharp croaking warning to anyone silly enough to interfere with them. There was one such, as his name betokened – Mungus, who although so stuffed with the spoils of the hunting that he had ignored the scraps, came at one bird yapping: *Kai-kai-kai-kai*! – to have no such victory as with the old-man crocodile. While that bird nipped him on the snout, another took him in the rear, right in the anus. Shrilling with pain, he went leaping into the creek. When his friends had done laughing at him, they all told him it should be a lesson to him, especially in the matter of barking. 'How many time I tell him you you got 'o keep quiet spone you wan' 'o be huntin' dog?' Prindy asked him when he came to him, shivering as ever with shame in his folly.

Nothing had been said about when they should go to the tin-mine; but such was the expressed longing of all three adults for tobacco as soon as the butcher bird incident had passed, that it was evident they wouldn't be wasting much time heading that way. In fact within an hour or so of being roused, that's what they were doing.

Breakfast was awaiting them just a little way up the creek in the form of a delicacy known in the patois as Stick Egg. It was no egg at all, but a gall growing on a miniature type of swamp bloodwood. The bit of dry swamp they came to was thickly grown with the small bushes, every one of them infested. The galls showed by their size (about that of a tennis ball) and colour, that they were at their very best for eating, according to George, packed with the lavae of the Gall Wasp, which would be fat with the syrupy juice that, by means of some marvellous natural chemistry induced by the parent fly in depositing her eggs, was supplied them from the sap of the tree. All you had to do was pull the gall off with a twist of the hand, then crack it open with a rock and suck out the squirming contents. The *munjongs*, which is to say the newchums, expressed their delight with it; and there was no doubt about Mungus's appreciation, despite his silence. Mungus was silent even when a family of kangaroos, drinking from the creek, came bounding out, to go thud-thud-thudding into the dense forest – except for some faint squeaking. There were other foods in plenty, such as yams of several types, cycad nuts, things that had to be prepared and cooked, even prepared for days in the case of the last, and fruit trees that in their season would be bearing. Altogether a fruitful land, despite the fact that it had been overrun some two-score years before by the *kuttabah* and that even worse despoiler, the Chinee-man, tin-mining, proving that the land itself, left to itself, could recover and re-establish its creatures, except the human. Soon they were seeing ample evidence of the mining, in the way of old gravel heaps and shafts and rusty bits of steel and broken glass – and weeds, weeds, Chinaman's and whiteman's weeds, that had perhaps once taken full possession of the creek banks, but now, what with floods and the greater resilience of native growth, were looking pretty poorly on it.

The rock of the country changed markedly as they progressed, from the hard granite into soft micaceous stuff, with consequent widening and deepening of the creek-bed, so that but for the poor little flow of water, it looked more like the bed of a river. Quartzy benches, grown with quite big trees of aquatic type, now stretched away from the stream on either side, to banks becoming higher and steeper as the country rose. The stream was getting muddier, too.

They had been going for some hours, when Prindy, at George's heels, clicked his tongue. George stopped. Jerking his jaw to indicate upstream, Prindy said, 'Injin.' Apparently not even Mungus could hear it, while they all stood listening. There was a lot of noise in the tree-tops from the wind. But George knew those supersensitive ears by now. He said they'd better get up on top. He chose the bank on their left, found a gutter by which to make climbing easy for his old enemy swinging along in the rear, led the way up.

The surrounding country was flat open forest. It would not be hard to spot a camp or homestead well ahead. All were soon able to hear on the gusty wind the beat of some kind of engine. Then there was glimpsed the shimmer of new galvanized-iron through the trees. They went warily. It proved to be a small homestead, comprising a verandahed dwelling built at ground level, a couple of sheds, a small elevated tank, a stockyard, fowl-run, all a little distance, say quarter of a mile, from the creek. By the creek was another tank and shed, and near these the low humpies of a blacks' camp. It was from the point beside the creek that the sound of the engine came. No sign of life, except a couple of horses sleeping under a tree.

George sent Prindy across the creek to see if there were anything to be avoided there, and when he came back to say Nutching, ordered him to take the women over there and follow the creek up to somewhere above the homestead, keeping out of sight, which should not be difficult, because of the screen the top-of-the-creek timber made along the banks, and there to sit down and wait for him. He held out his hand to Queeny for money. She got the wad from her drawers, tried to fob him off with a single One Pound Note. He demanded two, on the threat of abandoning them. Cursing him, she gave in.

Prindy already had an easy way down to the creek and up again. He led the way, and along up the other side; while the beat of the engine grew louder, and along with it came the intermittent sound of voices and the ring of tools. At length they came in sight of the source of the sounds, just a glimpse through the trees: a sluice box at the foot of a bush-timber chute built into the bank on this side, at which half a dozen men were working, a couple of them ruddy white, the others black, all clad only in shorts. The blackmen were shovelling the stuff from the chute into the box, while the whites, one tall and lean, the other nuggety, were cleaning up the concentrates with a device worked by the popping engine. A glimpse was enough for the trio. They drew away from the creek, skirted the region of operations, in the manœuvre crossing a road evidently made by the frequent passage of a heavy truck, came back to the creek-bank at least two hundred yards above, where the greater height and density of the timber below made a perfect screen. The most luxuriant growth was revealed as being due to a pool of clear green water stretching away as far on either side as could be seen from there. It looked very inviting, but in the circumstances must be viewed from afar, at least by the women. The banks were quite steep here, impossible of negotiation by Queeny. Prindy wanted to go down at once and get water for them in a coolamun made with paperbark, but was prevented by his mother. However, as time passed, she succumbed to his pressing, and he went, leaving Mungus struggling in silence in Queeny's strong brown hands. Before bringing the water up, Prindy went downstream to take a look, and saw that the water was dammed by a natural bar. The sluicing was going on below it. He didn't dare to go too close. He went back for the water and carried it up by an easier route than that by which he had gone down.

Soon after he came back to the women the engine down below stopped, and along with it the sounds of work, but not the voices. The difference in the voices could be distinguished, the loud harsh voices of the whites, the high whooping laughter of the blacks. It was noon. Evidently the workmen were having crib. That's what Queeny reckoned. 'I like a bit o' brea'n'beef,' she said, swallowing.

'Might-be *Nungalla* bring him,' said Prindy.

'You stop dat lingo!' his mother snapped.

'Got 'o talk lingo long o' bush,' he complained.

'By'n'by we back long o' Beatrice.'

'Me-two-feller *Nungalla* go long o' Mooragetaghee first-time.'

'No you don't. We go long o' railway line.'

Prindy broke the silence that followed by saying he could hear George's voice now down with the others. They waited. Still George did not come. The engine started up again, and the sounds of work. But no George. Prindy said he would go and take a peep, and without waiting for agreement, shot off to do so, along the top of the bank. Mungus dashed after him. He turned on the dog and ordered silence. Mungus appeared to understand, and trotted at his heels.

Prindy approached the scene of operations under cover of the contraption at the top of the chute into which the gravel for washing in the sluice-box below was dumped, brought from somewhere by means of that road they had crossed. It was a rough thing built of vertical saplings, just two L-shaped wings each side of the head of the chute, its purpose to feed the latter by gravity as the stuff was shovelled away below. As it protruded from the almost vertical bank, an easy and apparently safe way to get a clear view of what was going on below was to get into it and look through one of the wide cracks between its timbers. It was pretty well filled. One had only to drop down a couple of feet onto the red gravel and duck into the left-hand corner. Prindy did so, with Mungus on his heels – only to find the soft dry stuff sinking under him as even the slight impact of his jump set it flowing down the chute – and his struggling only made things worse. In a moment he and Mungus were out on the chute, and sweeping down as a couple of heaving heaps, to the astonishment of the couple of black shovellers at the foot attracted by their stifled yelps, who dropped their shovels and bolted. They crashed into the wooden sluice-box, now to be swept along in the muddy mess made by the ejection of a heavy stream of water from a wide pipe at the head of the sluice. Thus they were delivered onto the riffles, to the astonishment now of everyone, even a couple of large dogs. The two whitemen were no strangers, but the Knowles brothers, Nugget and Nobby, whom Prindy must know by sight at least. But familiar or not, Prindy was not staying. He struggled up, leapt off the plate, landed in a heap of wet tailings, bogged to the knees, was helpless again. A lean strong red-brown hand closed on a slender golden-brown arm; and the mean hatchet face came close to his own as Nobby, shouting above the din of the nearby engine, demanded, 'Eh . . . where'd you spring from?' Mungus fared no better. As he fled, *kai-kai-kai-ing* the big dogs leapt at him and stood over him while he lay on his back squeaking for mercy.

Apt pupil of Bobwirridirridi, Prindy slipped out of the grip, leapt out of the gravel, bolted for a road leading up the left bank through a cutting, his dog doing likewise. But there was something wrong with him, as everybody but himself saw, expressing their concern with sharp cries: 'Eh, eh, boy!' His right foot was shiny red with blood; and blood could be seen to spurt with his every step on it. He kept on, reached the road. The dogs went after the pair till someone shouted at them.

Then Nugget Knowles, shutting off the engine, yelled at King George, 'He one o' your mob?' and when George nodded, he added, 'Well, stop him . . . he's bleedin' bad!'

Prindy was scrambling up the rutty road. George put hand to mouth and called, '*Kokanjinni . . . danook . . . danook*!'

Prindy stumbled to a halt, looked back. George signalled him to return. Prindy turned, but still stood, grey eyes on the whitemen. George called, 'No more fright . . . him all right.'

Prindy came slowly, to stop again when Nugget came hurrying to meet him. Nugget said, ' 'S all right, sonny . . . gi's look at yo' *mundowi*.' Prindy looked down at his foot, apparently only now aware of the wound. A pool of blood was gathering round it.

George said, 'Boss all right, *Kokanjinni*.'

Nugget came up to him, sank down to look at the wound: 'Crise, you got a bad cut there. Here, sit down. I'll have to stop the bleedin'.'

The cut, evidently made by a shovel or some such thing he had struck in being hurtled along, was on the outside of the foot near the sole, almost from heel to toe, and deep as the bone the way it gaped and the blood pumped out of it. Prindy looked at George, who nodded, then sat down. Nugget pressed the gaping lips of the wound together, said, 'That'll have to be stitched.' He let go, to pull from the pocket of his khaki shorts a grubby handkerchief, which he folded quickly, while telling George to get a small stick. Then he applied the handkerchief as a tourniquet just below the ankle. The bleeding stopped immediately. 'Now, you hang on to it . . . tight now . . . and I'll carry you up.' Again Prindy looked for George's agreement.

The lanky Nobby, staring at Prindy, said as his brother took him up in his arms, 'I know him . . . he's from Beatrice . . . that right, eh?' he asked of Prindy.

Prindy met the narrow quizzing pale blue eyes, but didn't answer. Nugget took a look at him: 'Yeah . . . seen you Races, eh?'

Nobby added, 'Nelly Ah Loy's kid.' He looked at George for confirmation. When George appeared not to hear, he asked Prindy, 'Wha' name, you runaway or sumpin?'

George said, 'Lil bits walkabout, da's all, Boss.'

Nugget said, 'Where's his mother now?'

No answer. Nugget added, 'Better tell her . . . 'cause I wan' 'o take him up the house and put couple o' stitches in that wound . . . or he'll bleed to death.'

George made a sign to Prindy, who jerked his chin whence he'd come. 'Sing out to her,' said Nugget.

A nod from George and Prindy put hand to mouth and called: '*Ku*!'

No answer. Prindy called again, without reply. 'Come on,' said Nugget. 'She can come behind. Got 'o get this fixed. Got 'o get that twitch off, or it'll do damage to yo' *mundowi* . . . and you don' wan' that, eh?' He smiled at Prindy, who looking into the blue eyes, smiled slightly in response.

Then just as they set off towards the road up the other bank, there was a yell from the opposite side. The dogs barked. All looked. There was Nell at the top of the cutting: 'Le' my boy 'lone, yo' bastard!'

She was rushing down. 'Nelly Ah Loy, all right,' said Nobby. ' 'Ere comes trouble!'

Nugget waited for Nell, got in before she started her screeching for her boy: 'Now, don' be silly . . . he got a bad cut. Look at the blood everywhere . . . bleed to death if it's not stitched . . . ' He swung away each time she tried to take the boy from him. When Nobby tried to hold her, she struck him a blow in the chest.

'Bloody bitch!' snapped Nobby.

'Now look 'ere!' Nugget yelled at her. 'I'm not goin' 'o hurt him. I'm goin' 'o fix him. If you're runnin' away or sumpin, I don' care. Just let me fix 'im . . . then you can go . . . I won' tell nobody. Come on . . . have sense . . . don' be jitty . . . there's a good girl! You know me, Nugget Knowles. Right, eh? Okay, come on up the house. I'll give you a feed . . . give you new dress . . . looks like you need both . . . . ' Nugget's voice was kindly, a very different one from the harsh nasal snapping of his brother.

Panting, in tears now, stroking Prindy's blood-spattered leg, Nell gave in, followed Nugget as he swung back to resume the climb up the bank. A truck could be seen at the top.

Then the dogs, Mungus with them now that barking seemed in order, yelled again. Everybody looked to see Queeny swinging down to join them. The cry went up from the blacks: 'Eh, look out!' Nobby Knowles laughed, calling her name. Everybody knew Queeny.

Nugget called to his brother: 'Leave you to it, Nob.' Nobby went to the engine and restarted it, but stood watching the others up the hill. When Queeny came along he leered at her, bawling above the din, ''Ullo, tweet'eart!' She grinned at him, went loping after the others.

But Nugget was not waiting. Reaching the truck on top, he lifted Prindy into the cabin, then helped Nell up, then went round and started up and swung away towards the house.

At closer quarters the house could be seen to be a hotchpotch of old and new materials, iron and bush timber. It was an old place rebuilt, Nugget said as they came up to it. 'Belong to the Boss Chinaman in the ol' days . . . Hang Gong. Hang On, we call it . . . Hang On Creek . . . .'

He added with a guffaw, 'Only 'ope we *can* 'ang on to it . . . yaaaahaaa!'

They stared at him.

It was bungalow-built, on a foundation of stone and ant-bed, comprising four small rooms, to be seen on either side of a narrow passage. The front verandah, facing westward, that is towards the creek, was evidently the part most lived in by the present occupants. At one end were beds of saplings and hide strips, screened from outside with sacking. The rest of the furniture was likewise home-made, mostly from kerosene cases. Prindy, being carried in and placed in a sacking and sapling deck-chair, swung his head round to look at a large ornate radio set against the wall. Nugget noticed and said: 'Wireless . . . you like wireless, eh?' Prindy nodded. 'No good puttin' it on yet,' added Nugget. 'Can't get nothin' in daylight. Tonight, eh? Keep the *mundowie* up now, while I put a box under it.' He got a kerosene case and folded a sack to make a cushion for the small foot. 'Now I'll get the doings,' he said, and went into the passage and through to one of the rooms. Prindy looked out at Queeny swinging up the track from the creek, accompanied by the three dogs. Black women and children and dogs in the camp were out to stare at her, some waving and calling in the high, drawn-out way of their kind.

Nugget came out with a first-aid kit. Without any attempt at asepsis, he fished a length of horse-hair from a metal box and threaded it into a small curved surgical needle, bent over the foot, saying, 'Might hurt a bit . . . but you *kundirra-feller*, ain't you?' Prindy smiled. He winced only slightly as the needle pierced. 'Properly *kallum kundirra*!' said Nugget, tying the stitch off and snipping it. And going on to the next point, he asked, 'You savvy that language?' Prindy, biting his lip, watching the operation closely, shook his head. Nugget kept up the patter: 'This country language . . . mean proper strong man. That you all right.' He put in four stitches, then let go the ligature. Just a bubble or two of blood. Nugget said: 'She'll be right. Now we got 'o put sumpin on it . . . what'll it be?' He turned to the box, took out a bottle of iodoform.

Prindy was also not a *koornung's* apprentice for nothing. He said: 'Put him clee, more better.'

'Clay, eh? Blackfeller fashion. That's good, too. Got some pipeclay out the back, from makin' oven. I get some, wet him. Cover'm up first-time, though . . . don' wan' them flies gettin' on it.' He dropped a piece of gauze over it. Just then Queeny came up, and after greeting him, asked him for tobacco. He waved to a tin of it, with cigarette papers and matches, on a packing-case table. 'Help yo'self,' he said. He went out through the house.

'Properly goot man,' said Queeny. 'You know dat two-feller, eh?'

Nell, also helping herself, said, 'I been see long Beatrice.'

'Goot man all right.' Queeny peeped into the rooms. 'Properly shop,' she said to herself. For a couple of rooms held piles of stores and racks of hanging clothes, most likely stuff for paying the Aboriginal workers.

She took a peep out the back, where the verandah was semi-enclosed with iron and sacking, to make kitchen and dining-room.

Nugget was soon back, with chunks of white clay in a tin dish of water. He sat down to knead it into plasticity. He asked Prindy how he came to know blackfeller tricks: 'You ain't a blackfeller.'

'Da's right,' said Nell quickly.

Prindy started to tell of his *koornung* friend; but she interrupted him to say that he'd been stolen away by Mad Old Bugger, now in jail. 'Ah, yes,' commented Nugget. 'Saw it in paper.'

Prindy got in a word or two for Bobwirridirridi: 'He too goot, dat-one old man . . . can fix him up anysing, sore leg, broke bone . . . .'

'He no goot bugger!' snapped Nell.

Nugget chuckled. Then he asked did they want anything to eat, and being told yes, said apologetically that the bread was rather stale, that he was going to bake tonight; but there was beef, and butter and jam. Telling Prindy to stay where he was, he took the two women through to the kitchen. Getting food for them out of a home-made cupboard with legs standing in kerosene to beat the ants, he apologized again for the dry and doughy bread, saying he was no hand at making it, especially this cool weather, and lifted a cloth off a dish on a case-made table near the stove containing sponge for breadmaking. He asked, 'Know anything 'bout breadmakin'?'

Queeny whooped, 'Dis-one number-one baker!'

He looked at Nell with sheer delight: 'Are you, then? Well, how's this sponge . . . any good?'

Nell sniffed it. 'Gettin' lil bits sour . . . you keep him too long. Bake him now all right. No goot by'n'bye.'

He asked eagerly, 'If I make you up a fire'll you make the batch for me?'

She nodded. He leapt to the stove, stirred up the fire, threw in the couple of pieces of wood in the box, said he'd have to get more in, went rushing out to the woodheap. Queeny giggled, 'Dat man like him you, I reckon.'

Nell looked troubled. Queeny demanded, 'Wha's matter? He nice man, dat-one . . . young-feller, goot-lookin' . . . .'

Nugget was coming running back with an armful of wood. With the fire roaring and the kettle boiling, he suggested biscuits and cheese for the time being, and a grand supper tonight. They'd shot a buffalo yesterday, he said, and had some nice rib-roast stuff hanging in the meat-house. They had sweet potatoes, canned peas, canned everything, dried fruit. Would Nell cook supper for them? What about new dresses for both of them? Not such hot stuff, bought for the working-boys' lubras – but better than those terrible things. 'What you been doin' with yo'selves to get like that?' But he wasn't prying, wasn't doing more than talk to cover excitement. He took them inside and told them to pick dresses, and something for the boy. Then he got Prindy and carried him out to the kitchen, seating him so as to keep his leg up. When the women came out, carrying dresses, he said, 'Put 'em on.' But Nell said not until she had made the bread and put the dinner on. Queeny said they'd have to *bogey* first.

He showed them where the shower was, over underneath the tank.

They were seated at the table, drinking tea and eating biscuits, when there was a thud of bare feet coming through the house, and they looked up to see Nobby appear. He grinned, but rather crookedly, saying, 'Well . . . I like this . . . and me doin' a perish for smoke-o!'

Nugget reddened, said hastily, 'Sorry, Nob . . . forgot about you . . . sit down.'

Nobby leered as he took a seat: 'Thought yo' might be layin' off or sumpin . . . ha-ha!'

Still in the hasty tone, Nugget said, 'Found out Nelly 'ere can bake bread. Good cook too. Was cookin' the Compound . . . cakes, puddin's ev'thing. She can do our cookin' while the boy's laid up.'

Again the leer: 'That all?' His eyes were on Nell.

Nell avoided the look, said, 'Better I start bakin'.' She got up, went to the sponge. Nugget leapt up, saying he'd get the flour for her, the salt. Nobby's leer widened, and catching Queeny's eye he winked. Queeny giggled.

Nobby tried to get Prindy to talk, but without the slightest success. Queeny put him off quizzing by saying that they'd all been hunted out of Town by McCusky pending the building of the new Settlement and were simply having a walkabout, but had lost their swags when George's boat was wrecked. Evidently the Knowleses knew of the enforced exodus and had some of the ex-Compound residents there with them. But obviously Nobby was quizzing only for the sake of it. He scarcely took his eyes off Nell while she worked at the bread.

After a while Nugget said, 'You left the pump runnin'.'

'Came up see what you's doing'.'

'You know they won't do anything unless one o' us not there.'

'Wanted me smoke-o.'

'Better get back, eh?'

'Wha' 'bout you?'

'I wan' 'o do some butcherin' . . . big supper tonight.'

Nobby leered: 'Thought it's bakin' you's in'sted in.'

'Might pick up some hints.'

'Might pick up anything.'

Nugget shot him a sharp look. The leer faded. Nugget said shortly, 'Better get back, eh? Take a billy o' tea and a bit o' bread and jam down to 'em.'

Nobby sighed heavily, muttered, 'Okay, chief.' Given the provender, he went slouching out the way he had come in. They heard the truck start up and go.

Nugget said to Prindy, 'Well, young feller, I'll take you back to the front verandah. Fix you a bed up out there later. Got 'o get this butcherin' done now.' He picked him up. Setting him down in the deck-chair again, he said, 'There's some readin' matter.' He got him an armful of catalogues, left him. Prindy glanced at some pictures, then took to staring at the radio and hummed to himself, bits of those musics he had learnt from Miss Kitty Windeyer.

When Nugget appeared again on the verandah it wasn't all bloody from butchering, but shaved and scrubbed. He said, 'Come and let me give you a bit of a *bogey* . . . and then you can put on new clothes . . . right?'

Prindy rode out on the man's back. The bathroom was simply the bottom of the tank-stand screened with sewn sacks with a floor of the same material over ant-bed. There was a sack-screened privy close by, to which Nugget said he would carry Prindy whenever he wanted to go. Smilingly, Prindy let Nugget wash him, with the foot kept well out of the water. Nugget looked the golden little figure over with frank admiration: 'You's a real well-set-up young feller, ain't you. But you got a well-set-up Mumma, too.' Nugget had clean clothes for himself as well. Back in the house he himself put on new elastic-sides and polished them.

When, at somewhere round five, Nobby came back with the truck, in which the blacks were also riding, alighting and setting eyes on his brother, he chuckled, 'Shows what havin' women round the 'ouse 'll do, eh . . . even yeller ones.'

Nugget said shortly, 'Better go and wash yo'self.'

'Sure,' said Nobby. 'Think I'm goin' leave the lairin' up all to you?'

His brother's eyes snapped at him again as in the kitchen, and Nobby looked quickly away. He went in through the house, while the blacks went round to the back, King George amongst them. In the kitchen he paused, to leer at the females, done up in new floral dresses now. 'Lookin' real pretty, eh!' Then, sniffing at the odours of new bread and roasting beef, he added, 'Jees . . . that smells good!' Then he went out and across to the shower.

Nugget came out to give the blacks beef and bread and tobacco, with which they went off to their camp. Then he fed the three dogs, one of them Mungus.

Nobby reappeared looking even smarter than his brother, being a dressier type, and even smelling of hair oil. Nugget again looked at him sharply, but made no comment on his appearance. In fact they hardly spoke, and then only of their mining, while they set up beds for the newcomers, two camp stretchers in one of the rooms off the back, and on the front verandah a small one of kerosene cases and sacks and blankets for Prindy. After that, Nobby opened up the gramophone and put on a record: *Give Me My Boots and Saddle*, and grinned and winked at Prindy and tapped to the tune with a toe of his boot, while Nugget fiddled with the radio.

Then Queeny came tapping through the house, to announce in that rich contralto, 'Supper ready.'

Nugget caught Prindy up to carry him out, telling as they went that tomorrow he would make him a pair of crutches. They reached the kitchen to find the table set for only three. 'Wha's this?' demanded Nugget. The women were only waiting to be asked, but would not sit as Nugget tried to arrange it. They had set for the three males at the end remote from the stove, and now drew up cases for themselves at the other end – 'Handy gitchim anysing,' as Nell said. However, the gap of shyness was made up for by what was probably mostly responsible for it, Nugget's boyish exuberance. He talked all the while, even vociferated, but with no less appreciation of the good food, evident enough from his gorging and his ceaseless reference to it: 'Best cookin' I ever tasted . . . dinkum! Now, ain't that right, Nob?' Nobby, who seemed mostly amused by the situation, judging by his constant grinning and frequent winking at the newcomers, had to agree. It certainly was a good meal. Besides two large roasts of buffalo with trimmings, there was a pie made with canned apricots, the pastry of which would do credit to a professional.

Apart from the food, talk of which included descriptions of special dishes that Nugget had tried his hand at in desperation for variety only to end up dished himself, which produced loud guffaws from his brother and giggles from the others, the subject was the Beatrice River Races, as much the central point of the lives of these two young whitemen as of Nell and Prindy: the equine champions of the years, the outstanding events, comic and tragic, the wags. Queeny had never seen the Races, having come originally from a district too remote, and ever since the Alice River affair not having been away from Port Palmeston. She showed great interest in what was said of Barbu's business there, as if she would like to do something in the way of it herself. Also Nugget, as if talking to equals, told something of the business of himself and his brother here; or more truly his own business, since Nobby seemed to treat that as a bit of a joke as well, as indeed it might be judged. They were working a deposit of alluvial tin evidently passed over as of too low-grade by former miners, but with the advantage over their predecessors of financial assistance from the Government, and the ulterior motive of founding a stock run. This was not cattle country, at least not as a whole; but stock from the big stations further South wandered into it. The Knowleses were doing something like what the first generation of Delacy's had done on the country the Knowleses' own grandfather had been fool enough to abandon. Having a homestead lease included in their mining rights, they were collecting clean-skin beasts and branding them as their own, and getting together the makings of a herd. Not that stock was worth much at the moment. But Nugget was of the opinion that another great war was about to break out and that when it did, Vaiseys would reopen their long-closed meatworks; and of course the price of tin would rise. 'We'll be wantin' staff then,' said Nugget. 'We'll certainly be wantin' a cook . . . and we'll pay well.' He was looking at Nell, who dropped her eyes, surely because it wasn't as a cook he was seeing her with those wide blue ones of his. 'That right, eh, Nob?' Nobby answered with a nod and a leer that suggested that if he weren't as bright as his brother in conversation business, he was more aware of the immediate facts of life.

They were still at the table when it was dark enough to make Nugget think of lighting the acetylene lamp; dark enough inside, that is, because it was bright moonlight out. He was for leaving the dishes, enamel and tin, for later, while the whole company adjourned to the front verandah to listen to the evening news and afterwards have some music. The women wouldn't hear of it, nor of being helped. Nugget picked Prindy up again; and the three males went out to the moonlit verandah.

The radio came in with a twittering of static, which Nugget told Prindy was the voices of debil-debils flying about the sky. Prindy took it seriously, the way he quickly glanced up at Igulgul, peeping through a big woolly-butt tree just off the verandah. Then Chinese voices came in. Nugget mimicked them, causing Prindy to smile now. Nugget tuned, and got Radio Batavia and a Dutchman whom he also imitated, saying, 'I savvy plen'y language, see.' The Dutchman was announcing a high-class musical session. The opening bars of Wagner's *Prelude to Act 3 of Lohengrin* came in.

Prindy started forward in his deck-chair with obvious interest. But Nugget said, 'Bugger that stuff,' and tuned it out.

A Japanese voice came in, speaking English, talking of the China Incident and the success of what he called *Grorious Imperiya Japanese Army Soraja*. Nugget switched him off, saying, 'Slant-eyed bastards . . . not goin' 'o waste the battery on them. Somebody ought 'o stop them bloody Japs. If they don't, we're goin' 'o have to. We'll wait for the news from the ABC.' He pointed to the Evening Star, probably Venus from its brightness so near the Moon, asking, 'Know the name that big star there?'

Prindy answered promptly, '*Minaji*.'

Nugget chuckled: 'Real lil blackfeller, ain't you! Ain't nobody ever learnt you whitefeller way?'

Prindy just stared at him.

'Never mind,' said Nugget. 'You stay here with yo' Mumma, and I'll learn you everything. We call that star the Drover's Star. When that one goes down, you can stand camp-watch with one rider. You're a good rider, ain't you? I'll make a crackerjack stockman out o' you.'

Nugget switched on the radio again, this time to catch the marching tune, *The British Grenadiers*, which surely no one but an Australian would accept for what it was intended as, announcement of what the Australian Broadcasting Commission called the National News.

There was little that was national about the news, but much of international, and mostly concerned with intolerance and violence, the fratricidal war in Spain, the rape of China by the Japanese, bloody strife in Eastern Europe between Fascist and Communist, hints of terrible things happening to Jews, hatred and murder everywhere, for the betterment of the world, so each side said – the only Australian item of any interest being the statement by one of the leaders of the Commonwealth Government, just back from a visit to Europe and a meeting with Adolf Hitler, that he (Adolf) was truly a Great Man, the kind of man Australia needed to deal with the type calling the Great Man a Certifiable Lunatic.

'Understand any of that?' asked Nugget when it was over. 'Buggered if I did. Whiteman gone proper jitty by the sound of it.'

A News Commentary was to follow, but meantime music intervened: *Fantaisie Impromptue*, of Chopin. Nugget was about to switch off again, when he noticed the eager leaning forward again, and stayed his hand, asking, 'You like that kind o' music, eh?' Prindy was listening only to the music.

When it was over, Prindy sighed. So did the other two, but doubtless with relief, because when Nugget switched off the commentary by a man with a thick German accent, he said with enthusiasm, 'We'll get the gramphone goin'. We got a beaut lot o' records.' And Nobby fairly leapt up to get the records out of a tin trunk.

The first record was *The Man on the Flying Trapeze*. Nugget whistled it, while Nobby sang bits of it, both of them off beat, but keeping time with tapping boots 'Like that?' Nugget asked Prindy afterwards. Prindy was saved from answering, or not, by the arrival of his mother and Queeny. The brothers leapt up to receive them, or rather Nell, whom they ushered to a deck-chair, leaving Queeny to find a kerosene case, on which she sat with back to wall. Then Nugget put *The Man on the Flying Trapeze* on again. Queeny got into it now by singing it, so well that they clapped her. She said she'd had a gramophone and a lot of records, but had had to leave them behind: ''Cause dat bloody bastard Mick Cusky!'

So they sat, while the Moon streamed in on them till the place was ablaze with enchantment, and the records played half a dozen facile combinations of notes in a hundred tinkling or strumming varieties: *Frankie and Johnny were lovers, oh, lordy how they did love . . . An old spinning wheel in the parlour, spinning tales of the long long ago . . . A gal in Cherokee and she's waitin' there for me . . . I'm headin' for the last round-up, yoddle-doh, yoddle-dee, yoddle-doh yoddle-dee, yoddle-doh-dee-dee-dee* . . .

As the Moon went down behind the river trees, Nugget, stowing away the last record, said, 'Been a wondferul night. If only we'd 'ad a drop o' grog. We'll have some cocoa, eh . . . and some yo' new brownie, what say, Nelly?'

As Nugget rose to go through with Nell to the kitchen, where the acetylene still burned, Prindy asked him, 'Wirelitch?'

'You wan' some more wireless, eh? Sure thing!' Nugget switched it on.

Snap of switch, hum of warming apparatus – then a flood of silver sound, of flutes: Sibelius's *Entrance of the Little Fauns*. Prindy caught his breath, straining towards the little window of light from which the wonder seemed to come.

Nugget said, 'He sure likes that high-brow stuff . . . where'd he learn it?' He asked the question of Nell, who looking at her enraptured son, shook her head apparently at utter loss. Prindy was lost to them, anyway, lost to Nobby's and Queeny's laughing talk while the others were away, lost to everything but the undulating stream of silver that he seemed to see. When it was all over and a voice announced that that was the end of the session, Prindy looked up to find Nugget watching him. Nugget handed him the pannikin of cocoa and slice of buttered brownie that had been awaiting him for some time. He asked, 'Where'd you learn that kind of music, sonny?'

Prindy looked at him uncomprehending.

Nugget said, 'You must've heard it somewhere. Where you been hear him, eh?'

Prindy hesitated, then answered, 'Butcher bird.'

Nobby guffawed: 'Ask a silly question!'

Nugget said, 'Well's about bedtime. You wan' 'o go out the dunny, or have a pee?'

Prindy said he'd have a pee. Nugget took him out to a tree, held him while he did it. The dogs came out of their dust holes to join in, and Nobby, who guffawed over it, 'We'll 'ave to be puttin' up signs painted Ladies and Gents . . . aweeeah!'

When Nugget was putting Prindy in his made-up bed, the boy said, 'I like tchileep dere . . . long wirelitch.'

Nugget chuckled, 'So you can hear them butcher birds in the mornin', eh?'

'Yas.'

Nobby guffawed again. Nugget said, 'Come on, we'll shift his bed down there.'

Prindy was off to sleep soon enough. Not the others, however. It was midnight before the tossing, without talking, of the brothers ceased, and the whispering of the women. The wind had dropped. There was no sound in the world except the very distant calling of curlews. Then suddenly an odd whistling right there in the house, shrill and torn and hesitant, like the practice-singing of a young bird in the wind.

Nugget, the first to wake, lay listening, rose, and came to the radio, as if thinking the sound came from there, then discovered it was Prindy. As he bent over the boy another dark figure came up – Nell, wrapped in a blanket. Nugget caught his breath as he turned and saw her curly head against the stars. He whispered, 'He's dreamin'.'

She answered on indrawn breath, 'Like o' dat plenty time . . . I don' know wha's matter him.'

Prindy whistled again, the first notes of his Butcher Bird Song. Nugget gave a little laugh, leant near to her to whisper, 'He thinks there's a butcher bird in the radio.'

'I tek him inside, eh?'

'No . . . he's all right here. I like him here. I like him a lot.'

As if he heard it, Prindy sighed, turned over. Nell breathed, 'He's all right now . . . he tchleep properly.'

As she moved away, Nugget went with her, whispered, 'I'd like you to stay for good . . . will you?'

Without answering, she slipped into the passage.

He turned to find another dark figure. His brother's snicker came from it, and the thin nasal voice: 'Night-'orsin', eh?'

'Aaarh!' grunted Nugget, and turned his brother back along the verandah, adding, 'Kid woke us up, tha's all.'

'You was seein' 'er back to bed like, eh?'

'Aaarh . . . will yo' shut up.' Nugget stopped for a moment in passing Prindy to look down at him. Going on with his brother to their beds behind sacking screening at that other end of the verandah, he said softly, 'I like that nipper. He's got sumpin, sumpin special, I reckon, sumpin I'd like to bring out o' him.'

Nobby snickered again, and said as he settled down into bed, 'His mother's got sumpin special too . . . what I'd like to get into . . . eeeeeeah!'

Nugget was silent. Sounds of subdued mirth came from Nobby several times as they lay settling down. Then suddenly Nugget said, in a throaty voice, 'You don' mean nothin' what you said 'bout Nelly jes now, do you Nob?'

Again the snicker, 'Wha' you reckon, mate?'

Nugget heaved himself up in his bed: 'Now, listen, Nobby . . . you gi' me your word you wouldn't go playin' roun' with any woman while you's like you are . . . . '

'Who's playin' roun'?'

'Well, don' talk like that 'bout a nice girl.'

'You wan' 'er yo'self, you mean?'

'I don' wan' nothin' . . . only you don' go poxin' up anyone roun' here.'

'That's right . . . rub it in!'

'I'm not rubbin' it in. You's here so's you can get cured, 'cause you don' wan't to go to Town with it. I'll fix you. But you leave the women alone see.'

'Aw . . . shit!'

'I know you.'

'Aw, balls! Let a man go to sleep, will yo'?'

By the sound of them, it was a long while again before they slept.

Next day was Sunday. No work, as Nugget had said. Breakfast was no less festive than supper had been the evening before, with a great pile of steak and onions as its fragrant offering, along with that bread – 'Oh, that bread!' as Nugget kept saying, while stuffing himself with it. There was no hint of the tension between the brothers betrayed last night. After hanging about over the breakfast table for an hour or more, leering and winking, while his brother gabbled, Nobby went off to get a horse and go looking for stock. Nugget took Prindy over to the tool-shed, to make the crutches he had promised him, as well as a better one for Queeny.

Nugget talked all the while, showed all the tools and explained their uses, told Prindy how he would begin to teach him as soon as he got on his feet. Prindy sat gravely, apparently understanding what was said to him, but perhaps not even listening to the spate of words, interested more in this odd whiteman, surely like none he'd yet encountered. The business in the tool shed went on beyond the crutch making, was actually being concerned with the apparatus for cleaning the washed tin ore of mica, an invention of Nugget's of which he was very proud, when Queeny's contralto rang out across the yard, 'Smoke-ooooo!' They had a race to the house on the new crutches, with King George, at work on the wood-heap, cheering them on. Prindy won by a crutch.

There was a pile of buttered brownie of yesterday's baking and small buttery cookies hot from the oven. 'Ummmm!' was Nugget's delighted comment.

Nugget and Prindy went for a run in the truck to the place where the gravel was mined, to sample the stuff for taking more later. Nugget explained the process of what he called Bullin' the Ground, which meant to loosen it with explosive. 'Big bang', he said. 'You got 'o see that. Next week, after I been to Town. Like to come to Town with me, Friday?'

Then back to midday dinner, to find Nobby returned and joking with the women. Dinner consisted of cold beef with sliced onions and mashed sweet potatoes and currant slice with custard. 'Boy, oh, boy!' said Nugget to his brother. 'And you's always talkin' 'bout the good tucker you got workin' on the road . . . Wan' 'o go back the road now?'

Nobby snickered, 'Might pinch yo' cook and start a ranch-house on the road.'

Queeny asked, 'Wha' nam' rench'ouse?'

The term had but lately been introduced by itinerant construction workers now thronging the land. Nobby answered, 'Cook-house for big mob men. They pay good.' He added with a leer, 'Couple o' good sorts like yous'd make more'n a quid or two on the side, too.'

Nugget frowned at that, and growled, 'Cut that out, Nob!'

'Arrrh!' was Nobby's comment; but he grinned and winked at the women, who, by their expressions, may not have gathered what was meant, even though one was a procurer and the other had a conviction for soliciting, such being the ignorance of their kind of the civilized language of the land.

After dinner the men had what they called a Lay Off for about an hour. Then they both went out to bring in some cattle Nobby had found. They had a paddock somewhere up the creek. They came home to bath and dress up again, and to supper of steak-and-kidney pie and steamed pudding. Nugget said, 'We'll have to get a couple o' buffaloes a week to keep up with this.'

'What about some poultry?' suggested Nobby.

'Crise, no . . . . leave the chooks alone . . . Nelly'll be wantin' all the eggs she can get, eh, Nell?'

'I mean wild stuff,' said Nobby. 'Ducks and geese.'

'Good idea. We'll go out to the Duck Holes one day, eh?' Nugget turned to Prindy: 'Any good with a gun, young feller?'

Prindy answered, 'I goot wit' spear.'

Nugget laughed: 'Good on yo'! You can do all the huntin'. Save us ammo.'

So it looked as if the newcomers were already accepted as permanent members of the household. Another indication was Nugget's asking the women to make a list of the things they wanted when he would be going to Town.

Another musical evening on the moonlit front verandah, but with the difference that when the News Commentary was done with and the Concert Hour was announced, Nugget asked Prindy if he would like to listen to the radio rather than the gramophone, and getting an eager *yas*, had Nobby help him carry the radio round to the southern side verandah, where Prindy sat amongst saddlery to listen without intrusion. The radio music was classical waltzes: Tchaikovsky's *Waltz Serenade* and *Dance of the Hours*, Brahm's *Waltz in A Major*, Sibelius's *Waltz Krieg*. When it was over and talk resumed, Prindy switched off, as Nugget had instructed him, and lay back on his couch of pack-bags, evidently going through it all over again by his humming.

Thus Nugget found him when he came round to take a look. When Prindy said he wanted to stay there, rather than to go round to *The Man on the Flying Trapeze* and the like, Nugget said he'd try to get him another classical programme. As he tuned, *La Golondrina* came in, played on flute, the long notes like the swooping flight of swallows in sunlight. Prindy leant to listen so eagerly that Nugget, watching him, commented, 'Looks like I won't be makin' a shit-ringer out o' you after all. Maybe, 'stead you'll grow up to 'ave a dance band.' Prindy was listening only to the music, Nugget went back to the others, to tell them about it, to add, 'Must buy 'im a mouth-organ when I go to Town.'

Nugget next found him asleep, and carrying him round to his bed on the male side, asked him had he had enough music for the night, to which Prindy nodded, but perhaps in his sleep, because when the household settled down, he began to sing in his sleep, just a sweet, strained, soprano note or two, of *La Golondrina*. Nugget got out of bed and came and talked softly to him about getting the mouth-organ. Prindy sighed, turned over.

In the morning Prindy went down with the men to work on the tin, and helped with the concentrating. Nugget said that in a day or two they'd be finished sluicing this lot, and would dry-blow the ore in the shed and bag it, that he wanted as much as he could to take to Town to meet payments. But the very fact of expressing the want seemed to turn off the run of tin from the sluice-box. There was so little for three to do concentrating, that after smoke-o Nobby said, 'Bugger this. Jes waste o' time. I'm goin' 'o do a bit o' shootin'. Fancy roast duck. Can't wait'll Sunday.'

'Okay,' said Nugget. 'But you better ask Nell if she wants it. She may be cookin' sumpin else.'

'They'll keep'll tomorro' this weather. See yous.' Nobby set off up the bank.

Up at the house, Nobby changed into moleskin pants and put on a shirt and sandshoes, then got a shotgun down from the front verandah wall and a belt of cartridges, and went through to the kitchen, where the women were preparing dinner. He said, 'Goin' 'o get yous some ducks.' At the edge of the verandah he turned back, to say, 'Wha' 'bout comin' 'long with me, Nelly?'

Kneading dough, she dropped her eyes. 'Come on,' he urged 'Don' 'ave to walk. Go in my ute.'

She muttered, 'Cookin' dinner.'

'Leave it to Queeny. Do you good 'ave a break '

Nell said, 'Boss say we go Sunday.'

'Boss, is it? I'm boss, too, y'know. Come on.'

She went on kneading. He sighed: 'Okay . . . on'y thought you'd like a ride. See yous.'

When he was out of hearing, Queeny giggled, 'He don' mean ride in motor car.'

'Eh, look out!'

The battered old utility truck came backing out of the tool shed to round the yard, and then head off northward with noise and violence of movement suggesting an angry driver. Nell, looking after the vanishing dust, was plainly troubled. Eyeing her, Queeny said, 'You got 'o show dat man you like him brother more better.'

'Eh, look out!'

'Da's right. No goot two whiteman want one woman. He jealous bugger, whiteman. I know. Plen'y fight for me when I young feller. Spone you don' wan' dem two-feller fightin', you got o' mek him tweet'eart long o' dat-one Nugget quick.'

Nell showed her agitation in her kneading for a treacle rolly-polly.

Nobby was not back for dinner. The effect of his absence was marked. Although it was always Nugget who initiated the playful nonsense that so far had been part of the meal, without his brother, who had mostly guffawed and winked, he was serious now. He kept talking of Prindy's future, saying he must have some sort of schooling, couldn't just play about in the bush like a black kid. 'He's white,' he kept saying. 'He's as white as me, nearly . . . and he's got a lot more brains. What we goin' 'o do with him, eh? No good takin' him down the Beatrice. That Delacy mob . . . they won' do nothin' for him.' It was evident that he was trying to get Nell to say something, if it were only to tell the truth about why she and the boy were here, a subject so far not gone into. Nell would say nothing, despite some urging on the part of Queeny to listen to the Boss, because he was talkin' goot way.

It was a restless lay-off they all had after dinner. In fact Nell went on with her bread-setting, and Prindy sat out on the wood-heap, with King George and the dogs, sharpening up an old tommy-axe Nugget had given him, using the axe-stone. Then Nugget and Prindy went back to the sluicing.

Late in the afternoon Nell, with kitchen chores done in readiness for supper, went to shower and dress up. She was still in the bathroom, but bathed and dressed, in the act of finishing off the prettying up with brilliantine from a pot on the shelf, when she heard Nobby arrive back. He was already driving up to the shed before she heard him, the sound of his approach having been drowned so far by the tumbling of water into the tank as always at this time of day, being pumped up from the creek. She peeped. As Nobby drove into the shed, she grabbed up towel and discarded working dress and slipped out through the curtain that served as door. She was halfway across the yard, passing the woodheap, when he called to her, 'Hey . . . Nelly!'

She half turned, gave him a little wave, kept on.

'Wait on . . . come 'n' gi' me 'and with the poultry.'

She kept going. Queeny looked at her sharply as she came hurrying into the kitchen, to go through the house. As she was coming back into the kitchen, Nobby entered, carrying a bundle of slaughtered whistler ducks. He asked, 'Wha'd yo' run away for . . . frighten' I's goin' 'o ask you to pluck 'em?'

When she didn't answer, but went on to attend to things on the stove, he addressed himself to Queeny: 'I do me own pluckin'. Champion duck-plucker, me.' When she giggled, he added, 'Anything in the way o' pluckin' . . . that's me.' When she squealed with what was probably false mirth, he guffawed, and went and hung the ducks on a hook down the other end of the verandah. Then he went to the front to get shorts and singlet and towel. Coming out again, heading for the shower, he said to Queeny, 'Any time you wan' a pluck, I'm yo' man.' Again she squealed. Laughing he went out. Before he came back, Nugget and Prindy were there. Nugget complained about his not having plucked the ducks, saying it wasn't fair to leave it to the girls. Without any more play on the word Pluck, Nobby said he would do the ducks tomorrow morning.

It was curious how the manner of the brothers changed in and out of each other's presence. Over supper Nugget was as vociferously jocular as ever, and Nobby the same silent, leery observer.

The night was spent like the night before, only with the difference that Nugget tried listening a little with Prindy to a classical music session again from Batavia. He soon gave up, saying, 'No, I'm 'fraid I don' know what's it got, sonny. Leave yo' to it.' He went round the corner to *Frankie and Johnny*. Prindy was quiet that night, perhaps because it had been string music and it needed the flutes to reach his dreaming.

At breakfast next morning Nugget reminded his brother of the duck-plucking. He need not have bothered, even though Nobby pulled a face as if the idea irked him, because, as was soon revealed, he had it all worked out. He told his brother that he would get onto it at once, and come down to work afterwards. The others went off leaving him out on the woodheap with the ducks, chopping off their heads. As the truck halted in its usual place at the top of the bank, he watched. When the crew vanished into the cutting he rose swiftly, came to the kitchen, up to Nell, who was washing up, with Queeny drying the dishes for her. He spoke to Nell, breathlessly: 'I'll be wantin' 'ot water, love . . . for the duck-pluckin' . . . eeeee! Get's some, eh?'

Nell turned from his staring narrow eyes to the stove, saying, 'We been use'm all-lot for washin' up.'

He said, 'I'll put you on a can of it . . . and build up the fire . . . and you can bring it out to me, eh? We do a bit o' duck-pluckin' together, eh?' He was evidently excited. He grabbed up a kerosene can bucket, half-filled it from the tap, and put it on the stove. Then he made up the fire. 'There,' he said, 'that'll be boilin' in ten minutes. Soon's she's right, bring 'er out 'o me, eh?' He winked at Queeny as he went out.

When Nell looked at Queeny wildly, Queeny said, 'I been tell him you las' night . . . go walk in moonlight long o' Nugget. Wha's matter you wan' 'o play about two-feller man?'

Nell sighed: 'I don' wan' play about nobody.'

'You got 'o be tweet'eart long o' one feller. Which one I don' know. Dat you bijnitch. But I don' wan' trouble. Spone you tweet'eart long o' Nugget, might be dat-one Nobby tek me 'way start him dat renchouse he talk about. Spone you like him dis one more better, he can tek you long o' Beatrice . . . I stop here look-out 'nother one. You got 'o do sumpin, Tchister . . . you got 'o do him quick. Wha' 'bout you tek some fresh cake long 'o workin's smoke-o time . . . '

'You tek him hot water long o' 'nother one?' Nell asked eagerly.

'I can't carry-him-up hot water got him crutch. He can't do nothin' you now. Wha's matter you all-day fright' somebody puggim you? Spone I can do it . . . I do it all-time. Da's wha' for man wan' him you, ain't it?'

When the water was boiling, Nell went out with it Nobby was leaning back on the uncut firewood, hat over brow to keep off the sunlight, smoking. He sat up quickly at her step ' 'Ullo, love,' he said. She would have set the can down and gone; but he caught her hand, saying, 'No . . . sit down . . . talk to me while I pluck 'em.'

She breathed, 'Wan' 'o mek cake for smoke-o '

'It can wait. Sit down, I said!' He jerked her down onto a log.

He dipped a duck into the hot water, and while it hung there, said, 'You smell good. Been usin' my brilliantine, eh?'

She asked, 'Belong 'o you?'

'Yeah . . . but you use it much's you like. I get you a bottle for yo'self. What else you want . . . lookin'-glass, dresses? Wha' colour dress you like best?'

'I got dress.'

'That lubra rubbitch. I'll get you real white-girl's dress . . . shoes, too . . . comb, handkerchief . . . anything you like.'

He pulled the bird out and began to pluck. He repeated, 'Anything you like . . . 'cause I like you, see.'

She hung her head. He asked, 'You like me?'

She was silent. He urged, 'Come on, tell me . . . you like me?'

She nodded the hanging head. He drew a deep breath, reached and stroked her shoulder. 'I reckon' you did. You 'n' me go tweet'eart, eh?'

She shrugged free of the hand, muttering, 'No-more like o' dat.'

She moved to rise. He jerked her down again, breathing heavily now: 'You proper tweet one . . . I wan' you bad. You come to me in shed tonight, eh?'

'No-more . . . le' me go!'

He pulled her close, tried to kiss her. 'Tonight,' he insisted. 'When the mob's asleep. I'll be waitin' there. You promise . . . '

She broke away.

He leered at her: 'You been promise me. I wait for you.'

She broke into a run. He laughed after her: 'I wait . . . I wait . . . you goin' 'o come all right!'

When Nell went panting into the kitchen, Queeny, who must have seen it all and heard most, asked, 'Wha' you goin' 'o do?'

Nell could only shake her head.

'Mek dem cake, like I been tell him you. Tell him dat one Nugget you mek for him. Look him properly in heye, so he know you wan' 'o tweet'eart long o' him. You got 'o do it now, I tell him you!'

Nobby came in with the plucked ducks some twenty minutes later. He held one up, looking very pleased with himself: 'Didn' I tell you I'm champion duck-plucker . . . whaaaaa!' They were done nicely. Then he said, 'Wha' 'bout them cakes for smoke-o . . . I'll take 'em.'

Nell breathed, 'I bring.'

He leered at her, bumped against her deliberately, then winked at Queeny, and pinched her bottom as he passed her. Queeny gave vent to the false mirth. 'See yo' down the creek, then.' He went off.

Nell did take the cakes to the creek and say and do as instructed by that knowledgeable one, Queeny; but to no avail. Nugget didn't grasp the significance of her saying the cakes were for him especially, and dropped his blue eyes before the dark troubled stare. When she reported back, Queeny snapped, 'Wha's matter dat Nugget . . . he calico-cock?'

Nobby was all leers at dinner, and hung back afterwards to remind Nell about her promise, clearing off before she could protest. While his brother dozed during the lay-off time, he lay leering at the iron roof.

Things were similar over supper. But in the evening, after a bit of music, Nell said she'd like to go for a walk. Nugget asked in surprise, 'Not on your own?'

'No-more. You can come.'

'Okay.' Nugget leapt up, his delight obvious. But as they were stepping off the verandah he asked, 'You wan' 'o take the boy?'

It took Nell a moment to reply, 'No . . . him all right.'

'Okay.' But even with evidently still more delight in the situation, he had to ask, 'Which way you wan' 'o go, Nelly?'

'Aw . . . which way you like.'

Likeliest place for sweethearting would surely be down by the creek, in leaf-dappled moonlight, on a bit of couch grass, with a Willy wagtail singing and plovers peeping. But for walking, which was what she said she wanted, the other way was better, since much less used. Besides, the man had been called Calico-cock. Again, there was Igulgul, right above now, and big enough for magic business; and of course the business he dealt in was always Wrong Side, whereas surely this was Right Side. They went the other way, that is not the way of lovers but of mere walkers.

They walked the hard-packed wheel-tracks, a yard and a half apart, while he gabbled of the same old things: his economic hopes and plans, of the problem of Prindy's future, with a hint here and there for her to confide her own problem but never the frank demand for the truth that was needed. Such walking and talking would make anyone tired in a mile. That's when he asked her if she were, and getting a nod of the lovely dusky head, said simply, 'Okay,' and turned about. Even though she gave him her slim dark hand for the return, and he clung to it all the way, still he gabbled – while Igulgul, now looked them in the eye, leered for the joke of it. It was only as they came close to the house that he stopped, put his arm about her shoulders, and said, 'That was a lovely walk, wasn't it. What about tomorro' night again, eh? I wan' 'o talk you serious, too . . . real serious. You know what I mean serious . . . I mean not just play-about.'

'Yas,' she breathed.

Despite his sedateness during the walk, he fairly bounded onto the silent verandah, crying, 'What's wrong with everybody . . . let's have some music!'

His brother appeared to be asleep in his deck-chair. Queeny was sitting on her box like a graven image, but for the glint of the moonlight in her wide staring eyes. Prindy was asleep round the corner with the radio muttering in Malayan. Whether or not Nobby had been truly asleep, he might just as well have stayed so. Usually he sang to the gramophone music. Now he was silent. Nugget sang everything with gusto, especially bits like: *There's a girl in Cherokee and she's waitin' there for me, waitin' beneath the western Moon . . . Frankie and Johnny were lovers, oh lordy how they did lo-ove, swore to be true to each other, jes as true as the stars up above.*

He was still singing when he went out to the kitchen to help Nell get the cocoa and brownie. When suddenly he fell silent out there, which was in fact, when Nell scalded herself slightly and he leapt to get soap to put on her hand, Queeny on the front verandah, doubtless trying to make more of the situation than the pair had given evidence of, in order to discourage Nobby, said with a giggle, 'Wha' dem two-feller up to out dere, you reckon?' Nobby only grunted.

As they were retiring, Nobby managed to catch Nell in the passage, while his brother was out piddling. He was evidently waiting on her. He bailed her up, muttering, 'What game you playin'?' When she tried to dodge past him he caught her arm: 'You tol' me you like me. You promise me you come to me tonight.'

She breathed, 'Nutching promise you . . . le' me go!'

'You promised all right. I'll be waitin'. You come . . . or I make trouble. My brother don' wan' you. He tol' me . . . .'

Nugget's footsteps could be heard. The pair parted rapidly, Nell to slip into the room where she slept, Nobby himself to go out to piddle. Meeting him, Nugget said, 'Beaut night, ain't it. Pity to go to bed.' Nobby's reply was another grunt, but not unamiable sounding.

What Nugget had said about the night apparently he meant strongly, the way he tossed after getting into bed. The Moon was long down before his breathing told that he was asleep. Nobby, who apparently had been asleep almost since retiring, ignoring his brother's attempts to talk to him, rose at once, bent over the box beside his bed and took out what, by the glint of it, was a flashlight, then silently slipped out, went to the pee tree. The dogs stirred and growled softly, but assuming a normal condition of things, fell back into their holes with their fleas. After piddling, Nobby went round the house. Passing the back he flashed the beam into the passage, stood for a moment, then went across to the shed.

He lit up again in the shed, and propping the light on the hood of the utility, proceeded to gather up ore-bags from a stack, shake each one out, and spread them in the back of the vehicle. Then he settled down in the back with a cushion out of the cabin behind his head and his hands to prop it up, watching the dark bulk of the house against the stars. Curlews were calling down by the creek. No mopoke giving the all-clear regarding devilry tonight.

So many stars went down while he waited. From muttering to himself that she would come, would come, would come, must come, because she said she liked him, because he wanted her that bad, wanted her more than he'd ever wanted a woman before, he came to saying, 'The bloody bitch ain't comin' at all . . . the bloody yeller cock-teasin' bitch! But by the Christ I'll 'ave 'er . . . I'll poke 'er if I 'ave to knock the bloody gin-bitch down in broad daylight.' He fell asleep waiting. He started awake, must have been dreaming she'd come, because he exclaimed, ' 'Ere I am.' After a while he rose, stood before the shed, flashed the light on the house. He did it three times. Then muttering, he came slowly back across the yard, round the house, round it again, then gave up, went to bed, sighed, fell asleep.

Next morning Nugget, all exuberance himself despite lack of sleep, and unsuspicious as usual, took his brother's obvious lassitude and surliness for sickness, which Nobby let him believe when asked how he felt. However, when Nugget suggested that he give work the go-by for the day and stay at home, Nobby looked even alarmed. He said he'd rather work than lie about, especially as they wanted to finish the sluicing today. He even went on down to the creek ahead of Nugget, because today was that fixed for removing the stitches from Prindy's wound and the hanging of his crutches on the wall if all was well with the foot. In fact removal of the clay cast revealed that the wound had healed perfectly. The stitches came out; a bandage replaced the clay to protect the still tender skin; and Prindy, although hopping for a while from habit, went down with Nugget, singing with him *Give Me My Boots and Saddle*. Nugget went on singing it all morning to the beat of the pump engine, always with emphasis on the bit about the girl in Cherokee. Prindy, spared the worst of the cacophony through its being muffled by the engine's din, appeared to be singing to himself as he did his small bit with the tin. Nobby simply scowled and sighed. He did the same throughout the midday meal, so as even to get on Nugget's nerves and have him say, 'Now, for christ sake, you ain't comin' down to work this eve'nin'!' And so it turned out. When the others rose after the after-dinner camp, Nobby stayed stretched out on his bed. His brother tried to get him to take medicine. He said he would later. The bottle stood on the box beside him.

No doubt about it, Nobby was sick. Although it was quite warm there out of the wind, he lay covered with a blanket, and despite it, soon after the others left, was shivering. He tossed and turned, groaned and sighed. He sweated, flung off the blanket. At length he fell asleep.

He woke when Queeny came to him to ask if he would have smoke-o. He said he would have a cup of tea. As she was going, he called to her, 'Tell Nelly to bring it.' Queeny cast him a sharp look. As she disappeared, he sat up with a sharp intake of breath.

Queeny herself came back with the enamel pannikin of tea, saying that Nelly was busy preparing the ducks for supper. He muttered, 'Tell 'er I wan' 'er.'

Still Nell didn't come. He flopped back on the bed, to toss again. So for another hour. Then sounds in the house told of the women's coming from the kitchen to their room. He rose quickly, and clad just as he was, in pyjama shorts, slipped off the verandah as last night, and round the house, but this time to go to the dunny. He entered it, pulled down his shorts, sat on the box above the pit, blew off to rouse the flies in the pit below, while leaning so as to see through the slit of the sacking curtain. At long last there was what evidently he expected, Nell going with towel and clean dress to the shower.

He waited a little longer, then rose, pulled up his pants, peeped out, at the house first, then at the shower-room. No one looking. He came out, this time to head for the shed, for the back of it, which would take him past the back of the shower. Water was tumbling into the tank from the pipe from the pump. Coming level with the shower, he swung towards it suddenly. There were chinks where the sacking was sewn together. He applied his eye to one.

Nell stood under the streaming shower with arms raised as she squeezed water through her hair, so that the pale skin of her armpits with curl of glistening hair was to be seen in contrast to the gleaming chocolate rest of her. She ran the squeezing hands down over small breasts, slight curve of belly, slim loins, turned as she reached for the soap, to reveal her back in all the slender grace of form and carriage of Australoid womanhood. Breathing heavily, Nobby stole round to the front, took another look at the house, then lifted the screen.

Soaping an armpit, she was transfixed at sight of him. His eyes were popping, his mouth agape. Then as he met her eyes, he grinned, reached for the elastic of his pyjamas, pulled them down, leapt out of them. She gasped, 'No-more . . . no-more!' But he flung himself on her, went under the shower with her, snatching at her flailing arms, forcing them behind her, hissing in her face, forcing her down to the streaming floor, put an arm on her throat when she tried to cry out, in a moment had her overpowered, got to her. It was over in seconds. 'Christ!' he gasped. Then lying panting, while the water hissed over them, he chuckled, 'Done it . . . some places . . . me time . . . but never under shower . . . yaaaah!' He added, 'Wonder we wasn't drownded, eh? Aaaaah!' He got off her, reached for her hand to pull her up. She snatched it away. He scowled: ' 'Ere . . . that'll do you! Yo' me girl now.' He looked her over with darting little eyes as she drew away to where her dress hung. He said, still panting, 'Okay . . . finish yo' shower. See you tonight, eh? You should 'a' come las' night like you promised . . . then I wouldn't 'a' been rough. Anyway . . . gi's a kiss goodbye.'

She tried to avoid him; but he took the kiss, mauling her all over in the process. Then he let her go, and picking up his pants and stepping into them, said, 'That'll do till tonight. I'll look after yo' well . . . buy yo' anything. I'll take yo' 'way. I'll get a job on the road again . . . plenty money. 'By, tweet'eart!' Grinning wide, he slipped out.

'Bastard!' she muttered as he vanished. 'Bloody bastard!' She continued with her bathing, soaping the front of herself savagely, as if to wipe off contamination, now and again moaning, but with exasperation more than self-pity by her expression.

When she got back to the house the look she got from Queeny showed plainly that Queeny knew what had happened. She asked, 'Where dat bloody bastard?'

Queeny said, 'Go down creek now.'

'I kill him dat bastard he come humbuggin' me more.'

'Don' mek trouble, Tchister.'

'I wan' 'o go 'way from here.'

'Wait lil while. Wait'll after Nugget go Town.'

'Bloody puggin bastard!' Angrily Nell set about putting on the dinner. Queeny went off to bath.

But it was like old times at supper that evening, with Nobby adding his leer to the jollity of his brother. Even Nell giggled a couple of times when forced to it by Nugget's insistence. He called her Miss Modesty, because she hung her head over his lavish praise for her cooking of the ducks. The word modesty tickled them all. Prindy wanted to know what it meant. Nugget found he couldn't tell him. All he could say was: 'She's the best dook-cooker in the world . . . but she don't brag 'bout it . . . not like Nobby, 'ere, who's the best dook-plooker, an' got 'o tell everybody . . . aaaaah!'

Out on the verandah after supper, with the full company there, the radio news over and the musical arrangements made according to taste, a momentary revelation was given of the fact that things weren't so happy as Nugget in his simple way liked to have them, when he reminded Nell of that walk and talk they were to have, to be answered by silence so taut that he looked around, asked, 'Why . . . wha's wrong?' He had to ask of Nell herself, 'Don' you wan' 'o come?'

She answered with a sigh, 'All right.'

'Wha' we waitin' for, then?' He leapt up and took her hand and raised her.

Again they went eastward; and although he took her hand when they were clear of the house, and swung it in exaggerated arcs to the rhythm of their walking and probably the turbulence of his feelings, he gabbled as usual about what she had heard so many times and surely but half understood. Igulgul was glaring. A Willy wagtail was singing. They came round a bend to find a couple of curlews waiting for them. The birds clucked to each other and danced ahead for twenty yards or so before taking off. That stopped the gabble. 'Baby spirits,' he said. 'They lookin' out for baby spirits. That's what they reckon, eh?' She nodded.

He swung her hand high, then kept it down, arm stiff, and said, 'Yo' know . . . you never tell me nothin' 'bout yo'self. All the time I'm tellin' you 'bout me. Not 'cause I wan' 'o. I like you . . . yo' know that, don' you . . . eh?' She nodded. 'I think you like me, too, don' yo'?' Another nod. 'See . . . you never talk . . . tell me nothin'. I wan' 'o know . . . 'cause I wan' 'o help you. You in some trouble, ain't you?'

When she dropped her head, he said, 'Please tell me . . . Nelly. You can trust me, can't you?'

She breathed, 'Yas.'

'All right, then . . . tell me 'bout yo' trouble. Come on. You runnin' away, ain't you?'

She nodded. 'Then tell me 'bout it . . . so's I can help you.' He halted her. She drooped before him. He urged.

She breathed, 'Dey wan' tek my lil boy 'way.'

'Who's that . . . Cobbity and Co., eh?'

'Yas.'

'You can't go on livin' in the bush, though.'

'I tek him Beatrice . . . long o' Lily Lagoon. Dat Mullaka dere, he look out we.'

'Jeremy Delacy? What the Delacy mob done for you? That's Martin's kid, isn't it?' She nodded. 'Well . . . what you goin' there for?'

'Mullaka say my boy can go school dere. Das wha' for Mick Cusky wan' 'o tek him 'way . . . send him school somewhere long way.'

'I heard about 'em sending kids away . . . but halfcaste kids . . . with black mothers. You ain't black . . . an he's nearly white as me. Wha' 'bout them creamy kids with white fathers? They goin' to State School in Town. Wha's he wan' 'o take yours away for?'

'I don' know.'

'Maybe 'cause he ain't got a father now . . . now Ah Loy's dead.'

He started her walking again, swinging her hand again, said somewhat breathlessly, 'Look . . . how 'bout I marry you . . . and then he's got a father again . . . . ' He caught her swift look, turned from it quickly, to continue: 'I'd send him to the Convent School. He's a smart kid . . . he ought 'o be educated . . . . ' He seemed to run out of breath. They went on quite a way before he suddenly turned to her, blurting, ' 'Ow 'bout it . . . 'll you marry me?'

She breathed, 'I wan' 'o go Beatrice.'

'Beatrice's two 'undred mile . . . police 'll pick you up.' As she drooped her head he went on: 'And wha' you wan' 'o go there for, when them Delacy bastards done nothin' for you ever? That right . . . they ever look out for you and the boy?' She shook her head. 'Then wha' you wan' 'o go there for? When she only drooped again, he asked, ' 'Cause it's yo' country . . . that it?'

'Yas.'

They walked on in silence again, stiff-armed again. They disturbed a horse grazing, causing it to bolt. He remarked that it was a mare they were looking for. Then he stopped suddenly again and swung on her: 'Tell you what I'll do . . . I'll take you and the boy down to Lily Lagoons in the truck. You can't get there yo'self. Police'll be lookin' for you . . . specially down Beatrice. I'll run you down. Nobody'll know I got you with me. Then you can see what's what. If old Jeremy'll look after the boy, then it's okay. If you wan' o' stop there, it's okay. I only wan' 'o help you, like I said . . . but . . . but I'd like to marry you, too Nelly . . . I . . . I love yo' . . . . ' He snatched his eyes away from hers, swung her into a walk again. Still walking, after a while he asked, 'That suit yo' . . . I take you down?'

'Yas.'

'Good-o!' he cried, and swung her hand high again. He went on: 'Jes le'me go to Town first . . . get rid the tin. If yo' like I'll take yo' and leave yo' near the railway . . . some place where you'll be safe and comfy . . . till I get back. I'll be back same day. All right?'

'Yas.'

'Well, then, everything's sweet. Let's go back, eh? Get to bed early, we'll get early start on cleanin' and baggin'. Then we can get away early day after tomorro'. Sooner the better, eh?'

Igulgul, just ahead of them, seemed to be leading them – surely a dance.

Nell might have been thinking so, the way she kept her eyes down on her own dark feet and his paler feet padding the silvery dust. But not her companion, babbling again of how bright the future was, with world war looming and a chance to share in the spoils thereof with the Master, Lord Vaisey – she too, if she chose. Coming in sight of the house again, before letting go the dusky slender hand, he drew her to him, just enough to peck her cheek, covering his embarrassment with a guffaw . . . yaaaaah!

Nobby and Queeny were sitting in silence on the edge of the moonlight. Again guffawing, Nugget asked them if they'd had a row, then in their continued silence, suggested they all have an early night for an early start tomorrow. While Nell and Queeny got the usual cocoa and brownie, he told Nobby about the horse he'd seen: 'That bloody mare . . . must get her before she foals, or we never will.'

It wasn't until they were in bed that Nugget said anything about the arrangements he'd made with Nell. The hard creaking of the leather of Nobby's bed should have given him a hint of how Nobby was taking it. But he really needed no hint, as revealed, when, clearing his throat, he asked, 'Wha' you think o' that?'

Nobby took a deep breath first, then: 'I think yo' bloody well mad.'

Quite calmly Nugget said, 'Yeah . . . I reckon you would.'

'Wha' 'bout Mum and Dad?'

'Wha' 'bout 'em? 'S my life.'

'Kill Mum, you marry a yeller piece.'

'Where I goin' 'o get a white sheilah's goin' 'o live this kind o' life?'

'Plen'y other ways o' livin'.'

'Might suit you workin' on the road . . . but not me. I wan' a property, a stake in the land . . . . '

'Yo' goin' 'o do real fine with a yeller wife, ain't yo'!'

'I'll make a lady of 'er.'

Nobby sat up suddenly: 'You gone bloody insane or sumpin?' His voice was thick with feeling.

Nugget went on in the same tone: 'I don' care what anybody says . . . I'm goin' 'o marry 'er, if she'll 'ave me . . . . '

'A bloody Compound whore!'

Now Nugget sat up, snapping, ' 'Ere . . . careful what you say!'

'Well, it's right, ain't it? Wasn't she jailed for whoring?'

'No she wasn't. The paper said . . . . '

'The puggin' *Progressive* said . . . . '

'That'll do me. Now shut up and go to sleep.' Nugget dropped back to his pillow.

'No . . . by crise I won't. Listen, Nugget . . . listen, now . . . I'm only tellin' for y'own good. You don' know nothin' 'bout 'er. She's jes yeller shit. She's a whore . . . . '

Nugget shot up again and fairly yelled, 'You use that word again I'll crack yo'!'

Nobby, heaving for breath now, got to his feet: 'I tell yo' . . . I'm tellin' yo' for y' own sake . . . I know what she is, Nugget . . . they all the same, these yeller pieces . . . . '

Nugget leapt out of bed, advanced on him, grating now in anger, 'You dirty-minded bloody bastard . . . .'

Nobby snatched up the kerosene box beside his bed, scattering smoking things, thrust it before him to hold his brother off, panting, 'For y' own sake, Nugget . . . I . . . I been up 'er meself . . .'

'You . . . you . . . eh, what you say?'

Nobby backed away along the verandah. 'It's the truth. She's after me from the start. I couldn't hold her off. . . .' He leapt off the verandah, to stand out in the moonlight, a lanky bony figure. He set the box down, panting, 'Only for y' own sake . . . 'cause yo' me brother.'

Nugget yelled, 'Jees bloody crise!' and went loping down the verandah, sightless past Prindy whose pale eyes were luminous in the moonlight, two dark heads peeping from the passageway vanishing before him. He went down to their room, looked in at the open door. The women were pulling dresses over their heads. He stopped, to stand gasping and goggling, at a loss now. Nell drooped her head. He looked back at the figure out in the moonlight staring in, then again at Nell, and asked, in a voice comparatively high-pitched with strain, 'You . . . you 'eard wha' he said . . . my brother?' She remained drooped. He said, 'He's sick, yo' know. You'll be sick, too, now.'

She glanced up. He added: 'You must 'ave proper treatment. I'll take you in to Town to doctor . . . tomorro' . . . bugger the tin.'

Now as she drooped again, she turned her head sideways, as if to avoid a blow. As if he felt charged with delivering the blow he turned away quickly, came padding back, called to his brother, 'You goin' the doctor, too.'

Nobby took a moment to answer, 'Eh?'

Now Nugget was back to Prindy, whom he saw, and bent and touched the bright head, saying, 'I'll look out for you sonny. Go to sleep now, eh?' He went on to his own bed, dropped down to it with a groan.

Nobby came in, set up his bedside box, began to pick up the spilt things.

Nugget said hoarsely, 'I should'a' made you go to the doctor in the first place.'

'I'm gettin' right on what you givin' me, ain't I?'

'How do I know?'

'Well, you took on treatin' me with what the chemist give you.'

' 'Cause you whined 'bout not wantin' anyone to know.'

'Well, don't everybody know, the way them bloody Gover'ment doctors treat you?'

'So should everybody know when a bastard like you's got it and goes spreadin' it round. I see what the law 'bout reportin' VD and havin' it properly treated means now. And I ain't breakin' the law no more. You're comin' in with me tomorro' to report yourself.'

'I bloody well ain't!'

'If you don't, I'll do the reportin' for yo' . . . and you'll have the Johns after you.'

'Wha' . . . you'd do that y'own brother?'

'Wonderful bloody brother I got!'

'That makes two of us. Yo' only narked 'cause I got in before yo'.'

Nugget leapt up from his bed: 'You dirty-minded bloody bastard!'

Nobby snatched up the box again. Then seeing that Nugget was not coming at him, he set it down, but gathered the things from it, and also reached for clothes hanging on the wall beside the bed. Bundling them up, he started off down the verandah.

Nugget demanded, 'Where you goin'?'

At the second door, Nobby turned and snapped back, 'I'm pissin' off. You can go and get donkey-walloped, yo' bloody wowser.' He disappeared into the house.

Nugget shouted, 'Come back here, Nobby.'

Sound of thumping in a room inside. Nugget went after it. The room was half-lit with glancing moonlight. Nobby had a suitcase on a box, was throwing things into it. Nugget came up to him, saying, 'Nobby . . . you're goin' 'o that doctor.'

'Oh, yeah!' Knobby slammed the lid of the case, clipped the catches.

'Yeah . . . if I 'ave to pole-axe yo' to get yo' there.'

Nobby almost screamed, 'Try it!' and swinging the case up by the handle, hit his brother in the bare belly with the end of it. Then he turned and bolted out the back.

Nugget, sprawling for a moment amongst boxes, cases, hanging clothes, recovered, and bellowing, rushed after. Nobby, long-legged, was already passing the woodheap, with the dogs out of their holes, barking. Nugget yelled, 'Stop, Nobby . . . stop . . . or I'll belt crise out of yo'.' Nobby kept on, vanished into the shed.

Dogs in the blacks' camp were barking now. Nugget raced across the yard, entered the shed to find Nobby waiting for him with a raised shovel. 'You bloody mongrel,' yelled Nugget. 'Put that down and come out and fight like a man.'

Nobby panted, 'You le' me 'lone, Nugget . . . y'ain't goin' 'o bully me.'

'I ain't goin' 'o bully you, you bloody shit . . . I'm goin' 'o teach you a lesson you won't forget . . . teach you to be a bloody man, 'stead o' a puggin mongrel bastard. Drop that!'

'I'll give it to yo', yo' come near me, Nugget . . . my bloody oath I will . . . .'

'Will yo'!' Nugget leapt. If Nobby had intended to use the shovel he was too slow with it. Nugget snatched it out of his hands, sent it flying across the shed to strike the iron wall with a fearful clang that set the dogs fairly screaming. 'Outside!' roared Nugget, pummelling the bony body trying to keep him off with helpless flapping hands. 'Outside and fight like a bloody man!' Nobby was punched outside.

A mob of dark faces and yapping dogs surrounded them. Black hands tried to part them, voices crying in protest: 'No goot two-feller brother fight, Boss . . . eh, you stop!'

But Nugget hammered, never missing, spitting out foulness, fury, while Nobby flailed and sobbed and spat blood, doubled up when he could take no more. 'Take it like a man!' cried Nugget in a ragged voice, and grabbed at the skinny arms, which instantly grabbed his – and Nobby brought his bony knee up hard into Nugget's crutch.

Nugget gasped and fell to knees, while the surging crowd cried; 'Eh, look out!' Perhaps it was as much warning as comment. Nobby brought the knee up again, this time under his brother's sagging chin. Nugget grunted and sprawled out asleep. Nobby swung on the crowd: 'Get' t' 'ell out o' it, you black bastards!' Those in front of him leapt aside as he went loping back into the shed.

They were all standing jabbering over Nugget, when the engine of the utility roared. They looked. Grinding of gears – and there was the rear of the truck – and Nugget in the way of it. Yelling, the blacks dragged him clear. Nobby hung out, with bared teeth glinting in the moonlight. Someone said, 'Mad bugger!' He swung the truck round with savage tearing at the steering wheel. Then he was off. He was headed eastward. His dust rose edged with silver.

Nobby's going was only a sugar-bag drone when Nugget opened his eyes. He groaned and clasped his chin. He sat up and groaned again, clasping his loins. 'Where's he?' he gasped.

'He go, Boss.'

'Goo . . . good riddance, too.'

They helped him up, supported him in his unsteady going back to the house. By the woodheap were Nell and Queeny and Prindy and King George. Nugget said to them, 'No-good business, eh?' They only stared at him. He added, 'Come on . . . back to bed. Still got 'o make that early start for Town tomorro'.' He looked at Queeny: 'You and George can stop 'ere while I take these two-feller to Town.'

He waited to see them go, with what looked liked reluctance, to their beds. Saying goodnight to Nell, he added: 'Everything's goin' 'o be all right, girl. I know you don' wan' 'o go Town . . . but you got 'o. Women get that sickness a lot worse'n men. I got 'o see you properly fixed up. I'll take you to Dr Cobbity myself. Wan' 'o talk to him about the boy, too. Tell you 'bout it while we're drivin' in tomorro'. Right? Goodnight, Nelly, dear.'

She breathed, 'Goodnight . . . Boss.'

'Hey . . . what's this Boss business?'

But she was gone.

He sat on Prindy's bed for a while, as Igulgul flooded the verandah with light, telling him about their future together – till he discovered that Prindy was asleep. Then he kissed the pale brow and went off to his own bed.

It was dark when Prindy woke again, with someone touching him gently, stroking his eyes. As they opened the stroking finger slipped to his lips to silence them. His mother breathed in his ear, 'You come.'

He rose silently. She gave him his clothes that had hung on a peg, but pushed him into the house and through it. From the kitchen the first silver of dawn could be seen. She whispered to him to put on his clothes. He came outside to see the silhouettes of Queeny and King George. He whispered, 'Wha' nam'?'

His mother answered, 'We clear out now.'

'Where we go?'

'Come on.'

'I wan' him my dog.'

'Him dere,' whispered George.

'I wan' him my tommy'awk.'

He dodged his mother's clutching hand and went back into the dark house, through to his bed, got the tommy-axe from a box beneath it, along with a small bundle of other things. Then he came back: 'Where my dog?'

'I been tie him up dat-a-way,' said George, with a jerk of the dark bulk of his head westward. He added, 'We go now.'

The other dogs whimpered softly in the gloom. One gave a single yap. It was answered by a faint *kai-kai-kai-ing* from the creek.

CHAPTER EIGHT

At least as far as Njorjinga (also known as King George) was concerned, the trouble that put the runaways to flight again was much less the cause than the mere precipitant. He was fully prepared for it, not simply with all the necessities in the way of hunting appliances and other gear, but with assurance that their intentions should not be interfered with as before, through having these meet those of him supposed to be interfering at long distance, namely the Pookarakka back in Port Palmeston Jail. At first opportunity for privy male talking, George told Prindy he had made up a Letter Stick for sending to the Wise One, to say that they two would be going on to the Alice Country to await his coming when he freed himself. The message had been entrusted to one of the Hang On Creek blacks, who would be going in to Town with Nugget Knowles. He and Prindy would take the two women as far on their way to the Beatrice as need be for them to find the rest of it themselves, then desert them. They couldn't be mixed up with women in the bijnitch ahead of them. Mt Mooragetaghee was their immediate goal. They must reach it this first day, going by ridges to avoid leaving tracks for police. Once there they would have the advantage of the magic it offered. Climb to the top, and not only did you have a view of the country from sea to sea, but a hint of all that would be happening to concern you during this period of Igulgul. Then there was its stock of brush-tail wallabies. They would be wanting a couple of tails for their subsequent journeying. There were also the porcupines: 'Aw, mek'm spit come out!' said George, swallowing his saliva.

George chanted the legend of Mooragetaghee, the Echidna (or Porkypine to ignoramuses):

Burragin ga burragin
Widji getigheenya Mooragetaghee, Mooragetaghee,
Wudda baddah, wudda baddah, wudda baddah . . . .

Prindy joined in with a version of his own, despite the scolding of his mother and the mockery of his aunt Queeny:

Ol' Mooragetaghee, minji long o' water he.
Brolga come an' up him bum shove him spear . . . he he!
Proper minji bugger dat one Mooragetaghee – ee-ee!

The legend told of how Mooragetaghee was camped on a waterhole in dry country, when along came the Brolga People, very thirsty. Too mean to share the water, Mooragetaghee got on top of the hole and covered himself with mud, to make it look as if the hole were dry. The Brolgas said, 'There may be water down below. Let's try with our spears.' They all dug their spears into Mooragetaghee, who leapt out and fled, with the spears still sticking in him. He was crying to himself about the spears, when Wanjin the Dingo came along and offered to pull them out. But Mooragetaghee didn't like the way Wanjin was slobbering, and said, 'No thank you. I'd rather have spears in my back than myself in your belly.' Thereupon he dug himself into the ground; and the spears grew into the quills his descendants carry to this day. Likewise to this day do porkypines dig themselves in with amazing facility to avoid others creatures. Mt Mooragetaghee, or Finish, is where the Old Porkypine dug himself in for the last time, piling up a great heap of dirt and rock to mark the spot.

All that day they had glimpses of the fabulous mountain, seeming by their round-about-going to get no nearer, so that Queeny, toiling on stump and crutch, trying not to leave tracks, in extremes of thirst and fatigue and complicated belief, got the idea that she was being led a dance by what she called no-goot blackfeller bijnitch, and yelled about it. Through Prindy, King George replied that those who didn't like it could go back. She tried an old blackfellow trick of shortening hard travel by Singing the destination nearer, but did it to the tune of *Jesus Loves Me* and in Jesus's name: 'Jesus bring him dat place close, 'fore I knock-up, Jesus, please . . . . ' Nell might have been in it too, the way her lips moved. George whooped with merriment in telling Prindy how much notice that Old Mooragetaghee was going to take of Jesus Bijnitch.

Still, it was as if by magic of some sort that, in the vermilion and silver evening, from seeming to have lost Mooragetaghee altogether since the Sun went down behind a high intervening ridge, they topped the ridge to find him right before them, no more just a bit of peeping blue, but a mass, deep green and silver, very much like the bulk of a sleeping giant animal. The magic of it, like an emanation of its moon-silvered scales of rock, warm and iridescent, enveloped them as they went on down to the dark foot of it, causing Queeny to cry out that she wasn't going any closer. But George had been telling Prindy of the sweet sweet water they would find tumbling from those rocks. She stopped only long enough to utter a fervent prayer: 'You look out me, Jesus . . . I you goot girl, Queeny.'

The Shade of Mooragetaghee led them straight to water, to a winking pool fed by a streamlet tinkling out of granite that seemed to glow. Sweet sweet water! They sank sighing onto silky couch-grown sand. It was George said they were under the patronage of the Old One, directed by another, the Master, at the moment staring out of one red eye, as if he, Tchamala, were leaning over the silver wall of rock towering above them. Queeny must have her say, exhausted or not: 'Don' you believe dat, boy. Dat one heye belong Bible God. He lookin' out for you and me and my tchister . . . but no-more lookin' out rubbitch blackfeller.'

'Dis blackfeller country,' said George to Prindy. 'Too much *moah* for whiteman dis place. Anybody talk whitefeller way here get sick.'

'Yuuuurh!' commented Queeny, but nevertheless shut up.

According to knowledgeable whitemen, the red eye would be the planet Mars. George, the ignorant blackman, called up to it in lingo, while the others stared. Surely the eye winked in reply! George told Prindy that he had informed the Master that they would be climbing to the top tomorrow and would be wanting a couple of rock wallabies.

'You no goin' up dere.' said Nell to Prindy. He ignored her.

That the place abounded with brush-tails was made evident when they had their fire going and the creatures, bold in their magical advantage over common intruders, came leaping down over the rocks to take a look, not to be seen, since they were silver-grey like the rocks themselves, but to be heard, bounding, slithering, sending the small stones scattering. 'Cheeky bugger,' said George to Prindy. 'He don' savvy me-two-feller Tchinek Man.'

'My boy not Tchinek Man,' snapped Nell.

George chanted a bit of Snake Man stuff; and Prindy echoed him.

Poor Mungus, tied up, was squeaking with excitement, and not only because of the wallabies. There was scuffling and squeaking and rustling all around them. A particular sound, a sort of sighing and clicking, made, so George said, by porkypines. They would leave them till tomorrow night, when they would have a rock oven prepared for cooking them: 'Aw mek'm spit come out!'

For supper they had bread and beef and tea. Then they settled down to sleep – while smirking Igulgul sailed towards the wall of rock behind which the Eye of Tchamala had vanished. Igulgul had just taken his last look and slipped behind the mountain, leaving a weirdly glowing darkening world behind, when Prindy began to sing *La Golondrina*. It was rather different from any other of these odd outburstings of his spirit, probably by reason of the conditions of the moment. Queeny and Nell reached for each other and lay tense while it lasted; and Mungus lifted up his head and sobbed quietly in chorus. A hush fell even on the scuffling creatures. Only George seemed to be undisturbed.

George and Prindy were up at dawn. The women just took a quick look at things in the ruddy twilight, then buried their heads in their sacking bedding. Drinking tea with bread and beef, George remarked on the abundance of vegetable food thereabouts, yams amongst the rocks, some tall palms with hearts the length of your arm, cycad nuts for making nut-bread; stuff for women to collect, unless they wanted the men who hunted meat for them to do what Gurrawirrilyama, the Butcher Bird, did to his lazy-bone mob. No response from the sacking. But when George said that they would be off up the mountain, Nell sat up, saying sharply, 'You stop here, boy!'

Prindy looked at George, who looked aloft, saying that he was an old and broken-winded man who might die up there; and who then would lead the party to the Beatrice; and if he didn't go up, how were they to know who might not be following them or plotting to waylay them? Then turning his back completely, as a brother should when forced to address his sister directly, growled, 'Spone you no more let him my boy do it properly way long o' him huncle . . . den, all right, I leave him you . . . bugger you . . . you look out yo'self!'

Nell was silent, George waited a moment, then reached for his hunting gear leaning against a tree, and said to Prindy, 'All right, *Kokanjinni* . . . you come.' Prindy leapt to his own small weapons.

The only one to express any more concern about their going was Mungus, still tied up, and sobbing broken-hearted. As George had said, if he went with them he would run straight into the jaws of a python.

Prindy would have gone up over those shiny grey rocks like the brush-tails who kept them polished, and indeed did so till the waste of energy dawned on him after several trips back to sit with George while he recovered breath or to take his gear while he scrambled up pinches needing the strength of both his old hands. There was no sign of the riotous life of the night before. The wallabies would be in their nests asleep now, in nooks and crannies in sheer rock faces inaccessible even to the rock pythons, who would have to depend on the wind spirits to locate the sleepy beasts for them so that they might lie in wait when they emerged heavy with sleep in the cool of the afternoon.

It all went back to the magic dispensed by Tchamala and Mooragetaghee. The pythons were keeping out of sight, too, not because they were sleepy, their kind getting that way only after a huge meal, but from fear of Old Watagarra, the Wedge Tail, sailing up there in the violet, so easily, so peacefully, and minding his own business, it would seem, but all ready to drop out of the sky like a stone and strike dead with a blow of his mighty shoulder anything worth his while that moved. One thing did move, disturbed by the intruders, that must have filled the eagle with chagrin enough to come down to take it out on them, only for their spears. It was a large python, the best of twenty feet in length, with a couple of bulges in its middle that wouldn't have gone into a bran-sack. As it went sliding awkwardly down a steep slope of rock, George called to it, 'No-more fright, Jullungall . . . me-two-feller Tchinek Man!' The huge snake, with blue tongue flickering to pick up the sound, looked back as if in acknowledgement, then slid over the lip of the rock, the last of him running in a cleft between two rocks, like a sluggish stream of oil-streaked water, rainbow-hewed in the blaze of the Sun. George remarked, 'Spone dat old feller Watagarra up top dere been gitchim dis one, he can call up all-lot him mate, mek him properly *beeeg* tucker.'

It was a good thousand feet to the top. At last there they were, with the Wind Spirits jostling them and whispering around them, and with all the world laid out before them, north-west, south-east, as a blackfellow counts, needing but two points to his compass, those from which blow the prevailing winds. North-west a serpentine silver ribbon wound through emerald vegetation to the silver sea that stretched away to China. That was what the *kuttabah* called the Finish River, but was really the track made by Mooragetaghee when he came up from that hole he'd made when the Brolgas had filled him with spears. The hole was that bay of mud where they had been shipwrecked. So George informed Prindy as they looked around the world. Away west-west of North lay their ultimate destination, the Alice River Country. East-east of South was a shimmer of silver below the blazing blue, which was reflexion of the waters of Port Palmeston. South-south-south of East they followed a line of dust that obliterated the horizon that was the continent. George reckoned the dust was raised by the whitemen building the new road. As they watched they saw a pillar of the dust rising like a willy-willy, but was not made by frolicsome spirits of Tchamala's mob, as true willy-willies are, instead by whitemen, as evidence the faint *poom*! they soon heard from it. 'Dynamite,' said George. 'Whitefeller he don' like nutching in way. He got 'o blow-him-up.' Prindy asked could the *kuttabah* blow up Mooragetaghee. 'Can't do dat,' said George. 'Too-much *moah*, dis place. Whitefeller fright'. Das wha' for he call-yim Finish, I reckon.'

George listened to the Wind Spirits, and said they told him no one was following them, but they got to look out more far dat-a-way – he indicated due South: 'Might be trouble sumpin' . . . we got 'o look out. Come on, we go now. Wind him tell him which way we gitchim brush-tail.'

Ostensibly under occult direction then, George found the spot, one so obvious that anyone less conversant with the Laws of Nature might well have done it alone. It was about halfway down. Two huge bulbous boulders, joined to look like a giant's buttocks, lay beneath a sheer wall in which, some fifteen feet above the gluteal humps, just a nice hop-up for a rock-wallaby, was a ledge so well polished as to betray for certainty the cubby holes behind it. Likewise was the giant's posterior polished. As it was impossible from below to see anything behind the ledge, so was it from above to see anything below that didn't stand well clear of the base of the humps. Not that that would trouble a brush-tail, which dropping down into a dangerous situation, could as easily bounce up out of it. Hence the need for magical assistance. The next step was to sit under cover and out of range of super-sharp hearing and scenting, Singing Marmaroo out to do the silly things he must to die on the end of a spear.

Blue shadow rolled down the mountainside, to fill the gully below and rise up to the further ridge. The south-easter swept up against it, as wind over contrary tide, tossing the grass and scrub and a cloud of finches, and bringing with it the hint of smoke from the camp below. Everything to suit the strategy. Now was the time, said George, in response to windy advice giving in little moans and whines and whispers. They came out crawling to the base of the boulders, there to part, Prindy to go on hugging the rock to the windward side, George to stay. George had said that when the wallabies dropped down they would turn windward because of the smell of smoke and would pick up that of Prindy, and go warily to that side to take a look. They wouldn't be able to see him, but would know he was there. Bold as they were, one would try jumping over him to the rock beyond. He was to be ready with his spear to hit it in the belly as it went. No matter if he missed. The others would come the other way, and must land on a great flat slab where they would be sitting targets.

Thus it turned out. Soon half a dozen blackish heads were seen peeping down. Then as many furry forms flying through the air. A few minutes of tense waiting. Then a whitish belly flying over Prindy – *phwit*! The spear flew, struck with an audible thud. The little grey beast, woolly with winter coat, landed on a big sloping rock, tangled with the protruding spear, fell, to go skidding and clattering out of sight. Prindy stood. Then a call: '*Yu*!' He ran out, saw George going towards a thrashing bundle on the slab on his side, and other grey forms high-leaping far away. Then he ran round the other side of the big sloping rock. There lay the other victim of magic and primitive co-ordination of human hand and eye, killed by itself, in fact, through falling on the small spear that could have done little more with a boy's strength behind it than penetrate its hide, so that it was driven clean through. The stricken little animal lay on its side, with stream of blood pouring from the creamy belly, quivering, blue tongue licking at the sand. It raised its head slightly, to regard the boy with great dark eyes that seemed full of astonishment at his nearness. A tiny struggle. Then the eyes glazed, the head fell back. 'Poor bugger,' murmured the hunter, and bent and heaved it up, hooked an arm under its haunches, and with the head dragging on the ground, went back round the rock. George, looking, cried, 'Yakkarai . . . number-one strong womera-man!'

With string torn from a little hibiscus bush they tied each of their victims, hind foot to tail tip, thus making a loop to go over the shoulder. Then they went down. The Sun was down, Igulgul halfway up the sky, floating like a silver boat in a sea of vermilion. Butcher birds were singing at the camp for their expected breakfast. The air was sweet with the savour of roasting yams. Nell greeted the hunters with a tirade of abuse that surely expressed the anxiety she had been feeling for one of them, to be silenced by that one himself, flinging his share of the spoils at her feet, saying, 'Liver . . . you wan' him, eh, Mumma?'

They had grilled liver and roast yams to sustain them till the anticipated feast of porkypines became a reality.

Preparation for the feast had to be made with the firing of a ground oven, and for the hunting with the gathering of small termites' citadels and scraps of grub-ridden wood. These latter were scattered in a cleared space just off rocks where judging by last night's sounds echidnas abounded. Saplings were also cut for what were called crow-bars, which would be the only weapons used. It was truly night by the time everything was ready, and the porkypines on the move again. Then the entire party went to the clearing, to squat on the edge remote from the rocks. George, Prindy, and Nell had crow-bars. Queeny sat with Mungus on a lead. All that was required of them was to step lightly.

The echidna, invulnerable to all predators but man, evidently lives in constant fear of his single enemy, listening always for his tread, upon hearing which he freezes into what looks and feels like a lump of stone – if you're smart enough to get to feel him before he does that disappearing trick of his. He never moves in the open if he can help it except where the earth is soft and he can utilize his almost magic facility for digging himself into it. Digging under himself like a machine and with the strength of a machine, he can vanish before one's eyes and make a day's work for anyone fool enough to let things go to such a pass that he has to be dug out. Only a man can dig him out. Only on account of a man will he dig himself in. Only a man knows that his is the sweetest of all meats – a man and those creatures wise enough to wait on men's scraps, like those butcher birds clucking in anticipation up in the trees.

It wasn't long before the long snouts in amongst the rocks picked up the scents of termites and wood-grubs, and the weird sighings and clickings were converging on the little clearing. Then one appeared, an old-man who'd take up the best part of the space of a 70-pound sugar-sack, looking like a round ant-bed, black as shadow, save for a glint struck by the moonlight from his myriad little flat-lain spines. He waited, snuffling and clicking, full of suspicion for the moment. Mungus, in Queeny's powerful grip, nearly had a fit with stifled excitement. One yap escaped him, but apparently made no difference to the old fellow, who came on, shuffle-snuffle, following his nose. It must have been his assault on the bait that brought the others, the sound of his crunching, the odour of those delicacies that, although surrounded by them in profusion, they were limited in partaking of because of their suspicion of open spaces. There were seven of them on the pile when George gave the sign to get ready.

George had said that there was only one way to deal with them, which was to pounce with the crow-bar and roll each one over on his back and settle him with a whack on the belly. It must be done in a moment. Once he started to dig in you would never get the stick underneath him, because he would throw it out with his churning iron claws; and it was useless striking him on the mailed back. Invulnerable as he was otherwise, he was so vulnerable about the belly that a single blow would kill him. The pity was that Mungus hadn't understood the instructions. But then, being a *mungus*, he would have to learn the hard way.

George gave the signal *go*! The three leapt to it – and Mungus too, with so much strength despite his size, that he dragged Queeny to her feet without her crutch, hauled her reeling into the fray. Quite naturally, poor Mungus attacked his beast with his teeth – and got the shock of his life, yelped piercingly as the spines struck him in the nose, turned howling, swung round Queeny's peg, spun her, so that she fell, big bottom down, on top of the same heap of prickles, or at any rate as much as still remained above ground, which was quite enough to make her shriek at the top of her terrific voice. They got only four, the style of the three with the crow-bars being cramped not only by the mix-up but by the mirth it caused them. For minutes they were helpless with laughter.

The laughter went on, in bursts of giggles that worked up to shouts, throughout the couple of hours of cooking. Even Queeny joined in it after a while, and Mungus, and the butcher birds.

Seeing that one of the bag was that old-man porkypine, there was a good enough feed with the four. Those who hadn't so far tasted meat of the kind, the inlanders, mother and son, agreed that it was properly tweet-one, tweet-one, the best they had ever tasted. Igulgul was gone over the mountain before they went to bed. Perhaps it was the rich food that caused Queeny to dream again, still of the flying fox trying to take her. She woke screaming, 'You black bastard . . . you try kill him me, I kill him you!' She was upset even more than last time, so that it was a couple of hours before they were able to settle down again.

II

They stayed on at Mooragetaghee till Igulgul had passed his fullness and there would be less likelihood of meeting that threat ahead of them; or so said George, who was still troubled about what the winds had whispered. He and Prindy went aloft to check on that. It was still away there – southeast or southwest, it was hard to tell. 'Can't mek it out,' said George. 'Nutching belong 'o Old Man.' He showed he was referring to Bobwirridirridi by jerking his jaw east-east-northward. 'Deveren kind trouble.' According to Queeny, the scoffer at blackfellow logic, the real trouble was that the hunting was good and that a bloody blackfeller was having a blackfeller holiday at the expense of the discomfort of civilized people. There might have been something in what she said, because George and Prindy were out every day hunting, and George was evidently happy to be practising the ancient skills again and teaching them to an eager pupil. The hunting was all that could be desired, so much so that much of the game was spared after being stalked for the joy of it: great kangaroos, emus, brolgas. The western side of the mountain was climatically quite different from that where they were camped. Sheltered from the harsh winds of Dry

Season, it was largely grown with rainforest. Here were jungle-fowl and a camp of flying foxes. It was from this side that the Finish River had its beginnings in swampland as prolific in bird life as the billabongs of Lily Lagoons. Duck, goose, bustard, quail, yabbies, mussels, catfish, and always a porkypine or two, were hung about the camp, ready for tossing into the ground oven whenever anyone felt hungry, to be eaten with great cakes of cycad nut, which though it stank after fermentation in water so that all the bluebottles in the country came to camp with them, was so tasty as to be hard to leave alone. Along with the flies came the crows and the rest of the butcher bird population, and a couple of kites – to the perverse amusement of that old eagle, who sometimes swooped low over the crowded trees just to give the feathered bums a fright.

The women had really little to complain of, but so little to do as to need to complain. It was useless telling them they were loafers like the birds cawing and clucking and whistling around them and had never had it better, as George frequently did through his medium for talking to them, because their answer was that they were not bloody blackfellers and wanted to be on their way to the Beatrice and the civilized things belonging to it that became more and more alluring as talked about.

How long it might have gone on was anybody's guess, considering the pigheadedness on both sides. Anyway, it ended quite suddenly, even shockingly, by reason of what seemed to be involved, the cause of it an old-man goanna, of the large spotted rock kind, a *prindi*, called Warradabil by George.

The creature had been seen about for a couple of days, having come to join the feasting with the other bush scavengers. No one had molested it, because it was Prindy's Dreaming Mate and could not be killed without his permission, which he wouldn't be able to give unless the others were in real need of food. Mungus had had a go at it, but only to get a good fright when the three feet or so of its scaly white belly and throat reared over him, with claws extended and what looked like a hundred sharp teeth bared, and then to get a cuff from Prindy and lecture on the ethics of the thing. He repeated what George had said, that Warradabil might well be Prindy's dead Daddy's Shade, called *Lamala* in western lingo.

The birds were interested in the goanna only as a rival, he being much too big and ferocious a thing for any of them to tackle even in a gang . . . that is to say the feathered scavengers. For there was that other, the eagle, Watagarra. The great bird would know everything that was going on below and be biding his time. Then there he was, that morning, hurtling down over the rocks in a dive. The scavenger birds saw him and gave the alarm. The goanna, well out in the open, started a bee-line for the rocks. But it happened that Queeny was sitting on a rock just there, and not knowing what was going on, thought the huge lizard was attacking her, and leapt up with a yell and struck out with her crutch. But only lightning or an eagle could hit a goanna really on the run. With all that wood about her, he must have thought Queeny was a tree, and needing the first cover he came to, shot up her, hung for a moment staring into her face with talons hooked in her breasts, while the eagle went over. Then with her shrieking and spitting right onto the long forked tongue he was listening with, and her pounding his armoured back with the head of the crutch, he was moved to shin up further, grabbed an ear and a loop of her knotted hair, and there he was sitting on top of her head, forepaws extended and head turning from side to side, as if delivering a lecture, horny tail round her neck for better support. The three people watching whooped with sudden laughter. The birds took it up. Mungus barked. Queeny shrieked, 'Tek him 'way, tek him way . . . kill him!' But the others were helpless.

Now the goanna was watching his baffled foe spiralling aloft. Then Queeny raised the head of her crutch and started beating with it wildly. The goanna grabbed it, probably thinking it a limb of the odd tree, shifted onto it, and as it fell with his weight, came down in swift arc, to land on his back on a slab of rock with the crutch on his belly. He lay jerking, with the wind knocked out of him.

Queeny raised the crutch, screeching, 'You bloody bastard!'

George yelled, 'No-more!'

Prindy gasped, 'Don' you, Aunty!'

But with all her considerable strength she brought the crutch down and caught him in the side just as he was rolling over. Again he fell back winded.

'Eh! Eh!' yelled George and Prindy.

But she pounded the stricken creature with a succession of swift sharp strokes, so that his belly opened up and guts and blood came bursting out. With a mighty contortion he gained his feet, shot for the rocks again, reached them, went clawing up, got his trailing entrails caught on a projection, heaved himself round to get clear. Again the birds gave the warning. The great head came up. He tried to run for it. But there was Watagarra with great wings out to brake his dive and the wind whistling through them and talons outflung to grab. *Swish*! – and there was poor old Warradabil, with guts trailing behind him, having his first flight.

No laughter now. Even the birds were silent. Prindy, looking up, muttered, 'Poor-feller, my mate!'

Then George turned on Queeny, as a brother is entitled to in extremes of bad behaviour, and roared, 'Wha' for you do like o' dat, you bloody cranky rubbitch?'

'Shut yo' bloody puggin' mout', you black bastard!'

'I shut yo' mout' for yo' by'n'by, yo' bloody stink-shit woman.' When she raised the crutch to him he yelled, 'Yo' look-out . . . I give you spear!'

'Yo' try it, blackfeller!'

'I don' try it time I do . . . I *do* it . . . properly, yo' bloody halfcaste rubbitch!'

He turned to Prindy: 'We got 'o go. Spone dat-one daid daddy belong 'o you, he mek him trouble long o' we. Come on. Gitchim swag, lil bits tucker. I wipe him out track.' Even spirits need tracks to find those they would haunt. There was no doubt about the fear of those two unbelievers in Blackfeller Bijnitch, the care they stepped with in clearing out. George told them to stay behind and take the consequences. They ignored him. He was compelled to erase their tracks along with his own by means of his magic brush. Anyway, Prindy, working with his own brush would have done it for them, would have had no choice in the matter, indeed, so close did they stick to him during the exodus; and surely he would have wanted to do it.

The incident happened in mid-morning. By noon they were clear of Mooragetaghee and heading southward through open forest. Beyond, the view from the mountain top had shown a strip of plain with a line of billabongs down the middle of it, running southward to infinity. They would be following the billabongs, George said. They would camp on a billabong tonight. He spoke of the billabong country, travelled by him in youth, as a veritable Eden. 'Full up ev'ryt'ing, he said, meaning that it was a land of super-abundance.

The forest thinned out to the plain, a silver sea of mirage in distance, at close hand grey cracked mud with a stubble of bleached grass regrown from the annual burning off of the rank stuff of Wet Season by hunting Koong-yarrakuns. There was no water yet. Some of the first holes were damp enough to grow moss; but most were just hard-baked clay sterilized by rooting pigs. George had nothing to say about the vanished Eden, only that they must keep their eyes open for pigs, not only for food, but because the big ones were dangerous in places like this where there was no cover. Pigs, he explained, were reincarnated Chinamen. Certainly there were pigs about, judging by the stinking messed up water they first came to.

The Sun was red in the roadmaker's dust before they reached water they could drink, in a long thin pool with a scattering of red lilies and a few pandanus fringing reedy banks – and pigs. Mungus went racing to investigate the grunting, disappeared into reeds, came *kai-kai-kai-ing* out with a huge ridged-backed sow slavering on his very tail. George hit the monster with a boomerang, that bounced off as if it had struck rock. But the sow got a fright, swung away, and became a ball of dust racing and raging, evidently heading for the next billabong. The next generation of reincarnated Chinamen came out of the rushes in search of their coward mother, little fat balls of grey mud, squeaking and grunting. George took a quick look to see if they had a father, then gave the signal to attack. They got the lot, seven. Then when they made camp on the other side of the billabong, they ate three in chunks grilled on the coals of a fire made of pandanus pipes. Afterwards they dug a hole and shoved the coals into it, covered them with pandanus leaves, tossed in the other suckers, covered them with more leaves, and then with dirt, and left them to cook through the night. A purple night, and windless, and soundless save for the distant call occasionally of passing plovers. They lay armed in readiness for the return of the sow; but she never came. Only Igulgul came, sneaking red-faced and badly lopsided up the dusty eastern sky round about midnight.

As they proceeded next day, the billabongs became larger and more like billabongs than pig-wallows, even though the pigs were there in increased proportion to what there was to hog – not direct proportion, because they could not get at all of it, which was why it was still there. Where there was water of any depth above an adult pig's head there were blazing masses of lilies through which the ducks and geese swam and over which red-crested lotus birds trotted – it being one of the blessings of nature that the pig, as well as not being able to fly, is a poor swimmer, else Terra Australis would long ago have been overrun by pigs, might even have come to be ruled by them. Several times the party were challenged for the intrusion on their own heritage, and kept clear. At one particularly still-fertile spot they found traces of their own kind; but with the camp these others had used well back as precaution against the arrogance of the new owners.

George said the blacks who had been there were Koonyarrakuns who had come out of the utterly wild western region, a dozen or so, men, women, and children, evidently bound for the road-builders' camps, hungry for tobacco and tea and sugar, and a drop of grog, as even they, the freest people in the land, were wont to become. Their trading stuff was the narrow loins of their girls. George claimed to recognize the tracks of a couple of the men, and Queeny those of one of the women, Queeny adding, 'Dat bloody lubra owe me money . . . promise gitchim what I been lend him from Chinaman. She gitchim all right, I know. But she been gamble all-lot, playin' card. I belt him dat one.

They made camp that evening on the biggest billabong they had yet come to, where there were no pigs at all, but what was worse, the remains of several, piles of guts that were still being pulled about by kites and crows, and stinking to clean blue heaven. Also there were no water-birds, except half a dozen or so lying as little islands of bright blown-up feathers each with its cloud of blue-bottles, out amongst the lilies where it was dangerous for anyone but a black-fellow to swim. That the despoilers weren't black was evident from the tracks of motor vehicles, scattered beer bottles, a couple broken, newspaper in sheets and scraps, some of the scraps lying with a couple of heaps of what looked like squirming heaps of irridescent metal, so thick were they with happy blue-bottles, but were in fact what their owners would probably have called *coprus* – because, according to the knowledgeable Queeny, airing her knowledge in response to the little-literate Prindy's puzzling over the odd lettering on other bits of the paper, they were Greeks. Evidently the spoliation was the result of a weekend's recreation by road-workers. Still George had nothing to say about the change in conditions since his youthful vision of the place as an Eden. His main concern was in looking about for cigarette butts, to augment the almost depleted tobacco supply of the party.

Next day there was further evidence that human beings of one of the oldest civilisations had taken over the region from the pigs in a way to make it seem that the pig is a cleanly animal. Still no comment from George, only a tinful of second-hand tobacco that reaked of garlic, beer, and pyorrhoea.

That evening saw them passing out of the domain of the pigs and those who were coming to be called, officially at any rate, New Australians, – to spare them the hurt of such names as Dago, Ox-cheek, Hun, Wop, Balt, Pom, commonly used by Old Australians (white) – and entering that of horned cattle and the superior Old Australians who herded them for their lordly Pommy Master, Alfred Vaisey. The last of the billabongs were fouled with cattle dung and churned up mud out of which bleached bones and horns protruded. But they were not troubled about water, because on the very edge of the plain a windmill was rising up to meet them.

A few head of stock bearing the Vaisey brand were drinking at the iron trough, Corellas like a pinking evening cloud hovering over the spinning mill as if waiting for it to stop to let them perch, as indeed some were already perched on the yawing vane. On the fence of a small wire stockyard a few kites were preening, to sit erect and watchful when the cockies gave the warning of approaching humanity. A couple of spur-wing plovers swept up shrilly calling from the earthen tank behind a netting fence into which the pumped water shot in silvery spurts. It looked as if the party were going to pass by. But it was a stratagem. Round the other side of the tank the men dropped down by the fence, sheltered by tall weeds growing inside, while the women went on towards a couple of biggish bloodwood trees, watched by the corellas. The kites, now in the air, saw the men, but gave no signal, evidently thinking it all that the corellas deserved to be sneaked on when they had eyes to see and wings to fly if not the sense to mistrust every human being.

George raked four cockies off the vane with a boomerang, and put another up into the mauve cloud that swept over them to protest against the treachery of it, bringing down another two. With that the remainder left, and the kites whistled to each other and dropped back to the stockyard fence to await such pickings as would be. The women came to drink from the trough and fill the billy. Then camp was made under one of the trees; and the kites moved in to join the party. Prindy sang to all of them his song *Gilly Galah,* while the Sun went down and the mauve and crimson of the dead birds went up in smoke to join that of the sky.

They went on next morning into open forest. Everywhere now were signs of His Lordship's, the absent landlord's, stock: countless hoof-torn pads criss-crossing through the cropped clumps of rusty kangaroo grass and broken spear-grass; new pads, little rivers of dust, old ones, scoured out by Wet Season rains, miniature gullies exposing the conglomerate beneath the skin of grey talc. No more knee-deep Flinder's grass growing on the little flats that wound between the hummocks of raised ground as when only the kangaroo as herbivore roamed the land. The little flats were bare white patches. Every shady spot was now a dung heap.

The calling of cattle was now the music of the land. They had to be careful when they came on cattle camped in shade, because if disturbed the beasts would rise, first gallop off in alarm, then in curiosity turn and follow, bawling to each other, spreading the disturbance, till the original disturbers had to bolt to shake them off – not out of fear of the beasts, but fear of those who attended them. It was a statutory offence to disturb stock. That meant it was also an offence for Aborigines to travel over stock-runs, even if the region might have been their tribal ground – not statutory, perhaps, but no less a law of the land, introduced with settlement and well and truly laid down with the rifle, the stockwhip, and the hobble-chain. It wasn't that the stockmen, even if they owned the stock, loved their beasts so well as to be distressed over upsetting of their natural placidity, but that disturbance caused them to become restless, to herd, which meant to fight and rut and consequently to lose weight; and weight in saleable beef is the measure of the butcher's interest in his victims.

That night they camped on the muddy water of a stream that George said was one of the heads of the Caroline River. White cockatoos warned every creature in screaming distance of their presence. Nevertheless, a young wallaby came to drink within easy spear throw. George left it to Prindy. 'Poor bugger,' said Prindy, breaking the struggling beast's neck with a boomerang. Whether or not bovine beasts, being as it were New Australians, responded like indigenous creatures to cockatoos' vigilance, a mob gathered round them in the night to moo softly and sigh and chew the cud, so many that in the morning they, the indigenous ones, had to slink away in various directions to begin with, to prevent the cavalcade that would have been on their heels. Caroline Station homestead was not far away from here, according to George, who said that he spent a little time there after bringing cattle across from the Princess Alice for butchering for the gold miners. He said, 'Dat-lot whitefeller, Chinee . . . him proper mad long 'o dat-one goold. He been dig him, he been dig him . . . all day, all night, dig him . . . hot weather, cold weather, rain, no matter.'

'Wha' nam' goold?' asked Prindy.

'I don' know properly,' George confessed. 'Dey reckon for mek money. Dat time I young feller I ask old feller . . . '

Queeny protested: 'Gwan, rubbitch! Mek him money from silber, ain't it? Dat-one goold for put him rotten tooth, mek him weddin' ring.'

'Wha' nam' weddin' ring?'

'You see on white lady hand . . . some halfcaste . . . and lubra, too. I been get one box from Chinaman before . . . sell him two bob. Woman got him weddin' ring, da's mean she marrit . . . all-same some silly bloody blackfeller mob cut him off finger, knock him out tooth.'

'Goold for mek money,' said George stubbornly.

Queeny yelled, 'Don' you listen bloody mungus blackfeller, boy. Where you see goold money?'

'Arrhhh!' was George's comment. Queeny was even crankier than usual, because the tobacco had petered out and she had not got anything like George's share in those findings.

What had been done to the country they had passed through, by pigs and cattle, was nothing compared with what the gold miners of forty or fifty years before had done to the region they now entered. It was hereabouts that Civilization of the land had begun in force where the process known as Opening Up The Country had really begun. Quite literally had this country been Opened up. Disembowelled would be an apter term. Not a creek but its banks had been stripped to the rock, the detritus and humus gathered over a millenium and more put through the cradle and the dry-blower, washed away, blown away, its rock split with dynamite, its trees torn down for building and for firewood, seeds and seedlings dead for ever for want of earth to root in – because there was gold in that earth, to be got at only by destruction of the earth. Not a quartz-topped hill, some obvious symbol of the wonders of the Dreamtime which originally must have flashed to Sun and Moon like jewelled giants, but had been blasted into heaps of graveyard gravel for the gold in their hearts. The heart-stuff had been taken and ground to powder under the stamps of batteries now lying collapsed in rusty iron tangles amidst harsh thickets of whiteman's and Chinaman's weeds, looking like the ground-down molars of old men's jaw-bones protruding from upheaved graves. That powder had been reduced to cyanided sludge to leach out the last pennyweight of the metal so precious that a country had been stolen for it, and that country heedlessly destroyed along with its owners. They had piped away the poison sludge to silt the creeks and rivers and kill all life that these supported, to spread sterility without effort into places not considered worth effecting it with pick and shovel and dynamite. There were no more grassy flats. All that grew out of the level land, besides the weeds, the stinking-rodger, the castor-oil bush, the Chinee burrs, were the slow-decaying parts of the edifices erected by those who had brought Civilization into the land, their homes for the period of spoliation, their places of trading for greedy exploitation of the fruits of greed, the rusting iron, broken brick, shattered glass, of the shops and pubs.

Amidst the wreckage of what George declared had been the township of Golden Grove, where there was a pool of muddy water behind a weir across a waste of sand that had been the Caroline River, George called a halt in mid-afternoon. There were a few paperbarks and river-gums growing in the sand, all but dead, hanging onto the earth by one root and the sky with one branch. Evidently George wanted to recapture something of the wonder he had experienced in what had been the first town he had seen. 'Crise,' he said. 'Goot time here den. Plenty people . . . whitefeller, blackfeller, Chineeman, Scotty-man, Narishman, Germanman . . . any kind. Properly dat time. Ev'rybody drinkin', gamblin', playin'-up. By crise, yes . . . properly!' He sighed.

Evidently the fate of those of his breed who had been dispossessed of something they would have loved as only primitive man can love, his stamping ground, did not occur to him.

The water was bitter with the black concoction of macerated leaves and iron-rust. They drank it, made tea with it, camped in the sand under one of the mummified trees. No birds here to call the end of day. Even the *koodooks*, the vengeful Shades of tribesmen whose Dreaming Place has been destroyed since there was no calling of them in the night . . . *Koodook-koodook-koodook* . . . had abandoned it. There was scuffling round them in the early darkness, and tiny eyes to be seen like sparks. George said they were rats. Then in the middle of the night, as Igulgul was rising, they were wakened by a scream amongst the ruins across the way that had them up out of their sacking staring. Again: *Row-wow-wow — yee-yowl*!

'Pussy-cat,' said George.

The cats fought for all the rest of the night. The rats scuttled round the sand, trying to get at the bit of ripening wallaby hanging in the sugar-sacks from a bit of dead limb, only to be silently pounced on by Mungus. Igulgul was winking through the few leaves of the tree when Queeny woke them out of the bit of sleep they were at last enjoying, screaming again of the Black Flying Fox of Death: 'Le' me 'lone you black bastard!'

They left the ravaged country, to enter another shitty hoof-ripped tooth-torn stock-run, yellow earth and mean trees, a hint of inland, similar to Beatrice River country, on which fact Nell remarked with lively interest. George told Prindy that indeed they were getting near to the Beatrice, that tonight they would camp on the Princess Alice, from the head of which, where the railway crossed, it was only a good day's walk to Beatrice township. Prindy asked how far it was from here to the railway.

Distance is a relative thing, miles, the *mille passuum* of the Romans, the thousand paces, having as many meanings as modes of travelling them and moods of travellers. Primitive man's estimate is hard to beat: No-more long way, little-bits long way, lo — ng way, lo — ng way too much, for rough estimate – for accuracy reference to the passage of the Sun while one walks with purpose. George answered by turning his head to the brassy East, and fixing a point about thirty degrees from the zenith with his lips, swept them down to the horizon: hence two-thirds of a day's brisk walking, four hours, twelve miles.

They came to the Princess Alice River in mid-afternoon, in time for fishing for supper in a big hole where numerous cormorants showed the fishing must be good, a circumstance that caused annoyance to the women, who declared they wanted to go on to the railway. Queeny went so far as to start out for the railway, along the well-defined motor road they found following the river on the southern side – the road from Alice River Station, she and Nell declared, remembered from the old days; but she had to come back, because Nell would not go without Prindy, who ignored his mother as completely as George did. It was tobacco Queeny wanted. George, on the other hand, was not so hungry for the whiteman's weed as for a bit of fish he called Parunga, best of all fish, he declared, to be found only in the Alice and Queen Victoria Rivers, and always in holes like this. Queeny's assertion that the parunga was *Wahji* probably made Prindy all the more interested. George countered that by saying the fish was *Wahji* only when caught by women and boys, but not so if an initiated man gave it to them. The women cast themselves down in the shade of a big leaning paperbark to watch.

Catching the parunga required special technique besides the Singing of him. The great fish had a special weakness, an appetite for cormorants, the scourge of all other fish. Occasionally he would get one in a dive. What they needed was a cormorant. The fishing flock of about a dozen had moved upstream a bit at the arrival of the party, to sit in a line on the branch of a big submerged tree, watching. George got Prindy to walk slowly towards them along the water's edge, pretending to fish with his spear, while he himself, under cover of another tumbled tree trunk, went up the bank and worked his way along until he was just beyond them. He aimed his boomerang. The birds started at sound of its whistling rush, turned – too late. Two went down. Prindy came running to retrieve them. One disappeared as he was swimming out. He got the other. George told him to climb onto the tree and wait for him. George came out with spears and his sugar-sack. He took hibiscus string from the bag and tied it to the dead bird, tossed it into the water. He was certain that the other had been taken by a parunga and that all they had to do was to wait. They waited so long that Queeny and Nell collected witchetty grubs they found in large quantity in rotten flood timber and pencil yams, and having got a fire going to cook them, called Prindy to come and eat. Prindy ignored them.

It was sundown, with the hole becoming a lake of blood white-spotted with the reflexions of all the cockatoos in the country gathering in the trees to mock, and Queeny joining in with peals of nasty laughter – when there was a flurry in the green darkness down below, and spearman and henchman grew rigid again as countless times they had for flickering instants, but now held their poses – a great toothy cave of a mouth rising to snap – *tuk*! George's barbed spear shot past the floating bird. The mouth clamped over the spear. Spear vanished. George looked at Prindy with a grin: 'He come up by'n'by.' He looked up at the cockies, round at the women. All were silent. A blue crane high in a tree croaked whatever his opinion was, and then went flapping off, perhaps to spread the story of it.

The cockatoos yelled again when they saw the haft of the spear appear down by the bar, wag feebly. George said quick, they must get him, before he drowned and sank. The water was quite shallow where they got him, gasping his life out with his blood. He was a type of cod, a good three feet in length, and of such a weight as to need the pair to carry him and cause the heavy spear to bend. The cockatoos raised a great shout about it. The women only stared.

The fishermen cut great fillets from it and grilled them. Prindy offered the first piece to his mother, but to have her refuse it, saying shrilly, 'Dat no-goot tucker.' Prindy said his uncle had said he could give it to her, and that would make it right. She persisted, 'I don' wan' . . . and you leave him 'lone too . . . poison dat one . . . mek you blow up and get him sore all over. Don' you eat him . . . don' you, now!' But Prindy gobbled the fillets with his uncle, remarking over and over on its tastiness. The rest went into a ground oven, to taunt the hungry women all night with its sweet savour hanging over the camp like a haunting ghost.

Queeny, usually the last to rise, was first up next morning, bustling in the half-light to get her things together. Nell was up a little later, roused by the movement, likewise Prindy, to whom she said shortly, 'Come on . . . we go now.' She grabbed his arm, pulled when he would have turned to George, who still appeared to be asleep. Mungus came leaping into it, *kai-kai-kai-ing* in disapproval of trouble he suspected between his people. George grunted out of his sacking, 'You go, *Kokanjinni.*' Prindy looked surprised, bewildered. Without a word he took up his belongings. Queeny was already up on the road, calling, rousing the sleepy cockatoos.

It was luxurious going, following a silky pad after making your own road through the wilderness. How long since a motor vehicle had passed would be impossible to say, because cattle also used the twin tracks in what would be daily movements to and from water. The road pretty nearly followed the river, as would be necessary in the old days when waggon horses needed watering. Obviously there were short-cuts across the bends. But that would mean picking their way again. No need to hide their tracks, when invisible stock, already calling themselves together for the daily plod, would soon obliterate them. So easy was it that by mid-morning, Prindy, in the lead with Mungus, declared that he could hear motor car ahead, the sound not coming towards them but crosswise to their going. Then the others heard it – droning, constant, waxing and waning on the wind. Then suddenly – *poom*! It was a good way off. Still the air quivered to it, the leaves of the trees whispered, birds called alarm. It happened again, twice. The dust could be seen rising. Prindy explained to the women.

It was Mungus, out in front, who picked up the tracks first – a single pair of human footprints. Eventually he knew whose they were, by his quivering interest. Prindy also recognized them at once. As the others came up, looking anxious, he said, '*Ngangul.*'

Queeny exclaimed, 'How dat bloody old bastard get 'head o' we?'

Prindy said, quite seriously, 'Might-be he fly.'

'Don' be jitty,' snapped Queeny. 'Man can't fly!'

'You been tell him 'bout hangel.'

'Dat-one hangel long o' 'Eaven . . . no-more dis country. He daid feller.'

Prindy said, 'Dat-one Pookarakka can fly.'

His mother said shrilly, 'Rubbitch . . . dat old man he on'y gammon . . . bloody rogue. You finish long o' dat-lot now.'

Prindy turned away with a silent *Brrrp* of the lips, went on in old Njorgunga's tracks.

Mungus smelt George before they were anywhere near him, or perhaps more truly his cooking, because for a little while he trod warily, sniff-sniff-sniffing the breeze. Prindy with spear poised watched as warily. Then Mungus gave a yelp and dashed ahead and would not stop on the hissed order. Prindy ran after him while his mother cried in subdued voice for him to come back.

There was George sitting amongst dried cow-dung in the shade of a *mangun* plum, with a good coal fire, the billy boiling, and chunks of baked fish laid out on bushes. 'Goot-tay,' he said casually as Prindy came running up. 'You want him breakfas'?'

He had no weapons or dunnage of any kind with him. When he saw Prindy looking about, he said, 'Been plant him.'

As the women came up, Queeny demanded, 'Wha's matter you follerin' up we, old man? We finish long o' you.'

Nevertheless they all ate, while butcher birds gathered for the scraps.

They set off again, with George leading, not bothering to take short-cuts, as he must have on his own. Their progress towards civilization was soon to be measured not only by the waxing sound of it, the roar and rumble, but by the smell, the dust, the smoke of gasoline and dieseline and gelignite. Then they could see it, as a red haze hanging over hills to southward, whither the road was turning them. Now there was dust to be seen dulling the natural sheen of leaves evolved to reflect a blasting Sun and now tending to wither under it – dust, dust, dust – on everything. The guts of animals that ate the grass must be full of mud. It stung the eyes – or was it the fuming exhalations of the *kuttabah's* mechanical monsters?

The country was becoming rocky, the banks of the river high, the stream more rapid in its little flow. Signs of civilization in the form of tree-stumps, rusty cans, bottles, spent cartridges. Then suddenly there it was across the river, a very different place from that Nell and Prindy had looked out upon from the train half a year earlier – the couple of railway cottages, the shed in which their porcine progenitor lay dying. Now along the river bank stretched a township of tents, tin sheds, bush houses, laid out in orderly fashion, as it were in streets. As the timber on that side had been mostly felled, but was still thick on their side and thicker for regrowth from the stumps, the party were able to see without being seen, especially as the place was almost deserted and its few inhabitants preoccupied. Three or four people wearing white aprons, one a woman, were to be seen moving rapidly between a big tin building that was obviously the kitchen and a bigger one of bush materials that by the long table and line of bottled condiments and covered dishes was seen to be the mess room. Several dogs were sitting watching at respectful distances, and kites and crows from the few remaining trees.

Queeny said, 'Wha'you-call-yim Renchouse, eh? Dat woman white.'

The woman was really red, face and fat arms, as she moved back and forth through the slit of blazing sunshine between the two buildings.

Nell said, 'Close-up dinner-time, I reckon.'

Almost as she said it, the rolling mechanical roar that came like the sound of surf on a shore, waxing, waning, stopped dead. They turned towards the silence. A few minutes of nothing but the surge of the south-easter in the trees. Then mechanical sound again, the steady drone of an ordinary motor vehicle. There was increased bustle in the Renchouse. Soon there was the roaring of a truck going into low gear, its whining down a declivity, its howling up another. Out of the screen of spared trees a big red truck came rolling, its tray packed with yellow men, trailing a cloud of yellow dust that the wind swept across the river to smother more leaves. The truck drew up at another long bush shelter. The men leapt out of it, beating the dust from their clothes, went into shelter, to wash at a trough. Another truck, of indeterminate colour but with a similar load of men, rolled in behind. Soon a mob of red men were at the table, wolfing like starvelings, so that the clatter of their dealings with their provender was to be heard by the watchers, even though they were somewhat up-wind of them. Prindy declared that they were eating roast beef and puddin'. None of the party appeared to envy the men their provender. It was when the meal was done and the mob sat back and filled the mess room with blue smoke that there was swallowing and sighing. Half the men retired to their tents.

Then movement again. The trucks sounded their horns. The red men gathered slowly. All aboard. Then off again; and only the drone of their going; and at length again the roaring of their machine-monsters gouging the way to progress.

Dogs and birds in the camp came hurtling to squabble over the buckets of scraps being dumped in a hole behind the kitchen. More empty cans and bottles came rolling down the river bank. The kitchen people dispersed to separate tents. George said he would go see if he could get tobacco. When Queeny took money from her drawers and offered it he ignored her.

George was in no hurry. First he explored the river bank further up, then came back to cross by a shallow stretch, to saunter into the camp. The dogs bailed him up, until someone's head appeared at the fly of a tent. With the dogs called off, he went to speak with the head. After some minutes, he went on to another tent, remote from the rest, closest to the kitchen and beside a tin shed. Here he stopped for some time, evidently talking with someone inside who eventually passed him out a tin of tobacco. Rolling a cigarette, he then went to the woodheap, and after some luxurious puffing and surrounded by the dogs, he took up an axe and began, in leisurely style, to split skillets off sawn blocks. He was on the job long enough to take three spells and smoke three cigarettes, to the annoyance of Queeny, who kept saying, 'Bloody black bastard . . . mekin' me-feller do perish!' Prindy offered to go over and get a pinch for them, but to be quickly told *no-more*! What if George had taken a job there, intending to stay on? Then, the women said, they would clear out tonight and head down the railway. But Queeny sighed and moaned, 'By crise, I like him smoke too-much!' As if to taunt them, George kept a haze of smoke about him.

The Sun was halfway down the sky, when out of that end tent came a bulky red man wearing white singlet and khaki pants. The first thing he did was to scan the opposite bank as looking for something there, evidently through having been told about the presence of the others, which caused them to withdraw further into cover, muttering, 'Wha's matter him tell-him-'bout we?' He didn't see them. Then he went to the shed next door and opened it, and after a while reappeared carrying a sugar-sack containing something. From there he went to the kitchen, to be seen again heading for the woodheap with a sack now looking quite bulky. He gave the sack to George, who set down the axe and turned with him in another glance across the way. Then waving farewell, they parted, the man to go back to the kitchen, George to come strolling out of the camp. But instead of heading back to those awaiting him, George went the very opposite way, over the road and up the slight incline to the railway siding. He stopped at the water-tank to drink from a tap, then stood for a while in the shade, looking about, but never across the river. Queeny boiled over with annoyance: 'Dat bloody bastard all-day he been mek him sumpin trouble! I glad time I finish long o' him for bloody puggin goot.'

Behind the siding was a wall of rock, hacked out of the hill that there sloped south-westward, diverting the river sharply. The railway vanished into cuttings on either side. George set off down the railway southward, sack on his back, disappeared into that cutting. 'Where he go now?' moaned Queeny.

Now the road-camp was astir again, with those people beginning to bustle about the Renchouse. The party divided its attention between them and looking for George. First indication of George was a squeak from Mungus, who was promptly slapped by Queeny. Mungus had smelt him. Then Prindy heard him. Soon he was seen coming through the timber on their side of the river. George said they would go down the river a bit and back from it, so as to light a fire and eat. When they were settled down, he brought some of the stuff out of the bag: bread and beef and tea and sugar, tobacco, matches, cigarette papers. Queeny settled back in deep content to smoke while the billy boiled.

As they ate, George related through Prindy what, ostensibly, had passed between him and the big red man, who it seemed was the Boss of the Renchouse. Today was Friday. Tonight most of the road workers would be leaving camp, to spend the week-end at either the Beatrice or the Caroline townships. The red man himself would be going to Beatrice, but later than the others, because he had to see to the cleaning up after their meal and other things. George had asked him for a lift, explaining that he had a couple of wives, one a young halfcaste, whom he didn't want the mob of whitemen to see, because he'd heard they were a no-goot lot; not that he minded one goot whiteman having her. So the man had said, all right, bring her down tonight, and he would take them all down the line and drop them off where they liked.

Nell snapped at him, 'You been sell him me like lubra!'

George said to Prindy, 'Wha' two-feller you Mumma, Aunty, goin' 'o do? Dat long way yet long o' Beatrice. Plenty road-camp. Plenty motor car come. P'liceman, too. Dat man been talk p'liceman been come look-about you. One young colour boy, got him halfcaste mumma, he reckon . . . .'

Nell gasped, 'You been tell him dat man 'bout my boy?'

George said patiently, still addressing Prindy, 'Nutching I been tell him dat man . . . on'y 'bout woman wan' lift. Spone dat two-feller go long o' man tonight, get in truck, you'n-me two-feller meet him dere long o' crossing. You stop behind lil bits. He can't see you motor car light. All right, when he stop for pick me hup, you come out, jump up in truck behind. Man can't see you. I black him you face . . . Here!' He took up a lump of charcoal, crushed it in his fist, and as Prindy, grinning, thrust his face to him, daubed his cheek. Prindy chuckled. His mother scowled. Queeny was expressionless.

Just then their attention was diverted by a sound coming from northward, from amongst the hills. Prindy quickly identified it, 'Motor trolley belong to railwayman.' Soon, with engine popping and wheels howling, a section trolley burst from the cutting, to go right by. Prindy cried, 'Mist' Toohey!' It was, indeed, Tom Toohey, riding with one of his gang. They vanished into the southern cutting, in a moment were heard clanging over the little railway bridge, then lost in the din of the road machines. Nell said with a sigh that Tom Toohey was a goot man, with a coloured family, who would have given them a lift and not betrayed them.

'No matter,' said Queeny. 'We go long o' dis man, eh?'

Again Nell sighed.

Then that sudden silence fell again to southward. And soon the influx of the dusty men began, not merely two truckloads this time, but seven or eight, or nine or ten, it was impossible to see through their dust. Now there was a clamour of voices and banging of cans. The yellow men were darting about, lining up at a long shed where showers were streaming, and emerging from it as red-and-white men with towels about their waists.

The Sun went down. The sky behind the watchers blazed red, while that before them turned mauve against which the hills reared violet. Acetylene lights began to prick the gathering gloom. Some of the tents glowed with the light of lanterns. Then an iron clangour called the mob to mess; and they came like scurrying ants, khaki, white, blue.

After the meal the lights of trucks and cars blazed in the gathering gloom. The vehicles roared into life, went off with men in back and front, southward, northward. By the time it was fully dark, two-thirds of the men were gone and all but a couple of the motor vehicles. Obviously the others were remaining, sitting lounging at the mess table, or retired to lighted tents.

The light went out in the kitchen. Light came on in the Boss's tent. The silence that had hung for a long while over the watching party was broken by George's saying to Prindy, 'Come on . . . I mek him properly blackfeller you . . . den we go long o' crossing.'

The pale glow of Prindy's face and hair disappeared under charcoal, while the women watched. Then, taking up their belongings, the two set out the way George had come from up river.

Queeny called, 'Wha' 'bout dog?'

George answered without looking back, 'You tek him . . . put him truck.'

Mungus raised his voice in a thin howl as the males disappeared. '*Kaiatulli*!' snapped Queeny, and slapped him. He fell to sobbing softly to himself. 'We go, eh?' said Queeny, and heaved herself up, untied Mungus, but held the leash, took up her own sack of belongings. Sighing heavily, Nell also rose.

They went down and across by the way George had gone in the afternoon, but instead of heading straight for the Boss's tent, skirted the camp by going almost to the railway. Thus they got upwindward of the dogs, which came to them roaring. Mungus yapped in terror. Someone in the camp yelled, 'Shut up yo' bloody mongrels . . . lie down, there!' The dogs fell silent, let the intruders pass.

They came round by the wash-house and the stinking dunnies, struck back to the place they sought, came slowly up to it. For a moment they stood staring at the glowing canvas. Then Queeny coughed. A deep voice growled inside, 'Who's 'at?'

Queeny gave Nell a little shove. Approaching the fly, Nell said softly, 'Boss.'

Sound of creaking canvas and bare feet slapped on the ground, and the voice: 'Yeah . . . what is it?'

Nell hesitated: 'We . . . we come, Boss.'

A deep inhalation: 'All right . . . come on in.'

Slowly Nell lifted the fly, to behold the red man, redder than ever at close quarters and by contrast with his white sleeveless singlet, a fleshy biggish man, seated on the edge of a high camp-stretcher, the round face tight with cautious expectancy. The wide slit of mouth opened, revealing teeth in a grin: 'Ullo!'

Nell replied with a breath. The man said, 'Well, come on in . . . don' be shy.'

As Nell came in, she looked back at Queeny. The man asked, 'Who's out there?'

'My tchister.'

'Well, tell her to piss off . . . I don' wan' two yo.' When Nell hesitated, he raised his voice slightly: 'Go on, you out there. Your sister'll be all right. You go back your old man.' Then to Nell, as he rose, 'Come'n' sit down . . . we'll 'ave a drink . . . whisky.'

There was only the bed to sit on. The one chair was cluttered with smoking gear and an alarm clock. For the rest the place was packed with boxes, cartons, suitcases. A pressure lantern hung from the ridge pole. He took a bottle and glasses from one of a stack of kerosene cases serving as a cupboard. 'Sit down', he said again. She sat gingerly on the edge of the bed. He filled a glass, handed it to her, saying, 'Good lookin' girl, all right. Wha's yo' name?'

She breathed, 'Nelly,' taking the glass.

He filled his own glass, set the bottle on the chair, sat beside her. 'Here's fun,' he said, taking a swig. She took a sip. 'Come on, drink up!' She took another sip.

'Where'd you come from, Nelly?'

'Bush.'

'Wha's a pretty girl like you doin' livin' out'n the bush . . . and with'n old bloke like that? Come on . . . drink it up!' He swigged his off.

She muttered, 'Too sitrong.'

'Drop o' water, eh?' He reached for a water-bag also hanging from the ridge-pole. ' 'Alf an' 'alf, eh?' He filled his own, swigged heavily. Looking at her worn and rumbled dress he said, Need new dress. I got some there. Take that one off.' He leapt up again, to open a suitcase and rummage, and bring out several print dresses. 'Try 'em for size . . . and style, eh?' He chuckled. 'Take that one off, anyway.'

She muttered, 'No-more.'

'Gawn . . . don' be silly. S'pose yo' run naked roun' the bush. What yo' gettin' coy for now? Drink that up and then see what dress you wan'.'

'I don' wan' him dress, Boss.'

'Well, wha' yo' wan' . . . money?'

'On'y wan' go long o' Beatrice.'

'Eh?'

'You tek him me Beatrice, eh?'

'I'll take you some time . . . Races . . . but they ain't for long while yet . . . couple o' months.'

'I wan' 'o go tonight, Boss?'

'Eh?'

'You been promised old-man, ain't it?'

'I never promised him nothin'. I give him a swag o' tucker and tobacco for a lend o' you.'

She stared at him.

'What's wrong't you?' he asked irritably. 'Come on . . . get your dress off . . . .'

'No-more, Boss!'

As she made to rise, he pushed her down again: 'No, you don',' he snapped. 'I paid for it . . . I get it.'

'You tek me Beatrice . . . . '

'I'll take you bloody nowhere . . . 'ere!' He grabbed her. Then his voice changed, to wheedling, 'Come on, be sensible girl. Take off yo' clothes. I look out for you. I give you job in kitchen. Your old man can work on the wood'eap . . . come on, come on!' He dragged up her skirt. She had nothing under it. 'Oh!' he cried, and chuckled, and pulling the dress up about her waist, pushed her back on the bed. 'Oh!'

'No-more, no-more . . . . '

He was panting now, holding her down by a red hand on her chest, while, goggling at her, he tore open his fly.

'You tek me . . . .'

Her voice was smothered by the weight of him, his walloping about on top of her, so that the timber of the stretcher cracked.

Then he lay panting: 'Jesus . . . Jesus Christ!' He was slobbering. Now he giggled, 'Tha's good . . . eh, tha's bes' poke I ever 'ad. You goin' 'o be my girl, eh? My girl. I look after you good.' He heaved up from her, panting, quivering, reached for the tobacco. She sat up, pulling down her dress.

'Don' cover it up,' he said, licking a cigarette. He gave her the cigarette, lit it, turned to make one for himself, chuckling all the while. 'You work for me, eh? I look out for you good. You sleep with me tonight, eh?'

She said desperately, 'I wan' 'o go Beatrice, Boss.'

'Not tonight, sweetheart. 'Ere, 'ave some more grog.'

'Tomorro' you tek me?'

'No, I can't take you yet. I got to stay 'ere.'

'Old-man been say . . . .'

'If he said I was takin' you, he's a bloody liar. He asked me if I was goin' . . . and I said, No. I said I can't leave this place with all these thievin' bastards 'ere. I give him all that stuff for lend of you for the night. He said okay. Now, take off that dirty rag of a thing and I'll give you a new dress . . . and we'll 'ave a bit of a party, and then another naughty, eh? Yaahhhhh!'

She leapt up, eyes wide, mouth open. 'Eh . . . wha's matter?' he asked.

'I got 'o go,' she panted.

'No you don'!' He made a grab at her. But she jerked out of his grip, burst out of the tent.

The dim figure of Queeny could be seen sitting on a box near by. Nell rushed at her: 'Dat old man . . . he talk liar,' she said urgently 'Come on!'

'Wha' nam'?' hissed Queeny.

The Boss was at his tent-fly, peering out. In a lowered voice he called, 'Wha's goin' on?'

Nell seemed not to notice him, dragged Queeny to her feet: 'Dat old-man been steal him my boy.'

Queeny cried, 'Eh, look out!' Then, as she swung along after Nell, with Mungus pulling at his lead, she asked, 'Wha' for you talk like o' dat? Old-man say meet him long o' road.'

'Him talk liar . . . dat man been tell him me. I been all-day fright' dat bloody bastard goin' 'o tek my boy sometime . . . I been tell him you . . . I been tell him you . . . Now he gone!'

'Wha' you goin' 'o do, Tchister?'

'I got 'o run-him-up.'

'You can't gitchim dat-lot.'

'I gitchim all right. Where dat dog. Here, dog, you foller-him-up!'

Mungus gave a yap as if he understood, and straining on the leash, and with the other dogs roaring in the rear, took them back to the point where they had come from, then up along that bank of the creek where his other friends had gone. Easy going for a couple of hundred yards. Then they had to go down to the stream through a tumble of rocks where it swung towards road and railway, the foot of the hill across the way. It was slow going because of Queeny's disabilities and the deep darkness in there. They might as well have saved themselves the trouble, because that was the end of the trail as far as poor Mungus's faculties were concerned. It was lost in the water. He ran up and down either side of the star-streaked fluid blacker blackness that chuckled over and around the rocks, squeaking apologies for his limitations as more and more fiercely charged with them. Going on up further brought them to the concrete causeway on which the road, coming down through a cutting, crossed. Here things livened up for a minute or two when, a few yards up in the mud on the camp side Mungus found evidence that took him through another tumble of rocks to the railway. But evidently that was the way George had come during his leisurely walkabout of the afternoon. Mungus seemed to know it, and dragged Nell, the only one who could get through those rocks with him, back to the road crossing. They tried going up the other side, along the bank on top to right and left of the road. They came back and tried the rocky banks of the biggish pool spanned by the railway bridge. Mungus gave up with a dingo howl, in which Nell joined him: 'Oh, ow . . . where my lil boy . . . where you go, boy . . . where, where, where?' The camp dogs, not so far from the crossing, raised an echoing clamour.

All the while Queeny had been saying that George would have headed for the Alice River Country, that is the region further West where, joined by the Beatrice, the Alice truly became a river, the old man's own country. She said it again now, 'He been go Alice, all right. No goot look-about here. We can't find him track. He too goot, dat bloody black bastard. Two-feller got him dat-one brush, too . . . hide him tracks.'

Nell said promptly, 'We go Alice.'

'Eh, look out! Dat too much long way.'

'No-more long way. I been come dat road plen'y time, when I live long o' Mitchis Coon-Coon.'

'You ride long o' motor car dat time.'

'No matter . . . dat no-more long way.'

'Wha' you goin' do dere?'

'I tek him back my boy.'

'Might-be you can't find him dere.'

'I find him all right. I ask him dat station boss helip him me.'

'Might-be he tell him p'liceman.'

'I tchileep long him spone he want . . . I know dat man, Mist' Bolder.'

'Wha'bout ask him dat man dere tek we long o' motor car?' Queeny nodded towards the camp.

'He been say he can't go 'way from here.'

'Might-be tomorro' 'nother-one man.'

'No-more. I wan' 'o go now, Tchister. Come on, we go.'

Queeny protested, 'Too dark!'

'We can see dat road all right. Please you come, Tchister. I wan' my lil boy back. I don' wan' dat bloody black bastard breakin' him in. I tell him you before, I been dream dat-lot kill him my boy. 'Cause he not blackfeller dey wan' 'o kill him. Like dere behin' Catfish. I know dey goin' 'o kill my lil boy. You come now, please, Tchister.'

Queeny sighed heavily, then cried in sudden anger, 'All right, I come. Dis time I gitchim dat bloody black bastard I kill him daid . . . I get rifle from station . . . I buy him . . . I kill him daid, daid, daid!'

As they crossed the river again at that point lower down where they had gone to and from the road camp, the dogs started in on them again, roaring along the bank. The beam of a flashlight swept along the trees above. Then – *bang*! – *wheeee*! A bullet went screaming over them. The rocky river-bed rang to the explosion. The dogs were silent. The pair stopped in their tracks. Then a great voice rose up from the camp, 'Go easy with that rifle, you silly bastards!'

Another voice answered, 'Pull your 'ead in, mug.'

'I'll punch your bloody 'ead in!'

'Come an' try it!'

Uproar of voices of men and the dogs again.

Nell and Queeny and Mungus went scrambling up the bank, crossed the road and straight into the bush. They stopped again. The voices were still raised, but distant now. After a moment they swung to the right in the direction of the road, gained it, and went swinging away along it, with *Minaiji*, the Evening Star, palely lighting their way.

By the same dim light, across a pale-earthed plain grown only with stunted bushes and lank broken grass, parallel to the Alice road and about a mile to South of it, George and Prindy, heel to toe, were heading in the same direction. Somewhere away to southward of them dingoes were howling in doleful chorus.

But for those following the road was not the easy way it had been by day, because used now by stock for bedding down, the beasts leaping up in fright before the yapping onslaughts of a dimunitive debil-debil and the appearance of two grey ghosts, one with three legs, they were too astonished to move and had to be walked round. Queeny was scared of bulls, a couple of which were heard grumbling challenges. She told tales of acquaintances who had been chased by bulls. Nell kept on grimly, speaking only when Queeny complained of weariness, repeating shortly what she had said at first, that if they kept going, they might find those they sought camped where they had all camped last night. Queeny sighed and swung along, singing bits of hymns: 'Yas, Jesus luff me, yas, Jesus luff me, yas, Jesus luff me . . . de Bible tell me so . . . .'

After about two hours of it, with Minaiji down in the tree-tops, they came to a creek, one of many they'd had to cross, but this one with water winking at them. They stopped to drink. But Queeny said she couldn't go on without a drink of tea and a bite to eat. Nell agreed. They made a fire, boiled the billy, ate bread and beef with the tea. Meantime the star had gone, leaving a black black world behind, for all the blaze of other stars. Queeny said she was too done up to go on. Nell coaxed, screeched a bit, wept. But Queeny wouldn't budge. 'Stop worrit,' she said wearily. 'We gitchim all right. But no goot long o' dark.' Soon she was asleep. For a long while Nell whimpered crouched in the tiny glow of the fire, then sighing lay down in the cow-dung and slept.

Thus, while only a mile or so away up the same creek by another waterhole beside another tiny fire the quarry were sleeping. Dingoes were still howling away to southward.

Igulgul came up, winking through the trees, a skinny old fellow now, peeping, it seemed, at both parties, so near to each other and yet so remote. The dingoes got in between the two parties and howled to tell them of their proximity, so that they stirred in their sleep. Mungus woke, but made himself very small so as not to be seen or smelt. Evidently he didn't understand the lingo. Just before dawn the dingoes curled up in the way of their kind and fell asleep.

Both parties were up in moonlit lilac-tinted dawn, taking a hasty meal of the last of their bread, a swig of tea, then away. The Sun rose red behind them, turned to brass. The south-easter rose and lashed them on the flanks. The flies came to ride with them and drink their sweat.

In a couple of hours the women reached the point of long yesterday's beginnings. No sign there even of their own tracks now. Even the place where they had camped under the paper-bark was trodden over by cattle and torn about by birds after scraps. They paused only to drink. They went on till noon, when they came to a large stock yard that evidently had been worked only a day or two before. A couple of dead beasts, sick or maimed creatures that had been shot, lay behind the yard, attended by a large flock of kites and crows. Scraps of car tracks were to be seen amongst the hoof-prints, and horse-prints amongst the bovine. There was a shed by the river, in which hung a food-safe from an ant-proofed hook. Inside they found a heel of stale bread and a small can of treacle. They had bread and treacle for dinner.

Southward, now some five miles distant, the others were making their way over grey plain grown with stunted bushes and lank grass. Good *beinook* country. Everywhere grey heads of bustards popped up to stare. George said they would wait till they came to water before they took one. They saw the waterhole a long way off, by reason of the small birds clouding over it. Only a couple of small trees, the only trees in miles. George said they would get a *beinook* now. He had Prindy break a bough off a bush and, raising it high, go walking ahead with it. The silly birds began to follow the odd thing, the walking tree, forgetful of the man walking with spear poised in womera. Prindy stopped, to wag the bush slowly. The *beinooks* approached it warily. *Zip*! The spear flew. Great grey wings outspread. A croaking of protest against the treachery. The stricken bird ran with the rest, but could not take the air, fell, to be pounced on by Prindy and despatched with a boomerang, and the usual apology, 'Poor bugger.'

The water in the hole was white as milk with clay, but cool and sweet. They drank deeply. Then they grilled their bird and ate great chunks of it, and afterwards slept for a little in a bit of shade; while a couple of kites circled waiting for them to be gone. They went on, taking half of the bustard with them.

The southern plain ran almost to the Alice River, so that it was not impossible that those kites in their highest orbit would have been able to see both parties. At any rate, there was a windmill by the river that the women saw rise up out of the river timber; while the men saw it as what looked like a taller tree in the wall of trees away away to their right.

The women came up to the windmill right glad of the water in the trough they had to share with a small mob of cattle, because hereabout the bed of the river was sandy and its flowing underground. They reached it with the gilding of the sky, just ahead of galahs homing after a day of foraging along the river. They brought down one each with sticks, and had them, little bags of bones, for supper. Then they got through the fence of the earthen tank and lay down to sleep in the weeds.

Those across the plain kept going longer, drawn by a force much more powerful than a couple of hours' thirst and the prospect of laying weary limbs down, for all its remoteness. George had been looking for it since noon. The haze of the dusty windy day had hidden it until the western sky reddened and revealed it as a small blue speck. George, who had been singing softly to himself, suddenly cried, '*Ngah gunga . . . ngah gungah* . . . my country, my country!' He explained that the speck was a peak in the sandstone country, called Aldinbinya, The Head. They would be going there, into the very heart of Aldinbinya, into its Snake Caves. 'Properly Tchinek country . . . properly belong Old Tchamala.'

The last of the red light revealed a blue wall of plateau, made by Tchamala, in his burrowings that had resulted in the river system of the country, Beatrice Alice, Queen Victoria, so George said. He sang of his country:

Gubbalinga, gubbalinga, ngah gunga
Gubbalinga, ngah, ngah.

They were just about to camp, when away somewhere to the south-east Prindy said he could hear plovers. That meant water. They headed that way, by the light of Minaiji – and sure enough, there was a *gilgai*, a little clay-hole shaded by bushes. While the plovers ran round them, scolding, mimicked by Prindy, they made camp for the night.

In the clear morning air, The Head stood out more distinctly. George viewed it with face quivering. 'Long time I no see my country,' he said.

'*Gubbalinga, ngah gunga* . . . *ngah, ngah, ngah*!' As they went on their way westward he told of the wonderland it was, as so often during the long journey to it, but never with tears in eyes and voice as now. He pointed out where Alice River Station homestead lay, actually on the Beatrice River, just above the junction of the two streams. Nothing was to be seen there but the dark line of far off timber. He said they should reach the homestead by noon.

The other party, in trying to assess their own proximity to the homestead, made use of the windmill, up the twenty-foot ladder of which Nell went, to the great wonder and excitement of Mungus, to view the scene. She came down to report, 'Nutching . . . on'y tree, tree, tree.'

After a drink of tea strongly laced with treacle, they got on their way. Now the country was changing again from grey to yellow, the stunted beefwoods and mulgas that had lain between them and the plain that so narrowly kept them from what they were so widely seeking, giving way to open forest.

George now walked with sprightly step, telling Prindy how soon they would be entering upon their proper relationship of *Nungala* and *Wallanjinni*. Prindy must prepare himself for the ordeal of silence ahead of him for many a moon. The old men George would gather at the station would start the proceedings. One who stood in the relationship of father would give George formal permission to take charge of his nephew, one who was his father-in-law would impose the ban of silence. Then George might properly take him away to show him his Road, which would lead them right across the desert through the Frog Country and down to the mouth of the Queen Victoria and the people who lived there. They would meet Snake Men on the way, whom they would tell of the eventual rendezvous with the Pookarakka. Prindy would return as a Young Man. George said, 'I die finish dere, long o' my rown country. I never leave him no more . . . Goot-feller my country . . . *ngah gunga*!'

It was Prindy first saw the homestead, just a silvery flicker as of a breaking wave in the rolling violet sea that the dark line of the river timber ahead became with the climbing of the Sun. Then slowly, as if they built it in imagination as yearned they towards it over the miles of yellow dust and bleached grass and scant grey trees, it grew into a cluster of shimmering iron roofs, elevated tanks, a beef gallows, a radio mast, the darker green of alien trees.

The homestead stood in a wide clearing that would be the result of its own requirements in building material and firewood, extending on the western side of the timber of the river – Beatrice River, despite the station's name. The original homestead had stood at the confluence of the rivers, but had been too often flooded out. This place was built with the Vaisey take over. But surely that was the original material which made up the collection of hovels on the river bank below the tanks – the blacks' camp?

Still under cover of the surrounding bush, George and Prindy came to a barbed wire fence, slipped through it, kept going till it was likely they might be seen, then turned southward. Not that there was anyone in sight to see them, as to be expected at this time of day. Even the kites and crows on the gallows seemed to be asleep. George kept on, into timber of increasing density, so that soon the homestead was lost to view. They came to another fence, passed through. Still George kept on in the same direction, southward. Beyond the fence there were outcrops of sandstone, increasing in size. At a distance of a good mile past the homestead they came upon a place amongst the rocks that was clearly a Ring Place, *Kokulal*, as George called it, putting down his things and leaning on his womera to stare about, as if seeing it in ceremonial, at length saying, 'Big trouble here before.' There was no evidence of its having been used in a long while.

'Wha' nam' trouble?' asked Prindy

George only shook his head, then picking up his things again, said, 'We go long o' river.' He set out through the rocks, now at right angles to their former course.

Over and around the rocks and thick timber they went, for about a third of a mile, with the sound of the river waxing from a murmur to a steady watery roar, to come suddenly to where the ground fell away steeply to a flat grown with grass and patches of swamp reeds and large leafy trees through which the river could be seen glinting. They went down. Horses snoozing in shade woke and stared and snorted. They crossed the flat to the river, setting down their gear to walk in through the bit of ooze along the low bank and drink deeply.

The river, some fifty yards wide, ran swift and shallow, boiling over rocks. The other bank was steep, rising to rocks and heavy timber. The shallow ran up into the glare of the Sun. It ended a little below this point, where a long green reach began steep-banked on both sides, with aquatic trees clinging, their outer roots, arching down to the water, looking like the knees of a tribe of giants sitting washing their feet.

They went from the water to a shade too low to be fouled up with horse dung, and set their things down again. Then George said he would go down to the station to see his countrymen and get those men. Prindy could do what he liked, *bogey*, perhaps; but if anybody came along, he was not to let himself be seen if possible, and if not possible, must turn his back. George slipped out of the stinking khaki shirt and trousers he had worn to rags since leaving Hang On Creek, took the shirt and ripped the back out of it, to make a square. This he slipped between his legs and knotted on each hip. He told Prindy to do likewise with his clothes, remarking, 'We properly blackfeller now . . . chuck-him-out clothes.' Then, carrying only his womera, he set out, heading for the tree-lined bank. A well trodden path was cut into the earth behind the trees. He followed it.

The point below the blacks' camp was well marked. Two dug-out canoes were moored to roots; and roots served as drying racks for bits of clothing; and bits of soap were stowed in crannies. Several paths ran up the bank. George went up. He stopped short of the top to stand and survey the village of hovels, dog-high for the most part, and built of any rubbish, a score or more, grouped about ash-heaped hearths, some covered with bark or tin and with cans hanging from hooks, most with a skinny dog or two beside it dead to the world. No sign of life, except swarming meat-ants. George clicked his tongue. Dogs' heads rose on the instant. Noses sniffed. One blue-heeler bitch leapt up with a growl. In an instant the place was in uproar. Black heads poked out of blackness. George, made a sign. Black bodies, most in rags, some semi-naked, all children naked, a couple of adults decently dressed if badly rumpled, came popping out. George came to the top, to strike the conventional pose of visitor, stork-like, right foot against left knee, leaning on womera. He spoke a couple of words. A shout. Several of the men came running to him. First the whiteman's greeting, the handshake, then the touching, the smoothing, the frank delight of simple people in reunion. Then a crowding round, with babble of talk, and some weeping from women. An old woman laughing toothlessly from the doorway of one of the worst of the human kennels. George went to her, bent and took her hands in one of his, and smoothed her bony arms with the other, while she mumbled and wept and then snatched a hand free to stroke him. Others stared from a distance. Some dropped down by their firesides with backs turned. Then suddenly it became dignified. All but four or five old fellows withdrew. Those remaining with George led him away towards the tank-stand, to stop and squat in the shade of the tank and talk earnestly. Others in the camp began to drift back towards the homestead.

The talk of the grey heads went on for about an hour, when two left the group to go back to their humpies, to reappear after a little while wearing nagas only and head-bands, and carrying womeras and a couple of spears and a dilly-bag apiece, and one with a sugar-sack into which he put beef hanging in chunks in one of the fire places and a hunk of bread from a hanging safe. When these two returned the rest stood up and shook hands with George, who turned away, and with the other two on his heels, went back over the bank.

Prindy came out of the shade as the trio appeared, to stand awaiting them with head hanging, sunlight glinting on recently washed hair, glowing on golden skin. The intense interest of the newcomers was evident. As they came up to him, George addressed him, in the lingo of the country, in which he must have been instructing him. Prindy looked up, causing the strangers to exclaim on intaken breath: '*Ahgorru ghuli*!' probably the equivalent to *Eh, look out*! The grey eyes surveyed them gravely.

Then George named the elders: first Kadugo, who would be daddy, and who gave his hand in the whiteman's way, then kneeling, ran both arms up the slender golden arms to the cicatrices now perfectly formed at the shoulders, smiling, murmuring, 'Properly!' then breaking into lingo, as he brought his black hands up around jaws and ears caressing them. Prindy answered with a couple of words in lingo. 'Properly!' said Kadugo again, and rose.

The other was Ingaua – father-in-law, who for greeting turned his face sideways, as did Prindy. Neither looked directly at the other again.

Then George ushered them all into the shade, where they sat down, lit up a pipe and passed it round, the three men talking, Kadugo while he cut lines in a slice of white milkwood he had taken, along with a clasp-knife, from his dilly-bag. After a while George asked Prindy to relate what had happened at the Ring Place at Catfish Creek, that is to say the shooting, and then how the Pookarakka came to be arrested, while the strangers clicked their tongues over it. Prindy told it in Muttinglitch. By now Kadugo had his wand carved to suit his purpose, and took from his bag lumps of red and white ochre, starting with the white, moistening part of it in his mouth and then rubbing it into the engravings, after which he reddened the rest of it. This done, he tore a piece of paper-bark from the tree, and wrapped the talisman in it, bound it with a bit of fibrous grass, and handed it to Prindy with a flourish and some lingo. Again Prindy replied similarly. Then Kadugo motioned the boy to rise and go outside, and stood him with his back to the others, while he rubbed him about the head and shoulders with white ochre he had crushed in his hands and moistened with spittle, and then ran the red line down from brow to navel. Meantime, Ingaua and George slipped out from under the tree on the opposite side, and went quickly across the bit of flat and up the rocky wall, to halt at a spot amongst the rocks, from a recess in which Ingaua took a parcel, well wrapped in bark, that by its shape was a small Bull Roarer, and handed to George with a flourish and a string of words to which George replied. George placed the parcel in his own dilly-bag. Then they returned, to find Prindy painted and wearing a headband, and his daddy sitting on haunches, talking truly like father and son. The pair rose, Prindy to stand again with hanging head. Ingaua came close to the boy, and said to the others something in lingo, then placed the symbols of initiation, cane armlets and necklet of possum's fur, and with a hand on the boy's mouth pronounced the ban of silence to last till the end of his Road Following: '*Katjinga!*' Thus was renewed the *Jungara* broken by the catastrophe at Catfish.

Then George gathered up his belongings, and directed Prindy to do the same. Coming out of the shade, George shook hands with the other two. Kadugo patted Prindy on the head, while Ingaua turned away from him. Then George led the way to the tumbling water, entered it, with Prindy on his heels.

Nowhere was the stream deeper than Prindy's waist, and mostly only knee-deep, but flowing with such force that often he had to dig in his spears to keep erect or cling to rocks, and several times George had to come back to lend him a hand. Then they were across and clambering up the steep red bank. They stood a moment to look back at the pair watching from the other side. George waved, but not Prindy. The others waved. George said, '*Ngangulah.*' He swung away, headed into the tumble of rocks and twisted trees. Coming to a patch of sand, he stooped and took a handful, sprinkled some in his hair, rubbed the rest in his beard and the grey hair of his chest. He said, '*Ngah gunga* . . . my country . . . now belong 'o you country. You do all-same.' Prindy did it. George put an arm about him, chuckling, 'Properly countryman now, my *Kokanjinni.*'

Soon it was revealed that they were in a gully, with sandstone escarpments, not unlike the country back of Lily Lagoons, although the vegetation differed and the rock was brighter red. They made for a small creek running down the middle in a mass of ferns and reeds and palms, keeping to the bank above flood level for easy going. The Sun was down behind the inner wall and the sky gilding. A myriad birds were gathering for the night in the trees along the creek. A mob of white cockatoos flying over spotted the pair and wheeled back to tell everybody else that they had suspicious characters for company. Butcher birds and blue kookaburras carried on the alarm. Wallabies went crashing from the water back to the shelter of the rocks.

So on right up to the head of it, where there was a deep pool, and in the overhang above it a gallery of paintings, all sorts of figures, except the Snake. Evidently, by the blackened wall beside the pool, it was a favourite camping spot. The sky above was crimson now, fading to lilac back whence they had come. They lit a fire and grilled the beef and boiled the billy, then settled down in the soft red sand, Prindy promptly to fall asleep, while George crooned over him:

Marunga, marunga
Ma widji wa
Marunga . . .

While man and boy were bedding down, the women and the dog dogging them were wearily coming to their chosen camp, chosen perhaps for sentimental reasons, or because they thought they might find something there they wanted, or simply because the sound emanating from it lured them on long after sunset. The sound was that of another run of rapids, at the junction of the Alice and Beatrice Rivers, grown from a murmur to a roar. On the triangle between the streams the original homestead had stood. Nell said she was 'borned dere.' It was too dark to see anything by the time they arrived, too difficult even to get to either of the rivers to drink, because the intervening ground was swampy and by the sound of it thick with cattle. After floundering into a pool they halted, drank of its pissy water, then found a bit of thicket to lie down in safety. They fell asleep to the sound of the racing waters, the crying of plovers, the bawling of the stock.

Over in the sandstone gully, the butcher birds woke the men in the silver dawn. Prindy forgot himself to the point of raising his head to mock them, but to be stopped just in time by George. Anyway, the sharp rousing got them quickly on their way. George said he wanted to see Aldinbinya burning in the first sunlight, as he had first seen it as an initiate boy being shown his Road and last as a prisoner in chains, and because it meant that the Snake was hot with rage from being stared at by his old enemy, Kurrawaddi, as they called her here, Mother of the Earth. Also, he wanted to camp within its magic tonight.

Staying only long enough to fill their bellies with water for a long dry trip over the tableland, they climbed to the top. Sure enough, out of the purple of the West, as the crimson rose behind them, there was to be seen, just as if in fact it were a giant head rising to survey the wilderness, as legend told it was in the beginning, was Aldinbinya, the Snake's Head. That was how Tchamala, during the Dreamtime bijnitch of the Frogs, had popped his head out from his subterranean realms to see how things were going.

Back at the confluence of the rivers the women were also out with first light, and by reason of starting so early on their way might well have spent the day ahead of them hungry, but for finding a bull confronting them as they made their way back to the road. Just a black bulk though he was against the silver sky, there was no doubt about his mood, the way he tossed and growled and sent the dust flying. In haste they headed back into the thicket and made their way through it, and found that it was the remains of the Chinaman's garden that had supplied the old homestead. They smelt ripe guavas, and soon found them in abundance, and also cumquats. After gorging, they filled their bags. So they went up to the road, which since they had left it had turned from westward to southward. They swung along briskly, remembering how short a distance it was, or at any rate had seemed, to the new homestead. 'Close-up,' they kept saying. 'We gitchim, Sun like o' dat,' indicating the Sun just over the trees.

But the Sun climbed up and up, while they strained ahead for the first glimpse of their objective. The flies found them, more flies than ever, because more stock, and more stock meant giving the road up to them and taking to the river timber. But cockatoos discovered them, a great gang of the snowy pests who drowned out the sound of the river with their screaming. An embarrassing situation, when they expected to see the homestead round every bend and wanted to arrive so as not to put their quarry on the run again. They were still sure that man and boy had come this way, by some short cut known to George. The interference of the cockatoos with their strategy forced them to sneak back across the road into the scrub on the other side and to hide till the sticky-beaks had found something better to do with their idle time. Then they got back to the road, and kept to it as much as the meandering cattle would allow. Still the Sun rose up and up, to mid-morning, past it.

Then suddenly there was a white iron gate. But as yet no other sign of civilization, except tracks inside, where cattle had not trod: horse and human and car tracks. Careful not to leave obvious tracks of their own, they got through the barbed fence, took a look at the tracks. None that they knew. Keeping off the road now, they went on, warily.

Queeny saw it first: 'Look-it!' Glimpse of the homestead through the trees.

Like those who had gone ahead of them, they intended to skirt the place unseen, deciding that if the pair were there, most likely they would be camped on that flat up-river, since that's where visitors used to stay, at least in the old times. 'Old time,' said Queeny. 'Dat mek my heart jump t'ink-about . . . dem bloody muddrin' black bastard . . . kill-him-die my man . . . close-up finish me. Look-it me now!' She panted with emotion, with crowding memories, no doubt.

Nell, staring through the trees, became aware of Mungus's tugging on the leash she held. She jerked it angrily. But he tugged, straining with sharp nose darting about the ground, and let out a yelp of protest at the restraint. Queeny hissed at him, 'Shut up!' But she was also struck by his excitement over what seemed nothing, then a little ahead of him, in a patch of soft dirt, saw what he was seeing with his nose – two plain tracks, human, of an adult and a child. 'Look-it!' she exclaimed again.

Nell bent over the small print, gasping in her excitement, 'Da's it, da's it . . . my boy . . . my boy!'

Given his head, Mungus dragged them along with a rush, whimpering softly. So through the further fence, and on, into the stone, causing Queeny to become excited: 'Sunday Place . . . dis-a-way to Sunday Place . . . dat place . . . dat place . . . Oh, Jesus, oh, Jesus!'

Nell looked alarmed. They stopped, to stare ahead, while Mungus strained, whimpered. Queeny said, 'Better we go 'nother side, listen. Spone he mek bijnitch we hear him.' She meant down-wind.

So they went on again, wary now, troubled about Mungus, too, because, having been dragged away from the scent, he wanted to howl. Queeny threatened him with the crutch. Into the thick of the rocks, listening, listening; but no sound save the bluster of the wind in the stunted trees. Queeny kept whispering, 'Ring Place dere . . . dere. I know. Dis-a-way I come from homestead dat time . . . up from river flat . . . I been go . . . I been go . . . .' Her face was jerking with emotion. 'Oh, Jesus . . . eh, look out!' Mungus had found tracks again, the same tracks, of man and boy, distinct in the sand, going down towards the river.

They studied the tracks, stood debating what to do. If there were what they called a mob, they had best go and tell the station Boss. Queeny, beside herself with the old hatred now, kept saying, 'I kill him dat bastard die dis time. I don't care wha' Boss say. First chanst I get I brain him!' She swung the crutch viciously. The straining Mungus, taking fright at the movement, snatched the leash out of Nell's hand, and finding himself free, went flying through the rocks towards the river. The women looked at each other with horror. A moment. Then Nell cried, 'My boy . . . my boy dere!' She started off after the dog. Queeny called on her to wait. But she went running through the rocks.

Nell came to the steep wall, stopped, stared about the flat. The horses were there, snorting, disturbed no doubt by Mungus. Then she caught a glimpse of the little dog running round that low bush. She was starting to descend when Queeny came up, panting, 'Wha' nam'?'

Nell breathed, 'Nutching I see.'

'Wait, wait!' said Queeny. 'Might-be he sit down lil bits more far. Might-be he go long o' station camp. Better we gitchim dog first-time. Gi' me hand get down.'

They reached the little tree to see Mungus at the water's edge. They glanced at the tracks about the tree. There was a bit of ochre and a rag of khaki. Nell snatched up the rag, smelt it. Then Mungus, looking across the rushing stream began to bark . . . *kai-kai-kai-kai*!

'Bugger dat dog!' hissed Queeny. They both started out to stop him. He came running to them barking. They grabbed him, silenced him with thumps. Squeaking he dragged them back to where he had been barking at the water's edge. There plainly in mud churned up formerly by horses going to drink were the fresh prints of man and boy, heading into the water, and depressions in the ooze, and none nearby to show that they had gone there only to drink. Mungus dragged them into the water, and standing, staring across, raised his head and howled.

Queeny said, 'Dey go 'cross dere . . . on'y two-feller.'

'We go,' said Nell.

'Might-be water too deep.'

'I don' know. I never been crost dere. Dat *wahji* place, I t'ink.'

'Da's right. I 'member. I don' care *wahji*. Jesus look out me.'

'I got 'o get back my boy.'

'I got 'o kill dat old man die.'

So they crossed, having to pick Mungus up and carry him to save him from being swept away. Over and up the other side, and onto the scent again. The cockatoos weren't there today. They must have been the gang that harassed them back along the road. On up the creek they went. The day was well on, with the Sun over the rim of the escarpment. They reached the men's camp of the night before. Tired out, they rested, but intended to climb out and go on with the hunt. However, the cockatoos came in and spotted them, and made such a din that they decided to wait till the birds settled down, lest they go with them and betray them. It was dark when they made the climb. Then the waste of rock and stunted scrub intimidated them. They found a shelter from the wind, and settled down, made a supper of guavas and cumquats, and fell asleep

– if sleep it could be called, that fearful huddling together in a land of *moah*, where every rock, seen against the stars, seemed a crouching form, and the very stars in setting over the rim of the black flatness to be taking a last look in order to report to whatever menace lurked below.

Just over that rim, in comfort and at ease as those to whom *moah* held no terrors, the two males were camped in an overhang immediately opposite Aldinbinyah, which reared its head about a mile away, measuring down the steep gully intervening and up again. As a whiteman would see it, it was the headland of another projection of this plateau, a mass of rock that for some reason had better withstood the eroding effect of the ages which had levelled most of the rest of the high country thereabout. But it was not whiteman's country, and perhaps never likely to be, so that the blackman's reasoning that it was a Shade of the Old One, Tchamala, was the proper one. Indeed, reared against a purple sky, with the swinging stars, the Cross, the Scorpion, to give it fresh eyes as the others winked out, it looked remarkably like the flat head of a serpent rampant. George and Prindy had supped on a small wallaby, a whip-tail.

George told Prindy that tomorrow they must do a bit of painting in the Snake Caves over yonder. He said the Wind Spirits, to be heard humming round the Snake's Head, were on again about that trouble ahead. He couldn't make it out, since they were doing everything the Pookarakka would require of them, and were equipped to meet and pass any challenge that might be made to their going whither they were bound. However, a bit of painting might put matters right. It would certainly please the Wise One to know that his Mekullikulli had left his print here along with all the other Snake Men of the ages.

In the morning they waited to see the Snake's Head blaze back at the stare of Kurrawaddi. George said it was dangerous to be too close to Aldinbinyah when he was like that because the *moah* was too strong.

When it was safe and Aldinbinyah was just a mass of red and mauve and yellow rock, to all appearance, the pair descended into the gully. Here was a patch of rainforest, so that the sky was hidden by foliage, the ground overgrown with ferns. Orchids and staghorns hung from mossy branches. There were bushes of blackberries that George said were good eating; and they fed as they went. The trees were full of birds of many kinds. Water trickled through the mossy rocks. Aldinbinyah was completely lost to sight. It was a drop down of a good five hundred feet, into another world.

Then they began to climb and to catch glimpses of the brilliant rock, almost directly overhead, and as if looking down at them. The *moah* was very strong in here, George said. In thunderstorms the magic in the form of balls of fire rolled round the rocks. Suddenly they were out of the timber, and there was nothing but the rock. No birds up here. Even an eagle sailing down the gully was evidently keeping clear of it. Now the voices of the Wind Spirits were loud in their calling up there where round the scarlet head the very violet sky seemed whirling. So full of *moah*, so full of menace, the very air. *Oh, oh, oh*! the Spirits cried outside; and there was hollow calling back to them from the cracks and caves: *Moom, moom, moomba*!

The pair toiled upward through the rocks, where the only growth was a kind of lank spinifex, almost animalian in appearance, like spined creatures crouching. Up and up, diverging to the right, there being nothing ahead but the sheer upward curving face of the mass, the throat of the out-thrust head as it were. On the right the mass was less smooth, since eroded not simply by the south-east winds but by the north-west storms. Here at the base were overhangs. They reached the base and its comparatively level going, and halted, to rest and take the views of North and West. Mainly it was trees, trees, trees, hills at great distance: the Queen Victoria country, according to George. South-west was nothing but blue haze. There was the desert, George said, created by Tchamala when he let the water out of the great swamp where the Frog People had dwelt. They would go into the desert, see the Frog Men in rock.

They went on, turned a corner, to come suddenly upon an inward curving stretch of overhangs practically all of which even at distance could be seen to be painted galleries. George said, 'Tchinek Cave number-one,' meaning that this was the chief centre of the Cult of Tchamala. Perhaps that seeming red river of painting, the serpentine coil which made the background of all such galleries and suggested that the country was bound by it from sea to sea, ended here at Aldinbinyah, The Head.

They entered the galleries. Scarcely an inch of paintable surface that was not painted, from ancient times by the look of some of the least accessible of it, but for the most part even recently. No doubt Bobwirridirridi had been here, of all places, during the brief spell of liberty he had enjoyed through the unwitting indulgence of the King of England. In fact there was his stencilled hand in every section to prove it, as George pointed out. But no tracks. No human tracks at all, only a few bird-prints and those of reptiles and wallabies and a single dingo. There were still no human tracks, because George and Prindy brush-tailed theirs away behind them. The fact that the wherewithal for painting was obviously to hand in each gallery, the pigments in the raw, brushes, grinders, and so much evidence of recent work, yet no trace of who had done it, added to the weirdness of it. Then there was that *poom, poom, poom* of the wind outside. George spoke in whispers.

There were depictions of the Wind Spirits here, fuzzy-edged circular shapes in various colours, with the usual features of representations of occult beings, the black rings of eyes connected by the loop of nose, but also having each a projection on the left-hand side, which may have been their mouths, since they were more than anything gossips and messengers. George told Prindy what they were, but had nothing to say about other paintings not the conventional ones concerned with the Cult. Perhaps these told something of the history of the Cult, evidence for such a supposition being in a pictograph showing a group of standing human male figures surrounding a prostrate female with arms and legs distorted at the joints and a large snake-like thing entering her exaggerated vulva. Since it had been touched up recently, it might well record the event in which Queeny Peg-leg had been concerned. George stared hard at it. Another that seemed to show a huge snake-mouth vomiting human figures and also recently dealt with could have told that tale of Bobwirridirridi's first dealings with the Old One. There were others, some so old as to be scarcely visible. Since George said nothing of them and yet was so eager to relate the legends of the Cult, the history might have been regarded as something unmentionable, at least in ordinary terms. No ban on speaking of Cult Men, however. George told Prindy the names of others who'd confessed themselves by leaving their hand-prints behind, one of them Jinbul. And now Prindy had to leave his. White ochre was pounded in a crude mortar and wetted with water from the billy they had brought up stopped with paper-bark. Then the paste was put in the mouth, more water added and the mixture worked on with tongue and cheeks. Then with the right hand spread against the red of the river of the Snake, the stuff was sprayed between and around the digits and down to the wrist.

They both did a little touching up in several galleries, recording the event each time with a stencil as signature. By now the morning was well advanced. George said they had better get along and bag a couple of brush-tails, one of which they must leave for the pythons of the place, else the Old One might be *koolah*. So they came out from the last of the galleries and the blue shadow cast by the head on that side, into a wild tumble of great rocks that came down like a mane from the back of the head, and beyond which, at a distance of some half a mile, began the flat eroded surface of that arm of the plateau.

They stayed amongst the rocks, listening to the *Goondalaag*, the Wind Spirits. George told Prindy to listen for directions, and sure enough, soon the boy was signalling a spot. They camped to await the appropriate time. It was easy. Out came the Marmaroo – *Zip*! *Zip*! They got one each. Prindy could offer his apologies only with silent movement of his lips: 'Poor bugger!'

The one they would leave for their mates, the *Goolgoolgabin*, must first be singed, said George, to give the python who took it a good scent for finding it. They made a small fire and did the job, then hung the dead beast up by tied feet to a rocky projection under a ledge from which only a large rearing snake could take it down and carrion birds be scared to enter. Then with the other they set out to find a place to camp on water. Water did not look likely in that blazing wilderness of rock. It would be over the side, George said, and left it to Prindy to find it. So they followed the western rim. The Sun was fairly well down before Prindy saw and heard the signs, a cloud of little birds flitting about tree tops down about a hundred feet. They went down.

There was no sign of the water, only the smell of it and the greenery. They had to rake away leaves to find it, as a tiny well between the buttressed roots of trees, so small as scarcely to get the hand into it. A series of the little wells went down the steep hill. They drank and filled their billy, then had to look for a spot where they could camp without the risk of rolling down the hill. It was pleasant in there, out of sunlight and wind. They found their place under a shelf of rock, settled down with a fire and a feed, and watched the Sun go down over the country they would soon be going through, the desert land of the unhappy Frog Men.

Meanwhile the unhappy pursuers, following the nose of their tireless little guide, had crossed the northern arm of the plateau and come face to face, as it were, with Aldinbinyah, which even without their knowing of its *moah* troubled them so much that, although thirsty and presuming from the bird life down in the gully that water was to be had there and also food and presuming as they did that the pursuit could not lead up that sheer wall yonder but must go straight westward out across what looked like flat country, scared them so that they dared go no further that evening than the plateau's edge. The Head did not blaze an angry red for them with the sunset, but reared against the crimson sky, looked no less menacing for being purple. Queeny said of it, 'When Bible God mek de world in six day, I don' reckon he mek dat mountain. Satan mek dat-lot I reckon. No-goot place dis. No-goot all-away. Spone any goot, whiteman tek it.' Nell looked at the peak with equal distrust, but gave her attention mostly to the view straight ahead, looking for smoke, which a couple of times she thought she saw. They huddled closer than ever during the long night, while Aldinbinyah winked at them with his endless stock of eyes.

While Aldinbinyah was still black against the last of the night sky, the pair went down with their dog, found the camp of yesterday night in the overhang, and were so hungry as to vie with Mungus for the half-picked wallaby bones, sandy and anty as they were. Then on down to the water, to dally there gorging the berries and hearts of palms small enough to strip by hand – while the red *moah* glared above them. They missed it all. Again they emerged from the rain-forest, toiling up the steep, it was just a huge rock they saw, even though one frightening because it looked as if ready to drop on them like a giant hand and crush them. All the while, struggling, panting, they watched it, and sighed with relief when clear of it to the right, and again when free of the labour and on the level ground of the first overhangs. But then they turned that bend and saw the galleries, and stopped dead – those who were looking, not Mungus, who, free of the leash because of the difficulty of the going and seeing not with eyes but with nose, went sniffing on. The two women breathed together: 'Eh, look out!'

Mungus went some little way, actually to the entrance to the first gallery, before realizing that he was alone. Then he turned, and yapped. The women stood rigid with terror. Then he came trotting back, whimpering, seemingly afraid that he had done something wrong. They had been able to avoid looking at the other painted galleries they had seen on the other side of the plateau, and probably realized with some special faculty that they hadn't mattered so much, anyway, as these.

Queeny breathed, 'We can't go dere.'

'Wha' we goin' 'o do?'

They viewed the alternate route round through a frightful heap of boulders, impossible for Queeny to have negotiated; or go right down to the bottom again and then climb back up when the fearsome region was by-passed. They debated it, talking of singing to Jesus to protect them as they went through, but lacked the faith. 'Some-t'ing no-goot in dere, I know,' said Queeny. 'Jesus can beat anyt'ing, but not debil. Dat old debil Satan been beat' Jesus Gardener Heden. I t'ink it Satan live in dere all right. Come on, we go down.'

The descent was nearly as laborious as the climb had been, made more difficult by Mungus's dismay at being baulked, which he kept on expressing by refusing to budge and howling as he sat. The strange sound brought the birds around, amongst them some white cockatoos that made the caverns ring with their screeching. They were particularly worried because, as they were climbing up again, they smelt smoke, just a whiff, but unmistakable.

If only they had followed their own noses then they would have spared themselves a lot of labour and time and perhaps even a great deal more; unless, in the strange circumstances Chance could be utterly ruled out. For that smoke was from the still smouldering fire on which George and Prindy had cooked a late breakfast of brush-tail before going on downhill, finished with the plateau. It was no more than a hundred yards to the right of the women's toilsome climb, that deserted camp. But for the smoke Mungus might have picked up the scent of his male friends, since the wind was blowing from there. Perhaps his nose was doing less at the moment than his memory urging him to get back to that point from which he had been snatched off the scent that had become the sole purpose of his life. He whimpered with impatience as Nell dragged on the leash to prevent his rushing madly to the top and betraying them. As if the cockatoos had not done that already to anyone on top.

Reaching the top, Mungus at once dragged them back towards the galleries, which because of the tumble of rock were not to be seen from here. They were alarmed again, but for no reason, as soon revealed by Mungus's picking up the outcoming track of the men, and turning with it, to follow them over the course they had taken in their hunt, and so eventually to where the brush-tail had been left as a gesture to the pythons. If there were any pythons about, they were too well fed just then to have bothered with the gift. It still hung there, and not in any way to scare the hungry ones who viewed it now, because the tracks they knew so well were beneath it. The dead beast seemed to be quite fresh. Not more than half a dozen bluebottles were on it. The women did express wonder at why it had been hung like that, And for a moment looked about doubtfully. But hunger got the better of them. Queeny hooked it down with her crutch. They built up a fire on the spot where the wallaby had been smoked, and hacked the meat up with flints they had already gathered, and soon were gorging. Exhausted as well as replete with food they slept, slept long. The Sun was well down before they woke.

But this was no place to camp, even if they had time to tarry. They must have water. On they went again – and down, and found how close they had been to accomplishment of their mission. In fact they believed that the men must have been there when they passed, because the fire was only just dead when they reached it. Therefore, after drinking deeply and filling their can, they went on down. But night fell on them in dense forest. They had to stop. Still in sight of Aldinbinyah, who with ruddy countenance in the last light, seemed very definitely to be watching them.

George's determination for that same day was to get through the forest country below the plateau, and travelling South of West, make camp on a waterhole he called *Gubbindah Wiyan*, which was on the stony edge of the Frog Country. It went to plan. With the Sun on the one horizon, and Aldinbinyah as a ruddy spot on the other, they came out of the thinning timber into a region of great pinkish grey slabs of rock that lay like giant's paving, gently sloping to red infinity, it seemed. Mostly only small bushes and spinifex grew from the cracks; but here and there, standing starkly against the sunset, were so-called bottle trees, *Bamgulut*. Water was obtainable from a bottle-tree, of course, as George would show Prindy, who was now looking on the odd things for the first time; but the water they wanted was from a *gubbindah*, which meant a gecko. In many places throughout the rocks, according to George, were these holes, which led down to the great river through which Tchamala made his way about his nether world. Each was guarded by a *gubbindah*. Only certain. creatures favoured by the Old One, amongst them Snake Men, might drink, If others tried, the gecko in charge would call in his tiny voice, which became thunder down below; whereupon the Old One would suck the water back, and the intruder with it. One of the favoured was *Bilbilgah*, the Night Parrot of the desert country, who kept a look-out for Tchamala during the night and always reported to a *gubbindah* before dawn, when the flock went for the one drink they had from dawn till dawn of each day. The easiest way to find a *gubbindah* hole was to listen for the parrots coming to drink, because they made a lot of noise about it. However, failing that, you could pick out the spot by their *goona* on the rock. Because there was magic in the droppings you could see them in the dark. They would go look-about.

In this case, as so often, the blackman's idea of the geological history of the locality fairly fitted the whiteman's, while being so much more picturesque. Undoubtedly here had been a great lake, of which the mass of flat cracked sedimentary rock had been the bed. George's full story of its origin was that the Ol'Goomun-Ol'Goomun had made the great swamp for the Beral People, the Frogs. Living according to the rules she had taught them, the Beral had been as happy as the frogs of today are when the rains come, singing all day and all night long. Then Tchamala had come along and asked them what sort of life was it when you did the same thing all the while. The Beral asked him how to break the monotony. He said, simply by breaking those crazy rules – do a bit of *tchinekin* now and again. But the Beral, who were giants, did their *tchinekin* in such a big way that it led to a battle royal. Koonapippi (or Kurrawaddi) came along to stop it. Then it was that Tchamala made a hole in the swamp from underneath, so that all the water ran out into his river. The Beral perished. Prindy would see their Shades in rock away over there where the sand was. The swamp frogs of today, called *Gulladulla*, were a new lot made by the Ol'Goomun. She fixed it with them so that they would never go Wrong Side like the Beral. They didn't have husbands and wives like other creatures. The females simply laid their eggs; and the males came along and had a big corroboree to show that they were happy with the arrangement. But what a life, as the Old One had said so long ago!

The *Bamgulut*, the bottle-trees, said George, were people in the Beginning, the ancestors of the yam called *Miyakka*. They'd been mixed up in the great fight of the Beral, but had more sense than the Frogs in filling themselves with water before it disappeared. They were able to show a few of the Beral the trick in time, but very few, and these shrunk to mere handfuls. However, they continued to exist, and were to be found still, dug deep in the sand of the desert and came in handy if you were perishing for a drink; although you had to be a desert blackfellow to find them.

They went on out over the baked remains of the paradise that had been, carrying a few sticks of wood with them from the forest, and also a bagful of *larrama*, the pods of the so-called Kapok, the seeds of which make good eating roasted. Dark descended. It seemed a hopeless venture, searching for water there; and probably it was; but according to George they were not searching, but being called by a *gubbindah*, even if in a voice so tiny that it could not be heard. Sure enough, there at last in the darkness was a faint glowing. They headed for it. Spinifex grew profusely here between the rocks. George rolled a bundle of it about a stick to make a torch, lit it with a match. There was a widish space between slabs and a concavity beneath one of them. You had to crawl to get in; but inside was quite a cave, with a little hole in the bottom that showed the glint of water. And there, coming out of a crack in the wall ahead was a little white gecko, with bulging black eyes that flashed fire, challenging them in a tiny voice: *Gekk-gekk-gee*! George replied in lingo, at such length that the torch died. But the gecko remained glowing. *Gekk-gekk-gee*! the gecko said – and no doubt about it, a rumbling echo from below! George bent down to fill the billy. Prindy, behind him, stared. Then as George turned, Prindy backed out. They got into another hollow between slabs and built their fire and made their bedding-down places.

The wind moaned across the wilderness of rock. George said several times, 'I don' like it wha' dat-lot talk-talk. I can't-mek-it-out . . . but I don' like it.' Again he sang quietly to himself for hours while his small companion slept.

The night parrots woke them in coming to water, swooped over and around them in a twittering cloud dark against the stars, then went to water, evidently learnt from the gecko that all was in order, because, sitting the white rock while taking turns at the water, they were silent. Then, like a puff of smoke against the paling eastern sky, they were gone. George said that they dwelt in other caves in the ground during daylight, scared of coming out till dark, because the Ol'Goomun, for whom, like all the cocky species, they had been scouts in the Beginning, would blind them with that eye of hers, the Sun, for having betrayed her at the time of the Frog People bijnitch, by not reporting to her what Tchamala was doing with the waters of the swamp. It was because of this connexion with the Old One that they were permitted to drink of the secret waters.

After eating up the rest of their larrama seeds, they went down again to the water, filled their bellies to bursting for a long and perhaps waterless leg and took leave of little Gubbindah, the custodian, who duly came out of his crack and spoke. Then away again, west-south-westward.

The westward fall of the rocky waste was perceptible, but only just. That is in looking ahead. To look back was to see what looked like a purple mountain range, growing in size as they went, sometimes, as the Sun got up and mirage rolled everywhere, seeming even to be pushing after them. George said he didn't like it, that it might be a warning from the wind spirits that there were enemies behind. But who could be behind there? And what enemies could they have, now they were out of whitefellow country and had full warranty for passage through this domain of their own kind?

They came to another *gubbindah wiyan* just before noon, and went below to pay their respects to the keeper and drink their fill. Here was the beginning of the end of the region of flaggy rock. A short way off it ended suddenly, to become a red plain, timbered with the dwarf tough stuff of deserts, the gidjia, wilga, mulga, with here and there a bottle-tree looking over the tops of the others with tiny branches making them appear rather like old-men kangaroos taking stock of things. This was the proper Frog Country, George said. Soon they would see the petrified Frog Men. They went on. The earth they trod now was not merely red, but a mixture of reds of every hue, not merely mixed, but in streaks and patches, comprised of tiny polished granules that glistened so that every one might be an opal or an agate, heaped up, some of it, in large purplish mounds that were the nest of meat ants, the only ground creatures, apparently, to inhabit the waste.

Then suddenly there were the Frog Men peeping, blue humps in the distance: one, two, three. George named them: Karra Beral, the Boss, Barra Beral, Binga Beral. Then a whole horde peeping. Prindy, by his nodding head, was silently counting them, in the way of the *kuttabah*: around thirty. How would the *kuttabah* in his cleverness account for thirty large chunks of rock standing in the midst of a terrain where nothing else in stone was larger than a grain of rice?

The rocks reddened as approached, and took on very much the shape of squatting frogs, with heads all turned in the same direction: north-west. George said they were facing that way in expectation of the rain that at last would come to break their long long limbo. The rocks occupied an area of about half a mile square, the vegetation of which, although similar to that of the rest of the plain, was of much denser and bigger growth. There were numerous bottle-trees, all carved with aboriginal symbols, and kapok trees galore on the pods of which hordes of green lorikeets, hanging upside down and looking like half-ripe fruit themselves, were feasting. The lorries saw them and rose up in alarm, but settled down when it appeared that the intruders were not interested in them. George said they would bag what they wanted when good and ready. The birds would have to home to water, he said, a long way from here, on one of the heads of the Queen Victoria. He jerked his jaw west-north-westward. They would stop eating and sit preening a while before they took off in a flock. While eating they were watchful, like all other creatures. Preening they would be preoccupied, only waiting for the leader's signal. That would be the time to get them, each to find a bunch perched together, and simultaneously to put boomerangs into them. Meantime they would make camp under one of the bigger rocks, would get water from a bottle-tree, and collect *pituri*, which grew under the rocks, and which George had not had a whiff of in too long.

They chose Binga Beral whose belly was painted with many designs, but none concerned with the Snake. George got his *pituri* and made a cigarette of it and smoked happily, till he had to put it down, saying it made him drunk. He soon recovered. Then they went to get water. The trees were all bored, with plugs in the holes. It was like drinking from a tap, only something much more refreshing than water, slightly sweet yet tart to taste. 'Goot-feller, eh?' asked George. He often asked sudden questions like that, as if to catch the novice, but had not done so yet. Prindy smiled his appreciation.

They made a fire and gathered kapok pods knocked down by the lorikeets and put them on to roast. Then they sneaked out for the kill, came back with a round dozen of the lovely creatures, their emerald plumage crimsoned with their blood. The rest fled shrieking for their far-off home on water.

About the same time, those enemies of whose pursuing George had divined and yet forgotten, reached the bottom of that seeming purple wall and with the nose of Mungus found the secret water-holes and drank from them without incurring the wrath of Tchamala, even though watched by the geckos, and warned by the thunder below. They had moved fast, believed they were right on the heels of those they sought, but were intimidated by the red wilderness ahead in the red evening, and gave up.

There as the light faded from the sky was to be seen the newborn Igulgul, just hanging above the heads of those seeming ever-watchful old-men kangaroos. Queeny said, 'New Moon for luck. You wish for sumpin. Den I turn over my money, for mek more. Go on . . . wha' nam' you wish?'

Nell murmured: 'I wish I find my boy tomorro', and all dis no-goot bijnitch finish.'

'I wish all-same, on'y I wan' 'o gi' dat bloody black bastard hidin' so he go 'way die . . . pug him! Den I wan' go Beatrice River Races . . . and you'n me mek pie and sell him and mek plenty money.' She took the sweaty roll of notes from her drawers, and staring at the ghostly sliver of silver, solemnly turned it over, muttering, 'For Jesus Crise sake, hay-men!'

George squatting with Prindy under the painted red belly of Binga Beral, watching young Igulgul vanish with what looked like a sly wink hinting of lively Wrong Side things to watch for during his coming season, remarked to Prindy that the trouble he felt convinced was imminent might come from blackfellows away over where those lorikeets had gone. These would know that the birds had been disturbed, perhaps find a couple wounded amongst them, and think strangers were about and lay ambush for themselves, if they didn't do something about it. He reckoned that it would be a good idea to put up a smoke signal tomorrow, three smokes to show that they were coming in peace. They would gather up fuel first thing in the morning.

But Igulgul was in this, apparently, with his power over the Winds and his perversity. Starting with the dawn, they had three nice piles of smoke-producing stuff laid out about half a mile apart and all ready for the match, when the morning breeze that could be expected with the rising of the Sun, began to bluster, surely at the instigation of the invisible sly one just then taking to the eastern sky. It would have been useless to light the fires for the purpose designated, because the smoke would simply have poured as one stream and scarcely above the level of the ground. George said they would wait for the lull that might be expected at midday, and meantime would look around, do a bit of carving on the bottle-trees, and gather a quantity of *pituri* as a gift to those they were going to and have some in hand for the Pookarakka when he came along, he being very partial to it.

It was getting close to noon, and the wind dropping as expected, and George and Prindy back in the screened shade of Binga Beral, George singing softly, while Prindy gently clicked two boomerangs – when Prindy's hands stopped suddenly, his head cocked. George breathed, 'Wha' nam'?' The answer came from outside, scuffling, snuffling. Both grabbed for weapons; but before they could rise, they were overwhelmed by Mungus, flopping all over them, yapping his delight: *Kai-kai-kai-kai-kai-kai-kai*!

George flung the dog off, leapt up, ran crouching to the northern corner where Mungus had entered, stopped to peer through the screening bushes. Some fifty yards away, plain to see amidst the sparce vegetation, Nell stood, with her bundles, staring at the rock. He looked quickly elsewhere. No sign of anyone else. Nell dropped her load, but carrying a length of wood, began to approach. George breathed to Prindy at his elbow, '*Ngah pooropooro.*' Prindy fell back.

George fixed a spear to his womera, stepped outside. Nell stopped at sight of him. He gave another swift glance round, then looking at her, demanded, 'Wha' you want?'

She called hoarsely, 'Where my boy?'

'He all right. Wha' you doin' here? Dis place *tjungara*. Who been come long o' you?'

'Nutching. I wan' my boy.'

'By'n'by you gitchim. Now you git.'

She started towards him again. He raised the spear: 'I tell him you dis place *tjungara*. I let you have him spear you come more close-up.'

She shrieked, 'I wan' my boy . . . I wan' my boy . . . . Boy, boy, where you, boy?'

Prindy, inside, clicked his tongue. George ignored him, aiming the spear as if to hurl it, yelling, 'No more gammon . . . I kill-him-you-die, woman, spone you come more close-up!'

She stopped again. It wasn't on account of his mother that Prindy had given the signal. There within ten yards, to the left, was Queeny, emerged from behind a bottle-tree, taking aim at George with a length of wood in shape somewhat like a boomerang. Prindy clicked urgently. But it was Mungus who drew George's attention to the danger, by shooting out with a delighted yap to greet another old friend, one from whom probably he'd been forcibly parted not so long ago in order to effect just this strategy.

George looked just too late. As he swung the spear, the rough weapon came whirling towards him. He raised the spear to ward it off. But it was too heavy and the force behind it too great. It snapped the spear, and in doing so, veered up and struck him fair in the face, where otherwise it might have hit him in the belly.

George staggered, fell in a heap with his other spears. Yelling at the top of her powerful contralto, Queeny came in with her crutch: 'You bloody puggin black muddrin bastard, I got you now!' *Whack, whack*! The heavy crutch-leg smote his head. George rolled over, was taking it on the back of the head, when Mungus, yapping protest against this falling out of his friends, leapt into it took the most savage of the blows, howled and rolled over kicking. It gave George time to grab his big shovel spear, to roll into a sitting posture, and from there to drive it past the crutch rising again to deal with him, into the fat belly behind it. Queeny screamed, lost balance, fell on her back.

But there was Nell now charging in with her lump of wood, shrieking inarticulate in fearful rage, but to swing away as George snatched up another spear. George raised the spear without womera to aim, shouting, 'No-goot bloody halfcaste woman . . . you break him *tjungara* . . . you die finish . . . . '

Prindy leapt out, crying his first utterance in days, a croaked, 'Oh . . . no-more like o' dat!'

But the spear was on its way. Nell, now with back turned, took it between the shoulder blades. She screamed, flung up her arms, staggered a few steps, then fell flat on her face, with hands and feet beating the red earth, the upright spear haft swinging like a pendulum in reverse. Prindy staring great-eyed, glanced at a movement from goggling gasping Queeny, to see her pull the spear from her belly and a gout of blood follow it. George also turned, and as she struggled to her knees, gasping at him, 'Black bastard you die now!' bent to get another spear. But too late again. She caught him in the left side, driving the head of the spear out of sight up under his ribs. He coughed, fell sideways with blood gushing from his mouth. He looked at Prindy, raised his hand as if to make some peremptory sign – then fell on his back, mouth and eyes wide.

Queeny got her crutch, heaved herself up with it, stood over George, gasping, 'You daid, all right, old-man . . . now we square.' She turned to look at Nell, stared a moment, then swung towards her, reached her in a few long swinging strides, while clutching with a hand at her own bleeding belly. She bent over her, saw one eye glaring, bloody tongue fallen in the dust, and stood erect and howled like a dingo: 'Oh, oh, ow, ai-ee!' Then with her bloodied hand she tore at her own hair, tearing strands out of it, crying, 'Oh, my tchister, my lil tchister . . . daid, daid . . . she be daid . . . Oh, Jesus save my lil tchister . . . oh, oh, ah, ai-ee! I no-more been do it, tchister . . . I didn' done it.' She smote her own head hard.

She turned to look at Prindy, who was staring open-mouthed from one to other of those who had died so swiftly, as if he didn't believe it. Mungus was dead, with bloody tongue also in the dust and red meat-ants already at work on it. Prindy looked at Queeny, at the bloody mess below her waist. She gasped at him: 'You got him water?' He nodded. She licked her lips, adding, 'I thirsty too much. Gi' me drink.' He went in under the rock, came out with the billy that had been filled at a bottle-tree. She drank greedily. She muttered, 'I too hot. Wan' 'o sit . . . wan' 'o sit shade.'

She swung towards the rock. He looked alarmed, raised his hand in a sign of stop. 'Wha's matter you no-more talk?' she asked, and when he put his hand to his nose in the sign that he was bound to silence, she snorted, 'Blackfeller rubbitch. You talk my boy . . . you talk me!' She went into the shade, while he stared wide-eyed at her temerity. She let herself down slowly, moaning with pain, back to the rock, staring out upon the fearful scene. 'Muddrin bijnitch,' she muttered. 'I been dream dat, ain't it . . . dream about black flyin' fox. Gi' me more water, my boy. Oh, my tchister, poor daid feller . . . I didn't done it, my tchister . . . oh, ai-eeee!'

When she had drunk, she said, 'You'n me got 'o go p'lice.'

When he looked his opposition, she added querulously, 'Got 'o go gitchim p'liceman. Muddrin bijnitch no-goot. Dis 'Preme Court bjinitch. We got 'o go back Alice Station . . . oh, ah!' She fainted.

Prindy stood staring still: at his mother over there with the ants swarming over her dark side-turned face: at George with ants at his eyes, and the caked mass of blood about his side: at Mungus, so thick with them that they seemed to be moving him away.

Queeny recovered, croaked, 'Water . . . water . . . I thirsty too much.' She finished the can.

Prindy looked around again, then went off, past the rock, to a big bottle-tree, where he pulled a plug and let the fluid trickle in. There was his fresh cut in the bulbous trunk, a design dictated by George as a memento of his novitiate, so many marks for each moon of his Road Following, and only one so far. He took a long swig himself. Then when the billy was filled he returned with it, but slowly, with evident reluctance.

The scene was the same. He looked at it as if he'd been wishing it to be different. Queeny, in a weak voice, scolded him for being away so long, and hogged the water. She said they couldn't leave his mother like that; they must try to drag her in here and cover her up. He shook his head, and when she waxed querulous about blackfeller bijnitch, went off with his tommy-axe and cut branches from bushes, and gingerly went to his mother, and covered her. Then he went to do the same to George, and persisted with it, even while Queeny scolded, 'Let dem ant eat dat bloody puggin old bastard . . . Satan goin' 'o get him, burn, him long o' down-below.' She went on, rambling somewhat: 'Jesus goin' 'o look out my tchister . . . you mumma . . . Jesus love me, yest I know . . . de Bible tell me so . . . .'

Streams of ants were coming from everywhere, and to such activity that the leaves of the shrouding branches could be heard rustling to it. Queeny complained of feeling sleepy, and lay down. Prindy had to get more water for her, and hold up her head to help her drink it. She murmured that she would be all right after she'd had a sleep. She told him how she had crawled to the station homestead that time with broken legs and busted belly. 'Nobody can kill me daid,' she said. 'Cos Jesus love me . . . .'

Prindy went off to get kapok pods, having to climb for them today, since no lorikeets came back to drop them. Then he made a fire and cooked them, and tried to get Queeny to eat. She had little to say now. Mostly she slept. If she woke and he were there, she would look at him and smile and whisper, 'Lil Lord Jesus.'

The Sun went down on the other side of the rock. Igulgul went down, without being able to see how things were, but no doubt knowing all about it. Night parrots flew over, and came back to take a look, perhaps to report in the morning to their gekko on what had happened to those two intruders who'd made bold to drink the waters of the elect. Tchamala always got 'em, one way or another.

As night fell and Queeny complained of cold and that was the windy eastern side, she asked to be helped in under the rock, but didn't abuse him when he made no move to do so. She and Nell had brought their sacking with them. He covered her with the lot. Then he got into the cavity himself and dug into the sand.

Often Queeny woke him, calling for water. He went to her. Then a last time, but this time the call was to Jesus, whom she showed to him on the horizon: 'All dress' white . . . look-it . . . sweet Jesus . . . . ' It was the Pleiades, the Ol'-Goomun-Ol'Goomun's form of nights, probably the first appearance of the Constellation for the season, because the dawn was near, as witness the passing clouds of parrots. Then she got her religions mixed and babbled of Jesus and the Ol'Goomun as the one. 'Ol'Goomun Jesus,' she sighed. 'You look-out we. We foller him you. All-away we foller him you . . . Mumma-Ol'Goomun-Jesus . . . .' Then she fell silent.

Prindy, sitting near, watched the Ol'Goomun, who indeed seemed to be beckoning as she climbed the sky. She didn't get far before that part of her universal self faded with the dawning of that other self, the Sun. Prindy didn't have to wait for the Sun to come up to find that he was the sole survivor of whatever bit of devilry had led to the massacre. The ants, not out of the holes yet, hadn't started on Queeny; but there was no doubt about her being what he would call *warriji jeega*, completely dead. He took one long look at her, then went and got his things together, his own things only. These he took a little way off, then returning, with his brush-tail, he circumscribed the scene with a wide band of erasion that would be designed to prevent the Shades of the dead following him and making a nuisance of themselves, as the newly dead had a tendency to do. Then he set off, south-westward, as he had been going with George, and after covering only fifty yards or so, began to whimper and beat his head with a boomerang, muttering, 'I no-more been do it, daidfeller . . . no-more me . . . no-more me . . . .' For just a little while. Then quite quickly he sniffed back his tears, and in doing so, began to swing more southward, more and more, till he was travelling due South, heading for just such a purple wall as the day before yesterday he and George had left behind them. In mid-morning he reached the foot of it, and went on over the slabs, before long to come to one of those white patches and go down to see the gecko and get a drink. It was cool in there. Perhaps it was a dangerous place to tarry. But he'd had little sleep the night before, and who knew how much emotional stress. He fell asleep.

He was wakened by the gecko, standing on hind legs close to him and most likely telling him to be on his way. He drank deeply and went out. It was well past noon. Whether he did so aimlessly or because the sunlight was fierce and best turned full away from and the wind was fresh in his face, or from some deeper urge than any but the like of him would know, now he headed eastward. Night caught him still on the flaggy rocks. He got into a hollow, and watching Igulgul watching him, fell asleep.

He woke in the morning to find the Ol'Goomun beckoning from the eastern horizon. He gathered up his things and went obediently.

CHAPTER NINE

WHAT TURNED Prindy from those courses that might be considered obvious in his predicament, namely, to go back whence he had come or whither it had been so well arranged for him to go? It might be expected that he would be averse to returning to civilization, although it could hold no great fears for him. Fears lay more in the other direction, but surely not such as to intimidate one so well equipped in experience and inclination and actual talismanic safe-conduct as he. He had certainly started off in that second direction, perhaps not simply in compliance with discipline previously accepted, but on definite orders that could be classed as almost occult, since his mentor, George, made them in the act of dying, presuming the old fellow's final gesture had some such peremptory meaning. Yet it was evident that his ultimate choice was made with a degree of renunciation, since it followed his belated expression of grief. His mode of expression was the conventional one of the Aboriginal, which displays much less sorrow in loss of a loved one in the flesh than fear of gaining an adversary in the spirit. All the howling and head-cutting and hair-pulling conventionally indulged in is largely demonstration to prove non-involvement. As all death to such primitives is considered murder in some degree, the Shade of the victim is naturally vengeful in taking departure and must be appeased by those, who as it is put, *Didn't Done It*. Love amongst such people is a collective thing, ordered by rote. Somebody dies. He or she has died ten thousand times since the Beginning, and will be back.

Prindy's tardiness in honouring the convention was understandable in one so young and in such a predicament. But then, doing it as he did could be most significant. He was known for his tendency to solitariness, an odd thing in any child, but even preternatural in an Aboriginal, who is born not as an individual with his own destiny to meet, but reborn time and again as an unchanging part of Nature. That tendency of his was probably due to at least a degree of realization that he was not truly Aboriginal, while yet his being yearned for Aboriginal community with his environment, rejecting the patent empty alienness of the non-indigenous. Suddenly he found himself utterly alone, as perhaps he had always wanted to be, alone with a Nature not in entirety explained and ordered as for a fully Aboriginal child, but by reason of his difference of origin largely a thing of his own secret perception, although no less rich in mystery for that; hence his making his own songs, singing of his *Rown Road*. Yet blackman's rote had limited the expression of his spirit, especially of late. His mother had always mauled his freedom of spirit, because ultimately she must possess him as surrogate in her tragic love. Queeny Peg-leg surely could not have represented for him, beyond the conventional relationship, anything but the lunacy of blackman-whiteman involvement. Even poor yapping little Mungus must mostly have irritated an ear so sensitive. Then suddenly he was bereft of them, but with only momentary bereavement. At last he was free to follow his *Rown Road*. That could be in no direction but his own choosing, or rather the choice of the forces primarily dominating such a life as his – those of Nature. The seasonal wind was from the south-east, bringing the sounds and scents on which as a creature of the wilderness now his well-being would depend, as well as advantage over other creatures to windward of him. The Ol'Goomun-Ol'-Goomun made her first beckoning appearance in the south-east. Even Igulgul, by the angle of his sinking, would be making his rising for this season South of East. The very birds seemed to be heading that way.

Indeed, the heading of the birds his way may have been more in the way of collaboration than coincidence, the way they came to take a look at him, in flocks, in pairs, in families, or alone, according to their natures, surely struck by the sight of the small lone figure whose hairless skin glowed in the sunlight and wind-blown top-knot glinted, and who could speak their language, joining them in the caroling, twittering, chattering, cawing, whistling, croaking to each other about him. Where was he going? How could he find succour in that blasted land? Someone must show him. The parrots showed him the kapok trees he would otherwise have had to hunt for. The crested bell-birds showed him where the grasshoppers were lurking, ringing their tiny bells of voices. Crested wedgebills, delighting in his mimicry of their sweet song, and especially when they tried to trick him with a bit of ventriloquism and found he could do the same, showed him pods opening to shed seeds that made good nutty munching. Red quandong cherries were the spotted bower-birds' offering. The red-breasted babblers only wanted to talk about him, flying from bush to bush ahead and hanging upside down to get a different aspect of him to babble about. He got even with them when a *prindi* came scuttling along to take a look, nodded when given the sign that they were Mates, and led him to a clump of bushes where the babblers had a community of nests, and while those sitting the eggs chased him away, gave his young two-legged mate the chance to do a nice bit of thieving. Night parrots led him to water in the gekko-holes while he was still in the rocky wastes of the devastated land of the Frog Men. When he came out of that into the grey gijia, the finches, in their multitudinous breeds and multifarious hues, and the budgerigars in their singing myriads, took him to their little gilgais. Once when he hadn't been doing so well through the generosity of his new-found friends because of a bit of unbountiful country, he was about to commit the unforgivable by sneaking with his boomerang on a bower-bird he heard going through its repertoire in its bower, to be saved getting the reputation of Wanjin the Dingo by a black-breasted buzzard who, circling above, gave the warning, then called the would-be treacherous one away to show him a much more honest and satisfying meal in the shape of a clutch of emu's eggs in a patch of trampled grass with no one in attendance. There were a baker's dozen of them. The buzzard took one for himself, just hooked it up with his talons and flew a few yards to where some stones lay, and in leisurely style that surely meant he knew that Old Daddy Emu, who would be the custodian of the nest, was far enough away to make things safe, in that extraordinary manner of his kind, took up a stone and proceeded to hammer the thick shell of the great blue-grey egg till it broke, causing Prindy, who wouldn't have seen the like done in his part of the country, to stare. The buzzard, mopping up the tasty contents, stared back, with that boldness which is also a manner of his kind, as if to say: *So what*? Prindy could carry only four; but that meant four big baked meals. He shoved them in his gunny-sack and fled, leaving it to the buzzard to get the awful kick in the bum that someone was sure to get if Old Man Wallan got back to the nest and found anyone near it.

As if that bit of near-treachery had been noised abroad, after that his feathered friends dealt with him warily, or so it seemed; but it could have been the company he began to keep, which in itself could have resulted from his being taken for a kindred spirit by his new-found friend, a descendant of Wanjin's, one of those rare one's of his kind, an albino. Now dingoes like to attach themselves to solitary humans, and apparently without ulterior motive, since it has never been recorded that one has broken such a truce. It is always in the nature of a truce, because the dog's approach is very wary; and no doubt about it, he can read people's minds. He stayed with Prindy for quite a while, actually up to Igulgul's reaching his fullness; that is he stayed within sight of him, just out of the range the clever pink-eyed fellow reckoned those short skinny arms were capable of hurling one of those small weapons; while yet they were truly together. They shared the bustards and wallabies that one or the other brought down, this being better country. They shared their watering, which White Wanjin found. They camped together. At night Prindy would see the red eyes glowing like coals, reflecting the light of his fire. He would talk to him, sing to him. Wanjin never answered. Perhaps he expected Prindy to read his mind, too. Legend had it that the original Wanjin learnt to read others' minds from the Ol'Goomun, whose dog he was, of course. It was supposed that's why his descendants are prone to accompany lone travellers is through that early association. Wanjin always wanted to be somebody's dog; only he just couldn't take the servitude that goes with it. Prindy asked him, 'Wha' 'bout you be my properly dog, eh? You number-one hunter . . . me too. You quiet dog. I like dat. Wha' 'bout it, eh, Wanjin?'

It may have been that pressing; or Full Moon and a gathering of his clan for one of those dismal concerts they so love to indulge in when Igulgul is at his fullness; or the simple fact that he had done his bit in bringing this golden child who seemed to be specially favoured by Ol'Goomun Nature through the wilderness for delivery of his destiny; but the night of the Full Moon he slipped away. At no great distance he howled for the first time in his association with the boy. Prindy answered him, in lovely boy-soprano discords: *Oo-ee-ow-ooooo-ai-ee-ooooo*! Next morning in the red dawn he was not standing all shiny white as usual. Prindy called him. No answer. Prindy called him all day: 'Wanjin . . . Wanjin, where you been go?'

Perhaps the change of country had something to do with it. Soon after setting out that morning, Prindy came out of the flat red scrubby sandy region through which Wanjin had accompanied him, into one of chocolate loam so stony as to look as if it had been ripped up by rock-eating pigs or *kuttabahs* gone mad with machines, so that the very trees on it, stout little ghost gums and wattles and beefwoods, all had a twist or a lean to them. A rich place for growth when there was water, but not one for holding it, so that the profusion of grass was lank and dead. There were traces of stock, of cattle and unshod horses, but made months before, following the brief fertility after what hereabout would be a very light Wet Season, and probably made by scrub cattle and brumbies, since there was no sign of a shod horse's having come in with someone to herd them. A wild place; actually a region of transition between desert and fertile downs. It had to it the quality of downland in that although it was not really hilly you could not see far because of constantly rising and falling ground ahead. No sign of water. Yet water must be near because of the multitude of tiny birds of type that would never fly far from it: bright little creatures, robins in all their Australoid variety, chats, thornbills, Java sparrows, so-called, finches; all too busy with their little business amongst the twisted foliage of the distorted trees to take more than passing notice of something that, bright as he might be in comparison with others of his mostly unattractive species, was not in one wit arrayed so brilliantly as the dowdiest of themselves. Where was that water?

A little red-backed kingfisher, skimming just above the ground, led him to it just on sundown. There was no usual indication of water at the spot, no extra foliage; in fact none at all, the small trees of the vicinity being back from it some little distance, at what, to judge by the avenue of soil-less small stones leading to it, was the edge of the bed of a shallow creek that ran only during heavy rain, the setting one of those slight depressions between imperceptible rises. The little bird, fairly flaming in the ruddy light, sped like a flash over the stony stretch, more heard by his scolding scream of annoyance over intrusion than seen, so swift his going, to vanish suddenly. Prindy, heading for the rise, swung off course to see what had happened to him. It was a small reddish pool somehow scooped out of the stony bed and with enough clay about it to have retained the last of the water that had flowed that way. The kingfisher's home was a tiny tunnel dug in the clayey bank. When Prindy arrived he was peeping out of it. He gave another nasty little scream, then backed inside. Prindy was more interested in the water.

Having drunk, the boy retired to the further edge of the stony waterway where a spiny wattle made a fair shelter from the south-easter still blowing fitfully over the rise. He cast away what stones he could, made up a little fire, then settled down to watch day die in its glory, while gnawing on the hambone of a wallaby and nibbling the thin rosy flesh of quandongs and spitting out their great pitted seeds. Night fell. It was suddenly so dark that, having recently lived in company and in moonlight, he must have felt lonely, because he rose to knees and cupping mouth with hands, flung back his head and howled: *Oo-ee-ow-ooooo-ai-ee-ooooooo*! He cocked his head to listen. No answer. He cupped and called again. Still no answer. He sank back with a sigh.

But within a short while there was his other friend of the long nights, Igulgul; or at least to begin with the Shade of him, gilding the higher tree-tops beyond the water-hole. Prindy sighed again, watched the gilding turn to silver, saw more and more of the trees, and then the stony way light up as a stage for the dancing black shadows of the windblown bushes on the rise. Prindy, naked as he was born, cuddled into the dusty warmth of his Mother Earth.

Was it from dreaming of that all-abiding preoccupation of his that suddenly he sat up, and with head now gleaming in the moonlight, cocked to listen? He breathed, 'Musics!'

He turned towards Igulgul winking at him through the bushes.

For sure there was a tiny piping, rising and falling on the wind. He came out on knees, stared up at the sky, at the pale outline of the Scorpion, as if he thought it came from there. The wind died away. He sank to haunches, staring at the Moon. The wind waxed. Again the Musics.

He rose, went slowly up the rise, head cocked. Far enough up the rise to see beyond it, suddenly he stopped. A point of light on earth, distant about quarter of a mile, just about where the next rise began. He surveyed the scene. It was somewhat different here, less stony, more grassy, and with taller straighter trees; or so it appeared in the brilliance of the Moon. Against that brilliance, striking fairly in his eyes, which he shaded in his scrutiny, it was hard to see anything plainly where the ground rose again and the shadows were long; but there did seem a small black bulk where the light was. A camp-fire that light, for certain. But from what camp-fire would come such a sound as this tiny plaintive piping?

He went on warily, topped the rise, stopped to survey again. There was water some little distance away along the flat, a thin silver pool of it. Dark forms were near it. Prindy sniffed the dying wind. Horses. A *kuttabah's* camp, hence to be avoided. But the Musics!

He cocked his head more. Only ears such as his could have heard the continuance of it as the wind dropped away. He was listening as he came on down the rise heading for the fire – listening, listening, repeating with his lips. Magic in the notes that drew him, surely to draw such as he.

Still he was wary, moving from bush to bush. He reached the grassed flat. Horse dung and shod hoof-prints. Now he was within a couple of hundred yards of the camp and could see crouched beside the fire a dark figure. There was a vehicle of some sort covered with a dark tarpaulin. He got down in the grass to lean on elbows and stare, surely with hair glinting in the moonlight as the bleached grass of the Inland never could.

The music played on, so sweet, so sad. It stopped. A faint voice, hard to say whether male or female, sang, in the same minor key as the music, a whisp of words on the wind: *Gnara, genca nara . . . nara maka naragela* . . . .

Not whiteman's words – not blackman's chanting.

The piped music began again. The boy crept closer, down in the grass now like a true *prindi*. The grass was longish where there was a depression in the middle of the flat, probably a Wet Season extension of that pool. More than grass, there were several thin sticks stuck in the ground, not vertically, but leaning towards Prindy, which perhaps was why, with the blaze of moonlight in his eyes, he did not see them till amongst them and suddenly aware that they were somehow strung together and hence constituted some kind of trap. The music had stopped and the voice, a male alto, was singing, again: '*Genka kara, genka narela . . . nara maka maka naragela* . . . .'

Just like a goanna turning tail at a hint of danger ahead, Prindy swung on his belly, at the same time raising his head for a glance back, struck something, pliable yet taut, from the strange pressure of which he dropped his head swiftly.

Then he felt a net fall over him, and heard a tinny jangling in the direction of the camp. He lay still. The voice had stopped. He waited a moment, then essayed again to wriggle away. But the net was pressing on him now, and the jangling renewed. Again he stopped. A high-pitched voice cried out from the camp, '*Ho, permeshwar . . . kia hea ether*?'

What lingo that?

Prindy crawled carefully, inch by inch. Now the voice was closer, crying in English, 'Ho . . . . What dere in my net?'

Prindy glanced back. An approaching figure. Nothing for it but to up and run. But the net was pressing. He grasped it to lift it. The jangling broke out again. The high voice shouted. The net was being hauled on, boy being rolled into a ball. He fought furiously, felt the mesh give, but as quickly more of it about him. Completely meshed and immobilized, he found a thin dark form dancing over him, while the high voice wailed, '*Ho tu . . . mera jal alla krah dala*!' It was a skinny blackman, slight of build, clad in a long-tailed khaki shirt and white loin-cloth; or *dhoti* rather, since it was not an Aboriginal blackman, but one with a long sharp nose and tall and narrow brow, whom Prindy must have recognized at once, since he had seen him often enough elsewhere; he who was known generally as Ali Barba, Barbu the Indian hawker, of Beatrice River.

But there was no sign of recognition on Barbu's part. He bent over the boy, peering at him in evident amazement. He demanded: 'What you doing, poy, in my birdie net?' Then he raised his head and looked sharply across the way, up and down that rise over which Prindy had come, and asked, 'You got other blackfeller wit' you, eh? Where t'at other one?'

Prindy heaved up into sitting posture. Barbu looked at him again, bent closer: 'But you not blackfeller . . . you not halfcaste. You got t'e fair hair, t'e fair heye. But you not white poy. What you, golden poy, do t'is lonely place? What you do in my birdie net?'

Prindy began to struggle again, got an arm out, began tearing at the string. Barbu cried, 'Stop . . . you bugger-up my net. Vait . . . I let you free. Ho, you mek properly mess my goot net . . . *Mera jal alla krah*!'

The boy lay still. He had to be rolled over several times for disentanglement; while the old man whimpered of the damage to this net, speaking a mixture of his own language and his own kind of English, complaining that now his bird-catching was over for the season, and he had lost for ever the bird he had always been looking for, a Golden Finchee he was sure he had seen flying with the flocks: 'Ho, *Sunerhi Piddi*, my Golden Finchee to mek my fortune . . . and you come bugger-up my net! Who going to pay for damage? I t'e poor-man number-one . . . . '

As the last of the entanglement was peeled off Prindy's legs he leapt up. But a long black claw slipped round the thin ankle: 'No, my lil poy . . . you stop . . . you tell me where from you come?' Prindy stared at the black face level with his own as Barbu knelt, still maintaining that bracelet grip. The black crack of a mouth opened to reveal a few wide-spaced large teeth: 'What's t'e matter . . . you are deafy?' Still silence. 'You not spik English?' Only that grave grey stare. 'Haf you tongue? Show me . . . show me tongue.'

A tip of tongue showed.

'Ho . . . so you haf tongue and English you can understand. Den vy you not spik?'

Prindy, the pupil-escapologist, deftly snatched his foot free, leapt back out of reach. Still Barbu held his kneeling posture. He cried, 'Ho, lil poy . . . you no fright me! I am simple man. I am Barbu Ram, t'e bird-catcher. I do not net for lil poy . . . eeeeeee!' He giggled. Then he asked, 'How come you in my net? It is great mystery to me. Vun lil naked poy on edge of desert, come from novheres, vill not spik. You vont somet'ing from me?'

Prindy swallowed, perhaps with effort to overcome the long ban of speech to other humans, then said, low and vibrantly, 'Musics.' Barbu sank back on his haunches: 'Ho, ho! It vos my music call you to me . . . all-same t'e lil birdie?' The toothy grin grew wider: 'I call on my *bansari* for t'e *Sunheri Piddi* . . . and vot I get? I get a lil Golden Poy! Eeeeee!' Then the smile faded and the thin voice came doubtfully: 'But tonight I am not calling to tempt t'e birdie. I do not at night, because birdie in bush sleep. At night I play only to mek my poor lil catched birdie 'appy. Zey do not sleep so vell in cage at first. I play to t'em and I sing of what 'appy days for t'em in India later . . . might be in palace of Maharaja. I am sorry for my vork as bird-catcher . . . but vot is for me in t'is land where I, who am educate at middle school, am clerk and reader . . . vere I am only poor blackman, rubbish?'

Prindy sank to haunches too. Barbu said, 'You are very peautiful poy.'

Prindy said again in that same intense tone, 'Musics.'

But Barbu was staring at him now with dark eyes wide and luminous with some sudden exciting thought. A moment. Then he cried in a breathless voice, '*Ap pereshwar tu nehi, ho*?'

When the grey eyes grew round and luminous too at the music of the strange lilting language, Barbu came to his knees, and leaning forward, gasped, 'You are a god come to me?'

For some reason Prindy nodded.

Barbu leapt to his feet, took one piercing look at the boy, then turned towards his camp, crying in that high-pitched voice, 'Ho, Savitra . . . Savitra . . . I haf call a god from Paradise . . . a lil golden god . . . Ho, come you, come, my daughter!'

The old man turned back to Prindy, to sink again to haunches and place his hands in attitude of prayer, and bowed his head, saying, '*Ah nehi samaj-saktey meri zaban*.' He looked up again: 'You do not understand me, Master?'

The golden head, so golden to the magic touch of Igulgul, shook.

'My poor Hindustani is not fit for ears of god. But I am your servant, Lord. Vot can I do for you?'

Prindy murmured, 'Musics.'

'Music you vill haf, my Lord. Come you, please, to my 'umble camp. Lil haf I to offer. I haf tell you, I am poor man . . . and long time from my 'ome . . . even my holy language my tongue is losing. Come . . . come . . . come, *Meharban*!'

Barbu rose, and with hands still pressing, body bent in continual deference, walking sideways mostly, he urged the boy to follow him. Prindy went warily. Proximity revealed the well-know Barbu hawker's van, with tarpaulin rigged over it to form a tent. There was another similarly rigged fly, covering piled boxes evidently screened with hessian and housing the little captives that Barbu had excused himself for taking, judging by the sleepy twittering that greeted their arrival at the fireside. Barbu slipped in by the tented van, spoke softly and urgently there to someone who did not answer, and came out with a cushion, which he placed for Prindy, who staring in astonishment though he was, nevertheless sank down to it, to sit in exactly the right pose for the occasion, that is with legs doubled under him, which was an Aboriginal way of making oneself comfortable, as well as Indian. Barbu, with hands together again, made an obeisance: '*A Khunda kia mai ap key leay khurak laoon*.'

Prindy, looking up at him, said, 'Musics.'

Barbu spoke in English again: 'Musics you vill haf, Master . . . but you 'ungry must be. How far haf you come?' Prindy nodded northward. 'Of course, of course, from our Mother India. How how, *Meharban* . . . you not valk so far?'

Prindy said, 'I walk.'

'Ah, yas . . . ah, yas . . . over sea, over mountain, over desert. Not'ing is it to you, a god, But let me gif you tea. Poor man am I . . . but alvays t'e best of Assam tea. I vill mek. You vill play. You vill play to me, t'e musics of Paradise. *Bansari*, Lord.' He snatched up a bamboo flute from a kerosene case beside the fire, and wiping it on the tail of his shirt, handed it to the boy. Prindy looked at it eagerly.

Barbu dashed back to the van, this time to get things from inside it, mounting the step at the rear, at the same time calling to his daughter breathlessly, 'Savitra . . . daughter, you must come . . . I tell you I haf a god for guest.' The answer was a childish moan.

Barbu came back with china tea-pot and things, set them up, puffing with excitement, filled a billy from a waterbag, stirred up the fire. He asked, '*A khunda kia ap bja sakkey ho*?'

For answer Prindy handed the flute to him, saying, 'Mek musics, please.'

Barbu took it, but with a cry, 'Oh master . . . I haf talent so poor. I can play you only from my place of 'umble origins. It vill please you . . . a Kota song?'

From the van tent a child's voice said querulously, 'Papa . . . you go sleep . . . you wake me . . . I dream happy dream '

Barbu cried, 'Daughter, I tell you, I haf lil golden god for guest '

'Papa . . . you gettin' jitty again. Go sleep.'

'If I am mad, child, come 'ere to prove to me. He sit by our fire now.' Barbu flung out his hands towards Prindy: '*O, Mery piarey*! Jitty. It mean mad. I am mad Indian, to everyboty . . . even to my daughter!'

He raised the pipe, trilled a few notes in the minor key, then began to play. A couple of stanzas. Then the child's voice within the tent rose in quavering song:

Sandiramo vago, indaramaline dego,
Mainin moline anig amge puvine verigo . . . .

The voice stopped. The flute continued. Again the voice:

Rajammo vago, indaramaline dego,

Ainmolle ainigo alar sayine verigo.
Dari dari dari dari dari dari
Dari dari dari dari dari daro . . . .

Barbu stopped playing, called, '*Ao jigar key tukrey permeshwar key wastey foa*.'

'Talk me Henglish, Papa. I don' like it silly lingo.'

Barbu groaned, addressing Prindy: '*Maharaj meri jigir ki yukri Hindi mey charti hey*! *Meharban*. It is t'e vay of t'e country, vich contempt for all t'ing but race'orse and beer and bull.' He called to his daughter, peremptorily now, 'Daughter . . . you come ven your fader call . . . at vonce!'

A heavy sigh within, then: 'All right, I come . . . but you got 'o come bed after ve sing lil bits . . . I too sleepy.' A yawn; then the shuffle of feet. Out into the moonlight came a diminutive form wrapped in yellow Indian sari against which her face and bare arms appeared all but black. The child, about Prindy's age, stopped dead, staring at the naked golden figure on the cushion. Prindy stared back.

Barbu giggled, said, 'I am jitty, is it, my lil Savitra?'

After a moment Savitra answered in a toneless voice, while still her dark eyes kept on Prindy, 'Yas . . . Papa, you jitty all right. Dat no god . . . dat Prindy Ah Loy.'

Barbu cried, 'Ho, ho . . . vot you say? Ah Loy? He not Chinee!'

Girl sighed, spoke as if used to dealing here with patience: 'Not Chinee Ah Loy . . . but belong to dat halfcaste Nelly . . . muddrin bijnitch Catfish Creek.'

For a moment Barbu gaped in his gap-toothed way at the little figure sitting cross-legged on the cushion, then struck his brow, crying brokenly, '*Ruba*! . . . Indeed to gootness, I am t'e mad old Indian!'

But he stared and stared. So god-like was the figure in its slender beauty, all shiny gold of skin and towselled hair, so luminous of eye, so calm. He persisted, 'But if you are just colour poy . . . how come you 're . . . from desert . . . from novhere?

The luminous eyes regarded him.

'You haf somevone t'ere in bush . . . your mumma?'

The golden head shook.

'You are all by youself?'

Nod.

'T'en vere you come from?' The strained voice rose: 'Vy you not spik, poy?'

The little girl answered in that same dry tone, 'He runned away from Compound.'

Barbu demanded corroboration. When none was forthcoming, nothing but that shiny-eyed stare, Savitra put in her practical little spoke again: 'He been in Compound wit' his mumma. I been hear-'bout.'

'But t'at Compound two hunneret mile from 'ere . . . and t'e-vild, vild desert and t'e mountain in betveens! How vone lil poy . . . if he not a god . . . if a god don't 'elp him . . . Ho!' Barbu became all excitement again: 'I haf it . . . Mother Shasti, Goddess of Children, haf bring him for you, my daughter!'

'Jitty Indian talk!'

'Vot is jitty? Vos not I veeping for my harlot daughters, and crying to t'e gods . . . "Vere, vere in t'is land of red, white and blue, and blackman, can

I get 'usband for my *malli* flower?" Did ve not toget'er sing old Kadar song you like so much . . . *Talinjurdali*?'

Savita's eyes glowed now, her head cocked. Her father demanded, 'Did ve not sing of your marriage . . . did I not say if ve ketch t'e golden finchee I vill buy t'e golden *tali*, t'e sacred necklace for your marriage . . . and sing toget'er, ve?'

Savita breathed, 'Yas, Papa.'

'Vell . . . vot you talk about Jitty Indian? It is true. T'is god-like poy is prought to us . . . he is your 'usband . . . tek his 'and . . . daughter, tek 'and of your 'usband!'

Savita giggled, 'He got no pants on . . . eeeeee!' She hid her dusky face.

Barbu stared a moment, then went leaping to the tent again, rumaged in the van, came back with a white *dhoti*. He said to Prindy, 'Stand, *Jowatra* . . . my peautiful son-in-law, my son . . . and let me dress you to meet your *Dulhan* . . . your bride, my daughter.' As Prindy rose, the old man slipped the simple garment over a slim shoulder, knotted it. Then, taking the boy's hand, he reached for his daughter's, and as she gave it, passed it into Prindy's, 'From now you are marry in Gandharva . . . t'e plessing of all t'e gods be on you!'

The children looked at one another in surprise, in wonder, even – till Savitra dropped her head to giggle, 'Eeeeeee!'

Prindy smiled.

'Peautiful, peautiful!' cried Barbu, flinging out his arms. Then he snatched up his flute again, tootled a few notes, said, 'My daughter . . . you sing to your 'usband now . . . ve vill sing t'e *Talinjurdali*.' He rippled a flourish of notes, then began the sweet simple piece. The little girl began to sing:

Tana nana nana, tana nana nana,
Nana, nana nana, nana nana nana, coru.
Tomorrow We'n'sd'y . . . wit de flower going to my mother-huncle 'ouse.
De lil Tali, de lil gold Tali,
Is for my neck, de bride.
All pipple going my marriage feast.
De road stony and thorny.
My bridegroom come.
Must he be careful of way he go.
Other pipples wear cotton clothes,
Me and my 'usband wear silk from Palghat.
Tana nana nana, tana nana nana.
Tomorrow wit' de flower I go.

As the flute notes and the singing died away, Barbu sank to the kerosene case, dropped head into hands so that his long nose protruded through them, and wept without restraint. The youngsters stared at him. Then Savitra looked at Prindy. He looked at her. She giggled, – 'Eeeeeee!' snatched her hand away and rushed into the tent, there to cast herself onto a camp stretcher, and with face in pillow, gave herself up to mirth as liberal in expression as her father's weeping.

Prindy simply stood and stared, with that serenity of his in the midst of other people's twittering which had provoked some of those others to their several learned theories concerning his state of mind. What was preoccupying him was disclosed as soon as Barbu was able to control himself again, and looked at him with swimming eyes. He simply said, 'Musics.'

Barbu leapt up, snatching his flute, crying, 'Musics you vill haf, my poy, my son . . . musics all t'rough your 'appy life!' He played quite madly.

Prindy was obviously fascinated. Then Barbu finished, panting, he said, 'Ve vill haf music and feast and dance all t'is night of nights, your marriage night. But first ve must heat. I vill prepare t'e feast. You vill play to your bride. She vill sing to you . . . Savitra, my loved daughter . . . come to you 'usband . . . come, come, come!'

She came out still giggling.

Barbu said to Prindy, pointing to the kerosene case, 'T'at is your seat of boss. Tek t'e flute. Daughter, you sit on t'e pillow at your 'usband's feet.' The children obeyed. Barbu leapt away to the van to get food.

Savitra giggled, 'You can't play dat.'

Prindy put the pipe to his lips, blew a single note. She answered it with a scornful little laugh. But he had been watching Barbu's fingers. He moved his own. The sounds came sweetly. The laughter faded from the chocolate face looking up at him. He tried for scales. They were different here, but came in a minor run.

Barbu came running out with canned food – a curry. He cried, 'Sing him . . . sing t'e child song . . . t'e *Kabootran da Rag*. English if you want.' Prindy stopped, looking at her. For a moment she drooped her dark head under its slip of saffron cloth, then raising her eyes to Igulgul, who was beaming all his magic now from almost directly above, she sang in that sweet little voice:

Oh, Pigeon, I look-out you dat time of famine
Feed you de milk-curd, de milk and boil' rice.
But now plenty everyt'ing,
You wan' 'o go . . . tchinekin away.
But I not let you go, my Pigeon.
Where you go I foller him-you-hup.
No matter how high you fly,
By'n'by I gitchim you at Beatrice.

It was a simple little tune. Barbu, spreading canvas on the ground and making quite madly hasty preparations for the feast, panted, 'Sing to him slow, so he can ketch him.'

She did so. In no time Prindy had it. Again and again they went through it, she in the lingo belonging to it.

She sang other things, more difficult, and he tried with those, while Barbu, all the while at work on the strange smelling but savoury meal, kept saying that here was proof of all he'd said, of all he'd dreamt of: 'Ve vill sometay ketch t'e golden finchee for t'e Maharanee, and go to India and be so rich and 'appy, my children . . . ho, my peautiful children!'

The great meal of curry and rice and spices and sweets was too much for the children. They danced a little to Barbu's directing and fluting; but soon, falling against each other, fell asleep. Barbu, muting his flute, played to them, while staring at them and the sinking winking Igulgul, tears making his black face shine. At last he sighed, put down the flute, took the children gently apart, carried first his daughter in to her stretcher, and then his son-in-law, laying them side by side; but only to have them promptly turn their backs on one another. He sighed, went out, bowed down to the Moon, saying, '*Hey Chandarma Devta jerey ko lambi omar do*!'

Old Chandra Devta was well down the sky and showing the first sign of his seasonal decline, and no sound in the world but the far-off calling of a mopoke that all was well, when Prindy began to sing in that strained voice, *My Rown Road*: the usual words, but to something like an Indian tune. It lasted long enough to bring Barbu leaping out of his sleeping quarters with the birds and set there twittering. But then it was stopped by a sleepy little girl's groaning and saying, 'Oh, shut up . . . and go sleep!'

II

There was now no hope of snaring that Golden Finchee with the net so badly bugger-up as Barbu Ram declared it to be. Not that there was rancour in his declaration. The contrary. 'Haf I not ketch t'e Golden Poy?' he asked. Anyway, the lost bird might well have been a figment of the old man's yearning for the wonderful, there being no such creature as an Australian Golden Finch, the so-called Goldfinch being a rather mean importation like the Cockney Sparrow, and the only truly golden feathered Australian the delicate little Sunbird, which could never live in that harsh environment. This could have been confessed in some degree by his saying to Prindy, 'No matter, no matter . . . we got plenty ot'er t'ing do,' when the boy, perhaps by way of compensation, insisted on going looking for the bird while the others packed up during that day following the magic night of their coming together.

In fact, said Barbu, time in which to do those other things was pressing. In only about a month the Beatrice River Races would be on; and since the business he did during that festival constituted the best part of his livelihood, they must be back there on time. There was no question about Prindy's going along with the Barbus. Surely the arrangement had been made in advance by such forces as Mother Shasti, Chandarma Devta (Igulgul) and the Ol'-Goomun-Ol'Goomun, hence was unarguable. Nevertheless, there was some questioning. Aboriginal logic might accept a magical result simply as an accomplished fact; but the Indian mind, contaminated for so long, from Ghengis Kahn to Queen Victoria, must at least have the facts of the accomplishment. Where had Prindy come from and how? The boy would not say. It wasn't that he maintained utter silence as in the early association. By next day his tongue was loosened. But to that pressing question he simply said, 'I don' know. I been lose-him-head.' The latter expression was Murringlitch for *I have forgotten*. Barbu soon enough saw the logic in it that he needed. Naturally one would not remember dealings with gods, who would be much too subtle to be blatant about their acts. But little Savitra, so much a product of a culture of which the panaceas were Racehorses and Beer, was not so easily convinced. As far as she was concerned he had simply Runned Away from Compound, the logical conclusion of which she, the daughter and sister of several inmates of that institution of non-liberty, probably saw as keeping your mouth shut about it till such times as assured of your freedom. Even that rather crude interpretation didn't offend Barbu, who sighed and said he only wished those ladies of his might have sense and opportunity to do the same.

Those other things to do, were to be done while the turn-out travelled through three or four cattle properties (actually all with one proprietor, the Absentee Baron Landlord) on their homeward way. They would be calling at each of the homesteads, at once to make obeisance to His Lordship's underlords, who demanded it of itinerants, and to receive the conventional baronial hand-out. There would also be a bit of trading to do at homesteads and mustering-camps in the well-known Ali Barba lines, in the matter of goods, such as curries and condiments, especially the Mango Chutney, Indian silks, Indian fly-proof sunglasses (a type with tiny screens of gauze to keep out the pests) sandals and slippers, the *chorri*, or fly-whisks, medicines for those who wished to keep their ailments secret, like white stockriders with the clap they'd caught from riding the black stockriders' wives who'd got it from the white riders' mates, fat reducers and hair restorers (the bony Barbu was a great advertisement for the one but scarcely for the other, but sold each equally), *Rung*, those magic Indian hair-dyes that could change your personality in a moment, depending just what you wanted of the magician, anything from inky *basma* to sun-blazing *henna*; and in the matter of service, a discreet bit of fortune-telling with the crystal ball to the squatters' ladies, and even cutting the squatters' hair while amusing them by chuckling over their crude jokes about the morals of those black harlots of his.

Another line of trade with the stations was in something the station people could have collected quite easily themselves, but were evidently too proud or finicky to do so, namely horse-hair, used for stuffing saddlery. This came from dead horses, murdered horses, one might say, since this was a land of horsemen and the horse regarded as more than an equal to man if he had any value, because most of these beasts had been shot to save feed and water for animals that paid their way. Some of the horses had had their day as friends of man; but most were brumbies, creatures of the wild, largely runtish, which came in to the water-holes and the bores when things dried up where freedom lived. A preliminary to the end-of-season pleasures culminating with the Beatrice River Races was the slaughter of these nags. Usually it was done of Sundays as kind of recreation. Everybody turned out in a utility truck or two, armed with high-powered rifles. Bets were made on the kills. You dropped 'em on the run from the car – *bang, bang, bang*! Great sport. The Australians are a Nation of Sports. They used to shoot the blacks like that. The pity was that the blacks hadn't been able to breed like brumbies.

The *chorri*, the cow-tail whisks, were likewise taken from dead beasts. Most of these also had been shot, because diseased or maimed during mustering, and in odd cases for daring to turn on a man on horse-back flogging them whither they had no inclination to go. A grisly business – no, not the slaughter and the flogging, because those who did this were considered the very flower of the manhood of the land, but the collection of tails and manes from things blown up like bladders and crawling with maggots and stinking to the high heavens where flew the kites for the sheer joy of the effluvium. Barbu did it himself.

Prindy would have helped, but was refused. Savitra only wrinkled up her pretty little chocolate nose, so much broader than her father's, and said, 'Oh, pooh!' The stuff had to have the stink smoked out of it.

There was always a place for low-class itinerants to camp at the homesteads, somewhere down on the creek or lagoon that served as water-supply. The Barbus had their spot, used for years on circuits like this. No one troubled them. The whites regarded them as blacks; and the blacks had no kin with them. Barbu told Prindy he must keep away from the blacks' camps. Most likely Prindy didn't need to be told. The children stopped in their own camps while Barbu visited the homesteads. At Khartoum Station (so-named because its founder had served in Africa with the British General, Kitchener) they saw that a policeman was visiting the place. Prindy slipped away into the bush. He need not have. When he returned to the camp at night, Barbu told him that when the officer had asked him who was with him, he had said what they had spoken of doing in case of inquisitiveness, namely that he had his daughter Savitra and the son of a certain Indian who lived down in the Centre and who was his daughter's betrothed. The policeman had said he would take a look at the captive birds, in order to see if there were any prohibited by the Fauna Protection Law; but Barbu had overheard the man say to the Boss that he didn't know one small bird from another himself, to which the Boss replied that he shared the ignorance; and as they were sharing a bottle of rum, Barbu reckoned it didn't matter. Still, he said, they must be prepared. He'd had policemen pounce on him and free *all* of his birdies, apparently just for the fun of it; which might be fun for the policeman, but not for the poor birdies, which would quickly perish freed in a strange environment. That night, Prindy's hair was dyed with *basma.* Barbu said that now, with black hair and grey eyes he looked like a high-caste Parsee. Savrita declared that he looked like a half-caste Afghan, and that she wouldn't marry one of those if they gave her golden bangles for her ankles, because they treated their camels better than their wives. For several days she refused to speak to Prindy because he said he liked his hair black and was going to keep it like that. He spent a lot of time staring at himself in the mirror, often with a pair of fly-goggles on to hide his grey eyes from himself, too. Barbu, tickled about it, being something of a tailor as well as all else, while they were joggling along with the old horses, made him a pair of jodhpurs and a turban and dubbed him Shah Jahan, King of the World.

Prindy wasn't a bit troubled by being ignored by his bride. The contrary, she had been rather possessive and demanding and interfered with his practice of the flute and Barbu's story-telling. During the long days of jogging north-eastward towards home, Barbu related the Hindu Myths and Legends, to the boy's evident fascination. And during the dark nights of Igulgul's utter decline, sitting about their camp-fire he made up little songs about such deities as Ratri, one of the Goddesses of Night, who drove away the utter blackness with the shining of her eyes, the stars; of Apsarsis, the nymph, who lived in the Celestial Waters, and was the wife of Gandharva, who guarded the special grog they kept up there for the gods to drink, Soma, which is moonlight; of Ushas, Goddess of the Dawn, who roused everybody in the morning with light and beauty and the joy to live the day before them. Sometimes Savitra joined in, but often got sulky, talked of Jitty Indian Bijnitch, wanted him to make up songs for her or listen to her singing. Sometimes he called her Manthara, the Jealous One, and she went to bed and wept.

Thus it went, while they jogged homeward. There was Igulgul, or Chandra Devta, again, reborn to make more mischief, and plenty of opportunity for it this season, with all the chances for Wrong Side Bijnitch that would be offering through the Races, Igulgul hanging winking in the trees just after sundown. Yes – and there again were the familiar trees of Beatrice River, the glinting, murmuring river itself, with its tribe of cockies still arguing whose tree was whose to perch the night in. There were the couple of lights at the Toohey place. Then the House of Ah Loy, ancestral no longer to him who had become Shah Jahan. Then the goats ganged up in the red road, down which could be seen the Irish prodigality of Finnucane's lights and the Scottish meanness of McDodds'. The goats could be beaten off the road with the horsewhip; but their effluvium had to be suffered through. 'Oh pooh!' cried the fastidious bride.

And there, with rickety little shop-front verandah just visible in the bit of moonlight-twilight, looking so tiny and ramshackle against the great mango trees behind, was the House of Barbu. The weary old horses wickered with delight in the long journey's end. Barbu cried: '*Mai ap key leay tuffa laia hoon*!' which he explained to his son-in-law meant that the house was being told it was being brought a great gift, the Hindu custom in bringing home a newly married member to dwell therein.

The son-in-law dropped down to open the rickety gate, then shut it against the goats. Barbu drove under the mangoes, into the leaning coach-house. Prindy unharnessed the horses, which with renewed vigour went trotting out to their old familiar stamping ground. Barbu led the way to the back of the jerry-built huddle of iron structures that constituted his premises, carrying a lighted hurricane-lantern, which he swung to Prindy's fluting and Savitra's singing:

Tana nana nana, tana nana nana . . .
Other pipples wear cotton clothes.
Me and my 'usband wear silk from Palghat
Tana nana nana . . . tomorrow wit' de flower I go . . . .

With much unlocking and unbolting Barbu opened up, led the way in, through blackened kitchen, into the little shop, with its counter and shelves of multifarious wares, including snakes in bottles, herbs in bundles, astrology and palmists' charts on walls, nothing that anyone was likely to purloin while the master was away. He lit a glass-shaded lamp from the lantern. Prindy looked about with interest. Savitra snatched up the lantern and went out, through the passage behind, and into a room, the door of which she slammed hard behind her. As the others came out, she called shrilly from behind the door, 'I don' care he is my 'usband . . . dis my room, and nobody else!'

Barbu looked at Prindy and shrugged, saying, 'Princess Draupadi vos proud, too, vos not she, my son . . . yet did no she go vit Arjun to live in 'umble cottage in forest? T'ey all-same, vomen. Like young 'orse . . . t'ey got to play-up. You camp vit me for now eh?'

Prindy said, 'I like camp in van. I can play musics dere all night.'

'As you vish, my son . . . as you vish.'

Next morning soon after breakfast, all three of the Barbu household were in the coach-house, which was also the bird-house, putting the birdies into cages of many sorts, some to be sold locally by Barbu himself, others for trading to those who bought them for export – when Prindy breathed suddenly, 'Somebody come!' He was still in the jodhpurs of the Afghan outfit, but without the glasses, which were in the van. He just had time to leap into it. With badges and buttons flashing in the sunlight, Constable Stunke appeared in the doorway. He nodded to Barbu, saying, 'Gooday, Ali . . . seen your horses . . . take a look at your birdies.'

Cringing, bowing, smirking, Barbu cackled, 'Ho, yis Mist' Stunke, certainly yis . . . but no illegal ketching, my verd!'

'We'll see about that.' Stunke looked at Savitra, watching from under lowered brows. 'How you doin', young Satty . . . behavin' yourself?'

She said demurely, 'Oh, yas, Mist' Stunke.'

'Well see you keep it up . . . or you'll go along with your sisters'

There was no hiding in the van, with its mere canvas flap falling to tail-board level and the tail-board down. Directing his attention to the skinny jodhpured legs and small yellow brown feet plainly to be seen, the policeman asked, 'Who's that in there?'

Barbu hopped about like one of his birdies in fright: 'T'at is . . . t'at is . . . my son-in-law, Sir.'

Stunke stared now at Barbu: 'Your what?'

Barbu's voice quavered: 'T'e 'usband of my lil girl, 'ere . . . son of cousin relation of Centre, Sir . . . t'e Indian fashion, you know.'

Stunke said shortly, 'Let me see him.'

There was tense silence. Stunke broke it by calling harshly to the legs, 'Come out here, boy!'

Prindy didn't move. Stunke was stepping towards the van with a look as if to rip the flap down when he reached it. Barbu said sharply, '*Bahar ao, bahadar, puttar*.'

Stunke swung on Barbu: 'What'd you say to him?'

Barbu cringed: 'I honly tell him to hobey you, Sir.'

'Well, don't go speakin' any lingo with me . . . I told you before with your wife and daughter business.'

Barbu bowed: 'Yas, Sir . . . I am sorry, Sir . . . but poy is shy, and not spik so much Henglish.'

'Well, he ought 'o be speakin' English . . . it's an English country, ain't it, not bloody India?'

Prindy was lifting the flap, to look out, wearing the dark goggles. Stunke stared at him: 'Take those glasses off.'

Prindy looked poised as if to leap out and run. Barbu said quickly, 'He haf sore heye, Mist' Stunke . . . it is prevalentic in Centre, you know . . . .'

'Tell him to take 'em off.'

Barbu gasped at Prindy, '*Apnian akhan band rakho*.'

Prindy had learnt a lot of Hindustani during the month; but it must have been a shot in the dark, by the look of panic in Barbu's face. However, Prindy removed the glasses to show his eyes all squinty and blinky as of one with sore eyes having to expose them to bright light.

Stunke quizzed him closely, asking, 'What's his name?'

'Shah Jahan!'

'Got a bit of Abo in him, eh?'

'Might be just lil bits, Mist' Stunke.'

'Your son-in-law, eh?'

'It is Indian custom to marry as children, Sir . . . .'

'I know . . . and for dirty old men to marry bits of kids, too. But it's a good idea in this case . . . stop that kid of yours goin' the way of her mother and sisters.'

'Yes, Sir . . . t'ank you, Sir.'

'Well, let's look at the birds. I want a few for myself this time. Relatives coming to the Races.' He turned from Prindy towards the cages. Prindy promptly donned the glasses, and as the others moved further into the shed, jumped down silently, and seen only by Satriva, went sidling towards the house.

Half an hour later Constable Stunke was bowed out of Barbu's by the head of the household, carrying a brand-new gilded cage containing the pick of the finches, half a dozen or so, all of which began to twitter merrily, surely because they saw the bright world about them again, even if through bars, not because they felt better in the company of one whose calling it was to cage even his fellow men. Coming to McDodds' store, he entered, and by the bony square and ruddy-faced tight-expressioned Angus himself was given a parcel of goods he'd evidently already ordered. In showing the birds to McDodds he ignored the dry question: 'Hoo mooch did ye pay for 'em, mon?' Another admirer of the birds, but more discreet in respect of comment was another customer just then buying tobacco, Ozzie Burrows, the railway porter. But Oz was indiscreet in another way. When Stunke spoke of the new son-in-law and there was some small discussion of the barbarous customs of India and Stunke said that at least it would stop Barbu from selling this daughter in prostitution, Oz remarked that it would also stop, as he put it, the Old Bastard Pokin' the Poor Kid Himself. That roused McDodds: 'For God's seek, wha' are ye sayin', mon?'

Oz said, 'Course 'e pokes that kid o' 'is . . . poked all the others, too.'

Stunke asked Oz coldly, 'You got any evidence o' these allegations?'

'Course, everybody knows it!'

'I'm askin' you for evidence.'

Oz shrugged: 'Well . . . it's only what people say.'

'What people?'

'Aw, 'ow the 'ell do I know . . . Race Time mobs . . . 'cause 'e's an Injun . . . and everybody knows what Injuns're like with kids.'

Stunke said in a voice still colder, 'I'd be careful what I say, if I were you, Oz. As far as I know, and I know a lot more than you do, Ali Barba's been a good father to his kids . . . it was the mother . . . .'

McDodds interrupted, with square red jaw out-thrust: 'And I'd be muir than ceerful about sayin' things like that, Ozzie Burrows . . . I'd be damned well asheemed!'

Ozzie flamed: 'You can go and get stuffed, McDodds!' He flung the tobacco back on the counter.

McDodds grated: 'That meeks two of us, then!'

' 'Ere,' snapped Stunke. 'Cut it out.'

'Gi' me me money back!' snapped Oz.

McDodds turned his back, snapping, 'Once a thing's purchased in this store it's purchased. Teek your purchase and get oot.'

'I don' wan' yo' stinkin' tobacco . . . I wan' me money back!'

McDodds looked at Stunke: 'Constable, weell you kindly remove that man from my premises?'

Stunke said, 'Come on, Oz . . . get. Take your tobacco and get.'

'I don' wan' 'is flamin' tobacco, I tell you . . . I'll get it at Finnucane's in future.'

'And guid riddance to you, you foul-moothed ignorant slanderous loot!' yelled McDodds.

Oz turned on him; but Stunke got hold of him by the back of the shirt and bundled him out.

Shamus Finnucane was on his verandah, on a step-ladder, fitting the extra lights that would be needed in a day or two to make less dangerous the passage of those many feet that would be stumbling with less and less certainty to his greater and greater profit. Glimpsing the force of the law in action before Stunke, not expecting an audience in that empty street, had time to belay, he stared. To cover it up the pair came along together as if nothing were untoward, although not speaking. As they came up, old Shame-on-us, who had given the appearance of being very busy, stepped down: 'Ah, and a goot mornin' to ye, gintlemen. 'Tis a braw bricht day, indade, as me frind McDodds would say, if only he was friendly enough to pass the toime o' day wit' me.'

Stunke nodded greeting, murmured to Burrows, 'See you, Oz,' and went on towards his police station.

Ozzie made no reply, but stepped onto Finucane's verandah. 'Somthin' I can do for ye?' asked Shamus.

Oz said throatily, 'Tin o' tobacco.'

Finnucane led the way into the bar, saying, 'McDodds givin' up the sale of tobacco to deal in canaries is it? Remoinds me o' the moinin' days, whan he give up sellin' grog for water, because there was more profit in it, he says, there bein' a drought on and him with the only tank-cart for cartin' it.'

'The lousy ol' bastard!' grunted Ozzie.

Getting the tin of tobacco, Finnucane said, 'Well, now, I'll concur regardin' the former, but can't support ye in the latter, not knowin' his parentage. Ye got 'o be careful wit' these conclusions.'

'Now don't you start, too!' said Ozzie, setting down the second payment for one tin of tobacco.

'Start what, now, me bhoy?'

Ozzie told him. Finnucane listened without comment, except to say at the end, 'Well, 'tis noice to know we've got another fambly on the river . . . even if we'll have to wait the best part of ten years before we can really call it a fambly, to be sure.'

'Black bastards!' grunted Ossie, and went out and down to the station. He looked in on Col Collings the Station Master, as if he'd have liked to tell him; but Col, busy on the phone, waved him to go attend to the unloading of some waggons dropped off the last mail-train, goods wanted by someone in preparation for the Races.

Up and over the way at the House of Barbu, there was giggling over Barbu's painting the rims of Prindy's eyelids red with *gulal*, to simulate inflammation. Now Prindy would be able to go to the Races with the other two and serve in the booth. It was good to know how easy it was to take in those who had power, who were always the least perceptive because the least intelligent; and must be, since true intelligence would want power over none but itself.

CHAPTER TEN

BEATRICE RIVER RACES again; and a bigger spree than ever, swelled as it was by the ever-swelling population of the land under threat of war that nobody seemed to take seriously. At least nobody was serious about it, except those who thought they saw the chance to gain by war, or were aware enough of the reality of things, either through direct experience of what was going on where the dogs of war were already on the rampage, or having some version of it pumped into them by one or other parties to whom the slavering dogs belonged. At the moment things looked very grim, with the dictators of Germany and Russia hurling unforgivable insults at each other, and the Japanese frankly butchering the Chinese on account of some thing they trumpeted about in the name of Great East Asia Co-prosperity. Not that it made a bit of difference to the spree. The squatters and miners were those who talked of the gains they would make: the Extra Quid, as they put it; and the soldiers who were there in greater number because the Garrison at Port Palmeston was now in full establishment. Those with direct experience of the forces at work in Europe were the few of the foreign construction workers known as Reffoes, which meant refugees. These were even more rejected by the native-born than the other foreigners (the Oxes, Square'eads, Dagoes, Poms) for the reason that they put on airs, claiming to have been people of importance before fleeting their hearths, apparently for political reasons, since none of them looked, at least fully, like the Jews reported to be flying for their lives from the consequences attendant upon a grand idea the Dictator of Germany had in the matter of increasing the nobility of that noblest of breeds, his own.

There were no British aristocrats this time. Patron of the Meeting was to be Colonel Leon Chivvy, Officer Commanding the Palmeston Garrison.

Colonel Chivvy arrived in the same spectacular way that His Lordship, the Big Boss, had last year, by air, and in even more spectacular style, for reason that he had a pilot either less scarey or with a livelier sense of the spectacular than Lord Vaisey's man, namely, that wonder boy of the air, Fergus Ferris. They did a rip-roarin' tour of the town as a preliminary to landing. Colonel Chivvy, a brave man by the multiplicity of ribbons on his khaki breast, looked as if he'd had his closest call with death, but quite without glory, as, grey-faced, and trembling slightly still, even though with moustached upper lip properly militarily stiff, he took the hand of Lady Rhoda Eaton in genteel greeting. As the Colonel's 2-IC, before alighting remarked in aside to Fergus, 'You won't be flying the Old Man again in a hurry, feller.'

Fergus's split lip showed under the fair moustache in a leer: 'Teach the bastard for putting Security onto me to find out how I got this kite.'

'Well, you did get it from the Huns, didn't you?'

'I've got it on legitimate charter from the Junkers Company, friend. I wasn't aware of being at war with Germany.'

'We soon will be.'

'You hope . . . so's you can get in the Big Brass yourself.'

Fergus, having no such social status, however high he might literally fly, to be included amongst the guests at the Big House, of all those he had flown down, had to ask Clancy Delacy to run him in to the pub. It wasn't his first visit there, of course. He had come down with that anthropological team collecting data for assistance in the useless defence of Bobwirridirridi. Old Shame-on-us greeting him very amiably. Quite a lot of people hailed him similarly, among them one whom he greeted in return with open arms and open mouth, all of which closed upon her before she could do anything about it – Alfie Candlemas. She struggled free of him, but laughing, looking as elfishly lovely as he said she did. 'My fairy fay!' said he. Then asked if she were staying there, and being answered Yes, he said with an animal-like sound of deep appetite, 'Baby . . . you'n me's goin' 'o have fun!'

She chuckled, 'Frank's with me, of course.'

'Of course . . . didn't I mean the three of us?'

She laughed, saying she was going to Frank now, to join him in the lounge bar on the west-side verandah, and wouldn't Fergus come along too? He said he would, as soon as he'd found his room and parked his dunnage.

Fergus reached the lounge to find Alfie and her husband Frank sitting with Betty Bishoff, wife of the Stock Inspector, and Miss Kitty Wyndeyer, of the Telephone Exchange, Port Palmeston. Fergus, in greeting everybody, remarked to Miss Kitty, 'Didn't reckon you'd be one to play the horses, Kit.'

Kitty blushed, saying, 'I like my little flutter.'

Fergus winked: 'Maybe we can do a bit of flutterin' together, eh?'

She looked annoyed, saying, 'Don't be silly!'

'You misunderstand me, lady. I happen to be an expert judge of horseflesh, don't you know?'

Alfie remarked, as if she didn't believe it, 'He claims to have been a jockey.'

'Wrong,' said Fergus. 'I've made claim only to being an apprentice jockey.'

'Is that really true?' asked Betty Bishoff.

'Get your daddy to get me a mount, Madam, and I'll prove it in the Races.'

Frank asked, 'How on earth did you come from jockeying to anthropology . . . *and* aviation?'

'Shows all you know about human beings . . . except as dirty animals,' said Fergus. 'Jockeying is the easiest way to fame in this wondrous land of ours . . . and, like most people, I've yearned for fame. I grew up near Randwick Racecourse, Sydney, and used to see the boys taking the horses out of mornings, and by doing dirty work for them, often got a ride. Found I had talent with a horse. They're just like women, you know. You just have to have a cruel streak in you to master 'em.' The women looked annoyed; but Frank Candlemas chuckled. Fergus went on: 'So I decided to become a jockey. However, my father, who had no sense of sport at all, nor much sense of anything but his own importance, vetoed it completely. I was to finish High and go on to Varsity.

Now, since I went after the fame the easiest way, I did the same with scholarship, . . . for what's the biggest and easiest racket to work as an academic? Why, anthrop! Nothing to learn but how to sound off about the human race in terms that nobody can understand and therefore are intimidated by . . . nothing to do but go a-rovin' puttin' backward peoples in their place, on fat grants, with nice side-kicks from robbin' 'em of their most precious possessions for floggin' to museums. See? As to aviation . . . well, it just follows that a man who can manage a horse can manage an aeroplane. Didn't you know that the air-forces of the war, when they got going, were recruited from the officers of the redundant cavalry divisions? Here's a man who can tell you that . . . ' Jeremy Delacy was just entering the lounge with Charlie Bishoff. Rising to greet him and shake his hand, Fergus repeated what he had just said, adding, 'The Australian Air Corps was recruited from the Light Horse in Palestine . . . isn't that so?'

Jeremy gave his affirmative, at the same time taking Frank Candlemas's hand and bowing to Alfie with stiff dignity. Alfie was just as stiff with him. He plainly looked as if he regretted coming, since finding Alfie in the company. Their last dealings had been that time in Town, at the party she'd had at her own place, when overdoing Jeremy's advice on brandy-drinking, she had at first tried to monopolize him and then fled from him. He said now, 'Didn't know you were having a party. Just walked up with Charlie, talking shop. I'll be getting along back to my camp.'

Frank came to the rescue in his amiable way: 'No fear you won't . . . not till we get the real low-down on this little wonder horse of yours that's going to win the Cup. Please stop and have a drink with us, Mr Delacy.'

Jeremy submitted graciously. The talk was then of his mare, Golden Girl, favourite for this year's Cup. He talked of her pedigree and performance since a filly as another man might of his daughter, a fact that was remarked on by Betty Bishoff, who added, 'You don't have a daughter, do you, Mr Delacy?'

He coloured distinctly at the question, and surely noting the sharp look he got from both women, the way he dropped his eyes, answered with a slight chuckle, 'Well . . . not that I know of.'

Fergus came in with a guffaw: 'It's a wise daughter that knows her own daddy round these parts.' They all laughed.

What probably made Jeremy burn was the fact that Finnucane's daughter, Bridie, wife of Con Cullity, had turned up from down the Centre this year with a three-months' old daughter, about whom the whole Finnucane family were raving, in particular her nominal daddy, Con. On account of old Shame-on-us's granddaughter, the festival was being extended by a day, Sunday being the day of her christening, for officiation at which no less a personage than Monsignor Maryzic would be flying down from Town. Chief reason for Kitty Wyndeyer's being there was to play the organ at the service.

There was amusing talk by the Bishoff's and the Candlemases about their recent experiences amongst the squattocracy during the tour they had just made together round the western stations in their official capacities, or rather in those of Charlie and Frank. Alfie had had to be particularly careful not to show herself in any other than the wifely one, because of the suspicion that she would be, as they said it had been put, Writing People Up. The fact was that she was no longer a practising journalist, having fallen out with *The Palmeston Progressive,* or rather with Fay McFee, which amounted to much the same thing. Betty Bishoff said, 'In fact, such a success was she on the social side, that she'll be going on the Ladies' Committee tomorrow . . . what do you think of that, for one who so lately turned the snob circles of Port Palmeston upside down?'

Jeremy didn't laugh with the others. Alfie with several gins in her by now, met his blank look and, somewhat thickly, demanded of him, 'Not much, eh?'

He asked politely, 'I beg your pardon?'

'Betty asked what you think of that . . . and I said you don't think much of it.'

He reddened again: 'Well . . . I hadn't thought about it at all . . . .'

'Oh, yes you did . . . I saw the look in your eye.'

Jeremy glanced at Frank, who smiled as usual. Jeremy tried to avoid looking back at Alfie; but she demanded of him, 'You think I've let the side down, don't you . . . .'

Jeremy had to look, under his brows, just glancing, then fiddling with his brandy glass, murmured, 'What side would that be?'

'There'sh only one shide . . . shide o' truth an' honesty an' human'ty, isn't there?'

The others were silent, watching, as if a game; even Frank, with a slight rumple to his usually smooth handsome brow, but a light of interest in his eye. Jeremy took a sip of his drink, then said, 'Yes . . . I guess that's right. Well, if you'll excuse me, I'll be getting back to my camp . . . getting on supper time.' He rose, giving a little bow.

'Wait!' cried Alfie.

Frank laid a hand on her arm. She tossed it off without looking at him, saying to Jeremy, 'I want to talk to you . . . Mist' Delacy.'

Jeremy was turning away. He stopped, said without looking at her, 'I'd be glad to have you and your husband down at my camp sometime. Goodnight.'

Alfie leapt up and caught him by the arm: 'D'you think I went round with my eyes shut? D'you think I didn't do it all only to get to see more of what's rotten in the damn land?'

He looked at her now, saying, 'No . . . I'm sure you didn't.'

'I didn't either . . . and I tell you what . . . I'm goin' to write a book 'bout it and blow the whole thing sky-high.'

He glanced around. But really she was speaking only in a fierce whisper, and those about were too intent upon their boozing and making too much noise about it to hear. Still, half turning to her again, he said, 'Good on you . . . but if I were you I'd keep it to myself for a while . . . or you'll never get the best bit of all for your book.' He started off again. She went with him, still with hand on his arm.

'Wha'sh that?'

'A place on the Ladies' Committee of the Beatrice River Races.'

'Under chairmanship of your wife.'

They were at the door. He stopped, removed her hand gently, said coldly, 'My ex-wife. My wife is down in my camp on the river . . . waiting for me . . . so if you'll excuse me . . . .'

'Your Aboriginal wife.'

'Half Aboriginal.'

'Y'know . . . I can't un'erstand you . . . a man like you . . . married to a halfcaste woman.'

He met her watery black eyes, staring at him so intently, said, 'Women are all the same in the dark . . . Goodnight.' He was gone.

She stood for a moment staring after him, then swung back to the others who were eyeing her curiously. She said as she sat down and seized her glass, 'Y'know . . . I hate that man.'

Fergus said, 'Look out . . . hatred is akin to love, they say . . . and he's a bit of a lad with the ladies, so I'm told . . . .'

'Black ones!'

Betty Bishoff bridled: 'Now, that's not fair. He's not a bit like that. And his wife's a really lovely person . . . as sweet a woman as I ever met . . .'

'But black!'

Fergus asked, 'What's happened to our nigger-lover that rocked the nation with her Terrific Indictment of Official Callousness, and pulled poor old Cobbity down?'

'It's because o' that I hate him . . . because he refused to acknowledge that dear little boy as his grandson . . . so he's gone and run away into the bush with his poor mother to live like blacks. I can't forgive that. I won't forgive it. I hate him because he's Negative, as I said that night. He doesn't believe in anything . . . he's cold, hard . . . .'

Charlie Bishoff cried, 'Go on . . . he's just the opposite! D'you know, all the sick and wounded animals go to his place for attention?'

'Animals?'

'Blacks, too.'

'But not that little boy, that beautiful little boy!'

Kitty Wyndeyer sighed: 'Yes . . . that beautiful, wonderful, little boy.'

Fergus demanded, 'Hey . . . what's this, getting serious at a party? Let me tell you 'bout how I bunged the G's on the gallant colonel as we came in, and what he looked like as he got out.'

They were soon all laughing again.

That night while they all sat singing in the initial concert out the back amongst potted palms and under the coloured lights, they little realized that amongst the dark faces staring in at them was the lighter one of that same beautiful and wonderful little boy, standing beside his dusky little wife – not even Miss Kitty, who once when relieving Bridie at the piano, playing *Danny Boy* for Sergeant Cahoon to tax those tenor tonsils with, looked right at him, at his begoggled eyes, and smiled, or Eddy McCusky doing his stuff as usual as MC.

II

The job young Alfie got on the Ladies' Committee was that humblest yet most exciting of them all, the Golden Horseshoe selling. Not that she should have expected anything more exalted, her lowly social status and even somewhat dubious character notwithstanding, when she went to the Big House to receive her assignment quite improperly dressed, as she was warned by those who reckoned they knew. She was wearing a stock-rider's outfit. At least that's what it resembled, since no true stockman would ever have dared put on anything so natty. It was in white corduroy with red piping, red neckerchief silver-banded white wide-awake, the only common or garden bit about it being the tan elastic sides. But those knowledgeable reckoners were wrong. Even if Lady Rhoda did receive her first with a Look and then with the High Handshake, so far from being utterly disapproving was she that she remarked to someone that in fact the rigout looked quite fetching and was just the thing for the job the gal had to do. That started some of the Younger Set off saying that the next time *they* were going to trot along their Melbourne-tailored riding gear; but to be silenced by a *Duenna* who said tartly, 'And turn the affah into a vulgah stockman's Buckjump Show!' Hence the value of that hard core of social nicety to the festival. Her Ladyship, so recently having attained to true status by Letters Patent rather than to pretence of it through sheer hard striving on the social ladder, was probably only trying out a bit of *noblesse oblige*.

Indeed, so fetching was the outfit, that Alfie was fairly mobbed when she appeared in it carrying her tray of Golden Horseshoes and the gilded money-bag, on the Racecourse that first afternoon of racing. For those lolly kisses she gave to all and sundry with seeming pleasure she could have got the season's pay from most of the louts, old and young, master and man, who were game to take them. Quite a number blushed scarlet and fled when she offered her lips to seal the contract. They were the ones about whom the others guffawed in asides in the beery uproar of the bar between the dusty, sweaty, silk-and-tail-and-manes-flashing thunderous excitement of each race: 'She'd've 'ad to black 'er face before Billy Brew could'a' come at 'er . . . yaaaaaaaaah!'

Alfie didn't hear them say that, or any of the other bawdy things such as the way her pretty bum wobbled in those tight pants and those little tits filled her red-piped breast-pockets as nothing a stockrider ever carried could do to such effect . . . 'Yoo-hoo, boy . . . how' yo' like to pull them corduroys down, eh, get a feel under them pockets? . . . yaaaaaa-eeee-ah. Christ!'

If she had heard she might have thought there was something more than drollery in what was said about the Burnt Cork, and might have acted on it spitefully, in view of her outspoken opinion of Jeremy Delacy given the night before and what can be expected of a woman scorned, when she came face to face with him for the first time for the day. She would have ignored him, but for his asking her if he might have a Horseshoe, and on being sold one quite nicely, ignored the proffered lips. Both parties went red, but she the redder and with eyes ablaze, almost shouting at him, 'Are you afraid you'll catch something?'

They were in the midst of a shoving uproarious crowd. A race had just finished, the big race of the day, the President's Trophy, which had been won by Jeremy's colt, Red Rory. He had to all but shout back, bending to her, 'I take my kissing seriously.'

For a moment their eyes locked, grey with black. Then she answered, 'So do I!' and with a swift movement, kissed him squarely on the mouth. Then she was gone. Jeremy looked after her in astonishment.

Fergus Ferris, who had been with Alfie, showed his split lip in a wide grin, and leaning close to Jeremy, said behind his hand, 'Watch it, Daddy-o . . . she went through the boys up Town like a packet of salts . . . yaaaaa-eee!' He also in a moment was gone.

Someone else was witness to the scene, someone whose grey eyes would have been seen to pop with interest in both parties, only that they were hooded with Indian fly-proof dark glasses – he who was now joked about by the few who took notice of him as Ali Barba's son-in-law, selling fly-whisks in the Barbu booth.

Jeremy continued on his way, into the saddling paddock, to receive Red Rory and his jockey Darcy Delacy, after the weighing out, took some congratulations from those about, then went on with horse and jockey to the Lily Lagoons stables. There was Nanago, dressed as usual for these occasions, in a very smart frock of flowered silk, but with the inevitable black wide-awake with the silver band, and barefoot. Looking hard at Jeremy, she began to laugh, so that her plumpness shook. He looked surprised: 'What's the joke?'

She squealed, 'You got him lipstick all over mouth!'

Jeremy went redder than the rouge, wiped savagely at his lips. Still laughing, she got him a towel, wetted the corner of it, cleaned the stuff off for him. He muttered, 'That mad cowgirl who's selling the Horseshoes. Here's yours. Here's yours, Darcy.'

Nan giggled, 'Might-be dat cowgirl mad about you, eh?'

Jeremy grunted, 'Ugh!' Then he said, 'I'll take Rory down and give him a swim.'

He went with haste, and with a glance back, somewhat fearfully, as if expecting something like what had happened the last time he had brought Red Rory in like that. But there was no one following.

So the first day's racing came to a close; with the red Sun sinking in the dust of it and the crowd surging pubward through the dust to quench thirsts that the dust and the excitement and all the beer they'd drunk already only titillated because such thirsts as theirs, the Great Australian Thirst, is soul-deep, like the thirst of the damned in Hell; the thirst of people with a woeful past and naught but woe for the future. The Delacys in their bright camp locked themselves in to escape the dust, then came out to enjoy the freshness following the blowing away of the dust, the smoke, the stench of beer and sweat, and with no less pleasure evidently in their drinking, sat watching young Igulgul winking over the trees.

Up at Barbu's a bamboo flute was playing *The Camptown Races*, a piece played several times that day by the Military Band that was now an integral part of a festival that had been so truly rural.

Up at Finnucane's the beer was flowing as from a magic fountain, while the magician kept an eye on his sweating sons-in-law and an ear on the endless music of the cash-register. Out in the verandah lounge the Candlemases and Bishoffs and Fergus Ferris and others were enjoying the joke about that kiss. It was then Alfie heard the Burnt Cork joke; but, unpredictable little lady that she was, instead of laughing, she waxed indignant, and said, 'I'm going to apologize to him.'

Fergus cried, 'But that's an insult!'

'How is it?'

'If I kissed you, and then apologized, wouldn't that he a slight to you?'

'No . . . it'd be a blooming miracle!'

That restored the laughter. Nevertheless, Alfie meant what she had said, as proved later in the evening, when, suddenly tiring of the puerile fun and games under the coloured lights, she asked Frank to take her down to the Delacy camp. He looked dubious, but didn't demur. She said, 'After all, he did ask us down.'

So they went out, in time to catch the last glow of the Moon, to hear the last distant complaints of the dispossessed cockies, and the not-so-distant din of the cavorting of the common herd in the Dance Hall. Still, it was a relief from what they had just left, so much so, that Alfie, hugging her man's arm to her breast, commented, 'Lovely, isn't it . . . a lovely land . . . only unlovely people . . . Oh, what's that?' It was a gang of plovers flying low over their heads, probably scolding them as part of what she was complaining of as unlovely.

They came into the brightly lit circle of the Delacy camp, with its own noise the muffled beat and humming of the lighting plant, but with a mob of other people's dogs to sound uproarious warning of their coming. Only Jeremy and Nan were there, lounging in deck-chairs, with a brandy bottle and iced water on a low table between them, and a radio talking quietly on a bigger table. Both rose as the pair approached. Jeremy took Frank's hand and bowed stiffly to Alfie, and in formal fashion introduced Nan, who gravely complied. It was interesting to see the swift interplay of the women's eyes, the shiny black, the soft brown. Jeremy got seats and offered drinks. The others chose brandy. Nan got glasses. After a few preliminaries in talk about the camp, round which the visitors glanced with pleasure, Alfie said suddenly, 'I really came to apologize.'

Jeremy looked surprised, and hearing the reason, looked at a loss, turning to Frank. In his easy way, Frank said, 'Really only an excuse to visit you, I think.' Alfie was going to protest; but Frank got in again: 'I want to come out to your place, if I may. It sounds like effrontery, I know . . . '

'How so? asked Jeremy. 'It's your job to report on the health of every community in the country, isn't it?'

'But yours . . . with your reputation!'

Jeremy chuckled, 'Does that mean that with my reputation you thought you'd be chucked out?'

Frank chuckled in return, 'Could be . . . but I was going on what Charlie Bishoff's been telling me about it's being . . . well, a model place. It isn't to inspect it, I assure you, but for the honour of seeing what you've done.'

'Thank you. I'm afraid I don't get much honour paid me. When were you thinking of making the visit?'

'Well, right after the Races . . . if that would suit *you*!'

Jeremy stirred as if with slight discomfort: 'It doesn't really. I usually take a bit of a trip away when it's all over . . . But you could go out yourself . . . with Madam here, too, of course. My wife'll be there. She can do you the honours, and explain everything.'

'Thanks,' Frank answered. Now both he and Alfie looked uncomfortable.

Pouring drinks for them, Jeremy said, 'Surely you've been appraised of the fact that I have an alcoholic binge after the Races?'

Noting the increased discomfort, Jeremy said, although flushing to it, 'Sorry to inflict you with my unconventional forthrightness . . . but I know what these people say . . . I've lived long enough and hard enough with 'em. I guess you're not the conventional types yourselves . . . . '

Alfie cried eagerly, 'Ooh, we're not!'

'Well . . . there you are. I thought I'd be frank with you. I don't consider myself a drunkard . . . but I don't suppose any drunk does. Still, I don't drink anything near so much per annum as the people who'll tell you I'm a drunk. Besides, I conduct my binges in what I consider a scientific way. I'm a Druggist, you might know. I see alcohol as the most harmless of all the drugs used to physic a congenitally sick species . . . and use it, I think, to its best effect.' He met their staring eyes, made a wry face, shrugged, said shortly, 'Have a drink.'

When he remained silent after pouring for everybody and taking a sip of his own, Alfie said, 'Go on . . . please. I'd like to hear more about it.'

Jeremy chuckled, 'I've a faint recollection that I discussed the matter with you once before. Anyway, it isn't really a subject for a lady . . . . '

'I don't profess or want to be a lady. I don't see what difference it makes, anyway.' Alfie's tone was slightly indignant.

'I've also an idea I told you a man should never drink except with discipline or a woman except with a reliable male escort. But what I meant about its not being a subject for a lady was that women don't have the same need of drink as men.'

'Why?'

Jeremy looked at Frank, who nodded. 'We're both terribly interested in what you're saying, Mr Delacy. We've got our own ideas about drinking. They're probably all wrong. The boozing that goes on in these parts has, well, to be frank, rather appalled us . . . although we make a show of going along with it, well, knowing that it's something of a necessity. To hear someone talk about it sensibly . . . . '

'It doesn't only belong to these parts, Mr Candlemas . . . . '

'Frank's the name, if you'd do me the honour to call me that.'

'I will, son . . . . '

'I'm Aelfrieda . . . Alfie for short . . . . '

'Everybody knows what I think.' Jeremy said it so shortly that it silenced Alfie. He went on: 'It's not just a condition of these parts . . . it's a national state of things . . . if Australia can be called a nation . . . . '

'Don't *you* call it a nation?' Alfie demanded.

Jeremy shrugged: 'More to the point to ask me what I *think* of it. I prefer not to think of it as a nation, because of the pain it causes to a kink I have for nationality . . . because as a nation it's an abomination in the sight of the Lord. I prefer to regard it as a colony, a collection of colonies, of alien peoples who don't yet know where they are, or why they're here. To call it a nation now is to give up hope that it will ever be anything but a community of stupid greedy bastards . . . whereas to call it a colony . . . rather to think of it as such . . . is to retain a little hope that it might become eventually what alone will excuse the murder and robbery, the confidence-trickery and the bombast, the stupidity and the sycophancy it's been founded on.' Jeremy ended red-faced and somewhat breathless, grabbed at his glass and drained it.

His audience was breathless, too, with interest; especially the female part of it, the one with dark eyes staring wide and luminous, lovely lolly mouth agape, the other with the brown eyes watching the effect on the black-eyed one.

Jeremy drew a deep breath: 'Talking about drink . . . . '

Alfie cried, 'No . . . please talk about Australia . . . this's marvellous!'

Jeremy shot her a glance, then concentrated on replenishing the glasses, saying, 'Some other time. I get a bit worked up about it . . . and it's hard enough to sleep with all the row that goes on these nights. Tomorrow's Cup Day . . . and I have a horse to win. There's always a certain strain to it. I usually have to take something to ease the tension as it is. One can communicate one's feelings to a horse. I don't want my mare to lose on account of me. I'm going to ask you soon to excuse me, if you don't mind. If I can get off before the mob really starts their racket after midnight, I'll have had enough, and with what I can pick up, to put me right in the morning. In case you don't know, racing for horse and owner . . . a big race like the Cup . . . starts at first light in the morning, not at two-thirty in the afternoon . . . . '

'We'll go now,' said Frank, making a rise.

'Wait till I tell you the bit about booze. I don't think it will ever matter a lot to either of you . . . . '

'Why shouldn't it matter?' asked Alfie.

'Well, you seem to be a well-adjusted couple. You're an ambitious little lady. You've got talent. You're going to use it. You're evidently your husband's first interest in life . . . so you won't go wrong for help. So why should you have to bother about drink, except as a social appurtenance? The people it matters to are those who aren't adjusted.'

'Does that mean you're not adjusted?' Alfie asked.

Frank shot a glance at her.

But Jeremy only smiled: 'Did it sound like it just now, when I was blowing off about Australia Felix?'

'Do you mean to say you drink because you hate Australia so?'

He sighed slightly: 'You're referring to the binges, of course. My other drinking is medicinal. When I go on a binge to escape a certain sense of futility I have when all this's over . . . especially if what I've striven for all the year, for several years in every case, in fact, the breeding, training, seeing come to its natural perfection a noble animal. It may be that this's the time of year I have most to do with my fellows . . . the *'Strailyuns*, and at their very worst. I even contribute something to their meanness by what I've striven for. I know they love my horses . . . but out of greed for money, for excitement . . . never out of admiration for the beautiful beasts themselves. It all disgusts me somewhat. What for? I ask myself. For something to live for, is the answer. I don't want to die. I still have the hope . . . although it's fading fast, particularly with the news these days, which makes it sound certain that we're in for another war . . . . '

Alfie put in: 'But surely this war's got to be fought to stop the Fascists?'

'You mean the Italians?'

'No . . . all the brutes who are trying to walk jack-booted over the world.'

'That means any military body to me . . . . '

'Surely not the Army of Russia!'

'Are you a Communist, Madam?'

'No . . . most certainly not.'

'You make it sound that way. The Glorious Red Army is just as much a murdering machine as any other . . . and might be worse, because it has an element of religious mania to make its murder justifiable to itself. But please, I don't want to talk about war. I had enough of the last . . . not through personal suffering, but because of what I saw it do to my native land . . . put it into fiscal and moral bankruptcy. I'm now afraid, especially from what I've heard tonight about the likelihood of the appointment of a British General to become Commander-in-Chief of the Australian Army . . . . '

'No!' cried Alfie.

'That's what I just heard. It seems the rows of the local lads over getting power for themselves is worrying Prime Minister Lyons . . . or probably more likely, the Boss, Mother England, who might be wanting her death-or-glory boys, the simply Aussies any moment, with things as they are. But I was saying, that the Great War bankrupted us on the threshold of nationhood. To be dragged into another one will sell us out altogether. But, as I've said, I'd rather not talk about it. This drink business. When the Races are over, I see the family headed for home, then sneak off. I endeavour to get away where I'm not known, where I can drink with fools that I don't despise and don't know enough about to pity much. I can enjoy their lies for a while, and entertain them with some of my own. I'm a good liar when in the mood for it . . . I mean for the fun of it. Well, I usually can drink them all out . . . and know I've done a good deed doing so. Then I carry on alone till I see the floor coming up to hit me, or the landlady trying to get into bed with me . . . .'

Nan, so silent all the while, but so much there in her brown firmness, began to giggle. So did Alfie; then Frank, and in a moment all three were howling with laughter. When they had got control of themselves, Alfie wiping her eyes with a bit of lace, Jeremy said dryly, 'Nice to know you find it amusing and not disgusting. Actually one *does* come out of it with a sense of disgust. When I see the end coming, believing in the adage that the measure of a gentleman in drink is never to let anybody see you when you fall down, I get into my bus with a bottle and go off alone to some quiet spot on a creek or river, and flake out. I wake feeling pretty sick; but there's a lovely feeling of catharsis about it. So there it is. I can't see either of you having to do it.'

Alfie said swiftly, 'Take us along with you and try us out.'

Jeremy made a pretended grimace of being shocked, murmuring, 'Oh, dear!'

She said in the same swift tone, 'We heard about your taking Lord Vaisey's girlfriend off to do it last time.'

Jeremy's face stiffened. He asked shortly, 'What's this?'

Frank shot his wife another of those looks; but again she ignored it. 'Everybody's talked about it. Most of them thought it a great joke.'

Jeremy said in the same tone, 'Looks like another apology's pending.'

'How do you mean?'

'Talking of a lady friend of mine . . . .'

Alfie cried, 'Oh, go on . . . we know what really happened . . . she forced herself on you and Bridie Cullity shanghaied her away.'

'Where'd you get that?'

'Bridie Cullity's been telling everybody.'

'Indeed . . . I'll have to have a word with Bridie.'

Alfie almost snapped, 'That won't be hard. She's been looking for you. She's even put it round that you're going to be godfather to her baby at the Christening . . . . '

Jeremy went very red.

Alfie evidently had had just a little too much. 'People say you were lovers before she married.'

Jeremy could only stare.

Frank took Alfie's hand, saying gently, 'That's enough, sweetheart . . . an apology *is* pending now.'

Alfie's black eyes swam. She drooped her head, sniffed, then muttered, 'I'm sorry . . . but . . . but you do sound . . . sanctimonious at times . . . I'm sorry, really.'

Jeremy drew a deep breath: 'I guess I deserved it. You're right about my attitude, Mrs Candlemas . . . '

'Please call me Alfie.'

He drew another deep breath: 'Alfie.'

'Thank you', she breathed.

'Well, I think we'll be getting along, eh?' said Frank.

As they shook hands, with Nan first, Alfie kissed her, saying, 'They told me you're very sweet . . . you are.' Nan smiled easily. Taking Jerry's hand, Alfie said, 'May I come to your stable tomorrow?'

'Of course. Everybody's welcome . . . except likely nobblers.'

'What are nobblers?'

'People who interfere with horses to affect their performance.'

'I'm hardly likely to do that, do you think?' She laughed.

He didn't respond to the laugh, but added: 'To nobble also means to play any underhand sort of game.'

She bridled: 'What's that supposed to mean?'

Jeremy smiled: 'Only what the word means. You did ask me. Goodnight. See you tomorrow.'

They went off arm in arm, silent until Alfie muttered, 'Why did he say that?'

'I'm sure I haven't a clue, my love. He's a strange man. That's the kind of thing he does, so they say . . . says provocative things.'

'Did he mean I was trying to nobble him?'

Frank chuckled, drawing her close, 'Could be. I've seen you put a lot of likely lads off their performance.'

'Oh, don't be silly.'

'I'm not the silly one. It's the other fellows.'

'I've a good mind not to go near him tomorrow.'

'What . . . with that pretty blue dress and hat?'

She said bitterly, 'He'd probably prefer a woman in a stockman's hat and no shoes.'

'Now, now . . . this is where we came in! When somebody else said that . . . .'

'I wasn't referring to his halfcaste wife . . . although how such a man came to marry a halfcaste beats me.'

'For the same reason, I guess, as you said he'd prefer a woman who wore a stockman's hat and no shoes.'

'Why is that?'

'It was you who said it, darling. I presume you meant he wants just a bush-woman for a wife. They do say, you know, that the trouble between him and his ex-wife was that she wanted to be the lady, and he wouldn't be in it.'

'But a man with intelligence like that, having a woman like that! That's probably most of his trouble, why he goes on the booze like that. If he had an intelligent woman beside him . . . .'

'He did have one . . . You can't say Lady Rhoda isn't intelligent. What she did was quite smart, actually . . . . '

'I mean with his own kind of intelligence. He's a brilliant man. Look what Charlie Bishoff says about his scientific research. You can see it in his face. Hence the way he spoke of Australia. What he said is the exact truth. I hadn't seen it before. We mustn't let the old world drag us down with it. Here is the chance of the Brave New World . . . as Daddy used to say . . . .'

He squeezed her close: 'My daddy's girl. Do you want to go back into the pub?'

'No, for heaven's sake! Let's go for a long walk . . . out along the road.'

Passing Barbu's, above the din of the Dance Hall down the road a little, they heard faint music. Alfie took it up, humming it: the *Melody in F*. She said, 'Puts me in mind of the Compound kids. Poor little things . . . I wonder where they all are now . . . particularly that little boy of his?'

'His grandson, you mean?'

'Yes. That's what I can't understand about him . . . how he could reject that beautiful child, neglect him so that he's had to run away and live with the blacks.'

'But isn't that what his idea is, that the boy's better off growing up as a bush black than as a low-class crossbred?'

'He wouldn't be low class if he looked after him.'

'But would McCusky let him look after him?'

'If he fought. That's the trouble with the man. Everything's negative with him. Even winning races with fine horses he's bred. He has to run away and booze. I tell you, it's because he hasn't a woman beside him to make his life positive.'

'What are you going to do . . . try and get him one?'

'I'll try something. I'm not going to give up about that boy, McCusky or no.'

Speak of the Devil: there was Eddy himself, outside the Dance Hall, watching the common herd dancing, under the MC-ship of his rival, Pat Hannaford. The herd was much augmented this time with foreign road-workers, who seemed, in their innocence of or indifference to the conventions of the locality, to be doing so well with coloured girls, that more particular gentry, like the Knowles brothers and Oz Burrows, had been crowded out. The Knowleses, evidently friends again by their easy manner with each other, were talking with McCusky when the Candlemases came to take a peep at how the other half live. McCusky promptly dropped them for the newcomers. Asked why he had deserted his post at Finnucane's, Eddy replied that things were easing up there, because people were saving themselves for tomorrow's big things, himself included. He told them about the Cup Ball to be held here tomorrow night, in which, of course, Alfie would be playing an official part, at least to the extent of standing by the barrel out of which the winning numbers for the Golden Horseshoe prizes would be drawn and checking them with the names on her list of sales. First Prize this time was to be a handsome little chestnut colt named Golden Bobby, donated by the Eastern Pastoral Company, a British-owned rival of Vaisey's, and supposed to be a very likely laddy in future racing, being of the blood of Jeremy Delacy's famous stallion, Elektron. Speaking of this other devil, (Jeremy, that is, not his horse) started a lively discussion of him that was taken away from the Dance Hall by the trio and out along the southern road, Alfie evidently wanting to talk only of that subject, despite the rancour she had been expressing concerning it just lately and her inclusion of McCusky in it, surely glad now of the fellow's company since it silenced that tendency of her husband's to jest about her eagerness.

The discussion dealt largely with that school out at Lily Lagoons. Alfie wanted to know whether McCusky would permit its continued functioning under a properly qualified teacher. He at once demanded, 'Not thinking of taking it on are you?'

'Well, I hadn't thought of it till now . . . but if he'd agree . . . . '

'You know what his theory is . . . let the kids learn themselves, and for preference to live in the old style.'

'He might be talked out of it.'

'Him talked out of anything! Look, I told you all about the Euraustralia League business. Jumbo himself told you about it . . . reconstruct the ravaged country, get back to bloomin' nature . . while there's a fortune to be dug out of the ground. If he were genuine about wanting to help those halfcastes, there was the opportunity if ever there was . . . to form a co-operative. They'd've learnt what they're most lacking in for assimilation into civilized life . . . economic sense. He complains they only wanted money for booze. Maybe they did. But they did want money. The first step was to let them earn it by their own self-directed efforts. They'd have adjusted subsequently. Instead, what's he do? When they won't help him put the country back as it was as a gesture to the Old People, who they're trying like hell to forget, he calls them bloody mongrels. He claims he didn't mean it about their race, but about the type of people they were. The great Jeremy Delacy tact! The champion of champions for the dispossessed and downtrodden Aborigine . . . and when he has a row with a mob of halfcastes he's offering what he called dignity to, he calls them mongrels!'

Alfie sighed, 'He's a strange man.'

'He certainly is . . . round the bend, if you ask me.'

Alfie said hotly, 'That's not so . . he's a brilliant man . . . his only trouble is . . . is . . . . '

She faltered. Eddy asked rudely, 'What?'

She bit her finger, answered, 'I don't know, really . . . but listening to him talk . . . . ' Again she was at a loss.

Eddy chuckled, 'You want to look out for him. You know they say he's got a way with the ladies. He even pinched Lord Vaisey's fiancée.'

Alfie snapped, 'From what I understand, she chucked herself at him.'

Eddy guffawed, 'They all do!'

Frank came to the rescue with a sharp question, 'Have you any more news about the missing boy and his mother?'

Eddy, evidently brought up short by reminder of something that troubled him greatly, exhaled heavily: 'Not a squeak. Seems to be only one conclusion, that they tried getting away in a canoe from the Old Compound, and got drowned, like the police reckoned from the start. But I didn't believe it. The kid might've been a bit dim . . . but not Nelly. She was smart, wilful. She'd made up her mind to get back here, and hell and high-water wouldn't've stopped her once she got a start on . . . all those trucks running up and down the road.' He sighed. 'But if she had, she'd've turned up at the Races. They both would've. The kid had been coming here every year of his life, she most of the years of hers. That's the blackfeller way. The sentiment of the old familiar places . . . Poor Feller My Country . . . even if they know that gettin' caught means goin' to jail for life, they just got to go back. But there isn't a trace of 'em. Cahoon and his Man Friday've been out to Catfish, Lily Lagoons, up and down the river. If there was the slightest trace, a single track, Jinbul would find it.'

'Poor things!' murmured Alfie. 'I feel responsible for it all . . . . '

'What about me? I *am* responsible for it all. Any moment I expect your girlfriend, Fay, to come out with some sob-story that I hounded them to their death.'

They went on talking about Prindy and Jeremy and the strangeness of Jeremy's failure to do something for the boy, if only out of perverse desire to embarrass the Big House Delacys. Still on the subject, they returned to Finnucane's, to find it strangely quiet, silent almost, save for the clink of money in the den of Old Shame-on-us and the measured piping of divers drunks from the bedrooms. They parted.

As Alfie and Frank Candlemas undressed in their dark little box of a room, Frank gave a hand to his spouse, a hand that lingered lovingly in unhooking brassière and pulling down pants, without any demur from the owner of the dainties he fondled; but when they were in bed and he rolled over to her and proceeded to unbutton the pyjama jacket he had buttoned up with such care, she shrugged him away, murmuring, 'Don't.'

'Not in the moodies?' he asked gently.

'No.'

'Okay,' he sighed, and kissed her cheek and withdrew to his own pillow. For a while both lay awake in silence. He was first to fall asleep, rolling towards her, flinging an arm over her belly. Gently she removed the arm, lay for a long while staring into the dark.

III

Cup Day, dressing-up day for the ladies, if they had anything worth while to dress-up in, as at least most of the white ones did. Alfie Candlemas certainly had something worthwhile in that blue dress of hers, specially made for the occasion, a thing in blue and white with the colour and delicacy of design of willow-pattern china, with appurtenances to match. There it hung on its hanger as since unpacking and touching up with the iron, while with a degree of evident affection she regarded it, when after showering in preparation for the dressing-up at somewhere round nine-thirty, she slipped into fresh bra and pants, watched by her smiling husband. Yet it was not for the lovely thing she reached when ready for dressing, but for the stockrider's outfit hanging beside it, the white corduroy thing that had been such a success yesterday. But you don't have the same success with the same audience two days running; besides, this was dressing-up day for *Ladies*. Hence Frank's sudden change of expression as she cast the masculine rigout on the bed and proceeded to pull the pants off the horizontal bar of the hanger, and his question, 'Hey . . . what's this?'

She answered simply, 'I'm going to wear it instead.'

'Why?'

'Because I feel like it.'

She put the shirt on first, was buttoning it, when he said, 'You're going to look a bit odd in the grandstand with all the other dames done up to the nines.'

She waited till she was pulling on the pants to answer, 'I'm not going in the grandstand today.'

He only slightly frowned, and surely more in puzzlement than annoyance. He lit a cigarette. When she was ready to put on the riding boots, he rose and got them from the rack under the little wash-stand, gave them an unnecessary brush-over, brought them to her, and knelt to help her on with them as she sat on the bed. Concentrating on his task he asked, 'On account of Delacy?' When she didn't answer, but shoved her slim socked foot at him for the second boot, he looked up, met the black eyes, looked deep into them for a moment she allowed before dropping them to her foot. He dropped his to his task.

When the boot was on and she had her feet on the floor, she said, 'He told me I could come to his stable, didn't he?'

He backed away as she stood: 'Does that mean you have to dress-up for it?'

She went to the little dressing-table: 'I want to spend the day there.'

Their eyes met in the poxy little mirror. He asked, 'Will he let you?'

Fiddling with her dark curls she said, 'Why shouldn't he . . . if I make myself useful.'

He smiled, somewhat wryly: 'He might regard it as an attempt at nobbling.'

She avoided his quizzing eyes. 'I'd like to have the experience of spending a day like that at a country race-meeting . . . I mean with the people who're racing the horses, not the snobs in the grandstand. His horse's sure to win the Cup, they say. I'd like to be sort of part of the whole thing. Don't you think it's a good idea . . . for the book, eventually, of course?'

He sighed slightly. 'So long as my darling doesn't get hurt?'

Her voice was a little sharp: 'How can I get hurt? I'm not going to *ride* the horse.'

'You heard what happened to that Lady Lydia.'

'She threw herself at him.'

He responded a little dryly, 'Yes.' Their eyes met again as she was rouging her lips. He said, 'You won't be wanting me, I suppose.'

'You'll be all right . . . from all the ogling I saw you getting yesterday behind my back.'

'May I ask one little concession?'

'What?'

'That I take you there?'

She shrugged: 'What do I care what any of those snobs say?'

'It isn't the snobs I'm thinking of . . . it's Jeremy Delacy.'

'I can look after myself, thank you.'

'I know . . . but I like looking after you, too. Seems to me the best way to do it, for your sake, too, is for me to go along with you.'

'What d'you mean?'

'If you go alone, it *will* look like you're running after him . . . .'

She swung on him with black eyes wide: 'Do *you* think I am?'

He blinked: 'If you are, it's for a special purpose . . . and you know I won't interfere. I only want to see he doesn't offend you . . . as I think he's quite likely to do. But if I sort of deliver you into his hands . . . .'

She blazed: 'What do you mean deliver . . . as if I were some property of yours or something?'

He smiled that amiable smile. 'Sweetheart, you know me better than that . . . but you don't know this man . . . who's renowned for his provocativeness . . . no, listen! I'm insisting on this . . . not as your husband, but as your closest friend. You also are a provocative little lady. Just let me take you along, as if I'm interested in the stable too . . . then I vanish . . . into the arms of that pretty blonde from Brisbane. Okay?'

She nodded slightly.

The Bishoffs, waiting to go with them to the Racecourse in the big old Rolls, were much surprised by Alfie's choice of dress. Betty seemed to be inclined to argue the propriety of it; but Frank amiably stopped it by bringing up the subject of the book. 'Material,' he said. 'The artistic temperament's got no respect for respectability at all. But it's my guess she's saving the blue thing for the Ball tonight.' They were soon laughing.

And there soon they were with the surging mob helping to destroy the crystal clarity of the morning with dust and gasoline, and the sweet silence that had reigned for the night over the river there, so that tracks of regular habitues of the region of the Racecourse, the brolgas, plovers, curlews, were to be seen before the mob stamped them out.

There must have been lots of times in Frank Candlemas's association with his impulsive bride that the combination of his love and astuteness had saved the day for her in sticky situations; and surely this was one of them. The way Jeremy Delacy looked Alfie over in a swift sharp look, when the day before he had scarcely seemed to notice her get-up, was hardly a good omen, even though he received the pair politely enough. Then there was his abruptness in introducing those of his household not yet known to the visitors. He certainly excused it by saying it wasn't the best hour of the best day to be showing anyone around, with all the work to be done with the racing team and the tension of both man and beast. When she would have shaken hands with the blacks, he stopped her, saying, sharply, 'Don't do that!' When with flaming cheeks and hot dark eyes she turned on him, he added shortly, 'These people take physical contact much more seriously than we do. You only embarrass them by forcing false friendship on them . . . . '

She said breathlessly, 'I assure you it wasn't false . . . '

He cut in: 'How could it be otherwise, when you don't know the people, or they you? If and when they get to know you, if they like you enough, they'll even embarrass *you* by fondling you.' He looked at Frank, whose usual smile had been replaced with a tight mask. Then he said, 'I'm presuming that your wife wants to understand the realities in such matters . . . since she's writing a book about the country?'

Frank saw it as what it was, as near apology as could be expected. The mask relaxed as he answered, 'Yes . . . thanks for the tip.'

Alfie looked quite helpless, with black eyes ready to swim. Frank saw that too, and said quickly, 'As a matter of fact, it's on account of the book we're here so early.'

Both Jeremy and Alfie looked at him in surprise. He smiled at both of them, and then at staring Nan, and added, 'Material. We were hoping you might let her stay around a bit and watch . . . or even help, if she can. Country race-meeting stable . . . seeing the Favourite prepared for action, *et cetera*. Would it be asking too much?'

Both Alfie and Jeremy went red. But while Alfie looked blank, Jeremy smiled slightly: 'So that's what the ringer's rigout's for on Ladies' Day!'

Frank slipped an arm about his beloved's slim but stiff waist, chuckling, 'That's it. Greater love hath no woman for her art, than that she miss putting on a smart dress to serve it.'

Jeremy also chuckled, taking another but different look from before at Alfie. 'But I'm afraid that pretty outfit's going to get messed up if you really want to lend a hand.'

Alfie's eyes shone. 'I can always wash it . . . I'd be so happy to help.'

Frank said, 'Well, I can leave her with you. Thanks a lot, Jeremy . . . I'm much obliged.' He turned the smile on all and sundry, departed.

Jeremy remarked as he disappeared, 'Nice fellow, your husband. One of the nicest persons I've ever met.'

Alfie said, 'Yes . . . he is a dear . . . what can I do?'

Nan giggled, 'He handsome, too.'

Jeremy feigned a growl, 'That'll do you, *Ngunkomlalli* . . . I got a paper reckon I the handsome one for you.'

Nan squealed with mirth, as did Water Lily, her daughter-in-law and a couple of black girls. Alfie, looking at a loss, asked, 'What's that word mean?'

'Simply *wife*. Now, I'll leave you to her. Have to go and see them at the Committee room.' Jeremy went off.

'What you want to do, Missus?' asked Nan.

'Please call me Alfie, dear.'

'But dat boy name!'

'That's what they call me. I'll do anything . . . anything at all.'

'You like to curry-comb?'

'What's that?' When Nan looked incredulously over the stock-rider-girl, Alfie made a little grimace. 'Shows what a phoney I am, doesn't it. But you teach me, eh?'

Nan produced a metal comb. 'We try Golden Girl first. She de quietest one . . . if she like you. We see if she like you first-time, eh?'

The introduction between pretty ringer and beautiful chestnut filly was made, with complete success. Golden Girl so much liked the smell of Aelfrieda, the enchanted one, that she sought more of it by nibbling at the buttons of her shirt so as to undo them and nuzzle a little brassièred tit, much to the amusement of the other females present.

'She think you got him milk!' squealed Nan.

Alfie, just as tickled, said, 'Wait till I get round to that part of her . . . I'll take my revenge.'

It was all great fun. Golden Girl loved the fondling and fussing. The other horses got interested in the newcomer, too and whickered for attention. Nan gave Alfie some glucose squares to feed them as titbits. Jeremy cruelled things a little when he heard the titty-searching episode, which he did from the articulate one of those concerned, when he met her up at the course as the bulk of the household rushed up there to see the first race run with one of their horses in it. He didn't smile, but glancing over her swiftly, as one of his kind might a mare, asked, 'But you're not lactating, are you?' She evidently didn't like it, but giggled slightly, remarking that he was a real horse-doctor, wasn't he; to which he replied shortly: 'Yes,' and concentrated on the race with his binoculars. Still, it went pleasantly enough. Alfie got grubbier and grubbier and more excited with every race, to which she came rushing up with the rest, to stand beside Jeremy for all his apparent lack of interest in her compared with the equine performances.

She would have lunched with the Lily Lagoons people at the stable only for a request made to her at the end of the last race before lunch: that is to say before the Great Race, the Cup, which would follow lunch and end the serious business of the festival. It was Frank, coming to her, who made the request. He drew her aside and told her Lady Rhoda had been rather uppity with him when he had given her Alfie's apologies along with the reason for her absence from the company of the other Committee Ladies. He said, 'You'll have to make some little gesture, darling. Come to lunch with me, eh? Then you can make your own apologies.' Alfie looked annoyed. He insisted, 'It's important, sweetheart. They've got their rigid conventions, whatever we might think of them. You can go right back to your fun afterwards.' She agreed reluctantly, excused herself to Jeremy.

There was that polite bit of boozing to be done in the annex of the privileged under the grandstand before lunch. Alfie and her Frank went in to join the bleating throng. There was Lady Rhoda talking with the Patron, Colonel Chivvy, and his lady wife and the Widow Trotters who had at last made the Big House guest-list. Rhoda quickly caught Alfie's eye as she came smiling towards her. Who could have helped but see a dusty ringer walk in amongst that gathering of elegantly attired squatters? Alfie said nicely, 'Bit late with my apologies, Lady Rhoda, but . . . but . . . . ' Looking right past the vulgar intruder, Her Ladyship said to the Lady Patroness that she thought it time they adjourned for lunch. All swept by the red-faced big-black-eyed Alfie with a swish of silk and stiff-starched khaki linen. A moment. Then she rushed to the door and out, through the crowd swarming like flies over dung round those dispensaries to the gustatory needs of the common herd: Finnucane's temporary gold mine, Ah Loy's hot-pie and dim-sim foundry, Ali Barba's Russoyee. She was stared at sharply from the latter by a pair of small goggled eyes above busily working yellow-brown hands, but seeing nothing herself, not even those coarse fellows who took advantage of the crush and her haste to slap and pinch her wobbly bum, because her eyes were swimming with tears.

Back at the stables, under the bough shelter that served as dining-room, all were seated at the table eating, except Jeremy, who was standing, drinking from a bowl of soup. All stared in astonishment at the precipitate entry. Alfie halted just short of Jeremy, blinking her tears, strangling her sobs. Jeremy put down his bowl, asking, 'What's happened?'

Alfie panted: 'That . . . that . . . your wife . . . was rude to me . . . ooooooh!

Jeremy murmured, 'My wife?'

'I . . . mean . . . Lady Eaton . . . . '

'She's Sir What's It's Eaton's wife.'

Alfie's tears got the better of her: 'Oooooo . . . I know . . . I'm glad too . . . she's a . . . ooooooh!

Jeremy reached and touched her arm, drew her, saying, 'Come and sit down . . . have lunch with us.'

'Oooooo!' The corduroyed arms clutched at him, slipped round his neck, while the hat was knocked back to hang by its chin-strap as the curly head dropped on his breast.

Just then Frank came up. Gently disengaging himself, Jeremy handed Alfie to her rightful owner, saying, 'This's your job, man.' But Alfie was recovered now. She shook her curls, gave a weak smile, sniffed, planked her wobbly bottom on the space on the form available to her. Then, getting out the bit of grubby lace that was her hankie, and dabbing her tears, with laughter that sounded a little hysterical, she told what had happened. At Jeremy's invitation Frank sat beside her; while Nan leapt up to get them food. Jeremy's eyes twinkled in looking at Frank, causing Frank to smile slightly in return. When Alfie asked Jeremy what he thought of it, he shrugged, and picking up his soup-bowl, answered, 'Well, you could hardly expect anything else, when you deserted the table of the squattocracy for the stable of the one they call the Scrub Bull.'

Alfie cried, 'Give me the Scrub Bull every time!'

Nan, dishing out to her, squealed with a little laugh, but looked with searching brown eyes at those big black ones fastened so avidly upon her man, whose own grey eyes had taken flight to distance.

Whatever was being said about the incident around the squatters' table, there was no time for table-talk here. Finished his soup, and while the others made haste with their cold corned beef and mash, (except Darcy, who hollow-cheeked, nibbled a cracker and drank black tea and watched the gorgers hollow-eyed) Jeremy got out a stethoscope and went to Golden Girl, standing quietly enough in her special shelter, but with a dark stain of sweat here and there that betrayed her nervousness. The filly whickered at his approach, and nuzzled him to embarrassment as he went over her heart and lungs, listening,

listening, with eyes looking, as he kept pushing her velvet nose away, as if he *saw* those mighty mechanisms in actual rhythmic operation. Then there was his going over of every point of her slender limbs with searching fingers that seemed to have eyes in them, over her hoofs, her mouth, even a peep at what she had under her silky bridal-veil of tail. Alfie, who had soon leapt up to join him, boldly asked what the last inspection was in aid of. He answered off-handedly, 'To see if she might be coming into oestrus . . . the excitement could bring her on.'

'Would that make any difference to her performance?'

'Could even better it . . . with a good jockey to handle the situation. The trouble would be with the stallions running with her. Properly, she'd have to be scratched if she were . . . Objectionable Horse, is the official term. Sexual misbehaviour is grounds for disqualification. They're not machines, you know . . . but living, feeling intelligent creatures, essentially the same as ourselves.' He was not looking at her, didn't see the excitement growing in the pretty childish face. 'Well, she seems to be in perfect condition for what we want her to do. It depends on whether *she* wants to do it . . . and, of course, her opponents, the luck of the game, and all the other hazards.'

'What could go wrong?' asked Alfie.

'Anything . . . from a snake on the track to Darcy's losing his weights. Well, we must be moving.'

'Can I come with you?'

He looked at her. She added: 'I mean, to see everything this time . . . weighing-in, saddling . . . . '

'Of course,' he said shortly. 'Tag along.' He left her.

He bridled the mare and led her, with Darcy in his silks and carrying his tiny saddle on the other side of the beast's tossing head. Darcy's own head was cocked to listen to the Mullaka's final instructions. Alfie, as if understanding that she could have no place in this, came behind. Frank, as if realizing that he was not wanted, went with the household straight up to the spectators' flat.

They entered the Saddling Paddock. There was Charlie Bishoff looking the horses over. He eyed the trailing Alfie sharply, but ignored her while he made his inspection of the mare. He said to Jeremy, 'Although I says it as shouldn't . . . she'll romp in. Anyway, I've got my missus's year's dress allowance on it . . . or rather, she has. Good luck.' There were numerous sharp glances. Alfie ignored them, looked about boldly, followed Darcy to the door of the Scales Shed, watched him sit the big brass scales – while a battery of Committeemen's eyes watched her.

The mare was saddled carefully. She was excited now, snorting, quivering, rolling golden eyes, lashed a kick at one of her male rivals who took the liberty of a sniff. Alfie said with a chuckle, 'She's like a prima donna, isn't she?'

Jeremy, hoisting Darcy aloft, ignored her. A last word, a last pat; then horse and rider away, heading, prancing now, for the show-off of the Cup Parade. Jeremy headed for the gate leading to the flat where the common herd were swarming. Alfie darted after him. He looked at her as if he'd forgotten her. He didn't speak till they came up to the Totalizator: 'You having a bet?'

'Frank's betting for us . . on Golden Girl, naturally.'

'They've all got a chance . . . and the odds are better on the others.'

'You can't bet on your own horse, can you?'

'It isn't done, of course . . . openly. But I don't bet at all.'

'Why's that . . . one of your principles?'

'Not really. It is my opinion that the money business's what makes racing stink, probably worse than anything else human, except prostitution . . . but the reason is I'm not a gambler.'

'But you're a man who'd take risks?'

'Gamblers don't take risks . . . they just don't recognize them.'

'Isn't that the same thing?'

'Hardly. Gambling's a form of conceit.' When she eyed him with wide inquiry, he added: 'To be a true gambler you've got to think you're a special favourite of the gods. You can expect miracles simply by tossing for 'em, placing a bet at long odds. You don't curse yourself for a fool if you lose against logic, but the gods for letting down their white-haired boy.'

They were up to the rails of the course, amongst the Lily Lagoons people. She said with a cocky little smile, 'You know all the answers, don't you!'

'To questions mostly of little consequence, I'm afraid.'

'What are the consequential ones?'

'Shh! If you don't mind . . . this is the matter of most consequence of the moment.'

The horses were prancing and wheeling about, with Charlie Bishoff on his snowball patiently manoeuvring them to the barrier. The tension came from the horses to the crowd. Sweat was pouring, lungs straining.

Then: '*They're off*!'

That scatter of gravel and whirl of dust – the heaving rumps and flying tails – the Favourite at the rear. Alfie shrilled her dismay: 'Oh!' and grabbed at Jeremy's arm.

Gently disengaging himself, he said, 'He held her to stop her getting out in front.'

'Is that a disadvantage?'

'To some horses . . . the opposite to others. She's very lively, is our little girl. She'd lead the field, knock herself up before she'd done half of it.' He was looking through his glasses. He added: 'Where she shines is in the last two furlongs. All being well, she'll just tear away from 'em.'

'How do you know all this about a horse?'

'You breed the horse. You know what its progenitors have done. You study its own peculiarities . . . every little thing.' He was only muttering, intent upon the wave of colour disintegrating into the surf of rolling red mirage. He was silent till the field appeared across the way at the 4-Furlong. He gave her his glasses, saying, 'See if you can pick her out.'

After a moment Alfie cried, 'Yes . . . I see her . . . she's in the middle.'

'Her right place till she gets to the mile-and-a-half.'

She looked at him as she handed back the binoculars: 'If you could only breed human beings like horses . . . so that you'd know what they were likely to do.'

He grinned wryly: 'You can generally pretty accurately anticipate what the great majority are likely to do . . . something silly.'

'You *are* a misanthrope, aren't you!'

He was looking through the glasses again: 'Not really Man with his intelligence, and with his beauty when he's got it, is the most wonderful thing in creation.'

She touched his arm, saying swiftly, 'I'm so glad to hear you say that . . . Jeremy!'

He withdrew his eyes from the glasses to look at her again, met her wide dark adoring eyes, went red, and retreated with haste back to the glasses and the field now coming for the first time into the Straight in this gruelling race of two miles.

There was no talking to him now, as the wedge-like storm came thundering towards them and the mob gasped to the strain of striving flesh and sinew. Past in a roaring flash of colour, while the crowd shrieked its excitement and danced like lunatics – then gone again in dust She asked where the mile-and-a-half would be. But he ignored her, watching for the field to come into it as that strange rolling rainbow-hued wave across the way.

Then out of sight again, as only a willy-willy of dust, sweeping along as if all the Dust Devils in the land were in it. The wedge again – the thunder – the flying storm of flesh and hair and silk and hooves: 'Golden Girl . . . she's out in front . . . the Favourite . . . the Favourite . . . come on girlie, come on sweetheart, you got 'em . . . keep it up . . . keep it up!' With Golden Girl two lengths ahead the storm swept past the Flat, past the Post: 'Golden Girl . . . Golden Girl . . . the Favourite wins!'

Jeremy, red and breathing hard, found himself with an arm about a slender figure that was clinging to him, shrieking at him, 'She won, she won . . . the darling won!'

He blinked, went redder, pulled away.

Alfie didn't mind, even though there were tears in her eyes. Her gasping was joyful: 'Wasn't it wonderful!' She saw Nan staring, grabbed at her, kissed her. 'I never felt so excited. Aren't you excited?'

Nan smiled her comfortable smile. Still, the Lily Lagoons people were hugging each other. Alfie got into it. She came out of the huddle to see Jeremy heading for the gate by the Judge's Stand, leading onto the course, and in process of being opened. She asked those about her, 'Is he going to bring her in?'

They all answered, Yes. She looked at Nan. 'Could I go with him?'

Nan smiled. 'Da's all right, I t'ink.'

Alfie raced after the bulky fawn-clad back, caught up with it beyond the gate. Jeremy, watching his heaving champing champion returning from the little distance to which her terrific momentum had taken her, turned on finding someone at his side murmuring, with evident trepidation: 'I took the liberty. I did so want to be in this part of it . . . I . . . I asked your wife.'

He stared at her for a moment, so that she dropped her own eyes. He asked, 'What did you ask her?'

'If it would be all right for me to come.'

'All right for whom?'

She caught his arm: 'Oh, please, Jeremy!'

'I'm not objecting, girl. I'm just surprised.

'That your wife should be so sweet?'

'I hate that word used about Nan.'

'I'm sorry.'

He persisted, 'It always sounds like condescension.'

'I said I'm sorry.' She was still clinging to his arm.

He didn't shake her off as usual.

As Golden Girl came up, Jeremy said first to grinning Darcy, 'Good on you, lad.' Darcy giggled. Then Jeremy touched the sodden tossing neck of the mare, saying, 'Poor old girl . . . all that to prove what everybody knew you were . . . but it'll be nice to remember when you see your colts and fillies training, eh?' The mare, quite distressed, shoved her head against him as if to weep. There was no room in it for two clinging females. Alfie had to let go. Jeremy led the mare through the gate, then let her go to stand and wait while Darcy rode through to the Saddling Paddock for the Weighing-out, after which the mare, if declared the winner on the Numbers Board, must be presented to Patron and President.

'Why did you say that?' Alfie asked. 'Won't she race again?'

'Another race like that would kill her. Only a colt can do it more than once. She's had her shining hour. She can now settle down and become a mother and lead a normal life.'

'Half her luck,' said Alfie.

Jeremy, watching for the numbers, seemed not to hear. Then up went Golden Girl's number; and there in a moment was Darcy riding back. As Jeremy took the horse's head again, Alfie caught the bridle on the other side.

Jeremy seemed not to notice the act, in fact was looking up at the grandstand, where there was a little knot of women about the weeping Mrs Trotters, whose colt had been second favourite; but in a moment he asked, 'Why half her luck . . . on account of her settling down, or the shining hour?'

'I guess the shining hour.'

'Don't you think you'll get yours?'

'I hope so.'

'Then let's hope you recognize it and are content with it and don't go hunting greedily after more . . . like poor old Mum Trotters up there. She got it with the Cup last year and the inner circle this one . . . . '

'How would you know which is your shining hour?'

'I don't know . . . I haven't had one . . . yet.'

'Do you expect to?'

He shrugged. 'You mustn't expect . . . only hope . . . . '

Such was the effect of this tête-à-tête across the champion's blowing nose, at least upon those who had a grandstand view of it, as the mare was double-led to the grandstand, that even the relict of Piggy Trotters' was checked in her grieving for not having the hours shining for her always; although in the case of the Widow Trotters, it might have been her sensing of withdrawal of the interest of those who had been comforting her. Dead silence reigned in the grandstand, even while the common herd, whatever its closest members might be thinking. did the proper thing by clapping. Then the President bethought himself of the niceties and clapped; and appropriately the elite joined him – except for the most elite of all, his Lady Mother, who sat behind him, so wooden of face and form that it was impossible not to notice her amongst the applauding others, impossible for the two pairs of eyes, the grey and the black, on either side of the horse's head, not to meet her hard blue stare. Jeremy blinked and withdrew his eyes on the instant. Not so Alfie. She clung to the blue eyes for as long as they deigned to regard her, which was long enough for her to get her revenge with an elfin smirk.

Chairman and Patron rose from their special seats, came down the short flight of stairs, at the foot of which horse, rider, leaders, halted. Colonel Chivvy thrust his hand out to Jeremy, saying in clipped tones, 'Congratulations, Sir . . . great horse . . . great race . . . heartiest congratulations.' Then, even to the amazement of the lady herself, he thrust the hand at what he may have taken for a girl strapper – and, by jove, a pretty one, said a roguish light in his faded eye – and added in that military tone: 'And you, young lady.' The eyes swept swiftly up and down her neat if grubby figure in reconnaisance. Then he looked up at Darcy: 'And you, Jockey . . . damn good show!' and reached for the saddle-coloured hand. 'And, of course, you, my beauty!' He stroked the mare's nose. Then he stepped back, to let Martin Delacy do his stuff.

Martin did and said much the same, with the exception that he utterly ignored Alfie. He said to Jeremy, 'Grand little filly, Father. I've never seen a mare run a better race. Will you race her again?'

Jeremy replied amiably enough, 'Not likely, Son.'

'I didn't think so. But we might expect some of her blood, I hope.'

'Yes, Son.'

Alfie caught Martin's staring eye as she turned with the turning of the horse by Jeremy; and again that impish smirk, so evident as to make the young man turn red.

She kept her grip on the bridle right through the press of congratulating from the common herd, amongst whom there were lots of familiar faces: Eddy McCusky arm in arm with Kitty Wyndeyer and both somewhat under the influence, it seemed – Fergus Ferris, with his arm about a pretty silly-looking little thing, Miss Chivvy, the Colonel's daughter, Finnucane and his Bridie, and his son-in-law Con, in that order as they could get from behind the bar – even Barbu Ram, and some little fellow in a turban and dark glasses who was not noticed at all. Fergus and Eddy and a number of other boys kissed Alfie, till she was covering her face, but certainly not with annoyance, judging by the glowing of her eyes and her high colour and her giggling. But although as many hands as could reach touched the mare or grasped Darcy's hand, so few sought the hand of the one responsible for it all, he sometimes called the Scrub Bull.

They came through the press to the stables. There was Nan. Jeremy let go the horse to take her in his arms and kiss her. She smiled happily, turning her smile on the suddenly blank-faced Alfie, asking, 'You have good time, eh, Missus?'

Alfie took a moment to conjure the smile and the answer, 'Oh, yes, thank you . . . dear . . . it was marvellous.'

From a stable near by came some fluent bad language. Jeremy chuckled, addressing Alfie, 'If you don't want to learn all the swear-words in the language, you'd better trot along. That's my half-brother, Jumbo. He's always a bad loser.'

She glanced in the direction of the stream of filth, murmuring. 'Poor Jumbo!'

'Oh, it isn't so much a matter of hurt pride, but of wasted sacrifice.'

'Sacrifice?'

'He'd've been off the grog for a whole week getting ready for this.'

'You're wrong there. According to official information, since he's been made foreman of the McCusky ranch at Sweet Creek, he's been drinking very little.'

'Indeed! Well tonight'll prove how permanent the cure is. He starts making things hideous just as everybody else is beginning to settle down after the Ball.'

'Will you be going to the Ball?'

'No . . . I never attend any of the official functions.'

'So I heard.' She was staring at him.

He looked relieved when he saw Frank coming, said quickly, 'Well, here's your man come to collect you. You won't want to be mixed up in the rest of it. What you need most will be a long drink and a bath. See you later, eh?' He more or less shoved her into the arms of smiling Frank, who led her away towards the parked Rolls Royce.

The Lily Lagoons people, with a number of friends, were just settling down to their own Cup Banquet when the lurking dogs and plovers warned them of intrusion. Those of the household who were not black and preferring to enjoy themselves in the more natural way of sitting on the ground, were at a large trestle table set out under the high-sailing half-moon, the stars, and a couple of hanging electric globes. The provender was a couple of huge domestic turkeys, with sweetbucks, pumpkin, and other trimmings, a great fruit pie with cream, all sorts of dessert stuffs, and champagne, wine, beer. The friends were the Toohey Family, three or four down-country cattlemen, and the Jumbo Delacys, amongst them, Jumbo himself, and, miraculously, sober.

It was a dark-clad figure coming down the hill – a Lady, so breathed the sharper-eyes – and soon, more softly, 'Mitchis Elfie!'

Alfie was wearing the Race Day rigout, the willow-pattern china thing, as seen as she came into the bright circle of light. Jeremy and Nan rose to meet her, he greeting her, rather shortly, 'Hullo!'

She wasn't smiling, as a true intruder would be, but looking even anxious. She said, 'Sorry to butt in . . . but I wanted to see you . . . importantly.'

'Take a seat . . . have a drink.' He reached for glass and champagne bottle. Nan was getting a cane chair. Alfie said she wouldn't sit down, adding that she had something she wanted to tell Jeremy – in private, if he didn't mind. That Jeremy did mind somewhat, he showed with the reluctance with which he excused himself from his company. As they headed away towards the crossing, he said with a hint of a chuckle, 'I'd've thought a fire-eater like you would have braved the she-lion in her den.'

'How d'you mean?'

'Gone to the Big House banquet. As a Committee Member you were entitled to.'

She looked at him. 'Did you really expect me to go?'

'No . . . of course not. But Finnucane asked you to his, I suppose?'

'Yes . . . but I didn't go . . . because of what I want to tell you about.'

He halted as they reached the causeway, looking back at his camp as if to remind her of his responsibilities. 'Fire away.'

'Just before we were to go in to eat, that man Gilling, the Head Bookkeeper from the Station . . . he's Treasurer . . . came and said he wanted to talk to me privately . . . and I left Frank and the others. He said he'd come to get the list of names I had of the people I'd sold the Golden Horseshoes to. I was surprised . . . because when I gave him the money yesterday, he told me to keep the list . . . because I'd be helping the Patron with the drawing. He even told me to be careful with it. I reminded him of that. He said it was Lady Eaton's orders.'

'Oh!'

'I got mad at that . . . but didn't know what to say. I just said, "I can't give them to you now. I'm with my husband and friends." He was quite nice about it . . . said he'd collect it from me later . . . and went off. I couldn't go back into the lounge. When Frank came looking for me, I told him, and said I wanted to see you . . . and he could take that darling-of-the-regiment girl of his to the dinner instead of me.'

'Poor Frank!'

'He understood how I felt. Don't you?'

'You asked for it, you know. I think I mentioned that this morning. This social business has very strict rules. I'm surprised to find you take it seriously.'

'I'm taking it seriously on account of you.' He looked at her quickly. She went on: 'Of course she's doing it on account of my association with you.' Jeremy dropped his eyes, expostulating with a groan. She insisted, 'It's true. Everybody says so.'

'Who's everybody?'

'Well . . . Betty and Charlie . . . and Fergus and the others . . . talking about the lunchtime business. It is true, too. Didn't you see the way she looked at me when we went up to the grandstand with the horse?'

'I never see her.'

'Well, she sees you.'

He asked shortly, 'What's it you want to talk to me about?'

'I'm not going to give up the list.'

Again he looked at her. She was staring up into his eyes, her own dark eyes looking very wide in the moon-pale pixie face. Looking away again, he asked, 'Is that wise?'

'You asked me why I didn't go into the lion's den and defy her. I'm going to do it in the Dance Hall.'

He whistled softly to the distance, then asked, 'What's Frank think of that?'

'I didn't ask his opinion. I simply said I was coming to you.'

'What d'you want me to do . . give my blessing on what I think's a piece of folly?'

'No . . . give me courage to do what you'd do yourself.'

Again he looked at her. She went on rapidly: 'You've always defied them in their stupid arrogance. It's what you've done's inspired me to do the same.'

He looked away again, hooking a thumb in his belt. She seized the hand. 'If I give those things up to her, I'll give her a victory . . . not only over me, but over you. We're both in this. Let's finish it together . . . .'

'Now, look here!' He tried to get his hand free; but she clung to it.

'No, Jeremy . . . don't let me down. See me through it.'

'How?'

'Come to the Cup Ball with me.'

'Oh, hell!'

'I'm not asking you to do anything . . . only be there to back me up . . . '

'You have a husband . . . '

'It's you that counts. If you're there it'll be not just a piece of folly, as you called it . . . not just one woman refusing to be bossed by another . . . it'll be an act of defiance against the arrogance that woman stands for.'

He dropped his head, so that the moonlight glinted on the silvery mane. 'I understand now why you broke with her. People've said it's your arrogance. I know now that she's a woman ruthless for power, and only wanted to use you to get it . . . and that she represents a class . . . and . . . and . . . ' She finished breathless.

He said with a sigh, 'You know I never go to that silly Ball. I never could go now.'

'Not just to collect the Cup?'

'I haven't done that since it's become what it virtually is now, a Vaisey condescension . . . not for the best part of ten years . . . '

'Yet you run your horses in the races and collect the cups!'

'Where else would I run my horses . . . for what else would I breed 'em?'

She said angrily, 'That sounds like compromise to me . . . and I thought you didn't compromise?' He was silent. She said, 'I'm sorry.'

'That's all right. Life is half compromise, no matter how one strives for complete integrity. Didn't you go from the red raggers in Town to the squatters in the bush . . . . '

'For material for my book about what rotten bastards they are . . . . '

'Who?'

'Most Australians.'

He chuckled. 'I like that.'

She said eagerly, 'Well come to the bloody Ball . . . just to get the Cup. That'll rock 'em for a start. Then I come in and refuse to give up the things I was entrusted with till I met you. Can't you see we're in it together?'

He sighed, 'Only too clearly, my dear . . . . '

'Oh . . . you'll do it!' She shot up on her toes and kissed him fairly on the lips.

He pushed her away, muttering, 'Here . . . that'll do.' When she started babbling again, he interrupted: 'Leave it at that. I want to get back to my people. Come on. Come and join us.'

As he set off she grabbed his arm, swung into his stride, murmuring, 'Oh, Jeremy!'

He growled, 'Don't jump to conclusions. I'll have to think about it.' And he freed himself.

They came back to the table to find everybody busy eating, except Nan, who although she smiled her usual smile, was watching big-eyed. Jeremy said to her, 'She's going to eat with us. Some sort of row with the committee.' Then to the beaming Alfie, 'There's a seat next to Water Lily.'

Alfie didn't seem to care where she sat, so pleased was she with herself; so much indeed as soon to infect the company with her gaiety, talking about the wonderful food, fun she'd had at the Compound with the kids and everybody, her experiences as a *munjong* rider while recently out on the stations: 'I had to eat my meals off the mantelpiece for a week!' When some giggled and others stared uncomprehending, she asked, 'You know what's a mantlepiece?' Nan, squealing with laughter, explained to the ignorant ones. They whooped and slapped their thighs with mirth. Not so the rather grim-faced Mullaka. And Nan, for all her merriment, was still watchful.

Then the neighbours' dogs and the plovers sounded off again. It was Frank this time. They sat him down. He was his amiable self, ready with his laugh, but watchful like Nan. So it went on – till suddenly a burst of brassy music up at the pub. All looked, to see the glint of brass in the moonlight and Finnucane's glare, and surging people – *Roll Out The Barrel . . . pom-pom, p'pom-pom, pom-pom* – and there was the Military Band marching along the road towards the Dance Hall. Yet another innovation brought about by the stirring times, and probably the fact that Colonel Chivvy was Patron. The call to the Ball in former times had been merely the appearance of the Elite coming from the Big House in their cars. Almost all of the Lily Lagoons people and their friends leapt up to go witness the wonder of it. The plovers cursed; the dogs barked and howled; far away the dispossessed cockies were giving their opinion of it.

Jeremy said suddenly to Frank, 'You know what this lady of yours has in mind?'

'Not to give that list thing up, you mean?'

'Yes. How do you feel about it?'

Frank looked at his Alfie, who was regarding him haughtily, and smiled and shrugged. Then he asked Jeremy, 'How do you?'

Jeremy took a moment to answer, staring at his big hands fiddling with the silver, 'It was what was to be expected from Her Ladyship . . . and all of them. They need the stockwhip put round 'em now and again. They're too used to having it in their own hands . . . .'

Alfie interrupted joyously, 'He's going to back me up by going to the Ball with me . . . .'

'No, I'm not,' said Jeremy shortly. 'You're going to the Ball with your husband . . . if he wants to take you. I'll just be there to give the courage you said you need, but I'm sure you don't really need at all. Nevertheless, I guess my presence'll be a help . . . and it'll be something of a treat to see someone else showing 'em where they get off, instead of always Poor-bugger-me, as the blacks say. But we can't just barge into it. First, Frank, there's you to think of. These people are vindictive. They live by power and for it. Anyone who interferes with it is never forgotten . . . and they have the power to make those who defy them suffer. You've got your job to think of.'

Frank said, 'As a matter of fact, I'm in the process of chucking it. This Public Service set-up here's too much for me. We aren't able to do here what we came to do . . . except, maybe, with Alfie's book. It could be the means to bring down Cobbity and Co. utterly . . . and show up the whole rotten business of the ill-treatment of the Aborigines, the colonial arrogance of the squatters . . . .'

'The book's real, then?'

Alfie flamed, snapping, 'I told you about it.'

'I see lots of people from the South who tell me they're going to write a book about what they see. They've even been going to put me in their books, they've said. But I haven't seen any yet.'

Still snapping, she said, 'Well, you'll see mine in the New Year. It's nearly finished. Actually I only wanted to see these races to wind it up.'

'This Golden Horseshoe draw'll be in it?'

'Why not?'

'Law of libel.'

'No need to mention names . . . just tell the funny story . . . the horrible story.'

Jeremy said dryly, 'That sounds better. If you're doing it for fun . . . or fame . . . or anything but genuine anger over what your husband so aptly called Colonial Arrogance . . . .'

Frank cut in his clever way: 'Not my words, Jeremy . . . hers.'

It gave Alfie time to swallow what was making her eyes large and her face red and say humbly, 'I do assure you, Jeremy, that I was never more genuinely angry in my life.'

Jeremy sighed: 'Okay. But the thing's got to be planned, so that there can't be any failure. I happen to know the people you're dealing with a lot better than you . . . .'

'Of course,' she said eagerly.

'Although I haven't been in the Hall for years, I've often gone up to see who wins the horse in the draw . . . if it's a good one. This *is* a good one, as I think I told you. I'd like to have him. If he's got what I think he has, then combined with my filly's intelligence and courage, I'd have something pretty good in horseflesh . . . .'

'The breeder of classical horseflesh, who renounces his own kith and kin,' said Alfie.

Even Frank looked at her sharply. But her head remained high. 'Well, I've said it to you before, haven't I? This proves that I'm not sneaking to you to do me a favour.'

Jeremy searched the hot dark eyes for a moment, then dropped his own, and fiddling again, went on: 'I've bought a couple of good youngsters that way. Never won one . . . .'

Eager again, Alfie said, 'You might this time.'

He ignored her: 'Unless the winner has any real use for such a horse he's usually sold . . . on the spot, as a rule. It's a sort of ritual. I was going up in any case tonight in the hope of a bargain. Don't like bargaining for horses . . . but I'm not a rich man. So I'll be there, outside. No one will notice me . . . I mean the Elite. When the Cup's been won by a horse of mine, the Patron's always primed to say something like: "I understand the owner's rather shy of making public appearances," and gives it to Finnucane to stick up in the pub, as all owners let him do till the show's over. I'm told that sometimes there's a bit of a laugh over the remark. I'm never there to hear. Now, I suggest that Alfie keeps out of the way till the last moment . . . but not you, Frank. Gilling is sure to ask you where she is. You say she's around somewhere and will be along any minute . . . with what he wants. Any suspicion they might work up over her non-appearance'll be smothered by my appearance. Just as the

Patron's doing his stuff about my shyness, I'll stroll in . . . with Alfie. But you'll have to take Alfie off my hands at once. I'll get the blame for it all. Still, I don't want it to look like involvement. You stand with your arm around her . . . and well away from me. They'll then be busy with the other race awards. If Gilling should come to you in the meantime, put him off by saying, sort of whispering and all amiability, that she'll give it to him as soon as the draw begins. It'll follow the awards. Then Alfie marches up to the Patron, who'll be standing on the dais next to the President . . . and next to the President will be his Lady Mother. They might be too scared to ask you for the things after they've seen you with me . . . but if they do, as is quite likely, because Rhoda with her mind made up . . . well . . . anyway, what you do is refuse, addressing yourself to the President. He's the only person who can order you to hand the things over . . . I mean finally. You, Alfie, say they were entrusted to you with special injunction to take care of them, and that you won't give them to anyone but him. What he'll do is anybody's guess. It might depend on how much his mother has talked to him about it. He's afraid of her . . . but isn't above defying her in small matters. He won't be looking at her, but at you. I think he'd like to be gallant with you. But if his mother catches his eye, she'll have him, from my experience of watching them together. Still, you've got a trump. If he asks for the thing, say that first you'd like to know the *exact* reason why you're being done out of something you'd looked forward to with great pleasure. However it goes you should sink 'em . . . because everybody'll know what's supposed to happen, and if they haven't the courage to tackle it, the laugh is still on them. Got it?'

So overwhelmed by it was Alfie that the big black eyes swam, and she came and reached for the ruddy hands, choking, 'Oh, you're marvellous, Jeremy . . . you're wonderful!' He quickly got his hands off the table.

'Right,' he said, 'let's go.'

The band, now apparently ensconced in the Hall, was playing *Advance Australia Fair* and surely threatening to blow the rickety old tin place apart with its martial resonance. The music stopped as those who had designs on the social good order and discipline it symbolized joined the crowd outside. Those who presumed to control the order of things were arriving and taking the band's place on the red-white-and-blue decorated dais.

When the Committee was settled, President Delacy rose and started proceedings according to well-tried plan. He spoke of the great success of the festival, both as a gathering of devotees of what he called the Sport of Kings and a social event, and thanked everybody for their part in it, particularly the Ladies' Social Sub-committee, to whom he half-turned to bow, with an extra little bow to his Lady Mother sitting so straight and handsome beside him on his right. Then he handed over to the Patron, who rose amidst quiet applause, to say it gave him great pleasure to make the awards that the horse, the noblest of animals, had always had first place in Australian life, and always would, no matter how lesser people tried to glorify the machine; in fact one of these days Australia might find that she depended for her very existence on the horse, presumably meaning it in a military rather than an economic sense, seeing he was a soldier, not a knacker. He then eulogized the Cup winner, that is Golden Girl, getting a laugh by saying that it was a pity she couldn't be present to receive their congratulations, but they didn't have a chair big enough for her. Then, receiving the silver Cup itself from the hands of the President, he held it up for all to see, pronounced the name of the human owner of it, and was halfway through saying that he understood that the aforesaid was not one to – when, to the pop-eyed amazement of everybody, there was the man himself, looking very handsome and suave for one supposed to be an agoraphobe, accompanied by a pretty smiling girl in blue. Somewhat grim of expression, Jeremy halted before the Colonel, who, giggling with evident embarrassment, said, 'Ah . . . er . . . Mr Delacy . . . seems I was . . . er . . . misinformed . . . eeeeeee!' He thrust his hand at Jeremy, who took it gravely. Then he raised the Cup, which had been dangling from his left hand, and held it out, mumbling congratulations.

Jeremy took the Cup, looked at his staring crimson-faced son, who swallowed and said, 'Congratulations . . . Father,' and gave his hand. Again Jeremy gravely took the hand. Releasing it, he turned generally to the pop-eyed Committee, and bowed, then turned away, heading back towards the big main doorway. According to planned procedure, the Committee should have begun to clap as soon as the President had shaken hands. But, again it was the mob, crowding the doorway and falling back for his exit, that started the clapping. Then, somewhat feebly, the Committee took it up. But he was gone, in a way that made it seem doubtful if he had been there at all.

An awkward pause. Then Martin glanced at his mother, who seemed no less at a loss than himself. He turned away quickly, and announced that they would proceed with the Golden Horseshoe drawings. Evidently there was going to be no to-do about it. Mr Gilling brought forward the little brass-bound barrel on its slender legs and placed it before the Colonel. Alfie, burning and smiling, stepped up to the Colonel and from her satchel produced the box of celluloid numbers coinciding with those on the Horseshoes she had sold and the notebook of names. The Colonel returned her smile, likewise the President when she looked at him. She avoided looking at the Lady President. Assisted by Mr Gilling, the Colonel opened up the barrel and poured the numbers in, closed it, announced that the first draw was for the colt Golden Bobby, donated by the Eastern Pastoral Company, and turned the handle briskly, turned it back, turned it yet again. He opened the barrel, took out a number, read it, held it out for those near him to see, and called, 'Numbah forty-seven, foah seven . . . Who's the lucky one?'

Alfie consulted her book, raised her eyes to the Patron, at the same time handing him the book with thumb against the number, and turning toward the *hoi polloi*, called loudly and clearly, 'Ali Barba!'

There was the usual little silence that followed the announcement most of the crowd were waiting for with more than ordinary interest, indicating the disappointment of all but one, whose shout of joy was sure to come to start proceedings for good sportsmanship – and it came: 'Ho, ho, ho! Ali Barba? T'at me, ain't it?'

The burst of laughter that came with the hand-clapping rose up and up to a howl of mirth that surely didn't merely express amusement at the odd manner of the winner's response, but surely to the fact that such a figure of fun as Ali Barba, owner of a rickety van and two ricketier old horses, should become a racehorse owner, one of the Elite of the Nation! People round the door were already asking the old man if he would be running the colt in the Melbourne Cup as he came in, bobbing, smirking, ducking, cringing, babbling jocose inanities to cover his fear of the Masters of Mankind. Even the Committee were laughing, including that one who had called his name and worked the initial magic responsible for the miracle. He hadn't forgotten her. It was she to whom he first bowed, quite low, saying, 'Ho, peautiful lady . . . my many tan'k you for your most kind chenerosity . . . I moost mek you present.' It stopped Alfie's laugh, but no one else's. Back in the crowd they were hooting with laughter. Someone called, 'Gawd . . . there's no doubt about the old bugger, is there!'

Barbu turned to the Colonel, who shaking with laughter he was fighting down was holding out his right hand to him, in his left the rolled document in which was set out the colt's description, pedigree, brands, and particulars that eventually would declare his rightful ownership. Barbu bowed again, but not so low as to Alfie, and gave his black claw and took the scroll, saying, 'T'ank you, Sir . . . it is great honour and pleasure you pestow on me and my fambly t'is day.' Then he bowed, low again, to the Committee. 'T'ank you all-lot, gennelmen and leddies of Committments.'

Out of the laughing Committee someone bawled, 'Didn't you see it coming in your crystal-ball, Ali?'

A gale of laughter. Then as it fell and all craned forward for more, Barbu said simply, 'Yes, Sir . . . I did indeed . . . and see I too, my son-in-law, riding a race on t'is 'orse fit for a king, Sir.'

Barbu's show of astonishment at the continued mirth only made more: 'No doubt about him, is there . . . Haw, haw, haw!'

When it eased again, he asked the Colonel, 'May I dismissink now, Sir, and go gitchim my lil 'orse and tek him to my son-in-law?'

The Colonel waved him away, saying behind his hand, 'Go . . . go . . . before I have a fit!'

Offers to buy were flung at Barbu from all directions as he went back through the crowd, but most of them jocular – *two bob, ten bob, ten thousand pound* – since interest was still centred on the rest of the draw. He went out to the bright blur that was Golden Bobby stamping in fearful impatience under the milkwood tree, and spoke to him, as always to his own horses, in Hindustani. For answer the colt swung on his tether, presented his moon-dappled behind, and lashed out with a pair of nasty little hoofs. The old man leapt clear, to halt at safe distance, crying, 'Ho, ho! I do not see you do t'at in crystal. Wha' for? I am Barbu Ram, vit legality of ownershift. See! Turn your face to me, not your pretty arse. Am I not goot enough for you, because I am black?'

Jeremy came up and asked what was the matter, and while Barbu babbled, approached the horse warily, with coaxing words, let him sniff him, then touched and smoothed his shoulder. But when Barbu came up again he snorted and performed. Barbu wailed, 'It is my bad luck to vin a peautiful 'orse t'at hate me like a bought bride!'

Jeremy chuckled, 'He thinks you're going to put him in that van of yours. You better swear him you never will do that.'

Barbu proceeded to tell Golden Bobby that he intended him only as a racehorse for his own peautiful golden son-in-law. When asked by Jeremy if he really intended to keep the beast and being told yes, asked how he would train him, was told: 'My son-in-law haf mooch talent vit 'orse.'

'But he's only a little boy, isn't he?'

'He vill become big poy.'

'Meantime your colt will become a big horse, and it'll be too late to train him then. Better to sell him to me, eh? About time you pensioned off those I gave you and got new ones. I'll pay you enough to buy four good van horses, and give you a riding horse for your boy as well . . . how about it?'

But the drawing was over and the crowd pressing round. Golden Bobby began to snort and tremble and stir up the silver dust. Jeremy found himself with Alfie's arm linked with his. He seemed to suffer it. So they stood while the usual bidding started, in pounds this time, probably out of contempt for Ali Barba's knowledge of horse-flesh. Several young aristocrats were in it, including Clancy Delacy; but the rule was that they were not to throw their weight about in bidding, that if they really wanted a horse, they should wait till after the peasantry had decided the matter between themselves, and then descend in private on the winner. The Knowles brothers were also there, Nobby rather more sober than usual at this stage of the festivities. Nobby was the liveliest of the bidders, soon tossing at two pounds a pop. In vain did poor Barbu declare that he wasn't selling, that he wanted it for his son-in-law. Some wag got a loud laugh by saying that the old fellow wanted the horse for his son-in-law to ride instead of his daughter. Poor old fellow tried to lead the horse away. But it seemed as if even Golden Bobby was enjoying it, the way he was cocking his ears to the bidders, and then to the great delight of most cocked his hindquarters to his owner.

Thus till fifty pounds was reached, when Barbu began to look interested. It was now a contest between Nobby and that Road Works Renchouse Boss of Alice River Siding, Grayball by name. Fifty-five. Nobby kicked it to sixty; and Grayball fell out. Nobby yelled, 'Mine for sixty-quid, Ali.'

Barbu looked undecided, but didn't have to decide, because Jeremy called to him, 'That colt's worth a lot more than sixty, Barbu.'

Nobby, who had been in the act of going to get the horse, swung on him, all but spitting, the way it sounded: 'You keep out o' this, Delacy!'

Jeremy asked, 'Why?'

'You ain't biddin'.'

'Who says? I was just waiting till the price got up above what small-time shysters can afford to pay . . . I'll give you one hundred, Barbu . . . guineas.'

Nobby took a step back towards Jeremy, hissing, 'You call me a shyster?'

Jeremy, still in the grip of Alfie, said easily, 'Attend to your bidding, boy.'

'I hast yo', you call me a shyster?'

Looking past him, Jeremy said to Barbu, 'He's mine at a hundred guineas then, Barbu?'

Nobby swung on Barbu, 'I make it 'undred and five.'

Jeremy demanded, 'Hundred and five what . . . trouser buttons?'

Without turning, Nobby yelled, ' 'Undred and five quid . . . done?'

Because Barbu only gibbered, Nobby made another step towards the horse.

But Jeremy now shook Alfie off and set after him, got in front of him, saying, 'Not so fast, boy. You're still outbid . . . .'

'I bid 'undred and five 'gainst your 'undred!'

'You went to school, I know . . . but not for long. You bet in pounds, and I in guineas. You've only equalled my bid, not topped it.'

There was a loud laugh. Nobby swung on the crowd, then swiftly back on Jeremy, snarling now, 'Out o' me way, old-man . . . or I'll flatten yo'!'

Jeremy asked, 'Yes?'

'Yes!'

'You've been in the wars with me before, Nobby . . . and you were the bloke to hit the dirt . . . remember?'

Nobby shaped up, panting, ' 'S goin' be you this time, bozo!'

Nugget leapt at his brother, crying 'For christ sake no, Nob . . . you know what he's like.'

Nobby flung him off, snarling, 'I know't 'e's like with the dirt. But let him try it this time. Come on, Delacy . . . up with 'em.'

Others intervened this time, amongst them Clancy. Jeremy snapped at them, 'Get to hell out of it. Let the half-wit get it out of his system . . . .'

' 'Arf-wit am I?' cried Nobby. 'Well, cop this!'

He came rushing in bull-headed, arms flailing. Jeremy stepped aside, and as he blundered past, hit him hard in the midriff. Nobby gasped, grabbed at his gut, collapsed on his knees, fighting to get his breath back. Some men leapt on him, to pound his back and rub his stomach, stretching out his legs; but not among them Nugget, who came at Jeremy roaring, 'You dirty bloody bastard . . . you done it to 'im again!'

'Want me to do it to you, too?' asked Jeremy, heaving a bit for breath now.

'You try it . . . you dirty stinkin' rotten robbin' bastard!' Nugget came in in the proper style, left extended, right hand guarding his face, right elbow over that vital region his brother had left exposed. Now Jeremy shaped up. Nugget jabbed at the ruddy face with the left. Jeremy ducked. Nugget's right shot out and struck his shoulder. Jeremy's right shot out and hit Nugget in the midriff. Down went Nugget with a grunt like a pole-axed bull.

Now someone else yelled, ''E done it again!'

Jeremy said, 'Yes . . . it's the simplest thing in the world to do to fools . . . doesn't bust your hands, either.'

'Below the belt.' muttered someone.

Jeremy said, 'If you'll look you'll see it was fair in the solar plexus region. You can't drop anyone like that merely by hitting them in the guts. Anybody else like to try?'

Everybody except the very elite were there now. One of them, amongst the tallest, with dark pinhead silhouetted against the blaze of the hall, demanded in a strangely harsh yet not unmusical voice, 'Throwin' your weight about, eh, Delacy?'

It was Dinny Cahoon. He added, sharply: 'I'd get along back to camp if I were you.'

Jeremy said, 'If you were me, Sergeant . . . then pigs *would* have wings.'

There was a burst of laughter, that stopped as Dinny turned quickly on those about him. Then he pushed through those in front of him, and coming up to Jeremy, asked, 'Did you be any chance refer to me as a pig?'

Dead silence. Jeremy broke it: 'Are you on duty, Sergeant?'

'I am.'

'You're not in uniform.'

'I don't have to be in uniform to be on duty . . . so I'm telling you to get along home.'

'What I meant to infer was that, if you're on duty, you shouldn't be drinking . . . and to judge by your breath, you've had quite a lot.'

A gasp from the crowd.

'If you're not careful I'll run you in.'

'On what charge?'

'Disturbin' the peace. Those two men lying on the ground there were knocked down by you.'

'I've got a lot of enemies, Sergeant, including your noble self . . . but enough friends to bear witness that I merely defended myself when attacked. But by all means take me in. That'll give me the opportunity to call in the Police Superintendent and the Government Medical Officer to substantiate the charge I'd lay against you for drinking on duty.'

Another burst of laughter. Cahoon swung on the crowd, which fell silent again. Then he barked at them, 'Get moving . . . the lot o' yo' . . . .' and he took a couple of long strides towards those nearest, who at once fell away.

Jeremy turned to the gaping, cringing Barbu: 'Well, is he my horse, Barbu Ram?'

Barbu began to gabble, 'My son-in-law vill be mooch sorry if I sell 'im.'

'But you need money, don't you? I'll give you the money and a horse for the boy . . . and a couple of horses for the van, if you'll give me back those old ones to die in peace on my run.'

'You are a very goot man, Sir . . . but I tell my poy of vot I see in t'e crystal . . . and he vill be very disappoint.'

Barbu hung his head. Jeremy put a hand on his shoulder. 'You're a good man too, Barbu . . . if only you'd leave those little birds along . . . .'

'T'e 'awk tek t'e lil pird mooch more t'an I, Sir.'

'I know . . . you've given me that one several times before. It still doesn't make you anything but a destroyer of life . . . you a good Hindu.' Barbu drooped lower. Jeremy, still clutching the thin shoulder, went on: 'I'll tell you what I'll do. I'll let you have a pony for your boy . . . if you'll let me have this colt to train.'

Barbu looked up quickly. There were others looking, too, including the Knowles brothers, on their feet now, although somewhat bent from their usual erect postures. Jerry added: 'We'll make it all Legality, as you say . . . your properly horse . . . I the trainer. You can have him back after he's won his first race . . . with the prize.'

Barbu took the hand that lay on his shoulder and kissed it. 'That'll do!' snapped Jeremy, snatching the hand away. 'Let's take the horse up and show him to your son-in-law, eh?' He went to the horse, stroked his neck and nose, spoke to him gently, untethered him, took him by the halter. There in a flash to join him was Alfie, to take the other side. She was about to start a tête-à-tête again, but was interrupted by shouting from behind.

It was Nobby Knowles: 'We'll get you, Delacy . . . just you wait!'

He half-turned to call back, 'I first heard that from your old man, nearly twenty years ago. Can't a Knowles' mind run to something new?'

Nugget Knowles had his say: 'We'll get you all right, Delacy . . . just you wait!'

Jeremy said, 'Sounds like there's no such thing as a Knowles' mind.'

A burst of laughter from some of those behind.

'Shut up, yo' bastards!' yelled Nobby.

When Jeremy chuckled, Alfie asked softly, 'What was all that in aid of?'

'Tell you some other time. All went well, then?'

'Thanks to you.'

'No thanks to me at all. You started it alone, and finished it alone.'

'Inspired by you. I've never felt so strong in my life as in your company.'

'That makes me sound like a bad influence . . . and you can bet people are saying it right now.'

'What do I care?'

'Think of me!'

'What do you care?'

'I have my reputation as trouble-maker to guard. This country isn't big enough for two.'

She laughed, 'Oh, you darling!' and leant across the little horse's drooping head to kiss him. But he brought the head up smartly, so that she kissed the horse.

'Behave yourself,' he said. 'We're coming to the respectable house of Barbu . . . . '

'Not so respectable from what I've heard of it!'

'It was never declared a house of ill-fame . . . and never was that. The assignations alleged took place on the river bank. What man in this community is frank enough to have dealings with a coloured woman except like a furtive animal in the bush . . . except myself and Tom Toohey?'

That silenced her.

Barbu had run ahead, had opened the gate. There under the mangoes were two diminutive figures in white, one with covered head and black face, the other of much lighter complexion but inky hair and wearing dark glasses. Barbu cried out to the children in Hindustani, waving to the horse. Then to the white visitors he said, 'My daughter and son-in-law, Sir and Madam.'

Jeremy said, 'Here's your little horse, sonny. He's a little beauty, too. You want to make a racehorse of him, eh?'

The black head nodded gravely. Jeremy said: 'I'm going to train him for you.' Then he asked: 'Why're you wearing goggles in the dark?'

Prindy was silent; but Barbu answered, 'He haf t'e bad sore heye.'

'Let's have a look at 'em.'

'Oh, no t'ank you, Sir . . . it is not necessity. I am myself vit success treatink him.'

'Yes? Well, be careful you don't blind him. Better let the Flying Doctor take a look at him before he goes back to Town.'

'And so vill I, Mr Delacy, Sir, so vill I.'

The little horse, attracted by the little figures, strained towards them. Jeremy let him go. Alfie had already done so. He went up to them, sniffing. Prindy stuck a yellow finger out. The colt sniffed hard at it. The finger stroked the golden nose, then the hand. The colt whickered. The small hand ran up and along the gleaming neck. The muzzle sought the boy's jacketed breast. Jeremy said, 'Looks like they're going to get along fine. Right, old-man, we'll leave him with you . . . till Sunday. Then when my family go home, we'll take him along with us. The boy can come too, if he wants to.' With that he wheeled about.

As they went out through the gate, with Barbu bowing behind them, Alfie took Jeremy's arm again; but he shook it off, saying, 'Well, I've disposed of the colt for the time being . . . now I've got to get a filly off my hands.'

'What filly?' she asked.

He looked at her, and meeting the dark eyes wide with query, answered, 'You sound as dumb as the Knowles brothers.'

Then she caught the meaning, and flamed, so that the colouration could be seen even in the moonlight. He added: 'But it won't be hard. She's got a husband . . . a nice chap too. I think I even see him there outside the Hall. I'll hand her right over to him.'

She took a moment to speak, then asked huskily, 'Jeremy . . . when can I see you again?'

'Is it necessary?'

'Frightfully.'

'On account of what?'

'Everything.'

'You must have everything for your book by now?'

'I want to see Lily Lagoons.'

'You have my permission to go there whenever you like.'

'I want you to take me.'

'Sorry . . . nothing doing. Hello, Frank . . . here's your lady back. Thanks for the loan of her. She probably kept me out of trouble.'

Frank laughed, 'I guess you can look after yourself when it comes to trouble.'

Jeremy said loud enough for everybody round the door to hear, 'A man's a fool who can't. But having a lady with you is perfect assurance of peace around these parts, I do assure you . . . a white lady, that is . . . but it isn't gallantry so much that keeps thugs off your back, as fear of white women . . . yes, man, most of 'em go in holy dread of 'em.' There was some male guffawing and female tittering, in which Alfie and Frank joined.

Someone at the back of the crowd called out, 'That why you married black the second time, Jerry, eh?'

Another guffaw. Jeremy answered, 'No, man . . . because I didn't need a bodyguard.'

Only a chuckle over that one. Jeremy said to the Candlesmases, 'Suppose you'll be going to the Blackboys' Races tomorrow? See you there, then. Goodnight.'

He set off up the street. After staring for a moment, Alfie took her husband's arm, murmuring, 'Let's go for a run somewhere in the car.'

Frank responded with alacrity, and setting off with her in the same direction as the thick-set figure now only a blur in the moonlight, asked her where she'd like to go. She answered, 'Out to that place they call the Rainbow Pool.'

'Weren't we to go there with the Bishoffs?'

'I want to go alone. It's supposed to be a magic place.'

'Okay.'

Jeremy had to pass Finnucane's to reach the road that would take him directly down to the crossing and his camp near by; but on the bright-lit verandah, reclining in deck-chairs, saw a couple of persons he evidently wanted to avoid, so swung down towards the railway yards. However, he'd left the move too late, not having been able soon enough to see who the couple were because of bunting hanging at the end of the verandah. In fact there were three persons, the third cuddled up to its mother's breast. Jeremy heard his name called in a melodious soprano. He hesitated a moment in his stride, then swung to go as called. 'Hello, Bridie . . . Con,' he said, coming to the edge of the verandah. Con Cullity leapt up to take his hand in both of his, dragged him up to Bridie, who pulled him down with one hand and kissed him on the cheek. Con was babbling about where had Jerry been, never come to see the baby. Bridie said it was mean of him – and look what a wondrous darlint it was!

Rather red, Jeremy mumbled, 'Don't forget I'm the Scrub Bull . . . and bulls aren't interested in calves.'

'Go on!' cried Bridie. 'It's because you heard we want you to be her godfather.'

'For godsake, no!'

'Aw, plaze, Jerry,' cried Con. 'Plaze, man, plaze. 'Twould do us the greatest honour. Haven't we named the darlint after ye?'

'But it's a girl, isn't it?'

'Sure, 'tis a gurrl . . . and the most beautiful and wonderful gurrl that ever was, so help me gob!'

'Well . . . .'

'Jemima,' said Bridie.

'Hell!'

'What a thing to say about my baby!'

'I'm sorry . . . but . . . but . . . . '

'We'll call her Mimi . . . Mimi Cullity . . . isn't that a lovely name to go to bed with?'

Con guffawed, 'Sounds loike the name of an Afghan! But what's in a name, as Saint Patrick himself said whan he named the shamrock and t'others didn't loike the sham part of it . . . yawhawyaw! If she's Mimi to Bridie she's my little Jem, the gem in the crown of the king she's made me feel bein' her daddy-o, man. And you're surely not goin' to do us out of the great honour and goot fun 'twill be to have you shtand up there on Sunday in front of the Reverend Monsignor and everywan, and especially that slave-drivin' old splapeen himself, old Shame-on-us, who declares you an atheist, and say, "I do shtand godfather to this choild and renounce the divil and all his wurrks," or whatever . . . You'll do it old friend, for us . . . for me and me lovely Bridie, who wants it so bad, too . . . ye will, ye will? Den come'n' have a drink on it man . . . come'n' have a drink . . . and on the house, and divil care whet'er the old skinflint's got the contints o' the bhottle measured or no!'

Out at the Rainbow Pool, just the faintest iridescence hung where the water tumbled over the ferny rocks on the top side. Alfie declared to Frank that she *felt* the magic of the spot, despite the fresh litter of empty beer bottles and food cans and cigarette packets lying on grassy bank and shining bit of beach. They both remarked the fact that although the sand was well and truly trampled, only a couple of sets of tracks went into the water. Frank said, 'They talk about the blacks for being superstitious!'

She added, 'Jeremy believes in the magic of the place.'

'So the Bishoffs say . . . but I'd like to hear him say it himself. The Bishoffs're getting to criticize him like the rest, you notice.'

'He's a hard man to understand. Look, I'm going to clean up the rubbish. He wouldn't like it. He was telling me how the Races are turning the whole place into a rubbish dump. Come and help me.' They dumped the stuff into old flood debris beside the fall to the river, from where eventually it would be swept away. This done, Alfie kicked off her white shoes, then began to unbutton her blue dress, saying, 'Now I'm going to take a dip.'

'Eh . . . you know what they say about going in there?'

'That's why I'm going . . . and who was talking of superstition?'

'It isn't the hokus pokus I'm afraid of . . . it's supposed to be dangerous . . . and talking of superstition, *why* are you going in?'

She was out of her dress and standing in bra and petticoat. She said, 'Unhook me,' and as he slipped the bra free from behind, she slipped out of the petticoat, and then out of pants, to stand and stretch herself naked, so that the little tufts of axillary hair and pubes stood out like patches of jet on ivory. Eyeing her with head cocked, he remarked, 'Psyche at the magic well.'

She asked, 'You coming in too?'

He began to pull his shirt off, answering in a muffled voice, 'Course . . . didn't I for better or worse?'

Alfie went to the water's edge, stepped into it carefully. Dragging off his pants, Frank cried, 'No, wait for me . . . . '

But she took three long steps and flung herself down into the silver, to send it flying in iridescent spray. Frank was in after her in a moment. They swam only a little way, aware of the pull beneath, came back into the shallows, and played there. He, getting amorous, would have carried her up onto the beach. But she repulsed him vigorously, crying, 'No . . . no! It would be like sacrilege.'

He desisted at once, but asked, 'How come sacrilege?'

'This's been like a dedication . . . to . . . to what he calls the Spirit of the Land.'

'Hmm!' commented Frank. 'Well . . . we're dedicated. Let's get out and have a drink on it, eh?'

IV

Highlight of the Blackboys' Races was not any race at all, although an equestrian event in some degree. Prindy had ridden Golden Bobby to the Racecourse, not to ride him in a race, since the colt was as yet much too immature for anything but play riding (and surely Barbu, for all his simplicity, was too wary to let the boy show himself off too boldly) but simply to tie him up behind the Barbu turnout and feed him bread left over by the guzzlers of Barbu's curry who couldn't eat anything without a hunk of bread to stuff it down. It was during the luncheon break, between races and so-called Sports, when there was a goodly crowd at the curry, amongst them Nobby Knowles and that big Grayball fellow, both rather drunk. Grayball saw Golden Bobby and began to burble to Barbu about him, and so revealed the fact that the colt had not been sold at all. Nobby hearing it, whooped, and went round to inspect what he was declaring was his property. The little horse had his head in through the fly of the canvas curtain at the back of the turnout. When Nobby put a hand on his golden rump he lashed out at him. 'You little bastard!' exclaimed Nobby in that mean nasal voice of his, and made a wide and somewhat stumbling detour to get to the colt's head. Prindy, who could see through the fly, slipped the halter rope off the projection that had held it. As Nobby placed a hand on his shoulder, the horse backed out suddenly, saw him, perhaps recognized him, and lifting up his dainty hindquarters, pivoted smartly, and as Nobby turned to get clear, kicked with both hoofs fair in the backside, sending him hurtling into the crowd that had followed him round, causing them to stagger, so that he was without support, and fell sprawling in the dust, face down. There was a howl of laughter. A mob was gathering from everywhere: 'Wha's wrong . . . wha's a matter?'

Those who had seen it were too helpless with mirth to lend Nobby a hand. It was left to Sergeant Cahoon, in uniform today, since it was Blackboys' Day, to raise him, asking him what had happened. Clutching at his stern and grimacing with pain, Nobby panted, 'That bloody puggin lil bastard of a colt kicked me!'

Cahoon saw the horse, waved those intervening out of his way, and rasped at gaping Barbu, 'What's that horse doin' here?'

Barbu bobbed and simpered, 'Oh, not'ing, Sergeant Coon-Coon, Sir. Only ve brink him like pet doggy.'

'You know horses aren't allowed in the public enclosure.'

'He iss so lil, Sir . . . I t'ought it no matter.'

'Well it does. Get rid of him at once.' Then Dinny turned and looked at Nobby, still grimacing and clutching his behind: 'You could sue him for this, Nobby.'

'Got a bloody good mind to, too!'

Another voice came in, deep and quiet-spoken: 'Knowles laid hands on the horse twice before he was kicked . . . he wouldn't have a case.'

Dinny and Knowles looked. Dinny's thin mouth twisted. He said dryly, 'You, eh, Delacy, stickin' your bib in.'

'Somebody's got to keep an eye on the proper administration of the law.'

Dinny snapped, 'The law's my job, Delacy.'

'Maybe, Sergeant . . . but it's everybody's protection. You were advising your poxy mate here to take a liberty with the law that he had no right to . . . .'

Dinny's blue eyes, usually not much more than slits, popped, and the grating voice fairly split the air: 'What'd you say?'

'I think you heard quite clearly . . . and Knowles, too. Why don't you advise him to sue *me*, too?'

'By God I will!' cried the Sergeant, and turned to Nobby, who was pale now, and cringing, looking down at his dusty elastic-side boots, where something white was dangling by tape from his moleskins. Cahoon saw it, too, glared at it, then turned the glare on Jeremy.

Jeremy said quietly, 'See what I mean?'

Nobby bent and groped for the thing, pulled it out, crumpled it in his hand, shoved it hastily in a trouser's pocket. Cahoon saw the move out of the corner of a now slit of an eye, and turning back to Nobby, demanded, 'What was that?'

Nobby muttered, 'Bandage,' and began to turn away.

Jeremy said, 'It's a surgical dressing used to absorb urethral discharge in cases of venereal disease . . . commonly called a Nose-bag.'

Cahoon grated, 'What d'you know about it?'

'You forget I'm a Pharmaceutical Chemist.' Nobby was dodging away. Jeremy demanded of Cahoon, 'Aren't you going to do something about that man? Don't you know it's an offence for anyone suffering from VD not to be receiving proper medical treatment?'

'How d'you know he isn't?'

'Where's the treatment centre here? What doctor would let him get boozed while being treated?'

Silence. Jeremy broke it: 'If you don't look into the matter, Sergeant, I will. I'll go to your Superintendent and ask that in the interest of the health of the community Knowles submit to examination by Dr Fox. Are you going to?'

For a moment Cahoon, beetroot-faced, stared at Jeremy, then swung away, in the direction Nobby had taken, but swung back after a stride or two, to fling at Barbu, 'Get rid of that horse!'

As he went, someone in the crowd growled, 'Dead bloody nark!'

Jeremy asked, 'Meaning whom . . . myself or the policeman?'

No answer. But eyes turned away from him. He said, 'Teach you all to be careful how you tie on your nose-bags.' Then he turned from the crowd and went to the horse, now secured again, and spoke to it coaxingly, going to its head. Goggled Prindy was watching. Jeremy ran a hand along the pony's flank, causing the hind legs to jerk as if giving warning of more kicking. Jeremy withdrew his hand, and looking at the boy, said, 'The little feller's a bit too handy with that kick. Might be something wrong with him. I take a look-see, eh?'

The turbaned head nodded. Jeremy ran a hand down a front leg of the horse, talking softly all the while, got a fetlock, gently lifted the unshod hoof, touched the frog with a finger. The horse started, shivered. 'Hmmm!' Jeremy commented. He went to the other side, examined that hoof. Then, looking again at Prindy he said, 'Little horse got sore foot. They must've walked him too far and too fast coming here. Horse that young got very soft hoof . . . ought to be specially shod if he got to come long way. More better time we take him Lily Lagoons we carry-him-up, eh?' The goggles were regarding him gravely. He asked, 'How's the eyes?' No answer. He added: 'I'll take the little horse back for you, eh? Mustn't ride him for a while. You're lucky he didn't pelt you.' The turban nodded.

Jeremy led the colt away to the Lily Lagoons stable. Now that the racing was over they were packing up. The lunch table was also set, but not awaiting Jeremy, as seen when the other pursuits were dropped on the announced approach of Alfie and her husband. Then all came to the table. There was evidently a certain awkwardness never seen in this company before, surely having something to do with what had just now occurred up on the flat, and the reason, the newcomers' feeling about it. No word was said of it as the company settled down to eat. The first part of the conversation consisted only of jocular remarks about the Cullity christening tomorrow. It seemed from what was said that Old Shame-on-us, for all his allegedly having previously disapproved of Jeremy as godfather to his grand-daughter on the ground of atheism, was in fact so pleased with his acceptance as to be broadcasting the news of it. However, it was noticeable that Frank, usually so ready with his laugh, only smiled now and had practically nothing to say. Then Jeremy changed the subject abruptly, to say to Alfie, 'You said you wanted to have a last long talk . . . and also wanted to go out to Lily Lagoons with me . . . well, you can do both this evening, if you're free. I'll be running out there straight after lunch.'

Alfie expressed her readiness and eagerness. Jerry went on to explain that because of the condition of Golden Bobby's hoofs he would have to go home and get special gear for transporting him, hoof-cushions (a kind of boot for strapping over hoofs) and a vehicle specially fitted for hauling injured horses: 'That colt could be ruined as a racehorse for want of a little care. I'd like to know the mongrel responsible for knocking him up, and make him walk five hundred miles barefoot at thirty miles and more a day.' Jeremy's feeling was obvious in his mounting colour.

Frank then said, 'You have enormous compassion for animals, haven't you.' The tone was strangely dry. Jeremy looked at him quickly. Frank dropped his eyes. Alfie was silent. Jeremy made no reply. For a moment there was slight awkwardness. A few minutes later Jeremy and Alfie rose. When Jeremy looked at Frank inquiringly, Frank smiled, 'Leave me out. As it's to be the last long talk, I'd only be in the way.' Jeremy simply nodded, turned to Nan, pecked her cheek, saying he'd be back somewhere after dark.

Out of the Racecourse boundary and running northward, with Beatrice River homestead white-roofed through the trees across the river, Jeremy cut in on a pause in Alfie's excited chatter about her delight in what she was seeing, to ask, 'What was wrong with Frank?'

She looked at him quickly, then away. He added: 'If it was a private thing, no matter. I just thought it might concern me.'

She bit her lolly lip for a moment, staring ahead, then said, 'Well . . . as a matter of fact it was.'

He waited. At length she said, with another swift glance, 'He didn't much like what you did to Nobby Knowles back there.'

'Hmmm! A lot of 'em didn't. But I didn't see either you or Frank there.'

'No . . . we didn't see it. But . . . but, as you say, a lot didn't like it.'

'You too?'

She glanced again: 'Well . . . I wasn't there . . . and knowing you . . . .'

He waited, had to urge: 'Knowing me?'

'Well . . . you'd have a reason.'

'The reason was well and truly stated by the crowd . . . by one of them aloud, although out of my line of vision . . . but by the rest by their looks. According to them, the reason was that I'm, as the hidden bravo declared, a Dead Nark. Do you know the meaning of the term?' She nodded. He asked, 'Then tell me.'

'Well . . . it means . . . well, a spoil-sport.'

'That's the Australian meaning. The English dictionary meaning is a Police Informer. Comes from the Gypsy word *Nak*, meaning a nose . . . nosey. In English it's equivalent to the Australian term *Pimp* which, as anybody knows who looks up a dictionary, properly means a Pander, a procurer of women for prostitution . . . .'

She cut in: 'Is that the proper meaning of *Pimp*?'

'When I say proper I mean according to the English dictionary . . . which I take it is the one we have to go by, seeing that English is our language, that we don't have even an accepted Australian usage. You should know words better than that, being a writer.'

She smiled, but looked rather red. He went on: 'Misuse might land you in trouble . . . with the law, I mean. The King's English must be the language of the courts, however confused it might be made by lawyers . . . so you'd hardly be able to plead innocence through saying that you thought the language handed down to you from thieves, murderers, and guttersnipes, our noble ancestors, was quite proper to use without checking it . . . you, a writer.'

She looked at him somewhat bewildered. With eyes on the road he went on: 'I've been called a pimp as well as a nark . . . and've thought of taking court action for the fun of it . . . you know, claiming heavy damages for gross libel . . . but with the aim to show the awful ignorance of my fellow countrymen of the language they speak. I wouldn't have taken the damages . . . or would have given the money to the blacks. The curious thing is that I've never been called a Wowser, which is what I really am . . . and the word is good Australian, even if not in the English dictionary. Do you know what Wowser means?'

'Well . . . a . . . a spoil-sport . . . yes?'

'We're back to your definition of Nark again, eh? You'll really have to read your dictionary, literary lady.'

He flung a smirk at her red face.

After a moment he resumed: 'Well, we're back at Nark, in its local ignoramuses' usage, so let's discuss the condition of being such a type in those terms. Spoil-sport. Let's first take what spoil-sport means. I take it to mean one who through some perversity of nature spoils what more natural people would call innocent fun . . . right? Let's then take the great Spoil-sports of history. I think of Moses as the first . . . although there must have been lots before him. Read your Bible and you'll see what a Nark he was, with regard to the fun and games of his people. Then there was Jesus . . . the Biggest Nark of All. Literally Dead Narks, both. I'm called a Dead Nark . . . but the adjective has no meaning, as so much that our people say. I presume it means I stink in my condition of Nark . . . but why not say just that? Narkery, if there is such a term, is apparently a valuable thing . . . seeing that our very way of life is founded on the principles of the two dead narks aforesaid.'

He looked at her. Her eyes were round with what looked like fear. Turning from her, he said, 'You should have thought twice before coming out with me . . . seeing what you'd hear about me. Your husband, clever fellow, was too wise . . . .'

She said breathlessly, 'He didn't come, only so we could be utterly alone together . . . .'

He snapped, 'His idea or yours?'

She went very red now. After a heavy silence, but for the roar of the utility, he said, 'You confessed yourself to not much liking what I did to Nobby Knowles back there. Will you explain why?'

She swallowed, struggled, at last got it out: 'Well . . . it seemed like bullying, to tell the truth . . .' Her voice trailed off.

'Did you know why I intervened in the first place?'

'Something about the little horse, wasn't it?'

'When he found that Barbu hadn't sold the horse *he* proceeded to bully Barbu about it again. I happened to be going to take a look at the colt, because I'd seen the little boy on his back coming over this morning, and thought by his gait he was foot-sore. I saw Nobby handle him, and get kicked. Then Cahoon intervened and after bullying Barbu for having a horse in the enclosure, decided to make things worse by advising Nobby to sue the poor old man. Nobby said he bloody well might, too. I guess he wouldn't . . . but words are words, and the aim was to scare and bully a simple old blackman. Was it the act of a perverse and misanthropic person to chime in with the evidence that stopped the bullying . . . please answer me?'

Her big dark eyes looked near to tears as they met the grey. She muttered, 'Of course not.'

He waited a moment, then said, 'It's not that that's worrying you, though, is it . . . not what caused Frank to join the Dead Nark haters?' When she didn't answer, he went on: 'It was the fact that I exposed Knowles in public as suffering from gonorrhea, wasn't it?'

She nodded, eyes blinking on tears now as she stared at the road ahead. Again he waited, then said, 'I presume you don't know much about the matter, even though you were a Protector of Aborigines and in charge of a large number of women of Aboriginal blood, who if not actually suffering from VD were very much exposed to infection. You would not know that this country is rotten with gonorrhea . . . for one reason that the blacks, victims of the whiteman's lust and filthy dishonesty, have no comprehension of the disease except as some sort of affliction, for another, and most important, that the diseased whitemen will not seek proper treatment. If you knew enough about it you'd ask: Is proper treatment available? The answer is: No. The Medical Service is concerned only for the health of the whites . . . and the type of whiteman who gets Lit-up, as they call it, is hardly likely to infect a whitewoman. If it started to get about among whitewomen and hence among the whites of social standing, there'd be treatment enough then. Another thing is that types like Knowles are so proud of themselves as the Master Race, they just can't go and confess to a doctor that some poxy gin lit 'em up. They'd have to say, as the saying is: "Down the creek." They won't. What do they do? They go to the Chinese, who have all sorts of rubbish to give them. Some, I believe, get stuff from the

Government Pharmacist at the hospital in Town, on the sly. There is no proper treatment but that of segregation and constant expert surveillance and tests. It can be cured. I know. I'm a Pharmacist. I treat it myself . . . illegally . . . but only in the case of blacks, who wouldn't get treatment elsewhere, and in complete defiance of the law, because I would be glad to stand in court and take my punishment and make known to the Nation why I did it. The doctors and police know that. I'm too hot to handle in the matter.'

He paused a while, went on: 'Why didn't I report Knowles's condition privately? Because I know the bastard . . . because I saw him chasing after black girls only last night, because I know he's got no scruples. He must have howled like a hell-hound when he got his dose . . . but what would he think of passing it on? Any man might get it . . . but a man truly a man would seek treatment at once, even if it meant taking the first mail plane South to deal with a proper doctor. Why didn't I report his condition privately? To whom would I report it whom I could trust to do anything about it . . . policeman or medical man . . . when the information came from one known as a Dead Nark because he spoils sport that burns the life out of simple black women, sterilizes simple black men, blinds innocent black children?' Jeremy's khaki poplin breast was heaving, sweat on his brow.

For moments they both stared ahead. Then suddenly she shoved her curly head against his arm, one cheek against the back of the seat, the other clutched in a hand, and wept without restraint. He didn't even look at her, just stared grimly at the yellow road, swinging the wheel to its many bends, moving the streaming face a little with each movement.

When at long last she withdrew from him, dabbed her eyes, straightened up the mess she had made of herself, she said, 'I'm sorry, Jeremy.'

'What for?'

'For doubting you.'

'It was natural enough. I don't like spoil-sports myself. My trouble is I've got a different idea of what most of my fellows call sport. I truly hate this continued feuding with the Knowleses. My stomach turns over when I see one of them, knowing there must be trouble. Do you think I got any pleasure out of socking those two last night? I assure you I didn't. I know that no man can give me a beating. Those that could wouldn't want to. It's a very simple thing to knock a man down . . . unless you're a professional pug and dealing with your peers. The average man is a coward, and's driven by his fear to rage. It's glandular . . . adrenals. What a negative business to hurt people who can't help themselves! Yet, with the like of the Knowleses, what else is there to do? I'm their declared enemy because I picked up what they threw away, their Tantalite . . . and gave it to the blacks. That's what hurts them, and most of everybody else, worse than anything . . . I gave it to the blacks.

'If I'd put it to proper use, such as sold the mine to a big company, they'd have just said I was a smart bastard. But I've wasted it. I've given what it earns to people they consider utterly useless . . . because *they* can't use *them* . . . not as if, in fact, they haven't used the poor devils almost to destruction. But they wanted positive use out of them. They wanted them to become smart workers who'd make *them* rich . . . but hanging about like the lost souls they are is too much for them. There are people who, when they've knocked a man down just can't help but put the boot in. It's useless . . . but it's got to be done, because he's down and can't, or won't get up. The Knowleses are typical Australians. They are actually liked by everybody . . . Never had any luck, the poor bloody Knowleses, they say . . . and the devil of their ill-luck is me, Delacy, the Scrub Bull, the Dead Nark, the Bastard. They're all the same in their attitude to me. The only difference with the Knowleses is that hating me has become their justification for existence. Negative people that they are, they have to have something to fill the void . . . it's Delacy, the Dead Nark. The majority know it was fatal to sell out to Vaisey. Deep down they hate him . . . but dare not admit it . . . and so they hate me openly instead. It's the same with the RSL, the whole war business. They hated the dirty war . . . but it was all they had to brag about as achievement, having gone to it. Behind were the warmongers who profit by it, to cheer them, to call them heroes. They didn't dare say: "We're bloody fools." So they take it out on me. What do I do . . . call truce with them, the way I did with Finnucane to please his daughter, whom I happen to like . . . ?'

'She more than likes you.'

He shot her a wide grey glance at the sudden interruption. She added boldly: 'She loves you.'

He dyed red to the grey hair, turning back to the road, muttering, 'For godsake!'

She went on: 'Everybody says so. They say she was in love with you as a young girl . . . . after you left your wife.'

'I didn't leave my wife, as you call her . . . she left me.'

'Sorry . . . will you tell me about that?'

He glanced at her: 'For the book?'

'Of course not. So's I can understand you.'

'How'll that help?'

'They say it's on account of the break with her you're like you are . . . . '

His eyes were angry as he turned this time: '*They* say?'

'Now, don't get mad with me. You haven't told me about yourself . . . so where could I get my information?'

'If it's not for the book, why do you want information about me?'

'Because you're the greatest force in the land. Because you're a wonderful man. Because I admire you so much. Because you inspire me. Because . . . . '

'Oh!' he grunted.

She touched his arm: 'Tell me about it, Jeremy. They say that first you never got over your brother's being killed . . . . '

'Why the hell should I . . . the way he was killed!'

'Then they say that when you came home, bitter, hating the British and all that, and found your wife not only had sold you out to a British lord, but had a man who'd been a British officer lording it over your home . . . . ' She paused.

He said, 'Go on.'

'Is it true?'

'So far. Keep going.'

'Well . . . you offended her by throwing the Englishman out, so that she went, taking the children. Then you both got the sulks. She wouldn't come back to you . . . you wouldn't ask her. Then you took into your house one of her halfcaste maids, just to . . . well, nark her, was the word . . . and she was hurt enough to start a divorce, and you pigheaded enough to let her . . . .'

'Yes?'

'I'm still right?'

'Lots of small things wrong with it . . . but it'd be a fair interpretation of it for these people you call *They*. Any more?'

'Well . . . that the trouble with you is that you're a disappointed man. You won't compromise . . . so you lost your wife and family. That meant your purpose in life. That you then turned to doing what you have ever since, anything to annoy people . . . like putting the land back the way it was and giving it back to the blacks, and . . . and, well, I suppose, generally being the Dead Nark . . . but, and they say it quite kindly, really, that it's all because you're disappointed . . . disappointed in love.'

He swallowed, muttered, 'Christ!' He was very red.

'Well?'

He glanced at her: 'Well what?'

'*Are* you disappointed?'

'Yes.'

She swallowed, took a moment to ask, and then in a somewhat strained voice, 'In love?'

'What would you mean by love?'

She said a little sharply, 'Oh, please don't hedge, Jeremy!'

'I'm not hedging. There seem to be so many interpretations of Love. Give me yours.'

'Well . . . two people come into each other's lives who have a special meaning to each other . . . . '

'A male and a female, I presume?'

'Of course!'

'It doesn't follow. Human relationships are based on need. Some men marry women, but never cease to love their mother first . . . or their mates . . . '

'I said a special meaning.'

'You mean sexual attraction?'

'I mean everything between a man and a woman . . . that's love. Each fulfils the other.' When he didn't answer, she asked, 'Well?'

He shot her a glance: 'Excuse me . . . but it sounds rather vague to me.' Back to the road, he said, 'Love means something a lot different to men and women. It means something a lot different to men and women at different ages. It means something a lot different to individual men and women.'

'You make it sound very complex.'

'It is.' He added dryly: 'If I were you I'd leave writing about it till you've had a lot more experience with it . . . .' He blushed: 'I mean . . . after you've been around a lot longer . . . er . . . . '

She giggled at his being flustered, saying, 'I'm not ready to write of love yet.'

'Well that's a good thing. Stick to facts.'

'But I want to know about what happened with your wife . . . not to write about, but to know the truth. I want you to tell me about your brother, too . . . the war . . . everything.'

He sighed: 'It's a long and dismal story.'

'Tell it please.'

'Right . . . let's start with that filthy war. People are forgetting about it and getting ready for another. The next one will be the end of us. Write this, for godsake!'

'Why don't you write it?'

'I haven't the flair.'

'Of course you have! The way you talk . . . it's only talking on to paper.'

'I'm a disappointed man, don't forget. My expression would be only negative.'

'You said you weren't disappointed.'

'I don't recall it. I inferred that love had nothing to do with my disappointment, that's all . . . loss of wife and family, I think you said. You've met my wife and sons, of course. Can you see any cause why I should be disappointed in the loss of them?'

'I think the boot's on the other foot . . . they're disappointed in the loss of you.'

'That's their business. *They* left *me*.' He sighed, adding: 'I feel ever so glad about it too, every time I meet them.'

She laughed and caught his arm again. He went on: 'What I'm disappointed in is my country, my Nation. That's a terrible thing. Man may not be by nature a communal animal; but his very intelligence compels him to be so. Individuality is a thing to be fostered to bring out the fresh things, the new things, the advances, of the generations . . . but the purpose must not be selfish . . . or it cancels out. Every man must, in his maturity, dedicate himself to his species, his community, his Nation . . . but ultimately to his species. The beast creature does it blindly, in the rutting battle. Man must do it consciously . . . .' He broke off to look at her.

Her eyes were great and shiny as she regarded him, her cherry lips open with delight: 'Go on!'

'With what?'

'Your story of achievement.'

'It isn't a story of achievement, but of utter failure. My Nation, for which my brother gave his life in ignorance of the realities and I might have done the same but for waking up to them, is bankrupt of anything but what you have seen in miniature at this race meeting . . . stupidity, greed, guile, pettiness, cruelty. We, who could be the example to the world in intelligence, freedom, happiness, are bankrupt. Next war we'll be sold up, to become what we started as, Cockney and Dublin and Cardiff and Glasgow guttersnipes and hucksters . . . in Chains!' Another great sigh. Then: 'But, I'll start at the beginning . . . while there was still hope, while I and a few other fools like me could still dream of Australia Felix . . . . '

Yet again did Jeremy tell his bitter tale to a female, who by her expression, was listening as much to the deep male music of his voice as to his words. Thus did he show her those odd things to which he had given the energy, ingenuity, love even, of the maturity that he had preached should first be dedication to his community, his Nation, his Species . . . the crippled animals, the fossil humans, the land bursting with the wherewithal for busy modern man to meet the complex needs of progress, progress, laboriously remade pristine. He took her out for a peep at the billabongs, a glimpse at distance of the painted galleries. Then back at the homestead, while leaving her to look over the elaborate apparatus he had built up to keep the negation functioning to the limit of efficiency, the instruments, the books, he got out his animal ambulance and hooked it to the utility; and he collected the other things he needed to save a pony a bit of pain that could not matter much in the scheme of things, he who would, with a rapier word deliberately chosen out of the armory of his intelligence, pinion a fellow man and leave him with pride for ever bleeding.

Small wonder that while, as the Sun set, they sat in the lounge, eating a hastily prepared supper, she confessed that she couldn't understand him: 'You have so much intelligence, so much understanding, so much feeling . . . and yet it seems wasted.'

He replied, 'Take what you want of it and use it. You're young and not disillusioned. You might make something worthwhile out of it . . . . '

'Don't talk to me as if I were a little girl and you a hoary old man!'

'That's how I see it, my dear.'

'Well, I don't! You're a man in your full vigour . . . in your prime . . . . '

'Come on . . . it's time to go. I can't make much speed with that float behind.'

Away into the moonlight. She had told him about her visit to the Rainbow Pool last night, to his evident annoyance at the time. As they passed the turn-off again, she made bold to say that she would like to go and take another dip. He sounded quite angry in refusing, adding: 'You spoke of your first going there as a dedication . . . to what you didn't say. Now you speak of having a dip there, like one of those louts who come and foul the lovely place up with their litter. I think the significance of the pool that I tried to convey to you has completely eluded you.'

They were so silent thereafter that, like her female counterpart on the similar journey back last year, she fell asleep, and because of the swinging of the vehicle on the curves, more pronounced by reason of the other in tow, or perhaps from subtler causes, needing more stability in posture, she leaned towards him, on him, was soon snuggled against him, looking very young and elfin in the half-light. He gently nudged her awake as they came into sight of the lights of Beatrice Station homestead and the glow beyond it of the township in finale to the festival. She came awake smiling, stretching, yawning, saying she'd had a lovely sleep, looking and sounding very much like a little girl. Then suddenly her dark brows rumpled in a frown, and she said, 'But it's nearly over . . . all of it!'

'All good things must end, they say.'

Then like a little girl again, she cried, 'But I don't want it to end!'

He seemed to be ignoring her. She sat staring ahead as if in blank dismay. Thus till they were through the Racecourse and he was gearing down to make the descent to the river crossing, when she caught his arm again, saying urgently, 'Please, Jeremy . . . will you take me away on your bender?'

He swung on her: 'Eh?'

'I want to break the tension too . . . .'

'Don't be silly, girl!'

'I'm not being silly. I'm being wise. It's what we both want . . . need . . . Please!'

'I'm not going away this time. I have to take that colt back . . . and attend to it.'

'After that?'

Reaching the causeway, he accelerated violently, shot across, to pull in towards his camp, but not to go right up to it or to stop the engine. Darcy and his wife and Nan and others were sitting under the light. Jerry called, 'Darcy . . . come and unhook the trailer, will you, boy . . . I want to run the lady up to the pub.'

Darcy came running. Alfie said, 'I'd like to talk to Nan first.'

Jeremy said shortly, 'Plenty of time to do it tomorrow. We have to stay for this idiotic godfather business.'

Darcy called. Jerry slipped into gear, drove up the hill, over the railway tracks. Drunks seemed to be crawling everywhere. Jerry growled, '*Homo Australiensis Novis* . . . at the peak of his cultural achievement.'

'Jeremy,' she said urgently.

'The answer is No . . . .

'You don't know what I was going to say.'

'The answer's still No. I see your husband on the verandah. He's the boy to relieve you of your tensions.'

'Oh . . . Jeremy!' The great eyes were swimming. But the car was at the verandah, and Frank stepping up to open the off-side door. 'See you tomorrow,' said Jeremy shortly, the moment the door was opened. She had to get out, with Frank's hand on her arm. And as the door closed, waving, he drove away.

'What's wrong?' asked Frank.

She drew a shuddering sigh, muttered, 'He . . . he's inhuman . . . . '

'Didn't I tell you that?'

She swung on him, wet eyes now blazing, voice snapping, 'He's more than human . . . that's what I meant!'

'Shh, darling! Like a drink?'

'I'd like a lot of drinks . . . I'd like to get drunk.'

'Whoopee . . . here we go!'

It didn't take long to get Alfie drunk, because she was tossing off brandy; but drunk as she was, the Bishoffs and others who tried to get her to tell of her experience with the Scrub Bull could get little out of her, except that he was a mighty man, if an odd one, and a hint that she had bathed in the nude with him in the Rainbow Pool. Then Frank led her to bed. Curiously, when he had undressed her, she wouldn't let him put on her pyjamas, but falling naked on the bed, dragged him after her, hissing fiercely, 'Love me, Frank . . . love me like you never have before.' No doubt about it he tried, and she with him; but only to end up, she weeping into the pillow, and he sighing sadly over her rumpled hair.

V

The boozy mob had gone on their boozy way back to Town and to the Head of the Road, and much of the traces of their bacchanalia erased, at least the more obvious that might have offended the eye of Monsignor Maryzic over the route he would be taking in the course of his ecclesiastical activities in the locality. The Most Reverend gentleman arrived at Beatrice River, aboard Fergus Ferris's aeroplane that Sunday morning. It took a lot of really hard and smart work on the part of the Faithful able to be aroused by the shouts and boots of those two most ardent of them, Shamus Finnucane and Denis Aloisius Cahoon. It could never have been done in the little time available in the morning. Therefore Dinny, in his official capacity, had curtailed the final riot in the Dance Hall so as to get on with cleaning the place up last night. For that was to be the venue for the Cullity Christenin', which would be preceded, as all such events there and in similar places, with the Celebration of Mass and the accompanying practices concerned with the same according to the ritual of the Holy Church – *Glory Be to God*! as Old Shame-on-us himself would say.

A very different place the old hall looked with its mass of garish decoration down and replaced by the little permissible on the altar erected on that structure which served the several purposes of other events held here, the dais, for want of a proper word for the rough job it was. Not that there was anything rough and ready about the ecclesiastical adornment. Everything was of good quality and the proper order, kept for the purpose in a moth-and-rustproof chest at Finnucane's, and so for many a year. Here had been celebrated many a Mass, concerned with birth, marriage, death, and just plain sacerdotal bullying of faithful with little faith, the latter events being those annual visitations called Missions. The place was properly consecrated, despite its profane use. The Confessional was the little kitchen at the back. When the Monsignor himself was down to do the job Confessions were rendered rather more public affairs than the confessing liked, by reason of His Reverence's bull-roaring in reproof of sinners.

Most would prefer to forego the Sacrament in the circumstances, but had little chance against the power of his personality and the flexibility of his interpretation of religious procedure. Even the excuse that one had been drinking since last midnight, which properly precluded one from taking Communion and hence cancelled the need of Confession, would not work, because he would say something like: 'Who's talking about Communion? I vont to know vot you've be up to,' or, 'Did not the Blessed Saint Paul say, "Take a little vine for ze stomach's sake," mitout mention of midnight Saturday, and I take it you *did* drink for ze sake of your stomach, vot?' or yet to make a play on the aeronautical twisting of the rule that one must not fly an aircraft within twelve hours of consuming alcohol, to one must not consume alcohol within twelve feet of an aircraft, as he did on this occasion, perhaps having been appraised of it by that funny man, Fergus. He told a couple of would-be excusants: 'So long as you haf not drunk mitin twelf feed of ze altar.' He even tried to get Jeremy to Confess, telling him that his office of godfather could not be ecclesiastically valid without prior submission to the disciplines of the Church. Jeremy, who appeared to be on quite good terms with the jolly old fellow, the way they greeted each other, countered by saying that he had already Confessed himself, directly to God. The old man, probably well knowing how far he could go with Jeremy, replied, 'Direct dealinks mit Almighty God are not usual in our Faith, as you vell know, my son . . . but no doubt He vill make exception in ze case of vun so sufficient unto himself as Jeremy Delacy.' The sting made Jeremy redden; but he laughed with the old priest.

Along with the Monsignor came those two holy ladies, the Misses Cahoon, who brought a great basketful of flowers, as well as a change of shirts and socks for their little brother, a mission harmonium for Kitty Wyndeyer, and two small mission acolytes – full black and Aboriginal. By the way people stared at the little blackboys, the like had never been done before. When the Monsignor saw Jeremy staring, he winked at him slyly, as if to say: 'It vos der sort of t'ing you vood haf done yourself, ja?'

If the black altar-boys were something to stare at as they rode into town and up to the Hall seated in the back of Finnucane's big car on either side of the Monsignor, so nicely dressed in blue shirts and black shorts, with trim oiled hair, and leather sandals, they were indeed sight for sore eyes when they emerged from the kitchen-confessional-vestry clad in scarlet cassocks and snowy lacey surplices and with white birettas on their heads. Eyes fairly popped, all sorts of eyes, even one pair whose popping could not be seen for dark goggles. That hidden pair were inside the Hall with most of the others, because Monsignor Maryzic, before going behind for his own final investment, had got out amongst the mob who otherwise would have watched from outside and urged, and in many cases actually pushed, as many inside as could be got there, black and brindle for preference. He quickly pounced on Barbu, whom he knew, and his two children, and even found a place for them well forward on one of the forms. Prindy was dressed as usual, as the King of the World, but without the turban. He was sitting in full view of Miss Wyndeyer, who had her organ against the wall to the left of the altar-bandstand. She smiled at him and Savitra as she rolled out a Bach voluntary while awaiting the entry of His Reverence. Savitra smiled back; but not Prindy.

The blackboys, swinging their censers, chanting Latin in alto voices, led the Monsignor in – a magnificent figure in blue and white, a great blue flower-worked Y-shaped design decorating his silken white chasuble, with all the colourful appurtenances of his rank and order; such a sight, the three of them, as to turn the poor place into a cathedral and the drooping sweating beery-breathed mob into stiff worshippers at the Throne of God. They ascended to the golden cross and glittering candles, while the tin-pot organ did its stuff and the boys chanted of the Glory of God – *Gloria in Excelis Domine* – that a Bloody Boong could spout Latin!

So it went. Master of Ceremonies was, naturally, Sergeant Cahoon. He led the responses for the congregation, never missed a trick. Had he not himself been an acolyte to Monsignor Maryzic? His sisters looked at him as he stood with as much joy in their faces as had the Blessed Lord Himself appeared in his place.

Then when everybody who was qualified and could not escape the sharp eyes of His Reverence and Sergeant Cahoon had been effectively purified to take part in the act according to the canons of the Church, the Cullity Christenin' began. The font could have passed for a tall brass spittoon. It was set up just below the altar. The tiny red-faced silk-clad squealing bundle of humanity produced by the shining silk-clad mother and vouched for by the beetroot-faced tussore-clad godfather, with renunciation of the Devil and All His Works, became Jemima Mary, and fit to enter the Kingdom of God instead of hangin' about in limbo for eternity – *in der Name of der Fader, der Sohn, unt der Holy Ghost, Amen*!

It was all over bar the Head Wettin', to which those qualified to partake were pushing out of the holy place to get to. There was to be a grand dinner and booze-up at Finnucane's. Monsignor Maryzic and his boys had retired to the kitchen to disrobe. Miss Kitty Wyndeyer was rolling everybody on their way with a Bach fugue, rocking to the lovely rhythm of it herself and her own pedal-pushing and nodding and smiling to one with goggled-eyes who sat on longer than the rest and rocked slightly with her. Suddenly Miss Kitty stopped playing, rose swiftly, and came to the lingering little figure, said, 'Hello, you liked the music, didn't you?' The answer a nod. With a swift movement she snatched off the glasses, looked into the wide grey eyes, gasped, 'Oh!' As quickly as the glasses were snatched off they were snatched back by a small yellow hand and replaced – just in time, because there was Old Coon-Coon coming from behind, where he'd been to help disrobe His Reverence. The Barbus, father and daughter, were staring back in alarm at what they had seen. Barbu Ram cringed as Coon-Coon came up with them, staring sharply. But Coon-Coon was too full of his churchly duties. He went on past and out, pressing through the last of the mob. As Prindy turned as if to fly, Miss Kitty whispered, 'It's all right, Prendegast . . . I won't tell!' He looked back at her. She smiled in a wobbly way, whispered again, 'Goodbye, Prendegast!' He nodded. There was an open tin louver clear of people just beside him. He pulled at Barbu, who, grabbing at Savitra and ducking a bow to Kitty, followed him through it.

Now the unreliability of women in keeping others' secrets is proverbial. However, Kitty Wyndeyer had proved that doing just that was a basic principle of her existence. When she did depart from it in the past it was only where she was convinced that a more important principle was at stake. Then, what made her betray that secret she had herself declared – the whereabouts of him she called Prendegast? Was it true concern for him, for her own troubled conscience, or simply that natural female tendency released by a drop too much to drink?

The grand Christenin' Dinner was over and the proper Head Wettin' just getting under way, with the Tullamore Dew flowing loike the River Shannon and the Irish comin' out in all of us that had a drhop to boast of. It had been Champagne before that. Kitty had had her whack and got to the point of giggling, along with the Sisters Cahoon. She had been seated with them, perhaps as another maiden lady, while they were actually seated with their lanky little brother between them, and she had on her other side Mr Eddy McCusky. With what was bubbling in her mind and in her stomach and in the circumstances the temptation to tell must have been tremendous. Dinny's sisters, concerned more than any but official people in the existence of her known officially as Nelly Ah Loy, because as they said there and then, they had Grown the Poor Wretched Gurrl Up, asked their brother at table, this probably being the first opportunity they'd had for doing so, if he'd learnt anything yet of the whereabouts of the girl and her son. It so happened that Dinny had, and was loud-mouthed in saying so, because he had to shout above the din, for the reason that Eddy McCusky had to shove into it. Dinny didn't go into details, as was proper in such company and circumstances, but reported that he had definite evidence that the pair had been in the locality of Hang Gong Creek and heading this way. So Dinny, in his official capacity, must really have done his duty in dealing with Nobby Knowles. How much of the truth he would have learnt would be doubtful, Nobby being what he was. Dinny would want to know where he had got his dose of the clap and might have done a bit of arm-twisting to facilitate confession. Nobby was the sort of nobleman who would be more likely to tell who had given it to him, when the lady had not been as co-operative as he'd have liked, rather than to dob in the one who had donated it to him with at least a show of what to his like might be called Love. Dinny said he had sent his faithful Jinbul back by drunks' train, with instructions to drop off at Finish River Siding and go to Hang Gong Creek and work his way down from there. He himself would take another look round this district, because you never knew the pair might be smart enough to lie doggo till the Races were over. If he drew a blank again here, he would go to join Jinbul. Evidently McCusky had already been appraised of the situation and was very pleased thereby. As he confided to Miss Kitty: 'Those two made an awful goat o' me.' Surely that gleam in Kitty's eye meant: *If only you knew what I know*!

Despite the temptation, it wasn't to these people that she betrayed her self-imposed trust, nor there and then. As mentioned, the dinner was over and the Irishing on. Those not of the ilk or enough to become carried away wit' it, were either departed hence or in process of departing. Jeremy Delacy, perhaps loth to be suspected of likely to spoil the sport or maybe out of sheer guilt, was the first to go. He looked as if sneaking off, but was caught in the act by Alfie Candlemas, who primed with champagne as well as in what was obviously genuine grief over his going, made a demonstrative and weepy business over it; so much so that the mother of the cause of the whole business, Bridie, as primed as anybody, cried, 'I'm in this too!' and leapt into it with kisses and tears. Then when the object of so much affection had forcibly detached himself and fled, Fergus Ferris, about to depart for the airport with Monsignor Maryzic, who being no Celt was even impatient to be on his way again, leapt in to lap up the wasted kisses. Perhaps even this had an effect on Kitty, who standing out on the front verandah with the glowering Monsignor, saw it all. Anyway, when it was all over, Fergus called to heel by His Reverence and seeing to getting Finnucane to do something about transport, and Alfie standing staring wet-eyed after the broad-backed figure footing it as fast as dignity would allow for the river and his all-but-dismantled camp, Kitty walked over to Alfie and said to her softly, 'There's something I think I ought to tell you . . . but first you must promise not to tell anyone else.' Alfie looked at her angrily, perhaps thinking that an old-maid associate of an archpriest was expressing subtle disapproval. Undeterred, Kitty hastily told what she knew and feared, concluding, 'I don't know what should be done about them . . . but the authorities must not be told . . . not directly, anyway . . . not that horrible pair, McCusky and Cahoon. I thought you might be able to help them someway . . . with the grandfather. I've heard you speak about it. But if you tell anyone . . . I mean the police or anyone official . . . I'll never forgive you.'

Alfie, suddenly quite sober, breathed, 'Are you sure?'

'Positive.'

The Monsignor was roaring, 'Kitty . . . Kitty . . . do you vont to stay here und dance der Highlandt Jig till next train . . . or vont to come back mit me?'

'I must go,' whispered Kitty, pressed Alfie's hand, fled.

First Alfie looked down towards the Lily Lagoons camp, then up the road towards Barbu's. She put a hand to her mouth, nibbled rose-haw fingernails with cherry lips. Then she looked behind her. Although by the sounds the place was busting apart, there was no one in sight. She stepped off the verandah, went hurrying down to the river. She was crossing the railway when she saw the utility with the horse-float in tow swing out from the sapling frames that were all remaining of the camp. She began to run. But there wasn't a hope. No one was looking up; and in a moment the vehicles were on the road, on the causeway. She eased up as they went climbing the further bank. But she kept on. No one was left in the camp, she found, but some blackboys who told her the others had gone in the morning, except for the couple who had gone with the Mullaka, and that themselves would stay to stow away the camp-gear that was left here, then go home riding, maybe tomorrow, maybe tomorrow by'n'by.

She left them, to take a slantwise heading towards Barbu's, first along the mostly deserted river flat, then up the bank, over the railway beyond the station, to stop to reconnoitre from the shelter of the now work-a-day Hall, then to slip across the road to the little old shop, with its weather-beaten tin sign: *Barbu – Indian Herbalist & Gen. Merchant.*

The shop was open, Barbu behind the counter, bobbing servility. 'Vot is it your pleasure, Memsahib? So mooch am I in debts to you.'

Alfie looked over the shelves of herbs, the charts of fortune, obviously at a loss for the moment, then said, 'I didn't come for anything, really . . . I mean . . . I came to see the little boy.'

'T'e lil poy, Memsahib?'

Somewhat breathlessly Alfie said, 'The little boy you call your son-in-law . . . that's Prendy Ah Loy, isn't it.' It wasn't a question, but a statement merely wanting corroboration.

Barbu's black eyes blinked rapidly, but held the others steadily enough: 'I not understand you, lady.'

'Don't be afraid, Ali. I only want to help.'

'In vot vay help, Madam?'

'You know Miss Wyndeyer, the organist, recognized him. She knows him well. I do too. She told me. I won't tell the police or anyone. I only want to tell his grandfather, Jeremy Delacy.'

'Vot for you vont to do t'at?'

'So he'll look after him.'

'You not t'ink I can look after?'

'Yes . . . I'm sure you can. But you've got no legal right to him. They can take him away from you.'

'Nopody got legality for poy like o' t'at . . . on'y policeman, Mick Cusky, Dr Cobbity . . .'

'It would be fought in the courts.'

'I haf my rown vife and children tek from me . . . and in court t'e magistrate on'y call me dirty name.'

'You'd have to go to higher courts than you've been to. His grandfather'll do it. I'll ask him. He'll do it . . . I know. If necessary I'll abduct the boy and take him down South with me . . . and make the biggest row ever heard in this country over the wicked thing.'

'Abduct, Memsahib?'

'Steal . . . run away with.'

'Goodness gracious me!'

'It can be done. My husband and I are going away soon . . . overland. He can stay with his grandfather till we're going. Then we'll abduct him. His grandfather's gone home now. But I'll take him. I'll take him now, as soon as I get my car. Will you get him ready?'

'He not 'ere, lady.'

'What d'you mean?'

'After ot'er lady see, he runned avay.'

'Oh, lord! Where?'

'I do not know. He joost tek lil bits tucker and flute . . . and he is go.'

'Oh, they might catch him. Sergeant Cahoon's still here . . . and McCusky!'

'He is too clefer to ketch.'

'He's only a little boy.'

'But very clefer lil poy. Nefer do I see such clefer child for anyt'ing.'

'Where's his mother?'

'He say he do not haf mot'er.'

'But that's ridiculous. She ran away from the Compound with him. When did he come to you?'

'He not come to me. I gitchim in net.'

'You what?' Barbu explained somewhat. She demanded, 'Where did he come from?'

'To me he come from Paradise, Lady.'

'This is ridiculous . . tell me the truth!'

'Vy should I tell you liar, Madam?'

'I told you you can trust me. I swear I won't tell a soul about him except his grandfather. Don't you trust me . . . don't you?'

Barbu shrugged. 'Ze ot'er memsahib say she not tell nobody.'

'She told me only so I could help him.'

'And you tell grandfat'er so he can 'elp him . . . and who grandfat'er tell?'

'Oh, what's the use . . . you're not going to tell me anything, are you?'

Barbu shrugged again. 'I haf tell you everyt'ing I know, My Lady.'

Alfie's black eyes rolled desperately. For a moment she clung to the counter, then swung from it, crying, 'I'm going out to tell his grandfather . . . and get his grandfather to come and get him.' She rushed out, went running up the street, to the amazement of the goats just returned from their sojourn in the wilderness. She slowed down.

She found Frank, rather tipsy, looking for her. 'Where you been . . kissing the old boy goodbye all this while?'

She snapped, 'Don't be silly! Look . . . I have to go out to Lily Lagoons . . '

He shrugged, smiling mockingly. 'He's changed his mind, eh?'

'It's nothing to do with changing minds. He's already gone. But I have to go and see him about something urgent that's cropped up since.'

'Yeah . . . like what?'

'I can't tell you.'

'Can't tell your own old man?'

'Now, don't be silly, Frank. This is terribly urgent and important. Come along to the room, while I pack a few things . . . . '

'Won't just a tooth-brush do?'

'You'll make me mad in a minute. Is there enough juice in the car to take me out?'

'She's full up. But take *you*, eh? That mean I'm not wanted?'

'I can't take you.'

'May I ask why?'

'I can't tell you. I'm bound to utter secrecy.'

He stared at her, somewhat bleary-eyed, while she put a few things in a small case, among them the stockrider's outfit. When she was done, he took the case from her, and when she looked at him sharply, grimaced good-humouredly, saying, ' 'S all right . . . not stopping you. Have I ever stopped you? Just carrying it out for you.'

The old Rolls Royce was out in the parking lot behind, standing amongst a score of other and much smarter vehicles that nevertheless looked like dressed-up serving-maids around a somewhat battered but no less queenly dowager. As he shut the door on her he said, 'If he hurts you, I can't do anything about it but grieve, you know . . . not because he's an old man and could knock spots off me just the same . . . but because you're asking for it, you know?'

She turned wide angry eyes on him, 'Asking for what?'

He smiled, shrugged again, 'You'd know that better than I, sweetheart.' Then he planted a kiss fair on her cherry lips, hung there for a moment, then withdrew and waved her on. With face burning she started up, slipped into gear, and with a glance and a little wave, drove off. His face became quite sad as he looked after her. Then sighing, he went slouching back to the hotel.

VI

At Lily Lagoons, the winged watchers gave early warning of the approach of the big black car. Everybody was peeping when it reached the white gates. Identification was easy, of course, and not whispered through the place on indrawn breath as sometimes happened, but called quite gaily by most: 'Mitchis Elfie!' Only one of the household regarded the visit as intrusion, at least to judge by his tight expression and his shortness in speaking of it, and that the master himself, at the moment attending to Golden Bobby's feet in the veterinary hospital attached to the annexe. He dropped what he was doing to go to the telephone in the so-called den, and ringing the Big House, grumpily told Nan that he was not to be disturbed, that he would not see the visitor until he came over to dinner at six-thirty. It was then around four.

Nan came out smiling to greet the smiling Alfie as she drew up before the front of the house. Alighting, Alfie took the extended brown hand, kissed the plump brown cheek, said she hoped she wasn't intruding, bursting in on them when they'd only just got home, but she had something terribly important to tell Jeremy. Saying nothing about intrusion, only asking how she had found the trip out, Nanago led her into the lounge-room and seated her, then asked if she would like a cup of tea. Alfie said she'd love one. Then Nan went through to the kitchen, but to return within a minute or two, to seat herself and ask about how the party had been going and after Mist' Frank. Alfie, by her darting glances, seemed to be wanting to ask about Jeremy, but got no chance before there was the maid Cocky with a laden tray, dainty sandwiches and tea.

'What lovely bread!' said Alfie, nibbling.

'We been bake in camp-oven early morning.'

'I'd love to learn how to make bread.'

'I learn you. You stop tomorrow, eh?'

'I'd love to stop here for ever. But I came to see Jeremy about something very special.'

'He very busy now with horse. He come over for supper.'

When Alfie looked like expostulating about that business, Nan said, 'I get you room ready. I get girl bring in you swag. You like to read something?'

Alfie soon saw that there was no arguing against the rules of this household. When it was announced that her room was ready, she went up to it with Nan, set about bathing and otherwise putting herself to rights.

Jeremy arrived in the lounge, along with Nan, at exactly six-thirty, approaching the suddenly glowing Alfie with the outstretched hand and smile of the formally receiving host, as if they'd not met in a year and more, let alone parted only at midday this day with kisses and tears. He even said, 'Nice to see you.' Then when, burning with confusion she babbled that she'd come because she had something Terribly Important to tell him, he said, 'So Nan tells me. But you're staying at least a couple of days aren't you? Let's have a drink. Like one of my patent pharmaceutical cocktails . . . or a glass of my very famous beer?' They had cocktails, the three of them. When Alfie tried to broach the subject, he interrupted her again: 'We make it a rule here never to be serious while eating or drinking . . . especially drinking. Drinking should be done for the sheer fun of it . . . *The Subtle Alchemist*, you know.' He asked about the Christenin' party after he had left, and expressed disappointment when she replied that she hadn't seen any more of it than he: 'What a pity! It's sure to end up in a Donnybrook. Bridie and Colleen would probably start it . . they're ancient enemies . . . and Colleen's longest knife was the fact that Bridie had no babies. I could see the light of battle in Bridie's eye even while I mumbled the mumbo-jumbo at the font. Then the two boys'll get into it . . . then it'll be a free-for-all, with McDodds rushing in at last to shout of Eerish cloodhoopers disturrbin' the sabbath peace o' decent Protestant people . . . and getting a sock in the eye off Finnucane. Old Andy's always got to get out the Barley Bree when Old Shame-on-us get's out the Tullamore Dew. I'll have to tell you a few yarns about the private fun and games of the people of Beatrice River for your book.'

They went into dinner, where he kept up an amiable host's conversation. Then they came back to the lounge, for brandy and his special coffee and to listen to the news commentaries. When she tried chiding him for his interest in International Affairs when he had expressed indifference for the lunatic world at large only yesterday, he replied, 'I'm worried about Australia's involvement. Remember I told you that if we enter another war, as bankrupts, culturally and financially, we'll be sold up . . . and it looks frightfully as if we're going to be so involved.'

Well over an hour passed, while Alfie sat with dark brows rumpled, eyes troubled. Then, switching the radio over to soft music, he asked abruptly, 'Well, what's this urgent business?'

Alfie started, looked at Nan, said after a moment, 'I promised not to tell anyone but you.'

He gave a bit of a snort: 'If you mean you can't tell me in front of Nan it's silly . . . because I'd tell her, whatever it was.'

'But I swore.'

He quoted: ' "Was I sober when I swore?" ' . . . You certainly were in the party mood when I last saw you.'

The dark eyes swam, the lolly lips trembled. She muttered, 'Oh, Jeremy!'

He sighed, looked at Nan, who rose. He called to her as she headed for the middle stairway, 'Don't go to bed yet, dear. We won't be long. We all need an early night. Alfie'll probably want to be coming up to bed soon herself.'

The dark head drooped. He waited. At last she looked up, blinked at him, murmured, 'Why are you being cruel to me, Jeremy?'

He had to blink on that. He said slowly, 'I'm sorry . . . but I did tell you very definitely, you know, that I didn't want you to come out till I had gone.'

'I wouldn't have come, either . . . only for this.'

'No?' The question was dry.

'It's not just an excuse, Jeremy . . . it's . . . it's terribly important, as I 've said.'

He sighed. 'Well, tell me.'

'I've seen your grandson.'

They stared at each other for a moment. He said in the same dry tone, 'I have two grandsons . . . I think. One isn't accounted for . . . by law . . . .'

She blazed at him: 'Are you going to keep on repudiating that poor little boy?'

'I have never repudiated him. If in fact he's my grandson, it was his father who did the repudiation . . . .'

'Well, you've never accepted him as grandson.'

'How could I when there's no proof that he is?'

'You know very well he is.'

'I don't. He could easily be Dinny Cahoon's son, as some believe. But that wouldn't make any difference to me whose son he was . . . .'

'You still won't accept him!'

'Not till he accepts me.'

She was redder than ever and her eyes never so large. 'What a proud and stiff-necked man you are deep down! You don't accept anybody, do you?'

'On the contrary . . . I accept all who truly need me.'

'Well, this child needs you now.'

'Where is he?'

'I don't know . . . '

'For godsake, girl . . . what game are you playing?'

'I'm not playing any games. I'm trying to make you come down off your

Olympus and do something practical. I consider it the test of your life to fight for the custody of this little boy. If you fail it then . . . then . . . .'

'Then what?' The dark eyes welled, the curly head drooped. He said sharply, 'If you start crying, I'll get my wife down to deal with you.'

The head jerked up and anger flashed through the tears. 'Deal with me?'

'Sorry . . . badly put. I meant take care of you. Only a woman knows how to deal with a crying woman . . . the same as with crying children. Women and children cry for many things . . . it can even be from temper or artfulness. Men don't know. They can only guess.'

She sniffed and dabbed. When she had control he said, 'Now, without any histrionics, without any salvoes, tell me what you've learnt about the boy. I won't listen if you start your silly moralizing again. You know nothing about this boy, or me . . . or anything much at all, it sometimes seems to me. Now . . . please . . . the facts, and nothing but the facts.'

When she had told him what she knew, he sighed: 'Poor kid . . . so happy there with simple old Barbu, playing a game of being a little rajah . . . playing his flute. I heard him a couple of times . . . and you bloody harpies come along and drive him back into the bush!' He almost shouted the last, so that she stared at him, shocked.

He sighed again. 'Sorry. But I've talked about this to you before. If and when that boy needs me, he'll come to me. He might be coming now . . . running away from people like you, who're interfering with his life.' When her head drooped again, he said sharply, 'No tears . . . or the discussion's over.'

She asked weakly, 'If he comes to you, will you fight to have legal custody of him?'

'If he asked me to.'

'How could a little boy ask you that!'

'Madam . . . is it your intention to insult me?'

'I'm sorry, Jeremy,' she almost whispered.

'Now, let's have a last drink and go to bed. Tomorrow I should be able to find time to take you for a trip to the Painted Caves . . . .'

'Will you, Jeremy?' She was like an excited little girl.

He spoke to her as one: 'If you're good.' He raised his voice: 'Nan, dear . . . come and have a nightcap.'

Nan came smiling, in nightdress and dressing-gown. They had their drink, a special concoction. Then Jeremy pecked the cheek of each in turn, 'Goodnight,' and departed. Nan and Alfie went upstairs slowly, without a word round the moon-luminescent louvered verandah, to Alfie's room on the west side, at the fly-wire door of which they stopped, as if not sure what to do – till suddenly Alfie seized Nan, hugged her, kissed her, then fled into the half-darkness of her room. Nan went padding softly on bare feet round to her own room on the other side. It was a long while before either of them fell asleep. Likewise Jeremy, who sat reading in his den till midnight.

When Jeremy came across for breakfast next morning and found Alfie done up as a stock-rider, he suggested that she spend the morning learning to ride, with Darcy as her riding master. She was delighted with the idea, and added her own, which was that they might then ride out to the Painted Caves together. Jeremy chuckled, saying that part of the process of acquiring equestrianship was wearing-in the stern, so that not only would she be requiring an additional cushion for the truck ride out to the Caves, but a pot of ointment that was one of his famous concoctions. He delivered her to Darcy, but left abruptly to attend to his own business. He was almost as abrupt when, somewhere about eleven, she came to him walking stiffly and smiling ruefully and patting that wobbly bum of hers, asked for the ointment, but in such a way as might suggest to a man less circumspect that he might deal with the lovely thing himself. He sent her off to the big house, saying he would see her at lunch.

Immediately after lunch they set out for the Caves, by way of the little Vaisey stockyard beside the water-hole called Langunun, and up into the non-sacred galleries on the eastern side of that wide bay in the sandstone escarpment, to reach their object just as it was being presented to full advantage by the westerning Sun – as for how many suns in Time only the Sun herself, the Ol'Goomun-Ol'Goomun, would know. Jeremy went through the same procedure, as perhaps with all he took to see the show, namely that of sitting for a while in shade to accommodate vision to best advantage. But there was no such drastic effect on this lady visitor as the last. With hands in belly pockets, tossing curly head from side to side, pivoting for better angles of view on sharp-toed high-heel riding boots, her comments were mainly those of any knowledgeable art-gallery walker: 'Hmm . . . striking, isn't it . . . primitive, but striking . . . the colours of the earth itself. I like that one. What would it represent? A Dreaming Road? What's that? Oh! Look like a Catherine wheel spinning and shooting out sparks, doesn't it . . . eeeeeee! Colourful, though . . . complete mastery with the abstract.'

When they'd seen enough he showed her Terra Australis; or as he called it with a dryness of tone that was surely expressive of irony, The View. Her comment was: 'All those miles and miles of trees . . . a huge country, isn't it, our Australia . . . . '

'Ours?' When she looked, he said, 'Lord Vaisey's, isn't it?'

'Yes . . . the bastard!'

'Not poor old Alf who's the bastard . . . us.'

She nodded, 'Yes . . . us.' She caught his arm, drew close to him. He started moving.

As they were climbing down he asked, 'Well, how did it truly affect you?'

She answered at once, 'It was wonderful.'

'For what?' When she looked quickly, he added: 'I ask everybody that. It's interesting to hear the different views.'

'How does it affect you?'

'I'm in a very different position. I've seen it countless times. I've developed an attitude to it.'

'What's that?'

'I'm not helping you out in the matter, lady.'

Somewhat snappishly she answered, 'I don't need you to. I answered you by saying it was marvellous . . . that . . . that . . . . ' She boggled.

Not looking at her, he asked, 'Did it strike you as childish?'

'Of course not!'

'But you could hardly say it was sophisticated art.'

'It's abstract art.'

'Could you enlighten me on that term? I've read a lot about art . . . that stuff has made me, in trying to understand it . . . but the term Abstract as applied to it beats me.'

'It means expressing your individual self . . . not being concerned with any convention in the matter . . . you do what you feel expresses *you*.'

'Isn't that what children do with a box of paints or crayons?'

'Perhaps . . . but this is different. Children do the *best* they can without understanding what they're doing. This was done with real purpose . . . the Dreaming Road, for instance . . . or the Cloud Spirits . . . just the painter's own conception of it.'

'That's abstract art?'

'I should say the acme of abstract art.'

'Which is individual expression essentially, you said?'

'Yes.'

'How come there are literally hundreds of almost exactly similar paintings throughout this region . . . the convention . . . I suppose I use that word wrongly in my ignorance . . . changes only with what Anthropologists would call the Cultural Pattern?'

Again she looked at him, and more sharply than ever, and this time said, 'You're making fun of me, aren't you?'

He went red, murmured, 'Dear lady!'

Reddening herself, she said, 'You wouldn't, would you!'

'Truly . . . I only wanted to hear what you had to say to learn from it, if possible.'

'And you've learnt nothing!'

'On the contrary . . . '

'You mean you've learnt something about me?' She was angry again.

'I'm learning something about you all the time.'

'And I about you!' He avoided looking at the wide hot dark eyes. She broke the little silence: 'How did it affect your Lady Godiva?'

'You mean Lydia Lindbrooke-Esk?'

'I'm not familiar with the names of the British aristocracy.' He smiled slightly. She urged: 'Well?'

'As a matter of fact she bolted.'

'What d'you mean bolted?'

'Literally . . . like a frightened filly . . . she took to her heels in fright.'

'From those pictures?'

'Yes.'

'What on earth for?'

'She said she felt somehow rejected by them, by the country . . . .' He stopped.

Alfie said after a moment, 'Well, she was a Pommy, wasn't she . . . she was an alien in the land . . . the strangeness frightened her.'

'You don't consider yourself an alien?'

'Why should I . . . when I'm second generation Australian?'

'You beat me. I'm only half a generation . . . . '

'You *are* making fun of me, Jeremy . . . why?'

He reached for her hand to help her down a slab of rock, but kept it afterwards, saying, 'You're going to write this book, you know . . . and you need all the knowledge of the land you can. Any fool can write a book . . . too many fools *are* writing books. I want *your* book to be really worthwhile.'

She came close to him, to say suddenly and urgently, 'Help me with it, Jeremy!'

'Then it wouldn't be your book.'

'No . . . but it would be ours . . . which would please me more.'

'No, darling . . . I was never one for double harness.'

She cried, 'That's where you become negative . . . as soon as something positive's put to you . . . '

'This is where we came in, as they say. Remember our first meeting and first row, in Port Palmeston? And this is where we came in literally, too . . . see, there's the stockyard and the ute . . . our journey's end, you might say.'

Her eyes were swimming as she got into the utility. He remarked, 'Don't tell me I've been to all this last trouble to assist you on your way, only to bring you to tears!'

She bit her lip, blinked back the tears, muttered, 'No . . . Jeremy . . . I'm always a fool to cry.'

When she had recovered, driving homeward, he talked lightly to her of things she might use to leaven the heavy criticism of the country that was the main purpose of her book – Billy Brew, for instance. She said she had sought out old Billy on a station where she'd found him camped, and got nothing out of him but a dissertation on bush astronomy and native grasses. Jeremy chuckled, 'He was probably terrified of you because you weren't black. You'll have to get him boozing, and with a mob of other whitemen to protect him.' He told her some Brew yarns, made her laugh. But mainly she was silent.

Back at the homestead, he handed her over to Nan with a deliberate air of getting her off his hands, and in turning to leave them, directed his attention to Nan, saying that he had finished the business that had brought him home, and would be, as he put it, 'Off first thing in the morning,' – and would she have his tucker bags got ready? Then he was gone. Alfie looked utterly at a loss. Nan asked her, 'You have nice time?'

Alfie murmured, 'Yes . . . very nice, thank you.'

'I give you photo of cave, you like. I got plenty. People send 'em. Mullaka never take photo . . . not dat kind, only sick horse, or microbe, or sumpin like o' dat . . . but not country. He like to photo dat wit' his eye. Come, I show you, and you tek what you want. Den have bath, eh?'

Alfie was obviously at loss throughout the evening, despite the easy host and hostess manner of Jeremy and Nan. It lasted till about nine-thirty, when suddenly Jeremy said that, as he had an early start to make, he must ask to be excused. 'Keep on with the riding,' he said to Alfie. 'And the ointment, too, of course. In a week you ought to be able to get off old Bay Rum Betsy and ride a real horse. Darcy'll look after you . . . and Nan, here. Well, goodbye, my dear. Good luck with the book. We'll want to see it, of course . . . and you yourself again, someday . . . as is pretty certain, seeing you went swimming in Rainbow Pool.' He took her hand, and when she looked up at him miserably, planted a kiss on her rumpled forehead. Then he turned to put an arm about Nan's plumpness, to kiss her on the lips lightly, and say he'd be seeing her in a week or two. Nan clung to him for a moment. Then with a wave to Alfie, he was gone.

Alfie stood for a moment, staring with wobbly eyes, then, dropped back to her armchair, dropped head to hands, and wept softly. Nan also dropped back to her chair and watched her. When at last Alfie looked up with a shuddering sigh, Nan smiled, saying, 'You like him too much, eh? Plenty woman like o' dat. But he don't belong to no woman. He don't belong to nobody . . . on'y hisself.'

Sniffing, Alfie said, 'I . . . think I'll go to bed.'

'All right.' Nan went up with her, slowly, not saying anything. They paused together in the doorway of Alfie's room while she held open the fly-screen door, as if they had something to say. But perhaps it was only a politeness. Alfie murmured Goodnight, and went in.

Slowly, in the luminous gloom, Alfie undressed, was getting into pyjamas when she bethought herself of her bottom, and slipped down her pants and did a bit of anointing, sighing the while, as if the ache were less local than of the heart. Then into bed, to lie face down, dark head turned on the white pillow, one ear listening to the sad little thumping of her own heart, the other to the soft beating of the heart of this place that seemed to have no other but this central mechanical one: *Home, a-home, home, home, home*! To the synchronizing rhythm of what was not synchronized at all she fell asleep.

When she woke it was about midnight, and she lying on her back, and Igulgul just beginning to peep in, big enough for causing humbug now. Perhaps is was the Moon, maybe her bottom, that woke her. She rolled on her side to avoid the stresses of both. But she did not sleep. She lay a while staring – then rose, pulled her pants down and did a bit more larding, round and round the beautiful gluteal curves, up and down the smooth hot glacillic planes. Perhaps it was the nature of the operation, maybe something that had declared itself in the wilfulness of dreams; but she began to breathe deeply, and instead of going back to bed, stole out of the room, went round the North side, stopped to peep through a louver. There was a light in the den. She peeped only for a moment, then went into the bathroom just back of her, peed, took a drink of water at the washbasin and washed her hands, then out and back to her room for dressing-gown and scuffs. Then ever so quietly out to the outside stairway, to go slinking down in the blaze of moonlight, then to scuttle across the yard, with her short shadow bobbing along beside her like an attendant gnome. Somewhere in trees close at hand a mopoke was calling that the coast was clear, and afar a Willy wagtail singing of Wrong Side Love.

She stopped to stare for a short while at the fluted glass louver window with its light golden compared with the silveriness outside, then went to the porch-covered door, tried the handle, opened it, entered. Jeremy was in his den. An electric percolator was hubble-bubbling coffee, while he, in pyjamas, was taking stuff from a cupboard. He looked up as she appeared in the doorway, said casually, 'Hello.'

'Hello.'

'You timed it nicely. Sit down. Coffee'll be ready in a minute.'

As she came in she asked, 'You were expecting me?'

'More or less.' He was busy with the cups.

'Joyfully or otherwise?' She dropped into a lounge chair.

'One accepts the inevitable without much feeling.'

'You thought it was inevitable?'

He was getting out brandy. For answer he said, 'You'll have your coffee royaled, of course.' He put everything on a small low table between the chairs.

He poured brandy into the cups, then the coffee, then spooned in honey, handed her her cup. She sipped, said, 'It's strong.'

'Isn't that how you want it?'

'Yes.'

They drank in silence. He was first finished, poured strong brandies into glasses, waited for her, handed her the glass as he took the cup. She asked, 'Are you trying to get me drunk?'

'Isn't it your idea to get drunk with me?'

'I came . . . to say Goodbye.'

'I thought we said that last night . . . formally, at any rate.'

'Then why did you say you expected me?'

'I said more or less. Well, you did ask me to take you on my binge.'

Her eyes widened. 'Will you, then?'

'No.' Her eagerness fell. He added: 'We'll have it here.'

'But . . . how can we?'

'Why not? This is my den. My rights here are inviolable . . . except to pretty girls. Drink it up.'

Flushing, she downed the glass. He immediately refilled it. She asked, 'What about your wife?'

'Which one?'

She looked miserable, murmuring, 'Oh, Jeremy!'

'Now, no down in the mouth . . . down the hatch. Let's get properly steamed up, and see what comes out of it, eh?'

She drank again, shuddered slightly now. As quickly he replenished her glass. She said, 'You're not drinking with me.'

'I've had some already . . . besides, don't forget that the gentleman in the arrangement has to be perfectly trustworthy.'

'I trust you.'

'You've never been with me when I'm drunk.'

'Well, get drunk then.'

'I will . . . with you . . . with Alfie . . . Aelfrieda, the enchanted one.'

She smiled somewhat wetly, was already slurring a bit in speech: 'D'you think I'm enchanted?'

'Enchanting's a better word at the moment. Drink it. Come on . . . you've got to lay a foundation quickly, bring up the blood-alcohol content . . . then you can take it nice and molo.'

She drank again. She was blinking now. She leaned forward in her seat, said, 'You know why I came?'

'You said to say Goodbye. That was a fib, eh?'

'Yesh. I came . . . I came . . . I came . . . . '

'Yes, darling?'

'You call me darlin'!'

'Why not? You're quite dear to me.'

'Am I . . . Jeremy . . . darling?'

'Should be obvious. Come on . . . drink this one . . . and then you can take it easy.'

She swigged, coughed, then put her glass down very deliberately: 'Thash all I want.'

'Nothing more?'

'On'y . . . on'y to talk to you.'

'Okay . . . talk away.'

'I wan' 'o be near you.' She slipped out of her seat, came on knees to his knees, leant on them, chin on hands, bleary great eyes looking up at him, lifted her face to him. 'Kiss me, Jeremy.' When he bent to kiss her hair she pulled her head back so that he could kiss only her lips, and when he did, flung arms about him and clung with them and with mouth, until want of breath forced her to desist. Falling back to haunches, she gasped, 'I love you, Jeremy!'

He put hands on her shoulders, held her back when she would have come forward again. She cried, 'I shaid I love you. Doesn' it mean an'thing to you?'

'I find it most gratifying.'

'Don' be a bastard!'

'What else can I say?'

' 'T you love me . . . or you don' love me . . . do you, don' you?'

'Love's a very complex thing . . . . '

'Now, don' shtart philos-ph'los-fisin'.'

'I have to. They say a man's a fool or a philosopher at fifty. I'm well past fifty . . . and I don't want to be a fool.'

'You wan' me to be the fool.'

'That's just what I don't want.'

'Then love me, Jeremy.'

'One more brandy . . . . '

'No more brandy, I shaid . . . and you shaid . . . . '

'Just one more . . . and then you can come and lie in my arms and tell me about it.'

He rose and raised her and placed her back in the seat, and she fell back somewhat helplessly, poured her a stiff brandy, gave it to her. She swigged it, goggled, coughed, spluttered. He took the empty glass from her, set it down. She began to struggle up. He took her hand, helped her, went with her to his own chair, sat, and pulled her down onto his knees. She tried to kiss him; but he held her off, held her against his left shoulder. She took his right hand, and shoved it into her pyjama jacket onto her left breast. He left the hand there, fondling her gently. She smiled foolishly: 'I love you, Jeremy . . . I love you from . . . from . . . when . . . . '

'Why do you love me?'

'Why's anybod' love anybod'?'

'There are lots of reasons. But for a young woman like you to love a hoary old thing like me . . . . '

'You're not a hoary old thing . . . you're beau'ful . . . and that's why I love you.'

'Just for my beauty.'

'For yo'self . . . Jeremy Delashy. Le' me kiss you 'gain.' She devoured his lips wetly, released him, to pant, 'Take me bed, Je'my . . . take me bed an' love me . . . love . . . '

'All right.' He sat her up on one knee, holding her, because she was swaying. 'Just one more drink . . . and then off we go.'

'No more drink . . . . '

'But we're supposed to be having a binge aren't we? Come on now.' He slipped out of the chair while slipping her into it, filled glasses, gave her hers, and standing over her, said, 'Bottoms up!'

She giggled, 'My bo'm's all red . . . eeeeee!'

'I'm sure it's no less beautiful.'

'You ointment it for me?'

'With pleasure. Now . . . you right?' He drew her up. She swayed widely. 'Better carry you.' He slipped an arm under her thighs, lifted her. With arms about his neck, she sighed deeply, dropped her curls onto his chest.

Out of the den, into the passage, round into the other passage, and into the bedroom, twilit through curtained glass louvers. He lay her on the narrow white bed. She began to fumble with the belt of her gown. He removed her hands. 'Let me do that,' but instead of doing it, sank down on his knees beside the bed, and began to stroke her hair.

She smiled at him wetly, mumbling, 'Love me . . . I'm . . . . '

He whispered, 'In a minute. I want to look at you. Now lie still.'

She tried to speak again, but instead began to gasp and goggle. He asked, 'What's the matter . . . feeling giddy, eh? Turn over on your right side . . . that'll stop it.' She tried to turn towards him. 'No . . . the right side . . . or it'll get worse.' He rolled her over.

She caught one of his hands, breathing, 'Hol' me . . . Je'my . . . . '

He lay one hand on her breast, and with the other stroked her hair. In a moment she was sleeping, snoring softly. He knelt, caressing, for several minutes, then rose quietly, left the room. This time he went to the front door, looked out at the Big House, standing starkly white. Curlews were crying somewhere beyond it. After a moment he stepped off the porch, crossed on Alfie's tracks, climbed the stairs, went round to Nanago's room, paused at the screen door, whispered, 'You awake?' The answer was a soft Yu-ai.

He entered. She was sitting up in bed, her skin dark against the white of her nightdress. He sat on the edge of the big bed, sighed. She murmured, 'She all right now?'

'Yes, poor kid. I'll let her sleep till she's really out to it, then bring her over and put her back in her bed. She might wake up thinking she dreamt it.'

Nan giggled. Jeremy asked, 'Like a drop of fire-water?'

'Oh, yas.'

'Right . . . I'll bring the bottle up.'

When he came back with brandy and soda Nan was sitting on the edge of the bed, now wearing a dressing-gown of some pearly-glowing silky stuff with a faint Chinese pattern, and not the nightdress now, as could be seen by faint revelation of her breasts. Plump as she was, she had small breasts, like most women of Aboriginal race, not the flattish dugs of the half-starved of her age, but full, like a quite young white woman. He put the tray on a table by the bed, dispensed the drinks. They had two, while they talked of Alfie.

Nan asked, 'She chase every man like o' dat, you reckon?'

'I think she's used to being chased by the boys. Men like her very much.'

'You?'

'Yes . . . she's quite attractive.'

'Den what's the matter you don't sleep with her?'

'That'll do, now. You know very well I wouldn't do it for fun.'

'Might be good for her. She want you for somet'ing special.'

'Yes . . . some insecurity somewhere.'

'Den didn't you do wrong t'ing?'

'I don't think so. Anyway, stop arguing about it. I didn't come here to talk about her.'

'What you come for?'

'What you reckon?'

She giggled, touched his hand with her dark one, ran her hand into his pyjama jacket around his navel, an Aboriginal woman's trick. He pulled the jacket off. She released the cord of his pyjamas, rolled back on the bed and wriggled out of the pearly gown, while he pulled off his pants. He turned to her, chocolate against the bright whiteness of the sheet. She reached with dark arms for him. They strove in kissing, caressing – until at last they were locked together, panting and groaning in ecstasy. They fell limp, lay together, cheek to cheek, stroking each other gently, black hand on pale back, pale hand on dusky shoulder. They slept a little while. Then he roused, rose, kissed her awake, said, 'How about getting me breakfast . . . and I'll be on my way.'

VII

Alfie woke midmorning, lay blinking for quite a while before she saw beside her a tray of resuscitants: a thermos that proved to contain coffee, a long glass of some mixture of pineapple juice with brandy and cloves, two white tablets. She smiled wanly, rose with some difficulty to the edge of the bed to partake. Then she dropped back to her pillow. It was a good half an hour before she rose properly, went to the bathroom, showered. At last, looking something like her bright self again and clad as a stockrider, she came downstairs, although with careful steps, as if each gave her a whack on the head. Nan, evidently having heard the steps, came through the dining-room screen to greet her with the usual smile, to ask her did she want breakfast, and when being answered with a grimace, suggested a fizzy brandy, and led the way to the armchairs. Alfie sat down with a gusty sigh, while Nan did the dispensing. Nothing was said till Nan, with some dark and fizzy drink of her own also sat down. She asked Alfie would she go riding again. Alfie said with a rueful smile that her head might fall off, which made Nan giggle. Then Alfie asked, 'Where's Jeremy?'

'He gone.'

'Where?'

'Dat trip . . . he say Goodbye you last night. You forget, eh?'

Alfie blinked, furrowed her brows. 'But . . . but . . . . '

Nan said, 'You all right by'n'by.' She rose.

As she was going, Alfie said, 'Jeremy told me last night he wasn't going after all.'

'Oh, he gone all right . . . bee-fore deelight. I see him off.'

'You?'

Nan smiled: 'All-day like o' dat. He come tchileep wit' me lil bits . . . den he haf breakfast . . . den he go.'

Alfie went red. As Nan was turning away again she said, 'But I heard him say Goodbye to you last night too.'

Nan smiled. 'Dat only gammon.'

'What d'you mean gammon?' Then Alfie's voice, soft and somewhat hoarse till now, became suddenly harsh: 'I was with him last night . . . late last night.'

'I know.'

'How do you know?'

'I help put you bed.'

The brows ruffled again. Then the dark hot eyes blazed. 'You weren't there.'

'No . . . dat after he carry you over.' Nan started off again, heading for the dining-room. She looked back before entering it, to see Alfie rise suddenly. She stopped.

Alfie, heading for the stairs, without looking at her, muttered, 'I'm going after him.'

Nan asked quickly, 'Wha' for?'

'That's my business.'

'My business, too . . . he my old man.'

Alfie stopped and looked at her, said thickly, 'It's you that's the trouble with him.'

'Wha' trouble, Mitchis?'

'You hold him back.'

'I don' do nothing . . . only look out his house . . . tchileep wit' him sometime.'

'That's the . . . the inertia that's gripping him.'

'Wha' name Inertia?'

'Don't pretend you don't understand words. I know you can speak quite well if you want to. That's all part of it.'

'I don' know dat Inertia.'

'Well, look in the dictionary.'

Alfie, vigorous now, and determined looking, charged up the stairs. As she was packing her little case she kept saying to herself, 'He told me he loved me. We went to bed together.' She was down again in a few minutes, to find Nan still in the lounge. She would have ignored her, was heading for the front, where the Rolls stood.

Nan asked, 'What you runnin' after my old man for?'

Alfie flung back: 'To get him out of the dead grip of this place . . . to get him to do the great things he was meant to do.'

'What great t'ing?'

'You wouldn't understand.'

'Oh, yas . . . I understand all right. I live long time wit' dis man . . . . '

Alfie halted in the front doorway. 'I told you that's the trouble. I'm going to change all that . . . . Goodbye!'

She went out. But Nan came hurrying after her, called to her, 'You goin' 'o get hurt, spone you go chasin' after him. You can't catch him up.'

'We'll see about that.'

'You can't . . . 'cause he don't want you . . . I talk you true.'

Alfie, about to get into the car, turned. Coming up to her, Nan, now with arms folded on that small but somehow ample bosom, said, 'You tell me wha' for you want dat man . . . and if dat goot t'ing I help you. Spone he love you, he want you . . . I let him go. I never stop him.' Alfie stared at her. Nan urged: 'Come on . . . you tell me.'

It took Alfie a moment to get it out: 'He's too great a man to be stuck here doing nothing. There're great things for him to do. I can help him to do those great things. You can't.'

'Wha's dis great t'ings?'

'You wouldn't understand.'

'Why don't I understand. You reckon I can read-an'-write all right. You talkin' 'bout politics and t'ings . . . he not interested, on'y so dey don' hurt dis country . . . .'

'The great things are for this country.'

'He do 'em if he t'ink right. He done plenty. All the time he fight Vaisey's . . . .'

'That's not enough. That's a negative. He has to do positive things . . . and I can make him.'

'How?'

Alfie hesitated: 'With . . . with my love.'

'Wha' you know 'bout love?'

'What do you?'

'I don' know 'bout chasin' after man . . . and man chasin' after me . . . but I know plenty 'bout how I feel for dat man . . . and how he feel for me.'

'You? You're only his servant.'

'Might be . . . but I t'ink he like me lot more too. He tell you how I come to be his wife?'

Alfie said shortly, 'He took you out of a blacks' camp to annoy his first wife.'

'Dat not true. I was dyin' o' gonorrhea and starvation. Dat lot Delacy chuck me out. No matter who been chuck me out. Jeremy help me all-same. Plenty other black girl, halfcaste girl, he help like o' dat. He don't fix 'em up for pug 'em after. He fix 'em up like he fix up ev't'ing weak and sick and nobody else care about. He kind man . . . brave, kind, clever man. Da's what git him down . . . what you call negative . . . all meanness, unkindness, cruelty in country, in world. He don' wan' 'o go puggin no woman . . . on'y dat woman wan' him for some real, true, honest t'ing. You wan' 'o get him puggin you last night, ain't it? It didn't work.'

Alfie went deep red; and her eyes widened; and she was about to clamber into the car, when Nanago added: 'Jes minute . . . I tell you sumpin, you can put in you book.' Alfie paused, turned. Nan went on: 'Blackfeller reckon dere one kind debil-woman . . . *Min-minya* dey call-yem. Dat same name for Fly-catcher Plant . . . you know, dat lil gold and rainbow t'ing, got him honey dew, you see him dark place or night-time. Well, dat *Min-minya*, she wait for lonely blackfeller. Den she change into pretty girl . . . aw, tweet-one, tweet-one! Got'm tit like o' dat *Mangun* plum. Spone dat man too weak, he listen dat *Min-minya* sing him *charada*, love song, he finish. All-same dat Fly-catcher gitchim moth and flyin' ant and t'ing, she get him into *kumara* . . . ' She touched her pubic region. 'She suck him . . . she suck him dry. No matter he go home . . . he die finish. Das only blackfeller yarn. But plenty woman like o' dat properly . . . some black woman, but mostly halfcaste, and white woman. Dat first wife belong 'o Jeremy like o' dat. Dat one Lady Lydia, too. Might be you lil bits, eh? You wan' sitrong man . . . mek you sitrong. You husband, he weak man. Might-be you been suck him too much . . . oh!' Alfie's pale hand flashed out – *Slap*!

While Nan blinked and clasped the stinging cheek, Alfie leapt into the big car, started it with a roar, slipped into gear, swung round the turning circle, headed for the gate. The crowd of black kids who had been lurking waiting to open the gate since seeing Mitchis Elfie come out, raced to do their job, but gave no such squeal of farewell as might be expected, perhaps having seen what happened, but at any rate too observant to be taken in by the twisted smile and the little wave she gave them, and which was as much as they gave in return.

So fast did Alfie drive that great old juggernaut for the first couple of miles that it was a wonder she and it survived them. After a couple of near-misses of biggish trees on bends she eased up. She was going fairly slowly, brows ruffled in thought now, instead of arching in anger, when she came to the turn-off to the Rainbow Pool. She recognized it, which was a feat for a non-bush woman, looked along it as she passed; then, after having gone past some fifty yards, suddenly applied the brakes, went into reverse, and back to it, turned into it, drove the short distance to reach it. She sat a while staring, then got out, went to the little beach, stood staring some more, then retreated to shade back amongst the flood debris. She sat down with a heavy sigh. The pool was ablaze with noon. Perhaps her head was aching. She dropped it to her hands.

She had been sitting there for about half an hour when she became aware of a sound: a droning. But for the fact that the wind was blowing from the north-east and pretty fresh she might have heard it earlier. As it was, it was quite close at hand . . . obviously a motor vehicle slowly following the rough track in from the road. First surprise in her face; then excitement. She jumped up, was coming out of the shade, but stopped. When she heard the car stop, she went swiftly back to the spot and sat down again. A car door slammed. In a moment the sound of hurrying steps. Her husband appeared, hastening to the water's edge. The excitement vanished, she looked even annoyed. Frank looked at her tracks in the sand, saw them slanting back, looked, saw her. No doubt about his relief. The tense look was swept away by the usual smile: 'Hello!'

Her answer was barely audible. He went to her. She avoided his eyes, staring out across the pool. He asked, 'Something go wrong?' She was silent. He sank down beside her with a sigh. After a moment he said, 'Saw the old boy arrive in Beatrice while I was sitting out waiting for breakfast. He didn't stop . . . just waved and went on to Ali Barba's. That struck me as odd. But I thought he might be coming back . . . so I waited. After a while I saw him go on . . . heading for the open spaces, no doubt. That's what the others said, anyway. McCusky had a bit more to say. He was a bit hung-over from a party they'd been having to get over the christening party. He said, "You're lucky he didn't take your Missus along with him . . . like he did Lord Vaisey's girl-friend last year." I thought it better to laugh than hit him. Anyway, I thought you'd be along in the car sooner or later. But the way he did it . . . the old fellow, I mean . . . worried me. I went along to Ali Barba just to see if he'd have anything to say. But he looked positively frightened. McCusky and Cahoon had been bullying him the day before, I know. They're still looking for that little boy, Prendegast. So I thought I'd take a chance and come out and see how things were . . . and I sure did get a fright when I saw the old bus's tyre-marks coming in here . . . like on second thoughts.'

She asked dryly, 'Why should I want to drown myself?'

'I never said anything about you drowning yourself. I was worried about you swimming here alone.'

'I might have had someone with me.'

'Remember the second thoughts of the tyres.'

'Quite a detective, aren't you?'

He sighed. 'I can't afford to miss anything, when your welfare's at stake.'

She looked at him. He smiled. 'You look a bit down in the mouth, my love.'

'I had too much to drink last night.'

'That all?' She nodded to the pool. 'Were you on your way back?'

'Yes . . . I just came in to take a last look at the place.'

'Last look? I thought that once you'd been in that pool you'd always have to come back.'

She gave a sickly little smile.

'Where next?' he asked.

'I want to go back South . . . straight back South. I don't want even to go back to Port Palmeston. We left nothing much behind. I feel like getting on and finishing the book . . . but down there . . . not here.'

'Might be a good idea, too . . . to get it into better perspective.'

'It isn't that. I've got to hate it.'

'So suddenly?'

'No . . . I think I've rather hated it all the time. They're horrible people. That's what the book's about . . . horrible people, who think they're wonderful . . . .'

'Jeremy Delacy, too?'

'He's part of it . . . even in fighting the others. He only fights them for the sake of it. Negative, as I've said all along. The whole country's negative . . . the land too, I mean, the climate. It doesn't seem like Australia, does it? That's what we first said when we came into it, remember?'

He said slowly, 'Maybe Australia's really the civilized part of *Terra Australis* . . . the part we Europeans've made out of a wilderness. This's still Blackfellers' Country, as you hear some people who don't like it say.'

She looked interested, and then quite animated: 'Why, yes,' she cried. 'You've got something there. Being an Australian isn't being a blackfellow . . . just the opposite. That's where Jeremy Delacy's wrong. It's got to be civilized

. . . the blacks've got to be civilized. We've a continent to win . . . a nation to build!'

'Atta gal . . . the book's working!'

'Yes . . . let's go and do it.' She leapt up.

He leapt up and grabbed her. 'What about just a wee little swim in the nuddy first, eh? We mightn't ever get the chance again.' When she looked doubtful, he added: 'Just to defy that old Rainbow Snake . . . just to show he doesn't mean a thing to us Dinky-di Aussies . . . eh?'

She chuckled, 'Okay.'

They went to the beach. She let him undress her, caress her. They plunged in, swam close to the pull, came out. This time when he laid hold of her on the beach, her skin darkened in a flush all over, her eyes grew wide, her red lips fuller. He pulled her down, and while she lay with eyes closed, caressed her all over, with hands and mouth, until she reached for him, drew him onto her, into her, clasping him with what seemed like sheer ferocity, with arms, with legs – until he fell limp.

As they lay like that, after a while she asked, 'D'you think I'm a harpy?'

He raised his head quickly from her shoulder: 'Eh . . . why d'you say that?'

'Nothing . . . I just asked.'

'Did somebody say you were . . . the old fellow?'

'No . . . no!'

'Well . . . . '

'I was just wondering. They'd been telling me about black devil-women who catch men and make them make love to them, and steal their souls or something.'

'Who told you that.'

'Er . . . the blacks.'

'Sort of succubuses . . . or succubi, or whatever the plural is, eh? Nice way to lose your soul, anyway.'

'You think so?'

'I can think of no lovelier way of dying . . . except in your arms, my beautiful, my wonderful . . . harpy!'

She kissed him hard. Then struggled to get free of him, saying, 'Come on . . . we've got to go . . . nearly three thousand miles of a continent . . . a continent we've got to win!'

Book Two

AUSTRALIA FELIX

CHAPTER ELEVEN

There was no denying the combined astuteness and relentlessness of those man-trackers, Police Sergeant Cahoon and his Black Shadow, Tracker Jinbul. When they turned up again together at Beatrice River township, which was some six weeks after the Races, you could tell by their beards, their leanness, and their raggedness, that they'd travelled a long hard track in the meantime, and also by the smugness of their expressions that they had, as usual, accomplished what they had set out to do; or as near as dammit.

It was mid-November, which meant the height of the Mango Season, a very important matter to everybody in the country where they happened to grow; and not simply to human beings, but to manifold species of birds and beasts as well; such being the weakness of pretty well all creatures for the fruit's golden lusciousness in this mostly harsh and bitter land. Pretty well everybody and everything not too shy to come amongst men get the gripes from gorging. Still they gorged. And this season, probably no one gorged themselves more than those two hungry and thirsty wanderers in from who knew where, Coon-Coon and his Shadow. They dropped in for their gorge at Ali Barba's, where the fruit were not only the best in the district but in the whole country, because old Ali had grown his trees from seed specially imported from his native land for that most important of his several industries, the famous Barbu Chutney.

Barbu gave them the very special attention such powerful personages had a right to expect from such as he, offered them the pick of his pick, which were those got down with some difficulty by means of a net bag on a long bamboo pole to the top of which a knife was attached. He also offered them chutney to take home with them, since they would be going up on the next mail train. He was much too polite to ask how came they to be so unkempt. Anyway, they were renowned for coming in from the wilds looking like wildmen, and for maintaining the look as long as decently possible; this perhaps as a warning to would-be malefactors of what tough boys they were as manhunters, or maybe because they were just plain show-offs. But they were also polite to him, as never before, declining his offer of the special pickings, preferring to go round picking up for themselves those fruits, essentially somewhat bruised, knocked down by flying foxes, in so doing covering quite a lot of ground with hawk-eyes missing nothing of interest besides mangoes. On leaving, bowed out by Barbu, who promised to have a case of the specials and another of the chutney waiting for them on the train on Friday, Coon-Coon asked kindly after the little son-in-law, supposed to have gone back to the Centre after the Races, but sounded rather like his old self when, asking if he might expect an invitation to the christening when a grandchild should appear and being told that Hindus didn't practise baptism in the Christian way, he grinned and remarked, 'We can soon fix that, can't we!'

That was on Tuesday afternoon. On Wednesday morning, in the silver clarity of dawn, these bravos, along with Constable Stunke of Beatrice and Constable Kinnelly of Caroline River, and their trackers, 'moved in' on a shed a couple of miles down river that was the remains of one of those long-since abandoned peanut plantations established by the Government with Lord Vaisey's blessing for so-called White Russians. The conditions were perfect for a raid. Bright though it was, a colossus of a cloud, rearing from the north-west, almost overhung the place, with a battle going on behind it, as to be expected at this time of year, so that the still air shook with its reverberating; and ripe mangoes were dropping all about – plop, plop, plop! – and a few flying foxes were still there and all the more vocal for being late, and the true birds of the air were waking, but not wide enough to call alarm. Even a real goanna could not have got away, let alone a mere two-legged little brother to one. Still, he tried. 'No doubt about him!' as his Daddy-o chuckled, slipping that officially-declared most-humane of devices for restraint of his like, the neck-chain, about the slender golden neck. Then Daddy-o sounded hurt: 'Wha's a matter my little Sonny Boy go make that big-feller walkabout and knock his poor old Daddy-o up follerin' him?'

As usual Sonny Boy had nothing to say. But Coon-Coon was very amiable: 'Been lose him tongue again, eh? No matter . . . you got plenty time while you long o' jail for grow 'nother one . . . all-same that one lizard . . . what-you-call-yem, Yang . . . grow new-feller tail . . . aaaah-yaaaaah!' Then he asked him would he like to ride his Lily Lagoons pony back, adding: 'You smart feller with a ridin' horse and a racehorse, ain't you? Who goin' to race that Golden Bobby for you while you long o' jail waitin' for tongue to grow, eh? No good leavin' it to old Mullaka or Ali Barba . . . 'cause looks like they goin' 'o be in jail, too.'

Prindy said, Yas, he would like his pony – and also to keep the bamboo flute that they snatched off him perhaps on suspicion that it was some kind of weapon. Riding along with him, himself holding the chain, Dinny asked him to play something. Prindy obliged with some Indian music; but Dinny soon silenced that, asked didn't he know anything Irish, and on learning that he didn't, sang him *Danny Boy* till he got it. 'Arra!' he yelled to his khaki subordinates, 'Who say's the kid's *non compos mentis* now?'

Thus did Prindy again become a guest at the Beatrice River Police Station and under the same special patronage as before, but this time in different quarters, not the fuel shed with sack-covered cases for a bed; instead in a room of his own, one of those four little narrow ones in a row at the back, with their own netting-screened verandah, each with a tiny barred window high up at the rear, and a barred door with a dirty big lock on it in front, and an iron bed and all the rest of it in accordance with the regulations. That officially he was in fact a guest and not a prisoner was something he might have learnt for himself later in the day had he known enough English to follow a heated argument over the matter that took place in the office under the residence. This was when Jeremy Delacy came storming into the place demanding release of the child, not as someone for whom he himself claimed responsibility, but simply as a child, who even without a charge for any offence laid against him, was being treated like an adult felon. Sergeant Cahoon, who dealt with the matter, did not storm back, but even almost cooed in the certainty of his rights as a Protector of Aborigines, as he claimed. A heavy storm was about to break. The child must have shelter. He himself could not compel the district officer to take him into his private residence. Nor could the boy be kept there in the office where official business was being done and there was, anyway, no amenity for his comfort. He had every comfort in the cell, even his flute to play. He wasn't even locked in, as Mr Delacy might see for himself if he chose. In fact Mr Delacy could go and share the next cell with him if he liked for the next forty hours or so, and quite without cost to himself, because herewith he was charging him with complicity in the abduction of an Aboriginal Ward of the State, and would be requiring him to accompany him, along with the abductor, one Ali Barba, to Port Palmeston aboard the next train to face the charge in court. 'Ah!' said Dinny, with that crack of a grin probably wider than it had ever been before, 'Yo've several times said you'd like to stand in a court o' law with me. Now here's your chance. I'm doin' it as a kind o' favour to you. I'd like you to see it like that, Jerry . . . because I am grateful to you, you know. If it hadn't been for the dirty trick you did on Nobby Knowles that day we last had dealin's, I might never have got on the track of the boy and his poor mother . . . for, you see, it was from the mother, God rest her, that Nobby got his affliction . . . and one thing just led to another, as they say. But if you'd like to be locked up . . . . '

It was then that the storm broke. Through his open cell door, over the curly black head of Tracker Treacle, who was squatting out on the verandah probably officially only to keep him company, Prindy saw the Mullaka dash away into the driving rain. A few minutes later the train arrived, unheard even by the keenest ears in the terrific din going on away up top there – *Crash! Bang! Wallop!* – and the drum of the rain on the iron roof. The train looked like a procession of shades marching, into nothingness, because the station was lost in rain. It lasted only fifteen minutes, but long enough to set the dry yellow earth flowing with mud and hopping with frogs. But there was no devastation. Old Tchamala didn't by any means always win his wars with the *Waianga.* Probably the only untoward thing resulting from it was the suffering of the passengers off the train who'd had to wait that much longer in the stifling heat of shut up coaches or the station offices for the drink they'd surely been doing a perish for since heaving out the window the last bottle bought at the Caroline.

It was a sweet cool evening. Prindy had a great meal of beef and things and steamed pudding, brought to him from the hotel, no less, by his Daddy-o. It was a bright cool evening, with the stars shining like eyes washed by happy tears. Months of Lord Vaisey's dust had been washed from the air in those fifteen minutes. The frogs sang about it in vast happy chorus, Prindy tootled about it on his flute. When his Daddy-o looked in on him at bedtime reluctantly to turn the key on him, and asked him what it was he was playing, he said, 'Dat-one 'bout reen.'

'What about rain?'

'I don' know . . . I on'y hear him sumpin . . . I play him.'

'You're a strange little boy, you know. You're my little boy too, you know that, eh?' It sounded as if Dinny were near to tears as he said it. But he had been drinking up at the pub. To the evident astonishment of Jinbul, who was guard for the night over the little non-prisoner in a prison cell, he went and kissed the wide little forehead pale in the semi-darkness.

Next day was bright but stinging hot. Prindy and his Daddy-o went riding together, over the river, first to try the mangoes of the trees growing about the Racecourse. Prindy rode his pony as yesterday and wore his neck-chain, which Dinny had handcuffed to his own wrist. Unable to get Prindy to talk about his adventures since leaving the Old Compound that evening in the middle of the year – for the simple reason that the boy said: '*I been lose m' 'ead* – Dinny himself offered a fairly accurate reconstruction of the main details. Prindy simply ate mangoes and fed them to his horse. As they came back in the afternoon they were seen by Jeremy Delacy and Tom Toohey, the latter just in with his trolley from Running the Road. Dinny steered close to the pair in crossing the railway tracks, evidently with deliberate intent to show how the boy was shackled to him and by the wide split in his beard, wishing to provoke angry comment. Jeremy certainly stared, but did no more than raise a hand in greeting to Prindy and call, 'Goodday, young feller . . . how's the pony goin'?'

Prindy answered cheerily enough, 'He all right, Mullaka.'

Poor Tom Toohey, scared of most things, and especially of Coon-Coon, looked away down line from whence the returning train would soon be arriving.

That night, while Dinny taught Prindy some more Irish songs to play to his singing – *The Minstrel Boy, Erin Go Bragh, The Last Rose of Summer* – Jeremy sought out Pat Hannaford, who had been driving the train, in his quarters in the railway yards, bringing beer, which although accepted, was not enough to make Pat unbend much in his usual unfriendliness towards him. Nevertheless, Pat was very interested in what Jeremy had to tell him, and not only agreed to assist in what Jeremy proposed, but offered special service. When he heard about the neck-chaining of Prindy and Jeremy's prediction that as Cahoon had made so bold with it so far he would be sure to use the chain tomorrow on the journey to Town, Pat declared that he would not take the train till the Copper Bastard was put in his place. But Jeremy showed him that it would be all to their advantage if the Bastard got away with it to where they could make a big issue of it. His own trouble was to arrange the thing he had in mind for the Showdown. He had telephoned his lawyer about his own case and Barbu's, which latter he would see got the best of defence. That meant telling the world about it, of course, or at least that bit of it connected by phone from Port Palmeston to as far Inland as the gossips' interest went, five hundred miles, at least. There must be no gossip over this other matter. Pat grasped it, and said, Leave it to him. He and his Comrades had a method of communicating that had outwitted the Mocks and Master Bastards many and many a time. If things were as Jeremy predicted they would be, then the method would be put into operation tomorrow and there would be that Showdown without fail. Although no wit more friendly with Jeremy as they parted, Pat chuckled in seeing him out of his barracks hut: 'Yeah . . . looks like we got that Copper Bastard on toast!'

Jeremy returned to Toohey's where he was staying as usual. He would be required to report at the Police Station next morning for submission to custody.

What Jeremy had predicted about the lengths to which Cahoon would go in the sureness he had in his position exceeded expectations. Arriving at the train next morning, by no means of stealth but just before it departed so that all the world might bear witness, not only did he have one small boy on a neck-chain but a little blackish girl as well, while behind him, with the bearded Jinbul as indifferent escort, came his true prisoners, snivelling Barbu and erect but stony and ruddy-faced Jeremy Delacy.

The little journey from the Police Station, usually made with prisoners by truck, was made today on foot for better effect. The Coon-Coon beard split wide in silent greeting to the gaping crowd. The children looked happy enough, and were nicely dressed, in clothes that everybody knew Cahoon had bought from McDodds at his own expense, and carried bags of lollies. He had the last compartment of the last passenger coach reserved. He was entering it when Pat Hannaford came striding down from the engine looking very grim, causing the crowd to mutter and Dinny to grin wider and say, 'Hello, hello . . . looks like the Comrade Commissar isn't goin' to let us go!' As Pat came up he addressed him amiably, 'If you're not goin' to deign to drive us, Comrade, we can make the journey by truck, you know . . . only it's a bit rough on kids, all that long way and the state the roads're in at present . . . and looks like rain, too. How would they transport children in Russia?' A titter from most, and guffaws from several.

Pat answered, 'I wouldn' know that . . . but I know what they'd do with you.'

'Put me in the salt mines with the other poor buggers who don't believe Joe Stalin's God?'

'They wouldn't put you in a salt mine, mate . . . you'd turn the salt sour, and they'd transport you by night-cart.'

A weaker titter and guffaws only from those drunk enough to be reckless. But the beard kept split in the grin. 'Funny man, ain't you, Driver!'

Pat snapped, 'At least I am a *man*!'

The beard shut tight; and the narrow eyes widened in a blue blaze of anger; for the remark surely meant that worst of Australian insults to a policeman, handed down all the way from convict days: *Once a policeman never a man*. It was an offence to utter it. But had it been uttered? Cahoon turned to usher his charges and prisoners aboard. Pat called to Jeremy, 'If you see any Fascist basher tactics, Delacy, just send the word up . . . and this coach comes off the train . . . right?' Jeremy nodded.

Col Collings raised his voice: 'Driver Hannaford, are you going to take this train away?'

Pat shot his hand up in the Fascist salute, crying, '*Ja, mein Führer* . . . at vonce, toot sveet . . . but I vish you vhip me mit you little vhip, make me go quicker!'

That got a good laugh from pretty well everyone but Col. Even Coon-Coon leaned out of a window to grin and perhaps show his last manhunting beard of the season.

A minute or two of crowding aboard to the urging of Col and Oz Burrows. Then the bell – *Clang, clang*! – then the engine – *Boo-hoot*! – and they were rolling. Over the bridge with its leaping clangorous girders, but the water only a streamlet far below and scarcely muddied. Past the Racecourse, where the grass was already springing and the brolgas dancing again. Sweet pickin' everywhere; and plenty of things leaping and hopping and flying and strolling about to pick it. On and on, click-clack-clicking over the flats, howling and hammering through the cuttings panting up the grades and screaming down them: *Boo-hoot, boo-hoot*! Prindy tried for the notes. His Daddy-o asked him what he was playing. He answered, '*Treen*.' Dinny remarked to Jeremy that it was a funny way to play trains, then asked for *Danny Boy*. Water at Granite Creek. Then on to Alice River.

At the Alice, Mr Grayball came aboard with a couple of others, he himself keeping to himself and looking only half the man he was. His acquaintances whispered to others that he had a Bad Dose got from a young gin who came *tchinekin* into his bed about the middle of the year, and had sold out his Renchouse and was going South for treatment. Coon-Coon heard nothing of that, but remarked to his Sonny Boy that he knew this place, eh? Prindy, staring out, was silent.

So on again, to see the waters divide, to turn from West to East, what little there was of them now, and the rubbitch the Whiteman and the Narishman and the Germanman and the Chineeman had left behind in their quest of that unsolved mystery Goold. To Caroline and sandwiches and lollywater, and a lot of peeping from the populace. There Driver Hannaford was to be seen in earnest conference with Comrade Wally Walsh, who was the Water Pumper for that centre. Then on again, to halt for this and that: water for the engine or food or beer or both for passengers and crew, at the several sidings named to perpetuate the performance in bed of Good Queen Victoria with Albert the Also Good. On into red evening, into purple night; to bore into that grey-walled tunnel of trees now seemingly filled with flying ants through which the swinging gilded knife of the engine cut a track.

Then the hanging lights and the bumpy switches of the Loco Depot. There was the grey engine shed again, housing its sleeping iron elephants, the dripping water tank; but no nightmen; only the usual tiny crowd, to receive the few passengers who alighted there.

Soon on again to the beckoning glow of the Metropolis, with the windows of whitemen's houses winking along the way, the wobbly lights on the sea, the blaze of Captain Shane's affluence – and at last the glare of the terminal station, with its usual crowd in white linen and khaki and floral cottons and silks. However, the crowd was twice as big as usual, surely for the remarkable sight of seeing one called the Scrub Bull yarded, and twice as many policemen, amongst them Superintendent Bullco, the latter surely with his darbies in his back pocket for instant use should the glorious opportunity present itself – and, of course, the Press, in its two orders, but each no less on tiptoe and with note-books at the ready than the other.

The black beard, wide-split, was hanging out to give its location. The train stopped in just the right position, slap bang of brakes right before the Press. The owner of the beard said, 'Well, here we are!' Then he proceeded to detrain as usual from one of his successful manhunts to get the best dramatic effect for benefit of his superiors and the general public, as a true hunter does, standing, preferably with a gun, with the game stacked around him. He never just strolled off and shook hands with his waiting colleagues, leaving the hunted ones to be dragged out by trackers. He was always in the lead with the prisoners at his heels, and the trackers shoving from behind. Thus did he now step off the platform of the coach with the two chained children shackled to his wrist and the two elderly men, one a little old black man weeping into his white handkerchief, a step behind – *Pop! Pop!* – like little gunshots, but with the blaze of lightning – and again – *Pop! Pop! Flash! Flash!* – Everybody for the moment blinded, and too astounded to speak.

Superintendent Bullco spoke first, roaring, 'Here . . . what's this?'

They weren't used to flashlight photography in Port Palmeston, except at weddings.

Then Bullco woke up with return of his vision, seeing the cameras in the hands of Fay McFee and Rollo Ramstones, her editor, and yelled, 'Stop them men . . . confiscate those cameras!'

But that meant overcoming a squad of what the Superintendent would have called Bolsheviks, led by Billy Bellairs and Snowy Mack, leaders of what they themselves were pleased to call Progressive Society in Port Palmeston (although having little to do with *The Palmeston Progressive*, the name of which stood for an older form of progress) which suddenly formed up and covered the hasty retreat of the photographers to their car. Snowy Mack yelled, 'What's this . . . Nazi Germany?'

Bullco saw he was beaten, snapped at his poising khaki boys, 'Leave it men . . . leave it!' Then he turned his attention to the bearded bravo, and let him have it, *sotto voce*, but with such intensity of feeling that it was heard by most: 'For christ sake, Dinny, what'd you have to do that for?'

Dinny, realizing the significance, was at a loss for words.

Bullco went on: 'To bring kids on the chain . . . and at this juncture!'

Dinny said in a strangled voice, 'It was only for their protection, Sir . . . I didn't want 'em jumpin' out of the train.'

'And now you've got 'em jumpin' right into the front page of bloody *Truth* . . . "Police Brutality to Innocent Aboriginal Children" . . . you goddam, bloody, stupid, bastard! You must've realized that Delacy'd get you for it.'

'I didn't see how he could, Sir.'

'Well, it's your bloody baby. Let those kids go. You're not taking 'em to my headquarters to make a fool of *me*. Go on . . . do as I say . . . take those chains off 'em, quick!'

'They might do a bunk, Sir.'

'Let 'em. I'll call Cobbitty. They're his responsibility . . . not ours . . . . '

'I'm sorry, Sir.'

'What's the good o' being bloody sorry . . . except for yourself! Best bit of police work you've ever done . . . anybody ever done . . . and you had to cruel it all by putting kids in chains . . . Bah!' Superintendent Bullco strode away into the station office to use the phone.

A little later the children were placed in the station office, with their lolly bags, and a policeman only standing well outside. Meantime the real prisoners were conveyed to Police Headquarters in the police car, there to be formally received as the miscreants that allegedly they were, then released on bail put up by Jeremy.

Dr Cobbitty could not refuse responsibility for the children, but could easily delegate it, and promptly did, to Eddy McCusky, who was glad enough to accept – at least till he heard the sharp injunction that followed his saying that he would take the kids straight out to the Sweet Creek Settlement and lock 'em up in the jail-house there. Cobbitty snarled at him, 'If those kids are going to be locked up anywhere, man, it's in your house. Haven't you got the brains to see that the Bitch McPhee and the Bastard Delacy'll flog the thing to the limit? I know I'm on the skids . . . but I'm not going out with the reputation of a Boong Basher. Take those kids home with you, and treat 'em like your own . . . or I'll get someone else out of the office to do it . . . and you can give me your resignation from the Service to hand to the Old Man on Monday. Got it?'

Eddy answered weakly, 'Yessir.'

Thus it was that Prindy, who last time he saw the lights of Silvertail Point, as unofficially it was called, had done so as a fugitive from the exalted who lived thereon, rode the road to it that he had crossed furtively with his mother, now in a cosy motor car with one of those exalted ones telling him he was taking him home to make him his own little boy, with Savitra as his own little girl: 'So don't be fright'.' He and his dusky little bride were put up in the guest room of the McCusky residence, in luxury such as they'd never dreamt of. They hadn't heard the argument between Eddy and his sour-visaged wife that had preceded their ensconcement. She, who didn't like Aborigines of any breed, although their existence was her bread and butter, had wanted them put in the garage. When the Dirty Nigger line failed, she had tried the moral one, declaring that it wasn't decent that two people of opposite sex should share the same bedroom, young as these were, because everybody knew their kind were no more moral than animals. Eddy countered that by saying that it so happened that the couple were married, and explained. 'Call a Hindu ceremony marriage?' his missus screeched. 'This's a decent Catholic house!' Then Eddy had to confess the terrible fact that if they didn't put them up in a manner that could not be faulted by the Bitch McFee and her ilk, then they were out of a job, at least out of this wonderful job that paid so handsomely in money and prestige and would pay more and more so when Cobbitty got the boot and his successor would need his services to work his own racket on, and the racket would become more and more lucrative and prestigeful as the Aboriginal Problem became more and more complex with the Nation's becoming more and more aware of it – why, he might even end up as a Director of Aboriginal Affairs, even The Director of Directors – he who had started as a simple little Public Service office boy! He didn't put it quite like that. For instance, he didn't use the word Racket. It only sounded that way. Anyway, it convinced Mrs McCusky that she had no alternative but tight-lipped acceptance of the degradation of having a pair of Dirty Little Niggers fornicating under her Decent Catholic roof. The only thing she could add was that it wouldn't have happened in the first place but for Eddy's opening his Big Trap too wide to that Alfie Candlemas Creature.

Whereas the legal system of the land, apart from the sheer hounding of malefactors, which naturally went on all the while, normally dealt with its affairs in the same leisurely way as other Government Departments, which is to say between the hours of 9 a.m. and 4 p.m. from Monday to Friday, a state of emergency was declared for all those concerned in it over this weekend. Superintendent of Police, Clerk of Courts, Stipendiary Magistrate, Administrator, and lesser officials, conferred until late that Friday night and decided that there be a minimum of delay in presenting the cases of Abduction and Complicity Therein and the holding of the Coroner's Inquest into the presumed deaths of certain Aboriginal persons, to wit Nelly Ah Loy, Queeny Pegleg, and King George; so as to preclude as much as possible the embarrassment officially felt in the circumstances. To handle with proper official dignity something that had been besmirched by being previously adversely dealt with by such scurrilous rags as *The Palmeston Progressive* and *Truth* was impossible. But fortunately the slanders of the one would not be published till next Friday, nor of the other before the Sunday following. So Monday of next week was named as that for the Abduction hearing; and devil take anything else listed; and Wednesday for the Inquest. It was then left to underlings to sweat out the weekend in the elaborate business of preparation.

It could all have been saved, all the running to and fro and the labour, if they had only thought less about dignity and more about the kind of people who were out to rob them of it. Then it might have occurred to someone that, with modern methods of transport, the offices of *Truth* might be considered not much further than that of the plaguey *Progressive,* that an edition would be published in the meantime, and that their adversaries would stop at nothing to use it to their ends. Of course the air mail didn't come in from the South till midday Sunday or go back till Monday morning. But what of a chartered aircraft? And was there not one such, operated by a fellow who would come at anything for money?

That's how it happened. Fergus Ferris flew out with those photographs and the story at first light on Saturday: and there it all was in *Truth* that came off Sunday's mail plane, under headlines almost word for word as Superintendent Bullco had predicted: *Police Brutality to Aboriginal Children – Still This Evil Thing Goes On – Are We a Nation Without Shame*?

Prindy and his bride would never have known how famous they were, had not the youngest of the McCusky children, a boy of about Prindy's age, who having seen the paper when he went with his father to get it and been refused any further look at it and told that the huge picture on the front page, of the black kids with neck-chains was *not* of the kids in the house, early next morning stolen round to those kids while they were eating their breakfast on the side verandah and shown it to them.

Another sidelight to the affair was receipt of a telegram that same Monday morning by Jeremy at his hotel a few minutes after the Post Office opened and an hour or so before he was to appear in court: *Immensely proud of you stop put the boot in hard stop love love love Alfie.*

Stipendiary Magistrate Bundy made it clear in opening the case of Wilful

Abduction and Complicity Therein that the Defendants were for it, whatever their pleas or defence. He was renowned, of course, for his malice aforethought towards those arraigned before him on Monday mornings; by reason of his wife, as some said. But this Monday was after a weekend of enforced pre-occupation with this very matter, when probably he could have spent it fertilizing those orchids for breeding for which he was also somewhat renowned; a weekend wasted, as he saw it, since Waste of Time was the burden of his old-dog's growling preliminaries: 'I am not going to waste the time of the Court on a case that should never have had to be brought before me. The Law of the Land is explicit enough about the lawful custody of Aboriginal persons. It is vested in the Protector, pure and simple . . . and there is no gainsaying it except by illegal processes. One of the Defendants is an ignorant man, an Indian . . . but he cannot plead ignorance of the law in this matter because he has already been dealt with under it. The other is not ignorant by any means, and as far as I can see can only plead arrogance in the matter. I repeat that the issue is clear. The Protector can do what he likes in respect of his lawful assignment of protecting Aboriginal persons. That is the Law. Whether or not it is bad law is a matter for argument in much higher tribunals than this that I am empowered to preside over. This is a court of summary justice. I will not have it turned into a Banyan Tree for the airing of anti-social views by malcontents whose aim is to attract the attention of the doubtful media of publicity . . . .' That last bit left him breathless and with old-dog's jowls jerking. Getting his breath back he growled, 'Proceed!'

Sergeant Nullity, prosecuting, read the indictment. Barbu Ram, alias Ali Barba, entered the dock, bobbing and cringing, to plead Guilty. Sergeant Cahoon, minus whiskers now and with blue jaw bluer than ever for the rest it had had from the razor, but with no such confident grin as lately, took the witness stand to testify to how, by a long and circuitous and arduous search for a certain Aboriginal Person, to wit Prendegast Alroy, absconded from lawful custody, he had discovered that the said Person had taken up with the Defendant and travelled with him in the course of his hawking itinerary through several centres at which he could have reported the fact that he was harbouring a Ward of the State and at one of which he could have surrendered the Ward to a proper authority, instead of which he actually gave out false information regarding the Ward's identity. Subsequently he himself had found traces of the wanted Person on Defendant's premises at Beatrice River and then had located the Person and taken him into custody. Afterwards when he had charged Defendant with the offence of Harbouring, the latter had wept and told a cock-and-bull story of finding him in a bird-net and thinking he was a Hindu God sent to marry his daughter, a child of eight. Defendant admitted having told the other defendant in the case, Delacy, the true identity of the Person. He had then arrested him. The Sergeant made no reference to any assistance he might have had from Tracker Jinbul, also shaven and shorn now, and sitting on the bench reserved for black policemen.

Under examination by Sergeant Nullity, Barbu babbled of Prindies and Lil Golden Poys and Hindu mythology, to the subdued amusement of some of the court and the obviously growing irritation of His Worship. He claimed that the boy had never told him where he had come from, that he truly believed he had been sent by the Gods to be his daughter's husband, and that he would have incurred the wrath of the Gods had he tried to get rid of him. He knew him not as Prendegast Alroy or Prindy Ah Loy, but as King of the World. Loud laughter, until His Worship, with jerking jowls, threatened to clear the court. Barbu admitted that his daughter had told him the boy was one of these other persons, as he had told Sergeant Coon-Coon, that he had lied in saying the boy had gone back to the Centre after the Races, had known he was hiding down the river for some weeks, and had permitted him to visit him frequently and help with the pickling and bottling of the mango chutney – more laughter – but hadn't thought he was doing wrong, because he believed the boy was properly under the protection of Mother Shasti, Divine Protector of Children. Stipendiary Bundy had to hammer hard for silence. Yes, Mr Jeremy Delacy had given the boy a pony, but without knowing who he was. However, yes, Mr Delacy had asked him later if King of the World were in reality Prendegast Alroy, and he himself had told him that in fact he was.

Mr Billings, Counsel for Defence, took over Barbu and stressed the point of his being Hindu and how that affected his conduct generally; an exciting idea, at least to two or three of those present, among them Fay McFee, who forgot about her notes and sucked her pencil; until His Worship stopped it by almost yelling, 'Mr Billings . . . time and again it has been stressed in this court where Aboriginal lore has been raised as defence that this is a Court of British Justice, and that nothing but the basic principle of that justice, fear of God – the God of the Christian Bible – and honour for the King, will be tolerated. Extenuating circumstances, indeed, because of some hocus pocus this cunning old blackman professes to believe in! Next thing you'll be asking me to condone this abomination of child-marriage that the Defendant uses as excuse for breaking the law. When this man was last before me I called him a Dirty Old Man for permitting his wife and daughters to practise prostitution. I do so again . . . in respect of this filthy thing of marrying his little daughter to a small boy . . . and have half a mind to send him to jail for it, on a charge of Corrupting the Morals of Minors . . . so the sooner you limit your defence to asking me to be lenient because your client is an ignorant Indian, the better it will be for him, for yourself, and for the valuable time of this court.'

Mr Billings sighed, murmured, 'As Your Worship pleases,' and sat down.

Mr Bundy asked Sergeant Nullity if he had anything further to say, and being given a negative, asked the same question of Barbu – then promptly silenced the poor old fool for trying to say it. Mr Bundy went on: 'I have told you before, Ali Barba, that the filthy practices of your own benighted country will not be tolerated in our decent clean young Western society . . . and I warn you now, that if ever you come before me again, I will jail you without the option and recommend your deportation back to India. You are fined £100 . . . no time to pay . . . Call the Defendant Delacy!'

'Jeremy Deleon Delacy!' A stir in court.

Jeremy entered the dock, erect, red-faced, tight-lipped, his eyes on *Terra Australis del Espiritu Santo*, away there out of the window. Sergeant Nullity read the indictment of Complicity in the Case of Abduction Hereintofore: 'How do you plead?'

'Guilty.' That caused a stir.

Bundy took over: 'You are undefended?'

Without looking at him Jeremy answered shortly, 'I can defend myself.'

The jowls shook. 'You will use my title when addressing me.'

Jeremy said to the distance, 'Sir!'

'You will also direct your attention to me, Defendant.'

The grey eyes met the meaty red ones, to the evident discomfort of the latter. Blinking, His Worship growled, 'Have you anything to say for yourself?'

'Yes, sir . . . .'

'Then say it . . . and I warn you to be brief. As I said at the beginning of proceedings, I will not have this court made a soap-box orator's forum for airing their own grievances.'

'Even if one's grievances are legitimate, Your Worship?'

'Don't be impertinent! Several times I've ordered you from my court for conduct bordering on Contempt. Be careful I don't have you removed from it in the jail delivery van. Proceed!' The old dog's eyes dropped from the cold grey stare. The jowls shook.

Jeremy addressed himself again to the landscape: 'On learning from Barbu Ram that the boy who was passing as his son-in-law might be the quarter Aboriginal child known officially as Prendegast Alroy, I refrained from doing what I fully realized I should do according to the law, which was to report the matter to the Authorities, for the reason that I felt to do so would constitute an act of cruelty . . . .'

Bundy cut in sharply: 'What are you saying?'

Jeremy had been speaking slowly and deliberately, conscious no doubt that Fay McFee wanted every word of it. He looked at the Beak, asked, 'You wish me to repeat it, Your Worship?'

'I do not! I'm warning you to be careful what you say.'

'I assure you, Sir, that I'm choosing every word with the greatest of care . . . since from what you've told me you are more than ready to jail me for contempt.'

'I can also jail you for casting aspersions on the administration of authority in this area.'

'May I ask you to quote the act or ordinance that so empowers you?'

Bundy went purple, answered in a strangled voice, 'You may not! You've elected to do without Counsel. I will not have laymen . . . bush-lawyers . . . arguing law in my court.'

'As Your Worship pleases. I shall have to rely on my conception of what is called British Justice . . . which is that it is supposed to be based simply on Equity, on fairness of interpretation of the Statutes and Common law.'

Bundy looked as if about to have a fit. Fay's tongue was bulging her cheek as if she had a terrible abcess, so terrifically was she writing.

After a moment Jeremy asked, 'May I go on with what Your Worship asked me . . . namely if I had anything to say for myself?'

His Worship could only nod and blink at Fatty Doscas below him as if pleading for his help.

'I was saying that I felt that to betray the boy's whereabouts to the authorities . . . in the case, the local police officer . . . would constitute an act of cruelty.

I felt so because I'd seen how happy he was with the Barbus. I know the boy well. I have known him since his birth and had watched him grow up at Catfish Creek Out-station . . . where also he was very happy. I've not known a happier or more talented child of his breed and circumstances. He was removed from Catfish and placed in official hands. The result was that he ran away like a frightened animal . . . made a journey that is well nigh incredible in his determination to be free of what was imposed on him in the name of the Law . . . and seemed to have found his heart's content. I knew that eventually he would be located and dragged back . . . but hardly expected that he would be dragged back like a dangerous felon, or an animal, in chains . . . .'

'That will do!' snapped Bundy.

'How do you mean That Will Do, Your Worship . . . that I've said enough in defence of my action to convince you . . . .?'

'No . . . . that I won't have you using this court to air your views and bring discredit on the officers of the law. Any more, and I'll order you to stand down. Proceed!'

'There's nothing more to say, Your Worship, except that I'd like to have legal custody of the boy myself to ensure that he doesn't have to suffer this official bullying . . . .'

'I warned you!'

'Ever again, Your Worship, as I'm afraid otherwise a boy of his spirit is always going to have to . . . until something even terrible happens. That's all I have to say.'

For a moment the old dog was at a loss for words; then what he said was unexpected: 'I have no authority to give you legal custody of the boy . . . or even to recommend it. It's a matter entirely for the Protector.'

'I know, Sir . . . I'm only gratified that you should even think of it.'

The meaty eyes opened in surprise, then shut quickly to their squinting littleness. His Worship reached for his pen, and writing in his book said, 'You are fined £10 . . . in default one month's imprisonment.'

Jeremy bowed to the Bench, turned and swept his grey stare over the rest of the court, causing quite a lot of blinking or flight of hostile eyes. Pretty well everybody had crowded in or packed the verandah to hear this bit. There was Eddy McCusky, Superintendent Bullco, the Knowles brothers and their skinny old man, Miss Kitty Wyndeyer, and, of course, those so-lately-bearded bravoes who had been responsible for the whole thing.

Bundy snapped, 'The court adjourns.' And while everybody rose for him as the representative of *Georgius VI, Deo Gratia Rex*, he ducked out under that Most Worshipful One's garish insignia, as ever looking as if it had swallowed him up.

Jeremy took out his cheque book and approached the grinning Clerk of Courts, who gave him his fat hand, wheezing, 'Hello, Jerry, old man . . . . how you doin'?' Two cheques; one for £10, the other for £100.

Fay McFee was packing up as Jeremy passed her with chuckling Barbu beside him to go out. She hissed at him, 'Great stuff!'

He grimaced. 'Praise from you is praise indeed.'

She grinned, heaving herself up. 'Wait'll you see what I'm going to do with this!'

He looked at her inquiringly; but she shot out, was gone.

What Fay did with it became evident next afternoon, when Port Palmeston had a rare treat in the form of a bundle of leading Southern daily newspapers published that morning to read, brought up by Fergus Ferris. The Abduction and Complicity case made front-page news, not because of any particular Southern public interest in the thing itself, but by reason of the intrusion into it of the Indian Government Representative in Canberra, enraged by being told and asked his opinion of what Stipendiary Magistrate Bundy had said to Barbu about his country. The inner Government circle hadn't to wait for the news so long as the common herd. There was a rushing to and from between His Honour the Administrator's Office and the Crown Law Office and the Post Office from 8 a.m. to noon. Poor old Bundy was called out of Court to go on the mat, his place taken by Dicky Doscas, and Dicky's by Miss Williams and Miss Williams's by the temporarily-reappointed Miss Wyndeyer. First poor old Bundy was chewed up by Judge Bickering, his immediate boss, and when spat out, was passed on to the Old Man, who made such a job of him that he went home sick and took relief in poking his orchids.

At Wednesday's Inquest Mr Doscas sat as Coroner, looking like a British Buddha up there under the Holy British Sign. His own huge chair had had to be put up there for him; and he was too wide to use the hole in the Royal Belly for entrance and exit and had to come all the way round and be helped up to his place of dignity. It was a pleasant change in scene and proceedings, because he was a Smiling Buddha; even smiling, it would seem, at the amusement his odd appearance made. It was this amiableness and oddity doutless that loosened the tongue of the Chief Witness, standing again on books so as to be seen above the railing of the Stand. Already there had been some discussion of the witness Prendegast Alroy's unwillingness or inability to give the vital evidence. No one was able to decide what was the reason for the boy's continued silence. Sergeant Cahoon had to confess that he hadn't got a word out of him, but claimed he might have, had he not been denied access to him by the Aborigines Department. Mr McCusky had to make a similar admission, with the reservation that but for being rushed in the matter he could have got him talking, because they were becoming very friendly. Mr Doscas tried holding up a couple of the Exhibits for the boy to see, some bits of rag and what was undoubtedly a part of a wooden leg of the peg variety, but without getting any more than a nod to his question regarding the last-named: 'Do you know what this is?' Being pressed to say what it was only caused the grey eyes to seek the distance. Dr McQuegg testified to the effect that a very shocking experience could bring on a condition of amnesia in one so young, and stated that he now believed it was something like this that was responsible for the boy's non co-operation in a case earlier in the year, on account of which he had been declared *non compos mentis*. Dr Cobbitty was not in it. It was fairly well known in official circles that he had refused to be in it, saying that he had enough on his back without That Crazy Kid. So Mr Doscas tried leading the boy ever so gently into it.

Mr Doscas said, 'Now, young feller, what we want you tell us is properly Number-one bijnitch. We got to find out about this kind of think for put him in a book. Spone we can't put him in a book, well, we're . . . er . . . buggered, as you might say . . . .' No shouts of Silence or hammering in this court when there was laughter.

'Yes . . . you're the only one can help us. We give you prejent for that. What'd you like? You like make music, they reckon . . . you play the Indian flute all day, I hear. How'd you like a real flute, eh? No? Or a trumpet . . . yes, a real trumpet . . . we'll buy you one!' Eddy McCusky was heard to groan.

Attempted bribery didn't work. So Mr Doscas tried another line: 'Now, what about me-two-feller go walkabout like you did that time . . . gammon walkabout, I mean . . . like I'm 'nother little boy from Compound, like your mate, eh?' Dicky Doscas chuckled fatly, causing Prindy to chuckle too. 'That's the way! Right, we gammon walkabout. Me-two-feller run away from Compound. We got him Mumma there. Three-feller now. We go, go, go. We meet up two-feller . . . we can't talk dat name now, 'cause dat two-feller dead . . . but one him old man, been fisherman, 'nother one woman, got wooden leg . . . ain't it? Right, we go, go, go . . . .' Mr Doscas went over the ground that Sergeant Cahoon had covered in his evidence, all the way from Hang Gong Creek to the Frog Rocks; while Prindy watched him as if living it through again. 'Right,' he wound up. 'We there now . . . Frog Rock. Something happen there . . . what name that Something?'

So intense was the expectation at that moment that the boy, who'd so far scarcely seemed to notice the others in Court, turned on them wide-eyed, as if caught by it as something magnetic. Mr Doscas, sweating hard himself, had to recall his attention: 'Well, Prendegast?'

Prindy looked back at him. Doscas asked, 'Come on . . . what happened?'

Prindy said simply what he had said so often, 'I don' know . . . been lose him head.'

Mr Doscas gave up with a sigh. Mopping his huge face he said to Prindy, 'All right, sonny . . . you can go.'

Both Cahoon and McCusky leapt to grab the boy; but Eddy got him, simply by saying, 'Ah, no, Dinny . . . Boss's orders!'

Still mopping, Mr Doscas addressed the court: 'A difficult case . . . a *very* difficult case . . . and I'm afraid one that can only be left in abeyance until the amnesia or whatever it is has passed and we can get substantial evidence. A few bits of rag and bone scattered far and wide by birds and animals, a few bits of wood eaten by white ants, might at a stretch be taken as circumstantial to the fact that certain persons are now *non est*. But even proof of their non-existence is of no great importance, since nothing practical is involved, like insurance, inheritance. These persons were not even counted as citizens of the land. Their names appeared on official records, but only through involvement in official business. They had no birth certificates. They were not entered on any electoral roll. No mention of them is made in any census. Therefore, like all their race, for all practical purposes they never existed officially, and their non-existence can have no official import. But if their ceasing to exist was due to what is considered criminal according to the Law of the Land, it is another matter. Aborigines often die in the wilds . . . and no one knows anything about it but those close to them. Even here in this town the death of one of them means nothing but an unofficial interment. But if foul play is concerned we are bound by the rules of our society to investigate the circumstances to the limit. I therefore propose to adjourn this Inquest *sine die*. I thank you all for your co-operation.'

Eddy McCusky, bound not to let his Prendegast Alroy out of his keeping, took him straight from the Court into the offices of the Department of Aboriginal Protection. They had barely got in there, when Jeremy Delacy arrived and announced to Eddy that he wished to make formal application for adopting the boy. Eddy said it was not a matter for himself, but for the Boss, whom he would go and consult. The consultation took a good fifteen minutes, by which time Jeremy was looking pretty grim. Then Eddy appeared to say that the Boss had said it was Impossible. Jeremy rose, saying, 'I'll see him myself.' Eddy replied that he didn't think that would do any good. Jeremy snapped, 'Have another think!' and pushed past him, opened Dr Cobbitty's door, and went into his sanctum. Cobbitty's usually ruddy face paled. Jeremy said without ceremony, 'I wish to adopt that quarter-caste child known as Prendegast Alroy.'

Cobbitty swallowed, said with difficulty, 'I'm afraid you can't.'

'What do you mean afraid?'

Cobbitty straightened up, bold again in his official power: 'Well . . . simply that you can't!'

'Why?'

'I don't have to answer that.'

'Oh, yes you do!'

Cobbitty grinned in that way of his, but with a slight tremor to his thin lips. 'You might bully the bushwackers of Beatrice River, Mr Delacy . . . but you don't bully me.'

'If you don't give me a reason I'll take it further.'

'You can take it to Old Nick as far as I'm concerned . . . it'll only be referred back to me.'

'What a wonderful system it is!'

'I'm glad you think so. With all its faults it's the best that's yet operated in this country. Even you must admit that.'

'What preceded yours was pretty frightful. It couldn't last . . . any more than slavery in America could, Lincoln and Harriet Beacher Stowe and the rest of those given credit for stopping it notwithstanding . . . just as your bit of tyranny can't last.' Cobbity went very red, but still grinned. 'But I wasn't referring to your system particularly.' Jeremy went on, 'but to the bureaucratic racket in general. I'm going to establish that boy for what he is eventually . . . my grandson . . . despite the arrogance of you all . . . . '

'If you were his grandmother it wouldn't make any difference. The law makes such people Wards of the State exclusively . . . and made them so for their protection. You know what abuse was made of the Aborigines in the name of relationship with them . . . virtual slavery.'

'I know . . . but when people like you make a law in the name of Humanity, then that law becomes inhuman, too. All you've done is declare that there shall be no other gods but you.'

The doctor, a bit redder, but in so much control of himself that he was able to lie back in his swivel chair and press his fingers together and grin broader. 'That makes it tough on Olympian Dwellers like yourself, eh? You've never got over having your divine wisdom in the matter of dealing with the Aborigines passed over when you proffered it at our first meeting, have you?'

'What I've never got over is the stupidity of the Government in appointing a man with nothing but medical knowledge to deal with such a delicate matter.'

'Anthropology hadn't then reached the stature as a racket it does today, my dear fellow. Don't you know that the Anthrops are going to push me out? How will you deal with them? D'you think that showing them your collection of skulls and paeleolithic artifacts and your painted caves and re-established tribal grounds is going to have any more effect on their basic job of civilizing savages than it did on me?' Jeremy was at a loss. Realizing his victory, the doctor dropped forward again, with ginger-haired hands planking down to spread on the polished glass of his table: 'And speaking of civilizing savages . . . how come Jeremy Delacy, whose theory is leave 'em alone and they'll adapt themselves, those who want to . . . how come he suddenly to want to adopt his semi-savage grandson?'

Jeremy snapped, 'To save him from being buggered about by you and that up-jumped Melbourne guttersnipe you've set up to think himself an expert with people he had no more dealings with to begin than you.'

Cobbitty looked through the open door into the outer office, grinning still wider, saying, 'That's hard on poor old Eddy . . . he comes from Sydney.' Then placing his hands behind his head he swung back again. 'As a matter of fact, I was brought up in a country town where there were a lot of blacks . . . and I saw a lot of 'em, because my old man was a doctor there . . . and what I saw convinced me that it was a medical problem first. And speaking of that little town . . . there was an old fellow lived just outside it . . . The Hatter, we called him . . . who used to buy wild things the kids caught, birds, and wallabies, and bandicoots and things . . . so as to let 'em go again . . . and the kids'd catch 'em again and sell 'em to him again, and so well, if not *ad infinitum, ad mortem senis*. I trust you remember your Latin?' The green eyes twinkled in meeting the grey.

Jeremy swallowed, said, 'You haven't yet come to selling the wild things you're catching?'

'Not yet . . . Good morning!'

Jeremy swung away. In the outer office he paused to shake hands with Prindy, saying, 'See you by'n'by, young feller. I'll be lookin' out for your two-feller little horse all right. By'n'by we race him . . . win him Cup. *Mummuk yawarra, Mora*.'

The other grey eyes regarded him gravely: '*Mummuk yawarra, Mullaka*.'

As Jeremy disappeared McCusky asked Prindy, 'What mean *Mora*?'

The boy answered promptly, 'Dat-one gran'daddy call-yem young feller belong o' him.'

'But you don't call him him Gran'daddy, eh?'

Eddy didn't get the chance to hear the answer then, because Dr Cobbitty called him.

Cobbitty motioned him to shut the door, and when he had, said shortly, 'Get that kid out of the way as soon as possible. I don't want any more trouble with him.'

'I'll send him down the Centre next train . . . .'

'You won't. You'll take him down there yourself by car . . . and tomorrow. And no coppers. You'll stop at no police station. You'll put up at hotels or camp out . . . and keep that big trap of yours shut about the whole business.'

'What if he does a bunk on me?'

'Go after him . . . and unless you catch him, don't come back.'

Eddy answered weakly, 'Yessir.'

'What're you doing about the Barbu child?'

'I was thinking of sending her along to join her mother and sisters at the Leopold Mission.'

'Good idea. We can't let her go back to that bloody old lunatic, or he'll be getting to her himself on the orders of some Indian God or other.'

'They say he's been doing that already.'

'Eh? Jesus . . . if I'd known that I'd've examined the kid and seen that the dirty old bastard was put away for it!' The doctor's face was flaming.

'Aw,' said Eddy. 'Might be only just talk.'

Cobbitty snapped, 'I don't like that kind of talk. Incest is a serious crime. Anyway, I don't want to start anything now . . . not with this fool thing in the papers started by that crazy old orchid-poker, Bundy. Fix up about the girl's going on the next Mission boat . . . give her to the Convent right away. And get going with the other kid at daylight tomorrow morning.'

'Yessir.'

II

Eddy McCusky showed even a degree of subtlety in his handling of Prindy's disposal; at least to a point. He began by telling him that now the Gov'men' bijnitch was over he was taking him home, without specifying where home was; as indeed would have been difficult in Prindy's case. In accordance with the Boss's orders they set out so early on Thursday morning that Mrs McCusky refused to get up and make breakfast. That didn't trouble them. They called in at the Sweet Creek Settlement and had it with old friends, the Jumbo Delacys. Eddy's usual brash style could have put them in difficulties there, since in an aside to Jumbo and Possum, while Prindy was taking a look at the wonders of the new place, Eddy told where they were going, the result of which was to cause Jumbo to ask Prindy over breakfast to give him Golden Bobby now that he would be having no need for him. Eddy kicked Jumbo's shin hard enough to make it look for a moment that he was going to get one in return, and that one in the eye.

Perhaps it was what nearly happened at Sweet Creek that woke Eddy up to the dangers of his big mouth and kept him keeping it shut throughout most of the day; at least as concerned people other than his little companion, to whom he talked almost incessantly, but never about their destination. Thus did they speed past road-workers' camps, fettlers' camps, road-workers and fettlers at work, and even a couple of pubs with only a wave, when his natural style would have been to stop everywhere and have a pitch particularly if he saw anyone of Aboriginal breed about; and there were plenty. They went as far as Caroline River with stops only to pee or to drink from the water-bag, and then only in lonely places. They had to stop at the Caroline for fuel. There they also had refreshments at the pub, sandwiches and beer for Eddy, sandwiches and lolly-water for Prindy who sat out on the verandah within sight and sound of Eddy standing at the bar. Duggan the publican, who would have seen *Truth* brought down by yesterday's train, tried hard with inuendoes to learn something of the facts of the gossip he must also have been hearing over the phone, but completely without success. At last Eddy said, 'Well, Mick, we must be gettin' along?'

'Where to?' asked Duggan.

'Just down the road a bit . . . find a nice place to camp.'

They found what was one of the nicest spots in the country, despite the fact that the surroundings had been torn to pieces for gold nearly half a century before and there was a fair amount of fouling up done by modern travellers: Bamboo Creek, a place of clean quartz gravel and crystal water, a huge banyan and thickets of bamboo of the giant variety. Floods and the type of vegetation were most likely responsible for the rehabilitation; and floods would likewise soon clear up modern mess. Prindy was particularly delighted with the bamboo, a novelty to him, this being about as far South as it grew naturally. Although growing in profusion along the coasts, it was probably not truly native. Early voyagers from the Indies most likely introduced the coastal stuff, and Chinese this about the old goldfields.

Prindy showed McCusky how to make a flute, using the pocket-knife he always carried now, and taught him to play *Doh Re Mi*. Eddy was very much impressed, whereas formerly, perhaps influenced by his wife hostility to the boy, he had seemed to regard Prindy's bent for music only as nuisance noise-making. He got him playing, adding to his repertoire a couple of his own favourites, *The Road to Gundagai* and *The Old Sundowner,* stuff so facile – facile as the Australian Mind – that the boy was able to play it after practically one hearing. Prindy didn't say of the new pieces, 'rubbitch', but looked as if he might. Not that Eddy noticed. Leaning back on his unrolled swag, with knees crossed, one leg in the air, in true bush fashion, he said, 'You know . . . you're a real smart feller. You might go a long way. What you want to be when you grow up?' That took a bit of translating to convey its meaning to Prindy, who then replied that he wanted to play music and ride horses. 'Don't sound very ambitious to me,' commented Eddy. But suddenly he had second thoughts: 'But I don't know. If you could make up music like *The Road to Gundagai* and make a name for yourself as a jockey . . . By Christ, yes . . . Prendegast Alroy, the Musical Jockey . . . makin' up hit-tunes and ridin' Melbourne Cup winners . . . no, Aboriginal Musical Jockey! Jesus, boy . . . you might be famous yet! Play me the old *Road to Gundagai* again . . . .'

All this was fairly early in the evening, with young Igulgul winking through the bamboos and stirring up just enough wind to make them scrape and squeak as background music. When Igulgul disappeared they unrolled their swags, and Eddy built up the fire till Prindy drew his bedding away for fear of its catching. Maybe Eddy was afraid of the darkness. But nobody could be more afraid than a blackfellow, who makes the smallest fire possible, at once so as not to make his camp conspicuous, and to be able to see if anyone approaches.

However, it might have been that what he feared was that prospect of his charge's Doing a Bunk, with the terrible consequences such an eventuality threatened for himself; for he slept only in snatches, to start up and take a look at the small bundle on the other side of the fire, a couple of times even to rise and sneak across as if to see if there were really a boy in it and not just stuffing. Prindy himself slept quite soundly. Eddy's relief in finding him still there in daylight was surely shown by his promptly going off soundly himself. He had to be cooked out by the Sun.

They were having breakfast, of canned beef, canned beans and biscuits, when Prindy said he could hear the train coming. The track crossed there on a short but long-legged trestle bridge. They went to watch it. There she was, the mail train on her way home. The driver this trip was old Jack Tinball, who cock-a-doodled when he saw them, so that everybody else popped out their heads to see, and waved and cheered.

Then they went on their way, merely slowing down as they ran through the Alice River siding, simply waving to the dusty mob making more dust further South. The road skirted Granite Springs well to westward but soon came back to the railway; and there they were, just before noon, running past Beatrice River Racecourse, and seeing the old familiar scene. Down and over the river, up and over the railway, into the empty street, to pull up before Finnucane's verandah as the man himself came out to greet them; or rather one of them, although there was no doubt about his interest in the other. Where would they be goin'? Eddy had fairly to leap out to stop the bellowed questions. He went into the bar with old Shame-on-us, was out in a moment with a bottle of lolly-water. Then he drank with Shamus, while speaking in subdued tones and watching. Finnucane became quite conspiratorial. When after some twenty minutes they came out together, Finnucane said to Prindy, 'And so ye havin' a noice thrip wit' the noice gintleman, are ye, sonny? T'at's goot. You stick to him. He's your friend, ye know . . . your very best friend.' And he shook the boy's hand in parting.

They went on, past Barbu's, deserted, of course, since Barbu Ram had not yet had the chance to come home. Prindy hung out to stare at the poor little place, as if thinking it was for the last time. Eddy nearly hit the goats through watching him nervously. As they ploughed through the aroma he asked, 'You like that old Ali Barba too much, eh?'

Prindy, staring ahead now, replied, 'Him all right.'

'You like him bein' your father?'

'He not my father.'

'You know who your father is?'

Prindy was silent for a moment, evidently much less concerned with the anomaly of his paternity than with Aboriginal ethics, since he asked, 'When Critchmitch?'

Eddy looked astonished, this man who knew Aboriginal minds and ethics so well that he was not only second-father to all of the breed in this country but even aspired to become their Number-one Daddy-o. He answered, 'Aw . . . good while yet . . . pretty near one month. What for you ask me that?'

'No more dis one Moon . . . next one, eh?'

'Yes . . . that's about it. But why . . . . ?'

As Eddy should have known, before one could utter the name of a dead person a full year must elapse. Prindy had worked it out: 'My daddy daid-feller.'

After a while Eddy asked, 'You're goin' to let me be your Daddy for a while, aren't you?'

The grey eyes studied the thin profile for a long moment before the quiet little voice asked, 'Where we go now?'

Eddy also took a moment to answer, 'Aw . . . I take you show him you that Inland country . . . that Centre you know.'

Eddy glanced, to meet the steady eyes, and perhaps to read in them that indeed the owner of them did know, and that he himself had opened the trap too wide again, a realization that nearly put them off the red sandy road.

The Sun was down in the trees and the leaves gilding as they came to Charlotte Springs and ploughed through more goats and roused all the dogs and the human population of a score or so, all the whites of which were in the pub; or at least till the car pulled up before it, when they came lurching out. Stiff-lipped Colleen came out to rescue Eddy from the nosey ones. Evidently she had been appraised of his coming and its import. She told him to drive round the back and she would show them their room.

Thus did Prindy come to yet another stage in his compulsory rise up from savagery, to being installed in a hotel room; as poor a one as could be found in any civilized country in the world, to be sure, but such a one nevertheless and one where no one of his breed had ever been admitted before. There was a nice white bed, mosquito net, towel, a nice white pot to piddle in. What a long way had he come!

They went to the shower together, then to the dining-room, with its hissing acetylene lamp and pictures of mad horses in frightful storms on the wall. No one else came into the room except Colleen. The sounds from the bar made it plain that other people were more interested in drinking than eating. After the meal they returned to their room, where Eddy suggested Prindy amuse himself with his music until he came back, that he was just going to look into the bar for a minute or two. Eddy closed the door after him, and very carefully turned the key and pocketed it. He was away a lot more than a minute or two, but not so long that he could not tell Prindy, who had been asleep, that they were a rough mob in the bar, and they would be lucky if they got any sleep. Still, they did sleep, Eddy himself quite soundly.

Breakfast in the kitchen, again by acetylene; while Colleen, scarcely speaking, cut sandwiches and the place rocked with snores of patrons apparently sleeping everywhere. Then away into the red morning, tearing along to make the most of the cool, with the telegraph poles counting the chains in the miles with a sort of beating. There! There! There! like skinny fingers, as if to give emphasis to what Eddy yapped about for hours, that this was the Inland, a terrible place, waterless, trackless, tuckerless, its only inhabitants naked blackmen who would take your kidney-fat and eat it, if you were silly enough to try running away in it; this to a fellow who had crossed the blighted Frog Country and who now looked out at the water leaping in silver fountains to the thrust of the spinning windmills of the bores and never missed seeing one of the bustards peeping from the scrub or those old-men kangaroos that Eddy might have thought were antbeds. He might have asked whether the naked blacks ate one another's kidney-fat when there were no silly strangers going walkabout; but he had become his old uncommunicative self since that question of his yesterday: '*Where we go?*'

Except for one pee, they didn't stop till they reached York Waters Telegraph Station in mid-morning. The black mob in the camp, mostly naked and the rest in rags, afforded Eddy an opportunity to bring up the wild blacks business again. 'See what I mean . . . bad lookin' buggers, ain't they!' Then, as he went towards the linesmen lounging on the verandah of their residence, bearing with him the traditional offering of the bottle of OP rum, he warned the boy not to get out of the car, lest the kidney-fat takers make off with him. Prindy obeyed. But as soon as the gentry had disappeared into the house, he gave his Skin Sign to the dusky watchers, got the appropriate responses, including the turning away of some. After a while four middle-aged men came strolling across, two in loin-cloths of grubby flour-sack calico, the others stark naked, all bearing traces of recent painting, one with plaited beard; certainly as savage a bunch as one might wish to meet, at least to look at, from whom anyone particular about keeping their kidneys might easily have been excused for leaping out and running for protection to him who was so eminent a one in the protection business. But the grey eyes surveyed them quite calmly. It was the one with the plaited beard who spoke first, 'Good-tay, Julama.' This one was his Uncle, Jalyeri. He answered him accordingly.

Jalyeri tried him in local lingo; but he shook his head, and himself tried a bit out of his own vocabulary. The others shook their heads. Nothing for it then but Murringlitch. Jalyeri asked, 'Where you go, my-boy?'

'I don' know, Kamija.'

'Dat one Mick Cusky, ain't it?'

'Yu.'

The others held a lively and lengthy discussion in lingo. Then one, an Elder Brother, asked, 'Where you come from, Julama?'

'P'liceman been run him up me.'

Jalyeri asked, 'Wha' nam' . . . you myall bugger, eh?'

They all giggled. Then one asked, 'Him yard him you, eh?'

'I don' know.'

'Me-feller been see him p'liceman tek him halfcaste longa Tchenter . . . . '

They were interrupted by the appearance of Mick Cusky himself, yelling, 'Eh . . . what's goin' on there?'

Prindy's poor relations dodged out of sight behind a shed. At their action the whole camp vanished. Eddy, strutting somewhat and with hat over an eye, perhaps from having sampled the gift of rum, came to the car, the other men with him. He asked Prindy who the blacks were. Prindy said he didn't know, while staring at the whitemen who were staring at him no doubt because of what they had heard about him through telephonic gossip. Handshakes between the whitefellows; and then they were on their way again.

It was close to sundown when they pulled in at Mt Albert Station, the Knowles's place. The squatter and his wife were out on the verandah to greet the greetable one of them, and with them Nugget, who also greeted the ungreetable, calling; 'Goodday, sonny . . . how yo' doin'?' Father and Mother Knowles weren't dressed up on this occasion, nor had the guest-room been prepared. They told Eddy, when he came up to them on the verandah, that they were sorry, but couldn't have Niggers in their rooms or at their table, except as servants. You'd never be able to handle the creatures again if one of them were to be accepted as anything like an equal. Things were bad enough as it was, thanks to – er – well, Dr Cobbitty. They could camp on the water-hole. They would be sent down some bread and beef. Eddy went red, but said simply that he understood, his only expression of feeling in the matter being to retain the bottle of rum.

It was Nugget who brought the food down, quite a good meal, which he joined them in eating, but without making any apology for his parents' attitude. He frankly confessed his acquaintance with Prindy, and treated him like an old friend, and after a swig or two from the rum bottle declared to Eddy that he would have married Nelly, if she hadn't cleared out as she had; that is, of course, if Eddy himself had given permission: Would he have? Eddy answered promptly, 'Sure . . . you're just the right type we want to marry 'em off to.'

'But they reckon she's dead, eh?' said Nugget.

'Nothing's certain. Inquest was adjourned indefinitely.'

'But the young feller'd know. What happened your Mumma, Prindy, boy?'

Prindy, munching a huge sandwich of bread and roast beef with mustard pickles only stared at him. Eddy said. 'You won't get anything out of him.'

'Why?'

Eddy shrugged: 'Search me. They reckon it's amnesia . . . but I don't know. You know what they're like . . . .'

'Manesia? Sounds like sumpin for indigestion!'

'Loss o' memory . . . due to shock.'

'Aw . . . I see, Yeah . . . I remember he was a bit queer, used to wake up nights singin' . . . reckoned butcher birds taught him to make up songs . . . eeeeee-aaaaaaaah! Still makin' up songs, sonny?'

'Y' ought 'o hear him on the bamboo whistle!'

After the meal, Prindy entertained them, while they drank the rum, diluted with the chalky water of the hole. Soon they were singing with him, but not so happily as might be, because of Nugget's terrible voice. Nugget tried to blame it onto Prindy, even when Eddy told him he was tone deaf. 'Course I can sing!' declared Nugget. 'Ev'rybody can sing 't a few in.' He was no sort of drinker, even worse than Eddy, and was soon unable to sing at all. Then he wanted to talk – to Prindy – about those lovely moonlit nights at what he called Hang On Creek: 'Jes like t'night, washn' it, shonny . . . all shiny bright . . . 'n' pretty Mumma there . . . Aw, Jesus, why'd I let it happen?'

'What happen?' burbled Eddy.

'Huh-huh . . . ought 'o shot the bastard!'

'What bastard?'

'You know . . . don' yo' shonny . . . aw . . . I never had no luck!' Nugget began to whimper. 'First he busts that up . . . then he gets bloody coppers there . . . and they find a few clean-skins they reckon's Vaisey's . . . and I get hunted off me bit o' property . . . and just 's a war's breakin' out 'o make me rich man . . . aw, ah . . . Wha' 'appen' yo' Mumma, shonny boy . . . tell me . . . tell me . . . 'cause I love 'er . . . aw-aw-aw-aw-aw!'

Eddy fell asleep; and Nugget went reeling up home through the rocks and the goats in the last light of Igulgul. Somewhere away off a dingo was mourning.

They were off on their way soon after sunrise next morning, without paying their respects to the Knowleses; which they wouldn't have been able to, anyway, since it was Sunday, and everybody in the bush lies in of Sundays, if only to make it different from other days. They sped on their way, out of the barren hills, into the barren sandy mulga. It was only mid-morning when they came into sight of the mill of the bore beside which the Prospector's Alms stood, the settlement itself for a long while unseen, only that blur above the endless vista of stunted trees looking like an outsize one of them. Then when the tiny group of buildings began to consolidate out of mirage it was not that which caught the travellers' eyes, but what might have been taken elsewhere to be a great gathering of people, striving together for some purpose, raising the dust, and their voices, the latter coming like discordant snatches of song, of hymn-singing.

Eddy was the first to express his curiosity: 'They ain't goats . . . too big, ain't they?'

A moment more of staring; then Prindy got it: 'Donkey!'

'Yeah . . . yeah! For a moment I thought it must be the Salvation Army all gone balmy and come up here into the bloomin' desert.'

The donkeys were milling about the water trough. And there not far away from them was a huge waggon, with wheels even twice the height of the beasts surrounding it; and they were not small donkeys, but those very special animals bred by one whose name was uttered simultaneously by the approaching watchers: 'Billy Brew!'

Billy Brew was supposed to have five hundred donkeys, and to use as many as one hundred in a team at a time when he had a heavy load. There were all of the alleged five hundred of the creatures, black, white and brindle, and all of them Psalm Singin', as old Billy himself would say.

Eddy chuckled, 'We just got to stop here a while and hear old Billy. He's prob'ly tellin' yarns right now to a boozy mob o' miners from the Pisgah Field. Must be a fair mob in there. Look at the trucks . . . in for the weekend groggin', of course.

There certainly was a crowd at the hotel, although not so actively boozy at the moment, not yet having got a go on from the spell they would have had after the conviviality of yesterday, judging by the couple of dozen out on the verandah. They were in all sorts of attitudes, excepting those occupying the few chairs, from sitting with backs to the wall and legs spread out, some with heads drooping in sleep, to lying spread-eagled on the floor; only a couple with bottles and no one with an empty glass, and all who could see squinting like bandicoots caught out in sunlight. The bar was pretty well packed, too, but giving forth only the sounds of glass on glass and talk scarcely above hoarse whispers. They were proceeding to enliven themselves with the aid of that subtle antagonist who had floored them last night and would have most of them down again before the day was out. But they would need some purpose to get them properly on their feet to go through it all again – anything – and there it was, in the form of the new arrivals, or rather in one of them, the one usually not greeted elsewhere, even if hardly ignored. The arrival of the car roused only blinking interest, and the alighting of Eddy scarcely more. What brought the bloodshot eyes wide open and slouched bodies to their unsteady feet and burnt-out throats back into exuberant operation was someone's hoarse shout: 'Dat der lil poy vot's in las' Sunday *Truth* . . . look it!'

They were foreigners, a lot of them, Square'eads, Reffoes, and for the rest a very different class of person from the squatter and his hangers-on. They would have got last Sunday's *Truth* even earlier than the Port Palmestonians, because the mail plane called at Boulder Creek. Also probably they would have given a great deal more attention to the paper than the townies, having so much less to entertain them, and those who could not read English, particularly to the pictures in it; and not being Australians and bred to regard Aboriginal persons as not quite human, they might have had very different feelings from what generally would be felt about children chained by the neck and shackled to a lanky bearded laughing policeman. They flung Eddy aside in their uproarious rush to seize Prindy and haul him from the car and carry him struggling onto the verandah, ignoring Eddy's shouts of protest at their interference with his charge; except one huge fellow with hairless eyes, who shoved a peeling square red face down into his, to ask in a growl like a bear, 'Vot . . . you copper-man, ja?' Eddy fell back cringing.

Prindy looked scared, till amongst those bursting out of the bar he saw the tubby form and grey-bearded face of Billy Brew, towards whom he flung appealing hands, and who shoved through the others, reaching for him, roaring, 'Gi'm to me . . . I'm his huncle!' Billy got Prindy, embraced him boozily, then set him down.

'How you he honcle?' demanded someone 'He *mütter* you *schwester*, old viskers, ja?'

That roused the laugh that caused Con and Bridie behind the counter to line up the glasses.

Billy answered, 'Nein, nein, mein frient . . . I'm his tribal huncle . . . ain't it, young feller . . . blackfeller fashion.'

Some other waggish Square'ead said, 'So! It isht on *mütter* side you relate . . . but not by marriage, *hein*?'

Billy drew Prindy into the bar, picked him up again and swung him onto the counter, roaring to those behind it, 'Lookit I found . . . know him?'

Bridie stood gaping at the grey eyes staring at her, murmured, 'Course I know him.'

'Dead ring the Scrub Bull, ain't he?'

'Too right,' said Bridie, then looked, craning, as if to see if Jeremy were there.

'No . . . old Jerry ain't here,' said Billy. 'He come with McCusky . . . .'

Eddy came shoving in, demanding, 'Here . . . what you doin' with that boy?'

He would have laid hands on Prindy, only Billy Brew laid hands on Eddy, demanding, 'What *you* doin' with him, you mean?'

'He's in my lawful custody . . . .'

'McCusky's cuskody . . . haw, haw, haw!' There was a howl from those who understood.

Eddy dropped the official tone, for a matey one: 'Go easy, Billy. The kid's not supposed to be in a place like this.'

' 'Ear that, Bridie . . . Con . . . place like this, eh? What you runnin' . . . a moll-shop . . . Hey, where's them molls?'

Everybody laughing except Eddy, who appealed to Bridie: 'You know it's an offence for him to be on licenced premises, Bride . . . .'

'Offence me arse!' cried Billy. 'Where you reckon you are . . . the Queen Vic Hotel, or sumpin?'

'Fair go, Billy. Just let me put him back in the car . . . and then I'll have a drink with you.'

'You don' say, your lordship . . . you'll have a drink with me on them terms, eh?'

'I mean I'd like to have a drink with you . . . and the boys.'

'Make a bargain with you, Eddy . . . you can put him back in the car if you shout for the bar . . . 'ow 'bout it, sport?'

Eddy's eyes rolled as he surveyed the shoving roaring mob about him.

'You can put it down as expenses . . . travellin' expenses,' said Billy. 'That't you silvertails do, ain't it . . . travel at the public's expense?'

Eddy swallowed: 'Okay.'

As Eddy reached for Prindy and was lifting him down, Billy called to Con, 'Set 'em up, Cornelius, boy . . . scotch all round.' Eddy, as if making a swift count of heads, or rather of grinning faces, seemed to wilt. As he disappeared, leading Prindy, Billy said, 'Better watch the bastard don't do a bunk.' He leapt to the door.

Indeed Eddy looked as if he would have leapt into the car after putting Prindy into it, but for finding himself under observation. Billy grinned at him through his whiskers, and yelled, 'Don't forgit your cheque-book . . . Old Shame-on-us won't let 'em use the slate.'

Eddy came back, took the glass Billy handed to him. 'We goin' 'o drink to you,' said Billy, 'To good old Mick Cusky, as them's you keep in mickustody calls you . . . you know they calls you that?'

'I know,' said Eddy, assuming some of the old leeriness. 'You know what they call you?'

'Yeah, yeah . . . the Donk with the Biggest Walloper in the Team.'

What Eddy would have said was silenced by a roar of laughter.

Billy raised his glass and his voice: ' 'Ere's to old Mick and his Custody!'

Billy downed his whisky in a gulp, and amidst the uproar of the toast, unobstrusively disappeared. Eddy, rather slow with his drink, raw as it was and no doubt a double seeing who'd handed it to him, looked about for Billy. And there in a moment Billy was, pushing through the crowd, again with Prindy on his shoulder. Prindy had his flute. Eddy uttered a cry of protest, and would have snatched Prindy away, only for the intervention of a couple of dozen large red hands along with half that number of square red grinning faces. He almost whimpered, 'You reckoned . . . . '

Billy said, 'All I reckoned's we'd let you take him out the car if you'd shout. Now all you got 'o do's shout again . . . and you can take him out again . . . and so on.' Billy set Prindy on the bar again, calling to Bridie, 'Gi'im some lolly-water. . . Mick Cusky's shout.'

Eddy groaned, 'Aw, for chrissake . . . you'll get me into trouble!'

'Wha' for?'

'Permitting an Aboriginal Person to be on licensed premises.'

'Who's goin' 'o report you . . . yo'self? Christ, you blokes get pretty flamin' low mockin' on yo'selves!'

Eddy could only droop amongst the laughing mob. Billy pounded his shoulder. 'Cheer up, man. Have another drink. Look, you got 'bout forty drinks comin' your way to ketch up on that big shout. Fill'em up again, Con . . . my shout.'

Eddy protested, 'I don't want to catch up with the shout. You forced me into it . . . . '

'What . . . don't tell me you're one o' them's got to be forced to shout . . . a bloke't drinks't the bar'flies?'

'I got to get on me way, Billy . . . . '

'Where you goin'?'

Eddy jerked his head southward. Billy demanded, 'You ain't takin' that lovely kid down that bloody boys' home o' yours?'

Eddy screwed his face up, turning from Prindy, hissing, 'Shhhh!'

'What you shushin' for . . . you 'shamed the place?'

Eddy snapped, 'No I'm not ashamed of it. I don't want official business discussed here, that's all.'

'Well, you ought to be bloody 'shamed of it, seein' the last bastard runnin' the place was caught buggerin' the poor kids . . . . '

There was uproar in the bar, and more as Billy raised his voice to explain that a Superintendent of the Home for Halfcaste Boys had been dismissed for alleged sodomy, but never formally charged, and as Eddy, almost screaming tried to explain that there was nothing like that there now, that it was a model institution. It was stopped by the shouted intervention of Bridie and Con and the handing round of more drinks.

Billy said, 'Let the boy gi's a bit o' music. I heard him playin' that flute thing out there . . . and I never heard nothin' so sweet me life, fair dinkum . . . . '

Eddy tried to protest, but was ordered to drink. When everybody had drunk and another shout was on the way, Billy spoke to Prindy, who was looking scared, '*Koyada kumeri, Ngahgung* . . . play us that pretty toon you was playin' out there . . . Don't be fright' . . . your old huncle lookin' out you.'

Prindy raised the pipe. 'Shush, shush!' cried Billy.

The sweet notes were a little weak and tremulous to begin with, but soon found strength and clarity: Brahms *Lullaby*. Some of the Square'eads exclaimed in surprise; a couple began to sing in German.

When it was over there was great applause. Red hands reached to pat the musician, praising him in foreign lingo. Some pale blue eyes were magnified with tears. They were calling for more drink, all wanting to shout.

Billy said, 'Well, what d'you think o' that, from one so young, and classed as an Aboriginal Person not capable of managin' his own affairs . . . if he 'ad any.'

There was a burst of burbling talk about it, mixed with requests for more music, and mopping up the booze. Prindy rippled a scale or two.

Eddy had to take charge of it: 'I taught him a lot meself. Gi's *The Road to Gundagai*, Prendy.'

Prindy was already off into *La Golondrina*, with some Square'ead singing it in lingo. But Eddy stopped him, urging, '*Gundagai* . . . *Gundagai* . . . that's 't we want.'

Prindy stopped, looked reluctant, till urged by Billy Brew. Then he played it, while Eddy and Billy sang. When it was over, Eddy asked, 'Well, how you like that?'

Some Square'ead answered with a snort, 'Bloddy robbish!'

'Eh? That's a good Australian song!'

A mob of Square'eads shouted, 'Bloddy robbish!'

'Here, careful what you say!' cried Eddy.

Billy backed him up: 'Yeah . . . suits us!'

Eddy turned to Prindy: 'Give it to 'em again.' Prindy stared at him: 'Come on!' Eddy urged. Prindy looked at the Square'eads, then back at Eddy, and shook his fair head. 'Why?' demanded Eddy.

Prindy said simply, 'Bloody rubbitch.'

Even Eddy joined a little in the storm of laughter. They all had another drink on it, while Prindy concluded *La Golondrina*. But Billy Brew wanted something he knew, named a few, like *Annie Laurie* and *Silver Threads Amongst the Gold*, none of which was in Prindy's repertoire as yet. It was he himself made the suggestion, 'I play lil bits Narishman, eh?' Billy knew what he meant, that was certain from his guffaw, but not any of the others until he started so-called *Danny Boy*. That suited half the company, anyway. Prindy went through what he'd been taught by his Daddy-o, Coon-Coon. He went on to play things of his own – and Indian bits – and things that the boozy ones, getting boozier, came and took him aside and sang to him, Eddy amongst these and so boozy now as to have lost utterly his earlier scruples about the boy's being there; and so until the mob was roaring drunk and Prindy looking scared. Then Bridie unobtrusively whipped him off the counter and out through that half-door leading to the passage, and through to the kitchen, where she sat him down and gave him a plate of the curry and rice she had in huge pots on the stove and now proceeded to dish out into smaller vessels for taking up to feed the drunks without interruption to their drinking. While she worked she asked him questions about himself, out of a fair knowledge of his recent doings she would have culled, especially through her interest in his white grandfather, from the *Truth* story and telephonic gossip that probably had begun with Cahoon's apprehension of him. As usual, Prindy answered only what it suited his peculiar unfrankness to divulge. Naturally, Bridie wanted to know what had happened to his mother. He acted as if he hadn't heard her, simply went on eating, gazing out through the fly-wire of the window at the donkeys round the waggon and the trough. She left him, telling him to stay out the back. He sat on the back steps, amusing himself by imitating the donkeys and making up a tune from their odd vocalizing that might truly be called a Donkey Serenade, with the background uproar of the bar.

When Bridie returned after about half an hour with the empty dishes, accompanied and assisted and being fiercely talked at by Billy Brew, she appeared to be alarmed. Prindy glanced up at them. Billy signed to him to follow them into the kitchen. As the boy came in, Billy asked him, 'You savvy where that Mick Cusky takin' you?' Prindy made no vocal answer, but showed by his expression that he might have an idea. Billy went on: 'You want 'o go long o' him?' Prindy blinked, then shook his head. 'Would you like to come long o' me . . . dat-a-way?' Billy jerked his beard in the direction the boy had come. Prindy, mostly slow to answer, either from sharpness of wits or the opposite, no one had yet decided, looked into the pale blue eyes for a moment before giving a nod. Billy swung on Bridie, declaring, 'There!'

She said breathlessly, 'You're mad, Billy . . . you're drunk . . . playing a trick like that . . . '

'I tell yo' it ain't a trick, girl. Not't I wouldn't be glad to make a fool of the bloody blatherskitin' silvertail bastard. But puttin' this lovely kid in that lost-dogs' home of his is goin' to make jes another crazy mixed up yeller feller. This boy's been free right up to now. He thinks he's a blackfeller. They'll teach him there he's a bloody nothin'. I know it, Bride. Didn't I have yeller kids me own? Ain't I watched the rotten system most me life? A blackfeller, no matter 'ow crook things get for him, no matter he's starvin' and in rags, or even in jail . . . he's got the satisfaction of knowin' he belongs to sumpin . . . he's got dignity . . . and he needn't be true black, so long's he's been brought up black. Even if he's taken out of his country for good, he can lie down and die and send his Shade back to it. That's a blackfeller, no matter how dark or light in colour he is. But being a yeller feller, thinkin' you're a bit white anyway, and hatin' the black in you so's to justify the white, is being, as I said, a Bloody Nothin'. That's Jeremy Delacy's idea, too, you know . . . why he didn't take this kid before. He tried to take him now, 'cause now's the time . . . now's the time to save his very life . . . and I'm goin' to save it. If you won't give that big-mouth bastard knock-drops so's he jes don't know what happened to him today, then I'll give 'im a rabbit punch and knock him cold. He's belly-aching to go now. If we can't 'old him for another 'arf hour, he'll take the boy . . . 'Ere's the bastard comin' now . . . ' Billy glanced out at sound of footsteps.

Eddy, blinking bleerily and swaying, came into the kitchen, looked at Prindy, and said, 'Come'n boy . . . we goin' . . . hic!'

Billy said, 'Yo'll wan' a bit a tucker for the road, won't yo'?'

'We 'ad good feed.'

'You'll never get over Piss Ridge, Eddy, with all that booze aboard.'

'So long's we get goin' . . . I'm'n duty, not s'pose be boozin'. Camp 'long road.'

'So you'll want some tucker.' Billy looked meaningfully at Bridie.

She said, 'I'll get you a few sandwiches, Mr McCusky.' She leapt to do it.

'Sit down a minute.' said Billy. 'Sit down and 'ave one for the road. Ge's a drink, Bridie . . . '

'I 'ad 'nough,' said Eddy, but sat down. 'No more grog f'me.'

'Well, cup o'tea then . . . like a cup o' tea, straighten you up?'

'Yeah . . . I'll 'ave cup o' tea . . . no grog . . . no grog.'

'All right we'll have a cup o' tea . . . and finish our argyment.'

'What argumen'?' demanded Eddy.

Bridie was hastily making tea, getting cups and saucers.

'What you was tellin' them Square'eads about Aboriginal Hordinance . . . '

'I's just tellin' 'em . . . not arg'in' wit' 'em . . . I don' argue them bas'ds . . .

I don' argue any bas'd 'bout Ab'rig'nal Ord'nance . . . I administer Ab'rig'nal Ord'nance, my goo'd feller . . . admin'shter it, see?'

'Yeah . . . I see, mate . . . . '

'We got 'o go . . boy! Where that boy?'

' 'Ere he is . . . waitin' for his big boss. 'Ere's yo' tea, Eddy.'

They sat arguing boozily about nothing at all till suddenly Eddy declared that he'd got to go, and lurched up out of his seat, to stand swaying, while Billy steadied him. 'Come on, boy . . . we go'n!' muttered Eddy. Billy winked at Prindy as he guided Eddy out, and inclined his head as sign for him to follow.

As they went through to the front verandah, Eddy muttered, 'Feelin' bit crook . . . . '

'Now, don't you go puikin' all that good booze up,' said Billy. Eddy was swaying widely as Billy helped him off the verandah to his car. Opening the door and hoisting him in, Billy said, 'You can't drive like that, Eddy. Jest lay over and 'ave a bit of a kip . . . then you'll be right.'

'Where that boy?' demanded Eddy, blinking about as Billy settled him to lie down on the front seat.

' 'E's 'ere,' said Billy. 'There 'e is. You get in the back, boy, till your boss wakes up. You right now, Eddy?'

'Right . . Billy . . . old bas'd . . . . ' And with a snore Eddy flaked out.

Billy watched him for a moment, then took a quick look at the hotel. No one was watching. The few out on the verandah were asleep. He turned to Prindy, signing him to go round the far side of the car, where in a moment he joined him, then, with another look at the hotel, picked him up and set out with him towards his waggon, soon getting lost to view amidst his donkeys. He took another look at the hotel on reaching the high waggon, then bunked the boy up over the hanging tail-board, and climbed up after him.

It was like a great barn inside the waggon, empty of the loading it was made for, except for a few small bags of ore samples, containing only a jumble of harness, with cases and sacks of Brew's own stores. The hind end served as living quarters, with a bushman's bed made up on the floor beside a cupboard constructed of several kerosene-cases containing folded clothing and a goodly number of books that dealt with surprising subjects like Astronomy, Botany, Geology, History, Greek Mythology. Billy motioned Prindy to sit on the floor, while he himself sat on a case padded with sacking. As he sat down, Prindy looked about quickly. It was unlikely that he had ever been inside the waggon, or perhaps even seen it, since Billy rarely brought his team beyond the rail-head. However, he would know donkeys, because a few still roamed round about the Beatrice, which had been the terminus up till ten years ago, and were sometimes run in races on Blackboys' Day. Billy asked him, 'You can ride a donk, eh?' Prindy nodded. Billy then, speaking a mixture of Murringlitch and the lingos of the Beatrice Country and its neighbourhood, described how he intended to outwit Mick Cusky. The boozy miners would begin heading for home round about sundown, a truckload or two at a time, as they were able to bring themselves to it. There might be a couple who'd sleep till morning. Anyway, so many would be gone by the time Eddy woke, that when he started looking for Prindy it would be easy to make him believe that some of them had taken him along with them. Eddy would then dash out to the goldfields. How long he would be away was anybody's guess. Maybe the miners would have him scouring the whole district for the joke of it. One thing was certain, that he wouldn't call the police until utterly desperate, and then not without first getting his boss's permission, as Billy had learnt from what the big-mouth had dropped when complaining of being held up and expressing fear of losing his charge through letting him out of sight. It would be fun giving the fool the run-around. But what was more important, all-important, was that it would help to take suspicion off Billy himself. Mick Cusky might even begin by suspecting Billy, seeing he had a reputation for making goats of pompous asses. So Prindy must get away from here as soon as possible, and stay away for several days alone, because Billy must be here in all seeming innocence when the bloke came back from the goldfields. He, Billy, had only just come in from the fields himself, after delivering a load of heavy machinery brought down from the rail-head, and was known for the way he took things easy, hanging about places so long as there was feed for his donks and money for booze if there were a pub handy. There was no reason for his hurrying back to the railway. His next load was not due there from Palmeston for a couple of months. His only excuse would be that he wanted to get to the Charlotte for Christmas, which was a month away. He must show no signs of untoward activity whatsoever.

Now, this was what he wanted Prindy to do: take a bag of tucker to last him a week if need be – plenty of tinned stuff here – and a quiet riding donkey, and go to the next bore back, eighteen miles, then turn East and after a couple of miles he would come to half of Billy's donks feeding on the leaves of a type of kurrajong that grew there in plenty. 'The buggers can nearly climb trees, yo' know,' said Billy. He would make a camp out there. He could come in with the donks for water at the bore of a night as they did, He, a pupil of Bobwirridirridi, who it seemed was an old mate of Billy's, would need no advice on how to conceal his movements and otherwise keep a jump ahead of everybody. Anyway, it was easy to hide along with a mob of donks. When Billy reckoned the coast was clear, he would start moving northward, and when he reached that bore, would sent his blackboy, Barney Ninyarra, to bring him and the donkeys in. At the moment Barney and his wife, Nanitch, were over in the scrub there with the local blacks, boozing. Prindy need have no fear of betrayal by them, because they stood in relationship to him as father and mother. Still, it would be best they didn't know anything about the escapade till they were away from here. Right?

Within half an hour, mounted on a brown jenny named Becky, and with some mates of hers for company and to allay suspicion that a single set of fresh tracks might arouse, Prindy set out northward, unobserved by anyone except Billy, and with no one else except Bridie Cullity aware of the escapade, because Con, perhaps seduced by that Narishman piping, had taken to the bottle himself, to be sure 'be the nip' when it came to the accounting.

III

Thus began yet another phase of the career of him known variously as Prindy, Prendy, Ah Loy, Alroy, and such secret names as his black godfathers had conferred on him for use if and when he reached a degree of maturity and trustworthiness. He had been with the donkeys out in that patch of kurrajong country six days when Billy Brew's black boy came to fetch him and them. Barney Ninyarra came *tchinekin,* not out of malice or fear, but because he had caught a strange sweet sound as he neared, and thus come upon what must have struck him as a wondrous sight, the way he stared, and the way he related it to his master later: the boy sitting with his back to the bulbous trunk of a kurrajong playing on his bamboo flute to a packed semi-circle of donkeys whose attitudes left no doubt about their enchantment, although among them, so Barney reported, were some of the meanest of the team, like Bollocky Bill and Queen of Sheba. When Billy heard of it and asked Prindy, the boy said that he'd found the animals specially liked Indian music. Billy required a test, and saw the same effect for himself, on the whole team. Billy likened it to the quieting of restless cattle in drovers' mobs by the night-rider's singing to 'em or playing the mouth-organ; and being one who liked to delve into cause and effect he reckoned that it was some atavistic strain at work, because these donkeys were of the breed called Onager, originating in north-western Asia. Being also a resourceful man, he reckoned that the oddity might be put to good use in making the team easier to handle during harnessing-up. It was tried, but only to prove that a donkey isn't as silly as reputed. The intractable ones behaved even worse for having their musical interlude spoilt by the intrusion of rough hands and whirling whips urging them into the line-up for submission to collar and trace. An experimenter, too, Billy said, 'Try the bloody bastards with *The Road to Gundagai.*' Prindy began to pipe with extra vigour. Bollocky Bill started a bolt that held up the harnessing for a couple of hours. If Prindy supposed from that bit of cause and effect that he wouldn't have to play that Bloody Rubbitch again he was wrong, because the ever-resourceful Billy saw use in it: 'Y'know, we could keep that toon for huntin' the buggers away when they get crowdin' round the waggon o' full-moon nights a-psalm-singin'.'

Billy told an amusing tale of Mick Cusky's running about: 'Like a meat-ant full o' arsenic.' Sure enough, he had descended first on Billy, and even with Billy's show and proof of innocence, declared that he believed he had connived at Prindy's disappearance to make a fool of him. Still, he had acted on Billy's suggestion that the miners were responsible, and had gone after them, surely to have his leg pulled, because he made no less than three trips to the goldfields, dashing back each time to try to catch Billy by surprise. Then he had taken a trip to the Boulder, on learning that one load of miners had gone that way, heading for the South. Still he hadn't called the police, as the Cullitys would know, and more than that, had asked Bridie and Con to keep quiet about it in talking on the phone, confessing to them frankly his fear of his boss. It seemed that Dr Cobbity would be going South for Christmas and that Eddy would be getting his big chance by being appointed as his actual deputy with Dr McQuegg, who usually took over the Protectorship. But what hope would he have if Cobbitty learnt of this? In the end he'd had to ask even Billy to keep it dark. That was when he'd seen Billy harnessing-up. Billy reported, 'I says to him, I says: "You got the flamin' cheek to hask me to conceal your gross hinhefficiency after haccusin' me o' connivance?" . . . I'll teach you all them big words, *Ngahgung.* I'll teach you plenty . . . readin', writin', 'rithmetic. I ain't such a higgerant old bush-whacker as I make out, you know.' To secure his co-operation, Eddy had presented him with a bottle of rum at parting and hinted at a fairer go from the Aborigines Department than he'd had in the past. Nevertheless, they must keep constantly on the alert, not only in expectation of further investigation by Eddy, but by police, because you never knew what the erratic Silvertail Bastard might do. There was always a riding donk or two saddled and bridled ready for emergencies such as misbehaviour or mishap amongst the tailing mob or the intrusion of other animals, such as branded cattle, which must be hunted off as soon as possible to avoid complications with the law, or unbranded, which must be dealt with discreetly otherwise, or horses making a nuisance of themselves with their superior airs amongst their poor relations, or dingoes after foals. Prindy must be ready to mount and away the instant dust was reported on northern or southern horizons by day or the glow of headlights by night, leaving no trace behind him. Fortunately in this country you could see anyone approaching by motor vehicle a good five miles off; and no one would be travelling otherwise at this time of year.

They had half a dozen false alarms before reaching Mt Prince Albert, which took them as many days. They didn't go near the homestead (at least not with the team) but skirted it by following a track that took them to water a good two miles to eastward. This was for a combination of reasons, according to what Billy said, amongst them being the enmity of Ned Knowles towards him, another that he wanted a couple of the Mt Prince Albert goats, which were renowned as the best eating in the country, just as its bovine stock was considered the worst. Conditions were perfect for goat-duffing, Igulgul almost at the full and the season such as to have caused a concentration of dingoes in the vicinity with just such intentions as Billy Brew's. As Billy said, it was always best to share your thieving of small stock – goats, pigs, poultry – with the dingoes, since not only did they get all the blame, but made it easier by putting the victims into that proper state of accepting their fate which is the quintessence, the quiddity, the number-one principle of good hunting. A clever huntsman starts by Singing his quarry. Hence the dingoes' howling. But while you yourself may imitate this part of his procedure, you can't assume that Smell of Death which goes along with him. Therefore, you need a dingo downwind, while you come a-howlin' up-wind.

Usually Barney and Billy worked together with the dingoes on this kind of forraging; but since it was reckoned that the sooner Prindy got broken into it the better, it was decided that Billy would stay out of it on this occasion. Barney and Prindy set out soon after moonrise. The raid was more than a success. Prindy's talent with ventriloquism turned it into something that rendered Barney helpless with laughter, when later he came to describe it. Not only did they come home with three fat young wethers and a milking nanny, but two chooks and a muskovy duck, the former walking quietly, as their kind so conveniently do to their doom, despite their capriciousness in all other ways, the latter in a sack, a corner of which Barney had to keep stuffed in his mouth for some time to stifle his mirth. The great moment of the raid was when Prindy caused old Ned and young Nugget, who were sneaking about on different sides of the house with rifles, to believe they heard a dingo right in the house and to rush in after it from opposite directions and apparently to collide, judging by the bad language and the screaming of old Mum. However, Barney had to keep stuffing the sack into his mouth for much longer than expected, and the doomed goats kept walking further, because they got back to within Prindy's extra-long earshot of the camp to find that someone was there besides those they'd left, Billy, Nanitch, the two 'bully-dogs', and, of course, the donks. From reconnoitring, Prindy came back with the startling information that the additional presence was none other than that of Mick Cusky!

Eddy had come *tchinekin*. At least that's what Billy said the man had done, when at last the raiders were able to come home with their spoils, after hearing Eddy depart, not simply from the camp but from the neighbourhood in his car, which he had left up on the main road. It seemed that Eddy had told Billy he'd seen the fresh tracks of the turn-out and heard the donks and thought he'd just look in, leaving his car behind in case the track was too rough for it. Because there was a stiff little nor'wester blowing off a thunder-storm somewhere away up top, and he was down-wind from the camp, even the dogs hadn't become aware of his presence until he was right there in the camp. And there was Prindy's flute lying on the kerosene-case on which he had been sitting playing it by the fire after supper. Billy just had time to knock it off as Eddy went to seat himself on the box, by throwing a sack on it for him, and then with a kick had more or less covered it with sand. 'Yeah,' said Billy, 'the bastard come tchinekin all right. His eyes were all over the place . . . even took a look in the waggon sayin' it was a great way to live, jes wanderin' around the country like a gypsy. When I said I wasn't no flamin' gypsy, but a licenced carrier, he says: "You don't want to go doin' nothin' that'll lose you your licence, do you," then goes on to tell me how he's on his way to Town to take over from Cobbitty; and you never know, he says, Cobbitty mightn't come back, and he'll be the Big Boy in the Abo business, and anybody breakin' the flamin' Ordinances, he's goin' 'o break them . . . so, what's called Tacitly, which means out the side o' your mouth, mind yo' step, Billy Brew. If he'd'a'ad two-penn'orth o' bush-savvy he'd a noticed your tracks . . . look at 'em, all over the place. But he wasn't such a *mungus* about Barney bein' missin'. I told him Barney'd gone across to the homestead to look up relations. He says, 'What, a blackfeller go walkin' 'bout night-time on his rown?' I ups and says it's still daylight when Barney went. But I'm sure he didn't be'leve me . . . and starts talkin' 'bout you, young feller, bein' mates with Nugget Knowles . . . like he reckoned you'd gone over with Barney. I don' know . . . I might be too suspicious . . . that means I'm thinkin' too hard 'bout it . . . but I got a feelin' he's a wake-up. Still, don't you worry. We'll beat him. We just got 'o keep our eyes peeled all the while.'

It wasn't so much a matter of keeping eyes open as noses, it turned out, when next morning, as the team came back to the main road on the northern side of the Knowles's homestead, there was Mick Cusky tchinekin again. Fortunately that same wind was blowing. The dogs smelt him as he lurked in ambush, and growled, and the donkeys pricked their ears. Prindy was off like a shot. The team went on as if those who drove it hadn't the least idea that they were under observation; Billy up on the driving seat with his bullocky's whip and the name of every long-eared loafer ready on his tongue; Barney, mounted, trotting along cracking his stockwhip. Billy had called the dogs behind. He put on a show of great surprise at seeing Eddy appear as if out of nowhere, the hat tipped over an eye: 'Well, bugger me if it ain't Mick Cusky agin! What . . . you thumbin' a lift, or sumpin? What happen' yo' car . . . Knowles's goats eat it?'

Eddy grinned, casting an eye to the rear of the waggon, to which last night's spoils were tethered: 'Speakin' o' Knowles's goats . . . .'

'Wha' yo' mean by that?'

'Dingoes were supposed to have raided Knowles's goats last night.'

'Yeah . . . and they mistook old Ned for one of 'em, eh?'

Eddy chuckled, 'Not exactly . . . but lookin' round this mornin' Ned and Nugget found the dingoes'd left human tracks.'

'Well, wha' yo' know! Course everybody knows the critters'll pinch yo' boots you leave 'em lyin' round . . . to eat 'em. But I never 'eard tell of 'em *wearin'* the boots they pinched.'

Eddy guffawed, 'No, these dingoes left barefoot human tracks.'

'Well, blow me down! Them dawgs'll come at anything, won't they? I knoo a bloke one time, a drover, they raided his camp, pinched his boots, belt, pipe, pants, everything . . . includin' his cheque-book . . . and next thing he finds he's overdrawn at the bank.'

'No doubt about you, Billy!' said Eddy. 'But d'you mind if I take a look in your waggon?'

'Well . . . I'd kind o' like to know why. Not thinkin' o' gettin' one built to same specifications to go gypsyin' in, be any chance?'

'No . . . just to see if there mightn't be a dingo or two sneakin' a ride.'

'Yeah? Well, you can . . . but if you find one, don't go upsettin' him. I'm kind of partial to dingoes, as wild critters't never could be brought to lick a master's hand. If only the poor Abos'd had half the gumption 'o the dingoes, man . . . you wouldn't 'ave that cushy job o' yours 'oundin' 'em.'

'I'm not hounding anybody,' snapped Eddy, heading for the rear. 'I'm only carrying out the Law of the Land . . . .'

'Sound like old Coon-Coon, now.'

Eddy climbed up over the tail-board, took a good look through, came out by the front. Billy said, 'You didn't get bit, eh? I keep a couple o' death-adders in there to discourage sticky-beakin' . . . they must be gettin' too tame, I reckon. I'll have to chuck 'em out and get fresh ones . . . .'

Eddy took a stand on the bit of a platform below the seat, pushed his hat back, and looking very official and sounding it, said, 'Now look here, Billy . . . I've got a lot of respect for you in many ways . . . .'

'Now . . . ain't that a shame, when I got none whatsoever for you!'

'I'm talking seriously, Billy. I've always felt you had that boy . . .'

'What boy? Ain't we talkin' about dingoes and goats?'

'Yes . . . we are. And I've no time to be funny about it. I'm convinced now that you've got the boy. I've exhausted every other possibility of where he can be. This morning there are his fresh tracks following four goats from Knowles's . . . and you've got four goats tied on behind, which you never had when I came to see you last night . . . .'

'Think I keep the poor bastards tied up all night . . . like you keep your Abos?'

'I'm warning you, Billy. The boy's tracks . . . .'

'Who identified the tracks as this boy's yo' talkin' about?'

'Never mind. The boy was camped there with me a couple of weeks back. We were down the creek in a sheltered place. His tracks were still there for comparison. Nugget Knowles . . . . '

'Haw . . . if you're relying on the trackin' ability of Nugget or Nobby Knowles, or old Ned for that matter, all you'll be led to is the blacks' camp and the gins . . . . '

'I said I'm warning you, Billy. I know you've got that boy. I guess it's too much to ask you to hand him over to me . . . and, frankly, at the moment he'd be an embarrassment to me. But I want him. As I've told you, I'm going up to take over the Protectorship. What I'd advise you to do when you get to the Charlotte is hand him over to the police officer there. If you don't, I'll put Cahoon and Jinbul onto you. There won't be any silly chains this time, just the proper carrying out of the law . . . the law that treats abduction, kidnapping, as one of the most serious crimes in the book. Got the message?' Eddy began to descend the steps. At the foot he looked up, added: 'Be seein' you, Billy . . . hope it won't be in court.'

'It won't be in hell, either,' said Billy. 'I don't expect to go to the other place . . . but I'm sure they got departments in hell . . . and they'd never put me in with shit'ouse rats like you, McCusky.'

Eddy buttoned his face up tight, pulled the hat down lower, and turned and went away to his parked car, got into it, went off to his official exaltation in a cloud of dust. Billy waited till even the smell of his dust had blown away sou'east.

That afternoon all the dust was settled and for days to come by a heavy downpour from that southward-drifting war between Old Tchamala and the Cloud Spirits. And there was sweet pickin' now all the way to Charlotte Springs, not only to fatten the donks, but their drivers through the medium of those poor doomed trailers on behind. Minds could be broadened, too, without the former constant threat of disapproving authority. Not that alertness was dropped. But having some assurance of being left alone made a big difference to the intellectual communion so far something to be snatched in scraps rather than in the long luxurious indulgence that could be made of it both by preceptor and proselyte. They sat by day high above the trudging mass of flesh and blood that hauled them singing like yoked slaves, or by night by small camp fires that could not dim the glory of the wonder slowly rolling overhead in terms of astronomical science and Greek mythology. There was time to translate big words, to learn to count to one hundred, to show that every eightieth telegraph pole had a mark on it which meant a mile had been covered, to give some idea of what time and distance meant combined, even if you did travel in a way that had been described as jes wanderin' 'round the country, like a gypsy. What was a gypsy? Let's get out the big Webster's Dictionary. Well, what d'you know! The word meant Egyptians, but the people were originally Indians. The things you learnt! Every day you learnt something new and wonderful, if you had a mind to it. A wonderful world it was – only for the bastards in it. What did Bastard mean? Jesus – who'd believe it meant a Pack Saddle!

Yet despite the gypsy quality of their going, there they were on the outskirts of Charlotte Springs the night before train-day; and not by chance, as Billy revealed in a private talk with Prindy. He said he hadn't told him before what he had in mind concerning him, for fear of spoiling these last lovely couple of weeks of their relationship by setting a limit to it in Prindy's mind. But the reality was that they must part, for good, alas, since if what he had in mind came off, the boy wouldn't have any use for an old donkey skinner like himself. What he intended to do was to *ship* Prindy to his Grandfather. It was the only thing that could be done to beat McCusky.

He explained. Instead of shipping those ore-samples to the Mines Department in Town as he usually did (which was to place them just as they were in a railway waggon) he was going to empty out that big lock-up tucker-box of his and put some in, then Prindy on top of them with sacks for comfort. There were screened air-vents in the sides of the box. The box would be locked with its padlock, the key to which would be mailed to the Mines Department; but the nuts of the bolts that held the staple would be loosened so that Prindy might easily remove them and so get out when he got to Beatrice. But unless it was utterly impossible, he must replace the bolts and lock the box again so as to avoid creating suspicion that could bring in the police too soon. Billy would give him the other key. For sure the police would be in it before long; but it would be to Billy himself they'd come; and he would have much pleasure in misleading them. Time was what counted. If he were any judge of the weather, the Big Wet would be starting any day. The rain wouldn't matter, so much round here; but it would around the Beatrice. Finally, the police would take the hunt out to Lily Lagoons, but probably not until after the Wet by which time surely Grandfather Jeremy could have something working to beat them. Well, there it was. It was up to Prindy now to decide whether he was prepared to go through with what lay ahead of him: six or more hours in a box, because although the trip to Beatrice would take only three hours or so he would have to wait till dark to make his escape with safety . . . Or would he prefer to go to the Police Station at Charlotte and give in to the bastards for good? Prindy wasted no time in deciding: the Box!

They sat talking till midnight; or rather, Billy talked and Prindy listened; the burden of it the facts of life as they concerned Prindy, having to deal with procreation from a scientific point of view and hence Prindy's rights as a Delacy, things that Billy had been hinting about for some time, but only now came out with it as knowledge essential to the boy's well-being. Billy talked of race, of how inferior people made themselves feel superior by lording it over others, of how he himself would be humiliated, have his lovely life utterly spoilt, if he allowed himself to be taken in by it. He told of his own halfcaste children. There was that son of his, Brumby, as they called him; Inumbergo his proper name, from his Dreaming, the Red Kangaroo in his mother's lingo. Poor Brumby sneaked to the whites so as to be accepted by them, but only at last to kill in a fight a whiteman who had humiliated him, and go on the run South, where eventually another halfcaste killed him. His other son, Jerry, from his Aboriginal nickname Theralal, meaning sharp-eyed, because he could spot things like a kite hawk, hadn't had a chance to grow up as anything. He was seventeen when he went to the War. Before he was eighteen he was killed. Both boys had been properly initiated as blackfellows. His daughter, Skin Name Numija, called herself Millie, at fifteen ran off with a young whiteman working for a water-borer for whom Billy was hauling machinery at the time. What happened to her, Billy never learnt. She left the country. If she'd have come to anything but bad, surely he would have heard from her. They had loved each other. He had even been responsible for her getting mixed up with that young fellow, because she obviously loved the bastard and he, Billy, wanted her to marry like that. I taught 'em to be proud they belonged to the Old People. But that's not enough. I should've let 'em grow up with the Old People and learnt to be proud 'emselves. Your old *Mora,* Jeremy . . . he's got the right idea. He reckons it's better to be a blackfeller in this country than anything else. They the only truly 'appy people in it. You're a lucky boy you grew up like you did. Remember that. You're pretty well white . . . but that won't get you nowhere . . . only into trouble if you take it too serious. You belong to a new people, really, but people who ain't yet got a place. Old Jeremy'll teach you to be proud of yourself, *Nghagung* . . . like I'd have liked to do meself . . . proud of yourself as an Aboriginal. Never look down on your Old People. Keep going back to 'em. And if things go really wrong, put on a cock-rag and go right back and stop with 'em. Sleepy now, eh? All right . . . get into your nap. You got a big day tomorrow, little man. Here, gi' me your hand. We'll say *mummuk* now. Don't want to put on any show front of Barney and his missus tomorrow. Less they know about what we're doin', the best for them. *Mummuk yawarra, Ngahgung.*

'*Mummuk yawarra, Kumija.*' Old Billy bent and kissed the golden brow, blinked back tears, turned hastily to stir up the fire.

Billy had said that it was a wonderful world but for the bastards in it. The trouble was that a lot of people who seemed to be bastards in making things hard for others were only doing what they considered the right and proper things, as Eddy McCusky surely thought he was in respect of what Billy saw as hounding a little boy; and as another official, Oz Burrows, usually Railway Porter at Beatrice River but always acting Station Master at Charlotte Springs when the train was there, actually said he was doing when the hitch occurred next morning with the shipping of Prindy according to plan. Oz Burrows always came up to the head of the road on Thursday's train out of Beatrice to handle official business there, and went back with it. Billy went to his office on the tiny station when the train came in, driven by Pat Hannaford, at 11 a.m. and told him he had samples of ore for shipping to Town of total weight of three hundred and fifty pounds approximately. There was no question of weighing the consignment, nor any means of doing so, for that matter. One's word was taken for such transactions. If a thing was overweight they would soon check up in Town. Oz made out the consignment note, in the name of the senders, a mining syndicate; and Billy paid with a cheque, then posted the letter containing the advice about the ore and also the key of the box to the Mining Warden – again through Oz, who acted also as Post Master. Billy already had his waggon backed up to the loading ramp. When Pat Hannaford had turned the engine and the passenger coaches and brake van round on the reversing triangle in preparation for the return journey, he shunted a small open waggon up to the ramp for the loading. He and Billy exchanged curt nods only. They had fallen out long ago over Pat's having, deliberately, according to Billy, run down a couple of Billy's donkeys, which had had the habit of blocking the railway as they still often did the road. Matters had been made worse by Billy's dragging Pat's politics into the ensuing row.

Billy had been making these shipments of ore ever since taking to carting for the miners of Pisgah Ridge; thus it was rather a routine matter to deal with them whenever the train came in to find his waggon at the ramp. However, formerly the samples had been forwarded simply in their individual bags, not in a crate. He hadn't mentioned that to Oz Burrows. Nor did it appear to matter; at least to the train crew. Chas Chase, the guard, who came up with the engine and railway waggon, at once lent Billy a hand with the loading. Billy had all sorts of gear for handling his loads, and was running the box from his own waggon across the ramp on a rolling device, but was having trouble because the gravel surface was uneven, scoured by recent rain. They had just got it aboard when Oz arrived. Whatever brought him, an urge to help so as to facilitate the train's departure, or curiosity, his coming cruelled the whole thing. He promptly said, 'Hey . . . you can't consign that in an open waggon?'

'Why?' asked Billy.

' 'Cause it's locked.'

'What's the difference?'

'Anything't's locked or sealed's special freight, and has to go into the brake-van or a locked waggon.'

Rather testily Billy demanded, 'What difference't make if the bloody thing's locked already?'

'Somebody might tamper with it.'

'If anybody was that keen on gettin' at it, wouldn't they tamper with it in the flamin' van?'

'Guard's there to watch it in transit . . . and it'll be locked in the van for the night at Beatrice.'

Billy evidently was having trouble with his breathing; but it could be taken for annoyance. At length he said, 'Gi' me that letter back . . . and I'll take the key out and take the lock off.'

'Can't do that. The letter is posted.'

'Christ, you can take it out o' the bag, can't you . . . and I'll put it in a noo envelope?'

'Once a letter's posted it's the property of the PMG.'

Billy was red and sweating. 'Aw, balls!'

'Not balls at all . . . it's Rules and Regs . . . and I'm stickin' to 'em.'

'Well, I'll get a 'acksaw and saw the bloody lock off.'

'No you won't. It's not consigned in your name.'

'I signed the consignment, didn't I?'

'For someone else . . . you got some syndicate's name on it. And I guess they wouldn't'a' locked it, if it wasn't considered valuable. Now, come on . . . get it into the van. You're holdin' up the train. Chas . . . get 'em to run up alongside the van and shove the thing in . . . save time.'

Chas nodded, signalled to Pat, who with Porky Jones was hanging out listening. Pat turned to his regulator. Chas and Oz heaved up the waggon door, jumped into it. Billy cried, 'Wait . . . wait . . . I won't send it.'

Oz snapped, 'You've already consigned it . . . it's now the property of the Railways Manager.' The engine puffed. The waggon moved. Billy stood gaping, wiping a hand across his streaming brow. As the engine, running in reverse, passed him, Pat leered, evidently pleased with the consternation he saw in bearded face.

By the look of him, Billy was seeing nothing but what was in the box. Watching the engine and waggon make the swift short journey back to the van, he muttered, 'Christ Almighty . . . what've I done!'

As the engine stopped, he started out of his seeming trance, said to himself, 'Have to go on the train. Have to get him out o' that somehow.' He turned and ran into his backed-up waggon, tore open a tool-box, got out a hack-saw, then seized a suitcase, opened it and flung the tool into it. He came out to see the engine coming back. Then apparently a new idea seized him; and he ran to the edge of the ramp and held out the suitcase as a sign to stop. Pat looked as if he would knock it out of his hand, but suddenly applied his brakes, and rolling up, roared, 'What the bloody 'ell's wrong't you? 'Ere, wha' you doin' . . . you're not ridin' with me!' Chas Chase had stayed back in the van.

But Billy was already on the foot-plate, babbling, 'Listen, Pat . . . I know you're a good bloke at heart . . . listen . . . . ' He poured out the story as the engine rolled slowly to the points, from which it would come back to couple with the train. Porky was dropping down to switch the points; but Pat stayed him with a gesture. The engine stopped. Billy asked breathlessly, 'Could you get him out of the van at Beatrice?'

Pat answered dryly, 'He could get out himself. He only has to pull the bolts on the inside of the slidin' doors . . . or for that matter, open the door with the lock on it . . . it's only a Yale lock. He's got enough savvy to do that, ain't he?'

'He's got plenty savvy all right . . . but would you . . . would you keep an eye on things . . . see if he doesn't get out too quick, or anything?'

Pat cocked an eye at the northern sky, which was black almost to the zenith as if filled with rolling tarry smoke. He remarked, 'Looks like it'll be rainin' like hell in Beatrice. They won't notice him. But I'll look out for him. When we stop for water next I'll go back and give him a hint. I've got me oilskins hangin' in the van. I ought 'o be able to get a word to him. They got the box shoved up in a corner . . . Right Porky.'

Pat swung the wheel of the reversing gear. Billy muttered, 'Aw, Pat!' He shot out his hand, reaching for the grimy one as it left the wheel.

But Pat reached for the regulator, saying, 'You put in a complaint about me runnin' down your flamin' donks.'

'I 'pologize, Pat.'

'Don' bother. I'll run the bastards down agin, if they get on the track.'

'They won't.'

'And you reckoned Stalin was a train robber . . . and Adolf Hitler a great man.'

'Well, a man says these things . . . .'

'Don't go 'pologizin' . . . it don't become you. You better get off now. We'll be goin' in a couple o' minutes.' The engine was already back at the head of the train, Porky coupling up.

Moving to get out, Billy said weakly, 'Well, a Merry Christmas.'

'Merry-Kiss-Me-Arse! I'm a atheist.'

Climbing down, Billy persisted, 'Then 'Appy Noo Year!'

'Wonderful Noo Year your mate Hitler's goin' 'o make of it!'

Pat was looking back at the train. Oz had his green flag up. Pat reached for the whistle: *Boo-hoot*! The engine puffed. The train was rolling.

Billy stood by the track. There were a number of passengers aboard, hanging boozily out of windows, more than usual from the Head of the Road, because this was the Christmas train as well as the mail train, amongst them the Police Officer, Constable Gobally. They yelled at him as they passed, 'Merry Chrishmash, Billy . . . y'ol' donkey-wallopin' bas'ard . . . 'Ap Noo Year!' He responded automatically, eyes on the van as it sped past him, eyes on it all the way down the dead straight swaith through the stunted trees until it vanished into the sooty wall. Then, with a sigh, he turned and headed back to where his donkeys, still harnessed to the waggon but turned in a wide arc watching him, were complaining mournfully of his neglect.

IV

Prindy's deliverance was not nearly so simple as Pat Hannaford had even contemptuously predicted. Nor was it only circumstance that posed the difficulty, but Pat himself, with his own style of liberty-restriction in the name of liberty. True to his prediction, it was raining like hell when the train reached Beatrice, and no one there much concerned about anything but keeping dry. Left to himself, Prindy, with his by now quite highly developed faculty for doing the disappearing trick, might have got away with it easily. But Pat had had that quiet word with him, both in transit and again on arrival, and told him to wait till he came to his aid. Now, as always happened in such circumstances, passengers and crew were slow in leaving the train. But there was another predictable factor that had been overlooked. Because it was near Christmas the township was crowded with blacks, who because of their inability to provide shelter for themselves and their exclusion from private property to which they had no right of entry as employees, were always allowed temporary use of such railway buildings as were more or less open, like the station verandah, the engine-shed, the trolley-shed The back part of the train, left standing as usual where it had stopped, was in full view of these places, all crowded with people with sharp eyes. Surely it would have been better to leave it to a blackfellow to deal with his own kind. But Hannaford, for all he had done to buck the system denying Aborigines ordinary human rights, probably more than anyone else in that country, had little if any respect for them, as he often declared in anger to the people themselves, condemning examples of their stupidness. Even although what he did to get Prindy away was essentially a device, the anger expressed in it would be quite genuine, and certainly taken as what might be expected of him. Looking like a lanky debil-debil in his oilskins, alternately there and not there, as the lightning flashed, and vying with the thunder in his roaring, flinging squares of tarpaulin at them that he had hacked from big waggon covers, he told them to get to hell out of it and assert their rights as human beings by forcing themselves into the comfort denied them – at the Police Station, at the Hotel, at the Store, at the Cattle Station: 'But get to hell out o' it . . . and don't come back to sit like bloody half-drowned bandicoots shiverin' in a holler log . . . git, git, git!' They got. Pat then let Prindy out of the brake-van and took him, as he had promised to do, across to his own quarters behind the engine shed, and sat him down to a great meal. Porky Jones was up at the pub. But it would not have mattered had Porky been present, because he was in everything with his hero Pat. He came back later to report that no one of those whom Pat had driven forth into the rain to assert their rights had done so at the pub. 'Stupid bastards!' cried Pat. 'You can't do nothin' for 'em. This bloke's the same. He won't 'ave it on what we want 'o do for 'im . . . wants to stay in the bush, he reckons.' He dropped his head into his hands to show his despair. Prindy was the bloke referred to.

Porky took it up: 'But this's the chance of your lifetime, sonny. We sneak you up to Town. We hide you there till a West Coast steamer goes. The crew are all Party men. They smuggle you South. The Party takes you, schools you, does everything for you . . . even send you overseas, maybe . . . and you come back a big man and fight for your people . . . . '

Pat groaned, 'It's no good, Porky. I been over and over it with him. I asked him does he want 'o live like a blackfeller all his life . . . and he just ups and says Yes.'

'Did you say that, sonny?'

'Yas.'

Now Porky groaned. 'Well, for cryin' out loud . . . and he's as white as I am, nearly. What're we goin' 'o do with him now?'

Pat yawned. 'Forget about him till the mornin'. I'm going 'o bed. Go on, sonny . . . there's a rug for you. Make yo'self comfortable on the floor.'

The fact that Prindy had ideas of his own concerning his future was revealed as soon as it was evident from his would-be saviours' breathing that he could escape them. With the rain drumming on the iron roof there was little need for caution. Still, he went with stealth, opened the fly-screen door, slipped out onto the bit of verandah, leapt out into the roaring night. There was a wobbly square of light in a window of Col Collings's residence, a little distance away, enough to show the gleaming rails now that the lightning was gone. He picked his way carefully across the tracks. Up to the left was a largish luminescence that was the pub, and directly across the way a dim glow that would be the store, but nothing but blackness whence he was headed, evidently for Barbu's. He reached the road, crossed it, ran to the blacker patch of blackness, halted streaming and breathless under the sagging, verandah. The ground was awash. After a moment's rest he emerged again, to slip through the gate to the rear, to seek shelter again under the complex of roofing connecting the jumble of shop, residence, and kitchen, and to stand staring at the big shed where the van was kept, evidently with sharp ears hearing significant sound there above the roar of the rain, and to have his astuteness rewarded after a moment with sight of a flicker of light.

He went to the door leading into the residence, tried the handle. The door was locked. He knocked with care. Again. Again. A muffled voice within. He knocked louder. The voice was heard nearer. 'You go 'vay. You cannot come in 'ere. You gif me troubles, I call p'liceman.'

Prindy called, 'Papa, papa!'

Barbu spoke from the other side of the door: '*O, permeshwar kia hai eder?*'

Prindy answered in Hindustani. A pause, then the turning of the key, pulling of the bolt. As the door opened, Prindy slipped in. Barbu grasped at him, let go at the feel of his dripping wetness, voiced a stream of Hindustani, to which Prindy replied in a mixture of languages. Barbu ran off, into another room, lit a lamp, came out with it, staring. Prindy asked, 'Where Savitra?' Barbu babbled about her having been taken from him and sent to the Mission Island. Prindy jerked his lips to the rear: 'Who dere?'

They were blacks hunted from the railway, said Barbu. Then he asked, '*Apyahan kia ker rehey, ho*?'

Prindy gave only a slight explanation of his presence. But Barbu wailed, 'Ho . . . again you haf runned away.' He went on to babble about having made a promise to Mick Cusky, who evidently had dropped in while passing recently, not to report Prindy's escapade, but to threaten Barbu that should he ever harbour the boy again he would go straight to jail. 'Ten year jail, he say!' cried Barbu. 'If you efer come, moost pe I tell p'liceman at vonce . . . at vonce. *Oh, maiyahan kia karna hay. Kakah, kakah*!'

Barbu stared at the boy, then asked, 'You haf eat food?' Prindy nodded. 'All right . . . I moost tek you to p'liceman . . . .'

Prindy cried, 'Eh, look-out!'

'It iss on'y vay, Kakah. They vill come get you . . . and ve both jail go. Soon ve vill free you. I talk vit your Grandfader. He vill court-fight for you. But now moost you come. I vill get umprella and torch-light.' Barbu went off with the lamp, through to an inner room.

Prindy stayed for only a moment, then swung to the back door, opened it quietly, slipped out again, went back the way he'd come. It was a couple of minutes before Barbu reappeared. He stopped, to stare, flashing his light about the small room. The door was ajar. He went to it, flashed the light here and there. He muttered to himself. Then, setting one umbrella against the wall, he raised the other, went squelching out to the coach-house, flashed his light in there, to reveal a packed mass of what looked like grey-faced ghosts with glistening eyes, of all sizes, but none with fair hair. A tiny fire burnt in one corner. Barbu said, 'You careful vit fire . . . or you burney house down.' He turned back to the house, flashing to right and left. For a short while he stood on the back verandah making a moaning sound. Then he went inside, shut, locked, bolted the back door. As he entered the lighted room it could be seen that his thin black face was not only wet with rain. He bowed his head, croaked, '*Mata Shasti . . . ney mera puttah rakh lia* . . . . It is a cruel vorld!' Sobs shook him as he stood, bowed, leaning on his two umbrellas.

Crossing the railway tracks again, Prindy looked back several times, as if watching for the flashlight. Back there was only the dimmest glow from the lamp shining through the shop window. He looked back for the last time as he entered the engine house. He entered carefully, hugging the wall to avoid the ash-pit. It was warm in there with the engine. The contrast with his own wetness made him shiver. He went up past the tender, to stop just beyond the cab, where it was warmest. The comfort was somewhat spoilt by the fact that the corrugated iron walls didn't some right down to meet the cinder floor, which was sodden with the rain beating in. It took him some time to make bold to improve his condition in the simple way available, and then probably was driven to it only by exhaustion. He climbed up into the cab, stood there for a while hesitant in the darker darkness, then got down on the warm steel floor, at first to squat facing the unseen firebox door radiating its comfort, till the steam was rising from the front of him, then to lie down with a sigh, turn his soaked back to it, fall asleep.

He woke several times during the roaring night, peed out over the steps, found the tap in the water-tank in the tender and drank, found driver's and fireman's seats and sat in them. Added now to the drum and rush of the rain was the booming of the rising racing river. Prindy cocked his ear towards it. He found that the leather cushions on the seats were detachable, removed them and put them on the floor to make a bed, lay down again, slept soundly.

He woke on hearing voices, found it was grey dawn, was instantly on his feet, listening. Still the rain was roaring down. He caught a glimpse of a shiny sou'wester at the steps on the left-hand side, and leapt to the right, shot out and down so smartly that Pat Hannaford, climbing the other steps, was aware of his presence there only through stumbling over the cushions. He turned sluggish steam into the dynamo, lit the cab dimly, said, 'Poor little bastard must'a' camped here. Wonder where he is?' He looked out the other side. Coming back, he said to Porky opening the firebox, 'Keep your eye open for him. If he's round about before we hook her up, we'll grab him.'

When at length the engine came rolling slowly from its shed, Prindy saw the crew looking out for him as he sat crouched behind the batten doors of the shed used for storing tarpaulins and other gear. It should have occurred to Pat as a likely place to find him, since he himself had torn the padlock off the door to get at those tarps he had taken the liberty of ripping up and distributing last night to the homeless. But although Pat stared at it in passing, it was probably only with last night in mind, because he turned to Porky and grinned, as if in anticipation of the row it would cause and the powerful defence he had to meet it.

The engine disappeared into the rain. The train was only dimly to be seen. Prindy drew back to the stacked tarpaulins and stretched out on them, staring at the lean-to roof, so close to him that it must have seemed to be pressing down on him with the hammering weight of rain. He dozed again – waiting for what? The rain to stop, the train to go, for Mother Shasti or Koonapippi or Old Tchamala or Bobwirridirridi to come? What of his Grandfather Jeremy, to whom he had a sodden letter in his shirt pocket? He woke when the bell at the station clanged *All Aboard*. Then the engine whistled: *Boo-hoot*!

The train had not been gone more than five minutes when Prindy again was roused to sudden alertness by voices. He leapt to the batten doors, only to draw back instantly amongst the tarpaulins and hanging ropes and chains. Almost at the door he had seen four oil-skinned figures. Now he saw them stop at the door, drag it open and examine the damage done to it. They were Col Collings, Oz Burrows, Constable Stunke, and Tracker Treacle, all shouting above the rain, except the last.

'We got the bastard now,' shouted Collings.

'Case o' breakin' and enterin', all right,' was Stunke's comment.

'Destroyin' Railway property,' yelled Oz. 'He can't get away with that, can he?'

Nevertheless, apparently they hadn't dared charge Pat before he took the train away. Prindy was cringing down into a small gap in between tarps.

'Well, you'll have to give me an exact list of what's been removed,' Stunke bawled. 'No good just sayin' he removed tarpaulins.'

'I know 'ow many was there,' cried Oz. 'I got 'em in me book. I'll count what's left.'

They were coming in. Oz saw Prindy first, started, exclaimed, 'Eh!'

Prindy leapt up and shot through them. Treacle grabbed him by the back of his khaki shirt, pulled him down. Prindy landed face down in the cinders, but on the instant jerked out of the shirt. Stunke roared, 'It's that bloody kid again . . . stop him . . . christ sake don't let him get away!'

But Prindy was off like the *prindy* he was by Dreaming, heading for the river. All went after him, but without a hope, hampered as they were with their heavy clothing and lacking his natural speed. Besides, there was the mighty yellow snake of the river, almost filling the huge bed, bending the great trees with its might, heaving out of greyness into greyness. They saw him leap into it, strike through the bit of swirling debris-cluttered backwater at the edge, enter the current, go bobbing on it like a bit of rubbish, vanish into the rain.

Collings yelled, 'Mad little bastard'll get drowned!'

Stunke bellowed, 'Not him, the slippery bloody little pest. We'll have to get the boat out. Have to send word he's got away again, too. He's supposed to be down the Centre, according to McCusky. God·bugger it . . . just what'd happen in weather like this!'

Prindy's dabbling in other cults of late had evidently not denied him the patronage he might expect from the Old One, of whose power, of course, the raging river was only a manifestation. He had little difficulty in crossing, although he was carried so far downstream in the process as to be put to a long trudge back northward and thereby to difficulty, to get out of which he could count on nothing but his own resourcefulness. Down river there were the old White Russian farms, most of them with some sort of shelter offering and easily got provender in the form of wild-growing peanuts, sweet potatoes, and exotic fruits. But he had been caught there before, and certainly would be again if he stayed. It was the delay in doubling back that landed him in further trouble, because it gave time to organize pursuit to those who were bent on denying him that thing most precious to him, his complete freedom.

The boat Stunke had referred to was one belonging to Vaiseys kept for general use in time of flood. Stunke sent Oz and Mick Bolan, Railway Pumper and member of the fettling gang, off in the boat, while he got Tom Toohey, looking unhappy about it, to take himself and Treacle across the railway bridge on his trolley and set them down at the Racecourse, where the police horses were paddocked and at the moment stabled.

Prindy saw the boat pass him, but would hardly know who the oil-skinned crew were, dim as everything looked through the rain, and hardly consider duplication of pursuit, which was probably what caused him to use the road for its easier walking, although the risk of leaving tracks in the circumstances was minimal. Still, it was his unusual carelessness about leaving tracks that undid all the ease he had had so far. He was sharp enough to see the mounted policemen without their seeing him. Probably he first heard them, since the gusty wind was blowing with them. They were trotting down the road, watching the river. He, round a bit of a bend and out of their line of sight, at once ducked down and dodged away to the left into the thick stunted timber there that was regrowth of what was constantly being cut down to serve the Race Meetings. He kept to the bush for a while, then returned to the road, to run now, head down to the rain.

Thus to the railway and over it, and onto the Racecourse, through to that stretch of well-made gravel road leading to Beatrice Homestead's private causeway and the road to Lily Lagoons. He had it so easy now that he slowed down. While he was doing so, Constable Stunke, who was back at the Racecourse, having galloped back with Treacle after the latter's discovery of a couple of small oozing footprints, was speaking on the telephone to Beatrice Homestead. The Family were in Town, as usual at this time of year. The place in the charge of the Second Bookkeeper. Lesser lights were the Head Stockman and the so-called Engineer, the man who superintended mechanical jobs.

Prindy had just left the gravel road as it swung down to the submerged causeway, and was walking the road to the Lagoons, when suddenly ahead of him, bursting out of the light timber on the river side, he saw two other oil-skinned horsemen, easily recognizable as another pair by the colour of their horses, a chestnut and a white, the latter looking creamy with the yellow water of the river still streaming from its hide. They spurred after him as he leapt off the road, again to the left. And there on his left now, bursting into the scrub from the road behind, probably having sneaked up on him, were the policemen. In his surprise he collided with a small tree, fell sprawling in black ooze. 'Got him!' shouted Stunke, leaping from his saddle, 'Bring the chain!' The other two horsemen were halted together some twenty feet away. Treacle was turned away unbuckling his saddle-bag. No one stood between Prindy and the road he had come from – and the river. As Stunke, squelching in his water-logged riding boots, lunged to grab him, he leapt to his feet and raced for beckoning liberty.

Stunke collided with the same tree, yelling obscenities, calling on the others, 'After him . . . ride the little bastard down!'

The two station horsemen swung into action too readily, so that one of their mounts, the white, slithered onto his rump, spilling his rider, the Second Bookkeeper, and put the other off his purpose long enough to lose the quarry.

So fast did Prindy run down the steep river bank that he fell into the water, which here was racing wildly right against the bank because of a sharp curve. He went under, vanished as if pulled down, came up to be swept diagonally to the other side and then into a slowly swirling backwater packed with debris, welded with yellow froth. There was no getting out of here easily, even though the bank was not so steep as on the other side, the trouble being that here, at this level, it was undermined, the earth having been scoured from under biggish trees. Anyway, why want to get out, when there was hiding here, even if it must be shared with a myriad other homeless ones?

There were ants, spiders, caterpillars, centipedes and millipedes, grasshoppers, mantises, biggish lizards and tiny ones, beetles and bugs, prey of each other normally, but now indifferent to anything but the common doom, crawling over each other in masses rolling to their changing weights, enemy clinging to enemy in extremes of helplessness – children of superogative Nature, proliferated for the fun of it, now being exterminated in the same ruthless game. There were tiny marsupial mice, one with babies big as peas clinging dead to its pouch. There was a small bandicoot swimming in mad circles. Prindy, grabbing a root, reached for him, perhaps to succour him by lifting him up to temporary safety, but only to make him dive and never come up again. Prindy climbed up amongst the roots. It was warm in here, with the warmth of the earth, compared with the chill of the rushing river. It was quiet, too, with the external watery uproar sounding like that of the sea to be heard in a shell. A cosy place for a runaway; but a death-trap for any creature not able to take cognizance of the rising water. At length the doomed creatures were raised to the roots and began to overrun them. Prindy slipped out, coasted along in the slime, came after only twenty feet or so upon the big iron pipe through which water normally was pumped from the river to Beatrice Homestead. It was easy climbing here. He climbed up into the chilly rain, reached the silent pump-house on the flat above, to stand, shivering now, taking stock of things from behind it. Nothing to be seen through the grey rain sheeting in the wind, except a bit of fencing. He went to the fence, which ran parallel with the river, not to go through it, but to turn northward and trot splashing along the thin yellow rivulet that was the bridle-pad following it. Now above the dull thunder of the river could be heard the shrill hallelujah chorus of the frogs.

Not far away inside that fence was the road that ran to Catfish, as he would know, and as he showed by his frequent glances towards it and backwards along it. He passed several other fences running away towards the invisible road, must have trotted the best part of two miles before he came to the end of the fence. The heavy posts and rails of the grid by which the road passed through the fence as it now ran eastward could be seen; and the pad swung that way; but Prindy kept straight on, even though the going now was rough. Evidently no more road-running for him. It was slow going now. Often he eased up and walked, ran evidently to keep warm. Frogs in thousands, great and small, fell silent about him as he passed, leapt splashing out of his way. He came to a creek that was spilling its banks, was forced to turn up it because of its mid-stream fury, but went into it waist-deep when he saw a substantial paperbark, and tore sheets from it till able to get a piece big enough to make a hood. It was at this creek that the road turned away from the river, north-westward, to avoid the swampy country beyond. But he was not concerned with the road, apparently. As soon as able to cross the creek he did so. Beyond it the din of the frogs was ear-splitting.

Hunger was troubling him now, it was evident, from his stopping to turn over rotten wood and break it up, to extract here and there a grub and eat it. Coming into swamp, he had a feed of the corm of rushes before swinging round the area to avoid the probable impossibility of going straight through it. Always he came back northward when he could. The boom of the river was still in the background, but diminishing, to be replaced, apart from the louder-seeming shouting of the froggy legions, by a subtler watery sound, the chuckling of innumerable streamlets racing to become one with the great yellow snake raging roaring to the far-off sea. He splashed along, always ankle deep, sometimes down to the knees, sometimes to the waist and chest and having to hang onto tortured leaning trees for life. He soon lost his hood, walked with a waxy hand over eyes to peer ahead, into nothingness, just a hole in grey nothingness not much bigger than himself. Often he stopped and stood for respite behind trees, only to be fouled up by gobs of rank froth spat down from sodden trunks and branches. Time itself was a grey thing, getting greyer. The ground became a grey thing, a sheet of dirty water lashed into steam by rain. Water everywhere. No creeks now. Only one grey seething pulling mass. He floundered into holes, fell over submerged objects. It was swampland, grown with spindly tea-tree stuff that grew thicker, thicker, and allowed no way out. He came to moaning and whimpering with the effort it cost to go on, as he must go, or lie down and drown.

The greyness was such as to seem walled with blackness when at last he came to a fairly large paper-bark, too large for that water-logged earth, which at some similar season had collapsed, but continued to grow horizontally with half its roots, its substantial trunk held well off the ground with the stubs of stout broken branches, its branches of more recent growth, growing vertically up from the trunk. He went under it for shelter, saw that the under side was hollowed out by fire. It was dark inside, he was going to feel up inside, but backed out, broke off a length of stick, poked around. First a huntsman spider came out, ran along the belly of the tree, then a big black snake, which half hung out, challenging him with darting narrow head, then as if knowing they were kin, withdrew, and went slithering further up. Prindy ran his hand along inside now. There was quite a wide ledge where the snake had been. He was about to heave himself up into it, when he bethought himself of bedding, and on the lee side tore off strips of bark till he got to the dry understuff, collected one bundle of it, another, and another, tossing it up inside. Then clinging with elbows, and swinging up his feet, he got onto the ledge. It was quite dry, and wide enough to hold two of him. He spread out the bark, pulled some of it over him, lay down. It was snug in there, with the outside sounds muted. He sighed as with the luxury of it, was soon asleep.

He woke in utter darkness. The sound of water was so close that he reached down to feel for it. It was not so near as that. He reached several times, while lying with rumbling belly. Once he swung his feet over. Still safe. He slept again. When he woke next it was grey again. He hung over to see how the water was. Certainly it had risen, but not to within reach. When he dropped down he found it reached his thighs, and was pulling strongly. It was still raining, but nothing so hard as yesterday. Shivering again, perhaps more in thought of yesterday than from actual cold, because the wind had dropped and the air was muggy, he reached up into his recent refuge and pulled down paper-bark and wrapped himself about head and shoulders again. Then he set out, due East towards a glowing in the paler grey that would be the Sun just coming up. Soon he found the water coming from northward and getting shallower all the while; but he kept on splashing eastward. The silvery glow was halfway up the wet grey sky when suddenly he was amongst rocks, sandstone, getting bigger, until they appeared in a low dark ridge ahead. He climbed up, only half a dozen feet or so, onto red rocky earth, which although it streamed with water that went cascading down to the swamp-land, must have felt good to his water-logged feet. Here were substantial trees: bloodwood, ironwood, stringybark. He was watching the ironwoods, probably for sugarbag. And so going, with the ground becoming more and more sandy and the walking easier, swinging north-eastward, at length he came to the Catfish Road, just the pair of tyre-tracks each a foot or so wide filled with silky water-rippled sand, with springing verdure between. He tried the sand for its likelihood to betray his going. The drizzle wiped out his tracks almost at once, aided by the ooze beneath. He went on towards Catfish, surely a very long way from here, walking steadily, but with ears cocked all the whilc, and eyes, too. Several times he left the road to try rotten timber and was rewarded a couple of times. Then he spotted a likely iron-wood, searched round for a length of spear-grass that had not softened in the rain, found what he wanted, and shoving it through his pierced septum, went to the tree, and with arms locking round it and feet and knees gripping to each heave up, in a moment was up to the branch at the base of which he'd seen the tiny hole. Hanging onto the branch with one hand and legs about the trunk, he shoved the straw into the hole, sucked. A few little black bees came out to investigate, walked the straw and had a go at his golden flattish nose. He took no notice, sucking and swallowing. Several times he had to pull the straw out to blow it clear, and had to leave it in the hole while he changed hands and rearranged his legs and wiped off the bees. But evidently he got a bellyful, the way he sighed when he got down and went on his way. So on, with a spell here and there behind a tree that gave a little shelter with its leaning, past noon. He passed through a fence, by means of a grid, probably knew where he was by his hurrying – and there, suddenly, looming out of the rain, was the Corella Bore.

He halted for a moment, then went off the road and searched for a stout piece of wood, evidently for the purpose of dealing with some creature that could be used as food, the way he approached the place. But nothing was there. The birds would be away in the caves, and stock where timber afforded best protection. However, he made some useful finds; one a few wax vestas in a tin box, only three or four, melted into a corner as can happen with exposure to hot Sun, and a somewhat battered oilskin coat hanging in the engine house, as well as some cotton-waste. Although there was dry firewood in the camping shed, he made no attempt to light a fire in the antbed hearth, but retired at once to one of the hide and sapling beds, spread the oilskin, lay down and slept.

He slept for about an hour, starting awake as if having heard something, listened, rose and went swiftly to look out. Nothing but the rain, which was sheeting again in rising wind now blowing from the West, and the gush of the water from the overflow pipe of the earthen tank into the overflowing trough, and the groan of the furled windmill turning from the wind. He went back to the bunk and got the coat, tried it on. It was twice his length. Undaunted, he went with it to a projecting piece of the corrugated iron of the building, tore it, ripped the bottom off. Now it reached only to his calves. He did likewise with the sleeves. One of the lengths of hacked-off sleeve he tried on his head, which it fitted nicely. The scraps he bundled together and stowed, along with the match-box. Then with the waste he proceeded to erase his tracks. The waste also went into a pocket. A drink from the tap that ran in from the tank, then out into the rain again, a strange little figure in his capacious outfit billowing in the wind behind. For it was westward he was heading, not on towards Catfish now. Passing over the trackless circle made by the movements of stock, he came to the road to Lily Lagoons, this so much less used than the other that grass was growing high in the wheel tracks. He followed it, head in odd-looking black cap bent to the wind, and behind like a jinny donkey. Thus till the faint luminescence of the Sun was well down ahead of him and he came into the region of limestone outcrops. Then he swung away to the right, northward again. Soon he was amongst the limestone monoliths and the brawling milky streams. Here were turtles in plenty. He eyed them, but otherwise ignored them although he might have taken several, surely for the reason that he knew he would be able to have what he wanted later. Obviously, now, he was making for that cave where he had camped with Bobwirridirridi. It was coming on dark when he grabbed his turtle. It was quite dark when he reached the cave. He entered without hesitation, stripped off the dripping outfit, got out the matches and the waste, went groping, and found dry wood, as they had left it just a year ago, because termites do not thrive in limestone.

In no time he had a fire going and the turtle sizzling upside down in its shell. He looked about. There was everything as they had left it when dragged away in chains. Who would want to go in there where Snake Men had dwelt and Coon-Coon raided? Besides, other people's property in the form of weapons and implements, is as sacred as their Shades, to a blackfellow. Clothes are different things; not blackfellow things, anyway. After the meal Prindy curled up in the white dust with the old paper-bark bedding and slept. He had been asleep about an hour when he began to sing in that strangled little voice. *My Rown Road*, but did not wake for many hours. Even when he did wake it was only to stir the fire and then cuddle down again.

As regards use of an absent person's property, if it is deemed necessary and one stands in such relationship to the person as to make it proper, there is the simple process of asking permission of the property itself, in the name of the owner. Prindy wanted two light spears and a boomerang. He had to address each piece separately: '*Kooloo* spear belong to Pookarakka . . . you lend me, eh?' The fact that he must do so surely showed how slightly his recent experiences with what might be called Civilizing Influences had affected his basic attitudes. Simple as the process was, it carried grave responsibility. What one borrowed must be taken much greater care of than what was one's own, and returned. Failure in this respect exacted strict penalties. There was no dodging them. The spirit of the article itself would deal with you, if not the owner.

Dressed in his outlandish rig-out again and accoutred, he went out into the misty rain about midmorning, and headed northward, passed out of the limestone and into the sandstone, and by noon was close enough to the foot of the escarpment to feel its presence even although he couldn't see it. He followed the base of it a short distance westward, dodging amongst the great rocks, and then got what evidently he had come for – a brush-tail. *Zip*! – and it was dying on the borrowed spear. Such a spear could not miss, of course. Hacking the little beast in half with a sharp axe-head of stone, and fixing tail to haunch to make the natural carrying sling, he put the rest into a concavity that bore traces of recent inhabitance by a large snake, then shouldered his prize, took up his precious gear, and set off, heading directly back whence he had come.

He was well back in the limestone, splashing through the milky rivulets, slipping and sliding in grey mud in which he could see his own precious tracks – when suddenly he started, stopped, warned by that other self of his which would be looking out for him, perhaps by the *Yalmaru* of Bobwirridirridi, which must have been with him a lot of late, according to his understanding – and swung round, because the danger was all around him, – invisible as yet – but in a moment looming, piece by piece, out of the rain – the gleaming black riders on the streaming horses! How many of them? As many as the trees it seemed. He dropped the wallaby, darted for a narrow cleft between two marble monoliths. The harsh resounding voice of Coon-Coon followed him in like the man's long black-clad arm itself: 'No good, Sonny Boy . . . you can't get away . . . we all round you. Come on out o' there!'

Prindy had to drop down, because the cleft was too narrow above his hips. His oilskin caught on a projecting piece. He ripped himself half out of it, shed the other half when he got down to hands and knees – but did not let go spears or boomerang. Soon he was crawling, in the dark, shoving the weapons ahead of him; or more truly following where they led. One place was so narrow that he had to go through it sideways, and lost his pants and tore his bottom. Then he saw light ahead, and approached it warily. Bushes shielded the entrance, so that he could stand listening. The horsemen were galloping about, as if it were a cattle muster, shouting, Coon-Coon above the rest, 'Come on, Sonny Boy . . . don't be jitty! We ain't goin' to hurt you. I'm goin' 'o look after you meself this time. Me . . . your Daddy-o. Come on Sonny Boy . . . come on, my little boy . . . come to your Daddy-o . . . It's Christmas, don't you know? We had a good time last Christmas, didn't we, eh? We have better time this one. Come on boy!'

It was easy to hear their horses, because of their slipping in the mud and their puffing. No sound of them ahead now. He peered out. A glimpse of two of them to the left, turned the other way. He shot out, raced across the bushy open space, into the shelter of another clump of rocks. They did not see him. Coon-Coon was now swearing like the trooper he was: 'You stupid bloody bastards . . . let a bit of a kid beat you. Jinbul, you lump o' black shit, I'll flog the puggin' hide off yo'!'

They milled around the rocks. He left them behind by dodging from one mass to another, up and over some, under others. They kept picking his tracks up, but only to lose them. Then he seemed to lose them altogether, heard them shouting and galloping well behind. He could easily have swung then back towards the sandstone, beaten them to the escarpment, climbed up it and thumbed his nose down at them, helpless as they'd be with horses and lacking his agility and knowledge of the place – with a couple of hundred miles to put between him and them. But he had to put those borrowed things back. More than that, when at length he got back to the cave with them, he had to clean them of mud, store them as he had found them – despite the fact that near the spot was now a pile of police equipment!

He took a swift look at the pile: pack-bags of food, tarpaulin-wrapped swags. Then wiping out his tracks with the cotton waste, he slipped out warily, stark naked except for that mad cap of his, blood streaking from his lacerated bottom, washed down his yellow legs by rain. Now he walked warily, either in water or on rock, leaping from point to point where necessary, going north-eastward now, perhaps to double round the pursuers and get back to the sandstone. He must have been doubtful of his chances of escape, for all the effort he put into it, to have gone to such lengths to do the proper thing with respect to the borrowing. He certainly showed it in his scariness. Never had he been as jumpy as now. Hearing a horse snort he wheeled in near panic, seemed ready to rush anywhere. Then he heard stamping, and running to a wall of rock and peering round, saw that under a sheltering projection of it a couple of pack-horses were tethered. No humans. But he passed the place crouching, running from bush to bush and rock to rock. Sound of horse's hoofs again, but this time thudding and splashing. He turned from it, ran round a mass of rock, almost to collide with a horse and oilskinned rider. The horse reared. The rider yelled, 'Hey!' Stunke's face was clearly visible under the tilted-back sou'wester. Prindy turned his bare bleeding behind on the instant, rushed back where he had come, almost to do the same thing with mounted Treacle. Stunke coming from behind the rock yelled, 'Corner him!' He probably meant to get him up against the tall mass of rock. But there was a low flattish mass across the way. Prindy dashed for it. The ground was too slippery for the horses to get a quick start on. He was up on it and over it before they got near him. He fell over in jumping down, saw a narrow junction with another low mass, scrambled into it on hands and knees.

Bang! – Bang! The rocks rang to the sounds of the shots. He dropped down in the ooze, lay still.

Then away to north-westward: *Bang! – Bang!*

That's where he had left Coon-Coon and the others. Stunke and Treacle had probably come back to get the packs for moving up to the sandstone. He had almost beaten them without knowing it. But those shots were signals. They would be on to him again in a pack, with his tracks all too plain to lead them to him, wherever he might hole up.

A heavy silence followed the shots. The wind had dropped. The chuckle of small waters seemed stilled. Only afar the muffled thunder of the great water, of that turgid waste grown into an inland sea from the countless streams and the upwelling of the soakage from the Plateau, sweeping to the suck of that mighty yellow serpent, the river. Prindy rose as if the roar was a voice calling him, and ran straight towards it, seemingly careless of pursuit now. Soon he was splashing in water to his calves, to his knees. They were coming after him. They had found his tracks. Now in the comparative open where the rocks were left behind they could see him. He could have seen them had he deigned to look back, the long line of them, each a lurching shiny black monster in a cloud of spray. They were gaining, gaining fast.

Water halfway up his thighs now. He plunged into it, swimming although the flow was so swift that debris rushed past him. A couple of times he grounded, rose up beating at the water with his hands as he ran again. He was heading for that point where the Pookarakka had tried to deliver himself into the hands of the Master. Coon-Coon right behind him, yelled to those on the flanks, 'Keep him out of the deep water . . . head him off!'

Treacle was about level on the right, turned in, now on that strip of shallow over which the flood poured as over a bar. His horse was so close that its roaring breathing could be heard above the tumult of the water. Prindy glanced as he reached the edge, then went over, disappeared. Coon-Coon yelled, 'In after him!'

They were all leaping from their horses, ripping off their encumbering clothes. Treacle was first. As Prindy's fair head popped up some fifty years away, Treacle went in, arms thrashing in the preliminary turbulence. Others jumped in, went a little way, grabbed rocks or trees, watching the race – which was obviously with Death making the pace. For just down there was a kind of hill of water, sloping down to a wall of it; or so it seemed; an illusion for sure; but it could be taken for a great sucking mouth – the smooth slope the tongue, the leaping watery wall the upper lip.

The tongue caught the two bobbing heads, the fair and the black, so close now as to seem together. The maw opened to them. They vanished.

Coon-Coon, clinging to a swaying sapling, croaked, 'Oh, Mother o' God!' Then he hung his head and wept.

V

Christmas at Beatrice River was spoilt again, as so often in that country where it didn't belong. Even the Stunke Family, who with German wooden-headedness, seemingly got more out of it than anyone else with their Nordic Christmas tree and singing of *Stille Nacht, Heilige Nacht*, had a lousy time of it this year, what with the keening going on around them on account of the deaths of a couple of persons of so little account really that not only was there no need to pray for their souls, since they were not Christian, but not even to hold official inquiry into their departure hence, when legally they had not been citizens. Normally, Tracker Treacle's relatives, crammed into the smellful quarters that had been his home for many a year of faithful service to the whiteman's law at cost of betrayal of his own and for so slight reward, could have been told to shut up their yowling or take it elsewhere. However, that could hardly be done while a superior officer, even if being temporarily treated as a felon, at least to the extent of being locked in a cell, was doing his part of the mourning at the top of his powerful voice: 'Oh, oh, oh, my Sonny Boy . . . oh, oh, oh, oh . . . and whoy did ye doi, my little boy . . . oh, oh, oh, why did ye doi and leave all the good things behoint ye that ye Daddy-o was goin' to give ye? Oh, oh, oh, oh . . . no, no not me . . . as Almighty God and the Most Merciful Jaysus is me judges . . . it wasn't me, daid-feller . . . it wasn't me't done it . . . 'twas that divil yeself ye took up with, that Rainbow Snake . . oh, oh, oh, come back, my Sonny Boy . . . come back from beyant, before, in me grief, I go after ye . . . oh, oh, oh!

Dinny's sisters had been sent for, as usual to help with their Darlint's recovery. But they were coming for something more than that as well, like all who were Irish and proud of it who could make the journey to the Beatrice. For, belave it or not, there was to be held there, as perhaps through all the centres of what might truly be called the Civilized World if there were Irish living in them, an Irish Hogmanay.

Of course, Hogmanay properly is what the Scots call New Year's Eve, and is the one day in the year on which most of them will permit enjoyment of life. As long as Princess Beatrice River had been a township, Hogmanay had been celebrated with Angus McDodds as chieftain to any true Scots or such lesser ones of the blood, but not of the birth, who remained proud of it, as happened to be in the district; even to the drinking of a bottle of whusky without removing it from the lips and the smashing of it empty on the stroke of the passing of the year; which ceremony had originally taken place at the famous bottle-heap beside the hall, but later been transferred to Finnucane's front doorstep as a kind of challenge that old Shame-on-us had been too wise in the ways of the wurruld ever to take up; and anyway, being tidy people, the Scots always sent their blacks next day to pick up the glass.

Now the astonishing thing was that Finnucane, who hadn't exchanged a civil word with McDodds for years, had approached him as one Gael to another, offering to make an Inter-Gaelic affair of it, at least for this occasion – by raisin of the tremendous occasion it was going to be to the Irish, the expinse to be Finnucane's, and Divil take it, seeing what the great occasion was: no less than the declaration of the Republic of Eire at the striking of the hour of midnight, 1937! It was all rather sudden. There had been talk of the Republic since the middle of the year by those interested (they being interested in little else) but nothing definite until after Christmas, as if those concerned with it had been a little out of touch during the festivities. It left little time for arrangements, especially since when it was Tuesday in Old Ireland it was Wednesday over here. The telephone lines North and South were humming with Finnucane's blarney as he spread the glad tidings just in time for those interested in them to catch the mail train. He did say later that he would have chartered a special train if necessary; but, as they said, Old Shame-on-us had always been a grand liar. Anyway, a train of some sort was necessary, since while the great rain had passed for the time, the roads were left impassable.

McDodds had not accepted the international coalition suggested by Shamus, despite the prospect of free whusky, but had been nice enough to agree to forego the usual Scottish celebration, except as a private little function in his own home. To his cronies he had said, 'Let 'em hae their New Year shinnanigans. The Republic of Eire will be bankroopt by next New Year and crawlin' to the Bank of England for the wherewithal to hoold off anither famine, forbye. *A Nation Wanst Agin*, the ol' foo's shoutin'. It never was a nation. It was noothin' but a pack o' savages till the English took it over and colonized it with Scots.'

Such was the appraisal of what had been happening at the Beatrice lately that Jeremy Delacy got from Tom Toohey, when he arrived to meet that Irish-filled train, making his first visit to the township in a fortnight, and this time having had to make the trip in on horseback. He had left his horse, the stallion Elektra, over at the Racecourse and had walked across the railway bridge. It was the first he'd heard of Prindy's escapade. He was deeply shocked by the news, exclaiming, 'The bloody bastards . . . they hounded the poor little kid to his death! By God I'll have something to say about it to these roystering bloody Irish. McCusky's sure to be along. He's primarily to blame. As for Cahoon . . . But he can't have more than the mind of a child himself, to behave as you say he has been.' Asked by Tom if he would attend what he called Maginty's Gathering, Jeremy answered shortly, 'Of course not. Apart from this awful business, I wouldn't be able to help myself telling the clod-hopping bastards that it's their preoccupation with their lousy Emerald Isle and its troubles that's got us where we are today. Their hatred of the English on account of the Irish has only made the hatred all of us should have felt against Imperial tyranny a sort of Fenian thing. Bugger old Shame-on-us and his Irish Hogmanay . . . . ' He broke off as Toohey, looking alarmed, touched his arm. Jeremy glanced. There was Man Himself heading towards them, the blarney hanging in green wreaths about his broad red face.

'Ah . . . Jeremy, me boy!' cried Old Shame-on-us. 'Just the wan I'm lookin' for, now, and shame-on-us if I'm tellin' a loy. Didn't I tell you to tell him I wanted to see him if he came in, Tom?'

Toohey smirked, blinked. Jeremy was slow in taking the red hand thrust at him and held so challengingly to be taken, but did not answer the smile. Shamus went on: 'To be sure Tom's told you the wonderful news, and how we're going to celebrate it with the biggest New Year's party t'is country ever sayn.'

Jeremy answered shortly, 'I'm afraid I've been more concerned about the news of that little boy's death.'

The broad red face immediately assumed an expression of deep sorrow, the head falling a little to the side. 'Ah, yes . . . the poor little feller, now . . . and you were much attached to him, I know.'

Jeremy snapped, 'I was his grandfather!'

Shamus was too shrewd to get involved in a sticky thing like that. He murmured, 'Hmm! Ah, yes . . . a sad t'ing. But I'm hopin' to see you at our party, Jeremy. I'm thinkin' of your ould Da, and what it'd've meant to him, to see t'e Ould Country truly *A Nation Wanst Agin* . . . . ' He broke off, evidently not liking what he saw in the grey eyes staring hard at him, and seeing an opportunity to get away in the shape of the approaching police truck, with Stunke at the wheel and between him and his wife the gaunt face of Dinny Cahoon, and in the back the Stunke Children in the care of Jinbul and Constable Kinelly of the Caroline. He waved to them and went hurrying to meet them. Just then the cry went up: 'Here she comes!' No sound yet, but white smoke rising above the Racecourse trees. Then the sound of her: *Boo-hoot*! Then she was rumbling on the bridge. She burst into view; to show her smoke-box door painted in rings, green, yellow, and white, and green ribbons flying out like a dugong's whiskers from her cowcatcher; and her whistle sounding as if it were trying to play *The Wearin' o' the Green*!

'Tom Tinball's drivin',' Tom Toohey told Jeremy.

'What a pity it wasn't Hannaford's trip . . . he'd've painted it over with red.'

There were the Cahoon Sisters, waving to their Darlint, McCusky waving to Finnucane, and about a hundred more. For a moment Old Shame-on-us's wreaths of blarney vanished, to be replaced with a look like counting heads and reckoning up the cost of his Irish recklessness; and there were those to come from the Head of the Road as well! But in a moment the green wreaths were back in place; and as the train pulled up and the mob fell off, shouting that he was the Greatest Irishman of 'em All, he rushed to embrace them, himself shouting, '*A Nation Wanst Agin*!' They all took it up. Then there was Tom Tinball coming along to them from the engine with his cornet decked with green ribbons, and playing it; and they all began to sing it: *A Nation Once Again*!

As the visiting crowd went off up to the pub, with the Greatest Irishman of 'em All reared above most of the rest and roaring like an old boss bull in his pride in the midst of his herd, Jeremy and Tom Toohey went with the locals to collect the mail from Col Collings and Oz Burrows. Then the two together set out up through the railway yards towards Toohey's place, each carrying one of Jerry's saddle-bags. They hadn't gone far, when Toohey said, 'Reminds me . . . That poor kid had a letter with him that might've been meant for you.'

'Me?' asked Jeremy in surprise.

Tom related how he had seen Treacle tear the shirt off Prindy's back in the struggle that morning outside the tarpaulin shed, and how when the others had run down to the river after the boy, he himself had gone and picked up the shirt and found the sodden letter in the pocket. There was no address on the envelope. He had intended giving it to the police, but when they didn't come back, thought better of it, took it home and dried it out, and tried to read it. It had been written in so-called Indelible Pencil, the old bushman's favourite writing medium, which being brushed over with a damp cloth or even licked, gave the appearance of having been written in purple ink. The trouble was that further wetting blurred it utterly. Tom had been able to read only a word here and there, amongst these a couple that were started with a capital J and ended with Y, to be made out only because of the special flourish the writer had given to what went above or below the lines of the ruled paper. All that could be made of the signature was that it had two capital B's. Jeremy at once thought of Barbu, and left Tom, to go and speak to the old man, saying he would follow Tom home.

Jeremy found Barbu in a state only to weep and wail and beat his breast, blaming himself for the tragedy for not having gone straight to the police that night of Prindy's sudden coming and going. It appeared that he had gone to the Police Station after hearing of the return of the party, but had been hunted by the officers he found there, Stunke, Cahoon, Gobally and Kinelly, who were all drinking and didn't grasp what he was trying to tell them. However, he intended to tell McCusky when he could get him alone. On hearing the little Barbu had been told by Prindy, which mentioned the name of Billy Brew, Jeremy very forthrightly told the old man to keep his mouth shut, in order not to involve other people. Then Jeremy went hurrying back to the Railway Station, and caught Collings and Oz just as they were about to close up for the night and join the mob at the pub. He asked if they knew anything of Billy Brew's whereabouts. Oz reported on having dealings with him at Charlotte Springs last train, and hearing that he'd been heavily on the booze over Christmas. Jeremy asked Collings if he would oblige him by phoning the Charlotte to learn if the old fellow were still there. Col did so at once, to be informed that although Billy was still in the locality, seeing that his donkeys were there, nothing had been seen of him for several days, and it was presumed he was suffering a recovery. Jeremy asked if a message could be got to him to say that he would like to get in touch with him, would ring the Charlotte tomorrow morning. Hanging up the phone, Col Collings asked with a chuckle, 'What you cookin' up with old Billy?'

'Just donkey business,' said Jeremy.

'Not monkey business . . . connected with Finnucane's turnout, eh? Awaaaaaah!'

Oz lent his big mouth to the guffaw. Jeremy made a grimace as if he found it amusing, but turned and left them.

Over at Toohey's Jeremy studied the letter with a magnifying glass. No doubt about it, the indents under the blurring proved it to be a letter to him from Billy and one referred to several times as 'the boy'. Jeremy's assessment of the situation in the hours of that night he spent discussing it with the Tooheys was that Prindy must have escaped from the home at the Centre after McCusky had delivered them there, and somehow fallen in with Billy, who had somehow smuggled him to Beatrice for his keeping. He said, 'Perhaps he was coming out to me when this thing happened.'

Tom asked, 'Would you've kept him?'

'If he'd come of his own free will, of course. That's what I've always said . . . when he wants me. But was he really coming? What was he doing up in the Limestone? Besides . . . Barbu says he wanted to stay with him.'

'We'll never know now.'

'Billy might be able to tell me something. If I can get him tomorrow, I'll ask him to come up on the train. Can't talk about it over the phone.'

'What good'll it do now?'

'If I have proof that the boy wanted to come to me, then I'm going to jam it down McCusky's throat till it chokes him. I'll dedicate the rest of my life to breaking the power he and the rest of the bastards like him have over other human beings, just because they've been designated Protectors of Aborigines and the Bastard Country refuses to regard anyone that he and his like brands Aboriginal as human. It's a frightful situation, Tom. Nobody knows it better than you. But it's time a man did something real about it. This poor kid's death might be the turning point. You can bet McCusky's shitting himself. Notice how he avoided seeing me when he arrived? But I'll get him . . . by God, I'll get the rat!'

Later that night, after looking through his mail, Jeremy said, 'Here seems to be the very thing to get McCusky and Co. with, too.' It was a magazine entitled *Australia Free,* with a bright blue cover emblazoned with the stars of the Southern Cross, which as he took it from its wrapper, opened itself at a middle page in which was a sheet of written paper, the heading of the article revealed being: BLACK AUSTRALIANS TO DECLARE A DAY OF MOURNING ON JAN. 26, 1938, THE DAY WE WHITE AUSTRALIANS CELEBRATE OUR 150TH BIRTHDAY AS A NATION. ADVANCE AUSTRALIA FAIR OVER THE MISERIES OF THE DARK INNOCENTS WE STOLE THE COUNTRY FROM. Both article and letter were written by one signing herself, in the first place Aelfreda Candlemas, and in the second just Alfie. Jeremy glanced over the two pages of the article first. It told of how the remnants of the Aboriginal peoples of the South, living in squalor on the outskirts of the settlements built on their tribal lands without any more compensation than a system of rationing hardly fit to maintain dogs, were, with the aid of what was called the Free Australia Movement, determined to take part in the elaborate festivities planned for next Australia Day, dressed in their rags and wailing for their brethren murdered and their country plundered over the century and a half of white settlement. The article went on to describe what an Aborigine was: that is a person who had what some official without any qualifications at all except of being on some State or Federal Government payroll decided was of Aboriginal ancestry, unto the third and fourth or fifth or any generation, and hence must be 'Protected'; which meant denied the rights of ordinary citizens, except with the permission, which might be withdrawn at will, of the said official. 'Just the stuff to shove down McCusky's neck . . . and the necks of all the rest of the bastards . . . while they're celebrating the liberation of Old Ireland,' Jeremy growled, handing the thing to Toohey. Then he went on to read Alfie's letter.

It was an excited little girl's letter. Not only had she finished her book, but had seen it in print, (the proofs), and would see it as the finished thing before this year was out, so that it might be entered for an award in the Sesqui-Centenary Literary Competition. It was being published by the Free Australia Movement, of which she was a member now, and Jeremy himself, as he would see by the receipt for his subscription, a New Year's gift from her, enclosed. All her dreams were coming true, thanks to the Free Australia Movement, which was made up of the most wonderful people, Anglophobes to a man and woman. The old Imperial order was about to pass, the British Garrison to be ousted. Australia Felix was not a stillborn bastard after all, but a lusty little fellow about to spring into manhood – True Australian Manhood. So Jeremy's dreams also were coming true. Dear Jeremy! She had told the Movement all about him; and they wanted to meet him, wanted him as one of their leaders. The Chief himself sent his personal compliments. He was a Truly Great Man, the Chief, the Greatest Australian yet – except Jeremy. They must join forces. The Chief, who was in with the Right People, and these were Really Right – she ran off some names, including the Prime Minister's – was sure her book would win a high award and make a terrific impact on the Nation. She was keeping her fingers crossed. The day of the judging would be Australia Day. If she won they would have a terrific party. Would he come to it? The Movement would charter Fergus to fly him down – *and bring the boy*! To present the boy then to the Nation would be to win for him not only his individual liberty, but that of everyone of his breed in the country. Dear Jeremy! Would he please come? It ended with: *Love, love, love, Alfie.*

Jeremy set it down with a sigh.

Tom Toohey, glancing up from thumbing through the magazine, commented, 'Pretty lively stuff in it . . . certainly gets after the Poms . . . the British Garrison, as it calls 'em . . . and the Australian Crawlers. But it strikes me as being a bit what they call Fascist . . . sticks up for Hitler and Mussolini. Here . . . have a look at this hoist they give to Uncle Adolf . . . say he's the greatest man of the Century.' Tom laughed. 'Have to leave that round for Pat Hannaford to find . . . and watch his face . . . Haaaaho!'

Billy Brew was waiting at the Charlotte when Jeremy phoned next morning, and told him he had received his letter and would he put one of his best young jack donkeys on today's train and come up with it to Beatrice. Billy agreed very readily, becoming quite animated from having started the conversation warily. Jeremy had to cut him short. There he was on the afternoon train, riding with the donkey in an open waggon, to the great amusement of the boozy mob waiting to greet the boozy mob aboard. But one amongst the mob who didn't laugh was Eddy McCusky, who as the train stopped, shoved his hat over an eye and assuming that official strut of his, headed for the waggon, while the others crowded to take the hands of their fellow Irish. Another who wasn't amused was Jeremy, standing back a little with Tom Toohey. When Eddy moved off he went after him.

Billy stayed in the waggon, evidently waiting for it to be uncoupled and shunted to the stockyard or loading ramp. He stood staring at the two men approaching, the leader of whom was evidently unaware of the one behind. He nodded to Eddy as he came up, but got no such amiable greeting in reply. In the official tone, Eddy snapped, 'I want a word with you, Brew.'

Billy looked past Eddy at Jeremy. As Eddy swung round, Jeremy said harshly, 'And I want a word with you, too, McCusky.'

Eddy looked confused: 'Oh . . . hello . . . didn't see you . . . . '

'You've been at great pains not to see me since you've been here. What's the idea . . . you got a guilty conscience?'

Eddy's hat came down another inch, and the official snap back into his voice: 'Why should I?'

'Have a conscience? I thought people were born with 'em. Looks like I was wrong.'

'Well, what d'you want?'

'Just to tell you that in my opinion you're a bloody murderer.'

Eddy started, went red, cried, 'Hey . . . go easy!'

In the same level menacing tone Jeremy said, 'That's all I have to say . . . to *you*, at any rate. I'll have plenty to say elsewhere.'

Paled now, and rather breathless, Eddy said, 'You better be careful what you say. Remember there's a law . . . . '

Jeremy, climbing up into the waggon by the brake-lever, cut in: 'Only one law? I thought there were three . . . one for the rich, one for the poor, and the crookedest of all for the Aborigines.'

Eddy turned again to Billy. 'I said I want a word with you, Billy . . . if you don't mind getting down.'

Billy looked at Jeremy, who shook his head. Then he looked at Eddy and said, 'You come up here and say your word, mate . . . and you can get donkey-walloped the same time. Me colt here's pretty fresh.' It sounded like the Billy of old.

Eddy turned away, saying, 'I'll be seeing you later, then . . . maybe at the Police Station.'

Billy yelled after him, 'I'll bring me colt along . . . so he can wallop the lot o' you!'

But Billy's wide grin collapsed on the instant as he turned to Jeremy. Looking utterly miserable he muttered, 'Terrible business, that boy, Jerry . . . all my fault, too.'

'We're all saying that, man . . . except the one bastard it fits . . . that one!' Jeremy tossed his head towards the retreating strutting figure of McCusky.

'How'd it happen?' asked Billy. 'All I've heard is from what the phone gossips 'a' been maggin'. You got my letter, o' course . . . . '

'Wait. Here's Oz Burrows coming. You'll come and camp with me at Tom Toohey's, eh?'

The train did not go back to Town as usual next morning, but thanks to the power in the land of the downtrodden Irish in general and of that Greatest Irishman of 'em All, Finnucane, in particular, was delayed for a day. Tonight was to be the Night of Nights; as some called it, Irish Hogmanay, and others Maginnty's Gatherin'. As Jeremy Delacy was still about the township that day, the third of his stay this time, when usually he stayed only a few hours, it was natural the assumption should be made that he was staying for the shinannigans, as voiced by Shamus himself, when late in the morning the man appeared in the front bar of the Hotel with Billy Brew. Although Jeremy avoided actual committal, he was as amiable almost as Shamus himself, asking him to have a drink with them, adding: 'What about the gentlemen across the way?' He nodded to the corner where McCusky was having what looked like an official conference with Sergeant Cahoon and Constables Gobally and Kinelly, over beer. McCusky, who had been holding forth, faltered in his magging when he saw the newcomers and half-turned away. His mates looked at Jeremy and Billy under lowered brows. The suggestion was just what the blarney-brimming Shamus wanted. Quite joyfully he communicated the invitation. The trio looked suspicious to begin with, but relaxed to Jeremy's nod and grin, doubtless thinking he was liable to compromise on grand occasions as they were on any that suited them. Jeremy even gave the toast, the old Sinn Fein one: *Up the Republic*!

Then Shamus himself did the honours – then Eddy. Then Jeremy produced the copy of *Free Australia* he had rolled up in his back pocket, and spread it on the counter. The bright jacket was instantly arresting. Finnucane took a look at it, saying, 'And what's t'is? Very attractive from the outside, I must say.' Jeremy explained that it was a new political paper strongly advocating Australian interests first. 'And a goot thing too!' cried Shamus.

The trio in the corner were watching with interest. Jeremy held the thing up. Eddy commented, 'Very attractive, yes . . . good title, too. Heard something about it. Comms up against it, I think. Never seen it before, though.'

Jeremy, looking a little red and sounding a little breathless, began to move round to the group, saying, 'Perhaps you'd like to have a look at it. You should find it interesting.' They looked a bit suspicious again as he approached them, but made way for him as he breasted the counter to lay the bright thing down, and crowded round to look.

'The good old Southern Cross,' commented Eddy. 'Looks good without the Union Jack stuck in the corner, eh? I've always said that without that Union Jack, our flag would be the most beautiful in the world.'

Jeremy looked at him. '*You've* always said that?'

Eddy reddened, but gave a crooked grin, 'Well . . . yes, I think I did get it from you, Jerry . . . but I been sayin' it ever since.'

'Thank you,' said Jeremy. 'Imitation is the sincerest form of flattery.' He looked from one policeman to the other. They were still wary. Then, as they looked back at the paper as it lay, he opened it, at that article of Alfie's, with its headlines running over two pages. As the three pairs of eyes popped, he said, 'I'll leave it with you. You might find other things to interest you in it, too.

For instance, there's a review of Hitler's famous book, *Mein Kampf*, which discusses the matter of the superiority of the white race . . . Nordic Race, to be more precise . . . not against it, no! They're all for Uncle Adolf. Strange how this sort of thing got into it. But maybe they see it as a thing to whip the Nation's conscience with . . . that part of it that's got one . . . eh, Eddy? See you later.' He walked out by the side door.

Billy Brew came leaping out to meet him by the front door; and as they set off up the road, heading back towards Toohey's, he chuckled, 'Beautiful, beautiful . . . hit the bastards fair in the solar plexis! You're a genius, Jerry . . . the way you nutted it out. We'd 'a' never got nowhere just roarin' at 'em, like I would 'a'. But the way you done it lad . . . why, you just reared up like a thoroughbred and pissed all over 'em . . . hahahahahaaaaaaa!'

Angus McDodds, in the doorway of his shop, leered at them as they passed him, saying in answer to their nods of greeting, 'What hae ye go' to gaggle at, Billy Brew, at the end of a year of wurrukin' to feed a thoosand silly asses and get yesel' the DT's?'

Billy flung back at him: 'We was tickled at what we 'eard up the pub, 'bout a silly old bugger wurruks all year to get money to stuff his beddin' with.'

Jeremy said to Billy, 'It was just sheer luck, getting that paper, and catching them together. I'd like to hit the lot of 'em tonight, though . . . on the Irish business.'

Billy cried, 'I'm with yo' man, I'm with yo'. Jes you nut it out . . . and I'm there to sink 'em, the bigotted bastards!'

'I think I can see a way. While we were talking to Finnucane there about the new President they'll have . . . this Douglas Hyde, when everybody'd thought it would be DeValera himself . . . I remember reading something about Hyde in a digest thing I get . . . when it was first mooted, the Republic thing, in June or July. I always pass my reading matter on to Tom Toohey. If only he's still got it! I didn't take much notice of it at the time . . . wasn't interested . . . but if what I think I read's right, by golly we can sink 'em man, so that they'll go down for the third time and never come up!' Jeremy sighed, adding: 'Not a very nice metaphor, is it, when we've got the drowned boy on our minds.'

Billy also sighed. 'Speakin' of metaphors. That's one of the words he learnt, like I told you, "Metaphorically speakin'," I says to him a couple o' times: and he asks . . . "What's Metaphorically, Billy?" And I says: "Get the old Webster out;" and he does, and pores over it for hours, till he knows every *Meta* in the bloomin' thing, from *Metabasis* to *Metazoic* . . . Aw, Jesus, Jeremy!' Old Billy was near snivelling.

Jeremy and Billy and Tom Toohey, along with others not included in the Gaelic revels promised for this night looked in on the strongholds of the two rival clans, the pub and the store, somewhat late, knowing that the revellers had been saving themselves so as to be at their best at the witching hour. Both store and hotel had been closed for the afternoon, while their menfolk slept and their women sweated in the kitchens over the gustatory specialities without which celebration would be no more complete than Communion without the Eucharist. The excluded snoopers sniffed the strange odours of haggis and spiced boar's head.

It was about nine before anything started. Then a fiddle and a concertina were heard sleepily waking up in Finnucane's, and at McDodds's the squealing and groaning of bagpipes as old Angus blew out of his ancient set a year's work by mason-wasps and carpenter-bees and cockroaches. Round about ten the ancient ceremonial began. Mick Curry, Finnucane's son-in-law of Charlotte Springs, who was something of a fiddler, played the Boar's Head in from the kitchen, borne on a great decorated baking dish by Shamus himself and itself highly decorated with icing in the three new national colours – wit' a lolly shamrock in its tusky mouth and the new Tricolour flying from a hatpin in its head – to the laden table in the dining-room. 'Twas the way it was done in Ould Oireland on the grand occasions in the Ould Days: 'Far, far beyant the days o' King Boroihme,' as Finnucane explained to those Lesser Ones Without the Law peeping from the passage. 'And shame-on-us if we can't do the loike av it ourselves on t'is grandest of arl occasions!' Along at the store there was the Pipin' o' the Haggis, an annual event these many years and hence not of anything like so much interest to outsiders as the other turnout. But Jeremy and Billy and Tom were there, looking in through the back door of the room at the rear that served as kitchen and general living-room; while the McDodd of the McDodds, wearing a kilt for the occasion, but otherwise his inevitable white cotton shirt and sandshoes, and tootling what could have been any Scottish piece on his bagpipes, was marching round and round the much less lavish table, at the head of about a dozen of his clan, among them Oz Burroughs, with Maceachren, Chief Linesman of the OTL bringing up in the rear with the ancient *pièce de résistance* steaming in its offal bag, a big black dog at his heels, slavering over the rank smell – all this with a wide-shaded acetylene lamp flaring whitely overhead.

As they retreated, Jeremy said to the others, 'They're all the same, the bastards. They've never belonged here . . . and they've never let us who do belong, belong properly, dragging us along with their moth-eaten traditions. If only we could find a way to bust up this Jock show along with the Micks.'

'Yeah, yeah!' said Billy eagerly. 'How can we do it?'

'Something to do with bigotry. That's what they are first and last . . . bigots.'

'Yeah, yeah . . . let's nut it out.'

They got what they wanted as they strolled up to the pub again. Above the din that had risen considerably with the end of the gobbling and real guzzling of Tullamore Dew – concertina and fiddle and piano play and voices beefing *The Irish Exile*: 'There came to the beach, a poor exile of Ee-er-rin, the dew from his eyes, pour-hored down-how-how-ho-hown his chee-heeks . . . oh, Erin, my country, oh Erin, ghobrah'. They heard someone shouting, in what must have been a political group on the side, 'And now what we got 'o do's kick them yeller-bellied Presbyterian bastards out o' North. We'll never be a nation till that's done.' A chorus of Hear, Hear! Jeremy nudged Billy and winked.

It needed only some twenty minutes to midnight when Jeremy and Billy, Tom squibbing this bit, walked boldly into the Hotel dining-room, now cleared of its central furniture and being used for an Irish jig, the vigour of which in sound and action was like to bring the old place down. But it quickly stopped at their appearance, for the reason that the MC, McCusky, had seen them at once and stopped his calling. He had no hat to shove over his eyes, but made the movement as if to do so, as, tight mouthed, for all the swaying of his stance, he stared at them. Old Shamus came into it quickly, striding up as if to bar the way to what he was pretty certain must be Throuble. Nevertheless, it was politely, if also with a rumble of threat, that he asked, 'Ah . . . and what moight you gintlemin be wantin'?'

Jeremy said, 'We thought we'd just drop in and congratulate you all.'

'Yeah,' said Billy.

'Well, thin, if 'tis meant in arl sincerity and goodwill, we thank ye for it . . . although to my moind ye a little late in the day.'

'Midnight's the very time for it, isn't it?' asked Jeremy.

Silence and suspicious eyes, even if they were mostly bleary with booze. Cahoon, somewhat drunk, was muttering, but being held tightly by Sister Aggie.

Jeremy cleared his throat: 'What struck us as reason for congratulation, apart from the fact that at last you've got nationality, after living in Australia so long without it . . . . '

Finnucane raised the large red hand. 'I said if you come here in all sincerity and goodwill, which that kind o' talk don't make it sound to me . . . .'

'Wait,' said Jeremy. 'What I really want to congratulate you on is your great religious tolerance . . . . '

'We don't want religion talked here . . . . '

'I said religious tolerance. I've just been reading about the new Republic of Eire. The new Constitution declares it to be a Sovereign, Independent, Democratic, Catholic State, with a National Flag . . . . '

Mick Boland chimed in: 'Bein' a tri-colour, of green and white and orange, without anny indication o' the Union Jack whatsomever . . . '

'That's right . . . the very words. And the President is elected for a term of seven years, and is to be called *Uachtaran na h Eireann*, and the man chosen is Professor Douglas Hyde . . . . '

Now Mick Curry, who had been a schoolteacher home in Ireland before entering bondage as barman to Finnucane, came into it: 'A famous Gaelic scholard . . . the most famous in the wurruld . . . and's goin' to declare the use of the good Oirish tongue the only wan to be lawfully used in Oireland . . . . '

'I know . . . and he's also a Protestant . . . did *you* know that?'

Stunned silence, blinking and twisting of heads as if ears hadn't heard aright.

After a moment Finnucane asked, 'What's this, what's this . . . some idea of a joke?'

'No,' said Jeremy, 'As I said . . . cause for congratulation . . . that a country that declares itself a Catholic State puts up a non-Catholic as its first President. I must admit I was astonished at such tolerance . . . . '

Boland yelled, 'It's a loy!'

The yell was taken up all round: 'A loy . . . a bloody loy!'

Again Jeremy took from his back pocket a magazine, handed it to Finnucane, who ignored it, but with bushy brows shooting up, roared, 'Out of my house, you renegades, you throuble makers!'

Jeremy dropped the paper at his feet. Boland yelled, 'Down wit' the bastards . . . taich 'em a lesson for comin' here with their bloody loys!'

The voices rose up: 'Hear, hear . . . chuck 'em out!'

There was rush for them, sweeping the protesting Finnucane aside. Dinny Cahoon's long legs put him in the lead. Jeremy and Billy leapt for the door, but Jeremy to linger there long enough to hit Dinny in the solar plexus and lay him out for the others to fall over. By the din they left behind them, the yells and thuds and thumps, the celebrants were taking one another for the enemy. Then there was utter chaos, when Jeremy, running out the back way, threw the main switch in the little power-house.

'So far so good,' said Jeremy. 'Although I'd liked to have got in that bit about how the invaded and persecuted Irish never gave a thought to their own crime of invading this country and persecuting its simple inhabitants. Still, let's see what we can do with the other alien buggers.'

They went round to the back of McDodds's store again. The company here was also doing a jig, to Angus's boozy wheezing piping, and making so much noise, as they should be with all the empty whisky bottles on the table, that the pair came right into the back doorway without being seen, till the dog, cavorting with the rest, probably scented them, and raised the alarm. Angus's piping died with the usual death-cry. He blinked at the newcomers. Jeremy spoke first, 'No good wishing you a Happy Hogmanay, seeing you gave it away to the Irish.'

Maceachrin hiccuped: 'We ha'e gi'n naething awee tae the -hic- Irish, mon!'

Dodds advanced belligerently: 'Wha' would ye two trooble meekers be wantin'?'

'Just to take a look at the Scots holed up in fear of the Irish?'

A couple of Scottish road workers barged in: 'Wha's this afeared the Irish?'

'You let 'em have your Hogmanay . . . and now they're talking of driving all Presbyterians out of Northern Ireland.'

'The Deil ye say!'

'If you don't believe me, go up and ask 'em for yourselves. It's just midnight. Go and break your bottles on their doorstep the way you always did . . . and they'll be out and chuck you in the river . . . or are you too scared?'

Maceachrin roared, 'Hoots mon! Sceered o' Irish? A Scot sceered o' bloody bogtrotters? Come on, lads . . . we'll go and deal wi' 'em!'

There was a momentary scurrying round while the women tried to restrain them and McDodds tried to give warning that they might be Being Played for Foo's; but apparently the booze was at the stage of belligerence, and there was no stopping them, even McDodds when he got caught in the spirit of the thing and snatched up a bottle and joined the rush to do battle with the ancient enemy.

The lights were on again in Finnucane's, but voices high and angry. Jeremy and Billy dashed off to watch from across in the railway yards with waiting Tom. It started off ferociously with bottles hurtling through Finnucane's front windows, and the company within coming charging out like disturbed soldier ants and taking to the attackers on sight. But it was soon over, thanks to the shrieking of the women, and the shrewdness of the two chieftains, who after exchanging a couple of wild blows realized that they'd been had, and the passing quality of alcoholic belligerence as soon as activity begins to burn it up. The rival clans then joined forces to look for the real culprits. But these were in flight.

Billy panted, 'I won't be showing me nose in Finnucane's for a while, I can tell you.'

Jerry said, 'If he refuses to serve you, you can have the law on him. That'd be a real joke.'

'I've had enough jokes to do me for a long while, Jerry.'

'It really wasn't meant as a joke, any of it. They're down on it themselves if anyone else does it . . . the Greeks, the Pongs, the Japs . . . even the English, as far as the Irish're concerned, anyway. No. Billy . . . I never felt less like playing jokes in my life. But ridicule's necessary. It's the only criticism to get at fools with . . . make 'em look the fools they are.'

VI

At dawn on New Year's Day, a dawn so bright that the birds seemed to be waking with especial joy to it, while all those humans who had been expressing so much felicitation about the future snored on ignoring it, Jeremy left Beatrice township as he had come into it, by the railway bridge. Approaching the Racecourse, he whistled on his fingers, to get an immediate answer, and soon to have his great black horse coming trotting to meet him. He fed the beast a large chunk of Mrs Toohey's Christmas cake, and talking to him about cleaning his teeth afterwards and taking Bicarbonate of Soda, went with the horse butting at him with its great head in sheer love of him, to the shed used in Race-time for the weighing. Here his riding gear was stowed. Saddled up, he mounted, set off at a gallop, because that's the way the horse wanted it; out along the gravel road to opposite the station homestead, then onto the heavier home-track, where the damp earth flew in clods to the horse's striding, the heaviness soon pulling him up, leaving him tossing his head for breath. 'Not so good as you used to be, are you boy,' commented his master. As if knowing that he was being teased, Elektron swung back his head as if to bite one of the feet protruding from the stirrups. Soon they were being plagued by large brown and green marsh flies, for assistance in dealing with which, the horse took his rider to a bushy little beefwood. Jeremy pulled off a branch to use as a whisk. So they went on. Whenever the flies got too numerous, the horse broke into a gallop of his own accord and lost them.

Some ten miles out they came to the end of their tracks of the other day, since when it hadn't rained. Flood debris on the road showed that the river had been right over it and much beyond past that point. But knowing the road from years of experience, the horse chose to follow it now. There were still low patches into which the river swirled, some of which the horse avoided, others he went splashing through. Always there was the roar of the river. At length there was an extra note of vibrance in the roar, that steadily grew to distant booming. They came level with it on their right. Jeremy, cocking an eye at the Sun, said, 'Ought to be a great rainbow on the old pool today. How about we try and get in and have a look at it, eh?' As he always did when his master spoke the horse whickered, and again as if understanding what had been said, on coming to the turn-off to the Rainbow Pool, where the road had been well under water by the look of debris, turned right to go in. They were soon in slush, slipping and sliding, the horse relying on the skill of his rider to hold him up. But they got through.

A very different pool it was today; rather like that great tongue of water further North, except that it was lolling out, spewing its swallowings instead of sucking them in, the mouth hidden by a rainbow-tinted bank of mist and bellowing so that the air shook. Right from its hidden maw down the river-bed the mighty yellow-white tongue hung, not a fang of rock to be seen, level with the further bank, the vegetation of which bent shivering to the might of it. On this side it was banked with high-piled debris laced with froth.

Horse and rider stood staring for a while, as if trying to penetrate to the mystery behind that tinted mist. Then the marsh flies found them. The horse, impatient to be off, lashed with tail, scattered the debris with stamping. His rider sighed, pulled him round to the right to head away – when the horse shied violently, snorting, almost unseating the rider, who protested, 'Eh, look out!'

Then the rider saw what the horse had seen and stared. The horse snorted again, quivered. Some moving thing in the debris. Some crawling thing. A moment of staring; then Jeremy gasped, 'Jesus Christ!' and leapt from the saddle, went lunging through the oozy mass.

A small human thing, a skeleton almost, scarcely distinguishable from the rubbish in which, prone, it struggled feebly in striving towards the approaching man, skinny reaching arms, a death's head with gaping blackened mouth, but life in the deep eye sockets, life blazing as the sockets raised themselves to meet eyes of the same intense grey. The black lips strove for speech. Then the head fell in the dirt. Sobbing, Jeremy fell to his knees beside the form, raised it. The grey eyes were revealed for a moment, then shut. Jeremy ran a hand down the bony breast, down the belly that seemed to touch the backbone, down the right thigh, out of the boniness of which protruded an awful pussy mass. Pus oozed from a score of lacerations, and from cracked lips and nostrils. Even the marsh flies left the thing alone, settled on Jeremy, who seemed not to notice them. Turning the frail form over, taking care with that leg, he put his ear to the bony breast. The eyes opened. Getting control of his voice, Jeremy muttered, 'You all right now sonny.' He looked around. No sign of any other creature, alive or dead. Looking back at the boy, he said, 'Have to be careful of that leg of yours. Better splint it before I lift you. Just a minute . . . no, wait!' He held up a hand as the skeleton would have come after him again.

Jeremy went back to the horse, took shirts and singlets from a saddle-bag, tore a singlet into strips. Then back to the boy, to put splints on his leg from hip to ankle. The grey eyes kept closing, to start open again to stare, the effort too much to keep awake for more than a few seconds. Jeremy made a sling with a silk shirt, and by means of it lifted the frail form, carried it to the horse, which sniffing, drew away from the stench of it.

'Stand steady,' Jeremy said to Electron as he mounted with the bundle dangling from his left hand. The horse watched the move. As Jeremy raised it to lie across his knees the grey eyes looked up into his with a glint of a smile. Jeremy smiled back tremulously, muttering, 'You'll soon be home and right again. Come on horse . . . let's go! A fast amble. Can't go too slow. Looks like more rain coming up.'

In little more than an hour the custodians of the keep of hurt and hunted things announced their coming. With the gammy things, small black figures came running to open the white gates, all to stare at the odd-looking cripple being added to their ranks.

Jeremy rode to the front door, through the trellis porch, almost into the lounge, where he handed the bundle down to waiting Nanago. Looking at the skeleton face she breathed, 'Eh, look out!' The eyes opened to stare at her.

Jeremy took him from her. 'Make up a bed with cushions on the settee.' While she was doing it with flying hands, he added: 'Then make him egg-flip . . . with honey . . . warm it a bit. He's starving. He's got a bad compound fracture . . . but we'll have to feed him up before we can do anything much to it.'

She whispered indrawn, 'Where you find him?'

'Rainbow Pool.'

Her eyes grew wide. Then she rushed away to the kitchen.

Jeremy mixed brandy with the egg-flip when it came, and fed it to the cracked lips with a spoon, a slow business. He handed it over to Nan, saying, 'Keep it up to him, as much as he can take and as often. Got to build him up as much as possible. I'm going to load him with Sulphonamide, too. Have to set the leg by tomorrow, or he might lose it. Have to do it myself. The ground's too wet for Fox to land here . . . more rain coming, too. Still, I'd better radio 'em.'

Jeremy went over to his quarters, started up the rarely used radio transmitter. He raised Port Palmeston Radio Station, where the operator tried telephoning Drs Fox and McQuegg, but without success, as to be expected on New Year's Day and, the operator added, in the midst of a storm. Jeremy left word of what he intended to do, but without naming the patient.

That night Prindy, evidently much recovered, what with the feeding and the drugging, slept over in the annexe on a stretcher beside his grandfather, his leg strapped to a board. Soon after dawn, Jeremy had him into the dispensary and strapped to the table there, with Nan and Darcy and Water Lily assisting. There was to be no drugging him against pain for fear of weakening him, Jeremy said, and the use of a general anaesthetic too likely to frighten him. They must rely on his courage – and their own. He explained to Prindy what he wanted to do; and the boy seemed to understand. Perhaps things were helped by the flash and rumble of the storm that had arisen. As Jeremy said, 'That Old One, Tchamala, he lookin' out for his boy, I reckon.' Prindy smiled as if he believed that was exactly how it was.

During the retraction of the limb the boy fainted, making it easier for the sweat-streaming Jeremy to handle things. He came out of the faint staring as if he had been a long way off. Jeremy, splinting the leg so that it could be got at for draining and medication, chatted about how he would soon be hopping about, soon be training Golden Bobby. Prindy only stared, and was like that for some hours afterwards, while someone or other sat with him, watching anxiously, feeding him whenever he could be got to take the spoon.

Next morning the storm was gone. Jeremy got in on the Flying Doctor

Network and spoke to Dr Fox, reporting what he had done and saying that the patient appeared to be in good condition. Still he did not name him. Fox told him to carry on with his mode of treatment, saying that there was no hope of his seeing the patient himself for a long while.

VII

By next train day Prindy was so far on the way to recovery that, sitting with outstretched leg in a wheel-chair, he was occupying himself with making a bamboo flute and studying Webster and listening to high-class music from around the world. That morning Jeremy set out for the siding again on horse-back, arriving there just before noon, and went straight to the Railway Station and put through a telephone call to Dr McQuegg. McQuegg had always been friendly enough with Jeremy, in a guarded way. Now he greeted him in very friendly fashion, wishing him a Happy New Year, perhaps secretly tickled over what he must have heard about the shinannigans at Beatrice. He had also heard of the compound-fracture job, and congratulated Jeremy on hearing that the patient appeared to be on the way to a good recovery, but in the manner of his profession, supposing that Jeremy was seeking further advice from him, said that it was really a matter for Dr Fox. To that Jeremy said, 'It isn't the medical side of the case I want to discuss with you. The patient's Aboriginal, you know . . . and you're Acting Protector.'

'What difference does that make?'

'Rather a lot. I think I can reasonably say I've saved the boy's life . . . but he could easily be crippled for life by being buggered about with. I don't want anyone unqualified coming here interfering.'

'That's hardly likely to happen, is it? You've got Fox's permission to carry on with your treatment.'

'I want yours.'

'What d'you mean?'

'I want your permission as Protector, to hold the patient till he's fully recovered. He happens to be the boy known as Prendegast Alroy.'

The doctor was silent for a moment, then said, 'I see.'

Further silence, while a hundred or more ears must have been straining along the line, as two pairs were here in the Station Master's office while their owners pretended to be getting on with their jobs.

Jeremy broke the silence: 'Well, Mack?'

McQuegg was cagey: 'Cobbitty'll be back in about six weeks.'

'I'm only asking permission from you while you have the authority to give it.'

Another little ear-aching silence. Then McQuegg answered, 'Okay, Jerry.'

Jerry let out a pent breath: 'Thanks a lot, Mack. Will you pass the word along to your . . . er . . . colleagues.'

'Will do. But you'd better report to the local John.'

'I'll do that right now. Thanks, man . . . Goodbye.'

The Local John had apparently been listening in by the look on his face when Jeremy dropped in at the Police Station. He listened tight-lipped to what Jeremy had to tell him of the finding of Prindy, then put through a call to his Superintendent, ordering Jeremy to sit down and wait. Jeremy simply walked out.

Jeremy went next to Finnucane's, to breast the bar and smilingly ask for brandy, while old Shame-on-us glared under those bushy brows in a manner fit to strike him dead. Finnucane had to serve him, and did so, but baulked when Jeremy asked him if he would join him, when he roared, 'I'll be damned if I will!'

Chuckling, Jeremy raised his glass and toasted, 'Up the Republic!' Then, having drunk, still chuckling, he went out.

Next call was on Barbu, to suffer his tears and embraces. Next was to Billy Brew, still at Toohey's. Billy insisted on getting drunk. He went roaring to meet the train, to embrace Pat Hannaford and Porky Jones. He would have gone roaring up to Finnucane's too, had not Jeremy dragged him away with promise of a party at Toohey's that night. They had their party, just the conspirators, including Barbu, who after four beers fell down and went to sleep. There wasn't much to it, only bibulous expression of relief in not having caused the disaster after all that the defiance of authority of at least three of them seemed to have precipitated, together with that self-same spirit of defiance. Jeremy, the only one who stayed sober, kept things from getting too complex with his occasional shouts of: *Up the Republic*! They were all asleep by midnight.

Next morning Jeremy more or less poured old Billy aboard the train for the Head of the Road, on to the engine of which Pat and Porky had fairly to drag themselves. It was a hoarse-sounding *Boo-hoot*! she gave as she steamed away.

Then he headed for home.

CHAPTER TWELVE

THE EDUCATION OF CHILDREN by Aborigines, in the Aboriginal way, is based on the principle that one who is not mature is not responsible; maturity as they see it, beginning with puberty. Whatever the immature learn to prepare them for adult life is as they choose to learn it; which means that childhood is largely a game. There is no compulsion to do anything, even to give up sucking one's mother, no rebuking except as warning against harm, and no punishment of any kind. Perhaps all children would like it that way, and might be the better for having it so, but for the impractability of it amongst civilized communities, with their overcrowding and complexities of breeds and creeds and greeds. The school of Lily Lagoons was run essentially according to the Aboriginal principle, despite the fact that the curriculum was concerned with teaching the children what might seem to have little purpose in the old way of life, namely, what is known as the Three R's. Actually the purpose was to give the children a fuller life, while not disturbing them in their wholehearted acceptance of the old. Knowing that there was such a thing as what they themselves called *Read'n'write*, pronouncing it rapidly as one word, the children would have been at a loss without some knowledge of it, just as anyone of them who could not ride a horse or was scared of a train or motor vehicle was considered a *mungus* or a *myall*. They liked attending the school – when it suited them. Their elders liked the schooling of the children, too – so long as they were not involved.

The school had grown out of the elementary schooling of Darcy by his mother on their establishment in the household, Nanago herself having been similarly taught in a Protestant Mission school. Black kids who had become Darcy's playmates attached themselves for the fun of it. It was Darcy, a natural teacher and a very intelligent young man, really, for all his simpering silliness in public, who had made a true school of it. Influenced by his uncle Jeremy, he had departed from the simple Mission school system, to develop an institution of which the primary purpose was to enrich Aboriginal life as such. The purpose of the Mission system was primarily to Win Souls to Christ, as they say, secondly the more charitable one of equipping their charges in a way considered to render them less helpless in dealings with their mostly Christian conquerors; while that of such Government schools as were already operating for crossbreeds and mooted for full-bloods, was to train them to be what officials would call Useful Members of the General Community. The Lily Lagoons school's purpose, as its critics viewed it, was worse than useless, since it only encouraged the people to stick to their ancient ways. Jeremy's answer to that, of course, was that at least they had dignity as true blackfellows, and that so long as the whiteman could not offer them anything equally satisfying, they would continue to stick to it, even if in some debased form where, having had it destroyed on them, they made believe with it through the medium of grog and opium.

Teaching at Lily Lagoons was now not even in English, but in a native lingo that was actually a combination of the languages of an extensive region, now much depopulated, the tribes of which had had enough in common to cause them to think of themselves as one people, more or less. The combination of the languages was something fostered by Darcy and his uncle in the hope of overcoming the ancient diversities and antagonisms that proved the Aborigines' chief weakness in dealing with the white invaders, and establishing some sort of unity. The children were taught that. Probably it was the best thing they were taught. However, as the critics saw it, it was the worst, a means to causing trouble eventually – that is to the conquerors.

Because of the glosso-epiglottic quality of the language, the writing of it in ordinary Roman alphabet had presented difficulties in the beginning that had worried Darcy into inventing new letters, which had been used, much to the contemptuous mirth of those critics of the school who had seen the writing: 'What the hell's the good o' that, when only a few bloody boongs can understand it?' – until Jeremy discovered that there was, in fact, an International Phonetic Alphabet. But even with the introduction of that there were howls of derision: 'Only bloody Anthropologists'll be able to understand it!' At the back of it was the idea that those of the pupils who had a mind for it could go on to learn to write English in the almost idiotic way that much of the language has to be written, to pass the test of literacy. None had so far.

Reading and Writing was confined to Aboriginal matters. Darcy had collected many Old Yarns, as they were called, laboriously printed them in the new alphabet, and made them into little books with the aid of a *Roneo* machine. Jeremy promised to get him a typewriter with the alphabet whenever one became available in Australia. The children wrote their own stories, of small expeditions and walkabouts, which were passed round for others to read aloud. Sometimes one would tell on the blackboard, of some adventure and even be the cause of putting an end to classes for the day with his descriptive powers of, say, a sweet sugar-bag he'd had a hand in finding, or the proliferacy of yabbies discovered in a certain creek. There would be a yell of *dirralk gurruk*! – and the class would be gone, leaving Darcy sighing his resignation and turning to some other task.

There was no difficulty with arithmetic. It was only a matter of teaching the Tables, limited to ten – *Ten-tens-undred*! as they would conclude their sing-song recitation of it. It dealt with measurement and numbering as would be used in dealing with stock, simple money transactions, and the calculation of time. No Lily Lagoons kid had to ask how many weeks it was to the Races, how many days to Christmas; even if they still preferred to name the hour of the day at which something would take or had taken place by pointing with lips to the sky.

So simple a school could have no problem pupils; nor had it any until the attempt was made to include in it one who would be considered by many the most problematic of all children in the land, he known officially as Prendegast

Alroy, but here as plain Prindy. First problem concerning him was what he should be taught. As Jeremy said to Darcy, for certain they would be having an official visit from the school's foremost and most powerful critic, Mick Cusky, as soon as the road from Beatrice was trafficable again for motor vehicles. Luckily he was a *mungus* horseman; or they would have him along any time. As it was, they might expect some three months' grace. The great man wouldn't want to interfere with the school as it had been run till now, because he had nothing to replace it with as yet, and by the time he did, conditions in respect to Aboriginal welfare may well have improved enough to make him feel it better to leave it alone. He had seen it before and sneered, calling it a Play School and a Menagerie for Visiting Anthropologists. But what about Prindy? Was it likely that he would be permitted to stay on as one of the Performing Animals? Hardly. Surely the only way they would be able to keep the boy at Lily Lagoons was by proving that in every respect, and particularly that of schooling, he would be markedly better off there than where McCusky would want to take him; and the schooling must be of the kind Eddy and his mates in high places approved of, which is to say would equip him as a Useful Member of the General Community.

Jeremy discussed the matter not only with Darcy, but with Nanago, Tom Toohey and his wife, and even with Alfie Candlemas in a letter written to congratulate her on the publication of her book, *Australia Felix*. He asked Alfie as a schoolteacher for advice and books on the latest in elementary education, the books to be sent to Port Palmeston by air-mail, then brought on charter flight by Fergus Ferris and dropped, since he would be unable to land. In explaining the urgency to Alfie he had to tell her what probably he would rather have kept from her, although frank enough in confessing it to the others, namely, that failure to keep Prindy as a member of his household would be tantamount to failure of what he had given his life to. He had built Lily Lagoons as it was to stand as an example to the Nation of how honesty and wisdom could correct the hitherto accepted ravaging of the land and savaging of its owners. If McCusky could walk in with his hat over his eye and remove Prindy with the blessing of constituted authority, then he, Jeremy, must accept his enemies' evaluation of the place as nothing but a hide-out for misfits and outlaws, run by a misanthrope they called the Scrub Bull.

Meantime the Problem Child presented a second problem, the insoluble one enunciated by the adage that you can lead a horse to water but you can't make him drink. So rapidly did Prindy recover, perhaps thanks as much to his own insistence on the use of pipe-clay and honey in treatment of his wounds, as Jeremy's care (as Jeremy freely admitted) that, riding in a wheel-chair, he was fit to attend school within a fortnight of entry into the household. Because he had some conventional rudiments of the Three R's and it was considered that this was the stuff he would have to pass the McCusky test in, Darcy got to work on him at once to improve him. Now, while he might not look it, Prindy was no less a blackfellow than any other member of the school, and the rule of the school was that there were to be no rules, and pupils attended only when they had nothing better to do. At the time the school was working at full vigour, because it was raining like mad. But Prindy, the music man, always had something better to do. He was the only pupil in the history of the place ever to be compelled to attend. He went docilely enough when so ordered; but only to go to sleep; and sometimes in his sleep to sing.

Jeremy also talked to the boy about McCusky's practically certain interference, and got him to admit that he wished to stay there. But Prindy was quite unconcerned, no doubt having in mind his own method of dealing with Mick Cusky. As Jeremy said to his friends in discussing his difficulties with the boy: 'He'll simply bolt again . . . even if he's got only one functioning leg to bolt on. But there must be no more bolting . . . if possible. Next time will make him an outlaw. I've tried to tell him that . . . that there's one thing in being free, and another in refusing all restraint except what's imposed with chains and bars. He's won his freedom . . . of spirit, I mean. No one can ever take that from him. But he has to learn now that there are other ways of being free than with animal cunning and savage's magic. For godsake . . . what have I landed myself with? I remember when I first heard him singing that song of his, *My Rown Road*, at Catfish, year before last, before the trouble began . . . I thought of how remarkable he was, in originality, intelligence . . . he with his background, intuitively seeking a way of life of his own. Now when I hear him playing it on his flute, I know it's in rebellion against what we're trying to do with him. You can teach him anything. That's evident enough in the way he speaks since he's been with Barbu and Billy Brew . . . Indian Mythology, Greek Mythology, Astronomy . . . and the words he comes out with! Yet all he's doing at Lily Lagoons is waiting for old Bobwirridirridi to turn up. He hasn't said so . . . but I know. I've tried to convey to him that the old fellow might be a long while in coming, might not even be able to come. He's just looked at me . . . as if to say I don't know what I'm talking about. It was the same with the clay. If I hadn't got it for him and let him slap it on and eat chunks of it, he'd've crawled away into the Limestone and got it for himself. He doesn't give me any credit for having cured him . . . even for finding him that day and bringing him home. Whether he knows what happened to him or not I haven't a clue. When I asked, he just said, "Been lose him head." Could be true, being sucked miles underground and half killed in the process. But he believes it was the Pookarakka got him through, brought me to him, sent me home with him . . . and, God help us, the same master-mind will deal with Mick Cusky for him. What do I do? As I've said, if I fail with him, I fail with everything. It isn't the relationship. Truly, that means no more to me than it does to him . . . or perhaps that's going too far . . . I mean to compare *my* petty indifference to his . . . God, was anybody ever so aloof, and so smilingly so . . . "Yes Mullaka, no Grandfather" . . . so amiably obedient in everything that doesn't matter. He's learnt table manners, hygiene, so that he gets about the Big House like a true-born squatter's son. Yet you can see that every time the lightning flashes and the thunder rolls he's thinking of his true friends, Old Tchamala on Top, and the Pookarakka just biding his time to knock Blue Mud Bay Jail down and fly down to join him . . . .'

Those school-books from Alfie, along with a letter and a special edition of the magazine, *Australia Free*, arrived on the last day of January. The arrival was most spectacular, and could be taken as most auspicious, as Jeremy remarked, seeing that Fergus came flying under a perfect rainbow. Fergus made several circuits of the homestead, at such low level and steep bank that his split-lip grin could be plainly seen at his almost horizontal cockpit window, then dropped the package almost beside the wheel-chair, to shoot off again under the rainbow and disappear into a patch of blue. The Auspiciousness was suggested by Jeremy while they were unpacking the parcel in the lounge, and handing the bright primers to Prindy. He said, 'Looks like Old Tchamala let that aeroplane bring you these . . . so you'd better learn what they'll teach you, eh, or that Old One going to growl you properly with lightning and thunder?'

It was said with a smile, to which Prindy responded in a way that plainly showed he took it as a joke, even if it weren't exactly meant as one.

Alfie's letter was brief and hardly helpful, preoccupied as she was with the sudden tremendous success of her book, which had been awarded the highest prize in the Sesquicentenary Literary Competition and was receiving plaudits far beyond expectation when it largely insulted the nation. It was that she wrote of mostly. Concerning the problem Jeremy had confessed to her, she had only this to say:

> Silly old darling – didn't I tell you you'd have to take a positive attitude to things! But Lily Lagoons is only a tiny piece of your responsibility. You've got no problem with the boy. All you have to do is charter Fergus to fly both of you down here. We'll take care of him – the Movement. We have the money. We have the power. Who are McCuskys and other little creatures you're afraid of? I had dinner with the Prime Minister and his wife last night, and told them about their arrogant little men in far places. Not that I had to, because they'd read it in my book. So you see, you have no problem – except maybe little me, who am determined that you'll take your place in this nation you were born to. Give the books to your nephew Darcy. You aren't a teacher. You're a National Leader. I'm waiting for you, Jeremy darling. Don't keep me waiting too long. Things are moving too swiftly for delay. My true love to you – *Your wildly happy but grimly purposeful Alfie.*

The special edition of the magazine was to commemorate Alfie's award. Much of it was given over to reviews of her book, most of which were highly laudatory, the rest being dealt with by the Editor himself in comments that should shut them up for good, such being his verbal virulence in defence of the Darling of the Movement, as very evidently Alfie had become. There was also a large picture of the darling receiving her award from the Prime Minister.

When Jeremy showed Prindy the picture and asked if he remembered the lady, Prindy answered promptly, 'That Missus Alfie. She was teacher Compound School. She take we plenty picnic.'

Evidently seizing on what looked like another means to solving the pressing problem, Jeremy said, 'These books are present to you from Missus Alfie.'

Prindy's eyes opened wide. Jeremy went on, tapping the letter: 'She write in this letter that she want you to come down South soon . . . and she show you round.'

The grey eyes blinked. 'Eh, look out!'

'What's the matter?' Jeremy asked. 'You frightened to go in aeroplane . . . . . . to see big, big city?'

The eyes became hooded. Prindy murmured, 'Missus Alfie been tell Coon-Coon that time I sit down Barbu Ram place.'

'Eh? Now, you're wrong there. She didn't. Coon-Coon found you himself.'

Swinging the wheel-chair away towards the radio, Prindy said shortly, 'Barbu Ram say Missus Alfie.' He reached to switch on.

Jeremy looking at Nanago, said, 'Better I send a letter-stick to the Pookarakka tell this young man what is right thing.'

Prindy turned his fair head quickly, looked hard at his grandfather for a moment, then asked, 'How you send letter-stick to old-man?'

Jeremy assumed a knowing expression. 'I know plenty people I can trust.' He turned again to Nan: 'I think I'll do that.'

For a moment more Prindy regarded the pair, then turned away again, tuned, sank back in the chair with a sigh as the music came rolling in: *The Entrance of the Little Fawns*.

It looked as if Alfie's School books were to be ignored on principle, not only by pupil, but by teacher, who when told the sender, looked so troubled that Jeremy asked what was the matter. Darcy only shook his head. Of all the household, the head of it would be the only one who didn't know that Missus Alfie had concluded her last visit here by slapping her hostess's face. Nanago herself, hearing of Alfie's offer regarding Prindy, asked Jeremy would he do anything about it. He replied, 'Alfie's only interested in herself . . . particularly just now. Lord knows who she'd fob him off on. Besides, he wouldn't go. And even if he would, it'd mean much the same as his bolting. I'm afraid our only hope is through *Tchinek Bijnitch* . . . and damn me if I can see how that can be worked.'

But Jeremy, not being a Tchinek Man, did not know the power of the Old One.

It was just a week after that coming of Fergus's through the rainbow that had made things look as if Old Tchamala had finished his blasting and flooding for the season and the milder conditions ordained by Koonapippi prevailing, when a violent thunderstorm hit Lily Lagoons, doing some damage that included putting the Big House radio out of action. Prindy had just got onto crutches. Jeremy watched with interest his excited hopping about the place during the storm, showing none of the cowering fear of the rest of the household. Then, observing the boy's dismay later in not being able to listen to his musical programs, he remarked to him, showing him a fused coil, that since it was lightning had done it, Old Tchamala must be displeased with his listening to whitefeller rubbitch, so he wouldn't bother to fix it for him. Jeremy had his own smaller set in his quarters, which he used only for listening to news and such things. Prindy wouldn't expect to use that. Anyway, now that he could walk upstairs, he was living exclusively in the Big House. Although the boy said nothing in reply to Jeremy's remark, the effect on him was obvious. Jeremy told Nan about it, and suggested that something might come out of it.

For two days Prindy had only his flute to console him; and dismal did it always sound. Then while at dinner on the second evening, Jeremy, Nan, and Prindy, dining as they always did in squatter style, Nanago, following a wink from Jeremy, asked him was he not going to fix the radio. He answered that Prindy didn't want him to, because Old Tchamala had busted it so as to stop him from listening to white-feller music. Prindy at once protested, 'No-more!'

'But that Old One hit the place, all right. You saw him and heard him do it.'

After a moment's worried hesitation, Prindy said, 'I reckon he hit wrong place.'

Jeremy looked interested. 'Do you, now? I didn't think *he* could make mistakes.'

Prindy was silent.

Jeremy asked, 'Do you think he'd let you listen to music if it was fixed?'

Prindy blinked. 'That's all right, I reckon.'

'Well, if you think it is, you'll have to give me a hand to fix it. I'm busy with other things. Have to strip the old coil and rewind it. Slow job. But there isn't much to it. Got to measure the wire, of course . . . certain thickness, certain length. Reckon you could do that, with me alongside you?'

'Oh, yes, Grandfather!' No doubt about the meaningfulness of this affirmative.

'All right . . . we'll do it in the morning.'

Jeremy had tried to interest the boy in several of his own pursuits in the hope that it might lead him to realize the need for basic instruction; but in vain. Microscopy, chemistry, botany, zoology, revealed to him in simple examples, had held his attention only momentarily; then when permitted, he had gone off to play his flute or listen to the radio or look in Webster's for some obscure word that he would not try to spell properly. Jeremy had shown him the electric power plant and given him some slight idea of how it worked, and explained the rudiments of the functioning of radio. But Jeremy himself was not much interested in electricity, beyond maintaining the running of the household equipment of that kind. The results had been the same. However, that Jeremy felt there was something very different in the present circumstances was evident in the elaborate preparations he made for that simple job of rewinding a small transformer.

When Prindy went over to the Mullaka's quarters after breakfast next morning, amongst a lot of electrical gear he found set up for him on the bench in the special workshop, was a large spark-coil of the type used in early radio telegraphy. Jeremy explained that, for that winding job, it was necessary to have some idea of the nature of electromotive force running through a coil. Take this spark-coil, switch on, adjust the poles – and there it is! That flashing and crackling between the poles is lightning in miniature. Look that word Miniature up. Means Small Scale, means a Big Thing Made Little. Yes, lightning, exactly the same as Old Tchamala makes in a big, big way. Touch it – Whoops!

Prindy stared, amazed. But Jeremy jerked him out of it, saying they were here to rewind a coil to repair the radio. Now, here was a simple coil, called a Choke, for the simple reason that its purpose was to, well, choke down the liveliness of an electric charge, same as you choke down a colt or a micky-bull or some animal with a rope when he gets too rough. Switch it on. It only gets warm, taking out that wildness. Now let's shove the screw-driver in the hole in the middle. It's jumping about and growling like an old debil-debil in the dark – and look, it's grabbed the pliers! Try pulling them away. No, this won't give you a shock. It's cheeky in a different way. Right. Now here's yet another kind of coil. This is the receiver of a telephone. Even without connecting it up you'll find it grabs things. That's called Magnetism – same as the old debil-debil thing there, only it's there all the time. We'll deal with that later. Let it hold the tin plate. Put your ear to it. No sound. Now I switch on. You hear a hum. It's become alive with the stuff coming out of the battery. Now I'll connect up this talking-in piece. Look, it works much the same as the other. Get ready. I'm going into the lab. Hello, *Mora*! You hear me, my Grandson? So you see, a clever whiteman can do just the same as the Pookarakka with his voice. We've got wire on this; but it's just the same with radio. The music you hear, is played to you thousands of miles away. You know what a thousand is? Well, you know what's a hundred: ten times ten. A thousand is ten times a hundred. You've got to know numbers to know where you really are; except like a blackfellow in the bush. But you can't live in the bush all the time. You might's well be a kangaroo, eh? But we've got to fix this coil for the radio. Take a bit of the wire. We have to what's called Gauge it first. That's only another word for measure. We'll look all those words up later. Words are lovely things when you get to know them; like music, I suppose, different sounds. I don't know music like you. Maybe you can teach me music, and I'll teach you words, eh? But this wire. This is called a Micrometer Gauge, because it measures very small, like the microscope sees things very small – Micro means Little. Measure in what are called thousandths of an inch. See, that's an inch, on the ruler. A thousand inches is away over there – and a thousandth of an inch – *anth*, remember – is way back here. Must have pencil and paper for this. Here we are. Figures: one, two, three; they're really only pictures. Same with written words; only pictures you draw. Want to draw figure One? Right. Now figure Ten. Now figure One Hundred. One Thousand? That's it! Now, this's how you do One Thousandth. But you'd better leave that for a while. Measure the wire's thickness, then see if we've got it in stock. Then strip the coil and measure how much you took off or weigh it, to see how much you'll need to put back.

'You want to do this, son?' Jeremy asked at last.

'Yes, Grandfather.' Again no doubt of the sincerity.

That's how it began – with a fluke of interest that never waned.

In discussing it with others, Jeremy said he judged that it was the *Tchinek bijnitch* that started it, but the boy's natural bent that kept it going; not a bent for electrical phenomenon, but for the Miracle of Sound, since it was to what, taking the words from Webster's, he described as The Nature of Sound, his mind turned almost at once as means to deal with the Three R's; or more truly *vice versa*, since he realized he must have those to deal with the Miracle. While the repair of the transformer went on, the talk was mostly of Sound. Jeremy actually did most of the work, while Prindy consulted Webster on the subject and took notes. There was also the peculiarity, common to people of musical genius, Jeremy recalled having read, of facility with mathematical calculation. Within a week the boy was speaking of the mathematics of Sound and making notes:

> Sound travels in waves, like water. The waves act on the drum of the ear, like electric pulses on the diaphragm of a telephone. Sound travels at about 1,000 feet in 1 second in dry air at 0°C. Sound has Pitch, which is sharp or

dull, from what vibrations cause it. Pitch can be measured like speed of sound. Two kinds of sound, 1. Noise not regular, single like Bang, or lots of sounds like tearing or scraping or yelling. 2. Music, regular sound. Noise is harsh, means Make Sick the Ear. Music has Tone, from what is how fast and how strong vibration. Tone may be simple, as from Tuning Fork, or complex, as from stretched string or wire or wind blown note with pitch changing. Music has Harmony, which is mixing tones.

This sort of stuff was soon going into exercise books, the somewhat mature wording looking very odd in infantile handwriting. There were also diagrams of audio-electrical devices, childishly executed, but with use of conventional electrical engineering symbols taken from a book hastily procured from Port Palmeston, and a tracing of the structure of the human ear taken from Webster. But most interesting were the mathematical calculations. He had only to hear Square Foot to start squaring everything and extracting the roots, and proceeding to cubes, while yet he had to add up with the use of his fingers. When he found the word Comptometer with a picture of the machine in Webster's he was very excited, declaring that it must be possible to play figures like musical notes. That was just after the flute arrived for which Jeremy sent South for him. Jeremy promised to look into the matter of buying a Comptometer.

Probably Jeremy was only humouring the boy with the talk of the Comptometer, since the idea of a machine to do your figuring was a bit too much to take seriously in the circumstances, even by him; and just as well, when possession of one might well have been judged even sinister, seeing the way disapproving outsiders took to be a kind of transmogrification what they heard of Prindy's acceptance of civilized ways. Jeremy himself was largely to blame for the attitude of his enemies, since he was the one who, while in Beatrice a couple of times, reported on the matter with more loquacity than he usually indulged in. Perhaps he did it with deliberate intent to annoy his enemies. Still, there was no doubt about his delight in the phenomenon. To several people he declared, 'The boy's a genius.' One of these was Finnucane, to tell anything to whom was tantamount to telling it to the wurruld, and not to your credit if he were agin ye.

First indication of official interest came in the first week of April, when, with sudden changing of the wind to southward, the land began to dry and it was possible to make the journey from Beatrice by motor vehicle. The Watchers gave the warning of the intrusion. The Sharp-eyed ones peeped. The indrawn whisper ran through the place – not *Mick Cusky*, but *Coon-Coon*!

Here was the test of the civilizing influence. Jeremy in the annexe, receiving the warning by telephone, at once raced to the schoolroom, where Prindy was alone with Darcy, and told him to stay where he was, because Coon-Coon could do nothing to him. Prindy took it calmly enough, just a widening of grey eyes. The black kids were all away with parents on the walkabout that always followed cessation of the rains and the languishing of the land in fat fertility.

But Sergeant Cahoon's visit was unofficial; or so he declared, when Jeremy went out to meet him and curtly asked his business: 'Just dropped in to take a look at the boy. Quite unofficial, I assure you. Heard so much about him lately. Regular pocket genius. they're sayin'. Had to see for meself . . . '

Jeremy cut in 'I don't see how it follows that you had to see him . . . but just the opposite. It was through your hounding him he nearly met his death.'

'Now, don't go holdin' that agin me, Jerry. It was my very fear for his comfort and safety that brought that about . . . and all the wurruld knows how I suffered for it . . . and how thankful I am to Almighty God for delivering him.'

'I had a hand in it, too.' said Jeremy dryly. 'Well, you may see him, if I have your assurance you won't mention that day. As far as I can judge, he hasn't any recollection of what happened after you chased him into the flood. I reported the matter to the Beatrice Officer, who accepted my statement. I consider the matter not only closed, but strictly taboo.'

'I too . . . here's me hand on it.'

Jeremy turned away, saying, 'Your assurance is enough . . . provided I'm with you to see you stick to it. Come on. The boy's in school. I won't have you disturbing his lessons.'

Jeremy had ignored Jinbul, standing behind his master; but when the tracker moved to follow his master, Jeremy swung on him, saying sharply, 'You stay here, boy . . . right here!' Jinbul looked at his master, who narrowing his eyes and twisting his thin mouth, nodded.

The whitemen went on in silence, till they reached the entrance to the school, when Jeremy said to Cahoon, who was about to enter with his hat on, 'Seeing you're not here officially, you'll kindly remove your hat, Sergeant.' Dinny went red, but grinned as he complied.

Prindy was at his desk, Darcy at his table by the blackboard. Jeremy remarked, 'Usually Darcy has a crowd here . . . but, as you know, it's walk-about time.'

'Not for the buddin' genius, though, eh?' came that grating voice, while the green eyes fixed on the grey that rose momentarily to meet them.

Jeremy said to Darcy, 'The Sergeant here's interested in Prindy's education. He'll probably like to see his exercise books . . . do you mind?'

Darcy answered with wriggling and giggling as he hastened to gather up some books.

Coon-Coon was interested only in his Sonny Boy, up to whom he strode, with grin wide, holding out his hand, saying, 'Well, what d'you know . . . me Sonny Boy all dressed up and slicked and doin' schoolin'!'

Prindy was wearing a neat suit of good-quality khaki shirt and shorts, Chinese tailor-made for him in Palmeston, and had the fair hair, formerly mostly an unruly mop, nicely cut and combed. He didn't raise his hand from the desk, but looked at his grandfather. Jeremy said, 'You remember Sergeant Cahoon, don't you, son?' Prindy nodded. 'He wants to shake hands with you.'

Prindy slowly raised his right hand, to meet the green slits boldly as he did so.

'Nice to see you doin' so well,' said Dinny, and sat himself on a corner of the desk, adding: 'They tell me you've taken to the books like a bloomin' old goanna to sugar-bag, eh? Aaaaaah! Let's see what you're doin'.' He snatched up the exercise book Prindy had been writing in and the text-book. 'Eh, what's this . . . parsin' and analysis? Jees . . . but you have come on! I forget what it is, even. Spell it to me . . . spell that word Analysis . . . .'

Jeremy cut in: 'You assured me you weren't going to question him, Sergeant.'
Cahoon swung towards him: 'Only askin' him about his schoolin'.'
'You're not a school-inspector, but a police officer.'
'I told you I came here unofficially.'
'You'll always be a policeman to that boy.'
Dinny sneered, 'While he's under your influence, I guess.'
'I said always. I think it's useless your asking him questions. He wouldn't answer you. If you're genuinely interested in his schooling, you'll make the best judgement of it as a teacher would . . . by studying his exercise books. Darcy's got them here.'
Somewhat red, but still grinning, Dinny took the books, still without taking notice of Darcy, and thumbed through them. 'Pretty crook writer, I notice.' he murmured.
Jeremy said, 'Good writing only comes with long practice.'
'Spellin's not so hot, either.'
'How's yours . . . will you let Darcy test you?'
Dinny sniggered. Jeremy said, 'You're not really studying the work. Take a look at this.' He pointed out the piece, *The Nature of Sound*, whipped over the pages to show the diagrams and calculations, Wave Lengths, Frequencies, then demanded, 'Well?'
The green eyes fixed on Jeremy's grey in a hard quiz, as Dinny asked, 'That's all that kid's own work, eh?'
'Definitely.'
Cahoon swung to Prindy: 'You did that all yourself, Sonny Boy?'
Jeremy cut in: 'Don't answer him, Grandson.'
Dinny swung back, hard-faced, narrow-eyes: 'Here, what're you comin' at?'
Jeremy withdrew his gaze from the snapping eyes, to look at Prindy and say, 'In asking you that question, the Sergeant insulted me. I'll explain later.' Then he looked back at Dinny. 'Now, Sergeant . . . if you'll be so good as to let the boy get on with his lesson, I'll see that you and your tracker get something to eat.'
Dinny went very red, began to fold his arms as he sat. Jeremy also reddening, said, 'Will you please come at once? I wouldn't like to have to summon you for trespass.'
Dinny drew a deep breath, heaved himself to his feet. He looked down at Prindy, whose grey eyes met the green slits calmly. A moment; then he said, somewhat throatily, 'Be seeing you, Sonny Boy . . . be seeing you soon.' He shoved on his hat and strode out.
Jeremy watched him from the outer door, saw him join Jinbul and go striding, the lanky pair of them, back to their muddy utility. He remarked to Darcy at his shoulder, 'Sorry I had to do it like that . . . but I don't think he was here for any good. Couldn't let him make a fool of the boy with spelling. He naturally had to spot the weaknesses . . . .'
Prindy, peeping from behind, cut in: 'I can spell Analysis . . . ANALYSIS.'
Jeremy turned to him, smiling: 'I don't doubt it, son . . . but he'd've tried you with something else . . . something like Egg or Pig or Doggy . . . and you know you're not too good on the G's and Double-G's and such like.'

'But they are silly words, Grandfather . You say yourself there's no logic in English language spelling.'

Jeremy put an arm about the slender khaki shoulders, chuckling, 'I underrated you, son. You'd've probably sunk him a lot better than I. I'll leave you to do it to McCusky. I guess we'll have him along soon.'

'What's Under-rating, Grandfather?'

'Well, that's a job for Webster. Come on over and we'll consult the old boy, and have smoke-o the same time. Want to come, Darcy?'

Darcy giggled as he went with them: 'By'n'by he going to get head big's old Webster Dictionary . . . eeeeeeeee!'

McCusky was there within a week, taking them all by surprise by the manner of his coming. When they heard the drone of the aircraft, or Aeroplane Music as he who heard it well before the others called the tuneful sound, they first thought it was Fergus paying them a visit; and as many as could pack into the utility, went racing out to the race track to make smoke to signal to him that it was safe to land and how the wind lay. Then, as the plane came over the trees it was seen to be that of the Flying Doctor, presumably come at last to take a look at Prindy's leg. No one thought of McCusky till there he was, the first to come out of the plane as the stairway fell, a bit wobbly in the official strut for having been off the ground for a couple of hours, but making up for it with the tilt of his hat.

Eddy came marching straight for Jeremy, greeting him shortly, 'Goodday.'

Jeremy was as short: 'Goodday. What can I do for you?'

Eddy nodded to Prindy, standing by, leaning on his single crutch. 'I've come for the boy.'

'With what authority?'

'That of the Aborigines Department.'

'Something in writing?'

'I don't have to have anything in writing. I'm Deputy Protector . . .I stand in *loco parentis* to the boy.'

'You're official designation is Assistant Protector. I was given *loco parentis*, as you call it, over the boy by the Deputy . . . and it hasn't been rescinded as far as I know.'

'Well, it has . . . take it from me.'

'I'll take nothing from you.' Jeremy looked past Eddy at Dr Fox and another man, dumpy, gingery, bald, with odd-looking melanic spots and patches dotting his ruddy skin. Jeremy would have known him as Mr Fisher, Head Teacher at Palmeston State School and virtual director of education. He spoke to them: 'Goodday, gentlemen.' He added to Fox: 'You've come to have a look at the boy's leg?'

Fox looked somewhat uncomfortable, answering, 'Well . . . yes.'

'Right . . . we'll run up to the homestead . . . if you two gentlemen will get in front with me.'

Eddy said; 'The examination will be done at Palmeston Hospital.'

Jeremy glanced at him, then at Fox, asking, 'You're under orders, Doctor?'

'Not exactly . . . it's only the facilities . . . .'

'You know they're all here. I was given to understand by Dr McQuegg that the boy might stay till you declared him fit to travel.'

Eddy said, 'He looks fit enough to me. I saw him hopping about as we came in.'

'I'm talking to the doctor. I should think, Doctor that the important thing was *where* he was fit to travel. Is that right?'

'Well . . . I suppose so, yes.'

'Do you know where he was to go?'

'My business was only to take him to Town.'

'Well, I'm thinking past that . . . .'

'You don't have to,' snapped Eddy.

Ignoring him, Jeremy said to Fox, 'If you don't mind, Doctor.' He motioned to the car. Fox and Fisher went to it. Jeremy gave Prindy a lift up into the back, walked past the grim-faced McCusky, who hastily scrambled aboard as the car started up, packing himself in with the others, who obviously drew away from him.

In the hospital section of the annexe, they X-rayed Prindy's leg. The doctor declared that the healing was perfect, the only trouble some muscular atrophy that should be remedied by regulated exercise. Jeremy asked him, 'That can be done here?' Fox didn't answer. Jeremy pressed: 'Will you say it *can't* be done here as well as anywhere . . . with your direction?'

'Well . . . no.'

'All right . . . I take it that he's not yet fit to travel *anywhere* and that he couldn't be as well treated as here . . . .'

Eddy cut in: 'Now look here . . . .'

Jeremy continued to the doctor: 'You're satisfied with his physical condition, I mean the way he's been fed and generally cared for?'

'Oh, quite.'

'Would you like to see how he lives . . . with a room of his own in the Big House, the run of it like a squatter's son?'

'No . . . I can see he's healthy and happy enough.' The doctor was looking worried.

'Would you say he'd be better off in any place Mr McCusky's likely to take him to?'

Eddy butted in again: 'Now look here, Delacy . . . . '

'I'm talking to the doctor. Well, Doctor?'

Fox was getting nettled: 'Look . . . I don't want to get involved in this thing . . . .'

'But you are. You came here to examine the boy. You admit that he needs further care and that he can get it here . . . and that you don't know where else he'd get better, and for all you know, Mr McCusky might have in mind something much worse . . . . '

Now both Fox and McCusky expostulated: 'Now, look here . . . .'

Jeremy swung on Fisher, demanding, 'You're a witness to this, Sir.'

Fisher went crimson, so that his black spots turned purple and he swallowed and sweat burst from his brow.

McCusky came in sharply: 'There's the matter of schooling.'

Jeremy smiled: 'Ah . . . that's what you're here for, eh, Fisher . . . all the ends sewn up for an arrest?' He looked at Prindy, now standing by watching with wide-eyed interest: 'Boy . . . go into my den and get that *Australia*

Free with the picture in it . . . you'll find it on top of the desk.'

McCusky asked, 'What's that rag got to do with it? I saw the thing Alfie Candlemas wrote . . . it's bloody rubbish.'

'You saw the picture of her getting the prize from the Prime Minister?'

'What's that got to do with it?'

'You'll see.' There was Prindy with the magazine. Jeremy opened it at the Alfie part, where her letter lay as he had placed it. He handed Eddy the letter.

Eddy went pink as he read, then shot the thing back at Jeremy, saying, 'Bloody cheek! Suggesting abduction. Amounts to compounding a felony . . . d'you realize that?'

'We're not all as dumb as you silvertails think we are, Eddy.' Jeremy handed the letter to Fisher, then went on, to Eddy: 'Abduction on our part wouldn't be necessary. But if you were to use force, as you'd have to, to remove that boy when all the evidence proves he's far better off here than where you're wanting to take him and dare not say out of shame, then in the eyes of the Nation, from the Prime Minister down, *you* are the one who's going to be charged with abduction man . . . not me!'

Eddy went white, swallowed, then drew a deep breath and put on the official attitude, declaring, 'There's the matter of the schooling to be dealt with. Bill Fisher's entitled by law to decide whether or not the boy's getting proper schooling.'

'Right,' said Jeremy. 'Let's adjourn to the school.' As they went, Jeremy and Fisher leading, with Prindy swinging alongside, Jeremy explained the absence of the other pupils. Fisher replied mildly that he was only concerned with Prindy.

It didn't take long. Bill Fisher began by looking through the exercise books, hemming to himself with evident interest, then asked Prindy half a dozen questions out of what was written in them, then to write on the blackboard the squares of numbers up to ten, then to extract the square-root of 13 – to do the last by arithmetical calculation, when Prindy was going to tell him Three-point-One-Six-Two – then to write the words, Sugar, Soap, Salvation. Prindy wrote the last word Salivation. When Fisher said it was incorrect, Prindy looked at Jeremy, who suddenly smiled and said to the man, 'I think he misunderstood you. Ask him what the word means.'

Eddy put in here: 'No prompting, if you don't mind.'

Looking puzzled, but ignoring McCusky, Fisher asked the question. Prindy promptly answered, 'Spit.'

Jeremy chuckled at the evident bewilderment of the teacher: 'It's a house of scientific rather than religious thinking, Mr Fisher. I hope you don't expect him to have had religious instruction . . . .'

'Why not?' demanded Eddy. 'It's the regular thing in schools.'

Jeremy turned to him: 'In that school of yours down the Centre?'

'Of course.'

'Are Square roots and Cube roots and the Theorem of Pythagoras included in the curriculum?'

Very red, Eddy snapped, 'What's the use of stuff like that to . . . to . . . .' He floundered.

'Yeller kids, creamy kids?' asked Jeremy. As Bill Fisher cleared his throat,

Jeremy turned back to him. 'I understand, Mr Fisher, that on the Theorem of Pythagoras rests almost the whole weight of higher mathematics . . . is that so?'

'Yes . . . pretty well . . . by modern theories.'

'You might be interested to know that I got the information from the young fellow himself. He got it out of some new book he has.'

Fisher nodded: 'I'm not surprised. The boy's remarkably intelligent. You should see he goes on to university.'

Jeremy's face blazed and his eyes fairly popped: 'I?'

'Well . . . . ' Fisher, looking confused again, glanced nervously at Eddy.

Jeremy demanded of him, 'Does what you say mean you're perfectly satisfied with the way he's being schooled here?'

Fisher hemmed again, no doubt troubled by having to let his silvertail colleague down: 'I've said he's very intelligent . . . ha . . . he's . . . . '

Eddy snapped, 'What's you're official verdict on the school and method of teaching? That's the point we want cleared up . . . also, improper influence.'

'Well . . . I suppose the school must pass . . . to get those results . . . as far as the boy's concerned, I mean. It's not according to regulations . . . but there's no evidence of improper influence. The boy answered . . . . '

Jeremy cut in sharply; 'What's this improper influence you're talking about?'

Fisher screwed his face up, turned it towards Fox, saying, 'Well . . . that's really the doctor's province.'

Jeremy now swung on Fox. 'For godsake . . . what is this?'

Fox looked troubled now, but covered it up with a chuckle, 'Aw . . . something Cahoon thought up.'

'Cahoon . . . what?'

Fox answered with a sickly grin, 'He reported that he thought you had the boy hypnotized.'

Jeremy gaped, murmuring, 'Hypnotized?' Then his astonished face wrinkled up with merriment. He chuckled deeply. Fox joined the chuckle. Fisher grinned. A guffaw burst from Jeremy – and from Fox. Laughter seized Jeremy. He roared. The others roared with him; except poor Eddy, who red to the hair-roots, turned and strode out of the school. Prindy and Darcy also joined in, even without knowing what the joke was, in the manner of their Aboriginal kin, never likely to miss a good laugh, even if it were on themselves.

It took the men minutes to get over it. When they got outside, there was no sign of Eddy. At Jeremy's question, one of Darcy's boys said he'd gone walking back to the aircraft. Jeremy said, 'That's rather buggered things. I was going to have you over to lunch. Can't leave him out of it. Darcy, lad . . . . '

Fox cut in to say that they didn't have time to stay to lunch, anyway, that they were heading for the Missions, and had refreshments aboard. 'I'll be glad of some gasolene, though. Fergus Ferrus said he'd sent a bit of a stock out here, and that I could draw on it '

Out at the plane they found Eddy walking up and down with his hat well over an eye He just shot them a look and went on with his walking as they attended to the fuelling. It was only when Jeremy and Prindy were shaking hands with the others that he came near, and surprised everybody by holding his hand out to Prindy, saying, '*Mummuk yawarra*, sonny . . . it's good to see you doing so well.'

Prindy looked at Jeremy, who nodded. When Eddy had shaken the small yellow hand then given to him, he flung a crooked grin round the group, saying, 'Don't tell me there's no influence.' He was turning away to head for the door of the aircraft, when he swung back on the grinning Jeremy. 'Don't run away with the idea that you've got legal possession of him. You'll never get that. And the first bit of trouble, we'll take him off you. Get me?' He turned again.

Jeremy reddened, but still maintained the grin, saying, 'That might be dangerous, Eddy.'

McCusky swung back, demanding, 'What d'you mean?'

'Well . . . I could give him a post-hypnotic suggestion, every time he saw you to give you a kick up the arse . . . that right, eh, Foxy?'

The Flyin' Fox grinned as he leapt up the stairs, added a silent laugh from the cockpit window.

The engines were started. The plane was rolling. Thumbs up for Good Flying. She rolled away downwind, while the horses, the mules, and the one donkey in the wide oval paddock, from staring at a distance, scattered for the far fences with tails high. Then the roar and dust of the run-up. Then away in take-off – up, up, up, to swing back to make a turn in farewell salute to those waving below. Then off northward into the white-dappled blue above the slate-blue wall that was the Plateau.

Jeremy, with his arm round Prindy's shoulder, said as they turned towards the utility, 'Well, sonny . . . where do we go from here?'

'I want to go and get lunch, Grandfather . . . then listen to Batavia concert.'

'Right . . . but I meant something more than that.'

Prindy looked at him. 'What's hi-hi-potised, Grandfather?'

'Hypnotize? We'll look it up in Webster.'

'I hear that word that time they asking me about Pookarakka . . . Police Station in Town.'

'Ah, yes? Well, I suppose the old feller does do a bit of it . . . hypnotizing . . . in his own way.'

As they took their seats and Jeremy was starting up, Prindy asked, 'You send letter to Pookarakka yet?'

Jeremy looked at him quickly. Grey eyes held grey eyes for a moment. Then Jeremy answered, 'Haven't had a chance yet. But I will . . . I promise. It'll be necessary to go to Town to get someone we can trust to take the message. We'll go as soon as your leg's right. I've got some business to do, the leases and things.'

'Might-be we can bring old-man back?'

'I don't know about that. But we'll certainly get word to him that you're here and how you're doing.'

'He know that all right.'

Jeremy shot another glance as they sped along, then asked, 'How's he know that?'

The grey eyes were on the road. 'He know everything.'

'Well, why do you have to send him a message?'

'Tell him I wait.'

Jeremy bit at his lips, as if puzzling over the Aboriginal mind, particularly this one that could extract mathematical roots and understand the implications of the Pythagorian Theorem. He broke the little silence saying, 'Well, we've got to get this leg fixed first. Less study and flute-playing and more massage and exercise, eh? I'll make you an exercising gadget out of an old bike, I think. Must get those thigh muscles built up again, without putting too much strain on the bone. The bike'll show which ones are weakest. I think it's the *rectus*, mainly. You had bad infection in there. Can't have you limping round Town, can we. Want to put you in elastic sides, jodhpurs, the whole squatter outfit, to rock 'em. They saw you like a blackfellow before. Now it's going to be as what to them's a gentleman.' Jeremy turned smiling to the boy, to find himself being regarded with what looked like alarm. For a moment their grey eyes clung. Then, turning back to his steering, Jeremy said, 'It's all right . . . I know you're a blackfellow first. I won't take you away from that. I only want to prove to them that you and your people have as much dignity as they have, given the chance . . . and a lot more, maybe. You remember that word Dignity?'

Rather parrot fashion the answer came: 'From Latin *Dignus* . . . Noble, Excellent.' After a moment the little voice asked, 'Tell me about Hyp-not-ism now, Mullaka, please.'

'All right . . . this one comes from the Greek – *Hupnos*, Sleep.'

II

Before April was out they were on their way to Town in the utility, just the two of them, since it was a special occasion. But first they dropped in at Beatrice township to let the Tooheys and other friends, like Barbu and the Ah Loys, see the transmogrification for themselves, and subtly to let the wurruld know about it and about the joke connected with it.

It was exciting, to walk the streets with that stance of Nobleness and Excellence, beside the big man who carried those qualities so well, so that every head turned to look; to live in a big hotel, sleeping, eating at table, where no non-white had ever been accepted before and Mrs Morgan, the proprietess, so long a friend and admirer of Jeremy Delacy had to take to her bed for a day or two by reason of the effort it cost her; to be embraced and wept over and almost fought over by Kitty Windeyer and Fay McFee; to be taken to Church by Miss Kitty to listen to her handling what she had called Monsignor Maryzic's Wonderful Organ; and then to be presented to his Very Reverence and eat an apple with him; to go twice to the pictures, once down to the jetty and aboard the mail steamer; to buy a gramophone all of his own and order the list of records made up by Miss Kitty to be sent from South; and surely above all, to be embraced and crooned over by the Pookarakka himself.

This last and loveliest thing came about thus. Jeremy had tried to get Barney Bynoe to take Prindy's Letter Stick to the Jail for smuggling in to the old man; but Barney had been elevated to Overseer of the Sweet Creek Settlement and appeared to be offended by the suggestion that he should be thought capable of breaking the law, even though evidently thrown into some conflict by the offer of a substantial bribe. He said things were different now. Then while Jeremy was trying to work out another means, he and Prindy happened to meet Judge Bickering in the street. The Judge expressed his delight in the Transformation, as he called it himself, and his mirth over the joke connected with it, which he'd already heard, and asked Jerry would he not come and dine with him, bringing the boy. The Judge lived alone, having, as he put it obscurely, outlived his family. People said they had left him because of his excessive drinking and sarcasm in expressing his opinion of them. Anyway, over the brandy, Jeremy, perhaps on sudden impulse, mentioned the matter of the message, saying that as other prisoners were permitted some degree of contact with relatives and friends, why not an Aboriginal? 'Why not?' echoed the Judge. 'I'll take you out there myself tomorrow.'

Out at the Jail they were fussed over by Major O'Dowdy and his dotty Dotty. Evidently it was not unusual for the Judge to pay a visit to Bobwirridirridi; and naturally in the circumstances the rule governing supervision by some jail officer of prisoner and visitor was waived. Jeremy went in with the Judge and Prindy to meet the old fellow, looking as much the living skeleton as ever, and just as lively a one, despite his prison garb and shorn beard and hair. He embraced Prindy like a long-lost son, stroked him, jabbered over him in that cackling voice in lingo, having no more than a handshake and a grin for the others. Judge Bickering promptly said to Jeremy, 'Let's leave them to their Freemasonry, while we look around.'

Prindy and his Pookarakka were along in a corner of the exercise yard for a good half-hour. As the boy came out, more eyes than ever were on him, and eyes more knowing and more wondering, seeing him who not only walked with dignity with judges and squatters, but could talk with the earthly deputy of the Old One. Judge and grandfather were too wise to ask him what he had been talking about with the Wise One. Dotty had a go at it while they were sitting over the elaborate morning tea she had prepared for them, but to be silenced by a kick in the shins by the Major that followed a look in the eye he got from the Judge. She made up for it by kissing him goodbye as they left her, tears in her eyes, as she muttered that in just that place she had kissed his poor mother only a year ago.

The day after the visit to the Jail, which was something like a week since they'd arrived in Town, Prindy said to Jeremy, as they were standing in the vicinity of the Court House, looking out on the view they both had yearned to from within the dismal grey stone building behind, 'Young *Nuttagul* fly now.'

Jeremy looked at him. *Nuttagul* was the magpie goose. 'Why do you say that?'

Prindy sighed, his eyes fixed at a point beyond which Mooragetaghee would be.

Jeremy persisted: 'Old-man say that yesterday?' When the fair head nodded, Jeremy asked, 'It mean you want to go home?' Another nod. 'All right . . . we'll go. Tomorrow morning, eh?' Prindy turned to him and smiled.

As they went walking on towards the shopping centre, Prindy said, 'Pookarakka say . . . "You gitchim one young-feller gootch for me, *Mora*, cook him clay, put him there long o' hollit tree . . . my *lamala* come find him. Me toomuch hungry long o' gootch-fat".'

The first talk yet of any dealings with his master. Jeremy drew a deep breath: 'Did he now? We must get right out to the billabongs when we get back and get that fat young *Nuttagul* for him.'

They left at daylight next morning, Friday; and so good the road that was being built for war, that they did the trip in a single day, passing the homing mail train just North of the Caroline. But this time they didn't call in at Beatrice township, despite the jodhpurs and elastic-sides, but turned off the main road at the Racecourse, and headed straight for home, finishing the run in moonlight.

It was the second morning after their arrival home, Sunday, that they went out on the goose hunt, taking the utility and the big truck, because so many wanted to be in it, most of the household now being back from walkabout. The hunt would not be simply for that bird for Bobwirridirridi's other Self, but for stocking the cold-store. The billabongs would be teaming with geese, and ducks and pigmies. Many hands would be needed, because no shooting was allowed. Nor did you spear or boomerang birds like that, when you could get them without disturbance in any quantity you wished simply by swimming in amongst them in the way *Yingganga* the fresh-water crocodile did.

The utility, leading, had just passed the turn-off to the Painted Caves, when there suddenly appeared round a bend of the road ahead a running blackman, naked save for a *naga* of red calico and a pipe-clayed headband, his body ochred in red and white but with most of the paint washed off with sweat. He stopped at sight of the truck, to stand in the middle of the road, pumping for breath. Jeremy driving, Prindy at his side, slowed down. The man stepped to the right as the vehicle drew up to him. Jeremy said, 'Goodday . . . Narrama, ain't it?' The man, just greying, nodded. 'What's matter you run like o' dat . . . you trainin' for sports next Races?'

Narrama grinned slightly, then struggling to control his panting turning with lips pointing back along his track, he said, 'Man dere . . . got him gun . . . ' Man meant whiteman, and not necessarily one.

Jeremy asked how many. Narrama made a movement with his fingers to indicate that there could be as many as a dozen. He went on to say that the party was mounted and had not long ago arrived at the eastern end of the long chain of billabongs and stopped there. They were too far off for him and his mob, who were camped near the mine, to distinguish them; but they had caught the glint of silver buttons, and there had been one shot – in the air. He had come gallopin' to give warning.

'Hmm!' commented Jeremy. '*Tchinekin*, eh? They must've heard I was away. Wonder who they can be, though. Buttons like police. Might-be something wrong out Catfish and Stunke come *tchinekin* after young goose. Not like him, though . . . and you say mob, eh?'

'*Yu-ai*, Mullaka.'

'Well, we'll soon fix 'em. Stop here and tell Darcy wait till he hear *Poom*.' As he drove on, Jeremy said to Prindy, 'We haven't had anyone sneakin' in for a long while. Must be three or four years now . . . some road surveyors. But the buttons? Might be it's our old mate Coon-Coon trying to get even. He was away somewhere while we were in Town. Must take it easy so we don't raise any dust. We're down wind . . . they won't hear us. Want to get round the back of the hill and up to the mine and take a look at 'em through the glasses . . . then let 'em have it, if necessary.'

'What you going to do, Mullaka?'

'You'll see, son. We have an unfailing way of dealing with poaching on the billabongs.'

Prindy said in surprise, 'Poaching is cooking eggs!'

Jeremy chuckled, 'That old English language giving trouble again.'

A small mob of blacks were waiting by the open cut in the hill. Jeremy waved them to get clear of the region, then swung onto a track to the left that led round behind the hill, going only a couple of hundred yards, then pulling up at a stone building that was evidently an explosives shed. Slipping out of the car with the ring of keys from the ignition switch, he said to Prindy, 'Get the glasses and slip up to the top. and take a peep. I'll be with you in a minute.' He waved to the blacks who were passengers to scatter.

Prindy took binoculars from the panel compartment, alighted, went running up the almost barren hill. Jeremy opened the heavily padlocked door of the shed and entered, soon to come out with a loaded box he carried by means of a shoulder-strap. As he went up after Prindy two dull sounds were heard from afar: *Thud*! *Thud*!

Prindy, behind a rock on top, handed the glasses over as Jeremy came crouching to join him. 'What d'you make of 'em?' Jeremy asked, adjusting the lenses.

'I don' know. Little bit far. But all got khaki clothes . . . look like p'liceman.'

Jeremy, viewing the group, now walking beside the farthest billabong, a good mile-and-a-half away, remarked: 'They can't all be police. There's not that many in the force. There's . . . ten, I make it . . . and some back where they've left the horses.'

Thud! *Thud*! Then patches of white smoke in the blue air. A few birds rose in the distance.

Jeremy said, 'They're a hunting expedition all right . . . and after a big bag. They're driving the scattered birds down to the big mob in the middle. The birds are very tame. They'll just keep shifting. Then when they've got a mob and got'em a bit nervous, they'll scare 'em up. The birds'll come flying over in mass to see what's wrong . . . then Bang, Bang, Bang! That's the sportsman's way of doing it. You don't have to fish 'em out of the water . . . you've just got a great pile of dead birds to take back to your friends and brag about.' While he talked Jeremy gave the glasses back to Prindy, and busied himself with fixing explosive charges.

Thud! *Thud*!

Jeremy worked quickly, made up two charges, went with one, attached to wire, hurrying towards the head of the open cut, lowered it, came scuttling back, fixed the wire to the terminals of the firing box, snatched the glasses from Prindy and took another look. He said, 'They look like a detachment of troops . . . but they surely can't be.' He gave the glasses back. 'Well, here goes. Cover your ears, and keep down behind the rock. A bit of stuff might come flying up. Right?'

Jeremy raised the plunger, pushed it down: *BANG*!

It seemed as if the very blue sky wobbled to the blast. Grey dust boiled up from the cut. A scattering of pebbles. For a moment vision was lost; while away over at the Plateau the echoes rumbled like late thunder. Jeremy smiled at the wide-eyed boy, remarking, 'More Old Tchamala stuff. You don't know how much of that stuff the whiteman has . . . and doesn't he love to hear it going off, God help us!' He took up the glasses.

The dust had thinned quickly in the wind. The birds were up off the water, circling, but too far from the shooters, who were halted now. Jeremy chuckled, gave the glasses back to Prindy, cocked an eye at the birds, said after a moment, 'Have to do it again. They're not scared properly. They look like settling. Yes . . . they're going down. We should scare 'em occasionally. They get too tame. This'll be a bigger bang.' He went off again to the cut and dropped a charge, came back. Half the birds were down by now.

Prindy said, 'That lot coming again.'

Jeremy took a peep. 'Right . . . here she goes again.'

BURRRANG! The hill trembled to it. Rocks flew this time. The dust rose like a willy-willy. Through it the pair watched the packed mass of birds, honking, quacking, whistling, screaming, heading away North. Jeremy called to them, 'Sorry, old friends . . . but it was the only way. Come back soon.'

He stood up then, glanced at the distant khaki group, halted again, it seemed. Then turning the other way, he cupped his mouth, and hollowed down wind 'All right all-about . . . finish now. Tell Darcy come. Then better go plant yourself. Might be p'liceman there.'

He took another look at the group through the glasses. 'They're coming . . . so they must be police. No one else would have the cheek. Better come on down into the cut and pretend were're doing a bit of mining.'

Prindy asked, 'What will police do'

'They can't do anything. I've the legal right to blast whenever I want to.' Seeing Darcy pull up with the truck down at the open end of the cut. Jeremy shouted to him to bring tools for sampling. Then he and Prindy went down by a declivity. Down below he gave the glasses to Darcy, and told him to keep a look out, while he and Prindy and others proceeded to gather and screen detrius broken by the explosions.

After a while Darcy slipped in to say, 'Two p'liceman, Mullaka . . . Mist Stunke and Superintendent Bullco . . . tracker . . . other lot I dunno . . . but I think soldier.'

'Hmm . . . Bullco, eh? Must be some big brass around. Conducted tour. How far are they?'

'Getting close-up. Tracker and other man bring horse along. They all riding now.'

'Right. Come and give me a hand. Prindy boy . . . play with the kids. I don't want it to look like I work kids.'

The approaching party were to be seen from the wide mouth of the workings while still on the track beside the nearest billabong a couple of hundred yards away. Jeremy, geologist's hammer in hand, straightened up to stare at them. The party were riding in pairs, the width of the road, Bullco, in full uniform, leading, alongside a tall lean man, also in khaki of official-looking cut, but wearing a khaki flat-topped topee, of the kind called in jest a Lion-hunter's

Hat. There were a couple of similar topee'd riders behind them, then men in Australian soldier's slouch hats with sides let down; and Stunke, and his new tracker, Tipperary. They came riding into the cut by the track used by the trucks. Swinging his hammer. Jeremy went to meet them, saying as he came up to them, 'What's this . . . an expedition into the unexplored wilderness, a military exercise . . . . or just the usual periodic bit of police bullying of the unhappy people the land was stolen from?' He was red, and rather breathless, as though he had rehearsed it and given a lot of emotional effort to it. Still, he was smiling, and looking at the tall thin man in the topee beside the Superintendent, he nodded a bushman's acknowledgement of a stranger. The man was definitely a military type, straight and lean and brown-faced, wearing a clipped little moustache, his age about that of Jeremy. The man nodded in reply.

Meaty Bullco, red and sweating, wheezed harshly, 'Be careful what you say, Delacy.'

'I'm always careful what I say in the presence of enemies, Superintendent . . . but you haven't answered my question.'

'I don't have to answer your questions. I'm here to tell you that I'm going to lay a charge against you for a breach of the peace.'

Jeremy's eyes widened. 'Breach of the peace, Superintendent . . . when I'm minding my own business on my own property . . . . '

'You deliberately interfered with a perfectly lawful sporting activity.'

Jeremy laughed shortly. 'How d'you make that out? Here I am working my mine . . . .'

'You let off those explosions deliberately to disturb the birds and spoil our sport.'

'What were you sporting at, man . . . I've been working inside here . . . .'

'Don't waste time with being smart. I'm going to lay this charge.'

'D'you mean you're pinching me here and now?' Jeremy cocked an eye at the military man, whose lips had moved in a faint smile.

'I'm laying a charge through the proper channels in Port Palmeston. This interference of yours with people's activities in this locality where you've got no legal right whatsoever, except this mine, has got to stop . . . I'll see to that . . . I'll see to that . . . . ' Bullco finished breathless, strangled by his own verbal effort.

Jeremy glanced at the men behind, particularly at the two in topees, one short and thickset, crimson-visaged, popping-blue-eyed, with a large upthrusting fuzz of gingerish moustache, the other a lanky youth whose handsome girlish face was peeling from unaccustomed exposure to Sun and harsh sou'-easter, then back at the tall man just above him, saying, 'There speaks a man whose life is so dedicated to interference in other people's business, that having someone interfere with his, brings him to the point of apoplexy.' The lips beneath the small grey moustache twitched slightly.

Recovering his breath, Bullco demanded, 'Are you working these blacks in the mine?'

'If I were it would be perfectly lawful . . . there's no underground working . . . but as it happens I'm not working them.'

'What are they doing here?'

'Minding their own business, I guess . . . the same as you were, when you alleged I interfered with it.'

'What Aborigines do *is* my business.'

'Yes, I know that. But for hounding them, you policemen wouldn't have much to do, would you? Since you ask, though . . . they came here to take some ducks and geese . . . what I'd say was their lawful property'.

'And you've scared the birds away.'

'Wasn't that your aim, too?'

'We came here for a bit of sportsmanship.'

'Which would have driven the birds away, anyway. But don't be concerned about the poor buggers' losing a feed of birds . . . I feed them quite well.'

'Have you got permits to have them on your property?'

'Of course.'

'May I see them?'

'I don't carry them with me. You'll have to come to my homestead.'

'I intend to. I want to see all papers relevant to blacks, stock, leases.'

'You shall . . . but I warn you, don't take any of those horses past my boundary fence.'

'What's this . . . obstructing an officer of the law?'

'No . . . lawful precautions under Stock Department regulations. There's a horse back there coughing . . . and a couple snuffling. They've obviously got some infection. I've got very valuable horses. You're not infecting them. I'll be getting along, then, to get the papers ready. That'll just make nice time for it, because, in your condition, it's going to take you a couple of hours to make that two and a half miles from the top gate.' Turning, Jeremy glanced at the topee'd men, saying, 'Sorry, gentlemen, to spoil your sport . . . but I've been to an awful lot of trouble to preserve this bit of Eden. In fact, I transformed it from a dreadful wilderness.'

'Reahlly?' asked the tall man, evidently interested.

'It was just torn to pieces by the early mining here . . . the water drained . . just mud flats . . . not a bird or an animal about . . . You're English, aren't you?' Jeremy halted.

The man nodded. Jeremy went on: 'Then you'd understand . . . the fierce protection English people give their countryside . . . . '

Bullco cut in: 'In a developing country it's ridiculous . . . country's got to be opened up, settled . . . . '

'Torn apart and left to become desert?'

'There's plenty of it,' Bullco growled. 'It'll survive.'

'This little bit will, at any rate, so long as I can protect it.'

'You've got no right to protect it. It's a police officer's job.'

Jeremy addressed the Englishman: 'It took ten years of hard work to restore it . . . and ever since they've been trying to sneak in to destroy it again . . . small mobs of shooters, not really wanting the game . . . only wanting to beat me . . . and never once has any report I've made to the police been followed up . . . . '

Bullco snapped: 'Police officers've got more to do . . .'

Jeremy went on: 'I applied for an honorary rangership. It was refused . . . . '

Bullco cut in again, speaking to the Englishman: 'It's a police officer's job, General. This man's got a feud with the police. Don't be taken in with his talk. Everything he does is just to cause trouble.'

Jeremy asked the Englishman, 'General?'

Bullco snapped, 'General Sir Mark Esk, Inspector-General and Acting Commander-in-Chief Australian Commonwealth Military Forces.' Seeing the way Jeremy almost gaped at the General, Bullco added: 'That's whose sport you interfered with this time, Delacy. You've made a bad blue. You won't get away with it this time.'

Jeremy looked quickly at Bullco, stared at him hard, then back at the General, with lips writhing in a suppressed smile: 'Does this mean I'll be shot at dawn, General?'

The General chuckled, 'Have no fears, Mr Delacy . . I'm not the huntin', fishin', shootin' kind.'

'Not shootin'?' asked Jeremy, and when the General, misunderstanding, shook his head, added: 'A soldier not a shooting man?'

'Hmm, hmm . . . see what you mean. But not reahlly, old man . . . Inspector-General . . . Ordnance, you know . . . but I don't have to tell you that . . . you were a military man yourself, I understand.' Jeremy looked at Bullco, who blinked. Evidently the visitors had been appraised of the Scrub Bull, even if the appraisers had supposed he was not likely to be met up with.

The General added. 'Understand you spent some time up on the Euphrates and thereabout?'

'Where'd you get that information?'

'As a matter of fact, from your son Mr Martin Delacy. I've been staying there a few days. Thought I'd like to meet you and swap a campaign yarn or two. There myself, don't you know. But they told me you were away. May I have the pleasure?' He bent, extending his hand.

Jeremy stepped back to take it, but with another glance at Bullco, who blinked harder. Shaking hands with the General, Jeremy spoke to Bullco: 'What the blacks call *tchinekin*, eh, Lex?' Bullco went purple.

'Eh, what?' murmured the General.

'Only a joke, General . . . a rather dirty one.'

The General glanced at Bullco, for a certainty noting his discomfort.

'Well, I'll be getting along,' said Jeremy, 'I'll be seeing you in several hours, eh, Superintendent . . . if you survive that long long walk? No water on the track . . . only salt-licks . . . Goodbye, General . . . I presume you won't be wanting to make that quite unnecessary journey with the Superintendent . . . He knows quite well all my affairs are done with strict regard to the law . . . because he's been trying to get me out on the slightest ommission for years . . . sure he keeps a dossier of my dues, hoping and praying that I might someday miss paying 'em . . . So long!' Jeremy set off to return up the cut.

The General coughed: 'Ahhum . . . er, Major . . . .'

Jeremy turned quickly. The pale blue eyes were fixed on him. 'I understand that was your rank, old man?'

Jeremy grimaced: 'A long time since anyone called me that.'

'Field rank is permanent.'

'I tossed it in long ago, General.'

'Pity . . . but what I wanted to say was, I'd like to have that yarn with you . . . . '

'You mightn't like my ideas about military campaigning, General '

'I'll risk it, old man '

'Well . . . if you like to come out . . . without police escort.'

'I'd like to come along with you now, if I may.'

'I'm not on horseback . . . I've got a utility truck over the hill there.'

'Matter of fact, I'm a bit saddle-sore . . . the old seat a bit out of action these days, don't you know. Would you mind much?'

Jeremy glanced at Bullco, saw the look of hurt astonishment, then back to the General, and replied, 'I'd be delighted.' Then he turned to Darcy: 'Darcy, son . . . what about hopping over and saving our old legs by running the ute around?'

Darcy went darting off. The General alighted stiffly, looked up at Bullco with an apologetic smile, saying, 'Sorry, Superintendent . . . but to have done the full ride would have had me eating off the mantlepiece for a week.' Then he signed to one of the Australian soldiers, who had, with others, alighted as soon as the General had, as if it were improper to be mounted in the presence of a dismounted superior officer, calling 'Major.' The Major came scuttling, halted smartly: 'Sir?'

'Ah . . . er . . . have a car sent to pick me up at Major Delacy's place.'

'Yessir, when, Sir?'

The General looked at Jeremy, who said, 'Come as my guest, General. If you want to stay longer than today, there's a radio you can send a message . . . sorry, signal . . . by.' Jeremy grinned, somewhat impudently, it seemed.

'Well, that's too kind of you,' said the General. 'Would it be too much to have my aides along too . . . just two of them . . . you can put 'em up anywhere . . . do 'em good to rough it . . . I'm only thinkin' of their poor arses, which are probably in worse condition than my own, not bein' cavalrymen trained . . . eh, what, Malters?'

The man the General had addressed, also on the ground now, was the thickset fellow with the crimson face and fierce ginger moustaches. He replied simply by snapping, 'Sah!' evidently in affirmation.

'Certainly,' said Jeremy.

The General motioned Malters to him, saying to Jeremy, 'May I present Major Maltravers, Major?'

With another Sah! Maltravers, shot out a red hand.

Then General Esk motioned to the lanky boy, introducing him: 'Lieutenant Dickey. You might recall the name of Dickey . . . Colonel at that time, on the Euphrates . . . Denzil's pater . . . old campaign comrade of mine . . . retired list now.'

Jeremy said, 'I'm afraid I've put all military names and things out of my mind.' His tone was rather dry. 'Didn't they tell you that?'

'Ah-hum! commented the General.

There was the utility. As they went up to it and Darcy alighted, Jeremy introduced him as his nephew. Darcy chuckled and shook. 'My brother's son . . . killed on Gallipoli,' said Jeremy. And as the General made a sympathetic sound, Jeremy introduced Prindy, as his grandson, adding: 'You'll find we're a bit mixed in the matter of race round here . . . and rather proud of it . . . it gives us a sense of belonging, you know.' He said it loudly so that the staring group with their horses might hear.

'I'm sure it does,' said the General, as loudly.

As they were getting in, and Jeremy said that one of the aides would have to get in the back, since there was room for only three in front, Sir Mark Esk said, 'No . . . both of 'em . . . I want young Master Prindy next to me.'

'But what about those poor arses of theirs? No upholstery back there.'

The General chuckled, 'They can stand.' He gave a short wave to the watchers and got in. Jeremy ignored them. As they drove off Esk said, looking at Prindy between him and Jeremy, 'You're very much alike. I believe if I'd met either of you without introduction I'd've guessed a close relationship . . . father, even.'

Jeremy, with a glance at Esk, said, 'Curiously, your face seems familiar to me . . . but I'm sure it isn't a memory from Asia Minor . . . and I haven't seen a picture of you . . . although I've read a fair amount about your appointment . . . .'

Esk chuckled, 'The British Garrison, what?'

'You know about that, eh?' There had been a terrific attack on General Sir Mark Esk's recent appointment as Commander-in-Chief of the Australian Army in *Australia Free*, which had declared it a blatant return to Colonial Garrison days, since the man was an officer primarily of the British Army, with no associations with Australia whatsoever.

Esk said, 'There's been a lot of fuss. It's understandable. But conditions of defence are so bad here . . . the struggle for power between your own generals . . . no idea of the terrific realities, only personal ambitions that's the reason. *Your* Prime Minister's idea, not Britains's. And . . . well, the primary title's Inspector-General, which means seeing to defence . . . . '

'You're still Commander-in-Chief, though.'

'I detect resentment in you too, old man?'

'Why not? I'm Australian. Why not our own man?'

Esk shrugged: 'The condition of your military system has to be seen to be believed. You *haven't* a man, Delacy You've only got a gang of . . . of . . . but perhaps I'll offend you.'

'Not a bit of it. I'm intensely Australian . . . but I do remember the types I served with.'

'Perhaps it'd form a subject for discussion. I want to discuss it with someone intelligent *and* patriotic, someone with your strong views about the condition of things Australian.'

'Where'd you get this about my strong views?'

Esk smiled. 'As a matter of fact, I know you fairly well . . . no, not from the Euphrates, or talk at Beatrice River. You had the clue when you said my face seemed familiar. You know my daughter rather well. She's rather like me, they say.'

'Your daughter?'

'Lydia . . . Lydia Lindbrooke-Esk.'

'Oh!'

The General chuckled at Jeremy's obvious discomfort, and said, 'Must tell you about old Lyd, too. Would you know that she didn't marry the old man after all . . . thanks to you, she says . . . but the son? So the Vaiseys get their breeding and Lyd the millions.'

Jeremy drew a deep breath, staring at the road. They were coming to the top gate. Prindy said he'd get out and open it, and slipped over the General's bony knees, and stayed on that side thereafter.

They made a tour of the horse-paddocks before going on to the homestead. Esk was interested in horses not only as an old cavalryman, but raced at home, and said he would like to have an animal of good quality so as to pursue the sport as a diversion to his rather onerous military duties here. This was the part of Australia that was going to demand most of his attention, he said, confessing that the lack of preparation or even concern for the inevitable East-Asian War appalled him. He also said that he would like to hire horses for more or less private reconnaissances. Laughing, he said, 'I must keep people like your friend the Superintendent off my back. I must confess that I was awfully glad to get rid of him. It's been happening like that even since I came into the country, whether it's been by land, or sea, or even air, I've wanted to travel . . . there is the inevitable police escort . . . with Superintendent Bullco leading it. The trouble is, of course, that the military chaps up here have nothing but their parade grounds and messes and a couple of obsolete old shore batteries that would have to invite the enemy in to take a pot at him. Hence having to call on the civil authorities. I'd as soon do without your military chappies, too. If you don't mind my saying it . . . and I presume you don't, from what I've heard of your own attitude to the RSL and such odd things, I find your military men impossible . . . . '

'As gentlemen?' Jeremy cut in sharply.

The General chuckled, 'That old one!' and slapped Jeremy's knee. 'No, dear boy . . . I'm of the old brigade, I admit, but not of the brigade mess. No . . . your fellows aren't so much soldiers as policemen.'

'Aren't all soldiers in peace-time really policemen?'

'Not reahlly . . . keepers of the peace in the broad sense, let us say . . . which, unfortunately, happens to be preparation for war . . . .'

'So that there's more war!'

'I can see that we have a lot of food for discussion, Major.'

'Please don't call me Major. I don't like it.'

'Good. I don't like being called General . . . except when necessary.'

'I'm not going to call you Sir Mark!'

'Perish the thought, dear boy! Plain Mark will do . . . or Esk . . . whatever suits you. I feel we'll get along, despite our differences. One thing we have in common . . . besides horses and Lydia . . . ha, ha, ha! I know the story from her, old man . . . "He treated me like a father, damn him!" she said.'

'What's this other thing?'

'Australia.'

'How can you an Englishman be interested in Australia . . . unless you've got investments in it?'

'I have.'

'Oh . . . the Vaisey millions now, of course . . . .'

'Not a bit of it. The British Commonwealth which happens to be the be-all end-all of my existence, depends on the true patriotism of Australians . . . . '

'To go and fight for Britain, you mean . . . '

'No, old man . . . to fight for Australia. You are the bastion of the Empire in the East. If you fail . . . the old Union Jack comes down, and either the Rising Sun, the Stars and Stripes, or the Hammer and Sickle, goes up in its place.'

Jeremy asked dryly, 'What's the difference . . . to Australia?'

'Let that be the burden of a long discussion after I've had a bath, do you mind?' They were approaching the homestead. 'By George . . . what a fine place you've got!'

Jeremy set the visitors down at the annexe and gave them drinks, while he telephoned Nanango to prepare her. When eventually they went across, there she was, brightly but simply clad, the perfect smiling hostess in manner, while yet being what she was, as subtly confessed to with a red double-hybiscus in her dark glossy hair, a Chinese cane bangle on a wrist, silken Chinese slippers on her feet. The guests themselves were very formal in receiving their greetings, Major Maltravers even addressing her as Memsahib. She saw them each to a guest room, with a change of clothes and the facilities for bathing. Jeremy produced the famous ointment for novice riders. The General himself had no such need of it as he had pretended. The even extreme need of his aides he described as the first casualties to be suffered by Our Side in the Great East-Asian War. But even while, over drinks in the lounge before lunch, Esk jested so, he showed how seriously he thought of this war, already well and truly under way, as he averred, by reference to the sinking of the US Gunboat *Panay* in Chinese waters by Japanese, without anything but a mild protest from the USA and such indifference by Australians that he had found that even most of the military and naval men in Port Palmeston had forgotten it; although it happened only five months ago and so close to them; and few others he had spoken to about it had even heard of it. 'Strange people, you Australians,' he commented. 'Abroad you seem to be even offensively Australian . . . yet at home . . . . '

'Just offensive!' was Jeremy's dry comment.

Sir Mark protested mildly: 'Old chap!'

Another dry comment of Jeremy's was: 'I notice you speak of Australia as part of the British Empire in the East . . . not of the so-called British Commonwealth of Nations.'

'Ah . . . I would have thought that one so jealous of his nationality would know the truth of that!'

'What truth?'

'That in point of fact Australia is *not* a member of the British Commonwealth, but is still bound to the mother country to the extent of the autonomy allowed by the Balfour Memorandum . . . literally still governed from Westminster to the extent of what I think is called, somewhat vaguely, Function . . . . '

'But the Statute of Westminster of . . . when was it . . . '31?'

'Australia has never formally ratified the Statute of Westminster.'

Jeremy stared at him with a strange expression, a mingling of astonisment and hatred, it seemed. His comparatively fleshy face had turned quite pale.

Esk's thin face rumpled suddenly with anxiety. 'I say, old chap . . . hope I haven't offended you.'

But there was Nan come to announce lunch. She spotted Jerry's expression, eyed him keenly, asked, 'You don't want lunch, eh?' She turned to Esk, who had risen, while Jeremy had not, and smiling, said, 'My husband mostly not eat lunch.'

Jeremy rose, saying stiffly, 'It's all right . . . I'll come in . . . have some soup.'

'Thank you, old man,' murmured the General.

'Where dat other lot?' asked Nan. She went to a Chinese gong, rang it.

She meant Prindy and Denzil Dickey. Malters was there at the bookcase, with fierce moustache buried in a book on Australian exploration. The other two came running down the stairs, both looking excited. The young Lieutenant addressed himself to his General in appropriate style and stance: 'Sah!'

Esk asked, 'What is it, Denzil?'

'How long are we staying, Sir?'

'Good heavens, man . . . do you think you're in a billet?' The General was stiff and sharp-voiced. 'Apologize to your host!'

It could not be seen from the boy's sunburn whether he flamed with shame or not; but his blue gaze went scattering. Jeremy, going up to Nan to take her arm, asked, 'What's wrong?'

Denzil muttered, 'My humble apologies, Sir . . . but . . . but . . . you see, Sir, I'm musical and . . . and . . . .'

Jeremy looked at the dancing grey eyes of Prindy. 'You've found a kindred spirit, eh? I thought I heard the muted flute upstairs.'

'Yes Sir, yes Sir,' babbled Denzil, all eagerness now. 'I would like to teach Prendegast musical theory . . . his music should be written . . . if only we have time.'

Jeremy shrugged. 'It's up to your General how long you stay, son.'

Esk said again to Jerry, 'Thank you, old man.' Then at Denzil he snapped, 'It's up to your behaviour.'

'Sah!'

Lunch went easily, with Nan smiling over it, Denzil frothing about Indian music he had heard in India, Chinese music, Arabian music, while Prindy, or Prendegast suddenly come to life again, asked eager questions, Jeremy and the General talked horses, and Malters worked with masticatory precision on his cold buffalo tongue and salad and granadillo and cream and said nothing.

Coming out of the dining-room back to the lounge, with Nan gone to the kitchen, Esk took Jeremy's arm, murmuring, 'I'd like to put that matter right about the Statute of Westminster, old man. I'm afraid I gave the impression of having the old Damned Colonial attitude. I do assure you I haven't. Indeed, I've fought against it. I'm a Freedom for India man, if you want to know . . . which you can guess doesn't make one popular amongst the Blimps. I see the Imperial rôle as a guiding, not a dominating thing, and actually don't like this non-ratification thing I spoke of, because it puts Australia out of step with the rest of the Commonwealth . . . Am I annoying you, old man?' Jeremy's arm was rigid and his face blank.

He said, somewhat stiffly again, 'Not with your talk, General. My arm . . . if you don't mind. It isn't Australian practice for men to go arm-in-arm.'

The General withdrew hastily. 'Oh, I'm so sorry! Sissy business, I know. But, actually, we have a lot of old-world habits, we English . . . mean something different now.'

They stopped at the outside door, faced each other. Esk said, 'I'd very much like to talk this matter over with you, because I haven't had a chance to do so with any other person.'

'What matter's that?'

'The non-ratification of the Treaty of Westminster by Australia.'

'I'll have to tell you, General, that I don't give a damn about the British Commonwealth of Nations. I'm a citizen of the Commonwealth of Australia . . . and actually I feel deeply resentful that the people who run the country were so supine as to let you Imperialists pinch what was ours . . . our title . . . and bugger up, deliberately, I believe, our hopes of making a true Commonwealth out of it . . . now that it's called, as it is "a commonwealth within a commonwealth" . . . a meaningless thing now.' Jeremy was flushed and angry-eyed. 'When we spoke of The Commonwealth before, we meant our Nation . . . just as the Americans know what they mean when they say The United States. Now, thanks to the trickery of Westminster and the littleness of Canberra, we have to ask ourselves *which* Commonwealth.'

The General nodded. 'I see your point. Hadn't thought of it. But I think you should hear what I have to say about this Statute thing, because it means that you are *not* really a citizen of Australia, but a British Subject, inferior in status to Canadians, South Africans . . . even the Irish before they declared their Republic. It happens that I know a lot about it, because it was by reason of it that I received my dubious appointment . . . by Whitehall, *not* Canberra. I am *not* a mere liaison officer lent to help out with your military affairs, Jeremy, if I may make bold to call you that. Under the old Balfour Declaration system of limited autonomy, your Prime Minister asked Westminster for a C-in-C, to command that part of the British Army which is called the Australian Commonwealth Military Force . . . just the same as what is called by you the Royal Australian Navy, but by the Royal Navy quite legitimately the Australian Squadron, is commanded by a British Rear-Admiral . . . and the fault is not ours, my dear chap . . . but yours. I know this thing, because I've been made a bunny by reason of it. I'm puzzled by it. I'd like to know what it means. Shall we talk later . . . or would you prefer to avoid it as everybody else so strangely seems to want to . . . and we'll stick to what, after all, is a nobler animal than man generally?'

Jeremy swallowed, said huskily, 'Yes . . . we'll talk about it. I'd prefer it tonight. I'd like to look up a couple of things first. Do you mind?'

'Gladly, old man.'

'Right . . . I'll see you for drinks round about five.'

Superintendent Bullco didn't turn up for that declared inspection. Nor, so Jeremy said when the man was spoken of during the pre-dinner drinking, had he really been expected. Mention of him caused General Esk to recall how the fellow had raged when the birds on the billabongs had been disturbed by the explosions at the mine. Esk said, 'He declared that he was going to *get* you this time, that someone *had to get you*, because you were a menace to the country with your opposition to what he called Authority and Progress . . .

odd choice of words. I became very curious about them then. I'd felt there was something wrong when the shootin' expedition was mooted. As I've said, I'm not the huntin' type. I felt I was being pushed into it. There was something under-cover about it, don't you know. Naturally they couldn't be frank about it in the circumstances, your sons, your ex-wife, and all that . . . but I didn't understand how things were really then . . . picked up a lot from Bullco on the way out. My idea was that I was being got out of the way by the military chaps for some reason. Colonel Chivvy, OC Palmeston Troops, stayed back at Beatrice Homestead. Something they don't want me to see, I thought. It's like that in my job. You might call me the Imperial Trouble-shooter. I have to go out and clean things up that've got to stinking a bit. Well, it all came as a sort of climax . . . those shots, like bloomin' concealed artillery, Bullco's raging . . . and then yourself, so calm, so casual, impudent if you like, but so much in command of the situation, a man of strength and integrity and even humour . . . when I'd been led to think of you as a dangerous madman. Even Lyd, with her great admiration for you, classified you as, well, a bit of a crank. Believe me or not, but as I looked at you, I thought: "Here is the one just man in Sodom" . . . if you'll excuse the expression. You'll see what I mean by that when we come to discuss this amazing thing, Australia's non-ratification of the Statute of Westminster. Leave it at that, shall we? Cheers, dear boy! If I had your talent in beer-making I'd be a millionaire brewer, instead of a down-at-heel general dodging the Civil List.'

Jeremy asked, 'What about the Vaisey millions now?'

'Lyd's going to be as tight-fisted as the butchers-of-the-blood, I'm afraid. She's got very interested in overseas investment, I notice. Anyway, one good thing about it, it's taken her out of that British Union crowd.'

'You don't go for that?'

'Fascism? Good God, sir, I should think not! It's the aristocratic leaning to that damned thing's put us . . . Britain . . . where we are. Hitler and Mussolini, Franco, Tojo, would never have got where they are but for the pats on the back they've had from the British aristocracy, from Edward the Eighth down.'

'Does this mean you lean to the Left?'

'I don't lean any way, Jeremy . . . but march ahead to the reality of human brotherhood I believe has already been realized to a degree in our . . . with your permission . . . Commonwealth.'

'What do you think of Stalin?'

'Czar of all the Russians . . . only he's probably got only one valet instead of a hundred . . . and has pawned the Crown Jewels. Still, a valuable man.'

'Why do you say that?'

'He is the natural enemy of all other dictators. All pesky things have natural enemies to keep them in check. Stalin will settle Hitler, and vice versa, if left alone. If we interfere in Europe we're going to get involved with one or the other. Our business is the – er – Commonwealth and Empire.'

'What about Hitler's persecution of the Jews? I was reading that even Albert Einstein has had to flee for his life.'

'The fact is that Einstein had to be *dragged* out of Germany to *have* his life saved. That seemed to be the trouble with the Jews there. They were told to get out. They should have. The man Hitler stated clearly in *Mein Kampf* in 1925 that he would exterminate the Jews. Half of the German Jews have had the sense to leave. There's enough money and to spare in World Jewry to get *all* of the Jews in Europe out . . . if they're really interested in their people. It's the Jews' problem. I have a great admiration for Jews. I know them well. I've been C-in-C in Palestine. They are people who would be welcome anywhere, with their *gelt*, as they call their money, and their *chein,* their very special intelligence. You must know them from your Asia Minor days? There're many now settled in Palestine. They've bought the lazy, slave-driving Arab sheiks out, and turned sand dunes into blossoming gardens. They could do the same here, in Africa, in South America . . . anywhere but where mediaeval superstition reigns and they are regarded as the killers of Christ. But the Jews have a great weakness. They rely too much on their cleverness. They think they will eventually outwit the *goy,* the hostile Christian. Einstein . . . and Sigmund Freud . . . were both supposed to have said that the Hun would regard them as too valuable to persecute . . . the two greatest minds of the century, you might say . . . and they had to be virtually bundled out with the howling brown-shirted *judenhetzers* at their heels. Another weakness of the Jews is their tendency to go to extremities of opposite fanaticism when they renounce the faith of their fathers . . . Jesus, for instance, and Karl Marx. Their name is legion. The power behind Communism today is rationalized Judaism. That also has a lot to do with holding Jews back in Europe. The rationalists encourage the simpler ones to stay on with the promise of relieving them from persecution, while really all they want them for as is an opposition group. It's complete madness . . . because the Russian, being naturally stupid and brutish, is the arch-enemy of the clever Jew. If the Russians beat the Germans, *judenhetze* will become the *pogrom.* Really clever Jews see it, of course . . . and mistrust and fear Communism just as much as Fascism. Tell me, did you see anything of the *Kibitka* settlements Jews were making in Palestine?'

'No, I'm afraid I didn't.'

'They were making them even then. The clever Jews of South Russia, knowing the Ottoman Empire was collapsing, got in quite early. It's a Central Russian word, of course, meaning a camp. They got together in small groups and started plantations . . . oranges, dates . . . even planted your marvellous eucalypts. Since then, and especially of late the *Kevutzoth* movement, as they call it now, has grown enormously . . . to the great benefit of ourselves . . . I mean of the Commonwealth, since they now come under British rule. If only they'll stay under it . . . . ' Esk sighed.

'Why . . . don't they seem to regard it as the blessing you do?'

Esk smiled, tossed off his drink, then said, 'Your true Jew is like Moses standing on Mount Pisgah and viewing the Promised Land. Only Jews can share the Jewish vision.'

The gong rang for dinner.

There was roast goose with sweet potatoes and a pineapple pie, all eaten with relish by the guests. Afterwards a short adjournment all together in the lounge, for coffee (again a produce of the place) brandy, and the news. In the news was an item on the founding of a scheme for the large-scale immigration and settling of refugee Jews in Australia. Esk smiled. 'Speak of what the Chosen themselves would call *k'rubim*. You're lucky. You might get an Einstein or a Bruno Walter.' Jeremy made no comment.

Then, leaving Prindy and Denzil Dickey to their musical theory and Malters and his Memsahib talking of local native customs, Jeremy and Esk departed for the annexe, settled down in the den. Jeremy wasted no time in getting Esk onto the subject of the Treaty of Westminster, that agreement by which self-governing members of the so-called British Commonwealth of Nations, founded under the Balfour Declaration of 1925, were given complete and unequivocal autonomy over their own affairs, even to point of making their own individual declarations of war. Jeremy had a pile of papers, magazines, books, that he said he had been studying in the hope of finding something about what the General had obviously shocked him by declaring with such evident knowledgeability, but confessed that he had failed. He added wryly: 'I thought myself the great patriot . . . and now have to confess that I've got nothing on record about that most important event, except a few cuttings from papers and some angry comments I made at the time about that use of the term Commonwealth. I was going to write to Scullin, Australian Prime Minister at the time, about it. He'd been here on a visit. I didn't, because when my anger cooled, I realized that if he'd had any feeling in the matter he wouldn't have allowed it. So . . . well, please tell me the facts . . . Mark.'

It was the first time Jeremy had used the first name. Esk murmured, 'Thank you, Jeremy.' After drinking, as if to their established friendship, he said, 'As I've told you, old man, I was sent out here by the War Office, just as I would be out to India, Burma, any such place still ruled from Westminster. I'd followed the Statute of Westminster business closely, because of my all-abiding interest in the affairs of my country, and naturally thought Australia had ratified the Treaty, and queried the legality of my appointment. They showed me that Australia had simply not sought ratification. It seemed curious, when the cry at the time was that the limiting clause of Function in the Balfour thing literally gave the Government of Great Britain the last say in everything. Canada, South Africa, and Eire, immediately established their own citizenship as against common British citizenship, and established their own legations throughout the world. Are you aware of having any Australian Ambassadors anywhere?'

Jeremy shook his head, leaning back, staring at the lean face, so like Lady Lydia's in the shaded light. 'That should be proof enough,' Esk went on: 'At the time of the general ratification, Australia was in political turmoil. As you say, one Scullin was your Prime Minister at the time. He came back from Westminster to find one Lang, Premier of the State of New South Wales, in process of being sacked by the State Governor, one Game, an Englishman, of course, who was using the ancient and honourable Royal Prerogative. It seems to me a frightfully high-handed thing to do, evidently engineered by British banking interests, because this man Lang wanted to introduce some unorthodox fiscal policy to beat the effect of the financial depression, which would have ruined the banks, I suppose . . . at least in New South Wales. I missed that, because of a crisis in Egypt, where I'd been sent. But reading about it . . . well, it looked like a case for another Boston Tea Party. Of course you'd know it all. Your Lang was hailed as the Greatest of Australians . . . Greater than Lenin,

I believe was the slogan of his friends . . . or enemies . . . I couldn't decide quite which in what I read.'

Jeremy merely nodded, filled the General's glass. 'Thanks, old boy . . . cheers! Well, Mr Lang called on Mr Scullin to support him and throw the British Garrison into the sea. Scullin could have, too, quite lawfully, under the ratified Statute of Westminster . . . and they were both fellow Labor Party men. I've met Scullin, as you have. I did so deliberately to get to the bottom of this. He's a bookish man, a theorist, a coward, I'd say, politically . . . whereas Lang, whom I've not met, nor would dare to, because he's been one of my attackers, is just the opposite . . . an Australian of the Bulldog Breed. The other man is like an Irish priest. At the time his, Scullin's, Federal Labor Party was collapsing around him. There was fighting in the streets of Sydney, a Fascist-type uprising . . . New Guard, so called. It struck me that Scullin was deadly scared and deliberately let the Ratification slide, dodging the responsibility true nationhood would have left him with. His weakness cost him his head politically, of course. A split in the Labor ranks. Then the rise of this man Lyons with his so-called United Australia Party. An Australia so united that they had to call on Westminster to send a Commander-in-Chief! I asked the PM would he be ratifying the Treaty. He was so evasive, speaking of economic matters as having priority over all else at present, that I began to think there might be something in what the Left Wing papers, and this Fascist thing here . . . ' Esk waved to the bright copy of *Australia Free* lying on top of the stack of papers ' . . . were saying about my being appointed to protect Imperial financial interest with troops. However, I soon discovered that my authority as Commander was strictly limited . . . and, in fact, that the PM himself has little real authority. The real power seems to be in the hands of the Attorney-General, . . . groomed for eventual Prime Ministership, I've been told . . . his grooms, two former holders of that office, Messrs Hughes and Bruce . . . . '

'God help us!'

'I'm glad to hear you, Jeremy. I was becoming a little apprehensive of your silence. But why the invocation?'

'A Cockney runt and a Bunyip Lord!'

'Bunyip Lord, dear boy?'

'A term applied to Australian holders of Imperial titles . . . the Bunyip is a monster of Aboriginal legend, the only one to get into our own folk lore, but well used, I must admit . . . the Order of the Bunyip, as they say.'

Esk chuckled: 'If only I'd known that before I left London. I met Lord Bruce there as High Commissioner. He seemed so damned pukka, don't y'know. I'd have sooled the old Duke onto him. The old boy'd have got onto the subject of Bunyips with him, mark my words.'

'And put the Damned Colonial in his place, eh?' Jeremy's voice was dry.

Esk drank, asked coolly, 'You wouldn't approve even in the case of a Bunyip Lord?' Jeremy also drank. He said, 'Tell me about this other fellow. With such grooms as you mention, he might well turn out to be the worst political disaster we've ever had . . . and that's saying something . . . Fisher, who pledged us to the Last Man and the Last Shilling in support of British military ineptitude, and Taffy Hughes who would have utterly destroyed us in the squeeze to get them.'

'I can't say I know so much about him. He took to me while he thought I was a Blimp, but soon withdrew when he found I meant business in my appointment. The curious thing is that, while he's the complete Little Englander in outlook and didn't mind me as an Imperial figurehead, he actively supports the local lads who've made such a mess of your defence, in opposition to my having true command.'

Jeremy stared.

Esk went on: 'You appear to be as bemused about it as I, old chap. Your politicians are reckoned tricky fellows . . . by British standards. I was prepared for that. It's the same with your military men. On the one hand there's downright truckling to Imperial Brass, yet behind your back you're regarded as an interloper. I can't see any sense in it. In point of fact, that's why I'm here . . . with you.'

Jeremy, pouring brandy, looked up quickly.

' "The one just man in Sodom" if you remember? I want to know whether I'm dealing with a national characteristic of deviousness for its own sake, or have run up against something more sinister.'

After a moment Jeremy asked, 'What sinister purpose could there be?'

'Struggle for power in which I could be used as a pawn, perhaps. I've told you there are two military factions. Perhaps it's the same in the Government.'

'Well, that's your answer.'

'It's not. The British Commonwealth is in deadly danger. Its existence depends, in my opinion, utterly on the loyalty of this nation, or semi-nation, to the ideals the Commonwealth stands for. All these men appear to accept the Commonwealth without question . . . yet, as for doing anything practical to contribute to its strength and ideals, as the saying is, they couldn't care less. Even the PM after calling on the Imperial powers for me, when I've tried to thrash out the matter of the country's defence with him, avoided it. He just told me I had a free hand to do what I liked, see what was required to be done, and report on it, and he'd see that it was done . . . ever since which I've been bowed into every officers' mess in the country pretty well, had my questions about efficiency largely answered with the most polite No Sir's and my orders with the liveliest Yes Sir's . . . and yet not a damned thing to show for it!'

They stared at each other again for a while. Esk broke the silence: 'You can't help me?'

Jeremy swallowed: 'You put me in a very strange position . . . . '

'How's that, dear boy?'

'I'm the veriest Anglophobe, Mark. I mistrust everything the English do. I don't want to offend you . . . . '

Sir Mark shrugged, smiled. 'We are a much misunderstood people. We're not forthright. I think we're even clumsy . . . not with ourselves, but with the world. We judge the world by ourselves . . . fair play and all that. It's our fair play and honesty of intention that gets us where we want to go. But we have to put on masks to do it. We get dismayed by being misunderstood, and try to play the other fellow's game a little to show him we're friendly. Then he accuses us of perfidy. The Indians hate us . . . when we want them to love us. We become stiff with embarrassment. The situation gets worse. The Irish hate us . . . . '

'With every cause, surely!'

'Ah . . . you'd be of Irish descent, of course . . . .'

'And Welsh. The Irish in me doesn't matter that much . . . .'

'Are you so sure?'

'One of the things I hate most in this mostly hateful community is the heroizing of the Irish among us, who did nothing for their country's good but leave it, and nothing for us but teach us hatred of England.'

'Indeed!'

'You can easily check on that by a turn I put on at Beatrice River on New Year's Eve.'

'Tell me about it, dear boy.'

Esk listened intently to the story, commenting when it was done: 'Well, well . . . I've met your Shamus Finnucane. He did me the honour to treat me to a special Irish whisky he claims he's keeping for his wake . . . which I thought rather touching, although I didn't quite believe it. You see, I know the Irish fairly well. One of my less happy appointments was as a trouble-shooter during the Throuble, as they call it . . . therefore a Throuble-shooter . . . .'

'You were a Black and Tan?'

'Hardly, dear boy!'

'But the Throuble so-called . . . .'

'The Black and Tans were police, a lot of them English-born Irish. It was a bad political move to put them in the country . . . but the actual fact is that the Irish Government called for help. The country was in a state of civil war. The Sinn Feiners were attacking their own people as much as the British soldiery. I was sent rather to quell the excess of the Black and Tans . . . which in effect meant to save them from the IRA. Again no thanks . . . because we tried to be on both sides. Ireland couldn't live without England. For a long while we've regarded it as a trade-agreement, really. The trouble is a small band of violent men bent on violence against anyone for anything. Ireland is best dropped . . . as we've dropped her . . . but it leaves an awful gap in our family . . . because we've loved her ever since we civilized her. Do you believe we civilized her?'

'I'm not much concerned about it, Mark . . . believe me. Actually I was interested only in Finnucane's duplicity. He keeps his Tullamore Dew for the Absentee Landlord. Your . . . your . . . what would your relationship be to old Alf . . . . ?'

Sir Mark chuckled, 'Old Alf . . . that's a good 'un. Must tell him you called him that. He'd probably laugh. He claims to be Irish himself, the old scoundrel. But tell me about yourself, Jeremy . . . your ancestry, history. Your father was a Police Inspector, so the Superintendent informed me . . . rather like telling me that you'd sold your mother, seeing what your attitude is to policemen. Said your father was a Grand Old Man. I've done enough talking. Let me hear something about Australian character. For that's what I'm up against, I fear.'

'A drink first,' said Jeremy. Then he proceeded with his story.

They talked till midnight, drinking sparingly, as the intelligent do, just enough to maintain the illusion of bridging the gulf of personality. Esk also talked freely of himself and his ancient recorded lineage, pressed by Jeremy, whose frankly stated purpose was to show the utter alienness between the true

Englishman and the true Colonial. 'And never the twain shall meet, except in political falsehood,' as he said. Esk protested at that, declaring that without overcoming this alienness there must ever be bitterness between men, becoming bitterer unto Armageddon. Surely the British Commonwealth, of all institutions that had ever existed, had done more to bring men together as brothers than any other; and if blood brothers could not sink their differences in the cause of the progress of humanity, what hope was there for the human race? 'What hope, indeed?' asked Jeremy dryly.

They might have gone on, but for an arrangement made over dinner to have an expedition on horseback to the Painted Caves tomorrow. Jeremy took Esk out across the moonlit yard towards the apparently sleeping Big House. The General made a move to take his arm, but checked it obviously. Jeremy took him to the outside stairway, left him to go aloft himself.

The General, going quietly round the verandah towards the guest-side of the house, on hearing a faint sound like crying, cocked an ear, then stopped, turned back to a screened doorway. Here the moonlight was fairly strong. He stood listening. It was stifled singing. Gently he opened the screen, to see two figures, one small and on the white bed, the other, lanky, darkish in a dressing gown, bent over it. He stared a moment, then entered, hissing explosively, 'Dickey!'

Denzil straightened in a flash, swung round, gaped, gasped, 'Sah!'

The hiss was dropped to a whisper as Esk came up to his lieutenant: 'What're you doing?'

'N-nothing, Sir . . . it's fantastic, Sir. He's asleep . . . . '

'I'll give you fantastic! Come out of here.'

Denzil slipped out of the room. Esk stared at Prindy singing in the way of old, then followed. Major Maltravers was now with Denzil. He stiffened in pyjamas too big for him, softly barking, 'Sah!'

Esk made a peremptory sign towards the guest-side. The three went marching. Around the corner, Esk demanded quietly, 'Well, Dickey?'

Denzil gasped, 'On my honour, Sir. I heard the sound. It was like crying . . . a child. I thought it was he and . . . and went to comfort him . . . because . . . because, Sir, you see he'd been so emotional about the music. Sir, he was singing in his sleep!'

Esk looked at the Major, as if for corroboration, and got it in the usual word: 'Sah!'

Esk murmured, 'Sorry, Denzil . . . but you've only got yourself to blame for my suspicions.'

'Yessir.'

'Very good . . . Goodnight.

'Sah!'

When Jeremy went for his early morning run round the racetrack next morning, there was Malters pacing it out in pyjama shorts and singlet and sandshoes too big for him. There had been some talk over dinner about Jeremy's regular vigorous exercising, but not a word from the Major. Scarcely any words now, as coming together in their jog-trot side by side; simply a clipped greeting, then when Jeremy attempted friendliness by remarking on the fact that God had made the miles, like the night, too long, the inevitable: 'Sah!' After doing the two miles, Jeremy headed off without a word to see about getting the horses ready for the expedition.

The party went straight to the horse-yard after breakfast. First there had to be a lesson in mounting an Australian horse in the Australian fashion; that is with your left hip to the beast's left shoulder, left rein tight and on the pummel of the saddle, instead of your right to his left flank and his head free. A safer method, the Australian, since a fractious horse could only pull you into the saddle instead of off your balance; and anyway, Australian horses were used to it. Jeremy insisted on a couple of trials. Perhaps he sounded contemptuous of English riding manners. Malters was stiffly uncompliant until directed by his General.

As they rode off, with Prindy and the young men beginning with a gallop and the seniors taking it easy, Jeremy said, 'Hope you don't mind my saying so, Mark . . . but your Major Maltravers strikes me as representative of all that I've found wooden-headed in military men.'

Sir Mark chuckled, 'Yes . . . jolly old Malters is a typical British soldier in his manner. But you may guess that I wouldn't have him, if he didn't have some extraordinary talent. As a matter of fact, inside that wooden skull works the most amazing cerebral apparatus.'

'Can't say I've noticed it.'

'You wouldn't. He's a man of few words. One of the misfortunes of our breed, as I told you . . . generally a difficulty to communicate that leads to misunderstanding.'

'What's this talent of his . . . other than to limit conversation to one word?'

Again Esk chuckled, 'Well . . . he has the most extraordinary powers of observation, interpretation, and retention . . . in a military sense, I mean. There wouldn't be one facet of anything of importance that's occurred in his presence since I've been here . . . since I've been in Australia, for that matter . . . that he wouldn't be able to give me what he'd call an Appreciation of months hence, if called on. Do you play chess, by any chance?'

'No . . . I'm afraid the game of life's taken all my powers.'

'Well put! Malters is the best chess-player I've ever known . . . not that I'm one myself, but it's a favourite military pastime . . . .'

'With men if necessary?' asked Jerry dryly.

The General pinked slightly, but smiled. 'I was going to say that Malters isn't interested in life. He's unmarried . . . treats women as other-wordly, rather. Would have made a scientist, I always think if he hadn't come of a military family . . . .'

'You're all of military families. That's why you find our men hard to understand. You're bred to it. We use our militarism only in emergency.'

'By gad, Sir, you may be right! It may be what makes you better soldiers in the field than we are, too. But I do wish you'd see the dire emergency now . . . and act on it. Mind if I return to my all-abiding subject of the Japanese menace? I do so want to convince that "one just man in Sodom", you know.'

'Go right ahead,' said Jeremy.

'Before I start,' said Esk, 'Speaking of Malters and the Japanese in the same breath as it were, he delivered one of his Appreciations to me early this morning that might interest you.' Jeremy looked at him sharply. He went on: 'Your friends of the Free Australia Movement. You remember that they were the most vocal of all in denouncing me as the Old Gang. Malters would have checked 'em thoroughly. Seems he learnt through your Security . . . Civil, not Military, save the mark! . . . that they have pretty close connexions with the Japanese. The burden of Maltravers' report to me was a thing on the radio last night that we missed because of our talk. A Japanese speaking from Japan on trade with Australia, the great advantages to Australia that lie in her breaking her trade ties with Britain and transferring them to Japan, becoming a partner in the Great East-Asia Co-Prosperity Sphere, so-called . . . and mentioned the magazine *Australia Free* as supporting this.'

'So?' asked Jeremy somewhat dryly.

'I know you've said it's all a matter of trade . . . that Britain merely fears to lose her Eastern trade to Japan, that we've got no more right to it than the Japanese or anyone, that you're not fighting any more wars for Old Alf and his fat friends . . . . ' Esk paused as Jeremy looked at him hard, to go on: 'The point I want to make is that your patriotism will be seized on by the Japanese, and used by them through certain channels to show your advantage in being more friendly towards them than towards the British . . . . '

'Well, if there is advantage in breaking the economic stranglehold of the absentee landlords . . . . '

'Wait, please. You admitted yesterday in talking of the stranglehold that it is primarily Australians' own fault. They'll sell out at any price. They have no love of the soil. All they want is money, beer, sport, a good time. Don't you think that they'll sell out similarly to the Japanese if the Japanese come to dominate the trade of this part of the world?'

'No . . . because they hate the Japs.'

'What for?'

Jeremy was at loss, had to say, 'Just because they're Japs, I suppose. It's traditional.'

'I think it's instinctive. You came as Europeans into Asia, and wanted to keep your European identity . . . and saw the Rising Sun as something likely to burn you up.'

'The Japs could never get here to invade us. I've told you of the thousands of Chinese who were here and could have stayed . . and left to go home . . . . '

'We're talking of Japanese, dear boy . . . a ruthless militaristic nation, a tricky race of ju-jitsuists. Do you know that the Japanese now have a saying: "There are eighty million people in Japan . . . but they have only one head"? It doesn't mean the Mikado . . . it means the Purpose . . . *Dai Nippon* . . . meaning Greater Japan. But my point at the moment is that there are elements who, for power, will sell you into the hands of the Japanese, on any pretext, trade, patriotism. But enough of that . . . it was only to put in a word for old Malters, without whom, I'll confess, I would be utterly lost in this terrible job of mine, the worst I've ever tackled . . . because the threat of failure is so great and the thought of it unthinkable.'

Jeremy asked dryly, 'Has your Malters passed me as a good security risk?'

'As a matter of fact, with his Appreciation this morning he made one of his rare unasked-for comments in praise of you. Speaking of this Free Australia thing and their wanting to involve you in it, he said, what a pity you aren't still a serving soldier, since you'd make the perfect commander for this northern region, what with your knowledge of it and integrity, plus your ardent patriotism.'

Jeremy smiled grimly. 'But minus my enthusiasm for *Pax Britannica*. Does he know about that?'

'It's been pretty evident in your conversation, old man.'

'What's he know of my conversation . . . unless he eavesdrops?'

Esk frowned slightly. 'Can't say I like to hear my Old Faithful referred to as an eavesdropper. But he has long ears. It's his job.'

'To be checking on me while pretending to be reading!' Suddenly Jeremy turned on Esk, his face flaming with anger, grey eyes flashing. 'Look here, man . . . what *is* this? Am I under surveillance or something?'

'You're under particular notice as the "one just man in Sodom".'

'Is that what you're here for, purely and simply, trying to inveigle me into giving my life to your goddamned phoney Empire, the very beast that devoured my brother, bled and bankrupted my country to save its own skin, and then put the bailiffs in?'

The General turned pale before the sudden storm of passion, swallowed, took a moment to answer: 'Primarily, Jeremy, as I think I've frankly enough shown, my preoccupation is service to this thing you detest through, as I see it, a distorted image of it . . . but truly, there's much more to it, a feeling of attachment to you that I hope to be able to number amongst the few great friendships of my life. Will you believe me?'

Jeremy, who had been looking ahead with set expression, now turned, to meet the pallid thin face, the haggard eyes almost pleading, looking so much like the pale fair girl in the cave that day, who had fled, crying that the man and the country had rejected her. He stared for a moment, then said with a nod, 'Yes . . . Mark.'

Esk drew a deep breath, looked ahead, and in exhaling murmured, 'Thank you, Jeremy.'

They rode on, their horses ambling, a little while in silence. Esk broke it, saying, 'I hope you won't deny me talk of what presses my heart so sorely. The strength of your patriotism is in the bitterness you feel about the general lack of true love of country in your compatriots. So I can't offend you by my criticism of your countrymen. Besides, whatever your feelings about the *Pax Britannica*, its failure, which God forbid, is going to affect your country drastically. As a man of good sense you should know from an expert what the political climate is that creates the threat. I want Australia strong militarily to meet the threat against the British Commonwealth of Nations. I'm sure you want it to be the same, for the sake of your own Commonwealth. So, although we may not be speaking quite the same language, we're speaking about the same thing. I wish with all my heart to enlist you in my cause . . . and will try with all my might to impress you with its worthiness . . . but I promise to shove no Imperialism down the neck of a man who, having seen it at its worst, had had a gutful of it. But have I your permission to talk about it . . . if only aloud to my deeply troubled self?'

Jeremy smiled slightly. 'You have, Sir Mark.'

'Sir Mark? What's this . . . a subtle rejection of me?'

'No . . . the contrary. Your earnestness reminded me of your daughter . . . in her occasional moments of sincerity . . . very English, I think, and innocent, so different from the local . . . well, to give it its proper name, Bullshit. As to the title . . . it's your own, part of the usage of your own country. I object to such things only if held by my own countrymen, who must kowtow to the Imperium to get them . . . the Imperial Honours. Yours are not . . . just aristocratic tags. I was just trying it out on my tongue.'

Sir Mark looked relieved. After a while he said, 'I'd like to begin by telling you how Japan altered the whole picture of Imperial defence in this region by adoption of the aircraft carrier. Not their invention, of course . . . nothing ever is. But they are the world's greatest adaptors . . . the Clever Monkey-men, as the Chinese call them. By the way . . . presuming you hold no brief for the Japanese, such as *Australia Free* seems to have . . . . ' Esk looked at Jeremy inquiringly. Jeremy shook his head. 'Good, then, since it's a good joke . . . except from a Japanese point of view. It's the Chinese story of the origin of the Japanese Nation *Nippon*. Whether it's an old one, or come only out of recent events, I couldn't say. *Nippon*, you might know, is the Japanese name for Japan . . . I think the word Japan is a French or Spanish distortion of it. Anyway, it's a Chinese word, like most classical words of Japan, and means The East, or the Rising Sun. Now . . . a certain Chinese Emperor had a daughter of whom he was so jealous that he couldn't consent to her marriage to any man in the world, and fearing her abduction, because she was beautiful and so well endowed, had her removed to the uninhabited isles of *Nippon*, with none but female attendants. Supervision of whoever went to *Nippon* was frightfully strict. Not even a little boy could go there, and all females were stripped to prevent masquerading. The perfect *purdah*, it seemed. But, alas . . . while the island was not naturally inhabited by humans, it was by apes of both sexes . . . and the Emperor became grandsire to a little half-ape . . . and the Japanese Nation was born.'

Jeremy laughed heartily.

Esk kept the laughter going with more amusing stories, mostly of army life, to make it look ridiculous. Thus all the way to the Turtle Hole and yard. There they found the others, with a sugar-sack of turtles hunted while waiting for them. The party had smoke-o there, then climbed to the caves.

No such dramatic effect, either genuine or faked, this time as on former showing of the galleries to visitors. Esk confessed himself completely at a loss to find meaning in it; and if the supposedly so-perceptive Malters did so, he gave no Appreciation. Denzil Dickey tried to wax arty about it, using modernistic terms, but ended lamely by suggesting that it might make good design-motif stuff for modern household drapes. However, Prindy, also seeing this particular set for the first time, was obviously deeply affected, but only showing it with the intensity of his staring; for when asked by Jeremy what he thought of it, he merely muttered: 'Properly!'

When the show had been viewed and they were scrambling down, Prindy, alone with Denzil, said that the pictures had made him Sing Inside. Denzil became very excited, shouted to the others, and rushed Prindy to join them to tell them also. At the moment Jeremy was telling Sir Mark that while he himself did not presume to grasp the true significance of Aboriginal Art, he felt drawn to the Galleries as to holy places, shrines to the *Genus Loci* of Terra Australis, which only true Aborigines could feel at one with. Nevertheless, he said, he believed that it was only through the medium of it that the non-indigenous would ever come truly to feel at home. 'Teach it in the schools,' he said, 'so that children grow up to accept it as part of their own heritage . . . as they now do pictures of the Battle of Hastings or the Bayeux Tapestries . . . learn to respect it. This is something you don't understand, Mark . . . the awful emptiness of the colonial-born. You yourself have a country, and an Empire or Commonwealth or whatever you like to call it, as well. But it's your *country* comes first. As children we were taught at school . . . and I suppose it's still much the same, with King's Birthday and Empire Day and all that . . . *The Empire is My Country, Australia is My Home.* It used to hang framed on classroom walls. How can an Empire be anyone's country? And how can a man live without . . . a country . . . "Breathes there a man with soul so dead, who never to himself hath said, this is mine own, my native land?" Australia's filled with millions of men with dead souls. I believe that's what's chiefly wrong with us . . . . '

It was here that Denzil and Prindy arrived. Hearing Denzil's panted news, Jeremy asked Prindy what he meant by this Singing Inside him. Prindy answered simply, 'Like people singing long time ago . . . Aboriginal people.'

Jeremy drew a deep breath, then said, 'Yes . . . that's it . . . the answer I've been seeking for so long. No blackman could, or perhaps would, give it to me. The Voice of the Spirit of the Land. Thank you, sonny!' He turned his own grey eyes, shining, on the mildly staring other grey eyes. 'Thank you a thousand times!'

Esk looked from them to Malters, who was watching them with intent that well might be perceptive; or was just the fixed stare of the popinjay on parade. Catching his superior's questioning glance, he stiffened slightly, murmured, 'Sah!'

As they were riding homeward, the General, rather more urgently it seemed than even the emergency of things he stressed, got on with his statistical revelation of the might of the menace of *Dai Nippon*, for the most part secret, he said, because intelligence of the situation was hard to come by owing to this matter of the One Man with the Eighty-million Heads. They were not fiddling with designs for aircraft carriers, like Britain and the other signatories to the tonnage-limiting Treaty of London, but were actually converting their obsolete battleships to the purpose as they floated. Britain, France, America, couldn't take the aircraft carrier seriously. It was too vulnerable to attack, was the concensus of naval and aviation opinion. But from what attack after the blow of the first one to use it had been struck? What the Japanese were doing now rendered the Singapore Naval Base, keystone of British Imperial power in the Far East, a sitting duck. The Imperial Might must be switched at once from sea to air. Britain didn't need carriers yet. She had the land to fly her planes from – such planes as she had. Malaya and Burma must be filled with airmen and their aircraft, and ground troops, aerodromes built everwhere, even up into Fench Indo-China, where the first southern entry would be made by the Japanese when they had completely subjugated China. The Ju-jitsuist at the moment was playing lame. He was giving it out to the world that the cost of the war in China was embarrassing him. He'd lost half a million men, untold millions of yen. But what cared he for men? And the Chinese would give him the yen at the point of the samurai sword.

'Do you know anything about ju-jitsu, Jeremy? You have to know about it to know the Japanese. The expression means, literally, *the soft art*. Nothing soft about it, however, except your opponent's falling for your tricks. The whole art is to throw your opponent off balance . . . let him break his arm, his head, his arsebone . . . with his own weight and stupidity. The very approach to a bout of it is full of tricks, all bows and courtesy. The most polite people in the world, and most treacherous. They soft-arted us into making them a great naval power, the Germans into making them the most efficient army on earth. Then they turned against the Germans. Then they turned back to the Germans against us. What they count on now is our getting embroiled with the Germans again and drawing the USA in with us . . . then the sudden swift and treacherous blow . . . and we're a goner. Never forget that the Gentleman of Japan is first and last a ju-jitsuist . . . . '

'Or that an English Gentleman is first and last and always simply a gentleman, eh?'

Esk looked quickly. 'Do I detect a note of the sardonic, dear boy?'

'The Australian character, what little there is of it, tends to be sardonic, Mark. You want to understand Australian character, don't you, since I take it you want to use Australians to take the brunt of the Japanese Gentleman's treachery?'

'Dear boy!'

Esk left it at that. They talked horses again, and on arrival back at the racetrack paddock, went off to take another look at what Esk called Your Stable and Jeremy My String. Esk was much taken with Red Rory, and talked of buying him. Jeremy suggested that he ride him tomorrow on a picnic trip to the Rainbow Pool. 'He's a nice horse to ride,' he said. 'You could ride him on Anzac Day and give them a real treat in Town. He only gets mean where racing's concerned. Seems to like you, too. His grand-dam, by the way, was a direct English importation. Maybe he's descended from a line of aristocratic cavalry mounts, and'll race only for the glory of the regiment kind of thing.'

'In that case, I simply must have him.'

As they went on to the homestead, they arranged that the General and his men would go in with Jeremy to the Beatrice when he went to meet the train on Wednesday, instead of calling for special transport.

For dinner that night they had a curry made with the flesh of those turtles caught this morning. Such was the effect that Malters became even talkative at table. Curry-eating appeared to be his only vice. He knew a thousand recipes, but had never struck this one, nor one so delicately handled. Nan explained that she had found a book of recipes in the house and worked on it, adapting to local produce. Jeremy added to her explanation that his first wife had been a curry-maker for social reasons – 'The East, and all that, don't y'know' – hence the book of recipes; but Nan was natural with curry. He said, 'I live for the day when she curries a snake.' There was much laughter over it, except from one, whose silence went unnoticed.

After dinner Malters and Nan exchanged curry recipes; while the music lesson was resumed between Prindy and Denzil; and Jeremy and the General, after first taking a stroll in the moonlight, when Jeremy talked of the birds they heard and animals they saw, and of the Southern Stars, to his companion's apparent great interest, retired again to the den in the annexe. The talk there tonight was mainly of British Politics, following a report in the evening's news of a row between the Prime Minister, Chamberlain, and Winston Churchill, over Chamberlain's effort to avoid becoming involved in war in Europe. At last Jeremy and his guest found common ground in detestation of Churchill, although on grounds entirely different. Whereas Jeremy declared that Churchill was an Imperial adventurer, a cold-blooded scion of the British Aristocracy, Esk called him a loud-mouthed half-bred Yankee, whose lack of being a real Englishman made him want to appear as the Great Englishman, a man small in stature and outlook, so far from being an Imperial adventurer that he'd scarcely been out of England. Esk said, 'If we get involved in war in Europe it will be Churchill's doing . . . and simply to show off. He opposed intervention in the Spanish Civil War, which would have stopped the whole damned madness that's now raving in Europe. He supported Germany till Hitler came along out of the very things he supported, namely, acknowledgement of the Hun's grievances for having failed to conquer Europe before. He encouraged the arming of France to turn the Hun's attention westward instead of eastward where it would naturally have gone. It was the rise of the tin-god Hitler that maddened him. Hitler, a man with a big mouth, is what Churchill himself would like to be, *Der Führer*. Damn Churchill, Sir!'

'Do you know him personally?'

'I wouldn't Jeremy. But I've had personal dealings with him. All who work under him go in fear and trembling of the pot-bellied little giant's wrath. He was Chancellor of the Exchequer in 1925, when we were involved lunatically in mititary operations in the Middle East. He had no idea of the situation, no conception of the broad issues of the Empire . . . just England, England, England . . . and not even a proper Englishman!'

Sir Mark was wrath – an unusual thing – but Jeremy didn't seem to notice. Staring ahead, he said, 'I think I'd've killed him if I'd ever met him personally . . . if he'd ever come here, say with Vaisey, as the great and grand have on occasions . . . .'

'Churchill come here! He is the perfect Damned Colonial type. Colonials to be called on when Old England is in danger . . . to die!'

Jeremy looked round at that, stared. Esk said ernestly, 'Truly, Jeremy. It won't happen again to your Australians, if I can have my way. If there's dying to be done, it'll be in defence of your own country . . . .'

'In Burma . . . in Malaya?' demanded Jeremy.

'More realistic than in the mud of Flanders or on the rocks of Gallipoli or in the sand of Sinai, isn't it?'

'There's only one place a man should be prepared to die in battle . . . and that's on the sacred soil of his own country.'

Sir Mark, hollow-eyes again, stared at him for a moment, then sighed: 'Please God it never comes to that. And it won't Jeremy, I assure you . . . unless those military adventurers in Melbourne and Canberra can boot me out and get the power to lead boys back to the Brothels of Egypt, as you've so aptly put it, and leave Australia to the mercy of the most ruthless, cold-blooded, treacherous race on earth.'

They drank, sat in silence for a while, till Sir Mark, looking his suave self again, said, 'Tell me more about your life, Jeremy . . . particularly of late. You may not be typically Australian, but you do deal in Australian types . . . and I must know this Australian character.'

So they sat again till midnight.

Next morning was given to the horse-business and a definite arrangement that Sir Mark would buy Red Rory and take possession of him as soon as facilities were organized. He said he would be making a survey of the north-western part of the country during the next three months, would have a float built to haul the horse about, would ride him whenever possible, and perhaps run him in the minor station races. He had a military groom in England, for whom he would send as soon as he resumed his military contacts. The man was also a good jockey. Jeremy said he hated parting with a horse, but believed Red Rory might be better for getting away from the place. He didn't get along so well with Electron who when all was said and done was Boss Horse round here.

The General rode Red Rory to the Rainbow Pool to have lunch there, while Jerry rode Electron, as usual. As Jerry remarked, Rory looked stuck up already, with a titled General on his back, taking on a mincing military step, with much proud head-tossing, and then in an aside to his own mount, 'We've never been good enough for the bugger, old boy . . . that's the trouble.' Electron joined the laughter with a whinny.

There were the five of them again. At the Pool, Prindy insisted on taking a dip, despite Jeremy's saying that he ought not to, seeing that they had told the visitors it was a dangerous place. Prindy replied almost insolently, 'Not danger for me, Mullaka,' and dived in. The first time he had used that mode of address for a long while. There was still a menacing swirl of water back near the now gently tumbling falls. Prindy had not been there since that day of his deliverance. Jeremy watched him with a strange expression, as if wondering what the boy's motive was; some secret urge, or just wanting to show off? The General remarked on the boy's skill in the water. Prindy swam up to the lip of the menace, then showed his golden bottom in a dive. They stared. He burst from the water down in the shallows above the fall to the river. It was too much for Denzil. Behind the other's backs he slipped out of his clothes, and pink and white and bony, went loping and splashing to join him.

They had also talked of the superstition connected with the Pool. When at the General's sharp order Denzil came sneaking out, clasped hands hiding his genitals, Jeremy remarked to him, 'Now you won't be able to take over your father's field-marshal's baton, son . . . you'll finish up here as a ringer for Vaiseys.'

Esk said, 'I've a damned good mind to cashier him on the spot and ask your son to take him on as a jackaroo.'

That night there was another curry, a mystery to begin with, that Malters waxed eloquent over again – till told what it was, when he turned grey. 'Bandicoot,' said Nanago with a giggle.

'Bandicoot?' muttered Malters. 'A rat!'

'No-more rat!' cried Nan.

'But . . . but . . . a bandicoot is a rat,' muttered Malters.

Jeremy chimed in: 'It's a marsupial . . . nothing like a rat . . . and the sweetest of food. What gave you the idea of a rat?'

Malters, drawing a deep breath, evidently of relief, replied, 'In India the bandicoot is a rat.'

Jeremy exclaimed, 'Well, I'll be damned . . . another non-native name for a native thing! Emu is Portuguese . . . Jabiru's South American Indian, and Goanna a derivative of the Spanish Iguana. I wouldn't be surprised to hear that Kangaroo is Gaelic or something. We haven't even got a name for our Aboriginal people . . . except that stupid one. What sort of people are we?'

Esk shook his head. 'Strange, strange people in many ways.'

They all stayed in the lounge that night and heard an English comic show that caused much mirth. Even on that Jeremy had to comment: 'We have no real humour. What goes for professional humour is just childish imitation. The only real laughs we get are from sardonic comments. Deep down, I think we're bitter people . . . all of us . . . bitter for the want of a land to love.'

II

They set out for the siding after lunch next day, an unusual time, but not remarked on by anyone. Jeremy and Sir Mark were left to ride alone in the cabin. Neither had much to say. It wasn't to be a final parting by any means. They would be meeting again at the Races in September, after which the General intended to make a survey of the northeastern coast. Jeremy was up to something, the way he dawdled the last few miles, so as to arrive in the township almost simultaneously with the mail train, and contrary to custom drove straight up to Finnucane's. He said to Esk as they were alighting, 'I want to see how old Shame-on-us receives you.'

The bar was crowded, Shamus and his wife and daughter Peggy going for their lives. But Shamus dropped everything at sight of the General. 'Ah!' he cried, ' 'Tis yeself, Gineral Sir Mark . . . and Jeremy!' The great red face was wreathed in Irish amiability.

Over in the gentry's corner were some of those Esk had left the other day to go with Jeremy, among them Superintendent Bullco, and Martin and Clancy Delacy. All looked somewhat embarrassed, even though the General, and Jeremy with him, waved to them cheerily. Jeremy was holding Esk at the public bar. That was too much for Shamus, who leant over it to them: 'Now, you gintlemen would be wanting a little more privacy, I'm sure. My office, eh?'

Jeremy said quickly. 'No . . . over with the others'll do.' He nodded to the gentry. Then he added: 'But a drop o' the crayther for the gineral . . . he tells me he's tried it and's now what ye moight call addicted to it?'

The black brows shot up, exposing suspicious eyes. But Jeremy grinned like a boy. A moment. Then Shamus said, 'And whoy not . . . the t'ree of us. Come gintlemen!' He darted away and out of the bar; while Jeremy and the General walked round to join the others, or rather to enter the so-called Private Bar, and while nodding amiably to those already there, took a place apart at the end of the counter.

There in a moment was Himself, with a bottle of Tullamore Dew and three chased glasses, saying as he passed the others, 'You'll excuse us, gints . . . but a little private farewellin' loike.' He came beaming up to the waiting pair.

As Shamus was about to fill the third glass, asking about how did the General like his sojourn at that lovely place, Lily Lagoons, Jeremy said quickly, 'Not for me, Shamus.'

Finnucane looked at him quickly. Jeremy grinned. 'Many's the time you've told me that my old Da would turn in his grave at something un-Irish I've done. Perhaps he has, too. But I don't want him doing it through my drinking Irish whiskey with a British general who was in Ireland during the Throuble . . . no, sir!' It was said loud enough for all at hand to hear.

Finnucane gasped, gaped, turning purple, his popping eyes moving to the General. Esk was pale. Jeremy thrust his hand out to him, and as Esk took it weakly, said, 'Well, so long, Mark . . . see you at the Races. Nice knowing you.'

As Jeremy began to turn, Esk moved after him, muttering, 'Jeremy!'

Jeremy smiled. 'No offence to you, Mark. Only want to show you Australian character . . . and Irish . . . a lot of Irish about, you know. Guess you can talk yourself out of that bit of a war . . . you've nearly talked me into one with the Japanese.' He nodded to the hollow-eyed man, then to the others, then winked at Finnucane, and went out.

Malters and Denzil were standing by the utility, the latter with an arm about Prindy's shoulders. Jeremy told the men they'd better join the General, and shook hands with them. They shook hands with Prindy. Then suddenly Denzil stopped and kissed the boy on the lips, spun around, bounded onto the verandah. Prindy looked astonished, wiped his lips. Jeremy stared for a moment, then commented, 'Hmmm . . . these Englishmen!' Then, telling Prindy to hop in, he got in himself, drove down to the station to collect the mail.

In the mail was another copy of *Australia Free* and a fattish letter from Alfie Candlemas. As Jeremy stowed them in the glove-box of the car, he remarked, 'I'm supping with so many devils I'll have to buy a whole set of long-handled spoons.'

Prindy asked, 'What that mean, Grandfather?'

'Tell you later, sonny. Want to catch Tom Toohey . . . then off home. Do you know, we haven't been quietly alone at home for what seems weeks.'

CHAPTER THIRTEEN

SEPTEMBER AGAIN, and inevitably the Beatrice River Races. But could one be so sure any more about what had seemed inevitable? What changes in the old familiar scene! It had seemed odd enough having a few uniformed soldiers moving amongst the squatters, the ringers, the familiar townies, the boongs – astonishing to see them marching with a brass band. To be sure there was talk enough on the radio and space given in newspapers and magazines to threats of war; and the roads were being built in case of war; and the oil tanks and new rolling stock added to the railway. Still, even in Port Palmeston the Garrison was so far out of town it might not be there at all, and those who manned it didn't seem to do much more than booze in their messes. Likewise there were these Reffo types, a mere handful to start with, but ever increasing, who would tell you terrible tales of being driven from their native lands, if you'd listen to 'em, which you didn't, unless you were a Commo. Talk of bringing Reffo Jews into the country and settling them in a sort of New Jerusalem – Sheenies in elastic sides – did you ever 'ear anything so bloody silly?

But, for crise sake – this time there was a special train for the military, aboard it a titled British General who'd be running a horse for the Cup; and Nazi Germans, representatives of Fokker or Junkers or someone who made war-planes, and also of Krupp who made what everybody knew, staying at the Big House – and, believe it or not, the first of the Sheenies here, camped on the river!

This Munich business. You didn't hear anything else but that now. Everybody arguing about it, not simply Prime Ministers and Presidents, but men in the street, and not merely arguing, but fighting over it, and not away off in the streets of cities, but right here in the one street of Beatrice River, and on the night when everybody should be getting together to whack each other on the back, whether they were really mates or not, to booze and talk horses and the droll things that had been happening round the stations and the sidings and up in Town during the past year; violence in Finnucane's bar, with bottle throwing and yells of Commo Bastards and Fascist Shitheads, blows exchanged with similar and still choicer expressions out under the coloured lights and bunting on the verandah, wild brawling out on the gravel; and the Johns, who should have been boozing with the rest, having to run to the Police Station for batons and call on the military to help 'em! Strike me lucky, what was the country coming to?'

That's how it began this year. Fortunately, enough good sense prevailed to keep the like in check until the festival was pretty well over.

The Communists were blamed for it, and no doubt rightly, since what caused the provocation was their gathering in force at a function hitherto banned by them as a Boss's Beanfeast, and if attended at all only in the way of public duty, as in the case of Engine Driver Pat Hannaford. Still, they could claim that they were provoked into intruding by the political atmosphere in which this meeting was conducted. Those fiery leaders of theirs, Scotty McClaggity and Jordie Jenks, would not have travelled all this way at the Party's expense just to start a row, when they could start one any time in Port Palmeston, down at the waterfront, the railway yards, the oil-tanks, or out on the new road, without leaving that little old office of theirs. Besides, it was the act of one of their political opponents that precipitated the violence.

The political provocation was, of course, the presence of those Germans, members of Hitler's Nationalist Socialist Party, as they had quite proudly declared themselves in press interviews in Port Palmeston. The Krupps men, one a Von, the other a Herr Doktor, were here to see about increasing the supply of Tantalium ore they had been buying in small quantity from this region for some time; those representing Junkers Aircraft to demonstrate the efficacy of their machines and to hand one over for use by him who would be their local representative, Fergus Ferris. Such important people were naturally received by His Honour the Administrator, who, unless he had shared the politics of Messrs McClaggity and Jinks, could hardly be expected not to mention the impending carnival in the very region the Von and Herr Doktor wished to visit and to arrange for their inclusion in it, if only with intent to get a free and comfortable flight there for himself. As a matter of fact, the two big aircraft, one of them quite large, brought down *all* the Government Heads, excepting those of the Aborigines Department and the men of the Garrison. Dr Cobbity, of course, never attended the Races on principle; and his assistant, Mr McCusky, had been ordered to travel by train, for the reason that included amongst the flying Heads was Professor St Clair, famous Anthropologist, who along with Dr Fabian Cootes, was come to make an official survey of the condition of Aborigines, with a view to establishing a better system of dealing with the people; or as Dr Cobbitty put it, to boot him out. The Military Heads travelled as they did under orders from General Sir Mark Esk, as a military exercise. McClaggity and Co. had held a meeting in Town to tell the world that the visitors were here to get means to destroy the Workers' Fatherland and therefore should be declared black, but without attracting much more interest than that given by half a dozen policemen under the leadership of Sergeant Cahoon. Hence again it was a natural thing that these also should include themselves in this most popular gathering in the land.

The initial violence might be said to be only semi-political. It was done by Engine Driver Jack Tinball on his colleague Pat Hannaford, in consequence of the latter's having remarked derisively on a matter of such significance to the former that even with tears in his eyes as he got a few beers in he had been describing as the Second Most Wonderful Day in His Life. Old Jack it was who had driven the military train down. He had done much more than that. Having made it known to the General that he was an old military man himself and most likely had hauled him about the Western Front in military trains, he had the great man on the footplate, and for a considerable distance gave him the controls. That first Most Wonderful day in Jack's life was when he'd had Field Marshal Lord Haig as his pupil one day while they were pushin' Jerry back in 1918. 'Them were the days, General!' as he had said, and been overheard by his fireman. Also, in parting with his pupil, after shaking grimy hands, he had saluted. It was the report on the saluting that evidently had inspired Hannaford to make the remarks he did across the bar. Everybody knew that Jack had really lived those years in the Railway Corps in France and since had only existed on reminiscence of them, Pat more than most, who'd often tried to shut him up. It may have been that on this occasion Pat was inclined to be more forthright than usual by reason of having his Party Chieftains round him where he stood at the bar. Anyway, in making the sneering remarks about his colleague's boots being the only part of him that could be seen while he was in the presence of the General, he referred to the latter as an Imperialist Pommy Bastard. That was too much for Jack, who giving his opinion of communists, which condensed into 'Commo shit!' grabbed a beer bottle and let Pat have it with such force as to have brained a lesser man.

Such a job, indeed, did Jack do on Pat that Dr Fox had to be called from the Big House. Maybe Foxy wouldn't have come, seeing who it was and who the company he was having the Inaugural Dinner with, had the call not also included a request for his services to the mounting list of casualties consequent on the first. And maybe the doctor was lucky he didn't himself cop a bottle while attending to the bleeding, moaning first martyr to the class-struggle lying on the floor where he had been felled, judging by the way Con Cullity, behind the bar, looked at him while handling a bottle. For it happened that the Flying Fox was really in bad with Con, in fact with the entire Finnucane clan, by reason of his behaviour in the matter of the delivery of the latest edition to it, young Cornelius, at the moment yelling somewhere out the back, roused by the shinannigans out in front.

Nor was Fox's unpopularity just then confined to the House of Finnucane, but widespread amongst the common herd, who while hitherto liking him as a man though not much as a doctor, were now against the man because of the professional arrogance he had shown in respect to the Cullity Baby business. Most vocal of the common herd were those confessedly commonest of them, the Commos, in their case primarily as always for political reasons, because Fox's arrogance was directed against a refugee Jewish doctor, who it was generally believed had saved the life of both child and mother by taking them out of Fox's hands. To be a Communist just then meant also to be an ardent Judaeophile as opposed to the *Judenhasse*, or Jew Hating, of their Nazi enemies. The Jewish doctor, along with a handsome young Jewish woman about whose relation to him there was some doubt, were here too, brought along to the Races by Con and Bridie. They were the Jews, who to the wonder of so many locals who knew Jews only as something the Bible was largely concerned with or as Sheenies they'd glimpsed for a moment in the doorways of pop-shops while on visits to the cities of the South, were camped on the river – hardly to be regarded as evidence that the three hundred thousand Jews of Germany were, as often stated in the world's news, either fleeing for their lives or had already forfeited them or soon would do; but it was being said that they were come into these scarcely civilized parts to make a survey of likely sites for that mooted settlement for Jewish refugees.

This was the tale of the Cullity Baby, talked up and down the land wherever the gossips' blessing of telephonic communication reached. Bridie, probably owing to the masculine prowess she had predicted in her spouse as the result of finding himself somehow the father of the child called Jemima, had conceived again rather early, and perhaps from that reason had been prematurely brought to bed. The Flying Fox had been called, but had diagnosed her sudden and severe onset of labour as mere belly-ache, and had refused to come again when called upon by frantic Con in the Name o' God.

Dr Kurt Hoff, and his lady, had been out at Pisgah Ridge, either attracted by its Biblical name in their purpose or having contacts there. He had practised as a gynaecologist in Germany, but like all refugee doctors was prevented from legal medical practice of any kind in Australia, owing to what was generally considered the arrogance, arising out of fearful jealousy, of local medical talent. As people generally fear and hate doctors, they are mostly attracted to what the faculty call a quack, as Fox had called Dr Hoff. Hence the popularity of Dr Hoff in contrariety to the feeling for Dr Fox, when it was learnt that, having been called to the Prospectors' Arms or Alms by the frantic Con, Hoff had made contact with Fox and declared that the case was urgent, only to be told to keep his long Jew-nose out of it or he would be prosecuted, he had set to and by some special method effected the delivery safely. Evidently Fox would have had him prosecuted, too, only that the clever little Jew had countered by saying he had merely acted as adviser to his red-headed lady friend, who had stood in as midwife to the bedded woman, as any member of the sex was entitled to do in an emergency.

Fox had made matters worse by declaring to all and sundry, 'No wonder Hitler kicked the bastards out of Germany. Well, if this tricky little quack tries anything like that again, I'll see he's kicked right back?' This on top of the latest news that Hitler, having seized Austria, was also persecuting the Jews there. There was also this mad Munich business, which nobody could make out clearly unless they had only one eye to see things with, like Hannaford, or Herbert Stunke, or Col Collings and the like. But most important of all was Bridie's own statement, that she was beginning to see The Virgin and Angels and things, and was certain that but for Dr Hoff she would have died. Then there was old Shame-on-us to tell the Wurruld, all the louder for having Constable Stunke hint to him that Jews were notorious for doing ill to Christian babies, and therefore he shouldn't be so sure of his grandson Cornelius's future.

Another time Foxy, having finished his bloody job on Pat Hannaford and others, would surely have been treated to a dram or two of Tullamore Dew. Instead all he got this time was the presentation of Shamus's broad back.

There was also trouble for Fergus Ferris through his involvement with the *Herrenvolk*. That happened amongst the respectable ones not involved in the brawling, who tried afterwards to make something like the traditional whoopee out in the concert square at the back. The trouble-maker was Fay McFee, down for the Races for the first time in years, following her nose for news other than the social stuff she despised and disparaged. With a few drinks in, and before everybody, she told Fergus that he must be a Nazi agent to be taken up by these cold-eyed and bespectacled bastards; for sure he must, since also being involved with that renegade bitch Alfie Candlemas and the *Fascist Felixers*, as she called Alfie's new associates of the Free Australia Movement.

Fergus, more than a little drunk, replied, 'Fay, shweetheart . . . haven' I tol' you before you got 'o take your pants right off, not half off, 'cause like that they'll only hobble you and you'll fall, and get hurt a lot more that away than you would by takin' 'em right off and fallin' the way God made you for and you're so scared of.'

She didn't get a chance to deal with him further, because Eddy McCusky, although anything but a friend of hers, leapt in to champion her, snapping, 'That's no way to talk to a lady . . . you 'pologize, mate!'

Eddy also had had his share, and was probably fired with what had been going on out the front, although not a participant. Fergus turned to him, saying, 'Ah . . . the bull's arse speaketh!'

Eddy had no hat on, but seemed to tip one over an eye the way he cocked his head, demanding, 'You lookin' for lash, mug?'

Fergus giggled. 'There's an answer to that, o' course . . . but not fit for ladies' presence . . . and you reckon one's preshent. Nevertheless, Bull's Arse, you're at liberty to use your tongue in the manner of that unclean shuggestion . . . Ow!'

Eddy was into him. How it would have gone was anybody's guess, seeing that both were only fist-flaylers. They got as far as filling an eye for each other and bloodying noses. Then Dinny Cahoon, just cooling off from the grand fracas, leapt on them, dragged them apart, and little men that they were compared with him, held them so by the scruffs of their necks, grating, 'We've had enough o' this sort o' thing . . . now piss off to bloody bed, both of you, or I'll deal with you meself . . . and you too, you trouble-maker!' The last remark was addressed to Fay, as the belligerents slunk away. She answered with the protrusion of about a foot of tongue, but nevertheless obeyed.

In fact everybody retired early, a fact remarked on with expression of great relief by Jeremy Delacy down in his camp by the crossing: 'Thank heavens for that. We'll get at least one good night's sleep without having to dope ourselves. Might be a good idea to start a brawl every night to use up that alcoholic energy they mostly let off like engines blowing off steam.'

He was sitting up in his lounge tent talking to his next-door neighbours, the Jewish couple. The woman, or rather girl, because she looked so young, asked, 'Broll . . . vot isht?'

The doctor translated with a chuckle, *'Schlimozzel.'*

She giggled. She was a lovely thing, as everybody was saying; a redhead, as some of her race occasionally are, but with typical Jewish features: large hazel eyes that shone like jewels, full lips rose-tinted with natural colour, nose a little big perhaps, but perfect in shape, the planes of her face perfect. As she turned with a sweet smile to Nan who had echoed her giggle, the profile view revealed the secret of her beauty. It was the almost perfect semi-circle her features filled from hair-line to throat, without perceptible protrusion or inflexion of brows, nose, chin, as with most other types of face, in which the nose points outward or upward or is flat, the eyes sunken to give prominence to brow ridges, the chin jutting or receding, This was the perfect Semitic face. Also, despite the colour of her hair and a climate to which she would be quite unaccustomed, conditions that would have made a woman of so-called Nordic type coarse-skinned, her skin was as perfect as her features: a dark satin, natural, of course, in a race with desert origins. Nan was watching her with frank delight – and Jeremy surely with more than ordinary interest, the way he avoided the bright eyes when they turned on him. Her name was Rifkah, as called by the doctor.

The man, Kurt Hoff, aged about forty, was also typically Jewish of features, but with the perfection of the curve spoilt by too long and sharp a nose and compensating recession of chin. A somewhat foxy face, but pleasantly smiling. He was dark.

The pair had been more or less dumped on the Delacy household by Con Cullity and Bridie when they arrived. They had a car of their own, a huge old red thing, packed with camping-gear, and had put up a tent of their own, but could scarcely be treated as anything but guests. They were not husband and wife, and only laughed when it was suggested, the significance of their intimate association as it would be considered by local standards evidently being quite lost on them. The way they spoke, they had been thrown together simply by suffering at the hands of the Nazis; the SA, as they called them, or *Sturmabteilung*, a special force whose purpose was to seek out and persecute opponents to the regime, not necessarily Jews, although *all* Jews were taken, since declared anathema by the so-called Nuremberg Laws of 1935. You were classified as a Jew even if so slightly of Jewish blood as to have had one Jewish grandparent. Rifkah herself was only half-Jewish by blood, she claimed, her mother being Christian, but was brought up in true Jewish tradition by her father's parents, her *Bubbeh* and *Zaydeh*, as she called them in her quaint almost childish way. Both spoke English well, Kurt very well and with little accent, Rifkah with a heavy accent and much use of German or Yiddish and the help of Kurt in interpreting. Both had been in German prisons and had lost all known relatives and friends, either through murder, at which the SA were specially adept, or renunciation through fear. For instance, Rifkah's mother, who had been a prominent actress, through fear had betrayed her husband, a theatrical producer, hiding with his parents and daughter. The SA had shot him in front of her and the old people, Rifkah said quite calmly, after threatening to shoot her in front of him to make him give them information. Then they had taken her away. She learnt later that her *Bubbeh* and *Zaydeh* had committed suicide. When asked by Jeremy what had happened to her, she merely shrugged. Appalled, Jeremy asked how old she was then, she answered, with that sweet smile, 'I vos seventeen . . . *shaineh maidele*!'

'What's that mean?' asked Jeremy.

'I vos young Jewish virgin, vaitingk to be marry.'

'How old are you now?'

She shrugged again. 'Vot matter countingk year? Sometimes I feel old voman. But now I feel young and so 'appy . . . because I am free and in loffly country mit loffly pipple. Please not to talk about it now. Ziss ist fest, yes? Sometime I tell you, ven I am old *bubbeh* and sad . . . yes?'

The girl Rifkah, naturally as it were, became one of the strappers in the

Lily Lagoons stable, even though the animal she referred to as a *Ross* was evidently as strange to her as the *Schwartze* of the household, particularly the children, who by their continual peeping and seeking her smiles, appeared to be more delighted in her loveliness than anyone. The *rossen* also took to her, nuzzling her like an old friend. Jeremy remarked that it was a pity they hadn't kept Red Rory, since she might have been able to talk him into winning the Cup. The stable had no likely winner this time, except Golden Bobby for the Blackboys' Race on Saturday. Bobby, in meeting her, was not so well behaved as the others, but perhaps being jealous of the wealth of the colouring of her hair, a deep copper against his mere shining gold, tried to eat it.

It was in meeting Golden Bobby that she met his owner, Prindy, who had deserted the household to become again Shah Jahan, King of the World, all dressed up again, living and working with Barbu Ram. She was delighted enough with him as the little Indian she thought he was to start, but on learning who he truly was, embraced him, crying in that sweet husky voice, '*Kleine menscheleh*!' Prindy seemed no less pleased with her. Indeed, fascinated would be more apt expression, the way, in leaving to go back to his duties in Barbu's Khokha Rusoyee, he walked backwards, staring. Nan breathed to Jeremy, 'Look like he see his mumma.'

She had arrived in a mannish outfit, somewhat outlandish too; a German's idea of a bush-woman, maybe. Nan and Water Lily had put that to rights by getting her something more appropriate from McDodd's and amongst their own effects. She went to the Racecourse wearing white riding moleskins that fitted her trim figure perfectly, elastic sides, a grey silk shirt, a grey wide-awake, a red bandana round her neck. She was tallish, long-legged. Plenty of ringers were similarly outfitted. But there was no confusing her with them. Even the glasses of the silken ladies in the grandstand sought her out when she came up with each rush of the household to watch the races from the public enclosure. Even Lady Rhoda remarked on her beauty, moving General Sir Mark Esk to say rather loudly, probably for the benefit of the meaty white-clad and bespectacled *Herrenvolk* sitting amongst the very elite, that Jewish women were the most beautiful in the world. Shrewd eyes up there doubtless observed how much more interested Her Ladyship became in the Jew Gal, as she dubbed her, when standing beside her ex-husband, he so erect, so elastic of step, for a man of his age, and very evidently much interested in his lovely company. She even said, rather tactlessly in the circumstances (but for all her usual social talent she may not have been well enough aware of these) that they might have used her for the Golden Horseshoe selling, which hadn't been so good this year, left to a somewhat horse-faced young squatteress visiting from the South. Perhaps it was this bit of lack of tact that encouraged her son Clancy, also much interested, by the frequent directing of his binoculars towards the Jew Gal, to join the General when he declared that he must go have a word with Mr Delacy Senior about Red Rory, who was playing up badly.

The Hoffs, as generally they were being called, were together with Jeremy when Esk and Clancy approached them, Kurt having turned up from a round of the scene with the camera he was using to get material for his survey. Much of his time had been taken up by Fay McFee, who wanted to know all about the persecution business, and a little by the Comrades, whom subsequently he appeared to avoid. Jeremy, seeing the approaching pair, murmured, 'Hello, what's this?'

The Hoffs turned, as if still on the alert for danger, Rifkah asking, 'Vos ment?'

Jeremy muttered, 'General Esk and one of my sons.'

'General?' murmured Kurt, staring hard.

Jeremy nodded shortly to the two men as they came up. Already he had renewed acquaintance with the General when the latter had sought him out in the crowd yesterday watching the arrival of that oddity, the military train. Esk said, 'Excuse me, Jeremy, old man . . . but a word of your advice about Red Rory . . . playing up, don't you know?'

Jeremy grinned. 'Yes . . . I saw it this morning. Better have the band playing in his stable, I should say.'

Esk chuckled, eyeing the Hoffs. Jeremy introduced them, contrarily to proper usage, and no doubt deliberately, by presenting Esk, with full titles, *to them.* Not that the procedure appeared to affect the great man himself, who only smiled and extended his hand, saying, '*Shalom*!'

But despite the Hebrew greeting, Kurt was thoroughly Germanic in response, clicking his heels and bowing, murmuring, 'Excellency!'

Rifkah also bowed, answering, '*Shalom*,' and adding other words to it.

Esk said, 'I missed that bit. Afraid my Hebrew's got rather rusty.' He looked at Kurt, asking, 'What did she say, Doctor?'

Kurt shrugged. 'I am afraid also my Hebrew is rusty, Excellency'

When Esk looked again at Rifkah, she smiled, from being stiff-faced at first, saying that she had merely added that she was glad to know him, adding to this, 'How you come spik Hebrew, General?'

Esk explained, then asked, 'Have you been in Palestine?'

'A short time . . passing from Europe.'

'You didn't think of settling there?'

Kurt shrugged in his way. 'Zat is difficult.'

Esk smiled. 'In my official experience there, I found that the difficulty didn't deter so many Jews.'

Again Kurt shrugged. 'Ve are not Zionist.'

'I see. But I guess you'll have no less talent for settlement than your more zealous brethren.'

Rifkah asked, 'Jealous brethren?'

Kurt explained in German. Esk said afterwards, addressing her, 'You might be interested to know that the word Zealous has a Jewish origin.'

'Zat is so?' she asked with interest and looked at Jeremy.

Jeremy looked at Esk, who explained, 'The original Zealots were a Jewish tribe who most bitterly opposed the Roman occupation of Palestine . . . and, in fact, their fellow Jews who surrendered to them. There's much of the Zealot in all Jews. They can be very brave and steadfast people when roused. I'm wondering when they'll make a stand against Hitler.'

Kurt said, 'Ze whole vorld must make ze stand against Hitler.'

The General looked a little vague, 'Yes . . . I expect so.' He smiled when Kurt looked at him rather foxily. 'We have our problems, here, of course . . . the Japanese.' He looked at Jeremy, who was moving to leave the couple.

'Yes, Excellency, of course.'

'I only hope your people can settle quickly and lend their courage and intelligence to defending Australia.'

'You can depend on that, Excellency.'

Esk gave Kurt his hand again. 'I'm very happy to meet you, Doctor . . . and hope to do so again . . . by which time I hope our friend Jeremy, here, may have taught you not to call mere military men Excellency. *Shalom* . . . *Madame*!'

Clancy, all the while hanging in the background, stayed on as the others withdrew.

Out of earshot, Esk said to Jeremy, 'By jove, what a smashing girl that is! Never saw a better looker in my life.'

'Yes, she's handsome, all right,' said Jeremy, 'And as pleasant-natured as she's lovely.'

'If they all come like that, eh? They're making a survey, I understand. Any idea where they might be settling?'

'I've been telling them about the old White Russian settlement down the river. Vaisey could hardly refuse them that, after being so free with it to useless broken-down petty aristocrats.'

'We'll have to see he doesn't . . . a job for our Lydia, what? A test for her sincerity about breakin' with the Mosley Set.'

They came up to the Army stable to see a scatter of khaki-clad figures before the snapping teeth and lashing hoofs of Red Rory. The strappers were evidently all Australians, except one bandy little fellow, wearing military riding breeches and leggings, with a singlet and braces, his exposed skin flaming with sunburn, his face a ruddy ball, while yet he wore only a short-peaked British Army cap, instead of a wide hat like the others. All had their backs turned to the visitors. The little man, almost whimpering, declared to the others, in a strong West Country accent, 'It baint be no 'oss, it baint . . . it be a hoofed devil!'

Awareness of the General caused instant springing to attention. Esk addressed the little man, 'Still having trouble with him, Trooper?'

'Naithin' boot trooble, General . . . naithin' boot.'

'This is Mr Delacey, who owned him and bred him. Perhaps he'll quiet him down for you.'

The trooper whimpered, 'Boot I still got 'o roide him, General!'

'You did well enough before with him, man.'

'It moost be these 'ere flois, I think.'

'Well, start with the flies. I'm told he's a certainty to win the Cup if he behaves. If you let flies beat us for that cup, man, I'll break you . . . I'll have you sent home as a disgrace to the British Armay!' Esk winked slightly at Jeremy.

The Trooper mumbled, 'Yessir, thank you Sir.'

Red Rory whickered at Jeremy and nuzzled him when he went to him.

Having quieted the horse and given a few instructions about how to deal with him in his moods, and with the flies, Jeremy went off with Esk to have a drink at the bar. There was Clancy still talking to Rifkah, who was looking lovelier than ever, laughing, perhaps at Clancy, because he was looking so serious, Esk shook his head. 'Yes, indeed . . . a smasher, a stunner . . . if I were only ten years younger . . . no, twenty, thirty! How old is she, d'you know?'

'From what she's told me she can be barely twenty-one . . . and been through hell. Sometimes you can see it in her face . . . she looks quite old and hurt.'

'Jewish women are like that . . . as if they embody the gaiety and the tragedy that's so much a part of Jewish temperament and life.'

'This girl's certainly seen tragedy. She's scarcely talked about it, doesn't want to . . . what she has, murder, torture . . . her father shot before her eyes, and she a bit of a kid dragged off to God knows what . . . the Hun bastards!' Jeremy was ruddy with feeling.

Glancing at him with searching eyes, Esk asked, 'Speaking of Huns . . . what about our Kruppsers? I understand from my Malters that they're very keen to meet you and make a big deal over your Tantalite . . . but aren't pleased with your association with the *Juden*.'

'The bloody square-headed bastards . . . let 'em come near me!'

Esk chuckled, 'When it happens I must be at hand. Can't say I care much for the Herr Direktor and the Herr Doktor myself. The flying men aren't so bad. And speaking of the Junkers chaps . . . you know, I suppose, that young Ferris will be taking over one of their kites. I intend to use it for my survey of the northeast coast. Mind if I make a base of your place? Everything'll be paid for. I'd also like to bring along Professor St Clair. We've become quite pally. Quite a nice chap. Told him of your work for the Aborigines, the Painted Caves and things. Very much wants to meet you. Will that be all right?'

'Certainly.'

They were passing Barbu's stall, when Prindy, selling Chorry, saw them and waved. Esk stared at the yellow face beneath the turban, muttering, 'By jove . . . I know that face . . . it's not . . .'

Jeremy said, 'Yes . . . it is. He's a great friend of the old Hindu's, and helps him out.'

'Ah . . . the Indian music, eh?' Esk swung over to greet Prindy, to take his hand. The mob, gorging curry as absorbent and incentive for more beer, gaped at the lordly military man with his gold and red tabs, his flat topee, his swagger-stick, shaking hands with what to them was just a yeller-feller. Barbu, dishing the stuff out, also saw, and slipped in behind Prindy to bob and bow. Esk spoke to the old fellow in Hindustani: '*Kesey ho, desi doast.*'

A deep bow from Barbu with the answer, '*Ap kesey ho, Meharban.*'

'*Tum kahan say aiy ho?*'

'*Meha Suba Bombay say aia hoon.*' The crowd was pushing round, amongst them Cahoon, McCusky, Col Collings.

'*Ap kia phrokhat kartey ho?*' asked the General.

Barbu made an excited search of the fly-whisks, selected the best. '*Kia ap chorry tuhfa manjoor kergey?*'

The General smiled. '*Shukria. Agar Ap mera tuhfa manjoor kero.*' He slipped the encased field-glasses he wore from off his shoulder, handed them over, in return for the gift of the chorry.

Barbu's eyes popped as he took the beautiful pigskin in his black claws, saying in a trembling voice, '*Meharban, ma in key sath ap ko taraki kertey dekoon.*'

The General chuckled, '*Shukria. Hum fir kavi miley gey or bateny kerangay . . . khush hoonga Hindustani mey batan kerkey.*'

Barbu bowed low. The General bowed almost as low. They parted. Pushing through the crowd, Esk said to Jeremy, 'The old gentleman paid me a lovely compliment in taking the glasses . . . said "With these I shall watch your noble career for ever".'

Eddy McCusky, overhearing it, remarked, 'Well . . . I never thought old Ali Barba had it in him!'

The General swung on him, saying with a smile, 'There's an old English saying you ought to learn my friend . . . Never judge a sausage by its skin.'

That got a good laugh. Esk waved amiably to the mob, and parted from Jeremy to join Malters and Colonel Chivvy and others evidently troubled by his absence.

When Rifkah returned to the Lily Lagoons stable she had two escorts, Fergus Ferris as well as Clancy. She got rid of them both by telling them she was too busy to talk and actually running from them in amongst the horses. Talking about the young men over afternoon smoke-o, pressed by Nan, she laughingly said that they had both been wanting to take her to the party at Finnucane's tonight, that is to say separately. Catching Jeremy's glance at Nan, she asked why he had looked like that, and he replied, 'If you haven't yet heard about my relations with my sons you soon will. People like to keep you well informed in these parts. The fact of the matter is that I've never known either of them ever to come anywhere near this stable of mine before.'

'So? Zat is bad . . . for fader and sohn.'

Jeremy shrugged. 'You don't know the story, my dear.'

'Tomorrow maybe I know.'

'How's that?'

'Your Clancy haf ask me to come Big House tomorrow morningk . . . to see place, to meet his mutter.'

'Hell!'

'You not like?'

'You please yourself, my dear . . . better if you do go.'

'Zen I vill. I do not gif answer before. But tonight I say Okay. You vill tek me to hotel party tonight . . . you and Nan and all of us?'

'We never go?'

'Vot ist?'

'You'll get to know in time. I'll take you and deliver you there if you like.'

'No . . . I vill go mit zat flyingk young man. He ist funny. Also he ist mix up zose Deutschers . . . I vont to know vot for. Also, to mek Clancy jealous. He ist ver' jealous boy.'

'But he hardly knows you!'

'Perhaps I haf been free mit him because of you. He ist so mooch like you . . . even he spik like you.'

'Hmmm!' It was Nan who glanced significantly at Jeremy this time.

It was easy enough for so lovely a girl to fulfil her plans with men. She was fairly mobbed by men for the rest of that day, among them McCusky with his black eye hidden under dark glasses bought from Barbu, a number of young Australian army officers, ringers, squatters young and old, Dinny Cahoon even. She laughed with them all, and at the last moment told Fergus that he might take her to the party, in front of the glowering Clancy, whom she at once cheered up by saying she'd be glad to see him there too.

Thus it was. She charmed pretty well everybody in the place that night, including Himself, whose old biddy of a wife savaged him about it, and Fay McFee, who savaged all the men. She danced well and sang sweetly. Already Bridie knew a couple of Jewish folk songs taught her down Inland. Now she played them for Rifkah to sing. All the Irish had tears in their eyes after *Raisins and Almonds*, a children's song, which Rifkah told her audience first she'd heard children singing in a packed and stinking railway cattle-waggon. Fay also brought to tears, slapped Fergus's face when he, perhaps bitter over the fact that taking the lady to the party didn't mean anything like having sole possession of her there, remarked in an aside that she was falling for Yiddisher propaganda. Fay tried to pass on the information to Rifkah that she was in the hands of a Nazi agent, when she saw Fergus taking her home, but was rather too far gone in her cups to make herself understood. Not that it mattered much to Rifkah, who also had lined up as escorts, Clancy, Eddy and Dinny. She came home like Cinderella on the stroke of midnight. Not one of her escorts dared take her past the outer circle of bright light that poured from the pulsing portable plant, because in the middle of it, watching, sat that menace of the land, the Scrub Bull. They had to let the adored one go running to him, to see her kiss him on the brow as if he were her father, and sit down to tell him all about it with girlish giggles that surely made fools of them every one. Only one walked with any spring in his step back up the hill – Clancy, with the promise of tomorrow morning.

Cup Day tomorrow.

II

At the Big House, Cup Day always began as early almost, and certainly with as much general activity, as on the most climactic day of its functioning not as a mere social centre but of economic industry, which would be the beginning of what was called the Turn Off (when all that had been done in the way of husbandry throughout the year would virtually be turned into hard cash with despatch of the finished product bawling to the various points at which it would meet its doom). Today everybody was up for early breakfast and promptly to their various posts of social service; except those who had no part in the festival nor any more feeling for it than boredom, like the fat Kruppsers and Lieutenant Denzil Dickey. There were half a dozen in all who lay abed until a bobbing Chinaman came to tell them that 'late blekfus was leddy in blekfus loom.' Their boredom was expressed in their silence, when after formal greetings they sat down to the several dishes offered them; silence that is in the matter of verbal expression, because the *Herrenvolk*, in the manner of their kind, did slop and slobber over their portions, to the evident English distaste of daintily picking Denzil. Otherwise there was no sound but the whine of the electric fan, the faintest clatter from the Chinese waiter, and the hum of voices in last-minute conference coming from those regions where the several committees sat, such as big dining-room, side verandah, the office block. Denzil, perhaps seizing a unique opportunity to show his contempt for non-Englishness or because something had got into him to make him restless, left the table after a mere nibble at a boiled egg and a slice of toast, and betook himself to the deserted drawing-room, there to drop with a sigh before the grand piano, and opening it, strike a gentle note or two, then to drift into Chopin: the *Fantaisie Impromtue*. He played very nicely, and smiled boyishly in delight of his skill, looking out of the big window that gave the best view of the garden and beyond it the paddocks – until a sleek utility truck appeared, running along a road just beyond the homestead fence, when his fingers slowed stopped. Although a goodly distance off, the occupants of the car could be recognized by one sharp-eyed, by reason of its slow going and the fact that its occupants were viewing the homestead, one with brilliant copper hair, the other, the driver, leaning towards the copper, pointing things out: Rifkah the Jew Gal, and Clancy the Bullock Whipping Boor. That seeming to be how Denzil saw them, the way he drew his mouth down at the sight, and the things he murmured as, with disappearance of the car behind trees and sheds, he resumed his playing: 'Naughty, naughty . . . when Lady Mumma told you last night when you asked her . . . 'Don't be ridiculous, boy, you can't bring that gal heah!' Oh, what sharp ears I've got . . . sharp almost as my dear sweet Prendegast . . . sweet, sweet Prendegast . . . so lovely in his Indian clobber . . . oh, dear!' He sighed deeply.

So on with the *Fantaisie Impromptue*, ever so quietly, so as not to disturb the Boors and Boches, who should by rights come running in to hear, to stare, to acclaim it afterwards. No one to hear those sweet sounds so sweetly played. His face plainly told his frustration, and his voice went on to tell more, assuming now a sissy squeaking that was deliberate and expressive of a sissy's anger: 'Old bag, to stop me from having him here! "Reahlly . . . the boy is *no* connection of ours whatsoever . . . and I do *not* have coloured persons in may house, except as servants." Pooh to you, Lydy Wassis, up-jumped butcher's wife!' All the melancholy that can be in the *Fantaisie* fell from the long pink fingers.

Then another change of mood, that made the fingers fly and the chords come crashing, to drown a subdued screaming: 'And you, too, old Esky-mo . . . sack me, sack me! I'll go with him into the wilderness . . . and live on love and music . . . bugger you, Esky-mo, bugger you, bugger you old Brown-and-Malt, bugger you all . . . bugger, bugger, bugger! I'm going to get him and bring him and tell him I love him with Chopin!'

Crash! went the chords. Denzil leapt up, went loping out on long legs through the conservatory on the western side, out across the lawns to big car sheds. He got into a green military car, started up, backed out, swung round, out by the main gate and away towards Beatrice township.

Meanwhile Clancy, having taken Rifkah for a run round the perimeter of the homestead and up along the river a little way to show her the lush pastures used for stud stock, was with frank reluctance showing her through the blacks' camp. 'It isn't pretty sight, I warn you. They're primitive people. Don't blame us. We've done our best to civilize 'em.' He pointed to cement foundations, cracked and fire-blackened, evidently the remnants of burnt-down cottages. He explained that proper Native Lines, as he called them, had been constructed with the new homestead: 'Most of the iron those humpies're made of came off the good cottages, after they'd burnt 'em down . . . .'

'Burn down?' Today Rifkah was clad in a bright Austrian dirndl, with the bandana over her red head and tied under her lovely chin.

'Carelessness and stupidity. They can't sleep without a fire . . . a fire and a dog . . . security, warmth, enemies after your kidney-fat, devils prowling. You can't sleep with a dog on concrete. You've got to dig into the dirt with him. Then there's relationship. You can't live with this one or that one, can't eat with 'em, can't even look at 'em. So you see what you're up against trying to house 'em properly. They sort it out themselves. You've got to let 'em . . . and there you've got *their* idea of housing. You mustn't forget you're dealing with primitive people. Better if you don't look too close . . . it'll only disgust you.'

Rifkah was already obviously disgusted, the way her beautiful nose was wrinkling; but doggedly she carried on with the inspection. It would be worse even than usual, because the younger ones were away, preoccupied with the Races. Here were only the very old and the very young, lying in dust and ashes or on sacks and rags of blankets. Even the dogs were either old or crawling puppies. Bones lay about, encrusted with flies. Meat-ants ran in armies. Rifkah made no comment, except to say to one tot who had gone crawling in haste to the safety of the skeleton arms of a crone squatting in the ashes of a fireplace, 'Ach, dirty schnozzel . . . let me clean!' Long candles of snot were hanging from the baby's nostrils. Rifkah took out her handkerchief, reached for the child, which whimpered and ducked its matted gingerish head under the old woman's arm, who cackled with amusement, although keeping the child in hiding. An old brown and white mongrel showed a few teeth, growling deeply.

Clancy growled at the dog, 'Siddown, you mongrel!'

The old woman flung a stick at the dog, then held up the skinny hand to Clancy, quavering, 'Tobacco, Boss . . . lil bits.' Clancy drew his gold cigarette case, fished out a couple of cigarettes, flung them. The old woman skilfully caught them, promptly put one right into her mouth and began to chew on it. Rifkah looked appalled, then startled as other dogs looked out of dark little hovels snarling.

Clancy said, 'Have to have a dog shoot. Getting too many old uns and pups.'

'Shoot?' she asked.

'They never kill a dog. Part of the family. They get that many they start eating each other. Got to take the gun to 'em every now and again.' He seemed to take that as an example of how things were generally, adding: 'Come on away and I'll show you something nicer . . . the bulls.'

She looked at him in surprise. 'Bools?'

He reddened, smiling. 'Well, they're pretty to us. Most important thing on a station, of course, the bulls. The Bull's King, as they say. We've got some real royalty here . . . and not overseas stuff, either. These were bred from stock my father pioneered.' As he drove her away, to a special place of low shelter sheds and sprinkler-misty lucerne pastures, he told her how Jeremy had been the first man in the land to experiment with cross-breeding of the British types of cattle of the first settlers, which had suffered so badly under the harsh local conditions, with Asiatic. 'We breed all Vaisey bulls here,' he said. 'Look at those beauties . . . yearlings. Can't see much of the Zebu in them now.' He chuckled, adding: 'But old-time stockmen do . . . still regard 'em as a kind of buffalo . . . ha, ha! Father's first trouble was getting people to accept 'em merely on appearance, no matter superiority of stamina and weight. People don't like strange-looking things, do they . . . '

She looked at him. 'You are proud of your fader, yes?'

'For this . . . oh, yes! He's made a great contribution to cattle breeding. I understand what he's done's even been taken up in America.' He laughed again: 'Next thing the Yanks'll be claiming the beasts as theirs, and trying to sell 'em to us.'

'Only for zis you are proud?'

He looked at her, then away towards the homestead, frowning slightly. 'Well . . . my father's a difficult man. He's made things difficult for us.' Then he swung to her again, smiling, and said, 'But come on . . . I want to show you everything . . . then take you over the Big House to smoke-o . . . morning-tea, you know . . . and then you'll meet the Mater. Then we'll have to be getting to the Course.'

At the Big House, Denzil was sneaking Prindy in, coming from that direction where earlier he had seen Clancy and Rifkah pass, having left the military car out there. Prindy was dressed as King of the World. Denzil was leading him by the hand. Seeing the way Prindy looked about, he asked, 'Haven't you ever been here before?' When Prindy shook his turbaned head he added: 'But you know that the lady of the house was your grandfather's first wife, don't you?'

Prindy just stared. Denzil said, 'That enigmatic grey stare! Fancy calling you coloured . . . the old snob! Your grandmother's coloured, of course. Where is she?'

'Don't know,' said Prindy.

'You always say Don't Know about your family. That means Mind Your Own Business, I suppose. All right, I will. But it doesn't worry me . . . about colour, you know. You are more beautiful than any white boy I ever knew. Do you know you're beautiful?'

Prindy nodded. Denzil made a gurgling sound and slipped an arm about him and hugged him, and holding him thus, led him into the drawing-room. As Prindy looked about in surprise, the room being so different from what he'd previously seen, Denzil said, 'Not bad, is it? Must have been Sir Watsiss, the husband, who did it. He's English . . . very pukka . . . still, he's a bloomin' butcher to me . . . they're all butchers . . . even old Vaisey. Wonder they don't have His Lordship's picture hangin' on the wall instead of the King's, eh? Wearin' bull's horns instead of a crown . . . Eeeeeee! But come on . . . we're here to worship the god Chopin . . . I'm going to initiate you into Chopinism.' He swept Prindy along to the piano, and as he sat down, and drew the boy alongside him, drew him to him, whispering somewhat hoarsely, 'Initiate you . . . my dear!'

Denzil turned swiftly to the piano, began to play, this time the *Prelude in A*. He swung to Prindy after a while, noting his rapture, smiled, 'You love it, eh? I knew you would. Better than those bloomin' pipes you play.'

Prindy's eyes dropped before the ardent blue stare. Denzil turned back to his playing, softly, softly, and ever so sweetly, bending, caressing the keyboard, it seemed. When he looked again at Prindy he said, 'I'm going to sophisticate you. Do you know what Sophisticate means?'

The turbaned head shook. 'You soon will.' The long fingers sprang from the keys, to reach for the small golden-brown face, seize it, squeazing it so that the full rose-brown lips protruded. With his own lips protruding, Denzil bent to kiss, murmuring, 'Oooo!' but seeing alarm in the grey eyes, stopped, said huskily, 'No . . . I'll seduce you with Chopin first.' He turned back to the piano, 'Listen . . . listen with all your might.' He began with *Fantaisie Impromtue* again. Prindy was clearly fascinated. Denzil swaying to the tempo, softly crooning, turned again and again, smiling, eyes shining. He murmured, 'He hears . . . he hears at last something sweeter than the Indian Pied Piper . . . he hears the sweetest of all sounds, singing strings!' As he stopped with the end of the piece, he turned quickly and kissed Prindy fairly on the lips. Prindy stared, startled. Denzil laughed at him, chucked him under the chin, turned back to the piano, began a *Polonaise*.

The music completely changed his mood. His face contorted, blue eyes blazed. Both soldier and artist rampant now. On and on and on it went in its magnificence, seeming to make the very air a solidity of chorded sound. It ended with thunder like the voice of an angry god – Tchamala! He did not turn smiling now, but glaring, panting, to meet the unwinking grey stare. Then he leapt from the stool, fell on his knees, crying hoarsely, 'My darling, my darling . . . I have won you!' He seized Prindy, kissing him wildly.

Prindy woke, struggled, got free, only to be snatched back by a long reaching hand, dragged to a mouth croaking, 'Don't deny me, my darling . . . I love you, love you!' A bony hand began to drag at the jodhpurs.

Prindy yelled, 'Le' me go . . . what you do!' He slipped free again, ran for the door, dodged as Denzil leapt long-legged after him – CRASH! A table with a vase of flowers went flying. Denzil got him, bore him to the floor, while Prindy yelled and fought.

Someone else was there – elastic-side boots and fawn trousers, a male voice grating, 'Hey . . . what's goin' on here?'

Prindy found himself free, looking up at Clancy, who had Denzil by the scruff of the neck. Denzil hacked at his skins. Clancy smacked him across the mouth, sending him reeling, yelling after him, 'You dirty bloody bastard . . . what're you doing to that kid?'

Denzil, reeling, goggling, bloody spittle running from his mouth, panted, 'Just . . . a game . . . . '

'Game me fat aunt! I guessed you were one of them.' Clancy turned to Prindy, to find him slipping into the conservatory, at the moment looking back, then looking towards where the conservatory opened onto the verandah at the other end. Then he cried, 'Hey . . . wait a minute!

Prindy was out, heading for that door. But it opened, to reveal a stately grey-haired lady. Prindy turned back, to head for the further door, ran into Clancy's arms. Clancy pulled his arm behind him when he would have slipped away, stared down into the grey eyes.

Lady Rhoda came up, demanded, 'What's all this?'

Clancy swung the boy towards her. 'Look!'

'Who is it . . . an Indian boy . . . what's he doing here?'

Clancy said it sharply, spitefully, 'No . . . Martin's kid!'

Rhoda stared at the staring grey eyes, her own face greying. After a moment she asked hoarsely, 'How did he get here?'

Clancy, still with the small arm locked, turned towards the drawing-room door. Denzil was coming out, smiling with bloody lips. He answered Rhoda, 'I brought him.'

Her eyes grew wide. 'You?'

'I told you I wanted him to hear me play . . . he's my pupil.'

'How dah you!'

Denzil mocked her: 'Yes . . . how dah I disobey your royal command!'

Clancy grated, 'Don't you talk to my mother like that, you . . . you . . . . '

'What, stockman?'

Clancy in his anger pulled on Prindy's arm. Prindy kicked him hard, twisted to get out of the grip, went down to his knees in it. Clancy snarled at him, 'No you don't. You stop here and tell me whether you were a consenting party or not . . . oh!'

There was Rifkah rushing from the outer door, crying, 'Let him go zat little boy . . . vot you doingk to him?'

Clancy let the boy go. Rifkah grabbed him. Rhoda blazed at her. 'What are *you* doing here in my house?'

Rifkah, wide-eyed, pale, sweat on her lovely lip and brow, looked at her, then at Clancy, who had gone red and blinking. Clancy looked at his mother, cleared his throat. But Rifkah answered for him, to both mother and son by her darting fiery glance: '*Schtikfleish mit augen*!' Pulling Prindy after her, she went rushing off outside

Denzil laughed shrilly. Clancy, all confusion, swung on him, snapping, 'What're laughing at?'

'Eeeeaah, dear boy . . . at what she said . . . I understood it . . . eeeeaah!'

'What's she say?'

Rhoda snapped, 'We don't want to know!'

'I should think not,' said Denzil with a giggle. 'She called you chunks of meat with eyes . . . eeeeee! Good name for butchers, what?'

'You Pommy bastard!' hissed Clancy.

'Clancy!' snapped his mother.

'Veneer comes off these colonial aristos all too easily, doesn't it, Your Ladyship?'

'Will you kindly leave my house young man?'

'I'll leave with pleasure, Ma'am . . . but only after striking a little bargain.'

'What d'you mean?' demanded Clancy.

'Well, you see, I overheard . . . Martin's kid. Awful secret, or I'd've heard it before. You say nothing about myself and the boy . . . I don't tell the world about him and Martin, eh what?'

'You . . . . '

'Clancy!'

Clancy flung away towards that outer door. His mother leapt after him. 'Where're you going?'

'I'm going to take that girl back to Beatrice . . . . '

'No you're not . . . after what she called us!'

'I can't let her walk all that way.'

'Don't worry,' said Denzil silkily. 'I'll pick her up . . . and the boy. So long. Give my regards to the Boss Butcher, won't you, now . . . aaaaaeeee!' Denzil set his long legs into swift motion as Clancy turned on him.

Denzil, now with his baggage in the green car, caught Rifkah and Prindy up about halfday to the township. As they got in beside him, he asked Rifkah, 'Did you hear me playing Chopin?'

She answered shortly, 'No.'

'Pitay . . . I play it rather well, you know. Loveliest of all music, I think . . . with all due respect to the masters of your persuasion, of course. I'd like our young friend to come to think of Chopin like that, too. Are you musical, *Madame*?'

'I do not play, if zat vot you mean?'

'I'm told you have a sweet voice. Pity we can't get hold of a good piano, somewhere where the owners aren't stuffy cow-punchers. I'd like to hear you. Our young friend here is so full of music, he even sings in his sleep, don't you know? He's got great musical talent. But it's all primitive wood-wind as yet. I'd like to see him . . . hear him . . . converted to strings.'

Prindy was silent. Then Denzil fell silent, chewing his lips and looking troubled. He took them to the Lily Lagoons camp, to find it deserted, then took them on over to the Racecourse, set them down, staying only long enough to whisper to Prindy, 'Forgive me, Prendegast. It was the music. It won't happen again. Please don't tell. Please don't cut me . . . please!'

The grey eyes regarded him calmly as ever. Denzil made a movement to touch him. Prindy dodged, went running away into the gathering crowd to Barbu's Rusoyee Khokha.

The Lagoons people were sitting down to smoke-o. Jeremy asked Rifkah how things had gone at the Big House. In answer she shrugged, said with finality, 'Now mooch better I understand Delacy.'

'Hmm!'

Clancy was not amongst those gentlemen and others who again closed in on the Jew Girl whenever she appeared. She wasn't as merry as yesterday, but amusing enough, meeting their jests with that engaging accent of hers, itself a kind of merry jest when she demanded translations of their bushwhacker's vernacular – and even more beautiful for not being a ringer today. An addition to the admirers was Pat Hannaford, making his first public appearance since literally being knocked out of things by that first shot in the outbreak of class-warfare the other night, able to get a hat on at last and suffer the light of day. As an avowed enemy of the forces of which she was a victim he was inclined to take possession of her, had to be teased to stop talking politics, even gently threatened. Hearing that she had promised Fergus to take a flight with him tomorrow morning, he asked her to come with him for a run on his engine, from which she'd see far more, wild birds and animals even. She accepted, but on condition that there were to be no politics then or now. But in his zeal, getting her alone for a moment, he told her there was going to be demonstration of protest at the Cup Ball that night, in favour of her and Kurt and their fellow victims of Nazism, against those representative of the filthy thing who would be accessible to him and his comrades for the first time. The Party boys had tried demonstrating several times before the *Herrenvolk* up in the grandstand, but with little effect, since the mob they wanted to impress with the idea that the Devil was on their very doorstep were interested only either in the races while they were on or in beer-swilling or curry and dim-sim gorging in between; and Superintendent Bullco, rubbing shoulders with what looked rather like his kind, had his khaki boys on the alert to deal with anything unseemly. But tonight at the Ball, while the mob were crowded outside, and the Bosses and the Fascist Beasts packed inside, all you had to do was take a stand in the doorway and, as Pat put it, 'give 'em your true guts'; and there was this girl who should welcome the opportunity to leap in and spit in the faces of the bastards, crying out in protest of her own, 'No, no, no . . . ve vont no trouble, pliss!'

Rifkah told Kurt about the plan for tonight. That was evident, because Kurt told Jeremy when they gathered for lunch and asked him could he do something to stop it. Jeremy said that he rather liked the idea, although he didn't like those who were planning it; but since Kurt was obviously worried about it, saying that his people didn't want to start off with the prejudice that taking sides in politics would cause, he promised to tip off the General, who could be relied upon to warn the Kruppsers; and if they were arrogant enough to show up, then good luck to those who were after 'em.

Then there again was the bell calling the horses for the Cup. There was no excitement in the Lily Lagoons stable this year, because their entrant, a colt named Black Cloud, was merely a tryer, running chiefly to prove his stamina as a station sire, his only chance of winning by fluke, which was something the stable didn't care for.

Jeremy led the horse away as usual, with Darcy in silks, the difference this time the company: Rifkah, quite excited, and Kurt with his camera. All other owners were leading their horses, except General Esk, who had two soldiers at the head of his, because Red Rory was playing up so badly. Esk shook his head when Jeremy waved to him. Jeremy called, 'It's only at the Post you'll know what he's going to do, Mark. Don't give up yet. That fight's what he'll win with . . . if he wants to.'

They were in Saddling Paddock. Trooper Jorkins, Esk's jockey, went sweating, miserable-looking, bandy-legged, to the weighing-in. While waiting, Esk came over to Jeremy, who then quietly told him about the plans of the Communists for the night. Esk also said he'd like to see the Kruppsers humiliated, but agreed that it would do the Jews no good, therefore he would pass the tip on, through Old Malters. 'Don't speak to 'em myself, old man . . . just a stiff bow. I don't like the way they eat for a start. Slaves to prejudice, aren't we!'

Kurt and Rifkah were in demand at the moment by other owners, wanting Kurt to photograph them with their horses and Rifkah.

Trooper Jorkins came back with his riding gear, stared at by Red Rory surely with malice aforethought. While the other soldiers held the beast's tossing head, Jorkins flung on the saddle. He was stooped to grab the dangling girth, when Rory swung neatly round on his forelegs and let him have both his hind iron hoofs fair in the behind. Jorkins let out a yell, went sprawling face down in the gravel. Rory looked at him with a horse's grin, while most of those around laughed heartily, poor Jorkins' unhappy Pommy inadequacy being a general joke among the racing crowd. The laughter was all the louder for the wretched man's floundering about, trying to rise, now howling, 'Ow . . . ow . . . he's bruk me laig . . . he's crippled me . . . I knew the divil would . . . oh, ow . . . I should'a' desarted . . . ow!'

The only one alert to the seriousness of it was Kurt, who leapt to the stricken man's aid, knelt over him, felt him, looked up, crying, 'He is bad hurt . . . you got first aid? Zen kvik . . . splint and stretcher . . . splint, splint, splint . . . kvik!' Forcibly he kept Jorkins from moving. Jeremy went to his aid.

But instead of stretcher and splints came Dr Fox, striding, looking very much the Government Medical Officer, in bright white linen and white topee, but black-browed. 'What's going on here?'

Kurt looked up at him in evident surprise. 'Oh, Doctor!' Then he said, 'Bad femoral fracture . . . joost short of pelvic joint.'

Fox rasped, 'Take your hands off that man!'

Kurt looked helpless for a moment, then said urgently, 'I am compressing ze break. If I let go and he move, it vill compound.'

Fox roared, 'I said take your hands off that man!' His face was flaming with anger.

Kurt's face turned grey. A look like agony was in his large black eyes. He licked his thickish lips, said, 'No, Doctor . . . not till he is splinted. Pliss get splint.'

Fox was snarling now, 'I'm the one who gives the orders here . . . and if you don't do as I order now, you'll take the consequences.'

Kurt said hoarsely, 'I am doctor, too . . . and only consequences I care about is for zis man's leg.' He looked away from Fox to the others crowded round, to shout, 'Vere is splint?'

There were the splints, in the hands of Jeremy. It was to Jeremy whom Kurt addressed himself now: 'I want you slip splint under my hand, and tie.' He looked elsewhere. 'Somevun take him by shoulders. Jeremy . . . get your knees below his knees so he cannot move as you push . . . .'

'Here,' said Fox shortly. 'Give me the splints, Jerry . . . I'll help him.'

Both doctors worked swiftly and in silence. In a few minutes the moaning muttering Jorkins was splinted perfectly. Kurt and Fox and Jeremy and the man at the shoulders placed him gently on the waiting stretcher. Kurt looked at the still glowering Fox, and rising, dusting his knees, said, 'Thank you, Doctor,' and turned and pushed through the crowd.

Fox muttered, 'Take him into the scales-shed . . . I'll give him something for the pain.' He also rose, with immaculate knees all soiled. He looked at Esk. 'You've got first-aid men to look after him, General?' When Esk nodded, Fox added: 'I leave him with you, then. I'll keep an eye on him. Run him up to hospital in the plane tomorrow.'

For the moment the Cup Race had been forgotten. Even the President had come to see this strange affair. Now it was over – well, jockeys often come to grief. Another rider for Red Rory. Charlie Bishoff was calling through his megaphone, asking for a rider for Red Rory, weight about one hundred and forty pounds. There he was in a moment, asking the General for the job: Fergus Ferris. 'You?' demanded Esk.

Fergus showed the split lip in a grin. 'Started life as a jockey. Went on to the Winged Horse.'

'By jove!'

'You must know that the Royal Flying Corps was recruited from cavalry officers.'

'You're right man. The job's yours. Can you get silks?'

'I'll look after him,' said Jeremy. 'But it's going to depend on Rory, too.'

But already Fergus was making friends with Rory, who was sniffing him with evident interest. Fergus said with a wink for everybody. 'Horses know talent when they smell it.' There was some snickering. But he silenced it by putting an arm round Rifkah, saying, 'You can smell talent, too, can't you, sweetheart, with that lovely Yiddisher nose?'

'Yes . . . you go and vin!'

'There!' he said, grinning round the crowd. 'Now I've got the luck of the Jews with me too.' He set off for the scales-shed.

Red Rory certainly played up in the Parade and going to the barrier, but how much through his own and his rider's urge to show off compared with the perfidy of his nature could only be guessed at. Jeremy evidently thought it was more the former, since he said to Kurt and Rifkah, 'I'd back him if I were you . . . while the odds are long. It looks as if all he needed to put him in the mood for racing is to maim some human being.'

The Favourite was another roan colt, Blue Pigeon, belonging to one of the Eastern Downs Pastoral Company's stations, but smaller than Red Rory. The money was all on him.

Charlie Bishop had them all lined up: *They're Off*!

Rory was with them. The old familiar scene. The sudden surge of colour of hides and silks, the sense of the force of it in muscle and bone. The thunder. The enveloping dust. The old familiar scene that never lost its excitement. The thunder rolling with the dust-storm. Emergence of the flashing force that trailed the storm. Its coming up the Straight to complete the first easy mile – with the Favourite and Red Rory out in front and pacing it together, great loping strides to their mighty bellows-breathing. The crowd yelling for both horses. Rory's odds going down, the Pigeon's up: '*Red Rory, Blue Pigeon – Come on you beauts*!' Past in a flash. Then the trailing field, with Black Cloud leading, but never a hope of catching those two lightning flashes running neck and neck, eye and eye, white of eye to white of eye in trial of strength that only a horse can know.

Into the dust, and out of it – into the mirage – to come wobbling like a rushing dream-thing out of it, and into the Straight now for the mighty effort – '*Blue Pigeon, Red Rory – Rory, Rory, Pigeon, Pigeon*!'

But Red Rory had it, was only playing with the Pigeon, as Jeremy shouted – he and his smirking jockey playing a game – just shot ahead when the crowd was in ecstasy of suspense – and won by a length and a flowing ginger tail. '*Red Rory, Red Rory – what a horse – Fergus Ferris – what a horseman*!'

As people were saying during all the business going on out before the grandstand, the congratulating of owner and rider, the kiss that both got from the lovely Jew Girl, the genteel applause from the stand: 'He flew the horse in!'

There were two not so complimentary, Pat Hannaford and Eddy Mc Cusky. Eddy said to Pat, 'Lairy bastard, isn't he!'

'You can say that again, mate.' Then, after seeing Rifkah lift that lovely rose-mouth to meet the half-hidden bunny lip reaching down to her, Pat added: 'Y'ad a bit of a go with him the other night, they tell me. Why'n't you finish him off tonight? I got a feelin' there'll be more trouble tonight at the Ball. Pick the bastard again, and do him properly. He's only piss and wind. I'd do the shit meself . . . only he's a bit small for me.'

'Yeah,' murmured Eddy. 'Might, too.'

Well, there it was, the old Cup Ball again; and again in the new style beginning with the marching of the military band, this time playing *Waltzing Matilda*, and the common herd following. And as always the Elite came from the Big House in their big cars, done up like sore toes, to strut and mince their elegant way in to their special places while the mob merely gawped through the doors and open louvers; but tonight to be sniggered at for what they were, the Master Class who can Kiss Me Arse, by the elite of the proletariat. What a crowd of the stuck up bastards, too – Generals and Colonels and Professors and Doctors and Majors and all kinds of Upper Crust Shit! But where were the representatives of the Master Race, the Krauts, the Kruppsers, the Nazi Bastards? They weren't coming; that's for sure, because proceedings are starting, the President's spruikin'. They must'a' been tipped off. Somebody with a big mouth that'd have to have it stopped. The bloody bastards . . . but we're set for strife; and strife there's going to be. If it ain't goin' to be war on the enemies of the Workers' Fatherland, then make it a Class War!

Proceedings went as usual to the drawing of the Golden Horseshoe Prizes. The little black mare, Dusky Lassie, donated by Vaiseys, was won by Lieutenant Denzil Dickey, not present. The first shot in the Class War was fired then, when Jordie Jenks yelled, 'Bet it was rigged!' President, Lady President, Patron Professor, General, all looked in surprise towards the hidden accuser, and then when only jostling and muttering followed, looked scornful and withdrew their gaze to the business in hand.

Formality finished with, the Committee gave over to the military band, which struck up *Roll Out the Barrel*. Pat Hannaford, the one MC tonight, called, 'Select your partners for a foxtrot.'

There was a concerted move of young men towards the Jew Girl, just brought in by Jeremy Delacy and for the moment exchanging a smiling word with General Sir Mark Esk and Professor St Clair. Fergus Ferris was the only one bold enough to shove in and ask her to dance. His boldness may have been anticipated by those with ulterior motives. Anyway, it fitted nicely into the organization. Pat Hannaford, watching him all the while, allowed him two circuits of the hall, doing his stuff at full throttle with his partner, then right at the big front doorway, into which the usual mob of simpletons was packed, slipped up and tapped him on the shoulder, grinning widely at Fergus's surprise.

'Hey, what's this?' demanded Fergus.

'Bloke wants to see you outside . . . I'll take care of the lady.' Pat pushed in between them.

'What bloke?' asked Fergus.

'Go and see.' Pat gave a shove that sent him into the crowd. There must have been hands ready for Fergus. He vanished.

'Come on, dance,' said Pat.

But Rifkah baulked. 'Vot ist?'

'You don't want to dance with that cow. He's mixed up with them Huns.' He tried to force her into dancing.

She resisted him. 'Don't be *meshugeh*!'

'What's that mean?'

'Silly.'

'It's you't's bein' silly, gettin' mixed up with a type like that. He's a Fascist . . . belongs to a Fascist movement.'

There was a sudden movement of the crowd in the doorway – outward. Shouting out there now. Then the cry went up: 'A fight!'

Those inside, at least the vulgar, who heard it above the band, stopped dancing. A movement from there. Rifkah started to join it. Pat snatched her back. 'Don't go out there . . . there's trouble.'

She swung on him. 'Zat trouble you mek?'

'These bastards'a' got 'o be shown where they get off . . . .'

She jerked away from him, joined the rush that had now started with the stopping of the band. Uproar outside now, men shouting and women screaming, the crowd like a mob of goats milling about a billy-fight, dust rising in the moonlight. Policemen's hats bobbing amongst the mostly bare heads. Lanky Cahoon towering above the lot, his long arm swinging in rabbit-punching. Then someone insignificant in size came at Dinny from the side, hit him under the ear. He went down. The someone jumped on him, then several on the someone, with yells of Commo Bastards and Fascist Shit and much of the usual obscenity that seems the basic expression of the Australian mind. Other police were going down. Superintendent Bullco, in the doorway, was shouting, 'Colonel Chivvy . . . get your lads to help my men!'

Chivvy bawled, 'Major Martin . . . muster troops!'

Then the voice of General Esk was raised, in a tone never heard round these parts, cutting-sharp with power of personality and authority: 'Countermand that order, Colonel!'

The Colonel swung on him, gaping. The General added: 'This is a civil disturbance. Get your men out of the way.'

'But . . . but, Sir, we've always helped the police in trouble . . . .'

'I don't care what you've always done. It isn't a convict settlement any more. Countermand that order, man . . . or I'll do it for you, and relieve you of your command.'

'Sah!' Major . . . all military personnel back to quarters.'

'Sah! Sergeant-Major!'

'Sah!'

Bullco, his face twisted as with pain, gasped, 'General . . . my men are being bested. This's a riot . . . a Communist plot!'

'That's your business, Superintendent. Troops can't legally be used for other than military purposes without declaration of Martial Law.'

'Who'll declare it?'

'Not I, sir.' Esk marched off after his retreating marching men. Bullco, seeing his own men in full flight, slipped out, and with somewhat more dignity, for which he was better equipped, since not in uniform, followed them. The Master Class also slipped out discreetly, got into their cars, started up.

The mob were still fighting among themselves, but with no such zest for it; and soon it was over, save for exchange of insults. A score or more were on the ground, being attended by mates or comrades, amongst them Fergus, with a squashed mouth and the makings of a second black eye, and Eddy McCusky who was moaning that his jaw and several ribs were broken, and Kurt, silent but for his gasping, obviously in great pain from having been kicked in the abdomen. Rifkah, going to Kurt's aid, cried hoarsely, 'Ven I come I zink vot kindly happy pipples you are!' She wept over the panting Kurt. Jeremy came to her aid, raised the little man in his arms, carried him down to the camp.

The police were coming back, with batons and revolvers. The bravos scattered.

It was the end of the Ball. No use hanging about the place with no band and armed policemen watching every move. The crowd drifted away. A few got into Finnucane's by identifying themselves with shouting, because old Shame-on-us had locked himself and his family in. The others went back to their camps. The bravos gathered again to slang each other across the river: Trouble-making Commo Bastards – Scabs, Bosses' Men, Fascist Shit – and to sing the songs that stirred them, *The Red Flag, The Internationale, Solidarity for Ever, Rule Britannia, Australia Will Be There, The Road to Gundagai.*

Fights were common enough during the festival, with even general brawling on occasions. But there was something different about this, all those agreed who talked it over, something sinister, something suggesting that things would never be the same again. Some blamed the Communists, others the fools who had brought those Kruppsers here to cause provocation, a few those Jews for being here. None thought to lay the blame on Adolf Hitler or Josef Stalin or both. One thing there was general agreement on was the suggestion that the festival was as good as finished. Who wanted another day and night of it with this alien hatred amongst them?

When the factions got tired of their slanging match, things went peaceably enough, even when boozing resumed with Finnucane's opening his doors again. But that the end of the show was at hand and declared by an alien force, was announced by soldiers coming for a last drink, to say that they were under orders from the General to entrain next day at dawn.

Next day, just before the military train left, Esk came down to the Lily Lagoons camp to take leave of Jeremy and the others, to say that he hoped to see them again soon out at their place, to deliver a message from Denzil to Prindy asking him to take charge of his prize pony for him, and to ask Jeremy to look after Red Rory, then to ask Kurt and Rifkah what their plans were. Jeremy answered for the Jews by saying that they were coming out to stay with him, while negotiations were made with Vaiseys and the Government in the hope that the old Russian Settlement might be granted them for their own mooted settlement. Kurt was in such pain at the time that he could not talk at all. Esk said they should call Dr Fox. But Kurt wouldn't hear of it.

As the military train pulled out of the siding, with Jack Tinball cock-adoodling to the white campers on the up river side of the crossing, Sir Mark, with his aides, was standing out on the rear platform of the only passenger car on the train, waving to those down stream. The rest of the train was made up of stock waggons converted for the purpose, which as the General himself had said, was not simply to bring troops on an excursion but to prepare them for movement in emergency.

A short while after the departure of the military train another locomotive was heard puffing up towards the bridge. It halted where the road running up from the causeway crossed the tracks. Pat Hannaford was seen to alight, to come striding down, to come heading for the Lily Lagoons camp. He hadn't come to apologize, but to take Rifkah for that run on his engine promised yesterday. When Rifkah abused him for making the trouble last night, he snapped back at her that she was really the cause of it, since it must have been she who betrayed his confidence about the protest intended by his Comrades. 'We were after them Krupp bastards, that's all.' he said. 'If you hadn't given the game away, only them'd'a' got rough-'oused.'

'Vot are you talkingk about . . . game and rough house?' she demanded. 'Trouble ist not game for Jews!'

Pat sighed. 'Aw . . . you don't understand the English language . . . forget it. Now, how about this ride? The mob's goin' back today. I'll be pullin' out at ten.'

'No!' she cried. '*Na . . . nein, nyet, non* . . . any language you like . . . but *No*! Look at poor Kurt . . . from your doingk!'

Taking a look at Kurt, grey faced and sweating in his tent, Pat did apologize and declared that he was going to get the doctor, whatever they said. He left them at a trot.

Dr Fox was there within fifteen minutes. Grim faced he leapt out of the station utility, doctor's bag in hand, came striding up to Jeremy sitting with Rifkah and Nan, grating, 'I understand I've been called to attend to that Jew.'

Jeremy answered shortly, 'We didn't call you, Fox. He evidently needs medical attention badly . . . but he wouldn't have you called.'

'Then why have I been called?'

'It's your job to find out . . . and don't act like a pig.'

Fox glared, then grunted, 'Where is he?'

Jeremy rose and led him to the tent. Fox eyed the stricken little man with distaste, snapping, 'Well . . . what's wrong with you . . . you're supposed to be a doctor?'

Kurt gasped, 'Mein bladder, doctor . . . I haf stricture . . . pliss pass sound on me.'

Still snapping, Fox said, 'Syphilis or something, eh? Well, give's a look at you.'

Kurt was in pyjamas. Fox bent and slipped the bow of the cord, flung the flaps back to expose the loins, stared – stared – stared – whispered, 'Christ!'

Where Kurt's genitals should have been was only rawish flesh with little tufts of pubic hair – no new injury this. The new was a greenish bruise on the swollen belly above.

Fox swallowed, muttered, 'Who did that to you?'

'I did myself,' gasped Kurt, and when Fox's eyes widened, added: 'Nazis crush my genitals. I haf to cut off everyzing to stop gangrene.' He gave a wobbly smile: 'Not sooch goot surgery, I am afraid . . . but I haf only tobacco tin for job . . . and I am ver' sick zen . . . in ze dead-house mit ze dead . . . zey zink I am dead, too.'

Fox muttered, 'The bastards . . . I wouldn't've believed it!'

'Ze bladder sphincter ist veak. I haf to be careful of stricture. I get kick last night . . . you see. You vill pass sound on me?'

Fox tore open his bag, looked at Jeremy. 'I'll want a bowl and a bucket and towels and things.' Getting out his instruments, he asked Kurt, 'Do they do a lot of this sort of thing?'

'If zey don't murder uz zey sterilize uz.'

'The girl?'

'She is sterilize.'

Fox said it with half a sob, 'Jesus Christ!'

Jeremy, coming in, remarked dryly, 'Hardly a name to use before a man maimed like that by Christians, is it?'

Fox, fishing out the curving silver instruments, muttered, 'I'm sorry.'

'Zey are not Christian,' said Kurt. 'Zey have renounce Christianity because Jesus was Jew.'

'The mad bastards!' muttered the doctor. 'But bastards, bastards, bastards!

When it was over and Fox learnt what Kurt was going to do, he said he placed him in the hands of Jeremy, adding: 'But call on me if you want me. I'll be along like a shot . . . and, er . . . if you need any help medically, I mean when you've established your settlement . . . I presume you'll be the doctor there . . . I'll be glad to assist . . . with equipment and drugs and things, will have a word with the CMO. Well . . . I must be off. Flying that fracture of yours . . . the Pommy jockey . . . to Town. Couldn't let him make the long journey by train.' He held out his hand to Kurt.

Taking the hand, Kurt said, '*Danke*, Doctor Fox . . . goodbye.'

'Goodbye . . . Doctor Hoff.'

About half an hour later, Fox flew over the camp, dipped a wing. Kurt was out now, waving. Jeremy said to him, 'I wonder did he have anything to say to the Huns when he got back? If I know Foxy when he's got his Irish up, he did.'

They had scarcely sat down again under the striped awning, when another utility appeared on the road, running down to them. As it neared, Jeremy said, 'Speak of the devil!' Behind the windscreen could be seen the two round bespectacled faces of the Kruppsers.

The car halted at the causeway, the two occupants staring about. No one had seen them anywhere but at the Racecourse so far. The car moved again, swung in towards the camp. Again it halted. The driver called, 'Vere is Mr Delacy?' It was a strangely coloured face, pink yet pallid. Both men were youngish; in their thirties. Jeremy signed without rising. The driver opened his door and alighted, came loping. Quite a big heavy man, nicely dressed in some light material, wearing a panama hat. The other was following. The first man halted just short of the waiting sitting group, with glasses glinting to the quick movements of his staring from one to another. He removed his hat, bowed to Jeremy, saying, 'Ve are representative of Krupp. You are Mr Delacy?'

Jeremy cleared his throat: 'I am. What can I do for you?' Still he didn't rise.

The man bowed again, this time with more ceremony. His mate, somewhat similar in appearance and dress came up to him. The first said, 'Ve haf communicate mit you to inspect your miningk.'

'That's right.'

'Ven can ve inspection make, sir?'

'You're making no inspection. I want no business with you. Now go to hell!'

The man blinked. '*Was meinen*?'

'I told you to go to hell . . . now go!' Jeremy leapt up with a roar.

'You haf been listen to zis *Juden*.'

'Yes, I have . . . and I've seen things, too . . . things I'd never have believed civilized people could do. Now go before I become uncivilized and do the same to you.'

The man raised his voice: 'Zis *Juden* is liar and criminal!'

'*You* talk of criminals?'

'All *Juden* is criminal. Zey will you cheat and rob.'

Jeremy advanced on the two big men, his voice vibrant now, face and eyes blazing: 'Will you go . . . or will I get a gun and kill you for the murderous evil bastards that you are?'

The men exchanged glances and a muttered word or two. The man in the panama asked, 'You vill make enemy of friend for *Judische scheisse*?'

Rifkah leapt up, came crying in that strange hoarse tone of hers, '*Deutscher momzer*!'

The man raised his hand to strike her. Up shot Jeremy's arm and flung the hand down. Now he was shouting, 'You dare . . . I'll tear you to pieces, you square-headed bloody bastard!'

The man looked ready to fight. But the other grabbed his arm, pulled him away. The man in the panama tried to speak again; but Jeremy silenced him, shouting, 'I told you to get to hell out of it . . . now get!'

The pair stiffened up, turned and went with ponderous dignity back to the utility. As they reached it, as if doing something long rehearsed, they swung to face each other, stiff as timber, raised right hands, cried out together, '*Heil Hitler*!' Then without looking back at the camp they got into the car, started up, swung away.

Jeremy, staring, muttered, 'The bastards're mad!' He turned to the others, his eyes wide and wondering.

Kurt shrugged. 'It ist ze vay of ze German nation now – *Irren Nation*. Ze mad Hitler haf drive zem all mad.'

Jeremy exhaled heavily, 'They must've been mad to start with. You can drive only unbalanced people mad, can't you?'

Kurt shrugged again. 'I am not psychiatrist.'

Jeremy looked at Rifkah, who was staring after the car wearing that strangely old look in so young a face. As the car crossed the railway she suddenly blazed, spat after it, crying hoarsely, '*Momzer* . . . *Momzer*!' Then, turning to see Jeremy watching, she stared at him for a moment, then suddenly flung herself at him, her arms about him, shining head on his breast, gave way to wild weeping. He held her, murmuring soothingly. When it was over she drew away, sniffling, blinking, trying to smile, saying, 'I am sorry to cry.'

'Why?'

'Because only I want to laugh.'

'Well laugh . . . it's only ridiculous, really.'

'Ridiculous . . . vot ist?'

'Something to laugh at. I see I'll have to introduce you to Webster.'

'Who Webster ist?'

He gave her a hug. 'Leave it for now. But tell me what is *Momzer*?'

She looked at Kurt, who grinned. 'Ist like you call Bastard.'

'I like the sound of it. Must try it on someone sometime.'

It wasn't long before he got the chance to try it on the very persons it fitted. They were having breakfast, when they heard the roar of an aeroplane in starting and run-up. A few minutes later the big Junkers came roaring over the township, with everybody out to see. Jeremy cupped his hands to it, roared up at it, '*Momzer*!'

As the sound of it dwindled away northward like that of a passing storm, Kurt remarked, 'Callingk name vill not stop zem in zere madness.'

III

The untimely withdrawal of the Townies from the festival was blamed on Superintendent Bullco, who was said to be in a state of panic over what might happen without the troops to back his policemen. Nevertheless, it was evident that the mob, with a load of booze to see them through the journey, departed without much show of reluctance. Nor was there regret expressed by those left behind, the Bushies, who even remarked how like old times it was without that howling mob. Thus the rest of the program was gone through, the Sports, with a chance at last for bushmen to win the three-legged race and catch the greasy pig and the rest of it: the Black Boys' races, the dance in the night with room to swing partners in the vigorous old-time Bushie style, without having some Townie take a swing at *you*, plenty of space afterwards to fall down in and sleep it off with the mosquitoes getting drunk on your blood; and if you were young and unattached, with a bit of Black Velvet for a pillow. Just like old times.

But hardly like old times was what Jeremy Delacy was up to. What was he up to, exactly? Many asked the question. Instead of going off on the usual bender, the Alcoholic Absolution, he had gone straight home, taking those Jews along with him. The Scrub Bull, of all people, getting interested in settling the country – and with Jews! Maybe Hitler and Col Collings and Constable Stunke and others of their way of thinking were right about Jews' taking over if given half a chance. Or was it just the old Jeremy Delacy perversity, doing something that others were chary of? Or might it not be the Jew Girl? The old feller had an eye for the ladies, and they for him. Hmmm!

It was discussed at Finnucane's, where it was remembered that the last seen of him, he was walking with the girl in the moonlight, she clinging close to him, with red head shining, laughing merrily at something he was telling her. His yeller Missus? She'd be out lookin' for tracks at daybreak, eh? That caused a great laugh, went up and down the Telegraph Line, out on the Flying Doctor Network. It was an old joke of those parts. Aboriginal women with a stake in a whiteman's affections always took a quick look for the tracks of rivals round his camp.

Even old friends discussed it doubtfully. Tom Toohey and his wife, Billy Brew, the Cullitys, saying they'd found him markedly changed the last day or two of the Races. That old savagery was gone. He'd only laughed at the shinannigans instead of declaring them part of the lousy national character. And how angry he'd got whenever the subject of ill-treatment of the Jews came up, how he'd dealt with those Huns from Krupp's, out of whom he could make a fortune! They knew better than to talk of Nanago's looking for tracks. She was never a jealous one, they said. In fact, she seemed as happy as he with the Jew Girl.

But it had been discussed at Finnucane's; and so the Wurruld came to hum with it; the Scrub Bull's taken to the Scrub again – but this time with a lovely young Jewess!

CHAPTER FOURTEEN

THAT CLOSE-LINKED WALKING in the moonlight, one glimpse of which roused such widespread interest, was continued in comparative privacy at Lily Lagoons as long as the Moon of that September showed of early evenings, which was long enough for it to become a kind of ritual needing no light but that of the stars. But what a blaze that was just then, from the Scorpion, the Eagle, the Winged Horse, the Cross, the Milky River in the depths of which dwelt Old Tchamala, to name but a fraction of it! For whatever reason they clung so close, it was things like the stars they talked about, astronomically, astrologically, mythologically according to several mythologies; or about possums that shinned up stringy-barks at their approach and made comment on them in what sounded like apologetic little coughs; or tiny phalangers sailing squeaking from limb to limb above them; or koodooks, or bats; or the curlews who came to expect them and went dancing along the dusty road ahead calling, *Kweeluk, Kweeluk*! but not with the usual note of anxiety for disembodied souls in danger through too hastily wanting to live in the flesh again; instead joyously, it seemed, as if here in the flesh were something like what souls knew in the Nirvana.

It could only mean that they were in love. But there are all kinds of love.

Every evening, after a token listening with the others to the radio news session following the meal, they sallied forth, always the same way, southward, through the big white gate, down the long white road. Seldom did they speak of the news, even though the world at large was sitting with ears glued to radios worrying about what would be the outcome of all this running to and from Munich, accepting promises of peace and threats of war, threatening and wheedling in return, those who ran the world. Did those who ran the world do it for the world's sake or their own? That was the only sort of comment they made on what they had heard. The Jews were catching it wherever the Germans went; and they were, the Germans, going further and further beyond their legitimate boundaries; and the Jews of the world were screaming about it; that is those outside those boundaries, because the screams of those inside could not be heard. But when Rifkah spoke of Jews it was concerning the lovely simple things of Jewish life: the festivals, the foods; the Seven Candles, the tiny hut of the Feast of Succos; *Chuppah* under which one must stand to be truly wed; the *Mikvah* – the ritual bathing after menstruation; Rosh Hashanah, the New Year; the Passover; her silly sweet old *Bubbeh* in the *Sheitel* or wig she must wear instead of her true hair because a woman's hair is a snare to a man's holiness; her gentle old *Zaydeh*, in his kopple intoning over *Oneg Shabbat*, the meal you sat down to after two stars had come out on Friday night. Never of the persecution. Jeremy talked of the Irish, of the lovely ritual of the Catholic Church, but never of the meanness, the cruelty, the hypocrisy behind it all. He talked of the Aborigines, of their customs, their mythology, the perfection of their lives as children of Nature, not of the frightful reality of their dispossession. Both talked of horses, because she was eager to know the beasts. She was learning to ride, under the tutorship of Prindy, her mount as yet old Bay Rum Betsy.

Why the idealization of everything? Was it because they had found each other in complete despair of the realization of anything but disillusion?

The walks usually lasted about an hour, perhaps as long as perfection can last. They would return to the others sitting in the lounge – Nanago, Prindy, Kurt, sometimes Darcy and Water Lily, who would look at them as at people who had been to some secret place and might have some strange and lovely tale to tell. But although they came in always looking radiant, they acted always matter-of-factly just seemed to drop each other for the rest. Then Jeremy might ask Kurt what was happening in mad Europe, or listen to Prindy talking about something he had been reading or answer his questions. Rifkah might start talking cooking with Nanago, or take up some sewing, mending, at which she was very painstaking and so expert as to be able to make a rag of a garment last for a long while yet, a skill she said she had picked up from her old *bubbeh* and perfected as a mind-saving device while in prison. Jeremy would not stay so long, but in accordance with long-established custom take himself off to his own quarters, to read or to work at something in his scientific line of research. He would kiss both women, his wife lightly on the mouth, Rifkah as lightly on the brow, while the girl kissed him somewhat more ardently on the cheek, clinging for a moment.

What tales the gossips would have made of it had they known – about his doubling back later to sneak up the side stairs, or her to come sneaking down them and across the yard to jump into bed with him! Perhaps he might have wished it, the way he often sighed and tossed before going off to sleep alone – even without realizing it. But there were certainly no tracks to look for in the early morning, except those he had made in crossing from the Big House in the night and his early morning going to the race track to run with his horses.

Rifkah was always up at dawn, too, along with Nanago, to get things going in the kitchen. Soon they were sharing the kitchen. Rifkah confessed to a passion for cooking, instilled into her by her *bubbeh* and for so long stifled by circumstances. As if delighted to indulge her, Nan stood by most of the time, taught what she could, in the way of bread and brownie making and dealing with large chunks of meat and local fish and fowl, but didn't intrude on the innovating, the *tsymmise*, the *kugels*, the *bagels*, the *schnitzel*s, the *pfannküchen* and the rest of it, as if realizing that here was something more in the nature of ritual than domestic economy.

It was in between these culinary rites that mastery of the horse proceeded; or what was surely more correct, mastery of the self in respect of horses, since with all her expressed and evident delight in horses as creatures, Rifkah was admittedly afraid of them. In fact she was scared of all strange creatures, even of the crippled things and the blacks. There was much giggling on account of it at first. She made no pretence, giggled at herself. She was simply not venturesome in a strange environment, just as those who giggled at her would have been themselves for the most part out of theirs. Her preliminary dealings with the horses were made to please Prindy, who wanted a certain possession of her, and found this the only way he could get it. She would go with him to the race-track with bread to feed the horses, the donkey, the camel, perched on the rail for safety, and watch him showing off on various mounts. His urging her to get on to something herself met only with laughter: 'I moost only fall off and brek mein neck!' Jeremy was moved to tell the boy not to worry her with his urging, saying that it was not in some people's nature to do certain things. But plainly Prindy was disappointed. There were so many places he wanted to take her – alone, apparently.

Then suddenly there she was seen sitting astride of old Betsy, bareback, hanging on so hard to the old mare's mane that it was a wonder she didn't object, while Prindy led the old thing round with a mere finger hooked in her lip. How Rifkah got on no one quite knew. It seemed that the mare was pestering her for bread while she sat on the fence and that while trying to escape she had more or less *fallen* on her back. Once on Bay Rum Betsy's back it was pretty well impossible to fall off, so broad was it and so great the protuberance beneath. Prindy slipped the halter on and led them to the homestead, for everyone to see. So great was the delight of everyone that it could not be gainsaid with cowardice. Although it was with the sweat of fear on her lovely lip, since certainly there was terror in her great hazel eyes, Rifkah *climbed* off the fence on to Betsy next day, with a bridle to cling to instead of pulling out poor Betsy's hair, and was made to learn to use it. Next day the saddle, and Jeremy there to hoist her into it. So on, day after day, learning to trot; no cantering yet or change of mount, no matter how Prindy pressed. Prindy wanted to take her to so many lovely places where the utility couldn't go and where Betsy in her retirement wouldn't.

The equestrian accomplishment made no difference to the ritual in the kitchen. Smiling Nanago kept things going till the inspired one got back. There was also more than ritualistic cooking going on in the kitchen. Nan, product of a mission, knew about the ancient people called the Jews, of whom Jesus was one, and wanted to know more about them. As if starved for the faith of her fathers as well as for the spicy diet that was part of it, Rifkah took to telling stories in full that had been only touched on by the missionaries in their haste to get on with the Jesus Bijnitch. Sarah and Abraham and Jacob and Rachel and Rebecca and Isaac, Queen Esther, King David, all came alive as she told their stories while she cut and sliced and salted and peppered and sugared and cinnamoned and spiced and broiled and baked and fried. Like the Dream Time heroes of the Old People's yarns, during the enactment of the rituals of the bush. Prindy wanted to hear them. The school kids, too. Jeremy objected, to be roundly rated by Rifkah for confusing religion with legend. He gave in. He discussed it with Kurt, only to find him as hostile to Judaism as religion as he himself was to Christianity. 'Religion's got to be got rid of,' said Kurt. 'Zere can be no real progress of ze human race while superstition it is permitted!'

Kurt was not interested in the horses, nor in anything much but the statistics of the productivity of the land as set forth in a great pile of official reports, gazettes, and the like, along with maps, that Jeremy produced for him. The visitors had been run around the region in the utility, but for little better than glimpses, because that was all Kurt wanted: a photo here, a photo there, but with a mass of statistics to attach to them for eventual sending to those he called his Principals. Jeremy went on with his life seemingly as usual, the only obvious difference being in his mien.

But how different everything had become here in this place that for so long had been a very stronghold against change was suddenly and even drastically revealed after something like a fortnight of this idyllic condition, this little girl's play in the kitchen, fooling about with kids on horses, walking at night playing a game with love, while the outside world was climaxing to madness under the influence of the greatest set of madmen that had even lived. It was during that period that the Munich Agreement was signed, giving the blessing of half the world's lunatics to Hitler to indulge his frankly mooted wholesale homicide, while the other half cursed and spat upon the first and declared its intention to double the slaughter. It was there every night, issuing forth from the radio in subdued screaming in a dozen different languages, all of which the only one who really listened seemed to understand, the grey-faced Kurt: Fascist swine – Communist dogs!

One evening while Jeremy and Rifkah were walking, she remarked on the great good nature of Nanago, expressed especially in her own case by giving her the run of the kitchen: 'Jewish voman vood sooner share her 'usband zan her kitchen.' Laughingly she went on to tell how her old *bubbeh* had always said the trouble between Sarah, wife of Abraham, and Hagar, Abraham's concubine, really started in Sarah's kitchen. She was referring to the biblical story (Genesis 21) of the expulsion of Hagar by Sarah, traditionally because of the girl's overweening pride of having borne a son to Abraham before Sarah. 'Sabbath fry-fish . . . zat vas ze real trouble, mein Bubbeh say. Zat fry-fish is Jewish voman's special pride and secret, don't you know. Ze angels gif zat secret to Sarah. She moost not tell to ozzer voman . . . *shickseh*, strange voman, not Jewess . . . I tell you before. Zat Hagah vos Egyptian. She vont zat secret. So she got to go. She go mitt Ishmael, her son, start Mahomedan religion, to get . . . vot you call it . . . s'kvair . . . no, square . . . get square mitt, vit . . . I get goot accent yet . . . to get square vit Jews . . . hahahaaah!'

This was the sort of Bible Story that was causing so much delight to the simpler ones of the household, and even by now to Jeremy, who declared it so much more human than the namby-pamby Christian versions.

Rifkah went on with her comical tale, telling it just as if talking about known relations, about how Sarah had passed on the secret to Rebecca, wife of her son Israel, and Rebecca to her own son Jacob's wife, Rachel, and so on down the generations, as if it had happened a few years back, not all of five thousand.

Jeremy asked, 'Is that why you don't fry fish here . . . because a *shickseh* will learn your secret?'

'No, no! Nan isht not like *shickseh* to me. I loff her . . . like mein *tante*, what you call 'em . . . auntie.'

'Then why don't we have some of this marvellous fry-fish?'

'Ze catfish ist not *kosher*.'

'What's wrong with the poor old catfish . . . because it's got whiskers?'

'You are laughingk at me!

'No . . . you know I like you to do all the things you've been prevented from doing by those German dogs.'

She leaned to him. 'I know . . . dear Jeremy.'

'Well, why aren't catfish *kosher*?'

'No *schale*.'

'No scales? What difference does that make?'

She shrugged. 'I not know . . . only ist Jewish law. Fish got no . . . no skell . . . isht *treife* . . . not clean . . . *verboten*.'

'Just old-man been talk, eh?'

'Vos ment?'

'That's what the blacks say when you ask 'em why they practise some old custom. Means that's what the men of old decreed . . . not to be questioned . . . tradition. But there're plenty of fish to be had with scales . . . bream, barramundi, cod. Barramundi's a very tasty fish . . . best in the whole country . . . and got scales as big as shillings.'

'Vy not ve haf to eat?'

'Catfish team in the lagoons, and are easy netted. The others, in the creek, have to be hooked or speared . . . and barramundis, in the big holes, are particularly wary. There are some beauties, though . . . barras . . . twenty, twenty-five pound . . . up to fifty, even.'

'Vill you tek me vere zis vonderful fish?'

'Not much good my taking you. I'm no sort of fisherman. But get young Prindy. He's a marvel with a fish-spear . . . and the magic, too, of course.'

'Magic?'

'Can't do anything without magic in the hunting line. Why don't you go out riding with Prindy. It's time you got on a better mount than poor old Betsy and took a longish ride. It's only about five miles to the barramundi holes. Ride old Snowball. He's a big powerful animal, but very gentle-natured . . . why, you could go to sleep on him and he'd take you where you want to go by just telling first . . . yes, truly!'

'All right . . . I ride Snowball. Tomorrow . . . so ve haf fry-fish for Friday night. I vill gif you proper *Oneg Shabbat*, ze vay I haf tell . . . told you . . . about. Kurt vill ze Blessingk gif. Haha! I see his face ven I ask him. Pliss . . . don't you tell him. If you tell him he vill angry mitt me and not do. I surprise him. You do not mind, I do zis Jewish religious zing?'

'So long as it pleases you, my dear, I'm happy.'

'Dear, dear Jeremy!' She quickly kissed his cheek.

The fishing expedition eventuated as a horseback picnic, with Water Lily and her two tan children going along, as well as visitors they'd had with them since the Races; a blackish half-sister of Lil's known variously as Kujalinga, or Turtle, who also had two kids, chocolate-cream. Prindy was leader, despite the fact that Turtle's boy Tijit was older. There must be a leader for successful dealings with barramundi, one to enjoin strict silence, shadowless approach, to enact the procedure of enticement. Even the Singing must be done under the breath. The barramundi had but two enemies, the crocodile and man. The great size so many attained showed how successfully they dealt with both.

Mostly they could be taken only when the water was murky from the early rains. Here and now the big limestone pools were clear almost as the sparkling air. From where they lurked down in the weedy caverns, the big fish saw everything seeable that was going on, heard every hearable sound. Smaller species lived in constant terror of them, dodging amongst the weed masses nearer the surface, hiding also from fishing birds and their bigger brethren, while striving to make a living from whatever was to be picked up.

Prindy got out onto a projection of rock nicely shaded by an overhanging tree, stripped to the golden buff. His equipment was a magic fishing headband of woven hair, just a tiny strap of a thing, a tobacco tin of insects of various kinds somewhat maimed to render handling them easy, and a fish-spear. Similarly unclad but accoutred with only a spear, Tijit stood on another rock about ten feet away under the same shade. The rest, carefully placed, watched, scarcely breathing.

With an almost imperceptible movement, Prindy scattered a pinch of insects on the water. A moment, while the creatures broke the mirror surface slightly with their tiny struggling. Then a little translucent cloud of reckless fishy mites, followed by flanking slips of silver. The water boiled minutely to what went on below the surface and below again. Then below it all a shadow, black, silver, flickering. The surface heaved to the commotion of self-preservation. Grey eyes were fixed. The spear was poised: Zip! The spear-haft wobbled, leaned, ripped the surface for half a dozen feet, popped down, vanished. That was the sign that the spear held, the moment of release from tension. Pent breaths were freed in a subdued cheer: *Yakkarai*! No need for silence now, since you could get but one barramundi in one hole in one day – maybe one week, depending on the others' memories. Still, there were other holes, hence some restraint needed. The two naked boys slipped into the water. The others proceeded to strip with haste. The old barra might have to be hauled out of a cave; and how many caves might there be down there? Soon they were all in the water – tan and chocolate and chocolate-cream bottoms up in diving, faces of the same hues with red mouths wide and white teeth gleaming in coming up again for one gulp of air – all, that is, except Rifkah, who'd gone so far in stripping only to remove elastic sides and roll her grey moleskins halfway up her ivory-white claves.

It didn't take long to find the fish. Soon there it was shooting up out of the water, struggling feebly on the end of the spear, with Tijit-Tijit on the other end. The dark boy, all gleaming teeth and sparkling eyes, swam to plop the fish right at the white feet waiting in the shallow. It was a big enough catch to please anyone, a good ten pounds. Rifkah bent over it beaming with delight. She looked up, to see the others in a semi-circle, treading water, watching her closely. She said, 'Ist beautiful fish.'

Tijit came ashore, pulled out the spear, tossed the dying fish up onto the grass. It was intended that they should eat this first one for lunch, cooked in clay in the native style, along with bread and butter and a large cake Rifkah had made with cinnamon flavour.

Still the others watched Rifkah. Prindy said to her, 'Plenty mussel here. We cook with fish, eh?' Then he added: 'You swim, eh?'

Rifkah only smiled. Turtle said something in lingo. The others giggled, except Prindy, who replied shortly. Then the gigglers upended and went down after mussels. Rifkah asked Prindy, 'Vot zey say?' But he also showed his bottom in a dive.

Rifkah watched them, went to each one as he or she came up with cupped hands full of mussels. Thus till they had enough for lunch. Then the males went on down the creek to more fishing, leaving the cooking to the females. They returned in an hour or so with three fine fish, the biggest some fifteen pounds, over which Rifkah cooed for joy.

The cooking was done. The fish in its baked clay casing looked like a mummy in a sarcophagus, but smelt very different. That savoury steam issuing from the several blow-holes! Rifkah sniffed with appreciation. However, when the case was cracked open, to reveal fins, scales, guts as the offering, she showed no such gusto in pouncing on it as the others, but had to have nice clean pieces forked out for her to be eaten wrapped in bread. Still, she pronounced the firm dark-streaked flesh Loffly, perfect for fry-fish. She would not eat the mussels, baked in their shells, declaring them *treife*. The others understood readily. Water Lily told of how you must not eat turtle while your nose was healing after the ceremony of septum-boring, else your nose would rot and drop off. Turtle herself, who could not eat turtle at all because it was her totem, told of how, amongst her people of the coast, a pregnant woman who ate jungle-fowl or its eggs would have her baby stolen by such a bird at birth and taken and put into its huge mound nest to hatch out as a jungle-fowl.

They swapped yarns while they lazed with full bellies in the shade, each eventually telling the story of his or her own traditional ancestry, those too young to do so having it done by someone older. For instance, Water Lily told of her youngest's connexion with Widwidda, the Blue Kingfisher, and the story of how the little bird was always quarrelling with his big brother, Wadwadda, the Blue Kookaburra, about the places they camped in. Wadwadda, who was lazy, left it to Widwidda to build the camps, which the little fellow did to suit his size, causing Wadwadda to have to smash his way in with the nulla-nulla that became his powerful beak. So Widwidda grew wings and took to making his camps in the nests of tree-termites. Lazy Wadwadda also grew wings, and to this day goes about bursting open his little brother's nests. Tijit-Tijit told of how the little bird of that name will lead you to sugar bag if you belong to his clan. Rifkah's contribution was in like vein, telling of how her Biblical namesake had tricked her aged and purblind husband, Yitzchak, into leaving his property, a station where they ran mainly goats and camels, to her favourite son Ya'acov, instead of to Ya'acov's hairy twin brother, Esau, the elder by an hour or so and hence the true heir, but disliked by his mother because he'd given her a bad time having him. It seemed that it was this Esau, the Hairy One, who, to get even went off and started Araby Bijnitch. Rifkah began by telling the tale seriously, as though somewhat ashamed of the original Rifkah, but soon got caught up in the mirth it caused her audience, especially the bit about old Rifkah's getting Ya'acov to disguise himself with goat's hair. Prindy put the cap on it by declaring that old Yitzchak must have been a *mungus* not to have smelt that he was being had: 'Hair from billy-goat . . . ohaheeeee!' They were rendered helpless with laughter.

Then it was time to go home. They were getting the couple of sacks of fish, which had been lying in a cool spot in the creek where the small fry had been trying to get at them, to load them onto the pack-horse, when Prindy, grey eyes on Rifkah, suggested a dip before they leave. Off came the others' clothes at once, while Rifkah stood red-faced and slack-lipped, obviously miserable. They all shot a look at her before turning vari-coloured behinds to her and plunging into the big hole. They all vanished, came up again in a burst of silver bubbles and shiny dark skin and bright eyes and teeth, trod water looking at her. She uttered a little whimpering sound. Then suddenly she sat down, began to pull off her boots. She wasn't looking at the water-treaders now – but they at her, all eyes now, brown and black and grey, mouths tight. Still avoiding looking, her eyes up in the paperbarks, she slipped out of the brown silk shirt. It revealed the ivory whiteness of her torso from somewhat sunburnt neck, but not entirely, because she wore a bassière. She had to drop her eyes to take her pants off, but without meeting the others. Off came the moleskins. Long white shapely legs, but only as far up as the bit of lace on the skimpy drawers. She rose – the line of eyes rising with her. Now she met them. Here was the moment. White women who had no bathing costumes sometimes took a dip in the Beatrice in bra and panties. Her face was redder than the sun had made it, much redder. She dropped her eyes to the ground, came stepping to the water's edge. But her slim hands slipped behind her, up her back, unhooked the brassière, pulled it off. A slight sigh of released pent breathing, as small white slightly pendulous breasts were revealed. Still looking down, she stooped slightly, lifted a leg and pulled down on the drawers – and the sunlight caught the copper of her crotch. A deep inhalation on the water. The other leg out. She stood erect. A gasp. All white and gold! Not merely a naked woman, but something as lovely as a white crane poised immobile fishing. Still not meeting the wide wide eyes, she stepped daintily into shallow water, out into it to knees, then dropped down with a splash, looked at the dark faces, which at once broke into smiles. She smiled back. Down went the faces. Up came the arses. A swirl. Then up again and round, splashing, ducking. She stayed where she was, rolling over, showing white toes, knees, once or twice her bottom. Not that they took much notice of her now. Nor were they much concerned when they all came out together, just a glance or two as she got back into her things.

They went home singing Jewish folk songs that Rifkah had already taught Prindy and which he now played on his flute, swinging to the trot of his golden pony: *Rozinkes und Mandlen, Chosen Kalah Mazzeltov.*

Walking that night, Rifkah told Jeremy of the stripping, confessing to the effort it cost her, explaining how what was regarded as chastity in Jewish women was carried to such lengths as cutting the hair off at marriage and replacing it with the *sheitel*, as she had told him. Sex was never discussed by modest women. Young girls were left in total ignorance of bodily function until menstruation, at first appearance of which, in the old style, they were actually subjected to ritual beating, in the form of face-smacking by mother or grandmother, as punishment for reaching sexual maturity and becoming a potential snare to pious men. She said the Nazis used the public stripping of Jewish women, especially before Jewish men, as a form of torture, or sport, knowing how it affected them. Particularly prone to it were those Germans who obeyed the law concerning what was called the Crime of Shame, which was to have sexual intercourse with a Jewess and for which the statutory punishment was death. Rape was common enough, but had to be done in secret. But the raping, to those who'd suffered it, meant nothing so shameful as that public stripping. Not that she felt anything like that at the fish-holes, she said, 'Ist like . . . vell, if I don't do, somehow I offend zem. Vot you zink?'

Jeremy said, 'I don't know, really. They do put you to tests . . . to see if they can trust you. But then, it might've been out of sheer curiosity . . . to see what you look like underneath.'

'Zey are so strict wit' many law of relationship . . . you can't talk ziz vun, you can't look zat vun . . . but you can all go naked together!'

'Maybe there's more logic in their behaviour than in ours. Our faces are our distinguishing features. Bodies are all much alike. Maybe it was the Jews who first used clothing as more than mere protection . . . Thou shalt not look upon the nakedness of this one and that one, as it says in the Bible.'

Despite that legendary secrecy of the Jewish woman fish-frying, there was no suggestion of it in that first Friday's fry. Although it was evident enough from the way Rifkah went about it, starting as soon as the kitchen was clear after lunch, that she would have regarded assistance as intrusion, not only did she suffer all who were interested to watch her, but explained what she was doing. Such intricacy needed explanation: the precise filleting, to give uniform texture and size, slight salting, drying off with clean linen, making pale ghosts of the fillets with the finest flouring, batter of pure egg, broken so that it seemed even the skin inside the shell went in like a tiny sliver of silver, and the shells stacked neatly as if to be used, if only as witnesses to the perfection of the beating, to make a bowl of twenty-four carat liquid gold; a dainty two-finger job the dipping, second-timed, with a similar precision movement to the hot oil that must keep constant temperature for absolute results; again a dip that's like baptism of an infant lifted for dunking by the heel; the seconds again counted lest the lovely thing be destroyed instead of metamorphosized, as it surely is when lifted out faintly smoking and laid gently in pattern on white paper on a great dish, to render first a sweet savour to the God of Israel. Surely the way she flew about it was a state of religious ecstasy?

Even Jeremy came to take a look, ostensibly to see if the olive oil, which had been in stock for medicinal purposes for some time, did not Crack, as he put it scientifically, under heat. As if there could be any excess to crack anything in an operation so delicate! Even those eggs had seemed to deliver their substance up with volition. Prindy spent the whole time there, staring. No touching. It could not be eaten until cold and arrayed like Solomon in all his glory on the gleaming cloth on the *Shabbos* table under the twin candles that could not be lit before two stars appeared and the words were said in the Holy Tongue: *Blessed art Thou, O Lord, our God, King of the Universe, who hath sanctified us with his Commandments and enjoined us to kindle the Sabbath Light.* Prindy, by the silent movement of his lips, seemed to be singing it all, what she did, what she said. A new way to commune with Old Tchamala, perhaps, in Hebrew, so right-sounding a lingo for the purpose: *Eternal One, King of the Universe.*

It was hardly likely that Kurt could be kept in ignorance of what was going on, as it had been requested by Rifkah that he should be, when the house was redolent with it. However, it would seem that the request was quite unnecessary, since he showed no interest whatsoever. Pretty well all day he had been preoccupied with the radio news, sitting with greying head cocked and thin face pinched with worry, tuning from one kind of foreign gabble to another. His first words, when Jeremy came to join him at five-thirty were, 'Anozzer blow to ze 'eart! Benes, ze vun 'ope for Czechoslavakia, haf resigned. Looks like Hitler stooge, Henlein, vill be put in as Nazi *Gauleiter*. Poor, poor Bohemia! Again to become ze butcher-shop of Europe. Bismarck say: 'Who is master of Bohemia is master of Europe.' But ze Bohemian is traditionally ze freest of all men and do not take to masters easy. Poor Bohemia!'

But that long Jewish nose was not being excluded utterly from its natural functioning by the too-receptive ears was shown when after a couple of drinks Kurt sniffed appreciatively and grinned, remarking, 'Ze old Yiddisher Friday eveningk smell! Takes me back old times . . . bad old times, but seem goot zen. Zey say ve human beingks haf lost our olfactory sense compare mitt ozzer animal . . . but more memory come through ze nose zan ozzer vay.'

Nanago came to join them. She brought apologies from Rifkah, who wouldn't be coming at all. No word was said of the elaborate preparations for the forthcoming meal. Prindy also didn't come.

As it darkened, Prindy went outside to watch for the Two Stars. There at last they were in the pale saffron of the southwest – tonight the Pointers of the Cross, Alpha and Beta of Centaurus according to the Greek version, part of a broken fish-trap so the Snakemen had it, the trap set by Koonapippi to catch Tchamala as he came out of that hole in the Milky Way, but scattered by the Old One, its remnants the Southern Cross itself and other stars in the vicinity. Prindy ran inside, through lounge and dining-room to the kitchen, with the tidings, singing them, 'Two star, two star . . . two star to light two candle by, to bring in *Shabbos*.' Rifkah kissed him, snatched up matches, and with an arm about his shoulders, went hurrying with him into the dining-room.

Those in the lounge came at the ringing of the triangle – to stop and stare at the enchanted scene, even the two who'd seen the set-up in daylight, even Kurt who must have seen it many a time. Rifkah and Prindy, arms about each other, were part of it. Rifkah said, 'Goot *Shabbos*, dear pipple.'

Nan and Jeremy, schooled, returned the greeting. Not Kurt, who was staring at the head of the table, where within reach of whoever was to sit there was a small mound of mystery, at least to the uninitiated, something under a white table napkin, on one side of it a silver dish of salt, on the other a decanter of red wine. When Rifkah repeated the greeting, using his name, her voice sharpish, he looked at her quickly, stared a moment, then asked as sharply, '*Was meinen dieser*?'

The sweet smile was gone. She answered in English, 'To pliss zese pipple.'

He turned to the others, asked even rudely, 'So?'

Jeremy, looking somewhat alarmed, answered, 'I asked her, Kurt.'

Kurt's expression became surprise for a moment. Then he smirked, shrugged, looked again at Rifkah: 'You vont vot?'

She replied in Hebrew.

He elaborated the shrug, spread his hands in Jewish fashion, and grinning now, asked, 'Vot vill ze Eternal, Gott of Universe, et cetera, et cetera, zink of ze blessingk of atheist?' He moved to the head of the table. Rifkah went to the foot, where there was an array of serving dishes, the others to seats aside evidently allotted them, Nan on Rifkah's right, Jeremy next her and on Kurt's left, Prindy on Rifkah's right. They sat down.

Still smirking, Kurt reached for the napkin on his plate, shook it out, placed it on his head, and as Jeremy and Prindy did likewise, he said, 'Ve moost haf *Yarmulke* . . . no goot half do a zing.' He looked at Prindy. 'You know vot is *Yarmulke*?'

Prindy's covered head nodded. 'Ah! Soon ve vill haf *barmizvah*, eh?' Kurt turned the smirk on Rifkah, staring at him with great eyes, her face stiff. He grinned as he asked, 'Ze Blessingk in Hebrew, Yiddish, English, Polonski, Russki . . . Mumma?'

The great eyes flashed with anger. He dropped his own, drooped his head, pronounced in sing-song voice, 'Blessed art thou, O Eternal, our Gott, King of Ze Universe, who bring forth bread from ze earth.' He reached for the mound before him, removed the napkin, to reveal an oval loaf of bread, golden-crusted, crowned with a plait and pimpled with tiny seeds. He drew the loaf to him, bent over it, searchingly, remarked, 'Genuine Yiddisher *chalah*.' He looked at Jeremy: 'Truly is zis ze Promised Land. Who vood believe poppy seed here?'

Jeremy chuckled. 'I happened to have a couple of old opium-poppy heads. Got them for my father years ago. He believed in the superstition that if you put an opium-poppy capsule in the stuffing of your pillow it'll induce sleep. I suppose you've heard of it?'

Kurt nodded, then shook his head. 'Superstition, superstition, superstition!' He cast his big black eyes as if piously aloft, adding: 'Herr Gott . . . ven, oh ven, are you and all ze rest of ze devils goingk to get off ze back of humanity?' He said it with such feeling that his face became distorted, looking strange beneath the drooping napkin. Then dropping his eyes and seeing that the others were staring at him, he smirked again. 'Excuse. If I embarrass you . . . it is because I am myself embarrass mitt ze job.' He concentrated on the loaf, rather in the manner of a surgeon, muttering. 'Now . . . vot is it I haf to do.'

Again Rifkah spoke to him in Hebrew, sharply. He answered without looking up: '*Ken, ken* . . . Mumma!' Again the great hazel eyes beyond the candles flashed with annoyance.

Perhaps to ease the situation, Jeremy asked Kurt, 'Why do Jews use poppy seeds for this special type of bread?'

It was a most unfortunate remark, since in his obvious resentment Kurt could not help but seize on it as he laid hands on the bread, looking quickly at Jeremy: 'Karl Marx, a Jew in ze beginning, gave ze answer . . . "Religion is Opium of ze People". Ze poppy seed in ze holy *chalah bread* is symbol . . . '

He broke off at sudden movement from Rifkah. She was rising, staring a him, but with the great eyes now swimming with tears. With a stifled sob she swung from the table, went rushing out to the kitchen. The others just sat staring at the communicating swing-door swinging to shut. As it did so, Kurt said with a sigh, 'My apology. But I haf strong feeling about religion . . . Judaism . . . as you, Jeremy, about Christianity. She know zat. Vy moost she . . . . ' He broke off again as Nan rose hastily and went rushing after the girl. As she disappeared he sighed again: '*Yenteh*!'

'What's that mean?' asked Jeremy.

'Vomen . . . vomen as distinct from men. Literally mean Talkers. As if Jewish vomen only talk, vile ze men zink and act. Mumma scoldingk in ze kitchen . . . while Papa sittingk contemplatingk ze Infinite. It is a lie. Papa is smellingk ze fry-fish, ze *gefilteh-fish*, ze *tsymmis*. Ze 'Ouse of Israel is build about ze kitchen. Take avay kitchen . . . ze 'Ouse fall down. But for ze Yiddisher *nosh*, ze rich and ceremonial cookingk, Judaism vood haf died mitt Mithraism and Baalism and all ze rest of ze primitive devil-vorship . . . and ze vorld vood not be plagued mitt vot you call Jesus Business!' Kurt's usual expression, an amiable watchfulness, had suddenly changed to one of fierce animation, so that under the drooping napkin he looked like a ravening Bedouin. He must have become aware of the strangeness of his appearance as Jeremy stared at him, because he snatched the napkin off his head.

Uncovering his own head, Jeremy said, 'But surely religion based on practical things, like good food, clean habits, morality, instead of silly mysteries like the Ascension, the Trinity, the Virgin Birth . . . .'

'Is still religion . . . which means acceptance of supernatural control, vich moost stifle true progress in man. Besides . . . ze food, ze hygiene, ze moral law, is only part of Judaism. Ze Children of Israel are ze Chosen of Gott. Zey are ze elite of humankind. To believe you are elite is Fascist, for vont of better name. Judaism, alzogh ze declared enemy of Fascists, is only Fascism mit anozzer face . . . ze first Fascism and ze moost subtle, because its arrogance is disguise by mock humility.'

Kurt had risen, still talking emotionally, his hands waving. He stopped to glance at Prindy slipping out. Jeremy said then, 'But when you think like that about your own people, how can you work to found a settlement for them?'

Kurt's hands froze in the air. In an instant the Semitic animation was wiped out by that foxiness. He blinked. As he dropped his hands he shrugged, saying evenly, 'Settlement for refugees . . . refugees from any kind of madness . . . in ze hope zat might some community for progress be established.' His falling into silence then made it seem as if he felt he'd said too much.

Jeremy, rising, broke the silence: 'It was my fault, the religious business. I should have consulted you.' Kurt merely shrugged. Jeremy went on: 'She's had such a frightful time . . . and has seemed so happy being Jewish again.'

Kurt spoke in his usual polite and somewhat wary way: 'Vot do you vont to do?'

Jeremy hesitated, then waved to the table, 'She's given so much to this. I . . . I wouldn't like it to be spoilt for her.'

Kurt smirked, the way he had at Rifkah. 'Mumma's *gefilteh-fish*. Even if it gif you ze diabetes . . . a very common Jewish complaint, by ze vay . . . you must eat, so as not offend. But excuse my jokingk. You are master of ze house. You do vot you vont. I vill comply. Vot you suggest?'

'Well . . . only I'd like to get her back . . . .'

'I cannot to her apologize.'

'I know . . . I know. I told you the fault's mine. Surely we can do it without religion?'

Kurt shrugged again, smirked. 'You zink?' Then he added: 'If you vill take your proper place at head of ze table.'

'Yes . . . yes, I will. Now, I think I'd better go and get her. You'll stay . . . as if nothing happened?'

Kurt bowed slightly, but said, 'You sound like Englishman . . . not Irish-Welshman born in vild Australia.'

Jeremy seemed to be trying to work it out. Then he turned towards the kitchen. Out there were only the black housemaids, who said the others had gone out and up top by the outside stairs. He went that way, too, and straight to Rifkah's room, although there was no indication either by sound or sight that anyone was there. Only the verandah lights were lit. He stopped at the screen door, asked, 'You there?' A mumble in reply. 'May I come in?' He entered without invitation, to see three figures seated in line on the edge of the dim white bed. He asked, 'What about all that lovely food going to waste down there?' The answer was a sniffle. He added: 'You promised us Sabbath fry-fish. What are we going to do . . . chuck it out to the chooks?' The answer was a gasping sound. He came up to the bed and found Rifkah the middle one of the trio. He put a hand on her shoulder, asking, 'Aren't you going to come down and give it to us?' She snatched at the hand, pressed it to a wet cheek, mumbled something. 'What did you say?' He bent to her.

She muttered, 'Zat Kurt spoil ever'zing.'

'It's not Kurt that's spoiling the food. What about that *lochshen* soup . . . won't it be getting cold?'

Rifkah gasped, 'Oh!'

'Your first *lochshen* . . . and it'll have to be chucked down the sink. How can your *bubbeh* rest in peace, as you're always saying, if you do a thing like that?'

She uttered a little whimper, kissed the hand she held. 'Come on,' he said, raising her. Prindy flew to open the screen. With his arm tucked in hers as he led her out, Jeremy said, 'We can do without the religious bit.'

She halted. 'Ve must have Blessingk!'

'Now, now! You can't expect Kurt to do what he doesn't want to. Can't I give the Blessing?'

'No . . . it must be Jew.'

He urged her on. 'Now, listen, dear . . . you know this's not a religious house . . . you gave me to understand that you didn't care much about religion . . . .'

'Ist different mitt *Shabbos*. If you cookingk do for it, and light candle, and vish Gooten Shabbos . . . you moost have Blessingk!'

'Can't you give it yourself?'

'Only if I am vidow mitt no *barmitzvah* son.'

They were coming down the inner stairway. He asked, 'Can't you pretend to be that?'

She was silent for a moment. Then she answered suddenly, and, it sounded, grimly, 'Ja . . . yes, I can . . . I vill!'

Kurt was standing as Jeremy had left him. He bowed ceremoniously to Rifkah, who ignoring him, went straight to her place at the table and felt the soup tureen, lifted the lid and sniffed, then addressing no one in particular, said, 'Moost mek hot again. Excuse pliss. I call ven ready.' She took up the tureen and went off to the kitchen, followed by Nan and Prindy.

As Jeremy and Kurt went back into the lounge, the latter said with a grin,

'You see vot I mean, ze arrogance of Jewish voman, mitt basis of domestic economy. Anozzer voman . . . ze *shickseh*, ze stranger, as zey say in arrogance of beingk zemself elite, vood in circumstance compromise mitt cold soup . . . but not Jewess, no!'

Pouring more drinks, Jeremy chuckled, 'I think you're a little hard on your women, Kurt. Maybe we're all hard on things we know too well. My ex-wife had a different kind of fierce domesticity, as I've told you.'

'I haf not tell about my own ex-vife . . . first vun, Jewish. Yes, from experience I speak. Alzo I am already seeingk through ze falseness of Judaism, too mooch afraid vos I of zat mourningk ceremony my Mumma vood make my Papa haf, vile she herself vept for his hardness on her *kleiner menscheleh*.' Droll now, as he mostly was whenever, apparently, he felt called upon to be sociable, he told how his first marriage began to break up through his wife's emptying the *Shabbos lochshen* over his head because he had refused to don the *Yarmulke*, the ceremonial head-covering. They were chuckling over it when the triangle rang again, and went hastening in response, saying they must not risk the repetition of Jewish history, which, murmured Kurt just as they were about to enter the dining-room, 'Unfortunately haf been repeatingk itself for five t'ousand year.'

Now the *chalah* loaf and salt and wine were at Rifkah's end of the table. Sitting prim and stiff, that old-age look on her face, despite its youthful beauty, the complete matriarch, she dispensed the ceremonial, the male response to which was led by Prindy, who at once covered his head with his napkin. Kurt stole a wink at Jeremy while they did likewise. She broke the bread and salted it, poured the wine, all with appropriate muttering, to The Eternal, Our Gott, passed the offering to the others for solemn collaboration. Then with an entirely different mien, a sharp watchfulness for appreciation or lack of it in response to sweet savours that were the payoff to her invocations, she dished out and passed the soup, her own response rather one of dilation of her beautiful nostrils sniffing the heavenly steam – and then the golden fry-fish. The Galilean, said by non-Jews to be a Jew, and supposed by these to have organized a fish-fry on a gigantic scale, presumably on the Sabbath Eve and with the help of the very female angels who had instructed Old Sarah in the Dream Time of the race, could not have made a better job of it than this. To say that the aureate flakes melted in your mouth, as Jeremy, lacking the necessary piety and talent with words remarked, was to belittle their divine quality. Rather did one's mouth, one's whole being indeed, melt about the morsel, as the most inspired of those followers of the False Messiah, might feel about what they call the Blessed Eucharist. A very nice salad, of oiled lettuce, tomato, beetroot, went with it, but merely as unconsidered trimmings. However, as climax to the offering was what was lightly described by her dispensing it as *Nosh*, meaning a bit of something tasty, but proved to be no less than Manna from Above again: tiny pufftaloons, not much bigger than guineas and just as golden, made simply by dropping the last of that perfect batter in blobs into the oil in finishing off the ceremony of the fry. These were eaten with a touch of honey. It was Jeremy, using a bushman's term, who called them pufftaloons. The proper name was *Pfannküchen*. But religious in basis though the whole thing might be according to Kurt, Rifkah seized on the name Pufftaloon as the perfect one for them, a fact that hardly supported Kurt's contention that Jewish women were arrogant and conservative.

Out on the ritual walk that night, following the milky road that, so low hung the Milky Way in the southern sky, they seemed to be climbing to that bolt-hole of Old Tchamala's, Rifkah again refuted Kurt's contention while speaking of his intolerance to Judaism, saying, 'What you call Lose him Dreamin', eh?' The expression was used of such Aborigines as those in missions or towns who had renounced the old ways. She went on to say, 'Effer'body in zat refugee settlement goingk to be like zat. Zey intellectuals. Zey know more zan Gott. Might-be zey von't permit fry-fish. Zen I haf to come 'ere on Friday.'

Jeremy chuckled. 'I can't see them losing a cook like you, whatever their scruples about religion. I notice Kurt's didn't prevent him from eating more of tonight's lovely tucker than any of the rest of us.'

She cuddled up to him, sighed. 'I don't vont zis settlement now.'

'How's that?'

'I am so 'appy 'ere. I do not vont politic and economic and all zat intellectual stuff. Sure zey vill mek goot place . . . but it vill not be true bush place . . . and now I can be 'appy only in true bush place.'

'You're new to it. You'll get tired of it someday.'

'Nevair, nevair. I loff you all so mooch . . . ist . . . it is . . . like I have been far avay and I come 'ome.'

After a little silence she asked, 'Ven Kurt go . . . can I stop?'

'Stop as long as you like, my dear.'

'So I vill not be nuisance to Nan, I can do some job . . . teachingk school, if Darcy vill first teach me . . . or helpingk you in lab.'

'I'm sure Nan would never regard you as a nuisance . . . rather the opposite. Don't forget we've got this military and anthropology mob coming next week. You're going to be a godsend to her in the house. You might get the General off my back, too. He likes Jews, and's very partial to Jewish food . . . and you. With a combination of things, you might be able to get him to relive the old campaigns of Asia Minor, instead of trying to involve me in new ones he's dreaming of in Asia Major. Will you do that for me?'

'Ze only man I vont to talk to is you.' Suddenly she leant to him and kissed him on the mouth. How it affected him could not be judged in the gloom, except perhaps for momentary deeper breathing. She giggled, as if at her boldness, then said, 'But I am so 'appy Jeremy . . . *Kayn aynhorah*!'

'What's that mean?'

'Well . . . it is old *bubbeh* zing you say so not to spoil luck.'

'Like keeping your fingers crossed?'

'Vot is zat?'

'Oh, silly Christian superstition.'

'Tell me, pliss.'

II

That the interest of the Wurruld in the new condition of things at Lily Lagoons had not waned for lack of seeing anyone from there since the Races was evident enough when a truckload of the household arrived at Beatrice River in mid-afternoon of the first trainday of October, and heads popped out from everywhere as it came roaring up from the crossing. Jeremy, driving, remarked to Rifkah and Kurt sitting with him, referring to those nearest them as they came across the railway tracks, meaning the people of the Police Station, 'Better give 'em a wave . . . even though Hitler is their god.'

Constable and Mrs Stunke waved just as genially in response as their blacks already were waving to those in the back.

As Jeremy swung in towards the Railway Station, the two staring members of the staff there vanished. He chuckled. 'The other would-be Beatrice River *Gauleiters*. But don't let it trouble you. They'll be as sweet as pie. Don't forget what I told you . . . the only people Australians are rude to . . . when they're sober . . . are the boongs. Australians generally, I mean. If Pat Hannaford's driving the train you'll see him give Col Collings the Nazi salute as he comes in. I don't know if Pat himself takes it seriously . . . but no one else does.'

Kurt said, 'I zink politics only a game mitt you people.'

'Maybe you're right. Maybe everything's a kind of game . . . as it is to children. But isn't it time we grew up?'

'Pliss . . . not like Europe!' Rifkah protested.

'No . . . for godsake not like Europe . . . but by the same token, not stay like nasty children for ever!'

They entered the station to find Col Collings and Oz Burrows busy preparing for the train, ostensibly surprised to see the party, and certainly as pleasant in receiving them as Jeremy had predicted. Upon Col's saying he hadn't had the pleasure of being introduced to the doctor and the lady, Jeremy gravely did the honours; whereupon Col declared that Rifkah must meet his wife. Jeremy got in a wink while the accumulated mail was being got for him. There was also a telegram for Jeremy, which Col said he would have sent out by blackboy tomorrow if no one had come in today. Evidently Col was interested in that telegram. Looking at him, Jeremy seemed to be debating whether to take it away with the rest of the mail or read it then and there and see the effect on Collings. Col started to busy himself again. Jeremy opened the envelope. The wire read: EXPEDITION HOPE BASE ON LILY LAGOONS STANDING BY AWAITING YOUR CONVENIENCE TIME OF ARRIVAL IF NOT BEFORE FRIDAY PLEASE WISH YOUR JEWISH VISITORS SHABBAT SHALOM FROM ME TO YOURSELF AND WIFE MY KINDEST REGARDS ESK. Reference to the underlined words was made in the section of the form reserved for official data, with the word Hebrew, in accordance with regulations demanding identification of foreign or unusual wording. Jeremy looked up to catch Col eyeing him. He then passed the form to the others, saying, 'From General Esk. Mentions you.'

Kurt's eyes widened at mention of the name, and sought the telegram rather quickly. But having read, he smiled, nodded. Rifkah, handing it back to Jeremy, said, 'Zat is ver' kind of General.'

Jeremy nodded to Col, now looking indifferent. 'Thanks, Col.' Then he led the way outside. Out of hearing, he said with a grin. 'This's rather comical. They're all going to get steamed-up over using Hebrew. Must push it along by replying to him with some. What can I say?' The others only stared at him, not appreciating the comedy, since not knowing the ways of the country and its people. He had to answer himself, 'I know . . . I'll wire him to come for Sabbath Eve . . . fry-fish . . . *Oneg Shabbat.*' He looked at Rifkah. 'Do you mind doing another big fish-fry . . . there'll be six of 'em?'

Her face lit. 'I loff it!'

He chuckled. 'Yes . . . that's it . . . with all the trimmings, candles, *chalah*, salt . . . the Blessing! Would you mind, Kurt? Just for the fun. Good. Collings'll ask me what the language is. "Hebrew", I'll say loftily. They won't be talking about anything else in the bar tonight.' As they were heading back to the office he added: 'If only we could have old Shame-on-us Finnucane out to Friday night supper, within a week the country would be saying I'd turned Jew . . . hahaaaaaaah!'

Speak of the devil! As Jeremy entered the Station office, Col Collings rose from his desk with the telephone receiver in his hand, saying to him, 'Finnucane. He wants a word with you.'

Jeremy gaped. 'Me?'

He was wary; but without cause. The voice so well known telephonically to the Wurruld was dripping with blarney. The Finnucane household were just about to sit down to take a drop o' tay before the train arrived, and were wonderin' if the good doctor and his lovely lady would be carin' to join them – and, of course, 'Jerry, yeself, me boy.' Jeremy replied that he didn't doubt but that his guests would be glad to come, but excused himself because he had some telegraphic business to attend to before the train. 'Ah, yes, the Gineral,' said old Shame-on-us, apparently quite unashamed of the fact that he was betraying the confidence of another betrayer of confidences, namely he who stood beside Jeremy with an ear cocked towards the instrument crackling to the vibrations of the Voice. 'You'll be havin' him out wit' you anny day . . . which remoinds me, that I promised the good man a drop o' the cryather for his night cappin' away in the woilds . . . so if you'd be good enough to pick it up before you go home. An spaykin' of the Gineral and Tullamore Dew in the same breath, as ye moight say . . . that was a cliver one ye put over me about him and the Black and Tans, seein' he was there to stop the shpalpeens, as he explained to me most explicitly . . . and I did loikwise in regard to yeself, tellin' him that ye are a boy who must have his bit of divilment, high or low, no matter the company . . . hahaaaaaah! And you'll be sendin' the good Jews along, eh? They can rest assured, tell 'em, that there'll be nothin' to offind 'em in the way o' food. Remimber the couple o' Jew hawkers out at the tin-field in the ould days that we had to get goats for and let 'em kill 'em themselves and hang in a special place so's not to get contaminated by our Christian mate . . . and how in one o' your moods o' divilment you rubbed pork fat on the carcasses? But as I says to you at the toime, I says: "You can't take Sh . . . er . . . Jews in," . . . and we got left with two rotten carcasses we'd paid a lot o' money for. I'm presumin' you haven't told 'em that one . . . so I won't be repeatin' it.'

Jeremy, red, said shortly, 'Okay . . . I'll send them up right away.' As he turned from the telephone he muttered, 'My God, how that man can talk!' He caught Collings's quizzing eye. How much had those sharp ears heard?

Kurt and Rifkah accepted the Finnucane invitation readily, and went off at once, accompanied some of the way by Prindy. Prindy was heading for Barbu, who was standing outside his shop awaiting him. Jeremy then composed the reply for telegraphing to General Esk, using the term *Oneg Shabbat*, giving its derivation when asked by Col in the tone to be expected of him, but the tone of his own voice hardly the mock curt indifferent one that might have been expected when he planned the joke. Evidently Finnucane's joke on him had cramped his style a bit. However, to show that he took it in good enough part was the fact that soon after, meeting Tom Toohey as he arrived with his gang on the motor trolley, he told him how old Shame-on-us had got even with him, chuckling over it. Toohey was less concerned about the joke than the fact that Jews ate special food, perhaps for one reason that he would be putting them up with Jeremy that night at his place. He asked, 'Do they slaughter their own beasts and pray over 'em out your way?'

'Christ, no! They eat the same as us . . . only they prefer meat with the veins pulled out. Blood's what they don't like.'

'You wouldn't think smart people like Jews'd be fussy over their tucker, though.'

'Shows how shrewd they are. Blood's the main source of transmitting disease in meat . . . and also in its deterioration. Also, meat without blood's much better tasting. Since the girl's been there we've been having all game birds killed bled instead of having their necks wrung. You wouldn't believe the difference in taste. Your missus might like a few tips from her. Nan lets her just about run the kitchen now.'

Tom shot the speaker a sharp glance. Then he said, 'I see in that *Australia Free* paper of yours . . . .'

'*Christ* . . . don't call that anti-Jew rag mine!'

Another glance at the outburst of feeling. Tom went on: 'It says't the Jewish way of killing beasts is sadistic . . . and Hitler prohibited it the first thing he came to power.'

Jeremy leered. 'Course castrating Jews isn't sadistic.'

Again that look from Toohey. Now Jeremy was turned to look at Prindy, who was coming with Barbu. He remarked, 'Train must be coming, eh? Marvellous hearing that boy's got.' But then he turned towards Finnucane's, adding: 'She want's to see the train come in. Old Shame-on-us'll hang onto her till the last minute with his maggin'.' He looked even anxious, was moving as if to go across to the hotel, but turned again to Prindy and called, 'Go and tell Rifkah to come.' He turned back to Toohey to meet that quizzing look for the first time, but without appearing to consider it significant. He cocked his head on hearing the name Rifkah spoken in the group of halfcastes and blacks now crowded about those from Lily Lagoons – *Mitchis Rifkah*. He couldn't hear what they were saying about her; but it was the story of her swimming with them naked, received with indrawn exclamations of, *Eh, look out*! and *Properly*!

There was a Beatrice River Station utility pulling in, Clancy at the wheel. Father and son met each other's glance, nodded. As Clancy alighted he saw Rifkah coming hurrying with Kurt and Prindy. He went red, turned hastily away.

Just then the cry went up: 'Here she comes!' A plume of steam above the trees beyond the bridge – *Boo-oooo-oot*! – and then the rumble of wheels amongst the red girders.

Sharp black eyes of those who wouldn't have been told who was driving the train or, in their humility, have thought to ask, identified him as his engine burst bewhiskered with steam from the bridge – 'Patannaford!' – excitement in the voices, as if the name conjured the likelihood of exciting events. Pat cock-a-doodled at the road crossing, came rolling into the yards. Col Collings was standing by the track outside his Station, ready to take the running staff from Pat's hand and the insult of the Fascist salute that inevitably the hand would give afterwards. But Pat, glancing, grinning, over the waiting crowd, as was his way in pulling in, saw Rifkah. The casual grin changed to a smile of delight. He waved like a happy blackboy. She responded with equal animation. Thus he missed seeing Collings, who scowling and yelling, had to run after the engine, and when Pat did see him, have the staff chucked at him and the hand change its salute to the one of up-jerked thumb. A titter from the crowd. Then the engine disappeared in passing the Station. Freight waggons rolled slowly by with clanking couplings. The three passenger coaches, seeming to be bursting with passengers, the way they were hanging out of windows and platforms, drew up, stopped with a jerk as Chas Case applied his brake.

The little crowd was augmented by the mostly staggering passengers. People – white to the left, boongs to the right– were clasping and pounding and fondling each other. Then there was tall Pat pushing through them, black driver's hat on the back of his head, showing a forepeak of ginger hair, freckled face glowing. His green eyes were only for Rifkah. 'Hello!' he cried. 'Thought you'd gone bush with the Murris. How yo' doin', sweet'eart? Can't shake 'ands.' He showed his grimy paws. But then, grinning, he added: 'Me mouth's clean, but.' He kissed her fair on the lips. She laughed, looking radiant with a blush. He tried again. But she held him off. All who saw it looked amused – except staring Clancy, scowling.

'What 'bout that ride on the engine you promised?' asked Pat. 'Come on now, while I'm shuntin'. What . . . you got 'o ask permission?' She had looked at Jeremy. Pat also looked, belligerent now.

Jeremy said, 'It's okay . . . but we're going to Toohey's for supper.'

'I'll drop her right off at Tom's door for you. Come on, sweet'eart.' He grabbed her hand, dragged her away. Passing Collings and Guard Chase and Oz Burrows sorting out their waybills and looking up to stare at the couple, as everybody else was doing, Pat winked broadly. Collings scowled. Pat said, 'Come and un'ook us, Oz. We'll do the shuntin' ourselves . . . extra crew . . . ahaaaaa!' He was happy as a boy, rushed his flustered captive along to the engine, out of which Porky Jones was gaping. 'Give her a 'and up, Porky.' Pat got on the shiny steel steps behind her, hands grasping the stanchions so that his arms were about her shapely bottom as she climbed, although evidently he was being careful not to touch her.

Up in the cab, Pat got out clean cotton-waste and carefully cleaned the driving seat and helped her into it, all the while talking: had she ever been on a locomotive before, what sort of trains did they have in Germany, did drivers wear brown shirts with swastikas on their arms? She was too bewildered to answer much. Anyway, he didn't require it. He just talked and drove and occasionally cast her the unbelieving glance of an adoring boy. Thus while they ran to the goods shed and dropped off a couple of waggons, with Porky handling points and couplings. Then, 'light', as they say of a locomotive without a load, they headed for the main line southward, got onto it. 'We'll go for a burn,' said Pat. Burn it was literally, with Porky shovelling incessantly and sulphury steamy smoke pressing down on the cab and hanging like a grey screen over the tender owing to the suction of their speed. The engine rocked like a bolting horse. Wind howled through the ventilators. Pat stood swaying to the rocking, one hand on the fully open regulator, the other on a stanchion that Rifkah was gripping with all her strength by the look of her knuckles, his hand above hers, his arm almost about her, while he stared ahead through the bull's-eye window and sang the old engine-driver's song, *Paddy had an Engine but he Couldn't Make her Go*. Rifkah's face had something of that aged look. Her eyes were great with staring at the dead straight track, an arrow-head of silver lying on scarlet between folds of grey, and the purpling sky into which it bored. She heaved a sigh when at last he pulled off steam and let the engine roll out her momentum until she came wheezing to a stop.

'How'd you like that?' asked Pat.

She smiled weakly, shook her head. 'Don't tell me you were scared?' he demanded. 'What you been through . . . with them Fascist bullyin' dogs?'

She glanced round the barish box of steel, at the roaring fire, having to raise her voice above the bubble and the hiss: 'Ist different . . . like beingk carried away by storm.'

He chuckled. 'Safest things in the world, railway locomotives . . . properly handled, course . . . and a reliable track. You can trust old Tom Toohey.'

'Ve go back now? I do not vont to be late. Not before haf I had meal vit' Mrs Toohey.'

'You'll get goat. Jews allowed to eat goat?' Pat was turning the reversing gear.

She giggled. 'Did not old Rifkah in ze Bible cook kid goat for Ya'acov to gif to his old fader Yitzchak . . . you call Isaac?'

'One thing I'm not up in is the bloomin' Bible, lady. Religion's the opium of the people.'

'Not politic, too?'

He looked at her quickly, 'Depends on the politics. Right . . . here we go. Swing your seat round.'

'Pliss, not so quickly.'

'Can't go like that backwards . . . or we *would* come to grief. But what about you havin' a go pullin' her tail. Come on.' He drew her from the seat, placed her reluctant hand on the regulator. 'Hold it . . . press the little lever to get the movement. Right. I'll start you off. Away we go. But we ought 'o give a toot to let 'em know we got the right-o'-way. There's the whistle. Come on. Pull!'

Boot! They were on their way home, nicely and quietly now, so much so that Pat, swaying beside her, started talking politics again: 'A lot o' your mob're Comms, you know. Fact, Karl Marx was a Jew. Some o' best brains in Communism are Jews.' He leaned towards her. 'You wouldn't happen to be an undercover member yo'self, be any chance?' When she looked at him, he turned hastily away. ' 'S all right . . . forget it.'

He whistled a bit to himself, what, mixed up with the mechanical din, might have been *The Red Flag*. Then he turned back to her. 'What about takin' you along to the pub for a couple of hours tonight? When there's a lively crowd they have a bit of a sing-song . . . eh?'

'But I am guest of Tooheys.'

'What'll they do tonight? The two old fellers'll just sit up and drink and talk about yell . . . eh . . . halfcastes, or the news they don' know nothin' about . . . and the old girl'll go to bed after she's washed the dishes.'

'Still I am guest.'

'Tell you what . . . when I drop you there, I'll take you acrost, and ask 'em. You're young an' you ought 'o 'ave a bit o' fun.' She half smiled in answer, sitting now, with hand on the regulator, the regular engine driver.

He was silent for some time, staring along the track, frowning, biting a lip, as if chewing something over. Then suddenly he turned to her, came close, spoke in her ear: 'They reckon old Delacy's in love with you . . . that right?'

Her eyes grew great looking at him. Their eyes clung. He blinked, swallowed 'I only said what people're sayin'.'

'Vot pipple?'

'Aw, forget it. They'll say anything.' He swung away, to look at the boiler gauges.

And there they were back in civilization, goats along the line, glimpse of tents of laid-up drovers down by the river. Pat took over to stop before Tom Toohey's place. He went with her as arranged. Jeremy and Kurt were there with the Tooheys. Prindy was stopping with his father-in-law, Barbu. Pat told them that he'd like to take Rifkah to Finnucane's. When no one answered, he demanded angrily. 'What's wrong with yous . . . ain't I good enough for 'er?'

Jeremy said, 'Why ask us . . . can't the lady answer for herself?' He looked at Rifkah.

She smiled at him, then at Pat, saying, 'I mek up my mind later, Pat. If you like to come back. Zank you for engine ride.'

Pat blinked, swallowed, then muttering, 'Okay,' turned and went off back to his fretting engine.

The engine slipped in starting, snorted as if angrily in getting a grip of the rails, so aptly expressing the mood they supposed the driver was in that those who listened laughed over it, but without comment. It wasn't until they were eating that Mrs Toohey asked Rifkah why she didn't want to go to the Hotel. When told that it was out of consideration for herself, Nolly said that was silly, that she should go and have fun, a pretty young girl like her. The others agreed. Then Rifkah said, 'Ve vill all go together, yes?' An awkward silence. How tell a stranger to the ways of the country, and so friendly a one towards all kinds, the humiliating facts – that never in her life had Nolly been on what was called Licensed Premises, because the Law of the Land had for so long forbidden it to the like of her unto any generation decided upon by a so-called Protector of Aborigines, and still forbade it unless the party applied to such an officer for a permit to do so and was by him considered a fit and proper person to get drunk with the dignity of a pure white; something that Nolly, perhaps less out of pride than disinterest, had neglected to do. No doubt feeling the awkwardness, Rifkah added: 'No matter.' Jeremy said he'd take her along for an hour or so. No one seemed to think that Pat would be back.

It was about eight, and Rifkah and Jeremy just about to go out, when the dog began to bark, steps sounded on the front verandah, there was a hammering, and a shout, 'Well . . . you comin', lady?'

They had him in. He was nicely got up, in the uniform of his class in this classless society: cream silk shirt, black peg-top pants, patent dancing pumps, with ginger hair slicked with oil as no one had ever before seen it. To begin with he was a bit uppity, but relaxed with a beer and the sight of Rifkah and Jeremy's prompt surrender of his charge to him. Rifkah, wearing a bright dirndl and glowing herself in the soft reflection of the shaded brilliance of the pressure lamp on the table, looked lovelier than ever.

So black did the night appear as the couple were going off, seen out by the others, that Tom Toohey offered use of a flashlight. The darkness was worse for the footpath's being of railway cinders, and there being the wall of the tops of the tall river timber across the way, and perhaps because the heavens were so bright. At any rate, Pat declined the offer, saying that he had eyes like a cat in the dark and telling Rifkah to take his arm. As they went, following the main railway track, of which the stars gave a hint here and there, owing to Pat's recent lively polishing of them, he told her how he'd had often to drive of dark nights when the headlight failed, saying that he had developed this special night-sight of his through having trained in his calling on engines fitted only with kerosene lights, by which, he declared, you couldn't see further ahead than twenty feet. 'Yeah,' he added, 'I got eyes like a cat in the dark . . . ow!' He stumbled, fell on his knees, got up staggering, yelping, while she picked her way carefully over the rusty rails of the turning triangle: 'Jesus bloody Christ . . . bloody stinkin' bastard . . . I hurt me knee!'

She was giggling. Limping, he demanded, 'What's funny 'bout it?'

'Vot you sayingk.'

'What's wrong't it . . . don't you like bad language?'

'You call zat bad language?'

'Christ, no . . . but I couldn't let really loose in front o' you.'

'Vy?'

'Aw, Jesus!'

She took his arm again, 'Vy you call name of Jesus Christ, ven you don't believe religion.'

'Aw . . . just a bad bloody habit.'

'Vy you say bloody, bloody, bloody . . . everybody say?'

'Jees – hell – aw, I don' know. Don't Jews swear?'

'Yes . . . but wit' meaningk.'

Like what?'

'Vell . . . like, if you hurt yourself, or somezingk go vrong, you say "Fits on ze *Goyim*".'

'What's that mean?'

'Zat English.'

'Don't sound like it to me.'

'Of course. You vish all ze *Goyim*, ze Christians, to haf fits.'

He laughed. 'That's a good one. I'll have to use it. Fits on the bloody *Goyim*, eh?' He added: 'You could say Fits on the Fascists. I'll try it on Collings, the bastard. He pulled me up tonight for takin' that burn on the engine with you.'

'Because of me?'

'No . . . just usin' the per-way without his permission, he says.'

'Vot is per-way?'

'Permanent way . . . the main line . . . the Fascist bastard.'

'But he not belong to Fascist Party.'

'He's a bloody Fascist all the same. He's a bosses' man. He's a scab . . . .'

'You talkingk politics.'

'Well, what're you goin' 'o talk about?'

'Ve talk about stars. You know anyzing about stars?'

'What's the good o' knowin' anything about stars when our own bloody world's in the state it is?'

'Zen you can forget ze bloody vorld for leetle vile . . . and know how leetle ze vorld is, and yourself. See zat bright star up zere . . . zat is Altair, in ze constellation of ze Eagle. Do you know how many million miles it is avay, and how long it take light to reach us?'

'What's it bloody well matter when we got a social system like we have?'

'Mankind first begin to zing . . . stink . . . think . . . from lookingk at ze stars. Ze first true science vos astronomy.'

'It don't feed people. It don't stop Nazis persecutin' Jews.'

'Human intelligence vill do zat. Ven everybody look at stars and understand infinity of Universe.' The sort of stuff talked on those ritual walks at Lily Lagoons.

'You talk like that after the way you been treated by them bloody bastard Nazis!'

'I am free and 'appy now . . . in free an 'appy country . . . .'

'Says you!'

'Vot you mean by zat?'

'You'll find out, lady . . . you'll find out.'

She exclaimed suddenly, 'Vot's zat . . . all zose eyes?'

'Aw . . . only the famous heap of bottles. The biggest heap of bottles in the world, they reckon . . . stupid bastards . . . as if it's sumpin to be proud of, how much bloody grog you drunk!' He was starting off to give statistics on Australian drinking. She interrupted him.

'Listen!'

Across the road into which they were turning from the Hall, the sound of music.

He grunted: 'Silly old Ali Barba tootlin' on his bamboo flute.'

'No . . . ist not Indian music . . . it is Jewish . . . *la, la, la, la, lalala*!'

'What's he doing with Jewish music?'

'Not him . . . zat Prindy. Come, ve go see zem.'

'Eh . . . what about the pub?'

'Can vait. I vont to see my leetle boy.' She headed for Barbu's dimly lighted shop. Grunting reluctance, Pat had to go along with her.

The music stopped at sound of their footsteps in the shop. A moment, evidently for scrutiny through the peep-hole, then Barbu appeared, bowing low to Rifkah, while cocking a wary eye at Pat, asking what he might do for them. Rifkah said they'd heard the music as they passed and were just looking in to say Hello. Where was Prindy? Barbu, jabbering and gesticulating vaguely, appeared not to know anything. At length there was Prindy in the back doorway. Rifkah went to him, kissed him on the brow, told him how sweet the music had sounded. She said, 'You know Mister Pat Hannaford?' Prindy, eyeing Pat somewhat as Barbu had, nodded.

Pat said shortly, 'Course he knows me. Didn't I help him to get away from the Gestapo? Didn't I offer to help to send him to Russia?'

Rifkah looked astonished, murmuring, 'Gestapo . . . Russia . . . vot ist joke?'

'No joke,' snapped Pat, and briefly explained, concluding: 'But he wants to stop in the bush like a bloomin' blackfeller!'

Prindy appeared to be quite unmoved by the terse dissertation on his ingratitude. From looking at him, Rifkah turned to Pat. 'Better stay in bush, too. Zat vot I vill do. Who vont to go to Russia . . . cold, and hunger, and only vork, vork, vork.'

Pat growled, 'You ain't been to Russia.'

She snapped, 'You ain't, too!'

Pat glared. 'It's the Workers' Fatherland . . . .'

'Zat is vot I say . . . only vork. Blackfellers do not vork . . . not like slave vite pipple.'

'They're primitive people. You've got 'o work in the modern world. The Workers of Russia work for 'emselves . . . that's the difference.'

Prindy said, 'Worker of Russia work for lib'ration de masses of de world.'

They all swung on him. Pat exclaimed, 'Eh . . . where'd you get that?'

'I hear on radio.'

'Good on you, sonny!' Then when Rifkah giggled, Pat demanded, 'What's wrong't that?'

'So much he hear on radio. He hear Adolf Hitler ze ozzer night and imitate him beautifully. . . . '

'That yapping mongrel bastard . . . . '

'Also he hear Josef Stalin . . . and imitate him. He is very clever at imitation. He imitate King George, and Joe Lyons, and dingo, and donkey.'

Pat scowled. She said, 'He vill play us zomezingk . . . zen ve vill go. You vill play for us, *kleine mensheleh*?' Prindy nodded and went out. Pat swung on his long legs, evidently impatient to be gone. When Prindy returned after a moment with his flute, Rifkah turned to Pat. 'Vot you like him play?'

Pat grimaced his indifference – then suddenly leered: 'Yeah . . . how 'bout *The Red Flag*?' He turned the leer on Prindy. 'Know that one, Comrade?'

Prindy blinked, looked at Rifkah, who nodded, saying, 'Zat *Oh, Tannenbaum.*'

Prindy nodded, put flute to mouth. Pat demanded, 'What's this Tanninbum business?'

But the liquid silver was already flowing from the flute. Rifkah raised her hand for silence.

Pat became as entranced as Rifkah and Barbu. Then into the cascading sweetness came Rifkah's voice, softly, singing the German words of the original song. A sad song, so different from that through which, with voices and fists raised, so much satisfying defiance could be expressed by the oppressed – *The Master Class may kiss me arse, we'll keep the Red Flag Flying.* That's what Pat said in effect, when the last of it faded away like the last of bird's song in evening: 'Well . . . I never heard the old song like that before.'

'Zat is ze proper vay for it to play and singk,' said Rifkah. 'We go now.' She kissed Prindy. 'Vos beautiful. I see you later.' She smiled at Barbu, who bowed low. Prindy did likewise. Pat nodded amiably to them as, with Rifkah on his arm, he went out.

Out in the street, heading for the brilliance of Finnucane's some three hundred yards away, Pat asked, 'What you mean that's the proper way to play and sing the *Red Flag*? It's got 'o be militant . . . a fightin' song.'

'Maybe ze *Red Flag*. But *Oh, Tannenbaum* is of peace . . . people who vont peace . . . are tired from too much vor. Ze Communists tek zat simple song of peace and mek vot you call Militant.'

'Well, I didn't know that. But what's the use of havin' simple old songs o' peace, when there's a class war to be fought?'

She giggled. 'Vot's ze use of ze stars, yes . . . ven you can't eat zem?'

'Pokin' borak, eh?'

'Vot is borak?'

'I don't know, 'xac'ly. Just a sayin'.'

'You say so many zing you don't know.'

'Now . . . that's more borak. You go easy.'

She hugged his arm. 'I only play mitt you. And what you zink my leetle music master?'

'He's good with that flute, all right. But what a pity you can't do anything with him but tootlin' on a flute.'

'Vot you mean you can't do anyzing mitt him . . . wit' him?'

'You can't do anything with any of 'em . . . no matter how light their colour. The blackfeller's there always. You just can't get 'em to think in terms of betterin' their lot, of solidarity . . . .'

She snapped, 'Vot foolishness you talk!'

He snapped back, 'It ain't foolishness. I know 'em only too well. I suppose you've heard I got a halfcaste wife and quartercaste kids . . . or *did* have!' The addition was made with bitter emphasis.

'I 'ear.'

'Well, there y'are. Smart girl . . . out of a mission. I give her everything . . . every chance to better herself. What's she do? She prefers the yeller-fellers o' the town to me. Gets drinkin' and whorin'. When I put a stop to it, she picks up with this well-sinker . . . no-good bastard . . . just a lair and a Squatter's Stooge. They go bush. What's happened to her and the two kids, gawd knows. He's sure t've dropped 'em.'

'Did you try find zem?'

'What for? They don't want me.'

'Vy don't zey vont you?'

'Because they want to live like blackfellers. Talk politics to 'em, and they go to sleep. But tell 'em you seen native plums or applies or sumpin like that gettin' ripe down the line ... and they're on the next train with you, goin' to get 'em.'

'Pipple say you talk too much politics to zem.'

Pat's loud voice rose louder: 'Do they, the bastards . . . scabby bloody bastards are as bad as the scabby bloody blacks 'emselves . . . bloody bosses' men . . . . '

They were coming up to McDodd's, out of the dim-lit doorway of which popped the McDodd himself, cackling, 'Here . . . moderate ye language, ye foul-moothed larrikin!'

Pat grunted at him. 'Aw, shove yo'r 'ead in yo'r 'aggis bag!'

'Pay nae heed to his red- raggin' fashery, lassie . . . the mon's a fanatic . . . . '

'Up yo' tree, yo' Caledonian ape!'

'And off tae Rooshia wi' ye bog-trootin' sel' and pull barges up and doon yon Volga Reever wi' ye enlightened Comrades leeborin' under the Commissar's lash!' McDodd's voice rose so high that his fat wife came running out to see, and heads popped over Finnucane's verandah. Pat growled to giggling Rifkah, as he handed her up onto the verandah. 'See what you're up agin in this free and happy land, as you call it?'

They headed through the gaping group towards the passage leading to the lounge-bar. In the passage Rifkah asked, 'Vot is Caledonian ape?'

'Eh? A Scotch monkey.'

'But no monkey in Scotland?'

'Aw . . . just one of them sayin's. Let's get a drink.'

Four couples were in the lounge, compared with a score or more of males in the bar. At one table sat Constable Stunke and his colleague, Gobally of Charlotte Springs, with their wives, the Goballys also with two small children. The others were Station Master Collings and his wife, and one of Vaisey's small down-country managers and his. All eyed the newcomers with interest little short of rudeness, but as to be expected in those parts and the circumstances. Pat nodded, saying shortly, ' 'Night.' The others nodded and murmured in reply. Rifkah smiled and nodded and was similarly responded to. Pat chose a table, seated Rifkah somewhat ceremoniously, saying, 'I'll get sumpin . . . what you like?'

But there was Finnucane in the doorway, addressing himself to Rifkah: 'Ah . . . and ye did decoide to spend the avenin' wid us . . . but not the good doctor?' When Rifkah explained, he addressed the lounge generally: 'Let's have a bit o' gaiety, then.' He looked at Mrs Stunke. 'Hope you're in good voice this evenin', Missus . . . and you, Gil.' He turned to Gobally. 'So let's adjourn to the courtyard.' He went on out the back, bellowing to his spinster daugher Peggy to come and play and to Mam to stand by to attend the bar. There followed a general slow movement to the rear, with the men carrying bottles of various kinds of tipple. Clancy was amongst those who came from the bar, in company with the young Assistant Bookkeeper from Beatrice Station and a similar superior Vaisey type from off the train. He cast one surly glance at Rifkah and Pat, then with evident deliberateness avoided looking at them and concentrated on his companions. He talked rather too much for one not usually much of a talker, but when the singing started, kept out of it, even hanging his head when not swigging his beer.

Finnucane initiated the gaiety, as he called it, with his usual rendering of *Vive La Compagnie*, with his own bits added, insisting on the company's joining him when he roared the refrain to Peggy's extra thumping – *Vive la comp, vive la comp, vive la Compagnie*! – but without stirring them to the required state of liveliness that mostly he could with his flair for hostmanship. Perhaps they lacked the elements to make a lively crowd, and he would have left them to their own devices, but for wanting to make it a special occasion for Rifkah. Everybody who could contribute something did so under the compulsion of the blarney of old Shame-on-us, soprano, baritone, mezzo, and tenor – everything from Mrs Stunke's *Drink to me Only with Thine Eyes* to Shamus's own *Finnegan's Wake* – but only to have the audience, when the politeness of applause was ended, turn back into themselves and their glasses. Even Rifkah's ending a lively Polish-Jewish song with a bit of the dance called *Kezatzke*, in doing which she showed her shapely long legs a couple of times right up to her drawers, brought forth nothing but a few guffaws, in addition to the bit of clapping. The *Kezatske* was in response to a whispered appeal to Rifkah by Shamus for 'something to loiven 'em up'. As they stood looking at each other after it, baffled of expression, suddenly Rifkah's face lit up. She said she'd thought of something – just wait a minute. Pat seeing her running out, tried to stop her, asking where she was going. She laughed merrily, saying she vos not runningk avay – would be back in a minute.

She ran through to the street, turned southward, trotting. McDodd's was closed now; but not Barbu's, in the faint light flowing from which could be seen the herd of goats, evidently gathered to listen to Prindy's fluting and Barbu's high-pitched singing. Because the goats would not make way for her, probably through not being used to having anyone ask so nicely, she had to go through the gate into the yard and round the back. The concert going on in the kitchen stopped at her footfall. She rushed in, told Prindy she wanted him to come and play his flute at the Hotel: 'Your first publique appearantzingk,' she said. 'Come on . . . kvick . . . zey waitingk.' Barbu began to gabble protests. She didn't understand, nor try to. 'I bringk him back to you soon.'

As they trotted back to the Hotel they planned their repertoire, arriving there to present themselves puffing slightly, but otherwise with dignity that probably added to the gaping surprise of the gathering out in the beer-garden, whose bush-whackers' tradition demanded avoidance of the dramatic as something abberant. Beaming her pleasure in the effect, Rifkah guided her quaintly dressed young charge with a hand now on his shoulder towards the piano. Peggy and her father gaped and goggled no less than the rest. She pulled Prindy round to face the crowd, saying, 'Goot pipple, I present for you ze young Maestro of ze flute, Prendegast Delacy. First he vill play for my singingk some old Jewish songk. Zen for you he vill play anyzing you vish . . . from Bach to *Barney Google*.' A titter in response to her own giggle over the joke that probably no one saw. She turned to Prindy. 'Tek ze bow, Maestro.' Gravely Prindy bowed. That produced another louder titter, then a few hand-claps echoing those of Pat Hannaford. Failing to observe that some of the company looked anything but amused, she turned to Peggy, asking, 'You vill vont to accompany . . . now, or after?' Peggy had been looking at her father. The roll of her eye caused Rifkah to seek the cause of it. Shamus's eye was rolling too. He shifted it quickly to the police group. Obviously that's where the trouble lay, in those blank official faces, those disapproving policemen's stares. Rifkah's smile faded. She asked, 'Vot isht?' Stunke looked meaningfully at Shamus, who after a hesitation turned to her, came up to her, and with hand to mouth, said with comparative softness, 'Afraid we can't have him here, me dear.' Now it was Rifkah who gaped. He added: 'Agin the law, ye see.'

She murmured, 'Vot is meant?'

Finnucane grimaced, as if to dissociate himself from such a thing. 'A police matter.'

'Police? Vot is matter for police?'

Shamus turned back to the group, appealing for co-operation. They all exchanged glances. Then Stunke rose, came over. 'Sorry, miss . . . but it's against the law for that boy to be here.'

She blinked. 'I do not understand.'

'Aboriginal Ordinance. Take him away, please.'

'Vot is Aboriginal Ordinance? He is not black child.'

'He's barred from licensed premises just the same as if he was. In fact he shouldn't be out at night. Jeremy Delacy ought to know better'n to let you bring him here. Tell him so from me.'

Rifkah was going to say something, and evidently changed her mind, swallowed, said, 'Mister Delacy do not know I bringk him. I bringk him meinself.'

'Well, if you don't mind, take him back to Delacy. Delacy's got custody of him for a limited time. The boy's not supposed to be out of his custody. If I find him out of it again, I'll take him in.'

Rifkah's face went red. Staring into the heavy face she asked, 'You mean you put him jail?'

'I mean I'll take him into lawful custody.'

She asked sharply, 'Custody mean lock up?'

Stunke's face darkened. 'It means that, if anyone gives trouble. Now, get along, please.'

Rifkah reached for Prindy, panting, 'Must ve go, *kleine mensheleh*. It is not free happy country. I vos mistake.' As she took the boy's slim yellow hand, she looked round the staring crowd, repeating softly, as if she wanted someone to contradict, 'I vos mistake . . . I vos mistake.' They simply stared. Then suddenly her lovely young face took on that old *bubbeh* look, crumpled and quivered. A gush of tears made her great eyes grow greater. A strangled sob – then dragging Prindy, she rushed back across the courtyard to leave. Pat Hannaford came loping to meet her, caught her free arm, went with her. The staring eyes followed them.

Across the yard about to enter the passage leading through the Hotel, Hannaford halted his little group, while he swung round to face the crowd. He shot up his right hand, shouted, 'Heil Hitler!' Then with the arm going round his charges, he ushered them out of sight.

For a moment there was silence behind there. Stunke broke it, growling, 'Cheeky bastard.'

Finnucane sighed gustily. 'Sure, 'twas unfortunate . . . so nice a lassie. She should've been warned.'

Stunke said, 'She should be warned to keep away from Hannaford. Mixin' up with him won't do her or her mob any good.'

Col Collings came into it: 'Maybe they're hand in glove. There's lots o' Jews're Commos, what I read . . . .'

'Now, now!' boomed Finnucane. 'I'm sure there's no harm in that gurrl and that good little doctor. Let's have a drink. And let's have no scandal-mongerin' if you don't moind . . . or I'll be callin' the evenin' a day. This wan's on the house.'

Sobbing on Hannaford's arm, still clinging to Prindy's hand, Rifkah rushed them back to Barbu's, to get Prindy's things for taking to Toohey's. Poor old Barbu, in tears himself, said he had tried to warn her. He whispered to Pat that she had too big a heart. Pat only shook his head.

By the time they reached Toohey's she was only sniffling, but so obviously grief-stricken that all there stared at her in surprise. It was Pat told the story while she went off to rinse her face. After that she could only sit sighing, staring, staring. Soon she went off to bed. It was then that Jeremy blamed himself in speaking of the incident to the others, saying that he should have known better than to have let her go amongst the mob without him, checking the indignation that Pat was about to express by saying, 'In some ways she's very young and innocent. It's probably because she didn't get the chance to develop normally as a young girl. She's wanted to love everybody and everything here . . . in reaction to the hate she's known, I suppose. Is that right, Kurt?' Kurt only shrugged.

Next morning Pat stopped his south-bound train in front of Toohey's alighted, and while heads popped from passenger coaches and brake-van, came loping in. The household was already out to wave, including Rifkah, who smiled wanly at his asking how she was. He produced a letter he said Finnucane had given him to drop off, and told the company that he had heard from Porky Jones of Old Shame-on-us's shortness with the bosses and bosses' men last night. Then he said, 'Be seein' you later, eh?' and shoved his face at Rifkah in a clumsy kiss that made him go much redder than she, turned on Prindy and tousled the fair hair, waved to the others and went loping back to his engine – while the passengers cheered. *Boo-hoot*! A wave from Pat – and the train was on its way again – now with passengers and van-crew waving. Rifkah, waving half-heartedly, was suddenly in tears again, and had to go inside. The same mob who had sat and stared last night. Yet the cause of her humiliation then, the one truly humiliated, him of the tousled fair hair, waved with such enthusiasm as to have to hop.

Finnucane's letter, as ever a masterpiece of calligraphy and subtlety, was addressed to Kurt, expressing regret for last night's incident, and inviting him and the Lovely Lady Herself and that Beautiful Boy, and of course his old friend Jeremy, to take a Cup of Tay with the family before returning home. There was no gainsaying it, even by Jeremy, whose only comment was, 'There's no doubt about him. He never misses a trick. The dining-room of a hotel is exempt from the other restrictions on licensed premises.'

It was no mere Cup of Tay the homing party found awaiting them at Finnucane's. Old Shame-on-us must have had his female slaves up before the dawn to bake that varied spread, seeing they'd also had to prepare and serve a dozen breakfasts. When the guests protested at such lavishness so early in the day, he protested in return, 'Shame on us if we can't do for our personal guests in a stoil befittin' our regard for 'em!' The blarney was running full tap from the moment he received them to that when he bowed them into the truck to head for home. He was all apologies for last night, yet laid the blame on no one, nor even blamed the law of the land, although he made it responsible for making kindly people deal with simple ones in a manner they didn't choose themselves. The Aboriginal Problem was a very difficult one, he declared. But it would be solved, he said; sure 'twould be solved, and all the quicker for having in the community clever people like these new friends of his, helped by the great experience and intelligence of this old friend of his, Jeremy – Ah, yes, to be sure!

As the party swung away, farewelled with such a show of respect and affection, and passed the Police Station to find no one looking out from there, not even the Tracker and his family as if an order had been issued to that effect, Jeremy remarked, 'Well, at least you know how you stand with Germans. Last time that old Irish humbug mentioned Aborigines in my presence it was to say that but for Lord Vaisey's taking the country over, I with my views would have turned it into a black's camp . . . .'

Kurt cut in to say, 'Don't be so sure you can trust ze Germans. Ven Hitler first make ze trouble for ze Jews, my friends and colleagues express mooch concern, callingk him a madman and svearingk to make no difference in our relationship. But ven ze madman comes to full power . . . vot zen? Vere are my non-Jewish friends and colleagues? I haf none. And it is not fear. At least your Irisher make pretence at friendship. He doesn't turn his back on you, and call ze Gestapo.'

'The last thing I'd count on myself in dealing with the local variety of Gestapo would be the loyalty of our honey-tongued friend, Old Shame-on-us.'

Kurt looked at Jeremy searchingly. Jeremy went on: 'The informer's as strong in the Irishman as the rebel. It was probably the informer that put the Irish in bondage to the English for hundreds of years, and kept them there . . . till the English, who are only good at games that have rules, gave it up.'

Kurt laughed. But Rifkah had that haggard old look again. She said, 'I zink he truly loff Kurt for savingk life of his daughter Bridie and her baby.' She said it as they were running past the site of the Lily Lagoons camp beside the river, at which she cast a glance as if at some sweetness sadly lost. Jeremy, about to say something else in cynical vein to Kurt by the look of him, glanced at her as he leaned across, and plainly desisted, sat back, as they crossed the causeway, seeing a small cloud of cockatoos rise from a big plum tree up on the other bank, remarked, 'Plums must be early this yesr. We'll have to look for some along the way. There's a nice patch of them not far from the Rainbow Pool. Remember I told you you can make a lovely jam out of 'em?'

She smiled as if gratefully. He then talked of food, asking if she thought she could help Nan out in providing for the biggish party they were expecting for four or five days at least. He said he'd received a letter from General Esk saying that they intended setting up camp as soon as they arrived, so as not to inconvenience the household, but that he himself would rather have them in the house until they got used to roughing it, since none of them really had so far. Rifkah cheered up at that. Asked about fish for a big fry for *Shabbos*, she said there was enough in the refrigerator to provide for Friday evening, but that was all. 'We must do it properly,' he said. 'Must have enough for Saturday, too. I'll get them to go out for more first thing tomorrow.'

Coming at length to the vicinity of the Pool, they turned left, away from it, following a scarcely discernible track, to take a look at the grove of plums. No cockies, hence no ripe fruit. However, according to the knowledgeable ones at the back who ate a few green, among them Prindy, they should be ripe in about a week. Prindy suggested that he and Rifkah come there riding, and at the same time take a dip in the Pool.

Black at Lily Lagoons was that sanctuary for the little girl who had been snatched from her *bubbeh*'s arms while playing at housekeeping, in the like of it, the kitchen, and those gentle substitutes for *bubbeh*'s arms, Nanago's, into both of which Rifkah flung herself. Nevertheless, she was still subdued when she and Jeremy set out on the ritual walk.

Gently as they went, Jeremy got onto the subject of last night, confessing that he was puzzled by her being so upset when she must have known pretty well from his own talk what the law was regarding Aborigines and the attitude of whites generally towards them, Pat Hannaford himself being no lover of them, for all his defiance of authority on their behalf in flagrant cases of ill-treatment of them. She answered slowly, 'Ze vay zose pipple look, I am remind of German pipple ven zey see Jew marching wit' SS or SA. It is ze vorst zing zat look, I zink.'

'Yes?'

She drooped her dark-seeming head, so that the copper glinted in the starlight. 'Ze bullying of SA you expect . . . or some pipple spit at you. Zere vas alvays anti-Jew business. I know as little girl and my *bubbeh* and *zaydeh* tell me of bad times. But ven I am taken by Gestapo, and zey drag me avay and I am very frightened . . . I look at zose ordinary German pipple lookingk, and I see zey don't care . . . I am Jew. Zat is vorst zing, I say.' She looked up at him, the starlight now glinting in her great eyes.

'Go on.'

'Zen my heart . . . like stop. I tell you . . . I don't mind *polizei* so mooch . . . zat is job for zem . . . but zose pipple. Vy don't zey 'elp me? Vot is wrong? Vot haf I done? Only I am Jew. Vot is zat? Zey don't hate me. I do not see hate in eye. Vot I see is . . . is . . . zey don't care about me . . . because I am Jew. Don't matter I am young girl, or pretty girl, or . . . or . . . vell, zey don't care. I am some different.'

She sighed, drooped again for a while, went on, clinging close to him: 'I see after plenty time. Ve haf to vear ze Badge of Shame . . . ze Germans call . . . ze Yellow Star. Ve march t'rough street with SA guard. Pipple stare. Vot is in zere eye? Nozzing. You are Jew. Zen your heart . . . vell, like lead, so heavy. You have ozzer Jew. But you know zey feel same . . . lonely and lost. Ve are different kind. Ze vorld don't care about us . . . no matter ve are clean, goot, quiet pipple . . . ve are Jew.' She sighed again. 'Zat is vot I see in eye of zose pipple last night . . . not lookingk at me, because zey not like zat to Jew zis country . . . but at my leetle boy, my *kleine mensheleh*. He is most beautiful boy. He is most beautiful person in ze room, ze most *gebentchter* . . . most talent in country. But zey look at him like . . . like . . . .' Her voice grew, husky, faltered '. . . like in Germany.' She ended in a sob, drooped again on his arm. He reached and touched the dark glinting curls.

They walked in silence for a while, till he said gently, 'I'm going to ask you something personal. You know I'm not anti-Jewish . . . in fact I like you for being Jewish. But are you ashamed to be Jewish?'

Her head came up swiftly. 'Oh, no!'

'You are proud to be Jewish . . . you are happy to be Jewish, in spite of all you've had to suffer through being so?'

'If I do not vont to be Jewish, I change, yes?'

'You would never change?'

'Vy do I vont to change? I am happy to be vot I am. Vy do you ask me zat? I am not trouble now for Jews. Ze great Jewish capitalists of ze vorld and ze Communists vill save zem from Hitler. I vos trouble about Prindy.'

'You don't have to worry about him. He's not ashamed of being Aboriginal, I assure you . . . that's the remarkable thing about him, seeing he's only quarter, and that mother of his.'

'I vos trouble for Aboriginal pipple . . . zinkingk zey moost feel like Jews . . . vot you call it . . . nobody vont, nobody care?'

'Outcast. But Prindy's no outcast. He knows he belongs to the blacks. That's always been my theory . . . they grow up happily . . . the crossbreeds . . . if they're brought up close to the Old People.'

'But all ze time zey moost live close to vite pipple, and more and more need vite pipple, as you haf tell me . . . and zese vite pipple do not care, so Aboriginal pipple moost feel lost and lonely . . . outcast.'

He was silent for a while, staring intently ahead, while she, pacing with him, watched his dim profile. When he spoke it was with a strangely eager tone, for him, who usually spoke slowly, laconically, even warily: 'Do you know, what you've been saying makes me see the Aborigines rather differently from what I did. I've been thinking of them as clinging to their old ways as more satisfying, because there's nothing we have to offer them to replace these . . . nothing but work, semi-slavery, even on the level with the whiteman. But what you've told me makes me think of something else, something stronger even than tradition in man . . . dignity. You know that word?'

'Yes.'

'What you've said about the Jews . . . not only just now, but before . . . and what Kurt has told me, and what I've been reading lately . . . it seems to me that it is pride in themselves, in their individuality, in their dignity as what they are, that's kept the Jews going as Jews, through all the centuries of even frightful discouragement. The satisfaction of your ritual comes out of the satisfaction of your pride. Do I make that clear?'

'Yes . . . I zing it is right. Jews who change to Christianity are not happy pipple . . . no matter how rich and big zey come . . . . not like poor leetle pipple of ze ghetto.'

'Yet there's that loneliness you spoke of . . . being slighted, despised . . . no, that's not the word you used . . . you said what hurt worst was the world not caring for you in your suffering. How does this fit in with pride?'

She was still staring at him. 'I do not know.'

'I think I see the reason for the German people's not caring. That fits the not caring of Australians for the Aborigines. You have slighted them by refusing to be like them. Through the centuries you've made them look fools by being nice to them, giving them the best of everything you've got . . . but never imitating them. You suffer because you are Jews. You choose to be Jews. Therefore to hell with you in your suffering. Is that right?'

'I zink so.'

'The same thing with the Australian Nation. It can say to the Aborigines: "You have your chance. Become like us. Otherwise to hell with you." There's a saying amongst people who have a lot to do with Aborigines. "A blackfellow understands only two kinds of whiteman . . . the Cheeky Bugger and the Bloody Fool." You understand the Aboriginal usage of the word Cheeky, don't you . . . like Cheeky Yam, Cheeky Sugar-bag, Cheeky Snake . . . meaning something you've got to be careful of . . . full of bite, sting . . . in the case of a whiteman, a bully, and exploiter. Old Coon-Coon is Number-One Cheeky Bugger *Dookyangana*. The expression used to annoy me. I see now that there's real truth in it. The blackfellow doesn't hate the whiteman. He'd even like to help him, to co-operate with him. The explorers found that, even when intruding on wild tribes' hunting grounds. But like the Jews, he wants to be what he is, what he's proud of being . . . yes, even in the seemingly utterly degraded ones you find hanging about the fringes of towns . . . complete beggars, outcasts, social lepers . . . but still Aborigines, even the cross-breeds that have grown up with them. And that's why the whiteman . . . the Nation at large, when you get down to tin-tacks . . . can ignore what seems to be their frightful conditions. The black bastards only have themselves to blame, as they say. You'll find every squatter . . . pretty well everybody who has anything to do with them, even the police . . . will tell you what they've tried to do for them . . . only to be let down. God forgive me, I've done it myself . . . have been doing it in a way all along, I'm afraid. Even though I've bucked the stupid official policy of so-called Integration, I've still practised it in a way . . . teaching them to be white blackfellows . . . as against the official policy of making them black whitefellows.'

He sighed gustily. 'It's this strange fellow-feeling of yours for them that's shown me the truth. I've raged against their ill-treatment . . . plenty of people have . . . but I've never wept over the rejection of them for what they are . . . that subtle thing, practised by everyone in the land, even the missionaries trying to save them from exploitation, even myself . . . nor have I seen anyone else weep like that . . . nor had I realized that in their hearts there must be a great sadness on account of their rejection for what they are . . . the sadness like that in which they cry *Poor Fellow My Country*. I've pitied them only. So does every feeling person. But pity's the wrong feeling. They don't want it . . . only exploit it when it's given. They don't need it. They are proud people. Yes . . . these humblest of all the races of men, I see now, are amongst the proudest . . . thanks to you, and your own eternal pride of being . . . Bless you, dear girl . . . dear Jewish girl . . . dear Jewess!' He stopped suddenly, flung his arms about her, and for the first time in all intimate association, of his own volition, kissed her, fair on the lips, and with such purpose that when they drew apart they were breathless. That it wasn't mere sexual passion was evident from the way they both laughed, while still clinging, and her sudden little act of returning the kiss with the swift movement usual to her.

He looked around. 'Lord . . . how far we've come! We'd better go back . . .

or they'll think we've eloped.' As they turned they both laughed again, relinking arms.

As they went homeward he talked even more eagerly, saying how glad he was that this little miracle of revelation had happened before the coming of that Professor St Clair, surely the man who would become the Director of the mooted new Aborigines' Welfare concern and hence the one with more say in the matter of dealing with the people than any other in the Nation, since he now had a truly positive policy to put before him. This policy was primarily the protection of this people's pride, pride in their uniqueness, in themselves as themselves . . . which meant that the existing Aboriginal Reserves, so far maintained only by local ordinance that could be revoked by any petty official to meet the demands of commercial power, be written into the Constitution as inviolate, that the already dispossessed be prepared not for taking the lowest class place in the lowest class of a low-class white society, namely the Australian Nation, but for eventual inclusion in the still-proud tribes of the Reserves, that such assistance as these people would require would be in the way of scientific improvement of the productivity of their hunting grounds without intrusion on their own magical means of doing so . . . say getting pigs and buffaloes and other destructive alien creatures off them and replacing them with depleted native fauna and flora that would only be destroyed elsewhere. Ah, yes, a thousand wonderful positive things to do that would wipe out the original sin of the ruthless dispossession, and allow the Nation to become a thing of pride itself, instead of the thing of shame it was and always must be until such as this was done. There would also be the patronage of General Esk to count on. Then the Jewish Settlement, that could be on the fringe of the first Reserve, that of the Sandstone Country to the North here and the empty coastlands beyond, as a buffer of intelligence between the old ruthless gang of land-grabbers and despoilers, Vaisey and the rest of them. 'Ah, yes . . . ah, yes . . . thank you, dear girl, a million times, for your coming here, for your being what you are . . . for your doing what you did only twenty-four hours ago, scarcely thirty-six hours before these important people will be here. I feel you have saved my life. I'll confess I was just about beaten. The experience with Prindy was beating me. For all he's been showing in the way of being civilized, I've known he's only been waiting for Bobwirridirridi . . . and I must let him go . . . to what? To become simply an outlaw?'

He stopped her to say earnestly, 'You've got to help me, you know, girl. In fact you've got to do most of the active work with them. They've accepted you. You are the different kind, as they so wisely estimated. I'm still alien to them, the cheeky bugger and the bloody fool combined . . . the *Mullaka*, the Boss. They don't want bosses. They want *pookarakkas*, wise men, and someone they can look on as sort of Mother Goddess . . . a reincarnation of Koonapippi. You are the one . . . direct descendant of those earth mothers of your Bible . . . Sarah, Rachel, Rebecca. You *are* Rebecca, reincarnated, Mother of Israel, who fathered the Twelve Tribes and saw the ladder reaching from earth to heaven, and old Jehovah Tchamala up there on top! You've got to do it, Rebecca . . . Rifkah . . . you've just got to.'

She clung to him tightly, while looking up to him with the stars in her eyes. 'I vill, Jeremy, I vill. I know now zat is vy I am here.'

CHAPTER FIFTEEN

THE PARTY arriving by air at Lily Lagoons as arranged, were treated to something not in the arrangements for their entertainment. This was a poppy show; at least as he who was responsible for it called it, he being the pilot, Fergus Ferris. They were almost at their destination, dropping down the sky, when Fergus spotted something in one of the big holes of Knowles Creek that caused him to open his throttles and climb, then do a steep turn, and with throttles closed, came back like a swooping hawk, invisible in the eye of the mid-morning Sun, and almost as silent. Seeing now in full view what, keen-sighted though he must be to have spotted it at all, could have been only a glimpse of copper and ivory amongst flitting bits of jet and brown, he yelled from his cock-pit back at his puzzled passengers, 'Pin to see a poppy show!' and put on a bit of bank as he sliced through the lines of trees to give them all a look. It was naked Rifkah, running back to the water. A perfect view – at any rate for the hawk-eyed one, whose split-lipped grinning appreciation must plainly have been seen from the ground by those who could afford to look aloft; for very evidently it was only impending doom that at least a couple of the passengers saw, namely, Dr Fabian Cootes and Lieutenant Dickey, seeing how their complexions changed to match that of the leaves of the branches seeming to reach to rake them down – and the tightness of the faces of the others, Major Maltravers, Professor St Clair, and General Esk, suggesting that it was with fatalism rather than enjoyment that they looked. Then it was blotted out by the force pulling down eyelids along with entrails, as Fergus, his throttles wide again, climbed up out of what could be paradise.

They went in to land, doing a gentle turn about the homestead, came to earth. As the aircraft halted and the move to alight began, General Esk held up his hand, saying, 'A word, please, gentlemen.' Fergus coming from the cockpit to open the exit door halted. The General went on: 'I'd rather not have the incident that's just taken place remarked on to anyone we'll be seeing here. Agreed? Good!' Not that anyone gave him any assurance. But silent consent was surely to be expected from them all – except one, who as he moved again to open the door, Esk addressed directly, 'Mr Ferris . . . I've no doubt about your aeronautical skill . . . otherwise I wouldn't have engaged you . . . but I'm also aware of your excessive interest in females of our species and your propensity for talking, especially if the subject's bawdy. I'd like your word in this matter of keeping the little incident to ourselves. Do I have it?'

Fergus coloured, but showed the split lip grinning. 'What about swearing us all?'

'I'm sure of the silence of my own men . . . and can't demand it of our learned friends here, only expect it. I wouldn't like to terminate our contract . . . but would feel bound to, without your assurance. I repeat . . . do I have it?'

Fergus, quite red now, drew himself up in the manner of Malters dealing with his master, and in exactly the same tone snapped, 'Sah!'

Esk smiled slightly. 'Thank you. By the way, it was certainly a nice bit of flying, especially in view of the . . . er . . . . '

Fergus grinned again as he reached for the door. 'The view, eh?'

Esk chuckled. 'Exactly.'

Jeremy, greeting the party, asked what caused the diversion in flight. Fergus answered, saying he'd seen what he took to be members of the household and saluted them. Jeremy got the facts from Rifkah herself, when she popped into his den after lunch, having deliberately missed the meal. He turned red for a moment, then smiled and said, 'It'd be the cheeky young pilot, of course . . . but at least he was gentleman enough not to mention it. You should worry, anyway. Aren't you Queen of the Aborigines? That's the way I've been talking about you. Don't show any embarrassment at all.' She kissed him, saying she must hurry and get on with the fish-fry. He told her she would find in the store a case of *kosher* delicacies, canned stuff, that the General had had sent up from the South; and wonder of wonders, Kurt had offered to give the Blessing tonight. She kissed him again, went racing to the Big House.

There was no intrusion by the guests on the fish-fry. Perhaps Fergus would have tried it, the way he seemed to be yearning towards the kitchen while, with the house redolent of that sweet savour to the Lord, the guests were gathered with their host in the lounge as the ritual was reaching its climax. Indeed, he suggested, with a show of flippancy, that he should do so as a sort of crusade. This was the result of General Esk's telling the company that story, heard by himself in Palestine, of the angelic instruction behind the fish-fry and the secrecy surrounding it. Fergus said that, apart from the glorious smell, his scruples as a Christian demanded that he investigate. Esk said, 'I wouldn't advise it, young man. Your crusade would only end in Christian martyrdom. In her kitchen, a Jewess is a veritable lioness. Isn't that so, Dr Hoff . . . and Jeremy?'

Rifkah presented herself to the guests for the first time just before the meal, looking so lovely as to cause Fergus's face to twitch and the General to murmur softly, 'By George!' Her natural beauty was probably heightened by the fact of the achievement just wrought in cooking and table-setting and the challenge she now faced to preserve her dignity in that achievement. Dressed in a pretty dirndl and carrying a great tray laden with bits of those canned *kosher* delicacies to be eaten as hors d'oeuvres, as the men rose, she smiled, saying, 'I vill not be stayingk. I vill greet you in ze dining-room in proper vay. Anyvay, ve haf already met today . . . yes?'

Only Fergus sniggered, and stopped as soon as the great hazel eyes met his calmly. Smiling, she turned and left them.

The General declared, 'What a stunner she is . . . and poise, poise!'

Fergus, addressing those nearest him, Denzil and Malters, speaking under his breath and in mock Jewish accent, said, 'Poy's . . . vot's he mean poy's? Dat loffly vobbly bum ain't like a poy's!'

Denzil giggled; but Malters frowned.

Prindy, out looking for the Two Stars, found them, came racing in. The triangle sounded. The guests, and those who had surrendered hostship for the occasion, on going to the dining-room, found him waiting with the temporary hostess to enjoy the dramatic moment with her. With arm about her as she about him, in the golden candlelight looking, as Sir Mark Esk, momentarily halted with the others by the impact, whispered to Jeremy, 'Biblical . . . the Boy David . . . Esther the Queen!'

The meal, with its bit of ritual so nicely performed by Kurt and the incomparable dishes, went perfectly. Esk remarked, amongst much in praise of it all, 'There's no institution to compare with *Oneg Shabbat* in the simple grace that I believe is the proper expression of man's compromise between body and soul. I've had the honour of partaking of it in divers places, from the camel-hide tents of the Gypsy-Jews of the Russian Steppes, to palaces of multi-millionaires . . . and no matter the difference in fare or service, the same simple beauty was always there.' He raised his glass, glancing from Rifkah to Kurt: 'For this great *michayeh, toda rabbah*!'

Sir Mark was included in the ritual walk that night, with a new Moon to light the way, on account of which he with Rifkah recited a little prayer in Hebrew. Esk translated for Jeremy's benefit: ' "The beginning of the month hast thou given unto thy people as a season of expiation for all their generation". It really means that they've adapted the new Moon as substitute for the old burnt offering that expiates sin . . . clever . . . and very beautiful, don't you think, dear boy?'

Jeremy was delighted. Judaism remained so close to nature, he said, while those who practised it could rise to such heights of human intelligence. Eagerly he told of his discovery, through Rifkah, of the likeness between Jew and Aborigine in refusal to abandon their satisfying oneness with Creation, even under persecution by those who having lost it lived by lies. Esk was very interested, obviously more in Jeremy's new enthusiasm than in the theme. They talked it all the way.

The same theme dominated the talk in the lounge afterwards, with the word Ethos now flying about like a *Seraph* or a *Maiormu*, conjured up by those doctors of the science of man, St Clair and Cootes. The Professor, a gentle, rather nervous type of man, tall and thin and bony-headed, showed great interest in Jeremy's new theory. Not the Coot, however, who kept on declaring that it was dangerous to liken such diverse ethnic groups. Fergus wanted to know what the danger was; but there was something sly about his question, as if he were trying to catch Cootes on some point; and doubtless the learned gentleman had been caught by this angler after laughs too often to be drawn.

Fergus had the last word on the subject as he and the other newcomers were making their way round the upstairs verandah on the way to their rooms: 'D'you know, fellers . . . we're going to be lucky to get out of this place with our foreskins.'

It was received in gentlemanly silence by all except Denzil Dickey, who uttering a squeak of suppressed mirth, rushed into his room, where by the sound of it he had a fit of hysterics under a blanket. A little later it sounded as if the Coot who shared with Denzil, was similarly affected. Fergus then said to his room-mate, Maltravers, their room being next the other, 'That pair of poofters must be trying to wear out each other's foreskins before they lose 'em . . . what d'you think, old top?'

Malters' reply was a sniff of disapproval. Fergus chuckled as he settled down.

As a matter of fact that second outburst of mirth next door was due to Fabian Cootes's taking up the joke, although not in the spirit of sheer indecency in which it had been begun, as was hardly likely in such a man, whose even being jocular must be of rare occurrence. When Denzil had recovered from Fergus's bit, the Coot, or Fabers as Denzil was calling him, murmured that it would have been a good joke to have asked 'Old D.L.' (by whom presumably, he meant Jeremy) whether he thought the fact that Jews and local Aborigines practised ritual circumcision did not suggest an historic link: say Moses had brought the Children of Israel this way, and these were one of the Lost Tribes, or this was the truly Promised Land and the mooted Refugee Settlement the final rehabilitation of the Chosen, Fabers himself was so tickled over it that he had to muffle his mirth in a blanket. Perhaps it was really that which set Denzil off again.

Anyway, when Fabers recovered himself he was the man of science again, warning Denzil against being taken in by what he called Jeremy's amateurish balderdash: 'The old goat's had a couple of theories about how to deal with the Aboriginal question in the short time I've known him. This Jew thing's the result of his falling for the pretty Jew Girl. I only hope the Professor doesn't take him too seriously. That would ruin everything. There's the political side to consider first, if we're to get control. You stick to the books I've recommended you, my boy. You can't go wrong with qualified opinion before you.'

They went on talking quietly for some time, thereby revealing the fact that lately they had become quite pally, and for no such improper purpose as the bawdy Fergus had hinted at, but out of mutual interest in each other's callings. The subject first was anthropology, but soon became militaristic. Denzil said that his interest in anthropology didn't mean that he disliked being a soldier: 'Bred in me, I dare say, from generations of it. But I'd like to be something better than the . . . well, sort of political policeman you are in between wars. Our next war's sure to be with the Japs. That'll throw us in with a lot of strange primitive types. I'd like to be able to deal with 'em . . . well, like Lawrence with the Arabs . . . like to go into the military history books as Dickey of the Dacoits, or somethin' like that . . . eeeeeee! Sure to finish up as top brass . . . family failin'. Just like to be somethin' better than a Blimp . . . which is really what old Whiskers Eskers is, for all the suavity . . . if you understand what I mean, ...'

Fabers said he understood quite well, and sighed over Denzil's certainty of eventual generalship, saying that we in our dowdy colonial society had no such system where breeding counted – except in literal terms of peasantry, which after all was the true basis of our bastard society. Brawn was put before breeding and brains in everything. Certainly that was so in the selection of soldiers – real career soldiers, that is – as he himself knew only too well, confessing that a military career had been his primary ambition, that in youth he had sat for the competitive examination whereby entrance to the National Military College was achieved – had passed with honours, yet been turned down because he was short of the regulation height. He concluded bitterly, 'Napoleon also would have been turned down on that score.'

A moment. Then Denzil breathed, evidently with some excitement, 'By golly, don't y'know, old boy . . . you're the spittin' image of old Nap.'

'You think so?'

'Why . . . you've even got a way of puttin' your hand in your shirt when you're holdin' forth . . . er, talking, I mean.'

Fabers confessed that he rather thought he resembled Napoleon, and not merely in appearance. He said his grandmother, who doted on him, had harped on this resemblance in his boyhood and bought him several Lives of Bonaparte as presents, which he had read and re-read avidly. He added that of course it was the thing to belittle this Greatest Soldier of History, to sneer at him as a lousy little Dago adventurer. They had to belittle him because his true stature made them all look so puny. 'Anyway,' he muttered in the darkness, 'what's wrong with being an adventurer? Shouldn't life be an adventure? That's what I make of mine. Denied the military career, I took to anthropology because it would give me the chance to go into unknown places . . . not just as a roughneck, but as a scholar as well . . . because I'm that, too . . . and so was Napoleon . . . and Julius Ceaser. The adventures I've had, man . . . in New Guinea, the Solomon Islands, in parts here where no other whiteman has been . . . rubbing shoulders with naked primitive savages, crossing crocodile-infested rivers, finding poison snakes in my bed, and . . . and . . . well, things like that. But I'd rather have been a soldier . . . and a scholar in military science . . . and, as I've said, the opportunity may be just around the corner. War with the Japs. They don't worry about your height in war-time . . . and with *your* General's backing, *my* knowledge of this country, New Guinea, and the rest . . . and what I'm learning from you . . . man, oh, man, I might yet stand beside you as a general!' He ended breathlessly.

Denzil's comment was a soft, 'By jove, old boy . . . as these Australians say, "there's no doubt about you!"'

Doughty fellow though Cootes claimed to be, and to some degree proved by his tenacity of purpose, he was no sort of horseman. Now, this was something that the time, the place, and the circumstances demanded he must be, since not only was the horseback expedition into the wilderness his idea, but he its self-appointed leader. There's nothing in history to say that Napoleon Bonaparte was an outstanding horseman; but at least he could sit a horse. The revelation of this lack of Fabers' was made even brutally next morning, when pretty well the entire male company of Lily Lagoons gathered at the horse-yard for selection of those animals which were to be hired for the expedition. He did say to Jeremy that he would like a quiet horse to start with, not having ridden for quite a while. Jeremy replied that they were all quiet. It was, of course, the statement of a skilled horseman. Anyone knowing horses, as, for instance, Professor St Clair showed he did, would know that what is called a quiet horse by an expert is one that can be expected to behave with tractability when handled properly. The Professor, a natural horseman by his build, and somewhat experienced, having been brought up on a farm as he said, but confessing to being long out of touch with horses, went round the mob, talking to this animal and that, letting them sniff him, patting and stroking, evidently waiting for a horse to choose him rather, and came out leading a rangy ageing grey, Smoky. Jeremy said that the horse, despite his age, was a good stayer, and should do the trip nicely.

But big horses for big men, as they say. Fabers chose the biggest of the lot, Big Ben, a heavy-shouldered dark bay. Ben accepted docilely enough. What happened wasn't his fault. On being given his saddle at the harness-shed, Fabers had shown his knowledgeability by promptly measuring the stirrup-leathers with his arm, and adjusting them to suit his short legs. A wise thing to do if you know what you're doing. As it was, he made getting into the saddle on so big a horse as Ben by so small a man as himself a job for one of those mounting-blocks they use in riding-schools. With a foot in the high stirrup, straining to heave up his tubby bulk, he pulled hard on the near-side rein, causing the horse to wheel, so that he had to hop round with him, in the process losing a natty concertina-topped riding-boot and his balance and sat down heavily in the dungy dust in his nice white riding moleskins. Only Fergus laughed. A look from Jeremy stopped Prindy.

Malters and Denzil picked up the red-faced hero, brushed him clean, while Jeremy went after Big Ben and brought him back. It was the sort of thing that could have happened to anyone not accustomed to horses. But Ben knew better than that. Deciding that his would-be master was a *mungus* and most likely to become only a burden to carry, not what a rider should be to a horse, someone to add to his purpose in life, he refused to let Fabers touch him again, snorted, blew, reared. Jeremy saw the symptons and suggested another mount. The Coot agreed with alacrity. Jeremy brought him Black Andy, a much smaller beast, and very amiable the way he stood for the saddling and mounting. In fact Andy just stood. The Coot thumped him with his heels, so hard that Andy obeyed with alacrity, so much that he jerked his clumsy rider into the attitude known as 'Jockeying', which means with heels dug in and body leaning forward. Poor Andy, trained to instant response to changes of his rider's attitudes, would think he was being urged to gallop, which he did from almost a standing start. But there was nowhere to gallop. The gate was shut. Not getting any direction, Andy propped to avoid collision with the gate. Fabers went over his right shoulder, sprawling face down in the dust. Perhaps the most brutal thing about it all was the way Black Andy bent over him, as if out of curiosity, and sniffed his fat behind. There was a general ripple of giggling. Fergus and Prindy had to run away to explode their greater mirth.

Jeremy came to the rescue this time. Obviously the poor pompous fellow had ridden nothing better than jaded livery-stable hacks. But Jeremy didn't say so. He said that seeing Cootes hadn't ridden in a while, he'd better get his seat back with a bit of practice riding on a beast they kept specially for that; and he sent a blackboy for Bay Rum Betsy.

After the way the Coot looked at Betsy, as the first Napoleon must have looked at that nag he is eternally riding in the famous painting, *Retreat From Moscow*, and Betsey's nasty look at him, it said much for the man that he duly mounted her and suffered himself to be led away by him he called privily Old Goat and Old D.L., and despised as that lowest of all orders to a qualified Anthrop, a dabbler in the science without benefit of cap and gown. Jeremy took them away to the racetrack, and not knowing anything about those private opinions of the miserable-looking little fat man, did not stay to humiliate him, but telling him to take it nice and easy for a while, departed. Later Jeremy sent Prindy over on Golden Bobby to stir old Betsy up to better effort than she was making and tactfully to show the poor fellow a point or two. Soon after that, Betsy was trotting.

Again it said much for the man's character that he stuck to the trotting, round and round and round the racetrack, until Jeremy came out in the utility to bring him in to lunch; and when he dismounted stiffly it was to be seen that the seat of his white pants was blood-stained. Jeremy could not have missed seeing, but said nothing. So obvious was it that when Fabers came through the lounge, stiff-gaited and with gaze averted from the others gathered there for a pre-lunch beer, himself heading upstairs, Fergus remarked behind a hand, 'Looks like it brought on her monthlies.' Denzil, taken with hysterics again, but checked by a sharp glance from the General, rushed outside.

Hobbling back downstairs, wearing different pants, Cootes held his head high, declared that he was going to have another go this afternoon; although he declined the hard-bottomed chair offered by Fergus, and took his beer standing. In the dining-room he found a down cushion on his chair. Still he talked bravely of the expedition, which definitely would be setting out on Tuesday according to schedule. He surely must have messed up his schedule as well as his backside with his bravado, if not saved from it by the tact of Jeremy. When Fergus asked Rifkah to come for a flight with him sometime, and she replied that she would if the children of the place could come along too, and he agreed, Jeremy said, 'Why not make it this afternoon? All you fresh horsemen need to take it easy the first day . . . and the horses're sure to play up with the aeroplane flying about. Then you can have uninterrupted training afterwards . . . eh?' Instead of looking the gratitude he ought to have felt, Fabers actually pouted. Later on, Jeremy as tactfully induced him to come over to the clinic and have a dressing put on his fat, hairy, blistered and excoriated fundament: Sulphonilamide overlarded with the patent ointment and a thick pad of cotton wool. Still Fabers showed no gratitude. Perhaps it was simply shyness. Neither he nor his physician, himself face down on the clinic table, the other concentrated on the vast gluteal blush, realized that they had been peeped at. The peepers, through a slit of louver, were Fergus and Prindy, in the process of getting the utility truck out, while Rifkah had gone on to muster the crew for the flight. They had to bolt so as not to betray themselves with their mirth.

Fergus reckoned his load was a round dozen youngsters, as well as Rifkah, the former to be placed as pairs in each of the six passenger seats, she to ride beside himself. If there were too many kids for one flight, he said he would make another. That's the glib way he had put it. As Anthropologist as well as Aviator, he should know better. When he and Prindy reached the Aboriginal quarters and found Rifkah waiting for them alone, saying that no one wanted to come, he showed complete surprise. Rifkah looked at Prindy, who was giggling inordinately, and made him worse by asking him what was the matter? Fergus, thinking he knew the answer, replied for him, 'We just saw something very funny . . . the Coot's bum . . . ahaaaaeeeah!' But while there was all this mirth coming out of Prindy's mouth, his staring wide eyes belied it.

Fergus tried to get a crew himself, but failed utterly, even when he called those who only hung their heads and giggled, myalls and brumbies. A couple had already flown, he learnt, with Dr Fox. Why couldn't they fly with him then? They could hardly tell him the truth, which was that they regarded the Flying Fox as a kind of *dookyangana*. Getting back into the car with Prindy and Rifkah, he remarked, 'You can never understand 'em.' Then he asked Prindy, 'You're not frightened, too, are you?'

The grey eyes, already fixed on the silver thing away over on the race track, did not turn to meet the questioner. The answer was given on indrawn breath, 'Can't be fright'.' Fergus left it at that, not knowing enough about the manipulation of his own language by others who made use of it to know that the words could mean anything but what he would have taken literally. Rifkah, however, put an arm about the small shoulders, and surely responded to the tension in them, since she placed her cheek against the fair head.

Rifkah held Prindy while Fergus made an inspection of the outside of his aircraft, and while he himself looked blankly up into the blazing blue, void but for one small bright mass of cloud hanging over the Plateau. Then she shoved him along ahead of her when Fergus opened the door and dropped the steps. Fergus took him and led him up the sloping aisle, to set him in the front seat on the left, by a wide window looking out under the high wing. As he strapped him in, Prindy eyed him as he might a policeman putting on the neck-chain. Fergus then placed Rifkah in the right-hand seat of the cockpit, and settled into his own on the left, to begin at once to check his instruments.

Prindy stared ahead and upward, at the empty blue beyond the windshield. Had he looked out through his own window he would have seen the black and brindle mob, who had preferred to be called myalls and brumbies to voluntarily venturing into what to them was a medium of the greatest menace, since the realm of spirits, coming running to see do it the one who had been bedevilled by a *koornung*. He did look out when the port engine began its animal-like squealing and growling in being started, but evidently only to see the propeller spin into a blur. He turned away at the starting of the starboard donk.

In moving off, Fergus ran along the fence now draped with figures. Prindy didn't see them, now concentrated on that distant cloud as it swung into view ahead.

They went rolling away across the expanse of paddock, lurching over the little piles of horse-dung, the tiny attempts of termites to rebuild their constantly levelled cities. Horses, tails high, necks arched for the half-fun of it, were prancing away into a corner to which Fergus with his skilfulness of manoeuvring had headed them. Then as the further fence came close, the sky spun to Fergus's swinging into wind. Prindy looked out the side now, to find the propeller vanished, the grass flattened, the dung and dust flying as before the breath of Tchamala. A jerk. One's insides were left behind in the rush, as should be when one was becoming virtually disembodied. Grey eyes wide in concentration on the blue ahead, as if it were a hole in the sky into which the Old One was sucking them. Then suddenly the violence was smoothed out, the ear-shattering din becoming an harmonious drumming. There was the homestead, familiar scene: Big House, annexe, mangoes, garden, sheds, yards, cottages. Yet so unfamiliar; its denizens dwarfed to insect size, some waving, others bolting. The way the Old One must see it from on top, or the Pookarakka when he was moved to levitate. A turn of the homestead underneath, like a slowly spinning wheel. Then there ahead was the red wall of the Plateau and that cloud, seen from this height to have a purple belly.

In no time they were over the Turtle Hole, the little stockyard, the tumbled rocks, all so plain to see in miniature; and plain to see how Tchamala had made the Plateau by getting under it and heaving it up, then chucking those rocks over the side to clear a Ring Place, as the Pookarakka said he had, for initiating the first men into the secret rites he had stolen for them from the women whom only had Koonapippi instructed. Was that now a Shade of the Old One's travelling with them, just ahead of them and below as they flew eastward round the bays of the escarpment: a dark flickering bat-winged thing, leaping through and over rocks and scrub, sometimes leaping up a red wall as if with translucent wings to blot out some piece of those glimpsed bright substantiations of occult beginnings that were not to be seen by the uninitiated? It must have been Tchamala, because the thing beat them to that eastern horn round which were the Snake Galleries, found now to be blacked out by shadow the Old One had flung over it – just as the Kudijingera Men fling bark over the sacred objects if there is intrusion.

Again, when they lifted up over the rim of the Plateau, the Shade followed, dodging round the scrubby broken edges of the great silver-grey expanses of smooth rock that looked like the backs of turtles burrowing in mud. Brush tails darted out before the thing, to dash about madly on the rocks for fear then of the booming thing above. The ghostly follower was particularly in evidence when they came to a waste of yellow gravel that interested Fergus so much he dropped down as if to land on it, as he might have done without much damage in emergency, so sparcely grown was it with mere gorse and porcupine grass. But the black bat got right underneath them and with some angry heaving shouldered them off. Prindy covered his face. This would be the very *Woolahloo* where those first Koonapippi ceremonies took place, to which the Pookarakka had promised sometime to take his *mekullikulli*.

They rose to that hanging cloud, to find it nothing like the solid fat thing it looked at the distance, the coy coocoon of sleepy Waianga waiting for Wet Season, but the tenuous half-substance a gathering of spirits might be expected to be, which with old Tchamala's Shade flitting about, was spun into twin rainbows by those invisible forces in the wings. That they were no more wanted in the cloud than the Old One was on those stormy occasions of the Wet, was evident in the way they were tossed about, dragged at by whispy wet grey hands, at last flung back out into the blazing blue.

Now there was all Terra Australis to see as they circled high; a red-grey land that vanished on all sides into smoky infinity. But at hand were familiar things, if ever so tiny. Knowles Creek like a green whip-snake crawling. The Beatrice like a black adder. Lily Lagoons homestead quite plain. A glimpse of something away to southward that might be Beatrice township. The billabongs little emerald green pats in the red-grey. The white of the limestone country, with a glint of water here and there like sparkling eyes looking up out of the cavernous earth.

Then sudden silence, so that the ears rang with the memory of that humming engine music. Fergus was gliding down. Soon they were whistling like a swooping eagle. Down over the escarpment, to send a crowd of white cockatoos flying like blown petals, to see a black cloud of waterfowl pour like smoke from the billabongs, to circle the Corella Bore and see the corellas scattering and the insect cattle bolting. Then away southward, with engines singing again, synocopating as now and then they came out of synchrony – Ah-oom, ah-oom, ah-oom, ah-oom – low over the yellow dust that could so quickly become a raging yellow serpent of water when it pleased the Great Snake to make it so. Coming to the Knowles, Fergus dropped down again amongst the trees by that big water-hole, only scaring a couple of white egrets this time, remarking to red-faced Rifkah as he climbed again, his split-lip showing in a grin, that the view was not nearly so good as yesterday.

A turn over the Rainbow Pool, with the grey eyes intense in their staring search for what might be revealed of its secrets. Then along the yellow road for home. The white roofs and mangoes sliding to meet them, slipping under them, while the human ants and the equine insects ran hither and thither, and a wedge-tail eagle, glinting bronze in the Sun, hung in the blue ahead as if to challenge their progress. But they were going down, down, were down, with a tiny bump, and then a bumpity-bumping over the horse-dung again.

The rails of the race track were hung again with dark humanity as they drew up to it and stopped. Silence again. But no. Up in front there was a whining whisper, sounding like muted grief, as if this machine-thing were in fact a live thing and was whimpering in the disillusion of being bound to earth again. Fergus, coming to unbuckle Prindy, seeing the grey eyes staring, said, 'Those are the gyros . . . running down.' He added with a chuckle, as he had to pull Prindy up out of the seat: 'Looks like yours are running down, too.' Rifkah, shoving along, looking anxious over Prindy's evident state of daze, asked what was the matter with him. 'He's all right,' said Fergus, opening the door. 'Still up top in the spirit, that's all. Did you see how he took it all in? I was watching him in the rear-view mirror. Never saw anyone lap it up like him. Might make an airman of him.'

All eyes on the fence were fixed on the grey eyes that didn't seem to see them, that didn't seem to see anything, not even the utility towards which Rifkah was guiding him. Fergus, going round to the driving side door, jollied the crowd again for their cowardice, but now contrasting it with the courage of him he called their Little Mate. Again they only giggled. Fergus got in to find Prindy beside him, as when they had driven out, but now with head on Rifkah's breast and enfolded in her arms – asleep. He stared, would have spoken; but she raised a finger for silence.

The mob leapt into the back, making it sag and sway when the car got going. Those near enough, peeped through the little window at the back of the fabric hood or round the sides. All dropped off at their quarters. Fergus pulled up at the car shed by the annexe. He was going to speak again, but this time was stopped by a murmur from the boy, who stirred, sat up, still with eyes shut, lips writhing now and throat convulsing. Forth came the sweet strangled sound, unintelligible at first, but soon plainly to be recognized as imitation of the sound of aero engines in concert, rising and falling to make melody: *Ah-oom, ah-oom, ah-oom, ah-oom.*

Fergus breathed, 'Well, what d'you know!'

Prindy woke, blinked, looked from one to the other, then smiled, stretched, saying, 'I been sleep little bits, eh?' He moved to get out. Rifkah opened the door for him, and as he scrambled past her knees, kissed his cheek. He went running into the annexe.

Fergus leaned over as if for a kiss as well. But Rifkah got out. As Fergus joined her, there came the lilt of the flute from the annexe. She said, 'He is meking song of ze flight.'

'Strange kid.'

'He is very vonderful child.'

'What's going to become of him?'

'He vill decide zat. Come. It is time for smoke-o.'

Going with her, he asked, 'What about a walk with you this evening?'

'I alvays go wit' Jeremy.'

'Well, make it me tonight for a change.'

'You can come along, too.'

'No . . . I want you to myself.'

'Vell . . . you cannot haf.'

He tried to grab her; but she leapt away, went sprinting to the Big House, in by the kitchen door. Biting his split lip he followed, to enter by the lounge.

It was Jeremy who asked Fergus to go along on the ritual walk that evening. Fergus went eagerly enough, despite those last words to Rifkah, and behaved so circumspectly that the conversation might have been quite serious, but for Jeremy's constantly urging him back to the usual drollery. They began with talk of the Free Australia Movement, with which, evidently, Fergus was more than slightly involved. Whether or not he would have talked more of the involvement, he didn't get the chance, because Jeremy interrupted to say that from much of what he had read in the Movement's journal it seemed to him to be as lunatic as Hitler's brain-storms. Fergus agreed. He told about the pair who really ran the show, the Chief as he called the virtual boss, a monied man with a deep sardonic streak, who he himself believed was backing the Movement only with the idea of playing some mad joke on the Nation – that is by presenting it with a sawdust führer – and the Sawdust one himself, the nominal Leader, discredited Scholar, Writer, ex-Commo, ex all sorts of things, including barefoot bush-boy – the Bloke, as Fergus called him.

Still, Fergus went on to argue that despite that lunatic quality, there was value in Free Australia, properly handled. In fact he declared that Australia's future would depend upon its prospering. Establishment of Australia as truly a nation was now or never; and here was the means. He confessed then that he wrote for the magazine himself, and evidently would have talked about his writing, only that Jeremy steered him onto the subject of the Coot, about which he was sure to be droll. He certainly was droll, telling some very funny stories of the great man's academic life, of his being kidded, by Fergus and others, into believing himself a ladies' man. But again he got serious, saying, 'Don't underestimate the Coot, though. For all his lack of being able to see himself as others see him, deep down he's shrewd . . . and very ambitious. He knows exactly the right people to cultivate at the right time. Everybody thinks he's a bit of a joke, but knows at the same time he's a jump ahead of 'em in things that matter. If the top job of administering Aboriginal affairs eventually becomes worth having, eventually he'll have it. He's running St Clair. But his interest at the moment's really military. See how he is with the military boys? He believes war's inevitable soon. If there is a war, he'll leap into it as top brass, bet your boots. He won't even be a common junior officer. Field rank the day of enlistment.'

'Do you believe there's going to be a war?'

'If there is, Sir, it ain't going to be mine.'

'What about the Japs?'

'They don't want war with us. I know a lot of Japs well . . . top ones, too. Met a few down South . . . university, Free Australia which naturally has their official blessing . . . and up here, too. I belong to the Japanese Society of Port Palmeston . . . only non-Jap in it. I get on with 'em well. I like their manners. But they may be very useful, too. There's a hint of working for them flying . . . for the pearlers now working this coast from the Jap Mandated Territory Islands . . . Carolines. Good money in it . . . and the East Indies to knock about in to spend it. I'm learning the lingo.'

'Does General Esk know this?'

'Sure. Doesn't he know everything . . . through that super-sticky-beak of his, Maltravers?

'How's he take it . . . with his feelings about the Japs?'

'Rather keen on it, in fact. Naturally thinks I'm on the gentlemen's side, what, what!'

'Are you on the side of the Japs?'

'I'm only on my side, Sir. Anyway, I don't mind obliging. He's paying me extra for it. We'll be contacting the outside Japs at the watering places during the survey . . . and he's relying on me for the protocol . . . and any handy information on the side. Got to keep right with the Eskimo, as his boys call him. For the moment, anyway, he carries a lot of weight.'

'How do you mean . . . for the moment?'

'Well, the Coot, who as I've said's always a jump ahead of everybody, reckons this Government can't weather any sort of crisis, and things are certainly critical just now. A Labor Government will replace them. Then out goes Esk. Cootsey's already sucking up to Labor leaders, while being a white-haired boy of the others. But I think he's a bit out this time. My smoke-signals tell me a new party'll grow out of this Free Australia thing. People are sick of the common or garden party-line politicians. Hence my association with what, I admit, looks rather like a loony-bin at the moment.'

Jeremy said dryly, 'Strikes me you're all a jump ahead of yourselves even.'

Fergus laughed. 'Maybe you're right.'

The dauntless Fabers was up at dawn next day and out with Malters to the race track, where Jeremy was already running. But Fabers was there not to run but to ride. He found Bay Rum Betsy already with saddle on and saddle fitted with a felt pad. As if used to gnomes or fairies anticipating his needs, he said nothing to anyone about the courtesy. Another gnome, Prindy, came to dance discreet attendance on him after breakfast. He let morning smoke-o pass in his zeal for practice, and thus came with something of a stiff-legged strut to lunch on the down cushion. Hearing over lunch that the others had decided to go riding to the billabongs that afternoon, he declared that he would go along with them. When gently Jeremy remarked that such a trip would be rather much for old Betsy after all her recent work, Fabers flushed, said haughtily, 'Of course. I'll ride Black Andy.'

Fabers did just that, being the man of iron will he was, and Black Andy being a very amiable animal. Andy must have suffered from such grossly bad handling, but showed it no more than to droop and sigh whenever the flopping lump on his back permitted pause for it. While the others probably would have been content with trotting or ambling to make things easy for Fabers, he would persist in kicking Andy into bursts of cantering. Fergus, riding behind with Rifkah, softly sang to her a song out of his childhood: *Bumpity, bumpity, bumpity, bump, here comes the Galloping Major.*

The excursion also turned out to be a riding lesson for Rifkah, who with persistent cajolery from Fergus and his expert handling of the situation and the fact that all horses seemed to like her, was induced to get off old Snowball onto Fergus's mount Red Rory. Rory behaved like a perfect gentleman all the way, finished the trip with an easy gallop that left his lovely rider looking even lovelier with the joy of the accomplishment and earned the sly riding master a kiss that he would have made a meal of had the dainty dish not fought free.

When Fabers came strutting into the lounge for the evening drink, his gait was such that Fergus put Denzil in hysterics again by remarking behind his hand, 'Looks like she's pooped her panties this time.'

That night it was Professor St Clair who shared the ritual walk. He also shared in the talk at first, although it was evident that he would have preferred to listen to Jeremy on the subject of the Aborigines. Jeremy brought him to confess, honest man that undoubtedly he was, that he knew nothing of the people but from his reading and the reports of those he called his men, most valuable of whom, he was quick to say, was Fabian Cootes. His own field experience, he admitted, had been gained in other countries, particularly New Guinea, amongst people he freely owned bore little resemblance to Australian natives. Nailed by Jeremy about his likely appointment as director of the proposed new system of dealing with the Aborigines, he avoided a straight answer, perhaps quite truthfully saying that the thing was still in the talking stage, adding that he would prefer to stay in his University Chair.

Jeremy asked, 'Why appoint you, and not Cootes, who you say is the expert?'

The Professor shrugged his stooped narrow shoulders. 'Governments work in mysterious ways, I'm afraid.'

'There's hardly anything mysterious about the way any government of ours has been dealing with these people over the years.'

'I understand that there's to be a completely new deal for them.'

'Let's hope so. I'm only afraid your appointment may be a sort of sop. You're a distinguished professor of anthropology. What can critics of the system say to the Government then?'

St Clair said somewhat stiffly, 'If I'm appointed, I hope there'll be no need for criticism.'

'Hear, hear!' Jeremy then left the obviously troubled man alone, to talk of his own ideas on the subject, this being the first chance he'd had to do so to the Professor without argumentative intrusion by the Coot. St Clair listened closely.

Tomorrow St Clair was to be taken to see the Painted Caves. Jeremy said he was particularly interested in how he would be affected by them, more so than he had been in the case of anyone else to whom he had shown the galleries.

In fact the trip to the Galleries had been taken over by Cootes, who wanted to use it as what he called an Exercise, drawing on his new military vocabulary, to test the efficiency of his men, horses, and accoutrements. It was Jeremy who provided what, in bushman's parlance, he called the Plant, and who actually had plotted the route, or *rout* in local usage. Perhaps if he had used more dignified terms the Coot would have acknowledged his part in it, when, as it was, he seemed oblivious of it.

Certainly it didn't look anything like a horseback picnic or stockman's riding out, this cavalcade, strung out in pairs of riders, with pack-beasts running head to tail, horse-tailers bringing up the rear. The packs, which normally would have been running free, were roped. This was also Jeremy's idea, its purpose the fact that the early part of the planned expedition would be through the rocky gorges east of Catfish, the only means of getting horses over the sandstone Plateau, where it would be difficult to handle free horses that, fresh from home, would have turned for home at the first opportunity. Roping them early would get them used to it before the rough country was encountered. But Jeremy's idea of early had been the leg to Catfish, not this so-called Exercise.

In the circumstances it was proper that the Expedition Leader should lead the Exercise. Fabers made no announcement to that effect, but simply rode off ahead with Napoleonic dignity on his big horse, beside him his purloined aide, Lieutenant Dickey. Jeremy and General Esk, who had been about to take the lead as a matter of course, exchanged half-smiling glances, and followed. General Sir Mark Esk today was looking anything but what he was, wearing a rather old stockman's outfit, battered wide-awake and all, borrowed from Jeremy. Nevertheless, while it was academic anthropology that was being discussed by the military-looking men in front – Malinowski, Frazer, Margaret Mead – militarism was the General's subject, prognostications concerning that war he was spoiling for with the Japanese, more anxious than ever about it, while Jeremy apparently was no wit more concerned. Next came Rifkah, riding Red Rory again, in company with Professor St Clair, who with evident interest and surprise was listening to her telling of common Jewish ritualistic practices, going to show that preoccupation with savages can blind one to odd things one's contemporaries are doing under one's very nose. Then came Fergus and Prindy, mounted on Black Cloud and Golden Bobby respectively, talking of flying, by the way Fergus's hands were making the movements of ailerons, flaps, angles of attack; while yet his eyes kept on the gracefully swaying female figure just ahead of him, seeming to run over it, from ivory neck with the bit of copper peeping from under the black hat, down over the swell of trim buttocks to spreading thighs. Behind were Malters and Darcy, earnestly talking of the early official history of the country, which, perhaps surprisingly, Darcy seemed to have made a close study of, and Malters interested in because, as he said, his chief interest was history. In that clipped manner he had of speaking,

Malters explained that only by its history could you understand a community, adding sententiously: 'Of course history is always repeating itself.' Last came the four black horse-tailers, in fits over some private joke.

It wasn't so surprising then, that what ordinarily would have been the picnic lunch before the climb to the Galleries, turned out to be a kind of military bivouac, with tent-flies rigged, all cooking equipment unpacked and lined up, bedding laid out. Fabers had asked Jeremy if they might eat as though truly roughing it as an exercise for his men; and Jeremy had provided buffalo beef and lily roots and flour for damper making. Fabers himself made the damper, declaring himself a dab at it, but producing such a sod as to be uneatable even by the horses. He then declared that he would make another to prove himself, and that they should have it for smoke-o when they came back from the Galleries. The awful failure was probably what caused him to produce a part of the commissariat hitherto undisclosed. From a pack-bag in what might be described as the Mess Tent, be brought out a neat canvas satchel from which he took a packet of biscuits and a small can of raspberry jam, at the same time discoursing like a military lecturer, explaining that his experience in roughing it in the bush had taught him that small indulgences in the way of food worked wonders. 'It is no departure from the necessity to keep the commissariat down to the barest essentials, as is demonstrated by the fact that everything of the kind is of miniature size,' he insisted, emptying the satchel onto a ground-sheet, to show that besides biscuits and jams, it contained little cardboard boxes of triangular Swiss cheeses and anchovies. 'Every ounce counts, as I'm always saying,' he added, addressing himself to those he might call his Men. 'We must never lose sight of the fact that, as much an Anthropological Survey this expedition of ours is, it is also an exercise in the mobility that would be required in the event of guerilla warfare here. As experts in the way of living and thinking of the native people who are going to be the first consideration if this country is invaded, we must be able to advise on how to live in it indefinitely in harassment of the enemy. Now, experience has taught me that even the anticipation of a dainty bit of something will give you appetite for the poorest bush tucker. Of course it must be rationed according to strict military procedure . . . one biscuit per man, one dab of jam. So! Come on . . . who'll have one with me?' Only Prindy and Rifkah did. He addressed the others: 'Well, then, a nibble of *Schweitzerkase* . . . no? Very well, then. Away it all goes, not to be opened up again until we've crossed the Plateau.'

Jeremy, eyeing the uncanned stuff, as Fabers repacked, remarked, 'You'll have to be careful of ants. They'll find anything not canned in ten minutes. It's a wonder they haven't got at those biscuits of yours before now.'

Fabers smirked. 'You evidently haven't observed.' He slipped out one of the hooks from which the pack-bag was suspended from a sapling rigged for the bags under the fly, and brought it, showing that it was bound with a slip of adhesive cotton tape. 'Take a sniff,' he said. 'No self-respecting ant would cross that.'

Jeremy did so, handing it back, saying, 'Citronella, eh? Quite ingenious. Trouble with citronella, though, is carrying it around. It has the invariable habit, I find, of getting into everything you've got . . . and there's nothing fouler than food it's got into.'

Fabers smirked again, swung away and replaced the hook, then from another bag took out another satchel, a tiny one. Opening it, he produced a metal can with screw top, held it up, and at the same time held up the satchel, to show that it was printed in large letters with an indelible pencil: Citronella – NOT TO BE STOWED WITH FOOD. Then having satisfied everyone of his ingenuity, he said, 'Well, now I must prove my boast about that damper.'

He also made a lecture of his damper-making, not having opportunity for it with the last one, since the company was preoccupied with the bivouacking. He demonstrated the need for liberal kneading for effective aeration. All paid him close attention, perhaps mostly fascinated by his faculty for didacticism in all things – except Fergus and Prindy. Catching Prindy's eye, Fergus signalled him to withdraw; and the pair slipped away unnoticed, to confer behind the mess tent. The result was Prindy's stealing into the tent and, hidden by that hanging pack-bag, taking from it the Coot's patent satchels and bringing them to Fergus. After Fergus had poured a tot of citronella into that containing the delicacies, Prindy as unobtrusively returned the things. Then they joined the others to watch the placing of the camp-oven in ashes of just the right temperature to ensure a piece of culinary perfection by the time the party returned from the Galleries, estimated period two hours and fifteen minutes.

Perhaps Fabers might have presumed to leadership even in the trip up to the Galleries, only for being delayed in starting out by having forgotten where he had stowed his photographic and other gear required for what he called the Parietal Recordings he wanted to do, knowing the caves from that former visit, when he was here as expert in the case of the King Against Cock-Eye Bob. Thus Jeremy got away in the lead, with the Professor immediately behind him, then Rifkah who, also hadn't yet seen the Galleries, at least from the ground, with Prindy to help her up the steep pinches. The blackboys and Darcy, for reasons best known to themselves, remained behind in the camp.

Jeremy talked to the Professor of Aboriginal affairs as they went. Speaking of the Galleries, he said that one of the first reforms of the so-called new deal should be to declare the like of them not merely inviolate against destruction, as had been done in some Southern States where Aborigines now existed only as pariahs with no tribal life whatsoever, but against intrusion by anyone except Aborigines, who would have sole right to admit anyone else; and that preservation of such places as these here, where proper responsibility had ceased with disintegration of the tribes, be vested, at Government expense, in such tribesmen as still practised the ancient arts. As the law stood, these galleries might be despoiled by anyone choosing to have a day out in them, without even official censure.

Probably at no other time of year, in addition to the usual advantage of the time of day, could a better show of the Galleries, or at least of the main one, be expected. The reason was that there was extra lighting from the sunlight's striking rock faces below, which usually were in shadow. At least that would be the scientific explanation, perhaps necessary, since men of science were today concerned. A blackfellow would give other reasons, and perhaps quite good ones, since it would seem that for all mankind's advance, man still can't live by bread and measurement alone. To a blackfellow, of course, the Sun was Koonapippi, Mother Nature herself. Does the capacity to measure its distance from earth and its temperature make so much difference to any kind of man?

As usual, Jeremy called a halt outside the big gallery for accommodation of vision. He then remarked to the Professor that he always felt here like a devotee introducing proselytes to holy places. St Clair looked alarmed, and with his eyes searched away down into the tumble for Fabers lagging behind burdened as he was with Denzil – for Fabers and his scientific sanity.

Jeremy led the way into the Gallery. Both the Professor and Rifkah gasped and gaped. The Professor seemed to be seeing all of it, but with eyes rolling, as if he felt it crowding in on him. Rifkah was concentrated on a single piece, the great Moomboo Figure rearing almost from sandy floor to lip of the overhang, her great eyes rising with it in its upward curving, as if drawn, from splayed-out six-toed feet to the face directly above, the two blank yet seemingly all-seeing eyes created out of the single looping line that also made the only other feature except the nether-worldly bunny-ears. Suddenly she covered her own eyes, lowered her head, and with that posture turned towards those behind, saying in a tone strangely muffled by emotion and her hands, 'No . . . I cannot look!' She uncovered her face, to reveal that aged pained expression. She merely glanced at Jeremy, then concentrated on Prindy, extending a hand to him, saying in a hoarse undertone, 'Take me avay now . . . ve come back togzer ven I am ready.' She turned the haggard look again to Jeremy. He stared at her for a moment, then nodded. Prindy already had her hand. As she went with him she averted her head so as to see nothing more of the bright spectacle.

As the pair disappeared, Professor St Clair, who perhaps had taken relief from his own confusion to watch Rifkah's, murmured, 'What a strange reaction!' He glanced back at the paintings, concentrated on what might be taken for a lewd one, presumably depicting a sexual orgy, adding, turning to Jeremy, 'She didn't appear to look at anything that normally might be thought likely to shock her. How do you account for it?'

Jeremy shrugged. 'I've found strangers to the country more susceptible than ourselves . . . particularly women. She's also very much attached to the Aborigines, as you know.'

'Hmm! It'll be interesting to hear her explanation.'

'In the meantime I'd be interested to hear what you have to say, Professor.'

Again St Clair looked alarmed, shot a glance towards the entrance, as if in the hope of seeing the Coot, then another at Fergus, who looked only like a cat watching a mouse. Then with a little sound rather like a bleat, he swung on his long legs back to the pictures: 'Well, now . . . words are superfluous, really. It's . . . well, I'm not one for superlatives . . . but it's magnificent.'

'Do you mean as art or an anthropological or archaeological find?'

'Oh, come now . . . art, of course . . . primitive art.'

'Define Primitive Art for me.'

The Professor chuckled, although he looked troubled. 'What's this . . . are you having a go at me?'

'Truly, no. I've told you I'm most interested in your reaction.'

'But I'm sure a man of your intelligence and your interest in the Aborigines knows all these things.'

'As I've said to you, the more I see of these things the less I know I know.

But this matter of Primitive Art, as something different from just Art. My conception of the term Art is vague enough. Not my fault . . . the dictionary's. It seems to be simply something a man can do with some degree of skill. That's as near as I can get to it.'

'How much nearer could anyone get?'

'Then why differentiate . . . Art and Primitive Art? Surely not because of the use of crude materials and ignorance of rules of perspective and light and shade and such things? These people can draw quite realistically if taught.'

'I know . . . Namitjira and all that. But there you go . . . asking me what you already know.' The Professor chuckled again. 'Primitive Art is magico-religious, of course. You surely know that.'

'I know that everything these people do is . . . well, I prefer to call it simply bound by magic.'

'Well, there you are. You don't have to ask me anything. I should be asking you.'

'You're the expert . . . the man chosen by the Nation to clean up the hideous mess we've made, in our greed, of this other nation of people, who live by magic. I want to know what you feel about all this . . . should it be pulled down?'

St Clair's eyes popped. 'For God's sake, man . . . what're you saying?'

'I mean the whole structure of Aboriginal culture.'

'I know you do. And you know I'm not going to pull anything down, but preserve what's preservable, as I've told you.'

'That's why I want to know your true reaction to this.'

St Clair looked trapped, looked at Fergus, perhaps in the hope of help from a former pupil, but surely only saw a lout who'd never appreciated his teacher's wisdom and was waiting now with half a leer to see it pissed on, and to have to turn towards to entrance looking for succour from there. He looked back, almost haggardly, at Jeremy. 'What more can I say than what I have . . . that . . . that words can't convey one's feelings in such a matter . . . . ' His voice trailed off.

'Does that mean we can expect your feelings to be expressed in deeds . . . in what you're going to do about these people?'

The pale blue eyes rolled as if in agony – then shot towards the entrance and the sound of voices. Saved by the bell! He almost started towards the Coot as the plump one entered, seeming to bounce in, the way he was puffing and his accoutrements were swinging about him as he proceeded to unburden himself. Jeremy sighed, as if in resignation.

The Coot's voice, usually near-alto in timbre, positively boomed in the cavernous place: 'Well, Prof . . . what do you think of it?'

St Clair answered glibly, 'I was just telling Jeremy here that it's magnificent beyond words.'

'It's that all right,' boomed Fabers, beginning to set up his photographic gear with a mere glance at the blazing wonder. 'These parietals represent as perfect an expression of the Paleolithic ethos as you'd find anywhere in the world . . . . '

He was interrupted by Denzil Dickey, whipping out a large note-book and with pencil poised, piping, since that was the way his voice, being much nearer the ceiling, sounded, 'I say, Fabers, old chap . . . mind saying that again?'

Fabers, setting up his gear, took his time about it. When Denzil asked, timid as a child in class, what the term *Parietals* meant, he answered shortly, absently, out of the back of his head while writing on the blackboard, as it were, 'Wall paintings . . . from *paries*, the Latin, a wall.'

Fergus asked, 'Ever think of doing a paper on the parietals of the Sydney public lavatories, Cootsey?'

Squinting through his sectioning frame, the Coot ignored him. It was as the complete professional that he went about his preparations for photographing, with frame and light-meter, apparently as little concerned with what he was about to photograph as a true professional in that art would be with the bride and groom posing for him at a wedding, his only interest a good picture. At least that's the way it seemed from the scant attention he gave the paintings. Nevertheless he was able to deliver a lecture of sorts on them to Denzil, who stood at his elbow, snapping it up in short-hand: 'The concept is magico-religious, of course. You see in anthropomorphic form what constitutes the hegemony of Paleolithic Man, his occult background. Note the fact that some figures have six digits to the hands, others the normal five, some only three. Why, do you suppose? It isn't adventitious. You'll find the rubric repeated throughout the total art corpus of the region. It is patent, therefore, that you're dealing with a methodology, a mimesis, which is strictly controlled. Study the control. You'll find it's religious in its stringency. No matter the size of the figure, or its position, vertical, horizontal, slanted, ten metres tall or ten centimetres . . . all are exactly alike. That's methodology. Watch for it always. It is the clue to whether the depiction is sacred or profane. Take these male and female figures at the end here. Sexual differentiation is made with the finest simplism and partiality possible. Compare these with the crude dichotomy of sex depicted on the lavatory walls of our cities . . . .'

Fergus burst in with a guffaw: 'He *has* been studying shit-houses!'

Jeremy and the General looked at each other, reddening, evidently with the effort to control their mirth. Prindy giggled, surely only sensing the joke. The Professor frowned. He had been smiling, no doubt with the pleasure of drinking the old familiar juice of scholarship, after being dragged into a wilderness of self-doubting by an ignoramus. Fabers himself faltered by just a word or two in his dissertation: 'Er-what may be termed the cloacinean art of our cities . . . .'

Fergus shouted, 'Bravo, Cootsey!'

Fabian turned on him, snapping, 'Do you mind? This is important to our young friend.'

'I was congratulating you . . . *The Cloacinean Art of Woolloomooloo*. My thesis for my doctorate, Professor!'

St Clair joined the chuckling of the others, but with a shake of the head at Fergus.

Fabers finished what he was trying to say almost with a shout: 'To understand the difference between that sort of thing and this is funda . . . er . . . is primary in understanding Paleolithic Art. Whereas the former is mere unskilled, well, impressionism, if you like, and wholly individualistic, what plainly is sought here is presentation of the symbolic equivalence of sex as part of magico-religious existence, control of which is presumed to be gained thereby

. . . not for the individual, but for the sect, the tribe, the clan . . . . '

This last bit made the Professor fairly beam and turn from his star pupil to Jeremy, the unlettered iconoclast, with full self-confidence, saying, 'You wanted to know my reaction to it . . . primarily, I'm sure, to gauge how it would affect my attitude to our problem. On consideration, I'd say that, even if the work is essentially primitive man's cohibitive expression in service to the tribal ethos, the deliberateness of stylization, the controlled methodology as Fabian aptly put it, surely shows the self-discipline of the individual . . . and with that to work on, these people can be advanced to any degree of culture *Homo Sapiens* is capable of . . . with careful tutelage of course . . . the most careful tutelage. I hope you'll agree?'

The faded eyes pleaded so desperately for agreement that it would have been hard not to give it – and surely useless, too. Jeremy nodded slowly. Again the Professor beamed, looked even as if he were going to thrust out his hand to make a pact of it, but was diverted by tittering from Fabers and squealing from Denzil, as they came to the orgy scene, in which pudenda were depicted very realistically and in size to equal that of the figures to which they were attached. Fabers said, 'So that's what upset her! Jewesses, I'm told, are terrible prudes. Moses, of course, was the world's first wowser . . . ahaaaaaeeeee!'

Meanwhile, Rifkah had quickly recovered from whatever had upset her in the cave, and went along back to the camp with Prindy even gaily. She offered no explanation of her behaviour, nor was asked for it, as if what she had done was expected of her. Perhaps their gaiety during the descent, their constant hand-clasping and half-embracing expressed something of this, as if they had been brought still closer together.

They found the four blackboys and Darcy amusing themselves with that somewhat childish and womanish game of faking animal tracks. Rifkah and Prindy joined them eagerly. With expert assistance, Rifkah was perfecting what she already knew of the combination of piccaninny tracks with those of a couple of shepherding kweeluks. Prindy did an intricate one of a dingo's foraging about the camp, which culminated in the imaginary dog's rearing up to sniff at that pack-bag containing Cootes's dainties. This tickled the others greatly.

Then suddenly Rifkah sniffed the air, swung toward the fireplace, crying, 'Ze damper!' Prindy joined her in the rush, snatched up a stick and cleared the mound away and raised the lid. He would have hooked the damper out with the stick, too, into the ashes. She stopped him, grabbed the kneading sack hanging folded in military style with other regimented commissarial equipment, and lifted it out. It was but slightly burnt, charred only about the little crater in the middle that showed how nicely it was done. When she set it down on a stone, they squatted about murmuring their admiration, the blackboys and Prindy salivating in theirs. She was rising to get a knife to scrap off the char, when Prindy suddenly got an idea for playing a joke on 'Ol' Cootsey,' as he called him. There was concern for a moment on the part of the others as they heard what he had in mind, but soon laughter when he spoke of him as a Silly Bugger with a Big Head, evidently quoting Fergus. Then chuckling they set about doing what was necessary.

When the party from the Galleries came back into camp they found the place deserted. Nobody remarked on the fact till Fabers discovered that the lid was off the camp-oven, apparently *shoved* off and that it was empty and no sign of what had been in it. He almost screamed, 'My damper . . . where's everybody?'

The others came to the fire. 'They've taken my damper!' cried Fabers, a look of incredulity on his face.

From over in the rocks and scrub not far to eastward there sounded a howl as of a dog suddenly hurt. All looked in that direction. The staring eyes swung southward, as a yelping apparently travelled that way. 'A dog,' murmured several. They swung back again to where the howl had come from when a babble of human sound was heard from there.

Jeremy, who had been looking at the ground, said, 'By the tracks it looks as if a dingo sneaked in and pinched your damper, Doctor.'

'What . . . out of a hot camp-oven?' demanded Fabers.

'They'll snatch a bit of meat grilling on the fire, if you're not watching. Surely you've had experience of them?'

'Of course I have. I had my boots stolen from beside my swag one night.'

'Anyway . . . it sounds like the others caught him.'

'Caught him?' cried Fabers. 'Didn't you hear him running away. I'm going after him.' He turned towards the fly exercise-rigged for stowing bedding and such gear. A rifle lay ready for instant use on the neatly packed swags. As he grabbed up the rifle, Jeremy called to him, 'No shooting, please.'

The Coot swung on him: 'It's a dingo!'

'According to our reckoning here, dingoes've got more right to the place than we have.'

Fabers pouted, looking quite Napoleonic as he did, and snapped back, 'That one's got no right to my damper.'

'If you don't mind,' said Jeremy. 'I don't have shooting on the place.'

The Coot looked belligerent. General Esk saved the situation by calling, 'I say . . . heah they come . . . and with your damper, old boy, by the look of it.'

Fabers put the gun down. As he came out of the fly he met Fergus coming from the tree where the tucker-bag hung, who said to him, 'Lucky he didn't take your tucker-bag, too, Cootsey. Look at the track.'

Fabers took a look. 'By jove . . . yes. Cheeky bugger!' He looked at those he would be leading on the expedition. 'Now, there's a lesson for you. Never leave anything lying about a camp. Everything to be packed away, or hung high.'

Fergus said, 'Maybe what stopped him taking your patent tucker-bag, Cootsey, was the citronella. If you citronellaed everything, you wouldn't have to go to all the trouble of stowing things away by numbers.'

Fabers ignored him, going to meet those coming to the fireplace, foremost of them Prindy, carrying the damper in both hands, like an offering. Fabers took it without thanks, looked it over, asking, 'Did he damage it?' Prindy pointed to what might have been marks of canine teeth. Perhaps one less relieved than an old woman by recovery of a lost culinary masterpiece would have paid more attention to the slightness of the damage. Instead, Fabers held it up for all to see. 'A beauty, isn't it?'

Said Fergus, 'You don't expect us to eat it after it's been chewed by a dingo, do you?'

'Chewed be blowed . . . it's hardly touched.'

'That dog might have rabies.'

'Nonsense. We don't have rabies in Australia . . . do we Jeremy?'

Fergus winked at Jeremy, who replied gravely, 'No . . . but there is hydatids, of course . . . and dingoes carry it.'

Fabers looked at him quickly, he tittered, 'Go on . . . you're trying to pull my leg. We'll have it with raspberry jam.'

He went and got another tiny can of jam, oblivious of an excess of citronella till he came to opening it, when he sniffed it. He glanced round. No one was watching him, at least as far as he could see. Fergus and Prindy were behind him. Somewhat stealthily, he rubbed the top of it with a corner of the canvas ground-sheet spread for eating off, sniffed again, gave the top a rub in the sand and wiped again, then sniffed his fingers, and after another glance at those busy with making tea and laying cutlery, dealt with them likewise – to the silent delight of Fergus and Prindy.

The jam went nicely with the damper, or vice versa, without a hint of citronella nor a word about it from Fergus. The Coot was very proud, saying that this was nothing – he could actually make pastry, make a perfect meat or fruit pie – but his men needn't think they would be getting anything like that during the expedition: 'We've got to be tough,' he declared, 'This's an exercise in toughness . . . every ounce counts . . . only now and again a nibble from the special tucker-bag.' Fergus and Prindy looked at each other and dropped their heads and quivered.

As he had implied he would, Professor St Clair asked Rifkah, before all the others, what it was about the pictures in the gallery that had upset her. Jeremy looked annoyed and as if about to voice a protest, when she answered simply and smilingly, 'I vos frightened, because . . . vell, it vos so strange . . . so simple like children do . . . but so strong vit' magic . . . and meaning I do not understand. I must know zat meaning . . . because . . . . ' She reached towards Prindy, who came to her. She put an arm about his shoulders. 'Because zey are my children . . . and I must know.' She looked a little alarmed then, perhaps scared by the intensity of the staring.

Fergus said, 'Daisy Bates!'

She got a split grin when she looked at him, then looked at Jeremy, who explained, 'Daisy Bates is a famous old lady who lives with the blacks down in the Western Desert country.'

Cootes said, 'And what an old frump! When I saw her, she positively filled me with revulsion.'

Rifkah looked interested. 'She go naked wit' blacks?'

That got a laugh from the Anthropologists. Cootes said, 'Just the opposite. She dresses up like a mid-Victorian spinster . . . stays and all.' More laughter.

'Vot does she do for zese pipple?'

'No one ever found that out . . . but a book by her is said to be coming out before this Christmas.'

'A book . . . she is Anthropologist?'

'Ethnologist, I think is the word she uses,' said the Professor, with a hint of snicker.

Jeremy said: 'She started really as a journalist, writing about the ill-treatment of blacks for some English newspaper . . . way back, early in the century. She's been wondering about amongst them ever since. I've never heard or read anything she had to say about their ill-treatment.'

Rifkah said, 'I must read her book.'

Doubtless because of the bawdy joke the Coot had made of the incident of Rifkah's sudden withdrawal from the gallery-viewing, Professor St Clair didn't question her about it as he said he was going to do, or anyone else mention it, at least in company. It was General Esk who broached the subject, privily, while he and she, he having requested the pleasure, were riding home together. She answered readily enough, saying simply that the power she'd felt in the paintings seemed somehow to make her feel helpless. He pressed: 'Not rejected?'

'No. It is only I vont to help zese people. Like children zey seem to need help. Zen suddenly you see zey haf somezing you cannot understand. Ze painting is so much like zey are. It is like children do, you zink at first. Zen you feel somezing so strong and old . . . like Nature.' She laughed, adding: 'Like Jewish Ethos ze Professor and Doctor talking so mooch about. Zey spik of it as simple zing of past, kept as habit. But you know it is not. Ze ritual of ze synagogue, ze household . . . it bring Gott to you . . . ze Infinite . . . ze same Gott zat spik to Moses from ze Burning Bush.' Then she sighed. 'I moost learn to feel like zat for Aboriginal zing, or my feeling is not true. So I get fright' lil bits ven I see zat strong Aboriginal-gott-zing staring down at me.' She laughed again. 'You see, General, I am changing my religion. So far I am Proselyte of Gate, as Jews say, still outside. So . . . zat Burning Bush up zere . . .I moost go to it vit' my face cover up, and barefoot.' She ended with a giggle.

'Hmm!' Esk mused. 'I hadn't any idea you took it so seriously.'

'Now it is my life.'

They were silent for a while. Then General Esk said, 'From what I understand, proselytizing isn't encouraged in the Jewish faith . . . for the reason that it's mostly suspect as a means of overcoming the prohibition of marrying out . . . in short, that the motive isn't religious, but sexual.' When she looked at him quizzically, he smiled. 'I just can't see a lovely gal like you becoming like this old Daisy Bates they were speaking of.'

'Vy not?'

'Well . . . with a background like yours, where comfort is religious even, where intellectualism is revered . . . to aspire to live in conditions that, with all due respect to the Aborigine and his Ethos, are semi-animal!'

'I moost learn.'

'To what purpose . . . tell me truly?'

She looked at him again, raising her fine brows: 'Vood I tell you not truly?'

'Ah . . . the old Jewish trick of dodging an embarrassing question by asking another!' As she turned from him, ignoring the remark, he added: 'You spoke of proselytizing and didn't deny what I said about it's being suspect.' When she still ignored him, he went on: 'I'm suggesting that you are proselytizing not to the religion of the Aborigines, but to that of Jeremy Delacy.'

The great jewels of eyes swung on him. He smiled again. 'Please don't take offence at it. I'm sure your relationship's perfectly innocent. But it's obvious that you love each other.'

With face burning now, she could only swallow. It was he now looked away. 'Jeremy Delacy is quite a man. All women are attracted by him. My own daughter fell in love with him. The difference in your case is that the love's returned. He's never loved before. There're several reasons why you should be the first in his life . . . but, primarily, of course, it's yourself. Any man must be attracted to you . . . by your beauty, your essential goodness, your gaiety. Then you're Jewish. That's the chief quality. To have all those attributes and be Jewish is to have everything . . . the *Yiddishe Chein* . . . there's no other expression but your own that fits it. Next you have, in spite of youth, the maturity you've gained through intense suffering. On top of all that you have a certain air of helplessness. You are a refugee. That means you are looking for refuge. But you're a Refugee Jew, which is something different. You're not in flight through sheer fear, but through having the courage to be unable to come to terms with the persecutor. Helplessness in a woman has a special attraction for men. I don't know why . . . because in some men it brings out the knight errant, in others the brute. Perhaps it's because helplessness makes a woman accessible . . . and it depends on what a man wants access to in her. Anyway, with all these attractions, you come into the life of a man at the point of utter disillusionment. He's a man with a great capacity for love. Hence his deep disillusionment. This has bred in him a set of subtle hatreds. He's come to hate his country . . . through too demanding a love of it. He's long hated the countries of his origins, because he expected something of them they couldn't give. He would probably have come even to hating the Aborigines, to whom he's given so much for so little return, only everybody else hates them. He's perverse, you know. That mixture of Welsh and Irish. His last disillusionment, as I see it, was the boy Prindy. He speaks as if the boy is doing everything he expects and wants of him . . . which is probably intellectually true. But I'm sure he wanted the boy to accept him as his grandsire, to love him as belonging to him. The boy lives in a different world, of course. If he loves any individual at all, it's yourself, by the way I see him clinging to you and looking at you. Nanago loves Jeremy . . . in her own way . . . which to my way of thinking is as a slave-girl loves her kind all-powerful master.'

Esk looked again at Rifkah, but only to see her flushed profile, swaying to the steady ambling of Red Rory. Her eyes were fixed on distance. About the corners was a hint of those lines that could deepen to give her that look of age. He went on: 'The nearest to perfection most men can get in a love object is in the form of a daughter. But naturally, that's a very imperfect thing, since it smacks of incest, no matter how innocent. The matter of having scruples about incest is the essential difference between a man and an ape. For perfection, the daughter-object must be unrelated to you. Your proper father was taken from you even before the Nazis murdered him. Your mother, the *Shikseh*, took him. Your true mother was your *Bubbeh*, according to what I've learnt of your history. You've found your true father in Jeremy . . . and he, who never fathered a daughter in the ordinary way, has found his beloved daughter in you.'

When he fell silent, she turned to him, her face still flushed, eyes brilliant, but a certain hardness, shrewdness, to her expression, which he saw and chuckled over. 'Excuse me for saying it . . . but you look very Jewish, but in a very different way . . . that marvellous prescient way of the Jew sensing trouble with the *Goyim*.'

She swallowed. 'You intend to mek trouble for me?'

'No my dear. . .Why should I?'

'Vy zen you spik of Jeremy and myself zat vay?'

'I presumed you wouldn't be conscious of the implications, and thought you'd be better off for being so.'

There was something of a challenge in the hazel eyes now. 'So?'

He looked ahead again as he spoke: 'I presume you know all about my wanting Jeremy to take military command of this region?' When she didn't answer, he went on: 'You've heard me talking of the threat to the British Commonwealth and Empire by the Japanese, especially to this part of it. I assure you it's anything but idle talk. But whether or not you believe it, the patent fact remains that because *I* do, before long this country's going to be garrisoned to a degree that's certain to interfere with those Aboriginal tribes still living in the condition Jeremy wants them kept till it suits them to live otherwise. For the life of me, I can't see why Jeremy refuses the command I offer him, when the very chance of doing what he wants for the people depends on just that.'

She said shortly, 'He hate militarism.'

'I presume you mean military activity for its own sake. Don't we all, who have any intelligence? I admit I inherited and developed a military career . . . but I remain a soldier only to combat militarism. Armed agression can be met only with armed defence.'

'Jeremy believe zat as ze first purpose of any military business is destroy life and endeavour . . . alvays moost it be negative zing.'

Esk sighed: 'Let's forget military business as such for the moment, and concentrate on the practical issue I mentioned before. Someone's going to be given military command of this region. Can't you see, my dear, that without Jeremy's co-operation with me in the matter, his cause is lost before it's embarked on? Even eventual defeat of what he wants to do to make tribal country absolutely inviolate won't matter so long as he's able to do enough to bring home to the Australian Nation the true sense of responsibility they must have for these people they've dispossessed, without which it will never be much better than the convict settlement it began as. That's really what his cause is. Well, it's bound to be defeated, unless he faces this reality.'

When he stopped, she looked again with that seeming challenge. 'So?'

He drew a deep breath: 'I'm expecting you to induce him to co-operate with me.'

For a moment she stared, then swung away, to say breathlessly, 'Zat, I cannot do.'

'Why not?'

'You moost know him vell enough to know he vill do only vot he decide himself.'

'But because he loves you he'll at least listen to you . . . and see the unescapable logic of what I'm sure I've convinced *you*.'

'Because I loff him I cannot ask.'

'Even if you know it will destroy the basis of your love?'

'Vot is zis?'

'You love him for his strength and purpose. If he loses hope in his cause he'll become just an old man, defeated. He's too honest to cling to your young love to keep him alive.'

She swallowed again. 'He is best judge of vot vill defeat him. Vot he zink now is zat *you* are trying to defeat him, in clever English vay.'

Again Esk sighed. 'I know. That's the trouble. I've told you of his hatreds. One of them is of everything English.'

'He likes you as Englishman.'

'Personally . . . but not what I stand for.'

'Might-be he is right.'

'He's wrong. He's half aware he's wrong. He was listening to me till you came along. At least he listened and argued then. Now he's merely polite, waiting for me to give up. I can't give up. My cause is the peace of the world, which I'm convinced can be kept only by the strength and growth of the British Commonwealth, the *Pax Britannica*. We have a ruthless, efficient, treacherous enemy rising to challenge us. The time for action is now. Dear lady . . . I'm not merely asking for your help in what, I do assure you on my honour, is deadly peril to us both . . . I'm begging you.'

When, with eyes on the distance, she didn't respond, he added, now in a different tone, almost a whip-lash of military command: 'Madam . . . I'm fairly desperate. If you won't help me, I shall be moved to use even drastic means to prevent you from hindering me.'

She looked at him swiftly. Their eyes clung for an intense moment, hazel jewels to faded blue, both haggard at the corners now. She swallowed, turned away, paling. He spoke again, more gently, but still with that timbre of authority: 'Your Jewish Refugee Settlement will ultimately depend on my approval. If that doesn't move you, then consider your own position. You can't yet have qualified for British Citizenship . . . . ' He broke off when that old *bubbeh's* look was cast at him. As it was turning away again, he almost gasped, 'Dear gal . . . forgive me . . . but I am truly desperate . . . Rifkah, *maydle*!'

But she had dug her heels into Red Rory's flanks, flung herself forward on his gold and blue flecked mane. Rory shot away as on his best race days.

Fergus, riding Black Cloud with Jeremy on Elektron, next in the line and doubtless with eyes constantly on the slender form ahead, cried suddenly, 'That horse's bolting!' On the instant he was in the jockey's crouch and putting his mount in pursuit. The mounts of the self-appointed leader and his aide, already roused by Red Rory's thunderous passing, also leapt into it. Fabers sat Big Ben for a dozen or so yards, flopping wildly, then fell off, almost under the flayling hoofs of Elektron.

It was a fair test for the prowess of Rory and the Cloud, the first always the slow starter but magnificent finisher, the second the one to overhaul the field and lead till the strain set in. The winning post was the first gate, gleaming so white and solid, six feel of steel piping and mesh, or the six-foot netting fence, either of which Rory would surely have the horse-sense to swing away from. But you never know what a bolting horse will do. He might go over the gate. But whatever he did at that stride, his inexperienced rider, plainly out of control, clinging with hands and heels, must come to grief. It looked as if Rory was going to take the gate, the way he lifted his big head to sight it at barely, thirty feet. That was when he became aware of the Cloud coming up on him, rolled an eye. Fergus, initiate in the fine art of what is called Interference in horse-racing, somehow got Black Cloud's shoulder against Red Rory's flank and turned him to the left, so close to the fence that the wire rang, at the same time getting a grip on Rifkah's arm that saved her from going overboard, while shouting, 'Feet forward . . . head back!'

Rory eased up. Fergus grabbed the lost reins and stopped him dead. Rifkah, yellow-faced and shaking, looked at him. He gave her the split-lipped grin. 'Why don't you listen to papa? Feet back and head forward only when you're racing. Otherwise dead erect or leaning back. Don't blame the poor old horse. Better get off for a minute, eh?'

He dismounted and helped her, trembling, down, taking full advantage of the situation to embrace her closely. He asked, 'What happened? The old boy put the hard word on you? I thought he was more for the boys.'

But there were the others crowding up, at least those who hadn't fallen off in the excitement. A babble of sympathetic inquiry, most sympathetic of all the General, patting her hand, murmuring, 'Dear gal . . . dear gal . . . you're all right?'

When she was smiling again, if somewhat weakly, Fergus said, 'You know what they do with 'prentice jockeys who have a buster and haven't busted anything . . . and young pilots, too? They put 'em right up back again, so's they don't lose their nerve. Come on, sweetheart . . . up you go. You and me's going to have a burn round the race track.' He pushed her up into the saddle again.

Still following his advantage, Fergus, while walking her home after leaving the horses at the yard, asked again if he might have her alone on the evening walk, stressing the facts, when she refused, that this was his last night with her for some time, that he had something terrifically privately important to discuss with her, that, well, hadn't he saved her life or something? But to no avail. She even wouldn't tarry with him in the comparative seclusion of the mango grove, for 'just one little kiss', as he begged, but slipped out of the grip he tried to get on her, and finished the rest of the way at a run. Watching her shapely bottom wobbling in the tight pants to her going, he bit his cleft lip under the bit of hair then sighed. 'But I'll get you yet, Georgette!'

Fergus compromised again by sharing Rifkah on the walk, and seemed happy enough, by his talkativeness. He set out to tell a comical tale of how in boyhood he'd aspired to become a great writer: 'Lonely kid . . . stuffy parents and one priggish older sister. Remember I told you I was brought up in Randwick, Sydney, near the Racecourse. I could watch the races from a cubby I had up in a big Moreton Bay fig. I liked horses and horsey people, because I used to see 'em of early mornings exercising . . . and probably because the rest of the family thought it vulgar. Watching the big races, I'd identify myself with the winning jockeys, vice-regal handshakes and all, and when I got old enough to think about it, winning the girl who'd previously knocked me back, I took to writing it, as stories . . . eventually made it into a book, called *Wild Will Willnot, King of the Turf*. I was fourteen then. There were as many females of my own species in it as horses. My sister found it, gave it to my old man, who burnt it. It was after that I ran off to Brisbane, and got a job as a stable boy. I tried telling my yarns to my colt-brained colleagues. The result was useful. I learnt that you can escape from life by writing romances about it, just as you can by reading 'em. Those kids in the stables really did live. But when you came to think of it, what record did they leave of what they did . . . except in police headquarters? When the old man tracked me down and brought me home and I got back to proper schooling, I started reading about the really great adventurers, who'd written about what they did themselves . . . Richard Burton, Charles Darwin, Casanova. That's what led me into anthropology. I'd be all three. My trouble was in being born too late. You can fly over the Chilean Andes now in ten minutes . . . and take a bus to Mecca . . . and you don't have to get over the walls of convents or harems any more . . . and as for adventuring in the Australoid wilds, the fact is you can't get a grant for an anthrop survey without a letter from your local clergyman, like. The Coot and the Saint are perfect examples of the latterday bravos who face the perils of the untrod wilderness. I thought then that the Winged Horse would carry me to Parnassus. But Bert Hinkler, Lindberg, Kingsford-Smith, even Amy Johnston, beat me to it by a long way. Nothing left but to run guns to the Dyaks of Borneo to start a revolt against the Dutch and English . . . '

Jeremy asked, 'You're not seriously thinking of that, are you?'

'No one's asked me, more's the pity. All I get's an offer to spot uncharted shell-banks for Japs illegally pearl-fishing in Australian waters, and to keep an eye on the movements of the Coast Patrol boat. Might be something to write about that later especially if I can get to the Jap Mandated Islands, which they're supposed to be fortifying. Outsiders have been disappearing, it seems, for discovering too much of what's going on . . . .'

Rifkah cried, 'And you vill disappear, too!'

'Maybe to the relief of a lot of people,' said Fergus. When they'd done laughing, he added: 'Meantime my literary career's limited to more or less compulsory service to *Australia Free*.'

Jeremy asked, 'Compulsory service?'

'Financially involved with the Chief . . . old Claudius, who owns it all. I'm working it out.'

'Can't say I recall reading anything of yours.'

'Rather feeble *nom de plume . . . Phil de Terra*.'

'Ah . . . that you, eh? Quite good stuff, though, I thought . . . best in the rag.'

'Thanks.'

'I thought it was done by an Italian. I saw some objection to you as one, in letters published.'

Fergus chuckled. 'Yes . . . that was from the Eureka Stockade thing . . . about the chief rebel's being an Italian, and not Peter Lalor, the Irish Australian, who got all the kudos and finished up swearing allegiance to the Queen of England to get into Parliament. A number of people wrote, calling me a Dirty Insulting Dago, a Fascist Beast, Go Back to your Garlic, Giuseppe.'

'I enjoyed it very much. *Australians' Ten-minute Stands for Liberty*. Great title. Wonderful crack at how supine Australians really are, despite the everlasting boasts of love of liberty.'

'Glad you liked it. The crazy name had no connexion with the Italian thing, though. It's actually a feeble pun on the ideas of *Son of the Soil* and *Enfant Terrible.* I'd've liked to drop it, seeing it doesn't get me anywhere personally, only old Claudius, the Chief, was too pleased with the row it caused . . . and so I'm stuck with it, so long as I've got the old boy on my back.'

'What would you mean by that?'

'Well, it was through him I got in with the Junkers crowd. Naturally, as in the case of the Japs, the Huns've given the Free Australia Movement their blessing. Why shouldn't they, when the Bloke even wears his hair and mo like Uncle Adolf? The Junkers mob are flat out trying to make friends in aviation here. I understand it's the same in England, everywhere there might be opposition . . . trying to sell the invincibility of their new *Luftwaffe* and the nobility of its intentions, rather than their kites. Personally, I regard military aviation as the worst form of murder. I think any natural-born airman does. Even the so-called knightly personal combat business. Dog-fighting's a good name for it. It's just murdering your mate. Anyway, I played up to the Junks. They didn't want money, I found, only . . . well, again a sort of letter from your local clergyman. That happened to be old Claudius . . . as far as they were concerned. He'd got to like me. He's a sardonic old bugger himself, and . . . well, he likes the dry wit . . . ahem!'

Another laugh. He went on: 'So I got my lovely kite on what's virtually a gent's agreement, to use for an unspecified period . . . of course on the understanding that I advertise the invincibility and nobility of the *Luftwaffe* and say a Heil Hitler instead of a Hail Mary every hour. A gift from the gods. But you can't run even such an aeroplane on air alone. I had to put the hard word on the Chief. I offered him a partnership in my charter work. But he's shrewd. Nailed me down to what I could guarantee in such work. The result was another gentleman's agreement. He put up the money estimated to keep the kite flying for a year, put it in a bank, actually, fixing things so that only my creditors in the matter of flying expenses could draw on it . . . the condition in this case being that I write him a *Phil de Terra* piece for every issue of the rag for the period, and hand out copies wherever I go. I can say I've scrupulously stuck to the contract. You'll find copies of *Australia Free* hanging in every bush dunny in the land.'

When Jeremy chuckled, Rifkah asked, 'Vot is bush dunny?'

Fergus looked at Jeremy: 'You tell her.'

'No fear . . . you brought up the subject.'

'Vot is?' demanded Rifkah.

'Well,' said Fergus, 'You might describe the dunny as the intellectual centre of the average bush homestead . . . as the library, is, in a properly constituted residence. It's there the average bush Australian does his reading, broadens his mind.'

'He mek joke?' Rifkah asked of Jeremy.

'Not entirely.' Jeremy added to Fergus: 'I'll have to get back some of those copies of the paper I've lately been giving away without reading 'em, to bring myself up to date with this Phil the Terror.'

'What put you off the rag . . . the anti-semitism?'

'Partly. But there's that general air of insanity about it . . . stuff like yours excepted.'

'Why don't you contribute something of the kind yourself, and so improve the sanity?'

'I'm no sort of writer.'

'You express yourself very well . . . and writing's only a form of speech. You've certainly got the right ideas. You could tackle them on anti-semitism, for a start. No one's done it in an intelligent article yet . . only in wild letters from frantic Sons of Shem themselves, published for the fun of it.'

'Would they publish anything serious?'

'I'm sure the Chief would. The Bloke's the one who introduced the anti-semitism, along with all else he's borrowed from Der Führer. Old Claudius himself regards it only as a sardonic joke. He's told me he admires Jews, had lots of friends among them, till he got mixed up with the Bloke. He says he enjoys annoying 'em, especially the rich and intellectual ones he knows. They come to his office screaming abuse. Several times they've put bricks through his windows. He reckons they ought to have more sense.'

'Perhaps generally they have . . . and it's only the poor refugees, who're half mad with suffering and afraid of more, who do things like that.'

'Why not write just that, then? Why not write what you've learnt about Jews . . . or get the girlfriend here to tell you her tale and write it . . . and put a stop to it. It's cruelling the Movement as it is. Alfie Candlemas'd see you got published. She's one of the editors now. You say you'll start reading it again on account of me. Others'll do the same on account of you. I've said it could be a very good paper . . . could become the most powerful political force in the land. The same with the Movement. It's only a matter of getting the few ratbags out of it. I know the interest that powerful and intelligent people have in it . . . or did to start with. All it needs is men like you, without ulterior motive, with forthrightness, and sanity. After a bit of an introduction through the paper, all you'd have to do is go down and attend one of their inner circle meetings . . . Alfie'd get you into it . . . and I'll guarantee you'd have the Bloke and his handful of *Gauleiters* out with the first show of hands. If you were to take on the leadership yourself . . . . '

'Hey, go easy!' Jeremy laughed.

But Fergus was serious: 'I mean it. I'm thinking of myself, mainly. I'd like to be in on it, too. Under sane leadership, the Movement could have control of Australian politics within a year. People're waiting for it. The country's being run by Pommies from London, Commies from Moscow, con-men representing both sides within . . . . '

'I'm no politician, son.'

'But for the adventure of it! It could start a revolution . . . . '

'Not an adventurer, either, I'm afraid.'

'But you've got to do something to break this rotten racket. Look at these two cheats, the Coot, the Saint, knowing nothing about Aborigines, taking the thing out of the hands of the only man who does know anything . . . yourself. Look at Old Eskimo . . . a bloomin' Pommy aristocrat, organizing a war for us with the people who ought to be our best friends, our fellow Asiatics, the Japs.'

When Jeremy didn't respond, but only stared ahead at the golden lights of the homestead beckoning through the trees, the vague forms of limping, lolloping refugee things clumsily playing in the moonlight, Fergus said, 'Sorry, Sir, if I sounded cheeky. I do respect you, Sir. It's only . . . only . . . . '

Jeremy sighed. 'That's all right, son. I know I've got to do something sometime. Things're pressing a bit hard. Might write something, as you say. But I'll have to settle down a bit first. Been a bit hectic with all of you around. Used to quiet, you know. This's a quiet place, really . . . . '

'Might be a bit too quiet. You miss what's going on in the world.'

Jeremy looked at Rifkah. 'A lot of it seems to be worth missing, too . . . eh, Rifkah?'

She answered, speaking to Fergus, 'So true it is. You listen . . . you can hear zat loffly quiet.'

Only the soft heart-beat of the place . . . *Home, home, home, home*! . . . and a distant mopoke calling that all was well.

They went on some little way in silence. Then suddenly, with a rush of words that told of their being pent, Fergus, asked, 'Jeremy . . . would you much mind if I had a word with Rifkah alone?'

The question halted them. Both Jeremy and Rifkah stared. Jeremy slipped free of the girl, she of Fergus. It was Rifkah who answered, 'Vot is it you cannot say before Jeremy?'

Fergus was at a loss, blinking, biting his lip. Jeremy came to his rescue: 'Well, presuming that you're not going to annoy the lady . . . why not?' He began to move off.

Rifkah said, hesitantly it seemed, 'Jeremy . . . . '

He stopped and turned. When she said no more, he said, 'See you later.' He turned away, set off towards the house.

Rifkah stared after him for a moment, then swung on Fergus. 'Vell vot?'

He reached to take her arm, and when she pulled away, said, 'Only want to take your arm for a little walk.'

'I vill not valk. You tell me here.'

'There's a lot to tell you.'

'You said a vord.'

'This's the last chance I'll have to talk to you . . . . '

'Ze General vill be on ze coast till end of year . . . and coming in here often.'

'Fat lot of chance I get to talk to you alone, don't I!'

'You don't vont to talk . . . only play-about.'

'You're getting more a blackfellow every day . . . . '

'So?'

'Listen . . . I'm serious. I want you to be my girl . . . to come away with me.'

She laughed. 'I vill be ze co-pilot . . . or stewardess for General?'

'I mean when I'm finished with him. We'll clear out of here . . . go to the Carolines . . . . '

'Get killed for spying!'

'Don't be silly . . . I'm friends of the Japs. We'd live in real style . . . . '

'Vot about Germans who own your aeroplane?'

'You should worry about Germans!'

'I vorry about you . . . for being silly boy.'

'Then if you worry about me, you like me!'

'Of course I like you . . . but as *mein bruder.*'

'Now you're being silly. I want a mate . . . a girl . . . .'

'Plenty of girl for you.'

'I only want one . . . you. If you like we'll get married.'

'I am not goot for vife. I am sterilize!'

'I don't want kids. I want a mate. We could have a wonderful time together. I love you . . . if you want to know. Every day I love you more. You're everything I want in a girl. You're beautiful. You're a sport. Yes . . . and you're Jewish. I love you because you're Jewish. It makes you different . . . .'

'Ze SA men vont Jewish girl for difference. It is crime for zem. Zey get big trouble for havingk Jewess . . . but zey do. Zey say it gif zem goot luck . . . seventy year goot luck . . . rub off ze Jew-luck, zey say.'

'I know I'd be lucky with you. Look, I'll get a Special Licence and marry you next time I come here . . . take you over to one of the missions and get the Missionary to do it.'

'You are jitty. I cannot marry you.'

'Because I'm not a Jew?'

'Because I don't vont any man.'

'What about old Delacy?'

'You speak like zat I go.'

'Sorry. But what's here for you? It's all right now while it's new to you. But you'll soon get sick of it . . . the bush, the blacks. You believe the same as the old feller about leaving the blacks alone. Well, leave 'em alone. What do you intend to do . . go and live with 'em . . . like Daisy Bates?'

'I vont to help zem against vite pipple.'

'They don't want your help. Daisy Bates only follows them about. They probably don't want her . . . or only what they can get out of her. Anyway, she's just an old maid . . . run away from life. Like other old maids go looking after stray dogs and cats, she looks after stray tribes of blacks.'

'I vill be old maid, too.'

'You're crazy . . . you're what you call it . . . *meshugeh,* isn't it? You don't know what wild blacks are really like. You don't know the wild bush. You'd be dead in a month from sickness . . . if they didn't take you and rape you and then eat bits of you. I'm not going to let you do it. You're going to be my girl . . . .'

'Come . . . ve go in now.'

'No we're not!' He seized her, enveloping her protesting mouth with his own split one, grabbed at her fending hand and forced it behind her, forcing her back, back, with the greed of his mouth – and with his free hand began to drag up her skirt. She brought a knee up into his crutch. He gasped, released her, staggered, clutching at his genitals.

She panted, 'I am sorry.'

'You bitch! he gasped.

'It vos not hard I hurt you . . . but I am sorry, yes. You are all right?'

He nodded, getting control of his breath: 'You've had ex . . . perience . . . .'

'Too mooch experience. But I am sorry to hurt you.'

' 'S all right . . . I asked for it.'

'Still ve are friend?'

'Still I love you.'

'Still you are *meshugeh*. Come take my arm . . . but behave . . . or again I get rough.'

He laughed slightly. 'There's no doubt about you.'

'Vot is no doubt about?'

'That you're the girl for me.'

'*Ach*!'

A dull evening, with everyone wanting to get to bed, judging by the yawns. The Coot, that leader of men, led the way to bed by saying he'd like an early night for an early start tomorrow.

First leg of the expedition was to be the crossing of that stretch of wilderness to Catfish, required to be done in the first day, according to the plan of campaign. Not such an arduous undertaking, it might be considered by some, seeing it was no further than the trip to Beatrice, with pretty well as good a road to follow. Still, with military operations you can't leave anything to chance. Uneasy lies the head that bears command. So often did poor Fabers get up that night to go to pee, that round about 2 a.m. Fergus complained in a hoarse whisper as he passed his door, 'For christ sake, Cootsey . . . why keep going to the bathroom? Can't you piss in one of those fancy riding boots of yours . . . or Denzil's lion-hunter's hat?'

Nevertheless, the expedition set out as planned immediately after breakfast. Its departure was somewhat in the style of the early explorers, who perhaps because of realization that the odds were against their ever returning for it, had their heroic hour at the outset, escorted out of town by cheering crowds. Although there was no cheering for the Cootes Expedition, pretty well everybody turned out to accompany it as far as the top gate.

Professor St Clair, evidently ignorant of Delacy family relations, in taking leave of Jeremy, asked if he had any message to convey to his son Clancy. Jeremy merely shook his head. But Denzil, overhearing and being near Rifkah, said to her with a sly smile, 'You'd like your affectionate regards delivered at Catfish, I'm sure, *Fraulein*, eh what?'

She answered shortly, 'You know I like not ze catfish.'

Denzil giggled, 'Not *kosher*.' Then as she moved away, he whispered to Fergus, 'Not circumcised!' With that he took hysterics, which the cold if inflamed eye of his new commander had to quell before the party could get under way.

The Coot was properly condescending to Jeremy in taking leave, thanking him for his hospitality and help and promising to mention him in what he called The Appreciation he would be making to the Government. The Professor had nothing so encouraging to say. Taking Jeremy's hand he looked rather sad, as if losing a friend. That this was the termination of unofficial dealings between them was surely presaged by his saying, 'Goodbye, Jeremy . . . it's been a privilege knowing you. '

Then, with a snap of command and crack of stockwhips the Expedition was off, heading into the Never-Never. True, their progress would be checked from time to time by the General flying over them with Fergus. In fact Esk had offered to supply them with every need to make life easier, even a radio to call him, and their mail from home. But the Coot insisted on making it to the northern coast unaided by anything but the spirit of his own intrepidity.

Perhaps Esk wasn't thinking of Cootes so much as of his own untried men and the somewhat rickety old professor, as suggested by his saying to Jeremy, as they and the others rode back to the homestead, 'Well, it's to be hoped they make it safely.' Then he had yet another try at talking Jeremy into going with him on this trip, or at least to promise to make another with him. He concluded with a sigh: 'Sorry, old boy. Afraid I've rather pushed it *ad nauseam*. But I do assure you I share the sickness with you . . . although mine's sickness of the heart. Leave it for now. I shan't give up. I can't, of course. But I do hope you'll understand . . . and that it won't deny me the privilege of your friendship.'

There was more possession-yearning and promise-seeking further along the line of those trailing back from the brave departure. Fergus was at Rifkah again. Then, biting his lip as he set out to prepare his aircraft for flight, he hit on the idea of taking Prindy along, and while explaining the function of mechanisms he checked, talked about a wonderful trip they would soon make together, along with Rifkah, to Port Palmeston, and home again by way of the Queen Victoria River. Would Prindy like that? Vigorous nodding. 'Right . . . then talk Rifkah into it, son. You reckon I'm a good bloke?' Nod, nod. 'You reckon I'm number-one?' Fergus rumpled the fair nodding head. 'Okay . . . you keep telling Rifkah that . . . Fergus is number-one!'

The aeronauts waited for smoke-o, prepared in style for them by Nan and Rifkah as a send-off. The General took both females by the arms as they saw him to the luggage-piled utility, telling them how he had never been so happy in hostesses before: 'I'm going to take the liberty to send you both a little something. I'm telling you, so's you shan't be offended.' He kissed each on the cheek before they could reply, then was gone.

Fergus also kissed them both, one of them so as to leave her breathless and cause the other to giggle. But that wasn't the end of Fergus's farewelling. Airborne, he came in over the tips of the mangoes, and banking, flung down a last kiss from his split lip with his fingers.

Then silence, peace – only that soft heart-beat: *Home, home, home, home*! Nan and Rifkah looked at each other, smiled, kissed lightly, then sighing, hand-in-hand, went in to see to the great cleaning up after the departed guests.

Walking that Tuesday night in the ritualistic style of old, Rifkah told Jeremy of Esk's request for her help in inducing him to do what he wanted of him, however, without mentioning that veiled threat. But for the ommission, Jeremy probably wouldn't have chuckled over the information as he did: 'Poor old Mark! So desperately does the decent Englishman believe that his decency is God-given for sharing with the rest of mankind . . . the Lesser Breeds Without the Law, as their imperial poet so simply and frankly called the rest . . . that he'll come even at what he'd consider not decent in others to spread the gospel. That's why they're so dangerous . . . they're so sincere.'

She asked if there weren't some wisdom in what the General was saying, some value in what he was offering. Jeremy answered, 'He's taking himself too seriously. He's a political stooge himself. He realizes that the Australian military brass is made up largely of confidence tricksters and up-jumped bullying louts . . . but doesn't know that that goes for pretty well anyone who has power in this nation of con-men. Remember what young Fergus said about Coots's believing Esk will be out with the first change of Government. I believe that, too. But even if I didn't, I'd still be chary of putting myself in his hands . . . because that means the hands of the Imperial Brass, whom I know only too well of old . . . and I'll take a lot of convincing that they've changed. Of course he's right in saying the peace of the world depends on the *Pax Britannica*. Any power that dominated the world would have peace . . . by not permitting war. It's troops then become policemen . . . as the British are in so many parts of the world at present. That's what the Japs aspire to be, I suppose . . . super policemen. There's money in it too, of course. Napoleon didn't call the English a Nation of Shopkeepers for nothing.'

'Vot if vor wit' Japan?'

'I can't see them doing more in a hundred years than dominate Asia . . . which I think they've got more right to do than the Europeans dominating it now. They'd attack us, I'm sure, only if we were involved with someone attacking them, someone using Australia as a base, as Mark Esk wants to do. War with Japan's our chance of true independence and nationhood . . . to make the decison whether or not to fight them, make it ourselves. It'd take an enormous expeditionary force to invade Australia . . . and the size of it and the slowness of its approach couldn't match anything that we could put up if reasonably well prepared. Our northern wilderness is our first line of defence. The Japs know that even better than we do. No . . . I'm wrong. Our first line of defence is our true patriotism, true love of the land, determination for true liberty.'

'But vot about vot Cootsey and Professor vill be doing about ze blacks? Fergus is right, I zink, zat zey vill tek no more notice of you zan ozzer.'

'Fergus is also right about that Free Australia thing . . . as our one hope of acquiring the integrity to deserve nationhood. I'm going to try it out. I'll try 'em on that silly anti-semitism first. That should be a good test. If they accept what I say there's hope . . . and I'll go further.'

She looked at him, her face looking oldish with trouble in the moonlight. 'Vot vill you do about anti-semitism?'

'Write an article for them condemning it . . . for a start as barbarity, from the things you've told me about your sufferings . . . then as an example of Australian lack of originality. Let's concentrate on being what's to the point, I'll say . . . Anti-Britannic. What harm have Jews ever done Australia? Even those who've become leading citizens were the most honest and modest in power of anyone else we've had.'

'Vood not it be better to leave out Jews for start?'

'Why?'

'Might only mek trouble.'

He chuckled. 'That Jewish fear of offending the stupid cowardly *Goy*, who actually does what he does out of fear. No . . . as Fergus said, the silly anti-semitism is what's cruelling the thing. Australians at large aren't a bit anti-semitic. Don't forget we've got our own lost tribes to take out our meanness on. I'll work on that . . . the ethos business. I'll get to it right away . . . tonight. Glad of a night to myself. Might have a draft of it by morning. Then, if it's any good, I'll work on it carefully, and have it ready for next week's train.'

'You are not going to train tomorrow?'

'No. You can go with Darcy and his mob.'

'I don't vont to go . . . not for long vile yet.'

'Eh? Oh, I see . . . that business last time. It seems so long ago. But you mustn't let that worry you.'

She drew close to him as they walked. 'I cannot help vorry.'

'Why?' Lightly with his cheek he touched the glinting copper falling on his shoulder.

For a few steps she was silent, then said with a sigh, 'I am fright' somezing happen spoil my happiness.' She paused again, then added quickly: 'I must go svim in Rainbow Pool, so zey cannot tek me avay.'

'Eh . . . who's going to take you away?'

'I am not naturalize' citizen . . . . '

'Rubbish! What about all the Jews coming? They'll all have to wait for three years, or whatever the period is. Anyway, you don't swim in that pool till I'm there to watch you . . . . ' He broke off with a laugh, adding: 'And since I'm not a blackfellow, that means you buy a bathing suit first.'

She giggled, dropped her head, to rub it against his chest.

When on their return Kurt was told of the idea to challenge the anti-semitism of Australia Free, he also showed lack of enthusiasm, in fact more actively than Rifkah had. Frowning over it, he said more harm than good always came out of attacking anti-semites, since it only increased their antagonism – best to make them feel silly by ignoring it. Jeremy declared, 'Ignoring it didn't do you much good in Germany, did it?'

Kurt shrugged in his elaborate way. 'Australia is different. Zis zing is only small European influence.'

'It's the small influences we've got to get rid of, whether German, Scotch, Irish, Greek, Italian, as well as the big British.'

'But not Jewish?' asked Kurt with a sly smile.

Jeremy showed his puzzlement to their attitude with his expression. Still, he compromised by agreeing to tackle the thing not as an evil in itself, but something foreign to Australia, that, being so, must retard the Movement's avowed ideal of true nationhood. He said he would not mention the experiences of Kurt and Rifkah, or the mooted settlement. Kurt said that publicity in the first case could harm people who'd helped them out of bondage, and in the second embarrass those he called his Principals with too many importuning refugees.

It certainly made the job harder for Jeremy, who next morning red-eyed, confessed that he was far from having a draft to present for criticism. Still, he was also far from displeased with his efforts because he could see shaping a subtle use of the delicate subject to drive home that point of his about ridding the community of those ancient importations which retarded its growth and at the same time do something for the Aboriginal cause by comparing it with that of the Jews.

Kurt went along to Beatrice with the Darcys and Prindy, and returned to report that he'd received word from his Principals to say they would be along, flying their own aircraft, any day, if it suited Jeremy. In reply Jeremy sounded well enough pleased. But such was the effect of the news on Rifkah as to cause her to show but half-hearted interest in the bushel or so of ripe plums also brought back, when she had been so full of what she was going to do with them. Also, she scarcely seemed to hear the personal message Kurt had for her, from Clancy, who evidently in reply to something Denzil had said to him about her after all, sent his affectionate regards in return and hoped to see her again soon.

Rifkah's moody preoccupation persisted, so that out on the walk that evening Jeremy asked what was wrong. She sighed. 'Too many people come to us. I am fright' for my loffly peace.'

'They'll be calling you a Scrub Cow, if they find you're hiding from 'em.'

But she wasn't amused. 'It haf been so loffly, I am fright' it cannot last.'

'Why not use that magic formula of yours to ward off the demons of ill-omen . . . *Kayn Aynhoraḥ*?'

'Better I use ze magic of ze country and svim in se Rainbow Pool.'

'You just keep out of that pool, my lady, till I'm ready, and you're equipped, for proper and decent baptism.'

'Baptism . . . vot is?'

He explained, going on to tell of similar forms of primitive initiation ceremony, coming back to Christianity to express his old hatred and contempt. She was in a mood for that. She told him how her *Bubbeh* and *Zaydeh* in tales of the hardships of their early days told of being chased and caught by Christian children, who having forced them to confess that they had killed Christ the Saviour, baptised them with urine. *Tauchen* she called the ceremony of baptism. That made Jeremy blaze: 'The bastards! Was there ever anything so hypocritically low as a Christian?'

'Shush!' she murmured.

'Why . . . are you frightened of the dogs even out here?'

'I am alvays a lil bits fright.'

'Well, I'll see to it that you never have cause to be frightened again.'

'Zank you, dear Jeremy . . . I loff you!'

For a moment they clung kissing. Then he held her off, breathing heavily, starting to talk about his literary piece.

III

Do a thing three times running and it becomes a habit. Do it in company and it becomes an institution. So said Jeremy over breakfast on Thursday morning when he heard Rifkah and Prindy planning another barramundi fishing.

Again it was a picnic affair, with something like a dozen going along, counting those tots double-banking with grown-ups. Again with the use of infallible methods, the fishing was routine. They took only three big fellows, two for home, one for the *piendi* bake. The bake was on, and the entire company in the water, playing, when Prindy caught a sound and called for silence. With head cocked northward, he said, 'Aeroplane.' The adult females came rushing from the water to dress.

However, there was no aerial peeping-tom business this time, even though the aeronaut again was Fergus, according to Prindy's almost undoubted judgement. The aircraft was not even seen. Apparently it came in low over the Plateau and straight in to land. Rifkah was the only one to doubt, suggesting that it might be another aerial party that was due any day and arguing that the General had said it would be two or three weeks before he was back again. Perhaps her doubting was due more to fear than to lack of confidence on those marvellous ears, as betrayed by her look and her repeated question, 'Vy ze General vont to come back so soon?' The others noted her fear, that haggard look, new to all save Prindy, and exchanged covert glances over it. Prindy stared at her frankly, as if waiting for her to communicate her fear to him.

She ate but little of the tasty lunch, and as soon as it was over and the others settling for a nap, came out with the first of that communication to Prindy: 'I do not sleep. I vont to ride.' Prindy leapt up at once and ran to get the horses. She told the others that when they were ready they might go on home with the fish. When she was with Prindy saddling up, she said, 'I vont to svim in pool now.' His lips framed the inhalation: *Eh, look out*!

As they rode, she said, 'Might be ze General haf come to tek me avay. I moost haf ze magic to help me.' She went on to explain the half-threat and the intricacies of Naturalization and Deportation. Evidently he didn't understand much of what she was saying, but was no less forthright in declaring that he wouldn't let her be taken away.

At the pool they simply slipped their horses' bits, and left them, docile Snowball and Sugarbag, to graze on the bit of verdure behind the little beach.

As Rifkah stripped, of necessity much slower than her companion, she stared at the pool, at the mirror smoothness close in, unbroken till it met the rocks on the downside and poured smoothly down to become the river, at the emerald deep shaded by the rocky wall across the way and mysteriously flowing backward. A family of tiny sunbirds were bathing in the cascades constituting debouchment of Knowles' Creek, making tiny rainbows with ruffled plumage of purple and gold.

At last, in the ivory and copper-touched buff, she gave Prindy her hand. He would have rushed her in. She held back, and halted at knee-deep, plopping down when he tried to pull her, sat with water to her breasts, and took handfuls and dashed it over her shoulders. He insisted that she must come out to swim. She argued that she could not swim well enough, that it was sufficient to have a dip to ensure that bond between you and the pool, according to the Mullaka. Prindy argued that it was all right for ordinary white people to do that, but not she, who was to become his mother. When she questioned him about this, he told her that the Pookarakka had come to him one night and told him that she was not just a whitewoman but a Shade of Koonapippi and might become his *Koyu*, or Mumma, if she let the Old One take a good look at her up through his hole in the water there and he was pleased with her. She listened in astonishment, reassuming that haggardness which had passed off as soon as she'd entered the water. 'Come on!' he kept on saying, tugging at her hand. 'Come on . . . you got 'o come.' Almost moaning, she declared that she would drown out there. He said, 'Old One can't drown'd you. He want you for my *Koyu*. You come . . . you come . . . I Sing you come!'

Dazedly at last she let herself be pulled forward to knees, flopped onto her breast, began to swim, in her own fashion, breast-stroke. He swum around her, shepherding her. So out to the green, into the edge of the pull, pull, pull, and round it, with set face and steady stroke, stroke, stroke. The sun birds shrilled and came to hover and look. She seemed not to see them, to see anything. Prindy kept on the inside here, occasionally submerging a little, as if to see what was going on below. Stroke, stroke, stroke – till they were round, and heading for the shore. She crawled up the wet sand, onto the dry, to lie on her belly, weeping now. He came and sat on haunches beside her, stroking her quivering spine from the lank copper of her hair to the darkish patch in the ivory below which the cleft of her perfect buttocks began. So for a couple of minutes. Then she raised her head, resting on elbows, and looked round at him and smiled through tears. He pulled at her shoulder, causing her to turn right round and sit up. Staring at her gravely, he said, 'Now you properly my *Koyu*. You call me *Mullikirri*. Go on . . . you say.'

She breathed it, '*Mullikirri*.'

She reached for him, her lips projecting to kiss him; but he held her off, saying, 'Blackfeller don't kiss. You give me *kumilungornu*.'

'Vot is zat?'

'Titty.' He reached for her left breast, dusted the sand from it. When she held his hand, he urged, 'Come on.'

'Vot for?' she murmured.

'Blackfeller way. You my Mumma. Must I suck you.'

'But you big boy!'

'No matter. Spone I am not man yet. You give me.'

She released his hand. He dusted a little more, then bent and took the small nipple in his lips, all the while looking into her eyes as she looked into his, grey into hazel. Suddenly she wrapped her arms about him, drew him tight so that his cheek flattened on her breast like a baby's, the golden against the ivory; and she bent and kissed him between the eyes, breathing, '*Kleine mensheleh*!'

He got his lips free, corrected her: '*Mullikirri*.'

'*Mullikirri*,' she repeated, and rocked him.

They let go, to sit staring at each other. A snort from one of the horses. They swung round to see both beasts standing rigid peering towards the upper falls. Prindy cocked an ear. No sound but that of the waters and of the wind getting up with the declination of the Sun. The wind was blowing towards the falls. The sun birds had vanished. Now the horses moved towards what had attracted their attention, to halt after a few steps, in the manner of their kind, inquisitive but ever wary. He breathed, 'Something . . . I go look.' She rose as he did, grabbed up her clothes, ran with them to cover.

Prindy dived into the thick scrub at the end of the beach, where the ground rose steeply to the ridge that further in became the falls. He climbed up through the rocks, stopping at the top of the ridge crouching to reconnoitre. Nothing to be seen or heard. Here the noise of the water was louder. Still crouching, he advanced through the scrub that flanked the creek. Again he halted, this time at sight of fresh tracks of riding boots going to the edge of the ridge, diagonally towards the falls compared with the way he had come. He followed them, soon found that although they went on towards the falls, they converged with others, these of someone wearing ordinary shoes; a jumble of tracks, as if the two persons had run into each other there and stopped to talk. Evidently both parties had first been to the edge of the pool, perhaps unbeknown to each other until they'd met. The tracks went off together up-creek. Again he followed, came on tracks of a horse, which one man had mounted, while the other walked. More horse tracks and indication of mounting and of the pair's having ridden off together, away from the creek south-westward, no doubt to dodge the rough stuff lying directly between them and the pool, but making in that direction. He ran. Soon from the edge of the rough stuff he caught a glimpse of them, and surely recognized them: Fergus Ferris and Clancy Delacy, the former on Big Ben, the latter on a handsome bay. He then turned from them and ran directly to the pool. As he went he heard halooing from the men. Rifkah was standing waiting on the grass, fully dressed, but great-eyed with apprehension. Prindy panted his report.

Yodelling, in what must have been Fergus's voice was next heard. The horses on the grass got the scent and neighed. Back came an answering neigh. Then there were the riders coming in by the track, Fergus grinning and gaily crying greetings, Clancy looking serious and very much like his father mounted. As Fergus swung down to the ground he said, 'Having a quiet winky, eh?'

Eyeing him dubiously, Rifkah asked, 'Vot is vinky?'

'Vinky-vim . . . a swim. Nice spot for it, too . . . although they say it's haunted, eh?'

Clancy, dismounting, said stiffly, 'It's a very dangerous place.'

'Not so dangerous now, but,' said Fergus, and winked at Rifkah, who flushed. He added: 'I'm going to have a dip myself. Feel like coming in again, beautiful?' When she didn't answer, he looked at Prindy. 'How 'bout you, young feller?' Prindy nodded. Fergus looked over the golden nakedness: 'It's a free country . . . but I don't suppose I can go in like you.' He went off towards the scrub where Rifkah had donned her clothes.

Clancy said gravely to Rifkah, 'You shouldn't swim here, you know. Quite a lot of people've been drowned here.'

She ignored the remark, asking, 'Did you come in aeroplane?'

Rather too hastily and wordily, Clancy told her: no, he had been riding up the river looking for stock, heard the mob up there at the fish-hole, gone to investigate and learnt that she'd come down this way for a ride, and had thought to pay his respects: 'I got your regards from Lieutenant Dickey Tuesday evening. Thank you. I thought you'd be in to meet the train yesterday. Looked for you.' When she glanced towards where Fergus had vanished, he added: 'I don't know what he's doing here. Only met him on the track.' He scowled as he said it. The scowl deepened as Fergus appeared, clad only in cotton briefs, looking very hairy and athletic, if somewhat undersized. Finding all eyes on him, Fergus assumed the strut of a parading life-saver.

As Fergus came up, Rifkah asked him, 'Vy you come back so soon?'

'On account of you, sweetheart . . . just can't keep away.'

'Tell me properly. Is ze General come?'

'Ze General he is come.'

'Vy?'

'Tell you later. Private matter. Here goes!' He dashed into the pool, dived, vanished for seconds, came up in the emerald, laughing, dashing water from his handsome face. Prindy was there already. Fergus set after him. Prindy took him into the danger zone.

'Lunatic'll drown himself out there,' muttered Clancy.

But Fergus was a strong swimmer. He made the circuit easily, and made it again, even diving a bit with Prindy.

Rifkah asked Clancy, 'Don't you svim, Mr Clancy?'

'Drop the Mister, please. Oh, yes, I swim. Out at Catfish we've got the best swimming hole in the country . . . springboard, slippery dip and all. You must come out sometime.'

'You have svim in here?'

'No fear . . . that's strictly for lunatics . . . I'm sorry, I mean . . . of course you didn't know about it.'

'Oh, yes, I do know.'

He stared at her. She smiled and said, 'I vont to stop zis country alvays.'

'Oh, that,' he said, and shrugged.

'Don't you believe?'

'No. Blackfeller superstition.' Then with a rush he asked, 'Are you engaged to that pilot chap?'

'Engage?'

'Are you going to marry him?'

Rifkah stared for a moment, then laughed her lovely merry laugh. 'Vere you get zat?'

'He told me. He told me you're his girl.'

Another peal of laughter. He sighed in evident relief. 'I reckoned he was lying.'

The laughter brought Fergus out of the water, looking rather lewd with what the clinging cotton did to his hairy genitals. 'What's the big joke?'

Clancy sniggered, 'You, mate.'

Fergus flushed, but gave the split grin, saying, 'Yeah? Well just to make it funnier, what about swimmin' me round the pool three times for a tenner?'

'I'm not a lunatic,' snapped Clancy.

Fergus looked him over boldly. 'Hmm . . . I can see that. It's the other ticks you're interested in, ain't it. What would you be . . . Tick-dipper in Chief round here?' With a leer he marched off back to the bushes.

Ignoring it, except for getting very red in the face and somewhat breathless, Clancy proceeded to give Rifkah an account of the drownings that had occurred here. She appeared to be having a struggle to suppress an urge to giggle.

Soon Fergus was dressed and back. They went to their horses. As they mounted he said to Clancy, 'Well, so long, cowboy . . . be seein' you, I suppose.'

Ignoring him, Clancy said to Rifkah, 'I'll ride along with you if you don't mind.'

'Zat vill be nice.'

Fergus said, 'Thought you were looking for stock. None up this way, man.'

Still pointedly addressing Rifkah only, Clancy said, 'I want to have a look round the limestone and the billabongs. Besides, I want to have a word with my father about a sick horse. Thought I'd see him yesterday, too.'

'Didn't think you got along with your old man,' remarked Fergus.

Clancy blazed at him. 'How about minding your own business?'

Rifkah cut in hastily: 'Come, ve go home ... nice and quietly.' She broke the silence that followed by asking Fergus why he and the General had come back.

He answered, 'Tell you tonight while we're out on our walk, honey.'

'Zere is no trouble?'

'What trouble would there be between us?' His smirk evidently assured her that the matter was of small moment, the way she smiled again, the way she soon became her gay self. She rode between the two men, giving each her attention in turn. Prindy rode behind.

Thus they went, at an easy pace, trotting, cantering, walking, for the best part of the distance. Then suddenly bored Prindy kicked Sugarbag into a gallop, and passing the others, yelled, 'Race!' Rifkah put her mount straight into it. The others, after casting a dirty look across the suddenly vacated place, followed. It was no sort of race really, with Prindy holding in Sugarbag to let old Snowball keep up, and the others determined to keep close to the old fellow's lovely rider. However, it was enough to put the guardians of the homestead into a flap and bring out most of those they guarded. Anyway, it was a sight for knowing eyes to see Mister Clancy come galloping through the gateway. Eyes fairly popped.

Jeremy and General Esk were standing outside the annexe. The race ended before them in a scatter of gravel and drift of dust. Old Snowball, almost black with sweat, stood spread-legged, heaving for breath, gulping for it, head hanging and lolling about. Jeremy came striding up, ignoring Rifkah's smile, saying shortly, 'Get off. This horse's badly distressed.' He slipped the bit, and as she alighted, slipped off the reeking saddle.

'Vot is matter?'

'You've all but killed him. His racing days are long past.' Jeremy looked at the other riders, his face grim. 'You two ought've known better than to let her push an old horse like that.' To Prindy, he said, 'Come and give me a hand bed him down.' With that he turned away, leading the horse towards the annexe, the old horse now shivering, staggering, yawning for air. When Rifkah ran to accompany him, he said, 'Stay with them. Smoke-o's been rung.'

Rifkah looked as if about to cry. The General came up to her, took her arm, spoke to her soothingly, telling her she was not to know: 'A horse is a remarkable animal, don't y'know. You can be too considerate with him and be made to look a bally fool by him, or too demanding and kill him in his willingness to serve you. We'll go to tea, eh what?'

Nan was in the lounge to greet the party, nodding and smiling at Clancy as if his appearance there were every-day. Clancy on the other hand, looked very awkward, seizing on his formal meeting with Kurt as relief, babbling to him about the refugee settlement, declaring himself most interested. Esk kept possession of Rifkah, and over tea told her why he was there. At the Catholic Mission in the Leopold Islands Group, they had an influenza epidemic on their hands and very inadequate staff to deal with it. He himself had thought she might like to lend them a hand, while at the same time getting to know something of real bush natives: 'The mission there's quite newly established, set up as a civilizing influence on tribes as yet pretty well untouched by civilization. The natives drift in and out of the place as they wish. Very primitive. You need to know what you're up against in this new dedication of yours. Thought it'd be a unique opportunity, don't y'know.'

'But a Christian Mission . . . and I am Jew!'

'Matter of fact, m'dear, they're even very interested in you as Jewish . . . isn't that so, Fergus? Fact, they're awfully interested in the whole Jewish Refugee project . . . .'

Fergus cut in: 'They've laid in a stock of Holy Water for wholesale . . . .' But he stopped and grinned when Esk shot him a warning glance.

Rifkah didn't seem to notice the interruption, evidently deeply preoccupied with the General's proposal. He tried pressing her for an answer, but without success. She said she must think about it. He chuckled. 'Jewish caution.'

When the opportunity presented itself, with tea over and the men occupied with Kurt's maps, Rifkah slipped out with Nan to the kitchen, then across to the annexe. Old Snowball was in one of the animal hospital stalls, folded up in the way of his kind, asleep on a bed of straw. He was doped, Jeremy explained, to bring down his blood-pressure, which had been dangerously high.

Rifkah and Jeremy went to the den together, while Prindy went over to the house to eat. With her sitting on the arm of his easy chair, Jeremy asked about Clancy, evidently already appraised somewhat by Prindy. He pooh-poohed the idea that Clancy had come looking for cattle or to talk about a horse: 'See a man about a dog!' he grunted, then had to explain to her that the expression implied a false excuse for doing something. He added: 'Took him eighteen years to think that one up.'

'I help him to come by saying it vood be nice.'

'Why?'

'Is it not better you are friend . . . fader and son?'

He dismissed the subject with an impatient sigh, then asked, 'Did the General tell you why he's here?'

'Yes.'

'Will you go?'

'No.'

'Why not? Might be good experience, as he says.'

'First, I zink he only vont to get me avay from you.'

'Yes . . . I thought of that, too. He was a bit too eager about your getting to know about the blacks . . . after what he said before about not seeing you as a Daisy Bates.'

'Zen I don't vont to be mix up wit' Jesus Business. Blacks vill zink I am missionary, too.'

'Yes . . . that could spoil everything. They're spoiling everything as it is with that bloody mission. They'd've brought even the 'flu there . . . the gift of civilization, of Christ the Saviour. What'd you say?'

'Moost I zink about it. I am still zinking about it tomorrow, ven he go avay again. I vill tell him moost I be here ven Settlement pipple come.'

'Good idea. Now, about this bugger Clancy. He's evidently in no hurry to get on his way . . . which means he'll want to stay the night.'

'Vy not . . . it is custom of ze country, yes?'

'With strangers. He happens to be my son, turned up after shunning the place for eighteen years . . . and only because there happens to be a pretty girl here now.' Jeremy finished flushed and breathless.

She bent and put her own cool cheek to his hot one, murmuring, 'You are not jealous?'

'No . . . affronted!'

'You mean he cannot stay ze night?'

'No . . . we can't refuse him . . . but he'll get no invitation from me to stay. Nan can do it. Tell her, will you? Tell her to treat him just like a stranger . . . to ask him just before dinner is he going on, and offer him a bed if he likes.'

'But you vill not treat him like stranger . . . please!'

He met her pleading eyes. 'What's this? I thought you didn't like him.'

'Not ze vay he treat Prindy. Now moost he treat Prindy as his nephew.'

'Did you bring him here only for that?'

'No. He is your son. Ven I see him and hear him, I zink of you . . . '

'Sounds like you do like him . . . but it isn't much of a compliment to me . . . to have that supercilious, conventional, priggish . . . . '

'Now, please . . . you vill be kind to him . . . for me, Jeremy?'

He reassured her with a nod and a sigh of resignation.

When he came over before dinner to join the group in the lounge, Jeremy was hardly kind in his dealings with Clancy to begin with, dismissing his son's leaping at him to babble his reasons for being there with a short: 'I've already been informed,' and leaving him standing while he went to get himself a drink. Clancy was obviously embarrassed. Later, however, Jeremy made things easier by deliberately including the young man in his conversation occasionally and pouring him a drink or two. Clancy's gratitude for the gesture was as evident as his embarrassment had been. Thus it went throughout the drinking session, dinner, and the rest of the evening the company spent together in the lounge. Tonight no ritual walk, probably on account of Clancy.

As they were breaking up, somewhat early, in response to Jeremy's perhaps, pointed remark that they would *all* want to be getting away early tomorrow. Rifkah, getting Jeremy aside, told him she would like to have a walk round the garden with Clancy. It made him blink. Still, he nodded, and gave his cheek to be kissed when she reached for it.

Out in the moonlight, Rifkah took Clancy's arm, tucked up close to him, fell into that stride of hers which made men's walking with her so easy, and promptly asked him how he liked coming back to his old home. Taken by surprise, Clancy answered vaguely, dishonestly, that was certain, the way he worked up finally to saying that it was wonderful really.

She said bluntly, 'I zink you feel joost like stranger here.'

He answered hesitantly, 'Well . . . my father didn't exactly make me feel at home.'

'Vot do you expect . . . ven you tek eighteen year to come visit your fader?'

Still hesitant, he came to telling her that in fact he had often wanted to come, but had been afraid of all that would be involved. Although he very much admired and respected his father, there always was that uncompromising attitude of his. Every contact with him amounted to a challenge. He said miserably, 'I don't think he ever wanted to have anything to do with me, really . . . and I've had to think of my mother.'

'You moost zink of yourself. Vomen are very possessive, always. Your mozzer is ver' proud voman. Her pride is hurt from losing your fader. She moost keep you from him to get even.'

Somewhat bitterly be talked of his father's rejection of his family, over something that really didn't matter, as he saw it, at any rate not compared with keeping a family together: 'He'd come home from the war. He was a hero to me. I wanted him to tell me about the war. But he only hated the thought of it.'

'Vos zat so wrong?'

'War's a bad thing, I know. But he was my father, a returned soldier, someone to be proud of.'

'It is you, I zink, who von't compromise. You vont him to be *your* kind of fader . . . . like your mozzer vont him to be *her* kind of husband.'

'And what about him? He'd want me to see everything the way he does.'

'I do not zink he vood, but only zat you be honest vit' him.'

'How've I been dishonest? Just by sticking with my mother?' When she didn't answer, he sighed heavily. 'I wouldn't stick with her if I had a proper life of my own to live . . . if I . . . if I had someone . . . someone . . . like . . . . '

She swung him round suddenly. 'I zink ve go in now. Ve haf plenty of time to talk more anozzer time, yes?' He muttered affirmation, allowing himself to be led back to the house.

Under the leafy trellis before the front door she halted, released his arm, then suddenly kissed his cheek, whispered, 'Goodnight dear Clancy,' then was gone.

He hung there staring into the dim-lit and apparently deserted lounge for a while, then, sighing, turned about, headed back into the moonlight. As he emerged from the trellis a figure stepped up to him from beside it. It was Fergus, a different man from the usual comic, now spluttering with suppressed feeling, 'Didn't I tell you she's my girl?'

Taken aback, Clancy gasped, 'What . . . what you doing snooping around?'

'I'm keeping my eye on my property . . . and just you lay off it, boy!'

'Who says it's your property?'

'I do. D'you want me to call her down and prove it?'

Clancy hesitated, swallowed, muttered, 'No.'

'Right, then . . . pull your head in!'

'That doesn't mean I believe you own her . . . Only that I don't want to embarrass a lady . . . .'

'Aw, for christ sake . . . you've got the mind of a schoolboy! Well, just keep out of grown-up people's way, will you . . .'

'No I won't!' Clancy made a grab at Fergus, who by some sleight of hand flung him off, sent him staggering, to fall on his behind.

Fergus snarled, 'Want to make something of it?'

Clancy got up, panting, brushing himself: 'I'm not a common brawler. I know how to behave myself in someone else's house. But any other time, yes!'

'Right!' snapped Fergus. 'Till that other time, then . . . but in the meantime lay off!' He wheeled and went into the house.

There was a flicker of movement by a screen. Fergus went to it. It was the General, smiling. Fergus grunted at him, turned away. Esk followed him. 'How about a last drink, dear boy?' Fergus went with him to the sideboard, accepted the whisky and soda poured him. 'Cheers!' said Esk, and having swigged, added: 'I didn't realize you felt about the girl like that. Thought it was just fun and games.'

But Fergus wasn't talking. Finishing the glass, he headed for the stairs. Esk finished his, and murmuring to himself, 'Very interestin', very interestin' indeed, by jove!' followed.

There was no indication of anything untoward next morning. Fergus and Clancy went largely unnoticed, since that had been much how it had been all along. So early breakfast was got through. The trip to the race track and the aeroplane was saved from the likelihood of unpleasantness by Clancy's riding his bay behind the utility, on his way off like the rest of the guests. He came right to the aircraft to take leave of the General. Then he had to go, because his horse would surely be frightened by the starting of the motors. He shook hands with his father as well as Esk, and would have shaken hands with Rifkah, too, only she caught him by the shoulders and kissed him on the lips, to the interest of everybody, even the horse. Then he mounted with a flourish, set spurs, was off at a gallop, stopping just once to turn and take off his hat and wave it.

Fergus and the General got their kisses, too, fairly on the lips and in such a style as to cause both of them to flush deeply and look rather at a loss as they climbed aboard the Junkers and disappeared. Fergus did some more kissing by remote control out of the cockpit, and again, as airborne, he came hurtling back for a last one.

Then it was Jeremy and Prindy she kissed. That was the end of it. Briskly she said, 'Now, I moost get ready for fish-fry.'

CHAPTER SIXTEEN

THERE WAS NO WANING of the interest of the people of Beatrice River (and hence of all those in contact with them) in that very interesting business going on out at Lily Lagoons, generally suggested to be a virtual take-over of the place by Jews. Nor was there likely to be any waning while the chief topic of world gossip was what was being called the Jewish Problem, caused by the inexorable hostility to the race by the ever-rising colossus, Hitler, and reaching proportions of global hysteria. For local consumption there was Jeremy Delacy's contribution to the hysterics in the form of his article published in the November Issue of *Australia Free*, now in wide circulation throughout the land, in which he likened Anti-Semitism to the century-and-a-half of relentless persecution of the Australian Aborigines simply because they wouldn't accept the whiteman's gods.

As Fergus Ferris had predicted, this piece had been published in entirety, even with a eulogy on the author as a great Australian and champion of the Aboriginal cause. But what Fergus hadn't foreseen, as maybe he should have when he knew the owner of the paper to be drolly perverse enough to publish it, was the manner in which it was countered. Included with it was printed a copy of the so-called *Protocols of the Elders of Zion*, as if the thing were gospel instead of the fraud it had been completely exposed as years before. By means of these Protocols, the leaders of International Jewry were alleged to have worked out, sometime in the middle of the Nineteenth Century, a scheme for Jewish domination of the world. The document was first published by the Czarist Government of Russia towards the end of the Century, apparently as an excuse for savage pogroms against Jews at that time. The matter was specially investigated by *The Times*, of London, which proved beyond doubt that the thing was a fake, that in fact the material for the Czarist publication was culled from a satirical pamphlet circulating in France in the Eighteen Sixties, which was actually an attack on the re-established Bonaparte Regime and had as its theme a fanciful conference between Napoleon the First and his descendants and friends in Hades.

Thus Jeremy, as that other wise fellow, Kurt, predicted, had only made matters worse for Jews by mentioning them, slight as the mention deliberately was; for whereas *The Protocols of the Elders of Zion* remained a favourite weapon of confirmed Anti-Judaists everywhere, most people wouldn't have heard of it till now, and certainly few if any in these parts, including Jeremy himself who had to be put right in the matter by Kurt. Then it was Jeremy's job to put it right elsewhere, which done with his usual reckless forthrightness, probably made matters worse still, so that even Tom Toohey took to shaking his bald head over it and remarking to his wife, Nolly, 'They certainly got old Jerry by the balls, them Jews.'

Jeremy wasn't the only one they were talking about like that. Clancy Delacy was also showing himself as something of a Proselyte of the Gate, at first in speaking out in support of his father in the matter of the Protocols, then in his eager association with Kurt and Rifkah whenever thay came to the siding over the weeks, and the very true anger he showed over the news of the terrible pogrom that took place in Germany late that November in retaliation for the assassination of a German Official by a Jew. The assassination didn't occur in Germany or at the hand of a German Jew. A crazy Polish Jewish youth had shot an embassy official in Paris as a protest to the world against the persecution of Jews now taking place throughout all the countries now under the Hitlerian heel. As reprisal, ostensibly, *Der Führer* ordered the complete anathematization of all things Jewish within his realm, a task that his *Herrenvolk* fell to with such zeal that within a few days nothing remained to remind the New German Nation of the Shame its leader claimed had plagued it for half a millenium. No Jewish institution of any kind was left standing. Every book, picture, piece of sculpture or sheet of music or anything else that was the work of a Jew's hands or mind, no matter whether considered a masterpiece by the world at large even over centuries, was destroyed. Even the simple gravestones of the poorest Jews were reduced to shards. Nothing remained except that which was hardest to dispose of, for all the Hunnish efficiency in trying, namely, the unhappy perpetrators of the Shame itself, now being herded, branded, shipped as animals by special stock-trains – where?

News of the pogrom broke over the radio the night before train-day; so that Jeremy came in to the township fairly raving, that is according to those who watched his conduct and commented on it. 'For godsake, what a world!' he cried. 'The Spanish Inquisition, the Slave Trade, Van Diemen's Land . . . they're horrors of human cruelty you can forgive somewhat, because of the times, the general ignorance. But this . . . this frightfulness, in the Age of Reason, as it's called, as a legal enactment endorsed by the leader of what's supposed to be one of the most advanced communities of mankind, and a man being looked on by most of the rest of the civilized world as a genius in social leadership . . . For godsake, what a world!'

Tom Toohey, sounding a bit fed up with it at last, commented, 'This Jew business's really got you in, Jerry . . . no doubt about it.'

Jeremy blazed at him: 'Christ . . . how can anyone with common feelings of humanity ignore it?'

'I've heard you say same thing about the treatment of the blacks.'

'What the bloody hell's that got to do with it?'

'Well . . . remember when they started settlin' them White Russians, you said: "Why'n't they do sumpin for the blacks instead?"'

'Don't tell me you've joined the mob who're up against the Jewish Settlement?'

Toohey flushed. 'You know I'm always for the poor bastard's bein' trod on. I'm only surprised see how you've changed lately.'

'How've I changed?'

'Well . . . you've always preached charity begins at home, reckoned our first responsibility's to the Aboriginal race we robbed, said keep the land from bein' spoilt by settlin' people in it who don't give a damn for it, except to exploit it for cash.'

'You'll never hear me say anything different.'

'Then what about this Jew settlement you're makin' out the Lagoons?'

'Eh? Who says I'm making a Jewish settlement out there?'

'Well . . . you got them Jews there for months . . . you're expectin' more. People naturally wonder. Jews're smart people, what I been readin' about 'em lately. The general idea is they'll pick the eyes out of the land, and that you're helpin' 'em . . . Now, don't get off your 'orse, man . . . I'm only just sayin' what people're sayin . . . as yo' mate.'

Jeremy panted, 'What if the Jews do pick the best of the land? Why should it go to Vaisey's and the like, who don't even live here, and treat the native born for what they bloody well are . . . semislaves?'

Tom let it go at that, except to make that remark privily to his wife.

There was no doubt about a general sympathy for Jews suffering under Hitler. That was shown readily enough to Kurt and Rifkah, when at the siding people off the train they didn't even know nodded in a way to indicate their feelings, and some went so far as to address them: 'Things gettin' pretty crook for your mob over the other side. Sumpin ought to be done to stop them square-'ead bastards.'

Yes, there was sympathy aplenty. Elsewhere it was so vocal that the wide world rang with it. Sympathy and protest. But what more? Even the effectiveness of the protesting was soon being undone by making debate of it. For example, the BBC arranged a special broadcast in which a Mr Barney Sugarman, Member of the House of Commons, told of what he had seen of the condition of Jews in Germany during a tour of investigation from which he had just returned; while a Herr Sigismund Keitelling, an official of the German Embassy at London, was given the opportunity to counter with what he called the Facts.

Young Clancy heard this broadcast while at home in the bosom of his family. Already he had caused eyebrows to be raised here through his excessive concern for the reported plight of Jews. The session began with a statement by the compere that the BBC's sponsoring it in no way committed it or the British Government to an official stand in the matter.

Mr Barney Sugarman, MP, told of how, being refused entry into Germany under his true identity, had got in with a false one, ostensibly as a sailor ashore from a British ship. However, he had taken precaution to have his true identity tattooed on his person and make arrangements with British consular officials to check on his movements should he not report back within a certain time. He stated frankly that he had got round many obstacles with heavy bribery. He had a list of Jews to search for in several cities and towns. He found none of them, scarcely even a trace of any but a few. Jewish districts were to all intents and purposes completely depopulated, their former residents now herded into compounds in railways yards, to live like animals while awaiting shipment as the same to unknown destinations. He had got amongst them and talked. Some believed they were going to forced labour camps, others that it was to alpine border regions where they would be kicked out into someone else's country, a few that it was to their deaths, this last a logical enough conclusion, since *Der Führer* had declared it his intention to rid the earth of the like of them in that book of his, *Mein Kampf*, written back in 1925.

These people were all branded with numbers and many with the Shield of David, the latter as a mark of shame to those who put it there, but of great pride to the wearers: the *Magen David*, the Shield of David, the Star of Hope. They were permitted to travel in nothing but old clothes and with absolutely no possessions, these having all been stripped from them, often with torture for their disclosure. Every Jewish home and business in the land had been ransacked, not only by the Gestapo and other official thugs, but by many of the civil population, who according to the news, when questioned by foreigners, swore they didn't know that was going on under their noses. 'Wonderful people these Germans,' said Barney Sugarman, speaking with a Cockney-Jewish lisp. 'So innocent of guilty business when you charge 'em with it . . . but so happy to hold up hands dripping with blood when they can get away with it. You going to be taken in by the Germans again? I don't like Winston Churchill; and he doesn't like me; but he does say some smart things at times, and one of the smartest things was what he said of the Germans as a nation: "They are either at your throat or at your feet." Don't forget they are the people who invented those two very important words in war . . . *Strafe*, which means to destroy, annihilate, like the Wrath of God . . . and *Kamerad*, which is the cry for quarter, for mercy, the first to be shouted while they're at your throat, the second to be whimpered when they're licking your boots . . . The Boche, the Hun, *Ach*! Anything good he has ever done, the Jews have shown him how to do. Germany wasn't properly civilized when the Jews came into it. That's why they hate 'em. They hate 'em too much. Who thought of Einstein as a Jew first, till now? Of Ehrlich, Hertz, Wasserman, Mendelssohn, and all the rest of the geniuses who've made German science and art the best in the world? You know where Einstein is now? That wonderful man had to fly for his life to America. You know where the books and music of those other wonderful men are now? Torn to pieces, burnt in the streets. *Judenhassen* they call it . . . Jew-hate . . . and they are proud of it! Do you know that before this bloody business began, it was estimated that in three generations at most there would not be a practising Jew in Germany, so few were they in number, and so easily assimilated into the Fatherland? So much have the Jews loved the Fatherland that they adopted the old Gothic German language and adapted it to Hebrew script and usage to make the language called Yiddish, in which there is a great and beautiful literature. You know how many Jews were in Germany before this business start? I will tell you . . . three hundred thousand. How many Germans? Seventy-two million. If you're good at your arithmetic you'll see that makes less than one-half per cent of the total population. So if the Jews have been making all that trouble for the Germans that Hitler says, then that is one half a Jew making trouble for one hundred German Superman, and those Supermen must be all meat and no brains, don't you reckon? Maybe that's why Hitler declared anybody a Jew under the Nuremberg Laws who had any Jewish ancestry as far back as the year 1800, the best part of one hundred and fifty years, or five generations – so his New Germany won't look silly, eh?

Makes you want to laugh, doesn't it? That was one of the troubles with the Jews there . . . they did laugh too much at first. But, my friends, it isn't a laughing matter, as I shall tell you from what I saw with my own eyes. Now . . . .'

Sugarman went on to tell how every synagogue, school, orphanage, aged people's home, hospital, even cemetery, that had been Jewish had been reduced to ashes or rubble. Anyone who resisted the rapine or even protested was shot or clubbed to death, grannies, babies, whole families before each other's eyes, most aged and infantile, because they'd been systematically dragging away the younger folk for years. He had gone into quarters where a few desperate souls were still trying to fight it out, had heard the shots, the shouts, the screams, had seen bloodied victims hurled into the streets from upper stories, to have the life kicked out of them, if any remained, by proud-looking young men in smart uniforms, who shouted *Heil Hitler* and flung up their arms, as if invoking a god's approval of their carnage.

No one was immune; unless having enough gold or jewels on his person and the luck to strike someone worn out with slaughter, to buy respite, and maybe even a chance to get out. He had gone to a couple of border points where the lucky ones were getting away from it. It needed an awfully high price, because business was too brisk for those raking in the riches to be bothered with trifles. A handsome woman often had to pay with her body as well as with her jewels. *Both* sides of the frontiers were benefiting. Yet it was the Jew who had the reputation for demanding the Pound of Flesh!

Thus for several days of intense investigation; until Sugarman himself fell foul of the Gestapo and was taken to some chamber of horrors where, to the accompaniment of the shrieks and howls of others he couldn't see, he was beaten black and blue, in an attempt to make him confess that he was what the bullies believed he was, an agent from Britain there to gather hidden Jewish wealth and smuggle it out of the country. No matter his proof of British citizenship. As far as they were concerned he had no citizenship of any sort. He was a Jew. At what looked like the last moment, his arrangements with the British officials saved him. He was put aboard a special aircraft and whisked home.

But what did he strike at home? His parliamentary colleagues for the most part listened to him eagerly enough when he reported the horrors, but for the most part fled from him when he asked them what they were going to do about it. There were even some Jews who did the same. 'And what are *you* going to do about it?' he demanded of his worldwide audience now. 'You are mostly kindly people. You believe that charity is the first virtue. You believe what St Paul said: "And though I speak with the tongue of angels and have not charity I am as a sounding brass or a tinkling cymbal." Then what are you going to do about this extermination of a breed of your fellows whose only offence against the world is to stick to a way of life that they have followed with satisfaction for five thousand years and more and that has never done any harm to anybody – whose only crime is that they are Jews? If you can't think of what to do I will tell you. Start by demanding from your governments that they make official protests to this nation of bullies, and if nothing is done, for them to confer in the matter and take action even to the point of forceful entry into this den of inhuman monsters and the rescue of their victims. Will you do this . . . in the name of humanity? Or have you no more humanity than those German civilians who cannot see what is happening under their nose because it is happening to a Jew? Oh . . . . ' His voice broke in a sob, to be heard again in a hoarse cry, '*Shemah Israel*!'

Clancy, flushed and breathing hard, demanded of the company, 'Yes . . . what are we going to do about it?'

The faces of the others first looked surprised, then furtive. His brother Martin cleared his throat: 'There's the League of Nations, isn't there . . . sanctions and all that?'

Clancy snapped, 'What's it ever done, the League of Nations? Besides, Germany doesn't recognize it. It's like he said. Everybody must protest to their government. And if that doesn't work, an international brigade of some sort . . . . '

His mother cut in: 'The International Brigade was Communist.' Then, as the compere began to announce Herr Keitelling, she held up her finger for silence.

Herr Keitelling spoke smoothly, suavely, in excellent English, with more Oxford accent in it than German. He began by denouncing Mr Sugarman as a Left Wing Socialist, which was to say an unconfessed Communist; and as everybody knew, Communism was the first enemy of the Third Reich, and basically, as the *Führer* had proved, a Jewish plot to enslave the world. Actually the recent actions taken against the Jews in Germany had been precipitated by the Jews themselves. Previously, their dispossession and deportation, in accordance with the Nuremberg Laws of Shame of 1936, had proceeded smoothly. But the Jews were vengeful vicious people. They wanted violence, wanted to stir the world to war on their account. Hence the assassination of Herr von Rath of the Paris Embassy, revealed as the beginnings of a Jewish plot to stop legal proceedings against Jews in Germany through intimidation of German officials abroad, then within it, while crying of persecution to the world. The Jews had had plenty of time to remove themselves from the Fatherland, it being ten years and more since *Der Führer* had published to the world his manifesto that these mongrel people could be no part of the Reich that was to Stand for a Thousand Years – *Heil Hitler*! But they had hung on, still living like the parasites they were by ineradicable nature on what they had sucked from broken defeated Germany during the post-war years. Certainly Jews were being deprived of their property; and why not, when they had come by it through cheating decent Germans? But as to these tales of wholesale terror, the very fact that they were reported from regions where criminal elements congregated showed them for what they were: punitive actions by police against criminals, not necessarily Jews, but degenerate Germans who co-operated with them, and Communists. Not only had these criminals resisted lawful removal, but had fought amongst themselves for hidden spoil. Anyway, the world had only the word of dispossessed Jews for this terror. Had Einstein, Freud, Bruno Walter, complained of being beaten and robbed? They had not. Certainly they had been driven from Germany, because *Der Führer* showed neither fear nor favour in his determination to rid the nation of the insidious influence of their kind. After all, was not the British Union, led by the Baronet, Sir Oswald Mosely and supported by so many of the British aristocracy and upper classes, in complete agreement with German Nationalist Socialist Party policy in the matter of dealing with Jews? The manifesto of the British Union declared that when it came to power all Jews in Britain and the British Empire would be declared aliens, and those who were known to have put the interests of Jewry before those of the King and Empire, would be instantly expelled.

It showed, said Herr Keitelling, what sort of person this Jew Sugarman was when he freely admitted having entered Germany on false papers, procurable only through criminal channels, and had made his way by bribing criminals, until lawfully brought to book. Much of what he had stated in his broadcast was lies to be expected of a Jew. New Germany had nothing to be ashamed of in her treatment of these people. Let no one think that. What she was doing was actually purging herself of shame she had suffered ever since foolishly, out of misplaced kindness, committing herself to the cancerous evil of Judaism by admitting Jews in their flight into Europe during the Crusades. 'No . . . Germany is not ashamed. On the contrary, we have never felt so proud as we do today . . . *Heil Hitler*!'

That furtive look in the eyes of the rest of the Beatrice Big House company had disappeared as Herr Keitelling delivered himself, to become at last an answering challenge to Clancy's continued glowering. His mother put the challenge into words as the delivery ended: 'Well, there . . . you see!'

'See what?' growled Clancy.

'That these Jews have brought it all on themselves.'

Clancy sneered, 'What . . . by being Jews?'

Lady Rhoda replied stiffly, 'I'm afraid, my son, you've been seeing too much of those Jews who're trying to wish themselves onto us, too.'

Clancy flamed: 'If you saw more of the unfortunate people, and heard what they've been through, and came to understand their natural intelligence and kindliness, you wouldn't be taken in by the lies of murderous Huns!'

'Are you sure you haven't been taken in yourself . . . by a pretty face?'

Crimson now, Clancy leapt up and left the drawing room. Embarrassment was spared the others by the radio, from which lively music burst forth: *Orpheus in the Underworld*, surely a subtle British refutation of impartiality in the matter just dealt with, since the anathematization of all things Jewish by Hitler had declared the gay music of Offenbach the most morally insidious of it.

Next day Clancy was busy from dawn with the trucking of breeding bulls up country aboard the continuing train, and did not see his mother till she sent for him to join her at morning tea. Evidently she wanted to make amends for the contretemps of last evening. However, he remained sulky till she asked, 'Did your Jewish friends go back to Lily Lagoons or are they still around?' When he looked at her sharply, she added: 'I'd like to express my sympathy for what's happening to their people. Would you like to ask them for lunch?'

Clancy beamed. 'Thanks, Mater . . . that'd be nice. But they went straight back yesterday. What about next train-day? By the way . . . could you let me have some empty pickle-bottles . . . .'

His mother murmured. 'Pickle-bottles . . . whatever for?'

He flushed. 'Any sort of jar. I want 'em for Miss Rifkah. She's bottling mangoes . . . jam, chutney. She's mad on that sort of thing. All Jewish women are mad on cooking, I understand.'

'Reahlly!' murmured Her Ladyship. Then she added: 'See them in the kitchen and the store. There ought to be plenty.'

'Thanks a lot, Mater.' He kissed her cheek as he rose. As he went, Lady Rhoda exchanged a glance with Vivienne, Martin's wife.

That night over dinner, Clancy asked his mother, 'How about having Miss Rifkah up to Town for Christmas?'

Lady Rhoda blinked on it for a moment. 'We've got quite a lot of people this year . . . General Esk and his aides, ...'

'We always have a mob, and fit 'em in, either in the Town house or the beach house. She hasn't even been to Town yet.'

'I'll bear it in mind, dear. How did you get on about pickle-bottles?'

'They've been giving them to Ali Barbar. I got a few, but there're a lot of 'em out at Catfish, I remember. I'll get them, and run 'em across to the Lagoons tomorrow.'

'Tomorrow? Aren't you in a hurry?'

'Well . . . the mangoes are on, and the flying foxes at 'em . . . and you need fruit just ripening and unbruised for preserving, don't you?'

Her Ladyship shook her head. 'I wouldn't know, dear boy.'

II

Around about midday Friday, the watchers at Lily Lagoons had the unusual undertaking to investigate and report intrusion from northward, and not by air, as had become common lately. A minute or two of fluttering and scurrying, of listening to a waxing drone discernible at length as that of a motor, and of sharp-eyed peering; then once again the cry went up: Mitcher Clancy!

One judges one's welcome at a bush homestead by the number of people standing out at least to stare at one upon arrival. To find no one is surely portentious, although not necessarily a hint to get to hell out of it; for people who live in comparative isolation often have to go through a process of adjustment to the breaking of it, and even while quietly cursing an intruder to begin with, for the most part eventually come out smiling genuinely. Bush etiquette demands that, in the event of apparent unwelcome, one simply stands off at a little distance and waits. To shout, or toot your horn, is something only a Townie would do. Any noise you make, you make well back, to give warning of your approach.

Clancy did all the right things. He pulled up in the space between Big House and annexe, or rather on the edge of it, leaned on the steering wheel, glancing from one place to the other, as if indifferently, to show that he accepted privy scrutiny in the proper manner. However, as the seconds ticking from the expensive watch on one of the wheel-draping wrists grew into a minute or more, his glance sharpened, and in its flitting to and fro, came frequently to include the watch. Coming up a minute and a half. Now he was sitting stiffly, hands gripping the wheel. He moved impatiently in his seat. But whether he was about to stand on his dignity and depart, or to get out and humbly beg acceptance, was given no chance of proving; for just then the screen of the back door of the kitchen opened, and there appeared a female figure in a moment revealed in the blaze of the sunlight as Rifkah. At the flash of copper his face lit. He jerked open the door and leapt out, to go loping to meet her, babbling about his alleged reason for coming. She received him smiling. No doubt about his infatuation. He almost dropped one of the boxes of jars as he bumbled into the kitchen with it, he who normally would have left carrying anything to such as the black girls who came to do it. Jeremy and Prindy were watching from the laboratory over in the annexe, both stony-faced.

It was something like half an hour later that Clancy turned up at the annexe, to pay his respects, as he said. Jeremy received him coolly. Prindy, at work on an electrical gadget, appeared not to notice him. Clancy said that he had been kindly asked by the ladies to have lunch. Jeremy nodded shortly, saying that he wouldn't be lunching himself, since it wasn't his habit. He added to Prindy: 'Take your uncle over, will you sonny?' There was significant stress on the title, but without apparent effect on Clancy, who would be getting used to it through talking to Rifkah, no doubt.

Prindy said, 'I don't want lunch. Too busy.'

There was a moment's silence, broken by Jeremy, observing quietly, 'Nevertheless, take him over, eh?'

Grey eyes met grey eyes. Prindy nodded. Clancy, in obvious relief, smiled at Prindy, and went to see and ask what he was doing. Prindy, putting tools away, answered shortly, 'For fly'n' fox.' When Clancy pressed for details, Prindy threw a bored look at his grandfather.

Jeremy said, 'He's making a gadget to keep flying foxes away from the mangoes . . . rather hopefully. But explain it, sonny.'

Another quick exchange of glances. Prindy obeyed, speaking in the correct and stilted style he assumed at times. The device was an induction coil for producing high voltage to run through wires strung about the mango grove. The idea was based on the flying fox's weakness for taking a spell from eternal flying or jostling with his quarrelsome kind for precarious perches in trees, by grabbing anything that gave an easy grip and a clear view; hence the way the species fell victim to electrocution by the score every night on the power lines up in Town. 'This won't kill him,' said Prindy, 'Only give him big shock, knock him down silly for minute. I reckon that better way. That lot get killed up Town, they can't tell mates. This way they going to tell all-about . . . and they keep away . . . I reckon.'

Clancy laughed. 'Shrewd idea. You work it out all by yourself?'

'I see those fly'n' fox in Town.'

Jeremy cut in dryly: 'He used to eat 'em!'

'Yes?' asked Clancy innocently.

'When he was in the Compound. An addition to the starvation rations. The black relations of the cross-bred kids used to get the foxes for 'em.'

Clancy blinked, avoiding both pairs of grey eyes now, obviously aware that he was being got at. The triangle ringing over at the house saved him. Then Jeremy helped a bit by saying, 'You'd better not keep 'em waiting. You'd better have some lunch, too, sonny. You might be made up of electrons, according to that book of yours . . . but you can't live on 'em. You can keep on the job by telling your uncle about the electron theory. He probably thinks an electron's only a good name for a horse.' Clancy laughed, but looked bewildered. Jeremy grinned wryly at the pair as he watched them cross the yard. Prindy *was* giving a dissertation by the look of it.

In an hour or so the pair were back again at the annexe, not for Clancy to take leave of his father this time, as Jeremy appeared to think, (judging by his easier manner at first then abrupt return to the former stiffness) but to say that he was going to help Prindy with the rigging of the contraption. Jeremy remarked dryly, 'He's got plenty of helpers. Blackboys've been cutting him poles for a week.'

Clancy, happy as a boy with a mad idea himself, was undeterred. 'We're going to patent it if it works. Form a company . . . Delacy Deleters of Mango Eaters. How's that? *Aaaaaaaaah!*'

Prindy laughed, too, happy enough to be with his uncle at the moment. Jeremy grinned wryly, while quizzing the pair, perhaps wondering if it might not have been the subtle workings of a certain female who had brought them suddenly so close together. They went off to the grove with wire, insulators, tools. Jeremy returned to what he had been doing over the mere bowl of soup he'd had for lunch, namely the writing of yet another article for *Australia Free*, this in refutation of that on *The Protocols of the Elders of Zion,* based on information given him by Kurt, who declared that Anti-Semites would never publish it, while he himself argued that it would serve as conclusive proof of the paper's worth.

Prindy returned alone after about an hour, to say that he'd left Uncle Clancy superintending the erection of poles and stringing of wire, while he himself finished the shocking apparatus so as to try it out tonight. Jeremy asked him, 'Does that mean he's staying the night again?'

'I don't know, Grandfather.'

'I understood he came here just to deliver some jars. Did Nan say anything about him staying?'

'I never hear. I only know Rifkah hunt him away 'cause she want to fry fish.'

'What, was he hanging round the kitchen?'

'No-more. He say he hear how good her fry-fish, and want to try. She say he can try today!'

Jeremy sighed: 'Well, that's done it. I can't see the bugger going home with a bit wrapped up in paper. Blast him . . . coming here on *Shabbos*!'

Prindy, going off to his job, remarked, '*Shabbos* eve, you got to let anybody come to supper . . . Might be Messiah.'

Jeremy, catching the grey eye, asked quickly, 'Messiah, eh? You know that Christians call Jesus that, too?'

'*Yu*. Nan tell me and Rifkah.'

'That means that Messiah's already come.'

'No-more. Only *Goyim* reckon.'

'What's *Goyim*?'

'Silly bugger Christian.' Prindy vanished.

Jeremy sat staring out through the fly-wire of his window at the Big House, where there would be terrific activity going on in the kitchen in conformance with dealings Sarah, wife of Abraham, had allegedly had with angels so long ago. He wouldn't know what the mob outside were saying, that the Jews had taken over here, that in fact they Had Him By The Balls. Frankly charged with it at that moment, he might have found it hard to deny.

The rigging of the Delacy Deleter went on all afternoon, with smoke-o on the job, and co-mingled sounds of mirth and perturbation surely telling of the efficacy of it, at least as it affected humans falling foul of it. The Sun was setting when the newly associated partners came to report to Jeremy that all was ready for the trial tonight. Jeremy showed little interest, saying that he was still busy and wouldn't be going over to the house, asking Prindy to excuse him to the ladies and Kurt.

Then just before the Two Stars appeared to herald the Sabbath, there was the Mistress of Ceremonies, all dressed up for the occasion, bursting into the den, demanding to know of the titular head of the household why he wasn't in his proper place at the proper time. When he said he was too busy, she cried, 'But it is *Shabbos*!'

'I'm sorry, my dear . . . but I want to finish this . . . .'

'Nefair haf you miss *Oneg Shabbat* before. It is because of Clancy!'

'Now listen . . . I've always made it a point not to go to meals over there when there're guests I don't like.'

She stared at him great-eyed. 'You vill do zis to your son?'

'He's a stranger to me. And he isn't here to see me . . . but you.'

'Zis is ridiculous!'

He reached for her hand, drew her close to his chair. 'Why will you interfere in this? You must know I've given a lot of thought to my relations with my sons. They rejected me. The most they can expect from me is politeness. I've been polite to this one all day.'

'Be polite tonight, too, please.' She tried to pull him from the chair.

Resisting, he said, 'He's courting you. What's ridiculous about it, as you say, is that I'm expected to encourage it. I might as well encourage Knobby Knowles to come here courting you.'

'Jeremy!'

'All right . . . I apologize for the choice of lovers. But can't you see how silly it is? You say you don't care for him . . . don't love him, anyway. I believe you. I don't see how you could care much for a fat-head like him. But he's a young man . . . and you're young . . . and . . . and it's probably good for you to have young men friends. But let his one do his courting elsewhere . . . in at the railway, where he has been for the past month, or at his mother's place, or Catfish . . . anywhere but here!' His face flamed as he said the last.

The copper head drooped. Tears drowned the great eyes. The trim body shook. 'Now, now!' he said gently, and pulled her onto the arm of the chair, put an arm about her. 'You've involved yourself in a horrible business, something I'm prepared to admit I'm largely to blame for. But there it is. If I make this concession in this stronghold I've held so long against the gang he stands for, I might as well concede all the way. Don't you understand that? Now, now, now!'

She was sobbing against his neck. He took a loosely fallen hand, caressed it, went on: 'Remember you told me of the Jewish custom, where, when a son marries a *shickseh*, the father mourns him dead, with sack-cloth and ashes and all the rest of it . . . how your own grandfather mourned your own father when he married your Christian mother, and never really took him back as a son, although he took you as a daughter. The way you told it to me, it wasn't as if you thought your *Zaydeh* had done a terrible thing. What I took your story to mean was the great strength of Jews is non-compromise with what they believe will destroy the Law that makes them what they are. I'm sure that's what you meant. Yet you want me to compromise with these people who would destroy *my* laws, which is my integrity in certain matters . . . .'

'I do not . . I do not . . oh, ah!'

'Then what is it you want?'

'I only want you to eat my *Shabbos essen.*'

'Eh?'

'My fry-fish, my *pfannküchen*, my *lochshen soup* . . . oh, oh, oh! My poor lil *Shabbos* is ruin' if you do not come.'

He held her off, stared at her distorted tear-wet face. 'Is that all that's troubling you?'

'V-vot else? Haf not I v-vork all day to mek it beautiful?'

His face quivered. His lips moved. She snuffled, 'Vot you say?'

'I only said, *for godsake.*'

'Vy do you say?'

He rose quickly, raising her with him, saying 'All right . . . I'll come.'

A couple of blinks, and the tears were gone, the jewel-eyes shining, despite the redness of the whites. She flung her arms about him, was going to kiss his mouth, when a high childish cry outside, 'Two star!'

She drew back, disengaged herself. He said, 'Wait. Your face needs a wash. Your eyes are red. I'll give you some drops to clear them . . . .'

But she was already at the door. 'No . . . I must light ze candle!' She was gone.

Jeremy sighed, went into the dispensary to get the eye-drops. He crossed the yard to see young Igulgul winking through the trees, and the first of the flying foxes winging in from the limestone.

The meal, with its ritual a little too solemnly if just as briefly conducted by Kurt, as now the practice for the benefit of visitors, went perfectly. Clancy did full justice to it, not only gastronomically, but was frankly delighted with the ritualistic trimmings, confessing that lately he had been reading of the food laws in the Bible. Rather did he *boast* of his recent study, assuming a sort of superiority that even the dry comment of Prindy that they *all* had been reading the Bible Book could not discourage. But Prindy did at last put him in his place as up-jumped *Goyim*, when unwittingly he betrayed abysmal ignorance of what he was so rashly trying to identify himself with, through something that on the face of it had nothing to do with religion. They were almost finished the meal, when Clancy asked Rifkah if she would like to spend Christmas with his family and friends in Town. She looked embarrassed. 'It is ver' kind. But I am stranger to your family.'

'Not at all. Didn't I tell you the Mater wants you and Kurt to lunch. Only last night we were talking about having you for Christmas.' When she shook her head, he asked, 'Well, what plans *have* you got for Christmas?'

She looked more embarrassed, giggled slightly, looked at Prindy, who came up with the answer, almost contemptuously: 'Christmas not our *yomtov*.'

Clancy gaped at him, turned from the bold grey eyes back to Rifkah. She giggled again, 'Christmas is not Jewish festival.'

Still Clancy gaped. 'No?'

Jeremy couldn't keep out of that: 'Thought you'd been reading up on Jews?'

Clancy reddened. 'How d'you mean?'

Jeremy was red now. 'For godsake, man! Jews don't believe in Christ, do they . . . so how the hell can they be interested in Christmas?'

Clancy blinked and swallowed, then looked belligerent, and turned to Kurt. 'But Christ was a Jew, wasn't he?'

Kurt gave his shrug. 'I am not vot you call Up on religious matter, Clancy.'

Rifkah, watching Jeremy, turned swiftly to Nanago. 'Ve vill haf coffee in lounge, Nan yes?' She rose. They all rose. She went to Jeremy and took his arm, then swung him towards the disconsolate-looking Clancy, and took his arm too. So out to the lounge.

There was no more time for such involvement, scarcely any time for coffee, in fact, because of the din now coming from the mango grove – the shrieks of flying foxes in distress, the squeals and hoots of delighted black and tan humans. Prindy was off like a shot. The others moved to follow, more circumspectly, except Rifkah. When it was discovered that Rifkah was not with them, Jeremy and Clancy turned back, but Jeremy to go only to the door of the lounge, from which, after receiving a shake of the head from her and perceiving that *bubbeh's* look, he turned again, leaving it to Clancy to barge in. When Clancy asked her why she didn't come, she shivered, saying that she had seen people hanging on electric fences. He apologized so profusely that she caught his arm, and said, 'Ve vill valk instead, yes? I do not like to hear it. Ze poor fly'n' fox. It is my fault. I am too greedy for mango, and growl ven I see zem spoil so many. Zen I can't stop Prindy ven he start zis zing. He hate fly'n' fox. He say zey mek ze trouble zat kill his first mumma.'

'What's he mean first mumma?' asked Clancy.

She giggled, 'He haf adopt me as second . . . blackfeller vay.'

'What's he mean flying foxes made that trouble?'

'I do not know. Zat trouble is secret zing for him.'

They walked far, into the southern stars, and back into the northern, mostly talking of them, she in her new knowledge of astronomy and legend instructing him. Back home, she found that Jeremy had retired to his den, and went in search of him. His first remark was: 'Well, did he pop the question?'

'Pop?'

'Ask you to marry him?'

'Oh, Jeremy!' She sank at his feet, to lean on his thigh.

'Aren't I supposed to be interested in my son's doings?'

She giggled, 'I vos teaching him astronomy.'

'Isn't star gazing the first step to romance?'

She said rather shortly, 'I vos surprise' to find he had not been taught about ze stars as a boy . . . by his fader.'

He ignored it, asking, 'Well, has he settled in permanently? If he has, as a proper father I must find him something useful to do.'

Again she giggled, 'You *are* jealous. But, no, he goes avay tomorrow. I fix it by telling him I gif him fry-fish to tek home for lunch. Zat mek you happy again?' She kissed his cheek, rose, saying, 'Now I am going to bed. Moost early start to mek ze jam.'

III

Over breakfast next morning, Clancy confirmed the presumption that he would be leaving today. However, he made no haste about it. First he hung about the lounge, talking with Kurt of Vaiseys and the old White Russian Settlement, of how he would speak to his stepfather and brother about it. This brought the time to smoke-o. After dawdling over that, there was no alternative for him to do anything but say goodbye to those in the house and go to his utility. Still, there remained a final bit of hanging about to talk with Prindy over the erection of more of the Delacy Deleter apparatus. He was still talking to Prindy, when the latter cocked that ear of his, listened a moment, then declared, 'Aeroplane come.' He jerked his lips northwestward. Sure enough, at length there was the musical drone for anyone to hear, even Uncle Clancy. By that time Prindy was able to identify it, at least by naming the pilot: 'Fergitch Ferritch.'

Clancy scowled.

Prindy dashed away to the annexe to inform his grandfather, with whom he soon reappeared, to get into the utility and head for the landing-strip. Clancy, standing by his own ute, now looked as if buffaloes wouldn't budge him from the place.

It was the Junkers sure enough. However, there were strange faces at its cabin windows. Fergus winked from the cockpit. He was the first out, to come bounding down the steps, that usual glint of mischief in his green eyes, though his face solemn and his voice the same, as taking Jeremy's hand, he asked, 'The Land of Canaan, I presume, Sir?'

Jeremy, staring at him, murmured, 'Eh?'

The meaning should have been obvious in the faces now crowding the exit doorway. Fergus got closer to Jeremy and whispered, 'The first of the Chosen. And don't forget what their ancestors did to the Canaanites when they got amongst 'em . . . circumcised 'em to a man, if my recollection of my Bible studies serves me truly.' He stopped. Large suspicious eyes were on him. He reached for Prindy, rumpled his hair, asking, 'How are you, mate?' Then he walked to meet his descending passengers, saying, 'Well, here you are, ladies and gents . . . the Promised Land. This is the boss of it, Mr Delacy. Introduce yourselves while I get your luggage out.'

There were five men and two women, all very different from each other, in build and complexion. They were big and small, plump, lean, dark, fair, grey, bald, with eyes black, brown, hazel, blue, yet with a resemblance, something hard to define. Most would be in their forties. The youngest was a trim, tallish, black-eyed, inky-haired woman. The eldest was the other woman, flabbily plump and grey. All wore the conventional clothes of cities, except one in a riding outfit, breeches and top boots, a handsome young man, slender and dark. One of the other men wore a white solar topee. He was a massive man, clearly the leader. All were again alike in having briefcases tucked under their arms, and in hard-eyed staring.

Jeremy said, 'Gooday. I presume you're the people Doctor Hoff's expecting?'

The big man answered, in harsh thick tones, 'Doctor Hoff, ja, ja. Doctor Hoff isht vere?' He whipped out a large white handkerchief, to swipe viciously at flies singling him out as the bulkiest and juiciest prey, and then to mop his already streaming face.

'He's at the homestead. We didn't realize it might be you. I'll get him. We'll need his big car, anyway.' Jeremy turned to Prindy. 'Grab a horse and get Kurt to come, will you, sonny?'

As usual the horses were approaching out of curiosity after having bolted in alarm. Prindy, heading for them, whistled. Golden Bobby broke out of the mob trotting. The newcomers stared as he leapt onto the pony, and with nothing but knees to guide him, swung him to go galloping towards the homestead. Surely an unusual sight for them; but the look in their eyes was not so much curiosity as that same with which they had emerged from the aircraft, as if from experience always wary of traps. They turned the look on Jeremy, until the thumping of Fergus in the luggage-locker drew it that way, and all went marching thither. The big man snatched a polished wooden box from Fergus, to bring it to the utility himself. A small fat man took possession of the folded legs of a theodolite as if resentful of Fergus's touching it. Fergus, coming with the suitcases, and happening to catch Jeremy alone, nodding to the polished box, muttered, 'Bet that's the knives?'

'What knives?' asked Jeremy.

'Why . . . circumcising knives!' Pretending to struggle in placing the cases, Fergus went on: 'Haven't you read the Bible? Don't you know that the Israelites conquered the Canaanites by circumcising 'em first, then while they were sitting up holding their sore tossicks, sneaked up and cut their throats?' When Jeremy stared at him in astonishment, he muttered, 'Prepare to meet thy doom!' and fled.

A little later, while the company were walking about surveying the scene, ignoring Jeremy and Fergus utterly, to the evident displeasure of Jeremy, Fergus explained that such was their manner, that they had treated him like the cabman ever since taking up with him, and said that probably they would treat him, Jeremy, like the innkeeper. He went on to say that he happened to be flying them because, when he had received word by radio in Town from Leopold Mission that they were wanting to charter an aircraft, the General, at the moment involved with Japanese pearlers anchored off the Mission during spring tides, had gladly let him go. 'To get their guts,' he added. 'Like I get the Japs' guts for him. Old Whiskers sends his affectionate regards, *don't y'know?* and to tell you he'll be dropping in in a few days' time to meet your Israelites. I'll be going back for him tomorrow, then to pick up those wandering boys of his. By the way, I've got a parcel here, from him . . . present for Rifkah and your Missus. He asked me to pick it up in Town. Mind if I deliver it to 'em personally?'

There was Kurt coming in his old red juggernaut, with only Prindy beside him.

Either Kurt was a stranger to the newcomers, or subscribed to the same formalism that caused them to limit greetings to heel-clicking and nodding on the part of the men and stiff little bows from the women, with the minimum of verbal exchange in what could have been any East European language, harsh, terse, and sounding anything but friendly.

When Kurt formally introduced Jeremy, only the big man shook hands. His first name was Ernest, odd sounding as applied to him, the rest of the name surely lost on Jeremy through its foreignness; like the names of all the others, acknowledging him with stiff clickings and bows. With almost military direction Ernest bundled his squad into Kurt's car, while fighting a flank action with the flies, then himself got in with Jeremy. Fergus and Prindy got in with the dunnage behind.

As they drove off, Fergus said to Prindy, 'I'll get even with Colonel Cutcock in there, next time I get him up in the kite. He messed up my centre of gravity all the way by walking about.' Prindy, evidently familiar with the term, asked Fergus what he meant by *his* centre of gravity. Fergus replied, 'Explain it to you next time we fly together. But speaking of G, how's things going with my real C of G, Rifkah? You been buildin' me up, like we arranged, makin' my alley good, puttin' in a plod for me?' On hearing that Clancy was there, Fergus became angry, but soon relaxed with evidence that it was without the blessing or encouragement of anyone. However, he said, 'I'll have to think of a way to keep that snoopin' bloody dingo away from here . . . like this flyin' fox gadget of yours. Reckon you could rig me up a trap for him?' Thus when they came upon Clancy, still standing scowling by his utility, Fergus was able to greet him with a guffaw: 'Hi, cowboy! Still lookin' for strayin' stock?'

Rifkah, out from the Big House to greet the newcomers, did so with much the same stiff formality as they observed, to be addressed by Ernest, evidently in German, with as scant courtesy as a ranker by a military officer. In fact, for several minutes Ernest spoke and acted just like a military commander detailing a military operation, completely ignoring everybody but his troop. Most of his harsh alien speech was directed at Kurt, who all but cringed to him. Fergus cocked a wink at Jeremy, who grimaced in reply, and another at Clancy, who scowled. Then Clancy said to his father that he would like to stay and meet the people. Jeremy only nodded.

At length Ernest acknowledged Jeremy's presence by turning to him. Jeremy at once suggested refreshments and off with coats, and led the way to the lounge. Rifkah went back to the kitchen, watched by Fergus and Clancy. As she disappeared, Clancy started off after his father and the others, with Fergus calling softly after him, 'If you value your foreskin, brother, keep out of it.' Clancy ignored him. Fergus winked at Prindy, said he wanted to deliver the General's parcel, and with him went to the kitchen.

In the lounge the visitors drank the house brew with enthusiasm, comparing it with European beers of quality. Ernest finally declared for everyone that it resembled the *Einbecker* of Hanover, and therewith called for military action again. Kurt produced maps. Thenceforth the lounge became the centre of operations. Jeremy and Clancy were left out of it, except for an occasional apologetic acknowledgement by Kurt, usually only to tell them what were the qualifications of the one who at the moment was under the fire of Ernest's questions concerning some piece of expert knowledge required to substantiate a factor noted in Kurt's stack of research material. All were experts in some department of agrarian activity. Herschal, the bald man, was an Engineer specializing in irrigation and soil conservation, who had worked in South Russia, North Africa, Palestine. Zangwill, the fat one, was a Geologist, Baum the thin man, an Agricultural Scientist, Mendelewitz, the handsome fellow in the riding gear, a specialist in stock breeding. The ladies, Magda the young one, Catherine the plump old hen, were both Biologists.

Clancy was introduced by Kurt not simply as a son of the host, but an important man of the land as a member of Vaiseys. Since evidently neither Ernest nor his people knew anything about Vaiseys just then, the added information seemed only to render Clancy less important. Then he, trying to be helpful, barged into the map-reading with talk of the old White Russian Settlement, and caused a furore. Obviously the newcomers took it to mean that they had rival settlers to deal with, and dangerous ones at that, the way they reacted, especially Ernest, gesticulating and shouting at Kurt. Having learnt that the enemy had long since quitted the field, Ernest turned on Clancy a look that clearly dismissed him as *Schlemiel.*

Later on, Ernest's attitude to Clancy changed suddenly, doubtless owing to his having been appraised in an aside by Kurt of the significance of Vaisey. By the look of things it was just in time. Denied access to Rifkah through pressure of domestic affairs and with the alternative of having to suffer the doubtful company of Fergus now if he were to rejoin Prindy at work on the Deleter, Clancy, sitting moodily on the side-lines, might well have been thinking of going on his way. It would be during a hold up in the vigorous campaign-planning in the lounge, due to an argument over the matter of stopping proceedings for lunch, that the aside must have occurred. When it was announced by Nanago that lunch would soon be served, Ernest in his forthright manner declared that they didn't want it, for one thing because they'd not long had beer and sandwiches, for another that they were scheduled to make a reconnaissance flight as soon as their mapping was done. Rather coldly, Jeremy remarked that the ladies had been at great trouble to prepare lunch, and besides, it being *Shabbos*, there was fry-fish. Obviously it was the last bit that got Ernest in, stirring up gustatory memories. 'Fry-Fish?' he cried. 'All right . . . ve loncheon.' It was as they all went towards the dining-room that he slipped an arm about Clancy's shoulders, telling him that he would be glad to have any help he could give them.

There was no religious ceremony, or evidence that the newcomers even thought of it. Nevertheless, it was with zest little short of religious fervour that they gave themselves to eating food evidently long denied them. Rifkah and Nan beamed over it. Ernest pronounced the fish the best he had ever tasted, demanding to know what it was. When told about the Barramundi, its proliferacy under good conditions, the great size to which it grew, he declared, 'Moost ve farm zis ver' goot fish.'

It would be the first the locals had heard of fish farming, an idea that tickled them as they heard it elaborated, Prindy turned the chuckles into a laugh by saying to his grandfather, 'How we going to muster him up that barramundi and brand him?'

Ernest glared suspiciously at that, demanding, 'Vot ist foney?'

A quick remark from Kurt seemed to put the matter right; and Jeremy helped by asking how they would go about the farming in a locality like this. Little thin Baum, in very indifferent English, said he thought they had the very place for it in the extensive swampland they had seen to northeastward as they flew in. Jeremy said, 'The billabongs. But barramundi wouldn't live there . . . not with catfish.' Ernest wanted to know what a catfish was. When Jeremy explained that it had the power to sting and paralyse other fishes, Ernest asked if it could be eaten. Jeremy answered, 'Well, that depends.' He looked at Rifkah.

'Vot depends?' demanded Ernest.

Prindy gave the answer: 'Catfish not *kosher*. Got no scale.'

All stared at him. Fergus choked on a guffaw. This drew Ernest's attention to him, but not to show offence, rather to express impatience: '*Kosher*! Vot is *kosher* in new country like zis . . . in new society ve mek?' Then, perhaps concerned over the looks of surprise the locals gave him, he grinned. 'Haf you not ze dog-fish, too, to chase avay ze catfish?' So for all his heavy Teutonic manner he had the Jewish humour.

But no siesta for the like of Ernest. When Jeremy, perhaps ironically, remarked as they left the table that it was the custom of the country to take it easy in the middle of the day, his comment was one of disgust: 'Ach!' Then he spoke in lingo to his two women, with sharpness that suggested he was telling them that during his absence on the aerial survey they were not to join the rest of the household in sloth.

The males of the party, with Fergus, Jeremy and Clancy, headed straight out to the Junkers. In no time they were in the air. The survey was northward to the edge of the Plateau, eastward to Catfish homestead, southwestward across the Beatrice to meet the railway at Granite Springs, then swing southeastward back to the Beatrice flowing past the old White Russian Settlement site. They flew up and down the site at tree-top level, while Ernest dashed from window to window, giving Fergus a lot of trouble with the aircraft's trim. Kangaroos, wallabies, brumbies, brolgas, went flying through the grass before them. When they flushed a mob of emus Ernest all but put them in a spin with his excited leaping, shouting: '*Strauss, strauss*!' perhaps seeing himself in business selling ostrich plumes.

They did a turn over the township, with everyone out to see, and probably everyone knowing who they were, since Fergus had radioed his flight details to Port Palmeston and the community in its lust for minding other people's business was hardly likely to fail to take full advantage of modern methods of doing so. Shamus Finnucane was the only one to show any enthusiasm, standing out before his pub waving a bar cloth. Fergus dipped a wing to him, to the annoyance of Ernest, who was sent sprawling. Ernest's only comment on the civilized scene was: 'Ver' primitive.'

So up the river, scattering the cockatoos and white egrets, and home to land. Then back into the lounge and what might well be described as An Appreciation, by Ernest, taken down in shorthand by slim handsome Magda, while the others listened in silence. Although unable to understand a word, Clancy stayed. Not Jeremy, however, who slipped away, heading for the annexe through the kitchen, where Rifkah and Nan were up to their eyes in preparing a great dinner of roast bustard. He paused to ask Rifkah what was the Yiddish or Hebrew for Boss. She answered with a giggle, '*Macher*.' The voice of the *Macher* in the lounge could be heard right through to the kitchen.

When Jeremy returned for the drinking session, Clancy was the centre of talk of Vaiseys, and looking very pleased with himself. He told his father that he would be taking some of the party over to Catfish and then down to Beatrice homestead, but that those who would be going with him, Magda and Mendelewitz, both accomplished riders, would first like to look around on horseback; so would he mind letting him have horses tomorrow? Not a word about his staying overnight again, nor evidence of a thought about asking permission.

Again Jeremy merely nodded. Thus there again at the paternal board that evening sat the prodigal son, now looking and acting as if he had never left home, and doing much of the talking about the *pièce de résistance*, the fatted bustard, in answer to the eager inquiries of the new-come guests. With the bustard went baked sweetbucks and spiced pawpaw, followed by pineapple pie. The guests were particularly delighted with the information that none of it cost money, that either it ran wild in the bush to be taken in flocks as wanted or grew prolifically wherever planted.

Ernest demanded, 'Tell me more of zis bastard bird.'

When it was evident that Clancy knew little more about the great birds than how to shoot them, Jeremy cut in to say that Prindy knew more about them than anyone there. Ernest looked at Prindy as if seeing him for the first time, stared a moment, then asked, 'Zis bastard . . . how many *ei* he haf?'

Prindy looked at his grandfather, saw him buttoning up his face against laughter, but let his own brown face open in a wide grin, which he turned on Fergus, who looked fit to burst. It was too much for a boy. He tried to answer Ernest, but only squeaked, then squealed, and with a yell of laughter, slipped from his chair and rushed from the dining-room. That in turn was too much for the others struggling with mirth. They let it go. Among them were Mendelewitz and Magda, who spoke good English. But even the rest were caught in the laughter by sheer infection, except Ernest, who stared. But none laughed louder than Ernest did when the joke was explained to him. '*Ei* in German is *Egg*, ja? And German *Ei* sound like English *Eye*. And so of zis noble bird haf I mek ze vun-eye *momzer* . . . hahahohoho!'

Later, in the lounge, Cayley's *What Bird Is That?* was produced. Ernest fairly gloated over its vast variety of edible birds. Of what he was now calling Ze Momzer Bird, he declared, 'It grow to tventy pound in vild state. Zat ist ten kilogram. Oy, vot a bird ist zat! Vot a monster *momzer* ve can haf mit control foodink undt broodink . . . undt ze broodink season it ist all year round. Catherine, Magda . . . you ze expert are. At vonce investigation!'

Again no ritualistic walk, nor any hope of an alternative on the part of those who would have seized one: Clancy and Fergus, who obviously were jockeying for position, as it were. As soon as able to leave the lounge, Rifkah slipped away upstairs with Nan. Upstairs was something far more interesting for them than what was offering below, namely, those gifts from General Esk, as yet but glimpsed. They went to Nan's room, which for the time they were sharing.

The gifts were clothes for Nan and gramophone records for Rifkah. There was a handsome gown of Indo-Chinese style, made by someone of Bangkok, in mauve silk shot with silver and edged with it, high-collared, ankle-length, with silver sandals to match. The records were one of folksongs in Yiddish, the other of synagogue singing in Hebrew.

Rifkah had Nan put on the dress at once. It fitted perfectly, and suited her so well as to give her poise and dignity, in marked contrast with her usual dowdiness in European clothes; the kind of clothes she ought always to wear, as Rifkah said. She squealed at that, 'Eh, look out!' But it was true, going to show that dressing is involved with race, and that the General was wise enough to know it. When Prindy came in and saw it he tried hard to get her to come downstairs wearing it. Failing in that, he tried to induce Rifkah to bring the records down and play them on the radio-gramophone, no matter if it interrupted the yip-yap going on below. Rifkah had to sing him such of the folksongs as she knew. But it wasn't enough. She had to agree to play the records, softly, after the others had gone to bed.

Not even Jeremy was told about the proposed musical session. When he went over to the annexe upon the retirement of everyone about eleven, he did not know that Prindy, long since retired, was only pretending to be asleep, and that as soon as he himself had settled down, the boy slipped out. Nan and Rifkah were waiting in the bedroom. Prindy stole round the bedrooms checking on the rest of the household. Then they went below like mice.

They put on the religious record, Cantor and Choir renderings of the music of *Rosh Hashanah*, the New Year, and of *Yom Kippur*, the Day of Atonement. Rendering it truly was, of true believers to a god truly living as far as they were concerned. There was no instrumental music, simply the Cantor, with a tenor of sweetness possible only in one whose soul sobbed in the joy of being in the presence of the Creator, backed by an all-male choir whose perfect harmony rang seemingly far and near, like echoes of the Voice on Sinai. No musical instrument could have begotten such sweet sound, except that fashioned by the Divine Hand itself, the true *Vox Humana – Oov'shofar Gadol Yitakah – (The Great Ramshorn Bloweth!) – S'oo Sh'orim (Lift Up Thine Heads!) – M'louch Alkol Ho' olam (Reign Forever O'er They Universe, Oh Lord*!) – and the silver cry of the *Shofar*, the Ram's Horn, the Voice, as Abraham heard it, and as Jacob, Moses, and every true Jew had heard it ever since – the Four Cries: *Tekiah, Shevarim, Teruah*, and oh, again *Tekiah*, crying until its echoes were lost among the stars.

It was the cry of the *Shofar* if ever so muted on the toned-down gramophone, that brought the others. Only Prindy heard their ghostly footfalls. Rifkah, crouched before the set, with copper hair glinting like holy fire in the tiny light of the dials, on bent knees, head in hands, was softly weeping. Nan on heels beside her, erect, was invisible save for her glistening tears – *Hayom Harat Olam (This is the Hour of Earth's Creation!)*

The ghosts faintly materialized as those plump oldish ones, Zangwill and Catherine. They stood back for a while, till the *Kol* and *Nidre* and *Vehogein Baadeinu (Be Our Shield, Lord God of Israel!)* when Catherine sank to the floor with the others, and Zangwill's handkerchief appeared as a white blur to cover his bowed head, both rocking and weeping freely.

Yaaleh . . . Yaaleh . . . Yaaleh . . . Let Our Prayer Ascend.
We pray unto Thee at eventide. We cry unto Thee at dawn.
Redeem us till the eventide, pardon us with the dawn.
At last assure us of Our Atonement.

The recording ended. Prindy, crouching by the set, moved to turn the record over to play the other side, when arrested by a harsh voice sounding from the stairs, 'Vot isht . . . Midnight Mass?'

The others started. Heavy steps on the stairs. Then a bulky ghost seen in the little lights, from which issuing harsh guttural speech. Catherine rose hastily. Zangwill snatched the handkerchief from his head, pocketed it furtively, turned and vanished. Catherine, too, slipped suddenly away. Rifkah was slow to rise, and then only because the harsh voice put the lash round her personally. Sniffling her tears, she said to Nan, 'It is late.'

Nan rose. Rifkah took her hand. Both looked at Prindy, whose face was golden in the light as he stood over it. He was looking at the glittering eyes of Ernest. Then they, too, vanished. For a moment Ernest and Prindy stared at each other. Then Ernest spoke, with comparative softness: 'You like it . . . zat music?' The golden face moved in assent. 'Ist not strange zing for leetle boy like you . . . yes, no?' Prindy only stared. Then a fat hairy hand appeared, touched the golden hair, and then the slender shoulder. 'But time for leetle boy to bed, I zink.' The hand reached for the control panel, switched off the set. Ernest said, 'Ve all vont to be early risingk tomorrow . . . *Gutten nacht*!' He was gone.

Prindy sighed, stood a moment, then left the lounge, left the house by way of the kitchen, looked up at the stars as he crossed to the annexe, singing under his breath: *Oshamnu, oshamnu, oshamnu* . . .

Later in the night, Jeremy was wakened by the sweet straining little voice singing in sleep: *Oshamnu, Oshamnu*. He lay listening, perhaps wondering what language it was, surely never realizing that in English it meant – *We have trespassed*! For how could anyone, except who walked hand-in-hand with God, confess so joyfully to sinning, as if trespass were a part of righteousness, a part of God's True Purpose, which must be Life, not Death, as the *Goyim* have it? Life, Life, *L'chaim*!

IV

Despite Ernest's declared plans for the day and his being a superplanner and a Jew, he and his company might have been lazy-bone *Goyim* the way they lay abed that Sunday morning. No doubt the reason was the upset he had called Midnight Mass, emotional as well as physical, since obviously there was subtle conflict over the Voice that had been crying through the *Shofar*. Only the regular members of the household were up early, and peep-o'-day boy by calling, Fergus. Even Clancy the Cowboy was snoring his head off with the rest upstairs, as reported by Fergus when he joined those in the kitchen for a cup of tea.

Thus it was that Fergus was able to talk to Rifkah without intrusion by

Clancy or chance of her dodging him. He tried again to get her to come with him on the flight he would be making back to Leopold Mission after breakfast, and called on Nan to help him when Rifkah said she couldn't leave Nan alone to cope with this mob. 'Because of *kosher*?' he demanded. 'Big Ernest didn't seem so *kosher* last night when he broke up your midnight synagogue, now did he? Besides, you can leave all the *kosher* stuff to Prindy, by the look of it.' Mention of Prindy gave Rifkah the idea that Fergus should take him along instead of her. He argued: Prindy *and* her. At last he agreed to take the boy if she would declare before Nan that she was *his* girl and gave an assurance to have no hanky-pankies with Clancy. The deal was made, sealed with a kiss that she had to fight to get free of. Fergus went off to the annexe to clinch it with Prindy and Jeremy.

This time Prindy climbed the sky in the co-pilot's seat, raised on leather cushions for full viewing, and by the intensity of those grey eyes, missing nothing. The homestead, green, white, yellow, with its tiny scampering creatures, spun for a moment in the middle of the wide green-greyness under the blue, the blue, the blue . . . then vanished. The red wall of the Plateau was rushing at them. Up and over. A flicker amongst the rocks to westward showed that they had an escort. Thus there must be care not to look upon that Ring Place. As they approached it, the fair head dropped. Fergus noted the action, asked, 'Feeling sick?' The head shook. 'Frightened?' Another shake. There was no doubt about the fidelity of the responses when the head was raised again and the grey eyes leapt from rock to rock like the disturbed creatures belonging to them. The lips moved as if in silent song.

They climbed for smoother flying. Fergus suggested a lesson in handling the magic thing, saying when the eyes rolled in astonishment, 'Nothing to it, flying straight and level. Look. Hands off. She flies herself. Have a go.' It wasn't long before Fergus was sitting with arms folded, correcting little slips with occasional touches. How wide the grey eyes now in joy in the superhuman accomplishment!

Fergus said, (or rather shouted, since that was the mode of communion above the din), 'Head for that bit of cloud.' It was a tiny white puff where the green-grey of the earth met the northern blue. Soon it was revealed as the highest peak of a long cloud mountain. 'The Inter-Tropic Front building up,' remarked Fergus. After a while he asked, 'Know what means?' Prindy nodded. The split lip was revealed in a grin. 'Bet you don't!' But such was the look in the grey eyes turned on him, that he added: 'Bet's off. Maybe you know more about it than I do.' That was the Anthropologist speaking. Nevertheless, the Aeronaut had his say, telling of how the earth's biennial tilting in relation to the Sun caused the seasons. While a golden ear was cocked to take in the glib logic of the *kuttabah*, the eyes fixed on the dazzling heading were surely seeing something else; and what else was the Inter-Tropic front but the southward drift of the dreaming Cloud Spirits according to the eternal law of Koonapippi?

A silver glinting now between earth and sky. 'The sea,' said Fergus. Then first glimpse of those old pythons' tracks, wriggling in from the sea. 'Leopold River,' Fergus said. A nod. 'You been here before?' Nod. 'Not in an aeroplane, though?' No response. Did one need an aeroplane to see it, when the Dream Time Ones had left behind look-outs everywhere? Still, an aeroplane certainly helped. Fergus said, 'Let me take her. We'll drop down and follow the river, see a lot of buffaloes and crocs and things. Besides, we'd better take a look-see how the Coot and his boys're doing.'

As they swept down over the rain forest of the Plateau's northern slope, the nutmeg pigeons rose in their myriads to float like snowy clouds beneath them. Of several birds of prey high-hovering, one, a wedge-tail eagle, came gliding in ahead to take a closer look at the rival to his majesty of the air, halted in the blue to wait and watch, motionless save for slight working of finger-like tips of primary feathers of great wings glinting bronzily in the sunlight, occasional flick of wedge-tail rudder, serpent-like roll of big hook-billed challenging head. They passed within thirty feet of him. Fergus shouted, 'Ain't he a beaut?' And he waved to the bird: ' 'Ow are yo' mate?'

Prindy took a swift look back at the pigeons settling to their fig-gorging, at the line of concavities underhanging the sheer red wall of the escarpment about the trees. It wasn't the same spot where he and the Pookarakka had camped to watch Igulgul rise to work his Wrong-side magic on the world of night and the pigeons come like dawn-clouds with the rising of Koonapippi to put things right-side again. Not the same spot, but much like it.

The coastal plain was red and yellow patched with parched swampland awaiting the coming of those sleepy clouds; that is until it neared the glitter of the sea, where it was blue-green with maritime jungle. Dropping down to the trees of the upper reach of the Leopold River, in the comparative quiet of throttled-back engines, Fergus remarked, 'Just like a snake, that old river, isn't it? That's what it ought to be called . . . Snake River. Leopold was one of Queen Victoria's halfwit sons, I suppose. D'you know the blackfellow name for it?'

Prindy answered promptly, 'Snake.'

Fergus stared at him unbelieving, then muttering, 'Well, what d'you know!' He turned back to his flying.

They dropped down to about a hundred feet above the river, to follow its curving; while the egrets, the cranes, the cormorants, the cockatoos, the spoonbills, flying up ahead of them, took a look and scattered in ragged flight. What appeared to be black logs on a sandbank suddenly leapt into life, dived, left leprous-looking muddy patches on the green-gold mirror of the water. Then a strange sight to starboard that caused Prindy to crane that way, and Fergus, seeing the movement, to take a look and swing the kite. A billabong paralleling the river was strangely yellow and seemed to be bubbling. Fergus dropped down to approach it at about fifty feet. It was just as if a huge stone had been thrown into it. Great gobbets of yellow mud spilled over its outer banks, not to fall where they landed, but to go sweeping in glistening masses over the sparcely grown flat earth. Fergus laughed, 'Buffaloes . . . hundreds of the bastards.' He opened his throttles, got down almost on the backs of the stampeding monsters, yelling, 'Ride 'im cowboy!' Prindy laughed the high squealing laugh of the tickled blackfellow.

Up again with a rush, and back to the river, to disturb the peace, along with the black Shade hurtling along through the timber of the western bank, to stir up the blue air with white birds and the green water with the panic of crocodiles. The river was much greener now, much wider.

Then suddenly rounding a bend, they came upon other denizens of this noise-ripped Eden, these not nearly so timid, ready for what was coming at them, because they knew what it was; three canoes full. Nevertheless, there must have been something shocking about it – perhaps the Shade, since at the angle of approach it would be running ahead, because one of the canoes capsized as they passed over it.

'Hey . . . what'd I see?' yelled Fergus, opening his throttles wide and jerking aloft. Then he stall-turned and came sweeping back. 'Yeah . . . the Coot!' Yes, there was the chubby red face, plain to see amongst the black, the black faces split with gleaming grins, but not the red. Not so funny, for a certainty, to be spilled amongst crocodiles, without knowing anything about what to do except in *theory* – that is to say that, knowing a crocodile for a coward, *you* get after *him*, and having caught up with him, get on his back and stick your thumbs in his eyes; and not so easy for one primarily a theorist. But Fergus, turning again to make another swooping survey, only laughed. There were other red faces to be seen now, one in the water with the Coot, Denzil Dickey's, the others in another canoe. Denzil had probably just surfaced. He was clinging to his lion-hunter's hat as to a life-preserver. Perhaps those unspilled had been bobbed down so as not to show themselves before, on the orders of their commander. At any rate, that was Fergus's idea of the situation, as laughingly he talked about it while he and his mate went on their way again. 'The sneakin' bloody bastard . . . reckons he's going to make it right to the sea unaided. How long's he been in that canoe? You can come thirty or forty miles by that branch back there eastward. When I saw 'em the other day, they were that far away from here . . . with the horses. Hahahahhoho! The Coot'll never live that down. I'll see to that.'

Now the river was widening rapidly, its colour changing; from emerald to olive, to brown-streaked dull green opal; while the timber lessened in height, to become denser in growth, until it was impenetrable even for the attendant part of the Old One, which had to skim the top. Then suddenly they were over mangroves, the greenness of which turned the water silver, not just one wriggle of silver, but myriad veins of it, linking for miles, to turn the tree-growths into countless islets. Still the birds rose, to scatter like blown paper, with bigger ones amongst them now, pelicans, jabirus, sea-eagles. Still there was swirling in the deeps, not now by mere black logs of things, but of creatures roods in size by the extent of the disturbance.

Then as suddenly as everything had become dark green jade it changed to turquoise. The sea, the sea, the true blue sea. Just a strip of it to begin with, backed by those red-cliffed islands made by the Ol'Goomun for her nesting pigeons. The pigeons were there now, just as their mates were back in the rain-forest filling their crops for them and their fledglings, and rising just the same to float in snowy clouds. Beyond the islands – vastness – of turquoise, backed by that mountain-chain of sleeping cloud all but filling the northern sky. 'The Leopold Group,' said Fergus, nodding to what lay below. 'Pretty, isn't it . . . except for the name. Queen Victoria'll be forever looking over Australia's shoulder. Know what I mean?' But Prindy was too interested in the scene.

There were a score of islets in the group, only the bigger ones high-cliffed, and thus on the southern side, with white beaches on the northern and western and bits of mangrove swamp, and jungle-grown interiors. On some of the beaches were canoes and black figures running, waving. Fergus dropped down to zigzag through the jade channels, dipping his wings. Then up again a little when suddenly they were confronted with a small bay packed with anchored pearling luggers, trim black-hulled vessels with shiny varnished masts and crewmen waving. A biggish island backed the bay where the vessels lay. There was a long white beach, canoes and black figures on the beach. A fringe of casuarinas, behind it a double line of white-washed buildings making a miniature township by flanking a street of scarlet earth. They flew down the street, while what appeared to be penned children galloped about behind fences. They swung away over cultivated ground, a windmill, tanks, bush, to find a red slash in the bush rushing up to meet them as Fergus put his nose down. Trees rushed past them, small red antbeds, bleached grass. Bump-bump! They were down. Bumpity-bump. They were running the length of the gash, slowing down. They stopped, turned in their own dust, headed back a little way, to a track leading to a whitewashed shed, into which they turned.

There were figures waiting at the shed, with a motor truck. As they neared, it could be seen that only one of the faces of those who waited was what would be called white; a familiar one, that of General Esk. All but one of the others was black, the exception golden-brown as Prindy's, and again familiar. Fergus revved to charge his carburetters, cut his engines. Once again that strange silence in which the grounded spirit cried.

All eyes were on the aeronauts as they emerged, but the General's looking beyond them into the cabin, plainly expecting to see someone else, as proved when he spoke to Fergus: 'Neither of 'em with you, eh what?'

In a flippant few words Fergus explained the situation at Lily Lagoons, while Esk gave his attention to Prindy, taking his hand. 'And how are you, young man?'

Prindy responded gravely, watched intently by the dark eyes in the background. He took in the background scene at a glance, then appeared to dismiss it, even the smile given him by the familiar brown face, turning to the General to say that his grandfather had sent over a gift of Lily Lagoons beer and some brandy, and Rifkah some of her mango jam. 'Very thoughtful of them,' said the General, 'And most acceptable, I assure you.'

That familiar brown face came thrusting in, with a brown hand outstretched to Prindy. 'You know me,' said a whining voice. 'David. You know wet day Port Palmeston, we go ridin' truck with Miss Windeyer. I Catholic Missionary Man now.' Prindy took the hand, but evidently was not a bit impressed by the reunion. David made up for it by sharply ordering the blacks to see to the unloading of the aircraft, personally supervising it, declaring loudly to the superior ones that the Drink, as he called it, would have to be carried in the cabin of the truck: 'Dem Native cunnin' thief.' Fortunately the truck, a massive old-fashioned thing, had room in front for all the superior ones as well, with David driving.

A rough track brought them to the little whitewashed townshiplike Mission station. Young trees lined that one red dusty street: the usual poncianas and jasmins and coconuts. As should be, the church was the main building, built like any other tin bush church, except that it had verandahs on either side and cables slung across the roof to anchor it to the ground in case of high winds, a precaution that might be considered anomalous in view of the crosses on the roof-top fore and aft. The open door of the porch gave a glimpse of the altar, bright with candles, flowers, gilded fittings, but no worshippers. Still the place was not deserted. One verandah was packed with a gathering seated before a whiteman with a black beard standing by a blackboard. The whiteman waved to the truck. The others glanced, revealing themselves as Japanese. Seeing Prindy craning to see, David remarked, 'Father Glascock teach English Japanee pearlin' man.'

Obliquely across the road from the church was another building surmounted with crosses, this a bungalow of fair size with verandahs screened with bamboo lattice louvers an open one of which gave a glimpse of two pale peeping faces framed in nun's barbs and hoods. Back of this was one of those enclosures, against the high wire-netting fence of which small black girls in uniform clothing crowded. Next to it was what was evidently the kitchen, judging by the smoke pouring from a flue that took the place of a cross and aproned figures amongst those peeping. On the church side, further up, was another convent-like building with crosses, but no nuns, and small uniformed boys crowding the compound at the rear. Otherwise the buildings of the street were sheds, except for the last one, another bungalow with crosses, but with verandahs open and no one about. 'Dis Presbytery, where Father Glascock live,' as David explained to Prindy as they drew up before the place.

David saw to the unloading in his bossy way, himself carried the liquor to the rear, placing some of the beer, which had come in wet sacking, in a big charcoal cooler on the back verandah, the rest with the other stuff in a back room he unlocked and locked again. Then he took himself off, bowing obsequiously to the General and Fergus, simply nodding to Prindy and saying, 'See you by'n'by, young feller. We have big talk about Port Palmeston.' He headed for that building behind which the boys were herded and now shrilly playing.

Fergus, Prindy, and General Esk sat in deck-chairs on a side verandah evidently used for lounging and dining and with some slight view of the beach through the fringe of casuarinas. Prindy watched the activity on the beach, the movement of semi-naked blacks about their humpies and canoes, the play of naked children on the edge of the falling tide. Meanwhile Fergus and the General talked, of the Cootes Party, of things at Lily Lagoons, Fergus being mostly droll about it all, to the restrained amusement of Esk, occasionally calling on Prindy to bear him out in the drollery.

They had sat for half an hour or so, when there was seen movement through the casuarinas in the region of the rear of the church, accompanied by chattering as of a flock of noisy birds. Evidently Father Glascock's school was out and his pupils heading back to their luggers. But not all the pupils were leaving. Out in the street were other voices, and then their owners to be seen approaching: two Japanese clad in starched white linen, one even with a topee, between them the bearded priest, in khaki shirt and pants and wearing Japanese thongs, while his companions wore European shoes. The man in the topee was big for his breed, of a height with the stocky priest, the other a typical midget. All carried books under their arms. Behind them at a little distance was coming

David again. All turned into the Presbytery. Those on the verandah rose to meet them, the General with an arm about Prindy's shoulders.

There was no doubt about the priest's surprise in seeing Prindy, or at any rate one of his kind enjoying familiarity with a general. Esk was quite formal in introducing the boy: 'Your Reverence, allow me to introduce Master Prendegast Delacy. The Reverend Father Glascock, my boy.' By the slowness of his movement, it was pretty certain the priest wouldn't have shaken hands, only that Prindy, so used to introductions these days, thrust out his small hand, with a murmured, How d'you do. The priestly eyes ran over the tailored poplin clothes. The priest then introduced the General to the Japanese. The biggish man was Captain Okado, described as Number-one of the Pearling Fleet, the other Chief Engineer Sakamura. There was much polite hissing and bowing on the part of the two.

As the company settled down, David came from the rear with a tray bearing glasses and two bottles of beer and one of lime-juice. The priest frowned. Esk said quickly, 'My friend Jeremy Delacy kindly sent over a few bottles of his special brew, Father. Hope it's in order and all that.'

'Quite all right,' said the priest. 'Glad of it. Only I don't like this fellow's flunky ways.' He snapped at David, 'I've told you before, boy . . . I don't like being waited on.'

Quite undeterred, David set out the glasses, poured beer for the men and lime juice for Prindy, bowed himself away. The priest asked Esk, 'Do they get waited on like that over at the Protestant Mission?'

Esk chuckled, answering diplomatically, 'Well, I haven't seen alcoholic liquor being served.'

Father Glascock gave a grunt that might have meant good-humoured response, then raised his glass, saying, *'Banzai!'*

The Japanese leapt to their feet to the toast: *'Banzai!'*

They drank, remarked on the excellence of the brew, talked of beer and language. Esk remarked that he understood the term *banzai*, meaning may you live a thousand years, was reserved for acclaiming the Japanese Emperor. There was no true enlightenment from those who ought to know. Captain Okada's English was impossible to follow; and although Sakamura spoke the language reasonably well, evidently some formality prevented him from intruding unless ordered to do so by chief. Something of the complexity of Japanese formality was revealed with the coming of David with more beer and the priest's outspoken annoyance over it after ordering him not to do it again: 'He's immensely useful to me. But I can't stand that ingratiating manner of his. Whether he's been trained to it, or it comes natural I don't know and don't care. I just won't have it here!'

Captain Okada hissed politely, addressing the priest: 'Excuse Grascock, Sir. Meaning Ingshatink, pliss?' It was a strange, harsh, heavily masculine voice.

The priest groaned, reaching for a Japanese-English dictionary, murmuring, 'Why don't I learn to speak basic English always?'

When the word Ingshatink had been turned up, translated, discussed at length by the two Japanese and Fergus, with the others looking on, Okada said to Glascock, 'David iss some Japan-man, so humble man, must.'

Again the priest groaned, mumbling, 'God save us!' Then aloud he asked the Captain, 'How do you mean?'

It took the best part of five minutes to get the meaning, and then only through Sakamura, who could probably have given it pat, if permitted earlier. While it was going on, Glascock groaned to Esk, 'These endless verbal post-mortems. I've come to wonder if I can stand the strain.' The interpretation at last forthcoming was that David being of Japanese blood and lowly origin, was bound to act as servant to those whom he regarded as his superiors, not in duty but as a privilege. 'Ah!' sighed the enlightened priest. 'I see now that I'm doing him wrong by refusing him inequality . . . and in trying to stop him from bullying the blacks . . . . '

'Meanink Booryink, Sir?' asked Okada.

Reaching for the dictionary again, Glascock said, 'I'm afraid my English school isn't the bright idea I thought it was. Rather is it a penance for my sins.'

Since the remark was addressed to no one in particular, Sakamura, who understood it, chuckled, to be at once pounced on by his captain for an explanation. When he got it, Okada laughed uproariously, smacking his thigh with terrific wallops. Sakamura joined in. Soon everybody was laughing. After that the lingual struggle went on with better humour. Perhaps the beer helped.

Then a couple of young black girls arrived, wearing identical blue cotton dresses with white hemming, and bearing between them a huge basket covered with a white table cloth. They arrived giggling, but were very circumspect as they laid the table, acting as if they were not there. Then suddenly they were not there. Father Glascock rose and proceeded to seat his guests at the table, this time taking no notice when yet again David came with beer. Engineer Sakamura showed how he came to understand that humorous complaint of the Reverend Father's by emulating him when he crossed himself in saying grace over the pigeon pie and sweet bucks. It was poor fare. Even the Reverend Father apologized for it after thanking the Lord for providing it, although rectifying the seeming anomaly by blaming it on the cooks. The pie tasted more of onion than of pigeon, and its paste could have served as well as the base for the soggy treacle pudding that followed. Nevertheless, all but one of the guests expressed appreciation, Esk and Fergus with polite murmurs, the Japanese with genteel belching that couldn't have been hard to simulate. Prindy, who at least had the excuse of not having an appetite blunted with beer, merely picked at his portions. Fortunately for everyone, the portions were small.

The meal over, it was arranged that after siesta, for which the Japanese would be returning to their ship, Captain Okada would send a boat ashore to pick up the others, in order to return the hospitality. Then, hissing and bowing, the slant-eyed pair departed. The General and Fergus retired to the room they shared. Father Glascock eyed Prindy again as if surprised to see him there. 'What're we going to do with you?' he asked. 'You want to go over to play with the black kids?' Prindy answered simply by meeting the dark blue eyes and holding them. Glascock shrugged. 'Well . . . have a snooze in a deck-chair. I'll get you a stretcher for tonight.' He went off to his own room.

Prindy dropped into a chair, but certainly not to snooze. He saw a big hermit crab battling across the hot sand outside, evidently seeking a shady spot for digging in. He leapt up and out and grabbed it. The crab at once retreated into its purloined shell. As back in the days of life at the Compound and first playing on a beach, Prindy whistled softly into the shell, bringing the poor creature out begging for mercy from the torture of sound. He put it back where it would have to do the long hot haul all over again. Snores were now coming from the priest's room, real brass-reed snores that seemed to shake the very iron building. Prindy the sound-tormented one now, grimaced, and walked away, heading for the beach. He was in the casuarinas, when he heard something behind him, swung, and saw David approaching. 'Hello,' said David. 'Where you go?'

'Only look-about.'

'I take you, show-him-you, eh?'

They went through to the beach, of which there was now a vast expanse, the tide being well out. Not a sign of life, except that of the little creatures waging their eternal war out on the oozing sand. The blacks had retired to their humpies of bark and casuarina boughs. No dogs as might be expected to challenge intruders. David explained that dogs were prohibited here, as were many other things, like weapons that could be used in fighting, like people who caused trouble, like fornication, like all forms of blackfellow business. He used the word Fornication, and with something like gusto, for all his mincing way of speech and the primness he put into explaining what it meant: 'Dat puggin' when you not properly marrit in church. But dey all fornicate here, I tell you. Dey out dere on lugger now, dem young lubra, fornicatin' wit' dem damn heathen Japs.' He went on to say that Farther Glascock was a fool to trust the Japs, believing that by having them come in here during the spring-tide lay-ups he could keep an eye on them and so control the traffic in black velvet. But, according to David, all that was affected was to make the traffic easier, since otherwise it depended on the chance meeting of the wandering tribes of the mainland with Japs ashore for water and game. Now everybody knew where everybody would be at New Moon and Full. Why did the blacks always turn up here in force with their comeliest girls at such times? Plain as daylight though it was, Father would not see it, said that he had the word of Captain Okada that there would be absolutely no Humbuggin': 'Word of gentleman, he call it. Okada ain't no gentleman. He coloured man . . . like Chinee . . . like you'n'me. He good man, Father. But he don't know nothin' 'bout blackfeller and Jap. No dog, he reckon. Plenty dog dere. Dat lot hide 'em. Plenty shovel-spear, too. Plenty blackfeller business. Plenty fornication. Dem no good bloody black bastard! You t'ink dat bad talk for missionary-man? Well, it ain't. Not for Catholic Missionary. On'y bad talk for Catholic time you say t'ing like Jesus Bloody Christ, or God Bugger Me.' At that David crossed himself hastily, as if to show that his pronouncements were more in the way of religious instruction than blasphemy.

David said they would go out to the mission schooner, St Francis Xavier. The trim vessel lay out in the permanently deep water, apart from the pearlers. He claimed he was captain and engineer. Grabbing up a small dinghy and hauling it across the sand without apparent effort, he bragged of his usefulness and piety.

So out across the jade water and aboard the ship. She was well appointed, with two cabins and engine room, a spacious hold, fo'c'stle, all spick and span. When they went up in the bow David had Prindy lean over to touch a piece of varnished wood screwed to the bowsprit. To do so, he explained, would give him some of the good luck invested in the ship through carrying that bit of wood. It was a piece of the timber of the ship the great missionary, Francis Xavier, Apostle of the Indies and Patron Saint of Australia, as David described him in parrot-sounding phrases, had sailed in when bringing Christ to heathen Asia. That ship was so blessed that it had never rotted away like others, and so had been sawn into little bits for attaching to ships like this, which then shared its blessedness: 'Dat Saint Francis Xavier, too, he so bloody holy, when he die he don't rot neither. He dere now, in some big church, all-same when alive.' David sighed. 'I like to be like dat, too, meself. Francis Xavier, he not always good man. Like me before, he fornicator, drinkin' man, proper no-good. Reckon he might be a Protestant, too. But he seen Light, like me. Catholic Church wonderful t'ing. Better'n woman. I marrit dat church now. More better you come Catholic, too . . . chuck up dat no-good blackfeller bijnitch. I ask Father for you. Well, come on, now, I show-him-you church.'

Back to shore, and up through the casuarinas. The church was much more impressive within. They paused in the porch, where after dipping fingers in the holy water stoop, crossing himself, and genuflecting, David led the way in, pointing things out, with lips, naming them in a reverent whisper. It was sizeable, although having only a couple of sets of pews up in front, the rest of the seating the bare antbed floor, the polish of which testified to its use as such. Prindy was wide-eyed with interest.

They went up the left side, looking at the framed prints depicting the Stations of the Cross, and so to the Shrine of the Virgin. The statue was half life-size, of plaster, garishly painted in Italian style. David projected his lips to St Joseph's shrine in the recess of the other side, explaining that these were the actual parents of Jesus. Jesus himself, also in plaster and of similar size, but unpainted save for the nasty red of the wounds, hung, as ever, on the cross, up above the pulpit. As they came to look at the Crucifix, David said that Jesus was also the son of God, but without explanation or apparently impressing his companion. Still, Prindy was plainly interested in the Crucifix, probably the first he'd ever seen, and maybe seeing it as what he might have heard was called by Jews The Hanged God of the *Goyim*, which could have meaning only when the thing was seen.

David genuflected deeply to the altar, and drew Prindy to kneel with him at the communion rail, while he himself prayed in what might be taken for Latin, and the boy stared at the red lamp hanging before the altar, which well might be taken for the unwinking eye of some one-eyed god. Then they went round past the sad-looking Joseph, who it seemed shared fatherhood of the Hanged One along with God, somewhat in blackfellow fashion, followed the Stations back to the porch, where with more genuflexion and stoop-dipping and sign-language back to Jesus on the part of David, they went out.

Next was the Boys' School, where David said he worked as a teacher. The place was not a bit conventionally equipped. For a start, it was furnished rather like a bush-workers' camp, with saplings and antbed, and to judge by the eating gear stowed with scholastic materials, also served as dining-room. Books and pictures, slates and children's abacuses betrayed it as being at infant level. Yet it adjoined another building, a huge barn of a place, fitted out as a workshop, with everything from carpenter's chisels to oxywelding plant. What appeared most to catch Prindy's interest was a large garish Sacred Heart picture on the wall behind the teacher's table. Not only did the heart drip blood, but belched flames from the truncated *vena cava*, while yet the owner's face looked utterly benign, with a bleeding hand raised in benediction. David explained what it was, adding that he had one like it in his own quarters behind here, and that every Catholic must have one: to keep the Devil out, he said.

Further back was the boy's dormitory and playground, looking rather like the old Halfcaste Home back in Town, by reason of the fencing. Naturally it must be fenced, since wild things were being dealt with. Black kids lined the fence to stare. Prindy showed no interest in them. David led him back to the street, and across to the communal kitchen, where the clash of pots and pans and sound of voices told of cleaning up what had gone to cook that awful meal.

Evidently David had no intention of entering the place, and by the sharp looks shot at him as he and Prindy appeared in the doorway, would not have been a bit welcome. But the situation here was out of his hands. Of the several dark female faces that glared the swift hostility, one changed as swiftly to expression of delight, this the lightest complected of them all; and a voice shrieked from it, 'Prindy . . . Prindy!' A rush of bare feet. Bare sweaty brown arms enfolded him to an ample bosom. It was Nunji Barbu, spouse of Barbu Ram. She babbled her delight in seeing him, held him off to view his fine outfit, squealed with delight over his report on his being here. There also, chuckling with delight, touching him, was the eldest Barbu daughter, Paddi. They told him that the second, Indimali, had run away with a Malay working with the Japs. But Savitra was here, in the kid girls' compound. He wanted to see her, insisted on it; although they told him it was impossible. However, they showed him the place through the back door. It was something like that belonging to the boys, or vise versa, as one saw it. They told him that he would have Mother and Sister after him if he went near it. But there suddenly was someone breaking from the knot of girls in blue uniforms playing under the trees behind the high net fence. He broke from the kitchen and ran to meet it.

'Prindy . . . Prindy!' squealed Savitra, clutching at him through the netting, shoving her lovely little old-rose mouth and chocolate nose through for him to kiss. They had only a moment of it, when ripped apart by a sharp voice, female, sounding like a hen's high-pitched cackle of alarm: 'What's going on here, I'd loike to know?'

They turned to look. Bustling up on Savitra's side of the fence was a figure in voluminous white and black. Another of its like was following. Savitra leapt back from the fence. Prindy still stood, staring. The first of the nuns came up, puffing. She was old, with pale face seamed in segments like the belly-hide of a crocodile, the condition probably enhanced by the tight starched barb beneath the black hood. She demanded of Savitra in a voice with a hint of a brogue, 'And who moight this boy be, Barbara?'

In a tiny voice Savitra called Barbara answered, 'He my 'usband, Reverend Mother.'

The faded blue eyes widened. The leathery cheeks jerked. The cackle rose: 'Did I hear roight, choild? Say it again.'

Savrita murmured it to the ground, to a chocolate toe describing an arc in the ruddy dust. The Reverend Mother gasped, turning to her companion as she came up: 'Her husband she says it is, Sister Dymphna . . . her husband! Did you ever hear the loike?'

The other was much younger, and even beautiful, again with enhancement of her looks probably due to the constriction of her face. Her eyes, grey as Prindy's, met his in an astonished stare. The Reverend Mother looked back at the children. 'What haythen business is this?' When Prindy only continued to stare at her, at all of her, including the Hanged God in silver hanging from her waist on a string of great black beads, she demanded, 'Answer me, boy! Who are you? Where do you come from?'

But David was now there to answer, to explain, with cringing verbosity, evidently having learnt the facts from the kitchen. The old nun silenced him: 'Hold your whisht, man!' She turned to Sister Dymphna, to catch her smiling at Prindy, and frowning disapproval that instantly obliterated the smile, said, 'The doings of that black old divil, Ali Barba.' She swung back on the children. 'We'll have no such haythen business here. You, Barbara, back to the other girls.' Savitra, no doubt renamed to exorcise her heathen origins, with a swift under-browed glance at Prindy, obeyed. The Reverend Mother clapped her hands sharply to disperse the black and tan mob in blue who had been gradually converging. Then she turned to Prindy. 'You, boy, go back to your Gineral . . . and don't let me catch you hanging round here again.'

David placed an arm about Prindy's shoulders, turned him round. Prindy shot a last glance at Sister Dymphna, who being unwatched, smiled again. He let his lips move ever so slightly in response.

At the Presbytery they were up and yawning over tea Father Glascock had made, as he said, 'To be sure we've had a real cup of tea before they start serving that pale green piss of theirs they call *cha*.'

General Esk chuckled over the remark, but said, 'From what I understand of them, they're very fussy over their *cha*, even revering it somewhat . . . isn't that so, Fergus? I'm afraid, Father, we are in many ways the Hairy Barbarians they're supposed to call us behind our backs.'

'Hairy barbarian or not, General, I like my cup of tea my own way. Anyway, here they come.'

Hand in hand, like a couple of schoolgirls, two stockily diminutive men were emerging from the casuarinas. They wore spotless white singlets and khaki shorts and small towels wrapped about their heads, so that the bristly black hair stuck up like the tips of brushes, this the only hair apparent on their brassy bodies. Apparently they had no English, or as Humble Men could not use it in the circumstances. They merely hissed and bowed, then fell in behind the party as it went towards the beach, looking only confused when their superiors tried to have them with them. Thus out to a row-boat rolling on the edge of the now incoming tide. At the last moment the humble ones raced ahead to drag the boat in so that the others might enter it dry shod, then with strength amazing in men so small, put it afloat and leapt in to row.

No admiral's barge could have been more ceremoniously received than the row-boat when it reached the big lugger of Captain Okada, who dressed in white kimono but wearing a little black peaked nautical cap, bowed to the horizontal. To Esk, the first to mount the scrubbed-white little boarding ladder, he said, 'Werracoming, Generar Sir, in my poor humber ship-o.' He bowed to the other guests less formally. Sakamura and another small man, also in kimonos, but without the cap, also bowed. The rest of the ship's complement appeared to be standing at stations. The confessed poverty and humbleness of the ship was expressed with perfection of order and cleanliness. The visitors were bowed to a snowy awning slung amidships, to canvas chairs ranged about the hatch. When they were seated, the Captain and his aides stepped onto the hatch and sank down to squat on mats. Captain Okada clapped his large square brown hands, raised his harsh voice in what sounded like military command. In a moment two small men, wearing what appeared to be the uniform of crewmen, the singlet and shorts, but also in aprons, were there with laden trays and bottles, which they set on the hatch. There was Japanese beer and spirits and odd-looking bits in small bowls.

The Captain filled glasses with beer, had them handed round, then raising his glass, said, 'To great Hempirer of Japan and great Hempirer of British Hempirer!' The response came from the whole ship's company in a shout: *Banzai*! The guests, looking at a loss, merely raised their glasses.

Then Captain Okada gave another command, which caused a shining brass bell to be rung loudly. The result of this was the almost immediate approach of other small boats each bringing a white-clad figure dressed in European style. There were about ten of them, the Diver-divers, as Okada described them, or Chief Divers, as Father Glascock translated in a whisper to his fellows. The Diver-divers, although each as punctilious in acknowledgement of the visitors as the Captain had been, were not introduced, but having paid their elaborate respects, stepped onto the hatch to range themselves behind their chief and, except for whispered asides between themselves, remained silent throughout the whole odd procedure. In fact, Captain Oakada did practically all the talking for his side, but about what was anybody's guess, that is when he spoke in what seemed to be English, which was most of the time. The translating dictionary and Fergus's small knowledge and Sakamura's caste limitations did little to help. However, it would appear that the chief topic of conversation was The Great East Asia Co-Prosperity Sphere, which Okada seemed to regard as something religious rather than political. Thus while the tipple was swigged and the dainties consumed. Twice the Captain, who was drinking a lot of beer, rose, and with a bow to his guests, went to the rail and piddled over the side. No one else of his tribe appeared to have the right to do so, or at any rate the need. None of the others dared it, till at last Prindy did. Fergus then leapt up to follow him, and while peeing, whispered to him. As they came back, Prindy bowed to the Captain, and said, '*O mi o shobi, Sensei San.*' The Captain grinned, then slapped his thigh and uttered a guffaw, then slapped his other thigh and roared with laughter, with all his men joining in, and the guests as well, even though Esk kept asking what the joke was. Fergus eventually was able to explain what Prindy had said in literal translation: *Very honourable pissing, Captain Sir*. At least it had the effect of attracting a lot of attention to the boy. In asides to his companions, Fergus said that from what he could make out from asides of the others, there was debate about whose son Prindy was and that opinion favoured Father Glascock. But he could have been up to his tricks.

Thus till sunset, and the young Moon swinging in lilac. Then on a raucous order from the Captain a great meal appeared, consisting of all sorts of odd things, together with wooden buckets of steaming rice and pots of that beverage called variously *O Cha* and *Green Piss*. Prindy appeared to be fascinated by the way the hosts were able to *drink* the honourable green stuff off their chopsticks!

It was quite dark, except for the hanging Moon and the stars and the hissing pressure lantern that had been lit and the littler lights of the rest of the fleet, when with much bowing and hissing the party broke up, at least to the extent of the departure of the Diver-divers. What was to ensue was unexplained. Bowing, the kimonoed hosts went below. Father Glascock remarked on the lateness of the hour, the need of his getting ashore to conduct Vespers. 'Mother Mathias'll be ramping,' he said. 'She's an awful stickler for time. She missed her vocation, I think. She ought've been running a railway.' Although the others laughed, he looked troubled, adding: 'May the Good Lord forgive me for saying it, but not the least of the crosses I have to bear is the Reverend Mother.'

General Esk said, 'You're probably too closely confined together. It's a pity we couldn't have had the Jewish lady. The Reverend Mother seemed very keen on the idea . . . change, eh what?'

'Another woman to gang up on me,' growled the priest.

Esk chuckled, 'Actually, I've found the old lady very pleasant . . . a heart of gold, in fact, hidden beneath that stiff-starched habit.'

'Altar gold . . . which is largely brass. Besides, you're giving a gift of a hundred pounds to her convent.'

But there were Captain Okada and Engineer Sakamura back on deck, rigged out again in whites as earlier in the day, evidently for going ashore. Okada was carrying something, which in the light of the lantern was revealed to be a marine growth, a form of coral, looking rather like a small tree, having no particular colour, just a greenish brown, its attractiveness being in the extreme delicacy of its appendages. Okada bowed, saying, 'Present for Generah Sir.' He presented it to the General with both hands.

Evidently surprised, Esk took the thing as handed, murmuring, 'By jove, now!' His nose was seen to wrinkle slightly; and small wonder, when the thing smelt like a long-dead fish.

Okada said, 'Dry, you paint.'

'Oh, yes,' murmured the General, looking quite ill at ease, balancing the dainty thing, which was all of three feet in height, with a lump of rough coral at the bottom.

The rasping voice went on, 'Hithy hathom, that one.'

Esk rolled his eyes at Fergus, who said: 'They have difficulty with F's as well as L's. Might be Fifty Fathoms . . . the depth it was taken at, eh?'

Okada nodded and repeated the abomination, adding: 'Too dear.'

This time it was Father Glascock who came to the rescue of the rolling blue eyes: 'Pijin . . . meaning it's very valuable.'

'Oh, oh . . . thank you very much, Captain,' said Esk. 'I'm much obliged.

I assure you I'll treasure it.' Still, he could not hide that English look of distaste at an alien oddity or keep his nose from wrinkling.

'We go, yes,' rasped the Captain, and called an order.

It was a bigger boat this time. Okada took the coral tree again as the General was handed aboard by the crewmen and placed in the stern sheets, where he himself joined him. Now Sakamura took the coral and went forward to the small thwart there. Father Glascock and Fergus were seated amidships, with Prindy between them. The crewmen took their positions just ahead of the midships thwart, standing to row, murmuring some Nipponese fishermen's chant in measure with their long strong sweeping strokes, following the silver wake of the Moon. Phosphorescence trailed behind them, glowed around them with the struggles going on below. Prindy craned to look. Captain Okada sighed gustily, remarked, 'Like Inrand Sea, Japan.' Perhaps he was harking back, smelling again the scent of true jasmine, of cherry blossom, the hot sulphurous breath of that symbol of Nippon, that combination of beauty and menace, Fuji San, because he seemed to be looking far away, far beyond the dark line of the shore. Esk's eyes, looking troubled, were fixed on the silvery gossamer, as it was now against the Moon, of the coral tree, as if things he'd believed he understood had suddenly become deep mysteries. It might have been that everybody aboard felt like that through some magic of the night. The rowers fell silent, their only sounds now their steady breathing and the faint creak of rollocks and gentle splash of oars.

Prindy broke the spell by turning suddenly between his companions to cock an ear towards the shore. 'What's the matter, mate?' Fergus murmured.

Listening, Prindy took a moment to answer, 'Music.'

The others craned to listen. Fergus said, 'You can be pretty sure he's right. He's got the keenest hearing I ever struck.'

The priest grunted, 'I don't doubt he's right. I've also got a fair idea what it is too . . . a reception committee . . . for me.'

'How's that?' asked Fergus.

'The convent choir. The Reverend Ladies' little birdies never sing so sweet as when put to it for the purpose of reminding me of a neglected duty . . . rising late for early Mass, or otherwise not running to Mother Mathias's time-table. It is singing, boy?'

Prindy nodded, and began to sing softly to himself: 'Ah-ah-ah-ah . . . ah-ah . . . '

'Schubert's *Ave Maria*,' said the priest. 'You've certainly got good ears, sonny.'

Okada asked, 'What's matter you?'

'Children singing ashore, Captain.'

Okada stilled his rowers, cupped an ear: 'Must my ear no good. Too much deep dive, I stink.'

But only one pair of ears could hear it as yet; while the voice repeated the hearing in a whisper. It wasn't easy hearing, with the breeze rolling inshore with the tide.

Then there it was for everybody's ears, rising, as the breeze waned, waning as it waxed, faint as far bird-calling to begin with, at length to become that sweetest of all sounds on earth, and surely in the universe, the singing of children in harmony, sweeter because it is always somewhat sad, as if children know deeply that it is expression of their innocence, of a loveliness that cannot last: *Santa Maria, Maria, Maria . . . ora pro nobis . . . ora, ora, ora pro no-o-bis . . . ave, ave, ave . . . Ave Mar-ee-ee-ah*!

Tears glistened in the eyes of Captain Okada. Father Glascock saw them and drooped his dark shaggy head. Esk also drooped his silvery head, murmuring, 'How unutterably sweet!'

Okada muttered thickly, 'Hive rirra one I have at home.'

While the crewmen pulled softly to the beat that seemed to come dancing in sparkling leaps across the sea, to strike against the small golden face now fully turned to it and drinking it in with silent-moving lips: *Ave, ave, ave Mar-ee-ee-ah*!

As the boat neared the shore, with the Moon now in the casuarinas, the choir was to be seen only as a darker patch in dappled shadow reaching almost to the water's edge – except for her of the white habit, whose silver hands controlled the singing and brought it to the final softly fading note – *Ah — vay*!

It was Sister Dymphna, easily recognizable by her stately slenderness compared with her dumpy superior, and then by a pearly glimpse of her lovely face as she turned at the beaching of the boat.

Father Glascock, barefoot and with pants rolled to the knees, was first out of the boats, saying, evidently to Fergus and the General, 'Must away. I leave friends to you. Excuse, Captain.' He went trotting up the beach, keeping to the left to pass the ranked choir, bowing slightly to the nun, but addressing the children: 'Good evening, children. Your singing was very nice. I'll give you a present for it . . . mango jam . . . that all right?' They giggled.

He passed them, was amongst the first of the casuarinas, when a shadow stirred and startled him with a cackling old voice: ' 'Tis ayvenin' you call it, Father?'

Halted, he bent to put on the Japanese scuffs and roll down his pants, grunting, 'We've discussed the usage of the word *Evening* before, Reverend Mother . . . which in English, the language we teach, is that period between the onset of darkness and normal bedtime . . . .'

The cackling voice rose: 'Depending on what you call normal, Your Reverence. Bedtime for my children tonoight is going to be annything but that.'

Rising, he hissed at her, 'Madam . . . keep a hold of your tongue! There are gentlemen behind us.'

The cackle dropped to a fierce whisper, 'Don't *Madam* me . . . I've a toitle of my own!'

He sighed gustily, went on his way – but with her beside him, still at it, even if with the dry old voice subdued: 'And if it's the Orientals you'd be referring to as gintlemen, then I'm remoinded that it's not so long since Your Reverence was calling them Slant-eyed Despoilers of the innocents of your flock . . . and with all due respect to your cloth and your English usage, Bloody Spies into the bargain!'

He broke into a run, caught a scuff in a root, fell to hands and knees. The old woman chuckled deeply, calling after him as he rose and went on, 'Haven't I always said those Japanese shoon were made only for cloven hoofs?'

She turned at sound of steps behind her. General Esk greeted her, 'Good evening, Reverend Mother. A lovely set of song birds you have.'

'Goodnight, Gineral. Yes, indeed . . . if they were as good at everything else as they are at singing, the instruction of them would be another story. Now, if you'll excuse me, I'll be seeing to getting them along to Vespers.'

'We'll be along, too, Your Reverence.'

'Indeed . . . and that'll be a high honour for all of us . . . including yourselves.'

The church was lit with two pressure lamps, one hanging in the porch, the other behind in the sacristy, combining to make a holy twilight in which the altar candles burnt reverently, touching things as it were with tiny tongues of fire, even the bent knees and drooped jowl of the Hanged God. David, wearing scarlet cassock and lace-edged alb and black biretta and an air of deep piety, placed the visitors in a front pew. The other front pew was occupied by parti-coloured females, including the two Barbus from the kitchen, with Mother Mathias sitting dragon-like at the inner end as if to protect them from the Haythens across the bit of aisle. Other respectably clad adults filled the rest. The captive boys were packed in a mass, sitting on forms, with St Joseph to keep an eye on them. The girls were on the other side, more carefully watched by Sister Dymphna, since the Virgin before them looked too smug with beatification to care what anybody did; and doubtless anything was likely to happen to those black maids, to judge by the glittering eyes in black faces crowded behind and peering through the louvres from outside. Sister Dymphna was seated alone, looking over an harmonium, which was crying softly. Prindy, seated with the visitors, every now and then craned to see over that other side, perhaps interested only in the little organ, and not the fact that his wife was there in the choir, as the sharp intervening glances of Mother Mathias seemed to suggest.

Then there was Father Glascock, brilliantly gowned in white and gold and purple, tasselled biretta on his head, looking a very different person, indeed not looking a mere person at all, but a priest, and acting it, the way he walked, with eyes downcast, hands piously folded. Behind him came David, swinging the censer, the smoke of which rushed to the candles like holy breath, causing them to flicker – as it were, to genuflect. Behind David were two boy acolytes, similarly attired, but with faces black as their small birettas. As all made obeisance before the altar, the harmonium's crying rose into the shout of the *Te Deum*, which the choir took up, so much more powerful of voice with the rearing corrugated iron roof to give resonance.

The priest went through the liturgy, mumbling and murmuring, with incomprehensible and seemingly inconsequential asides from his aides, all three bowing and kneeling and crossing over. Then he climbed into the pulpit beneath his dead white god, and proceeded to harangue his flock in a mixture of English, Murringlitch, and local lingo, the burden of his address being the benefits this thing he represented offered to everybody with the savvy to accept it, but with some cracking at those who weren't playing the game as far as practical contracts were concerned. These contracts would be those entered into whereby youngsters of the tribes were hired by the Mission from their elders for a price until they reached maturity. It would seem that some of the hirers were pressing for further payments, since having disbursed the primary one in profligacy, and others were breaking the contracts by sneaking the objects contracted for away. But none of this no-good bijnitch would work, for the simple reason that Him Up Top There was watching all the while and telling him, Father Glascock, exactly what was going on and who was doing it. So look out!

In all it lasted about forty-five minutes, perhaps cut down because Mother Mathias, who would be keeping the time, if what Father Glascock had said of her and her timetables was correct, came to heaving about and sighing. Then as the choir sang *Faith of My Fathers*, to somewhat different words from the original, as was only to be expected, first the boys marched out, led by Brother David, and then the choir itself, led by Sister and tailed by Mother, both parties heading for their dormitories. The blacks vanished like grey ghosts. The visitors waited while Father Glascock became a man again, then went with him to his presbytery.

With the Gift from the Deep standing like a talisman between them, so fairy-like in the glare of the hissing lamp and yet so fish-foul, priest and guests sat drinking brandy, and talking, talking. They talked as it were out of corners, half-hidden, out of shyness, awkwardness, suspicion of each other, such their appearance about the table in the overbright half-hooded light and the manner of their having to pass the conversation in bits from one to another to make sense of it; if indeed true sense were got from it at all, what with the difficulty of language and the subjects. These latter were those usually avoided in merely friendly company: religion and politics. In the circumstances, perhaps, there were no others.

To the evident astonishment of the Europeans, it was revealed that the religion of Japan was what was summed up by both Japanese as Shinto-Buddo-Christo. Thus it seemed that the Japanese had religion to serve them in all ways, or as Father Glascock declared, while inclined to argue about it, a Hotchpotch Religion. Perhaps it was the amount they drank while trying to work out the religious conundrum that rendered them all somewhat drunk by the time they got onto politics. Captain Okada, drunker than the rest, for one reason that he swigged the firewater much as he had the beer, and perhaps for another that he had stated later, was much more forthright in declaring his politics than the others. Becoming bombastic, he declared that there was only one Japanese, *Tenno*, known to lesser breeds as the *Mikado* – but he had eighty million heads. At least that's how his vociferating was finally interpreted. A nicely poetic way of claiming perfect national unity, as the General said – although evidently the idea appalled him. Not that the British Hempirer had anything to fear from this, apparently, the way Okada went on. It was the United States of America the myriad-headed *Niponjin No O Kata Gata* was set on bringing to its knees. No mere politeness to present company this, as evident in the Captain's raucous condemnation of American arrogance towards Japan dating from the middle of the last century, when a ship of the US Navy broke the stately isolation of what he called the Japan Ord Rion, by bombarding Yokohama without provocation. Japan Ord Rion was, at some pains, interpreted as Japan the Old Lion. He shouted. 'Ord Rion sreep quiet in Sun. Rong time sreep quiet. By'n'by from West come Tiger . . . *Brrr! Grrr!*

Yrrr! Now Ord Rion say: "Must that bugger Tiger eat him me, spone I not do nothing. Aw right, I put on tiger skin–*Brrr! Grrr! Yrrr!* I give him back." What you stink o' that, eh?' Whatever his audience thought, he began to roar with laughter: 'Ho, ho, ho!' Soon they were all laughing with him, although for probably a different reason, except Sakamura, who only giggled and looked rather troubled, perhaps because he feared his chief was saying too much. Prindy also, long since retired to his stretcher on the other verandah, was not amused, rolling and groaning in interrupted sleep.

Okada wound up his tirade against the Americans with a story of something purported to have happened recently in Shanghai. It seemed that Japanese and American naval ratings, meeting in a bar, took to vying in acts of strength and endurance, in which the Japanese outpointed the Yanks easily. Finally, a brawny Yank, having bared his forearm, took out a sharp knife and, tossing it aloft, as it fell, took the point on his tensed muscle, causing the knife to bounce off. He then picked up the knife, offered it to the rivals, saying: Beat that Jap! One Japanese promptly took the knife, bared his left arm to the biceps, into which he plunged it to the hilt. Thereupon the Americans left. 'What you stink o' that?' Okada demanded again, this time rising, as if to challenge someone to try it out with him. But he staggered. Sakamura leapt to hold him up. The Captain guffawed feebly, 'Too much drink hit my head now . . . from too much deep dive.'

They swayed off the verandah together, turned, goggling with oily slant eyes at the others. Sakamura bowed, said, '*Sayonara.*' Then he swung his chief around and marched him off into the darkness, while the others blinked after them in silence.

It was not for a good half-minute and after they heard Okada burst into raucous song somewhere in the casuarinas, that any of the others spoke. It was the General, saying stiffly, 'Well, there it is . . . *Dai Nippon*, in all its . . . its arrogance.'

'Fanaticism!' grunted Glascock.

'So long's they use the knife on 'emselves,' murmured Fergus. 'The old *hara-kiri*. And speakin' o' *hara-kiri*, I'm off to disembowel myself down the dunny. All that seaweed and bird-shit and stuff they fed us has given me the gripes. Then I'm off to beddo. Got 'o fly tomorrow . . . that right, General . . . or is it today? *Sayonara*!'

'I think I'll retire too,' murmured the General. 'Thank you, Father, for a very pleasant evening . . . .'

'It's noight, man . . . noight . . . even accordin' to proper English usage . . . hic!'

The priest didn't rise as the General went off with exaggerated dignity, but dropped bushy head to arms on the table.

Apparently in any position Father Glascock was the grand snorer. The very bottles and glasses on the table tinkled to the vibrations he soon was sending through it. The cacophony woke Prindy, who after lying under his net listening for a while, got out and stole through to take a look. Evidently completely wakened, returning to his own verandah, he sat in a deck-chair and watched the southern sky. Now the stars there were blotted out by a cloud-mass in which lightning flared and thunder grumbled. The *Waianga* had drifted inland, to be caught by the Old One, who was giving them a bit of hurry-up in the old style. Prindy sang of it softly as he watched, songs he had sung with the Pookarakka, but into which there soon was popping hints of what he had heard in last night's session – *Oshamnu, bogadnu, gozalnu* – until he was singing only that. He rose and went to his bed, got out of pyjama shorts and into his poplin clothes. Then from his suitcase he took the flute, and with it slipped away, going round the back of the house, and heading for the sea. It was noisy away there out on the sea, with the tide rushing through the many channels. Hidden Igulgul up to his tricks. He entered the casuarinas, but to turn about hastily when fiercely attacked by mosquitoes and sandflies, and made his way to the street.

The white buildings looked like phosphorescent night-growths of rain-forest, believed to be spirit-things that glow and fade in signal to each other; as these did in response to the far off fireworks in the sky and the passing of so odd a thing as a lone small golden boy at midnight. Undaunted he made his way up the street, past convent, kitchen, boys' school, all soundless and in darkness. But there was no passing the church. A red eye was watching from it, suddenly to be seen staring unwinking through the open porch. He stopped, to stare back, At length he was drawn to the porch.

Save for that red eye, the sanctuary lamp, inside it was utterly dark. That is to begin with. Slowly things took ghostly shape. Then he entered, slowly, but purposefully by his movement, because, coming to the pews, he chose the one in front across the aisle from that he'd sat in at the service, seating himself at the left end of it, almost directly before the Crucifix. This thing was even plain to see now in the ruby darkness: the sagged knees, the drooped thorn-crowned head, the helpless hopeless spread of arms, the impaled feet: bloodied ghost of Man's dead dream of identifying himself with God?

Strange irony of chance that caused political upheaval on the other side of the world, a boozy party, and hungry mosquitoes, to send a semi-savage boy to lay the ghost by playing to it the very music expressing the ancient wisdom against which, in flesh, it had heriticized at cost of being pinioned for ever. Over ond over, ever so softly, he played the pieces he had come to know of *Yom Kippur: I have Trespassed*, and *Prayer for the Dead*, mingling them, eventually making them into something of his own, in final accomplishment of which he made bold to give it *full voice.*

Then he fell silent, to listen. Still no sound anywhere, except the murmurous violence of the sea and the faint rumbling of that distant warfare in the sky. But that magic in here was at an end. He did not put pipe to lips again, but yawning, shook his spittle from the mouthpiece, then rose, turning his back without ceremony on the dead things of Jesus Business, and headed for the street.

There could be no doubt about what moved him to his next performance: the sheer impishness of the prentice to a sorcerer. The idea must have struck him as he emerged into the street and found, apparently still dead to the world, the community he had risked rousing in the sudden boldness of achievement; for he stopped in his tracks and stared at the signalling ghosts, which alone seemed aware of him. A moment. Then he put pipe to lips again, and softly began to play the vague opening bars of Schubert's *Ave Maria,* which are like the shy approach of a lover to the beloved to whom, after a moment, he is pouring his heart out: *Hail Mary, full of Grace*. The piping rose, clear as the crying of kweeluks. With his ears filled with his own sweet rendering, he would not have heard the almost-instant scuffling, bumping, fearful whispering, which betrayed the fact that his audience was wakeful enough, only so far stunned by his first effort. *Ave, ave, ave* – the flute cried in ecstacy – *Ave Maree-ee-ah, or-or-or-or-or-ra pro no-o-bis . . . beatificat supra omnes muliro-or-or-um . . . Ave, ave . . . ah - - - vay*!

That last long note dissolved, leaving the void of silence deeper than ever – say for five slow breaths. Then pandemonium, subdued, but no less intense: thumping, bumping, squealing, squeaking. Lights glimmered in convent and quarters of kitchen-staff, blazed suddenly. Lights flickered in the girls' dormitory, with a hubbub of young voices rising like the exchanges of scared birds – till quelled by an old bird's peremptory cackling. Silence again. A listening silence now.

The watching imp raised the pipe again. *Ave, ave, ah-ah-ahvay Mar-ee-ee-ah.* Just that much.

Stationary lights leapt again. The louvers of the convent front verandah leaked with light. A fireball of light burst into the street with the opening of the verandah door. Shadows lurched to the swing of a pressure lantern with voluminous draperies. A dimmer light popped out of the staff quarters. Kitchen and convent women were converging. There was also flashing of light from the boys' quarters, clack of voices, thud of feet.

The imp bolted, first for the cover of the church on the northern side, then to the casuarinas. He looked back to judge how things were going. By sights and sounds, an excited advance was being made on the church. Also through on the beach human voices could be heard above those of the returning waters. He slipped into the grove of trees, not to pass through, but to head towards the Presbytery.

Father Glascock was sleeping as before, although not now with nearly so much suggestion of abandonment of priestly dignity. With falling pressure in the lamp and smudging of the mantle, the glare of it had faded to a mere twilight, so that bottles and glasses were mostly hidden, and Japanese-English dictionary and accompanying scribbling-pad close to the dark curly head made it look like that of a worn-out student. Prindy gave him only a glance as he passed, by way of the rear verandah, to his own side. Back at his stretcher, he put away the flute, got into pyjamas again, and under the net. But scarcely had his head touched the pillow, when he sat up quickly at sound of voices in the street. Light was also dancing towards the presbytery.

Feet scattering gravel. Then a cackling voice, high with excitement: 'Father . . . Father!' Steps slapped on the concrete floor before there was a grunt in reply.

'Father . . . there's been a miracle!'

'Eh? Eh . . . what you talking about?'

'An angel in the church, Father . . . .'

'Wha's up . . . you walking in your sleep?'

'An angel, Father . . . as Almighty God's me witness!'

Sister Dymphna's voice, added, shrill as an excited child's: 'An angel playing a flute . . . a divine instrument . . . playing *Ave Maria* . . . .'

The cackle: 'Didn't you hear it?'

'You been dreaming, ladies . . . awp!' The priest's voice ended in a yawn.

'Dreaming, is it? When all these others heard it too? We all heard it plain as . . . as the choir singing . . . plainer, because 'twas hivinly music!'

Father Glascock yawned again: 'Nice to know they play Schubert in Heaven . . . specially when Schubert was probably a Jew – ee-awp!'

'There was other music . . . divoin music, the loike of which I never did hear. I tell you, Father . . . .'

'Tell me in morning . . . when you're properly awake.'

The cackle rose sharply: 'And whan you're properly sober!'

'*Madam*!'

'Don't you Madam me! I tell you . . . .'

'No you won't. I'm off to bed.' Scrape of his chair. Slap of his scuffs.

Mother Mathias fairly screamed, 'Oh, ye of little faith!'

The priest's retort came from his room, 'And you of too much yap!'

'Oh dear, oh dear!' cried the Reverend Mother. 'We have a miracle . . . and no credence even from the one who should be the first to believe. What shall we do, my children? We must have guidance. We can get nothing here . . . only the smell of drink. Come . . . let's go to the church, and ask our Blessed Lady for it . . . come!'

There was some murmuring between the other occupants of the presbytery, on the other side of the iron wall from Prindy. But he wasn't interested now. He dropped back to the pillow, was soon asleep, and remained so, despite the renewed organ recital in Father Glascock's room.

Next morning there was more talk of the disturbance between the presbytery guests, Prindy included. Fergus asked him, 'You've got good ears, mate . . . did you hear any bloomin' angels?'

Prindy answered briefly, 'Kweeluk singing-out middle-night.'

'That's it!' declared Fergus. 'Curlews . . . ahaaaa!'

Father Glascock wasn't there to join in the laugh. He was away at early Mass. Nor was he inclined to laugh when he returned and they discussed it over a breakfast of watery porridge and slimy rissoles, after his reporting that he'd found the church packed with convent females when he went there at dawn, along with a great swarm of mosquitoes that they'd had to smoke out with an extra burning of incense. 'It isn't funny, really. What we're fighting is superstition. This sort of thing only makes what we're doing a turning from one devil-devil to another. With all due respect to Her Reverence . . . she's a bloody old fool!'

General Esk and Prindy heard a first-hand account of the angelic visitant from the Reverend Mother herself, when in midmorning they called on her to take their leave. The General took the precaution to enjoin Prindy not to laugh when he mentioned the matter, saying that to do so would not be The Thing, don't y'know. Prindy took advantage of the injunction to tell the General about Barbu's people and to say that he'd like to say goodbye to them for Barbu. 'Of course,' said Esk. 'We couldn't face our old friend Barbu Ram again without being able to report that his family are well and happy, eh what?' That's how he put it to Mother Mathias. She pursed her seamed old mouth over it; but in view of the extremely polite hearing she had to her story of the Visitant, to say nothing of that fat gift the General was making to the Convent, she could hardly refuse.

Thus Prindy had a last clinging moment with his bride, in the comparative privacy of the kitchen. If there were to be any true reporting back to Barbu Ram, it could only be of the abandonment of his family's grief at this moment.

Father Glascock went with the departing ones to the air-strip, not simply out of politeness, but to give them the benefit of his connexion with Certain Powers by making the sign of the cross over them as they entered the Junkers.

Again Prindy sat with Fergus, the General having said he wanted to ride in the cabin to do some writing. So thumbs-up to Father Glascock and Brother David on the ground, and roll away down wind. A minute of standing on brakes, raging like the Old One at his worst, in the pre-flight run-up. Then away upwind at full gallop, to lift up out of the dusty clutching hands of Mother Earth, into the realm of the Old One; but not yet to climb higher than to make sure that all donks were doing their stuff, and then to swing back in salute to Father and Brother, to clip the tree-tops across to the Mission station, run down the street just above the roofs, with everybody out to wave, even Mother Mathias. Then over the casuarinas and along the beach, to scatter the laughing blacks and uncover their dogs. Out to sea then, and up over the pearling fleet already heading back to their grounds, with the crews waving like human beings, instead of stiff-bowing like wound-up dolls. Over the islets and the whirling snowy clouds of disturbed pigeons. Then the islands were behind, and ahead the southern vista, the green-brown land, backed by the dun wall of the far-off Plateau, and domed by the blue – the blue, the blue.

V

That determined fellow, Fabian Cootes, had reached the sea. From the Junkers, there could be seen his smoke signal rising from a bit of beach, the first dry land to eastward of the involuted debouchment of the Leopold River. A sweep round the locality by the aircraft revealed that it could have been reached easily enough from inland after the river had been crossed higher up. Therefore, whether the Coot could claim that he had made it under his own steam, as he had insisted he was going to do, would be debatable; for judging by the number of canoes on the beach and the crowd of blacks and the fact that the dunnage was still in a heap, the last twenty-five miles or so must have been travelled in pukkah style, and the party not long arrived. No sign of horses, or of the Lily Lagoons blacks, according to sharp-eyed Prindy. Fergus declared that the horses were with the party when he saw them the day before yesterday. He added, speaking over the intercom to General Esk, 'They're going to be mad when they get your message. They were probably going to wait here for the horses, gorging on fish and crabs. Maybe they'll get the blacks to piggy-back 'em to our rendezvous.' The message, or Signal, as the General called it, dropped to the party, instructed them to be waiting at a certain point some thirty miles southwest of here, where the aircraft would be landing in three or four days' time.

The signal acknowledged, the aircraft turned eastward, flying low and over the clear jade of the deeps just beyond the muddy shore line, competing with the sea-eagles for a view of what was going on below. Most interesting and even exciting viewing, revealing creatures some of which were well worth turning back for another look: a mighty devil-fish that surged up from below like a new-born island, and dugongs big as bulls, and basking old-man turtles, and, wonder of wonders to the young co-pilot, a sporting school of young whales. Less interesting denizens of the region were three or four small groups of blacks, either camped on beaches or paddling canoes between the mostly mangrove-cluttered shore and small scattered islands each with its frosting of nesting pigeons.

Thus for about a hundred miles. Then there appeared ahead what at first looked like a sharp northward turn of the coast, but proved to be a substantial island, divided from the mainland by a passage some five miles wide and now white with tide boiling over a maze of reefs. 'Lady Beaumont Island,' yelled Fergus. 'Wonder who the lady was . . . wife of the boss of the toady who reckoned he'd found it, I suppose? You know this place?' Prindy shook his head. Fergus went on: 'All the halfcaste kids from the Old Compound here now . . . the girls, anyway. You might find some old sweethearts. Careful I don't tell 'em you got a wife back on Leopold . . aheeeeah!'

The Mission Station was on the shore of a bay on the eastern side, a much more substantial settlement than that in the Leopolds, since much older. Fully grown coconuts lined the wide white beach; and substantial exotic trees sheltered the neat squares of white buildings. But more interesting, at least to Prindy by the look of him, was the shipping lying in the bay. No mere pearling luggers here. There were two naval vessels, one large and grey, with three funnels and the Union Jack at her bow as well as the White Ensign at her stern, the other by comparison small, white-hulled, with one yellow funnel, well-known as the Australian naval survey sloop *Arafura*, operating out of Port Palmeston. Also there were two trim white schooners, each flying the Cross of Jesus from her peak.

No untidiness on the beach here, like canoes and native humpies. Facing the beach were the bigger buildings, on the verandah of one of which could be seen a line of white-clad figures, as Fergus did a nicely proper fly-past. He remarked, 'Old Tusker Tasker's there, Chief Wow of the local Wowsers . . . and the Naval Brass.' Whether or not he said it as excuse for not doing his usual aerial play-about or merely as information was not disclosed. He swung away, over broad and fertile-looking gardens where black workers stood to wave. Then in a moment they were down – with gyros whimpering.

As one enchanted, Prindy would not be surprised by any of the odd things that continued to happen to him. That his enchantment was accepted by pretty well everyone he had dealings with was evident enough, even if, as usual, most believed they accepted nothing but the work-a-day. The awed peeping and whispering of old acquaintances was acceptance, anyway. None of these presumed to speak to him. He didn't give them a chance, seeming not to see them. Even the Reverend Mr Tasker must have felt looked-through by the calm grey eyes when, on being introduced, he said he was already acquainted with the Young Man. Nor did Mrs Tasker fare any better. As if in an attempt to break the spell, she remarked, in an aside, while seeing to seating at lunch with the company literally glittering with white linen and gold braid, 'My . . . we have become big for our boots, haven't we!'

Mr Tasker had another try by suggesting that the Mission take care of the Young Man while the General went about his business with his naval colleagues. A reasonable enough suggestion; but in it an unmistakable note of vindictiveness. Thanking him, the General said that, apart from feeling responsible for his young friend as the grandson of a man he held in such high esteem as Jeremy Delacy, he was sure no boy of ten would be anything but broken-hearted to miss the chance of spending a couple of days aboard warships. Mr Tasker, with what seemed like a slight sneer, remarked that it would depend on the boy's background. The General countered that with a chuckle, 'This young chappie's background didn't prevent him doing most of the flying to get us here . . . eh what, Fergus, dear boy?'

The official business was to include a conference on coastal defence matters aboard H.M.S. *Durbah*, and a short oceanographic cruise in H.M.A.S. *Arafura*.

Immediately after lunch, the official party adjourned for their business. accompanied to the jetty, where a pinnace lay, by the Missionaries, that is the local Superintendent and his wife and Mr Tasker and his, and peeped at by numberless dark eyes wide with wonder at the sight. What a sight: to see one who had shared the squalor and ignominy of their breed, walking so easily in such proud company, to be received as part of it by the stiffly standing crew of the pinnace, to be handed aboard the sleek vessel as if he were a princeling!

Indeed, it was as a prince or some such exalted being that Prindy was received aboard the cruiser. Captain Silskin himself handed him over to a special steward for conducting to a stateroom he was to share with the General. Having bowed him into the cosy place, stowed his luggage and shown him bedroom and bathroom, bowing himself out, the steward said, 'Hif yer 'oiness wishes summink, jes' ring, sir . . . there's the bell.' He meant it, too, the way his pale blue English eyes rolled and his paler forehead rumpled.

A little later, while Prindy was contemplating the view from one of the numerous portholes, a knock at the door. A man in trim white uniform, with red and blue badges and peaked cap under arm, was there, who said, 'Chief Petty Hofficer Wilkins, Sir. Captain's orders . . . you would like to make tour inspection of ship, Sir. Hif yer 'oiness is ready nah . . . '

Thus did the sorcerer's apprentice see things in the way of wizardry in doing violence comparable only with what the Old One himself was capable of. It was a pity, perhaps, that his privilege, although undoubtedly regarded by his several guides as something very special, didn't extend to firing one of those great guns or a torpedo or two, to prove the powers they boasted of.

Back in the stateroom, he found General Esk, who told him they would be dining with the Captain, and later, at a gathering of officers of both ships, seeing motion pictures of Imperial Defence activities North of Australia.

After the picture show, Captain Silskin had Esk and Prindy to a private sitting in his own quarters. There Prindy was given a large illustrated book on warships and ginger beer to beguile him, while the men drank brandy and smoked cigars and talked of local naval defence in a manner to suggest that their very meeting had been arranged because of their fears for it in emergency in the hands of those they referred to as the Awstralians. The General said, 'Really, old man, you have to see it to believe it . . . which is why I've got you heah. Complete irresponsibility. These survey sloops have been working this coast for the best part of twenty years . . . and still they're using native pilots who learnt their navigation of the locality from the Japanese. This Commander fellow freely admits it. As I see it, the surveys are only annual naval picnics . . . .'

The Captain cut in with a laugh, 'I understood the Australian Squadron's concentration on Melbourne every November was that.'

'What's this concentration?'

'The whole shebang converges for exercises in Port Philip Bay . . . which means to be at hand to see the running of the Melbourne Cup . . . races, don't y'know . . . Australian equivalent of our Derby.'

'Gad, Sir!'

'Rather shows 'em up as horse-marines, what?' Both laughed. The Captain went on, 'But, of course, they have no real naval tradition, as with us . . . or the Yankees, even who, after all, took it from us . . . out of Devon . . . *Mayflower* and all that. These people came out of the gutters of London. Any nautical tradition they have belongs to the convict ships. I know 'em, old man. We train their officers. There's only two kinds of 'em . . . the toady and the cad. They may make great soldiers . . . but never sailors.'

The General sighed: 'If only I could believe they'd make *real* soldiers, not the mere shock-troops they've only shown as. You fellows can do the naval part of it for 'em . . . you'll have to. But they'll have to defend 'emselves on land . . . and I can't see 'em doing it. Wait till you see this utterly undefended country tomorrow . . . thousands of miles of coast, known only to the Japanese . . . and not a bally Australian concerned about it!' He sighed again: 'You'll see it all tomorrow.'

There next day it was to be seen in the first glimpse of the faces hanging over the rail of the *Arafura*, as the cruiser's pinnace drew up to the gangway, bringing Captain Silskin, the General, Prindy. The faces of guttersnipes, one might easily be moved to call them, at once shrewd and sycophantic, now looking on their betters as such while still holding that they had no betters, an ambiguity that was probably what made the faces look shut, as compared with the open, pinker faces of those below. From street-loafers' lounging there was sudden springing to disciplined attention at a sharp nasal order from the bridge.

Amongst the faces there were familiar ones, too. However, these were very different from the rest, although quizzing no less: black faces, under jack-tar caps. The Aborigines used as what the General had called Pilots were of that tribe of islanders who'd had ruthless control of the Old Compound cook-house at the time of Prindy's induction. A couple of these had been cooks. One raised a hand as if to give sign-language, but dropped it when the grey eyes slid off him as if wiping off his existence.

Aboard the pinnace was the *Durbah*'s Chief Petty Officer Wilkins, still in charge of Prindy, it seemed, and either in accordance with naval formality or his own inclination, bound to transfer the responsibility to his opposite number on the sloop. This was C.P.O. Pickles, as Wilkins named him in introduction. Prindy he named as ' 'Is Young 'Oiness.'

C.P.O. Pickles accepted the responsibility readily enough, although with mean face shutting rather more tightly. However, at first opportunity, when the sloop was under way and he returned from seeing his men settled to their duties, to Prindy standing where he had left him near the roaring funnel, he asked, 'Wha's this 'Ighness business them Poms is givin' you, young feller-me-lad?'

The grey eyes met the quizzing slits of blue in that disconcerting stare, which probably meant no more than it usually did, that the question was not properly understood. It made the slits sheer off, even if it did not immediately quell the gutter-snipe cheekiness: 'Mean to say, you's on'y a creamy Abo kid . . . now ain't you? So 'ow can you be an 'Ighness?' The lean nosy Aussie face swung back, twisted with a grin. ' 'Less you's the son 'o King Billy o' the Brinkins . . . awawawah!'

Prindy looked away, towards the swiftly moving mangroves of the mainland, a couple of miles to starboard, red haze above them, hint of the red wilderness behind.

The man looked at a loss. After a moment he asked, 'Wha's yo' name, anyway?'

Whether it was Aboriginal wariness of betraying identity to a stranger, or a degree of awareness of the situation's implications, Prindy answered promptly, 'Munda Khan.'

'Eh . . . what kind o' name's that?'

'Indian.'

The slyness of the face turned sycophantic. 'Aw . . . I see . . . that's 'ow the 'Ighness comes into it, eh?' A pause. 'But you don' wan' me callin' you Your 'Ighness, do you?' The slits again avoided the questioning grey eyes. 'Them crawlin' Pommy buggers . . . they love that kind o' thing. Different with us. 'S all right callin' officers Sir, and Governors Yo'r Excellency, and things like that. But callin' kids Yo'r 'Ighness . . . aw, strike me pink! 'Less you's real royalty, o' course. But you ain't that, are you?'

Prindy smiled in reply to the ingratiating chuckle, and asked, 'Will you show me engine working?'

'Why, sure, sure . . . come right on down!'

After a couple of hours of steaming eastward, the sloop came to anchor in a bay of small islands. The sloop's pinnace, a roomy vessel, since it did most of the so-called survey work, was lowered. A demonstration of the quality of the work was immediately forthcoming, when the sloop's captain, Lieutenant-Commander Toby, told his guests that he was taking them to the islets for a bit of pigeon shooting. The shotguns produced looked well and truly handled. The General and Captain Silskin went readily enough. Prindy also went, still under the wing of C.P.O. Pickles, who skippered the launch, with one of the ex-cooks swinging the lead in the bow. Pickles instructed his charge in steering, once taking the liberty of putting his cap on the fair head, as reward for his skill and to show how matey they were. But it was not just a picnic. Soundings were made that showed that quite big ships could use the bay; although they would need to have more forthright commanders than Lieutenant-Commander Toby, who declared that whatever the lead said, he wouldn't risk his own ship in there.

Having returned their bag of pigeons to the sloop to be made into pie for dinner tonight, the pinnace headed for the coast, sounding along the edge of the tidal mud, which the Lieutenant-Commander declared he would never trust, even if the soundings did show that some of the channels would take the battleships *Ark Royal* and *Prince of Wales*. Then it was lunch time; and they went up a creek through the mangroves to eat at a spot the Commander promised as a Little Paradise, and where they would be able to bag some more game: geese and duck. Bottles and cigarette packs and rusty cans showed that the paradise was well known, and not only to the like of those now enjoying it, as revealed by the fact that some of the beer bottles were Japanese. Here Captain Silskin somewhat dryly remarked that the Japs would make a happy hunting ground of these parts if and when they invaded. That caused Toby to guffaw, 'If and when they get past *us* you mean, Sir!'

Even more dryly the Captain answered, 'Of course, of course.'

That was the limit of any directly spoken criticism.

From there they returned to the sloop. Up anchor then, and back to Lady Beaumont, where they arrived soon after dark, but to find anything but darkness, what with the blaze of H.M.S. *Durbah*, lights ashore as for some fête, and Igulgul at half his fullness. The fête, it was revealed, was a treat being put on for the Mission by the *Durbah*, including a picture show. Prindy watched the pictures as one of the white-clad elite. Afterwards there was a teetotal supper at the Mission House. Then back to the cruiser and resumption of the status of 'Oiness to go to bed with, while watching through the portholes Igulgul, low over the mainland, swinging to the swing of the big ship to his Shade, the tide.

Next morning, old acquaintances, crowded on the sloping beach, had a grandstand view of how big for his boots a certain one of them had become, when, with General Sir Mark Esk, he was saluted off the *Durbah's* pinnace, and came along the jetty past a line of sailors standing in a stiff row as you did only when Mr Tasker came to look you over. Mr Tasker himself was one of the watching crowd, and evidently so much impressed that he gave his hand readily this time. Not Mrs Tasker, however. Even if she didn't mention the size of one's boots with her mouth, she did with her eyes. Not that it mattered, when His Highness paid her as scant attention as he did the rest. The handshaking was in farewell. Almost at once the departing ones were whisked away to their aircraft.

VI

Fergus Ferris should have known better than to make the Cootes Expedition appear to be only a joke, the way he spoke of his observation of it from the air, when he himself had uttered the warning that, for all his seeming silliness, the Coot was really a shrewd fellow in getting what he went after. This was evident when the rendezvous was made with the party at the spot to which Fergus had suggested its members would have to be piggy-backed by the blacks, to find a situation so far from fiasco that General Esk was impressed not merely to the extent of congratulating the hero, but of agreeing to make official what the shrewd one described as the Appreciation he would be making of the Exercise. As Fergus remarked in an aside to Denzil Dickey, 'Herewith the Coot lays the foundations of his military career.'

Fergus may have done better to try out the drollery on Major Maltravers, since evidently Denzil was still too preoccupied with ethnology and blinded by his temporary leader's brilliance in that direction to see faults he had in any other. Not that Malters appeared to be any better disposed to Fergus. Still, obviously he had come no closer to Fabers, since he took no part in the lively discussion between this temporary leader of his and his proper chief on the subject of the utilization of the inhabitants of the region in the event of war. Natural warriors, Fabers called the local tribesmen, still living much as of old, by virtue of their prowess with arms, disciplined to the limit by their own code, requiring only to be given an inkling of proper military discipline and to have rifles put in their hands, to make them the best guerilla force in the world. Denzil echoed this, almost hysterically.

Nor was it mere talk. Fabers put on a parade of a score or so of young men out of the hundred or so natives they now had with them, who, even if their uniforms were only *nagas* of flour-sack calico, performed with such guardsman-like precision in response to their commander's quite professional parade-ground barking that Fergus remarked to the General, 'Can't you get him busbies for 'em? They look kind of naked as they are.' Esk smiled, but mostly out of politeness, so intense was his interest. He was even more interested when a demonstration was given of the squad's adaptability to firearms, with use of the expedition's only rifle. The target, a little tea-tree, was at three hundred yards, the limit of accuracy for the weapon. Each man was given but one shot. No need for more, when none missed the mark, and without one of the marksmen's seeming to take aim. All that each man did when given the rifle was to raise it breast-high, and with the butt under his arm instead of at his shoulder – *Bang*! – the narrow trunk jumped and showered a little cloud of fragmented bark.

Fabers said the men had no idea of the use of the rifle's sights. 'Nor any need of 'em, by jove!' the General commented 'The blighters are equipped with in-built range-finders. Marvellous, old man, marvellous!'

Further evidence of this adaptability was the camp itself, set up by his black squad, according to the Coot: bush-houses for accommodation, a mess, a cook-house, no mere blackfellow humpies, but neat jobs done with the axe. Even the bark humpies of the others, hasty shelters from the rain of the other night, were placed with some semblance of order about the water-hole; although, as Fabers stressed, with due consideration for tribal convention. 'To get maximum co-operation,' he said, 'we must operate with a minimum of interference with their way of life'. He went on to say that the majority of the blacks were gathered for an annual Increase ritual concerned with the *Booroo-looloogun*, or Nutmeg Pigeon Totem. A big corroboree was due to be held at a site at the foot of the Plateau, only five miles or so from here. It would already have been under way, only that he had induced the performers to wait for the coming of the Number-one Soldier Man, the idea being not merely to entertain him, but more importantly to win the people's certain allegiance through showing interest in their ways, as opposed to the usual coercion to the white-man's.

When Esk expressed himself as delighted over both the compliment to himself and the cleverness of the move, Denzil, dithering with excitement in new knowledge, leapt into it: 'If only we'd done this sort of thing in the early days of the Empire, Sah . . . in the Sudan, Somaliland, Afghanistan, everywhere, pretty well . . . so much unnecessary bloodshed, Sah!'

Esk chuckled: 'If your gallant father heard you saying that!'

'Sah?'

'Might kill him. There's still a lot of glory attached to that bloodshed, don't y'know.'

'But, Sah . . . .'

'Mainly jokin', dear boy. I congratulate you on your modern outlook. Brains rather than blood and guts, what, Fabers, old man?'

It was then the shrewd Fabers saw his chance to ask that his Appreciation be submitted to Army HQ: 'To give me immediate status, in the event of hostilities . . . if you see what I mean, General.'

By the look that Esk gave him, he saw clearly enough the ambitious boy, but seemed no less impressed.

Then military business went by the board, at least as far as the ambitious boy was concerned, at mention of the fact that amongst what had been brought to reprovision the expedition was fresh stuff from the Mission and the warships: beef, vegetables and fruit, bread and butter, and – Fabers let out a whoop at the naming of it, 'Boy, oh boy!' – a pot of English raspberry jam, specially procured from H.M.S. *Durbah*. He lost no time in preparing a large panful of steak and eggs and onions – for himself. As he explained to the General, when he found him staring while he wolfed it and Malters was cooking for the rest, 'I always do my own cooking, when possible.' He added with a greasy smirk, 'I don't know a better cook.'

Fergus remarked, 'Should put some of the lard back on you, Cootsey, old piggy.'

It was a fact that the Coot had lost an awful lot of the upholstery that formerly had helped him to look Napoleonic. The flesh hung on him in sadly depleted bags. Had Bonaparte been truly depicted in that famous picture of his retreat from Moscow he must have looked rather like that.

Indeed, all four white members of the expedition looked much the worse for wear. Denzil and Malters were shadows of their former well-fed selves, their pink Pommyness in sunburnt rags. Professor St Clair, although as a bushman born less obviously battered by the wilderness, looked so wearied that Esk tried to induce him to give up and come back with him to civilized comfort. St Clair sighed; 'I'll be getting enough of that in a Public Servant's chair. I'll see it through. The least I can do is to get to know these people in their natural state, if I'm to direct their destiny. We're lucky we fell in with these Pigeon People. I'd like to do an academic paper again, before I get caught up in officialdom.'

An example of the finesse demanded of anyone dealing with people they might be inclined to regard as simple savages, was almost immediately forthcoming in the matter of sharing the good things brought by the aeroplane. There was plenty for everybody: at least a hundredweight of meat, several sacks of flour, treacle, trade-tobacco. The Coot, as the most knowledgeable, should have been equal to the demand. As it was, of course, he was preoccupied with his own belly at the time of the dole-out to the blacks, which he left to Denzil, perhaps as a kind of Anthropological Exercise. Nevertheless, had he been as wise as he pretended, he surely would not have indulged in roaring like any bullying *kuttabah* as a preliminary to settling the dispute over distribution, which, fortunately for him, was noisy enough to hide his *faux pas* from his fellow *kuttabahs*, at the time preoccupied with their turn at feeding. Thus he was able to lay the blame for it on Denzil, who seemed happy enough to accept it, the way he dropped knife and fork for pencil, to take down the clever Fabers' dissertation on what he claimed were the Facts, delivered between nibbles at Denzil's neglected bread and butter, plastered with raspberry jam.

According to the Coot, the cause of the dispute was that the black mob generally were bound to pay the Pigeon Totem People, the Boorooloologun, for the right to conduct the ceremony and to gorge on their spiritual kinsmen during the season of their stay amongst them, and that the Boorooloologun had decided to settle the matter of the fee then and there by taking *all* of the *kuttabah's* largesse, while the others argued that it couldn't be done with what amounted to foreign currency. It seemed that the parties already were at loggerheads over outstanding payments. Prindy helped with the translating, having some knowledge of the local lingo, while the disputants had practically no English and others not enough for subtleties. However the Coot failed to acknowledge this assistance in reporting back to his comrades, giving the impression that he had handled it pretty well alone. Thus he missed a very important ethnical point raised at the very end of the disputation, in fact the very terms of settlement. Prindy confided this to Fergus only. It was that unless granted what they demanded, the Boorooloologun would immediately return to the coast, and thenceforth the others wouldn't be able to eat a nutmeg pigeon without becoming mortally ill. Still, the Coot's report was enough to show that but for his cleverness the whole thing might well have been cruelled, and to cause General Esk to say, 'Thanks, old man. What you've done might prove to be of inestimable value in the event of military action here. To impress these people now with our generosity, friendliness, and tact, when they seem to be getting anything like it only from the Japs themselves, could be vital.'

Hence it eventuated that the Boorooloologun, men, women, children, dogs, settled down to a great feast of charred steak and sod-centred damper and lashings of treacle, while the rest, empty-bellied and carrying nothing but their usual impedimenta, somewhat disconsolately broke camp and headed for the site at the foot of the Plateau. After all, their part of the ceremonial was due to begin in the middle of the afternoon, with the rising of Igulgul, while that of the Pigeon People would not be till night, when they would come to dance and cry in mourning for their totemic kinsmen, who by then would be digesting in the swollen bellies of those sitting around sleepily watching them.

The whites waited till about an hour before the appointed time, then set out for the green and red wall that was the rain-forest-hung northern escarpment, on horseback, and also taking along a couple of packs with camping gear, because it looked likely to rain. They had been instructed where to go, but could have got there anyway, with Prindy leading instead of Generals

Esk and Fabers, since it was that same spot where he had camped with Bobwirridirridi. He didn't mention the fact to anyone.

The site was in its usual frenetic state for this time of day at this time of year, with cliff-hanging trees fairly heaving to the activities of the gobbling gossiping pigeons – *Wallaka-woo, wallaka-woo* – the blue air flickering with the manoeuvrings of the wheeling diving feathered predators, but with the addition of the human elements, the black crowd milling about on the sandy red earth, making no more show of stealth in their preparations for predacity than their counterparts above, preparing the *piendi* ovens, decorating themselves for ritualization of the slaughter. If the pigeons noticed the additional menace, they showed no sign of it, wallaka-wooing away without let, perhaps accepting it as part of their existence. The miracle of it was that a species so indifferent to survival and burdened with such limitations for it, as the odd mode of feeding their young, should be in existence at all. This was the burden of the talk of the whitemen settling down to watch.

Fergus, knowledgeable in Australiana because of his greater mobility, told the others of how, in fact, with the coming of intense white settlement, the species had been virtually exterminated on the Eastern Coast, where it had been even more numerous by reason of the much greater rain-forest areas and multiplicity of off-shore breeding islets. An odd thing about the discussion was that, although there were three qualified Anthropologists and one half-baked in the company, it didn't appear to occur to any one of the company that the difference between the situations, that is on North Coast and East, might be the very thing they were gathered to witness, namely, the Increase Ritual, long since unpractised on the East Coast, where the Aborigines had been the first of the indigenous species to be eliminated. Could not one suppose that, in dabbling in magic as these experts did, even if only out of curiosity, some sense of it in the scheme of things would not have rubbed off on them?

All this pother went on for about an hour, while the Sun, still holding off that cloud-mass drifting in from the northwest, got down into the tree-tops, so that by the direct light of it a scarlet glimpse could be had through the trees of the flat to eastward of a bare patch of escarpment where it swung northward in a bit of a bay. Still the preparations continued on the ground, the firing of the *piendis* and the gathering of baking clay by women and children, the painting of themselves and one another by the men semi-concealed amongst the rocks about the wide Ring Place. The *kuttabah*, not used to sitting about on rocks with nothing to do but outdo each other with airing of their knowledge, were becoming restless – 'When's the bloody thing going to start?' Prindy relieved the situation, speaking for the first time, by announcing that the start must be imminent because the Moon was coming up. The others looked for the Moon, but could see nothing but trees and rock. Then they looked at him.

Fergus asked him how he knew. He swung his lips round the trees of the flat, which from having been drooping in a lull in the wind, were tossing again, and answered, 'Wind change.' Sure enough the wind, which had been blowing from nor'west before, was now sou'easterly.

The Coot remarked, 'Well, it'll blow the rain away.'

Fergus guffawed, 'Balls, Cootsey! A thunder-head always advances *towards* the wind.' He turned to Prindy. 'Ain't that right, mate?'

Although probably not understanding what was said, Prindy nodded gravely.

The Coot looked annoyed, snapped at Fergus, 'Give the reasons for your theory.'

'It ain't no theory, man . . . it's just plain meteorological fact.'

'Well, state it as such . . . and not in the terms of an ignoramus.'

'Aw, pig's arse, Cootsey . . . . '

What might have become a nasty argument was stopped by a sudden ululation from amongst the rocks – *Woo-woo-woo-woo-woo-woo-woo*! – which signalled movement on the part of everybody. The *piendi* attendants left their fires, to take up positions round the Ring, the *Tjaina*, while the men vanished, except for the musicians, some half-dozen, who with didjeridoos and minga-minga sticks came to squat on a flat expanse of rock beside the Ring.

For a short while there was no sound save the din of the pigeons. Then a distant shout. The musicians set to: *Boombooloom, boombooloom, click-a-click, click, click, boombooloom, boombooloom, boombooloom, boo*!

Suddenly into the *Tjaina*, as if from nowhere, sprang a tall and stringy figure, painted red from head to ankles, white-footed and white-headed, with a sinuous white streak running from throat to snake-skin-covered pudendum, and the spiky crown of the Snake Cult as a head-dress. His actions were also representative of a snake's: head thrust forward and darting from side to side, dancing circuitous and furtive. His interest was divided between the pigeons in the banyans and an invisible following to which he kept turning to make furtive signs to join him; while the musicians boomble-boomed and click-a-clacked and the pigeons kept up their insane chorus: Wallakawoo, wallakawoo!

Then the Snake Man swung right round to those behind, put hand to mouth and wobbled it: *Woo-woo-woo-woo-woo-woo-woo*!

Now they came, from all directions on that far side, in small groups strung out follow-my-leader, those following clinging to the waists of those ahead, all decorated like the skinny initiator of the proceedings, and doing a similar snake-like dance, weaving in and out about him while he stood swaying in the middle, now chanting, while they came in with responding chants – *Goorook-wah, Goorook-wah . . . woo-ee-ah, woo-ee-ah . . . goorook-wah . . . ai-eeeee*! – the women and children joining in, with clapping of hands, thighs, buttocks – and boombooloom, boombooloom, click, clack, click!

'The Snake Dance,' explained the knowledgeable Fabers. 'These are the pythons who preyed on the Pigeons in the Dream Time . . . . '

Prindy cut in: 'They not proper Snake Man . . . that not proper snake dance.'

Fabers snapped at him, 'What d'you know about it? Only what that old humbug Bobwirridirri taught you.'

'That proper way.'

'It isn't. It's only *koornung* gammon.'

'Hey!' cried Fergus. 'Anthropological polemics. What would we anthrops do if we ever came to agree?' He turned to Prindy. 'How about you do a proper snake-dance mate?'

'Can't do it,' Prindy answered promptly.

'Why?'

'All this lot get frighten' . . . bolt.'

'There you have it!' declared the Coot, turning now to Professor St Clair. 'That's all that's at the bottom of this Rainbow Snake business, as I've always said. It isn't anthropological . . . just a racket introduced from time to time by shrewdies, the so-called *koornungs*, to put it over the mob . . . . '

His attempted dissertation was interrupted in the sudden rising of the chanting and the musical accompaniment to *staccato* crescending to a concerted screaming and a general rush towards the banyans.

Out came the pigeons, fluttering in alarm. Up went the throwing-sticks. Down came the pigeons and a rain of feathers. Women and children pounced on the lurching wounded, wrung their necks – *Wallakawoo, wallaka-woo*! – the silly survivors after wheeling aloft, wheeled back again, looking for mates. Up went the sticks again – and down the birds – *Wallaka-woo, wallaka-woo, wallaka-wooooo*!

Goorook-wah, goorook-wah, woo-ee-ah, ai-eeeee!

The pigeons woke up, fled back to the safety of leafy branches and tangled aerial roots. Hastily the murderers gathered up their victims, flinging them into heaps beside the ovens, kicking away the dogs who would have helped themselves. Then all rushed, pseudo Snake Men with the rest, to take their places on the sidelines to watch the next act.

Again the drone of the pipes and the click of minga-minga, the strange compulsion of the syncopated rhythm seeming verily to conjure up the dozen figures suddenly there in the *Tjaina*. They were utterly black, smeared from breast to feet with greased charcoal, and stark naked, save for white yokes of birds' down stuck to their flesh and pipe-clayed head-bands. Dancing in line, facing the banyans, stamping, crouching, executing movements of swallowing and flying and feeding one another from their mouths, rising to make half-turns in perfect unison, pointing with lips towards the sea, they mimed, as the Coot explained, the telling of the Borroolooloogun by the Googoowinji, the Cormorants, how to save their nestlings by stuffing their crops and flying home to feed them.

But for the musical accompaniment, the first of it was done in silence – until one of the Cormorant Men leapt out before the others, chanting: *Burrin derrinjin, burrin derrinjin.* – to which the others gave response in chorus: *Wirrianga, pisht, pisht, pisht*!

Tempo of dancing and voices rose – rose – *Burrin derrinjin – Wirrianga, pisht*! – until all were shouting: *Pisht, pisht, pisht*!

Then, for all the world, as if they'd got the message, the pigeons rose – not just to flutter round within range of the *mumbarma* as before, but to whirl aloft; and not just those from the trees of the locality, but from everywhere along the cliff-face, in that vast cloud, which the sinking Sun touched with gold as if with a blessing for its journey. A turn or two high up to make formation, then away with a storm-rush of wings. Black necks and white necks craned to watch. A rosy cloud above the tree-tops now. Dulling to sepia against the rosy horizon. A mere line of smoke. Then it was gone. The Googoowinji announced it with a yell that rang around the wall of hidden rock: *Iai-o . . . kai-o . . . kai-oh-oh-oh-oh-oh*!

It was the signal for release from ceremony. Now the feast. The crowd converged on the *piendis*, the women and children to wrap the birds in clay, while some men raked the ashes from the ovens and others squatted to watch and converse and laugh – laugh, till the moonlit twilight rang with laughter. Old Igulgul himself, all lopsided, seemed to be laughing too.

The Coot spoke to his fellows in the brisk tone of one who has accomplished something for others less clever: 'Well . . . how'd you like it?'

General Esk answered, in a voice of which the constrained quality would have betrayed his feelings even if his words had not, 'Amazin'. Absolutely bally amazin'. I hadn't realized the power that man can get from living so close to nature.'

'Well, of course it's largely mnemonic, ethnic memory converted to, well, what one might term traumaturgical dramaturgy, I suppose.' The Coot chuckled, 'Quite a mouthful that, eh?' He looked at Denzil.

But Denzil, although he had his notebook open and had been eagerly noting the Master's utterances up until lately, did not note this one, instead, asked, 'What's it mean?'

'Eh? Well, in blunt terms, that a racket is made out of magic for entertainment. Same in all religious practice.'

Denzil's voice was constrained too: 'A racket?'

'You've seen the economics of it . . . and there's power for certain individuals . . . .'

Now there was protest in Denzil's voice: 'But the way those birds left when they were told to!'

'The Coogoowinji have been doing it from time immemorial. They know the exact minute for take-off. They think they do it by magic. But that doesn't make it any less a racket. They get a special share for that.'

'But the oneness with Nature. Isn't that magic? Because natural phenomenon amounts to magic, doesn't it?'

Cootes grinned. 'Look out you don't get taken in by this magic stuff, boy.'

Denzil blinked, looked at Prindy, who was staring at him with great eyes luminous in moonlight. He muttered, 'But I am . . . I am.'

Cootes guffawed, 'Look out . . or you'll get taken in by our young con-man friend and his Rainbow Snake.' He pulled a face when the glowing eyes were turned on him, and swung away, saying, 'Come on . . . we'll go watch the culinary business. I want to cook our own damper, too . . . don't want one of their sods.'

Despite rejection of the native way of cooking damper, the Coot was voluble in praise of their mode of baking in clay. He addressed himself to the General, not only because the others would have heard it long since; but Fergus, and even to a slight degree Denzil also, was flippant about his recent show of obvious preference for civilized food and cooking. Ignoring these others to begin with, he said. 'You can eat pretty well anything in the bush, from roots to rats. Of course, you must have a stomach for it. Food prejudices are the first we form, and about the hardest to get over. Overcoming them's simply a matter of ignoring them. A native can eat a thing . . . well you can. That's what I've been trying to teach Denzil here, to make a real bushman of him. He's never been able to eat anything with pleasure cooked with the guts in it . . . although the fact of the matter is its the guts that gives it its special flavour . . .

like seasoning, as you'll find when you come to eat these pigeons. Of course, you don't have to eat the guts . . . although the blacks do, with relish, especially if fatty . . . and I assure you that some of it's quite nice.' Here Denzil made gagging sounds, and when sniggered at by his mentor, made bold to say that he'd never seen *him* eating guts. The Coot replied, 'Only out of consideration for your finicky stomach, boy.' Asked by Fergus if he would eat some pigeon's guts tonight, Cootes snapped, 'If *you* do . . . yes!'

In no time the savour of the cooking was in the air, and the black mob dribbling in anticipation, as plain to see in the bright moonlight. This caused the whites some amusement, and the Coot to remark to the amusement of the blacks, '*Ga breumba wuduk*.' Rather grandly he translated what he'd said, 'Make spit come out, eh?'

In little more than an hour, so swift was the mode of cooking, the ovens were opened, and the football-like cones of hard clay lifted out with forked sticks, to be grabbed by impatient hands protected by leaves, and taken away for eating in family groups. The whitemen retired to their rock with a couple each – too many, surely, as expressed by Fabers. 'Bags I what the rest of you can't eat!'

Fabers opened the first one for the General, showing how the feathers, skin, legs head, came away with the clay, leaving only the plump savory-steaming flesh. 'By George,' exclaimed Esk. 'It certainly meets with the approval of the old sniffer, what?' Eating with fingers, Esk peeled a slab off the breast, tried it, smacked his lips. 'Hm-um . . . very nice . . . gamey . . . but tasty.' He ate more. However, he couldn't get past the breast. 'A little too rich inside,' he confessed. 'Must be that natural seasoning of yours, what?'

'Give it to me,' said Fabers.

He proceeded to pick it down to the bones and guts. He was about to toss the remains away, to the dogs hunting about for scraps, when Fergus said, 'Wait on, Cootsey . . . what about that deal?'

'What deal?'

'You'll eat the guts if I do.' Fergus held up a little lump of what appeared to be swollen intestines.

The Coot hesitated, said, 'You'll make yourself sick.'

'You should worry. Come on . . . down the hatch together!'

The Coot swallowed saliva. 'I . . . we might upset the others.'

'No squibbing, Cootsey, What's happened to the tough bushman you were telling us about just now?'

Cootes was sitting fairly with the moonlight on his face, so that the sweat could be seen to pop out of it glistening. Fergus's face was shaded. Cootes said, in somewhat constricted tones, 'No tricks. Turn round and let's see you.'

Fergus swung round, opened his mouth wide, then popped the lump into it, chewed vigorously, swallowed, with all eyes fixed on him, then wiping his mouth, declared, 'Not bad. Now . . . Cootsey!'

The eyes turned on the Coot. He was sweating harder. He swallowed his spit again. Then, with a determined movement, he tore the gut from the carcase, stuffed it in his mouth. However, his chewing and swallowing were nothing like so lively as Fergus's. So hard did he swallow on it, that it must have been the obvious effort that caused Esk to murmur, 'Bravo!'

Denzil gagged, turned away. Prindy and Fergus chuckled. Malters sat wooden, staring at these two, perhaps suspecting Fergus of not having played fair.

Fergus belched heavily, then said, 'Excuse me . . . but, well, it's a bit hard to keep down. You're right, Cootsey . . . you've got to have a stomach for it . . . urgh!'

The Coot's baggy jowls quivered. Fortunately, the light was less intense, with the Moon at last becoming entangled with the cloud mass. He looked up at the rags of moon-rainbow.

Fergus persisted: 'Afraid I was a bit hasty in my judgment. Fact is . . . well, it tastes rather like a suck of a chook's arsehole . . . '

Denzil fled gagging. Esk said stiffly, 'Reahlly, old chap!' Malters sniffed.

Igugul vanished into the flickering blackness of the cloud. In the gloom the Coot muttered thickly, 'Better go and see how Denzil is.' He slipped off the rock.

'Looks like we might have rain after all,' said Esk. Malters agreed and suggested they put the tent up. Fergus, rising to lend a hand, snatched Prindy aside, whispered in his ear. Prindy slipped away like a shadow.

Sure enough, there behind a rock, with the rumble of thunder to drown the sounds of his travail, was the Coot – vomiting, alone. Prindy watched for a moment, ran back. Denzil was already back and helping with the tent. The wind was now blowing stiffly from the West, the black curtain of which was being ripped by lightning.

Soon the Coot turned up, carrying an armful of firewood, saying they would be needing it, so perky now as to add, 'Wind's in the right direction to rain now . . . *if* you care to notice, Captain Ferris.'

Fergus shot back, 'Wind, eh? Yes . . . I suppose you brought up a bit with the rest of it . . . the pigeon shit, the raspberry jam, and all . . . yes?' Cootes ignored him. But Fergus persisted: 'Nothing like a good puke, is there, Cootsey . . . after it's over, of course.'

Cootes snapped at him, 'What're you yapping about. If we don't hurry we'll get caught in the rain.'

'I admit that gut-stuff tasted shitty . . . but I didn't bring it up, now, did I?'

Rather breathlessly, Cootes said, 'If you're trying to be funny, Ferris, try it on the boy here. He's about your intellectual level.'

'Yes . . . he is a smart, kid. Smart enough to wake up that you went away for a puke . . . and followed you. That right, ain't it, mate?'

All were looking at Prindy, including the Coot. Prindy nodded. 'Yas . . . I see him *barcoo* . . . there.' He jerked lips towards the spot.

The Coot gasped. Then stiffening into sudden rage, he fairly screamed, 'You damned little liar!' And he leapt, and taking Prindy by surprise, slapped his face, hard.

Prindy staggered against Denzil, who caught hold of him. The Coot, beside himself, came in for another slap. But Denzil knocked his hand away, crying, 'Heah . . . reahlly . . . I say!'

The Coot screamed, 'Let me get at him. I'll belt hell out of him . . . the lying little mongrel dog . . . ' But the others had him pinioned.

Now the blacks were crowding round. For a moment Cootes suffered himself to be held and stared at, while he slavered and panted. Then with a wrench he freed himself, went rushing off into the gloom, vanished among the rocks.

Fergus called after him: 'Going to have another puke, Cootsey?'

The General expostulated, 'Now reahlly, Fergus . . . . ' But what he might have been going to say was stopped by a blinding flash – *Zip*! – followed almost on the instant by – *Crash*! – a detonation that with its barrage of echoes made it seem as if the whole cliff-face were falling down.

Behind it all a rising roar. Then like the blow of a mighty hand a hot wind smote, flattening the tent, stripping the trees, whipping the little fires of the blacks into flares that showed masses of grey spidery limbs and buttocks and backs flying for the shelter of rocks. Flash and crash! Then the rush of rain, like a breaking wave, lukewarm to start, then chill and breathtaking as a mountain waterfall, gouting over rocks, gushing under them. Black and white, male and female, piccaninnies and dogs, huddled together, with the spiders and the ants and the lizards crawling over them.

Although it seemed interminable, it lasted no more than fifteen minutes; and indeed could have lasted no longer without tearing everything apart and washing the bits away. The rain drummed steadily for another fifteen minutes, then eased off, to become a silvery mist through which Igulgul kept peeping, until at last he came out beaming, laughing at the sodden crowd turning out shivering. Just one of his little jokes, along with the Old One, stirring up those silly sleepy Waianga. The frogs were out in their myriads now, yelling hallelujah; while kweeluks and plovers loudly rejoiced over what they were going to do to the happy ones.

No thought now for the Mourning Ceremony of the Booroolooloogun People; who, anyway, had had their decorations washed off them, and were complaining over loss of much of the collected fee. No thought on the part of the blacks for anything but getting their fires going again and themselves warmed up. But the preoccupation of the whites, who should have been mustering their hobbled horses and saddling up for getting back to dry clothes and beds, was that one of their number was missing and not answering call upon call – old Fabers. Useless calling, anyway, because the answer always came back from the frogs or birds. Useless also to look for tracks in the scoured earth; and no hope of starting a wide search, despite the numbers available, in country notorious for its devilry. At last it was decided by old Fabers' friends that, bushman as he was, of course he would have headed back to his HQ. Only his two enemies dug each other in the ribs over that one.

Fabers' enemies knew him better than his friends. There was no one back at the camp, except the Lily Lagoons boys left to guard it. Poor old Fabers, soaked to the skin, with nothing but the damp earth for a bed, and surely no sleep to be had what with that froggy chorus and the seething masses of flying-ants popping from the grounds and the mosquitoes that had come out with the frogs! Shaking their heads in sympathy with his plight, his friends, after a stiff whisky as a nightcap, retired to their cosy netted beds. But there was consolation, as the General said: if he didn't turn up, they could soon locate him with the aircraft. 'You mean when we can take off,' corrected the hard-hearted Fergus. 'It's going to take at least two days for that clay-pan to dry out . . . if it doesn't rain again.' He and his young mate went to bed in the aircraft, chuckling.

It didn't rain again. Next day was blazing hot, with marshflies now out in swarms. It was thirsty country between here and the Plateau, too, being mostly sandy, sucking up early rain almost immediately. That poor old Fabers was out there suffering was certain, because his friends went back to the Plateau next day, and along it for some distance, in the hope that he would have the savvy to make for it and the comparative luxury of the rain forest. But not a sign of him. Another night without him, and with the mosquitoes worse than ever. 'Poor old Fabers,' the General said over the nightcap. 'This is getting serious.'

Then that final humiliation, soon after breakfast the second morning, to be found within five miles of his HQ and on the wrong side of it, that is the seaward side. Not that he showed any resentment at first, the way he danced in a clearing, waving his shirt to attract the aircraft. But he must have felt it, to see his two enemies grinning down at him. There was no landing to pick him up at once. Fergus took a bearing, and went back to give it to Denzil, who went out on horseback with two blackboys. The relief party took with them water and a thermos of tea and sandwiches of stalish bread spread with raspberry jam.

However, it wasn't any poor old Fabers who turned up at his HQ a couple of hours later, despite his appearance, his being shrunk to positively flabby bags, spotted with insect bites, torn and sunburnt, his clothes in rags and only able to hobble when he slid from his horse. It was still the Coot, the unsinkable Napoleon. Ignoring greetings and outstretched hands, heaving with indignation, he cried hoarsely, 'I demand an apology.'

All stared at him, except Denzil, who knowing the score, hung in the background, drooping.

General Esk broke the surprised silence: 'Apology, man . . . what for? Gad, we've been worried stiff about you.'

The Coot swung on Fergus, pointing a peeled red finger at him. 'I demand an apology from this . . . this racecourse lout . . . and . . .' The finger swung on Prindy ' . . . from this up-jumped half-bred little beast who's . . . who's caused nothing but trouble . . . everywhere . . . .' He ran out of breath.

'Apologize for what?' asked Fergus. 'For finding you? Did you want to win ultimate glory by dying walking round in circles like Ludwig Leichhardt?'

The Coot got his breath back: 'For the filthy lies you told the other night.'

'For christ sake . . . what lies?'

'The lies you put that kid up to telling . . . that I vomited.'

Fergus and Prindy looked at each other. 'Well?' demanded the croaking voice.

Fergus asked Prindy, 'That really true he been *barcoo?*'

Prindy nodded. 'That true all right. I watch him.'

Again the Coot flew into a rage, as the other night, but with scream cracked now: 'You dirty lying little black bastard . . . I'll . . . .' But Fergus stopped him as he lunged to hit the boy.

Fergus struck him in the chest, and as he reeled back, struck a fighting attitude, snapping, 'Deal with me, you bullying bastard!'

'Gentlemen, gentlemen!' General Esk protested.

The Coot turned on him. 'General . . . I demand that you make these two apologize.'

Esk looked dismayed, exclaimed, 'I say, reahlly!'

'I'm demanding it. If I don't get it, *you* don't get that Appreciation . . . and what's more, I won't have your men continue with me.'

Esk went crimson, but answered coolly, 'Reahlly, Doctor Cootes!'

'I mean it!'

'But this is ridiculous, man! It's a matter between you and these two . . . and a pretty petty one, if you ask me . . . . '

'I'm not asking you. I'm demanding that you order an apology from these two who have damaged my prestige. This . . . this Ferris fellow, he's your employee. The boy's just an Aboriginal waif he's using to undermine me. But he's got to be put in his place. If you value my prestige. . . . '

'Reahlly, old man . . . aren't you rather over-valuing it yourself?'

'My prestige can be of the utmost importance to your plans. . . . '

'Don't be ridiculous, Cootes!'

'I warn you, General . . . that I happen to be in a position, with Government people and others, to make what you want to do in this country a success or a dismal failure. I know how you stand . . . even if you don't . . . although I guess you do . . . and that's pretty precariously. If you make an enemy of me . . . '

The General exploded: 'Damn your enmity, Sah . . . and you yourself for a conniving rogue! Goodday to you!' He turned about with almost military precision, signalled to his aides, snapping, 'Pack your kits, gentlemen.'

They clicked to attention, answered together, 'Sah!'

At Fergus he snapped, 'Be so good as to prepare for flight, Mister Ferris.'

The Coot, physically and emotionally exhausted, fell into the arms of Professor St Clair, who supported him to a tent.

The General's indignation lasted till he was packed and about to go, when suddenly, turning to his aides, he said, 'The fellow's insufferable, I know. But perhaps he's even a bit deranged now by his ordeal. Go and ask the Professor to come and see me.'

St Clair came, looking as miserable as a man could be. No, he said, he didn't think his colleague was deranged – only mortally offended. If only he could have some sort of apology. Impossible, the General declared. He was sure the boy was speaking the truth, because he himself had seen that the man looked sick that night. No doubt it was due to Ferris's uncouthness. But that was a matter between the two of them. Still, as for himself, he didn't want to cut the fellow off like this. Not that he was afraid of him, by jove! 'Tell him, Professor, that there's no one sorrier about the whole wretched business than I . . . and what about coming to Lily Lagoons for a few days . . . or the Beatrice . . . and having a bit of a spell. Then he can whip back here in the aircraft, and carry on . . . eh what?'

The Professor came back looked as miserable as ever, to say, 'He wants straight-out apologies . . . and one from you, too, for calling him a conniving rogue.'

The General fairly shouted, 'God damn the man for a pompous ass! That settles it. I'm off.' He was marching off, when he turned back to the Professor. 'I can't take you along with me, old man?'

The Professor sighed, shook his head.

Perhaps the Professor was prevented from doing so; for he was not out to wave as the Junkers flew over the camp in departing. Only the blackboys were out. A little later, there were the other blacks, still at the foot of the Plateau, but somewhat further westward, waving. Fergus dropped down to them, did a turn or two – then up, up – to scatter the falcons and challenge the eagles, to defy the signs on the red wall that marked it off as a region of *wahji*; then to sweep on over the grey waste of rock, with only that for horizon, with only the compass to steer by, according to the pilot-in-chief, unwitting of the fact that there are some who don't need clever instruments to show them the way home, no matter how far the going.

VII

Although everybody at Lily Lagoons was out to greet the Junkers in the sky, only Jeremy came to receive her company as earthlings. He was his usual self: polite, restrained, watchful. Still, it was evident that his response to General Esk's frank show of affection was something more than politeness, rather like an elder brother's meeting with a younger, whose need of him he did not share, but accepted out of regard for him. Quite readily he agreed to Esk's suggestion that they let the others go in the utility, and they themselves walk. 'To stretch the old legs,' said Esk, 'and hear about your Jews, before they can pull the wool over my eyes.' When Jeremy showed surprise at the remark, Esk added, 'Jews never really like us, Jeremy. They might even want to. They might even love us to a degree . . . but only for our not hating them. But that's not liking. In my experience, ultimately they don't trust us.'

'But you've been a kind of policeman amongst them.'

'Not necessarily. Many of the Jews I knew in Palestine had reason to want my friendship. Then, I've known some very high placed Jews at home. They're included in our aristocracy now, don't y'know. Eager to make friends, even . . . but always that quality of distrust.'

'How do you account for it?'

'Ah . . . I see you've become aware of it! I suppose, ultimately, it's because we don't belong, and . . . well, they're shrewd enough to know we resent it. Anti-Semitism is, of course, primarily due to resentment at their exclusiveness. I've observed that the more Jewish Jews are, which means to say the more exclusive, the less disposed they are to be friendly with the Gentile. But the average Jew will act in the way he shrewdly judges you want him to. Hence what I mean by being prepared to have the wool pulled over my eyes.'

'What you say hardly applies to this lot.'

'No?'

'They're not very Jewish, really . . . certainly not in a religious way . . . the opposite. If they have any resentment, it's against conceding that they're Jews . . . I mean in the matter of food and things.'

'That could be a defence . . . and a concession to you, their host.'

Jeremy made a mocking little sound: 'I'm afraid they regard me rather as the innkeeper. They insist on paying their way. They see me when they've got time to notice me, that's all.'

'But surely they want your expert knowledge of local conditions?'

'They don't need any expert knowledge at all. They're all experts in some line to do with development of wild poor country. They can buy and sell me in everything. They could do in a year, what I've spent most of my life only fiddling with . . . .'

'That's Jews, my friend. But to ignore your local knowledge. . . .'

'Kurt had it all on paper for them.'

'I see. And are they really going to settle hereabouts?'

'I've told you I'm not very close to them.'

'Knowing my Jeremy, I'd hazard a guess that that was more his doing than theirs. From what I understand, from pumping young Prindy, that your son Clancy is more their mark.'

'Yes . . . he's pretty thick with them. As a matter of fact, they've only just come back this morning from Beatrice Homestead . . . been entertained there, no less . . . some of them.'

'Naturally the Vaisey interest would come first with them. Anyway, that suits you well enough, doesn't it? You don't want them despoiling your part of the country, do you?'

'They wouldn't do that . . . at least not as other settlers could be expected to. I mentioned the matter pretty early . . . to their boss, a big fellow named Ernest.'

'Ah, yes, Ernest. I heard about him from Prindy and Fergus. Odd name for a Jew, I must say.'

'He's an odd type. Anyway, he just cut me short, saying, "Spoil ze land and kill ze bird and animal? Vot you think ve are – *Schlemiel*?" You know the expression?'

The General chuckled, 'Yes . . . but I haven't heard it in a long while. Very meaningful, really. Means so much more than Fool . . . rather Born Fool, Fated Fool, Fool Without End . . . .'

'Yes . . . I've gathered that from Rifkah.'

'By the way . . . how's the dear girl? In her element now, I take it.'

Jeremy answered, a little stiffly, 'In the kitchen, as usual. The settlement business doesn't interest her.'

Esk shot him a glance. Jeremy had his eyes on the horse-yard not far ahead, where there was some kind of struggle going on between horse and man.

Esk remarked, his tone dryish, 'I expect it came as something of a surprise to your visitors to find a virtually Jewish household awaiting them?'

Jeremy coloured slightly, and was constrained in his tone in answering, 'As I've said. they're not so keen on the *kosher* business.'

'I'd judge that a bit of a pose. I've yet to meet the Jew who doesn't prefer *kosher* to *treife*, no matter how renegade he might be. As our redoubtable Doctor Cootes remarked, just before the bust-up, food prejudices are primary and the hardest to eliminate.'

'Tell me the facts of the Cootes business while we've got the chance.'

Esk told it drolly, so that Jeremy laughed a lot. However, Esk concluded wryly, 'Ridiculous fellow, of course. Still, I don't like the situation. From what old Malters tells me, he's got an eye on military command of the country in the event of hostilities. Cheek of him! The only pretension he has to a military background is as a Boy Scout. Hence that Appreciation he wanted me to submit for him. You can imagine the private indignation of old Malters. But, according to Fergus, who seems to know his background pretty well, he's in with the politicians . . . both sides. Well, the Coot made that evident enough in what he flung at me. He's the type that politicians go for in dealing with military maters: the opportunist, through whom they can undermine the real soldier, with whom they can never get along. Then there's the matter of the rivalry for power between the local military brass. He could be useful to either side there for political leverage . . . perhaps in levering me out, as he pretty bluntly hinted. If you don't mind my harping on it, dear boy . . . more than ever now do I . . . and Australia . . . need your military services.'

Jeremy was silent. Esk let the silence hang, perhaps in the hope of breaking something in Jeremy with it. They were coming through the mangoes now. He gave up with a sigh: 'Perhaps it may turn out to be a matter for Jews to defend the land. They're quite capable of it. Historically they're a warrior race. Do you think this Big Ernest of yours might make something of a Joshua? From what Prindy and Fergus told me, he sounds like true officer material . . . Prussian, no less!'

Jeremy chuckled, 'How Hitler ever got a man like that on the run beats me.'

Indeed, as so much a military man did Ernest strike General Esk on introduction, with his heel-clicking, that he remarked on it frankly. Ernest replied, 'Haf not ve all military man been zis generation, Excellency?'

'That's a melancholy truth,' said the General. 'But please don't call me Excellency. It's not a title we bestow on mere generals. By the way . . . with what army would you have served? I saw something of you fellows on the other side during the Occupation, don't you know.'

'I like not to spik of it, General. I vos not 'appy in defeat.'

'Understandably, my good chap. My apologies.'

On the other hand, Mendelewitz, every bit as military as his boss, confessed to having been a subaltern with the Polish cavalry and after hostilities to have done a spell as an airman. 'Then you were on our side, of course!' cried Esk, and wrung the lean brown hand like that of an old comrade.

Wool was certainly being pulled over eyes now, if what Jeremy reported of the guests' preoccupation with their business to the point of ignoring him were not an extension of his own withdrawal. Not only were they most amiable with the newcomers, but also with Jeremy, of whom Ernest spoke to Esk as Our Host, Our Patron, Our Wise Counsellor. Anyway, their immediate task was just about concluded, according to what they said in answer to the General's curiosity about their business. It seemed that they had been assured use of the old Russian Settlement site as an initial step to an establishment of their own, but also wished to be permitted to do some experimental work here at Lily Lagoons. 'Ze dog-fish farm,' explained Ernest, grinning.

Conditions for amiability were greatly improved by the first serving of Rifkah's mango wine before lunch, and then by the lunch put on by her and the fat Catherine and Nanago. Speaking of the wine, Ernest addressed the maker very much as her boss: 'You vill learn chemistry from Catherine, and be ze brewery of our settlement.' However, so far from appearing to be bossed was she, that her answer was a wink at the others.

In fact, such was the change in conditions as had been reported by Jeremy, that Ernest even permitted his crew to join the household in what formerly he had denounced as the practice of savages, namely siesta, and retired along with them. Maybe it was the mango wine.

Rifkah herself forewent siesta, as always of Friday afternoon. Catherine joined her in the fish-fry. There would be chemistry in what they did between them, since it is the very basis of cooking; and no doubt the learned Catherine would know about all the chemical processes taking place; still, it was not a bit like a chemist that she gave herself to her share in the intricate proceedings, but as a true daughter of Sarah acting under angelic instructions, her great eyes shining with the joy of it.

There was a general tendency in the company to pair off, beginning with their congregating after siesta.

Jeremy became involved with the elderly Zangwill, who now revealed himself as being much less interested in the practical application of Geology, his speciality, as in the pure science of it. Over in the laboratory, he expressed himself as envious of Jeremy's freedom to give himself to science completely as he chose, saying with a sigh, when Jeremy suggested that it shouldn't be long before he had a lab. of his own and leisure to conduct the research he so eagerly talked of, 'I am afraid it vill nefer be for me, my frient. So mooch zat iz of first importance to ze human race moost accomplished be. Ah . . . but for ze moment, let me live in 'appy private vorld of science mit you. Zis strange rock formation 'ere . . . ze Trias. It moost produce unusual mineralization. I haf specimen tek from ze Rainbow Pool, vich I am sure is Lime Uranate. If only ve haf time to mek ze scintilloscope . . . sure I am ve vood find radioactive mineral in limestone region . . . alzough theoretically absurd, zey vood say. But so much before called absurd in theory is revealed as logic in practice, and vice versa. Our Einstein! Radioactivity now is ze great interest of best brains of geological vorld . . . . '

Fergus found a kindred spirit in Mendelewitz, since learning that he had been concerned with aviation. He said to him, 'You're a dark horse. Why didn't you tell me before and be my co-pilot?' Mendelewitz merely shrugged his shoulders, screwed up his handsome face, as if to say there were things one doesn't talk about. That's how the gesture must have struck Fergus, since he protested, 'I've never yet struck a flying man who made anything of a secret of it. Most of our flying time's spent flyin' 'em in talk . . . usually holding a bar up.' They went out to the Junkers together and took to the air, to do things with her away up in the blue that everybody came out to watch – except the two ritualists in the kitchen. Prindy, forgotten by Fergus, looked forlorn. Ernest looked annoyed, and expressed it, demanding to know what his party was going to do if the *verdamt* thing fell apart, and whether he would have to pay for the flying time being used up so recklessly.

Ernest and the General found a way to vie as strategists without resort to militarism upon learning that they were chess-players. Jeremy produced the wherewithal for them, with which they plunged into campaigning that kept them eye to eye throughout much of their subsequent association.

Herschel was revealed as a music lover, in fact as a very accomplished flautist, which threw him in with Denzil, and also with Prindy for a while, through Denzil's enthusiasm was for his talent. However, Prindy had to drop out, because Herschel had no enthusiasm for what he called the Primitive. Indeed, he said that the proper instrument for that sort of music was the clarinet. Bach was Herschel's great love. He played Bach on Prindy's flute. Now it was Prindy who lacked enthusiasm. He left them with the instrument, and went off to play Jewish music to Rifkah and Catherine on his Indian flute, tucked away with them in the room Catherine shared with Magda. They had ample time alone together there, when the *Shabbos* ritual was finished, because Magda had found a mate in Malters with whom she went riding.

It wasn't riding that brought these last together, but the subject of History. Magda had lectured in it at the University of Prague, while Malters had majored in it at Sandhurst and aspired to return there at the end of his active military career to teach the subject. But surely more than so dry-as-dust a thing kept them riding for miles, and later sitting for hours sipping whisky and looking into each other's eyes, black into blue, even while they talked pedantically of Albemarle, Charlemagne, Marlborough, Kosciusko, Ivan the Terrible, Queen Anne. Asked about Magda by Denzil, Malters replied in his stiff fashion, 'Damned intelligent woman, old chap. Mind like a sword. Attractive, too, by George!'

Unfortunately, Malters made that remark within hearing of the irrepressible jester Fergus, who said, 'D'you know it's worth seventy years good luck to win the love of a Jewess, Malt? Good luck to you! But take my tip . . . if you value your foreskin, don't go to bed with her without searching her for razor-blades . . . yaaaaaaaah!'

Denzil fled, with hand to mouth. Malters went red and rigid, muttering, 'You cad!'

That was just before the Two Stars appeared, when the trio ran into one another going to and from the bathroom prior to going to the dining-room for *Oneg Shabbat*.

What a supper that was, and what a surprise for most who partook of it, for all the evidence of its elaborateness in the way of scents and sounds coming from the dining-room for an hour or so before it, while those not concerned in its preparation sat in the lounge drinking the mango wine and talking, talking. Curiously, those most surprised were the ones who oughtn't to have been, who must have seen the like so many many times, even if not so often of late. Ernest's blue eyes fairly popped, and again curiously, with a look not at all of delight, but rather of consternation, as if being confronted with a reality he had forgotten and would prefer to keep so. There was something more like alarm in the faces of Magda and Mendelewitz. But in those of the older Herschel and Zangwill there was obvious wonder, as in the faces of children at sight of a laden Christmas tree.

It was the same scene, familiar enough here now, of comestible abundance and beauty, with the ritualistic touch given by candles and draped bread and wine, but elaborated because of the larger company, and perhaps subtly also in female defiance of that heavy male disdain of such preciousness already expressed: *Vot is kosher in a new country*?

To make it more impressive were three hostesses, all glowing with pride, and with a touch of naughtiness, each, by having a hibiscus in her hair. Catherine looked naughtiest of all, perhaps because feeling most defiant. Nan looked particularly impressive in her Indo-Chinese costume. Prindy was with them. The four spoke the greeting together, this time in Hebrew, no doubt for the special occasion: *Shabbat Shalom*!

Only Ernest didn't respond. Only the General commented, 'Well, now, isn't that wonderful! I was hoping for it . . . in spite of the attitude of . . . er . . . well, *Haskalah*, is the word for Free-thinking, eh what? I confess I'm really hungry for a little show of the old orthodoxy. If you've done it for *me*, thank you, ladies, and my heartiest congratulations on it. But I'm sure that it's effrontery to think that all you good Jewish people won't appreciate it a hundred times more than I, a poor benighted *Goy*, will . . . for all my love of your most beautiful ritual.'

An odd thing to say; but oddly necessary, it would seem. The others, excepting Ernest, looked at him with something like gratitude. Ernest looked at a loss.

Jeremy had the head of the table, as usual; while as on other formal occasions, Kurt had the bread and wine and salt set before him. However, this time Kurt looked at Ernest, as if for direction. Ernest just stared at him Then as Kurt, with a shrug, moved to cover his head, Ernest shook out his own napkin, and covered his large squarish head completely, as if going into hiding. Kurt mumbled the *Kiddush*, broke and salted the bread, poured the wine. There were responses, but only murmured. The embarrassment was stiff.

Then the food was served. Away went the embarrassment before its magic. In no time even Ernest was shouting his appreciation in English, German, Yiddish, Hebrew, and perhaps other lingos, and soon making everybody laugh with his talk of taming dog-fish to round up the *treife* catfish so that they could start their farming of Barren Mondays and breaking in *Straussen* for Muster-him-up ze *Momzer* Bird . . . Ho, ho, ho!

The happy state lasted right through to retirement at midnight. Only two of the company didn't share it, Fergus and Clancy, paired now by mutual love for one they could not get possession of and hatred of each other. Rifkah conceded them only a short walk, after the meal, both together and with Catherine, too. Retiring for the night, disgruntled, Fergus remarked to Clancy, as he had to Malters, about the reward for winning the love of a Jewess, but without the bawdy addendum, saying instead, 'The seventy years that goes with Rifkah are mine, bozo. You get yours from Magda. I understand you've been pretty thick with her, taking her home to Mum and arranging to have her for Christmas and things. So you're set. Just lay off mine.'

Clancy's comment was a hissed, 'You little bastard, I'll belt the shit out of you!'

'Like you belt it out of the cows, eh, cowboy? Just happens I ain't a cow.'

Fortunately, it happened that General Esk, perhaps even concealed for the purpose by a screen in the lounge, the only other person left there, overheard them, and intervened. He was waiting for Jeremy, who was seeing Nan and Rifkah to their room. When Jerry returned and they were walking over to the annexe, he did not mention the incident, but in response to his host's saying it had been the only jolly day they'd had in the week the party had been there, said, 'Jewish, perhaps, eh what? Six days of hard work . . . rest the seventh. Don't forget the example of their God. But it's hardly religious with them, I think . . . anyway, certainly not with Big Ernest. I wonder about him, Jeremy. Of course he's playing up to me. I expect it. But I suspect something, also.'

'Like what?'

'That remains to be seen. Do you know that he did something no good Chess player would ever do . . . and certainly no Jew without ulterior motive . . . he let me win our game tonight, when it was one that could have been of immense interest in proper finality.'

'Is there anything wrong with that? You look tired. Maybe he was only letting you get off to bed.'

Esk yawned behind his hand. 'Yes, I am tired . . . several bad nights and busy days . . . glad to hit the old palliasse. But I've a feeling he wanted to see how I'd take the faked win.'

'How did you?'

'With a pretence of triumph. But I'm sure he knew I knew he'd let me win . . . for all the subtlety with which he'd worked it.'

'Where does that get you, Mark?'

'Exactly nowhere, dear boy. I started out by saying that I wonder about him, if you remember. I've been wondering if you've wondered too.'

'You're getting a bit muddled by the sound of it. Better call it a night, eh?'

'Thank you, dear boy. See you tomorrow.'

Saturday passed pleasantly enough for everybody, paired as they were. Even Fergus and Clancy were at least well occupied with vying for their beloved's attention and, as revealed, privily plotting to get it exclusively later on. The hopelessness of getting what they wanted here and now was shown them by General Esk, when once again he came upon them at a moment of confrontation. They were bristling like a couple of dogs out under the grandillo vine on the western side of the house, whence they had retreated separately after having been shoved out of the kitchen following separate approaches to the beloved one. He said, 'Chaps . . . to a Jewess there's very definitely a time and a place for everything . . . and I do assure you that the worst possible time and place to choose to make love to one is when she's working in her kitchen.'

Frankly curious now about the seriousness of the rivals' interest in the girl, Esk subequently got each one alone and chatted to him about it. Neither admitted much. Nevertheless, he did learn of those privy plots of theirs. Fergus intended to take Rifkah along with him for the trip when he flew the Settlement Party out tomorrow. He would certainly be overloaded, what with the excess of luggage the party had foisted on him; but the wind would be nicely in his favour. Clancy's idea was to take her in to Beatrice River homestead tomorrow, to stay with his mother till train-day. Something of the sort, apparently, had already been arranged with his mother, who had quite taken to the urbane Magda and Mendelewitz when he had them to meet her and his stepfather. Evidently as curious about the effect of the scheming on Jeremy, Esk told him about it, closely watchful, for all his making a joke of it. But Jeremy wasn't amused. He growled, 'Bloody pests! The girl's shown them plainly enough she doesn't want 'em.'

The way Rifkah dealt with the schemers, when at length, seizing separate opportunities, they put their propositions to her, could hardly be called plain rejection. In fact, for anyone not blind with love, it was something subtly much worse. She told Clancy that she would be glad to go with him – if Prindy went along, too. He tried to get out of that by saying that he would have to ask his mother first, but was sure she'd agree, and that meantime the boy could stay with his friend Barbu. Rifkah giggled over that, saying, 'But ve can go to Barbu ourself any time. I vait for your mumma's invitation card.' She dealt with Fergus similarly. When he pleaded that to take both of them tomorrow would grossly overload the aircraft, she countered, 'All right . . . overload only leedle bit by taking only Prindy. I come vit' you . . . wit' Prindy too . . . ven you take ze General to Town.' Fergus was shrewd enough to leave it at that. Ernest and his party would not be returning to Town to catch the mail plane back to the South, but going down to the Centre to do so, it being financially wiser to do so, as shrewd Ernest had worked it out.

So Clancy had betrayed himself as that worst kind of laggard in love, the one who lets his mother intrude on it. He was glum for the rest of the day. Nevertheless, he was ready enough to go walking with the crowd after dinner and kept as close to the beloved one as made possible by possession of her by Esk, Ernest and Jeremy, and the jockeying for position of his 'Racecourse Lout' rival.

Straight after breakfast next morning, the Settlement Party departed, with the entire household and much of the stock out to farewell them. Catherine, Herschel, Rifkah and Nan wept openly, Denzil behind the fuel shed. Malters shook hands with Magda with more than his usual stiffness, then without waiting to see the party enter the aircraft, marched himself off to the fuel shed, but not by any means to do what Denzil was doing behind. He had a camera planted in there. Through the half-open iron shutter he took the mementoes denied those left behind by Ernest's objection to his party's being photographed, a principle strictly maintained by refugees, the reason for which, it was stated, being that photographs could lead to betrayal of the means by which they gained their freedom.

So they went. Prindy was not co-pilot this trip, but Ex-Lieutenant Mendelewitz. Not that it could make much difference to one who had travelled the red swathe of the Telegraph Line in circumstances so different from now. Catherine had him next to her, giving him the outside seat and hence getting the benefit of his knowledge of the geography. How wonderful – how much in keeping with the expectations of a sorcerer's apprentice, to skim so easily over a road formerly so hard and beset by hazard! Charlotte Springs – Ilfracombe Station – Mt Prince Albert, the Knowles's lousy place, with its rocks and goats, and blacks and all of them out to gape and wave, with never an idea of who it was looking down at them – the long empty stretch, with its occasional windmill drawing silver water with the brisk nor'easter – and then the Prospector's Arms (or Alms), with Billy Brew's donks milling about the water-trough, looking like a sprawling mauve growth on the red earth – yes, and Billy himself, white-bearded, out waving with the Cullitys and the boozy weekend mob in from the mines. Again it would never be guessed who was up there looking down with the others to be glimpsed at the windows, as Fergus did a turn.

Then on southward, up over Piss Ridge, and in a matter of minutes to see the straggle of civilization about Boulder Creek gather itself out of the wilderness to form the little township. Down, down, down, to hit the red dust and start a little dust-storm that whirled away on the hot wind just as if it were something done by a familiar of Tchamala's.

As that wind which had brought them so far so swiftly would be anything but a help on the return trip, Fergus told Prindy they would go into town with their passengers and have lunch and wait till the wind eased off, as it should after midday. So Prindy, at last, came into this town that so nearly had become the centre of his existence, as one of the hundred or so male crossbred waifs who lived in the so-called Home on its barren outskirts.

Yet, while the place was strange to Prindy, he was not an utter stranger there, as soon proved. They went to the Princess Marina Hotel, to be bowed in by Nikko the Greek as if they were Vaisey People, which perhaps he thought they were, seeing they travelled by chartered aeroplane, instead of a mob of Reffoes.

They were just settling down to lunch, when into the dining-room, with that official strut, and even with the hat tilted over an eye, as if he were a Jew and had to keep his hat on at table, a familiar figure came. He was going to sit at another table, but in accordance with the custom of the land, turned towards the strangers to pay his respects. He fairly gaped at what he saw. Coming up, he cried, 'Hello, hello, hello! What's this?'

It was Mr Eddy McCusky, Assistant Protector of Aborigines.

Fergus leered, looking as if about to cut his old enemy down to size, but did not do so, instead, amiably explained the situation, introducing his passengers. But Eddy was not to be put off official business: 'You had no right to bring that boy. Lawful custody of him is, for the moment, invested in Jeremy Delacy. You're committing an offence, Ferris . . . and not only the matter of unlawful transportation of an Aboriginal Ward of the State, but in bringing him onto licensed premises.'

Fergus growled, 'Aw . . . pull your head in, Adolf!'

Eddy flamed: 'Right . . . I take custody of him herewith!' He laid a hand on Prindy's shoulder. 'Come on, my Scarlet Pimpernel. I'm going to put you away where you ought to been long ago.'

'No you don't!' cried Fergus, and leapt up and snatched Prindy away, at the same time hurling Eddy back so that he collided with another table and sent the cutlery crashing on the concrete floor.

The others rose hastily. 'Vot ist?' demanded Ernest.

'The local Gestapo,' said Fergus.

'Gestapo? Vot . . . zis is secret *polizei*?'

'No . . . only a mug silvertail who big-times himself bullying defenceless blackfellows.'

'Careful what you say, Ferris . . . or I'll take an action against you. And hand over that boy . . . or I'll get the police . . . . .'

Nick the Greek came rushing in, yelping, dancing about, imploring everybody not to Mek de Troubles.

Fergus said to Eddy, 'Listen, big-boy . . . he stays in my custody till I hand him back to those who gave him to me.'

'You have no authority . . . .'

'No, you've got it all . . . up your bum! Now, just keep your bum shut for a moment, and I'll tell you something that'll keep it shut for a week. This boy's been with me for the past week, in the company of Professor St Clair and Dr Cootes, on an official survey. These blokes're now virtually your bosses. You want me to go back and report to 'em that you're playing the same old game of protection with your boot? Then there's your old mate, Fay McFee. Wouldn't she like to have it for the papers . . . Gestapo tactics with coloured kids, in front of Jewish Refugees . . . wow!'

Eddy blinked and swallowed, seemed to shrink under his hat. But with all eyes on him, and perhaps especially those little quizzing black beads of Nick the Greek, he had to do something. He worked his narrow jaw, thrust it out, pulled the hat down a fraction, turned on Nick, 'You're committing an offence having an Aboriginal on licensed premises, Nick. Get him off at once . . . or I go for the police.' He turned back to Fergus. 'Sergeant Cahoon happens to be here.'

'Oh, pliss, pliss, Mist' Ferritch!' Nick yelped. 'Tek 'im 'way. I don' want de troubles.'

Fergus considered for a moment. 'Okay. Come on, son.' He turned to the Jews. 'You see the unpromising Promised Land you've come to, Australia . . . the Land of the Anzacs, the bold and the free. It may be pretty tough for Jews where you come from, brothers . . . but it could never have been tougher than it has been and still is for kids like this . . . and all his black and brindle breed. So long . . . and *mazel tov*!'

As they headed out, followed by Eddy, Ernest shouted, 'Vy you let ze *momzer* boss you? Speet in 'is eye!'

Fergus only grimaced. But Eddy demanded, 'What he mean *Momzer*?'

Fergus exchanged a glance with Prindy. He grinned. 'You tell him, mate.'

Prindy looked at Eddy. 'That a turkey.'

With a whoop of laughter, Fergus snatched him away, leaving behind the dining-room awhoop and bewildered-looking Eddy in the doorway.

Up the street a bit, Fergus said. 'We'll go back to the kite . . . and nip over to Con Cullity's and have lunch there.'

So they went back over the Ridge, chased Billy's donkeys and the Cullity goats out of the way, then landed so as to pull up right before the pub. Great was the astonishment of those watching from the verandah when they saw who had come to them out of the blue. They rushed him. Bridie and Billy had to fight the Reffoes for him, and then each other. Everybody won, really, since he spent most of the time he was there sitting on the bar playing the flute for them.

The wind dropped as Fergus had predicted. However, Fergus, by then roaring with the rest, everything from *Shlaaf Mein Princeling* to *The Road to Gundagai*, didn't notice it. He finished up in the huddle, now bellowing in sleep, on the front verandah, with Igulgul smirking as he dropped down to the deserted goldfields. Prindy spent the night with Billy in his waggon.

They were so slow in getting away next day, what with Fergus's hangover and the reluctance of everybody to lose them, that the wind was up again, and now blowing from the North, which would make the going slower still. Fergus made his headache worse with having to work out whether his fuel would last the journey, and finally had to abandon the job to Bridie. There was much embracing and some shedding of tears at parting. Fergus was lucky in having a co-pilot and easy navigation in the form of the Telegraph Line. He spent much of the flight asleep. In fact he only took the aircraft off the ground, and put her down again at Lily Lagoons.

It was nice to be home again, and with such a droll tale to tell, but spoilt a bit by finding Clancy still there. As Fergus muttered to Prindy when they saw him, 'We'll have to do something drastic to get rid of that bastard for good.'

VIII

In the lounge that Sunday evening, after coffee and brandy and the news session, it was not Jeremy or Rifkah who suggested the walk, as was invariable if there was to be walking, but General Esk. He came out with it quite suddenly, looking at Jeremy and Rifkah with what was more than a smile: 'Shall we walk?' Both blinked, then turned towards Fergus and Clancy, who from scowling suddenly brightened. But as if anticipating it, Esk also turned to the young men, saying quickly, 'If you don't mind, chaps. This'll be my last night with 'em for quite a while. Be off South in a week or so, don't y'know. You can drop in any time . . . eh what?' Even wooden Malters looked surprised. Nan's and Kurt's eyes widened with watchfulness. Although there could hardly be objection, Esk acted as if to forestall it, rising quickly and going to Rifkah, giving her his arm while still she sat. Slowly she rose to take it, looking at Jeremy. Esk turned the toothy smile again on Jeremy. There was certainly objection in the expression that met him. Undaunted, Esk turned with Rifkah and headed for the door. Jeremy drew a deep breath, heaved himself up and followed.

Igulgul, at his fullness, well up the sky already, held the world bewitched. Not a sound in the world, but for the soft heartbeat of this odd little part of it – *Home, a-home, home, home*! A great cloud that filled the northwest sky blazed like a wall of scrolled silver. The General, manoeuvring to get Jeremy to take Rifkah's other arm, exclaimed, 'By jove, what a perfect night! But all your nights are perfect . . . even in a storm, as I saw the other night. How shall I ever get used again to the poor little drizzly pale nights of my native heath?'

The others made no comment. Still in command, he swung them towards the mangoes, saying, 'Let's go take a look at the horses, what? Must say a chin-chin to my dear old Rory.'

Still no comment. Esk cleared his throat: 'Ah-hum! Sorry for the way I went about it, but . . . well . . . you did bring Clancy along last night, and you avoided the toddle I proposed this afternoon . . . and, really, it's most important that I speak to you both together, and with complete frankness.'

They went on and through the jet and silver of the mangoes in silence. Emerging, Esk turned to Rifkah. 'I know, my dear, that you never knew Ernest Boch or any of his people before they came here. However, I feel certain that you know *what* they represent.' He paused. As she didn't anwer, but only stiffened on his arm, he asked, 'Is it any use asking you are they Communists?'

She answered breathlessly, 'Nozzing do I know of zem.'

He nodded to the distance. Then turning again, swiftly, he asked, 'Are *you* Communist?'

She swallowed first, but answered readily enough, 'I am not Communist.'

'I don't mean an actual member of the Party. You have worked for the Communists?'

He waited for her. At length she answered, with difficulty, 'My fader was Communist. I vos put prison for Communist and Jew. It vos Communist people save my life . . . not ze English!' She spat the last.

'I accept the rebuke, my dear.' He was silent for a moment. 'I take it you have worked for the Party . . . because Communists never do anything for nothing.'

'I do not vurk for Communist now. I am free.'

'As I understand Communists, there is no getting free of them. If you're not with us, you're against us, don't y'know . . . .'

Jeremy cut in, his tone quiet, but intense: 'Tell me, Mark . . . is this an official interrogation?'

'Anything but, dear boy. I tried to tell you that last night, when you rebuffed my attempt to broach the subject . . .'

'Then, your purpose, please? I told you I wouldn't have the girl badgered or embarrassed under any circumstances.'

Esk cleared his throat again: 'Hem . . . my purpose, Jeremy, is to avoid these very things. I've hinted to you already that I suspect Ernest and his people of being Communists planning to establish a Communist Cell, as it's called. As I'm responsible for the defence of this country, I'm vitally concerned. I'm bound to have these people investigated. I want to spare Rifkah this . . . and Kurt . . . and you yourself . . . .'

'I don't give a damn. When you hinted at it, I told you I'd prefer such people to those aliens who already hold the land and are only concerned with exploiting it and its people.'

'But I *do* give a damn, Jeremy. You don't understand Communists. Nor do you really understand this vicious Government of yours, which already regards you as an enemy, and will destroy you if it can. I told you I have reason to believe that the Communist Party is about to be declared illegal in this country, and have hinted at the danger to you of suspicion of involvement . . . Wait, please! I don't doubt for a moment that what Rifkah has said about herself is true . . . she's not Communist and wishes to be free from Communist business . . . . '

'She *is* free . . . and *I'll* see to it that she remains so.'

'Good for you! But, as I've said, you don't know Communists. You mustn't judge them by the poor local ignoramuses. If need be, you'll both be used . . . and destroyed when you're no more use. I repeat that my purpose is to save you this . . . both of you . . . because of my regard for you.'

They were greeted by those sitting outside their houses in the Aboriginal quarter, and called back. They were silent till they reached the horse-yards.

Esk said, 'No doubt Kurt's an active member of the Party . . . or he wouldn't be entrusted with his special task . . . .'

'What task?' demanded Jeremy.

'My purpose is not to convince you of anything, but simply to warn you so as to help you. Please remember that I have had much to do with Jews and Communists, officially. I suspected Kurt from the first, when I met him at the Beatrice and had no idea that he would be likely to become involved with you. It was his outright denial of Zionism. Although the average Jew is not a serving Zionist, and may even hate Zionism a bit because of the dangers inherent in it, he has a sneaking regard for it . . . well, it's the essence of being a Jew, the return to Zion's Hill. When a Jew denies Zion out of hand, he denies he's a Jew . . . and, as Jews don't usually do things by halves, this type will have taken on, in place of his Judaism, what will make equal demands on his capacity for community dedication, which in these days is Communism. After all, Communism, as we know it, is an extension of Jewish Socialism, which had its origins in the Haskalah Movement, the revolt of Enlightenment, the struggle against the tyranny of unworldliness that the Jew's closeness to God tends to subject him to. At least Hitler is right in blaming Communism on the Jews. But if Communism had been left to the Jews to develop in their own way, as a faith, a science, and a brotherhood, combined, it could well have meant the salvation of mankind, the factual coming of the Messiah. Unfortunately, it fell into the wrong hands . . . into the cruel hands of people bred for ages in tyranny of their own making, whose tradition compels them either to tyrannize if they have the strength for it, or to accept tyranny as the right of the strong if they themselves are not . . . .'

Jeremy interrupted: 'If Jewish Communism would be the blessing you say, why spoil a unique opportunity to establish it here?'

'There is no such thing as Jewish Communism . . . except as expressed in the theory of Zionism, which can only be practised in the Holy Land. I told you that what the Jews had created in their own faith and brotherhood and intelligence had been seized upon by people who only know that might is right. Ernest and his company are the victims of those others. They came here not as Jews, but as Communists pure and simple, as members of the soulless Party, sent by the Party, which actually is Anti-Judaistic, since headed by as savage an Anti-Judaist as ever was, Josef Vissarionovich Dzhugashvili, rascal monk originally, now neo-Czar or all the Russias, and would-be Czar of all the world, so-called Stalin, or The Man of Steel. They are his minions . . . at the cost of having renounced their birthright as Jews. They *pretended* to come here as Jews, because that was seen as the opportunity to infiltrate them as seemingly innocent, hapless, homeless refugees from tyranny. What better opportunity than this to create the all-important Cell?'

'This is all supposition of yours . . . born of hatred of anything that opposes your own form of wanting power over the minds and bodies and possessions of simple people!' Jeremy said it so forcefully that Esk looked at him startled. Both turned from each other hastily.

After a moment General Esk said huskily, 'It isn't simply supposition. I've already had some investigation made. I didn't want to say that. I've told you this is completely unofficial. All that I want to do is what I think proper as a friend . . . to see that you people aren't hurt.'

They went on in silence towards the racetrack. Jeremy spoke first: 'If you supposed that Kurt was sent here to establish a Communist Cell, why didn't you say something sooner?'

Esk was silent. They came up to the race track gate. Jeremy pressed: 'Well, Mark?'

Esk still had time to delay the answer, because horses in a bunch came whickering to greet them. Stroking an extended snuffling muzzle, he murmured, 'I assumed that you could deal with it yourself.'

'Then why didn't you let me?'

Esk breathed deeply: 'Because of your involvement with Rifkah.'

Rifkah looked at him with great eyes, drawing a shuddering breath. He looked down. She turned to Jeremy, who was staring at her. For a moment they stared into each other's moon-luminous eyes. Then suddenly, with hands and lips she reached for him, clung to him, but as he began to put his arms about her, broke away from him, and with a sob, turned and ran away, back towards the homestead. The men stared after her. The quiver of her shining head, the jerking of her silken slender shoulders, told of wild grief restrained. She vanished in the shadow of the horse-yards.

Esk looked miserably at Jeremy. 'I'm sorry, Jeremy.'

Jeremy swallowed, took a moment to ask, huskily, 'What for?'

'For hurting . . . both of you.'

The horse Elektron was stretching his glossy black neck for his master's hand. Stroking, Jeremy muttered, 'All in a good cause, though, isn't it?' Esk didn't answer. Jeremy drew a deep breath, and exhaled it harshly: 'Your bloody Commonwealth!'

He slipped through the rails.

Esk leaned over the gate. 'Jeremy, I assure you that's only a small part of the purpose now. The enthralment can do neither of you any good. It can only steal your remaining manhood . . . .'

'Which you want to press into your Imperial service!' As Elektron shoved against him, Jeremy grabbed his mane at the withers, heaved himself up onto his back.

'Jeremy . . . .'

For answer Jeremy dug a heel in the glossy flank to turn the horse, then kicked with both. Elektron leapt into a gallop. The other horses snorted, swung, stared at the racing pair, shot off in pursuit. Esk, staring at the receding cloud of silvery dust, sighed. For a while he hung on the gate. Then, sighing again, he turned and headed towards the homestead.

The Moon was close to the zenith and that mighty cloud when Jeremy returned. Coming through the mangoes, he saw Fergus on the driveway, as if coming from a lone walk in the other direction. Fergus waved and hastened his step. Jeremy only half waved, and hastened his own step towards his quarters. There was a light in the room that the General still occupied in the annexe. Jeremy went to his den. He had just got out the brandy bottle and settled in his arm-chair, when Esk appeared in the doorway.

The two men eyed each other in silence for a while. Then Esk said, in subdued tones, 'Sorry to intrude, Jeremy . . . but I don't intend to do anything about the girl . . . or Kurt.'

Only a blink of the grey eyes.

Esk swallowed. 'I said I'd already done some investigating. They were only inquires about the settlement business. There *is* an authentic settlement scheme . . . but it's for the far northwest. I saw some of the principals over there. They know nothing of anything's being done over here.'

Another blink. Esk added: 'My inquiries were discrete, I assure you. Anything I do about Ernest and his people will be the same.' His stiff lean face quivered ever so slightly. 'That's all, Jeremy . . . except to say again, I'm sorry . . . Goodnight!' He withdrew.

Jeremy blinked again, then opened his mouth, and called after the retreating steps, 'Mark!'

The steps stopped. A moment of hesitation. Then they returned. Jeremy rose as Esk reappeared in the doorway. He asked, 'Care for a nightcap?'

Esk's face quivered again. He cleared his throat slightly: 'Hem! Well, yes, thank you, old man.'

Jeremy waved him to the other armchair, and proceeded to pour the drinks. Taking his glass, the General raised it, saying, '*L'chayim*!'

Jeremy responded: '*L'chayim*!'

They drained their glasses. Jeremy set about refilling them. Esk sighed: '*L'chayim* . . . *To Life*! A perfect toast, isn't it. No people enjoy life like Jews . . . and yet none have such restrictions on enjoyment. An Orthodox Jew doesn't live by a mere Ten Commandments but Six Hundred and Thirteen . . . do you know?'

Jeremy, sipping, shook his head. Esk went on: 'I've presumed to understand Jews, but . . . well, thinking about it this evening, I see how little I do know. I suppose it's the impossibility of knowing Jews that makes them generally hated.'

Jeremy said, somewhat stiffly, 'They seem simple human beings to me.'

'There's nothing simple about them, Jeremy.'

Jeremy looked away. Esk was silent for a while, then asked, 'May I talk, old man?' When Jeremy looked at him quickly, he added: 'About myself.'

Jeremy took a swig first, then answered, 'Go right ahead.'

'I've hinted to you of a marriage . . . well, not unlike your own . . . your first. I'd like to be frank with you about it.'

Jeremy nodded, but was wary-eyed. He placed the bottle where Esk could help himself. Esk replenished his glass, sipped, began: 'As I told you, I married early in the war. Excitin' times. Sort of thing I was bred to, don't y'know. Pamela . . . daughter of a General et cetera, high-steppin' filly . . . and war. I supposed I was very much in love. In the matter of marriage it's so dashed hard to tell what's made in heaven and what in the mind . . . By the way, would you know that the saying, "Marriages are made in Heaven", is originally Jewish?'

Jeremy shook his head. Still that wariness. Esk avoided the eyes, looked at the ceiling. 'Clever Jews,' he said. 'They blame everything on Heaven . . . so there's no arguing against it. Traditionally, of course, Jewish marriage is arranged, on very practical grounds. Their conception of love is something entirely different from ours. *Mazel Tov*, as they say to bride and groom, merely wishing them the best that may come out of it . . . with no illusions about the realities.'

Esk drank, moved in his chair. Clearly he was beating around whatever it was he had to say. Jeremy, as if to help him, withdrew his gaze, turned sideways in his chair, hung a leg over an arm.

Esk seemed more at ease. Settling himself, he went on: 'Our illusions, Pamela's and mine, lasted the war out. The product was our Lydia. Whether I had the capabilities to become a family man was never put to the test, because of what was revealed to us in our disillusionment of the difference of our conceptions of the meaning of family. My own family's a pretty old one. But we've never been grand. We're proud of our ancestry . . . rather, I should say, of our history, which is really only one of serving the Crown, loyally. We would have been Liberals always, long before there was any idea of what has come to be called Liberalism. That was what Pamela had against us most . . . against me, because she scarcely recognized my family. A Lily-livered Liberal. That was her final denunciation of me. There was nothing worse to her. It was we Liberals who had betrayed the natural rulers of mankind, the aristocracy, of which we were hangers on, to all the lousy things now crawling about the earth . . . the Lenins, the Ghandis, the Lloyd-Georges. I rather spoilt things by entering politics . . . at her behest. She wanted the world cleaned up. So did we all. But I didn't realize that she wanted it put back the way it was, with a new Czar of Russia, a new Kaiser of Germany, the Delhi Durbah, and all that . . . and, of course, the British Labour Party declared a treasonable organization and extirpated. I got into Parliament very easily. One of my relations, rather doddering, resigned his Conservative seat to me. I promptly went over to the Liberals. It wasn't out of vindictiveness, I assure you. Things were bad. Men who had served under me, many of them hideously maimed, were begging in the streets, after all they had suffered to get rid of the very things Pamela wanted back. But it was quickly brought home to me that politics had no place for me. Parliament was exactly what it was meant by the name . . . Talk . . . the meeting place of the loudest talkers in the land. All talk. The General Strike sickened me. Nothing but Talk . . . while people starved. Shoot the strikers, shoot the bosses, at the two extremes, and us in the middle begging both sides to behave themselves like Englishmen. I resigned my seat and went back to the Army . . . largely because I saw extremes entering there, too: The Blimps were quite ready to shoot down the men who had so faithfully served under them. Fortunately, my super-Blimp of a father-in-law had placed me so well up in the service that no one could pull me down, except at the risk of causing a fearful row.'

Esk sipped, went on: 'I think I can claim the honour of having introduced something like democracy into the British Army at last. You didn't have to be a gentleman to hold rank . . . or rather to assume it. You didn't have to be white to have command of coloured troops in your own coloured country. Of course there was a lot of heart-burning over it. I was accused of being a Bolshevik . . . I'd had a strong hand in withdrawing our Army of Intervention from Russia. I was accused of giving the Empire away . . . when I was only honouring the promises made to Indian leaders for more say in the running of their own country for dedication of their services to us in our travail.'

Another swig. 'I've told you much of this already, Jeremy . . . I mean what I've been doing in my job. But I've never told you *why* I did it . . . hence the repetition. The fact was that disillusionment, or disappointment, in marriage.

Rather like your own case, as I say. I was tending to do all the things that Pamela stood against. One does those things, believing one has a pure motive. As I've said, it's hard to judge what's made in Heaven and what's perhaps even the product of the other place. This, of course, alienated me utterly from Pamela. But we English aren't as honest as you. The pretence had to be kept up. I went home on all the special occasions. Even hunted with her and her family . . . although I'm sure they'd have been much happier baggin' me than the fox, the stag, or the grouse.'

Jeremy chuckled. Esk was evidently encouraged, changed his position, now leaning forward, elbow on knee, hand cupping chin, as if coming to the gist of the thing he had to say: 'There was young Lydy, of course. Always a strong bond between us. She never knew of the estrangement, at least not as a child . . . although no doubt she felt it. Our reunions made the concessions to convention bearable. I didn't see so much of her. She was pretty soon away at school. But there were grand occasions together . . . London, when I'd come home from somewhere, doing the rounds of the bun shops and the cinemas. A trip to Paris . . . another to Rome. The relationship was frowned on at first by Pamela, who naturally wanted her daughter to share the Dukely ermine. However, as Lyd showed more and more of a tendency to have more of the Lily-liver than the blue blood, she let her go, concentrating her efforts on helping down-at-heel Russian aristocrats with their futile litigations against the Soviet, helping organize British Union, oppose the Balfour Agreement on Jewish rehabilitation, and all the misanthropic rest of it that goes with the fight to retain power and privilege. By the time Lyd left school she was as much estranged with her mother as I.'

Esk paused, and when Jeremy glanced at him, added: 'D'you know, dear boy . . . I believe the same sort of thing would've happened to you, if you'd had a daughter?'

It was half a question. Jeremy turned his head away from it.

Esk leaned back now, sighed, put hands behind head and crossed his knees, looking up again. 'After that, Lydia was with me all the time. I took her away on all official trips. But for the . . . um . . . well, the horrible consequences, it was the happiest period of my life. I'd tried to solace myself with other women. There are always women for solace, of course . . . they're seeking it themselves in some way. But solace isn't love. Love is the identification of yourself with someone. What closer identification can one have than with one's own daughter? The honeymoon is perpetual, because there's no satiety to it. The relationship is pure because there is no ulterior motive. It is simple, pure, unadulterated love.' Esk dropped his arms, and head, to meet Jeremy's eyes. His tone became sharp as he added: 'Love, I said . . . because that's what it is . . . love between a man and woman. One imagines oneself safe from the suggestion of abnormal relationship, because it's unthinkable to oneself.'

Jeremy removed his eyes from those hard-staring blue ones. Esk took a drink before going on: 'The truth was brought home to me in Palestine, where I had her with me to begin with. There was a young subaltern pursuing her . . . cheeky young pup. She didn't encourage young men, except of such a type that she could help, mother as it were . . . the weaker ones. These she brought to me . . . for me to help them. This fellow was quite different. He wanted no help. He wanted her . . . and the aristocratic connexions that went with her. He made no bones about it. First he told her that she was virtually my tart . . . and then when I dressed him down for it, he called me a Dirty Old Man.'

Jeremy shot a glance at the stiff face. Esk added, in the same sharp tone: 'Yes . . . a Dirty Old Man . . . keeping my daughter to myself . . . like Dirty Old Lot, he added, very aptly, in the circumstances, because at the time we were living very close to the Bible. Of course you know the story of Lot and his daughters. Hardly nice is it. But one tends to blame Lot rather than the daughters, because he did remove them from other men.'

Another swift exchange of glances. Both drank. Esk went on: 'That young puppy saved me a lot of embarrassment by asking to be relieved of his duties immediately, and to be sent home. I also have cause to be grateful to him for advising me, as he left me, to read Freud. I did. But whereas Freud was plain enough speaking about unconscious incest, he had nothing to say about how one who has indulged in it should handle the situation he has created when he becomes aware of it. In my ignorance, I simply packed Lydia off home. Well . . . it was hardly simple. Naturally, I didn't confess my guilt to her. I simply withdrew. In fact, to discourage her, I took a Jewish mistress . . . not a young one, but a very capable woman, name of Leah, who rather forthrightly told the poor kid to go get a man of her own, when she showed signs of struggling for me. Poor Lydy rushed off home to Mumma then . . . and quickly became everything Mumma was, and more, in her vengeance as a woman scorned. No . . . first she took to a fast crowd of aristocratic youngsters, drank, drugged, raced about in sports cars . . . till she ended up in a smash that cleaned up everybody except herself. It was after that she settled down to the true ruthless patricianhood, in which you saw her. But, I understand, as in your own case, she never got over the affair with Daddy. Do they ever?'

Jeremy shifted uncomfortably Esk emptied his glass He continued: 'I've naturally paid a lot of attention to the Electra Complex, as it's called . . . the father-daughter relationship when it gets out of hand. I've observed that it's always the man unhappily married and with one daughter, who falls into it. Old Lot had two, or course . . . but those were the days of multiplicity of wives.'

Esk paused, with so much significance that Jeremy met his eyes again. Esk added: 'I'd say the essential difference between a man and an ape is his capacity to give his daughters to other men. I think the Sororate, the primitive social system of sister-exchange in marriage, was probably the first law men made. Out of it came the cessation of the rutting battle and the saving of all that energy for mental development. So up the scale we came, making more and more laws about sex. The man who lies with his daughter is classed as a degenerate. Even where his incest is unconscious he is a Dirty Old Man.' Another significant pause, fetching another swift glance. 'Perhaps even where the girl isn't related to the man, but young enough to be his daughter, it's something similar. Speaking of Jews again . . . in my experience it's rare if not impossible, for an old Jew to take a young wife or mistress. Whether there is any law about it, or it's simply a matter of Jewish wisdom, I don't know. The wisdom of it is plain to see in Asia Minor, in the comparison between the rich old Jew who is content with his old wife, living out his age in dignity, and the high-caste Mohammedan, with his young wives and concubines, holding his power by means of violence and treachery, while becoming more and more a travesty of a man the longer he lives. For that matter, you don't have to look beyond our own society . . . at the bloated capitalist with his young mistresses, paying only lip service to any kind of morality, and his opposites, the scholars, the scientists, the men of dedication to the species and true dignity in age.' Esk paused, to add: 'I've thought that my Lydia's break with old Alfred was brought about much less by her seeming wilfulness than his shrewdness . . . for old Alfred isn't wanting in dignity, you know, however much you have cause to hate him otherwise.' He paused again. 'I suppose true dignity in age is really the reward for having gone through the perils of living . . . would you say?'

The question was put with a deliberateness that demanded an answer. Jeremy was slow with it, his tone somewhat husky: 'What do you mean by Dignity?'

'Well, surely . . .' Esk stopped. 'Sorry . . . I was forgetting that words mean a lot to you.'

'Why shouldn't they . . . to everybody who uses them?'

'Of course. I expect I've got the word wrong. Will you be so kind as to define it for me?'

'It's a misused word, of course. I'm prejudiced against it, because of its use by the Imperium to dominate my country . . . *Our Sovereign Lord, the King, his Peace and Dignity.* Don't forget I've also seen your Mohammedan sheiks and satraps . . . and dignity, the pomp and ceremony, the sun-canopy, the slave with the fly whisk and the fan, were the last word with them . . . as the Orb and Sceptre are with His Imperial Majesty, your Boss. I don't see that as any reward except for a rogue or halfwit.'

Still Esk smiled. He said gently, 'What I really meant was Integrity, Jeremy . . . something I think you have in greater quantity than any other man I've ever known.' He rose, stepped up to Jeremy, who had reddened now. 'May I take your hand on that, to show you how much I mean it?'

Somewhat awkwardly, Jeremy rose and gave his hand.

'Thanks, old man,' said Esk, wringing the hand. 'Thanks for everything. Knowing you has been a great privilege. I only hope this won't be the end of our association.' Releasing the hand, he said, 'Well . . . I'll toddle. Goodnight, dear boy!'

Jeremy replied thickly, 'Goodnight . . . Mark.'

Esk paused at the door, to look back and wave. Then he was gone. Jeremy stood staring. A slight sound at the window caused him to turn to look. Nothing to be seen save the sparkle of the moonlight on the fluted glass of the louvers. He sighed and sat down.

There was nothing to be seen out there, because the cause of the sound, Fergus, was gone, slipping along in the shadow of the southern wall, making for the eastern end of the annexe. He turned the corner into moonlight, swiftly, as if fearing to be seen from the Big House, hurried into the shadow of the garage, then across to the mangoes. He stood looking at the Big House, in darkness, except for the moonlight. Then he started to head for it directly, strolling, as if just returning from a walk. As he emerged from the shadows, there appeared out of the eastern door of the annexe another figure, its identity unmistakable by the glint of copper hair. She looked towards him, but with the blaze in her eyes must have missed seeing him. Then she slipped round the annexe the way he had come. He halted momentarily, broke into a run.

Rifkah, now to be seen heading across the yard, heard him, light as his running was, whirled about and stared, but only for a moment. She turned away again, hurrying now. He caught her before she could reach the kitchen door. She hissed in protest at his grabbing her hand, 'Pliss, pliss!'

'I want to talk to you.'

'I can't talk to you here . . . tomorrow.'

'No . . . come for a little walk.'

'No . . . no . . . pliss, Fergus!'

'It's important. It's urgent. Round here, then.' He pulled her round to the shadowy western side, under the trellis. He went on: 'Did you hear what they were saying over there? Old Whiskers wants to get rid of you, you know. I've heard him talking to Malters . . . about you and the Mullaka . . . .'

'Pliss, Fergus . . . I vont to go to bed.'

'Tell me what happened when you were out walking with the old blokes . . . No, I'm not going to let you go. You're in trouble . . . and I want to help you.'

She sighed: 'You cannot help.'

'Yes I can. The only way Esk can get you is through your lack of citizenship. I can fix that in two ups by marrying you.'

'I tell you and tell you, I do not vont to marry you.'

'Well, how're you going to get out of it?' When she was silent, he went on: 'I saw you come running home. I was having a walk. I was going over to the annexe to ask you what was wrong, when I saw Whiskers coming back, too. I thought he was following you. I went to listen. But you dodged him, didn't you? I waited for you to come out. But I reckoned that you'd got out the back way . . . and I'd missed you.'

Still she was silent. He asked, 'You know he reckons you're Commos . . . you and Kurt . . . and the others?'

'Ve talk in the morning.'

'Okay. You're coming with me to Town, don't forget.'

'No.'

'You promised.'

'Now it is different.'

'Why is it?'

'Let me go . . . pliss. Ve talk in morning.'

'Give me a good night kiss, I'll let you go.'

She gave her cheek. 'That's no good.' He pulled her round to him. She gave her lips. He took them as if to possess them permanently, clasping her close, gripping one of her hands when she tried to fight free, twisted it. In her pain she got her mouth free, uttered a sharp cry. He silenced her with his mouth again. She got rid of him only by bringing her knee up into his crotch. He gasped, 'Ow!' . . . staggering back. 'You bitch!'

Panting, she turned towards the outside stairway, but stopped at the clatter of footsteps coming down. A male figure in pyjamas leapt down to the quartz gravel. The voice of Clancy rasped, 'Hey . . . what's he doing . . . molesting you?'

'Pliss . . . it is nuzzing,' she gasped.

'It's something, all right. That dingo's been dogging you all night. I been watching him.' He addressed Fergus, who was straightened up and glaring: 'You lay hands on this girl again, you bunny-lip mongrel, I'll tear the tripes out o' you.'

Fergus exploded: 'You will, eh?'

'Yeah . . . I will!'

'Try it now, you cow-dung plodder . . . . '

'Right . . . cop this!'

They leapt at each other, banging, bumping, wrestling, hissing, equals in ineptitude if not in build, hence able to hurt each other equally. Blood was soon spurting, dripping on the quartz gravel that flew like hail to their wild footwork. Rifkah whirled about them, but apparently without even being seen by them. She herself was so preoccupied that she didn't see the intrusion of others, till these leapt into the fray and stopped it, hurling the combatants apart.

Jeremy demanded of the slavering, bleeding, heaving pair, 'What's all this about?'

As if it were necessary to ask. Jeremy cut short their babbling: 'Shut up!' He turned to Rifkah. 'Did anyone molest you?'

Weeping softly, she shook her head.

'That's not true!' panted Clancy. 'I. . . . '

'Shut up!' roared Jeremy. 'Don't add to your loutishness by calling the lady a liar.'

Jeremy turned to Nan. 'Take her inside . . . and make some tea.' Then he looked at the other intruders on the hostilities: 'If you gentlemen don't mind retiring . . . I'll handle this. Goodnight!'

In a moment they were all gone, except Prindy, lurking at the corner.

The belligerents started up again to explain themselves. Again Jeremy silenced them. 'Now, listen. Neither one of you is a formally invited guest. But that doesn't mean you're not entitled to the hospitality of the place . . . until you abuse it with bad behaviour. You've been doing that for some days. Now you've forfeited it completely with behaviour that'd get you kicked out of a back-street bar. You,' he said to Fergus, 'once told me that at places you go where you feel you're not welcome, you camp in your aeroplane. You can feel like that right now. You're welcome to come back for breakfast.' He spoke to Clancy: 'And you . . . you don't live that far away that you'll be inconvenienced getting along back there without delay. It's a good night for driving. Matter of fact, by the look of the weather, it could be the last night for driving for the season. So take advantage of it. Right . . . get going. Both of you.' He swung away, motioning to Prindy, then swung back. 'If you feel like finishing that billy-goats' brawl of yours, do it well out of hearing of this place . . . or you'll have *me* to deal with . . . and when you've picked yourselves up, you might know a bit more about how to use yourselves than you do now. Goodnight!'

Rifkah was seated at the big table in the kitchen, bright head lying on arms curled on the linoleum cover. Nan was at the range, with the tea-pot, waiting on the kettle already singing on the stirred-up fire. Jeremy sat down opposite the girl, Prindy beside her. Jeremy reached and touched a slim tear-wet hand.

Without raising her head, she pushed the hand towards him. Laying his own on it and stroking gently with a finger or two, he asked, 'Is anything terribly wrong, dear?'

Shuddering with suppression of her grief, she muttered, 'I vill haf to go avay.'

'Who says?'

She lapsed back into weeping. Nan came with the tea-things. Jeremy glanced at her. She smiled. But there was the glint of tears in the deep-set eyes. He turned back to Rifkah, raised her hand and shook it slightly. 'Tea's ready now. What about sitting up . . . and getting rid of those sniffles. Here's my hanky.'

The copper head rose. The great eyes blinked on the welling tears.

Jeremy said, 'I see no reason for your having to go away . . . unless you *want* to.'

She shook her head vigorously. He went on: 'Matter of fact, Esk told me he wouldn't do anything about you and Kurt . . . in that investigation thing he said he's making.'

She snuffled: 'I hear him. I vos vaiting for you in annexe when he come back. I was hiding in lab.'

'You naughty girl! But if you heard what he said, what're you crying about?'

'He expect me to go . . . because . . . because it is not goot for you to haf me here.'

'He didn't say that.'

'He tell you about his daughter to say it.'

Jeremy swallowed, turned when Nan began to pour the tea. 'Well, let's have some tea. Nothing like tea to cheer you up, as they say . . . a shot of Caffeine to clear the vision. What's there to bother about? They'll all be gone after breakfast. Then, by the look of it, we're going to have a spell of real wet . . . and nobody able to get near us for quite a while. You've been saying you want to see the Wet. It's a bit early . . . but listen to that!' A long roll of distant thunder. He added, 'Real rain behind that . . . eh?' He looked at Prindy, who had giggled.

Prindy said, 'That motor-car . . . Clancy go.'

Jeremy chuckled. 'Well, now . . . we all make mistakes.' Nan also giggled. But Rifkah looked troubled. Jeremy said to her. 'It's all right . . . I hunted 'em both.'

They drank tea. The true rumble of thunder was soon heard. It gave them something to talk about. Heavy rain too early meant a poor Wet Season. Worse than that, as Prindy reminded them, it meant no Blackfellow Christmas. Jeremy said to that, 'I thought Christmas wasn't your *Yomtov* any more?' That got them laughing.

Thus for the best part of an hour, by which time Rifkah's tears were completely gone; but the great eyes were blinking with sleepiness; and Prindy's fair head nodding. At last, at a signal from Jeremy, Nan got the pair up, and with them snuggled against her yawning, led them away to bed. She also got a signal from Jeremy to come back to him. While he was waiting, he went into the kitchen storeroom and brought out a bottle of brandy.

When Nan returned, Jeremy asked, 'Sleepy?' She shook her head. He said, 'Well, have a drink. Then how about we take the bottle, and go for a run in the ute?' She eyed him quickly. 'Lovely night,' he said. 'Pity to waste it . . . seeing it'll be about the last fine moonlight night we'll have for a while. Right?' She nodded.

They went out arm in arm, across the blazing yard. Old Igulgul was past the zenith, and shoving back the northwestern clouds, evidently because he wanted a clear field for his magic-making. Jeremy made Nan giggle by murmuring to her, speaking the argot, as rarely he ever did to her, 'Like that old Igulgul make him me-two-feller go tchinikin Wrong-tchide bijnitch, eh?'

When they were in the utility and Nanago asked where they were going, Jeremy said they would have to go South, since Clancy had gone the other way and they didn't want their drive spoilt by his dust. However, that his choice of direction had nothing to do with Clancy's was shown when they were gone along the Beatrice Road that nine or ten miles to where the track to the Rainbow Pool ran off it, and without hesitation he turned into the track, while talking of the events of the evening. Nan interrupted him, exclaiming. 'Eh, look out!'

'What better place for a bit of Wrong-tchide bijnitch than the pool?' he asked.

'Why you take me dere?' she demanded.

'Aren't we going to play-about lil bits?'

She stared at him for a moment, then said, 'You know I don't like dat pool.'

'I know. But you know very well it can't hurt you to go there . . . with me, anyway. Besides . . . I want you to go there for a particular reason.'

'What dat?'

'I tell you when you get there. Meantime, you say *Our Father* and *I Believe* and all the Mission stuff, so's the *wahji* can't hurt you.'

They reached the pool, got out with brandy bottle and glasses, went to the bit of silky beach. The pool lay as shimmering silver. There was only slight tinkling from the waterfall and murmuring from the overflow, but that same mysterious hissing whisper from where the silver turned upon itself to make the challis lip. She eyed it apprehensively. He chuckled as he pushed her down to sit on the sand: 'That Old One can't hurt you and me. Didn't Prindy tell us that he told him he regarded us as mates, because we're looking our for his boy? Have a drink.' He poured the brandy. Raising his glass, he said, 'To life . . . *our* life!' She stared at him, the moonlight glowing in her deep dark eyes.

After sipping, she asked, 'What dat particular t'ing you say you come here for?'

'Drink that brandy off, and I'll tell you.'

When she had drunk, he took the glass, then reached for her, taking hold of her skirt at the hem, attempting to raise it. She stopped him by locking her dark arms round her legs, crying, 'What you doing?'

'I want you to have a dip with me.'

'Eh, look out!'

'Come on!'

'No-more. I can't go in dere!'

'But I want you to. You've never been in there. I want to make sure you stop here.' When she stared at him, he went on: 'I had a dream a while back. I dreamt you left me . . . went away back to the Mission.' As she stared, he continued: 'It worried me . . . not only in my sleep. In the dream, when I lost you, I felt I lost myself, too . . . well, I didn't know where I was, although I wasn't alone. It wasn't a very distinct dream . . . but, as I say, it worried me, and I thought, I'll make her take a dip in the pool, and then she can't run away.'

'Run away?' she murmured.

'I heard you talking to those Jewish women one day . . . telling them you'd been a teacher at the Mission . . . and you said you might run away sometime and do it again. Yes . . . you said Run Away. That's why I noticed it. So. Well, what about stripping off . . . and we'll have a little dip . . . and then a little play-about . . . . '

She said quite sharply, 'No!'

'Eh? What's that mean?'

'I mean dis not right time.'

'What for?'

'For anyt'ing.'

'Come on . . . out with it?'

'You love dat girl, Jeremy.'

'Now, don't be silly . . . . '

'Yas . . . you do. You know you love her . . . but you frighten' love . . . . '

'She's young enough to be my daughter.'

'She *not* your daughter.'

'All the same . . . she's young enough for it.'

'Young girl good for old man. Make him young again.'

'Make a fool of him!'

'Dem old blackfeller in wild country all got young wife. They all strong man.'

'Only because of the *Kudijingera.* And the young fellers play about with their wives behind their backs. Besides, that's what's kept the Aborigines back. An old man should have dig . . . er . . . integrity.'

'Da's what General say, eh?'

'What're you talking about?'

'Da's what Rifkah say . . . General he's talking 'bout his daughter. Dat one run after old man . . . . '

'Now, listen . . . . ' He tried to lay hands on her again.

'No, Jeremy . . . le' me 'lone. I don't want swim dis place. By'n'by might be you *want* me go away. I know dat time. I go. Spone properly you want me . . . dat old pool don't have to keep me here. But you don't know yet. You only fright' lovin' dat girl. You want to run away to me. But you can't do it like o' dat . . . not Jeremy Delacy. Spone you don't want to love Rifkah, you got to stop you'self. Nobody can stop you . . . only you . . . . '

He asked, huskily, 'What about her?'

'She is woman. She love you cos you kind and strong.'

'Like a father. Don't forget, her father half-deserted her from the start. Then she lost him when she most needed him.'

'No matter she love you like father . . . she love you . . . and spone you want her, she got to give herself to you.'

Jeremy caught his breath. She reached and touched his arm. 'I talk true, Jeremy. I know all dat lot woman get after you. I know how much chance dey got, cos I can see how much *you* want 'em. Before it all play-about for you. Not dis time.'

He sighed, stared at the slowly whirling corner of the pool. He asked, 'Do *you* love me?'

'Yas, course.'

'Aren't you jealous?'

'Only white woman get jealous . . . only woman she want to be boss of man.'

'What about Rifkah . . . is she jealous of you?'

Nan giggled slightly. 'No-more. I am like her auntie. But if you want her . . . if you marry her . . . den I reckon she start get jealous, spone I stay round. But I go first-time.'

'What on earth are you talking about . . . marry Rifkah?'

She touched his shoulder, pressed and heaved herself up by means of it, saying, 'We finish dat talk now. No-more talk about dat, pliss, Jeremy. Now I want go home. Early breakfast for dat lot. I get it. More better Rifkah stay in bed.'

He rose, reached to kiss her. She turned her dark cheek, began to move towards the truck. He put an arm about her plump waist, leaned towards her glistening dark curly hair, whispered, 'Bless you, dear Nan . . . bless you!'

She swung to him, clung to him, with arms and lips – for a moment – then broke away, gasping, giggling, 'Gwan, you . . . old night-horse! Come on . . . we go!'

In a minute they were running home. It was getting dark now, with Igulgul slipped into the cloud, his job done, perhaps, or perhaps done for him. Soon they were going through the gate, with the crippled animals whimpering and jostling round them, and the heartbeat welcoming them: *Home, home, home, a-home, home*!

CHAPTER SEVENTEEN

JEREMY'S PREDICTION of early heavy rain proved right, but not his supposing that the condition, dubious blessing as he considered it otherwise, would mean relief for his household from the intrusions upon its usually happy seclusion that lately had become a veritable plague. However, they did get a week or so of the old happiness, a spell enjoyed by everyone (excepting those who saw the rain first as a threat to the Christmas festivities) but by none nearly so much as by Rifkah. Nor was it simply the fact that the place again had become a haven that gave the girl the fairly bubbling joy she showed during the period, but the rain, the rain, the rain! Already in love with the land in its most unattractive state, drought-stricken by months of Dry Season, having heard so much about its sudden transformation by rain, she lapped up the change in conditions eagerly as a child does happy variation, and lapped literally, often with tongue out-thrust to drink of the stinging sweetness.

Jeremy warned her that this seeming bounty could be disastrous to the natural economy, that grasses could be roused to sprouting out of suspended animation only to be exposed to the solsticial ferocity to be expected at that time of year but normally from which growing things in their frailty were protected by the tempering conditions of the Intertropic Frontal System: the massive clouding, the dripping humidity, the sheeting rain. If the freakish rains ceased and drought struck the land again because the proper frontal movement had been checked, buds could wither on the bough, roots give up hoarded moisture for lack of which a tree could die, a myriad creatures unprepared for sudden dehydration left to perish in cracked mud. Absolute evidence that conditions were not normal, he said, was the fact that the Giant Cuckoo, so-called, properly called *Googoomara*, was still about, waging noisy mock battles with his mates to divert the crows and magpies and the like from their nesting so as to cuckoo 'em. *Googoomara* invariably came with the first thunderstorms, and cleared out before the rain set in properly, leaving his victims to suffer the discomfort of it while rearing his fobbed-off progeny. The fact was, you could just about estimate when it was Christmas with cessation of all the yelling, screaming, fluttering that accompanied this annual piece of dirty work. Prindy corroborated his grandfather's reasoning as far as *Googoomara* was concerned, but contended that only Tchamala was responsible for the abnormal conditions. Rifkah appeared to accept it both ways.

She spent most of the period out of doors, along with Prindy, splashing about on foot in rubber boots and oilskins. Riding was out of the question, because all of the horses were too fractious for safe handling, as always the case at the onset of continuous rain. Thus did she roam the neighbourhood, watching the pools fill, to spill into streamlets, to set the creeks trickling, racing, roaring – helping where possible the creatures scrambling and struggling to adapt themselves to the too-sudden change in the state of things and rescuing where disaster threatened – taking note of all that was shown her: the sprouting and budding, the shedding of old bark to reveal the wonder of what had been created in secret meanwhile, the frantic masonry of termites and engineering of ants and forth-popping of so many lovely things metamorphosed from deep-lain pupation – and, joy of joys, spying on the large white flowers, white-feller named Morning Glory, during the couple of hours of their exquisite blossoming before the dawn. It did, in fact, seem as if the rain always eased off to mere mist to permit the blossoming, as local legend had it.

In lingo the Morning Glories were called *Gringelli*, which also meant stars. The legend told of how the Bandicoot Sisters, Iyuwuk, were fleeing from that old reprobate Wanjin, the Dingo, who declared that he wanted them for wives, but secretly intended to eat them, as everything he could get his sharp teeth into. It was Wet Season. Wanjin manoeuvred the sisters into a swampy region, where he knew that they, helpless in mud and water and in want of their own kind of food, would soon give up. But the Ol'Goomun-Ol'Goomun, watching from the sky, felt sorry for them, gathered some little stars, which are celestial flowers, and scattered them along bits of ridges in the swamp, to show them the way out and also to feed them in the process, since she attached a sweet little yam to every flower as a root. The stars shone only during those couple of hours before daybreak when Wanji has to sleep, and vanished completely with the dawn, so that he could not track them, baffled as he was by the onset of rain again.

In fact, the diaphanous stuff of the swamp morning glories surrounds a silver star. As the rain eases with approach of dawn, the tightly furled buds, pointing like long slim fingers since midnight, open while you watch, unfurling into perfect pentagons in which shape they glow and shimmer as with inner light and seem thus to float along the ground – 'Like leedle ballerina,' as Rifkah said. With daylight they fall into rags, to dissolve like wafers in the ooze created by rain now falling like warm tears shed for the reality that beauty is for ever transient. Prindy made up a song about it, which they sang together while gathering mushrooms.

It began to rain the night before the first train-day of the happy period. Only Darcy and his family went in to the siding. They had to use skid-chains to make it home again.

Although Jeremy's prediction from studying his meteorological apparatus was that the rain would be over by next train-day, when that day came it was raining so hard that Darcy, to whom the trip was left again, had to make it in the dray, with two draught horses pulling. As usual he took his family, who under the low-hung tarpaulin looked and sounded rather like a load of Ah Loy's pigs being taken for shipping up to Town for Chinese New Year, as with mirth it was stated by those watching them go. Since it would take them the best part of the day to get to the siding, they would be spending the night with the Tooheys and returning tomorrow. When next day they reached home again, it was raining even harder. Thus was the Mullaka, for all his cleverness in other directions, exposed as knowing no more about the weather than any other *kuttabah* did about natural phenomena, which any fool blackfellow knew had no more to do with barometers and thermometers and such things than a high-tension coil had to do with lightning. At least, that was the way in which Prindy, whom Jeremy had been instructing in meteorology according to the book, privily expressed himself to Rifkah. Similarly, that supposition of Jeremy's that at least the otherwise dubious blessing of the rain would give them back their old happy isolation was shown up as fallacious, because the seeming load of pigs that drew up in sheeting rain at the back door of the Big House on Thursday afternoon had increased by one, and one so little welcome, that when Jeremy was informed of the intrusion by Nan's telephoning him at the annexe, he groaned, 'Oh, lord!' The intruder was Fay McFee, news-hound, of the *Port Palmeston Progressive*.

Fay was come to look into the matter of the Refugee Jews' Settlement, having been waiting, it was revealed, for the return of Ernest and his party to Town to interview them, learning of their departure only the other day from Fergus. When Jeremy heard of her arrival, she was already in the kitchen of the Big House, drinking tea that had had to be forced on her, more or less, because of her reluctance to accept anything in the way of hospitality from her old enemy. Nan informed him that it was Fay's intention to camp in a shed, sustained by rations she had brought along with her, while getting what she wanted from Rifkah and Kurt. Jeremy told Nan to give his greetings to Fay and tell her he would be right over, but that meantime he wished to see Kurt and warn him about Fay and would she ask him to come over unbeknown to the lady. When Kurt came, Jeremy growled, 'She's a pest, really. I wish I could put her up in a shed. Oh, she means that, all right. Last time she was here, she camped like a drover, under the mangoes. She came here about that Euraustralian thing I tried . . . with the halfcastes . . . my Dictatorship, as she called it in that rag of hers. She's a fool . . . but a clever journalist . . . which means that she can do a lot of harm. I know you're clever enough to handle her. But you don't want publicity . . . and so I thought I'd better have a word with you first. She's madly political, but in the stiff Centre style of official Labor. Talk socialism . . . but with a small S . . . and you'll have her eating out of your hand. I guess Rifkah will get her in by having her eating off plates. She likes her tum, does old Fay. I used to torture her while she was camping out there with bully-beef and biscuits by having the roasts that are sent over from the Big House kitchen to the Aboriginal section carried right under her nose. She also has a weakness for the female of her species . . . so they say.'

Jeremy had to be all but abject to induce Fay not to leave his roof. In fact he settled the matter only by saying that she might regard herself as the guest of Kurt and Rifkah. Quite ungraciously, she acceded, saying that, anyway, she would be staying only one night.

Fay stayed a week, 'The happiest week of my life,' as she described it, not only in words spoken in farewell to her hosts, but in what subsequently she wrote of the experience and had printed nationally. Other superlatives she used were that Kurt was the most charming and intelligent man she'd ever known, and Rifkah the sweetest and most beautiful woman, and a cook *par excellence*. Even if the pair did begin by beguiling her deliberately, it would have cost them small effort to win her extreme regard, political dreamer and inverted virgin that she was. Half the time she spent at the feet of the sexless Socrates, listening wide-eyed and open-mouthed to his nostalgic dissertation on what would be so much more satisfying to her essentially romantic nature than the crude reality of the domestic politics in which she had to root for a living like a pig, namely, International Socialism, told like a fairy-tale in a foreign accent, with names of places that conjured up visions of barricaded streets, noble fighters for the Brotherhood of Man being trampled under the hoofs of hussars' chargers, and the Shades of prophets of the proletariat less troublesome than Marx, Engels, Lenin. The rest she spent either playing house with her red-haired girlfriend, cooking, cooking, or out in the rain, the rain, little-girl nature-studying, or sitting cosy of nights singing Jewish folksongs to the music of an Aboriginal child who made the true sap of womanhood rise warm in her ample bosom – 'Little Boy Pan,' as she called him, not knowing that he mimicked her braying voice and jenny donkey's waddle when reporting to his grandfather.

Jeremy himself mostly kept out of the way, joining the others only for drinks and meals, when he acted the Squatter, which by her own stiff formality in his presence evidently she wanted. It was only at parting that she unbent to him, saying that she regretted the unfriendliness of the past and hoped they might be friends in future.

The rain was gone and the earth baking, when next Thursday morning Fay departed from Lily Lagoons. She rode in the utility, with Rifkah driving and Prindy between them. Behind them came all the other vehicles on the place, because all those who recognized Christmas as their *Yomtov* were going to be able to celebrate it after all. This latter circumstance was generally believed to be due to Prindy, who had been approached by his brindle cousins to do something about the rain, seeing that he was supposed to be in the business. Whether or not he did any actual Singing was not clear. Anyway, when asked if he had stopped the rain he gave a solemn affirmative. This greatly tickled Fay. Nevertheless, she did say that she could believe anything of Little Boy Pan, and showed her credulity further when on the way to the Beatrice they turned off to take a look at the Rainbow Pool, and she said that she would like to take the magic dip, 'Just for the fun of it,' since, of course, she didn't believe in such nonsense.

If Old Tchamala were watching from down below, as Prindy suggested he well might be, there being a hint of rainbow hanging over the now cascading falls, the Old One certainly saw a sight in that mass of human female flesh wallowing and puffing like a pink and white buffalo. Prindy tittered behind the ample back – but only to get a disapproving look from Rifkah. Fay herself, staring frankly at the lissom golden nakedness of her companions, expressed her delight in them with a bovine sigh.

They were at the siding to see the train come in from the Head of the Road, an event usually of interest only to railwaymen, police, blacks, even when it would be a full train, as this one loaded with people heading to Town for Christmas. There would be plenty of time to see who was aboard, since it would be staying the night. However, Pat Hannaford was driving, and seeing

Rifkah for the first time for a while, came in with such a din of whistling as to bring everybody out to see. When Rifkah laughed and waved acknowledgement, Fay scowled, grunting, 'That bloody larrikin!' When Pat, immediately on stopping, leapt down from his engine and came loping towards them, Fay snapped, 'I don't talk to the lout. See you in a minute.' She set off towards the alighting passengers, turning to add, 'Don't let him spoil our last lovely evening.'

Pat might easily have spoilt things. He began by saying to Rifkah, 'You wan' 'o look out that old bitch. She's a lez, for a start. She put the hard word on you?' Rifkah giggled, probably not understanding. Then he proceeded to make arrangements for the night. First he would take her shunting, then for drinks, then to dinner – and, afterwards, well – She told him of the arrangements already made, how she and Fay and Prindy would be having a curry supper at Barbu's and afterwards Indian music, and then Tom Toohey would be taking her home. The only concession she would make was in the matter of the shunting – provided he took Prindy along too. Pat acceded, even let Prindy do a bit of tail-pullin' and whistling while he himself disinterestedly lent a ginger hand, while otherwise almost completely preoccupied with his other passenger.

As they puffed up and down the yards, Pat said to Rifkah, 'You're mad to let her write anything about you. She's a wizard for dobbin' people in. Beats me why you had anything to do with her at all, seeing that Committee mob o' yours dodged her when she tried to interview 'em up in Town. Didn' yo' know? If I'd'a' been drivin' last mail train she'd never got out there to see you . . . if I'd'a' had to shanghai her to the Head o' Road and dump her there. She'll put you in the poo if she writes anything 'bout you . . . sure as Lenin lived, girl.'

Rifkah explained that she and Kurt had been most careful in what they had said, and had Fay's assurance that no mention would be made of the Settlement and no identities disclosed – only a Pen Portrait. Moreover, Fay had promised to let them see what she wrote before she handed it to the press.

Pat shrugged. 'Well, at least you were wise in tyin' her up like that. I wasn't when she did one of her famous Pen Portraits o' me. Christ, the trouble I had! Nearly booted out of the Party . . . suspended from me job . . . could'a' landed in clink, only that the bosses hate her guts. And, d'you know . . . she still thinks she done me a favour! I tell you, when it comes to dobbin' anyone in, old Fay's a sheer genius.' Rifkah only smiled, surely still understanding but half of what he said.

Pat left them to their Lovely Last Evening. They ended it by walking with arms about each other's waists from Barbu's, where Prindy was sleeping, down to the roaring crossing, in darkness that glittered with stars and fireflies and Finnucane's lights and reeked of the cracking mud and the goats. Parting at last at the door of Fay's room at the hotel, Fay clung and kissed hungrily, then dashed away to hide her tears.

There were more tears and kisses next morning at the train. Perhaps that was why Pat, seen to be hanging out of his cab, sounded so impatient with his whistling to get the passengers aboard, and then, in moving off, gave that seemingly spiteful jerk which sent those leaning out of windows for a last touch of hands flopping into seats.

II

True to her word, Fay McFee sent the script of the Pen Portrait by next mail, along with a letter for Rifkah. The letter was largely a rather lyrical recounting of the joys of the recent interlude, for the rest a report, penned with the ironic gusto for which Fay was famous in lampooning the local aristocracy. It concerned the Boxing Day Party held at the Delacy place on Rainbow Beach, one of the grand social events of the year, Very Posh, Don't You Know, but which this year had ended in a vulgar brawl. 'Scratch a squatter,' Fay wrote, 'and you'll find that beastly common fellow the squattocracy so despise – the ringer.' I'm going to call it *Scratch a Squatter*. It'll be in next week's issue – provided my heroic editor doesn't get the Libel Shits.'

It seemed that the fracas began as a clash between those two bravos, Clancy Delacy and Fergus Ferris. Half of the other gents had become embroiled through trying to separate them, and then some of the ladies going in to stop their men and seeing a chance to settle old scores. 'They'll never live it down,' wrote Fay. 'Lady Rhoda's gone into smoke – booked on the next plane for the South, I hear, and the Festive Season only halfway through! Next on the list is Captain Shane's New Year's Party. I must disguise myself and crash it. Best disguise at the moment as one of the elite is a black eye. But the biggest laugh is that it all started over *you*. There's a whisper that the two louts fought over you down at Lily Lagoons. I can't believe it – but is it true? I wouldn't mention it in the piece for the paper, of course. I hope you'll like the Pen Portrait. It's all ready for whizzing away to *Truth*. If you have any objection to it, wire me at once.

As if anyone could object to something written with so much love! It was entitled *Rebecca the Refugee*, and told of a lovely Jewish girl, who'd come through the hell of Nazi persecution, to find complete happiness in an environment that would be considered utterly alien to her, amongst people quite strange – this surely vindication of those who supported the idea of offering this empty land as refuge for the like of her, the bravest, healthiest, most intelligent and adaptable immigrants any country could wish to have. It went on to tell of Fay's own sweet experience in company with the lovely gentle girl, away there in the wilderness, where she had come to love everything, from butterflies to blackfellows – and being loved in return. Every intelligent creature turned to her: horse, dog, the injured creatures of the wild that, like the sweet girl herself, had made the place a refuge. There was also something about the Jewish Doctor, with the face and the gentleness of Christ – and about a Little Boy Pan, an Aboriginal waif rescued from the hell of official semi-neglect, to prove, under the guidance of Rebecca, to be a Musical Genius no less. Such was this lovely influence that the squatter, the Big Boss, on whose property this wonderful thing was taking place, from having been the hardest, bitterest man in the land, now sat at his own table with head bowed and covered, while prayers were said in Hebrew on Sabbath Eve.

That bit about the Big Boss was all Fay had to say about Jeremy – and quite enough, according to him: 'Just what Fay would do. With one stroke of that pen of hers, make me the laughing-stock of the country.'

Rifkah asked, 'Vot is laughing-stock?'

'Oh . . . well, to tell you the truth, I don't know. Just an expression.'

'You do not like vot she write? I vill ask her to stop it.'

'No, no, my dear. Leave it as it is. What she's written about you is inspired.'

III

Next train day, in at the Beatrice, waiting for the train, Rifkah, with Prindy and Kurt, found Clancy beside her. She was surprised. He looked wary, muttered, 'Happy New Year.'

She echoed the greeting, adding, 'You 'ave goot time in Town?'

Avoiding her eyes he answered, 'Oh, the usual.'

Further embarrassment was avoided by the coming of the train. As she came roaring over the bridge, they talked of the weather. Pat Hannaford was driving again. He quickly saw Rifkah and Clancy, and after staring at them for a moment as he came rolling in, withdrew from his customary leaning out of the side of the cab, but almost immediately to appear again, with something in his hand, with which he climbed down the steps of the now very slowly moving locomotive – not to alight, but to lean out to the crowd to the limit of his long arms and legs, and thrust the thing into the hands of staring Clancy. It was a copy of *The Port Palmeston Progressive*. Clancy took it, gaping now. Winking at Rifkah, Pat hauled himself back, and clambering up into the cab, looked round and back at Clancy, yelled, 'Read all about it, Squatter-boy!'

Still gaping, and with many eyes on him, Clancy watched the engine disappear beyond the station, then looked at Rifkah, who was peeking at the paper, then looked at the paper himself. The *Progressive* never ran a headline wider than a column; but this one was plain enough to see, even blurred a bit by Pat's engine-driver's thumb: SCRATCH A SQUATTER. He couldn't have read more in the glance he gave it, or have guessed at the import till he looked up again at Rifkah, to find her eyeing him quite guiltily. She proved her guiltiness by saying hastily, 'Moost get ze mail,' and started off into the crowd, with Prindy and Kurt following.

Clancy watched them disappear, then looked again at the paper, read while his face flamed and rumpled. He looked up again. Everybody was occupied with something. He twisted the paper in his hands as if to tear it, then folded it with a slap, grasped it on one hand, turned and went walking quickly away.

Hannaford, coming from his engine, found Rifkah and pulled her out of the crowd, saying, 'You're famous . . . you've hit the National headlines.' He had the latest *Truth*, which when they had got clear of the crowd, he opened for her, to reveal a banner headline: REBECCA THE REFUGEE. Sub-heading declared: From Nazi Prison to Freedom in Never Never – Jewish Girl Becomes Bush Woman Overnight.

Pat guffawed, 'Does she wrap you up! Look . . . "This sweet and lovely creature." Told you she was a lez. If you'd a been a man she'd a tore the tripes out o' you. You should see what she wrote about the Scrub Bull. Sittin' up at the table sayin' prayers like an old Jew . . . Ho, ho, ho! He'll never live it down.'

Apparently quite heedless of the ruffling of the lovely brows, Pat went on, after a glance about, 'Yo' boyfriend skedaddled, eh? So him and the pilot bloke had a go in at Lily Lagoons, eh? 'S all right . . . Ferris told me 'bout it himself.'

She said shortly, 'Pliss . . . you talk about my friend!'

'Eh? Rubbish like that your friends?'

'Zey are my friend . . . as you are my friend. I vill not let zem talk about you in such vay.'

He stared at her. 'Okay, okay . . . Well, what about a run on the injin . . . then a drink! I got a paper in German . . . supposed to be underground. Like to know what it says. Where's Kurt?'

They couldn't ride with him, because they wanted to get back home. However they had a drink with him and read bits of his paper to him. There was no sign of Clancy at Finnucane's. Prindy spent the waiting time at Barbu's, practising on a brand new clarinet sent him as a present from General Esk. No doubt the instrument had been recommended as a better medium for his own music by Denzil Dickey, passed on from the old flautist, Herschal – perhaps from the latter as subtle protest against use of the flute for the Primitive he abominated.

IV

Storm clouds began to gather from the North again, but only to be dissipated in dry fireworks over the Plateau, the din of which of sultry evenings roused the tree-frogs round about Lily Lagoons to flat-toned croaks that surely were protests, like the angry shouting of the nuttagul geese on the billabongs, which was so loud as to be heard at times at the homestead. The gathering of geese so early for nesting was taken by weather prophets as yet another indication of a poor Wet Season. When the rain did come, they said, it would last no longer than it took the geese to hatch their eggs.

It was on such an afternoon of dry rioting of the elements while the mocked world wilted that a new sound was heard. Naturally Prindy heard it first, announced, 'Aeroplane come . . . Fergus!'

There soon was Fergus grinning down at them as he banked over the mangoes, but only a glimpse of what appeared to be a boy's face at a cabin window. 'Who could it be?' they were all asking. Anyway, only Jeremy and Prindy went out in the utility to be the first to see. Both got a surprise on seeing the face of the trim female figure in light brown that stepped out of the aircraft, smiling and waving, that came running with a twinkle of white legs and shiny high heels and a toss of brown curls, crying, 'Jeremy . . . Jeremy, darling!'

It was Aelfrieda Candlemas – Alfie!

She flung herself into Jeremy's arms, fastening her red mouth to his, clinging, clinging. When at last she drew back, she laughed in his purpled face. 'Surprised?'

He gasped, 'What d'you think?'

Her lovely mouth was wide with laughter, her little teeth gleaming. 'My same dear darling dry old Jeremy . . . mmmm!' She kissed him again.

Fergus, coming with a single suitcase, grinned. 'Sorry you put that strip down now, eh, Mullaka? You'll have to get an anti-aircraft gun.' When he saw Jeremy looking expectantly at the plane, he added, 'Nobody else.'

Jeremy asked Alfie, 'Where's your husband?'

'Frank's in Sydney. He isn't in this. It isn't exactly a social call.' When he looked at her questioningly, she added, 'I mean that I came for a special reason . . . but, of course, first to see you.'

'Where'd you come from?'

'Sydney. Fergus was down with that General of yours. So I hitched a ride back . . . . ' She broke off on noticing Prindy, stared, cried, 'No . . . it can't be . . . but it is! I thought when I heard that it must be . . . Prendegast!' She grabbed him, hugged him, kissed him, held him off to stare at the good clothes, the stance, and turned to Jeremy. 'I knew it would work. Didn't I tell you? I knew it would work. But isn't it wonderful!' Then to Prindy again, saying, 'But you lost your poor mother. Fergus told me.'

Prindy blinked, was silent for a moment, then, because she was staring, turned his face with lips projected towards the homestead, said, 'Mumma there.'

'What?' she demanded, and looked at Jeremy.

He gave a slight warningful shake of the head. She asked, 'Why, what?'

He murmured, 'Another mother.' Then: 'That all your luggage?'

Alfie said, 'It's really only a flying visit . . . figuratively, as well as literally. I want to catch the mail plane back on Monday.'

'Hmm! Must be important, to bring you all this way for a couple of days.'

'It is!'

The answer was made with such emphasis that Jeremy looked at her quickly, but meeting the black eyes, wide with challenge, as quickly looked away, at Fergus, to whom he said, 'You'll put up at the house too, eh, son?'

'Thanks, Mullaka,' said Fergus, and swung away to get his own valise.

As Jeremy turned back to Alfie to hand her into the utility, she said, 'I understood you had some people here . . . Jews.'

He didn't look at her, or answer till he'd got her seated: 'A Jewish doctor, and a . . . young lady.' He hesitated slightly in saying the last, and coloured a little. He added quickly, turning away to look at Prindy and Fergus getting into the back, 'Refugees.'

As quickly she asked, 'Are they staying permanently?'

He didn't answer, but went round to get in on the other side.

As he started up, she said, 'I asked you if your Jews are staying permanently.'

With eyes on the track as he drove off, he answered, 'Permanent's a longish word, isn't it?'

She gave a little giggle, and pushed her curly head against his shoulder. 'My same dear darling Jeremy, quibbling about words.' Then as she straightened up, she spoke crisply: 'Speaking of words . . . we haven't had anything from you lately.' When he shrugged, she asked, 'What's that mean?' He shrugged again, this time with a grimace. She demanded: 'Means you're not writing, eh?' When still he remained silent, she asked, in the same tone, 'Why not?'

He shot her a glance, looked away. She said, 'Meaning mind your own business, eh?' When he smiled slightly, she said sharply, 'It *is* my business, Jeremy . . . if it's something that's wasting your talents.'

He half-growled, 'What talents?'

'You've already shown it tremendously in what you've written.'

He looked at her fully and in surprise. 'Attacks on Anti-Judaism in an Anti-Semitic rag!'

'Your articles were far more than that. That's why they were published.'

'I wasn't aware of anything else in them.'

'You wouldn't be . . . because of your natural genius. What you were doing, was speaking with the true Voice of Australia. It inspired us all . . . as I wrote and told you at the time . . . .'

'And the contempt I expressed for your Anti-Semitism?'

'The Anti-Semitism is rather something of a mistake.'

'I haven't noticed that you've cut it out of subsequent editions.'

'That would be *your* job.'

He looked again in surprise. She went on, somewhat breathlessly, and with pretty face bright with excitement now: 'I mean it, Jeremy! Your talent's needed now as never before. Even to rectify mistakes, with the great common sense you have as well . . . a rare thing in men of genius.'

He flushed. 'Now, go easy . . . .'

'I'm not going easy. This is the *Time*, Jeremy . . . for all of us . . . and for *you* most of all of us.'

'Time for what?'

'Being Australian.'

He sighed: 'Haven't I been Australian all my life . . . God help me!'

'You've got to teach other people to be as Australian as yourself.'

'Haven't we been through all this before?'

'We only just got started on it before.'

'Is this another session?'

'Any objection?'

He shrugged. 'You are my guest, my dear.'

'But uninvited, eh?' Then when he didn't answer, she leaned against his shoulder again, murmuring, 'You called me My Dear. I like that.' When he stiffened, she withdrew, but ran a slim hand down the bare of his arm, adding with a sigh, 'Because you are dear to *me*, Jeremy.'

They ran on in silence to the homestead, came through the mangoes, were slowing down in the run across the yard to the front of the Big House, when she said, in a voice that sounded strained, 'I hear there's a beautiful Jewess involved.'

He swallowed, waited till he had stopped the car to answer, 'In what?'

She almost snapped it, 'In you!'

He alighted, went round to help her out. But she was getting out already. For a moment she stared into his eyes as he stood waiting. Then as her feet touched the ground, she smiled her wide smile, swung to Prindy who was climbing down, looked around, exclaiming, 'Dear Lily Lagoons! It's like coming home again.'

He took her arm to lead her in, perhaps to prevent her from taking his.

Rifkah was waiting, with Kurt, in the lounge, not in the usual mannish outfit she affected, the stockrider's pants and shirt, but in a floral dress, and looking very feminine, and was flushed and a little out of breath, perhaps through having changed in haste. Why should she change, if not at a hint from someone who knew something of the visitor and thought the move tactical? That is to say Nanago who was not in evidence herself.

The eyes of the two young women seized upon each other at sight, the hazel eyes of the one seeming to grow wider as if in apprehension, the other's black eyes to narrow calculatingly. Jeremy, apparently, was aware of the tension between the two, judging by his awkwardness in introducing them. Alfie, flashing her wide smile when the introductions were done, spun on her high heels to look round the room with a proprietorial air, saying, 'This dear place . . . I do miss it . . . the peace!' She turned to Jeremy. 'I could never live permanently in the South again.' Then she giggled: 'Of course, I've got to come back eventually for good . . . because I've swum in the Pool. I was telling Fergus, as we flew over it. He says he's swum in it, too.' Then she turned quickly on Rifkah. 'Fergus says you've done it, too.'

Rifkah coloured, shot a glance at Fergus, who looked down. She looked back at Alfie, swallowed, and murmured, 'Yes.'

Alfie's colour rose too. Her eyes narrowed: 'Did you know that if you do that, you'll have to die here?'

Again the murmured answer, with a slight nod, 'Yes.'

Now Alfie swallowed, 'Then why did you do it?'

Rifkah drew a deep breath. 'I like it here.'

Alfie took another swing round, but to look at the others in the room, then back to Rifkah. 'How can you really like it, when you don't belong here?'

Another swallow. 'I belong here now.'

Alfie made an impatient gesture. 'But that's ridiculous. You're a stranger. You come from something quite different. You've got to be born here.' She turned on Jeremy. 'You can't really love a place unless you belong to it . . . you've got to grow out of it . . . like a tree . . . be part of the soil itself . . . and its tradition has got to be yours. Isn't that so, Jeremy?'

Jeremy, looking rather red, turned to get drinks. Alfie flung after him. 'Well, that's what you taught me . . . Master!'

Jeremy, quite red now, glanced at her sternly, but only to say, 'I presume you still drink alcohol?'

'Of course . . . didn't you teach me that too?' And she came after him, adding: 'But what's happened to so suddenly change your opinions?'

Getting the home-brew out of the ice-box, he growled, 'What opinions?'

'Of love of the land . . . of the spirit of the place.'

He looked right at her, snapping, 'Perhaps reading that rag, *Australia Free.*'

Fergus gave a loud guffaw. Now Alfie went red. But she summoned up the smile. 'Well, so long as you read it . . . and, write for it.'

Jeremy set the drink on the table. A little silence. Alfie broke it, doing another of her flings around: 'But where's Nanago?' She looked at Rifkah.

Rifkah answered promptly, 'In kitchen . . . I vill get her.' She started off.

'No . . . I'll go myself,' said Alfie quickly.

For a step or two they went shoulder to shoulder, eyeing each other with that primary intensity and similar expressions. Then Rifkah halted. She looked back, at Jeremy who was staring. A moment. Then she said, 'All right. I go get rooms ready.'

Alfie threw a smile back at the others, surely of triumph the way her eyes shone. Then she went into the dining-room, through to the kitchen, hailing Nan loudly as she entered.

Nan, also dressed up, and with a hibiscus in her hair, looked startled for the moment. Alfie smiled easily, looking her over, saying, 'My, but you look nice!' And she kissed her. 'No troubles?' she asked.

Nan smiled in answer and shook her head.

'Nice to see you again, Nan, dear . . . . But how're you getting along with the Jew-girl . . . what's her name?'

Nan met the quizzing black eyes. 'Rifkah all right.'

'That's nice. You're still the boss, then?'

'On'y one boss . . . Jeremy.'

Again their eyes clung. Then Alfie swung away, to speak to the black girls. As she was turning to go back to the lounge, after some minutes of playful talk and looking about the place, she said to Nan, 'Prindy's come on marvellously, hasn't he! Who's responsible for the . . . for breaking him in?' Alfie giggled at her own way of putting it, adding, 'You or the Boss?'

'Nobody break him in. He jes come quiet, himself-himself.'

'Ah . . . I knew he would! But what's this about his having another mother . . . that you, eh?'

Nan shook her head, so that the hibiscus shed its laden pollen on her silky hair. 'I can't be his Mumma.'

'Who then?'

Again their eyes locked. Nan projected her lips towards the lounge. Alfie's eyes widened. 'You don't mean the Jew-girl?'

Still holding the other dark eyes, Nanago asked, 'Don' you know dat girl name yet?'

Alfie blinked, and reddened slightly, took a moment to answer, '*Well*!' With that she left the kitchen.

It was a somewhat different Alfie who re-entered the lounge. Gone that new arrogance, that impatient swinging-about of the woman of the world with more to do than play at social niceties. Her smile was less wide, her manner more that of the engaging little girl of old. Seeing the drinks out, she said, 'Ah . . . that's what I want . . . something to relax me. Coming back here by plane's too quick. Coming from a place like Sydney, you need to go through some sort of decompression chamber, like divers do. Ah, this lovely Lily Lagoons brew! The nicest stuff in the world.' She looked fondly at Jeremy, adding, 'Except brandy with you!' She sighed.

Rifkah wasn't there to hear it.

Then Alfie concentrated on Prindy, drawing him to her armchair, putting an arm about him, asking about his music, of which she had heard from Fergus. He answered readily enough. She cried, 'Marvellous! Of course, you're nationally famous already as a musician . . . *The Little Boy Pan*!' She laughed merrily.

Rifkah came back to have a drink just before dinner. Alfie was very polite to her now, telling her how she had read of her in *Truth*. On the subject of riding, she laughed over her own poor showing on a horse, telling of her sore bottom and how Jeremy had made her an ointment for it, making it sound rather as if he had done more than the dispensing in treating her. Then the gong rang.

The meal went pleasantly enough, even animated by Alfie's talkativeness. She talked mostly of the constructive things being accomplished by the Free Australia Movement, such as no one could object to, the urging of the establishment of a National University, the development of the Commonwealth Literary Fund from the mean Pensions for Poverty-stricken Old Writers Scheme it had functioned as since its inception with foundation of the Nation to true subsidization of national talent to break the power of British Commercial Imperialism wielded so ruthlessly by the great British publishing concerns, appointment only of born Australians to the Vice-Regal positions so far held by Englishmen responsible only to the Crown of England. On this last score, she seemed even ignorant of the fact that the reform had been effected by the Scullin Labor Government back in 1931, with appointment of Chief Justice Isaac Isaacs to the Governor-Generalship, only to have it rescinded when the British Garrison, as she called it, got back into power with the betrayal of the Labor Party by Joseph Lyons, and the replacement of Isaacs with General Lord Gowrie – surely a nice point in her argument. But perhaps the fact that Isaacs was a Jew precluded him from mention in any matter concerning reform by Australia Free. It seemed for a moment that Jeremy was going to raise the matter, when he mentioned the fact that the reform was one of the Scullin Government's ideals. However, he took it no further, maybe as a good host, or it could have been by reason of Alfie's looking so childishly innocent in her enthusiasm for her cause. Both Rifkah and Kurt showed lively interest. Fergus, usually the life of the party, had little to say.

After dinner they all returned to the lounge. No walk tonight, by unspoken mutual consent, it seemed, even though it was a perfect night for walking, with Igulgul at first quarter sailing the ragged edge of the northern cloud mass. Perhaps it was preoccupation with the news that kept them in. The radio news and comments all concerned Hitler's now blatant disregard for the promises he'd made in the Munich Agreement concerning interference in Czechoslavakia. Only Alfie had much to say about it, not supporting Hitler by any means, but harping on the vital need for Australia to keep out of the certain trouble brewing: 'This is our one chance of nationhood,' she kept saying, 'Our last chance. If we're dragged into another war with the British it will be the end of us . . . financially, morally, in every way. Isn't that so, Jeremy?' He agreed, but with nothing like the enthusiasm that might be expected, and even went so far as to say that constitutionally there was no gainsaying involvement, since Australia was not a truly Sovereign State, not having ratified the Treaty of Westminster. That piece of information, unknown to Alfie, and evidently not to her superiors in her Movement, fairly fired her. She became quite hoarse trying to get him to commit himself to write an article on it, to do what she called, Expose the Dastardly Lie we Live Under. He argued that if he she called the Chief couldn't do it, the Movement wasn't worth tuppence. The arguing was stopped by the coming of Prindy with his clarinet, to play for Alfie, as she had earlier requested.

Prindy played quite unselfconsciously. Alfie was delighted, and said that she must see to doing something about getting his compositions published through *Australia Free*. 'We're doing this for poetry,' she said. 'Of purely Australian tradition, of course.' When Jeremy asked if the obvious Indian influence might not disqualify Prindy's work, she cried, 'Why should it? The Indians were amongst the first of our pioneers.'

In the same dry tone, Jeremy asked, 'Then what about Jewish influence?'

Alfie blinked, looked quickly at Rifkah, who was watching her, then back to Jeremy, with colour mounting, and rather demanded, 'Why Jewish?'

'Well . . . that *Morning Glory* thing you liked so much, is very much in the tradition of the Yiddish folksong, I understand. Isn't that so, Kurt?'

Kurt nodded and smiled. But it was on Rifkah again that Alfie's dark eyes, narrowing, lit. She turned away from the gazing great jewels with half a shrug, back to Jeremy. 'I was speaking of Australian tradition . . . . '

'If you concede Indians a right to have contributed to it, why not Jews? They were amongst our first citizens, in chains and out of them. As a matter of fact, our richest slang is derived from Yiddish . . . *shikker, cobber, kleiner, spieler* . . . didn't you know?'

Alfie looked so much at a loss that the black eyes hinted of tears

Prindy, perhaps, saved the situation, at least for the moment, by rising and saying he was going to bed. Rifkah sprang up and went to him. Jeremy also rose, saying, 'About time we all adjourned, I think. You people must've had a long day.'

'I'll say,' said Fergus, also rising, stretching, yawning. 'I've been on the go since four this morning.'

They were all up now, except Alfie. When Jeremy looked at her, she said, 'I've got something for you to read.'

He stifled a yawn: 'Okay. Let's have it.'

She said it was in her suitcase, and rose and went hurrying to get it, ignoring Rifkah and Prindy about to mount the stairs, ran up. When she came down, which was after a little delay, there was no one left in the lounge except Jeremy. She handed him a long envelope. He glanced at it, put it in the back pocket of his trousers. She said, 'I'd like you to read it tonight. It's actually why I came.'

'Okay. I'll read it over in my den. Goodnight, dear!'

She said quickly, 'But I want to be with you while you read it.'

He looked into the black eyes, regarding him earnestly, hesitated for a moment, then said, 'No, dear . . if you don't mind. You hop off to bed. I'll give you my opinion in the morning. Best for me to sleep on it, too.'

She cried, 'But it isn't something to sleep on. It's urgent!'

She caught his arm. He stiffened, to hold her off, saying gently. 'If it was so terribly urgent, why didn't you give it to me at once?'

'What chance did I have with that . . . with those . . . with . . . . ' Tears welled in the eyes like a disappointed child's.

He said quickly, 'In the morning, dear. Good night!'

But she flung herself upon him, pressing into him, seeking his lips. He held her off, looking red, but saying gently enough, 'That was naughty. Now, off you go. See you in the morning.' He pushed her back into an armchair, then wheeled and went off quickly, through dining-room and kitchen.

He sighed as he went out into the night, dim now, with Igulgul up to some mischief in the clouds. He entered his den, poured a brandy, settled down in his armchair, opened the envelope. It contained a single typewritten sheet:

> THIS INFORMATION IS FROM AN OFFICIAL SOURCE AND IS COMPLETELY RELIABLE.
>
> Report on histories and political activities of Communist Party Agents, Kurt Kaufmann and Rebecca Rosen, posing as Jewish Refugees from Germany, being sought by Commonwealth Immigation Authorities for illegal entry into Australia.
>
> KURT KAUFMANN, 45, born Stuttgart, Germany, Jewish origin, Doctor of Medicine, member of German Communist Party from 1929, actively opposed to National Socialist Regime. He was arrested first 1933 in connection with Reichstag Fire. Escaped from prison and fled country, but soon returned to continue Communist activities. Subsequently arrested and imprisoned on three other occasions, escaping each time with aid of Communist machine, finally in 1937, when smuggled out of Germany, to conduct subversive activities in various European countries in guise of dispossessed Jewish Refugee. Eventually travelled with other agents of Commintern to South America, organizing Communist Cells wherever Jewish Refugees were being admitted. In May 1938 he left Mexico, and under the name of Dr Hoff boarded a ship coming through the Panama Canal bringing Jewish Refugees to Australia. Aboard this ship was a young woman, later identified as Rebecca Rosen.
>
> REBECCA ROSEN, age about 22 born Leipzig, Germany. Father Jewish, mother Christian. Father, Gershon Rosen, theatrical producer, mother second-rate actress. Subject was reared by father's Orthodox Jewish parents. Father exposed as high-ranking undercover Communist with suppression of German Communist Party 1933, and fatally shot while resisting arrest. Subject suspected as involved in father's activities and imprisoned. She spent five years in various corrective institutions in Germany. At length her escape and flight from Germany were engineered by Communists, under whose direction she travelled through Europe and to Middle East in manner similar to that of Kaufmann, her job chiefly to make things easier for her superiors by seducing officials. Became known in dossiers of various Intelligence Bureaux as Red Rifkah. Red-haired, very beautiful, and possessed of innocent-seeming girlish charm. Joined Kaufmann on voyage from Central America to Australia.
>
> With connivance of Australian Communist Party, many members of which are Jewish and former refugees, these agents formed a team for the establishment of Communist Cells in remote parts of the Australian Continent, as Kaufmann had done in South America. The names and histories of their associates in this apparatus are also known.

Jeremy had been sitting with the screed on his knee for some twenty minutes, occasionally taking a sip of brandy and reading the thing again, but mostly staring blankly at his bookshelves – when the latch of the outside front door clicked, followed by light steps in the passage. His eyes turned to the open doorway of his den, which in a moment framed Alfie, clad in pyjamas and blue silk dressing gown. She stopped, meeting the grey stare. He did not speak. She swallowed, muttered, 'I had to come, Jeremy.'

Still he didn't speak. The black eyes dropped to the paper on his knee. 'You've read it?'

His face remained as stony. She began to enter slowly, saying, 'I want to help you, Jeremy.'

She stood before him. He picked up the script and handed it to her, still looking into her eyes. The eyes began to swim. She mumbled again, 'I want to help you.'

'Thank you,' he said coldly.

She asked, 'May I sit down?'

He nodded, waved to the other chair, but did not rise.

'May I have a drink?'

Now he rose and got another glass. 'Brandy do you?' he asked.

'I always drink brandy now . . . please, more than that. I'm pretty used to it now. Drink a fair amount down there. One needs it.'

As he added water to her stiff drink he asked, 'Why?'

'Why do you drink brandy?'

' "The subtle alchemist", I think I told you once.'

'Well, I do for the same reason.' She tossed it off at a gulp.

'I thought you'd be happy . . . with your fame . . . and your fine-feathered friends.'

'But not you. Give me another.'

He gave her a small one, ignored her plea for more. She tossed it off as quickly as the other. She said, 'You're still not happy, either.'

'Says who?'

'It's plain to see. I was told you were in love, too.'

'Who told you that?'

'A journalist never tells. Please, another drink . . . I can take it.'

He poured her a small one. She swigged it at once again.

'You haven't learnt to drink it.'

'I'll go easy now. I only wanted to . . . to . . . .'

'What?'

'To get the courage to . . . to beard the lion in his den.' She giggled.

He poured for her again. This time she sipped. He sipped. They sat in silence for a long while, she staring at him, he out through the door. At last she asked, 'What're you going to do about these Jews now?'

'What d'you mean now?'

'Since you've found out what they are.'

'I've known all along.'

'That they're Communists?'

'That they're Refugees.'

She finished her glass, and when he made no move to replenish it, boldly reached for the bottle and helped herself. He merely watched. She drank again, but more sparingly. She said, leaning forward, 'Jeremy, darling . . . I told you I'd come to help you.' He nodded, sipped his own drink. 'Well, that's true. When this thing's published, I want you to be in the clear.'

'Who's going to publish it?'

'*Australia Free* of course.'

'What about libel?'

'They haven't a leg to stand on. This stuff is from the Commonwealth Investigation Service.'

'What're *you* doing with it?'

'The paper got it somehow. I don't know. It was shown to me because you were mentioned.'

'I'm not mentioned there.'

'That's only what I copied about these people . . . for you. It's a big thing. It involves the whole Communist plot. When I saw it I was shocked. I asked them not to publish it, till I'd warned you.'

'What difference will warning me make, if they're going to publish it?'

'You could get from under.' She drank again.

'From under what?'

'Suspicion that you're implicated with these people.'

He drank, too. 'But I am. They're my guests.'

'They're notorious Communists, known to be here for subversive reasons.'

'They're here because I asked them. I met them at the Races.'

'And they've been here ever since?' The black eyes flashed. She swigged, declared, 'Then it is true!'

'What?'

'That you're in love with the girl.'

He went very red and swallowed on it, but answered in his usual calm way, 'Well, what business is that of yours . . . or your lousy Fascist rag?'

She cried, 'They've been getting at you, all right!' She stared. 'I didn't think you'd ever make a fool of yourself . . . over a woman . . . oooooh!' Her face crumpled, eyes filled. She dropped her head while searching for a handkerchief. He made no move to help. She wiped her eyes on the lapel of her gown, then shoved her glass out for refilling.

'Sure you can take it?' he asked.

'Only one . . . but make it a big strong one, to last.' Taking the drink, she sipped, sniffled, sighed: 'I've expected such great things of you. Now's the time for the great things. And . . . and . . . Oh, I just can't believe it!'

'What?'

'That this girl . . . this . . . this foreign woman . . . this . . . this Red Rifkah, a . . . a Communist Jew-whore . . . could steal your great strength from you . . . like Samson and Delilah.'

She sniffed back more tears. 'Now's the time Australians're becoming conscious of themselves . . . their country . . . their nationhood. But the resurgence will have to be fought for. There are the enemies. Not only the British Raj now. There's internationalism . . . International Communism. Already the Comms're getting into it . . . into our nationalism, I mean. They're sponsoring national literature . . . have a Book Society and prizes . . . have formed Eureka Youth . . . are going round the country singing the ballads of the pioneering days, marching with the Five-starred Flag . . . . '

'What's wrong with that?'

'You know very well why they're doing it. There's only one nation and one flag for them. The Hammer and Sickle'd be put in the corner of the flag to replace the Union Jack . . . .'

'What would your crowd put in . . . the Swastika?'

She drank again, looked like swigging, but stopped when he said, 'Go easy.'

She looked at him fiercely. 'That's the sort of thing *you* could stop. It's what's wrong with the Movement, what's spoiling it. The Chief's a great man . . . a genius . . . but . . . but he's not truly Australian . . . I mean like you. None of us are. That's why we need you. I keep telling the others about you . . . keep saying: "Wait till you hear Jeremy Delacy!" Even the Leader. He doesn't know the real Australia. He's a scholar . . . a bookman. It's theory with him . . . and most of them. What we want's not politicians, but fighters . . . like you . . . like you fighting Vaiseys, Cobbity and Co., even the lousy Knowleses. It's *you* we want, Jeremy . . . you with your power . . . your manhood . . . your honesty . . . your vast love of our vast and lovely land . . . Oh, Jeremy!' Again the eyes swam, and the head drooped, and there was a searching for hanky. This time he produced his own handkerchief. She would have taken his hand with it; but he snatched it away.

Now she looked fierce again. 'And I come back here and find you throwing your life away on an alien whore . . . a Communist decoy-woman . . . a bloody Jewess!'

'Steady,' he murmured.

She tossed off the drink. They stared at each other for a moment. Suddenly she burst out, 'What're you going to do, Jeremy?'

He answered slowly, 'Right now, my dear, I'm going to ask you to go back to bed.'

She gaped. He rose. She sprang up and seized him. 'No, Jeremy . . . no . . . you've got to listen . . . .'

He pulled her arms from his shoulders, held her off, saying, 'You're very tired . . . and you've had too much to drink. Beddo!'

She struggled to free her hands. 'No . . . no . . . I'm determined to have this out!'

'We've had it out, my dear . . . as far as I'm concerned.'

'You mean you're going to keep this Jew-bitch here . . . and ruin your reputation as an Australian . . . as a man . . . as a man of dignity?'

Gently he was pushing her back towards the door. 'I mean I'm going to do exactly what I think proper according to my own ideas . . . without interference from anyone.'

She shrieked, 'Except Communists . . . and Jews!' She wrenched free.

He was breathing heavily now. She tried the little-girl tactic: 'Jeremy . . . Jeremy . . . I want your help, too . . . I want . . . .'

He growled, 'What you want's your behind slapped . . . and if you don't go, I'll call Nan over to make you!'

She shrieked again, 'Nan . . . Nan . . . a black woman . . . and a Jewess! What kind of man *are* you, Jeremy Delacy?'

'You've been talking as if you knew.'

She was panting: 'I thought I knew . . . the man I could have made the Greatest of this Nation . . . .'

'You drink your brandy too quickly . . . .'

He had her out in the passage, backing to the front door.

She kept on: 'The man I could have made . . . with my own youth and beauty . . . but it's . . . it's . . . but even if I can't make you what you ought to be . . . no, I'll never let that ginger Jew-whore ruin you . . . no, never, never, never . . . Oh, Jeremy, Jeremy, Jeremy, darling . . . don't send me away!' Her voice rose to a scream.

They were at the front door. He got it open. She was sobbing wildly now. He shoved her out, puffing, 'Get a good night's sleep . . . . ' and shut the door in her straining face, snibbed the lock.

She hammered on it. 'Jeremy . . . Jeremy . . . Jeremy!'

The lights in the annexe snapped off. She fell against the door, weeping. 'Oh, oh, oh, ooooooh!'

Igulgul was in the trees, laughing, winking. She turned from the glare, whimpering, staggered drunkenly, went reeling across the yard towards the black and white bulk of the house.

Out of the shadows at the eastern end of the annexe another shadow came flitting, to stop at the glitter of the fluted glass of Jeremy's bedroom window. A dark hand knocked gently. A soft voice called, 'I get you drink o' tea, Mullaka?'

The answer came muffled, 'Okay, dear.'

Nan turned away and went hurrying across the yard, into the kitchen, to put on lights and stir up the fire, draw hot water and put on the kettle. Having got things under way, she stole through the dining-room and peeped into the lounge. Alfie was in an armchair, under a standard lamp, with a brandy bottle and a glass on a small table beside her. Nanago returned to the kitchen. She had the tea made and was placing the pot on the tray, when the screen-door to the dining-room burst open and Alfie entered. They stared hard at each other for a moment. Then Nan smiled. 'You like cup o' tea?'

Alfie blinked at the tray. 'What you makin' tea thish time night for?'

'Mullaka like cup o' tea time he not sleep good.'

'How you know he's not sleepin' good?'

'I see light.'

'You were over there lishtenin', weren' you?' Nan nodded amiably. Alfie exhaled heavily, brandily: 'Ahhh . . . lubra lookin' for tracks of other lubra . . . well, I'm not a lubra, see!' She wheeled about, went back through the swing door.

Nan raised her heavy brows, then picked up the tray and went out.

From sitting brooding for some twenty minutes, with consumption of three stiff brandies and progressive rumpling of black brows, Alfie suddenly rose, snapping, 'Yes . . . I will too!' She poured herself another brandy, downed it at a gulp, then started for the stairs. She stumbled on the first step, but was careful thereafter, deliberate, holding the rail. She was breathing heavily, through her nose, drunk, but with an occasional snort that betrayed deep anger. To the top, and round, swaying somewhat, bumping the walls, but being very careful, to Rifkah's room. She took a good look at it, as if to be certain where she was, then jerked the screen-door open, letting it bang shut with its spring, as she groped for the light-switch. The light flashed on, leaving her blinking, swaying.

Rifkah woke at once, blinking like a startled child, raised on an elbow. Then as the dark-haired figure approached the bed, she sat up quickly, asking, 'Vot is matter?'

Alfie, standing beside the bed, folded her arms, her red lips, then ground out, 'S'you't's matter here, shister . . . get up!'

'I don't understand?'

'Oh, yes you do . . . Red Rifkah!'

Rifkah stiffened, swung feet to floor, while not taking her wide eyes from the black ones goggling at her. She reached blindly for the dressing-gown folded over the back of the chair beside the bed. Alfie snatched it away. 'Leave that 'lone. Get yo' clothesh on.'

Rifkah rose, looked at the dark screen-door, muttered, 'It is late night . . . . '

'Get yo' clothesh on, Jew-girl. Yo' goin' out thish housh tonight.'

'You are drunk.'

'I'll give you drunk you don' do wha' I tell you . . . you stinkin' bloody Jew-whore!'

'I vill call for help if you do not go.'

'No one's goin' help you here . . . dirty Jewish proshtute. They know 'bout you now . . . wha' you been, wha' you here for . . . an' next thing police'll be here to pick you up an' chuck you out thish decent clean lovely country you preten' you love . . . you . . . . ' The drunken voice rose high ' . . . you Jew Comm'nist lyin' whore of a bitch . . . No you don'!'

Rifkah tried to slip to the door. Alfied pounced on her, with red claws extended. Rifkah screamed. 'Scream, yo' red bitch!' screamed Alfie, slashing with one claw, grabbing at the red hair with the other. Rifkah fought back. Shrilling and wrestling, they fell over the chair, tangled on the floor. Alfie getting on top, hooked the claws into the distorted face beneath her, dripping her streaming bloody spittle onto it, was getting a knee into the soft belly – when her own dark mop was jerked up and back, and she found herself staring up into the dark distorted face of Nanago. She tried to turn on Nan. But male hands seized her, dragged her to her feet. Her rolling eyes looked into the grim face of Fergus. She tried it on him, but only to get her hands locked behind her, to be spun round, and rushed to the door and out.

Kurt and Prindy were at the door. They gave way, then rushed into the room.

Nan took Rifkah in her arms, kneeling beside her, stroking her hair, crooning to her in her wild-eyed sobbing distress, 'All right now . . . all right now . . . she on'y drunk, dat one. De cat, she scratch you deep, but. Come on. Get up. I wash you face. We get Mullaka put you somesing make better. Come on, my little girl. Den I mek you nice cup o' tea.'

Jeremy came to them in the bathroom, asking, 'Everything in order?'

Nan answered, 'Yas, Mullaka . . . want some medicine for scratch.'

Rifkah turned from him with a sob. He patted her shoulder. Nan said, 'Dere, now, you see. Mullaka don' tek notice dat one. I know. I been talk-about long o' him. Come on, now . . . you stop crying.'

Jeremy said, 'Don't wash the wounds, Nan. It'll spoil natural healing. I'll get some Sulphonilamide.'

'Got 'o keep dat pretty face,' said Nan. Rifkah buried her head in the ready breast.

In Alfie's room there were more tears, as Fergus, looking not a bit interested in the pretty things revealed, pulled off her pyjamas and dressed her in whatever he could lay hands on, while she lay sobbing on the bed. He shoved her shoes on, bundled her remaining clothes into her suitcase, then quite roughly dragged her to her feet and forced her to come out of the room with him. Down in the lounge he left her while he went to pack his own bag. When he came back, she was stretched out in an armchair, snoring. He slapped her awake, got her to her feet, marched her out into the darkness.

At peep of day, the household was wakened by the roar of aeroengines starting. It was too early for sleepy black heads to come out to see; and other heads knew it would not be proper. Soon there was the roar of take-off. Now the household turned out. Fergus came over the roof in the usual salute and banked to show his split-lipped grin and upthrust thumb. However, there was no sign of his passenger.

When Jeremy came across for breakfast, he found Kurt and Rifkah in the lounge, standing as if waiting for him as for one expected to deliver a momentous verdict. Kurt was stiff and grave-faced, Red Rifkah drooping, her face puffed and streaked with the rawness of scratches and the white of medicament. Jeremy came in as usual by way of the kitchen, where usually Rifkah was to be found cooking one of the several breakfast dishes she had introduced to him. He said gruffly, 'What's wrong . . . no eggs and onions?'

But Rifkah only looked miserable. He came up to her, looked at her wounds, turned to Kurt. 'I don't think she'll be that ugly in future, do you, Doctor?'

Kurt smiled slightly. But Rifkah uttered a sob, dropped face to hands. Jeremy asked, 'Why the tears?'

Still she shed them. When Jeremy looked again at Kurt, the little man cleared his throat: 'Ze . . . er . . . lady, she gif you certain information . . . .'

Jeremy chuckled: 'You can hardly call her a lady in the circumstances.' But as Kurt still looked serious, he added: 'Yes . . . she gave me what purports to be a copy of an official statement. I have it if you want to see it. But I'd rather have breakfast, first. I'm not concerned about it myself.' Kurt held out his hand. Jeremy put his arm about Rifkah while Kurt read. She only half leaned on him.

When Kurt was done with the paper, she reached for it. But Jeremy grabbed it, saying shortly, 'No!'

She gasped, 'But it is about me . . . I know.'

'What's it matter? I want you to know that I don't care what's said here. Why should I? You told me most of it yourself, practically the first day we met. Whatever your reason for coming here in the first place, I'm sure it's true love of the place that's kept you. It's your home . . . so long as you want it to be. That applies to both of you.' Now she snuggled against him.

Kurt, staring intently at Jeremy, said, 'I beg your pardon for ze deceit. I vood haf like to confide in you.'

'I've guessed, Kurt. You made it pretty plain from the start where your sympathy lay.'

'You are very generous, Jeremy. A man who does not like Communism . . . vich is not itself generous.'

'That lack of basic humanness should convert you, an essentially humane man.'

Kurt sighed: 'Zere can be no conversion until ze goal is vun.'

'It'll be too late then. Things like generosity, the essential human things, will have been destroyed.'

'You can never destroy humanness . . . but you moost check it to fight vot is bad in humanity. Communism is ze cold hard fight against ze inhuman, so zat true humanness vill at last prevail.'

'Sorry, old man . . . but I can't believe it.'

'I am sorry too . . . because I can't mek you belief in vot is inevitable. Only troo control of human passion can the hell man has alvays made on earth be destroyed. It vos fashion of old religion to pretend hell vos ozer side of life, and to torture ze veak on zis side. It is fashion of new religion of Fascism to set up Satanic Elite and mek no pretence about ze hell on earth. Communism haf many fault . . . for it is human. But it is built on ideal of brudderhood. Alvays zat . . . brudderhood.' Kurt sighed again: 'Of course, ve vill haf to go at vonce.'

'Why?'

'Ze security police. It is true ve are illegal immigrant. Ve cannot involve you, goot friendt.'

'Be careful with your generosity, Kurt! But where will you go?'

'It vill be arrange. I haf only to send code telegram or letter.'

'Well, there's nothing much to worry about at the moment. The rain'll set in again within a week. I'll bet on that. You'll be safe here for a month at least. They're hardly likely to come looking for you in rain the way it falls here.'

'If you pliss, ve vill leave as soon as possible.'

Jeremy raised Rifkah's chin. 'You want to go?'

The answer was plain enough in the swimming hazel eyes. When Jeremy looked at Kurt, the man shrugged and turned away. Jeremy turned back to Rifkah, and shrugging her off his arm, said, 'Well, seeing you're stopping . . . what about getting on with the job?'

She looked at him with agonized puzzlement. He said gruffly, 'My bloomin' breakfast, girl . . . I'm starving . . . eh, eh!' She flung herself on him, clung for a moment, then detached herself and went flying to the kitchen.

Kurt had turned on the radio. A mincing English voice was saying that one Dr Emil Hacha, newly appointed President of Czechoslavakia, summoned to Berlin by Herr Hitler, had signed a declaration placing his country under German protection, and German troops were already marching in as protectors – a flagrant breach of the Munich Agreement, according to Mr Chamberlain, British Prime Minister, and one that Germany in the end would bitterly regret, so he said.

Kurt commented, 'Ze Skoda Munition Vorks, ze biggest manufactory of lethal veapons in ze vorld, now passes into ze hand of ze biggest gangsters in history.'

Jeremy asked dryly, 'Wasn't it already owned by gangsters . . . Schneiders of France?'

Kurt shrugged. Jeremy went on: 'It all stinks rather badly, doesn't it? Where there's power there's corruption . . . in the true sense of that word.

Why don't you stay with us . . . and put your idealism and intelligence to something that won't be exploited by rogues. You and I and Rifkah, giving ourselves completely to this Aboriginal thing?'

'I haf not ze legal right to stay.'

'I'll sponsor you for legal entry. Immigration difficulties have been overcome like that . . . even in the case of Asiatics. Good lawyers . . . . '

'I vood be in jail and declared *non persona grata*. Zat has been done, too . . . in spite of best lawyers.'

'There's the law of *habeas corpus*, supposed to be the basic principle of British Justice.'

'British Justice is not for alien. Besides, I am Communist. Zey vood deport me before any court action could be taken. Zey haf done zat already many time.'

'Leave the Party, then. That'll make a hero of you to them. You're too intelligent not to know that it's as rogue-ridden as any other movement concerned with having power over people.'

'It is ze only movement zat does not have power over people as its end. No, my dear friendt, I must go . . . not simply to escape, but to fight ze goot fight. Ze bugles are sounding in Europe for Armageddon. I am soldier in ze fight. I moost go.'

V

Kurt's departure from Beatrice was organized very simply, but so nicely for its purpose that no one knew of it except the engine-crew. He and Rifkah and Prindy had attracted little attention through being on the footplate with Pat Hannaford during the shunting. Obviously no one noticed that when the Lily Lagoons truck set out for home it was lacking one of those who had come in with it.

CHAPTER EIGHTEEN

There are many ways of predicting rain: from noting the behaviour of ants to invoking one's corns; but all unreliable to some degree, surely, from the very fact of their multiplicity. However, one sign generally regarded as infallible in these parts was the nesting of the nuttagul geese, which evidently was impossible without a prolonged spell of rain. In normal times it did not begin until Wet Season was well advanced. If it did not begin at all, it was safe to say there would be no Wet to speak of. It was also a sign that could hardly be missed where geese were to be found, which as yet was just about everywhere there was still water, even on the outskirts of townships, because of the row they always made over it. Always noisy birds, at mating time they were positively uproarious. At Lily Lagoons, the hullabaloo could be heard at the homestead if the wind was right. At Beatrice River, those on the billabongs beyond the Racecourse could even be a nuisance to light-sleeping residents of the township of nights – and this despite the depredations made on them throughout the years, good eating that they were, and especially the toll taken of late by the road-workers. Still, they were a species that bred prolifically.

The din of the nuttaguls' breeding was not caused so much by the contentiousness usual in most species in their season, but rather by a sort of frenzy in looking for mates – not fighting for them. At least this was how native legend explained it. According to this, the First Geese, Nuttagul-jul, the male, and Nuttagul-nul, his wife, were tragically parted soon after mating – actually while they were building the seasonal nest in the manner they established for their kind, which is by dancing together on a clump of weeds out in a billabong or swamp, to form an island. The tragedy was due to that meanest of creatures, Dagoolya, the Crocodile, who sneaked up under water while the pair were dancing and pulled Nuttagul-jul down by a leg without his mate's being aware of it, the trick also used ever since by black humankind. Nattagul-nul learnt what had happened only when Nuttagul-jul's Shade came to her in a dream and told her to carry on regardless, to lay her eggs and hatch and rear the young – but never to mate again until he returned reincarnated and claimed her. The injunction stood for all nuttaguls who came after. They could have but one mate for ever. Hence for ever there must be this frantic search for lost mates, because of the great wastage to which so delicately fleshed a species was doomed.

Now the geese were shouting everywhere, day and night, and knowledgeable people saying, 'We'll have rain in a week . . . a real Old Man Wet, be the sound o' them bloody geese.' They might also have referred to the look of the sky, which to northeastward had come to look like a sooty tunnel. But perhaps they had as little faith in sky-signs as formerly it seemed the geese had. Anyway, to bear everybody out, there one day the radio was telling of an intense cyclone, 890 millibars at the centre, sweeping the Gulf, from where it was expected to advance inland as a deep rain-depression.

That week's mail train brought to Beatrice a crowd of road-workers who had been able to continue their operations under the abnormal conditions preceding, but now convinced of a spell of enforced idleness, wished to spend it within staggering distance of a pub.

Pat Hannaford was the driver again, hanging out of his cab as usual as his train came rolling in, but without that leery look he mostly had for the waiting crowd. In fact, he looked even anxious. No doubt about whom he was looking for, with eyes seeking out the Lily Lagoons people, and not finding her with them, leaping elsewhere in search. Only Darcy and his family and a couple of blackboys were there today. Clancy, also, was in the group, but seemingly unnoticed by Pat, for all his scowling back at him. Instead of the Lagoons utility, they had the big truck today, no doubt for an easier run home if caught by rain.

Pat ran on past the Station, applied his brakes rather hard, causing a clanging of couplings and a muffled roar of protest from those who would have been thrown off balance while preparing to alight. Apparently quite unconcerned, he dropped from the cab, to come hurrying back along the train, shoving through the crowd. Col Collings sniggered at him, 'Looks like you ought to be back on the shovel, stoppin' like that.'

Pat hissed out of the corner of his tight mouth, 'Get tore!'

He also passed Clancy, and this time swapped scowl for scowl. He paused for a moment to look at a couple of passengers off the train, strangers like so many of the others, but outstanding in build and dress. They were big men, wearing the clothes of Southerners, but without coats, and evidently were feeling the heat, since one was fanning himself with a pork-pie hat and the other was mopping his fleshy red face. They were talking to Constable Stunke. Tracker Tipperary was also in the group, along with another of his kind, but handling suitcases. Pat slipped round the end of the station, screened by a stack of empty fuel drums, and made his way to where Darcy and his people, knowing their place better than to join the white crowd in its heading for the Station office and distribution of the mail, still stood. Without coming right up to them, Pat attracted the group's attention, then quietly asked of Darcy, 'Miss Rifkah not 'ere, eh?'

Darcy giggled, 'No, Boss. Stop home . . . cos big rain close-up.'

'When're you going back?'

'After I pick up mail.'

Pat took a peep at Stunke and his bulky friends, who were now headed for the police utility, preceded by the trackers lugging the baggage. He drew Darcy back behind the drums. 'Look, I'm goin' out with you.' Darcy's eyes widened. 'It's very important . . . for Rifkah. Wait for me at Ali Barba's. Don't tell nobody . . . not even that I talked to you. Savvy?'

Darcy, still gaping, nodded. 'Right,' said Pat, and turned and slipped back into the crowd, through it, heading back to the engine. Nearly there, he halted, to pop in between waggons to uncouple them. Then he went on.

Porky Jones was leaning out of the cab. As Pat climbed up to him, he said, 'No, Porky, she's not there. Didn't come in. I'm goin' out to get her.'

Porky's little eyes were popping. Pat went on: 'Our luck to get her away might be right in. They can fix it out at the Lagoons to make it look's if she's gone bush, when the bogies go out for her. When I bring her in tonight, I'll leave her at Toohey's. She can hide there till we get back from the head of the road tomorro'. In the night we'll whip her up to Granite Springs on a tryke . . . and pick her up on our way on Frid'y.'

Porky breathed. 'Jesus!'

'Mustn't miss a chance like this. Better'n anything else we could do to beat the bastards. Come on. Let's kick them couple o' waggons off. You take 'er. I'll 'andle the points. I want to keep an eye on 'em. I'm pretty sure they won't go out there tonight, when they got all day tomorro'. Still you never know.'

Glancing at the sooty sky, Porky said, 'Rain might make 'em go out while they can.' Then he asked, 'What about if you get caught in the rain and can't get back?'

'I'll get back, boy. It'll take a lot o' rain to close the road after that long dry spell. But if they go out tomorro' and go huntin' round for her, they could be stuck out there for a week. Give us a good chance to get her right away out o' the country.'

Riding the brake-lever of a waggon while they shunted, Pat watched the Police Station. The trackers had retired. Through the wide-open louvers of the front verandah of the residence the company could be seen, Stunke and his wife and the two big strangers, the latter sitting, while the former were dealing with bottles and glasses on a table. He growled, 'Copper bastards . . . Gestapo shit!'

Pat fumed somewhat while waiting for Darcy to get the mail: 'Stupid yeller bastard, waitin' for everybody else to go through . . . and that bloody Führer Collings maggin' to everybody. Trouble the bloody boongs, that docility of theirs. Christ, Darcy . . . hurry up and get that friggin' mail and let's get goin'!'

There at last was Darcy driving up to stop at Barbu's. Pat had the engine placed so as to make a quick move across under cover of stacked rails and sleepers. As he left he said to Porky, 'Now, remember, anyone asks for me, I'm in the barracks readin' . . . got a shitty on the world. People're sure to be askin' at the pub about them bogies. Not a word, mind, to anyone.'

The creamy Delacys were astonished to see Pat climb stealthily into the back of their truck and cover himself with a tarpaulin. Thus did they run down to the river crossing, over through the light spill of water, up the other side. As they passed the Racecourse, Pat appeared, streaming with perspiration. He looked at the sky, his watch. The time was four-forty. The Sun flickered like a ghostly face through the grey rags in which the black menace rolling from north-eastward ended away to westward. The trees were billowing to hot gusty wind. Pat got up in front. Soon he was yelling at Darcy to get a move on. Fifteen miles per hour seemed to be what Darcy considered a reasonable speed to get them home. Threatening to take the wheel off him, Pat forced it up to twenty, which was all that could be done with safety with the big vehicle on the winding narrow road, much of which was still scoured out by the earlier heavy rain, leaving deep holes now filled with fine dust and the roots of big trees exposed, negotiation of which at much speed caused havoc amongst the passengers.

They had covered about seven miles, when there was hammering on the hood from behind and squeals from the kids, 'Motor car come behind!'

They were just then rounding a bend and thus had a rear view clear of their own dust. There was another dust-cloud amongst the trees, looking rather like some furry beast foraging: a puffball of bright yellow for head, the body the rising cloud behind. Darcy slowed down to look back with the others. Asked by Pat who was likely to be coming out this way, Darcy replied, 'Might-be Mist' Clancy. He say he come out sometime . . . tell Miss Rifkah.'

Pat grunted, 'Well, we don't want the bastard out there now. Go on . . . get a move on! Give him your dust to slow him up. I want 'o talk Rifkah before anybody else can.' He yelled back at the kids. 'Watch . . . see who it is.'

They went on, roaring, lurching, bouncing.

Then hammering again on the hood, and those behind shrilling, 'P'lice truck . . . p'liceman!'

'Aw, Jesus!' cried Pat. Then as Darcy slowed down, he yelled, 'Keep goin' . . . keep goin' . . . we got 'o beat the bastards!'

Darcy shot him a scared glance, but obeyed.

For several wild minutes they carried on as fast as Darcy dared under the incessant lash of Hannaford's tongue, which while enough to keep the passengers behind in a bouncing heap, proved of no avail in shaking off that hunting yellow-headed animal behind. There soon were its eyes glinting. Then its strident voice could be heard above the din of the truck: *Bairp, bairp, bairp, bairp!* Darcy's eyes were rolling with fear, now not so much of the hazards ahead but the menace behind. Still Pat urged him, 'Give 'em enough dust they'll drop back!' That's the way it was beginning to look, too – when, turning a sharp bend at too much speed for the clumsy vehicle and the scary driver, the truck skidded in deep bulldust, all but capsized, recovered by the grace of circumstances, but crosswise on the road and with engine stalled.

At the moment they were out of sight of the pursuer. But the roar of his engine was close enough to set Pat fairly screaming when Darcy failed to restart. The engine was so hot that steam from the radiator was turning the dust on the windscreen to mud. Pat took a wild look into the dust behind which the menace was snarling now right on their heels. He leapt out of the cabin, dashed into the scrub.

The police truck also almost turned over in its sudden stopping to avoid collision with the other. Only a glimpse of those aboard, before they were obliterated by their own dust, but enough for sharp eyes to pick them out: Constable Stunke and those two hulkers earlier referred to by Hannaford as Bogies and Gestapo Shit, in front, and Tipperary and his tracker mate with complexions the same colour as their khaki shirts, clinging to the hood behind. Out of the pall of dust came the bully-bellowing of Stunke, 'What the bloody puggin' 'ell . . . .'

The high wind whipped the dust away. Now the Bogies were revealed as having shirts khaki-spotted instead of white, and yellow eyebrows. No doubt about those hard-staring eyes – they were policemen's. Stunke, leaning out, yelled at shaking Darcy, 'What's idea givin' us your dust? I been blowin' the horn at you for a couple o' mile. Get off the road and let us pass.'

Poor Darcy's face was jerking as he flogged the starter. A frightful moment. Then the engine started with a roar, blasting the policemen with a cloud of smoke that started them off roaring, too, and coughing and spluttering. Darcy bumped a tree in backing, then nearly hit the utility. 'You stupid bloody bastard!' Stunke yelled.

Then the road was cleared for the law, which with savage glares departed.

Pat came out of a konkaberry bush, stared for a moment at the receding dust of the enemy, then came up to Darcy and said, 'No good me goin' out there now. Take me back to Beatrice.' He waited till Darcy got back to the road, then climbed aboard. No word was said.

Nothing was said till they were passing Beatrice Station homestead, the white roofs of which across the river showed starkly against the inky background. The Sun was gone, whether sunk or lost in the liver-coloured cloud now filling the western sky could not be judged. But it was close to darkness. Coming out of black-browed brooding, Pat said, 'You can drop me at the Racecourse. Don't want anyone sticky-beakin' 'bout you coming back. Now, listen. Those blokes're coppers from the South. They come to take Rifkah away.' Darcy's eyes grew large. 'I was tryin' to get to her first. I want you to tell her I tried to get out . . . but not to worry, because we'll be doin' sumpin to beat 'em. If you can't talk to her herself, tell the Old Bloke. We'll be doin' sumpin, remember. And not a word to the coppers. Right?'

Exhaling fearfully, Darcy nodded.

II

Finnucane's, always lively of train-day evenings, was doing such a roaring trade tonight that Old Shame-on-us had Col Collings and Oz Burrows to help him behind the bar, as well as that old-maid daughter of his, Peggy. Most of the customers were strangers. However, these were showing just as much interest as the locals in the subject that fairly had the latter by the ears: what was going on at Lily Lagoons to send Stunke dashing out there with his trackers and that pair of mysterious strangers who everybody was now convinced were Johns. It seemed that the pair had attracted attention on the train with their aloofness, but had been taken for official spies of some sort, to do with the Railway, the Telegraph, or the Road-building, since they had not spoken to any policeman along the route. Hush-hush business, it was being said. Might be something to do with them Jews, eh?

When Pat Hannaford arrived with Porky Jones just after dark, he was mobbed, because, he was told, he had been seen riding in the Lily Lagoons truck by the Engineer at Beatrice Station homestead, who at the time was working on the pump on the river. Pat, no doubt already informed of this by Porky, answered easily, 'Balls! How the 'ell could I be out at Lily Lagoons, if I'm 'ere?' As the Engineer was not present to refute it, the mob was satisfied with so pat an answer, but still pressed him for his opinion of what was going on. His answer to that was, ' 'Ow the 'ell should I know?'

Chas Chase, the guard, said, 'You was watchin' them plain-clothes coppers all the way down.'

That roused the crowd again. But Pat had his answer, 'That's 'cause I reckoned they was Railways Department Inspectors . . . and I was watchin' to see if you dobbed me in to 'em.'

The crowd roared over that one. Red to the ears, Chas departed. Soon afterwards Pat and Porky did the same, Pat's excuse to the protesting Finnucane, who offered to shout, being that he didn't like his barmen. 'Likely to put arsenic in me beer.'

Although he departed leaving mirth behind him, it showed how far from feeling mirthful himself was Pat the way he dealt with Clancy Delacy, with whom he almost collided out on the verandah. Clancy, who had been over in the Squatters' Corner of the bar and staring hard at Pat throughout his stay, evidently had whipped out and round to meet him as he left. Scowling in reply to Clancy's staring, Pat demanded, 'What's wrong with you, mug?'

Clancy bridled. 'Nothing. I was just going to ask you a civil question.'

'There's nothin' to be civil about between the likes o' you'n' me.'

Clancy swallowed, said with difficulty, 'No . . . I don't suppose there is. You don't know what being civil is.'

Pat sneered, 'No?'

'No!' Clancy flamed as he said it.

Pat also flamed: 'Wan' make sumpin of it, Mug Squatter?'

Clancy panted, 'If you want to . . . Mug Commo!'

Those near the door of the bar had heard, were surging out, crying, 'Fight!'

The cry went up in the bar, 'Fight!'

Finnucane slipped under his flap and came barging out in his apron, to find the pair glaring at each other. He leapt in between them. 'Ah, now, me boys . . . two intelligint laddies loike yo'selves behavin' loike common navvies . . . .'

Pat snarled at him, 'Get donkey-walloped!' He turned away suddenly, stepped off the verandah, went off into the wind-tossed darkness towards the railway, followed by Porky.

The mob tried to capture Clancy and get an explanation. He flung them off, also stepped off the verandah, and went walking up towards Barbu's.

Down in the barracks, Pat and Porky were preparing supper from food from their tucker-tins, when to the surprise of both, Clancy appeared in the doorway of their quarters. Clancy's face was hardly friendly, as he said, 'How y'doin'?'

Pat scowled. 'Still lookin' for lash?'

Clancy swallowed. 'I wasn't looking for it in the first place. I told you I wanted to ask you something.'

'Nobody's stoppin' you now.'

Clancy glanced at Porky. 'I'd like to talk to you alone.'

'If you can't talk front o' me mate, you can go and get . . . . '

'This is very confidential.'

'Nothin's too confidential for me mate to 'ear.'

Clancy hesitated, then cast a glance behind, as if to be assured no one else was near, then in turning, approached by a step or two and gripping the door posts, said, 'I've been down to Ali Barba's.'

Pat snapped, 'I don't care you been up in Annie's room. State yo' business . . . and then 'op it.'

Clancy swallowed. 'You were seen in the Lagoons truck . . . .'

'By your scabby engineer. He must'a' been on the rum again.'

'Old Ali told me he saw you get into the truck.'

Now it was Pat who swallowed. 'Did 'e, be Jesus!'

'He also told me that you took Kurt Hoff away.'

Pat jumped up, his face distorted. 'What . . . you joined the Gestapo or sumpin?'

Clancy looked haggard, shifted his grip on the door, licked his lips. 'I'm only worried about Rifkah. Those two who went out with Stunke . . . were they police?'

' 'Ow should I know?'

'Well, you tried to go out there ahead of 'em . . . I reckoned you must've wanted to warn her.'

Pat stared at him for a moment, then asked, 'What d'you know about Rifkah?'

Clancy swung by one hand in the doorway, looked back again. Pat grunted, 'Better come in,' and waved to a canvas stool. As Clancy sat down, Pat asked, 'Well?'

Clancy cleared his throat. 'Only that she's a refugee . . . but I guessed she was worried about something.'

'Like what?'

'She did tell me she'd like to get Australian citizenship . . . and when I said it oughtn't to be hard, she sort of hinted that she didn't have the proper qualifications. That Lieutenant Dickey, too . . . he dropped something about illegal immigrants.'

Pat was silent for a while, then said, 'She's an illegal immigrant all right.'

'How do you know?'

'I'm likely to tell you!'

'Why not? I'm her friend. I was a friend of Kurt's.'

'How much of a friend?'

'There's only one kind of friend, isn't there?'

'I don' know . . . there ought 'o be. But would you lend a hand gettin' her away from them Bogies, if they're takin' her away?'

'Bogies?'

'Secret police . . . Commonwealth Investigation Service. They come up on Sunday's plane. They got reservations for four to go back on next Monday's. They got half a coach reserved for Friday's trip back to Town, too. I guess they think they'll be pickin' up Kurt, too.'

'Where's Kurt?'

'Well and truly out of the Country . . . where Rifkah could'a'been, if she had any savvy and wasn't stuck on hangin' round with your mob.'

'She loves it here.'

'Well, she's got no bloody hope o' stopping, what I see . . . unless . . . . ' Pat paused, then asked, 'Can I trust you?'

'Why not?'

'Because you're a bloody squatter type . . . Now, don't get off yo' bike! You said you were a friend of Rifkah's. All right . . . the fact that you *are* a bloody squatter might help.'

'How d'you mean?'

'Look . . . I'm trustin' you, bozo. You let me down, I'll find a way o' killin' you . . . yes, killin' you! What we aim to do . . . '

'Who's we?'

'The Party.'

'What Party?'

'What d'you think, yo' silly bastard . . . the United Australia Party, or the Australia Free Party?' When Clancy looked properly chastened, Pat resumed: 'There's been too much o' this deportin' business of people with progressive views. We got a real case 'ere. We can make it one o' persecution o' Jews, we reckon. I start the ball rollin' by refusin' to take a train that's bein' used like the trains in Nazi Germany to take Jews to concentration camps. Course that won't stop 'em takin' 'er up to Town . . . on a bloody fettler's trolley, if they can't go by car 'count o' rain. But it'll start sumpin . . . sumpin big . . . through the press. This bloody Federal Government'll fight us to the limit, o' course. Still, so long's we can hold things up. We'll bung on a general strike up 'ere. They won't be able to take 'er on the plane, 'cause we'll pull out the mechanics and fuel men at the 'drome . . . and if necessary stop the mail. Just delayin' tactics, see. Our idea's to get 'er away from 'em. Once we done that we're right. We can get 'er out the country, same's we got Kurt out . . . '

'How was that?'

'Mind your own business . . . . '

'It is my business . . . anything't happens to that girl . . . . '

'Right. Glad to 'ear you say so. But you was askin' about Kurt, which's Party business. Now, we got to stop 'em from lockin' her up. I think we can do that all right . . . with the persecution business. But we might need some, what they call Respectable Citizen, to stand security for her. That's where you could come in. Once she's released, we whip her away.'

'Where?'

'Party business again.'

'What's she got to do with the Communist Party?'

'Everything.'

Clancy gaped. 'You . . . you mean . . . . '

'That she's a Communist. Yeah. That make any difference to you, Squatter Boy?'

Evidently it made a lot of difference, the way Clancy paled and swallowed. Pat sneered, 'Won't 'ave it on now, eh?'

Clancy cleared his throat: 'Course I will . . . any . . . anything to help her.'

'Good on yo', boy! I didn't think y'ad it in yo'. 'Ave a beer.'

While they drank Pat went on to say that there was nothing to be done till they saw how things were with Rifkah. 'Yo' never know.' he said. 'They mightn't 'ave enough on her to bring her in tomorro'. Then, she might do a bunk on 'em there. Others'a' done it. That creamy kid o' your brother's is smart enough to get her away. But what you can be doin' tomorro', while I'm doin' the rest o' the run, is to find out all you can, if they come in. Okay? Listen . . . here's that bloody rain comin'. You better do a bunk. We're goin' to 'ave supper. See yo'.'

The rain was coming with the roar of a tidal wave, and with almost as much obliterating force struck the township. Clancy all but swam the last hundred yards to the water-wavering beacon Finnucane's had become. Breathless, he flopped onto the pub verandah, where the mob out to watch the deluge drew back as from a wet dog bound to shake itself.

III

At Lily Lagoons, the Big House was quivering to the monstrous lash of the rain, rocking to the cannonading back over the Plateau. Comfortably at dinner, the tiny household of these days of normal refuge from the world, expressed commiseration for Darcy and his family out there battling what they might well have missed, but for what Jeremy called Darcy's Funeral-coach Driving. Rifkah said 'Poor dollinks . . . and ve so cosy!'

Scarcely had Rifkah said that when what at first had seemed to be the flashing of lightning, proved to be headlights cutting across the yard, to swing towards the house and glare directly in through the eastern windows. The company cried together, 'Here they are!'

Nanago, Rifkah, and Prindy jumped up, to head for the kitchen, to the back door of which the truck normally would go to unload. Jeremy called after them, 'Tell him not to bother to get out . . . but go on home. We can get the things in the morning.'

But the vehicle had stopped, with lights still beaming into the dining-room. Jeremy blinked at them. There was a glimpse of oilskinned figures alighting. He looked surprised, then turned at the sudden opening of the swing-door from the kitchen and the entry of Prindy, crying, 'That not Darcy . . . whiteman, I think.'

'Eh?' Jeremy rose, was going to the windows, when there was hammering at the front door of the lounge. He swung to go there, growling, 'Who the hell've we got on our backs now?'

In the front doorway stood a bulky figure in oilskins – the caped oilskins of police. There was another lurking behind. Jeremy stared. The first man spoke: 'Good evening . . . I am Inspector Ballywick, of the Commonwealth Investigation Service. Would you be the person in charge here . . . Mr Jeremy Delacy, I understand?'

Jeremy had to clear his throat: 'That's right . . . what can I do for you?'

'We're concerned with a foreign couple . . . a Doctor Kaufmann, and a woman, Rebecca Rosen. We understand they're staying here.'

Jeremy swallowed: 'Nobody of that name here.'

'Perhaps you know them under aliases . . . Doctor and Missus Hoff?'

'A . . . a Doctor Hoff was here . . . but he's gone.'

'Indeed? And the woman?'

Jeremy hesitated: 'I don't know any woman of the name you mention.'

'But I'm sure you know the woman we mean, sir.' When Jeremy was silent, the Inspector asked, 'May we come in?' He motioned to the other man, who had come closer: 'This's Sergeant Bugsby.'

With evident difficulty, Jeremy said, 'There's a rack there to hang your things on.'

'Thanks.'

As the two men removed their rain-clothes, Jeremy withdrew slightly, glancing out of the eastern windows, where still was to be seen the glare of the utility, as well now as the criss-cross beaming of flashlights, revealing other oilskinned figures.

Coming in, Inspector Ballywick, took papers from a wallet, extended them towards Jeremy, saying, 'My identity, Mr Delacy, and authority to search. Would you be so kind as to lead me to these people?' The tone was dryly official.

'What people?'

'Come, now, sir . . . I've told you who these people are, and know they're under your roof.'

'I told you Doctor Hoff had gone.'

'We'll soon make certain of that. Please don't deny the presence of the woman. We saw her just now at your table.'

Jeremy breathed deeply: 'What's your business with this woman?'

'I'm afraid, sir, it's just that . . . *our* business.'

Jeremy went red. 'It's my business to protect the people under my roof.'

'Not such people as I have authority to apprehend. I ask you again . . . please lead me to these people . . . or I'll use my authority and go and seize them myself.'

Jeremy almost gasped, 'Seize?'

'A purely official term. I've no wish to deal with the prisoners roughly . . . unless they're non-compliant.'

'Prisoners?' demanded Jeremy. 'Why . . . you haven't even laid a charge . . . '

'They became my prisoners the moment I was entrusted with the duty of delivering them into the hands of the authorities seeking their custody. Now, if you'll . . . '

'You haven't even identified this girl . . . yet you call her your prisoner! You sound like an agent of the Gestapo or something . . . . '

'How dare you, Sir!'

'You object to being identified with anything so abominable as the Gestapo.'

'I resent being called an agent of any service but what I serve.'

'Which is?'

'I told you . . . Commonwealth Investigation Service.'

'But virtually you are acting as an agent of the Gestapo.'

'I tell you I resent that . . . and warn you that insults to an officer in the course of his duty are actionable . . . . '

'Act and be damned to you!' cried Jeremy. 'This girl you call Rebecca Rosen is a refugee from Gestapo persecution. Since childhood, when she saw her father murdered before her eyes, knew her grandparents had to kill themselves, was herself dragged away to become the helpless victim of these monsters . . . she . . . she's been nothing but bullied and hurt, imprisoned, dragged around like an animal, for no reason but that she'd been anathematized by a madman because of her race . . . No, shut up . . . I'll have my say!' Jeremy was beside himself. Crimson and strangling for speech, he went on: 'By the grace of God she managed to escape, managed to find refuge, safe from the brutality . . . .'

Ballywick cut in: 'I know nothing but that she's an illegal immigrant, and as such is my prisoner until delivered up to the proper authorities.'

'Does that mean that without questioning the right or wrong of what you're doing you'll drag her away, to see her flung back into prison, to have her given back to you eventually to escort to some ship that will take her back, stateless, into a world that doesn't want her . . . except for one dirty purpose?'

Ballywick was red now and heaving for breath: 'I'm here simply to carry out my orders . . . . '

'Whose orders?'

'My chief's.'

'Who's he?'

'That's no concern of yours.'

'Is yours a secret service, then?'

'I've told you it's the Commonwealth Investigation Service.'

'Run by anonymous persons.'

'Certainly not!'

'But you won't name them.'

'It's a matter of security.'

'To secure what . . . the fact that you take your orders ultimately from the Gestapo of Germany?'

'Really, Mr Delacy . . . if you persist in this line . . . . '

Both swung towards loud sounds in the dining-room indefinable against the din of the storm, but the cause of which was revealed in a moment. Out into the lounge through the hanging screen burst six struggling streaming figures – Rifkah in the combined grip of oilskinned Stunke and Tipperary, right behind them Prindy held by the hair and an arm by the other tracker, and Nanago beating this other on the back – the women sobbing wildly, the men gasping, grunting, growling.

For one long moment Jeremy stared. Then with a bellow, he rushed at the group, grabbed Stunke, flung him off so violently that he collapsed in a shiny heap, turned on Tipperary, who let go the girl and skipped clear. Rifkah fell into his arms. But the embrace lasted only seconds. The Inspector and his Sergeant leapt on Jeremy from behind. Sergeant Bugsby got a lock round his throat. Inspector Ballywick grabbed his arms and forced them down. Rifkah fell into the swiftly reaching arms of Nan and Prindy.

'What's this?' demanded Ballywick.

Stunke, rising, gasped, 'She tried to do a bunk . . . with the kid. They gave us a chase.'

Ballywick turned on Jeremy. 'So that's what the talk was for . . . delaying tactics?'

Jeremy, half-throttled, could only gurgle.

Ballywick went on: 'I told you I didn't want to deal with you roughly . . .

but you've brought it on yourselves. I warn you all if you don't submit to my authority, I'll put you in handcuffs. Let him go, Bill,' He pulled Rifkah away from those who held her, pushed her against the wall when she staggered as if about to fall, demanded, 'Are you Rebecca Rosen?'

The copper head hung, jerking to unrestrained sobbing.

'Answer up!'

Jeremy croaked, 'For christ sake, man . . . let the girl recover . . . let her sit down . . . she's . . . she's . . . let me take her . . . .'

'I warn you . . . .'

'There's no need. You've got her. Only for God's sake don't torture her.'

'She tried to escape . . . .'

'Probably because she heard you talking like a Gestapo bully. Please, please, let me have her. I know what she's been through. You've frightened her to death.'

Ballywick reluctantly let Jeremy take her. She fell against him again. He led her across to the armchairs, seated her in one, stroked her bright sodden hair for a while, while she wept into his other hand. Then he bent and said he would get her a brandy.

The police were standing round. Ballywick asked Stunke, 'Did you see anything of the man?' When Stunke replied that they hadn't looked, being preoccupied with the girl, he said shortly, 'Well, see to it with your men. Search all outbuildings, question occupants. We'll attend to things here.' He turned to Jeremy. 'I'll require all keys to the place, if you don't mind, Sir.'

Jeremy rose from attending to Rifkah. 'I *do* mind. I mind every high-handed damned thing you're doing.'

'I'm doing nothing but my duty.'

'Duty?' Jeremy's voice rose. 'What crimes aren't committed in the name of duty?'

'Kindly give me the keys . . . or I'll be obliged to arrest you for obstruction, put you under restraint, and have everything I consider might conceal a criminal or evidence of crime broken open.'

Jeremy gasped, 'You horrible official bastard!'

Ballywick's heavy face darkened. But he swallowed it, turning to his sergeant. 'Put that down, Bill.' He added. 'You stop here and keep an eye on things while I make the search.' He turned back to Jeremy with outstretched hand. 'The keys.'

Jeremy heaved for the breath to answer, 'There aren't any . . . At least, there's nothing locked. We live here in a world where locks aren't necessary. At least we thought we did. But you're wasting your time. Doctor Hoff's been gone a fortnight and more.'

The Inspector turned from him to his man. 'Watch this man, Bill. He's got a reputation for trickiness and contempt for the law . . . .'

Jeremy shouted, 'It isn't contempt for the law I have, but for the brutes and bullies like you who use it for the power they weren't born with!'

'I'm doing my duty . . . .'

'You're doing what some other brute and bully, whether he wears a top hat or a judicial wig, tells you to . . . and because you *want* to do it.'

'To protect the public from law-breakers . . . .'

'To perpetuate the power of those who seize it . . . the destroyers of true human values . . . . ' Jeremy's voice, wild as the storm now, cracked.

'Take that down, Bill.'

But Bill looked so much at a loss, with pencil poised over his notebook, that his master said, 'Okay . . . leave it. But watch him.' He added to Jeremy: 'I warn you that we're armed.'

'I don't doubt it,' panted Jeremy. 'With rubber truncheons, too, that leave no bruises.' As Ballywick swung away from him glowering, he said to Nan, 'Go with him, dear . . . don't let's have to suffer the last indignity of that creature's invading our privacy unwatched.' But as Nan moved to follow the Inspector lumbering towards the stairs, he added: 'No. We'll have to get Rifkah out of these wet clothes.' He looked at Prindy, hanging over Rifkah from the back of the chair. 'You go with him, sonny.' Prindy leapt away.

'Now, little girl,' said Jeremy to Rifkah, helping to raise her with Nan. 'Everything's going to be all right. I'll get you out of it somehow . . . if I have to blast Hell open to do it. Now come on.'

Still sobbing wildly, Rifkah moaned, 'I vill kill meinself.'

'No you won't. You're going to live . . . and be as happy as ever. Trust me.'

'If I go from here my heart vill die.'

'Now, now, now my darling.'

It was a slow sad procession upstairs, with Sergent Bugsby plodding at the rear. Prindy broke away from the foraging inspector to come and help Rifkah into her room. Bugsby would have gone in, too, only Jeremy blocked his way, snarling, 'No you don't, you ape. You're supposed to be watching me . . . not a young girl dressing.'

Bugsby concurred without verbal comment, but wrote something in his notebook.

Rifkah stayed in the bedroom. When Jeremy was told by Nan that she had put her to bed and was staying with her, he said he would go below. Bugsby promptly told him to stay where he was, and when Jeremy ignored him, came after him, tried to place a hand on his shoulder, only to have it flung off. Bugsby stopped at the corner of the verandah, seemingly at a loss what to do.

Jeremy went down, to find Ballywick going through the broom cupboard under the stairs. They merely glanced at each other. Jeremy went and poured himself a brandy, turned on the radio, sat down. Soon Ballywick came across, but to look out through the rattling windows at the roaring flashing night. He was still looking out, when Jeremy called to him, 'When're you taking the girl in?'

The Inspector swung round, approached, saying, quite amiably, 'Tomorrow, Mr Delacy.'

'I want to pack some things, then. My quarters're across the way.'

Ballywick stopped. 'Your presence will not be required.'

'Nevertheless, you're going to be plagued with it.'

'I tell you, Sir . . . . '

'Don't waste your breath, man. I'm going to Port Palmeston to see what I can do to prevent you by legal action . . . and failing that there, I'll be going all the way . . . to see that that poor persecuted child isn't pulled back into the clutches of the monsters whose dirty work you're carrying on for them.'

'I've warned you, Delacy!'

'Keep your warnings for the poor little people you live to browbeat. I want to go to my quarters.'

'You may go when an escort's available.'

'Am I a prisoner, too?'

'No, Sir . . . you're merely under surveillance as a suspicious character.'

'Suspicious for what reason?'

'It's alleged that you've given shelter to wanted criminals on several occasions.'

'If you're referring to unfortunate Aboriginal people, who've not only had everything taken from them, but in trying to maintain the last shreds of human dignity have come to me . . . .'

'I'm talking about wanted criminals.'

'The Aborigines I gave shelter to were like this unhappy girl . . . whose only crime in her own country was to be born a Jew, and whose crime here has been to think that this is a free country with its arms open to the hunted . . . .'

Ballywick fairly roared, 'Wanted criminals!'

Jeremy stared at him for a moment, then shrugged. 'Oh, what's the use of talking to a hunk of meat like you . . . *Shtick fleisch mitt augen* . . . how appropriate!'

'What did you say?'

'Like to put it in your notebook?'

But Ballywick's eye was caught by the flash of a torch outside. He went to look. In a little while Stunke came striding in by the front door, heading towards Ballywick with water streaming from his outfit. Jeremy yelled at him, 'Take those clothes off and hang them in the porch!'

Stunke merely glanced at him, and coming up to the Inspector, said, 'The man Kaufmann isn't here. It's pretty evident from what I learnt from the native staff that he left a couple of weeks back . . . .'

Jeremy leapt up, roaring, 'Get out, you German pig . . . or I'll throw you out!'

Stunke swung on him. 'You lay a hand on me, Delacy . . . .'

Jeremy did, shouting, 'You've got no warrant to come into my house!' and began to hurl him backwards.

Ballywick rushed up to intervene. But Jeremy flung him off, got Stunke outside. Ballywick roared, 'Unhand that officer. He's under *my* authority.'

'Well, use it, you bastard, and make him act like a civilized human being . . . or, by God, I'll throw the whole lot of you out, and be glad to take the consequences, for the opportunity of showing the Nation the animals it employs to keep its peace.'

Ballywick choked on it for a moment, then snapped at Stunke, 'Take it off!' As they were coming back from the door, he said to Jeremy, 'I was given to understand that your own father was a police officer.'

'That's right.'

'Then I'd've thought you had more respect for the police.'

'I saw nothing my father ever did as a policeman to respect him. He was just as big a bully as the rest of you. But at least I never saw him lay violent hands on a woman, black or white.' As Ballywick turned away from him, he added: 'I understood you people are properly called not police but Peace Officers.'

Ballywick snapped, 'That's correct.'

Jeremy said, 'I like the term. It shows the basic goodness in the Constitution of our Commonwealth . . . just the same as we have no War Office, jingoistic thing in proper name, but a Department of Defence . . . and no King's Crown or depradatory animal in our coat-of-arms, but two of the gentlest creatures on earth surmounted by a star . . . Star of Hope for Better Things, as I like to think of it. But you so-called Peace Officers have certainly brought no peace to this haven of peace, my household . . . and may God damn you for it, and you and the mongrel bastards that have seized control of my lovely country!' His voice gave on the last of it. He swung away, went striding to the dining-room, disappeared.

For a moment the policemen stared after him. Then they looked at one another. Stunke shrugged. 'I told you he's a rat-bag as well as a trouble-maker.'

'Have you got someone handy to keep an eye on him if he goes over to his quarters?' Stunke nodded. Ballywick went on: 'He insists on coming in with us . . . in going all the way, if he can.'

'Christ . . . that'll mean trouble!'

'He won't give any trouble to me! But, man, I don't know about you . . . I'm starving.'

'I'll get rations from the truck.'

'No . . . there's a roast and some wonderful bread in the kitchen.'

'I told you he never lets us eat here. We always have to bring our own.'

'You don't know your way about as a policeman, son. You can take what you want, if you leave a chit for it, saying it was commandeered in course of duty. Any court'll uphold you in that.'

'But you don't know what a bastard Jeremy Delacy can be in trouble-making . . . .'

'I know what a bastard I can be, though, in dealing with trouble-makers. Come on . . . we're having a feed. Then you can go and relieve old Bill.'

Jeremy, coming over later with Prindy, to spend the night in the Big House, found the signed chit on the kitchen table, rolled it up and stuffed it in the range. In the lounge he found Ballywick and Stunke seated in armchairs, listening to the radio. He was about to climb the stairs, when he wheeled about and came to the pair, who rose. Laying hands on Stunke's chair, he dragged it back savagely, saying, 'I can't keep you out of my house . . . but I can out of my favourite chairs.' He then hauled the other away. 'There are other chairs.' He glanced at the radio, as if about to deny them that, too, but after listening for a moment, said, 'Sounds like your Master's voice. Better listen. Last time I heard him, he was calling Hitler a Great Man. Seems to be back-pedalling now that the British Prime Minister's decided he's a cad after all. Will that cramp your style with the Gestapo?'

Any satisfaction Jeremy may have felt in acting thus didn't last long. Upstairs, inquiring at the door of Rifkah's room of Nan about the girl's condition and being told that she was still weeping, he produced a bottle of tablets, saying they were barbiturate and telling her to give a couple. He had to speak loudly because of the rain on the roof. Sergeant Bugsby, with ear cocked, snatched away the bottle as it was being handed over, growling, 'No you don't. She doesn't get anything without the Inspector's permission.'

So Jeremy had to go down and ask. Ballywick promptly said, 'No . . . how do I know it isn't poison?'

Jeremy cried, 'Would I want to poison someone I'm trying to protect?'

'You might. She was heard to say she'd kill herself. Anyway, it's against regulations for a prisoner to be given any medicine, unless prescribed by a legally qualified medical officer. I understand you're only a horse-doctor.'

Jeremy ground his teeth on it: 'I only hope you never have a good night's sleep again . . . you fat-headed official feelingless bastard!'

Ballywick only snickered, and went aloft to instruct his Man Friday.

Jeremy, in the room he was sharing with Prindy, later gave a couple of the tablets to Prindy, who had been able to pass in and out of the prison-room unhindered. Prindy suggested that they give them to the police instead, in a drink of tea or something, and when they were sleeping, he would whisk Rifkah away. Patting him, because the boy had been showing deep distress all evening, Jeremy said, 'I'd like to, sonny . . . but it wouldn't do any good. I'd only go to jail and be stopped from helping when you were caught.'

'They can't catch me,' declared Prindy.

'They did at last, you know. And you were on your own . . . and you belong to the country, and can live as easily in the bush as in a house. But she can't. She hasn't even spent a night in the bush yet . . . and listen to this rain. Country'll go under water in a couple of days.'

'I can look out for her, Mullaka.'

'No, son. She'd get sick. There's fever, and all sorts of things for people not used to it. Trust me. I promise to do everything I can. There is goodness in most people . . . more than badness. We've got to fight for that . . . people's goodness . . . to save Rifkah.'

Prindy snivelled, 'I been promise I take her away if policeman come.'

'And I've promised to get her free again.'

Unconvinced, Prindy dropped fair head to hands and wept. Stroking the head, and sounding close to tears himself, Jeremy muttered, 'D'you know . . . I've never seen you cry before. I reckoned you were too much *kullum kundera* for that.'

Prindy sniffed hard. 'Too-much my *gawang* cry.'

'Right . . . now, how're you going to carry these tablets, in case that ape Bugsby wants to take a look?'

'You put in little bit paper. I carry-him-up in my toe,

'Good idea. Now, put on your pyjamas, and make it look as if you're going to say goodnight.'

Bugsby did run his hands over Prindy's slight person, even to feeling in his hair, but didn't even glance at the stubby bare brown feet, with the little brown-paper packet between big toe and the next.

So soundly did Rifkah sleep that at dawn she had to be roused with shaking, and thereafter was drowsy, drooping, withdrawn, still tearful, but no longer sobbing. It looked as if she had resigned herself to things. However, most likely Jeremy had doped her heavily to ensure just such a state, and might even have got Nan to sneak her another dose in the little breakfast she would take. The police, trackers and all, ate breakfast in the kitchen, at Jeremy's orders. The morning was as wild as the night.

Soon after breakfast and a tearful farewell of Rifkah by all who would not be going with her, the start was made for the Beatrice – and what beyond? Rifkah was placed in the police utility, between Stunke, driving, and Inspector Ballywick. The other police rode under tarpaulins behind. Jeremy, Prindy, Darcy, and some blackboys, followed in the big truck. Both vehicles were fitted with skid-chains.

Thus they travelled through the sheeting rain, having to stop from time to time for the removal of downed trees or branches from the track, or to be manhandled out of mud, or in the case of the utility, shoved or towed out by the truck. The journey took till mid-afternoon. Already the train was back from Charlotte by the time they arrived.

As the trucks came roaring up from the still-unflooded river, Pat Hannaford, in oilskins, was waiting at the railway crossing. Rifkah's bright hair could be seen through the streaming windscreen. However, it was doubtful if she would have recognized him, for all his waving, even if Stunke did, as was pretty certain the way he scowled through the celluloid side-screen. Pat jumped onto the running-board of the big truck to go with it as it followed the utility to the Police Station. Jeremy told him he had got his message from Darcy and had passed it on to Rifkah, and thanked him for his effort.

There was nothing they could do at the Police Station but stand outside and stare. The police truck was run into its shelter under the residence, and the gate quickly shut against intrusion, by Tipperary. Then Rifkah was pulled out of the vehicle by Ballywick, who taking one of her arms, while Bugsby took the other, hurried her out to the stairs and up to the front door of the residence, which was opened on the instant by Mrs Stunke, and almost as quickly closed again. She went drooping, evidently unaware of those outside. Stunke shot these a hard enquiring glance, then went into his office.

Pat said, 'The bloody bastards!'

'Yes,' murmured Jeremy.

'But we'll beat 'em,' declared Pat.

'I hope so.'

'Hope?' demanded Pat. 'We got to . . . or admit the bloody Gestapo's taken over!'

'That's right. I'll do everything in my power.'

'Such as?'

'Invoke the law . . . the press. Have you got any ideas?'

'Plenty.'

'Let's hear them.'

Pat eyed Jeremy cautiously. Then he said, 'Come down to my quarters.'

'What about you coming along to Tom Toohey's? We're wet through and up to our eyes in mud. Want to wash and change.'

'Okay.'

Prindy was standing at the gate that had been shut against them, grasping it as if to pull it down, while his lips moved as if he were talking or singing. Jeremy called to him. He looked back, eyed those behind with a strange hard look in his vivid eyes. Then after taking one more glance at the shuttered house above, he turned and came to join them.

IV

It seemed as if everybody in Beatrice township, temporary and permanent residents alike, and white, of course, since others perhaps knew better how to mind their own business, converged on Tom Toohey's when the news of Rifkah's arrest and incarceration and of the presence there of people from Lily Lagoons got around. Even Shamus Finnucane turned up, battling the storm in oilskins some said they'd never seen him in before. Perhaps he did the unprecedented thing, which included leaving his bar when there was drinking going on there, to test his famous powers of blarney in a feat where everybody else had failed. Still, it could have been out of genuine concern as well, since above the roar of the rain on the verandah roof, he bellowed through the door shut these several hours against the curious, 'I understand yer feelin's. Shame on us that a lovely gurrl loike that should be locked up like a common criminal . . . and for what? In God's name, for what?'

But for the select few who knew, no one was telling – especially to the Biggest Ears belonging to the Biggest Mouth in the Country, and more especially when by then they were concerned not so much with what had happened as what should be done to counter it. By now they constituted a conspiracy, the leaders of which were, in order of vehemence of expression of purpose, if not in actual feeling in the matter, Pat Hannaford, Jeremy, Clancy.

Already Jeremy had telephoned his lawyer in Town, Bill Billings, asking him to make preparations for the issue of a writ of *habeas corpus* on behalf of one, Rebecca Rosen, allegedly unlawfully detained, and if necessary to brief a leading lawyer from the South, all done without giving away more of the game than absolutely necessary to the many ears that would be listening in. Pat had got in contact with his local Party principals, Scotty McClaggity and Geordie Jenks, and talked to them in a jargon that would have little meaning to an outsider, but had that pair fairly shouting for glee in promising to organize, or perhaps more properly to *dis*organize, things immediately. Clancy would have rung Dicky Doscas, who besides being Clerk of Courts and many other things, was Registrar of Births, Deaths, and Marriages, to ask for the Special Marriage Licence considered as a useful adjunct to the claim he would make to being Rifkah's fiancé, in seeking her release from custody pending legal proceedings. The idea of Clancy as fiancé was Pat's idea, a matter of sheer subterfuge and expediency, as frankly he declared by saying that if it came to having to marry Rifkah off to beat the law, it would be done through Party processes, as on other occasions, which would leave her completely free in fact from the outset and secure her freedom in law at the earliest possible time. How Clancy took it would be hard to say. He went very red when the matter was raised. But this could have meant several things: embarrassment at being involved in more than he bargained for, pleasure in it, or resentment at being used as a mere stooge in a matter he considered delicate. To begin with, Jeremy also looked embarrassed.

By local law, a period of three days must elapse between the issue of a Special Licence and actual marriage. Hearing this from his father, Clancy suggested that the sooner he applied the better. However, Jeremy argued that although Dicky Doscas was the soul of discretion in official matters, he might not take this as one, seeing what it implied without his knowing the circumstances, and gossip might be started, at least by his female staff, that might contribute to forestallment of their plans – and how could Dicky be asked over the telephone to keep it to himself?

'Better leave it till you get to Town, son,' said Jeremy. 'Dicky'll be in his office on Saturday morning. He's got so much to do he's always there. Anyway, he's such an obliging bloke, he'd go there if you asked him. I never knew a fat man so helpful and so kindly. Very fat people've usually got a mean streak in 'em.'

The conspirators had been left to themselves for a couple of hours, but were still behind locked doors, when, soon after ten, they were startled by Tom Toohey's wife's screaming from her bedroom that there was an intruder in the house. They came rushing with the pressure-lamp to the kitchen, where a clatter had followed Nolly's shrill announcement. It was Prindy, presumably gone to bed this long while, but certainly not looking dressed for it now. He was wearing wet oilskins, and at the moment of discovery was snatching a bundle of similar clothing from the table. Evidently he had been in the act of taking food from a cupboard, and would have fled the kitchen by way of a partly open tin shutter if not headed off by Jeremy. Even when cut off, he tried to dodge round Jeremy, who then grabbed him by an arm, causing the bundle to fall and spill its contents – a sou'wester, a small pair of elastic-sides and socks, and a towel. Jeremy, staring into the wild-looking grey eyes, asked in surprise, 'Why . . . what're you up to, sonny?'

The other grey eyes became defiant. 'What's wrong?' asked Jeremy. He released the arm. Immediately Prindy swung back towards the shutter. But Jeremy leapt ahead of him and slammed it shut and bolted it, then turned on him. 'Tell me what's the matter?'

They stared at each other. The defiance turned to something like desperation. At length Prindy said, so low in the uproar of the rain that Jeremy had to ask him to say it again and to bend to hear, 'I go back home.'

'Eh? Why?'

'I don't like here.'

'The truck'll be going back tomorrow as soon as the train goes.'

'I don't want see train go.'

'All right. But what've you been doing out in the rain?'

'I go get horse.'

'You'll never catch a horse in this rain.'

'Tom got two horse in shed.'

Jeremy looked at Toohey, who nodded. Then Jeremy picked up the stuff from the floor. 'What's this? Who're you taking with you?'

The grey eyes rolled, as if looking for a way to escape. Jeremy drew a sudden breath, put a hand on the small shoulder. 'What're you doing, son . . . not trying to get Rifkah away from the police, are you?'

That look of desperation again. Jeremy went on, in a gentle tone: 'You can't do it, sonny. They've got her locked up.'

Prindy blurted it out, 'I been do it now!'

Jeremy gasped. The defiant look came back, flashed round the others crowding in to hear. Jeremy swallowed. 'Tell me what you've done . . . come on . . . you can trust me.'

Prindy said, somewhat truculently, it seemed, 'You all talk-about get him 'way from police. I been go get him.'

Hannaford's narrow green eyes widened. 'Good on you, kid! That's what's called direct action . . . the *fait accompli*.'

But Jeremy looked worried. 'Tell me what you did? Where's Rifkah now?'

Prindy explained that he'd gone out to do what he called Sing Goodnight to My Mumma, and found that there was a sort of party going on in the Police Station residence, loud talk and laughter and the clink of glass, a situation that, combined with the fact that the trackers were shut up in their quarters against the roaring rain, emboldened him to sneak into the house by way of the back stairs to see if he could speak to Rifkah, whose voice he hadn't heard amongst the others'. He heard her in a room used by the Stunke children when they were at home, still crying. The door was locked, but the key in the lock. Apparently neither Rifkah nor he had thought of anything but the freedom offering when he opened that door, and had seized it on the moment. As Prindy added with a smug smile at the faces staring at him aghast: 'Old One been do it all right.'

He and the girl had run straight to the rising river, crossed and headed straight for home. However, they'd had to stop at the Racecourse, as Prindy put it: 'She been knock-up foot. She got no shoe. Missus Stunke been take away her shoe to dry. Road up from river too rough from wash out by rain.' Evidently she had cut her feet quite badly, not being used to walking barefoot. Hence his return, leaving her in the shelter of the grandstand.

When the story was told, Jeremy was the only one to comment, 'God . . . what do we do now?'

Tom Toohey, looking troubled as usual, said, 'They'll be buzzin' round here like bloody hornets.'

Jeremy said, 'We'll just have to get her and take her back to them.'

Prindy went rigid, crying shrilly, 'No-more . . . you can't do it!'

'Now, listen, laddy,' said Jeremy gently.' 'You know we've got it all worked out to get her back. It's got to be done properly, you know . . . white-feller way . . . .'

Jeremy was proceeding to give the latest details of the plan, when Pat Hannaford interrupted: 'Bugger it . . . this is a *fait accompli*! Never go back on a *fait accompli*, they say.' Perhaps it was a Communist tenet. Eagerly he went on to say that, having her free, the most important thing, they must keep her so until they secured her freedom legally. He was for Prindy's taking her, as he'd first tried to do, away into the Sandstone, where with his nous he could baffle the police for weeks even.

But Jeremy argued the dangers of the girl's inexperience of the bush: 'You don't know anything about the real bush, Pat . . . you only see it from an engine. I've seen it kill strong men. Look what's happened to the girl's feet after walking only half a mile or so. These boots and clothes he's got for her won't last a week in this weather. As it is her feet'll turn septic. For a certainty she'll get a fever out of this rain. Even the blacks suffer in this kind of weather. If he takes her into the Sandstone she'll die. For christ sake be sensible!'

'Then we'll take her to Town,' snapped Hannaford.

'How?'

'While they're lookin' for her. Let 'em think the boy took her. Let him go himself. They'll go after him. Then we'll sneak her away. It's *fait accompli*, I tell yo' '

'How're you goin' to sneak her away?'

'I snuck away people before, ain't I?'

'You're not putting her in any coal-tender!'

'Won't be necessary with the Johns out o' the way. If we take her up the road a bit, I'll pick her up in the mornin' . . . and we can easily keep anyone off the injin, or plant her under a tarp worst comes to the worst. We got a tarp there to keep the rain out while we're shuntin'. Tom here can give's a hand. You got a pump-car over the other side the bridge, Tom. What about we run her well up the road on that tonight. We could run her far as Granite Springs and pick her up while we's waterin'.'

Looking haggard, Tom swallowed. 'With them Johns runnin' round like hornets . . . '

'Not askin' *you* to do it. Me'n Clancy here . . . '

Jeremy interrupted: 'Better leave it to me and Clancy, Pat. She mightn't go with you . . . '

'Eh . . . what's wrong with me?'

'What I mean's she'll have to be talked into going. I'll go over with the boy . . . with the horses. Clancy can come with us, and get the pump-car out of the shed. Anyway, Pat, when they wake up and start hunting round, and they find you gone, they'll immediately take a jerry. Better for you and Porky to get back to your camp right away. If they catch me and Clancy, we can say we caught the boy taking the horses, and went straight out to get the girl and bring her back to 'em.'

'Okay,' said Pat, reluctantly. Then he became vigorous. 'Right . . . we'll get along. First we'll take a look see everything's normal at the Cop Shop. If one of us ain't back in five minutes, you'll know the coast's clear. See yo's!'

That five minutes of waiting weren't wasted. While Nolly made up a bundle of dry clothes, food, and stuff for dressing Rifkah's feet, Jeremy, Tom and Prindy went to get the horses, two old campers, used by Tom to keep an eye on the handful of stock he ran along the river, which while making some objection to being dragged out into the rain, proved docile enough in capable hands. The only precaution taken was to see to it that, where human tracks might be left, those of the men were superimposed on Prindy's, to support the subterfuge that the boy had done everything unbeknown to his elders. Outside it didn't matter, because all signs were washed away practically as made. Toohey, utterly miserable with the prospect of being bullied yet again by police in search of fugitives he was suspected of harbouring, agreed no less readily to tell the man-hunters, should they come before Jeremy's return, that he had gone looking for the fugitives himself. Within ten minutes, Jeremy, Prindy and Clancy, were mounted and away, heading along the railway track so as to avoid running into anyone along the road. Jeremy had Prindy up behind him.

By the look of things at the Police Station, the little party was still proceeding happily. The horsemen dropped down to the river, to find it knee-deep on the causeway.

Jeremy found a very different Rifkah from the stricken one who earlier in the day had scarcely seen him for her flooding tears. The great eyes revealed by his flashlight were quite dry, and glinted with suspicion as he outlined his intentions. There was no clinging to him. It was evident from her behaviour that, but for the condition of her feet, some of the wounds which Jeremy declared should be stitched for proper healing, and the fact that he told only half-truths in answer to her inquiries about what was planned for her eventual freedom, most likely he would never have got her to go with him to the railway. Particularly did she resist the idea of going without Prindy. As for Prindy, but for being told that, as likely as not, she would be back with them utterly free on next week's train, he might well have cruelled the whole scheme by refusing to be parted from her. It was evident that they did not trust him as before. Even his final instructions to Prindy, to make contact with him secretly at Lily Lagoons after losing the police party that would surely pursue him into the Sandstone, was received in silence.

Never had physical contact between Jeremy and the girl been so close as tonight, when he humped her on his back to the railway to save her feet, with her thighs about him and his hands on the bare flesh of them at the knees, her arms about his neck, belly and breasts pressed against him; yet so far from being the Rifkah who had clung to him and kissed him so recklessly in the past was she now that she scarcely responded to his trying to jolly her by reference to their ridiculous posture, even giving a buck or two. She seemed even relieved to be taken in Clancy's ready arms and placed on the waiting pump-car.

Clancy reported that he had taken a peep from the bridge and seen what he took to be lights flickering in the vicinity of the Police Station. Jeremy went to look for himself. It was hard to see anything through the lashing curtain of rain. Even Finnucane's appeared as a faint luminescence. But unmistakably there was another hint of light, now moving about the railway yards. He returned to say that evidently the police were out, and that it would be best for him to stay behind to deal with them and leave it to Clancy to get Rifkah to Granite Springs alone. In any circumstances it would be a tough job for one man to handle a cumbersome vehicle like that, designed for operation by the co-ordinated efforts of two, but in such as prevailed was positively formidable. Yet Clancy leapt to it with eagerness that was even indecent, almost ignoring his father when enjoined to make the trip up and back as soon as possible and himself scarce when he got back. With barely a nod, bending to his task like an argonaut, he shot away. Jeremy was left standing, staring into the roaring darkness that almost on the instant had swallowed his love. He hadn't been given the chance even to touch her hand in farewell. Heaving a great sigh, he turned, headed towards the bridge.

A white-painted cat-walk ran between the rails on the bridge. In the utter blackness made by the walls of latticed steel it seemed to float like a magic carpet. Already the steel was beginning to hum with the pressure gathering below.

Indeed the police were out and in the mood of angry hornets – worse, as hornets probably would be, from being disturbed on such a night. Jeremy went to them, to be pounced on at once and accused of engineering the escapade. When he was able to give his version, telling them that he had just come from finding fresh tracks up at the Racecourse, they yelled at him for not having reported to them before he went there He growled, 'How the hell did I know she wasn't with you? I was only thinking of the boy, clearing off back home with a broken heart'

'That little black bastard,' snarled Stunke. 'I'll see he pays for this.'

Jeremy said, 'D'you know, Stunke . . . the other night when I called you a German Pig I could've bitten my tongue off. I don't like prejudice against people for their breed. Germans are just as good as anybody else . . . and as bad. It was only this Gestapo business that made me say it. I was going to apologize to you some time. But I won't now . . . after what you've just said about that sorrowing little boy, whose real mother you had a part in depriving him of . . . Wait . . . I do have an apology to make . . . to the Germans . . . and the pigs, for classing *you* with 'em.'

'Ahhh!' exploded Stunke, and swung away towards the utility, standing with lights staring like watery eyes. He told one of the trackers to stay behind and search and, 'Watch that man!' Inspector Ballywick also told his sergeant to remain.

Stunke started up, swung for the road down to the causeway. Jeremy watched the lights till they went out. After a while Stunke and his mates came up the hill again, tramping now, and getting onto the railway, headed off towards the bridge.

Jeremy turned and headed through the yards towards Tooheys'. There was a crowd in the shelters of the lighted station. Some called to Jeremy. He ignored them. Then one came after him. It was Pat Hannaford, wanting to know, when they were out of hearing, how things had gone. When he heard that Clancy was handling the pump-car alone, he railed, 'That lily-white handed bastard! He'll knock-up in the first mile.'

'I think he'll be all right.'

'You ever pulled one o' them things on your own?'

Jeremy answered dryly, 'Yes. So has Clancy. You've forgotten the time you got derailed in the big flood of Thirty-Four? We had to take the pump-cars out single-handed to leave room to bring you mob back . . . and the water was two feet deep in places.'

When Pat fell silent, Jeremy said, 'Best you're not seen with me too much, I reckon. See you in the morning.'

'Okay,' muttered Pat, and turned about.

Apparently, Pat didn't know the super-power of a man in love, perhaps, being an idealist, didn't know that love – love of man for woman – is a power at all.

What, to Clancy, meant those back-breaking, muscle-cracking, hand-skinning miles to Granite Springs, that heaving to the limit of strength upgrade against the eternal resistance of gravity, the hair-raising rushing with it down into what looked like nothingness, the drag of the howling bind of steel on steel on the curves, the bellowing counter-blasting of the wind in narrow cuttings, the lash of the wild wet wind on the inky plains, the menacing roar of unseen waters, while a beloved object, so black in the blackness as to be utterly invisible, yet oh so vividly there, crouched beside him? He even had the breath to sing at times: 'She'll be comin' round the mountain when she comes – Along the road to Gundagai.'

'Vy don't you rest?' Rifkah called up several times, not knowing, even from his laugh in answer that she was calling to a superman.

But his love was not left just for guessing. When the long miles of his conquest lay behind like the coils of a slain dragon, and at Granite Springs he had borne his beloved in his arms to the shed beside the water-tank and lain her on the heap of old tarps used by loafing fettlers, and she, looking at him by the light of the torch lying where he had dropped it on the streaming ground, thanked him for all the trouble he had taken for her sake, telling it with lips against his ear because of the din of falling waters, he laughed, and shouted above the uproar, 'How can it be a trouble when I love you?'

He would have kissed her, had she not caught his face in her hands, and holding it, cried wildly, 'No, dear Clancy . . . it is not goot you loff me!'

He must have misunderstood, because he bawled back, 'Yes . . . I love you!'

Then his lips would not be denied, and drank of them – raindrops, tears, the essence that is woman, and perhaps an added sweetness no other man would ever savour – till suffocation broke the bond.

She gasped, 'You must go.'

'Yes . . . my darling . . . but only till the morning.'

He would have kissed her again. She pushed him away. He rose laughing, gave her the light, the directed beam of which he followed to the door. He turned, kissed his hand, shouted, 'Good-night!' shut the door on her, drew a great breath, and climbed back aboard the pump-car.

Proof of a man's love is not what he says to his beloved, but what he finds himself saying, sighing, singing as he leaves her. Clancy sang love-songs now as he slugged homeward: 'I love you, I love you, that's all that I can say.' Now he had the wind on his quarter astern, and fairly bowled along.

What time he got back to the bridge was of no moment in the circumstances, save to Eternity. At any rate, no sign of life was to be seen in the township, or sound of life when he had crossed the bridge and was making his way through it towards his home. He went whistling under his breath. He did not let it go till he reached the first gate: 'Love me, and the world is mine!'

The cattle-dogs heard him when he reached the homestead, and challenged him till they caught his scent. He went straight to his quarters, hung his oilskins out on the verandah, stripped to under-shorts and singlet, dried face and hands, dropped on his narrow bed, was asleep immediately.

It was breaking day when he woke. He leapt up, went to shower and shave, all in haste. Back in his room he added a couple of things to a small suitcase already packed. The rain had eased considerably. Still, to cross to the Big House, he donned the oilskins again. Tramping along the side verandah of the detached kitchen, he signalled to those at work inside who looked out at him. Then in to the house and to the dining-room.

He was just finishing his steak and eggs, when his brother entered. They grunted at each other. Then Martin, unrolling his napkin, asked, 'Off to Town?'

'Yeah.'

'What for . . . this weather?'

'Business.'

'What business?'

'Mine.'

Martin's ruddy face darkened. 'Happens to be my business what staff does in the Company's time.'

'You don't say?'

'I do say. As soon's the rain stops, the stock at Catfish'll have to be checked.'

Clancy, rolling his napkin, answered shortly, 'Nice job for you.' As he rose he added: 'Take some of the fat off your arse to get back in the saddle.'

His brother stared at him, not in anger, but in evident surprise, perhaps because of the easy insolence compared with the usual bluster in such circumstances. As Clancy headed for the door, Martin called after him, 'You're not mixed up in this Jew-girl business, are you?'

Now Clancy looked belligerent as he swung back. 'What d'you mean?'

'Police here last night looking for her . . . asked where *you* were. Where were you?'

Clancy's breast heaved. 'Minding my own bloody business!'

'It's my business what you drag the family name into while the Mater's away . . . . '

'Balls!'

'Now, listen, Clancy . . . you were seeing too much of that girl before . . . and Mater didn't like it . . . . '

Clancy snapped, 'What a bloody pity!' With that he turned and stalked out.

Martin's blue eyes were wide as he stared at the empty doorway. Surely such words had never been uttered under that roof before!

Clancy was driven to the railway by the Second Bookkeeper, who also told him of the visit by police, and when pressed, added with a little cough of apology that Martin had told them he supposed that he, Clancy, would be at Ah Loys, as usual. Evidently the police were satisfied with the word of a Vaisey Manager, because there they were at the station, all eyes, but giving no more attention to Clancy than to anyone else.

Jeremy was waiting. After Clancy had bought his ticket and was going with his case to a coach, his father elbowed him out of the crowd and asked him how things had gone. Clancy answered as if the question sounded unnecessary, 'Okay.'

Dryly Jeremy added: 'Well, let's hope the rest of it goes the same.' Then when Clancy moved towards the coach, he caught his arm, murmuring, 'Just a minute.' Clancy looked, to see the face changed, the broad face redder, the grey eyes strangely fixed in expression. Jeremy glanced away. Pat Hannaford, no doubt bent on waylaying Clancy, too, was examining a journal box of the coach. Jeremy kept his eyes on Pat, while he said quickly, 'I told her she wouldn't have to leave the country. She doesn't want to. But Hannaford's hell-bent on getting her away to the Comms down South. When you get that Special Licence . . . why not use it properly?'

Now he looked at Clancy, whose blue eyes had widened. Jeremy swallowed, looked away again, went on, his voice now throaty: 'You can always get a divorce if it doesn't work out. Old Maryzic would marry you without asking too many questions. Even if he knows, he's got no time for the police . . . and he'd know Jews, and sympathize with 'em.' He looked back again at Clancy, swallowed again, 'It'd solve the whole problem.'

Now Clancy swallowed, looked down, murmuring, 'Yeah . . . I have thought about it.'

Pat was approaching. 'How yo' doin'?' he said casually. Then after a glance around, he asked Clancy, 'How'd it go?'

Clancy answered in that same indifferent tone he had used in reply to his father's question, 'Okay.'

Pat's green eyes quizzed him, then he took another look around, muttering as he did so, 'Wēll, you know the drill . . . any suspicious movement towards the injin when we're stopped and you don't see one of us lookin' out . . . you come beltin' up the other side the train to tip us off.'

'Okay.'

'See you later, then.'

When Clancy turned to the coach again, Jeremy went with him. Casting a glance towards the police. Clancy murmured, 'What're they doing here?'

'Just killing time, by the look of it. They've searched through everything. They're waiting for the trackers to catch the police horses. I'll go back with 'em.'

That was the end of private discussion. Oz Burrows was ringing the bell for All Aboard. Father and son parted with slight gestures.

Chas Chase blew his whistle. Pat responded with his. The engine let out a blast as she slipped in too-hurried starting that made the wheels spin. Then they were away. Clancy glanced again at his father, who nodded. Then he saw Lucy Ah Loy, pantalooned and standing under a huge umbrella, looking very pretty in a wooden Chinese way. She waved to him slightly. He replied.

Out of the railway yards with a clatter of points, and onto the bridge, and over the now raging yellow snake of river. The police trackers were over the other side, having trouble with a dozen fractious horses near the little shed that housed the pump-car. Whereas other passengers watched the equine mêlée Clancy had eyes only for the innocent-looking vehicle standing on its twin lengths of rail. He smirked as he drew back inside to settle down. Everybody else looked amused as they settled down, because one of the trackers had been thrown from his horse. As one of them chuckled, 'There's nothing so funny as seein' a boong pelted . . . all bloody skinny arms and legs flyin', like a spider with a hornet onto him . . . aheeee!'

V

The abduction of Rifkah went almost perfectly according to plan, from the plucking of her out of the mist of rain and spray at Granite Springs, to setting her down in what seemed like a deliberately discreet moment of darkness given by the Moon at the planned destination, the 10-Mile Lagoons, outside of Port Palmeston. For abduction virtually it was, seeing that she would have been elsewhere but for the interference of those presuming they knew what was best for her. Also, it was rather like one abducted that she behaved, than one being whisked away to the wonderful things Pat Hannaford brayed about through the journey, blind to her obvious misery, and Clancy, just as blind, yawped of in innuendoes the couple of times he was able to talk to her.

Pat was frank about her going to join the ranks of those he called their Comrades, in the South, to help establish the Workers' Paradise he declared he saw Australia as within five years now that Fascism and Capitalism were bound to go to war and destroy each other. She just sat in the lurching cab, staring great-eyed, the haggard *bubbeh's* stare, as mile after mile they cleft the wilderness ahead, surely all too fast for her who believed it was her refuge; while above the roar of fire and steam and the clamour of whirling rods and wheels, Pat vociferated in her ear.

Clancy, during his couple of visits to the engine, while Pat was oiling her up and Porky Jones watering her, hinted at the advantages of being a Vaisey Delacy, with a town-house and a beach-house, a huge launch that would even take them for a trip to the East, where he wouldn't mind going if he had someone nice as his companion. He was too much in love to see the *bubbeh*'s lines round the lovely jewels of eyes.

The weather improved with every mile; until beyond the Caroline, out of the area of the cyclonic influence, the conditions were those of normal Wet Season, with the Sun popping in and out of fat cloud masses, so that the verdant landscape varied in hue between vivid malachite and hazy cobalt, sometimes backed by silver curtains of rain, occasionally obliterated when the train passed through such a curtain.

There were only three untoward incidents throughout the journey. The first occurred at Helena Springs, while the engine was watering and most of the passengers boozing in the pub and Clancy was paying his second visit to his beloved. His first visit was made back at the Caroline, while his fellow-passengers were having dinner along with their booze, and he had strolled up to report to Pat at his oiling that all was well, that there was a lot of talk going on about the Jew-girl, but nothing in it to suggest that anyone knew anything like the facts or had the slightest suspicion that she was travelling with them. He had then gone round to the far side of the engine and climbed aboard, to find Rifkah eating sandwiches and drinking tea, beside the tarpaulin draped over the tender for instant use as concealment. When he came up again at Helena Springs, he didn't trouble to report to Pat, but climbed straight up into the cab. He was deep in talk about that trip through the Isles of Spice, when Pat, oil-can in hand, came up from the other side. The green eyes in the smudged freckled face snapped at Clancy with hostility. Pat demanded, 'Anything wrong?'

Clancy answered easily, 'No . . . she's right.'

'Then wha' yo' doin' 'ere?'

Clancy flamed at the tone, snapped back, 'Just came to see how things're going.'

'You don' 'ave to see 'ow things are 'ere, mate. Your job's keepin' an eye on things back there.' Pat jerked his thumb in a manner clearly ordering Clancy off.

Clancy blazed: 'Who d'you think you're talking to?'

'I'll stop talkin' and swing into action, you don't get crackin'.'

Rif kah got between them, crying, 'Pliss . . . oh, pliss!'

Porky, hearing the voices above the gushing of the hydrant, came leaping over the coal, dropped onto the footplate. 'For christ sake, you blokes . . . wha's wrong't yo'?'

The belligerents looked at Rif kah, who laid a hand on an arm of each, smiled a wobbly smile. Then they looked at each other, narrow-eyed. Pat grunted, 'Got 'o keep your eye skinned all the time.'

Clancy grunted back, 'Okay.' Backing to the steps, he winked at Rif kah, stepped down, vanished.

The next incident was at the 40-Mile, where they stopped for water. The Sun had just gone down, leaving the cloudy West looking like the burning breast of a phoenix. The East, however, was clear almost to the zenith, as if Igulgul, just popping, almost in his fullness, from the trees, had blown away the clouds the easier to see and gloat over Wrong-side Business. Porky Jones, up on the tender with the hydrant, called to Pat who was oiling in between his driving wheels, that Chas Chase was coming. Pat came back to the step and called a warning to Rif kah. As Chase came up, he asked, 'Well, wha's wrong?'

'What the hell's wrong't you?' demanded Chase. 'Bloody hour and fifteen behind now . . . and you're crawlin'.'

'Don' blame me,' snapped Pat. 'Blame the bloody coal.'

'They're goin' 'o blame me. Gi's a sample to show the bloke.'

Chase began to climb up to the cab. Pat grabbed him by the shirt and pulled him down, demanding, 'Where you think you're goin'?'

'I wan' some bloody coal, don' I?'

'I'll get your bloody coal.'

'I wan' 'o get it meself . . . a fair sample.'

'You'll get only what's given to yo', mate. Chuck him a couple o' nuggets, Porky.'

Porky Jones was suspiciously long in throwing down the few chalky chunks. However, Chase only scowled as he picked them up and headed back to his van. Climbing into the cab, Pat chuckled, 'Just as well we had a bit o' rubbish to give him.' Then he saw Clancy peeping in over the foot-plate from the other side, and scowled.

Clancy said with haste, 'I couldn't beat him here. I was afraid if I ran he might hear me.'

Pat's scowl cleared. He grunted, 'She's right. I been 'oldin' her back. Had to 'ave an excuse. I reckoned on it being cloudy enough to be properly dark when we get to the 10-Mile. It'll be dark enough now . . . if that bloody Moon don't spoil it.' Pat cocked an eye at smirking Igulgul, adding, 'If the Moon's out, I won't be able to stop close to the road, like I said. I'll 'ave to keep goin' to a curve 'bout half a mile on. Whenever you pull up, the bastards all hang out to see what it is. So might be you'll 'ave to go lookin' for her when you come out to pick her up. She mightn't be able to make it on them feet of hers to the road. You better get back now. We'll be off in a minute.'

But Igulgul might have been in the plot, the way he ducked into cloud just as the train was coming to the point planned for the stop. The plan was that an act would be put on as if kangaroos were on the track. While the usual procedure of whistling, light-dowsing, blowing off steam, was gone through, Pat would lift Rifkah down and rush her to the cover of thick scrub just off the track there. That's how it turned out, with Porky doing the stuff on the engine. The only difference was that there was no rush about it. After sitting all day, Rifkah had to be almost carried. Pat gave her a squeeze in parting, saying, 'Good luck, Comrade . . . till we meet again . . . hey!' She had kissed him quickly. He stood for a moment. But Igulgul was about to pop out again. He turned and sprinted back to the engine.

The headlight blazed again. The steam hissed, billowed into a moonlit cloud. Silver in the moonlight, the train went rolling on.

As suggested, it might have been, according to some reasoning, that Igulgul came out deliberately, being in the conspiracy all along, because it must have been pretty scary to be suddenly alone at night in the bush for the first time, too much so in darkness – with all those things crowding round, scuffling, hopping, flapping, snuffling, croaking, squeaking, coming to look at one who with moon-pearly face and flaming hair – surely the Earth Mother, the Ol'Goomun-Ol'Goomun, looking ever so young and lovely, but her aged-agelessness to be seen in her great eyes, come back to her children.

Rifkah was amongst old friends, whose like she had been introduced to on those night-walks at Lily Lagoons, or on daytime rambles when the magician Prindy had given her glimpses of them curled up asleep in hollow logs or pipey branches. There was old Mininjorka, the Bandicoot, with his wife and his pack-bag testicles, talking about her – K'nitch, k'nitch, k'nitch – through long sharp nose, making bold little runs towards her and timid retreats again through the silver-jet-emerald grass-tussocks. Murrimo, misnamed Possum by whitemen, always a cheeky one, came slithering down from the tip-top succulence of a tall stringybark, to swing out onto the lowest limb, from which, for better view, he hung by the long jointed finger at the end of his glistening black bushy tail, eyes apop and aglitter in the glare of Igulgul. In a nearby bloodwood Mud-burrabah, called Wildcat by the Misnamer although not in the least like a cat, having broad yellow stripes down his black back and furry triangles between legs and body that came in handy for getting about without the trouble of using his claws, took a peep, then came volplaning across to land on that same stringybark branch, causing Murrimo to abuse him deep-throatedly, but answering only with a snicker. Someone coming through the tussocks, dodging as usual, because never up to any good, snatching away other people's forraging or stealing their eggs, betraying himself with the flash of his long white whip-tail, Boin-Boin, called the White-tailed Rat, while no more like a rat than Mininjorka was like the Malayan pig the silly *kuttabah* had named him for as 'Bandicoot'. The flapping, or rather swishing, since the wings that made the sound were spear-swift in motion, came from three circling shadows that called their own names – Karra-Keera, Karra-Keera, Karra-Keera! Plovers they could be rightly called, perhaps, since they belonged to that species – yet why so-called, unless out of some spite against anything native, spite born of guilt of robbery with violence? The birds landed with the grace of sprites, to go trotting round and round the shining visitant, bobbing their wattled heads, still calling their names – Karra-Keera, Karra-Keera, Karra-Keera!

But sight of old friends seemed only to stir up memories contrasting so sadly with present realities that the great eyes swam. Igulgul, turned the tears to pearls as they streamed. Now there was sound all round like tiny clicking of tongues in sympathy, culminating in the distant cry of Kweeluks: Kwee-luk, Kweeee-luk, even the Mother of the Land is lost! We are all lost who are native to it by birth or love . . . Poor Fellow, Our Country!

Igulgul only stared and stared, even gloating, perhaps, since his business was forever Wrong-side, Negative.

Two or three motor vehicles passed along the main road, so far away it did not matter to the peace of the place, the beast-like roaring no more than a drone, and only the slightest reek of their foul breathing and a little silvery powdering of their dust coming drifting with the tang of the sea on the evening breeze. Then there came a droning that was different, rising, falling, waxing, waxing instead of waning, with a glitter of lights soon, and – *toot, toot, toot*! The friends vanished in a flash.

Clancy slipped out of the car, to come bounding to prevent her walking to him. She tried to prevent him from taking her up, but failing, gave in with a wobbly smile. Looking into her face as he carried her, he demanded, 'What . . . crying? When everything's going to be all right?' He added, as he placed her in the front seat: 'God-forsaken place to leave you, I know. But it was safest. I'd've been here earlier, only that old fool Hanno'd let a tyre go flat . . . and I had to wait'll he changed it.' He got in himself, started up, swung back towards the main road, telling her that while they were hardly likely to meet anyone this time of night, she had better be ready to bob down. 'That copper knob of yours,' he chuckled. 'I saw it at fifty yards. Just's well no stock around here . . . or you'd 've had a bull after you. Bulls go wild when they see red, like the song says. You know that song – *Lulu*?' He hummed a bit. Then he went on to say that they would soon turn off the main road to follow back tracks most of the way home, as he called it. He talked rapidly, excitedly. When she asked who Hanno was, the only time she spoke, except a Yes or No to his swift questions, and he explained that Hanno was the Japanese factotum employed by the family in Town, he went on to tell how the man was eternally obliged to the family through having been extricated from serious trouble with the Law and his own compatriots by Grandfather Delacy, in his capacity as Police Inspector. 'Murder, no less,' he said. He chuckled, 'No doubt about old Gran'pa Delacy when it came to cashing in on anything. He never missed a trick.' He talked of the old man with real admiration. 'He was a real man . . . in every way. I mean, he knew what's what about everything. That's how people took to him . . . blacks and whites, Asiatics. Like old Hanno. He's still serving Gran'pa, although he's been dead all these years. We're all part of Gran'pa to him. He'd lay his life down for us. Even the Mater.' He chuckled again. 'Can be a bit embarrassing . . . because he still regards her as a Delacy . . . so you'll know who he means when he says *Missus Delacy*. Missee Delacy . . . that's Martin's missus. Reckon he'll be calling you Missee Delacy Number Two, eh? Awaaaah!' He guffawed loudly, but shot her a glance that looked a bit scary. He covered it up hastily, by adding: 'Fortunately, mostly he calls the Mater Ma'am-San. He's a wizard cook, too. I got him getting a special supper . . . fish, because it's Sabbath, don't forget . . . Good Sabbath, by the way!' He turned and kissed her swiftly, then let out another guffaw. 'But it isn't fry-fish. It's a fish-stew he makes . . . aw . . . it's . . . well, you got to taste it. You'll have to teach him to fry fish your fashion. I can see you two having some great old fights in the kitchen . . . aaaah!'

All she did was look at him from time to time as they swung through the winding back-tracks. Every time he looked at her he laughed, like a boy, crazy with first love, flung into the presence of his beloved unprepared.

He was too voluble, obviously very excited. To begin with his talk was of his family, the family of today, that is, and with pride, despite the showing of rebellion this morning. She sat silent, mostly watching his face. Often he glanced at her, and always with a sudden happy grin.

They were soon approaching the sea, as evident by the glare of it through the scrub. He told her that at the point where they would come out they would be able to see Rainbow Head, behind which was Rainbow Beach, where they would be going tomorrow. Then suddenly they were out and running across the stretch of clearing above Blue Bay, with the Jail, looking like a mausoleum in its stark whitewashed whiteness, to the North of them. Clancy mentioned what the building was in two short words, as if such an institution meant nothing to him, and as, indeed, doubtless it meant to him at the moment. However, her eyes widened at sight of it, and she stole a couple of glances at it while he talked about the harbour as if he owned it: 'Port Palmeston . . . one of the best harbours in the world . . . but for that awful tide . . . twenty-eight foot rise at spring. It's spring tide now. Look at it running in . . . like a river. There's Rainbow Head.' He drew up, pointed to the glistening mass across the harbour to southwestward. Then he swung northward, pointing to the black line beyond the harbour's mouth. 'The open sea . . . and just across the way there is the East Indies . . . the Isles of Spice . . . nearer to us, in fact, from here, than Beatrice River is. Wouldn't believe it, would you! Good weather, you can nip across there in twenty-four hours in our big launch. Done it several times.' He looked at her intently. 'But I'd like to do it with you . . . go right through all the islands. Would you be game?'

She dropped her eyes from his. Suddenly he seized the hands on her lap, and seeming to crush them in the stress of his feeling, began to babble, 'Listen . . . I'm supposed to be engaged to you . . . to be going to marry you . . . getting a Special Licence tomorrow . . . .' He went on to tell of the scheme to get her out of custody, and how they would stick to it in case of accidents. She heard it all while staring at him great-eyed. He stopped as suddenly as he had started. A moment of breathless silence, while he still clung to her hands and she stared at him. Then he blurted out, 'I've decided to make the Licence dinkum . . . and marry you!'

She blinked at him. He blinked back, wringing her hands in his. After another little silence he said with a rush. 'It'd save all the bother. You don't want to leave the country. You don't want to get mixed up with the Comms again. So there it is. If only they can be kept down the Beatrice looking for you for the next three days . . . and they don't know about it up here. I don't think they do. It's been strictly hush-hush, apparently. Anyway, I'll soon find that out when I got to Fatty Doscas in the morning . . . .'

He seemed to be stopped by her staring. He stared back for a moment, then demanded, 'Well . . . what about it?'

She dropped her eyes, swallowed, looked up, was slow to answer, 'It is . . . it is . . . too impossible . . . .'

He interrupted: 'Why . . . how'd y'mean? As long as they're not looking for you here, old Fatty and old Maryzic'll help us do the trick.'

'I mean I am no goot for wife for you.'

'Why?'

'I cannot haf children.'

'Who wants kids? I want you!'

'Later children you vill vont.'

'I tell you I'm not interested in kids. I don't want to be like my brother Martin, stuck in one place with a family.'

'But you are very strong for your family . . . Your *mutter* vood not like . . . .'

'I'm only interested in you. I love you. I told you last night I love you. I've loved you ever since I saw you. I never loved any girl before . . . .'

'It is talking mad . . . .'

'It is talking love.' He stopped. Then in a strained voice he asked, 'Why . . . don't you love *me*?'

'Lof is . . . lof is . . . .' She was at a loss.

'Don't you even like me?'

'Oh, yes . . . oh, yes.'

'Well, that's it, then! You like me's enough. I love you. I'll make you love me, too. I'll make you so happy . . . I'll . . . I'll . . . oh!' He snatched her in his arms, drew her to him, and devouring her lips, twisted her so that she had to turn and lie across his lap. He withdrew with a gasp, to stare down at her. 'Oh, but I love you . . . I do, I do . . . oh!'

When he released her mouth again, it was to smile down at her. There was fear in her face. He said, 'Don't be afraid. I won't let anyone take you from me.'

She began slowly to withdraw herself. He kissed her lightly, helped her up, said, 'Come on . . . I'd better take you home. Someone'll be coming out. This's a favourite courting spot . . . aheeee. Same down the beach there.' He nodded towards the shimmering stretch of Shelly Beach. Here's my hanky. She was wiping her slobbered mouth. 'You've got a coal-smudge on your nose, too . . . eeeeah! Your beautiful nose!' He kissed it swiftly, and in drawing away, sought the ivory glimpse of ear amongst the tangle of copper, and kissed that, settling back in his seat then with a sigh and wide smile.

He slipped into gear, drove on, singing, 'Home, James . . . and don't spare the horses . . . .'

Down the hill and along behind Shelly Beach, through the coconut grove, where their shadows on the white road looked like the splayed feet of giants – past the Cemetery, where the dead slept decently in their separate divisions according to race and religion – round past the site of the old rubbish-tip, formerly called Long o' Coconut, where upon the buried rubbish, human and otherwise, now stood, all silver in the moonlight, looking like moons themselves, in fact, like moons come to earth to rest, the Shell Oil tanks. Clancy drew attention to the tanks, sounding proud of them, despite the proximity of them to what he called Home – perhaps because of the progress they represented, or interest as a Vaisey Man in what was financially involved, since powers like Shell Oil and Vaiseys seem to interlock, at least as far as mutuality in exploitation of the earth and its inhabitants are concerned. But his pride fell on deaf ears, as he discovered when the swing of the car brought the shining head onto his shoulder, and he saw that its owner was asleep. He smiled, murmuring, 'Tired out, poor pet,' and bent and kissed the copper.

They reached the hill-top, swung in by the wide gateway, up the drive through the grove of leafy East Indian trees planted this long while by the Chinaman old No-Doubt-About-Him Inspector Delacy had chiselled the place away from, to draw up at the massive stone stairway with its guardian Chinese dragons on either side. Out of the shadows of the trellised and creeper-grown verandah a diminutive white-clad figure popped, to come down bowing – Hanno, dressed like an East Indian servant, with white tunic to the throat but compensating for his race with the incongruous addition of black Japanese canvas sneakers with division for the toe. Rifkah, only now roused and only half awake as she was helped out, was introduced as Missee Rifkah-San. She smiled sleepily, while Hanno bowed so low as to reveal the flattish back of his bristly grey skull. He was quite old, judging from his wizened brown nut of a face, but as nimble as a monkey the way he leapt back up the stairs, leading the way for the bridegroom to carry in his Missee-San. They didn't enter the house by the big front door, but went round the verandah, to a bright-lit bedroom into which Hanno bowed them.

It was a pleasant room, furnished in rosewood, with a narrow white bed above which a mosquito-net hung furled. Clancy sat her on the bed, and telling Hanno to go run a bath, dropped to knees and proceeded to remove the grubby sandshoes she'd worn all day. Gently stroking her swollen bandaged feet, he said, 'Bandages stuck, I'm afraid. Better wait to soak 'em off in the bath, eh?' He rose, went to a shiny chair and took from it a neatly-folded little heap of clothes. He placed them on the bed beside her, detaching a dark green satin kimono-like dressing gown, and handing it to her. The other things were pale green silk pyjamas. He said, 'Get out of that grubby dress, eh . . . and put on the kim. I'll come back in a minute and take you to the bathroom. You don't mind having supper in pyjies and kim, do you? I'll get you a complete outfit at Fang Chong's tomorrow morning. Right?' When she smiled up at him, crookedly, sleepily, he bent and kissed her lightly, then saying he'd be seeing her, turned and went out, shutting the door.

She sat for a minute, holding the kimono, staring at the door. Then, with obvious effort, she rose, to stand awkwardly, and pulled the coal-grimed print dress over her head, flinging it over the end of the bed. Her underclothes were scanty lace-edged silk drawers and a short cotton shift. She sat down again, yawned, reached for the kimono where she had placed it in the middle of the bed, found she was sitting on part of it, tugged, overbalanced, to fall backward. She lay there, with legs dangling from the knee over one side of the bed, red hair falling over the other. Her eyes rolled backward, so that she could see her face upside down in the long wardrobe mirror. She stared for a moment. Then her eyes shut. A moment later she was breathing softly in sleep.

When at length there came a tapping at the door she did not hear, or the calling of her name. Clancy opened the door, stood staring at what could be seen from his position. Then he came slowly in. Now what he saw caused his breath to catch – the slight-spread ivory thighs, bare almost to the crotch, the outline of what lay beneath the tight-drawn silk there plain to see, above that the goblet of the navel in the strip of white belly revealed by updrawn shift, a small breast half-revealed, the other almost as evident under a slip of the flimsy kimono, the whole beautiful landscape made astonishingly vital by the slow rhythm of the breathing. Clancy stood with eyes popping, mouth agape as if his own breathing were suspended. A long long moment of complete enthralment. Then he started slightly, breathed deeply, swallowed, licked dry lips, began backing to the door. His breast was heaving and his voice husky as he called from outside, 'Rifkah . . . Rifkah!'

She stirred, muttered – then sat up quickly, exclaiming, 'Oh!'

He smiled weakly from the door. 'What about your bath?'

Now she smiled, and stretched, murmuring, 'Lil sleep.' Rising with the kimono half-concealing her, she turned her back to don it.

As she tied the waist-band he came in. 'Let me carry you?'

She smiled, took up the pyjamas, slipped into his arms. He tried to kiss her mouth, but was given her cheek. Undaunted, he hugged her to him as he went with her round and into a passage and along to the bathroom, murmuring, 'I love you . . . I love you . . . I love you!'

Reluctantly setting her down in the white-tiled bathroom, breathless, he said, 'There's stuff there of Hanno's to put on your feet . . . and slippers. Can I do your feet for you . . . after you've bathed?' She nodded. 'Well sing out when you're ready. Don't go to sleep again . . . in the bath . . . aheeeeaah!'

When she did call he was so close at hand he had to wait a decent interval before coming. He found her seated, in pyjamas and kimono, her feet bare. Scarcely with breath to say it he said, 'Green suits you. I thought it would.'

He talked again about the clothes he would buy her, while he salved and bandaged her feet. Looking at the feet when he had done, squatting on his heels, he chuckled, 'Like a Chinese bride.' He looked up at her. 'Don't suppose you've ever seen a Chinese woman with bound feet? They don't do it any more, of course. But there're still a couple of old girls hobbling round Chinatown here on child-sized feet. Strange customs people have, don't they?' He bent and kissed the feet, then put them into slippers.

He would have carried her again, but for her insisting on walking, clinging to his arm.

They went to the big dining-room, where the end of the great table was nicely set for them, with Hanno waiting to receive them, to place the chair for Missee-San. There was wine. Clancy tried to press her with it. She only sipped. There was the Japanese fish stew, which she said she liked, and proved her words by eating quite a lot. There followed pawpaw and cream.

After the meal they went to the drawing-room and sat before the radio. However, it was not long before she was nodding and blinking and asking to go to bed. He took her eagerly, refusing to let her walk this time, and setting her down on the bed, having helped her off with the kimono, looked as if he would be staying, the way he bent over her, clinging and kissing. She pushed him away, looking frightened, muttering, 'No . . . no . . . pliss, Clancy, dear! I vont to sleep.' He withdrew with a shaky smile, to which she responded, giving him her hand. He kissed the hand, then reached and pulled down the net, blew a kiss to her through it, and wishing her good-night and sweet dreams, departed, putting out the light. She sighed, curled up like a child, in a moment was asleep again.

VI

In a great Malayan Chekka tree in that grove of the Vaisey-Delacy townhouse a Willy-wagtail sang all night of *gulli-gulli* love – while the One responsible for the sweet madness sailed the sky, winking whenever he saw his victims, either as they strove together in thraldom, or if not yet come together in it, yearning, yearning. Igulgul winked at the white-roofed Vaisey-Delacy house, where out on the front steps, between the dragons, Clancy sat in pyjamas, sighing, absently swatting at mosquitoes mad for his fevered blood, staring at the silver smirk that *gulli-gullied* him more and more. Twice he rose, and panting from the stress, went round the verandah with stealthy haste, only to have the seeming burning intention quelled at the door, where he hung with heart hammering so loud it was a wonder it did not rouse the house, let alone have so little effect on the sleeper within that her soft breathing did not falter – such breathing as to him must have meant so much more than rhythmical intake of oxygen, since after listening to it he came away shivering as if its suggestion of the soft ivory fleshcape had caused an earthquake in his own taut flesh.

At last he fell asleep in a deep canvas chair not far from her door, giving himself up to troubled dreaming of the wonder and the worry of it all – while Igulgul slid smirking down the sky, a-winking now at the Old One's watery Shade soft-roaring out to join him down in that hole behind the horizon – and Kirrikijirrit sang and sang and sang – *Kirri, kirri, ki-wirri-jittit* . . . Sweet Pretty Plaything, Love!

He woke in heliotrope dawn, scratching at his myriad bites, rose quickly, went to the screened door. A soft voice called from within, 'Goot morning!'

He rushed in, breathless, to seize her as she sat up to greet him, but just to hold her by soft shoulders and look into the pale blur of her face and breath deeply the bed-warm female fragrance of her. He panted, 'I thought . . . I mean I dreamt . . . you'd run away.'

She put her hands on his arms, perhaps deliberately to hold him at a distance, since there was no such excitement in her voice as his, but rather a dry wariness: 'Vere vood I run avay?'

'I don't know. But you won't . . . will you?'

'You are vishingk?'

'What d'you mean?'

'Dreamingk is vishingk . . . zat is vot Freud say.'

'Blow Freud! What do I want to wish you to run away for . . . when it's been such a job to yard you?'

'Yard me?'

'Excuse the crudeness. But it's a compliment, really. When I was about fourteen I had a chestnut filly. You remind me of her.'

She giggled, 'A horse!'

'She was very beautiful . . . and I loved her as . . . as if she was a girl. But I'm sorry if it sounds crude. I only mean I . . . I love you!'

'Dear Clancy!' she murmured, but held him off when he pressed. 'Vait, vait! I vont to get up. I vood so much like a cup of tea.'

'Right . . . right!' he cried, stabbed a kiss at her, and went rushing out.

When he returned she was out on the verandah in the canvas chair, with kimono over pyjamas. Again he remarked on how well green suited her, and went on to talk about those clothes he would buy her today. She was inclined to protest; but he argued, 'Even if I can't take you to the altar in a veil and all those things, I want you looking like nothing they've ever seen in that old church. Old-man Maryzic's a bit of a lad with the ladies, too . . . or used to be, they say.' But mostly he was circumspect during the talk, the nervous bridegroom now, rather than the excited lover of earlier. He was even more so at breakfast, which they also had out on the verandah, off trays. He advised her to keep close to her room while he was away, in case some friend of his, having heard he was in Town, might call. Hanno would deal with such callers.

When at length he was ready to go to Town, he came and kissed her lightly, and as his last words said, even a little desperately, 'Keep your fingers crossed!'

As expected, Dicky Doscas, Clerk of Courts, was in his office, and alone, since it was Saturday. He greeted Clancy in very friendly fashion, and, rather pointedly, asked after one he called Your Dad. However, he showed frank surprise and even consternation at mention of the Special Licence. 'What's this? Runaway marriage, or something?'

With obvious embarrassment Clancy said he'd met a nice girl and – well, he wanted to get married without fuss.

'With your mother away?' Piggy eyes quizzed him.

When Clancy, swallowing and paling, avoided the eyes, Doscas demanded, 'Is she coloured?'

Clancy looked quickly. 'Oh, no!'

Still the eyes quizzed. 'Do I know her?'

Again Clancy swallowed.

'What's her name?'

Clancy drew a deep breath before answering, 'Rifkah Rosen.'

The huge body sagged in its outsize swivel chair to a wheezy sigh. 'Ah . . . the Refugee-Jew girl.' Clancy blanched again. 'The girl our Fairy Fay's been writing about, eh?'

Clancy uttered a strangled affirmative. Dicky Doscas stared for a little longer at the drooping averted face, then drew a deep breath that blew him up like a toad again, swung in his chair to his vast cluttered desk, reached with a small fat hand into the seeming chaos of pigeon-holes and piled ledgers and official forms and tape-bound papers: 'Well . . . I hope you're doing the right thing, son.' He got what he wanted with ease that was astonishing in the circumstances: a book of forms, a ledger, a receipt-book. 'Three days before you can get married . . . cost you a fiver. Sign, eh?'

As Clancy signed, betraying his agitation with his clumsiness, Doscas remarked, 'Very pretty girl, I hear.'

Clancy breathed, 'Yes.'

'Ah, well . . . so long's it doesn't land you in trouble.'

Clancy met the piggy eyes swiftly, fearfully. Dicky Doscas smirked. 'I mean with your mother. Your Dad agreeable?'

Clancy gasped, 'Oh, yes!'

Doscas chuckled fatly; 'Well, he'd know a good filly when he saw one. Where's she now? I didn't hear about her coming on the train.'

Clancy said quickly, 'Still down the Beatrice.'

'You'll be getting married down there, eh? Who'll be doing the job. Let's see . . . you've got two JP's down there . . . Constable Stunke and Finnucane . . . no, three . . . there's your brother Martin, now . . . but you'll hardly be having him eh? . . . awaaaaah!'

Clancy blinked. 'Old Shame-on-us, I guess.'

'Then you'll be having quite a party. Don't forget to bring her to see me sometime.' The fat hand was extended. 'Well, son . . . all the best. From what Fay says, anyway, you're getting something pretty good. Our own girls aren't up to much when it comes to living in the bush. Strange that a Jewess should take to it like Fay says she had.'

Clancy said, eager now, 'Don't forget the Jews started as graziers . . . you know, old Abraham and Jacob and the rest in the Bible, with their flocks and herds. A lot of Eastern European Jews are farmers, too . . . and look what they've done to the deserts of Palestine.'

'Yes, you're right there.'

Clancy went on in the same tone, while the piggy eyes quizzed him: 'There were some experts down our way looking over things for that Settlement Scheme . . . all agricultural scientists . . . could buy and sell us for knowledge of stock and land.'

'Hmmm! Maybe this settlement business'll be a godsend to the country.' The moon-face rippled with a grin. 'Anyway . . . you'll be right, marrying into the family like . . . eeeeeesh!'

Clancy turned in departing, to say softly, 'If you don't mind keeping it dark . . . I don't want the mob . . . well, you know what they're like . . . '

'Mum's the word, son . . . mum's the word!'

Round at the Catholic Church, Clancy was directed by the black gardener to Monsignor Maryzic's quarters in the old Mission bungalow. As he went through the well-kept garden he had a glimpse of the sea beyond the cliff. The Mission schooner *St Francis Xavier* lay straining at anchor in the falling tide. Away in the western distance could be seen the backbone of Old Tchamala, seeming to be heaving as the rushing waters danced in mirage. Walking one verandah of the bungalow, clad in white cassock today and with breviary in hand, was Father Glascock, in from his mission station. Clancy raised a hand in slight greeting, which was answered with a movement of the breviary.

Clancy found the Monsignor in his study, reclining reading in a deep canvas lounge chair, with black cassock unbottoned so as to expose bulbous hairy chest and rotund belly to the blast from a small fan humming on his littered desk. The old man looked up at the presence in his doorway. Clancy was standing slightly stooped, with hands hanging down clasped before him, in a proper reverential stance, which did anything but impress the arch-priest, the way he pulled his glasses down his Slavic nose and stared with evident suspicion. Clancy cleared his throat: 'Good morning, Monsignor.'

The old priest gave a slight heave of his massive body, but without changing position. 'Goot morning, young man . . . and vot vood you be vonting?'

Clancy reached with the pious hands to clutch at the door-frame, swallowed. 'My name's Delacy.'

'Zat I can see from your face. You haf come for me to baptize you?'

Clancy looked surprised. 'Oh, no . . . you baptized me when I was a baby.'

'So! Zen it is zat you are ashamed of your Christian name you cannot tell me?'

When Clancy blinked, confused, the old man grunted, 'But come in. Take seat.' Then as Clancy seated himself circumspectly beside the desk, he went on: 'Many people are ashamed of Christian name. Zey should not be. Ze fault is not of zem, but of parents and godparents. But in our Faith, of course, ve haf ze remedy . . . ze Confirmation Name of our own choosing, ze name of our Patron Saint. Who is your Patron?'

Clancy muttered, 'Thomas Aquinas.'

'Ah! And you have followed in ze steps of Ze Angelic Doctor . . . you are teacher and scholar?'

Quite at a loss, Clancy mumbled, 'No, Sir.'

'And mit vot name I baptized you?'

'Clancy.'

The old man heaved a little. 'Ah . . . so zat is your shame! Tell me . . . who wos zis Clancy I find so many people of zis county vont to name zere children for?' A purely rhetorical question, since he who asked it went on immediately: 'He is no prophet of ze Bible, no saint of ze Calendar. All I can find, mit mooch investigation, is a legendary character of ze bush, vun, Clancy of ze Overflow. Vy moost people inflict zere innocent little vuns so? And vorse and vorse it gets, zis misnoming. Now it is ze moving picture vich is ze inspiration. Last veek I am ask to baptize a baby girl as Greta. I ask ze parents and godparents, who is ze Bible heroine of zat name, who is ze female saint? Vot do zey answer? She is name from Greta Garbo.' All this while the slaty blue eyes, stared and stared out from under craggy Slavic brows, so that Clancy must lower his own. At last: 'Vell, Clancy, my son . . . your business?'

Clancy fumbled for his Licence, mumbling, 'I want to get married, Monsignor.'

'A very natural vont in a young man. But vot is zis . . . a Special Licence. Marry in haste, zey do say, and repent at leisure. *Rifkah Rosen*. A Jewish name, I zink. Zis vood be ze young lady Fay McFee has made famous mit her pen?'

Clancy muttered, 'Yes, Father . . . Monsignor.'

'It is not alvays goot to be made famous by our talented Miss McFee.' Clancy dropped his eyes again from the craggy stare. The old man asked, somewhat sharply now, 'Vy haf you come to me to marry zis voman?'

Clancy swallowed. 'You married my brother Martin . . . and my father, too.'

'Zey marry Catholic girl.'

'But Catholics can marry non-Catholics behind the altar, can't they?'

'It can be done, under certain conditions . . . but zese presume zat ze non-Catholic haf Christian belief.' A tense little silence. Then: 'I tek it zis voman is of Jewish Faith?'

Clancy nodded, breathing, 'Yes.'

Now the old man's fleshy ruddy face darkened, and his voice rumbled: 'Zen how dare you, a Christian, ask a Christian priest to gif blessing of ze Church on union mit vun who rejects our Blessed Saviour?' He dropped his slippered feet from the leg-extensions of the chair, thumping the floor hard, to sit up, glaring.

Clancy went red, dropped his eyes, fumbled with hands before him again. Silence till he got the courage to look up to meet the glare again.

'Vell?' demanded the priest.

Clancy swallowed. 'Then . . . then it's impossible?'

'It is not impossible . . . it is simply unthinkable!' The old man handed back the Licence.

Clancy, drawing a deep breath, turned away. He was at the door, when the archpriest called to him, 'Vait!'

He turned. The old man asked, 'You haf some special reason for coming to me, is it?'

Clancy blinked, nodded.

'Vot is it?' When Clancy swallowed and looked down, the priest added: 'You are running avay from somezing?' Clancy was silent, drooping, utterly miserable. 'You are stealing zis girl avay from her people?'

Clancy muttered, 'She has no people.'

'She has a whole race of people.' After another little silence, the Monsignor said, 'Do you know zat Jews are more hard on intermarriage even zan ve . . . zat zere is no behind-ze-altar compromise . . . nuzzing but complete ostracization?'

'I . . . I don't know much about it, Father.'

'Do you know mooch about ze girl?'

Clancy roused. 'Oh, yes! I've known her ever since she arrived in the country . . . more than six months ago . . . and have seen a lot of her. She loves this country . . . and wants to stay here. She's not interested in the Jewish Settlement.'

The old man stared and stared. 'Is it trouble about citizenship you vont to overcome mit marriage?'

Clancy blinked. 'Yes, Father . . . partly . . . .'

'She is marrying you for citizenship?'

'Oh, no . . . we love each other!' Clancy was looking expectant at the broad face with its long snout.

A moment. Then the old man held out an age-freckled hand, evidently to have the Licence back. Clancy came hurrying to give it. Taking the paper, the old man said, 'I vill marry you . . . if ze voman agree to be baptized.'

Clancy looked surprised, murmured, 'Baptized?'

'If she is of Jewish Faith she is not baptized. Don't you know zat?'

Clancy shook his head.

The deep voice rumpled again: 'You call yourself Christian . . . yet do not know zat ze first Article of our Faith is Baptism into ze Church!' When Clancy dropped his eyes again, the voice went on, as menacing: 'You vill yourself fulfill your duties as a Catholic in preparation for ze Sacrament of

Marriage . . . Confession, Communion . . . and vill svear on your immortal soul to bring up your children in ze Faith.'

Clancy looked up again quickly. 'Yes, Father . . . Monsignor.'

'Very vell. You cannot marry before t'ree day. Ven is it you vont?'

'Could we make it Monday, Monsignor?'

'Provided ze voman is properly prepared. She is here?'

'Not with me here . . . but in Town.'

'Bring her to me zis afternoon.'

Clancy was beaming now. Then his face clouded slightly. 'Couldn't we make it tonight?'

The eyes were boring. The answer came curtly, 'No, ve couldn't. Zis afternoon at t'ree.'

The cloud vanished. Clancy cried, 'Thank you, Monsignor . . . thank you!' He rushed out. He kept on rushing, so that Father Glascock and the black gardener stared after him.

He leapt into his car, went roaring round to Chinatown, to stop with a scattering of gravel at Fang Chong's high-class drapery. Such was his excitement as he bought the things listed, as well as other bright bits that caught his eye, that the fat young Chinaman serving him remarked slyly, 'Velly nice plesent . . . must for velly nice lady, I stink, Mist' Clancy, hey?'

Clancy guffawed, 'You're stinkin' right, Gong . . . awaaaaah!'

He rushed out with his large parcel, almost into the arms of Fergus Ferris, who was coming into the store with an armful of packages with Southern labels. Evidently Fergus had just arrived back from the South. He glared at Clancy, but only got an amiable grin. He turned to see Clancy start up, and got another grin and a wink with it.

As Clancy drove through the middle of the town, approaching the squatters' hotel, the Queen Victoria, he slowed as if to stop, but then accelerated and went on, soon fairly racing. Thus back home, to stop at the front steps with another scattering of gravel.

The sound of his steps coming round the verandah must have told Rifkah of his elation well before his bursting in upon her with it, to toss the parcel on the bed and grab her, crying, 'Worked like a charm . . . married Monday . . . oheeeeah!' He silenced himself by planting his lips on hers. At length withdrawing, breathless he laughed joyously in her staring face, unwitting of the lack of reciprocity. 'So everything's set . . . and you're as good as Missee Clancy Delacy . . . wow!' Again he kissed her. Then he turned his attention to the parcel, snapped the string and ripped the paper, causing the bright things to burst out onto the white counterpane like a gaudy opening flower. When he looked at her with shining eyes, this time she smiled – to have him seize her again, panting, 'When you smile I could . . . eat you, eat you!' He proceeded to do almost that. Then again to the things, to separate them, babbling of his certainty that they would suit her, his hope that they would please her.

One of the articles was a beautiful Chinese tea-gown in black and red satin. He snatched the kimono off her to replace it with the lovely thing, kissing her swiftly in the process, then swinging her to the wardrobe mirror. When she smiled at his smiling image behind, he seized her from that direction, kissing the back of her neck, and would have taken liberties with her bosom, but for her taking possession of his hands. He showed no resentment at the check in his ardour, only swung away to fish from the bright heap on the bed what he called a Play-suit, trousers and jumper in apple-green, with silver sandals to go with it. 'Wear this this arvo to go round to see old Maryzic,' he babbled. 'He's got an eye for the ladies. You'll rock him! We'll go by launch. Not likely to run into anyone that way. Anyway, there's football at three, and a wedding. Nobody'll be on the water. After we've seen the old bloke, we'll take a run over to Rainbow Beach . . . and come back in the moonlight on the high tide. Like that? I'll get Hanno to pack us a picnic tea. I was going to get a couple of bottles of bubbly to celebrate . . . I thought I'd better keep clear of the mob, who'd sure to be in the pub.'

She smiled again. He was proceeding to deal with her again in response to that cannibalistic urge he'd confessed to – when loud sounds outside arrested the attention of both. A motor vehicle was coming up the drive. Loud male voices could be heard as it swept past the house. They stood listening. The car stopped at the steps. The skurr of feet on the gravel, scraping on the steps. Raucous voices bawling, 'Clancy . . . Clancy o' the Overflow . . . Where're you, ol' bastard, Clance . . . Wha' yo' up to?'

Clancy groaned, 'The mob! It's all right. I'll get rid of 'em. Just stay put.' He kissed her quickly, went out, shutting the wooden door. She stepped after him and locked it.

Getting rid of the so-called mob proved no easy business. Evidently they were drunk. Their vociferating could be heard in the bedroom: 'Great party last night . . . where'd you get to, Clance? You got a girl here, eh? Who's she? What's she? Creamy piece, eh? Gi's look at her! Gi's a drink! We ain't goin' till we 'ad a drink . . . . '

There was tramping through the house. By the sound of it they'd settled down in the breakfast-room, if settling down could be called that stomping about, scrape of furniture, whooping, harsh laughter, and incessant babble. Rifkah sat on the bed facing the direction of it, arms folded across her bosom and hands clutching nervously at her shoulders, the attitude of a woman fearful of molestation, of brutal manhandling only too well known, the fear plain in her wide eyes. How often had she heard such raucous hilarity as preliminary to the bestiality that only man of all the beasts is capable of?

It lasted more than an hour. Then it ended in clumping back through the house to the front steps, a boozy farewelling, crash of car doors, roar of motor and swish of whirling wheels. Clancy's footsteps sounded wary as they came back round the verandah. She opened up when he knocked and called.

He flung himself on the bed, smelling of booze but evidently not what could be called Boozed. 'Lord!' he sighed. 'Thought I'd never get rid of 'em. Come and sit by me. What . . . did you get a fright, eh?' She sat primly on the edge of the bed. He took her hand and tried to pull her down to him. She resisted. He did not seem to mind, just kept clinging to the hand, and talking: 'They guessed I had someone here. That bunny-faced Ferris told 'em. He saw me come out of Fang Chong's . . . and must've asked the Pong who served me what I'd bought . . . and then round to the pub and told 'em I was buying clothes for a gin. I didn't think Pongs had such big mouths. I'll have to have a word with old Fang about that son-in-law of his. I let 'em think it. It'll keep 'em away.' He sat up. 'Now . . . how about trying the things on. Here's some nice Chinese-silk undies . . . like 'em?'

He looked as if he intended to stay to watch the trying-on. However, when she made no move, he took the hint, gave her a kiss, and said, 'Okay . . . leave you to it. Put the play suit on, eh? We'll be going straight after lunch. Getting a bit late.'

So nicely did the play-suit fit and suit her, together with the silver sandals and a large multi-coloured straw sun-hat Clancy found for her, that she herself was cheered up, and suffered Clancy to show her off to the only one possible at the moment – Hanno, whose little oily eyes popped for a moment, after which he bowed deeply, saying, 'Ver' bootchifoo raidy.'

Hanno had prepared them a roast-chicken lunch, and had packed chicken and salad and other things for their picnic tea. Soon after lunch they set out in the car, going by way of the Old Compound site, where now the New Hospital was building, and round to skirt the Old Hospital, to come out at the edge of the cliff above a deep little bay where the big Delacy launch lay at moorings. A stairway led down to a small pontoon jetty to which a dinghy was moored. Rifkah made the descent easily enough, with Clancy's arm about her. She limped only a little, quite comfortable, as she said, in the rubber-soled sandals. On the jetty, as he was hauling in the dinghy, he stood off and looked at her, exclaiming, 'I'd like the whole town to see you like that. Jees what a shock they're going to get after Monday . . . *on* Monday . . . 'cause I'm going to take you straight into town and let 'em see. You'll knock 'em cock-eyed!'

She had to stop him from kissing her. The Hospital was just across the bay there, pretty well hidden by trees, but with a fair view of what lay below. He got his kiss secretly as he lifted her into the dinghy. Then with eyes shining at sight of her as she sat in the stern, with great strokes he rowed them to the launch.

Aboard the launch a marked change came over Rifkah. The haggardness of days past lifted almost instantly. Her eyes shown like jewels again. Her face, revealed fully when she removed the floppy sun-hat, glowed. It certainly wasn't the luxury she found aboard that affected her, because she merely glanced at what Clancy proudly showed her of the vessel's appointments. Clearly it was the wide vista – of jade sea, emerald shores, far-off sapphire hills – that kept catching the shining eyes and holding them. But it was something more that made eyes shine, something expressed in her exclamation, 'It is so . . . so vide and free!'

Still, one even so freedom-craving, surely would have lost the joy of even the illusion of it had she understood what Clancy told her when she asked what a certain place was shimmering away whitely in the green of the mangroves southward. It was the Leper Lazaret, the only sign of civilization in that direction. If she had understood the words and known the fact that this single spot in what looked so wide and free was the filthiest and most hopeless of all prisons imaginable! She showed she didn't understand by giving a questioning glance to his answer. But even if he had interpreted the glance and been any more interested in the place than all the rest of the like of him who took it for granted, he would hardly want to talk about a thing so utterly unlovely in the sight of such loveliness as hers. As he steered the vessel the little distance they had to go, just round the next headland to the bay below the Catholic church, he scarcely took his eyes off her, while she stood gazing, gazing – dreaming?

They passed the *St Francis Xavier* swinging abandoned at the buoy. When Clancy told her the ship belonged to the Leopold Islands Mission, Rifkah's eyes shone again – just for a moment, as if happy old memories were stirred – then took on that haggard look again, as if she were yearning for that old happiness again in face of the fading of the illusion of freedom with the looming of the cliff before them. As if to remind her of the menaces surrounding her reality there came a great roar of human voices from somewhere back of the cliff-top. She started, stared in the direction of it. Clancy chuckled. 'Only the mob at the footie. It's a good way from where we're going. We go straight up those steps there.'

At the foot of the stairway was a pontoon-jetty similar to that they'd come from, and sufficient water under it, according to Clancy's reckoning of the tide, for them to tie up there during their stay ashore.

They climbed the stairs, stood for a moment under a shady tamarind to reconnoitre. Across in the street from the mission-house, outside the church, was a line of cars and crowd of people, only to be glimpsed from here because of intervening shrubbery. 'Wedding,' said Clancy with a grin. 'Ought've been ours, eh?' He took her hand as they headed towards the bungalow. There was no chance of their being seen from the church, with garden and other buildings obtruding as they went.

However, they did not make the little journey completely unobserved. They had just reached the back verandah at the western end, when round the other corner came Father Glascock, still breviary-walking. Again he raised his book in answer to Clancy's wave, but stared so intently that at the distance of fifty feet or more the blue of his eyes could be seen beneath the bushy black brows, doubtless arrested by the sudden splash of colour, verdigris and burnished copper. Coming out of the sunlight and the risk of being seen again, Rifkah had removed the cumbersome hat. An ivory hand came up to give the inevitable feminine touch to hair as she met the blue eyes. The meeting was only momentary. She and Clancy went straight on up the side verandah towards the Monsignor's quarters. 'That was the Missionary from the Leopolds,' Clancy explained. 'Well . . . here we are.'

Monsignor Maryzic was in his study, now seated at his desk. He looked up over his glasses. 'Ah, der bridal couple. Come in.'

They entered shyly, to take chairs he indicated. He stared hard at Rifkah, who lowered her own gaze. With a sort of wriggle of his massive body, he said, 'You are ver' 'andsome, my daughter.'

She looked up quickly, evidently startled by the term of address. He went on: 'I haf read of you in der papers. You haf been cruelly treated. Your people haf been cruelly treated. Der *Deutscher* still largely is der barbarian of der forest . . . like der Russki.' He paused. 'But sufferingk for der Jew is nuddink new, is it? To suffer sufferingk is der strength of Israel, is it not? Der *Judenhassen* is silly. Der best vay to deal mitt Juden is mitt pity.'

Her eyes widened. Slaty and hazel eyes held each other for a long moment. As she lowered hers again, he asked, 'You are of Jewish faith?'

She murmured, 'Yes.'

'Jewish tradition mitt regard to marriage ver' strict is, yes?'

'Yes.'

His tone became sharp suddenly: 'Den vy you vont to marry dis young man who is Christian?'

The hazel eyes blinked back at his stare. The harsh wheezy old voice went on: 'You vill cease to be Jewish. Your people vill scorn you.' When she remained silent, he demanded, 'Vy do you not spik?'

Clancy put in: 'She isn't really religious, Monsignor . . . . '

Maryzic silenced him without looking at him: 'Let der girl spik for herself.'

Rifkah swallowed. 'I am not of strict religion.'

'Den prepared you are to become Christian?'

She started, blinked.

He went on: 'You understand dat baptized moost you be before I can marry you?'

When she looked uncomprehending, the old man looked at Clancy. 'You haf told her der condition I marry you?'

Clancy reddened. 'Well . . . as a matter of fact, Monsignor . . . '

The slaty eyes swung back to Rifkah. 'I haf told dis young man dat you must be baptized. Evidently he haf not told you.'

She glanced at Clancy, murmuring, 'Baptized?'

The priest cut in shortly: '*Tauchen.*'

She stiffened, paled.

'You vill submit to *tauchen*. I haf make arrangement mitt nuns for your instruction.' Now there was terror in her face. He demanded, 'Vot is der matter?'

She swallowed, licked her lips. She muttered, 'I cannot do.'

The fleshy old face darkened. 'Vy cannot?'

She swallowed again, said miserably, 'I am Jewish.'

The old face purpled. A large hand slapped the desk. The voice came rumbling: 'Jewish? Dat you say like it is someding you cannot 'elp . . . like apology you mek for your difference . . . vile alvays it is arrogance. Your cursèd unbelief you fling in Christian face like mud!'

Her eyes rolled as she turned to Clancy. He, red with embarrassment, asked throatily, 'What's the matter?'

Maryzic gave the answer with a roar: 'Der matter is der voman refuses to be baptized!'

Clancy dodged the eyes, now glaring at him redly, looked at Rifkah, asking, 'Why not?'

She breathed, 'Zat I cannot.'

'But . . . there's nothing to it . . . just put holy water on you . . . . '

The hand banged the table again. The roar rose: 'Noddingk to it? You . . . you pretender to der Grace of der Lord Jesus Christ! Shut your silly mout', boy! I vill do der talkingk.' The slate smote Rifkah again. 'You vill not baptized be?'

She drooped her shining head, shook it.

The priest shot to his feet, flinging up a hand to point to the door, bellowing, 'Den go, Jew voman . . go from dis Christian house!'

She rose at once, turned to the door. Clancy leapt up, grabbed her arm, held her while he turned back to the priest, panting. 'There must be some mistake, Father . . . . '

The old man rumbled, 'Der mistake is yours, my son. Tek dis voman avay. I vill not again see her . . . unless she haf been baptized in der Christian Faith. Here your Special Licence is. Take it. It is not licence to insult der Holy Name of der Lord Jesus!'

Rifkah was drawing away. Clancy looked back gaping at the priest to the last.

With haggard eyes on the blaze of sea and sky, Rifkah limped back along the side verandah. The clinging Clancy muttered, 'The old bigot! I didn't think he'd be like that.'

They reached the back verandah to find Father Glascock just around the corner, looking at them with even sharper interest than before, surely having heard something of the roaring that must have reverberated through this old sounding-board of a building. Rifkah did not seem to see him, but stepped as it were blindly off the verandah, to go heading back to the cliff, and was deaf to the burst of cheering and clapping from the vicinity of the church. Clancy looked across to the street, to see the confetti flying. Turning back to her, still clinging to her arm, he said, 'I forgot about what he said about your getting baptized. I didn't think it mattered really. ' His voice trailed off, since it was evident that she was not listening.

Nevertheless, when they reached the stairway and she would have gone hobbling down without his assistance, staying her, to get a grip on her arm, he asked, 'Can't we do something about it, darling? It's nothing, really. It's usually done to babies. They just make the Sign of the Cross over your brow and mumble something, and . . . well, you're in, like. Couldn't you put up with that?'

She looked across the sea, towards the lazaret, with old *bubbeh's* eyes that now seemed to know what it was, what it meant, in a world where compassion must for ever be cancelled out by the urge to dominate. She answered shortly, 'No.'

As he helped her down the stairs he went on: 'It's such a simple way out. Otherwise you'll have to go to the Comms.'

She said, 'I vont to go to ze bush.'

'But where?'

'Anywhere . . . vit' blacks . . . who vill hide me . . . . '

'Not them! They'd betray you for a stick of tobacco.'

'I do not believe it. All haf been goot friendt to me. Pliss vill you tek me in ze launch somevere zere are blacks?'

'That's mad, darling . . . you can't live with blacks!'

'I cannot live free vit' vites . . . . '

'Now, be reasonable . . . . '

'Pliss, Clancy . . . pliss!'

They reached the launch. Sighing he helped her aboard, started his engines, cast off, swung out to sea. But he kept looking behind, and before they were were out of the bay, while she was staring at *St Francis Xavier*, said, 'Sure you won't change your mind?' When she shook her head, as if himself taking inspiration from the tall-masted ship, he added: 'That Father Glascock, the missionary . . . that's his boat. He might be able to help. He's a nice chap . . . not a bit like a priest. What say we go back and have a word with him?'

Now her eyes were back on the lazaret. 'No.'

He sighed again. 'Okay. Well, we'll go over to Rainbow Beach, just the same. We can think about it there.'

They were silent until they had turned the headland and were heading into the jade and silver blaze of the west. Then he remarked, 'I thought you were only particular about Jewish food. Why can't you get baptized?'

'Zat mek me Christian.'

'Does that matter so much?'

'I am Jew.'

He sighed. 'I still don't get it.'

She said, 'For Jew, ze *tauchen* . . . that is German word . . . is ze vorst zingk.'

'But you were telling me at the Lagoons about ritual baths and things that Jews have. Isn't it much the same thing?'

'Ze Jews haf suffered mooch from *tauchen*.'

'How do you mean?'

'It is vay Christians haf to hurt Jews. In ze *pogroms* . . . ze persecution . . . zey vill catch Jews and *tauchen* zem . . . sometimes vit' *pissen*, urine. My *Zaydeh* tell me of ven he is little boy, some Jewish children are drowned in *tauchen* business. I have been *tauchen* vit' stinkingk urine in Nazi camp . . . .'

'The bastards, eh! I see what you mean. But . . . well, old Maryzic wouldn't do an awful thing like that. It's only that it means a lot to him . . . .'

'To me it means a lot to be Jew.'

'But I thought . . . .'

'For Jew to give up beingk Jew is like blackfellow give up Dreamingk for viteman vay . . . it only mek him what blackfellow call Bloody Nutching. You understand?'

He didn't. That was evident in his turning quickly away. Another little silence while they cut the jade tide with purring engines. Then he said, staring ahead, 'There's still a chance with Fatty Doscas. I'll get in touch with him early Monday morning . . . ring his house. I'll be able to tell if he's heard anything from the police about you. If he hasn't, I'll arrange for him to marry us as soon as he opens his office.'

She didn't answer. Her eyes were on the turmoil, exaggerated in mirage, of the tidal waters on the Rainbow Reef.

He overcame the silence, for himself at least, by pointing out the features of the harbour and talking again of its potentialities as a great seaport but for the perversity of its tides. He showed her where lay the best points for fishing, crabbing, prawning. He told how his family had scored a point on the tides by having a passage blasted in the reef so that they might have access to their beach resort at all times – only, as he laughingly confessed, to create a shifting sandbank problem at their front door. 'Almost makes you believe in that old Rainbow Snake, doesn't it?' She appeared to be listening to him, while dreaming over the distant places. When eventually they made the passage, passing through walls festooned with dripping seaweeds, she was plainly fascinated by the myriad sea-creatures scuttling from their noisy intrusion, among them a red octopus, that having with amazing facility packed itself into a crevice a fraction of its extended size of a square yard or so, regarded them balefully with golden eyes. Clancy shouted above the clangour of their passing, 'Greeks eat 'em. Greeks'll eat anything.'

The western shore was now revealed, but still as something of a realm of fantasy by reason of mirage, the bush behind and the Delacy buildings appearing to be perched on white cliffs cut with purple bays beaten by sweeping silver seas. In fact the seeming cliffs were Those Blasted Sandbanks, as Clancy called them. 'You never know where they are. They shift about with the tide. What's needed's an extension of that wall of rock there . . . see, to the South of the houses . . . to make a groyne. Trouble is to get labour these days. Blacks won't work since they've been feeding 'em so well in the Sweet Creek Settlement . . . and the Greeks and the rest're all on the defence works, the oil-tanks and the road. There's some Greeks there . . . see 'em away there on that big bank?' He pointed to elongated stick-like figures. 'Fishing. They can't live without fishing. Lot of 'em been imported lately by local Greek contractors. They come over here weekends to fish and booze and . . . .' he chuckled ' . . . chase the gins.' He added: 'Better take a look at 'em, I think. The old halfcaste women we got there as caretakers can deal with 'em usually. Still, it's best to show 'em the Boss's around. Greeks can get cheeky.' He swung the launch southward.

Soon two small launches were to be seen lying in a channel between sandbanks. The so-called Greeks, who were really Aegean Islanders, had a net across the channel. There must have been a score of them. Assisting them were some naked blacks. More blacks, mostly women and children, were well back on the besch, sitting in the shade of the first line of scrub, the casuarinas. All watched the approaching vessel, evidently much more interested than afraid. Clancy quickly guessed the reason. 'They've spotted your hair. They're fascinated by red-haired women . . . blacks, I mean . . . you know, the old Koonapippi business, and all that . . . and I suppose the Oxes are, too, being dark people.'

Clancy was the happy boy again, evidently having forgotten what had happened to his romance so recently. Swinging the launch so as to give the watchers a full view, he grabbed her, put an arm about her. The blacks, at least, fairly hopped with excitement. He let go the wheel to wave. Everybody waved back vigorously. He looked at her smiling. She smiled back. He kissed her. They missed the effect of that. Nor did it interest them, he glowing, she looking as if surprised and perturbed by his sudden renewal of ardour. He guffawed, 'That's what I like to see . . . that smile!'

He swung the launch back northward. He said, 'That mob'll be along to take a closer look at you, don't worry. But wait'll they hear you're a new Mitchitch Delacy!' He met her eyes. 'Because you're going to be that after all, aren't you!'

Her eyes rolled slightly. Still, she smiled. He kissed her again.

They entered a wide channel, to see two female figures coming towards them down the steep beach, accompanied by a brace of dogs. 'The old girls,' said Clancy. 'Don't bother to take anything ashore. They'll bring everything . . . except you . . . that's my job.' He chuckled gleefully.

They ran in for about a hundred yards before the launch grounded. 'That's it,' said Clancy. He took a boat-hook to depth the sand-murky rushing water, then removed shoes, tucked up trousers, and slipped over the side. He extended his arms to her. Without hesitation she slipped into them.

As they approached the women, now splashing towards them in the shallows fed by streamlets bubbling from the sand, Clancy murmured, 'Let me kiss you. It'll give 'em a great thrill.' He did it without waiting for agreement. The dark wizzened faces split into grins. Leathery claws came up to hide eyes in pretence of not seeing. Beaming, Clancy said, 'Goodday Loochee, Mylee. Look what I been bring him you . . . new Mitchitch!'

The pair squealed with delight behind their hands. When they peeped, Rifkah smiled at them, saying, 'Hello!'

Guffawing his delight now, Clancy continued on his way with his bright burden. 'You simply got to marry me now!'

Once again her mood changed utterly, in coming to land now as when formerly she had left it. Her eyes shone with delight at what she saw about her, no less than his at sight of her. As they came out of the water, she slipped from his arms, to bend and touch the satin-shiny micaceous sand, patterned as it was with tide-ripples and the tracery of tiny claws. She pounced on the little denizens of the region, laughing when they so skilfully dodged her. He caught her a largish hermit crab and showed her how to whistle it out of hiding. She would have stayed there on the water-line, marvelling at the life, but for his pulling her towards the house. Then she found more childish delight in the form of a scattering of bright seeds under a large abrus tree. He could stop her from gathering them in large quantity only by telling her that she would disappoint the old servants, who would want to give her one of the many necklaces they'd strung with them. She was then diverted by the variety of tropical fruits, mostly fruiting: tamarinds, jacks, monstereas, and a rose garden, and bougainvilleas of many hues. 'Vot a loffly place!' she sighed when at last he dragged her away from it all and made her lie in a hammock under the trees before the house, while he swung her.

'Lovely place for a honeymoon, eh?' he said. 'D'you know, there've been lots of honeymoons here. We've often lent it to couples. And yet, there's never been a Delacy honeymoon. Would you believe that?' He smiled eagerly. 'What about we're the first, eh?'

When she smiled at him he bent and kissed her, then snatched her up, and ran with her to the house, across the front verandah, into the big sitting-room into which the front door directly led. She was alarmed, struggled, protested, while he only laughed. When he set her down and saw the alarm in her face, he asked, 'Don't you know the old custom of carrying the bride across the threshold?'

She shook her head.

'Don't Jewish bridegrooms do that?'

Perhaps because he looked downcast now, she smiled again, saying, 'I zink moost it be cave-man custom, yes?'

He glowed again, grabbed her, kissed her, let her go, panting, 'Oh, I do love you!'

Another delight she found was an ancient phonograph with cylindrical records of songs popular about the time of the instrument's manufacture. She played *White Wings, Thora*. Clancy chuckled, 'Gran'pa Delacy's idea of music.'

She said it was very sweet, and had him take it out onto the verandah. There was a large box of records: *Nelly Bligh, Killarney, The Exile of Erin, Will You Stop Your Ticklin' Jock*. He played them to her while she lay on a cane lounge, looking out across the now flooding harbour at the town extravagantly high-perched on its cliffs because of the light effect. Windows there were already blazing in the level light of the Sun.

The musical session was interrupted by Clancy's crying out, 'What'd I tell you!' He pointed to that rocky wall of quartz which shut the Delacy place off from the stretch of beach to southward. At the top end the quarters of the servants stood under trees. The blacks were crowded there, peeping across. Seeing the Boss laugh, the bolder ones came out to stare frankly. Clancy said, 'I'll call 'em over, so they can have a good look at you and put it on the bush-telegraph. But I'd better get some tobacco. They never fail to put the nips in, given the chance.' He signalled to the blacks to come, then ducked inside, to return in a moment with a box of trade tobacco.

The crowd hung well back from the verandah, except for two old fellows wearing loin-clouts of flour-sack most likely put on for the occasion, who came with what they described as Prejent for Mitchitch. The present consisted of a pair of huge mangrove crabs, alive, with murderous claws bound, carried in a bag of paperbark.

Clancy asked them, 'How you like him my Mitchitch?'

They answered together, 'Properly!' The sentiment was echoed by a murmur from the others, staring hard. There was an audible indrawn gasp as Rifkah smiled at them.

Then Clancy handed out the tobacco and told the admirers to clear out, which they promptly did, well knowing their place in the scheme of things. As they went, Clancy remarked, 'Those two old yeller pieces didn't waste any time marrying us, did they?' He guffawed, and called the women over, not to chide them, but also to give them tobacco and the crabs to cook for the picnic tea. Rifkah confessed that she had never yet tasted crab, that she guessed it wasn't *kosher*, but that didn't matter, because she wished to try.

While they waited for the crabs and the setting of the fixed table out under the trees the Sun went down, causing the town windows to blaze with gold.

They had tea in twilight that became moonlight as Igulgul, hanging in turquoise above the town, took over. For a few minutes the town looked enchanted, like one of fairy castles. If only Igulgul could do that occasionally to the inhabitants, they might have got used to living less meanly, since, as it is said, use is second nature. As it was, it being Saturday evening, at least half the town would be getting drunk and the rest preparing to take the consequences. So it was over here, too, where sounds coming from down the beach told of the beginnings of those revels for which Clancy had said the Greeks came over of week-ends. Although he had laughed over it then, now he growled, 'Sounds a bit close. Have to have a word with the police about it. If they start making a habit of that sort of thing, it could spoil our own parties over here.'

With the tide at the full by now, the launch looked a long way off, lying out in the blaze, like something detached from time. The dinghy, moored to an oar stuck in the sand, was actually hugging the shore-line of the moment, broached to the little lap of the tide, gently moving, as if breathing against a gleaming white mothering breast. Here and there a big fish leapt as a momentary fiery flash, plopped back to its fight or its fate. Quiet plop-plopping everywhere in the stillness. Scented smoke from smudge-cans of cypress sawdust, lit at sundown by the halfcaste women to discourage the sandflies and mosquitoes, rose like incense.

Clancy and Rifkah sat on deck-chairs, out in the moonlight, just clear of the trees. He held her hand, talking most of the while, but softly, as the conditions demanded. She just sat staring at the sea, half-smiling. He talked mostly of his boyhood, how he had loved coming home to this sort of thing from school down South and had always hated going back: 'The South's like a foreign land to us Northerners. Even the country people're like townies compared with the townies here. I'm so glad you like it and want to stay here. I never want to leave it myself. What I'd like's a small place of my own, to get away from Vaiseys. Father was right not to give into 'em. I can see that now. I only wish he'd take me in with him and teach me stock-breeding. I could take the place over from him when he dies.' When she looked at him, he gave a little laugh, 'Well, he can't last for ever, can he?'

He raised her hand to his lips. 'How'd you like to be mistress of Lily Lagoons?'

She smiled. 'You are dreamingk.'

'Maybe . . . but my dreams all seem to be coming true.'

The slow swinging of the launch to the change of the tidal flow caused Clancy to talk again of that trip to the East, as he called it, meaning northwest to the Isles of Spice. The breeze started by the outward movement of the vast silver mass brought the sweet smoke drifting through the trees – and louder sounds of what was going on along the beach to southward.

Soon it became evident that it was not simply the breeze making the sounds of revelry louder, but approach of the revellers. They were singing. A musical instrument was playing. Clancy growled, 'If they think they're coming in here they've got another think coming.' He sat stiff now, eyes on that natural barrier against intrusion on aristocratic privilege, the gleaming wall of rock.

It was an accordion that was making the music. Mingled with music and singing was the mirthful squealing of blacks. The dogs of the halfcaste women began to yap, to be silenced by their owners. 'Wonder what the bloody fools are up to?' said Clancy. 'Come and have a look-see'. He helped her up, supported her with an arm about her waist.

They had gone but halfway to the rocks, while the riot beyond increased, when the sparkling mass close to the halfcaste quarters became alive with leaping figures. They were pale-skinned, with black heads, most stripped to the waist and wearing only shorts or drawers, and all seeming to have in hand masses of vegetation, creepers, some of which they waved above their heads. The accordionist leapt onto a peak of rock and stood there swaying to the wild music he was pumping from the snorting squealing instrument.

Clancy roared, 'Hey . . . what the hell you think you're doing?'

The mob answered by coming racing towards them, babbling their lingo, waving the wreaths, which proved to be lengths of the beach convolvulus, so-called Bindweed.

Clancy kept on roaring, 'You got no right here. I'll get the police . . . .'

But undeterred, the intruders formed a half-circle round the couple, while one of them, a tall well-built young man wearing khaki trousers rolled to the knees, came right up to them, laughing and gesticulating, speaking a mixture of his own language and what went for English in the local Greek community, from which it could be gathered that they were there to wish the newlyweds luck. 'Belong Greek fashion!'

The blacks were showing at the rocks now, but staying there.

The young man shouted, 'We-lot dance-dance!'

'Dance-dance!' yelled his mob.

He threw an end of his garland to one of his mates, measured out half of it, then handed the middle of it to Clancy, grinning widely and saying something in his own language. Clancy took it, but scowling, muttering, 'What's this business?'

The rest of the mob did likewise with their lengths of bindweed. Stretched out, silvery green with big red flowers nodding, it looked very pretty. Clancy accepted a few proffered strands, said to Rifkah, whom he still held about the waist, 'All right with you? They evidently only want to be friendly.' She smiled, although looking a little scared. He said to the leader, 'No rough stuff, now.'

But the leader was only concerned with his preparations. He let out a shout that started the mob prancing round the couple, while himself leaping in to grab up the strands that Clancy had let drop and force them on him. Then he yelled at the accordionist, who stood outside the circle, and who started a wild sort of tarantella, to which the mob, the leader among them, began to circle the couple, prancing a dance-step and singing to the music.

'Hey, what's this?' cried Clancy, but laughing.

It was a sort of maypole dance, the design of which soon was seen to be to bind the couple with the garlands, which in spite of Clancy's good-humoured efforts to prevent it, happened in no time. There they stood, embraced and immobilized, while the mob pressed round them, still clutching their ends of the bonds and shouting their wild song and now to their prancing adding definite erotic movements.

The blacks, emboldened, were now crowding in, but to stop at a respectful distance.

Again the leader shouted above the uproar. Someone brought him a bottle from one of a couple of wet sacks lying on the sand. He turned to the couple, waving the bottle, crying, 'Drink-drink!' It was beer. He tore the metal cap off with his teeth, then shoved the bottle at Clancy, again with the cry, 'Drink-drink!' which the mob echoed. Trussed as he was, Clancy couldn't take the bottle. The man put it to his mouth, and avoiding all attempts to dodge it, made him drink, made him drink half of it. Then the man gave the bottle to Rifkah for a couple of sips. This done, he put the bottle to his own lips and guzzled off what remained, to hurl the bottle away. 'Now how about letting us go?' demanded Clancy.

But there was more to it. Again the leader gave the cue. While the others formed up he addressed the couple in his mangled language which suggested that a nuptial dance was about to be performed for them. He struck a pose, extended arms sideways, began to click fingers. The others followed him. The accordion wailed and coughed in rapid rhythm. The dancers kicked up the sand in intricate steps with which they weaved in and out amongst each other, with tempo increasing to the frenetic, until the leader, with the last of his breath, gasped, 'Hey!' when they all stopped dead. For a moment they hung pumping for breath. Then up went the cry again: 'Drink-drink!' There was a dive on the bottles.

Panting and laughing, the leader and a couple of others disentangled Clancy and Rifkah, but before letting them go, hung small garlands about their necks so that they remained linked. The leader thrust out his hand, saying, 'Good lucky.' Others coming with bottles did the same. A bottle was given to Clancy to drink a toast that all shouted, 'Good lucky!'

Then the leader said, 'Okay, finish. You go bed!' Someone else said something that raised a whoop of laughter.

Clancy laughed, tucked his arm under hers, looked at her, saying, 'Looks like we got married sooner than we expected.' She giggled.

'Goodnight!' cried the leader. The others echoed him, grabbed up their wet sacks, turned back towards the rocks. Some rushed in amongst the blacks and grabbed girls, to drag them off squealing. In a minute all had vanished.

Clancy chuckled, 'Well, what d'you know!' He added: 'Seeing we're married, what're we going to do about it?' She shrugged and smiled. He would have kissed her. She dodged away. He said, 'Looks like we're stuck here for the night, anyway. Look . . . the launch's on one of those mad sand-banks. You mind?'

She smiled. 'I like to stay here.'

He drew a deep breath. 'Ah . . . that's fine!'

He kissed her lightly. 'Let's have a drink of our own cold beer, eh?'

They went back to the table under the trees, to sit with Igulgul winking through the leaves, looking for Wrong-side even here, perhaps, when there was plenty of it going on behind the rocks, judging from the sounds from there. Clancy showed annoyance over the evident cavorting of black-haired satyrs with black-skinned nymphs, saying he ought to hunt 'em, but doing nothing more than cast scowling glances in the direction of it. He kept hold of Rifkah's hand, caressing it, kissing it now and again. He was evidently restless, far from tired himself, but kept on asking if she was tired. She sat seemingly content, looking out on the rapidly shrinking sea, the rising backbone of the Old One's Shade and his head with its myriad eyes.

At last Clancy said, 'Come on into the house. I can't stand that billy-goat business over there any longer.' On the front verandah, he suggested that they take beds on the northern side verandah, where they wouldn't be disturbed. 'Ready for bed-o yet?' he asked. She nodded.

The latticed verandah was grown with creeper, but bright enough from moonlight to need no other lighting. She chose one of four beds there, as yet not made up. He went inside for linen, brought only that. He insisted on making the bed for her, dropped the net, even hastily, but showed no haste in departing to let her strip. He set about fixing the next bed for himself, saying, 'Better keep an eye on you, case that handsome big Ox comes snoopin' round . . . aheeee!' It was not until she asked where she could undress that he took the tip and said he'd better go and undress himself. Quickly she slipped out of the play suit, hung it on a chair, and clad in silk shift and pants, got into bed, pulled the sheet to her chin, despite the muggy warmth.

He was soon back, wearing only pyjama shorts. He peered through her net, asking, 'Comfy?'

She murmured, 'Zang you, yes.'

He hung there for a moment, then said, 'I didn't kiss you Good-night.'

She was silent. He sank to haunches, shoved his head in under the net. Now the lovely face was plain to see, dark ivory against the whiteness of the pillow, the large eyes, looking dark, fixed on him. The arm that pulled up the sheet lay bent across her bosom, enticingly bare to the neck, to the little ear peeping whitely from the blood-dark spill of hair, except for a slip of silken shoulder-strap. His hand, comparatively dark, reached to fiddle with the bit of silk. He breathed, vibrantly, 'I love you, you know.' The dark eyes blinked.

The fingers went caressingly up her neck, round behind it. As he bent to her lips he drew her head up, slipped the other arm over and round her, clasped her close, kissed her fiercely. She did not struggle, but was plainly resistant in expression when at length he withdrew from her, while still keeping hold. She swallowed, murmured, 'Goodnight.'

He swallowed too. 'You're not sending me away yet, are you?'

She moved to slip out of his arms. He held on, bent again, this time lying across her bosom to keep her down, and kissed her again with ardour. When he released her lips, she pushed him back. Complainingly, he asked, 'Why . . . what's the matter . . . don't you like me kissing you?'

'You are too 'ungry. You eat my mouse . . .. '

He gave her a hug, chuckling, 'You lovely mouse! I told you you make me want to eat you.'

'You haf mek my mouse sore.'

'Oh, I'm sorry . . . poor little mouse!' This time he kissed her shoulder. A tiny wisp of dark axillary hair was showing now. He drew back to pluck at it gently, then inserted his finger into the fold, and withdrawing the other arm from round her, raised her arm to expose the axilla, and bending, vented his ardour on that. He looked up, chuckling, 'Ate you with salt that time. You taste lovely!'

She smiled at him, but quickly held him off when he would have kissed her lips again. He sank back to knees, holding the hand that had checked him, staring at her. Then he said, 'You must be hot under that sheet.'

Promptly she said, 'No,' and repeated it sharply, 'No, no!' when he grabbed the top of the sheet and pulled it down over her bosom. She grabbed and held it.

'What's the matter?' he asked. 'You're quite decently clad.' But he heaved for the breath to say it. What lay under the film of silk was all too evident. She tried to pull the sheet back. He restrained her, muttering, 'No . . . don't cover yourself up. I . . . I . . . . ' He took a deep breath, added with a rush, 'I've seen you naked, you know!'

After another long moment of staring, he asked tremulously, 'Wouldn't . . . couldn't . . . I see you . . . like that . . . again?'

She breathed, 'Pliss . . . no.'

'But we're going to be married.' He drew again at the sheet.

Still she clung to it, murmuring more urgently, 'No, no . . . pliss.'

He laughed feebly, 'They all think we're married already.'

Again the spell of staring, of laboured breathing, while the hands counter-clutched. At length he muttered, 'I'm not going to hurt you. I love you. I . . . I . . . I only want to see you.' Then with a swift movement he snatched the sheet completely off her.

She gasped, 'Oh!' and sat up quickly.

As quickly he pushed her down again, himself gasping, 'No, no . . . don't get up.' He held her down by the shoulders, looking into her face now wildly staring. 'Truly I'm not going to hurt you. I . . . I only want to . . . worship you. I love you!'

When she relaxed, he drew his hands down from her shoulders to her breasts, which he fondled, while staring at her. Although rigid again, she made no move. When he smiled she only blinked. He lowered his cheek to the breast near him, still looking into the great watchful eyes. He raised his head and smiled again. Then, as quickly as he had pulled down the sheet, now he pulled up the chemise, exposing her from throat to navel. She grabbed at the silk at her throat, but could do nothing with it because at once he obstructed her by dropping his head, to apply lips to the near breast, a hand to the other. When he lifted his head, he slid his hands up so that the silk slid over her head, even while she kept hold of it. He was trembling now, his voice quavering: 'I told you I'd seen you naked. I've loved you ever since. You're so lovely. No, I loved you before that . . . when I first saw you. You're so lovely. Don't be mean with your loveliness!' He pulled the shift away from her, leant on it with elbows, on the edge of the bed, looking her over, sighing, saying tremulously, 'So lovely . . . lovely!'

She tried to bring down her arms, still bent where he had pulled the silk over them, down to cover her breasts. He immobilized one arm with an elbow and the other with the same hand. Then with his free hand he caressed the glowing loveliness from breasts to belly, ran a finger round the navel, stabbed it gently, looked back from what he was doing at her stiff face. He smiled, at the same time slipping his hand down under the elastic of her drawers. She started, but could not raise herself. He chuckled shakily. 'Take 'em off, eh?'

Her bosom heaved. 'No . . . no!'

'But I've seen you naked already . . . . '

'No, no!'

Fondling her down below, he faltered, 'But we're getting married . . . .'

'No . . . pliss . . . Clancy!'

'Someone'll marry us. No one'll take you away from me . . . .'

'Oh, Clancy . . . you vill spoil . . . oh!' Her voice rose up as he pulled the pants down. As she heaved up against the pressure of his imprisoning arm, he yanked at the pants, tore them clean off her, hurled them away, and on the instant had his hand between her legs at the crotch. Forcing her back, not looking at all he had revealed, but at her distorted face, he panted, 'Don't struggle, darling . . . don't fight me . . . .'

She gasped, 'Let me go!' She tried to tear his hand from her loins.

'But I love you . . . I want you . . . . '

She was sobbing now: 'Pliss, Clancy . . . you vill spoil . . . pliss . . . so mooch haf I been hurt . . . oh, pliss!'

'I'm not going to hurt you . . . I love you!'

'No, pliss, no pliss . . . do not spoil!'

He turned from her to look below. She heaved up against his relaxed restraint, broke it, reached with a hand for the edge of the bed, swung a leg over it. The action suddenly maddened him. Hissing now, he flung her back to the pillow and raising a leg from the floor, thrust the knee between her widely parted thighs. She tore at his restraining hands, shrieking now, 'No, no, no!'

Ignoring her, pressing her down with the weight of his bare torso, he turned again and began tearing at his own pants.

She shrieked, 'I vill kill meinself you do!'

He grunted, 'Shut up!'

He got entangled in his pants, had to pull away from her a little thus freeing her inner leg. She brought her knee up into his engorged genitals. He gasped, heaved up, fell back clutching the net, half-slid out of the bed. Quick as a flash she drew up her legs, swung them under the net, ducked under it. Her chemise tangled with her feet, nearly tripping her. She snatched it up, went running down the verandah towards the blaze of the sea.

She stopped at the edge of the front verandah, looked back. Sounds of scraping and mumbling there. She would be silhouetted. She dodged out of line of sight from the side verandah. Amongst the cane furniture she shook out the chemise, pulled it over her head, then looked about, as if for something to add to this flimsy thing that barely reached her hips.

'Rifkah!' Sound of scuffling steps.

She ran along the verandah to the other end, turned as she reached it, looked back to see him come round the corner. She leapt off on to the sand. He called to her, 'Where you going? Don't be silly!'

She started running towards the halfcastes' quarters. She came out of the shadow of the trees to shine like a wraith in the full blaze of moonlight. He bawled after her, 'Come back here!'

She went racing, for all her awkwardness on sore feet, for the trees on the other side. She reached them, to be greeted by the dogs, snarling, yapping. She halted, panted, 'Goot tog . . . goot tog!' But the bigger, a shaggy blue cattle dog, came at her with flashing teeth, leapt for her throat, missed as she started back, ripped the chemise down the front. She screamed, wheeled, rushed back into the moonlight, now heading for the sea. She screamed again as teeth nipped her heel.

Black heads popped over and through the glistening wall of rock. Naked white bodies and black bodies leapt out behind her. A shout went up. A yelp as the dogs were kicked off. Then laughter, whooping: 'Aphrodite, Aphrodite.' Howls and squeals of mirth and sound of pounding feet.

There in what looked like a gully amongst the sandbanks was the dinghy, tethered to the oar, and still floating on a strip of silver. She flew to it, scattering the tiny hordes foraging in the ooze above the water-line, went floundering through water and quicksand. She fell into the dinghy with white bottom presented to smirking Igulgul above and the howling mob crowded to a halt at the water's edge. She snatched at the mooring line. It came in, but without the oar. The tide snatched the boat away. Running stern-first, the boat rounded a bend, to meet doubly swift water from another channel. It spun. She grabbed up the oar lying on the thwarts, tried to control the boat, only succeeded in turning it broadside to the stream, which flung it into a crumbling bank and nearly capsized it. She fell into the bottom of the little vessel, to sit clutching the gunnels, gaping.

The tiered walls of the channels were left behind, with only an island or two of sand about. The shore was lost to view in the westerning moon-glare – all except the winking head of Tchamala. Now the tide-stream was running like a river, parallel with the shore, as if drawn to the headland, then as if spurned by it, to swing sharply away, inevitably it seemed, towards those shadowy serpent-like humps of the reef.

Soon little boat and helpless voyager were caught in the play of the Old Ones, Tchamala and his mate Igulgul, drawn into a wild race, in which ran flank to flank, frail timber and frailer flesh, with those slimy iron humps that bounced them off and sucked them back – at last to engulf them, drag them down into luminescent chaos, tear them apart.

A silver surge flung the lost voyager as a lump of whiteness onto a flatish hump, rolled her in weeds that held her from being washed off. Another surge. Another. The weeds entangled her more. The surges fell away. The creatures popped out, with glistening eyes and gaping maws. Meat? The clutching weeds relaxed their grip with deflation of air-bladders. The tiny monsters came circling. Time was subordinate to Tide out here. Back would come the surging waters to fling the Meat to hungry others. They came circling. The Meat moved. The creatures scattered.

She raised her head, coughed, sneezed, puked, heaved in the agony of pumping out the water. A strange sight, that writhing whiteness amongst the black and silver weed, with glints of burnished copper. So strange a sight that a brace of sea-kweeluks, winging over, wheeled back to take another look, circled, landed on the beacon a rock away, screamed above the tumult of the waters: *Kwee-luk, kwee-luk . . . Somebody is lost*!

The great eyes of the lost one regarded them blankly.

Igulgul smirked. The Head of Tchamala seemed to be looking back along his monstrous swimming length, winking. The tiny monsters began to advance again – for there was the tang of blood, blood!

Out of the dark mass of her wet hair with its fringe of fire, blood was running down a pale cheek. Blood was running down the right arm from a bloody mess that was torn white flesh and the remaining rags of the chemise. She struggled to rise, fell back to haunches, causing another retreat of those who had designs on her.

She groaned, dropped head to hands, so that the blood streamed over them. She swayed, keeled over, went through a spasm of ague. When at length she fell still, the impatient waiting ones grew bold again.

She was not dead. That was to be seen in the gentle rise and fall of whiteness under shroud of weeds. But the Tide, the Tide, already on the turn, and all that meat and blood, blood! The boldest of the creatures tackled her torn feet.

Unwaking she kicked them off. Some tried her shoulder, others her head. At last they swarmed over her. She started up, with bloody mouth opened to what should have been a shriek, but came out only as a croak. She sat up, blinking.

Igulgul was well down now. The Snake's Head was black against a blazing sky. The beacon across the way now stood stark, a barred triangle against snowy cloud. The tide was running fast, hissing, gurgling, licking the rock with long silver tongues.

She rose to knees, struggled to feet, only to drop down again groaning. On hands and knees she went to the edge of the rock. The rock of the beacon was higher. Intervening was a lower stretch, already submerging. The creatures, despairing of keeping her, surged over her feet and legs. She had to tear them off, take refuge from them by sliding down into the weedy shallows below.

The shallows were where she found them. The floating weeds often meant bottomless holes into which she vanished, to emerge as a weedy monster herself, floundering to the succour of some projecting rock that as often was denied her scarcely before she had recovered breath through submergence by the relentless tide. Igulgul in his slow sliding down the sky watched her hideous progress, seemed to hang above the horizon to see it out.

She was almost across, was in the shadow of her goal, when a new sound came into the uproar of the waters and her breathing for her very life, a throbbing. She was in water to her neck, when a black form shot into view from behind the beacon rock, no further than fifty feet away. The Delacy launch, not crewed by one man, but half a dozen, all black men against the moon, all staring anywhere but where the Old One had her hidden. She called to them – with a croak. They went on, southward, following the reef – towing the lost dinghy. Igulgul got another glimpse of her through a split in the rock as she reached it, winked at her over the horizon, vanished, but left her enough light to climb by and to see, when she reached the top, the triangle of the beacon looking doubled against a silver cloud, like the Shield of David, the magic *Magen David*, and the steel rungs leading to the safety it offered – if only she had life left in her to make it, instead of like poor Lucy Bynoe, who managed only half of it and so left half of herself for the sharks. The sharks were round already, as to be seen by the boomerangs of phosphorescence hurtling about the rock, perhaps only now having got the tang of that incentive to their monstrous living – blood, blood!

VII

The Mission ship, *St Francis Xavier*, had slipped her moorings when Father Glascock came aboard after early Mass, and was heading for home, that is for the islands called Prince Leopold, was running out with the tide and the mist the tide was bringing from the countless reaches it had sneaked into in the dark, mist now gilding with the rising Sun. Father Glascock, back in work-a-day khaki shirt and shorts, was standing by the foremast, watching the smoking water with its tide-lines of debris, the flotillas of migrant mangrove shoots, the islets of pumice that having come all the way down from the volcanoes of the Indies were heading back again. Perhaps, if true to his vocation, he was contemplating the Mystery so-called in which he had just taken part before the altar of his Hanged God, or if more the realist he seemed to be, was pondering the Inscrutable in the simple marvels before those intense blue eyes. Anyway, his attention was suddenly seized by commotion amongst his crew. He looked aft.

At the wheel was a blackman, wearing only a red loin-cloth, while others were attending the stowing of the dinghy just swung inboard; and Brother David, in blue overalls and wearing a Japanese officer's cap, stood halfway in the companion of the engine-room, arms folded in dignified fashion, while evidently controlling his engine with prehensile toes. The engine was put-put-put-ing softly, leaving it mostly to the tide to give the vessel way. All eyes were staring directly ahead, in evident alarm. As he turned to look at what they saw, the ship swung hard astarboard, and the beat of the engine simultaneously increased. He had to swing contrarily. They had been approaching the beacon on the Rainbow Reef that would give them their heading straight out through the harbour's mouth. Still a good hundred yards off, it was seen as a vague shape in the mist. He turned away from it, doubtless thinking that it was sudden realization of their proximity to the reef that had caused the alarm, until he looked at them again and saw that although they had turned from the beacon they were still watching it and even more fearfully. Again he looked that way, this time to see the beacon struck by sunlight with momentary thinning of the mist about it. He stared at the vague shape it had become again almost instantly, then swung back towards the crew, bawling, 'What was that there?'

The answer was a rolling away of dark eyes, not only from what had filled them with alarm but from his blue quiz. Coming aft, he demanded, 'What's matter you-lot?'

Heads drooped a little, while still eyes remained fixed on the golden mistiness ahead. He eyed them for a moment, then snapped, 'Go about. I want to take a look-see at that beacon.'

The answer was a gasp, soft in expression, but expressive enough to one who knew it well: *Eh look out*!

He roared, 'Go about, I said!'

Still no response, only that scared looking out to sea. He leapt to the wheel, snatched it from the helmsman, who cringed away. He spun it. As the ship yawed widely when broadside to the tide he yelled at David, 'Engine!'

But David only gaped at him. When he repeated, angrily 'Give me more engine, man!' David shook his head. The priest roared, 'What's got into you all?' He left the wheel, to come leaping to the engine-room, leaned down past stiff-standing David, opened the throttle to make the engine fairly bellow from its exhaust. As he came up and headed back to the wheel he leered, crying mockingly, 'Blackfeller business, eh? Old Tchamala. Call yourselves Christians!'

He snatched the wheel back from the helmsman who had taken it again. As the boy fell back, he muttered, 'Properly no-goot bijnitch dat-one, Father.'

'Balls!' snapped the priest. 'Bloody *panganis*. Ease off the engine a bit, David. I'm surprised at you, anyway. Half-speed!'

They were coming on the beacon diagonally. The mist was denser, so that it could scarcely be seen. Then suddenly the Sun broke through again. A glint of copper – of ivory! A gasp from everyone.

The figure hung from a brace of the alternating climbing-spikes, on one side by a knee hooked over, on the other by a wrist wrapped round with a loop of rag. The copper head hung drooped over the shoulder of the loose-hanging arm. The mist closed in again. As if in reaction to it, the beat of the engine fell. The goggling priest looked quickly at David, shouted, 'What're you doing?'

David, looking back with slant eyes rolling, called back quaveringly, 'Dat's devil, Father.'

The priest yelled, 'You fool . . . give me way!'

The helmsman panted at Glascock's side, 'Dat Ol'Goomun Dibble from rock, Father.' He jerked lips in the direction of the Garrison Point.

'Pagans!' roared the priest. 'Open that throttle, David . . . or I'll open your silly head with this boat hook!' He snatched the instrument from where it lay on the hatchway before him.

David turned away terrified, bobbed his foot down. The engine bellowed again. Above it Father Glascock roared, 'There's some white person up on that beacon. Now stand by your posts. If you're frightened of devils, then pray to Jesus. Here, boy . . . take the wheel!'

With the boat-hook he went running forward. As he reached the bow the Sun struck again. He gasped, 'Mother of God!'

Almost absently he sounded for depth as they nosed up to the beacon, his blue eyes never leaving the hanging female figure, revealed as they neared as much black and red with bruising and abrasion as ivory white. Likewise did engineer and helmsman perform their tasks. They were able to get right up to the beacon, so that the priest could grab it with his hook. As he did so, the eyes in the face above him opened, to stare down into his. Time was suspended in that moment, even for ship and tide, it seemed.

Then the copper head jerked up. The eyes swept over the ship. Hanging hands and feet came to life to grab for grips. The ship came to life. Glascock yelled for engine, for rope. As a boy came with the rope the priest yelled, 'That canvas off the hatch, there.' Then he looked up at the staring blood-stained face, and asked in a strangely matter-of-fact tone, 'Think you can climb down?' Rifkah answered by lowering a grossly swollen foot to a lower rung, and a hand.

There was only a side view of her from here. When down she would have to turn right round to face the priest. Too much for such as he. He snapped at the blackboy, 'Get aft!' Then as she reached the bottom rung and let go with hands to grab the stay beside her, he raised the sheet of canvas to hand to her in such a way as to obscure his vision of her. It was delicacy wasted. She almost fell into the sea in stepping aboard, and lost the canvas. He caught her naked in his arms. Staggering aft with her, he shouted, 'Get a blanket!' He stopped at the forward cargo hatch, holding her till the boy came running with the blanket. Then, wrapping it about her, he lay her on the hatch. As she looked up at him, in the same matter-of-fact tone he said, 'Hello . . . I know you.'

Her swollen lips moved. For a moment he looked into the eyes that, for all the blood-shot whites, still shone like jewels. Then, swinging to look around, he asked, 'Is anybody else out here?' He had to repeat the question before she answered with a shake of the head. He went on: 'What happened . . . did you get wrecked in Delacy's launch?' Shake. 'How'd you get out here, then?' She struggled for speech, but could only swallow painfully and shake and shake her matted copper head. He stared at her for a while, then said, 'Well . . . we'd better get you to the Hospital . . . .'

At that she heaved up to sitting, croaking, '*Nein*!'

'Eh . . . what's wrong?'

She struggled again to speak, but could only shake her head, grasping his hand and looking at him with fear. 'You don't want to go to hospital?' She shook her head hard. 'But you're badly knocked about . . . .' She interrupted by pulling at him, shaking her head, croaking.

'Well . . . what d'you want me to do with you?'

She got it out with a gasp: 'Tek bush . . . .'

'Take you to the bush?' Nod. 'Where?' She could only goggle at him.

He asked, 'What about Delacy . . . aren't you going to marry him?' Shake. 'But you can. Monsignor Maryzic's sorry for yesterday. He said he'll marry you without baptism.'

She croaked, 'No, no!'

'You don't want to get married?'

'No.'

'You want to go to Delacy?'

'No, no.' She was finding her voice, panted a whisper: 'Tek . . . me . . . bush.'

'Where?'

'Any . . . place . . . any . . . .'

'But I can't put you ashore in that state.'

'Let . . . me . . . stay . . . .'

'On the ship?' She nodded. 'I'm going to my Mission.'

She clung to his hand. 'Tek . . . tek . . . tek me.'

He stared. She whispered, 'Pliss . . . goot . . . man.'

He stared still, then swallowed. 'All right.'

The jewelled eyes flooded with tears. Still grasping the hand she sank back, pressed it to her lips. He tried to withdraw it. She caught it with the other, drenching it in tears. He turned from her to shout at the gaping crew, 'Put on the Primus. Make some tea.' Still she clung, while her body quivered to her sobbing. He shouted at the helmsman, 'Take her to sea!'

VIII

That strange, strange Sunday, which had looked like being Clancy's Wedding Day, even with no other ceremonial to initiate it than that of going to bed with the bride! Strange, strange day, which must have seemed to him to have no beginning and to be going to have no end! It saw him come back to the Vaisey-Delacy townhouse in the middle of the afternoon, exhausted from futile searching the harbour and its shores for his lost love.

The Japanese servant, Hanno, greeted him on arrival home, with the information that Monsignor Maryzic had phoned during the morning and left a message asking him to come to see him and bring New Missee. Clancy's only response to the message was a grunt. Hanno, the perfect servant, seemed not to notice the haggard bloodshot eyes, the desperate mien. He simply asked was there anything the Master wanted. Clancy replied that he would have beer and sandwiches in the lounge. He ate those sandwiches as if he'd not eaten since the crab of the evening before – first feed of crab for her off whose ivory and copper loveliness the crabs themselves might now be feasting! It may have been something like that which, when he'd finished the sandwiches, made him go out to drink the beer on the front verandah, or rather to sip it, while he sat staring at the sea, the sea, the jade and silver flood, still flowing – in, or out? What did it matter? It was always flowing, except for a menacing moment, that moment of its turning, when it seemed to drag the whole world and its hopes back to where things had started or stopped or never begun. He was still seeing the sea when he fell asleep. That was plain from blink-blink-blinking of his too-tight-shut eyes, while all the rest of him sagged so utterly weary.

Yet so soundly did he sleep, that he did not hear even the arrival of the weekly mail plane, always a noisy business, since the crew seemed to know that most of the town was sleeping the booze off just about then and delighted in rousing them by doing a low turn over them before going in to land. Nor did he hear the footfalls of one coming to him with no show of stealth but rather, by expression of narrowed green eyes and tight-shut trap in freckled face, in frank hostility. The visitor was lanky Pat Hannaford, coming up from the direction of the Oil Tanks, as might be expected of one who would be making anything but a social call to a place like this. Clancy didn't wake even when Pat came scraping up the stairs, stamping onto the verandah. Pat had to wake him, grating, 'Hey!'

Clancy blinked up into the green eyes. Without waiting for him to wake fully, Pat demanded, 'What the 'ell's goin' on?'

Clancy sat up, licking his lips.

'Where is she?'

That woke Clancy. He caught his breath, then breathed, 'I don't know.'

'Wha' you mean you don't know?'

'I . . . I took her over to . . . . '

Pat cut in: 'Don't try tellin' me she's at Rainbow Beach . . . 'cause I been there.' Clancy blinked. Pat went on: 'I been out in a launch with some mates. I went ashore behind Rainbow 'Ead, and along the back way to your joint. I see your launch pokin' around . . . but didn't think you'd be silly enough to have her out with you. So I go to see 'ow she's doin' and tell her the latest 'bout the arrangements for gettin' her away. But she ain't there. She ain't *been* there. Now, where is she?'

Clancy panted, 'She was there, but . . . but . . . but I don't know where she is now.' He reached for the bottle, poured the remains of it into the glass.

Pat leant over him. 'Now listen 'ere, mate . . . I want 'o know what's goin' on. You supposed to take her over there and hold her till we was ready to get her away.'

Clancy took a swig, grimaced his displeasure at the flatness and temperature of the beer, then said, 'I did take her, too . . . yesterday afternoon . . . . '

'Then 'ow come them yeller women o' yours reckons no one's been there?'

'I told 'em not to talk about it to anyone.'

' 'Bout what?'

Breathless, Clancy said, 'She . . . she disappeared . . . last night.'

The green eyes opened wide. 'What d'you mean . . . bolted?'

'No . . . I'll tell you. Sit down and have a beer.' Clancy was eager now, as if to get something unpleasant off his chest.

'I don't want your bloody beer. I wan' 'o know 'bout that girl. I'm responsible for her.'

But already Clancy had clapped his hands. Hanno may have been lurking in the hall with the loaded tray, so quickly was he there. He didn't appear to notice Pat, who scowled at him. When he had gone, Pat growled, 'Anybody here besides that Jap?'

'No. Sit down. I want to explain how it happened.'

Pat complied ungraciously. Clancy gave his own version of what happened, blaming it all on the dogs and the Greeks, particularly on the Greeks, one of whom, snooping, so Clancy suggested, must have panicked the girl. It didn't seem to occur to Pat, listening intently, to ask why she'd had to seek protection from halfcastes. But perhaps, as seemed likely by the look of his narrow eyes and tight lips, he was holding it back for spitting out in full force when the story was told.

Clancy said the Greeks and the blacks hadn't been much use in the search when at last he was able to embark on it, the former being silly drunk and the latter too scared of the reef by night. However, they'd quickly enough found the dinghy, on the rocks at the western point of the harbour's mouth. In daylight they'd found the oars, one in a backwater behind Rainbow Head, the other in mangroves of a narrow swamp where she might have got through to the bush without leaving tracks. He told how she asked him to take her away somewhere she could live with the blacks, but without mentioning how the request had come about, that is following the breakdown of the plan to marry. He said nothing about his intention to marry the girl at all. He'd had blacks looking for tracks along the western shores since dawn, but without avail.

There was one interruption, when the phone in the hall rang. Clancy ignored it. However, Hanno who answered it eventually, came out to say that it was the Monsignor ringing again. Clancy growled, 'Tell him you can't find me.'

When it was finished, Pat did spit out: 'Nice bastard you were to trust her to!'

Clancy bridled, but meeting the blazing green eyes, looked hastily away – out to sea, to sea. Pat joined him in looking, with eyes now seeming to be searching. Pat broke the long silence that followed: 'Bugger me if I can believe she's dead . . . not after all she's been through . . . with them Nazi bastards, and these bloody Federal Security Dicks.'

Clancy sighed: 'Neither can I. But there it is. The dinghy knocked about . . . the oars miles apart. I suppose we just got to face it.'

Pat looked at him. 'Face what?'

'That, well, she's missing, anyway . . . and report it.'

'We?'

Clancy flushed, blinked. 'Well, me.'

The green eyes were narrow. 'What you goin' 'o say?'

Clancy was hesitant. 'Well . . . as a matter of fact . . . I thought of seeing my lawyer first.'

'You bloody bastard!'

Clancy looked astonished. 'Eh . . . what's wrong with that? Got to protect myself don't I?'

'From what?'

'Well, wasn't she wanted by the police? They'd want to know what she was doing with me.'

'And what would you say?' The tone was menacing.

Clancy swallowed, answered rather feebly, 'That'd be up to my lawyer.'

Pat's tongue, though obviously kept under restraint, was no less stinging: 'You'n' your bloody lawyer . . . you rotten bloody boss-bastard! You're goin' to dob *me* for this.'

Clancy, pale and sweating, panted, 'No . . . why should I?'

'To get out o' the shit yo'self.'

'It was your idea I take her over there . . . . '

The restrained whip lashed venomously: 'There you are! You tell your lawyer that. He tells the cops . . . how the gallant young squatter got himself involved with the dirty Communists, tryin' to help a pretty girl. They'll grab that. That's what they want. They're your mob, paid by you to put down my mob. You won't take no rap . . . Oh, no . . . you dirty, sneakin', shit'ouse, bloody, product-of-capitalism rat!'

Clancy glared, but with eyes that rolled somewhat and voice that had a quaver to it, as he protested, 'You be careful what you say.'

'And you be careful what you do, squatter-boy! 'Cause, be the livin' Jees, you dob me . . . and it's the last bit o' dobbin' you'll ever do. My mob don't take dobbers easy. I'm tellin' you, boy . . . it'll be more than your testicles're worth for a start. Got that?'

Clancy's glance wavered before the green lightning of those eyes. Pat had to get the breath back to go on: 'You said nobody knows 'bout this but them Greeks, who know they're to blame, and your boongs, who you can keep quiet.'

Clancy panted, 'Someone's sure to let it out sometime . . . . '

'Well, let 'em!'

Clancy turned his eyes to sea again. Pat went on: 'You said she might'a' got ashore. I got a couple o' days off. I'll get out in that launch again. I know an old yeller-feller'll track for me. You just keep out of it . . . and your trap shut. I'll be gettin' along now.' Pat tossed off his beer. As he rose he leaned over Clancy. 'Jes one thing more.' His voice shook slightly: 'That was a nice girl. Don't matter 'bout the Commo business. She was the nicest thing I ever seen in female flesh. Boy . . . if she's dead, I ain't never forgivin' myself for puttin' her in your hands to die . . . and I certainly ain't never ever forgettin' that it was in your hands she died . . . . ' He straightened suddenly at sound on the drive. A car was coming. He asked quickly, 'Who'll that be?'

It was one of the town taxis, driven by a Chinaman, with Monsignor Maryzic as passenger. The Chinaman leapt down to help His Very Reverence to alight. The young men, both now on their feet, stared.

The old man, wearing yellow tusser-silk, with beaded black vest, dog-collar, clerical black hat, dismissed his driver with a wave of his stout walking stick, then headed for the steps. As the car swung away and he was climbing, darting sharp glances at those above, he cried wheezily, 'Vot ist I see . . . der Proletariat hob-nobbing mitt der Master Class!' He chuckled deeply as he reached the verandah, 'Not for der classical purpose of kissingk der arse, I hope . . . eeee?'

Clancy only blinked. Pat scowled. The old man made his way to the seat Clancy had vacated, and eased himself down into it, still chuckling, 'Anyvay . . . nice it is to see der lion lyink down mitt der lamb . . . even if only to get up ze appetite to eat him . . . aaaaah!' He sighed gustily.

Pat grunted, 'Well, I'll be off.'

'No, no!' cried the priest. 'You are joost der man I vont to see.'

The green eyes glinted with suspicion, which swung from the priest to Clancy, then back. He snapped, 'What would *you* want to see *me* about?'

'This,' said Maryzic, and took from a capacious pocket a folded copy of what, by its vivid blueness, was obviously a copy of *Australia Free*. 'You voodn't haf seen it, I suppose. It haf joost come in der mail. But for luck . . . or Divine Providence . . . I vood not see meinself . . . only der name catch my eye . . . see?'

He held up the spread-out cover, on which in large red letters were the words RED RIFKAH, and under them, in the usual black-on-blue: COMMUNIST-JEW PLOT TO TAKE OVER OUR EMPTY NORTH. The pair goggled at it. Hannaford reached for the magazine. The priest withdrew it, saying, 'No . . . you can read it in goot time. All I vont you to do is answer me straight: Iz ze girl a Communist?'

Pat swallowed, blinked. The priest continued: 'I full vell know ze vord of Communist is govern only by expedience. Still, I vont your honest answer. I haf zis zingk read and do not belief. It is malicious. I vont to 'elp zis girl. I am bound to 'elp zis girl, because I half uncharitable been to her in anozzer vay. But if she is of Communist Party, she do not need my 'elp. So. You haf no need of expedience, *Kamerad* Hannaford. Yes . . . or No?'

Pat swallowed again, muttered, 'No . . . she isn't one of us . . . never has been, as far as I know.'

'Goot! I zank you from my 'eart for zat. Now you may depart from my obnoxious presence, mitt its reek of ze Opium of Ze People, and go dispense your soothing syrup of All Men are Equal Under ze Commissar. Goottay.'

But Pat hung there. 'Tell me . . . what'a' you got 'o do with Rifkah Rosen?'

Monsignor Maryzic shrugged, looked at Clancy, who showed embarrassment so plainly that Pat demanded of him, 'Wha's goin' on?'

Clancy cast a glance at the sea as if wishing himself away on it. Maryzic chipped in, 'Yes . . . vot ist goingk on?'

Clancy swallowed hard, looked at the priest, at Pat, and then back to the sea, muttering, 'We were going to get married.'

Pat gaped. 'Eh? You and Rifkah?'

Clancy suddenly looked belligerent. 'Well, wasn't that the idea . . . that I was her fiance . . . that I get a Special Licence? Well, I thought I might's well make it fair dinkum. I asked her if she would. She said Yes. I took her to Monsignor, here.'

Still astonished, Pat asked, 'Is this all since we got here Friday night?'

'Well . . . yes. I asked her that night. But . . . but . . . well, I'd always wanted to . . . . '

Clancy broke off as the green eyes blazed. It burst from Pat in a pent breath: 'You lousy little bastard!' Then heaving for the breath again, he resumed: 'Behind me back . . . while I and others were riskin' jail to arrange things for her . . . you . . . you go and put the hard word on her when she can't say No. Jesus Christ!' Pat looked as if he were about to leap at Clancy.

Maryzic raised his stick. 'Zat vill do! Vot ist zis about behind ze back and jail and arranging zingks?'

The pair looked like schoolboys checked in a quarrel, and as likely to confide in the one who'd checked them. The priest waited a moment, then demanded, 'Vere is ze youngk lady?'

The young men eyed each other. There was that rumble in the old man's voice now: 'I am askingk, vere is ze lady. I vont to see. I haf apology to mek.' Then when they both looked at the sea, the voice roared, 'Vot is ze mystery? You, boy . . . Delacy! Vere ist zat girl you vont to marry yesterday?'

Clancy met the slaty eyes, licked his lips, faltered, 'I don't know, Father. She . . . she's disappeared . . . . '

Pat snarled, 'You bastard! You done it after all!'

Clancy flinched. Maryzic roared at Pat, 'Vy is he bastard? Vot haf he done?'

Pat showed his teeth at him. 'You mind your own bloody business!'

The old man pressed on his stick, shot to his feet, bellowing, 'How dare you spik to me like zat! Ist all my business . . . vot has happen to zat poor, hunted, frighten' Jew-girl. Tell me vot you haf done . . . or . . . or I vill beat it from you!' He raised the stick. Pat stepped out of reach, looking alarmed.

Clancy looked at Pat, who said quickly, 'You tell him, he'll tell the police.'

The old man roared, 'Ze police I vill tell if you do not tell me!'

Pat glowered at him for a moment. Then he said, 'Give your vow as a priest that you won't repeat it . . . your Confessional Vow . . . . '

Again the bellow: 'Vot, Confession from atheist? I vill vow nuzzing . . . only zat if any vun of you haf hurt zat sveet girl, I vill . . . vill . . . . ' The massive frame shook. Tears drowned the slaty eyes. The old man struggled for speech, got it out hoarsely: 'Yesterday . . . I vos guilty of ze moost un-Christian charity to zat child. I vos zingkingk she vont only to marry for citizenship. If zat so . . . if she ist vot zis dirty paper call her . . . Communist and Whore . . . she vill get vot she vont at any cost. But she vill not gif avay ze faith of her fathers. I insult her. I drive her from my door in her vonting . . . . ' He choked, hung his head for a moment. Then up it came, tossed like an old bull's, roaring, 'Damn you both! Tell me vot has happen zat Child of God?'

Clancy let it out in gasps, 'I think . . . I think she got . . . drowned . . . Father . . . . '

'Drowned you say . . . drowned . . vot. . . . vere?'

Clancy began to mumble the story, his version of it, while the old man, red in the eyes now, leaned menacing towards him on his stick. Clancy was telling of the futile search, when suddenly the old man's face changed remarkably, and he stood erect, crying, 'Vait . . . vait!'

They stared at him. He said. 'Zis morningk I get radio message from ze Mission ship. Ze AWA station isht goot to us like zat. Ze ship haf limited radio range. Mostly she call only ven comingk in. Zis morningk she leave at dawn. Father Glascock is aboard. At nine o'clock I get message in Latin. Vot for, I vunder . . . about vot? It is in Morse Code. You do not know Latin, of course. You do not know anyzingk! Ze message say: *Ze lost lamb of Israel isht safe mitt me.* Vot can it mean but zat he haf pick up our Rifkah?'

'God!' exclaimed Pat.

Maryzic snapped at him, 'Yes, *Kamerad* . . . ze sort of zingk zat Gott do . . . not Marshal Stalin!' Then, while they stared at him, the Monsignor went on excitedly: 'I am sure ist true. But ve moost vait for confirmation from Mission radio ven Father Glascock get zere. I vill call him. If it is by der Grace of Gott he haf found her, I vill proceed to secure her citizenship.'

'How you goin' 'o do that?' asked Pat.

'Ah . . . now ve do come to mindingk my business! You Communist haf your secret vays. Ze Church also . . . but for mooch more truly humanitarian ends. Ve do not vont to rule ze vorld . . . ve vont to save it.' Maryzic looked challengingly at Pat, who appeared to be about to answer mockingly, but refrained. The old priest continued. 'Now I am askingk a vow of silence from both of you. Not vun vord to anyvun . . . you understand? Ozzervise you might spoil my plan. I haf your vow?'

Both nodded. 'All right. Gif me some beer. I am t'irsty from too mooch talk. Zen I vont you tell me all about zis business. Vy is ziz girl here? Vy ze secrecy? Moost I know everyzingk to do vot I haf in mind.'

CHAPTER NINETEEN

THAT SAME strange Sunday afternoon (or Evenin') away in the Sandstone beyond Lily Lagoons, in fact well back on the Plateau, young Prindy was still leading Inspector Ballywick and his posse the dance arranged to divert them. They had been there for a full three days, mostly spent struggling through the very worst of the maze of caves and chasms supposedly created by the Old One for the hell of it. Those not frankly sick of it were they who simply would not be frank about it, the two Federal Officers, the Inspector and his Sergeant Bugsby. Already one member of the expedition had fallen out, and he one of the least to be expected of such weakness. This was Tracker Splinter, who had fallen victim to acute diarrhoea. His immediate master, Constable Stunke, declared that it was due to the too-soft living his Black Bastards had been enjoying back at his station, a condition of things he swore to put an end to forthwith.

Splinter's own diagnosis of his complaint, privily communicated to and shared by his dusky colleague, Tipperary, was that he was a victim of the *moah* of the region and as likely as not would die of it. Tipperay himself hung on, perhaps because being more used to breaking the blackman's law to maintain the whiteman's, he got some kind of satisfaction, above his miserable pay and little status, by being able to get away with it. Nevertheless, with Splinter's falling victim to disregard for what was *wahji*, he became very wary, never entering any place he considered might be dangerous for the like of him, except when in the company of his alien superiors, who could be blamed for the intrusion. When sent off to track and hunt alone, he made only a pretence of it.

Splinter had been sent back to what Inspector Ballywick called Base, meaning Lily Lagoons homestead, carrying a note to the head of the household there, requesting medical attention for his man, and also verbatim instructions to watch for anything fishy going on about the place. Poor Splinter, being told not to forget that he was a policeman even while his bowels were in a state of flux! It must have been a tough trip for him, not simply because he was ill and afraid and the first half of it was through the worst kind of terrain, but besides having to erase his tracks wherever possible to ensure his not being followed by hostile devil or man, had to remove all trace of his frequent defecation, since for a pursuer to have found the least bit of his *goona* would mean he could be dealt with without the trouble of pursuit.

Sergeant Bugsby also had a touch of diarrhoea, or as he called it in making light of it, the Tom-tits, the term being rhyming slang, a crude form of Cockney humour still indulged in by the transplanted Cockneys of Australian cities.

He put it down to what he called the Bad Water, which actually was very sweet stuff, filtered through the rocks, but lacked his native tang of chlorine and the rust of pipes. He carried on quite cheerfully, evidently well compensated by the joy of man-hunting. Constable Stunke, however, while apparently well enough, was not happy. A single day of being made a fool of by that voice which could come from anywhere and those tracks leading nowhere caused him to declare that the hunt, as they were conducting it, was waste of time and energy. 'You'll never get that slippery, yeller-haired, grey-eyed, little, black bastard without Dinny Cahoon and Jinbul,' was his verdict.

Whether the Inspector himself suffered even chagrin could not have been guessed at, so grimly set in his purpose did he remain always. He silenced Stunke at once by saying, 'Constable, you'll never get anywhere as a police officer by admitting that anyone else can do what you can't. You've got to make up your mind to get your man yourself . . . and, by God, get him!'

Meanwhile, he who was leading them the dance was acting in no way like the man Inspector Ballywick was sworn to get, which is to say like a human being. For much of the three days and even some of two nights the rocky wilderness had rung to his mournful crying: *Moomboo, moomboo, moomboooo! . . . Amerrna, amerrna, amerrna kumeri! . . . Where you go-oh-oh-oh-oh!* It could seem to come from right behind one, but when one turned to grab it, was half a mile away in another direction. Often distinct tracks of two pairs of feet, one small and bare, the other in smallish riding boots, led to where a voice was singing sweetly in female timbre, only to vanish completely when those who followed reckoned they were at the point to pounce. Inspector Ballywick was moved at the beginning to express admiration for the elusive one, saying that he must curry favour with the kid to learn how he did it. Later he spoke of braining the Pesky Little Bastard, although quite without anger in his tone.

As for the Pesky One, so bored with the game had he become by this afternoon as to fall asleep gorged on brush-tail cooked in an overhang of a cliff-face in which was a crevice to disperse the smoke in many directions blown by the rising westerly. The wind was wet, heralding *Mokorrnbo*, the last heavy rain of the season. It was not the kind of day when anyone but a complete *mungus* could be sneaked up on even from downwind, let alone across it. Yet, Sergeant Bugsby, with all his bulk, got right into the overhang, and would have got his man, but for breathing like a winded horse from the climb from the rocky ledge below.

Prindy was up and off like a brush-tail, to vanish into the crevice so swiftly that a more imaginative person than the Sergeant might have doubted if he had been there at all. The Sergeant's lack of imagination plus his bulk, useful as they might be to him as a policeman, proved his undoing in this odd chase. With a bellow that must have been heard half a mile away, he dashed after the seeming wraith, did not see the crevice that cut his path till too late to halt the momentum of so large a person, went down feet first, through jagged rocks, spiky timber debris, thorny scrub, thirty feet. Fortunately a good clip on the back of the head spared him from knowing anything much of the mess the precipituous descent had made of him. He was fortunate again in having bellowed as he did. Otherwise he might never have been found in such a place.

Such a place was it, that it was dark before his comrades reached him, having to traverse that tumble of rock which formed the ledge where the crevice ended, with another thirty-foot drop for anyone who missed his footing. It was Full Moon tonight, but of no advantage here under a cliff facing westward and the western sky inky. There was no moving Bugsby that night. His mates did what they could for him with bits of stick and rags of his ripped clothing. He had a left foot like a football, a right leg like a boomerang, bruises to the trunk that suggested anything might have happened beneath, and that bleeding emu's egg at the base of his skull. Yet actually he had it better than any of the others, at least for the time, since he must have the only bit of flat available to stretch out on, and wasn't troubled by the glare of Igulgul when he topped the cliff at midnight and hung so long there as if out of heartless curiosity, nor by the creature somewhere up top that kept up an unearthly laughing sound – Hoo-hoo-hoo-hoo-hoo! – a Laughing Owl so Stunke said, although without conviction in his voice and certainly without impressing either of his comrades, Tipperary who fairly cringed whenever it let loose, or Ballywick, who kept muttering that it was getting on his nerves. Then when the Moon dived into the black wave heaving up the western sky and the creature ceased laughing, it rained, heavy and cold. Sergeant Bugsby snored through it all.

In the murky morning light Prindy, watching from a cosy cave above, saw them go get saplings to make a carrying device for their mate and stuff from their camp of yesterday for breakfast. When they'd gone back to the crevice, he also paid a visit to their camp, and helped himself to a can of corned beef, a packet of biscuits, and a bottle of tomato sauce. He breakfasted in a spot where he could keep them in view. He watched them struggle with their burden along that terrible ledge, then lie down to rest when it was over. He watched them start off again, in a direction that showed they would be heading for their advanced base, the Turtle Hole Yard, in which region they'd left their hobbled horses, instead of for Corella Bore, which was much nearer and from where they could have got help quicker by someone's going on to Catfish Homestead. Evidently that was what he was waiting for. At once he rose and headed that way, too, but at a more acute angle to the straight line that would have taken them to their destination, had they been able to do anything like follow it. This gave him a direct heading for Lily Lagoons homestead. He set off at a lope. It would be a good day's walking for legs as short as those golden brown ones still were.

It began to rain again. When Prindy reached the flat below, he might have followed the road home without much fear of leaving tracks. Perhaps it was days of caution that kept him so. He kept to the bush, at least with the advantage of finding things to nibble on as he went: fruits, shoots, roots. Thus into the afternoon, by which time the rain had eased again to drizzle. He was coming up to the top gate when he heard a sound that caused him to swing in the direction he had come. It proved to be the thud of hooves. Soon into view came an oilskinned horseman, riding so hard that he had to pull his mount to haunches to stop him at the gate. It was Tracker Tipperary. Through the gate, he resumed the urgent pace.

The light was failing when Prindy reached the racetrack paddock and there heard another sound, ahead this time. The hum of a motor. He planted himself in long grass, to see the big truck belonging to Lily Lagoons go roaring by, flinging up a haze of yellow mud with its whirling skid-chains. Darcy was driving, with Tipperary as passenger.

The boy crossed the paddock to westward, and followed the fence on that side to the orchard, through which he went to where a concrete culvert drained from the homestead to the creek. Ankle deep in rushing water, he went up the culvert, and so came to the rear of the annexe. By way of the little stockyard there, he entered what constituted the animal hospital, the several stalls on the back verandah. With a sigh of accomplishment he halted here, removed his sodden khakis, and shivering, grabbed a horse-rug from a rail and wrapped himself in that. Thus attired, he went inside. The place was lit. He took a wary look into the clinic, which was empty, However, the sound of hawking was to be heard from the little ward adjoining. He went on to the master's den. The man himself was there, standing before his bookcase, a large book in hand. Prindy clicked his tongue.

Jeremy looked, startled for a moment by the odd shape. Then as the boy came in, he raised a finger and nodded towards the clinic. Putting the book down, he came to the boy, put an arm about his shoulders, and guided him along the passage to the room that was his whenever he chose to live in this part of the homestead. He didn't speak till they were inside with the door shut. Then he said. 'Hello! I was wondering if you might come in. Know what's happened?'

The damp fair head nodded. Jeremy removed the horse-rug. 'You're cold. Let's warm you up with a towelling, eh?' He went out, to return with a big bath-towel. Vigorously rubbing, Jeremy told of having Tracker Splinter in the ward, physically recovered, but otherwise in even worse condition than on arrival since hearing what had happened to Sergeant Bugsby: 'He's pretty badly hurt, eh? I'll have to do something for him, dog though he is. I'll try and get 'em off to the siding as soon as I can. They'll have to get a move on, anyway. The road'll go out again by the look of things. From the message I got, they'll have to get the Flying Fox down to him . . . on the train.' Finished the towelling, Jeremy said, 'You'd better stay put here for the time. They shouldn't be long turning up. I'll get supper sent over, and dry clothes. It's best they don't see you till everything's clear.'

Prindy asked, 'You been hear him?'

'About Rifkah? Not yet. I'm hoping to hear from Clancy. I've been listening-in on the radio skeds all day.'

Wrapping himself up in the towel, Prindy asked, 'She come on train, you reckon?'

Jeremy hesitated. 'I don't know about this week's train . . . but she'll be along sometime . . . don't worry.' He patted a small shoulder, went out.

When the truck came in it was quite dark and raining heavily. Jeremy waited in the rear door of the clinic, while the four oilskinned figures came with the stretcher on which the bulky tarp-covered figure lay. He gave no greeting. When they halted, he asked curtly, 'What would you be wanting?'

From under one of the sou'westers came the cold precise voice of the Inspector: 'I sent you a message, Sir.'

'I sent what you asked for.'

'My Sergeant's in a bad way.'

'All the more reason to keep going to the railway while you can. If it's urgent, you can get the doctor down by rail.'

'It is urgent, Sir. I'd like you to take a look at him, if you'd be so kind.'

'Why me?'

'You're skilled in such things.'

'You denied me the right to use my skill on that unfortunate girl you upset with your bullying. Besides . . . you're police . . . you must have had training in first aid.'

'You've got special equipment here . . . X-ray.'

'If you think I'm going to let you monkey with my X-ray . . . .'

Ballywick cleared his throat. 'I meant yourself, Sir . . . *if* you'll be so kind.'

'How dare you ask kindness of me . . . when through your callousness a frightened girl's suffering God knows what!'

The Inspector swallowed hard, said with difficulty, 'Come now, Sir . . . my Sergeant's been unconscious for more than twenty-four hours. My own limited knowledge tells me he could be at death's door. I intend to get him to a doctor as soon as possible . . . but, meantime, some skilled attention might well save his life.' The voice became hoarse: 'Surely you wouldn't be so vindictive as to put a man's life at risk?'

'Nor a woman's!' snapped Jeremy.

Silence, while all stared, and the covered burden snored. Jeremy broke it: 'I'll agree to give him such attention as I'm capable of . . . on one condition . . . .'

The hoarse voice broke in harshly: 'I'll make no bargains where my duty's concerned. The search for the wanted person will go on.'

Jeremy's voice became harsh, too. 'You stinking hypocrite . . . still sanctifying your bullying by calling it duty! I'm not striking a bargain. I used the word Condition.'

Ballywick drew a deep breath. 'Name your condition, Sir.'

'When preventing me from giving a sedative to that distraught girl you called me a Horse Doctor . . . . '

'No insult was intended. I was only informing you of the regulations in such a case.'

'Good. It's regulations *I* want to stick to now. I'm qualified only to treat animals and take a fee. You did say that you want to regulate any call you may have to make on my goods or services by proper requisition, didn't you?'

'I did.'

'Right. If you'll agree that I'm dealing with an animal in this case, I'll do what I can for him . . . as for any stricken animal.'

Even the rain on the roof and Bugsby's snoring seemed to be stilled in the next long moment. Scarcely able to get it out, Ballywick at length replied, 'To save the life of my officer, and friend . . . I agree.'

'Okay. Put him down and take off your coats and things. I won't have any more police arrogance in my house. Then bring him in.' Jeremy backed in, disappeared. He was back from his den with a sheaf of bluish forms to wave the party with the stretcher to place their burden on the operating table. Then he said to Ballywick. 'This's an official form for services rendered to a Government department . . . in triplicate, you see, in accordance with Government love of wasting paper. I'll require you to put your signature to it . . . and Constable Stunke to witness it.' Ballywick held out his hand for the fountain pen Jeremy took from his pocket. 'Wait,' added Jeremy. 'You'll observe that it says here *Species of Animal*. What're we going to put? You call yourselves Peace Officer, I understand. But that written would look even more ridiculous than it sounds. Besides, that mysterious boss of yours might want you to be more specific in identifying the creature, in case it looks like you're rigging the ex's. So, say . . . *Species of Animal*, a 'Sergeant of Secret Police. Answers to name of Bugsby' . . . that suit you? Then I'll write it in first . . . and you can sign.'

The Inspector's hand shook slightly as he signed, and his voice with it: 'As a police officer, dealing with people whose egotism makes them naturally hate the law, I've run into a lot of vindictive men in my time, Mr Delacy . . . but never one like you.'

Taking paper and pen to hand to Stunke, Jeremy answered, 'You have the advantage on me, Inspector. I've run into too many types like you . . . whose need for ascendancy over their fellows is what, in my opinion, is wrong with the law, with the world.' His face was dark with feeling, but his voice steady. He added when he got the paper back: 'I'll fill in the details later and give you your copy. One I'll send to . . . the Attorney-General's Department, I think you said . . . the other to the Press with the story of this poor hunted Jewish girl. And now, if you'll be so good, you can leave your man to me. You'll find quarters prepared for you in the harness-shed, with clean dry clothing, and food. It's of the kind I issue to my blacks, of course . . . but you'll find it all of good quality . . . as I'm sure Constable Stunke, who knows the usual quality well, will vouch. Goodnight.'

When the police were gone, Jeremy turned to look over Bugsby, saying to Darcy, 'Hmm . . . we've got a job on here, son. Take us all night, perhaps. That ankle's bad. Could be gangrenous already. Poor old Bugsby. Looks like your days as a paid bully are over. They won't want you chasing your fellow-men with an artificial foot.' He added: 'You'd better get a feed and some dry clothes, Darcy. I'll give him some sulpha, and get things ready in the meantime.'

For most of the night Jeremy and Darcy worked on the still-unconscious Bugsby. The fractures of femur and tibia were set and splinted, the pus and lymph drained from under the scalp, dried blood cleared from nasal passages, the football foot kept under constant fomentation, all to the effect that the Animal answering officially now to the name of Bugsby not only looked more comfortable, but sounded so with easier breathing.

Once they were interrupted in their quiet work by a strange sound within the building, faint above the steady roar of rain, like kweeluk-crying. Their eyes met. A groan was heard from the ward. That was not where the sound came from. Also, both knew the sound well, even if one of the hearers was surprised to hear it now, as shown by the rolling of his dark eyes in sweaty scarred yellow face. Jeremy murmured, 'Yes . . . Prindy's here. Came in at dusk. I'd better go and quiet him.'

It was the strained sweet sleep-singing, the song *My Rown Road*. Jeremy waited at the closed door, awaiting the opportunity to intrude into the magic of sleep in the proper way:

I follow, follow, follow, follow Rown Road
I find him by'n'by
Kill dat whiteman, kill him die
Dat my Road, my Road, my Proper Road
My Rown Road . . .

When the little voice trailed off, Jeremy said softly, 'Prindy, sonny.' Twice he repeated it. There came a sigh from within, faint sound of turning over. Jeremy waited a little longer, then with careful tread returned to the clinic. Thus into the small hours.

Jeremy was asleep in his bedroom and Darcy gone home and Nanago watching over the patient, when in the weeping dawn Inspector Ballywick, despite orders to await reports, called to see how things were with his Bugsby and also to say that when radio contact was made with Town he wished to make an official communication. Nanago told him that the first Radio Schedule would not be till eight and her husband not available before that time.

Ballywick was in the radio-room while Jeremy got through to Dr Fox. The procedure in such circumstances was for the AWA operator in Port Palmeston to act as intermediary between the parties in communication by means of the town telephone system. Thus he relayed back to Jeremy the information that Dr Fox would be leaving for Beatrice River by section-trolley as soon as he'd had breakfast. Before calling out, Jeremy read an ordinary Post Office message for delivery to Clancy, just a few words to say that he was waiting to hear from him. Then he handed headset and microphone over to the Inspector, but remained standing there, as the man had himself, despite a glance that clearly showed Ballywick would have preferred to be alone.

Inspector Ballywick called Police-Superintendent Bullco, giving a skimpy account of what had happened on his expedition, and requesting the assistance of certain officers whom he had been informed had special ability in tracking and also experience in dealing with the Aboriginal boy who was causing all the trouble, namely Sergeant Cahoon and his Tracker Jinbul. By the time it took, Bullco was being difficult, perhaps piqued by having something done over his head and now saying Told You So as nearly as it could be conveyed with official dignity through a third party who was not concerned. Anyway, the reply was that the required officers would be coming down on tomorrow's train.

As Jeremy ushered Ballywick out of the radio-room, he remarked that he would be sending the big truck in to the railway to pick up the doctor as soon as it could be got away, and asked if the Inspector wished to go in with it or send any of his men. Ballywick looked at him suspiciously, asking, 'Why should I?' Jeremy shrugged and replied that he was only considering the matter of loading.

In fact Jeremy was considering a great deal more than he said, as revealed as soon as the coast was clear and he was able to go to Prindy and tell him of the coming of his old enemies. He said, 'I think you'd best go in with Darcy. I won't send anybody else. No good you going back to the Sandstone. They'll be led a dance just the same. All we want is time. Let's hope we hear from Clancy to say we've got all we need. Go to Barbu. Tell him that if there's trouble over having you there, I'll get him out of it. Better make a start right away. You can get out without 'em seeing you, can't you. I'll keep nit for you. Wait down the road a bit . . . say on the bend where the big mangun is. I'll tell Darcy to stop for you there . . . if all's well. Just to be on the safe side, don't show yourself till he stops. Right?'

The fair head nodded. Jeremy pressed a small shoulder. 'See you by'n'by, then. *Mummuk yawarra,* and *mazzeltov*!'

Although it was only drizzling when Prindy slipped away from the homestead, he managed it without detection, even clad in oilskins. He hadn't long to wait at the plum tree. There was the waxing-waning drone of the motor soon to be caught by his sharp ears above the roar of rising waters eastward. But wax and wane though the motor did to the driver's negotiation of the slippery road, there was no hint of its slowing down in approaching the rendezvous, as expected. The contrary – it loomed out of the rain, came roaring to the bend, round it. The sharp eyes peeping from within a leafy bush would not have missed the identity of the passengers, Stunke up in front with Darcy, sick drooping Splinter standing clinging to the cab at the back.

Prindy stood till the sound was lost in the watery roar, then, with a sigh, set out to follow it. What meant another thirty miles to legs so well exercised of late as those golden brown ones fairly twinkling because of their wetness beneath the oilskin?

The rain set in again, as yesterday, to pour all day. He walked the road without caution, because it soon was a lot of little rivers filling little lakes that spilled away eastward to feed the monster that roared the more it was fed. When he came near the Rainbow Pool about noon he went in to take a look. There was nothing to see, only boiling mist, but everything to hear – the Voice, in the measured thunder of which all other sounds in the world sang. Prindy sang into it:

> *Tjeritju wijeru, wijeru agula,*
> *Alga agula, Numeriji ga!*
> *Look out you-lot,*
> *Old One proper koolah now.*
> *No-more Snake Man you,*
> *All right, you look out.*
> *Alga agula! Look out, look out, look out!*

He splashed on into the afternoon, nibbling when food was offered by unseen hands, taking his few spells always by the river, always by some bend where, perhaps, he could appraise its serpentine might, where he could feel its brown spittal shower him as it lifted one of its myriad yellow tongues.

It was darkening when the truck came roaring back, making heavy going of it by the look of the steaming radiator. Only Dr Fox aboard with Darcy. Across the Old One's heaving yellow back was to be glimpsed the fence of Beatrice Station's northern bullock paddock. That meant ten miles from the homestead. Good going for those small legs. But they'd had enough. He found one of those horizontally growing paperbarks with a burnt-out under-belly, poked its hollow gut with a stick to make sure he would have it to himself, then stripped off bark for bedding, and in the process got a handful of large white grubs for supper. He tossed in the bark, climbed in. The Voice was deep and muffled in there, with new over-tones. He sang himself to sleep – sang in his sleep: Follow, follow, follow my Rown Road.

The dawn was a silver mist, beyond which, invisible, the Old One bellowed like all the bullocks that had ever been lifted out of that great paddock in their season to die, with the note of resigned despair of that last bellow and of the bell of the Coacher who led them to the slaughter. Prindy went to look, found the Old One laughing, licking, down the road. *Alga agula, Numeriji ga*! he sang as he went on his way through ghost forest, where from round every unsubstantial trunk some sort of *Moomboo* peeped. But what should he fear, who could sing: No-more Snake Man you, all right you look out!

The mist lifted slowly with the Sun, till it was hanging only in rags in the distance by noon. He was back on the road by then, or rather walking beside it, just about where those *kuttabah* and their horses had tried to ride him down the last time he was round these parts on foot. To the Old One's thunderous accompaniment, as if recalling that event, he sang:

I find him by'n'by
Kill dat whiteman, kill him die
Dat my Road, my Rown Road!

He came to the Racecourse in watery sunshine, reconnoitred. No one was about, except half a dozen horses that from having a race of their own, probably in relief from having spent so long kicking and biting under rotten bush shelters, came to stare at him, odd little man coming out of nowhere when men were all tucked away! He went up into the grandstand, which offered the best viewpoint of the locality, chose the President's Box, surely only because it was the best of the best to suit his needs, not through any feeling of identifying himself with the dignified figure he was used to seeing sitting there surrounded by whisky bottles and field-glasses and other dignitaries with red faces and white suits – his sire according to the lore, if not the law exactly, of the *kuttabah*, since he was still humming to himself *My Rown Road*. No cane lounge-chairs here today. He lay on the floor, propping his head up on folded oilskins. Mostly, while his eyes were open, he gazed away northwestward, perhaps seeing in imagination the mail train pounding, squealing, screaming through the verdant watery wilderness, with one beloved head already hanging out in impatient anticipation of first glimpse of his, with its burnished copper flying in the wind. Yet even when, in his weariness, he dozed off, he kept his head cocked slightly to the left, listening to that sound which had become the background of his existence: the Voice of the Old One, more clamorous than ever here, raging against the arrogance of the *kuttabah* who had presumed to intrude upon the Dreamtime with a contraption he could roll into a bundle if he wished and bury to rust away back to the ochre the fool had got it from in the first place – the railway bridge.

The Sun was halfway down the sky when he woke startled out of dozing by a sound that ears only sharp as his own could have detected, and looked directly towards the straight dark line of the railway to be glimpsed through the straddle of trees beyond the Racecourse fence, to see the fettlers' trolley flickering on its way towards the bridge. He rose then, gathered up oilskins, went down and out, heading for the railway. Fortunately the horses came after him, to obliterate his tracks. Only going through the belt of weeds beside the railway embankment had he to be wary. For these were very thick, the first crop having been burnt off by the fettlers during the dry spell, only to produce a second more prolific and stinking in their alienness when the rain set in again. Sometimes the fettlers poisoned them, but without lasting success. It was only the native things, vegetable, animal, human, that succumbed to the *kuttabah's* bane.

He climbed the embankment, stood looking up the empty track for a while, then turned and headed for the bridge, his small feet feeling through steel rails and sleepers, the way he stood a couple of times and eyed them, the quiver of the bridge in fearful anticipation of the some-day inevitable. From here there was a magnificent view of the Old One raging round the bend from the vicinity of Beatrice Homestead, his raised hackles flashing golden in the sunlight. It was still better to look down from the concrete buttresses and see the great tongues licking the red piers, trying a lick for the rails, to see the whole thing shaking with dread – and better better still to hear the Voice, and sing with it: *Look out, him proper koolah . . . no-more Snake Man you . . . .*

He also kept looking for the train. There at last she was – a grey feather above the green. He went back well clear of the comparative growthlessness in the vicinity of the buttresses, to where the weeds were thickest, again on the Racecourse side, which was that from which passengers always looked to catch their first glimpse of the white roofs of the township, and planted himself.

The train came rumbling, wheezing, wary in approaching the bridge, since not in the hands to day of any brash young bravo, but in those of that old iron-war-horse, Jack Tinball, who boasted having saved his trains from many a broken bridge in peace and in war. Jack was hanging well out to get a good look at everything. In fact everybody was hanging out. There were black heads, white heads, grey heads, fair heads, even a ginger head or two – but not one of burnished copper. There were plenty of familiar faces – Uncle Clancy's, Gran'pa Ah Loy's – even one to which one would perhaps have liked to show one's own –Billy Brew's – and old Coon-Coon's and his mate Jinbul's. Both these latter were out on the platforms on their coaches – different platforms of necessity, in accordance with the rules, but adjoining. Coon-Coon's narrow blue eyes were ranging far, perhaps making an estimate of the conditions he'd have to reckon with on his man-hunt. The hidden black eyes of his fellow man-hunter, as to be expected of one whose part was to look for those tell-tale little things close at hand which his clever master would blunder over, perhaps caught by a glint of wet oilskin in the weeds, looked right into the grey eyes.

Jinbul hurled back the black crowd pressed about him, jerked open the little safety-gate, and yelling to his master, leapt. As the tan elastic-sides hit the soft gravel of the embankment, Prindy was up and off. Jinbul lost his hat and one boot. He was unconcerned. He kicked off the other boot, and leapt into his long-legged stride in pursuit of the quarry, scooting like a brush-tail, heading for the only avenue of escape, the raging river. The train rocked to the sudden excitement of the chase.

Oh, Master Snake . . . a Snake Man calls you in extremity . . . Deliver me from mine enemies . . . Nugunga, nugunga, I come . . . Your coils my refuge, Numeriji!

The yellow legs sent frothy spillage of the shallows flying in yellow spray. The small figure reached the deep, slid into it, vanished.

Jinbul tore off his policeman's shirt as he splashed through the shallows, was black to the waist when he dived.

Prindy came up to see the red girders above him and the score of faces peering through, was spun underneath and out, battled for control, looked back, saw the black face above the leaping golden water not ten yards behind. He dived. He came up again just about where the causeway was, close to the left bank because of the swing of the current there. He looked behind. The black face was gone. He swung round, striking out to get back to the wild race of mid-stream, to see the face pop up within a yard splitting with a grin at sight of him. Again he dived. But now it was into the clutches of what under water looked like a grey spider. He was yanked to the surface by the hair. Now the grin in the black face was so wide you could see the gaps in the white teeth made by the *kuttabah's* diet. He struggled, ready to leave his golden scalp behind. But the black claw holding it forced down his head, while the other clamped his hands behind and the spider's legs wrapped round him. The golden yellow of the water must have blazed to crimson before he fell limp in the spider's grip.

Jinbul jerked the fair head to the surface, took a look at glazed grey eyes and gaping bubbling mouth, then keeping only the grip on the hair, lashed out for the shore. They were just below the station. A laving tongue flung them against the pipe running up to the pump-house. Jinbul grabbed it, got his feet down, and with the pipe to help them, dragged his limp captive up and out of the water.

The train was rolling into the yards, with everybody hanging out this side now. Jinbul paid it no attention, but releasing the hair, let the head drop, to catch the legs behind the knees and lift the inert body so that the head hung, gave the whole a jerk, then clamped the midriff with his skinny khaki-clinging knees, released, clamped again, released, clamped. A gasp. A cough. Yellow water jetted from the hanging gaping mouth. He flung the body on the ground then, face down, jerked the head sideways, then straddling, pumped mightily on the skinny little ribs. A groan. A feeble attempt to scramble away. Jinbul let go the ribs to grab the hair again, to jerk the head up and look into the eyes again, wide and rolling now. He grinned again. 'Close-up dat Old One been gitchim you.' When the grey eyes blinked, he added: 'You Shade been come out from top you head. I been grab him, pushed him back . . . aaaaaaaah!'

Prindy struggled feebly in the grip of the hand on his hair, raised his own hands. Another hand grabbed them, twisted them behind, forcing him round to look towards the Station. Now the train was stopped, and a crowd coming leaping over the intervening rails, well out in front of them a tall figure in khaki. 'Look-see,' said Jinbul. 'Dere you old Daddy-o come. He got him prejent for you . . . aaaaaheeee!

Sergeant Cahoon was swinging a length of neck-chain.

Jinbul's wide grin faded as Coon-Coon drew near enough for the signs of his mood to be read – and who, in all the world could have read those signs better than he whose marvellous faculty for sign-reading had made him this man's slave? Cahoon had his tight eyes fixed on Prindy, but as he knelt before the boy, to lock the padded steel collar about the slender neck, spoke to Jinbul, with a sound of terrible menace in the harsh so-masculine voice: 'Spone you been bugger-up this boy, you black bastard, I'll shoot you!'

Jinbul, releasing his grip on the fair hair, muttered, 'Him all right, Boss.'

'He'd bloody-well better be!'

Jinbul withdrew slightly as the long hands moved upward from the collar, as if expecting to be struck. However, the hands, one holding the clinking chain, only came up to touch the yellow cheeks. Looking into the wide grey eyes, Cahoon asked in a voice strangely gentle now for all the harshness of tone, 'You all right, Sonny Boy?'

The grey eyes only blinked. Cahoon touched the still-streaming brow with the back of a hand, remarking, as if generally to those pressing around, 'Injury of the brain can be caused be bein' half drowned. Good job that doctor's round.' With that he reached for a back pocket, withdrew handcuffs of the ratchet type, one cuff of which he fastened to his own left wrist, the other to the chain. Then, stretching out his long arms with their stripes of rank, he took the boy in them, sopping as he was, rose with him, turned and pressed through the crowd, snapping in a policeman's voice, 'Make way!'

All fell back quickly except one, tubby and white-bearded, Billy Brew, who evidently rather drunk, defied him: 'What you doin't that kid on chain?'

Dinny shouldered him out of the way, growling, 'Put you on, you not careful.'

Billy made a grab at the striped sleeve. 'Le' him go! You know you got no right . . . . '

Constable Stunke laid hands on Billy, shot him into the gaping crowd, who held him up from falling and restrained him when he would have returned to the fray. He yelled, 'Ain't none you bastards goin' do nothin' 'bout it?

'Go easy, Billy,' someone said.

Someone else said, 'They'll only yard yo'.'

Billy bawled after the retreating policemen, 'Yard me, you khaki bastards . . . yard me . . . an' I'll tell yo' all night wha' stinkin' rotten bloody dirty bullyin' puggin bastards y'are! Where's Jeremy Delacy? Jerry, Jerry . . . look't what they doin' our golden boy!'

Meanwhile the police reached their utility. Cahoon got in front, hugging his burden, all but crooning over him now, saying how cold he was, but soon would be warm as toast, how skinny he was, but soon would be fed by his Daddy-o till fair bustin': 'You goin' 'o be my lil boy from now on, y'know . . . . '

As they drove to the Police Station, Stunke asked, his tone dry-sounding, 'What about the Jew-girl, Dinny?'

Cahoon answered, not even half interested, it was evident, as if already he'd been pressed about the matter, 'Go and see if she's over there if you want 'o . . . but I'll bet she's not. Anyway, you can get the horses yarded. I want to get away as soon as possible, get Foxy take a look at this boy. He's cold as charity. You got brandy?'

In fact Prindy was shaking now.

Mrs Stunke, by her tight mouth and hooded eyes, didn't like the idea of having what privily she described to her husband as a Boong Brat towelled with one of her best bath-towels, rigged out in some of her son's best clothes, fed on bread-and-milk and egg-nog she had to prepare and for which there could be no hope of reimbursement since nothing of the like was listed as Aboriginal Rations; all while having to listen to the yap of this madman who was her husband's superior officer about how he'd got permission from the new Director of Aboriginal Affairs, Professor St Clair, to adopt the brat. She sniggered a little, hearing of all the wonderful things Sonny Boy and his Daddy-o were going to do when Daddy-o got his leave next month and they took a trip down South together. Perhaps the snicker was due to the incongruity of such paternalism while father and son remained attached by a police-chain and the latter hadn't a single word to say. She also had to suffer them at her dining table, as yet never debased by having any but a white face sitting at it, and again in her lounge-room, where, of necessity, the pair sat in her biggest and best lounge-chair, listening to the radio. Finally, there was the humiliation of having to make up the double-bed in the guest-room for the Siamese Twins, as rather bitterly she called them in a last word to her husband.

Next morning, soon after early breakfast, Mrs Stunke got what was almost a genuine laugh out of it, on seeing her Siamese Twins go to the dunny together.

There were to be only three in the party riding out to Lily Lagoons. Constable Stunke took them only so far as the Railway Station to board Tom Toohey's trolley for the run across the bridge. Poor timid Tom! He was at such pains to avoid the grey eyes that were surely begging some question of him. Even as they parted, when he put them down at just about the point where yesterday's chase had begun, he would not meet the eyes, when squinting along a rail as if looking for faults in its alignment, he said, 'Everything'll turn out all right, sonny . . . you'll see.'

With the horses ready, it took no time to get on the way. Again a misty morning. Still shackled together, but with a yard or so of extra chain to facilitate horsemanship, Prindy and his Daddy-o rode in front, while Jinbul, as if in perpetual disgrace for having done the only thing possible in his way of duty and actually with great skill, brought up so well in the rear with the pack-horse as most of the time to be invisible. For several hours you could feel the Sun if not see it. The rain was finished. 'But listen to that old river!' as Coon-Coon said. 'Must'a' been a lot o' rain up where you and them Southern coppers were. Bet they was glad of the excuse of that feller Buggery's hurtin' himself to chuck it up. They're all right chasin' burglars and molls, them blokes . . . but put 'em in the bush, they're rooted. Silly bastards to think they could get anywhere near a brumby-colt like you . . . aheeeeyay!'

Prindy responded readily enough to the merriment – as any black-fellow will, when he finds the boss in a merry mood.

As they rode along, speaking of policemen, Coon-Coon remarked that he would be getting his Inspectorship when he came back from leave, the Boss having as good as promised it, if he brought this job off and taught them Federal Flatfoots a lesson for shovin' their beaks into other people's business. He went on to explain rank as it concerned policemen, an important thing for Sonny Boy to know, since he would be a policeman himself one day – could easily become the best officer the country had ever seen, what with his inheritance and experience and the fact that his tutor would be the best so far: 'Y'know, you got 'o 'a' be a bit of a law-breaker yourself to understand the law-breaker and deal with him effectively. When I was growin' up I was a bit of a larrikin. Used to drive me poor old sisters nearly jitty with the things I used to get up to . . . with mobs, o' course . . . the young law-breaker always belongs to mobs, unless he's partic'ly dangerous, and then he's not just a law-breaker but an outlaw, a very different thing.' Coon-Coon looked at his Sonny Boy. 'I could'a' been an outlaw . . . in the old days . . . like Ned Kelly, and Starlight. Given a chance, that type can lead. You're like that. But not them rats o' Tooheys. They're just law-breakers.' He went on: 'My sisters were scared stiff me gettin' into Reformatory. I nearly did once. But policemen know their types. They put the others away, but showed me which side the law it pays to be on. Ned Kelly could'a' been the greatest trooper in the country . . . like I am, Dinny Cahoon. You know about Ned Kelly? Well, I'll have to tell you . . . '

Prindy was very interested. Even if he mostly answered with gestures and monosyllables, his grey eyes showed his interest. It seemed as if he were seeing his Daddy-o Coon-Coon differently. It couldn't have been simply that Daddy-o was being especially pleasant, because he had often tried to be like that before. Whereas formerly Prindy had been always wary, he seemed even inquisitive.

Cahoon had been talking about Jews last night with the Stunkes, while listening to the radio. Sheeny Bastards Cahoon had called them. Stunke had said they deserved all they were getting from Hitler now for what they had done to Germany after the Great War. Now Coon-Coon brought up the Jews again: 'No-good bastards, them Jews, Sonny Boy. I must say I got a big surprise when I heard you'd run away with that Jew-girl. All right with your mother, o' course . . . God rest her soul! That was natural. But this Jew-piece was only using you . . . like they use everybody. They're tryin' to take over our country . . . for the Commos.' He paused, to look seriously at the boy. 'O' course you know they killed our Blessed Saviour. Yeah . . . they murdered our Lord Jesus Christ.' The staring grey eyes then popped to see Daddy-o whack himself in the chest with a manacled fist. Noting the wonder, Daddy-o explained: 'You've always got to strike yourself when you speak of the Blessed Lord. You'll learn all about it. You'll be goin' to a great Catholic college someday, for the sons of the Catholic gentry. But, o' course, we got 'o gitchim that Jew-girl first. Now, how 'bout a song . . . *Danny Boy*, eh?

They sang many songs, solo as well as in chorus. Daddy-o was pleased to hear some of Sonny Boy's own, declaring that he would buy him a violin, since that was the instrument he himself liked best: 'Gets to your very heart-strings, a violin.'

So they went on, following up the roaring river, but seeing little of it, making good going despite the heavy ground, since, in accordance with good police practice, they didn't have to spare the horses.

They looked in at the Rainbow Pool. A rainbow hung in the mist today, the real one, circular, just like a great snake-eye, always to be found there at the end of Wet Season. Prindy gazed with obvious reverence, perhaps not hearing his Daddy-o's confession that he himself had bathed there and done so out of sheer superstition: 'I was in a bit o' strife at the time. They were tryin' to get rid o' me . . . after all I'd done for 'em in the Twenty-eight riots. I reckoned I'd beat 'em, accordin' to the old superstition that if you take a dip here you're here for keeps. Well, I am y'see . . . me'n me Sonny Boy!'

At Lily Lagoons the alarm was sounded as usual, but without the usual active response. Invested already, as the Keep was, no point was there in going into bolt-holes. Besides, as it was known already that Coon-Coon was on the way, those with cause to fear him more than just fear of the man himself were gone. Nevertheless, a wary peeping. Then that familiar gasp sounded, in its strange breathed-yet-seemingly-shouted way: 'Eh, look out!'

As the cavalcade was passing through, heading for the mango grove, through which Inspector Ballywick and Tracker Tipperary were coming to meet it, Jeremy emerged from the annexe. He stood gaping in obvious surprise. Cahoon grinned across at him, waved a manacled hand, bawled, 'Day, Boss!' went riding on.

Then Jeremy came striding, loping, demanding harshly as he came up, 'Here . . . what's this?' His grey eyes shot from the narrow slits looking down at him with amusement, to those other so much like his own and now wide with inquiry, and back to the slits.

Evidently it was just the way Dinny had wanted it and anticipated. His horse had stopped, as well-trained beasts of their kind will, knowing that their masters like to meet and chat. But Dinny kicked it on, glancing back with the grin, to ask, 'What's what, Boss?'

Jeremy shouted, 'This boy on the chain!'

'That's all't's worryin' you, eh? Come on . . . giddap!' Cahoon had his eyes on his colleagues now waiting at the edge of the grove, at what might have been a line of demarcation.

Jeremy, red and panting now, keeping pace with the horse, declared, 'It's going to worry you, if you don't take him off right now.'

Without turning, Dinny answered, 'Well, that'll be my worry, won't it.' Then he spoke to Ballywick, 'Inspector Ballywick, I presume.'

'Are you going to take that boy off the chain?' roared Jeremy.

Dinny introduced himself to the Inspector, who stepped up to take his down-reaching hand. 'Glad you could come,' said Ballywick, but out of the corner of his mouth, and with policeman's glances darting at all concerned.

'Always on the spot where the law's to be upheld,' said Dinny, dismounting. He turned to his shackled mate, raising his hands to lift him down. But Prindy, with eyes on his grandfather, slid down himself.

Jeremy got in front of the chained pair, grinding in his speech now. 'If you're so concerned with the law, Sergeant . . . what've you got that boy on the chain for, when you know it's against the law?'

Dinny grinned at him to the limit of the elasticity of his wide mouth. 'Show me it in the Statute Book, Boss.' He turned back to the staring Ballywick. 'Well, Inspector . . . I've got the first and most important of the party you're lookin' for. Without him, the other's practically in the bag.'

'Congratulations, Sergeant. You've really done a marvellous job . . . .'

Jeremy broke in, shouting, 'You must be mad, Cahoon, after all the trouble you've been in through chaining children . . . .'

Completely ignoring him, Cahoon went on talking to Ballywick: 'But I want you to understand you can't charge the boy with anything. He's only been used. He's officially in my care . . . and stops in it. That clear, Sir?'

Ballywick eyed him shrewdly for a moment, then nodded. 'So long's I get the woman.'

'I'll have her for you tomorrow.'

Jeremy, breathing heavily, spoke to Prindy, who was still questioning him with his eyes: 'It's all right, sonny. I'll get you out of it. I'll get you out of it. I'll radio Town right away . . . .' He was about to lay a hand on the boy's shoulder, when it was jerked by the chain out of his reach.

Cahoon snapped, in the official tone now, 'No talking to prisoners.' Then he addressed Ballywick: 'There's a doctor here to see your man that's injured. I want him to take a look at the boy.'

'He's over with my Sergeant.' Ballywick nodded towards the annexe.

Cahoon snapped at Tipperary, 'Go'n' tell the doctor I want him, boy.'

Jeremy demanded, 'What's wrong with the boy?'

Cahoon spoke to Ballywick: 'I presume that in accordance with the famous hospitality of this here place, you're campin' in the harness-shed?'

Ballywick answered with official crispness, 'That is correct.'

'Okay . . . well, let's adjourn to our quarters. Go'n, boy . . . go and get Dr Fox, before I boot you up the bloody black arse!'

Casting a sidelong glance at Jeremy, Tipperary trotted away. Jeremy didn't look at him, was eyeing Prindy, whom he asked, 'What's wrong with you, sonny?'

That long-sought question of the grey eyes was voiced now: 'You been hear him?'

Jeremy blinked before the intense stare, swallowed before he could answer, 'No . . . not yet.'

The expression of the stare changed to blankness, as if the man before him had suddenly ceased to exist, so that it was with obvious indifference that he turned away when the chain was jerked again and the official snap repeated, 'I said no talking to prisoners!'

The policemen and Prindy set out for the harness-shed, while Jinbul, all but riding Jeremy down, took charge of the horses. Jeremy dodged clear, to find Dr Fox approaching. 'What's up?' asked Fox.

'Cahoon wants you to look at the boy.'

'What boy?'

Jeremy swallowed on it. 'My grandson. He's got him on the chain again.'

Fox whistled, then went on after the retreating group. Jeremy went, with what looked like faltering in his steps, back to the annexe, through to the radio-room.

Dr Fox was back well before Jeremy could do any radio-calling. He reported that there appeared to be nothing wrong with Prindy. Evidently he was being well treated, and content. He related what Cahoon had told him of the boy's arrest, which sounded rather like a piece of rashness in which kindly policemen had intervened to the great good fortune of the rash one. It seemed that the boy was on the chain simply to prevent him from doing something similarly rash again. As to making an official protest, it would be useless, because Dinny had written authority from Professor St Clair, assigning him complete guardianship of the boy. Jeremy said nothing, simply stared at the doctor to begin with, perhaps because he sounded very much like another policeman sticking up for a colleague, then dropped his eyes. Fox concluded: 'Ballywick asked if he could come over and sit with his man, now there's no hope for him. I told him I didn't think you'd mind.' Jeremy looked up at that, to meet the doctor's doubtful gaze, then nodded, and with a sigh turned and went off to his den. He found Nan awaiting him.

At dusk Nan herself went with food and clothing for Prindy. She came back to report to Jeremy, who was sitting, hunched, in his den: 'He all right. On'y too quiet. Like before . . . when he first come. Coon-Coon reckon he going to adopt him. Got it all fix up. What you going to do 'bout dat?'

Jeremy shook his head. 'I just don't know what to do about anything at the moment. He's rejected us, I'm afraid . . . me, anyway. I couldn't help Rifkah . . . and stopped him, when he thought he could. Now I can't do anything even to help him.'

'Come for dinner.'

'No, thanks. I just couldn't stand Fox . . . with his know-all doctor's manner. Hitler might be a certifiable lunatic . . . but why didn't the German doctors, the best mental specialists in the world, certify him while they had the chance, instead of running away from him? Why doesn't Fox certify Cahoon? Tell him I don't like leaving Bugsby till he can get back.'

'Bugsby going to die, eh?'

'Fox says he'll die tonight.'

Nan clicked her tongue in sympathy. Jeremy added: 'Yes, there's a sad side to it. Ballywick tells me he has five young children, the eldest just entered university to do law . . . and he's very much attached to them. Ballywick's almost crying. It's just too much of a bloody puzzle . . . their humanness and inhumanity all mixed up together.' He sighed into cupped hands.

Her slim dark hand touched his thick grey hair lightly. 'I send you over dinner.'

'Only a little bit. I'm not hungry.' As the hand withdrew he caught it, squeezed it. The dark eyes flashed a smile at him. Then she was gone.

Sergeant Bugsby died in the early hours of Friday, while Igulgul was taking a lopsided look at him through a window. Igulgul had every right to be in it, since according to some, the phenomenon of death was initiated by him, only he reserved the right to resurrection – that is, of course, until Jesus Christ came along.

Bugsby's dying was simple business, as should be for one whose Shade had virtually left him some five days before, at that moment of his sighting and trying to apprehend what someone less sterilized by civilization of the marvel of imagination might well have left alone. He relinquished his slight hold on it with a shuddering sigh, as of resignation, conceding that the Unknowable had won. His eyes, so long shut tight, opened, just a little, but enough to seem by their stare to be trying to tell his superior officier something. Inspector Ballywick was alone with him at the time. He went to rouse the doctor, since death is an official thing, unless concerned with animals or blacks. Left alone again with the remains of him he'd described as friend and comrade, he answered what he must have supposed was the message of the eyes, as gently he closed them with finger-tips, saying huskily, 'All right, Bill, old feller . . . I'll see they're looked after.' He then put his hand on the waxen brow, leaving it there for a moment, as if in court and swearing as so often he must have, even if slanting things somewhat to see that Justice was served, to Tell the Truth, the Whole Truth, and Nothing but the Truth, So Help Me God!

Over at the harness-shed, the Inspector found his fellow-residents there already astir, packing up by the light of a hurricane lantern. Cahoon, still linked to his bed-mate, looked up from what he was doing. 'How's your mate?'

'Dead,' Ballywick said flatly, then added, as if to confirm it to himself: 'Yes . . . poor old Bill's dead.'

'Bad luck!'

'Yes . . . he was a good officer.'

Cahoon resumed his packing. After a little silence, during which Ballywick stood blankly watching the others, Dinny asked, 'Will you be coming with us, now? We want to get away as soon as possible.'

Ballywick cleared his throat: 'Er . . . no, I don't think so. As you said, it isn't really necessary . . . and I . . . want to bury Bill.' He swallowed on the last of it.

'Where you goin' to bury him?'

'Certainly not at this place. I only wish I could get him away somewhere he'd have a proper funeral . . . police honours. He's been a police officer since he was twenty-one.'

'Pity you couldn't'a' got him to Town. If the road'd been right you could'a caught this mornin's train. But you'd have to take a dray . . . and that'd take all day . . . Corpses go off here pretty quick.'

Ballywick swallowed on that. 'There's a cemetery at Beatrice River township?'

'Yeah . . . quite a nice one . . . War Memorial and all. You could prob'ly make a bit of a police show out of it, too, by getting the officers down from the Caroline and up from the Charlotte . . . fettlers' trolley . . . and there's Herb Stunke, o' course.'

'Yes . . . I'll do something like that. Old Bill'd'a' liked it.' Ballywick's voice became husky: 'Always said he wanted to die with his boots on, doing the job . . . and have the boys take a noggin or two farewelling him . . . .'

Dinny came to the rescue: 'That's how I'd like it meself.' Then he said, 'Well, we'd better be seeing about a bite of breakfast. You, Tipperary . . . over the Big House.' As the tracker went, Dinny said, 'I'll leave that boong with you, Inspector. He's not much use to us. He's got the wind up about devils and things now. The Big Brain here,' he jerked his head towards Jinbul, 'told him that Splinter's dyin', too. When they get like that they're worse'n useless. But he may be some use to you . . . save you lowerin' yourself askin' for help off his Nibs across the way. I guess you'd rather be independent.'

'You're right. I hold Delacy largely responsible for the whole thing . . . along with this one here.' Ballywick nodded at Prindy.

Cahoon bridled at that. 'Eh, go easy! He's only a kid. He was used, as I said.'

Ballywick, staring at Prindy, who was as boldly staring at him, drew a deep breath: 'He's something more than a kid as I see him. You can have him as far as I'm concerned, Sergeant . . . and good luck to you!' With that he turned away sharply, went out, to stand staring at the marvel of the dawn; or perhaps more truly at what surely would have attracted his attention more, the shadowy figures of a man and a horse running side by side round the distant race track.

II

So confident was Sergeant Cahoon of a quick capture, that he was taking along with his small party, comprising himself, his Sonny Boy, his Man Friday, a spare horse for the captive. As he said to Sonny Boy when they set out, 'Can't have her tailin' along behind like a black gin . . . pretty girl like that, even if she is a Jew.'

He had every reason to be confident. First of all he was the complete egotist, lacking that faculty which makes the more humble warier of the likely opposition of chance. Then again, he supposed he had a fair idea of where his quarry was laying up, from having, in his own shrewd way, quizzed the only one who knew. Why should the boy lie to him, when the Jew-woman could mean nothing to him while himself everything. 'A lousy Commo Jewess,' he said. 'Y'ought'o see what they got about her in that paper Alfie Candlemas runs now!'

Anyway, from the bits that Sonny Boy had given away, it was plain that the Yiddisher Piece was over in the Limestone, not in the Sandstone, as these Federal Mugs had been led to believe, in one of those caves, maybe the same one, where they had taken Cock-Eye Bob that time. Thus did he deliver himself privily to his Man Friday, concluding: 'Smart little bastard, y'know. No chance leavin' tracks in the Limestone in weather like they been havin' down this way. He's goin' 'o put you out o' business as Number-one Tracker one these fine days . . . you know that, boy?'

Jinbul readily agreed to everything his master said. That was only the *kuttabah's* due from a blackfellow. Or so it might seem to the *kuttabah.* Perhaps from a blackfellow's point of view it was only what any fool might expect from someone he didn't know. To the blackfellow, what others would condemn as treachery would be considered only the due of whoever was *mungus* enough to be taken in. What's wrong with approaching an enemy with a smile and a spear in your toes with which to kill him? If he's smart enough he'll have one, too, and beat you to the throw. What's wrong with sending a pretty *kweeai* to distract the *kuttabah* who's despoiling your country and intimidating you with a rifle, then while he's in the clip, shoving a spear up his bobbing *loonga*? It was wrong enough for the blackfellow to earn the arsenic-spiced gift of flour from those who condemned such ways, the poisoned water-hole, the punitive expedition that shot the tribe out to the last piccaninny. But did he ever complain? No, he just took it as part of the dangerous game he called *Muddrin' Bijnitch,* a normal diversion of humankind, if not generally admitted; took it till at last he saw he could not win against the *kuttabah,* and either kept out of his way as much as possible, or if inclined to keep on with the game, joined him in it like Jinbul and his ilk, or if madmen like Bobwirridirridi, play it to extermination. That was all understandable to blacks and whites who knew each other as much as it is possible to know. But what of that odd creature, for whose existence there was no more explanation according to the blackman's logic (and who would believe a whiteman?) than for such monstrosities as twins, pigs, buffaloes – the Yeller Feller? Some said he was part whiteman. No true blackfellow ever said that. To such he was a Bloody Nutching . . . Brrrp!

All Yeller Fellers? What of this kid who had been adopted by the cleverest *koornung* in the land. Could you wipe him off as Bloody Nutching? There seemed to be doubt about it in the mind of Jinbul, judging by the way he revealed himself to his master as they went their way to this supposedly so easy capture that the master was talking of being back to go to Bugsby's funeral. He made bold to warn his master to look out for tricks.

When they came to that wide expanse of water, the merging of all the streams flowing from out of the Limestone and Sandstone Country, into the vast tide-like sweep towards the Rainbow Pool, Jinbul reminded Coon-Coon that it was in crossing here that Bobwirridirridi had tried that trick which might have drowned some of them. Prindy had led them to the crossing, the easiest means of reaching the limestone caves, the long shelf of marble above which were the treacherous shallows and below the murderous deeps, but itself completely safe, as distinctly delineated as a weir – unless someone tried tricks. Coon-Coon only scoffed at first: 'But old Cock-Eye Bob didn't get away with it, did he?'

Going any other way meant a long journey round the back. Coon-Coon continued to scoff a bit: 'Spone you fright' that Old Snake, boy, you can go round behind . . . we see you next week . . . or you can go back and shit yo'self long o' Tipperary.'

Jinbul said quietly, 'I no-more fright', Boss. You know I no-more fright' nutching. I no-more trust him young-feller, da's all.'

'What's he goin' 'o do?' Coon-Coon asked it with a grin of the Young Feller himself, who was listening intently.

'Might-be he pull him off'n horse.'

Cahoon chuckled, 'A bloke that size!' Then he asked Prindy, 'You thinkin' o' tryin' 'o pull your ol' Daddy-o into the drink?'

Prindy smiled back at him. Daddy-o stared at him with the slits for a while, then said, grinning broader, 'Well, there's nothin' like makin' certain, is there.' He turned to Jinbul. 'Right . . . get out another length of chain and cuffs . . . and we'll hook him up between us.'

There was much less mist this morning; at least hereabouts, where the atmosphere was warmer. Down towards the Rainbow Pool it was well enough blanketed. Here it was only in rags, ripped out of pockets by the racing water, touched by the rising Sun into shreds of rainbow that went swirling away, no doubt to build the solid rainbow of the Pool. Jinbul, dismounting to do his master's bidding, looked away towards the Pool, warily, it seemed. Not that there was anything sinister about the scene. The sound of the water was like laughter, in which was faintly mingled music, which was the carolling of butcher-birds somewhere back amidst the limestone masses.

Getting the things from his saddle-bag, Jinbul locked the length of chain to Prindy's collar, to do so hauling the boy's head down quite urgently, and locked a handcuff to the other end. He was about to lock the other cuff onto his slim black wrist, when Cahoon snapped, 'Onto your ankle . . . and round the stirrup, too.' He leered at Prindy, adding: 'See'f he's smart enough Snake Man to pull a horse over.' Prindy smiled back at him.

Jinbul did as told when he was mounted again, cuffing his skinny right shin to the stirrup-leather. The horse objected to begin with, because the length of sawtooth ratchet left over was raking its flank like a spur. Jinbul had to pull it round so that it raked his moleskin-clad leg.

'Right!' said Coon-Coon when all was set. He rode ahead, with Prindy behind him, Jinbul behind again, each separated by the regulation length of chain, which would be about a dozen feet, or two fathoms, as chain-measurement is properly designated and which was appropriate since they were embarking on what might be called an acquatic venture. The spare horse, carrying the little gear they'd brought along, came last, on a lead lashed to Jinbul's saddle.

They went splashing in to make the crossing. It was never deeper than to the horses' knees and mostly not much more than hock-deep, even though the strangely irridescent limey water swept over the ledge with the same smooth strength everywhere. Here was practically no rough, the rock mass having been worn smooth as a weir by the wash of ages. No trees at all on the crossing. There were biggish trees upstream a bit, but down only the permanently dwarfed and hump-backed things, just now but shivery islands of foliage. Immediately over the ledge the water was not so deep, as could be seen by the swirling weeds there and whiskery masses of moss. The deep was over another ledge.

It was out about the middle that the Pookarakka, that time while crossing slung broken-legged on a pole, had tried to do his famous disappearing trick again. Here the water was knee-deep. They reached it. Was it the fact that the horse Prindy now was riding had taken part in that event which caused it to play-up now? Whatever it was, the beast's rearing jerked Coon-Coon's manacled hand and startled *his* horse, causing him to yell above the watery din, 'Hey . . . what's goin' on?' He swung round, to see Prindy sliding out of his saddle on the off-side, that is the down-stream side, the right. He wheeled his horse round, to the left, the only way he could. That slacked the chain. Prindy took a flying leap over the ledge. He probably wouldn't have heard Coon-Coon yell, 'You treacherous little bastard!' With both chains tautening, what began as a dive ended with a gutser. He went down. But almost on the instant, Coon-Coon, taking a grip on his end of the chain, jerked him up again, this time so that he floated on his back.

'Haul him in!' Cahoon bawled at Jinbul.

Jinbul had to lean well over to reach his chain. As he did so, Prindy grabbed his end of the chain, jerked. Jinbul, already almost overbalanced, came flying out of the saddle. His startled horse reared, slipped, could not recover its footing, since shackled to its rider, fell on its side, with helpless Jinbul half under it.

Cahoon, fairly screaming now, moved back to lend a hand. 'You bloody little bastard . . . I'll belt Christ out of you for this!'

The Little Bastard was only a small yellow face with wide grey staring eyes. What with the pouring water and the dragging weight downstream, the fallen horse hadn't a hope of rising, especially with the led-horse performing behind.

Cahoon went first to the led-horse, slipped the clip of the lead-rope, then swung back, yelling at Jinbul, who was lying on his back, flapping the water to keep his head up, 'Pull your foot out, *mungus*, and slip the stirrup-leather off the catch-bar.'

The stirrup-leather was only semi-attached, for the very purpose of easy release of a rider pinned by his fallen horse. However, it meant being able to bend sufficiently to slip a hand under the saddle. Jinbul, looking strangely grey of dusky face, only kept beating the water with his hands, calling back to his master, 'Break him my artch-bone, I stink, Boss . . . .'

He had to say it a couple of times before Coon-Coon heard, when he howled, 'Jesus bloody Christ!' and this without any of that breast-striking.

Coon-Coon dismounted, leapt off the ledge, braving the fallen beast's thrashing hoofs, flung himself on its belly, tore up the saddle-flap, snatched at the girth-buckles. The horse went mad again with release of the pressure of the girth, tried to rise. Coon-Coon stilled it with a boot in the guts. He had yet to free the surcingle. He was a bit slower with this, bawling curses over the strap. Then the surcingle gave. Pressure of water against the upraised flap and the pull of Jinbul beyond, tore the saddle away. Jinbul went with it, and Prindy ahead of it, all with a jerk that pulled Coon-Coon over the horse's slippery wet body and after them all.

It was all so swift. There in a moment were they all, out in smooth shining water, riding the long swell of it, past the hunchback trees that bobbed to them as if in deference, while they looked back in astonishment at the distance-dwarfing horses that stared as astonished at them.

Strangely quiet out there, the only sound a sort of continuous hissing, but beyond it somewhere a growing roar. Perhaps it was this that roused Coon-Coon from what appeared to be a stupor of unbelief. He yelled at his Man Friday, 'Get the chain round a tree!' Several biggish ones were coming up. He himself struck out across the current, to make sure of their being caught. But Jinbul, the grey-faced, accepting the inevitable, had sunken eyes only for what lay further ahead, a dark line, like a thin lip, and instead of striking oppositely, went drifting after. So they missed the tree, all of the trees. Cursing, Coon-Coon saw the staring, not only of the black eyes but the grey, and turned to look. Plainly it was a lip, quivering as if with suppressed laughter over the presumption of little men who thought they themselves so powerful, over the retribution always the due of traitors. But blind as he must ever be to the realities of the Unknowable, he saw it as a rock, and screamed 'A rock, a rock . . . let's get to each side of it . . . swim, man, swim!'

No need to swim. As the lip opened to reveal the maw, those on the extremities of the chain were swept around as if sucked from both sides, leaving the chosen one, the mid-link of this magic chain, to fetch up against what for a fact was a shelf of rock even if serving as a laughing lip.

Prindy, slammed up against the lip, looking over it, saw it all. So near were they, the wanted ones, measured by man's reckoning, a couple of fathoms, plus a half for that outstretched three-striped arm and a bit more for the leg with its whipping saddle attached – and yet as far as Eternity, as could be seen by the agony of death in those eyes, blue and black, gazing up at him in the long, long, little moment it took for their engulfment.

No, they were not gone clean away. There were their Shades hovering.

The maw was like the throat of a flower, shining with light, to trap unwary creatures – like *Gwangu*, the Fly-catcher. The Shades hovered down inside like insects digesting in the false nectar that had trapped them.

The Sun rose up and up.

The water was falling.

Bits of the sugary marble peeped.

The sky was vivid blue, with white clouds sailing.

A straw-necked ibis came sailing along from where the flooded billabongs would be, saw, croaked with alarm, turned and went flapping back. A flight of white cockies, heading down from the Sandstone glimpsed, shrieked, wheeled and went screaming away eastward towards Catfish.

The Sun climbed up. The water fell.

Suddenly the chain on the right hand slackened. That meant being jerked sideways, dragged along the slippery rock a little way to the left, till the taut chain jammed in a crevice. It could be seen, silvery in the green whiskers. Now there was only one ghost below.

It was a long while before Prindy dared to haul in to see which it was had left him. It would have been that of the late Tracker Jinbul, because the handcuff was fairly wide open and a rag of moleskin hung on the saw-tooth projection like bait on a hook from which a fish has broken free.

How long would Daddy-o Cahoon's Shade be in taking itself off? Where would it go to? He might be right with his Old Jesus, but what about Old Tchamala, and Old God, who it seemed was a Jew – and Coon-Coon called Jews Sheeny Bastards?

What were the thoughts of the small executioner, as he lay against the marble lip, with hair now flying golden in the breeze, while he was chained by the neck to a dead man who probably had loved him?

Then Daddy-o went with suddenness that caused the chain to jerk out of the cleft. Prindy wasted no time in pulling in this time, because it was getting hot there with the Sun directly overhead and the water steaming and beginning to stink. But he stopped dead when a waxen hand appeared, outstretched as if in waving farewell, giving a blessing, or Heiling Hitler. He stared at it for a long while before he dared again. First the handcuff, well back on the black-haired wrist. Then the buttoned cuff of a khaki sleeve. Then the sleeve with the three chevrons of the sergeant who might have become an inspector. Then rags of cloth and flesh.

Who could trust the hand of Coon-Coon close enough to grab, even if it had no more than a torn-off arm behind it? Prindy could only keep it at a distance, and stare.

The problem was suddenly solved by a rush of wings. Prindy looked up, to see a brown white-breasted osprey diving to grab what he mistook for a fish. The buggers would often snatch one off your line. The long black talons seized it, raised it to the limit of the chain, which snatched it back, so that it came hurtling down and struck the hard rock – *Crack*! It was the cuff that struck. The lock was sprung. The manacle opened. The arm pulled by the waiting

Shade drew the hand out of it, down into the maw. It was gone so quickly, that the osprey, hovering for another strike, whistled in protest. Prindy looked up to meet its angry yellow eye.

Now the ledge that was the crossing could be plainly seen as a dark ridge. The crippled trees were straightening up as best they could. The horses could be seen in the higher country to eastward, moving about amongst the timber there, with the angry restlessness of their kind when hungry but unable to crop properly with bitted mouths. From staring around, Prindy looked back at the maw. It was gone. All that lay before him was flat water, bound on the other side by a slab not dissimilar to that he was on, water that in its running round the rocks seemed to be laughing, perhaps over his having been tricked out of seeing how the magic had been wrought.

Bottom could be seen now. He gathered his chains together, slid down from the rock, began to work his way from shallow to shallow towards the horses, but looking back often whence he had come, as if expecting to see something odd. There was nothing. The falling water reflected the blue and white and silver of the sky.

Catching the horses was a simple matter. They wanted to be rid of those bits. Then, surely, they knew that this diminutive one, who kept popping up in the most extraordinary circumstances, was no ordinary pesky human. Apart from these conditions, there was that of his being a Delacy, the best horse-handlers the country ever knew. He behaved as if he owned the beasts, despite their Government brands; unsaddled them, hobbled them out. Then he settled down to help himself to what was in the tucker-bag. All of it he did without his usual caution in avoiding betrayal of his doings, as if presuming he had no further need for it, having done for good with others' interference in his business.

Having stuffed himself with canned food, he settled down to sleep, doubtless tired out by the ordeal of days. Yet, despite the appearance of sleeping heavily and that evidence of self-assurance, after only an hour or so he woke suddenly – to sit up listening, while still the horses, quick enough creatures to catch a sound, continued with their cropping. That it was not imagining was obvious from the intensity of his staring away southeastward, of the movement of the stare as with the moving of a sound. He was up and grabbing a bridle, before the horses, from taking a look to see what he was up to, turned prick-eared to listen as he had. He caught the horse he had ridden before, a good ambler, saddled up, set off at an amble – not in flight from what he'd heard, but in pursuit of it.

The Sun already was well down behind him, along with the breeze spinning his hair to gold that caught the attention of the birds busy with their final forraging. The Sun was almost down when he came into sight of the Corella Bore, with its windmill golden as a sunflower and the corellas, at their evening squabbling for roosts, like golden bees about it. He was interested in neither bore nor birds, but made straight for the road, which even at distance could be seen to have been used recently by a motor vehicle with skid-chains. The fling of the mud showed that it headed towards Catfish Station. That was the way he went, too, after stopping at the bore only long enough to water himself and horse. Again he took it at an easy amble.

It was quite dark when he reached the first gate. From the second he could see the glow of the homestead. That was about a mile off. He dismounted here, slipped the horse's bit and tied him with the lead-rope to a fence-post. Then he slipped through to continue on foot. But although this showed caution, he boldly walked the muddy road. It was not till close to the homestead that he became truly wary, skirting it now so as to approach upwind, to avoid betrayal of his presence to sharp noses.

Thus he came to the Big House, stole into the garden. There was light above and below. Clancy was down in the latticed lounge-room, stretched out in a canvas chair, apparently listening to popular music on the radio, but by his set staring at the ceiling, preoccupied with thought that only bored him, the way he yawned from time to time. There was light also in the kitchen, from which came sounds indicating preparation of bread for baking next day. The wind brought the beat of *minga-minga* sticks and chanting from the blacks' camp. Prindy took up a position on the concrete base of one of the radio masts, from which he could see into the lounge. However, it was not so much to mount a vigil as to have a dry spot for dozing in, as shown by his carefully setting down his bundle of chains and dropping head to knees, the head a faint pale blur in the reflected light. He woke wide when he heard the radio switched off. Clancy was up and yawning deeply. Prindy watched him mount the stairs. Then he rose and slipped across to the door of the lounge and waited there in shadow.

For a while footsteps clomped about up top. The gaslight began to fade. Soon there was only the starlight. Prindy entered the lounge, went softly up the stairs, and round the verandah to Clancy's bed.

Clancy should have seen the form against the starlight, even through his net. However, Prindy had to attract his attention: 'Pst!'

Clancy growled, 'Who's that?'

Prindy murmured, 'Uncle Clancy.'

Twang of bed-springs. 'Eh . . . who's that?'

A fumbling. Then the glare of a flashlight through the net. A gasp at the sight revealed. The light-beam wavered, to show the net's being pulled. Again it struck Prindy, causing him now to shield his eyes with dangling chains. Clancy demanded breathlessly, 'What the bloody hell're you doing here?'

'I come find out Rifkah.'

'She's not here. But what 'a' you been up to?' The flashlight was approaching.

Prindy muttered, 'Where she?'

'She's all right. What're you doing in those chains?'

'Policeman put him.'

'Where's the policeman?'

'Been lose him.'

Clancy lowered the light, and Prindy his hands.

'What d'you mean?' demanded Clancy. 'You did a bunk?'

'Policeman get drowned.'

'For christ sake!'

'Tell me where Rifkah.'

'I'll tell you bloody nothing! You tell me what's happened.'

Prindy swallowed, 'Spone you don't tell me where Rifkah . . . I go tell policeman.'

'You're going to tell policeman, all right. Where'd the policeman get drowned? Who was he?'

'What I going to tell policeman is you been take away Rifkah.'

'Eh?'

'You been take her away on trolley. Where she now?'

'I told you she's all right. I can't tell you where she is.'

'All right . . . I go tell dat policeman.' Prindy moved to go.

Clancy gasped, 'You little bastard!' Then he added hastily: 'Wait a minute!'

Turning back, Prindy asked, 'Where Rifkah now?'

Panting now, perhaps from anger, or guilt, Clancy answered, 'She . . . she's in a good place . . safe and well.'

'Where dat place?'

'I can't tell you the place . . not yet . . . later on. But it's a good place.'

'I want to go dat place.'

'Eh? Well, I suppose you can . . . yes.'

'What time I go?'

'Go easy! Not yet. Next week might be. I'll tell father . . . your grandfather . . . and he can fix it up to send you there. But you got to tell me about this policeman getting drowned. This is serious . . . bad business.'

Apparently satisfied, Prindy told a simple story of a horse's shying on the limestone crossing, the spilling of the party into the flood, his own fetching up against a rock, while the others were swept away.

'How come they didn't get to the rock, too . . . seeing you were chained to 'em?' asked Clancy.

Prindy shrugged. Clancy answered himself, 'Must've unlocked the cuffs, eh?' Apparently he'd noticed that only one was unlocked. He added, 'So they wouldn't pull you after 'em. Rather decent really.' Then he asked, 'Anybody here see you come?'

'No-more.' Prindy told of leaving his horse back at the gate.

'We don't want too many knowing about it,' said Clancy. 'But something's got to be done about reporting this. You just can't let a sergeant of police . . . expecially Cahoon . . . drown and walk off.' He pondered a moment, then said, 'I got an idea. You say no police are at Lily Lagoons now. I'll take you over there. The old man'll know what to do. Look . . . you get back to Corella and camp the night there . . . and I'll ride over first thing in the morning, and pick you up. Right?'

Prindy agreed, and slipped away.

III

At Lily Lagoons, Jeremy, having been warned in good time of the approach of horsemen from the North, naturally believing he knew who they would be, took little notice. However, when appraised of the facts by a breathless informant, he fairly flew out to meet the party. In reply to Clancy's quite filial greeting, he demanded, 'What the hell's this?'

It was left to Clancy to explain. Prindy just met the grey-eyed staring with his own. Concluding, Clancy said, 'I reckoned it'd be better if you reported it.'

Jeremy asked, 'Where is Rifkah, then?'

Clancy coloured slightly. 'I made a promise not to divulge it till the proper time. Anyway, you'll be informed.'

'She's in safe hands?'

'The best, I'd say.'

'You couldn't get to marry her?'

Clancy went redder, hung his head. 'No . . . that part didn't work out.'

'Why?'

Clancy was obviously embarrassed. Avoiding the quizzing grey eyes, he answered, 'Look, father . . . I can't say any more . . . only that she's safe.'

'I only hope so. We'll be having the police out again. Will you be staying to see them?'

'No . . . I'd rather be left out of the whole thing. If you'll let me have a fresh horse I'll be getting back to Catfish.' A rather different Clancy this from the one so hard to get rid of recently.

Giving him a glance that inferred as much, his father said, 'Well, have a bit of lunch first. You, young fellow . . . have to get the hack-saw to work on you. Then a big feed, eh? You look as if you need one.'

After the big feed, Prindy settled down before the gramophone to play that record of the Cantor's singing *L'Shanah Tovah*, snatching bits of it with his clarinet. Then he fell asleep, deeply asleep for the first time in so long.

While Prindy slept, Jeremy worked the radio to rouse officialdom from its Saturday afternoon indulgences. The AWA Station in Port Palmeston got him both Superintendent Bullco and Professor St Clair to speak to personally. Bullco, shocked to hear of Cahoon's presumed drowning, was much easier to deal with than usual. Evidently the death of Sergeant Bugsby, already known to him, hadn't caused him much concern. Now he was blaming Inspector Ballywick for the loss of his own Sergeant, the best man he had, as he declared. The death of Jinbul didn't seem to trouble him at all, although he would be truly the best man he could ever hope to have. Far from dealing with Jeremy with the usual hostility, he said he would be obliged if he would make a search immediately in case there were a chance that Cahoon might still be alive and in need of help and also to provide him with means to get out to Lily Lagoons as quickly and easily as possible, as he intended to come down tonight by special train to investigate the matter himself. Jeremy said he thought it would be possible to take the truck in to Beatrice by tomorrow morning. It was about Prindy that Jeremy spoke to Professor St Clair, telling him that the boy had been involved in no way in any guilty business, but only scared into running away, and asking that he be returned to the custody of himself until such times as it might be proved to the boy's actual detriment. St Clair, perhaps through not having his official Advising Anthropologist, Dr Fabian Cootes, beside him at the moment, agreed readily enough.

Jeremy went off at once mounted on Elektron to take a look at the Rainbow Pool and such other spots further back as were accessible and likely to yield any evidence. There was nothing. The country was draining fast. He got back to the homestead just on dark.

An early start for the Beatrice was made in the big truck next morning. Jeremy himself went along with Darcy, perhaps making a concession to

Superintendent Bullco's amiability, or for some politic reason not usual in his dealings with police. Prindy was left at home.

The journey took five hours, as against the little more than one when conditions were good. They arrived at the Racecourse to see the special train, driven by Jack Tinball, puffing across the bridge to meet them. An odd thing, as Jeremy remarked to Darcy, when those who were coming could have nipped over on Toohey's trolly, if too tired or scared of the river to walk. Jeremy exclaimed again at the mob aboard. Soon the reason for the oddity was revealed. Most of the mob leapt out to converge on a bundle of black being helped out by others – the Cahoon Sisters, large and small, clinging to each other in abject grief and being supported in blind movement by as many hands as could get to them, closest of which were those of Shamus Finnucane, towering above all and looking as melancholy as a well-paid undertaker. 'God . . . do we have to have them?' muttered Jeremy.

Yes – the sisters would be coming to Lily Lagoons, Superintendent Bullco whispered to Jeremy, after coming up to him and shaking hands like an old friend. 'Terribly cut up, as you can imagine. Want to see where it happened. Hoping against hope that it didn't. But there can't be any hope, can there, seeing you never sent me word?' Jeremy shook his head, and meeting the eyes of the sisters raised for a moment from large white handkerchiefs, gave a sympathetic nod. All he got for his courtesy were terrible red-eyed glares and a betrayal of how well the stricken pair could operate under their own steam if they wanted to, by the suddenness and stiffness of their turning their backs on him.

Finnucane surrendered his place of honour in conducting the sisters to the truck in order to descend on Jeremy, still looking lugubrious, but with that light in his eyes that told he was after information. There was no avoiding him, because he was holding out as bait the red envelope of an urgent telegram, booming, 'Jerry, me boy . . . just given to me for ye be Col Collings.' That he knew what the telegram said was evident enough in his utter lack of interest in Jeremy's opening and reading it, while he muttered, 'Terrible thing, terrible business. Haven't you got the young feller wit' you? Terrible thing!' Still, he couldn't have missed seeing the effect the message had on Jeremy.

Jeremy went red, blinked hard, swallowed. It read: HAPPY INFORM YOU HAVE ARRANGED RIFKAH BE GRANTED CITIZENSHIP STOP ONLY MATTER OF BEING SWORN SORRY IF DISTRESS CAUSED STOP ASSURE YOU FAULT NOT ENTIRELY MINE STOP HOPE SEE YOU BOTH SOON STOP AFFECTIONATE REGARDS MARK.

Having permitted the reading, Finnucane got down to business: 'Indaid 'tis a terrible thing . . . wit' them poor souls besoide 'emselves wit' grievin', and that inspector feller ravin' in drink of the Divil himself behint it all and set on wipin' out all policemen . . . which doesn't help much, you may be sure, wit' two simple and religious ould biddies like themselves here. They're naturally antagonistic, Jerry. I want to warn ye. But it's all but out of their moinds they are. Be koind to 'em, Jerry, me boy. A terrible thing. But might I ask what exactly it was that happened, now?'

Jeremy met the avid eyes with brows arched high above them, answered dryly, 'It's been reported. Simply an accident.'

'But so many accidents, man! There's a limit to credence in coincidence, ye know . . . o' course I'm only speakin' o' the common person . . . but there it is, and what wit' one thing and another, there's a lot o' talk goin' on. And the gurrl, that lovely gurrl, and all this chasin' after her and men getting killed, for nothing. How is she, be the way . . . well, I hope?'

'So do I,' said Jeremy, and walked away to see to the loading of the truck.

Besides the Cahoon Sisters and Bullco, only two young policemen from Town and two trackers who were strangers would be coming out. Jeremy left it to the solicitous mob to place the sisters in front. Then he found that they wanted to get out again and ride in the back when they found they would have to ride with him. He promptly gave the driving seat up to Darcy, and got in the back, where Bullco quietly congratulated him on his forebearance, adding: 'They thought the Sun shone out of Dinny, you know.' As if that were excuse for vindictiveness in the depth of grief.

That wasn't the end of the vindictiveness by any means. When they arrived at Lily Lagoons, towards evening, and the truck pulled up before the porch of the Big House, the sisters refused to alight with the others, declaring to all the world, except Jeremy, and Nan who was waiting just inside, that just as their Poor Brother had never accepted the hospitality of this place, neither would they.

Jeremy spoke to them then: 'Look, ladies . . . I respect your constancy in hating me. But isn't this taking things a bit far? There're comfortable beds waiting for you. You needn't eat with us if you don't want to. Believe me, you have my true sympathy.'

Miss Kitty answered with a tearful shriek addressed to the world again: 'Our Dinny always said that the place was only a blacks' camp, anyway!' What was inferred was made plain by a toss of the silly little old-fashioned black velvet hat towards the plump figure in the doorway. Jeremy went red, but only shrugged, and told Darcy to take them to the harness-shed, then turned to usher Bullco and the young policemen in.

Most likely Nan was there for the very reason of acting the hostess to Bullco in the approved style, instead of her own usually shy appearance after guests had settled in. Jeremy said with ease, 'You know Superintendent Bullco, dear?' Nan nodded, smiling her sweet plump-cheeked smile. The fact was that while she and Bullco knew each other by sight, they had never spoken. She wisely refrained from the somewhat unladylike custom of the land of giving her hand like a man.

Bullco, all amiability, nodded and smiled too. 'How d'you do, Missus!'

The constables did likewise when introduced.

Bullco was equally amiable with Prindy, who rose with squatterling dignity at entrance of the guests. 'Hello, young feller! Been through some pretty tough business lately, eh?' Then he added, bending with a sort of confiding air and placing a hand on a small poplin shoulder, 'You'll help us, won't you?' Prindy nodded gravely.

The bit of a drinking session to begin with and then dinner went well enough, even if there were some strain of over-politeness. However, the rest of the evening was made easy by a momentous announcement in the radio news that gave scope for lively discussion without heart-burning, as no doubt it did throughout the Nation. The Prime Minister had died suddenly. Despite what a legion of mealy-mouthed so-called Leaders of the Nation had to say in simulated sorrow and tribute, the first thought in the minds of most people concerning the Departed One would be summed up with the word Rat. Even those who gained through his betrayal of the principles by mouthing which he had started on his way to political power, namely those ideals of a true Commonwealth of Australia as dreamt of by the Australian Labor Party, had despised him for his arrant opportunism. His Pegging Out, or Turning Up His Toes, as those here more honestly called what the lugubrious legions were calling His Passing, wouldn't mean so much to the Nation generally, since he had sold out to interests that during his five years or so of office had entrenched themselves too securely ever to be dislodged again except by force such as did not exist in the lousy make-up of Australians as a whole. However, it was likely to affect conditions in these parts drastically, as every change of Government did, even if only nominal, this being a region dominated by bureaurocracy that needs must change with the inevitable replacement of bosses, however petty. Bullco was much concerned about that. It might well presage complete reorganization of the local Administration by appointment of a new Administrator.

Jeremy expressed interest in eventualities likely following the death of a strongly Catholic leader of a predominantly Protestant Junta, the ingrained bigotry of Australians being what it is. Everybody knew that it was the Catholic Church broke the old Labor Party, the formation of which it was largely responsible for through its early Irish anti-British-Imperialism, and that the just-dead Sawdust Caesar owed his elevation to it. Now the Church was militant in the very opposite direction, supporting even Imperial vested interest rather than let the Labor Party reach the degree of radicalism inevitable with the encouragement of the Church's old enemy, Communism. Jeremy's outspokenness in the matter offended no one, since none of the guests was Catholic, a rather odd circumstance when policemen were mostly of Irish origin, and perhaps in this case due to deliberate policy on the part of Bullco, choosing his men so as not to risk making a Finnegan's Wake of his investigations. Anyway, none of them liked politicians, and so were at one in expressing contempt for the scramble for power manifest even in the drooling of those who were come to praise their Caesar prior to burying him.

As the guests were tired, the evening wound up fairly early. Perhaps as a precaution against interference, Prindy was taken by his grandfather to the annexe to spend the night. Before retiring they had a long talk in the den. By no means all of it was about the smart way to deal with the situation. There was that red telegram to discuss. Prindy went off to bed with it in his pyjama's pocket.

What the Cahoon ladies thought of being served excellent meals in the mean quarters of their vindictive choosing was not disclosed. Perhaps, since served as usual by black hands, they reckoned it simply as service to the superiority of their breed. Anyway, sustained with porridge, omelette, coffee, next morning they went forth, again driven by Darcy, but this time in the utility, to the nearest point reachable on wheels to where, as they put it, their Darlint had been taken from them into the arms of Our Lord Jesus Christ – with a whack in the stomach for the liberty. Prindy, who travelled with the others in the big truck, had a glimpse of them at their whacking and bead-telling, as they knelt at the spot where the party had gone overboard. They could not get nearer to the exact point of Dinny's delivery because of the intervening ooze, or he nearer to them to see what they were up to because of their having shown a tendency to break off whatever they were doing, no matter how devout, at sight of him, and to scream, 'Halfbred spawn o' the Divil . . . you were the cause o' this!'

Prindy, with his grandfather always close beside him, showed the police the exact spot. Not that anything was to be seen there but smelly slabs of rock under which water could still be heard pouring. Back on the mossy rock of the crossing was ample evidence to corroborate the boy's simple story of the fall off the horse and what followed. Still, Bullco, in what sounded like a kindly way and might well have been a policeman's ingrained habit of talking during investigation, did seem to be trying to trap him and also to get him to speak of Rifkah. Here it was that Jeremy would intervene, saying that there was time enough for elaboration of the story when it came to making out the proper statement – and as for the business of Rifkah, that was Inspector Ballywick's. Bullco desisted each time without demur.

Bullco said that he wanted, if possible, to get everything cleared up today, so as to be able to make a definite report to Town tomorrow. As an inquest into the death of Sergeant Bugsby was pending and best held at Beatrice, where the witnesses Stunke and Tipperary would be available without further disruption of the police services of the region, and Inspector Ballywick, too, since surely they would have him Dried Out by then, he saw no reason but to have the Coroner down on the next train, to clean up both cases in the same Court Sitting, on Thursday. To that end the investigation was conducted.

While the ladies were returned to the homestead and their hide-strip beds in the harness-shed and their alternate keening and cursing in the good old Irish way, the others went to the Rainbow Pool. Nothing was found but the rainbow – nothing. As the sisters wailed when Bullco went to them with a funereal air and a bottle of brandy to relate the sad news, if only they had something to Remimbrance By of his Last Moments. If only that chevroned arm giving the Hitler Salute could have been found for them!

But Bullco had something for them, at least as a promise. Since Dinny died doing his duty he would be entitled to that highest of awards to policemen, the Medal for Devotion to Duty. That would be something for them to be proud of. So affected were they by the thought of it and the brandy that they wept in a different way. Then the fathead Bullco spoiled it all, probably owing to his helping himself to the brandy too liberally too, by adding that since there was evidence that the boy had been released from the drag of the chain to save his life at the expense of Dinny's, why not also the much-coveted George Medal for Bravery? He did not know the Irish. That started them shrieking again, worse than ever by reason of the brandy: 'If only that yeller imp of Satan had drowned instead of our Darlint! A curse on that divil-child and on this house that shelters him!'

Hearing of the arrangements to have the Inquest got over this week, the sisters asked Bullco if he would also ask that a priest be sent down on the train so that their Darlint might be consigned to the Hereafter Daycently, in accordance with the Faith of his Fathers. As it was considered that his mortal remains must be lying somewhere along the bottom of the Beatrice River (no one dared think of crocodiles) the idea of holding the Burial Service beside the River at the township seemed quite proper. As they said, but raising their voices again to make it heard far and wide, 'We don't want it held here . . . amongst haythan blacks and yeller divils and atheistic halfbred Irish!'

Bullco, rejoining Jeremy in the annexe, was inclined to apologize for the unseemly yelling. Jeremy put him at his ease: 'The Irish have relentless memories. The wake only adds fire to the feud. They're realists, I guess.'

When Bullco got in touch with Town by radio to arrange things as he wanted them, Jeremy also made contact with Bill Billings, the lawyer, whom he asked to come down to hold a watching brief for him and Prindy at the Inquest. When all this was done, including the drawing up, typing, signing, and witnessing Prindy's Statement, it was decided that the party had no further business here at Lily Lagoons, and would best be getting back to Beatrice.

Thus on Tuesday morning, after a substantial smoke-o to sustain them for the trip, the visitors departed, unfarewelled by the household for fear of rousing the Irish of the tearful sisters to deliver a parting shot. Darcy drove again. Jeremy and Prindy would be following tomorrow, as usual in time to meet the train.

IV

Uncle Clancy also was there to meet the train, nodding amiably to his father and nephew, but keeping his distance, as of old. They let him. Hadn't he frankly said he wanted to be left out of this messy business? Plain to see how messy it was, the way everybody else kept their distance from them. Even scary old Tom Toohey, with whom they would be spending the night, did no more than pay his respects and then busy himself with railway duties. More so that fearless one, who normally would have braved a lion's den to be able to Tell the Wurruld what the lions were up to, old Shame-on-us, had only a nod for them, as he came rolling across from his pub when the train came rolling in. The fact that Finnucane was meeting the train rather than standing by to meet the rush from it of those perishing with thirst meant that there was someone very special aboard.

Well, here she was, with Pat Hannaford hanging out as usual, but without the grin either of amiability or mischief. He ignored Clancy, as in former times, his class-enemy. However, he nodded to Jeremy and Prindy, eyeing them sharply. As ever he gave Col Collings the Fascist Salute, but, curiously, bestowed it on old Shame-on-us as well, to the evident surprise of the bushy eyebrows.

As a matter of fact there were *several* important people aboard. The numerous policemen waiting pressed in to receive him they would regard as most important, the Coroner, dressed in white linen and fanning himself with a panama hat, while assisted, wheezing with exertion, down the steps of the car platform by many hands from behind. It was that amiable mass of humanity,

Dicky Doscas. It was to the other end of the car that Finnucane went, along with Mick Bolger and other Irish faithful of the locality, but strangely not the Cahoon Sisters. Here was another massive figure being helped with deference down the steps, he in tusser-silk and black hat: Monsignor Maryzic.

Finnucane took possession of the old arch-priest, crying, 'Ah . . . and a grand pleasure indaid it is to be havin' Your Lordship back wit' us ag'in . . . even be it an occasion of sad sorrow as well!'

Monsignor Maryzic rumbled, 'If I do not know der Irish misuse of der English language, Shamus, moost I zink you qvite mad . . . And haf not I told you vun hundret time I am not Lordship?'

Finnucane drooped with humility. 'Ye Very Riverence, sure, it leaps to me tongue ahead o' me thinkin' . . . . '

'Like your famous blarney, man!'

'Not at all, Father. As oft' I've told you . . . 'tis a bishop ye ought've been long since, and therefore as His Lordship the Bishop ye are long established in me moind.'

'Is all zis blarney worth der awful risk of excommunication it vood mean if der Hierarchy got to hear of your interference in zere judgement?'

'Ah, now, Ye Very Riverence . . . . '

'Don't bother! Vere are ze Cahoon ladies? I vood expect zem to be vaitingk, seeingk zey send for me?'

Finnucane got his mouth up under the black hat. 'As a matter of fact, Ye Riverence, I want to give ye toimely warnin' . . . . '

'Zat zey do not vont a clergyman so mooch as an Irishman to conduct der service, yes? In zat case, vy not yourself to conduct ze Burial . . . it vood be quite in order?'

' 'Tis not exactly that, Ye Very Riverence . . . although I'll admit they were rather expectin' Father Ryan down. 'Tis that they're in a bad way, poor souls . . . cryin' 'tis Divil's Business and such koinds of unholy nonsense, through one thing and another bein' too much talked about round here, and which, to be sure, you'll put a stop to. But they're simple old biddies . . . and their loss has unhinged 'em more than somewhat . . . . '

Maryzic stopped the patter by waving his walking stick to Jeremy and calling, 'Goottay to you, Jeremy Delacy! I'll be vontingk a vord mit you, as soon as you can spare der time.'

Jeremy nodded.

Another voice said, 'I'll be wanting a word with you, too Jerry.' It was Eddy McCusky, hat over eye, the official strut in his walk, as he went on with the rush of the perishing for the pub.

'We're in demand,' said Jeremy to Prindy. 'Too much, methinks. Come and get the mail and make ourselves scarce.'

But there was no escaping the demand, it seemed. Before they could get into the Station office, Pat Hannaford, grubby handed and surly, came up muttering exactly the same phrase as the others, and drew them clear of the crowd. He said, 'You know about Rifkah, I suppose?'

'That they've given her citizenship after all?'

'Yeah . . . and that it's the Micks got it for her . . . and'a' grabbed her as cons'quence?'

'I only know they've called off the hunt. I don't even know where she is.'

To Jeremy's evident astonishment, Pat explained his version of Rifkah's translation to the Leopold Mission. Pat concluded, 'Catholic Action's behind this, o' course. The bastards'a' been running the country ever since Scullin. The fact the Party was helpin' her was enough to set 'em in action, once they got old Maryzic's say-so that she didn't belong to us. He got the dope about her out o' me . . . with his Jesuitical trickery. Well, they ain't goin' 'o beat us. Will you lend's a hand . . . get her back to Lily Lagoons?'

'I presume she'll be coming back herself, when everything's fixed.'

'Not on your life, man. Maryzic reckons he's been talkin' to her on the radio . . . and that she wants to stay there . . . workin' for the boongs. Y'ever hear the bloody like . . . a Jewess brought up with Communists, wantin' to be a nun!'

'A nun? Did Maryzic say that?'

'Well, no . . . but you know them bastards. They've talked her into stayin' . . . they'll talk her into becomin' a black beetle. That's 'cause I was silly enough to tell him we was gettin' her away aboard the *Koolpinya*. It's all fixed for her to sail week-end after next. The Party members're goin' 'o kick up a row she don't go, after all the trouble to arrange her passage.'

'But there's no need for it now . . . and she never wanted to leave the country.'

'She won't be leavin' the country. The idea was only to ship her down to Port Hartog. The meatworks just opened now, and the mob up from the South. They were goin' 'o look after her. She'll have to make the trip. Otherwise we're goin' 'o look bloody bunnies. They're waitin' for her. They want her to tell 'em about conditions in Germany.'

'What can I do about it?'

'Get her overland.'

'It'd take a month.'

'No matter. She could go on the next *Koolpinya*. So long's we don't have to tell 'em Catholic Action pinched her under our very noses, to make her a black beetle . . . Jesus!'

A flicker of a smile passed over Jeremy's face. Pat saw it, and scowled. 'You were ready enough for our help before. Now give *us* a bit. I got 'o do a bit shuntin' now. See you later . . . tomorro'. I won't be takin' the train to the Head. I'm leavin' it to Porky and Bill Bolger. Goin' off sick. Want 'o see the Inquest.'

As Pat went off, Jeremy and Prindy looked at each other, grey eyes into grey. Prindy's were shining. He drew a deep breath. 'Rifkah Leopold Mission, eh? I been dream dat. I been dream she been sing out me from dere, when I stand up on Sandstone, looking away at sea. We go and get her, eh?'

'I don't know, son. Sounds a bit mixed up to me. Old Whiskers says he got her free . . . now Pat reckons it's Maryzic. Wait'll we hear more from Maryzic. Let's get the mail now and get our gear over to Toohey's. You want to see Barbu about hearing the record, too, don't you?'

They stopped at Barbu's. Prindy had the record of the Cantor's singing, evidently promised for Barbu's hearing this long while, along with Prindy's accompanying it on the clarinet. As Barbu had no gramophone, he was to come over to hear the record on Toohey's after supper.

So it was. The music session was still in progress, when Jeremy and Tom Toohey, who were sitting out on the verandah overlooking the railway and the invisible roaring river, heard slow heavy footsteps on the clinker path outside. Soon against the blaze of the southern stars a bulky figure appeared. It became a yellowish blur as the light leaking from inside the house caught it. The sitting pair could easily see who it was by the time the visitor reached the gate, but made no move, in accordance with the proprieties regarding uninvited callers. Anyway, everybody knew that Tom had quarrelled with Monsignor Maryzic over his children, whom the priest had wanted to put in one of the missions he then administered to save them from what he called Going to the Bad.

The old man entered the gate, came crunching up the path, puffing and pushing hard on his stick, evidently tired by the long walk. In his free hand he carried the black bag of the priest going to perform an Extreme Unction. He it was who gave the greeting, wheezing, 'Goot night, gentlemen. I presume I am intrudingk. Still, I did ask Jeremy to see me . . . and ze poor old mountain haf to come to Mahomet.'

The others only mumbled greeting, still without rising. The old priest addressed Toohey: 'How come it I hear psalm-singingk in ze house of Toohey ze free-zinker?'

Tom grunted, ' 'Tain't psalm-singin', Father . . . it's Jew music.'

'And vot is a psalm but Jew music?'

The walking-stick rose to wave like a baton to the Cantor's cadence and cascading melody of the clarinet. 'Zat is Psalm Tventy-Four . . . *Lift Up Your Heads*.'

Then clarinet ceased, and the volume of the music fell. 'Oh,' said the old man. 'But it moost not stop. Ist too beautiful. Ze boy ist playingk ze flute, Jeremy?' When Jeremy nodded, he added, 'Vill you tek me to him, zat I might compliment him . . . and ask him to play me more?'

The two men rose at last. Toohey led the way in. Seeing Barbu, Monsignor Maryzic rumbled, 'How come you to be interest in zis kind of music, Barbu Ram?'

Bobbing, Barbu answered, 'In all gootness am I interest, Your Graciousness.'

'Vell said . . . efen if your idea of gootness does not conform mit recognize moral standard.'

'Sir?'

'I haf but a little private joke, Barbu Ram. Now, boy. You know me. Do not look at me as if I am policeman. I vish to tell you how sveet your music. Vill you not play more for me?

Prindy glanced at his grandfather in the doorway. Jeremy nodded.

The priest asked, 'Vill you not play ze record from ze start? I hear but little outside.'

Prindy responded readily, and when he played, did so quite unselfconsciously, even while keeping grey eyes fixed on the smiling, nodding old man. So truly wrapt was the priest, perhaps as much in study of the young face as in the music, that he started when Toohey asked him to take a seat. He shook his head, stood leaning on his stick until the first piece was played through, and Prindy lowered his instrument. Then he clapped his hands lightly, saying,

'Bravo, my little genius! Please keep playing for me vile I am outside mitt your grandfader . . . I vill be listeningk.' He turned to Jeremy. 'I can spik to you alone?' Then he glanced at Tom, who looked at Jeremy. The old man chuckled, evidently at the show of wariness. Jeremy turned to go back to the verandah. The old man nodded to Prindy, followed.

Seating himself, with the sigh of one making himself comfortable for a goodly spell, with eyes on the stars, the old priest said, 'Ze boy haf mooch talent. Pity to vaste.'

Jeremy, also seated again, eyes on the flatish Slavic profile, answered somewhat dryly, 'It won't be wasted . . . if I can help it.'

'Ah . . . but *can* you help it?'

Jeremy took a moment to ask, while the old man lay back in the canvas chair waiting, 'What is it you want to say, Monsignor?'

The priest took a deep breath. 'Vell, first I haf message for you and ze boy . . . in Yiddish, vich I am told you vill understand. *Ess Gezunter hait.*' The stars twinkled in their eyes as they turned. When Jeremy nodded, the arch-priest chuckled. He turned back to the stars.

Again silence. Then the priest began: 'You are avare zere ist conspiracy to tek ze boy avay from you?'

Jeremy swallowed. 'I'm always aware of the resentment there is over my having him.'

Maryzic talked to the stars: 'Now, as zey say, ist cut and dried to tek him.'

'That's why McCusky's here?'

The profile nodded. Monsignor Maryzic went on to say that McCusky had been blabbing to him on the train, having some drink in. Since then he had heard more boozy talk, while himself sitting in Finnucane's office and officialdom gathered in the private bar next door. He mused, 'For whitemen who so despise ze blackman, ist surprisingk to hear zem spik of zis silly Devil Business as if legal evidence. Of course, der purpose ist to use against you. But, at least in drink, zey more zan half belief der boy haf Satanic power.'

'They can't talk that sort of nonsense in court.'

'Zey can hint at it. Der verdict in boze case ist foregone – Death by Misadventure. But how can der misadventure happen mitout zis boy of Satanic Power acquired tru beingk left in contact mit Blackfellow Business, ven he should be in Mister McCusky's special school for makingk good stockboy for Lord Vaisey?'

Another silence till the old man resumed: 'From vot I gazzer, as soon as der verdict in der Cahoon Case tomorrow is giffen, Mister McCusky vill rise . . . he vill haf possession of der boy already, in his legal right as Protector . . . he vill rise after der Coroner haf say No Blame Attachable to anyvun, and vill confess zat blame attach to some degree to himself for havingk permit zis boy to fall into wrong hand.'

Jeremy breathed explosively, 'The bastards!'

'Vell . . . ist zere business to boss people. Howeffer, I zink I can beat Mister McCusky for ze boy.' The old man waited, with the stars in his eyes, till Jeremy was driven to ask how. Maryzic glanced. 'You may not approve. You may call it Jesuitical.'

Jeremy grunted, 'You are a Jesuit, aren't you?'

'Of course. But to belong to Society of Jesus does not mek vun suspicious character, vich vot Jesuitical mean. Vot I haf in mind is for sake of ze boy.' Again silence, which at length the old man broke himself: 'My idea is to forestall our McCusky by risingk in der court before him and sayingk mooch der same zing as he vood . . . only mitout inference zat der fault ist Jeremy Delacy. I vill blame ze native influence. I also am Protector. I am Missionary. I am member of great institution for savingk soul and succouringk life. I vill spik of der talent of zis boy, his intelligence. I vill say zat under proper care he might efen show vocation for der priesthood.'

The old man swung quickly at the sharp intake of breath beside him, demanded, 'You object?'

Jeremy took a moment to answer, 'Tell me straight out what your intention is.'

'I haf several intention, Jeremy. Der first ist get der boy avay from McCusky, who vill only mek outlaw of him. I vill ask him, before der court, for custody of der boy. I do not zink he can refuse. He ist free-zinker in his talk . . . but deep down a Catholic. Der Church is der background of born Catholic. Like nationality. But efen zose who are not Catholic moost be impressed by idea of vun call Satanist becomingk a Christian priest.'

The old Jesuit took to contemplating the stars again. Jeremy waited. Maryzic resumed: 'But moost I not look ridiculous in my claim. Moost I appear to know more of der boy zan in fact I do. He haf been at Leopold Mission, I am told. Who here knows vot happen zere? Who know he ist not baptize Catholic? In court I vont to go to him and place my hand not on Imp of Hell, but on vun of mein flock who haf strayed.'

The square face turned again. 'I vont to tell der court zat I am usingk zis boy as accolyte in der sacrament of layingk to rest der soul of der man it is implied he haf kill.'

A smothered gasp from Jeremy.

'But I am not goingk to stand in der court and lie, Jeremy Delacy. I cannot haf accolyte to serve me in my Christian service who ist heathen.' A long pause. Then: 'You follow me, my friendt?'

Jeremy swallowed, said huskily, 'You mean you want to baptize him?'

'Exactly.'

Jeremy stared into the eyes that seemed to glow with the starlight. 'You yourself were baptize, Jeremy. I do not see vere it haf done you harm.'

Jeremy swallowed again. 'There's the boy to consider. He hasn't been brought up to respect any religion . . . .'

'Not der Jewish?'

'Well . . . I mean . . . .'

'I know what you mean . . . zat you haf taught him only atheism . . . but zat his longingk for God has first turn him to Blackfellow Business, and zen to Judaism. Der boy is ripe for conversion.'

Again a deep breath from Jeremy. Again the glowing eyes turned to the blaze of Eternity, to which the old voice, spoke wheezily: 'I haf der bait. I understand he is ver' mooch attach to der Jewish girl and she to him. First I vill ask him if he vish to go to join her at Leopold Mission. Zen I vill tell him of McCusky. Finally I vill name der price. I zink zat only your influence vood prevent him from accepting.' The old man turned to look at the effect of his words.

Jeremy answered, rather weakly, 'Don't overestimate my influence on the boy. I've said he's strong-willed.'

The old man's voice became suddenly harsh: 'Vood you do anyzingk to interfere mit any influence I might establish?'

Again Jeremy took a moment to answer, 'No.'

'Ver' vell. Ve vill talk to him. First ve vill talk of Rifkah. I intend to sail to Leopold next Sunday for der citizenship. I am Justice of Peace. I haf only to get der form from Immigration Office in Port Palmeston and tek for her to sign. You know, of course, she haf been grant citizenship? Zat was zrough der goot office of der Church.' He met Jeremy's stare, resuming: 'Ve haf our man at Head of Government zen. It vos easy. But zing haf change. I understand zat der most likely vun to become new leader of Government is zis Attorney-General who gafe order for arrest of der girl. A vain and arrogant man, I am told, alzough capable of cleffer diplomacy. He could not gainsay der request of der late Prime Minister. But he did try. Zat he do by callingk in Military Security. Fortunately der matter was referred to General Esk, who actually start der investigation, but not on account of der girl. He is friendt of der girl zrough you. Who is to say vot zis Attorney-General, become his own Prime Minister, and oppose to General Esk, I am told, vill not do in der vindictiveness of power? At present he is preoccupy mit der scramble for power over der corpse. No time must be lost to haf zat paper sign and seal. So I go next Sunday. Vot better zan zat I tek my little acolyte mit me . . . mit his grandfader's blessingk . . . mit his grandfader goingk along, too, if he vish?'

It was Jeremy who studied the stars now, while the old priest studied him.

At length Monsignor Maryzic asked, 'Yes?'

Jeremy nodded, breathing, 'Yes.'

'Goot! Can ve haf him out? First I vill talk music to him, and haf him play for me.' As Jeremy rose the old man added, 'May I haf a drink. I am ver' zirsty from so much talk. But no alcohol . . . because I haf religious task to do.' As Jeremy went inside, the Slav face turned back to contemplate the alien stars, the Crux and Corona Australis. He sighed deeply.

The old priest proved himself very clever in handling Prindy. To begin with, he could play the clarinet, and pleased the boy with some gypsy-like pieces of his origins, and surely gratified him by his genuine praise of his own skill. Then there was talk of Rifkah, implying that she was now under this fatherly wing and that there was room there for more who might be in trouble. How would it be if they all went in the magic ship *St Francis Xavier* to look her up at the Mission? Getting onto the subject of the opposition they might expect to their happy ideas was a simple matter: Hadn't Old Mick Cusky always opposed any form of natural enjoyment of life, and outwitting him been a prime factor of existence? As to the idea of taking part in the Bijnitch of laying the Shade of Coon-Coon according to what sounded very interesting rites, even if *kuttabah's*, what could be more alluring to the one who had parted the spirit from the flesh? Would he wear the lace and scarlet and swing the censer? Prindy, about to become *Prendegastus, in Nomine Patris, et Filii, et Spiritus Sancti*, nodded right readily.

Within a couple of hours of the beginning of the Jesuitical talk, they were back in the sitting-room, Monsignor Maryzic now wearing a violet stole and biretta, and with the salt and the oil and the holy water out of his black bag, and that Free-zinker, Thomas Toohey, standing by as godfather. The name Prendegastus was hardly in keeping with the canons of the Church, His Very Reverence had to admit. But, as he said, there was so much latitude in Baptism, so many forms of Baptism, for that matter, that you needed an almanac to do the proper thing, and this occasion was hardly formal. Besides, who knew but what there had been one Prendegast amongst the early British Martyrs to the Faith who had been overlooked in canonization?

'*Prendegastus, quid petis ab Ecclesia Dei?*'

Tom Toohey answered rather as if the words were choked out of him, 'Faith.'

'*Fides quid tibi praestat?*'

Again the strangled response, 'Life everlasting.'

Three slightly whisky-blessed breaths upon the golden face to form the Sign, while the deep voice Latinized like the notes of an organ: '*Exi ab eo, immunde spiritus . . . et da locum Spiritui Sancto Paraclito*'

So Old Tchamala was hunted out

A touch of oil with the thumb to broad brow and bared breast: '*Accipe signum Crucis . . . sume fidem caelestium praeceptorum . . . ut templum Dei jam esse possis.*'

A little salt on the red tip of tongue to cause relish to ingested grace and at once to preserve it: '*Prendegastus . . . accipe sal sapientiae . . . propitiatio sit tibi in vitam aeternam.*'

A sharp glance shot over glasses at Godfather Tom, who gasped, 'Amen.'

A touch of priestly spit on ears and nose, to open them to divine knowledge and the breath of Faith – all such good stuff in the way of Bijnitch as to cause the grey eyes to be wide with interest. Then a change of purple stole to one of white and gold. The holy water poured to form the Crucis, while the priestly throat gave forth its deepest notes: '*Prendegastus, Ego te baptizo . . . in nomine Patris . . . et Filii . . . et Spiritus Sancti* . . . Tom!'

'Amen.'

Then a little lighted candle put into a small yellow hand. The voice changed its tune: 'See zou guard der grace of zy baptism mittout blame . . . keep der commandments of Gott, so zat thou may meet him in der Heavenly courts, and zere liff for effer and effer . . . *Vade in pace, et Dominus sit tecum.*'

Tom sighed with relief this time, 'Ah-men!'

Now was the time for the non-ecclesiastical ceremony of Head-wetting. Tom got the whisky out. While the others sat about the table drinking, slowly the fair head on which Grace had been set drooped, till it was right down. His new mentor asked the privilege of putting him to bed. Jeremy thought it wouldn't work. But it did, simply. A start when hands were lain on him, then a sleepy smile to see whose they were. Monsignor Maryzic carried him out to his bed on the verandah, stripped him, bent to kiss the blur of gold on the white of sheet, made the Sign of the Cross over it, sighed, pulled the mosquito net.

The Monsignor himself also spent the night at Toohey's, despite the fact that he had been given the best room at Finnucane's. Reason was that he liked his Sleep, as he said, and as Tom said, 'They're wakin' Dinny already. They'll be at it all night . . . and for a week.'

The venue of the Coroner's Court was, as usual on the rare occasions when judicial issues were dealt with out of Town, the Police Station: the underneath part where normally the utility and other gear was kept. However, such was the attendance that Dicky Doscas remarked to his official assistants that they should have hired the Hall. Of course he was joking. Everybody knew that the Hall had been rigged out for Dinny's Requiem this afternoon. The crowd consisted largely of up-line passengers who ought to have gone on with the morning train, but, bearing out Tom Toohey's prediction about waking Dinny for a week, had let it go without them. It wasn't that Dinny had become any more endeared to the community generally through having ceased to be of it. As it was put in endless boozy repetition: 'Yeah, he was a bastard, all right . . . but he's dead.' Even Finnucane, with ear ever cocked and brows ready for any desecration of the Wake's uncoffined corpse, could not object to that.

There were no untoward incidents to interfere with Proceedings. The booziest of the audience were kept to the rear and in many cases slept through it. The Cahoon Sisters merely wept through it, except during the period when the little star witness gave his simple bit of evidence, which they gave to staring so intense that they might have been hoping to get their revenge in the hope of there being some truth in the old adage, *If Looks Could Kill*. Inspector Ballywick seemed like letting loose at times, and in fact, insinuated bitterly about certain people. However, as an experienced officer of the law, he knew better than to blow his top in a witness-box. Those Certain People might have meant the local authorities, or even those under whom he worked. Or it could have been, as one of the drunks at the back remarked over an especially irrascible outburst, 'Poor bugger's got the dry-horrors.'

Thus the verdicts in both cases were as generally predicted. Likewise, Monsignor Maryzic acted according to his Jesuitical predication, and with such success that he was applauded even by those he had left red-faced by out-pointing them, when he told the Court that it was his hope to make a priest of him he was so easily able to go up to and put his arm about in unassailable possession. It lasted till noon. It ended in rush to the pub, a rush all the more headlong for having Monsignor Maryzic's blessing go with it: 'Savages! Anyvun who come drunk to my Mass vill be forcibly enjected. Savages . . . and no reflexion on der blackman!'

It was just as well that most took heed of the forthright old priest, if that was what kept the majority away from the Requiem, since the couple of drunks, whose excess of faith or lack of savvy caused them to defy him, made such a hullabaloo in sympathy with the utterly distraught Cahoon Sisters, that a pack of them would have made it a bedlam. Prindy was there, but well out of their line of vision, they being up front beside the black gold-fringed pall lying on the floor to represent a non-existent coffin containing a vanished corpse, while he was right at the back with his grandfather and godfather. No doubt about the interest in the ritual the way those grey eyes stared and darted. There were two black acolytes. He would be wearing the colourful outfit of one in taking part later in the simpler ceremonial of the Funeral. The Burial Service was to be conducted above the river just outside the Cemetery, at a spot on which, so it was being said, eventually the Sisters would have erected a life-size Crucifix in bronze.

Everybody went to the Funeral, as they were calling the hearseless, coffinless, corpseless procession to the Cemetery. Included were those just off the train back from the Head of the Road, too dry to cry. Amongst these latter was Billy Brew. He walked at the rear with Jeremy and Toohey, surely a subtle mark of disrespect. Fetching up right behind were the goats, but only because they had been denied presumption to lead. Leading was Monsignor Maryzic with black stole and wooden cross, attended by his fair-haired acolyte in scarlet and lace and bearing the golden holy water bowl and aspergillum. Behind them came the Finnucanes, supporting the Sisters and singing the Processional to the accompaniment of their sobs. The singing, augmented by several other of the more Faithful, was ragged, but perhaps even more to the pathetic purpose for being so:

May the Angels lead you into Paradise
May the Martyrs await your coming
And bring you into the Holy City
The Heavenly Jerusalem.

Only the McDodds were missing. Still, they made concession by closing their door, but whether out of respect for the dead or disrespect of Irish Popery would be known only to their Presbyterian selves.

Thus to the spot that for ever was to be sanctified in the name of Dennis Aloysius Cahoon. It sounded as if the racing Shade of Old Tchamala roared with laughter as Monsignor Maryzic boomed out the Burial Service above it: *Absolve quaesumus, Domine, animam famuli tui Dennis Aloysius Cahoon ut defunctus saeculo tibi vivat* . . . Dead to the world . . . *atque per flagilatem carnis humanum commisit . . . per Christum Dominum Nostrum.*

A sweet boy's soprano responded so that all lowered eyes were raised: *Oh, Deus cujus miseratione animae fidelium requiescant, hunc aqueum tumulum benedicere dignare.*

A slight signal, and the golden brush was passed to the white lace-fringed hand. The holy silver droplets flew – *Pater noster secreto usque ad.*

The soprano almost perfect in its echo: *Sed libera nos a malo.*

Requiescat in pace.

Amen.

'Eternal Rest grant him, Oh, Lord.'

Those who knew how to joined the response: 'And let perpetual light shine upon him.'

Requiescat in pace.

Amen.

'May his soul and der souls of all der faithful departed, tru der mercy of Gott, rest in peace.'

'Ahhh-men!'

So it was over – for Eternity. Most of the living who thought themselves immortal, and perhaps really were so until reality caught up with them, galloped back to the pub to deliver their panagyric: He was a bastard, but he's dead.

Monsignor Maryzic moved out of the Hotel permanently, with the cringing apologies of the host. Doubtless he could not have stood another night of Waking. However, it was not for that reason he left, although he did not help Finnucane by telling him the truth, which was that he was going out to Lily Lagoons, with Jeremy and Prindy, who wanted to collect things for taking to Leopold Mission. They would be back to catch tomorrow morning's train to Town.

V

To depart hand-in-hand with one so personable as Monsignor Maryzic was surely enough to attract the attention of most people to a little coloured boy, no matter how attractive in himself. However, it was pretty evident that the interest taken in Prindy on his departure from Beatrice that return-train-day was largely on his own account. To people like the blacks and halfcastes, the Ah Loys, Billy Brew, who crowded round him for a last touch, the Monsignor was only a Missionary Man, a kind of policeman. Not all these simple ones could touch the boy, some not even look at him, and others again who despite the right preferred not to exercise it. Who could not but have some fear of one invested with the power to rid them of the worst blight of their so-blighted recent history, Coon-Coon and Jinbul? Some awe of one who despite his immaturity could take a leading part in the *kuttabah's* laying of the Shades? The air was sibilant with indrawn comment on him. Even old Shame-on-us came to take his hand. Billy Brew wept a little. That made it seem like a long farewell. Such a farewelling of one renowned for popping up at any time from anywhere!

The grey eyes took it all in with customary calm, the last of it from the moving window of the coach, with the grey heads of those who had presumed to his guardianship, old guardian and new, on either side of him. Then Beatrice township was swallowed by the girders of the bridge, as if by the jaws of the Shade winking beneath. A last look at the Shade. A last wink back. Then there were those police horses, back from the Limestone, where they had seen so much. They saw him from across the Racecourse fence, flung up heads and tails, and did a furlong of their best beside the train. Then the familiar wilderness again – the autumnal russet of seeding grasses tipping the limitlessness of new greenery – lilies purpling still waters – far hills blue-blue – the milky blue of cloudless horizons.

Familiar sounds, too – song of wheels to *minga-minga* click of rails, and the deep dijeridoo of the engine, with an occasional shrilling of ecstacy: *Yai, yai, yai, yakkarai*!

Familiar places. Granite Springs and Bamboo Creek. The Alice River siding, deserted now by southward-pressing roadmen, peopled now only by the railwaymen, their black slaves, and memories. The torn country of the Caroline, with much of its destruction hidden for the nonce under Whiteman's and Chinaman's weeds.

Prindy ate with his Monsignor and grandfather at a special table in the hotel at Caroline River. Everybody stared. Outside they stared, the brindles and the blacks, with that wonder-whispering. He did not return to the coach with his guardians, because just as they were about to leave, Pat Hannaford came loping along, first asking him personally if he would like to ride with him, next more or less challenging the guardians to say No. It was only the Monsignor who could object, anyway. He did not, merely saying that he presumed Pat had an Ulterior Motive. Pat snapped back at him, 'Course *you* ain't!'

Pat's immediate motive was to congratulate Prindy on what was the wonder and joy of everybody else who had no cause or inclination to hold authority in respect: 'Christ . . . the way you cleaned up that mob o' coppers . . . four in a bloody row! Son, you're goin' 'o be a great asset, *Comes de Revolutions*, as they say. Tell me 'bout it?' He tried hard to pump Prindy, bawling in his ear above the mechanical din, so as to make him wince. Prindy kept his eyes on the twin silver ribbons rushing at them from ahead. Even that drew a compliment from Pat: 'You sure know how to keep the trap shut. 'Nother great asset. You were born to be a Comm.'

Pat told Prindy at the top of his voice, how within five years everybody left standing would be a Communist, by which time he, Prindy, should be ready to take his place in organizing the Aborigines for the Workers' Millenium. He told how he had taken Rifkah to Town on this very engine, sitting in that very seat, where he hoped to have her again someday, in fact the two of them together, as he'd had before. He waxed confident in the wincing ear: 'If only I can track down that yeller moll of a wife o' mine and get shot of her, I'll marry Rifkah, and adopt you as my son. How'd you like that, eh?' Prindy nodded readily, perhaps in the hope of stopping the torture of those sensitive ears.

When in late afternoon they were approaching Helena River, Pat came out with what must have been the ulterior of his motives. He took from the pocket of his black shirt a grubby but otherwise unmarked envelope, which he explained to Prindy was a letter to Rifkah, which he wanted him to deliver secretly. He buttoned it into a pocket of Prindy's beautiful tailor-made shirt, grubbying the material a little in the process. 'I know I can trust you,' he shouted, and gave his hard hand on it. Grey eyes met green. Then Pat patted the fair head, and turned away to give his attention to bringing the train into Helena siding.

Back in the coach, with the Sun down amongst the trees and gold and violet hurtling through the windows like flights of startled birds, making it hard for anyone to keep awake without a bottle and an argument to sustain them, Prindy mostly slept. From one lap to the other of the grey old men who guarded him he rolled in half-waking, perhaps dreaming through their talk-talk-talk, perhaps singing it in dreams:

Catholicism, Communism,
Anachronism, Despotism,
Christians, Pagans, Fascists, Jews,
Dominus vobiscum, and same to yous!
Hey, out the way there, Kangaroos,
Here come de Revolutionism!

Igulgul woke him, peeping through the window. He knelt on the seat to watch the engine's headlight swinging round the curves to burn a track for them through the bush. Thus till lights appeared ahead. Pin-pricks at first. At last a blaze.

Yet again Port Palmeston. Policemen waiting as usual, but eyes and hands ready for a gang of black miscreants who, manacled, had been poked aboard at Caroline. There was Fay McFee again, but without the camera and flash-light, only open arms, which she flung about Prindy as he stepped down, muttering between kisses that they must have a quiet talk in which he'd tell her all about it, eh? But also there was Kitty Windeyer, who snatched him away, and with the aid of another old acquaintance, Brother David, held off the unholy opposition. Said David, holding one small hand while Kitty held the other in taking him to the presbytery car, 'You belong our Catholic mob now. Finish no-goot pagan blackfeller bijnitch and rubbitch Communist. I learn him you Catechism.'

Yet another *Ism*?

David placed him in the front seat of the car, and got in himself to drive. Kitty got in on the other side. Monsignor was helped into the back seat by many willing hands. Jeremy joined him. So up into the blazing town with its residents of many breeds scurrying like meat-ants. They stopped at the Queen Victoria Hotel to drop off Jeremy, who in parting with Prindy reminded him that they would be shopping together tomorrow for things to take to the Leopolds.

At the Catholic mission house they found a nice supper awaiting them. Kitty left them to it, with an arrangement for Prindy to join her tomorrow at the church, to hear her play the big organ for a wedding. That night the other occupants of the mission house, Monsignor Maryzic, Brother David, and Black Bartholemew the gardener, were roused by strange sweet sounds from the netted bed on the verandah outside the Monsignor's rooms, and for the first time heard *My Rown Road.*

On the list for Saturday morning's shopping was first a gramophone for Rifkah, so that she might play her Jewish records without offence to Christian instrument or ears. Other such records would soon be coming from the South. Jeremy also bought some he thought might be pleasing to the Mission people.

While they were dealing with this matter of the gramophone, they found themselves confronted with another old acquaintance, who hailed them with gusto and that deceiving wink of his. It was Judge Bickering. Rumpling Prindy's hair, while winking at Jeremy, he said he'd been hearing a lot of things lately that he'd like to know the truth about, and insisted on their coming to lunch at his home. It was agreed.

Later they were buying a fishing net, for presentation to the Mission, were out at the back of the store, Jeremy with the salesman in a back room, Prindy out on the back verandah idly examining things stored there, when there appeared still another old friend. This one was black, and peeping round a shed. It was him called Kadjugo, or Daddy in the Alice River lingo, one of that pair who, by the river that day so long ago in experience if not in time, had given his blessing to the final fatal leg of Prindy's journey with the late Njorjunga, generally known as King George. He gave the Snake Sign, then vanished. Prindy hesitated only so long as it took him to estimate the occupancy of those in the net-room and to make a swift survey of the yard. Then he slipped across to the shed.

Kadjugo was fresh out of jail, as obvious from his stiff new khakis with the store-folds still in them. He grinned, and did the *Properly T'ing* by dropping on a knee and running slim hands over the tailor-clad small person. Then from out of a pocket of his store-stinking outfit he produced a small paper package, which he unwrapped to disclose a Letter Stick, saying, 'Pookarakka been send him.' He didn't hand over the missive at once, but in the manner of those delivering such things, traced out the glyphs, explaining: 'Pookarakka talk you come look-him-up.' Then rewrapping the stick, he gave it to Prindy, who buttoned it in with that other message he had received in secret. Kadjugo touched him again, but now without bending, grinning widely, saying, 'You too goot, eh? Properly my-boy. All-same Old Man been talk. All-same all-about talk.' He shook his grey head, no doubt expressing incredulity with the proven – the demons Coon-Coon and Jinbul despatched at a blow by a boy! Then he sighed, said '*Mummuk yawarra*,' turned, vanished.

Prindy came back across the yard to find Jeremy awaiting him. No questions asked, just an exchange of grey glances.

Judge Bickering was alone as usual, already slightly drunk and full of witty talk about the advantages of having wives and families sensitive enough to find one hard to live with. Still, he did not forget why he had them there, and over lunch tried many lawyer's tricks to get at the facts of those matters he'd hinted at, nor forget that he was a lawyer and show nothing but appreciation for being outwitted, and winked and winked. His wink was more than a *tic* when he talked of Monsignor Maryzic, that was certain. He laughed deeply over the Very Reverend gentleman's intrusion into things. 'Old Jesuit fox!' he cried. 'It's true the saying that the fox can be beguiled by his own scent in season. The reek of casuistry outstunk that of Awld Reeky himself. Ha! ha! He's been and gone and baptized an Imp of Satan, a 'prentice Snake Man, neophyte to Cock-Eye Bob . . . because that's what you are boy, that's what you are, aren't you? Ah, how cleverly he holds that tongue! But wait till I have His Very Reverence round to dinner next . . . Ha, ha, ho!'

Was it just coincidence that the Judge should suggest a trip out to see the Pookarakka? He did say that he hadn't been out to the Jail for some time and would be glad of the run this afternoon to get away from the mob who would make it hideous with their bawling during the football match. 'Why can't football be played with the seemliness of cricket?' he demanded. 'You might answer that the former is the sport of louts while the latter that of gentlemen. Then tell me the difference between a gentleman and a lout? You may say education. Then what are we but troupes of performing apes, performing according to the methods of some particular ringmaster somewhat more intelligent than ourselves . . . and where is that Divine Spark that we call Human Intelligence? Yes, Prendegast, my boy . . . we'll pay our esteemed friend, Bobwirridirridi, a visit. You needn't look alarmed, Jeremy. We'll be going alone. Therefore His Very Reverence will not be able to charge *you* with stealing a march on him, and your own indestructible Catholicism will be preserved to get you past St Peter. Of course you're still Catholic. Don't the Jesuits say: Give me a child to the age of seven, and he's mine for ever?'

Was it just coincidence, or another lawyer's trick, this one to get Prindy away on his own? But there was that Letter Stick in Prindy's pocket, a magical thing from the Master of Magic!

'Come, boy,' said Judge Bickering. 'Let's get out to the Jail while I've still wits enough not to drive us into the sea.'

Thus did the Pookarakka again lay those claws of his, though in nothing like depredation but the softest touch of love by the look of their caressing motions, on him he called *Mekullikulli*. They were left to talk for a good hour alone in a corner of the exercise yard. Judge Bickering, knowing when he was beaten, getting nothing from them singly or together, left them to it, to go suffer afternoon tea with Dotty O'Dowdy, the Major being a football fan and absent. Officials were told to leave them alone. Who would want to intrude upon them having heard of the recent doings of the apprentice?

The Judge himself delivered Prindy back to the Mission house, telling Monsignor Maryzic, who met the winking with a hard suspicious eye, that they had gone for a long drive to get to know each other better. 'Ah,' said His Very Reverence dryly, 'I haf been vonderingk if he might haf fallen in mitt bad company.'

Monsignor had no time to do any quizzing of his own, because no sooner was the Judge gone, when there was Kitty Windeyer come to scold Prindy for failing to keep his appointment with her at the organ, and to tell Maryzic that now the wedding was over people were lining up for him to hear their Confessions. She snatched Prindy away, this time to join her in partaking of the wedding breakfast in the church hall. 'You never saw such a cake!' she cried. As they went and she showed him the crowd waiting in the church, she told him how Monsignor was preferred by other priests as Confessor, despite the fact that as likely as not a Confession might be made public by his roaring in castigation. She said with a little giggle, 'I think it's because he understands sin as something human. I'll bet he's been a great sinner himself in his time.' She sighed, as if sad to think that time was over.

Before dawn on Sunday morning, Brother David roused Prindy to come join him in service to Monsignor Maryzic serving early Mass. Prindy, again in scarlet and lace, did no more than kneel on the sidelines, swinging a censer, watching. Thenceforth David kept him under his wing. They had breakfast at the Mission house with Jeremy, whom they found awaiting them, then boarded *St Francis Xavier*, to slip moorings as the Sun rose. David as captain had Prindy beside him at the wheel. He brought the ship close to that beacon on Rainbow Reef. Everbody wanted to see it, stood staring, the blackboys as if seeing again the wonder of that misty morning. David giggled in Prindy's ear under cover of the engine's beat, 'Dem silly-bugger blackboy been reckon she dibble from rock . . . eeeeeee! What you reckon, eh?' An unanswerable question, probably not requiring answer, but betraying a deep preoccupation with Rifkah that made much of the conversation between the pair throughout the voyage.

Two days and two nights they ran, mostly east-by-north, in Autumnal calm. David rigged hammocks for the pair of them up amongst the bowsprit shrouds, the quietest and pleasantest part of the ship, for anyone with stomach for the pitching and not minding an occasional douching with spray. Here

David talked religion and Rifkah, while Prindy lay watching the unfamiliar places rise out of the jade-green sea – the emerald islets, the terracotta cliffs, the violet ranges, all to vanish as if only dreamt of – at night watching the stars dip down almost close enough to grab, only to snatch themselves away, with glimpses of young Igulgul aloft, dragging after them on a cable of gold.

Dat Jewish Woman, as David called Rifkah, every now and again dragging her out of Limbo or Heaven or Hell, the Communion of Saints, the Forgiveness of Sins, the Life Everlastin', *Dominus Vobiscum et idem ad te*. That-lot Jew belong to Bible Book, like Dream Time people in Blackfeller Humbug. How come they still knockin' round? Father Glascock reckon they's a big mob yet, very clever, and holy, only trouble they ain't Christian. On the other hand, Sister Dymphna reckon they get kick-out of Holy Land by God, for Muddrin the Blessed Lord Jesus Christ (Got 'o hit yourself in the guts every time you say that name). Sister don't like Rifkah. Jealous, I reckon. But Mother Mathias like her all right, say on quiet, 'By'n'by we baptize her . . . but don't matter now . . . she good cook, and we want cook more'n we want convert.' She was running the kitchen now. Properly good tucker!

David said he was thinking of giving up celibacy and marrying Rifkah and later starting a cook-shop for Asiatics in Town, with her as cook. He'd wait till she put a bit of fat on. As yet she was skinny as a lubra, from being pretty sick when she came to the Mission: 'I like woman got plenty fat. What dis Jewish woman like before . . . got him fat arse? Father reckon dey fat woman mostly. I don' know . . . sometime I don' b'lieve him. But dat no-good t'ing say 'bout priest. I got 'o do a penance now for dat. Wha' name Penance? All right, I tell him you . . . . '

Two days – two nights – and there they were in the Leopold Islands, battling the tide through emerald channels. No pigeons – no Japs. A few egrets, cranes, cormorants, a great flotilla of pelicans, and a couple of sea-eagles. No canoes or campfires on the bits of beaches. The plumes of smoke on the mainland, bending to the beginnings of the Sou'easter, told of the concentrations there for the bounty, and the ceremonial supposed to be the means of producing it, following Wet Season. As Brother David put it: 'Walkabout Time. You can't keep dem black bastard for Jesus Christ (whack!) when plenty tucker long o' bush.'

Then there at last were the white roofs of the Mission, seeming to be floating behind the green-brown wall of the casuarinas. Dots of colour moved before the wall. A flash of copper amongst the dots. Prindy hopped with excitement.

Prindy, in the bow of the boat going ashore, was first overboard, at touch of bottom. Rifkah was first into the water to meet him. They met in a fling of spray, embracing – '*Mein kleine menscheleh . . . Koiyu, koiyu!*'

How the others stared!

A very different-looking Rifkah. She might have been taken for a halfcaste, so lean and brown was she, barefoot and clad in a shapeless mission dress. The girlish look was gone. The *bubbeh's* lines about the eyes seemed permanent, while yet the jewels themselves sparkled as of old, as if harsh experience with man and circumstance had taught the final lesson the wise old *bubbeh* learns, that in the midst of joy we are in terror, in the midst of life in death. It was no lost little girl who greeted Jeremy. She didn't fly to *him*, but met him with that sweet smile she had for all who were not her active enemies, placed hands on his shoulders, looked into his face so much aged since last she'd seen it, shook the copper head slightly, then kissed his ruddy slightly jerking cheek. Then she turned to give her hand to the Monsignor, as to an old friend. He bowed over it, touching it with his lips.

The staring crowd!

Father Glascock watched the Monsignor's courtesy with eyes screwed like an oaf witnessing something he would never have the finesse to do. Mother Mathias stood with arms folded on flat chest and seamed moustachioed old lips pursed and eyes twinkling, as only seeing advantage in it. Sister Dymphna looked sullen. Indeed, Mother Mathias wasted no time in telling Monsignor that now they had this girl who was proving such an asset to them they would be needing more money, money, money. Monsignor Maryzic murmured in reply that, besides advising the Bishop, he would also try touching Mr Delacy: 'So be a little bit more tactful zan usual, dear Reverend Mudder, yes?'

But there was no time for talking business now. This was a holiday for the Mission. News of the good things for the great picnic on the beach had been radioed ahead. The second boat came ashore so heavily laden with cases of soft drink, tins of cake, biscuits, stringed sausages, as to be, to fearful eyes ashore, almost awash.

That this holiday was a long long day for Jeremy was plain to see in his face as he sat out the picnic, watching the children at their play and feasting, hen-mothered by Rifkah, on whom the Reverend Mother beamed and the Reverend Sister scowled, watching these two in their private striving, watching the two priests in theirs. There was much talk between the priests on Judaism, with mouthings of Seminary Hebrew, excluding him – as if he knew so little of Jews that the knowledge had not completely changed his life! He saw nothing of Rifkah privately all day.

It looked as if the night were going to be not dissimilar, with the clergymen settling down after supper at the presbytery to argue ecclesiastically, politically, philosophically, their differences the more stubborn for those in their age, status, nationality, and the liberal supply of liquor donated by Jeremy. Then there on the moonlit road appeared the glint of copper. Rifkah came in with a smile, excusing herself, saying she'd just got her kitchen clear, declining Father Glascock's invitation to join them: 'I come for Jeremy. Alvays at Lily Lagoons ve go valkingk after supper. Ve have mooch to spik. It is permitted?'

'Of course, of course,' said Glascock.

Both priests eyed her with curious intensity. Jeremy looked at a loss.

She was wearing one of the good dresses brought to her, but still wore no shoes. As they went off together, Jeremy remarked on the latter fact. She told him that her feet had been so badly lacerated and infected that she had been unable to walk properly until a week ago, having got about on crutches after recovery from her initial illness, and then found that she preferred to go barefoot. She asked, 'Vot matter? It mek me more like ze ozzers. Zat is how I vont to be.'

She took his arm as of old, guiding him down through the casuarinas to the bright beach. But there was not that tendency to lean against him now, to draw close in looking into his face. In fact she did that only twice, the first time for only a second in response to his asking was she never coming back to

Lily Lagoons again. She had been talking eagerly of how she liked it here, making shift on the poor supplies available to make everybody satisfied. The gesture was perhaps a form of renouncing the old sweetness of refuge in him. She sighed before answering, 'Of course, moost I visit sometime. I vill ride overland. But I cannot stay zere. It was only *playing* house zere. Here I haf real job to do. Zese holy vomen do not know how to housekeep properly or look out for children. Zey are so different from ze children, zey fright' zem. Zey are not fright' of me.' She giggled. 'I zink zey do not look on me as vite voman. So no shoe. By'n'by ven I haf ze lingo and can go bush wit' ze blacks, maybe no clothes.' She giggled again. 'Ven I tell zat to ze nuns, I zink zey are goingk to fall down faint . . . eeeeee!'

He said, 'Look out they don't baptize you.'

She answered, 'I do not zink zey are mooch interest. Zey call ze house I haf ze Synagogue, because I light *Shabbos* candle for myself zere. Zey like me to tell ze children Old Testament Bible story. Father say ze kids pick it up from me like Dream Time story. I mek myself useful to zem. Zey are happy. I am happy, too.'

'How do you feel about Prindy's being caught by them?'

'He is not caught.'

'But he seems to like it.'

'It is ceremony to him. He like zat. It mek music for him. He is Snake Man. He is little bit Jew. He is Christian. Better like zat, because I can keep him wit' me. I haf ask Monsignor. He say he vill tell me tomorrow. Ze old man vont ze boy for himself, I zink. He loff him. But I zink he vill let him stay. He say if I do not interfere vit' him beingk Christian. I say, "How can I, a Jewess, mek a Jew . . . except in kitchen?' He is goot old man. Zey are all goot. Truly are zey zinkingk of zese poor people as nobody else I know. It is not to mek zem Catholic, but to save zem from vot zey call Barbarous Practice. Somezing ze blacks do are ver' cruel . . . .'

'That's Aboriginal Ethos. I thought we were pledged to preserve it?'

'I do not know now. Mooch I haf to learn. Prindy vill help teach me. He haf become very vise little boy.'

'Did he tell you what happened after you left?'

'Only Old Tchamala kill policemen. Vot is true story?'

'I know no more than that. Perhaps that *is* the true story. So much is strangely wonderful in life.' He sighed. She looked at him, closely this time, into his eyes, clung a moment, then withdrew, to remain stiff for the rest of the walk.

He returned her to her place of residence, a converted storeroom, the so-called Synagogue. Prindy was there, piping in the doorway, perhaps for the secret entertainment of the girls in the convent dormitory across the way. Rifkah kissed Jeremy's cheek lightly in parting with him. He kissed her hand, then turned away abruptly. He was heading back to the presbytery, but nearing it, hearing voices raised in ecclesiastical argument, swung away, to go back to the beach. He walked the beach, following their dual track of earlier but without sullying it with his own steps as if wishing to preserve it, till the Moon was gone. Then he sat on the beach below the presbytery and watched the sinking of the stars. When at last he got back, there was but one sitter at the table on the verandah, and he with dark head lying amongst the glasses, palely lit by the dying pressure lamp – and snoring hard.

Early next morning Prindy assisted at Mass, with a little more to do, directed by Brother David. He moved with special dignity, perhaps not merely by reason of added experience but through having on him the eyes of two unbelievers. Jeremy and Rifkah were seated in that pew formerly occupied by the Japanese. Otherwise there were only the nuns present. Both priests officiated, Monsignor as Celebrant. When it was over and Rifkah going to officiate in the kitchen, she had Prindy with her, an arm about him, and her expression showing nothing but pleasure in what she had just seen. Jeremy watched from the porch, Monsignor Maryzic from the sacristy.

Soon after breakfast at the presbytery, Monsignor declared he wanted the Naturalization Business got over and himself away home. Rifkah came with Prindy and Mother Mathias. To begin with, it looked at if it would not come off, because Rifkah refused to swear allegiance to the King of England, no doubt inspired by having heard Jeremy talk of his shame as a modern man, son of a so-called democracy, in having, according to the law, to bend the knee to the anachronism of monarchy. She looked to him now, as if for support, when the old man, perhaps suffering somewhat from last night's ecclesiastics, became irritable, grumbling in much the same way that Pat Hannaford had, about all the trouble they had been to on her account. Jeremy was silent. Monsignor Maryzic growled, 'You are not ask to svear by book or candle. All you haf to do is mek affirmation you vill vell and truly serve His Majesty ze King. Ist not matter of conscience, but discretion. You vont to stay in zis country. For zat you must be British Subject, because it is rule by British Crown. You can aftervard argue der politic of it . . . if any zere is. Now please not to vaste time. Ve vont to catch tide. You vill mek der affirmation, yes?' With a sigh Rifkah gave in.

They had a nip of whisky to seal it. Monsignor sighed over his as if he needed it as badly as his bleary-eyed confrere. Then he told Prindy to get his things and come to board the boat. Prindy stared at him. 'Vot's matter?' asked the old man.

Prindy said simply, 'I stop here.'

The squarish old face darkened, quivered. The voice rumbled, 'I ask you come back mitt me.'

The grey eyes sought Rifkah's. The slaty old eyes did the same. Her brow rumpled.

After a moment the old priest swallowed, asked huskily, 'You vont him stay?'

She breathed, 'Pliss . . . yes.'

He blinked rapidly. Then with sudden harshness he declared, 'Der boy vill liff as Christian . . . ist understood?'

She reddened, but nodded. Then with softness as swift as the harshness had come, he said, '*Danke, Mädchen* . . . I leave him mitt you.'

He was turning away. But she grabbed him, flung her arms about him, kissed his cheek. He put an arm about her, squeezed her, rumbling, 'Eat more of your goot food, *Mädchen*.' Then he shoved her away. He looked at Prindy. 'You stay. But first you come mitt me to der church and pray.' He reached for the boy's hand. Prindy went readily.

Maryzic kept the boy's hand, telling him as they went that he expected him to be ready for Confirmation when the Bishop came, which would be about Race Time: 'Father Glascock vill instruct you. I vood like meinself to do zat. Please Gott I haf der privilege of instructingk you furzer.'

In the church Monsignor saw to it that Prindy crossed himself properly at the holy water stoop, that he genuflected to perfection. Then he sat him in the front pew, while he went himself to the altar-rail, knelt, dropped grey head to hands supported by elbows. He prayed for some ten minutes, while the grey eyes behind him gravely studied the equipment of this cult of his new initiation – the gilded brass of the altar, the mock eye of God, the Poor Bugger on the Cross, the petty idols that so demeaned the Great One with their lousy humanness. All this could bring so big and powerful a man as Monsignor Maryzic to his knees!

The old man turned and beckoned. Prindy slid across the little space to join him, was pulled to knees, manipulated into the attitude of prayer, golden fingers to golden chin, eyes closed to exclude reality. The old man had him follow him in the *Pater Noster* in English: Our Father, who art in heaven ... our daily bread ... our transgressions ... temptation ... deliver us from evil ... Amen. Always *Amen* to anything you say. What for? Evidently it was too rudimentary for the more sophisticated to bother to explain. David's explanation had been: I don' know dat one properly. Might-be like whiteman say, time he finish sumpin, Daddle-doo.

Monsignor said, 'I vont you, my dear boy, promise me, effery morning ven you vake you say zat prayer. You promise? Prindy did so. 'Now Sign of der Cross. Zat is moost important ... to keep der shadow of der sacrifice of our Lord Jesus Christ (thump) alvays on you. You understand me?' Nod. They rose, genuflected beautifully, went out.

Everybody was at the beach to see the visitors off. The nuns knelt the children for a special Blessing by Monsignor. Rifkah brought Prindy for an extra-special one, and a kiss on the forehead. The old man also kissed her forehead. She kissed his hand. Then she kissed Jeremy, not on the cheek that he presented, but on the mouth, clinging to him for a moment in such a way as to cause eyes to pop, then letting go, dropped face to hands. All over in a moment. She looked up with a wobbly smile, with jewels of eyes just a little too shiny. Jeremy, lobster-faced, nodded even curtly to the smile, then turned suddenly away to the waiting boat.

The grey hairs of the two passengers sitting amidships blew in the rising sou'easter as they waved their hats, the squatter's wide-awake, the cleric's black, to the waving crowd ashore. Not a word between them as the blackboys rowed them and David steered them to the schooner. No word even aboard ship, while they stood in the stern and waved till those they'd left had merged with their background. Still they stood staring back, till with the curving of the channel the dream-thing behind vanished like a dream. Then they looked at each other, grey eyes and slate, as if in challenge, as if in former association they had ignored the reality of each other, disguising it with formality, but with reality now thrust upon them and each having to justify his part in it or die of heart and soul. Jeremy broke the long silence: 'I've some brandy.'

The old priest sighed. 'Zank you, Jeremy ... I vill be glad.'

It followed that, while they sat and sipped and watched the passing scene of seascape, landscape, bird and fish and acquatic beast, they, being men with minds rather more than with bellies and cocks, should escape into polemics and that these largely should concern religion.

Their religious argument was no mean scrap between scoffer and bigot. In fact the priest revealed himself as more the unbeliever, if still faithful to what formerly he had unquestioningly believed. As he put it: the mass of humanity was stupid, dishonest, cowardly, and needs must have something to support it that belied these negative forces in it. Otherwise the negation would destroy the species, which even the bitterest cynic must admit was the supreme achievement of Creation. He himself having known the solace of religion, felt it his duty to give it to these weaker ones. On the other hand, Jeremy, the avowed atheist, talked with reverence of the Spirit of the Land and the Aborigines' kindred with it, spoke eagerly of the closeness of Jews to God without what he called the complications of *Christus* and *Paraclete* that only drove the needy man further from the god whose hand he sought to cling to. Maryzic pinned Jeremy's argument down here as spurious, declaring it simply refusal to accept the ultimate exaltation of Man, expressed in the Christ as in no other revelation.

An intelligent man, argued the old priest, need not accept Jesus literally as the Messiah; but not even to accept the fiction that the Messiah had been among Man was tantamount to insisting that the Rainbow was only a revelation of the consistency of the Sun's rays, more easily produced with a lens in the laboratory. Even to believe, he said, in what was negative and mean in Man as a spiritual force outside himself, personified as Satan, gave Man the impetus to resist it. As for Judaism's closeness to God, the Jews made God actually Boss of the Jews, with no interest in anyone else. The Christ Idea forced the God of Abraham to take cognizance of his other children. Again, rejection of Christus by Jews, while yet they clung to the hope of the Messianic Coming, denied them the miraculous in life, left them isolated and unsatisfied. A Christian could say, even if with tongue in cheek, that the Messiah *was* here. A Jew had to keep on hoping: 'Tomorrow, tomorrow,' which never comes. Take a parallel with the Aborigines' Dream Time. The Aborigines knew that the Totem Heroes had been here. There must be happiness for them so long as they followed in their footsteps. That brought Jeremy in to damn all those who would destroy the Dream Time fiction and leave the blackman a husk of non-believing. Maryzic countered: 'Der Dream Time fiction must go of necessity . . . Ve, der Christian Missionary, try to direct der lost footstep in der vay of Jesus Christ.'

So it went on, by the hour, while they sipped their brandy for the only real solace they got for all their vociferating, staring astern, as ever since they themselves had become husks of men – one in loss of the son he had always yearned for, the other in loss of his never-found bride. They saved the last of their daily ration of brandy for a stiff nightcap to sleep and dream on.

Then, at last, there was something to look ahead to, although rather like the blank prospect of their remaining years. To begin with it was a wide space of silvery nothingness, into which vague things grew like mushrooms of promise, only to become commonplace, revealed as the edifices of that commonest of places hereabout – Port Palmeston. They entered the harbour in midmorning glare.

As they were chugging in, running smoothly with the inrunning tide, passing the white jail on its red cliff, as if casually Monsignor Maryzic remarked on Prindy's visit there last Saturday. Jeremy was taken aback. The old man said, 'I know you haf nuzzing to do mitt it.' Asked how he had learnt of it, Maryzic smiled. 'Missus O'Dowdy is confessary of mine . . . and not only to confess her sin. After I hear, I telephone der Judge.' He sighed: 'Ven der boy not tell me himself, I know he ist not for me.'

The engine seemed to take that up and sing it like repetition of the thoughts of two old men for whom each a dream had faded: *Not for me, not for me, not for me*!

They rounded the beacon, came into view of the town proper. At the big jetty lay the West Coast steamer, *Koolpinyah*, with Blue Peter flying, a feather of steam at her blow-off pipe, evidently about to sail. They were staring at her as they rounded the point to go to moorings, when Jeremy said suddenly, 'I think I'll take a trip down to Hartog. Mind taking me to the jetty?' Monsignor Maryzic looked at him quickly, perhaps cognizant of the Delacy Bender, the flight from disillusion.

All was bustle aboard the steamer. On the jetty beside her the little locomotive that did the haulage there, the Sandfly, so called, was bringing up the passengers' luggage. Pat Hannaford was the driver. He stared at the schooner as she came up to the small-boat landing, got down from the engine to see her berth and put Jeremy ashore. He cupped his hands and bawled down at them, 'Where is she?' Jeremy, handling suitcase and swag, only shrugged. Pat bawled at the Monsignor, 'What you done with our girl, you bloody black crow?' Maryzic turned his back on him. The schooner was slipping away again.

Pat met Jeremy at the top of the steps from the landing, demanding, 'Why'n't bring her back?'

'She didn't want to come.'

'Balls! What's she want to stay with that mob for?'

'Said she likes it.'

'Don' gi' me that! You've worked it between you to keep her away from us.'

Jeremy looked surprised, then sour, grunting, 'Don't be silly!'

The steamer's whistle roared. Jeremy set off towards it. Pat followed him, asking, 'Where you off?'

'Just taking a bit of a trip.'

'What for?'

'What the hell's it got to do with you?'

'A lot. *She* was supposed to be goin' down on this ship.'

'So what?'

'You'll have to do a lot of explainin' to the crew . . . and the boys in Hartog . . . .'

The whistle blew again. Jeremy climbed the gangway, made for the purser's office to book his berth.

VI

Within half an hour Jeremy was back at sea, but heading in a different direction now and with only one glance towards what he'd lost. He then took up with a couple of meat buyers, urbane men, one English, the other American, and good drinkers, with whom he settled down in the smoking saloon. Thus he spent the rest of the day.

It was evening, dinner over, and Jeremy taking a stroll alone on the boat-deck, when out of shadow into the moonlight stepped a man in the rough clothes of a member of the crew. As Jeremy eyed him, the man asked, in a thin nasal tone, 'You Delacy?'

Jeremy took a moment to answer, staring into the slit eyes, 'Suppose I am?'

'Where's that girl?'

'What're you talking about?'

'You know bloody well. Where's she?'

'As I presume you're one of Pat Hannaford's mob, you'd know all about it.'

'I wan' 'o hear it from you.'

'Who are you, anyway?'

'Bo's'n.'

'Okay, Mister Bo's'n . . . I'll say Goodnight.' Jeremy turned away.

The man grabbed his arm. ' 'Ere!'

Jeremy flung off the hand, swung on the man menacingly. The man stepped back swiftly. After a moment the man asked, 'What you doin' on this ship?'

'Isn't the Bo's'n informed of such things?'

'Why you goin' 'o Port Hartog?'

'You ask so many questions that you seem already to know the answers to.'

'If you're goin' there with some trick up your sleeve, don't try it. They're a militant mob in the meatworks. They'll tear you apart.'

'Seeing you've got all the answers . . . what trick should I have up my sleeve?'

'Whatever it is you've cooked up with that British General and the Jesuits.'

'You're talking through your hat, man.'

'Am I? Then why didn't that girl get clear with the Jewish doctor when everything was organized for her?'

'Simply because she didn't want any more truck with your mob.'

'You mean because you wouldn't let her go. You was keepin' her to ride her . . . .'

'Eh?' Jeremy took a menacing step. 'What're you saying, rat?'

'What everybody's sayin'. You had the girl in your power. She was scared to leave, 'cause you'd put the Security Bulls onto her . . . like you did at last.'

Jeremy's flame of anger was extinguished by obvious astonishment. 'For chrissake . . . when I've been fighting like hell to keep her free!'

The man sneered. 'How come your Fascist cobbers of the Free Australia Movement blow the gaff on her?'

'Where'd you get all this bullshit?'

'You turned her in 'cause she was tryin' to get away from you. You let 'em put her in the lock-up, reckonin' you'd help her through the courts. Balls! It was Pat Hannaford got her away. So then you call in Catholic Action . . . '

'Did Hannaford tell you that?'

'We know everything's goin' on.'

'Then why waste time asking me?'

'I ain't askin' you . . . I'm tellin' you. Keep on the ship, mate. The mob at Hartog's expectin' the girl. When they hear you dobbed her 'cause she wouldn't let you root her . . . ' Again Jeremy advanced and the man stepped back. Jeremy's fist was raised this time. The man added from safe distance, 'Don't try any that stuff on me. *I* run this ship. My mates run Port Hartog, too.'

Jeremy exhaled heavily: 'I don't doubt it, from what I've heard. But listen, bilge-rat . . . if I ever get you alone you'll never be able to crawl up past a rat-guard on any ship again.'

The man almost squeaked, 'You been warned.' Then like a rat he vanished.

Jeremy saw the Moon down, walking the deck, sighing, clenching and unclenching his fists. When at length he returned to the saloon, he found his former companions too far ahead of him in drink to be good company, and after a single drink more, retired to his berth.

At dawn next morning they were in Hartog Sound, which from the ochreous mud for ever being churned by monster tides, looked as if it ran with the blood of the thousands of bovine innocents that met their fate in the great slaughter-house at the head of the waterway. Soon after breakfast the ship berthed at the meatworks wharf, to take on meat. Meat, meat, meat! The place reeked of it. Fresh meat still jerking with the last of life in it. Meat boiling in vast vats for canning. Meat dried with blood and crushed bone and being bagged as fertilizer. The passengers fled, to take a bus into the tiny township a mile away. Jeremy went with them, booked in at the one hotel. Later he looked up a couple of acquaintances, a stock and station agent, a Chinese storekeeper.

Before lunch he returned to the hotel, there to rendezvous with his meat-buying friends from the ship, who were joined by the Meatworks Manager and the ship's captain. He stayed with them till they went back to the ship, which was due to sail in mid-afternoon. Then he joined up with some boozy drovers. Soon he was the Jeremy Delacy known for his dry wit in down-country pubs, keeping the place in fits with his tales of odd characters like Billy Brew, Neddy Knowles, Piggy Trotters, his own policeman father. They were fed in the bar, as was usual when what was called a Session was on.

It was high moonlight when Jeremy left the bar to cross the yard to the latrine. He was almost there, when from behind it and a nearby shed a number of men suddenly appeared. They were all big fellows, Southerners by the conventional dress of black pants, striped shirts, black patent-leather shoes. Boozy as he was, Jeremy looked about quickly, swung round to have the wall of the privy at his back, demanding, 'Whash thish?'

The biggest man, a fair bull, with close-clipped bristly hair that shone in the moonlight and a butcher's face and belly, growled, 'You were told you ain't wanted here.'

'Tha'sh so? I haven't been informed by the mayor yet.'

'Cheeky bastard, eh?' growled the man, and with surprising swiftness in one so big, aimed a blow.

Jeremy was too slow to avoid it, took it on the shoulder, but to be spun round so as to deliver his famous left into the man's fatty midriff. The big fellow grunted, sagged at the knees, gasping for breath now. Jeremy got in a few hard hits at the others as they fell on him, sent a couple down, but in no time went down himself to a well-placed rabbit-punch. As he lay they set about him with their shiny shoes, till the bull-man, with breath recovered, heaved up and flung them back. Nevertheless, the bull-man bent over him, pulled his lolling head up by the hair, and growling at the senseless face, ''It me below the belt, would yo'? Fascist bastard? Cop this!' he smashed his huge fist into it. Then he let the bloodied thing drop to the gravel, and rose, saying, 'Okay, bring him along.'

The others raised Jeremy. A couple of the biggest got shoulders under his arms, and with the bull-man leading, dragged him round the far side of the hotel and out into the street well beyond it. Out of the dark doorway of the stock and station agent's a tall lean figure stepped. He met the procession, took a look at the hanging blood-streaming face. He asked, 'You weren't too rough with him, were you?'

The biggest man growled, 'No. He put up a fight. Had to KO the bastard.'

'Better wipe some that blood off him. Give's y' handkerchief.'

Then the lean man said, 'Right . . . bring him along.' He set off in the direction of a blue lamp not far down the road. That meant a police station in these parts.

The policemen were in their office, a sergeant and constable, taking it easy, smoking, with feet up. They assumed more decorous attitudes as the lean man entered. The sergeant spoke: 'Goodnight, Mister Secretary . . . what can we do for you?'

'Bit o' trouble, sergeant. Chap off the boat . . . passenger. Throwing his weight round amongst my members. Boozed. Brawling. Thought you'd better take care of him. If he stays here, there's sure to be more trouble . . . and none of us want that, eh?'

'We certainly don't. Where's this chap?'

'Boys've got him. Had to KO him to stop him.' The man turned and beckoned to those outside. When they dragged Jeremy in, the sergeant signed to them to drop him into a wooden armchair, receptacle for many an incapable prisoner, no doubt. The sergeant asked the constable did he know him. The man replied that he'd seen him boozing in the pub, heard him magging about things over the State Border. He jerked his head eastward.

'Right,' said the sergeant. 'We'll put him back over the Border.'

The tall lean man said, 'Thanks, sergeant.' He and his mates went out.

Rising, the sergeant said, 'Let him sleep it off in a cell. Better see if he's got any belongings at the pub.'

Between them, as the other men had, the policemen raised Jeremy, dragged him out to the cell-block, into a cell, dumped him on a plank bed, left him, turning the key on him.

The Moon was well down before Jeremy was recovered enough to take intelligent interest in his surroundings. A door of bars, revealing a blaze of stars, a stretch of ruddy water lit by reflexion from the meatworks ablaze and roaring at its never-ending seasonal orgy of slaughter. At length he rose, approached the bars, examined them, shook them, shouted. He was silenced by a distant voice, 'Shut up and go to sleep . . . let you out morning'!'

He sighed, searched the dark place, found a tap, drank greedily and laved his sticky face. At last he returned to the plank bed, removed shoes and stripped to underwear, made a pillow of sorts of what he'd doffed, stretched out, slept.

Soon after dawn the constable came, with a hunk of bread and dripping and a pannikin of tea. He ignored Jeremy's questions, locked the door again. But he was back in about half an hour, growling, 'Come on . . . out!'

Jeremy followed the man through the station office to the street. The police utility was at the curb, engine running, the sergeant, in bright blue shirt with silver buttons, behind the wheel. The constable shoved Jeremy in with the sergeant, himself climbed into the rear. As the car moved off, heading out of town, Jeremy asked, 'What's going on?'

The segeant grunted, 'You.'

'What d'you mean?'

'You're on your way home. I understand you're from across the Border?'

'I am . . . but what've I done to get run out?'

'We don't like troublemakers here.'

'What trouble've I made?'

'Take a look at yourself in the rearview mirror.'

Jeremy looked. He said, 'A mob got to me.'

'You started it.'

'Who says this?'

'Listen, man . . . don't waste your breath. You got a long dry walk ahead o' you.'

'But you haven't even asked me what happened!'

'I know.'

'How can you know when I didn't tell you? You've not questioned me. You've not charged me. Yet you're running me out of the country I paid my fare to come into and my board to stay in for a while.'

'I told you we don't want your kind here.'

'What kind?'

The sergeant's voice rose. 'Will you shut up?'

'No I won't shut up. I'm in my own country . . . not Germany, or Russia.'

'You're not in your own country . . . but you soon will be. Now shut up!'

'I demand to be charged.'

'If you don't shut up, I'll put the handcuffs on you and chuck you in the back.'

'By God, you'll pay for this, sergeant!'

'You talk to me like that, I'll give you such a bloody beltin', you'll have to crawl the rest of the way home!' So did the sergeant glare that the car almost ran off the narrow track.

Jeremy subsided, muttering, 'I have come to Germany after all . . . or Russia.'

'Shut up, shut up . . . unless you want that beltin'!'

Jeremy sighed, looked out on the desolate scene. They were running along a scrubby gravel ridge, the only means of permanent passage through the waste of salt-arms. Through the mean tea-tree and withered maritime growth could be seen the silvery upper reaches of the Sound, beyond miles of salt-pans already glistening in the rising Sun.

After a while Jeremy asked, 'Are you a Communist, Sergeant?'

The man looked at him sharply, snapped, 'Don't give me cheek!'

'No cheek was intended. I just thought you might be . . . seeing you let me be beaten up by Communists.'

'Who says you were beaten up by Communists?'

'I do.'

'Who're you?'

'You haven't even troubled to find out my name. But you'll soon know when I've laid a complaint to your Commissioner about my treatment at your hands.'

The sergeant looked as if about to roar, but only gave a harsh laugh. 'You can lay a complaint to Old Nick, if you like . . . it won't get you anywhere. I'm here to keep the peace during the season. That's what the Commissioner wants. That's what the Government wants. That's what everybody wants . . . except the likes of you . . . which is why you're getting run out.'

'In effect the Communists run this town while the meatworks're working?'

'*I* run this town.' The sergeant was glaring again. 'Didn't I tell you to shut up?'

Jeremy subsided, dropped head to a hand to cover his bunged eyes.

After a while the sergeant said, 'At Invercargill Station they'll give you some steak for them eyes.' Jeremy glanced at the hard profile, intent upon the rough track, said nothing. The Sergeant made several other remarks of friendly nature, such as that this part of the country was only fit for blacks, that it got better further on, that he should be able to join a returning droving plant at Invercargill to make his way home, that he'd take him all the way to the station homestead, only he hadn't the time, had a court case this morning. To the latter remark, Jeremy responded, 'Do you hold People's Courts in there?'

The hard eyes searched his. 'What you mean People's Courts?'

'Where the Commissars have condemned someone, but hand it over to a mob to give the verdict and carry out the sentence.'

'That meant to be funny?'

'Not really. I don't feel in a funny mood.'

'Then shut up . . . like I've told you a hundred times!'

They ran the best part of an hour, fast, because the sergeant was skilled and knew the road. The country changed suddenly from gravel and clay to grey sand, thickly grown with scrub of all kinds. Soon they came to a creek. The car stopped.

The sergeant said, 'Well, here we are. It's only fifteen mile to the station . . . best part o' fifty the other way. Water here. Water on the road. You ought 'o make the station by sundown. Right . . . get out.' He leaned towards Jeremy as he obeyed. 'If you come back, you'll only be put on the wood-heap for a week and then run out here again . . . this time with a boot up the arse to start you movin'. Got it?'

The constable tossed Jeremy's dunnage down to him, then got down, dusted himself, got into the front. The car swung round, was gone.

A couple of crows flapped in to land in a bigger tree and watch Jeremy go down to a stagnant pool of water, raucously muttering about him, perhaps about his chances of survival with a face like that and all the flies in the country starting on him. He sat for a while by the water, fighting the flies with a switch of leaves. Then he opened swag and suitcase and rolled bare necessities in the former, to make what was called a Cigarette Swag, fixing a towel through the straps for easy carrying. He put the case in a tree. A good drink; then off towards where he had been told to go. The crows farewelled him: Bastard, bastard, why couldn' yo' die heah, heah, heah?

Harsh country. Still, it abounded in many things that interested him, to which he waved his fly-switch, when they peeped, or spoke to if they did not bolt. A goanna, a frilled-lizard, kangaroos, an emu with chicks. Perhaps even a bounteous country for anyone who knew how to live in it. There were plovers on a little billabong, brolgas on a bit of plain – then the criss-crossing tracks of cattle. At length a fence, a gate. More tracks here, and the distant calling of cattle going to late afternoon watering.

Another gate. Then through the trees a glimpse of white homestead. The Sun was down in the trees. The radio-masts were gilding. It was a small homestead, comprizing only half a dozen buildings, the Big House only so-big, and looking smaller for being built on the ground and surrounded by an unusually extensive garden. The big kitchen behind, another bungalow, was already lit artificially. Somewhere a power-plant sang. Jeremy headed for the Big House, opened the gate of the garden, went up the gravel path, cigarette swag still hanging from his sweat-soaked shoulder.

On the front verandah two men lounged in canvas chairs, with a bottle between them on a table, glasses in hands. One was nuggety, grey, the other lanky and young. It was the young man who spoke, shortly, jerking his head, 'Kitchen's behind there.'

Jeremy kept on, said, in a voice hoarse with weariness and slurred with broken lips, 'Like to see the Boss.'

The young man drew in his long legs, leant forward, snapped, 'I told you where the kitchen is.'

The older man, obviously the Boss by his wooden magisterial expression, met the glance Jeremy gave him with glassy bloodshot indifference. Jeremy, now at the step, husked at him, 'What . . . the Boss do the cooking round here?'

The man's face flamed. But it was the young man who answered, 'Don't be cheeky!'

Jeremy looked at him, then back to the Boss, who stirred uncomfortably now, grunting, 'They'll attend to you in the kitchen. If you want work, see the Head Stockman tomorrow.'

Jeremy inhaled deeply, took another look at the young man, who was leaning forward now with blue eyes blazing and in an attitude as if to leap to his feet. Then he turned about, marched back to the gate.

Now the evening was red. Jeremy made for the kitchen. Those within it were plain to see: the cook in whites and cap, a whiteman, almost as white as his clothes, a lanky cadaver of a man, the staff halfcaste women. A woman directed the cook's attention to Jeremy when he came to the door. The man approached, stared, nodded to Jeremy's greeting, said in a thin sour voice, 'Where I seen you before?'

Jeremy shook his head, asked in a mumble if he could have a drop of soup and slice of bread. The man quizzed a moment longer, then saying, 'Been in the wars, eh?' turned and called on a woman to fill a billy with soup. He himself got a couple of slices of bread, put them on a tin plate, handed them over, asking, 'What happened to the other bloke?'

'He got the shielah,' mumbled Jeremy, adding, 'Where can a man camp round here?'

Grinning like a death's head, the cook directed him to the men's quarters across the way. Jeremy went. There were men out on the long verandah who nodded to him, staring hard, a dog that snarled at him till toed by its owner. He went to an empty room at the far end of the long row of rooms. While he ate his spare meal, sitting on a kerosene-case that was all the furniture outside the room, the other men crossed to the kitchen in response to the supper-gong. Afterwards he went to the shower, washed his clothes as well as himself, reducing his covering to the towel from the swag. Then, having hung his stuff on a wire on the verandah to dry, he went into the room and made up the bare iron bed by laying his swag-cover on it, dropped down on it, was soon asleep.

Next morning Jeremy breakfasted with the other men, was amiably enough treated to begin with and amiable enough himself, but blocked all efforts to satisfy their curiosity about him. The Head Stockman said he reckoned he knew him and tried to work out how and where. Jeremy merely answered that it was a Big Country. He showed he knew something of them by speaking of the cook by name: 'See you got Poor Bob poisoning you.' It was hardly fair, seeing that Poor Bob had gone to the trouble to make him a special mince, although evidently not without the motive of getting him to talk about himself. At length the men punished him by ignoring him. He returned to his quarters.

Later on, in badly rumpled if clean clothes, unshaved because it would be days before he could put razor to that puffed, lacerated, black-and-blue face, he crossed to the office building. As he entered he was met by the hard blue eyes of the young man of last evening, evidently the Bookkeeper. The man was seated at a desk. As Jeremy breasted the counter, the man snapped at him, 'Well?'

Jeremy had to husk to speak: 'You do the postal business?'

'I do.'

'Like to send a radiogram.'

The blue eyes glinted, as with anger at being forced to do something for an enemy, class-enemy asserting rights under the lunacy of democracy. He rose with deliberate slowness, it seemed, came slouching across, produced a form from under the counter, slapped it down, eyes all the while fixed on the scarcely visible slits regarding him. Jeremy concentrated on the form, wrote: FERGUS FERRIS PORT PALMESTON. STUCK OUT ON INVERCARGILL STATION PLEASE COME SOON AS POSSIBLE PICK ME UP. J DELACY.

He shoved it at the watching man, who although obviously interested, evidently was not impressed, beyond being somewhat less rude in naming the price. Jeremy paid without a word, walked out, back to the quarters.

Some twenty minutes later, while sitting reading an out-of-date copy of the *West Australian*, Jeremy looked up at hearing steps, to see the stocky man of last evening, the Boss, approaching. The man waved to him, and still at a distance hailed him: 'Jeremy Delacy, eh? Didn't expect to see you out this way.'

Jeremy neither answered nor rose. The man came up to the verandah thrusting out a ruddy pudgy hand. 'You remember me . . . Alec Smither . . . had a horse run second your stallion, Elektron, Beatrice Cup, Thirty-two.'

Jeremy nodding slightly, took the hand limply.

The man leant against a verandah post. 'Sorry about last night, old man. Should've said who you were.'

Jeremy's tone was dry, for all its thickness: 'Didn't get much chance, did I?'

'Aw . . . that Bookkeeper. Newchum. Doesn't know the ropes.'

'What ropes?'

'Well . . . you know . . . took you for a bagman . . . .'

'Didn't you?'

Smithers chuckled, but avoiding the slits, looked afar. 'Tell you the truth, I did see something familiar . . . but, with the bunged up dial and the . . . and the cigarette swag.' He looked back with a chuckle. 'The cook reckons he knew who you were all the time . . . but you know what bloody liars cooks are. Anyway, I'm dead sorry, old man.' The pale blue eyes blinked as if hurt.

Jeremy husked, 'No need to be, Mr Smithers. I *was* a bagman to all intents and purposes.'

'Aw, go on! Anyway, come on over the house.'

'I'm waiting for an aircraft.'

'Wait at the house. You need something on that face. Missus'll see to it for you. You could probably do a drink, too, eh?'

'Thanks . . . but I'm quite comfortable here.'

'Don't take offence, old man. Genuine mistake.'

'I'm not offended. I looked like a bagman. I know the custom of the land . . . especially on Vaisey stations. It was my fault for going to the Big House. It was only I thought there might be a special sked I could get the telegram through on.'

Smithers heaved away from the post. 'I know how you feel about Vaiseys . . . about me, too, I suppose. But for my missus' sake. She'll be offended.'

'Give her my compliments. Tell her I still regard myself as a bagman till I get aboard that plane. I'll wave to her out the window.'

The man went deeply red. A snap came into his voice. 'Don't be bloody silly!'

It was difficult to see a colour change in Jeremy's multi-hued face. However, he rose at once, saying with what sounded like anger, 'No, I won't be silly any longer.' He went into the room, grabbed up rolled swag and hat, and emerging, asked, 'You won't mind if I camp on your airstrip?'

'Eh?' Smithers blustered, 'That 'a way to treat a man offering you hospitality?'

Jeremy stepped off the verandah. 'I've been taking your hospitality . . . or Lord Vaisey's . . . long enough. I'd prefer to have no more than's absolutely necessary . . . thanks all the same. Goodday to you.'

Smithers let him go some twenty yards, before bawling after him, 'You *are* an intolerant bastard . . . like they say. Get stuffed!'

Jeremy kept on, waved to the obviously peeping kitchen staff, who must have heard that last remark. The billowing wind-sock in the distance showed the way to the air-strip with its little fuel-shed floating in mirage. As Jeremy trudged towards it, limping somewhat from yesterday's blisters, he kept repeating under his breath something of what had just been said: 'Intolerant bastard . . . intolerant bastard,' and adding to it, 'What exactly does Intolerant mean? From the Latin, *Tolerare*, to Endure, to Permit, to Bear. How much does one have to refuse to permit or bear what one considers obnoxious in others to be justly deemed intolerant? That poor stupid bastard was only trying to save his face. Why didn't I let him? Because I wanted to save mine? But I hate the things, the principles, the prejudices, he stands for. So I am an intolerant bastard. Christ, I could've done with that drink!'

Fergus arrived just before noon, doing a turn over the homestead before landing, but without bringing anyone out of the Big House. His first question, as his eyes popped at sight of the battered face and unkempt dress, was unspoken. Then he asked, 'Boss not home, eh?'

Jeremy grimaced as best he could. 'Not home to us.' He explained briefly, concluding: 'I even turned down a much-needed drink in the process . . . which is taking principles a bit too far, I'm afraid.'

Fergus chuckled, then said, 'If you could do a drink, I've got some?'

Jeremy licked swollen lips. 'My oath I could!'

Fergus ducked back into his plane, to reappear with a bottle of whisky, a pannikin, a water-canteen. He said, as Jeremy mixed himself a stiff one, 'Matter of fact, I'm doing a perish myself, Got terribly full last night. All I could do to drag myself out to the aerodrome. If it hadn't been you, I'd've turned the trip down.'

'That was good of you. How d'you find it flying with a hangover?'

'Actually it's good for it. You've *got* to pull yourself together to handle the crate. Then, up top, it doesn't seem so bad . . . rarefied air, or something.' Looking across at the homestead, Fergus remarked, 'Looks like we're not going to get any help with refuelling. Have to do it ourselves. But better fuel ourselves up first, eh? Have another.'

They drank half the bottle between them, while Jeremy talked of what had happened to him recently. Fergus knew, as he explained, that he had come here straight from the Leopolds, because he had himself come from there only the day before yesterday. He said, 'Pity I hadn't caught you there. We could've flown out together and gone on a proper scoot.' He paused, looking into the peeping bloodshot eyes. 'I presume your trouble was the same as mine – Rifkah?' Again it was impossible to see how it affected Jeremy, except that the bunged eyes looked swiftly away to the fuel-shed.

They were silent as they rolled out the drums of fuel and set up the pumping equipment. Fergus mounted the ladder with the hose, while Jeremy pumped. The fuel had just started to gush into the tank when Fergus said with a rush, 'I went to the Mission to marry Rifkah.' He looked down at Jeremy, who held his gaze, steadily pumping. Fergus turned back to his task, went on: 'Didn't know they'd worked citizenship for her. Thought I could work the double, like.'

Silence again for a little while, save for creak of pump and gush of gasolene. Jeremy broke it this time: 'Tell me, son . . . did you have a hand in putting the Commonwealth Police on her?'

Fergus reddened, bit his bunny lip.

Jeremy added: 'I'm not criticizing you. I knew you wanted to marry her. Matter of fact, I talked to her about marrying you . . .' Fergus looked at him quickly. Jeremy, pumping, looked away, sighed: 'Anyway . . . she's all right now.'

Addressing the gushing stream, Fergus said, 'Actually, it was General Whiskers and Co. started it. You know they were flat out to break your interest in her. I overheard Whiskers and Malters discussing it a couple of times. They'd already started something when they looked into the Jewish Settlement business . . . with Security. I admit I tipped off Alfie Candlemas. But I didn't expect anything so mad as what happened. I knew she wanted you for Free Australia . . . as we all do . . . it's your job . . . only you can do it. But you couldn't do it the way things were. I didn't know Alfie was in love with you. I didn't have any idea she'd rouse the Canberra mob up like an ant-heap. I thought there'd be a ton of time. Matter of fact, it was my intention to come down to the Lagoons as soon as I could make a landing there, with a Special Licence, to make my proposal in front of you . . . with the stipulation that it could wait as long as she liked for consummation . . . so long as she got the citizenship, and your blessing. I reckoned on your collaboration, because . . . well, I knew you weren't keen on her marrying your son, or she either, for that matter . . . and although you might have liked her for yourself . . . who wouldn't? . . . you're first of all a man of dignity, in my opinion. I didn't think you'd ever have her for more than a daughter . . . whatever the bastards said. I reckoned on everything, as a matter of fact, except the first friggin' thing a pilot ought to reckon on . . . the weather.' Fergus looked again at staring Jeremy, and sighed: 'Yes, the bloody weather. That's what beat me. If it hadn't been for that bloody rain depression, I'm sure I could've worked it . . . even with those bogies after her, I could've whipped her away under their very noses . . . but for that bloody rain!' Fergus sighed again. After a while he signalled for the pumping to stop.

As he came down to Jeremy and began to unscrew the gear, he gave the split-lip grin, saying, 'Well . . . we lost our little darling . . . where do we go from here?'

Jeremy was silent. As they were putting the gear away, Fergus said, 'What you were telling me about your experience in Hartog would make a wonderful piece for *Australia Free.*'

'Anti-Communist stuff, you mean?'

'Not exactly . . . Australian bastardry. They're pockets like this down South, where the Comms are allowed to be boss because it suits the proper bosses, who're all outsiders . . . coal-mines, shipping, steel-works.'

'Matter of fact, while I was sitting here waiting for you to come, I made up my mind to go back to Hartog, get myself a good suit of clothes and a revolver, and go round to the Police Station and ask the Sergeant to give me a licence to carry the gun, because I was being attacked by thugs.'

'Phew! That would have bowled him over.'

'Maybe . . . even seeing me there. But where'd it get me in the long run, seeing the Government, Vaiseys, and all the rest's behind it? It was only the dry horrors that made me savage about it. Now I've had a drink I can see the futility of it. Best to put it into print, as you say, so's Australians can see how their country's run. These other bastards'd only hush it up . . . and even might connive at the Commos' bumping me off.'

'Will you write it?'

'No . . . I leave it to you, son. You write a good piece.'

'So do you . . . and you've got more than I have . . . the capacity for leadership.'

'You know I don't like that rag's mad Anti-Semitism and Hitlerism.'

'I told you they're the things we want cut out . . . and you're the man to do it. This Free Australia Movement's the only chance we've got. Who's running the place? Here's the Commos, telling the police what to do, under Lord Vaisey's orders . . . or Lord Someonelse's somewhere else. There's bloody Catholic Action can get Rifkah citizenship with a flick of the finger. And old Whiskers, with his *Pax Britannica*, organizing us for a war with people who could be our best friends. I ask you . . . what chance have dinky-di Aussies got . . . except through this Free Australia thing . . . . '

'Run by Adolf Hitler!'

'That's where we came in. We've got to stop that. We've got to get rid of the Fascist element that's ruining it . . . . '

'Is there any other element in it?'

'I told you before . . . some of the best brains in the country've been looking to it as a means to establishing true liberalism and honest intelligent government.'

'Why don't they take it off that stupid bastard who's aping Hitler, then?'

'You don't know Southerners . . . and intellectuals, Jeremy. They haven't got the forthrightness of Northern bush-people . . . . '

'I haven't seen anything so forthright about my fellow Northern Bushies, crawling up Lord Vaisey's arse . . . . '

'There is a great difference . . . take it from me . . . I mean with people like you . . . old Billy Brew. There's plenty like you. But you're the man with the intelligence and strength and dignity. It needs a man who can stand up and ignore that Bloke's specious arguments on political philosophy. He's Oxford, you know. He intimidates the intellectuals. They'll say he's mad . . . but they'll concede he's a scholar and a genius, and leave it at that. That Oxford bullshit wouldn't go down with you. You'd stand up and talk like an Australian bushman, which is what Australians understand, bush bred or not. You'd shoot the Bloke's arguments down in flames simply by saying something like, . . . like, "The bloody country's like a beast that's bogged down, with a mob of alien crows onto it, trying to pick out its eyes".'

'Sounds like you don't need me, boy!'

Fergus said huskily, 'I do. It's from you I've learnt to talk like that. I need a drink, too. Let's have a swig.'

Having drunk and handed the stuff to Jeremy, Fergus resumed: 'Where are we governed from? Not Canberra . . . but from Westminster, Moscow, Rome . . . . '

Jeremy paused before he downed his drink. 'Berlin!'

'Right . . . Berlin if you like, too. And any day we'll be mixed up in a war with any or all of the bastards.' Fergus's speech was somewhat slurry. He blinked at Jeremy. 'Where you want me take you from here?'

Jeremy hesitated, licking his lips over the last of the whisky. 'Well . . . I suppose home.'

'Wha' you going to do there?'

Again Jeremy hesitated. 'Well . . . I got to put my face right, need some new clothes.'

Fergus said eagerly, 'Listen . . . I got to get back South in a week or so to pick up old Whiskers. I only sneaked back up here to fix things for Rifkah . . . . ' The name caused him to boggle, to blink. He swallowed, and went on: 'What about you coming back with me . . . seeing for yourself this Free Australia thing . . . .'

'Take me home first, son. I need a bottle of brandy . . . and a big deep think.'

'Right . . . away we go.'

CHAPTER TWENTY

UNDER HIS OWN medical treatment, even though X-ray revealed some small bone damage and the likelihood that at last he would lose the teeth he had so long and so well preserved, and even with a goodly consumption of brandy during the treatment, Jeremy recovered so quickly from the immediate effects of that lesson he learnt in the Brotherhood of Man from those expert exponents of it at Port Hartog, that he was able to go in to meet the first mail train to come down since his return home. By his declaration his going in was not nearly so much to get the mail or meet his kind in something like mass, as to confront Pat Hannaford, due to be driving again, with his steamed-up opinion of Communism. However, as likely as not it was simply for the flight with Fergus, who was still around, helping him to drink the brandy and make his mind up about the trip down South.

It was evident that Jeremy was not keen on the trip South, but that, affected by the emptiness so resonant here now in its new silence, he was tending to cling to the young man. Anyway, the futility of bawling out Pat Hannaford had already been well and truly expressed by the pair in their long talks on Communism, a persuasion made up only of rogues, fools, and madmen, surely, since it aspired to establish the Millenium on a basic tenet of *End Justifies Means*, the philosophy of a common criminal.

No doubt about it, young Fergus worked overtime to keep his host's inflamed hostility burning with intent to induce him to commit himself to what was, for better or worse, the only logical answer to Communism in this country, Australia Free. At the same time, it was evident that his zeal for the cause was not without ulterior motive. Brandy is a good drink in that it doesn't impair the wits like most other alcoholic beverages, but just like the rest will loosen one's tongue, and if one is secretly distressed, drop some of the secret, no matter how wary one may be. Fergus dropped bits that anyone as astute as Jeremy must instantly have seized on, had he not himself been afflicted similarly. If only he might have had Rif kah's love he would be in no such jam as now, he said, and in no such other spots as his rashness would lead him for sure.

Fergus long ago had confessed, in his jesting way, that he'd got considerable concession for use of the Junkers by impressing on everybody possible and flying-types in particular the invincibility of the German Air Force, while advertising *Der Führer*, as the Aryan Messiah. However, anyone listening carefully now must suspect that the involvement was considerably deeper and could include this purest seeming of causes, Australia Free. Tantalite, which meant Krupp's, was mixed up in it. Fergus had often talked Tantalite to Jeremy, but mostly in jest, in view of Jeremy's pronounced view of the matter since the clash with the Kruppsers last Race Time, still with enough serious intent occasionally to suggest that the working of the mine to capacity might well benefit the Cause: 'The good earth itself giving us the means to make it free from the exploiters . . . and who's it matter who we sell it to, so long as we get the dough?' So Free Australia virtually could be financed by *Der Führer*? Jeremy obviously missed the implication. Probably he was just not interested, his interest being centred then, pretty well to the exclusion of all else, in her Fergus had called Our Little Darling. Still Fergus tried it: 'If only I could kid those Hun-Dun bastards there was a chance to get the Tantalite, I'd get 'em off my back.' Still Jeremy ignored it.

At length it came out that Fergus hadn't made this last trip up from the South solely with intent to marry Rifkah and get her citizenship, but that he was also in flight from his German creditors. In fact, since coming to Lily Lagoons this time he had made arrangements by radio with an aviation-engineer friend of his at Palmeston Airport to send him immediate warning should the Hun-Duns drop in there enquiring his whereabouts. In that event he would fly the Junkers to a hiding place where even the mighty Goering directing his invincible Luftwaffe wouldn't find it in years.

According to Fergus, the Junkers people now were so convinced of the imminence of war in which Australia would be ranged against Germany that they wanted all outstanding contracts met with despatch. In the event of war, of course, if the aircraft were still here and registered in the name of its rightful owners, it would be seized as enemy property. However, it seemed that Fergus had a deed of sale with him, which required only dating and witnessing. That didn't mean the Germans had been silly enough to put such a document in his hands, but only that he had been smart enough to take signatures from less important transactions he'd had with Junkers and transfer them to it. Forgery? Who's going to bother to check the transactions of enemy aliens who have flown the land? All's fair in war. The clever thing to do was to keep a jump ahead of the Duns till the war broke out, seeing to it that when they took flight it was in some other aircraft than this one.

Far from striking a moral attitude to the patent dishonesty, Jeremy was even tickled by the idea of it, and when Fergus followed it up with the confession that his prospective hiding-place was the ancient Ring Place just over the escarpment on the Sandstone Plateau and asked if he would lend him the utility and tools to go and clean the spot of the few bushes and ant-beds and things, not only agreed readily, but said he'd lend him a hand. Fergus did not want even the blacks to know of it.

They went and did the job in a single day. Next day they flew across and landed there, and took off again without hazard. Next day they flew in to Beatrice, alone, because there now was no one at Lily Lagoons who wanted to forsake the safety of the ground for the realm of birds and devils.

They flew over Beatrice Homestead, of necessity, because it was under their flight-path in the prevailing wind, but made no circuit as a call for transport from the strip, because they had no intention of using it. They dropped down to the Racecourse, while the household stared after them.

Perhaps it was the obvious slight that caused Clancy to turn from them scowling as they came towards the Railway Station from the bridge. Still, he could have been feeling somewhat guilty, as well as just as miserable as they about the loss of that Little Darling of theirs, knowing that at least one of them had lately talked with her.

As the train came in, and Pat Hannaford gaped his surprise at seeing Jeremy, Jeremy gave him the Communist salute, changing it suddenly with upjerking of the thumb to the indecent gesture of contempt it then meant. Pat went crimson and missed his customary Fascist salute to Station-master Collings.

Having got the mail, and finding Pat pretending to look at wheels and couplings, Jeremy gave him not the tale of his adventures amongst his comrades he evidently wanted to hear, but a loud dissertation on those worthies, how they worked in dingo packs, with the connivance of their supposed enemies, the police, whose purpose was to keep the peace for the greater profit of their worst enemy, the beef baron. 'The great reformers!' he jeered. 'The End Justifies the Means, they say. So does a bloody crook. Get what you want . . . no matter how you get it!'

Pat tried blustering, but was obviously outpointed from the start and being made to look not only the associate of criminals but a fool into the bargain before a goggling crowd that even forgot the call of the grog in wonderment what it was all about, stopped it by playing the good old Commo trick of the Diversionary Tactic, spotted Fergus grinning at him, and leapt away from his too-powerful assailant, to snarl, 'What you grinnin' at, Bunny?'

Fergus paled, but maintained the grin. 'Don' know quite . . . trying to figure it out . . . .'

'Maybe this'll help yo'!' Pat aimed a ginger sooty fist that could have put another split in the bunny lip. But Jeremy was after him, shouldered him aside. Pat swung on him. Jeremy squared up. Then Pat dropped his hands, growling, 'I ain't fightin' an old man.'

'Not without your dingo mob, eh?'

'You know bloody well I don't need no mob to do me fightin'.'

'But you pick your marks, eh, Comrade? That boy's only half your size.'

'I'll 'ave him and your squatter-bastard son on together!'

The Knowles Family, just off the train and somewhat the worse for wear, Ma Knowles the worst since not having the alcoholic capacity of her males. She screeched, 'Give it to 'em, Pat . . . father son and . . . .'

'Holy Ghost!' laughed Fergus.

She turned the screech on him: 'Shut your bunny mouth, you dirty German spy!'

Everybody looked surprised at that. Ma liked it, tossed her flowered squatter-ess's hat. 'Yeah . . . that's't he is. Trying to get that Tantalite o' ours for the Huns. Tried 'o get Dad mixed up in it, too . . . and him a Returned Soldier.'

Fergus, quite red, snapped at her, 'You bloody old liar . . . he'd've been right in it if he could.'

' 'Ear him, 'ear him?' she squealed to the mob. 'He admits he tried it. He admits he's working for the Huns!'

Oh, the look in the eyes of the crowd! Fergus took it in, grunted, 'Aw!' went off up the line.

Pat yelled after him, 'Nazi bastard!' Then he had a shot at Jeremy: 'Great mates *you* got!'

But Jeremy had no time to answer, because of another diversion. Now Fergus was embroiled with Clancy. He rushed to fling them apart, yelling at them, 'Bloody fools . . . couldn't fight your way out of a green-ant's nest . . . '

However, Mrs Knowles wanted to fight, and leapt to it, screeching to her men, 'Come on, boys . . . give 'em the beltin' o' their lives . . . this Hun spy and this claim-jumpin' dog Delacy.' Her men were tardy about it. But she struck a blow for the family and its ancient grievance, with the back of her bony ringed hand across Jeremy's still tender eyes. She would have given him more, only Stunke grabbed her.

Blinking tears, Jeremy hastened away to where Tom Toohey, who was to take him and Fergus back over the bridge on his trolley, was waiting. Fergus came on his heels.

As they set off on the trolley, Fergus yelled in Jeremy's ear. 'That Krupp business was before I got to know you. I didn't hear any screaming about spies when I took the Kruppsers down to Mount Prince Albert. Matter of fact, I happened to overhear old Ned trying to explain to them that the easiest way to deal with you, seeing you had it all tied up with law, was to pay someone to shoot you . . . and because you've got no heirs and successors who have legal rights, it would go to your sons, who he reckoned would be glad to do business with 'em. Trouble was, the Kruppoes didn't have enough of the Knowles' kind of English to savvy . . . and the way they spoke to me afterwards, thought he meant that if they went near you you'd shoot *them*.'

Jeremy didn't laugh, only growled, 'Bastards! What sort of species does a man belong to?'

'Eh?' howled Fergus above the pop-and-clang. 'Haven't I heard you say . . . a very noble one, only wanting the opportunity to grasp his nobility?'

'I must've been drunk.'

So over the bridge, back into the plane, back into the air. No waste of time on saluting the township of Beatrice today.

They got home in time for the last radio-sked of the day, on which came a message for Fergus: *The Hun-Duns are in town*. Over dinner Fergus told Jeremy: 'I'll have to get going in the morning, to pick up Whiskers. While I'm with him, I'm safe from 'em. Besides, they'll want me to be with him to find out what he's up to. When they turn up, will you tell 'em I'm away on a military survey with him . . . only you don't know where. I won't give any flight details out tomorrow till I get out of the area.' Jeremy agreed.

However, over breakfast next morning, Jeremy delegated Nanago to deliver that message, because he would be going South with Fergus.

Fergus raised a little cheer. Nan smiled her sweet fat smile, saying 'Dat's good you go.'

'Why . . . you want to get rid of me?'

'No . . . I want see you come back de properly Jeremy.'

'Is there such a person?'

'I reckon.'

'Hear, hear!' said Fergus.

II

They flew some fifteen hundred miles the first day; over the great grey inland seabed, miscalled The Downs, where the sea had sunk into great cracks to form the world's vastest prairie of sweet grasses so that Lord Alfred Vaisey and some others like him might run their kine there to grow fat and make them richer; over the great inland river systems, at this time of year only narrow lines of darker green of coolibah and watergum against limitless grey-green of mulga, only a flash of water here and there, where in season it would stretch for miles, rushing from a thousand miles away to revive the grasses that fat the beasts that fatted Lord Vaisey and the other absentee landlords of this land that Jack the pioneer stole from those who'd thought they owned it; over the homesteads built by Jack with a gun in one hand, only to be sold for a song to Their Lordships while now Jack held in that other hand a bottle; over the little towns that had grown up in the tradition of the never-to-be forgotten Homeland each as a sort of tenantry to the Manor, little one-pub affairs, the pub the centre of culture, or social gravity, about it clustered half a dozen iron shops and sheds, from it diverging dusty crossroads leading to meaner and meaner shacks till nought left but the dog kennels of the dispossessed owners.

Fergus, mocking at these first sights of civilization, was surprised to hear Jeremy say, 'These little townships have the virtue at least of being original. You'll see nothing like them anywhere else in the world. Overseas, I used to yearn for them. Walking country lanes and fields, I'd round a bend or come over a hill, to be surprised to see the spired church, the shingled inn, the thatched cottages, instead of the old familiar scene. I suppose you've got to be born to it to find any charm in it. Still, the pioneers had a way of working even with stringy-bark and saplings. If only they could have gone on making truly Australian-looking things like that with better materials and taste, instead of the Hollywood abominations that are springing up in the new places, like Mount Isa and Alice Springs.'

In late afternoon they dropped down to spend the night at such a one-pub town that stood beside a salt lake, its salinity declared by the lack of growth around it and its crystalline shores that turned from silver to vermilion as they descended.

The salt lake was of primary importance to the town, so they learnt from those they found in the bar of the pub and with whom they drank till bedtime. It was not so much its saline waters, which only the goats and dingoes drank, the rest of the population living off tank-water or what the Council hauled from Five Mile Creek in dry weather – and beer. Rather, beer should have had priority, because the value of the lake was its effect on the atmosphere, which put such a fine edge on a thirst for beer that far more was consumed here per head than anywhere else in Australia. The publican had the exact statistics, running into decimals. It was this that brought the drovers, fencers, shearers, doggers, 'roo-shooters, ringers, well-sinkers, and all the rest of rural workers and loafers, to take a spell there, hence literally was the settlement's means of subsistence. The only trouble was that the regular citizens themselves were similarly affected, so that all profit from the boon went down their gullets also, for which reason liberal strangers were always more than welcome, like this pair o' flyin' gents. What was it they said their business was, again?

Thus did what is called the Bullshit, chief delight of most Australian males, get started, and the evening made a complete social success. The pair made their full contribution. In answer to the sly inquiries regarding their business, they declared that they were representatives of the great brewing monopoly, Carlton United, which had heard of the fabulous atmosphere of the town and wanted samples of the lake waters so as to be able to synthesize the contents and, in accordance with their well-known concern for the Nation, establish lakes of the kind throughout it. This so tickled the mob as to check the resentment that otherwise must have met their dodging accounting for themselves. Jeremy quickly advanced the good feeling by answering the usual question as to whether the Catholic Church owned CUB by saying, 'Sure! And every brew's blessed personally by the Apostolic Delegate. Ask my mate, here. He has to sometimes fly the old boy in from his favourite convent when he's behind time and they want a brew out in a hurry. A blessing in every bottle, you might say.'

Fergus was surprised to find Jeremy so accomplished a Bullshit Artist, and tackled him on the matter when they retired to their little iron box of a bedroom. 'A serious man like you,' he protested, somewhat boozily but with the rationality of developed intelligence that succumbs only when clean bowled. 'Mob o' bloody morons, really . . . ev'thing you don't like in 'Stralian character in 'em . . . mean bastards, ev' one of 'em. Yet you really enjoyed that Bullshit session, didn't you!'

Jeremy answered, 'I always do. I wouldn't go on the booze . . . but for the company, and the fun . . . and that's it . . . the Bullshit. That's the actual catharsis of drinking for me . . . not just getting rotten. I think it's the same with most bushmen. They certainly finish up in the gutter, or in the goat-shed, or on the police-chain . . . but it's the company . . . the old Australian mateship.'

'Yes . . . but a solitary like you . . . the ol' Scrub Bill? You're an idealist, driven into himself for the lack of anything approaching idea . . . idealism . . . around him.'

'A solitary wanting identification with his fellows, eh? Sure, I hate 'em for their stupidity, dishonesty, laziness, or whatever it is makes the average Australian what he is. But I want to love 'em, too . . . my countrymen, my comrades. The Bullshit with Booze maybe's the only way to conjure up that ideal of ours, the mateship. Confession of failure, I s'pose you might call it. But, well . . . when I get into a session I always feel it's a form of realism . . . not just an escape from harsh reality, in boozy sentimentality as you find the English do, or cock-sureness as you do the Yanks, or sheer brutality as you do so many others . . . but rather a game you actually face the facts of your existence in, and make fun of 'em. What do you think?'

But Fergus, having lain down, and having had a hard day behind him, could only mumble sleepily. Jeremy shut up, set about undressing, by the light of Igulgul peeping over the goat-yard, was soon asleep himself.

Next morning Fergus had to do some telephoning to prepare for their flight. As soon as it was done, they were off, to beat up the appreciative town in farewell, and away.

Now they were to see civilization as larger and larger infestations of the innocent dreaming landscape. Bigger and bigger townships pocked the plains, abcessed the woodlands, carbuncled the hills, binding themselves to the host they'd settled on with an increasingly intricate system for sharing their sucking of its substance: roads, railways, waterways that mocked the meandering old rivers with their engineer's geometry. Then suddenly, soon after noon, as they came out of that almost-still-pristine backdrop to it, the Blue Mountains, and overcame the dazzle of the five thousand miles of blue Pacific beyond, there was the very centre of the rash, the focal point, stretching to the sea and North and South as far as eye could see even at five thousand feet – Sydney. As they dropped down to it with whispering engines, Jeremy remarked, 'Looks like a huge cemetery from here, doesn't it!'

'You're dead right,' said Fergus. 'No pun intended. I've often wondered what it reminded me of looking at it from on top.'

'Graveyard of our hopes, eh?'

'What hopes?'

'That the Australian community will be anything much better than it started as . . . the sweepings of the gutters of London.'

'Eh? Is that the spirit to start the crusade to nationhood in?'

'Where'd you get this crusade idea. I'm coming to take a look-see.'

'Alfie Candlemas' words.' After a moment Fergus added, 'Have to tell you . . . I was talking to Alfie on the phone this morning. She'll be waiting to take charge of you.'

Jeremy reddened, muttered, 'For christ sake!'

'Sorry . . . but I've got to get on the move again as soon as I set you down. Got to get to Whiskers and his protection. Otherwise the Duns down here will be onto me. And I can't just leave you to find your own way about. Someone'd sell you the Harbour Bridge within an hour.'

'D'you think I'm that bushy?'

'It's meant as a compliment . . . but you look the typical bushman. Anyway, it's a long while since you've been here . . . and I happen to have been born here, and know the style of the inhabitants. But what've you got to worry about? Nobody can handle little Alfie better than you.'

Down over rusty roofs, acres of dumped rubbish, blocks of belching smoke-stacks, tangles of roads with motor vehicles streaming like meat-ant runs to a carcass . . . down . . . down . . . down . . . to the good earth, to almost exactly the spot where the first whiteman trod it some one hundred and seventy years before and since had for the most part trodden it out of recognition. They swung from the runway to the apron. There was Alfie, in her impatience, or whatever it was, evidently having weedled her way through the barricade, all trim and citified in autumn brown with pretty little face glowing like a ripening fruit, coming running to meet them.

Alfie flung herself on Jeremy as if their last lamentable experiences together might never have happened, kissed him on the mouth with such frank sensuality as to make him burn, and releasing him with lips, gripped him with arms, crying on his breast, 'Oh, oh . . . it's so good to have you again!'

Fergus, with a wink and a split-lip grin, took himself off to official business. Alfie whisked Jeremy away to her car.

Alfie was showing off, no doubt, the way she handled the car in what to Jeremy would be a snarl of traffic, but which she said was nothing to what it could be. She laughed at his obvious fearfulness, taking shining black eyes off what she should have been watching to look at him, a hand off the wheel to caress his tight-drawn arm. Thus into and through the heart of the city, while she gabbled of all sorts of things, from Lily Lagoons to Langham Court (the latter the exclusive block of flats beside the Harbour where she had arranged his accommodation), from Monsignor Maryzic to Mussolini, for both of whom she expressed admiration. Evidently she knew a lot about how things were Up Top, as she called it, spoke of Prindy, Nan, and others – but never of Rifkah. Jeremy seemed too much preoccupied with the hazards of their journey to be listening more than to answer in monosyllables.

Then there, miraculously, they were at Langham Court. The flat was on the ground floor, if such it could be called, when descent had to be made to it from street level. It was practically on the water's edge, with only a strip of lawn and a sea-wall intervening, deliberately chosen for the perpetual warmth of the water, she said. 'You're going to find it cold. The westerlies've started. We can't have you getting sick or running away because of the rotten climate. You'll be able to keep fit. There's a little park just round the corner where you can run. I'll show you when I take you home. Everything for dear Jeremy . . . even brandy. Let's have a nip to warm the house, eh?'

They had three before she left him so that he might bath and change and rest in preparation for her coming to take him to dinner with her and Frank, her husband. Now her chatter was of Free Australia and all there was for him to do for it. She didn't seem to mind his silence, kissed him, laughing gaily in his blank face.

She returned to him in moon-silvered dusk, looking like a lovely thing belonging to it, fluorescent in semi-evening-dress, dark of face and curly hair. 'Like me?' she demanded, pirouetting on silver heels. Then, without waiting for answer, which perhaps was in his eyes, she said, 'How smart and citified you are!' Actually he was looking as uncomfortable as any Northerner does when first trussed up in the trappings of the South. He wore a dark serge suit, with white shirt and blood-dark tie, and shiny shoes. She went round him, brushing proprietorially. She wanted a drink, accepted his limitation to one, took his hand and led him up the terazzo stairs into the violet and silver and the fragrance of local high-class cooking. Hanging on his arm, making stride for stride with him, she guided him, showing him this and that. She pulled the Moon down to them, as if it were something belonging to them, properly located at Lily Lagoons but as properly following them about. She sighed: 'Those moonlit nights at Lily Lagoons . . . the Rainbow Pool . . . the Caves!' Had she been there in moonlight? Did it matter with such a one, who could so easily create the pleasant and forget the rest?

She told him that after dinner they would be joined by two important members of the Free Australia Movement, who would prove to him the worthwhileness about which he seemed dubious. One was a practising Economist, the other a retired Banker. She said that if she could get up in time she would join him on his run in the morning, but snuggled up to him to show how much she liked bed and someone in with her to make it snugger.

Frank Candlemas was warm in greeting, taking Jeremy's hand in both of his, putting an arm about his shoulder, proving his sincerity by turning from smiles to gravity when Alfie went off to the kitchen, and from saying how glad he was to see him again to how necessary it was to have him there: 'I know you'll fix things with the Movement . . . one way or an other. If it's only a lunatic thing, you'll expose it. If it's what I hope it is, you'll inspire us to make it better. But it isn't only of the Movement I'm thinking. It's Alfie mainly. She's terribly involved. If it's a flop, she'll be heartbroken. But better that than being destroyed . . . as I'm afraid she might be. You'd help her over it. Yes, Jeremy . . . I was never more pleased to see anyone in my life.'

Alfie came back, with cocktails borne for her on a tray by one she introduced as Mrs March, her helper, a plump, jolly, middle-aged female, wearing an apron, but also smart clothes and an expensive hair-do. It wasn't as mere servant that Mrs March came, but to meet the guest. ' 'Erd lot 'bout yo'.' she said. 'Real bushman from the wild bush, eh? My old dad was one of 'em . . . a bullocky . . . and swear! 'Ow you on swearin', Mr Delacy?'

'Only in front of bullocks,' said Jeremy gravely.

'Aw-eeee! You's a wag, too . . . jes like my old dad. I like a man with a sense of humour . . . and a big appetite. Got a lovely dinner for yo' . . . not goanna, course . . . eeee-ow!' She had a drink with them, returned to the kitchen.

'That's Australia for you,' said Alfie proudly.

'What d'you mean, exactly?' asked Jeremy.

'The democracy. A servant's as good as her mistress. You'd never get old Dolly to truckle to any boss.'

'Then why the need for Free Australia, if we're already so bold and free?'

Alfie laughed. 'Trust Jeremy to chuck a spanner in! Still, that's what you're wanted for. We are bold and free . . . but only in our estimation of ourselves. We've got to make it a reality.'

It was a large and tasty meal – casseroled lamb with a fruit pie – to which Jeremy did justice such as to have Dolly bending over him, leering even lasciviously, as she cleared away.

The trio were just settled down to their brandy when the expected visitors arrived. They also greeted Jeremy with enthusiasm, the Banker, an oldish man, quite frankly saying that the bushman with intelligence was the ideal Australian. Jeremy laughed. 'The catch is there aren't that many bushmen with intelligence.'

The Banker, for all his look of the shrewd old businessman and evidence of that shrewdness in his talk, yet had about him an air of innocent eagerness, like a Boy Scout rearing to do his good deed, which somehow cancelled out respect for his mature judgment. Likewise there seemed something wrong with the young Economist, suave and factual though he was – just too much so. The Banker's denunciation of control of Australian finance by foreigners, although expertly substantiated, sounded like hysterical declaiming against a bunch of caddish outsiders rather than exposure of a nation of nitwits being exploited by people much smarter than themselves. The Economist was similarly critical of the fiscal racket, but talked nationalism as if a nation were not a band of brothers bound by the mystery of earth-kinship but a limited company – The Commonwealth of Australia Inc..

Evidently Jeremy was very interested, having little to say himself, except in questioning. Alfie, most of the while hovering about the arm and back of his chair, plying him with brandy, tried often to rouse him to something like patriotic fervour, but without success. He answered her simply, 'I want to hear facts.'

The visitors, although obviously strongly enough bound together in service to the ideal, also differed widely in their opinions of those controlling the Movement, the pair they called, as everybody did, apparently, the Chief and the Bloke. The Chief, a very wealthy man, was instigator of the Movement, an admirer of that strong man in the midst of national diffidence, dishonesty, moral dissolution, as some believed him to be, Benito Mussolini. Jeremy asked, why the instigation? Not for personal glory. That was for his chosen mouthpiece, the Bloke, if he could make it – the Bloke, reputed to be a genius. In what? Whereas the Banker sounded as if he even worshipped the Chief, for his astuteness, forthrightness, purposefulness, financial wizardry, he made no bones about his choice, the Bloke – an opportunist, renegade Communist as likely to revert as not if it suited him to the Communist Party, an erudite wrangler who pandered to the same weakness in the Chief, flattered him, was likely to lead him into a morass of verbosity, then by some act of treachery bring him down. Thus the Banker. On the other hand the Economist dismissed both as madmen. The Chief was a plutomaniac. He had so much money he believed he was a sort of god with divine right to sport with mortals. The Bloke was a born paranoic, whose only real talent was his capacity to believe that he could rule the world. 'This man's no brilliant opportunist, like Mussolini or Hitler,' the Economist said. 'If he were, he wouldn't have to plagiarize from them. He hasn't got a single original idea of his own. And as for economics . . . the way he talks, when he's the Great Dictator, gnomes will mint money for him in the basement.' At least the pair, the Banker and the Economist, were at one in believing that control of the Movement must be wrested from these two runaway forces as soon as possible in order to save it from disaster.

The party broke up at eleven, with all seeing Jeremy to his flat. Tomorrow, Saturday, Alfie would be taking Jeremy to visit the Banker at his home at a seaside resort, to spend the day not merely in idleness, but in study of ample evidence the man had of Australia's enslavement to overseas financiers, and more, of the lack of any attempt on the part of any Australian Government of any sort to discourage it; in fact the reverse. It seemed that there had been a move to have Jeremy presented to the Chief and the Bloke tomorrow, but which had fallen through because of the former's preoccupation with his racehorses of Saturdays, and the latter's habit of spending weekends in seclusion somewhere. When Jeremy asked if it might not be taken as a rebuff, Frank answered, saying that city people lived so much by rote that it cost mighty effort to break it. Alfie said the great ones otherwise had been most enthusiastic about meeting him – Monday.

Having parted from the others, Jeremy, at the foot of the stairs, before entering his flat went out onto the strip of lawn. He was just in time to hear the others talking as they walked along the road above. The Banker was saying, with boyish enthusiasm, 'Our man . . . our man, all right. Strong silent bushman. He'll save the Movement.'

Alfie's little voice sounded like the alto of a flute: 'He'll save the Nation.'

'What I like about him,' said the Economist, 'is his appreciation of the economic facts of nationalism, as against silly emotionalism.'

That brought Alfie's fluting up higher in protest and Frank's bass into it evidently to stop an argument. But they were out of clear hearing now.

With a sigh, Jeremy turned to look at the strange skyline: ragged black bulk of city and twinkling towering arch of bridge, against the gilt of the setting Moon. Igulgul would still be well above the timber at Lily Lagoons, peeping in at western windows. At Leopold Mission he would be casting long shadows across the single street of poor little buildings, perhaps peeping into the one now called the Synagogue to reveal a glint of copper, a sheen of gold. He sighed again, turned to go in.

Alfie's sole possession of Jeremy for the trip to the Banker's next morning was not due simply to her wanting it, as, more or less, she confessed as she drove him. It seemed that Frank could not stand the dyspeptic consequences of the Banker's hospitality, or more truly his wife's, since she ran the show. 'Poor old Dickey's a chronic dyspeptic himself,' laughed Alfie. 'She ruined his insides in the first year of marriage. Doesn't mean her food's bad. Just the opposite. She lives for cooking . . . and eating . . . she's immense! Like old Dolly, she likes a man with a bit appetite, she says. You can live for a week on one of her dinners.'

It was a region of the rich they went to. Alfie pointed out the mansions of people even Jeremy had heard of for their achievements in commerce: great drapers, grocers, butchers, one famed for a couple of generations as makers of WC china. No names of writers or artists, as Alfie remarked with bitterness. The biggest stood on a peninsula, from the backbone of which were millionaires' views, of rolling blue ocean on one side, on the other a deeply-indented silver inlet backed by timbered hills. The Banker's house was right on top. It was of Spanish-American style, blue-tile-roofed, somewhat incongruous amidst bloodwoods and wattles, perhaps, but the anomaly somewhat rectified with a cactus garden.

Old Dickey's massive spouse looked Jeremy over in shaking hands with him like a man, saying in a great voice, 'Hope you've got a bushman's appetite. I've prepared a big dinner for you. I was brought up in the country, don't y'know . . . sheep station . . . used to big-eating men. Like to see a man act big, eat big . . . like my father and brothers. How I came to get mixed up with banking I don't know.' This she said before Dickey, as if he didn't exist. No doubt it was mortgage that had brought her down; that being the general way of the squattocracy. Anyway, she went on booming about the superior ways of the bush to those of the city, which included that of having dinner in the middle of the day, as they would be doing today out of consideration for their bushman guest. Jeremy had little to say to her, nor much chance of a say if he'd wanted it. Snatching Alfie away to assist her in the kitchen, which by the sound of it meant hounding servants, she left him alone with Dickey to sip beer and take the views.

Jeremy, much interested in the surroundings, remarked on the preservation of so much that was pristine so near a great city. Dickey told him it was owing to local private policy: 'Land values are kept far too high for Tom, Dick, and Harry to get in and spoil it.' He went on to describe how the bush abounded with koalas, lyre-birds, possums, the sea with marine life. 'There'd be nothing if the herd got in.'

Jeremy went on to say that it must have been a rich preserve of local Aborigines, and asked if any were still about. Dickey shook his head. 'No . . . the only Aborigines in the Sydney area would be those living on the La Perouse Reserve.'

'That's near the airport, isn't it? Pretty poor country, by the look of it from the air.'

'Oh, they only live on Government hand-outs these days. No hunters left. They only make spears and boomerangs to sell 'em to whites.'

'Wouldn't it be more correct to say there aren't any hunting grounds left?'

Dickey looked at Jeremy. 'They wouldn't hunt while they get a hand-out, would they?'

'Pretty lousy hand-out, I understand . . . mere subsistence.'

Dickey picked his nose nervously, as he had when his wife had talked over him. 'I understand how you feel about Aborigines . . . but isn't it a fact that they booze everything more than sheer subsistence?'

'Do you know much about them?'

'Can't say I do. They're more a problem for you people of the North.'

'Not for the Nation as a whole?'

Dickey picked harder, frowned. Jeremy went on: 'You say you understand how I feel about the Aborigines. My articles in *Australia Free* did stress the point that the first thing we've got to do to become a nation of any worth is to realize our responsibility for the people we stole the country from. Wasn't it taken seriously?'

Dickey reddened, docked some hair from his nose. 'Well . . . yes . . . but the consensus of opinion was . . . well, it's impractical.'

'How impractical?'

'Well . . . you wrote that there should be a tax put on all property owners, according to property owned, and a percentage taken from transfer fees and such . . . to keep the Abos.'

'What's wrong with that?'

'Well . . . they wouldn't work, would they . . . sort of live on their investments?'

'Why should they work? Do people round here work? Don't *they* live on their investments?'

Dickey drooped his head, much as he had when his wife had run down city folk. After a little silence, Jeremy asked, 'I don't want to be rude . . . but could you give me a rough estimate of the worth of this property of yours here?'

'Oh, round about fifty thousand.'

'A lot of money. Have you any more?'

'A bit here and there.'

'How did you come by it?'

Dickey sat up straight, answered rather shortly, 'I worked for it. I started in banking as a common office boy.'

'I mean, from whom did you acquire it?'
'Former owners of a large area here.'
'Blacks?'
Dickey's pale eyes widened as they looked into the intense demanding grey. He swallowed, mumbled, 'The blacks'd been gone a hundred years.'

'Still, it was theirs originally . . . and not paid for when taken over.'

Dickey drooped again. Jeremy continued: 'Buying something that's been stolen makes one accessory . . . no matter how long ago the theft took place.'

Dickey went red, but roused up again. 'You've got property yourself!'

'Not land. I have a leasehold . . . but hold it really in trust for the blacks who aren't, by law, allowed to hold it. They can use it as they like, make any demands on me that are within my capacity . . . .'

'Yes . . . but you live where there're a lot of blacks. Ours are all gone . . . .'

'To the La Perouse Reserve . . . to all the other mean reserves in the country.'

Dickey pulled so hard at the hair in his nose that he winced.

Jeremy's voice was even, slow: 'You see what I mean. Nothing personal. I'm speaking of the Nation. To be an honest people we must absolve ourselves of that primary guilt. We don't object to paying tax to the Crown for the right to possess property. Why should we object to an infinitely smaller tax to square our conscience? The Crown was the original thief, I know. It tries to square off with the reserve and the hand-out. But each of us compounds a felony with the Crown so long as we don't make personal restitution.'

Dickey stared at him. Then suddenly he burst out with the Boy Scout enthusiasm: 'By God, man . . . you're right, you know!' He smote a pink palm with a pinker fist. 'We must make it the first plank in our platform. *You* must . . . for you're our man . . . Our Man, Delacy!' He shot the pink hand out to grasp the brown one. Jeremy shook with him gravely.

Dickey, breathless now, asked how they could go about fixing this Guilt Tax, as he called it. They must lobby for it; but in which Parliament, State or Federal? Jeremy quieted him down, saying that there was much first to be done to rouse people to awareness of the lousy thing the Commonwealth of Australia really was. The financial racket was the one that would rouse most interest. The mass of the people still recalled that the Great Depression was the result of the machinations of International Finance: 'Let's see those figures of yours. From what you've told me, they'll reveal the truth of our bondage like flashes of lightning.'

Dickey whooped like a Boy Scout: 'Flashes of lightning . . . yes, yes, yes!'

Although in a tone much more subdued, at the dinner table, he kept on whooping similarly. His wife growled at him through the handles of her carvers, as she dealt with a huge muscovy duck: 'What on earth are you talking about, Dickey? Lightning at this time of year! Why . . . it's Winter.'

Dickey was too excited to shut up. He told Alfie about their their primary responsibility to the Aborigines. His wife, intent upon estimating Jeremy's stowage capacity, took no notice at first; but satisfied that she had a Man to feed, she fixed her pop eyes on her spouse and raised her voice: 'Don't be ridiculous, Dickey! Taxes to keep dirty blacks . . . what next? Aren't we taxed already to keep them in idleness and booze they aren't supposed to have?

Out on the station we knew how to deal with 'em . . . no work, no tucker. If they got cheeky and reckoned they'd go back to bush-tucker . . . all we had to do was organize a district kangaroo and emu shoot . . . and poison the carcasses . . . for, of course, the filthy creatures'll eat meat rotten. They'd soon be back begging . . . "Give it lil bits tucker, Boss." You know how to deal with 'em, I'll be bound, Mister Delacy.'

Jeremy winked his off-side eye at choking, blazing Alfie. Her ladyship, ringing for the *crêpe suzette*, continued, addressing the somewhat puffy duck-stuffed Jeremy: 'Don't let this crackpot Free Australia thing of Dickey's take you in, Mister Delacy. What's wrong with the country, anyhow? The Depression's over. Once we'd kicked the Labour Party out, everything was all right again. Dickey's the last person who should talk about financial rackets. He got some good cheap property through others' going bankrupt and committing suicide and things while the Depression was on. Ah . . . you certainly are a true bush eater, Mister Delacy. I only hope you won't think my *crêpe* too sissy. I'd've given you a good steamed pudding . . . ah, those good old suet puds! . . . only I'm very proud of my *crêpe suzette*!'

Soon after the huge meal, Jeremy, Dickey and Alfie were sitting out on the patio, drinking brandy, while her ladyship was hounding her staff at the washing-up, when a car came skittering up the gravel drive. Alfie groaned, 'Oh, Lord . . . the Colt!'

There was no time for explanation. A shortish thickset man of fifty or so alighted springily, wearing the golfing outfit called Plus-fours. 'Hello, hello, hello!' he cried with cheery raucousness, and came to Jeremy with hand outstretched. 'Delacy, eh? Mighty glad to meet you. From the wide open spaces. Might come up there look you up some time . . . do a bit o' shootin'. Crack shot in my time . . . sniper, AIF.' He turned to Alfie. 'Hello, sweetheart . . . that long-overdue kiss for Uncle Tom, eh?' He would have taken it. However, with a grimace that could have meant anything, she dodged his assault on her, ducked inside. He shrugged. 'Gratitude in women! Y'know, I did the advertising of her book for nothing . . . and in a big way, too. That's my line. Ad-man.'

He flopped into Alfie's seat. 'Brandy, eh? Don't mind if I do . . . although I been beering a bit at the Nineteenth. And how d'you like our neck o' the woods, Old Timer? But I better introduce myself, seeing old Dickey here's forgotten his manners . . . Tom Colt. Usually known just as the Colt . . . ha, ha! . . . don't know whether they mean I'm a young stallion still . . . .' He gave a poor imitation of a neigh ' . . . or am a straight shooter. Well, here's cheers!'

It seemed that Mr Colt's arrival wasn't mere coincidence, but that Dickey, doing an early round of golf for exercise had met him and told him of his coming guest, and that he happened to be a foundation member of the Free Australia Movement, but was an active critic of it now. Promptly he began to vociferate about the chaotic state of the country, the threats of Communism and Catholicism, advocating a militant counter-force, backed by the RSL to take drastic action to do what he called Put Dear Old Aussie Back On Those Feet She'd Marched So Proudly On From 1914 to 1918. Very definitely he wanted the Movement to get rid of the Bloke, and had heard enough from Dickey to reckon Jeremy the man to oust The Hun-loving Bastard. 'Down-to-earth bushman-returned-soldier type . . . that's what we want. None of your Masters of Arts and Cambridge Dons . . . with the taint of Commo! Getting the Jews' backs up, too . . . that's plain silly. The Jews've got the dough. Besides, we've got smart Jews, good dinky-di Aussies, too. Look at Monash! Best soldier in the war. Liked what you wrote about the mad bastard's Anti-Semitism. Now . . . what's your policy about other things?'

Jeremy hedged, saying that all he wanted for the moment were facts to base a policy on. This irritated the Colt, who said what they wanted was Action. Dickey got into it, waving his hand about the landscape, as if seeing it again thronged with dusky warriors, and declared that their basic policy must be concerned with the Aborigines, and had babbled out just about all that Jeremy had inspired him with, before the Colt, till then staring at him in growing astonishment, jumped on him: 'Where'd you get that bull-shit?'

'Why . . . from Delacy here,' faltered Dickey. 'He wrote about it in *Australia Free*, remember?'

'No . . . I don't remember tripe like that. I remember he wrote about Anti-Semitism and our being too bloody nitwitted to run our country ourselves, which is true.'

Jeremy said quietly, 'I did write that. Also, Alfie Candlemas wrote it in that book you say you sold for her.'

Colt stared at him, frankly puzzled. Then suddenly he grinned. 'I get it! Now I remember. Alfie told me. You got a black wife, eh?'

Jeremy coloured slightly, Dickey deeply. Jeremy answered stiffly, 'My wife has Aboriginal blood.'

The Colt returned cheerfully, 'Same thing, eh?'

Jeremy maintained the stiffness. 'May be . . . but what difference should my wife's complexion make to my believing our first responsibility is to pay for the country we stole?'

'I didn't steal any country, mate.'

'Do you own any property?'

'I certainly do. Dickey here'll tell you I got the biggest place on this peninsula. But I'm not paying any tax on it to keep a tribe of no-good niggers!' He looked belligerent.

Jeremy held his brown-eyed challenging stare for a moment, then shrugged, looked away at the view.

Colt resumed in a tone quite amiable: 'Sorry, old man . . . but you'll have to change views like that if you want to be our leader.' When Jeremy looked at him, he chuckled: 'We know you boys Up North. The old Burnt Cork, eh? Half your luck. I'll try a bit of it myself when I get up there. But it doesn't go down here. We got strong views on race, you know. That's what holds the country together, really. White Australia. It's basic.'

Jeremy nodded. Then he said, 'Well . . . if you'll excuse me. I was going for a bit of a stroll. Rather heavy lunch.' He rose.

The Colt chuckled again: 'She does stuff you, doesn't she?' He tossed off his brandy, also rose. 'Look, I'll give you a run around in the car.'

'Thanks . . . but it's the walk I'm needing.'

'Well, let's run you down the hill, anyway. See my place from down there . . . show place of the district.' There was no gainsaying it, without bluntness inexcusable in another man's house. The Colt fairly shoved him into his huge car.

They went winding down the inlet side, with the Colt talking all the while, mostly about the Movement: The Bloke, whom he detested, the Chief, whom he seemed to fear, finishing up with Alfie: 'You seem to be doing all right there, feller. See her hanging over you when I arrived. Way she used to talk about you, too. You'd be a fair bit older than me, too. What you got, Dad, that I ain't?' He guffawed. 'I been trying to knock her off ever since the book. What's the secret?'

They were down on the waterfront, halted near a jetty running out into the inlet. Jeremy, opening his door, answered dryly, 'Maybe it's the burnt cork.'

'Aheeeeah! No doubt about you. But wait a bit.'

'I want to take a stroll out on the jetty . . . '

'I'll come with you. Haven't shown you my place. Can see it from there.' The Colt leapt out. Jeremy gave him a look that would have discouraged most people. Not so Colt, who trotted along with him onto the jetty, telling him how good the fishing was there. Some half-dozen fishermen were squatting with lines.

Out at the end, Colt pointed out his Hollywood-type mansion amongst several acres of gum trees. He laughed: 'Expect me to take in a tribe of boongs as boarders to give me proper legal title . . . Aheeeaaaah!'

Jeremy answered with a good-humoured grimace, but a surprising statement: 'I presume you can swim, Mr Colt?'

'Eh?' The Colt looked quite surprised. 'Swim? Yes, course I can . . . got a special shark-proof enclosure across there . . . see! That big ketch there, too . . . she's mine. Why d'you ask?'

They were close to the unrailed edge. Jeremy answered, 'Oh . . . just to make sure. Let's see you.' He gave the Colt the slightest shove. Over he went.

No one seemed to notice till the Colt came up, gasping, shouting. Jeremy glanced down at him, grinned, waved, started back for shore. The Colt was screaming, 'Bloody bastard . . . sue you . . . help, help, sharks!'

There was no sign of sharks. Still, the fishermen were running, one of them with a lifebuoy. Jeremy went on his way, reached the shore, glanced back to see the knot hauling on the rope of the buoy. Chuckling, he went on strolling.

It was a couple of hours later when Jeremy got back to the Banker's, to find the household waiting for him with a sumptuous afternoon tea and happily agog over the news of the event on the jetty. It seemed that the Colt himself, in haste to tell them they were harbouring a dangerous lunatic, had reported it by phone. Evidently all detested the man. Jeremy's answer to their eager questions was simply that he had thought the fellow could do with a ducking. That especially delighted the lady of the house, who boomed, 'Just what my father and brothers would have done to a cad like him . . . dump him in the horse-trough . . . ha, ha, ha, ho, ho!'

Dickey chuckled: 'He swears he'll sue you for assault. But he won't be game. He'd be scared of making a fool of himself. He's got too many enemies . . . aheeeah!'

Alfie said, 'That makes up for all the bruises he's put on my bottom.'

After another huge meal called Tea in bush style, Alfie and Jeremy set off back to Town. Jeremy insisted on being set down at his flat and left alone there. Alfie agreed, on condition that she could come and fetch him tomorrow afternoon to eat with her and Frank and meet some politician friends.

Sunday morning he went roaming the empty city, looking at the shops – so obviously bushy, despite the neat grey business suit and pork-pie hat, that thrice he was accosted: by booze-reeking beggars muttering for the price of a meal, which he gave liberally without comment: by a battered young prostitute, who when he gave her the fee she asked but declined to go home with her, yelled after him, 'What's wrong't yo' . . . can't raise one, eh?'

End-point of one hundred and seventy years of the greatest chance for social advancement ever offered mankind – *Australia Felix* in reality!

He peeped into each of the great cathedrals, with their well-dressed congregations, their hidden organs thundering like the Voice of the Almighty Boss, whimpering like the souls of sinners who'd lacked the price of prayers for Indulgence, their hidden choirs wailing of Pie in the Sky, their clergy quaffing the Vinous Blood, with fat ornate silken backs turned on the world of reality.

Two thousand years of hypocrisy imported along with the blatant evil of all history.

He took the steamer trip to Manly, looking at the view with an expression to suggest that he was seeing not so much the bright modernity of shore and islet as the past, a natural enough thing in a thoughtful person not familiar with a locality but well knowing its history. A landmark that interested him particularly, as it does everybody unused to it, and one that had changed but little in all the years, was the fastness built on a rock and into it: Pinchgut, as our convict forebears called it, where those who dared rebel against the hideous inhumanity of the day were confined to starve in dungeons, with a periodic feast off their own blood drawn by the wire cat. Mediaeval dungeons set up in view of those shining eucalypt-clad shores, from which the free-roaming blackman and the leaping marsupial in its vast variety had first peeped in wonder – then in terror – then had run for their lives. Pinchgut – eternal monument to the horror of our beginnings that fathered the squalor of our destiny.

Australia Felix!

Jeremy must have been thinking of so much as he stood and stared and stared; and the blade of the ship's bow cut the blue silk of the water and the screws churned it out as creamy lace.

If only Captain Phillip and his First Fleet had foundered with all hands, on the reef near the Heads called the Sow and Pigs, that morning of January 26, 1788 – or Captain Cook had gone down in the maze of the Great Barrier Reef, as by all that's nautical logic he should have, that Sunday, April 29, 1770 – would there have remained for ever the magic land mariners dreamt of as the Southern Land of the Holy Spirit – or would some other and even stupider bastards have come along and made an even worse mess of it? The grey eyes roved the length, the breadth, even the deep depths, it seemed, of Port Jackson. Who was Jackson, anyway, that his name in perpetuity should supersede whatever red-gum-scented, wattle-blossom-tossed-in-southerly-buster name the blacks had for it? That name lost for ever of course – like the God-given opportunity for *Australia Felix*.

He returned to his flat to find Alfie in possession. Clever girl had bagged a key for herself. She took him utterly by surprise, in that way of hers. However, she went easy with her amorousness on finding him in a negative mood. He declared that he felt it was hopeless trying to do anything positive with a nation so ill-begotten. She took him home.

The politician visitors were already there: massive men, rather like policemen in build and hard-eyed staring, but exceedingly amiable, almost taking Jeremy to their bosoms in greeting him. Both were of the Labor Party, Federal Representatives. One had been President of the Senate, the other a Senior Minister, in the Government brought down by the recently deceased Prime Minister's treachery to his Party. There was no doubt about their interest in Jeremy personally and his association with Free Australia. Instead of pontificating in the usual way of politicians with those not having the privilege of being called Honourable whether having honour or not, they questioned him eagerly. It was also evident that the Senator, a handsome oldish man of about Jeremy's age, was interested in Alfie. Although she held his overt fatherly affections at bay in company, a number of times she was out with him in the kitchen preparing drinks over-long.

These potentates came out with the pontification after dinner. Both declared that nothing of value could come out of a mere Movement. The Senator said, 'You've got to have a Party with an aim to govern. Nothing gets anywhere, unless spouted in the National Gas House. Even with only a single Rep in Parliament, you've got a voice the whole country hears. Otherwise, no matter how good and necessary your reform, you're a voice crying in the wilderness. Even with one Rep you can gain power by aligning yourself with one or other of the major Parties. In our Governments the balance of power is always so fine that any voice is welcome in a vote . . . and the payment is a word of support for your cause. That's the great aim of the Comms . . . to put men into Parliament. No matter about swearing allegiance to the King and the Constitution they're sworn to overthrow . . . anything to get that voice crying from the sanctified benches of the House. British people . . . Anglo-Saxons, if you like . . . have a holy respect for Parliament, and a deep suspicion of anything else. Even if they know the elected Government is largely a facade for Public Service bureaucracy, there's always one's power to break that bureaucracy through one's elected representative.'

The M.H.R. said, 'We need reform. For godsake we need it! Look how we were chiselled out of power last time. Labor will welcome anything you've been talking about, Mr Delacy . . . proper treatment of the Aborigines, elimination of outside financial control, absentee landlordism, a real say in Foreign Affairs. The name Free Australia's good . . . couldn't be bettered to attract attention to our enslavement from outside. But how'll you get rid of the Fascist stink that's got attached to it? Old Labor stalwarts lean well to the Left, you know . . . even if they don't like the Comms. And the Comms won't let you get away with your ideal at the expense of theirs. Already they've pushed Internationalism into the background and talk Australian Nationalism . . . since Free Australia started. Instead of shouting now of the Octobrist Rising, the Glorious Red Army, and all the rest of it on May Day and such occasions, it's the Eureka Stockade. Before it was Communist Youth and the Hammer and

Sickle. Now it's Eureka Youth and the Five Starred Flag. The Australian Labor Party's always been strongly nationalistic. It had to be to get the social solidarity to break the Imperial grip. We started with Eureka, don't forget. You may be sure we'll welcome you . . . if you can found a Party declaring itself for Australia and Australians first. Liberty, equality, fraternity . . . for your Aborigines before anyone else, if you like . . . but a nation without class, caste, privilege. Found your Party . . . but first get rid of that Fascist stink.'

How get rid of it? These warriors of the hustings had the answer.

They said that when Jeremy attended the special meeting of the Movement next Tuesday, after his formal admission, Alfie should call on him to make a speech, in which he should propose formation of the Party. Someone should second him, and the proposal put to the vote. If, as Alfie said, she could pack the meeting with dissidents to the present regime, it should be carried easily. Then and there arrange another meeting, for formulating a constitution and allotting offices. With all this done, the Party's platform should be made public at an open meeting as big and as well advertised as possible. Meantime, the whole idea should be kept secret from those masterminds, the Chief and the Bloke, whose declared policy was opposition to party politics.

The Senator said, 'At the public meeting you must somehow denounce or discredit or dissociate yourself plainly from those two. That'll win you a lot of kudos . . . look as if you've overthrown the would-be dictators in the name of democracy. Once you've done that, we'll be right alongside you.'

Thus through the afternoon, dinner, and a bit of a boozy session afterwards. Jeremy stayed on after the politicians were gone. Alfie was glowing. 'Isn't it wonderful?' she cried. 'I knew they'd be a great help.' But then she bridled at finding Jeremy unimpressed. He said he felt they were only using him, wanting ideas to throw about Parliament themselves. He called them Bower Birds. Alfie waxed indignant, as the daughter of a politician should: 'Of course they have to think of their own party first. But politicians can be as sincere as anyone. You do what they say . . . and I'll bet they keep their promise. We have to have a Voice, as they said. You're not going to turn down the idea of a Party, are you?'

'No . . . I'll give it a go.'

'Bless you, darling Jeremy . . . bless you!' She tried to kiss him. He held her off, telling her that she stank of the Senator's cigars. She laughed gaily: 'You're jealous!'

Jeremy saw to it that his being walked back home was a Candlemas family affair.

Next day, in midmorning, Alfie, very smart in a blue tailored suit and little felt hat, came to take Jeremy to the rendezvours with the Chief and the Bloke. They were all to lunch together. She took him to one of the largest buildings in the city – owned and built, she declared with what sounded like pride, by the chief himself.' A remarkable old man,' she said. She had said it several times.

Curiously, instead of going up from the palatial foyer to something perhaps even more luxurious, hauled by the plush elevator, they went down, by way of plain concrete stairs, into a basement, into a very rough and ready place of business, partitioned into sections with unpainted plywood, where lights glared without shades, and stacks of blue-covered copies of unsold *Australia Free* stood about untidily with reft-lidded packing cases and packing, and harassed-looking people were bent over various tasks.

Chief and Bloke were waiting in one of the cubicles, amidst a pile of literary junk of all sorts such as to make movement awkward. They leapt from their chairs as the visitors appeared. Again the effusive greeting of cityites. The Chief was quite an old fellow, tubby, almost bald. The Bloke was biggish, stoutish, aged about forty, with small moustache and lick of corn-white hair over forehead, so that he looked rather like *Der Führer*, and was just as wooden-faced, despite all the yelping and gesticulating of his greeting. Chairs were drawn up for the visitors. Jeremy was watchful, sparing with words. The others were watchful, too, but quite vociferous. They asked him questions, then proceeded to answer themselves; or rather to conduct small debates between themselves on each subject. They seemed to be knowledgeable on all subjects, from Aborigines to Determinism, Religion to Rationalism, with just enough difference of point of view to make debate of it. Thus, till suddenly the Chief hauled from his waistcoat pocket a large old-fashioned gold watch, and announced that it was time for lunch.

The elevator was called down for them by the doorman. The driver cringed in admitting them, and passed people waiting on other floors, but without even a glance for his sycophancy. They were delivered with deep deference into the heart of a large restaurant. A lanky man in black came rushing to greet them, only to turn and rush away to stand by their table. He properly seated Alfie first, although with lackey's eyes fixed on the Chief, to settle whom he positively leapt. He took their order, departed.

Their table would be the best in the place, in the only windowed corner, with wide views of the city. The Chief set about showing Jeremy the landmarks. Then suddenly the Chief whipped out his Hunter again, shoved it back, clapped his hands and shouted, 'Service there . . . service!'

The clatter of tongues and tools eased off as nearby people stared. He took advantage of the lull to shout even louder. The tall man in black came running again. The old man demanded of him, 'Why aren't we served?'

The man panted, 'Sorry, sir . . . rather rushed . . . at once.' He raced away. The place was packed.

The gustatorial din arose again. The Chief resumed his entertainment of Jeremy. But still no service. Suddenly he flamed into anger, thumped the table now, and roared, 'Service . . . service!'

Now a waitress came, tight-faced, eyes glinting. She was clumsy, slopped soup in serving. The Chief snarled at her, 'Why did they send you?'

She flushed, tossed her pile of silly synthetic waves, snapped, 'Why shouldn't they?'

'Don't be insolent. You don't know your job. I've been waiting fifteen minutes.'

'The place's packed. You's last in. You expect to be first served?'

'Yes, I do. Stop serving. Get me the manager.'

The girl looked alarmed, faltered, 'What for?'

He roared, 'I said get me the manager!'

She vanished. The lanky man appeared in her place, cringing. 'Sir?'

'That girl was grossly impertinent. Dismiss her . . . and send me a senior waiter.'

'Yes, Sir . . . sorry, Sir . . . the girl's new . . . . '

'I said dismiss her and send me a senior waiter . . . with fresh soup!'

'Yes, Sir,' The manager fled.

Meeting Jeremy's surprised eye, the Chief said, 'Slipshod's anathema to me.'

Jeremy swallowed. 'You own the restaurant?'

'No . . . but I own the building.'

A male waiter came with finely balanced tray. 'Ah, that's better,' commented the Chief, watching the swift expert service. When the man was gone and they were settled to their soup, the old man caught Jeremy's eye again. 'You don't approve, Mr Delacy?'

Jeremy flushed slightly, lowered his spoon, said shortly, 'Well . . . since you ask me . . . no.'

A glimmer of amusement in the faded eyes. The ghost of a grin. 'May I ask why?'

Jeremy drank another spoonful, looking uncomfortable. 'I'm unused to city ways.'

'Please don't hedge. I like frankness. I think you're a frank man. Why don't you approve?'

Jeremy flushed. 'Well . . . you admit that you don't own the restaurant . . . yet you interfere with its management, simply because you own the building.'

'You're wrong there. I'd've done the same at any restaurant when I was kept waiting at a reserved table and served so badly. I told you I abominate the slipshod.'

'Was there any need to demand the waitress's dismissal?'

'It was meant as a dressing-down for the manager. How dare he send me a novice!'

'The girl will be the sufferer, though.'

'The lesson will teach her to wait on people properly . . . if that's the job she chooses to do. I find that stupid people learn only by drastic lessons . . don't you?'

Jeremy concentrated on his soup.

The Chief, slopping his soup, went on: 'This whole Nation needs drastic teaching. That's why I formed our Movement. Australia as a whole is slipshod. I thought we would be agreed on that.'

The waiter was hovering to take the soup plates and serve a silver grill he had under a dome on a dumb-waiter. When Jeremy declined the portion offered him, the Chief exclaimed, 'Come, come, Mr Delacy . . from what I've heard and read of you, I'd hardly think you were a man to get in a pique!' But the eyes were glittering with amusement, the thin mouth twitching with a grin.

Jeremy met the eyes calmly. 'I'm not piqued, Sir. I'm not in the habit of eating in the middle of the day. Mrs Candlemas will tell you that.'

'I beg your pardon. Very wise. You look a fit man. It's true we dig our graves with knife and fork, most of us. But don't deny me the pleasure of contentious debate. I see I haven't won my argument for efficiency. Where did I fail?'

Reddening again, Jeremy replied, 'Well, Sir . . . your demands on others seem to amount only to arrogant assertion of your power over other people.'

The eyes gleamed with pleasure. 'Why should I not assert power when I have it?'

Jeremy turned quite red. 'I beg your pardon, as your guest . . . but you sound like the supreme egoist.'

The grin split wide. 'You compliment me with the word Supreme. Aren't we all egoists? Isn't egotism the primary incentive to human endeavour?'

'You may have a philosophical point there. But I'm sure the majority of people, however precious their ego might be to them privately, are simply bewildered about it, thinking themselves of no account at all.'

'They *are* of no account if they think so. Are we, who are aware of the fact that we account and can increase our accounting, to truckle to these what'd you call 'em . . . bewildered No-accounts?'

'At least be kind to them.'

'Explain yourself. The word Kind is vague in usage, I find. It means actually to do with Kin . . . the natural feeling one has for one's kindred. Are No-accounts *my* kin?'

Jeremy blinked, fiddled with his napkin, while the old fellow chewed his steak and watched his discomfort with evident glee. At length he said, 'Well, take the case of the young woman. In her inexperience she thought you lacked consideration for others there . . . last in, want to be first served. Presuming the manager's been callous enough to carry out your order to sack her . . . Callous being my word for the opposite feeling to kindness . . . and presuming that kinship basically is identification with one's species . . . what if she has domestic problems, drunken husband, children to feed . . . I presume she wouldn't be working for the sheer love of it . . . .'

'So much presuming by an obviously logical mind! If she has such problems, can she not come and state her case?'

'And grossly humiliate herself!'

'Humility's part of her job. That's why I said she'll be a better waitress for the lesson.'

'Suppose she can't get a job after this . . . has to Go On the Town, as they say?'

'I'll suppose nothing but that she's a fool if she can't get herself out of this difficulty.'

Jeremy drew a deep breath. 'I must say, Sir, that for one advocating a Free Australia, you sound to me like some old English overlord.'

The old fellow laughed merrily, glanced at his tame *Führer* who was eating as if numbering the chews, and who, as if feeling it required of him, raised his wooden face, to glare at this one taking liberties with his Chief.

Jeremy, still red, said, 'This Brave New Australia of yours sounds like being what they call Tough Country . . . at least for some.'

The old man cried eagerly, 'Naturally, my dear fellow . . . for those who, because they can't make the ranks of the Elite, kick against the traces.'

'You make it sound like dictatorship.'

'What else could it be?'

Jeremy blinked. The old man pressed: 'You're a patriot . . . you want to be proud of your country . . . well, how do you envisage it?'

'As a brotherhood . . . with the land the bond.'

The Bloke broke in with a laugh and a spurt of spittle: 'Egalitarianism? It died on *La Guillotine*!'

The Chief chuckled and twinkled: 'I guess the Eskimos have brotherhood . . . only the bond is ice.'

The Bloke roared with laughter. Alfie giggled. Jeremy's face didn't change. When they fell silent, he said dryly, 'Your conception of Free Australia is evidently very different from mine.'

'You've read our published views,' said the Chief. 'And as you've experienced yourself, we're quite prepared to publish others' . . . provided they're rational. By the way . . . this's a good subject for literary debate in the paper . . . How Would You Have The New Australia Run . . . eh?'

Here Alfie cut in quickly: 'There's the meeting for him tomorrow night. Jeremy should be given the chance to voice his opinions there!'

'Of course, of course!' cried the Chief. 'It could be the liveliest meeting we've had yet. I understand a lot of people want to meet our hero here . . . some simply because he chucked the Colt in the drink . . . ha, ha, ho!'

The Bloke echoed the laugh, then looked dreamily away as if at a vision of himself as having the power that the Chief was telling Jeremy the Colt had but such as in which no one would dare throw him in any drink. That incident tickled the Chief very much. Evidently, for all the Colt's power, which included even dictating to the Labor Newspaper because he had a financial lien on it, he despised the man. 'You ought to be afraid of him,' he said to Jeremy, 'But I guess you're not . . . ho, ho, ho!'

After the meal the two great ones went back to what Jeremy, while he and Alfie went to the Hotel Australia for a drink, called their Fascist Forge in the basement. Calling their hang-out a forge was due to the Bloke's having claimed that his father was a country blacksmith. Jeremy remarked that he was more modest than Mussolini, who claimed to have been a blacksmith himself. 'Don't you believe it?' asked Alfie.

'Not after hearing that he also claims to tame wild horses. The two things suggest the strength to mould powerful objects to one's will.'

'You can't say Mussolini isn't a strong man!'

'I'll bet my boots he isn't a horseman of any kind. He hasn't the build for it. You've got to be long in the legs to stick on anything but some old jade. He's the same build as Napoleon . . . who was so poor a horseman, I understand, that horses had to be carefully selected for him so he wouldn't make a fool of himself falling off.'

'Don't you think Napoleon was, in his way, a great man?'

'I suppose Ned Kelly was.'

She squeezed his hand, laughing. Whether it was the brandy they drank, or the infection of Alfie's enthusiasm for what lay ahead, Jeremy was in much brighter spirits than he had shown since his arrival. When they went home to her place, Alfie got busy with her planning on the phone.

That night there was quite a big gathering at the Candlemases'. Eager talk went on till midnight, with Jeremy the centre of it. He looked different tonight, not appraising, but lending himself for appraisal. Alfie flitted about like an excited moth, one that has got the wavelength of a mating male.

Nevertheless, all the organization of this momentous meeting was hers. She had mustered the most worthy of those interested in Free Australia, many of whom had dropped the idea completely in disapproval of the course the Movement had taken. She'd had to convince them that Jeremy was their true Messiah. Now in her knowledge of the inner circle she had to tell them what must be done to overthrow the false prophets. Jeremy must be declared Leader tomorrow night. Every available hand must be there to hail him; and the opposition must be taken completely by surprise. Yet she could act the love-excited little girl.

Next day she was a little bee in her busyness. So much had to be done to follow up last night's decisions. She did it. Over early dinner the trio had at the Candlemases' flat that evening, she declared that she was positive every available member of the Movement, some two hundred, would attend tonight's meeting, all with a sense of great expectation, although few would know of what. Many times she cried, 'This is really living, isn't it!' She told of some lively campaigning with her ex-politician father, but added: 'It was never like this! This is really living . . . with all that's involved!'

Again it was to that large building belonging to the Chief they went. This time it was straight into the elevator and up again to the top floor, now into a compact conference room. Already the place was filled, with the principals on the rostrum. The Bloke had the Chairman's place. He leapt up to give Jeremy the Sydney Hug. The Chief remained seated, but reached for Jeremy's hand and wrung it with no less hearty insincerity. Jeremy was seated next to him. On the other side of the Bloke was the Secretary, a bald wisp wearing pince-nez and crouched over minute-book.

When the place was full, proceedings began with the usual rigmarole of Secretary. Then the Bloke rose to announce, in his somewhat high-pitched but flat and echoless voice, that this meeting was special in that its purpose was formal induction of one already well known to the Movement for his forthright contributions to their organ – a Nominator, please? Alfie sprang to do the job, fairly shining as she told of the candidate's patriotism and his courage in dealing with all who negated that precious thing, concluding rapidly, so as to beat the sob the eulogy in its crescending emotion threatened to use as a full stop: 'Not only the truest, greatest Australian I've even known . . . but . . . but . . . the greatest . . . truest . . . man!'

Such was the emotion of it that it compelled silence for a long moment – except for a small nanny-goat bleat from right at the back. Eyes on those on the rostrum focused on that point. It wasn't a goat at all, but one who fancied himself as a stallion, Mr Colt. Then the applause broke forth, as perhaps never before at one of those flat-voiced *Fuhrer*'s meetings. There was even stamping. Alfie, dropping back beside Jeremy, blinking on tears, whispered, 'There . . . I told you they'd love you!'

The Bloke restored order with a Hitlerian thumping of the table with a fist. Then he barked, 'Seconder!'

Dickey the Banker rose, and would have given a Boy Scout's breathless forecasting of the wonders the new Scout Master was bound to work for the Troop, only the Bloke intimidated him with an irritable gesture, and took advantage of his faltering to pipe to the audience, 'All those in favour?'

Almost every hand shot up.

Alfie was on her feet as the hands came down, crying, 'Speech . . . speech!'

The crowd took it up. 'Speeeeech!'

Jeremy was rising. But there was Mr Colt, already up and shouting, 'Wait on . . . what about those not in favour?'

The Bloke snapped, 'Those against?'

Only the Colt's hand. The Bloke snapped, 'Carried almost unanimously.' The bald little scrivener wrote.

But the Colt wasn't done: 'Opposition has a right to state objections. If the majority knew what kind of man the candidate really is, they'd think twice . . . .'

The Chief called through cupped hand, 'We all know he chucked you in the drink last Sunday, Tom. You advertised it too thoroughly . . . ha, ha!'

There was a general laugh, above which the Colt fairly screamed 'That shows what a thug he is! But what I want to tell you is . . . he's got a black wife!'

Dead silence. The Colt looked round, grinning now. But old Dickey leapt up, he the screamer now: 'Shame . . . shame!'

The crowd took it up: *'Shaaaame!'*

There was tussling round the Colt. He appeared in the aisle, apparently about to deliver an address from there. The Bloke hammered for order. The Colt yelled, 'I'll have my say!'

The Chief spoke to the Bloke. He hammered again, crying, 'Sit down, Mr Colt . . . or remove yourself!'

The Colt gaped. 'Eh?'

The Chief whispered again to the Bloke. He passed it on: 'Sit down or get out!'

'Right!' yelled The Colt. 'Accept my resignation . . . and no more ads in your dirty Hun rag!'

'Let us weep!' bawled the Chief.

The Colt swung round towards the entrance, glared over the audience watching him in silence. At the door he wheeled, yelled, 'I'll ruin you, you bloody bunch of cranks . . . ruin you!' He vanished.

The Chief flung back his shiny white-fringed head, laughed uproariously. In a moment everybody was laughing; except the *Führer*, who stood wooden-faced as ever. When it was over the Bloke turned to Jeremy. 'You are duly elected to membership of the Free Australia Movement, Mr Delacy. Do you wish to say something in acknowledgement?'

Jeremy rose, to loud and long applause. The *Führer* hunched himself, assuming the Hitlerian scowl. *Vos ist das* – a Rival *Führer*?

Jeremy spoke slowly: 'Fellow countrymen . . . .' It brought more applause.

He resumed :'It's good to have my mode of addressing you so well received . . . in a country where compatriotism has so little meaning . . . .'

Another burst.

'Believe it or not, it's the first time in my life I've ever used it . . . .'

Someone in the audience shouted, 'First time I've ever heard it used!'

'As a matter of fact, Aborigines use it . . . or rather, simply the term Countryman . . . in addressing one another. Once it would be applied only to one belonging to one's own tribal area . . . but lately, with so many tribes broken up, I've noticed that they use it in speaking to strangers of their kind. I take it to be a good sign of some growing fraternalism amongst them. Their tragedy has been largely due to their lack of identity beyond what the Anthropologists call the Horde, a relationship grouping that's not easy to understand. I begin with this reference to Aborigines, not because of my alleged tribal connexions through my wife . . . . ' A ripple of laughter ' . . . My wife, by the way, although of Aboriginal descent, is hardly what anyone except a complete fool would call black . . . . ' What had been a ripple became a roar, not merely of laughter but of applause. When it ended he said, 'I hope your enthusiasm is based rather on sympathy for Aborigines than for me. Intermarriage with these people can be a very complex business. It would take a lot of explaining to you . . . .'

Someone called: 'It's sympathy with the Aborigines. We want to help them.'

'How?'

'By raising them to our level.'

Jeremy cried, 'God save them from that!'

Silence. He went on: 'What is our level that we can be, as a Nation, proud of it?'

'Hear, hear . . . hear, hear!'

'I'm not here to discuss the Aboriginal problem. When I began I wanted simply to say that I made mention of the Aborigines because I believe that no talk of Australian nationalism can be made without including them, in fact without considering the case of their ruthless dispossession by us before all else . . . . '

The place vibrated to the applause. Even Chief and Bloke were hard at it.

When it ended he said quietly into his microphone, 'That's good. It shows that conscience is dawning where there was only blank indifference before . . . Now . . . I've been given the privilege of membership of your Movement . . . . ' A ripple of applause. He stopped it with upraised hand: 'Wait . . . observe that I didn't say The Honour.'

Silence. The Bloke and Chief, from lounging in their seats, stiffened.

'I can't feel honoured . . . because I can't accept much of what purports to be its ideals . . . . '

'Hear, hear . . . hear, hear!' It came from scattered quarters. These would be Alfie's strongest recruits. Some people looked askance. The Bloke scowled. The Chief eyed the audience sharply, as if noting the identity of the dissenters.

Jeremy resumed: 'I'm glad so many of you approve of my objections. If Free Australia can't be originally Australian, with policies entirely our own, but borrowed from other countries, whether Imperial Britain, Imperial Japan, Nazi Germany, Fascist Italy . . . . '

'Hear, hear . . . hear hear!'

The Bloke, wooden-faced again, rapped hard, and when Jeremy turned to him, demanded, 'What's this?'

'You asked me if I wanted to make acknowledgement, Mr Chairman.'

'That doesn't mean giving you permission to stand up and criticize . . . .

'The right to criticize is exactly what we want!' shouted someone.

'Hear, hear!' The support was greater than ever.

The Chief leant towards the Bloke, speaking behind his hand. The Bloke cocked an ear, then said with wooden severity, 'You will refrain from taking advantage of this situation to criticise, Mr Delacy . . . or sit down . . . . '

Uproar in the audience. Even some tussling. Jeremy stopped it with a gesture: 'I refrain. I never used the word criticism. I want to construct . . . not pull down.'

'Good on you!'

'What I want to say is what I've learnt through careful observation and inquiry since coming into these parts. Undoubtedly there's a strong feeling *for* Australia by Australians, and deep concern over mismanagement of the Nation, worse, over ruthless betrayal of it even by some entrusted with the power to run it . . . . '

'Hear, hear!'

The Bloke cut in: 'We've said and published all that long ago.'

Jeremy did not turn to him. 'It is also very evident that mere club debating and discussion in a magazine of limited circulation will achieve little . . . in fact the reverse . . . since I understand the Movement has lost considerable ground it gained at first through debating itself into involvement in contentious issues that have nothing to do with this country, even in the matter of religion . . . . '

The Bloke leapt up, red of face, and cried something that was drowned in the roar of applause. He sat down, to intimidate them with the Hitlerian scowl.

Jeremy continued: 'My careful study of the matter, along with expert advice, has convinced me that there isn't a hope of getting what we want, without formation of a political party to take its place with other parties in Parliament . . . . '

A great stir in the audience, with more drowned protesting from the Bloke and an audible shout from the Chief, 'Our policy is against party politics!'

But Jeremy, so evidently having the majority of the audience, ignored them. 'We Australians, for all our contempt for politicians generally, are great believers in Parliament. It's Parliament ultimately that we trust . . . because we know that if we take the trouble to be wise in our choice of candidates, *our* voice will be heard . . . . '

The Bloke, on his feet all the while, shouted into Jeremy's pausing for breath, 'Parliamentary government is discredited, outdated, outmoded . . . . '

A yell from the audience, 'Shut up . . . we want to hear him!'

'Yes . . . we want to hear him.'

'I'm Chairman!'

'You think you're Adolf Hitler. Sit down!'

'I'll declare the meeting closed . . . . '

'What do we care? We'll carry on regardless. Sit down!'

'Sit down, Adolf!'

The *Führer*, wooden but very red, sat down.

Jeremy went on: 'Parliamentary government, in its true sense of the unrestricted talking-out of things by freely elected representatives, is essential to democracy . . . and democracy is essential to people like us, who haven't come so far from our humble origins that we can afford to put on airs, any of us, as Elite . . . . '

'Hear, hear!'

Chief and Bloke were now slumped in their chairs, looking as if now they dissociated themselves from the proceedings.

'I propose,' said Jeremy, 'that out of this Free Australia Movement, the Free Australia Party be formed . . . with an ordinary political platform like any other party, with concern for all the things that ordinary people want, like reform in taxation, pensions, education, and the like, and the same primary aspiration, which is to get our representatives into Parliament to plead our special causes to the Nation, and, let's hope, eventually to govern and see that our cause is served.'

This was received only with a murmur. Now the Bloke perked up, sneered. But no one was looking at anyone but Jeremy. 'I've talked to Parliamentary representatives. They've assured me that they'll be glad to voice any constructive opinions of ours till such time as we can do so in the House ourselves, and when we can, will give our representatives all support. The Communists haven't just sat in back rooms debating Marx and Lenin, or slanging Fascists in their newspaper. They contest every possible seat with what looks like not the slightest hope of winning .. but never give up. We'll have to do the same . . . . '

Someone called, 'The Comms get money from Moscow . . . as much as they want. Where are we going to get ours?'

'That will be the test of our sincerity. I understand that you're all comfortable people. I'd say I'm that . . . by dint of saving. We can surely make some small sacrifice to start with. We don't aspire to anything yet but formation of the Party and presentation of it to the public. As I see it . . . it's now or never for the True Australia, *Australia Felix,* that we and our immediate ancestors dreamt of. Another world war is pending. The last one cut off our growth like cutting off our legs. If we're dragged into this one, it will mean cutting off our hands, our heads, will spell our utter ruin as anything but a dump for surplus population of the world, a quarry for raw materials for an overpopulated world. I don't say we have to keep *out* of it. Maybe we won't be able to. I said Dragged Into It. We must never again be dragged into war like the colonial oafs we've always been, to bleed ourselves to death for some Imperium, be it British, American, Russian, German, Japanese, or any other . . . . '

The applause was deafening. When it had subsided, Jeremy said, 'All we need to begin with is the money to advertise our coming into existence and then for hiring a hall to show ourselves. I'm sorry now that I succumbed to the urge to push Mr Colt overboard. He could have been a great help, perhaps.'

Loud laughter. The Bloke took advantage of the pause to sneer, 'You'll be the first candidate for election, I take it?'

Half-glancing at him, Jeremy replied, 'It's unwise to judge others by oneself.'

He turned back to the chuckling audience: 'I certainly won't be standing for election. For a start, I'm too old for such a departure from my quiet life. For another, your climate would kill me . . . . ' A laugh. He said, 'For the time I'll take on the job of Chairman . . . . '

The Bloke leapt up, screaming, 'Will you, by God . . . I'm the Chairman!'

Without looking at him, Jeremy said, 'I'm not talking about the Free Australia Movement . . . from which, herewith, I resign. I'm speaking of the Free Australia Party, an entirely different thing, which will publicly dissociate itself from the Movement. Those of you who are prepared to assist in forming a steering committee and all the rest of it, I'd like to meet in another place. This is no inspiration. We've got things well organized already . . . .'

'I'll bet you have!' screamed the Bloke. 'I knew there was something fishy about you coming down here . . . '

'It's your Movement that's fishy,' someone yelled. 'It stinks!'

Laughter – but with some protesting.

Jeremy, moving from the table to the steps of the rostrum, now without aid of microphone, cupped hands over mouth to amplify his voice: 'All that's required now is to know the strength of your approval. May I ask for a show of hands from those who say Aye to formation of the Free Australia Parliamentary Party?'

At least two-thirds of the hands shot up.

The Bloke, hoarse now, croaked, 'You can't do that . . . this's my meeting! All those not in favour?' The rest of the hands, a poor showing against the others, were raised somewhat feebly, except his own, which shot up like Uncle Adolf's up and out – *Heil*!

Alfie, rushing after Jeremy as he descended the steps, cried joyously, 'Almost unanimous!' She grabbed him, kissed him, clung to him as he made his way through the crowd shoving out to shake his hand and pat his shoulders and pledge their support and say, so many of them, 'The man we've always wanted. A man of true strength and honesty . . . a dinky-di Australian!'

Thus to the door and out and down in the crowded lift. Strangely, the Chief came down immediately after them and offered use of the foyer of the building for the business of collecting names and addresses, and even put his own name on the list. Jeremy was suspicious. However, Alfie and Frank and Dickey said it was like him to do such a thing, that he never bore malice, treated life as a game. As Frank said, 'He can afford to.' This was as they went home, just the three of them, to crack a couple of bottles of champagne that Alfie had in the refrigerator as part of her expert campaign.

The Steering Committee of the Australia Free Party was formed at a meeting at Jeremy's flat next afternoon. It would have been earlier had those others concerned been able to locate their Chairman. As it was he walked into the flat at noon to find them waiting. He said he had been out on the Harbour again, this time to learn how the ordinary run of people felt about what they themselves considered vital. The depressing result was plain enough in his face, let alone his words. He began by saying that he found Sydney people honestly approachable only on ferry boats, giving it as his opinion that only under the influence of the hypnotic rhythm of engines and blinding marvel of their waterway were they ever relaxed. He had talked to passengers and crew, even to one captain, leading them into giving their views on the state of the country. Practically all frankly stated that they thought it stank, but in what way no one could say exactly. When one talked money to them, suggesting that the trouble lay in the stranglehold of foreign finance, all showed fear. Monkeying with the finances was the last thing they wanted. They'd had too much of it, 'In Jack Lang's time,' as they put it. All they wanted was security. What did it matter who held the money, so long as they got their little whack? As to patriotism, to Australia's need to think first of itself in case of war, most had said, 'Well, we've got to stand by Old England if she gets in strife, haven't we?' Some added: 'Hasn't she always stood by us?' and looked indignant when he had suggested, 'Hasn't she rather stood over us?' Nearly all had volunteered that 'We Could Do With A Strong Man' . . . a Mussolini, according to passengers and that captain, a Stalin in the opinion of a couple of members of crews.

To that Alfie cried, 'It all means they want a leader, someone to *tell* them what they want and show them how to get it!'

The others, who were Dickey the Banker, the Economist, a retired Judge with liberal reformist leanings, an ex-Senator, and a writer of some repute, agreed.

They began their business over an *al fresco* lunch, carried it through till dark. Dickey declared that there would be plenty of money, producing a substantial cheque of his own to start the kitty. The Economist took it as Treasurer. Whether he was appointed as such by acclamation or by his own eagerness would be hard to say. There did seem to be a little doubt about it, as Jeremy, who mainly listened and watched, must have observed. Dickey himself took on the job of Research Officer, in which capacity he would look into all matters that stank nationally and come up with the facts for publicizing them with purpose. The Judge promised to chair all meetings and so lend his prestige, and also to lend his very efficient secretary. Mr Rumple, the writer, became Publicity Officer. Alfie was formally inducted as Campaign Director, for which purpose the Treasurer would secure her an office in the centre of the city that would also lend prestige to the Party. He himself would include the Party's business with his own accountancy practice, for a modest fee, if they would not mind.

When it was done, the Judge took them all off to dine at an Italian restaurant, where the Secretary, a handsome willowy and evidently quite clever young woman, was awaiting him. There and then Mr Rumple sketched on the back of the half-a-yard-square menu the first of the series of the quite clever pieces that thereafter appeared in the press as quasi-news-items but were in fact expensive advertisements, the expense increasing as the Party's declared policy differed from the paper's own.

Despite Jeremy's own dismal success in sounding out the populace, the response to ordered campaigning could well be described as Tremendous, as those concerned put it. Offers of support and inquiries for more information began to pour in the moment the location of Alfie's plush office was made known. It could be quite truly said that the interest represented all sections of the community, since amongst the correspondence were abusive and sometimes even obscene letters and phone-calls from Communists who called them Dirty Fascists and Anti-Communists who called them Filthy Comms. The Communist Press wiped it off as only the Fascist Free Australia Movement waving a bunch of wattle to try to overcome the stink it had caused with its German Anti-Working Class and Anti-Semitic filth. The Jewish Press had something to say, warning its readers to be wary of what declared itself to be at war with Anti-Semitism, but which was led by one who had encouraged false prophets to besmirch the name of decent Jewry with that faked settlement for Refugee Jews. *Australia Free* took it up, not to condemn it, but far worse, to give its blessing and remind everybody that the new Party had its beginnings in the Movement. One could almost see that impish grin of the Chief's behind the words of fatherly advice that declared that Socialism is Socialism and Nationalism is Nationalism, and never the twain shall meet satisfactorily save when hyphenated by some Great Man, like Adolf Hitler or Benito Mussolini, between whose colossal forms it was hoped eventually the Party Leader would rise up truly to make Australia Free.

In fact, the Movement's interest was more than an exercise in impishness. The Chief caught Jeremy at his flat. He was quite humble in approach, saying, 'I'm prepared to kill the Movement, Delacy, if you'll let me in with you . . . and I'll back you to the limit of my means.'

Jeremy, although he had been dodging him since knowing he was seeking him, sat him down and gave him brandy. The old man said, 'I've got this nationalistic bug like you. I've always felt humiliated by being denied nationality . . . proper nationality, that is. I haven't travelled abroad for years . . . because I refuse to do so on a passport that declares me British-born, when I'm born Australian. I know the Movement stinks. But so does every innovation that forces the mob to face reality.'

Jeremy demanded, 'Do you call your printed support of Hitler's lunatic theory that Bolshevism's a Jewish plot to rule the world *reality*?'

The Chief grinned broadly. 'It was largely a joke . . . but I'll admit that it was somewhat unfortunate.'

'As I see it, it was even fatal. It might cruel any chance we have of winning a Free Australia.'

'At the time I never thought we had any hope of winning a Free Australia . . . not till I met you. Saying the things that infuriated doctrinaire fatheads like Communists and clever people like Jews, simply amused me. Give me credit for publishing your objections to our Anti-Semitism.'

'Why did you persist in it after publishing my objections . . . which meant tacitly admitting you were wrong?'

'I've told you . . . for fun. I found it amusing as well as instructive that such clever people as Jews should take on so. Don't forget, we attacked the Catholic Church at first, and then the Anglicans, and the Salvation Army. Judaism is primarily a religion. One must be fair. As people, I admire Jews, for their generally superior intelligence, and for their courage in standing against the world throughout history, as you yourself wrote. I never expected them to throw bricks through my windows and yell abuse at me in the streets.'

'Not when their kith and kin are being murdered according to law by what purports to be a civilized country? Not when they might have escaped with their lives themselves?'

'The Jews have survived plenty of this . . . will survive plenty more. But, listen . . . I'll drop all this sort of thing to support you.'

'What about your Little Hitler?'

'I'll drop him, too.'

'Just like that! And I take his place?'

'So I would hope. You have everything that man lacks to be a true leader of this country. But, of course, you have your own lackings to rectify.'

'Such as?'

'Your Democracy. Mob rule is what it means. That's a fallacy for a start . . . because a mob can't rule themselves . . . never have, never will. The Superman, even if only a bonehead, always takes over. Your Socialism is tommy-rot. Bureaucracy controls all so-called socialized concerns . . . and bureaucracy breeds hierarchy . . . and hierarchy means a Big Boss at the top. A man with your intelligence and experience can't believe that men are equal!'

'I believe they could be, in a well-ordered society.'

'In a dream!'

'Call me a dreamer, then . . . and let me go my way.'

The old man suddenly became haggard, swallowed, said almost breathlessly, 'I would like to come with you.'

'Why . . . when we have such different views? Do you imagine you can convert me, make me a creature of yours as it seems to me you've made that poor mad bastard they call the Bloke?'

Again the Chief swallowed, said huskily, 'I'm an old man, Delacy . . . and far from well, despite my appearance. But I love life. I want to live out my last days with vigour. I can see all sorts of troubles ahead for Australia, as for the rest of the world. We're about to enter the Forties. My love of my country and my love of life make me want to take a hand in shaping the destiny of this country . . . which I'm sure is going to be decided, for better or worse, in the next two or three years.'

'I'm not a Man of Destiny, as they say. I came here just to see the reality of things.'

'Ah . . . as I thought! You will see through the airy-fairy dream. You will be snatched up to serve the destiny of the Nation . . . you are already. And I want to be with you. Will you have me?'

'No.'

'I will keep in the background so as not to embarrass you.'

'No, Sir . . . no! I'm dreaming of national dignity . . . while all you want, really, is to use the power you have in your money. Why not let your madman free to form an SS or SA private army, like Hitler, and burn down the Federal Parliament and blame it on the Communists and Jews, and murder them for it? I want nothing to do with you.' Jeremy rose. 'Goodday to you, Sir!'

The Chief, ruddy and heaving somewhat for breath, rose, too, somewhat falteringly followed as Jeremy led the way to the door. He muttered, 'National dignity? Man . . . go out into the working-class suburbs and see the material you've got to work on. Go to the races on Saturday, the Stadium on Saturday night . . . the pubs any time they're open.'

Jeremy opened the door. The old man had regained his composure. He grinned. 'No ill feelings, eh?' He held out his hand. Jeremy hesitated, then took it.

The Chief shook it heartily, saying, 'Nothing will please me better than if you succeed. I'll be watching you all the while. *Au revoir*!' He was gone.

Jeremy heaved a great sigh as he went back to his chair, saying aloud, 'Mad

. . . mad with money!' He swigged his brandy, went on musing, 'Are the people behind Hitler like that? Is it madness . . . or a form of badness . . . rising out of frustration . . . having everything, yet nothing?'

Later he talked it over with Alfie, who again showed she had a sneaking regard for the Chief, and more, that she was not above their making the use of him that he had offered. She argued that his declared Nationalistic Bug might well outweigh his rich-man's oligarchic arrogance eventually and make him a true patron of democracy in that Well-ordered Society of Jeremy's dreams. Jeremy remained of the opinion that all the man wanted was power of a perverse kind, adding that the like of him were probably by no means rare and need not be wealthy but able to wield their power by other means, and that these might be their chief opponents. Still, far from depressing him, the incident with the Chief seemed even to have stimulated him to action, at least by the interest he showed when Alfie told him that the Leader of the Opposition of the Federal Parliament was in Sydney and had expressed a wish to meet him. Alfie arranged the meeting, and went along with him, being well known to the Leader, as the old warrior Silas Tripconny's girl.

As the meeting was at the Federal Members' Rooms, Jeremy met other members of the Labor Party than their leader, men whose names had been on everybody's lips a few years back, either in praise as the Nation's saviours, or in execration for bringing it to the brink of ruin. All told him they would welcome him, if he were elected to join them in the Gas House, but insisted that his ideas were also theirs. Still, they said, fresh voices were useful for making old ideas sound new. When he told them he had no political aspirations himself they looked incredulous.

Alfie, bred amongst them, became one of them. Hence later, when they went off together to the Hotel Australia to talk over the experience and he expressed anything but enthusiasm, she was disappointed. He said he thought the leader had the mind of an adolescent, filled with Nineteenth Century Parlour Social Reform stuff: 'He talks as if he's practising elocution for a Young Labor rally . . . with the emphasis not on what you say but how you say it . . . sort of *Storm the Barricades, Brothers*! when he's talking of a thing like reform of the treatment of Aborigines. God help us if he ever becomes Prime Minister! The others struck me as just con-men turned respectable through having pulled the great trick.'

She got hot about it, especially his decrying the Leader of the Opposition: 'He's been a tremendous fighter for freedom. He went to jail during the Anti-Conscription campaign.'

'For Ireland . . . not Australia. It was Irish hatred of England behind that . . . not Australian love of Australia.'

'Of course it was Australian love! You weren't here to see it.'

'And how old were you to be able to take in the truth of it . . . three or four, eh?'

'Harping on my age again! First I'm too young to have a right to love you. Now I'm too young to have any brains. Don't you think I've been listening to talk about the realities of the Conscription Issue most of my life? Everything's going so beautifully . . . but you've always got to knock it!' There were tears in her eyes.

'Too much brandy, again,' he said. 'Come on. Let's go for a ride on a ferry and get some fresh air . . . and you tell me about these things you've got lined up for me. I'm seeing it all through. I'm enormously interested. But I reserve the right to my own opinion, which, by the way, you always ask me for.'

'Oh, darling!' she sighed tearfully, grabbing for his hand.

It was a fact that Jeremy was doing all that was required of him readily enough, even if he would not show exuberance. Alfie arranged that he should meet all local Labor Party potentates. Only from the Labor Party could they expect even sympathy, since no other was inclined to true Australian Nationalism. He was asked to show himself at several important metropolitan branches, to listen to formal executive meetings then have a few beers and a chat afterwards. There were other such invitations from the industrial centres of the North and South Coasts of the State. 'Getting my guts', was how Jeremy cynically described the interest shown in his ideas. Alfie countered the cynicism by saying that what they got obviously did them good, and in turn would benefit themselves when it came to political support. Here again he always found incredulity in response to his saying that personally he was not interested in election.

Alfie's father, bedridden at home in Melbourne, stricken with cancer, all the while kept up a steady flow of advice by letter. As Frank Candlemas said, there was nothing the old man did not know about politics. It was understood that they were to go down to meet him as soon as possible. Then suddenly he was demanding that they come down immediately, not merely to visit him, but because the regional Labor hierarchy had become interested, and that meant insistence on Jeremy's presenting himself. Melbourne was the headquarters of the Labor force of the land, he wrote. To ignore the hierarchy would destroy all hope of the new Party's being recognized as anything but a Sydney racket.

Jeremy took convincing that the well-known rivalry between the States of Victoria and New South Wales (what woeful names for perpetuation, as he remarked!) and especially between their capital cities, was anything more than a national joke. Frank Candlemas enlightened him. Frank said that the difference was based on the historical fact that Melbourne, having been established by men who were free, even if most of them ought not to have been, considered itself as the National Capital of Worthiness, while Sydney still remained the Sydney Town of the Lags and Lashers. Even a Melbourne criminal had class compared with the up-jumped pickpockets of Sydney Town, Frank said. If Ned Kelly had not operated in territory that eventually became the State of Victoria (God Save the Queen!) and been hanged in Melbourne, he would have gone down in history simply as an executed criminal like the far wilder Colonial Wild Boys who finished on the Sydney gallows, instead of risen to become the National Hero: 'It's serious, Jeremy . . . particularly in politics, where all the Parties had their origins, or at least are claimed to have had them by the Victorians. The old fellow's right. He's always got his ear to the political ground, even if these days he has to listen-in through his pillow.'

So one morning, from the wide windows of the train the Victorians proudly called the Spirit of Progress and with which passengers from Sydney were picked up at the Border emerging grubby and rumpled and half-asleep from the dowdy dirty clangorous turn-out that had dragged them through the night, Jeremy saw the compact spired Queen City of the South, as the tourists' brochures called it, rise out of the violet mists of plain and inland sea, very much like a queen, wearing a jewelled crown of winking glass. Jeremy remarked to Alfie, snuggled at his side, 'Doesn't look like Australia, does it, eh?' He would be referring to the English-type hedges, the English trees, which had replaced the leagues of familiar post-and-rail fencing and eucalypts. The nearer you got to it the more English it became. Even the shops had the bare facades of those where the Sun shines meekly.

Delegates of old Si's met them. They were supposed both to go to stay at Si's. Jeremy declined, went to put up at a hotel, said he'd be along to meet the old man as soon as possible.

Silas Tripconny received Jeremy with an embrace that put the Sydney Hug to shame. But it was sincere, as Si explained when he saw that Jeremy was much embarrassed and learnt the reason. Jeremy was frank, saying that bushmen, for all the tradition of open-handedness attached to them, are slow to make friends and suspicious of those in a hurry about it. Silas replied that Melbourne people weren't like the Sydney-siders in that respect, and that he himself already knew him well through the Enchanted One, as he called her: 'As well as if you were my chosen son-in-law,' he added, in front of Alfie, and much to increase Jeremy's embarrassment, but only to tickle the old fellow this time and cause Alfie to giggle.

Later on, after several remarks of Si's plainly suggesting that he considered Jeremy and his Enchanted One more than good friends and heartily approved of the relationship, Jeremy tackled him in private forthrightly: 'Now, listen, Si . . . your daughter's a married woman . . . and I'm a married man . . . and what's more, for godsake, I'm pretty well as old as you, her father!'

Si, a yellow-skinned skeleton under his blankets, was no less forthright: 'Aw . . . come off it, man. You were made for one another . . . my little girl and you. You are what she would've liked me to be. But I've been too smart. Si the Sly, they used to call me. I liked it. I've never had your masculine strength and integrity. That's what she loves in you. That's what she wants to give her the completeness to make her great . . . for she's talented, my Enchanted One . . . never forget that . . . and that we're all bound to serve true talent, because it's the only proof we have of human worth. As to your age . . . age is a relative thing. You're only a boy compared with me. I'm a wreck. I wrecked myself years ago . . . while you were building yourself for your destiny. I'm a wreck . . . and quickly breaking up and going down.'

It wasn't sympathy Si sought. He waved it away when it was offered. Mostly he was jesting, even when his face twitched with pain.

Certainly politics was Si's first concern in his dealings with Jeremy. But weren't the politics rather for Alfie's fulfilment? He said, 'You'll establish your Party all right . . . but not *Australia Felix*. Only someone who can share the dream of it with the mass of Australians can do that . . . and that one's our Enchanted One, Aelfrieda. The Pen is ever Mightier Than the Sword, Jeremy.'

He would talk politics, and then Aelfrieda: 'The great thing that happened to her was finding you. That released her talent. I always knew she had it, urged her . . . but she said she had nothing to write about. You gave it to her. That was the great thing. Now comes the greatest thing, in your reunion.'

Jeremy argued that it was Frank Candlemas who'd seen her through her now famous book, that he himself had actually driven her away.

'After you'd inspired her, my boy. Your honesty, your integrity . . . *and* your fear of women!'

Si broke away from politics on one occasion to say, 'Do you realize the desperation women feel in striving to fulfil themselves? It's different with us . . . simply a fight for power and the love of women, as Freud says. That's where you're lacking. You hide from these things. There's no hiding from them and truly living too. But whereas we accept the love of women as merely reward for achievement, women need the love of a man to achieve.' Jeremy argued that Alfie had the love of Frank. Si dismissed Frank with a shrug: 'A nice chap. But what she wants, needs to desperation, is mature strength. In so many ways she's a little girl. If she weren't she wouldn't have that beautiful thing, her talent. The little girl must be fathered . . . not simply indulged, but disciplined, led. Her love will give you a new lease of life and add to your strength.'

Jeremy's protesting, always argued down, at last was silenced when Si, in the midst of telling him of the involvement of the Labor Party with the Catholic Church and having to suffer more protesting over this for insisting that Jeremy must also seek The Blessing, as he called it, suddenly seized one of his hands in his own skeleton claws, and clinging, cried brokenly, 'Don't squib, Jeremy, son . . . don't squib! You must see this thing right through for the sake of my little girl. Don't abandon her. Swear to me you'll never abandon my darling in her need!' The hollow eyes were swimming.

What does one say to a dying man, Si the Sly though he may have been called? Does one answer a last request by saying: *Man, you're on the brink of hell already . . . what about getting along and stop dragging me with you?* Jeremy bent over the death's head and let the withered lips seal the one-sided contract with a kiss on his brow.

Then as quickly as he had swung from politics, Si swung back: 'Yes . . . you must get The Blessing without delay. You were brought up a Mick. You ought to be able to cope with the old boy. Personally I, brought up Cousin-Jack-Methodist, always found it hard. But the Archbishop holds the trumps, man. You've said it's illogical that a man with his heart in Ireland should dictate the destiny of Australia to Australians. How much more illogical it is for the present Prime Minister, an Australian born, elected to guide that destiny, to say, as he has, that his heart is in Old England? Logic or no logic . . . if the Archbishop vetoes your party, he vetoes all we've dreamt of from the beginning who are capable of dreaming . . . *Australia Felix*.'

Preparing Jeremy for the meeting with the Archbishop that had been arranged for him, Si said, 'It's Socialism the Church is afraid of. They and their rich parishioners still think they'll be able to get their money-bags through the eye of that camel or needle or whatever it is they prate of from their pulpits. As the majority of Catholics vote Labor by tradition, because it's voting against British Imperialism and our Catholicism's based on Irishism, the Church wants an alternative popular party to curb our growing Left Wing element. His Grace, cunning old Jesuit fox, sees it in your idea, I guess. I know you're truly socialist. What man worthy of the name isn't? But don't talk socialism when he quizzes you. Stick to the things you know and feel most strongly about . . . the country, its magic and richness . . . the ruthless exploitation of it, especially by outsiders . . . the Aborigines.'

Jeremy duly arrived, alone, at the Episcopal Palace, to find His Grace awaiting him outside, seated on the northern side verandah in the slanting scarcely warming winter sunshine, a rug about his long thin legs. He extended the ringed hand. Jeremy bent over it as if to bestow the kiss of orthodoxy, but stopped short of it.

The Archbishop eyed him with keen if faded blue eyes, while an Irish smile played about his wide thin lips. 'Delacy . . . Delacy. Now that remoinds me of the ould song . . . *And they say that it's Frinch for her name*! It was common Lacy back in the Ould Sod, I'll be bound.' Jeremy acknowledged it. The old man chuckled, 'Sure, 'tis noice to come so far up in the wurruld that you nade to change your name to mate the new circumstances. You'd be a drinking man, Mr De-lacy?'

Jeremy had been prepared for this. 'Yes, Your Grace . . . and I took the liberty of bringing along a little something.' He had given a case of the best whisky to the servant who admitted him.

'Sure, and it was thoughtful of you.' The long thin ringed hand reached for a small bell. A hunched old man in black appeared, bearing a tray with the wherewithal.

Sipping and savouring, the Archbishop began his sly quizzing. Jeremy stuck to instructions.

'Patriotism,' said His Grace. 'A much bandied and misused wurrud. *Patria solum omnibus carum est*, says Cicero . . . The soil of their native land is dear to all men's hearts. Or, according to Field, Patriotism has its roots deep in the instincts and affections. Love of country is expansion of filial love. Yet Dr Johnson, who was nobody's fool, declared for posterity, Patriotism is the last refuge of a scoundrel. What say ye to that, my son?'

Jeremy shook his head. 'I don't know what to say, Your Grace. I only know that my own feeling for my country is all-abiding, however it may be judged.'

'An honest answer, from one I'm sure is an honest man. As to Dr Johnson, I think we may ignore him on the ground that he was Cockney. Dwellers in great cities have no love of country as we peasantry have. Their city is their fatherland. They are more like soldiers in a garrison . . . with the surrounding country to support them. That has not yet come to our own cities. We are still at heart frontiersmen . . . I mean those of us who don't come from great cities abroad.'

Evidently the old priest loved to talk, and having satisfied himself about his visitor, let flow the Irish wit and the subtle savagery that can go with it: 'Spayking of Cockneys, Patriotism, and Scoundrels . . . we have the perfect example of it all in that one of dubious fame a few years back, our own Cockney who called himself also a Welshman and an Australian . . . if indade he was true Cockney even, and not, as I suggested one toime at risk to my liberty, born on wan of those garbage barges that ploy the River Thames at a toime whan it was out of the traditional sound of Bow Bells. You may be interested to know that my saying that at a public meeting during the First Conscription Referendum was wan of the raysons the Commonwealth Police, or Peace Force, was formed. There was no State police officer prepared to swear that I had said it. The other rayson, as is well known, of course, was that of his being hit in the eye with a rotten egg during the same lively period of our history. Do you know, that funny little runt of a man made himself so powerful that we're lucky we still haven't got him dictating our lives . . . and deaths . . . for he was a great advocate of death . . . The Last Man, the Last Shilling, for King and Country . . . what country? The crayture didn't have one. Sure, the scum that roises to the top in this benoited country of ours! I look forward, Mr De-lacy, to what you moight do with your Party to put an end to it.'

Thus did Jeremy get The Blessing. The benefits were forthcoming almost immediately. Labor leaders dropped in at Si's. Jeremy was asked to executive meetings. He received what Si called The Accolade in being asked to attend a meeting of the Ballarat Branch of the ALP. Si said, 'Every true reform has to start in Ballarat . . . according to the Ballaratians.'

It lasted a week. Old Si would have kept it going indefinitely. But there was that Party Initiation Meeting to be dealt with in Sydney. Si had himself taken to the train in a wheelchair, carried into their reserved compartment, along with a basket containing two magnums of champagne and decorated with a Good Luck horseshoe tied with ribbon. He grinned in toasting them, saying, 'Happy honeymoon!' Alfie giggled. Jeremy burnt. It looked as if he would be burning more, since Si's intention evidently was that his last words were meant to bind the couple together as irrevocably as a marriage service – when the situation was saved by someone's stepping into the doorway from the corridor, perhaps with no more intention at first than to give way to someone passing, but after a moment of staring, coming right in, with hand outstretched, booming, 'Why, Si . . . up and about again!'

It was a big man, aged about fifty, handsome in a flabby way, Mephistophelian, with hair sticking up at the side like little horns, eyes slanting and mocking, mockery in his laugh, so that Si answered rather appropriately when, taking the plump small hand, he cried, 'Speak of the devil!' He had mentioned a little earlier, referring to a certain official-like bustle that he guessed the new Prime Minister, the Spieler, as he called him, this old Yiddish-Australian slang-word for a clever but none too honest talker, evidently being what the gentleman was called by those of his calling, was on the train.

The Prime Minister sat down, showing genuine interest in Si's health. 'Shows I'm out of the running,' laughed Si. 'When I was on the Ministerial Benches you'd've been glad to see me dead.'

'Now, now . . . that's unkind. I've always admired and liked you, Si. And how's Alfie? Your book's a greater and greater success they tell me. If I'd've been PM when they gave you that prize I'd've made a condition that you gave me a kiss in public. How about it now?'

Flushed and laughing, she leant with her lips to meet his.

Then Si introduced Jeremy. The Prime Minister was interested at once: 'Oh, yes . . . I've heard of Mr Delacy. Very glad to meet you. Like a bit of a chat with you, as a matter of fact. You're travelling right through, I suppose? See you on the train the other side of the Border, eh?' He rose then.

Si said to Jeremy, 'He's going to try to talk you into joining his mob. Be careful . . . he's got the silver tongue!'

The Prime Minister went off laughing. Si laughed, too, with evident pleasure in dealing with his kind again. His kind? Jeremy was staring at him as if surprised. What had Si *not* said in derogation of this man he contemptuously called the Spieler before and now called the Silver Tongue and whose hand he grasped with such warmth, a hand he had declared would always be against the common people, against Australia as anything but a colony ruled over by a king! Si had said, 'The bastard will drag us into war at the drop of the British Prime Minister's top hat. *He* won't call for a referendum on conscription. He's already got his manpower trap set. You've got to get behind us, Jeremy, to help get that bastard out . . . or we'll have him on our backs for years . . . and that will be the stone end of any hope of an Australian Australia.'

So excited was Si by the meeting that he delayed his homily too late. There were the bells ringing, the whistles blowing. All he could get out as they carried him away was a choking cry, 'Look after my little girl, Jeremy . . . look after my Enchanted One!' Only a glimpse of him waving from his wheelchair – a wave back as they sped away into the night.

So obviously was Jeremy affected by the anomalous behaviour of Si in the presence of the Prime Minister that even Alfie, bubbling with champagne and excitement, noticed his set expression as he sat watching the flaring glimpse of things within range of their bright windows, and despite his vagueness, divined what was troubling him. She told him that the etiquette of parliamentary politics demanded inviolate truce off the hustings, as in law all lawyers are comrades outside the court. He tended to be ironic about it. She silenced him, saying that the alternative was perpetual civil war. No doubt about it, she was a politician's daughter.

At the Border, with change of trains they parted to go to their respective sleeping cars. Jeremy found himself sharing a berth with a little bald man, who without delay told him the Prime Minister was travelling with them: 'A great man. Certainly a silver-tongued orator, but a great statesman, too. Now we'll be safe from the Unions. That's what's wrong with this country . . . Unionism. No man's allowed to do a decent day's work for a decent day's pay any more. They're stopped by the bloody agitators that live on their gullibility. I'm a Manufacturing Chemist. I'd make twice the money with half the trouble if it weren't for these damn Bolsheviks. D'you know, five years ago I could get a qualified Chemist for a fiver a week and work him any hours, *and* get a first class job done. Now I'm paying ten and fifteen . . . for a forty-hour week . . . and getting what they deign to give in service. Make you sick, wouldn't it? But our silver-tongued boy'll fix all that . . . mark my words!'

Jeremy had so little to say in reply, that his companion lapsed into suspicious silence, perhaps thinking that he may have chanced to unburden himself to one of those very agitators travelling First Class at the workers' expense. He got into striped silk pyjamas and red bed socks and was just climbing up to the top bunk, when a young man of official mien came and asked for Mr Delacy, saying that the Prime Minister would like to see him in his berth if he would care to come. The little Chemist hung on his ladder like an astonished monkey.

Jeremy found the PM alone, already in pyjamas and dressing-gown, but by no means ready for bed, judging by the array of beverages set up on the collapsible table, together with cheeses, biscuits, cigarettes, cigars. He greeted Jeremy simply: 'Brandy-man, I understand. Help yourself.'

Pouring himself brandy and soda, Jeremy asked, 'Do you keep such close tabs on citizens that you know their drinking habits?'

The other's growing chins shook in a chuckle: 'No. But I'm interested in a man's choice of drink. It often betrays his character. And I happened to learn what yours is from a friend of yours.'

'Yes . . . and who might that be?'

'General Sir Mark Esk.'

'Oh!'

They were silent for a while, eyeing each other as they drank. Then the PM said, 'It's this military business I wanted to talk to you about. Tell me, how interested, really, are you in getting the Northern Area Command?'

'Not a scrap.'

'Ah . . . I thought as much!'

'Did General Esk tell you I wanted it?'

'Not exactly. He said *he* wanted *you* for it. He was vague about your aspirations. What he insisted on was that you're the perfect man for the job. Would you consider yourself that in the event of war?'

'That's a tough question for any ordinary man to answer. But war with whom?'

'Anyone.'

'Are we likely to go to war with anyone?'

'Anything's likely these days.'

'If we were attacked by any nation, I'd serve in any capacity.'

'You'd wait to be attacked?'

'I'd wait for war.'

'Defence?'

'I'm always on the defensive myself.'

Smiling, the Prime Minister raised his glass to him: 'Spoken like a politician . . . although you hardly strike me as the type.'

'I'm not.'

'Then why have you entered the political arena?'

'I want to see my country free from outside interference. I always have. Apparently the only way to make the Nation aware of it is by shouting about it from the National Parliament.'

'What you call outside interference . . . where do you think we'd be without it?'

'We would be independent . . . and by being so would have the self-respect we utterly lack now as a Nation.'

'Do you realize the enormous task that complete independence would throw on an undeveloped unprotected country like ours?'

'I spoke of self-respect as the issue. Without that we'll never amount to anything '

'How many of our nine million people do you reckon have any sense of what you call self-respect?'

'I haven't any idea. I come from remote parts.'

'With a dream, I'm afraid, my friend. Do many people where you come from have self-respect?' When Jeremy was silent, the silver voice went on: 'Alfie Candlemas in her book, which I understand you inspired, tells of the surrender of your pioneers to the great outside interests, the absentee landlords. Where's the self-respect there? How much less will be in the cities, where all the masses want is a home of some sort, a job, a little pleasure.'

'You don't have a very high opinion of the people you're responsible to.'

'I'm responsible to the Nation, not the people.'

'Do you have so much respect for that?' Jeremy coloured as he said this.

The PM eyed him curiously. 'Why do you say that?'

'I understand that it's through you the Treaty of Westminster was never ratified.'

'Why didn't the Labor Government do it after signing the Treaty?'

'They might have been too preoccupied with politics.'

'Maybe I am, too.'

When Jeremy was silent, the Prime Minister added: 'Where would ratification get us?'

'It would give us the independence that we only have in token now . . . '

'You're on that independence again. I've said that we can't afford to be independent. We've neither the population nor the quality of people fit for it. We are still colonial people. The Empire is our country. Let us stick to our countrymen as long as we can. We make a formidable force standing together. Divided, we fall. That's the ideal I walk the high-wire of Prime Ministership for every day . . . . ' He broke off with a yawn.

'I'll go,' said Jeremy.

'No . . . no! Just recollection of the high-wire, the eternal balancing. I've had rather a hard day of it today. Tell me something I don't know about and should. Damn politics. What about the Aborigines? I'm surrounded by experts, each with a different theory. I'd say you're an expert without claiming to be one.'

'Do you want to help the Aborigines?'

'I want to set right a condition that's giving us a bad name throughout the world, and particularly at Home.'

'You mean Britain?'

'Of course.'

'But you're Australian born.'

'To me Britain is spiritual home. But this is politics. Can't we talk of Aborigines . . . as people, not as political pawns?'

'But you spoke of our bad name in what struck me as a political sense.'

'I'm always a politician first. But you tell me about them as people . . . and I'll see them as that. Politics regarding them can follow. Give me the credit for heading a Government that's implemented sweeping reforms in Aboriginal administration since having Aborigines presented to us more as human beings than we'd seen them before, thanks directly to our Alfie, and indirectly to yourself . . . . ' Another yawn. 'I'm afraid I will drop off if you stick to politics, old boy.'

Jeremy proceeded to explain his ideas of maintaining the Aboriginal Ethos. To begin with, undoubtedly the PM was interested. However, as it went on, the lids fell lower, lower. Time after time the bulky frame shook itself awake. *Aborigines, Aborigines, Aborigines* – the lips were framing the words as if in sleep. At length Jeremy broke off, saying, 'I think we'd better call it a night.'

The bulk became alert. 'Yes . . . yes . . . but I heard it all . . . most instructive. Glad to have met you.' The neat plump hand was extended. The silver voice shook off the husk of sleepiness: 'Take my tip, old boy . . . keep out of politics. You're not the type. If you persist . . . I'm afraid you'll come to grief . . . Good-night!'

Back in his own cabin, Jeremy found the little Chemist reading in bed, ready to pounce. Gravely, as he undressed, Jeremy told how the Prime Minister said he was going to ban both Unionism and Communism in Australia. The red bed socks, hanging over the side of the bunk, fairly danced: 'I told you so . . . I told you he's our man!' Then as Jeremy got into his own bunk he added that the great man also had said that he was dissatisfied with the efficiency of Australian industry and intended to encourage the establishment here of branches of the big British monopolies, like Imperial Chemical Industries. 'What?' squeaked the Chemist. 'After we've done all the spade-work? I'll get my Association onto this. If this's the kind of thing he's going to do . . . out he goes! Politicians . . . bah, you can't trust one of 'em!'

Early next morning, Jeremy rose, got a cup of tea, and went through to the Parlour Car. He was standing out on the observation platform, watching the countryside tumble in on the vanishing silver tracks, hill and gully, homestead and siding, to become embroiled like yarded cattle, herd upon herd, when Alfie found him. When she remarked on the stripped bare hills, the eroded gullies, he answered, 'But it's still alive . . . and could be brought back to full living with a little love. It's got like that because it was hated. If only they'd asked the blackman about it, how it was named, why it was named, and seen it as he did, as the sleeping beasts of the Dream Time. Perhaps, through your pen, they may yet see it.'

'You sound a lot more optimistic than you did last night,' she said. 'What happened? Did you see Silver Tongue?'

'Yes. He spoke of you and your writing.'

'That's nice of him. I'll have to kiss him again when he gets off at Goulburn to go to Canberra.'

'We've passed Goulburn. He also told me to keep out of politics.'

'He would! He's shrewd enough to know that you're the only one to topple him.'

'I don't want to topple anyone. I only want people to love this country . . . so that I can have countrymen.'

'You won't get *him* to love it.'

'I realize that. But he asked me about the Aborigines.'

'He did that?'

'Yes . . . mentioning you. Admittedly he said he wants to put things right with them because our treatment of them's giving us a bad name abroad. But it's the first sign of guilt . . . the first sign of hope for the future.'

'No wonder you're in a different mood!' She kissed him quickly, then snuggled up to him, whispering, 'Put your arm around me . . . I'm cold.'

III

Every politician should have some gift of prescience, even if only enough to fake what he had predicted. Undoubtedly he known variously as Silver Tongue and the Spieler was so gifted considerably, but could have been nothing less than clairvoyant to know that Jeremy would come to grief through meddling with politics as quickly as he did. On arrival back in Sydney, Jeremy found on his doorstep duns from whom he learnt that owing to his political activities he was deeply in debt. It wasn't that those promised Party Funds hadn't materialized. They had, even lavishly. Perhaps it was the lavishness that tempted the Treasurer to do a bunk with them. Jeremy was the only one really shocked. Shamefacedly his Committee, among them Alfie, confessed that they had known the Economist had been in trouble over mishandling of trust-funds before. Their excuse for not speaking out about it in time was that the man seemed so truly dedicated to the cause.

Anyway, no one offered to replace the Treasurer, or the money. Perhaps it was generally felt that Jeremy's early statement that he was anything but a wealthy man himself had sounded rather like crying poor, coming from one reputed to hold broad acres, breed racehorses, and employ black servants. There was no emulating the Treasurer. The debts were in Jeremy's name, and the duns armed with writs of attachment. Nothing for it but that he should go to the Commonwealth Bank and turn the Government Bonds that constituted his life-savings into cash.

What price National Dignity in such trying circumstances? Jeremy in his preoccupation with the economics the Economist had left him with as a taste of reality, had nothing to say about it during those first few grey days, while those close to him evidently were mostly silenced by their shame. Only Alfie expressed fear that he might not go through with the program. He assured her, somewhat grimly, that he would, there being no point in not doing so, since by reason of the Economist's efficient management, the advertising must go on to the bitter end, that is to the date of the Inaugural Meeting, and the hall, the most expensive in the city, be paid for, used or not. Alfie and Frank were the most concerned, knowing something of the facts of his financial condition, which he was too proud to speak of to others, but could not help beyond suggesting that he give up his flat and come live with them. Frank was working in some unimportant position in the city's health service. Alfie's book, although quite famous, measured in financial success only up to the mean standards governing Australian literature. Jeremy declined with thanks, using that somewhat dubious expression: 'In for a penny, in for a pound.'

Then suddenly there was Alfie, the Enchanted One, coming running to dispel the gloom with her little girl's excited brightness, crying, 'Wonderful news . . . a mining agent's looking for you to buy your Tantalite . . . to give you a large advance on the assurance of a large supply of it.'

Jeremy promptly asked, 'Krupp's?'

'No . . . a Frenchman . . . Félix Beaucoup, quite well known in the city. You see, *Terra Australis* herself has come to our aid. She's giving her substance to our Cause. Koonapippi, the Earth Mother, at work for Free Australia . . . Hooray!'

A hard thing to pooh-pooh by one so recently the inspiration of such sentiments, no matter how changed his attitude to the value of the Cause in practical terms.

Jeremy made contact with Monsieur Beaucoup and met him at the Hotel Australia. He proved to be a very pleasant fellow. He said he was buying for an international company, which he wouldn't name, but hinted at the French concern of Schneiders, which also owned the great Skoda Works in Czechoslovakia, now controlled by the Germans. Suffice it to say that he was buying large quantities of the ores of Tantalum and Nickel from the French Islands of New Caledonia. He shrugged widely: 'You are man of ze vorld, Mr Delacy. You know zat in armaments manufacture zere is no *nationalité*.' He went on to say he had heard that Jeremy was in financial difficulties. If Jeremy would permit his principals to mine his ore in a big way, he could promise him a big advance in cash.

Jeremy replied, 'We'll see.'

It was what Jeremy did *not* see to begin with that caused the trouble. Whisked in a taxi to the place for meeting M. Beaucoup's principals, out of his element when cast amongst the hurrying herd of cityites upon alighting, observant though he mostly was he missed what the biggest of the many brass plates on either side of the wide doorway of the office-block proclaimed. A uniformed commissionaire saluted them, escorted them to the elevator, where they joined another shoving throng. They were whisked to the seventh floor, debouched with a mob into a mob, and hence again missed, on the directory-plate on the wall of the corridor, what, had he seen it, surely would have stopped Jeremy from being ushered along it by his companion. They turned through an open door, to be received by a pretty smiling receptionist, and at once shown into a large luxurious room with great windows looking out over the city. Behind a shiny desk sat a smiling handsome man wearing rimless spectacles, who rose at once with hand extended to Jeremy. He was a stranger, foreign, obviously, by his looks. Behind him, on the wall, was a face only too well known, foreign to pretty well everything though it might be – a large picture of the *Führer* of all *Führer*s. Gaping at the picture, while M. Beaucoup introduced the man as Herr Konsul-Generale, Jeremy, quite at a loss, sank into the leather chair indicated to him.

Herr Konsul-Generale asked, 'You vill haf visky and cigar, yes?'

Jeremy shook his head. Then, coming to himself, he turned quickly to Beaucoup standing over him, demanding, 'What's this?'

M. Beaucoup smiled and bowed. 'I vill leave you.' As he turned, a side door opened, and there entered a big stiff-moving man bearing a tray with bottle, siphon, glasses. Jeremy looked back at the Consul, now seated. As the man with the tray set it down, the Consul spoke in German. The man bowed and withdrew, leaving the side door open.

The Consul, smiling, twinkling amiably through his glasses, remarked, 'You do not drink, Mr Delacy?'

Jeremy shot another glance at Uncle Adolf, then met the spectacles, asking shortly 'What business have I got with you?'

'Some gentlemen vish to meet you here.'

'Who are they?'

But there they were, marching stiffly through the door, the two big Kruppsers, last seen Heiling Hitler beside the Beatrice River. Jeremy stared at them. The Consul-General said, 'Zese gentlemen already you haf met, I zink, yes?'

'Yes,' grunted Jeremy, rising. 'And I've no wish to meet them again, thank you.'

He was turning towards the exit, when the Consul, rising quickly, said, 'Vait, Mr Delacy . . . be reasonable!'

Jeremy paused, half-turned. 'I told these two I'd have no dealings with them under any circumstances . . . and I resent the trick to involve me with them.'

'It is no trick. It is to help you. Ve know you are short of money for your political campaign . . . and ve approve of your politics . . . . '

Jeremy growled, 'Are you Krupp's, too?'

'I am representative of my country. I only vont to bring you together.' The Kruppsers were standing, wooden, by the Consul's desk.

Jeremy snapped, 'You haven't a hope in hell!'

'Explain your reason. You haf change your vay of life. You are fighting Communism and British Imperialism. You are close to bankrupt. Ve offer you mooch money . . . . '

'I don't want your dirty money.'

'Vy do you say dirty?'

'Because you stole it from Jews . . . and from people whose countries you've invaded like wolves '

The handsome face flushed deeply. It took a moment for the Consul to find his voice: 'Your friends ze Jews first stole from us.'

Jeremy snapped, '*Judenhasse* . . . go to hell!' He swung away again.

But the Consul came leaping to head him off. Jeremy cried angrily, 'I told you I won't do business with you.'

'Because of Jews?'

'Because of Jews.'

'You know nuzzing of ze trut' of ze Jewish situation in my country.'

'The whole world knows . . . that cares to know.' Jeremy's voice rose: 'Out of my way . . . . ' Evidently he was struggling for words to express the anger flashing in those grey eyes, words learnt in recent times. As he got them, he brought them out with all the harshness and contempt that can be expressed in German, making a single expression of it as Germans do: '*Judenmurdervolk*!'

The Consul stiffened. 'Be careful vot you say!'

'Why should I? I'm in my own country. You Germans . . . you're . . . you're . . . . ' Again the struggle for a moment – then: '*Irren nation*!'

The Consul's face was flaming now, his voice harsh: 'You insult my Nation by calling it Lunatic?'

'I do. That's your trouble. Intelligent people though you seem to be, some madman only has to yell *Achtung*, and you *all* go mad. There's your latest madman!' Jeremy flung a finger at the scowling picture.

Smack! The Consul's palm smote Jeremy's cheek. His voice came grating with fury: 'Pig-dog . . . you vill not insult *Unsen Führer*!'

For a moment Jeremy blinked on the tears the sound smack had started. Then he, too, grated, 'Hun bastard!' and shot out his left in his usual style.

As the Consul reeled, gasping, grasping his flabby midriff, two big men, one of them the waiter who'd brought the tray, leapt from nowhere, laid hands on Jeremy. He flung them off. As they came at him again, the Consul, supported by a Kruppser, gasped out, '*Verprugelt ihn . . . die . . . polizei . . . rufen . . . .* '

The two men got hold of Jeremy, forced him to the wall, beat him down. The other Kruppser snatched up the telephone, spoke rapidly, then dropped it, to go leaping to join those dealing with Jeremy. Soon they had him overpowered, sat on him, spat in his face. The Consul-General, lolling gasping in an armchair, while his attendant Kruppser massaged his middle, watched with evident satisfaction.

Within a few minutes, led by the receptionist now looking like an angry whore, the police arrived, a sergeant and a constable. The sergeant took a quick look around, demanded, 'What's going on?'

The Consul, mopping his face now, exaggerating his breathlessness, panted, 'Zat man . . . he assault me . . . insult my Nation . . . I gif him in charge.'

The sergeant looked at the pinioned Jeremy, who gasped up at him, 'The bastard cracked me. I cracked him back. Then they all piled on me. It's them did the assaulting.'

The Consul puffed, 'He lie. He come insulting my country, my Leader. He call me Hun Bastard. He hit me . . . so zat nearly I am knock-out. My men moost overpower him. Zis . . . zis is violation of Diplomatic Protocol. Moost serious. To your Prime Minister I vill complain. I charge him, Sergeant . . . arrest him.'

The sergeant glanced at the hard square faces of those holding Jeremy. He grunted, 'Let him up.'

The Kruppser said, 'He is violent man. Look at my face . . . my clothes.'

The sergeant said to the constable, 'Handcuff him.'

Jeremy fought as the constable bent over him. 'Don't you put those things on me!'

The sergeant's face became like the others. He snapped, 'D'you want me to bring the squad to deal with you? Give him your hands!'

Jeremy obeyed, struggled up. The sergeant turned to take notes from the Consul, who said he didn't know Jeremy, hadn't seen him before. Jeremy tried to get into it, to say he had been brought there. The constable shut him up. All the sergeant asked of him was his name and address, told him he could tell his story at the Station. 'Come on,' he said.

As they went through the door, the Consul-General called after them, '*Er hat Deutsch von seiner Judische Hure gelernt*!' It caused the others to chuckle.

The sergeant asked Jeremy, 'What'd he say?'

'I don't know . . . something about Jews.'

Out in the corridor, the sergeant looked at Jeremy. 'You ain't a Jew?'

'No.'

'Commo, eh?'

'No.'

'Well, whatever you are, you're in strife. Don't you know these people have special privileges? There've been several cases of assault like this. If you're not Aussie born you're likely to get deported.'

They fell silent as they approached the group awaiting the elevator and were all eyes at sight of the handcuffs. They went down in silence. There was more staring in the street while they awaited a taxi. Then, within a few minutes, they were at the Central Police Station, where the prisoner roused so little interest he might not have existed except as a name written down in the charge book. The desk-sergeant gave him a single glance. No questions were asked of him. He was searched, certain things taken from him. Then a policeman who didn't seem to see him ushered him to a tiny empty cell.

The afternoon wore into evening – with the only relief the comings and goings outside the barred door of men in uniforms and out of them, of men in handcuffs, bowed and snivelling or erect and giving cheek. He called to a couple of uniformed men, who ignored him. The lights came on, one high in the ceiling that glared like a watchful eye. Then uniformed men came with a trolley loaded with sliced bread and pannikins of tea. As he was given his portion, Jeremy asked, 'How do I get in touch with someone outside?'

The man who stood with key in lock grunted, 'You don't.'

'But you can't just keep me locked up here!'

'Watch me!' The key clicked in the lock. The trolley went on its way.

Later the pair came back, tossed in a blanket and a piece of towelling too small to throttle oneself with. No more visits. Only the tramping up and down the corridor, with the snivelling and the snarling. Jeremy, rolled in the blanket on the bench that served as bed, watched by the unwinking eye above, slept in snatches.

Dawn, and breakfast of tea and bread, served by hard blank voiceless faces. Tramp, tramp, tramp – till suddenly, in midmorning, there was a uniformed man unlocking the door to someone whose face, if no less hard and blank, was familiar. Inspector Ballywick, in neat grey suit and pork-pie hat, stepped in, saying coldly, 'We meet again, Mr Delacy.'

Jeremy stared at him, growled, 'What's the idea of this?'

'You're charged with an offence under Federal Law. You're my prisoner.'

'I want to see a lawyer.'

'I understand that one's been engaged for you. Meanwhile, you must accompany me to a special place of detention. Your wrist, please.'

'For christ sake . . . what's all this handcuffing for?'

'You're considered a violent man. I know you for a tricky one. Your wrist!'

Back to the desk-sergeant, to be signed out and have the things taken from him given to Inspector Ballywick. Then out to a court-yard, where a big black car waited with a uniformed driver, and a red C on its number-plate. C for Commonwealth – Commonwealth of Australia – Southern Land of the Common Good. Inspector Ballywick got into the back, perforce with his reluctant companion.

A swift silent journey, past towering buildings, dirty little shops, mansions, slums, factories, sandy wastes. Out in the wastes there was even a string of ragged blacks, walking built-up tram tracks, as if denied ordinary thoroughfare. Thus to a great grey jail that might have been Darmoor or Broadmoor or some such prototype of transplanted inhumanity. A door opened to swallow them. At another desk the Inspector surrendered his prisoner, with a last glance at him that plainly told of a devil's cave in the Northern wilderness, a sheeted corpse, a lonely grave, never to be forgotten. Then march to another cell-block, and other tiny empty cell.

Solitude till mid-afternoon, when a tiny carroty man of uncertain age was ushered in. He gave a hot little hand and introduced himself as Sorbee, Solicitor, appointed by Alfie Candlemas, who sent her love. Alfie had tried to arrange bail. 'But Commonwealth Law is peculiar,' Mr Sorbee said. 'They seem to be able to get away with just about anything by simply invoking the right to it. Now, tell me what happened.'

When Jeremy was finished, Mr Sorbee shook his head. 'Only your word against theirs. Your association with Jews is known. Jews have been in trouble for the same thing. Only in their case, of course, they were intruders. The Germans admit you went there on business, are able to prove that you had done business with Krupps previously, so that it looks as if you went there of your own free will and simply became abusive, for reasons they claim they don't understand. Unfortunately we can't plead that you were tricked into going there, because this Beaucoup fellow has vanished . . . is in New Caledonia, according to his staff.'

'What's at the back of it?' asked Jeremy. 'Conspiracy of some sort?'

'Since you've entered politics you can expect political chicanery, of course. No, I don't know what's at the back of it . . . unless it's that you happen to be in bad with Commonwealth Security and by a stroke of bad luck fell into their hands. Anyway, don't worry. You've a lot of influential friends behind you. By their efforts they'll make you too hot to hold for long. We'll have you out in time for this meeting of yours.'

'Damn the meeting!' growled Jeremy. 'All I want is to get out of here and back to where everything doesn't stink of phenyl, gas, and dishonesty.'

'You must come from a nice place, Mr Delacy. Now, don't despair. I'll be in every afternoon . . . anything you want . . . . '

It lasted five days, which must have seemed like as many weeks to Jeremy, pacing his little cell, or running it sometimes, pacing the small exercise yard where he was permitted a glimpse of the sky for a short period each morning, but not running there, because his fellow prisoners wouldn't have it. These fellows of his were no ordinary prisoners, but like himself all victims of the seemingly all-powerful Common Weal. There were usually about a score of them, their numbers varying as some went out and others came in. Those who went out, it seemed, did not simply depart the prison walls, but the shores of this Land of Liberty. Most were Jews. However, there were others, with all sorts of accents, including some of those of the British Isles, who called each other Comrade and spoke savagely of what they were going to do when they got back here after the inevitable fall of Capitalism in the great war that was imminent. Jeremy got to know a lot about them during the first brief session. They wanted to know all about him, too. However, he merely shook his head at everything asked of him, till they gave him up with shrugs and the nickname *Shtumer*.

He would have done better to have talked a little while he could with credibility. By next meeting they had their own version of him through their grapevine. They pounced on him: 'You beat up the German Consul-General!'

'What for?'

'For vot?'

'They say you clobbered 'im 'cause he wouldn't pay you the price you asked for minerals you've been sellin' 'em for armaments.'

'You been sellin' stuff to Krupp for years?'

'Krupp?'

'Ja, Krupp!'

'Ach! He is Anti-Semitic.'

'He's National-Socialist!'

'He's a dirty Fascist!'

'*Shtum, shtum*! He betray us to ze guard.'

'*Shtum*!'

They wouldn't let him run for exercise in the yard because they complained that it distracted them. He complained that he felt the cold. They complained about his running in his cell in his shoes and disturbing their sleep. He had to run in his socks.

It was on the sixth morning that the guard who used to take him to the exercise yard snapped instead, 'You're going out.' He was marched to the office, given back what had been taken from him, shoved through the Dartmoor door.

Terra Australis – in a blaze of blue and silver. He stood blinking at it.

A tram was coming lumbering along that built-up track from southward. Close to the jail was a tram-stop with a shelter-shed. He went to it, had time to see that its wood was scored beyond the limits of the surface offering with initials and names, probably cut to celebrate the freedom symbolized by return to the owner of the knife that had done the work. The driver of the tram winked at Jeremy as he pulled up for him. Did it need only six days in the cage to make one look like a jail bird? The other passengers gave him interested looks, while the conductor offered him a cigarette after taking his fare and lounged beside him for a moment as if expecting him to try communication with his fellows in a way perhaps long denied him. Jeremy sat taciturn, watching the scene roll back to seeming chaos of the city centre. He took a taxi back to his flat. Someone had been through his belongings in his absence, and left them in a state to declare the fact. Any policeman might have done it, seeing that they'd had possession of his keys till this morning – but who more likely than Inspector Ballywick?

Jeremy had not long shaved and bathed when Alfie burst in, in such a state that he had to take her in his arms and sit with her in an armchair petting her like an hysterical little girl. She knew nothing of the circumstances of his sudden release, was interested in nothing but that he should not abandon her and the Cause. Whatever he may have said to Mr Sorbee while in jail, to her sobbing relief he assured her that he would present himself at the meeting tomorrow night. In her state she would not notice the grimness with which he said it.

He went home with her, and spent the rest of the day there, mostly with his Committee around him. They did most of the talking. They told him that all debts had been paid and his bonds redeemed. Some of this was due to the generosity of a few would-be members of the mooted Party, but largely to that of an anonymous donor, suspected by Alfie and the Banker as being the Chief. Despite the evident pleasure the pair had in naming the unknown one, Jeremy was cold about it although hardly vocal, saying merely, 'Sounds like we've been bought out.'

In parting with the others in the night, Jeremy said he wanted to be alone tomorrow, to think things out. He would not see anyone until just before the meeting. He also would not let anyone see him home. Alfie clung to him at the last, asking, 'You won't let us down, will you, Jeremy, darling?

He answered shortly, 'If by us you mean my countrymen, I assure you I'll give all that's wanted of me.'

'Bless you, darling!'

'Good night!'

Next morning he ran in the little park for so long that an old fellow who exercised his dogs there asked, 'What . . . you wound up this morning? Missed your trot the last week, I noticed. Making up for it, eh?'

This was said as Jeremy passed him. Jeremy called back, 'Yes . . . I've been in jail.'

The old fellow, staring, made himself scarce before the jailbird came round again.

But was it the restrictions of the jail behind him or the ordeal before that kept him going? His face was expressionless.

After breakfast he went into the city, to the Public Library, where he consulted *Webster's International Dictionary*. Then he crossed the Harbour again, to Manly, to walk the deserted ocean beach, talking to himself in the way of the bushman on his own and no doubt giving his thoughts away, but having the snatches of revelation drowned in the thunder of the surf. He returned to the city in mid-afternoon, went to a silver grill to eat. He emerged as the great baracoons of commerce were releasing their slaves for the night and the streets were swarming with what goes for humanity in a city but to a countryman looks so much more like communal insects. He walked back to his flat, got into pyjamas, into bed.

He slept a full hour. It was seven when he rose. The meeting was timed for eight. He made coffee, laced it with brandy, dressed, set out.

He walked some of the way in the still cold star-glittering night. He stared at those old friends of his, the stars, perhaps as relief from the winter skeletons of imported trees that lined the way, plane and poplar. One thing the immigrants had not been able to do was to pull the Southern Stars down to replace them with replicas of the comparatively mean display of the Northern Hemisphere. Still, it was interesting to see what had been done with the stars. Those first moved to identify themselves with the land had taken the Southern Cross to make their flag of. What happened? John Bull in England, or his agents on the spot, had turned the lovely thing into travesty by sticking the Old Fellow's waistcoat in the corner.

He hailed a taxi, arrived at the hall on the tick of time. He found Alfie and the others waiting tense in the foyer. All cried, 'We thought you'd let us down!'

There was a goodly crowd; surely more than the most optimistic would have expected. The Committee bore their champion to the rostrum. There the Five-starred flag draped the speakers' table, but so arranged that John Bull's Waistcoat was out of sight and it looked as if, indeed, there were an Australian

Flag. The Judge was there as Chairman. He rose to take Jeremy's hand and seated him beside him.

But though those who would be described officially as Disloyalists might play dirty little tricks with the flag to assert a semblance of independence, there was no getting round the obligation to acknowledge true ownership of the land as embodied in the playing of the British National Anthem. It was the law that the proceedings of all organized public gatherings be preceded by the musical rendition of this piece. A lady sat at the piano on the rostrum for this very purpose. A sergeant of police and several constables stood at the rear to see that it was done. In Britain they play it *after* such proceedings, as a mark of respect for their Monarch. Likewise had it been done in this lesser part of His Britannic Majesty's Realm, until, during the War of 1914–18 and the troubles that beset the so-called Commonwealth because of it, notably that a large part of the population refused to sacrifice their lives for the Absentee Landlord under compulsion, it was remarked by a certain potentate of the period and of doubtful nationality himself – Cockney, Welsh, Australian, take your pick – that large sections of audiences showed so little respect for the Annointed One as to walk out while the Anthem was being played or sung, instead of standing to attention, as convention demanded. So convention was made law and in procedure reversed. The curious thing was that there appeared to be no legal obligation to stand. Perhaps it was because of a legal loophole. One could always claim physical disability.

When everyone was seated and the appropriate solemnity assumed, the pianist struck the opening roll of notes. Quite a large number of the audience did not rise, amongst them, *en masse* two sections occupying the front of the hall for a dozen or so rows of seats on either side of the aisle. Likewise on the rostrum, Jeremy and most of the Committee remained seated. The Judge rose and stood rigid. That was one of the valuable things about having him on any committee, his ability to be in everything without giving offence to anyone. A few who had stood, as it were automatically, sat down again upon seeing how things were.

Send him victorious, happy and glorious,
Long to reign over us,
God save the King!

The Judge stood risen to open proceedings. He didn't say much. That was another virtue of his as a Chairman. He spoke of the need for greater national awareness in Australia, but also of the dangers of nationalism. He even said, 'You can be national without being nationalistic.' This brought solid applause from that front section sitting on the left, their choice of position doubtless made through Leftist tendency in politics by the look of them. There was no applause at all from those on the right, but rather something that sounded like snickering. No doubt about their leanings, with the Bloke sitting in their midst looking very much *Der Führer*, arms folded, face wooden with a scowl under the Hitlerian cowlick. The Judge in his social wisdom threw the ball to the Right: 'At the same time, great things are done in nationalistic resurgence. There was the foundation of the United States of America. The greatness of Ancient Rome, whose institutions probably had more advancing effect on mankind than any other human movement, was based on the pride of the Romans' being Roman . . . . ' A burst of applause now from the Right. But some fool spoilt it by yelling, 'Viva Mussolini!' which others took up. The Left glared. Some shouted, 'Fascists!' The Judge was quick with his play: 'And although every modern Russian is an Internationalist, his first thought is for Mother Russia.' Thunderous applause from the Left, not merely of hands and voices, but of heavy boots. Then with nice discretion he brought Jeremy into it: 'A man of deep patriotism, uninvolved in the factionalism that tends to spoil the good intentions of us who live too close together, a man who because he lives so close to this good earth of ours that he can inspire us with the proper love of it which we've tended to lose by smothering it with concrete and steel and ideas brought from too far away . . . a man of the deepest integrity, a true man . . . Jeremy Delacy!'

The Judge always got a good hand, no matter whom or what he talked about.

Jeremy rose, to strong applause from the body of the hall, some from the right-hand block, including a contribution from the Bloke, but none from the left at all.

He bowed. His voice came grating through the amplifiers, the voice of an angry man: 'Fellow-countrymen . . . . '

The effect was the same as when first he had used those words in public, only so much more so because of the much greater crowd. The applause became a veritable storm. Only those on the left were unmoved, many sitting back with arms folded as if locked against applause of any sort.

Jeremy himself was moved. Even had he not admitted it as he proceeded, it was evident in the softening of his tone: 'I'll confess that I came here tonight with intentions other than expected of me by those concerned with this bid to form a political party with the purpose of making this country of ours not a Commonwealth merely in name but in fact . . . a true Commonwealth . . . '

Loud applause from the main body. He stopped it with an impatient gesture. 'I was telling you that I came with other intentions. They were to decry the thing, not support it.'

Silence. After a moment he resumed: 'My experience since coming into what, from a practical point of view, one must admit is the Real Australia, has done anything but change my opinion that such a party, if a possibility, is an absolute necessity. It is concerning this matter of possibility where my opinion has changed. The effect of the experience has been to make me feel that it is too late, much too late, to realize the dream of *Australia Felix* . . . that the rottenness the whole thing started with has become gangreous, cancerous . . . is impossible to stop . . . . '

Cries from the main body, and from some of the Committee on the rostrum, amongst them startled Alfie: 'No . . . no . . . no!'

He took a sip of water. 'You are so used to it that you don't see it as I, a stranger to it, do. You're like people who live in slums, compared with someone who happens into what the slumites at least find tolerable but that revolts the stranger . . . .

'We don't find it tolerable!' shouted someone in the body.

'Hear, hear!'

'We ain't goin' 'o tolerate it!' came from the left-block, to be followed by the first enthusiasm from there, stamping of feet added to the clapping.

Jeremy continued: 'But it's what has happened to me lately that has . . . or I should say had, in view of what I'm going to add . . . stifled the hope in me. You'll most of you know that I've just come out of prison.' It caused a murmur all round. 'What I was imprisoned for no one bothered to tell me. I know I hit a man who first hit me. Probably it was against the law . . . but surely not more serious than to have cost me more than a few minutes' wigging by a magistrate and a small fine. I faced no magistrate. I was simply handcuffed, dragged to prison, chucked into a cell, and left *incommunicado*, except for occasional visits from a little lawyer, whose contribution to my condition was to tell me that he'd soon have me out, while at the same time warning me that Commonwealth law was something that could be manipulated to pretty well any ends that those who had control of it chose. I was, I must tell you, a prisoner of the Commonwealth, not of the State . . . our Glorious Commonwealth, which we believe is the freest institution in the world! The only difference between the treatment meted out to me and what I might have expected under absolute autocracy like that of Germany or Russia . . . .'

Someone on the left yelled, 'They don't do things like that in Russia!'

' 'Ear, 'ear!'

A burst of heckling from all over the place, and particularly from the right. Jeremy raised his voice above it: 'I say the only difference was that I was as summarily chucked out of the place as into it . . . .'

Someone in the body of the hall called, 'You could sue!'

'Maybe I could . . . but to what end? Such a system would only become more oppressive for being thwarted. It either has to be accepted . . . or overthrown . . . .'

'Overthrown!' yelled a leftist.

'But not by National Socialism!' yelled another.

' 'Ear, 'ear!'

Stamping, clapping, cheering on the left. Hooting on the right. Savage exchange of glances between the factions. The Chairman rapped and called for Order. The police sergeant was coming down the aisle.

When order was restored, Jeremy said, 'What I set out to say is that I came here in a spirit of utter pessimism, dejection, even contempt, that I addressed my first words to you in that spirit . . . but that your response to being called *Fellow-countrymen*, instead of the usual Fellow-Australians, renewed my hope . . . . .'

Loud applause from the main body.

'The enormous difference that word *Countryman* makes!'

'Wha' dufference?' a Scottish voice demanded from the left.

Jeremy turned that way. 'You wouldn't understand, Jock.'

Laughter from other quarters than the left.

'Wha would nae I oonderstan'?' the same voice demanded.

'Because you're not a fellow-countryman of ours.'

'Hear, hear!' from the main body and the rightists.

'Ye nae a blackmon!' the voice went on.

Jeremy raised his voice: 'Oh, shove your sporran in it! When I used the term Fellow-countrymen I was addressing only the native-born. What I have to say will be of no interest to others . . . except perhaps negatively. You others kindly keep your negativism to yourselves.'

Boos from the left, with yells of Fascist, National Socialist, Nazi! People of the main body were yelling, 'Shut up . . . shut up give him a fair go!' The Chairman was hammering, the sergeant bawling.

When silence was got, Jeremy said, 'An interesting interlude, because it highlights what is perhaps our greatest trouble . . . the resentment of outsiders to our pride in being native born . . . . '

Applause and abuse again. Now the other policemen joined the sergeant. Abuse was being hurled across the aisle between right and left.

Jeremy was red now and somewhat hoarse as he resumed: 'This is anything but new. That resentment started back in the days of the Currency Lads and Lasses . . . remember?' He swung on the still-muttering restless left, leant towards them, flinging out a finger to where the invisible Scot had spoken from. 'You, Jock . . . do *you* know who the Currency Lads and Lasses were?' Silence. He looked the block over, about a hundred of them, all tight-faced in watching him. 'How many of the rest of you know? Hands up those who do?' About ten hands came up, and these reluctantly. Jeremy shouted now, 'There! That shows how little you know of the country you've got the cheek to come into throwing your weight about, telling us how to run it . . . and you can't even speak our language!'

'Hear, hear!' from the mass.

Turning to the body of the crowd again, he went on: 'There was a deliberate policy of disparaging the Currency Lads . . . as a sort of bastard breed . . . and it still goes on . . . . '

Applause.

'Natural enough, I suppose, from the immigrant colonists . . . as from the immigrants here . . . . ' He flung a hand to indicate the leftists ' . . . natural enough to react on finding themselves regarded as somehow inferior when they'd thought themselves god-almighty superior . . . . '

A burst of anger from the left that had to be quelled by threats of ejection from the police.

Jeremy got a hearing again: 'But what I say is *un*-natural, is how the spirit of those Currency Lads and Lasses, so strongly assertive at first, has gradually been lost . . . until today we find that it hardly exists at all . . . . '

Prolonged applause from everywhere but the left with its tight faces and tight-folded arms.

'While I was in jail I had plenty of time and need to think . . . and gave my thoughts largely to this matter of love of country . . . Patriotism, Nationalism . . . . '

'National Socialism!' was shouted from the left.

'Shit Commos!' came from the right.

'Shut up . . . or out!' bawled the sergeant.

Jeremy kept on at the main body: 'Patriotism, of course, comes from *Pater*, Father, one's Fatherland. Although I've called myself a patriot in the past, I'm inclined to reject it now as jingoistic . . . despite the fact that its dictionary meaning is "One zealous for the freedom of one's country." Nationality comes from *Natus*, Birth . . . so, the land that has borne me. But that's come to stink somewhat, too . . . . '

'And it's yoour jab to stop stink, ee?' a loud voice demanded from the left.

Jeremy swung to it. 'What d'you mean by that?'

'Sticks oot a mile, choom!'

'I'm not your chum . . . but explain yourself. I'm sure there's a meaning behind your words. Enlighten me . . . and stand up and do it . . . like a man!'

A big hard-faced man rose slowly. He looked official somehow, at any rate better dressed than most of the others. He said in a grating voice, 'You can't poot it o'er uz, snoozer.'

'I'm not trying to put it over anyone. Come on . . . out with it!'

'Yoou're heere to wheetwash the Free Awstreelia Fascist Movement.'

'Aw, rubbish!' Jeremy turned back to the mass. 'I was talking about those words, lovely words, really, but distorted by rogues and fools . . . and therefore I'll avoid them, and use instead the simple expression Love of Country, clumsy though it is. I don't think anyone can object to that . . . even our immigrant friend over here who can't shut up and can't sit down . . . what a pity I called on him . . . I should've known better than to call on a Liverpool-Irish Commo!'

The man was still jabbering and gesticulating. The sergeant had to go halfway in to where he sat to shut him up.

Jeremy added: 'They decry nationalism . . . but I've yet to meet the Scotch or Irish or Welsh Communist who ceased to identify himself with his native heath by dropping his accent in favour of one showing he now belongs to the Worker's Fatherland.'

Loud laughter – except from the left block.

He continued: 'Speaking of objections to such a simple natural thing as national identity, let me remind you of all the efforts that are made to deny it to us. You had the example earlier in the compulsory playing of the British National Anthem. You have it in the practise of making school-children salute the Union Jack before going into school, of having the picture of the British Monarch hung on classroom walls. You have it in what I think is its worst example in the Passport. There, despite the fact that the Australian Coat-of-Arms, which, by the way, is not surmounted by a crown but by a star, is on cover, even if you were born in Boorooloola or Wyalcatchem, inside you are classed as *British Born*. In fact, there is *no such thing as being Australian, legally*. We are British Born, British Born, British Born *ad nauseam*! This is all flagrant denial of that simple thing I now call Love of Country. This is the sort of thing, the supine acceptance of it, that we have to overcome before we can hope to become a nation, before we can hope . . . . '

The Liverpool-Irishman was on his feet again, shouting, 'Before you can start yoour Nationalist Soocialist Party.'

Jeremy looked at him, and perhaps somewhat tired, despite the ruddiness of his face and the shine of his eyes, sighed, 'You again, Geordie!'

The man shouted, 'You coom 'ere to launch yoour party. All reet . . . gi' uz yoour party policy.'

'I belong to no party. I'm here to talk of Love of Country . . . . '

'This 'ere meetin's advertoised to launch yoor Free Australia Party.'

'Don't you believe in a free Australia?'

'I doon't believe in no dirty National Socialist Fascists workin' their way in to teek o'er country loike bluidy Hitler.'

Cheers from the left. Hoots of anger from the right.

'You sayed yo'self this Love o' Country stoof's only anoother neem for Nationalism . . . . ' It ended in a compact *Plop* and a gasp, as an egg, thrown from the right, hit the speaker fairly in the broad face. Amidst the howls of wrath the action roused in the man's supporters were whoops of disgust at the smell. The egg was very rotten.

But it was not only the right who were armed for conflict. An egg went flying back from the left. More eggs from the right. Both factions to a man were on their feet. Tomatoes and other vegetables were flying – and abuse – *Fascist Bastards – Commo Shit*! The police were hurled aside or trampled down. The factions were at grips. People at the back were shouting, screaming. Those on the rostrum were on their feet, staring, gaping like actors on a stage who suddenly see the drama stolen from them by the audience. Press cameras were flashing and popping at the back.

Then there was the drama back on the stage, its actors not the staring ones to begin with, but the Bloke, with that big Liverpool-Irishman after him, the Bloke all eyes and mouth, squealing, 'Help, help!' the other all eyes and teeth and reeking egg-yoke, grabbing at his flying coat tails. The coat came off in the pursuer's huge hands, with the sleeves ripped out and dangling foolishly down the *Führer's* arms to make them look like a chimpanzee's.

The Bloke gave a last strangled cry of *Help*! as the huge hands spun him and one fastened on his shirt at the throat. They were right before Jeremy, the other side of the table. The Bloke's bulging eyes looked into Jeremy's. Jeremy vaulted the table, shot his arm in between them so as to strike the big man's throat and force him back. The big fellow howled his wrath and came in shaped to fight. Jeremy dodged the blow aimed at him, and as the mass of man lumbered by, gave him his favourite poke in the midriff. The man went at the knees. The Bloke grabbed at Jeremy, who promptly flung him off to face the mob surging up the steps. But perhaps it wasn't for help the Bloke was grabbing. The Judge was shouting, 'Jeremy . . . come on, quick . . . this way!'

Jeremy looked round. The manager of the hall was there, urging the Committee out through a back door. The Bloke was already flying through it. Jeremy flung off a couple of would-be assailants and followed. The manager held off pursuit with a heavy chair, and when Jeremy passed through, flung the chair at those behind, then leapt to the door, slammed and locked it. All went clattering down a narrow stairway.

At the bottom of the stairs the manager said, 'Out that door, and into the lane. Turn right. When you come to another lane turn left. That'll bring you out into Hunter Street. Quick. They're breaking the door down. I want to go to my office and call more police. Damn you and your National Socialism!'

Out in the lane, Jeremy found the Bloke grabbing at him again, panting, 'Thanks, mate . . . the good old Aussie mateship!' Jeremy flung him off again.

Out in Hunter Street, there was the Bloke plucking at Jeremy's arm again. Jeremy turned on him angrily. 'What d'you want?'

The other, with his high-pitched voice, sounded like a pleading little boy: 'To come with you.'

Jeremy roared, 'No, by God, you don't! You're the one responsible for all this.'

'I? Why, it's you've done all the harm!' In indignation the Bloke's immature voice cracked like an adolescent boy's: 'Everything was going smoothly till you poked your ignoramus nose into it.'

'You're as mad as the bloody lunatics overseas you worship! Can't you see that it's because of your silly aping of Fascist and Nazi systems that the whole idea of Free Australia now stinks?'

'Here . . . I say! What do *you* know about social science, human bionomics . . . you *horse-doctor*!' The high-pitched tirade ended in a neigh of a laugh.

'Gentlemen!' cried the Judge.

Jeremy's voice came thick with anger: 'You bastard . . . with your nit-wit conceit you've fouled up for ever any hope we had of true nationality!'

'It's you're the bastard.' Again that neigh: 'The Bastard from the Bush. Get back where you belong!'

'Gentlemen, gentlemen!' the Judge protested. 'This is most unseemly.'

Dickey the Banker also was calling for propriety. He tried to take one of Jeremy's arms, Alfie another. He shook both off. He was turning to leave them, when the Bloke called after him, 'Back to your black wife . . . and your Jews!'

Jeremy swung back. Now he was fairly hissing with subdued anger. 'Listen, you . . . you Aryan Storm Trooper, you white-haired alien in my brownland . . . .'

With most of the group behind him, the Bloke must have felt braver than he had appeared to be back at the hall; and perhaps had it in mind that he had to do something to put that little matter right; or it may have been the taxi approaching looking for fares; but his hand shot out, to catch Jeremy fairly across the face – *Smack*!

He turned to the taxi now halted just clear of the curb, took the necessary couple of steps, laid hold of the handle of the door, looking back as he did so, to pipe at blinking Jeremy, 'That'll teach you to keep your place, bushwacker. In future just keep out of my way!' He opened the door, was about to enter, when Jeremy leapt at him, grabbed him by an arm. He took a swing at Jeremy, who ducked, and drove home that punch of his. The Bloke grunted, sagged at the knees, collapsed in the trickle of water running downhill like quicksilver in the moonlight.

'For godsake!' cried the Judge. 'Brawling in the streets!'

The blow must have been one of Jeremy's best, or the Bloke's solar plexus particularly sensitive, because the Bloke lay utterly insensate in appearance, white-faced so that his strange wheat-white hair looked dark against his skin, eyes wide, mouth agape. The Judge looked at him, let out a howl, 'You've killed him!' The group leapt to attend the stricken one.

Not the Judge, who looked aghast, looked around, as if struck with the thought that he had taken his liberalism too far. It must have seemed so when he heard Jeremy growl that he hoped he had. That made him start and stare at Jeremy, who having glanced at his victim and seen that he was in no worse condition that many another he had dealt with similarly, began to get into the cab.

The Judge expostulated, 'You can't go away, man . . . and leave him like this!'

'Can't I!' grunted Jeremy, and stepped inside.

Jeremy was just too late in closing the door behind him. As he reached for it, Alfie rushed up, panting, 'Don't leave me!'

He said shortly, 'I want to be alone.' His arm barred her way.

But she ducked under the arm and flung herself against him, wailing, 'Oh, don't abandon me, Jeremy.' He fell back to the seat with her clinging to him. The taxi driver, indifferent as ever, reached back and slammed the door.

Then the taxi was rolling down the hill. Those left behind shouted something. Alfie, still clinging, wept unrestrainedly. Jeremy sat like stone. The cab swung into Pitt Street.

When they reached his flat, Jeremy would have sent Alfie on to her own, and actually paid the driver to take her – only to find her out behind him. As he tried to induce her to get back in, she sobbed, 'If you send me away I'll die.' There was nothing for it but to wave the bored driver away.

Jeremy suffered her clinging to him down the stairs and into the flat. That was plain by his expression. Perhaps he was thinking of the Desperateness of a Woman's Love, as described by the knowing one, the father of this woman; perhaps of the desperateness of a dying father's love for an immature daughter. He sat her in an armchair as one does someone sick, got her a brandy and held it to her lips while she sucked at it and salted it with her flooding tears. The drink steadied her. The wild storm of weeping abated to snivelling. He got her another drink, but left her to drink it herself, poured one for himself and with it dropped into the other armchair, close enought to be able to reach across and give her his big handkerchief. She muttered, 'Am I a wreck?' She dabbed and sniffed, and sipped her brandy. After the second glass she got out her compact and began to set herself to rights.

It was a long job, and none too rewarding with those puffed and blood-shot eyes. Taking a last look, she did not ask if she were a wreck, but asserted it. However, the very act of shutting her compact and putting it away changed her mood. For the first time she raised the curly head and looked at him. He met the black shiny eyes for a long moment, then reached for her glass and proceeded to recharge it. She spoke then, low-toned, husky: 'It's what you wanted, isn't it?'

He took a swig of brandy. 'How could I want anything as lousy as all that?'

'But anything . . . so long as you could give it up.' When he said nothing, she went on: 'You gave it up before you started. You admitted you didn't come to form the Party . . . only to talk Love of Country.'

'What else had I to offer? I've always said I'm not a politician. Wasn't it only my inspiration, so-called, that you all wanted?'

'The purpose of the meeting was to start the Party.'

'I don't recall doing anything to stop it. The stoppage was planned, apparently. You people, with your experience of the meanness of politics, should have foreseen something of the kind and been prepared for it.'

Her face quivered. A moment more of staring at him. Then suddenly she rose, came and flung herself at his feet, head on his knees, arms reaching to get around him. He dropped a hand to her silky dark head, smoothed it while she wept out a second storm. When it was over, she lifted her wet smudged face to his, muttering, 'What're you going to do now?'

'What is there for me to do? I've done all I ever could. I couldn't go ranting up and down the country indefinitely . . . .'

'It's not ranting. It's inspiring people with love. Look how they loved you tonight!'

'Yes . . . particularly that big Liverpool-Irishman, or whatever he was . . . and the Bloke!'

'They were a minority . . . .'

'But they had all the say, didn't they?'

'You always get opposition in politics.'

'I don't regard this as politics. I've had a dream of a Nation I could be proud to belong to, not as something like a football team to barrack for, or an organization of clever-dicks to plunder and murder other tribes of men . . . but a grouping of people who by the example of their own honest and dignified living could be an inspiration to the world, a contributing factor to the high destiny I hope for for my species. From my experience since I came down here, it strikes me that I'm the only one with the dream . . . and that makes me the odd man out . . . a freak.'

'But that isn't true. So many of us have the same dream.'

'How many?'

'You heard how they went quite mad when you called them Fellow-Countrymen.'

'What's the population of this city . . . a couple of million? There might have been five hundred people there tonight . . . two hundred in violent opposition . . . .'

'No . . . only the Communists. The others would have listened to you, I'm sure. I was watching them.'

'How comes the Bloke, then, to treat me with contempt afterwards, to tell me to get back to the bush?'

'He tried at first to be friendly with you. You told him he was the cause of all the trouble. You hurt him.'

'Hurt his vanity. That's what I'm up against in my dreaming . . . the reality of the conceit of others who have another dream . . . one of personal power . . . and the vast majority with no dream at all but of filling their bellies. Maybe the couple of hundred in opposition are all there are in this city. But three hundred out of two million who bothered to come along and give support! And that three hundred. What supporters! What did they do when the fun started? Skiddadled to a man.'

'They need a leader.'

'To leave him to be torn to pieces when things go wrong!'

'Oh, Jeremy!' The black eyes welled again; the head sank.

He reached for her glass. 'Here . . . have a drink. You've got yourself all messed up again.' He reached for his handkerchief, dabbed, while she raised her face to him like a child, eyes closed. She still kept her eyes closed when he had done. A moment. Then he bent and kissed her lightly on the lips. She grabbed him at once, clinging with arms and mouth. When he got free and his breath back, he said, 'Now, pretty yourself up again.'

'Why?'

'Because I like to see you looking pretty.'

When she sat back to stare at him, he reached for her compact, gave it to her. She began on her face again, squatting on haunches now. He leaned back, watching, sipping his drink. After a moment, he said, 'You know . . . it's really up to you now.'

She stopped her tissuing to stare again. He went on: 'As your father insisted . . . The Pen's Still Mightier than the Sword. All the great reforms were done with books. *Uncle Tom's Cabin* freed the American Negroes. Tolstoy's *War and Peace* freed the Russians . . . at least from Czarist tyranny . . . someone else will have to get rid of the present one for them. There's your own book, which in a year or so has had more effect on the conscience of Australians about their treatment of the Aborigines than all that's been preached in pulpits, and spouted by others who saw the evil, in a hundred and fifty years. The old order's on the skids on account of it. Now's the time for you to put the skids under those who won't let us white Australians be what we want to.'

She looked up from her mirror. 'How am I going to do that?'

'That's your job. You did the other pretty well.'

'Inspired by you.'

'Inspired by no one but Alfrieda.'

'That isn't true. I haven't got the strength to do it alone. I'll have to have you to help me.'

He sighed slightly, said quickly as her eyes widened, 'Finish that off and let's have a drink. Let's get drunk, eh? We've never been drunk *together*.'

Her face lit up. She squealed, 'Wheeee!'

She was finished in no time. Then, drawing the little table close so that he could handle the drinks more easily, she slid herself onto his lap, put an arm about his neck. With her free hand she stayed his handing her the charged glass, and looking into his eyes, asked, 'You won't humiliate me again?'

He held the black eyes for a moment, then swallowed, answered, 'No.'

She kissed him quickly, then took the glass. He took his up, clinked it with hers, saying, 'Your book!'

She corrected him: 'Our book!' They drank.

Now she snuggled up to him, kissed him in a different way, slowly, not now snatching something denied, but enjoying ownership. She smoothed his brown seamed cheek and silver hair, smiling at him tenderly. She murmured, 'I love you.' She kissed him again.

His breath quivered in a sigh. He said, 'We're going to get drunk.'

'I'm drunk already . . . with happiness.'

'After so many tears?'

'I was afraid I was going to lose you.' She kissed him again, lingeringly. He joined in the sensuousness of it, rolling her back into his arms. She shrugged out of the sleeves of her jacket, unbuttoned her blouse, heaved up to release the brassiere, offered her little breasts to his lips, rumpled his hair and kissed his ears while he attended to them.

He withdrew to see her laughing face, her sparkling eyes. He asked breathlessly, 'Why are you laughing?'

'Because I'm happy . . . because I'm getting what I've wanted for so long . . . Oh!' She dragged his lips down to her, kissed him wildly.

He rose with her in his arms, carried her into the bedroom half-lit by the light from the lounge. She kissed and clung and moaned while he undressed her – dragged at him while he slid out of his own clothes – dragged him onto her, into her – sobbed for joy while they rocked in union.

Afterwards, still clinging to him, she fell asleep. He tried to move. Still she clung. She slept for minutes, breathing deeply. Then suddenly she woke, began to jerk her loins, just three or four times. What seemed like tension went out of her then. She relaxed with a gusty sigh. She smiled up at Jeremy, reached and smoothed his face and hair. She whispered, 'It was wonderful.' She kissed him. When he moved she let him go.

He went to the wardrobe, took out two dressing-gowns, one heavy, the other a light silk for the tropics. She was sitting up unashamedly on the edge of the bed when he came back. He was going to put the heavy gown on her. She chose the silk. With arms about each other they went back to the radiator-warmed lounge, again into the one armchair.

Sipping brandy, with thick brows now rumpled, she said suddenly, 'What are we going to call it?'

He stared at her. 'The baby?'

She laughed delightedly, pressed brow against his as she kissed him. 'No . . . the book. But I suppose you can call it our baby.'

'I won't be in this book business, you know.'

'Oh, yes, you will. You have to be.'

'Why have to be.'

'I can't do it myself. I know I can't.'

'But I can't write anything . . . only those stilted articles. I can't even talk well. I can only get angry about things.'

'That's what I want . . . your angry strength.'

He sighed, reached to pour brandy. She became wrapt in the book. She hit on the title of *True Commonwealth*, decided that it should be a novel, a huge novel, about a family – going back to its founders here, Eureka, the early idealism, the hotch-potch history of the land laced in with that of the family, to show the rottenness, the struggle against it, the subtle opposition to the idealism, the growth of the rottenness through frustration – while he plied her with brandy and biscuits and cheese.

Then she was drunk, burbling, getting her story mixed up with their own. Suddenly she forgot the story, seized him, hissing that she loved him, loved him, loved him. He carried her back to the bedroom. This time, when it was over, she lay relaxed completely. He rose and got pyjamas, dressed her while she lay blinking at him, muttering, 'Am I dreaming . . . Jeremy . . . am I . . . dreaming?'

She fell asleep almost as soon as he had tucked her in, clinging to him as he bent over her. Gently he freed himself, tucked her hands in under the bedclothes, kissed her on the brow. For a while he stood looking down at her childish little face, truly the face of an Enchanted One, glowing against the whiteness of the pillow and the darkness of hair and brows. He turned and went quietly back to the lounge, through it to the kitchen.

He made coffee, brought it into the lounge and laced it with brandy, drank. Then he took pad and pen from the sideboard, dropped with them into his chair. For some time he sat staring, thinking. At length he began to write:

Little Sweetheart,

It is proper, it is wise, that I go out of your life with the honey taste of you on my lips. The wonder would be spoilt by my hanging about, to become old through aging when by your enchantment I have become young again and shall remain so in my memory of you. You have conceived 'Our Baby'. Now only you can gestate it, give it birth. Only the weak need the strength of others. It is a tremendous task you have to do. But you have strength, courage, ability, youth. I leave you to it with my love.

J.D.

Having written, he left the missive on the table, held down by a brandy bottle beside which were two pink tablets. He went back into the bedroom, stealthily got together his belongings, his suitcase, stole out again. The sleeper was softly snoring. Packed and dressed, he looked in at the bedroom door, at the dark head on the white pillow. He sighed slightly as he turned away, went softly out of the flat, onto the stairs, and up.

It seemed as if he were walking right into the Cross as he emerged on top. The Moon was not yet down, but out of sight behind the black city. A telephone booth was blazing with light not far away. He went to it, found an advertisement for an all-hours taxi company, and rang.

A cab was along in no time. He asked to be taken to Central Station, and learnt from the driver as they went that the first train going northward would be the Paper Train to Newcastle, departing at five. At the Station he made himself more or less comfortable on a bench, slept a little.

Suddenly the huge sleeping place became clamorous with the arrival of the papers and those who would be travelling, the shunting in of the train. The news-stand was opened up for its share of the papers, still damp and reeking off the press. Jeremy bought a paper, took it to the Refreshment Room, opened it on the counter while the sleepy waitress got his coffee and a sandwich. There was a large picture of himself perpetuating the perfection of that punch of his. It had been taken from the foot of the rostrum at the moment the big Liverpool-Irishman was sagging at the knees, hanging as it were on the fist of the stiffly-outstretched left. It was a photographer's masterpiece. The adversaries had been caught in profile. To right and left of them were standing, or rather crouching, all agape, Alfie and the Bloke. Half the front page was taken up with it and the letter-press concerning it. The heavy heading was: POLITICAL MEETING ENDS IN WILD BRAWL. Beneath it stated: NEW NATIONAL-SOCIALIST PARTY'S INAUGURATION BROKEN UP BY COMMUNISTS. Jeremy glanced at others drinking and eating and reading all about it. He folded the paper, finished his coffee, went to the train. Because few passengers were travelling first-class he easily got a compartment to himself.

He read the piece while waiting for the train to start. His name was mentioned with that of the Bloke, as if they were associates, fellow-travellers the Way of the Crooked Cross. *National-Socialism, National-Socialism.* The report flogged the term, as if aiming to anathematize it as dirty a word as

Communism. Yet, on the same page was a small piece praisefully reporting on the unity and productivity of National-Socialism in Germany resulting from a system of youthful recreation called Strength Through Joy. Apparently neither Nationalism nor Socialism nor anything else but British Conservatism could be classed as decent in Australia. It stated that the two *National-Socialist* leaders were not to be found when sought for interview, with the inference that they had taken to funk-holes. No mention was made of the fact that the audience was largely respectable and to some degree distinguished. It was described as 'Made up of factions obviously spoiling for battle from the outset.' Not a line reporting what Jeremy had said about Love of Country, only something concerning his complaint over having been imprisoned without trial under Federal Jurisdiction, and that in such a way as to suggest that the extraordinary powers of Federal Law were designed for dealing with just such as he.

Jeremy's muttered comment was: 'The bastards, eh? They've got it all sewn up!'

The bells dinned. The engine hooted. They were off. They went picking their way through a maze of gleaming tracks and coloured lights, to enter cuttings that were the backs of mean tenements, in many windows of which lights burnt and in some figures moved, as preparation was made for the certain meanness of the day ahead, wage-slavery at the best, the misery of pinch-pensioned invalidism at worst. They passed out of this pocket of poverty, only one of so many, in the land of greatest plenty and human opportunity in the world – into one of neat little houses on pocket-handkerchief lots, in a land three million square miles wide most of which was empty space. Only a few lights here. Then into a region where the lights were only those on the street poles and the grand houses stood well back from that vulgar thing, the railway, separated from it by common-land and golf-course. Here the inhabitants would be fast asleep, not having to go to work till their wage-slaves were well settled down, or perhaps having no more to do all day but wander about a golf-course with an allegedly fellow creature to tote the clubs. So much for plenty, space, equality, in this land that so loudly boasted these things. At least that must have been what this disillusioned patriot was thinking as with set face he watched from his window – unless it was of an abandoned little girl, still dreaming that she had found what her nature craved and her woman's desperateness in love had striven so long for, father and lover combined to perfection in the one man.

Coming into hilly country, they stopped to drop their first bales of papers and to take on another engine for the winding climb. Few lights beyond this point. Jeremy watched the flare of headlights and fireboxes on the curves ahead. It was still too dark for him to see the road the railway mostly followed, that was cut through the great rock-masses by the Father's of the Nation, yoked and flogged as the first beasts of burden of the settlement never were, since considered far more valuable. Such a sight must stir up history in the mind of one not inured to it by use or heedless of the fact that a nation's future is, for better or worse depending on the intelligence of its people, eternally bound to its past.

They rolled down at last to the Hawkesbury, dropped papers and extra engine, to go thundering across the bridge. Now dawn was silvering the wide reaches seaward. There was mist on the water, drifting with the tidal stream in detached patches that might, in the strange light, have been taken for trudging gangs of men, or rather the ghosts of them, the clank of their chains drowned by the roar of wheels on girdered rails.

Why is the unauthenticated death of the presumed Christ made an annual ceremony of deepest solemnity in Australia, while commemoration of the first marching on these shores of those skeletons in chains who had survived the frightful journey from the brutal society that had condemned them and to which we still bow down, Australia Day, is made occasion for skiting about what a Wonderful Mob We Are? A stranger might well be moved to ask that question.

Beyond the river, as day dawned on the swamplands, there were revealed the small homesteads of poverty-stricken landholders, so many of them with dwelling houses but half built, although the majority were of long standing. A common enough sight to be seen throughout rural Australia, as perhaps nowhere else on earth. The builders had built the essential back part first: kitchen and a bedroom. Thus they faced the world with strange squashed faces: just a door in the middle that was never opened because it led to nowhere but the vanished dream of the parlour, the best bedroom, the front verandah from which to sit and view the passing world. The stranger might ask again: Why were these buildings never completed? Had their builders, those who had settled the land, lost heart? Was it symbolic of the character of the Nation to do things by halves? Or was it the Banks, pressing for mortgage-money from their London counting-houses? Damn fool Colonials – what did they want with anything save the bare necessities of life? Damn fool Colonials! You can do anything you like with 'em.

At Newcastle, Jeremy booked a room in a hotel, slept in it till noon. Then he walked the few streets, looking at the faces. Men coming off shift in the coal mines or the foundries, grimy, seamed with exhaustion, worry, bad nutrition, might have been doing the like in Newcastle-on-Tyne, for all the blue and silver above, the shimmering river rolling to the sapphire sea from far-away mountains, some of those mountains peeping purple above grey bush. Likewise their women lugging their shopping, bitter-mouthed, blowzy, sag-bellied, dowdy, shrill. No one noticed him as the tight-faced fighter against the stupid bullying of frustrates, whose face stared out at them from the papers. Eyes for nothing but the usual. At what age did they cease to see what was not essential to their little living? How many knew what phase the Moon was in, even though it now was peeping over their shoulders of late afternoons? How many knew anything, except what was the best beer, what would win next Saturday, what the woman next door said to the woman next to her about her old man's getting drunk and belting her? Free Australia! Free for what? It was a Commo Town. Here they didn't want even the freedom to cheek the Boss. Let's have a Boss who'll put us up against the wall and shoot us!

The evening was well advanced when the Brisbane Mail came in. Jeremy boarded it. He had a companion in the sleeper, who looked up from the evening paper he'd brought from Sydney, stared hard, but evidently only to judge whether he could say what he wished without dispute: 'Goodnight. Getting cold. Bloody country's in a hell of a state. What we need's a dictator . . . but none o' National-Socialist bullshit.' Jeremy only grunted. The man grunted back, returned to his paper. Soon afterwards the steward came to ask about making up the bunks. Jeremy, who had the top one, said he would have his done at once.

IV

On arrival in Brisbane next afternoon, Jeremy sought out the terminal of the Northern Aerial Service, made a booking for next Sunday. He sent a telegram to Fergus for passing on by radio if necessary: ARRIVING BOULDER CREEK SUNDAY COULD YOU PICK ME UP. He then established himself in a quiet hotel. Fergus's reply reached him next afternoon. Fergus would be there.

The intervening days were spent in shopping for what, evidently, were presents for members of the Lily Lagoons household, for books on the things he was concerned with in his practice as veterinarian, and a couple of books on new aspects of Anthropology. Thus it looked as if he were returning to the old work-filled seclusion. He looked older, grimmer. There were bushmen staying at his hotel who gave him the sign that they guessed he was one of them and might join their sessions of Booze and Bullshit. He ignored them.

Sunday. *Truth* was on sale at the aerial terminal when the passengers assembled there before dawn. The paper featured the incident at the hall in Sydney as front page, too; or at least in part, beginning with a half-page headline; NAZI MOVEMENT IN AUSTRALIA and introductory stuff about what it called the Riot, neatly boxed in a frame of tiny Swastikas, then continuing the story on an inner page. On the inner page was another picture of Jeremy dropping his man, who was named as Secretary of the Communist Party, a well-known identity. Jeremy was also named. The trouble was that the angle and the moment at which the picture had been taken made it look as if he had struck Below the Belt, as so often accused of doing by his enemies. These were in for a feast this week! A large bundle of *Truth* went along with other cargo and the passengers to the airport. One of the enemies, a Vaisey Manager, was amongst the passengers. By the looks Jeremy got from others, information on his identity was quickly passed around.

The flight began in the red dawn – with cranes and egrets taking off ahead to fly in echelon with the aircraft till outflown. Slowly, with the hours, they overhauled the wilderness, letting drop behind, first the raped coast region, then the near inland with its millions of acres of grey ghosts of trees destroyed for sheep that had their short existence chiefly to fat the Absentee Landlord, to give the millionaire Bradford spinner his wool and the titled butchers of Smithfield cheap meat to sell to the poor, the drained swamps, dried rivers, eroded plains, the centres of the noble national art of Bullshit, to which they kept dropping down to make their deliveries and take on fuel, growing meaner with the distance. Then it was grey wilderness. Then wilderness where only the Dust Devils dwelt. At last over Boulder Creek – and down, down, down to the red earth itself.

Fergus was waiting. He greeted Jeremy with his split grin, saying as he took his hand, 'Doctor Bullshit, I presume!' He added as they got Jeremy's luggage and packages: 'Do we have the Bullshit Session here or over at the Prospectors' Alms?'

Jeremy answered, 'I never felt less like shooting the bull than I do now, son.'

'Yes? From the bit I heard on the radio about how things wound up, I'd've thought you'd've been rearin' for it. What is it . . . Home James?'

'Not exactly. I don't feel like facing anybody yet . . . except you.'

'That's an honour. But I more or less booked you in with the mob at Cullity's. They heard the radio, too.'

'God save us! I'll write 'em a note to drop to them. Drop the papers to them, too. *Truth's* full of it . . . well, their version of it. I don't want to go straight home. Let's get aboard your kite and head in that direction . . . and I'll explain on the way.'

So up again and away, over Piss Ridge, down to the Prospectors' Alms, to do a low run before the crowd, among whom was Baby Jem in her mother's arms, to drop the papers and the note of apology, then on again up the Telegraph Line, fairly sweeping the poles up beneath them with a stiff sou'easter on their tail. Jeremy took over the simple task of keeping the aircraft straight and level while Fergus read the pieces in the papers. His comment was: 'Pity it hadn't been the Bloke you were shown dropping. Not only will the Commos make capital out of it, but that white-haired bastard, too. Certainly you're right when you say he's made Australian Nationalism stink for good. Still, we just can't walk off and leave it to the Poms, the Comms, and that mad bastard.'

'I don't know, son. The Real Australia, the Nation as it is in fact, shocked me so deeply that it just seemed a lost cause to strive for anything better . . . that is for me. Don't forget I'm first a Bushie . . . and a bit out of date. I've never looked squarely at the Nation before. My previous acquaintance with it . . . and its reality as seen in the Southern Cities, the Capitals, where two-thirds of the population live . . . has been more in the nature of short excursions into what I accepted as strange territory. This time I went, you might say, reversing the old proverb, to pray . . . but didn't stay to mock . . . I bolted, from what was alien to me . . . made alien by aliens in great numbers, as the bush could never be. Remember, also, that I belong to a generation brought up on the idea of *Australia Felix* as a foregone conclusion, more or less . . . because there was then hope for it. What could I preach but a Bushie's love of the bush to Townies? They received me well . . . all who hadn't an ulterior motive for opposing me. But I'm convinced it was as a sort of freak they took to me . . . something out of the past for which they felt nostalgia. The way those that night of the big meeting . . . the one's supporting me, applauding me . . . bolted when the reality presented itself in the form of the faction fight, convinced me of my freakishness. Those two factions represent the idea of *Australia Felix* now. As yet they're fakes, because they're dominated as much by overseas interests as the others. Maybe they'll always remain fakes . . . because a place begotten in such rottenness can't throw anything to the top but rubbish. I saw I was the odd man out. Didn't the Bloke tell me that when he called me the Bastard from the Bush and told me to get back to it?'

Glancing at Fergus, who was biting his bunny-lip and frowning as if deeply chagrined, he placed a hand on his knee. 'It's up to you now, son, if you want something better. Alfie's idea of a book is a good one. Maybe you could help her. You're a clever writer yourself . . . and could bully her where she's wanting. She's got talent . . . if not strength to do great things with it. There's a job for you. Only leave me out of it.'

Fergus asked, 'And what's going to happen to you?'

'I've got plenty to keep me busy till I'm ready to die. I want to do something to save the blacks from the obliteration that threatens them now in place of the old extinction. As I see it . . . the new deal for them is much the same as Cobbitty's old one . . . breed 'em out, make 'em white. Then I've got more to do about conservation. With militarism marching into the land it'll be torn apart with roads and camps and fortresses.'

'Then why not take over that command to get control of it?'

Fergus went on to say that lately he had been talking to Rifkah, and she, while displeased with his having taken to politics, was all in favour of his taking the command for the sake of the blacks. Leopold Mission felt the same. He said he had gone there with Old Whiskers immediately after the General's return to the North. Esk had gone there primarily to apologize to Rifkah for the trouble he had caused her, and as an earnest gift had presented her with ownership of Red Rory, whom he wanted her to run for the next Cup. He went on to say that Whiskers himself had heard of what had happened to Jeremy at the meeting and was pleased with it, evidently as something that would drive him back to do what he wanted of him. Rifkah and Prindy were quite happy at the Mission, he reported. Both would be over for the Races.

Speaking again of the effect on him of having to abandon the dream of a lifetime, Jeremy told how he had thought of setting out for home from Newcastle on foot, to beat his way across country, avoiding as much settlement as possible, as he said: 'To walk it out of my system. The idea of the rush home, by train and plane . . . or rather, the walking in home after such a rush and in such a state of mind . . . was too much to contemplate. I felt it would do me some harm, crush me somehow. But there didn't seem much sense in battling as a bagman for six months or so only adding to my burden of disappointment in my fellow-countrymen the bush-bastardy I was already only too well acquainted with . . . because I'd have to rely on homestead hand-outs. So I arrived at a sort of compromise. I reckoned that if I got you to fly me the last of the way, and put me down in some truly wild place not so far from home, battling the rest of the way, living off the land, would do the trick. I bought an outfit for the purpose. What about that hide-out of yours for the plane, up on the Plateau? If you'll put me down there, you can take the rest of my gear on home . . . with a note for Nan explaining. Okay?'

They were well up the Telegraph Line, about halfway between Ilfracombe Station and the Railhead, when they spotted Billy Brew's plant pulled up at a bore. The old fellow was out before his great press of donkeys staring up. Jeremy said he'd like to drop down and give Billy a wave and toss him out those newspapers. Fergus said that they could easily land there. But Jeremy stuck to his resolve to see no one yet. He wrote a note for rolling in with the papers: *Largely bullshit. Will give the facts when I see you Race Time. Bring four quiet donks – jacks and jennies. J. Delacy.* As they flew on their way again, Jeremy explained that he wanted the donkeys as a gift for the Leopold Mission.

Reaching the railway, they kept well to eastward of it, and so in coming to the Plateau, avoided Beatrice River township and Lily Lagoons homestead. An hour before sunset they landed on the ancient Ring Place.

Jeremy changed into his bushman's outfit. Fergus was troubled by the fact that he had no food or any means of getting it except a large clasp-knife. Jeremy said, 'If I can't live off this country as I am, son, I don't deserve to live in it.'

Fergus took off. Jeremy stood watching his dust, all that could be seen of him, as he flew into the sou'easter, straight over the edge of the Plateau. The dust dispersed as the engine-sound diminished. Then the sound ceased, as Fergus cut his motors to glide down to Lily Lagoons, a good day's walking from here, but only a matter of minutes in the style of the Old One. Silence – like a Presence. Jeremy looked around. That silence must have poured into his ears after all the dinning they had suffered during past weeks. He heaved a great sigh, started for the gilding Sun now balanced on the Plateau's rim. Then, as if with his moving a spell was broken, the silence broke. The evening orchestras of the insects burst forth. Somewhere, half a mile apart, butcher birds were carolling a chorus. Down in the timber below the escarpment white cockatoos were starting the eternal dispute about night perches. The wind was dying with the day. As Jeremy went, it seemed as if his long blue shadow had leapt out of the sacred earth behind and was following, stride for stride at first, till the flat gave way to the slabs of rock, when it took to dodging and leaping and lurking, scaring the peeping brush-tails.

With a last flaring that lit things strangely, the Sun vanished over the escarpment. Then the long shadows rushed together, as if to whisper of the business of the night. Against the luminous sky a flock of small birds was seen to fly in from eastward, to halt in their progress, to circle, to hover, then to dip down to a clump of bushes bigger than most of the poor growth hereabout. Water would be there. Jeremy headed that way, but veered off as a new sound came into the twittering of the birds, telling that he had been seen. Best to let them settle down. He went on to the edge.

The Sun was down now, and all the world blue, save the tumbled rocks below, which still glowed with the colours, the crimson, scarlet, orange, of the horizon. The blue was darkening, rocks paling to mauve, West's ruddiness taking on the tinge of green of showy petals where they meet the calyx. The flower died in its green cup. The bush turned black. The rocks aged grey. A star winked on the ragged western horizon. It would be Sirius, considering the hour and the time of year, as anyone should know, except those fool enough to ignore the glorious things of earth of which the heavens are a part. It was called Nyang by local tribes, and supposed to be the Shade of the Fly, who vanished at this time of year because of the onset of what was called Cold Weather Time. One should be able to tell the date by the stars – even the time. One should know the stars as well as the lineaments of one's own hand. Sun, Moon and Stars – yet Jeremy, the knowing one, looked surprized when he turned from West to East to find Igulgul up and peeping at him through the scrub.

He watched Igulgul climb the silvery blue a little way, while Igulgul watched him, as if calculating how to deal with him on this night of his own fullness and Wrong-side magic. Then he moved towards the water. His coming was greeted by sleepy twittering of protest. He moved slowly, quietly, to avoid undue alarming.

The clump of bushes shaded a small rock-hole, probably fed by a spring from the mass of rock behind, but in wet weather part of what must be a brawling stream, judging by the sandy channel winding past. He bent to the water, tried a handful, then put his new hat to its first bushman's use by dipping it in and drawing a quart. Now a Kirrikijirrit was singing down below. Also down there was a Gogal calling that the coast was clear of No-good bijnitch: *Mopoke, mopoke, mopoke*!

Jeremy left the hole, to follow the channel a short distance to a spot where there was a stretch of sand wide enough and clear of rock to make a bed in. He dropped to knees, dug a hip hole and with the dug stuff built a pillow, in such a way as not to have Igulgul staring him in the face all night. He sat down, removed boots and socks, put the latter in his hat and folded this over the pillow-mound, then with a sigh stretched out. Last night he had gone to sleep to the clang and scream of trams, the revving and tooting of cars, the yelping of Saturday night's boozers. How different to do so to the love-singing of the Willy wagtail and the quiet calling of the Mopoke that all was well!

It was near midnight when Jeremy woke – startled – although there was no sound in the world. No Mopoke!

He didn't move. Only his wide staring and the rigidity of his body showed that he had been startled – by something on the left of him, the way he had been lying, and above him. Not Igulgul. The Old One was looking over his shoulder. A moment of this intense immobility. Suddenly he sat up. His eyes dropped to the sand beside him. It was untrod, unmarked. He had made his bed from the other side. He looked upward again, to about that point to which he had been attracted on waking, then beyond the low left bank of the channel . . . Nothing. He looked right round slowly, searchingly. He glanced at the Moon. He muttered, 'But I could swear to it!'

He looked at his own short shadow, at the shadowy right bank. There was nothing near to throw a shadow longer than a foot or so. Again he looked around, and muttered again, 'I wasn't dreaming. I was wide awake. I saw the face distinctly, the glint of the eyes . . . the shiny blackness of the face . . . like a polished boot.'

Then the Mopoke started up again: *Mopoke, mopoke – de coast is clear*!

That roused the Willy wagtail to his silver *kirrikijirriting*. Far away a dingo called. Another, still further, answered. The birds in the bushes twittered sleepily.

Jeremy seemed not to hear, sitting staring at nothing now, or perhaps at the memory of what he had seen, or now conceded he had imagined seeing, since he muttered, 'Halluncination . . . the first I've ever experienced . . . wonder what that means?'

At length he rose. Even now he looked about as if expecting to see something to corroborate his fancy, again at the ground, as if for tracks. Then he went in the direction of the water-hole. The birds began to twitter again. He moved more slowly, took a drink, then returned to his hip-hole.

He sat again, but did not lie, sat for a while, then got out his socks, shook the sand out of them, donned them and his boots, took up his hat, looked around again, still expectant in his mien. He stepped out of the channel and headed for the cliff edge. It was easy going in the brilliance. Soon he was seated again, on a rock overlooking the silvery world below, his shadow now a series of blacks blobs on the rocks below. A brush-tail down there went to investigate a blob when it moved. He raised an arm. The Marmaroo shot into the air, to land twenty feet away and vanish. 'Shadows,' he muttered. 'But that wasn't a shadow I saw. At least, it was a shadow cast by my own mind. But I wonder why? Why a huge blackman?'

After a while he rose, evidently went looking for a way to get down from here, since when he came to it, he set about descending. It was slow going and not nearly so easy here in the shadow of great rocks. He disturbed a python in one shadowy place, halted while it fled from him with dry slithering and clatter of dislodged stones. Further down, where there were substantial trees, a couple of possums spotted him, but far from fleeing, followed him for a while, travelling from tree to tree, swinging by tails, flying through the air, scolding him. That he was anything but depressed by the experience that had aroused him was evident enough in his comical answering the scolders back: 'Look out I'm not a *moomboo* and jump up and grab you by the tails and eat you.' The word *Moomboo* seemed to fascinate him for a while thereafter, by his constant breathing of it. Then it was the word *Hallucination*. He repeated it many times.

He headed down towards the Turtle Hole and eventually reached it, drank from it, stretched himself out on the grass there, and stared at Igulgul getting down close to the western shoulder of the Plateau, over near the Snake Caves. With hands behind his head, he asked himself, 'What's an hallucination? Seeing something that doesn't exist. No . . . rather, it exists only to the person who has it. The hallucinations of delerium are real enough. In DT's people try to kill the things they imagine, try to escape from them. An hallucination is a manifestation of a state of mind, then.' He seemed to doze on that. But it wasn't long before he roused, rose, went on his way, which was along the road.

Thus he came to the turn-off of the Limestone. There he seemed undecided what to do, and sat down. Still the matter of the hallucination was troubling him: 'Why should I have a manifestation like a blackfellow? Why see a *moomboo*, when I should be seeing monsters like the Archbishop, Silver Tongue, the Chief, the Bloke? Strange that I haven't seen anything like this before . . . and then all of a sudden, when I come home . . . must be something significant. I never felt closer to the land before.'

After a while he murmured, 'Billy Brew hinted once of seeing something, I remember. I said it was because he lived like a blackfellow, he thought like one. He didn't like it. I was only joking. I didn't take him seriously. I must ask him again . . . carefully.'

He rose, still undecided, by his standing, looking in either direction. Igulgul, with a wink, went over the edge of the escarpment. Then suddenly he said, quite loud, 'Yes . . . I think I will. I don't feel like wanting to be on my own now. It'll be a better way of coming home. I should've thought of it at the time

. . . but then I wouldn't have had that experience to share with him. Yes . . . that's what I'll do. If I move, I ought to catch young Fergus.'

He swung in the direction of Lily Lagoons, fell into a long stride.

Coming clear of the escarpment, he soon had the moonlight again. Igulgul watched him all the way to the top gate, vanished, to leave it to his old enemy, the Ol'Goomun-Ol'Goomun, already with the faint glow of her coming getting the butcher birds out to rouse the rest of the world. As he entered the racetrack the horses saw him, whiffed him, came galloping to greet him. He was able to give them all a touch before Elektron snapped and kicked into full possession of him. There was the Junkers standing as a grey blur by the fuel shed.

Jeremy left the horses at the inner gate, passed the Aboriginal quarters, where no one was yet abroad, since it is contrary to Aboriginal custom to get out before full daylight, unless forced. He passed through the mangoes. Light in the kitchen of the Big House, as always at piccaninny daylight. He headed for it. Through the fly screen, Nan and Fergus could be seen seated at the table drinking tea.

Jeremy knocked, and as the others glanced, called in a mendicant blackfellow's whine, 'Mitchitch!'

Taken in, she answered, 'Wha' name you want?'

'Me hungry, Mitchitch . . . you gi' me lil bits?'

She rose, saying, 'Who dat come wantin' tucker be-fore deelight?'

She came to the door, opened it, gaped. He smiled, opened his arms to her. But she was a moment in coming to him. From surprise her expression changed suddenly to searching. Then she came, kissed him, dropped her curly head on his breast, clung for a moment, then quickly withdrew and looked searchingly at him again. He asked, 'I meant what I said just now. I'm starving.' She giggled, wheeled about to rush to the store-room.

Fergus, also, was gaping. Jeremy came up to him, saying, 'Captain Bullshit, I presume. Have you been shooting the bull all night or only just started for the day?'

Fergus was looking searchingly, too. 'You didn't take long to get it out of your hide.'

'No,' said Jeremy, sitting down and taking a finger of buttered toast.

'You look a different man,' said Fergus.

'Maybe I'm just the same man as before . . . only I was different yesterday.'

'No . . . you look different altogether.'

'How?'

'Can't say, really . . . less . . . well, forbidding . . . I mean, you used to have a look that scared us lesser mortals . . . and yesterday you looked set against the world. Say . . . you must've travelled to get here so quick!'

'I wanted to catch you. Will you be able to fly me back a bit of the way we came yesterday?'

'What's this . . . a session?'

'No . . . it struck me the best way to come home is have a spell with another old Bushie. I'd like you to drop me down with Billy Brew. I'll travel up to the Charlotte with him. I want some donkeys off him, you know. I'll bring 'em up myself. Suit you?'

'Sure. I can nip back to Whiskers on the Gulf from there.'

'I'm not making a session of it . . . but I'll need some grog for Billy. He's a rum hound. Would you mind first nipping over to Finnucane's and getting a small case for me to take to him. I don't want to be seen there.'

'Okay. I'll nip over right now, if you like. When d'you want to leave?'

'As soon after breakfast as possible. It takes the old bloke hours to yoke up . . . but he starts before dawn. Want to catch him while he's still at the bore and you can land.'

Nan was coming with a slab of steak and a bowl of eggs. 'Steak and eggs?' she asked.

'Bless you,' said Jeremy.

V

Billy Brew's plant was already on the move when the Junkers reached it. The landing wasn't the simple thing it could have been yesterday, when the worst to be expected to happen if scary ones amongst the donkey mob took flight at the aerial monster's coming to earth would be a general scatter that a couple of hours' rounding-up would rectify. No one concerned had any experience of how donkeys would behave in the eventuality, not even old Billy, who boasted he knew the creatures so well that he could tell when they were expressing their opinion of him in their sing-songs. He and they were well enough used to aircraft flying low over them, since the Flying Doctor always paid his respects in passing and others took a look out of curiosity. However, none had yet landed near them. Billy himself thought that this was merely a salute, the several low runs made to signify intent to land, and merely pulled up his team and stood up on the driving seat to wave. As yet his assistant, Barney Ninyarra, was not helping to control the team on horseback, but having got the team started, was behind with his lubra getting the spare beasts, the Tail, so-called, on the move away from the bore. Fergus had to scatter the milling Tail to ensure a safe landing.

When the Tail saw the huge bird amongst them, raising enough dust and din for a thousand donks, they bolted – not just anywhere, but up the track after the waggon, passed it at full pelt and, as Billy put it, 'Singin' to beat the 'Eavenly 'Ost beefin' it out round the Throne o' God.' Naturally the team joined in – with a jerk into action that knocked old Billy off his perch and left the turn-out completely without control. All went bush, the team to finish its wild careering in a heap of tangled harness and torn scrub and the waggon sitting on an uprooted kapok like a bustard on the nest, the Tail to keep going, 'Headin' for flamin' India, where their bloody puggin ancestors come from!' according to Billy Brew. Comical as these remarks of Billy's sounded, so that Jeremy, coming to his aid had difficulty in restraining his amusement, they were uttered in no comical mood. When Jeremy did lose control for a moment, the old man turned on him with white beard bristling, pale blue eyes blazing, yelling, 'What's so bloody puggin funny 'bout buggerin' a man's plant for a flamin' month?'

Fergus didn't come near, except to fly at a respectful height to take a look at things in departing. Billy shook a fist at him, then turned on Jeremy. 'What're you doin' stoppin' behind. Not 'lectioneerin' for your loony party, are you?'

Jeremy explained that he'd come to get the taste of it all out of his mouth by spending a few days with a true old mate, and that he had brought a nice drop of grog along to help. Although Billy must have been Doing a Perish, as he'd have called it, after the long dry haul from the Prospectors' Alms, as betrayed by his swallowing and licking his lips over that last bit of news, he was not to be appeased by it yet. He answered savagely, 'I never drink while I got work to do . . . and, Sweet Jesus, jes take a look-see at the work you got for me to do!' Then, turning his back on Jeremy, he added. 'I ain't a piss-pot like others I could name!'

He remained intractable for hours, taking it out on Jeremy as they worked side by side putting things to rights, mostly by scoffing about his adventure in politics: 'To think I'd ever live to see the day when Jerry Delacy turned politician! Christ Jesus . . . gettin' mixed up with them mongrel bastards! And here's me all these years thinkin' you's the most hintelligent man in the country. Hain't I told you a 'undred times there hain't no 'ope for that *Australia Felix* lunacy? We're an Asiatic country. It follers that some kind o' slant-eyed bastards, Japs or Chows, are goin' 'o grab the place someday . . . same's we grabbed it off the poor Abo's. Only 'ope I'm 'ere to see it. 'Oly bloody 'olocaust . . . but wouldn't I love to see them squatter bastards and silvertail turds takin' poor ol' Jackie's place with the stock-whip round 'em . . . doin' the dirty work for five-bob a week and 'avin' to live on stewed dawg and bird-shit, eaten with chop-sticks . . . Pohetic justice!'

He harped on Jeremy's adventure, refusing to acknowledge the assertions that much of what was in those papers was incorrect: 'Jesus wept . . . to think o' Jeremy Delacy bein' pelted off a political platform with rotten haigs! Don' know whether to laugh or cry. No wonder you're ashamed to face nobody but an old bushwacker like me! Still I'd'a' been a lot better pleased if you'd'a' spared me that . . . the way you went about it . . . you and your bloody bunny-faced haeronautical mate. Strike me bloody black . . . look at them hames? I'll be blacksmithin' for a puggin month to straighten 'em . . . thanks to a pair o' flamin' flyin' ijits!'

Jeremy took it cheerfully, seeing to it that the old fellow had a good lunch of fresh Lily Lagoons bread and butter with spiced beef and cake, even if he could not induce him to join him in at least slaking his alcoholic thirst. He also saw to it that the brace of geese he had brought and the sweet-bucks were put in the huge camp-oven to cook ready for supper, attended by Ninyarra's lubra.

Things weren't nearly as bad as the old fellow made out. They had the plant well enough to rights to be able to take it back to the bore before sunset. Billy steadfastly refused to drink until camp was made. Then he had a long rum and lime-juice, and immediately began to unbend. Nevertheless, when after the good meal they were settled down by the camp-fire to a bit of steady drinking, he became perverse again when Jeremy broached the subject that was the real reason for his being there: 'Bill, would you remember an occasion, a few years back, when you were out my way buying a horse, and talking of Aboriginal superstition, you mentioned an experience you'd had yourself of

. . . well, of a supernatural kind?'

Billy's answer was a bristling of the beard and a suspicious glare.

Undeterred, Jeremy took a swig from his pannikin, went on: 'You told me how you'd seen a *Moomboo* . . . remember?'

Billy snapped, 'What you getting at, Jerry?'

'Nothing offensive, I assure you. In fact, I'd like to say I'm sorry I stopped you from telling your yarn. Would you mind telling me now?'

Billy growled. 'That time you told me you wasn't hinterested in superstition except from a scientific point of view. What's happened to you in your old age? Is it the politics . . . or them young white girls you get mixed up with?'

'Now, that's unkind. You know I'm a burnt-cork man. I've said I'm sorry. At the time I thought you were shooting some of your bullshit. We were talking seriously of the effect of magic in the lives of Aborigines. We're both non-believers in supernatural things. You know how silly whites, although mocking at everything else a blackfellow does or thinks, still has a tall story of some magical event concerning them. Well, I thought you were putting the same thing over . . . but as one of your leg-pulls. It's occurred to me I was wrong.'

'Why the sudden change? Not so long. Cahoon's funeral. Something to do with that?'

'No.'

When Jeremy remained silent, Billy asked, 'It's about this you come to look me up, ain't it?'

'As a matter of fact, yes.'

'I thought there was more behind it than you reckoned. What . . . you writin' a book on Aboriginal Superstition, or sumpin? If so, you leave me out of it, mate. I don't go for this Anthropology stuff . . . no more than Politics. They're both rackets. Those that go for both them things are only in it for what they can get out of it.'

'No, Bill. This is purely personal.'

Billy waited this time, almost challengingly, until Jeremy came out with it: 'As a matter of fact, Bill, I've had a similar sort of . . . well, supernatural-like experience.'

The beard split in a grin. 'Don't come under the headin' o' silly tall-stories in your case, I don't suppose.'

Jeremy replied somewhat stiffly, 'I inferred that I didn't regard it as supernatural. I realize that it was an hallucination . . . or, better, a metempirical experience. Do you know the word Metempirical from *Websters International?*'

Billy asked, 'Anything to do with Metaphysics?'

'No. A metempirical experience is one such as a saint has . . . seeing Christ, or the Virgin, or some such thing . . . or a blackfellow has when he sees a *moomboo*. It's more than an hallucination, which can be due to a physical condition. It's not just a fancy or a dream, either. It's a concept arising from some deep emotional state . . . a need for a manifestation of a belief, I guess . . . conceived as actual experience.'

'You're talkin' like a book, even if you ain't writin' one, Jerry. We'd have to get the Dictionary out for me to follow you properly.'

'It isn't necessary. I'm using words I looked up in trying to understand it myself. The explanation of it isn't important. It's what was seen . . . and whether others . . . bushmen like ourselves, who live close to the real country . . . have had similar experiences . . . otherwise it could be just freakish. I remembered that experience of yours that I so rudely and unwisely interrupted you in telling.'

'Okay . . . apology accepted. What'd you see?'

'I'd rather hear that experience of yours first.'

Billy was silent for a moment. Then: 'It's hard to tell about these things. That's why you're cagey. I've never told anyone . . . a whiteman . . . about mine. You were the only one I ever broached it to . . . and you laughed . . . . '

'I didn't exactly laugh, Bill. I just told you to cut out the bullshit with me. I realize now that you did me a great honour. It *is* hard. I couldn't tell any whiteman but you . . . doubt if I could tell even a blackfellow yet. So . . . if you don't mind. . . . '

'No, Jerry . . . I reckon it's up to you to tell me yours first. By the way, it wasn't any *moomboo* I saw. A *moomboo's* a spirit, either good or evil. This was something different. Right . . . what'd you see?'

Jeremy took a swig first, took a little while to get going, gazing away into the moonlit scrub, as if conjuring the scene again: 'Well . . . I was camped in a bit of a wash up on the Plateau last night. I'd been sound asleep some hours . . . tired after a long day. It was about midnight when I woke. I'll swear I was awake when I saw it . . . wide awake. I remember distinctly how I lay there staring at it, trying to figure out what it was. I'd remember the face again. . . not the face of anyone I knew . . . a blackfellow's face . . . truly Aboriginal, and with all the beauty and nobility you can often see in the faces of some of them.' Jeremy stopped to take a deep breath.

Billy drew a deep breath, too, leaned forward, beard upthrust, eyes wide with staring. Jeremy only glanced at him, then away again: 'He was tall . . . taller than any man I've ever seen . . . and blacker. He was standing with arms folded, looking down at me. I could see the glint in his eyes. His skin shone like polished boot-leather in the moonlight. I wasn't scared . . . only startled . . . just as when someone you know comes on you suddenly. I was even going to ask who he was. I just opened my mouth to do so . . . when he . . . well, he just wasn't there . . . only the empty sky. But so convinced was I that it was real, that I got up and looked for tracks. Nothing, of course. An apparition.' Another deep breath. Then Jeremy looked back, to see the eyes fairly popping at him. He added, now sounding matter of fact, whereas his voice was vibrant before: 'Well, that's all . . . except how it struck me.'

Billy all but breathed the question, 'How did it strike you?'

'Tell me your experience first.'

Billy inhaled deeply. 'Nothin' to tell now . . . 'cause it was practic'ly the same.' They stared at each other. Billy broke the silence: 'Like I told you that time, I was camped on a waterhole over the Murranjai. The donks were a fair bit away, where there was grass. Moonlight. Just like you did, I find meself awake lookin' at this big blackfeller watchin' me. Real as real. Only thing is I *did* speak to him. I asked him, "Who're you?" Then he vanished. I was so certain it was someone, that I roused Ninyarra, who says right off it's a *Lamala* . . . what the mob over your way call *Yalmaru* . . . a man's second Shade . . . *my Lamala.* I want him to look for tracks. He won't look. He explained to me how your *Lamala* or *Yalmaru* doesn't live in your body, like your ordinary Shade, the one you're born from, your soul . . . but a familiar spirit that attaches itself to you through all your lives, to look out for you, warn you of danger, tell you what to do in trouble. Not so silly when you think about subconscious and unconscious and all that sort of modern stuff, which's only dealing with ancient things. The only thing was . . . How come I, a whitefeller, to get a *Lamala*? That's what I asks Ninyarra. He says, "Now properly you belong country. That *Lamala* belong to some old blackfeller before, finish now for good. He lonely. He grab'old o'you. Now you all-same blackfeller . . . belong country!"

Jeremy drew a long shuddering breath, breathed it out, repeating the words, 'Belong country!' He looked half around, into the distance, murmuring, 'That's what struck me . . . if I see things like a blackfellow, then I must belong like one.'

'Yeah . . that's it . . . belongin'. I used to feel ashamed o' belongin' . . . even with halfcaste kids. Livin' in a blackman's country, with blackmen . . like a parasite. After that experience I felt completely different.'

'I do, too . . . sort of at peace with it.' Jeremy reached and took up a handful of dust, let it fall, sparkling in the moonlight, through his fingers. Then he asked, 'Tell me . . . did you ever see your . . . your *Yalmaru* again?'

'Not like that. But I sort o' know he's round all the time. Sometimes I nearly catch sight of him . . . sort o' vanishin'. He speaks to me, too . . . in my mind. It was him told me to look out for young Prindy.'

Staring into the staring eyes, Jeremy murmured, 'How wonderful!'

'You know Shakespeare, Jerry . . . 'Amlet? "There are more things in 'Eaven and Hearth, 'Oratio, than dreamt of in your philosophy".'

Jeremy shot out his hand. Billy gripped it.

'Countryman!' whispered Jeremy.

Billy Brew breathed it back, 'Countryman!'

Then, releasing each other's hands, they grabbed for their pannikins, drank.

Book Three

DAY OF SHAME

CHAPTER TWENTY-ONE

SURELY in the history of human affairs, never were the changes rung more rapidly nor with further-reaching percussion than in the year 1939. How, otherwise, could occur a circumstance so drastic in its little way as postponement of the Beatrice River Races? In that Year of Destiny, what a lot of postponing of events long established there must have been – and not simply to a Date to be Fixed, as the Beatrice Race Club's announcement stated; but forever! As a matter of fact, the Beatrice Races need not have been put off at all. It was only that the Committee agreed that they ought to Make a Gesture in view of the Seriousness of Things. Not that anything really serious was happening thereabout. The trouble was a good ten thousand miles away. Still, that's the way the Committee felt. They didn't go into it. They didn't have to, being all of one mind in such matters. The implication was that if they didn't make a showing of some sort they wouldn't have been doing the Decent Thing. We were at war again – or at any rate, Old England was, which amounted to the same thing.

As to the Seriousness of Things, the event that precipitated the war in Europe – that most astonishing piece of political jugglery, the suddenly declared Non-agression Pact between the former arch-enemies, Hitler and Stalin – in effect removed the threat of war in this region so much harped on of late by dismal Jimmies like General Sir Mark Esk, which is to say the expansion policy of the Japanese and their hostility towards the British Empire. So angered were the Japanese by the somersaulting of their ally in the bullying of weak nations, Germany, that promptly they broke the alliance, changed their policy to one much milder, and turned back towards their traditional friends, the British. If any proof were needed of how unwarlike things were on the Home Front, surely it was to be seen in the conduct of General Esk himself. Whereas, immediately on Britain's declaration of war on Germany, as Commander-in-Chief of the Australian Military Forces, he had hastened from the North to General Headquarters down South, excusing himself from the role of Patron of the Race Meeting again assigned him, here he was wiring to say that he would be returning to attend the festival after all.

The Meeting, formerly always held in the first or second week of September, eventually was fixed for late October. This put it to the hazard of the first thunderstorms. However, there was great compensation for the risk. At least, that's how most saw it. The interlude had encouraged a number of young men to offer themselves for enlistment in the Second Australian Imperial Force, a recruiting depot for which had been established at the Garrison, Port

Palmeston. Thus a very special feature of the festival this time would be the honouring of Our Boys, as the recruits were being called. Arrangements had been made for their being granted final leave to attend the Races before embarkation for the South to join the so-called Sixth Division. Although this Division was in fact the First, it was being called the Sixth with the idea of preserving continuity with the original AIF of 1914–19, which had consisted of five Divisions. The idea emanated from that august body of Lest-We-Forget-The-Gloryists, now called the Returned Soldiers', Sailors' and Airmen's Imperial League of Australia, or for somewhat short, the RSSAILA, whose idea behind it was that these young men already might feel themselves comrades of the scores of thousands of their kind of the last generation, of whom it was so truly stated on the Anzac Memorials and mouthed with boozy solemnity on the Day of Days, *They Shall Not Grow Old*. A goodly portion of the profit expected from the Race Meeting already had been spent on a so-far secret presentation to Our Boys at the Cup Ball, which, in effect, would be their Send Off.

Local lads who had become Our Boys were, in order of social grading, Clancy Delacy, Knobby Knowles, Ozzie Burrows, a young fettler named Tim Healy, and the younger of Tom Toohey's quarter-caste sons, Brumby. Although Martin Delacy declared that he would Give Anything to be in it, he was precluded as a married man, such not yet being accepted. Again, the General Managership of Vaiseys Australia had devolved on him with resignation of his stepfather, Sir Clement Eaton, to go home to England and rejoin his old corps, now with the rank of Brigadier. In much lesser degree it was the same with the Knowles Brothers. Nugget lately had married Miss Phyllis Lilyponds, former teacher at the Old Compound School, in which state of respectability he had been appointed to take Clancy's place as manager of Catfish.

Brumby Toohey's enlistment was motivated by more than patriotism. Vanishment from the scene of those worse enemies of his, Sergeant Cahoon and Tracker Jinbul, had emboldened him to pay a sneak visit to his parents. Then when recruits were called for, he saw further advantage in answering the call, since being a soldier would put him out of reach of civil law completely. That's how he declared himself to Jeremy Delacy when tackled on the subject. Jeremy said, 'You've beaten the bastards so far with your wits. Why risk your life to do it now?'

Jeremy should have realized that there was greater advantage in it for Brumby than he declared. An example was his being treated like a whiteman the night before the local boys entrained to go up to enlist and were fêted at Finnucane's. Apart from being coloured and a wanted man, Brumby was also not exempted from the Aboriginal Act in respect of partaking of intoxicaing liquor. It did look as if Constable Stunke would have said something about it, only for Finnucane's swift intervention. Finnucane declared, 'Shame on us, if a man who's considered good enough to foight for us can't take a drink wid us!'

Jeremy, who was present at that impromptu little send-off, subtly scored off Finnucane for what he said by remarking, 'Who's this *us* you're talking about, Shamus? I thought you were neutral.'

It was a fact that, at outbreak of war, old Shame-on-us, in his delight as an Irishman in Eire's asserting her independence of Britain by declaring herself neutral, had boasted a bit about the war's having 'Nowt to do wid me.' However, since then, patriots had been saying that those who were declaring themselves Irishmen first should be compelled to register as aliens. It was typical of Jeremy to have that shot at Finnucane. Still, it was done with a grin, which was returned, along with a general chuckle. Jeremy's amiability these days had been noted. He had not spoken out against the war as expected, even when provoked a bit by people like Col Collings and McDodds. As people said behind his back: 'The Scrub Bull's not nearly so hard to get along with these days. Must've been what happened to him down South. They must've de-nackered him or sumpin.' That was before it was heard that the lovely young Jew-girl was back at Lily Lagoons, when the old smirking innuendoes were resumed.

Rifkah and Prindy, along with Savitra Barbu in Rifkah's care, were brought across from the Leopolds by Fergus a week or so before the new date fixed for the Meeting. Thus Lily Lagoons was brought back to something like that bright life it had known during the spell of magic following last year's Races. Even if there is no recapturing magic, the glow of it remains.

Nanago would have handed the kitchen over to Rifkah again. However, the girl had no need of such a shrine as formerly. Cooking had ceased to be the essentially ritualistic thing it had been to her, since becoming aware of the primitive reality of food as basic means of survival. She told Jeremy as much, while remarking on the strangeness of the fact that while the people she came from were learning the same truth in the concentration camps now spread over the greater part of Europe, she herself had discovered it through rubbing shoulders with simple savages whose no-less precious ethos had been bludgeoned to the point where they sold their wives' bodies and their children's souls for food. The intensity of her feelings in the matter took the music out of her voice whenever she expressed them. It wasn't that she criticized anyone. She even praised the Mission for its dedication, even if it stole far more than it gave since its motive was ulterior. She did not damn the despoiling Japanese, even for spreading gonorrhea with the largesse, because, as she said, the whiteman did the same, but with comparative lousiness. Her own dedication was surely demonstrated by her disinterest in the war and even in the plight of the Jews suffering worst in it of all others, of whom she said, 'For five t'ousand year ze Jews haf suffered. Zey can take it, zose who suffer now. Zere are plenty more not suffering. Zey vill help ze ozzers . . . and all vill rise up stronger zan effer. But my poor black children . . . vot is zere for zem but extermination of ze spirit if not of ze body. Ze pox of Shinto is blinding ze babies, sterilizing ze muders . . . vile ze Blood of Christ . . . urrgh! but maybe I still haf old Jewish horror of blood as unclean. Moost I finish wit' old Jewish t'ing.'

Nevertheless, the household was treated to the miracle of fry-fish each Jewish Sabbath of her stay.

Otherwise Rifkah was preoccupied completely by day with the training of Red Rory, and also of herself in co-operation with him, because she was to ride him for the Cup. Such a thing as a woman's riding in any race but the occasional Ladies' Hack that got into the program, if there were a number of horsey women on the Ladies' Committee, was without precedent. Still, as Jeremy had told her when she named her jockey in applying for nomination of her horse, there was nothing in the rules against it. Only eyebrows could be raised in objection, and since she had not been asked to join the Ladies' Committee, no doubt these were already raised on her account.

There were two reasons for her wanting to be her own jockey – or rather, perhaps, just one twofold reason. She was almost frantically concerned about the horse's chances, which in the opinion of those experts, Jeremy and Fergus, would be greatly enhanced by her ability to handle him in the race, because his special liking for her decreased that worst of hazards against him, his unpredicable crankiness. However, the basis of her concern was her blacks. She wanted the money that went with the Cup – two hundred and fifty guineas.

Fergus popped in to instruct her whenever free from flying. He was not now flying General Esk, who since the outbreak of war had been accommodated thus by the Royal Australian Air Force. That suited Fergus, so he said, since he didn't want too much attention attracted to the aircraft he had literally purloined. He was doing well enough with private charter work, especially through the postponement of the Races, which had caused a number of people to seek his services to obviate the inconvenience of traditional modes of getting to the festival. Although he kept on telling Rifkah of his love for her, he had become sufficiently aware of her dedication not to pester her with it as he had in the past. He took training her as seriously as she did, knowing the horse and her purpose.

She wanted the money to buy two things she considered essential to the success of her vocation, namely, an easily portable and operable motion-picture projector along with some film, and a similar machine of phonographic-recording type. The first was to cause the blacks to attach themselves to her with no other motive than pleasure, the second to help her in the very difficult task of mastering their several lingoes. She had learnt at the Mission how, of all the things the whiteman had to offer, none delighted the blackfellow like the motion-picture. Evidently it didn't matter what the picture was about. The magic of seeing life reproduced on a screen was enough for complete enjoyment. Few tribes people of the Leopold District had seen pictures. However, the delight of those who had was such as to be one in which the rest lived in anticipation. She had got the idea from Father Glascock, who told her that he would like to have an outfit for showing religious pictures, but that the Hierarchy in its wisdom frowned on it as interfering with proper Christianizing of primitive peoples by reason of the suggestion of magic. He himself had no objection to her doing what she wanted, provided the films were not of any kind his superiors could object to or their showing in any way intruded on the Mission's purpose. While such apparatus ordinarily would be priced far beyond her capacity to buy it, she had been given to understand from a concern in the South with which she had corresponded that owing to the great advances made in recent times in the technology of the systems of cinematography and phonography there should be obsolete gear that one could buy quite cheaply. It was only a matter of finding out where to locate these old things. She wanted help in this matter; that is in the finding, but very definitely not in the matter of buying it.

She explained to Jeremy: 'Moost I not look like I am rival to Mission or Government . . . 'specially vit' help of Jeremy Delacy. If I do it myself, only zey can say, Mad Jewess . . . like Mad Daisy Bates. Zat I vont to be, also, to do all by myself. So zese people become my children . . . and I can votch over zem. Zere own pride I vont to save . . . from everybody. I vill cure zere body sickness if zey vill let me. But I vill not be doctor to zem . . . only Mumma. Moost I stop zat bloody pox. Zere you can help me. I vont your magic Suphanilamide, and all advice. Maybe, by'n'by, ven zey trust me as Mumma, you can gif me microscope. But ze ozzer t'ing moost I buy myself in my own vay . . . mad vay, zey vill say, and laugh. I vont Eddy McCusky to laugh. He haf been out to Mission to question me like ze Gestapo . . . "Vot you up to, you and zat boy and Jeremy Delacy?" he ask me. So you see. Only ze medicine from you . . . and by'n'by, two leedle donkey from Billy Brew for packing my picture-show round ze bush. You like it . . . yes?'

They talked like this on their evening walks. There was no clinging now as formerly, of lost little girl to love-starved father-lover. They walked arm-in-arm, but with circumspectness that baffled Igulgul ready to wink and silenced Kirrikijirrit ready to tell the world about it in song.

One night while they were walking and could see lightning flickering away to the northwest, Rifkah expressed fear of a thunderstorm on Cup Day to upset Red Rory. Jeremy laughed: 'Don't let that worry you. A thunderstorm could win him the race. He was born in one . . . as I remember only too well . . . because his mother nearly died delivering him, what with his size and her fright. I do believe he thinks thundery weather's the normal condition of things. If we happen to have a storm while we're training, just you watch the difference in his behaviour from the rest. He'll gallop with 'em. But you won't see fear in his eyes . . . his tail will be up instead of down. He enjoys thunderstorms, I'll swear. If you can't handle him on Cup Day, get young Prindy to call up his old mate, Tchamala . . . or doesn't he do that any more, since he's become a Missionary Man?'

A little stiffly, Rifkah replied, 'I tell you he is joost ze same. No matter he mek Sign of Cross at table, Jesus is only 'nother-kind *bijnitch* to him.'

Jeremy chuckled. Much of her talk was in Murringlitch these days.

Then, out of a little silence, he began, haltingly, to tell her of that experience in *bijnitch* he had that night on the Plateau. He gave no explanation, made no mention of the sequel, simply stated the facts, if such they could be called, keeping his eyes fixed on distance all the while, probably because aware of how intently he was being watched. When at last he turned to meet the jewel-eyes, wide and shiny, he said with a smile, 'Got to be quite an old blackfellow since you left, eh?'

She leaned on him then, saying with soft intensity, 'But zat is vunderful!'

'I'm glad you think so. I thought it wonderful, too. It's made me feel I truly belong here at last.'

'Ah . . . zat is ze difference I see in you!' Then, after a slight pause, she added swiftly, 'I also haf see.'

They stared at each other as they walked, closer now. She went on: 'Zat night on ze Rainbow Reef. I see ze Ol' Goomun-Ol' Goomun in ze sky. She is black, vit' red hair. I see her face plainly. It is ver' smooth and loffly. She . . . vot you call sign me vit' ze finger . . . beckon . . . beckon me to come. Zen she is gone.'

He signalled complete acceptance with a nod, then asked, 'Do you know they thought you were the Ol'Goomun when first they saw you?'

She smiled. 'Fader Glascock tell me.' Then, looking ahead as he had, she said, 'Tvice I haf seen . . . vun night at Mission ven I am trouble' because Sister Dymphna don't like me. Zat day she mek row about I tell children Bible Stories of Old Testament, so zey don't vont to hear about Jesus. Do I haf to go avay? I don't know vot to do, and valk on beach, and lie down and go sleep. Zen I vake at calling of my name . . . softly, like my *Bubbeh* use to call me in morning . . . *Rebkin, Rebkin*! I look . . . and zere from sea come ze Ol' Goomun . . . all shiny black now from vater, but hair like fire in ze moonlight. She stop back at vater. I can hear her vord but not her voice. She said: "Don't run avay. I vont you. I vill show you ze vay, like ze Bandicoot Sisters". Zen, like before, she is gone. But I am not dreaming . . . no!'

Now both were looking ahead, still close. After a while he asked, 'Did you tell anyone about it?'

'How can I tell it in Mission . . . vere superstition is vickedness?'

He gave a short laugh. 'Superstition! If you'd told them you'd seen the Virgin Mary come out of the sea . . . .'

'*I* also zink she might be ze Virgin . . . who zey call Star of ze Sea. She also is muder of ze vorld. But zis vun is black . . . and vy is Virgin come to a Jewess, Sister Dymphna vill ask?'

'The answer is that Mary was a Jewess, too.'

'You tell me before she is Greek.'

They both laughed. Then he asked, 'But why this trouble with Dymphna, when you say the priest himself likes you to tell the Bible stories and's become so interested in Judaism he's brushing up his Hebrew and going to study the *Torah*?'

'He does not know. He does not haf mooch to do vit ze vomen. Alvays he is ver' stiff vit' me, but kind.'

'Well what about the old girl? You say she's nice and kind to you. She's the boss. Why let the other make your life a misery?'

'It is not misery . . . not now . . . only for leedle vile, ven Dymphna is all-day vonting to argue about Christianity, saying ze Old Testament only keep people in darkness. I am only svopping my own tribal Dream Time stories vit' the blacks for zere's, she say. Mother Mathias belief zat, too . . . but she don't mind. It is true. So I stop telling ze stories . . . till by'n'by, I tell all-about.'

'What about Prindy . . . didn't you tell him about the Ol' Goomun?'

'He is being goot Missionary Man. Soon he vill be taking First Communion. I do not vont to upset him.'

'But you've both said you're going bush together later. How can he go with you if he's a Missionary Man?'

'Nefer properly vill he be zat. He is beliefing in Jesus only like vot he call Dat Lot On Top . . . like Tchamala and Ol' Goomun. He like ritual. He is mooch Tchinek Man, leedle bit Jew, leedle bit Christian. I promise not to interfere wit' zey mek him Christian. It cannot hurt him. You vill come to church in Town and see him tek First Communion?'

'Hell!'

'Please. Also . . . vy don't you tell him about how ze Shade come to you.

Zat vill be goot for him. Zat vill draw him close to you. He like you mooch as Mullaka . . . but still you are *kuttabah* to him. I zink if you tell him, he vill loff you.' '

'Hmm! I might do it, too.'

The opportunity for it occurred a couple of days before the household set out to make camp at the Beatrice. Jeremy and Prindy were alone together, training Golden Bobby to stand before the barrier, a thing he did not like doing. Bobby was to run his first race this Meeting, with Prindy Up, as they say. Jeremy was mounted on Elektron, who was helping to discipline the colt by nipping him occasionally. They were spelling the little horse, and remarking on a hint of thunderstorm away over the western Plateau. Jeremy reckoned the storm might reach them, seeing that the wind was blowing towards it. Prindy shook his head. Jeremy asked, 'Why're you so sure . . . because you're a Tchinek Man, eh?'

Prindy met the grey eyes quizzing him, nodded, answering shortly, '*Yu*.'

Jeremy pressed him: 'How can you be Tchinek Man and Missionary Man, too?'

Prindy answered, 'Das all right.'

'Yeah? Shade of that Old One still come to see you?'

'Sometime.'

Then, with eyes on the Plateau, Jeremy said, 'One time up there . . . after you go away . . . I was camping the night . . . and a Shade came to me . . . my *Yalmaru*, I reckon.' He turned to find the other grey eyes wide with interest. He went on, as if casually, to describe the event, while listened to with intensity that scarcely permitted blinking of the staring eyes. From looking away again at the Plateau, he turned in conclusion to ask, 'You reckon that *Yalmaru*?

Instead of answering, Prindy asked, 'What he say?'

'He didn't talk at all. Shade doesn't talk, does he?'

'Got 'o say sumpin. Don't come for nutching.'

'Well, he didn't.'

'He don't talk wit' tongue. He tell you inside head.'

'I see. Come to think of it, he did tell me something inside my head . . . something very important.'

The grey eyes met again and held for a moment. Then Prindy turned away, as if it were the proper thing to mind one's own business about other people's dealings with the occult. He said, 'We have 'nother-one go, eh? I reckon better let him turn right round himself first-time. He pig-headed bugger. Spone we let him do what he want first-time, might-be he do what we want after.'

'Might be good idea.'

II

Thus, despite what was going on out in what would be called the Great World – the murder and mayhem, the ruthless destruction of Man's kindlier creativeness throughout the centuries of his apparent rise above brutality, all in the cause of the urge of individuals and groups to prove themselves Second-to-None

– there again was the old familiar scene of Beatrice River township *en fête*, if so pretty a term might be applied to so mean a little show, really – the camps on the river, mostly built of dying boughs, the brawling dogs and swarming flies, the blowzy bushwomen, the hipless, toothless, lean, lanky, bandy bushmen – the dispossessed denizens of the region watching from safe distance, cockatoos, wallabies, goannas, goats, the cockies giving voice to what the others might be feeling, what all non-human animate creation might be feeling with them: *The bloody business is on again! Oh, when will Mankind die out and leave the world in peace, but, please, Creator, not in pieces?*

The people from the camps and the township were waiting by the Station for the train, for the arrival of the uproarious mob that would signal true beginning of the festival. As usual, they were talking of who would be on the train, or rather, of who they *supposed* would be, according to Col Collings who was supposed to know everything about a train once it left the Caroline. This had never been a place for secrets. Still, it was wartime, a time for secrecy, as Col Collings himself more or less stated in a notice stuck up outside his office door: HOLD YOUR TONGUE. THE ENEMY HAS LONG EARS. But every public office throughout the land had a notice like that, just as every sizable bridge had an armed guard on it. Rather were these things reminders of the fact that We Are At War, which a lot of people found exciting. Thus the waiting crowd were able quite openly to discuss the reason why the Military Band would not be coming this time. The information came from that advocate of the Held Tongue, Col Collings himself. Port Palmeston Garrison was alert because an enemy raider, a so-called Pocket Battleship, was believed to be prowling adjacent seas. Some asked: What the hell's wrong with the Navy? Others wanted to know didn't Britannia still Rule the Waves? Others again said it was bloody silly to involve the Band, when what use would they be with guns blazing, even playing the new hit which made rather a fool of the enemy: *We're going to hang out our washing on the Siegfried line, have you any dirty washing, Mother dear?* So it would be the Coloured Boys' Band again, as of old, augmented, so it was being said, by that Creamy Kid with his clarinet, who'd been entertaining the campers these last couple of nights. And could that kid play! Where'd he got it from – Delacy or Cahoon? Old Dinny had been musical.

Speaking of Dinny, meant talk of the Cahoon Sisters, who were also aboard the Race Train, bringing down the bronze Crucifix to be erected to Dinny's memory. There was to be a Memorial Service conducted by Monsignor Maryzic on Sunday morning. Some said it would be a fitting way for the festival to end, seeing that Our Boys would be departing immediately afterwards, perhaps to pay the Supreme Sacrifice themselves, as the elder Knowleses, here to greet and farewell their hero, Knobby, tearfully had said with a drop in. However, others, who may have had reason to remember Dinny Cahoon without the aid of a monument, declared it a damn nuisance, since it must cruel the binge with which the turn-out always ended and which they believed would be more to the liking of Our Boys.

Formerly it was always That Creamy Kid who heard the train first. But here was the war intruding again. The sentry on the bridge, being a good half-mile nearer and with a view up-line three times that distance, beat Prindy to it, as was evident from his coming out of his canvas shelter, and with bayonet flashing in the sunlight, taking a quick look round for lurking Huns. Then he stood himself in appropriate military style beside the track to show the driver that all was well. However, there could be no doubt but that the soldier, as the train came up to him and past, was surprised to see that this civilian train was being driven by one of his own kind. Still, since he was not a local man, the sentry could have been nothing like as much surprised as were the locals when they discovered not simply that the driver was a uniformed soldier but his identity. Naturally, it was those sharpest eyed though least considered ones amongst the waiting crowd who made the discovery, which they announced in sharp indrawn chorus – 'Patannaford!'

Sure enough, it was Pat Hannaford hanging out grinning under a slouch hat bearing the badge of the Imperial Force. Jeremy, standing with his household, stared as hard as any, but remarked, 'Surely wonders will never cease!'

As the engine came up it could be seen that actually it was in charge of that old war-horse, too old for warring now, Jack Tinball, who was letting one who formerely had mocked him for his militarism pull her tail for the auspicious occasion, while keeping a grimy hand on the khaki shoulder to show the world how things had changed. Pat waved vigorously to Rifkah beside Jeremy, and shouted that he would be along to see her. Then as he passed the gaping Collings, instead of giving him one of his old-time insulting salutes, he only winked. Thus had been kept the first secret ever to be brought down by train, no doubt because Pat had insisted on it to begin with, but surely also because of the sheer incredibility of it.

The boozy mob poured from the train, amongst them the other rookie warriors. Three of these latter were denied the heroes' welcome they would have got from the waiting crowd, except for a bit of cheering and slapping on the back, through being snatched immediately to maternal bosoms and whisked away. One of the bosoms was that still-trim one of Lady Rhoda, suddenly here as from nowhere in her big car, into which, with remarkable dexterity, she bundled her flushed, glassy-eyed, hoarse, unsure-footed Clancy, even while he was having his back pounded. No one had ever seen Her Ladyship expose herself to the common herd like that before. Mum Knowles did similarly but with much less finesse, not having it to start with and then a less broken colt to deal with. She fairly had to drag Knobby away, with the help of his brother, Nugget, also just off the train, down towards the Knowleses' camp. Behind them came old Ned, also somewhat the worse for grog, with the brand-new addition to the family, nee Philly Lilyponds, who by the look of her was not that proud of the family she'd joined, even if she might now claim to belong to the squattocracy. Tom Toohey had his trolley at hand to help his Possum whisk away their roaring soldier boy.

There were the Cahoon Sisters, still wearing the blackest black, being helped from the rear coach by fellow-travellers of the staider kind, like Kitty Windeyer, Monsignor Maryzic, and Superintendent Bullco. Most of the congregated policemen were also there to help, and Shamus Finnucane, whose concern was for His Very Reverence, as usual. There was another to help down, too – not animate, yet hardly to be called inanimate by what Shamus, doffing his hat when he saw it, would dub a Daycent Christian, and certainly not handled as such by the four policemen who took charge of it. The Crucifix, for sure, by the shape of it under its shroud, about half life-size. The Sisters went, supported, to another car from the Big House, waiting to pick them up, along with the Monsignor and the Superintendent. However, His Very Reverence, spotting the Lily Lagoons group, or perhaps more truly Prindy in his colourful Indian trappings, headed that way. Finnucane was coming with him, and Eddy McCusky, too.

The attention of the Lagoons people themselves was drawn by the precipitous arrival amongst them of Pat Hannaford. Although Pat took in the group with a wave and a wink, there was but one he was interested in. He grabbed Rifkah, kissed her, held her off to look at her and exclaim, 'You got thin . . . ain't they feedin' you?' He gave her no time to answer, telling her that he'd arrived back from the South only on Sunday's mail plane, that he'd enlisted while down there: 'To get even with them Nazi bastards for what they done to you and your mob. Heard you's here. So here I am. Got sumpin terribly important to tell you.' When she asked what it was, he answered, 'Strictly private.' He tried to draw her away. But she wouldn't go, telling him to come down to the camp with them. By that time the others were up to them. Pat scowled, and growled, 'See you later, then. Come to the dance with me.' He headed for the pub.

The others shook hands amiably with Jeremy and Rifkah and Nan. Monsignor concentrated on Prindy. 'So, it is a Hindu ve are on the eve of our First Communion, is it?' Eddy gave scant attention to Prindy, as if repudiating him, concentrating that official paternalism of his, hat over eye, on Savitra, even more brilliantly Hindu than her young husband. She clung to Rifkah to show how much she trusted her official Daddy-o. Kitty quite gushed over Rifkah, saying how wonderful it must be to work at the Mission, and how soon she hoped to be out there with her. Old Shame-on-us clearly was more concerned with what was going on up at his gold-mine without himself there at this richest moment of its yielding, trying to work the double by getting the company to come along and Have a Drap wid Me.

The little interlude was interrupted by the arrival of an aeroplane – not the Junkers nor Flying Fox's Moth, but a smart-looking thing wearing camouflage paint and the bull's-eyes of the Royal Australian Air Force, or rather of the Royal Air Force of Britain, since the former existed in name only. The aircraft, of light bomber type, circled the township at roof-top level, roared over the railway to reveal in banking the face of General Esk at a window.

The party broke up at that. Finnucane went rushing to his pub with Eddy, the Monsignor with Kitty headed towards the waiting car, the Lily Lagoons people down to their camp.

So the festival was on.

The dance that night was more than the poor little affair previously left to the humbler of the lower castes as their part in initiating the festival. It started as usual in that mean little way, but in no time, through what seemed to be sheer spontaneity, into a generally attended entertainment for Our Boys. Although the farewelling of the Boys had been well considered, no one concerned with organization had understood what was involved in their homecoming. Ostensibly they had come home to say Goodbye to home, while in effect they already had done that in going off to become soldiers. General Esk understood it, and perhaps had something to do with getting it going. He showed up at the Hall with the rest of the gentry, and shook hands with the Boys. It was really a great moment for the whole gathering. After all, was he not General Sir Marcus Esk, Bt, K.C.M.G., D.S.O. etc., etc., Commander-in-Chief of the Australian Army?

When Old Whiskers got the chance he sneaked away, to go down to the Lily Lagoons camp, where Rifkah told him Jeremy was, alone. By that time the old Hall was rocking to unrestrained dancing and singing of the music danced to, which was all of the war-variety, the newest with the oldest: *We're going to hang out our Washing on the Siefried Line, Kiss Me Goodnight, Sergeant-Major, Run, Adolf, Run, Keep the Home Fires Burning, Australia Will Be There, Tipperary.*

Whiskers, sipping brandy with Jeremy, said, 'In wartime, a soldier alone with civilians is lost. With even one other soldier he finds himself again. Young Clancy was a perfect example of it over there with his family. He would have clung to us . . only, he's already intimidated by rank, and, of course, our being Regulars makes a difference. Naturally his mother wanted to cling to him. I explained to her She's over there at the Hall now . . . seeing a very different boy from what she thought she had. You'd remember that sort of thing from the old days, dear boy?'

Jeremy answered shortly, 'I prefer not to recall those days.' When Esk responded with a slight cough of evident embarrassment, he added, 'You know how I feel about all this lunacy, Mark.'

Whiskers took a swig, drew a deep breath, said in a tone so short for him that Jeremy's eyes opened in inquiry, 'However you feel about it, Jeremy, you're involved . . . and rather more than you realize.'

The grey eyes grew wider. Esk coughed again, this time without the note of embarrassment, but rather with a hint of a forthright pronouncement: 'Just now when I arrived, you expressed surprise at my returning for such a seemingly frivolous purpose at such a time. You missed the point in my reply that I was here to see you. I meant that it's solely on your account I made the journey.'

Jeremy frowned slightly, was about to say something, when the General interrupted, saying quickly, 'I have to inform you, Colonel, that you're on active service.'

The frown turned to a gape. Then the mouth shut tight, to open again, snapping, 'What the hell's this?'

'According to the records, your resigning your commission was never ratified. Evidently things were rather anyhow at GHQ for some time after the war. Anyway, finding you on the Reserve of Officers, I promoted you . . . and posted you. . . .'

Flaming, Jeremy burst out, 'Well . . . of all the bloody cheek!'

Whiskers' lean handsome face could be seen in the bright electric light to flush. He answered somewhat curtly, 'Apart from the great good use I myself can make of you, but which only you can agree to co-operate in, there's the fact that your country is at war . . . .'

Glaring, Jeremy grated, 'My country has made no war with anyone . . . or, as far as I know, has had anyone declared war on it.'

Esk sighed as he said, 'Nevertheless, according to the constitution of this country of yours, you are involved in a war . . . and are liable under law to be declared a traitor to it if you refuse to acknowledge the fact . . . .' Esk's shoulders heaved with a sigh: 'Please Jeremy . . . regard me first as your friend. Even without military involvement, you're still bound to serve the War Effort, as they're calling it, under the new Manpower Regulations . . . or suffer the consequences. Do you imagine that your enemies aren't going to take advantage of the National Security Act to harrass you, if they get the chance? Aren't you much better off as a ranking officer under the wing of the Commander-in-Chief?'

Jeremy growled, 'I don't want to be under anyone's wing, thanks.'

'Notwithstanding your independence, you're under the shadow of war . . . with all the drastic things that can be done in the name of it. Won't you take my word for it that much of what I've done's been with genuine desire to benefit you rather than myself?'

Jeremy drew a deep breath. 'What is it you've done?'

'I found that the gang at GHQ had already put into operation their plan for regional commands, and that the GOC Northern had been appointed. There was no gainsaying it, without a first-class political row, because the new Prime Minister's behind them. The man picked for the job's an exceptional soldier . . . but of that war-anywhere-with-anyone type we've talked of as typically Australian . . . and hence in my opinion useless for the job. All he's doing is filling in time till he can get a division to take overseas. However, I could veto their machinations in respect to appointment of actual OC Troops for the region, because I had the very man, and their man's not so well in yet as for them to risk a row over him. So, with the substantive rank of full Colonel, you are 2-IC Northern. As soon as possible, you'll be raised to Brigadier, so that no one can out-rank you here. The force deployed into the region will be of brigade strength, nominally if not numerically to start with. How you handle things is a matter between you and your GOC. You won't have any trouble with him. He's pleased with the appointment . . . yours, I mean . . . to get it off his hands. There're two factions fighting it out to see who's goin' to be king of the castle. He's leading one, and daren't turn his back on the other. Guess who the chappy was whom I threw out for you?'

Jeremy, looking deflated by now, only staring and gulping the brandy he had twice replenished, muttered, 'I'm in no mood for guessing.'

'Our old friend Fabian Cootes. To all appearances he's a civilian, working as an expert on Japanese Affairs in the Department of Defence. Seems that during his academic career he did a short course in Oriental Studies, in the hope of landing a cushy job the Government was offering at the time for better relations with Japan. He missed out . . . well, for the time. I find, also, that he holds the rank of Subaltern with the CMF, evidently without even having attended a parade . . . another card up that sleeve of his to play when real rank is offering. He'll be the only one annoyed. The others are concerned only with mustering their precious AIF, and, as you would say, heading for the brothels of Alexandria at the earliest possible opportunity. They're not even bothering about anything but basic training before embarkation, saying that it's useless to train men in Australian conditions, when they might be required to fight anywhere from the African deserts to the Russian Arctic. They've already got tentative plans for embarkation of a contingent in the New Year . . . and this in spite of the Imperial High Command's telling me and my telling them that Australians will only be an embarrassment if sent over before called for. The Canadians will be supporting the BEF for a start.'

Esk paused to drink, then went on while Jeremy, haggard now, sat and stared at him: 'At the same time High Command tells me to be careful not to antagonize anyone with heavy objections. Thus they've been able to take things out of my hands rather, by forming this infernal Imperial Force of theirs. It's as if it were a private army. I'm only C-in-C Australian Military Forces . . . a completely different thing from a legal standpoint. While the AIF is composed entirely of volunteers and can go anywhere its C-in-C, whoever that's going to be, chooses, with Divisional Commanders responsible only to British High Command, the AMF is a conscripted army that can't be sent beyond Australian shores. Your men will be AMF. At least that should please you.'

They stared at each other. After a while Esk spoke again: 'If you don't want to do it, Jeremy, you've only to present yourself before the Military Board at GHQ and ask to be exempted on some ground that won't prejudice you as a civilian. You're not over age . . . because they've advanced the age-limit for service in field-rank to secure their own jobs. But you could say you feel too old for the responsibility. They'd gladly grant it to you, as a man of mine . . . if you don't mind that description.'

Again Jeremy sighed. 'Has one a right to mind anything said by a superior officer?'

'Will you not regard me first as your friend, Jeremy?'

For a moment Jeremy looked into the pale blue eyes, then nodded. Esk thrust forth his hand. Jeremy took it. Esk's face quivered slightly, and his voice was husky, as he murmured, 'Thanks, dear boy.' Then he seized his glass. 'Let's drink to it!'

Jeremy asked dryly, 'To what, exactly?'

Esk didn't have to answer. Footsteps and voices were approaching. Beyond the ring of light of the camp it was dark, with the Moon not yet risen. They could not see beyond the ring, nor those approaching see them, seated as they were. Then there they were – a man and a woman, the one in military khaki, the other in gay print. Rifkah and Pat Hannaford.

Pat halted, exclaiming, 'Eh, look out!'

He grabbed at Rifkah as she proceeded. She pulled away. He snapped at her, 'Okay . . . see yo',' turned to go.

'Jeremy called, 'Care for a drink, Pat?'

Pat looked back, grunted, 'Company's a bit too 'igh class for me.'

Jeremy glanced at Esk, who immediately took the cue: 'Join us, Soldier.'

'Yes,' said Rifkah, and turned and caught Pat's hand and drew him. He came ungraciously, scowling at the two men as they rose for Rifkah. Placing a chair for him, Jeremy said, 'I don't know if you two gentlemen know each other.'

'Yes, of course,' said Esk, but extended his hand.

Without responding, Pat said, 'We shook 'ands up the 'all.'

Whiskers kept his hand out. 'That was a formality.' Reluctantly Pat took the hand. Then, dropping into the chair, being asked by Jeremy what he'd drink, growled that he'd have beer.

Bringing a bottle from the refrigerator, Jeremy broke the silence that had fallen: 'Lot of water's run under your bridges since I last saw you, Pat.'

Pat looked at him suspiciously, but only came out with a grunt, 'Yeah.'

Jeremy mixed brandy and soda for Rifkah. Silence hung again, till he raised his glass, saying, 'Well, Pat . . . all the best.'

Still Pat could only grunt. He took a long pull at his beer. Esk asked him, 'What are you thinking of doing in the Army, Soldier?'

That roused Pat. He leered. 'Getting pushed round, I guess.'

'You don't get pushed round if you've got an aim in service.'

'Ain't the aim just to kill the other bloke?'

'The aim's to equip yourself to give the best service to prevent the enemy from overrunning you and forcing his will on you. You don't have to be in the front line killing. There're plenty of just as important jobs at the rear.'

After another swig of beer, Pat leered again. 'You make it sound like a picnic. Prob'ly is . . . up your end of it.'

The General's voice was even: 'You sound disillusioned already. How long have you been a soldier?'

Pat reddened. 'You don't 'ave to go soldierin' to know about militarism.'

'Then why did you join up?'

Because Pat was slow to answer, Esk added, 'You must've gone to some trouble about it, because up here where you're known they'd've turned you down as being in a reserved occupation.'

Pat snapped, 'I wan' 'o 'ave to go at them Huns.'

'That's the fighting spirit . . . militarism, if you like! But, tell me, isn't Having a Go at the Huns contrary to the Party Line these days?'

Pat's green eyes narrowed. 'What Party Line?'

'I understood you were a member of the Communist Party.'

'Who says I'm not still?'

'I'm merely showing personal interest, old boy. Like everybody else round here who's known you in your real job, I'm interested. How could you have joined the Imperial Force without disaffiliation from the Party? After all, the Communists are actively campaigning against enlistment.'

Pat swigged off his beer, then rising, snapped, 'Nobody tells me what I got 'o do, if it don't suit me . . . not even generals.'

Esk said quickly, 'That doesn't exactly tie in with your declared purpose for enlisting, my friend. After all, you can legally have a go at the Hun only under the direction of generals.'

Pat sneered. 'What's this Friend business in aid of?'

'Well . . . Comrade, if you prefer it.'

'You're shootin' the Party Line now!'

Still Esk's voice was calm and amiable: 'No, merely the military one . . . a more sincere one than the Communists' in respect, I'm sure. The Communist's comradeship is merely conventional. You can hate a fellow-traveller and still call him comrade. When a soldier uses the term he uses it in true brotherhood . . . even to an enemy in distress. All soldiers serving the same cause as myself are my comrades. Rank is only a degree of responsibility. They have it in the Red Army, as in any other . . . with much more enforcement of obedience to it, too, I understand.'

Pat answered with an off-hand, 'Yeah?' Then he added, 'Well, I'll be gettin' back to the 'all. Thanks for the beer, Jerry. See yo', Bekky.'

General Esk rose, saying, 'I'd like to come along with you.'

Pat looked at him sharply. 'Wha' for?'

'To prove that I'm your comrade, irrespective of rank . . . and perhaps to give you a tip or two about Army life. Had a lot of it myself, don't y'know. Any objections, Private Hannaford?'

Pat looked nonplussed, shrugged, grunted, 'Okay.'

Esk smiled at the others, saying, 'Be seeing you at the Races tomorrow, eh what?'

As the soldiers went off, Esk said to Pat, 'Hear what they're playing . . . *Old Soldiers Never Die*. Know what an Old Soldier means in military jargon? Not simply grown old in service . . . but one who knows the ropes, knows that the basic principle of army life is Good Order and Discipline, and how to get round it without losing your individuality . . . in point of fact, how to get round without being pushed around . . .'

As Esk's voice faded away with the two tall slim military figures, Rifkah remarked, 'He is nice, ze General.'

Somewhat shortly Jeremy replied, 'I haven't served under him long enough yet to know.'

She looked at him quickly. 'Vot means zat?'

He explained. She expressed her pleasure. However, he did not respond to it. He said, 'Although I think he's quite honest at heart, I can't trust him . . . because of his British Commonwealth, or Empire, or Heaven on Earth, or whatever it is . . . the British Sense of Destiny. It's the most powerful thing on earth . . . and the most dangerous . . . the cause of all the world's troubles. They're so Decent, to put it as they do, about everything. He did it more for my sake than his own . . . and I can't gainsay it . . . while I can't help thinking he might have cooked those records himself to catch me.'

'But is only for defence of Australia, you say he say.'

'There's nothing Australian about a Commission. It's the King's Commission . . . that's what it's called.'

'Ven haf you to start duty?'

'Not till I'm ready. I've got things to do at home. Besides, I don't want to get mixed up with that AIF gang at GHQ. Let them get out of the way first. Isn't it amazing, that after all that happened to us in the last wretched business, which everybody was aware of . . . the waste of men and money at the hands of utter incompetents . . . the country should be fairly rearing to get into the same lunacy! Even the same title . . . AIF . . . even the same silly cocked hat!' Jeremy heaved a sigh. 'And I thought I was free of it all!'

She laid a hand on his. Then, clasping the slim brown hand, he smiled, and said, 'But you're home early. What happened?

She explained that Pat had been pestering her all evening with a proposal of marriage, resenting her dancing with other men.

'But,' said Jeremy, 'He's still a married man.'

'He tells me zere is new law for soldier going oversea to get qvick divorce. He haf applied. Poor fellow . . . zat is vy he come back. He try to bribe me vit' allotment pay and don't have to go to bed vit' him . . . and pension if he get killed. He is desperate, because he haf lost a dream vit' zis Stalin business. He so mooch love Stalin before . . . like Christ, or Moses. Now he hate him like death adder.'

'What happened between him and the Commos?'

'He don't tell me straight . . . only zat he haf big row vit' Party Bosses. He say ze Party haf been fighting Boss all ze time, but now haf made ze new Bosses, vit' ze Death Adder on top. He alvays hate any boss, you know.'

'He's going to get plenty to hate now, from Lance-Corporals up. If you ask me, he'll do most of his service in the brig.'

'Brig?'

'Military prison. Like me to take you back to the dance?'

'No . . . I am finish'. Clancy vill only grab me if Pat not. He is ver' excited.'

'He doesn't want to marry you too, does he?'

'No. He is only showing off as soldier-boy. He is ver' proud of himself. Nefer before haf I see him so . . . vot vill you call it? . . . vell, joost proud, I zink. He is taking no notice of his lady muder at all.'

Jeremy sighed. 'That's the trouble with the rotten business. Boys . . . and men with boys' minds . . . suddenly become men through hero-worship.'

'He vood ver' mooch like to show himself to you as soldier-boy, I zink. He vos talking mooch about you. Vait till he hear you are soldier-boy too!'

'God help us!'

'You vill not be cruel to him?'

'What do you mean . . . as a colonel?'

'No . . . his fader. He is sure to come to our stable tomorrow. He say he vill. Please, you say you vill be kind to him?'

Jeremy clasped his grey head and sighed again. 'I can't give him a show of hero-worship. Being the sort of soldier he is, a colonial-oaf trapezing off to an imperial war isn't a hero . . . he's a fool.'

She took one of the hands as they were lowered. 'You vill not say zat to him tomorrow?'

Meeting the jewel-eyes, he smiled. 'No, dear, rest assured I won't.' Then, looking away hastily, nor'westward, where distant lightning flashed and thunder rumbled, he added, 'Looks like we could have a storm in the night. If we do we'll have to go over and see to the horses. Better have your rain things ready.'

It didn't rain. By morning all threat of rain had disappeared.

Next day's activities began with an odd little ceremony not listed in the official Program of Events. Not many people were involved in it. In fact, properly there were only about ten. The handful of others, who were those camped near enough to the river crossing to see what was going on up on top of the bank in the vicinity of the Cemetery and up and capable of seeing things so early in the morning after a lively day like yesterday, were really intruders. Amongst these latter, probably the most interested and certainly the first to pop up for a closer look and the smartest in concealing himself so as to keep on looking after the former showed resentment to the intrusion, was Prindy.

It was a gathering of policemen, the full force of those here for the festival, acting in quasi-military style, under the command of Superintendent Bullco. They had come, primarily, to cement the Cahoon Crucifix into the sandstone cairn already erected for it. This they had accomplished before being spotted. Now they were lined up before the edifice. Those in line had their back turned to the sticky beaks, but not the Superintendent, out in front. He quickly dispersed the intruders with a policeman's peremptory wave of the hand. Then he called his men to attention, smartly about-turned himself, that is to face the shrouded monument, and came to the salute, to be followed in this gesture on the instant by the squad. For seconds they stood thus, stiff as guardsmen. Then the commander dropped his hand, relaxed. Without further ceremony the lot of them broke into a mere khaki group and so went heading back towards their Cop Shop.

What was it in aid of? That's what the few peepers asked themselves. Why the privacy? One would think that if they were going to Bung Something On they'd do it at the unveiling ceremony. It didn't look like a rehearsal, in the case of which they would surely have done it several times. Was it some private sentiment – Coppers mourning their dead from their hearts, something they could not do in the presence of their enemies, the Public? Jeremy, and Billy Brew, who was camped with him, were those who discussed the matter thus analytically. Billy Brew's father, also, had been a policeman. Both confessed that they did not understand the policeman's mind, and spoke of the odd circumstance, which many a time they must have discussed during their long friendship, that policemen's sons rarely ever become policemen, that there's even something wrong with them if they do so, yet most policemen's daughter's become policemen's wives. Still, these two were no more interested in the event than anyone else. When, by the time the crowd had gathered at the Racecourse and it had become generally knowledge, it was the chief topic of conversation.

Another matter of general interest was the appearance of Lady Rhoda, not in the feminine finery that always had been an essential part of the festival for those who could afford it, but in the uniform of a Red Cross officer. Not that she looked less dressy. In fact, in tailored khaki gaberdine, offset with red tabs and a semi-slouch hat that was no common general issue but a piece of high-class Southern millinery, she made the dressed-up look overdressed. Nor did she sit out the day in state in the grandstand as hitherto, but went out amongst the common herd, chatting to all and sundry with gracious amiability, while shoving a Red Cross collection-box under their noses. No – it was *not* to all and sundry. She missed out the people of Lily Lagoons. Whether she would have done so, knowing that the head of the clan was now one of Our Boys, couldn't have been guessed. People had long ago given up guessing about her feelings towards him. Obviously she did not know. That was evident in the fact that Private Clancy made no mention of it when he came to the stables, ostensibly to have a look at Golden Bobby, being prepared for his race. Old Whiskers must have decided to leave announcement of the new order of things to Jeremy himself.

This was Jeremy's first meeting with Clancy in uniform. When Clancy came up to him, grinning with outstretched hand, he grinned back, saying, 'That fits you too well for a general issue. You must have had it altered.' Clancy swore he hadn't that it was just as he had, as he put it with pride in his voice for now being able to speak such language. Drawn it from the Q Store. Jeremy added, 'Then you must be the perfect soldier. They only make 'em in one size, worked out in accordance with military statistics.' Clancy liked that. Judging by his continued animation during the rest of his stay with them, it made up for his father's showing no further interest in his wonderful new condition, but stuck to the subject of horses.

When Clancy was gone, Rifkah smiled at Jeremy, saying, 'Zat you do ver' nicely. Everybody haf been telling him how good he look in uniform . . . but he could not be true 'appy wit'out his fader blessing.'

Jeremy, full of sighs since last night, remarked, 'I would have felt more like his father telling him that military statistics aren't concerned with a soldier's brains.'

All these strange new things, because two super-madmen on the other side of the world had decided to try their devil's luck together in a game with a thousand million other people's lives.

Nevertheless, when the show got going properly, it was just like old times.

The milling, boozing, vociferating mob. The dust. The flies. The prancing, whinnying horses. Jockeys' colours mingling with gleaming hides of mounts. Charlie Bishoff in his coat so gay. The Parade with thoroughbreds doing their stuff. The turmoil of silks and tossing manes and tails at the Barrier: '*They're off*!' – manes and tails and silks now billowing above a heaving sea of rumps and thundering surf of flying hoofs. All to disappear in its own dust – to reappear as a spectral cavalcade riding in the sky – to materialize on the home-run as bettors' hopes storming in to realization: '*Wonder Lad, Bonny Lassie, Maid of Montijinni, Brunette Boy, Golden Bobby – Golden Bobby – No, the Maid – No, it's Bobby – Come on, little 'orse – little Bobby – Golden Bobby you little beauty – Golden Bobby wins*!'

'Christ, can't that Creamy Kid ride!'

'All them Delacys's born riders.'

'Gern . . . Dinny Cahoon was a great rider, too!'

Prindy went, mounted, led by her he now called Mother, whose hair flaming in the sun as it fell from under her wide-awake, was exactly like that of the colt's main tossing in his striving to regain normal breathing, to receive congratulations from the President, as both owner and rider. He was grave. So was Mr President. The applause, both from mob and élite, was most hearty – perhaps not so much on account of owner-jockey's youth, as the President's squattocratic *aplomb* in dealing with his half-bred bastard, because there was whispering behind hands – 'Be-jeesus, they look alike!'

Then it was all over for the day – and just as well, with that inky storm-cloud rising. Once again the time-honoured rush over to the pub in a cloud of dust by the mob, and the more sedate withdrawal of the élite by the back road to the Big House and cocktails.

The evening was spent more normally, much as it would have been in the old days, with initial getting together of people, according to ideas of propriety, either at Finnucane's, the Big House, or the Dance Hall. The Lily Lagoons people stayed in camp, celebrating the victory of their young champion, with such odd company as Barbu, the Ah Loys, the Tooheys, Billy Brew. It came to an end with Tchamala's putting on the first real show of the season. For an hour the heavens cracked wide open, revealing chaos that rocked the very earth, turned streaming fire to sheeting water. So heavy was the downpour, that when it was over and the timid stars and hump-backed Igulgul came peeping out, the frogs came up out of their deep hide-outs and set up the Hallelujah Chorus: *De Wet has come, Now we have fun, Gi' money, gi' money, Two Bob*!

No dust tomorrow, anyway – even if the bush-flies would be worse and the marsh-flies also along to lend them a hand annoying people. Also, a nice cool night for sleeping, drunk or sober, with a partner, or alone.

Cup day began as anticipated. The marsh-flies emerged from their *pupae* in such numbers and so avid for blood that dung-fires had to be lit to protect the horses. Weather-prophets were saying that when the pests swarmed like that with the first storm it meant there would be thunderstorms daily till the end of the year, after which the rain would cease completely for the season. Others declared that the blood-hunters were no more numerous than usual, but only appeared so because of the unusual concentration of victims, that, in fact, the only sure indication of excessive early storms and a curtailed Wet was if the frogs began spawning with the first of them – and, look-see, no spawn in the puddles! – but yes, there was, take a look here – but a different kind o' frog – bet yo'!

Interest in the controversies betwen experts was taken lightly generally, until when in mid-morning a great cloud rose in the blue of the West and quickly took on the shape of a thunderhead. Then people began to bet not only on the races and their savvy of the species of frogs, but on whether or not a storm would break to cause cancellation of the Cup Race. The Committee rather spoil-sportingly intruded here by cancelling the last of the minor races, so as to advance the luncheon recess and the time of the running of the big race. Mean as it might be considered by some, it was a wise move. By the time the mob were guzzling Barbu's curries and Ah Loy's dim-sims with their beer, and the élite their tongue and salad and sparkling hock, the betting on rain within an hour was Odds-on.

The thunderhead was now fully formed and directly overhead, while the West was a black wall towards which, sure indication of a storm, spiteful little gusts of wind came blowing from the East to cause embarrassment to ladies by lifting their skirts and spoiling the enjoyment of gentlemen by snatching off their hats.

It was one thing to advance the time of the race to beat the elements, but quite another to get compliance in the matter from those who mattered most in the circumstances – the horses. The champions, already worked up by anticipation of what was required of them and irritated by marsh-flies and smoke, now disturbed by the condition of the atmosphere, were all playing-up badly. Worst of all was Red Rory, probably unconcerned about the weather, as Jeremy had predicted, but driven to such ill-temper by his old enemies the flies, that because of his attempts to deal with them once and for all, he had to be put in restraining harness to prevent him from tiring himself out, only to put him in worse temper. He wouldn't let Rifkah near him in her brand-new silks, maroon and silver, very nicely made for her by Nanago. Rifkah was in tears. Things looked so bad when they got him to the saddling-paddock that

Fergus said he'd better borrow an outfit himself and ride him. However, Rifkah insisted on going herself to the weighing-in. Then, as if having the saddle put on him made all the difference, Rory became more tractable. He took a sniff at Rifkah, nuzzled her a bit, let her mount him without objection. In fact it could be said that he was the best behaved horse in the Grand Parade, although that wouldn't be saying much for the others. As someone in the crowd on the rails yelled, 'Like a mob o' bloody brumbies yarded to be shot . . why don' you shoot 'em, Charlie?' Poor Charlie Bishoff looked as if he were trying to round up a herd of scrub bulls.

Other people on the fence were yelling to Charlie to get them off before it rained. Odds were fluctuating like the sudden little spiteful gusts of wind that embarrassed the ladies with their dresses. Rory, who as Favourite had been at odds-on and had reached Tens with his performance in the paddock now made a most interesting betting proposition. People were yelling at Rifkah to 'Bring the bastard in if you got 'o kill 'im!' They were calling her *Bluey*, from the copper curls popping out of her maroon cap. They were calling her the Jew-girl, too, amongst themselves, marvelling that a Jew could even mount a horse, let alone sit one as well as this female of the species.

'Didn't they use to ride asses, accordin' to the Bible, Jews?

'It's the Scrub Bull's taught her to ride.'

'Thought it was her teachin' him . . . eeeeeah!'

'Easy . . . he's just there with his mob!'

But Jeremy and his mob were too intent on what was happening out there in the Parade against the back-drop of blue-black, down the towering wall of which rivulets of lightning were running.

Charlie Bishoff gave up trying to get order for the start, gave the signal for it: '*They're off*!'

Half the field were facing the other way, Red Rory among them. But, electrifying as that cry is to a race-crowd, the effect on such is nothing compared with that on horses trained to the limit of sinue, heart, and nerve to hear it. The glowering mouth of hell could not have stopped the champions from swinging straight into stride. There they were racing – not in the colourful bunch of the usual start – but racing – strung out – manes and tails streaming and glossy hides agleam – and the billowing silks. Soon they were lost in the dust pounded out of last night's mud by other races. But this time there was no riding in the sky as they came into view on the other side. The back-drop showed them as a bright meteor trailing a red tail. So, round to complete the first mile, to go lung-roaring by into the telling second, bunched now, with no thought, no feeling, no purpose, but to get up there in front – in the lead, the lead!

Again the dust-cloud – the meteor – then the leaders on the home-run, coming up and up. Who was it out in front, in front? '*Red Rory, Red Rory – the Favourite wins*! *Good-on-you, Jew-girl*! *Whacko-the-diddle-o – I won a 'undred fids*!'

All while a giant black head hung above as if watching.

When it was all over, and the quiet of reaction set in, it was realized that the world was still – menacingly still. Eyes cocked to the sky. Everyone had an eye on the sky as the sweat-soaked Cup-winner with his lovely drooping-weary owner-rider was led by Private Pat Hannaford to receive the President's congratulations.

The President had barely said his little piece, was still holding the slender hand, when – *ZIP*! – a fiery spear ripped through the heavy air, and – *CRACK*! – like the Crack of Doom. A stunned moment. Then all the Bells of Hell pealed in echo.

People turned to look across the river to see what had been struck, since obviously it was something near the township. There was a babble of guessing. Finnucane's little power-house? God forbid, when it meant flat beer. The Hall? Then no Ball tonight. The Police Station was out of line of vision. The Cop Shop gone? Hooray! But there was little time for gawping or yawping. The black wall of the West had tumbled with the crash, releasing a silver wave now sweeping, roaring in across the course. Scramble for shelter, any shelter, even the sacrosanctity of the grandstand and its exclusive dunnies, even the tiny space of Barbu's booth.

One there was quite unconcerned about dodging the elements, standing out in Hindu finery as the rain came swamping down, grey eyes fixed on a point across the river located either by his exquisite hearing or some other still subtler sense. Prindy had been watching what was going on at the grandstand, standing on top of Barbu's van. Now he was on the flooding ground. He snatched off turban and silken slippers, tossed them into the van, then went racing away into the silvery chaos, following his nose towards that point.

He passed invisible stables where frightened horses were stomping and shrilling, entered the ghostly company of the river timber, went slithering down the bank. The river was boiling in the rain. He slipped into it, swam the few strokes to cross its little width, climbed out amongst the camps of the *kuttabah*, where their chained dogs raised angry voices above the roar of rain – *There goes a nigger*! Up the other bank – to that spot where yesterday the policemen had performed their secret ritual on their feet and this morning early the Cahoon Sisters on their knees.

The monument to Daddy-o? Nothing but a scatter of splintered stones and a hole in the ground from which steam was rising.

He approached the hole warily. It wasn't deep. Only a depression about some shapeless black thing. No – it was not shapeless. There to be glimpsed as the steam thinned, was a hand – extended – not shackled, but nailed – only a small hand, but so bespeaking in its gesture: *Oh, Sonny Boy*! So short a glimpse it might have been illusion – to vanish in a slide of mud.

The rain stopped dead. Ghost trees came back to vivid life with leaves gleaming silver in the sudden sunlight. Frogs were hopping, piping. Prindy looked round. All sorts of things behind trees, beginning to take shape as steam rose from the earth. He looked into the hole again. It had stopped steaming. The black lump was drowned under muddy water.

Over on the Racecourse motors began to roar. Prindy turned from the hole, began to race back down the bank. As he crossed the river again, he saw Finnucane's utility slithering down to the crossing, the Map-of-Ireland face twisted in agony, as if he were pissing himself over thoughts of a shattered power-house and hogs-heads of ruined beer.

He climbed again, went to the Lily Lagoons stable, where there was everybody, as well as Fergus and Pat Hannaford ranged alongside the slim red-haired figure in maroon and silver. All stared at him in surprise, as anyone would, seeing so bright a costume so bedraggled. Rifkah met the grey eyes, made the Aboriginal sign: *Where you been*? Prindy answered with twisting of the lips.

Jeremy, feeding Dextrose to Red Rory, had read the signs. When the grey eyes met his, he asked, 'What'd the lightning hit?'

For a moment grey eyes looked into grey. Then Prindy answered shortly, 'Coon-Coon.'

Dark eyes widened. Audible intake of breath.

Jeremy pressed the question: 'The Crucifix, eh?'

Prindy nodded. Now the lighter eyes widened. Pat Hannaford's green eyes then squinted with cynical amusement, and he said, 'That'll kill the old girls.'

Jeremy said, 'Wouldn't mind betting it kills the rest of the shivoo.'

'Why should it?' Pat demanded. 'It's nothin' 'o do with the mob.'

'Mob's not running this. If I know the Committee, they'll have a meeting and solemnly declare that as a gesture of sympathy to the old girls, there'll be a purely formal gathering for presenting the prizes – no Ball. Old Shame-on-us'll probably cancel his Winning Owners' Dinner, too . . . so you two chaps can stop arguing about who's taking Rifkah.'

'Bloody lunacy,' growled Pat. 'On account of a silly effigy.'

Jeremy said dryly, 'You ought to know there's been an awful lot of bloody lunacy . . . literally bloody . . . on account of that same effigy. This one's only a bit more loony, because the old girls've probably got Christ mixed up with Dinny by now.'

Jeremy was probably right about the Committee, but, as it turned out, quite wrong about old Shame-on-us. When Finnucane heard the news, at the same time hearing that it had not yet reached the Big House, he wasted no time in taking charge of the situation. He telephoned Lady Rhoda, and in the process of telling her of the dreadful event and predicting the effect of it on the Sisters, dropped the hint that, as tonight's proceedings were very special in the way of being mostly concerned with Our Boys, it would be no crime to keep the Poor Unfortunates in the dark about it till tomorrow. Her Ladyship agreed. She said she'd heard enough of their grieving already. Even over in the quarters Clancy had given up to them they could be heard crying themselves to sleep every night. However, she insisted that Shamus himself break the news to them, and do it early in the morning so as to beat them to going to pray there again as they had this morning. Poor dears would not be coming to the Ball, of course.

Thus was Cup Night saved for Our Boys as a memento of what happy things they would be fighting for. The other memento, kept secret right up to the moment of Lady Rhoda's opening the box, was a gold wristwatch for each, inscribed with the Race Club's arms. Fortunately she had ordered a couple more than there were Boys already enlisted. Thus Pat Hannaford got one, too, along with an aristocratic peck on the cheek that so obviously embarrassed him that the crowd laughed.

Other interesting interludes were, to begin with, presentation of the Cup to the Jew-girl, who looked so lovely in fluorescent green taffeta with the copper mane, that the louts outside expressed appreciation in a popular new form of doing so called Wolf Whistlin'. General Esk, as Patron, kissed her with rather more warmth than seemed patronly. The President looked as if he might have done the same, but for the hard watchful blue eyes of his mother beside him. Pat Hannaford and Fergus Ferris came near to a tussle to do just that when, with that smile of hers, she came away from the dais with the Trophy and the Cheque.

Lady Rhoda's eyes were just as watchful when Martin presented his Bastard with the Trophy for the Novice Stakes, perhaps because that one in his golden beauty looked even eatable by anyone who had any feeling for him. Certainly Prindy was chewed up a bit by others, females, that is, including Kitty Windeyer, before his little wife, resplendent in Indian costume, shoved in and snatched him away.

Then there was Knobby Knowles's drawing the prize in the Lucky Horseshoe sweep, a handsome little filly. It wasn't simply that Knobby had made his reputation as the Unluckiest Poor Bugger in the World, through having declared it so often, that made a special interlude of it, but that his exuberance caused what was really the only unseemly event of the evening, at least in public. Knobby's new sister-in-law, Philly, had been Horseshoe Seller this season, and hence the caller of the winner's name at the drawing. When Knobby, who was rather drunk, heard his own name, he whooped for joy, came bumbling in, and burbling, 'You lil beaut,' grabbed her and kissed her. She smacked his face. Later on, outside, Mum Knowles, also under the influence, smacked Philly's face and called her a Stuck-up Bitch. Nugget took Philly away weeping.

The only unseemly event, with so much grog flowing that the music of Finnucane's till never ceased till two a.m. Clever old dog, people said about Finnucane, when his saving of the night for their enjoyment was discussed. He himself, despite that music, remained lugubrious, declaring that he didn't look forward to the payment he would have to make for it all tomorrow morning. But that also only made people laugh. Was ever there one who could break bad news as tactfully as old Shame-on-us? The tale of him and the Rigger's Widder was resurrected. Billy Brew told it best: 'When they was buildin' the railway bridge. This rigger . . . terrible booze-artist . . . falls off and gets himself killed. They left it to old Shamus to tell his wife, 'cause, after all, he was the one most benefited by the bloke's bein' in these parts. He puts on his best dark Southern clothes. When the widder seen him and how solemn he looked, she thought he was there 'cause the money her old man owed him. Old Shame-on-us grabs his chance, talks about what a hard life she's had with a man like that, and really how much better off she'd be without him, 'specially as they was havin' a whip round to give her a benefit. When she woke up to it, she was so well prepared, she only blinked . . . and then thanked him for his trouble. He used to brag about that for years. You were always on a free drink askin' him about it.'

Shamus duly did his duty early on Saturday morning. However, according to subsequent reports of the performance the Cahoon Sisters put on and the fact that the master-of-tact had to get Monsignor Maryzic to help him out, it wasn't anything like as easy as the Rigger's Widder's case. Nevertheless, thanks to old Shame-on-us, the festival was saved completely for the festivity it of all others demanded. Soon after the news was broken to them, the Sisters, along with Monsignor Maryzic and Miss Kitty, were whisked away to Town aboard

Fergus's plane. Thus did Saturday go off normally, with its Blackboys Races, hilarious Boozy Sports, and the rest of it, and the free-for-all dance to wind up.

There were several fights at the dance, most interesting being that between the Knowles Brothers, over Philly and the Filly. When Nugget heard that Knobby was going to give the little mare to Selina Ah Loy, he asked for it for his wife, only to be told something so unpleasant that they were soon at it. However, as usual they finished up in each other's arms, weeping, but this time with more than boozy tears, because Knobby said he had a Feelin' he'd Never be Comin' 'Ome. Then there was a bit of a scrap between the two ladies in question over who in fact now owned the filly. Mum Knowles settled it by snatching off her old man's belt and putting Selina to flight for what she called a Chinee-whore. Clancy, the only representative of the Big House there, went off after Selina to comfort her. Prindy, a member of the Coloured Boys' Band, also made a hit with his solo playing of old favourites: *Waltzin' Matilda, The Road to Gundagai*.

Next morning the mob for Town were poured back onto the train in time-honoured style. The only difference was that the departure was also honoured by distinguished company to see Our Boys off. All the Big House big-wigs were there. Lady Rhoda embraced, her own soldier-boy, blinking while his face wobbled, and Selina Ah Loy wept frankly behind a pile of sleepers. Pat Hannaford embraced and kissed Rifkah and told her he'd be back to marry her: 'So don' go doin' it with any other bloke!' Then he climbed aboard the engine with Jack Tinball. Jack had to get her away, since it was always a delicate business with passengers likely to fall off with the slightest jerk, and Pat was only sober enough to blow the whistle. But how he blew that whistle! He had his old mate, Porky Jones, bent on the shovel giving him steam for it right out of sight and hearing.

The Lily Lagoons people had just got back to camp, when General Esk, who had been with the Big House party, came down and drew Jeremy aside, saying, 'Haven't seen much of you, dear boy . . . thought you'd prefer it. Something important, however. Hope you won't mind . . . but, assuming that you'll be wanting to use Lily Lagoons as something of a base, I'm having a powerful radio-set brought back by Fergus . . . There'll be a Signals man along to install it. Any objections?' Jeremy only shrugged. Esk went on: 'I'm sure you'll be glad of it eventually. It'll put you directly in communication with people that matter. Another thing . . . as I'll have to be installing myself rather more permanently at GHQ, I'd like to have you accompany me over the ground I've covered in working out the defence strategy. Quite likely you might have your own ideas. As it's your job, essentially, you're at liberty to reorganize as you please. Still, I'd like to have it on paper. We could do the trip, with Fergus, while the set's being installed.'

Jeremy said he had promised Monsignor Maryzic to have Prindy in Port Palmeston for his First Communion next Sunday, and intended going himself, along with Rifkah, and then delivering all back at the Mission.

Esk said, 'I know, old man. We'll all go together. If I get the set down tomorrow, as I hope, we can start our survey at once. Fergus will drop in for me at Beatrice Station. I'd like to proceed straight out to your place.'

'Just as you like . . . Sir.'

'That'll do, Jeremy. There's going to be no rank between us at any time. I've told no one about your appointment. Have you?'

'No . . . Mark. I'd rather it just leak out . . . if it has to. It mightn't come to anything at all.'

'What d'you mean by that, old boy?'

'Well . . . already they're calling it on the radio Twilight War, Phoney War. It may be no more than an adjustment between Hitler and Stalin, and token on the British side. Could fizzle out.'

'Nothing as complicated as this can fizzle out, Jeremy.'

'Maybe . . . but nothing so alienly complicated can involve me, Mark. I'm in this purely for the defence of my country, you know.'

Esk nodded, putting an arm about Jeremy's shoulder and patting the other, saying, 'I know, dear boy. Well . . . cheery-o, I hope, only till tomorrow.'

III

Things turned out as General Esk said he hoped they would: which is to say that Fergus, bringing the military radio for installation at Lily Lagoons and the military man to do the job, picked Whiskers up at Beatrice Station the day after the Race Meeting wound up, and brought him across to the Lagoons homestead. It also turned out that more than Whiskers's hope was involved. Within twenty-four hours of the arrival of the aircraft, by which time it had gone again on that tour of inspection planned for himself and Jeremy, Rifkah was saying that the soldier there to install the radio, one Signals Sergeant Sims, had come in answer to her prayers.

Sergeant Sims, a fleshy gingerish man, no more than twenty-five but well on the way to baldness it was revealed when not wearing his badged slouched hat, was not introduced to the household, nor really into it. Ignoring everyone, he gave himself immediately to his task, proceeding to the annexe when told that's where the radio-room was, not simply to work, but also to eat and sleep there; until, at least, his military superiors were gone. It was his attitude to military superiority, in this case General Esk, Major Maltravers and newly promoted Captain Dickey, that was responsible for his complete withdrawal. This was known from the start, explained by the General to Jeremy when the Sergeant brusquely declined full hospitality of the house. Whiskers said briefly, 'He's got this Australian thing about rank rather badly.'

Relieved of This Thing by departure of the cause of it, Sergeant Sims showed himself to be anything but the stiff-neck he first appeared to be. When Nanago made the same offer as Jeremy, he accepted with alacrity, and entering the Big House for his first meal there, introduced himself to the assembled company – Rifkah, Prindy, Savitra – in military style: 'Sigs Sarge Sims,' adding, 'Better known as Dim-sim, Zig-zag-zim, or just plain Sarge . . . take your pick.' They laughed. After that he made them laugh a lot. He himself was always either laughing, singing, or talk-talk-talking. When they showed they were puzzled by the change in him, he explained his attitude to rank: 'First thing you learn in the army is your place. An officer's an officer . . . an OR an OR.' Asked what OR meant, he replied, 'Other Ranks, according to the book . . .

but in the minds of officers, 'Orrible riff-raff . . . hohoho!'

Sims was well spoken and knowledgeable in many ways, in particular in those of his calling. He wasn't simply a military signaller, but a trained electrician. On learning of Prindy's interest in electrical phenomena, he took him under his wing, made him his assistant in setting up the new radio. It was when, during his first evening in the lounge in the Big House, he was asked by Rifkah if he knew anything about the showing of moving pictures and he replied, 'Just about everything. You might say I cut my teeth on movie films,' that he was declared the answer to a prayer. Thereupon he began to call himself, The Answer to the Maiden's Prayer, a name he used often and with evident pleasure.

Obviously he was smitten by Rifkah. However, it was not simply to impress her that he claimed to know everything about cinematography. With evident truthfulness he told of how his family were in the moving picture business in a small way, engaged in the itinerant form of it called Country Circuits. He said he'd got to know the faces of the filmstars of his childhood before that of his old man. He proved this by mimicking Charlie Chaplin, Harold Lloyd, Rudolf Valentino and others, to the delight of his audience. When he heard what it was Rifkah wanted, he declared that it was as good as got. The first thing he would do when he got the radio going, which he expected to do experimentally by next day, he would call Sigs Sarge Solomon, a mate of his at Sigs HQ (and, as he put it to Rifkah, 'One of your mob') and get the ball rolling. He knew people in the motion-picture equipment trade. Such out-of-date gear as Rifkah wanted could be had practically for the asking. The biggest expense would be the cost of freighting. They might as well arrange to have it sent by mail-plane so as to get it while he was still about to set it up for her. Part of his duty while here in the North, he said, would be to inspect the radios at the Mission stations, all now under military authority.

Sims and Rifkah talked of little else but the movie outfit. She didn't give him a chance to do otherwise, never letting him get her alone. His amorousness, expressed in singing love-songs at her, in rarely looking anywhere with those pale blue eyes save at her, was only too plain. To make it plainer still, he talked about it to Prindy while they worked on the radio: 'Never saw anyone as beautiful . . . or so nice in every way. My family's strict Catholic and'd throw fits over me wanting to marry a Jewess. But blow 'em. Anyway, you never know, living out on the Mission there, and you a Catholic, she might convert. Put in a plod for me, mate. I'll take you, too, as my son. After the war we'll start an electrical contracting business in Port Palmeston. Good opening there, I reckon. I'd apprentice you. Tell her that . . . and for christ sake, mate, make yourself scarce tonight, so's I can get her alone to put in a moan for myself.'

Prindy reported all this to Rifkah. She only giggled, and saw to it that if Prindy made himself scarce as requested, Savitra took his place as gooseberry.

Despite the discouragement, Dim-sims, Zig-zag-zim, or The Answer to the Maiden's Prayer, never appeared downcast, and just as eagerly talked of Rifkah's picture-show. He had an ingenious scheme for making the outfit the simple portable thing she wanted. He said, 'You've got to have good light for good projection. But lumen requirement is proportional to distance of projection and screen area. *You* need project only a few yards onto a bit of a sheet. I've seen small projectors, like churches use for showing religious films, fitted with ordinary incandescent globes. Course they used to use the magic-lantern . . . slides with an oil-lamp. It's reflection that counts. But you don't want to be carting round kerosene in the bush. You want electricity, and without batteries or any generating power but hand. I once saw a travelling preacher with a projector with a ten-watt dynamo geared to the crank. Took a bit of turning. But I reckon, that with a good reflector you could do it with five watts . . . which is what those little bike dynamos give. All you need's a bit of a bike and someone in your audience to crank for you. Soon's we get to Port Palmeston I'll have a rake round the bike shops.'

This happy state of things lasted four full days. It ceased suddenly on the Friday afternoon, with return of those snakes in this soldier's arcady, the officers. By then The Answer to the Maiden's Prayer was so enamoured of the maid that he was telling her himself what an asset her natural Jewish astuteness would be to that business he was going to start in Town and how he would like to leave his Sigs Sergeant's pay, along with a dependant's allotment meantime and how, in fact, he might overcome his prejudices in the matter and try for a commission. Yet, even the savour of her fried fish in his soul and anticipation of eating it by the light of Sabbath candles, could not overcome that Thing he had about rank, which immediately drove him back into seclusion in the annexe. When Rifkah came, along with Prindy, to ask him to join them at her 'leedle *Shabbos*', for the first time he sounded other than the cheerful soul they'd known, grunting, 'Eat with a General? It'd choke me!'

Next morning, after breakfast in solitude, Sergeant Sims marched himself across to the Big House, and in military hob-nails bashed to attention in the front doorway of the lounge, barking at those within, while looking at no one, 'Sigs Sarge Sims reporting!'

The lounge was lively with preparations for the departure for Town. Luggage was being stacked ready for taking to the air-strip. Everybody looked at him in surprise. He stood like a guardsman on parade. General Esk broke the silence, saying amiably, 'Good morning, Sergeant . . . all present and correct, I take it?'

Still without meeting an eye, Sims barked, 'Previous orders carried out. Further orders?'

'Thank you, Sergeant. We'll be leaving in an hour or so. If you'll be good enough to pack your kit . . . .'

'Sir!' Sims about-turned himself with crashing boots, marched off.

Esk shook his head. 'This Australian attitude to rank never ceases to amaze me.'

Jeremy said, 'As I've told you . . . the easy-going Anzac is a fiction. This Thing, as you call it, is a complex. It's all the same, whether expressed the way you've complained of with the Garrison people, all rushing round saluting you, sycophantly . . . or cheekily, like Pat Hannaford, or embarrassed, as in the case of Clancy . . . or veiled hostility, like this man . . . it expresses only one thing . . . a deep feeling of inferiority mingled with resentment.'

Esk sighed. 'Thank heavens I've got you to deal with it.'

'Me? I'm all the types rolled into one.'

'All the better, dear boy.' Esk patted Jeremy's shoulder. 'Well . . . I expect we'd better be marching.' He turned to clasp Nanago's hand. '*Au revoir*, dear lady. Hope it's not long before I shall be seeing you again. Meantime, God Bless!'

Sergeant Sims literally marched himself to the airstrip. When his superiors turned up later in the utility and truck, he lined himself up as if to give the General Salute. However, the General took no notice of him. Still he stood with military propriety, At Ease, kit at his feet, awaiting embarcation orders. Perhaps it was only because none of his superiors bothered about him; but his regimental attitude collapsed on the instant when Rifkah called him to come. He fairly leapt out of the military strait-jacket, snatched up his kit, came running. She told him they would sit together.

That was The Answer to the Maiden's Prayer's first chance to be alone with the maid. Virtually they were alone in the crowded cabin of the aircraft, since that is the way of individuals or pairs in flight, pocketed in space, as it were. He gave himself with vigour to what he called Putting in a Moan, telling her how much he liked her. She had to lean to hear above the roaring engines, whereupon she would lean away again, to look out of the window, and maybe to direct his attention to something more important: a mob of brumbies, a herd of buffaloes, a flight of ducks or cockatoos.

For most of the flight they were in the hands of that young master of so many arts, Prindy, who although directed by Fergus, most likely was following the Shade flitting over hill and gulley just ahead of them. The Shade left them when, on arrival at Palmeston Airport, they turned over Blue Mud Bay Jail to go in to land, seeming itself to dart into the jail.

Lieutenant-Colonel Chivvy was waiting with a staff-car and a stiff salute for the General and a stiff bow to Jeremy that hinted he must know something of what lay below the civilian clothes. He would have taken General and Colonel with him, only Jeremy declined. Esk and his aides went off with him. For Sergeant Sims there was a utility-truck driven by a soldier of equal rank. Zig-zag himself clung to Rifkah as long as possible, assuring her that he would get after those bits of bikes at the earliest opportunity, and asking with a last gasp as she got into the taxi with Jeremy, Prindy, and Savitra, if he might take her to the pictures tonight. With a smile she assented.

In the taxi they went first to the Catholic Church, to drop Savitra at the convent into the care of the Mother Superior, who smiled very sweetly at Rifkah, then to Mission House, to give Prindy into the outstretched hands of Monsignor Maryzic. Rifkah took Prindy back for a moment from His Very Reverence, to draw him to her breast and droop her head over his head while smoothing his back, as Aboriginal women do in parting with young sons. The old priest watched closely, as if seeking significance in it – this Jewess handing her son over to Edom and doing it like a black gin!

Jeremy and Rifkah left Prindy, saying they would see him in Church tomorrow.

A Jewess and an Atheist in Church tomorrow to see one almost as notorious for outlawry as Ned Kelly and past-prentice to a Witch-doctor take his First Communion? 'Would the roof fall in', as the common herd would say?

Jeremy and Rifkah went on round to book in at the Queen Victoria Hotel. Mrs Morgan, the proprietress, soon stopped the bawdy whispers it started in the bars: 'A gentleman like Jeremy Delacy and a nice sweet girl like that? A double room, indeed! And as if I'd have such goings on in my house!'

IV

On Sunday morning the Catholic Church was packed for First Communion Mass. It always was so on such occasions, but more so on this because the Bishop was new. Quite glorious the Bishop was to look upon, robed in ivory and silver with a touch of scarlet, with the gems in his mitre sparkling in the blaze of altar candles like the Stars in the Crowns of the Saints about the Throne of Thrones, the ruby of his office glowing like Faith itself as with lace-cuffed exquisite hands he ministered with pious grace fit for display before the Throne itself – *Gloria in Excelsis*! – yet he was *not* the centre of general interest!

What caught and held the interest of the congregation at large was surely the most incongruous group of participants in a Holy Mass imaginable. They were divided between the front pew and the Communion Rail immediately opposite. Small wonder Monsignor Maryzic and Reverend Mother Mercy were flanking them! Why? Never out of tolerance of such, but in readiness to deal with any Old-Nickism, for sure. Those in the pew were Delacy the Scrub Bull, Red Rifkah his fancy Jew-girl, and (Mother of God!) that meanest atheist this side of Hell's Gate, Fay McFee. Those at the rail were as sure a brace of Imps of Hades as ever slipped into human hide. It was not white hide, of course. How different they looked from the sweetly pallid innocents kneeling on either side of them. The Creamy Delacy Kid – or was it Cahoon? – and one of those young chocolate whores of Ali Barba's (Pray for us!).

The whispers flew from pew to pew. Pious eyes were raised to the roof (now and in the hour of death, Amen!). Perhaps the old tin roof really would have fallen in, had the Cahoon Sisters, beginning to raise their first whispers of astonishment to squeaks of protest that must crescendo to shrieks of fury, not been gently but firmly ushered out by sidesmen and taken to the Convent.

New as the Bishop was, he would not know about the doubtful things behind those intense grey eyes in the golden face into which he looked as he lay the jewelled hand in blessing on the golden head, as he placed the Host on the rosy tip of tongue, murmuring, *Corpus Domini nostri Jesu Christi custodiat animam tuam in vitam aeternam . . . Amen.*

Kyrie eleison.

The Voice of God, unutterably sweet, sobbing to Kitty Windeyer's manipulation.

Christe eleison.

Angel voices ringing in the roof.

Kyrie eleison.

God's Voice now thundering till the roof-tree shook.

The Bishop's voice rose like that of a sacrifical bull, quavering: *Pater Noster*!

Oh, how the grey eyes stared, the golden ears strained – to catch the magic of it all?

Afterwards there was Communion Breakfast in the Church Hall. Then followed a picnic to the ocean beach at East Point. The Point itself was now out of bounds, since mounted with big guns. Prindy was in it all, with his people. They delivered him back to Monsignor Maryzic at sundown. He was to assist the Monsignor at Vespers, to be conducted tonight in the presence of the Bishop watching from the Throne. Prindy was given the honour of helping with His Lordship's disrobement. Would it be disenchanting to find pants and braces and pot-gut under all that glory? But perhaps true magicians are realists, knowing that the trappings are only for the mob, that the true *koornung* is the Force beneath the ochre. At any rate, when asked by His Lordship if it were so that he intended to become a priest, Prindy answered promptly, 'Yas, My Lord.' For that he got a special inscription put in the brand-new gilt-edged Missal bought him as First Communion present by his mother, Red Rifkah, and a special Blessing in parting: *Deus Vobiscum*!

Prindy was blessed again, as well as kissed, as, tired out, he was put to bed in his netted stretcher on the Mission House verandah by Monsignor Maryzic.

It was an hour or so later, when the Monsignor, reading in his own bed inside, was startled by a sound outside: faint crying it seemed. Then, realizing what it was, the old priest smiled. That sweet strained singing in sleep. Soon the self-immolating words and the wild sacrificial notes could be made out: *Kyrie eleison . . . Kyrie eleison . . . Christe eleison . . . .*

The old priest muttered, '*Pater noster.*' He rose, only to sink to knees and lean on the bed and pray.

Kyrie eleison . . . Lord have Mercy!

The singing ceased. The old man climbed back into bed, soon was snoring steadily.

Igulgul, close to full, climbed the sky, looked down on this den of sleeping magicians, winking, went over, and in westerning peeped in at the prentice. Prindy stirred, turned from the stare, only to have to turn back to it, to open eyes and meet it. For a while the two stared at each other. Then Prindy drew a deep breath, lifted the net, slipped out. He went to the verandah's edge, and clasping a post, stared fully at Igulgul. He wore only pyjama shorts, glowed satinly golden in the blaze of light. The world was asleep, except for some flying foxes squabbling over the first ripening mangoes in trees by the Convent, and the distant bellow of the Shade of the Old One away out on the harbour waters. A minute or so of such staring. Again Prindy breathed deeply, but this time on a whisper, 'All right, old-man.' He turned and headed for the open door of the Monsignor's bedroom. He stopped. Inside was dimly bright with moonglow. The old man's netted bed was a tall ghost in a corner. The rumbling roar that came therefrom was a miniature of that other voice across the water. Prindy's clothes were flolded on the back of a chair. Silent as a shadow cast from the brilliance outside he entered, took the clothes, faded out with them. Back at his bed he dressed.

Barefoot now, in contrast with his gentlemanly getting-about during the day and evening, he slipped off the verandah, headed noiselessly up the gravel path to the street-gate, out into the street, No one about, except a couple of flying foxes who came flapping softly over to see what the bright apparition was. The long yellow gravel road, the old familiar road to the Old Compound, stretched away through its line of silver-topped trees, into moonmist. That was the way he headed, in the middle of the road, past the dark houses of the sleeping *kuttabah*. Not even their dogs sensed him. Thus should a *koornung*, old or young, be able to travel.

At length he came to the old familiar site of that Home officialdom in its kindness had found for him and bound him to with barbed wire. Now the brand-new *kuttabah* hospital stood there. A few lights shone in its many otherwise glittering windows. How the *kuttabah* must have sterilized that ground of the taint of the boong to make it fit for his kind to walk on! But he hadn't got rid of the Shades of those dead unclean who had been brought too far away from their country ever to find their way back again. *Koodooks* were scolding everywhere. Some swooped on the diminutive traveller, probably thinking him too bright of colouring to be any but one of the Enemy, but saw the features upturned to them, wheeled away.

Northward now, with a glint of the sea. Familiar sites changed hands about here, too. The Shell Oil Tanks, aluminium-painted, glowed like bits spat down upon the earth by Igulgul. They were enclosed by barbed wire now, in which was a gate with a lighted sentry-box in which the sentry, nursing his bayoneted rifle, slept.

So on, and up the hill past the Meat Works, out onto the flat back of Blue Mud Bay, with sudden blazing revelation of the limitless sea. There further back, like another lump of Igulgul's spittal, stood the Jail, lightless of itself. Prindy paused, to look back towards Rainbow Reef, now at the height of uproar. Igulgul winked – at Reef, at Jail, at Boy. Prindy went on towards the Jail. Kweeluks in the moon-mist, cried as in alarm: *Kweeluk, kweeluk . . . that is the place of the lost*!

He went through the line of sleeping guards' residences, following the driveway to the entrance. The great iron door in the high iron wall was a white square in the moonlight. He reached it, pushed on its rigidity, then tried the handle of the wicket. Locked. He looked aloft. Climbing here was a job for a gecko. He pushed against the great door again, as if hoping that the ability of the complete *koornung* to pass through things might have come to him. It hadn't. With a sigh he sank down, to squat with back against the door. He yawned. With Igulgul watching him, he fell asleep.

He slept for hours. He woke with a start at sound of steps. Igulgul was gone. Clouds in the West were silvered with dawn. The steps were inside. He jumped up. Jingle of keys. Rattle of lock. The wicket opened. A head in a peaked cap appeared, and shoulders, and a flash-light. The light found Prindy. A gasp. Then a gruff voice, as a form stepped right out, 'What the hell you doin' here?'

Prindy blinked against the nearing light, answered under indrawn breath, 'I come look him old-man.'

'Eh?' asked the guard, leaning towards him.

'Ah! I know you now. Delacy, ain't you? Yeah . . . I remember the Judge bringin' you. But where' the Judge now?'

'He sleep, I reckon.'

'I reckon, too. What . . . you come here on your own?'

'Old-one send me.'

'What old one?'

Prindy jerked his lips skyward. 'Old God.'

The guard stared at him for a moment. 'Well . . . you just can't come in here like that, sonny.' He added, 'The old feller's pretty sick.' Then, after another pause, he said, 'Wait a bit. I got to get things goin' here.' He gave his attention to the big gate, pulled a lever, opened it. The inner courtyard was revealed, with stores and offices about, one lighted, the light glinting on the bars of the inner door. The guard turned to go back in, beckoning to Prindy to follow.

They went to the lighted office. The guard dropped behind a desk, waving Prindy to a form along the wall. He opened a big ledger and wrote in it. Then he looked at Prindy again, and after a moment's contemplation, reached for the telephone. After a while a voice answered, plain to anyone of good hearing, 'Hello?'

'Baxter, Major. I got a kid here . . . that Delacy kid . . . you know, came with the Judge to see old Cock-Eye Bob. Wants to see the old feller again. Remember him . . . creamy kid . . . Cahoon, some say.'

'Yeah. Judge not with him, though?'

'Oh, no. Matter o' fact, he said God sent him.'

'Eh . . . God? Hell!'

'What'll I do . . . hunt him? I hung onto him, because I thought it might do the old feller good to see him . . . seein' he's been singin' out for him . . . *Mekullikulli.*'

The guard looked at Prindy. 'That's you, isn't it, sonny?'

Prindy nodded.

The Major said, 'Yeah . . . might be a good idea, too. The Judge'd approve it, I'm sure. Can't very well ring him this hour, though. Better send him over here to wait . . . No, hang onto him there. I'll come over.'

Guard Baxter went about his duties, leaving Prindy. A big bell tolled. Soon the place was astir inside. Prindy craned out to peep through the barred gate.

The Sun was up by the time Major O'Dowdy came, smelling of soap and coffee. He was hearty: 'Goodday, young feller. Come to see the old Doctor, eh? What's this about God sending you? You want to convert him . . . aheeeah! You Missionary man now, aren't you. My Missus tells me she saw you take your First Communion yesterday. Really come on, haven't you, eh? And going to be a priest, too, they tell me. Well, well!'

The Major regarded the small figure approvingly for a while, then went on: 'The old feller's been pretty sick. Hasn't eaten anything for a couple of weeks. No matter brandy in his bre'milk, as he calls it . . . or even the brandy raw. He's sendin' his Shade home, I'm afraid. I wouldn't like him to die on my hands . . . not with him being the pet of the Judge he is. They won't have him in the big hospital, of course. They don't want him in the hospital out the New Compound. The doctor reckons there's nothing more wrong with him than there ever was. But he's been singin' out Poor Feller My Country, and wanting you . . . so we worked out. You're his special little mate, aren't you?' Prindy nodded.

'Right . . . then maybe you might be able to get him to take his bre'milk and brandy. Come on . . . we'll give it a go.'

As they went on their way, through the barred gate and along white-washed phenyle-reeking corridors, the Major explained that the old man was in what he called Solitary, for the reason that his spells of howling were disturbing to the other prisoners. They reached the cell, a mere concrete box, bare of furniture save for a wooden bench on which lay huddled what, at first glimpse with the opening of the door by the accompanying guard, looked like a heap of dead black flying foxes. Bobwirridirridi himself might have been dead for all the movement or sound he made. He made no response to the guard's sharp calling him, 'Up, Bob . . . someone to see you!'

The old man, completely naked, was curled up to face the wall. When the guard lay a rough hand on a skeleton shoulder and jerked him round, he came as supinely as any dried-out black corpse and almost with the same dull rasping sound as might be expected. The death's head simply flopped. The shrivelled lids closing the caverns of the eyes did not flicker, until the guard slapped the face lightly. Then the flicker revealed no light of life behind.

Major O'Dowdy said to Prindy, 'You talk him, sonny.'

Prindy said, '*Pookarakka, n'gangah.*'

A slight quiver the fleshless skin. Prindy added, '*Ajat, guga mugugari.*'

A glint in the caverns. Then a sudden blaze of that deep fire. A moment. Then a rasping feeble cry: '*Mekullikulli*!' A claw came reaching. Prindy took it. The claw ran up the golden forearm. The skeleton strove to sit. The guard jerked it up. The skin-and-bone arms sought to embrace the golden vision. Prindy moved into them. The claws grasped and smoothed, smoothed and grasped. The clipped grey skull fell against the golden hair. The skeleton shook with sobs. The whitemen stood staring blankly.

A full minute. Then O'Dowdy spoke: 'Old-man.' When Bobwirridirridi took no notice, the Major added sharply, 'I talk you, old-man . . . listen!' He pulled Prindy away from the clinging claws. 'This young-feller been come for make him you good-feller again. Spone you want him stop talk-talk long o' you, first-time must you tucker something.' When the red eyes met his, he asked, 'You savvy?'

The Pookarakka nodded.

'All right . . . we gitchim you bre'milk-plendy, eh?'

The Wise One swallowed with a jerk, nodded.

'Okay . . . then come out and sit in the sun.'

The Major and the guard took hold of the old man, pulled him to his feet. He could not stand unaided. They supported him between them as they led him out, remarking on the smell of him. O'Dowdy said to him, but in an amiable tone, 'You old bugger, when you get better, we goin' to put the hose of you . . . Pooh!'

Bobwirridirridi cackled weakly, cast a gap-toothed grin back at Prindy at his heels. The eyes were red-hot coals again, even though the old feet dragged with weakness.

The Sun was peeping over the wall of the exercise yard. The yard was empty. They sat him down against the wall where the Sun could bathe his dingy hide. Prindy dropped down with him. The others went off.

To begin with, little was said between the pair. The Pookarakka wanted only to continue the interrupted embrace, the stroking that is so important in Aboriginal affection, to which now was added tears that streamed down the grey-black parchment of the cheeks into the grey bristle of beard.

Then the guard came with the bowl of bre'milk-and-plendy and a spoon, and stood by while Prindy fed it to the old man. Old Bob had difficulty in getting it down at first, belching and griping. But when the brandy took hold, he took the spoonfuls eagerly, at last seizing the bowl and finishing it off with greed. The guard laughed, told Prindy he was better than a doctor, rumpled his hair, took the bowl, departed.

From then on the Pookarakka was even animated. What he talked about so eagerly might not be known even to one who could understand the mixture of lingos and signs since these were of a kind whose signs were secret, as was evident several times, when Prindy responded to some sign-language with the Murringlitch word *Wha'nam* and after whispered explanation repeated it a couple of times till he got a nod of approval. But some hint might be got from the import by the old man's gesticulating in a way to suggest the obliteration of what restrained him when it suited him at some time in the future and his going hence, a lo — ong way, judging by the backward throwing of his cropped skull and projection of his lips to the utmost, along with his *Mekullikulli*, as shown by that grasping him about the slender shoulders.

Thus for a good hour without interruption. Then Major O'Dowdy himself came, to say that Prindy must come, because the Monsignor was there to fetch him, that he would be flying back to the Mission that morning. But O'Dowdy also tarried to congratulate them both on the transformation of the Pookarakka, whom he assured that he would not go off his food again and told that he would have another bowl of bre'milk sent him. The pair embraced and parted. At the gateway to the yard, when Prindy looked back, the Pookarakka made a sign to him not unlike that in which the Bishop had blessed his future as one of *his* cloth last night, a flourish with two fingers of the right hand.

Monsignor Maryzic was in the O'Dowdys' quarters, for the moment trapped by Dotty, to judge by the sound of her incessant chatter and his dead silence and his sudden seizing relief on the appearance of the Major and Prindy. He hailed the latter loudly: 'Vell, vell . . . you are truly der Christian Zealot . . . to start your Missionary vork so early . . . First Communion vun day, and der next out mittout breakfast to convert der heathen!'

Prindy only blinked. The Major guffawed. Dotty took it seriously, also addressing Prindy: 'You haven't got a hope of making a Christian out of old Cock-Eye Bob. You might as well try catching the Devil and baptizing him.'

The old priest chuckled: 'I guess der Devil haf many times been baptize' . . . and mittout anyvun hafingk to catch him.'

The irony was lost on Dotty, who asked, 'You really think so, Monsignor?'

He was saved elucidation by the appearance of the current prisoner-serving-maid, who was none other than Wilhelmina Whitehead, fellow inmate of the old Halfcaste Home, who in a roundabout way had contributed so much to Prindy's fortunes. They exchanged a secret sign of recognition. Wilhelmina brought tea and fresh-baked biscuits and also a plate of sandwiches, which last Dotty passed to Prindy, saying, 'Seeing you missed breakfast for your missionary work and you've got a long journey before you, I had them make you these. Aren't you a lucky boy, now . . . with everybody looking after you! I saw you Confirmed yesterday. And the Bishop autographed your Missal for you, eh?

My, my! Now, eat those up . . . and I'll give you a nice cup of tea to wash them down.'

Prindy looked right ready to eat the sandwiches. But the one he took up so eagerly got no further than his nose. He sniffed it, put it back. Dotty saw, gaped, then turning pink, demanded, 'And what's wrong with it?'

The grey eyes met the popping blue. He answered simply, 'I can't eat.'

'Indeed! Isn't it good enough for you?'

'Not *kosher*.'

'Not what?'

'Not clean.'

Dotty flamed: 'How dare you say my food's not clean!' Nevertheless she grabbed the sandwich, opened it, sniffed, then turned her pop-eyed glare on him. 'It's perfectly all right. It's the same pork I donated for the Communion Breakfast. You dare to sniff *my* food, you . . . you . . . . '

Monsignor Maryzic stopped it with a guffaw. She swung on him indignantly. His belly was shaking with much greater mirth than he was expressing vocally. She stiffened, said with a duchess's dignity and accent, 'Reahlly, Monsignor!'

He spluttered, 'Mein apologies, dear lady . . . but ist not insultingk der boy refusingk. Ist matter of food prohibition . . . . '

'Blackfellow business? I thought he was supposed to be a Christian? I've never known his kind to refuse pork before, anyway. We always give it to them at Christmas . . . and . . . and . . . . ' Tears were now starting in the pop eyes. She ended in a sob. ' . . . . I've never been so insulted at my own table . . . ooooooo!' She fled.

The Major was turkey-red, his white military moustache bristling. The priest said to him, 'I am sorry, Major. Actually, der boy is following der precepts of der Bible in refusing pork . . . . '

The Major burst out: 'Refusing the hospitality of my house . . . the likes of him!'

The old priest made a clucking sound, and rising, signalled to Prindy to do likewise. Turning towards the front door, he said, 'I refer you to der Old Testament, Major . . . Leviticus. Dank you for lookingk after der boy. Goot-tay to you.' He slipped an arm about Prindy's shoulders, led him out and down the steps. A taxi was awaiting them.

As they drove away, the old man gave himself up to laughter so hearty that it involved Prindy and the Chinese driver. Recovered, he asked Prindy, 'You keep Jewish food-law, yes?'

'Yas.'

'You keep at Mission?'

'Yas.'

'Vot does your religious instructor say to zat?'

'Father Glascock keep de law, too.'

The old man stared. 'Vot do you say?'

'We study Bible together. He is reading in Hebrew. To help me wit' English it help him wit' Hebrew. He say de old law is for Christian same as Jew.'

'So! And Rifkah . . . she is in zis study, too?'

'No. Hebrew is language of Jewish man . . . to read de holy books. Woman's language is Yiddish . . . *Mumma-loshen*, you call. Rifkah keep away from us. It is like I am learning de Law in *Beth Hamidrash.*'

'Vot is zat?'

'De place of Jewish religious study. Only man can do.'

'So! Moost I come out to see zis new *Shtettel.*'

'What is *Shtettel*, Monsignor?'

'Ah . . . I haf catch you on *Judische* vord! It is Jewish settlement . . . in East Europe.'

They were nearing the aerodrome, where the Junkers could be seen with a group of people standing by. The old priest said, 'Last night you tell me you vont to come to see der Bishop off on mail-plane zis morningk. But I get up to find you are gone. Vy so?'

'I go see dat old-man.'

'Zat I know. But you tell zem Gott send you.'

Prindy nodded, said simply, 'Yas.'

'Now you tell me truth.'

As simply, Prindy answered, 'God call me.'

The priest stared, urged, 'Yes?'

'He call, *Mekullikulli.*'

'That mean My Little Boy, yes?'

Prindy nodded. Maryzic asked, 'Vy does Gott call you by blackfellow name, ven you have Christian name?'

Prindy looked wary. The old priest urged: 'Pliss you tell me. I am ver' interest'.'

Prindy breathed, 'God is blackman.'

The priest merely blinked, asked, 'How do you know zat?'

'I see.'

'You see Gott?' Again that wary look. Maryzic urged gently: 'You tell me. You are mein *Mekullikulli*, too.'

Prindy swallowed. 'I hear God call. I look-see . . . dere outside verandah.'

'Vot Gott say to you?'

'No talk. I look-see. He gone.'

'But you say he tell you go see old man.'

'My foot tell me dat.'

'You foot?'

'Yas. My foot go. I reckon God make my foot go. I foller-him-up.'

'I see!' The priest sighed. 'Well . . . . here we are . . . . Vot a crowd! Also, I see, our friendt Mr McCusky. Let us pray he ist not come to mek trouble about you.'

By the aircraft were Jeremy, Rifkah, Savitra, General Esk and his aides, Lieutenant-Colonel Chivvy and some other military men of varying rank, and Signals Sergeant Sims standing by his kit in his usual rank-conscious way. McCusky, having just alighted from a police utility and in company with a uniformed policeman, was approaching the others.

As Monsignor and Prindy were alighting, the former said, 'I haf not time to tell you zat der movingk-picture projector and film arrive by der mail-plane yesterday, and because der General and your grandfader go to mek military inspection of der mission stations, efferybody is in hurry to go. I suppose you vont to go too?'

'Yas, Monsignor.'

McCusky, after giving a few short greetings here and there, concentrated on Rifkah, speaking in the official voice: 'I understand, Miss, that you've got some cinematographic film you intend to show to Aborigines. Is that so?' She answered affirmatively, looking both surprised and alarmed. He went on: 'Presumably you're unaware of the Ordinance covering such showings?'

'Ordinance?' she murmured.

'Section Seventeen lays down that all books, films, media of entertainment or instruction, must have the approval of the Protector . . . Director of Native Welfare these days, of course.'

Fergus, appearing in the cabin doorway of his aircraft, said loudly, 'The old order passeth . . . but its ordinances linger on.'

A titter.

Eddy snapped at Fergus, 'What's wrong with you?'

'The more pressing question, mate, is what's wrong with you? And what are the *Polizei* in aid of. Going to have her jailed?'

'Careful what you say, Ferris!'

' 'Cause it may be taken down in writing and used as evidence at my trial, eh? But I didn't think the Gestapo bothered about trials.'

McCusky turned from him with a show of contempt, to Rifkah. 'I'm afraid, Miss, you'll have to hand over those films for censorship.'

The lovely face was now drawn with that suffering *Bubbeh's* look. She breathed, 'Censorship?'

Sims snapped out of his military trance and came striding to the rescue. 'I can assure you, Mister, there's nothing censorable in these films. They're just scraps mainly . . . comics . . . passed by Commonwealth and State censors years ago.'

McCusky looked him up and down, thrust the official jaw out a little and pulled the hat down a trifle more. 'They haven't been censored by *me*, Sergeant. I assume you're the person who secured these things for the lady. You should have consulted me before you became involved. You've been in contact with Bill Norrish. Surely he told you the rules and regulations?' (Norrish was proprietor of the local picture show.) Eddy concentrated on Rifkah again. 'If you don't mind letting me have those films, Miss. They'll be returned to you after I've viewed them.'

Fergus, descending the steps, called to her. 'Tell him you want it in writing.'

Ignoring him, McCusky said, 'It's the law, Miss.'

Fergus came up. 'I'll bet the law is that any act made in the name of the Director has to be signed by the Director. That's why I said get it in writing. Professor St Clair would never do such a lousy thing . . . especially to you.'

Eddy went red, but still ignoring Fergus, said to Rifkah, 'This matter has the authority of the Director. When I heard what was going on, I informed him of the Ordinance . . . and he told me to go ahead. You can phone him if you like.'

Fergus let out a groan, saying, 'How have the mighty fallen from their high estate . . . the pure in spirit been contaminated by the bugs of bureaucracy . . . .'

Eddy turned on him flaring: 'If you're not careful, I'll lay charge against you for interfering with me in the course of my lawful duties.' He swung his anger back on Rifkah, snapping, 'If you don't hand over those films at once, I'll have the constable seize them.'

Fergus cried, 'Let any copper try seizing cargo off my aircraft without a warrant!'

The policeman was Constable Gobally. He said sharply, 'I have a warrant. What's more, Flight Control's been informed not to clear you for flight till informed.'

Fergus, who had been boozing with the mail-plane crew the night before, yelled, 'They talk about the Gestapo and the O.G.P.U. . . . and it's all on account of a few bits of second-hand film to amuse poor blackfellows in the bush!'

Rifkah said urgently, 'Pliss, Fergus . . . I vont not trouble. Please open locker.' She turned to Eddy. 'You can haf ze film, Mr McCusky.'

That brought Eddy's jaw out a bit, his hat further over his eye. His tone was more conciliatory even if the question was officious in the extreme: 'What exactly is your intention in showing these films, Miss?'

There were tears in the jewels of eyes. She answered huskily, 'I . . . I only vont mek ze poor people 'appy.'

'These people you're dealing with are still tribalized and likely to cause trouble. It isn't so long ago since they were murdering Japanese. If I find evidence of your stirring up disaffection amongst them, I'll clamp down hard, I warn you.'

She blinked on the tears, looked at Jeremy, who looked as if carved from rock, murmuring, 'Disaffection?'

Fergus, tearing open the cargo locker, flung the answer to her: 'He means don't do anything that'll make the blacks detest him more than they do already.'

Eddy flared again: 'I'll have you for slander, Ferris . . . . '

'And I'll have you for breakfast, mug lair!'

'Pliss, Fergus!' Rifkah pushed him away. Fergus stamped forward to look at his engines.

Eddy and Gobally began to lift out the metal cannisters and place them on the ground. They had got some half a dozen, when Sigs Sarge Sims intervened again: 'That's all that came from the South. The rest's damaged stuff given to me by Bill Norrish.' Nevertheless, Eddy took hold of another cannister, labelled *Anna Karenina*. Sigs quickly pointed to the stamp of the Aborigines Branch super-imposed, with a scrawl of signature that was probably Eddy's own. 'Look, you've passed it already . . . you surely don't want to do it again.' When Eddy jutted his jaw at him, he said, 'Be a sport. We went to a lot of trouble and expense to get the gear up here. Let her have *something* to take. I want to get things going for her while I'm at the Mission.'

Eddy thought it out officially, then said shortly, 'Fair enough.' Still, he looked the rest over for his stamp. Satisfied, he said to Rifkah with an air of magnanimity, 'Well, you've got a fair bit to go on with.'

'Zank you, Mr McCusky,' she said humbly.

He nodded. 'Be out to see sometime. So long.' He turned, and with Gobally, took up the half-dozen cannisters and went strutting through the staring crowd.

Rifkah gave Sims a peck on the cheek, murmuring, 'Zank you, Zig-zag . . . zat vas ver' sveet of you.' He glowed, went back for his kit with eyes on his military superiors that seemed not even to see them.

There was a sharp snapping to attention and saluting as the General, an arm linked with the obviously embarrassed Jeremy's, moved to board the aircraft. Esk murmured, 'D'you know, dear boy, I used to think this censorship thing of Australians was a hangover from Victorian times . . . but I begin to see it now as rather a passion for officiousness. Am I correct?'

Jeremy rather mumbled the reply: 'I've always told you we've the traditions of a convict settlement. The jailer's always officious. Whereas you might call Russia and Germany Police States, ours is a Prison Bureaucracy.'

Esk chuckled: 'How you love to malign what you really love so well!'

The seating was much as on the way up from Lily Lagoons. Again Rifkah sat with Dim-sims, as was only proper in view of that smart act of his. That act, in fact, was much smarter than she understood till, Putting in his Moan as best he could above the roar of the engines, he explained what was involved. The cannister labelled *Anna Karenina* contained only a scrap of that film, badly buckled. For the rest the contents were bits and pieces of so-called Westerns actually cut out by McCusky because they showed whitemen being bested by Indians, a circumstance that gentleman evidently calculated as likely to Stir up Disaffection if seen by those for whose welfare he was responsible. Sigs said that Bill Norrish, a friend of his family's, properly should have destroyed the cuts, but had kept them out of resentment against the Aborigines Branch, because their piddling authority actually interfered with the film-seeing of all citizens. He reckoned that the bits and pieces, stuck together in some sort of sequence, should make a classic of Aboriginal vengeance on bullying colonists.

Prindy was up in front again. Soon he was using as guide to his flying them northeastward the Shade that, although it seemed to join them by slipping out of the Jail, surely to one so recently Confirmed in the Faith, must look, with ever-outstretched arms, more like the Symbol of Sacrifice of that Faith. So, following the Shape, along the green jade swamplands of the coast, over the red and yellow tumble of the hinterland, to the silvery serpent windings made in the Dreamtime, and out over the blue jade of the sea to those refuges of the ancient Boorooolooloogun, so cleverly called the Prince Leopold Islands by the *kuttabah*.

Fergus did a bit of fancy stuff over the Mission settlement to the hopping delight of most of the crowd out to wave them greeting. Then down to the strip and out of their dust, to find Father Glascock and Brother David awaiting them.

There was marked contrast between the priest's greeting of the males of the party, with all of whom he shook hands heartily, and the two females, Rifkah and Savitra, whom he almost utterly ignored. Obviously Rifkah was used to such treatment, since her smile of greeting, which he met with a curt nod, remained while she introduced Sigs Sarge Sims to him. Evidently he had been appraised of the sergeant's coming. From the introduction onward, Rifkah might not have been there for all the notice he took of her. On her own insistence and with no objection whatsoever from him, she rode in the back of the truck.

Again there was contrast in behaviour when they reached the settlement.

The men went on to the presbytery. Rifkah and Savitra were seized by a waiting crowd, or rather a large section of it, since there was a small one that merely watched. Mother Mathias was in the middle of the mob. Sister Dymphna had the others about her, only about a dozen, all of them the bigger halfcaste girls. Whereas the Reverend Mother kissed and embraced Rifkah, Sister gave her a wan smile. Nevertheless, everybody was equally interested in the boxes and packages unloaded from the truck into the girls' dining-room.

Having saved so much from her win at the races through the generous help of the Answer to a Maiden's Prayer, Rifkah had been able to buy many things that the Mission, compelled as it was, by those who controlled it from distant comfort, to temper charity with rigid economy, could not afford. A sewing-machine, bolts of cloth, cotton, buttons, braid. Pots and pans and household implements. Laughing, she confessed that she had driven hard bargains with those who had supplied her, even to getting some of the stuff very cheaply through finding flaws in it. There was also a great tin of lollies for the children.

Mother Mathias pressed her seamed old face against the young bosom. However, she expressed herself troubled about the effect the pictures might have on the children's sleeping, seeing that they were hard enough to settle down of nights already. Sister Dymphna took advantage of this to say with too-sweet a smile, 'But I shouldn't think we'll be able to go to Miss Rifkah's pictures too often?'

Rifkah asked innocently, 'Vy not?'

'Well, with your good business sense, you're hardly likely to let us in for nothing, are you?'

Rifkah went red. Mother's puckered old eyes opened wide, and her mouth, too: 'Sister . . . how dare you!'

The sweet smile was torn away. The lovely face looked haggard. Sister Dymphna muttered, 'I'm sorry, Mother.' But she turned away without saying the same to the other one.

At the presbytery, the men sat down to beer and talk of war. That is to say, those of the party did so who had no bias about whom they ate or drank with. Sigs Sarge Sims, with Prindy as assistant, immediately began his inspection of the radio. Latest war-news was the invasion of Finland by Russia. As General Esk put it: 'Czar Stalin's wasting no time in re-establishing the Holy Russian Empire broken up by the Revolution against it in 1917. First Lithuana, Latvia, Estonia, all enjoying autonomy for the first time in centuries . . . and now poor Finland!' It seemed he knew a lot about these countries and their fierce desire for independence they could never keep, through having served in those regions with the Army of Intervention following cessation of hostilities with Germany in 1918. Talk of war brought Father Glascock to asking Jeremy why he would not take military command of these parts, as he himself wished he would. Jeremy went so far as to say he was in the process of making a decision.

The party lunched off food brought with them. Sigs Sims had his out in the kitchen with David. Immediately afterwards, the exalted ones went back to the aircraft. The arrangement was that Sigs should stay on here for another two days, after which Fergus would come to fly him to Lady Elliott Mission.

Sigs had no scruples about accepting the full hospitality of Father Glascock alone, as he said, when the priest, on his way back from seeing the military gentlemen off, called at the boys' schoolroom, where Sigs and Prindy were working on the projector, to ask if he would like to stop with him. Sims said with a grin, 'But I warn you I'm not what you'd call a Good Catholic, Father.'

Rather coldly, Glascock asked, 'What would *I* call a Good Catholic, Sergeant?'

'I don't know. But you know what I mean.'

'Can't say I do. Anyway, we've several long nights to put in together . . . so you've got plenty of opportunity to explain. When d'you reckon you'll be able to give us our first picture-show?'

'We ought to be able to give a trial run tonight.'

The trial showing that night turned out to be what the showman himself, using the cant of theatricals, called a Gala Performance. Although it was made a public affair, at Rifkah's request, no one had thought of more audience than those properly belonging to the Mission. Even Rifkah, whose whole plan was based on the interest she'd heard that all Aborigines had in pictures, hadn't thought of the mob of pagans on the beach, there to await the presumed coming in of the pearling luggers for the spell during spring tide, not knowing yet that, owing to War Precautions, the Japanese were now denied landing without naval escort. Even those who had never seen moving pictures had heard enough about them from the few who had to regard them as the best of the *kuttabah's* magic, next to grog. Because of the roll-up of tribes-people, such was the attendance at the trial-run, with the schoolroom packed tight and the louver-openings simply jammed with black faces, that Sigs Sarge Sims declared, 'We could've filled the Sydney Regent.'

In fact, such was the quality of the performance, with trial and error, with Prindy's forgetting in enthralment to keep the bike-pedal turning and hence the power to fail and the picture to fade, that a Regent Theatre audience probably would have wrecked the joint. But no audience anywhere could have been more appreciative than this, of the fragmented doings of Cowboys and Indians, Riffs and *Légionnaires*, and a full adventure of Felix the Cat all missed by Mick Cusky – even including the nuns, the younger of whom would not have seen the like since Taking the Veil and the elder never.

Mother Mathias was proved quite wrong in fearing that the excitement would upset the children for the rest of the night. On the contrary: probably it was lack of excitement in their lives that took them usually so long to settle down, while tonight, although they went to their dormitories as noisily as galahs battling for perches, they were just as quickly asleep.

It wasn't really late – just after nine, or as Sigs Sarge Sims insisted on his assistants', Prindy and Rifkah, counting the time with him, 2100 hours. Here was the first of those long nights mentioned by Father Glascock. However, His Reverence erred badly in supposing that his companion for the period would want to spend it in religious argument, or even in his company.

Sims stayed on with Rifkah after the show to give her further instruction. Prindy, weary from yet another arduous day, went straight away to the presbytery and bed. Alone with the Maiden, Sigs wasted little time before resuming his role of Answer to her Prayer, and declaring that they'd had enough cinematography for the time, suggested a walk along the beach in the moonlight.

She went readily enough, probably since now knowing how populous the region was. She even let him take her hand as they went through the casuarinas. Obviously he hadn't expected and didn't appreciate the warm welcome he got on the bright beach. Black figures popped up from everywhere to hail him: 'Goot-feller picture-man . . . properlee . . . Number-one!' He would have had her keep going on to where they might have some privacy. However, as she showed him, there were mangroves not far ahead, the mosquitoes and sandflies from which were already coming to greet them. He was quite willing to turn back when she explained that too much attention from the creatures could bring you down with fever.

As they came through the casuarinas this time, he made bold to put his arm about her. She suffered it without demur until they reached the road, when she shook him off, saying, 'Look . . . Fader!' The priest could be seen with his bright light on the side verandah of the presbytery. It was the same when, reaching her quarters, the little whitewashed shed converted to her use, 'the Synagogue', he tried to kiss her Goodnight. The presbytery was even nearer, the priest plain to see, communing with a book and a bottle. She shook his hand, went in hastily, shut the door.

Sigs turned away with a sigh, not towards the presbytery, but up the road and past the line of white buildings, out along the track on the airfield. When at length he did come home, Father Glascock eyed him sharply. He explained where he had been, saying that he liked a good long walk before retiring. That was fair enough hint that he wanted no arguing. He accepted the drink of whisky the priest offered him, then went to bed. Still, he was awake and tossing on his bed on the verandah long after Glascock was settled down and snoring.

Next day Sigs Sarge Sims and Prindy perfected the projection apparatus, and made up those Cowboys and Indians cuts of McCusky's into a sequence of sorts that Sigs declared a Classic that ought to be titled *See The Conquering Heroes Come A-Tumblin' Down*. Prindy showed frank pleasure on having the title explained to him. Zig-zag took advantage of this to get information on how and where to take a lady for a strictly private chat. Prindy suggested a trip in the rowboat to the beach beyond the mangroves. Pressing the advantage, Sigs sought assurance that there would be no gooseberrying if Rifkah tried to make it a threesome.

There was more than perfection of the machine to do. Because of last night's success it was decided to hold tonight's showing out of doors. Anyway, that's how it must always be done eventually. A screen was rigged on the beach, with an alcove of bushes to obviate the interference of Igulgul.

Why should that Old One interfere? It was only a technician's term. That night Igulgul was well up, this the night before his fullness, to watch the gathering of the crowd, and smirked no less for not being able to see what was going on that drew such wrapt attention from those who knew no other magic of light at night except his own till now.

Everybody got good viewing. *See The Conquering Heroes* was a great success, perhaps not nearly so much by reason of its subtle inference as its packed action – that is as regards the less sophisticated of the audience – its success with the others being expressed in amusement over its patent absurdity. These latter got more positive enjoyment out of a length of *Quo Vadis*, which showed what purported to be their early Christian predecessors' being thrown to what were very evidently trained circus lions by huge blackmen. 'Big-feller dog!' those unsophisticates with English shrieked. No doubt the reason for Mick Cusky's cutting the piece was this manhandling of whites by blacks. However, the fake was so obvious that knowledgeable ones yelled, 'No-more blackfeller . . . him white feller paint him black!'

Prindy was as good as his word in removing himself as soon as the show was over. Conditions were perfect for Sigs's romantic excursion; except that the boat was much too high up the beach for him to handle it himself, so that he had to have help, amongst which was David, who after the launching climbed in and took the oars. In vain for Sigs to protest that he could quite well handle a boat himself. Both David and the Maid stressed how dangerous these waters could be for anyone not experienced in sailing them. From babbling joyfully as he had been, he fell silent, leaving it to David, who said he wanted to learn how to operate a radio. 'I savvy dat telephone, Sergeant-sir. De talk go long o' wire, like you talk-talk long o' bit o' string and two milk-tin. Spone you put ear to telephone pole in Town you can hear all dat white lady talk-talk-talkin'. But I can't mek-it-out dat radio . . . how you mek talk jump all dat long way long o' nutching?' Under pressure from the Maid, the Answer to her Prayer was forced into giving a sulky dissertation on the basic principles of electro-magnetic radiation.

David's sheer enthusiasm for the subject was the means of relieving Sigs at last. He asked to be taken as Sigs's helper on the rest of the tour of the Mission Stations, saying what a handy-man he was. Sigs, swiping at the mosquitoes that came at them out of the mangroves as they passed, asked sharply, 'Why are you so keen on seeing all the Mission radios?'

'Keen, Sergeant-sir?'

'Why you want see all these radio stations?'

'For learn him to be radio engineer.'

'Not to tell Japs, eh?'

'Wha' for I tell Japs?'

'You're half a Jap yourself, aren't you?'

'I was stinking you not like other whiteman to look down on colour man.'

'I mean you might be a spy for Japs.'

'What is spy, Sergeant-sir?'

'Aw . . . put a sock in it . . . which means, don't talk so much. And turn the boat around and go back. Too many mozzies. I don't want to get fever.'

David didn't have to shut up, because Rifkah encouraged him to talk, to ask questions, which seemed his favourite form of conversation, by telling him about the Races. Thus Sims, deep in the sulks by the time they disembarked, quite cruelled his pitch as the Answer-man, that is to Praying Maidens. David accompanied them right up to Rifkah's door, which she shut on both of them with a smiling *Goot-night*. As they turned away, David asked if Sergeant-sir would not give him a lesson in radio-operating now. Sims grunted, 'Aw, go to buggery!' and stamped away to the presbytery.

Father Glascock, sitting reading and drinking as usual, didn't make things any better for Zig-zag, who joined him in a drink, by replying to his complaints about David's limitless inquisitiveness, 'I know what a pest David can be . . . but isn't the greatest thing about having knowledge, to share it?' At that Sims finished his drink and went off to bed.

Next day, working with Prindy on the radio, Sims was frank about his desperate love of Rifkah and his hopeless chance to tell her. He asked Prindy to tell her for him and to add that he would like to marry her, tomorrow if Father Glascock would do the trick for them. Prindy agreed. In the course of their tests they picked up Fergus in the Junkers somewhere the other side of Lady Elliott. Fergus said that he would be there about smoke-o time tomorrow morning. Sigs made him translate the casual timing into proper radio terms, to which Fergus responded, 'ETA, GMT, Zero, Zero, Three, Zero . . . and you may kiss my quoit.' Dim-sims betrayed the fact that, for all that boyish fun he often indulged in, his sense of humour was not so deep, through ponderously telling Prindy that one could lose one's Radio-operator's Licence for taking such liberties on the air.

Pictures again that night. This was no mere dummy-run, but the real thing, the Big Night, with Rifkah as operator.

'Pictures *every* night,' as Sister Dymphna remarked with something of a snicker. 'My . . . aren't we getting civilized! We'll have to get posters printed . . . or is it going to be the same program always?'

In general, the audience was even more appreciative with repetition, as if it brought them into closer identification with the actors since able to predict the action. At each critical point yells of warning or advice arose. Quite contrary to the knowledgeable Censor's idea of things, nothing but sympathy was expressed for those whites bested by rampaging savages, this in the universal way of tongue-clicking – *Tchit, tchit, tchit* – but which comes so explosively from the cavernous mouth of an Australoid.

When it was over, Rifkah, silver and gold shining under the magic of Igulgul, was moved to say a few words to her audience, using Murringlitch, Lingo, and a bit of Yiddish. To describe the joy she felt in their happiness she used the word *Nachas*, probably because she could find no other to express herself fully. It is a derivative of the Hebrew, *Nachat*, meaning the special joy one has in one's children. If not even Father Glascock understood the meaning, it was shown plainly enough in her face, glistened in her eyes. It was Sigs Sarge Sims they really had to thank, she said – 'Dear Sigs Sarge Sims!' – with which, to his dumb astonishment and the indrawn breath of the crowd, she embraced and kissed him. Then, overcome, she fled – home to her little Synagogue.

Far from being smug about the praise and the public reward that went with it, Sigs Sarge Sims was obviously distressed. With the priest and Prindy he brought the cinematographic gear to the presbytery, not from choice, but because Glascock ordered it so, somewhat sharply, saying, 'You could see how it affected her. She probably wants to be alone.'

The priest got out the whisky bottle. Sims had a long-sleever. Glascock was setting out to tell him about the Japanese, how they had been murdered here by blacks before the Mission was founded, how – but Sigs was not interested. He had to interrupt to say he felt bad about having the projector and things here, when Rifkah might have expected to have them brought to her quarters, that he would like to find out. Quite irritably, the priest said, 'Her light's out. She'll be in bed.'

'She can't be asleep yet. I'm going to ask her.' Ignoring the priest's groan of disapproval, Sims rose, headed for the Synagogue.

There was no answer to his first knock, to his second: 'Who zat?'

'Sigs Sarge Sims.'

Silence, as if the situation might have been anticipated. He told her he wondered if she wanted the gear brought over. She replied shortly, 'Zank you, no, Sigs. Better for Fader to kip.'

'I didn't get it for him. I got it for you.'

'Ist for blackfellow.'

'It's for you.'

When she kept silent, he asked, 'Can I have a bit of a talk with you?'

Sound of the creak of her canvas stretcher. 'Not now, Sigs.'

'What other time is there? I leave in the morning.'

'Not till mittle-morning. Ve haf hours to talk.'

'Not for what I want to say.

Silence. He drew a deep breath. He asked, 'Did young Prindy give you my message.' Again silence. It was some time before he spoke again, now with a stridence in his voice: 'Now you've got what you want, you don't care, eh?'

'Pliss, Sigs . . . zat is foolish . . . . '

'I'm not such a fool as you think.'

'I zink you are ver' nice man.

'Well, then, come out for a walk with me.'

'I can't. I am tired, I vont to sleep. Pliss, goot night, Sigs.'

His voice came harshly: 'But I love you.'

Silence.

'I want to marry you.'

Sound of a sigh. 'Ist impossible for me to marry.'

'Why . . . you're not already married?'

'Ist impossible. Pliss, dear Sigs . . . do not spoil. It haf been so ver' nice to know you. You haf been so kind . . . .'

'Let me come in for just a minute.'

'No, no!' Nevertheless he tried the door. It was somehow shut from inside.

He said bitterly, 'Lock yourself in, eh?'

'Pliss, Sigs . . . zis is religious Mission . . . . '

'So everybody's got to lock 'emselves in . . . the women . . . what . . . against the priest?'

'You vill mek me angry vit' you, Sigs . . '

'That'll make two of us!' He sighed sharply, then said, 'All right. I know when I've been played for a mug. Goodnight . . . Goodbye!' He swung away, went stamping across the road.

It was not back to the presbytery he went, but with a marching soldier's step directly across the road and into the casuarinas. Kweeluks were crying on the beach. Perhaps their seeming sadness drew him. They were not up where the blacks were camped, but on the bit of beach to southward. He turned that way. Their crying became excited at sight of him: *Kweeluk, kweeluk – here is a lost one*! But they took wing, and like silver wraiths, became part of the silver sky, vanishing towards the near black wall of mangroves. He sat down in the silky silver sand. Igulgul, smirking at him from behind, showed him his own Shade, a poor little butter-ball thing, writing in misery in the sand.

The simplest way to meet failure is to blame it on someone else. That Sigs Sarge Sims was doing just that was soon evident with his sighs' turning to growls: 'Bloody Jewess . . . bitch . . . stringin' a man on!'

Hermit crabs came up from the blaze of the sea to see if his dumpy Shade were worth a nibble. He kicked at them, hurled sand. Scouting mosquitoes and sandflies found him, signalled for the squadrons. For a while he let off steam on these intruders on his solitude. At last he grunted, 'Not getting fever for any Jew-bitch!' He rose, jumped on some hermit crabs, swiped at the whining dive-bombers, went back up through the scrub, to the presbytery.

Father Glascock was still at his table. He merely glanced at the khaki figure as it came onto the verandah, returned to his book. He did not look up at scrape of a chair, the heavy sigh of sitting, but waved a hand, murmuring, 'Help yourself.' Sigs reached for bottle and glass, poured himself a stiff one, added a little water. 'Cheers!' he grunted. The priest looked up, nodded, took up his own glass, sipped sparingly as Sims took a long swig. Then he turned back to his book.

Sigs finished his glass, replenished it, growled, 'Not very sociable this evening.'

Glascock raised his head. 'Meaning you or me?'

'Who d'you think?'

'You have a tendency, I notice, to throw the onus for some ill-considered statement you've made on others.'

'Meaning what?'

'There you go again! You come in obviously with the hump about something . . . then blame me. Then when I attempt to defend myself you want to put me in the wrong for doing so.'

Sigs took a swig, demanded, 'What've you got against me?'

'For God's sake, man . . . nothing! I'm only too glad of what you've done.'

Again Sigs swigged. 'You're in the game, too eh?'

'You're talking in riddles.' Then when Sigs finished off the second glass and reached again for the bottle, Glascock added: 'Better go easy with that grog, man.'

Ignoring the remark, Sims replenished his glass, just as stiffly. 'Been played for shucker all way through.' Already his voice was slurred.

'Still talking riddles.'

Sigs's little pop eyes glared. 'I'm talkin' 'bout bein' kidded 'long by that Jew-bitch . . . Shtrikes me y'all in it . . . to get a bloody picture show!' The voice was harsh with anger.

Glascock's ruddy face darkened. He swallowed, said with an effort, his voice vibrant, 'You wouldn't be talking about Miss Rifkah?'

'I bloody would!' Sigs took a swig.

'Well . . . don't!'

'Won' I! I been kidded to, led on, cock-teased . . . . '

Glascock shot to his feet, voice rising to a shout: 'Will you shut up . . . you drunken fool?'

Sims sprawled back in his chair, hiccuped, 'No . . . I won' shu' up . . . and don' you call me fool . . . . '

'Go to bed!'

Now Sims joined in shouting, lurching forward to glare up at the priest. 'Don' you gi' me orders! Priests don' mean two bob to me.'

'I'm not talking to you as a priest, but as a man. You've insulted a lady under my roof . . . .'

Sims sprawled back again, guffawed. 'Lady? That! She's a bloody Reffo Jew-whore on the make . . . Hey!'

Glascock sprang round the table, seized him by the bosom of his shirt, shouting, 'You foul-mouthed bastard!'

Sims lashed out with a boot, caught Glascock on a shin, but overbalanced himself backwards, went crashing with the chair.

Glascock, after a hop or two, clinging to his shin, came back to the momentarily helpless Sigs, tangled with the chair and trying to rise, not to help, but to bend over him, roaring, 'Now get . . . before I do something I'll regret!'

'You?' howled Sigs, getting his feet on the ground and a grip on the table and heaving himself up. He goggled at the angry bearded face thrusting close to his. Then he let out a loud guffaw, turned away, flinging back. 'On with the bitch yo'self, eh?'

Glascock grabbed him by a shoulder, swung him round, snarling now, 'Put 'em up!' He fell back, to strike a fighting pose.

Sims gaped for a moment, then leered. 'I'm not fightin' a priest.'

'I told you to forget the priest. Put 'em up . . . or I'll give it to you straight in the moosh!'

'You will, eh?'

'I bloody will!'

Concentrated as they were, they saw nothing of the three figures racing across the road, or of the small fair head peeping at them round a corner.

Sims backed off without raising his hands. Glascock leapt at him, driving for his mouth as declared, got home. Sims hooted, crashed against the table, sending the bottle over. Then up come his hands, and down his head, and he came back roaring. Flailing of arms, thuds, grunts, hisses. The table rocked. Prindy leapt in to save the lamp. He swung it towards the figures now on the verandah. Rifkah, clad in light dressing-gown, was leading. The two nuns wore shapeless gowns and towels over their heads.

'You dog!' gasped the priest, driving hard.

'Bloody hypocrite!' hissed Sigs, trying to get into a clinch.

'Pliss . . . pliss!' cried Rifkah.

'Father . . . Father!' Mother Mathias's voice was shrill as a shrew's.

Glascock threw Sims off, sending him crashing against the iron wall. Then as he rushed with upraised fists to deal with him again, Mother Mathias snatched up a chair and thrust it in front of him. He turned on her, glaring, demanding, 'What're you doing here?' He tried to fling the chair back.

She held the chair, got between him and Sims, shrilling, 'What wouldn't I be doin' here . . . wid drunken brawlin' the loike of Donnybrook Fair goin' on. For shame on you, Father.' She swung on Sims. 'And for shame on you, Sir . . . darin' to lay hands on a priest!'

Sims wiped blood from his mouth, gasped, 'He started it. I said I didn't want to . . . . '

'The fool's drunk!' panted the priest.

'Drinkin', drinkin' . . . I knew it'd come to the loike o' this!'

Glascock raised his voice at her: 'Madam!'

'Sir?'

'Will you . . . kindly . . . remove yourself?' He swung on the other women. 'And you, too, ladies!'

The Reverend Mother, snapped, 'Not till I see this thing settled . . . whatever 'tis.'

Sims, now dabbing his mouth with a khaki handkerchief and evidently much sobered, said breathlessly, 'Settled far as I'm concerned. I'm off.' He turned away, to head down the verandah, looking back to snap, 'And you can all go to bloody hell!' He went into his room.

Priest and Reverend Mother eyed each other sharply. Glascock faltered first, glanced at the other women, then turned away, to proceed to put the disarray of things to rights. The Reverend Mother turned to the two young women, waved them away. They withdrew. The old woman herself, with withered face buttoned tightly, stood by watching. Prindy replaced the lamp, helped the priest pick up the broken glass.

Perhaps ten minutes. Then there was Sigs Sims, pack on his shoulder, tool-kit in hand, stepping off the verandah. He paid no heed to those who watched him, but made for the road, and noithward, evidently heading out to the airfield. As he disappeared, the Reverend Mother said, 'I'll be layvin' you now, Reverend Father . . . to go to Bloody Hell on your own . . . wid your bahttle!'

Glascock ignored her. She went scuffling away in slippers.

Finished the clearing up, the priest asked Prindy, who was watching him, 'You all right, sonny?'

'Yas, Father.'

'You'll be able to get to sleep?'

'Yas, Father.'

'Well, you'd better get off. If you can't sleep, we'll make a cup of cocoa.'

It was Glascock needed the cocoa. He sat a long while over his book, a *History of Jewry*, now without drinking. Then he dowsed the light. He looked across the road. The mean little shack, the Synagogue, under the spell of the Old One, almost directly overhead now, looked like a bower of ivory. A Willy wagtail was singing of love in the casuarinas quite close by. He sighed, went to his room, changed to pyjamas, knelt in prayer at his prie-dieu, got into bed. But he tossed for an hour. Then it was he rose and made more cocoa. He took it round to his place on the verandah, sat in a deck-chair to drink it and stare at the ivory bower, in which slept a princess with copper hair, perhaps only needing to be kissed awake to that love the wagtail was still singing of so sweetly: *Kirri-kirri-kirriki-kirriki-jirritee*!

Kirie eleison . . . Lord, have Mercy!

He rose quickly, went rushing to his room, to drop at the prie-dieu again, striking his breast – *Kirie eleison* . . . *Kirriki-kirriki-jittit* . . . what a night for love . . . Lord, have mercy upon me, a miserable sinner!

A small golden head was peeping from the door.

Out at the airfield another Kirrikijirrit was singing of love, while Sigs Sarge Sims sat huddled in a strip of shadow beside the fuel-shed, with tears mingling with the blood of his broken mouth, as was plain to see in the glare flung back by Igulgul straining to see, to smirk at the power of his Wrong-side Bijnitch.

V

When in midmorning Fergus arrived, coming straight in from the sea to do a low turn over the settlement, everybody turned out to wave, but none moved to go to meet him. He came out of the dust of his landing to stare from his cock-pit at the solitary Sigs Sarge Sims lined up with kit at feet, one hand behind in the at-ease position, the other involuntarily breaking good order and military discipline to wave the flies away from his black eye and swollen mouth. When he alighted, he asked, 'What happened?'

'Bit of a blue.'

'Can see that . . . but who with?'

'The bloody priest.'

'Jesus! What for?'

'That bloody Jewess!' As Fergus gaped, Sims poured it all out as he saw it, concluding: 'Never dawned on me that he was on with her . . . although it sticks out a mile when you see it. They never speak in anybody else's company . . . avoid one another. Yet he's always watching her joint. She warned me about it, when I tried to put in a bit of a plod with her. Then when I let him have it straight, he didn't deny it . . . just went bloody mad. Priest or no priest . . . I had to defend myself.'

Staring at him hard, Fergus asked rather coldly, 'Sure you haven't got it all wrong?'

Sigs spat out blood. 'Never so sure of anything in my life, dig. I've been played for the biggest mug this side o' the Black Stump.'

Fergus drew a deep breath. 'Well, not much use my looking 'em up, I suppose. Here, put your gear in the locker . . . and get aboard, while I take a look around the under-cart.'

Returned from his inspection, Fergus found Sigs standing waiting for him in the cabin. 'Better sit well aft,' he said. 'She's a bit nose-heavy flying light.'

'Couldn't I come up the front with you? I've never flown with a pilot before. Matter of fact, flying up from the South was my first time in an aeroplane.'

Fergus, looking tight-lipped, stared at him for a moment, looked like refusing bluntly, but then said, 'Okay . . . but you might find it a bit rough. I always beat the place up a bit to amuse the kids.'

'Suits me,' said Sigs cheerfully.

It was rough. Fergus bunged on just about every manoeuvre the aircraft would stand, to conclude by flying out across the sea upside down. Back into normal straight-and-level, he turned his split grin on Sigs, whose complexion was pea-green, asking, 'Well, how was that?'

Sigs only swallowed for answer. Then Fergus's grin was wiped off. He sniffed. He leant towards Sigs sniffing. He drew back with a grimace of disgust, exclaiming, 'You've shit yourself!'

Sigs drooped in utter misery.

Fergus leant over again, slipped the buckle of Sigs's harness, and drawing back, cried, 'Jesus wept! What a job you're going to do in the face of the enemy. Get out of that seat and right down aft. . . . oh, pooh . . . get moving!'

Stiffly poor Sigs rose, went stumbling out of the cockpit, while Fergus, tight-faced, tore open his side window.

CHAPTER TWENTY-TWO

EXCEPT for those people who, as individuals, ethnic or political groups, nations, had been obliterated by the rush of events of 1939, for all the human uproar that had been accompaniment to its passage, the year ended on a note of anticlimax. The War that so many Dismal Jimmies had predicted as certain to be the worst in history if those spoiling for it were not put down, had become an international joke. From being called the Twilight War, as in the halcyon calm following the initial carnage and conquest, it was now being called the Phoney War. The word *Phoney* in itself was in the nature of a joke, being a take-off of the pronunciation of *Funny* by refugees from the earlier frightfulness. The Reffos naturally did not mean that they found it amusing, but the casual attitude to it by those amongst whom they took refuge bewildering and dubious in the extreme, in view of their declared hostility to those who had caused it all.

At Beatrice River, they still had the armed guard on the bridge, and on the Railway Station that notice telling you to keep your mouth shut because of the long-eared enemy. However, the guards were now more concerned with the fish in the river than with likely lurking saboteurs, the gossips back on the old familiar themes. Still, the War was not completely dropped from gossip. There was news from the doings of Our Boys, still in their training camps Down South and getting rather fed up with the mere marching-up-and-down-again, some more than others. For instance, Brumby Toohey had gone more or less permanently Ack-willie, and had the Provosts after him now, instead of the Johns as of old; and Pat Hannaford was in the brig for striking an officer – guess who? – well, naturally Lieutenant Clancy Delacy.

Speaking of the Delacys (between you and me and the verandah-post as old Shame-on-us said) what was this about the Scrub Bull's being mixed up with Military Intelligence? Imagine it – when he had been so anti-war that he'd stuck that stuffed french-letter on the concrete Warrior atop the Anzac Memorial in Town! Yet how account for that high-powered radio installed at Lily Lagoons by military experts and his dashing about the country by air along with General Esk, and his fancy Jew-girl's being installed at a Catholic mission, showing propaganda pictures to the boongs and learning their lingo? There had been a whisper a year or two back of the Pommy General's being interested in the recruitment of the Black Bastards in the event of war. If that was the game, arming the Bush Boongs, then for godsake, that was the stone-end of everything!

That chieftain of the gossip clan, the Finnucane of the Finnucanes, tried to get a clue to the mystery by having the Scrub Bull in for a private drop of the Tullamore Dew to toast the New Year. Afterwards he had to confess himself even more baffled, telling his cronies, 'When I fished for a hint of what's goin' on he took the bait too aysily. Yes . . . a Secret Service Man he'd have us belave he is . . . which means, o' course, that he isn't. T'in what the divil is he? And so amiable! Sure, ayven his ould Da wasn't half as amiable as he these days . . . and I'll tell ye, Ould Pat was the most amiable man in the wurruld . . . when it suited him.'

Probably, of all the people in the district who knew what was going on, or thought they did, Jeremy was the least concerned. Tom Toohey tried pumping him privily, telling him what was being noised abroad. Normally, perhaps, he would have confided in Tom. However, Tom was much changed since Brumby's enlistment, first filled with pride in his Soldier Boy and tending to run with the mob in his feeling about the War, and now utterly ashamed of the boy's dereliction and hardly likely to be anything but embarrassed in the presence of one he knew for a high-ranking officer. Jeremy put him off, saying simply, 'I told you the General wants me to take command of the area. It might be necessary someday. It certainly doesn't look like it at the moment. It's my bet that the business in Europe will peter out with the onset of the Northern winter. As for the Japs . . . they've shown how they feel about Germany and Russia getting together. With things like that, they're going to have their hands full in China for a long long while '

Actually, Jeremy's Secret Service amounted to the daily receipt of a coded signal from GHQ formally requesting a report on the military situation in the area and the routine reply to it: *Situation normal.*

It was a couple of weeks after that attempt of old Shame-on-us's to elucidate matters for the public benefit that Jeremy, just home again from meeting the mail train, perhaps for the last time by motor-vehicle for the season by the look of the weather, took a look at the tape hanging out of the relay that printed the signals coming through the radio, and saw that the latest communication was obviously different from the routine one. He got his code-book. The message decyphered: *Request your attendance GHQ earliest possible date repeat earliest kind regards signed Mark.* Although the ending was not at all in keeping with military procedure, as might be expected in the circumstances, the repetition was hint enough that the message was an order to be obeyed.

Speaking to Nan about it, when he asked her to get out some Southern clothes for him against his catching Friday's train to Town, suggesting that he would want only one suit, he said ruefully, 'Looks like I was wrong saying I couldn't see myself ever wearing a uniform again.'

Catching the train on Friday, he told the sticky-beaks that he was only running up on business. It was a fact that in Town on the Saturday he attended only to matters concerned with Lily Lagoons, except that of booking a seat on Monday's mail plane, which he was able to do with a clerk from the South who did not know him.

Judge Bickering met him at the hotel, and failing to get him home that first day, was not to be gainsaid the next. Jeremy went round to lunch with him. No doubt but that the Judge had it on good authority, probably from Lieutenant-Colonel Chivvy, that Jeremy was somehow involved in military matters.

However, Jeremy dodged the leading questions, quite without offending the Judge, who only winked that eye and said finally, 'Well, after all, a soldier isn't supposed to talk.' The Judge was more interested in talking about war, in a philosophical fashion. He said, 'I was too cowardly for the First . . . or, at any rate, I thought more of getting an honours degree in law than a medal or a glorious death . . . and now I'm too old. Still, I'd like the experience . . . immoral as the act may be. Rather like an old chap in his dotage, too scared or scrupulous to go to a brothel, eh?'

II

So up into the milky blue of the dawn sky, with day already blazing golden in the valleys of the cloud-mountains of the North – to swing away from these and set course for the crystal violet of the South. Almost before the big mail plane had reached flight-level the silver northern sea had vanished – while *Terra Australis* bared her vast neuter-coloured bosom.

In an hour there was the Beatrice River, only a whip-snake from away up here. Beatrice Township was only a couple of white dots. A single white dot, seemingly next door, was Lily Lagoons homestead. Away northeastward the neutral emptiness fading into the hazy nothingness of the horizon was the Sandstone Plateau, so full of secret places, alive with secret life, sacred to the memory of so many things; but as such only to this passenger, who stared at it with intense grey eyes. By the way he half-frowned, perhaps Jeremy was wondering whether modern means of getting about his environment would so demean it to Man that he would not scruple to destroy it. If eventually our kind come to be born of synthetic wombs it will mean nothing to us to see the cradles of our existence disposed of as waste when they've served their purpose. Yet is destruction of one's true mother's womb even thinkable? And is not one's country one's mother, too, since one takes one's first substance from it? Are not its features as much to be beloved? So might Jeremy have been thinking, being the man he was, and that the reason he raised his hand to what he knew so well as if in farewell to it, as it passed from view with his being rushed by unnatural means towards the source of the unnaturalness that to the like of him must seem like a blight fallen upon fairness.

In the evening, they broke through bloody weeping rain to land at Brisbane. There was the synthetic Womb of Environment opening. It glittered with artificial light. It teamed with artificial children jostling for space. Jeremy, the bushie, used to natural darkness and leisurely movement, blinked and blundered his way in. He hired a habitat for the night. Even the blinds and shut window could not keep out the incessant glare and shackled restlessness of this, by comparison with others, small city.

Next morning he betook himself to the Interstate Railway Station, to book the rest of his passage by rail. The city was gay with War. Flags flew on most buildings – mostly Union Jacks, as was seemly, seeing that it was an English War. There were bright posters about war-like things – how to invest your money in War Bonds and do your bit while making a bit – how to invest your life so as to Be A Man, like the three young heroes in Army, Navy, and Air

Force uniforms depicted beckoning to you to join them. There were hundreds of these heroic laddies in the flesh, temporarily a lot of them, crowding the pavements, mostly outside the pubs, few if any as handsome as those in the posters, but no less cheerful about the investment, except a couple puking in the gutter. People smiled and nodded at them, however they were behaving. Why not – when they were Our Boys, keeping up our pride as the People of Anzac. Without such as they there would be no Anzac Day. Without Anzac Day, what would we do? Like Old Soldiers, we'd Simply Fade Away. Such might have been Jeremy's thoughts, as with a glint of mockery in his eye as compared with that troubled look of former times, he made his way through the plastic thoroughfares imported from Trinidad.

At the Interstate Station Jeremy learnt that he hadn't a hope of getting anything but sitting-up accommodation aboard an Interstate train within a week of booking. The booking-clerk said, 'There's a war on, mate, you know. Priorities go to the Services.'

Near the general booking-office was another, a temporary frame structure, with the inscription: *Railway Transport Officer. All Travelling Service Personnel Report Here.* Jeremy went to it. In the outer section a couple of young soldiers were lounging at a desk behind the counter. They merely glanced at Jeremy, went on yarning. Jeremy had to call their attention again: 'Excuse me.'

One of the soldiers, a corporal, half-yawned, 'Yeah?'

'I'd like to see the Railway Transport Officer.'

'Yo' can't.'

'Why not? I'm service personnel.' Jeremy's face had reddened slightly. Still, his voice was even.

'Why ain't you in uniform?'

'I have my reasons.'

'What's yo' rank?'

Jeremy took out his military wallet. The corporal made an effort to get to his feet and come. He glanced at the wallet lain open for him to see, started, gasped, 'Yessir!' wheeled about and went marching through to another section. The other man at the desk dropped his head and hands to work.

In a moment the corporal was back, at the double, to lift the flap of the counter and say breathlessly, 'RTO see you at once, Sir.'

'Thanks,' said Jeremy, and strolled in.

The RTO was a captain, a thin foxy-faced man of middle age, with a slick of long lank hairs over ivory baldness. He was standing at attention behind his desk. The waste-basket beside him bulged with a newspaper still expanding from having been crushed into it. 'Good morning,' said Jeremy. 'I'd like a rail-warrant . . . if that's what you still call 'em. I'm on my way to GHQ.' He handed the wallet to the captain, who only glanced, then, handing it back, leapt to get a chair, stood behind it like a flunkey while Jeremy seated himself, then back to the table, to get out forms with bungling haste.

Having got the warrant, Jeremy pocketed it and rose, saying, 'Thank you, Captain Smollet . . . good day!' He turned to the door.

Captain Smollet beat him to it, leapt through the door, to stand to attention and bark, 'Stand fast!'

Corporal and private in attendance were ready for it. Two soldiers at the counter sprang to it. All stood glazed-eyed, as Jeremy, with a wave, went out. Outside he broke into a chuckle. An over-painted girl, perhaps waiting for those inside, met his laughing eye and scowled, snapping, 'Who you laughin' at?'

He looked surprised, then said, 'Not you, my dear.'

The thin scarlet lips writhed. 'Don't you Dear me, y'ol' prick!'

Jeremy paused to look at her, reddening now. He said, 'No . . . it would be silly, with all the boys about.'

'Who yo' callin' silly?'

'Everybody, lady . . . everything!' He fled.

That evening a different RTO received him, to send a private soldier marching ahead to place his suitcase in his reserved compartment. The soldier looked as if he could have been any sort of tough self-reliant Aussie workman formerly. Now, in answer to Jeremy's murmured thanks, he stiffened to attention and used the English flunkey's ever-ready answer to his master: 'Very good, Sir!'

It was easier to sleep during the journey through the night because of the rhythm of the mechanical din and the natural darkness mostly outside. Waking, there were the old familiar things: the Beasts of the Dreamtime sleeping against the Eternity of the Sky – the Ol'Goomun-Ol'Goomun, humping her Dilly-bag of Souls and trailing the Cat's Cradle of their Relationships – the Fly, buzz-blazing, brightest of all – Igulgul, striving with shrunken magic to rouse the craggy hills to do something as in *Alcheringa, Kurnallun*, the Beginning of Things.

In Sydney, Jeremy went strolling through the city, as much as it was possible to do such thing in contrariety with the mad rush of urban humanity. He came to Circular Quay. There was the usual ferry-boat traffic, a couple of smallish steamers berthed at the wharves of the further shore. But what caught the eye, not only his but of individual starers and groups, was the glimpse of a great ship riding the Harbour just behind the glimpse of Garden Island Naval Depot to be had across the ships and wharf-sheds opposite. Only mighty masts and three funnels like factory stacks were visible. It wasn't hard to identify her, from what the other starers were saying: '*Queen Mary* . . . biggest ship in the world.' But don't Cunard Liners have red-and-black funnels? These were warship grey.

A Manly ferry was blowing off the full head of steam about to move her. Jeremy hurried, boarded her just in time. There soon in full view was the majestic ship. She was all warship grey, and to be sure a warship, flying the White Ensign and with a six-inch gun atop her fo'c'stle and A-A's on her boat-deck. Naval pinnaces were plying between her and Garden Island Naval Depot, looking like shiny water-beetles by comparison. The big ferry-steamer was dwarfed to a bum-boat as she passed. The ferry passengers crowded the rails to stare up at her.

Being on their Harbour, the Sydney-siders were relaxed enough to talk.

'Biggest ship in the world.'

'But never been nothin' like this one in 'ere before.'

'Tykes a war to bring the biggest things to us, eh?'

'Yeah . . . she's a troopship now.'

'Long time since I seen a troopship.'

'Like ol' toimes, ain't it. I 'member 1916 when I syled in the *Medic* . . . same line's this 'un.'

'She's 'ere to tyke the first contingent of Our Boys, they reckon.'

'She'll take a 'ole flymin' Division . . . biggest ship in the world.'

Jeremy murmured, 'Biggest ship for the biggest fools.'

A heavy-faced man swung on him. 'What's that?'

Jeremy looked at him. He was about his own age and size and one used to having his opinions respected, with fists if need be. He wore an RSL badge. He demanded, 'What was that you said?'

Jeremy held the glaring eyes for a moment, then gave an elaborate shrug, said, 'No spik English.' He turned away.

Someone mumbled, 'Bloody Reffo.'

The RSL man growled, 'Bloody Bolshie!'

Jeremy escaped to the deserted bow, to stand taking in the view on the other side. Every garden ashore was bright with flowers. They would be a-hum with bees, too; not with the little black native bees, but the big slave types imported by that slave himself, the *kuttabah*. However, in the bits of bush yet clinging to points not yet given over to the realtor, no doubt cicadas would be drumming out their ear-splitting joy in waking after sleeping seven years, as in pretty well every native tree still standing on the Continent, this being just their time of emergence. Out here on the slave ship all that could be heard was the roar of the forward propeller.

The train for Melbourne was due to depart at what Jeremy's Warrant called 2110 hours. He was there well ahead of time, with another heel-clicking RTO's man to put him into his reserved compartment. Again he wore that new expression of half-mockery as from the spacious isolation thrust on him by reverence for rank, he watched through his half-open window the scramble of lesser ones for accommodation already paid for but still requiring a fee, judging by the forking-out to porters and conductors. Service personnel of lowly orders were being herded by RTO's men and military police. Officers were being saluted into place. All this in a country priding itself on its lack of class distinction!

So many of the passengers were in uniform that it might well be described as a troop-train. Would the guards on the bridges along its track be fishing? They might well be, since still further away from the Phoney War by a couple of thousand miles. But away down here the bellicosity was livelier. Hence for want of something better to do in that way, the sentries might pass the time honing their bayonets against the happy day when they might be able to use them for their proper purpose.

Perhaps Jeremy was thinking of the Australian preoccupation with what was called The Bayonet with a kind of reverence. Australian troops claimed to be the Best in the World With The Bayonet. Speaking now of the War of 1914–18, currently referred to as The Last Turn-out, to say, 'We got to 'em with The Bayonet,' was tantamount to declaring, 'The Victory was Ours.' Old enemies were honoured or despised according to their readiness to be disembowelled: Johnny Turk was a great fighter . . . met you with The Bayonet man to man. But Fritz didn't like cold-steel. He only had to see The Bayonet . . . and up'd go his hands and *Kamerad*! The preoccupation is to be seen in the Australian Military Emblem, the so-called *Rising Sun*, introduced with the establishment of the Australian Military Forces along with semblance of nationhood, which in fact is a semi-circle of Bayonets cropping out of a Crown. Yet so far are Australians from having a propensity for gut-slitting in normal life that their chief dislike of non-British immigrants is their readiness to use a knife in violent disputation. Judges and Magistrates continually rant: 'We will not tolerate use of The Knife in this country.' The bottle, the axe, the gun, the boot . . . but never the foreign Knife!

Jeremy may have been dreaming over such an anomaly when he became aware of a face staring at him through the window. It was a man's face, youngish, handsome, leanly dark, topped with a military officer's cap – a familiar face. It smiled. Then it dropped down to peer through the opening, and a slim hand came through.

'Jeremy!'

Jeremy, staring, took the proffered hand, murmuring, 'Frank Candlemas!'

There was no doubt about the immediate pleasure of both in meeting. But even as they wrung hands, embarrassment smote them both, causing them to blink, to avoid eyes, to release each other. A little silence. Jeremy broke it, with evident effort: 'How come *you* to be mixed up in this lunacy?'

Frank was wearing the pips of a lieutenant. He grimaced. 'You said you got caught up yourself in the Last Turn-out. Anyway, I'm not really a combatant.' He explained that he belonged to a new type of unit whose job was to survey zones of combat for endemic diseases, particularly malaria.

Jeremy said it was about time something of the sort was thought of, adding that the casualties from malaria in Asia Minor had by far exceeded those wrought by the enemy. He remarked, 'That's where you'll be heading, eh?'

'They don't tell you anything, you know.'

Another little silence, while Frank stood hunched in the window. Evidently he had more purpose there than simple exchange of greetings, judging by his expression which changed instantly on Jeremy's asking, somewhat constrained of voice, 'And how's the little lady?'

Frank smiled. 'Wonderful, actually . . . but . . . but being Alfie . . . ' There was a look of appeal in his eyes.

'How's she occupying herself these days?'

'The book.'

'Book . . . she's on another?'

'The great work . . . the one you told her to write.'

Jeremy blinked, cleared his throat. 'That's nice to hear. How's it progressing?'

'Nearly done.'

'That's going some.'

'That's the way she's been going . . . ever since she found she was going to have the baby.' Frank smiled at the reddening, gaping face. 'She calls them her twins . . . says they'll be born together . . . couple of months' time.'

Jeremy asked, with evident difficulty, 'Should you be going away at such a time?'

Again the smile. 'Not wanted . . . in the way.' Then a slight frown: 'I've been going to write to you since we've had movement orders . . . just as well I didn't.' The fine brows rumpled more. 'I'm afraid the book might get her into trouble. She really should have the stuff taken off her as she writes it. That's what I was going to ask you. She'd only take notice of you.'

Jeremy asked, warily, 'How d'you mean?'

'Well . . . National Security and all that. She's really gone to town on it . . . all the things you inspired her with. She'll never get it published while the war's on . . . and I'm scared that if the script fell into the hands of Security just now . . . . ' The look of appeal returned. 'Will you go and see her while you're down?'

Jeremy blinked.

The starting bell rang. Frank seized Jeremy's hand again, said urgently, 'The baby's yours, Jeremy . . . and the book . . . it's about the You she's always dreamt of since meeting you . . . . '

The engine's whistle was hooting.

The hand clung. 'Will you, Jeremy . . . please!'

The train jerked. Jeremy swallowed, nodded. The anxiety of the peering face vanished in a smile. The train was moving.

A last squeeze of the hand. 'Goodbye, Jeremy . . . God bless!' Hand and face vanished. There was scuffling on the platform as RTO's men and MP's seized the belated officer to shove him aboard. Doubtful if Jeremy saw any of it, sitting staring blankly as he was, saw even the line of pallid faced and flapping hands past which the train was running smoothly, inexorably, it seemed.

Still he stared as they entered the maze of glittering tracks, gantries, coloured lights, click-clack-clacking, gathering speed. He was still staring, when, with the glare of the city fragmented into mere flares and pin-points, the conductor came and asked about making up the bunk. Jeremy told him to do it at once, and betook himself meantime to the lavatory.

Back in his compartment, he prepared for bed, but not for sleep. For hours he lay propped on pillows staring out into the roaring and occasionally light-slashed darkness.

At dawn, changing trains at the Border, evidently he was looking for Frank. No sign of him. However, when on the other train they'd run for about an hour it stopped at a small station beyond which a large encampment could be glimpsed through trees, he saw him amongst a crowd of soldiers who alighted. Frank was now looking for him, but only from a distance and to wave and then to vanish into khaki anonymity. The train went on.

Then there again was the Queen City of the South, looking so regal – until you saw the rags of her outer raiment. Then journey's end at the Interstate Station. There was General Sir Mark Esk, resplendent in khaki gaberdine with red tabs and gold braid as Jeremy never yet had seen him, walking across the platform, oblivious to the rigid immobility about him caused by the call to *Stand fast*!

'How are you dear boy?' Esk asked, taking Jeremy's hand. Then he linked arms with him and led him towards a luxurious staff-car ringed about by graven images in khaki.

They were whisked away through the city, towards a hotel where the General had a suite and where he had booked a suite for Jeremy. Chuckling, he whispered that the 'C-in-C properly has a mansion near GHQ. I've never been in it. It's been under repairs ever since my appointment.'

Jeremy was left to settle himself into his own quarters, with an arrangement to meet the General in his: 'At 1100 hours. Have a perfect brandy . . . present from a feller from South Australia . . . Major Light Horse . . . vintner, don't y' know. Makes the stuff specially for himself and friends. Mentioned you as a likely friend . . . eh, what?' Whiskers also sounded much more the soldier now.

At 1100 hours a military flunkey, wearing white jacket and black red-striped pants, came to escort Jeremy. The General's quarters were quietly luxurious to the limit. The large windows of the sitting-room overlooked an English-like park. Deep leather chairs were drawn up to take the view with the brandy. Esk allowed the flunkey to pour the first of it, then dismissed him.

Esk toasted: 'To the continuation of our friendship in uniform, dear boy!'

Jeremy responded with a nod, but having drunk, said rather shortly, 'I don't have a uniform, Mark.'

'Anticipated, dear boy. Maltravers wore your things at Lily Lagoons, and with customary thoroughness knows your measurements. So we had a few things made. Didn't you find them in your wardrobe?'

Jeremy, reddened somewhat, answered, 'I didn't have that much to unpack that I needed the wardrobe.'

Esk was staring at him over his brandy glass, wondering, it was obvious. Jeremy took another pull at his glass, then, setting it down, said almost harshly, 'Right, Mark . . . out with it. Why'm I here in such a hurry?'

Whiskers blinked, took a sip, smiled wryly. 'My forthright Jeremy! I'm not used to bluntness these days.'

But Jeremy's face remained set, his eyes demanding. 'Very well,' said Esk. 'I want you to go to Malaya.'

It was blunt enough to cause Jeremy to catch his breath. Having delivered himself, General Esk turned to the view. 'I'll give you the map. I've been almost completely outflanked politically. This new Prime Minister, while very suave, actually has all those elements of what it is that you've told me go to make a successful Australian. This is what makes him so popular . . . even with many of his opponents, in a grudging way . . . and, of course, what makes the larrikins in military high places agreeable to him. You understand these people better than I . . . but, I expect it follows that his sycophantic pro-Anglicism is part and parcel of the type. Mark you that I say pro-English, and not pro-British. That's what appeals to the Blimps at home. That's how he and his laddies are able to outmanoeuver me. High Command would like to do exactly what I recommend . . . but have this sycophancy, which in my mind is a sort of confidence trick, all the while diverting them. They truly believe that Australia is behind the Old Country out of sheer identity. The fact that in high places the motive is political and military adventuring is beyond them. By gad, it was beyond me . . . until you taught me that this is no nation at all, but a haunt of confidence-tricksters!'

Esk sipped, glanced at Jeremy, who still was watching him. He resumed: 'You may know that they've the liner *Queen Mary* here to embark the first contingent to the Middle East. If you don't, you'd be one of very few.' Jeremy nodded. Esk said, 'There's been no attempt at secrecy about it. On the contrary.

It's a show-off . . . nothing less than the Biggest Ship in the World for the Bravest Men. Some more brandy?'

Jeremy finished his glass, met the watchful blue eyes as he handed it.

Having drunk, Esk said quite sharply, 'I've got to stop this bleeding of this country of every man worth tuppence as a soldier. Let them throw away their first recruitment. For the most part they'll be mere adventurers and no-hopers. I predict that with their larrikinism they'll bring nothing but discredit on themselves . . . and on the British Commonwealth.' The last was said with anger that brought up the colour of the thin aristocratic face and made the blue eyes flash.

Whiskers swallowed the affront to English decency with his brandy. Then, his suave self again, he resumed: 'It is subsequent recruitment that will count. They'll be men of responsibility, who've had to take time to put their affairs in order before committing themselves to the drastic demands of war. The Seventh Division, Jeremy, *must not go out of this region*!' The force of the last words left Esk breathless. He grabbed his glass.

Jeremy asked, 'You mean out of Australia?'

'I mean out of the region in which danger to this country, and with it the British Commonwealth as a whole, really lies. If Australians, lacking imagination to live adventurously in their own country or in the wider Commonwealth, as you once said, must seek military adventure abroad, then let it be to places that have meaning in the defence of their homes and the Commonwealth.'

The General paused, as if expecting comment from Jeremy. Getting none, he turned again to the view. 'I was brought here, and sent here, to establish the defence of an utterly defenceless part of the British Commonwealth, against the only true enemy that institution has . . . and I'm not going to be put off by any European conflict that can only end, as ever, in the reshuffling of European power blocs. These Colonial Australians you hate are hand-in-glove with the Little Englanders *I* hate. The local Larrikin Brass counters my otherwise irrefutable contention that our defence is a local matter by declaring that the European war offers Australian troops essential battle-seasoning. But in what way? If the European war goes on, it will be a tank war. Fritz has concentrated on his Panzer. It was our tank that threw him off balance last time. Look how they've used their Panzer squadrons this time. Were any of their mechanized cavalry war-seasoned before they rolled over Poland? There's only one way to stop a tank . . . and that's with a tank. They soon found that out in Poland. If Fritz keeps at it . . . as I don't doubt he will, because by nature he's a military marauder . . . it will be with his Panzers. How will Australians, famed only as shock-troops handy with the bayonet, meet these? How will they be seasoned? They will simply fertilize ground that doesn't belong to them. Britain and France are preparing for a tank war. Leave it to them, I say. I've succeeded in my contention to this extent . . . I've had a company detached from the Sixth Division, ostensibly to form the nucleus of an Armoured Unit, which will be kept behind here to train, with a few tanks I hope to have for them soon. The ostensible part is that the the Brass expect they'll be sent after them when trained. I do really hope to establish a full armored Division, with mechanization built here. But I assure you that none of these men or their armour will go to Europe or the Middle East.'

Esk paused to drink, waiting as if for Jeremy to say something, and when still he didn't, went on: 'Whatever the Jerry's initial success, he must eventually overstrain his lines of communication. Like all marauders, he's equipped only for what he calls the *Blitz Krieg*. Eventually he must stop. By then we are dedicated to putting him back where he belongs. The same old thing. The different thing is with the Japanese. If there's real conflict in Europe, as I don't doubt there must be while Fritz is crowing, Japan will have to take advantage of our preoccupation with it . . . or give up the dream of *Dai Nippon*. The sign for her to go ahead will be the preoccupation of Australia with this war, since that will mean the Commonwealth is not yet properly consolidated, that it's still a colonial system and has all the weaknesses of such a system, the first of which is that All Roads Lead to Rome, that without Rome there can be no Roman Empire.' Again Esk paused as if for comment, but got only wary watchfulness.

He continued: 'Now, while the Germans have concentrated on the Panzer for the type of terrain he aims to overrun, the Japanese have put their crack troops to training for yet another new type of warfare . . . that of the jungle. Intelligence reports intense activity in the jungles of Formosa. What for? It's obvious. A vast jungle lies South of him . . . from the back door of China to the front door of Australia. The jungle is a wonderful place to fight in . . . for those trained for it. Who, in all the British Commonwealth, is so trained . . . except a handful of bandits operating in their native lands and who owe allegiance to no one but their chieftains? Isn't the obvious training for our men jungle warfare, too? We have our own jungles . . . yet not a single man trained to fight in them. I intend to place my Tank Corps handy to the northern jungles. They'll train in them first as infantry. The tanks I've asked for are of the light reconnaissance type. I hope to develop a type of our own, specially suited for use in jungle warfare.'

When Esk stopped and sipped, he said, 'You're too silent, my friend.'

Jeremy also sipped, answered dryly, 'I'm waiting for that bit about my going to Malaya.'

Whiskers pinked. 'Very well,' he said. 'I shan't keep you waiting. I've been giving you the map, as I said. Now to pinpoint. I've been able to justify the training with tanks. Now I have to prove the worth of jungle training and so keep all further Divisions raised from going, as you say, to the Brothels of Alexandria. To do this I have to convince the High Command of the threat from the North and our inability to meet it. First factor in our inability is the weakness of British defence already established in the area. I've had Maltravers up there. He's just back. His report is appalling. Things were bad enough at Singapore when I was there . . . but the war's made it worse. Everybody wants to go home and fight for Mother England. It's natural enough. Even your countrymen would want to come home if their country was threatened. Morale is down to zero. The Japs will know that. But if Malaya were to be garrisoned by Australians, things would be very different. First, that longing to get away from their own country would be served. There's plenty of banditry to keep them militarily busy . . . they could operate right up through Cochin China. Second, and most important, is the fact that the Jap would see that the Commonwealth is truly that, a fraternity of nations, and intends to remain so whatever happens at the presumed centre of it. There is no centre to a Commonwealth.' Esk met the still demanding eyes. He said, 'I'm coming to it swiftly as I can. Give me your glass.'

He continued: 'I've seen the Singapore Base . . . and like everybody else, was impressed. That is, everybody except our Argus-eyed Malters. Of course the guns were placed to meet the threat of Japan as a Naval Power, which she was supposed to be, because most of her population were fisherfolk and she licked the obsolete Russian Navy with ships a degree less obsolescent gifted her by Britain. Malters considered: Why does a pre-eminently Naval Power have five million men in its Army? He asked: Could the guns be turned to meet an invasion from across the narrow Straits of Johore? He was told: No . . . but who was likely to attack from there, except bandits? No one but bandits could negotiate the jungles, he was told. He asked himself: Why are there half a million men being trained in jungle warfare in Taiwan? No good asking that of the people of Singapore. All they want is to be relieved and go home. Now, somebody's got to do something about this with the War Office. I want to do it, but can't, because I'm C-in-C Australian Military Forces. I can't do anything unless I can show that my work here is nullified by the conditions in Malaya. I can show that by sending a responsible officer to the area, and on his report offering to send a Division of first-class troops to help out. In no time the area would extend from Burma to Tasmania, commanded from the natural focal point – Australia.' Esk stopped, stared at Jeremy.

Jeremy said, 'You've just sent a responsible officer into the area, you said.'

Esk shrugged. 'With all his virtues, old Malters is a Pommy. *You* may think we Pommies believe we are the anointed. It isn't so. I've hinted to you several times that we should admire our colonial brethren beyond all other men, but for their awful weakness for denigrating themselves. To call you Great Soldiers but Impossible as Gentlemen was, in our opinion, to praise you as something somehow better than ourselves. You can't see it. But the High Command will. The report of Brigadier Delacy, my right-hand man as they already know, will do the trick. I'm positive.'

Jeremy said thickly, 'The arrangement between us was that I was not to be sent out of the country.'

'As a commander. I would gladly give you command of the Division I hope to God I'll have in Malaya within six months . . . because no man could handle it better, or deal with the British Brass you'd have to take over from more effectively. I also hope to God that what you see as my special intelligence officer may make you want to take that command. Still, I made that pact with you. You will not be required even to wear uniform there. In fact it's better that you don't. We don't want any clashes with the Brass there until the deal is signed and sealed. A special branch of British MI will look after you while you're there.'

Esk waited. Jeremy simply stared. At last, sounding nervous, Esk asked, 'Well, Brigadier?'

Jeremy drew a deep breath, exhaled it with a rasping sigh: 'What can I say but *Very Good, Sir*?'

Esk pinked: 'I'd like it put better than that.'

Jeremy went red. His broad breast heaved. He said shortly, 'Not being in uniform, I can't salute you, Sir. Shall I get up and bow?'

Esk frowned. 'Don't be foolish, man. If you wish to refuse, you're quite free to do so. I'm not asking you to do something against your conscience. Even if *my* motive is primarily to serve *my* Commonwealth, if effective it will save the rest of the hundred thousand or so of your countrymen who are going to offer themselves for service overseas from going to be butchered through their own recklessness and the heedlessness of their immediate leaders. I ask you again . . . this time as my friend Jeremy Delacy. Jeremy . . . will you go?'

Again Jeremy breathed deeply, but answered in a different tone, 'Yes, Mark.'

He reached for his glass. Esk beat him to it, filled it, offered it, saying, somewhat breathlessly, 'Let's drink to it.'

But as their eyes met over the glasses they were stuck for a toast. Jeremy relieved the situation, raised his glass: '*L'chaim*!'

Esk chuckled, as if in relief, responded: '*L'chaim*!'

When they had drunk, General Esk said, 'There are some preliminaries to go through. I've had to talk about this assignment of yours with the opposition . . . of course without mention of the immediate intention to divert a Division. They're compliant enough, seeing it as something that draws my attention away from them, and also, in spite of the sycophancy, a laugh on their betters out of Sandhurst. As for its military significance, they don't care a hang. Anyway, you must meet them. We have a Staff Corps meeting tomorrow for your presentation. However, I know these laddies by now. Anyone not met at a bar or party is never quite accepted. Therefore, I've arranged an informal meeting at a dinner-party tonight . . . .' Esk broke off when Jeremy frowned. He added with haste, 'This's quite a decent affair, I assure you . . . our hostess a titled lady. There'll be other important people there . . . Prime Minister, most likely . . . for certain Minister for Defence . . . .'

Jeremy cut in sharply: 'You know I don't got for that social sort of thing, Mark.'

'Yes . . . but I've told you its purpose. All you need do is suffer introduction, They know you for a bushman, the strong silent type. They'll be all the more attracted because of your difference . . . especially in uniform . . . . '

Jeremy, crimson, barked, 'I won't wear uniform.'

The General pinked again, but answered mildly enough, 'Deah boy . . . you're on active service, which requires you to wear uniform at all times . . . . '

Jeremy's voice was thick again: 'Regulations, as I know them, require a soldier only to wear field-dress in wartime. I'll put on nothing but what's issued to any soldier at a Quartermaster's Store.'

'Jeremy, old boy!'

'I mean it, Mark. Besides, your first instructions were that I am to go to Malaya ostensibly as a civilian. Regulations, as I know them, make that allowance regarding civilian dress, if ordered by a superior officer.'

Esk sighed, sipped, then, with a slight smile, said, 'Failing giving you a Division, I might appoint you Judge Advocate . . . with your knowledge, so long retained, of MR and O's.'

Jeremy remained grim.

Esk said, with a note of pleading, 'Dear boy, bear with me. I've explained the reason for the affair tonight. You can't very well go wearing field-dress . . . and since the idea is to meet them on their own terms, as it were, civvies are out of the question . . . .'

'With all due respect, Sir . . . .'

Esk snapped, 'Oh, cut that out, Jeremy!'

Jeremy swallowed. 'Excuse me from the party, Mark.' When Esk only stared, he added sharply: 'Look, I'm not dealing with anyone on any terms but my own. I'll meet whoever you present me to in the course of my duty, treat them with proper deference . . .'

Esk sighed wearily. 'Very well, Jeremy. You're excused the party. It's only that I'm counting on you to help me beat these people. Your countrymen are at the mercy of them. A little tact . . .'

'I'm sorry, Mark . . . but I won't truckle or use guile. You suggest that the Prime Minister is hand-in-glove with the others. He happens to be the representative of the people. You say he appeals to the Nation because of his subtle larrikinism. Likewise, I believe, does military Brass he favours. Generally, my countrymen aren't at the mercy of anyone. Whatever the faults of this Nation, it is a true democracy. If what stinks is tolerated, it's either because the majority have no sense of smell or like stinking things. It's only people like myself who suffer . . . and our suffering, for the want of decency and honesty in the land, only makes the others laugh.'

Esk dropped his narrow aristocratic head to hands, muttering, 'Jeremy, Jeremy . . . we've been such good friends. I want to keep it that way . . . even with this damned war . . . .'

Jeremy rose. 'They used to say in the Last Turn-out . . . as the fools are now calling the last blood-bath, as if it's been a bloody picnic . . . that you don't have friends in the Army . . . only comrades . . . because it hurts too much to see your friends die. I'll help as much as I can, Mark . . . and be as friendly as I can. But you're a real soldier . . . and I . . . well, my country's involved, and so am I . . . but very much against my will. May I go? I'd like to do a bit of thinking.'

Esk looked up at him, haggardly. He nodded, but rising himself, added: 'Give me your hand first.' Wringing the hand, Esk said earnestly, 'On your terms, Jeremy.'

'Thanks, Mark.'

The General put a hand on his shoulder and turned him towards the door, murmuring, 'If only all Australians were like you, dear boy.'

Jeremy did not answer till he was going out, when he turned: 'If they were, Mark, you wouldn't be here . . . except, maybe, as an immigrant.' He went.

Outside it was quite hot. A battering nor'wester was blowing, a wind known locally as a Brickfielder, a name betraying how tenuous was the grasp of these people on the Continent they had presumed to have won. The wind, from desert perhaps a thousand miles away, was the Continent's panting under heat that would kill such people as these. Yet they, though native born for several generations knew it only as some uncomfortable condition of the locality, a mere intrusion of the heat of brick-kilns that, without their realizing it, converted *Terra Australis* into a form in which it was possible for them, for ever alien, to live.

Jeremy removed his coat as he walked the street, causing the passing sweating overclad mob to stare at him as a freak. He went to the Art Gallery. There he had to don the coat again, for a start because the attendant, doubtless thinking he intended to sneak out something wrapped in it, wanted to take it from him, and then because the usually chilly climate of these parts was trapped eternally in the mass of the place. Here again was the sun-loved substance of the land, its granite, torn out to make igloos for the cold-blooded aliens.

Whether because of his mood of the moment, or the fact that the pictures of battle were the biggest and most spectacular and he no connoisseur of art, he gave most of his attention to these. Surely the artists who had painted them had never seen actual warfare, since even while exposing homicidal mania with skilful depiction of facial expression, they showed nothing of the filthy reality: the burst intestines, clotted severed limbs, agony so frightful that there could be none of the final courage implied by the nobility of the faces of the dead. Maybe true artists don't go to war, or going, don't return. Maybe you couldn't get your picture hung in an art gallery if you painted the truth. That seemed to be what Jeremy was thinking, as, with quizzical expression, he went from one handsome lie to another. Occasionally his lips moved, perhaps repeating those recent words of his: 'You don't have friends in the Army. It hurts too much to see them die.'

He came out in mid-afternoon, to find things drastically changed climatically. It was still hot, but, as the locals would probably say, with the heat of a boiler-room as compared with that of the kiln. A vast black cloud filled the northern sky, looking rather like a hugh black face – the Spirit of the Land in vengeful mood. There seemed to be guilt now in the haste of the crowd.

Then a wind came whistling in from the South. People hanging onto their hats and dodging the flying rubbish, bawled at each other, 'Southerly buster!'

The black face above suddenly showed features with a glowing within – great fiery eyes, great cavern of mouth out of which fire belched with sound like booming sardonic laughter – *BOOM, BOOM, BOOM-a-BOOM – CRASH*!

The black air rocked. The wind howled. The rain from the South came bucketing, soup-warm for a moment, then chill as the ice it soon turned into. Black air turned white with hail.

Jeremy, jammed in a doorway with fifty others who growled about having neglected to bring umbrellas and things watched the storm with evident interest, perhaps wondering what the Snake Men he knew, particularly a certain young one, would think of this other weapon of the Old One's, which in their locality they never would have seen, this hurling of great chunks of the stuff the *kuttabah* made in the fridge, with such force as to dint the steel of cars and shatter glass. Anyway, it was good to see they hadn't destroyed Old Tchamala, with all their bent and power in destruction of what was alien to their immigrant ways.

When the hail ceased, the rain took over, now coming in chill sheets from the Antarctic, of which these denizens of London, Limerick, Naples, Nicosia, even unto the third and fourth generation removed, were scarcely more aware than of the desert. The deserts of the Sahara were nearer to them, the icebergs of Greenland. Jeremy took refuge in a picture show, viewing the deserts of Arizona.

He returned to the hotel to dine, found awaiting him a note from General Esk asking him to take breakfast with him tomorrow in his suite. He retired early.

Next morning the military flunkey came to march Jeremy to the General's suite. Whiskers looked his suave self again. He told of a successful social evening, of having impressed the Larrikins by telling them of the Absent One's social reserve. 'They liked that,' he declared. 'Having no reticence themselves, understanding nothing but self-assertion, they take it for weakness in others. You're the kind of man they want . . . who'll hide his brilliance under a bushel and so not outshine their own merely ugly glare. However, I'm still of the opinion that your first dealings with them should be as informal as possible. You can be rather intimidating acting formally, don't y'know. Therefore, I've changed the order of the day. You meet them not in stiff conference, but over a drink and lunch in the Staff Corps Mess. Any objections?' Jeremy agreed readily.

Major Maltravers and Captain Dickey were in attendance when Jeremy was called down to the waiting staff-car. They greeted him with military stiffness now, despite his easiness as of old with them. Denzil sat in front with the driver, Malters in the rear, where the place of honour, in the middle, was given to Jeremy, perhaps because he was in civvies. Then away to GHQ.

Properly that institution was called Victoria Barracks. Such a citadel, similarly named, stood in every State Capital, relic of the day when the States were separate Colonies, each with its British Garrison – if that day really could be said to be past, when each State still had its Governor, appointed by the British Crown, living in regal isolation under the Union Jack and possessing all the privileges and prerogatives of the Sovereign, even to taking over Government if need be, and the vision of most citizens was confined to their State Borders.

It was a massive place, built of local granite, but looking as if each block had been cut in English prisons and imported as ship's ballast along with the first chained immigrants. Indeed, it looked rather like an English prison – or an Australian prison, for that matter, since the main ones were built on the good old English plan. Originally, no doubt, it had had its prison-like equipment: the flogging-triangle, gauntlet-running alley, cells, and gallows, for dealing with those who breached the Honour of the Regiment.

Ancient cannon squatted each side of the wide stairway, grinning like a pair of British Bulldogs. Above the doorway was the Royal Coat of Arms, with the Alien Beasts and the Royal Boast, *God and my right*. In the doorway stood a sergeant with gold stripes, whose job it was, apparently, to do what now he did as General Sir Mark Esk and his party came up the stairs, scream for all the world round here to hear – *Stand fast*!

In a corner of the panelled and polished hall stood a marble bust of the Good Queen who had originally owned the place and whose expression still said: *Flog 'em*! Seemingly wooden soldiers of varying rank stood staring at nothing as the procession passed. They climbed a wide wooden stairway and entered a corridor, passing more graven images in khaki. Thus to the front of the building and into a spacious office. Wide windows overlooked a wide road of several traffic lanes divided by bright flower-beds and park beyond, so that the view was again rather like that of a botanic gardens. A couple of wooden soldiers were there. The General dismissed them with a casual wave. They dismissed themselves with proper ceremony.

Esk seated Jeremy in a wide leather chair, then himself behind the great desk, with his aides on either side. At once he got onto the matter of conditions in Malaya, and had Malters produce his report and read it, item by item, while Esk discussed each with Jeremy; and Denzil, tapping buck teeth with a pen, gazed out upon the flower-beds as if in fancy plucking them to make a nosegay. Thus till Esk suggested tea. Then Captain Dickey flew into action, seized the telephone, soon captained a squad of flunkeys in white coats and red-striped pants marching in with laden trays. He commanded another detachment later bearing a huge map of Malaya and trestles on which to set it up. These were the only breaks they had from the task in hand. Jeremy looked interested enough, asked questions, made notes. He even showed some interest in drill proceeding on a parade-ground to be seen from side windows, remarking on the difference from the mode of his day: 'Good to see they've got rid of that idiotic Forming Fours.'

At noon a bugle rang from the parade-ground:

Come to the cook-house door, boys, come to the cook-house door,
Pig-swill's ready, pig-swill's ready,
Come to the cook-house door.

An hour later the bugle rang again, a different call:

Officers' wives have puddings and pies,
And Sergeants' wives have jelly,
But Privates' wives get nothing at all,
But a stiff prick in the belly.

At that General Esk said, 'Righty-ho . . . we mustn't keep 'em waitin'. It's their Mess . . . but they won't even enter till I have . . . these Democrats of yours, Jeremy, old boy!'

The Staff Corps Mess occupied almost an entire rear quarter corner of the great building. Its spaciousness was now divided with movable partitions, which evidently would be removed on special occasions. The polish of its floor and hangings hinted at Regimental Balls. Glimpses through the partitions could be had of dining-section, reading-room, bar. Inside, over the wide door, flanked by folded Union Jacks, was a portrait of the Present Owner, whose slack mouth and vacant eyes made him look as dim-witted as his great-grand-dam looked grim.

There was no one in the bar but the barmen, in white monkey-jackets and striped pants, and another, similarly attired, but wearing three gold stripes, who stood at the entrance, for the same reason as the gold-striped sergeant was stationed at the main entrance – *Stand fast*! The crew became wooden. Esk nodded to the sergeant, who screamed, 'At ease!' Normal business of setting up bottles and glasses on the counter was resumed.

The second scream, apparently, was also signal for a rush of natty khaki figures from the outer door – rush, that is, in respect of haste, since the movement must have been in strict accordance with precedence of rank, when those who first entered the bar wore the insignia of British Generals of varying degrees of generalship (no such thing as Australian insignias, of course). The first was a tubby chubby figure, with bristly white hair and moustache and ruddy chubby countenance and shrewd blue eyes. Despite his gleaming sambrown and scrambled-eggs-and-tomato mass of campaign ribbons, he looked rather like an undersized butcher. Those at his heels looked like grocers or schoolteachers or accountants. Not a warrior-type among them, and most undersized, as if that were in itself a primary in qualification for generalship since established by that General of Generals, Napoleon Bonaparte.

The fat little leader came up to Esk grinning, saying with what was obviously false heartiness, 'Ah, General!'

Esk bowed slightly, smiling, answering, 'General!' Then he said, 'I've taken the liberty of bringing a guest, General. May I present Brigadier Delacy?'

'Ah!' exclaimed Tubby, extending a small plump butcher's hand, but flicking his shrewd little eyes over the civilian-clad figure as if subtly discounting the asserted rank thereby, before meeting the grey eyes as Jeremy took the hand. 'Welcome, Brigadier . . . heard a lot about you.' It was a quick clipped voice.

Jeremy bowed slightly, murmuring, 'Thank you, Sir.'

'What'll you have?' asked the tubby one.

'Something with a touch of brandy.'

A deep chuckle, while the keen eyes quizzed: 'Here's to the good old brandy, eh?' He turned to snap an order at a barman who was waiting as if expecting to be tossed the Golden Fleece

While the drinks were being prepared, General Tub introduced his retinue. There was the Mil. Gen. Sec., the GDMI, the AG, the QMG. All were interested, amiable. Meanwhile the place was crowding, although decoriously, so as to leave the Top Brass ample room. All soon had drinks. But no one drank. Herein lay a great formality. It began with a sharp tap from somewhere. Silence on the dot. Then General Tub raised his glass, snapping in his precise schoolteacher's voice, 'Gentlemen . . . "The King"!'

They swung in a body towards Silly Billy enthroned between his flags above the door, and as solemnly as a congregation in *Amen*, intoned: '*The King*!'

It was over. Down the hatch!

In the midst of the clinking, glugging, and clap-trapping, one of the little Generals, a slight accountant-type thin, wiry, sharp-featured, sharp-eyed as an auditor, staring at Jeremy, remarked, 'Delacy . . . wouldn't happen to be related to a Flash Jack Delacy?'

Jeremy, who till now had looked withdrawn, showed sudden sharp interest. 'Yes . . . my brother.'

The little general smiled, in a tight way, as if not used to doing so. 'Well, well! I hadn't thought of Flash Jack for years, until the name . . . yes, and the face . . . brought him back to me.'

Jeremy swallowed. 'He . . . he isn't alive, you know.'

The small squarish grey head nodded. 'Yes . . . I know . . . I saw him die.'

Jeremy's eyes widened. 'You did? You served with him?'

'He served under me. As gallant a soldier as ever was.'

Jeremy blinked. 'Served under you?'

'On Gallipoli. Landed with me . . . with the first. Pity he wasn't able to come off with us who had the luck in the end . . . and to have shared the glory ever since.' The General heaved a gusty sigh, shook his head sadly.

Jeremy looked at the grey hair of the head searchingly, after a moment asked, 'Would you have been red-haired younger?'

The General looked surprised. 'Yes.'

Jeremy suddenly was heaving for breath. He almost gasped, 'Would . . . would you have been called Bluey . . . by your men?'

Again the thin smile. 'I believe they did call me that . . . behind my back. Why do you ask?'

Jeremy got control of his breathing. He swallowed again, hard. He said, in voice of which the vibrance caught even further interest than that already roused, 'My brother wrote about you . . . in the last letter I got from him.'

'Indeed, now! That's interesting. Written from the Peninsula?'

Jeremy's voice shook: 'Where else . . . except from Hell?'

The General's face changed. He was a man who knew danger, and saw it in the quivering face, the staring grey eyes. His own face tightened, eyes narrowed.

Jeremy laboured again for breath. 'I came several contingents behind my brother . . . landed El Kantara. That's where . . . I heard of his death . . . and got the letter.'

The General swallowed, made a sympathetic bunch of thin lips, opened it to say, but warily, 'I say, eh! Nasty shock!'

Jeremy got control of his breathing with an effort that turned his face crimson and brought the sweat beading on his brow. He said hoarsely, 'He told me he was about to die . . . and asked me to look after a halfcaste girl he'd left behind with a child. He . . . .' His voice now whistled like a flying stock-whip, to crack,' . . . he told me he was serving under a homicidal maniac called Bluey . . . who had a charmed life himself . . . and was proving it, by forcing every possible hazard . . . in the process wiping out all the poor luckless bastards that had to follow him!'

The lean brown face of the little General had turned grey as the hair above it. But the eyes held boldly. The jaw was out-thrust.

Jeremy drew a deep breath to conclude: 'Would you be the homicidal maniac called Bluey . . . Sir?'

A gasp from all round.

Now it was the little General who strove for breath. Getting it, he answered through clenched false teeth, curling thin lips back, 'Your . . . brother . . . was the most gallant officer . . . in my unit. I . . . I tried to get him a posthumous VC.'

Rage blazed in Jeremy's eyes now, was thick in his voice: 'Just as well you didn't . . . Sir!'

Colour was coming back into the grey face. There was anger in the snapping voice: 'Why do you say that?'

'Because *I* was his next of kin . . . because, in effect, his murder murdered the rest of our family . . . and so you would have had to give it to me . . . Sir!' Spittle flew from Jeremy's lips as he thrust his face close to the other grown grey again to roar, 'And I would have shoved it up your bloody arse . . . you military murderer!'

Everybody seemed to be in a trance. The tubby General was the first to snap out of it. He touched Jeremy's elbow, saying sharply, 'That's enough!'

Jeremy swung on him. 'Enough, is it? Nothing's enough for you bastards. I know you. You tried to send me to Ireland to kill my kinsfolk. You tried to smother me in the mud and blood of France, as you did scores of thousands of your own countrymen . . . while you sat in the War Office, in London, suck-holing the British Brass . . . you filthy fat little runt! What did you get those campaign ribbons for? Sitting at that Staff Corps desk . . . or rooting in a brothel?'

The blue eyes popped. The purple face split with a bellow, 'How dare you!' '

Esk had a grip on Jeremy's arm before Jeremy could take it further. Jeremy took one look at the haggard imploring face, then, shaking off the hand, turned towards the entrance. The crowd fell back before him as if he were a monster. He seemed to see no one, not even the imbecilic inbred face of the Symbolic Superman above with outer door.

Hatless, he made straight for the stairs, went down, was challenged at the entrance by the gilded sergeant: 'Your pass, Sir.' Jeremy stared at the wooden-faced man for a moment, then thrust his hand into an inner pocket, drew out his military wallet, handed it over, went bounding down the granite steps, past the guns of the bulldog breed. He was at the great front gate when the sergeant shouted to him. He didn't look back, went out, turned into the street, went striding the slate-slabbed footpath towards the city.

A squad of old soldiers, marching in old-style column-of-fours, some in natty business suits, others in the poor rumpled best of workingmen, with their regimental flags and wreaths of poppies, were heading down the road towards the Anzac Memorial, no doubt in annual commemoration of some battle ordered by a Brass Hat with his feet on a Staff-Office table, which had reduced them from a battalion to this boy-scout's squad. In memory of those for whom they would lay the wreaths they would quote what was graven on the plinth of the Memorial: *They Shall Not Grow Old as We That Are Left Grow Old.* Jeremy's face quivered at the pathetic sight of them. Other passer's by doffed their hats.

On the bridge over the dirty river, ensconsed in the little alcoves designed for those with leisure to view the passing rubbish from the factories upstream, were guffawing soldiers taking scarcely concealed liberties with giggling girls. A great banner stretched across it between lamp-posts: AUSTRALIA WILL BE THERE – ARE YOU GOING TO BE THE ODD MAN OUT?

Poor fellow my Country!

Jeremy returned to the hotel, to his suite, began at once to pack. He was almost finished – when a knock at the door. He called entry. It was Mark Esk – not General Sir Marcus Esk, Bt, DSO, etc – because no military nobleman could look so haggard, so near to tears. Jeremy's set face did not change, except for a tiny furrow as of pain between his eyes. After staring at the beaten man for a moment, he said shortly, 'I'm sorry, Mark . . . but no post-mortem, if you please.'

Esk replied in a flat voice, 'I'm glad you realize that a death's concerned.'

'Death of your scheming for your Commonwealth?'

'If I've been doing what can be classed as scheming, it has been in all honesty for what I've deemed the greatest hope for the progress of mankind. It's that hope that's just died, Jeremy . . . at your hands.'

Returning to his packing, Jeremy remarked, 'The last thing I expected of you was melodrama.'

Esk took a moment to answer, husky now, 'Is it melodrama to mourn the destruction of what you've given your life to?'

Jeremy snipped the locks, clinched the buckles. As he took up the suitcase and turned again to Esk, the latter said, again in that flat tone, 'You gave them exactly what they've wanted the whole time I've been here . . . a chance to discredit me so as to get rid of me.'

Standing with the case, Jeremy said, 'You only have to disown me to get your credit back.'

'The Australian way. Yes . . . but disowning you, to me means disowning the "one just man in Sodom".'

'Another thing I didn't expect of you, Mark, is casuistic clap-trap.'

'I myself didn't expect that I'd ever have to explain myself to you. What I meant was that without you I can't defend Australia . . . and without Australia defended by its own people and their kindred, our Commonwealth goes down.'

'You know I don't give a damn for your Commonwealth. Nor do the mob back there . . . nor even legally belong to it, in fact, nor want to. The old bullying Empire . . . God Save the King and Bless the Lee-Endfield Rifle will do them.'

'You also evidently don't give a damn for your own country.' Jeremy's eyes became hard again. Esk went on: 'You know that *they* don't . . . that they'll make no effort to defend it. Hence, either it will be overrun by the Japanese eventually, or someone you'll have to yell for help to . . . the Yankees, who never do anything for nothing. Your alternative is to become part of the Japanese Empire or the U.S.A. . . . or perhaps the U.S.S.R.'

'My alternative, Mark, is to die fighting any bastard who tries to intrude on the bit of country I now consider I belong to, even if I can't claim it belongs to me.'

Poor Whiskers drooped. Jeremy, advancing towards him, said more gently, 'I'm truly sorry to disappoint you, Mark . . . but I would have had to eventually. I've felt all the while lately that you've had me trapped. Better now than later . . . .'

'If it'd only been later . . . I might have got enough done to have carried on . . . have recruited enough of the other Jeremy Delacys there must be about. We haven't been nearly strong enough for the Larrikin Gang, just the two of us.'

'You never would have been strong enough, Mark. Don't forget this is a convict community . . . and its symbol of authority the Cat-o'-nine-tails. As you can't flog 'em, you can't beat 'em . . . and, as the old saying has it: If you can't lick 'em, join 'em. They're really so dumb, for all their con-man shrewdness, that you could feasibly outwit them in the end.'

Esk sighed: 'No . . . having lost you, I've lost the battle. There's nothing for it but for me to resign as C-in-C and go home to become a Little Englander. That's what's wanted, of course. I left them gloating over the victory.'

'Have you resigned?'

'Not officially. I'll do that on a plea of ill-health or something . . . to satisfy the High Command and the political hypocrites here. But in effect I've done so . . . in defending you.'

'There's no defending my action. Militarily it's indefensible . . . .'

'Of course. But it wasn't your action I defended . . . it was you.'

'What d'you mean?'

'I had to defend you against their malice. You could be court-martialled for your action . . . if truly a serving soldier. I had to tell them you were not.'

Jeremy gaped. 'Eh?'

'I lied to you about there being no record of your resignation of commission. It had been duly dealt with, as you supposed. With promotion, I bribed the records man to expunge it. I confessed as much to the Larrikins just now. Thus, in effect, did I sign and seal my retirement from the fight.' Esk ended in a gusty sigh.

Jeremy stared at him. Whiskers' face wobbled in a weak smile. 'Anyway, since I couldn't do without you, I'm better out of it.' The narrow head drooped again for a moment, to come up with a different expression, the old suave one. He said, 'I can't go on loving you, since you've destroyed what's been so dear to me . . . but have no right to hate you, when it was I involved you . . . and, anyway, I couldn't hate anyone I've loved as well as you. Goodbye, dear boy.' He thrust out his hand.

Now Jeremy's face quivered as he took the hand and met the smiling eyes. He could only mutter in reply, 'Goodbye, Mark.'

Releasing the hand, Jeremy snatched up his case, went swiftly out. He waited for no elevator, but almost ran down the wide stairs. A long-coated flunkey at the bottom saluted him, asking if he wanted a taxi, then flew ahead to get him one. Within a minute he was settled in one, heading for the Interstate Station.

At the station he learnt that it would be days before he could find comfortable accommodation on an express train: 'There's a war on, sport, y'know.' However, he was told that he might make the journey in half the time of waiting by doing it in stages aboard local trains, a convenient one of which would be leaving in half an hour.

Thus, in half an hour he was on his way, standing out on the car platform, watching the Queen City glittering in the afternoon sunlight, fading away into summer haze, gone for ever from his sight – and good riddance to her, to judge by his expression.

III

Jeremy arrived in Sydney in mid-afternoon on the Saturday. After establishing himself in a hotel close to Central Station, from his room he telephoned the reception desk and asked if a call might be made for him to a number he gave, to inform a Mrs Candlemas that he was in Town and would like to see her. Within a few minutes he was informed that Mrs Candlemas was expecting him, and to come at once. Evidently Alfie had heard from Frank. Jeremy went out at once, got a taxi, gave Alfie's address.

Despite the initial hurry, he had the taximan set him down short of his destination. It was at the little park where last visit he used to take his morning run. Perhaps it was sight again of the *Queen Mary*, in full view from here, that caused him to curtail the trip. Still, when at length he went on his way, it was with steps showing no sign of eagerness.

The same elfin face presented itself to his ringing the doorbell, the smile as wide as ever. However, there was a glitter in the black eyes rather like that of a snake about to strike, which probably was what caused Jeremy to drop his own as he took the outstretched hand. 'Well, hello!' she cried merrily. Then seeing that his eyes flitted away again, now from what they had fallen on, she laughed: 'Looks like triplets, doesn't it!' Certainly the bulge beneath her maternity gown looked enormous, seen for the first time by one having known her only in girlish slimness. 'Come on in,' she said.

He had a package of wine, brandy, cigarettes. She said, 'We'll save it for the head-wetting. I'm off booze and tobacco. I'll make some tea.'

She had everything ready. While she made the tea, he remarked, somewhat feebly, 'You're looking very well.'

She smirked. 'The flowering of womanhood . . . or fruiting, is it? Makes every woman bloom . . . till she's had two or three. But I'm afraid I can't say the same about you. What've you been doing to yourself?'

He shrugged. 'Just getting old. You know I met Frank, of course.'

'I'd hardly have expected you to come if he hadn't asked you.' She said it easily, and with a smirk that said *Don't Care*, even while the snake's eyes struck.

'I wouldn't have needed asking if I'd known about the book.'

'It isn't finished. But you'd have got your copy when it's published.'

'I understand that's hardly likely in these times.'

'You never know.' She settled down with the teapot.

'I understand it could get you into trouble if published during the war.'

She became shrill. 'The bloody bastards and their war! But you can always publish things secretly. The Commos do.'

'They'd go to jail for it now. Do you want to go to jail?'

'It'd advertise my book.'

'Not in these days. Nobody would know anything about it . . . or about your book. They'd simply lock you up, with the powers they now have . . . and destroy your book.'

'Some books would survive . . . for reproduction.'

'You say you haven't got it finished yet. They mightn't let you finish it.'

'Let them try to stop me!'

'Don't be silly, girl. Under their National Security Regulations they can do anything . . . and *will* do anything if their purpose is crossed . . . and I presume you're not writing something that'll get you the O.B.E.'

As she laughed, he glanced at her writing table by the window, on which, with typewriter, books, and scattered notes, was a pile of typescript. He asked, 'What do you do with the script as you finish it?'

'Stash it away.'

'Where?'

'I've got a hiding place.'

'Good enough to beat the best sniffing-out noses in the land?'

'I'm not silly enough not to keep a copy, in case anything happens.'

'*Keep* it?'

'Well, take it . . . and give it to a friend.'

'What friend?'

'You're asking as many questions as Security. You didn't go to Melbourne to join them did you? If you can't lick 'em, join 'em, eh? Eeeeeah!'

'It isn't funny, my dear. You've got a heap of script there. Is there anything in it that could be taken as subversive?'

She gave a squeak of mirth: 'Is there ever! I'll give it to you to read afterwards.'

'I didn't come here to read your script . . . but to take it off you . . . what you've done.'

The black eyes struck. 'Oh . . . Frank's orders, eh?'

'More my own inclination. I guess it's a red-hot security risk at the moment . . . and also that it's something too valuable to be lost to this Nation at the hands of the bastards at present in control of it . . . .'

'Thank you, Sir!' She bowed ironically. 'I didn't think you had so high an opinion of me.'

He answered, stiffly, 'You seem to have forgotten it was I started you on it.'

She reached to touch his knee, softened, murmuring, 'No, dear Jeremy . . . only . . . only . . . you've been so silent.'

'Will you give the script to me to look after?' When she stared at him hard, as if trying to read his thoughts, he added: 'I've got hiding places where no one but myself could find anything.'

'Including me?'

'Yes . . . until it's safe to be published.'

She turned from him to pour more tea. Giving him his cup, she said, 'It's about you, largely, you know.'

He half smiled. 'Then it ought to be burnt.'

She shot a swift dark look. 'You might burn it, too. You mightn't like the you I've made out of you.'

He chuckled: 'I couldn't have a lower opinion than I have of the present me.'

'That's your trouble. But I've made the *You* you could be . . . only for that self-rejection complex of yours.'

'Hurrah for that self-rejection complex. It'll make you famous . . . unless you foolishly let the snoopers get hold of it first.'

'Over my dead body!'

'What's the good of that? Please let me have all you've done, to take away with me.'

'Where?'

'Back home to Lily Lagoons.'

'What about the rest? I've got at least another month's work on it.'

'You can send it . . . .'

'With the mail being censored?'

'I've thought of that. Tom Toohey gets parcels from down here . . . from the catalogues the big stores send, you know. We'll do it like that.'

The black eyes regarded him gravely, in that childish way of old. She asked, 'Why not take me along, too ... and save the postage!' The first simplicity was swept away by a smirk.

'I'm afraid I'm not going to be so secure from Security myself. Then we'd both be involved. That's why I've thought of Tom Toohey.'

The black eyes became snake-like again. She flung a hand towards her desk, saying haughtily, 'The Jeremy Delacy there isn't afraid of involvement.'

'He doesn't live in the real world. Besides . . . he isn't concerned about his creator. If necessary, I can get you a secluded place to live in while you finish it.'

'Where?'

'You know the pub down in the Centre . . . Cullity's place . . . . ?'

'Bridie Cullity . . . Finnucane's daughter . . . your old flame, eh?' When he coloured, she laughed. 'As if she'd have me!'

He frowned muttering, 'What're you talking about?'

'As if I don't know! Her jealousy of me was the give-away.'

He asked stiffly, 'Well, will you let me have the manuscript?'

'I'll think about it.'

'You'll have to think fast. I'm off tomorrow.'

She looked dismayed. 'Oh, no!'

'I don't want to stay round these parts. For a start I don't like them . . . and then, I've had a bit of trouble with the Army . . . .'

She bent to him eagerly. 'Tell me about it.'

'When you give me the script.'

'Well . . . I'll have to get it together. I'll have to take notes. You forget things . . . like names and things . . . you're apt to change them as you go along. I have to get the copy back, too.'

'How long will that take?'

'Several days. My friend lives in the country.'

'Then that could be sent to Tom Toohey.'

'You *are* in a hurry. I'd like you to read some, too, before you go.'

'I'll be glad to.'

'Well, I'll get it for you right away. You can be reading it while I'm finishing off the day's quota. You'll stay to dinner?' He nodded.

Big-bellied, she lumbered away, not to the writing desk, but to the sideboard, which she opened to reveal a stack of script. She took out some of the script, came with it, looking eagerly childish again. He remarked, 'Is that what you call Stashing it Away?'

'I told you I had to keep it at hand for reference. I hide it at night.'

'It's to be hoped Inspector Ballywick makes his raids by night.'

The raised child's mouth fell. Probably Jeremy realized that it was a sacred moment, because his voice changed on the instant, and he reached for the script with a reverent movement, saying, 'The dream come true, eh?' He read aloud the outer page, which was inscribed in large letters with black ink: '*The Last Australians – A Novel by Aelfrieda Tripconny* . . . hmm!'

She giggled: 'Our first born . . . in the making. One of the twins . . . eeeee!'

As he turned the outer page, to read, she swung away, took up the tea-tray and went out to the kitchen, whistling: *If you Wish Upon a Star*.

When she returned, it was silently, to seat herself at her typewriter, and soon to become as absorbed in what she wrote as he in his reading.

Sounds from the kitchen a little later told of someone's being there. Jeremy looked up, looked at Alfie. Evidently it was not Inspector Ballywick sneaked in by the back way. Soon this fact was proven by the opening of the swing-door to the kitchen and the emergence of the lacquered goldilocks of Mrs Marsh, the Helper. The woman smirked and nodded recognition of Jeremy, then went through a dumb show that clearly implied that she was nursing this little-girl genius of theirs with complete understanding of the case, but finished with a hard sharp little look straight at him, surely betraying Alfie's madcap frankness about things that were, well: *Leave it at that*! her eyes snapped as she withdrew. Alfie did not notice her, sitting with colour heightening as her story-weaving fingers flew faster with passing time. Withdrawal of each finished sheet was done with a flourish and an impish smile, as if each time she gave an enemy a back-hander he could not hand back.

It was getting dark; so that Jeremy had to put on the light beside his chair. Alfie, with her young eyes, still worked on by the light from the window. The sky behind her curly head was pink. Already lights were blazing at the Garden Island Depot.

Mrs Marsh came, this time, right in, to announce in a tone of maternal authority, 'Enough's enough. Dinner'll be ready in 'alf hour.'

Alfie came out of her trance, smiled at her. 'All right, dear . . . set up.' She turned the elfin smile on Jeremy, then back to the typewriter, to tie up the last threads of her spell-weaving. She sighed gustily, dragged fingers through curls like a tired man, rose, came to Jeremy, and as he set aside the script, asked, 'Well?'

When Jeremy only pulled a face, she asked, 'What's that mean . . . lousy?'

'Means words of praise don't come easily to me. Anyway . . . it's what I expected.'

She eyed him. 'I suppose you *are* praising it. Anyway . . . wait till I get something to drink.' She went to the kitchen, to return with beer and a soft drink. He was reading again, and kept on until she had poured the drinks and was seated.

She asked, 'Do you like my hero?'

'Charles Belamy, I presume. I don't know yet. Seems a bit of a stuffed shirt . . . well, compared with your other very human characters.'

'He's you, of course.'

Mrs Marsh came in to lay the table. Alfie called her over to have a drink. Mother again, the woman gave the toast: 'Here's to the two babies . . . ought 'o be born 'bout same time. 'Er twins she calls 'em . . . eeeeeee!' Instantly she became serious: 'Wonderful bit o' work, though, ain't it? So real . . . just rotten like everything really is.'

'You've read it?' asked Jeremy.

'Well . . . not really. The words're a bit 'bove me edification. But dearie 'ere reads me bits and fills the gaps. In fac' she started it be tellin' me what she 'ad in mind to do . . . didn't you, dearie? Jes the way she tells me she's goin' 'o 'ave the baby . . . eh . . . what'm I sayin'?' She went red, swigged off her beer. 'Now I got to dish out.' She departed hastily.

Jeremy sat stony.

Alfie, staring at him, chuckled: 'Charles Belamy to perfection!'

Now he went red. She reached to touch him. 'Meant as a compliment . . . the uncompromising enemy of stupidity.' She lowered her voice: '*She* is that, of course . . . Sydney-stupid. Don't I show Charles ranting against all the effort put into education . . . yet they remain *Unedificated*, as rather aptly, if unwittingly, she puts it?'

'Ranting's right, if I may say so. Perhaps I'm prejudiced . . . but you make your Belamy a bit of a pontificator . . . rather like our friend the Bloke . . . or ex-friend, rather, as I presume he is.'

She retorted sharply, 'He isn't.' When he stared at her, she added: 'I know politically he's a fool . . But he does know literature . . . and has sustained me. For that matter . . . but for him and *Australia Free*, where would I be?'

'Has he seen this?'

'Of course. And he'll see it's published when possible. Who else would publish it in this benighted country . . . war or no war?' She said it all quite frankly in Mrs Marsh's hearing.

Jeremy said, 'It doesn't read anything like as dangerous as I'd expected . . . only people trying to make reality of that old *Australia Felix* dream . . . '

She interrupted with a whoop: 'Wait till you get into it!' She heaved herself up, to go back to her desk, search amongst the script, and came back with a couple of sheets. Handing them to him, she said with a smirk, 'There's something to give you a taste. Although it's near the end, there's plenty of stuff like it earlier on.' She turned and went out after Mrs Marsh to the kitchen.

Jeremy's eyes widened, jaw sagged, as he read. He read on, enthralled, while the two women concluded the laying of the table. Mrs Marsh went out. Alfie stood by the table watching, arms folded above her other offspring, her expression impish.

Jeremy was lost in a description of how Charles Belamy, with a squad of young daredevils, apparently part of a private army of his, while others of them diverted attention by acting as a launch-load of drunken louts clamoring to board the *Queen Mary*, were fitting magnetic mines to the vessel's hull the night before troops were due to go aboard.

As he finished what there was of it and looked up, she came across, took the sheets from him, went back to the desk. As she came back to him and he rose, she demanded, 'What about it now?'

His answer was scarcely audible: '*Christ!*'

She said, 'Come on and eat,' and took his arm. 'I'm starving these days. I'd love to eat and eat . . . but can't while I'm writing, 'cause it makes me sleepy. Have to stick to two meals . . . like you. Starve one of my twins all day to feed the other. I make up for it at dinner. Watch me!'

They ate in silence for a while, she quite greedily. Then she said with a smirk, 'Shocked, are you?'

He replied warily, 'It's certainly a dramatic scene.' Then with a wry smile he added: 'Anyone'd think it was written by any old-hand saboteur.'

She became excited. 'I've spent hours reading on explosives . . . mines and things. I even went in for a secret swim the other night to get the effect of the phosphorescence.'

He looked aghast: 'In your condition?'

She laughed: 'Scared your baby'll grow-up to be a saboteur?'

He went red, dropped eyes to plate.

She resumed her guzzling.

At length she said, 'That great ship out there didn't simply sail into Our 'Arbour . . . it was towed in for me by Golden Bunyips. I so badly needed a terrifically dramatic scene in which the group . . . . '

'What group?'

'The Last Australians. You'll find that Charles forms this group . . . to defy the Britishism that's putting the last stranglehold on us by getting us into this war. Charles and his group refuse to consider themselves belligerents, because they've been denied a say in the declaration of war . . . have been tricked into thinking Australia's a true Nation, instead of still a British Dominion because those bastards haven't ratified the Treaty of Westminster . . . .' She choked over her food with anger.

Recovered, she set knife and fork aside, to go on excitedly: 'They're declared traitors, naturally, by the Britishists . . . and like our ancestors who first had the guts to rebel against British tyranny, have to take to the bush . . . bushrangers . . . but with the difference that they don't have to rob Judge McEvoy and other bastards. They've got the sympathy and help of at least half their fellow countrymen. They've got an aeroplane, fast cars, radio, spies everywhere. But they've got to make some terrifically bold move to prove themselves . . . and with a minimum of violence and no actual hurt to their own countrymen or country. Well, think of a better way than to sink the biggest ship in the world, which the Britishists've had the bloody effrontery to bring right into the heart of the land itself, you might say, to take away the cream of our manhood. I'd thought of scores of ways . . . blowing up Army camps, sinking warships flying the white ensign . . . but it meant killing Australians, hurting Australia. Then there she is, towed almost to my front door by the Bunyips . . . Her Britannic Majesty, *Queen Mary*! I saw her arrive through that window. I was amazed. I thought I was dreaming. It was the postman told me what she'd come for. He's a bit of a rebel . . . and we often yarn. He said, "Pity we couldn't put a sticky-bomb under her."

'It didn't strike me that *I* could put a bomb under her, that a story-teller is God and can do anything in imagination . . . till I woke up next morning. I get up about one a.m., you know . . . go to bed with the kookaburras. There she was out there, in the late moonlight . . . just a black bulk with only a light or two . . . and there was the marvellous idea, too!' She was quivering with excitement. Mrs Marsh, coming in with dessert, scolded her.

But Alfie couldn't be shut up. She went on: 'What the group do, when they've got the mines fixed and ready to detonate by remote control, is radio the ship and tell the crew it has ten minutes to get off, that an electrical device will intervene if they try to get at the mines and will set them off at once. Imagine it . . . *BOOM*! . . . and down it goes, the symbol of Britishism, down into the depths of Sydney Harbour, never to be recovered!' The black eyes were shining. She belched with the indigestion she was giving herself.

She met Jeremy's stare, asked, 'Shocked?'

'No . . . scared, rather.'

'What of?'

'Same thing as Frank . . . what might happen to *you*.'

She became shrill: 'Everybody's scared. That's how the bastards get away with it.'

'Would Frank know about this piece?'

'Yes . . . I was just starting on it when he left.'

'What'd he have to say about it?'

'You know Frank . . . the little ironies. He only said, "Well don't sink her before I get aboard and well out to sea." '

'Poor Frank!'

She flared. 'Why do you say that?'

'He's very worried about you.'

'I know. That's why I didn't want him round. Looks like I'll have to get rid of you, too.' She became shrill again: 'I can look after myself!'

'That's just what you're not doing.'

'Do you expect me to give up writing this thing that takes the very lid off the rottenness of our country, just because I might get jailed under the National Security Bloody Britishist Regulations? You told me yourself, long ago, and told hundreds of others here last year, that if we enter another war not of our deliberate choosing, we're sunk. And yet you expect . . . '

'I expect nothing but that you do it discreetly . . . or rather, I hope . . . no, I don't expect or hope anything. I'm just going to see to it that no evidence of your indiscretion's left lying about.'

'Is that all you can call my lovely book . . . an indiscretion?'

'No . . . I call it your lovely book, too. It's your behaviour over it . . . telling everybody . . . the postman, the helping-woman . . . worse, that lunatic the Bloke, who'll sell you up the river to make capital out of it for himself. He's mad enough to act on what you've written.'

'And why not? That's what it's for. To inspire people . . . to revolution, if necessary. We're the only people on God's earth who've never had a revolution. Our great patriots never get past starting a riot . . . and then go into Parliament on the strength of it, and swear allegiance to the sworn enemy . . . or go off and hide in the bush.'

'I can see I'll have to take you and hide you in the bush, too. You don't understand there's a war on . . . and that these people can do anything to you, *anything*. War's something you've never experienced.'

'I'm experiencing now. Frank wanted me to hide, too. If I had I'd've missed everything . . . this biggest ship in the world come to take the flower of our country, and those running the country bragging about it as if it were an honour. Christ . . . what's going on's incredible!'

'It's what went on before.'

'And what'd any of you do about it? Did anyone write a great book about the filthy thing *as a filthy thing*? The best you did was to form the RSL, originally to protect the men who'd been sooled off to war and came home to be chucked on the scrap-heap . . . and then grabbed by the Britishists to make the stinking thing it is today, sooling men off to another Britisher war. And Anzac Day . . . inaugurated to make the Nation aware of the frightful thing that happened that day, but glorified by every fat politician, general, parsonical sod, into . . . into . . . the abomination it is . . . ' She choked with emotion now. 'And you . . . even you . . . with all your hatred of it all and your strength and courage to stop it . . . what'd you do? Go off into the bush to become the Scrub Bull . . oh!'

She dropped burning face to hands. But in a moment up it came, with eyes flashing all the brighter for having been washed with tears. 'I'm not going away anywhere. I'm going to see it through. Everything that happens now goes into the book. Tomorrow there's the first big march through the city. I'm going to see it, drink it in to the last drop . . . to bring it out in words that'll be bayonets to stab the Britishist bastards to the heart!'

Jeremy could only stare, overwhelmed by the passion of the artist. She went on: 'The first part of the contingent will be going aboard that thing out there tomorrow . . . their crack regiment . . . all recruited in Sydney. They'll detrain at Central . . . then march through the city, to be saluted by the military brass, the Lord Mayor, the clergy, at the Town Hall. The city will be *en fête* . . . to see the young manhood of the country herded like cattle into the world's biggest cattle-boat. They march to the Domain . . . from where they'll go down to the wharves to be taken out to the Queen of Cattle-boats. After that, to add insult to injury, there'll be a grand recruiting rally in the Domain . . . to call for more cattle. That Jasper Jemeson, the singer, will be there to sing *Goodbye* to the boys who're going . . . and to stir up those who haven't. He's just come home from England, where he's lived ever since he became famous. He's been singing on the radio, *ad nauseam*, so-called patriotic songs . . . and at recruiting rallies . . . and talking, too, the bastard! . . saying it makes him feel ashamed to be Australian to see all the young men walking about in civvies. He's one of the heads of the Recruiting Committee. And who d'you think's in it too . . . and the loudest mouthed of all the soolers . . . your old mate, the Colt.'

'The Colt?' murmured Jeremy.

'The creature you chucked in the sea that Sunday. You ought to hea· him . . . the Old Digger. He's another who declares himself sickened with shame over what he calls the Slackers, Shirkers, Skulkers. Haven't you heard either of them on the radio?'

'I don't listen to that kind of thing.'

'Well, you ought to! Come with me tomorrow . . . and get as sick as me about it . . . and then you might do something!'

'You *will* get sick in that condition.'

'Rubbish! I never felt stronger physically in my life. Besides, it's an asset to be like this in a crowd.'

'How?'

She laughed: 'It gets me up the front. Tomorrow I'll tell'em my baby's daddy's in the march.'

He shook his head. She shrilled: 'Does that mean you won't come?'

He sighed: 'I'll come all right . . . if only to keep you out of trouble.'

'Bless you, darling Jeremy!' She rose clumsily to reach and embrace him, sent her half-eaten dessert flying in the spoon so that it spattered him. 'Oh, I'm sorry!' she cried, grabbing a napkin to clean him. 'I get carried away after I've been working. It's all so exciting . . . the power it gives you . . . to make or break things.' She kissed his brow, his lips, met his alarmed resistance with a loud protest: 'But you're the father of my babies . . . my lovely twins!'

He groaned, with rolling eyes on the kitchen door.

She laughed merrily: 'My Charles Belamy . . . scared of women . . . but what a man!'

Dinner was over. She went to sit with him on the settee, leaning against him, yawning like a sleepy little girl, saying how tired she was, but keeping on babbling about her story. Before long, Mrs Marsh came from the kitchen saying, 'Now how 'bout beddo, dearie?' Looking at Jeremy the woman said, 'Wears herself out.'

Jeremy handed her into the strong arms stretched out to her. He offered his cheek for the kiss. Alfie said, 'Don't go yet, Jeremy, darling. Stay and keep on reading me. Stay all night. We'll have coffee when I get up.' Yawning, she let Mrs Marsh lead her away.

Jeremy read till Mrs Marsh, having put everything to rights, came to say she was going home. Then he put the script down, saying that he was tired himself from much travelling and would like to go. The woman took the script from him as if she owned it, stowed it back in the sideboard, which she didn't even lock. When Jeremy asked her wouldn't she also put away the small stack by the typewriter, she answered, 'Can't touch nothink she's workin' on.'

They left the house together. He offered to take her in the taxi he intended to call from a phone booth. She declined, saying she still had work to do in the neighbourhood. While waiting for the taxi he stared across the water at the dark bulk of the mighty troopship, her lack of lights, if the condition was regulated by some rule of war, contrasting idiotically with the blaze of the Naval Depot. He had the taxi take him back to the hotel. Soon he was in bed.

The early part of next morning, Jeremy spent at Central Station, bribing his way to getting a berth to Brisbane on an express train leaving that night by the old inland route. Evidently he had learnt much about train-travelling these days. Afterwards he gave himself to securing the services of a taximan who would see him through the afternoon's commitments. He found an amiable fellow who assured him he could make a simple matter of it. Then he telephoned Alfie, to be answered by Mrs Marsh, who said the Little Lady was Hard at It. He left a message with her to say he would arrive at two. Time of the March was three.

Alfie was ready when he arrived, excited, and looking very lovely – at least the top half of her. She was bursting with what she had just now been writing: about the Britishist Government's collapse in the face of the furore caused by the sinking of the *Queen Mary*, with resultant taking over office by the Labor Party under the leadership of a famous anti-Britishist who had suffered persecution during the Last Turn-out for fighting against conscription, but even this hero operating only under the tacit patronage of the invincible and still elusive Charles Belamy. Her chattering of events that had to her become realer than reality sounded strange, with the great ship lying out there, smoke pouring from one of her funnels, no doubt signalling preparation for the thousands of men who soon would be disappearing into her mighty maw. The taximan became interested, asked questions, looked disappointed upon learning that it was only in a book. He growled, 'Wisht some'un *could* get rid of this damn Government . . . and be strong enough to keep Labor from makin' the mess o' things they al'ays does. I don' like them Dictators . . . still, we sure need a Strong Man in this country.'

'You anti-British?' Alfie asked recklessly.

'Lady, I'm anti-everthink's not Aussie . . . and Aussie's got no business in this flamin' war.'

Alfie clapped him on the shoulder, crying, 'Good on you, mate!'

Very cleverly, the taximan took them by back ways that avoided the mile-long railed-off route of the march, to drop them right beside the Town Hall, with the need only to climb a low grassy bank to get a grandstand view. He left them with arrangement to pick him up again at a point up Park Street, which, simply ducking under the barricades, they could reach within a few minutes after the parade had passed. The Saluting Stand, right before the Town Hall entrance, was only twenty yards or so away.

There were few people here on the lawn, compared with the crush below on the street. Even without having to tell that fib about her pudding's daddy, Alfie was let through to the front, and was even able to get a spot to sit down while waiting. Music of the moment was coming through amplifiers hung on lamp-posts: what sounded like *Soldiers of the King*, and then *Colonel Bogie* – no certainty about it, owing to some acoustical freak.

The music stopped suddenly. Then the flags screening the short corridor leading to the stand from the Town Hall portico began to bulge with invisible passengers. First onto the stand was a small nosy man wearing the uniform of the Municipality, who darted round amongst the potted palms and microphones, like a terrier in search of intruding cats. Then he leapt back to the entrance, to stand at attention as the first of the party appeared: none other than His Worship the Lord Mayor, in full regalia, fur-trimmed robe, chain of office, weird fore-and-aft flat-sided hat. Behind His Worshipful Lordship came the aldermen, as hard-faced a gang as one would have seen in chains in the old days, despite their frock coats and striped trousers, and their ladies, richly-gowned as successful brothel madames.

Alfie murmured to Jeremy, 'Why must the mayors of Australian capital cities be called Lord Mayors? Is there something diocesan about municipal administration, so that His Nibs is like the Bishop, while the others are mere parish parsons?'

'I wouldn't know, my dear. Isn't knowing such things more in your line?.

'Isn't it knowing the Nation? I've never found out. But I suppose, like everything else, it's just slavish copy of English things.' She added with a giggle 'I wonder did the first Lord Major of Sydney wear a ball-and-chain as well as his chain of office?'

Jeremy squinted to see if anyone had overheard. If anyone had, the interest immediately was lost as the amplifiers began to crackle with different versions of the Lord Mayor's speech: 'Leddies, gemmen, gemmen . . . gethered 'ere . . . t'die . . . t'die . . . 'istoric koishion . . . stirric poison . . . Sy'ney lads . . . dads . . . ow-er boyees . . . boyees . . . bower boidees . . .'

Alfie had her note-book ready. She shut it, saying, 'Damn . . . I'd've liked to hear what the fool said.'

Jeremy grinned .'Can't you guess it? Anyway . . . his accent should do for the record, shouldn't it?'

It was the authentic Sydney-sider accent, vestigial of Cockey-convict origins. Old Perce as he was being named in cat-calls might well have had a symbolic ball-and-chain hidden beneath his fantastic Cockney clobber.

Presumably it was a kind of civic blessing of this city's noblest sons. It lasted about five minutes, to end in cheers from the common herd, along with a few rude remarks about the city's finances. Old Perce withdrew with dignity, giving his place to one of the Military Brass who were mingled with aldermen, clergy, madames. The last movement caused Jeremy to exlaim like a blackfellow, 'Eh, look out!'

'What is it?' asked Alfie.

Jeremy's answer was drowned in the burst of clapping that greeted the leading military gentleman's saluting the crowd. It was General Tubs from GHQ.

It was all nicely timed. Into the silence that fell on the clapping came the strains of a distant band: *Poom-pom-pom-boom . . . boom-pom-boom.* Faint cheering came with it. General Tubs, on the very edge of the red-carpeted stand, drew himself to stiff attention.

The band was approaching rapidly, as proper, when it led the Pride of the Nation, quick-marching in its eagerness for death and glory – *Pompom-a-pompom, pomboom-a-pompom, boompom-a-boompom-a-pompom-a-mee* . . . .

'Good Christ!' muttered Jeremy.

'What is it now?' demanded Alfie.

Because of the approaching storm of sound, he had to bend to her. 'What the band's playing.'

'What is it?'

'Listen.'

She cupped an ear.

Pompom-a-pompom, pompom-a-pompom, pomboom-a-pomboom-a-pompom-mee . . . .

She looked at him with black eyes wide. '*Waltzing Matilda*?'

He nodded. The crowd back along the street were singing above band and cheering: *Waltzing Matilda, waltzing Matilda, who'll come a-waltzing Matilda with me* . . . .

'Made into a march!' cried Alfie, shining with pleasure. 'Who'd've believed it!'

Others about them were commenting, too. Yes – who'd believe the favourite old bush ballad would become Our Boys Marching Song?

Jeremy soon checked Alfie's pleasure, bawling in her ear, 'It was originally a marching song.'

Staring at him, she said, 'No . . . a camp-fire song from Queensland!'

'A marching song from England.' He drew away.

Not the way it was being sung all round them now: *And he sang as he shoved that jumbuck in his tucker-bag, who'll come a-waltzing Matilda with me* . . . .

Alfie hauled him back, howled at him, 'Are you sure?'

Close to her ear again he sang with the crowd: '*Marching with Marlborough, marching with Marlborough, who'll come a-marching with Marlborough and me . . . and we sing as we shove our halberds up the Frenchy's arse, who'll come a-marching with Marlborough and me*. According to General Esk, who ought to know.'

She had turned quite pale. Then the blood rushed to her face. Her eyes blazed, mouth opened to give vent to anger. He grabbed her close, saying swiftly, 'No . . . not here. Keep it for your book. Here they come.'

She shrank against him, trembling.

The crowd were roaring it as the band came up blaring it . . . *Pompom-a-pompom, boompom-a-boompom, pomboom-a-pomboom, a-pompom-a-pom, and he sang as he sat and waited while his billy boiled, who'll come a-waltzing Matilda with me* . . . .

Behind the brazen blare were two tall bannermen with flags: the Five-starred Banner in which the Southern Cross is cancelled out by the crossword puzzle of St George, St Andrew, St Patrick, and St David – and the Puzzle itself, in all its ancient arrogance. A few paces behind these came the Senior Officer, with naked sword at the slope. At his heels were a squad of fellow gentry similarly accoutred. Then the gleaming forest of bayonets, a suspended flickering forest of flame.

General Tubs came to the salute as the flags drew level. Simultaneously the Senior Officer screamed, 'Eyeeees left!' and with the swivelling of his own eyes, brought his sword to the Present.

A flourish of other swords, and surely a score of cricked necks.

The scream went down the fiery line: *Eyeeees left . . . Eyeeees left . . . Eyeeees had a good home and Eyes left!*

Streamers flying and confetti cascading while tramp-tramp-tramp the Flower of the Nation passed to the beat of the one song they could call their own:

Who'll come a-marching, who'll come a-marching,
Who'll come a-marching with Marlborough and me,
And our ghosts will be heard when you stand beside the Cenotaph,
Who'll come a-waltzing with Blamey and me!

Passing, passing – out of sight – out of hearing. The crowd hung as if stunned by it. Even General Tubs was slow to drop his hand, as if in momentary acknowledgement of the silent army of the past that trudged behind. Then he about-turned right smartly, marched himself out with chubby dignity.

Alfie looked stunned. Jeremy took her arm. 'Let's get a move on.'

But she pressed against his shoulder.

'What's the matter?' he asked.

She sobbed, 'Poor fellow my country! Isn't there anything any good in it at all?'

He got her moving. Already the crowd about them were dispersing, while down in the street the police were dismantling the barricades. He said, 'I thought you'd worked that out. Isn't that what your *Last Australians* is for . . . to show the lousiness?'

She kept her head against his shoulder. Nothing unusual about a weeping woman there and then. But surely the others wept for very different reasons, some perhaps even for show. Sniffing back the tears she said, 'I've been hoping that showing the lousiness might rouse up those who are capable of becoming the First Australians . . . those who'll want to build a True Commonwealth, not just exploit a lovely land and one another.'

'Don't despair of it.'

'I do now . . . after that. It looks as if we've got no originality, no special quality at all, nothing that'll be of any use to mankind . . so no reason to become but a dumping-ground for excess populations not wanted elsewhere, and a farm and a mine owned by outsiders to supply outsiders first . . . .' She broke off with a sob.

While she was dabbing her eyes he said, 'You'll see something even worse round at this recruiting rally. What about cancelling it?'

She drew a deep breath: 'No . . . I'll see it through.' She began to put her face to rights. She added: 'Then you can take me away to that place in the desert. That's where the book ought to be finished . . . in a desert . . . in despair.'

'All right then. But we'll have to move. Otherwise we'll never get there.'

They found the taxi waiting. By more clever manoeuvring they were taken to the Domain in a few minutes, set down amidst great Moreton Bay figs within twenty yards of the stand erected for the recruiting rally.

As yet the stand was deserted, except for a single policeman lounging in one of the cane chairs amidst the hanging bunting and the standing microphones. The usual Sunday-afternoon Domain mob were crowded along the road leading up from the city and round and down to the wharves of Woolloomooloo, to watch the passing troops. Already the troops were in the region. Now the band was playing something less ambiguous: *The British Grenadiers*. Already the glint of bayonets could be seen above the wall of the crowd.

Not everybody was interested in the passing troops. Under one of the big trees was a group of about fifty, standing round one of the portable rostrums that of ordinary Sundays were to be seen all over the Domain, but today were missing because of all-powerful opposition; except this one, belonging to a *coterie* brooking competition from no one – the Communists. That it was the Commos was announced by Alfie, who said that ordinarily they had held this best of all pitches and were very sore about having been ousted by the Soolers and interfered with recruiting rallies as much as they dared. Jeremy need not have been told who they were. On the rostrum stood that big fellow he had called Geordie, the one whose protuberant gut had made his locally famous straight-left to the solar nationally infamous as a foul blow. Doubtless his keen bushman's eye would have spotted the man. However, it was unlikely that the Pommy townie Geordie, trained only for spotting trouble he could exploit to the advantage of his Cause, would have recognized him at that distance. Geordie was haranguing his mob with belligerent gestures, perhaps annoyed because some were stealing glances at the marching Stooges of Capitalism. Nevertheless, Jeremy drew staring Alfie out of his line of sight. They halted under a fig tree quite close to the recruiting stand.

The band swung out of the procession, to stand aside and play the Stooges past, now with *Goodbye Dolly Gray*. Then when the latter were gone, to thump out the rest of their contact with their native land to the rhythm of their own foot-slogging, they shut up, formed themselves into marching order, and with trombone and trumpet at the slope, came marching towards the recruiting stand. Behind them came the small squad of officers and OR's of the Three Services, so-called, who would deal with those taken in by the ballyhoo from the stand. You have to act smart, before the mugs get time for second thoughts. Sign 'em in while they're coy with the public act of heroism, then whisk 'em away for the medical and swearing in. An Army truck stood by.

At the stand, the band formed itself into the order of the Salvation Army outside a pub, while the recuiting personnel settled themselves at flag-covered trestle-tables ranged behind barricades in front of the stand. The band's leader flourished his baton with a one, two, three: and it broke into what probably is the only truly Australian folk-tune, since it so truly expresses the people's simple faith: *Australia Will Be There.*

The crowd came pouring like meat-ants. Alfie and Jeremy were right against the barricade.

'There he is . . . the fat little sooling bastard!' hissed Alfie, as on to the stand by way of a rear stairway came a middle-aged man in expensive grey suit and trilby, but with left breast ablaze with beribboned medals.

A murmur from the crowd, too: 'There he is . . . Jasper Jemeson!'

A flutter of hand-clapping rose to a crashing wave. The plump little red-faced man, coming to the edge of the stand, removed his hat, to bow as if taking a curtain-call for one of his La Scala performances. Behind him was another man in civvies hung with medals, this one in blue serge and black homburg. Jeremy and Alfie recognized him together. Alfie would have hissed again, only Jeremy grabbed her, drew her back a couple of ranks from the rail. It was Tom Colt. Still the band was playing.

The Famous Baritone rose out of his bow to favour the audience less formally, with a wave and a larrikin grin, then turned towards the band, and signalled *diminuendo*, got it, waited till the refrain recommenced, and burst into magnificent song:

Rally round the banner of your country,
Take the field with brothers o'er the foam,
On land or sea, wherever you be,
Keep your eye on Germany,
Old England, home and beauty, have no cause to fee-ah,
Should old acquaintance be forgot? No, no, no-no-no!
Australia will be there-ere-ere-ere-ere, Australia will be there!

From the last deep resonant note, Jemeson raised his great voice and short arms: 'Now, all together . . . one, two, three . . . *Rally round the banner of your country* . . . come on, come on! That's better . . . *Wherever you be, keep your eye on Ger-her-many* . . . that's the stuff to give the troops . . . *Should old acquaintance be forgot* . . . now into it!' He signalled the band *crescendo*. It came crashing from the brass and a thousand throats:

Australia will be there-ere-ere-ere-ere,
Australia will be there!

The short arm silenced the band: *finito*!

In the sudden silence Jemeson leered at the crowd. So often had he held multitudes with that big voice in the little body. All the roaring had not frayed it by a fibre. It came booming forth like organ music: 'Thank you, friends, fellow Aussies, brothers in arms. I've told you before . . . but I'm never tired of telling it . . . how good it does my heart to sing to you like this under the blue skies and the golden Sun of our own good country. All the grand theatres in the world, all the grand audiences of kings and queens and dukes and duchesses, are nothing compared with this . . . the stage of the great Australian outdoors, and the audience my fellow Australians.'

A burst of applause, with yells of, 'Good on you, Jasper!'

He stopped it with a wave. 'But joyous as it is to my heart, it's not for the simple joy of it . . . .'

'No . . . it's for the dough!' yelled a voice from the back.

At once a howl from the crowd: 'Shut up!'

The chubby man drew himself up with dignity to glare at the point of interruption, resumed: 'I have a purpose . . . a great and urgent purpose. My friends, we are at war again . . . and with the same brutal enemy who mauled us so badly in the Last Turn-out. This time we mustn't let him get the advantage . . . .'

From another quarter at the rear another yell: 'He's already got it. You and your Capitalist mob give it to him at Munich, reckonin' he'd attack Russia . . . .'

The great voice rose even above the hubub rising to support him. 'It's thanks to *your* mob, Comrade, he's got an advantage.' A finger shot accusation at the point. 'Thanks to the treachery of the Workers' Fatherland!'

The crowd generally roared approval. There was scuffling.

The chubby hand called quiet. The rich baritone dropped to a tone of beguilement: 'Prepared to the hilt we must be . . . with every man capable of bearing arms trained and ready to use them. We don't want it like last time . . . with half our boys over there giving their lives, while the other half stayed at home bludging on their sacrifice . . . not even able to be shifted off their cowardly behinds by two referenda to conscript them . . . .'

Stir amongst the crowd; some angry shouts and scuffling. Alfie, flaming suddenly, raised her voice with other protestors: 'What a thing to say!'

A big woman, oldish, whiskery, standing at her shoulder, said, mildly enough, as if putting someone right on a point not understood, ''S right, too. Skulkin' mongrels wouldn't even go when they was conscripted.'

Alfie swung on her blazing. 'They were never conscripted!'

The hairy face puffed ruddily. Now the woman snapped, 'No . . . the dogs *wouldn't* be conscripted!' She added, with sudden drooping of jowls and sagging of corners of baggy eyes: 'My boy was killed in France.'

Alfie shrilled: 'So you'd have *all* the boys killed there, too!'

The eyes straightened up to glare. The voice was growling now: 'What . . . you a bloody Commo?'

The attention of those close was caught, and even that of Jasper Jemseon, halted in his delivery by the stir. Jeremy took Alfie's arm to draw her away. She pulled against him, to shriek up into the hairy face, 'No . . . I'm an Australian . . . not a transplanted Pommy!'

The woman showed false teeth under her fluffy moustache, shoved her face down, yelled in a hoarse alto, 'Don' you call me a Pommy, you dolly-faced bitch!'

The baritone boomed from the stand, 'What's the trouble down there?'

Those blocking his view drew back, as if it were his right to see. The big old woman turned to him, waving a great flop-muscled arm, raising her great voice: 'Commo piece 'ere, stickin' up for bludgin' slackers!'

Jeremy tugged at Alfie, growling, 'Come on out of here.'

Alfie would have gone with him now, pressing back through the crowd. But the old woman grabbed her other arm. 'No you don't!' Jerking Alfie away from Jeremy, she swung her so as to present her to those in front, those on the stand, the recruiting officers. 'Take a look at 'er . . . 'fore she goes underground wi' the rest the Commo rats . . . I 'ad a lovely boy killed in France by the likes o' 'er . . . IWW's and Sinn Feiners . . . . '

Jeremy lunged back, seized the wrist of the big restraining hand, twisted it to free Alfie, barking at the woman, 'Hands off, you bloody old fool!' He gave her a shove that sent her staggering back into the crowd, which had to grab her to stop her falling.

The woman yelled, 'Bill . . . Bill!'

Bill must have been the huge old man who came shouldering through the press, rumbling, 'Dong me wife, would yo'!' He aimed a blow at Jeremy that caught him on the left collar bone. Jeremy raised the arm and swiped the old man with it sideways. Thereupon the whiskery woman uttered a hoarse scream, jerked out of her helpers' hands, fell upon Alfie with hands clawing, Alfie grabbed at the hands. One of them, snatching free, lashed out backward, with a flash of a heavy gold ring, smote her across the face. Alfie fell back against the rail, goggling, blood beginning to burst from nostrils. The old woman raised the hand to give her another, but was grabbed by someone. Jeremy was flinging the old man off again.

Jemeson boomed, 'Ladies, ladies . . . this's a man's war!'

A burst of laughter. But Tom Colt, now at Jemeson's side, didn't laugh. From hard staring, he raised a finger and pointed, shouting, 'They're not Comms! . . . they're pro-Germans!' It came bellowing out of amplifiers in the trees.

Jemeson leant towards the Colt to speak. The Colt answered in a shout for everybody, 'Belong to the pro-Nazi Free Australia Movement . . . I know 'em!'

Jeremy grabbed Alfie again. But there was the old woman again, fairly mad now, spittle flying to her cracked-voiced screaming, 'Bloody 'Uns . . . killed my boy!' She came in battering. Jeremy tried to stop her, but was grabbed behind, hauled back into the crowd. Old Bill gave him a parting crack in the mouth, then turned to join his wife in dealing with the now collapsed Alfie.

The Colt's voice crashed out of the Moreton Bays, 'Pro-Germans . . . chuck 'em in the drink!'

Uproar rose – *Pro-Germans – Huns – Nazis*!

Jeremy, well back in the crowd, and pinioned, saw another heavy face before him, red and sweaty, but not berserk, cold and calculating even in its expression, the ruddiness and sweat probably due only to the exertion of getting through to this point of scented trouble. It was Geordie. He even grinned as he lifted his big fist, growling, 'Cop this, yo' Fascist bawstid!' He smashed the first into Jeremy's solar plexus. Nothing below the belt about this. As Jeremy sank breathless in the hands of those who held him from behind, Geordie brought his boot up into his crotch. Goggling Jeremy fell to the ground. Other boots dealt with him there.

Someone yelled, 'Fair go . . . fair go!' The voice stopped suddenly, as if silenced with a fist. There was female screaming from where Alfie was. Policemen and soldiers could be seen on the edge of the milling crowd. Fists were flying everywhere. Jemeson's voice boomed vainly through the amplifiers, 'Order . . . order!'

As if by prearrangment, a group of four snatched up senseless Jeremy, barged with him through the crowd, which gave way to them as if they had authority of some kind. They passed right through the crowd, dropped their burden when Geordie appeared from behind the wide root-buttressed trunk of a fig tree. All looked round. No one was watching. All other interest was centred in the brawling crowd. No doubt that was how Geordie and his men had planned things. Geordie bent over Jeremy. 'He's only knocked out,' he said. 'He can take a bit more.' He reached for the left hand, caught the wrist, brought the arm backwards over his own bent knee, gave it a jerk that made his own eyes pop with the effort and brought Jeremy's open – *Snap*! As Geordie dropped the arm inert, he grinned at the grey staring face. 'You won' be usin' that dirty left o' yourn in a 'oory, choom.' When Jeremy tried to struggle up the big fist shot out again, this time to take him on the chin. Jeremy dropped back with a grunt.

Geordie took another swift look round, then, rising, said, 'Chook the bawstid in the drink . . . loike 'is Fascist mate said. It'll bring 'im round. Get a move on. I'll keep nit.'

The water was close – just down over a grassy slope, over a pathway, a low sea wall. The four took up their burden as before, the one on the broken arm not gentler than before. So down – and a heave-ho up on to the wall. The tide was well down. The shore-line was another wall, steeply sloped, of weed-grown boulders. They lowered him over. He went skidding down the slimy slope, splashed into the opaque green water. The contact revived him on the instant. He floundered for a moment, then grabbed at the rocks, looked up, to see the four faces watching. A second – and they were gone.

It was only with the right hand that he gripped the rocks. He kept trying to bring up the left, but could do no more than raise the upper arm. Also, he was breathing badly, in short gasps that jerked his body. By his grimacing, all effort was at cost of considerable pain, of which, evidently, he was not yet fully aware. His clinging seemed to be little more than instinctive, to prevent his being pulled away by the tide. Rubbish floating in the murky water, a great flotilla of it, consisting of ice-cream cups and lolly-packets and the like, tossed from the lawns of the Botanic Gardens round the corner, showed the run of the tide here as parallel to the shore, flowing towards Woolloomooloo Bay. A couple of times, in dazed striving to use the useless hand, he lost his grip with the other and went along a yard or two with the rubbish, instinctively to grab at the rocks again.

Perhaps five minutes passed before there was indication in movement and expression that he had somewhat more regained his faculties. Sudden din of ship's whistling close at hand may have helped to rouse him. He looked towards the bay, to see come into view a ferry-steamer so heavy-laden as to look, at that distance of about quarter of a mile, like a piece of wood in a flood carrying a seething mass of meat-ants. It wasn't coming towards him, but heading straight out of the bay, which lay slantwise to his position, out of sight round a point.

The ferry was *Cock-a-doodling* so hard the fireman must have been hell-bent to give her steam. The khaki ants aboard were waving antennae at black ants on roof-tops of high buildings on the further shore and at others, invisible from.

here, who would be crowding the sea-wall of the Gardens. He turned from it, now to take note of his dragging arm. With right hand and hip, he got into a position where he could sit on the rocks. He applied his good hand to the injured elbow. Already it was swelling. He felt throat, ribs, scrotum, wincing at each touch. Then a slanting little wave lifted him off his behind, dragged him out a yard or so, causing him to lose more yards to the tide while he floundered back to get a grip again. When he looked again, the ferry was stern-on and heading for the passage between the further shore and Garden Island. That wave was probably the wash of her turning.

More tootling from the bay. There was another ferry steaming out. He was not interested. He set about crawling up the rocks. It could not be done, what with the steepness and the slime and particularly his condition. Besides having but one hand for it, he hadn't the breath. Advance of a mere foot left him exhausted, gasping for breath with bloody bubbles bursting from his lips, groaning with pain. He got his shoes out of the water only to lose his grip, and because he had made the slime slimier, slid right back again. He let himself drift a little, to what looked a likelier spot with rocks projecting. Again he struggled up, reached the projection, but couldn't get over it because of the hurt to his ribs, apparently; and whimpering now, he went sliding back again.

He hung there, staring up. No sight or sound of succour. He opened his mouth as if trying to shout. Only a croak came with the bloody bubbles. The only sound was that of the water, its lapping, sucking. Then more tootling from Woolloomooloo Bay. He looked that way. He had drifted a fair distance towards the point. Just a little further on the sea-wall above gave way to the high steel pickets of the wharfage enclosure. There was a peep of wharf-shed roof above the point. Succour must be surer round that point, with its wharves and ships and these ferries and the mob surely congregated to see the ferries off.

He found hip-hold again. Now with a struggle he got out of his jacket, flung it up on the rocks. The wet silk shirt sleeve showed such swelling as could only mean fracture of the elbow bones. Carefully he palpated it. Then he drew up a foot, and one-handed, removed shoe and sock, to let the water take them. Likewise with the other. Again he examined the broken elbow, felt his ribs. He pondered a little while. Then he undid his belt and trouser's top, and lying back, took the wrist of the useless arm and shoved it down past his loins. Buttoning and belting up again, he had the arm immobilized as effectively in a splint.

The ferry came out of the bay. He shoved himself clear of the rocks into the muck of the tide-stream and went with it, swimming awkwardly side-stroke, gasping and grunting with every movement, soon having to give up and roll over and float. The tide drew him well out. It was swinging away from shore now. Just as Woolloomooloo Bay revealed itself, another stream, this heavily laden with the garbage from ships tied up there, joined it, to turn it directly outward. No more ferries. Four big ships, but all well down the wharf on this side, and only a few khaki figures at the point where embarkation must have been made, all busy by the look of them, and too far away, to see a grey head floating amongst rotten cabbages and broken fruit cases, or to notice the momentarily upraised hand. He tried swimming up the bay. No hope against the tide.

Anyway, the tide itself appeared to offer hope of effortless salvation, since the rubbish marking the course of the stream was heading directly for the further shore. There on the point stood those tall blocks of flats, on the roofs of which, and from the windows now it could be seen, the black ants were waving to the khaki ones aboard the ferry. Over there it was easy climbing up the shore. There were even little beaches. Just round that point was where Jeremy had lived when last here and the little park. It could not be more than half a mile across. Sharks? But the Port Jackson Shark was not a man-eater. Could there be others that ate Port Jackson Sharks? Sydney was notorious for its sharks. Or had the waters become too befouled, as by the look of them here, to support any life but that which subsisted on filth?

The ferry was running through the passage now, screaming to the shore. The White Ensign flying from a yard-arm on Garden Island dipped in salute to her, or more truly to her khaki complement – momentarily half-mast, perhaps, for those who never again would look upon Our 'Arbour. The ferry disappeared behind the island. The people disappeared from windows and roofs.

Fast as the tidal movement seemed, those windows were already gilding to the last shafts of sunlight able to reach them through the maze of the city opposite. By the time he got within distance of them from which anyone reasonably might have seen his waving, there were lights behind them and their occupants evidently at the evening meal. The eastern sky was purpling, the northern pinking. Then, within thirty yards of that long promised shore, the tide-stream swung again, as if shouldered off because of its filthiness, to join the race of waters through the passage across which was Garden Island. On the island the White Ensign was already down for the night, and lights shining.

There was the *Queen Mary* again, ghost-grey against the violet background of northern shore and pink sky. Pin-pricks of navigation lights, ruby and emerald, above the indigo sea, showed the never-ending erranding of the naval pinnaces. The great ship was dark, but surely buzzing like a gigantic beehive tonight. The tide seemed to be heading for her. What irony if the inspiration for the figment Charles Belamy should be carried to her and seized for trying to sink her with a sticky-bomb! But would a man who gasped for every breath and grunted and groaned with agony at every movement be capable of ironic thought, of any thought at all, indeed, beyond that of succour – succour?

Indigo night rolled in through the Heads like a counter-tide, to be met by the glare of Garden Island, where the sea-tide slacked. Jeremy strove now to reach the glare. Aeons of striving, blindly following blinding pathways of light. A stroke or two – then float with exhaustion, sink a little with forgetfulness, to be roused by the gurgling laughter of Death about to make the coup – then stroke again – float, sink – fight up, and on, and on. A dream of rocks beneath his feet, which he seemed to walk as in a dream, sinking sometimes to walk them on his knees, to try to lie down on them and sleep only to be roused again by that mocking laughter. So on – on until there was no laughter to disturb his sleep.

No laughter for a long while. In unconsciousness he found the strength to roll on his back to take the pressure off his broken chest and battered loins and even while still struggling for every breath by the sound of it, seemed to draw comfort to the limit from his bed of broken rock, the way he sank into it. But there at length was the chuckling again in his swollen ears. He woke with a start. He sat up suddenly – cried out hoarsely with the pain it cost him – fell back. But the tide was spilling in. This time he rose with care, rolling on to knees, rising from that position slowly. Still the blaze of light ahead. Like a wounded insect he blundered towards it.

His shins struck an obstruction. He pitched forward, saved his hurts more hurt with good arm extended. He was on grass. He nuzzled it, like a beloved thing. He lay upon it loving it, till pain drove him over on his back again.

Had he his wits about him, he could have told the time by the glittering heavens. The Ol'Goomun-Ol'Goomun was abeam to northward. Where he knew her best, twenty-five degrees of latitude less, she would have been nearly overhead. Her Dilly-bag of Souls was tangled with what appeared to be tall radio antennae. The northeastern sky blazed with her Cat's Cradle of Human Destinies. Perhaps he did have the wits. At any rate, he showed awareness of a humming of machinery somewhere beyond where that radio-mast would be rooted, turned his head that way, and after a while struggled up, and swaying on his way, headed towards it.

With all the light, it was hard to see anything clearly. Shrubs grew along the grassy verge obscuring much of what lay beyond, and that so crowded, sheds and stacks of material, as to be indistinguishable. From the grass he stepped onto asphalt. Beside the asphalt was a high barbed-wire fence. He stopped for a moment, to stare and sway, then turned towards the hum again.

'Halt . . . who goes here!' A male scream – a leaping figure – fiery flash of polished steel.

Jeremy stopped dead.

A mean Sydney-Cockney voice demanded, 'Gi' password!'

The shape against the glare was that of an accoutred sailor. The voice lashed, 'Up y'ands!'

Jeremy raised one hand, making a gesture towards the other as he did so, and uttering a croak.

'Both 'em . . . or I let y'ave it!'

Making the croaking sounds, Jeremy essayed to step nearer.

'Gi' back . . . and take other 'and out yo' pocket . . . or'll blow yo' liver out!'

Still striving for speech, Jeremy turned sideways, to show the position of his arm and the gross swelling.

Momentarily the sentry was at a loss. Then he said, 'No tricks.' With that he raised his rifle high – *BANG*!

Almost on the instant the smoking cartridge was ejected, the bolt snapped home, the bayonet presented again, while the voice yelled above the echoes of the shot, 'Next un's for you . . . yo' try anythink!'

Rush of footsteps on the asphalt. In a moment a bayonet-menacing squad was there.

The first man addressed his fellows out of the corner of his mouth as they crowded round and he kept at the ready to deal with the swaying enemy, 'Copped 'im snoopin' lookin' through the fence.'

Then one of the other sailors, evidently a superior, took charge, confronted Jeremy, snapping at him, 'Both 'ands up, snoozer.'

Again Jeremy croaked and showed his condition. But yet another was barging in to take command, this one in the uniform of a petty officer, demanding, 'Wha's up 'ere . . . wha'sup?'

The first sailor explained, adding, 'Don' seem savvy Henglish . . . 'urt, too, be looks it.'

'Hatch!' snapped the PO. Then, raising his voice almost to the pitch of song, he ordered the squad into escort formation, in which the first sentry posted himself with a bayonet at Jeremy's back, as if it were his privilege to have first poke if need be. The PO then placed himself in front, to set the squad marching: 'Keeokak, keeokak, keeokak!'

But doing it according to the Blue Book would not work, even with a bayonet pricking the prisoner. The PO had to call halt and have two of his men support the tottering prisoner.

Thus to a gateway in the wire fence, through to a bright-lit office. The PO was there already, seated at a desk, speaking into a telephone. The supporting sailors ranged Jeremy before the desk, stood back to guard him in the proper style. The PO, eyeing him as he stood swaying, remarked, 'Looks like 'e been on shore-leave a'ter six mon's at sea.'

Steps outside. The PO sprang to attention and the salute. The guards came to stiff attention. Jeremy only blinked puffed eyes and grasped at his gasping swollen throat. Four officers came in, one, a Commander, who took the place the PO surrendered to him at a bound, the others to stand beside the table staring at the prisoner.

The Commander demanded in an affected drawl, 'Well, whet's all this?'

The PO standing stiffly on his left, gabbled the information.

The Commander demanded of Jeremy, 'Well, may man . . . what've you got to say for yourself?'

Jeremy croaked, reeled a little. A bloody bubble burst from his lips.

'Speak up, man!'

Jeremy indicated his throat.

'You speak English?'

A nod.

'Well . . . how come you to be in a strictly prohibited areah?'

Jeremy flung out his right hand, lurched towards the desk.

'Hold him!' snapped the officer, and grabbed up the ebony ruler.

The guards grabbed Jeremy, one of them by the swollen elbow. He uttered a hoarse cry, fell against the desk, scrabbled for support for what lay on it, gasping so that blood spotted the papers. He slid back with a groan, to knees, rolled over, sprawling on his back, eyes closed, One of the sailors, bending over him, looked up at the craning Commander. 'Out to count, Sir. Knocked about pretty bad, I think.'

'Hmm! Bettah get him to Sick Bay.' He reached for the telephone.

IV

When next Jeremy opened his eyes, it was evident that awareness came to him much more slowly than last time. He was lying in a white bed in a white room.

Seated not far from his bedside was a big man, half-bald, reading a newspaper. The man was in civilian clothes; that is shirt and trousers, his coat hanging on the back of his chair. It was daylight and hot. Through an open door and a window and beyond them a stretch of wire mesh, could be seen clear blue sky. But all that Jeremy saw for a long while was the corniced ceiling. Not so much would be seen of Jeremy himself, bandaged as he was about head and neck, and but for that square of bruised face, only his hands protruding from the strapped cuffs of the device used in hospitals called a Restraining Sheet. Even when his eyes dropped down to window level, by their blankness they marked nothing of the significance of things: the fact that since nothing was to be seen but sky meant they were high up, that the mesh outside meant an enclosed balcony.

It was not till the man with the paper rattled it in turning a page that Jeremy was anything like roused. He glanced to the right, and after a moment tried to turn his head, but failing because of the bandages, rolled that way, causing the bed to creak slightly. The man lowered the paper. Bloodied grey eyes met clear quizzing brown in a long stare. Then the man dropped his paper on the floor, turned to his coat and took a notebook from it, looked at his watch, made a note. Again he looked at Jeremy. Another long stare. Then, as if exhausted by it, Jeremy rolled back to his pillow, shut his eyes. His breathing, which was shallow and with a light rasp to it, had quickened at sight of the man. Now it slowed again. Asleep again.

For some minutes the man in the seat watched, then reached for his paper opened it. Again the crackling roused Jeremy. Likewise his movement attracted the man. Now while Jeremy stared, he became aware of his restraint, gave attention to his hands, which he flapped, to his hidden straddled and strapped feet, which he waggled. The man rose with his paper, stepped towards him. Jeremy opened swollen cracked lips, struggled for speech, came out with a hoarse whisper, 'W-w-what?'

The man turned from him, stepped towards the inner door, revealing the shape of a pistol in his back pocket. Jeremy rolled to watch him. The door was shut; a glass door but with glass moulded over mesh. The man did not open it, but reached for a push-button on the wall there. As he came back, headed for his chair again, Jeremy whispered again, stronger of voice now, 'W-where . . . where'm?'

The man answered with a voice like a growl, 'Better not talk. Someone coming t'attend to you.' He sat down.

Jeremy persisted: 'W-who . . who . . . you?'

The man shut out conversation with his paper.

The whisper rasped: 'Police . . . police.'

The paper didn't move.

'W-why'm I . . . re-strain'? You . . . listen . . . tell me . . . . '

A rattle at the door. The police officer, if such he were, rose, folding his paper. He didn't got to the door, but watched it open. A youngish fairish nurse entered, shutting the door again with a swing of her hip. She smiled in friendly fashion at the officer, then concentrated on the square of face, giving it the distant sort of smile of those professionally attendant on the sick. 'Hello,' she said. 'Wakey-wakies at last, eh? And talking, too! Let's hear you.'

'W-where'm I?'

'Good!' she exclaimed, and turned to the locker to take out a thermometer. As she was about to thrust the thermometer between lips he repeated the question. She answered, 'In hospital, of course. Now, that'll do for talking. Open, please.'

She then gave attention to taking his pulse.

The whisper followed removal of the thermometer, 'How . . . long?'

Now she addressed the chart above his head: 'I told you not to talk any more. Doctor'll be along soon.'

The policeman leapt to open the door for her. Returning, perhaps because he saw in the staring grey eyes that he was in for more questions, he grabbed up paper and chair and went out onto the balcony, settling himself where he had full view of his charge but was out of range of the whisper.

After a while Jeremy fell asleep.

He was wakened by noise. The policeman was coming in. The inner door was being opened. Two men in doctors' jackets entered, one tall and gaunt with bristly grey hair, the other comparatively short, slight, dark and young. Behind them came two nurses, the young one who had been here earlier, carrying a tray, the other a good deal older. The women bustled past the doctors to pounce on Jeremy and strip him of sheet and dressings. The doctors were talking, evidently still with the last patient, having no eyes for this one yet, staring unseeingly through the outer door, the elder with one hand tucked under an arm, the other hand stroking a lean furrowed jaw with long thin fingers, the younger with hands in pockets. In fact it was the elder who did the talking, murmuring in a preoccupied way, while his junior answered with monosyllables and nods.

Jeremy lay exposed to below his loins, lying on a waterproof sheet, naked except for a jacket of adhesive plaster binding his chest and a plaster-of-paris cast on his left arm. His throat bore the unhealed scar of an incision from which numerous black stiches struck out like whiskers on a tight-shut mouth. His scrotum lay in a pad of gauze looking like a huge blowfish, mottle-skinned, black and blue and red and green. It was the senior nurse who uncovered this part of him, her lined eyes growing wide with concern at the sight.

The silence of the waiting nurses brought the senior doctor from the last case. He turned, glancing with long yellowish eyes, seeming to be reckoning what this case had to do with him, then, when his eyes lit on the swollen testicles, exclaimed, 'Ah!' and fairly sprang upon them. A long forefinger extended to probe the mottled mass. Jeremy winced. The tall spare figure was bent almost double, as if the scimitar nose were sniffing diagnosis while the finger probed. The young doctor followed it all with sharply mobile black eyes. Almost a leap and a gasping in response to an extra deep dig woke the senior doctor up to the fact that someone was attached to the fascinating thing. The yellow eyes slid up to meet the grey looking out of their meaty sockets. The thin lips opened to speech that was harsh-sounding yet kind enough: 'Not too good this end, I'm afraid. But we'll get you right. How's the rest of you?' The doctor moved up, to lay a great wax-yellow ear against the chest, rose up, saying, 'Doing nicely. And the throat?' Another long finger poked at the scar. 'Ah, healing nicely. Let's hear you speak.'

The hoarse whisper: 'Why'm I . . . un-der . . . re-straint?'

The thin flap of mouth widened in a happy smile. 'Good! We weren't too sure of saving your voice. Should come good slowly.' Then the long fingers came up to run the hollows of the cheeks, erasing the smile. 'But I don't like those old knackers of yours. Best have 'em out, I think.'

The yellow eyes met the staring grey, narrowed as the grey widened in obvious protest. The doctor looked away towards the blowfish, stroking his chin now, said musingly, 'It's not as if you were a young man. Sooner or later you'll be having a prostatectomy, anyway.' He swung back with the smile again. 'So what about it, old feller?'

The hoarse whisper came sharply, 'No!'

The yellowish face reddened slightly. The trap of the smile closed. The yellow eyes left the grey to flip over the medical colleagues, with a look that plainly said: *The things we've got to put up with from 'em*! All three pairs of eyes agreed. Then he bent over the blowfish again, had another good look, and took another good poke, making Jeremy gasp. Having made his point, he looked back at Jeremy. 'You've heard of gangrene?'

It took the whisper a moment to get out: 'I . . . veterinary surgeon.'

The doctor looked pleased again. 'Ah . . . then you'll know what I'm talking about.'

'I . . . I won't be . . . castrate'.'

The doctor pulled his long lower lip, let it flip back into place. 'You came to us in a pretty bad way, you know . . . or, rather, you don't know. Fact, you're lucky to be alive . . . and wouldn't've been, but for this wonder-drug, Sulphanilamide.' He had another pull at the lip while it sunk in, looking down, frowning benignly at the upstaring grey eyes. 'You were brought in with a roaring empyema. You have three costal fractures, one with deep penetration of the left lung and the grossest infection I've ever seen. We had to pump the pus out of you while we mended the ribs. Trouble was that those who first had you didn't realize the extent of your injuries till too late . . . concentrated on a slight cranial fracture and the arm. As I say . . . Sulphanilamide saved you . . . your throat, your arm, your thoracic condition . . . . '

'Then . . . then . . . let it save . . . my testes.'

'It won't . . . or it would have done, with load of it we gave you. You have an emphysema there . . . certainly turning gangrenous. As you must know, there's no cure for gangrene but revitalization of the affected tissue, or excision of it. There's no hope of revitalization . . . in your condition and at your time of life. Without excision, I'd say your chance of survival is . . . well, two per cent.'

The eyes held. Again it took a struggle to get the whisper out, such as to bring sweat bursting from the square of bruised face, 'No!'

Now the doctor looked annoyed. 'For godsake, man . . . after all the trouble we've taken to save your life . . . . '

'No!'

Now the doctor was angry. He almost shouted, 'You're not going to die on me for the sake of some silly notion of being castrated.'

'Rather die . . . than be . . . eunuch.'

The mobile face changed from anger to pleading, and with it the tone: 'Look, old man . . . I'll do my best to . . . to Cut You Proud, as you fellers say . . . leave what I can to maintain some glandular functioning. How's that?'

'Then I'd be . . . a rig . . . doctor. No . . . no . . . no!'

The doctor's narrow head drooped, to sway from side to side, while he muttered, 'Then you'll die. You'll be dead within a week.'

'You said . . . you said . . . two per cent chance.'

'One per cent.'

'I . . . take . . . it.'

The doctor swung away again towards the others, with an expression of dismay that if not genuine was consummate acting. A moment, then he turned back. 'I'll give you time to think of it. But you'll have to be quick about it. Gangrene doesn't wait. No . . . no more talk. You've talked too much already.' He glanced at the scarred throat, adding with a sigh, 'Not that all the good work I put into it'll matter, if you're going to let gangrene beat us.'

He turned away completely now, heading, stoop-shouldered, for the door, muttering, half-indifferently as he went, 'glycerine-belladonna to the scrotum for the time being.'

The dark little doctor cast Jeremy a look of deep reproach as he followed. The young nurse also went out. The senior, redressing the neck, spoke remotely: 'You're a very foolish man if you don't do what doctor says.'

He whispered through her hands, 'Please let . . . me . . . get up.'

'Don't be foolish.'

The nurse came back with a bottle of treacly manure-smelling stuff. The senior soused lint with it, packed it about the blowfish, with an expression as if she were dealing with a poison snake. As they began to adjust the restraining-sheet again, Jeremy whispered, 'Please let me out of . . . this thing.'

'I'll ask doctor,' said the senior. 'Can I tell him that you agree to let him do it, too?'

Again the hoarse whisper came sharply, 'No!'

Buttoning up her mouth, the senior turned, went out. The younger nurse hung for a while, to give him a sad look and a shake of the head. Then she was gone. The presumed police-officer, who had been watching from the outer doorway, retired to his seat on the balcony.

Far from lapsing into sleep again, Jeremy showed signs of deep agitation: flapping his hands, waggling his feet, heaving himself up from his pillow as much as encased chest and arm would allow. However, before long, purpose came into his movements. Evidently he was trying to reach his loins with his right hand. By then the policeman had become disinterested, returned to his paper.

By dint of straining, at length Jeremy was able to pluck at the sheet above the bulge of his swollen testicles. Clinging to it, he wriggled, gasping and grunting surely with pain. Then with a great sigh he relaxed, with sweat pouring from his face.

A few minutes later the door opened again. The policeman leapt up and entered. It was the young nurse, carrying a tray. She was quite pleasant to Jeremy now, saying she had brought him some tasty high-protein broth to replace the intravenous feeding they'd been giving him. The policeman lent a hand to prop the patient up, adjusting the slope of the barred bed-head. However, when the nurse approached with the feeding cup, Jeremy turned his face from it, whispering, 'Want feed myself . . . free my . . . hand.'

'Can't do that.'

'Why?'

She shrugged. 'You're under restraint.'

'W-what for?'

'You were delirious for several days. Might've hurt yourself.'

'Not de'rerious . . . now.'

'Can't help it. Come on.'

'Sister said . . . ask doctor.'

'Sister didn't say anything to me. Now, come on. I've got lots to do.'

He gave in. When she had done feeding him, she smiled. 'Feel better with something in your tummy, eh?' He belched. 'Now to make you comfortable,' she added. She pulled the sheet clear of his right shoulder, reached for her tray, swabbed the shoulder with spirit.

The whisper, 'W-what . . . you do?'

She didn't answer, but from a covered dish produced a hypodermic syringe and ampoule. When she came to him he asked, 'W-what?'

'Just something for the pain.'

'Morphine?'

'Something like that. Now . . . what are you doing?'

He'd shrugged this shoulder back under the sheet. He shook his head, breathed, 'No . . . no.'

'Don't be silly!'

'Won't have.' He drew his shoulder away from her searching hand.

'You've got to have. If you don't stop struggling, I'll get the policeman to hold you.'

The whisper fairly roared as Jeremy heaved up from the inclined pillow, 'Illegal . . . my restraint . . . injection . . . illegal . . . without . . . my permission.' The meaty eyes swung to glare at the ready policeman.

Nurse and policeman exchanged glances. The nurse gave an impatient shrug. 'Okay . . . I'll get doctor.' She put her things back, swished out.

Jeremy challenged the policeman: 'Show credentials.'

The man only blinked, retired to stand in the outer doorway.

In no time the door rattled again, now to admit the dark young doctor, the nurse, the sister. The doctor was frowning. 'What seems to be the trouble now?'

Jeremy hoarsed with some strength, 'No seem 'bout it . . . illegal restraint . . . medication . . . won't permit . . . .'

'You're in police custody.'

'W-what for?'

The doctor shrugged. 'That's not my business.'

'Your business as access-access-ary . . . I take . . . action.'

The doctor looked at the policeman. Jeremy hoarsed again, 'Ask . . . what charge?'

The doctor asked the question with his black eyes only. The officer answered with a blink of non-committal. The whisper did the answering, 'Illegal cus-custody.'

The doctor turned to Jeremy. 'Go easy . . . your throat's far from healed.'

'How going . . . heal . . . lying trussed . . . want see chief . . . doctor.'

'I'm chief at present.'

'Who you?'

'Surgical Registrar.'

'You respons'ble . . . le' me out . . . . '

'Stop talking . . . or you'll ruin all our work.'

In fact Jeremy's voice was fading to faintness. Still he persisted: 'Die if don't . . . get . . . free.'

'You'll die if you don't get those testes out.'

Jeremy heaved up, eyes blazing, voice coming back again: 'You tie me up . . . for that?'

'Of course not.'

'Then . . . le' me out . . . le' me out . . . damn you!'

The doctor sighed, pulled at his smooth round chin. 'You've got a reputation for violence.'

'Who say?'

'Police.'

'What police? I . . . I ask that . . . that . . . for credentials . . . won't show. I done . . nothing . . . only help Jew refugees . . . Com'wealth police . . . hunting. You Jew . . . I help your people . . . make this trouble myself . . . help . . . name of Jews . . . help me . . . live . . . .' The last word was scarcely audible. The bandaged head fell back. The eyes closed with weakness.

When Jeremy opened his eyes it was to meet the black eyes of the doctor, who said, 'If you give me an undertaking not to be violent . . . . '

Jeremy struggled up again, whispering, 'How can . . . violent . . . my con . . . condition . . . . '

'All right. But no more talk.' The doctor nodded to the sister. Sister and nurse began to free the points of restraint.

Then it was discovered that the belladonna dressing had been dislodged. As the sister was about to replace it, Jeremy jerked up, thrusting out his hand, husking, 'Don't want.'

'But you've got to have it for the pain.'

'Bel'don' retard . . . periph'ral healing.'

The doctor thrust away the staying hand, saying rather sharply, 'You might be a vet, but . . . . '

'Also pharm'cist . . . and what you know . . . 'bout bel'donna . . . doctor?'

The smooth face flushed slightly, glossy brows rumpled in a frown. The urgent whisper went on: 'You surgeon . . . ask physician . . . bel'don' only . . . only advance . . . gangrene.' The whisper faded out.

The dark eyes stared into the grey for a moment. Then the doctor turned to the sister, muttered, 'Leave it. I'll check.'

As they turned from him, Jeremy swung his feet to the floor. The effort made him gasp and droop. The doctor turned back to him quickly, put a hand on his shoulder, exclaiming, 'What d'you think you're doing?'

The policeman came loping. The doctor waved him back.

Jeremy just managed to breathe, 'Feet . . . on ground . . . please . . . please.'

The doctor released his grip. He spoke to the nurse: 'Get him pyjamas.'

When he looked at Jeremy again, Jeremy breathed, 'Thank you . . . thank you, doctor!'

'Now, you must take it easy.'

'Must exercise.'

'Later on.'

Jeremy let himself be pushed back gently to the pillow. The sister covered him with the sheet. Having done so, she asked, 'Will you be wanting me any more, Doctor Solomon? I've got . . . .'

'Okay, Sister.'

As the sister departed, Jeremy whispered, 'I knew a . . . Doctor Solomon . . . but he . . . Syrian.'

'I'm of Syrian descent.'

'Not Jewish?'

'No.'

The nurse came with the pyjamas. When she would have set about putting them on him, Jeremy stopped her. The doctor waved her away, helped Jeremy himself. Thanking him, as he sank back to the pillow, Jeremy added: 'Old Doc Solomon . . . used to travel country . . . turn-out . . . South Australia . . . when I . . . a kid.'

The doctor looked interested. 'That would be my grandfather. He wasn't a qualified doctor, though.'

'No . . . herbalist . . . but best physician . . . the country . . . knew well . . . used to camp our place . . . my father . . . policeman.'

'Is that a fact? I've heard my father talk about the old days. My father's a qualified physician. Used to travel with the old man sometimes.'

' 'S right . . . family. We used . . . to play together . . . kids. Your father still . . . alive?'

'Oh, yes . . . and practising. He'll be interested. I'll tell him. Now, you've got to keep quiet . . . you've got to make up your mind about those testes.'

'Mind made up.'

'Doctor Paton told you he'd leave some gland if he could. Besides . . . nowadays there's Testosterone . . . implants.'

'Still castration . . . no . . . old bull . . . he's bull to last. If I die . . . I die . . . entire . . . as we vets . . . say.'

The doctor stroked his chin as if to crease it like his master's. He asked, 'And you don't want anything for pain?'

'Want all will . . . to heal.'

The dark head shook. 'Going to take more than will, old chap. Well, don't overdo it. Sleep a bit. I'll be back to see you later.'

'Thank you . . . son.' The eyelids drooped. Before Dr Solomon was out of the room, Jeremy was sleeping.

It was the changing of the guard that next woke Jeremy. A new policeman came in with a new nurse. It was dusk. The light was switched on. The nurse had more gruel for him, and vitamin tablets. He refused to be fed, having to use hands to express himself to begin with, because the whispered words came slowly. Then, taking the tablets from the nurse, he sniffed and tasted them before swallowing. Both nurse and fresh blue-jowled officer watched him blank-faced.

When the nurse was gone he swung his feet to the floor again. Now he essayed to rise, only to have to sit down again at once, panting. The policeman watched from the outer doorway. Jeremy tried again, held the stance a little longer, before dropping back, with sweat streaming from his face. Evidently he was suffering great pain in the loins, the way he clutched at them. Still he tried again, this time to totter a few steps. He stood swaying, looked like going at the knees, swung, grabbed at the locker beside the bed. It was on castors, and moved at his touch. He came down on his knees, clinging to it, gasping with pain.

The policeman came to him, placed a hand under his good arm. He jerked free of it, whispering hoarsely, 'Le'm'lone.'

'Only helping you up.'

'Le'm'lone.'

'What you trying to do, anyway?'

With his one hand Jeremy dragged himself up with an effort that left him hanging over the locker breathless.

The policeman said, 'Let me help you back to bed.'

The whisper came stronger, hoarser: 'Hand off me . . . illegal custody.'

The man shrugged, retired to the doorway. Jeremy turned to the bed, fell upon it groaning, was soon asleep again. The policeman settled down with the evening paper.

Night fell. The sister came to take temperature and pulse. When she was gone, Jeremy rose again. This time he took hold of the locker for support, shuffled a few steps after it, came back with it. A rest. Then another and better excursion. Thus till he was able to reach the other wall, hang there for a while, return to the bed. The policeman watched, as one might who was in charge of a dangerous animal doing unaccountable things. Jeremy acted as if the man did not exist, even later to massaging his testicles. When at midnight the guard was changed again, the two officers had a long conference out on the balcony, evidently about the peculiarities of their charge, the way they stared in at him while talking.

Completely ignoring the newcomer, Jeremy proceeded with his seeming lunacy throughout the night: exercising, sleeping, massaging, sleeping, exercising, despite expert warning, pitting his will against – what was it, the exterminating hand of Death or the extirpating hand of a Surgeon? When at dawn a nurse brought tea for both prisoner and guard, the latter looked as if he had lived through a nightmare, and the former through a dream.

Young Dr Solomon looked in quite early with nurse and sister, very friendly in his manner. He told Jeremy that he had been to see his physician father, who sent word to say he remembered the Delacy family well and would like to meet Jeremy again, and more, here was a dosage of a special Gas Gangrene Antitoxin not available to the hospital. Jeremy got a shot of the antitoxin then and there. Then young Solomon rather spoilt things by saying, 'You'll have to get rid of the necrosed tissue, you know. The antitoxin can only prevent the spread of it. What about it?'

'No,' whispered Jeremy. 'No.'

As the doctor was turning away shaking his head, Jeremy grabbed his sleeve. 'Your father . . . he would remember . . . what your grandfather . . . did . . . with honey.'

The young man stared at him. The hoarse whisper went on: 'A case . . . third-degree burn . . . blacksmith . . . surgeon wanted amputate leg . . .

declared gangrenous . . . old Doc cleaned it up . . . in a week . . . with . . . honey . . . and . . . raw wool-fat.'

Young Solomon had a go at creasing his cheeks.

Getting back the breath for it, Jeremy hoarsed, 'Let me try . . . inunction . . . honey in hydrous Adeps Lanae . . . honey . . . truly wonderful stuff . . . '

The doctor chewed his lips, then said, 'You'll have to talk to Doctor Paton about it.' He departed.

As soon as he and his nurses were gone, Jeremy got out of bed and started again on his rounds with the locker. He was still at it, when the door opened, to reveal, with the nurses, an all too-familiar face, which tightened with annoyance at the sight, then snapped open, demanding, 'What's this?'

The face was that of Inspector Ballywick. Jeremy halted, to stare, panting, sweating. The Inspector turned on the guard. 'What's the prisoner doing out of restraint?'

Glancing at the sister for corroboration, the guard replied, 'Doctor's permission to exercise, Sir.'

Ballywick snapped, 'Well, he hasn't mine. Put him back to bed . . . and handcuff him to it.'

Jeremy's whisper came stronger than it ever had, 'How dare you call me . . . prisoner!'

'You are my prisoner.'

'I'm not charged.'

'You've been charged by Naval Authorities with being in a prohibited area.'

'Mad . . . I was thrown . . . in sea . . . washed up . . . hardly remember . . . want lawyer . . . '

The Inspector cut in: 'You are also charged by me, under National Security Regulations, with being party to an act of subversion.'

Jeremy goggled at him. 'You must be . . . mad . . . I was attacked . . . by Communists . . . . '

'The evidence is that you were attacked by loyal citizens while disrupting a recruiting rally. Investigation revealed that you were associated with one, Aelfrieda Candlemas, in preparation of a document advocating sabotage of the war-effort.'

Jeremy gaped.

The Inspector went on: 'I warn you that anything you say may be taken down and used in evidence at your trial. However, a voluntary statement of facts will serve in your favour. Have you anything to say?'

Jeremy found his voice, the hoarse harsh whisper: 'Only . . . you . . . same Gestapo dog . . . '

Ballywick snapped, 'I've warned you before that such insults are actionable. I promise you now that I'll prosecute you for them to the limit of the law . . . '

'You call it law . . . that you . . . represent?'

Ballywick looked at his subordinate. 'Handcuff him.'

The sister protested, 'Doctor's orders . . . .'

Already the officer had his handcuffs out, and in a moment had one cuff snapped on Jeremy's right wrist. As Ballywick himself closed in on Jeremy and grabbed him quite ungently by the plastered arm, the sister cried to the nurse, 'Get Doctor!'

Jeremy was propelled towards the bed.

The sister hovered, panting, 'Don't be rough with him . . . he's a very sick man.'

'Then what's he doing out of bed?' growled Ballywick.

Jeremy was made to lie down. The officer locked the free end of the handcuff to the bedstead.

Ballywick growled again at the sister, 'I warned you that this man's got a reputation for violence.'

'We haven't found him so.'

'You don't know him.'

The hoarse whisper cut in: 'You don't know him . . . either . . . you Gestapo dog . . . . '

Dr Solomon burst in, demanding, 'What's going on here?'

Ballywick said, 'I warned you about this man, Doctor.'

'Take that handcuff off him.'

'He's my prisoner, Sir.'

'He's my patient. I've found no tendency to violence in him. I think you lied to us. I think you're persecuting him for something . . . .'

'How dare you, Sir! I'll report you to the Hospital Superintendent.'

The black eyes were wide and hot, the smooth cheeks flaming. 'Take that thing off him, before I report *you*. This's outrageous. This man's dangerously ill . . . '

'I found him . . . . '

'I don't care how you found him. You have no authority here but to have patients you bring here kept under guard. You've no right to interfere with them in any way not countenanced by the hospital staff . . . .'

'I'll remind you, Sir, that there's a war on, that under National Security Regulations we have extraordinary powers . . . . '

'There's no power on earth going to let you chain a patient of mine to a bed without my permission. I don't have to even refer the matter to the Superintendent. Take that thing off . . . or I'll send for the hospital engineer to cut it off with a hacksaw.'

Ballywick stood for a moment bristling. Then, between his teeth he said, 'Very well, Doctor . . . but the responsibility is yours . . . . '

'That's what I've been telling you all the time.'

Ballywick signed to his man. Then he looked at staring Jeremy. 'I'll be dealing with you later.' He turned towards the door, looking back as he reached it, to fling, 'If you're still alive!'

'Phew! Certainly got the knife into you,' said Dr Solomon. Then he waved the policeman outside, and nodded to the nurses to dismiss them. He sat on the bed. When Jeremy thanked him, he said, 'Least I could do . . . especially for an old friend of the family.' He smiled. Then, stroking his cheeks he said, 'I spoke to the Super about that inunction idea of yours.' He paused, looked away, to go on: 'Naturally he's against anything empirical . . . . '

'Everything's empirical . . . start with . . . I've . . . studied honey . . . under microscope . . . bacteriostatic action . . . don't know why . . . and tissue feeding . . . blacks use for . . . bad burns . . . bad ulcers . . . your grandfather got idea

. . . from blacks . . . anti-inflamatory . . . nutrient . . . Nature's own cure . . . damaged tissue . . . . ' Jeremy ran out of breath.

The doctor was looking at him again. He said, 'Dr Paton said he'll make a bargain with you. He'll permit the inunction, provided that if there's no sign of improvement after forty-eight hours, you have the testes out.'

Jeremy swallowed, answered with a strangled, 'No.'

Solomon shook his head. 'That's silly, you know. You can give your treatment a go . . . . '

'It'll work . . I know.'

'Then why not make the bargain?'

'No.'

'I'll bring you a book on Gangrene.'

'No . . . please bring me . . . the ointment . . . twenty-five per cent honey . . . in absorbent . . . lanolin . . . base . . . cholesterol in lanolin . . . stimulation . . . tissue . . . . '

The doctor regarded his panting patient for a moment, then said, 'Right . . . I'll see what I can do.' He reached and touched the thick brown hand beating betrayal of desperation on the encased breast, then rose. 'Twenty-five per cent you said, eh?' Jeremy nodded. The doctor went out.

Half an hour later the nurse came with a pot of the ointment. The moment she was gone, Jeremy set to work. A blob of the creamy stuff worked in ever so gently but with grimaces of pain, until it vanished – another – another – until the skin would take no more. A little sleep. Some more exercise, following the locker about, or sitting on the bed-edge tapping his feet. Then more inunction. By mid-afternoon the one hundred grams or so of ointment was down to a mere lick. He asked for five hundred. But so much on the mend was he that he asked for buttered toast with his gruel.

Dr Solomon came in late afternoon, took a look, a probe. The blow-fish was distinctly deflated. His black eyes grew wide. 'By God!' he muttered. Then he asked, 'What about pain?'

Hoarser and stronger the whisper now: 'Gone.'

The smooth fingers stroked the smooth cheeks. The eyes looked wary now. 'Could all be auto-suggestion, you know.'

Jeremy nodded, husked, 'Auto-suggestion's . . . good medicine.'

'If it can be maintained . . . and there're no lesions to cancel it out.' The black eyes blinked. Then somewhat hurriedly the doctor said, 'Well, keep on with the good work . . . and good luck.' He departed.

Jeremy kept on with it, between spells of sleep and exercise, all night, to the fascination of his several guards, who still might not have existed for all the notice he took of them.

At the appropriate time next morning, there was Dr Paton, the Superintendent, with his retinue, including Dr Solomon. The long yellowish eyes had only a glance for the owner of the testicles before the long fingers sought them. 'Hmm, hmm, hmm!' he droned. When at last he looked up he seemed at a loss to know whom to address, the way he looked round, so addressed himself ultimately to the now-even-shrunken organs themselves: 'Certainly improvement . . . hmm, hmm! But could be due to manipulation . . . and some auto-suggestion . . . not forgetting the antitoxin. Hmm! But I still can't see how we can avoid debridgement.' Then he looked squarely at the owner. 'Another twenty-four hours, eh? That's our bargain, isn't it?'

Jeremy rolled his eyes to Solomon, who winked quickly. Jeremy said nothing.

Dr Paton then gave his attention to the throat, this time using a laryngoscope for an inside view. He chuckled with satisfaction: 'No auto-suggestion about that. Feed him up, Sister. He ought to be able to take pretty well anything now.' Then to Jeremy: 'How's the voice?'

'Don't get much practice . . . Doctor.' Still the hoarse whisper, but stronger. It added. 'Don't like . . . the company.' Jeremy rolled his eyes towards the staring policeman.

The doctor followed the glance, slid the thin lips into a wide grin. 'Just as well . . . not too much talk yet. Right. Twenty-four hours then.' He and his crew withdrew. Jeremy got out his pot and worked with vigour.

Late that afternoon young Solomon came alone. 'How's things now?' he asked, and took a look for himself. He made the Master's comment, Hmm, hmm! but also frowned.

Jeremy asked, 'Wha's matter?'

'Seems as if you've done the trick.'

'Don't seem so pleased.'

'Because it is a trick.'

'Don't see it.'

Solomon sat on the edge of the bed. 'We don't know for certain what did it.'

'I'm certain.'

'You're an empiricist . . . if you don't mind my saying so.'

'But . . . everything has to be . . . experimented with.'

'We can hardly call this an experiment . . . when we weren't even certain of gangrene.'

'Superintendent was.'

The young man shrugged slightly. 'Busy surgeon. He didn't really commit himself, you know. Said, Looks Like It.'

'But . . . he'd have . . . had . . . my balls out.'

'He did say, remember, that it'd be different if you were a young man.' But this young man avoided the old man's eyes. Stroking his cheeks again in his Master's style, he said, 'There's always a struggle between the physician and surgeon . . . in the doctor, I mean. It's all right with you vets. If you're uncertain, you can shoot 'em. Medicine is largely empiricism. In case of urgency, surgery is the simple and often the safest way out.'

'But a man's testes . . . . '

'We've got drug-replacement therapy these days . . . . '

'A eunuch's a eunuch . . . for a' that.'

Solomon laughed lightly. 'You take those old balls of yours dead seriously, don't you!'

'Don't . . . don't you take yours . . . seriously?' When the young man only laughed again, Jeremy asked, 'You made . . . that bargain . . . with him?'

Solomon flushed, but grinned. 'I had to . . . to get you what you wanted.'

'Thanks . . . but . . . what if it hadn't . . . worked?'

A shrug. Then a chuckle. 'I suppose you'd've died with your balls still on.'

The doctor rose. 'You're not out of the wood yet, you know. If there's necrosis, complications could set in. That's what the Super's going to say tomorrow. You're not going to get *him* to believe in the magic properties of honey.'

'Does . . . does that mean . . . *you* believe?'

Another shrug and smile. 'I'm the grandson of old Doc Solomon.'

He departed. Jeremy returned to his routine.

Next morning it was as Dr Solomon had predicted. Dr Paton, while obviously impressed by the difference he found in what had looked like decaying blow-fish, nevertheless turned from probing and palpating to fix the grey eyes watching with those yellow ones, saying, 'They're not going to be much use to you, you know, old chap.'

The hoarse whisper replied, 'Useful . . . as ornaments.'

The wide mouth grinned, then pursed: 'Could be dangerous ornaments. Any necrosed tissue, and the slightest injury could bring on a fatal sepsis. I'd have 'em out if I were you.'

The grey eyes held the yellow, 'If you . . . were me . . . Doctor?'

A moment. Then Dr Paton straightened up, drew a deep breath. 'Well . . . a bargain's a bargain.' But as he turned towards the door he flung back, 'Put not your faith in miracles, old man . . . they're commoner than cures. I'll always be ready when you are.' Again the retinue went out.

Dr Solomon dropped in again in late afternoon. He said that he had been talking to his father about the alleged honey cure and that his father was deeply interested. He said, 'The old herbalist dies hard in us, I'm afraid. My father's an empiricist if ever there was one. That's why I took to surgery. The old man does seeming miracles. But it's only faith-healing. Most sickness is psychosomatic. As a surgeon, at least you know what's going on, however it might have started, and have a real chance of stopping it. Anyway, my dad would like to see you . . . when you come out.' The young man flushed slightly, dropped his eyes. 'He can't come here. He doesn't get on so well with the profession.' He looked up, grinned. 'They still regard us as Syrian herbalists . . . unto the third generation. I'd never have had a chance myself . . . only for Paton. He's a big-hearted man, Paton.' He chuckled, adding, 'Even if he did want to de-ball you!'

Jeremy said, 'I'll be glad to meet your father . . . but . . . more than a medical case . . . what need most . . . just now's . . . good lawyer. Got any lawyers . . . in family?'

'No. But I can put you onto a good one. Syrian descent. We all stick together, you know. They make us. I'll speak to him. What exactly happened to get you in here?'

Jeremy was telling what he knew, and had got to Alfie and her book, when the doctor interrupted: 'Candlemas. There's a young woman patient in here of that name . . . '

'To have a baby?'

'This one had a rather bad abortion.'

'Oh!'

Staring at the wide grey eyes, Solomon asked, 'Would that be the one?'

Jeremy took a deep breath: 'W-what happened . . . to her . . . I mean . . . was she . . . hurt?'

'Yes . . . rather badly. I understand that she was mixed up in a brawl . . . why, it would be that recruiting rally you were talking about! She was with you?'

'Yes. Tell me . . . what happened . . . to her.'

'Some fiend jumped on her . . . a heavy-weight of a woman, by the marks. She was pretty close to term. Haemorrhage killed the baby. Nearly killed her, too. Only just off transfusions.'

Jeremy's voice had faded to the whisper: 'God almighty!'

Solomon said, 'You were telling me about a book she was writing.'

Jeremy shook his head, inferring that he could talk no more about it. The doctor prepared to go. Jeremy asked, 'Could you . . give message?'

'Surely.'

'Tell her . . . how sorry I am. That Commonwealth . . . Inspector . . . must've charged her . . . is . . . is she . . . under restraint?'

'Yes, come to think of it . . . yes got some sort of policewoman guarding her.'

Jeremy's restrained breast heaved: 'That . . . bastard!'

'Now, you take it easy. I'll see her for you. You'll probably see her for yourself when she's well enough to be moved. She's sure to be brought up here to Refractory. There are male and female sections . . . but only wire in between.'

'Poor dear . . . poor dear!' breathed Jeremy. Then he heaved up again, hoarse with anger: 'That bloody . . . bastard . . . .'

'Now, take it easy. Don't go setting yourself back, when you've done so well. I'll see her for you. And I'll get you Melrose . . . the lawyer.'

V

Mr Hector Melrose, Barrister at Law, was of much more the Syrian type, a fusion of ancient Levantine tribes, than Dr Solomon, the more or less pure Semite. He was fleshy, kinky-haired, of no determinate complexion, grey-eyed. But so un-English did he look that it was no wonder Jeremy asked him how he came by his very English name. He answered with a shrug, 'We live in a country of English prejudice. A rose by any other than its English name smells not so sweet in our English courts of law. My name translates that of my forebears. Now, this case of yours.'

A smart fellow from the outset.

Like that Mr Sorbey, who so ineffectually had guarded Jeremy's rights in his brush with Commonwealth Law, he admitted that under this peculiar jurisdiction one had practically no right at all. Nevertheless, said he, he could guarantee Jeremy and Alfie a very great deal of protection from the tyranny of which the system was capable. He said, 'Since bureaucracy lusts for power only for its own sake, the simplest means of combatting its machinations is to make a show of acceding to them.' When Jeremy objected, saying that this was no sort of combat at all, but surrender of rights, the lawyer declared, 'You must not look for rights under Commonwealth Law. Australia, as a national entity, has no Bill of Rights, as has the United Kingdom of Great Britain or the U.S.A.. Commonwealth Law is by decree, which can be made to meet expedience at the drop of the Chief Justice's wig . . . and, of course, His Honour's wig is the property of the Attorney-General's Department. Without a doubt you're guilty of subversive activity, as they see it, and as, in fact, they could probably charge you for failing to wave a flag in a patriotic procession. Don't forget the powers wielded and exercised under the War Precautions Act of the last war. It is on record that you've said that Australia's entry into another war not of its making will ruin it. You'll have to recant that when it's levelled at you. Your late friends of the Free Australia Movement have done that. Of course their rabid anti-Communism has been useful in their case. If only you'd've been attacking the Commos at that Rally, instead of them attacking you, as you allege. From inquiries I've made they actually say they've nothing against you.'

Mr Melrose went on to outline his tactics: 'Basis of the charge against you and Mrs Candlemas is this unfinished manuscript of hers. Mark the term Unfinished. The fact that it's unfinished constitutes incomplete evidence. A fair claim can be made that what's already written is only preliminary to the book's ultimate purpose, which is one diametrically opposed to subversion. In effect, we claim that Mrs Candlemas, wife of a serving soldier, had no other intention than to point a moral. By creating a band of saboteurs, she wished to show how easily it could be done . . . and if given the time to complete the book, would have given the scoundrels their deserts. Fortunately, I've been granted the first interview with her, and have already established with her the fact that such was her intention. Likewise with Mrs Marsh, her former servant, who can be quite helpful to us as a witness. I've read the manuscript. It was rather hard to get hold of. However, I managed it through contacts in the Attorney-General's office here. I'm afraid, though, the cost of doing so is going to add rather to costs generally.'

Jeremy was hard to impress with the efficacy of such patent deception.

In answer Mr Melrose said, 'You must realize that it's deception you're up against. The thing started with Ballywick. He chanced to find you, an old enemy, involved in something. He and his boys have nothing much to do just yet as watch-dogs of the Nation's internal security. They have extraordinary powers. They want to exercise them. They won't be so much concerned with convicting you. In fact I am convined that legally they've got no case against you. Nevertheless they have the power to punish you to some degree. You'll be tried by Special Court. Such courts don't follow the normal course of the Legal Calendar. They are convened . . . and only at someone's convenience. Both you and Mrs Candlemas are bound to do a term of imprisonment. That's normal Commonwealth Legal procedure. Commit 'em before trial. Dr Solomon assures me he'll hold you both here as long as possible. I assure you I won't let you languish in jail too long. There are ways and means. What I advise is that you try to forget the whole thing. Your affairs at your home apparently are in good hands. I've written assuring your wife that all is well with you. You're a man of science, I understand. Why not an absorbing course of study? I'll see to it that you get the books. This will help you not to fret and cause further vindictiveness. Remember this . . . you can't win with them. To antagonize one bureaucrat is to antagonize them all. Whatever the protestations of the political party in power . . . the same bureaucracy holds the standard bearing the Kangaroo and Emu.'

Jeremy raved for a while, but not loud enough for his guard to hear. There was raving in his eyes when able to take his first look out through the linked-wire screen of the balcony. There wasn't much to see from away up there: only a rising ridge of tiled roofs, with scarcely a tree amongst them, but a sliver of azure sea beyond, and silver clouds in which Waianga slept, silver clouds in the blue, the blue. He calmed down when able to express his feelings in walking the fifty feet of balcony. This he was able to do fairly frequently, despite the rule that only one prisoner at a time was allowed out for such exercise. There were some half-dozen ward-cells abutting it, most with a prisoner-patient and a separate guard, all the other guards being uniformed officers of the State Police. Fortunately for Jeremy, his fellow prisoners were all too sick or too used to confinement to exercise their privilege. Thus he had the balcony to himself for most of the day. He was unable to walk fast because of the condition of his lungs. He wheezed and puffed continuously. He made up the necessary exercise with distance. Otherwise he was engaged with the books brought him by Dr Solomon. These were mostly on Animal Diseases. He had a large loose-leaf notebook, inscribed on the outside: *Effect of Diseases of Imported Plants and Animals on Indigenous Fauna and Flora.*

It was a good three weeks after his hearing of Alfie's being in the hospital that he was told of her now being an inmate of this section called Refractory. He kept a lookout for her on the balcony. As Dr Solomon had said, a mere mesh barrier divided male and female sections. There was hardly chance of male and female shenanigans with all those guards about. However, it was three days before he saw her, and then in the corridor outside, when they both happened to be going under escort to the male and female lavatories that adjoined. Although they came within a dozen feet, for all their staring, it was evident that they didn't recognize one another, so greatly changed in appearance were they both, till there was time only to give a little gasp and a wave, before being headed off by their guards and ushered into their separate lavatories.

Two days later they met on the balcony. He was swinging away from the barrier, walking in the warm level sunshine of early morning, when he heard his first name called by a female voice. He swung round to see her coming running. They crashed against the wire together, linking fingers, pressing lips.

'Here . . . none o' that!' It was a harsh male voice from behind Jeremy, who turned to see a uniformed policeman pop out of the nearest cell-ward.

But the man stopped, to look through the wire beyond the couple. Jeremy also looked, to see a few feet behind Alfie the squat blank-faced female guard he had seen her with before. Evidently a signal had passed between the officers. The policewoman was halted. Turing back to Alfie, seeing her mouth open to say something, Jeremy jerked a finger away from her hand to place it against her lips, whispering, 'Careful what you say . . . looks like this's rigged.' Aloud he said, 'And how are you feeling now?'

The black eyes were swimming. Brokenly, she replied, 'Awful. It's a . . . .'

He cut in: 'The doctor tells me you're getting better every day.'

Her face was pinched and lined, her dark eyes hollow, like a starvding child's. She tried hard to stem the tears, but in a moment dropped curly head against the wire, snivelling, 'Oh, Jeremy . . . Jeremy . . . I feel . . . as if I'd died.'

He fingered and kissed a protruding curl. 'You'll soon be all right again. Everything soon'll be right again.'

'No . . . never . . . now . . .'

'Have you heard from Frank?'

She struggled, whispering inaudibly. Her guard called out, 'No whispering. Speak up!'

Alfie panted, 'He . . . he's in . . . Egypt.'

He chuckled: 'Dear old dirty Egypt. He'll have the lesson of his life there in un-hygiene.'

'Why must our men be sent to Egypt?'

He countered: 'Why must the oldest civilizations be the dirtiest?'

Still she didn't respond, sobbing, 'It's like a . . . an awful . . . dream.'

He squeezed her fingers. 'Life's like that . . . when you're really living it. Only the dull everyday things seem real.'

When the beaten-child's face wobbled again, he bent quickly, offering his lips in a kiss. Then, having kissed her, he drew back, saying, 'Better go now. Chin up. See you later. I've got a lot of things to talk to you about . . . animals. I'm writing something. I want your help. Right?' He turned to find his own guard at about the same distance from him as the female from Alfie. He passed him as if not seeing the man, returned to his room.

There, now, he had a canvas lounge chair. On the arm was that note-book of his and a bound volume entitled *Diseases in Swine*. He picked up the note-book. However, it was a long while before he wrote in it. He sat staring out through the wire of the balcony, by the look of him, thinking more about human agony of soul, surely the worst disease in the world.

Nevertheless, when he saw Alfie again later in the day, and she came to meet him at the wire, at once he began to dissertate on how utterly the Australian Continent must subsequently be changed, not simply by human immigration, but even more so by that of other creatures. Giving her no chance to vent her obviously overflowing self-pity, he said, 'We've always thought of *Terra Australis* as more or less permanently like the way our forebears found it . . . there being so much of it. Of course we're all aware of the ravages of well-known pests like rabbits and rats, of weeds, erosion, river-silting, deforestation . . . but as things to be remedied by common sense. But when you consider the vast ramifications of the changes wrought from the very start of immigration, remedy is out of the question. The first known immigrants were the pigs released by Captain Cook while he was repairing the *Endeavour* in 1770. Pigs, while hardy things, are prone to all sorts of diseases, contractable by other creatures, man included . . . and you can be sure that Cook's pigs were a pretty seedy lot . . . maybe that's why he committed the seemingly idiotic act of releasing them in a wild unknown land . . . to be rid of 'em. Well, there are millions of those pigs now through the North. Captain-Cookers they're called, to distinguish them from less wild domestic pigs that have taken to the bush. Captain-Cookers are truly feral animals . . . the most dangerous creatures in the bush.'

When she drooped as if it were too much for her, he urged her: 'Listen, darling. This is important. We have to face facts. *Terra Australis* is our first consideration. Politics mean little more than weather patterns. Won't you join me in this? It's lonely doing it on my own.'

When she looked up again, puzzled now, he went on eagerly: 'Now, take pigs. The pig, like the rat, has great powers of survival, because it can live on practically anything under pretty well any conditions. You'd wonder how a pig, the barn-yard wallower of the old world, could flourish in our stony and mostly waterless wildernesses. In need of water, it will uproot the kind of tree that stores it in its roots. Goodbye tree, of course. Goodbye even to all species of water-storing trees eventually . . . likewise all edible tubers. The dingo, himself non-indigenous, I suppose, but with a very lengthy claim to the territory, while useful in checking over-proliferacy of other species, is helpless against the pig. To begin with, the dingo's hunting method is to isolate large individuals of his quarry. You can't isolate pigs. They never break herd in danger. Then there's the savagery of the mature ones. The dingo is too wary to take them on. So any territory a pig lays claim to is his. That means progressive and irreversible destruction, complete destruction, because of their omnivoracity. A family of pigs can reduce an abundant billabong to a sterile hogwallow in a week. Everything's eaten . . . birds eggs, turtles, fish, yabbies, even the rushes and the roots of trees. My worst enemies in fighting for the restoration and preservation of the so-called lagoons back home have been pigs. Because they're very intelligent animals, they soon saw what they were up against and lay off to a great degree, so that control of them now is easy. But what about all the other billabongs and lagoons . . . all the rest of the couple of million square miles of wilderness so far undestroyed? I feel like doing something about it on a bigger scale, even a national scale. Say I can find a method, through disease, of wiping out the whole of the wild pig population of a defined area of the North . . . a method against which domestic pigs can be immunized. You could help me, by reading with me, and listening to my yip-yap about it. Then when we get clear of this, you can come to Lily Lagoons and help me with research. How does that strike you?'

She took a deep shuddering breath: 'It sounds like retreating into a laboratory . . . to find out what someone's dying of . . . and doing nothing about their dying.'

He blinked, at a loss for a moment, while she stared at him great-eyed. Then he said, 'Death is a process of life. It's only negative when the life has been futile. You can make a negative death positive by discovering the cause of it.'

Again the shuddering breath: 'My baby died . . . my book . . . .'

He cut in: 'Research for the truth of things is the highest human endeavour . . . .'

'You said, Courage, Kindness, and Awareness.'

'This is the Awareness part of it. And you're a bit down on Courage at the moment, if you don't mind my saying so. But listen. There's a special job I'd like you to do for me. The Indian myna, a bird related to the common European starling that's proliferated so tremendously in these southern parts, is establishing itself in the North in numbers that could easily menace native bird life there. Like the starling, it's a great carrier of bird diseases. Heaven knows how many native species have been wiped out here by the starling, and not simply by being pushed out of habitat. I'd like you to make a study of the myna and the starling for me. Our Melrose will supply the books. Now . . . don't look glum. It can be interesting, and even amusing. Mynas are really remarkable birds, with an intricate social system. They're much more interesting than starlings. You can drop the starlings if you like . . . till we get onto their diseases.'

When she still stared glumly, he touched her pointed pixie chin, chuckled and said, 'Let me tell you a yarn about mynas that takes us back to the things we know and love so much. Mynas can be taught to talk. You remember old Billy Brew, of course. He had a couple of the birds that he'd caught to keep for picking ticks off his donkeys. Delousing cattle is one of the bird's more useful attributes. Anyway, being Billy, he taught them to talk . . . or, at any rate, they picked up the bad language he uses when driving his donks. Mynas, being social creatures, are quarrelsome . . . and particularly so amongst themselves. When Billy's birds fell out, they used to swear at each other. Well, eventually they cleared out and joined other mynas. According to Billy, if you listen carefully to any row between mynas, or Myna-birds, as they call them up there, you'll hear the best of his donkey-walloping language.'

She smiled only feebly, and with a negating shake of the head.

He chucked her chin again. 'Chin up, sweetheart. Make the best of it. It won't be for long.'

To express such optimism when, either through other ears or some phonographic device, these too-easy chats were being monitored by Inspector Ballywick, according to Jeremy's suspicions, and to use such expressions in them in seemingly innocent talk of pigs and starlings as *Spiroptera strongylina, Distomum* in its varieties, *Filaria clava, Mecator suillus, Trichostrongylus, Trichenella, Myna Lice*, which could hardly mean anything but secret code to a policeman's mind, was hardly wise. If indeed the Inspector was eavesdropping, he got sick of it after a fortnight. That was when he turned up, after weeks of non-appearance, with a doctor of his own to check on Jeremy's condition.

Still, Ballywick's sudden move might have had to do with the sudden change just then in the war situation. The lengthy Phoney War had become a menacing reality. The Germans had invaded Norway. Although it might seem a silly thing to do with Norway half a world away, local people classed as enemy aliens but so far permitted the leniency of mere periodic reporting their whereabouts were being rounded up for proper internment. Perhaps, by reason of the elasticity of Commonwealth Law, Jeremy could be classed as an enemy alien, being the declared enemy of most of what the so-called Commonwealth stood for, and surely alien in the truest sense of the word, which is Wholly Different in Nature from the Common Herd.

At any rate, there that day was Ballywick, accompanied by a long stick of a doctor who, judging by his fiery ruddiness and white hair in a youthful face must have been an albino. Although the doctor did not appear to see with those strange almost colourless eyes, he made a thorough job of the examination. Jeremy may have been a cadaver for all the notice he took of him. He wrote a lot of things down on a form, but uttered only one word, and that at the end of the examination: 'Fit.' He then departed with his form.

Ballywick then spoke for the first time to Jeremy since last hurling that remark from the door about the likelihood of their not meeting again. He said shortly, 'You're finished here.'

Jeremy asked, 'What's that mean?'

'You're coming with us.' The guard was standing by.

'Like this?' asked Jeremy. He was in pyjamas, as he had been for weeks.

'You'll be provided with suitable clothing.'

Jeremy moved towards the locker. 'I've got some books and papers in there.'

'Leave them.'

Jeremy reddened, heaved a bit for breath, then said, 'I'd like to take leave of my friend, Mrs Candlemas.'

'You'll come with us without delay.'

Jeremy's voice, always hoarse these days, only sounded a little rougher: 'You'll find those notes of mine useful.'

Inspector Ballywick's curiosity got the better of him. 'Indeed? I understood you were studying veterinary science.'

'Yes . . . pigs.' Jeremy set out for the open door, at which the guard stood waiting.

No Alfie out in the corridor. They headed the other way, to a room at the end, where Jeremy was set to changing into an outfit of slops. Thus attired, he was marched to an elevator. As soon as they entered, Ballywick took out handcuffs and reached for Jeremy's right hand, cuffed it, and then his own left. Thus they descended, to come out of the hospital by a discreet back door.

A large black car was waiting, with a driver who wore the uniform of what was called the Commonwealth Peace Force, and number-plates that described it as being in the service of the Common Weal.

Away and through the tangle of masonry and frenetic human movement that had supplanted the groves of blue-gum and wattle and the little bands of corroboreeing freemen who had counted time not in pence but in the flowering and fruiting of trees and the spells in the spirit between incarnations. Jeremy may have been visualizing the vanished scene, the way he looked out blank-faced on what stood for Human Progress.

Soon it was evident that once again they were on their way out to that replica of Dartmoor Jail standing amidst the sandhills near where Captain Cook started it all in the name of His Britannic Majesty, George III. Perhaps the mass of stone stood as something in the way of a monument to what it all really meant.

Again through those great doors that clanged shut on what would generally be opined the first attribute of the Nation sprung from Cook's bit of petty thieving that Sunday, April 29, 1770, for the Royal Crook who employed him – Freedom. Again through the rigmarole of being signed over like other people's property, then marched away by a warder with a face like a pig, again into that section reserved for prisoners of the King of England as deputized by Ministers of the Commonwealth of Australia rather than of this State called by James Cook, New South Wales, no doubt because of the collieries and miners' hovels he dreamt would soon be standing smoking on its dreaming hills. Was Jeremy thinking such things as he trudged along with his porcine keeper? Or was he thinking: How many Departments of Administration are there in Hell, how many Deputies to His Satanic Majesty? Or: is this pig in the peaked cap carrying *Trichinella spiralis* in his fat flesh?

The block to which he was taken was uproarious with guttural voices raised in talk and song. A musical people, the Germans. It was said that each of the centres, now known to be established throughout the German-controlled regions of Europe for the systematic extermination of all Jews laid hands on, had its *Liedertafel*, so that the exterminators might indulge their simple love of music out of hours of duty.

The pig-warder halted Jeremy before a cell of which the barred door was crowded with fresh-complexioned blue-eyed rather handsome faces. He unlocked the door, shoved Jeremy in.

There were five men in the cell, young or youngish. They surrounded Jeremy, asking eager questions in German. He replied, 'I don't understand German.'

One asked, 'Vot your nation ist, *Meinherr?*'

'Australia.'

The blue eyes popped and stared. One ventured: 'Vy for internment you are, yes, ven Awstrahlien you are, no?'

Jeremy shrugged. 'I guess its because I really am, as you say, Awstrahlien.'

Fair brows rumpled in puzzlement. Then blue eyes exchanged doubtful glances. They asked no more questions. Nevertheless, it was with extreme politeness that they showed him the vacant bunk, even with the suggestion, that as he was an old man and disabled with that left arm, he choose whichever one he liked.

It was difficult to imagine that such as these, who would behave with courtesy and kindness so spontaneously, should become as barbarous as the news showed their nation to be these days. That these were no different from the rest of their countrymen was evident from their gloating over the news coming in of the success of the German soldiery in their rape of innocent neutral Norway. Either as right, privilege, or by means of bribery, every edition of every newspaper was brought in to them. The only prohibition on them was use of radios, perhaps because it was feared they might call in paratroopers from twelve thousand miles away to free them. But the newspapers were enough to keep the place resonant with their *Hoch, hoch, hoching* and their singing of *Horst Wessel* and *Deutschland Uber Alles*.

Those with Jeremy let him have their papers, but were too polite to discuss the good news with him.

VI

Those Happy Huns were soon gone – to sing out the rest of their conviction that the Fatherland truly was Above All, behind barbed wire. Their places were taken by a less numerous and mostly quite unexuberant bunch of what were described as Suspected Enemy aliens. These people called themselves Czechoslavs, Austrians, Hungarians, Letts, Finns, Switzers, with anything but sympathy for the German cause, and well might have been telling the truth, the surly way they took their confinement.

For reasons best known to the authorities, Jeremy was not locked up with these new prisoners, although included with them at exercise. With the clearing of the place of the happy ones, he had been moved to a small cell and left to himself. He was also left to himself in the exercise yard, but now by his fellow-prisoners, who since he was not a foreigner, treated him like one. He was not alone in this respect, there being a number of young Australians awaiting Special Court for failure to comply with the demands of the National Register of Manpower, under which they were liable to compulsory military service at home. Some of these were just artful dodgers of any kind of authority, but a goodly number genuine haters of war and bureaucracy. There was no difficulty in learning their business, because their exercise was mainly vociferation. Obviously they regarded Jeremy as a spy. Just as obviously he was unconcerned about their attitude, using all time allowed for exercise for that purpose, so that he returned to his cell always exhausted.

He was comfortable enough in his small cell, thanks to Mr Melrose, who saw to it that he had better clothes and bedding and food than was issued, and newspapers and books. He never got back his notes on Diseases of Pigs. Mr Melrose said that he had learnt that these had been confiscated under suspicion that the purpose of the study might be sabotage of the pig-raising industry of the Nation. He stopped Jeremy from laughing over it, declaring, 'You must learn to regard the official mind objectively. It's that you're up against. If you want the acquittal I'm sure I can get you with my strategy, you must accede to any suspicion levelled at you as quite properly conceived, and answer it with due respect to the powers of your accusers, even while denying guilt according to the law. In short, old man, *Don't Give Cheek*. You are dealing with power where it is valued for its own sake. Please, Mr Delacy, mark my words.'

Through the agency of Mr Melrose, he was able to keep in much closer contact with Lily Lagoons than would have been possible through communication properly controlled by prison rules. All was well at home. Two matters of great importance had been attended to satisfactorily: these the re-registration of leaseholds and of permits to keep Aborigines on the place. Fergus Ferris had done this with Power of Attorney vested in him for this very purpose. Jeremy had asked Melrose to call on him as the one truly intelligent person in the country to be relied on in the circumstances. It seemed a strange choice to make, in view of Fergus's poor showing of responsibility in their early dealings. However, Fergus turned up trumps. As he reported frankly to Jeremy in communication smuggled in by Melrose, the commission suited him well. Because he was not doing so good in his aviation business, since the Air Force had established a base at Palmeston and for sheer practice flying were depriving him of official flights that had meant much to him, he needed to watch expenses. Therefore, taking advantage of Jeremy's need of him, he had established himself at Lily Lagoons, at once to save board and lodging and the too-ready availability of convivial companionship, and to be nearer the points that favoured him in bush-flying. In his droll way, he said he was Earning his Oats by keeping the racing team up to training for next Beatrice River Races. Everybody was expecting him home for the Races, he said, and that included Rifkah and

Prindy, still at Leopold Mission and happy enough and intending to be over for the festival. A report of special interest concerned a visit to Lily Lagoons by Inspector Ballywick, with a warrant of search. Fergus himself had transported the Inspector, picking him up at Boulder Creek, where he had left the mail-plane. So secret had Ballywick made his mission that he had never discovered his, Fergus's connexion with the place. He had gone through all of Jeremy's books and papers and removed some of the latter, most of which concerned animal diseases. Fergus had been able to compile a list of all that was removed. Apparently nó one in the country, except those at Lily Lagoons, knew that the man had been there. Fergus had taken him back to meet the plane at the Boulder. The only indication to what Fergus called The Wurruld that anything untoward was happening was the sudden descent of troops from Palmeston to transfer the big military radio from Lily Lagoons to Beatrice Homestead. It had been pretty well established in gossip circles that Jeremy was away on secret military service for his patron, General Esk, and was virtually Officer Commanding Northern Force. Then came the nationwide news that General Esk had resigned as C-in-C and gone back to England. Next it was announced officially that OC Northern was Brigadier Chivvy, formerly merely Commandant of the Palmeston Garrison. The Finnucane of the Finnucanes was fairly hopping with thwarted curiosity. It was rather a strain standing up to the quizzing, Fergus wrote, especially when it was plied with such sublety and so much free grog. He would be glad when Jeremy was back to relieve him of it, even if it did mean his having to go camp elsewhere, say with Ali Barba.

Thus for several more weeks.

Then suddenly this special department of the prison filled again with joyous Germans. These were the last permitted liberty, because of apparent harmlessness. Amongst them were even some Australian born and bred. This was the result of Hitler's *Blitzkrieg*, whereby, in a matter of hours, simply by again flouting international convention and invading the innocent neutral countries of Holland and Belgium, the Germans were able to bypass the impregnable Maginot Line built up over years to keep them out of France, and with their Panzers roll into that country practically unhindered. The new-comers arrived shouting, *Nacht Paris*!

Jeremy learnt what the shouting meant from one of the new men, who was locked up with him. A tall handsome man he was, in his early forties, so far from being downcast by having the barred door shut on him, that immediately he grasped Jeremy's hand and laughingly greeted him in German. When he got over his surprise in finding that Jeremy didn't understand him, he introduced himself as Bruno Schroeder, better known to his Australian friends as 'Browny'. He was Australian himself, 'A Dinky-di Aussie,' as he put it. On hearing Jeremy's name he shook hands again, saying that he had read his articles in *Australia Free*, that in fact he had himself been a member of the Free Australia Movement. Laughing, he said he had dropped out of the Movement when it took to supporting Hitler. He roared over that, confessing that, like many another, he had been taken in by the Jewish-Communist lie that Hitler was a lunatic. He said, 'They said that of Napoleon . . . and afterwards hailed him as a genius. But I tell you, Napoleon's genius was nothing compared with this man Hitler's. We'll be in Paris in a week.' He then explained that the cry,

Nacht Paris had been the toast of every German regiment since the days of the Franco-Prussian War.

He went on excitedly: 'That's what brought me here. Although I'm Aussie born, I served in the German Army in the Last Turn-out. We used to toast it then . . . *Nacht Paris*! Lately I've been hearing it in broadcasts from Germany . . . and now that German victory's certain, it's proved too much for me. I couldn't face my Australian and British friends without embarrassment. So I asked the Big Boys I've always been in with to intern me.' He laughed: 'Not as easy as it might sound. I belong to a rich and internationally famous family. The Big Boys didn't like it. There's a lot of riff-raff in the internment camps. Besides, I have a young family of my own.' He laughed again. Just then he was laughing most of the while, so happy was he. 'I had to tell 'em I'm a dangerous man to have at large . . . potential number-one saboteur. Of course you know Schroeders is a great chemical concern, being a chemist yourself. I'm a trained chemist, too. I told 'em how I could carry out first class sabotage with bits of things out of the kitchen and the bathroom medicine cupboard . . . a bit of sugar and some throat tablets, a pinch of Condy's and an ounce of glycerine . . . anything from sawdust to soap. They only laughed and slapped me on the back, saying they knew I'd never do anything like that.'

Dryly, if hoarsely, Jeremy asked, 'Would you?'

'Of course not! Aren't I a Dinky-di Aussie? Would I want to hurt my own country?'

'But you fought against it before. How'd that come about, when you say you were born and bred here?'

'I'll explain that later. We've plenty of time to talk. I want to get things organized here. By the way . . . my Aussie friends call me Browny. I'd like you to . . . and I'd like to call you Jerry . . . ha, ha . . . I supposed you feel more like calling *me* Jerry, eh? But, to tell the truth, I find my German friends rather stuffy. That's why I asked not to be put in with'em. I don't want to talk war. The damn thing's nearly over. I'd rather talk chemistry. Suit you?'

'My word! How are you on the new Physical Chemistry. I'm a bit out of date on that.'

'Right up my alley, mate! Speaking of Phys. Chem . . . our Company's very interested in that Tantalium of yours. We've found traces of radio-activity in the ore.'

Jeremy looked surprised. 'What do you know about my ore?'

'We process for Krupp's.'

'I dropped Krupp's long ago.'

'I know. But it won't be wanted for war soon. I'd like to research the stuff here . . . with you. Radio-active materials are going to be in great demand. Our German scientists are on the eve of harnessing nuclear energy, do you know?'

Schroeder was most up-to-date in his chemical knowledge, and eager to share it. He even paid warders to procure him chalk and ignore the fact that he made blackboards of the tarred lower halfs of the cell walls. He said, 'You can't do justice to chemical formulae, except on a blackboard.' As it would take another coat of tar to erase his merely wiped-off masses of hieroglyphs, it would be interesting to know what subsequent inmates made of them, and even more the effect on the suspicious authorities. When they moved to the spacious and cosy quarters that Schroeder boasted those he was Well In With would soon see provided for them, perhaps Inspector Ballywick moved straight in after them with a cypher expert.

Schroeder reckoned it would be about a month before capitulation of the Allies would affect their release. Optimist though he might seem, he certainly had sound knowledge of what was taking place in Europe, as evidenced in the tardy revelation of the truth of things in the news. Like those other Happy Huns, Schroeder had all the papers delivered at the cell-door. Along with them also came the best of food, and even a little beer and wine, all of which Browny shared equally with his cobber, Jerry. The good things were sent in by Schroeder's wife, Brünnehilde, or Browny F as he called her. Jeremy would be meeting Browny F, the Female of the Species, as Browny M explained – 'And, oh boy, oh boy, what an F of the S is she!' – as soon as they had accommodation fit to receive her. Then, said he, and broke into song in a very pleasant tenor, to explain the prospect: 'All through the night, you will hear two Brown Birds loving . . . ha, ha, ho!' He said, 'Of course you'll be sharing the new quarters. with me. I'll fix that . . . just the two of us . . . with Browny F along to brighten things up occasionally. Although she's as German as Brünnehilde the Valkyrie, there's nothing stuffy about my Brown Bird . . . unless, well . . . ho, ho, ho! But speaking of German stuffiness, I must tell you the yarn about the first Aussie I met after being a German by compulsion from August 1914 to November 1918, and how proud it made me feel to know I was an Aussie, too.'

The man's story of that period of his career was to the effect that, after boyhood in Australia, where his father represented the Schroeder Concern, he had been sent to Germany, for tertiary education and induction into the firm as both executive and technician, such being the family tradition. When the war broke out, as an Australian, he said, 'Naturally I wanted to get stuck into it. Never thought about Australia coming in. We Aussies are naturally war-like people, like the Germans. I only thought about fighting the Frogs and the Poms. Matter of fact, I don't think the Dinkum Aussies of the AIF gave two hoots in hell who they were fighting, so long as they got stuck into it. That's the way I felt about it. And I'll tell you this . . . if I wasn't sure Germany was going to win this Turn-out, I'd offer my services to the Second AIF.' He laughed. 'Wonder how they'd feel about taking someone who'd been an officer on the other side before . . . even if he could claim to be a native son?'

Jeremy said dryly, 'I understand they've taken quite a number of men who held German commissions like you . . . and were German born.'

Schroeder grinned: 'Jews, eh?' Then he added: 'They won't be much good to 'em.'

In the same tone Jeremy said, 'There were some very good Jewish officers in the First AIF, the best of them, Monash, of course . . . finally considered the best of all the Allied officers and the man who beat Hindenberg and finished the war.'

'It was the Communists who beat us, old man . . . Jewish Communists.' Schroeder laughed. 'That's probably how Monash cashed in . . . he knew what was going on inside.' When Jeremy went red, Browny M clapped him on the shoulder. 'No offence, Dig. I know how you feel about Jews. We've all got our own opinions . . . and cobbers like us mustn't fall out over ours. Let me tell you about that first Aussie I met after the war . . . . '

It was at Cologne, he said: 'I was still in uniform . . . as most of us were, because we couldn't get civvies. I happened to come down to the river one day to take the ferry . . . and just missed it by a whisker. You know how strict Germans are about regulations. Gangway up . . . so *verboten* to board . . . not like here!' He laughed: 'Watch any ferry at busy times here . . . and half the passengers do the long jump . . . often into the drink . . . ha, ha, ha . . . the good old careless Aussie!'

He went on: 'Well, there was an Army of Occupation sentry on the wharf . . . an Aussie, cocked hat and all . . . rifle and bayonet. There was also another passenger just missed, ahead of me, an old woman with bundles. When the Aussie saw the man at the gangway wave the old woman off because the whistle had blown, he yelled, "Hey . . . fair go!" Of course they only stared at him. But that was too much for him. Seeing me near him, he said, "Here, Jerry, grab this," and tossed me the rifle. Then he rushes to the boat, shoves the gangway back in place, and says to the old woman, "Go on, Auntie . . . go for your life." Ha, ha, ho, ho! You should've seen those Jerries' faces! Apart from breaking the *Verboten*, there was a sentry leaving his post, and maybe most astonishing of all, shoving his arms into the hands of a disarmed enemy . . . and a common soldier doing it to an officer! But to me it was so Dinky-di Aussie that I roared with laughter. When he came back for his rifle he growled at me, "What's so bloody funny?" I explained . . . spent hours yarning with him. When he was relieved, we went off together to a boozer . . . and boozed and talked Australia till we finished up crying in each other's arms.'

That wasn't the only tale or talk of Browny Schroeder's that caused Jeremy to stare at him, surely wondering over the man's strange duality. There could be no doubt about his Germanness. He fairly gloated over the attrocious warfare being waged in the cause of the *Reich that will Live a Thousand Years*, as he was fond of saying, parroting his acknowledged *Führer*. He whooped for joy over the reduction of the ancient, innocent, and lovely city of Rotterdam. His only excuse to Jeremy's protests being, 'Well, the Dutch should have come in with us in the first place. They could have been our allies. Now, for first rejecting us and then defying us, they'll be our slaves.' Yet this philosophy didn't apply to the Russians, who made all this glory possible by Coming In With Us. Every German knew, Schroeder declared, that as soon as continental Europe and Britain capitulated and were ready to follow their conqueror-friends, the Sub-human Bolsheviks would be eliminated, along with the Non-human Jews. Jeremy said nothing to that, but seemed to be searching for some expression. Perhaps it was that one he had learnt from Kurt Hoff, the man they had castrated under the solemn edict of the Nuremberg Laws of Shame, the phrase turned into one horrible guttural word in the Germanic style of oral gymnastics – *Irrenation* – *Nation of Lunatics*!

While the other *Herrenvolk* were marched off singing to await acknowledgement of the world's homage elsewhere, Mr-Herr Schroeder remained with Jeremy, sure enough soon to be moved to much better quarters, and to take him along, too.

The new place was situated in a block remote from all the rest. It was even a pleasant place, despite its bars. It comprised half a dozen roomy cells comparatively comfortably furnished, with its own exercise yard, which they were able to use at leisure, because they were the only occupants and while locked within the block itself were not locked in their cells. There were even decent toilet facilities. As they soon found out, it was the section that had housed condemned prisoners awaiting execution. This fact tickled Browny's sense of humour. You could see why when, true to his prediction, his Brünnehilde came to spend a day and a night. Both said next morning that now they would be able to boast to their friends that they had slept together in a Death Cell.

Browny F was just as unbrown as her corn-silk-haired spouse. She was very handsome, in the too-smooth-faced German woman's way, and inclined to be naughty. She played up to Jeremy to the point of coquetry. Anyone knowing him would easily have guessed he didn't like it. Still, he took it in good enough humour not to give offence. Doubtless, harsh experience and wise Mr Melrose had taught him that it was too dangerous to give offence to those Well In as to the ones they were Well In With. Just how Well In were this pair was revealed by the fact that, simply on Jeremy's telling the man that he was troubled to hear from Mr Melrose that Alfie Candlemas was in the women's section of this same jail Brünnehilde had secured her release. Brünnehilde told him that she had visited Alfie, found her deeply distressed by news that her father was at death's door and she could not go to him, and promptly reported the matter to the right quarters. Alfie had been freed on bond put up by Brünnehilde herself, until called to trial. She had gone to Melbourne. Jeremy could hardly do other than express his gratitude.

Brünnehilde came with the news of Alfie's release in a particularly happy mood, not merely by reason of her charity, but because her visit coincided with the Battle of Dunkirk. She and her Bruno were convinced that Britain would capitulate in a matter of hours. She brought a radio-set with her, so that they might follow the battle, Ball-for-ball, as Browny M put it in good Australian cricketing cant. They had the bilingual advantage of being able to hear the versions of both sides, the BBC's and Radio Berlin's. While Browny M himself took the dogged British resistance for granted and as something of a joke, his Brown-bird eventually became so exasperated as to resort to vehement German – '*Einredung!*' she kept screeching. Browny M explained to Jeremy that the word meant Self-delusion, that his little girl, being German born, was a realist, and couldn't see how anyone could consider themselves invincible in flight. It rather spoilt that Brown-bird's Loving of which Bruno had spoken slyly and the pair had said they would be able to boast later as having taken place where other's had had a Honeymoon with Death, because All Through The Night Browny F kept the radio playing that idiotic refrain of *Englandische Einredung*. She departed next morning somewhat jaded, leaving behind the radio, prison rules to the contrary in that respect notwithstanding.

Thus were Jeremy and his Cobber Browny M able to keep up the Ball-for-ball vigil. There could be no doubt about the fantastic goings on at Dunkirk and beyond, with the versions of both sides to hear. Finally Bruno himself got exasperated, but did his shouting in good Aussie English: 'The stupid bloody ning-nongs! Can't they see they're rooted? Running home in motor-launches and rowing boats! You wouldn't read about it! The stupid bastards don't have to surrender. They only have to capitulate. Then they can take an honourable place beside us. What's wrong with the British? On the one hand they own up they're effete . . . yet they listen to this bullshit of Churchill's about fighting on the beaches, in the streets. Tell me what's wrong with the British, Jerry . . . it beats me!'

Jeremy said, 'You're not dealing with the British now . . . but with the English.'

'British . . . English . . . what's the difference?'

'Enormous . . . but don't ask me what it is . . . I don't belong to the breed.'

'Anyway . . . this dog Churchill's not English. He's half American, which means half mongrel!' Browny ground his teeth over that in a very un-Australian way.

When it was over and the BBC announced it as a Famous Victory, winding up the broadcast with the song – *We are the Boys of the Bull-dog Breed, who made Old England's Fame*, poor Brownie was stricken. 'Now we'll have to wipe 'em out,' he said miserably. 'I didn't want that to happen.'

It was soon after Dunkirk that the war-song *There'll Always be an England* was introduced. Browny heard it through once, expressed his contempt for both English sentiment and musical talent, and declared that it should be silenced whenever played, which just then was pretty often. A couple of times it came on while Browny was on the WC. Then, despite his shouting for the Damn Thing to be switched off, Jeremy even turned it up a little:

There'll always be an England, while there's a country lane,
Wherever there's a turning wheel, a field of standing grain.
There'll always be an England, and England shall be free,
If England means as much to you as England means to me.

Jeremy's excuse was that he wanted to get that bit about the Empire. As he said, 'Nothing about the Commonwealth.' It sounded reasonable.

The Empire, too, we can depend on you.
Freedom remains, these are the chains, nothing can break.
There'll always be an England, and England shall be free,
If England means as much to you as England means to me.

But was there need to turn up the volume? The look in Jeremy's eye as he listened might easily suggest that he was even enjoying the idiotic song – or at any rate, the idiotic situation.

Then Browny was made happy again, with the news that it was truly *Nacht Paris*. The Frogs had capitulated. The Supermen were marching through the *Arc de Triomphe*. He cried, '*Gott* . . . what a wonderful thing to march into a great city as a conqueror! If only I were there to share!'

Brünnehilde was soon back, with so many good things with which to celebrate the victories that it took two warders to carry them in. Although Jeremy partook of the feast, he declined to join in the toasting, saying, 'I don't happen to be on the winning side.' Challenged by Brünnehilde to declare his side, he replied with a shrug and a smile, 'Just mine, I guess.'

She also came with news of Bruno's imminent release. Those he was In With had worked it out that all that was required in *his* case to meet National Security Regulations was his not permanently residing within one hundred miles of the sea during the duration of hostilities. What better example of the democratic flexibility of the laws of the Australian Commonwealth! To meet the conditions, Brünnehilde had bought an orchard in the Central Highlands, a beautiful and bountiful place, a bit run down because its former owner was at the war and his wife had run off with another man, but the better for being so, since it made the purchase a bargain and would give them something to occupy themselves till the British came to their senses. Jeremy must come and stay with them as soon as free, as Alfie Candlemas would be doing also. As to getting his freedom, his cobber Browny would see what he could do to get things moving in that direction.

A couple of days later Bruno Schroeder departed, leaving everything behind, so that Jeremy might continue to live in clover. However, the comfort lasted only a couple more days longer, perhaps because his patron had forgotten to leave some of his bounty with the jail authorities. Quite unceremoniously, Jeremy was bundled back to the old block. Still, it might have been proper contingency that was behind the move, since suddenly the place had become crowded again with entry of Italy into the war. Jeremy returned to the other block to find it uproariously Italian, but not in the happy way of its former occupants, despite the fact that Italians are also a singing people and were on the winning side. Certainly there were some shouts of *Viva Mussolini*! but the commonest were *Bloddy Bastano*! Evidently the Italians, always realists, saw no reason why they should be locked up simply through having belonged to the Australian Fascist Party, an organization that had given them a bit of the dignity of their ancient origins to offset the humiliation of being called Dago by the low-class descendants of tribes their highly civilized ancestors had found as savages. They sounded angry almost to a man – *Bloddy Bastano*!

However, Jeremy was not locked up with Italians. His cellmates were three youngish men who were obviously Australian. Not that they declared themselves to him, nor even spoke to him except when necessary, and held their own conversations in his presence toned to the lowest possible key. He guessed that they were probably Communists, having heard on the radio that with the Fall of France, the Commonwealth Government, exercising its Punch-and-Judy powers, had declared the Party illegal and all confessing adherents of it liable to imprisonment. Apparently he had no more inclination for intercourse with them than they with him.

He didn't have to suffer his surly compatriots for long. One day there was Mr Melrose, to say that the Special Court would be convened this week, and taking him to the private room reserved for the purpose, finally briefing him in the conduct calculated to secure him acquittal. But perhaps even this had been fixed for him by ex-German Army Officer Bruno Schreoder in collaboration with those mysterious people he was obviously Well In With. Was it money that put Kapitan Schroeder in so powerful a position in such extraordinary circumstances? Money knows no frontiers, they say. Yet the Australians have that notorious weakness for lick-spittling foreigners of wealth or rank or note.

Then one morning after breakfast he was informed that he was required to prepare himself for going to trial. This meant taking a shower, submitting to the prison barber, dressing in a new good-fitting suit of clothes no doubt provided by Mr Melrose. Within an hour of dressing up, he was called to the reception desk, there to meet again Inspector Ballywick, whom evidently he expected, since he seemed not to see him, but who showed a lively interest in his, Jeremy's, appearance while the signing-over was being done. Handcuffs again, and the Black Car of the Common People. No word was exchanged between the manacled pair.

Their destination was in the heart of the city, the great polished granite and shiny-windowed Commonwealth Office Block, the base of which is the head office of that most democratic of financial institutions in all the world, or so they say, the Commonwealth Bank of Australia. They stopped before a great doorway, above which was the insignia of the Nation: not the King's Beasts as seen on State Government buildings, but the Kangaroo and Emu dexter and sinister of the Shield of the States atop which the Star of Hope in which the idea of True Commonwealth was conceived, the Star still preserved despite general acceptance of the fact that the brave conception resulted in bureaucratic abortion. Citizens of the Commonwealth hurrying by stared at the handcuffed man being hauled into the ostensible citadel of liberty, which looked so unlike court house or jail.

Not so surprised was the uniformed Peace Officer on guard inside, who saluted and greeted the Inspector and accompanied him and his prisoner to the elevator, perhaps to ensure no funny business on the part of the latter. Escape would have been possible through glass swing-doors giving side entrance to the Bank. However, it would have meant taking the Inspector along, too.

The elevator driver also saluted the Inspector, and talked to him about the weather, disregarding the prisoner. So up with a rush, to be let out somewhere on high into a cosy corridor, grey-carpetted, panelled in red Australian cedar and lined with glass welcoming-looking doors on which plain black lettering described what was behind: *Attorney-General, Secretary of the Attorney-General, Ladies, Court Room No. 1.* The sort of thing one might expect in a well-ordered democracy, going to show either that the fiction of one still prevailed or a glimmer of Hope still shone in that seemingly dead Star.

They were met by another Peace Officer, who took Jeremy off Ballywick's hands, literally, and without recuffing him, escorted him to a room marked *Private.* It was a pleasant room, with nothing to show that it was used for confinement, except the fact that its glazing was reinforced with wire mesh and its good-quality furnishings anchored so as to prevent their use as weapons of assault. The door was locked on him. On the wide table was a stack of good-quality magazines and illustrated brochures, all the work of the Commonwealth Government Printer, and giving the same information, which in effect was what a pretty happy land was this Australia.

Lost in a wonderland of lush forests and broad rivers, of verdant pastures dotted with fat cattle and sheep, of mines and factories whose smoking stacks seemed only to add to the purity of the blue and white above, Jeremy was roused by the unlocking of the door. It was Mr Melrose, just popping in to say all was well and that they would be in court in half an hour and, 'Remember . . . don't argue. Leave all that to me.'

In half an hour the Peace Officer came. They went to Court Room No. 2.

It was a chamber not much bigger than a substantial drawing-room, into which it might easily have been turned by rearrangement of the furnishings. The Bench was merely a long table with three chairs, the middle one taller backed than the others and set beneath the Commonwealth Coat of Arms.

Alfie was there already, seated at a table with Mr Melrose, who now looked more imposing in wig and gown. At another table were the Prosecution, two gentlemen wigged and gowned and Inspector Ballywick. In one of the comfortable chairs lined up behind, and adding just the right bit of colour to the place with the imitation violets encrusting her small hat, sat Alfie's former servant, Mrs Marsh. Jeremy was handed over yet again, to Mr Melrose. He nodded to Alfie, murmuring, 'Hello.' She merely nodded in reply, but eyed him searchingly. A very different Alfie. Evidently she had quite recovered her health, was even plump. However, that elfin look was gone, to be replaced by something still impish but perhaps cruelly so. Her black eyes, usually so frankly wide before, now had little wrinkles at the corners as if from being narrowed too often in such a look of suspicious quizzing as she gave Jeremy, and her full childish mouth become tighter.

Jeremy, seated, leaned across Mr Melrose to ask her, 'How's your father?'

Alfie answered in a flat tone, 'Dead.'

Jeremy swallowed, momentarily at a loss for certain by the shortness of the reply. Then he said, 'I'm sorry to hear that.'

In the same tone she replied, 'It was a release.'

He withdrew. Mr Melrose did a little whispering to each about the case, to be interrupted by a movement by the Peace Officer standing near a door to the left of the Bench. The Clerk of Court, at a table directly before the Bench, with a typist beside him, rose and said, 'The Court will rise.' Everybody rose. The officer by the door opened it. In a moment there appeared a tall man in gown and legal cravat and with a grey short-bottomed wig perched on a pin head. He looked like a dyspeptic suffering a sour stomach at the moment. He swept to his seat, clutching his gown as an old woman does her wrapper. Behind him came two younger men, wearing gowns but not wigs. The Peace Officer leapt to be ready to slide the Judge's chair under him. But before sitting down, His Honour bowed to Counsel on both sides. He sat. The Court sat. He shuffled papers before him, gave a little belch into his hand, and in an indifferent voice said, 'This Court is now in sitting. Proceed.'

First move was the Arraignment. The Clerk turned to Mr Melrose, who whispered to Jeremy and Alfie. The Peace Officer who had attended the Judge stepped up to them, motioned them towards a small church-pew-like stand on the left of the bench. As they stood together, the Clerk addressed them, reading from a large legal-looking document, to inform them that they Stood Charged Under Section 13 of the National Security Act, to wit, with Conspiracy to Publish a Document Calculated to Endanger the Security of the Commonwealth of Australia – 'How plead you, Guilty or Not Guilty.' Both murmured that they were Not Guilty. The typist tapped.

Jeremy was stood down, leaving Alfie, chief culprit, to face the music alone.

One of the gentlemen of the Prosecution rose, with Alfie's typescript in his hands, now neatly bound and tied with red tape until he freed it. He proceeded to question her about her writing This Book, as he termed it. He didn't get far. Mr Melrose rose to challenge the description of the Exhibit, which he claimed to be not a Book but a Manuscript. Here was a pretty point in law. That was evident from the way His Honour and Associates perked up from bored drooping. It took lengthy and lively argument. In point of fact what was a Book? There seemed to be no legal ruling on the matter. According to the Oxford Dictionary it might be considered to be what originally it was, a piece of Beechwood on which something was written, Buk, the Anglo-Saxon rendering of the Gothic *Bochus*, Beech, being what it derived from. However, according to His Honour, who had all the say here, it was now generally accepted that a book was a compilation of printed matter contained within covers of some sort. Therefore the Exhibit could hardly be described as a Book. All right, conceded Prosecution, This Typescript. But Mr Melrose stuck to Manuscript. Why? Because a Typescript might readily be considered something compiled deliberately for dissemination, as in fact such scripts were by means of various copying devices, whereas a Manuscript could be claimed to be a private documentation of thought of which the purpose was search of truth with complete absence of what might be termed *amari aliquid*, the essence of a disquisition of which the aim was pernicious. Poor Alfie, author of it all, stood drooped, forgotten. Jeremy sat hunched, expressionless. The Peace Officers stifled yawns. The Clerk appeared to be getting on with other business. The typist dozed. When His Honour, with a peep at his watch, apparently reckoned the legal game had gone far enough, he ruled that, since Manuscript, from the Latin, *Manu Scriptus*, meant Written By Or With The Hand, and to all intents and purposes an original Typescript amounted to the same, the Exhibit would be called a Manuscript.

Then Mr Melrose, with a fat sigh, settled back in his chair, to rouse only when Alfie sounded like getting rattled under examination and needed a cough to remind her of the pact of humility, or the Prosecutor seemed to be stealing a legal march. Alfie was for the most part duly humble, contrite, while sticking to her story of having intended only to fill in the period of her pregnancy with writing what in effect would have amounted only to a sort of spy-yarn, in which the miscreants eventually would have been brought to book. At last she was allowed to stand down.

Jeremy took her place, expressionless, apparently emotionless, answering the Prosecutor exactly as Melrose had directed. One thing Melrose had not foreseen was the bringing up of that incident at Victoria Barracks, Melbourne. However, Jeremy got over it easily enough, explaining that he had been upset by reference to the death of his brother by the General in question in a manner that had seemed feelingless. Asked if he would offer his services to his country as an officer after all, he replied mildly, 'I doubt if they'd want me now. These things aren't readily forgotten. Properly I'm not commissioned . . . and I'm too old to enlist and start at the bottom again.' Pressed to say whether he would offer his services, he replied, 'If I'm wanted in emergency I shall be more than willing.' Still the Prosecutor kept at him, wanting to know why he, a veteran, did not belong to the RSL. Here Mr Melrose, seeing him go red, came to his rescue, declaring that the question was akin to asking someone why they did not belong to the Freemasons. The Judge ruled for Mr Melrose.

Examinations and arguments were nicely timed to bring the first part of the sitting to a close right on lunch-time. The Court adjourned. Jeremy was returned to his nice cell, to be served there with tea and sandwiches.

When the Court resumed, it was first Mr Melrose's turn. He began by putting Mrs Marsh on the stand. She was rather too glib in defence of Alfie's innocent intent, so that in cross-examination Prosecution demanded to know if she had been Put Up to tell this story. She handled it neatly: 'Why, no, Sir. I wouldn't be smart enough to put a clever girl like Mrs Candlemas up to tellin' a story. But, mind you, I did 'elp. Her idea o' books, o' course, is rather classy. She 'adn't read them books like *Bulldog Drummond* and *The Saint*, and Edgar Wallace and all that, which was my kind o' readin'. I dare say you read that kind o' book yourself, Sir, and'll know what I mean . . . .'

If the Judge were truly dyspeptic and liable to prove difficult after having lunched, this bit cured him. He smiled broadly over the Prosecutor's obvious embarrassment. Even before the Prosecutor was halfway through his Address, His Honour said he'd heard enough. Thereupon he retired with his Associates, ostensibly to Consider the Verdict.

No doubt about it, an hour had been allowed for Consideration, which perhaps was spent on other matters, because almost exactly to the minute of that period His Honour was back. He wasted no time over Summing Up. He said he could not accept the plea of absolute innocence of the Accused, the histories of both of whom showed them to have subversive tendencies. However, he considered that there was more folly to their act than the coldly planned subversion charged by Prosecution. The Accused Candlemas obviously was politically immature. Besides, her Condition at the time of the offence must be taken into consideration. On the other hand, although the Accused Delacy could prove that he had taken no part in compilation of the Exhibit, he showed either complete lack of or regard for social responsibility in not seizing the Manuscript after reading the first few pages and demanding its immediate destruction in his presence, on threat of submitting it to authority. He then asked Inspector Ballywick how long the Accused had been under restraint – as if he didn't know! That was the first time the Inspector had been called on, although reports accredited to him were a large part of Evidence for the Prosecution. He replied that the period was almost exactly six months.

His Honour addressed the Accused, standing side by side in the pew: 'Although I've conceded your misdemeanour as largely one of indiscretion, you are no less guilty according to the Citation. Had you come before me earlier, I should have had no hesitation in sentencing you to a term of imprisonment to bring home to you the gravity of your acts and as a deterrent to others of like irresponsibility. This is no time for any sort of indiscretion likely to hamper our struggle for the Democratic Way of Life. But since already you have had time to rue your unlawful conduct, I will do no more than have your convictions for contravention of the Act recorded and your persons detained until the rising of this Court. Let this be an abiding lesson. The gravest war in history is in progress. You are involved in it. Give your very best to it, like decent citizens . . . or take the consequence of betrayal of your country, which, I assure you, is not light.' He turned from them to Ballywick again. 'Your prisoners, Inspector.'

With that His Honour addressed the Court generally: 'This Special Court now rises.' He rose himself, bowed to Counsel, belched, marched out with his wrapper held and his henchmen at his heels.

Mr Melrose came to his clients grinning, but with grin directed first at Inspector Ballywick now standing by the convicted parties to see that the law was carried out to the letter, to whom he first spoke. 'The Court is risen, Inspector.' Ballywick nodded shortly, marched out of the courtroom. After congratulating his clients, Mr Melrose asked to be excused, because he had other business with his Learned Friends here. 'See you later,' he said, adding, 'At the office,' as if to hint that it would not be for purely social reasons.

Jeremy and Alfie went out together, went heading for the elevator, with the corridor to themselves. Jeremy said, 'A brandy's what I'm needing right now. Will you join me?'

Rather shortly she answered, 'Of course.'

'There's a catch in it. I don't happen to have any money on me. Will you stand shout?'

'Of course.'

He eyed her sideways, as if wondering at her curtness. She did not look at him. They rang for the elevator. The driver now bowed them in. He was just closing the door when someone else came running. He opened it – to admit Inspector Ballywick. All three were momentarily taken aback. It was Jeremy who spoke first: 'Ah, Inspector . . . we meet again.'

Ballywick answered no less dryly, 'Yes, Mr Delacy. As a matter of fact, I was just wondering when the next time would be.' With that he turned his back, to continue his early discussion of the weather with the driver.

Down below, Alfie marched out with head erect. Jeremy followed a pace or two behind, and cast a glance back at the Inspector, who met it blankly. Alfie reached the front doorway as Jeremy reached the doors of the Bank. He stopped there, turned to the Inspector, and said, 'Excuse me, Inspector . . . may I have a final word with you?'

Ballywick looked wary, answered slowly, 'Very well . . . what is it?'

'Do you mind coming in here?' Jeremy pushed the swing-doors open.

Ballywick looked suspicious, glanced at Alfie, who was looking back, at the Peace Officer who was close at hand. Then he followed. Inside the bank they were close to a counter with the sign *Interstate Accounts*. Jeremy got close to it before he turned to Ballywick, saying, 'You could always identify me, couldn't you, Inspector?'

Still wary, Ballywick answered, 'Have no doubt about that, Sir.'

'Right!' exclaimed Jeremy, and seizing his arm, drew him up to the counter, where a clerk stood staring. He smiled and nodded at the clerk. 'I have an account here, but need to be identified. This gentleman . . . . ' Ballywick snatched his arm away. "This gentleman's Inspector Ballywick, of Commonwealth Police. He's prepared to identify me.'

Ballywick went very red.

Jeremy added, 'Will you show him your credentials, Inspector?'

The surprised clerk said, 'It's all right. I know the Inspector.'

Jeremy smiled. 'Good. Then, will you let me have the signature form?' As the man turned to get it, Jeremy turned a grin on Ballywick, gave him a nod. Ballywick answered with something like a snort, wheeled about, almost colliding with Alfie who had come in staring, went marching out. Jeremy turned the grin on Alfie, who, however, met it stonily. He turned back to deal with the clerk.

Alfie turned away, to go to the great windows looking out on the street.

Having completed his business, Jeremy joined her, saying, 'Now I can treat you. We'll make it champagne, if you like.'

The black eyes were smouldering. She asked shortly, 'Why?'

'I thought you might be in a mood to celebrate.'

They were moving to go out by the swing-doors. Coldly she asked, 'Celebrate defeat?'

He shrugged. As they reached the crowded pavement he said, 'It's nice to walk the streets without manacles. I don't suppose they did that to you?'

'I wouldn't have cared if they had. I wouldn't have cared what they did. *I* would never have crawled to them.'

He turned her into a side entrance of the Hotel Australia, standing just as if part of all this mass of masonry erected for the Common Weal.

He asked, 'Do I detect a note of condemnation?'

The dark head tossed. 'You asked that creature to do you a favour.'

He was silent for a moment, pondering. As they entered a lounge of the hotel, he chuckled, 'You mean the identification?'

'Yes.'

'Actually I didn't ask him . . . but tricked him into it . . . made him look a bit of a fool, in fact.'

She stared at him. But there was not time for comment. A waiter came to them, ushered them to a table overlooking the street. Jeremy ordered double brandies. As the man went off, Alfie, staring at Jeremy, said, 'The Jeremy of old, eh?'

'Do I still detect condemnation?'

She leaned to him across the table and fairly hissed, 'Yes . . . that's what Jeremy Delacy was chiefly renowned for when I first met him . . . making fools of people.'

He reddened slightly, but answered easily, 'I think I did it only when they deserved it.'

'It's a negative thing.' She fairly spat it, then withdrew as the waiter came.

Raising his glass, he asked, 'Well, what shall we drink to . . . our liberty?'

She sneered: 'Our liberty gained at the price of letting those dogs browbeat us the way they did today?'

'Well . . . my liberty, then.' He raised his glass and took a good swig, putting it down with a sigh of satisfaction. She fairly gulped hers. As she set her glass down, he said, 'What we did was simply to obey the instructions of a good lawyer.'

She snapped, 'I was obeying *your* instructions.'

'How do you make that out?'

'Melrose told me that you wanted me to take it quietly, so that you could deal with them.'

'Did he? And how was I supposed to deal with them?'

She snatched up her glass and finished at another gulp, putting it down with a clatter, gasping at him, 'For godsake . . . what's happened to you?'

He took a sip, said, 'I don't follow you, my dear.'

She was hissing again, 'If I'd've known you were going to give in to those dogs, I'd've told 'em what I thought of 'em to their faces . . . and you too!'

He sipped again, murmured, 'I begin to see Melrose's strategy now. You were going to fight them, eh?'

'Of course.'

He sighed, finished his drink, signed to the watching waiter. He said, 'I'm a free man. I've been locked up for half a year . . . . '

'Free?' she demanded, aloud now. 'What freedom is there in this cursed country?'

'Shush!' he breathed, and took a swift look round.

She sneered again: 'Scared, eh?'

But the waiter was there again. When he was gone, Jeremy said, 'You've got to be sensible, you know, dear. The dogs, as you call them, happen to be having their day . . . . '

'Yes . . . and they'll always have it while cowards run away from them.'

He reddened again, took a sip. Again she gulped. He said, 'I did a bit more time behind the bars and with the stink of tar and phenyle and caged humanity in my nostrils that are used to clean air, than you, you know.'

She snapped. 'From what I've been told, you didn't have it so bad!'

'The Schroeders, eh? As a matter of fact, I think that was about the worst part of it, being stuck with those Huns . . . listening to them gloating over the brutality of their mob.'

'Why shouldn't they gloat? They've put our enemies on the run.'

He took another glance round, murmuring, 'You really must be careful, Alfie. Even the Schroeders won't be able to save you from another stretch.'

'Oh, yes they will! Their side's winning hands down. We can win with them . . . those of us who've got the guts!' She tossed off her drink, turned to look for the waiter, signalled him. Unseen by her, Jeremy shook his head at the man, who nodded, and withdrew. She turned back, to lean across again, breathing fire with the brandy fumes: 'I've been treated like an enemy in my own country. I *am* an enemy in my own country, too, while it's being run by those dogs. I thought you would be, too. How sadly I was mistaken. They've knocked all the fight out of you . . . . '

'They nearly knocked the life out of me . . . and you too . . . and who were they that did it?' He got in before she could answer: 'The Comms got me. I take it that who got you was that big whiskery woman who would be called a Loyal Citizen. Then the Commonwealth of Australia got both of us. What for? All had different excuses . . . but the same motive. The Germans and the Russians have entirely different excuses for having torn the Poles to pieces. But their motive's the same . . . brutality. What we're up against isn't differences of political opinion . . . it's the sheer urge to brutality that in some people, people of all nations, is all-powerful. In the majority of people the same urge seems to be latent, only able to come out when those others give them an excuse for it . . . otherwise gentle people . . . who can become Huns . . . '

'I don't like that word!'

'I'm not using it simply against your Schroeders . . . but against all who practise brutality. Brutality, brutality, girl . . . you can't fight against it, girl . . .

at least not with its own weapons. It only gets worse . . . .'

'What weapons would you use?'

'I don't know. I only know about the brutality so far. I'm going home to think it out.'

She sneered again: 'With your black woman and your Jewess!'

He reddened. 'That's unkind. Don't tell me my Aelfrieda, the Enchanted One, has become brutal too?'

She raised her voice again: 'Why shouldn't I be? They killed my baby . . . destroyed my womb . . . my book . . . my . . . my . . . ' Her voice broke. The curly head dropped to her hands, elbows on the table. She croaked it out in sobs: 'Made a coward of . . . of . . . my Jeremy . . . oh, ah!'

A moment. Then the head came up, to look around, while she sniffed back the tears, muttering, 'Where's that waiter?'

'I think you've had enough.'

She swung on Jeremy. '*You* do?'

'Yes . . . let's get out of here. I want to book in at a hotel. Are you living somewhere?'

'What's it to do with you?'

'I want to take you with me.'

'Where?'

'To Lily Lagoons. You'll only get yourself into trouble here.'

'But not as part of the Scrub Bull's harem!'

'Alfie!'

She leaned across again, hissing, at the same time reaching for her handbag lying on the table, 'You *are* a decadent man, Jeremy. Bruno Schroeder judged you right. And he was right in saying that it was the Jews that made you what you've become.'

He reached for her hand. 'Now don't be silly!'

She snatched her hand away.

Her voice rose: 'Jews . . . that damn Jewess . . . Red Rifkah! If it hadn't been for *her*, for *her*, with *my* help you would be master of this country today . . . .'

'That's foolish talk, girl . . . Free Australia talk, Schroeder talk . . . . '

'It's the truth. I could have made you a hero!' She almost shouted it, rose, swung away from the table.

He rose, too, whispering, 'Alfie!'

The black eyes welled with tears. She turned from him, went rushing from the lounge. People were looking. Jeremy stood for a moment, then went after her. But out in the foyer was a great crowd, herding because the place would close at six. She might have gone in any of three directions. After standing looking about, he headed out the way they had come. He stood on the steps looking out on the street, which was crowded now with people pouring out of offices.

At last, with a sigh, he stepped down to the pavement. A taxi pulled in to set down a fare. He got in, asked to be taken to that hotel near Central Station that had been his last abode in freedom in this so-civilized place where he had known little but savagery.

At the hotel they found the record of his having stayed there and also his baggage. It seemed they had notified the police of his disappearance, and been told it was known where he was. He allayed suspicion by saying he had been concerned with National Security business. They let him book in again.

After dinner he paid another visit to those central parts of Central Station, and by devious means booked a berth on a train leaving for Brisbane next night. From there he went to the GPO to wire home, asking for whatever help Fergus could give him to facilitate the journey. Thereupon he strolled to the Quay and bought himself a ticket for a trip to Manly. Perhaps there was some idea in him of looking his last on what was so essentially Australia while yet so alien to him who had featured in a fantasy as the Last Australian.

As they passed Garden Island he showed an interest in the place that surely must have aroused suspicious interest of his few fellow passengers at such a time as this, had he not chosen a spot to sit alone and those who were near not been engrossed in their newspapers and perhaps the war they were involved in on the other side of the world if not next week-end's races. Even more so, when they rounded the island, and suddenly were abeam a mighty ship, towering black against the Southern Stars, seeming to rake them down with her rigging, her three great funnels. He stared as if living in the fantasy of the *Last Australians*. Or Jeremy might have been wondering how often H.M.T. *Queen Mary* had been in and out of this harbour, by way of which had come in chains those who had sired a Nation so odd that its sons were even eager to give their lives for the Motherland that had dealt so brutally with their forefathers as to deserve to be remembered here by no other symbol but the Ball and Chain. It was freely said that the great ship was so fast she could deliver her passengers for their rendezvous with death within a fortnight.

VII

With the help of Fergus Ferris, Jeremy reached Lily Lagoons, that refuge surely as meaningful to himself now as for those weaker ones for whose protection from the brutal world he had established it, well in time to join in preparations for the Beatrice River Races.

Rifkah and Prindy were already there, working their own horses, but right ready to confess that doing so without the Mullaka wasn't easy. Fergus also conceded that training horses here was something that couldn't be done properly without the Boss about. There could be no doubt about that, the way he was received by animals as well as humans. He had scarcely stepped from the Junkers, and was still being clung to by weeping Nanago and Rifkah, when the beasts, led by Elektron, rushed him. They were not only the horses, although only they got near enought to sniff him and a sniff was all that jealous Elektron would allow. The old stallion himself nuzzled him, even chewed him a bit, and by the way he eyed him, might have been as aware of the great change in his condition as the snivelling women. It was not only Nan and Rifkah who wept over him. Tears streamed down many a black and brown face. From their whispering, the simpler ones evidently though he was come back wounded from the war, because they were using the term *Rotten Sodjer*, long used in Murringlitch to denote a veteran of *kuttabah* wars.

Jeremy soon dispelled all grieving for him with his cheerfulness, his obvious delight in being home. He went round looking at everything. He entered his den as if it were a holy place. That night over a great dinner of roast bustard and sweet-bucks and pawpaw, with jack-fruit pie and honeyed coffee, he declared that nowhere on earth could anyone eat more sweetly or wholesomely than here at dear Lily Lagoons, and that he'd have his Head Read if he ever left the lovely place again. After that dinner, they had a jolly evening out under the mangoes, with lights strung in the branches, pulsing to that heartbeat of the place, that soft *Home-home-home-home*! Jeremy had brought gramophone records for everyone. For Rifkah there was a huge one packed with Children's Folk Songs in Yiddish, for Prindy a selection of light classics, including *La Golondrina*, for Nan some new Cowboy stuff. There was a surprise also for Jeremy. Prindy, on the verge of puberty, was at the fullness of his boyhood voice, a very strong and sweet soprano, a fact that it seemed had been taken full advantage of at the Mission both for religious and entertainment purposes. Lately he had foregone much of his playing music for singing. He sang *La Golondrina* for them, to the subdued accompaniment of the record. It roused the sleeping butcher birds and started them off, so that he was bound to sing back to them his *Butcher Bird Song*. He also sang duets with Rifkah, including a brand new one off the record, and in Yiddish, so quick were those ears to master sounds, *Rozinkes Mit Mandlen. Raisins and Almonds*, a lullaby:

Unter Yiddele's vigele, Shteyt a klor veis tzigele . . .
Under Baby's crib is a tiny white goat, Baby and goat grow up together . . . .
Shlof-zhe Yiddele, shlof.

Jeremy plunged into activities for which he had come back with the latest in equipment. Most of it was concerned with veterinary practice. However, a very important part of it was primarily for human use. This was the wherewithal for manufacturing Sulphanilamide and derivatives of the drug, concerning which he had received instruction from Hugo Schroeder, whose firm had dealt in it, the original, called Prontisil, being a German patent. While in hospital Jeremy had learnt that supply of the drug in Australia was now limited to military use. He also had learnt from Schroeder much about the pharmacology of the Sulphanilamides not yet known here. As he told Rifkah, when she reported on her lavish use of what he had supplied her with for treatment of the gonorrhea the Japanese had left behind them on the coast: 'If your patients weren't about the toughest people on the earth you'd have killed most of 'em by now.' But apparently she'd had great success, and was most eager to learn all he had to tell her about the drug's toxicity and how to remedy it. She and Prindy helped him set up the intricate apparatus required for the manufacture, a job beyond him, limited as he was in use of his left arm. They also helped him build a contraption designed to train the arm to better functioning.

Thus with manifold interests was he able almost utterly to ignore what just then had practically the entire civilized world by the ears if in no closer grip, as nothing ever had it before or has since; namely that combat in the sky, as it had to be between the two races of Supermen, the Irresistible German and the Immovable English, already being called The Battle of Britain. Only the local newspaper brought news of the world's madness, as Jeremy called it, and that already stale enough not to count.

But it isn't easy to hide from the world in these days. Along with the stale papers, one mail-day there was a letter for Jeremy with an English stamp and post-mark, it read:

For Jeremy Delacy,

I cannot address you in the conventional manner, because at this moment of all persons, I bear you the deepest resentment. I write only to strike you, only hoping that you have anything in you sensitive enough to feel the blow. I consider you responsible for the futile death of my gallant, talented, and noble father. As no doubt you will have learnt by now, dear Daddy died on the beach at Dunkirk. But for your shattering his dream of a great and glorious British Commonwealth with your Irish-convict-colonial treachery, he would never have been involved in the Little England lunacy which has caused this frightful debacle. At least he has been spared the humiliation of defeat that inevitably awaits those of us who have so far survived. That is not meant as amelioration for *you*. Had my father lived, as he should have, had you served him faithfully, he would have formed that Commonwealth, which in collaboration with the victorious Third Reich, would soon have put down the mongoloid Japanese, the semi-Tartar Russians, and all other inferior races that presume equality with us who raised them out of barbarism. Daddy's word to the High Command here to avoid conflict with the *Führer*, so as to concentrate on Imperial Power, would have been taken, and his old and noble comrades would not have resigned themselves, as he did when he returned to them a broken man, to the madness of the Little Englishism that put the half-bred Yankee Churchill where he is and England where he has dragged her. We are in even direr straits than at the time of the Armada, having no Elizabeth or Drake or anyone like them any more.

England will fall before this year is out, to become a vassal of the Reich 'That Will Stand a Thousand Years', when as brothers in blood and culture we might have stood as its closest ally. Australia will soon enough fall to the Japanese, to become a slave State, which is all the wretched country and its low inhabitants are fit for. I only hope you may survive to bear the chains, and know that you yourself forged them, by betrayal of my darling daddy.

I have no more to say to you, no mind even to think of you again. I spurn you for what you are – a dirty damned colonial.

Lydia Vaisey.

Mad as the letter might have been, it cast Jeremy down for days. As he told those close to him, it reflected the awful madness abroad in the world today. The Germans were not the only *Irrenation*. When he heard from Fergus that there was official talk of cancelling the Race Meeting because of the desperate plight of Britain, he said, 'It's to be hoped so. I'd cancel my part in it, only for my people here. They live by recurring ceremonial. This is the grand annual one for them now, where the Making of Young Men used to be before. No Beatrice Races would mean the end of the world to them.'

Fergus said that most whites he'd talked to sounded as if they felt like that about it, too, only they thought of Britain's being beaten as certain end of the world and any sort of pleasure impossible while the abyss yawns, as it were: 'Mad bastards! I never realized how stupid my countrymen are, almost to a man, till this Battle of Britain thing. Even those you know have some degree of radicalism are identifying themselves with the Old Dart. I can't make it out. The fact is that we're not at war at all. We're involved politically because we've no true political identity of our own. We have men standing by to go into battle who've sworn allegiance to the King of England. But we're still not actually at war, and won't be till someone actually declares war on us. D'you know that even Finnucane, who started out boasting about his neutrality, is worried about the likely defeat of Britain? He's a changed man. They say he spends most of his time listening to the radio . . . .'

'Wishing, maybe,' Jeremy commented.

'No . . . he's really worried. You can tell by the look of him. Anyway, he's one who says the Meeting should be called off, the one who benefits from it most.'

'He's only being Irish.'

Jeremy would not comment on anything Fergus had to say, except flippantly. Of the reported growing hysteria in the land as the distant battle neared the climax that everybody was predicting for it about Race Time, he said, 'I think it's the rule in madhouses that when one loony starts raving they have to sedate the lot.'

The idea that the Battle of Britain would be decided coincidental with the Beatrice River Races, that is about the middle of September, was not just a bit of the local lunacy of the time. Perhaps Winston Churchill had sown the seed for it with his frequent broadcast exhortations to his people to gird themselves to meet the unconcealed intention of the enemy to invade Britain by air and sea as soon as the weather suited the adventure. Perfect weather for war in Europe was traditionally just before the Northern Autumnal Equinox.

Then Fergus, in a rush because he was back in business to fulfil bookings he had made to fly the more remote and affluent bushies in to the Races, was there again to say that the Meeting was to take place as usual – well, hardly as usual, as he explained: 'The Service Heads want it . . . to Boost Morale, they reckon. Seems like the Army, Navy, and Air Force boys, all dressed up to kill and nobody to kill or kill them, are getting browned-off, as they say these days. Captain Toby's going to be Patron, instead of the Administrator. They're going to put on two special trains, for Army and Navy Personnel . . . and the Air Force'll fly their men in. Then they're going to have regular race meetings in Palmeston. Seems like the boys're boozing too much and doing their dough on swy and poker. Everybody's saying it should be the biggest turn-out yet. But old Shame-on-us doesn't look any happier. I don't suppose he'll cheer up till he's certain his old enemies are licked. I wonder will he put on free beer that day?'

Captain Toby, commander of what was called, H.M.A.S. *Palmeston*, was he who formerly had captained H.M.A. Survey Sloop *Arafura*, with the rank of Lieutenant-Commander. His new command was not a ship, as made to sound, but the Port Palmeston Naval Depot, centre of which was a block of offices even remote from the sea. Fergus told the Lily Lagoons people an amusing story of how the place was run just as if it were a ship, even to having a Bos'un piping and the staff's – no, crew's – saying they were Going Ashore or Aboard according to their movements out on to Smith Street or off it. 'No doubt about it,' he said. 'The bastards're mad. You should see the moustaches the Air Force blokes're sporting now. The higher the rank the bigger the mo . . . commissioned rank, of course. The shit aren't allowed to wear 'em. You'd think at least flying an aeroplane would bring a man down to basic realities. But, of course, for the most part these blokes are only bomb-jockeys. I've struck only a couple who regard an aeroplane as anything but a weapon of war. The fact that I won't have it on as a means of murder's declassed me completely with 'em. Since this latest lunacy's been on I'm regarded as a sort of moral leper. They're all just rarin' to go and get killed in the Battle of Britain.'

Thus, just when it looked as if, indeed, the end of the world had come, and at long last the white cockatoos of Beatrice River might yell their kingship of the river timber unchallenged the year round, and the Beatrice goats wander at happy will scavenging what they could from their two-legged kin without having to suffer that hideous banishment to the mercies of the dingo and the eagle in the bush, there was the dispossessing human mob again, shattering the pristine peace with axe and hammer in camp-building, with its discord of communication, its roaring motors, howling aircraft, screaming trains. Beatrice River Races on again!

Official beginning of the Meeting was, of course, declared by the President of the Committee at the Racecourse on the Thursday morning. But of course, it was always accepted that the Festival itself began with that classic influx from the train and the storming of Finnucane's all-too-ready-to-capitulate citadel. Thus it began this time, festive enough and to spare, with all those boys in khaki, naval ducks, Air Force blue. But was it really a time for festival, despite the brave showing?

Even in booze the mob were arguing the Battle of Britain.

'Next couple o' days'll tell.'

'What d' yo' reckon?'

'Poor old Poms coppin' it.'

'Yo' mean they'll get beat?'

'Did I say that, sport?'

'Say't you mean.'

'You tryin' 'o make some'n' out of it?'

'You pro-bloody-Hun, eh?'

' 'Ere, break it up, you two . . . keep the stoush for the enemy.'

' 'E said . . . . '

'I never said nothin'. Course there'll always be an Englan'.'

'Yeah . . . so long's she can hang on till our mob get there.'

'There'll always be an Englan' . . . an' Englan' shall be free . . . . '

If Englan' means as much to you as Englan's means to me. Red, White and Blue, whaashit mean to you . . . .

Finnucane, tapping a new barrel, looking nothing like Mine Host of former days, his eyes hooded, bushy brows rumpled in a frown that could have meant anything – anger, perplexity, distress – felt a touch on his arm, turned to see his daughter Bridie. She screeched above the din, 'Telephone!'

He dropped what he was doing, and wiping great hairy hands, went to the office. It was the Big House calling, the speaker Martin Delacy. He said 'Shamus, we've just heard something on the big radio . . . a speech of Churchill's . . . that makes us feel a bit . . . well, we felt it wouldn't be proper to carry on in the usual way . . . . '

Old Shame-on-us cut in with a sort of gulp: 'England's had it?'

'Eh? Oh, no . . . nothing like that. But things look pretty grim. There's sure to be a re-broadcast of Churchill's speech . . . y'there, Shamus?'

Finnucane had removed the handset from mouth and ear, as if to get air. His hand was quivering, face jerking. He brought the instrument back into place, to gulp again, but almost inaudibly now, 'Yes, Martin.'

'We've decided we ought to have a mass meeting tonight . . . in the Dance Hall. Can you stop 'em boozing, and get the word round. We want everybody there. Right?'

Shamus hung for a moment, then asked hesitantly, 'You couldn't give me some idea of what to tell 'em?'

'It'd take too long. Besides . . . well, it's nothing definite . . . rather an appeal. We don't want to break up the show, now everybody's here. But it's hardly a time for . . . well, kicking up. See what I mean?'

'Yes, Martin.'

'Right . . . I leave it to you. Meeting to start about ten, say. See you.'

For a good minute the old man sat, with head lowered sideways to a hand, the fingers of which tore as if in unconscious worry at the silvery mane, while the black eyebrows worked above eyes that might be struggling to hold back tears. Then with a great sigh he heaved his bulk up, went back to the bar. Now his expression was savage. He roared and thumped for silence. Getting it, he told the news quite shortly, silencing the babble of questions that followed with another roar: 'I'm closin' the bar. Ye've ahll had enough dhrink for the whoile. I'd advoise those of ye that've had a drhop too much to put your heads under the tap. Shame on us, but it's no toime for shinnanigans. Out wit' the lot o' ye!'

Surely the End of the Wurruld was at hand when old Shame-on-us would do such a thing as empty his bar at the height of its liveliest trading. Although no one was heard actually to mention the phenomenon, it was implied in the general mode of the expression as they headed for the Hall: 'Things must be pretty crook.' The sobering effect of Finnucane's announcement was all but miraculous. No more than a dozen of the mob failed to pass that strict scrutiny of those who set themselves up to judge who was fit to take part in so serious a business. It was interesting that Finnucane himself took no part in this vigilance, and did not even seek a place in the Hall. The vigilantes who culled the hopeless ones and lured them away to a fictitious booze-party down the river, were chiefly servicemen of non-commissioned rank, no policemen taking part, probably to avoid antagonism. One of the civilians was Eddy McCusky, at his best at such operations. Another of them who was familiar was Chief Petty Officer Pickles, formerly also of H.M.A.S. *Arafura,* now skipper (or Coxwain as properly ranked) of a small naval patrol boat, and quite a friend now of Prindy's, and also Rifkah's, as revealed when he shoved in to stand with them in the

Hall. No doubt he had got to know them together through visiting the Mission. Nanago was with the other two, but not Jeremy, who stayed outside with the packed mob of blacks. Finnucane saw him there, as was easy in the blaze of the Moon almost at the full, and joined him. They exchanged no word except in greeting.

The Elite arrived from the Big House, and took the places reserved for them as usual. The Committee took their usual places on the rostrum. However, there was no other formality. Rising as soon as all were settled down, the President said, 'Ladies and gentlemen . . . this is an extraordinary meeting to meet an extraordinary situation. We're gathered together for our annual festival of indulgence in the Sport of Kings, our own favourite sport. But it's hardly a time for festivity and indulgence, is it, with the Old Country fighting for its life? I am your chairman because I'm a racing man. But the job's really one for a man of the Armed Services in these circumstances I've mentioned. Fortunately, we have as Patron a fighting serviceman of the Senior Service. I propose to hand over command to him. Command's the word he used himself when we discussed the situation, and the right word, when really the proper thing for us to be doing right now is bear what share we can in the Battle of Britain, even if what we can do is no more than cheer our fighting brothers on to victory. Ladies and gentlemen . . . Captain Roger Toby, commander of the Naval Forces for the Northern Region . . . and our special commander for the time being.'

Martin sat down amidst a thunder of applause, leaving Captain Toby to rise to it. The Captain was in full naval whites, with gold braid and service ribbons, only minus his gold-encrusted cap, which lay so close to his hand on the cane table beside him that it looked as if he were going to grab it and jam it on his bristly iron-grey head to assert command as he would from the bridge of his ship, which with his megaphone voice and blunt manner he appeared to do: 'Comrades! For that's what we are . . . and I don't hesitate to use that honourable mode of address now that the treacherous scum who besmirched it as their pass-word have been discovered for what they are and put where they belong . . . .'

Loud applause – perhaps even from some secret Commos if there were any still about.

'Comrades I call you, because we are all fighting this war together . . . man, woman, child . . . in uniform or out, and whether we like that sort of thing or not, because our ruthless enemy makes no distinction. We are all in the line of battle. Unfortunately, we're not in the front line with our brothers overseas, much as we'd all like to be, those of us who're worth our salt as Britishers . . . and as for the rest, they ought to be put up against a wall and shot . . . .'

Loud cheers.

"We're here for the Beatrice River Races . . . but, God dammit! . . . how can we think of racing when our grand old Empire is fighting for the life as never since the days of Drake?' At this moment the bridge of the Ship of Empire, the mighty City of London, the very nerve-centre of our existence, the magazine of our power and our pride, is under attack by the most ruthless and methodical enemy ever known. Every night the watch on that bridge faces the full fury of the aerial blitz. Every day they pick up the pieces and make things shipshape

. . . and bury the dead. Don't forget that . . . bury the dead . . . for night after night our comrades there . . . our brothers and our sisters by blood and culture and everything else . . . die by the hundreds, fighting to keep the grand old ship afloat. What if she sinks? It's unthinkable! But the odds are great and terrible. Not long ago we heard a broadcast by our beloved leader, dear old Winny. I won't go into it, because you'll be hearing a repeat of it. Enough to say that it chilled us to the blood. The enemy is poised to strike the final blow. Now's the hour we British face our destiny. Never, never, never will they break our will and chain us, of course. But superb as we are in every way, as never any other race of men has been or ever will be, we are but flesh and blood . . . and that's about all we have at present to meet the Hun's steel and fire . . . but we are steel and fire in our resolve, and will fight to the end, bitter or sweet. Please God, who has always stood by us in our hour of need, it will be sweet!

'That's how things stand at the moment. Even as we stand here now our last brave Spitfire may be falling from the sky, shot down by the Hun's Armada . . . and the invasion he has ready mounted from the sea in progress. It is like that now . . . at any hour . . . at any minute. How can we do anything but sit with our ears glued to our radios and our minds and hearts in the fight? I know I speak for you all. There couldn't be anyone so low and mean and despicable amongst us who could feel otherwise.

'Now, we are gathered here at Beatrice River, representative of every section of our country. Our country is at war. So why not fight this greatest battle of this war, of all history, together . . . if only with the only means at our disposal, our ears and our hearts? The big military radio at present installed at Beatrice Homestead gives direct contact with London. The BBC has pledged itself to twenty-four hour service. Britain is on constant Red Alert. I propose to put the whole community on Stand By, and to that end am having the radio transhipped to the Racecourse, the point of muster.

'At the moment all military action within the British Isles is confined to the hours of darkness, the enemy having found that for all his numerical superiority he can't beat our skimpy but superb RAF, and wanting to weaken the will of the British people as much as possible while at the same time conserving his forces for the final shattering blow that will be followed by invasion. Of course, if it may be permitted a jest at such a time, as the song says, *When it's Night-time in Italy it's Wednesday Over Here*, by which I mean we're nine hours ahead of 'em . . . that is in terms of siderial or solar time . . . because actually we're synchronous with them in terms of heart and mind. Thus, until the invasion actually comes, we'll be doing most of our listening by day, during the period One Thousand Hours to Sixteen Hundred, which is to say Ten a.m. to Four p.m., the hours usual for racing. Of course racing's out of the question. But we won't just sit glum. There'll be the bar and refreshment stalls and the Band . . . and speaking of the Band . . . Bandsmen, there . . . if you'll be so good as to form up . . . I'll be needing you for a bit of music when I've done talking.

'Yes . . . well . . . there it is, Comrades. My technicians will rig amplifiers so that everybody can get full hearing without having to crowd round. We'll sit round in our groups and listen . . . and in between times sing . . . the way they do it At Home in the Underground and such places . . . listening, singing, but ever on the alert . . . and joking, too. The good old British humour has never failed. Listening to the BBC broadcasting under fire, sometimes you'd think you were listening-in to a commentary on a cricket-match or something, and expect someone to yell *Get a Bag*! . . . only, of course, the English don't yell like us at cricket matches . . . .'

Laughter.

'That's the stuff,' roared the Captain. 'Laugh! We'll laugh the Hun out of existence. Now . . . these are the orders . . . all hands muster at Racecourse One Thousand Hours tomorrow, Thursday. Don't bother to bring riding-boots. Only kit required is ears to listen with and tongue to sing the praises of Old England. Let us begin our singing right now, with that grand old song that has sustained our Motherland throughout many an ordeal, *Rule Britannia* . . . Band!'

As the Band struck up, the Captain led the singing with his in-built megaphone. Soon the flimsy old Hall was rocking to it:

When Britain fir-ir-ir-irst at Heaven's command,
Aro-ooo-o-ose fro-o-om out the ay-ay-ayzure main,
This was the Charter, the Charter of the Land,
And Guardian Ay-ay-ay-ay-angels sang this refrain:
Rule Britannia, Britannia rule the waves,
Britons never, never, never shall be slaves!

Jeremy withdrew, so unobstrusively that only the blacks noticed it. He went down to the still-lighted but deserted camp. First he took a look at the quietly-running power-plant, then entered the shelter used as lounge and dining-room, took brandy and water from the refrigerator. Still standing, he was pouring a drink at the table, when he heard steps, turned to see the massive figure of Finnucane, bright as a wraith in the moonlight with his immaculate whites and silver mane. He came up to Jeremy with his usual amiable greeting, but without the engaging smile: 'First I've seen of you in a very long whoile.' Jeremy asked him what he would like to drink. The silver head shook. 'I'm not drinkin' just now, Jerry.'

Raising his own glass in silent toast, Jeremy asked, 'What, saving yourself for the big moment?' Jeremy took a swig.

Eyeing him with head a little aside as when he was fishing for special information, Shamus countered, 'And what big moment would that be, now?'

Jeremy finished the drink, returned with the bottle to the refrigerator. 'I'm only going by what seems to be the general anticipation.'

'Ah . . . and what, then, would be your own anticipation of events?'

Coming back to the table, Jeremy asked, 'What would we be talking about, Shamus?'

' 'Tis yeself who raised the subject, Jerry.'

Jeremy regarded the quizzing black eyes for a moment, then said, 'Well, in that case I drop it.' He added: 'If you'll excuse me . . . I'm off up to the Course. I want to let my horses run.'

As he moved off towards the crossing, Finnucane went with him, saying, 'I'd be obloiged to go along wit' ye. It's a beautiful noight for walkin', sure.' When Jeremy gave him a look that plainly hinted that he would prefer to be alone, he added hastily: 'Besoides, yon music's not to the taste av me ear.'

Back at the Hall they were now blaring and roaring *Sons of the Sea . . . All British born, Sailing every ocean, laughing foes to scorn . . . .*

The pair went on in silence. As they crossed the causeway, the Shade of old Igulgul winked at them from the shallows of the river. They did not speak until they were climbing the further bank, when Jeremy's hard breathing became so obvious that Finnucane remarked on it: 'I hear'd that ye're but half the man ye went away, Jerry . . . but I didn't think 'twas as bad as that.' When Jeremy made no reply, the old man went on: 'Although it's a matter of deep consarne to me, I wouldn't have the impertinence to ask ye what happened to ye, seein' ye've made a point avoidin' me . . . although for whoy, I can't for the loife of me imagine.'

Jeremy managed a little laugh, which caused Shamus to say with a note of indignation, 'Ye regard consarne for the son of me dearest friend, God rest him, as a laughin' matter?'

'No,' panted Jeremy. 'I was thinking of the old man, as a matter of fact . . . and his way of asking questions as a policeman . . . "I wouldn't be worryin' ye about so small a matter, Mick, only Knowles claims the hoss is his . . . so would ye be koind enough to settle matters be producing your proofs of ownership?" ' He chuckled.

Shamus sighed: 'Ah, your dear old Da! If only he were here today to confoide in. Niver in me long loife have I wanted a trusted confidant the more.'

Jeremy made no reply. They reached the top, went in silence to the Lily Lagoons stable. Scraps of the warlike fervour of the community came to them across the river on little gusts of wind like bits of old rag . . . *Oh, God our help in Ages Past, our Hope in years to Come . . . .*

The horses came crowding to Jeremy. He let them out, led them up to the flat and across and through onto the track, and slipped a rail so that they could go into the inner paddock. They waited for him, but when he replaced the rail and waved them off, went off at a gallop, to become a silver cloud of dust.

Finnucane was waiting at the gate to the flat. He said as Jeremy rejoined him, 'Could we have a little bit of a tahlk, man.'

'On what subject?'

'There's but wan at the moment . . . as is all too plain to hear.'

Lest we forget, Lest we forget . . . .

'The least subject I'm interested in, Shamus, is politics'

'Politics?' cried Finnucane 'You call the changin' av the course av history politics?'

'What's politics mean but the so-called science and art of government . . . and isn't what's going on just a climax to the lunatic business?'

'Ye've no consarne for the defeat of England?'

'Is England defeated?'

'Sum up the news of the wurruld, man . . . and the answer's Yes. D'ye listen-in to wurruld news?'

'I've been much too busy with neglected things, since I came home, Shamus.'

With hands and eyebrows Finnucane made a gesture of despair, and almost groaned, 'I was countin' on ye as the wan and only hope of disburdenin' meself av what's fairly tearin' at me heart.'

'Unburden yourself as much as you like . . . so long's you don't involve me.'

'In what?'

'Now listen, Shamus . . . I know you want to talk to me . . . and I can guess about what. You don't have to beat about the bush. You know I'm no informer . . . unless I see a gross injustice being done that I can't rectify myself . . . . '

'Infahmer? Begob, that a day should come whan I regarded the son of me ould friend as an infahmer!'

'Cut it out, Shamus. I was brought up on Irish bullshit. It's the Irish bullshit that's smothering you now, I'll be bound. Come over to the grandstand steps. I get tired standing too long these days.'

Loudly clicking his tongue in sympathy, Finnucane went with him. As they sat down, with Igulgul peeping over the roof at then, Shamus said, 'I don't suppose ye'd be up in Irish news at all at all.'

'You know I have no interest in Ireland.

'Shame on you to say so, the son of a great Irishman, and ould Ireland bein' the single wan of all England's vassals to stand out agin her!'

Jeremy simply leaned back with arms folded and referred it to Igulgul.

Shamus went on after a moment: 'I have meself now a grand and powerful radio be which I can pick up Americy. So I know a lot that doesn't come through our censorship. For instance . . . Churchill has inflamed the English public agin what he calls De Valéra's Republic, wit' transparent intent to invade Ireland if it becomes necessary to break the German blockade of southern England. All the ould tyranny is there. The craytur's already expressed indignation at not bein' allowed to use Irish ports . . . whan he should be thankful Dev doesn't let the Germans use 'em. The only thing stoppin' him from invadin' is fear of American opinion. Although Roosevelt's a bloody Dutchman, as indaid was William of Orange, he knows the strength of Irish opinion in Americy. Forbye, Americy, loike the rest of the civilized wurruld that's not taken in by British conceit, is doubtful that England can hould out.' Looking at Jeremy and changing his tone from what had sounded belligerent to wheedling, he said, 'That's whoy I was wonderin' what ye moight be thinkin' yeself about England's chances.' When Jeremy sat straight and eyed him back, Shamus added quickly: ' 'Twas only to disburden meself of me own doubts and difficulties, as I was tellin' ye.'

Jeremy said, 'I don't think anybody can predict these things. There's no science or art about war. The weather can upset the best planned campaign. The British have been saved by their notoriously bad weather before. Probably the Romans pissed off and left them on account of the lousy climate. Already this invasion thing's been put off because of bad weather. Maybe the good weather they're hoping for will never come.'

'I think there'll be invasion, man.'

'All right, then. What d'you want to consult me about?'

'If the English are licked, ould Ireland will be free at lasht.'

'Don't you think the Huns will grab Ireland, too?'

'Let 'em troy! We'll foight 'em on the beaches . . we'll foight 'em . . . . ' The vociferation trailed off as it dawned on Shamus whom he was quoting.

Dryly Jeremy rubbed it in: 'In the bogs.'

Recovered, Finnucane replied as dryly, 'Exactly.'

The grandstand gave some refuge from the vociferation across the way. Still, with little bursts of wind that Igulgul dragged after him, it came – *There'll always be an England* . . . .

Shamus took a deep breath, exhaled: 'We would doy foightin' wit'out chains . . . those Chains of Ulster we'll niver shake off till the stuffin' that makes an Englishman is knocked out av him.' He sighed again: 'But the throuble is to stand by and see'em licked. They're foightin' the way we've fought 'em for four huntret years. 'Tis the God's truth that they'll niver give in. They put us in chains . . . but havin' lived so long in chains oursen, we don't wish it on another . . . and particularly on Ould England. That's what I mane when I say the heart's bein' torn out av me. Niver in me long loife have I been so confused and bewildered . . . in the wan breath wantin' to see 'em go down, wit' the next wan prayin' for the spalpeens to win. And niver so lorn. No wan in the woide wurruld to tahlk to, not ayven the woife av me bed. Begorra, man, 'tis for that rayson I've shtopped drinkin'. I was startin' to drink too much . . . just settin' be me radio . . . listenin' and drinkin' and seein' the ding-bats craypin' on me if didn't pull meself together. It's been fair droivin' me mad, man . . . the unsartinty av it . . . what wit'out havin' annywan to tahlk to. Manny's the toime I thought of droivin' out to you and throwin' meself on your mercy . . . as the son of me ould friend, who'd've been feelin' the same.' Shamus stopped wih a sign.

As Jeremy said nothing, the brogue went on: 'I know ye be no lover av ould Ireland, Jerry, me boy . . . but ye love your own counthry as if 'twere the Ould Sod itself . . . and as of times ye've said yeself, 'tis the same chains that shackle it, the same slander of disloyalty livelled at annyone that's loyal to it as a native son should be. 'Tis for that rayson that I've wanted to confess and relieve meself to you . . . and whoy I'm now doin' so.' There was a quaver in the voice. Jeremy glanced to see tears glistening in the eyes.

It took a moment for Shamus to find further voice for it. 'I was hopin' the Races would be cahlled off . . . in fact suggested it to Martin. I had hopes when I got the message this ayvenin' that such would be the case, and they'd ahll be goin' home tomorrow. I wasn't reckoning on the British lunacy, or whatever it is. Och, man . . . they're goin' to make another Dunkirk out av this! Ye may think I'm mad . . . but 'tis more than I can shtand . . . wit'out somewan to turrn to.'

Jeremy, from another contemplation of staring Igulgul, looked again at Shamus, who lay a hand on his arm, saying almost shyly, 'Would ye do me the grace, Jerry, me boy, to let me see this thing through in your company?'

Jeremy looked surprised. He murmured, 'How d'you mean, Shamus?'

'Well, there's this mad death-watch thing they've organized. I can't very well absent meself from it entoirley. There's suspicion and fear and British bullyin' abroad. You can see it in in the oyes of men ye wanst trusted. No one will expect *you* to take part in annything. What was your intintion for tomorrow, annyway?'

'Hadn't thought of it. My mob will want to be in it, of course. I suppose I'll spend most of the time in the stable, as I usually do race-time.'

'Ah . . . then would ye be after havin' me wit' ye . . . and we could drink a drop . . . and ye could kape an oye on me so's I don't overdo it?'

The great face was working with emotion. For a moment Jeremy regarded it, then murmured, 'Okay.'

The great hands seized one of his, pumping and squeezing. 'Thank ye, me boy, thank ye . . . you don't know what it means to me.'

'I think I do.'

Finnucane leaned eagerly. 'You do?'

But Jeremy was not committing himself further. He released his hand, and hearing what the wind brought, said, 'Sounds like they're winding up, over there . . . so we can get back and have a sleep.'

They were singing *God Save the King* at the Hall, and not making the usual skimpy mere declaration of what was called Loyalty, but really beefing it, giving it in its fullness:

Oh, Lord our God arise, scatter his enemies,
And low them bring.
Confound their politics, frustrate their knavish tricks,
Smash them to bloody bits.
God save the King!

Jeremy said as they went back down to the crossing, 'There'll be some dry gullets after all that. You'll have to hurry and open up, or they'll have the door down.'

Shamus whooped for joy, slapped Jeremy's back: 'Ah, Jerry, me boy, God bless ye! 'Tis the firrst toime I've had a laugh since Dunkirk.'

They parted at the Lily Lagoons camp, with arrangements to meet early next morning, when Finnucane would bring along his radio, which he hoped to bribe one of the service technicians to hook up to the main set.

Thursday morning's trooping across the river to the Racecourse looked like any other in all the years of Beatrice Race Meetings – of course with the usual increase in numbers and greater disturbance of the peace and the purity of the atmosphere with the advance of humanity towards ultimate complete disuse of pedal appendages. For an hour the region lay under the pall of dust that was as ever just so much thicker than last year. The reek of gasolene was just so much more powerful. The small creatures of the surrounding bush scuttled away just that bit further, and the smothered trees drooped a little lower to the ordeal.

But how strange and new the Initiation of Proceedings as the Committee had termed it. On the stroke of 1000 hours C.S.T. a military bugler, standing on the grandstand steps, sounded *Reveille*, while a sailor beside him ran the bundled bunting to the masthead on the roof and broke it out in true naval style – of course the Union Jack, Flag of Freedom, as Winston Churchill recently had described it to the world. Another Jack draped the table in the President's box, where now stood Captain Toby, alone and rigidly at attention. He came to the salute as the Band on the flat before him struck up *God Save the King*. Likewise all other servicemen. Male civilians doffed their hats, even the black ones when they saw what their betters were doing. Even the horses, all now out in the centre paddock, were in it, crowding the rails, heads high, eyes and nostrils wide, beside themselves with curiosity over the antics of their masters. A couple of dogs sang to the band. Of all the gathering, the only ones who were At Ease, to put it in military terms, were Jeremy and Finnucane, seated in cane chairs in the human section of the Lily Lagoons stable. That they were not at ease literally was shown by Jeremy's hasty reaching to turn down the volume of the radio, connected as it was to the general amplifying system. He turned it up when the music ceased and Captain Toby began to speak:

'Comrades . . . as no doubt you are aware, the modern method of specifying warlike action is by means of code-names that can easily be abbreviated. Our own action is to be styled Operation Beatrice Ear-watch, abbreviated to O.B.E.'

Jeremy groaned. Finnucane took a gulp of Tullamore Dew from the glass beside him.

The megaphone voice went on. No doubt it could have been heard from here even without electronic boosting: 'The letters, of course, also mean Order of the British Empire, being that honour bestowed on individuals by our Gracious King . . . but in our case they mean no less than that. With the use of it we are acknowledging the Great Honour bestowed on us by birth, the grand and glorious Order of British Citizenship. I call on you one and all to initiate this action of ours by raising caps and voices in a cheer that will ring as far as our beleaguered Motherland . . . as, without exaggeration, I assure you it will, because I intend to make a despatch of this action, which eventually will reach the British Admiralty and Winston Churchill and His Majesty the King himself. Stand by to cheer!'

Jeremy remarked, 'He's probably after the the O.B.E. himself . . . . '

His voice was drowned by the thunder of the cheering. When the echoes had died, the sharp-eared might have heard the cockies complaining as again they shifted camp. The horses had vanished into dust and mirage. All the flies seemed to have come for refuge with those two solitaries in the Lily Lagoons stable. Shamus had to fish several drunk as Donnybrook Irishmen out of his Tullamore Dew.

Whether by accident or design, the Action was timed nicely for reception of the final regular news-bulletin of the day from the BBC, that is of yesterday in local terms, it still being Wednesday Over There. The broadcast was typical of the period, given in that 'varsity drawl which long ago had given the enemy the impression that vanquishing the English was a walkover and which still must puzzle him with reporting the life-or-death struggle as if it were a jolly old game, don't y'know – 'Score at last postin', one hundred and forty-eight for twenty-two. But as Jerry heads for home after that last nasty bit of sneak-bowling, he'll be running into bright moonlight . . . so look forward to good opening figures for tomorrow's innings. Today's bag again . . . one hundred and forty-eight . . . not runs, but Huns, which means wickets, of course . . . for twenty-two of our bowlers. Rather foul havin' to twist the jolly old rules round like this, I must say . . . but you all know what I mean, knowing the game. Jerry should have learnt the jolly old game before he took us on, what?'

Then followed the Churchillian speech that had sparked off Captain Toby's Action, its typical ponderosity so much at variance with what had gone before as surely to puzzle the enemy still more: 'Whenever the weather . . . is favourable . . . waves of German bombers . . . often three or four hundred at a time . . . surge over this Island by daylight . . . to be met by our fighters . . . and their losses average three to one in machines and six to one in men.

'This effort . . . of the Germans . . . to secure daylight mastery of the air over England . . . is the crux of the whole war. So far it has failed conspicuously. There is no doubt . . . that Herr Hitler is using up his fighter force . . . at a rate . . . that if he goes on . . . will wear down this vital part of his Air Force. That will give us great advantage.

'For him to try to invade this country . . . without having mastery of the air . . . would be a most hazardous undertaking. Nevertheless, all his preparations . . . for what he calls Operation Sea Lion . . . which means invasion . . . move steadily forward. Every Continental harbour . . . from Norway to the Bay of Biscay . . . is crammed with vessels for this purpose. No one should blind himself . . . to German thoroughness and method.

'This invasion cannot be long delayed. The weather will break at any time. Besides . . . he cannot keep these gatherings of ships and men . . . waiting indefinitely . . . expecially when we continually harass them from the air . . . and from the sea.

'Therefore we must regard . . . the next few days . . . as perhaps . . . the most important . . . in our history. They rank with the days . . . when the Spanish Armada was approaching our shores . . . and Drake was playing . . . his famous game of bowls . . . or when Chatham stood between us and the Dutch . . . in the very Thames Estuary . . . or Nelson beat off the might of Napoleon . . . at Trafalgar. But what is happening now . . . is on a far greater scale . . . and of far more consequence to the life and future . . . of the world . . . and its civilization . . . than what took place . . . in those brave old days.

'As I told you . . . after the tragic Fall of France . . . the whole fury and might of the enemy . . . will be turned upon us. Herr Hitler knows that he will have to break us . . . or lose the war. If we can stand up to him . . . the life of the world may move forward . . . into broad sunlit uplands. But if we fail . . . then the whole world as we know it . . . and care for it . . . will sink into the abyss of a new Dark Age . . . one made more sinister by the lights of perverted science.

'Therefore . . . let us brace ourselves to our duties . . . and so bear ourselves . . . that if the British Empire last for a thousand years, men will still say . . . "*This was their Finest Hour*!" '

The session ended with *God Save the King*, for which everybody leapt to their feet, except the pair lurking in the stable and a few of the more disloyal and somnolent of the dogs. When it was over, a strange silence fell on this region which had just now been so vibrant with electronic sound, so that anyone not deaf could have heard the cockies. Finnucane poured himself another whisky, gulped it, muttered, 'Their foinest hour, begob! 'Tis loike a drame.'

Jeremy said nothing, only looked at the troubled face with its ordinarily fearsome eyebrows rumpled again in misery.

Again Captain Toby spoke from the bridge, but now with what might be called a parsonical note in the megaphone, as if he were standing cap-under-arm, hymn-book-in-hand, delivering Sunday Service at Sea: 'We will all join in singing the *Doxology* . . . will you oblige at the piano Mrs Cullity?'

Finnucane uttered a whimpering sound – perhaps because involvement of his flesh and blood added to his burden, as suggested by still more miserable rumpling of those formerly fearsome brows. If so, it was his own fault, since it was on his recommendation that the piano was brought over from the pub, so as to lend some of the old-time flavour to the singing. A shrewd move, no doubt, not merely politic, but to cramp the martial style of the band. Another reason for it may have been Andy McDodds's attempt to get into the act with his bagpipes as the proper instrument to cheer a beleaguered garrison. The fact that Captain Toby showed little or no respect for McDodds's offer of service caused the old fellow to button his face up tight and retire to his store and stay there. Still, in practice it must have run deeply counter to anything Finnucane could have envisaged in his pride in his daughter's playing music of sentiment so different from what was being demanded of her now. Something similar might have been felt by Jeremy, too, when later he heard that sweet boy's soprano in which lately he had much delight, singing the airs of *There'll Always be an England*:

The Empire, too, we can depend on you.
Freedom remains, these are the chains
Nothing can break . . . .

While the crowd beefed the choruses.

As the day wore on, with glimpses in fantasy created out of electronically translated words spoken of what was happening on the dark side of the world, Prindy's singing became more and more in demand. There was not only the attraction of his voice, but of his appearance, since while he was leaving the Barbu booth to his father-in-law and wife, he was dressed as usual at this time of year as King of the World. That the demands on him were more in the nature of relief from the strain of belligerence was evident in the requests not for war-songs so much as those reminiscent of old times – *Danny Boy*, *The Road to Gundagai*, *The Wild Colonial Boy*. The yearning for what had been was expressed when during intervals newcomers asked about Prindy and in telling of his doubtful origin the old-timers conjured up the Shade of Daddy-o Cahoon in a guise so sentimental that, had the Sisters Cahoon been there and not fled the country, they could not have been but pleased. That silver soprano was sure proof, some of the old-timers said, of those claims old Dinny had often made in drink – for listen to that bull-frog croak of Martin Delacy!

Prindy was also in demand for singing duets with those famous for their singing at Race Time: Eddy McCusky and Constable Stunke and Bridie and Rifkah. He also sang trio with Rifkah and Chief Petty Officer Pickles, who had a goodly tenor, and who evidently had practised with the pair at the Mission. It was also evident that the CPO had a crush on Rifkah, the way he tried to shoulder off other men interested in her.

So the nightmarish day wore through, its distant murder and mayhem, destruction and devastation, described ball-for-ball by several seemingly *blasé* BBC types, who occasionally had to raise their voices, wearily, above a background of cannonade that beat the sound-proofing of their watch-stations: 'Well, that makes the bag for tonight forty-eight . . . Come on, you Raff cads, make it an even fifty before day breaks and brave old Frankenstein cuts and runs for home. I say . . . I wonder whether Aunty Hermann doubles his count of what gets home, so's not to start Uncle Adolf chewin' up the jolly old carpet in a fit, as they say he does when things go wrong, by telling him the truth about our baggin' 'em . . . what?'

Then the sirens came in joyfully sounding the *All Clear*.

The last news dealt with the weather, which apparently was still not the kind to encourage invasion. Day was dawning over there, while here the West was gilding. The last item of war-like information was given with a yawn: 'Usual enemy reconnaissance just shot down over Guildford. When will they ever learn that we've given up goin' to bed since they forced us to adopt the twenty-four hour time system? Well . . . I expect that wraps it up for the night. Be seeing you . . . Good luck meantime.'

Thereupon Captain Toby declared End of Watch for Day. All hands on deck tomorrow, 1000 hours – unless Red Warning sounded.

By then Finnucane was well and truly drunk, slouched in his chair, muttering to himself, 'Out'n their feet . . . poor bastards . . . dead, but won' loy down . . . hic! Foinest Hour, says he . . . t'hour o' their death, says I . . . poor bastards . . . now and at hour o' death . . . Amen . . . .' Tears were trickling down the fleshy ruddy cheeks.

When the other Lily Lagoons people came to the stable, Jeremy headed them off, telling them to go home to the camp, that he would join them later. He also headed Bridie off when she came after closing the bar. He told her that her father was in no fit state to go back to the hotel, that he would look after him.

Bridie asked, 'Why are you doing this, Jeremy? You don't like him that much.'

'He asked me . . . as his old friend's son.'

'You didn't like your father that much, either . . . nor Ireland . . . and England . . . which is what's upsetting him.'

'I assure you there's no ulterior motive, my love.'

The endearment made her blink and blush slightly. But her voice was even: 'I didn't suppose there'd be a bad one. Only, you've always been so unmovable on principles.'

'Maybe I've changed.'

'That's what everybody says. But I don't believe it. They say that it's because you were knocked about so. Did it make all that difference?'

'Only so far as teaching me more reality of things.'

'And what's that?'

'What a lot of questions?'

'Why not, when . . . when we're friends . . . even if you have been avoiding me.' When he avoided her questioning eyes, she asked, fiercely, 'Who *were* the bastards who hurt you?'

He shrugged. 'Just people with a grudge.'

'I'm sure you never gave them cause for grudge.'

'Look at all the grudges I've built up here.'

'Only by being yourself. Don't stop being yourself.'

He smiled. 'Can anybody really do that? But how's Con?'

'Latest letter from Jerusalem . . . of all places, when he thought he would be popping in on the old folks at home. Do you think our boy'll get home all right if we lose the war?'

'Who says we're going to lose it? Anyway . . . how're the kids?'

'You'd've seen for yourself if you'd come up.'

'Bring them down to the camp. I've kept away on account of all this business.'

'Thank you for seeing Da through it. It's had me worried.' With a quick movement she kissed his lips, spun about, hastened away.

Jeremy went back to look at old Shame-on-us, found him asleep, He roused him: 'Better get to bed, I think.' He got him up, grumbling, supported him to a discreet little corner where ordinarily the blackboys slept who watched the horses of nights. There were two hide-and-sapling bunks. He lowered Shamus onto one, took off his shoes. Stretching out, the old man groaned, 'How long, oh Lord, how long?'

'Won't be long now,' said Jeremy.

But Shamus was asleep again. Jeremy left him, went down to the camp.

Next morning, at piccaninny daylight, Jeremy was back in the utility, with a vacuum flask of coffee and tablets. Finnucane partook greedily, muttering his thanks. Jeremy suggested driving him over to the hotel at once to clean up, and offered another day of his company watching with what he called the Noble Order of Beatrice Earwigs. But there was no tickling the old fellow. He groaned: 'Shame on us for crackin' jokes at a toime loike this . . . wit' them poor arrogant bastards goin' jokin' to the death av 'em, and ourselves it is suffering' to see 'em humbled in the dust the way they humbled uselvin. Musha, God help us! How long 'twill it be lastin'?'

Of course it lasted for days more – long long days, which were, in the reality of this utter unreality, long long nights – out of each of which the bewildered Order of Earwigs emerged with the *All Clear* ringing in their ears, as the Sun rose on the smoking ruins of the lunatic side of earth, while setting here on what should have been sanity.

Black Friday.

Blacker Saturday.

As the sirens hooted the *All Clear* on Saturday evening, Finnucane, far gone in whiskey, howled, ' 'Tis the keenin' o' the damned in Hell!'

There was no easy bedding him down tonight. Jeremy, with Darcy's assistance, kept him in check till the crowd were gone. Then he got him into the utility and whisked him away out to Lily Lagoons.

Out there, Jeremy doped the old fellow heavily with Paraldehyde. Shamus was soon asleep, going off muttering of the shame of wishing destruction on a gallant enemy: 'Huns they moight be in their way . . . but niver Squarehead childer-murtherin' Huns loike av them others . . . on which bad cess, says I, says I . . . . '

Finnucane was well recovered in the morning. Jeremy was for leaving him behind. Finnucane roared in protest. Nevertheless, he would have no more of the O.B.E. Watch. 'I can't shtand anny more of it, Jerry,' he declared, and went back to the pub and locked himself in so that no one would bother him. Being Sunday morning, there was to be a Naval-type religious service conducted by Captain Toby at the Hall to begin with.

Finnucane wasn't the only one who'd had enough of it. A good half of those who attended the service refused to follow the Captain when he called the order for Action Stations again. They were for having Driver Porky Jones and his youthful fireman get up steam at once for heading back to Palmeston. 'We can hear what's going on there just as well as here,' they argued with the Captain.

Before marching himself and his halved band of O.B.E.'s off to the Racecourse, he roared at the faithless ones, 'I tell you it'll happen in the next twenty-four hours . . . because the weather report indicates it. You lousy lubbers . . . you won't even have the doubtful honour of deserting in the face of the enemy, but bolting like bandicoots at the very moment of victory. I give you the Sailor's Farewell . . . Goodbye and Bugger You!'

The deserters only snickered: 'The bastard s mad. It's goin' on for ever. We'll all end up with him in the Loony Bin if we stop any longer. How long before you can have steam-up, Porky?'

They were in the midst of their arrangements for departure, when their attention was caught by an odd sound coming from beyond the railway yards westward, a squealing and moaning that caused some to exclaim, 'Pigs!' All popped out – to behold what must have been one of the oddest sights ever seen in that place of oddities: McDodds, clad in kilt and sporran, but otherwise as usual in white sleeveless singlet and sandshoes, swinging down the road to the river crossing, with true Gaelic swagger, playing his bagpipes, and actually followed by a small herd of pigs that must have broken out of Finnucane's stye. What he was piping could be heard now:

Wha wouldna fight for Charlie,
Wha wouldna draw a sword,
Wha wouldna up and rally,
At our Royal Prince's word . . . .

Someone with the Scot strong in him declared, 'That'll do me!' and marched swaggering away to join the pigs. Perhaps it was the hypnotic power of Scottish lunacy, that crying the Weal and Woe so eloquently through the bagpipes, which broke the sane resolve of the rest and in the moment had them pouring through the railway yards. Only Finnucane, locked in his office with his Tullamore Dew locked out of his mind with a wave of the hand, failed to respond.

Thus Action Stations were fully manned again. In the circumstances, Captain Toby could hardly object when McDodds seized every opportunity to take the initiative whenever belligerent musical expression was called for, having the advantage over the Band in not having to wait for the conductor's beat. The anomaly of the fact that practically everything he played had its origin in defiance of much the same ruthlessness perpetrated against the Scots by the English as now was being dished out to them by their brother-Huns seemed lost on everyone.

But for all this brave showing at the start, the Action turned out to be much the same deadly monotonous thing of past three days – the sirens wailing, wailing, the bombs a'whistling and a'booming, the guns crashing, the aircraft screaming dives to death–and the casual reporting – 'Sixty-three for twenty-six. When will Jerry wake up and realize that not only can we take it, but have come to like it in a way? What're we going to do of nights when this show's over?'

When it's over?

Yet again the long night-by-day watch ended with the sirens' happy hooting and a yawn from the Boy at the BBC – 'Aheeee! Usual Jerry rekky downed . . . over Start Point this time. D'y'know, I do believe they do it deliberately, dropping in for a British breakfast of bacon and eggs. Speaking of breakfast . . . I do hope that last egg of mine survived the dirty big one that sounded awf'lly close to my digs. Don't like 'em scrambled. Score again . . . sixty-three for twenty-six. How'll you twist that round, Hermann, old boy, to preserve the carpets of Berchtesgarten? Be seeing you all at tonight's show. Cheery-ho!'

If McDodds had led the weary crowd away with *The Lament*, it would have been more appropriate than his standing, as they straggled by, glaring his contempt over blowing cheeks, while piping them defeated off the battle-field as it were with *Scotts Wha Hae*:

Noo's the dee and noo's the oor,
See the front o' battle loor,
See approoch prood Edward's poower –
Chains and slavery!
Noo's the dee and noo's the oor,
Torch the fure on Davie's Toower,
Liberty's in every bloo,
Death or Liberty!

McDodds played all off save one, and that one looking even dourer than himself: Captain Toby, who stood at the salute all through the squealin' o' it, and then, like unto Bruce, retired to brood alone in a darkening corner of the grandstand. McDodds, his defiance done, let his baggie collapse with a dreadful moan of drone-pipes, then tucking it under his arm, fairly sprinted after the mob. It wasn't that he wanted to catch them, but to pass them; for warrior though he might be, he was a canny mon and not forgetful of the considerable business to be done with the campers at this hour.

Finnucane was in the bar to receive the dispirited mob, and although looking no less low himself, ready enough to try to revive them. He asked no questions. Anyway, the answer was there without the asking in the general assertion, 'Off home straight after breakfast tomorrow . . . that's for sure.'

No one drank much. In fact by 8.30 p.m., which was how they were telling the time again, not more than a dozen were left in the bar. The grand old last-night jag of the past evidently was a thing of the past.

Despite the quite large population, at the time the place was almost dead silent, the only sound being the soft cry of Prindy's flute, as with Barbu and Savitra, he sat out on the front verandah of Barbu's shop, playing a Hindu folksong, and Savitra's little-girl singing:

Krishna-ah-ah-a you have throw too much colour water on me, on Radha,
On Radha-ah-ah-a,
That mean too much you love me,
Krishna, Krishna-ah-ah-a . . . .

Igulgul, halfway up the sky, peeping in.

That mean too much you love me?

Perhaps the populace was listening, sick of the din of war and its glorification in brass-blaring and discordant squeal.

But Prindy stopped suddenly. No doubt but that even above his own music he had heard that strange sound first of everyone. He cocked an ear – as everyone soon was doing. It was coming from across the river.

'Donkey,' said Barbu.

'No-more donkey,' said Prindy. He put down his flute and ran.

Other people were running. Those who were nearer to the sound had caught its import. They were running towards the causeway to cross the river.

Chief Petty Officer Pickles, down at the Lily Lagoons Camp, said to the company he sat amongst, 'That's the Old Man . . . talkin' through a megaphone.'

The strange braying came on a bit of breeze: 'You lubbers, it's on . . . the great battle's on . . . action stations . . . action stations . . . . '

'That'll do me!' cried Pickles, and grabbed Rifkah's hand and went racing.

McDodds was well behind the mob, having to change from pants to kilt.

Finnucane came last of all, having to put his money away. He found Jeremy with his household on the edge of the crowd packed before the grandstand, from which Captain Toby was bellowing through a horn he had torn from a loud-speaker, giving the preliminaries missed by his tardy crew:

'One Thousand Forty Hours, G.M.T., warning system showed enemy formations, ten-plus, twenty-plus, fifty-plus, up to one hundred-plus, forming up over Calais and Boulogne. It's a fine bright day, as I told you was forecast. The Hun's out for the decisive stroke. He's mustering a veritable Armada. Our boys are already up and waiting for him. Attention, all hands! Listening Watch commences.' He reached for the whispering radio, turned the volume up.

Big Ben, unperturbed as ever, rang the quarter-hour: *DING-DONG DING-DONG*. The BBC Boy was still drawling, but with an edge of excitement to it now: 'Last Sunday we thought we were for it, too, when he came over in daylight. But this time, evidently, he really means it, judging by what he's putting into the air . . . everything he's got, apparently. He must think we still sleep in of Sundays. Napoleon made the same mistake at Waterloo. Because it was a Sunday he thought the English would be caught napping . . . he, he! . . . excuse the pun. But, 's' matter of fact, friends, it was just that gave rise to our term *Go Nap*, which means to put everything you've got on one desperate throw, as poor old Boney did at Waterloo . . . and lost! Looks like Adolf's going to do the same. But how could a man named Schicklegruber have any better luck than one named Bonaparte? Of course you know that Adolf's proper name is Schicklegruber . . . or rather, I should say, that was his father's name . . . Herr Schicklegruber. I wonder what he thought when he first set eyes on Adolf – if he ever did set eyes on him?

'Anyway, here they come, according to observation reports, in one blundering mass . . . no attempt at feints, surprises, tactics. I tell you, Jerry's not right in the head. Even on the ground he's crazy, marching up and down and calling himself Superman . . . but at fifteen, twenty thousand feet up! Their bombers have got their fighters all round them. What for? It'll be too late to tackle our boys when they strike. Perhaps they're really there as a sort of gun in the back of the bombers, to see they really do the jolly old job. Adolf must have been getting suspicious of all those reports Aunty Hermann's been putting in about finishing us off every night. Let's hope Adolf's come along with 'em to see for himself . . . because I'm pretty sure an awful lot of these aren't going home again.'

'Ah . . . things are happening! Over Canterbury. I've got a beautiful view. A glorious autumn day. There's the Armada . . . like a black cloud in a golden sky. What a pity to break that nice formation up . . . but it's happening. Our naughty boys are diving on 'em from way up . . . you can see the tracers . . . you can see the Jerry's coming down . . . like red roses blossoming.'

'Here's some more of our boys . . . two . . . three squadrons . . . tearing 'em to pieces . . . our chaps breaking off to tackle groups of 'em single-handed . . . shootin' 'em out of the sky . . . . '

The voice broke off, to resume after a moment with a note of hysteria: 'Too many getting through. Where are our chaps . . . where? Ah . . . coming in from the West . . . but only a single squadron . . . and all those Huns . . . Hurricane fighters I think . . . where are the Spitfires? But . . . by God! . . . the Huns are turning from them . . . the boys are into 'em . . . the Huns are blowing up with their bombloads!'

'Parachutes now . . . white roses amongst the red . . . not paratroops . . . only homeless Huns. Lord, we'll have to feed 'em . . . and sausages are so hard to get! The others've gone . . . done a bunk . . . listen . . . the *All Clear*! How long's it been? Ah, thank you, Big Ben . . . . '

DING-DONG, DING-DONG . . . DING-DONG- DING-DONG . . . DING-DONG, DING-DONG, DING-DONG . . . DONG, DONG, DONG, DONG, DONG, DONG, DONG, DONG, DONG, DONG, DONG, DONG.

'Dear old Ben . . . he never fails us. Now let's see if there's any news. Ah, yes . . . here it is. A bomb fell in the kitchen garden at Buckingham Palace. The King and Queen are at home, of course. This sounds a bit tall . . . but it's here . . . it says that when Her Majesty saw the mess, she said, "Well, it will save shelling the peas for dinner".'

'Here's another. A whole Luftwaffe squadron landed with parachutes on the cricket green at Kennington, and surrendered to the men in the pub there. The publican was going to make it drinks all round . . . only their squadron leader was silly enough to say that the English can't make beer like the Germans. I told you they've got no brains . . . even on the ground. Yes . . . and one of our own boys, coming down by parachute, landed stern-first in a dustbin at Chelsea. They didn't take him to hospital . . . but to a plumber . . . . '

Finnucane, at Jeremy's shoulder, drew a shuddering breath, turned away. After a little while, Jeremy slipped away after him. Finnucane had brought a bottle of whisky and planted it in one of those bunks. Jeremy caught him swigging from it, but said nothing, merely looked, then went and seated himself and poured a brandy. Shamus came to join him, bringing the bottle, sat down with a gusty sigh, but not to drink then. He dropped his silver head to a hand and groaned. Neither spoke.

The BBC dismissed the war for the time, put on another announcer, who did the proper British Sunday midday thing and played light classical music, all of it German, on which occasionally he commented with deep respect for the composers, however, rather spoiling it for those Germans who might be taking comfort from it, by including a couple of Jews without bothering to differentiate. The Earwig Watchers weren't much interested. For the most part they crowded the bar and the eating booths.

Finnucane finished his whisky rather quickly, and took to Jeremy's brandy. All he had to say was an occasional, 'I wonder will there be anny more of it?' Jeremy's only answers were shakes of the head.

Then Big Ben chimed the hour again – then struck: *DONG*!

Not for old Ben to break with tradition and give the twenty-four-hour-time of Thirteen.

It was like a talisman that stroke. Out of its overtones seemed to grow the wail of the sirens again: *Oweeee, oweeee, oweeee*!

That midnight *Moomboo* howling to Igulgul beaming full magic from above.

Here the Hour of Zero, according to the new count of time. Over there the Hour of Thirteen – and the Unhappy Hun, so close to the Devil always, rising compulsively to meet his doom.

Captain Toby turned up the radio. A new commentator was speaking: 'Well, it looks like this is his last toss. He's not coming *en masse* this time. It must have been a bitter lesson that last one. Jerry learns with bitter lessons. He's in for another. He's coming in three waves from different directions . . . but, of course, our boys are up waiting for him.'

Poor blundering Hun – still not a wake-up to the obvious fact that the British must have some device by which, beyond ordinary human viewing, they watched his every movement beyond the Channel. Up and up he rose, and then came heading for the inevitable. He knew he was beaten, according to reports, which came in swiftly to tell of the jettisoning of bombs in the marshes short of the obsessive objective, London, of fighters landing to surrender on cricket pitches. Finally the fiasco of the only formation that got through to London, there to be swooped on by one lone Hurricane, from which they all turned tail. While the announcer was laughing over it the *All Clear* sounded. He said, 'Looks as if it's all over bar the shouting.'

But as there was no shouting there yet, there was none here. Captain Toby kept his crew quiet, or rather they themselves did, since most fell asleep waiting, even with Igulgul staring them in the face and the mosquitoes up from the river feasting on them. It wasn't until the river timber was standing black against the silvering eastern sky and Igulgul was winking an eye through the western tree-line and news came in of a silly little raid at 1800 G.M.T. in the vicinity of Southampton, the anti-aircraft guns of which chased the silly ones off to drop their bombs in the sea and the announcer said, 'Well, good evening to you all, and God bless,' that the Captain rose up and roared through his megaphone, 'And now those three cheers that will echo round the world . . . Hip, hip . . . . '

HOORAH!

It roused the cockies and the butcher birds five miles away.

The Captain declared that they would form up and march over to the pub, but in good order and discipline till they got there. 'Band!' he bellowed.

But McDodds was ready. Even if the Sassenach had licked his kith at Bannochburn, noo doot aboot it, there would hae been moore Scots in this English victory, as in every English victory since Scots discovered the principle of: '*If ye canna lick 'em join 'em*. He leapt to the lead, and without having to suffer the delay of tuning up, since there was not so much tune to what he played, swung away with jaunty swish of kilt, piping *Cock o' North.* Captain and Band and crowd fell in behind him.

The Lily Lagoons people came to the stable. Jeremy motioned them away to follow the pipes.

Finnucane, quite drunk again, was weeping freely. He refused to be put to bed. 'Le' me dhrink meself to death, man . . . Ould England's won for ivver, to the etarnal defeat av Ould Ireland . . . nivver, oh, no nivver, niver, will we get off av us those last chains they boind us wit' in Yeller Ulster . . . Oh, take me home wit' ye, boy . . . me own boy, Jeremy . . . me son be what ivver soide av the bed it was . . . and I'm proud av it, because always have I wanted to mix the blood of Finnucane and Delacy . . . me darlint Bridie tell me, and 'tis no sin as I see it . . . so, Jerry, me son . . . take me home wit' ye . . . and le' me drhink and drhink meself into the forgetfulness of the Beyant . . . and bury me be the soide o' me ould friend, your Da . . . and put upon me shtone what I'm croyin' in me heart loike a lorn blackfeller . . . Poor Feller My Counthry . . . my poor Ireland now for ivver in chains . . . . '

Jeremy went to the utility. Before starting it, he cocked his ear to the procession climbing the further bank. Now the crowd were singing to the piping:

Bonny Mary caught a canary
Up the leg of her drawers.
Half a croon to fetch it doon,
And mind what ye do wi' ye paws!

When he'd pulled the car in close, he called to Shamus. But the old man was asleep now. He got out and went to him. The radio was still operating, perhaps switched onto its own power by the distraught Finnucane. As he reached to switch it off, Jeremy paused, recognizing the well known voice: 'Never . . . in the long history . . . of human conflict . . . was so much . . . owed . . . by so many . . . to . . . so few.'

CHAPTER TWENTY-THREE

NO ONE would deny that the Battle of Britain decided the issue in what came to be called World War II, even if it by no means stopped the conflict at the time. The issue could be made very complex by delving in economics, history, sociology, but in fact primarily was the very simple one of whether the nation calling itself Deutschland was in reality what it had boasted so long in song of being: *Uber Alles*, or *Above All*. Now, that even the Deutschers themselves conceded the famous victory, tacitly at least, surely was made manifest by what came to be dubbed the Hess Escapade. Rudolph Hess, Deputy to Adolf Hitler, attempted privately and secretly to treat with England for peace. That his *coup d'essai* was in truth quite unofficial was quickly proved by Hitler's promptly disowning him. However, that he embarked on it as the inspired representative of most of his countrymen and that such humanness finds no favour with those given to rulership must be acceded as being borne out by history.

Hess, a strangely simple man to hold so high a place in a gang like Hitler's Nazi Party, sought to treat only with the King of England, whom he believed to be a Man of Peace and true leader of his people, refusing to have dealings with him he called the War-monger Churchill or his Ruling Clique. In disowning him, his Führer at first declared him an Idealist Suffering Illusions. Churchill's first estimate was that he was the cunning emissary of a wily enemy, whose aim was to weaken that purpose he himself had declared as England's, namely to bring Germany to her knees, by encouraging a movement for peace already extant in England. An interesting sidelight was Joseph Stalin's opinion of the Escapade, which was that it was connivance between Hitler and Churchill to stab him, Joe, in the back. Thus do the mighty reckon: who lives by the sword in the hands of others must ever be wary of its coming anywhere near him.

But what was most significant about the Escapade was the way it affected the world at large. It was top news everywhere for a fortnight, sustained by the idea that something of a miracle was taking place simply through one man's having the courage to stand up in the middle of mad mass slaughter and cry, *Enough*! Was the day of miracles really past?

Beatrice River and locality, for all its remoteness and former contribution to the belligerence, seized on the idea of imminent peace no less eagerly than most, and perhaps even more so than some. It happened that the Hess Affair took place at the height of that part of the war which claimed most of their attention, namely the Greek Campaign, in which, to judge by the little news available from our side and the lot from the enemy's, Our Boys were being badly mauled. According to Winston Churchill, Our Boys, called by him Those Gallant Australians, were Fighting a Rearguard Action of Inestimable Value as a Contribution to Ultimate Victory. It was he who had sent them into Greece, as he had sent their fathers into Turkey. The region seemed to have some special fascination for him. He even had a special name for it – *The Soft Underbelly of Europe* – on which he harped in his broadcasts to the world, as if relishing it as something to slit; as if he were, as Jeremy Delacy made bold to say, 'A Jack the Ripper.'

Jeremy, taken in like the rest, and still more because he saw the thing as token that the *genus* he belonged to was not generally utterly insane, talked out during that strange period as never in a long time. In fact, ever since the Battle of Britain, he had turned his back on what he considered the lunatic sequel, to prosecute that little war of his own, more important to Australia than any other at the moment, as he averred, against the Feral Pig.

Jeremy did some straight talking about Man's being the only *genus* in the Animal Kingdom that deliberately killed its kind. Unnatural as murder was, he said, perhaps it could be claimed as natural to a degree in Man, since undoubtedly the acme in achievement was the taking of a brother's life, and Man with his intelligence could perceive that fact. Other animals would have no such urge, since they obtained no perceptive personal satisfaction at all. The vying of the lower animals in combat is instinctive service to the *genus* or species, obedience to the natural law of Survival of the Fittest. Hence the reason animals in combat mostly stop short of the *coup de grâce*, a killing when it did occur being rather accidental. But even if Man's murdering may be considered as natural, it is no less perverse for being expression of his intelligence above his instincts, hence cannot be condoned. That there is a sense of guilt attached to it is surely shown in the general ban on killing without the faked excuse of tribal sanction, as in legal execution or war. Even then guilt is betrayed, with elaborate trials and religious ceremonial and the salutation of the fallen foe as comrade after the reek of war has blown away. The savage warrior *eats* his fallen foe to put things right with a show of ingesting his victim's valour.

Jeremy held forth like this at Finnucane's on the nights of the couple of train days that fell over the period, not going straight home as usual after the train's arrival, but hanging on and even getting a little drunk, on the strength of the expectation of the miracle. He had pretty attentive audiences, too. A couple even took notes, one of these being the new constable who was working with Stunke, who had lately been promoted to sergeant. The other, a stranger, might have been only philosophically interested. Perhaps the least attentive one, excepting the plain dim-wits, was old Shame-on-us, who formerly would have been Master of Ceremonies, even if with the aim only to silence what he might have judged dangerous talk. Poor old Shamus, after a lifetime of self-restraint with what he called The Bahttle, had scarcely been sober since the Battle of Britain. Not that he was incapable of carrying on his business. His hard drinking was done in private. In public he behaved like an automaton, simply dispensing his wares and raking in the cash and looking as if he would be only too glad when alone again – he who had acted Mine Host to perfection.

Of the Escapade, Jeremy declared: 'Many a madman has arisen to put the world right . . . but this is the first time to my knowledge that someone simple and sane has done it. Now, it only remains to be seen how many other people in Britain and Germany are sane enough to accept him. The British can do it through their Parliament. A mere vote of no confidence in Churchill to conduct their affairs sanely any longer is all that's required. Then the new Government, instead of sending over the bombers with the thousand-pound bombs and the poison gas that Churchill's been telling the world he is building up for the annihilation of the German race if they don't surrender unconditionally, ought to send over a hundred million leaflets, signed by King George and Hess, saying, "You had twelve months as Supermen. Surely that's enough. It is enough for us that we put you back in your place as ordinary human beings like ourselves. We have got rid of the man who inspired us to stand against you, before he can go mad with self-importance and drag us to the destruction that's all a megalomaniac can ultimately achieve. Now you get rid of your Messiah-turned-Mephistopheles. Then we can get together, unarmed, and talk over the grievances that started this damn thing, and maybe once and for all solve the problem of war".' He went on: 'It may be natural enough for us to get involved in mortal combat, tribe against tribe, just to break the monotony of things, as blacks do . . . or to try to overcome our doubts about ourselves as being as good as we'd like to be . . . but internecine war is an evil that there's no excuse for at all, except the negative one that we hate ourselves and want to destroy ourselves and all the things we've been at pains to make as intelligent animals. Surely we had enough of self-destruction in the Last Turn-out? You can't blame it on the homicidal maniacs who drive us to it. They are in the minority. The people of Europe have far less to fear from defying their blood-lusting masters than they have from one another doing the blood-letting at their masters' behest. As I see it, here is Man's chance in all history to face up sanely to his first problem: how to make his theoretical brotherhood work.'

But what a squib of a thing it turned out to be!

What a poor little thing is Sentiment compared with Destiny. Both Hitler and Churchill were Men of Destiny. In all modesty they had told the world so, and were mostly so accredited, although for good or ill according to viewpoint. How deal with a silly yet potentially dangerous bit of sentiment like Hess's? The well-tried method of all Grand Turks in silencing criticism that might appeal to reason is to declare the critic a madman. Perhaps its efficacy is due to the fact that only autocrats themselves are sure of their sanity. At any rate, Churchill, who had possession of Hess, put him away in a madhouse, with a kindly British injunction that he be given everything he wanted – except access to other lunatics like himself. Hitler concurred by putting away Hess's relations and friends, or rather, to use the emphemism, Putting Them Down, since the Nazi system precluded the continued existence of any kind of lunatic except such as could with unfeigned fervour scream *Zieg Heil*!

Thus was the way cleared again for the havoc so thoroughly inaugurated and so well planned for progression to the limit of human endeavour by what might be called the Best Brains of the most civilized nations of the world, meaning not merely Britain and Germany, but also the United States of America, Russia, Japan, all now spoiling to be in it to the knife. Poor Rudolph Hess! In his innocence he made matters only worse.

At Beatrice River again it became dangerous to talk of Peace. Jeremy shut up, and went back to warring with the pigs, but gave himself to the latter with no such purpose as formerly. As he said to the one safe confidante he had left outside his simple household, Fergus Ferris: 'By tradition the genus *Sus scrofa* is the greediest, dirtiest, most destructive creature on the earth. I'm coming to doubt if it's any worse than *Homo sapiens* in these respects . . . and to concede that it's better in one . . . it isn't *self-destructive*. Maybe I'm wasting my bacteriological efforts on pigs, and would be doing a more useful job finding a less painful and more dignified way of wiping out our own race, than the accepted one, which amounts to the sort of suicide practised by some poor old disappointed prospector, who lets off the last of his stock of gelignite with a three-inch fuse.'

Perhaps Fergus could be called one of the household now, since he spent most of his time at Lily Lagoons. It wasn't only that it was a more convenient base for his shrunken aviation business, but a refuge from the ever-increasing pressure people were putting on him to get into the war. He told Jeremy: 'If only the bastards'd charge me with cold feet, it'd be easier. I could tell 'em to go to hell. But the attitude is that a pilot with my experience could turn the bloody scales. They're fascinated by aerial warfare now . . . Churchill-inspired, of course. The Battle of Britain was won by The Few. A Few More, and we'll win the bloody war. One of our pilots is worth ten of the Luftwaffe. Tom Toohey more or less blames the Greek debacle onto me . . . "If only Our Boys'd had air-cover by a few flyin' men like you, it'd never 'a' 'appened." Bitter like. No good telling him Churchill ought've thought of the air-cover . . . because he knows all about it . . . how the RAF there had to be in half a dozen places at once . . . and after all, it was a job for our own Air Force to look after our own Army. No good telling him our Air Force doesn't have the kites. "What about your own?" he says. "In the Last Turn-out a lot of the Light-horsemen took their own horses with 'em . . . Jerry's brother Jack, for one." Is that right?'

'Yes,' said Jeremy. 'All the smart squatter-boys did that. Jack took a couple of good horses . . . one, King Cole, was as fine a beast as I ever saw, and out of a brumby mob. Matter of fact, he was grandsire to old Elektron. I've often wondered what happened to him after they dismounted Jack's troop . . . probably finished up carrying some brass hat who couldn't ride a donkey . . . and then got shot like the rest. We lost a lot of good horses in that Turn-out, too.' He sighed: 'Old Tom to become a Sooler, eh! Who'd've dreamt it? It's on account of Brumby, of course. Poor old Tom's hoped he'd come back covered in glory, join the RSL, and be accepted as a worthy citizen, instead of hounded as the mongrel outlaw, as he's always been. He had a crack at me, too, over Clancy. He asked me if I'd heard from him. I said, "Why should I?" He called me an unnatural father, especially when I would know what my son was going through. As a matter of fact I had a letter from Clancy, and suspected that Tom knew and might even have a hint of what was in it. That new Station Master is a worse sticky-beak even than Col Collings. Clancy wrote to me just before going to Greece . . . poor kid . . . bragging about his soldiering . . . one old soldier to another, sort of thing. He happened to mention that Brumby Toohey was in trouble with the Brass and he'd been trying to put in a word for him. I felt that Tom was fishing. I couldn't very well answer him straight, in case he pressed me. I just walked off. He's gone crazy like the rest of 'em . . . with mixed grief and pride and doubt. He's probably heard that rumour you picked up from the Air Force about the sell-out in Greece.'

Fergus had heard at Air Force Base in Palmeston that the Command had virtually bolted from the Greek Debacle, leaving Our Boys to the mercy of the enemy. The source could be judged reliable. Evidently the flying man's contempt for the foot-slogger lent savour to spreading the unsavoury tale. It had become widely known and a source of some bitter argument. The RSL in Palmeston had gone to the length of advocating jail for anyone overhead repeating it. No Australian officer would do such a thing, the League declared, let alone the AIF's beloved General Tubs. Still, it was a disturbing fact that Tubby was still being reported as alive and kicking, mostly in news from luxurious Cairo, while most of Our Boys who had fought the Greek Campaign remained listed as Missing. The General wasn't kicking about the monstrous failure of the AIF in Greece. He was concentrated now on Churchill's latest game with the Knife, and was greatly angered by what he called the Callous Indifference of the Majority of the Australian People. He wanted more men – more and more men. Jack the Ripper now saw Italy as the softest part of the Underbelly. The trouble was that to get at it when about a million Italians and Germans under heavy arms in North Africa, had first to be brought to their knees. He particularly wanted the Gallant Awstralians in it. You could always count on them. As a nation of gamblers they never counted risks or costs. Not that General Tubs was classed like this, to judge by news of strife he was having with British High Command. Evidently by them he was considered more the Bookmaker. A more apt designation would be Ringkeeper in the Two-up Game, only the British would not understand the low-class colonial jargon. The Ringkeeper is always the first away when things go wrong.

Such was the defeat of our soldiery in Greece that nothing exact was known about the fate of most of the men for a very long while. This was not to be blamed entirely on the utter breakdown of command and general ineptitude of Australian official administration, but to a degree on Australian character. Many of Our Boys, with the tradition of bush-ranging behind them and that individualism and resourcefulness therefrom (which is perhaps the only Australian characteristic Worth a Dump) instead of surrendering to the Hun, joined up with bands of brigands and the like or took refuge with Greek peasantry. Astonishing that an Aussie could come to rub shoulders so intimately with the alien he probably most despised, his utter contempt expressed in the appellative *Ox*! Imagine one of Our Boys, when the Huns were hunting for them, hiding beneath a frousy bed in which a Greek had slept with his garlic and salami sausage, nose all but in the Greek's piss-pot! Yet all but beyond credence though it was, rumours of this sort of thing sustained a lot of fearful hearts at home, even for years. No such luck, however, for those waiting back at Beatrice. Within a few months they had the grim facts concerning their heroes from the sole survivor of them, Pat Hannaford, back home with one arm, one leg, one eye, and as he put it himself, One Arse'ole. As people said, with bitterness or pride, according to how they were disposed to him, it just had to be Hannaford of all the others who would get out of it.

Later there were people bitter enough to say that it was a pity Pat hadn't lost his tongue as well, when he began to wag it to the detriment of their pet illusions. Apart from reporting how some of the heroes died in circumstances hardly heroic, he claimed to have seen General Tubs go off in the seaplane with his officer son and his pet poodle, while the Aegean waters were staining with the blood of his dying men. Fortunately for his own prospects, he hadn't begun to talk out like that from the beginning. He came home as a hero, and acted it, and was taken to the community's bosom. They even all but gave him his old job back. He was now unfit for engine-driving officially. However, so that he might still have authority to ride the foot-plate, as soon as he was discharged from the Army, they appointed him an Engine Inspector. This even gave him the right to run the length of the road, because the stationary engines used for pumping came under his inspection. Curiously enough he owed this chiefly to his old enemy, Col Collings, now Acting Railways Superintendent, in the absence of Superintendent Broadbeam, now a Colonel of HAD handling the maintenance of war-tanks in North Africa. It was a time of advancement for everyone smart enough to take advantage of it.

People said it was nice of Col to do what he had for Pat. However, when Pat came to speaking out, he suggested that it was less out of regard for himself as for the fact that the political climate lately had changed drastically. The Prime Minister, he of the Silver Tongue (who so rashly had committed Our Boys to a war in fighting which they were likely to fall, as their fathers had, into the doubtful hands of Old Jack the Ripper, had outlawed the Communist Party without thought that the notorious fortunes of war might land us with Russia as Our Gallant Ally, in fact had been so unheeding of reality in a working-class country as to declare all things working-class subversive except sheer unprotesting hard work) was tottering out of office, to give way to the Labor Party, which was pledged to reinstate their comrades of the Class Struggle. It was utterly silly of Silver Tongue to have maintained the ban on the Commos, when since Russia switched from the other side to ours, they had become the greatest Soolers in the land. Pat who had gone away all but spat on by his former Comrades for a Capitalists' Stooge, returned a Hero of Democracy.

Pat returned home in August, just before Silver Tongue was brought down. A lot had happened since May and the Hess Escapade. Eastern Europe was ablaze with the Russian War, North Africa with Churchill's latest game of tin soldiers. The Japanese had seized Indo-China from the Hun-humbled French.

Anybody could have had French Indo-China. Anybody was entitled to it, seeing that the rightful owners had long ago surrendered to imperial mastery. Yet the British, Americans, and Dutch, who had their own imperial possessions round about, told the Japanese to get out at once, at the same time imposing economic sanctions with which they must comply to survive even at home – or go to war. More than that, the Americans, who were supposed to be keeping the peace by supplying everybody with the means to make war, told the Japs to get out of China – pronto! The Japs had been in China since 1933. Upstarts! The Yanks had been in there since the Boxer Rebellion, which they put down, in 1900. The Japanese made no move to do what their betters told them. As

Jeremy said when he met Pat and talked over the war with him: 'We'll be at war with the Japs before the bloody year's out.'

Pat reappeared at the Beatrice in the old style, leaning grinning out of the cab of the engine of the mail-train, winking a glass eye, waving an artificial arm, but with his good hand on the brake. At his shoulder was the official driver, Porky Jones. He was given a hero's welcome. All took his hand – from the lowest, who also stroked his good arm shyly, proudly calling him *Rotten Sodjer*, to the aristocrats of the Big House, who had him over to tea. It wasn't all that pleasant for him, just the same. He had those unpleasant reports to make to bereaved relatives. Of the three mothers he had to tell the sad news to, only one had not made it hard for him. He had gone also to Tooheys for tea. Possum had suddenly smashed a cup and cut her head and howled like a lubra. Unfortunately, he had told Tom the truth about Brumby's death, believing that it would anger rather than grieve him and likewise his missus when told. He had seen Brumby die in AG Hospital, Jerusalem, as a result of having been beaten up by a particularly vicious type of AIF military police, unofficially known as Jerusalem Screws. Mrs Knowles, stopping at the pub, at first was only stunned by what he told her of Knobby's end on a beach in Crete. Then apparently she got on the bottle, and came at him in the bar, screaming about the like of him, a Mongrel Commo, getting away, while a decent law-abiding clean-living boy like hers must die. Of the third he said, 'You know I don't go for them Squatters, male or female . . . but old Rhoda certainly took it like a real lady. She made me give her more details than I cared to. Poor old Clancy was shot to bits by a low-flying Jerry while climbing into a fishing boat he'd swum out to. She only went white and bit her lip, and muttered, "It's what we had to expect, of course." Then, bugger me, as I'm leaving, she takes me in her arms and kisses me, thanks me for my kindness, and gives me a silk scarf she made herself for Clancy.' Pat had to bite his own lip relating that.

Pat was proud enough of himself as a *Rotten Sodjer*, and ever ready to talk of his campaigning, even though frank in his contempt of what he had fought for. However, he would not comply with what was demanded of him to win that greatest of Australian martial honours, and in fact the only indigenous one, since the others are Imperial, namely, membership of the RSL. The local branch of the League was always presided over by the Administrator, always a man with a military background, officer caste, of course. The present Administrator was but newly appointed, but an old acquaintance. He was Major Bullco, formerly Superintendent of Police. As stated: everybody was getting ahead these days. Major Bullco had served in the Last Turn-out as a Military Policeman. He was no less incensed than other members of the Branch by what he heard of Pat's damning contribution to that slander against the Command, but more so against Pat personally for what he was saying about Brumby Toohey's fate at the hands of the Jerusalem Screws. When Pat applied for membership there was a special conference. Then he was hailed before the Committee and requested to recant. According to Pat, he replied simply by making an indecent gesture and walking out. That there was truth in it was surely borne out by the fact that that old iron-war-horse, Jack Tinball, subsequently refused to have him on his engine. Of course, Pat and old Jack had never been friends. Still, there had been that moment of comradeship between them, when Jack had given Pat, as a soldier, the pride of bringing the Race Train into Beatrice in 1939 – what turned out to be the last of those famous trains.

A special train came down in this year '41 about the time the Races normally would have been held. However, this one ran for a very different purpose. It came bringing people to the Memorial Service for Our Boys who would not be coming home, or as the RSL, which organized it, described it, For Our Glorious Dead.

Because Jack Tinball, wearing his medals, was driving, Pat Hannaford had to ride with the common herd. As medals for general service in this Turn-out had not yet been struck and Pat was not entitled to the *For King & Country* badge of the RSL or even to ride in the coach reserved for old soldiers, he had only the glass eye and aluminium arm and leg to show for his warring. Nevertheless, his tales of it were so much more interesting than the mouldy ones being told in the veteran's coach, that even some of those worthies sneaked along to listen: 'Them bloody Hun paratroopers . . . suddenly-like the sky . . . and they got clear sky in them parts like here . . . was filled with clouds . . . bringin' everything with 'em . . . guns, light tanks . . . yes, and be jees, even the bloody kitchen stoves! They reckon they was drugged . . . our MO's . . . but 'ow they found out I don't know . . . them bloody Chocko Commandos were well in the lead in the evacuation . . . that's why so many poor bastards died.' He had a wondrous tale to tell about how, loaded with Sulphanilamide and entirely treated by himself, he had made his way to the coast of Asia Minor aboard Greek fishing boats, sometimes hidden under fish when German patrols assailed them. 'Don't let me hear anyone runnin' down the Oxes again,' he declared. 'They're filthy bastards . . . they're only half civilized . . . but, be jees, they got guts, and fought bloody Jerry like none of us did.' When someone reminded him that the Greeks had been fighting on their own soil, he said, 'Yeah . . . but if we can put up half as good a show if ever we're invaded, I'll join the friggin' RSL.'

The Memorial Service was held on what would have been Cup Day. Despite the precedent set last year in the Battle of Britain Watch and the fact that the Races were mentioned in the Panegyric as an Imperishable Bond between this community and its dead heroes, it was not held on the Racecourse. There was some talk of it in view of the Bond and last year's immortal gathering there. However, the chosen venue was the Anzac Memorial in the Cemetery. Some said that to have held it elsewhere would be a slight to the memory of the heroes already honoured there. Nevertheless, it was whispered that the choice was really made because the officiating clergyman objected to breaking a lifetime's vow that he would never set foot on a racecourse. The cleric was another old acquaintance in a new guise, Captain-Chaplain Tasker.

It was a properly solemn affair. Naturally, considering the place, there were small hitches that might have made it ludicrous elsewhere. Here they went properly unnoticed.

There was no band, because the Palmeston Garrison was on stand-to again because of something Admiral Tojo had said about Japan's being strangled by the Oil Embargo. But there was always Andy McDodds, quite famous now for his pibroch renderings. So that he might perform to best effect, a complete Scotty's outfit was brought down for him. Unfortunately, his bunions could not take the fancy brogues, so that he had to wear his usual sandshoes. Still, having the show to himself, except for Jack Tinball's bit of bugling, he excelled himself with his piping:

But aye the tear comes in me ee,
Tae think on him tha's far awee . . . .

The procession formed up at the Hall, according to rank. The McDodds had the lead, of course. Behind him came His Honour the Administrator. Then Lady Rhoda, in white Red Cross uniform with official black arm-band, leaning on the arm of her surviving son, Martin. As Rhoda stepped up to take her place, passing close to the Lily Lagoons people, she happened to meet Jeremy's eye. As it was her ancient habit *not* to see him if they happened to be thrown into proximity, it might have been that her glance had been caught unwittingly by the sudden gleam of Rifkah's hair as she came out into the sun. Rifkah was there with Prindy, brought over from the Mission by Fergus, as was now customary at this time of year. Holding her eyes, Jeremy removed his wide-awake and bowed. She replied stiffly, turned away, went on.

Next in line was Mrs Knowles, in black splashed with purple, as had been the fashion in hero-mourning in the Last Turn-out, leaning heavily on the arm of her frail old man. Then came Nugget Knowles and his bride, who was pregnant, but looked no less the squatter's lady. The veterans followed, the leader carrying a Union Jack, behind him Jack Tinball with tasselled corded bugle slung over his shoulder, his mass of medals swinging to his proud stride. Old Jack had more medals than anyone else. As everybody knew, one time he had driven Field Marshals Haig and Foch on special tours of the rear lines of the Western Front, and let both of them drive the engine. Pat Hannaford was not with the veterans. It wasn't that they weren't prepared to forego principles in concession to the solemn moment. They asked him to join them nicely enough. He replied as he had at that committee meeting, and marched with the people of Lily Lagoons, near the tail. The actual tail was the goats.

The ceremony followed almost exactly the time-honoured pattern of Anzac Day. Indeed the only difference was the placing of a temporary list of the names of the newly fallen, printed on white asbestos sheeting trimmed with artificial poppy leaves, alongside the marble plaque to which eventually they would be added. The usual poppy wreaths were laid upon the plinth. Originally the poppy was the symbol of the warrior dead left behind to fertilize the Fields of Flanders where the flower grew naturally. It was said to have fairly blazed with the flowers in the first Spring following the Last Turn-out, come as it were to symbolize bloodshed anywhere in the Glorious Cause of War.

They shall grow not old, as we that are left grow old:
Age shall not weary them, nor the years condemn.
At the going down of the sun, and in the morning,
We will remember them.

Last Post rang out, the last sad notes to be taken up in mournful chorus by the dogs.

It was over. Adjourn to the pub.

Now, according to Anzac Day tradition, with the matter of the Glorious Dead settled, those who'd had the misfortune to grow old, should have been fighting their battles over as they boozed. However, it was not so on this occasion, and not because it was not really Anzac Day. The fact was that the very Tradition of Anzac appeared to be in jeopardy. The old soldiers were saying that this might even be the last time they would be able to foregather, at least lawfully, in the happy comradeship of the RSL. The reason for this was that Prime Minister Silver Tongue at last had been ousted, had been replaced by the Leader of the Labor Party, who was not only frankly Anti-Imperialist, but during the Last Turn-out had been jailed for so being by that darling of the AIF (they'd even given him their wondrous hat to wear) the Rt Hon. Taffy the Cockney-Welshman. The new man at once had restored legality to the Communist Party. Was it not reasonable to suppose that he would transfer the ban to the Commos' opposite number, the RSL, especially when he was at loggerheads with its top men over his demanding recall of the Second AIF from abroad and the presence of General Tubs to see to the defence of Australia? Thank God he had that grand old friend of the Digger, Winny, to deal with. Churchill was saying flatly, No. Likewise was good old Tubby digging in his toes in Sister Street. As Jack Tinball roared, 'Dishloyal bashtard! Anyone'd think the British was our enemies and not out kith'n'kin. The bastard's a Bolshevik . . . a Rev'lutionary. You only got 'o lisen way he blows his bags . . . ev'thing he says' like *Storm the barricades, Comrades*! Be a rev'lution all right, he tries bannin' us an' bringin' home Our Boys jus'n ol' Winny needs 'em . . . eh, Diggers, eh, me ol' sodjers?'

'My bloody oath!'

It was a fact that the new Prime Minister's every utterance (and he made a lot these days, new as he was to having control of the National Broadcasting System) did sound rather like Storm the Barricades! But it could have been due less to intensity of feeling than to training in some Labor Debating School that still clung to the traditions of William Morris and the Tolpuddle Martyrs of the 19th Century. In fact, a prominent British Minister and outspoken critic of the man in his demand for the return of Australian troops, had said that Australian Labor Politics were a century behind the times, and also that the new Leader had the Mind of a Schoolboy. This was brought up in the angry discussion in Finnucane's pub. It was countered by Pat Hannaford, who quoted another noted Englishman as having said that the Prime Minister just ousted had the outlook of a Seventeenth Century English Tory. He also dragged up the ever delicate matter of Silver Tongue's having squibbed the Last Turn-out, for all his imperialistic sooling.

Pat couldn't be kept out of it, since the place was a public house. Naturally he supported Storm-the-barricades. On one point he needled them mercilessly was the fact that while a fundamental part of RSL policy was what they called Upholding the Constitution, here they were slandering and threatening the very constitutional head of the Nation. At last he went too far, countering their endless eulogy of Jack the Ripper by bringing up the old furphey of his being suspected of having connived, as First Lord of the Admiralty, in the sinking of the liner *Lusitania*, in order to get America into the Last Turn-out. That was too much for Jack Tinball. Declaring that he didn't care whether Pat had only one arm, one leg, one eye, and one arse'ole or not, he was not going to stand for that kind of desecration, and would have lain hands on Pat if not restrained. Actually it was Finnucane put an end to it, coming out of his lethargy to roar, 'I won't be havin' the arguin' of religion in my house . . . out t' big mout' Protestant lot o' ye!'

So much for the Beatrice River Memorial Service held in lieu of the Races of 1941 – a fitting end, perhaps, to what might be called the Ancient History of the settlement, since such drastic changes were wrought upon it so soon afterward. As well the Service was held then and not after the incident that caused the change, since from it Pat Hannaford had a fresh furphey to cause the name of Jack the Ripper to stink to very Heaven, and for a certainty would not have been able to get away with voicing it as lightly as he had in the case of the sinking of the *Lusitania*. The incident was, of course, that one which, to date, ranks as the most devastatingly treacherous in history, and has come to be known simply as *Pearl Harbour*.

Pat got into a lot of trouble with his furphey here, and but for his status as a War-hero of a class ranking only second to that of the Glorious Dead, would certainly have copped it a lot worse. As it was, he was soon compelled to be careful in choosing those he would enlighten. Amongst these was Jeremy Delacy, who was even more careful in listening than Pat in telling.

Where Pat got his astonishing story was anybody's guess. He talked as if it were on the best authority, but could give no more that sounded authentic than that the Russians claimed they had picked up and decoded a message from Admiral Tojo to Adolf Hitler giving a hint of the Pearl Harbour atrocity several days before it took place and had passed it on to their new Comrades, the British. Something like that could have come to him from the Communists, who were still fawning on him as a Hero of the People, despite his continued contempt for them in their new role of Soolers. Nevertheless, it would not have been confided to him by the Commos with anything like the suggestion of the evil he put into it: for just then, with their Glorious Red Army in headlong retreat, they were yelling as hard for a Second Front as their master, Joe Stalin, himself, and wouldn't have cared any more than he how and where it came from, since *The End Justifies the Means* is a basic Communist concept.

What he said was that Pearl Harbour was another piece of Churchillian connivance and for the same purpose as that other, but this time carried out in conspiracy with President Roosevelt, who everybody knew was just bellyaching to get into the war with his old pal Winny. To those who argued or wanted proof, he would say: 'Now, for godsake, how's that great Jap fleet going to sail halfway across the Pacific, through some of the busiest shippin' lanes in the world, with the Asiatic fleets of the British, the Yanks, and the Dutch keepin' watch as they must be at such a time . . . and not a bastard's a wake-up till the Japs're droppin' their bombs on Honolulu Sunday mornin'? What'd bring the Yanks in quicker? Even if they did'n wan' 'o come in . . . they'd bloody 'ave to.'

Jeremy also had opinions he had to be careful of voicing, even to Pat. Fergus was his only confidante. The fact that Storm-the barricades had fairly screamed for help from America within hours of the outbreak of the Pacific War made Jeremy fairly groan: 'God help us! That stupid bastard gets us free of British Imperialism, only to hand us over to the Yank, the most ruthless stand-over merchant in the world. He's offered Australia as the base for the Pacific War. That means it'll become in perpetuity an American colony, like every other place they ever went into with their dollars to spend and their rapacious capacity to get 'em back fifty-fold. I had a lingering hope that what looked like his Australianism would have brought us at last to stand on our own feet. Maybe the old leg-irons hang too heavily on us for us ever to be able to stand alone.'

Jeremy had to tell his household that he feared the traditional Blackfellows' Christmas at Beatrice would not be held this year. The reason was that the locality was in turmoil over the arrival in Port Palmeston of the first of the Americans – as refugees from the Philippines. That brought the land into the zone of war. Already people were packing up and heading for the comparative safety of the South. There was talk of official evacuation, of putting all civilians and civil industry behind a barrier that was to be called the Brisbane Line. A new command had been formed, with Australian authority seemingly having small say in it. The title of the command was ABDA, in accordance with modern military style. It was abbreviation for American, British, Dutch, Australian, in that order. Jeremy remarked: 'It's a wonder they bothered to include us at all . . . and I don't suppose inclusion's worth tuppence, anyway, seeing that in fishing round for a C-in-C for it they haven't made mention of a man of ours.'

II

Eventually the C-in-C, ABDA was named. He was Field Marshal Lord Wavell, a man of considerable titular aristocracy and hence military honours, formerly C-in-C Middle East.

Jeremy and Fergus heard the announcement while listening to the midday news in the lounge at Lily Lagoons. Jeremy was struck with the inappropriateness of the appointment, not as it affected Australia, which actually delighted in crawling to such people, but America, which after all had bagged first place in the junta. He said, 'The Yanks have always been distrustful of the English . . . they understand the kid-glove arrogance better than we do . . . yet here they are submitting their men to the very worst type of British Brass Hat. It must be Churchill . . . half a Yank himself . . . and having that strange fascinating influence he evidently has on the crippled would-be benign ruler of the world, Roosevelt. What are Wavell's attributes for the job, anyway? He chased a mob of half-hearted Dagoes out of Ethiopia and Somaliland and the Western Desert of Egypt . . . then ran into the Hun and went back to Cairo. Now he's to conduct a jungle war against an enemy that has the only army in the world trained for such warfare. How right was poor old Whiskers!'

Jeremy had scarcely spoken, when the Watchers of the Keep shrilled their warning of Intrusion. Nanago came bursting from the kitchen. Jeremy and Fergus rose to look through the windows towards the gate and the road beyond.

A distant cloud of yellow dust. Soon a flash of glass in sunlight. Then a car appeared, a military vehicle, as easy to see by the camouflage painting effected these days. When it halted at the gate, a soldier leapt out to open up. It came on in. The same man leapt out again to open a rear door. A round ruddy face under an officer's cap appeared. Fergus gasped, 'For cryin' out loud!'

The officer was Fabian Cootes. He was in tropical kit, which is to say, cotton khaki shirt and shorts and so-called top-socks, the last particularly striking, since bright yellow, as also were his suede boots, a new military type effected by officers, called Desert Boots. He was accoutred for action, with officer's webbing and a pistol at his hip. Out after him came another officer, no less tubby and ruddy but of bigger size. Again Fergus exclaimed. The second was known here as Sigs Sarge Sims, but now wearing the insignia of a Lieutenant. The Coot was a Lieutenant-Colonel, no less. There was still another to appear, out by the other rear door and unaided – another old acquaintance, Eddy McCusky.

Jeremy went slowly out to meet them. The Coot greeted him heartily, thrusting out his pudgy little hand. 'Good to see you again, Jeremy. Long time no see . . . eheeee!' Cootes waved to his companions, that is those out of the back seat, saying, 'You know these chaps, I think.' Both shook Jeremy's hand, babbling pleasantries.

Jeremy asked, 'To what do I owe this unexpected honour?'

Cootsey made a moue with his little Napoleonic mouth and shrugged, as Bonaparte might have done, even answering in the language, *'C'est la guerre.'*

A moment of hesitation. Then Jeremy said, 'Well, you'd better come in.'

Nanago had vanished. Fergus was standing in the middle of the lounge with arms folded. His eyes flitted over the trio, coming to rest on Cootes, to whom he gave his split grin, saying, 'Well, you made it, eh, Cootsey . . . congratulations!' He didn't unfold his arms.

Cootes, eyeing him warily, nodded shortly. 'Thanks.'

Fergus added, 'You certainly knew which way that cat was going to jump.'

There was a military snap in Colonel Cootes's voice: 'What cat?'

'Political pussy.'

Cootes frowned in the Napoleonic way. 'I presume you're being your usual facetious self?'

'Not at all, mate. How many people were as astute as you in predicting a swing to Labor in the midst of a state of war?'

'I've always been a keen student of politics . . . and of military science. You know that.'

'I know you're a smart boy, Cootsey . . . hence the congratulations.'

Cootes turned from him. Jeremy said, 'Well, I suppose you could do a drink.'

Cootes smirked. 'The famous Lily Lagoons brew, eh . . . my word!'

Jeremy seated the visitors. Fergus still stood. When Jeremy had served them, he raised his glass. 'Well . . . *L'chaim*!

Cootes stood for a moment puzzled, then smiled his chubby smile. 'Oh, yes . . . *To Life* . . . old Whisker's toast. After sipping, he added: 'Poor old Whiskers . . . I suppose you know he's dead?'

Jeremy nodded, sighed: 'Just as well, poor fellow, I suppose. It'd've killed him to see everything he predicted happening, and not be able to do anything about it.'

With evident surprise Cootes remarked, 'I didn't know you were so well disposed to him.'

'On the contrary . . . I had a deep regard for him . . . as a man . . . and maybe as a soldier. too, because I don't think he was the destroying type.'

'Then why did you let him down?'

The grey eyes snapped. Reddened slightly and stiff of tone, Jeremy asked, 'What's this about letting him down?'

Cootes read the signals, shrugged, murmured, 'Only quoting the Brass.' He drank off his beer.

There was an awkward little silence while Jeremy replenished the glasses. Cootes broke it with a nervous giggle, saying, 'Well, what about a toast to victory?'

In the same tone Jeremy replied, 'Yes . . . we're not getting so much of it, are we.'

Cootes became his military self again, putting on the Napoleonic frown, and the voice as he raised his glass: '*La victoire!*' At the same time he raised his left hand with first two fingers spread to make the V sign popularized by Churchill.

Fergus chuckled, and when Cootes shot him a suspicious glance, said with that grin of his, 'You know what that sign used to mean, don't you?'

Obviously Cootes didn't. Fergus went on: 'Of course you know that the Thumbs-up sign originally meant *Up Your Bum, Bertie*?' Cootes frowned. Fergus chuckled again: 'Well, the two fingers were for the girls . . . *Up Your Snatch, Susie*! . . . yaheeeah . . . . Funny how everything's got mixed up lately, ain't it!'

Cootes flushed, swung away swiftly to glare at Sims, who'd guffawed. Then to his glass he remarked, 'Still the same puerile-minded Bunny, eh?'

Fergus, always sensitive to that nickname, flushed now, and flung back, 'Still the same prurient squirt, Cootsey.' Then he added: 'You wearing those boots and socks for camouflage, eh?'

Cootes looked at him sharply, questioningly, but was too wary to ask. Fergus let him have the answer with the grin: 'In case you shit yourself in face of the enemy . . . they won't notice it . . . aheeeeeah!' He swung away laughing towards the dining-room.

Cootes stared after him, face aflame. But as Fergus reached the curtain the scowling warrior had asserted himself. He barked, 'A minute, Ferris!' He strode after him with little fat man's dignity, broad beam asway.

Jeremy intervened sharply: 'Gentlemen!'

Without looking at him, Cootes answered shortly, 'This's official.'

Fergus had turned to lounge insolently. Cootes halted out of reach of him, snapped, 'Are you aware that this area's been declared a Combat Zone?'

Fergus dropped smirking eyes to the yellow socks. 'Hence the camouflage!'

Cootes drew a deep breath to control himself. Evidently he had become used only to respect. He said heavily, 'I'd advise you not to take liberties with me, Ferris.'

Fergus grinned at him widely. 'Now, you know I'm not a boy like that, Cootsey.'

Cootes swallowed hard on it, then shot out a demanding hand, saying with difficulty, 'Where's your permit . . . to . . . operate in this zone?'

Fergus regarded him for a moment, then asked, 'What's that got to do with you?'

'Everything. I happen to be MI One in this area.'

Fergus snickered: 'What's that mean? If you told me you were calling yourself IM one, that would be easy . . . . '

'It means I'm chief of Military Intelligence here.'

'Well, we all know what military intelligence is . . . . '

'Your permit, please . . . otherwise I'll have to deal with you drastically. The country's in a state of war.'

The grin vanished. The greenish eyes snapped with anger. But evidently Fergus saw what he was up against. He only growled, 'I've authority to operate, granted by the Director of Military Intelligence, GHQ.'

'You *did* have such an authority.'

'I've still got it. It's in my nav-bag on my kite.'

'It's become null and void since the area's been declared a Combat Zone.'

Fergus snapped, 'With the DMI's signature on it, it'll do me.'

'But it won't do me. I'm the DMI's deputy here . . . and what I say is what he wants done. Only service aircraft can operate in this area from now on.'

Fergus swallowed it, then snapped, 'Put it in writing!' With that he swung into the dining-room.

For a moment the Coot stood, then turned back to the others. He said, 'Smart alec!' As he came up to them, he said to Jeremy, 'You know, he's an awful bloody fool. As an airman he could've had really high rank in the RAAF now, if he'd only played his cards right. The Raff tell me they'd even have bought his plane at a high price . . . . and he probably got it for nothing.'

Jeremy answered dryly, 'Fergus isn't a gambling man . . . and he doesn't like war. But what's this about a Combat Zone?'

'It's been declared so by ABDA. That's what I've come to see you about, actually.' Cootes turned to Sims, addressing him with superior's shortness: 'My map-case.'

'Yessir.' Sims snatched up the khaki-bound satchel, opened it on the low table.

Cootes pointed to the map revealed, a small-scale one of the northern half of the Australian Continent, a goodly section of which was stamped in purple in several places COMBAT ZONE. The zone extended almost from coast to coast, its southern boundary at this longitude a line that cut the Telegraph Line somewhere about the Prospectors' Arms Hotel. He ran a chubby finger along the line, saying, 'Southern perimeter. All persons, stock, plant, et cetera, not deemed essential to military ops in the area must be moved out as soon as possible . . . . '

Jeremy cut in: 'But isn't this the Brisbane Line Strategy . . . condemned by the new Government?'

'Not exactly. See, practically the entire eastern sector's excluded.'

'That'd be the very region where evacuation and scorched-earth tactics would be of value in case of invasion. The geography of this country would be its first defence.'

'Geography doesn't count in modern war.'

'Then why bother to evacuate any place?'

The Colonel shrugged, as an expert might dealing with an ignoramus.

Jeremy pressed: 'Are you expecting a *blitzkrieg*?'

'We have to expect anything. We're up against a tricky and ruthless enemy.'

Jeremy drew a deep breath, asked, 'Well, what is it you want of me?'

Cootes said it quite blandly, 'Oh . . . just to get out with the rest.'

Jeremy gaped. Cootes avoided the intense grey eyes, addressing himself to the map-case as he closed it: 'Everybody else is going who's got nothing to contribute . . . all women and children, of course . . . but also people like Finnucane, McDodds, Barbu . . . and Billy Brew. You can't have pubs and stores and donkey teams in the midst of military operations . . . . '

Jeremy's face had darkened, his husky voice become a rasp: 'But, dammit . . . I'm not keeping a pub or a store. I can contribute militarily.'

Handing the case to his Lieutenant, Cootes said dryly, 'You haven't tried very hard to do that so far.'

The rasp deepened: 'What do you mean by that?'

The Coot met the eyes boldly now. 'Well . . . you had rank, and an important appointment . . . even if it was rather snide . . . . '

The grey eyes blazed. The voice rose to a hoarse roar: 'How dare you talk to me of snide rank, you . . . you up jumped political opportunist!'

A quiver of scare in the chubby face. A blink or two. Then Lieutenant-Colonel Cootes remembered who and what he was, put on the Napoleo-Churchillian scowl, and while yet avoiding holding the angry eyes too long, said with dignity, 'Mr Delacy . . . you are required to leave the Combat Zone with as little delay as possible. I'll give you ample time . . . say till the middle of January.'

Jeremy had control of his utterance, but was breathing hard. He asked, 'What of my household? It's mostly comprised of Aborigines.'

'That depends on Eddy, here.' Cootes half-turned to McCusky.

Eddy thrust his jaw out importantly. 'I'm mustering the entire Aboriginal population, Jeremy.'

Jeremy swallowed that, asked again with difficulty, 'What for?'

'Get 'em out of the firing-line, of course.'

'What firing-line?'

Eddy avoided the eyes, to look out through the side windows towards the Aboriginal quarters, peering somewhat, as if to show how much what was there was his lawful business. 'You never know. But the first thing is, you can't have blacks wandering up and down a country occupied by troops . . . . '

Jeremy almost croaked it: 'So you're going to overland 'em with the stock?'

Eddy shot him a hurt glance, then grabbed his jaw as if to support the official set of it. 'You know I wouldn't do a thing like that. They'll be kept in settlements as close to their country as possible. The males'll be given lucrative work . . . like road-making, timber-cutting . . . . '

'You're going to herd all these people together, with their tribal differences?'

'We want to get rid of tribal differences . . tribalism . . . . '

'And create Bloody Nothings like ourselves!'

Eddy became annoyed. 'For christ sake . . . you've got to have some system of confining 'em, controlling their movements! D'you want me to leave the women at the mercy of the thousands of troops that'll be crowding in here soon?'

'Mercy? Is that what you think of your countrymen as soldiers . . . rapists?'

'They'll be men away from home for a long while . . . and, besides, there'll be others . . . thousands of Yanks of all breeds . . . Negroes.' Then suddenly Eddy looked desperate, spoke appealingly: 'There's a bloody great war on, Jerry . . . the war we've always feared. Everything's changed. Look . . . I've had to break up my home, send my wife and kids away. It breaks my heart to have to break up the tribes, too. But it's the bloody war, man!'

A moment of silence. Then Jeremy, calm now, said, 'If you're making settlements, what's wrong with making one here . . . and letting me stay on to help run it.' Eddy blinked. Jeremy went on: 'There's a nucleus of my own people. I'm known to blacks for a hundred miles around. You'll have to have people with experience of blacks to run your concen-er-settlements.'

Eddy swung on him. 'He isn't with us any more. He's gone back to New trouble with your reputation with those on top.'

'What for?'

'Well . . . causing disaffection amongst the natives . . . .'

Jeremy exploded. 'Oh, balls! I'm going to put it to Professor St Clair.'

Eddy swung on him. 'He isn't with us any more. He's gone back to New Guinea . . . Army appointment. I'm Acting Director.'

Jeremy exhaled heavily: 'Jesus!'

Out of the silence that followed, Colonel Cootes came in with the military tone: 'Army wouldn't approve of your being here, anyway. Rear HQ will be established on the Beatrice.' When Jeremy looked at him, he added quickly: 'You're not considered a good security risk, you know . . . . '

Jeremy exploded again. 'You bastards . . . get out of my house . . . before I throw you out!'

All stared at him. Though evidently but half the man he had been, he looked as if quite capable of doing just what he said. A moment. Then Colonel Cootes swung away, snatched up his cap, jammed it on his head, while pressing the boyish curls back with a hand, went marching to the door. The others more or less slunk after him.

In the doorway Cootes halted and turned back. The scowl was in place again, and the voice coldly Churchillian: 'I'll give you now till the First of January. After that I'll be wanting this place for my own HQ. If you're not out on that date, I'll have you removed by military police.' He marched off, with the others at his heels.

Jeremy stood where he was, getting only a glimpse of them through the creepers of the porch as they climbed back into the car. He was fighting for breath. As the car started up, he felt a touch, looked round, to find Nanago at his shoulder. He put an arm about her, drew her to him, stroked her dark head as she wept softly on his breast.

After a minute or so, Jeremy said easily, 'Well, let's have a brandy, eh?' Fergus came to join them, saying he'd heard it all. Jeremy said, 'I don't think anything would've been gained by truckling to them. I guessed they'd come to throw their weight about in their new importance and would have something to embarrass me with. Neither ever liked me.'

Fergus asked, 'Who would the bastards ever like . . . except 'emselves?'

Sipping his brandy, Jeremy mused, 'I wonder why it is . . . that most people will hate you simply for not accepting them at their own valuation?'

'Obvious . . . jealousy of the little for the big.'

'I don't see it like that. Both of these two positively revere ruthless masters. Look how McCusky grovelled to Cobbity, who was just an arrogant bureaucrat, while more or less despising St Clair, who's really a nice intelligent chap. And I guess the Coot must have fawned on the HQ Brass, as he calls them, to get where he has. I've heard him speak well of Hitler and Mussolini . . . . '

'Birds of a feather.'

'It still doesn't make sense to me. In nature you find fawning and domination . . . and jealousy, too. But only those creatures of proven superiority show jealousy . . . of their rights, not of individuals. Inferiors can presume on a superior's rights . . . but always back down when challenged. There's no evidence of resentment, vindictiveness, as in humans. There two men are in position of considerable power now. I felt no resentment . . . although I was suspicious. I couldn't congratulate them because of the obviousness of it all. Maybe I should have . . . I mean out of kindness to fools.'

Fergus said, 'I'm afraid I didn't help much with the famous wit.'

'If Cootes had any intelligence he would have expected it from you. But at the same time he *is* intelligent. That's what beats me. He was looking for an excuse to throw his weight about, to *prove* to us that he really is a big man . . . and he seized it. He has to call me a bad security risk because I declined rank he's chiselled for . . . and McCusky to say I can't be trusted with Aborigines, when he knows quite well they'd do what I told them while they'd run from him. But why? That's what I'm trying to get at. It seems to be the fault in human nature. For my part, if I'm wrong on some point, I'm grateful for being put right . . . . '

'You're a perfectionist, Jeremy . . . in an imperfect world.'

'I won't have it that our lovely world's imperfect . . . or that our wonderful genus isn't capable of overcoming its meanness.'

'What . . . in the face of this?' demanded Fergus. 'These bastards are turning you out of house and home.'

Jeremy breathed, 'Yes!' and swigged his brandy.

After a little silence, Fergus asked, 'What happens now?'

Jeremy answered promptly, 'For my part, I'm staying put.' When the others stared at him, he added: 'I don't mean here. That's impossible. But I can't let them hunt me out of my country . . . and at such a time. That would be cowardice. If it's invaded, I want to meet the enemy. I'll fight my own war, if necessary.'

Fergus asked, 'You mean you'll go bush?'

Jeremy jerked his lips towards the Plateau. 'There're countless hide-outs over that way. There'll be no police, no trackers, no bushmen . . . only fool soldiery like Cootes . . . . '

'Can I go with you?' Fergus asked quickly. 'I could plant my kite in that possie we chose. I'll have to, anyway. I couldn't make a living flying down South these days. The Raff want the kite. They'll take it off me. I'd rather prang it than let them have it to destroy.'

'I'm afraid it'd rather complicate things . . . two's a crowd when it comes to taking to the bush. But chiefly there's the fact of our circumstances. This isn't just a temporary thing. The old order passeth . . . and we old ones pass with it. My act of defiance is largely one of despair. What can I expect, except to die the way I want to . . . either defending what's really indefensible in the long run, or hiding from the ruin of what I've loved, which is sure to come . . . because, even if we're not invaded by the Japs, we will be by all the others . . . and every invasion of this country, from the first convict settlement, the various mining rushes, the railway, Vaiseys, the road, has scarred it beyond remedy . . . so what is there left for me, but to become truly one with what's left? Your defiance must be positive. There's no point in your living like a hunted blackfellow . . . and dying like one. Plant your aeroplane, by all means. You might have use for it . . . and at least will have the satisfaction in not giving it up . . . then get South . . . or anywhere you can make your protest have some value.'

Fergus bit his lip, said with difficulty, 'I don't like parting like this. We've got pretty close lately. If I'd had a father like you . . . '

'You'd probably have turned out like one of my sons. Let's be realistic about things. You've got a life to lead . . . I only a life to end. I'd like to go out thinking that you're doing something to make our countrymen love the place instead of hating it, to want to make it a place of beauty in the world instead of destroying it pandering to humanity's greed. You can give me a lot of help organizing things right now. There's Nan here and the others to be got away and set up in comfort . . . .'

Nanago shrilled: 'No-more . . . I stay wit' you!'

He raised a finger. 'You can't, dear. You've promised to let me die on my own . . . . '

'What for you want to die now . . . when you not sick and only war . . . .'

'Shush, now. It would spoil everything . . . I having to look after you, you having to look after me. Besides, you've got the mob to look after. What's going to happen to everybody without someone to watch over them?'

'I can't go away from my country!'

'You certainly can't go into one of McCusky's concentration camps. That'd suit him down to the ground. I'll fix it with Bridie Cullity for you to set up camp near her. I'll arrange with the bank for finances. I'll see if I can get Rifkah to go with you. I might be able to get messages to you . . . and if all goes well, you can come back. That all right?'

She nodded, blinking back the tears.

Jeremy said to Fergus, 'They're sure to be clearing the Missions out. They can't leave 'em in the Front Line. We'll just have to get hold of Rifkah. We don't want her becoming a refugee a second time. There's young Prindy, too. Either the Catholic Church gets him . . . or McCusky . . . unless we get in first. I'd like to fly over to Leopold and have a talk with Glascock . . . and bring 'em back and send 'em down with you and Nan in the motor vehicles. Let's start nutting things out. There's a hell of a lot to do. Must get all the rations out of here. There's the horses . . . .'

'What'll you do with 'em?' asked Fergus.

'I'm certainly not going to leave 'em here to be hack-ridden by soldiery. Run 'em over to the coast country through Catfish Gorge. At least they'll put good blood back into the brumbies there. Now, first the matter of going to the Mission. Will you take me tomorrow? Let's get a load of canned stuff to give them for Christmas . . . . '

It was next morning, Friday, soon after breakfast, while the truck was at the rear of the Big House, being loaded with the stuff for flying over to Leopold, when again the warning, *Intruders*, was sounded. But now there was no sound of an approaching engine, and the approach so slow that scouts had to go take a peep. These latter returned with the news that the vehicle was Barbu's van, the intruders old Ali and Billy Brew. Jeremy groaned: 'Complications! Poor old buggers probably want me to take 'em in.'

Although the situation was actually much worse than that, it proved less of a complication to his plans than Jeremy supposed. Billy Brew had been badly injured in what amounted to a freak accident, and had got Barbu to bring him to Lily Lagoons less for treatment to continue living than for succour in dying. 'I'm goin' 'o die, Jerry,' was Billy's greeting as Jeremy helped him from the van. He couldn't walk. They had to carry him to the little hospital on a stretcher.

Barbu was only concerned about his family. He'd come to try to get Jeremy to get in contact with the Mission by radio. Evidently he'd tried it at Beatrice and refused to believe that by war-time regulations ordinary use of radio was prohibited, or that his wife and daughters would not be left to the mercy of the Japanese, who he supposed were practically upon us. When he heard that the Junkers was about to fly to the Mission and would take a message for him and bring one back, he had to be restrained forcibly from getting into it. Fergus would have taken him. However, Jeremy thought it unwise. 'They don't like him there. He could easily mess up everything, running round hysterically. As it is, Glascock might take some talking into it. Look, I won't go with you. I'll write a note to Glascock, and to Rifkah . . . and leave the rest to you. It might even look better that way . . . just as if we've got it all arranged with McCusky and Cootes. You might even get the Barbus. They'll be better off with the Indians down the Centre the old fellow wants to take them to, than in camps. Glascock'll see that. Leave it to you, son. If you can't work it, come back and get me and I'll see what I can do. Meantime, I'll have to look after poor old Billy. He won't last more than a few hours . . . ruptured liver, by the look of it . . . and he wants me to see him out.'

Fergus went.

There was no treating old Billy, except by giving him sips of rum, which Jeremy said would only make him worse. Jeremy wanted to give him opium for the great pain he was suffering. Billy gasped, 'Too weak's I am, Jerry. Want all me strength . . . tell you 'bout it. Rum, Jeremy, ol' friend . . . the ol' familiar . . . juice.'

Jeremy gave it to him in sips, while, lying waxed almost to the hue of death, he whose face and bald head had always flamed like the rising desert Sun, told the strangest of all the tales told of his freakish adventures in defiance to bosses, bombasts and bullies. In between administering the one acceptable specific, Jeremy mopped the sweat of death oozing from the domed brow, trickling down through the ragged white beard.

Billy said that even before he'd been told he had to leave the zone he'd had trouble with troops now stationed at Caroline Springs: 'They got ammunition dumps there now . . . guarded be the . . . the lowest class o' Southern mongrel. They'd been interferin' with me donks from . . . the start . . . copper give's 'em open . . . slather. Ridin' 'em, knockin' 'em . . . about. When I get marchin' orders from that . . . that Coot . . . I'm told I can't take me team. So's really open slather now. Them mongrel military bastards . . . they start target practising on the donks. That ain't enough, neither . . . hand-grenades . . . Jesus!'

Often Billy's voice faded away to a whisper. Then it was he wanted the rum. He struggled on, most of the time clinging clammily to Jeremy's free hand: 'Some me donks come 'ome to the plant . . . cryin' to me to 'elp 'em . . . trailin' their guts . . . oh, ah!' The tears streamed from the dimmed old eyes. ' 'Ad to shoot 'em meself . . . me own . . . oh, Jerry!'

'Take it easy, Billy.'

'I'd no 'tention goin' away . . . I reckoned on beatin' crost country . . . jes with the donks . . . to the Alice Sandstone. I get what's left the team on the move. But you know me . . . al'ys got o' get square. I goes back on one the donks . . . makes up a bomb with gelignite I left at the plant. There's a guard-room at the biggest o' the dumps . . . bastards guardin' it al'ys boozin' or playin' cards or sleepin' . . . never seen one with a book. Night-time, I comes up on far side the dump. Inside 'igh barbwire fence . . . ammunition packed around with sandbags. I got a long enough fuse . . . long's me arm. But you can't trust old fuse. Maybe it landed so's the fuse hit the detonator and percussed it. I don' know. I don' know much 'bout what 'appen' after I chucked it. I just 'ear them bastards laughin' round the front. I lights the fuse, chucks, was swinging away on the donk . . . Christ . . . fire and bloody brimstone . . . all I remember's the donk's boltin' through burnin' bush . . . and must 'a' fetched up 'gin a tree . . . oh . . . oh!'

'Easy, Billy.'

'I come to . . . find the bush smoulderin' round me . . . men yellin' somewheres . . . me donk dead. Next I'm back at me plant, drinkin' water. Next I'm under a tree in the bush . . . and someone callin' . . . "*Billy, Billy Brew*". I wake up and look, and there standin' off a bit's that old *Lamala* o' mine . . . jes like before . . . big blackman . . . but it's daylight now. He says, "*You come, Billy.*" I get up. He's gone then. I don't see him no more . . . but I know he's leadin' me . . . cos I hear him callin' . . . "*Billy, you come!*" Then I'm on the railway track. I'm headin' North, I know . . . cos there's me shadow West o' me. Then there's the train. I didn't 'ear it. I'm perishin'o' thirst. Porky Jones and his fireman's helpin' me onto the injin . . . goin' up to Town . . . givin' me water. I can't talk to 'em. Only I 'ear 'em talkin' about explosion. Men killed. I ain't never before killed a man, Jerry. I been dreamin' 'bout that. But I ain't sorry . . . like them mongrels was Huns or Japs. You reckon that's bad?'

'It was your war, Billy.'

'Yeah . . . tell 'em that yarn for me, Jerry . . . Billy Brew's War.'

The whisper was getting fainter: 'They wan' 'o take me . . . get doctor. I 'ear meself talkin' 'nother voice . . . like that *Lamala* talkin' . . . "*Put him off Tom Toohey's.*" They do that. But I don't see Tom. *Lamala* call me crost to Barbu's . . . sayin', "*Take him out to Jerry . . . Jerry find him good place for leave him bone.*" You goin' 'o do that, eh, Jerry . . . find place for my bone? There Old Man now . . . *Lamala* . . . I come, Old Man . . . I come . . . I come . . .' The whisper faded away while still the lips moved slightly.

Then the lips were still. Jeremy felt the pulse, rose quietly, went out. He called Darcy, 'Get the ute out . . . put in some tools. Old man close-up finish. We'll take him up to the foot of the Plateau and bury him.'

He went back, sat again, wiping away the sweat, occasionally taking the pulse. In about an hour the eyes opened slightly, the mouth, too, as if about to speak. But both eyes and mouth stayed like that. Jeremy felt the pulse. He placed the limp hand beside the once-plump body that in its tattered and charred khaki bushman's outfit had suddenly sagged. He reached and so placed the other. Then he rose, looked down at the set dead face. He breathed, 'Poor old Billy . . . the first casualty . . . on our side.' After a moment of staring, he bent to the head, whispered into the waxen ear, 'Go after your *Lamala*, Billy. I'll see to your bones.' In rising he brushed the pale dome with a kiss. He then busied himself with strapping the corpse to the stretcher. This done, he went out and called Darcy.

They started for the Plateau immediately, just the two of them, the living, in the front, Billy Brew under canvas at the back. It looked as if they might run into rain. The sky above the Plateau was filled with a squall-line that looked like breakers of an inky sea, the thunder of which could be heard in a continuous menacing roll.

They made haste to beat the rain, since a burial in a tropical downpour can be more like a drowning, even in good sandy sloping burial ground like that at the foot of the escarpment. They reached the chosen spot still dry and with time to spare for digging, judging by the set of the wind, even though the red wall was quivering to the rioting of the Old One up beyond. However, as they were about to begin the job, Jeremy said, scratching behind his ear, 'I don't know . . . might-be that old *Yalmaru's* telling me something . . . but I feel we ought to plant him more in blackfellow fashion.' He looked around, musing, 'Can't do it in a tree, just two of us. How about a cave? That's what he'd've crept into himself to die. Yes . . . let's find a overhang for him. His last words were, "*Find a place for my bone.*" Come on. We don't need any tools.'

It might well have been a sprite that led them to the spot, such a dance was it. The rain caught them before they found it, drove them to shelter, while it poured outside like a cataract. It wasn't lack of good niches for burial that put them to the trouble, but finding one to meet the special circumstances. As Jeremy said, 'We got to make dead certain of beating the dingoes. Old Dead Feller had a feud with 'em for years . . . account of his foals. They're sure to sniff him out and know who he is. Wanjin's got as good a memory as he has a nose. I reckon they'd've got him before he got here, only for his *Yalmaru*, or *Lamala*, as he called it in his lingo.'

Perhaps first noting his uncle's careful avoidance of the dead man's name, a matter of extreme importance even to Aboriginal people of quite limited respect for the old beliefs, and one rarely conceded to by even the best disposed of the *kuttabah,* Darcy giggled nervously, 'All the time more like blackfeller you get, Mullaka.'

'What's wrong with that, son? A blackfellow's religion's just as good as a whitefellow's . . . and maybe better. Look at the whiteman's world today. Hang on to what you can of the old ways, son . . . and watch the kids . . . don't let 'em become Bloody Nutchings.'

'I watch all the time, Mullaka. That my new job, I know.'

It was tough going, with Jeremy having to stop so often to get his breath and to ease the strain of his weak arm. The Dead Feller was no light weight, and the terrain the worst possible for such a procession. At last they found the perfect place, in an overhang. They could reach the crypt by both standing on a narrow ledge in the face of the painted wall of rock. Not even the original Old Wanjin himself would be clever enough to get up there. Jeremy was a bit troubled about the fact that the place was painted, but rationalised it, saying, 'If the old Shades object, I guess his *Yalmaru*'ll be able to square things with 'em.'

From the ledge they were able to push the stretcher a little into the crypt, then slide old Billy off it, in out of sight. They dropped down. Looking up, Jeremy said, '*Mummuk*, Dead Feller. You lie quiet, now. We never forget you. *Mummuk . . . yawarra*.'

Darcy echoed him. It was the ancient ceremonial. Just one more bit, which Jeremy forgot, but not Darcy. That was the erasing of their tracks in the dry sand, so that the Shade could not follow them.

It was now close to sundown. The Sun went down in a clear sky just as they reached the utility. It was tough going home, too. The road was so slippery they had to fit skid-chains. It was dark when they came up to the homestead, gleaming through the garden and the mangoes. Jeremy got out at the last gate, leaving Darcy to run on and put the car away, finishing on foot, as if wanting to capture for ever sight of the place as the haven he had kept it so long, and the sound of its heartbeat – *Home, a-home, a-home*!

III

At Leopold Mission, already they knew of the order for general evacuation, and were preparing for it, at expense of the usual preparations for Christmas. They were still in radio contact, their set being classed as a Service Unit, and its operator, Father Glascock, as a Coast Watcher.

Father Glascock explained things to Fergus. He said he had been informed that the patrol-boat, H.M.A.S. *Melville*, skippered by Warrant-Officer Pickles, would be calling to pick up the evacuees a few days after Christmas. All, except full-blood blacks of the locality and himself, would be going. Although at first the priest demurred at the propriety of handing over some of his charges to Fergus without official sanction, when he heard about the high-handedness of McCusky and Cootes and had partaken of some of the grog Jeremy had sent over, he agreed to what was requested, even to the inclusion of the Barbus. Referring to those who would be coming in the patrol-boat, he said, 'They'll probably be glad to be saved some passengers, anyway. They'll be packed tight as it is . . . and the weather looks like breaking any time.'

Fergus, while waiting for his passengers to pack, saw to it that his stock of fuel kept on the air-field was buried in the scrub. He said to Brother David, 'No bugger's getting that . . . so-called friend or foe.'

Rifkah, saying her farewells, was embraced and wept over by those who loved her, and coolly dismissed by the few who didn't. Mother Mathias gave her a Rosary: 'Not to intrude on your own Faith, m'dear . . . but just so's Our Lady'll come tó your help if you're in throuble. Ahll ye've got to do is say a few *Hail Marys*. God bless ye and kape ye and bring ye back into me ould arms again someday after.'

Sister Dymphna wished her a Happy Christmas.

Rifkah left the priest to last. He came to greet her as she stepped on to his verandah, extending his hand well before they met, as if in haste to be rid of her, grinning at her, saying, 'Well, this is it, eh . . . after all your efforts. Hardly say Man Proposes and God Disposes . . . rather the Devil in this case . . . Tojo, eh?'

She smiled that smile, making him go red from it. 'Might be Mister McCusky.' She took his hand.

Giving a man-to-man shake, he said, 'Well, I only hope you'll be back to finish the good work you've started.'

Keeping his hand, holding his blue eyes, she said, 'Ze vork vill not stop . . . because I do not go.'

He gaped. 'Eh?'

'I am leaving only to go to Lily Lagoons to see Jeremy. I vill come back overland.'

For a moment his face blazed with obvious excitement. Then he frowned. 'What's this nonsense?' He withdrew his hand roughly.

'Jeremy is not going avay. He vill go bush. Also, Prindy . . . . '

'But this is madness, girl. The country's under martial law. Don't you understand what that means?'

'No . . . also I do not care. All law is cruel . . . not human. I vill not leave my poor people for soldier and McCusky.'

He groaned, running a hand through his curly mop of hair. Then he said, 'Jeremy didn't say anything in his letter about staying . . . or about your staying. He says he wants you and Prindy to go with his people.'

'He vill not send us avay. He know zis is my country now . . . zis is my life. I vill come back.' When he groaned again, she reached for his hand, clasped it in both of hers, fixing him with those jewels of eyes. 'Pliss . . . Stephen!' He blinked as if struck. No doubt it was the first time she had called him by his first name. She went on: 'I haf before been driven from my home . . . from my loved vuns. Not again. I vill fight to stay . . . and die if zey try to tek me. But only you vill know I am here. Pliss . . . you vill let me come back to you . . . my loved vun?'

He was flaming, sweating, breathing hard. For a moment they stood staring into each other's eyes. Then suddenly she smiled, pulled his hand up to her lips, kissed it. He gasped. She released his hand, gave a little laugh at his gaping, said merrily, '*Mummuk* . . . *yawarra*.' wheeled about, went running away, to the truck awaiting her outside the convent.

She looked back out of the truck to see him standing watching from the verandah, gave a last wave. Then in a little storm of farewelling and wailing, she and the others set out for the airfield.

Fergus had Rifkah up front with him. Prindy sat back with his Indian relations, his little bride beside him. Savitra alone of the Barbu's was happy about the flight. Eager as they were to leave the Mission, they had to be shoved into the aircraft, and then cringed and whimpered during take-off, and fairly howled their heads off during the farewell beat-up, while the two experienced ones squealed with laughter.

A last whirling glimpse of white-washed roofs and dark upturned faces, then away across the waters of multi-coloured jade, heading for the blue line of the Plateau. Fergus remarked to Rifkah, 'I wonder when we'll be seeing that again.' Then he gaped as she leant to him and told him that she would be coming right back.

Fergus was quite deeply concerned about Rifkah's intention to defy the evacuation order. While he didn't say so directly, it was evident from his preliminary outburst against it that he'd been cherishing the hope of taking her away with him. When it became plain that nothing would discourage her, he tried persuading her to let him stay along with her. He argued: 'You don't know what you're letting yourself in for. You see these people . . . *your* people, as you quite erroneously call them, because they're *nobody's* people . . . you see them as simple Arcadians . . . and their Arcady as some lovely thing to be preserved as an example to the brutal world. The fact is they're no more Arcadian than Nazis, and no saner in their beliefs. Listen . . . I'm an Anthropologist, trained. I don't go round claiming to know these people like the others. I *don't* know them . . . even though I've been round amongst them for the last couple of years, and pretty close to all kinds of 'em. But I know savages from intense reading about them. You yourself know from bitter experience how even civilized people can act in the most barbarous way when chanted to about Tradition . . . "*The Jews killed Christ*" . . . . "*The Jews are poisoning our sacred blood, tainting our holy culture*!" Then what can you expect from people who live entirely by the dictates of Tradition . . . who can find virtue even in eating their own dead? It's one thing to study them to try to make sense out of the rest of human lunacy . . . and to protect them from halfwits like McCusky in normal times when someone might be interested in their wretched condition and make it easier . . . But it's a very different business for a girl, whose only equipment is thwarted motherhood or love or something, to go and live with them in their primitive condition, hunted like they'll be, if McCusky gets after them, or the Japs, if they come. No . . . it's unthinkable. Jeremy won't stand for it. You can bet on that. Come with me . . . and I'll see you're brought back when there's a chance . . . or if you won't listen to sense, for Christ's sake . . . or Moses's . . . let me stay and look after you!'

An example in miniature of the complexity of savage culture and the brutality that could go with it, was forthcoming even as Fergus gave up the argument as they neared their destination and gave himself to preparing for the landing. They were still over the Plateau, now descending from the fair height at which they had been flying to avoid the turbulence caused by the heat from the vast rock mass, when Fergus, with the thoughtlessness of the *kuttabah*, decided to show Rifkah the hide-out he planned for his aircraft, and made a circuit of it. Prindy grasped the significance of the situation at once, yelled to his fellow passengers, '*Kumali*!' and as they all covered faces with hands, himself bent down so as not to see the forbidden. Thus he caught Savitra taking a peep. He lashed out, striking her face aside. Even though she yelled to beat the engines, the others didn't uncover till he called, '*Kala*!' Then they only stared at her streaming tears and bloodied nose. Nor did she do more than whimper after that first yell. When they were down and Rifkah came aft and pounced on the child and, cleaning her up with a handkerchief, asked what had happened, no one volunteered an explanation. In fact it was Fergus, in his knowledge, who gave it, as he opened the door to let them out: 'Copped a bump, eh, kiddo? Sorry.'

The incident was forgotten in the excitement of the reunions. The whole household was there, and the horses. Barbu was hopping about like a *Iwuyuk* laughing and weeping. His large females appeared to treat him like such a little animal. Rifkah wept on the breasts of Jeremy and Nan, and gave herself for stroking and nuzzling by everyone. She insisted that they all have a picnic lunch under the mangoes, with the last of the fruit made into a huge fruit salad with the first of the granadilloes.

Fergus was wrong in predicting that Jeremy would not countenance Rifkah's remaining. In fact, Jeremy appeared to have been prepared for it. All he did was to shake his head and say it added complications to his own plans, which he would not let her intrude on, and that he would have liked her to go to be a help to Nan. He said with a sigh, 'Our cause is lost, of course. Our Arcady is soon to be raided by a rout of bully-boys. Our Arcadians will be scattered.'

She flung back, 'Vot is zis Arcady? Zis is your beautiful country . . . zat your loff for made my country too. Zese pipple are human beings hanging onto zere own country. Many are sick pipple. Many are hungry pipple. Zey vill more hungry and sick get, vot effer soldier come . . . Japanee or Australian. Ze same after soldier go.'

Then she told him she had a present for him, something she had made. She would not show it till she had explained: 'It is like ze *Jeripunga* . . . Jeremy's *Jeripunga* . . . ze symbol of his Dreaming.' She went on: 'At ze Mission zey all sewing mad for long while . . . meking clothes. After it is say moost ve evacuate, ze sewing is all zing for soldier. Sister Dymphna haf brother and two cousin soldier. Zey only half see vot I am sewing . . . and zink I am ver' patriotic!' She giggled.

She showed it to him in his den, tossing it up to hang from the half-closed door. It was a full-sized flag – would have been the Australian Flag, but for the fact that John Bull's Waistcoat was missing, its place in the top corner taken by a big star, replica of that beneath, thus giving the smaller stars of the Southern Cross the two Pointers belonging to them in the heavens but denied them on earth – by what? The blame could not be laid entirely on John Bull.

She stared at him staring. When he looked at her, she came to him, saying, 'I see I haf done ze trick. It is vot long ago you tell me is your dream of flag of your True Commonvealth . . . the Star of Hope at ze top, to balance ze Star of Commonvealth, of bruzzerhood, at ze bottom . . . and ze Cross, complete, as emblem of *Terra Australis*.' He reached for her, drew her to him, kissed her shining hair. She added: 'Ven ze Jap Var start, I am vondering how you are feeling . . . and zink . . . Now moost Jeremy haf his Dreaming as nefer before.'

He squeezed her, saying huskily, 'Bless you!' She kissed him on the lips.

That night the flag hung in the dining-room during dinner. It was a cheerful meal, despite the fact that enough had already been said of their plans to declare it tacitly their last dinner here together. As usual, Rifkah and Prindy had a stock of droll tales to tell about the Mission. As usual Nanago appeared to enjoy the stories most – but surely with a betraying shrillness to her mirth. Another betrayal of general unspoken sadness perhaps was the reluctance shown by the company to leave the table. So long did they sit, that Nan told the black maids to go home and leave the last of the washing up. Go home? Tomorrow was Christmas Eve, and before the day was out, every member of the household, except Jeremy and Fergus, would be gone, most likely for ever.

There followed another long sitting in the lounge. Primarily it was concerned with the complication of Jeremy's plan to outwit the authorities now that Rifkah and Prindy had become involved. However, secondarily it became evident that the prolongation again was due to reluctance to face the reality of dispossession, mostly on the part of Nanago, who kept going over points of the plan obviously settled, herself showing no sign of weariness, even when the others were blinking sleepily and stifling yawns. These others were Jeremy, Rifkah, Fergus. Prindy and the Barbus hadn't been included in the elaboration of the plans. The Barbus, wearied by the excitement of reunion and lured by what to all except Savitra was the wonder of being bedded down like squattocracy, retired early.

The reason for the rushing in to Beatrice tomorrow was that Jeremy had assumed patronage of the Blackfellows' Christmas, which otherwise definitely would have been off. The traditional patrons were, of course, the people of Beatrice Station. The ladies of that household already had evacuated themselves. The gentlemen were preoccupied with the decreed reallocation of stock before the Wet set in. Jeremy had sent word of his intention to Sergeant Stunke, saying that he wished both to settle his blacks down while they awaited McCusky's arrangements and to dispose of surplus stores. Stunke had replied that he Very Much Appreciated the Gesture, adding that all the blacks of the district needed settling down, bewildered as they were by the New Order.

Jeremy's gesture was genuine as he had described it to Stunke. However, his deep purpose was to divert suspicion from his non-compliance, and attention, too. They would set up camp on the river as at Race Time. Then after the Christmas shivoo, but while the excitement was still high, those who were going on down to the Centre would pack up again. They would be travelling in the big truck. It would be given out that he himself and some others would be following in the utility, after he had formalized the commandeering of Lily Lagoons. He would harp on this formalization to Stunke during the Christmas festivities, although, in fact, as he told the others, the Army could do just what they liked, apparently. No one would know exactly who had gone South, except themselves. Actually it would be only Fergus who went in the utility.

and it could be suggested that he and those supposedly going with him might turn East from the Telegraph Line instead of going right down to the Centre to leave the Combat Zone.

Jeremy's original intention had been to make a show of final departure from Beatrice a day or two after New Year, only to have Fergus drop him off just outside the township. He would then make his way across country to the billabongs, pick up the horses, and head for Catfish Gorge. Now that there were Rifkah and Prindy to sneak away, too, they must elaborate. He suggested that, during Christmas, Prindy work some of the horses always to be found about the Racecourse, down-river to the old Russian Settlement. Then, after the departure of the others, the pair could make their way down there unobtrusively and await his coming, and they would make the trip to the billabongs on horseback. Given her way, Rifkah would have avoided going in to Beatrice. However, Jeremy insisted that she go and help Nan out as hostess, and to attract attention, make even a show of it. He said, 'If this is to be the last of squattocractic *noblesse oblige* in these parts, I want Nan to have the honour of it. Her Ladyship is sure to hear and be sour about it.'

The sitting ended with Rifkah's nodding off to sleep. Nan took her up to bed. Fergus took himself off. Jeremy yawned deeply, but sat waiting for Nanago, who had not said Goodnight. Soon she was back, to seat herself on the arm of his chair. Pouring her a little brandy, he said, 'You should get a bit of sleep. It's going to be a bit strenuous during the next few days and nights. Like me to give you something?'

She nodded as she took the glass, slipping her free hand round the back of his neck, to smooth his grey hair. After sipping, she said, 'I can sleep only wit' you.'

'What's that mean . . . you want me to sleep with you?'

'No-more . . . only if you close-up. Tek me to annexe?'

'Don't you want to sleep the last night in your own house?'

She shook her head. 'I have no own house.'

He took the hand from his hair, pulled to round his neck, fondled it. 'This house is yours as long as it stands. They can commandeer it, order you out, while this business is on . . . but they can't deny your ownership or compensation for damage. Keep that in mind always. Unless the Japs take the country, which I very much doubt, whatever might happen in the meantime, it's yours to come back to as mistress.'

She sipped. 'I am not mistress . . . I am servant.'

He looked at her shocked. 'Eh . . . what's this?'

She removed her hand, to resume stroking his hair, looking at him with the great calm of broad, sweet, dark countenance that was usual when she spoke seriously. 'Always you have been my master . . . I your servant.' The patois was dropped.

He burst out: 'But this silly! I made you my wife. You have been full mistress here ever since I brought you to the place.'

'For all other people I am mistress. For you I am servant.

'You mean that's all I wanted you to be?'

'No . . . all I want to be for you. I tell you before like this. You don't listen.'

'I told you that you're my wife in every way.'

'What is wife . . . to man like you? You have one before. You don't like it.'

He stared at her, after a moment urged: 'Go on.'

'What for?'

'I want to hear the truth about your feeling for me.'

'You know my feeling.'

'How can I . . . when after all this time you've been my wife, you tell me you're only my servant?'

She finished her glass and set it down, put her arm round his shoulders, looked away to say, 'You bring me from blacks' camp . . . because you are kind.'

'Because you are my dead brother's responsibility, as I told you long ago, when you talked about going away again.'

'All-same.'

'It isn't. I loved my brother. I loved what belonged to him. Also, as I've told you before, if you hadn't been Jack's sweetheart, you would have been mine. Didn't you believe that?'

She looked at him, nodded.

'Then what's this servant thing? Does it mean you could only be Jack's wife?'

She took his weather-and-age-beaten hand and pressed it to her smooth chocolate cheek. 'You know I love you. But I am Aboriginal woman. I am servant to man I love. White woman who is boss don't love her husband. Only partner.' She kissed the hand, nuzzled it, murmuring, 'Always I am servant of Jeremy Delacy. Time I can't be his servant, I don't want to live.'

He pulled her somewhat roughly into his lap. 'Now listen . . . we've had all this out. You promised to go away and look after the others.'

She kissed him, with passion, then relaxed, saying, 'I do dat, because you tell me . . . and I am your servant.' She pushed her face against his shoulder.

He was silent for some time, holding her close. Then he said, 'You're rather heavy. Let's go over, eh? We'll both take a Barbitone, and have a good sleep.'

They crossed the dark yard, arms about each other. They sat in the den to take the tablet and another brandy, sitting as before, she on his lap.

He talked of what he wanted her to do to maintain the pride of race that had been taught here as religion to crossbreds ever since it had been made a refuge for them, that now was the time when degeneracy could set in through her like having the opportunity to identify themselves with whites and being tempted to seize it, only to become as low as the lowest whites: how he wanted her to fill in her empty time with showing herself in her pride to those who would be sympathetic towards her and learn from her the problems of being Euro-australoid – to distinguished people to whom Fergus would introduce her; how he relied on her to teach the difference between yellow-fellow and black-fellow and stop the destruction, moral or otherwise, of those the country really belonged to, before it was too late and they became part of the community of riff-raff the Australian Nation was doomed to become unless this fundamental evil of the Dispossession was honestly dealt with. If she were his beloved servant, here was her service.

She fell asleep listtenting to his droning. When he realized she was asleep, he rose with her, and with a good deal of puffing, carried her to his room, lay her on his narow bed. Still sleeping, she groped to pull him down with her. When he sat beside her, she groped for his hand and drew it up under her skirt and into her drawers. He played with her till by her breathing he knew she was sleeping deeply. Then he rose, went to the press, got out bedding, made up a bed on the floor beside her. Soon he was sleeping, too.

Despite Nan's disavowal of mistress-ship and her apparent cheerfulness, next day with the last of the packing and locking away of such of the household effects as it would be a sacrilege to leave to the tender mercies of the usurpers, she surveyed and handled a lot of things in a manner surely betraying secret bereavement. The big truck, starting out soon after breakfast and loaded the first time as for a Race Meeting, made two trips to Beatrice in the morning. The third and last trip was made in mid-afternoon, with the personal belongings of those who would be going beyond Beatrice. With this went Rifkah, Prindy, Fergus, originally supposed to follow with Nan and Jeremy in the utility. Rifkah insisted at the last minute that Nan and Jeremy must leave the house last and alone. Both women wept a little in each other's arms at the front door, not saying simply Goodbye, since they would be reunited within an hour or two, but Goodbye to some sweet thing they had shared, which was gone herewith for ever.

Jeremy and Nanago stood together in the lounge, at the foot of the bright polished stairway, arms about each other, taking a last look. Only the most fragile and precious things had been locked away. As Jeremy had said, there would be more respect given to a house that looked as if it still belonged to someone. Then they embraced closely, kissed Goodbye to it. As they parted, she would have headed for the door, only he checked her, asking if she wouldn't like to take just a last look alone. She blinked, nodded. As she mounted the stairs he went out.

She was smiling when at last she came to him waiting by the utility, much as if nothing untoward was happening. However, he took her in his arms, kissed her eyes first, and then her mouth. She said she would walk to the gate, to pat the cripples gathered about the grid, as usual during the Race Time exodus. He drove through. She closed the gate, leaning on it for a moment to stare at the house. Then quite briskly she got into the car, sighed, and still with matter-of-factness, said, 'All finish. Now we go.'

But it was not all finished. They had passed the turn-off to the Rainbow Pool, had swung in towards the river, the shimmer of which, reflecting the last of the Sun to be able to reach it through the river timber, struck through the wind-screen. Thereabouts was the first big hole. She said quickly, 'We swim.' He glanced at her. A strange glitter in her eyes. He slowed down, geared down, turned off the road towards the hole.

When they stopped at the top of the steep bank she slipped out like a kid in her eagerness, fished under the canvas at the back and got out a basket from which she took a towel. Then without waiting for him, she went scampering down. Again he reached the bottom, she had her bare chocolate bottom presented as she stood on a bit of couch grass beside the pool. She looked shapely, despite a bit of padding above the broad hips. If her bottom came from the white side, the slenderness of back and shoulders and the grace of arms with one hand tucked into its axilla, the other grasping its shoulder, was from the other side of her inheritance, as did the stance. As he shed his own clothes on top of hers, he stared, revealing his interest when he dropped his trousers. She looked back then, saw the elongated *darra*, smiled, then turned away again, dived. In a moment he was in with her.

They played for a while like boy and girl lovers, he displaying a full erection as he rolled over, although his breathing was hardly that of a lover. Then suddenly she struck back to shore, climbed up to the grass, to swing towards him, dashing water from her eyes, her breasts, laughing like a lubra, showing white teeth and rosy inner-lip. He came after her, presented himself rampant, grabbed her. A moment of slippery embrace. Then she drew away, staring down at his *darra*, which had collapsed. She reached for it. But he caught the slim dark hand, and as she raised wide velvet-dark eyes to his, breathed, 'No darling . . . only in gladness, never in sadness.' The brown eyes blinked, then fell. The curly wet head drooped, fell against his grey-haired breast.

He got the towel. She blinked and sniffed away her tears as lovingly he towelled her, even giggled a little as, drying her loins, he tickled her *kumara*, kissed it. She appeared her cheerful self again as, dressed, they climbed back up to the truck, hand in hand.

As they went on their way he talked chiefly business with her, banking and the law. He also talked of the war as of not so great concern generally as he saw it personally. He said the issue must be decided within six months, as all wars were, that seeming to be as long as any nation could delude itself as being invincible. The Japs would have to take Australia, now the bastion of the Americans' war against them. It seemed hardly feasible, when the Americans had so many more men than the Japs, to say nothing of Australians and others they could throw in, and technology for any purpose that was unsurpassable. Hence it was very likely that by the middle of the year the Japs would be fighting as desperately to hold their illusion as the Germans were. But if they weren't here by then they never would be, and perhaps those who were now being hunted out of the country might be allowed back again. It sounded quite cheery. However, Jeremy didn't look at her while he talked thus, but kept eyes on the winding road. Nor did she look at him, staring ahead as if thinking her own thoughts, despite her ready responses.

He also talked of Bridie Cullity, who happened to be in Beatrice, as they knew from a note she had sent Jeremy with the returning truck. He said he would be able to tell Bridie things that he hadn't dared in the letter he'd written her. With her kindness and shrewdness, Bridie would be a great help.

Actually it was Bridie asking for help at the moment. She had written to say that the Finnucane Clan had planned to have Christmas together at her place, but that her father had jacked up at the last minute and now was raging in drink. Her mother and sister had sent for her as the only one the old man would listen to. She had failed utterly. Could Jeremy do something?

So to Beatrice. The camp was already up. Nanago, with Rifkah's help, at once set to the task abandoned by her social betters. Jeremy went on to the Police Station.

Sergeant Stunke was stiffish in the old attitude towards the Scrub Bull, despite that amiable note about the Blackfellows' Christmas. By his tight expression he looked as if he was expecting defiance of the order to evacuate.

Jeremy acted the Scrub Bull. What sort of country was it, he demanded, when civilians could be pushed around by their own army as if they were conquered enemy, and their paid civil protectors just sat around and watched? He said he wanted to submit an inventory of the property he was being dispossessed of to Stunke. The sergeant said he could do nothing, that liaison between civil and military authorities could be effected only through an officer called Town Major, an appointment not yet made for the Beatrice district. Jeremy said he would hang on till the officer was appointed. Stunke replied to that grimly, 'The order is for you to be out of the place by January the First. If you're not, and you're in strife with the military authorities, don't come to me.' Jeremy left him as if in truculence, but stopped at the gate and came back and asked amiably if Stunke would care to drop in for Christmas dinner tomorrow, seeing his family was gone. Stunke swallowed on it, answered – Well, he'd drop in for a drink, anyway.

Jeremy went on to Finnucane's, the hullabaloo from which could be heard from afar. The place was shut in front, not as normally out of trading hours, but with windows and glass doors boarded up; a face shut for ever against the world it had once so eagerly welcomed. He went round the back, came up through the courtyard. At his steps, three female faces looked out of the kitchen: old Biddy's, sour-spinster Peggy's, Bridie's. Out rushed Bridie, to fling herself into his arms; while the others watched narrow-eyed. The din, the bull-roaring and banging and crashing, was coming from the direction of old Shame-on-us's office.

Tearfully, Bridie told how the old man had now been standing siege so long that blue-bottles were popping in and out under the door of his den – and the stink! She hadn't seen him, or been able to talk rationally with him. If he took notice of her at all it was to talk to her as he had when she was a child and sing *Eileen Alannah.* The voices of the other two only made him rave. Forceful entry could only mean that someone must get badly hurt. Already he was waging what sounded like a war to the death with a figment of his delirium he had created out of hatred of Winston Churchill. Bridie explained that recently he had been much upset by something he had read in an Irish paper about Churchill's having been trying all along to wheedle and bully De Valéra into joining Britain in the war, with promises of total independance for Ireland later or vows of never, never – *It's Now or Never*! – and now filling Ulster with American troops ostensibly to prevent invasion by Eire, but in fact to invade her. On top of this had come the order to evacuate. If only they could do something without having to call in Stunke.

It took a while for Jeremy to get a response to his calling and hammering at the door. Shamus was in the midst of a bout with his Figment, using various weapons by the sound of it, probably the remains of the fine furnishings he'd been so proud of: 'Now or niver, is it, ye crocodile-bellied bastard . . ye Protestant Church on a hill in Hell . . . got ye . . . got ye . . . got ye . . . och, the slippery spalpeen's got away agin!'

When at last he heard, Shamus shouted, 'Ah, Pat Delacy, me dear ould friend . . . and so ye've come back to me . . . as I knew ye would . . . or is it meself is come to ye? Come in, Paddy, man-dear . . . and have a drap o' the crayter.'

When Jeremy asked him to open up, he said he daren't: ' 'Tis the Churchill thing, Pat. 'Twill git out on me . . . and then, musha God help us! Kill it I must, to save ould Oireland and the wurruld.' He began to sing in hoarse snatches as he banged about: '*There came to the beach . . . a poor exoile av Erin . . . he sang the bould anthem av Erin Go Bragh . . . oh, Erin, my country . . . oh, Erin, Go Bragh* . . . . '

Jeremy got tools, and proceeded to cut a hole in the heavy door to get at the lock. Then there was the job of getting at the lock with a mahogany chair-leg striking at his hand as an appendage of the Churchillian reptile with which Shamus continued to do battle: 'Snaykin' out be the keyhole would ye be at . . . take that, Sassenach!' All in vain. The door was not only locked, but bolted.

A group had gathered: railwaymen, some travellers camped for the night, Stunke. Jeremy kept them back. But now he had another idea, in which they could lend a hand. There was another means of entry: the small trap-door communication with the private bar. It was bolted tight, but should give way easily to assault with an axe and without the danger certain to accompany smashing in the big door and might well be means to raising the siege bloodlessly, if the besieged one could be kept preoccupied at the big door. Jeremy conferred with Tom Toohey and Sergeant Stunke. Their job was to attack the big door with an axe and a crow-bar, while he tackled the trap, backed by other men, both efforts to be timed so that one or other assault took Finnucane off his guard.

It worked. They had the door off its hinges with old Shame-on-us holding it up with the strength of a bull, when Jeremy, shoving through the trap a long-legged-bar-stool as shield, took him in the rear. They let the door fall out. Poor old Shamus, mother-naked, his hairy flabby mass fouled with his own filth, fell face down on it. They pounced on him, pinioned him. Jeremy raced to the kitchen for what he had ready there, came back with it: a hypodermic in a covered bowl. He cleaned a bit of Shamus's hairy behind, gave him the needle hard. Shamus bellowed, 'The bastard's bit me . . . help, help . . . I'm pysened be a voiper!'

They had to hold him hard for ten minutes, during which he raged even worse, seeming to believe that the Churchill Thing had him in chains and was dragging him down to Hell – 'The harp he loved ne'er spake agin . . . 'twill niver sound in slavery . . . oh, oh, Mother o' God!' He started vomiting. He fairly puked his heart up, so that they had to let him get up to hands and knees so as not to smother in the alcoholicy slime he was disgorging. When he stopped, he would have fallen into it in instant sleep, had not they hauled him clear. Jeremy said, 'He's right now. Let's get him to the bathroom.'

Jeremy himself bathed him, while he snored under the tap, dried him, put him in pyjamas, saw him into bed. Asked by Stunke what he had given the old man, Jeremy replied, 'Apomorphine. Its chief use is as an emetic. Very powerful. Useful in cases of poisoning. But it also has the happy effect of calming delirium quickly and completely. The old fellow should sleep like a log for a good twelve hours . . . and wake up quite sober and refreshed.'

The Finnucane women were for taking advantage of the log-like condition to whisk their chieftain away at once. Jeremy wouldn't have it, arguing that for him to wake and find himself virtually shanghaied most likely would set him off again. As much of his trouble was due to his having to do something against his will, the best thing to do would be to mitigate the feeling of dispossession as much as possible. Hearing them say that the old man had said he wanted to have what he had called Me Last Christmas in the Land o' the Livin' in his own house, heading his own table, Jeremy suggested that a world of good would be done him by giving him just this. For a start, after long subsistence on alcohol alone, feeding him up with food was essential; and how better do it than with a tasty Christmas Dinner with Himself presiding? He assured the doubtful women that even if his lordship got on the grog again in celebration, he would see to it that he went off with them tomorrow as quiet as a lamb.

Therefore, sucking pigs and fowls were got from Ah Loys, a ham and such canned Bush-Christmas goodies as pudding, cake, dessert, from McDodds, grog broached from the crates packed ready for transference to the Prospectors' Arms, and invitations sent out to those remaining of the old hands and such as were passing through who could be considered as worthy to sit at the Finnucane board. The latter condition, of course, ruled out all of the Lily Lagoons household except the head, and Fergus, if now he were to be included. On another occasion it would have ruled the head out, too. However, he promised the troubled-eyed Finnucane women that he would be there, to act as it were, as the power behind the throne of old Brian Boru.

McDodds was invited, but didn't even deign to decline. For one thing, as a Good Scot, he didn't believe in the Pagan Shoneenin' imposed upon decent Presbyterian Christianity by his Norse ancestors, and for another hadn't set foot in Finnucane's since their declaration of war an age ago and wasn't one to let a piddling world war interfere with his private hostilities. As regarded the exigencies of the piddling business now disrupting the community, he had declared his intention of staying on till the dead-line for evacuation, New Year's Day, to see out what he grimly predicted would be the last Hogmanay ever to be celebrated here according to decent tradition. As he said, 'Moot tis nae the heathen Jap the bye, 'twill be summat nae mooch lessen veecious . . . twite yon khaki lootin' loons!' The bitter reference was to passing soldiers, some of whom had robbed his fowl-house, and a couple had bought things over his counter, telling him to send the bill to John Curtin.

So Beatrice River had its two traditional Christmases after all, even if in circumstances very different from those of long-established tradition. Gentlemen of the Big House had always topped Finnucane's list of guests: these the lesser of the staff's hierarchy: Second Bookkeeper, Head Stockman, Engineer, and such. In the past, of course, the top ones had always gone to Town for Christmas and New Year. However, with all truly social events channelled into the War Effort and the local ladies fled to do their bit where it was safest, the gentry were all here this time. Hence heading the list was Mr Martin Delacy, O.B.E.

To the evident momentary astonishment of Jeremy, down in the camp just before noon on Christmas Day, Martin called in there. Jeremy was alone, the others of the household being busy in the bush kitchen built for cooking for the blacks, and Fergus already up at the pub. It would be the first time Martin had set foot in the camp. But the way he approached his staring father, smiling and walking with complete ease, it might have been everyday. No doubt the years of success had taught him that he could be at ease much as he chose. He was the Big Boss. He looked it, every inch of him, in his good olive poplin clothes, shiny tan elastic sides, fine Stetson. He had grown to be a bigger man than his father – unless his father had shrunk. But there was something gross about the bigness. Even his handsome ruddiness looked more like a flush of self-satisfaction than of health. He addressed his father easily as he came up to him holding out his hand: 'Goodday, father . . . Merry Christmas.'

Jeremy took the hand, as he often had on formal occasions, and likewise mumbled a reply that could have meant anything. Unaffected, Martin looked away at what was going on concerning Blackfellows' Christmas. The mob of blacks were already in brand-new Christmas clothes and sitting in their family and horde groups waiting for the feast. He looked again at his father. 'Good of you to take over this business. We just couldn't manage it. I appreciate it very much. You can charge it all to us, of course.'

'Of course,' said Jeremy. 'Have a drink?'

'Thanks . . . yes.' Martin sank with a big man's sigh into the canvas chair he was waved to. 'A beer'll do nicely.'

Turning to the refrigerator, Jeremy also signalled to Nanago and Rifkah and Prindy, who were staring. They came slowly. As the women and the boy came up and Jeremy set out bottles and glasses, he said, 'You know these ladies, of course.'

Already risen, Martin bowed gravely, saying, 'Merry Christmas.'

Nanago returned the compliment with a smile. Rifkah, her eyes somewhat narrowed, merely returned the bow. Martin concentrated on Prindy. 'And how are you, young feller?'

The response was rather startling, by reason of its raucous tone, like a cockerel's crow, 'All right, thank you, Sir.'

The somewhat piggy eyes opened wider. Then Martin chuckled: 'Voice breaking, eh?'

As the company sat and took their drinks, Prindy a lemonade, Jeremy said, 'That beautiful soprano gone for good.'

'It happens to us all,' said Martin.

Jeremy raised his glass, toasted: '*L'chaim*!'

The others echoed him; except Martin, who blinked and made a mumble.

A little silence. Martin broke it, looking again at Prindy, saying, 'Getting whiskers, too, I see.' He looked at his own father, away from the grey eyes of his son so much alike, gave a little guffaw: 'You give him a razor for Christmas?'

Jeremy grimaced slightly, shook his head, turned from the closed smooth red face of the father, to the open golden one of the son with its soft fuzz of glinting gold about the chin.

Martin also looked again at Prindy, chuckled: 'What say *I* make you a present of your first razor?' Still chuckling, he gave attention to a tunic pocket of his beautiful shirt, took out a wallet. Opening the wallet and fishing out notes, he said, 'A Rolls Razor. They're the best. As a Christmas present from me.' He held out what looked like a fair sum. Prindy cast a swift glance at his grandfather, who merely blinked. 'Here,' urged Martin.

Prindy looked at him, squeaked, and then rumbled, 'No thank you, Sir . . . Christmas not our *yomtov*.'

Martin's ruddiness darkened. 'Eh?'

Jeremy cut in: 'We don't go for Christmas, you know.'

For a moment Martin was at loss, his blue eyes rolling between the two pairs of grey. Then, shoving the notes back in the wallet and the wallet in his pocket, he said, now in the dry tone of the disapproving Boss, 'I understood he was going to be a priest.' He looked up and met Prindy's eyes. Prindy nodded. Martin asked, 'Then how come you don't go for Christmas?'

For all its dissonance the breaking voice was precise: 'Christmas not Christian properly.'

Again a moment of loss, by the change in colour, the blinking. But the Boss was ready to hand. 'Go on with you! Christmas is the Birth of Christ.' Martin looked at his father, chuckled again: 'Fine priest he'll make! We'd better make him a Vet, I reckon.' So natural-sounding was that expression of shared responsibility. Yet it might have been only the Big Boss's way of having a hand in everything.

Jeremy answered dryly, leaning forward to refill Martin's glass, 'As a matter of fact, Christmas has its origin in an old Nordic festival celebrating the return of the Sun after its couple of days' disappearance during the northern winter solstice . . . and there's no authenticity about the date of Christ's birth.'

Martin went quite red, swallowed. Jeremy raised his glass. 'Well . . . a Happy New Year. anyway . . . however grim the portents.'

Martin took refuge in drinking. Lowering his glass, Jeremy said to the others, 'Well . . . I suppose you'll be wanting to get back to your job . . . I'll be trotting along to Finnucane's in a minute, too.'

They all rose. Jeremy rose. Martin rose, too, just a fraction behind.

Nanago smiled at him. 'Excuse us.'

'Certainly,' he said. 'And thank you for doing everything. My mother will be glad. I'll write and tell her.' They went off.

Jeremy said, 'I suppose you're going to the pub?'

'Yes. I heard you made a wonderful job of the old man. Come in the car with me.'

As they headed for the car, Martin said, 'I hear the Army're taking over your place.' When Jeremy murmured affirmative, he added: 'How do you feel about it?'

Jeremy's voice was dry again: 'How would you?'

They paused beside the car. Martin said, 'Maybe I could do something.'

'Such as?'

'Well . . . from what I understand, your occupation's not considered essential. What say I appointed you Company Vet . . . and we could work round to saying we wanted the Lagoons for, say, quarantine purposes?'

'You only understand half of it. I'm also considered a security risk.'

'Eh? But that's absurd!'

'Not really. I've already been twice jailed for alleged breaches of National Security.'

Martin stared at him, utterly at a loss now. But again he struggled to be the Big Boss: 'I'll see someone about this. I'll fix it.'

Jeremy chuckled now, turning to get in: 'Thanks all the same. But you don't know these boys playing at war. The only thing that'll take their power off 'em is a gun bigger than the one they're packing. You wouldn't be able to do any good, even if you got old Alf to have a word with Winston Churchill. It's war, man, war . . . something I know a lot more about than you.' He got into the big car for his first and last ride in it.

As they drove up to Finnucane's, Martin said to the road in a rather strained voice, 'I would very much like to do something to help, father . . . I could, you know.'

Jeremy looked at him quickly. Martin turned. Genuine concern was in blue eyes. Jeremy reached and touched his knee lightly. 'Thanks, son . . . but I've got things working my own way. I'll be right.'

They entered the pub, to join the male crowd about towering old Shame-on-us and the table laden with all kinds of grog under hanging paper Christmas bells out in the courtyard. The place was redolent with the pagan smells of Christmas: booze, rich food, cigars.

Jeremy took charge of old Shame-on-us. He was easy to handle, well and truly drubbed by the Demon Liquor as he had been and right ready to take it now in sips and with a drop of Paraldehyde along with it. He was content to talk, to tell old tales, for corroboration in which he often called on Jeremy. He harped on that good old one which had laid the foundations of the Finnucane and Delacy fortunes: 'A pound o' beef for a pound o' tin . . . ye can't ate ye tin, boys . . . but a pound o' beef bought wid a pound o' tin will give ye muscle to get a bag o' the stuff . . . Come on, there . . . A pound o' beef for a pound o' tin! Rimimber it, Jerry, me boy?'

Jeremy was able to get Bridie aside to tell her of his intentions and his requirements of her. She was appalled by the revelation of his secret, but readily agreed to keep it and to do all she could for his people.

She had a secret of her own to share. She'd had a letter from her mother-in-law, Cullity, in Ireland. It wasn't hard to read between the lines that it had been dictated by Con himself. Con had been listed as Missing for some time, but not along with the rest of Our Boys, because he hadn't gone into Greece with them for Jack the Ripper. Soon after going away he had got into the Canteen Service, with promotion to Sergeant. According to the insinuations of ex-Private Hannaford, because all Canteen Sergeants made fortunes, he probably retired into the wilds of Arabia with a harem. However, officially it was thought likely that Con had been taken prisoner by hill-tribesmen in Syria, where he had been sent with other Australians to fight the French, Churchill's only true enemies. Judging from the letter, he'd used his fortune to do exactly what he'd enlisted for, to go see his Old Mam. She had written an extraordinarily cheerful letter, saying how delighted she would be to see Bridie and the children when it became possible for them to make the journey – and that she had a bonny surprise for her.

Jeremy's response was: 'Good on him. That's the only way for a true man to fight a war . . . his own way.'

But Bridie was troubled over Jeremy himself, making him promise that if he found things too hard in the bush to sneak down to her.

The shivoo ended at about three, with the cutting out of the grog. Old Shame-on-us was maudlin, but no more. He raised no objection to his women's urging to be on their way. A heavy thunderstorm was threatening from the northwest. He took affectionate leave of everyone, even of McDodds, who unbent before his blarney to the point of taking his hand. The other Finnucane women went ahead in the big truck with the heavy dunnage. Himself travelled alone with Bridie in her utility. The last Beatrice saw of him was his great red face turned back to them gleaming with tears.

McDodds was mean enough to sneer after him: 'Och . . . for all his craikin' o'er the yearn o' his sobriety in the feece o' turrible tempteetion, he gangs awa' a ceese for the Hame for Inebriates!'

Nugget Knowles was the only one to take umbrage, and that perhaps only because there was an ancient fued between the Knowles and McDodds clans: 'You lousy old bastard . . . I can see you turnin' on the grog like he did at the last . . . I don't think!'

McDodds struck a fighting attitude. 'Forebye, I'll breek the bone heed o' ye for tha'!'

It was stopped by Nugget's catching a look from his Big Boss that clearly told him, sozzled as he was, that if he wished to remain of the true squattocracy, he'd better act it.

Jeremy dispersed with the others, leaving behind the House of Finnucane, more shut-faced than ever. He went down to his camp, where he found Nan and Rifkah resting after the labours of their own shivoo. Most of the blacks were sleeping it off in huddles under bush and bough. A few who had got grog were over the other side of the river hurling insults and bamboo spears at each other in brave mime of ancient feuds.

Jeremy suggested to Nan that they go for a walk. As they came out, she looked at the inky sky. 'Big rain tonight.'

'Yes. I'd better be getting back before sundown . . . or the road might be out for a couple of days.'

She sighed and reached for his hand. 'Last walk together.'

He put both his arms around her and drew hers about himself, fell into step with her. 'Who says?'

She sighed again. 'Mullaka.'

They dodged the sleeping crowd of blacks by going up the bank and skirting the railway yards. Then they dropped back to the river, to follow the horse-pads that, cut in the thick couch beside the shallow stream. meandered with it. She kept him talking about the Finnucane party, wanting every detail. When that was exhausted he tried to get her onto the subject of her own affairs; but without much success. They fell silent, walking hand in hand, not letting go even when bushes cut their separate paths, either swinging hands over them or coming round. A couple of times when they came thus close they kissed swiftly. Occasionally they looked at the sky. The storm was holding back, apparently. The Sun was on the edge of it, turning the boiling black surf to silver. So they kept on, as if drawn by something, till they were close to where the old Russian Settlement clearing began. Here the river was wider and the banks lower and less steep. She said, 'We go up, eh . . . take last look?' Up on top there, before the Russians had come, had been the blacks' camp in which he had found her, a skinny bit of a thing, scarcely more than a child in age, with two dying children – twenty years ago. Was it to recapture that grim scene?

They climbed the soft micaceous bank. On top was comparatively clear of trees, all the bigger ones having been cut down by the alien settlers and the secondary growth retarded by the termites that had taken over the abandoned place. A myriad antbeds crowded the flat to the clump of dark exotic trees that marked the centre of the settlement, reared amongst saplings and spear-grass like head-stones in a neglected cemetery. The Sun, getting clear of cloud, blazed fiercely. 'Too hot,' said Nan. 'Come, we sit down lil bits.'

The only substantial shade was under a mangan plum, a well-grown tree near the edge of the bank. Without comment on the significance, they went to it.

It was a snug spot for a camp; used as such by wallabies, judging by the mat of flattened grass. They sank down sighing. He tumbled up sand and grass and placed his hat on it to make a pillow, then, stretching out, drew her to him. She put head on his right shoulder, undid his shirt to push her hand across his breast, forced his thighs open to insert her own leg. Lying thus, they kissed lightly a few times. She stopped it, saying, 'We tchileep lil bits.' Both relaxed, sighed, shut eyes. In fact soon both were breathing steadily in sleep. Two bustards that must have been watching all the while, stole out of the long grass to take a peep, stole away again. A pair of fairy wrens, called *Biaiuk*, the male vivid blue, the female russet, arrived, to peep from branches, to twitter faintly, fluttering wings at each other.

The pair below slept soundly for perhaps ten minutes. Nanago woke first, saw the birds with eyes for a moment wide with surprise. Then she smiled. She looked at Jeremy. Carefully she withdrew the hand from his chest and touched his cheek with a slender finger. He twitched, as if to dislodge a fly. Her lips moved in soundless utterance. The wrens twittered and fluttered. Still with lips moving, she passed her hand down to his waist, with scarcely perceptible movements slipped the buckle of his belt, undid each fly-button, slid her hand inside. That woke him, blinking.

From staring at her, he glanced aloft at the now excited birds. *Biaiuk* were supposed to be concerned with *Charada*, Love Magic. He lowered his eyes to meet the brown awaiting them, half-growled, 'What's this?'

She giggled: 'What you reckon?'

'Eh!' he cried, in response to the liberties she was taking, and tried to sit up. She stopped him with a kiss, and held him down, to smooth his face with hers in the Aboriginal way of making love, while still at play with her right hand.

He managed to say, 'You been sing me.'

She giggled again, withdrew from him quickly, to rise to knees, in which position she whipped her dress up over her head, dropped it, then with two more swift movements was out of her drawers. She only had a shift on now. He sat up, muttering, 'Eh, look out!'

She was breathless as she swung on him. 'Wha's matter look out?' She grabbed at his trousers, hauled them down his thighs, brought her hand back caressingly over the erect *darra*. 'Blackfeller fashion,' she panted.

He pulled off his boots. She didn't wait for him to remove his pants, but stood up, straddling him, so as to bring *kumara* level with his mouth. Seizing her by the buttocks, he drew his feet in under him so that he was squatting on heels. As he put mouth to *kumara*, she grabbed his hair, pulling at it while gurgling her delight. He ran hands up her back, round to her breasts, down to her jiggling belly. She dropped her head to bite his scalp.

Suddenly, crying out, so that the *biaiuk* flew up, grasping his shoulders, she lowered herself to her own haunches – down – down onto what awaited *kumara*. They clutched each other, rubbed faces as before, now wildly while they jigged in union – till suddenly she shot her feet forward, locked legs about his back, drew head and shoulders away from him, dropping backwards, dragging him on top of her. A spasm of complete union. They lay quivering, gasping. The *biaiuk* swept up twittering, sped away. Back came two sticky-beaking *beinook*.

It was the soft clucking comments of the bustards that roused the human pair.

Shyly they put themselves to right. Now the Sun was obliterated, a wind stirring from the South. She said, 'Rain close-up.'

'Yes . . . better be getting back.'

Before descending the bank they stood to look back at the mangan tree, staring as if to imprint it on their hearts, or to project their hearts to it in blessing. They kissed. She clung for a long moment. Then down, and back along the river now running purple, reflecting the sky ahead. They walked as before. But now mostly she went with hanging head.

At length he asked, 'Are you crying?'

She shook her head, but blinked hard. He stopped, to raise her face, to kiss the welling eyes. He whispered, 'Please be brave, my dear.'

She choked: 'I got to cry lil bits . . . I lose my country.'

'You'll be able to come back to your country some day.'

Her head fell again. 'You are my country.'

They went on. They came to a place, just below a sharp bend, where the river ran shallow over a wide bank of pebbles. She stopped suddenly, saying, 'I stop here.' When he looked at her in surprise, she added: 'I wash myself. You go.'

Still he stared. She flung herself into his arms, straining to him. As suddenly she released him, gasping, '*Mummuk*,' and swung to face the water.

He caught her hand and tried to pull her back. She jerked her hand away, panting, 'You go now.' She headed towards the water, stepped into it while he stared, calling back without turning, her voice strangled, '*Mummuk* . . . my husband.'

She went on splashing to the middle, stopped, but did not turn.

A moment. Then he called huskily, '*Mummuk* . . . my darling wife . . . *yawarra*.'

Her answer was a quiver of the shoulders. Still he waited. She remained rigid. He drew a deep breath, turned to go on his way. Twice he looked back before he reached the bend, and again before turning out of sight. Still she stood as he had left her, watched by a white crane as immobile as herself, perched on a snag, watching the white crane, if there were sight in her eyes.

She turned after he had vanished, stared for a moment at the void he had left; then uttering a high cry, she sank to knees in the water, groped in it whimpering, brought up a sharp-edged stone, smote her brow – smote and smote again – then dropped the stone and drooped her dark head, and howled like a mourning lubra while her blood and tears dripped into the widow's blackness of the stream.

IV

Out at Lily Lagoons, Jeremy and Fergus accomplished to the last detail what they had planned so precisely to outwit their first enemy, that authority bent on ordering their lives without concern for any idea they themselves might have about it. The big jobs were: first, to fly stores and gear over to the other side of the Plateau: second, to stow the aircraft. The landing on the other side was that where the Coot had made his bivouac. They were lucky in finding blacks near at hand with whom to leave the stuff for packing back to the escarpment for dry stowing there. Jeremy rewarded them well and promised more rewards when he returned. At the same time, as he told Fergus, he expected a certain amount of pilfering. Subtle thieving from the *kuttabah* was practised as a kind of etiquette, he explained, the proper response to which was to pretend not to suspect it. Many a fool whiteman, he said, had lost his life in the early days by making a fuss over a few pounds of flour, sugar, tea in ounces, delicately extracted through tiny holes bored in containers. You only lost respect now – but true respect from the blackman was the rarest thing.

Returning, the Junkers was landed on the old Ring Place, and hidden camouflaged under nets Fergus had purloined for the purpose from the Air Force. One would fairly have to bump into it to find it. She was left with tanks full and all parts liable to deterioration sealed. Fergus reckoned she would be safe to fly after a good two years.

The pair became very close in their association. On one occasion Fergus was moved to say again he wished he'd had a father like Jeremy, that having a father you can't fully respect is an everlastingly painful thing. To that Jeremy said, 'I'd've liked a son like you, too, boy. But what's this about fully respecting your father? Isn't it part of the racket of religion? Everlasting honouring your old man is surely a form of escape from being a man in your own right, isn't it? Isn't it more the natural thing to see your father's weakness and want to be a stronger man than he? The father-worshipper . . . male, I mean, because it's natural in the female . . . is always a craven. I suspect those two sons of mine of having a sneaking respect for me that compensated for their own lack of manhood, surely shown in their switching from me to the authoritarianism of their mother. Probably father-worship's the fault of our Nation . . . John Bull always the Boss . . . or up to now, when it's a switch to Uncle Sam. The Yanks showed their superiority over us by quickly declaring themselves independent of the Old Man.'

At one as they were in defiance of authoritarianism, even to fight it to the death, they were markedly different in their attitudes. When Jeremy offered Fergus his choice of the armory he had maintained throughout the years with no more use for it than to kill pigs or put doomed animals out of misery, the young man picked the prize weapons, a heavy automatic pistol and automatic rifle, fingering them with obvious satisfaction and saying, 'Now, any bastard tries to take me goes first!' For himself, Jeremy took only a shotgun and a light rifle with telescopic sights, declaring that he had never yet killed a man and hoped never to do so. When asked what he'd do if the Japs came, he replied that if there were killing to be done, he guessed he could leave it to the blacks. As for killing animals, he hoped to be able to leave that to the blacks, also, except in the way of small creatures prolific in numbers that could be despatched with a stick.

Speaking of fighting the Japanese, he said, 'It will only be to defend a portion of my country to live as I like in. If they come here, it'll be because they're forced to. I haven't any quarrel with them. I'll endeavour to outwit them the same as these other bastards. Resort to arms in self-defence means only to increase vindictiveness. Knowledge of the cause of vindictiveness is the only way to overcome it . . . if ever it's to be overcome and Mankind persist as a blessing to Earth instead of a curse.'

Fergus tried hard to be allowed to stay on, offering his youthful vigour as inducement, even rather asserting it to impress Jeremy with his own failing strength when it was declined. Jeremy settled it, saying, 'With the difference in our purposes, it could only serve a negative end, son. I want simply to stay on in my own country, to die in it, sooner or later, loving it as an old blackfellow does when he dies . . . his love born of his knowledge of it. I've got much to learn through unhurried observation to get that knowledge. My defiance isn't vindictive, it's imperative. I'm an old bull that's left the herd . . . to die. That's why I had to deny my poor dear Nan's wish to stay with me. She said she wouldn't intrude on me . . . that she never has. Subtly she has . . . snaring me with the comfort she's provided. She'd do it again. All women will. Emasculating the male is the female's business. I felt very mean in leaving her . . . still do. She'll be very unhappy for a long while. But there's a positive alternative for her . . . if she can take it. There's one for you, too. If you stayed with me it would only be as an outlaw. No one can justly charge me with outlawry. I'm only insisting on the right of an old man to die where he chooses and in perfect peace. Your youth would drive you to impatient, angry acts. You'd soon be in strife that would hamstring you. You have a nation to build, man. Give all you've got to that . . . till it proves too much for you. It's proved too much for me at last . . . but I still believe it's possible . . . to make out of this community that True Commonwealth that'll be an example to Mankind. So leave me to make myself one with the good earth . . . and you go back to teach others to love it, too . . . not for mean nationalism . . . but for the true salvation of men's souls, which I believe can come only through all-abiding love for the wondrous thing he owes his origin to . . . Mother Earth.'

They talked of the tantalizing differences in men, taking the differences in their own temperaments as example. Jeremy spoke of having himself grown up under the very shadow of constituted authority as a policeman's son, of how he had never thought to question it till shocked by the stupid abuse of it as revealed by his brother Jack's death; while Fergus, reared in indulgence of conventionality, had rebelled from the start and for no apparent reason. Jeremy wanted to know: 'Why the difference and yet the sameness between us? Why the sameness of your upbringing and that of Cootes, and yet the utter difference? That's what I'd like to find out before I turn my back on civilized man . . . so that I can think about it and have the sweetness of truth in my mouth when I die. Will you be pleasant to Cootes when he comes . . . if only for my sake?'

'I won't find it easy. I can't stand the awful fake the fellow is.'

'Well . . . keep out of the way. I'd like to get to the bottom of the fake. Anyway, quarrelling with him won't do any good. Don't forget, I want to put him off the scent.'

They saw the Old Year out, sitting tippling in the lounge, listening with interest to what surely must have been the first bit of news concerning Australia even to seize world interest enough to rouse comment. This was the controversy between the new Australian Prime Minister and Churchill over bringing home Australian troops fighting Churchill's war in North Africa so that they might fight for their own country. What made it world news was the Common Enemy's seizing on it as the first sign of the cracking of the British Empire. The Japanese, in a special radio session now being beamed regularly to Australia from Saigon, were advising Australia that now was their chance to get out of bondage to Britain and keep out of getting into it with America, by dropping out of this war they had no say in fighting and in which certain Japanese victory would be all to the advantage of the friends of Japan. The Germans were telling the Australians in North Africa that the Yanks Churchill told them were arriving in thousands to defend their country were already getting to bed with their womenfolk. Churchill broadcast to Australia that the Gallant Australians would throw away their Place of Honour in Military History by Letting the Old Side Down with such a craven thing as running home. Taffy the Welshman, who as Prime Minister himself, had jailed the new Prime Minister as a Traitor for resisting his Conscription for Britain Campaign, was screaming *Traitor* again. The new Prime Minister was yelling *Storm the Barricades*. Australia itself was split down the middle with Nationalism and Imperialism. Jeremy's comment was: 'We're not a Nation but a madhouse of schizophrenics.'

The Coot was as good as his word about dispossession As From January 1. He arrived shortly before noon on New Year's Day. The Watchers gave warning as usual, not knowing that they were doing so for the last time, that at long last the keep had been breached. When the alarm sounded, Jeremy and Fergus were together in the Big House as before. Jeremy repeated his injunction to Fergus to behave with restraint, and as a precaution sent him over to the annexe, saying that he thought he could handle things better for a start by doing it alone.

This time there were two military vehicles: a staff-car and a type of van specially built for military use and lately introduced into the country. It was from the latter that the first of the newcomers alighted. They were a brace of big soldiers, a sergeant and a corporal, armed with pistols, wearing caps instead of hats. So Colonel Cootes had kept his threat to bring along Military Police. Out of the other came the Colonel himself (but not in yellow boots and socks today) and his Sigs-Lieut Sims. Evidently trouble was anticipated, since it was left to the policemen to make the advance on the front porch, while the others appeared ready to duck for cover. Jeremy spoilt things militarily by emerging before the challenge could be called, countering it by calling himself, quite amiably, 'Goodday.'

A moment of obvious disconcertment. Then Cootes returned the greeting, and approached. Jeremy said easily, 'Are New Year greetings in order?'

Cootes smirked: 'Well . . . I must say . . . hardly what we expected . . .

but a Happy and Prosperous New Year.' He extended a chubby hand.

Jeremy took the hand readily, saying, 'I'm rather like a Chinaman about New Year . . . like to think of it as the time for wiping out all debts and difficulties and starting afresh. If only it could be made universal and binding, eh?' He took in all the others with a glance and a wave of the hand. 'Happy New Year.' Then he addressed himself to Cootes again: 'What was it you expected?'

Cootsey giggled somewhat: 'Well . . . at least a shotgun blast . . . eeeee!'

Jeremy eyed him with seeming gravity. 'You should know the rule here against discharging firearms.'

Cootes squealed with mirth: 'Aheeeeeah!' Then he looked serious, cleared his throat: 'Of course I'm here to take over, you know.'

Jeremy answered matter-of-factly, 'Of course. But let me do the last honours. Come in and have a drink. I've saved some beer for you.'

The Coot looked utterly relieved, said even humbly, 'Thanks, Jeremy.'

It looked as if he would have left the others outside, only Jeremy called all in. He poured for them all while they stood in an awkward semi-circle. He raised his glass: 'To Nineteen Forty-two . . . may it see the beginning of the end of all tyranny!'

Having seated them and refilled their glasses, Jeremy asked the Coot if other troops would be coming. 'Oh, yes!' Cootes answered eagerly. 'My entire unit.' Jeremy's eyes widened at the term. Cootes went on: 'I'm here now only to make a Rekky . . . and, of course, take over officially.'

Jeremy asked mildly, 'What's the official procedure of . . . er . . . taking over?'

Cootes shook his boyish curly head. 'I really don't know. Matter for the Judge Advocate's boys, I presume. All I did was tell GHQ I need this place . . . and they signalled OK.'

Jeremy said, 'In the Last Turn-out there was a procedure for commandeering. An officer was detailed to arrange things. Actually the unit CO signed a paper assuming full responsibility.'

The Coot shrugged. 'Of course you were in other people's countries, weren't you, where I suppose some sort of international law had to be observed.'

Jeremy pursed his lips. Cootes turned to his men, and with regimental peremptoriness told them to see to the unloading of the dunnage. As they went out, Jeremy asked, even with a note of deference, 'Mind if I stay on another day?' Cootes looked at him suspiciously. He added: 'Won't get in your way. Just want to clean up a couple of things.' He smiled. 'Won't feel so much like getting kicked out . . . if I can take my time.'

Cootes coloured slightly. Jeremy waved a hand about. 'Been the centre of my little world for the best part of my life, you know . . . and my wife's. She's left things for you much as they were, you see . . . .'

The Coot cut in: 'I didn't ask for furniture . . . only buildings and the site. You ought've taken your things out.' He blinked before the intent grey eyes.

Jeremy sounded as easy as ever: 'Where could I put 'em?'

Cootes, quite red now, bit his pretty lip. Jeremy came to his rescue: 'No matter. As you've enjoyed the hospitality of the house yourself, I'm sure you won't forget us away somewhere waiting to come back.'

Cootes replied with haste, 'No . . . of course not. This bloody war. Thrown us all out of balance.'

Jeremy nodded. '*C'est la guerre*, as you've said before. The French used to say it a lot during the Last Turn-out . . . even as an excuse for their women giving our men the pox.'

The dark eyes grew round with suspicion again. But Jeremy stopped it by saying, 'Having some more beer. By the way . . . I've left you a couple of dozen bottles in the cellar under the kitchen floor. And speaking of the kitchen . . . I haven't any staff now . . . Fergus and I have been batching.'

'That's all right. Sims and I have our batmen. But what's this about Ferris? He was told he couldn't fly here.'

'He isn't flying. He disposed of his aircraft. He's travelling South with me by road.'

'What'd he do with his aircraft?'

'I think you'd better discuss that with him yourself. He's over in the annexe. You'll find him friendly enough. We've all had time to adjust ourselves. If you like to go over now, I'll show your men the ropes of the kitchen and upstairs. I've got a couple or rooms locked up. Hope you won't mind. Some valuable things. I'll be obliged to you if you'll see there's no wanton busting in. Soldiers can do silly things . . . .'

'Not mine, Jeremy. I've got a very special team.'

'Well, that's comforting to know. See you for another beer before lunch, then, eh?'

At lunch Jeremy presided, at Cootes's insistence. However, that the new master was already in command was made evident by his vetoing Jeremy's idea of having everybody sit down to the meal as he'd had them in for that drink. The Coot said, 'This is to be my Mess. Good order and military discipline should be observed from the outset. The men know their places . . . and prefer to keep them. They'll eat in the kitchen.' Thus there were only Jeremy, Fergus, Sigs-Lieut Sims, and he who before long would have the power to keep other men waiting on his entry here and the glory of being able to raise his glass to that Silly Billy Face which surely would hang here, as in every other Officers' Mess throughout this Commonwealth, perhaps in the very place where, as a last despairing gesture to the Commonwealth that might have been, had so briefly hung that secret starry symbol of it, Rifkah's flag. Cootes asked after Rifkah, saying he'd been informed that Fergus had flown her over here, while the rest of the Mission people had gone by boat to Palmeston. Jeremy said that by now she would be down the Centre with his family, or perhaps gone on still further South.

Cootes wasn't left to concentrate on the doings of Rifkah. Fergus got him on to the much more interesting subject of his Unit; or as he called it sometimes, My Team, My Mob, My Men, My Boys. It seemed that out of his Intelligence Corps he intended to form a Commando unit, by which he meant a true guerilla band such as the Boers had had in South Africa and no one had had since, those units of the British Army called Commandos being mere hit-and-run saboteurs, according to him. *His* men would hold their ground if they wanted to, independent of the battle ebb and flow of either friend or enemy. *His* men would be mounted to fight in the only way truly effective in this country, on horseback. Let the enemy bring in his tanks, his trucks, his sneaking bicycle-riders. Nothing they had would be worth tuppence against the sudden unpredictable onslaughts of his bushmen-horsemen. No arms manuals for them. A sniper's rifle each and a few machine-guns would constitute their armour; unless you counted gelignite for booby-traps and cyanide for water-holes and common or garden matches for setting fire to the grass on the plains, and the scrub on the hills, after luring the enemy into such places. They'd finally round 'em up and yard 'em like cattle. Whole divisions of troops not familiar with country like this could be held by his mere four companies. Let the Nip land and make his bases. They would only serve as sitting shots for the Air Force later on. One thing was certain: with *his* men to deal with, they would never penetrate more than a score of miles, and then wish they hadn't.

Asked by Jeremy if he were recruiting his men from the locality, this brave defender of the land made a Napoleonic moue with that pretty mouth, then said, 'You know yourself that the so-called bushmen of this country have always relied on the blacks. Deny 'em their black guides and they're buggered. And who's going to rely on blacks that have had far closer contact with Japs than with whitemen? No . . . I'm getting my men from the wild parts down South . . . Snowy River Country, Gippsland . . . even Tasmania. These are *real* bushmen. In fact I've got 'em . . . all in camp down South now. It's only a matter of getting the transport to bring 'em here. We're expecting a shipment of our own brand-new four-wheel-drive type MT any day.'

'Thought you were only going to use horses?' Fergus murmured.

'Horses in the line of battle. MT of our own to make us completely independent in the matter of supplies. MT will be based here. This will be my Rear HQ. By the way, Jeremy . . . what horses have you got available?'

Jeremy said he was sorry, that as his were all blood stock, the first thing he had done was to see to getting them out of the zone. 'Pity,' said the Coot. 'I was rather looking forward to having Red Rory as my own charger . . . great horse, that. Still . . . I guess I'll be able to get what I want from your son Martin.'

During the afternoon, when Jeremy and Fergus were able to exchange a word or two in private, they recalled that bit of bushmanship of the Coot's following the Pigeon Corroboree. Evidently the bravo himself had quite forgotten it. Fergus explained how easily he had taken Cootes in by telling him he'd handed the Junkers over to the Air Force. He said, 'Such a deep bastard in many ways . . . and yet such a simpleton in others. Imagine what his Commandos are going to be like! Any man worth tuppence out of those places he's talking about has been recruited long ago. If he gets any, they'll be jackeroos and cooks. But most likely what he'll get's a bunch of poofters whose only riding's been one another in the Sydney Domain and Hyde Park.'

'Yes . . . I can hardly see him getting bushmen to follow him. I must get a bit of a talk with him to see whether what he intends to do might clash with my own intentions . . . and to see what makes him tick. I consider him a classical case in that difference between people we've been talking about.'

That night Jeremy was able to get Cootes to himself while the others, according to their respective castes, amused themselves, with games Jeremy fished out of cupboards for them. Fergus played checkers with Sims. Jeremy introduced the Coot to brandy, well-diluted with a gingerish cordial of his own making for consumption largely by his blacks. The Coot was delighted. 'Ah, that's my drink!' he cried. Jeremy told him there were flagons of it in the cellar.

Under the glowing influence of the drink and Jeremy's shrewd questioning, Cootes told much of his history, evidently with a fair degree of truth, as might be expected of one who saw his destiny all but fulfilled and as star-shiny as he had dreamt it as a child. He was convinced he would die in battle. But this was to be no tragedy, even if his voice quavered and cheeks quivered in declaring it, because his eyes shone with the glory of it: 'It's what I foresaw as a little boy playing with my tin soldiers . . . dying at the head of a regiment of my own men, at the moment of victory. My old Granny, who brought me up, you know, foresaw it, too. The Little Corporal, she used to call me . . . Napoleon, you know. I think I mentioned she gave me a book on Napoleon's life . . . such a huge advanced work for a kid of my age . . . but I fairly mopped it up . . . struggling with a dictionary at my elbow. What a pity dear old Gran didn't live to call me Colonel! It's a pity you couldn't be with me, Jeremy. You'd make a good 2-I-C. Only, of course, it would be impossible, with that anti-militaristic kink you've developed through the death of your brother . . . a glorious death, actually, I understand.'

Jeremy responded to that somewhat dryly: 'You'll have no crazy brother to get a kink over your own glorious death.'

The Coot missed the irony, sighed: 'No . . . I leave no one.'

'How come you've never married?'

Evidently the Coot had considered it – with academic ladies. But no female had ever meant much to him, excepting his Granny. He was bitter about his own mother, who had abandoned him to her own mother while his father was away in the Last Turn-out. He was vague about his father. Anyway, he wouldn't have known much about him, since the man had never come back to claim him. As previously he had related, he'd tried to establish himself in a military career from youth, and had taken up Anthropology as an adventurous alternative. Not for him the sissy Grove of Academe, but a Man's life in the wilderness, taming the Savage. Nevertheless, Jeremy pressed him as a Student of Man, since that's what Anthropologist means. What was his opinion, he asked, of the anomaly of men's being so different when possessed of so much in common, even blood brothers, say? The Coot answered airily, 'Simply a matter of genes. One man is born better endowed than another.'

'You mean just as there are the strong and the weak amongst animals?'

'Exactly.'

'But the endowments of a man are so much more complex. A man who's physically a runt . . . . ' The Coot blinked over that ' . . . may be a giant intellectually . . . and vice versa.'

'Your vice versa chappy could be a moron.'

'He could also be quite intelligent in many ways . . . yet stupid in others.'

'One uses one's intelligence in accordance with the urges of one's genes.'

'Don't you believe in education, then?'

'Of course . . . but only of those capable of the full benefit of it.'

'How do you select them?'

'That's the educationalist's job . . . the result of his urge to educate . . . eeeeeee!'

'But we all have something of a didactic urge. Couldn't the wrong types seize power in this way . . . having it merely accepted that they were educationalists, or any other specialists in dealing with their fellows, by nature?'

'Wrong types don't last. Take the wrong type of man who shoves himself in front of an army for the power of it. What happens? *Débacle!*'

Jeremy didn't go into that. This gave the Coot the chance to put aside the boring questioning of an amateur philosopher, one whose academic achievements amounted to licenciatship as druggist and horse-doctor, and swing the talk to war – war – war! The word made his eyes shine to begin with. But after a while he got maudlin over his impending death. When his eyes glazed, Jeremy tactfully left him.

Jeremy went outside. Igulgul, a couple of days off full, was high in the sky, taking broad glimpses through masses of cloud drifting southward. He went across the yard, heading for the mangoes. He passed through the grove. Who would be eating the fruit next season? Perhaps it would be left largely to the flying foxes, since Southerners mostly had English habits in the way of fruit-eating, as in anything. That might cause the new masters to cut the old trees down, to obviate what they considered the nuisance of the seasonal nocturnal rioting of the bats, which to a Northerner was only proof of the season's bounty. Not infrequently Southerners did that when they came North. Lily Lagoons without its mangoes! Igulgul looked down through the trees and winked.

Jeremy glanced at the lightless Aboriginal quarters as he passed. The desertedness could be *felt*. He was standing staring, when he heard soft scufflings. Creatures that would have been hanging around their human brethren in refuge came to seek a touch from him. Some followed him to the horse-paddock, where others, now without fear of being bullied by jealous equines, attached themselves to him. He crossed to the creek on the western side, with a small crowd shuffling and snuffling and squeaking and croaking around him. Did they know the Mullaka was about to leave them and were gathered to say *Mummuk*?

He stopped beside a shiny hole, went down to drink. Some of the creatures went down with him, one a brush-tail who'd had his marvellous agility torn off him with half a haunch and most of his tail by dingoes. Jeremy sat down beside the pool, sighed, murmured, 'The sweetest waters in all the world, the waters of home.' The wallaby nuzzled him who had patched it up to continue a half-life. He fondled it, continuing his sighing and his murmuring, 'Where else are creatures for ever being driven from their home waters as we are?' A few creatures settled down around him, others went off to forage or play in the moonlight. Igulgul peeped down through the paperbarks and the leichhardts, while his Shade glared up from the water. 'Will all this quiet loveliness be laid waste to satisfy the *kuttabah's* insatiable technology, which is really only a craze for artificiality, a hatred of what is natural because Nature makes him feel too small? Will it become a desert place, exhausted of everything that can be made use of . . . or a site for an equally sterile modern settlement?'

He continued his musing to his silent listeners: 'I feel deeply guilty about you, my friends. What have I done to you, in my whiteman's arrogance and ignorance of Nature? Now that I have to abandon you, do I make your misery greater for having postponed it? I leave you confined here, perhaps at the mercy of louts of my kind who'll even make a sport of torturing you . . . while to open the fence for you will only be to let your natural enemies in. Should I've left you to your true patron, Nature, to give you the *coup de grâce*? You won't have to charge me with your agony, when it comes. I'll be charging myself, thinking of you . . . as of all the others . . . sweet Nan, gentle Darcy, the poor old blacks . . . all, like you, victims of dependence on one too weak to support them ultimately. But what would real strength be in the circumstances . . . to have given you all the *coup de grâce*, and when condemned for it, put the blame on those who condemned me . . . or give you all the chance of fulfilment by a miracle? Is that what I'm expecting for myself . . . a miracle?'

So musing for a couple of hours. He fell asleep at it. The creatures drifted away. Igulgul watched him as he went down through the trees. He was wakened by the Moon's hard staring. He rose, drank again, headed back towards the homestead, this time by way of the orchard and kitchen garden. Only one light to be seen at the homestead now, that in the little power-house, where the heart of the place still throbbed as usual: *Home-ahome-ahome-home-home*!

As he came through the orchard, flying foxes swept up from gorging on papaws and bananas that normally would not have been left for them. Futile guilt. Jeremy sighed, as if affected by the futility of everything. He paused in the kitchen garden, to sit for a little on the steel garden-seat he had made and which was polished from Nanago's sitting there often, as she said, 'To watch him Chinee cabbage grow'. How these Chinese cabbages did grow, under her loving care! Now they would grow to seed. The sugar ants would steal the seeds, the white ants eat the roots. The alien weeds that had lurked waiting ever since the ravishment of the mining days would pop out again in full vigour. Goodbye, Nan's garden! He rose.

Igulgul was down, the West aglow. The Big House stood black against it. He did not head that way, but towards the harness-shed, that long established shelter here for unwanted ones. Where else to go? The New Master had said he would be using the Big House for his officers, the annexe for his WO's and sergeants, the Aboriginal quarters for OR's. The MP's and batmen would be bedded down tonight in the annexe.

He stopped at the power-house, looked in. Throbbing green engine and humming dynamo gleamed spotless in the light of two bright lamps above the switch-board, on which meters told of the state of the spirit of this place: normal, although actually at the hour of death. He stood for a minute or so, staring as if in unbelief. Rarely was the plant ever stopped, because it kept the big refrigerator going. Suddenly he moved in, grasped the two main switches, opened them. The lights dulled. The heart-beat faltered, slowed. The dynamo whined. The engine gasped to a stop. Darkness – save for the golden glow without. Again he stood. Then with another swift movement he reached for the board again, pulled the two main fuses. He was turning with them, going out – when he stopped. A moment. Then he went back, replaced the palely gleaming china things. Futility. Sigs-Lieut Sims was an electrician.

He went out, on to the harness-shed, into it. Already his swag lay unrolled on one of the hide harness racks. In the gathering darkness he stripped to underclothes, lay down.

Butcher birds were the alarm-clocks here at dawn as well as the alarmists during the day. Jeremy had dozed off. He rose hastily, dressed, rolled his swag, shouldered it, went out. Through the mangoes. The Big House still bulked dark, but with windows of mother-o'-pearl. He went to the garage of the annexe, tossed the swag into the back of the already loaded utility. Then into the annexe, walking softly. Loud snores were to be heard in the little hospital. He went through to what had been his own bedroom. It was now occupied by Fergus, who woke easily to Jeremy's touch, and rose. Jeremy went out again, to stand by the utility staring at the Big House as it came into everyday being with the growing light. Soon Fergus was there. Jeremy said to him, 'You drive. She's yours now. Let's get going before anyone wakes. We'll have breakfast at the Rainbow Pool.'

As they went through the gate he looked back, breathing, 'Goodbye, dear home . . . goodbye, I fear, for ever.'

They drove on for a couple of miles in silence. Then suddenly Jeremy broke it, saying in a voice so unexpectedly lively that Fergus glanced quickly at first sound of it, 'D'you know . . . Cootes has the mind of a child!' He stared at Fergus, who had to look back at the road. After a moment Jeremy asked, 'I wonder if that's what's wrong with humanity . . . that the majority of people never really grow up, never become anything more than children made vicious with experience?'

Fergus remarked: 'There is a theory that the intellectual development of people stops at varying ages . . . like seven in the moron. The average age is supposed to be about sixteen.'

'Yes . . . I've read that. It struck me as significant, too . . . as having something to do with sexual development. But I didn't think much about it at the time.' Jeremy paused, to go on after a moment with increased eagerness: 'Now it strikes me as highly significant . . . I mean this sexual maturity idea. It's a fact that animals are easiest to train before sexual maturity, in most cases impossible afterwards. Blacks are similar . . . I mean in the matter of educating them in our ways. It's generally accepted that their capacity for schooling collapses utterly at puberty. Generally it's put down to natural stupidity . . . even though that's obviously gain-said by the fact that they start off learning our ways easily . . . and, of course, in their own ways can be so astute as to leave a whiteman marvelling. My idea for a long while has been that what interferes with black kids at puberty is the pull of the Aboriginal ways . . . because that's the age when education in the so-called primitive style begins. Now . . . . ' He swung on Fergus with eyes ashine.

Fergus took a quick interested glance. As he turned back to his driving, Jeremy said, 'In Aboriginal life, the sexual taboos are introduced with cultural education . . . Initiation. I'm speaking of males, of course. Women must be left out of it, because their part in cultural activity is only background . . . which I suppose you could say of most women in all societies, anyway. Women are the true keepers of sex. It's their business to see that it's kept to rules. That's particularly so in Aboriginal society. But we're speaking of the male. With a male Aboriginal . . . that is a mature one and one living in the true Aboriginal way . . . continence in sexual matters is paramount . . . or rather, the strength to be continent. Sexual desire is considered due to woman's magic. To withstand it shows strength. No ceremony of any importance is conducted without strictly enforced periods of continence . . . even if some end in a veritable sexual orgy. A blackfellow's life, indeed, is ruled by this continence factor . . . beginning with the long one of Initiation, which can last two or three years in the period of a youth's greatest sexual potency . . . ending with the permanent one of the top-class cult-man, the Pookarakka, who, properly, is a celibate. Whereas entry into manhood is proclaimed with the Circumcision, a symbol of castration and so a drastic introduction to control of sexual behaviour, Subincision, a still more drastic symbol of castration, declares full manhood. The price of inability to pass through these ordeals was death . . . and now rejection as Rubbitch. Probably that's the reason for the female mourning ceremony when a boy's taken away for Initiation . . . originally there was a very good chance that they would never see him again.'

When Jeremy paused, Fergus cut in: 'Not all tribes practise circumcision . . . and few subincision.'

'That's right . . . but from what I can judge, these were practices in process of becoming general when the whiteman came . . . in fact, there's even increased adoption of it since, amongst those still able to follow the old ways, while having the closer contact with each other forced on them by us. The practices seem to have spread from the Northwest. It isn't uncommon for some blackboy out of an uncircumcised area who's gone, say droving, into regions where it's practised, to come back cut . . . and with special kudos for being so . . . and even set himself up cutting the others. That old Bobwirridirridi used to go round circumcising and subincising. You'll find that the tribes who practise it are those with the more disciplined . . . and richest . . . cult-life. But I'm not concerned with blackfellow business . . . except to exemplify this idea that's struck me regarding the root cause of differences between ourselves that the blackman doesn't suffer.'

After another pause, Jeremy continued: 'The impact of puberty on all fully hung men must be tremendous. I'm sure I'm not much different from the rest of my fellows physically . . . and I know how it hit me . . . .'

'Me too,' said Fergus to the road.

'You're the first man I ever heard admit it. Perhaps even the prurience of concealing it indicates an almost instinctive urge in human beings to exercise control. There are even crude forms of initiation into manhood practised by civilized boys . . . as jokes, ostensibly, but I'm sure with this urge behind it. Of course it would have to be conducted by mature men to be effective, and all idea of dirty pranks removed from it. Such serious initiation as there is is left to namby-pamby institutions like Boy Scouts and Y.M.C.A., who really only make repression worse by preaching guilt and fear.'

Jeremy collected his thoughts again: 'What I'm getting at is this . . . Couldn't it be that at this time of his life the mind of the average youth . . . civilized, I mean, becomes fixed on sex . . . that it becomes his permanent preoccupation, underlying all he learns thereafter, in effect cancelling out all the value of what he learns . . . except the superficial . . . except, say, what indirectly serves his sexual ends . . . hence this sixteen-years-of-age mental fixation? Freud says that men strive only for Power and the Love of Women. He was preoccupied with sexual neurosis. What he meant were those not intellectually developed beyond puberty . . . don't you think?'

'Maybe . . . but how does all this apply to Cootsey? He doesn't appear to have any sex at all. In fact he doesn't seem to have much in the way of cods. Have you ever seen him stripped? He's hard to catch . . . ashamed of that little-boy's dicky of his, I guess. He's also not a bit interested in the female of the species.'

'An example of the same thing . . . differently. No doubt he's sexually underdeveloped. In a primitive society, he'd either be killed, or rejected as a runt from male society. In our own, with present medical knowledge, he could be treated for the lack. Not unlikely his sexual development's been retarded by non-descent of the testes through ceoliac malformation . . . not an uncommon condition, in animals as well as men. It can be treated surgically and with the use of hormones to effect normality. As he is, he probably yearns for proper manhood.'

Fergus chuckled: 'It would be interesting to see him become a bull . . . following his cock around . . . aaaaaaahaha!'

Jeremy wasn't amused. He went on: 'In puberty . . . or, rather, in the prepubital stage, probably the most sensitive period of life, as exemplified by young Prindy's behaviour up to just now and his sprouting whiskers . . . he dreamt of himself . . . I'm talking of the Coot . . . as a great soldier. His father was a soldier . . . and especially through being deprived of him, would make a soldier symbolic of complete manhood. This isn't uncommon. The traditional officer type is a fop. Even the traditional courage of the type . . . the sissy young subaltern . . . is some vain-glorious personal drama. Cootes wanted to be a soldier. Unable to be, for reasons he's stated frankly . . . couldn't pass the physical test . . . he decided on what he saw as a life of high adventure, but what to a drover, a sailor, a man like yourself who took to the air, seems just sissy. Even some of the great explorers, like Leichhardt, Burke, weren't in the true sense men of action. I guess the Hitlers, the Mussolinis, the Stalins, the Churchills, are much like Cootes . . . preoccupied with sexual inadequacy . . . or, better, lack of proper masculine adequacy . . . and so have to get power over men to compensate. Even the well-hung male can have it . . . through having his natural adequacy distorted . . . like a priest, say . . . or a Dinny Cahoon. Poor old Dinny was brought up in an atmosphere thick with sexual repression, although quite a man in his way. Maladjusted as he was, he became a man-hunter. So it could apply to all those who seek power over their fellows . . . could be the key to all this lunacy we see in the midst of sanity, this stupidity in the face of fine intelligence, which has been puzzling me for years. Sexual aberration . . . distortion . . . oddity of some kind, sexually . . . in the male . . . the civilized male. What do you think?'

Fergus grinned: 'I'm afraid I bear out much of what you say by thinking mostly of the female of the species . . . and what about *her*, anyway, in the scheme of things . . . isn't she distorted, too?'

'I think mainly only in so far as the male distorts her. She'd be all right but for the brutal weakness of the average male. She trades on it. She has to.'

'Why don't you come South and start lecturing on it . . . that war's due to boys whose balls haven't descended . . . you might stop the bloody thing.'

'Don't you think I've been in enough strife already blowing my bags? Why don't you do it?'

'Me? Lecture on the glorious rewards of sexual continence! Half the whores in Sydney would turn up to laugh.'

Jeremy laughed. They were approaching the turn-off to the Pool. Slowing down to make the turn, Fergus said, 'It's good to see you laughing, in the circumstances.'

'I'm feeling better now about the whole business . . . less bitter about harassment, feeling I know it can't be helped . . . or rather, perhaps can be helped – someday.'

'How . . . through seeing that all little boys' balls come down in time to stop them becoming tyrants?'

Jeremy chuckled, then said seriously, 'Through intelligent direction of the most marvellous thing in the Universe . . . human intelligence.'

They reached the Pool. The place was looking its best in strange brooding beauty, as usual at this time of year, freshened by recent rain, yet not roused thereby to hint of the violence of which it was capable. Jeremy expressed concern about what the coming soldiery might do to it. Fergus remarked that it was more to the point what it would do to them, considering the lives it had claimed of foolhardy miners. Jeremy said he had asked the Coot, as an Anthropologist, to guard the sacred places hereabout from the natural spoliation of the civilized lout, had got his assurance readily, but doubted it, seeing how callous he had been about the dispossession that he'd appeared not even to hear when Jeremy had talked of the effect of it on old natives who'd been here for years. Fergus said, 'He might put a ban on this place, though, because he's scared of it.'

'Don't tell me he's superstitious!'

'No. He'd heard about the drownings here. He's scared of water . . . deep water. I tried to get him in . . . but, the champion bullshit artist, he pretended it was desecration of a place sacred to other people. He just can't swim, of course . . . but won't own up to it, naturally.'

'I don't see anything natural about it. That's the odd thing I'm talking about . . . that intelligent people can be so childishly dishonest about trifling things.' Jeremy looked about for sticks to make a fire to boil the billy. He added: 'Anyway, if there's anything in the superstition that anyone who *bogies* here must die in the country, we're safe from a Japanese invasion.'

'How come?'

Jeremy told how the Coot was convinced he would die in battle, hence his glorious death could not take place in these parts.

Fergus commented: 'Poor old Cootsey! Makes you feel sorry for him . . . bastard and all that he is.'

'Yes . . . I felt that way about him. But later, when I was walking round the place and thinking of the misery he and his like visit on other people with their pathetic silliness, I wondered where the compassion should start, and how.'

Fergus said suddenly, 'Let me stay with you . . . and we'll work it out together . . . and write a book about it.'

'No, son. We'll each work it out in his own way. And it's you who'll have to write the book. Come and have a dip while the billy boils . . . to make sure you'll be coming back someday. Maybe you can write the book at Lily Lagoons . . . if it's till there.'

After breakfast they went on. At Beatrice they went straight to the Police Station. Stunke received them amiably, wishing them a Happy New Year, taking the document Jeremy had prepared on his dispossession, and promising to pass it on to the Proper Authority. He even gave them his hand, wishing to see them back someday.

Tom Toohey was working with his gang in the railway yards. Jeremy went to him alone. It was a very different Tom from the mate of old. He did commiserate thinly on Jeremy's dispossession, but let it be known that he knew he could have stayed on by the grace of Martin but for his perverseness. Jeremy didn't argue, didn't prolong the parting. Back with Fergus in the utility, he said, 'Poor old Tom! I don't know whether the life was kicked and batoned out of him, by the Jerusalem Screws along with poor Brumby's, or only some silly pride I didn't know he had, by the bastards here. It's strange that he hated Cahoon for hounding Brumby . . . yet now, I think, hates poor Brumby for doing the same thing in a uniform as before he did in rags . . . simply defied an oppressive authority. The things war does to people!'

They went on their way. The township was deserted now, save for goats camped on the hitherto prohibited areas, the verandahs of pub and store. Barbu's shop was shuttered, but to no purpose, because the door had been knocked down. A convoy of troops was bivouacked in the hall, its members sitting about eating breakfast from mess-tins. Toohey's was deserted. Horses were gobbling up the Ah Loy's garden. Goodbye to Old Beatrice!

Then they were on the new straight road that ran between lanes of drooping dust-suffocated bush to red haze in the distance. Even though their own wheels were the first to churn the dust since yesterday, the acrid taste of yesterday still hung in the air. When, about a mile and half beyond the township, Jeremy called on Fergus to stop, he suggested the young man make the rest of the journey wearing a cloth over his face like a drover. He wouldn't let Fergus get out with him, saying that one pair of footprints were enough to have to erase. He hauled out his swag, gave his hand. 'Goodbye and good luck, son.'

Fergus's greenish eyes blinked on tears. Teeth seized his bunny lip. His brown head drooped in shame, till the lips touched Jeremy's hand – and kissed it. For a moment Jeremy stood, troubled. Then he bent and kissed the head, muttering, '*Mummuk, Igeiyu.*'

As he withdrew his hand, Fergus's tearful face came up to answer huskily, '*Mummuk, yawarra,* Mullaka.' A weak smile. Jeremy smiled in return, backed away, erasing his tracks with the side of a boot. At the edge of the scrub he smiled again, waved, heaved swag onto shoulder, turned and marched off into the red bush. It was a good couple of minutes before he heard the truck start up and go on its way.

It took half a mile of walking to get clear of the blight of the road dust. Then the subtle colours of the bush came into their own again. Soon ahead was the greener line of the river timber topping all, itself topped by a cloud of white cockatoos.

He reached the river bank so close to that magic mangun plum tree of

Christmas Day that he swung towards it. It must have been out of sheer sentiment, since he could not have an inkling at the distance of what was going on there. First indication was a flutter of russet and blue above it, as on that day – then a flash of two tints of brown, golden and chocolate, as two slight figures, hands clutching clothes, dashed from under it, to vanish over the bank – the little wrens of *Charada* – and Prindy and Savitra!

He stopped dead, staring. No sound, save those cockies, who had spotted intrusion. He went on his way towards the mangoes. The cockies were announcing his coming. They came to escort him the last of the way. He put hand to mouth, called, '*Ku-i* . . . Rif-kah!'

There she was – at first a flash of copper in the sunlight. She was running to him, dressed in her stock-rider's outfit, minus hat. She flung herself into his arms.

When able to disengage himself, he asked, 'Everything okay?'

'Yes . . . only waiting for Prindy bring in horses. He go ven he hear you coming. He hear you cross ze river.'

'Hmm! he murmured.

She noted his tone, his look, asked, 'Vot is?'

'I saw him . . . with young Savitra.' When she blinked, he asked, 'What's she doing here?'

She caught his free hand. 'Come . . . I gif you smoke-o. I tell you zen.'

'Her family aren't here, are they?'

'No, no. All haf gone. But come . . . sit down. You are sveating and tired.'

Under a mango was a heap of packed dunnage and saddlery and a fire with a steaming billy. She saw him seated on his swag, back to the tree-trunk, then, while making the tea, told him what had happened to encumber them with Savitra. Not that she spoke of the girl as encumbrance. Jeremy showed his feeling about it by his set expression, causing her to say, 'Please, Jeremy . . . don't be *koolah*. It is ver' loffly zing. It is Nature. You cannot stop it.'

She told him the others had left for the Centre on the morning of the second day after Christmas Day. On Boxing Day, Prindy had sneaked off, to go down the river, alone, to see what horses were available at the Russian Settlement. The tale he told her was that, at the Settlement, he had been lured by a pair of *biaiuk* wrens to a mangun plum, where he had found Savitra. *Charada*, of course. He hadn't told Savitra about his staying behind. Right to the last minute she had supposed that he would be going with her and the party. When, according to plan, Rifkah had announced that she and Prindy would be waiting to travel in the utility, Savitra promptly had declared she would wait, too. In the argument that ensued to try to get her away, in which the other Barbus had supported Rifkah, it came out that the young couple had become husband and wife in fact. That settled it. Barbu immediately changed his tune, declaring that under no circumstances must those blessed by Kamadeva be separated in the flower of their love. Only bad luck could result. Either Savitra stayed with her lover or he came. Rifkah said, 'Ze old man become all vork up, dancing about and singing out, to mek me fright' Sergeant Stunke vill find out. So, moost I say, all right, she can stay.'

Jeremy still looked disapproving. She begged him, 'Pliss, Mullaka . . . it is true loff . . . it is magic. Zey are like leetle bird . . . so 'appy, and singing togezher. Zey are ver' shy about it. I haf to sneak up listen to him playing on his flute to her . . . Indian loff music . . . and sometime singing his rown song . . . "*My sveet'eart haf titty like mangun plum . . . kumara like hot honey*" . . . so beautiful, it mek me, for first time in my life, vont loff. Pliss don't be *koolah* vit' zem.'

'I'm not *koolah*. I'm thinking of the complications.'

'Is vot?'

'You're going back to the Mission with them?'

'Yes.'

'I gave Glascock an assurance I'd send the Barbu women away.'

'I vill take care of zat.'

'What about his Aboriginal status? You want him to go bush with you to help you?'

'Yes.'

'Well, this will deeply complicate the Initiation he'll have to go through to have proper blackfellow status.'

'You tell me yourself nobody stop Aboriginal children from any kind of play, only might-be zey hurt zemself.'

'Children, yes. But these aren't children any more. They're sexually mature . . . otherwise they wouldn't behave like you're saying. It's not just play. The blacks judge puberty as the time for strict sexual restraint . . . in a man . . . and for proper behaviour in a woman, because it's then she's allotted to a husband. A boy becomes a man then. He's taught, most harshly, to withstand the temptation of women. He can't have a wife till he's fully spiritually developed as a man . . . and then it isn't one of his own choosing. See what I mean?'

'Yes . . . but, maybe zis pass soon . . . like mating of leetle bird. Pliss not to spoil it, Jeremy. I zink true loff moost belong to children. Nuzzing greedy . . . nuzzing cruel. Pliss to gammon you not see . . . like I do.'

Jeremy sighed. 'Okay. Maybe you're right and puberty's the proper time for love.' He sipped his tea. He mused about it: 'Romeo and Juliet were only kids . . . and theirs is the great classic of love. Maybe if sex were got over before it can become a neurosis . . . maybe . . . maybe that would stop the sickness of the world.'

Sound of horses – hobbled horses in their clumsy driven gallop. They burst through the grass and scrub, half a dozen of them. On their tail was an unhobbled beast, ridden by those two slight figures, the golden-brown and chocolate, but clothed now. Their saddle was a sack. The chocolate one rode behind, with slim arms about the other's waist, lizard-like sharp head peeping bright-eyed round his arm. By comparison, Prindy's usually alert gaze was blank, like a little boy dreaming. Savitra, child of a week ago, had become a shrewd-eyed woman. Prindy responded gravely to Jeremy's smile of greeting, and as gravely answered him, in a man's voice, 'Goodday, Grandfather.'

The children slid off their horse, to separate at once, to take the tea and cake Rifkah gave them and sit separately eating it each as if the other didn't now exist.

While they ate, Jeremy, as matter of fact as everyday, told how they would head straight across country eastward of the river, to make camp in the

Limestone. They would need shelter tonight for sure, by the look of the northern sky.

Within half an hour they set out. The bridal pair found each other again, got back on their sack saddle and took the rear to tail the packs. Jeremy and Rifkah rode ahead, going back over Jeremy's tracks. Already there was traffic on the road and the dust rising; so that they had to wait a little to cross without exposing themselves. Then they were on their way, with no road to cross again till they reached the vicinity of Corella Bore.

It was a hot dry ride, with a squadron of marsh flies to make them keep the pace and not prolong their spelling. Round about noon they camped for crib on the only water on the way so far, a bit of a clay-hole in a creek. A great thunder-head was building up over where Catfish Homestead would lie, but with no hint of storming yet; while the air hung dead. Horses and riders ran with sweat. At least it made things harder for the marsh flies, which wanted blood, not salt-water, and a good grip while drawing their portion. Even sun-down brought small relief. Mosquitoes, now that they were in the vicinity of the limestone swamps, took over from the marsh flies. As the Sun went down they crossed the Catfish road. Rain would surely wash out their tracks before many hours. Still, they'd heard a motor vehicle going out there, and it well might be coming back before the storm broke. Prindy dismounted to erase their tracks with his magic brush-tail.

Igulgul rose over Catfish, under the thunderhead, the bottom of which he set on fire. He was at the Full tonight. There would be fireworks for sure when he got aloft and joined his old mate Tchamala in harrying the *Waianga*. The Old One stayed in the clear long enough to light them through the labyrinth of the Limestone and to reunion with the Lily Lagoons horses, which would have picked up their scent and the Mullaka's whistling on the breeze now blowing from the East. They had to dismount at once and unhobble their own horses and get rid of the strangers that had brought them, because their own objected to these. The stallions sent the strangers galloping for home. They saddled up their own horses, and went on to the caves, their way now lit with almost continuous lightning.

Prindy found a cave for them. They made a meal, then tired out, dropped to their swags. Prindy and his bride shared the one swag in a corner. The riot in the East had begun. The wind was roaring from the West to join it. Nearer and nearer come the storm, but without disturbing them, so snug were they. It struck about midnight. No one could sleep through that. They rose and made tea. Then it was over. Igulgul blazed above triumphant with his Mate streaked across the sky as the Milky Way. The air was cool. The frogs were in full Hallelujah. The campers went back to sleep.

In cool bright dawn the butcher birds came to call them. The horses, by Lily Lagoons custom, ought to have been along for pickings too, but were otherwise occupied, as stamping and whinnying somewhere just out of sight of the camp betrayed. Jeremy reckoned that one of the mares must be in season. In that event, he said, they would have to be a bit hard and break up the fun to get them moving: 'A bit of the stockwhip for a start, and then the rough going through the gorge should quiet them down. Elektron'll take charge of things as soon as he knows what we want to do. Despite his age, he's still the

Boss. I think the others regard him as sort of my deputy.'

'Vot vonderful animals horses are,' Rifkah remarked.

'I suppose all things are . . . if you can get to know them.'

Prindy, who had gone to bring in the horses that were to be saddled and packed, came back without any, to report that the mare was a stranger, and no mere brumby, he reckoned, but that chestnut filly won by Knobby Knowles at the very last Race Meeting. They all went to see.

It was the same mare, Knobby's Luck, as poor Knobby had named her before going to his doom. 'Nice bit of horseflesh, too,' said Jeremy. 'Poor old Knobby might have done all he wanted with her.' He cracked his whip to stop the horseplay.

Old Elektron was playing the gallant, prancing about, challenging the other stallions, while the filly showed all the signs of her kind in season, ruffled sweating coat, the nervousness, wild eyes and hard breathing, yet snapping and kicking at the gallant whenever he came too near. The other stallions seemed to be making only a show of accepting the challenge. The rest were watching with interest.

At the crack of the whip the filly kicked up her heels and did a short bolt away. Elecktron arched his neck and shook his great black head and snorted at his master, in a show of challenging him, too. Then he reared, swung after the lady. Jeremy called him. He only flung back an ear. But when Jeremy cracked the whip again, he wheeled to face him. Jeremy approached him, saying, 'You're hurt. Let's have a look at you.' The horses stood.

The stallion's breast and front legs were caked with blood and flies. Examining the wounds, Jeremy remarked, 'You busted in to get her, eh? How many times have I told you not to do that till you've learnt to use wire-cutters?' The horse flicked ears and whickered, as if he understood, thrust his nose out for fondling. Jeremy turned to Rifkah. 'Get the Sulpha and Benz. Co.. He could get a bad infection this time of year.' To the horse he said, 'You old fool, you've messed things up properly this time. About time you acted your age. The brumby bucks over on the coast aren't going to be as nice to you as our own mob, you know. Or would you rather stop here and be king of the castle for Vaiseys . . . or Knowleses . . . till they've got what they want from you, and shoot you like a brumby?' The horse snorted.

Rifkah came back with drugs and dressing. Jeremy looped the whip round Elektron's neck and gave it to Rifkah to hold. Attending the wounds, he said, 'If only the dressing'll last three days. The biggest hazard would be if she bit him on the breast . . . a favourite place . . . but the Benz. Co. might discourage her. She won't have him on for at least three days. But she might lead him a dance through timber that'll tear him.'

Rifkah asked, 'You are going to leave him?'

'He won't leave her till she's finished with him.'

'But you say you can hold till ve get ozzer side.'

'We couldn't take her with us. Nugget'll sure to come looking for her. They'll find shod tracks and know the stallion wasn't a brumby. Even with rain we'll leave some trace. You can't clean up every heap of dung. If they find him round here with her, they shouldn't bother to follow us to the gorge. They'll probably think he's come home from wherever I was supposed to have taken him . . . as stallions often do . . . and probably only too pleased to see her mated with the best blood in the country.' As he varnished the Sulpha-packed wounds with the balsam and the horse winced to the sting, he said, 'Serve you right, you old bugger . . . doing us out of your standing fee . . . and giving a champion to the Knowleses, of all people!'

Knowles's Luck stamped and shrilled with impatience. Finished the dressing, Jeremy said, 'Off you go, you old fool . . . this might be your last chance. I'll come back for you after the Wet . . . all being well.' The horse rubbed his head against him, then turned to the filly, to go prancing with tail high. Jeremy remarked: 'He's still got his faculties about him. He must have picked up her scent on that bit of an easterly we had after sundown . . . at a good seven miles.'

Rifkah giggled: 'Might-be she sing him *Charada*.'

'Might-be. Let's get out of here . . . before someone else gets sung.'

'Who zat somevun else?'

Jeremy glanced at her. 'You never know. You were saying the kids had made you think of love. Suppose Nugget Knowles were to turn up looking for the mare. You said one time you liked him. His missus is away . . . .'

'G'on you!' she cried in a lubra's voice.

V

The trip through the gorge took the best part of two hard days, with a dry night camp spent almost shelterless and sleepless battered by a hot wind ripping through it from the North: the breath of Tchamala, according to Prindy, who told how the Old One had gouged out the gorge following the Boorooloo-loogun Bijnitch, the mica that winked about them like a myriad eyes being his shed skin. Here the rock was quartzite, the result of some vast compression in a fault between the sandstone masses, the first outcropping of the mineralized mass that appeared again at the old-time tin-field near the Lagoons. There was no rain during the trip nor any residual water, so that drinking had to be rationed from the pack-canteens. The only water-hole was at the extreme end, where the climb up to the Plateau had to be made, a secret and sacred place, according to Prindy, through which access could be had directly to the head of the Leopold River far below – but only for Tchinek Men, naturally. It was up that way the Old One had come from directing his Pythons in their Bijnitch. Certainly it was a secret place, hidden amongst a tumble of sandstone and a tangle of banyans that took their substance from it. Prindy went alone to fill the canteens.

They had their midday meal up there. They were about to start the climb to the top of the Plateau, when Savitra, who had been whinging all the way about the heat, asked why they couldn't go down to the river through that hole. When no one answered, she screeched at Prindy, 'I not going over no more hot rock. You take me down through dat hole.'

He answered mildly, 'Can't do it.'

'Wha's matter can't do it? I you wife. You take me now.'

'Only Tchinek Man can go that way.'

The screech rose: 'Tchinek Man rubbitch!'

The grey eyes widened, became intense as he looked at her. Still she went on, like a beserk lubra, even with arms stiff at sides, fists clenched and outthrust: 'Bloody blackfeller gammon!'

His hand shot out. She gasped. The tears welled, blood burst. That sharp Indian nose was not adapted to take an Aboriginal wife's traditional putting in her place easily. Jeremy checked Rifkah when she would have gone to commiserate the girl. Prindy simply turned away, took the halter rope of his horse to lead the way.

Savitra snuffled and sulked for the rest of the afternoon. However, when in the evening they made camp on the northern edge of the Plateau, with a purple view of what might be taken for the sea, she was ready enough to pop into her lord's swag as usual.

But there was the white shrew as well as the docile Indian and the slave-rebel lubra in the little lady. Hence there was more domestic trouble next day even when the going was lovely compared with what it had been. They descended the escarpment during the morning, made the head of the Leopold by midday. Savitra wanted at once to *bogey* in the big hole they made camp on, despite Prindy's saying he wanted to fish it first, and stripped off. As she moved to dive in, he back-handed her. This time she was smart enough to take it on the cheek and skip out of reach. Letting her go, he set about his fishing. Watching him stalking with fish-spear poised and lips moving in incantation, she laughed shrilly. He signed to her for silence, only to get louder derision and an opinion: 'Silly bugger blackfeller!' In a flash he reversed the bamboo spear and sent it flying butt-end, to catch her in the naked belly. She fell with a shriek. She grabbed at the spear as he bounded round to retrieve it. He snatched it from her, raised it to lash her with the flat of it. For a moment she stared at him terrified. Then, rolling over on to hands and knees, bare-bottomed she scuttled away into the scrub, and stayed there till the fishing was over. Jeremy remarked to Rifkah: 'Whatever the blacks are going to think of his having a wife, they won't be able to object to the way he treats her . . . strictly according to the rules.'

Savitra was beside her man to eat the tasty supper Rifkah prepared with the fish: steamed in the camp-oven with onions and canned butter – a Jewish way of cooking, even if the fish was *treife*, catfish. They had to sleep that night under nets again. But, as Rifkah remarked there was something specially cosy about that hum outside, so long as you didn't shove your feet up against the end of the net in your sleep and suffer the bastinado of a thousand stings.

By rights the horses should have been spelled for a couple of days before being pushed further, hard as the going had been of late and the beasts unused to hardship. So said Jeremy. At the same time, he said, there wasn't time to spare for such consideration. By the look of the mountain-range of cloud far away to sea, the rain would set in in earnest within a week, to render the trip of the others to the Mission most uncomfortable and even impossible, if it caught them. They could not go at once, because he needed the help of Prindy (apprentice to Ex-Sigs Sims and assistant to Coast-Watch Radio-Operator Glascock) in rigging his own radio at the base camp he would set up.

Therefore, straight after early breakfast next day, they set out eastward for that point at the foot of the Plateau to which the blacks engaged by Jeremy a week ago should have packed the stores by now. It had been arranged that the spot be marked with a strip of red calico hung in a conspicuous tree, in case Jeremy should not be able to contact the blacks immediately on return. As it was, smoke seen away to eastward, a distance of about twenty miles according to Jeremy's estimate, was well to northward of the Plateau. Probably that marked the location of the blacks. Anyway, they did not head for it, but kept going parallel to the escarpment. Sure enough, in late afternoon there was the red rag fluttering against blue sky high in a dead leichhardt pine that reared above a growth of banyans. Undoubtedly banyans had killed the great tree, because substantial little ones were growing in the interstices of the great bare horizontal branches.

It was a pleasant spot for a camp, with a ferny waterhole fed from a spring above, and with a plentiful supply of easily gotten food, to judge by the evidence of recent blackfellow feasting on banyan figs and flying foxes. The stores were found up in a weather-proof overhang easily reached, neatly packed and apparently intact. Swags were carried up to give the place a house-warming, because Jeremy declared he would make it his home.

The flying foxes arrived at sundown, in a veritable Churchillian Vengeance-on-the-Hun flight, darkening the sky. When Prindy brought a couple down for cooking on the coals, using a mere stick as weapon, Rifkah declared that she'd like to try cooking them in more civilized fashion, deciding that, singed and gutted and dewinged, they might go nicely as a sort of casserole with the figs and butter and seasoning, done in the camp-oven. They did indeed go nicely. As Jeremy said, it was just as well the blacks weren't there, or having tried that dish, there would be no getting rid of them. Instead of giving the usual musical recital after supper, Prindy cut his grandfather a couple of throwing sticks of approved shape from banyan roots, to ensure him easy flying fox felling for the future.

It was good sleeping in the cave, cool because at this season the Sun's track was South of the wall of rock, and without mosquitoes. Bats popped in to take a look at them. A mopoke stationed himself in the pine tree, dead white in the moonlight, to call the watch. A python had been here at some fairly recent time, as Prindy pointed out. Twice in the night Savitra woke squealing and clinging to her man with the illusion that the creature was come back. As if the wife of a Tchinek Man should need to fear snakes! Or might she not fear them all the more?

The radio rigging began straight after early breakfast next morning. The dead leichhardt made a perfect mast. Prindy shinned to within ten feet of the towering top of it to fix block and halyard for hauling the aerial aloft. Then he went up the escarpment, with a roll of wire, pliers, insulators, and made the fixture up on top in a stout ghost gum near the edge. Then the business of getting the right tension for aerial and lead-in. While this last was going on, Rifkah suggested fixing the True Commonwealth Flag to the halyard. It was acted on when they ran the aerial up for the last time. There on the breeze floated the flag so naturally, like a patch of the sky itself in which stars were shining in daylight, as scarcely to be noticeable – so unlike John Bull's garish Waistcoat, which might well suit a Royal Palace or a Barrack Square, or Uncle Sam's Stars and Bars that look like the trappings of a circus, or Joe Stalin's semi-European adoption of the bilious phallic symbol of Islam, or most of the other over-spectacular others – so naturally part of the land as to put them in no mood for ceremonial, but simply to look up at it and say it looked good.

Next to get the radio working. For power they had dry batteries, a whole case of various kinds having been bought from McDodds on pretence of taking them for use down in the Centre. After some fiddling, they were getting almost as good reception from ABC and BBC as at Lily Lagoons, and far better from Radio Saigon, which last already had proved itself more trustworthy in reporting than the others, since having only victories to announce, not defeats. They tuned in to hear the ABC admit what Saigon had announced three weeks before, namely that all Borneo was in the hands of the Japanese and the natives thereof accepting their new masters no less amicably than they had the even more alien British and Dutch. Jeremy remarked sardonically on that bit of news: 'It was Royal Dutch Shell, and what appeared to be an entirely different concern, the Shell Oil Company of Britain, that owned the oil-wells formerly. I wonder will it now be Imperial Japanese Shell? For men may come, and men may go . . . but Shell goes on for ever!'

They had the job done by noon. Still Jeremy would brook no respite. The cloud mountains were perceptibly nearer. They must press on to the sea, he said, wasting not one hour. After a bit of dinner they saddled up again and headed North.

Still without meeting blacks, they reached the maritime region in exactly forty-eight hours, that is with two night-camps and one full day of travel from dawn till dark. Jeremy insisted that they must think in terms of hours, with that cloud mountain looking nearer, darker, every time they raised eyes to it from the immediate view. Prindy took them to water he knew from his aerial jauntings, and finally to the exact spot in the maritime jungle from which access through the mangroves could be had to the bit of more or less permanently dry land, really an island itself, mostly used by natives as landing in their voyaging to an from the Leopolds. He had been here before and evidently knew the passages through the islands well, so that he was able to make light of Jeremy's doubts about their making the Mission before the certain storm. There was no sense in Jeremy's going any further with them. The passage through the mangroves, of indeterminate distance so did it wind about, was by way of a ridge of sorts built up by opposing tide streams, and mostly under water. As it was they had to wait for the tide to fall. Although used from time immemorial, nothing more had been done to facilitate passage than to break off the branches of the mangroves that would have closed it. Anyway, for feet that had known it from infancy, the tangle of roots, the holes, the slimes, would have meant slight inconvenience. So long had it been trodden by such feet that in bigger roots, hard almost as iron as the root of the mangrove can be, deep dents were worn where these had been used as steps across the more oozy stretches. Jeremy, taking a look at it and trying to reckon how long it would be before the three could negotiate it, declared that he would wait for at least twenty-four hours, in case they were forced back.

While waiting on the tide, Prindy and Rifkah and Savitra prepared themselves for the rest of their journey. They stripped to the minimum of clothing. Rifkah to shorts and shift, the youngsters to mere nagas, promptly having to lard themselves with citronella cream because of the onslaught of sandflies and mosquitoes. Their other clothes they stowed in gunny-sacks, together with their bushnets and hard rations for a couple of days.

Then it was time to go. Rifkah and Savitra embraced Jeremy. Prindy took his hand in manly style, easily assuring him that he could look after the females. Not that Jeremy was foolish enough to express doubt about his ability, saying merely he left it to him. Still, perhaps his insistence to the last on worrying about the storm was hardly discreet addressed to one of Tchamala's men, even if finally so mildly expressed: 'Anyway, you've got plenty of islands to lay up in if the storm beats you to it.' The answer was worthy of a Tchinek Man, even one with grey eyes. The eyes met the other grey ones with complete self-assurance.

Prindy led the way, with Savitra as close to his heels as she could keep, often with a hold on him, as often having to be helped out of difficulties by Rifkah at the rear. Savitra was the first to be coloured blue-grey from toe to tip. They all had their spills, tripping over hidden roots, sliding into waist-deep slimes, floundering into murky deeps. Savitra whimpered and swore a bit. The others only laughed, when they had breath for it. Often they had to spell to get their breath, with a haze of blood-suckers about them whining for a sip. It was then they could hear the myriad sounds of the swamp: those mysterious clickings and clackings, supposed to be signals between the spirits that haunt such places, the trilling of the mangrove robin, the carolling of blue-black butcher birds calling to their brown voiceless mates, the ceaseless gurgle of moving waters. The pressing wilderness of unrelieved olive-green soon became all the more forbidding for darkening of the sky with the Sun's reaching the cloud-mass and being doused by it, showing that the mass was moving aslant across the sea and would already have reached the coast to westward.

At last a lightening of the gloom ahead. They cried out for joy, slipped and slithered like mad. Trees above the mangroves: only the slight growths of maritime jungle, but in a variety of colour, and some with great bright flowers. Sand under their battered feet. Hermit crabs scuttling, only to roll over and slam tiny doors upon the intruding world. A coucal sped with neck outstretched like a snake and hissing like one, to rise and tangle on awkward wings amongst the thick vegetation. Jungle fowl set up a cackling. But the party were interested in nothing but the glint of the sea ahead. Bursting from the jungle onto the open beach, they dropped their muddy bundles, raced to the water, flung themselves in. First to get off that grey skin which made them all of one breed, and then the greasy bit of clothing, wash it out and fling it ashore, then a happy bit of play in the limpid water, while in its hurry to meet tidal appointment it swept them along the crumbling bank of the beach. Suddenly they found themselves being swept back into the mud of mangroves. They floundered out, to dash dripping up the steep slope of the beach, unaware of their gleaming nakedness – until the blood-suckers scented them, came upon them fairly howling with hunger, when swiping and slapping they raced back to their bundles, and in haste got out the citronella and their damp all-covering clothes.

Only then did they look upon the scene before them: the violet islets across the streaming pewter of the channel, against the sooty wall of the cloud mountain with its dingy white peaks toppling to the flaming violence beneath, the sound of which could be heard like the continuous drumming of an invincible rolling army, brought on gusts of heavy air. They stared for a little while, then turned to go to drink.

The water supply was in a huge turtle carapace set up to catch rain on a rude platform rigged between trees on the edge of the jungle. There were other similar platforms, on which were lashed canoe paddles and rigging and dilly bags and baskets and crab-hooks and other Aboriginal gear. Although there was a fair litter from savage picnicking here – shells of crab and mollusk, bones of turtle, dugong, bird, fish – nothing like the kitchen middens of ages of Aboriginal feasting was to be seen, hence it was probable that in great storms the sea swept over the little islands, which was why the trouble had been taken to make those platforms, why the several canoes were lashed to trees with rope made from beach hybiscus; for people who lived so close to nature would never take trouble to gainsay its whims unless it was not more trouble not to do so, as say, in having to spend a year making another dugout canoe.

While the women got firewood and rigged the two nets, Prindy chose the canoe, one into which a mast could be stepped. Then he stepped the mast, to which was rigged a crude sail made of sacking, put in baler and paddles, dragged her to high-water mark for swift launching in the morning.

It got dark quickly with that blackness filling the West. They ate their iron rations by the light of their fire and in a cloud of smoke from a smudge fire. Then into nets, and watching the play of lightning in the sky and on the sea, they were soon asleep. Day dawned darkly, with Igulgul, who should have helped, already gone to join the battle in the sky. First-light served only to make the sea to northward and westward a black mirror shattered anon by reflected lightning. Now the rumble of the storm was somewhat muted by change of wind, which was running towards it; sure sign, according to some, of imminent advance of weather against it. Rifkah, eyeing the threatening signs, mentioned the theory. Prindy dismissed it shortly, saying, 'Him all right.' He was more interested in the tide, which was behaving quite contrarily to what might be expected from last night's set; that is, it was flooding instead of ebbing and flowing from northwest instead of southwest. This could only mean that the storm was creating tidal conditions of its own, and hence was of considerable force. Not that he looked troubled in the least – as who should, whose familiars were the Spirits of Wind and Sea?

They stripped again to the skimpiness of yesterday; then with haste to dodge the whining horde, they stowed their other clothes and shoved off. Less a launching was it to begin with than a flight – and then a consignment of themselves to inevitability, judging by their attitudes. In fact there was nothing much to do but just sit and stare. Each had a paddle, but not in hand. Prindy, who might use his for steering, had it gripped between his knees as he sat crouched in the wedge of the stern holding the sheet of bark-twist attached to the leg-of-mutton sail. The others sat amidships, back to back against the rude thwart, part of the substance of the vessel itself, burnt and scraped out of a log, into which the mast was stepped. They sat on the washy bottom, Savitra facing her lord, Rifkah the blue islet ahead. Such craft, the stability of which depends much upon their ballasting, aren't made for sitting up in.

With a bellyful of wind in her sail and the contrary tide to stop her from luffing, the canoe headed straight across the channel, leaving a fine wake that divided the sea astern to make it look like a pearl oyster, bright irridescence to starboard, shimmering dark blood to port, a truly wondrous sight to see when touched with the first hint of rose. Then it was all vermilion. The islet became copper. So swift the changes. And swift the progress now, as the wind swung them off that islet into a crimson channel running between it and another still sleeping violet. White egrets rose in small flocks from mangroves, wheeled and dropped back again to perches, as if only to show how white they were and how black where these brave ones were heading. Below the black was a line of lilac, which would be rain. Against the lilac the many violet isles. Then all was golden, the rain like vibrating harp strings. Then the Sun came up, turned the rain grey, the black to soot, the islands to green-grey.

Through channel after channel they sped, past islet after islet. Dugongs surfaced near them to blow and take a pig-eyed look. Turtles sounded in haste. Cormorants on the tallest of the mangroves ignored them, stretching long necks to watch the weather. The egrets did likewise. That hint was enough. Now look to your own safety.

It was not simply a matter of going to whim of wind and tide. Shrewd handling of sail and paddle, judicious back-tacking, kept them generally heading towards their destination, northeastward.

Thus through the morning. It was near noon. Savitra was whimpering of hunger and thirst and weariness of sitting. Prindy made no response to that, in fact said little more than his one answer to the many demands to know how far the Mission was: 'Close-up.' Occasionally they sang, all three of them, but, mostly Rifkah and Prindy, their old favourites in Yiddish: *Raisins and Almonds, In the Fireplace, This is the Way the Tailor Sews.* It looked as if he intended to keep going till they got there – when suddenly, as they were passing an islet with a stretch of beach and a bit of jungle, he cried, 'Fresh tuttle-egg for omlette!' Pointing with lips to fresh turtle tracks, he swung the craft in. The pull of the tide was evident on the beach, which it was deeply eroding in rushing past. They had to pull the canoe well up for safety.

The turtle had shown consideration for safety, too, going right up to the edge of the jungle to dig her nest. The wind was bellowing through the jungle, stripping it of leaves. It all seemed much worse there than on the sea. Rifkah remarked on the fact while she and Prindy dug for the eggs, anxiety in her voice and face. His answer was that early one which dismissed all argument: 'Him all right.'

Savitra went off to look for water.

They got some sixty eggs, laid only last night, according to Prindy, who sampled several raw. The others waited to eat theirs cooked, a couple of dozen between the three of them. Savitra had found water and made a fire. Prindy sprinkled sand on the coals glowing in the wind, placed the eggs, then covered them up with a heap of sand. The cooking took about fifteen minutes. They ate the savoury yokes spread on biscuits. The rest of the eggs, packing conveniently in their soft tough shells, they stowed in the bow of the canoe. The casual stowing was surely indicative of Prindy's continued assurance. Anyway, they must have been near their journey's end, since his answer to their questioning him now about the distance to go was changed to a jerk of the lips that would mean it was practically to be seen – as a blackfellow sees things, by what is associated with them, landmarks in the case of places. There was no telling when they would get there by lip-pointing reference to the position of the Sun, because it was now obliterated by the black crepe flying high across the western sky.

The tide was pulling harder than ever when they shoved off again, so that all had to paddle with might to get clear of its sucking into the tumbling sand. They nearly went over when Prindy set the sail by the simple means of unfurling it off the mast. Thereafter, the vessel heeled so that they had to hang out to windward, and Rifkah kept busy with the baler. The water boiled behind them, but ahead looked like black flesh purpled and goosed with cold. The wind that drove them was still the hot wind from the mainland.

They rounded the island of the turtle to have revealed to them their first unobstructed view of open sea to northward since entering the island group, and hence full view of the monster advancing upon them, now so close that the waters could be seen boiling beneath it. The tide flowing from it seemed, as they saw it through a passage, to be pouring in a black stream downhill. As if maddened by the sight, the wind screamed through their little rigging, snatched the sheet from Prindy's hand, sent it whipping with the flimsy sail. The tide seized the craft, whirled it. The sail was torn off from the top, to fall trailing, while the canoe ran with the tide as if over rapids. Prindy tried to steer. They were heading for the mangroves of another islet, which themselves, almost totally submerged, were heaving like a dark green sea. There was no going now but where the tide listed. They came almost within touch of the tossing tangle of trees, which surely must have drowned them were they engulfed there, when the tide swung them to race along beside it, stared at by pop-eyed gobies up from the mud to see what was going on. The canoe was half full of water. Prindy leapt to grab the bailer from Rifkah's slower hands, himself bailed furiously, floating turtle eggs and all.

HISSSSSSS . . . CRACK!

The air was ripped. The sea ran fire. The wind fell dead. Strange ear-ringing silence. Then a vibrant humming that in a moment became a mighty roar. What looked like a monstrous gaping mouth was bearing down on them, its top lip a great curl of blackest cloud, the boiling sea its gnashing teeth, its throat a grey void from which icy breath soon smote them. And then an icy wave of rain – with great combers of the sea. The canoe rolled over, spilling its crew, scooping them up again as it rose with the pull of mast and sail, hung like that for a little, shoving them along as they scrabbled for grips on the gripless gunnel, then as a surge roared over and tore out the mast, righted itself, to wallow awash. Prindy scrambled in first, using care not to roll her again, then helped the others, first his lissom bride, and then Rifkah, who had such difficulty, what with the surges, that the buttons were torn from her shorts, which were dragged down to hobble her. Inside the heaving vessel there could be no use for hands except to cling for dear life to the one hold, the thwart. So they clung, while they coughed water, goggling at each other like gobies. The canoe turned with her natural streamlining to ride the breakers, buried her bow in them, giving her crew respite from the icy rain under fleecy blankets of warm water.

They were bumping on bottom. A crumbling wall of sand loomed up beside them. The bow caught. A wave flung them sideways up a beach. The canoe was being sucked back again, when Prindy leapt out, grabbing at Savitra. Another wave struck the craft, sent it sliding on its side, sucked it back. Rifkah still clinging to the thwart, goggling, saw the beach vanish, was back in grey chaos, alone – alone.

No – not alone. A great grey eye on a black stick popped up to stare into the wide hazel eyes – an eye on a stick that was like the scabbard of a sword and that cut the water like a sword – and vanished, with the hint of a black mass under the seething water.

Still the chill rain and the feathery blankets of warm breaking sea – but with the wildness abating – more a roll to the waves than wild leaping – less sting in the rain – less plunging of the canoe – but still the grey chaos – and again the eye, caught by that blob of sodden copper-red in the grey, cutting the water at a different angle this time, so perhaps the other eye of the shadow, and as it disappeared this time, a black triangle of fin.

Evidently because gripping the thwart was becoming too much for her, she hooked an arm about it, and tiring of that, hooked the other, and at length, changing from one to the other, worked her shift up over her head, looped it round, with difficulty that nearly had her out of her refuge a couple of times and once looked like drowning her in it, tied it, so as to hang on by one or other elbow.

The grey eye appeared once more, so close as fairly to stare into the soul of the other seer. It went straight down. A hammer-head shark, more renowned for the curiosity that had caused Nature to endow it so monstrously than for savagery.

While the grey silvered – the rain became mist – the sea turned jade.

Still she was alone, alone. She cried to the invisible sky, '*Lieber Gott*!'

Watery Sun in her eyes. She blinked. She sat on bare haunches, still with elbow fastened. The Sun glinted on her wet hair, on the ivory of her breasts. Glimpse of an island, emerald glimpses above the heaving jade. But alone – alone. She cried again to glimpses of blue above, '*Lieber Gott . . . Lieber Gott*!'

The island came close – within quarter of a mile – in glimpses of greenery and snowy sand – then fell away. Her head sank on the thwart. Her shoulders shook to her lonely misery.

A bump. She looked up quickly, gasped, '*Gevalt*!'

Peering at her were blue eyes under a shock of dark hair, above a spray-sparkling wind-parted fuzz of bronzy beard. An oar gripped in a strong brown hairy hand was clamping the submerged canoe to a high-riding dinghy. She hove up out of the wash, freeing her arm. Both vessels rose on a wave, looked like being wrenched apart. The hairy hand let go the oar, and with another grabbed at her, caught her under the armpits. The vessels bumped again, the gunnel of the dinghy to force that of the canoe down. She grabbed his shoulders as the canoe went under. He drew back to balance the tipping dinghy, heaved mightily, dragged her in, slopping and floundering, with half a wave. She fell on her knees between his hairy shanks, seized him round the waist, pressed the tangled wet copper of her head into his singlet clad belly, sobbing wildly. He placed hands on the trembling slender shoulders, crying against whip of wind and slap of sea, 'Easy now, easy . . . you're all right now.' The blue eyes rolled at the sight of the spreading perfection of the ivory back to the cleft of buttocks. Catching his breath he released her, to grab the trailing oars.

The dinghy rose high on a comber. The copper head came back, with face lifting to his. A glimpse of hazel eyes, parted red lips, ivory breasts brown-tipped. Again the blue eyes rolled. He tried to look away. But she rose, clasping him high, crying, 'Oh, Stephen!' and buried her mouth in the beard. Groaning, he let go the oars, flung arms about her, giving her his lips, all of himself.

A broaching wave flung them apart. He grabbed oars again, dipped, pulled, eyes on the sea. She sank back to haunches, arms round his calves. Having righted the boat, he looked back, eyes ashine – but in a moment to assume an expression of agony at the wondrous sight, to turn from it, bawling hoarsely at the sea, 'Let go of me!'

But she only let go his legs to put arms back about his hips and force herself in further to prevent him from forcing her away, pressing her bosom against the obvious bulge in his pants.

He fairly screamed, 'I want to turn my back on you!'

She drew herself closer screaming back, 'I loff you, Stephen!'

Still with head averted, he gasped, 'For God's sake!'

'For Gott sake I loff you!'

He strained on the oars. 'Best get you ashore . . . .'

She looked under his arm. 'Vere ve are?'

Pulling till his sinews cracked, he panted, 'North of Mission . . . bit of beach . . . put you ashore.'

So for a minute or so – when suddenly he dropped the oars again, and still without looking, dropped hands to grab at his singlet above her hands and haul it up, hauled it up over his head, exposing his hairy torso, but with any but urge to share her nakedness – dropping the garment to her without looking, crying, 'Here . . . cover yourself!'

She dropped back to haunches. Instantly he closed his thighs. She used the singlet to dry her hair. He glanced – then away with rolling eyes. A moment of fighting with the oars, then he roared above sea and wind, 'What happened?' He bent an ear, but not an eye, to hear her short explanation. She finished, saying she thought Prindy and Savitra were safe.

Then, rising to knees again and clutching his waist-band and pressing against the resistant hairy knees, she cried, 'Gott send me to you.'

He would not look, but heaving, answered, 'The blacks thought it was Tchamala.' He paused, added: 'They saw the canoe passing . . . saw your hair . . . knew it was you . . . but said it was Snake Business . . . so wouldn't come out with me in the big boat to get you.' He glanced.

She smiled. 'Might-be Tchamala is Gott.'

He swung away flaming. She cried. 'I haf offend' you?'

'No, no!' he shouted. 'No . . . you might be right.' He pulled madly.

'I loff you, Stephen!'

He raised eyes to the sky, howled, 'Oh, God!'

The oars fell from his hands. His arms swept in to embrace her, to draw her in to him, up to his mouth.

A wave broke over them. He released her to grab the oars again, to look wildly round. They were close to shore. The tide was running out now from the badly eroded beach, while still the wind flung the waves high up the glistening slope. A wall had been cut in the beach at the very roots of the casuarinas. He fought to get a wave to run them in. They hit bottom, slewed. He leapt out, hauled her out, shouted at her as another wave came rushing in knee-deep, 'Run!'

She struggled up in the sinking sand to the wall. The wave rushed out. He heeled the boat to empty it, shouted, half-turned to her, 'Stay here, while I go and get you clothes.' Another wave swept in, whirling the empty boat up further. He leapt after it, had to look at her, as she stood facing him, unashamed in her ivory copper-touched loveliness. He goggled at her.

She called, 'Do not leaf me, Stephen.'

His eyes rolled to her feet. The feet moved towards him. He looked up, groaning, 'But clothes . . . .'

'You haf see me no clothes before.' She extended her hand.

'Oh!' it was a croak, as he took the hand. The other hand came round him. He seized her, buried her face again in his beard, bending her backward so that she would have fallen, only he let go her right arm, to lift her from her feet to leap with her to the three-foot wall, drop her on the silky sand above. He was climbing the wall on a casuarina root, when he saw the boat spinning away. He rushed after it, hauled it back, snatched out the anchor, came running to hook it in the roots.

She was sitting on haunches as he leapt up. He stopped dead, staring as if in unbelief. She smiled that smile at him, extending a slender hand. Breathless, he came and took it. His own hand was shaking. She drew him down to her. He clumped awkwardly on his behind beside her. She put a slender arm about him, drew him to her, to her mouth, to her breasts. He panted and slobbered, got to knees. She herself undid his buttons, got under him as he kicked off his pants, took the wildly pulsing rigidity of him in her own hand, and enveloped him with all her being while he bucked and sobbed.

It was too soon over. He lay panting in her ear, 'My darling . . . oh, my darling.'

She stroked his tangled wet hair.

'Did I hurt you, my darling?'

'You cannot hurt me if I loff you.'

'So rough and clumsy . . . I . . . I've never done it . . . before.'

'I have nefer done like ziz . . . in happiness.'

'You are happy?'

'Oy, oy, oy!'

'My Jewish angel . . . my Rebecca at the Well . . . I love you!'

'I loff you, too.'

'I've loved you always . . . since I first saw you at the Mission House in Town . . . and then when I saw you that day . . . on the beacon . . . and always . . . it has seemed like . . . like the Will of God.'

'Not of Tchamala?'

'Might-be they're the same.'

She giggled. Then she kissed his eyes, and said, 'Zat is Jewish blessing.'

'Let me give you my blessing . . . pagan blessing!' He bent and kissed her breasts.

'Oh!' she cried. Then, 'Suck my titty!'

She tousled his head while he did so. He went lower, slobbered over her navel – down to the gleaming copper *mons*. She cried out in delight, seized his renewed rigidity, wrapped herself about him, strove with him, kissing and moaning, this time in long ecstasy. They tossed in spasm – fell limp, quivering – to lie cheek to cheek again.

At length he murmured, 'That was more wonderful than anything I could ever dream of.'

'It was *Mechaieh*.'

'What's *Mechaieh*?'

'Ze moost great 'appiness . . . like Paradise.'

He kissed her, sighed, 'My angel from Paradise . . . my darling, oh, my darling darling!'

She slapped her thigh, exclaiming, 'Mosquito in Paradise.'

'You're right,' he said, and reached to slap his own hairy bare behind. Then he rose on his elbow, saying, 'I'd better get along and get those clothes for you. It'll soon be dark . . . and the mozzies . . . . '

She pulled him back on top of her. 'So vot is mozzies to us? Ve vill slap zem on vun anozzer. Ve vill go togezzer ven it is dark. Loff me, Stephen. I am 'ungry for loff.'

'Oh, my darling . . . and how hungry for love am I!'

CHAPTER TWENTY-FOUR

As there is no idyllic state known to Australian Aborigines (except perhaps that in which the Shade languishes in its Dreaming Place awaiting reincarnation) no indigenous legend provides comparison with the idyll established at Leopold Island Mission with the violent onset of Wet Season of 1942. Or perhaps the religious designation of the place now should be eschewed and it be called simply Leopold Island, since religion had fled it with those of its *religieux* compelled to abandon their ministrations, the dispersal of its communicants, and its Prior's having cast his curacy literally to the winds. In fact the very heart of the place as a religious institution, its Chapel, its House of God, was still, because there was no Man of God to keep it beating with faith.

What is a church without a priest?

What is a priest without faith?

However, so idyllic was the situation there during those weeks of rain, rain, rain, with nothing much else to do but love, love, love, that it might be said the place fairly cried out for comparison with some Happy Land of Legend. Yet where, in *all* legendry, was ever such a place of undiminishing love-enchantment? Even Avalon, that *Ocean Island* of mediaeval romance, said to be located, *Not Far This Side of Paradise*, suffered disillusion, bitterly. Did not the *Idyll of a King* begin to fade with Fay Morgana's whispering to her brother Arthur of hanky-panky 'twixt Guenevere his Queen and his beloved Sir Lancelot, and vanish with the tragedy of the Lily Maid, Elaine?

Thus it would seem that *Amour*, for all people of all times, is, as for those who come nearest to being Arcadians, the Australian Aborigines, surely a magical business, but for all practical purposes a nuisance and therefore to be declared Wrong Side and discouraged except in that sphere in which it can do no harm, Legend, Romance.

Certainly, those languishing in Love Idyll on the Ocean Island of Leopold were Wrong Side. Since they were in love and in no apparent danger therefrom, it would not worry them. Still, there was someone to do the worrying for them; at least to begin with. The Nark in Arcady was Brother David. The Reverend Father, holy keeper of the Confessional in which the unanointed must bend their backs to the rod of Penance for Unchastity – boldly bedding down with an unbelieving Jewess in the Presbytery! The pet Acolyte and Novice Priest Prindy shacked up in the Convent with a black minx known to be still a Heathen Hindu, for all the Blessings the Church had laid upon her pretty head – and just as bad, by Aboriginal Observance, the censer-swinging sinner's tribal sister!

Merely Wrong Side Bijnitch? Surely worse than that. Hadn't His Reverence, when properly entitled to be called so, often likened Old Tchamala to Old Lucifer? Eh, look out! *In nomine Patris, et Filii, et Spirutus Sancti . . . Amen*!

Exactly how Brother David was affected was beyond knowing from his behaviour, beyond guessing, indeed, so odd was it. Anyway, those he would have embarrassed with his muddled disapproval were too far gone in rapture with each other to bother about him and, despite the lengths he went to, dismissed him with chuckles and shrugs.

Naturally, Stephen Glascock bore the brunt of it. David, from primary hesitancy in charging his former Father Confessor with sinfulness, soon became a righteous pest. Obviously, Glascock did not want to shake the poor fellow's faith by defending his own disavowal too stoutly. He excused himself as being too weak to maintain his vocation. His own happiness in weakness should have given the lie direct to that. But the effect of his kindness in the matter was only to rouse David to a sense of responsibility for the morality and religious fidelity of the community. He took over the pulpit of the Chapel himself, when the priest himself failed to turn up the first Sunday. In fact Glascock hadn't been into the place since that night he came home with his naked bride. He raised no objection when he heard from Prindy what had happened. After all, rations for the blacks were issued after the general Sunday service; and it was David's job to conduct the hand-out. David wore his acolyte's outfit to officiate. He tried to get Prindy to wear his, too, and to dançe attendance on him. However, Prindy would do no more than play the organ for him and sing with Savitra the hymns dictated. Most of the service was taken up with David's ranting against sin in much the same manner as his former pastor, the Reverend Mr Tasker would have done. In fact, David may have reverted towards Protestantism somewhat through Stephen Glascock's telling him, in answer to his insistent questioning about his lapse from Chastity, that perhaps the Protestants were right in rejecting sacerdotal celibacy, that as he saw it now, one did not have to repress natural desires to be chaste. Anyway, the following Sunday David put on the full priestly regalia, and even tried to bully Prindy and Savitra into taking Communion at his hands. When Glascock heard of this, he said nothing to David, but quietly went to the Chapel and locked away the vestments and such other of the furnishings the unauthorized handling of which might be considered sacrilegious.

Glascock found it no easy matter to explain this matter even to himself. While declaring, at least to Rifkah, complete disrespect now for the Church, here he was concerned to prevent what amounted to a good joke on what he called its Hocus-pocus. In fact, he joked to Rifkah about it, saying that it showed how mad Catholicism was when its trappings had the same sanctity as the magically invested things blackfellows hid in hollow logs, while the custodians of these objects must hold a certificate of competency issued by a properly constituted institution of learning – in fact how mad all Christendom was, even that part of it which didn't believe in trappings and diplomas, but leapt about like lunatics when, as they put it, *The Spirit Moved Them*. For her part she didn't see it as a joke, but rather showed evidence of being glad he could still show some degree of respect for what he wanted only to mock at now. Indeed, by the way she talked, it would seem she would have been pleased even to see him continue with his sacerdotal duties; going to show how little she understood them, as he himself remarked.

He couldn't talk like that to David, when that righteous one descended on him in high indignation over being deprived of what probably the blackfellow in him suggested was now his by right of cult-succession. Glascock had to say that he was afraid the Church authorities might make trouble over use of property they might even go to court to prove was theirs. Then he talked of the austerity of the form of worship of the Early Christians, how it had been superseded by elaborate ritual actually adapted from the pagan polytheism of Ancient Rome. David's lay preaching, he said, would bring him no less credit in Heaven than all the ceremonial of an ordained priest, and perhaps even more. The matter of celibacy came up again. Evidently the fornication that was going on around him was upsetting David. He spoke of getting himself a wife, but of the difficulty of finding a suitable one now that only black girls were available. Glascock went so far to appease him as to suggest that he would do no wrong in a tribal way by going over to the mainland and getting a girl he was entitled to, and offered him use of a dinghy and a bride-price in stores to facilitate matters.

With the state of the weather, it was small wonder David chose his own alternative. A couple of days after that talk with him he still called His Reverence, he came to him again, with a proposal that left the reverend gentleman speechless for a while. It was that he, David, marry Rifkah, seeing that His Reverence was prevented from doing so by reason of his vows, and also because David actually had proposed marriage to her first. It could be made quite regular with a proper ceremony. But that wouldn't mean David would claim exclusive right to her. With Father's new attitude to Chastity, a bit of *tchinekin* on his part could be winked at. Glascock nearly choked over it, but got out of it gently enough by saying that he intended to resign his priesthood and marry the girl himself, and sharing women wasn't whiteman's way. He urged David more strongly to get himself a black girl. Still the weather was against it.

David did the next best thing. He approached Prindy on the same terms as he had His Reverence, although much more forthrightly. He told Prindy that by fornicating with Savitra, not only was he committing a Mortal Sin as a Catholic, but outraging Tribal Law. He himself, who stood in tribal relationship to Savitra as *cudjin*, had some right to her. He could simply take her, but being a Good Christian was bound to marry her with the Blessing of the Church. He would get Father to marry them. If Prindy came *tchinekin* now and then, he wouldn't mind. A bit of Wrong Side Bijnitch in the blackfellow way was nothing like this wanton wickedness.

How Prindy took it at the start was as difficult to judge as any state of the odd boy's mind. He simply stared with those grey eyes into the almond eyes before him. He didn't have to give the answer. Savitra did so, when poor unwitting David turned those Oriental eyes amorously upon her and reached to touch her as his. She shrilled, 'You bloody black-Japanee bastard . . . you try puggin me, I cut you cock off!' A carving knife was handy. She snatched it up. David fled. The pair fell into each other's arms to giggle over it for hours afterwards.

No one saw anything of David for several days. Then suddenly the weather cleared, as it was likely to do for a matter of hours or days now and then. He came to the Presbytery again, somewhat surly this time, and told Glascock he would have the boat and things he'd offered. Glascock agreed readily, only too glad to get rid of him to waste time asking his intentions. David didn't confide. In fact, when seen off at the beach by both pairs of lovers, he didn't even turn to wave to them.

Glascock sighed: 'Good riddance. He's always been a damn nuisance. I hope he goes back to the Proddies . . . whatever it is he has to tell them.'

Leaning against him, Rifkah murmured, 'Poor zing . . . so mix-up is he in ever'zing.'

The four took advantage of the situation to go off in the cutter on a prawning expedition. It was the season of *Gadeeia*, the King Prawn.

The wild wet conditions of the Intertropic Frontal System lasted the usual six weeks or so. Then the wind fell, rain turned to mist, sea to jade glass, green and blue. The idyll at the paganized Mission had continued untroubled since David's departure. True, there were spats between the youngsters, but more as a form of self-assertion on Savitra's part than antipathy. Prindy was inclined to neglect her, to go play music on his own or listen to it, or to sit with the grown-ups participating in talk beyond her comprehension. Religion and language were the chief topics of these talks. Glascock obviously was not only in love with a Jewess, but with Jewry. Whatever the urge to his intensive study of Talmud and Torah in the beginning, now he was trying to identify true Judaism with his conception of it as got from the Old Testament of the Christian Bible. While he was quite contemptuous of the Christian Ethic now, he seemed ready to accept almost any Judaistic hocus-pocus, or at least to excuse it as legitimate human groping for truth; whereas he dismissed Gospel as the yammerings of halfwits, worse than the lunacy of Mohammedanism, since that was frank at least in the classification of men and admission of their irremediable weaknesses.

At first Rifkah showed disconcertment over this change in him, until convinced of his assertion that he had been doubtful of Christianity for a very long while. Then quite joyfully she indulged his eagerness to know of the human practice of Judaism, as compared with the academic – the reality of the fast and feasts, of a Jew's homely attitude to the awful Yaweh of the Law. He laughed to tears over the old Jewish joke she told him: that if God lived on earth He'd have all His windows broken. It was so human, he declared. A Jew could be at once so respectful and disrespectful – so different from the constant whining abjection of the Christian in guiltiness, or in hypocrisy. There was the lovely joke of the fact that the disrespect couldn't be expressed in Hebrew, the Holy Tongue, but must be in Yiddish, a language made up for this purpose out of a hotchpotch of languages salted with the inimitable accidence of Hebrew. 'Talking behind God's back, as it were!' he laughed.

Thus while the world was tearing itself to pieces. Occasionally they listened to the news. The Japs were even riding bikes in their easy advance on that last bastion of the Glorious British Empire, Fortress Singapore – as the little fat man who still bossed it called it, shouting across the world from his dug-out deep under London, *No Surrender*!

But Singapore, not so far away as distance was measured in those parts, seemed as remote from the Ocean Island as London. Likewise Canberra, where the Prime Minister in vain stormed-the-barricades to get his Commander home from Sister Street, Alexandria. The Russians, with the help of their frightful winter, were now beating the Germans back, and, so 'twas rumoured, starving, eating their fallen foes just as they had when they had put Napoleon's *Grande Armée* on the run. Not only remote, but unreal, like the convoys of ships that passed within a few miles of the Island, going to and from Port Palmeston, sailing as dream-ships in the hazy sky.

Not, however, that they were lost utterly to grim realities of the madhouse world. Glascock averred that they'd been left alone this long only because the patrol-boat, H.M.A.S. *Melville*, would have been kept away by the hazards to navigation to be expected in bad weather in these tricky waters. She should be paying them a visit any day now, but hardly likely to surprise them, when there was only one safe approach for a vessel of her size, which would bring her into sight a good half-hour before she would drop anchor. Besides, Sub-Lieutenant Pickles never failed to announce himself with a hearty tootling on his siren. The radio could not be used these days except in dire emergency. Nevertheless, everything was ready for a quick get-away by those not supposed to be there. Even the indulgent Pickles could not be expected to turn a Nelson's eye to such a flagrant breach of wartime regulations as would be revealed by being frank with him – especially when his indulgence was largely due to his own infatuation with her who was chief of the delinquents.

At a landing on a creek up in mangroves about half a mile to southward of the Mission Station a canoe waited fully equipped for a passage, if necessary, all the way back to the mainland. If they needed to put to sea, they might do so by way of a back channel out of sight from the main one and even, if navigated shrewdly, from the station itself.

Well, Singapore fell. The doleful tone in which its knell was tolled by Jack the Ripper sounded silly after all the blather of *No Surrender* – or would have, were the futile cost of life in obedience to an idiot command not counted. Following it, was a nasty hint from Storm-the-Barricades that, despite his insistence on having every Australian soldier home, Old Jack was covertly diverting the convoys already on their way, in a last desperate hope of bolstering the tumbling ruins of his Empire by submitting them to slaughter in Burma. Perhaps the first real crack in the Imperial Edifice was this necessity for the Imperial Master to have to try to do a sneak behind the back of a Damned Colonial.

Two days after these historic proclamations, there was H.M.A.S. *Melville* coming into view of the Mission. Rather slow with her siren on this occasion. A blackfellow off the beach was already well on his way to the presbytery to report before its banshee wail sent the white egrets and the black cormorants whirling aloft from the islets – *Whoop-whoop-wheeeeeeeep*!

The planned procedure of the delinquents was put into operation at once. Rifkah ran to change and get her ready bundle, while Glascock got rid of the messenger, saying he would be coming to the beach. She changed into slacks and man's shirt and wide-awake and sandshoes. Ready to run, she clung close in last embrace with the rough and hairy male flesh that had given her her only joy in being woman – while he'd had the same from her female softness to give him fulfilment as a man – and all in the name of Sin, which perhaps is another name for Nature. As she withdrew, he said huskily, 'Don't come back if you don't want to, my darling . . . but I'll be always waiting.' Then she was gone, racing to join the others already out and looking for her.

Whoop-whoop-wheeeeeeep!

They trotted away into the scrub, into the mangroves. The robins and butcher birds gave warning so sweetly that Prindy's grey eyes rolled with pleasure and his mouth so red in the golden skin about it moved as if he were mimicking the melody in breath as he would have in voice before he grew those whiskers. The fiddler crabs gave them the Nazi Salute and bolted to their holes, as no doubt the Nazis would someday.

Whoop-whoop-wheeeeeeep! The sound was subdued in here, cushioned by the dense greenery and the trickling ooze left by the falling tide.

So low was the tide that they had much more difficulty in launching the canoe than anticipated, and while they drifted down to the sea, had to give their first attention to washing off the mud.

Whoop-whoop-wheeeeeeep! The patrol-boat was still a good way off by the sound of her siren, but close enough for her engines to be heard distinctly, an acoustical oddity that might be due to the intricate pattern of land and sea here, not lost to the sharp ears of Prindy, the way he cocked to listen as, paddling at last, they made their winding way out of the mangroves.

The last reach of the creek ran southward, that is parallel with the mangrove-cluttered shore, but with no glimpse of the waters beyond. However, these waters were hidden from view from elsewhere, too. Eastward lay a long island entirely grown with mangroves and jungle. The patrol-boat would be behind that. It was from eastward came the sounds of siren and engine. Ahead of them, sparkling in mid-morning sunlight, was the channel by which they would slip away into the maze. Now they were moving at a spanking pace, with the tide and all three dipping paddles strongly as they sat on wet behinds in the muddy bilge.

They fairly shot out into open water, startling a couple of egrets perched on the last of the mangroves with attention fixed elsewhere – fixed on what those in the canoe had suddenly revealed to them, not plainly for the instant because of the art of camouflage, but once seen, as monstrously visible as the diving hawk must be when too late the victim becomes aware of it. It was a pinnace off the *Melville*, quietly roaring up the back channel from eastward, and barely quarter of a mile away. The paddling hands froze in their strokes. The eyes, grey, hazel, black, popped. In their insignificance of size and camouflage of muddiness, would they be seen against that background of grey and green? Perhaps they might not have been, had not Rifkah left off her muddied hat to dry after the washing. But what would concealment then have availed them, when the hawk was so obviously hunting them? A shout across the water. The egrets swung from seaward to the safety of mangroves elsewhere. The bow-wave of the pinnace was seen to swell, the engine heard to raise its voice. Prindy made a few wild instinctive-seeming dips with his paddle – then sat still. So fast was the pinnace overhauling them that the features of her crew could be recognizedl

The coxswain could be seen red-faced beneath his sailor's cap at the wheel in the cockpit. Standing on deck on the right was another even redder of face, but soldier, not sailor, a sam-browned officer – Sigs Lieut Sims for certain. Even more certain the identity of the one who stood opposite, clad only in shorts and singlet, brown-skinned, almond-eyed as anyone who knew that figure well would know.

The pinnace headed them off, as it were, then swung round to come slowly alongside them, with engine throttled back to a murmur. Sailors fore and aft secured the canoe with boat-hooks.

A long moment of staring, with all faces expressionless, except Brother David's, which wore a smirk. David could not blink and purple like Sims under the captives' stares, but changed his smirk to a frown of righteousness. Then, surprisingly, Sims saluted Rifkah, mumbling, 'How do you do?'

Her answer was cold blink of those lovely eyes, that made him blink harder. But still he strove for gallantry, stepped down from the deck into the well of the vessel, and bent over the gunnel offering his hand to help her aboard. She looked past him at a sailor. He stood back and gruffly told the man to help the lady. She took the sailor's hand readily.

Sims then concentrated on Prindy, nodded to him. Prindy nodded back. Sims asked, 'How you doing, young feller?'

'All right, Sigs,' said Prindy amiably.

Sims said, 'Better hop aboard. We'll take your canoe in tow.' Then when Prindy rose and gave his hand to Savitra, he too gave a hand, saying, 'Is it true this young lady's your wife.' Prindy nodded gravely. When the two were aboard Sims put hands behind their backs to impel them in fatherly sort of fashion towards the cushioned stern, where Rifkah was already seated. Then, as if he were running it, although none of the crew paid any attention to him, he made a show of seeing to the passing of a tow-line to the canoe, and nodded when the coxswain revved up his engine, slipped in the clutch, and swung towards the glimpse of the Mission Beach now to be seen to northward. He then walked aft, halted before Rifkah who made him blink with her stare again, and clearing his throat, said, 'Sorry about this . . . but Boss's orders, y'know.'

Coldly she asked, 'Who is Boss?'

'Colonel Cootes . . . head of Intelligence round here now. You know him, of course.'

When she looked away, in the direction they were heading, he looked, too, and went on to talk, awkwardly, of the war. He spoke as if he expected invasion to be imminent: 'The Japs have command of the seas to North of us!' He waved dramatically.

She might not have heard, her gaze intent now on the roof of the Chapel peeping above the distant casuarinas. His talk fell flat. Still he remained, staring with her. Then suddenly he turned to her again and almost panted, 'I'm afraid I owe you an apology.'

The lovely eyes turned on him, making him blink hard. In the same distant voice she asked, 'Vot are you afraid of?'

He heaved for breath: 'Well . . . I didn't behave so well last time . . . did I. So . . . so I'd like to apologize.'

In the same tone she said, 'It does not matter.'

He looked eager. 'That means I'm forgiven?'

She addressed herself to the distant beach, where a knot of figures could be seen against the casuarinas. No sign of the sea off the beach from here, because the wide low-tide flat intervened. She said, 'It mean only zat anyzing you say does not matter.'

He swallowed hard on that. Still he couldn't accept dismissal. He puffed: 'I want to tell you . . . you know my sister . . . . '

She was watching one of the group in a white shirt detach and head towards the sea. It would be Glascock, the others the blacks. She said, 'I do not know your sister.'

'You know the one who helped us get the movie gear. I thought you could look her up down South. I'll write to her.'

The hazel eyes met his. He became animated again. 'How's the movies, by the way?'

She looked away without answering. He hung for a moment more, then drew a deep breath, turned away. Glascock passed out of sight behind the screen of the point of the islet to starboard, beyond which the silver sliver of sea was widening slowly.

Some minutes. Then they were rounding the point and having the wide expanse of wet tide flat revealed to them, and the jade of deep water, and another knot of people ashore at low-water mark disembarked from another pinnace. Then there was H.M.A.S. *Melville*, lying at anchor. Glascock had reached the knot. Soon it was to be observed that he appeared to be arguing with some of them, the way he was waving an arm about. Also, Prindy was able to name some of the others, in an indrawn whisper: 'Monsignor . . . Mick Cusky . . . Mist' Pickles . . . Cootsey.' There were a couple of common soldiers, too, and some sailors.

The pinnace ran on, ran in, to beach gently beside the other, bow into the shelf of sand that fell away steeply into deep water. A sailor leapt from the bow to hold her head. David also jumped overboard, but to head for Cootes, who was approaching. Cootes looked past David at Sims, calling to him, 'Jolly good show, old man. Take 'em out to the ship.' Ignoring those he referred to, he turned to signal the two soldiers on the beach to go along with them, but swung round suddenly on finding Glascock coming at him.

Glascock demanded harshly, 'Here . . . what's this? Why aren't those people to be allowed ashore?'

The Coot's chubby face jerked with fright. He gabbled, 'Sorry. Father . . . but I can't take any risks with them.'

'I tell you those people were blown ashore here in a storm. I'm not going to see them dragged away like criminals . . . . '

Cootes went red. 'They're my prisoners . . . . '

'Prisoners be damned! You're not a policeman . . . . '

Cootes's voice rose shrilly: 'I told you I'm I-One for this area . . . '

'I don't care if you're I-One-Bloody-Hundred . . . you're not going to treat these people like the Germans treat Jews.'

'These people have defied the official order that all *Bouches Inutiles* be removed . . . . '

Glascock grabbed the neck of Cootes's pretty khaki shirt, dragged him so that he bellowed in his frightened face, 'You dare use that brutal Churchillian expression speaking of that girl who's giving her life to working for the people *you* were supposed to work for? *Yours* is the *Useless Mouth*, you up-jumped bastard!'

Eddy McCusky and Monsignor Maryzic laid hands on Glascock. He shrugged them off, still roaring: 'Lousy little runt!'

The Coot got his wobbling eyes on his soldiers, squeaked at them, 'Men . . . men!

They came leaping to obey. Glascock was too quick for them. He gave the Coot a shove that sent him staggering backwards, over the tide lip, there to lose his balance on the steep soft slope, and fall on his back in the water – *Splash*! All gaped, except the scowling perpetrator. Cootes went right under, to bob up again gasping and flapping wildly and looking scared to death, perhaps thinking he was out of depth, giving no heed to his beautiful cap floating away, but struggling for the shore, only to find that he could kneel on it. His men grabbed him, hauled him to his feet, while he coughed water. Glascock looked past him to Rifkah, to whom he called, 'Do you want to come ashore?'

She shook her head.

The Coot became articulate, bubbling, 'You're . . . under . . . arrest . . . . '

Glascock would have leapt at him again, but for those restraining hands, which held now. He roared, 'You'll be under the water for good!'

Cootes gasped to his soldiers, 'Seize that man . . . .'

Monsignor Maryzic also raised his powerful voice: 'Don't be ridiculous . . . zis man is priest. You haf pipple you vont.'

Cootes squeaked, 'Acts like a priest . . . doesn't he?'

'Silence! I vorn you zat if you exceed your duty you vill pay for it.'

The old Napoleon swelled up. 'I am I-One!'

'You vill be I-Nuzzing if I report you to General Vavell. Now go!'

For a moment the Napoleonic scowl tried to master the natural authority in that square old face under the clerical panama. Then the Coot swung away, to order that the pinnace with the captives be swung in broadside so that he could board her. He had to be bumped up by his soldiers and hauled in by his lieutenant, looking so ridiculous that most of the observers grinned, including Prindy and Savitra. Nevertheless, once aboard he assumed command, ordered the pinnace under way. The Coxswain took the order from his Chief ashore, who winked as he nodded. The engine roared. The screw kicked up sand as she swung away. Glascock jerked free of his captors to wave. Rifkah and the others waved back. Oblivious to those about him, he stood and watched that bright head receding across water instead of coming closer as formerly. He looked as if he expected the miraculous again. It did not happen. A last wave from the deck of the *Melville* – and it was gone. It still did not happen, even though he waited minutes. At last with a sigh that sounded more like a stifled cry and with blue eyes rolling as if refusing to see any other thing except what was burnt into them, he turned, stumbled about as if undecided where to go. Then he saw what was part of the vision, the canoe pulled up high and dry. He went to that, stared into it. After a while he lifted out the bundles, came back with them and gave them to Sub-Lieutenant Pickles, muttering that they would be wanted. Then he wheeled away, went striding homeward across the tide-flat. Homeward?

Monsignor Maryzic was ready waiting, now with a canvas bag in hand. He nodded to Pickles, went striding after, and with long legs soon caught the other up – and kept up with him, even though it was evident his company wasn't wanted and the effort cost him all his breath.

No word was spoken until they were trudging through the soft dry sand above water mark, when the old man puffed, 'Steady for vun minute, Stephen.' Glascock halted, but would not look anywhere but ahead through the casuarinas, even when the arch-priest shook his bag to make liquid sounds and said, 'Some excellent Bourbon giffen me by American admiral.'

Getting his breath, the old priest moved off again, holding the pace down now, and able to talk: 'On voyage I am torture' by sin of uncharity undt t'irst, because I cannot open a bottle for drinking alone. Zerefore I come Doing a Parish, as zey say. You know zat ver' expressive Australianism, I presume?'

The young priest glanced under heavy brows, grunting, 'The word is Perish.'

'Zat is vot I say. Do you know, der Protestants haf vun hymn, *Rescue Der Perish In*? I hear zem singing. I vunder is it der state of der parochial finances or of der parson's cellar zat is vorrying zem.' Anyone who knew Monsignor would guess he was up to his drollery. Glascock ignored it. The old man sighed; 'Vell, I hope you haf cool vater in your vater-bag.'

They reached the presbytery. Glascock saw his unwanted guest into a canvas chair, went off to get water and glasses. He was so long in coming back, that the slatey eyes quizzed him sharply. The blue eyes looked blank, glassy, like one not yet properly conscious from having been stunned, or recovered from grief that had necessitated washing the eyes.

There were two black bottles on the table. Monsignor took hold of one to do the pouring – a stiff one and a thimbleful. The latter he shoved across the table to Glascock, saying, 'You can get drunk ven I am gone. Meanvile, I vont your full intelligence.' He watered his drink sparingly. On the other hand, Glascock soused his modicum as if with contemptuous deliberation. The old man raised his glass: 'Your health, Stephen.' Glascock only grunted in reply. The old man took a long pull, sighed, settled back in his chair.

A brittle silence; till Monsignor asked gently, 'Vell, my son . . . haf you not somezing to say to me?'

The man answered coldly, 'I supposed you wanted to say something to *me*.'

'I haf so . . . but can I initiate mitout appearance of asserting aut'ority of superior?'

'Aren't you here in the role of disapproving superior?'

'First I am here as your friendt.'

'And then?'

'I can zink of nuzzing but our friendtship.'

Glascock swigged his weak liquor. The old man finished his drink, poured another stiff one for himself. When he had taken a pull at it, and fastened the slatey eyes on the glassy blue, he breathed, 'So?'

Glascock almost sneered in reply: 'I assume you've been appraised of my ecclesiastical misconduct by the Very Reverend David?'

The old priest clucked his disapproval, rumbled, 'Vot haf happen' to your charity zat you mock a poor pagan you haf both inspired undt disillusioned?' He sipped, looked up to meet the blue eyes now looking hot with defiance. He said, 'You are behafing like a naughty schoolboy, Stephen.'

Glascock snapped, 'Why not . . . when you come to me as *dominie*?'

'I say I come as friendt.'

'The *dominie*'s dodge . . . *It hurts me as much as you.*'

The old man drank again, sank back, avoiding the hot eyes to stare away to the silvery glimpse of sea beyond the casuarinas. Still staring away, after a moment he asked, 'You intend to marry zis girl?'

That was a blow between the blue eyes, the way they blinked. Glascock's voice was husky as he answered, slowly, 'No.'

Monsignor glanced at him, then away again. 'So I vood suppose. She is goot girl . . . undt goot Jewess vill marry only mit her people.'

Glascock's voice took an edge: 'The reason she won't marry me is because she can't have children . . . because of what those Nazi bastards did to her. She wants to dedicate her life to looking after Aborigines.'

'Der Jewish voman is alvays mutter first. She is der mutter of mutters. Der Mutter of Gott vos Jewess.' Then the slatey eyes bored the blue. 'You vill marry some ozzer voman?'

Again Glascock was taken aback. He swallowed, muttered, 'No.'

'Vy not . . . ven you haf renounce your vow?'

'I . . . love this girl.'

The old man nodded. '*Ja* . . . I cannot see you indulging for lust.' The blue eyes dropped. The rumbling voice went on: 'Vot vill you do now she is tek from you?'

The dark head dropped. Glascock muttered, 'I don't know.'

'You vish to follow?'

'She wouldn't want me to.'

'Vize young voman . . . Jewishly vize.'

The blue eyes rose, hostile again. The slate held them compellingly. The voice rumbled: 'You do not expect me to ignore der very significant fact zat she is Jewish?' The heavy brows above the blue eyes rumpled in a frown. Still the rumble continued: 'Ever since she vos so strangely to come into your life, more undt more haf you lean to Judaism . . . until now I vood call you vot der Jews vood . . . Proselyte of Der Gate . . . vun of der Unchosen who yearn outside . . . you, a Priest of der People!' The last was barked.

Glascock flamed. 'I'm a priest no longer.'

'Vot are you, zen . . . vot blacks call Bloody Nutching?'

Glascock snorted, shot to his feet.

Maryzic looked up into the angry face, to say quite mildly, 'Only am I testing you, my son. Pliss to sit down.'

Glascock breathed hard: 'I'll not submit to hierarchical bullying. I'm finished with the Church.' His voice rose: 'Understand that, Your Right Reverence . . . *I'm finished with the Church*!'

The old man sighed: 'Because of a daughter of Israel . . . . '

Glascock's voice was too sharp: 'No . . . she has nothing to do with it. She didn't like it . . . wanted me to keep my faith. But I see it as a false faith.'

The old man turned to his glass. 'Pliss to explain.'

Glascock was still breathing hard: 'I've always doubted the Dogma.'

'Alvays?'

'From the age of reason.'

The old priest sipped, sighed, ran thick peasant's fingers through white hair. 'Doubt is der Cross all *religieux* bear . . . fait' is our strengt' to bear it.' He now doubled the other's ration of whisky, and pushing the glass towards him, said, 'Pliss to sit, Stephen . . . undt listen to me for fifteen minute. I am not here to discipline . . . nor to preach or plead. All I vont is to test der reality of your renunciation . . . undt also to test der value of mein own fait'. You need not spik. Pliss to sit and mit me drink.'

Reluctantly the young man complied. They drank in silence.

The old priest gazed away again as he spoke: 'Vile ve are sailing here, zinking mooch about you, I recall vot you tell me of your call to der priesthood . . . how you vere so mooch affected by your own fader's brutality undt lechery, his cruelty to your mutter . . . how you are move' to gif solace to suffering pipple . . . der solace only a priest can gif . . . and how der goot Gott grant you der grace to minister to your penitent fader on his death-bed. Of all telling of vocation I haf hear, I know none zat is so pure example of Christian Charity. You haf show zat same charity here in choosing zis poor curacy, because you belief der Aborigines are more in need of ministration, temporal even more zan spiritual, zan any ozzer . . . .'

Glascock cut in: 'I was a boy of thirteen when I received my vocation. I was still a boy when I went to my father's bedside. The fact is that my mother was a weak personality, incapable of dealing with my brute of a father as she should have, if only for her children's sake. As to my father, he was a stupid egoist, actually so insecure that he stayed with my mother for the security she gave him and the means to compensate for his weakness by torturing her . . . and he was so scared of Hell that he believed I, his own son, might be able to get him out of it better than another priest.'

'Poor simple pipple like zat are first responsibility of der priest. Zat solace you brought to your fader, voteffer you zink of it, vos true Christian Charity.' After pausing to drink, the old man went on, again to the distance: 'Let me tell you of my own vocational experience. It should be of special interest to you, because concerning Jews. It vill also explain somezing of mein attitude to Jews, vich lately you haf hinted, ven I haf spik of your preoccupation mit Judaism, as Anti-Semitism.' A little pause. 'I haf tell you before zat zere vos large Jewish community in town vere I grow up . . . .'

Glascock cut in sardonically: 'You mean *outside* that town . . . *Beyond the Pale* . . . in accordance with the Christian Charity of your good Catholic country!'

The old priest was unruffled: '*Ja* . . . *Beyond der Pale*. Der Jews live in *Judische Shtettel* . . . as der Chosen of Gott, vich zey do not consider us poor Christians . . . .'

Again Glascock interrupted: 'There would be no Anti-Semitism but for Semitism, eh?'

'Exactly. But you did not vish at first to spik. Pliss to let me tell my story.'

Glascock swigged his drink. Monsignor went on: 'I also vos t'irteen at time of vocation. A ver' impressionable time in life of boy . . . der moost. To Jews it is year of *Bar Mitzvah*, ven a boy properly become a Jew . . . *Son of Der Covenant*. I presume you know all zis. Vell, it happen in my year t'irteen zere is special festivity in *Shtettel* because of *Bar Mitzvah* of several boys. Jews haf more joy in festivity zan ozzer pipple. I zink it is because zere feasts are truly part of zere 'istory . . . and each is proof of a continuity of existence in vich zey don't qvite belief. Anyvay, a Jewish festival vould alvays irritate der Christians . . . .'

'Christian charity!'

The old man appeared to ignore it. 'Passover, der Feast of Esther, Jewish New Year, undt der rest, vos alvays special time for pulling out Jew's beard, force-feeding him pig-meat, baptizing him in piss. It sound bad . . . but actually in my experience zere vos nefer der terrible brutality of der *Pogrom*. As I see it, der *Pogrom* happen' only ven der Jews lose zere usual vonderful control of zemself in petty persecution, and by hitting back gif excuse for der cruelty nefer too deep down in peasants and petty officials of zose days and place. But zis time I spik of vos vun ven Ivan der Peasant vas feeling too mooch his own ineptitude because zings vere bad in agriculture. Zings vere bad for Jews, too . . . vorse . . . but nuzzing can stop a feast for zem. Vun Jew is in town, too happy because of his *nachat* in his son become *Son of Der Convenant*. Maybe he is a little drunk. Anyvay, zose who set on him kill him, and zen crucify him, upside-down, on a dunny door . . . . ' Glascock groaned aloud. Maryzic commented: 'You have to see zese stupid peasant pipple as zey are . . . ignorant, superstitious . . . .'

'Good sons of the Catholic Church!'

'So zey belief. Der Crucifixion and Jew are effer in der front of zere mind.'

'It was the Romans crucified Christ.'

'Der Testament say, *Der Jews cry out: "Avay mit him, crucify him!"*' The old man added with a sidelong look: 'But you do not credit der New Testament now?'

'How can a rational person believe what is mixed up with the silliness of the Resurrection and Ascension . . . as silly as any primitive Mohammedan's belief that the Prophet's spirit rode to Paradise on a stallion, while his mortal remains are in a golden coffin hanging perpetually between heaven and earth?'

The old priest sighed: 'Rational person . . . primitive person. Vos I not telling you about primitive pipple . . . pipple *not* rational? Let me continue. Zese primitive, irrational, wretched pipple, who med up moost of zat Christian community I grow up in, kill a Jew because he is happy. Did I say more? Vell, zen, let me tell you zat Jews are not super-human. Zey can get vicious, too . . . *Life for life, eye for eye, toot' for toot'*, to quote zem. Because of zis *Bar Mitzvah* festival, zere are in der *Shtettel* some big, strong, not-so-pious Jews. Zese are voodsmen, who vork mit axe undt horse-team. Zey demand revenge, march on der town mit axe undt goad. Der town-pipple are ready vaiting. So vill begin der *pogrom* zat vill at last leaf der *Shtettel* a smoking ruin, men, vomen, children, old volk, torn to pieces . . . because to Jews to be afflicted is to come close to Gott, undt sooch strange holiness drive mad zese ozzers who not yet know Gott but vont to so mooch, until zey are like volves for blutt. But zere is no violence.

Der Parish Priest get between. He spik not to his own pipple, but to der Jews, in Hebrew, telling zem his pipple vere brutal t'rough ignorance and fear and frustration. He quote from Old Testament, saying: "Vill you, in defiance of your teaching, mek convenant mit Death undt mit Hell agreement?" He ask zem on zere charity to depart in peace. Zis I know, because as young priest myself I ask him.'

The old man sipped, sighed: 'I myself am ver' mooch relief to see zose Jews go avay, because I also am infected by zat fever of frustration and hate of vot I cannot understand, vich vos against my training, because my fader was merchant undt vos friendtly to Jews. But it is only relief I feel zen. Der full significance of der power of der priest for goot did not come to me till I see him use it on our own pipple. After zose Jew voodmen go avay, der vorst element of der town start drinking undt soon come to t'ink zey haf been made fool. Zey rouse up der town undt go march on der Shtettel. But zere, vaiting outside der Pale is Fader Haenke. He say: "In name of Lord Jesus Christ you vill not pass. If pass you do, moost you kill me, der Vicar of Christ among you, vich vill mean killing Christ again, and proving to zese Jews zat our Fait' is empty." He make Sign of Cross. Der mob do same, turn and go home. It is zen I see more zan power of vun man for goot, but of der Church. Zat is zat man's power. So did I get my call.'

The old man drank, but with eyes fixed on the other's face, which was hard with unacceptance. Setting down his glass he said, 'You are not so impress' mit mein call as I mit yours.'

Glascock answered stiffly, 'I'm not impressed by the way your Christians acquitted themselves. First it was the intelligent constraint of the Jew that checked their barbarity, which was stopped finally only through superstitious fear.'

Monsignor asked quietly, 'Fear of vot, my son?'

'Of what you've already named . . . the power of the Church.'

'Der name I use is Power of der Church for Good.'

'By bringing up the Crucifixion, making the Sign of the Cross . . . in short, by means of hocus-pocus!' The effort left the young man pale, sweating, breathless.

The old man merely blinked, then asked quietly, 'Do you not know of hocus-pocus in Judaism?'

Glascock growled, 'Judaism is a simple relationship between Man and the unknown quantity called God.'

Monsignor Maryzic pondered it a moment, then with a slight shrug as if dismissing it, said, 'Der ram's horn, or *Shofar*, blown in der synagogue on Day of Atonement is rich in symbolism. It is reminiscent of Gott's reprieve of Isaac, ven his father Abraham vood sacrifice him to prove his fait'. Der bend of der Horn represent der humility of Man before der Almighty. Zere are many notes to be blown, each mit own sacred name undt meaning. Der purpose of der ram's horn is to call on der pipple as der Voice of Gott: *Hear, oh, Israel, remember t'y Gott*! Hocus-pocus if you like. Call der Elevation of der Host in celebration of der Mass hocus-pocus . . . but find me more inspired symbol of vot is basic in religion. Man's need to feel bot' humility before der Infinite and union mit it. Call der Crucifix hocus-pocus . . . but show me vot can mit greater force express Man's Inhumanity to Man, vich is our primary sin and veakness, der fault zat mek dark der bright image in vich der Almighty haf created us.' A pause to drink.

The old priest went on: 'You say Judaism is simple relationship betveen Man undt Gott . . . by vich I infer, from your expressed hostility to der Church, zat it is unemcumber by ecclesiasticism. Vell,let us get back to der synagogue undt der ram's horn. You know, of course, of der *Minyan*, der gazzering of ten male Jews, over der age of t'erteen, Sons of der Covenant, mitout vich no ritualistic religious service can be held? Zat is a congregation far in excess of ecclesiastical requirements of der Church, in vich efen the most holy Sacrament of der Eucharist need only single Celebrant and Communicant. But vy congregation in any fait'? Der answer vos giffen by der Lord Jesus Christ . . . *For vere two or t'ree are gazzer togezzer in My Name, zere I am in midst of zem.* Vich mean, of course, zat few men are able to commune mit der Infinite alone. Hence der Church, der Synagogue, der ceremonial zat you call hocus-pocus. Der difference betveen der Church undt der Synagogue is zat der Church is Catholic, for all Mankind, vile der Synagogue is for vun tribe only, der Jews. Ritual is Art. Appreciation of Art and ability to practise it is giffen only to Man. In religion Art reach its highest form because it is selfless. Der priest is der keeper of zis art . . . the Catholic Priest the moost dedicated, because his curacy is for all his bredren. I repeat to you zat der vast majority of Mankind is simple as savages. Only der Church, adapting itself to Man's need alvays, efen in der name of Gott, slow to change as Man is, but ever changing, can gif Man solace in der agony of his struggle tovards his Divine Destiny . . . can assure him zat Destiny.'

The old priest tossed off his liquor, drew in his long legs. 'I say no more, my son, except to advise you to stay here as Priest of der Pipple, if only because zat is your vun chance of staying at all . . . undt I presume zat you vont to go on mit der verk of zis sveet girl, who maybe haf brought you to der true manhood you moost haf to be truly of der pipple. Zis is not to dishonour celibacy. True priest dare not haf vife and family to distract his loff from its catholic dedication. He dare not lif for sexual indulgence . . . moost alvays regard it as veakness. Marriage is Sacrament . . . so also, *in parvo*, is every sexual act. If you choose to stay, I vood suggest you return to sacerdotal duties, if only to try to discover der beauty of der hocus-pocus undt der visdom behindt it . . . zat is if you haf appreciation of true art in you.' He rose, easily for an old man, probably from long exercise in the obeisances of his calling, as does a dancer or acrobat who has taken life-long pleasure in graceful movement. He moved to depart without ceremony, stepped off the verandah before looking at Glascock, pausing to say, 'If you accept my suggestion, come mit me to der beach . . . undt tek leafe of me as normally. If not, I vill go alone, undt tell zem you are putting zings in order and vill vont zem to come get you later.' He raised a hand, perhaps to bless, or merely to wave farewell. He had to do neither, because Glascock rose and joined him.

They went a few steps together awkwardly. Then the old man linked his arm with the other's. Still, it was in silence they went through the casuarinas.

The pinnace was waiting, now well in with the flowing tide. The blacks were squatting by their humpies, amongst them David, who jumped up when he saw the priests, but did not approach. Then Monsignor Maryzic spoke: 'May I leave David mit you?' When Glascock looked at him, he added: 'He is perfect specimen of der simple man.'

A moment of slate eyes staring into blue. Then Glascock nodded. 'Goot!' exclaimed His Right Reverence. 'I moost gif him my blessing.' He beckoned to David, who came racing, but to follow them like a dog when he came up, so that Monsignor Maryzic had to speak to him over his shoulder. 'You vood like to stay mit Father, David . . . or do you vont to go back to der Protestants as you haf tell me?'

David breathed out heavily: 'Oh . . . I want stay very much, Your Right Reverence, Sir.'

'Goot!' Striding along, the old man murmured to Glascock, 'Be sure zat I vill tek effery care of my daughter in Gott.'

'Thank you,' breathed Glascock.

They reached the pinnace. Sly eyes were watching them, but saw nothing, more than the parting of a young priest with his clerical superior: a handshake, a blessing. A sailor humped the Monsignor aboard dry-shod. Then the vessel started up, swung away. David, beside His Reverence, wept openly.

No sign aboard H.M.A.S. *Melville* of the captive trio – until Monsignor boarded her and for certain demanded freedom of movement for them. Then they were waving: a copper head, a golden head, an inky black one, plain to see in the midday sunshine. Glascock and David waved.

Then the *Melville* was under way, with siren whooping: *Whoop-whoop-wheeeeeeee! . . . Goodbye to Avalon . . . Mummuk, mummuk . . . Goodbye!*

David and His Reverence waved her out of sight – the former frankly grieving, although for what, for what? – the latter's face a blue-eyed mask. As they turned away at last, David asked timidly, 'I get dinner for you, Father? I got him tuttle-hegg for homlette.'

'Thank you, David. But first we'll go to the church and ask a safe voyage for our friends.'

II

H.M.A.S. Melville's voyage to Port Palmeston was eventful only in that it was the first time she had run at full speed for aught but testing or temporary emergency. It was emergency drove her now, the whole way. Certainly emergency was only assumed while the voyage lasted, but proved real enough at the end.

This state of affairs had nothing to do with the captives aboard her. No one would have taken them for any but very special passengers after they'd settled down. In fact the treatment given them was all that Naval Top Brass could have expected. The girls were bunked in the VIP stateroom. Prindy shared the Captain's cabin with the skipper himself and Monsignor Maryzic. No one badgered them officially. Even if this had been permitted by Monsignor and Pickles, the conditions of the trip would have dissuaded the officious ones.

The ideal sailing conditions attending commencement of the voyage lasted only a couple of hours, after which they deteriorated through combination of adverse weather and the fact that the presumed emergency precluded the kind of navigation a good captain would have seen to for the comfort of his passengers. There was no wind, but a downpour of rain such as to be expected anywhere and at any time just now, together with a heavy ground swell rolling from bad weather they must have had away to the North – or could it be to the whole fleets of ships the Japs were sinking? At ordinary speed, the rain would have run off the awnings down the drain-pipes, and the rollers could have been ridden easily with altered course. As it was, the rain was swept into every unbattened corner, along with sheeting spray the bow tore from waves into which often she ploughed deep.

To anyone used to rough sailing it was even good fun to be tearing along like that. Such, of course, were the captives – but certainly not their captors. While the former stayed on the glassed-in bridge with the captain, enjoying it all till ready for their bunks, those land-lubbers, the Coot, Sigs Sims, Mick Cuskey, had been stuffily cabined since it started, puking and groaning in misery. Monsignor was no great sailor, but experienced enough to get out on deck, discretely spew his dinner, and spend the rest of the night in oilskins riding the pitching and yawing with the ship herself. While Pickles had the party on the bridge he told them how sorry he was to be involved in their capture, saying how he had done his best to warn them by making such a fuss with his siren, much to the annoyance of the Coot. He told Rifkah that he would like her to look up his sister when she got down South, and would be writing immediately to prepare the meeting, also that he very much hoped he might see her when he came home on leave.

Pickles also gave Rifkah more information about the emergency that was driving them so hard than he had given to the others. These he had simply told that he had received radio orders to make port as soon as possible, because, as he put it, 'Things look crook.' Cootes had pressed for more, but less than half-heartedly, being already in the grip of *mal de mer*. In any case, probably Pickles would have been niggardly in collaboration with the Coot, since it was evident that he didn't like the man and that already there had been friction between them.

Pickles told Rifkah that things looked really grim as regards the war hereabouts. The message he had received with orders to make full speed to base included news that while they were at Leopold Island this morning an American cargo ship had been attacked by enemy aircraft not a hundred miles to east'ard of them, that the plane probably came from a carrier, a force of which was known to be steaming this way through the Indies, and also that an aircraft, suspected of being Japanese, had flown high over Port Palmeston. Then he proceeded to assuage her alarm by telling her that the Slant-eyed Bastards would never get past our Navy and Air Force. Nevertheless, he spent the night on the bridge.

Day dawned sweet and clear. However, as the swell was running higher than ever as they wested to the region of the greater tides, the call to breakfast and the greasy oniony reek of it awafting from the galley only had the effect of laying lower those already stricken. They did not appear till the ship was slowing down to enter harbour. It was then mid-morning. The long haul was surely a record for that region of leisurely sailing, done in less than twenty-four hours.

Any civilized habitation on those long low shores was hard to spot without special knowledge of the locality. Much difference had been made to the entrance to Port Palmeston lately, but not obviously, in keeping with the circumstances. In fact it had become a fortress. Still, the eastern headland, where most of the fortification was concentrated, looked much the same as when used simply by canoodling couples. A submarine-boom, strung from point to point, blocked entrance except as controlled by those on watch, but might have been taken for a string of flotsam streaming out on a king tide. Hence, anyone who really knew the place, looking through to glimpse the ghostly blur of the Jail above Blue Mud Bay and to see Rainbow Head reared in a mirage to many times its actual height so as to appear to the superstitious very much like the Old One on the look out, should recognize it at once.

Perhaps poor Cootes was still confused from his night of horror. After all, he had come out of this same place only a couple of days ago, and as the bushman he boasted, if not completely familiar with a place he would be returning to, would have done what any bushman worthy of the name would, that is take a look backward, since landmarks have as many aspects as approaches. Still, his silliness could have been due simply to that essentially simply little-boy's way so often in evidence. Anyway, as the vessel swung suddenly to make directly for the boom-gate, from standing just below the bridge, grasping a stanchion as if still he didn't have his sea-legs, first he looked up at the bridge, then climbed up to it. On the bridge were Pickles and a couple of members of his crew, and also the three captives.

Pickles looked at Cootes suspiciously. Cootes asked, 'Why're we going in here?'

Suspicion turned to surprise. 'Why the hell shouldn't we?'

Cootes blinked, asked now with curtness, 'What place is this?'

Pickles' face changed again, to narrow-eyed meanness. 'Thought you knew this country like the back of your 'and?'

The Coot saw his mistake, flushed slightly, but kept his dignity and curtness. 'Not being of the nautical persuasion, I don't know it so well from the sea.'

Pickles blinked on it, but in a moment saw a way to score, looked sly, cast a glance to see if Rifkah might overhear, then put a hand to his mouth to say it softly as he could, 'Naughty-cal persuasion, eh? Sounds like puttin' the 'ard word on a sheilah . . . ahaaaaa!'

How the Coot would have dealt with that, beyond a momentary widening of black eyes in what might be taken for horror of such vulgarity, was not to be discovered, because at the moment, a sailor standing with a signal-lamp in the port wing of the bridge, called, 'Urgent signal, Sir.' Pickles swung to him.

Amongst the innocent-seeming yellow rocks a bright light was winking. All watched it. When the message was spelt out, Pickles himself took the lamp to answer. He then swung away to the engine-room telegraph, which indicated *Slow Ahead*, and jerked it over to read *Full*. Almost instantly the ship leapt into her stride again, causing the unsteady Cootes to stagger close to Pickles, of whom he asked, 'What'd they say?'

Pickles snapped impatiently, 'Who?'

'People ashore.'

'Can't you read? That was given clear.'

'I can't . . . . ' But Cootes corrected himself, to add stiffly: 'I don't read Morse. I leave it to my sigs men.'

'Then more fool you. They probably play you for the mug you are.'

The plump face assumed the Napoleonic scowl. 'I've warned you before, Mr Pickles, that I've a mind to report you for gross insolence.'

Pickles leered now: 'Go right ahead, snoozer . . . and add this to it . . .' with voice rising to a nautical bellow ' . . . get off my bridge!'

He did not bother to watch the dignified if somewhat waddling retirement, but swinging to his chart-table, snatched up the phone from it, and while waiting for an answer, remarked to the others, 'Looks like a Red.' When a voice was heard crackling in the receiver, he asked, 'What's cookin', Sparks?'

The answer could be plainly heard: 'Furpheys flyin' round like seagulls after breakfast, Chief. Nothin' Navy yet . . . but R Tok from Apsley Island started to report large flight unidentified aircraft, then went off air like jammed. Air Force took it up, reckons must be Yanks who went North rekky this mornin' comin' home . . . but I heard the Yanks quite a while back natterin' as they come in to land.'

'Well, see'f you can wake Navy up. Just got a signal from Port War. Reads like a Red Warning to me. They must'a' got it from somewhere.'

They swept through the boom, leaving bow-waves that sent the floats bobbing as if Old Tchamala himself were caught in the net.

Speaking of the Old One (or thinking of him, as Prindy must be by the intense darting of those grey eyes) there was the Jail abeam now. No winking light from there. But do magicians need outward and visible signs for intercommunication? Surely the Pookarakka would know that his *Mekullikulli* was passing by.

The others were concentrated on the scene as more and more of the inner harbour was revealed. Pickles remarked, 'Christ . . . look at that shippin'! Twice as much as when we left. What a sittin' bloody shot, eh? Why the hell don't they disperse more?'

Probably it was fear of Rainbow Reef that was the cause of the shipping congestion. A number of ships even lay moored in couples, evidently to obviate fouling each other's anchorage with the swing of the tide. West of the Reef, where was quite deep water had they known it, there was no ship at all. There as ever beyond the headland was the Delacy place showing up as a wobbly bit of red and white.

Prindy looked as if he would be staring the Jail out of sight. However, as they were coming abeam Shelly Beach, he turned suddenly, to look up into the sky eastward. No one else heard the sound for seconds, above the roar of the ship's engines, and then as likely as not looked only because of the intensity of his staring – to see breaking through the whisps of silver cloud, all silvery themselves in slanting sunshine, looking rather like a great flight of migrating white ibis, which invariably fly high on such excursions. A moment of staring. Then Pickles cried heartily, 'Thank Christ for that! At last we'll have proper air cover.'

Naturally they would be ours, coming from sou'east'ard.

But, as swiftly they swept in to cross harbour and town, what was that odd streaking-down to be seen against the high white wall of cloud above the southern horizon – surely not rain?

Suddenly the answer was given in the most wondrous sight a devotee of Tchamala could hope to see this side of that hole to mystery in the Milky Way. It was as if, in fact, the Old One had been baffled by the submarine-net, as in the Dream Time he had been when they tried to trap him with the Southern Cross, and now was back in the inner harbour venting terrible rage. For the green sea heaved up, spouting sky-high, spouting not only water, but fire, smoke, great chunks of ships, and what by their wild spinning might have been puny men.

WHAM!

The shock-wave keeled the sloop over to port rails, sending her complement sliding, staggering, sprawling, all silent with astonishment.

Then as she righted – *BA-HOOM!*

To port abaft, the country formerly known as the Compound Gully, between the New Hospital and the Garrison, erupted in a cloud of smoke and flame and dust and debris, a scattering of the latter of which almost reached them, whipping the smooth silver of the inflowing tide – as if a giant hand were pelting them.

Then *Bam*! and *Boom*! a mile or two further back – and flecks of white amongst the black and red upward billowing, that surely must be the white-washed iron of the Jail wall. Hadn't the Pookarakka declared he would have the old wall down someday?

Prindy's attention, from what the intent staring suggested went beyond the reality of sight into the magical, was torn back by the harsh clamour of the ship's alarm bells: *Brangarangarangarangarangarangarang*! Crewmen on the bridge were snatching life-jackets and steel helmets from racks. All over there was a racing to action stations. Prindy looked further, to see ahead the awful results of the leviathan's strike at the harbour.

The nearest ship, a large squat merchantman with four gantrymasts and flying the Stars and Stripes, was leaning towards them so that they could almost see down her belching funnel. Nor was it only her funnel that was smoking, but many other parts of her, along with savage licks of flame that were also tonguing the water in which a horde of men struggled like tossed ants. Just ahead of her another smaller vessel was lifting her stern like a duck about to dive, while smoke and fire bubbled from her vanished bow – then she was gone, leaving a water-borne hell of fire on which burning men seemed to be dancing. How many ships in that ill-fated roadstead sinking or ablaze? All, it seemed – all. Nor the shipping alone stricken. A pall of black smoke limned with red dust was rising from the promontory on which the town stood, unseen from here.

Pickles leapt from his alarm button to the telegraph and rang for *Slow*. Then snatching up his loud-hailer he bellowed, 'Pinnaces away . . . two men to each . . . foam extinguishers . . . pick up survivors!'

Survivors? In that Hell where even the sea burnt – from whence came the wailing of the doomed in hideous chorus – *Ohhhhhh . . . ahhhhhh . . . ohhhhhh . . . ohhhhhh . . . ohhhhhhhhhhhhh!*

Slim efficient-looking little guns with a seat for the gunner to ride in and an arched butt for his shoulder were mounted fore and aft. Atop the bridge was a heavy machine-gun on a column. All before had looked of no more account than covered winches and the like, straight-jacketed in canvas as they had been while all was sanity about them; but now in a flash they were unleashed and revealed bristling with the purpose for which this very ship and crew existed, namely, to deal out death to any other fellow spoiling for the reckless game of war. Two men were on the machine-gun, one on the trigger and the big round sights, the other with a coil of cartridges, neat-patterned as a carpet-snake, ready for feeding the spiteful apparatus when the fun began. There were two approaches to the bridge-top, one by steep steel ladder from the front on the starboard side, a short one running up from the rear of the bridge decking. Prindy shinned up the latter to watch the unlimbering of the machine-gun. As the gunner lifted the barrel to the vertical the boy's eyes went aloft with it. Then he saw something beyond, stared a moment, then slid back to the bridge, yelling to Pickles who was seeing off his pinnaces, 'More aeroplane come!'

Pickles followed the direction of the projected lips, snatched up his binoculars.

They were rounding the Garrison point, getting an almost complete view of the inner limits of the harbour. Now that the first vapourous blanket of the strike was lifting, thinned by the rage of the spreading fire of which it was the first suffocating breath, the jetty and adjacent foreshores could be seen, and the as-yet-unsullied sky southeast of the smoke-obliterated town. Three ships were at the jetty, all looking knocked ashew, and one redly ablaze from stem to stern. Yet the shunting engine was puffing along as usual, the only difference being that a man was standing up on the coal-tender with what was evidently a rifle levelled at the sky. But those things would be taken in only at a glance. In the clear space above, not so high above the pleasant greenery of the intervening bush, were to be seen about a dozen aircraft, dark against the wall of cloud, obviously climbing.

Pickles didn't look long. Lowering his glasses he said, 'They're ours. The Air Force 'drome's over there.'

But he had scarcely let the glasses dangle and was turning again to see to his ship, when Prindy cried again, 'Look-see, Mist' Pickle!'

No need of binoculars this time. Amidst those climbing aircraft was a rosy bloom, which an instant later opened wide with spurting black edges, like an hybiscus unfurling in sudden sun, as which it came floating down. Another such blooming! Then the cause was visible in the form of a flight of what seemed vengeful hornets, diving out of the Sun's eye. Pickles raised his loud-hailer again: 'Enemy aircraft attacking from east'ard!' He reached for the telegraph, at the same time turning to the captive passengers and bawling to them, 'Put on life-jackets and get below. I'll put you ashore soon's possible.'

But they were looking at the falling flowers – a rain of them now – and the hornets, seemingly undeterred, were swooping in to take revenge on everyone – on Captain Shane, by the look of it, he who had lorded it over their kind as semi-slaves so long, since spikes of flame were leaping from the locality of his pearling-station along with chunks of things that could have been his shattered grandeur and maybe even bits of the grand old man himself – all lost in smoke and dust, as were railway station and railway yards and approaches to the jetty

– then all obliterated by a fireball that seemed to gather from the four corners of the view and meet at the stricken ships and shunting engine – *WHAM*!

Wide-winged shadows on a boiling sea – and *BRRRRRAAAAT*! like a shower of great stones – and holes gaping in the roof above and through one of them blood pouring as from the cut throat of a bullock. Rents in the deck, too, and shattered windows. Blood was streaming down Pickles' cheek. Rifkah stepped towards him. But he waved her back, roaring, 'Get below . . . the three of you!' He made a menacing move at them as they stared. They grabbed each other and staggered towards the stairway, went down in a bundle, slid on blood, fell and rolled into the concrete drain behind the bulwark that was the base of the bridge.

They stared at what the blood had come from: Eddy McCusky lying flat on the deck amidships. Also staring, from the other side, were the other passengers: the Coot, Sigs Sims, Monsignor Maryzic. Monsignor came from the cover there, approaching Eddy, looked up to see Pickles looking down, wiping his bloody face with a white handkerchief. Reading the slatey eyes, Pickles bawled, 'I'm okay. Just a bit o' glass. He's dead, eh? You better keep under cover, Father . . . till I get you ashore.' Pickles turned to Cootes and Sims. 'You use a machine-gun?' Sims nodded. 'Well get up top here . . . the crew's been killed . . . ladder just be'ind you.' Sims moved slowly, disappeared. Cootes only stared, stunned, perhaps. Pickles raised his voice at him: 'You, too. Feed him ammo. They might be back again.' The Coot lurched after Sims as if an invisible hand had hauled him.

Monsignor Maryzic bent over Eddy, closed his eyes, signed his bloodied brow with the Cross, while his lips moved soundlessly in the engine din and the dying din of war in the background. He was climbing the stairs to the bridge when Pickles looked again, and waved him back, crying, 'Get below and into cover. You'll 'ave plenty to do ashore.' The old man hung there for a moment, then stepped down, went to join the three cowering on the port side.

They were close to the point now round which lay the Mission Landing. But no one was looking that way at the moment. Out of the holocaust to starboard a Yankee destroyer had come bursting, down by the stern so deeply that her greyhound bow was clear of the water, but with all guns cocked aloft and some still blazing at the sky. Also to be seen now was what remained of the jetty and its shipping and its railway – nothing but a heap of ruin from which smoke billowed black as from a funeral pyre and fire leaked to make a lake of Hell.

They rounded the point. There was the Mission Landing intact, and apparently the buildings back of the cliff-top. Another floating landing had been built in the locality, off what was called Residency Beach, a couple of hundred yards further in, beyond a clump of mangroves. Evidently it was now a seaplane base, since a couple of craft, one with the insignia of the Royal Air Force, the other with that of the Netherlands, were riding at buoys. The beach was now crowded with small buildings of military kind.

They swung towards the Mission Landing, slowing down. With the tide at almost full they could run right in. Pickles leant over again, to tell his departing passengers to be ready, and to loud-hail his men to see to their swift disembarkation. He disappeared. The telegraph tingled. The ship boiled the water in reverse. Pickles appeared again, to shout, 'Look after yo'selves. Get into cover. See you later.'

Prindy called back, 'I leave my clarinet in cabin.'

Pickles answered, 'I'll look after it for you, sonny. Go on ... get going.'

They were helped through the rails onto the pontoon.

The telegraph rang again. The iron heels kicked hard astern. Pickles looked over the bridge to wave. But those ashore weren't watching for him, at the moment concentrated on someone else in the act of disembarking, a tubby man in khaki, with a stockinged leg and suede officer's boot already on the pontoon, but too big in the behind to slip through the rails. A dicey position with the ship already on the move. Then the loud-hailer bellowed: 'Stop that man going ashore!' A couple of sailors pounced. It was the Coot who stood goggling in their grasp, still looking like Napoleon, but Napoleon very young and very scared, as that bravo must have looked for at least a moment that day at Waterloo. The hailer blared again: 'Get on that gun with your mate, you yeller bastard!' The sailors shoved Cootes at the vertical steel ladder, left him, to attend their proper duties. Those ashore saw him grasp the ladder, not so much, it seemed, to scale it, as to support him. Then the sloop swung him out of sight as she turned sharply to head for the Yankee destroyer.

But there was Sigs Sims standing bravely by his gun. He waved. They waved. Then they turned and bolted for the cliff-face – for there on the sea again was the shadow of death and the sea behind boiling with its obliterating magic. As they fell into a concavity at the base a shower of splintered rock and earth and torn bushes came down like the first hot flurry of a thunder-storm.

Then the thunder – *CRACK*!

Huddled, they stared out.

The strike had been to the left of them, the seaplane base, the seaplanes, which were now only tarry smoke and flame like the setting Sun.

Whee-whoop! The familiar sound called them.

What had happened to H.M.A.S. *Melville*? Her foremast down, bridge looking like a crushed hat. No Sigs Sims on top. But the gun in the stern was spitting and barking at the sky – and still she was heading for the Yankee and able to yell encouragement – *Whee-whee-whoop . . . Hang on, Brother Swabbers*!

But how hang on now, when only the bow of the destroyer was pointing to Heaven and the Lake of Hell was licking down those who clung to it?

Whee ———— It never finished – because above the crimson lake the very mouth of Hell blazed, with the sloop steaming right into it.

Sight, blinded by the blaze, did not recover till hearing was assaulted by the blast – *WHAM*! Down came another shower of cliff debris. Then it was seen that the blaze had been dowsed by a great pillow of black smoke. They watched the smoke thin out, to become drifting feathers of grey. By then the pontoon was bouncing like a dray behind bolting horses that, white-maned, were leaping up the rocks.

No Yankee warship. But still the *Melville* was there, now looking like a red-backed whale with her bottom up. Dots abobbing on the smoking water beside her would be men – dead men or live men it did not matter, since all would be wearing life-jackets. The watchers drew a single breath, heaved out of hiding, as if impelled together by some futile impulse to help. Fire was leaping up again on the other side of the red hull.

But real help was coming. Quick-eyed Prindy saw, and cried, 'Pinnace come!'

She was coming with a great bow-wave, as mid-morning yesterday years ago she had come to drag them from the felicity of Avalon. As she rounded the now rearing bow of her stricken mother ship, it could be seen that she was already so crowded as not to be able to save another soul – mostly crowded with a pile of dead, it seemed – yet those who stood, together with the coxwain, were bending to supplicating arms, making it look certain that they must capsize her.

'Oh!' the watchers gasped.

For suddenly the sloop heaved her bow up to the perpendicular, sending a great wave that tossed the pinnace high and her able crew overboard, then went down like a sounding whale, dragging everything after her, except the pinnace, which still under way, ported her helm herself and left them to it.

Where to now? She swung in a slow arc, set her course for that wall of fire behind which the mass of destruction lay. Where else for a shipload of deadmen to go?

The watchers gulped. Then suddenly they breathed again: 'Ah!'

Someone was struggling from the heap of dead, getting to feet, a figure in khaki, not Navy whites, stumbling over the inert passengers, making for the cockpit, assuming command.

'Ah!'

The pinnace was swinging from the fire. She was heading this way, zigzagging, as if her skipper were coming back from shore-leave. No – she was veering away to starboard, heading for those sunken pontoons further in and tangled bits of seaplanes floating off them. For there the awkward skipper would have seen people. They could not be seen from here, because of the mangroves, but could be heard shouting. Yes – and there were some in a dinghy rowing out to meet him.

As the pinnace passed so as to give a rear view of the new coxswain, Prindy said, 'That the Coot, I reckon.'

All stared.

The men in the dinghy were lucky the erratic skipper didn't run them down. They jumped aboard, took over from him. Steering a straight course now, the pinnace disappeared behind the mangroves.

Prindy said, 'I go look-see.' Savitra would have followed when he started out, only he turned on her, saying sharply, 'You stay behind.'

Monsignor stirred, as if coming out of a trance, asked, 'What are you going to do, boy?'

'See who come. Might-be Pickle.'

'You're in my charge, remember.'

Starting to run along the track, Prindy flung back over a shoulder, 'I see you Mission House.' In a moment he was out of sight of them behind the mangroves.

He skirted the mangroves, hung in the last of them to reconnoitre. The numerous small buildings appeared all to be deserted, the people of the place all down by the beach attending the stricken ones off the pinnace. To see who these latter were needed much closer approach, which was possible without exposing himself by slipping from shed to shed. This he did, till halted by sound of voices in the very last place. He would have to pass the entrance, and in doing so be seen. There were open canted windows, shoulder-high to him. He peeped through one, started at what he saw, popped back out of sight, but to stand rigid listening. The voices were very familiar – likewise thc faces he had seen.

The Coot was there, sitting sagging in a cane chair, attended by Major Maltravers, Old Malters of happier days, and Denzil Dickey. Prindy hardly would have noticed that though these old acquaintances looked much the same as before, according to the insignia they wore they were greatly changed in status. Denzil was a Major, Old Malters no less than a Major-General. Much less acute hearing than Prindy's easily could have followed their talk.

Malters, of old usually the silent watchful one, was now even voluble, evidently in anger over the prevailing military state of things. Evidently he and Denzil had lately come from Singapore or some such place, aboard one of those flying boats, the destruction of which he was not cursing the enemy for, but those he was calling, 'These impossible local fellahs . . . goddammit!' In that stiff clipped way of his he was saying, 'This complete lack of comprehension of the military situation is going to give the enemy the cheapest victory heah he's so far had anywhereah . . . goddammit, mark my words! Something will have to be done to take command of this rabble . . . from General Staff down . . . and not by this Yankee, MacArthur . . . ridiculous, absurd . . . a defeated man, and a Yankee, goddammit! Must get to Australian GHQ as soon as possible and put a stop to all this. But now I've lost my means of rapid transit, thanks to these damned colonial muddlahs, what am I going to do? It's a certainty amphibious assault will be made heah . . . otherwise why did they spareah the oil-tanks . . . every damned oil-tank intact, when *everything* was just a sittin' shot for 'em! Six ack-ack guns of obsolete type, when Imperial Staff advice, based on Battle of Britain experience, was thirty six . . . . '

Denzil cut in, speaking to Cootes, 'I say, old boy . . . you're wounded, don't y' know?'

Cootes answered feebly, 'No . . . I'm all right.'

'But blood's runnin' down your legs, dear boy. Let's get your jolly old pants off and see what's happened.'

The Coot's voice grew feebler, sounding as if he were about to sob, 'No . . . no . . . it's only . . . haemorrhoids.'

'Ow!'

'Oil is their greatest need at present,' snapped Malters.

Perhaps to justify the strain that had been put upon his bowels, Cootes whimpered, 'It was bad out there.'

'Of course, old boy,' said Denzil soothingly. 'Jolly good show you put up . . . jolly good show, eh, what, Sah?'

'Jolly good show.' agreed Malters. 'If I get my way I'll see you get recognition for it. Only wish I had you with me. For a start you'd be handy as liaison dealing with those bounders at GHQ . . . especially now with this anti-British socialist Government. You were good in the political game, I recall.'

The Coot's voice changed: 'Could you really use me?'

'My bally word . . . but not much hope of that, eh, what?'

'I could work it.'

'But this commando thing of yours they tell me about. Gad, man, you're going to have your work cut out if there's invasion. I'm all for return to the Brisbane Line strategy myself, That's what I'll press for . . . that's what I'll get, goddammit!'

Cootes's voice became a little boy's pleading: 'I could hand over that command, Malters . . . General . . . and I would so love to be with you. I . . . I've had enough action . . . for the time.'

'Fair enough,' snapped Malters. 'We've had our share, too. Staff Corps from now on. Now, if you can get me transport . . . .'

The Coot said eagerly, 'I've got my own MT here. I could get you to my Rear HQ . . . Lily Lagoons, you know . . . facilities for direct contact with GHQ from there . . . and getting you an aircraft . . . two or three days at most . . . .'

'Jolly good show! Consider yourself on my staff as from now . . . Liaison Officer, Full Colonel. Shake on it!'

Prindy took another peep – to look straight into the eyes of Denzil, whose eyes popped. Prindy withdrew in a flash, to go running back along the iron wall. Hurried stamp of feet inside. But the corner was near, and round behind it the road that run up to the town, and beyond the road thick scrub to hide in. He whizzed round the corner – 'Oootch!'

He had run into a mass of white, which on the instant locked him to it. He drew back his head, to see the ruddy face with blue pop-eyes under bushy black brows of Captain Toby. He tried to pull free; but the Captain hung on, booming in that voice which never really needed a megaphone, 'Don't panic . . . everything's under control . . . *my* control.'

They stared at each other. Still keeping his grip, now on the boy's upper arms, Toby tilted his head, said, 'I know you. You're from Leopold Mission. You were one of those *Melville* brought in . . . right?'

Prindy only blinked. The Captain shook him. 'Speak up! I want to know what happened to the sloop.'

Prindy muttered, 'I don' know properly. Mist' Pickle put us lot ashore.'

'He did, eh?'

But there was Denzil, so excited that, without seeming to see Toby, he grabbed Prindy as the other released him, took him in his arms, kissed him on the mouth, withdrawing to gasp, 'Oh, my dear, it's true, then . . . thought I was seeing things!'

'What's this?' demanded the Captain. 'Sod Street, Smyrna?'

Becoming aware of him, Denzil went very red, said stiffly, 'Sah!'

The Captain snapped, 'I know you, too. You're aide to that Pommy General who was throwing his weight about at our Service Dinner last night . . . telling us how to run things . . . when all he's been doing is running since Dunkirk.'

Denzil looked indignant. 'Reahlly, Sah!'

The megaphone boomed: 'I'd've told the pompous Pommy donkey, too, but for presence of junior officers . . so you can tell him for me . . . *Swaddy*!' The last word was uttered with all the contempt it expresses by a sailor for a soldier.

Trembling now with outrage, Denzil declared shrilly, 'Reahlly, Sah . . . I must protest!'

'Protest and be damned to you. I've had a ship sunk and a crew lost through the propeller-footed likes of you.' Toby turned to Prindy, now standing by staring. 'You, boy . . . did that up-jumped schoolteacher, Colonel Cootes, go ashore with you?'

Prindy shook his head then jerked it towards the shed, saying, 'He in there now.' Perhaps it was said with intent to shake the Captain off. He seemed about to add something, but broke off at sight of another white-clad and familiar figure approaching from the road . . . Judge Bickering.

Captain Toby didn't notice. The megaphone bellowed: 'He is, is he? Well, I'm going to have a piece of him . . . because this would never have happened, but for that Schoolmaster Swaddy going over my head to use my ship. That's all this bloody Army consists of, poofters like this one here, schoolteacher prigs, and lawyer pricks . . . .'

The Judge, now just behind, announced himself: 'Present company excepted, I hope, Captain?'

Toby swung on him, scowled when he saw who it was. 'All lawyers are pricks as far as I'm concerned.'

The Judge's tic jumped for the joy of a battle of words. 'As far as you're concerned, Captain. But on the evidence, there are pricks in all walks of life. You surely have pricks in the Navy?'

Captain Toby roared, 'No, Sir, we do not!'

The tic was turned on Prindy and Denzil, as if on opposing counsel to prepare them for a neat one, then back to the square red face that appeared to be about to remove itself with irate abruptness. 'Ah . . . then you still continue that practice of the ancient captains?'

Captain Toby swung back. 'What practice?'

'Of unmanning their crews with the castrating iron, so as to keep them at the galley-oars for life.'

The Captain spluttered with the rage of having been caught. As he swung away again, His Honour added: 'My reading of Naval Law does give me the impression that it hasn't changed in barbarity since the days of Drake . . . but never did I dream that you still cut off your sailors' jocks.'

The megaphone boomed: 'Bah to your legal barratry!' The Captain vanished round the corner.

The Judge chuckled at the others, then put an arm about Prindy's shoulder: 'Well, young man, and how come you're mixed up in this terrible business? I'd have thought you would be amongst those evacuated.'

'Just now we come . . . on *Melville*.'

The Judge stared. 'Good God! But I was told just now she'd been sunk.'

Prindy nodded. 'That after we put ashore.'

'Who's we?'

'Rifkah and Monsignor and Savitra.'

'Monsignor, eh . . . is he all right?'

'Yas.'

'That's good. I suppose he's looking after you, will take you South? I must say Goodbye to him . . . Tell you what . . . I have to go out to the Jail to release the prisoners. Come with me . . . and say Goodbye to that mutual friend of ours, Cock-Eye Bob . . . and we'll drop in on Monsignor on the way back . . . right?'

The grey eyes widened with the nod.

'Right then,' said the Judge. 'Just want to have a look at things down here, while I've still authority.' He dismissed Denzil with a nod. Moving Prindy still with arm about his shoulders, he said, 'Martial Law will be declared at any moment. As head of Civil Law I want to do what I can before that rather inhuman condition is imposed.' He chuckled. 'Not that Civil Law has much dignity left. We were bombed out of court. Everybody bolted, leaving me with the prisoner, who showed me to a drain-pipe they were about to put under the road. We finished the trial together, head to head. He was obviously guilty. I sentenced him to the Rising of the Court.'

They didn't approach the dead and dying too closely. With tic jerking violently at the sight of the terrible maiming wrought by fire and explosive, the Judge drew Prindy away, murmuring, 'Man's inhumanity to man is beyond believing. Come, let's get my car . . . presuming I still have one.'

As they began to climb the steep road leading to the administrative part of the town, the Judge mused: 'What is it in us that can make us do such things? We can't accuse the Japs alone of barbarism . . . because worse things are happening in Europe. And would the Jap be here practising European barbarity, if not forced to adopt it by the brutal Yankee Trader who forced Yokohama in Eighteen whatever it was, and blew his ancient dignity to smithereens . . . for Trade? Perhaps all mankind had some dignity and honour before the Yankee Trader came into being. But the Yankee Trader is something we had to expect in our evolution, it may be. The Republic of Vulgar People . . . the U.S.A. Perhaps it is the Age of Vulgarity . . . in which there is no nobility even in the illusive chivalry of war. I wonder, if the Jap should win, whether he would consider his outraged ancient dignity avenged, and go back to it and set us all the example . . . .'

Prindy interrupted by saying, jerking his lips to the left, 'Light there . . . in ground.'

A strange sight: a luminous streak amongst the rocks and scrub. The Judge stared, then said, 'Ah . . . the famous Silvertails' Funk Hole. I've never seen inside. All mod. cons, they say. Let's take a peep.'

There was no need for over-cautious approach, because of the noise beyond the slit, which was a ventilator with its steel shutter open. Nor had they need to go right up to see in, because the slope of the ground let them look right in from a little distance. It was a big chamber, cut into the rock and cement-walled, entered by a stairway descending from the other side. An incandescent pressure lamp hung from the ceiling. It looked cosy, and at the moment was packed with a goodly number of the local Civil Service elite. A conspicuous one was Fatty Doscas, Clerk of Courts. A bar at the end was being operated by a Police Sergeant. The Judge whispered, 'Amazing! What more convincing proof that we are a Bureaurocracy? The Bureaurocratic Masters guzzling in safety, while the people bleed! God, I wish I could throw a stone in at that light and give the bastards a real good fright. They'd come running like rabbits out of a dynamited burrow.'

They exchanged glances. The Judge asked, 'Could you hit it?' Prindy nodded. 'Good,' said the Judge. 'But wait a bit. Let me get up top to bear witness to the noble exodus. Wait till you see me stop in the square there. Don't be scared when they come up. I am still head of the Law.'

Prindy selected a missile while he waited.

Through the trees he saw the white-clad figures halt in Anzac Square. He threw the stone.

Crash!

A moment of blackness and silence. Then a burst of flame – and pandemonium. He ran to join the Judge.

The result was as His Honour anticipated. The Bureaurocratic Bunnies dashed right into the square, before realizing, at sight of the well-known practical joker, that they'd been had. When they halted, looking foolish, Judge Bickering addressed them dryly: 'Gentlemen . . . there's a war on . . . right here in this town. Thought you'd like to know. Goodday to you.' He held out a hand to Prindy, to go sauntering away to a pall of heavy smoke that had been his background.

The smoke didn't come from the wrecked Government buildings, which were of stone and had soon burnt out. It was in the region of the Post Office. Nothing could be seen till they got close. No Post Office. But these ruins weren't giving off the heavy smoke, because they were of similar material to that of other Government buildings. It came from sheds at the back, causing indistinct figures working amidst the ruins to cough. They approached the figures, climbing over scattered stone and splintered timber. The Judge asked of those delving in the wreckage, 'Is anyone under there?'

One coughed and puffed, 'Whole staff . . . telephone exchange, too.'

'My God!'

One of the men moaned, 'My wife was working on the exchange . . . my wife.'

'Where're the police?'

Sergeant Nullity, wearing only pyjama pants, came out of the smoke, gasping, 'Police here, Judge.'

'Where're the others?'

'Can't say. Came from home. Night duty. Blown out o' bed.'

Prindy had seen something under the wreckage near at hand. He said, 'Somebody there.'

Nullity and the Judge looked, tore away the wreckage. It was a plump figure in male attire, lying face downward, with a scattering of stamped letters about it. No movement. Nullity turned the head. Fay McPhee looked at him with a glazed blue eye. All caught their breath. Nullity raised his voice: 'Hey, Doc . . . here!' Then he murmured, 'She protested hard against evacuation. Must've put on this outfit to beat us.'

Dr McQuegg came up, puffing, reaking of booze, red-eyed, blotchy-faced. He took a look at Fay, said what was obvious, 'She's had it.' He looked at the Judge, adding, with a nod backwards, 'Her mate, Kitty Windeyer, too.'

'No!' breathed the Judge. Then he sighed: 'Poor Kitty. I was speaking to her on the phone only an hour or so ago, while I was in chambers. After putting me through, she told me rumours of a raid were flying about. She came back to the exchange because it was a way to beat the evacuation. Poor Kitty!' His voice shook slightly.

The man digging for his wife howled, 'If the bastards'd only given us proper warning . . . someone will pay for this if my wife's dead . . . oh, Peg . . . oh, Peg!'

The doctor muttered to the Judge, 'Jesus, I could do with a drink!'

The Judge whispered, 'Come along home and I'll give you one . . . presuming I've still got a home.'

It was only up to the next corner. The Judge still did have a home, amidst ruins. The doctor said it was because the Devil looks after His Own. The Judge said it was likely, but that the doctor was the one the Devil had in view just now. He gave him a slug of whisky, had one with him, and gave him the bottle to take away. Then he got out a bottle of brandy, 'To put our old friend on the road,' as he said to Prindy, as he wrapped it in a copy of the *Palmeston Progressive*. He paused in the wrapping to read a little. It was a criticism of the defences of the region, undoubtedly in the style of Fay McPhee if signed by Rollo Ramstones. *Who is in command?* it demanded. *Are we a Regiment or a Rabble?* 'Poor Fay's parting shot,' he commented. 'Well, come on . . . let's get out the car and on our way. This isn't the time for words, but deeds . . . everyone his own commander till we get one for us all.'

They got out the car, drove off. There was no traffic in this street, lined with shattered burning houses, but glimpses down cross streets showed them numerous cars on the main thoroughfare leading out of town. It was close enough to see that the cars were piled with luggage and at least of what breed the hurrying travellers. 'Greeks and Chinese,' said the Judge. 'Rats leaving the sinking ship. Still, I don't suppose you can blame them, seeing it's not their country and they haven't been so well treated in it. They wouldn't show such arrant cowardice in their own. Both are noted for their patriotism.'

Soon they discovered another stream of outgoing traffic, similarly laden but very differently manned, as His Honour observed with evident expression of shock. It was coming out of the better class section of the town. Not only would he call these fellow-countrymen, but even friends and colleagues. There was the manager of the biggest bank, manager and accountant of the biggest store, the Crown Solicitor. Judge Bickering had to pull up, such was the stream. He fairly gaped in unbelief – until there was Fatty Doscas. That must have been too much. The Judge drove in and stopped him, yelled at him, 'Where the hell d'you think you're going?'

Fatty hung all his chins out of the window and answered mildly, 'South, Your Honour.'

'What for?'

'Going to be invasion, they say.'

The cars behind were tooting.

'Who says?'

'Everybody. Japs didn't hit the oil-tanks . . . means they want to use 'em.'

'And you'd let 'em?'

'Can't do much . . . no command.'

Cars at the back were coming round Fatty's.

'Better come along, Your Honour,' Fatty said. Seeing no one was immediately behind now, he backed.

It was unnecessary. The Judge bawled, 'Rabble is right!' He let in his clutch, shot across the road.

He was still heaving with anger, his tic jerking violently, when several hundred yards further on, as they approached the hill running down past the old Delacy place, he demanded of Prindy, 'Is this to be Australia's Day of Glory, or Day of Shame?'

When the grey eyes met his gravely, he added: 'You're too young and too ill-informed to realize it, I know . . . but let me tell you that you are witnessing the testing of the worth of this social entity we call Australia. What is a nation but a great family, bound together by a special identification. You start with the blood-brotherhood of family. Then you have the brotherhood of the tribe. Ultimately we hope for the brotherhood of mankind. The family that breaks up at a threat of its identity, that cries *Every Man for Himself*, is not a true family at all, but a gathering of rabble, which is another term for a herd of beasts, with no higher feeling than the instinct of self-preservation.' The tic worked furiously again. 'What you saw back there, my boy, was the scattering of a rabble.' His voice was hoarse with feeling as he concluded: 'What you have witnessed, I fear, is Our Day of Shame.'

If Prindy were following it, his attention was distracted as they passed the old house and he caught a glimpse of a diminutive figure slipping into the cover of the trees of the drive. It was Hanno, that supposedly most faithful of servants, who had but one loyalty, so it was said, to the family he served. Despite the obvious furtiveness of the little Japanese, Prindy said nothing of seeing him. However, a moment later, spotting something hanging like a moon of green cheese above the silver Shell tanks, craning through the windscreen, he asked, 'What that something?'

Judge Bickering looked. 'Meteorological balloon. They have little radios in them . . . for telling weather conditions at a distance.' He added bitterly: 'Air Force uses them . . . but not much use to *our* Air Force now.'

He went on as they passed the deserted Oil Tanks: 'It's not three-quarters of an hour since the raid . . . yet everybody's in full flight. Perhaps even the native-born will use the excuse that they don't belong to these parts, that they come from Melbourne, like Doscas, or Sydney, like McSawley. But is it conceivable that an Englishman born in Birmingham would run away from Dover if it were attacked? God Almighty, if these people are representative of the Nation as a whole, then none of us is less alien to the soil than a Greek or Chow and no more right to tenure to it . . . and if we are overrun, may the conqueror show us no more mercy than we did the poor ill-armed innocents we seized the land from and who *did* fight for it, and who I'll now set free and arm to fight again for it . . . to the eternal shame of the whiteman!'

Prindy eyed the jerking tic.

The Council Depot was deserted, too. A repair job on the road had been abandoned with such haste that the tea-billy for smoke-o still boiled. Yet there was no damage hereabout, perhaps owing to the proximity of the Tanks – or Hanno?

They didn't come on damage again until they came within sight of the Civil Aerodrome, which with a couple of small aeroplanes, had been completely wrecked and gutted. From that same point they also got first glimpse of the

Jail, so odd-looking with most of the wall down, like a secret revealed. Yet without a wall, the figures to be seen were all *inside*. Because of wide-flung debris the Judge had to stop well away from where normally he would before the entrance. There was Major O'Dowdy coming to greet him, skirting the wreckage, awkwardly climbing over some.

'Your Honour, Your Honour!' panted the Major coming up.

The Judge eyed him as he might a witness he was summing up, asked shortly, 'You have control?'

'Yes, Your Honour. Only a couple of white prisoners unaccounted for.'

'Casualties?'

'Only slight injuries. The prisoners in question escaped.'

'Record them as jail-breakers. The rest are to be set free.'

The Major's pale blue eyes popped. The Judge went on: 'You and your guards report to whatever authority remains in town. You could be used for police duty.'

'Begging your pardon, Sir, I'd prefer to be relieved of duty, so that I may return to military service.'

'At your age . . . and in the face of invasion?'

The Major drew himself up. 'I am first and last a soldier, Sir.'

'Hmm! Last will probably be right. Look, there'll be martial law proclaimed within a matter of hours. That leaves me free to be a soldier, too . . . .'

The Major gaped. 'You, Your Honour?'

'Why not? I'm not for the mayhem and murder of war, as you well know. Nevertheless, any creature that won't fight in self-defence, to the death if need be, isn't deserving to live. Our country's facing a ruthless enemy, Pat. I don't want other men to die defending *me*. They say we were Blooded as a Nation at Anzac. With all due respect to you as an old Anzac, I say we were only *Bloodied* then, like louts in their first push-fight. It's in this we'll be blooded truly . . . *if* we fight. This is the test of our true courage as a people. Leave it at that. My last word as your superior. Seeing that I'll make a hell of a bad soldier . . . except, I hope, in the heat of battle . . . will you take me under your wing to start with . . . .'

The Judge was interrupted by swift movement near by, turned from the Major, to see Bobwirridirridi, spider-legged, coming leaping over the debris, and Prindy as eagerly going to meet him. With interest he watched the Aboriginal embrace, the fondling that is like the so-called Grooming of apes, so naturally expressive of fellow-feeling that the whiteman seems to have lost, particularly odd-looking in view of the difference between the pair, the old scarecrow with a black death's head topped with a fuzz of grey bristles, the beautiful golden-headed boy.

When the old man looked across, the Judge beckoned him. He came, with a black claw of possession on the boy's shoulder. He came up grinning widely, answered the Judge's greeting with a nod, gave his slim black claw to meet the extended lumpy ruddy ginger-haired white-feller hand, but without the ingratiating way he had received this Big Boss Man's favours formerly. The Judge said, 'You finish jail now, old-man. I come let you go.'

The grin widened. The Judge blinked. Whether the absurdity of his generosity struck him it would be hard to say. Anyway, he seemed to cover embarrassment by saying hastily, 'Bottle *plendy* there for you in car.'

Even then there was none of the old *Tahng You, Boss* of the mendicant blackfellow. The sunken red coals glowed. The Pookarakka went to the car as if it were his right.

Perhaps the Judge was a simpler man than he appeared to be and very much wanted to show that he had the power to free men as well as imprison them, because he said to O'Dowdy, 'I'll have a word with prisoners.' They went off together, leaving Prindy with Bobwirridirridi.

Again his seeming magnanimity failed. Only the guards were impressed with it. The white prisoners shuffled. The blacks, who should have understood because he talked Murringlitch, were curiously silent. So anticlimactic was it that the Judge's speech trailed off at the end. No cheers. He turned to Major O'Dowdy and said, 'I could do with a drink, Pat. Hope you've got some.'

Judge and Warden were just settled down on the latter's front verandah, with a bottle of whisky and a dazzling azure view of the open sea beyond the boom, when Prindy appeared on the steps, and asked if the Pookarakka might have some milk to go with his brandy. The Major told him to take the old fellow round to the kitchen and give him anything he wanted.

Prindy turned to go, but stopped, to cock his ear northward. So evident was his attention, that Judge Bickering asked him what it was. Prindy answered, 'I hear . . . *Boot-boot-boot* . . . what that?'

The Major rose, came to the steps and cupped an ear. It came on a faint puff of midday breeze: *Boot-boot-boot-boot-boot-boot-boot*! He said, 'That's the Naval air-raid warning . . . from the Boom Defence. Maybe they're only practising. They often do.'

'Queer time to practise after an air-raid,' remarked the Judge. He also rose. His tic jerked mildly. 'Perhaps they've only just heard of the raid. There does seem to be some disparity in co-ordination between the Services.'

An exclamation by Prindy: 'Aeroplane . . . big mob!'

Prindy leapt away, for a view of the eastern sky through the ruins of the jail. The two men came running down to join him. Over in the jail there was movement, too. Evidently there had been a line-up at the store.

Prindy jerked his lips towards where the Air Force Base was. High in the sky silver birds flew again in massed flight. An instant later fire began to run in a ragged leaping line along the horizon. Then the sound: *Boom-boomble-boom-boom-boomble!*

The Major breathed, 'Japs. They're tearin' the Raff 'drome to pieces . . . to stop opposition to a landing, I suppose.'

The line of leaping fire was describing an arc towards the town. The birds were diving. The earth was heaving up beneath. 'Comin' this way,' cried the Major. 'Better take cover.' He cupped his mouth and shouted to the milling crowd, 'Take cover!' Then he turned to the Judge, 'Down over the cliff, there, is a search-light post. Sandbagged. Nobody there. Only come nights . . . practise. Machine-guns there, too . . . have a pot at the bastards.' He started to run.

Boom-boom-booble-boom!

'In my car,' said the Judge. He beckoned to Prindy and Bobwirridirridi.

All piled in. As they drove across the little flat to the edge of the cliff, the Judge vociferated as on the journey out: 'Goddammit . . . what's wrong with us? Did you ever hear of such damned colonial ineptitude? This Jap war's been going on three months, with the enemy fairly rolling down on us, an enemy we've been waiting for for forty years . . . and there isn't even a trained troop of Boy Scouts to meet them!'

The Major said stiffly, 'Don't forget we've been fighting a great war on the other side of the world.'

'Urgh!'

They reached the cliff. Both men went down at once; while the others tarried to watch the fireworks over the town. The six-out-of-thirty-six anti-aircraft guns were in this.

The searchlight post was a gap in the cliff, built amongst a tumble of yellow rock that had been cemented into a platform. It was the perfect military botch. A good storm would have swept it away in an hour. It was protected from human assault from the sea by a thick wall of sandbags. From the air it would be a sitting shot, especially at night with the light on. The big light stood in the middle, shrouded in camouflaged canvas that made it stand distinctly against the rock. Into the cliff was built a shed for the power-plant. It was locked with a great padlock, but with the key hanging from a nail above with a big tin tag so that no one could miss it. The Major opened up.

There were two machine-guns. Watching what the Major did, the Judge assembled one, ignoring the Major's disputing the legality of his bearing arms since not a sworn soldier, saying, 'Balls! These bastards're out to kill us. Bugger your rules of war . . . there never were any except in theory . . . there never will be. Help me set the bloody thing up.' Then when he got it on its stand, under the Major's direction he fired a short burst into the sky, and cried, 'Lord, send one of those slant-eyed Sons of Heaven down close enough for me to blast him into Hell!'

As the echoes of the gun died away, the sounds of combat over the town came to them strongly: *Boom, boom . . . boom-boom . . . boom!*

Then Prindy came flying down, crying, 'Aeroplane come!'

A roar like an approaching storm. Then shattering flattening din as the flight swept overhead, so close that the exhaust flames could be seen as little red darting tongues and the oil streaks striping silver bellies and those red spots that were the insignia of the Sons of Heaven, looking down like malevolent suns in drought. But they weren't close enough. Although the machine-guns poked back fiery tongues, apparently their spite went even unnoticed. The flight was rising, heading out to sea, home to the conquered Spice Isles, where these mere captains now lived as kings.

But no!

One aircraft was breaking formation, banking to port to return, in a moment running past them, over the sea, out of range, but close enough for them to see the helmeted pilot looking at them through his perspex. They swung to watch him, saw him bank to port again somewhere off Shelly Beach, then vanish. It was hard to follow the sound of his going with the roar of the departing flight still beating on cliff and sea.

Then they heard him, coming at them from the back – the rising roar.

Then there he was – with his phosphorescent storm of death rushing ahead of him. They opened up their guns to meet him. Only for a moment could they be heard – *BRAAAAAAAAAAAAAHP*! – before he overwhelmed them – *WHAAAAAAAHM*!

He was gone over – climbing to the Glory of *Dai Nippon*.

The Major, his khaki torn to shreds and dyed with blood, staggered from his gun to the tattered sandbags, to cling to them, watching the departing foe, while his blood ran with the flowing sand, counting the seconds of his life remaining. The Judge seemed welded to his gun with blood and guts and white rag – but watched. Prindy watched from the shelter of the concrete wall, unscathed. The Pookarakka was still invisible.

Over the boom the foeman swept, out of the stricken South Land. What would he call it when he came to conquer it? Could any sweeter name be found than Australia? But what would it matter, if after sullying it with his brutality, he despoiled it with stupidity?

Out over the sea he flew – climbing to the Glory of *Dai Nippon*.

But he lurched. He rolled. He spun. He hit the sea – *Splash*!

So big a splash – but no sound to it. No sound in all the world now, it seemed, but the drip-drip-drip of blood.

The Major turned his head to look at his comrade. Blood was running from his mouth. Yet he smiled. The Judge could answer only with his tic, which after a violent spasm froze into a wink, in which it stayed as he slid down the gun into his entrails. The Major sighed, fell, to let the spilling sand bury him.

A sound out of the silence – *Tcht*! – Aboriginal signal for attention. Prindy looked up at the cliff, to see materialize out of the yellowness the khaki-clad Pookarakka, much as he had seen him do as grey out of greyness that first time of setting eyes on him long ago. Bobwirridirridi signed for him to come up. Prindy hesitated, turned to look at the dead men, stared a moment, then Signed them with the Cross. The Pookarakka saw, but said nothing when he came up.

Over at the remains of the Jail there was scurrying as of a nest of yellow ants. Some of the khaki-clad figures were already in flight, heading for the scrub across the golf links behind. A few were to be seen at guards' quarters, rushing downstairs with packed baggage. A car was being loaded out in the road.

The Pookarakka gave only a glance that way, then westward, to stare at a speck of blue that surely was Mooragetaghee. As if reading his thoughts, Prindy said, half questioning by his tone, 'More better we go motor-car?'

The old man looked at him, stared a moment, then grinned, lay a claw on the slight shoulder, murmuring, 'Pro-perly!'

The Judge's car had been struck, but had suffered slight damage, only a few holes in the roof at the rear and back window shattered. Prindy got in, switched on, started the engine. It ran perfectly. He opened the off-side door for the old man, who entered warily, probably never having ridden in front of any motor vehicle before.

Prindy headed diagonally for the road, townward. No one appeared to notice their going. No one was seen on the road, all the way back to that cross-roads, where still cars were heading out, with even more haste now for more devastation around them. Much of the damage was due to the flimsiness of the buildings. Nothing much of the town had been build to last, like a concession to the alienness of those who'd built it, hoping to get out of it as soon as possible, or expecting to be dispossessed of it as a thief of his booty. Not a peculiarity of the place, of course, but of the whole wide land, the so-called Nation, a community without a sense of future, without a right to it.

Where only a few buildings showed signs of direct bomb damage, many had simply been blown apart by blast. Not many were burning, for all the smoke.

They ran into thick smoke as they approached the Catholic Precincts. Prindy slowed down – stopped with a sudden squeal of brakes and a cry, 'Oh!'

The church was a smouldering heap.

At last that shaky old roof had fallen in, as so often people had declared it must for this or that unholy reason; but no one had thought of one like this. Evidently it had taken a direct hit. Even without the incendiary effects of a bomb it must have caught fire, with all those hazards of candles and sacrum-lamps. Apparently it had fallen like a house of cards, then as the timbers burnt, the iron roofing sprung up to fold peaked like praying hands. It smoked like a great censor, every ounce of incense in the sacristy going to feed it in last vast supplication to the Most Merciful who had given it to a grinning heathen to destroy what Faith in Him had raised.

In a moment he knew what had happened, when from the gateway of the half-wrecked Mission House, Rifkah and Savitra came to fling themselves on him, weeping and babbling of *him*, of *him*, of *Daid-feller*. He could no more ask the name than they pronounce it. When they had come up from the landing, they said, *he* had gone at once to the church to pray. They had been told by the old black gardener, now decamped, that Father Gorgan had gone to the Hospital as usual, but had not come back. Everyone else was gone. They themselves had gone with him to the church. When the alarm sounded announcing the second raid, *he* had told them to go back to the Mission House and take shelter in the slit trench. *He* wouldn't go with them.

Prindy waited for no more, went racing through the wreckage of the presbytery, to get as near to the altar as possible. Some of the shattered blackened marble could be seen. Nothing else. But yes . . . for a moment, through the curling smoke, yet again a nailed hand. The grey eyes blinked rapidly. For a long moment he stood. Then he raised his hand, made the Sign of the Cross, murmured, '*Requiem Aeternum*.' He was about to turn, but stopped to tear a small branch from a scorched hybiscus, with which to erase his tracks as he backed a yard or two. Then flinging down the branch, he called softly to the smoking ruins, 'You lie quiet, old-man . . . *Mummuk* . . . Amen!' He ran back to the others gaping at him from the street.

He said, 'Better we go. Might-be Japanee soldier come.' Savitra howled and would have grabbed him, only he pushed her away. 'Tucker in Mission House?' he asked.

Rifkah asked, 'Vere ve go?'

'Back to Mission, I reckon.'

Savitra shrilled, 'How you go Mission you only got motor-car?'

Ignoring her, Prindy said to Rifkah, 'We go down Beatrice way, go find Mullaka, first-time.' He took a look in at the fuel-gauge of the car, which read very low. He said, 'Must get benzine. I go look-about, time you get tucker. He added as they turned away, 'Give Pookarakka milk and brandy.'

He looked all over for gasolene, even went down to the boatshed; found nothing, but saw dead men running out with a stream of rubbish on the tide. He returned to find the others at the car with a box of food. He said that they would have to try to get fuel down town.

Although for the most part the town was under a pall of smoke, there was a clear view down this street that even gave a glimpse of the innermost arm of the harbour and the mangroves beyond, looking much as usual. Even the big Shell sign at the Queen's Service Station was to be seen, although no hint of anyone in the vicinity. He said they'd go to the Queen's, and asked Rifkah if she had money. She said she had. The place was opposite the Queen Victoria Hotel.

They got in, Prindy to drive again, with the Pookarakka beside him, the girls in the back. They set off, past the oldest and most substantial houses of the town, mostly unharmed, but all abandoned.

However, that not all the citizens were lily-livered was soon startlingly revealed to them. They reached the service station without seeing any more sign of life than one poor crying cat, suddenly to find at least one important institution fairly bursting with it: the Queen Victoria Hotel. Often enough a lively place, never, never had it been like this. In fact, it far less resembled a tavern at the height of a carouse than a behive in the uproar of swarming. The furore was not only in the packed bars, all three of which could be seen into through their half-doors. The old place simply rocked with it from top to bottom. It couldn't be seen what was going on upstairs, because the verandahs were latticed. Nor could it be guessed, except as destruction to the accompaniment of wild hilarity. Such was the din, of shouting, smashing, stamping, laughing, that the arrival of the car across the street had not been noticed.

It was not noticed even from upstairs when someone opened a louver in the lattice and a couple of men presented themselves at it, soldiers by their hats, struggling to shove out something large. Soon the thing the two men strove with with much laughter was seen to be the drawer out of a wardrobe or other large clothes-closet and was bulging with clothing of a sort, a scattering of which preceded it before it came hurtling down to strike the foot-path – *Crash*! – and splinter, scattering its odd contents widely.

Men came bursting from the swing-doors of the bars, soldiers and civilians in about equal number, all staggering drunk, gawping, burbling, 'Wha's matter . . . christ sake!'

A whoop of laughter from above. The others looked up. One of the soldiers up there shouted, 'Help yourselves to stays . . . millions of 'em.'

The other heaved out an armful. 'More of 'em . . . ho, ho, ho!'

Then the booze-witted ones below grasped the fun in it, pounced on the pile of corsets, which must have included every style invented, from the steel and whalebone armour of the beginnings of this cult in feminine falsity combined with masochism to the kinder elastic girdles of the day, all well shaped through having been worn by a form that had stretched them to the limit. One soldier stepped into one of the more primitive devices, which another proceeded to lace him into while pressing a boot into his behind, causing much mirth and a scramble to do likewise. Others tore the things apart, shooting slips of springy steel aloft, assaulting one another with lengths of stretched elastic. A civilian amongst them was hopping about in a purple girdle, yelling, 'Old Mum Morgan's . . . always trussed up like a flamin' old chook . . . too bloody mean to chuck 'em away, eh? Ho, ho, ha!'

Another civilian shouted, 'Always drippin' with di'monds, too . . . thievin' old bitch.' He looked aloft, shouted to the grinning faces there, 'Find any 'er jewelry . . . she 'ad 'ole bloody jeweller's shop?'

Nods from above.

Crash! of splintered glass – and again *Crash*! – of china now, as a chamber-pot that had been hurled through a bar-room window struck the other side of the road. A burst of foam – a spreading of dark seething liquor. The mob howled with mirth. Evidently someone had been drinking beer out of the pot.

Then the mob became aware of the car and those in it. Savitra was particularly noticeable, hanging right out of her window, all darkly shiny bright with curiosity. Someone yelled, 'Young gin!'

It was taken up by many: 'Yeah . . . gins . . . creamies!'

Perhaps they took Prindy for a girl. They surged forward.

Rifkah, too well used to ramping satyrs, leant forward and struck Prindy on the shoulder, crying, 'Qvick . . . go!'

A yell: 'Red-'eaded moll!'

Prindy was instantly alert, slipped into gear.

But the mob was on them, pawing at shrinking Savitra, grabbing at the car as it moved, babbling, 'Don' go . . . don' go, girls!'

Prindy trod on the accelerator, so that the engine roared. But the car only crept forward, now in the grip of the mob.

'Don' go, girls . . . stay'n'ave good time!'

'Plen'y money . . . plen'y booze!'

'Look the jewels I got, sweet'eart . . . all yours . . . don' go!'

'Don' let 'em go!'

'Pull 'em out!'

The engine almost stalled – when – 'Ow, Jesus!'

'Christ . . . look't his hand . . . cut off his fingers!'

Someone had grabbed hold of the broken back window. Blood spurted like a fountain. The diversion gave the engine its chance. It roared again into full power. The car leapt forward. A few still hung on, shouting, but had no chance. Prindy changed to second gear. They let go. There was a cross-street only fifty yards away. Prindy swung into it, right.

One last cry they heard as they passed out of sight of the staring mob – '*Ohhhhhhhhhh*!' It was like the howl of a pack of rutting dogs when the bitch is taken.

The going was not so easy here. Iron and timber littered the street. Prindy had to gear-down to negotiate it. Further down was another hotel, this with a crowd already outside. He avoided it by swinging into the next street. This was the main street out of town. It was littered, too, but offered no human obstruction. Soon they were clear of the wreckage. Soon they were at that cross-road which would put them on their way. As they swung into it, Prindy said they would get their gasolene at the Three-mile.

As they approached the bridge that spanned the railway they saw smoke in the cutting on the town side – *two* plumes of smoke – a double-headed train.

Prindy slowed down. All stared as if prescient of the fact that there must be something very special about this train – the last out of Palmeston.

Certainly no odder train had ever run on that ragtime railway. It was made up of what must be just about all the functioning rolling-stock that could be marshalled in the shortest possible time. No consideration had been given to the usual balance of load. Vans, open waggons, cattle-cars, flat-tops, passenger coaches, were just anywhere. The only things in place were the engines and the last brake-van. It was entirely a passenger train. Its packed passengers must have been the last of the lily-livers unable to get away by other means, servicemen as well as civilians. Porky Jones was driving the leading engine, eyes fixed on the iron road ahead as if, like those earlier scary ones in the cars, he saw that Cowards' Castle at the end. Most of the passengers were looking at the sky. They surely constituted an aerial bombardier's dream as now located. None noticed the car plainly visible on the bridge approach, not even Chas Chase, the guard, and Col Collings, Acting Manager, both leaning out of the caboose looking for the Sons of Heaven. Then the train was past, leaving the watchers snuffling and blinking in the smoke of its hard going. They went on, turned into the main South road.

They got another glimpse of the train, stopped at the Three-mile station, taking on more passengers, apparently, but wasting so little time about it that most of these were still clinging to the outside as with engines hooting their impatience and filling the southern sky with their pent breath she went on her way.

Just as the train disappeared, the engine of the car conked out. Prindy said he must go and get gasolene. He alighted at once, to go heading for the station.

Only one person had remained at the station when the train left. He was a tall man, dressed like a civilian, in dungaree overalls, but obviously accoutred like a soldier, with rifle slung over a shoulder and web-equipment. He was now heading away towards the railwaymen's quarters, walking with a curious lope. It took Prindy only a moment of staring to discover who it was. He broke into a run, yelling, 'Patannaford!'

Pat Hannaford halted, stared. It was probably the red head that promptly popped out of the car that attracted him more than the fair-haired running boy. He swung towards them. He grabbed Prindy as they met, gave him a hug, asked him what he was doing there, but with attention really only on that racing figure with the flashing copper top. He opened his arms as Rifkah reached him. She fell into them, wept on his breast relief from fear that up to now had not been evident. He kissed her hair. When she raised her face he kissed her wet eyes. He asked, 'For christ sake . . . what you doin' here in the middle of a war, and everybody else done a bunk?'

She gave a little explanation, promising more later, saying that they wanted fuel for their journey. He said they'd look for some, although he wasn't so sure of finding it easily: 'The cowardly bastards were fillin' up everything they had with benzine last I saw of 'em. Try the Maintenance Inspector's joint here. He blew through so quick he couldn't've had time to see if his tyres was blown up.' He led the way to a biggish bungalow amongst the quarters, talking: 'The Japs blew up a bit of the tracks while they was straffin' the Raff. Old Clarry gets order to repair it at once for a special train. He gets everybody on the job . . . then comes back, grabs his car, and off. The fettlers weren't too far be'ind him, neither . . . takin' the trolleys. You never seen a fettlin' job done so quick. In half an hour they done what normally'd'a' taken 'em a week.'

They went into the garage. Nothing but oil. They went to a shed. Only kerosene. They headed for the house. Pat said, 'Beats me, this bolt. You can understand the Greeks and Pongs and others doin' it . . . although the Greeks I seen in Greece weren't like that . . . standin' up to the Hun with shotguns, and riskin' terrible things hidin' us blokes. But Aussies behavin' like this mob today . . . well . . . who'd believe it! Looks like we're still only bloody immigrants, no better'n Oxes and Pongs and all the rest. Jesus!'

Rifkah asked, 'You are not going avay, Pat?'

'What you take me for?'

'But you are badly crippled man.'

'I'm a trained soldier . . . and I got arms . . . and them slant-eyed bastards come, I'll 'count for at least a dozen of 'em before they get me. See this rifle. Know where I got it? Jes a while back. The Raff mob were in a panic, stopped the train to get on. I abused 'em for deserters. But they reckon they been told by their command it's *Every Man for Himself* . . . that means full retreat, without discipline. So I promptly disarms one of 'em.'

In the house they found a pressure lantern filled with gasolene. Pat declared that it was enough to get the car to the Depot, where they might find some left by the decamping fettlers. As they went to the car, he told them more about what he had seen of the panic bolt: 'Believe it or not, but they even used the two nightcarts . . . not the poor bloody yeller-feller nightmen, but high-up silvertails, with their high-class luggage stowed in the shit-can compartments. You wouldn't read about it, would you? I'll bet that when it comes out, no one'll believe it. It'll be considered a furphey. But I can tell you it's God's truth . . . and it proves that deep down the great warrior Aussie is nothin' but a shit-house rat!' Pat went red with feeling, spat.

They reached the car. As Prindy was pouring from the lamp into the tank, Pat said, 'Wait on . . . it's runnin' out.' He bent down awkwardly, swinging out his artificial leg, rose, saying, 'There's a dirty big hole in it only a couple inches from the bottom. Looks like a bullet went through the top, come out there. She wouldn't 'old 'alf a gallon as she is. Have to fix it. That ought to get us to the workshops. We'll take the tank off and oxy-weld it.'

They all got in.

At the shops they were dismayed to find the difficult job confronting them in the first task of removing the tank. All bolts were badly rusted and would have to be cut out. They were about to settle down to it, when Pat, from grumbling, suddenly said eagerly, 'I got a better idea. The old Sandfly?' Then he called on them to follow him to another shed, where they found the little old shunting engine, normally used for work on the jetty, but laid up for repairs. He declared that they could effect these repairs in half the time it would take them with the tank, not have to bother about getting gasolene, and also be free of the refugee mob who'd be sure to be cluttering the road. 'I'll run you down in her,' he said, 'Then I'll bring her back and make an armoured train out of her and fight the bloody Nips me own way.'

The Sandfly was quite tiny compared with the locomotives in general use, with only a bit of a coal-scuttle for a tender and water-tanks flanking her boiler. Stroking her work-worn flank with more than affection, Pat said, 'You wouldn't credit she's the best part a 'undred years old, would you? She's one the original locos used when this railroad was laid. The others gone long ago. She's certainly got nine lives. Twice she's been overboard at the jetty and had to be lifted out with a ship's crane. She's been off-agin, on-agin, to beat Flannagin's old injin to hell. Normally she'd've been workin' the jetty today. She'd'a' never got out o' that. Old Jack Tinball was drivin' there today. He and the injin jes vanished, they say . . . him takin' a pot shot at the Japs with a rifle he took from a sentry done a bunk. Way he'd'a' wanted to go, I s'pose. Was always singin' *Old Soldiers Never Die, They Simply Fade Away*. Poor old bugger! I never got on with him . . . but it was 'count that stinkin' RSL. He could never see that it really wasn't a veterans' organization, the thing it had been at the start to protect their rights, but a rort, taken over by the Exploitin' Class, for the very purpose o' keepin' down the man who *did* want his rights. Echt!' He spat. He moved to a small pile of parts from the little engine stacked on a work-bench beside her, and described them.

The link of the link-motion mechanism had cracked and been distorted by subsequent operation. The workshops fitters had been waiting for a new link to be made down South. 'Lazy bastards,' he growled. 'If I's a fitter I'd make every part of an injin meself . . . in fact, I'd make a whole flamin' injin.' He went on: 'I s'pose it needs a new link in the long run . . . but I reckon this one could be mended to do the job for quite a while, simply be straightenin', weldin', grindin', temperin'.' He turned to Prindy. 'I'll want your 'elp. Know anything about black-smithin', young feller?' Prindy answered that he had worked with his grandfather in the smithy at Lily Lagoons. 'Okay, then. Let's get to it . . . case there is an invasion.' Pat turned to Rifkah. 'If you could organize gettin' up steam, eh? With that old blackfeller o' yours. There's kindlin' and kerosene in the big injin shed.'

Already the Pookarakka had found the kindling, a couple of lengths of packing-case pine, and was beating them as *minga-minga* as he sat singing softly in the shade of the water-tank. They didn't ask him. Rifkah and Savitra did the job.

While Pat and Prindy worked together, Pat gloated over the fact that he was about to own an engine of his own. No one could deny him ownership, when authority had fled, crying *Every Man for Himself*. It was the impossible dream of every engine driver to own an engine and run it as he pleased: 'Like them first old drivers did . . . the blokes who drove for Stephenson . . . before they invented time-tables and runnin' rules and regs and all the bloody rest that ties a man down to the orders of a 'undred bosses, not one of 'em knowing a link-block from a fire-bar, or for that matter one end the bloody coal-shovel from the other.' He went on: 'There must be plenty guns lyin' round . . . machine-guns, light ack-ack. Must make up that armoured train when I get back from puttin' you on your way. Get a crew from somewhere. Old Porky'll come back if I talk to him. Might-be you'd like to be in on it? Remember that time we's ridin' together, and I reckon you and me's likely to do big things together someday?' This last to Prindy.

Like all things born of true inspiration, the fitting of the Sandfly, for what surely promised to be the liveliest adventure in her long career, was accomplished without a hitch. Repair and replacement took just about the same time as to get up steam: some four hours. Rifkah attended the boiler as she might the kitchen range at Lily Lagoons of a Friday afternoon, with such loving care that when at last the safety-valve announced full-head, the plume that arose from it was like a Sweet Savour to the Lord – and she coal-smudged to the line of her bright hair.

In the circumstances, it was natural that Rifkah, in the considerable conversation that passed between foot-plate and workbench, should confide much of the truth about the doings of herself and companions of late. In fact, by the time the job was finished, she had told Pat just about all; excepting the Love Idyll, which Pat, by the way he looked at her from time to time, was hardly likely to take as sympathetically as he did the rest. She also omitted to say that it was their intention to return to the Mission, making it sound rather that they were going to join Jeremy.

The confession made a difference to what Pat had started planning. Reckoning himself now above Rules and Regs, he had included the others with him. First learning that they did not intend bolting to the South Pole like everybody else, he said he would find them a nice safe spot on the railway for a permanent camp, and in his peregrinations in his own little train would keep an eye on them. But the case was altered with Rifkah's admission that she was regarded as a Security Risk, at least so long as those who so regarded her remained in the country. Pat had seen Cootes *Blowin' Through*, as he called it, along with his Pommy mates. Hence they'd best start by keeping Rifkah out of sight as much as possible. It didn't matter with the others. Even Prindy, smudged with grease, could be taken for a boong. 'Matter of fact,' said Pat to Rifkah, 'With a bit more coal-dust on your face you'd pass . . . only for the hair.' She laughed and said she'd cut off her hair. He said, 'You do . . . I'll turn you in!'

But it was an idea to assume some degree of disguise. She had need only to blacken her face, wear a hat, and keep out of the way.

Soon it was put to test. Bobwirridirridi slipped in to announce the approach of two whitemen. Pat flung his hat to Rifkah, then went to hold the intruders outside.

The men were oldish, known to Pat. One said, 'Heard you hammerin'. Wondered what's goin' on. Thought all the railway blokes'd sold out.'

'Quickest and cheapest sell-out in history,' said Pat.

'I'll say. But what you hangin' round for?'

'Puttin' the Sandfly in runnin' order . . . case I need her.'

'What you need her for?'

'Never know. She's only injin left.'

The men craned in. But Pat offered no invitation. One asked, 'What . . . you got boongs for offsiders?'

'Who else is there?'

'Still a few old-timers hangin' on.'

Pat said, 'Thought you'd 'a' been evacuated.'

'They tried it. But we been camped over Willy Lee's. Goin' back home now.'

'Reckon you still got a 'ome? Awful lot o' damage.'

'Yeah . . . we seen it. We been in. Only come out to get our swags. Fair mob still in town . . . drunk, lootin' . . . soldiers mostly. Nice lot of bloody bastards we bred up since Last Turn-out! Couldn't be any worse if they was Japs.'

The other said, 'Japs wouldn't carry on like that. I don't like the slant-eyed bastards . . . but they always been the best behaved people in this town, barrin' none.'

Pat asked, 'What'll you do if the Japs come?'

The skinny one of them spat. 'Depends what they do. We got the makin's of a Home Guard. We got arms. We'll try hang on till the Yanks come.'

'The Yanks? They was right in the lead in the big bolt.'

'I mean the proper U.S. Army . . . what Churchill and Roosevelt promised to defend us. Don' worry. We'll carry on. We're all old soldiers.'

The other growled, 'Looks like we'll have to start by puttin' down that lootin' mob.' He turned to look away towards the town. 'Here's some of 'em comin' now. They been patchin' up old trucks and loadin' 'em with loot. Don't know what they reckon they're goin' 'o do with it . . . bloody thievin' bastards!'

Already a couple of loaded trucks from the town had passed, but without attracting much attention from those preoccupied in the workshop. This one announced itself not only with the sick roaring of its ancient engine, but with the bellowing of its crew. As it approached it was seen that they were all soldiers. Small wonder the engine protested, when loaded to the limit with goods and men. The load appeared to consist largely of things like household refrigerators, radios, gramophones. The men at the back were perched on top, drinking beer from bottles. They waved their bottles cheerily to those watching from the shed.

The thin old fellow growled, 'Lootin' like the common enemy. We'd'a' got shot for doin' that kind o' thing in the Last Turn-out . . . wouldn't you, in your mob, too, Pat?'

Pat said dryly, 'We was runnin' too hard from the common enemy to pick up anything but our *mundowies*.'

Both men frowned at this reminder of Pat Hannaford, the traducer of the Glorious AIF. One hawked and spat. The other said, 'Well, we'll be gettin' along. See you round.' Then as they started off, this one added, casting a sly glance back: '*If* you're not goin' chasin' your *mundowies* again.'

Pat grinned. 'I'm an injin driver again, Chris. Any travellin' I do'll be on wheels in future. Besides . . . I only got one *mundowie* now.' He shoved his artificial foot forward. 'Thanks to your mates Churchill, Wavell, Tubby Tubs, and Co.'

The others departed scowling.

It was a fair test, because the engine was only twenty feet or so inside the shed, with only that little bit of a coal tender screening Rifkah. Pat returned to be surprised to see her face entirely blacked. He laughed at first, then growled, 'No . . . take it off. I'll admit I married colour once . . . but it wasn't for the colour, but because I was silly enough to think it a social responsibility. I got a feeling there's sumpin wrong with marryin' out o' your colour. All right in the early days . . . and like old Jerry Delacy says, it might'a' been a good idea if we'd'a' crossed with 'em then . . . but colour to colour and white to white, I say now.'

Rifkah declared that she would remain black until the coaling for the journey was done.

They did some test-runs up and down the yards to prove the job done on the link-motion. It appeared to be perfect. Next they marshalled a little train, three two-ton coal-hoppers, a small open waggon, a little brake-van with accommodation normally used for breakdown work. Pat said that, apart from use as mobile bunkers, the hoppers, at least a couple of them, would make first-class emplacements for guns, with protection for the crews. Coal could be got from them to feed the tiny tender simply through opening the chute at the side and catching it by the bucketful. Pat did the driving, while Prindy and Rifkah handled points and couplings. Then there were the hoppers to fill at the big bunker. After that there were supplies of oil, kerosene, and carbide to lay in. The latter was for the old-fashioned headlamp. They did it all without interruption. The Sun was setting as they rolled their little train, ready for the road, into hiding behind the Goods Shed.

It looked as if it would be a bright night. Anyway, if it rained, it would be only a light shower or two, as had fallen during the day. Igulgul, close to First Quarter, was just past the zenith. Pat reckoned they would have a moonlight trip till ten. It was good travelling like that, he said, because you had less trouble with animals on the track. Besides, they would have a better idea of what they were passing. He believed they could expect to find people camped at all the main stops, which meant the watering points, except their destination, Granite Springs, which was off the road. He reckoned that the double-headed train wouldn't get beyond Helena River tonight. With a train like that he wouldn't care to tackle those long stretches of water-logged plain beyond the Helena. Old Porky would be even more reluctant. Anyway, before they left, he would telephone through to estimate the situation. If Porky was at the Helena he would have a word with him.

They went across to Pat's place to have a meal and collect whatever they might need for the journey and beyond. Daylight was gone by the time they were ready. At the station Pat got on the telephone, cranked – *Two Longs, a Short.* A couple of crankings. Then a flat official voice spoke: 'Helena River . . . working.'

Pat said, 'Thought you'd be at the Head o' the Road be now, Col. What happened . . . you run out o' panic?'

The voice of Col Collings snapped, 'Who's that?' Then in a moment: 'Hannaford, eh?'

'Porky there?' asked Pat.

'Where you speaking from?'

'I don' know what they call the place now. They renamed Singapore right away, 'cordin' to the radio . . . Queen City o' the South, or sumpin.'

'You mean the Japs've landed?'

'Ain't that what you expected?'

A moment of silence. Then Collings asked, 'What're you calling for?'

'Told you I want to speak to Porky Jones.'

'I'm in charge. I handle anything official.'

'Who says it's official?'

'If it's not, what're you speaking on a railway telephone for?'

'The Post Office ain't open.' Then Pat raised his voice: 'Listen, Collings . . . I said I want to talk to Porky. What I got to say to him's no business of yours. Nothing's no business of yours no more. You did a bunk, remember. I'm the one official left in this place dealing with railway matters. If you don' get me Porky right away, I'll take the matter to a higher authority.'

Another silence. Pat appeared to be about to break it angrily, when Collings' voice could be heard somewhat muffled: 'It's that mad bastard Hannaford. He wants to speak to Porky Jones. Where is he?'

Porky was soon there, puffing: 'Yeah, Pat . . . wha's happen' . . . they landed?'

'Tell you when I see you. Jes wanted to know where you are. You campin' the night there?'

'Yeah . . . providin' everything's okay up there. Is it?'

'If I said they was here, would you blow through?'

'You're kiddin' . . . they ain't there.'

'Not for the moment. But look, we're organizin' a way to deal with 'em when they do . . . fittin' out an armoured train. Like to be in it?'

'Jesus Christ!'

'Think about it. What I really want to know is can I get past you if I come down tonight?'

'What in?'

'The armoured train, o' course.'

'You been boozin', Pat?'

'No. Now listen. You don't know what's been goin' on up 'ere. We got this train all fitted out . . . 'cept for guns and things . . . .'

'Who's we?'

'All top secret. We want to give her a trial run tonight . . . .'

'But there ain't an injin up there runnin'.'

'Will you listen? This is dead hush-hush. Are you clear of the points so's I can go through there without stoppin'?'

'Why ain't you stoppin'?'

Pat bawled, 'Because it's top secret, bugger you! Can I bloody well get past you?'

'Well . . . if it's that bloody important, I'll see you can.'

'Thanks, mate. Be seein' you.'

'Wha' time?'

'For christ sake . . . do I have to keep on tellin' you it's hush-hush? Now, not a word of what I've told you to anyone . . . *anyone*, you hear?'

Porky groaned: 'Jesus . . . the things you get me into. I thought it'd finished when you got off the foot-plate.'

'I'm back on it again. Now, I'm relyin' on you, mate . . . and you ain't never let me down yet. So long.' Pat hung up, grinned at Rifkah.

She asked, doubtful, 'Is it all right?'

'She's sweet, girl.'

'It von't mek trouble for you after?'

'Who's going to be game to make trouble after the way they bolted? Come on . . . let's get goin'.'

Bobwirridirridi and Savitra were put into the accommodation section of the brake-van. However they felt about one another was not evident. Each acted as if the other didn't exist. Savitra made a fuss at first, wanting not to travel on the engine, of which she was scared, but Prindy to travel with her in the van. She was quieted by being told that he would be coming back from time to time to operate the brake to facilitate stopping.

They started off very quietly, merely whispering out of the yards onto the main line. In fact, it was not till they were past the smouldering ruins of what had been the Air Force Depot that they really got going. Pat pulled the whistle-cord. For all its size, that big brass whistle crowed like a bantam: *Keek-a-keek-a-keeeeee*! They laughed at the squeak. Igulgul came out of a silver cloud to laugh. *Keek-a-keek-a-keeeeeeee*! But when Pat opened the regulator, she showed that like all bantams she lacked nothing in spirit. Her drivers fairly chewed up the silver track, spitting it out in a long gold-spangled cloud from her long skinny funnel. Pat sang to the hammer of the piston-rods:

Patanna 'ad a hinjin, and be jees he made her go,
Took him 'xactly sixteen minutes, Ballarat to Bendigo,
Bendigo-ho, Bendigo-ho,
Start to stop jes sixteen minutes,
Ballarat to Bendigo!

They all sang it. It became the theme song of the magic journey.

Pat himself said it was magic – without realizing that magicians were aboard and that their way was lit for most of it by the Master of Magic. In no time they were at the Palmeston River water-tank, taking a long long drink that must serve them a hundred miles. Soldiers were camped not far away, on the river crossing, no doubt those riotous ones they had seen passing the Three-mile. These would have come to see what was doing, only Pat, with bayoneted rifle, met them at the pump-house and telling them that it was a top-secret train, held them till he heard – *Kee-ee-ee-ee-eek*!

Then on again, *keek-ing* at the creatures of the wild that became too venturesome in their curiosity over the astonishing sight. Kangaroos tried to race them. Curlews flew up over them to try to take a peek inside. Frogs in the billabongs yelled to try and drown the rival music of panting cylinders and whirring wheels. Mopokes called of magic abroad. Igulgul smirked his way down the sky.

Helena River announced itself with a spot of green light. So the way through was clear for certain, said Pat, because the distant signal of a siding need not be set at clear. It was the home signal that said Yea or Nay to admittance. 'Old Porky give us that green light,' he declared, 'Jes to show us we're sweet. Good old Porky!'

There were sentries on the bridge with blades flashing in the last of the moonlight, but without challenge in their stance. Pat yelled for them as they passed, 'Pass friend!' The steel bridge took it up in a rolling shout: *Pass Friend*!

Then they were racing through the siding, on one side of the double-headed train, on the other its multitude of passengers and more. Numerous familiar faces were seen gaping in the acetylene glare: good old Porky, and some would say good old Col Collings, and His Honour the Administrator reduced to such dishonour, Major Bullco, and the Coot, and old Malters; too many to recall, so swiftly were they swallowed in the smoke, obliterated as if it were part of the magic to create them for the moment for their several purposes and leave them as nothing but laid-ghosts.

Over the down-line points and out on the main line again, the engine-crew embraced and laughed. Old Igulgul had a last laugh as he vanished behind the western trees.

First stop was to be the 120-Mile Siding. A fettler's camp there. But stop they must, or *Drop Their Plug*, as Pat said. The Plug, he explained, was a soft-metal device set low in the boiler. Let your water get too low and it would melt and let the steam blow into the fire-box and dowse the fire. To *Drop Your Plug* was the worst thing that could possibly happen to an engine driver. Anyone who did it got straight down from his engine, walked to the nearest water-tank, and there hung himself under it either with his belt or braces – 'So keep your eyes on that bloomin' gauge!' he cried. 'And easy with that bloody banjo. We got plenty o' coal . . . but coal don't only 'eat water, but eats it . . . if you get what I mean. Watch the gauge . . . or I'll have you out bucketin' water from a creek!' But the threats were accompanied with hugs.

They made the 120-Mile all right, pulled up at the hydrant. The fettling gang would have sticky-beaked like those soldiers back at the Palmeston. But again Pat left the watering to his firemen, and came loping back with his rifle and his talk of Top Secret. The gang would have heard all about it on the telephone. That was soon made manifest by Ganger Walsh's remarking, 'They reckon you gone round the bend, Pat.'

Pat answered readily, 'That's nothin' new. They'd'a' certified me years ago if they'd'a' got the chance.'

'They reckon you're bomb-happy now.'

'Maybe I am Mick. But I'd rather be that way than shit-scared like them. They left a trail o' *goona* you can smell for a hundred mile. Tell 'em that when you ring 'em . . . and tell 'em, too, that that old smell'll be hangin' around for a hundred years and more to come . . . . '

The clanging of the engine's tank-lids told him the job was done. Then – *Ker-ee-ee-ee-eek*!

So on their wondrous way again, tunnelling through the darkness, singing again of those heroes of railway legend, Paddy of Nanty Glo, Casey Jones, Pattanaford – *So he pulled her by a string all the way to Nanty Glo, Nanty Glo-ho*!

Now they had water to take them to their destination, and only Caroline River Siding remaining as a human hazard. The distant signal at the Caroline showed red. That need not mean anything, of course. Then the home signal showed up green. 'She's sweet!' cried Pat. Caroline either had decided or been instructed to let them pass. Who would want to bar the way of a Locomotive Loony, anyway? as Pat asked. But that didn't mean the population was indifferent to their passing. Everybody was there to see them pass: white, black, and brindle. Again a flash of faces, of upturned astonished eyes. Then back on the open road.

Only thirty miles to go, and all hazards behind them – provided the magic held. The 'prentice magician fell asleep over his coal-shovel – his banjo, as called by Pat. Pat stopped, roused him, sent him back to sleep beside the brake in the van. Because his other fireman began to nod in her seat, Pat had her over into his, and stood with artificial arm behind so that she could not fall out. At last she let her head fall on his shoulder. How the copper gleamed in the little light of the kerosene lamp above the gauges! He kissed it. He talked to her softly of the magic ride and of how he wished it would never end and hoped that it might be renewed for ever by her soon getting sick of the wilds and coming back to be his. She would not be able to hear him above the din. Yet sometimes she smiled, as if she liked what he said. So he kissed her again – not only her hair, but her brow, her cheek, and at last, as the rocks of Granite Creek loomed out of the blackness, on the mouth. As she started awake, he called in her ear, 'Brakes!' She fairly leapt to her job. He reached for the whistle: *Kee-ee-ee-ee-eek*! In a moment there was responsive grinding of brakes from the van.

A flashing light below, and voices. Prindy and Savitra were there, bringing the dunnage for the trip across country. Pat and Rifkah got down. 'Well,' said Pat, 'Better give me a bit of coal in the tender to take me on to Beatrice . . . she's jes about out. Then clean up all tracks. You never know, as I said, the buggers may be follerin' us on a trolley.'

Soon everything was done, and the trio were standing on the rough wet stairway leading up to the water-supply. Pat took their hands in last farewell, saying, 'I 'spect to wake up any minute find it's only a dream.' Then suddenly he asked, 'Where's the old bloke . . . I ain't seen him?'

Prindy answered, 'He get off long way back.'

'Where?'

'I don' know properly. When I go back van one time I find he gone. Pookarakka like that always. He go . . . he come . . . nobody know.'

'He wouldn't go and tell white people 'bout Rifkah, would he?'

The blur of fair hair was seen to shake in the glow of starlight. 'He can't talk white people. He go bush tell him all-about blackfeller whiteman finish now.'

'Hmm . . . that's the way he sees it, eh? He might be right at that. Anyway . . . this is the finish for us . . . for the time bein', I mean. Don't forget by'n'by . . . don't forget it's only *Mummuk, yawarra*.' He reached to squeeze their hands.

'*Mummuk, yawarra*, Pat,' they all said.

He climbed aboard the engine, gave her steam. Her wheels spun on the wet track, bit when he gave them a spill of sand. Then she was on her way – *Keek-ee-keek-ee-keeeeee*!

In a moment she was out of sight round the bend. In a minute or two she was out of sound amongst the gullies and the hills.

Strange silence now after all the din of this long long day. Only the soft music of the tumbling water. The eyes of the trio sought the clear sky, where the story of the Dream Time was being told eternally. There was the Ol'-Goomun-Ol'Goomun slipping over the West, trailing her Dilly Bag of Souls, her Cat's Cradle of Right Side Relationship. The Broken Fish Trap, the so-called Cross, was swinging up from South, futilely, as for ever, trying to block that bolt-hole in the Old One's Road, the Milky Way, from which now his red eye was taking a peep to see how things were before he came forth to dominate the sky in that pattern of brilliance called by the *kuttabah* The Scorpion – the *kuttabah*, who did not realize that he still lived largely by folklore, too.

A sound – up over the rocky wall – *Mopoke* – *Mopoke*! So the way was safe in that direction.

Prindy began to lead the climb. On top he caught another sound. It came from southward, from those hills beyond which lay the flats stretching to the Beatrice. A faint breeze brought it a little louder. It would be the Sandfly, perhaps climbing that last long bank. What was she saying?
Yawarra, Yawarra, Yawarra, Yawarra . . . Farewell till we meet again!

III

Yawarra happened to be the last word spoken between this trio doomed always to be runaways and Jeremy, for them their only certain refuge. That was when they had parted with him at the edge of the mangroves of the Leopold River estuary, not so long ago in time, but what a little age in experience!

The end of a spell of *Yawarra* is, of course, reunion, conventionally announced, where approach to other people needs must be circumspect since always potentially dangerous, with the call – *Ku*!

There was the call now, three months and more later, ringing echoes from the northern escarpment of the Sandstone Plateau in the region of Jeremy's permanent camp – *Ku . . . u-u . . . u-uuuu*!

Jeremy heard, and looked out from his new keep, through the tumbled rocks and banyans, northward. The action betrayed him as a *kuttabah*, as little else might, because the source of the call was at variance with the direction of his seeking it by a good ninety degrees. However, the lapse from his usual astuteness might be excused on the grounds that he was used to looking that way for visitors, which is to say the Aborigines of the maritime plains, and also that at the moment he was listening to the radio with obviously intense interest.

The radio was giving the ABC midday news broadcast, much of which concerned the official appointment of the American General, Douglas MacArthur, as Commander-in-Chief of the South Pacific Zone of War (dubbed *Sowpak* in the usage of the day) and hence C-in-C of the Australian Military Forces. No mention was made of who had appointed the man. Unnecessary, no doubt, when only the President of the United States could have done so. The Prime Minister of Australia could hardly have any say in the matter, when he had hollered so urgently to Uncle Sam for help – *help*! In fact, the news, made it sound as if Australia had become the Forty-ninth State in the Union and should feel profoundly happy about it. Even with the enemy practically at the gates all fear of him seemed to have been banished by the appointment – so confident was General MacArthur. The fact that he'd had to fly for his life from the Philippines made no difference to his presumption to have the Jap on his knees in no time. He was bringing in men and equipment from the U.S.A. as fast as fast ships and planes could carry them. His men would do the fighting. All that would be required of Australians militarily would be to stand guard here and there. Otherwise they would be profitably employed in behind-the-lines service to his legions. Money was no object. Instead of having to raise money to raise men, as had always been the case in fighting Old England's battles, the U.S.A. had an easy-going system called Lend-Lease, by means of which you could have what you liked on security so vague that it didn't seem to matter. Apparently all you did was to tie yourself to the U.S.A. for ever.

What arrangement could be happier for a people who had never been free or aspired to freedom?

Small wonder, then, that a man like Jeremy should be so preoccupied when that reunion call rang out the first time as to look northward instead of eastward, away into the flat country, instead of up to the cliff-top. But he got it the second time – *Ku-uuuuu*!

There were the trio, standing out distinctly against a sky as blue as the Flag that was flying as when they had helped him hoist it for the first time. Since they were well away from easy descent, they must have been reconnoitring. Certainly they took him by surprise, as betrayed by the long moment of his staring before shouting back and waving to them to come down.

When at length they reached him he first stared hard at them, doubtless astonished at their appearance. Gaunt and ragged, but for their lighter colouring they might have been taken for mendicant blacks. There was astonishment in his greeting: 'For God's sake . . . where've you sprung from?'

Rifkah answered with a squeal of happy laughter, rushing to fling herself into his arms. Savitra came on her bare heels, to share one of the arms and lay her tangled black head on it and weep a little. Prindy, the complete blackfellow with a handful of spears and a womera, leant on the latter and smiled happily at his grandfather.

The girls began to babble explanation. Jeremy listened for a moment, then silenced them: 'Now, wait a minute . . . what about sitting down and starting at the beginning . . . but you'll want something to eat . . . bone-buggers! Come on . . . sit down in civilized style at the table. I've just made a damper. Wait till I get butter and canned stuff. Prindy, boy . . . stir up the fire and put the billy on.'

It was gobbling rather than gabbling after that. The talk was left to Jeremy, while the trio ate enough to feed a mustering camp for a day. The new damper, scarcely cool, vanished. They finished off with cracker biscuits and jam.

Jeremy told them how he had heard from blacks about their having been seized and transported by Cootes and McCusky, but had been unable to place the date, hence had not thought of their having become involved in the Port Palmeston *débâcle*. He said that although he had an idea that Prindy might turn up someday, never had he dreamt it likely that he should see them all there. He knew of the air-raid, both from the ABC and Radio Japan. He said he gave more credence to the report of the latter, because it gave very precise details, whereas the ABC had cried down as a mere nothing what, by the very fact of its being the first attack on *Terra Australis* since the *kuttabah* came, was an enormity. But he knew nothing of the Great Bolt, till told now. He stared as if incredulous as, light-heartedly, they told him of it, his only comment a whisper: 'My God!'

His informants believed that the country must long ago have fallen to the Japanese. Jeremy easily disabused them: 'No . . . the Americans beat them to it. They patrol the coast every day in planes.' He glanced up at the Sun. 'They'll be passing in an hour or so . . . and you'll be able to see them with the glasses.' He knew who they were, he explained, because a couple of times they had come close enough for him to distinguish their markings. The blacks had told him that they had been shooting up buffaloes in the maritime swamps, apparently for target practice. 'I wish they'd shoot up the bloomin' pigs, too,' he said. Asked if they might not land on that strip of Fergus's near by, he replied that he reckoned the planes were much too big for that.

The talk didn't last much longer than the great meal, because the travellers were soon heavy with sleep, and being excused by Jeremy, in the manner to which lately they had become accustomed, sought soft shady places in the crimson sand. Jeremy watched them from his deck-chair, mostly Rifkah, lying curled, head on arm, mouth pressed open like a sleeping child's, but looking so unchildlike in her gauntness, even unrecognizable now as the lovely creature he had known, except for that gleaming copper spilled on the sand.

They slept for about an hour. Rifkah woke first, came yawning to sit on the ground beside Jeremy. The first thing she asked him was what day it was. He said Friday. She cried out, 'It vill be *Shabbos* . . . oh, I haf been vonting to come on Shabbos and fry fish.' She rose, asking excitedly, 'You haf oil still?'

'Have everything . . . even candles . . . .'

She leapt up and kissed him. 'Fish?'

'Bream in the billabong.'

'Eggs?'

'Preserved goose-eggs.'

She swung on Prindy, who was awake but still lying down. 'You vill get fish?'

He jumped up at that, and came to get his fish-spear. Then he grabbed up a gunny-sack and set out. Savitra went on his heels. Rifkah called, 'Don't be long. I haf not mooch time.' She looked at the Sun.

Jeremy chuckled: 'You go living like a blackfellow for weeks and even tell the time like one . . . but still think of your fish-fry.'

She looked at him. 'You do not vont me to mek *Shabbos*?'

'Of course . . . I'll love it.'

'Zen ve vill mek ze moost loffly *Shabbos* ever vos!' She kissed him, then whirled away quickly. 'Moost mek 'nother-one damper . . . for *chalah*. Vere is flour? Vere is baking-powder? Oh, vot sort of *Kashrut* can I expect, ven I don't know vere anyzing is in my kitchen?'

She looked so truly troubled that Jeremy, who looked as if about to make a jesting remark, obviously desisted and went off up to his store in the cave to get what she would be wanting.

Those two angels supposed to check every Jewess's Sabbath Making to see if it conforms to *Kashrut* would have been mean indeed not to have passed this one. Perhaps they were amongst the gang of butcher birds that came at sundown to sing for their supper over a sight and a savour such as to add to the liquidity of their fluting with salivation.

Jeremy had foreseen such an occasion. Hence there was a gleaming white cloth to cover the bush-table topped with kerosene-case timber and a napkin for that bushman's *chalah* and brass sticks for the candles standing ready to be imbued with the Spirit of Light which is the Breath of the Lord, as soon as those Two Stars appeared. There was the fried fish, spread on a tin baking dish instead of the best china, but looking and smelling no less like an Offering to the Lord. The *pfannküchen* made a golden pyramid on an enamal plate. The beetroot and fruit, out of cans, were in enamel, too. But surely the *Kashrut*

Angels sang in the voices of the butcher birds the Psalm for Inauguration of the Sabbath: *The Eternal Reigneth, Let the Earth be glad*!

It happened that Igulgul, making his first appearance for the month, got into the act: as he had every right to do, meaning so much to Jews, whose Calendar he keeps, that the Faithful must ask a special blessing on his resurrection. Prindy, watching for the Two Stars, spotted him peeping through the western trees, ran to tell Rifkah. She and he and Savitra joined hands:

Blessed art Thou, the Eternal, Our God, King of the Universe.
Bless us especially on this Night of New Moon.

Igulgul hung peeping to see the candles lit, to see the maker of the magic draw it to her breast with ceremonial movement of the hands, to bend her head so that the magic was struck from it in flashes of fire:

Blessed art Thou, Who commandest us to sanctify Thy Sabbath with Light.

It had been decided to follow the meal with a sing-song and Prindy's playing a bamboo flute he had made. However, with washing-up done and everything stowed, as proper in the bush where proper observance of the Sabbath would mean capitulation to the ants, the newcomers, filled with food again and used to going to bed like pythons after a feed, were yawning their heads off. Jeremy saw them into swags made up in the cave, then came back to the fire-place, to sit and watch the candles burn away.

Next morning began with talk of going on to the Mission as soon as the travellers were well rested and fattened up a bit. Rifkah said Stephen Glascock would surely be concerned about what had happened to them. She gave no hint of the reason why there should be this mutual concern. Apparently Jeremy knew nothing about her relations with the priest. Perhaps the blacks who had reported to him had their information so much at second-hand as not to know themselves, or knowing, saw it as no business of theirs or his. Anyway, Jeremy suggested that they complete the journey to the coast on horseback, since even if it took time to muster the horses, that much would be saved in foot-walk, and they wouldn't lose again the condition he hoped to put back on them. Chuckling, he said to her, 'You don't want even a priest to see you looking Bone-bugger, do you?' He didn't seem to notice the blush under her deep tan.

Jeremy said he was not certain where the horses were, not having seen them since the rains set in or having heard anything definite from the blacks. His own assumption was that the Lily Lagoons beasts had split up with brumby mobs and dispersed. According to the blacks, the brumbies favoured two distinct regions of hilly country during the Wet: one eastward of here, the other westward. He wanted to muster the horses to look them over after their unaccustomed spell of running wild. All would need attention, he reckoned, if only to their hoofs. Besides, he would like to have some about him again. During the talk he said he must go soon and get Electron, who would be fretting for him. When he said this, Prindy and Rifkah exchanged a covert glance.

There were blacks in the locality now, said Jeremy. He'd had a visit from them the other day and made tentative arrangements for a horse-hunt with their assistance. Tomorrow, say, he would put up a smoke to tell them he wanted them.

Later in the morning, Rifkah, after looking over Jeremy's kitchen garden down below the spring, declared that she would like to do a tasty roast for tomorrow's dinner, and asked Prindy were there ducks or geese to be got from the billabong. He said there was nothing, that evidently the blacks had taken their toll recently and the rest had flown. He had come on a brace of *beinook* that were very scary, but reckoned he could get one or both for her. Prindy then asked Jeremy for a Turkey *naga*. Jeremy winked at Rifkah as he went to his store to get the piece of stuff.

Turkey twill, the native's choice in material for use as a loincloth, was supposed to be imbued with hunting magic, especially in respect to the *beinook*, or bustard, the supposition being based on misunderstanding of the word Turkey, which of course means here the bright red colour, because the *kuttabah*, the maker of the magic, mostly calls the bird Plain Turkey. There could be some logic to it, too, since the bustard, otherwise a wary bird, is easily lured by bright objects, especially red. Savitra was another little bird whose eye was caught by the magic as Jeremy cut from the bolt of cloth a piece to make the conventional male *naga*, which merely slips between the loins and knots on the hips. She came and felt and sniffed the cloth, then asked if she could have a piece large enough to make a *sari*. Jeremy gave her the scissors to help herself.

Attired and accoutred for his expedition, carrying a gunny-sack in which were a knife for dealing with his victims to meet the demand of *kashrut*, a packet of fried fish and *pfannküchen*, and his flute, Prindy set out, farewelled by only Rifkah and Jeremy. Savitra was fitting her *sari*. Then just as her man vanished beyond rocks and trees, there she was, a vision in black and red, dashing after him. The others only stared. In a little while raised voices could be heard. Evidently Prindy did not want company. However, there was no return of the spectacular vision. Jeremy, turning with Rifkah to the deck-chairs, remarked, 'The trials and tribulations of matrimony!'

Jeremy went on to discuss the pair, this being his first chance to do so, asking Rifkah how things had gone with them over the months. She replied that they hadn't changed a bit in their attitude to each other, adding in a tone that suggested she believed this explained it all, 'It *Charada* business, you know.'

Jeremy shot her a keen glance, which she met with one of innocent inquiry. Then he remarked, '*Charada*'s usually only a temporary state. When it lasts it always leads to trouble. As I told you before, the blacks won't like it . . . if they're going to mix with them. How've they got on with blacks so far?'

'Vell, zey haf not mix.'

'How did Bobwirridirridi take it?'

'I do not know. He vos vit' us only few hour . . . and he does not talk to voman.'

Jeremy was silent for a while, then said, '*Charada* is woman's business, of course. A man's victim of a woman's magic. Women supposed to possess power in it usually make trouble through the wilfulness it stirs up in them. Aboriginal women aren't so well treated that they won't take advantage of anything they can. I've noticed she rather clings to him and tries interfering in what he does and says.'

'Yes, she like to boss him. Ve haf bit trouble over zat vile ve are coming here . . . vot mek us slow coming.'

'How was that?'

She explained that when they reached the rough country below the southern edge of the Plateau, Savitra refused to go on, saying that her feet were sore and that she was sick of the bush and wanted to join her people. Of course she wanted Prindy to go with her. Rifkah herself was agreeable, confident of reaching Jeremy by following the Gorge route, and really wishing to be rid of Savitra and certain that Prindy would rejoin her eventually. But despite his obvious infatuation, Prindy could be stubbornly and even brutally resistant at times. He told Savitra they would be glad to be rid of her. In a pique she departed. Convinced that she would be back within a few hours, but doubting her ability to follow them if they went on, Prindy said they should wait for her. Rain was threatening, but not in that quarter. However, when it fell, it swept right across the path the girl had taken. Prindy decided then that she would be utterly lost and that he must look for her. In fact, so badly lost was she that it took days to find her. She had got away into the swamps to eastward of the Beatrice, close to the Rainbow Pool. They found her quite ill, not simply from exhaustion, privation, fright, but from having been stung by some poisonous creature. She had a large swelling in her groin and fever. Prindy rather brutally declared that he had sung her sick to punish her for giving them so much trouble. Nevertheless, he had gone to Lily Lagoons in the hope of getting some of Jeremy's fever mixture to physic her.

'Did he get any?' asked Jeremy. When she shook her head, avoiding his eyes, he added, 'There was a great stock of it in the annexe . . . ready bottled for the blacks. Couldn't he get at it?'

The copper head drooped. She murmured to the ground, 'Vos no annexe.'

'Eh?'

She looked at him quickly. 'Burn' down.'

He only blinked, reddened slightly, took a moment to speak: 'What about the rest of the place?'

'Full of soldier, Prindy say . . . and ever'vere barb' wire . . . .' She faltered so obviously that Jeremy stared hard at her. She dropped her face to her hands.

He asked, a trifle harshly, 'What else?'

The brown fingers spread across her eyes. She muttered, 'Elektron.'

He waited a moment: 'What about Elektron?'

She quivered, looked up, now with eyes swimming, muttered, 'Dead . . . ve do not wont to tell you . . . but . . . but you say you are going looking.' She drooped her head again.

Now his voice was really harsh: 'How'd it happen?'

'Joost terrible accident vit' barb wire, I zink. Poor dear moost try come back home and get tangle up and bad hurt . . . and soldier shoot.'

The broad ruddy face contracted with pain. Then Jeremy sighed: 'Poor old fellow . . . he was always in trouble with barbed wire. Another casualty. We've got to expect things like that now, I suppose.'

She rolled her lovely eyes, murmuring, '*Kayn aynhorah*!'

Meanwhile, Prindy and his bride were making their way southeastward. It hardly could be said that they were together, so great was the distance between them, he slipping along like a hunter, all eyes and ears and as these organs demanded treading his way, while she, despite the brilliant vision she made, dragged along sullenly, not wanted or considered, but determined to hang on. A couple of times she hissed her annoyance – 'Bloody blackfeller!' – but without getting even a glance back from him – 'Bloody bastard!'

They were approaching what must be a creek, judging by the uneven line of taller trees beyond the generally stunted scrub. Suddenly he stopped, raised his hand. She obeyed on the instant. But now he wasn't looking or listening, the way his fair head was lifted and his beautifully moulded nostrils dilating. Savitra also sniffed. He turned and signed to her to come. She came quickly, only to be handed the gunny-sack. Taking it with a grimace, she muttered, 'What's matter?'

'Smoke. Must be blackfeller camp.' He turned from her, now with spears held horizontally, warrior-fashion, instead of at an angle like the hunter, the womera in his right hand.

She snapped after him, 'Where you go?'

'See blackfeller.'

'Wha' you want see blackfeller for?'

' 'Bout horse.'

'I don't want see blackfeller. I tired. I want camp and have dinner.'

Ignoring her, he went on. 'Black bastard!' she hissed, and followed.

They were heading for the tallest timber of the creek, where there would be a water-hole. A few minutes of walking. Then the squeal of a lubra's laughter. Prindy slowed his pace, raised his face, called, '*Ku*!' A man's strong call.

The answer was the yap of a dog, evidently stifled with a slap.

After a moment he called again, '*Ku*!'

Another minute of walking; and there through the green scrub was the brown of humpies of dead branches. To the right of the direct track the scrub was thinner. He veered to it. Then there was the camp in almost full view. He stopped. There were half a dozen humpies, and just as many blacks, all adult males, grouped together by a fireplace, two standing, four squatting, all staring. Prindy leaned his spears against a tea-tree, stood with the womera, and while the men still stared in silence, did the proper thing for a stranger, lowered the womera to lean on it, raising the right foot to rest against the inner left thigh. In that stance you can't pick up a spear from the ground with your toes.

Not a sign from the staring blackmen. They were all naked and to some degree painted. A couple were old, the others middle-aged. Not a move. Till at last one of the men standing stooped and spoke to the squatters. Ochred and banded heads came together in consultation, while slowly backs were turned. Still Prindy stood, knowing that part of his heritage well enough not to expect anything to be done in a hurry, except in dire necessity. Even the answering of a question requiring a simple Yes or No could take an hour, a day, a week, a tribal convention. A visitor without special privilege might easily be kept waiting a full day for the invitation to enter a camp. A group of visitors could be kept for a week.

Savitra became impatient, muttering, 'Wha's matter dat silly-bugger?'

Prindy breathed sharply, '*Kaiatulli*!'

The Sun was at the zenith. The men in the camp were under a bough shade. They passed a pipe round between them. Savitra, behind Prindy, stepped further back into shade. Prindy stood rigid, now running sweat. The world was still, with birds and animals camped as usual in midday heat. No doubt the invisible rest of the camp, women, children, dogs, were napping somewhere in shade. By now they would have tired of peeping.

Then two of the blacks rose, and without a glance towards the visitors, made for the water-hole, disappeared. It was the sign of a protracted wait. Prindy relaxed, turned to shade. Savitra would have joined him, only he waved her off with his womera. She sank back, put the tucker-bag under her head for a pillow. He sat straight with back against the small tree. The men at the fire stretched out to sleep.

After a while Savitra started complaining that the ants were at the tucker-bag and getting in her hair. He ignored her till she tore up a little bush and began to lash about her savagely. Then he rose and snatched the bag away, returned to his tree and hung it up, dropped down again. Savitra then complained of feeling thirsty, of being hungry, asked for the bag back. He ignored her. 'Bloody puggim black bastard!' she squeaked with subdued passion, then fell silent, perhaps fell asleep.

Prindy sat waiting, waiting, while nothing moved but Sun and shadow. Several times he had to move. Several times Savitra moved, looked up, distorted her prettiness with silent rage, returned to bury it in her chocolate arms.

Waiting, waiting, according to the rules.

Then a sound to the left. He looked quickly. A moment. He leapt to his feet. Dogs were coming tearing through the scrub, a great pack by first sight of them, but proving only to be seven or eight when they stopped in a snarling line twenty feet away, stopped as if by silent command. Dogs of all sorts and sizes, with only one thing in common, which was that they all had a strong dingo strain that glared yellow fire out of their eyes and shot like sparks from golden bristles in their mongrel hackles and grinned menace with gleaming teeth. Not a bark out of one of them, only the long rolling scurl of the snarling.

Prindy looked towards the camp. The dusky sleepers still apparently slept. He turned to get weapons and tucker-bag. The dogs made a feint, causing Savitra to shriek and run to him. He growled at her in his new old-man's voice, 'Shut up . . . he only gammon!'

In fact the dogs hadn't advanced an inch. There is no animal more obedient to a master's will than a blackfellow's dog. All they did was to raise the pitch of the chorus – *Ngabadaua – Gidardavit*! – as the unwanted pair withdrew.

When a goodly distance from the scene, Prindy paused to look back, Savitra at his side all the way now, panted, 'Dat lot been hunt him we wid dog.'

He shook his head.

She demanded, 'Wha's matter like o' dat?'

'I don' know,' he muttered.

He was setting off again, when she whimpered, 'Me t'u'sty . . . me hungry!'

He kept his heading for a few paces, then swung diagonally for the line of creek timber well above the camp. He made a good mile of it, causing Savitra to complain about her thirst and in addition about her feet: 'Wha's a bloody matter you race . . . my foot knock-up.' He continued to ignore her.

Where they reached the creek it was dry, a narrow channel with a bed of fragmented sandstone cut deeply in the clayey loam. He followed it up. Another couple of hundred yards brought them to water, a pleasant little hole, all emerald under drooping paperbarks. Savitra, who had been limping, stumbling, whimpering, broke into a run. By the time Prindy reached the hole, she'd finished drinking, and was unpeeling the *sari*. 'Come on, *bogey*,' she said. But his eyes avoided her dusky nakedness, fixed on the sandy shallow end. As she leapt into the pool, he went round it, dropped down to the strip of sand. Horse-tracks, some of them shod.

He followed the tracks up the bank, looked to see the general direction of their coming and going, then surveyed the landscape in that direction. Obviously the ground was rising gradually, because the meagre timber, mostly of about equal height, appeared taller. It was not the rise of the Plateau, because that was southward, and this was eastward. Savitra recalled his attention. She was out of the pool, standing naked, drying herself with the *sari*, saying she wanted to eat. He still had the tucker-bag. He went round to her.

Savitra flung the *sari* over a bush to dry, dropped down, folding legs in the manner of a lubra, a heel to guard her vulva. He dropped to haunches beside her, dipped in the sack, brought out Rifkah's cloth-wrapped package. There were two large fillets of fish and four *pfannküchen*. He gave a fillet to Savitra, put the other aside, rewrapped the cakes.

She ate her fish before asking, 'Gi' me cake.'

He went on eating his fish. When he had finished she asked again. He said shortly, 'Want him for horse.'

'What horse you talk-about?'

'Station horse dere somewhere.' He jerked his head eastward. Then, gathering up bag and weapons, he rose.

'Where you go?' she demanded.

'Look-about horse.'

'You come for look-about *beinook*, you reckon.'

'Da's all right . . . I got to look-about horse.'

'I knock-up now. I wan' 'o camp.'

'You can camp. I come back.' He moved to go.

She got to her knees, voice rising: 'I can't stop here wid dem blackfeller.'

'He can't hurt you.'

'You goin' 'o stop here, you bastard.' Her voice rose to a lubra's shriek: 'You can't never run away from me . . . I got you *Charada*!'

His grey eyes were grave as he met the blazing black. After a moment he said, 'I got 'o look that horse for Mullaka. We got 'o have horse for go Mission, ain't it?'

'My foot too sore. Look my foot!' Certainly they were puffed.

He said, 'I gitchim horse, you ride him back camp, then. You wait lil bits.'

She leapt up shrieking, 'You can't go leave him me. You carry-him-up me gitchim horse.'

'Eh, look out!'

She snatched for *sari* from the bush, rushed at him. 'You carry-him-up me!'

For a moment he stared at her slender nakedness, quivering with the intensity of her feeling. Then he murmured, 'All right,' set down his spears, knelt.

Her scowl changed instantly to a smirk as she flung the *sari* over her head as a hood, and cocked a slim dark leg over his golden-brown shoulder. His left hand shot out to remove the spears, evidently to prevent the defilement they would suffer if bestridden by a female. As she brought the other leg round to clasp his neck with thighs, he handed her the tucker-bag. Then with her feet tucked under his armpits he rose, with obvious ease, and evidently untroubled by her light weight and probably not unused to it, set off. She placed the bag on top of his mop of fair hair.

The tracks fell into a pad heading for the rising country. The creek wound about, split off. No more water. That was probably the last hole of any permanency.

Savitra tried talking coyly. He told her to keep quiet in case horses were at hand. She tried singing softly an Indian song: *Okale pusili payra.* He threatened to buck her off. She contented herself with rubbing her vulva against the prominent bone at the nape of his neck, giggling to see the bulging and leaping behind the tight red *naga.*

The bush thinned, revealing ahead a grassy hillside. It was not part of the Plateau, the red and green wall of which could be seen a couple of miles away to northward. They crossed a little gully, to come into tall grass and skinny little trees and peeping antbeds. They had just got into it, when he stopped suddenly, pressing her ankles tight with elbows.

She breathed, 'Wha' nam'?'

He breathed, '*Beinook.*'

The hunting instinct in her kept her rigid. Imperceptibly almost he turned to the left. There only twenty feet or so away, popping above the grass like odd-shaped pods on thick grey stalks, were a brace of bustards, peering in their strange way with heads cocked so that they can see all round, suspicious of everything, cursed as they are with such delicate flesh, yet curious about everything. That blaze of scarlet suddenly risen out of the gully. The male spoke to his mate: a couple of drumming grunts.

Slowly Prindy sank down till Savitra's feet were on the ground. '*Danook*!' he breathed, and slowly withdrew from under her, moved further to the left, crouched on haunches, invisible because the same yellow-brown as the grass and so delicate of movement.

The male spoke again and advanced slowly to see what that pretty thing was, while yet keeping an eye on all the rest of the world, although perhaps now more out of habit than purpose. A small break in the grass revealed the plump grey bodies, the strong yellow legs. Spear ready in womera, Prindy aimed from haunches – *ZIP*!

The male went down with a hoarse croak, rose flapping great wings, overbalanced with the spear in his rump. The female took one quick look, then turned, ran into the grass, rose crashing from it, wings beating hard. The male got to his feet again, turned to bite the spear. Prindy leapt back to get the tucker-bag, snatched out the knife, pounced on the bird now belligerent in the face of doom, grabbed the head, slit the bristling gullet. The blood shot out. He dropped the bird to flap itself to death while he tore at a twig of a sapling and got a ribbon of bark. The bird was dead when he returned to it. 'Poor bugger,' he muttered as he withdrew the spear. He tied the great steel-like feet together, and with the ribbon looped, heaved the bird up to the broken twig, and hung it there.

Wiping blood off his hands and off the spear and the knife with grass, he returned to staring Savitra. Taking up bag and weapons, he said shortly, 'You stop here.'

'Eh, look out!'

'I only go up over hill there. Spone no horse, I come back. But horse here all right . . . look-see.' He jerked his lips towards where the hen bustard had taken off. There was horse-dung, scattered as if the birds had been at it, and fresh.

She protested: 'You can't leave me behind!'

He growled, 'Spone you foller me, I gallop that horse back camp . . . leave you behind altogether.' He turned away, leaving her standing, still draped with the hood, gaping after him. He did not look back.

He reached the top of the slope. Under a clump of small trees he found a brumby stallion's dunghill, recently trodden. The hill rolled gently down to a gulley, climbed up again eastward, red with kangaroo-grass. A mob of kangaroos, the same colour and distinguishable only by the bobbing of heads against the violet sky, were grazing away to northward. He took off the *naga* before descending warily. A flying mob of kangaroos could send a mob of brumbies heading tail-high for the horizon even with the thud-thud-thud of their panic-progress.

Just as well he had taken the precaution. He topped the next crest to see a dozen or so horses grazing only a couple of hundred yards away. The wind favoured him. He dropped down, to crawl to the cover of a bush.

There were only two Lily Lagoons beasts – those oldsters, Bay Rum Betsy and the gelding Snowball. The rest were brumbies, mares with foals, all poor specimens, and one rangy old stallion, grouped no doubt through common decrepitude.

Still hidden, he rose to knees, put fingers to lips, gave that whistle with which his grandfather was accustomed to call the horses. Heads were flung up. Ears flicked rapidly. Particularly startled were those who knew the call. But none moved. Prindy waited. The old stallion did not like it, began to ring his mob, tail-up, looking for the menace, looking everywhere, as were the others. Prindy whistled again. The heads swung towards it. Again. Betsy wickered. The others snorted. Betsy began to head that way, cautiously. Grabbing up the *pfannküchen*, he began to work his way into the open, but so carefully that only the keenest of eyes could have seen him.

Betsy was within thirty feet before she saw him. She stopped dead, ears flapped forwards, nostrils flared. He spoke to her, using the Mullaka's form of addressing her: 'Hello, Betsy, womany!'

The head jerked. He rose very slowly, with a cake held out as the lure of a piece of bread was. She sniffed. A moment. Then she whickered, came with a rush. She gave him one good sniff, one rub with her forehead, then snatched the piece. While she munched he embraced her neck, smoothed her shoulder, crooning to her, 'Dear old Betsy . . . how you doing? Eh, look out! You *binji-binji*, ain't it?' Poor as her condition was otherwise, Betsy's belly was rather too full, and her udders were not the shrivelled things they had been before.

The other horses had seen enough. The stallion whistled, wheeled his mob, put them on the run. But there still stood Snowball. Prindy called him by name. He neighed, came at a trot. Prindy had a job to share the rest of the *pfannküchen* between them. Looking them over, he clicked his tongue. 'Proper bone-bugger, eh? How Mullaka goin' 'o get you fat again?'

He tried to mount Snowball, but was butted away by Betsy. She whickered with pleasure when he mounted her. So the three of them went off back along his tracks. The kangaroos were back in the gully, staring this time. Up and over and down to Savitra, awaiting them wearing the *sari* again. The horses wouldn't come up to her till she had removed it. He would have put her on Betsy, because old Snowball, for all his bone-buggery, was more fitted for his weight and the weight of the *beinook*. Betsy settled it by trying to bite her. So he had to bump her up onto Snowball and force her to carry the bird on threat of leaving her behind, because she objected to the blood. Now the Sun was well down in the trees along the creek. Prindy said it would be dark before they reached Mullaka's camp, but there was Igulgul to help the horses pick their way over the last rough stretch of the way.

They returned to the water-hole, where the horses wanted to drink, and Savitra wanted to *bogey* again and this time getting Prindy in with her to play-about, got to wanting more. With eyes ashine, lips moist and wet and quivering, she dragged him by a hand up to the soft spot where they had camped briefly on first coming there, forced him down into that position in which to have herself served by him in so-called Blackfeller Fashion. Primitive it might be considered, yet actually the only way a human female may have coitus with satisfaction and dignity completely becoming a human being. The horses stood staring at them. Igulgul smirked at them out of a lilac sky. Wrong Side Bijnitch so early in his monthly round of encouraging it! But what really could be wrong with something that caused so much delight, as expressed by their gasping cries, when at length they fell locked in orgasm? Near by a Willy wagtail sang of it: *Kirrikijirrit, kirrikijirrit . . . kirri, kirri, kirri . . . sweet, sweet Wrong Side Love*!

Drugged by the magic, they slept into the silvery darkness left by Igulgul's vanishing. Savitra, waking hungry, as any healthy female should from fufilment of her function, demanded food of her spouse, wanted the bustard cooked. He said he had no matches for a fire. She complained: 'You reckon you smart bloody blackfeller . . . wha's matter you can't make him fire from stick?' He replied that he couldn't find the necessary things in the dark.

She complained till he silenced her with his flute, to which soon she was singing, and sleepy birds twittering:

Okale pusili payra
Dodhi dudhoch bhatoch go . . .
Oh, Pigeon, I look-out you hungry-time,
Feed you my milk, my kunni.
I never let you go, my Pigeon.
By'n'by I gitchim you in Nankura Town.

When he fell silent she thought of food again: 'Dem bloody horse get my supper. All you-lot t'ink about, horse. All right . . . you can puggim dat old mare now . . . I hold him, up tail for you . . . you can't have me no more. Oh, me hungry too much!'

He played again:

Talinjurdali, talinjurdali,
Ponnek kuru pontala coru.

She sang:

Dis lil Tali,
Dis gold Tali,
For my Hindu sweetheart,
For my Hindu bride.

Finally he silenced her by curling up with her, to fondle her with lips and fingers – till with the limitless appetite of adolescence they were in the clip of love again, this time entwined like mating lizards, stared at by the stars. They fell asleep as one. When they woke again the Cat's Cradle was gone and the Snake high in the East. When she whimpered again, he appeased her yet again, so that she sighed snuggled up to him and slept again. No mopoke about. But curlews were crying near – about a baby?

At piccaninny dawn the butcher birds woke them. Prindy bounded out of the slim hands that held him, went to pee, to drink, to sluice, then went off to look for the horses. The beasts were not far away.

'Me hung-greee!' howled Savitra like a lubra.

'All right,' he said. '*Kulli-kulli* . . . come on, get on old Snowball . . . we get back camp for breakfast.'

Within an hour they were within hailing distance of the camp – '*Ku*'!

The mature male voice answered not only caused the horses' ears to flick, but their nostrils to dilate as if sniffing for a familiar scent. When the voice rang out again – *Ku–u*! – old Betsy flung up her head and neighed, and would have broken into a trot, only the going there was much too rough for her overgrown hoofs, and Prindy checked her by grabbing an ear. However, there was no holding her when she saw the beloved figure coming down through the rocks. Prindy slipped off and let her go whinnying for joy. Embracing her while she bumped him with her head, Jeremy sounded close to tears as he talked to her: 'Dear old Betsy . . . dear old womany . . . it's good to see you again.'

Snowball knew better than to shove in for his share too soon.

By the easy way the youngsters were received, it was evident that no concern had been felt for their protracted absence. In fact, Jeremy spoke as if he'd expected Prindy to accomplish something concerning the horses. No mention was made of contact with the blacks till after breakfast, when Savitra came out with it in a few sharp words. Jeremy had just said he would put up that smoke to get the blacks to locate themselves, so that he and Prindy might ride out to them and save the inevitable weary wait till they made up their minds to come. Tossing her dark head, Savitra snapped, 'We been see dat lot. Dey been hunt him we . . . wit' dog.'

When Jeremy looked at Prindy, the grey eyes met his with a blink, then swung away to look down towards the horses busily munching oil-cake. Jeremy looked at Rifkah, who was wearing that troubled old *bubbeh* look. Prindy rose, saying, 'I get tools for shoeing, eh?'

For a moment Jeremy sat silent, then also rising, said, 'I'll have to show you where they are. Must get some more oil-cake, too . . . they've just about cleaned up that lot. Got to feed 'em up.'

It was not till a couple of hours later, while Jeremy and Prindy were working on the horses' hoofs, that, breaking a silence following Prindy's giving further lively details of how he and the others were taken at the Mission, Jeremy asked, 'Are you going to stay now all the time at the Mission, and be a missionary?'

Prindy answered promptly, 'No-more . . . I go bush with Rifkah.'

Jeremy, seemingly concentrated on the trimming of one of Snowball's jagged hoofs, asked, 'What about Savitra?'

Prindy, filing a shoe to fit old Betsy, stole a look at him. Jeremy looked and caught him. The other grey eyes flicked away. Giving attention to the hoof again, Jeremy persisted, 'Don't you reckon the trouble you had with the blacks yesterday was because of her . . . Wrong Side business?'

Prindy filed vigorously. But Jeremy kept on: 'I don't want to boss you . . . you know that. I don't want to boss anyone. I want to live quietly here. I want to see you and Rifkah sometimes. I want to see you happy working with these blacks. I want to see the blacks happy. Only I don't want to see trouble.' A little silence, only for the scraping and filing and gusty breathing of the horses. Jeremy added: 'More than anything, I want to see you to . . . to go a straight road . . . that doesn't mean I'm worried about Wrong Side or anything . . . only, there's your song about your *Rown Road*. Don't matter what road you go . . . only it's got to be straight. See what I mean?'

Prindy spoke to the horseshoe: 'Yas, grandfather.'

After a moment Jeremy said, 'If you'd like the girl to go down to her people, I'll help you to get her away . . . or if you'd like to take her, and come back on your own . . . whatever you like.'

No answer. Jeremy added: 'But you can't keep her and be right with the blacks, too. They hunted you like strangers . . . the way they do halfcastes or low-class whites who come hanging round camps . . . .' His voice trailed off, perhaps because the rasp had begun to sound impatient. But he finished: 'Any way I can help you . . . you just ask, eh?'

Still working, Prindy answered calmly, 'That old-man make it all straight, Grandfather.'

Jeremy stopped to stare. 'What old man?'

The other grey eyes met his frankly. 'Pookarakka.'

Jeremy blinked before the gaze. Prindy, turning back to his work, added: 'He come by'n'by.'

For a moment Jeremy continued to stare, then resuming his own work, he mused, 'Hmm!' He repeated it a couple of times, as if conceding the point that there was no arguing anything with one who had a magician as patron.

The talk turned to horses. Jeremy said he was troubled to find old Betsy in foal after all the years of infertility. He foresaw a bad foaling. 'I'll be needing your help then,' he said. 'I'll have to work out about when it'll be. Luckily I've got a fair quantity of Vitamin E. That might help her.'

When much later in the day Jeremy was able to have a private word with Rifkah, he heard from her the details of the youngsters' encounter with the blacks, as she'd been told by Savitra. He told her of his own talk with Prindy.

Rifkah wanted to know how Bobwirridirridi could solve the problem. Jeremy answered, 'I can't see any way, except by somehow frightening the two kids apart.'

Rifkah said, 'I'll haf her on my hand zen. She might be hafing baby zat time. I don't understand vy not she is pregnant yet.'

'The human female is slow to come to bearing-maturity, despite coming to sexual activity comparatively soon. Most species gestate from the first oestrus. Yet, while the average girl reaches puberty between twelve and thirteen, she won't bear before fifteen. Notice how those black kids married off after first menstruation don't have babies for several years? You'd think it's intellectual development that Nature's concerned with first in the case of human reproduction, wouldn't you. The better the intellectual quality is likely to be, the longer fecundation is delayed. Still, you never know. The Ol'Goomun seems to make rules only to break 'em at will . . . unless it's Old Tchamala that does the breaking. Look at our Betsy . . . never in season for the past five years . . . and now she foals in circumstances ripe to kill an old mare so gently reared.'

'It vill be all right to tek her horse-hunting?'

'She'd only be upset if left behind. Besides, gently handled, exercise should do her good.'

Jeremy and Prindy set out on the horse-hunt three days later. It was mid-morning, with the sou' easter just starting to sweep down over the lip of the escarpment, like a cool wave breaking. They had gone no more than a mile, when Prindy, in the lead on Betsy, drew rein, raised his hand to stop, and cocked his head towards the red wall. After a moment of listening, he called back to waiting Jeremy, 'Aeroplane!'

Jeremy looked back towards the camp, perhaps to see if the flag were conspicuous. He had left instructions for it to be pulled down if any aircraft came close. Not that those at the camp could have heard, when he himself looked incredulous when Prindy, swinging back to him, added the information: 'Sound like Fergus aeroplane.' By the looking, as he sat his horse with ear cocked, Jeremy still hadn't heard, when Prindy reached him and said, 'Junkers all right.'

Then there it was, the *pijak* hum so well known of old.

Jeremy stared for a moment at the violet skyline, then said, 'Better take cover. Can't be Fergus, surely. Someone must've found the plane.' He dismounted, led the conspicuous Snowball under a tree.

In a moment there was the Junkers, almost in line with them, shooting aloft from what must have been near tree-top level, now to avoid the downwash of the wind, with a roar that seemed likely to bring the red rocks down as it was sending the white birds up. Just short of them, she banked steeply to port, to turn to fly westward parallel with the escarpment. They saw only the glint of the Sun in cabin windows. She flew on, dropping to the level of the banyans, went only a short distance past the camp-site, then turned to starboard, came heading back. Obviously her captain had known the location of the camp. 'Must be Fergus,' said Jeremy.

Then just short of them again, the aircraft banked to starboard, so that the pilot could be seen. Prindy cried, 'That Fergus all right!'

No faces at the cabin windows.

Fergus made a 180° turn, to run back to the camp. Jeremy said quickly, grabbing at the matches-pouch on his belt, 'Better make a smoke.' Prindy leapt out and tore up a tussock of dry grass, then as Jeremy lit it, got more and dry leaves. As Fergus was coming towards them yet again, Jeremy tore a branch from a small eucalypt. The leaves blackened in the flame. The oil-cells burst, to send up a spiral of blue-grey smoke. Prindy had another branch. Fergus saw it just as he was on the point of turning again. He swung back to heading, came over them, banking to grin and wave, then climbed, to make a stall-turn and come sweeping back to them, now giving them a view of the starboard side, a glimpse into the cockpit as he turned to head now northward. Prindy yelled in the din. Jeremy shoved his head closer to him as the uproar receded. Prindy repeated it: 'Mitjis Elvy!'

Jeremy looked astonished. He looked away after the plane. It had climbed somewhat and was turning again. Just about there was the clay pan Fergus had used in landing here last time. He was making a circuit now to land. Then the sound of his motors waned. He vanished behind the trees.

The two pairs of grey eyes met, the boy's inquiring, the man's puzzling. Jeremy said, 'I'll go over and meet him. Nip back to the camp and tell Rifkah, will you, son? She probably kept planted. Then you can come and join me.'

Jeremy mounted, set Snowball ambling off in the direction his ears were pointed, murmuring to himself, 'Alfie, eh? Now what the hell!'

Soon there through the scrub was to be seen the Junkers on the ground, looking like some huge hump-backed animal. He drew rein, to approach more warily. Only Fergus and Alfie Candlemas were to be seen, which surely meant they were the entire complement. There was no luggage to be seen, only some of those small cans of gasolene with which Fergus had loaded the Junkers. He called: *Ku*!

Only Fergus waved when he appeared, and then not as cheerily as might be expected. Indeed there was something strange in the way the pair watched his approach. Certainly their appearance was such. They looked like a pair of bushies, stockmen just flown in from a mustering camp. Jeremy's laconic greeting made it seem as if he regarded them as sueh: 'Goodday!'

'How's it, Jerry?' Fergus answered, and came to take his hand, wearing the split-lip grin, but nothing of the former cheeky self-assurance of expression. It was only the lips that grinned. His face was set, eyes drawn. Alfie, wearing a similar expression did not move, except to fold her arms. She nodded like a man, and looked like one, in grey working pants and shirt.

'Well,' said Jeremy. 'This's unexpected.'

Fergus shrugged. 'What isn't these days?' A pause. Then he said, 'We're headed for Portuguese Timor. Thought we'd look you up.'

Jeremy stared his astonishment, turned it on Alfie. Her lips turned down in a scowl, and black eyes snapped like her voice: 'They were going to intern me . . . the bastards . . . in my own country!'

Jeremy breathed, 'Intern?'

Fergus said, 'They've interned the Free Australia Party.'

Still scarcely audible, Jeremy commented, 'So that was it. Heard something on radio about internments.'

Alfie sneered: 'Did you think it was the Communist Party?' When he blinked at her she added savagely, 'The Comms aren't interested in the war against Japan . . . because Russia isn't in it. In fact they've howled against our men coming home. All they want's a second front in Europe, to help the Russians.' She stopped breathless, to go on: 'They were declared a subversive organization by the Conservatives . . . for being pro-German while the Germans were allies of the Russians. Then Labor, the Great Australian Party, the moment they came to power, lifted the ban, gave them their blessing to be Russia First. But when it comes to us, the True Australians, not only do they declare us subversive, but class us with enemy aliens and put us behind barbed wire. That's enough for me. The Commonwealth of Australia stinks as far as I'm concerned. The Yanks have got it now. Let 'em keep it. I'm getting out!'

Still looking at a loss and sounding it as he spoke, addressing them both, Jeremy asked, 'Did you escape or something?'

Alfie, panting from her last effort, answered, 'The dogs didn't get the chance to lay hands on me. I was tipped off . . . by an uninterned German, no less!'

Jeremy concentrated on Fergus, who said, 'They were going to draft me.'

'Into the Air Force?'

The grin split the moustache. 'Into the Choco Commandos.' Seeing Jeremy's puzzlement, Fergus added: 'Civil Construction Corps. Sort of slaves to the Yanks. Road building, et cetera. That's how I got back up here . . . with a lot of bluff . . . in your ute. Alfie came to me on the lam. So here we are.'

'But . . . Timor!'

'Should be easy enough. I've done the trip several times, know people there. With the sou'easter, couple of hours night flight.'

'But you can't just fly out of the country in wartime!'

'I've checked on things. There're Yanks at Beatrice now, building a big air-base. Got talking to some flying types, about local conditions, easily got out of them the set up round here. Apparently they haven't got sufficiently well organized yet to make more than a scratchy patrol of the coast . . . and no navy at all yet.'

'They seem to have a regular aerial patrol from Palmeston and back along the coast.'

'How regular?'

'As clockwork, it seemed to me. Struck me as mad as the German patrols of the English Channel . . . when the Pomms always rendezvoused with 'em and shot 'em down. If there're Japs about and they don't know their movements by now they're pretty slow.'

'Half these Yanks are of Hun descent, by their names, and the look of 'em . . . the other half Dago. It's no wonder it took the Japs to get 'em into the war.'

Alfie cut in bitterly: 'So that if they beat the Japs and hang onto the country, we'll have been beaten by the Germans and Italians after all . . . without having had cause to make war on them, or anyone else. This country's a lunatic asylum!'

Jeremy said dryly, 'You can hardly call a man with the name of Douglas MacArthur a Dago or a Hun.'

Fergus said, 'The way he talks, the Huns'll have nothing on him when he comes to dealing with the Japs properly. Have you heard him broadcasting his boasts and threats to the Philippines, after doing a bunk for his life from there . . . *I will return*!' Fergus assumed a brassy Yankee accent.

'Yes . . . I've heard him.'

'Don't tell me you're for him now?'

'I'm not for any leader I know of . . . or I wouldn't be here.'

Alfie cut in again, shrilly: 'All you're here for is the Jews, isn't it, Jeremy . . . or at least the one you're shacked-up-with in your cave?'

Jeremy went very red, swallowed hard, with difficulty asked her, 'I beg your pardon?'

Alfie opened her mouth wide. However, Fergus got in first: 'We spotted Rifkah at your camp.'

Jeremy now had control of himself, demanded sharply, 'Well?'

Now Fergus was flushed and cutting of tone: 'I understood she was to operate from the Mission and keep clear of you.'

Alfie uttered a trill of nasty laughter. Disregarding her, Jeremy briefly explained the circumstances to Fergus, concluding, 'As a matter of fact, Prindy and I were just off horse-hunting to get them back to the Mission as soon as possible. Perhaps you'd be good enough to spot 'em for us from the air.'

Nodding agreement, Fergus asked, 'There's no naval or military establishment at the Mission, then?'

'I couldn't say that for sure. But I listen to Glascock giving his skeds, and sometimes speaking to ships and planes. I haven't heard any other voice . . . and the Morse is always his slow stuff.'

'Wouldn't the blacks know?'

'Only those who've been there recently. Rifkah and the others hope to contact them . . . otherwise they'll go *tchinekin* in a canoe to see for themselves.'

'If possible I'd like to take off from there. I left a fair plant of fuel.'

'What about Glascock? Won't he be bound to report what you're doing?'

'I hadn't intended to tell him exactly. He hasn't dobbed you in. I'd make out I was here only to join you, and wanted my gas.'

'Why not make that a fact . . . instead of making this hair-brained trip?'

Alfie intruded: 'And hide in a cave!'

'I'm standing by to fight the war my own way, if need be . . . . '

She cried, 'If MacArthur lets you! We'll he's not stopping us.'

'Unless you're very lucky, any fool with his finger on a trigger on either side will stop you.'

'Then we'll go down fighting whoever it is . . . because we're armed!' Jeremy looked at Fergus, who blinked. Then Fergus said, 'There's always been a gun aboard the old crate. Huns had it in a secret compartment. Operates under the floor of the cockpit, through a false venturi.'

Jeremy breathed, 'God, you're looking for trouble!'

Alfie cried, 'We're not running away from it!'

'The Portuguese will intern you . . . . '

'Let them! So long as I'm not interned in my own country as an alien, simply for defying the tyranny of the U.S.A. and exposing the spinelessness of Australia . . . . ' Alfie choked over the last words. Tears flooded the black eyes, but to be blinked back with harsh effort. She went on with rising passion: 'I intend to broadcast to Australia . . . the truth . . . about our bravoes who've become lick-spittles to the Yank with his Almighty Dollar . . . about our women whoring with the Yanks like the women of a conquered country. Listen, Jeremy . . . if I weren't here, I'd be behind barbed wire, with people called the enemy. If I'm caught here, I'd be dragged away to the barbed wire . . . only they'd never take me alive. What about you? If they get you . . . and they will in time . . . will you let them take you?'

'Of course not. What I'm objecting to is your leaving your country in time of war . . . '

'The only place I can fight for my country at present is outside it . . . pouring scorn on it for what it is, a rotten mongrel colonial community. What happened to my last effort . . . my book . . . and to me? No . . . this is my chance, and Fergus's, to show true courage. If we can't make it, it's too bad. We'd be better off than if we stayed, because we would have died with honour, as Australians refusing to fight a war forced on us from outside, who would rather go outside and die free than stay and rot as eternally damned colonials!' The passion of her delivery left Alfie panting and quivering.

Jeremy looked at Fergus, who half-shrugged and turned away, looking as if he'd heard a lot of it. Then, as if on sudden thought of a way to get relief from it, he said, 'I'd like to see Rifkah.'

'Take the horse,' said Jeremy. 'I want to talk to Alfie.'

Snowball remembered Fergus, nuzzled him. Fergus mounted, rode away.

Alfie asked coldly, 'What would *you* want to talk to *me* about? Not Jews, I hope . . . because to me the subject stinks.'

He uttered a slight groan, said, 'Don't tell me you're still anti-Semitic!'

'Why not? Isn't the whole trouble in the world over the damn Jews? Didn't their Communism and capitalistic greed combined start it all off . . . and then their lies and propaganda about the way they've been unjustly treated bring in the Americans, and war right to our own shores?'

'For God's sake, girl. I thought it was only Rifkah the woman you hated.'

'Rifkah the harpy, you mean . . . who with her Communist mob, destroyed our hope of our True Commonwealth.'

Jeremy made a despairing gesture. 'I wanted to try to talk sense to you . . . .'

Alfie's voice rose: 'And I'm going to talk truth to you! But for your falling into the hands of that creature, you'd have been our leader . . . and we'd not be the defeated slave people we are today.'

He flamed: 'But for that stupid anti-Semitism of *your* mob, with your Movement you might have got a real leader and done some good . . . . '

'The leader was *you* . . . and only you. With your love of the land, your power to inspire others with it . . . . '

'Things only invested in me by your romanticism . . . . '

'Things invested in you by the Spirit of the Land you used to talk so much about. Things that *I* could have brought out . . . if only you'd accepted the love I offered . . . if only you'd *dared* to accept!' He blinked, swallowed. She kept on: 'You seduced me . . . yes, with your passionate talk of *Terra Australis*, filled me with hope of our *Australia Felix*, as you did with our child. You took me as an inexperienced girl, and pushed me into war against your declared enemies . . . yes, but when the war really started, you abandoned me, left me to be torn to pieces . . . . '

He cut in sharply: 'If you really believe I've let you down, you can join me now.'

It stopped the wild tirade, smoothed those hard lines of bitterness from eyes and mouth. For a moment the little girl Alfie looked out of the wide black eyes. A moment of expectant black eyes staring into defensive grey. Then the tight mask was drawn again, the voice came more shrewish than ever: 'Join you in *what*?'

Caught at a loss, he half mumbled, 'In staying with me here.'

The black eyes snapped: 'Sitting round that cave of yours, doing the washing for your Jewess? I understand they give such jobs to Christians, but won't let them touch food or even dishes. Is that right?'

The grey head drooped wearily. She went on: 'Doing that either till the Japs come and murder us who never had a say in declaring war on them . . . or old friend Inspector Ballywick turns up to cart us off to the barbed wire for refusing to be in the undeclared war. No, Jeremy . . . *I'm* at war . . . with a bastard colonial community that besmirches a beautiful name by calling itself Australia . . . and if necessary, I'll go down fighting . . . . '

She broke off at a peal of flute-like sound from the scrub: like butcher birds in song, only it ran on into true melody. Jeremy glanced with her, saying quickly, 'Young Prindy . . . with his flute.'

Prindy was playing his *Butcher Bird Song*. In a moment there he was, astride Betsy, swaying to the rhythm of his playing. He was in fresh khaki shorts and shirt now. Hardly the little boy whom Alfie had known. She stared wide-eyed. He played only a little, put the flute away in his saddle-bag. No doubt the bit of tootling was to announce himself to people he'd heard in disputation. He came on with face blank of expression, with only a glance for the waiting pair, then concentrated on the Junkers, running his eyes over her.

Alfie cried, 'Prendegast!' He looked at her, slid from the saddle.

She came with a rush, seized him by the upper-arms, stared into his startled face for a moment, then kissed him hard on the mouth. It was he who withdrew. Still holding him, she gabbled, 'Where's that little boy I knew who used to sing so sweetly? You're a man . . . you've got whiskers!' The interest was real. The Alfie of old was glowing in her face. 'And, oh, aren't you a Delacy . . . those eyes!' She turned to stare at Jeremy, then back to Prindy again. 'You were my little boy once, you know. Remember our picnics . . . down the beach . . . down the harbour?'

His voice came growling, 'Oh, yas.'

'An old man's voice, too!' She laughed merrily. When he smiled, she kissed him again.

Jeremy broke in: 'You can look after Mrs Candlemas, son, eh? I want to have a word with Fergus. He'll look for the horses for us.' He glanced at Alfie. 'I presume you don't want to come to my camp?'

By the sudden twist of her lips she was about to say something savage, but perhaps checked by the intensity of two pairs of Delacy eyes, only muttered, 'No.' Pulling Prindy, she said, 'Come and sit in the shade and play for me. I believe you make up wonderful songs.'

Prindy went readily enough to get the flute.

Jeremy said, 'See you later.' Betsy trotted up to him. He lengthened the leathers, mounted, in a moment was good.

The shade Alfie sought was under the Junkers' port wing. She dropped down, to sit clasping legs, chin on knees. Prindy folded up feet and legs like a blackfellow. She said, 'Play me something from the dear old Compound days . . . one of those lovely classics the Bible Bashers had the cheek to pinch to make silly hymns out of. *God is Love*, eh?'

'*Melody in F*,' he said, raised the flute.

Staring at him soft-eyed she softly la-la-la'd in accompaniment. Again the child Alfie. When it was over, she sighed: 'Those were dear days for me. . . the dearest days of my life, I think. I was really fighting for something . . . and winning!'

He played Mendelssohn's *Spring Song*. Then *La Donna è Mobile*. She laughed over the latter: 'How ridiculous to make *Praise Ye The Lord* out of *The Woman is Fickle*! Yet it brought beautiful music to those who'd never hear it otherwise . . . and particularly to you . . . so we can forgive the Bible Bashers. Now some of your own.'

After a while she sighed again: 'Such talent wasted . . . and only one person to blame for it!' Her brows rumpled again in anger. 'If he'd've done what I wanted, you'd be nationally famous now. By now you'd probably have composed our National Anthem, that would have us marching in pride . . . instead of cringing in spineless abjection, still singing *God Save the Bloody King* . . . and now as well *The Star Spangled Banner*!' That roused her, so that her face flushed and eyes flashed. Then bitterly she added: 'God, how I hate that man, Jeremy, sometimes!'

After a moment she asked eagerly, 'Would you come with me, Prendy?'

The grey eyes became wary. 'Where you go?'

'To a place where you won't have to run away all the time . . . where people won't despise you for being coloured, but love you for being beautiful, and respect you for your talent. Do you know where Timor is?'

He jerked his lips northward. She went on: 'Fergus and I are going there. Come with us. There's no war there. We'll get you a proper flute. You can play all day. We'll have your music published. You'll become famous. Will you come?'

Prindy looked interested, but answered, 'I ask Mullaka.'

Her black brows rumpled. 'Why ask him? He doesn't care about you. I tried to get him to look after you years ago, when you were only a little boy, and the police were hunting for you. He said you'd have to go your own way, because that's what you wanted. You were playing about your Own Way just now. But you've got to have someone to show you the way . . . .' She stopped as he swung quickly away from her.

On the edge of the scrub was Savitra, wearing a bright print dress, standing staring. Alfie turned and stared, asked, 'Who's that?'

'That one Savitra.'

'Ah . . . the little Indian girl! Fergus said you're married to her. Is that true?'

'Oh, yas.'

'And you love her, and . . . and . . . ' Alfie broke off, to look across at Savitra again, and beckon to her, calling, 'Come on, dear.'

Savitra waited for Prindy's signal, then came warily, even sulkily, so that

Alfie laughed as she got to knees to greet her: 'Did you think I was stealing your hubby?'

Savitra's black eyes looked into the other's. She kept hands locked behind her, so that Alfie had to drop the one she had extended in greeting. Still, Alfie's tone was merry: 'I'd've been more careful if I'd realized what a big girl you are now. You were only a little thing last time I saw you. I knew your sisters, too, and your mother.'

Savitra only blinked, twisting invisible fingers; not shy, not hostile, but certainly not eager to be friends. Evidently baffled, Alfie turned back to Prindy, saying with a nervous little laugh, 'Matter of fact, I was trying to steal you away, wasn't I?' Prindy's expression was much like that of his bride.

Alfie dropped back to haunches, looked again at Savitra, asked even breathlessly, 'Would you like to go to India?'

Savitra gave a big blink, stared, nodded.

Alfie rose to knees again, saying brightly, 'Well, that's where we're going ... to the beginning of India, anyway ... East Indies. Will you come with us ... Fergus, Prendegast, and me?'

Savitra glanced at Prindy, who was concentrated on Alfie. She turned back as Alfie gushed: 'You could be a true little Indian girl then, wear a *sari* ... and a jewel in your nose ... eeeeee! We could be so happy, don't you think? You would be my children.' She reached to touch the girl, only have her draw away, to stand beside squatting Prindy.

The brightness faded from Alfie's face. In a constricted voice she asked, 'Why ... don't you like me?'

Savitra's answer was to pull at Prindy's shirt to make him rise. He shook her off. Alfie asked, harshly now, 'Have you been taught to hate me?'

Again Savitra pulled. This time Prindy growled at her, 'I got 'o stop look-out Mitjis.'

Alfie rose on one knee, eyes flashing 'You don't *have* to stay.' Then she shot to both feet, crying shrilly, 'In fact I don't want you ... go away!'

Still they stared. Her voice rose: 'I said go away!' She swung away herself, towards the steps into the aircraft's cabin, rushed up them. She could be heard to slump into a seat. A sob – another – then a storm of weeping.

The pair under the wing eyed each other. Now when Savitra pulled, Prindy rose, hung for a short while staring at the doorway, then let the dark hand draw him away.

Back at the camp, Jeremy found Fergus drinking tea with Rifkah. Both looked dejected and received him awkwardly. He said, 'Surely we can do better for a guest than tea. How about a brandy, Fergus?' He got a bottle from his store.

'How's the fire-water hanging out?' asked Fergus.

'I've hardly touched it. I get little pleasure from drinking alone. In fact it's a couple of weeks since I had a drink ... till her ladyship, here, turned up.'

'I've been trying to talk her ladyship into coming along with me. If anyone's got a right to leave the damn country, it's her.'

After they'd drunk, Jeremy asked Fergus, 'Whose idea exactly was it to leave the country?'

'How do you mean?'

'Has Alfie talked you into it?'

'I didn't think you'd think I was a bloke to be talked into things.'

'I mean, the poor girl's quite crazy with what's happened to her . . . understandably . . . and you might be being rash on her account.'

'I'm not inclined to be chivalrous, either, Jeremy. No . . . I involved myself I might not've come at it if she hadn't happened to turn up on the run, as she did. But I'd often thought of the kite up here . . . only needing me to have the guts to get into it and flying out of the lousy hole. You have to see it down South now, to realize what a low-class people the Australians are. They're not even much interested in war with their old enemies the Japs, now. The Yanks are here. You hear it everywhere . . *The Yanks'll get us out of it* There's a sort of gala spirit . . expressed in the song they're all singing . . . *Drinkin' Rum and Coca-Cola . . . Workin' for the Yankee Dollar.* The rich have opened their houses to them. They're the new aristocracy, the officers. They've taken over anything else they want . . . the big hotels, hospitals, office-blocks, for their exclusive use . . . Off Limits, as they call it, to the local yokels, under the Stars and Stripes. The only objections you hear down back streets, where the local troops can't get into the brothels for the conquerers. A few fights. But they're soon stopped. It perhaps wouldn't be so bad, this grovelling, if there was anything superior about this Master Race. But from what I've seen of 'em, high-ranking and low, they're inferior even to our mob . . . physically and mentally . . . drooling hill-billies and loud-mouthed cheap-skates from the Bronx and Chee and Filly and such semi-brute communities of Our Great Yew-nighted States, man. Ahhhh! To live in that atmosphere I just find impossible, Jerry. To stay in it a moment longer than necessary when I have the means to get out would amount to acceptance of it. I'm only surprised that you, of all people, Jerry, don't see it like that.'

'It's . . . well, the idea of deserting the country that bothers me. There is this kinship with one's country, if not with one's community . . . . '

'Is it really one's country? I'd always despised it as a colonial dump, till I met you. Contact with you taught me to see the bush and to love it. But already it was being destroyed by exploitation from outside. Now it'll be destroyed with a rush, won't it? It's always been the ambition of every intelligent person born in the place to get out of it, to become part of the mature world. Those who come back are those who couldn't make it out in the big world . . . like the Bloke, who didn't become a Patriot till he had to come home broke and beaten. But for you . . . and this one here . . . . ' Fergus grinned wanly at Rifkah ' . . . I'd have been gone long ago.'

He took a swig at his replenished glass, stared moodily across the northern wilderness, while the others stared at him. He went on: 'Very few people are really Australian. I've talked to them lately, especially since I've heard of the bolt from Palmeston. Actually a similar thing has taken place right down the East Coast . . . and the West, for all I know. You can buy mansions within big-gun range from the sea for a song now. It's not a nation, Jeremy. It's never been any better than a federation of British Colonies. Now the Old Dart's lost her grip, the Yanks have moved in. I don't feel as if I'm deserting anything anyone with any quality wouldn't have deserted long ago.' He drew a deep breath, turned back to take hold of his glass, exhaled savagely: 'It might have been a beautiful land in its primal state . . . but never since the White Bastards moved in . . . the Lags in chains with their guards wielding the cat-o'-nine-tails, the Scum of the Earth herding in to get rich quick by tearing her guts out for the gold, then those lowest class people in the world, whose own countries were glad to get rid of, the Immigrants. The Australian community, Jeremy, as I see it, is bastard by origin and bastard by tradition, so that I can feel nothing but shame in confessing that I was born into it!' So passionate was he in final declamation that his face was jerking. He raised his glass, drained it at a gulp. The effect of his feeling was plain in the flushed staring faces of his audience.

Jeremy broke the strained silence that followed: 'When do you intend to make the flight?'

'As soon as possible. I'm pretty sure I got away without anyone's hearing us over the other side there. They'd already started roaring up their track-vehicles . . . and I waited till the wind got up strong. But you never know, with radar and things . . . if they've got it at Beatrice yet. Seems you can beat 'em by gully-raking. I raked the whole Plateau at tree-top. You say that coast patrol will be passing about now, and back about 1300.' Fergus looked at his watch. 'I'd like to be over on one of those salt-pans near the mouth of the Leopold well before dark, and with the kite camouflaged. Rifkah says she'll come with me, with the kids . . . that is to the coast . . . and go on to the Mission by canoe and see how the land lies. If it's safe to come over, she'll get Steve Glascock to give me a short R-tok call. All being well, I'd like to leave the Mission somewhere after midnight, to make landfall at first light . . . '

'Midnight tonight?' asked Jeremy.

'Hell, no! They've got to get to the Mission first. According to Rifkah that can take anything from a couple of hours to a couple of days, according to tide and wind. I'll wait the two days, if necessary. So long as I've got the kite as close to the sea as possible and the tanks full and the engine tuned, I'll go ahead notwithstanding. I've got enough fuel to make the trip as it is. Still, it could be dicey . . . with no weather info', and the things that can happen over sea . . . wind-changes, wind-shears, even storms. I'd like to have my tanks right full, and the emergency tank as well. We've even got to think of getting there ahead of time and having to hang about burning up gas for light enough to get down . . . . '

'*Ku*!'

They looked down through the rocks. Again the call. Jeremy said, 'The youngster's coming back already. Wonder what happened?' He gave the answer.

Prindy, coming with Savitra on his heels, eyes on what could be glimpsed of the camp above, was diverted by a slight sound above him to the right. Here was a great block of sandstone almost entirely enveloped by roots of a big banyan. It was a sound only the keenest of hearing could have heard: the merest *Click-click*. His eyes flew searching. He halted, turned on his bride, who from looking down picking her way, looked up at his movement. His stood aside for her, saying, 'You go on up. I want to look horse.'

They had passed the horses in their little yard. Eyeing him sharply, she said, 'I come too.'

But the intensity of the grey stare was too much for her. When he repeated, shortly, 'You go on up,' she obeyed, sulkily.

Indeed he went to the yard, but only to skirt it and come back to the rock on the other side. As he came up, a spider grey figure emerged from the web of grey roots. A soft cackle answered his subdued cry of joy. They rushed to embrace.

Bobwirridirridi, smoothing his *Mekullikulli*, talked swiftly in the mixture of lingo, *Murringlitch*, and signs, evidently with the aeroplane as chief topic: '*Haeroplane ngaiya koregoro . . . Misminara long o' haeroplane . . . minara minara haeroplane . . . Nigari Haeroplane Man.*'

Prindy nodded gravely and made signs in answer. At length the old man cackled, indicating his stark nakedness with a wave of a claw, '*Nogoro ngeinyima Mullaka trowjis.*'

Nodding as gravely as before, Prindy turned away and headed for the camp, going round the rock, so that he came closer to those above without being seen. He paused to listen to what was being said. Evidently the subject was Alfie, no doubt reported on by Savitra. Fergus was saying, 'She flies off at anything . . . bundle of nerves.'

Rifkah commented: 'Poor zing! I know vot ve do . . . ve pack up dinner and tek to eat at aeroplane vit' her . . . yes?'

Prindy made his appearance. Jeremy asked if the horses were all right. Nodding, Prindy went to the water-bag to drink, staying there till he caught Jeremy's eye. Jeremy asked, 'What is it, son?'

The boy's grey eyes held his grandfather's for a moment before he answered, with a jerk of lips hindward, 'Pookarakka there.'

Jeremy blinked, nodded, then said, 'Tell him to come on up . . . tell him I've got some brandy for him.'

'He can't come yet.'

'How's that?'

Still grave, Prindy replied, 'He got no trousers.'

Jeremy blinked again, reddened, pursed his lips before saying, 'Well, come and we'll get him some.' Turning, he gave the others sitting under the shelter what could only be taken as a warning glance. Fergus looked ready to crack a joke. Rifkah had merriment in her eyes. He said to Rifkah, 'Could you make a big egg-flip, dear?'

Soon Prindy was hurrying down with a neat fold of khakis, topped with a red bandana. Jeremy grinned at the others. They had their chuckle. Jeremy remarked to Fergus, 'It's marvellous how that old fellow can get about. Last heard of him was on that train they came down on with Pat Hannaford . . . just dropped off somewhere, to go on a great walk-about.'

Rifkah said with a smile, 'Zey reckon he can fly.'

Fergus said, 'If only he could . . . we could get him to make a rekky of the Mission.

'If you could get him to go with you to the coast you should make good use of him, said Jeremy. 'He has a remarkable faculty for getting about unseen . . . makes himself invisible, they say. The trouble would be to get him into the plane . . . unless the fact of Prindy's going might induce him.'

There were the two khaki figures coming up, the taller one looking very odd with its topknot of ochred hair and plaited goatee. Also, Bobwirridirridi wore the bandana tied round his right leg above the knee, as a bush blackfellow might some decoration made of woven material and feathers, which could serve also for carrying something.

Jeremy went to meet the pair, grasped the old man's hand, said it was good to see him again, asked him where he had been. Bobwirridirridi only cackled in reply, and spoke but one word, which was in appreciation of the appointments of the camp: 'Prop-er-lee!' Being told that brandy with egg and milk awaited him, he expressed his appreciation with a smack of the lips and a deep sigh.

Bringing him up to the shade, where the others all stood to receive him, Jeremy said, 'You savvy all this lot, eh?'

The Pookarakka nodded, but looked only at Fergus, whose extended hand he took. When Fergus asked him if he remembered their brief association during the old fellow's trial, Bobwirridirridi answered, 'I savvy you plenty time you hon top dere long o' haeroplane.'

'Flying over the Jail, eh? Yes, I often did that. But you must have pretty good eyes to know it was me.'

The few teeth showed in a grin. 'You learn him me dat haeroplane, allsame you been learn him my-boy?' A nod towards Prindy.

Fergus looked surprised, but answered readily, 'Sure. We go salt-water. You come?'

'*Yu-ai.*' But now the attention of the cavernous eyes was on the enamel bowl of brandy-flip, and the wide nostrils flared in sniffing. Jeremy got the bowl from the table. The old man took it in both hands, sniffed at it deeply, then as if the others had ceased to exist, turned from them, to go to the fireplace. He dropped into blackfellow sitting posture, sipped, smacked. He swigged, belched. Then with a deep sigh he settled down to enjoyment. The others left him alone, the men to sit again, while the women and Prindy saw to the packing of the stuff to go to the Junkers.

When the bowl was empty and the death's head turned, Jeremy asked if the Pookarakka wanted more. The topknot shook, and the head turned back towards the antbed stove with nostrils flaring again. The cracked voice cried, 'Tchoop!'

A saddle-pot stood giving off a sweet savour. Jeremy looked at Rifkah, who nodded and got another bowl and a spoon and came to the fireplace. As she stirred the giblet soup the scraggy old throat jerked convulsively. She filled the bowl, handed it over. But again the topknot swung towards the table. Jeremy rose and came and took the bowl and passed it on. As the old man took it from him he said, 'Brett.'

Rifkah came with a wedge cut from the semi-circle of camp-oven baked bread about to be packed. Jeremy gave it into the claws, which tore it up and dropped it in the soup, then fished it out again. A deep sniff to savour it, then down that wide hatch. How he smacked and slobbered! When he had tongue for it he cried, 'Number one . . . number one!'

Bobwirridirridi cleaned it up to the last finger-lick. Then with a great belch he rose, set off whence he'd come, vanished. The others returned to their packing. When after about half an hour they all went down to the horse-yard, they found him awaiting them, still decently attired, but otherwise equipped for the bush with dilly-bags and weapons. When they were ready to set out, he handed all of his equipment to Prindy, except one spear and the womera. Prindy took them readily, and deferentially fell into line behind his Master and his grandfather as they walked together. Fergus and Rifkah led the way, with Savitra behind them, casting an eye back now and again longingly at her man, apparently not daring to walk with him in the circumstances.

Also with evident deference to the Master, Jeremy questioned him concerning his recent peregrinations. Bobwirridirridi, with a backward roll of the topknot to take in just about everywhere but the country ahead, answered with equally vague and sweeping assertion of his power to get about, 'All-a-way.' However, through Jeremy's gentle persistence, he named one locality – Beatrice township, or rather encampment, as now more properly it might be called. This came out through Jeremy's carefully asking, 'You reckon *kuttabah* finish this country now?'

The old man sucked in parchment cheeks till they seemed to touch and considered it. Then he replied, 'Dat old lot bee-fore, him finish now. New lot come behind. Him dere now . . . long o' Beatritch.'

'Wha' name new lot?'

'What-you-call-him Yengis.'

'Yankees?'

The old man said deliberately, 'Yengis.' He went on: 'Big mob dere. He been bring him 'nother kind blackman wukk long o' him.'

'What about countryman . . . him altogether go bush, eh?'

Now the cheeks blew out to express contempt: 'Him dere . . . wukk all-same long o' jail . . . cuttin' woot, breakin' shtone . . . lock him up night-time.'

The old man then got onto the subject of aeroplanes and the attack on Palmeston, obviously excited by the destructive power of what he must see as a magical contrivance. 'Boom, bam, burrup!' he kept exclaiming as he gave an almost incoherent description of the air-raid, using as much lingo as *Murringlitch*, talking rather to himself, it seemed. By his expression, Jeremy soon gave up trying to follow him. At length it became evident that he had finished his air-war and was talking about the Junkers, which he had found in her hiding-place and looked over. It might be assumed that he believed she was here for his convenience and that he was mightily pleased about it. When they came into sight of her, hump-backed above the scrub, he cried out, '*Yakkarai*!'

They came into full view of the aircraft to see Alfie's dusty bottom disappearing through the cabin doorway, obviously in rebuffment of Rifkah, who was standing staring with brows drawn. Rifkah looked round at Jeremy, but without waiting to consult him, at once turned again and went heading for the cabin door. She climbed the steps, halted in the doorway. Alfie was in the cockpit, in the pilot's seat, out of sight of those below. Rifkah called, 'Alfie!'

Dark head and shoulders stiffened, but did not turn.

Rifkah cleared her throat: 'Ve haf brought picnic dinner, Alfie.'

Alfie's head may have been a dummy's.

Rifkah stood for a moment, then stepped inside, said as she began to move slowly up the aisle, 'It is nice stew of pigmy-goose . . . .'

Without turning, Alfie snapped, 'Nice and *kosher*, I presume.'

Rifkah halted, drew a deep breath, answered in a constrained voice, 'As mooch as possible.'

The snap became strident: 'Well, it would be just *too mooch* for an unclean Gentile like me.'

The copper head drooped for a moment. Raising it, its owner said carefully, 'You go to great danger. It is not goot to go hating ev'body . . . . '

The black head swung round, with black eyes blazing. 'I wouldn't have to go into danger, out of my own country . . . if it weren't for you, you Jew-whore, directly, and your evil race, indirectly. Not good to hate you, and all your filthy mob? It's the breath of life to me now. Yes . . . I hate and hate and hate you . . . and will till the day I die!'

That old *bubbeh's* look fell upon the bright young face that stared back. A moment. Then Rifkah turned, went hurrying out so fast that on the step she stumbled. Fergus leapt to her aid, handed her down. All eyes were on her, because all ears must have heard that last tirade.

Fergus climbed the stairs, looked in to meet the black eyes, scowled and said, 'You're mad . . . the girl was only trying to be kind to you.'

'Trying to take me in like she's taken the rest of you . . . like her dirty race has taken the world in for ten thousand years . . . . '

'Aw, shut up! She's coming with us.'

'She's not coming with me!'

'Then you'll have to get out. I'm taking them to the Mission. And if she'll come, I'll take her to Timor, too.' Fergus withdrew.

Jeremy, standing staring glumly, as if moved by sudden impulse, went quickly to the steps, mounted. Alfie was staring out of the windshield again. She sat rigid till he reached the cockpit, then swung on him with a smirk: 'So you've come to fighting her battles for her now . . . not like last time!'

He stopped with hands on the backs of each seat, looking down at her. The smirk widened, although the black eyes blazed and the small bosom heaved: 'Last time you put your halfcaste woman on to me.'

He bit his lip as he met the challenge of her eyes. Still standing, he said, 'If I could be sure your antipathy's only personal, some woman's thing . . . . '

She screeched at him, 'If you could be sure my bitterness over your rejection of my love and all it stood for, for me, for our country, is only *Some Woman's Thing*!'

He went red, blinked, utterly at loss.

She went on, almost spitting up into his face, 'You only understand cows. No wonder they called you the Scrub Bull! Driven out of the herd because you refused to conform . . . but it was only bull's stubbornness, not courage. Go to your Jew-cow and back to the scrub and die defeated!'

'For God's sake, girl . . . . '

'For God's sake leave me alone! I loved you, loved you . . . like a god . . . and you call it *Some Woman's Thing*!' She was shrieking now, and rising with small fists clenched and quivering. 'Now I loathe you. Go away . . . go . . . before I hit you!'

No doubt about the loathing in those black eyes. He drew back.

'Go, I said!' she screeched.

He backed away, muttering, 'Goodbye, Alfie . . . don't . . . . '

'Don't tell *me* what to do . . . *you* who don't do anything. Go, I said!'

He nodded, swallowed, muttered again, 'Goodbye,' turned away. At the door he glanced back, to be smitten by the eyes again. Heaving a great sigh he went out.

That awkward meal eaten beneath the starboard wing hardly could be called a picnic dinner, despite Rifkah's seemingly compulsive efforts to make it so by pressing her food on the others and jollying them for lack of appetite. Only the horses responded. The others, even while they nibbled, kept glancing towards the source of the tension, silent behind the cockpit window. Even the Pookarakka, sitting under the other wing gobbling more bread and soup, although he could have understood hardly a word of the bitter outbursts, appeared to be little less affected by it. He could see the source, and kept his sunken eyes fixed on it. Nor could the youngsters have grasped much of the significance of the situation – unless all of it lay in that simple sentence, *I loved you*!

Jeremy looked aghast, as if confronted for the first time with vivid sense of the awful responsibility one has for one's fellows. His grey eyes were blank, as if their vision were drawn back along the years, seeing the havoc he had wrought in the smugness of his own self-sufficiency.

Fergus must have read the look, because when soon it was time to depart, taking Jeremy's hand, looking something like his old cheeky self, he said, 'Don't let our troubles get you down, Jerry . . . or else you might's well come along and share 'em.'

Was it a covert way of begging patronage? Jeremy might have thought so, the way he avoided the hard stare of the greenish eyes.

Rifkah kissed him lightly in farewell, then at the steps turned back and flung herself into his arms and clung a long moment with lips and hands, breathing as she released him, 'Dear Jeremy!' The grey eyes rolled in the burning face. Some Woman's Thing – sealing possession to spite a mean rival – or the act of an insecure child setting seal on security? If the rival saw it, she gave no sign. But Fergus saw it, with narrowed eyes. How much is one responsible for others? Is the measure reason or compassion? Is the demand made on one's strength, or one's weakness?

The cabin door shut on it with a soft bump.

Inside, Fergus ushered Bobwirridirridi to the cockpit, where he said to Alfie staring at the scarecrow in surprise, 'Old medicine-man friend of mine . . . going to the Mission . . . wants to add aviation to his talents. Mind riding in the cabin to the coast?'

Without comment she rose, came into the cabin, completely ignoring the others there, seated herself alone, buckled herself in.

Up in the cockpit, how those red coals in the dusky death's head with its topknot glowed as the engines erupted into bellowing life. The topknot danced as the head, like that of an inquisitive bird, followed the flitting of Fergus's hands over the controls. When the claws would have done likewise, Fergus shouted to him to wait till they got On Top. The Junkers rolled.

In the storm of the run-up at the end of the strip, the sunken eyes watched the magic motors spin silver webs about themselves and start dust-devils leaping from the earth, which they swallowed and farted out as flame and smoke. Then away, seeming to swallow the very strip – and up, to swallow the trees, then bore into the blue. The whole world spun beneath them. There was a midget man with tiny horses – then the *koornung*'s trance-state of level flight, one's seeming to hang there while the green-brown wilderness tore along beneath like waters of a mighty flood – violet distance far ahead rushing to meet them.

Fergus called, 'All right . . . you want to have a go?' He explained lightness of touch of hands and feet, demonstrated roll and pitch. 'You follow me through . . . foller-him-me up. Now, easy . . . easy!'

Soon Fergus took off hands and feet, and the Pookarakka came into his own, cackling for joy.

'You're a natural!' shouted Fergus.

'*Yakkarai*!'

There was another topknotted death's head mirrored in the windshield by a trick of light. Both grinned at each other – '*Yakkarai*!'

Thus straight to the Leopold River, reaching it about ten miles from the mouth, following its python-windings down just above the trees, scattering the white birds, the blue birds and black birds, as a Cock-Eye Bob does – '*Yakkarai*!'

Then out over the emerald and brown opal of the estuary, with sea stretching away with islands seeming to float on a tide stream, jade green shallows deepening to saxe blue and indigo, creamed by the sou'easter.

Fergus took over, to bring them low along that stretch of beach from which those going on to the Mission must embark. The canoes were there, but no person. The tide, in neap, was only halfway up the beach and on the turn.

Back over the mangroves, so swiftly that the distance seemed only an easy boomerang-throw, then down to land on a glittering salt-pan.

Alighting, the Pookarakka embraced his *Mekullikulli*, cackling, 'Prop-er-lee, prop-er-lee . . . number one!'

'No doubt about you blokes,' said Fergus. 'If there wasn't this bloody war on, I'd start a flying circus with you.'

'*Yakkarai*!'

Fergus, with chart and compasses, was telling how best the voyage to the Mission could be made with set of tide and wind – when he became aware of the steady staring of those who would be doing the navigating, the almost imperceptible glowing coals, the intense grey. He shut up, folded up his chart, murmured, 'How silly can a whiteman get!' He contented himself with giving Rifkah written details of the mode by which he wished to communicate with Glascock, and then with seeing them on their way, to the passage through the mangroves.

Those Spirits of the Mangroves, with their secret click-click-clicking, how urgently they spread the word – *Koornungs*! And the *koornungs*, the young one leading, the old one as rear-guard, mocked them – *Clickety-click*! Igulgul, peeping through the tips of the mangroves, looking in daylight like a white-ochred face in profile, got into the game, scaring spirits and gobies and one-armed crabs by tossing his Shade into pools where it shook with laughter. Blue and black butcher birds, blue kingfishers and red robins, protested melodiously over the intrusion. It was hard going, with the tide half in, but no taking it easy, when the only one who dared call a halt was, for all his skinny ancientness, indefatigable.

Muddied to the ears, they reached the beach with still a lot of daylight to spare. Still, no time was wasted, even though they found a turtle's nest and the women were for cooking a meal. The men left the women to dig the eggs while they prepared the canoe. The eggs were loaded for eating raw. The canoe was launched. The Pookarakka now was in the lead, sitting in the bow, singing softly to Igulgul smirking out of a gilding sky while working his magics on wind and tide. Prindy handled the sail in the stern. The women sat amidships bailing.

Thus through the islets, purpling in the failing daylight, through channels of flowing gold and silver, till Igulgul had the sky to himself and flung them a shiny towline to haul them, so that the islets parted to let them through – and there in no time were they in view of the little lights of the Mission, a few campfires on the beach, the presbytery winking through the casuarinas, and then in the back creek, still on the silver line, even though the haulier now could be seen only winking Goodnight to them through the mangroves. They ran up onto the corduroyed landing, to the skirl of the hordes of bloodsuckers joyously piping them in.

The women were left to the welcoming party, while the men went on to reconnoitre, up out of the mangroves, along the darkening street with its humps of deserted buildings, to the blaze of the presbytery.

Stephen Glascock appeared to be alone, on his east-side verandah, reading as usual by the light of the pressure lamp, sprawled in a deck-chair.

Prindy, just out of the ring of light, signalled, 'Pst!'

Glascock looked up at once, searched the grey gloom of the casuarinas, till he caught faint movement. 'Who's that?'

Prindy let himself be seen. Glascock gaped, breathed, 'Prindy!'

The boy came warily, eyes darting, asking on indrawn breath as he came up, 'Anybody stop with you, Father?'

Glascock rose and grasped the boy's shoulders. 'No . . . only me. But where'd you spring from.' Prindy made a vague movement of the head. 'Who's with you?'

'Rifkah there.'

'Where?'

'Leave behind at creek and come look-about. Where David?'

'I don't know. We had a bit of a row and he cleared out again. But we must get Rifkah.' Glascock started off up the verandah. 'Tell me how you got here. I heard you got off the *Melville* before she was sunk . . . but nothing after that.'

Prindy panted his tale, so fast was the pace the man set. Yet, for all the preliminary haste, as they were coming up to the mangroves. Glascock slackened pace, interrupting Prindy, to say, 'You all must be pretty hungry, eh?'

'Yas . . . pretty t'usty, too . . . like drink o' tea.'

Glascock stopped suddenly. 'Look . . . you go on and get Rifkah. I'll go back and light the fire and get supper going . . . eh?'

Prindy stared at him as he stood bulked against the starry sky. But the man waited for no answer, wheeled about, went off now at a lope.

That Glascock, from simple eagerness, had been thrown into a state of perturbation, was obvious enough in his not coming from the kitchen at sound of the arrival of her he had on impulse gone rushing to meet. In fact, he didn't even turn from the flaming stove till she called him from the doorway: 'Stephen!'

It was to be expected that he should turn red-faced and blink, but not that when she ran to him with open arms he caught her hands, and although smiling, held her off. Certainly she was a messy bundle to embrace, clad only in shorts and shift, still grubby with mud and stained with egg-yolk. Still, it was only at her face he looked. His breast was heaving, his voice strained, as he spoke, 'Well . . . this is a surprise!'

This time she breathed his name, and in evident protest: 'Stephen!' She tried to free her hands. When he clung she asked, with eagerness changing to anxiety, 'Vot is ze matter?'

He gasped, 'Nothing . . . oh, nothing . . . only . . . . ' When she strove against his grip again, he bent and kissed her hands. Then she buried her face in his mop of hair.

He looked up, releasing her. She stood staring, asked, 'You are not 'appy to see me?'

Still finding speech difficult, but still smiling, he said, 'Do I really see you . . . or are you a dream?'

She caught his hand, drew him to her suddenly, but only kissed his cheek, released him, stood back to stare again.

Flaming, avoiding looking at her now, he muttered, 'I've dreamt of you so much . . . too much.' Then he swung away back towards the stove, vociferating now, 'I'm getting you something to eat . . . you must be starving . . . what'd you like?' He began to leap about. 'I've got all sorts of tucker. The boats . . . the Yanks . . . bring me everything you can think of. Look . . . I've got a kerosene fridge now. Can you beat it? All mod. cons. What about steak and eggs and onions?'

She watched him, a little smile on her lips, but puzzlement in her eyes.

Then he looked at her. 'But you can't sit down to a slap-up supper like that! Have to shower and change. Still got your clothes. Come on . . . I'll rig the shower for you.'

He dodged round her, ran out ahead, came back with a hurricane lamp and a towel and a fold of clothes, went racing to the outside bathroom. He waited only long enough to fill the shower-bucket and haul it up on its pulley, then bolted.

Such was his swift concentration on the task that he had the cooking well under way before Rifkah returned and tried to take a hand in it. He let her set the kitchen table for four and make a bowl of bread and milk and whisky for Bobwirridirridi to take away somewhere. Otherwise he insisted on her keeping out of his way and confining her effort to giving him a detailed account of her experiences. She complied docilely enough. Soon the youngsters were there to help him divert two-thirds of the bit of attention he'd been compelled to give to the company. Over the meal, he gave them nearly all of it.

It was a great meal, with fresh bread and hard butter and odds and ends the like of which it had taken a world war to bring to these parts: like canned sauerkraut, pickled cucumbers, stuffed olives, maple syrup. While the kids only picked at the oddities, Rifkah ate so heartily as to confess herself sleepy when the host said she must be, as a preliminary to declaring the guests too weary to help with the washing up and hunting them off to bed. The youngsters went off to their former bridal bower in the convent.

Where Rifkah retired to was not disclosed, until, when after about an hour with all chores done, he returned with the pressure lamp to his lounging post on the eastern verandah. There in a canvas chair drawn up beside his own she sat, or rather by the utter relaxation of her posture, lay suspended, sound asleep. He almost blundered up to her, perhaps dazzled by the light, or maybe by the sight. No doubt she was truly sleeping. Her head hung to one side as if too weary to hold erect. Her lips were open like a child's, just visible, because a great hank of gleaming hair hung over that side. The rest of her hair, dragged as her head had fallen, and spread upon the canvas, blazed like the radii of a monstrance in altar candle-light, the glimpse of beauty it encompassed the holiness within, to a holy man, as this one looked to be as he stood staring, the consecrated flesh and blood. He had come silently on bare feet, with the lamp, needing pumping, barely hissing. One sleeping so soundly should not have been wakened by his very careful turning away. Perhaps it was some subtle thing like that which caused his blue eyes to roll as if in agony while he was watching her. He had only turned his back, when she called to him sharply, 'Stephen!'

He stood like a rock before turning back. Then he was frowning, and his voice was a growl: 'You're supposed to be in bed.'

She smiled naughtily. 'You haf mek convent bed-time rule again . . . like Reverend Mudder?'

The frown became darker with darkening of the skin above the beard. 'You're tired out.'

She yawned luxuriously, raising arms in a stretch that revealed a glint of axillary hair and tight-fitted the print convent dress over her young torso. The blue eyes rolled again. She sighed, still smiling, 'I am all right now . . . I haf loffly sleep . . . ahhh!' She yawned again, showing the pearl and coral of her mouth.

His growl was tremulous now: 'Anyway . . . you've got to go to bed.'

The smile became naughty again, as she extended a slim hand towards him and said, 'I vill go to bed ven you go to bed . . . vit' . . . you.'

The shock made the lamp leap in his hand so that it almost flicked out.

The naughtiness changed to a look of concern. Dropping her hand, she asked, 'Vot is matter, Stephen . . . you go back to sacerdotal vow?'

He tried to speak, but failed, hung his head. She extended her hand again. 'Come sit vit' me.'

He came blundering, not to the chair, but to the table, to set down the lamp and pump and pump it, till she reached and caught at his belt and drew him. Looking dazed, he slumped into his chair. She sought his hand and held it, looking at his set profile, as he stared into the starry sky above the grey rags of casuarina. She asked softly, 'Now you are sorry for vot ve do . . . for our loffing?'

He swallowed, took a long time to answer: 'Only as one who has lived in paradise must feel to find himself in hell.' Still he regarded the stars.

Her brows rumpled. She gave a little tug at his drooping hand. 'Explain to me, Stephen.'

Now he licked his lips, breathed deeply as if to make a great effort, began hesitantly: 'I understand . . . now . . . now I know what celibacy means . . . the vow unbroken . . . what you never have you never miss.'

'You vish to be celibate again?'

'How can a drone bee that's flown the nuptial flight do anything but die . . . only I didn't die . . . I just fell and fell and fell from the heights . . . into hell . . . . '

As his voice trailed off in a sigh, she raised his hand to touch her cheek, murmuring, 'My poor Stephen . . . you haf been too much alone.'

He looked at her quickly. 'I told you I had those damn Yanks here all the time.'

'Too mooch alone to dream.'

Now his eyes devoured her, only to turn suddenly away again.

She went on: 'You are not alone now. You are not dreaming. I am vit' you . . . to loff you again.'

His breast heaved. He panted to the stars, 'Then to leave me in hell again.'

'I vill not leaf you.'

Still to the stars he declared, 'Then I'll only make you hate me with my importuning.'

'Vot is Importunink?'

He swallowed. 'It is following you around . . . only wanting your love . . . because it's become the meaning and purpose of my life.'

'Is zat ver' bad zing?'

'We said before that our love was a gift of God . . . or Tchamala or something . . . and we used to say it was too wonderful to last for ever, but we didn't care because we would die together like Romeo and Juliet when it ceased. But you were snatched away from me. When I realized the loss of you I tried to die. I went swimming in the sea that had thrown us into each other's arms . . . so far out that I was too exhausted to come back . . . . '

'Oh, Stephen!'

'But the sea wouldn't let me die. It brought me back. Three times it brought me back . . . and left me on the beach . . . to cry in misery . . . once on that beach of ours . . . where I thought I saw you, all golden in the sunlight . . . but it was only the salt water in my eyes . . . and the tears.'

She slipped over to his knee, knelt before him, breathing up at him, 'Oh my darling . . . oh, my Stephen . . . my dear, dear loffer!'

But he sat rigid, his audience the eternal stars, his breast heaving, his voice hoarse: 'It is too hard, my love, to go back. I have come so far now in self-discipline. I couldn't go through it again.'

'Zrough loffing me?'

'Through the agony of losing you.'

For a moment she stared up at the set bearded face. Then she said, 'Stephen . . . you haf become ze priest again!'

He dropped his eyes to her, wide with protest: 'I haven't! I rowed with that fool David over it, when I found how lost I was . . . and he tried to flagellate me . . . .'

'Flagellate?'

'Whip . . . for penance . . . fool had been reading something and only half-understood it. No . . . the vow I took with myself . . . for my manhood . . . that you should be a lovely dream.'

'But I am real, Stephen!'

His eyes were rolling again as he looked down at her. 'The sea gave you to me. The sea took you away. Only the sea can give you back . . . and I must die in the sea for it.'

For long moments they stared at each other.

At last she said in a quivering whisper, 'You are fright' of such vonder . . . and I am fright' too.'

He swallowed, nodded, blinked on what looked like the beginning of tears.

She went on in the same tone: 'Spone ve go back to sea . . . go back to zat beach . . . '

'Oh!' With a hoarse cry he seized her, drew her up, smothered her expectant mouth with his own.

Both wept as they clung and kissed – wept, wept, till they were laughing, embracing wildly.

'Oh, my darling!'

'Oh, my dollink!'

'Oh!'

'Oh!'

He had her on his knees in his arms when at last he was able to say, 'We'll take blankets and things . . . all mod. cons this time.'

She laughed and kissed him, and withdrawing her mouth, laughed, 'And citronella.'

'No . . . the Yanks've got something better than that . . . and no stink . . . I've got a big pot.'

'Vell . . . come on . . . ve go . . . to the sea . . . and our beach.'

And so they went, in the rowboat, through the phosphorescent waters of the magic Island of Avalon, said to be on the Edge of Paradise and to have a Castle of Lodestone on its shores so that hearts magnetized by love were drawn to it inevitably. A billion stars went with them aloft – below a myriad denizens of the deep like herding comets. The beach – the nuptial bower, all chased with the cool fire of breaking wavelets. Silver cased their legs as they stepped ashore, as they stood for a moment in embrace, as he lifted her and bore her up to the faintly glowing bridal couch.

But love is always Wrong Side in Avalon – and the price of Wrong Side Love is Death. Or is it that Death is the Price of *Right* Side Love, like that which takes the King of the Bees to Heaven to fertilize his Queen, and that Wrong Side Love is really that stodgy semblance of the real thing which by obeying all the rules lasts until it becomes a dirty joke?

It was piccaninny daylight, and they were rolled tight together in a blanket, when the blue and the black butcher birds woke them: *Lulla-lull-la-la, lulla-lull-la*! Glascock roused first, raised dark head and looked about, looked down at the other head with a strange gleam in its darkness turned from him on the pillow, and bent and kissed it lightly. Again he looked further, at the sea, which was a ghostly blur hidden under a thin wad of mist the whispy top of which could be seen drifting as purple smoke against the faint gleam of the opening oyster of dawn.

Carefully he withdrew from the blanket, palely naked, and getting to his feet, stole over the little tide-lip down onto the wet sand. He stood straddle-legged, piddling and yawning. The boat was afloat, dimly rocking, pulling on the kedge. He turned back, was about to leap up the tide-lip, when he halted. Faint luminiferous movement in the gloom. Then sound of swift soft gushing. He smiled, drew a deep breath. Again the movement. When it ceased, he jumped up onto the dry sand, loped to the bed, crawled under the blanket, whispering. Whispering, gasping, a last wild flight to the dazzling Edge of Paradise.

When they came back, and sat up, and flung off the blanket, it was comparatively quite light. They laughed at each other. He rummaged amongst a heap of things, produced a towel. Holding it between them, they jumped up and ran to the sea. They dipped and danced, scattering silver and grey smoke. Then out on the wet sand he towelled her. He did it as a sort of religious rite, from tip to toe and back again; while she stood as if receiving it as such, only with an occasional movement of her hands when he bent low, to touch his head as if blessing him. Twice he murmured, 'I love you.' Twice she answered softly. Then the butcher birds took it up and kept it going while they dressed, while they got into the boat, as they went sweeping away in sharp silhouette against the morning: *Lull-lull-lull-luv-yu*!

As he rowed with joyous strength and she played with the little waves he made as if he made them for her, they talked matter-of-factly about Fergus and Alfie and how to dissuade them from their dangerous escapade. He said, 'If it's the Yankee take-over that's driven them crazy, they could do no better than to stop here and fight it . . . because it's here that the great grab's going to be made.'

He went on to talk of his American visitors, whom he described as quite unlike officers one would expect to find in other navies and armies: 'Seems like those in powerful social positions . . . I don't mean mere snobbish social grading, but position in business and profession . . . simply walk into high rank in their services, and judging by their talk and their activities, remain exactly as they were, except that they're in uniform. Their first interest here isn't military, but rather commercial. They talk as if they've won the war already. And it isn't just based on their boundless self-assurance. To us it looked as if the Pearl Harbour business knocked the U.S. Navy right out of existence. That's far from fact. They have their large Asiatic Fleet intact, and their Atlantic Fleet . . . and the capacity to turn out other ships like Ford turns out his motor cars. They regard the Jap Navy with contempt, and frankly say their strategy is to force it into a great sea-battle as soon as possible and cripple it and deal a death-blow to what is the very heart of Japanese pride. The Japs will face it in their pride, they reckon, even though their lines of communication are stretched to the point of snapping. While the Japs haven't got one substantial base or ally to fall back on, the Yanks have them all round the globe. They're only waiting for this battle, the Yanks. They say it'll take place in the Western Pacific any day. Meantime, those round here are seeing what this place is worth to them. All the ships that come this way put parties ashore. That's reasonable enough, seeing they're here to defend it. Still, they come back with bags and boxes of stuff they frankly gloat over. They say there's aluminium and iron and manganese and what-not round about here to supply the world for a century. They say there's oil under the swamps and rare metals in the beaches. As one of 'em said to me, "Mairn, what's wrahng with you guys? You bin sittin' on a billion bucks for a hundred years . . . and only gaht corns on your butts to show for it." '

Glascock told of how he had protested that the region was an Aboriginal Reserve, only to be laughed at and told that half of America was once Indian Reservation: 'They're quite ruthless about the rights of simple people. One of 'em said to me, "Who's going to let Stone Age savages play about with stones the blast-furnaces of the world are roaring for?" Our people are bad enough. But you have to see the Yank in action in the matter of race to really know a whiteman. They have Negroes doing the most menial of tasks, and treat them as if they weren't human. On one occasion, when a naval padre assisted me at Mass and I asked if there weren't any Catholics amongst the Negroes of the crew, he said, "Yes . . . but we'd have to hold a separate service for them . . . or the whites would walk out of the church!" '

Pulling even harder, he said, 'It's a job for us, too, girl, to keep these greedy grasping dogs from taking the country over. If we can map the sacred sites, and see to it that the Government recognizes them as sacrosanct to their owners in perpetuity, we've got something real to live and love for, haven't we? Well . . . if we can talk this crazy couple into joining us in it . . . . '

The Sun was rising as they landed, setting fire to the tallest of the mangroves of the islet across the channel and burning out the egrets and the shags. It made a golden grove of the casuarinas for them to walk in, caused the nervous hermit crabs to cast long blue shadows of themselves in which crazily they tried to take refuge. The triangle of the radio antenna looked like new-spun spider's web with – oh! – the cross on the church looking like a St Andrews Spider. Smoke was rising from the flue of the presbytery kitchen.

The youngsters came out of the kitchen, stared at the bundles the pair were carrying. Savitra asked, 'Where you been go?'

Rifkah replied gaily, 'Fishink.'

When the quizzing eyes sought for the catch, Glascock said as gaily, 'We felt sorry for the fish and chucked 'em back. Got anything cooked for breakfast?'

'We been open tuttle-hegg to mek omelette.'

'Lovely! Come on, Prindy boy . . . leave the omelette to the girls, while we go and call up Fergus.'

The official radio set was still housed in the shed beside the Boys' School and Dormitory, but in a much more spectacular way than when last seen by Prindy. Not only was the place now surrounded by a barbed-wire fence with padlocked gate, but encased in sandbags. Noting Prindy's stare, Glascock told him the protective devices had been installed soon after the raid on Palmeston. An alarm system was connected to his own quarters to give warning of sneaking intruders, to deal also with whom of nights or if he were away the place was booby-trapped. The trap was set now, he said, and they must go to the church to switch off. 'Yankee idea,' he said. 'They put it in for me only recently, because Jap submarines have been detected close at hand. Quite ingenious, with a counter-device to stop *me* from being the booby. Look.' He attempted to unlock the gate. 'Won't work unless the switch in the church is opened. The lock's easily enough busted by raiders . . . and the door of the shed. But, get inside there with the switch closed, and . . . *Boom*! They let off a charge down on the beach to show me. Terrific. They say that here it would kill at twenty yards.' As they went on to the church, the priest continued: 'See what a lovely business war is . . . all that flag-waving and cheering and medals and things . . . and they leave things lying round for simple people to pick up and get their heads blown off. The Yanks are past masters at it, the way they talk. They probably invented it. They brag that the poor silly Nip, as they call him, is a real Sucker for the booby-trap. Makes you think the Nip, for all we hear of him, has a much more chivalrous view of war than our gallant allies, eh? But I suppose he'll learn.'

Whether Prindy was able to follow the discourse closely would not matter to Glascock in his gay expansive mood.

The booby-trap switch was rigged inconspicuously under the holy-water stoup. It could be manipulated as one signed oneself with the cross, as indeed Glascock did, although with so little show of reverence as at once to walk out again. Prindy was more circumspect, and looked in through the door of the church at the Red Eye of God. Before turning, he genuflected.

They opened up and entered the radio-shed. Seating himself before the set, Glascock switched on his batteries, and while things warmed up, studied the slip of paper Fergus had sent over with Rifkah. The calls were in Clear, which is to say weren't coded, but so simply worded as to cause little curiosity if overhead, being the usual test-calls operators all over the place made to test their equipment.

Donning ear-phones, he spoke into the microphone: 'Zono to Fergo . . . Zono to Fergo . . . over.' He had to call several times to get an answer. Then he said, 'How do you read me, Fergo? Over.' He replied to the answer, 'Loud and clear this end, too. Repeat, *Clear*. Over.' A moment more of listening, then, 'Roger, Fergo. Out.'

They went out again, merely closing door and gate behind them, no doubt because Glascock must soon come back to make his scheduled calls. The sou'-easter was rising with the Sun. Glascock sniffed towards the presbytery. 'Do I smell that turtle omelette?' Prindy said it was only the sea-smell. Glascock chuckled: 'You might have a better nose than mine, son . . . but my *binji* tells me it's omelette. Come on!'

They had not long been finished their tasty breakfast, a portion of which was set aside for Fergus and Alfie, and were all doing something about clearing up their own mess, when Prindy announced the approach of the awaited ones. A moment or two of listening by the others: and there it was, the deep drone of the Junkers. Then there she was in sight, flying so low as to seem to be hopping from islet to islet, raising a great scattering of birds. They all came out into the street to greet her. Bobwirridirridi, greasy to the waist with omelette, fairly hopped for joy at sight of her, the complete scarecrow in his flapping khakis.

Fergus came in by way of the back channel, at barely a hundred feet, swept in over the station, but with none of the old bravura, only a slight roll of salute.

Glascock, Prindy, and Bobwirridirridi, the last with all his gear, evidently thinking he would be boarding the plane again, got into the truck and set out for the air-strip. They found Fergus with the aircraft not at the usual parking point, but over the other side, close to the scrub, evidently as close as possible to his cache of fuel. They drove round to him.

Fergus was surprisingly short in returning Glascock's cheery welcome, going on with what he was doing in preparation for fuelling, saying dryly, 'Thought you reckoned the coast was clear?'

Glascock stared. 'Why . . . did you see someone?'

'Launch in the mangroves . . . couple of miles down the passage there. Your people?'

'No. Our launch's on the slip. Was it big or small?'

'Quite small. Couldn't see much of it. Looked like they'd ducked into the mangroves to dodge me. Flying so low, I didn't spot 'em till right on top of 'em. It was really the mud they'd churned up caught my eye. I didn't dare go back for another look.'

'That's queer. There'd hardly be a small launch about without a ship of some size. Any sign of ships?'

'Nothing.'

'Anybody aboard the launch?'

'They'd hardly be likely to show 'emselves when they took the trouble to hide the boat.'

'Well, it licks me,' said Glascock. 'Unless it's from Beaumont and they took you for a Jap. There've been Jap float-planes about lately, according to reports . . . supposed to be launched from submarines.'

'They'd need a lot more gas than that little hooker could carry, to come all the way from Lady Beaumont.'

'Might be that crazy David come back . . . pinched a launch from them, the same's he pinched a dinghy from me. He might've sailed it.' After a moment the priest added: 'What about refugees from occupied islands? I hear some small boats are still making it.'

'Whoever it is, I'm getting out as soon as I'm fuelled up.'

'To go to Timor?'

'Go along the coast a bit and wait till midnight.'

'I was hoping you'd stay a few days.'

Fergus shook his head, went on with his task.

'Mad what you're doing, you know.' The green eyes shot a sharp look. Glascock sighed: 'Okay. But have another think before you take off.' When Fergus concentrated again on his job, Glascock added: 'I'll be getting along, see what's doing. I'll get these boys to reconnoitre. If it's dangerous I'll send young Prindy over to warn you.'

Fergus only nodded. Glascock got only a short nod from Alfie, as, passing her to go back to the truck, he bowed.

As they ran back to the station, Glascock explained the situation to Prindy, who said he would take the canoe down the back creek and see what could be spotted from the mouth. Glascock set him and Bobwirridirridi down at the entrance to the track through the mangroves, then went on to the presbytery.

Rifkah and Savitra were alarmed at the news. However, Glascock calmed them by saying that he was convinced the intruders would turn out to be refugees: 'So don't go bolting clean away. Hole up in the convent till Prindy gets back. If you have to go, we'll easily sneak you out . . . and maybe you won't have to go right back to the mainland, but camp on one of the big islands till they're gone and I come out for you. Let's get you some tucker ready . . . some of the Yankee canned stuff . . . and, of course, a pot of that marvellous mozzie cream.'

Prindy and the Pookarakka, in the canoe, approached the mouth of the creek warily, with ears cocked to engine sound to be heard distinctly in the passage beyond. Taking no risks this time, Prindy called a halt short of the end of the horn of mud, because the tide, despite its being just past the neap, was running swiftly enough to carry them out. He stopped their progress with a paddle stuck in the mud, jumped overboard with the mooring line, and knee-deep, fastened to the nearest mangrove root. Then he climbed up the roots, reached the top, stopped – to stare.

There was the small launch, about quarter of a mile away, packed with men in white with brown faces, not heading this way, but swinging into the northern passage that would take them to the Mission beach . . . and what else? That strange craft coming up the southeastern passage, so swiftly, yet looking as ungainly as a pelican treading water with wings outstretched. It was that from which the engine noise came, drowning out the motor of the launch. The grey eyes stared unblinking in intensity. The red mouth gaped. Then the spy came clambering down, to hiss on indrawn breath, although such caution was unnecessary, 'Japanee come, I think. *Ngangula* . . . tell him Father *umbborera jeriminji*.' He slipped the mooring as the Pookarakka dipped paddle to hold the canoe, leapt in, applied his own paddle to swing the craft. Dip, dip, dip — stripling and ancient — but making her fairly fly. Out to the middle where the bobbing line of mangrove-shoots showed slack water — dip, dip, dip! — while Prindy explained that the pelican-thing was a seaplane.

Back at the landing, Prindy left it to his master to moor the craft, went racing to the presbytery.

Glascock was standing out, listening to the engine-hum, distinct and coming from straight ahead, so that already the plane would be off the southern end of the beach. As Prindy told the news the hum went on northward.

The priest's first comment was: 'Fergus will have to take you and the girls now.'

'What you goin' 'o do, Father?'

'First I'll have to get on the radio and give the alarm . . . then blow it up.'

'I give you hand.'

'No time, boy. Go on . . . off you go now. Girls are in the convent. Go on foot, so's not to give the game away. Go the back track.' Glascock cocked his head to the hum, murmured, 'Wonder where they'll land. Might be going right round the island, eh?' He turned back to Prindy: 'Fergus is not to take you to Timor. Tell him take you back to the mouth of the Leopold . . . .'

Prindy interrupted: 'I give you hand with wirelitch, we all-lot go Fergus.'

'No . . . listen . . . they must be landing. Quick . . . I've got to get to the radio.' Glascock started running for the road. Rifkah ran out of the convent. He waved her back, but stopped when she came on.

'Vot is matter?' she asked.

'We think it's Japs . . . not sure. Prindy'll tell you. Go with him to Fergus . . . back to mainland.'

'Vot you do?'

'I've got to radio.'

'You come vit' us.'

'If I can catch you up . . . but if I don't, I'll follow in row-boat . . .'

'No, Stephen.' She tried to hold him.

He kissed her quickly, saying, 'You're holding me up, darling . . . please!' He pushed her away, saying to Prindy coming up, 'Take her!' He went racing up the road.

'*Kulli-kulli*!' cried Prindy, grabbed her hand and tugged. One last glance with *bubbeh*'s eyes after the nuggety racing figure; then she turned with Prindy and ran.

They took nothing from the convent; only called Savitra out and ran to the back track, Prindy in the lead. They had just entered the scrub, when Prindy halted, cocked his head. No need for concentrated listening. The sound was a roar. Fergus was starting up. Prindy shot away. Scarcely a hundred yards more covered when the other engine bellowed. He tripped over a root, came a buster, rose half-dazed, to be driven on again by the moving of the sound.

Prindy reached the clearing to see the Junkers already at the far end of the strip and swinging to line up for take off. As he went racing to it an engine howled in run-up. Fergus would be concentrated on his instruments. The other engine raised its voice. The dust and grass flew out behind. Prindy was within twenty feet when the aircraft shot away. Fergus saw him, answered his wave with a nod, went storming on his way, smothering Prindy with his dust.

The dust cleared to reveal the Junkers over the station, but not flying straight and level at a hundred feet or so as usual in taking leave of those below, instead up to five hundred and climbing hard with all the power of its donks. The reason became evident in a moment. The seaplane was in the air, looking like a pigmy-goose striving for its second element, seeming to be kicking off the first in silvery cascades from cumbersome webs. By comparison the Junkers was an eagle.

Obviously the midget was rising to challenge the eagle, since it was cutting across it flight path; a presumptious thing to do, with much less power and the encumbrance of floats, but being done cleverly, at an angle so as to have the aid of the sou'easter. Perhaps the presumption was that the Junkers, evidently unarmed, would swing away sharply to avoid attack and hence in the turn lose enough speed to bring it into range. But the Junkers kept on, flew over the midget with a couple of hundred feet of clearance. The pigmy spat venom upwards. The wind caught the phosphorescence of its tracers and spun them like flying spider-webs. The eagle went over, high into the blue. The midget turned after it, but with no hope of catching it. But, no – the Junkers was stall-turning, was coming back, hurtling down a stream of phosphorescence of its own. It pulled out of the dive just short of the pigmy-goose, leaving it in the act of what seemed like folding up its wings, swung away to a southward heading, as the little thing vanished in a ball of flame and smoke. The ball blew away, to reveal bits and pieces like rubbish being chucked out of the blue heavens into the sea.

The Junkers would be well over the back passage and a couple of thousand feet up when smoke was seen to burst from her. She appeared to halt in flight.

She rolled. She was in a spin. Her engines howled in agony. She vanished. A sound – *Clop*! Then dully – *Boom*!

Egrets and cranes and cormorants could be seen rising high, to wing away to quieter waters than those now about the Ocean Island, Avalon.

Prindy returned to the others, at a trot, but slow enough to betray the perplexity that they, too, showed in their blank staring at him when he reached them. They all turned their staring to the sky where the astonishing thing had happened – as if expecting it to happen again – and were astonished again, to see a sudden growth, like a spiky-branched tree, storm-tossed, arisen from where the station stood, a rusty red.

BOOM! The tree vanished, leaving only faint red haze.

Booble-boomble-boomble. Echoes rolling. More birds rose and fled.

Prindy spoke: 'Father been blow up wirelitch.'

Bobwirridirridi murmured, 'Properlee!'

Again the others stared at Prindy. He blinked, after a long moment said, 'Father reckon he clear out long o' rowboat . . . meet him we Leopold River.'

Rifkah asked, 'Vot ve going to do?'

Prindy considered a while: 'We go *tchenekin*, gitchim canoe, clear out.' He pointed with lips southward. 'Come on . . . we go now.'

He led them through the scrub to the mangroves, then along the edge of the swamp towards the station, reached the track through to the landing. No view from here, except the back of the Convent. No sound to be heard. Prindy told the girls to go through and wait, while he and the Pookarakka went and got the things they'd left at the convent, and to 'Look-about'.

The reconnoitring pair reached the convent to hear harsh voices raised in the direction of the church. They got their arms, and under cover of the various buildings, made their way to the kitchen. Still the vociferation continued as they slipped through to the front to peep. Prindy breathed, 'Eh, look out!'

A group of men struggling, amongst them several old acquaintances. Stephen Glascock was in the grip of two Japanese sailors, while shouting in his face was Captain Okada clad in naval whites with gold braid: 'You talk me riar . . . you pray me trick.' He slapped the priest's face.

Glascock, struggling violently gasped something.

The Captain's henchman, Sakamura was there, too, also in officer's uniform. And there was Brother David, clad as a common sailor, and but for his height looking very much like the others in white duck, with quaint-looking knee-breeches and a flat cap from which long black ribbons fluttered.

Okada roared, 'You Cristo man-o'-peace . . . you gammon me!'

As he swung his hand at Glascock again, the priest shot out a leg and tripped the man who held him on the right. All three came down. Okada leapt into the struggling group, struck Stephen on the neck, knocked him senseless.

Okada rasped at his men. They picked the priest up, pulling his arms over their shoulders, started off down the debris-littered road with him hanging between them head lolling forward, feet dragging in the dust because of the difference in his height and theirs. Okada, talking loudly in Japanese, followed with his Lieutenant. The other two sailors followed, David fetching up the rear. They came down past the ruins of what had been the Boys' School and radio house, then swung off the road into the track that led through the casurinas to the beach.

David stopped, looked down the road, looked into the very eyes of the watchers, had he known it, looked over the tracks left by Prindy and Rifkah in taking leave of the priest, which he must have spotted if he had come on. But perhaps it was only a fleeting sentiment that halted him. He turned after the others, disappeared.

Still the watchers stayed where they were, eyeing every visible point, listening. Okada's voice could be heard all the way to the sea. In fact it was drowned out only by the starting of a motor: *Pop, pop, brrrrup, brrrrrup!*

Soon could be heard the steady drone of a motor-boat under way.

'Must be him clear out, eh?' said Prindy.

The old man nodded, said, '*Ngangula, porrunna.*'

They emerged warily, slipped across the road, into the casuarinas, through to the beach. No one on the beach. Even the few old blacks had gone, with their canoes, fled like the birds from the savagery of civilized men.

The launch was now well down the main passage and out of hearing, heading for what looked like a black rock, a mile and a half away. It was evidently the rock-like object that the Pookarakka referred to when he asked, '*Gurruk*?'

'Call-yim su'marine, I t'ink. Boat him go down-below *burrulka*.'

'Properlee!'

There was no other expression in either face than intense interest as they watched – seeing the launch dock with the submarine, and soon the rock vanish. Bobwirridirridi clicked his tongue in appreciation, no doubt of another way for a *koornung* to get about.

They returned to the road, inspected the ruin done by the explosion, over which again the Pookarakka clucked with pleasure. They also examined the tracks thereabout. Evidently Glascock had got to his radio unmolested and also into the church and out by the back of it, to be seized in the casuarinas and dragged back to the road.

They returned to the convent, there to talk for a while. As there was now no haste about leaving the island, Prindy said they should get more tucker and use the rowboat. Then he went off alone to the mangroves. At the landing he found the girls plastered with mud and slashing at the still-avid bloodsuckers, but wide-eyed with wariness, looking their surprise at his leisurely approach. He greeted them casually: 'No-more fright'. Dat-lot been clear out.'

'Zey vos Japanee?' asked Rifkah.

'*Yu-ai*. He been here before, diver-diver ... what-you-call-yim, Okada. Dat-one David bring him.'

'Where Stephen?'

'Japanee been gitchim ... take him 'way.'

Rifkah gaped, to blink hard as Prindy, in the same casual tone, told briefly what had happened. That old *bubbeh* look as never before. As he began to tell of the new arrangements, she uttered a low cry, flung past him, to go running back up the track. The cry stayed in her hard breathing.

She came out onto the road by that little house of hers, called the Synagogue, stopped there, but not even to look at it. Her haggard eyes were fixed on the presbytery, looking so deserted. The cry in her breath grew louder. She looked up the road, all the more deserted-looking for the litter up there. She started towards it, walking now. She saw the tracks left in parting, her own bare prints toe to toe with the beloved ones, paused over them, incredulity in her expression now. Then she went on, faster now. She came to where the party had turned to the sea, studied the tracks again, then swung that way, and now with eyes on the sea, again broke into a run.

The empty sea. Still, she ran to it, crying on her breath, crying. The tide had receded from the point of embarkation. She halted in the last of the tracks, looking wildly from islet to islet, then at last straight down the passage, staring as if projecting her being that way.

She turned at a sound. Prindy was coming, running hard. She only glanced, turned back to the sea, but now withdrew eyes from it, to look at the trampled sand, at the ruts cut by the dragging feet. She sank to knees, and with a groan, took a handful of sand that had had contract with the beloved feet, raised it to her mouth.

Prindy came up panting, 'Aeroplane come!'

She raised *bubbeh*'s eyes to him.

'Big mob aeroplane. We better clear out.' He reached for her arm.

She raised the sand above her shining head, let it fall, crying '*Lamah Sabakhtani*'.

She rose to the urging, and now weeping, went blindly to his leading her by a hand. He headed towards the presbytery. The drone of the aircraft could be heard distinctly now. He hurried her. They were in the casuarinas when the flight passed over – half a dozen machines at height. They reached the shelter of the presbytery verandah as the flight came back, now down to a couple of thousand feet, making the iron building ring to their passing.

Prindy was peeping out. She went on faltering steps to the doorway of Glascock's bedroom. The aircraft were swinging round the island. Prindy called, 'He going to land, I t'ink.'

For a moment she hung in the doorway, then rushed in, dropped to her knees before the prie-dieu, dropped hands and head to the polished wood, hands clutching blindly at the breviary still in its place, sobbing, 'Stephen . . . Stephen!'

Prindy came, slipped a hand under her arm. She rose, still clutching the book, went with him blindly, weeping.

CHAPTER TWENTY-FIVE

THE JOURNEY back to the mainland was comparatively slow. First there were hunting aircraft to hide from, and next the pinnaces of a couple of warships, none of them Japanee, by what the hidden watchers could make of the faces of the crews. Then came the spring tides and the consequent blustering sou'easter.

But perhaps tide and wind behaved as the leader of the expedition, the Pookarakka, wanted. Certainly he made no complaint, but rather good use of the dawdling progress to acquaint himself with the reality of places he would have known previously only in legend. He sang the legend stuff, and had Prindy put it to flute music. That the magic of the legends still lingered was shown by the old man's coming back to camp one day with what he claimed to be a *Mawnyinga*, or Mosquito Shade, tied up in a sugar-sack. He said he had caught it and now held it through the magic of that wondrous new insect repellant of the Yankees, Dimethyl Phthalate Cream. Bobwirridirridi had been greatly interested in the stuff from the start of seeing its efficacy. Capture of the *Mawnyinga* so far enhanced the value of the cream to the old fellow that forthwith he commandeered the whole lot, and no doubt because he considered it deserved better treatment than to be housed in a *kuttabah*'s tin can that was already rusting, made for it a container from a length of giant bamboo found as flotsam, which he inscribed with the motif of the Mosquito Dreaming. Thereafter he wore the container slung about his neck with other magical appurtenances, doling it out to the others on request.

Although Bobwirridirridi held the *Mawnyinga* captive for three days, during which the party was camped in the one place, none of the others actually saw it. This was during the height of the springs, when it would have been senseless to go battling sea and wind. They were camped on a cosy islet with its own bit of mud flat beyond the jungle. In the camp, where as always the Pookarakka placed himself well apart from the others, he kept the sack up a tree. When he went wandering he took it with him. Undoubtedly the sack contained something, because it could be seen to move sometimes. Also it made sounds, squeaks and squawks, as if in answer to conversations he held with it in lingo. However, since he was known to be a ventriloquist, this hardly proved anything. The movements of the thing were slow and spreading, just as might be expected of a mosquito about a foot across cramped in such a way. Evidently having learnt all he wanted from the creature, one day he came back without it, and the sack palpating vigorously with, instead, mud crabs. That night he got Prindy to help him rig himself up for the Mosquito Dance, which he did on the beach for all to see, by the light of rising Igulgul.

The girls might have been black lubras for all the share they had in anything but the chores, and apparently were content enough to be left alone together. Obviously Savitra was too scared of the spidery old man to try to assert her marital rights as usual, and doubtless also was still somewhat subdued by the shock of recent experience. She talked much of her family to Rifkah, giving the impression that she would be glad to be back with them as soon as possible. Rifkah herself was much as usual again, calm and mostly smiling, even though her eyes retained the old *bubbeh* look for some time. Not a sign of the wild grief since leaving the Mission. Not a word about the lost ones from anyone.

Thus did they dawdle their way for somewhat more than a week before coming into sight of the mainland. One fairly easy leg would finish the voyage. However, it was more than just a journey to him in command. As they were about to set off on that leg before the rising of the sou'easter, the Pookarakka told Prindy that the *Mawnyinga* had told him of a camp along the coast westward, where he would find men with whom to do the Mosquito Dance as it should be done. He gave the direction with lips. Nothing to be seen across the green sea that way except sepia haze, whereas southeastward there were the mangroves of the Leopold River estuary floating in islands of mirage seemingly just across the way. Prindy, the captain, set his sail and plied his steering paddle as directed.

It could have been a fearful journey for a crew not used to rough passages and without faith in their league with the forces responsible. Soon the wind was up, and the sea, clear of the lee of the islets, became a chaos of snowy-ridged mountains tumbling into their own valleys of pellucid green. On the ridges they flew like the silver scud itself, to fall into the valleys and see their own pale images staring out at them like corpses in glass-walled graves. They had to use some sail to beat the pull of the tide, East then West, hence suffer continual capsizing. When they went under, the only way to bail was in the blackfellow way of rolling their vessel sideways down a wave, then getting her half-afloat, leave the rest to the flying cupped hands of the lubras. Their bailing tin, like everything else they had been unable to lash down, was soon lost.

They were still a long way from the point to which, it must be in those conditions, a magic compass was leading them, when the slow-slow rising land turned from blue to grey – to gold, crimson, violet – disappeared. The wind fell. Still the sea tossed them, now to the stars. Then there was Igulgul, somewhat misshapen, popping up out of the pool of gold he'd prepared for his appearance, and seeming for a spell to do a Mosquito Dance thereupon. After that he got behind them, and fairly *shoved* them on their way, so that in no time sandbanks were rising like white whales, and they were in a tideway that swept them through high banks – until suddenly the magician pilot cackled, '*Yakkarai*!' There on the moon-side of a bank lay two canoes. Prindy swung the bow in. Their own canoe beached with a sound like a heavy sigh.

The pilot went up first, took a look around, signalled the others.

No sign of life on top – that is discounting the teeming existence of tiny crustaceans. No sign of human beings other than the canoes; and the reason soon forthcoming – Mosquitoes! Small wonder the region was noted for its specialists in Mosquito Dancing. Within half an hour the place was fairly howling with them. But, of course, they had the magic to beat them. The Pookarakka had lost none of his gear. He handed out dabs of cream, those to the girls through the hand of his 'prentice. He had matches, and soon had a fire going on the edge of the jungle. The meal was that poorest known to maritime blacks, hermit crabs roasted in the shell, and brackish water dug for on the edge of the jungle where the tide-arm entered it, and drunk along with slimy sand from a rusty bailing tin taken from a canoe. After the meal the old man went off with a fire-stick to set up camp on his own. The others settled down where they were, dug into burrows in the sand. They were soon asleep watched over throughout the night by Igulgul.

First light saw them up and out. In fact it would have been impossible for any but the stone deaf to sleep through the din arising from the expanse of silver that the tide-arm was become. In progress was one of those piscine internecions only to be seen in remote waterways such as this, when a run of smallest fry starts a rush of fish of all sizes and species bent, it would seem from the indescribable havoc, on exterminating all but the very largest and most voracious sharks, which themselves stopped short of suicide only through utter repletion. The water was boiling, lilac-streaked already, although there was no colour in the sky. Prindy leapt up to take a look. The water was almost up to the high-beached canoes. Fish in their extremes were even landing themselves, only to be snatched back by others big enough to handle themselves better in both mediums. Prindy ran to rouse the Pookarakka.

But no Pookarakka, nor smallest trace of him. Prindy looked about warily, went to where a track led into the jungle. There a fish-spear stood erect in the sand. Prindy took it, went racing to the fray.

They breakfasted hugely on the sweetest of the catch, grilled on the coals and eaten off tea-tree bark. Now the mosquitoes had to be kept off with smoke. Savitra waxed bitter because they had been left no cream, and, convinced that the old man had deserted them completely, wanted to get into the canoe and make eastward for the Leopold country. Prindy, as certain that the Pookarakka would be back, explained that he had taken all his gear simply because it was all too *mahraghi* to be left lying about. Savitra yelled at that, 'Dat mosquito cream nutching magic. Dat belong whiteman. Dat belong we!'

He solaced his bride somewhat by building a separate shelter for her and himself and letting her accompany him on the fishing and crabbing and ibis-nest robbing expeditions with which he filled the four days of waiting. Rifkah spent the time making dilly-bags of shredded hybiscus bark, and in gazing sometimes northeastward across the jade sea with haggard old eyes.

They were lying off in siesta when the signal sounded from the jungle. Prindy was up in a moment. He found the Pookarakka well inside on the pad, fully decorated and accoutred. They embraced. They dropped down to the sand to talk; or rather the Master to talk and 'prentice mostly to listen. Most of the weapons the old man had were for Prindy, to take him and his companions across country to the Mullaka's camp. There was a spot along this track, marked, where he should turn off eastward to head for good camping for tonight. The Pookarakka would follow at some unspecified time. Prindy should wait with the Mullaka until he came for him. The talk didn't last long.

The old man ordered his *Mekullikuli* on his way, then vanished into the jungle. Prindy returned at once to the girls. They were only too glad to break camp.

As Bobwirridirridi had predicted, or ordained, they were soon in pleasant open forest country, and reached a big billabong with plenty of time left for Prindy to go out and bag a wallaby and the girls to get lily tuckout and mussels and to be cooking before darkness fell.

Next day's leg brought them to the Leopold. From then on for several days they followed the river up, taking their time, enjoying its bounty, and having it all to themselves, because the tribes-people, as the smoke of distant fires showed, were still taking the seasonal offerings of the plains while it lasted. Sometimes the fires were not so far away and too small and temporary to be those used by hunting parties. Hence it was likely that their passing was known and noted. Yet in all the way to where, within plain sight of the Plateau, they cut away, heading for Jeremy's camp, they met no human being.

That Jeremy was at home was signalled by the starry flag. Still, they approached warily, Prindy first to make a reconnaisance, then all of them to call at distance –*Ku*!

It was a strange reunion, at first a mixture of merriment and shyness. Jeremy was the shy one to begin with, because, as he said, he hadn't spoken to another human since they'd left and must find his tongue. That made the others awkward. Then it all changed suddenly with Jeremy's asking how thing had gone with them. The change in Rifkah's expression caused him to ask in his rusty voice, 'Why . . . something bad?'

Rifkah's lovely eyes, from sparkling, had turned blank and haggard. She blinked hard. But the flood burst. She flung herself on his breast howling her grief again. At first he showed astonishment, trying to hold her off, asking what was wrong. She only clung and howled and wept. He sat down with her, taking her onto his knee, to soothe her like the heart-broken child she seemed.

When at last exhaustion silenced her and she shook her head at his invitation to talk about it, he suggested that she go lie down in her bed, and sent Savitra and Prindy up to prepare it for her. She went clinging to him to the cave, dropped from his arms into her bed to bury her face in the pillow and give way to the storm again. He bent and kissed her neck, motioned to the others, left her alone.

The youngsters told Jeremy what had happened, making much more of the fate of Fergus and Alfie, since having little comprehension of that of Stephen Glascock. Again they made no mention of Rifkah's relations with the priest. Thus Jeremy must presume that it was the whole frightful affair had shocked her, as suggested by his saying, 'After all she's been through, that had to happen in the place she chose finally as her refuge.'

Rifkah kept to her bed for the rest of the day, unintruded on. In the evening Jeremy visited her to ask if she wanted anything, refusing to accept her whispered negative, and gave her a barbiturate with brandy and milk. She was sound asleep when the others retired.

Next morning, when they gathered at sunrise for the early cup of tea, Rifkah was much as always, a little heavy-eyed, but no less cheerful. When Jeremy told her he had heard the story and understood how deeply she was shocked, she only looked at him. Holding the lovely eyes for a moment, he asked, 'You don't want to talk about it?' She shook her head, and when he nodded, surprised him by taking his hand and kissing it.

He asked her if she would not rather now go back to civilization. She answered promptly, 'Oh, no!'

He said, 'But if the Japs come even only raiding, how do you know you won't run into them again somewhere . . . I mean if you still intend to work with the blacks?'

'I zink zey are too fright' to go to blackfeller camp. I see at Mission zey are fright'. I hear zat before, from . . . .' She stopped, with eyes clouding. Perhaps she had been going to say something that Glascock had told her.

'Yes, I think you're right there. They do fear the *Binghai*, as they call him. The blacks have killed a lot of pearlers over the years . . . Japs . . . A lot more than is known officially, I guess. Rather strange, that. There's an analogy to it in New Guinea. According to the news, they're frightened to go into the jungles because of the natives . . . which has meant a lot of whites have got away and are able to hang on keeping tab on their activities.'

He went on to say that the news these days mainly concerned manoeuvring of Japanese and American naval forces for evident confrontation in what was being called the South Western Pacific, although actually it was Mid-Western: 'It looks as if the showdown's at hand . . . and it's going to be naval . . . as the other one, the Battle of Britain, was aerial. The Japs are boasting that they have command of the region as far south as Sydney. Certainly they got a midget submarine into Sydney Harbour and shelled Sydney from the sea for a few minutes and sunk a hospital ship off Brisbane. But that could all have been done by one big marauding submarine. The Yanks undoubtedly have a considerable fleet deployed off our northeastern coast. Their naval chief, Admiral Nimitz, boasts that he'll have the Jap fleet at the bottom of the sea within six months of Pearl Harbour. That's really shooting off your mouth, as the Yanks themselves say, seeing there's only about a month to go. And then, says Nimitz, he'll ride a white horse through the streets of Tokyo. Can you beat a Yank?'

Can you beat a Yank? That was the big question of the times.

It was soon answered.

Just a week after the reunion at the caves, the Battle of the Coral Sea was joined. It was easy enough to anticipate it, with both sides as vocal as they were in telling the world. Jeremy declared it the first time he had yet heard the Japs really boasting, adding that it might suggest that for the first time they were unsure of themselves. The Movement of a great task force southward from their main base in the Carolines might have been a peacetime manœuvre, so frankly did they report on it. Not that such a vast movement of ships could easily be kept secret. On Our Side, the general opinion expressed in news was that the enemy intended to invade Southern New Guinea and so be in a position to dominate Australia. The Japs themselves declared that they would add Port Moresby to the many cities of the New Japanese Empire before the month of May was out. Jeremy, now listening to the news by the hour, as at the time of the Battle of Britain, expressed doubt about what the Japs were up to. Why, he asked, make so much effort at so much risk, namely, passage of the archipelago constituting the southern tip of New Guinea, perhaps the most hazardous in the world, when he had command of all other parts of the great island and need only send a force of his as yet unbeaten jungle warriors over the Owen Stanley Ranges to get what he wanted practically without opposition?' He soon had the answer: 'Why . . . the Coons, as they call them there . . . the natives!'

He went on to talk to Rifkah about this strange fear of black savages seemingly felt by all Asiatics: 'It was that definitely kept the Malay types out of this country over the centuries. The Chinaman was similarly scared. The blacks used to give them hell round here in the early mining days. On the northeast coast during the gold rushes the Chows were fairly massacred . . . and eaten, too! Comparatively, the killing of whites was a rare thing . . . and I never heard of them eating a *kuttabah*. Strange, isn't it!'

But the trend of the news supported what Stephen Glascock had learnt from his Yankee associates, namely, that the wily Yank, trading on the Jap's conceit in naval prowess, was luring him on to stretch his lines to breaking point. The news of the actual Battle of the Coral Sea was as confused as the engagement itself proved to be, being as much aerial as naval in eventuality and fought in such a crazy place and in such mad weather. Both sides immediately claimed the victory, and not without right when it came to counting losses. However, the great weakness in the Japanese claim was the fact that those who survived turned back. It was the first retreat in Japanese military history. How they justified it to themselves was not disclosed. But what soon became obvious was that they were now confused. Their broadcasters talked stupidly of leaving the next onslaught until July, while still claiming that the U.S. Fleet was at the bottom of the sea, and having to admit the bombing of Tokyo by aircraft of the same non-existent force. Then they took to declaring that they were about to take the war to the North American Continent itself.

All the newsmongers of the world got onto this line of a final confrontation on the western seaboard of the U.S.A., to begin in the region of the Aleutian Archipelago. The rest of the month of May was taken up with prediction concerning it. The Japs were as frank about it as the Yanks. Admiral Yamamoto declared that he would repay violation of the Sacred Soil of Nippon by laying waste the land of the Hairy Barbarians. The Hairy Ones stated grimly that they were concentrating all their forces to defend their homeland from a race of hairless apes. Jeremy suggested that there was rather too much frankness in it. Still, the Japanese had surely betrayed their naivete to the world by broadcasting as truth President Roosevelt's jocular naming of the base from which Tokyo was bombed as *Shangri-la*. Also, the Yankee's frankness about defending his native hearth sounded honest enough, even to anyone inclined to doubt a Yankee's veracity in anything.

Then suddenly, at the beginning of June, there they were at it full blast – right in the *middle* of the Pacific. The Battle of Midway Island. Where the proud Yamamoto was at the time was not stated. Sufficient was it to confess that his deputy, Admiral Nemura, had to abandon his fine flagship, in which he had scourged five of the Seven Seas for half a year, and run for home in a humble little destroyer – surely to effect the Happy Despatch to be expected of any *Nipponjin no o kata Gata* in the circumstances. If Admiral Nimitz went home after that conclusive battle, it was probably to procure the white horse with which to make a Yankee Wild West Show out of the humbling of a proud people *for the second time.*

So the Second World War was over – that is, but for the wholesale slaughter, mayhem, destruction of vast collections of the works of Creative Man and wide stretches of the beauty and bounty of Nature, the inevitable climax to the periodic madness of war. Convinced as Jeremy was that the so-called enemy was beaten on all fronts, he had no illusions about early peace. He told Rifkah, 'Apart from the Military War Lords, who have to justify their cry of *havoc,* till it's taken to the extreme where they begin to fear it will turn on themselves, there are the Merchant Lords, who've Geared the Economy to War, as they put it, and won't pull it out of gear till they've got their maximum return in dividends.'

Again he suggested that Rifkah might like to return to civilization, at least to get some legitimate place before the lifting of restrictions on movement in the district, which he predicted soon. An added reason was that it was evident, now, that Savitra was pregnant, and hence would be easier got rid of if they went about it wisely. Jeremy's idea was that they cross the Plateau again as before, but travel as far South as possible without being seen. They should be able to make Charlotte Springs if they set out before the country got too dry. Then, if questioned about their movements, they could say they were hunting for blood-stock lost in the early exodus.

Savitra was ready enough to go and have her baby with her people, provided Prindy went along with her. Prindy was agreeable to go, and to sneak back with Rifkah when the opportunity offered – provided he first spoke with the Pookarakka, as arranged.

Now the time dragged. Jeremy, with the preoccupation of the war past, evidently wanted to be alone again for the solitary communion he had got used to. Often he went walking alone, leaving Rifkah to study of the medical matter he had instructed her in, and the youngsters to their devices. He was frank in saying that he must prepare himself for a solitary end to his life, since he could see nothing but what would make him mostly unhappy back in the society of his fellows. He said, 'I haven't lost my hope that the wonder that is Human Consciousness will ultimately prevail, and am pretty sure I'll not die in contempt of the ideal of mankind . . . but to maintain hope and ideal I must keep clear of the common herd, especially what I'm afraid is the commonest of the herd, those who call themselves Australians.'

Rifkah was also irked, filling herself with knowledge she couldn't use, because those who might benefit by it would not come near. The hunting fires on the plains and then along the line of the river were a taunt to her, the way she watched them – approaching, approaching, only always to recede again.

Prindy also watched the fires eagerly, but evidently without impatience. His spare time went into hunting for the camp and music. He helped Jeremy with a lot of jobs, including the baling of dry grass for hay and the construction of a hay-loft. Savitra fretted frankly, sick of following her man about, yet being loth to leave him out of her sight. She wanted to be with her people. Thus while Dry Season asserted itself in harshness they must all feel irksome from not being used to living through such conditions so close to nature. The sou'easter, at full blast now the winter solstice was passed, blew cold and dust-tasting from the

Interior. The lush land as they had known it wilted visibly. Still the fires kept their distance.

One day Prindy was on the way out to hunt, with weapons hooked over the left shoulder with arm clear so as to have both hands free for tootling on his bamboo flute. He was clad only in the red *naga*. A little distance behind him, scowling her displeasure, came his bride. She wore a dress of green and brown printed calico, and carried the lubra's dunnage: a sugar sack in which were tommy-axe and knife and cut lunch. They were about half a mile from the camp, well clear of the rocks and heavier growth below the escarpment. They were entering dense tea-tree scrub, when suddenly a startled exclamation from Savitra: 'Oh!' Then a shriek.

Prindy swung round, to see leaping upon her from the scrub on both sides, what, on the instant, looked like a mob of striped stick-insects, tall as men. Painted blacks, of course. But no sign of black could be seen in any of them. Their heads were hooded with conical caps of grass. All the more did they look like attacking insects, multi-membered, because wielding thin saplings stripped of leaves.

As the boy turned, he was himself pounced on from behind by two hooded figures. They snatched away his weapons, immobilized his arms. He rolled grey eyes at them. Then as a din of whooping arose whither he had been looking, he looked again, to see the hooded pack belabouring screaming Savitra with their switches, driving her back and back, till with a piercing shriek she turned and ran for home – with the whoops and whistling sticks in pursuit.

Savitra's terror and the din of the assault made her outrun her pursuers a goodly distance before she realized that no longer was she pursued. Still running, she glanced back. She slowed down, stopped and turned, heaving for breath, wild-black-eyed, dark face wet with sweat and tears. She bent to listen. No other sound than the rising wind in the trees. She gasped, 'Prindy!' She tried again, with more strength, and again and again, till she reached a cracked screech of despair: 'Prind-eeee . . . where you . . . Prindeeeee!'

Then she dropped her face to blubber. A lizard running over her feet startled her. Small birds were peeping at her out of bushes. She stared miserably back into the thicket she had come through, then blubbering again, swung away as she had been going, towards the camp, began to run again, whimpering, 'Black bastard . . . I tell Mullaka . . . Mullaka gitchim rifle . . . shoot 'em daid . . .black bastard . . . black bastard . . . taken him 'way, my Prindy . . . oh, ah!'

Jeremy and Rifkah were at the table under the shade, working on some pharmaceutical concoction, probably for dosing Bay Rum Betsy, who was in the horse-yard, evidently sick. When Savitra rushed up to them babbling incoherently, they looked at her rather with indifference, no doubt thinking she was only reporting one of her increasing rows with her man. Then, as the import dawned on them, after an exchange of glances, they took hold of her, sat her down, soothed her as they questioned her. 'You shoot dem black bastard!' she sobbed and sobbed. 'Dey kill him daid . . . I know! For Wrong Side.'

When her fear and rage had subsided to mere misery, Jeremy talked to her gently: 'Now, you've got to be sensible. It's only blackfeller business . . .

now, now, you know that he likes business. If they were going to kill him, they'd've killed you, too.'

'I runned away.'

'They hunted you. Women can't be in business.'

'Dey stop him come back, for Wrong Side.'

'You're too young yet. Later on it'll all be fixed up . . . and he'll be able to come back to you.'

She cried fiercely, 'He got 'o come back now . . . cos I got him wid *Charada*. Spone you no more gitchim back for me, I gitchim long o' *Charada*.'

'Now you're being really silly. You're going to have a baby. We'll take you to your family. Then when business finished, Prindy can go to you.'

She howled, 'He got 'o go wid me . . . you got to go gitchim!'

'I can't do that, girl.'

'Course! You whiteman . . . boss. Dey fright' you.' When the grey head shook, she leapt up and began to pound him with dark little fists, shrieking, 'You tek him rifle shoot dat bugger . . . .'

Rifkah drew her away, taking the thumping and the tears that went with her. Jeremy fixed things by getting her brandy and water, and when she sipped, slipped a barbiturate between her lips. At length, when she was crying herself to sleep, Rifkah took her gently and led her to her bed.

The girls had no sooner disappeared, when Jeremy, back at the dispensing, was arrested by a slight cough, looked towards the fireplace, to see standing there, in grubby khakis, leaning on his womera, Bobwirridirridi. Jeremy stared for a moment, perhaps not sure of his vision, because above the khaki the death's head was freshly white-ochred and the hair tied up in ceremonial style. The cavernous eyes showed no glimmer of recognition, until Jeremy called greeting, 'Goodday, Pookarakka!'

The coals glowed momentarily. The topknot nodded. A wide grin. 'Goottay, Mullaka!'

Jeremy went to greet him, offered his hand. As the old man took it, Jeremy asked, 'You want him something . . . bre'millik, brandy?'

The lips smacked. Jeremy went back to the shade, got the requirements from the kerosene-case cupboards. The old man stayed where he was. Mixing, Jeremy talked across the little distance, talking of what he had heard of the Pookarakka's adventures since last meeting and asking what he'd been doing since last hearing of him. The answers were chiefly in nods and grins and gestures. Jeremy brought the bowl, along with brandy and water for himself.

Bobwirridirridi snatched the bowl, muttering, 'Tahng you, Mullaka.' He seated himself on a case and at once fell to with fingers. Jeremy also seated himself, to sip from his pannikin.

Nothing was said till bowl and fingers were licked clean. Belching his satisfaction, the old man declined more. Jeremy took the bowl, came back with another pannikin of brandy and water. The Pookarakka sipped and sighed. Still silence, till Jeremy asked, 'What you do now, Pookarakka? You been walk-about too much. Now you spell little bits, eh?'

The red coals fixed the grey quizzing eyes, The cackling voice spoke deliberately: 'No-more spell. Too-muchee bijnitch.'

'Ah!'

A long holding of eyes. Then: 'You give it prejent, Mullaka?'

'Present, eh? Long o' you?'

'Long o' bijnitch.'

'Ah!' Jeremy swigged off his brandy.

Tradition demanded that those formally responsible for a boy about to be initiated must pay those who gave their time and talent to it. Jeremy asked, 'What you want?'

The black claws rose to count off on fingers. The cackle changed to something more like the drone of the calculating blackfellow: 'Plour, dry-dea, tchugar, tobacco, pipe, metchitch, tom'yawk . . . millik belong o' meself-meself.'

'All right. How much you want?'

The counting began: 'T'ree bag plour . . . one bag tchugar . . . one bockis tobacca . . . . '

When it was concluded, Jeremy asked, 'When you want him?'

'I tek him now.'

'You can't carry-him-up all that lot. Where you mate?'

'Me-two-feller carry-him-up horse, eh?' The coals glowed as if in challenge.

Jeremy grinned and nodded, rose and went up to the store-cave. When he came back, carrying a calico sack of flour on each shoulder, puffing rather hard, the old man rose to meet him, took over the sacks, and with seeming effortlessness, despite his apparent frailty, went on with them down towards the horse-yard, while Jeremy returned for the other things. Besides what had been ordered, Jeremy added a can of treacle, a couple of clasp-knives, a small bolt of the magic turkey twill.

While only Betsy was in the yard, a number of the station horses were close at hand, some fossicking for spillage from the feed-trough, others dozing in the shade. The hay-loft stood just behind the yard, erected in the limbs of a couple of convenient ghost-gums. There was also now a plot of tropical lucerne, bright behind a stout wire fence. Jeremy brought in Big Ben and Black Andy to pack, and Red Rory to ride. The Pookarakka shook his head when asked if he wanted a mount, and when the cavalcade was ready to start, went loping ahead with his own sugar-sack of stuff and a couple of spears.

They travelled about three miles, towards the high-climbing Sun. Bobwirridirridi halted, put his sack in the fork of a tree. They unpacked, with no more conversation than a couple of jests about their age, 'Flour-Bag', as they called themselves, with reference to the white in their hair. When they were done, the Pookarakka wasted no ceremony on taking leave, merely saying, '*Mummuk, yawarra*, old-man.'

Jeremy asked, 'How long *yawarra*?'

'No-more long time. I come tell him you time finish.'

'You bring him young feller then?'

'Eh, look out!'

Jeremy must know that an initiate remained under a ban of silence and isolation for a long while after the ceremony, and must go on the long journey called *Look Him Road*. The red eyes were quizzing him. The old man said, 'You give it tucker for walk-about, time finish bijnitch?'

'Yes . . . when you come. *Mummuk, yawarra.*' He mounted, waved, headed away.

Bobwirridirridi watched him out of sight, heard him out of hearing, then turning towards the near escarpment, put claw to mouth and gave the call *Tjangaluma*. It was answered from back in the rocks. He proceeded to strip off his sweat-soaked khakis.

Before long, there again were the painted mantis figures of the morning, now unhooded, and recognizable, a couple at least, as the same men who had rejected Prindy with his Wrong Side bride, indeed perhaps the same as had shown such interest in him as the protégé of General Esk so long ago. They pounced on the pile of stores, looking it over, talking in lingo. The Pookarakka more or less ignored them, soon turned from them with his own supplies, heading for the escarpment.

He came through the great rocks to where the fig trees began, into a bit of clear space that was evidently an ancient camp site. On one side was a pool of water under a leaning slab of rock, on the other a similar rock formation, but dry beneath, with two figures squatting in its shade, one behind the other. The outer figure was slight and white ochred from top to toe, wearing only a small *bulkung* belt and brow fillet, and on upper arms cane *delera* with tufts of dyed feathers. Despite the paint and the fact that he squatted on heels and knees with head drooped so that his face was unseen, his identity was made plain enough by a tuft of fair hair from which the ochre had been shed. He sat still as stone, with hands on knees. The other, painted like the rest, was sitting at ease, with an arm on a knee supporting his head, in his hand a switch like that used to beat Savitra. He was that old Googoowonjin, Boss of the Pigeon Bijnitch. He would be known now as *Pirri-Pirri*, guardian of the neophyte.

The Pookarakka only glanced at the pair, and stooped at the pool to drink. The *Pirri-Pirri* yawned, stretched. Prindy did not move. Nor did he move when the others came with their loads, although Googoowonjin dropped his switch and rose to join them. The newcomers dropped down in the shade, to open the tin of treacle and pass it round for licking off sticks with evident relish, and then to broach the box of trade tobacco and pass the pipes around. Bobwirridirridi went over to take the place of *Pirri-Pirri*. None of the others seemed even to see the boy.

After about an hour of lazing with such abandonment to ease that it looked as if they intended to stay there, in the manner of their kind, the idlers sprang into activity, loaded themselves up again, this time to the limit with addition of their own belongings – weapons, dilly-bags – those with the sacks balancing them on their heads. The proper *Pirri-Pirri* resumed his role, at least to the extent of rousing the boy with a sharp word, setting him on his way, and following, himself well laden. Prindy carried nothing. Bobwirridirridi took the rear.

Through the tumble of rock and tangle of roots, up the red wall, they went almost with the facility of rock wallabies, scarcely faltering, despite the heavy burdens, the balanced sacks, which, even while hanging only by toes on some ledge they deftly passed from one to another when passage with them became otherwise impossible. The smaller white figure showed distinctly against the red. Perhaps it was that caused the buzzard-kites to gather, used as they were from the Dream Time to attending on initiations, lending their magic eyes in watching for intrusion, in return for pickings of the accompanying feasting, They would even know where the Ring Place was and be there wheeling, whistling welcome.

The party did not stop till it reached the top, then dropped down in shade again, to smoke and laze as if the journey were over. The great grey smooth-humped masses of rock, seeming to quiver in the heat, to burrow under the masses of wind blown bushes about them, truly might have been the creatures of the Dream Time they were supposed to be, come to life again. Then that sudden access of activity again, with the heading South of East, over and round the rock masses. Soon ahead there was seen to rise a mass of different shape and colour, a sort of rampart, reddish black, a harder bit of the country, lagging behind the general weathering of the ages. The kites wheeling above it showed it as the party's destination. Soon they came up to it, a long wall as it seemed, disappearing into the scrub North and South, some forty feet in height. They did not have to climb it. Hidden by a clump of spiny wattles was a cleft, barely wide enough to let a skinny man through or a wallaby, as to be seen from the ancient polish on the walls. Again they had to pass weapons and sacks from one to another. Thirty feet or so of cramped passage brought them suddenly into the open; not such a region as they had come from, but a little country of its own, walled all round, the middle a sandy flat grown with coarse grass and stunted trees, a couple of hundred yards across by twice that in length. That there was water was indicated by a goodly little growth of pandanus at the southern end and sudden whirring upflight of small birds.

The procession headed for the pandanus. There was water aplenty. They dumped their burdens to drink. As Prindy came up, the *Pirri-Pirri* signed him to drink, and when he had done so, directed him to go to a solitary tree close by the rock wall. Prindy dropped again into that statuesque posture. The others carried their loads to the wall, which here was riven by numerous clefts, somewhat like that by which entry had been made, only horizontal instead of vertical and not giving passage through. Some of these clefts were quite wide at the outside, serving as good shelters, like the overhangs of the cliffs below, and were painted. However, the paintings were not of striking quality, appearing to be more recording of events than traditional, not done with much care. Mostly it comprized stick-insect drawings of what might be taken for Ring Place proceedings. There were a couple of what looked like battle scenes, which might have recorded some time when the celebrants fell out. There were numerous stencilled hands; in fact layers of them, the signatures of generations of tribesmen. It was evident that for some reason, perhaps its inaccessibility, the place hadn't been used for several years.

Another spell of idling – then a springing into greater activity than ever. Now the task was to clear the middle of the arena. Small trees were uprooted, then chopped up and the branches thrown into heaps. When cleared of such growth, some men went in search of more branches and saplings, while the rest stayed to clear the grass. When the last of the grass was out, digging began in the middle with sticks and hands. All except Pookarakka and *Yalunga* the initiate, laboured, the latter still sitting under the tree, the former watching from the rocks.

The hole was dug to a depth of a couple of feet, just big enough for someone to crouch in. Then the diggers got saplings and bent them in the ground above the hole to make the frame for a whirley. Boughs were heaped on. Then attention was given to setting up half a dozen lean-tos of boughs about the perimeter of the Ring. Thus while the Sun went down behind the wall through which they entered, and the day rusted away. But there was Old Igulgul, almost at the full, beaming over the other wall.

Fire leapt near the waterhole. A couple of men who'd left off work about sunset were back with a kangaroo and were chopping it up with the tommy-axe. The hair of the squatting *Yalunga* could be seen gleaming fair through its shedding paint.

Conclusion of work on the Ring Place was announced by a great *Tjangaluma* to which the rock walls rang. Then the workers came trooping to the camp, to drink, to dash water on their sweaty dusty bodies, then come to the fire, which already was a heap of coals. A sack of flour had been opened. The men began to make small dampers, working in pairs, one extending cupped hands, while another, having filled these with flour, added water from the billy-can, the first then kneading. The dampers were tossed on the coals, as well as lumps of meat. When the billy was finished with, it was filled to boil for making tea. Still no one took notice of the ghostly figure now squatting in the full glare of Igulgul. It wasn't until the rest were stretched out to sleep off repletion and surely fatigue that old Googoowonji, the regular *Pirri-Pirri*, came to his charge with a couple of dampers and the billy. Prindy ate and drank eagerly. Afterwards he resumed his posture, but soon dropped head to knees, and in that position at last rolled over and slept. The *Pirri-Pirri* himself already was asleep.

Prindy was wakened by a cut of the switch. Now Igulgul was high, the loafers up and setting about redecorating themselves. The *Pirri-Pirri* signed his charge to rise and follow, and took him to the Ring Place where he directed him into the *wirrianwah*, the whirley over the hole in the middle, to squat facing westward, then shut him in. A mopoke was calling away beyond the western wall . . . *Mopoke . . . Mopoke . . . the Coast is Clear*!

Igulgul was at the zenith when the men, fully decorated and accoutred, went to the Ring, severally and silently, to take up positions around it. Bobwirri-dirridi, painted in a way of his own and carrying a brace of boomerangs, stole in behind the *wirrianwah*. A long pause. Then with a shout to make the rocks ring, the standing men leapt with levelled spears at the heap in the middle, thrust their weapons through the top of it, and bursting into a chant in which the Pookarakka joined with accompanying clash of boomerangs, danced back to the perimeter, only to shout and rush again. Once again they did it. After that each man did an armed dance about the hidden *Yalunga*, while the rest clapped, stamped, chanted; except two, who squatted with didjeridoo and minga sticks, to give the accompaniment. The Pookarakka had disappeared.

So it went on, each celebrant doing a different turn, acting out his own Dreaming and the Great Traditions of their Cult, in song and dance. Igulgul joined in more and more, by casting lengthening shadows, Moon Shades, of the active participants to move with them, foot to foot, in magic-woven patterns.

The Old One was halfway down the sky when there was *Tjangaluma* in the background. At once the dancing stopped. The dancers swung to answer: *Yoodle-oodle-yoodle-oo-doo-doo!*

As the ululations died away, another sound intruded, a whizzing, buzzing, moaning, seeming to fill the arena like an invisible whirlpool: *Bidooz, bidooz, bidooz, bidooz, bidooz* – while out of the blaze of moonlight came the Pookarakka, swinging the magic source of it, the *Bidu-bidu*, symbol of the Voice of Koonapippi, Creator of All Things, The Earth Mother, so oddly purloined to be set up as the Deity of Masculinity – *Bidooz, bidooz, bidooz, bidooz, bidooz – All Weak Things, Women, Children, Tremble at My Voice* – as indeed the very earth seemed now to do.

The Pookarakka marched round the ring, swinging the invisible thing by its long cord of hair with such vigour that it seemed to re-spin the moonbeams, while the others followed him in procession ululating – *Yoodle-oodle-yoodle-oo-doo-doo – Bidooz, bidooz, bidooz* . . .

Chanting cut into it:

Marunga, marunga
Ma widji, widji ma
Koonapippi, Koonapippi
Koonapipeeeeee!

And interminably the Oldest Voice in Creation: *Bidooz, bidooz, bidooz* . . . Igulgul saw it out, tired of it before they did, having watched it so often, and really being of another persuasion, given to encourage the breaking of laws instead of ruthlessly enforcing them, dropped out of sight behind the wall, causing the silver mushrooms that grew thereon to blacken and wither and become rags against the blaze of the Celestial Snake. At that last moment, the celebrants, with a final *Tjangaluma,* broke off, went back to the camp, all except the Pookarakka, who remained, with *Bidu-bidu* hidden in the coil of hair-string on his knees, as *Pirri-Pirri*. The others had damper and tea, were soon asleep. The mopoke could be heard again.

Soon day dawned. The little birds, after a wary survey, flitted in to drink. The Sun rose. The kites rose with it from their scattered roosts, floating in their lazy way on the first heat-eddies in the air, circled into congregation over the arena. They saw the scraps, whistled, then came spiralling down silently to snatch and go aloft again, gobbling on the wing. Nobody stirred below.

It took the Sun, almost literally, to burn the celebrants back to activity. They came-to slowly, drank, ate, touched up decorations. Thus while the Sun climbed. Then sudden activity. Accoutred as at last night's opening ceremony, the group converged on the Ring Place, and again with a yell that even rocked the sailing kites above, charged the *wirrianwah*. The ceremonial continued much as last night, only with increasing tempo, despite the growing heat. The billy-can was replenished many times and passed around.

With the Sun exactly overhead, the dancers massed again, to go prancing round the *wirrianwah*, yelling and clashing weapons, reaching a seeming pitch of frenzy at which it seemed their frequent simulated murderous assaults on the *Yalunga* must culminate in bloody reality – when the regular *Pirri-Pirri*, who had disappeared, was suddenly there amongst them with a blazing fire-stick. With a flourish he put it to the shrivelled leaves of the whirley – *Poof*!

The eucalyptus-charged leaves exploded in a ball of fire and smoke, leaving only the burning frame with full view of the sacrificial figure crouched head down in the hole. His behaviour at that fearful moment would establish the worth of his manhood. A boy who would leap out in panic – well, they had a name for him, *Nutching*. The dancers shouted their acclamation while whirling about and snatching at the frame and tearing it from the ground to extinguish the embers with bare feet. Smoke snd dust for a moment obliterated everything, except the Voice – *Bidooz, bidooz, bidooz* . . .

As the air cleared, the dancers formed themselves into a compact squad, facing the bowed boy and chanting:

Marunga, Marunga,
Ma widji, widji ma
Koonapippi, Koonapippi
Koonapipeeeeee!

One from each side peeled off, to come leaping to the hole, stooped and seized Prindy by the armpits, hauled him up and out. He staggered between them, tears and mucous streaming. The squad opened to let them in its midst, the men from either side then falling in behind, to drop to hands and knees, and with the adroitness of much practice, form themselves into a kind of table, a sacrificial altar, onto which, almost as it was formed, the neophyte was pushed, so that he fell with legs dangling to the ground. As he fell, the rest shouted and rushed round to form a half-circle facing him. Behind the circle the Pookarakka appeared, whirling the *Bidu-bidu*. One of the two handlers flung the boy's arms backwards, where ready hands of the living altar grabbed them. The other parted his legs, while hands at this end fastened about his ankles.

The chanting rose high:

Ma widji, widji ma
Koonapipeeeeee!

The Voice shook the air – *Bidooz, bidooz, bidooz*!

One of the handlers fished from his *bulkung* a package wrapped in paper-bark, took out a blade of quartz, handed the bark to his mate, who formed it into a little bowl. Standing between the divided legs, the man with the knife flung back the apron of the boy's *bulkung*, to reveal white-painted genitals. Without ado he seized the *dara* with left hand, inserting his little finger into the prepuce to pull it from the *glans*, then with the right made four deft and deliberate cuts, each causing the whitened body to wince, and so in a moment removed the foreskin.

The other man shoved the little *coolamun* forward to receive the bloody bit of skin and knife, whereupon the operator took the vessel and held it under the stripped member to catch the trickling blood. Flies joined in, no one bothering about them, except the initiate, who shivered to the contact. Perhaps an ounce of blood ran before clotting set in. Then the operator raised the bowl to his lips, blew the flies away, and sipped, passed it on to his mate, who sipped and passed it on.

Someone handed the operator a dripping dilly-bag, from which he drew the healing pipe-clay, waved off the flies and encased the bloody *glans*. Then someone gave him a roll of fine paper-bark to apply as bandage. With the *dara* dressed, he turned it back to lie on the boy's belly, pulling over it a looped piece of the belt to hold it in place, pulled down the apron. Both custodians then drew the boy to his feet. This was greeted by a great shout and the instant disintegration of the altar, and a wild dance about the dazed boy. The Pookarakka stood clear, whirling the *Bidu-bidu*. Through the dancers, the custodians led the boy to an open bough shelter bigger than the rest, where he was seated again, now with head up, facing West.

The dancers divided into two lines on either side of the shelter, stamping and chanting – *Ma widji, widji ma . . . Koonapippi* – and ululating; while the Pookarakka advanced on the wide-staring *Yalunga*, still with Bidu whirling, to a point where, with a deft movement brought it spiralling down, to catch it, and then reverently wrap the long flat carved elipse of polished ironwood in the hair string. Thus with the sacred symbol lying on upturned hands, he advanced on the shelter, knelt before the boy, offered the thing. Obviously trembling, the boy took it on extended palms, while the Pookarakka said, '*Barumba, birrini, wirrana*.'

At that another shout arose, and the dancers ranged again in a half-circle, stamping, chanting: *Djeninalua, djeninalua, Djeninalu-ah-ah-ah*!

A moment. Then the Pookarakka reached and took the *Bidu-bidu* back. As he rose he touched the boy's head with it. Thereupon the crowd shouted, and as the old man withdrew, came each to touch the head, while the grey eyes stared entranced. That was the end of proceedings for the time. The Pookarakka retired to the next bough shelter, while the others filed off, still shouting and yodling, to the camp.

The kites were to be seen spiralling down, knowing that cooking would be on again. The Sun was down behind the wall. A couple of men went over it with spears, were soon back with rock-wallabies. The fire blazed in the sunset. The high laughter of blackmen rose. There was a howl of mirth as one fellow tripped and fell into the fire, saving himself from much injury through his incredible alacrity, himself laughing, indifferent to hurt. Igulgul came up on the feasting. The kites snatched and fled to roosts. Soon everybody was asleep.

Igulgul was halfway up the sky when they roused again. Now they washed off the paint of former proceedings, and assisting each other, assumed new decorations, of various designs. Thus did they occupy themselves till the Old One was directly overhead. Then, ready, they took from the caverns behind the dilly-bags and packages they had brought up from below, and with them trooped to the Ring. Here they stowed their things in the unoccupied shelter. Then some went to the *wirrianwah* hole and filled it in. All this done, those two men who had acted as handlers for the initiate, brought him from his shelter and placed him out in the open close to where the hole had been. Again he squatted, but with head erect.

Proceedings began with group dancing, to which Bobwirridirridi kept accompaniment with boomerangs, assisted by another with didjeridoo. The group danced itself to the sidelines, there to stamp and clap, while individuals, after having gone to a shelter to get his particular sacred artifact, came and danced before the boy. displaying what he had. The first man had a thin piece of wood carved like an elongated bird and decorated as he himself was. The next had a stone about as big as an emu's egg held in a net bag. The boy's eyes glittered in the moonlight as he viewed the things. So each danced and sang of his Dreaming and displayed the symbol of it, the import perhaps to convey to the initiate the responsibility of tribesmen to what was their own, as a lesson in the responsibilities he himself would be assuming.

It went on, repeated again and again – till Igulgul got sick of it, and ducked down behind the wall, leaving it to the Sun, always Right Side. But the magic vanished with the golden blaze. Halt was shouted. Prindy was placed back in his shelter. Bobwirridirridi went to his and had a swig of brandy and water. The others returned to the camp to cook and eat and sleep. The kites came down for their pickings.

Those kites, in wide wheeling, could be seen from Jeremy's camp. Jeremy pointed them out to Rifkah, while they were down at the horse-yard taking a look at sick Betsy. The movement was no more than a flicker in the violet sky, of sunlight striking the sheen of dark wings. He said, 'Lend me your young eyes. Are those kites . . . or am I developing cirrhosis through too much brandy?'

Rifkah shaded her eyes, after a while answered, 'Kite all right.'

'Hmm. Then that's where the Ring Place will be. Kites always join in. They get the scraps for nix.' Jeremy glanced towards the camp. No one was in sight. Turning back to Rifkah, he went on: 'I saw them when we were down here yesterday afternoon, but didn't say anything, for fear of starting her ladyship off.' Giving his attention to the mare, who was lying groaning, he continued: 'There's what looks like an old Ring Place just about there . . . a rather marvellous place, with cave paintings, shut off by a circular wall of rock, so that you feel you're in a dream world in the middle of it. Wish I could take you to see it sometime . . . only it wouldn't be proper. Anyway, at least we know they're handy. The old fellow should be along for his rations as soon as the show's over. Then we can get her little ladyship going on the pretence that she'll be able to join her boy over on the railway after his walkabout. We'll have to stop this mad *Charada* singing of hers . . . or she'll have a breakdown. It's Full Moon tonight. She'll probably be sitting up all night singing, the way she's lying in this morning.'

Rifkah commented with a sigh: 'Poor dear!'

Jeremy talked of the mare, saying he had a suspicion that her condition was not uterine but intestinal, the cause fermented hay: 'In spite of our care in drying it, a bit of damp could have got in. The by-products of hay ferments can be quite toxic to animals. Must have a look at that hay.'

Had he gone to take a look right then, he would have found more than ferment in the hay. Had he even looked up at the loft instead of towards the camp, he would have seen a dark face looking down at him. It was a pleasant place to 'lay-off' in, out of the blustering wind, without being back amongst what to one in her state must have been the constriction of the rocks and wall. She must have heard what Jeremy said, because she withdrew at once and slipped across to the other side, to stare at the sky southwestward. Then, avoiding the ladder, she climbed through the fork of the tree on that side, slid down the smooth trunk. For a moment she hid behind the trunk, peeping at those in the yard, then backed away to the cover of other trees. Hidden, she looked at the sky again. Here it was too close in to see. She went on up to the kitchen shelter, took a drink from the water-bag, then flung herself into a chair, facing southeastward, staring up into the violet sky cut by the top of the escarpment. Soon she began to sing softly to herself, tapping fingers like *minga-minga sticks*:

Kowe breiju, I sing you now
Kowe breiju, you my sweetheart
Kowe breiju, must you come
To my Charada, Charada, Charada . . . .

Over and over, as if entranced herself by the spell-binding. Yet, hearing the others coming while still a long way off, she fell silent, and in a moment was up and off, to take refuge in the rocks beyond. While Jeremy and Rifkah set about preparing smoke-o, she went to the sleeping-cave, flung herself down on her bed. When later Rifkah came to ask her to join them, she appeared to be asleep.

That Savitra was far from sleeping was shown by the alacrity with which she rose as Rifkah disappeared. She slipped out of the cave, made her way westward through the rocks, soon to reach the track by which ascent to the top of the escarpment usually was made. She stopped often, out of breath from her haste, but always where she could not be seen from below. She stared at the Flag of Lost Hope. She watched Jeremy and Rifkah drenching Betsy. She didn't look upward much, probably because, by the way she blinked, it made her dizzy. But on and up she went, and at last with a sigh cast herself down on top, back from the edge, in the shade of a wind-bent larrama.

Now her eyes were fixed on the sky eastward, where the kites could be seen as black dots above the horizon. She began to sing:

Kowe breiju, Must you come
I sing you Charada . . . .

At length she rose, drew a deep breath, started eastward, with the wind pressing her floral cotton dress tight on those most vital parts of her, her growing breasts and belly. Gorged breasts and pregnant bellies of rock all round her, like symbols of the Earth Mother's fertility. Round and through and over she went, panting, sweating, sometimes cursing, often singing her *Charada*, which the wind snatched from her lips as improperly directed and flung it the other way. She scratched herself on rock, got torn by spiny bush, shouted, 'Bloody bastard!' She nursed bruised feet, whimpering, 'Wha's matter he no-more come, all-time I sing him? Blackfeller magic can't beat *Charada*. Nutching beat *Charada* . . . *Kowe breiju*, must you come . . . .'

On and on, while the Sun climbed high, watching, watching – the Ol'-Goomun-Ol'Goomun, who throughout the ages had seen so many women recklessly trying to win back the magic she had given them but they had let men steal behind her back. The kites rose with the Sun. They spotted the intruder, swung westward to take a better look. She hid when they came too near. Not that she seemed worried by their attention. She sang back at them from hiding:

Kowe breiju, must you come
I sing you Charada.

She projected her sharpish Indian nose into the wind, sniffing. Smell of smoke if not sign of it. Then there was the darkish wall of the arena rising. In the wilderness it had the look of some sort of habitation, at least to one whose eyes would long to see such things. Her step became brisker. She was in more open country, with the rock masses smaller, the trees bigger and more plentiful. There were huge red ant-hills amongst the trees. Suddenly she stopped, staring at the ground. A blackfellow's footprints. She looked about with black eyes wide with alarm. The tracks crossed her path. She peered carefully in each direction. No sign of life except those wheeling birds, now above the mass behind which could be a station stockyard. After a moment she moved on, reached the wall.

It was easy enough to climb. In no time she was at the top, but to be startled by the unexpected sight of the amphitheatre. On the instant she dropped into hiding amongst grass and scrub. She sniffed. Here the smell of smoke was strong. She peeped. Nothing living to be seen. But, yes – the small birds were back at the water. Staring at the pandanus palms, she licked dry lips and swallowed. She wriggled into a better positition for viewing. That it was a camp of some sort and occupied, if at the moment deserted, was obvious. She would have little if any idea of its significance. Even the women and children of the wilds knew nothing of Ring Places, nothing more than that certain places were *wahji*, whether because used by devils or men, and to be avoided as one loved life.

But was the place utterly deserted? Her sharp eyes spotted the white figure squatting in the shelter almost directly facing her. She stared and stared. Her lips moved. The song came under her breath:

Kowe breiju, I sing you now
Kowe breiju, you my sweetheart
Kowe breiju, must you come
To my Charada, Charada, Charada . . . .

Again, and again, and louder. She rose to knees singing. She leapt to her feet. The whiteness stirred. She screeched, 'Prindy!'

No movement.

She stood a moment, then in a different tone, shriller, a little girl's voice, at once expressing fear and anger, she screeched, 'I know dat you. You come here. You come here now.' When there was still no movement, the screech became higher, more ragged: 'You got 'o come, you bastard. I been sing you *Charada*!'

Movement now, if ever so slight.

Another moment. Then the voice became a woman's, a black gin's, the scream of defiance of denial of a woman's right: 'All right . . . I don' care 'bout blackfeller bijnitch . . I come gitchim you!' As she came leaping down from projection to projection, her voice rose again, screaming now that song she could sing so sweetly:

Okale pusili paya
Dodi dudhoch khatock ho
Feed you my milk, my kuni
My Pigeon, I never let you go!

On reaching the bottom she halted, wary again, looked about, breathing hard. Not that she could see even the Ring Place now through the intervening scrub. Then she started off towards it, at a run, crashing through the growth, came out on the sacred circle, but with eyes for nothing save the squatting pipe-clayed figure. She leapt to it, flinging herself on knees before it, grabbed at its feathered arms, babbling, 'Prindy, Prindy, Prindy!'

The grey eyes were so wide with horror that she was silenced momentarily. Panting likewise, he tried to shake her off, and when she only clung the fiercer, heaved up to knees, croaking the first words he would have uttered for days, 'Go 'way!'

She found her voice, screeched, dragging at him, 'You got 'o come wid me . . . Mullaka say!'

'Go 'way!'

It seemed like the sudden obliteration of the Sun by a storm-cloud in a high wind, so swiftly did the great shadow fall upon them. An instant under the menace. Then black hands appeared, snatched at the slender chocolate arms. Savitra shrieked as she was yanked away, heels dragging in the sand. One moment of goggling of black eyes into grey. Then both looked up. Again the hooded mantis figures, although this time not with switches. She tried to fight against restraint. The blade of a black hand struck her neck. As she fell limp, the handling of her was left to a pair of the stick figures, who hauled her by the wrists across to where the human altar of initiation had been formed, there dropped her unceremoniously.

The group strolled over and formed a circle. No one carried any sort of weapon, except one tall fellow who had a heavy nulla-nulla stick, which, upon reaching the prostrate form, he set up in the ground by the sharper end. Then this same man bent and took the floral dress by the neck and jerked as if to rip it away, only to drag the girl with it. Another man put a foot on an outstretched arm. The dress was ripped off, showing the plump little chocolate body wearing only a pair of cotton drawers. The man had these off in a swift movement. The clothes were tossed away.

The crowd stood silent, till the tall man put hand to mouth and gave voice to the *Tjangaluma*. As all took it up, he stopped, reached for the nulla-nulla, took a grip on the light end with both hands, swung high, brought it down with full force on the girl's right knee cap. Savitra woke with a gasp, goggling. Up went the stick again, to come down on the left knee. She sat up with a shriek. Two other men leapt from the circle to seize her upflung arms. With a dexterous backward movement, the bone-breaker swung his stick to catch the right arm at the elbow, and as it was dropped shattered, swung to do likewise with the left. Screaming at the top of her lungs, heaving, trying to rise, the victim got into a sitting posture. A black hand shot out and silenced her with another swipe on the side of the neck.

Still yodelling, the group danced into a squad as it had done to receive the other initiate, in a trice formed the human altar. The senseless sacrifice was raised and dumped onto it. The man with the nulla-nulla had used it to dismantle a shelter, the boughs of which he brought to cover the naked chocolate body. Whatever tradition demanded in one circumstance, it could not be violated in another. She might be Wrong Side to someone. So long as they could not see her.

Again the bone-breaker stood his stick in the ground, to go take up a position a few paces from the spread chocolate thighs. Then, leaping into a dance in which he jerked erotically, he drew his black *dara* from the apron of his belt and masturbated to the rhythm and the ululating of his fellows till he had erection, when suddenly he rushed the victim, penetrated her, jerked to orgasm, after which he wheeled away, now with hand raised to join the *Tjangaluma*, while another man who had been dancing as he, replaced him. The victim roused, howled into the din – Oooooooooooo! The men of the altar had her fast. Soon it was their turn. The only one not in it, watching with great grey eyes, could not have seen much with all the crowding, not until it was over, and as the altar collapsed the man with the nulla-nulla grabbed the black hair of the falling howling victim, and with another deft stroke caught her in the back of the neck. She fell quivering. The group ceasing yodelling, to drop to haunches.

The man with the nulla-nulla still stood. Again he dug his stick in the sand, and this time went off towards the camp, alone. The others sat in silence staring at the now still victim, what could be seen of her beneath the boughs. The kites were wheeling low, as if they'd done a job and expected a reward.

Soon the executioner was back, with a fresh bit of bough and one of the clasp-knives donated by Jeremy. He gave the leaves to another man, who quickly formed them into a sort of dish. He stooped over the victim, bared the right breast, seized it in his left hand, while with his right he sliced round and removed it to the depth of the white rib bone. As the man with the dish held it towards him, he cut the slightly quivering flesh into some half dozen lumps, letting them fall. He stepped over to the left breast, did the same. The flies swooped into the oozing holes. He stepped to the crutch, took a grip of the tuft of pubic hair, sliced from back of the *mons* right round the *vulva*, removed the whole, again cut it into pieces into the fly-filled bowl. Finished, he raised his bloodied hand to give the *Tjanguluma* again. The others leapt up to join in. He took the leafy platter of sacrificial pieces from his mate, turned and headed towards the camp, with the rest following in line still keeping up their din.

At the fire the executioner set down his platter, took off his hood to disclose himself as one of those men at the water-hole that day. He flung it into the smouldering fire. The others did likewise. The fire was stirred up, to blaze, to fall to coals. The kites whistled at the rising of the savour of cooking human flesh.

Prindy sat staring at what could be seen beneath the boughs and the busy busy flies. The mother Sun stared down. How often since the Dream Time had she witnessed the like?

Soon five men appeared from the direction of the camp. The leader was the executioner, now carrying spears and womera, but not bent on more execution, evidently because he only took up his nulla-nulla and headed for that gap in the western wall. The others, apparently not Wrong Side, kicked the boughs from the corpse, and taking it up by wrists and ankles from which it dangled in a strangely flaccid way, set out to follow. It would be the burial party, the nulla-nulla for gouging a hole in an ant-hill, the customary place for burial of such as whose remains held no sanctity.

The grey eyes under the shelter stared trance-like – suddenly to become alert at movement to the right of the shelter. There was the Pookarakka. The red coals met the grey eyes in a long stare. The old man was fully accoutred and freshly decorated with the motif of The Snake. Jerking his lips in direction opposite to that of the camp he said in his cackling voice, '*Ngangulah.*' The boy rose at once.

At the moment, down at Jeremy's camp, there was consternation, owing to the discovery that Savitra had slipped away and fear of what might by her purpose. Jeremy was not expert enough to judge with exactness how long it was since the girl had left the camp. Nor was Rifkah sufficiently knowledgeable of Savitra's awareness of Aboriginal lore to say whether her purpose was as reckless as might be. Jeremy said, 'Well, we can't take risks. If she's headed for the Ring Place, it's going to take her hours to get there. It's also going to take as long to follow her through that rough stuff up there. I think the best thing to do is for me to take a horse to where the old fellow left me, then climb the cliff. There must be some sort of track there for them to have gone up with all that gear. If she hasn't already got there, I'll be able to see by tracks, and come back along the top and head her off . . . and if she has, and's in trouble, can buy her off. You go up top and scout round a bit. She might be only sitting on a rock singing her *Charada*. If so, persuade her to come down, telling her I've gone to get Prindy. But don't follow if she's gone. Come back and wait here.'

Rifkah eyed him anxiously. 'You vill be all right climbing? Your arm not so goot lately, I see.'

'I'll be travelling light . . . a few presents in case there's a fine to pay . . . and the rifle.'

Her eyes widened. 'Ze rifle?'

'It'll come in handy for the climb . . . as an alpenstock . . . and, although I hate the idea, I might have to use it to come the whiteman over them, if the little fool's fallen into their hands. Let's hope, if she's got close enough to annoy 'em, they'll only give her a belting again and hunt her. But don't you go getting a belting, too. Promise?'

She nodded.

He said, 'Come on . . . help me to get going. I'll take your horse again, because he knows the track and can move. I'll send him straight back to you, because whether I beat her to it or not, I'll be coming back the top way. So don't be alarmed to see him. I'll take tucker and water for just one day . . . and a bottle of brandy, a drop to help me up the jump-up, the rest for the old fellow.'

She clung to him at parting, saying, 'Be careful, Jeremy. I feel fright'.'

He chuckled: 'On account of me? Go on! The old boy and I are old mates. As for the others . . . well, they're bush blacks and used to doing things their own way and know the *kuttabah*'s law isn't anything like it was to fear . . . but still, I guess, the old fear will still be there when the *kuttabah* raises his voice.'

He kissed her, mounted Red Rory, called, '*Mummuk, yawarra.*'

He had split-bags, lightly filled, hung across his pummel, the rifle slung across his broad khaki back. He put the horse straight into a canter, saying to him, 'Sorry to push you in the heat of the day, old boy . . . but it might be urgent.'

In no time he was at that point where he had parted with the Pookarakka. He did not stop there, but rode on as far as possible to the foot of the escarpment. He then fixed stirrups and bridle, gave Red Rory a slap on the rump and sent him home. Without delay, he shouldered split-bags and rifle and made his way through the tangle and tumble.

Even if those who'd gone ahead of him had left any sort of track, he would never have been able to follow it exactly. He had to pick his way, often had to retrace his laboured steps and try another way. Several times he clung trembling and panting, telling himself that he was too old to take risks. Clinging in some precarious place on the red wall, he swigged at the brandy, breathing, 'Too old at last, eh? It's hard to admit. The natural thing is not to admit it, I suppose, but to go down striving.' When the kites found him and flew level squinting with predatory eyes, he called to them, 'I'm not going to fall off and leave you the pickings . . . so don't look so expectant.'

After a terrific struggle he made it, to lie exhausted for a time in a bit of shade and under his hat. Then he muttered to himself, 'Dare a man die just because he's feeble and lost his pride as a physical man, when it's courageous intelligence that's the most valuable contribution one can make to one's fellows?' He rose, took a swig of brandy, shouldered split bags and rifle again, started on his way. The darker stone of the Ring Place could be seen from where he was. However, he did not approach it, southeastward as it lay, but went directly southward into the wilderness of rock, eyes on the ground, darting at every open space, surely in search of tracks.

Thus after a while he came into sight of those red ant-hills. He saw a freshly broken bush, examined it, looked about, saw a stretch of sand, went to it, stopped and stared. Small footprints, coming from westward, going towards the dark bulk to be glimpsed eastward through the rocks and trees. Drawing a long hissing breath, he set out to follow them. He lost them several times amongst the rocks. He was searching for them where the rocks began to give way to more timbered space, when a movement to his left attracted him. He looked, gaped, to see a few paces away the Pookarakka, decorated as the Snake Man, armed. The cackled greeting was as easy as if it had been made down at the camp: 'Goottay, Mullaka.'

Jeremy swallowed hard before replying, 'Goodday, Pookarakka.'

The death's head cocked in that sly-looking way of the blackfellow asking of a stranger a question to which already he knows the answer: 'Which way you walkabout, Mullaka?'

Jeremy came out with it with a rush: 'Young Indian girl from my camp . . . been get lost long o' bush, I think. You been look him?'

The head held the pose, while the red coals burnt into the anxious grey stare. But not a word or hint of comprehension. Jeremy waited, then burst forth again: 'Look, Pookarakka . . . that girl no-more lubra. You savvy him daddy, old-man Barbu . . . Ali Barba. I got to look out that girl for daddy.

Two-three day more I take him back long o' daddy.' Still no hint. Jeremy's voice became hoarse with urgency: 'You'n'me old friend, Pookarakka. All-day I look out for you. I give you anything. I got brandy . . . big mob long o' camp. I got him here.' He slipped the split-bags from his shoulder, set them down, stooped and took out the brandy bottle, handed it, saying with a forced grin, 'I been drink lil bits . . . knock-up climbin' that jump-up . . . gettin' too muchee old.' The black claws rearranged the arms. Then one was extended to take the bottle.

'Tahng you, Mullaka.' The wide mouth pulled out the cork. The little finger of the claw with the bottle removed it as the bottle was raised. A long pull. A gasp and shudder. Then a sigh as the bottle was lowered: 'Proper-lee!'

'You keep him', said Jeremy quickly. Then as quickly he added: 'Now, you tell him me which way that girl, eh?'

The coals fixed the grey eyes again, but now without the cock of the head. The cackle was harsher: 'More-better you go back you camp, Mullaka.'

'Eh?' Jeremy looked at a loss, blinked hard.

The old man pulled a spear from the bundle under his arm, not to point it, but to reverse it, dropping the butt-end to the ground, beginning to draw a line in the sand with it. Watching the procedure wide-eyed, Jeremy again said with a rush of speech, now with an hysterical note to it, 'I been do it good way long o' you. I been helip you from start. I been good friend long o' all-about blackfeller. I been 'shame for my rown countryman do it wrong thing long o' you . . . . '

The cackle cut in, harsher: 'You goot friendt all right, Mullaka. Dat what for me talk goot-way long o' you now. I tell him you . . . more-better you go back long o' you camp.' The red eyes dropped to the spear in the sand. The skeleton figure began to back away, while the cackle went on: 'You savvy dat kind bijnitch, eh?' Evidently he was referring to what he was doing. Jeremy could only stare at the extending line.

The Pookarakka had retreated a couple of full paces drawing his line where the ground would take it. Not that it mattered how long or how distinct it was. Such a line, drawn by one who had the authority for it, was virtually limitless in the direction in which it ran, and absolutely uncrossable for anyone who saw it drawn. The red eyes came up, fixed the grey for a moment. Then their owner said easily, '*Mummuk, yawarra*,' turned about, and now trailing the spear, vanished amongst the rocks. Jeremy opened his lips as if to cry a protest, but closed them on a groan.

Slowly he turned to look at the dark wall from which the line debarred him, his eyes drawn and haggard, his tanned face twisted with worry. He looked along the line again, into the rocks, searching. He drew a deep breath, shouted, 'Pookarakka!' Only the echo from the rocks replied. He muttered, 'The old bastard . . . he's put it over me. I shouldn't have let him.' Then he cupped his mouth and shouted, 'Pookarakka . . . you can't do it blackfeller way long o' that Indian girl. I'm going to get him. You hear that? I'm going to get him!'

Again only the echo. He turned again and looked at the wall beyond the intervening rocks and scrub. He growled now, 'No . . . damn me if I can allow it . . . bugger his line!' Slinging the rifle on his shoulder again, he stepped across what would have been the extension of the demarcation, went heading for the wall, grim-jawed and resolute of step.

He was close to the wall, eyes on the tracks, when he looked up quickly, as if something had caught his eye. He searched the rough mass of rock above with darting glances. There was movement, but only of bushes thrash-thrashing in crevices. He dropped eyes again, went on – in a moment to look up. A dark form leaping over the rocks from South to North! In an instant it was gone. He heard the whistling of kites, looked back and up to see them wheeling between him and the westerning Sun. He reached the wall, lost the tracks there, but saw where the small feet most likely would have picked their way in climbing. He started up.

About halfway up he was startled again, looking this time at a crevice some distance to his right and up. Leaning on the rifle, he stared hard. Something could have been in the rift, screened as it was with dried grass and bushes. He put a hand to cup his mouth, called, 'Who's there?' No answer but the swish and rumble of the wind gusting over the rampart of broken rock. He called again, 'Is that you Savitra?' He headed for the crevice, muttering, 'I'll swear I saw something . . . a black face watching.' At the crevice there was no sign of anyone's ever having been there. He zig-zagged away from it to resume the easier climb to the top, but twice looked back quickly. The second time he breathed, 'Perhaps my *Yalmaru*.' As he was coming to the top he added: 'If it's you, old fellow, for God's sake show me the right and proper thing to do. They have their own way . . . but I have mine. I don't want to live out my life regretting something I ought or ought not to have done.'

He reached the top at the same point as Savitra had, saw the depression where she had hidden in the vegetation before he observed what it was had sent her to ground. Then he looked, gaped. It was a very different sight from that the girl had seen.

The Ring Place was anything but deserted now. At the end nearest the camp, the southern, stood a semi-circle of armed and painted men, facing northward. In that direction the scrub beyond the Ring had been cleared further, to make a passage about as long as the Ring was wide. At the end of it stood a solitary slight figure, wearing the regalia of The Snake, but accoutred with a single boomerang, one so brightly painted that it flashed like a swift bright bird in darting to meet a spear that at that moment came hurtling from one of the group still standing out in front crouched with womera extended. The boomerang turned the spear to the right, so that if finished in the ground with haft vibrating above the scrub beyond. Two other such hafts were to be seen. Speech broke from Jeremy as a croaking: 'Oh, God . . . a trial by ordeal!'

Another spearman had stepped from the semi-circle, weapon hooked in womera, crouched. As the spear flew, a mere line of air-disturbance in its fleetness, Jeremy croaked again, 'Jesus Christ!'

Up came the bright boomerang again and met the hurtling death, causing the wooden blade to split away from the haft, the latter to go spinning over the fillet-bound head that in the last rays of the Sun upon the western rampart glittered gold. The slight figure staggered slightly from the impact. The arm with the boomerang fell heavily, betraying weariness.

Here was another man out with spear and womera. How many more before the outrage done on tradition was vindicated either with death or the magical prowess to defy it? How much longer could a scarce-bearded boy beat skill and strength and indignant purpose that themselves were in the realm of magic?

As the marksman, that tall thin Executioner, swung to give full force to right arm and to the arm's magical projection, the womera, a yell burst from Jeremy: 'Hey!'

Even the spearman looked. Jeremy started to leap down, shouting now so that the rock behind him rang his words all round, 'Cut that out!'

Cut that out . . . Cut that out . . . Cut that out!

But he gasped and halted in his headlong rush to see that flicker of the air as the spear flew, and gaped as he watched the boomerang come up too late, and the slight figure stagger back impaled. The figure swayed, sagged at the knees, collapsed, while the haft of the missive of tribal justice wagged its triumph in the air.

Jeremy sprang out of immobility, turned on the group now turned from him, and got their attention again on the instant, shouting, 'You bastards!' As he started leaping down again, they swung as if to meet him. He stopped again, and from using the rifle to aid his progress, threw it up to grasp in both hands, slipped the catch, and without aiming, pulled the trigger – *BANG*!

A small burst of dust from the further wall. The rocks rang all round – *Bang, Bang, Bang*! The kites whistled and flapped for height. With a single movement the arc of warriors swung towards the camp, bolted *en masse*, except for the Executioner, who was late off the mark. Again a flicker in the air. The Executioner staggered, fell to knees, with a spear-haft waving between his shoulders.

Jeremy looked to left. Risen out of the scrub was a tall skeleton figure in the insignia of The Snake, womera still extended from the throw. He looked again to right, to see the fallen man rise and with swaying steps vanish after his brethren. He raised the rifle and fired again at the opposite wall – *BANG*!,

In a moment there were the warriors to be seen leaping up the split part of the southern wall, a couple dragging their wounded mate between them with the Pookarakka's spear still wagging like a tail behind him. Then they were gone.

Jeremy turned towards the fallen boy, started for him at a run, did not pause as he passed the Pookarakka, but glaring at him, yelled, 'What's matter you no-more look-out that boy?' He burst through the scrub to the cleared space, reached Prindy to have the grey eyes so like his own fix him with the light of recognition and see a slight sweet smile move lips and release a bubble of blood. The spear had penetrated the painted breast just above the heart.

Struggling with his breathing, Jeremy stooped – only to jerk erect again with a sharp cry: 'Oh!' He staggered to the right, tripped over the rifle, fell to knees. He goggled at the watching grey eyes as he swung to his left, hands groping that way, his own eyes staring astonishment. The long haft of a heavy spear protruded from his side backward, swinging out of sight as he turned, the blade buried to the hilt just above his hip. He grasped both haft and hilt. It was a shovel-spear of the modern kind, with broad blade of thinly hammered steel. He looked up to see the Pookarakka approaching, gaped at him, gasped, 'What's matter you?'

How fiery the coals and harsh the cackle as the answer was given: 'You been kill-him my *Mekullikulli*, Whiteman!'

The red eyes were directed at the prone figure towards which the long spidery stride was headed. With a groan Jeremy turned, to see the Pookarakka bending over his grandson, to see the grey eyes glaze, the smile obliterated by the sag of the bloody jaw. He groaned again, then suddenly drew breath and yelled, 'You bastard . . . why you let that mob make boy stand-up?'

The red eyes were raised from the pale dead face, to fix the living grey. The voice was not a cackle now, but a harsh scream: 'Wha's matter you come bugger-him-up bijnitch?'

Jeremy's face had turned yellowish. Sweat oozed from it. Still he clutched at the spear with both hands, but as if unaware of it now. He struggled for breath, panted, 'He only young boy . . . must . . . they kill him . . .?'

The Pookarakka swung and reached for the painted boomerang, and seizing it, rose and lunged and shoved it before Jeremy's eyes, crying in the same tone, 'Nobody can beat him dat *Mahraghi* . . . spone you no come bugger-him-up!' There was froth on the wide lips.

Jeremy's eyes rolled.

The voice went on: 'Me been tell him you right t'ing . . . g'won, you go 'way. No matter, you whiteman, you do it wrong t'ing . . . you come . . . finish *Mahraghi* . . . finish belong me *Mekullikulli*!'

Jeremy breathed, 'Oh, Jesus Christ!'

For a moment the coals burnt into the grey eyes, then the old man, setting the boomerang down with his accoutrements, bent again over the boy. He touched the forehead, muttered something in lingo, then placing stubby toes on the slender shoulder, took hold of the fatal spear and with a wrench removed it. For a moment he stared intently at the finely barbed bloodied ironwood blade, then dropping the blade to the sand while holding the haft, stamped in the middle of the latter and broke the weapon in two. With that he flung it aside. He turned as Jeremy heaved himself groaning to his feet, stared at him for a moment, then at the protruding spear, then stepped up with a hand outstretched, evidently to remove the weapon. Jeremy swung away from him gasping, 'No . . . leave him!'

The red eyes sought his. The cackle back to normal asked, 'Wha's matter you?'

Holding himself askew, a hand on the haft, Jeremy panted, 'Spone you pull him out . . . I fall down dead-feller.' He struggled for speech, while the sweat ran down his lips. 'You been gitchim me . . . long o' spleen . . . blood-bag.'

The coals burnt into his eyes. Jeremy reached with right hand for the clasp-knife in the pouch on his belt, gasped, 'Here . . . you cut him off.'

The Pookarakka's reluctance was obvious. A spear that gets its mark proves its magic. To damage it is to destroy its powers. But the Wise One saw his way round the problem, set to work on the little knob of fibre cemented with fire-hardened gum that bound split haft to blade. Such joints often had to be repaired . . . Perhaps guessing at the reason, Jeremy panted, 'Take too long that way . . . I pay you for . . . spear.' But the claws worked steadily at the joint. When at long last blade and haft were parted and the latter snatched away to toss on the Pookarakka's heap, Jeremy, groaning at every breath now, said, 'You can't get that iron out . . . till I . . . die finish . . . and you can't take thing from dead man . . . can you . . . old-man!'

Bobwirridirridi turned from him to the dead boy. Jeremy also turned, asked, 'What you . . . going . . . do with him?'

Without looking, the old man answered, 'Plant him long o' rock . . . come back by'n'by, gitchim bone.'

'Half-half that boy belong . . . 'o me.' The eyes came up. Jeremy added: 'I . . . got to helipim you plant him.'

The red eyes dropped to the widening stain of blood on the left side of the khaki shirt. Jeremy stepped closer, tried to bend, gave up with a hoarse cry: 'Oh!'

He staggered, would have fallen again, only the skeleton leapt and grabbed him, held him up. A claw came up to touch his face, not sweating now and grey of hue. 'Too-muchee hot,' said the cackling voice.

'Yes,' breathed Jeremy. 'Too-much blood . . . I lose. But . . . but . . . must be I helipim you . . . I pay you. Where . . . which way . . . you plant him?'

For a moment the red eyes stared. Then the lips jerked towards the abandoned camp. The old man said, 'More-better you go dere wait. Me come behind, bring him. Gwon, you go. Water dere.'

Jeremy licked dry lips, swallowed, nodded weakly, reeled away. He crossed the Ring with dragging feet, stumbled his way to the water-hole. A billy hung in a bush, making it easier for him to get the water he so badly wanted, the way he drank. He was drinking again, when the Pookarakka came, with his burden slung over a shoulder like a kangaroo, blood dripping from mouth and beautifully shaped nostrils. The old man, showing no exertion, gently set his burden down, went to drink. Again he touched Jeremy's face, looked into his eyes, then looked down to stare at the dead boy's face, as if comparing. He stooped to take up his burden again. As the Pookarakka moved off, Jeremy caught at a dangling dead hand, and when the old man turned, gasped at him, 'Close-up I finish . . . old-man . . . please . . . you . . . you plant him . . . me-two-feller together . . . I send . . . message . . . Missus . . . pay you . . . ah . . . ah!'

Again the red stare for a moment. Then the old man nodded, cackled, 'Foller-him-up.'

He went on, to climb the expanse of split rock. Jeremy followed, dragging each foot. Soon the old man vanished amongst the cracks.

Jeremy started to climb, got no distance before he was on knees, on belly. He rolled over in his agony, groaning, 'To die like this . . . but . . . how better? The debt . . . the . . . the ancient debt . . . paid . . . . Old *Yalmaru* . . . come . . . get me . . . . '

He was babbling to the reddening sky when Bobwirridirri came down to him. With astonishing strength, the old skeleton got a shoulder under his arm and raised him, dragged him up, and along, to a horizontal slit, not more than a foot or so in width outside, narrowing in to darkness. Well inside could be seen the pale form of Prindy, lying on his back. The Pookarakka lowered Jeremy. Flat on his back again, Jeremy rallied. The old man grinned at him, jerked his lips, cackled, 'Properly goot place, eh?'

Jeremy rolled his grey head to look. He tried to roll in, but fell back fighting for breath. The old man began to shove him in, with a claw against his left shoulder and hip, but eyes on the protruding end of the spear-blade. Jeremy breathed, 'Thank . . . you, Pookarakka.' His right shoulder was touching Prindy's left. With an effort he lifted his right arm, scraping it along the rock so close above, let it fall behind the filleted faintly gleaming head. He struggled for speech again, could only whisper, 'You no hurt Missus Rifkah.'

'Can't hurt him Mitchis, Mullaka.'

'Tell him . . . tell him . . . two-feller can't come back . . . *Mahraghi* business . . . he savvy . . . pay you . . . .' Jeremy slipped his arm under the head beside him. His legs were pushed in. The claw ran up his thigh, passed the hip, snatched out the magic iron. Jeremy gasped, 'Oh!'

The Pookarakka looked like a black spider against the dying light. Jeremy tried to say something, but sagged, with rumbling belly and rattling breath.

The cackle came softly: '*Mummuk, yawarra*, Mullaka.'

Jeremy gagged on a breath, fell silent, still.

For a moment the Pookarakka stared, then from his *bulkung* fished the magic track-eraser, the brush of a brush-tail, and brushing, backed away, crooning as he did so:

Padinya ngeinya, murrummarrum
Amininimmi kwalli goyai
Kwalli tjerritjeru
Amininimmi, aminimmini
Padinya, Padinya
Mummuk.

II

It was midmorning of next day when Bobwirridirridi, again in khakis, carrying the inevitable womera, but also Jeremy's rifle, came into view of the camp below, for the first time announcing his arrival – *Ku*! *Ku*! Rifkah, in stockrider's outfit, came down to the fireplace to meet him, evidently surprised. Also for the first time, he addressed her, cackling as he came to a halt on the other side of the fireplace, 'Goottay, Mitchis.'

Her answer was wary: 'Goottay, Pookarakka.' Her eyes sought beyond him.

Propping the rifle against the post on which pots and pans hung, he said easily, 'Been bring-him-up.'

She eyed the rifle, then met the scarcely discernable flicker of the coals, asked in a constricted voice, 'Vich vay Mullaka?'

He rolled his head with lips protruding to indicate pretty well anywhere.

She asked, 'He come behind?'

He looked past her to the kitchen shelter, cackling, 'Can't come behind, dat one.'

She drew a deep breath, took a moment to press the questioning: 'Wha' for can't come?'

The coals met the wide hazel eyes, flickered to the fire, which he began to stir with the butt-end of the womera, cackling now in a different tone, rather as if talking to himself: 'Dat one been send him word . . . "Mitchis pay you . . . anysing prejent." '

She swallowed. 'But vere's he now? Vere Prindy? Vere zat Indian girl?'

He addressed the fire, 'Me too-muchee hungry for bre-millik-plendy.'

Again she drew a deep breath. 'All right . . . I get you . . . but you got to tell me.'

Their eyes met for an instant as she turned away. He dropped his to go and sit on a case.

While she mixed the bread and milk for him she kept glancing towards him, anxious-eyed, and sometimes looking further. Now he was singing softly to himself. Along with the bowl of stuff for him she brought a pannikin of tea for herself. She sipped while he gobbled. Nothing was said till he had finished and thanked her. Then, taking the bowl, she demanded, 'All right, you tell me now. Vot's matter Mullaka can't come?'

The coals met her demanding stare, flicked back to the fire. He gave a smack of the lips before answering, 'Dat one die-finish . . . two-feller all-same.'

She swallowed hard, quivered slightly, then spoke with evident control of voice: 'Vot name two-feller?'

'Dat old-man . . . dat young feller . . . Whuuup!' He belched.

She blinked as if struck, turned yellow under her tan. Again she swallowed, took a long while to ask in a husky whisper, 'Vot happen?'

Black lips and red tongue smacked again before answering, 'Old-man been talk, "Tell him Mitchis, belong *Mahraghi* Bijnitch been finish him two-feller." ' When she made no sound or move, he raised his eyes to meet her haggard stare, asked, 'You savvy?'

A moment of mutual staring. Then she rose slowly, breathing hoarsely: 'You talk liar. You been kill him . . . because of girl.'

The coals blazed for an instant. Then they looked past her at the kitchen. Mildly enough he cackled, 'Can't talk liar long o' you. Old-man been send him word . . . "Tell him Mitchis *Mahraghi* . . . tell him Mitchis pay." '

A long moment. Then when the coals came back to her, she asked hoarsely, 'Vere are zey?'

'Him all right, dat two-feller. Me been plant him. By'n'by I come back gitchim bone, tek him 'way.' He looked away, after a moment adding, speaking to the kitchen distance, 'No goot you go look-about. No goot like o' dat.'

She swayed as she stood, reaching for her own jerking throat, as if only something within herself could give her support.

The red eyes were on the brandy bottle standing on the kitchen table. The voice cackled, 'Old-man been talk you give it me plendy. You give it me now, eh? Me go.'

After a moment she swung away, went with crazy steps, got the bottle, came back and handed it to him, her eyes wide and wild. He looked into the eyes as he took the bottle, said, 'No-more fright', Mitchis. Nobody can hurt him you. Me go now. By'n'by me look-him-up you. *Mummuk, yawarra.*'

As he turned, she croaked, 'Ven you come back?'

He cocked his head to the sky, swung it as if calculating passages of Sun and Moon, cackled, 'Dat time Pigeon Mob come . . . Rain Time start.'

He went, vanished in that way of his, leaving her staring haggard-eyed, slack-jawed. Then slowly her features crumpled. Slowly she crumpled bodily, hands clutching for support now gone, came down to knees in the scattered ashes, drooped brow into the ashes, groaned to the earth, '*Ach, Lieber Gott* . . . all gone . . . all gone . . . *ach, Lieber Gott*!'

III

More than keep his word to return with the first rain, Bobwirridirridi was actually waiting for Rifkah. Long since she had gone looking for blacks to whom to attach herself, and came back to the Plateau with the Booroolooloogun and Googoowonjin, the Pigeon and Cormorant Peoples, for their annual festival. But for the whisps of copper to be seen peeping out of the dirty rag she wore around her head, she didn't look much different from the rest of the lubras with whom, bearing all burdens except arms, she tagged along behind the tribesmen. She wore only a hip-knotted loincloth of flour-sacking, and although in reality nothing like so dark-skinned as the rest even with deep tanning, wore enough billabong mud from daily delving for lily tuck-out and the like and a variety of the natural colours of the earth through spending so much time in close contact with it and having learnt that water was mainly for drinking, to go unnoticed. No one would have recognized the lovely Red Rifkah who had roused such a storm of admiration and other interest on arrival in the land. She was skinny as a gin. The perfectly formed face appeared to be elongated by its gauntness, the nose lengthened, sharpened, hooked, the great eyes, from constant squinting in the sun and battling flies when hands were occupied, narrowed and deeply wrinkled at the corners. As well as numerous dilly-bags and digging-sticks, she carried split-bags that gave a glimpse of medicines and surgical instruments.

As they reached the banyans and were preparing camp, Bobwirridirridi appeared as suddenly as ever, now the old grey skeleton *koornung*, laden with his magic bits and pieces. No one looked at him with pleasure. In fact no word was spoken to him, and any communication between him and the menfolk confined to an exchange of signs. Not that he was interested in the crowd. He made straight for Rifkah, cackling as he came up to her, 'Goottay, Mitchis . . . properly you go blackfeller walkabout, eh . . . eeeeeee!' The cackle ended in a giggle.

She said, '*Yu-ai*. I go look-out sick pipple.'

'Me been hear him. You go back long o' you camp now?'

They were some five miles westward of the late Jeremy Delacy's camp.

'No-more. First-time I look him Pigeon Bijnitch. By'n'by I go camp gitchim anyzing you want.'

'Me been gitchim.'

She eyed him. It wasn't like a blackfellow to help himself – at least to do so frankly. The old man might have read that as her thought, the way he added promptly, 'Halfcaste been give it.'

She stared. 'Wha' name halfcaste?'

'Belong old-man whitefeller before . . . sit down Lu'lu'lagun.'

She gaped a moment, then asked, 'You mean zat one Nanago?'

'*Yu-ai.*'

Her eyes became great again, showing the pallor in the wrinkles. She cried out, 'Nanago . . . moost I go see now!' She turned to the other women, all staring at her with the *koornung*: '*Ngai areya* belong me camp. *Ngaiuma koiyu* . . . *yawarra*!' She snatched up her split-bags.

The Pookarakka cackled at her easy use of lingo. 'Proper-lee!'

She asked him, 'You come?'

'No-more. Me finish long o' dis country now.'

She hesitated. 'You . . . gitchim . . . bone?'

'*Yu.*'

'Vot you do wit' zem?'

He jerked his head to show a journey across the Plateau. 'Tek him long o' dat one Rainbow Pool.' While she stared, he added: 'From dere me-t'ree-feller go hon-top.'

She murmured, 'Hon-top?'

Now he jerked his lips to the southward sailing clouds. 'Long o' sky.' The giggle came into the cackle again: 'T'ree-feller star. Spone night time you look up, might-be you look-see . . . eeeeeee!' For a moment the red eyes held her. Then he said, '*Mummuk, yawarra,*' swung away, did his disappearing trick.

From staring after him, she turned on the staring crowd, called to them, '*Areya*!' She swung away, shouldering the split-bags, found a horse-pad, broke into a trot.

It was all of five miles in afternoon heat and rising thunderstorm. Still she kept on at the trot, slowing only where wash-aways and gullies and rock masses hindered her. In less than an hour she was in familiar surroundings. There was the horse-yard beyond the scrub, and familiar horses, the old geldings Snowball and Big Ben prancing about, tail high for some reason.

Coming into full view of the yard she was confronted with the reason, gasped, 'Oh!' halted. On the ground outside the yard a bay horse lay on its side, lashing with hoofs and snapping with teeth at a ring of dingoes crowding in on it. The two geldings were trying to help, but only to be driven off with counter attacks by members of the pack.

A moment of staring. Then Rifkah shrieked, 'Bay Rum Betsy . . . haffing foal!

She went racing. The dingoes took fright at her approach. Rifkah screamed when she saw the foal struggling in bloody afterbirth. Betsy raised her head, evidently recognized her, whinnied, let her head drop. By her heaving flank and lolling tongue she was having a bad time of it.

Rifkah leapt into the mess, dropped her bags, set about disentangling the panting colt, got his long legs free of the blood-spirting cord – only to hear a snarl behind her, and swing to find a huge dingo menacing her with bared fangs. She reached for the bag, perhaps to fling it, to see others darting in again low-crouched. Her voice rose in a piercing scream: 'Oweeeeee Nanagooooooh!'

The dogs were ringing again, all glaring yellow eyes and gleaming teeth. The big one snapped at the bloody bag as Rifkah struck at him. She screamed again: 'Nan-a-goooooh!

BANG!

The air leapt – and with it the dingoes.

BANG!

The dingoes turned tail, vanished.

There was Nanago, in a print dress, stockman's hat, rifle in hand, coming running. Rifkah rose with outstretched arms. Nanago dropped the rifle to meet the embrace. Like lubras they howled on each other's shoulders – till a small wet form entangled with their legs. They drew apart, stared at the wobbly standing foal. It collapsed on baby knees. Rifkah shrieked, 'My split-bags . . . scissors . . . catgut!'

Nanago snatched up the bags, tore them open. In a moment they were on their knees together, sniffling back tears, while with flying fingers they set to work. Bay-Rum Betsy raised her old head again to take a look, to see her son butting against the bare brown breast of Rifkah as she cut the cord close to his silky belly. Then with a sigh she dropped her head again, to look with great eyes at the other horses crowding round staring.

CHAPTER TWENTY-SIX

OF COURSE the Yankee Trader soon brought to conclusion that conflict he himself dubbed World War II (just as he had called the Last Turn-out World War I after taking part in it, although nothing like all the world was involved in it either – it being the nature of the Yank to make everything he is concerned in appear to be grandiose, or to use his own language, *Superduper*). Indeed, only a Yankee super-superlative could do justice to the way he stopped his World War II. Not all the military murderers of history combined in one grand alliance could even have *dreamt* of havoc so sweet and swift as *Hiroshima*. Only those masters of the Negative in Nature, the Old Ones, Satan, Ahriman, Tchamala, could have equalled it. Yet, almost as soon as he had brought to their knees the survivors of those who had presumed to empire like his own, he raised them up, healed their wounds, fatted them from starvation, put tools and money in their hands, set them up again as rivals to himself – in Trade, which has no meaning to a Trader without the incentive of Competition.

In no time, all signs of the war were built over by the ant-heap industry the Yankee urged – except for soldiery he still kept under arms and in occupation, lest the industry take a turn not acceptable to his philosophy of *Do Others Or They'll Do You*. Not that there was anything about the behaviour of the Yankee Soldiery to suggest the tyranny of conquest, as evident in the fact that they occupied the territory of former friend and foe alike. The intention was quite benign – simply to *Americanize the World*. And so successful was it, that within a decade the World was changed as not in the couple of centuries of marked change since the Yankee Trader came into being. Indeed, some parts of the Globe were changed almost beyond recognition, amongst them that region which has been the main location of this tale, namely, Princess Beatrice River and its district.

Appropriately (according to the negative turn of things) the greatest change hereabout had been wrought in the very centre of the location, Lily Lagoons as known formerly, now again called Knowles Creek. Some would say it was poetic justice that gave the place back the name by which the primary disturber of its pristine peace had sought to immortalize himself. Not that there were many about now who knew the history of the place or, of the multitude of strangers, who cared even about its future. As to its future, that was already foregone, as that of every place upon which strangers converge simply to exploit what can be torn from it.

The boom in exploitation of the entire country had begun here. That was soon after the war ended, when Nugget Knowles, still employed by the still existent Vaiseys (Aust.), acting on a tip from Yankee Army Geologists, discovered that it was rich in that mineral then prized above all things on earth since the smart Yank had shown that in clever hands a chunk of it had the might of a Bolt of Jove – Uranium. It was ironic that the same tip had been given to the interloper Jeremy Delacy (by the Jewish Communist Zangwill) when it had no value, just as the Tantalium that had caused the ancient feud between Knowleses and Delacys had none during the former's tenure.

Most likely the old feud had much to do with Nugget's luck. Surely it was that made him watch for the opportunity to pounce on the lease of Lily Lagoons the moment it lapsed. From rags of gossip still fluttering about, it would seem that Nugget had become aware of Jeremy's defiance of the evacuation order (from having found the tracks of the cavalcade in the region of Catfish Gorge when he went there in search of his mare, Knowles' Luck, lured away by the stallion Elektron) but had been prevented from betraying it to the authorities by his boss, Martin Delacy. Subsequently he could scarcely have cared about revenge, since the discovery of the Uranium brought him a reward of £20,000 from the Government, along with an O.B.E., and another large sum from sale of the lease to Vaiseys.

Last heard of Nugget was in a full-page report in *Truth* of divorce proceedings taken against him by his wife Philly (nee Lilyponds) for adultery with a halfcaste girl. The affair was no mere bit of bush play-about. Nugget was described as a wealthy man, resident in Sydney, and the girl one he had taken out of the lousy Aboriginal Settlement of La Perouse and installed in Kings Cross luxury as his mistress. As it was said at the time, Nugget must have had to use a burnt cork on Philly to get her with those couple of kids for which she claimed princely maintenance. That was long ago. Probably no one now of the thousands dependent on the luck of Nugget Knowles had ever heard of him.

Knowles Creek Uranium was no longer a Vaisey enterprise. For that matter, the name Vaisey was now only a cypher in a business consortium of the kind that had come to be called Multinational, the full title of which was Matsu-Arkansas-Vaisey Inc. (Aust.) generally called MAVIS. Germans had a hand in it, too.

To the ordinary simple citizen it was understandable that the Yanks should have control of the country, seeing that it had been handed over to them in sheer funk to defend, but a mystery how the others got into it, after their frightful beating. The grand old warmongers who had started it, like Krupp and Mitsubishi, had become masters of those who had supposed they were the victors. Now, along with the generous Yank who had discovered the spoil for them, they were exploiting the natural wealth of the country from the desert to the sea. How right were those Yanks who had complained to Stephen Glascock of the sloth of his countrymen getting corns on their butts sitting on a billion dollars' worth of Alumina, Manganese, Iron, Copper, Calcium, Platinum, Molybdenum, Uranium – name it, and all you had to do was pull down a hill, drain a billabong, level a forest, tear up a beach, to become a millionaire! What matter if you left a desert behind, when you didn't have to live there?

The original Uranium find was made a little to southward of the so-called

Lagoons, on the line of fault dividing sandstone from limestone. In fact it was revealed by intensive blasting that the two sedimentary formations shallowly overlay a mass of thermal origin of which the red micaceous hill that was the site of the early Tin and Tantalite mining was the only outcrop. The blasting also disclosed that mysterious underground stream which was the real head of the Beatrice River. The stream, which was perennial, draining the southern immensity of the Plateau hereabout as it did, was diverted to supply the great Uranium Treatment Plant set up on the site of Lily Lagoons Homestead. That meant the end of the Rainbow Pool, at least as the Place of *Moah* it had been from the Beginning. Except during Wet Season it was now dry. The fact that it was still subject to flooding made it a useful rubbish dump, since it was scoured out annually. By now the western river system must have been bedded with insoluble rubbish all the way to the sea, and not only owing to the efforts of the populace of Knowles Creek, but of the entire district. Beer cans especially were to be seen winking in shallows everywhere when the river was running clear. Indeed the beer can had become symbolic of the final conquest of the land. Travellers now carried them as the pioneers had their water-bags and pack-canteens, blazing their trails with the empties, even the Aborigines, what few of them still wandered.

A spur of railway now followed the river to its head from the boom-town called Elizabeth that had replaced the old township of Beatrice. Diesel-electric trains bright-coloured and ear-splittingly rackety like everything else in the modern style, had long since driven the cockatoos away. In fact, native birds and animals of most species had vanished, mostly not because they had cleared out in dudgeon like the ever-irascible cockies, but had fallen victim to the new economy, either through unwitting contribution to it or inability to survive beside it. For instance, since the population explosion of humanity at large (following the period of decimation through wholesale slaughter) had created critical food shortage and rendered anything eatable marketable, the hunting of the bigger marsupials had become such big business that the breeds hereabout had been all but exterminated. And as the poor of the world got poorer, so did the rich get richer, causing such a demand for fancy leathers like those made from the skins of reptiles that even a kookaburra would be hard put to find a snake or lizard of any size. Not that there were so many kookaburras about, either, they having been cleaned up by so-called New Australians of Mediterranean and Balkan types who weren't so fussy about what they ate. Also, a lot of these newcomers, never having had living creatures other than humans to destroy before, killed for the human joy of it. Most active of these killers were the Germans, young Germans, perhaps outletting blood-lust denied them by youth in that grand orgy enjoyed by their elders.

A first-class road also ran up the river, not as a mere artery of commerce, but for the convenience of the tourists who, as everywhere now, came in droves, and particularly to this region, because the Uranium Plant surely attracted them not only as proof of the advancement long sung-for with *Advance Australia Fair*, but as symbolic of Man's having beaten God to the power to destroy the Earth And All That In There Is. For those who came not fully appreciating the devastation that could be wrought with Uranium, along with bits of the pretty green ore that could be bought as souvenirs, were picture postcards of nuclear-bomb-blasts and of the ruins of Hiroshima. Also of interest to tourists was the Plant Manager's Residence, a beautiful old two-storey house set in a bright garden and screened from the Works by a grove of ancient mangoes. If few visitors came in season to enjoy the edible bounty of the great trees, this was made up for with the liberty to carve mementoes in trunks and limbs, which were for ever weeping milky tears for the attention—or was it for the past? Postcards of the Big House and its garden also were on sale. However, these made no mention of its origin.

Another Tourist Attraction of the locality was the Painted Caves. These were now part of a National Park, under the caretakership of Aboriginal Rangers. No old timer would recognize the Turtle Hole in its new surroundings – a wide expanse of playground with swings and things for kids and Department-of-Works-built picnic shelters and lavatories. The Hole was still there, although certainly without turtles, which could never have survived along with the pump that supplied the reticulated system. Anyway, of those who sojourned there now, anyone seeing the long neck of a *Kudjerlinga* popping out of the reeds and lilies probably would have yelled *Snake* and bolted – even the Rangers, who were just as much strangers as the rest and not much nearer to being blackfellows except in breed.

Generally, the only blacks who worked these days were from Southern centres, people far removed from old tribal ways, having regard for the *kuttabah's* economics, hence not content with the Social Service Payments. Social Service had become the blackman's livelihood since the acquirement of citizenship, which, although designed by benign authorities to keep unemployed citizens in reasonable comfort, was barely enough to keep in booze such booze-artists as the Aboriginal Race had proved to be with the lifting of restrictions. Those who worked, like the Rangers here, wanted the things that *proved* their emancipation – fine clothes, radios, guitars, motor-cars – above all motor-cars. Above their wages, the Rangers profited from the sale of Aboriginal Artifacts, which were in such demand since the Nation had come to feel fully guilty about its former ill-treatment of the blackfellow that they were mass-produced in factories, even imported from Japan. However, there were occasions when these smart fellows reverted to type, went in to Elizabeth and got on the booze with their happy-go-lucky brethren from the Aboriginal Settlement popularly known as Boongville, and joined in the new Aboriginal sport of calling whites White Bastards and telling them to get to hell off their sacred soil. Thus visitors to the Painted Caves had the freedom now and then to identify themselves with the Dreamtime by making their own contributions to the paintings, or even to hack out chunks to take home. Notices declared that defacement of the galleries or removal of any part thereof was a serious offence. Still, no one had ever been charged therefor – and for good reason. Officialdom was in a difficult position here, it being well known that Professor Fabian Cootes, in his capacity as Director of Aboriginal Culture, had had the very best of the paintings chopped out by experts, to ensure their perpetual preservation in museums. The catch was that not all of the collection went to Australian institutions, or the price the others fetched into revenue. There was a national row about it. The Coot was not sacked, but, expressing high indignation over the defamation of one who had served his country so well as he, as scholar, soldier, public servant, resigned, to take the Chair of Anthropology at a leading university overseas. No doubt about him – as old acquaintances of his would have said.

The Plateau afforded yet another attraction for visitors, although in a negative sort of way; which is to say as something luring, awesome, but forbidden. For here the Army of Occupation had set up one of the many Super Sentry Boxes with which Uncle Sam had been moved to gird the Globe since forces stupidly antagonistic to his benevolence had stolen his Jove-given secret of how to strike Divine Fire from Uranium. The entire Plateau was now classified as a prohibited area, as notices proclaimed. Although not fenced, except for a bit located in the Catfish Gorge, the region was safe enough from intrusion, watched over as it was by electronic devices sensitive enough to record the movements of birds and beasts – supposing such life had survived the experimentation therein with the holocaustic contraptions now accepted as engines of war. Anyway, no one but a lunatic would venture past those notices, since it was well known that such experimentation rendered the localities where they took place as uninhabitable as the Moon. Why they bothered to fence the Gorge was a mystery, when the Australian people had proved to be so unconcerned about the alienation and devastation of vast tracts of their country by foreigners as scarcely to have raised a voice in protest. In fact, the only protestors were Communists, who probably were only doing what ordered to do by their own masters beyond the seas. Speaking of seas: those of the North Coast in the region of what once might have been thought to resemble *The Ocean Island, not far this side of the Terrestrial Paradise*, were now under electronic taboo.

Still Australians sang *Advance Australia Fair* (*For we are Young and Free*!) and with even more solemn fervour, since it had been adopted as the Australian National Anthem. The British National Anthem still had its place – For Occasions, as it was declared. That, too, now had special significance, since the Monarch (currently a female) had metamorphosed from a mere symbol to a glorious reality by having set gracious foot upon this long benighted region of the Realm. Her Gracious Majesty, Elizabeth II, had been right here, which was why old Beatrice (named after her great-great-grand-aunt) had been renamed.

No one who had known the old township and not been witness to its transition, if dumped there from afar (as was possible now it was a major port in the National Airways) would ever have known it. Even that landmark which might have been expected to last indefinitely, so solidly had it been constructed, the railway bridge, was gone. Old Tchamala at last had had his way with it. This was in the so-called record flood of Fifty-two, when the township had been all but obliterated. Cluttered with a huge amount of debris that was the result of wholesale timber-cutting up-river, the bridge had acted as a dam, causing the river to cut deeply into the curving bank on the town side and to carry away those other seeming permanencies, Cemetery, Police Station, Railway yards, leaving the formerly easy-sloping bank almost sheer, and a long deep reach in place of the former camping ground.

Camping was a thing of the past, even though the Race Meeting remained the main social event of the year. The élite stopped at the Royal Hotel. There were three good hotels. A fourth, commonly called 'The Boongs', catered almost exclusively for Aborigines, who while not denied service in the others (there was now a strict law against what was called Discrimination) evidently preferred their own company. Likewise these people preferred a residential area of their own, so-called Boongville, which was situated downriver, in the old style as regards location, but constructed in nothing like that style, having been established by the Government as a model for Nationwide acknowledgement of the guilt for ancient wrongs now freely expressed. The site was that of the long-forgotten White Russian Settlement, which also had failed in its purpose. Officially it was called Weeanjingalla, meaning Running Water, the significance being that here the river ran shallow and swift. The common name was not entirely undeserved, when all its establishment had proved was that a blackfellow's natural habitat was still the bush. Despite tremendous efforts on the part of experts of all kinds, it had quickly degenerated into a slum, and not only as regards domestic squalor, but social.

The centre of Elizabeth comprised some half a dozen blocks of modern shops, offices, restaurants, and the like. It now lay between the river and the railway, instead of vice versa as formerly. A pleasant park now occupied the space between built-up area and river – Queen's Park, where stood a fine memorial to the visitation of Our Sovereign Lady. It was grassed and planted with flowers and exotic trees, and kept remarkably well ordered, considering the fact that it was a haunt of the denizens of Boongville when they came to town, who in trading on the guilt of the *kuttabah* were never much concerned about their behaviour these days. It was the scene of black brawling pretty well every night. If things got so bad as to move the police to intervene, there was a handy escape route for the boisterous ones by way of the river. All you had to do was slide down the curving concrete bank and float home to Boongville.

The railway bound the city blocks on the up-river side, crossing the river now by a handsome suspension bridge that also carried traffic. No railway yards with ugly whitewashed sheds and coal hopper and stinking stockpen here now, but a neat station that, with potted plants and bright tourist posters, would have done credit to a scenic railway in Bavaria or some such place, whence its efficient and courteous staff had its origins. Perhaps it was that passion of theirs for order that had caused the Germans, after eliminating the native animals that might have seemed to them pesky things like the Jews and Gypsies their elders had dealt with so efficiently in essaying to establish the Reich that was to last a Thousand Years, to take over the running of that hitherto ragtime show, the railway system of these parts. Most of the Running and Traffic staffs were now Square'eads. Maintenance was now largely in the hands of Italians, who perhaps saw fettling here as easy means to fulfilling their poor-peasant's passion for ownership of land, since most of them had taken up blocks in the vicinity of their camps, to work in spare time. Yes, the ragtime railway system, so much a part of the outback Australia of old, was gone for ever.

The Railway Yards were now situated on the other side of the river, upstream from the Racecourse. Railway workers, as indeed all working-class types, lived over that side. The middle class was distributed in suburban blocks close to the centre. The upper class mostly had river frontages, except in the vicinity of what had been the site of the old Beatrice Homestead, where dwelt the Master Class who ran the show on which the new economy was based, MAVIS. The homestead had been replaced by a complex of modern offices and laboratories. The name of Delacy meant nothing here now. Martin had departed when MAVIS took over, to live in Sydney, where he died soon afterwards of heart failure, but with the merit of being named in his epitaph *Sir Martin*. His mother had gone to her second husband's home in England. No one now knew of the Pioneer of the District, Patrick Delacy, it not having been thought worth while to replace his monument lost in the flood. The only record of the name was on the new War Memorial, at the river end of Beatrice Street: two inscriptions with crosses against them, one in the World War I panel, *Lt. Jack Delacy*, the other in that of World War II, *Lt. Clancy Delacy*. There were two other inscribed panels, for the Korean War and the Viet Nam War, and a blank fourth that well might be awaiting World War III, the way things were going in the world. Anzac Day was still celebrated in much the same old way, the only difference being that the Germans and Japanese discreetly lay their wreaths on the memorial while the Anzacs were boozing in the RSL Club.

Another memorial, and the most interesting because of the legend attached to it, was that standing in Railway Square, outside the station. It was a diminutive locomotive, rather garishly painted, mounted on a concrete plinth, with a bronze plaque describing it as one of the original engines of the railway system. The history of the system was given, but not that of the engine, officialdom not having changed that much as to make public what might make officialdom appear ridiculous. For the little old thing was the *Sandfly*, whose last run must surely be one of the most famous in railway annals. However, the official ommission didn't matter much, because picture postcards of the memorial had a ready sale at the Manager's Residence at Knowles Creek and the Painted Caves, and as the old love of gossip still prevailed, those who sold them often told the tale. The story was made more interesting by the fact that two of those involved were still around to be pointed out, a couple of old fogeys known as Lopsided Pat and Red Rifkah, the old fellow swinging along on a single crutch, his withered spouse tailing him, always dressed in stockrider's outfit except for boots, still copper-haired, despite her crone's appearance otherwise.

The old couple lived out of town, down-river, on a bit of a farm opposite Boongville. They had established the place in order to help their neighbours across the way, before these became better off than themselves with the granting of all forms of Social Service to them tacitly as a sort of pension. There had been a great foregeathering of blacks at the settlement following the official decree that Aborigines were to be paid wages according to award, when the squatters, now largely Yankees, had hunted them off their runs. Pat and Rifkah had tried to organize the blacks to make a lively show of protest, to return to the stations (now called Ranches) and claim their old camp sites as their own property, while calling on the Government for support. To begin with, the people had no will to protest. Then there got amongst them cross-breeds who were emissaries of the Communist Party, from whom they learnt that someone from afar called Karlmarkus would soon be putting them back on the stations as bosses, provided that on every possible occasion in public places they shouted the slogan: *Land Rights*! Any hope of giving real help to the helpless was ruined by Pat's hostility to the crossbreeds, whose like he had detested ever since being done wrong by his first wife. For his abuse of them as Mongrel Yeller Bastards he might well have come to grief, bred as many of his adversaries were to extremes of violence in reaction to extremes of social injustice in Southern cities. However, he was known for a dangerous man himself. He and Rifkah also had as opponents the Government Welfare Officers, who preached the millennium for the Aboriginal Race with the slogan: *Integration!. Only learn to live like whitemen and you'll be saved.* These branded the pair as Trouble Makers.

Indeed, that was how most of the community regarded Lopsided Pat and Red Rifkah, despite the general tendency to dismiss them publicly as superannuated cranks. Pat had established himself as a public nuisance even before civil administration was resumed. He had been run out by the military authorities following the *Sandfly* incident. Then, returning with the Peace and being refused readmittance to the Railway Service, he became a savage critic of just about everything done in the way of rehabilitation, particularly as it concerned the railway. He was right ready for the Germans and Italians when they took over. He never saw a train out without reminding the crew and station staff of the efficiency of the German railways in carrying Jews to the Death Camps by the million. Fettling gangs fled from him, because he wanted to talk to them only of what a brave show the Italians had made in fighting the Australians and how they had sold their daughters to both Huns and Yanks. There was no answer to his vocal savagery but violence, for which he was always more than a match with his crutch. The police did no more than get between him and his opponents. His ready plea of honest comment and self-defence made convicting him impossible. A move was made to get rid of him by having him declared insane. Curiously enough, he was saved by the RSL, which even while he still feuded with it, gave him no less credit as a hero, since of all hereabout, none bore more scars in testimony to the Glory of Anzac.

Pat began his campaign as public nuisance alone. Rifkah did not join him for some five years, having spent the meantime in the North Coast country, along with Nanago. Her intention to become a sort of Queen of the Blacks had not been the success her prototype, the late Daisy Bates, had made of it. The blacks had not wanted her, except in extremes of illness or trouble with the missionaries of the several mission stations now dotting the coast. Perhaps Mrs Bates's blacks would have been the same, only that being desert people they depended more on her stores, which she was able to replenish, that she had the backing of police, and that, being English, she might be less sensitive about not being wanted. Finally, Rifkah was expelled from the country, in which she had no legal right, it being an Aboriginal Reserve. She was forcibly removed to Palmeston by officers of Aboriginal Welfare. However, her expulsion was initiated by the missionaries, whom she had annoyed all along with un-Christian interference in their business on behalf of the blacks and ultimately angered by charging them with collusion with the mining people when these intruded. They countercharged her with being a troublemonger. Enough was remembered of her career to make her suspect to any decent-minded citizen. There was even a rumour that she had been immorally involved with the missionary at the old Catholic Mission in the Leopolds, who had been abducted by Japanese during the war and subsequently executed. Nanago was not taken with her, but aging and ill as she was, stayed behind at Lady Beaumont Mission, as she wished to do, to work as a teacher.

If only Rifkah had realized in time that all she required to give her legal access to an Aboriginal Reserve, not being either a Government Officer or an Accredited Missionary of the Gospel, was a Miner's Right. For the Act concerning such Reserves waived the defined inviolability in case of the discovery of workable mineral deposits therein. To get a Miner's Right she had only to step into the Mines Office in Palmeston. But probably it would have been denied her legally, because soon after her arrival there she was again declared an Illegal Immigrant. So vehemently had she protested to the local press about the violation of the Reserve by the mining boom that, chiefly by reason of the oddity of her career, she became national news. The authorities then discovered a flaw in that hasty naturalization of hers, rescinded her citizenship, and ordered her deportation. Now she could be departed without causing any heartburning, because, being of Jewish origin, automatically she had become a citizen of the newly founded State of Israel. The process of deportation was just slow enough to enable her to beat it by marrying Pat.

Thus, with a Jewish wife who only too well knew true German character, Pat was all ready for the Square'eads when they arrived with all that amiability which Winston Churchill, in his own understanding of that peculiar character, had described as the alternative to the Hun's being *At Your Throat* – '*Either At Your Throat or At Your Feet.*'

Of course, Beatrice River Races, as the grand annual social event of the country, was one of the first casualties of World War II. After the war, racing was resumed, but only as a local pastime. Even with the establishment of Elizabeth Town and the reintroduction of a Cup Meeting (Queen Elizabeth Cup) as the main social event, it remained chiefly a matter of local interest. Booming Elizabeth had no need of other communities to liven it up. The Cup Meeting was held in October, over the Labour Day holiday weekend, the races being but a one-day affair, held on the Monday. There was nothing like the boisterous behaviour of old times. Just as much booze was consumed as ever, (and maybe more, since statistics showed that the Nation as a whole was steadily progressing towards chronic alcoholism) but with a good deal more circumspection – or it might have been that the several pubs and numerous dwellings hid what formerly, of necessity, took place largely in public. Anyway, the boongs made up for the loss in bacchanalian frolic.

When the Germans came in force, being used to lavish festivity in season and ever ready to share their genius for organization, they told of their own glorious *Oktober Fest* and suggested that they incorporate it in the holiday. The idea was well received, naturally, when it meant free beer, and no common local swill, but some Nectar of the Teutonic Gods being especially imported as a gesture of *At Your Feet*. Already the Square'eads had their *Klub Germania* and had proved what pleasant hosts they could be. A great crowd turned up at the *Klub Halle* that Saturday night of the first and only *Oktober Fest* ever to be held. Pat was there, and was well received, despite the fact that his hostility was already well known, such being the essential simplicity of German character.

He waited till things got nicely under way, then got to work with his crutch, shouting, 'You dirty bloody Jew-murderin' bastards . . . you think after what you done, murdered six million Jews, men and women, young and old, babies in arms, and crise knows how many other poor helpless buggers by the million . . . and got the world into the stink it is in . . . you goin' to take us in with your smoodgin'? As if you won't do it all over again when you get the chance! Well, I'm gettin' in first, you square'eaded inhuman bloody monsters . . . cop this!'

Pat was not alone in the rampage. A sufficiently large number of others with memories deeper than their bellies, mostly foreigners who had suffered the Hun in war, some Greeks, helped him wreck the joint and put a dozen Deutschers in hospital. It looked like Palmeston Jail this time. The RSL could not be expected to help, now that it permitted the gallant enemy to lay wreaths to the Glory of Anzac and was even planning joint excursions with him to visit the old battlefields of North Africa (but never those of Greece!). However, an equally powerful benefactor appeared in the handsome buxom shape of Mrs Bridie Cullity, proprietor of the Royal Hotel and of several other down-country hostelries, an exceedingly rich old lady, and more than that, mother-in-law of Mr Barnabus Bugsby Q.C., husband of her lovely daughter Jemima, and Crown Law Officer. The charges were quashed.

II

It was during an October Holiday weekend that this tale concludes, a very special occasion in the history of our locality – in fact, in general opinion, second only to that of the Visitation of Her Most Gracious Majesty. Indeed, it was a very close second, because the Personage who made it so special was the First Prince of the Blood. His Royal Highness came as world-leader of the so-called Conservation Movement that lately had come into active being through the all-too-obvious realization that the destructiveness of Human-kind had reached a point where the race stood in danger of destroying itself. The Prince's particular line was to preach preservation of what was left of unspoiled wilderness, perhaps really more for something to do to justify his otherwise useless existence than with genuine concern, but still with a show of purpose, coupled with personal charm and the mystique of Royalty, that gave the Movement credit it could not hope for otherwise. Who else could have got the entire population of an Australian town dependent for its existence on exploitation of country so recently pristine to pack Queen's Park that Sunday afternoon? Black, white, and brindle were there – Aussies, Pommies, Square'-eads, Ox-Cheeks, Yanks, Japs – even Wops, neglecting their weekend ring-barking, blasting, ploughing, and otherwise contributing to the making of another Sahara, as their ancestors had so long ago – already the Racecourse billabongs had ceased to exist owing to Italian zeal for labour and the *lira*.

His Royal Highness had just come from a tour of the North Coast Country, of necessity made in haste, mostly in aeroplanes and cars, and always with a retinue that generally was concerned rather with pleasing than displeasing him with what was revealed. However, not even the smartest guys in the world (nowadays well represented hereabout) could hide the league upon league of havoc wrought by monster machines and high explosives: the pumped-out billabongs, looking with heaped bones of perished animals and withered wreaths of lilies like forgotten cemeteries, fouled rivers flowing to sully the jade and sapphire of the *Ocean not far this side of the Terrestrial Paradise*. He was most eloquent as he stood on the flag-draped dais under his own personal standard (Oh, what a breathless effort had been made by officialdom to get that Standard here in time!) telling of deserts he had seen about the world that were not the work of Nature but of Man foolishly defying her, and how easily it could happen here. He told of water shortage due to destruction of Nature's means of dispersing this most precious of all the Good Earth's bounty – to such degree in same places, he said, that waste including even the inhabitants' bodily effluent had to be what he called Recycled to maintain supply. He stood before his microphones, tall, slim, handsome, as a true aristocrat should be, in such contrast to most of the males of the press of important people seated behind him. Gone for ever was that affected English bleat, perhaps bombed out of them by their would-be conquerors, the Huns, or laughed out of it by their real conquerors, the Yanks.

He said, 'Water is a blessing bestowed on our Planet as perhaps as on no other in the Universe. It is from water that the life of Earth burgeoned. Water is the life-blood of Earth. Where it dries up permanently Earth withers, dies. If our beautiful Earth is doomed to die completely, like the Moon, then it will be through destruction of its capacity to maintain Nature's marvellous cycling of water . . . and perhaps through Man's interference with that marvel.'

His striking blue eyes were fixed on the river, to be seen beyond the crowd because it was running rather high for the time of year, owing to abnormally heavy early rain – and running milky white, as always now from the earliest rains, since the mining of the Limestone. He could hardly be aware of the significance of its discoloration, when it wasn't likely that, while being shown around the settlement, he would have had pointed out to him the filtration plant now necessary to make the river water drinkable.

He was saying that he had been distressed to find how little had been done to prevent disturbance of the ecology of the country in the rush to exploit it economically, and how he would like to see co-operation between exploiters and conservationists – when out of the respectful, even reverent silence with which he was being heard, the piping voice of a woman was heard, located about halfway back in the crowd towards the river-bank, as to be seen by a fluttering hand. He stopped, eyed, cocked his narrow princely head to catch the words: 'Vot about ze people . . . ze Aboriginal people?'

All eyes focussed with the Prince's.

The voice rose higher: 'You talk of saving tree and vater and animal . . . but vot about ze pipple zose zing belong to?'

A murmur of annoyance from the white part of the crowd, which largely intervened, the darkies being further back, many perched on the river-bank railings. Far from showing himself annoyed, the Prince raised a hand to cup an ear.

'Ze Aboriginal people . . . who are part of zat country, and zat country part of zem . . . from Dream Time . . . now pushed out vit bulldozer . . . to die in spirit!'

His Highness blinked and bit his lip, turned his head from the interrupter, but without dismissing her, as shown by keeping hand to ear. His glance was directed to those on the right behind him, the heirarchy of officialdom: His Honour the Administrator, Superintendent of Police, Military Men, Equerry, Aides. Superintendent Gobally turned snowy eyebrows on the District Inspector of Police, who at once sprang from his seat and came, to inform his chief in a stage whisper that was caught by a microphone: 'That mad Jewess . . . Red Rifkah.'

The voice from the crowd came back: 'Zat country is last bit of dignity left to Aboriginal Race.'

Superintendent Gobally also rose, to come sidling deferentially to speak to the Prince. Again it went through the loud-speakers: 'A rat-bag, your Royal Highness.'

His Highness murmured, 'Rat-bag?'

Gobally simpered apologetically: 'Loony . . . but a trouble-maker, too. I'll get rid of her.'

He turned away and signed to several policemen lining the foot of the dais. Then a voice was heard from amongst the élite on the left of the platform – again female, powerful, mature, and vibrant with indignation: 'She's *not* a rat-bag!'

The Prince swung thither, to meet the dark eyes of Bridie Cullity, which in her flushed fleshy old face under heavily pencilled brows were reminiscent of that glare of Old Shame-on-us in wrath. She addressed him boldly: 'A brave woman, too. Lived for years with the blacks, trying to help them . . . hunted out by Yanks and Japs and Germans . . . . ' The effort left the ample bosom heaving.

His Royal Highness eyed her for a moment, then with a slight bow turned and looked back at the interrupter. Now the crowd was in hubbub with policemen pushing into it. Without another glance at cringing Gobally he spoke quickly, curtly, as one used to authority: 'Silence, please . . . silence!'

Obedience at once. The policemen stopped. He added, 'I want to hear what the lady has to say. Pray continue, Madam.'

Perhaps through surprise, the voice now came too weak to catch the words. He put his hand to ear again, calling, 'Speak up!' Then with a wave of his free hand he added, 'Stand back from the lady, if you please.'

Rifkah was revealed, dressed as always, in shirt, trousers, wideawake. Gaunt as she was, judged by her face with high Semitic cheek-bones and sharp hooked nose, and by her flat bosom, in conventional woman's clothing probably she would have looked a scarecrow. At her shoulder, lean almost as she, standing spread-legged, supported by his crutch, his artificial leg and arm apparently not much use to him, by their stiffness, was Pat. Only by his snapping green eyes would anyone have known him. He nudged Rifkah, saying in that same harsh voice of old, 'Go on, love . . . give it lip!'

Her voice rose with strength: 'Vite pipple of Australia have only vun chance left to cure ze Black Pox zat is vages of sin zey have commit' against ze Aboriginal Race. Give back to ze blackman a vorthvile piece of ze stolen land, and let him live zere as he likes. Zat North Coast Country is ze only vorthvile piece left. If ze *kuttabah* . . . ze stranger, vich mean everybody not belonging, and zat mean halfcaste, too . . . if zey get out and keep out, ze truly native people, if left alone, vill go back to old vay, ze only vay zey really know. Change moost come. But let ze blackman change himself. Do not count zese ozzer blackfellows in numbering ze Aboriginal Race. Zey have lost zere Dreaming, vitout vich zey are like cripples . . . to be helped vit pity. Do not count halfcastes even vit cripples . . . because zey are really *kuttabah*, only pretending to be Aboriginal ven it suit zem . . . .'

She was drowned in a howl of protest from the crossbreeds in the dusky crowd. But her voice came through again: 'Like Jew who is not brought up to Judaism is not Jew, but what blackfellow call Bloody Nutching . . . blackfellow who has lost his Dreaming is Bloody Nutching . . . .'

'Bloody nutching yo'self!'

'Shut up . . . bloody puggin white bastard!'

They were shoving towards her. Pat turned on them, brandishing his crutch, roaring, 'Shut up yo'selves, you mongrel bastards, and give her a go!'

Again the voice of Rifkah, cracking now with the strain: 'Not only have zese poor vuns here lost zere Dreaming, but zere dignity, too. People cannot truly live vizout dignity. Still ze people of ze North Coast have it. Leave zem alone, and zey vill make a nation. Zey vill become proud people . . . like ze Jews now zey have ze dignity of owning again zere ancient land of Israel. All Jews zroughout ze vorld share zat dignity . . . even if so many have lost zere Dreaming, too. So vill zese poor ozzer blackmen become proud again, knowing zat zere is a black Australian Nation . . . *Murrinbidui* . . . .'

Someone yelled, 'Land Rights!'

It was taken up: 'Lan' Right . . . Lan' Right . . . Lan' Right!'

Pat bellowed, 'Shut up, you bloody *munguses* . . . and listen to sense for once!'

Rifkah got in a last hoarse word: 'Land Rights vill only make ghettos amongst ze vites. Ze blackman living vit ze viteman moost alvays feel he is rubbitch . . . .'

Up went another cry: 'In'egration . . . In'egration . . . In'egration!'

And yet another: 'Karlmarkus . . . Karlmarkus!'

The darkies were on to Pat – and he on to them with the crutch – *Crack, crack, crack*!

They snatched it from him, overwhelmed him, in a huddle that looked like a spider in the grip of a swarm of furious ants. No whites interfered, but rather drew back to avoid involvement. Rifkah started to his rescue. They were dragging him towards the river-bank. She fought her way through the black and yellow press, positively seering a path with her she-hawk's screaming and the blaze of her hair now divested of the hat. She almost got to him before they shoved him through the rails, reached the rails herself to see him go sliding down the curving concrete wall – Swish! – and he shot out into the milky stream – Splash!

He sank. He came up further out, thrashing with one arm. Hanging on the rail, great-eyed, she wailed, 'He cannot svim!'

Again he sank, to come up now a distance down, caught by the current. She screamed till her voice cracked. 'Float, Pat, float . . . do not struggle!' But Pat went down again.

She croaked, '*Gevalt*!' She slipped through the rails, let go, went sliding down on her belly – *Splash*!

Her head came up like a bubble of dark blood above the milk. Pat was out in racing midstream now and well away. She struck out, was soon in the flood-race. Pat had vanished. But there ahead of her, retreating at the same swift rate as she advanced, was a strange sight – a quadrigeminal pattern of four bubbles. She stared, stopped swimming, swept on.

Were the great eyes behind the flared nostrils really intense grey, or only appeared to be so upon the racing white water? Her mouth opened wide, to give forth a cry that rang to the very tops of the few remaining river trees: 'Prindy . . . Prindy . . . *Ngoornberri* . . . *ngungah* . . . *ngungahhhhhh*!'

Down went the pattern of bubbles. Down went the copper head that looked like a bubble of blood. Nothing else for the gaping world to see. Only the *Moah* of the river to be sensed, by those with senses not yet too blunted by the jack-hammer logic of the *kuttabah* as still to be aware of the all-pervading *Mahraghi* of this ancient land, *Terra Australis del Espiritu Santo*.

POOR FELLOW MY COUNTRY

GLOSSARY OF ABORIGINAL TERMS

Bamgulut—bottle-tree
Baranga—brother
Barcoo—sick
Beinook—bustard
Beraga—'bring here'
Beral—Frog People (*myth.*)
Biaiuk—fairy wren
Bidu-bidu—bullroarer
Bijnitch—activity (general)
Bilbilgah—night-parrot
Binji—belly
Bogey—bathe
Booroolooloogun—nutmeg pigeon, also name of tribe
Bornji—tail of brush-tail wallaby
Bulkung—girdle of human hair
Burrulka—the sea
Burruwa—sister

Charada—love magic

Danook—silence!'
Darra—penis
Delera—armlets
Dibble—evil spirit
Dirralk garruk—'spit come out' (it makes my mouth water)
Dookyangana—policeman

Gadeeia—king prawn
Gogul—mopoke
Googoomara—giant cuckoo
Googoowingi—cormorant
Goolgoolgabin—*see* Jullingaal
Goona—dung
Goondalahg—wind spirits
Goorawundangi—salt-water crocodile
Gooruk bambulla?—'who is that person?'
Goydai!—'come!'
Gringelli—white morning glory (*Convulvulus*)
Gubindah—gecko lizard

Guliyurik—night heron
Gully-gully—crazy
Gungu (Ingornu)—fire-lighting equipment
Gurrawilliyuma—pied butcher bird

Igaiyu—'my boy'
Igulgul—The Moon God
Ingornu—*see* Gungu
Iwuyuk—bandicoot

Jalyerri (Julama, Jumbajinna)—totemic skin name or sign
Jeripunga—symbol of totem
Jitty—silly
Joey—small boy
Julama—*see* Jalyerri
Jullingaal (Goolgoolgabin)—python
Jumbajinna—*see* Jalyerri
Jungara—taboo business

Kaiu kahlu—'no good like that'
Kala—all right
Karrarra—plover
Kirrikijirrit—Willy wagtail
Kokanjinni (Ngaggun)—'nephew' (maternal uncle speaking)
Kokulal—secret ceremonial ground
Koodook—nightjar (departed spirit)
Koola—angry
Koonapippi—*Kurrawaddi, Ol'Goomun-Ol'Goomun*) The Earth Mother, The Sun Goddess
Koornung—witch-doctor
Kowee!—'come!'
Koyada kumeri—'don't be frightened'
Koyada namyul Koynainjil—ban on speech (during period of initiation)
Koyu—'mother' (son speaking)
Kudijingera—tribal elders
Kudjalinga—salt-water turtle
Kudjingah—songs of the Dream Time
Kulli-kulli!—'quick!'

Kallum kundirra—good hunter, strong man
Kumali—*see* Wahji
Kumara—Female genitals
Kumbitji—ironwood tree
Kumija—*see* Mora
Kumilungarnu—female breast, mother
Kundirra—strong
Kunjan—*see* Woolahloo
Kurrawaddi—*see* Koonapippi
Kuttabah—white man
Kwee-ai—young girl
Kweeluk—curlew

Lamala (yalmaru)—spirit-double
Larrama—native kapok
Loonga—backside

Mahraghi—magic
Makoon—nephew
Mangan—native plum
Marana nunga (Mundinjana)—song-man
Marmaroo—brush-tail wallaby
Mekullikulli—'my boy'
Minaji—the evening star
Minga-minga—music-sticks
Mininjorka—bandicoot
Min-minya—fly-catcher plant, devil spirit-woman
Miyakka—yam
Moah (Tulli-tulli)—bewitched
Moomboo—evil spirit
Mora (Kumija)—paternal grandfather or grandson
Moya—native apple
Muddrin bijnitch—murder
Mukkinboro—banyan tree
Mullaka—elder, boss
Mullikirri—'son' (mother speaking)
Mumbarma—throwing stick
Mummuk—'goodbye'
Mundinjana—*see* Marana nunga
Mundowi—foot
Mungus—stupid person
Munjong—a new chum, novice
Murri—native term for full-blood Aborigine, *also* adj., cf. Murringlitch
Murrimo—possum
Murringlitch—Aboriginal dialect of English
Myall—wild

Naga—loin cloth
Nainjil—tongue
Ngaggun—*see* Kokanjinni
Ngangula—'we go'
Ningari—initiate
Numeriji—*see* Tchamala
Nungyardil—'who are you?'
Nuttagul—goose
Nyang—'The Fly', the star Sirius

Ol'Goomun-Ol'Goomun—*see* Koonapippi

Pam—palm tree
Piendi—ground oven
Pijak—native bee
Pookarakka—wise man
Poot-poot—tick (insect)
Poorunna—'look see'
Prindy—goanna
Puringa—cod fish

Sunday bijnitch—sacred ceremonial

Tchamala (Numeriji)—The Rainbow Snake *(myth.)*
Tchillip—sleep
Tchinek—snake
Tchinekin—acting with subterfuge
Tilbyuk—duck
Tjaina—non-sacred dancing ground
Tjala—catfish
Tjangaluma—sacred call
Tjooloo—spirit of an unborn infant
Tjungara—taboo, forbidden
Tjuril—fresh-water turtle
Tulli-tulli—*see* Moah

Wagga—urine
Wahji (Kumali)—taboo
Waianga—The Cloud Spirits *(myth.)*
Wallan—emu
Wallandak—pelican
Wallingerra—newphew (sister's son)
Warriji jeega—dead
Watagarra—wedge-tail eagle
Winyan—waterhole
Wirrianwah—shelter for an initiate
Woolahloo (Kunjan)—ring place (secret ceremonial ground)
Wurrak—bad

Yakkarai!—'hooray!'
Yalmaru (Lamala)—spirit-double
Yalunga—initiate
Yang—skink lizard
Yawarra—'until I return'
Yerrilgeenah—galah
Yinganga—fresh-water crocodile
Yu, Yu-ai—'yes'